THE NORTON ANTHOLOGY OF

WORLD
LITERATURE

SHORTER FOURTH EDITION

VOLUME 1

THE NORTON ANTHOLOGY OF

WORLD LITERATURE

SHORTER FOURTH EDITION

MARTIN PUCHNER, *General Editor*
HARVARD UNIVERSITY

SUZANNE AKBARI
UNIVERSITY OF TORONTO

WIEBKE DENECKE
BOSTON UNIVERSITY

BARBARA FUCHS
UNIVERSITY OF CALIFORNIA, LOS ANGELES

CAROLINE LEVINE
CORNELL UNIVERSITY

PERICLES LEWIS
YALE UNIVERSITY

EMILY WILSON
UNIVERSITY OF PENNSYLVANIA

VOLUME 1

W. W. NORTON & COMPANY | New York · London

W. W. Norton & Company has been independent since its founding in 1923, when William Warder Norton and Mary D. Herter Norton first published lectures delivered at the People's Institute, the adult education division of New York City's Cooper Union. The firm soon expanded its program beyond the Institute, publishing books by celebrated academics from America and abroad. By midcentury, the two major pillars of Norton's publishing program—trade books and college texts—were firmly established. In the 1950s, the Norton family transferred control of the company to its employees, and today—with a staff of four hundred and a comparable number of trade, college, and professional titles published each year—W. W. Norton & Company stands as the largest and oldest publishing house owned wholly by its employees.

Editor: Peter Simon
Project Editor: Taylere Peterson
Editorial Assistant: Katie Pak
Managing Editor, College: Marian Johnson
Managing Editor, College Digital Media: Kim Yi
Production Manager: Sean Mintus
Media Editor: Carly Fraser-Doria
Media Project Editor: Cooper Wilhelm
Assistant Media Editor: Ava Bramson
Editorial Assistant, Media: Joshua Bianchi
Marketing Manager, Literature: Kimberly Bowers
Art Direction: Rubina Yeh
Book Design: Jo Anne Metsch
Permissions Manager: Megan Schindel
Permissions Clearing: Margaret Gorenstein
Composition: Westchester Publishing Services
Cartographer: Adrian Kitzinger
Manufacturing: LSC Communications—Crawfordsville

Permission to use copyrighted material is included in the backmatter of this book.

ISBN: 978-0-393-60287-6 (pbk.)

Library of Congress Cataloging-in-Publication Data

Names: Puchner, Martin, 1969– editor. | Akbari, Suzanne Conklin, editor. | Denecke, Wiebke, editor. | Fuchs, Barbara, 1970– editor. | Levine, Caroline, 1970-editor. | Lewis, Pericles, editor. | Wilson, Emily R., 1971– editor.
Title: The Norton anthology of world literature / Martin Puchner, general editor ; Suzanne Akbari, Wiebke Denecke, Barbara Fuchs, Caroline Levine, Pericles Lewis, Emily Wilson.
Description: Shorter fourth edition. | New York : W. W. Norton & Company, 2019. | Includes bibliographical references and index.
Identifiers: LCCN 2018033851 | ISBN 9780393602876 (v. 1; pbk.) | ISBN 9780393602883 (v. 2; pbk.)
Subjects: LCSH: Literature—Collections.
Classification: LCC PN6014 .N66 2019 | DDC 808.8—dc23 LC record available at https://lccn.loc.gov/2018033851

W. W. Norton & Company, Inc., 500 Fifth Avenue, New York, NY 10110
wwnorton.com
W. W. Norton & Company Ltd., 15 Carlisle Street, London W1D 3BS

1 2 3 4 5 6 7 8 9 0

Contents

II. ANCIENT INDIA   621

III. EARLY CHINESE LITERATURE AND THOUGHT   689

IV. CIRCLING THE MEDITERRANEAN: EUROPE AND THE ISLAMIC WORLD   733

V. MEDIEVAL CHINA 1179

VI. JAPAN'S CLASSICAL AGE

Preface

They arrive in boats, men exhausted from years of warfare and travel. As they approach the shore, their leader spots signs of habitation: flocks of goats and sheep, smoke rising from dwellings. A natural harbor permits them to anchor their boats so that they will be safe from storms. The leader takes an advance team with him to explore the island. It is rich in soil and vegetation, and natural springs flow with cool, clear water. With luck, they will be able to replenish their provisions and be on their way.

In the world of these men, welcoming travelers is a sacred custom, sanctioned by the gods themselves. It is also good policy among seafaring people. Someday, the roles may very well be reversed: today's host may be tomorrow's guest. Yet the travelers can never be certain whether a particular people will honor this custom. Wondering what to expect, the thirteen men enter one of the caves dotting the coastline.

The owner isn't home, but the men enter anyway, without any compunction. There are pens for sheep and goats, and there is plenty of cheese and milk, so the men begin eating. When the owner returns, they are terrified, but their leader, boldly, asks for gifts. The owner is not pleased. Instead of giving the intruders what they demand, he kills two of them and eats them for dinner. And then two more the next day. All the while, he keeps the men trapped in his cave.

A wily man, the leader devises a scheme to escape. He offers the owner wine, enough to make him drunk and sleepy. Once he dozes off, the men take a staff that they have secretly sharpened and plunge it into the owner's eye, blinding him. Without sight, he cannot see the men clinging to the undersides of his prized sheep as they stroll, one by one, out of the cave to graze, and cleverly the men cling only to the male sheep, not the females, which get milked.

* * *

This story of hospitality gone wrong comes from the *Odyssey*, one of the best-known works in all of world literature. We learn of this strange encounter of Greek soldiers with the one-eyed Cyclops named Polyphemus from Odysseus, the protagonist of the epic, when he recounts his exploits at the court of another host, the king of the Phaeacians. Unsurprisingly, Polyphemus isn't presented in the best light. Odysseus describes the Cyclopes as a people without a "proper" community, without agriculture, without hospitality. Is Odysseus, who has been wined and dined by his current host, trying to curry favor with the king of the Phaeacians by telling him how terribly he was treated by these non-Greek others? Reading the passage closely, we can see that Polyphemus and the other Cyclopes are adroit makers of cheese, so they can't be all that lazy. When the blinded Polyphemus cries out for help, his associates come to help him as a matter of course, so they don't live quite as isolated from one another as Odysseus claims. Even though Odysseus asserts that Polyphemus is godless, the land is blessed by the gods with fertility, and Polyphemus's divine father comes to his aid when he prays. Odysseus says that the Cyclopes lack laws and custom, yet we are also shown the careful, regular, customary way that Polyphemus takes care of his household. In a touching scene toward the end of his encounter with Odysseus, after he is blinded, Polyphemus speaks gently and respectfully to his favorite ram, so he can't be all that monstrous. The one-eyed giants assist one another, they are shepherds and artisans, and they are capable of kindness. The passage's ambiguities suggest that perhaps it was partly Odysseus's fault that this encounter between cultures went so badly. Were he and his companions simply travelers badly in need of food, or were they looters hoping to enrich themselves? The passage suggests that it's a matter of narrative perspective, from whose point of view the story is told.

Scenes of hospitality (or the lack thereof) are everywhere in world literature, and questions about hospitality, about the courtesies that we owe to strangers and that strangers owe to us (whether we are guests or hosts), are as important today as they were in the ancient world. Although many writers and thinkers today are fond of saying that our era is the first "truly global" one, stories such as this episode from Homer's *Odyssey* remind us that travel, trade, exile, migration, and cultural encounters of all kinds have been features of human experience for thousands of years.

The experience of reading world literature, too, is a form of travel—a mode of cultural encounter that presents us with languages, cultural norms, customs, and ideas that may be unfamiliar to us, even strange. As readers, each time we begin to read a new work, we put ourselves in the role of a traveler in a foreign land, trying to understand its practices and values and hoping to feel, to some degree and in some way, connected to and welcome among the people we meet there. *The Epic of Gilgamesh*, for example, takes its readers on a tour of Uruk, the first large city in human history, in today's Iraq, boasting of its city walls, its buildings and temples with their stairways and foundations, all made of clay bricks. Like a tour guide, the text even lets its readers inspect the city's clay pits, over one square mile large, that provided the material for this miraculous city made from clay. The greatest marvel of them all is of course *The Epic of Gilgamesh* itself, which was inscribed on clay tablets—the first monument of literature.

Foundational Texts

From its beginnings, *The Norton Anthology of World Literature* has been committed to offering students and teachers as many complete or substantially represented texts as possible. This Shorter Fourth Edition emphasizes the importance of *foundational* texts as never before by offering new translations of some of the best-known and most-loved works in the history of world literature. *The Epic of Gilgamesh* stands first in line of these foundational texts, which capture the story of an entire people, telling them where they came from and who they are. Some foundational texts become an object of worship and are deemed sacred, while others are revered as the most conse-quential story of an entire civilization. Because foundational texts inspire countless retellings—as Homer did for the Greek tragedians—these texts are reference points for the entire subsequent history of literature.

Perhaps no text is more foundational than the one with which we opened this preface: Homer's *Odyssey*. In this Shorter Fourth Edition, we feature the *Odyssey* in a new translation by our classics editor, Emily Wilson. This version captures the fast pace and rhythmic regularity of the original and offers a fresh perspec-tive on cultural encounters such as the one between Odysseus and Polyphemus that is described above. Astonishingly, Wilson's translation is the first transla-tion of the *Odyssey* into English by a woman. For centuries, commentators have remarked that the *Odyssey* is unusually attuned to the lives of women, especially in its portrait of Odysseus's wife, Penelope, a compelling and powerful charac-ter who cunningly holds a rowdy group of suitors at bay. Wilson's translation pays special attention to the poem's characterization of this remarkable woman, who is every bit as intriguing as the "complicated man" who is the eponymous hero of the tale. Other female characters, too, are given a new voice in this translation. For example, Helen, wife of the Greek king Menelaus and (accord-ing to legend) possessor of "the face that launched a thousand ships," is revealed through Wilson's translation to speak of herself not as a "whore" for whose sake so many young Greek men fought, suffered, and died (as she does in most other translations) but instead as a perceptive, clever person onto whom the Greeks, already eager to fight the Trojans, projected their own aggressive impulses: "They made my face the cause that hounded them," she says. The central conflicts of the epic, the very origin of the Trojan War, appear here in a startling new light.

This example highlights an exciting dimension of our emphasis on new trans-lations. The first half of this anthology has always been dominated by male voices because men enjoyed privileged access to literacy and cultural influence in the centuries prior to modernity. Our focus on new translations has allowed us to introduce into these volumes more female voices—the voices of translators. So, for example, we present Homer's *Iliad* in a new translation by Caroline Alexander and Euripides' *Medea* in a new, specially commissioned translation by Sheila H. Murnaghan, and we continue to offer work in the first volume translated by female translators such as Dorothy Gilbert (Marie de France's *Lais*), Sheila Fisher (Chaucer's *Canterbury Tales*), and Rosalind Brown-Grant (Christine de Pizan's *Book of the City of Ladies*), among others. This commit-ment to featuring the work of female translators extends beyond these early centuries as well, for example in the brilliant new translation by Susan Bernofsky of a foundational text of literary modernity—Kafka's *Metamorphosis*. The result throughout the anthology is that these works now speak to today's readers in new and sometimes surprising ways.

Our emphasis in this edition on new translations is based on and amplifies the conviction expressed by the original editors of this anthology over fifty years ago: that world literature gains its power when it travels from its place of origin and speaks to people in different places. While purists sometimes insist on studying literature only in the original language, a dogma that radically shrinks what one can read, world literature not only relies on translation but actually thrives on it. Translation is a necessity; it is what enables a worldwide circulation of literature. It also is an art. One need only think of the way in which translations of the Bible shaped the history of Latin or English or German. Translations are re-creations of works for new readers. This edition pays keen attention to translation, featuring new translations that make classic texts newly readable and capture the originals in compelling ways. With each choice of translation, we have sought a version that would spark a sense of wonder while still being accessible to a contemporary reader.

Among other foundational texts presented in new translations and selections is the Qur'an, in a verse translation that is the product of a collaboration between M. A. Rafey Habib, a poet, literary scholar, and Muslim, and Bruce Lawrence, a renowned scholar of Islam. Their team effort captures some of the beauty of this extraordinary, and extraordinarily influential, sacred text. Augustine's *Confessions* are newly presented in a version by Peter Constantine, and Dante's *Inferno* is featured in the long-respected and highly readable translation by the American poet John Ciardi.

We have also maintained our commitment to exciting epics that deserve wider recognition such as the Maya *Popol Vuh* and *Sunjata*, which commemorates the founding of a West African empire in the late Middle Ages. Like the *Odyssey*, *Sunjata* was transmitted for centuries in purely oral form. But while the *Odyssey* was written down around 800 B.C.E., *Sunjata* was written down only in the twentieth century. We feature it here in a new prose translation by David C. Conrad, who personally recorded this version from a Mande storyteller, Djanka Tassey Condé, in 1994. In this way, *Sunjata* speaks to the continuing importance of oral storytelling, the origin of all foundational epics, from South Asia via Greece and Africa to Central America. Throughout the anthology, we remind readers that writing has coexisted with oral storytelling since the invention of literature and that it will continue to do so in the future.

A Network of Stories

In addition to foundational texts, we include in this edition a great number of stories and story collections. The origins of this form of literature reach deep into the ancient world, as scribes collected oral stories and assembled them in larger works. Consider what is undoubtedly the most famous of these collections, *The Thousand and One Nights*, with its stories within stories within stories, all neatly framed by the overarching narrative of Shahrazad, who is telling them to her sister and the king to avoid being put to death. What is most notable about this story collection is that it draws its material from India, Persia, and Greece. There existed a continent-spanning network of stories that allowed storytellers and scribes to recycle and reframe what they learned in ever new ways; it proved so compelling that later writers, from Marie de France to Chaucer, borrowed from it frequently.

Expanded Selections

Along with our focus on making foundational texts and story collections fresh and accessible, we have pruned the overall number of authors and are therefore able to increase our offerings from major texts that feature in many world literature courses. *Don Quixote* now includes the compelling "Story of Captivity in North Africa," in which Cervantes draws on his own experiences as a slave in Algiers, where he spent five years after having been captured by pirates. Other major texts and authors with increased selections include the *Iliad,* Sappho, Ovid, the Qur'an, Murasaki's *Tale of Genji,* Machiavelli's *The Prince,* Baudelaire, Tagore, and Borges, and we have introduced complete new texts, such as Aphra Behn's *Oroonoko,* Wole Soyinka's *Death and the King's Horseman,* Mo Yan's "The Old Gun," and Orhan Pamuk's "To Look Out the Window." We are particularly excited to now close the anthology with a story by the Nigerian writer Chimamanda Ngozi Adichie called "The Headstrong Historian," which, since its publication in 2008, has already become a favorite in world literature classrooms. This compact work introduces us to three generations of Nigerians as they navigate a complicated series of personal and cultural displacements. A thought-provoking exploration of the complex results of cultural contact and influence, this probing, searching journey seemed to us the most fitting conclusion to the anthology's survey of 4,000 years of literature.

The Birth of World Literature

In 1827, a provincial German writer, living in small-town Weimar, recognized that he was in the privileged position of having access not only to European literature but also to literature from much further afield, including Persian poetry, Chinese novels, and Sanskrit drama. The writer was Johann Wolfgang von Goethe, and in 1827, he coined a term to capture this new force of globalization in literature: "world literature." (We now include the "prologue" to Goethe's play *Faust,* which he wrote after encountering a similar prologue in the classical Sanskrit play *Śhakuntalā.*)

Since 1827, for less than 200 years, we have been living in an era of world literature. This era has brought many lost masterpieces back to life, including *The Epic of Gilgamesh,* which was rediscovered in the nineteenth century, and the *Popol Vuh,* which languished in a library until well into the twentieth century. Other works of world literature weren't translated and therefore didn't begin to circulate outside their sphere of origin until the last 200 years, including *The Tale of Genji.* With more literature becoming more widely available than ever before, Goethe's vision of world literature has become a reality today.

In presenting world literature from the dawn of writing to the early twenty-first century, and from oral storytelling to the literary experiments of modernism, this anthology raises the question not only of what world literature is but also of the nature of literature itself. Greek tragedies are experienced by modern students as a literary genre, encountered in written texts; but for the ancient Athenians, they were primarily dramas, experienced live in an outdoor theater in the context of a religious and civic ritual. Other texts, such as the Qur'an or the Bible, are sacred pieces of writing, central to many people's religious faith, while others appreciate them primarily or exclusively as literature. Some texts, such as those by Laozi or Augustine, belong in philosophy, while others, such as Machiavelli's *The Prince,* are also political documents. Our modern conception of literature as imaginative literature, as fiction, is very recent, about 200 years old. We have therefore opted for a much-expanded conception of literature that includes creation myths, wisdom literature, religious texts, philosophy, and political writing in addition to poems, plays, and narrative fiction. This speaks to an older definition of literature as writing of high quality or of great cultural significance. There are many texts of philosophy or religion or politics that are not remarkable or influential for their literary qualities and that would therefore have no place in an anthology of world literature. But the works presented here do: in addition to or as part of their other functions, they have acquired the status of literature.

This brings us to the last and perhaps most important question: When we study the world, why study it through its literature? Hasn't literature lost some of its luster for us, we who are faced with so many competing media and art forms? Like no other art form or medium, literature offers us a deep history of human thinking. As our illustration program shows, writing was invented not for the composition of literature but for much more mundane purposes, such as the recording of ownership, contracts, or astronomical observations. But literature is writing's most glorious by-product. Literature can be reactivated with each reading. Many of the great architectural monuments of the past are now in ruins. Literature, too, often has to be excavated, as with many classical texts. But once a text has been found or reconstructed it can be experienced as if for the first time by new readers. Even though many of the literary texts collected in this anthology are at first strange, because they originated so very long ago, they still speak to today's readers with great eloquence and freshness. No other art form can capture the human past with the precision and scope of literature because language expresses human consciousness. Language shapes our thinking, and literature, the highest expression of language, plays an important role in that process, pushing the boundaries of what we can think and how we think it. This is especially true with great, complex, and contradictory works that allow us to explore different narrative perspectives, different points of view.

Works of world literature continue to elicit strong emotions and investments. The epic *Rāmāyaṇa*, for example, plays an important role in the politics of India, where it has been used to bolster Hindu nationalism, just as the *Bhagavad-gītā* continues to be a moral touchstone in the ethical deliberation about war. The so-called religions of the book, Judaism, Christianity, and Islam, make our selections from their scriptures a more than historical exercise as well. China has recently elevated the sayings of Confucius, whose influence on Chinese attitudes about the state had waned in the twentieth century, creating Confucius Institutes all over the world to promote Chinese culture in what is now called New Confucianism. World literature is never neutral. We know its relevance precisely by the controversies it inspires.

There are many ways of studying other cultures and of understanding the place of our own culture in the world. Archaeologists can show us objects and buildings from the past and speculate, through material remains, how people in the past ate, fought, lived, died, and were buried; scientists can date layers of soil. Literature is capable of something much more extraordinary: it allows us a glimpse into the imaginative lives, the thoughts and feelings of humans from thousands of years ago or living halfway around the world. This is the true magic of world literature as captured in this anthology, our shared human inheritance.

About the Shorter Fourth Edition

New Selections and Translations

Following is a list of the new translations, selections, and works in the Shorter Fourth Edition, in order:

VOLUME 1

A new translation of Homer's *The Iliad* by Caroline Alexander and Book XVIII newly included • A new translation of Homer's *The Odyssey* by Emily Wilson • New translations of Sappho's poetry by Philip Freeman, including ten new poems • New translations of *Oedipus the King* by David Grene and *Medea* by Sheila H. Murnaghan • A new selection from *The Aeneid*, including Book VI and an excerpt from Book VIII • New selections from Ovid's *Metamorphoses*, including the stories of Jove and Europa, Ceres and Proserpina, and Iphis and Isis • A new translation of Augustine's *Confessions* by Peter Constantine with a new selection from "Book XI [Time]" • A new translation of the Qur'an by M. A. R. Habib and Bruce Lawrence with new selections from "Light," "Ya Sin," and "The Sun" • A new translation of Marie de France's *Lais* by Dorothy Gilbert, including the new selection "Bisclavret" • John Ciardi's translation of *The Divine Comedy*, newly included • Selections from Christine de Pizan's *The Book of the City of Ladies*, translated by Rosalind Brown-Grant, newly included • New poems by Li Bo • Selections from Sei Shōnagon's *The Pillow Book*, translated by Meredith McKinney, newly included • New selections from *The Tale of Genji*: "*Sakaki*: A Branch of Sacred Evergreen," "*Maboroshi*: Spirit Summoner," "*Hashihime*: The Divine Princess at Uji Bridge," "*Agemaki*: A Bowknot Tied in Maiden's Loops," "*Yadoriki*: Trees Encoiled in Vines of Ivy," and "*Tenarai*: Practicing Calligraphy" • A new prose translation of *Sunjata: A West African Epic of the Mande* by David C. Conrad • New selections from *The Prince*: "On Liberality and Parsimony," "On Cruelty and Pity," "In What Ways Faith Should Be Kept," "On Avoiding Contempt and Hatred," "[The Best Defense]," "[Ferdinand of Spain, Exemplary Prince]," "[Good Counsel vs. Flattery]," and "[Why Princes Fail]" • A new selection from *Don Quixote*, "[A Story of Captivity in North Africa, Told to Don Quixote at the Inn]"

VOLUME 2

Aphra Behn's *Oroonoko; or, The Royal Slave*, newly included • A new translation of Sor Juana Inés de la Cruz's *Response* by Edith Grossman • A new selection from *Faust*, "Prelude in the Theatre" • New poems by William Wordsworth and Charles Baudelaire • Nguyễn Du's *The Tale of Kiều* • A new translation of *The Death of Ivan Ilyich* by Peter Carson • Anton Chekhov's "The Lady with the Dog" translated by Ivy Litvinov • Rabindranath Tagore's *Kabuliwala*, translated by Madhuchhanda Karlekar • A new translation of *The Metamorphosis* by Susan Bernofsky • Eric Bentley's translation, new to this edition, of Pirandello's *Six Characters in Search of an Author* • Chapter 2 of Virginia Woolf's *A Room of One's Own* • Jorge Luis Borges's "The Library of Babel," translated by James E. Irby • W. B. Yeats's "Among School Children" • M. D. Herder Norton's translations of Rainer Maria Rilke's poems, newly included • Seamus Heaney's "Digging" • Wole Soyinka's *Death and the King's Horseman* • Mo Yan's "The Old Gun" • Orhan Pamuk's "To Look Out the Window" • Chimamanda Ngozi Adichie's "The Headstrong Historian"

Resources for Students and Instructors

Norton provides students and instructors with abundant resources to make the teaching and study of world literature an even more interesting and rewarding experience.

With the Shorter Fourth Edition, are pleased to launch the new *Norton Anthology of World Literature* website, found at digital.wwnorton.com/worldlit4pre1650 (for volume 1) and digital.wwnorton.com/worldlit4post1650 (for volume 2). This searchable and sortable site contains thousands of resources for students and instructors in one centralized place at no additional cost. Following are some highlights:

- A series of eight brand-new video modules are designed to enhance classroom presentation and spark student interest in the anthology's works. These videos, conceived of and narrated by the anthology editors, ask students to consider why it is important for them to read and engage with this literature.
- Hundreds of images—maps, author portraits, literary places, and manuscripts—are available for student browsing or instructor download for in-class presentation.
- Several hours of audio recordings are available, including a 10,000-term audio glossary that helps students pronounce the character and place names in the anthologized works.

The site also provides a wealth of teaching resources that are unlocked with an instructor's log-in:

- "Quick read" summaries, teaching notes, discussion questions, and suggested resources for every work in the anthology, from the much-praised *Teaching with* The Norton Anthology of World Literature: *A Guide for Instructors*

- Downloadable Lecture PowerPoints featuring images, quotations from the texts, and lecture notes in the notes view for in-class presentation

In addition to the wealth of resources in *The Norton Anthology of World Literature* website, Norton offers a downloadable Coursepack that allows instructors to easily add high-quality Norton digital media to online, hybrid, or lecture courses—all at no cost. Norton Coursepacks work within existing learning management systems; there's no new system to learn, and access is free and easy. Content is customizable and includes over seventy reading-comprehension quizzes, short-answer questions, links to the videos, and more.

Acknowledgments

The editors would like to thank the following people, who have provided invaluable assistance by giving us sage advice, important encouragement, and help with the preparation of the manuscript: Sara Akbari, Alannah de Barra, Wendy Belcher, Jodi Bilinkoff, Daniel Boucher, Freya Brackett, Psyche Brackett, Michaela Bronstein, Rachel Carroll, Sookja Cho, Kyeong-Hee Choi, Amanda Claybaugh, Lewis Cook, David Damrosch, Dick Davis, Burghild Denecke, Amanda Detry, Anthony Domestico, Megan Eckerle, Marion Eggert, Merve Emre, Maria Fackler, Guillermina de Ferrari, Alyssa Findley, Karina Galperín, Stanton B. Garner, Kimberly Dara Gordon, Elyse Graham, Stephen Greenblatt, Sara Guyer, Langdon Hammer, Emily Hayman, Iain Higgins, Paulo Lemos Horta, Mohja Kahf, Peter Kornicki, Paul W. Kroll, Peter H. Lee, Sung-il Lee, Lydia Liu, Bala Venkat Mani, Ann Matter, Barry McCrea, Alexandra McCullough-Garcia, Rachel McGuiness, Jon McKenzie, Mary Mullen, Djibril Tamsir Niane, Johann Noh, Felicity Nussbaum, Andy Orchard, John Peters, Michael Pettid, Daniel Taro Poch, Daniel Potts, Megan Quigley, Payton Phillips Quintanilla, Catherine de Rose, Imogen Roth, Katherine Rupp, Ellen Sapega, Jesse Schotter, Stephen Scully, Kyung-ho Sim, Sarah Star, Brian Stock, Tomi Suzuki, Joshua Taft, Sara Torres, J. Keith Vincent, Lisa Voigt, Kristen Wanner, Emily Weissbourd, Karoline Xu, Yoon Sun Yang, and Catherine Vance Yeh.

All the editors would like to thank the wonderful people at Norton, principally our editor Pete Simon, the driving force behind this whole undertaking, as well as Marian Johnson (Managing Editor, College), Christine D'Antonio and Kurt Wildermuth (Project Editors), Michael Fleming (Copyeditor), Gerra Goff (Associate Editor), Katie Pak (Editorial Assistant), Megan Jackson (College Permissions Manager), Margaret Gorenstein (Permissions), Catherine Abelman (Photo Editor), Debra Morton Hoyt (Art Director; cover design), Rubina Yeh (Design Director), Jo Anne Metsch (Designer; interior text design), Adrian Kitzinger (cartography), Agnieszka Gasparska (timeline design), Carly Fraser-Doria (Media Editor), Ava Bramson (Assistant Editor, Media), Ashley Horna and Sean Mintus (Production Managers), and Kim Bowers (Marketing Manager, Literature). We'd also like to thank our Instructor's Guide authors: Colleen Clemens (Kutztown University), Elizabeth Watkins (Loyola University New Orleans), and Janet Zong (Harvard University).

This anthology represents a collaboration not only among the editors and their close advisers but also among the thousands of instructors who teach from the anthology and provide valuable and constructive guidance to the publisher and editors. *The Norton Anthology of World Literature* is as much their book as it is ours, and we are grateful to everyone who has cared enough about this anthology to help make it better. We're especially grateful to the professors of world literature who responded to an online survey in 2014, whom we have listed below. Thank you all.

Michelle Abbott (Georgia Highlands College), Elizabeth Ashworth (Castleton State College), Clinton Atchley (Henderson State University), Amber Barnes (Trinity Valley Community College), Rosemary Baxter (Clarendon College), Khani Begum (Bowling Green State University), Joyce Boss (Wartburg College), Floyd Brigdon (Trinity Valley Community College), James Bryant-Trerise (Clackamas Community College), Barbara Cade (Texas College), Kellie Cannon (Coastal Carolina Community College), Amee Carmines (Hampton University), Farrah Cato (University of Central Florida), Brandon Chitwood (Marquette University), Paul Cohen (Texas State University), Judith Cortelloni (Lincoln College), Randall Crump (Kennesaw State University), Sunni Davis (Cossatot Community College), Michael Demson (Sam Houston State University), Richard Diguette (Georgia Perimeter College, Dunwoody), Daniel Dooghan (University of Tampa), Jeff Doty (West Texas A&M University), Myrto Drizou (Valdosta State University), Ashley Dugas (Copiah-Lincoln Community College), Richmond Eustis (Nicholls State University), David Fell (Carroll Community College), Allison Fetters (Chattanooga State Community College), Francis Fletcher (Folsom Lake College), Kathleen D. Fowler (Surry Community College), Louisa Franklin (Young Harris College), James Gamble (University of Arkansas), Antoinette Gazda (Averett University), Adam Golaski (Central Connecticut State University), Anissa Graham (University of North Alabama), Eric Gray (St. Gregory's University), Jared Griffin (Kodiak College), Marne Griffin (Hilbert College), Frank Gruber (Bergen Community College), Laura Hammons (Hinds Community College), Nancy G. Hancock (Austin Peay State University), C. E. Harding (Western Oregon University), Leslie Harrelson (Dalton State College), Eleanor J. Harrington-Austin (North Carolina Central University), Matthew Hokom (Fairmont State University), Scott Hollifield (University of Nevada, Las Vegas), Catherine Howard (University of Houston, Downtown), Jack Kelnhofer (Ocean County College), Katherine King (University of California, Los Angeles), Pam Kingsbury (University of North Alabama), Sophia Kowalski (Hillsborough Community College), Roger Ladd (University of North Carolina at Pembroke), Jameela Lares (University of Southern Mississippi), Susan Lewis (Delaware Technical Community College), Christina Lovin (Eastern Kentucky University), Richard Mace (Pace University), Nicholas R. Marino (Borough of Manhattan Community College, CUNY), Brandi Martinez (Mountain Empire Community College), Kathy Martinez (Sandhills Community College), Matthew Masucci (State College of Florida), Kelli McBride (Seminole State College), Melissa McCoy (Clarendon College), Geoffrey McNeil (Notre Dame de Namur University), Renee Moore (Mississippi Delta Community College), Anna C. Oldfield (Coastal Carolina University), Keri Overall (Texas Woman's University), Maggie Piccolo (Rutgers University), Oana Popescu-Sandu (University of Southern Indiana), Jonathan Purkiss (Pulaski Technical College), Rocio Quispe-Agnoli (Michigan State University), Evan Radcliffe (Villanova University), Ken Raines (Eastern Arizona College), Jonathan Randle (Mississippi College), Kirk G. Rasmussen (Utah Valley University), Helaine Razovsky (Northwestern State University of Louisiana), Karin Rhodes (Salem State University), Stephanie Roberts (Georgia Military College), Allen Salerno (Auburn University), Shannin Schroeder (Southern Arkansas University), Heather Seratt (University of Houston,

Downtown), Conrad Shumaker (University of Central Arkansas), Edward Soloff (St. John's University), Eric Sterling (Auburn University Montgomery), Ron Stormer (Culver-Stockton College), Marianne Szlyk (Montgomery College), Tim Tarkington (Georgia Perimeter College), Allison Tharp (University of Southern Mississippi), Diane Thompson (Northern Virginia Community College), Sevinc Turkkan (College at Brockport, State University of New York), Verne Underwood (Rogue Community College), Patricia Vazquez (College of Southern Nevada), William Wallis (Los Angeles Valley College), Eric Weil (Elizabeth City State University), Denise C. White (Kennesaw State University), Tamora Whitney (Creighton University), Todd Williams (Kutztown University of Pennsylvania), Bertha Wise (Oklahoma City Community College), and Lindsey Zanchettin (Auburn University).

THE NORTON ANTHOLOGY OF

WORLD LITERATURE

SHORTER FOURTH EDITION

1

Ancient Mediterranean and Near Eastern Literature

THE INVENTION OF WRITING AND THE EARLIEST LITERATURES

The word *literature* comes from the Latin for "letters." "Oral literature" is therefore a contradiction in terms. Most modern Westerners assume that literature is something we read in books; it is, by definition, written language. But people told stories and sang songs long before they had any means to record them. Oral types of poetry and storytelling are quite different from those produced by writing, and it is difficult for us, living in an age dominated by printed and digital language, to imagine a world where nobody could read or write. Preliterate societies had different intellectual values from our own. We tend to think that a "good" story or essay is one that is neatly organized, original, and free from obvious repetition; we think of clichés as a mark of bad writing. But people without literacy tend to love stock phrases, traditional sayings, and proverbs. They are an essential mechanism by which cultural memory is preserved. Before writing, there was no such thing as an "author"—a single individual who, all alone, creates a text to be experienced by a solitary, silent reader. Instead, poets, singers, and

King Priam asks Achilles for the body of his son, Hector. From an archaic Greek bronze relief, ca. 570–560 B.C.E.

storytellers echoed and manipulated the old tales and the inherited wisdom of their people.

Of course, without either writing or recording equipment, all oral storytelling is inevitably lost. The tales that were told before there was writing cannot be collected in any anthology. But they left their mark on the earliest works of written literature—and many subsequent ones as well. As one would expect, literacy did not take hold all at once; the transition was partial and gradual, and in much of the ancient world, poetry and storytelling were less closely associated with written texts than they are for us.

Writing was not originally invented to preserve literature. The earliest written documents we have contain commercial, administrative, political, and legal information. It was in the region of the Tigris and Euphrates rivers, Mesopotamia (which means "the place between the rivers"), that writing was first developed; the earliest texts date from around 3300 to 2990 B.C.E. The characters of this writing were inscribed on tablets of wet clay with a pointed stick; the tablets were then left in the sun to bake hard. The

characters are pictographic: the sign for *ox* looks like an ox head and so on. The bulk of the texts are economic—lists of food, textiles, and cattle. But the script is too primitive to handle anything much more complicated than lists, and by 2800 B.C.E. scribes began to use the wedge-shaped end of the stick to make marks rather than the pointed end to draw pictures. The resulting script is known as cuneiform, from the Latin word *cuneus*, "a wedge." By 2500 B.C.E. cuneiform was used for many things beyond administrative lists: the texts preserved historical events and even, finally, literature. It was on clay tablets and in cuneiform script that the great Sumerian epic poem **Gilgamesh** was written down. This writing system was not, however, designed for a large reading public. Each sign denoted a syllable—consonant plus a vowel—which meant that the reader had to be familiar with a large number of signs. Furthermore, the same sign often represented two or more different sounds, and the same sound could be represented by several different signs. It is a script that could be written and read only by experts, the scribes, who often proudly recorded their own names on the tablets.

There was one ancient writing system that, unlike cuneiform, survived, in modified forms, until the present day. It was developed by the Phoenicians, a Semitic trading people. The script consisted of twenty-two simple signs for consonantal sounds. Through trade, the Phoenician script spread all over the Mediterranean. It was adopted by the ancient Hebrews, among others. The obvious advantage of this system was that it was so easy to learn. But there was still one area of inefficiency in this system: the absence of any notation for the vowels made for ambiguity. We still do not know,

An administrative tablet from Mesopotamia, ca. 3100–2900 B.C.E.

for example, what the vowel sounds were in the sacred name of God, often called the Tetragrammaton ("Four Letters"). In our alphabet the name is written as YHWH. The usual surmise is Jahweh (*yá-way*), but for a long time the traditional English-language version was Jehovah.

One thing was needed to make the script fully efficient: signs for the vowels. This was the contribution of the Greeks, who, in the eighth or possibly the ninth century B.C.E., adopted the Phoenician script for their own language, but used for the vowels some Phoenician signs that stood for consonantal combinations not native to Greek. They took over (but soon modified) the Phoenician letter shapes and also their names: *alpha*, a meaningless word in Greek, represents the original *aleph* ("ox"), and *beta* represents the original *beta* ("house"). The Greeks admitted their indebtedness; Greek myths told the story of Cadmus, king of Tyre, who taught the Greeks how to write, and, as the historian Herodotus tells us, the letters were called Phoenician. The Romans, who adapted the Greek alphabet for their own language, carved their inscriptions on stone in the same capital letters that we still use today.

ANCIENT NEAR EASTERN AND MEDITERRANEAN CULTURES

Modern, postindustrial societies depend, economically, on machines and sources of energy to power them. We use complex devices to produce food and clothes, to build roads and cities, to excavate natural resources (such as oil and coal), to construct nonnatural materials (such as plastics), to get from place to place, and to communicate with others across the globe. In the ancient world, most of these machines did not yet exist. Though

metal was mined and worked, there was no heavy industry as we know it. Coal and oil were not exploited for energy. War galleys were propelled by sail and human oarsmen; armies moved, sometimes vast distances, on foot. People therefore relied far more heavily on the kind of natural resources that can be easily accessed by human labor: no ancient city could be built far from fresh water and fertile soil on which to grow crops and graze animals for meat and wool. Where we use machines and fossil fuel, all the advanced civilizations of the ancient world depended for their existence on slaves, who worked the land; took care of animals and children; dug the mines; built houses, temples, pyramids, and cities; manufactured household goods (ranging from basic tableware to decorative artwork); performed housework; and provided entertainment. Modern Western societies exploit natural resources and harness them by using the cheap human labor available in less "developed" countries; most of the time, we do not even think about the people who make our clothes, phones, or cars or about the energy it takes to produce them and dispose of them. Similarly, elite ancient Hebrews, Greeks, and Romans seem to have taken slaves almost entirely for granted. The existence of ancient slavery should remind us not to idealize ancient cultures (even those of the "great Western tradition") and to remember how easily human beings, ourselves included, can be blinkered about the forms of injustice and exploitation that are essential to their cultural existence.

Because ancient societies depended on the proximity of natural resources, especially well-irrigated, fertile soil, the first civilizations of the Mediterranean basin developed in two regions that were particularly receptive to agriculture and animal husbandry. These areas were the valley of the Nile, where annual floods left large tracts of land moist and fertile

A relief from the Palace of Sargon, from the eighth century B.C.E. It shows the transport of large logs propelled by human rowers.

under the Egyptian sun, and the valleys of the Euphrates and Tigris rivers, which flowed through the Fertile Crescent, a region centered on modern Iraq. Great cities—Thebes and Memphis in Egypt and Babylon and Nineveh in the Fertile Crescent—came into being as centers for the complicated administration of the irrigated fields. Supported by the surplus the land produced, they became centers also for government, religion, and culture.

Later, from the second millennium B.C.E. onward, more cultures developed around the Mediterranean, including those of the Hebrews, the Greeks, and the Romans. These societies remained distinct from one another, and each included many separate social groups; we should be wary of generalizing about what "people in antiquity" believed or did. But it does make sense to consider the ancient Mediterranean and Near East as a single, albeit complex, unit, because there were large-scale cultural exchanges between these various peoples as a result

of trade, colonization, and imperialism. Greek sculpture and architecture of the seventh century B.C.E., for instance, owes a heavy debt to Egypt, and striking similarities between Greek and Middle Eastern myths are probably the result of Mesopotamian influence.

Most ancient cultures were polytheistic (they believed in many gods); and since crosscultural religious influence was common, gods from one place were often reinvented in another. Ancient texts that emphasize a single deity over all others are rare: the most important exceptions to the polytheistic rule are the Egyptian *Great Hymn to the Aten*, composed at a time when the Egyptian monarchy was developing a new cult to the sun god; and the **Hebrew Bible**, which featured the singular and "jealous" god who is now worshipped by many of the world's populations. But neither of these texts suggests that other gods do not exist—only that the creator deity is by far the most important and powerful. The Hebrew Bible is also unusual in

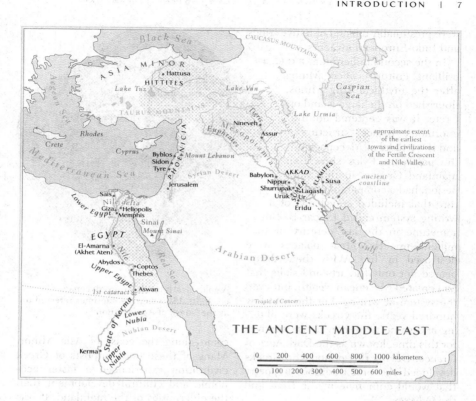

THE ANCIENT MIDDLE EAST

approximate extent of the earliest towns and civilizations of the Fertile Crescent and Nile Valley

suggesting, in the Ten Commandments, that religious observance is closely connected with the observance of a code of behavior. Ethics and religion were not necessarily linked in the ancient world, and gods of ancient literature often behave in obviously immoral ways. In many ancient cultures, religious practice ("orthopraxy") was more important than religious belief ("orthodoxy"). Religion involved a shared set of rituals and practices that united a community in shared activities such as festivals and song; few ancient cultures would have understood the idea of a religious "creed" (a formal statement outlining the specific beliefs of a particular religious community, to which all members must subscribe). Cult practices were often highly localized. We should, then, be wary of assuming that the stories about gods that appear in ancient literary texts are necessarily a record of the religious beliefs of a whole culture. Myths circulated in many different forms, changing from one place and time to another; in most ancient cultures, composing alternative stories about the gods does not seem to have been regarded as "heretical," as it might seem to a modern Jewish, Christian, or Muslim reader.

THE GREEKS

The origin of the peoples who eventually called themselves Hellenes is still a mystery. The language they spoke belongs clearly to the Indo-European family (which includes the Germanic, Celtic, Italic, and Sanskrit language groups), but many of the ancient Greek words and place names have terminations that are definitely not Indo-European—the word for "sea" (*thalassa*), for example. The Greeks of historic times were presumably a blend of native tribes and Indo-European invaders.

In the second millennium B.C.E., a brilliant culture called Minoan, after the mythical king Minos, flourished on the large island of Crete. It was centered around enormous palace structures, and the citadel of Mycenae and the palace at Pylos show that mainland Greece, in that same period, had a comparably rich culture that included knowledge of a writing system called Linear B. But sometime in the last century of the millennium, the great palaces were destroyed by fire. With them disappeared not only the arts and skills that had created Mycenean wealth, but even the system of writing. For the next few hundred years, the Greeks were illiterate and so no written evidence survives for this time, known as the Dark Ages of Greece. During this period, the Greeks developed the oral tradition of poetry that would culminate in the *Iliad* and the *Odyssey*.

The Dark Ages ended in the eighth century B.C.E., when Greece again became literate—but with a quite different alphabet, borrowed, as noted earlier, from the Phoenicians. Greece was still highly fragmented, made up of many small independent cities. These were known as "city-states" (a rendering of the Greek term *polis*, from which we get "politics"), because they were independent political and economic entities—not, like modern cities, ruled by a centralized national government. The geography of Greece—a land of mountain barriers and scattered islands—encouraged this fragmentation. The cities differed from each other in their customs, political constitutions, and even dialects: they were rivals and fierce competitors with one another. In the eighth and seventh centuries B.C.E., Greeks founded many new cities all over the Mediterranean coast, including

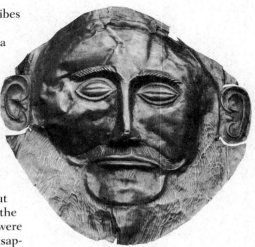

A gold "death mask" from Mycenae, ca. 1550–1500 B.C.E., sometimes referred to as the "mask of Agamemnon."

some along the coast of Asia Minor. Many of these new outposts of Greek civilization experienced a faster economic and cultural development than the older cities of the mainland. It was in the cities founded on the Asian coast that the Greeks adapted to their own language the Phoenician system of writing, adding signs for the vowels to create their alphabet. The Greeks probably first used their new written language for commercial records and transactions, but as literacy became more widespread all over the Greek world in the course of the seventh century B.C.E., treaties and political decrees were inscribed on stone, and literary works were written on rolls of paper made from the Egyptian papyrus plant.

In the sixth century B.C.E., the Persian Empire dominated the Middle East and the eastern Mediterranean Sea, eventually becoming one of the largest empires in the ancient world. Millions of people lived under Persian control, and the ruling dynasty of Persia (the Achaemenids) conducted an expansionist policy, extending their domain from

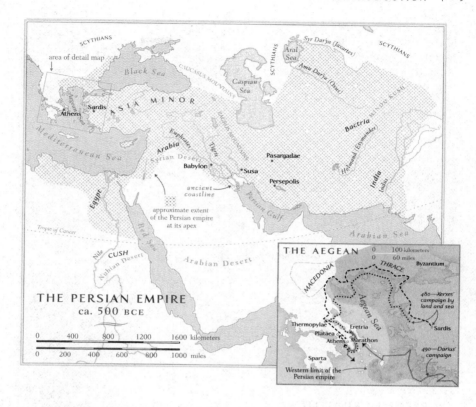

THE PERSIAN EMPIRE
ca. 500 BCE

THE AEGEAN

their capitals in Pasargadae, Susa, and finally Persepolis (in modern Iran) eastward, as far as the Indus river, and westward, into Egypt and Libya, as well as into the eastern parts of Greece, such as the cities of Ionia (in Asia Minor). The Persians had a sophisticated and globalized culture, influenced by elements from many of the other cultures they had encountered; their art was rich and intricate, and their architecture was impressively monumental. The empire was governed by a complex and highly developed political system, with the emperor at the top. The Persian army was huge and expertly trained, and it included vast numbers of skilled cavalrymen and archers. By the beginning of the fifth century B.C.E., the Persian Empire must have seemed all but unstoppable; it would have been reasonable for the Persians to assume that they could dominate

the remaining parts of Greece. But surprisingly, the Greeks—led by Athens and Sparta—managed to repel repeated Persian invasions in the years 490 to 479 B.C.E., winning decisive land and sea battles at Marathon, Salamis, and Plataea. Their astonishing victories over Persia boosted the confidence of the Greek cities in the fifth century. In the wake of this success, the Athenians produced their most important literary and cultural achievements.

Sparta was governed by a ruling elite, an oligarchy ("rule of the few") that used strict military discipline to maintain control over a majority underclass. By contrast, Attica—the city-state of which Athens was the leading city—was at this time a democracy, one of the first such states in the world. *Democracy*, which means "rule by the people," did not imply that all adult inhabitants had the chance

THRACE

Black Sea

Byzantium

Sea of Marmora

Philippi

MACEDONIA

Thasos
Samothrace

CHALCIDICE

Hellespont

ASIA MINOR

Troy (Ilium)

Thracian Sea

EPIRUS

THESSALY

Lemnos

PERSIAN EMPIRE

Corcyra

LYDIA

Leucas

Phthia

AETOLIA

Lesbos

Sardis

Ithaca

BOEOTIA

Delphi

Euboea

Chios

Ephesus

Cephalenia

ACHAEA

Thebes
Eleusis Athens

Andros

Samos

Aegean Sea

Gulf of Corinth

ATTICA

Peloponnese

Corinth

Miletus

Olympia

Zakinthos

Argos

Cyclades

Delos

Naxos

MESSENIA

LACONIA

Pylos

Sparta

Kos

Melos

Rhodes

N
W   E
S

Sea of Crete

GREECE DURING THE
PELOPONNESIAN WAR

ca. 425 B.C.E.

Crete

Mediterranean Sea

| 0   50   100   200 kilometers |
| 0 20 40 60 80 100 120 miles |

Athens and	Athenian allies		neutral Greeks
members of	and conquered	Spartan	
the Delian League	tributaries	confederacy	non-Greeks

to vote; "the people" were a small subset of the population, since women, slaves, and metics (resident aliens) were all excluded from the rights of citizenship. The citizens of Attica in the fifth century B.C.E. probably numbered only about thirty thousand, while the total population may have been ten times that. Slaves had no rights at all; they were the property of their masters. Women, even free-born women, could not own property, hold office, or vote. The elite women of Athens had less autonomy than those in most Greek city-states, including Sparta (where women were allowed to exercise outside in the gymnasium); in Athens, they were expected to remain inside the house except for funerals and religious festivals, and were rarely seen by men other than their husbands or male relatives. Moreover, even among citizens who participated in civic life on a roughly equal political footing, there were marked divisions between rich and poor, and between the rural peasant and the city dweller. Still, Athenian democracy represented a bold achievement of civic equality for those who belonged. Since

A contemporary artist's reconstruction of the Acropolis in fifth-century Athens.
The Parthenon temple is the large structure near the top of the image.

the voting population was so small, it was possible for the city to function as a direct, not representational, democracy: any citizen could attend assembly meetings and vote directly on the issues at hand, rather than electing a representative to vote in his place.

Athens's power lay in the fleet that had played such a decisive role in the struggle against Persia. The city rapidly became the leader of a naval alliance that included most of the islands of the Aegean Sea and many Greek cities on the coast of Asia Minor. This alliance, formed to defend Greece from Persia, soon became an empire, and Athens, with its formidable navy, received an annual tribute from its "allies." Unlike Athens, Sparta was rigidly conservative in government and policy. Because the individual citizen was reared and trained by the state for the state's business, war, the Spartan land army was superior to any other in Greece, and the Spartans

controlled, by direct rule or through alliances, a majority of the city-states in the Peloponnese. Athens and Sparta, allies in the war of liberation against Persia, became enemies when the external danger was eliminated. As the years went by, war between the two Greek powers came to be accepted as inevitable by both sides, and in 431 B.C.E. it began. The war ended in 404 B.C.E. with the total defeat of Athens.

During the fifth century, Athens changed culturally and politically, as the self-confidence roused by Persian victories, and celebrated by monumental displays of civic pride (such as the famous Parthenon temple to the city's patron goddess, Athena, completed in 438 B.C.E.), gave way to increasing social tensions and anxieties during the war years. But throughout this century, Athenian democracy provided its citizens with a cultural and intellectual environment that was without precedent in the ancient world. In the sixth century, Greeks on the Ionian coast had already begun to develop new, protoscientific ideas, alternatives to the old myths about how the world was made and how it functioned. Now many of the most original thinkers and writers from all over the Greek world began to gather in Athens. The fifth century was also the great age of Athenian theater: both tragedy and comedy developed and flourished at this time, and drama provided an essential outlet for the cultural confusions of the age.

In the fourth century B.C.E., the Greek city-states became involved in constant internecine warfare. Politically and economically bankrupt, they fell under the power of Macedon in the north, whose king, Philip, combined a ferocious energy with a cynicism that enabled him to take full advantage of the disunity of the city-states. Greek liberty ended at the battle of Chaeronea in 338 B.C.E., and Philip's son Alexander inherited a powerful army and political control of all Greece. He led his Macedonian and Greek armies against Persia, and in a few brilliant campaigns became master of an empire that extended into Egypt in the south and to the borders of India in the east. He died at Babylon in 323 B.C.E., and his empire broke up into a number of independent kingdoms ruled by his generals; modern scholars refer to the period that followed (323–146 B.C.E.) as the Hellenistic age. One of these generals, Ptolemy, founded a Greek dynasty that ruled Egypt until after the Roman conquest and ended only with the death of Cleopatra in 30 B.C.E. The results of Alexander's fantastic achievements were surprisingly durable. Into the newly conquered territories came thousands of Greeks who wished to escape from the political futility and economic crisis of the homeland. Wherever they went, they took with them their language, their culture, and their most characteristic buildings—the gymnasium and the theater. The great Hellenistic cities, though now part of kingdoms, grew out of the earlier city-state model and continued many of the city-state's civic and political institutions. At Alexandria, in Egypt, the Ptolemies formed a Greek library to preserve the texts of Greek literature for the scholars who studied and edited them, a school of Greek poetry flourished, and Greek geographers and mathematicians

A detail from a mosaic (dating from ca. 80 B.C.E.) discovered in Pompeii that shows Alexander the Great on horseback in battle.

made new advances in science. The Middle East became, as far as the cities were concerned, a Greek-speaking region; and when, some two or three centuries later, the first accounts of the life and teaching of Jesus of Nazareth were recorded, they were written in the simple vernacular Greek known as *koine* ("the common language"), on which the cultural homogeneity of the whole area was based.

ROME

When Alexander died in 323 B.C.E., the city of Rome was engaged in a struggle for control of the surrounding areas. By the middle of the third century B.C.E., Rome dominated most of the Italian peninsula. Expansion southward brought Rome into collision with Carthage, a city in North Africa that was then the greatest power in the western Mediterranean. Two protracted wars resulted (264–241 and 218–201 B.C.E.), and it was only at the end of a third, shorter war (149–146 B.C.E.) that the Romans destroyed their great rival. The second Carthaginian (or Punic) War was particularly hard fought, both in Spain and in Italy itself. The Carthaginian general Hannibal made a spectacular crossing of the Alps, and remained in the peninsula for years, while Rome's southern Italian allies defected to Carthage and had to be slowly won over again. Rome, however, emerged from these wars not merely victorious but a world power. The next two decades saw frequent wars—in Spain, in Greece, and in Asia Minor—that laid the foundations of the Roman Empire.

Unlike Athens, Rome was never a democracy. Instead, from around 509 B.C.E.—when, according to legend, the last tyrannical king of Rome had been overthrown—the state was governed by a complex political system (which changed and developed over time) known as a republic. Power was shared among several different official groups of people, which included the Senate, a body that controlled money and administration, traditionally dominated by the upper classes; the Assemblies, gathered from the people, including lower-class or "plebeian" citizens; and elected officials called Magistrates, the most important of whom were the two Consuls, elected every year. The system (one of the most important models for the United States Constitution many centuries later) was designed above all to prevent any single person or group from seizing total control. The republic would last until the time of the Roman civil wars, in the first century B.C.E.

The Greeks believed that arguing, strife, and competition can be good, since they inspire us to outdo others and improve ourselves. The Romans, by contrast, saw conflict as deadly: it was what, in Roman mythology, led the founder of their city, Romulus, to kill his twin brother, Remus. Whereas the Athenians prided themselves on adaptability, versatility, and grace, the Roman idea of personal and civic virtue was based on a sense of tradition, a myth of old Roman virtue and integrity. "By her ancient customs and her men the Roman state stands," wrote Ennius, a Roman epic poet, capturing an ethos that emphasized tradition (known as the *mos maiorum*, the custom of predecessors) and commended "seriousness" (*gravitas*), "manly courage" (*virtus*), "industry" (*diligentia*), and above all, "duty" (*pietas*). Roman power was built on efficiency, and strength through unity. The Romans organized a complicated yet stable federation that held Italy loyal to them in the presence of invading armies, and they developed a legal code that formed the model for all later European and American law. The achievements of the Romans, in conquest and in organizing their empire after victory, were due in large part to their

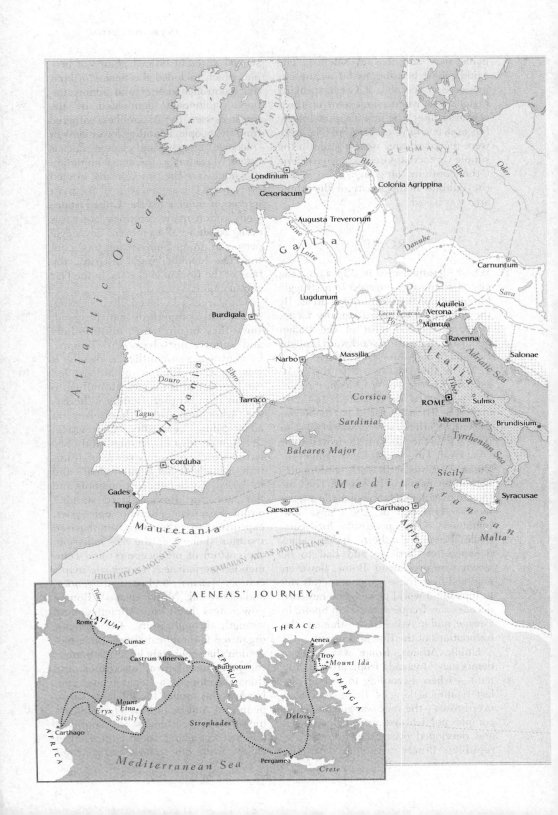

Londinium
Gesoriacum
Augusta Treverorum
Colonia Agrippina
GERMANIA
Rhine
Elbe
Oder
Britannia
Atlantic Ocean
Gallia
Seine
Loire
Danube
Carnuntum
Sava
ALPS
Lugdunum
Lacus Benacus
Po
Aquileia
Verona
Mantua
Ravenna
Salonae
Burdigala
Narbo
Massilia
Italia
Adriatic Sea
Hispania
Douro
Ebro
Tarraco
Corsica
Sardinia
Tiber
ROME
Sulmo
Misenum
Brundisium
Tagus
Tyrrhenian Sea
Corduba
Baleares Major
Mediterranean
Sicily
Syracusae
Gades
Tingi
Caesarea
Carthago
Africa
Malta
Mauretania
HIGH ATLAS MOUNTAINS
SAHARAN ATLAS MOUNTAINS

AENEAS' JOURNEY

Tiber
Rome
LATIUM
Cumae
Castrum Minervae
Buthrotum
EPIRUS
THRACE
Aenea
Troy
Mount Ida
PHRYGIA
Mount
Etna
Eryx
Sicily
Delos
Strophades
AFRICA
Carthago
Pergamea
Crete
Mediterranean Sea

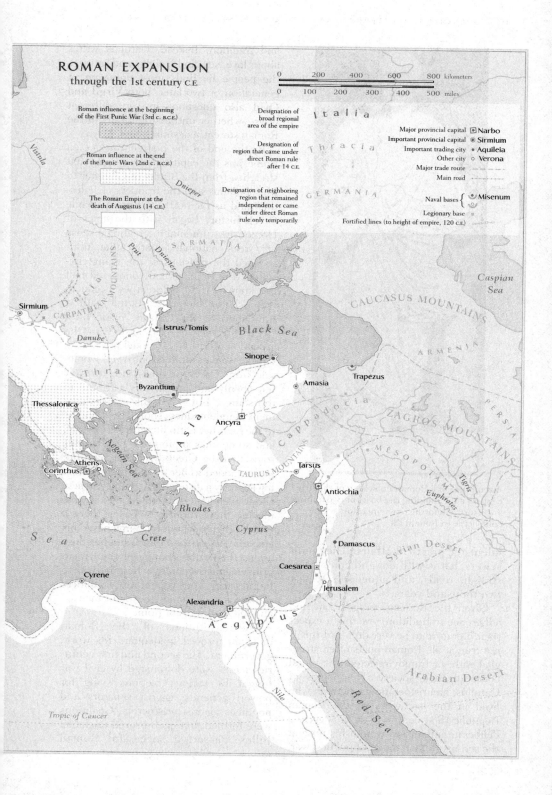

ROMAN EXPANSION
through the 1st century C.E.

Roman influence at the beginning
of the First Punic War (3rd c. B.C.E.)

Roman influence at the end
of the Punic Wars (2nd c. B.C.E.)

The Roman Empire at the
death of Augustus (14 C.E.)

Designation of
broad regional
area of the empire

Designation of
region that came under
direct Roman rule
after 14 C.E.

Designation of neighboring
region that remained
independent or came
under direct Roman
rule only temporarily

Major provincial capital	⊡ Narbo
Important provincial capital	◉ Sirmium
Important trading city	• Aquileia
Other city	○ Verona
Major trade route	
Main road	
Naval bases {	Misenum
Legionary base	
Fortified lines (to height of empire, 120 C.E.)	

0   200   400   600   800 kilometers
0   100   200   300   400   500 miles

Vistula

Italia

Thracia

GERMANIA

Dnieper

SARMATIA

Prut   Dniester

D a c i a
CARPATHIAN MOUNTAINS

Sirmium

Danube

Istrus/Tomis

Black Sea

Caspian
Sea

CAUCASUS MOUNTAINS

T h r a c i a

Sinope

Amasia

Trapezus

ARMENIA

Byzantium

Thessalonica

A s i a

Ancyra

C a p p a d o c i a

ZAGROS MOUNTAINS

PERSIA

Aegean Sea

TAURUS MOUNTAINS

Tarsus

MESOPOTAMIA

Athens

Corinthus

Antiochia

Tigris

Euphrates

Rhodes

Cyprus

S e a

Crete

Damascus

Syrian Desert

Cyrene

Caesarea

Jerusalem

Alexandria

A e g y p t u s

Nile

Tropic of Cancer

Arabian Desert

Red Sea

A sculpture of a Roman nobleman of the first century B.C.E. holding the busts of two of his ancestors. Honoring one's ancestors was a core virtue in Roman life.

talent for practical affairs. They built sewers, baths with hot and cold water, straight roads, and aqueducts to last two thousand years.

Given the Romans' pragmatism and adherence to tradition, one might expect their literature to be very dull. But this is not true at all. Roman poets often struggled with, or frankly rejected, the moral codes of their society. The poems of Catullus, an aristocratic young man who lived in the last years of the Roman Republic (first century B.C.E.), suggest a deliberate attempt to thumb his nose at the serious Roman topics of politics, war, and tradition. Instead, Catullus writes about love, sex, and feelings and satirizes the people he finds most annoying. A generation or two later, both **Virgil** and **Ovid** also question—in very different ways—whether unthinking loyalty to the Roman state is a desirable goal.

By the end of the first century B.C.E., Rome was the capital of an empire that stretched from the Straits of Gibraltar to Mesopotamia and the frontiers of Palestine, and as far north as Britain. While Greek history began with the epics of Homer (instrumental in creating a sense of Greek national identity that transcended the divisions of the many city-states), the Romans had conquered half the known world before they began to write. Latin literature started with a translation of the *Odyssey*, made by a Greek prisoner of war; and, with the exception of satire, the model was always Greek. Roman authors borrowed wholesale from Greek originals, not furtively but openly and proudly, as a tribute to the source. But this frank acknowledgment of indebtedness should not blind us to the fact that Latin literature is original, and sometimes profoundly so. Catullus translated the Greek lyric poet **Sappho**, but he added to her evocation of agonizing jealousy a distinctively Roman anxiety about idleness. Ovid retold Greek myths, making them funnier by giving them a Roman rhetorical punch. Virgil based his epic, the *Aeneid*, on Homer, but he chose as his theme the coming of the Trojan prince Aeneas to Italy, where he was to found a city from which, in the fullness of time, would come "the Latin race . . . and the high walls of Rome."

The institutions of the Roman city-state proved inadequate for world government. The second and first centuries B.C.E. were dominated by civil war fought by various factions vying for power: generals against senators and populists against aristocrats. Coalitions were formed, but each proved unstable. Julius Caesar, a successful Roman general, seized power (although he refused the title "king"); but he was assassinated in 44 B.C.E. by a party hoping to restore the old system of shared rule. More years of civil war followed, until finally, in 31 B.C.E., Julius's adoptive nephew, Octavian—who later titled himself Augustus—managed to defeat the ruler of the eastern half of the empire, Mark Antony, along with Antony's ally and lover, Cleopatra, queen of Egypt. Augustus played his hand carefully, claiming that he was restoring the Republic; but he assumed primary control of the state and became the first in the long line of Roman emperors.

For the next two hundred years, the successors of Augustus, the Roman emperors, ruled the Mediterranean and Middle Eastern world. The empire covered a vast area that included Britain, France, all southern Europe, the Middle East, and the whole of North Africa. Some native inhabitants in all these areas were killed by the Romans; others were enslaved; many, both slave and free, were Romanized, acculturated into the norms of the Roman people. Roman culture stamped this whole area of the world in ways that can still be discerned today: the Romans built roads, cities, public baths, and theaters, and they brought their literature and language—Latin—to the provinces they ruled. All modern Romance languages, including Spanish, French, and Italian, developed from the language spoken throughout the Roman Empire.

But controlling so many people, in so many different areas, from the central government in Rome was difficult and expensive. It could not be done forever. Marcus Aurelius (121–180 C.E.), who in his spare time wrote a beautiful book of thoughts about his struggle to live a good life (the *Meditations*), was the first emperor to share his power with a partner; this was the first official recognition that the empire was too big to be ruled by one man. The Romans fought a long losing battle against invading tribes from the north and east. When it finally fell, the empire left behind it the idea of the world-state, later adopted by the medieval church, which ruled from the same center, Rome, and which claimed a spiritual authority as great as the secular authority it replaced.

THE EPIC OF GILGAMESH

ca. 1900–250 B.C.E.

The Epic of Gilgamesh is the great-est work of ancient Mesopotamia and one of the earliest pieces of world literature. The story of its main protag-onist, King Gilgamesh, and his quest for immortality touches on the most fun-damental questions of what it means to be human: death and friendship, nature and civilization, power and violence, travel adventures and homecoming, love and sexuality. Because of the appeal of its central hero and his struggle with the meaning of culture in the face of human mortality, the epic spread throughout the ancient Near East and was translated into various regional languages during the second millennium B.C.E. As far as we know, no other literary work of the ancient world spread so widely across cultures and languages. And yet, after a long period of popularity, *Gilgamesh* was forgotten, seemingly for good: after circulating in various versions for many centuries, it vanished from human mem-ory for over two thousand years. Its redis-covery by archaeologists in the nineteenth century was a sensation and allows us to read a story that for many centuries was known to many cultures and people throughout the Near East but has come down to us today only by chance on brit-tle clay tablets.

KING GILGAMESH AND HIS STORY

Gilgamesh was thought to be a priest-king of the city-state of Uruk in south-ern Mesopotamia, the lands around the rivers Euphrates and Tigris in modern-day Iraq. He probably ruled around 2700 B.C.E. and was remembered for the building of Uruk's monumental city walls, which were ten kilometers (six miles) long and fitted with nine hundred towers; portions of these walls are still visible today. We will never know for sure how the historical king compares to the epic hero Gilgamesh. But soon after his death, he was vener-ated as a great king and judge of the Underworld. In the epic he appears as "two-thirds . . . divine" and "one-third . . . human," the offspring of Ninsun, a goddess in the shape of a wild cow, and a human father named Lugal-banda. By some accounts, *Gilgamesh* means "the offspring is a hero," or, according to another etymology, "the old man is still a young man."

Gilgamesh was not written by one specific author but evolved gradually over the long span of a millennium. The earliest story of Gilgamesh appears around 2100 B.C.E. in a cycle of poems in the Sumerian language. Sumerian is the earliest Mesopotamian language. It is written in cuneiform script— wedge-shaped characters incised in clay or stone—and has no connection to any other known language. About six hundred years after Gilgamesh's death, kings of the third dynasty of Ur, another Mesopotamian city-state, claimed descent from the legendary king of Uruk and enjoyed hearing of the great deeds of Gilgamesh at court; the earliest cycle of Gilgamesh poems was written for these rulers. As in the later epic, in the Sumerian cycle of poems Gilgamesh is a powerful king and an awe-inspiring warrior. Gil-gamesh's shattering realization that he will die and can attain immortality only by making a name for himself appears already in this earliest version of the Gilgamesh story, where he exclaims:

> I have peered over the city wall,
> I have seen the corpses floating in
> the river's water.
> So too it will come to pass for me,
> so it will happen to me . . .
> Since no man can avoid life's end,
> I would enter the mountain land
> and set up my name.

The Sumerian poetry cycle became the basis for the old version of *Gilgamesh,* written in Babylonian, a variant of the Akkadian language—a transnational written language that was widely used throughout the ancient Near East. The traditional Babylonian epic version of *Gilgamesh,* which adapted the Sumerian poems into a connected narrative, circulated for more than fifteen hundred years. It was read widely from Mesopotamia to Syria, the Levant, and Anatolia and was translated into non-Mesopotamian languages such as Hittite, the language of an empire that controlled Turkey and northern Syria in the latter half of the second millennium B.C.E.

The definitive revision of the epic is attributed to a Babylonian priest and scholar named Sin-leqi-unninni. He lived around 1200 B.C.E., and by his time King Gilgamesh had been dead for about fifteen hundred years. He carefully selected elements from the older traditions, inserted new plot elements, and added a preface to the epic. His version, included here in translation, is divided into eleven chapters recorded on eleven clay tablets. New fragments of *Gilgamesh* continue to surface from archaeological excavations; some pieces are still missing, and some passages are fragmentary and barely legible, but thanks to the painstaking work of scholars of ancient Mesopotamia we can today read an extended, gripping narrative.

THE WORLD'S OLDEST EPIC HERO

The Gilgamesh of the epic is an awe-inspiring, sparkling hero, but at first also the epitome of a bad ruler: arrogant, oppressive, and brutal. As the epic begins, the people of Uruk complain to the Sumerian gods about Gilgamesh's overbearing behavior, and so the gods create the wild man Enkidu to confront Gilgamesh. While Gilgamesh is a mixture of human and divine, Enkidu is a blend of human and wild animal, though godlike in his own way. He is raised by beasts in the wilderness and eats what they eat. When he breaks hunters' traps for the sake of his animal companions he becomes a threat to human society and Gilgamesh decides to tame him with the attractions of urban life and civilization: for seven days Enkidu makes love to a harlot (prostitute), sent out for the purpose, and at her urging he takes a cleansing bath and accepts clothing and a first meal of basic human foodstuff, bread and beer. Shamhat, the prostitute, leads him to the city of Uruk. Although he and Gilgamesh are at first bent on competing with each other, they quickly develop a deep bond of friendship.

Their friendship established, Gilgamesh proposes to Enkidu the first of their epic adventures: to travel to the great Cedar Forest and slay the giant Humbaba, who guards the forest for the harsh god Enlil. With the blessing of the sun god Shamash they succeed, and they cut down some magnificent trees that they float down the Euphrates River to Mesopotamia. But their violent act has its consequence: the dying giant curses them and Enlil is enraged. Their second adventure leads to a yet more ambiguous success, which will set in motion the tragic end of their friendship. Gilgamesh, cleansed from battle and radiant in victory, attracts the desire of Ishtar, goddess of love and warfare. Instead of

This modern impression of an ancient cylinder seal shows a bearded hero, kneeling and raising an outstretched lion above his head.

politely resisting her advances, Gilgamesh makes the fatal error of chiding her for her fickle passions and known cruelty toward her lovers, and heaps insults on the goddess. Scandalized by Gilgamesh's accusations, she unleashes the Bull of Heaven against the two friends, and it wreaks havoc in Uruk. After the heroic duo kills the Bull of Heaven, a council of the gods convenes to avoid further disaster. In a gap in the text, the gods decide that Gilgamesh and Enkidu have gone too far; one of them must die. The lot falls to Enkidu, because Gilgamesh is the king.

Enkidu's death brings Gilgamesh face to face with mortality. He mourns for Enkidu bitterly for seven days and nights and only when a worm creeps out of the corpse's nose does he accept that his friend is dead. Terrified that he too will die, Gilgamesh forsakes the civilized world to find the one human being known to have achieved immortality: Utanapishtim, survivor of the Great Flood. Like Enkidu in his days as a wild man, Gilgamesh roams the steppe, disheveled and clad in a lionskin, and sets out on a quest to ask Utanapishtim for the secret of eternal life. He braves monsters, runs along the sun's path under the earth at night, encounters a mysterious woman who keeps a tavern at the edge of the world, passes a garden of jeweled trees, crosses the waters of death, and finally arrives at the doorstep of Utanapishtim and his wife. Utanapishtim's dramatic account of their experience and survival of the flood resembles the biblical story of Noah and the Great Flood in **Genesis**. At his wife's request, Utanapishtim gives Gilgamesh the chance to attain immortality by eating a magic plant, but he is afraid to try it and a serpent steals the magic plant and gains the power of immortality for itself. In the end Gilgamesh returns to Uruk, empty-handed. Although in the final moments of the epic he proudly surveys the mighty city walls of his making, he is a profoundly changed man.

AN ANCIENT EPIC

The word *epic* is originally Greek and refers to a long poem narrating important historical or cosmic events in elevated language and involving a panoramic sweep of action and a cast of protagonists who straddle the human and divine worlds. Some epics, like **Homer's Iliad**, tell of the foundation or destruction of civilizations or cities, featuring noisy battle scenes, in which the heroes can prove their strength, wisdom, and understanding of the workings of the divine order. Other epics, like **Homer's Odyssey**, focus on the travels and adventures of a central protagonist. Greek epics usually invoke the Muses, goddesses in charge of the arts and a poet's inspiration, who inform the poets of past events and the world of the gods. Epics often include long speeches, in which protagonists remember past events or justify future actions. And they rely heavily on the repetition of lines with variation and on a rhetoric of parallels and contrasts. Scholars of Homeric epic have argued that repetition and formulaic expression helped the bards to remember and recite extensive storylines and pointed to the poems' oral and performative roots.

Gilgamesh shares a few fundamental features with Greek epic. True, there was no concept in Mesopotamia corresponding to the Western literary genre "epic," and *Gilgamesh* has no equivalent to the strict hexameter of Greek epic. A verse line in *Gilgamesh* is not defined by a fixed number of syllables or stresses but varies in length, which can only be inferred by context, such as patterns of parallelism. Still, in contrast to the literary works of other civilizations of the ancient world that had no epic, like China and East Asia, *Gilgamesh* can be considered part of a larger Near Eastern and Mediterranean epic tradition. Although *Gilgamesh* was only translated into cuneiform languages and never directly entered the epic repertoire of alphabet languages like Greek, it shared with the Greek tradition a number of classically epic motifs. In Achilles'

mourning for his friend Patroclus (in Homer's *Iliad*) we can recognize Gilgamesh's desperation at the loss of Enkidu. Just as Gilgamesh finally returns to Uruk after challenging adventures, Odysseus (in Homer's *Odyssey*) returns to Ithaca from the Trojan War in the guise of a destitute stranger after performing dangerous feats. In *Gilgamesh* and Greek epics, scenes featuring councils of the gods who decide the fate of their heroes reflect religious beliefs about the intersection between human limitations and divine powers but are also astute plot devices that sharpen the profile of the heroes and their ways of confronting divine antagonism. We can see a parallel to the wiliness of the Greek gods and their personal preferences in the opposition of Shamash and Enlil, in particular in Enlil's argument that Enkidu should be sacrificed and Gilgamesh spared.

In contrast to the orally rooted Homeric epic, *Gilgamesh* was from the outset conceived as a literary work. With its elevated style, geometrically parallel phrases, and moments of complex word play, *Gilgamesh* was addressed to the sophisticated ears and minds of scholars and members of the royal court. We know that it was used in Babylonian schools to teach literature. This hypothesis is further supported when we look at the nuanced use of speech registers in the epic's portrayal of its protagonists. Utanapishtim speaks in an obscure archaic style that befits a sage from before the Great Flood, and he has a solemn way of rolling and doubling his consonants. The goddess Ishtar appears in an unfavorable light, talking like a low-class streetwalker. In contrast, Shamhat, the prostitute who brings Enkidu to the city, speaks with unexpected eloquence and distinction.

Shamhat is a thought-provoking example of the several powerful female protagonists in *Gilgamesh*. Much of what Gilgamesh accomplishes is ultimately due to women: his mother's pleas with the sun god Shamash allow him to kill Humbaba; the wife of the scorpion monster persuades her husband to give Gilgamesh entrance to the tunnel leading to the jeweled garden; and the mysterious woman he finds at the end of the world, the tavern keeper Siduri, helps him find Utanapishtim, whose wife persuades her husband to give Gilgamesh the plant of rejuvenation. In some of Gilgamesh's encounters there are touches of wit and parody. It is stunning to find this blend of epic grandeur and comic sobriety in the world's earliest epic. Part of the epic's subtlety is invisible today, because we know so much less about the historical and literary context of *Gilgamesh* than we know about the context of Greek epic. Still, the glimpses we get show the sophistication of the early Mesopotamian states and the art of literary narrative they developed.

Like Mesopotamian civilization and its cuneiform writing system, *Gilgamesh* eventually disappeared. In the seventh century B.C.E., when an invading force of ancient Iranian people called Medians sacked Nineveh, one of the capitals of the Assyrian Empire, copies of the epic written on clay tablets, which had been preserved in the palace library of Ashurbanipal, the last great Assyrian king (reigned 668–627 B.C.E.), vanished in the destruction. Although the epic did not disappear

completely and still circulated until the third century B.C.E., it was only rediscovered in the 1850s, when an English explorer, Austen Henry Layard, dug up thousands of tablets from the site at Nineveh. They were later deciphered at the British Museum in London, and when the young curator George Smith made the stunning discovery that this epic contained a version of the biblical story of the flood, which had hitherto been considered unique to the book of Genesis, this challenged conceptions about the origin of biblical narrative. *Gilgamesh* was suddenly propelled into the canon of world literature.

The Epic of Gilgamesh took shape many centuries before the Greeks and Hebrews learned how to write, and it circulated in the Near East and Levant long before the book of Genesis and the Homeric epics took shape. The rediscovery of the names of the gods and humans who people the epic and of the history of the cities and lands in which they lived is a gradual, ongoing process. And the meaning of the epic itself is tantalizingly ambiguous. Has Gilgamesh succeeded or failed in his quest? What makes us human? Can civilization bring immortality? Whatever we decide to believe, the story of Gilgamesh and his companion Enkidu, of their quest for fame and immortality, speaks to contemporary readers with an urgency and immediacy that makes us forget just how ancient it is.

The Epic of Gilgamesh[1]

Tablet I

He who saw the wellspring, the foundations of the land,
Who knew the ways, was wise in all things,
Gilgamesh, who saw the wellspring, the foundations of the land,
He knew the ways, was wise in all things,
He it was who inspected holy places everywhere,   5

---

1. Translated by and with footnotes adapted from Benjamin R. Foster.

Full understanding of it all he gained,
He saw what was secret and revealed what was hidden,
He brought back tidings from before the flood,
From a distant journey came home, weary, at peace,
Engraved all his hardships on a monument of stone,   10
He built the walls of ramparted Uruk,[2]
The lustrous treasury of hallowed Eanna!
See its upper wall, whose facing gleams like copper,
Gaze at the lower course, which nothing will equal,
Mount the stone stairway, there from days of old,   15
Approach Eanna, the dwelling of Ishtar,
Which no future king, no human being will equal.
Go up, pace out the walls of Uruk,
Study the foundation terrace and examine the brickwork.
Is not its masonry of kiln-fired brick?   20
And did not seven masters lay its foundations?
One square mile of city, one square mile of gardens,
One square mile of clay pits, a half square mile of Ishtar's dwelling,
Three and a half square miles is the measure of Uruk!
Search out the foundation box of copper,   25
Release its lock of bronze,
Raise the lid upon its hidden contents,
Take up and read from the lapis tablet
Of him, Gilgamesh, who underwent many hardships.
Surpassing all kings, for his stature renowned,   30
Heroic offspring of Uruk, a charging wild bull,
He leads the way in the vanguard,
He marches at the rear, defender of his comrades.
Mighty floodwall, protector of his troops,
Furious flood-wave smashing walls of stone,   35
Wild calf of Lugalbanda, Gilgamesh is perfect in strength,
Suckling of the sublime wild cow, the woman Ninsun,[3]
Towering Gilgamesh is uncannily perfect.
Opening passes in the mountains,
Digging wells at the highlands' verge,   40
Traversing the ocean, the vast sea, to the sun's rising,
Exploring the furthest reaches of the earth,
Seeking everywhere for eternal life,
Reaching in his might Utanapishtim the Distant One,
Restorer of holy places that the deluge had destroyed,   45
Founder of rites for the teeming peoples,
Who could be his like for kingly virtue?
And who, like Gilgamesh, can proclaim, "I am king!"
Gilgamesh was singled out from the day of his birth,

---

2. City-state ruled by King Gilgamesh. It was the largest city of Mesopotamia at the time and among its important temples featured Eanna, a sanctuary for the goddess of love and warfare, Ishtar.
3. Lugalbanda, Gilgamesh's father, was an earlier king of Uruk. His mother was Ninsun, a goddess called "the wild cow."

Two-thirds of him was divine, one-third of him was human!   50
The Lady of Birth drew his body's image,
The God of Wisdom brought his stature to perfection.

He was perfection in height,
Ideally handsome

In the enclosure of Uruk he strode back and forth,   55
Lording it like a wild bull, his head thrust high.
The onslaught of his weapons had no equal.
His teammates stood forth by his game stick,
He was harrying the young men of Uruk beyond reason.
Gilgamesh would leave no son to his father,   60
Day and night he would rampage fiercely.
This was the shepherd of ramparted Uruk,
This was the people's shepherd,
Bold, superb, accomplished, and mature!
Gilgamesh would leave no girl to her mother!   65
The warrior's daughter, the young man's spouse,
Goddesses kept hearing their plaints.
The gods of heaven, the lords who command,
Said to Anu:[4]

> You created this headstrong wild bull in ramparted Uruk,   70
> The onslaught of his weapons has no equal.
> His teammates stand forth by his game stick,
> He is harrying the young men of Uruk beyond reason.
> Gilgamesh leaves no son to his father!
> Day and night he rampages fiercely.   75
> This is the shepherd of ramparted Uruk,
> This is the people's shepherd,
> Bold, superb, accomplished, and mature!
> Gilgamesh leaves no girl to her mother!

The warrior's daughter, the young man's spouse,   80
Anu kept hearing their plaints.

[*Anu speaks.*]

> Let them summon Aruru,[5] the great one,
> She created the boundless human race.
> Let her create a partner for Gilgamesh, mighty in strength,
> Let them contend with each other, that Uruk may have peace.   85

They summoned the birth goddess, Aruru:

> You, Aruru, created the boundless human race,
> Now, create what Anu commanded,

---

4. The sky god who is supreme in the pantheon but remote from human affairs. Uruk

was known for its temples for Anu and Ishtar.
5. Goddess of birth.

To his stormy heart, let that one be equal,
Let them contend with each other, that Uruk may have peace.   90

When Aruru heard this,
She conceived within her what Anu commanded.
Aruru wet her hands,
She pinched off clay, she tossed it upon the steppe,
She created valiant Enkidu in the steppe,   95
Offspring of potter's clay, with the force of the hero Ninurta.[6]
Shaggy with hair was his whole body,
He was made lush with head hair, like a woman,
The locks of his hair grew thick as a grainfield.
He knew neither people nor inhabited land,   100
He dressed as animals do.
He fed on grass with gazelles,
With beasts he jostled at the water hole,
With wildlife he drank his fill of water.

A hunter, a trapping-man,   105
Encountered him at the edge of the water hole.
One day, a second, and a third he encountered him at the edge
   of the water hole.
When he saw him, the hunter stood stock-still with terror,
As for Enkidu, he went home with his beasts.
Aghast, struck dumb,   110
His heart in a turmoil, his face drawn,
With woe in his vitals,
His face like a traveler's from afar,
The hunter made ready to speak, saying to his father:

   My father, there is a certain fellow who has come
      from the uplands,   115
   He is the mightiest in the land, strength is his,
   Like the force of heaven, so mighty is his strength.
   He constantly ranges over the uplands,
   Constantly feeding on grass with beasts,
   Constantly making his way to the edge of the water hole.   120
   I am too frightened to approach him.
   He has filled in the pits I dug,
   He has torn out my traps I set,
   He has helped the beasts, wildlife of the steppe, slip
      from my hands,
   He will not let me work the steppe.   125

His father made ready to speak, saying to the hunter:

   My son, in Uruk dwells Gilgamesh,
   There is no one more mighty than he.
   Like the force of heaven, so mighty is his strength.

---

6. A god of agriculture and war. Son of Enlil.

Take the road, set off towards Uruk,   130
Tell Gilgamesh of the mightiness-man.
He will give you Shamhat the harlot, take her with you,
Let her prevail over him, instead of a mighty man.
When the wild beasts draw near the water hole,
Let her strip off her clothing, laying bare her charms.   135
When he sees her, he will approach her.
His beasts that grew up with him on the steppe will deny him.

Giving heed to the advice of his father,
The hunter went forth.
He took the road, set off towards Uruk,   140
To the king, Gilgamesh, he said these words:

There is a certain fellow who has come from the uplands,
He is mightiest in the land, strength is his,
Like the force of heaven, so mighty is his strength.
He constantly ranges over the uplands,   145
Constantly feeding on grass with his beasts,
Constantly making his way to the edge of the water hole.
I am too frightened to approach him.
He has filled in the pits I dug,
He has torn out my traps I set,   150
He has helped the beasts, wildlife of the steppe, slip
    from my hands,
He will not allow me to work the steppe.

Gilgamesh said to him, to the hunter:

Go, hunter, take with you Shamhat the harlot,
When the wild beasts draw near the water hole,
Let her strip off her clothing, laying bare her charms.   155
When he sees her, he will approach her,
His beasts that grew up with him on the steppe will deny him.

Forth went the hunter, taking with him Shamhat the harlot,
They took the road, going straight on their way.   160
On the third day they arrived at the appointed place.
Hunter and harlot sat down to wait.
One day, a second day, they sat by the edge of the water hole,
The beasts came to the water hole to drink,
The wildlife came to drink their fill of water.   165
But as for him, Enkidu, born in the uplands,
Who feeds on grass with gazelles,
Who drinks at the water hole with beasts,
Who, with wildlife, drinks his fill of water,
Shamhat looked upon him, a human-man,   170
A barbarous fellow from the midst of the steppe:

There he is, Shamhat, open your embrace,
Open your embrace, let him take your charms!
Be not bashful, take his vitality!

When he sees you, he will approach you,   175
Toss aside your clothing, let him lie upon you,
Treat him, a human, to woman's work!
His wild beasts that grew up with him will deny him,
As in his ardor he caresses you!

Shamhat loosened her garments,   180
She exposed her loins, he took her charms.
She was not bashful, she took his vitality.
She tossed aside her clothing and he lay upon her,
She treated him, a human, to woman's work,
As in his ardor he caressed her.   185
Six days, seven nights was Enkidu aroused, flowing into Shamhat.
After he had his fill of her delights,
He set off towards his beasts.
When they saw him, Enkidu, the gazelles shied off,
The wild beasts of the steppe shunned his person.   190
Enkidu had spent himself, his body was limp,
His knees stood still, while his beasts went away.
Enkidu was too slow, he could not run as before,
But he had gained reason and expanded his understanding.

He returned, he sat at the harlot's feet,   195
The harlot gazed upon his face,
While he listened to what the harlot was saying.
The harlot said to him, to Enkidu:

> You are handsome, Enkidu, you are become like a god,
> Why roam the steppe with wild beasts?   200
> Come, let me lead you to ramparted Uruk,
> To the holy temple, abode of Anu and Ishtar,
> The place of Gilgamesh, who is perfect in strength,
> And so, like a wild bull, he lords it over the young men.

As she was speaking to him, her words found favor,   205
He was yearning for one to know his heart, a friend.
Enkidu said to her, to the harlot:

> Come, Shamhat, escort me
> To the lustrous hallowed temple, abode of Anu and Ishtar,
> The place of Gilgamesh, who is perfect in strength,   210
> And so, like a wild bull, he lords it over the young men.
> I myself will challenge him, I will speak out boldly,
> I will raise a cry in Uruk: I am the mighty one!
> I am come forward to alter destinies!
> He who was born in the steppe is mighty, strength is his!   215

[*Shamhat speaks.*]

> Come then, let him see your face,
> I will show you Gilgamesh, where he is I know full well.
> Come then, Enkidu, to ramparted Uruk,

> Where fellows are resplendent in holiday clothing,
> Where every day is set for celebration,   220
> Where harps and drums are played.
> And the harlots too, they are fairest of form,
> Rich in beauty, full of delights,
> Even the great gods are kept from sleeping at night!
> Enkidu, you who have not learned to live,   225
> Oh, let me show you Gilgamesh, the joy-woe man.
> Look at him, gaze upon his face,
> He is radiant with virility, manly vigor is his,
> The whole of his body is seductively gorgeous.
> Mightier strength has he than you,   230
> Never resting by day or night.
> O Enkidu, renounce your audacity!
> Gilgamesh is beloved of Shamash,
> Anu, Enlil, and Ea broadened his wisdom.[7]
> Ere you come down from the uplands,   235
> Gilgamesh will dream of you in Uruk.

[*The scene shifts to Uruk.*]

Gilgamesh went to relate the dreams, saying to his mother:

> Mother, I had a dream last night:
> There were stars of heaven around me,
> Like the force of heaven, something kept falling upon me!   240
> I tried to carry it but it was too strong for me,
> I tried to move it but I could not budge it.
> The whole of Uruk was standing by it,
> The people formed a crowd around it,
> A throng was jostling towards it,   245
> Young men were mobbed around it,
> Infantile, they were groveling before it!
> [I fell in love with it], like a woman I caressed it,
> I carried it off and laid it down before you,
> Then you were making it my partner.   250

The mother of Gilgamesh, knowing and wise,
Who understands everything, said to her son,
Ninsun the wild cow, knowing and wise,
Who understands everything, said to Gilgamesh:

> The stars of heaven around you,   255
> Like the force of heaven, what kept falling upon you,
> Your trying to move it but not being able to budge it,
> Your laying it down before me,
> Then my making it your partner,
> Your falling in love with it, your caressing it like a woman,   260

---

7. Shamash was god of the sun and of oracles, overseeing matters of justice and right dealing; Enlil was supreme god on earth; Ea, a god of wisdom and magic, is known for his beneficence to the human race.

Means there will come to you a strong one,
A companion who rescues a friend.
He will be mighty in the land, strength will be his,
Like the force of heaven, so mighty will be his strength.
You will fall in love with him and caress him like a woman.   265
He will be mighty and rescue you, time and again.

He had a second dream,
He arose and went before the goddess, his mother,
Gilgamesh said to her, to his mother:

    Mother, I had a second dream.   270
    An axe was thrown down in a street of ramparted Uruk,
    They were crowding around it,
    The whole of Uruk was standing by it,
    The people formed a crowd around it,
    A throng was jostling towards it.   275
    I carried it off and laid it down before you,
    I fell in love with it, like a woman I caressed it,
    Then you were making it my partner.

The mother of Gilgamesh, knowing and wise,
Who understands everything, said to her son,   280
Ninsun the wild cow, knowing and wise,
Who understands everything, said to Gilgamesh:

    My son, the axe you saw is a man.
    Your loving it like a woman and caressing it,
    And my making it your partner   285
    Means there will come to you a strong one,
    A companion who rescues a friend,
    He will be mighty in the land, strength will be his,
    Like the strength of heaven, so mighty will be his strength.

Gilgamesh said to her, to his mother: 290

    Let this befall according to the command of the great
      counselor Enlil,
    I want a friend for my own counselor,
    For my own counselor do I want a friend!

Even while he was having his dreams,
Shamhat was telling the dreams of Gilgamesh to Enkidu,   295
Each was drawn by love to the other.

Tablet II

While Enkidu was seated before her,
Each was drawn by love to the other.
Enkidu forgot the steppe where he was born,
For six days, seven nights Enkidu was aroused and flowed
    into Shamhat.
The harlot said to him, to Enkidu: 5

You are handsome, Enkidu, you are become like a god,
Why roam the steppe with wild beasts?
Come, let me lead you to ramparted Uruk,
To the holy temple, abode of Anu,
Let me lead you to ramparted Uruk,   10
To hallowed Eanna, abode of Ishtar,
The place of Gilgamesh, who is perfect in strength,
And so, like a wild bull, he lords it over the people.
You are just like him,
You will love him like your own self.   15
Come away from this desolation, bereft even of shepherds.

He heard what she said, accepted her words,
He was yearning for one to know his heart, a friend.
The counsel of Shamhat touched his heart.
She took off her clothing, with one piece she dressed him,   20
The second she herself put on.
Clasping his hand, like a guardian deity she led him,
To the shepherds' huts, where a sheepfold was,
The shepherds crowded around him,
They murmured their opinions among themselves: 25

    This fellow, how like Gilgamesh in stature,
    In stature tall, proud as a battlement.
    No doubt he was born in the steppe,
    Like the force of heaven, mighty is his strength.

They set bread before him,   30
They set beer before him.
He looked uncertainly, then stared,
Enkidu did not know to eat bread,
Nor had he ever learned to drink beer!
The harlot made ready to speak, saying to Enkidu: 35

    Eat the bread, Enkidu, the staff of life,
    Drink the beer, the custom of the land.

Enkidu ate the bread until he was sated,
He drank seven juglets of the beer.
His mood became relaxed, he was singing joyously,   40
He felt lighthearted and his features glowed.
He treated his hairy body with water,
He anointed himself with oil, turned into a man,
He put on clothing, became like a warrior.
He took his weapon, hunted lions,   45
The shepherds lay down to rest at night.
He slew wolves, defeated lions,
The herdsmen, the great gods, lay down to sleep.
Enkidu was their watchman, a wakeful man,
He was tall.   50

He was making love with Shamhat.
He lifted his eyes, he saw a man.
He said to the harlot:

> Shamhat, bring that man here!
> Why has he come?
> I will ask him to account for himself.

55

The harlot summoned the man,
He came over, Enkidu said to him:

> Fellow, where are you rushing?
> What is this, your burdensome errand?

60

The man made ready to speak, said to Enkidu:

> They have invited me to a wedding,
> Is it not people's custom to get married?
> I have heaped high on the festival tray
> The fancy dishes for the wedding.
> People's veils are open for the taking.
> For Gilgamesh, king of ramparted Uruk,
> People's veils are open for the taking!
> He mates with the lawful wife,
> He first, the groom after.
> By divine decree pronounced,
> From the cutting of his umbilical cord, she is his due.[8]

65

70

At the man's account, his face went pale.

Enkidu was walking in front, with Shamhat behind him.

When he entered the street of ramparted Uruk,
A multitude crowded around him.
He stood there in the street of ramparted Uruk,
With the people crowding around him.
They said about him:

75

> He is like Gilgamesh in build,
> Though shorter in stature, he is stronger of frame.
> This man, where he was born,
> Ate the springtime grass,
> He must have nursed on the milk of wild beasts.

80

The whole of Uruk was standing beside him,
The people formed a crowd around him,
A throng was jostling towards him,
Young men were mobbed around him,
Infantile, they groveled before him.

85

8. This means that by his birthright Gilgamesh can take brides on their wedding nights, then leave them to their husbands.

In Uruk at this time sacrifices were underway,   90
Young men were celebrating.
The hero stood ready for the upright young man,
For Gilgamesh, as for a god, the partner was ready.
For the goddess of lovemaking, the bed was made,
Gilgamesh was to join with the girl that night.   95

Enkidu approached him,
They met in the public street.
Enkidu blocked the door to the wedding with his foot,
Not allowing Gilgamesh to enter.
They grappled each other, holding fast like wrestlers,   100
They shattered the doorpost, the wall shook.
Gilgamesh and Enkidu grappled each other,
Holding fast like wrestlers,
They shattered the doorpost, the wall shook!
They grappled each other at the door to the wedding,   105
They fought in the street, the public square.
It was Gilgamesh who knelt for the pin, his foot on the ground.
His fury abated, he turned away.
After he turned away,
Enkidu said to him, to Gilgamesh: 110

>   As one unique did your mother bear you,
>   The wild cow of the ramparts, Ninsun,
>   Exalted you above the most valorous of men!
>   Enlil has granted you kingship over the people.

They kissed each other and made friends.   115

[*Gilgamesh speaks.*]

>   Enkidu has neither father nor mother,
>   His hair was growing freely,
>   He was born in the steppe.

Enkidu stood still, listening to what he said,
He shuddered and sat down.   120
Tears filled his eyes,
He was listless, his strength turned to weakness.
They clasped each other,
They joined hands.

Gilgamesh made ready to speak,   125
Saying to Enkidu:

>   Why are your eyes full of tears,
>   Why are you listless, your strength turned to weakness?

Enkidu said to him, to Gilgamesh:

>   Cries of sorrow, my friend, have cramped my muscles,   130
>   Woe has entered my heart.

Gilgamesh made ready to speak,
Saying to Enkidu:

> There dwells in the forest the fierce monster Humbaba,
> You and I shall kill him   135
> And wipe out something evil from the land.

Enkidu made ready to speak,
Saying to Gilgamesh:

> My friend, I knew that country
> When I roamed with the wild beasts.   140
> The forest is sixty double leagues in every direction,
> Who can go into it?
> Humbaba's cry is the roar of a deluge,
> His maw is fire, his breath is death.
> Why do you want to do this?   145
> The haunt of Humbaba is a hopeless quest.

Gilgamesh made ready to speak,
Saying to Enkidu:

> I must go up the mountain forest,
> I must cut a cedar tree   150
> That cedar must be big enough
> To make whirlwinds when it falls.

Enkidu made ready to speak,
Saying to Gilgamesh:

> How shall the likes of us go to the forest of cedars, my friend?   155
> In order to safeguard the forest of cedars,
> Enlil has appointed him to terrify the people,
> Enlil has destined him seven fearsome glories.[9]
> That journey is not to be undertaken,
> That creature is not to be looked upon.   160
> The guardian of [. . .], the forest of cedars,
> Humbaba's cry is the roar of a deluge,
> His maw is fire, his breath is death.
> He can hear rustling in the forest for sixty double leagues.
> Who can go into his forest?   165
> Adad is first and Humbaba is second.
> Who, even among the gods, could attack him?
> In order to safeguard the forest of cedars,
> Enlil has appointed him to terrify the people,
> Enlil has destined him seven fearsome glories.   170
> Besides, whosoever enters his forest is struck down by disease.

---

9. It was believed that divine beings were surrounded by an awe-inspiring radiance. In the older versions of *Gilgamesh*, this radiance was considered removable, like garments or jewelry.

Gilgamesh made ready to speak,
Saying to Enkidu:

> Why, my friend, do you raise such unworthy objections?
> Who, my friend, can go up to heaven?   175
> The gods dwell forever in the sun,
> People's days are numbered,
> Whatever they attempt is a puff of air.
> Here you are, even you, afraid of death,
> What has become of your bravery's might?   180
> I will go before you,
> You can call out to me, "Go on, be not afraid!"
> If I fall on the way, I'll establish my name:
> "Gilgamesh, who joined battle with fierce Humbaba," they'll say.

You were born and grew up on the steppe,   185
When a lion sprang at you, you knew what to do.
Young men fled before you

You speak unworthily,
How you pule! You make me ill.
I must set my hand to cutting a cedar tree,   190
I must establish eternal fame.
Come, my friend, let's both be off to the foundry,
Let them cast axes such as we'll need.

Off they went to the craftsmen,
The craftsmen, seated around, discussed the matter.   195
They cast great axes,
Axe blades weighing 180 pounds each they cast.
They cast great daggers,
Their blades were 120 pounds each,
The cross guards of their handles thirty pounds each.   200
They carried daggers worked with thirty pounds of gold,
Gilgamesh and Enkidu bore ten times sixty pounds each.

Gilgamesh spoke to the elders of ramparted Uruk:

> Hear me, O elders of ramparted Uruk,
> The one of whom they speak   205
> I, Gilgamesh, would see!
> The one whose name resounds across the whole world,
> I will hunt him down in the forest of cedars.
> I will make the land hear
> How mighty is the scion of Uruk.   210
> I will set my hand to cutting a cedar,
> An eternal name I will make for myself!

The elders of ramparted Uruk arose,
They responded to Gilgamesh with their advice:

> You are young, Gilgamesh, your feelings carry you away,   215
> You are ignorant of what you speak, flightiness has taken you,

You do not know what you are attempting.
We have heard of Humbaba, his features are grotesque,
Who is there who could face his weaponry?
He can hear rustling in the forest for sixty double leagues.   220
Who can go into it?
Humbaba's cry is the roar of a deluge,
His maw is fire, his breath is death.
Adad is first and Humbaba is second.
Who, even among the gods, could attack him?   225
In order to safeguard the forest of cedars,
Enlil has appointed him to terrify the people,
Enlil has destined him seven fearsome glories.
Besides, whosoever enters his forest is struck down by disease.

When Gilgamesh heard the speech of his counselors,   230
He looked at his friend and laughed:

Now then, my friend, do you say the same:
"I am afraid to die"?

Tablet III

The elders spoke to him, saying to Gilgamesh:

Come back safely to Uruk's haven,
Trust not, Gilgamesh, in your strength alone,
Let your eyes see all, make your blow strike home.
He who goes in front saves his companion,   5
He who knows the path protects his friend.
Let Enkidu walk before you,
He knows the way to the forest of cedars,
He has seen battle, been exposed to combat.
Enkidu will protect his friend, safeguard his companion,   10
Let him return, to be a grave husband.[1]
We in our assembly entrust the king to you,
On your return, entrust the king again to us.

Gilgamesh made ready to speak,
Saying to Enkidu: 15

Come, my friend, let us go to the sublime temple,
To go before Ninsun, the great queen.
Ninsun the wise, who is versed in all knowledge,
Will send us on our way with good advice.

1. "Grave husband" plays on the words for "bride" and "interment" (grave); the phrase seems to portend Enkidu's death.

Clasping each other, hand in hand,   20
Gilgamesh and Enkidu went to the sublime temple,
To go before Ninsun, the great queen.
Gilgamesh came forward and entered before her:

> O Ninsun, I have taken on a noble quest,
> I travel a distant road, to where Humbaba is,   25
> To face a battle unknown,
> To mount a campaign unknown.
> Give me your blessing, that I may go on my journey,
> That I may indeed see your face safely again,
> That I may indeed reenter joyfully the gate of ramparted Uruk,   30
> That I may indeed return to hold the festival for the new year,
> That I may indeed celebrate the festival for the new year twice over.
> May that festival be held in my presence, the fanfare sound!
> May their drums resound before you!

Ninsun the wild cow heard them out with sadness,   35
The speeches of Gilgamesh, her son, and Enkidu.
Ninsun entered the bathhouse seven times,
She bathed herself in water with tamarisk and soapwort.[2]
She put on a garment as beseemed her body,
She put on an ornament as beseemed her breast,   40
She set [. . .] and donned her tiara.
She climbed the stairs, mounted to the roof terrace,
She set up an incense offering to Shamash.
She made the offering, to Shamash she raised her hands in prayer:

> Why did you endow my son Gilgamesh with a restless heart?   45
> Now you have moved him to travel
> A distant road, to where Humbaba is,
> To face a battle unknown,
> To mount an expedition unknown.
> Until he goes and returns,   50
> Until he reaches the forest of cedars,
> Until he has slain fierce Humbaba,
> And wipes out from the land the evil thing you hate,
> In the day, when you traverse the sky,
> May Aya,[3] your bride, not fear to remind you,   55
> "Entrust him to the watchmen of the night."

> While Gilgamesh journeys to the forest of cedars,
> May the days be long, may the nights be short,
> May his loins be girded, his arms strong!
> At night, let him make a camp for sleeping,   60
> Let him make a shelter to fall asleep in.
> May Aya, your bride, not fear to remind you,

2. A medicinal plant used in cleansing and magic.
3. Goddess of dawn and wife of Shamash, the sun god, often called upon in prayers to intercede with her husband.

When Gilgamesh, Enkidu, and Humbaba meet,
Raise up for his sake, O Shamash, great winds against Humbaba,
South wind, north wind, east wind, west wind, moaning wind,   65
Blasting wind, lashing wind, contrary wind, dust storm,
Demon wind, freezing wind, storm wind, whirlwind:
Raise up thirteen winds to blot out Humbaba's face,
So he cannot charge forward, cannot retreat,
Then let Gilgamesh's weapons defeat Humbaba.   70
As soon as your own [radiance] flares forth,
At that very moment heed the man who reveres you.
May your swift mules [. . .] you,
A comfortable seat, a bed is laid for you,
May the gods, your brethren, serve you your favorite foods,   75
May Aya, the great bride, dab your face with the fringe of her
     spotless garment.

Ninsun the wild cow made a second plea to Shamash:

O Shamash, will not Gilgamesh [. . .] the gods for you?
Will he not share heaven with you?
Will he not share tiara and scepter with the moon?   80
Will he not act in wisdom with Ea in the depths?
Will he not rule the human race with Irnina?[4]
Will he not dwell with Ningishzida[5] in the Land of No Return?

[*Ninsun apparently inducts Enkidu into the staff of her temple.*]

After Ninsun the wild cow had made her plea,
Ninsun the wild cow, knowing and wise, who understands everything,   85
She extinguished the incense, [she came down from the roof terrace],
She summoned Enkidu to impart her message:

Mighty Enkidu, though you are no issue of my womb,
Your little ones shall be among the devotees of Gilgamesh,
The priestesses, votaries, cult women of the temple.   90

She placed a token around Enkidu's neck:

As the priestesses take in a foundling,
And the daughters of the gods bring up an adopted child,
I herewith take Enkidu, as my adopted son,
may Gilgamesh treat him well.   95

His dignitaries stood by, wishing him well,
In a crowd, the young men of Uruk ran along behind him,

---

4. Another name for Ishtar and a local form
of the goddess.

5. Literally "Lord of the Upright Tree," a
netherworld deity.

While his dignitaries made obeisance to him:

> Come back safely to Uruk's haven!
> Trust not, Gilgamesh, in your strength alone,   100
> Let your eyes see all, make your blow strike home.
> He who goes in front saves his companion,
> He who knows the path protects his friend.
> Let Enkidu walk before you,
> He knows the way to the forest of cedars.   105
> He has seen battle, been exposed to combat.
> Enkidu will protect his friend, safeguard his companion,
> Let him return, to be a grave husband.
> We in our assembly entrust the king to you,
> On your return, entrust the king again to us.   110

The elders hailed him,
Counseled Gilgamesh for the journey:

> Trust not, Gilgamesh, in your own strength,
> Let your vision be clear, take care of yourself.
> Let Enkidu go ahead of you,   115
> He has seen the road, has traveled the way.
> He knows the ways into the forest
> And all the tricks of Humbaba.
> He who goes first safeguards his companion,
> His vision is clear, he protects himself.   120
> May Shamash help you to your goal,
> May he disclose to you what your words propose,
> May he open for you the barred road,
> Make straight the pathway to your tread,
> Make straight the upland to your feet.   125
> May nightfall bring you good tidings,
> May Lugalbanda stand by you in your cause.
> In a trice accomplish what you desire,
> Wash your feet in the river of Humbaba whom you seek.
> When you stop for the night, dig a well,   130
> May there always be pure water in your waterskin.[6]
> You should libate cool water to Shamash
> And be mindful of Lugalbanda.

Tablet IV

At twenty double leagues they took a bite to eat,
At thirty double leagues they made their camp,
Fifty double leagues they went in a single day,
A journey of a month and a half in three days.
They approached Mount Lebanon.   5
Towards sunset they dug a well,
Filled their waterskin with water.

---

6. Travelers carried drinking water in leather bags.

Gilgamesh went up onto the mountain,
He poured out flour for an offering, saying.

> O mountain, bring me a propitious dream!   10

Enkidu made Gilgamesh a shelter for receiving dreams,
A gust was blowing, he fastened the door.
He had him lie down in a circle of flour,
And spreading out like a net, Enkidu lay down in the doorway.
Gilgamesh sat there, chin on his knee.   15
Sleep, which usually steals over people, fell upon him.
In the middle of the night he awoke,
Got up and said to his friend:

> My friend, did you not call me? Why am I awake?
> Did you not touch me? Why am I disturbed?   20
> Did a god not pass by? Why does my flesh tingle?
> My friend, I had a dream,
> And the dream I had was very disturbing.

The one born in the steppe,
Enkidu explained the dream to his friend: 25

> My friend, your dream is favorable,
> The dream is very precious as an omen.
> My friend, the mountain you saw is Humbaba,
> We will catch Humbaba and kill him,
> Then we will throw down his corpse on the field of battle.   30
> Further, at dawn the word of Shamash will be in our favor.

At twenty double leagues they took a bite to eat,
At thirty double leagues they made their camp,
Fifty double leagues they went in a single day,
A journey of a month and a half in three days.   35
They approached Mount Lebanon.
Towards sunset they dug a well,
They filled their waterskin with water.
Gilgamesh went up onto the mountain,
He poured out flour for an offering, saying: 40

> O mountain, bring me a propitious dream!

Enkidu made Gilgamesh a shelter for receiving dreams,
A gust was blowing, he fastened the door.
He had him lie down in a circle of flour,
And spreading out like a net, Enkidu lay down in the doorway.   45
Gilgamesh sat there, chin on his knee.
Sleep, which usually steals over people, fell upon him.
In the middle of the night he awoke,

Got up and said to his friend:

> My friend, did you not call me? Why am I awake?   50
> Did you not touch me? Why am I disturbed?
> Did a god not pass by? Why does my flesh tingle?
> My friend, I had a second dream,
> And the dream I had was very disturbing.
> A mountain was in my dream, an enemy.   55
> It threw me down, pinning my feet,
> A fearsome glare grew ever more intense.
> A certain young man, handsomest in the world, truly handsome he was,
> He pulled me out from the base of the mountain,
> He gave me water to drink and eased my fear,   60
> He set my feet on the ground again.

The one born in the steppe,
Enkidu explained the dream to his friend:

> My friend, your dream is favorable,
> The dream is very precious as an omen.   65
> My friend, we will go [. . .]
> The strange thing was Humbaba,
> Was not the mountain, the strange thing, Humbaba?
> Come then, banish your fear.

At twenty double leagues they took a bite to eat,   70
At thirty double leagues they made their camp,
Fifty double leagues they went in a single day,
A journey of a month and a half in three days.
They approached Mount Lebanon.
Towards sunset they dug a well,   75
They filled their waterskin with water.
Gilgamesh went up onto the mountain,
He poured out flour as an offering, saying:

> O mountain, bring me a propitious dream!

Enkidu made Gilgamesh a shelter for receiving dreams,   80
A gust was blowing, he fastened the door.
He had him lie down in a circle of flour,
And spreading out like a net, Enkidu lay down in the doorway.
Gilgamesh sat there, chin on his knee.
Sleep, which usually steals over people, fell upon him.   85
In the middle of the night he awoke,
Got up and said to his friend:

> My friend, did you not call me? Why am I awake?
> Did you not touch me? Why am I disturbed?
> Did a god not pass by? Why does my flesh tingle?   90
> My friend, I had a third dream,
> And the dream I had was very disturbing.

The heavens cried out, the earth was thundering,
Daylight faded, darkness fell,
Lightning flashed, fire shot up,   95
The flames burgeoned, spewing death.
Then the glow was dimmed, the fire was extinguished,
The burning coals that were falling turned to ashes.
You who were born in the steppe, let us discuss it.

Enkidu [explained], helped him accept his dream,   100
Saying to Gilgamesh:

[*Enkidu's explanation is mostly lost, but perhaps it was that the volcanolike
explosion was Humbaba, who flared up, then died.*]

    Humbaba, like a god [. . .]
    [. . .] the light flaring [. . .]
    We will be victorious over him.
    Humbaba aroused our fury,   105
    we will prevail over him.
    Further, at dawn the word of Shamash will be in our favor.

At twenty double leagues they took a bite to eat,
At thirty double leagues they made their camp.
Fifty double leagues they went in a single day,   110
A journey of a month and a half in three days.
They approached Mount Lebanon.[7]
Towards sunset they dug a well,
They filled their waterskin with water.
Gilgamesh went up onto the mountain,   115
He poured out flour as an offering, saying:

    O mountain, bring me a propitious dream!

Enkidu made Gilgamesh a shelter for receiving dreams,
A gust was blowing, he fastened the door.
He had him lie down in a circle of flour,   120
And spreading out like a net, Enkidu lay down in the doorway.
Gilgamesh sat there, chin on his knee.
Sleep, which usually steals over people, fell upon him.
In the middle of the night he awoke,

    My friend, did you not call me? Why am I awake?   125
    Did you not touch me? Why am I disturbed?
    Did a god not pass by? Why does my flesh tingle?
    My friend, I had a [fourth] dream,
    The dream I had was very disturbing.
    My friend, I saw a fourth dream,   130
    More terrible than the other three.

7. Mountain ranges along the Mediterranean coast of present-day Lebanon.

I saw the lion-headed monster-bird Anzu[8] in the sky.
He began to descend upon us, like a cloud.
He was terrifying, his appearance was horrible!
His maw was fire, his breath death.   135

[*Enkidu explains the fourth dream.*]

The lion-headed monster-bird Anzu who descended upon us, like a cloud,
Who was terrifying, whose appearance was horrible,
Whose maw was fire, whose breath was death,
Whose dreadful aura frightens you.
The young man you saw was mighty Shamash.   140

[*It is not clear how many dreams there were in all though one version refers to
five. A poorly preserved manuscript of an old version includes the following
dream that could be inserted here, as portions of it are fulfilled in
Tablet VI.*]

I was grasping a wild bull of the steppe!
As it bellowed, it split the earth,
It raised clouds of dust, blotting out the sky.
I crouched down before it,
It seized my hands, pinioned my arms.   145
Someone pulled me out,
He stroked my cheeks, he gave me to drink from his waterskin.

[*Enkidu explains the dream.*]

It is the god, my friend, to whom we go,
The wild bull was no enemy at all,
The wild bull you saw is Shamash, the protector,   150
He will take our hands in need.
The one who gave you water to drink from his waterskin
Is your god who proclaims your glory, Lugalbanda.
We should rely on one another,
We will accomplish together a deed unheard of in the land.   155

[*Something has happened to discourage Gilgamesh, perhaps an unfavorable
oracle. Shamash comes to their aid with timely advice, just before they hear
Humbaba's cry.*]

[Before Shamash his tears flowed down]:

Remember, stand by me, hear [my prayer],
Gilgamesh, scion of [ramparted Uruk]!

---

8. Monstrous bird with the head of a lion. He appears in a mythological story, where he steals
power from the god Enlil but is defeated in battle by Enlil's son Ninurta.

Shamash heard what he said,
From afar a warning voice called to him from the sky: 160

> Hurry, confront him, do not let him go off into the forest,
> Do not let him enter the thicket!
> He has not donned all of his seven fearsome glories,
> One he has on, six he has left off!

They charged forward like wild bulls.   165
He let out a single bloodcurdling cry,
The guardian of the forest shrieked aloud,
Humbaba was roaring like thunder.

Gilgamesh made ready to speak,
Said to Enkidu: 170

> Humbaba [. . .]
> We cannot confront him separately.

Gilgamesh spoke to him, said to Enkidu:

> My friend, why do we raise such unworthy objections?
> Have we not crossed all the mountains?   175
> The end of the quest is before us.
> My friend knows battle,
> You rubbed on herbs, you did not fear death,
> Your battle cry should be dinning like a drum!
> Let the paralysis leave your arm, let weakness quit your knees,   180
> Take my hand, my friend, let us walk on together!
> Your heart should be urging you to battle.
> Forget about death,
> He who marches first, protects himself,
> Let him keep his comrade safe!   185
> Those two will have established fame down through the ages.

The pair reached the edge of the forest,
They stopped their talk and stood there.

Tablet V

They stood at the edge of the forest,
They gazed at the height of the cedars,
They gazed at the way into the forest.
Where Humbaba would walk, a path was made,
Straight were the ways and easy the going.   5
They saw the cedar mountain, dwelling of the gods, sacred to the
    goddess Irnina.
On the slopes of that mountain, the cedar bears its abundance,
Agreeable is its shade, full of pleasures.
The undergrowth is tangled, the [thicket] interwoven.

[*In older versions, they begin to cut trees and Humbaba hears the noise. In the standard version, they meet Humbaba first.*]

Humbaba made ready to speak, saying to Gilgamesh: 10

>How well-advised they are, the fool Gilgamesh and the yokelman!
>Why have you come here to me?
>Come now, Enkidu, small-fry, who does not know his father,
>Spawn of a turtle or tortoise, who sucked no mother's milk!
>I used to see you when you were younger but would not go near you.   15
>Had I killed the likes of you, would I have filled my belly?
>You have brought Gilgamesh before me,
>You stand there, a barbarian foe!
>I should cut off your head, Gilgamesh, throat and neck,
>I should let cawing buzzard, screaming eagle, and vulture feed
>   on your flesh.   20

Gilgamesh made ready to speak, saying to Enkidu:

>My friend, Humbaba's features have grown more grotesque,
>We strode up like heroes to vanquish him.

Enkidu made ready to speak, saying to Gilgamesh:

>Why, my friend, do you raise such unworthy objections?   25
>How you pule! You make me ill.
>Now, my friend, this has dragged on long enough.
>The time has come to pour the copper into the mold.
>Will you take another hour to blow the bellows,
>An hour more to let it cool?   30
>To launch the flood weapon, to wield the lash,
>Retreat not a foot, you must not turn back,
>Let your eyes see all, let your blow strike home!

[*In the combat with Humbaba, the rift valley of Lebanon is formed by their circling feet.*]

He struck the ground to confront him.
At their heels the earth split apart,   35
As they circled, the ranges of Lebanon were sundered!
The white clouds turned black,
Death rained down like fog upon them.
Shamash raised the great winds against Humbaba,
South wind, north wind, east wind, west wind, moaning wind,   40
Blasting wind, lashing wind, contrary wind, dust storm,
Demon wind, freezing wind, storm wind, whirlwind:
The thirteen winds blotted out Humbaba's face,
He could not charge forward, he could not retreat.
Then Gilgamesh's weapons defeated Humbaba.   45

Humbaba begged for life, saying to Gilgamesh:

> You were once a child, Gilgamesh, you had a mother who bore you,
> You are the offspring of Ninsun the wild cow.
> You grew up to fulfill the oracle of Shamash, lord of the mountain:
> "Gilgamesh, scion of Uruk, is to be king."   50
>
> O Gilgamesh, spare my life!
> Let me dwell here for you [as your . . .],
> Say however many trees you [require . . .],
> For you I will guard the myrtle wood [. . .].

Enkidu made ready to speak, saying to Gilgamesh: 55

> My friend! Do not listen to what Humbaba says,
> Do not heed his entreaties!

[*Humbaba is speaking to Enkidu.*]

> You know the lore of my forest,
> And you understand all I have to say.
> I might have lifted you up, dangled you from a twig at the entrance
>   to my forest,   60
> I might have let cawing buzzard, screaming eagle, and vulture feed
>   on your flesh.
> Now then, Enkidu, mercy is up to you,
> Tell Gilgamesh to spare my life!

Enkidu made ready to speak, saying to Gilgamesh:

> My friend! Humbaba is guardian of the forest of cedars,   65
> Finish him off for the kill, put him out of existence.
> Humbaba is guardian of the forest of cedars,
> Finish him off for the kill, put him out of existence,
> Before Enlil the foremost one hears of this!
> The great gods will become angry with us,   70
> Enlil in Nippur, Shamash in Larsa.[9]
> Establish your reputation for all time:
> "Gilgamesh, who slew Humbaba."
>
> May the pair of them never reach old age!
> May Gilgamesh and Enkidu come across no graver friend to bank on![1]   75

---

9. Nippur and Larsa are cities in Babylonia with important temples to Enlil and Shamash, respectively.

1. This is one of the elaborate, sometimes obscure wordplays in *Gilgamesh*. In Humbaba's curse, *cross* sounds like *friend* and *bank* echoes *grave*, so that the giant's words can mean either "May they not cross water safely to the opposite bank" or "May they not find a friend to rely on."

[*An old version contains the following exchange between Gilgamesh and Enkidu concerning the seven fearsome glories of Humbaba.*]

Gilgamesh said to Enkidu:

> Now, my friend, let us go on to victory!
> The glories will be lost in the confusion,
> The glories will be lost and the brightness will [. . .].

Enkidu said to him, to Gilgamesh: 80

> My friend, catch the bird and where will its chicks go?
> Let us search out the glories later,
> They will run around in the grass like chicks.
> Strike him again, then kill his retinue.

[*Gilgamesh kills Humbaba. In some versions he has to strike multiple blows before the monster falls.*]

Gilgamesh heeded his friend's command,   85
He raised the axe at his side,
He drew the sword at his belt.
Gilgamesh struck him on the neck,
Enkidu, his friend, [. . .].
They pulled out [. . .] as far as the lungs,   90
He tore out the [. . .],
He forced the head into a cauldron.
[. . .] in abundance fell on the mountain,
He struck him, Humbaba the guardian, down to the ground.
His blood [. . .]   95
For two leagues the cedars [. . .].
He killed the glories with him.
He slew the monster, guardian of the forest,
At whose cry the mountains of Lebanon trembled,
At whose cry all the mountains quaked.   100
He slew the monster, guardian of the forest,
He trampled on the broken [. . .],
He struck down the seven glories.
The battle net [. . .], the sword weighing eight times sixty pounds,
He took the weight of ten times sixty pounds upon him,   105
He forced his way into the forest,
He opened the secret dwelling of the supreme gods.
Gilgamesh cut down the trees,
Enkidu chose the timbers.
Enkidu made ready to speak, said to Gilgamesh: 110

> You killed the guardian by your strength,
> Who else could cut through this forest of trees?
> My friend, we have felled the lofty cedar,
> Whose crown once pierced the sky.
> I will make a door six times twelve cubits high, two times twelve
>   cubits wide,   115

One cubit shall be its thickness,
Its hinge pole, ferrule, and pivot box shall be unique.[2]
Let no stranger approach it, may only a god go through.
Let the Euphrates bring it to Nippur,
Nippur, the sanctuary of Enlil.   120
May Enlil be delighted with you,
May Enlil rejoice over it!

They lashed together a raft
Enkidu embarked
And Gilgamesh [. . .] the head of Humbaba.   125

Tablet VI

He washed his matted locks, cleaned his head strap,
He shook his hair down over his shoulders.
He threw off his filthy clothes, he put on clean ones,
Wrapping himself in a cloak, he tied on his sash,
Gilgamesh put on his kingly diadem.   5
The princess Ishtar coveted Gilgamesh's beauty:

Come, Gilgamesh, you shall be my bridegroom!
Give, oh give me of your lusciousness!
You shall be my husband and I shall be your wife.
I will ready for you a chariot of lapis and gold,
With golden wheels and fittings of gemstones,   10
You shall harness storm demons as if they were giant mules.
Enter our house amidst fragrance of cedar,
When you enter our house,
The splendid exotic doorsill shall do you homage,   15
Kings, nobles, and princes shall kneel before you,
They shall bring you gifts of mountain and lowland as tribute.
Your goats shall bear triplets, your ewes twins,
Your pack-laden donkey shall overtake the mule,
Your horses shall run proud before the wagon,   20
Your ox in the yoke shall have none to compare!

Gilgamesh made ready to speak,
Saying to the princess Ishtar:
What shall I give you if I take you to wife?
Shall I give you a headdress for your person, or clothing?
Shall I give you bread or drink?   25
Shall I give you food, worthy of divinity?
Shall I give you drink, worthy of queenship?
What would I get if I marry you?
You are a brazier that goes out when it freezes,   30

---

2. Mesopotamian doors did not use hinges but were made of a panel attached to a post. It was this post, or "hinge pole," that rotated when the door was opened or closed, some- times on a piece of metal, or "ferrule," at the bottom. The top of the post was cased or enclosed so the hinge pole would not slip off its pivot point.

A flimsy door that keeps out neither wind nor draught,
A palace that crushes a warrior,
A mouse that gnaws through its housing,
Tar that smears its bearer,
Waterskin that soaks its bearer,   35
Weak stone that undermines a wall,
Battering ram that destroys the wall for an enemy,
Shoe that pinches its wearer!
Which of your lovers lasted forever?
Which of your heroes went up to heaven?   40
Come, I call you to account for your lovers:
He who had jugs of cream on his shoulders and [. . .] on his arm,
For Dumuzi,[3] your girlhood lover,
You ordained year after year of weeping.
You fell in love with the brightly colored roller bird,   45
Then you struck him and broke his wing.
In the woods he sits crying "My-wing!"
You fell in love with the lion, perfect in strength,
Then you dug for him ambush pits, seven times seven.
You fell in love with the wild stallion, eager for the fray,   50
Whip, goad, and lash you ordained for him,
Seven double leagues of galloping you ordained for him,
You ordained that he muddy his water when he drinks,
You ordained perpetual weeping for his mother, divine Silili.
You fell in love with the shepherd, keeper of herds,   55
Who always set out cakes baked in embers for you,
Slaughtered kids for you every day.
You struck him and turned him into a wolf,
His own shepherd boys harry him off,
And his own hounds snap at his heels!   60
You fell in love with Ishullanu,[4] your father's gardener,
Who always brought you baskets of dates,
Who daily made your table splendid.
You wanted him, so you sidled up to him:
"My Ishullanu, let's have a taste of your vigor!   65
Bring out your member, touch our sweet spot!"
Ishullanu said to you,
"Me? What do you want of me?
Hath my mother not baked? Have I not eaten?
Shall what I taste for food be insults and curses?   70
In the cold, is my cover to be the touch of a reed?"
When you heard what he said,
You struck him and turned him into a scarecrow,
You left him stuck in his own garden patch,
His well sweep goes up no longer, his bucket does not descend.   75

---

3. Shepherd god. He was a youthful lover of
Ishtar, who let him be taken to the netherworld when she had to provide a substitute for
herself.

4. According to a Sumerian myth, Ishtar
seduced a gardener named Ishullanu whom she
then sought to kill.

As for me, now that you've fallen in love with me, you will treat me
   like them!
When Ishtar heard this,
Ishtar was furious and went up to heaven,
Ishtar went sobbing before Anu, her father,
Before Antum, her mother, her tears flowed down: 80

> Father, Gilgamesh has said outrageous things about me,
> Gilgamesh's been spouting insults about me,
> Insults and curses against me!

Anu made ready to speak,
Saying to the princess Ishtar: 85

> Well now, did you not provoke the king, Gilgamesh,
> And so Gilgamesh spouted insults about you,
> Insults and curses against you?

Ishtar made ready to speak,
Saying to Anu, her father: 90

> Well then, Father, pretty please, the Bull of Heaven,
> So I can kill Gilgamesh on his home ground.
> If you don't give me the Bull of Heaven,
> I'll strike [. . .] to its foundation,
> I'll raise up the dead to devour the living,   95
> The dead shall outnumber the living!

Anu made ready to speak,
Saying to the princess Ishtar:

> If you insist on the Bull of Heaven from me,
> Let the widow of Uruk gather seven years of chaff,   100
> Let the farmer of Uruk raise seven years of hay.

Ishtar made ready to speak,
Saying to Anu, her father:

> The widow of Uruk has gathered seven years of chaff,
> The farmer of Uruk has raised seven years of hay.   105
> With the Bull of Heaven's fury I will kill him!

When Anu heard what Ishtar said,
He placed the lead rope of the Bull of Heaven in her hand,
Ishtar led the Bull of Heaven away.

When it reached Uruk,   110
It dried up the groves, reedbeds, and marshes,
It went down to the river, it lowered the river by seven cubits.
At the bull's snort, a pit opened up,
One hundred young men of Uruk fell into it.
At its second snort, a pit opened up,   115
Two hundred young men of Uruk fell into it.

At its third snort, a pit opened up,
Enkidu fell into it, up to his middle.
Enkidu jumped out and seized the bull by its horns,
The bull spewed its foam in his face,   120
Swished dung at him with the tuft of its tail.
Enkidu made ready to speak,
Saying to Gilgamesh:

> I have seen, my friend, the strength of the Bull of Heaven,
> So knowing its strength, I know how to deal with it.   125
> I will get around the strength of the Bull of Heaven,
> I will circle behind the Bull of Heaven,
> I will grab it by the tuft of its tail,
> I will set my feet on its [. . .],
> Then you, like a strong, skillful slaughterer,   130
> Thrust your dagger between neck, horn, and tendon!

Enkidu circled behind the Bull of Heaven,
He grabbed it by the tuft of its tail,
He set his feet on its [. . .],
And Gilgamesh, like a strong, skillful slaughterer,   135
Thrust his dagger between neck, horn, and tendon!

After they had killed the Bull of Heaven,
They ripped out its heart and set it before Shamash.
They stepped back and prostrated themselves before Shamash,
Then the two comrades sat down beside each other.   140
Ishtar went up on the wall of ramparted Uruk,
She writhed in grief, she let out a wail:

> That bully Gilgamesh who demeaned me, he's killed the Bull of Heaven!

When Enkidu heard what Ishtar said,
He tore off the bull's haunch and flung it at her: 145

> If I could vanquish you, I'd turn you to this,
> I'd drape the guts beside you!

Ishtar convened the cult women, prostitutes, harlots,
She set up a lament over the haunch of the bull.

Gilgamesh summoned all the expert craftsmen,   150
The craftsmen marveled at the massiveness of its horns,
They were molded from thirty pounds each of lapis blue,
Their outer shell was two thumbs thick!
Six times three hundred quarts of oil, the capacity of both,
He donated to anoint the statue of his god, Lugalbanda.   155
He brought them inside and hung them up in his master bedroom.

They washed their hands in the Euphrates,
Clasping each other, they came away,

Paraded through the streets of Uruk.
The people of Uruk crowded to look upon them.   160
Gilgamesh made a speech
To the servant-women of his palace:

> Who is the handsomest of young men?
> Who is the most glorious of males?
> Gilgamesh is the handsomest of young men!   165
> Gilgamesh is the most glorious of males!
> She at whom we flung the haunch in our passion,
> Ishtar, she has no one in the street to satisfy her.

Gilgamesh held a celebration in his palace.
The young men slept stretched out on the couch of night.   170
While Enkidu slept, he had a dream.

Tablet VII

My friend, why were the great gods in council?

Enkidu raised,
spoke to the door as if it were human:[5]

> O bosky door, insensate,
> Which lends an ear that is not there,   5
> I sought your wood for twenty double leagues,
> Till I beheld a lofty cedar.
> No rival had your tree in the forest.
> Six times twelve cubits was your height, two times twelve cubits was
>   your width,
> One cubit was your thickness,   10
> Your hinge pole, ferrule, and pivot box were unique.
> I made you, I brought you to Nippur, I set you up.
> Had I known, O door, how you would requite me,
> And that this your goodness towards me [. . .],
> I would have raised my axe, I would have chopped you down,   15
> I would have floated you as a raft to the temple of Shamash,
> I would have set up the lion-headed monster-bird Anzu at its gate,
> Because Shamash heard my plea
> He gave me the weapon to kill Humbaba.
> Now then, O door, it was I who made you, it was I who set you up.   20
> I will tear you out!
> May a king who shall arise after me despise you,
> May he alter my inscription and put on his own![6]

---

5. Because there is a gap in the text, it is unclear why Enkidu curses the door so violently. Since it is made of cedar wood from the forest, it might embody the adventure that results in Enkidu's death.

6. These concluding words of Enkidu's curse of the cedar door parody traditional Mesopotamian inscriptions affixed to monuments, which called the wrath of the gods upon anyone who damaged, removed, or usurped the monument.

He tore out his hair, threw away his clothing.

When he heard out this speech, swiftly, quickly his tears flowed down,   25
When Gilgamesh heard out Enkidu's speech, swiftly, quickly, his tears
  flowed down.

Gilgamesh made ready to speak, saying to Enkidu:

> My friend, you are rational but you say strange things,
> Why, my friend, does your heart speak strange things?
> The dream is a most precious omen, though very frightening,   30
> Your lips are buzzing like flies.
> Though frightening, the dream is a precious omen.
> The gods left mourning for the living,
> The dream left mourning for the living,
> The dream left woe for the living!   35
> Now I shall go pray to the great gods,
> I will be assiduous to my own god, I will pray to yours,
> To Anu, father of the gods,
> To Enlil, counselor of the gods,
> I will make your image of gold beyond measure.   40
> You can pay no silver, no gold can you [. . .],
> What Enlil commanded is not like the [. . .] of the gods,
> What he commanded, he will not retract.
> The verdict he has scrivened, he will not reverse nor erase.
> People often die before their time.   45

At the first glimmer of dawn,
Enkidu lifted his head, weeping before Shamash,
Before the sun's fiery glare, his tears flowed down:

> I have turned to you, O Shamash, on account of the precious days
>   of my life,
> As for that hunter, the entrapping-man,   50
> Who did not let me get as much life as my friend,
> May that hunter not get enough to make him a living.
> Make his profit loss, cut down his take,
> May his income, his portion evaporate before you,
> Any wildlife that enters his traps, make it go out the window!   55

When he had cursed the hunter to his heart's content,
He resolved to curse the harlot Shamhat:

> Come, Shamhat, I will ordain you a destiny,
> A destiny that will never end, forever and ever!
> I will lay on you the greatest of all curses,   60
> Swiftly, inexorably, may my curse come upon you.
> May you never make a home that you can enjoy,
> May you never caress a child of your own,
> May you never be received among decent women.
> May beer sludge impregnate your lap,   65
> May the drunkard bespatter your best clothes with vomit.

May your swain prefer beauties,
May he pinch you like potter's clay.
May you get no alabaster,
May no table to be proud of be set in your house.   70
May the nook you enjoy be a doorstep,
May the public crossroads be your dwelling,
May vacant lots be your sleeping place,
May the shade of a wall be your place of business.
May brambles and thorns flay your feet,   75
May toper and sober slap your cheek.[7]
May riffraff of the street shove each other in your brothel,
May there be a brawl there.
When you stroll with your cronies, may they catcall after you.
May the builder not keep your roof in repair,   80
May the screech owl roost in the ruins of your home.
May a feast never be held where you live.

May your purple finery be expropriated,
May filthy underwear be what you are given,
Because you diminished me, an innocent,   85
Yes me, an innocent, you wronged me in my steppe.

When Shamash heard what he said,
From afar a warning voice called to him from the sky:

O Enkidu, why curse Shamhat the harlot,
Who fed you bread, fit for a god,   90
Who poured you beer, fit for a king,
Who dressed you in a noble garment,
And gave you handsome Gilgamesh for a comrade?
Now then, Gilgamesh is your friend and blood brother!
Won't he lay you down in the ultimate resting place?   95
In a perfect resting place he will surely lay you down!
He will settle you in peaceful rest in that dwelling sinister,
Rulers of the netherworld will do you homage.
He will have the people of Uruk shed bitter tears for you,
He will make the pleasure-loving people burdened down for you,   100
And, as for him, after your death, he will let his hair grow matted,
He will put on a lion skin and roam the steppe.

When Enkidu heard the speech of the valiant Shamash,
His raging heart was calmed,
his fury was calmed: 105

Come, Shamhat, I will ordain you a destiny,
My mouth that cursed you, let it bless you instead.
May governors and dignitaries fall in love with you,
May the man one double league away slap his thighs in excitement,
May the man two double leagues away let down his hair.   110

7. That is, may anyone hit her, drunk or not.

May the subordinate not hold back from you, but open his trousers,
May he give you obsidian, lapis, and gold,
May ear bangles be your gift.
To the man whose wealth is secure, whose granaries are full,
May Ishtar of the gods introduce you,   115
For your sake may the wife and mother of seven be abandoned.

Enkidu was sick at heart,
He lay there lonely.
He told his friend what weighed on his mind:

My friend, what a dream I had last night!   120
Heaven cried out, earth made reply,
I was standing between them.
There was a certain man, his face was somber,
His face was like that of the lion-headed monster-bird Anzu,
His hands were the paws of a lion,   125
His fingernails were the talons of an eagle.
He seized me by the hair, he was too strong for me,
I hit him but he sprang back like a swing rope,
He hit me and capsized me like a raft.
Like a wild bull he trampled me,   130
"Save me, my friend!"—but you did not save me!
He trussed my limbs like a bird's.
Holding me fast, he took me down to the house of shadows,
    the dwelling of hell,
To the house whence none who enters comes forth,
On the road from which there is no way back,   135
To the house whose dwellers are deprived of light,
Where dust is their fare and their food is clay.
They are dressed like birds in feather garments,
Yea, they shall see no daylight, for they abide in darkness.
Dust lies thick on the door and bolt,   140
When I entered that house of dust,
I saw crowns in a heap,
There dwelt the kings, the crowned heads who once ruled the land,
Who always set out roast meat for Anu and Enlil,
Who always set out baked offerings, libated cool water from
    waterskins.   145
In that house of dust I entered,
Dwelt high priests and acolytes,
Dwelt reciters of spells and ecstatics,[8]
Dwelt the anointers of the great gods,
Dwelt old King Etana[9] and the god of the beasts,   150
Dwelt the queen of the netherworld, Ereshkigal.[1]

---

8. Reciters of spells were learned scholars, while prophets, or "ecstatics," were people who spoke in a trance without having studied their words. Ecstatics were sometimes social outcasts or people without education.

9. Ancient king who was said to have flown up to heaven on an eagle to find a plant that would help him and his wife have a child.
1. Queen of the netherworld and jealous sister of the goddess Ishtar.

Belet-seri,[2] scribe of the netherworld, was kneeling before her,
She was holding a tablet and reading to her,
She lifted her head, she looked at me:
"Who brought this man?"   155
I who went with you through all hardships,
Remember me, my friend, do not forget what I have undergone!
My friend had a dream needing no interpretation.

The day he had the dream, his strength ran out.
Enkidu lay there one day, a second day he was ill,   160
Enkidu lay in his bed, his illness grew worse.
A third day, a fourth day, Enkidu's illness grew worse.
A fifth, a sixth, a seventh,
An eighth, a ninth, a tenth day,
Enkidu's illness grew worse.   165
An eleventh, a twelfth day,
Enkidu lay in his bed.
He called for Gilgamesh, roused him with his cry:

> My friend laid on me the greatest curse of all!
> I feared the battle but will die in my bed,   170
> My friend, he who falls quickly in battle is glorious.

[*Enkidu dies.*]

Tablet VIII

At the first glimmer of dawn,
Gilgamesh lamented his friend:

> Enkidu, my friend, your mother the gazelle,
> Your father the wild ass brought you into the world,
> Onagers raised you on their milk,   5
> And the wild beasts taught you all the grazing places.
> The pathways, O Enkidu, to the forest of cedars,
> May they weep for you, without falling silent, night and day.
> May the elders of the teeming city, ramparted Uruk, weep for you,
> May the crowd who blessed our departure weep for you.   10
> May the heights of highland and mountain weep for you,
> May the lowlands wail like your mother.
> May the forest of balsam and cedar weep for you,
> Which we slashed in our fury.
> May bear, hyena, panther, leopard, deer, jackal,   15
> Lion, wild bull, gazelle, ibex, the beasts and creatures of the steppe,
>   weep for you.[3]
> May the sacred Ulaya River[4] weep for you, along whose banks we once
>   strode erect,
> May the holy Euphrates weep for you,
> Whose waters we libated from waterskins.

2. Literally "Lady of the Steppe," scribe and bookkeeper in the netherworld.
3. This refers to an episode that does not appear in the extant portions of the epic.
4. Karun River in the southwest of modern Iran.

May the young men of ramparted Uruk weep for you, 20
Who watched us slay the Bull of Heaven in combat.
May the plowman weep for you at his plow,
Who extolled your name in the sweet song of harvest home.
May they weep for you, of the teeming city of Uruk,
Who exalted your name at the first [. . .]. 25
May the shepherd and herdsman weep for you,
Who held the milk and buttermilk to your mouth,
May the nurse weep for you,
Who treated your rashes with butter.
May the harlot weep for you, 30
Who massaged you with sweet-smelling oil.
Like brothers may they weep for you,
Like sisters may they tear out their hair for your sake.
Enkidu, as your father, your mother,
I weep for you bitterly. 35

Hear me, O young men, listen to me,
Hear me, O elders of Uruk, listen to me!
I mourn my friend Enkidu,
I howl as bitterly as a professional keener.
Oh for the axe at my side, oh for the safeguard by my hand, 40
Oh for the sword at my belt, oh for the shield before me,
Oh for my best garment, oh for the raiment that pleased me most!
An ill wind rose against me and snatched it away!
O my friend, swift wild donkey, mountain onager, panther of the steppe,
O Enkidu my friend, swift wild donkey, mountain onager, panther
   of the steppe! 45
You who stood by me when we climbed the mountain,
Seized and slew the Bull of Heaven,
Felled Humbaba who dwelt in the forest of cedar,
What now is this sleep that has seized you?
Come back to me! You hear me not. 50

But, as for him, he did not raise his head.
He touched his heart but it was not beating.
Then he covered his friend's face, like a bride's.
He hovered round him like an eagle,
Like a lioness whose cubs are in a pitfall, 55
He paced to and fro, back and forth,
Tearing out and hurling away the locks of his hair,
Ripping off and throwing away his fine clothes like something foul.

At the first glimmer of dawn,
Gilgamesh sent out a proclamation to the land: 60

Hear ye, blacksmith, lapidary,[5] metalworker, goldsmith, jeweler!
Make an image of my friend,
Such as no one ever made of his friend!

---

5. Gem carver.

I will lay you down in the ultimate resting place,
In a perfect resting place I will surely lay you down. 65
I will settle you in peaceful rest in that dwelling sinister,
Rulers of the netherworld will do you homage.
I will have the people of Uruk shed bitter tears for you,
I will make the pleasure-loving people burdened down for you,
And, as for me, now that you are dead, I will let my hair grow matted, 70
I will put on a lion skin and roam the steppe!

He slaughtered fatted cattle and sheep, heaped them high for his friend,
They carried off all the meat for the rulers of the netherworld.
He displayed in the open for Ishtar, the great queen,
Saying: "May Ishtar, the great queen, accept this, 75
May she welcome my friend and walk at his side."

He displayed in the open for Ninshuluhha,[6] housekeeper of the
    netherworld,
Saying: "May Ninshuluhha, housekeeper of the crowded netherworld,
    accept this,
May she welcome my friend and walk at his side.
May she intercede on behalf of my friend, lest he lose courage." 80
The obsidian knife with lapis fitting,
The sharpening stone pure-whetted with Euphrates water,
He displayed in the open for Bibbu, meat carver of the netherworld,
Saying: "May Bibbu, meat carver of the crowded netherworld,
    accept this,
Welcome my friend and walk at his side." 85

Tablet IX

Gilgamesh was weeping bitterly for Enkidu, his friend,
As he roamed the steppe:

Shall I not die too? Am I not like Enkidu?
Oh woe has entered my vitals!
I have grown afraid of death, so I roam the steppe. 5
Having come this far, I will go on swiftly
Towards Utanapishtim,[7] son of Ubar-Tutu.
I have reached mountain passes at night.
I saw lions, I felt afraid,
I looked up to pray to the moon,
To the moon, beacon of the gods, my prayers went forth: 10
"Keep me safe!"

---

6. A netherworld deity in charge of ritual washing.
7. Akkadian name for the sage who, together with his wife, survived the Great Flood and became immortal. He resembles the biblical Noah and his name literally means "He Found Life." He is called "Ziusudra" in Sumerian and "Ullu" in Hittite.

[At night] he lay down, then awoke from a dream.
He rejoiced to be alive.
He raised the axe at his side,   15
He drew the sword from his belt,
He dropped among them like an arrow,
He struck the lions, scattered, and killed them.

[*Gilgamesh approaches the scorpion monsters who guard the gateway to the
sun's passage through the mountains.*]

The twin peaks are called Mashum.
When he arrived at the twin peaks called Mashum,   20
Which daily watch over the rising and setting of the sun,
Whose peaks thrust upward to the vault of heaven,
Whose flanks reach downward to hell,
Where scorpion monsters guard its gateway,
Whose appearance is dreadful, whose venom is death,   25
Their fear-inspiring radiance spreads over the mountains,
They watch over the sun at its rising and setting,
When Gilgamesh saw their fearsomeness and terror,
He covered his face.
He took hold of himself and approached them.   30

The scorpion monster called to his wife:

     This one who has come to us, his body is flesh of a god!

The wife of the scorpion monster answered him:

     Two-thirds of him is divine, one-third is human.

The scorpion monster, the male one, called out,   35
To Gilgamesh, scion of the gods, he said these words:

     Who are you who have come this long way?

[*The scorpion monster apparently warns Gilgamesh that he has only twelve
hours to get through the sun's tunnel before the sun enters it at nightfall.*]

The scorpion monster made ready to speak, spoke to him,
Said to Gilgamesh, [scion of the gods]:

     Go, Gilgamesh!   40

He opened to him the gateway of the mountain,
Gilgamesh entered the mountain.
He heeded the words of the scorpion monster,
He set out on the way of the sun.
When he had gone one double hour,   45

Dense was the darkness, no light was there,
It would not let him look behind him.
When he had gone two double hours,
Dense was the darkness, no light was there,
It would not let him look behind him.   50
When he had gone three double hours,
Dense was the darkness, no light was there,
It would not let him look behind him.
When he had gone four double hours,
Dense was the darkness, no light was there,   55
It would not let him look behind him.
When he had gone five double hours,
Dense was the darkness, no light was there,
It would not let him look behind him.
When he had gone six double hours,   60
Dense was the darkness, no light was there,
It would not let him look behind him.
When he had gone seven double hours,
Dense was the darkness, there was no light,
It would not let him look behind him.   65
When he had gone eight double hours, he rushed ahead,
Dense was the darkness, there was no light,
It would not let him look behind him.
When he had gone nine double hours, he felt the north wind,
Dense was the darkness, there was no light,   70
It would not let him look behind him.
When he had gone ten double hours,
The time for the sun's entry was drawing near.
When he had gone eleven double hours, just one double hour was left,
When he had gone twelve double hours, he came out ahead of the sun!   75
He had run twelve double hours, bright light still reigned!
He went forward, seeing the trees of the gods.
The carnelian bore its fruit,
Like bunches of grapes dangling, lovely to see,
The lapis bore foliage,   80
Fruit it bore, a delight to behold.

[The fragmentary lines that remain continue the description of the wonderful grove.]

Tablet X

[*Gilgamesh approaches the tavern of Siduri, a female tavern keeper who lives at the end of the earth. This interesting personage is unknown outside this poem, nor is it clear who her clientele might be in such a remote spot.*]

Siduri[8] the tavern keeper, who dwells at the edge of the sea,
For her was wrought the cuprack,[9] for her the brewing vat of gold,
Gilgamesh made his way towards her,
He was clad in a skin,
He had flesh of gods in his body.   5
Woe was in his vitals,
His face was like a traveler's from afar.
The tavern keeper eyed him from a distance,
Speaking to herself, she said these words,
She debated with herself: 10

> This no doubt is a slaughterer of wild bulls!
> Why would he make straight for my door?

At the sight of him the tavern keeper barred her door,
She barred her door and mounted to the roof terrace.
But he, Gilgamesh, put his ear to the door,   15
He lifted his chin.

Gilgamesh said to her, to the tavern keeper:

> Tavern keeper, when you saw me why did you bar your door,
> Bar your door and mount to the roof terrace?
> I will strike down your door, I will shatter your doorbolt,   20

Gilgamesh said to her, to the tavern keeper:

> I am Gilgamesh, who killed the guardian,
> Who seized and killed the bull that came down from heaven,
> Who felled Humbaba who dwelt in the forest of cedars,
> Who killed lions at the mountain passes.   25

The tavern keeper said to him, to Gilgamesh:

> If you are indeed Gilgamesh, who killed the guardian,
> Who felled Humbaba who dwelt in the forest of cedars,
> Who killed lions at the mountain passes,
> Who seized and killed the bull that came down from heaven,   30
> Why are your cheeks emaciated, your face cast down,
> Your heart wretched, your features wasted,
> Woe in your vitals,
> Your face like a traveler's from afar,

---

8. Literally, "Maiden" in Hurrian, a language of northern Syria and northern Mesopotamia that was not related to Sumerian or Akkadian.

9. Some Mesopotamian drinking cups were conical, with pointed bottoms, so they were set on a wooden rack to hold them up.

Your features weathered by cold and sun, 35
Why are you clad in a lion skin, roaming the steppe?

Gilgamesh said to her, to the tavern keeper:

My cheeks would not be emaciated, nor my face cast down,
Nor my heart wretched nor my features wasted,
Nor would there be woe in my vitals,
Nor would my face be like a traveler's from afar, 40
Nor would my features be weathered by cold and sun,
Nor would I be clad in a lion skin, roaming the steppe,
But for my friend, swift wild donkey, mountain onager, panther
   of the steppe,
But for Enkidu, swift wild donkey, mountain onager, panther
   of the steppe, 45
My friend whom I so loved, who went with me through every hardship,
Enkidu, whom I so loved, who went with me through every hardship,
The fate of mankind has overtaken him.
Six days and seven nights I wept for him,
I would not give him up for burial, 50
Until a worm fell out of his nose.
I was frightened.
I have grown afraid of death, so I roam the steppe,
My friend's case weighs heavy upon me.
A distant road I roam over the steppe, 55
My friend Enkidu's case weighs heavy upon me!
A distant road I roam over the steppe,
How can I be silent? How can I hold my peace?
My friend whom I loved is turned into clay,
Enkidu, my friend whom I loved, is turned into clay! 60
Shall I too not lie down like him,
And never get up forever and ever?

[*An old version adds the following episode.*]

After his death I could find no life,
Back and forth I prowled like a bandit in the steppe.
Now that I have seen your face, tavern keeper, 65
May I not see that death I constantly fear!

The tavern keeper said to him, to Gilgamesh:

Gilgamesh, wherefore do you wander?
The eternal life you are seeking you shall not find.
When the gods created mankind, 70
They established death for mankind,
And withheld eternal life for themselves.
As for you, Gilgamesh, let your stomach be full,
Always be happy, night and day.
Make every day a delight, 75
Night and day play and dance.

Your clothes should be clean,
Your head should be washed,
You should bathe in water,
Look proudly on the little one holding your hand,   80
Let your mate be always blissful in your loins,
This, then, is the work of mankind.

Gilgamesh said to her, to the tavern keeper:

What are you saying, tavern keeper?
I am heartsick for my friend.   85
What are you saying, tavern keeper?
I am heartsick for Enkidu!

[*The standard version resumes.*]

Gilgamesh said to her, to the tavern keeper:

Now then, tavern keeper, what is the way to Utanapishtim?
What are its signs? Give them to me.   90
Give, oh give me its signs!
If need be, I'll cross the sea,
If not, I'll roam the steppe.

The tavern keeper said to him, to Gilgamesh:

Gilgamesh, there has never been a place to cross,   95
There has been no one from the dawn of time who could ever cross
    this sea.
The valiant Shamash alone can cross this sea,
Save for the sun, who could cross this sea?
The crossing is perilous, highly perilous the course,
And midway lie the waters of death, whose surface is impassable.   100
Suppose, Gilgamesh, you do cross the sea,
When you reach the waters of death, what will you do?
Yet, Gilgamesh, there is Ur-Shanabi,[1] Utanapishtim's boatman,
He has the Stone Charms with him as he trims pine trees in the forest.
Go, show yourself to him,   105
If possible, cross with him, if not, then turn back.

[*Gilgamesh advances and without preamble attacks Ur-Shanabi and smashes
the Stone Charms.*]

When Gilgamesh heard this,
He raised the axe at his side,
He drew the sword at his belt,
He crept forward, went down towards them,   110
Like an arrow he dropped among them,
His battle cry resounded in the forest.
When Ur-Shanabi saw the shining [. . .],

---

1. Servant of Utanapishtim, ferryman who crosses the ocean and the waters of death.

He raised his axe, he trembled before him,
But he, for his part, struck his head [. . .] Gilgamesh,   115
He seized his arm [. . .] his chest.
And the Stone Charms, the protection . . . of the boat,
Without which no one crosses the waters of death,
He smashed them and threw them into the broad sea,
Into the channel he threw them, his own hands foiled him,   120
He smashed them and threw them into the channel!

Gilgamesh said to him, to Ur-Shanabi:

> Now then, Ur-Shanabi, what is the way to Utanapishtim?
> What are its signs? Give them to me,
> Give, oh give me its signs!   125
> If need be, I'll cross the sea,
> If not, I'll roam the steppe.

Ur-Shanabi said to him, to Gilgamesh:

> Your own hands have foiled you, Gilgamesh,
> You have smashed the Stone Charms, you have thrown them into
>   the channel.   130

[*An old version has the following here.*]

> The Stone Charms, Gilgamesh, are what carry me,
> Lest I touch the waters of death.
> In your fury you have smashed them,
> The Stone Charms, they are what I had with me to make the crossing!
>
> Gilgamesh, raise the axe in your hand,   135
> Go down into the forest, cut twice sixty poles each five times twelve
>   cubits long,
> Dress them, set on handguards,
> Bring them to me.

When Gilgamesh heard this,
He raised the axe at his side,   140
He drew the sword at his belt,
He went down into the forest, cut twice sixty poles each five times
    twelve cubits long,
He dressed them, set on handguards,
He brought them to him.
Gilgamesh and Ur-Shanabi embarked in the boat,   145
They launched the boat, they embarked upon it.
A journey of a month and a half they made in three days!
Ur-Shanabi reached the waters of death,
Ur-Shanabi said to him, to Gilgamesh:

> Stand back, Gilgamesh! Take the first pole,   150
> Your hand must not touch the waters of death,
> Take the second, the third, the fourth pole, Gilgamesh,
> Take the fifth, sixth, and seventh pole, Gilgamesh,

Take the eighth, ninth, and tenth pole, Gilgamesh,
Take the eleventh and twelfth pole, Gilgamesh.   155

With twice sixty Gilgamesh had used up the poles.
Then he, for his part, took off his belt,
Gilgamesh tore off his clothes from his body,
Held high his arms for a mast.
Utanapishtim was watching him from a distance,   160
Speaking to himself, he said these words,
He debated to himself:

Why have the Stone Charms, belonging to the boat, been smashed,
And one not its master embarked thereon?
He who comes here is no man of mine.   165

[*In the fragmentary lines that follow, Gilgamesh lands at Utanapishtim's wharf and questions him.*]

Utanapishtim said to him, to Gilgamesh:

Why are your cheeks emaciated, your face cast down,
Your heart wretched, your features wasted,
Woe in your vitals,
Your face like a traveler's from afar,   170
Your features weathered by cold and sun,
Why are you clad in a lion skin, roaming the steppe?

Gilgamesh said to him, to Utanapishtim:

My cheeks would not be emaciated, nor my face cast down,
Nor my heart wretched, nor my features wasted,   175
Nor would there be woe in my vitals,
Nor would my face be like a traveler's from afar,
Nor would my features be weathered by cold and sun,
Nor would I be clad in a lion skin, roaming the steppe,

But for my friend, swift wild donkey, mountain onager, panther
     of the steppe,   180
But for Enkidu, my friend, swift wild donkey, mountain onager, panther
     of the steppe,
He who stood by me as we ascended the mountain,
Seized and killed the bull that came down from heaven,
Felled Humbaba who dwelt in the forest of cedars,
Killed lions at the mountain passes,   185
My friend whom I so loved, who went with me through every hardship,
Enkidu, whom I so loved, who went with me through every hardship,
The fate of mankind has overtaken him.
Six days and seven nights I wept for him,
I would not give him up for burial,   190
Until a worm fell out of his nose.
I was frightened.
I have grown afraid of death, so I roam the steppe,

My friend's case weighs heavy upon me.
A distant road I roam over the steppe, 195
My friend Enkidu's case weighs heavy upon me!
A distant path I roam over the steppe,
How can I be silent? How can I hold my peace?
My friend whom I loved is turned into clay,
Enkidu, my friend whom I loved, is turned into clay! 200
Shall I too not lie down like him,
And never get up, forever and ever?

Gilgamesh said to him, to Utanapishtim:

So it is to go find Utanapishtim, whom they call the "Distant One,"
I traversed all lands, 205
I came over, one after another, wearisome mountains,
Then I crossed, one after another, all the seas.
Too little sweet sleep has smoothed my countenance,
I have worn myself out in sleeplessness,
My muscles ache for misery, 210
What have I gained for my trials?
I had not reached the tavern keeper when my clothes were worn out,
I killed bear, hyena, lion, panther, leopard, deer, ibex, wild beasts
    of the steepe,
I ate their meat, I [. . .] their skins.
Let them close behind me the doors of woe, 215
Let them seal them with pitch and tar.

Utanapishtim said to him, to Gilgamesh:

Why, O Gilgamesh, did you prolong woe,
You who are formed of the flesh of gods and mankind,
You for whom the gods acted like fathers and mothers? 220
When was it, Gilgamesh, you [. . .] to a fool?

You strive ceaselessly, what do you gain?
When you wear out your strength in ceaseless striving,
When you torture your limbs with pain,
You hasten the distant end of your days. 225
Mankind, whose descendants are snapped off like reeds in a canebrake!
The handsome young man, the lovely young woman, death [. . .]
No one sees death,
No one sees the face of death,
No one hears the voice of death, 230
But cruel death cuts off mankind.
Do we build a house forever?
Do we make a home forever?
Do brothers divide an inheritance forever?
Do disputes prevail in the land forever? 235
Do rivers rise in flood forever?
Dragonflies drift downstream on a river,
Their faces staring at the sun,

Then, suddenly, there is nothing.
The sleeper and the dead, how alike they are!   240
They limn not death's image,
No one dead has ever greeted a human in this world.
The supreme gods, the great gods, being convened,
Mammetum, she who creates destinies, ordaining destinies with them,
They established death and life,   245
They did not reveal the time of death.

Tablet XI

Gilgamesh said to him, to Utanapishtim the Distant One:

As I look upon you, Utanapishtim,
Your limbs are not different, you are just as I am.
Indeed, you are not different at all, you are just as I am!
Yet your heart is drained of battle spirit,   5
You lie flat on your back, your arm idle.
You then, how did you join the ranks of the gods and find eternal life?

Utanapishtim said to him, to Gilgamesh:

I will reveal to you, O Gilgamesh, a secret matter,
And a mystery of the gods I will tell you.   10
The city Shuruppak,[2] a city you yourself have knowledge of,
Which once was set on the bank of the Euphrates,
That aforesaid city was ancient and gods once were within it.
The great gods resolved to send the deluge,
Their father Anu was sworn,   15
The counselor the valiant Enlil,
Their throne-bearer Ninurta,
Their canal-officer Ennugi,[3]
Their leader Ea was sworn with them.
He repeated their plans to the reed fence: 20
"Reed fence, reed fence, wall, wall!
Listen, O reed fence! Pay attention, O wall!
O Man of Shuruppak, son of Ubar-Tutu,
Wreck house, build boat,
Forsake possessions and seek life,   25
Belongings reject and life save!
Take aboard the boat seed of all living things.
The boat you shall build,
Let her dimensions be measured out:
Let her width and length be equal,   30
Roof her over like the watery depths."
I understood full well, I said to Ea, my lord:
"Your command, my lord, exactly as you said it,

2. City in Babylonia reputed to antedate the   written.
flood, long abandoned at the time the epic was   3. Minor deity in charge of water courses.

I shall faithfully execute.
What shall I answer the city, the populace, and the elders?"   35
Ea made ready to speak,
Saying to me, his servant:
"So, you shall speak to them thus:
'No doubt Enlil dislikes me,
I shall not dwell in your city.   40
I shall not set my foot on the dry land of Enlil,
I shall descend to the watery depths and dwell with my lord Ea.
Upon you he shall shower down in abundance,
A windfall of birds, a surprise of fishes,
He shall pour upon you a harvest of riches,   45
In the morning cakes in spates,
In the evening grains in rains.'"

At the first glimmer of dawn,
The land was assembling at the gate of Atrahasis:[4]
The carpenter carried his axe,   50
The reed cutter carried his stone,
The old men brought cordage,
The young men ran around,
The wealthy carried the pitch,
The poor brought what was needed.   55
In five days I had planked her hull:
One full acre was her deck space,
Ten dozen cubits, the height of each of her sides,
Ten dozen cubits square, her outer dimensions.[5]
I laid out her structure, I planned her design: 60
I decked her in six,
I divided her in seven,
Her interior I divided in nine.
I drove the water plugs into her,
I saw to the spars and laid in what was needful.   65
Thrice thirty-six hundred measures of pitch I poured in the oven,
Thrice thirty-six hundred measures of tar I poured out inside her.
Thrice thirty-six hundred measures basket-bearers brought
        aboard for oil,
Not counting the thirty-six hundred measures of oil that the offering
        consumed,
And the twice thirty-six hundred measures of oil that the boatbuilders
        made off with.   70
For the builders I slaughtered bullocks,
I killed sheep upon sheep every day,
Beer, ale, oil, and wine
I gave out to the workers like river water,
They made a feast as on New Year's Day,   75

---

4. Literally, "Super-wise," another Akkadian name of the immortal flood hero Utanapishtim.
5. The proportions of the boat suggest standard measures of both ship building and the construction of ziggurats, pyramidal temple towers.

I dispensed ointment with my own hand.
By the setting of Shamash,[6] the ship was completed.
Since boarding was very difficult,
They brought up gangplanks, fore and aft,
They came up her sides two-thirds of her height.   80
Whatever I had I loaded upon her:
What silver I had I loaded upon her,
What gold I had I loaded upon her,
What living creatures I had I loaded upon her,
I sent up on board all my family and kin,   85
Beasts of the steppe, wild animals of the steppe, all types of skilled
    craftsmen I sent up on board.
Shamash set for me the appointed time:
"In the morning, cakes in spates,
In the evening, grains in rains,
Go into your boat and caulk the door!"   90
That appointed time arrived,
In the morning cakes in spates,
In the evening grains in rains,
I gazed upon the face of the storm,
The weather was dreadful to behold!   95
I went into the boat and caulked the door.
To the caulker of the boat, to Puzur-Amurri the boatman,
I gave over the edifice, with all it contained.

At the first glimmer of dawn,
A black cloud rose above the horizon.   100
Inside it Adad[7] was thundering,
While the destroying gods Shullat and Hanish[8] went in front,
Moving as an advance force over hill and plain.
Errakal[9] tore out the mooring posts of the world,
Ninurta[1] came and made the dikes overflow.   105
The supreme gods held torches aloft,
Setting the land ablaze with their glow.
Adad's awesome power passed over the heavens,
Whatever was light was turned into darkness.
He flooded the land, he smashed it like a clay pot!   110
For one day the storm wind blew,
Swiftly it blew, the flood came forth,
It passed over the people like a battle,
No one could see the one next to him,

---

6. The references to Shamash here and below suggest that in some now lost version of this story, Shamash, the god of justice, rather than Ea, the god of wisdom, warned Utanapishtim of the flood and told him how much time he had to build his ship. This substitution of one god for the other might be due to Shamash's role in the epic as protector of Gilgamesh. In the oldest account of the Babylonian story of the flood, Ea sets a timing device, apparently a water clock, to inform Utanapishtim of the time left before the onset of the deluge.
7. God of thunder.
8. Gods of destructive storms.
9. God of death.
1. God of war.

The people could not recognize one another in the downpour. 115
The gods became frightened of the deluge,
They shrank back, went up to Anu's highest heaven.
The gods cowered like dogs, crouching outside.
Ishtar screamed like a woman in childbirth,
And sweet-voiced Belet-ili[2] wailed aloud: 120
"Would that day had come to naught,
When I spoke up for evil in the assembly of the gods!
How could I have spoken up for evil in the assembly of the gods,
And spoken up for battle to destroy my people?
It was I myself who brought my people into the world, 125
Now, like a school of fish, they choke up the sea!"
The supreme gods were weeping with her,
The gods sat where they were, weeping,
Their lips were parched, taking on a crust.
Six days and seven nights 130
The wind continued, the deluge and windstorm leveled the land.
When the seventh day arrived,
The windstorm and deluge left off their battle,
Which had struggled, like a woman in labor.
The sea grew calm, the tempest stilled, the deluge ceased. 135

I looked at the weather, stillness reigned,
And the whole human race had turned into clay.
The landscape was flat as a rooftop.
I opened the hatch, sunlight fell upon my face.
Falling to my knees, I sat down weeping, 140
Tears running down my face.
I looked at the edges of the world, the borders of the sea,
At twelve times sixty double leagues the periphery emerged.
The boat had come to rest on Mount Nimush,[3]
Mount Nimush held the boat fast, not letting it move. 145
One day, a second day Mount Nimush held the boat fast, not letting
   it move.
A third day, a fourth day Mount Nimush held the boat fast, not letting
   it move.
A fifth day, a sixth day Mount Nimush held the boat fast, not letting
   it move.

When the seventh day arrived,
I brought out a dove and set it free. 150
The dove went off and returned,
No landing place came to its view, so it turned back.
I brought out a swallow and set it free,
The swallow went off and returned,
No landing place came to its view, so it turned back. 155

2. A goddess of birth, who in one version of the flood story was said to have collaborated with the god Ea in creating the human race.

3. High peak sometimes identified with Pir Omar Gudrun in Kurdistan. Landing place of the ark in the Gilgamesh epic.

I brought out a raven and set it free,
The raven went off and saw the ebbing of the waters.
It ate, preened, left droppings, did not turn back.
I released all to the four directions,
I brought out an offering and offered it to the four directions.   160
I set up an incense offering on the summit of the mountain,
I arranged seven and seven cult vessels,
I heaped reeds, cedar, and myrtle in their bowls.
The gods smelled the savor,
The gods smelled the sweet savor,   165
The gods crowded round the sacrificer like flies.

As soon as Belet-ili arrived,
She held up the great fly-ornaments that Anu had made
    in his ardor:
"O gods, these shall be my lapis necklace, lest I forget,
I shall be mindful of these days and not forget, not ever!   170
The gods should come to the incense offering,
But Enlil should not come to the incense offering,
For he, irrationally, brought on the flood,
And marked my people for destruction!"
As soon as Enlil arrived,   175
He saw the boat, Enlil flew into a rage,
He was filled with fury at the gods:
"Who came through alive? No man was to survive destruction!"
Ninurta made ready to speak,
Said to the valiant Enlil: 180
"Who but Ea could contrive such a thing?
For Ea alone knows every artifice."

Ea made ready to speak,
Said to the valiant Enlil:
"You, O valiant one, are the wisest of the gods,   185
How could you, irrationally, have brought on the flood?
Punish the wrongdoer for his wrongdoing,
Punish the transgressor for his transgression,
But be lenient, lest he be cut off,
Bear with him, lest he [. . .].   190
Instead of your bringing on a flood,
Let the lion rise up to diminish the human race!
Instead of your bringing on a flood,
Let the wolf rise up to diminish the human race!
Instead of your bringing on a flood,   195
Let famine rise up to wreak havoc in the land!
Instead of your bringing on a flood,
Let pestilence rise up to wreak havoc in the land!
It was not I who disclosed the secret of the great gods,
I made Atrahasis have a dream and so he heard the secret   200
    of the gods.
Now then, make some plan for him."
Then Enlil came up into the boat,

Leading me by the hand, he brought me up too.
He brought my wife up and had her kneel beside me.
He touched our brows, stood between us to bless us: 205
"Hitherto Utanapishtim has been a human being,
Now Utanapishtim and his wife shall become like us gods.
Utanapishtim shall dwell far distant at the source of the rivers."
Thus it was that they took me far distant and had me dwell at the
    source of the rivers.
Now then, who will convene the gods for your sake,   210
That you may find the eternal life you seek?
Come, come, try not to sleep for six days and seven nights.

As he sat there on his haunches,
Sleep was swirling over him like a mist.
Utanapishtim said to her, to his wife: 215

  Behold this fellow who seeks eternal life!
  Sleep swirls over him like a mist.

[*Utanapishtim's wife, taking pity on Gilgamesh, urges her husband to awaken him and let him go home*].

His wife said to him, to Utanapishtim the Distant One:

  Do touch him that the man may wake up,
  That he may return safe on the way whence he came,   220
  That through the gate he came forth he may return to his land.

Utanapishtim said to her, to his wife:

  Since the human race is duplicitous, he'll endeavor to dupe you.
  Come, come, bake his daily loaves, put them one after another by his
      head,
  Then mark the wall for each day he has slept.   225

She baked his daily loaves for him, put them one after another by his head,
Then dated the wall for each day he slept.
The first loaf was dried hard,
The second was leathery, the third soggy,
The crust of the fourth turned white,
The fifth was gray with mold, the sixth was fresh,   230
The seventh was still on the coals when he touched him, the man woke up.

Gilgamesh said to him, to Utanapishtim the Distant One:

  Scarcely had sleep stolen over me,
  When straightaway you touched me and roused me.   235

Utanapishtim said to him, to Gilgamesh:

  Up with you, Gilgamesh, count your daily loaves,
  That the days you have slept may be known to you.
  The first loaf is dried hard,

The second is leathery, the third soggy,   240
The crust of the fourth has turned white,
The fifth is gray with mold,
The sixth is fresh,
The seventh was still in the coals when I touched you and
    you woke up.

Gilgamesh said to him, to Utanapishtim the Distant One: 245

What then should I do, Utanapishtim, whither should I go,
Now that the Bereaver has seized my flesh?
Death lurks in my bedchamber,
And wherever I turn, there is death!

Utanapishtim said to him, to Ur-Shanabi the boatman: 250

Ur-Shanabi, may the harbor offer you no haven,
May the crossing point reject you,
Be banished from the shore you shuttled to.
The man you brought here,
His body is matted with filthy hair,   255
Hides have marred the beauty of his flesh.
Take him away, Ur-Shanabi, bring him to the washing place.
Have him wash out his filthy hair with water, clean as snow,
Have him throw away his hides, let the sea carry them off,
Let his body be rinsed clean.   260
Let his headband be new,
Have him put on raiment worthy of him.
Until he reaches his city,
Until he completes his journey,
Let his garments stay spotless, fresh and new.   265

Ur-Shanabi took him away and brought him to the washing place.
He washed out his filthy hair with water, clean as snow,
He threw away his hides, the sea carried them off,
His body was rinsed clean.
He renewed his headband,   270
He put on raiment worthy of him.
Until he reached his city,
Until he completed his journey,
His garments would stay spotless, fresh and new.

Gilgamesh and Ur-Shanabi embarked on the boat,   275
They launched the boat, they embarked upon it.
His wife said to him, to Utanapishtim the Distant One:

Gilgamesh has come here, spent with exertion,
What will you give him for his homeward journey?

At that he, Gilgamesh, lifted the pole,   280
Bringing the boat back by the shore.
Utanapishtim said to him, to Gilgamesh:

Gilgamesh, you have come here, spent with exertion,
What shall I give you for your homeward journey?
I will reveal to you, O Gilgamesh, a secret matter,   285
And a mystery of the gods I will tell you.
There is a certain plant, its stem is like a thornbush,
Its thorns, like the wild rose, will prick [your hand].
If you can secure this plant, [. . .]

No sooner had Gilgamesh heard this,   290
He opened a shaft, flung away his tools.
He tied heavy stones to his feet,
They pulled him down into the watery depths.
He took the plant though it pricked his hand.
He cut the heavy stones from his feet,   295
The sea cast him up on his home shore.

Gilgamesh said to him, to Ur-Shanabi the boatman:

Ur-Shanabi, this plant is cure for heartache,
Whereby a man will regain his stamina.
I will take it to ramparted Uruk,   300
I will have an old man eat some and so test the plant.
His name shall be "Old Man Has Become Young-Again-Man."
I myself will eat it and so return to my carefree youth.

At twenty double leagues they took a bite to eat,
At thirty double leagues they made their camp.   305

Gilgamesh saw a pond whose water was cool,
He went down into it to bathe in the water.
A snake caught the scent of the plant,
Stealthily it came up and carried the plant away,
On its way back it shed its skin.   310

Thereupon Gilgamesh sat down weeping,
His tears flowed down his face,
He said to Ur-Shanabi the boatman:

For whom, Ur-Shanabi, have my hands been toiling?
For whom has my heart's blood been poured out?   315
For myself I have obtained no benefit,
I have done a good deed for a reptile!
Now, floodwaters rise against me for twenty double leagues,
When I opened the shaft, I flung away the tools.
How shall I find my bearings?   320
I have come much too far to go back, and I abandoned the boat on
    the shore.

At twenty double leagues they took a bite to eat,
At thirty double leagues they made their camp.

When they arrived in ramparted Uruk,
Gilgamesh said to him, to Ur-Shanabi the boatman: 325

    Go up, Ur-Shanabi, pace out the walls of Uruk.
    Study the foundation terrace and examine the brickwork.
    Is not its masonry of kiln-fired brick?
    And did not seven masters lay its foundations?
    One square mile of city, one square mile of gardens,   330
    One square mile of clay pits, a half square mile of Ishtar's dwelling,
    Three and a half square miles is the measure of Uruk!

THE HEBREW BIBLE

ca. 1000–300 B.C.E.

The sacred writings of the ancient Hebrew people are arguably the world's most influential texts. They have remained the sacred text of Judaism and have inspired two other major world religions: Christianity and Islam. Because these texts have been so influential in human affairs, and have become central to so many people's core religious beliefs, they are not often read in the same way as "literary" texts. But studying the books of the Hebrew Bible as literature—paying close attention to their narrative techniques, their imagery, characterization, and point of view—is not incompatible with religious faith. Close reading enriches our understanding and appreciation of these texts as supremely important cultural and historical documents, for readers of any religious background or belief.

The Hebrew Bible encompasses a rich variety of texts from different periods, composed in both poetry and prose. One of the obvious differences between the Bible and most works of "literature"—such as **Sophocles's** *Oedipus the King* or Virgil's *Aeneid*— is that no single human hand composed the whole Bible, or even the whole of Genesis or Job. Traditionally, Moses is thought to have been the author of the first five books of the Bible and also, according to some traditions, the book of Job. But modern Bible scholars agree that these books, in their current form, must have been woven together from several different earlier sources. This theory explains the otherwise puzzling fact that there are often odd contradictions and repetitions in the narrative. For example, God tells Noah to take two of every kind of animal into the ark; but a little later, the Lord tells Noah to take seven pairs of each animal. The simplest explanation for this kind of discrepancy is that the text we have is a collage built of several earlier narratives, put together, or "redacted," into a single master story. Many scholars believe that it is possible to distinguish between the different original strands, each of which has its distinct stylistic features and perspectives on the narrative. For instance, one strand of the text is identified by the name that it uses for God, YHWH (a personal name for the Hebrew god: in English, Jehovah, and hence the strand is called *J*); in another strand (dubbed *E*), God is called Elohim (which comes from the standard Semitic term for any god, *el*).

The various sources have been put together with great skill, and the result is a text of extraordinary literary, philosophical, and theological richness. The lengthiest selections included here are abridged versions of the books of Genesis and Job. Perhaps the most important element running through the two is a complex ethical concern with how human suffering and prosperity come about and what role God plays in shaping human lives. The books resist easy answers to these questions. We might expect that God would simply punish wrongdoers and reward the righteous; and indeed, he does punish Adam and Eve for their disobedience. But often the relation between human behavior and divine favor is shown to be deeply mysterious. God favors Abel over Cain, blesses Noah and Abraham over all other humans, seems to pay more attention to Isaac than Ishmael, favors Jacob over Esau and Joseph over his brothers, and blesses the Hebrew people over all other inhabitants of the Middle East; but in none of these cases are we given an explanation, let alone a moral justification. Moreover, God allows even his favorites, such as Jacob, Joseph, and Job, to suffer terrible hardship before restoring them to prosperity. The book of Job brings this issue explicitly to the forefront. God's ways are mysterious, and instead of reinforcing a simple moral (like "Be good and God will bless you"), the Bible constantly undercuts it. But throughout these texts, we see that God's power is the major force in all of human history.

It is no accident that the book of Genesis—unlike other ancient creation stories—begins not with earth, sky, and sea but with God himself, the originator of everything.

GENESIS

The first book of the Bible takes its name from the Greek word for "origin" or "birth"—*genesis*. The book tells a story of how the world, and the human race, came into existence; how humans first disobeyed God; and how God began to establish a special relationship with a series of chosen men and their families: Noah, Abraham, Isaac, Jacob, and Joseph. The book was probably redacted in the fifth century B.C.E., a period when the people of Judah were in exile in Babylon. One can understand Genesis in this context as an attempt to consolidate Jewish identity in the midst of an alien culture.

The first section (chapters 1–11) recounts "creation history"—God's creation of the world and of humankind, and the development of early human society. Human beings occupy center stage in this account of the world's origin, as they do not in, for example, Mesopotamian and Greek creation stories. This early age is marked especially by God's anger at humanity, from his expulsion of Adam and Eve from Eden to his destruction of the Tower of Babel, which scatters human beings and divides their single language into many languages. God's decision to destroy humanity is presented as a reversal of the original act of creation. The flood mixes together again the waters that were separated on the second day of creation, and it destroys almost all the different kinds of animals created on the fifth and sixth days, together with almost all humans.

But not quite all animals and humans are destroyed. Noah and his family, and the animals taken onto the ark, are spared, because Noah has found favor in God's eyes; Noah's various wives and the chosen animals, it seems, have attracted no particular divine attention but benefit by association with Noah. This dramatic demonstration of God's power and willingness to favor certain members of the human race while destroying others leads to a new beginning. The second part of Genesis (chapters 12–50) moves from humanity in general to the stories of four men and their families: Abraham and his wife, Sarah; Isaac and his wife, Rebekah; Jacob and his wives, Leah and Rachel; and Joseph and his brothers. The transition is marked by God's first declaration of his commitment to the people of Israel. When he tells Noah's descendant Abram (who will be renamed Abraham) to leave his home in Mesopotamia, he declares, "I will make you a great nation and I will bless you and make your name great, and you shall be a blessing." Showing him the land of Canaan, he promises, "To your seed I will give this land." This positive covenant builds on the merely negative promise God has already made to humanity in general: that he will never again destroy the world by flood (chapter 9). Now there is a purpose in history: other peoples will be blessed through the people of Israel, who are chosen for a particularly close relationship with God.

Many complications arise that seem to threaten the fulfillment of the covenant—and add narrative excitement to the story. God has promised "this land" to Abraham's children, but repeatedly, Abraham's descendants must leave the land of their fathers, deferring the hope of a settled home in the promised land. The pattern of exile from home recurs again and again in the book of Genesis and recalls the expulsion of Adam and Eve from the Garden of Eden, while the strife between family members, especially brothers, and the theme of the triumph of a younger brother over an elder, constantly recall the story of Cain and Abel. Repeatedly, we see God's covenant fulfilled in unexpected ways, revealing his power and his surpassing of merely human expectations.

God himself can be seen as the most vivid and complex character of the book of Genesis. He, like the humans made in his image, enjoys an evening stroll through a cool garden; he is willing to scheme and make deals; he has his particular friends and his favorites; and he is capable of emotions: pleasure, hope, anger, and regret. But the human characters in this book, both men and women, are also strikingly vivid. They are people of intense feelings, and their relationships with one another, their loves, hatreds, fears, and desires, are evoked in compelling detail.

It is worthwhile to pay close attention to the way the text brings people's feelings, characters, and motivations to life in just a few simple words. We often seem to be invited to ponder several possible layers of meaning in what people say, as when Abraham loads up Isaac with wood for the fire, takes the cleaver in his hand, and leads him into the mountain. Isaac says simply, "Father!" Is he scared? Does he know what his father plans to do? Does the word fill Abraham himself with guilt and horror? Or is he unshaking in his resolve to obey?

Like the *Odyssey*, the book of Genesis is about the search for a homeland, a special place of belonging—although here the quest belongs not to a single man but to a whole people. As in the *Odyssey*, hospitality plays an essential part in the value structure of the text. It is often through human hospitality that God's plan can succeed. Abraham, sitting by his tent flap in the alien land of Mamre, passes a test of his hospitality with flying colors when he offers a lavish feast to the "three men" who

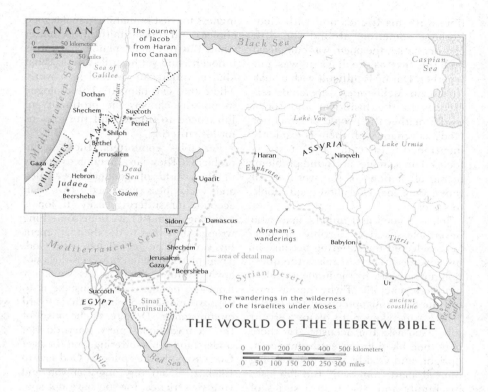

THE WORLD OF THE HEBREW BIBLE

turn out to be messengers of the Lord. The descendants of Abraham negotiate their relationships with the various other peoples who inhabit the area that God seems to have promised as their inheritance. At the same time, they must try to avoid total assimilation; in terms of culture, worship, and "seed," the people must remain distinct. Circumcision, which God enjoins on Abraham and his family, marks this male line off from its neighbors.

EXODUS

After the death of Joseph, the Hebrew people remain in Egypt and multiply, and the Egyptians become increasingly hostile toward this alien population. Moses, along with his brother Aaron, is chosen by God as the savior of the people, the man who will lead them out of slavery and exile and back to their homeland in Canaan. They escape from Egypt, crossing the waters of the Red Sea, which miraculously part to let them through and then wash back to drown Pharoah and his army. In the wilderness, Moses goes to hear the word of God at the top of Mount Sinai, and the Ten Commandments are revealed to him: ten rules of ethical and religious conduct, to be carved on stone tablets, that will form the basis for the new law of the Hebrew people and their covenant with God.

JOB

The book of Job draws on an ancient folk tale about God and his Accuser (the Hebrew term is "Satan") testing a just man, who finally passes their test. But the biblical story makes this motif into the prose frame for an extraordinary poem recounting Job's conversations with his friends and with God. Perhaps sometime around the fifth century B.C.E., the poem was composed and the text as we have it was put together. Dating is difficult with a book that seems deliberately to exclude references to the historical and social world: neither the people of Israel nor God's covenant with them is explicitly mentioned. Instead, the text is focused on a single, profound problem, facing all nations of the world at all times. Why does God allow good people to suffer?

Job is a good and upright man who nevertheless suffers horribly—in fact, he is selected for suffering because of his goodness. The text raises the question not only of why the innocent suffer but more generally of why there is misfortune and unhappiness in the world. "Have you taken note of my servant Job," God asks the Accuser, "for there is no one like him on earth: innocent, upright, and God-fearing, and keeping himself apart from evil?" But Job loses his family and wealth in a series of calamities that strike one after the other like hammer blows and is then plagued with a horrible disease. In a series of magnificent speeches, he expresses his sense of his own innocence and demands one thing: to understand the reason for his suffering.

From the beginning, we can see a little farther into the problem than Job. In the prologue, the Accuser challenges God's praise of Job by pointing out that Job's goodness has never been tested; it is easy to be righteous in prosperity. Because we see that Job's afflictions originate in a test, we know that there is a reason for his suffering, but we may not find it a valid reason and may feel that Job is the object of sport for higher powers. If so, what we know from the prologue only makes the problem of innocent suffering worse. Alternatively, we can see God's wager as a sign of his respect for Job and his will-

ingness to trust humanity to make good choices and remain faithful no matter what. But the fact remains that Job is innocent, and yet he still suffers. What kind of order can we find in a world where that can happen? The prologue in no way cancels the profundity of Job's need to understand the reasons for his suffering.

For Job's comforters, there is no problem. They are anchored solidly in the world of goodness rewarded and wickedness punished. They can account for suffering easily. If Job is suffering, he must have done something wrong. All he has to do, then, is repent his sin and be reconciled with God. Their pious formula, however, does not apply to Job's situation. As we know from the prologue, their mistake is to confuse moral goodness with outward circumstance. Despite or because of their conventional piety, they do not understand Job's suffering, and they get God wrong. In the epilogue, God says to Eliphaz, "I am very angry at you and your two friends, for you have not spoken rightly about me as did my servant Job." Job has spoken rightly by insisting on his innocence and not reducing God's ways to a formula. He also avoids identifying goodness with his fortune in life; unlike his friends, Job acknowledges that good people sometimes suffer dreadfully, and he is appalled by it. But he fulfills God's expectations because he does not curse or in any way repudiate him. Instead, Job wants God to meet him face to face. But he is mistaken to think that he and God can meet on such equal terms and that he can get an explanation. In the end, God does speak to him, but only to pose a series of wonderful but entirely unanswerable questions, such as "Where were you when I founded the earth?" There is no reciprocal conversation; Job simply, briefly, acknowledges his error and recognizes the vast, incommensurable greatness of God.

The text culminates in God's magnificent speech from the storm, which ranges over all of creation and its animal life. The contrast with the account of creation in the first chapter of Genesis, which puts human beings at the center, is dramatic. Here there are beasts whose might far surpasses that of humans, who seem just a part of the created world, and the poetry of this speech conveys the awe and mystery that are attributes of God. The book of Job does not explain innocent suffering, but it does leave us with a sense of what we cannot understand.

PSALMS

The book of Psalms is a collection of 150 poems or hymns. Traditionally, King David was imagined as the author, though modern scholars believe that the various poems come from different time periods, some from before Jerusalem was besieged and finally destroyed by the Babylonians (in 587 B.C.E.), while others (such as "By the Rivers of Babylon") were clearly composed afterward, at a time when the Hebrew people were exiled to the city of their conquerors. Most were composed to be used in worship, and they range in theme and mood, from hymns of praise or joyful thanksgiving to desperate songs of lament expressing the sorrows of a people in exile or the bitterness of a person unjustly wronged. The rich, vivid imagery of the Psalms—memorably conveyed in the language of the King James translation, used here—has had an essential influence on the development of literature in English.

A NOTE ON THE TRANSLATIONS

Except for the Psalms, presented in the King James Version, the biblical text given here is from the recent modern translations by Robert Alter. Alter's language is mostly contemporary, but he is conscious of the need to be faithful to the poetic rhythms of the original—both in the verse of the book of Job and in the rhythmical prose of Genesis (which includes short passages of verse). Far more than other translators, Alter preserves the simple syntax and verbal repetitions of the Hebrew—for instance, by repeating *and* no less than twenty times in the first eight verses of Genesis. The lack of subordination is an essential feature of the original text's style, as are other kinds of word order that Alter tries to imitate in English, like emphatic inversion (God says, "To your seed I will give" rather than "I will give to your seed"). The Bible tells its complex story in a surprisingly small number of words, and nouns may take on greater power through their repetition in a number of different contexts: it is worthwhile to trace, for example, the use of *hand* or *house* or *brother* throughout the book of Genesis. Alter does not manage to retain every repetition or verbal effect of the Hebrew, but the translation comes close to mirroring the Bible's combination of simple, colloquial vocabulary (with occasional uses of archaic or peculiar phrasing) and vivid concrete metaphor. Alter uses *seed*, for example, to reflect the Hebrew imagery, instead of changing it to *children* or *offspring* (as the New Revised Standard Version does).

Genesis 1–4[1]

[From Creation to the Murder of Abel]

1. When God began to create heaven and earth, and the earth then was welter and waste[2] and darkness over the deep and God's breath[3] hovering over the waters, God said, "Let there be light." And there was light. And God saw the light, that it was good, and God divided the light from the darkness. And God called the light Day, and the darkness He called Night. And it was evening and it was morning, first day. And God said, "Let there be a vault in the midst of the waters, and let it divide water from water."[4] And God made the vault and it divided the water beneath the vault from the water above the vault, and so it was. And God called the vault Heavens, and it was evening and it was morning, second day. And God said, "Let the waters under the heavens be gathered in one place so that the dry land will appear," and so it was. And God called the dry land Earth and the gathering of waters He called Seas, and God saw that it was good. And God said, "Let the earth grow grass, plants yielding seed of each kind and trees bearing fruit of each kind, that has its seed within it upon the earth." And so it was. And the earth put forth grass, plants yielding seed, and trees bearing fruit of each kind, and God saw that it was good. And it was evening and it was morning, third day. And God said, "Let there be lights in the vault of the heavens to divide the day from the night, and they shall be signs for the fixed times and for days and years, and they shall be lights in the vault of the heavens to light up the earth." And so it was. And God made the two great lights, the great light for dominion of day and the small light for dominion of night, and the stars. And God placed them in the vault of the heavens to light up the earth and to have dominion over day and night and to divide the light from the darkness. And God saw that it was good. And it was evening and it was morning, fourth day. And God said, "Let the waters swarm with the swarm of living creatures and let fowl fly over the earth across the vault of the heavens." And God created the great sea monsters and every living creature that crawls, which the water had swarmed forth of each kind, and the winged fowl of each kind, and God saw that it was good. And God blessed them, saying, "Be fruitful and multiply and fill the water in the seas and let the fowl multiply in the earth." And it was evening and it was morning, fifth day. And God said, "Let the earth bring forth living creatures of each kind, cattle and crawling things and wild beasts of each kind." And so it was. And God made wild beasts of each kind and cattle of every kind and all crawling things on the ground of each kind, and God saw that it was good. And God said, "Let us make a human in our image,[5] by our likeness, to hold sway over the fish of the sea and the fowl of the heavens and the cattle and the wild beasts and all the crawling things that crawl upon the earth.

---

1. Excerpts from Genesis are translated by Robert Alter. The notes are indebted to Alter's annotations.

2. The translator combines a rare English word (*welter*, meaning chaos, or the turmoil of rolling waves) with *waste* to render a phrase that is very rare in the Hebrew, *tohu wabohu*.

3. The Hebrew word for "breath," *ruah*, may also mean "spirit."

4. The water below the vault, or sky, is the ocean; the water above the vault is the rain.

5. The Hebrew word for "human" is *'adam*, which also means "dust"; it is not the first man's name, but the noun denoting all humanity. It does not necessarily imply that the human is male.

> And God created the human in his image,
> in the image of God He created him,
> male and female He created them.[6]

And God blessed them, and God said to them, "Be fruitful and multiply and fill the earth and conquer it, and hold sway over the fish of the sea and the fowl of the heavens and every beast that crawls upon the earth." And God said, "Look, I have given you every seed-bearing plant on the face of all the earth and every tree that has fruit bearing seed, yours they will be for food. And to all the beasts of the earth and to all the fowl of the heavens and to all that crawls on the earth, which has the breath of life within it, the green plants for food." And so it was. And God saw all that He had done, and, look, it was very good. And it was evening and it was morning, the sixth day.

2.[7] Then the heavens and the earth were completed, and all their array. And God completed on the seventh day the task He had done, and He ceased on the seventh day from all the task He had done. And God blessed the seventh day and hallowed it, for on it He had ceased from all His task that He had created to do. This is the tale of the heavens and the earth when they were created.

On the day the LORD God made earth and heavens, no shrub of the field being yet on the earth and no plant of the field yet sprouted, for the LORD God had not caused rain to fall on the earth and there was no human to till the soil, and wetness would well from the earth to water all the surface of the soil, then the LORD God fashioned the human, humus from the soil,[8] and blew into his nostrils the breath of life, and the human became a living creature. And the LORD God planted a garden in Eden, to the east, and He placed there the human He had fashioned. And the LORD God caused to sprout from the soil every tree lovely to look at and good for food, and the tree of life was in the midst of the garden, and the tree of knowledge, good and evil. Now a river runs out of Eden to water the garden and from there splits off into four streams. The name of the first is Pishon, the one that winds through the whole land of Havilah, where there is gold. And the gold of that land is goodly, bdellium[9] is there, and lapis lazuli. And the name of the second river is Gihon, the one that winds through all the land of Cush. And the name of the third river is Tigris, the one that goes to the east of Ashur. And the fourth river is Euphrates. And the LORD God took the human and set him down in the garden of Eden to till it and watch it. And the LORD God commanded the human, saying, "From every fruit of the garden you may surely eat. But from the tree of knowledge, good and evil, you shall not eat, for on the day you eat from it, you are doomed to die." And the LORD God said, "It is not good for the human to be alone, I shall make him a sustainer beside him." And the LORD God fashioned from the soil each beast of the field and each fowl of the heavens and brought each to the human to see what he would call it, and whatever the human called a

---

6. Here and elsewhere in the translation, the indentation marks a shift into a brief passage of verse in the translation, reflecting a shift in the original.

7. This is the beginning of a different account of the Creation, which does not agree in all respects with the first.

8. There is a pun in the Hebrew on 'adam, "human," and 'adamah, "humus" or "soil."

9. A fragrant tree.

living creature, that was its name. And the human called names to all the cattle and to the fowl of the heavens and to all the beasts of the field, but for the human no sustainer beside him was found. And the LORD God cast a deep slumber on the human, and he slept, and He took one of his ribs and closed over the flesh where it had been, and the LORD God built the rib He had taken from the human into a woman and He brought her to the human. And the human said:

> "This one at last, bone of my bones
> and flesh of my flesh,
> This one shall be called Woman,
> for from man was this one taken."[1]

Therefore does a man leave his father and his mother and cling to his wife and they become one flesh. And the two of them were naked, the human and his woman, and they were not ashamed.

3. Now the serpent was most cunning of all the beasts of the field that the LORD God had made. And he said to the woman, "Though God said, you shall not eat from any tree of the garden—" And the woman said to the serpent, "From the fruit of the garden's trees we may eat, but from the fruit of the tree in the midst of the garden God has said, 'You shall not eat from it and you shall not touch it, lest you die.'" And the serpent said to the woman, "You shall not be doomed to die. For God knows that on the day you eat of it your eyes will be opened and you will become as gods knowing good and evil." And the woman saw that the tree was good for eating and that it was lust to the eyes and the tree was lovely to look at, and she took of its fruit and ate, and she also gave to her man, and he ate. And the eyes of the two were opened, and they knew they were naked, and they sewed fig leaves and made themselves loincloths.

And they heard the sound of the LORD God walking about in the garden in the evening breeze, and the human and his woman hid from the LORD God in the midst of the trees of the garden. And the LORD God called to the human and said to him, "Where are you?" And he said, "I heard Your sound in the garden and I was afraid, for I was naked, and I hid." And He said, "Who told you that you were naked? From the tree I commanded you not to eat have you eaten?" And the human said, "The woman whom you gave by me, she gave me from the tree, and I ate." And the LORD God said to the woman, "What is this you have done?" And the woman said, "The serpent beguiled me and I ate." And the LORD God said to the serpent, "Because you have done this,

> Cursed be you
> of all cattle and all beasts of the field.
> On your belly shall you go
> and dust shall you eat all the days of your life.
> Enmity will I set between you and the woman,
> between your seed and hers.

---

1. "Man" is *ish* in Hebrew; "woman" is *ishshah*.

He will boot your head
and you will bite his heel."[2]

To the woman He said,

"I will terribly sharpen your birth pangs,
in pain shall you bear children.
And for your man shall be your longing,
and he shall rule over you."

And to the human He said, "Because you listened to the voice of your wife and
ate from the tree that I commanded you 'You shall not eat from it,'

Cursed be the soil for your sake,
with pangs shall you eat from it all the days of your life.
Thorn and thistle shall it sprout for you
and you shall eat the plants of the field.
By the sweat of your brow shall you eat bread
till you return to the soil,
for from there were you taken,
for dust you are
and to dust shall you return."

And the human called his woman's name Eve, for she was the mother of all
that lives.[3] And the LORD God made skin coats for the human and his woman,
and He clothed them. And the LORD God said, "Now that the human has
become like one of us, knowing good and evil, he may reach out and take as
well from the tree of life and live forever." And the LORD God sent him from
the garden of Eden to till the soil from which he had been taken. And He drove
out the human and set up east of the garden of Eden the cherubim and the
flame of the whirling sword to guard the way to the tree of life.

4. And the human knew Eve his woman and she conceived and bore Cain, and she
said, "I have got me a man with the LORD." And she bore as well his brother, Abel,
and Abel became a herder of sheep while Cain was a tiller of the soil. And it happened in the course of time that Cain brought from the fruit of the soil an offering
to the LORD. And Abel too had brought from the choice firstlings of his flock, and
the LORD regarded Abel and his offering but He did not regard Cain and his offering, and Cain was very incensed, and his face fell. And the LORD said to Cain,

"Why are you incensed,
and why is your face fallen?
For whether you offer well,
or whether you do not,
at the tent flap sin crouches
and for you is its longing
but you will rule over it."[4]

---

2. "Boot . . . bite" represents a pun in Hebrew:
the word for trampling, or "booting," is repeated
to refer to the snake's reaction; it may refer to
the snake's hiss just before it bites.
3. The name *Hawah*, Eve, is similar to the ver-

bal root *hayah*, "to live."
4. Obscure; it seems to mean something like
"Sin shall be eager for you, but you must
master it."

And Cain said to Abel his brother, "Let us go out to the field." And when they were in the field, Cain rose against Abel his brother and killed him. And the LORD said to Cain, "Where is Abel your brother?" And he said, "I do not know. Am I my brother's keeper?" And He said, "What have you done? Listen! your brother's blood cries out to me from the soil. And so, cursed shall you be by the soil that gaped with its mouth to take your brother's blood from your hand. If you till the soil, it will no longer give you its strength. A restless wanderer shall you be on the earth." And Cain said to the LORD, "My punishment is too great to bear. Now that You have driven me this day from the soil and I must hide from Your presence, I shall be a restless wanderer on the earth and whoever finds me will kill me." And the LORD said to him, "Therefore whoever kills Cain shall suffer sevenfold vengeance." And the LORD set a mark upon Cain so that whoever found him would not slay him.

And Cain went out from the LORD's presence and dwelled in the land of Nod east of Eden. And Cain knew his wife and she conceived and bore Enoch. Then he became the builder of a city and called the name of the city, like his son's name, Enoch. And Irad was born to Enoch,[5] and Irad begot Mehujael and Mehujael begot Methusael and Methusael begot Lamech. And Lamech took him two wives, the name of the one was Adah and the name of the other was Zillah. And Adah bore Jabal: he was the first of tent dwellers with livestock. And his brother's name was Jubal: he was the first of all who play on the lyre and pipe. As for Zillah, she bore Tubal-Cain, who forged every tool of copper and iron. And the sister of Tubal-Cain was Naamah. And Lamech said to his wives,

> "Adah and Zillah, O hearken my voice,
> You wives of Lamech, give ear to my speech.
> For a man have I slain for my wound,
> a boy for my bruising.
> For sevenfold Cain is avenged,
> and Lamech seventy and seven."

And Adam again knew his wife and she bore a son and called his name Seth, as to say, "God has granted me[6] other seed in place of Abel, for Cain has killed him." As for Seth, to him, too, a son was born, and he called his name Enosh. It was then that the name of the LORD was first invoked.

Genesis 6–9

[Noah and the Flood]

6. And it happened as humankind began to multiply over the earth and daughters were born to them, that the sons of God saw that the daughters of man were comely, and they took themselves wives howsoever they chose.[7] And the

---

5. This is the first of many lists of genealogies in the book of Genesis. Genealogy is one of the major ways in which the text evokes and orders historical time and creates a connection between past and present.

6. The pun in Hebrew is between the name

Shet and the verb *shat*, "granted."

7. The passage is based on archaic myths (perhaps from an old Hittite tradition) about male gods ("the sons of God") having sex with mortal women.

LORD said, "My breath shall not abide in the human forever, for he is but flesh. Let his days be a hundred and twenty years."

The Nephilim[8] were then on the earth, and afterward as well, the sons of God having come to bed with the daughters of man who bore them children: they are the heroes of yore, the men of renown.

And the LORD saw that the evil of the human creature was great on the earth and that every scheme of his heart's devising was only perpetually evil. And the LORD regretted having made the human on earth and was grieved to the heart. And the LORD said, "I will wipe out the human race I created from the face of the earth, from human to cattle to crawling thing to the fowl of the heavens, for I regret that I have made them." But Noah found favor in the eyes of the LORD. This is the lineage of Noah—Noah was a righteous man, he was blameless in his time, Noah walked with God—and Noah begot three sons, Shem and Ham and Japheth. And the earth was corrupt before God and the earth was filled with outrage. And God saw the earth and, look, it was corrupt, for all flesh had corrupted its ways on the earth. And God said to Noah, "The end of all flesh is come before me, for the earth is filled with outrage by them, and I am now about to destroy them, with the earth. Make yourself an ark of cypress wood, with cells you shall make the ark, and caulk it inside and out with pitch. This is how you shall make it: three hundred cubits, the ark's length; fifty cubits, its width; thirty cubits, its height. Make a skylight in the ark, within a cubit of the top you shall finish it, and put an entrance in the ark on one side. With lower and middle and upper decks you shall make it. As for me, I am about to bring the Flood, water upon the earth, to destroy all flesh that has within it the breath of life from under the heavens, everything on the earth shall perish. And I will set up my covenant with you, and you shall enter the ark, you and your sons and your wife and the wives of your sons, with you. And from all that lives, from all flesh, two of each thing you shall bring to the ark to keep alive with you, male and female they shall be. From the fowl of each kind and from the cattle of each kind and from all that crawls on the earth of each kind, two of each thing shall come to you to be kept alive. As for you, take you from every food that is eaten and store it by you, to serve for you and for them as food." And this Noah did; as all that God commanded him, so he did.

7. And the LORD said to Noah, "Come into the ark, you and all your household, for it is you I have seen righteous before Me in this generation. Of every clean animal take you seven pairs, each with its mate, and of every animal that is not clean, one pair, each with its mate.[9] Of the fowl of the heavens as well seven pairs, male and female, to keep seed alive over all the earth. For in seven days' time I will make it rain on the earth forty days and forty nights and I will wipe out from the face of the earth all existing things that I have made." And Noah did all that the LORD commanded him.

8. This appears to mean "the fallen ones." The allusion seems cryptic, perhaps because the monotheistic writer is avoiding explicit discussion of multiple semidivine or divine figures, although the idea of such beings would have been familiar to the ancient reader.
9. "Clean" and "not clean" refer to the catego-ries of animals that might or might not be sacri-ficed; it does not refer to dietary restrictions, which came later in the tradition. There is clearly a discrepancy in the narratives here, between the previous chapter's specification of "two of each thing" and this chapter's require-ment of "seven pairs."

Noah was six hundred years old when the Flood came, water over the earth. And Noah and his sons and his wife and his sons' wives came into the ark because of the waters of the Flood. Of the clean animals and of the animals that were not clean and of the fowl and of all that crawls upon the ground two each came to Noah into the ark, male and female, as God had commanded Noah. And it happened after seven days, that the waters of the Flood were over the earth. In the six hundredth year of Noah's life, in the second month, on the seventeenth day of the month, on that day,

> All the wellsprings of the great deep burst
> and the casements of the heavens were opened.

And the rain was over the earth forty days and forty nights. That very day, Noah and Shem and Ham and Japheth, the sons of Noah, and Noah's wife, and the three wives of his sons together with them, came into the ark, they as well as beasts of each kind and cattle of each kind and each kind of crawling thing that crawls on the earth and each kind of bird, each winged thing. They came to Noah into the ark, two by two of all flesh that has the breath of life within it. And those that came in, male and female of all flesh they came, as God had commanded him, and the LORD shut him in. And the Flood was forty days over the earth, and the waters multiplied and bore the ark upward and it rose above the earth. And the waters surged and multiplied mightily over the earth, and the ark went on the surface of the water. And the waters surged most mightily over the earth, and all the high mountains under the heavens were covered. Fifteen cubits above them the waters surged as the mountains were covered. And all flesh that stirs on the earth perished, the fowl and the cattle and the beasts and all swarming things that swarm upon the earth, and all humankind. All that had the quickening breath of life in its nostrils, of all that was on dry land, died. And He wiped out all existing things from the face of the earth, from humans to cattle to crawling things to the fowl of the heavens, they were wiped out from the earth. And Noah alone remained, and those with him in the ark. And the waters surged over the earth one hundred and fifty days.

8. And God remembered Noah and all the beasts and all the cattle that were with him in the ark. And God sent a wind over the earth and the waters subsided. And the wellsprings of the deep were dammed up, and the casements of the heavens, the rain from the heavens held back. And the waters receded from the earth little by little, and the waters ebbed. At the end of a hundred and fifty days the ark came to rest, on the seventeenth day of the seventh month, on the mountains of Ararat. The waters continued to ebb, until the tenth month, on the first day of the tenth month, the mountaintops appeared. And it happened, at the end of forty days, that Noah opened the window of the ark he had made. And he sent out the raven and it went forth to and fro until the waters should dry up from the earth. And he sent out the dove to see whether the waters had abated from the surface of the ground. But the dove found no resting place for its foot and it returned to him to the ark, for the waters were over all the earth. And he reached out and took it and brought it back to him into the ark. Then he waited another seven days and again sent the dove out from the ark. And the dove came back to him at eventide and, look, a plucked olive leaf was in its bill, and Noah knew that the waters had abated from the earth. Then he waited still another seven days

and sent out the dove, and it did not return to him again. And it happened in the six hundred and first year, in the first month, on the first day of the month, the waters dried up from the earth, and Noah took off the covering of the ark and he saw and, look, the surface of the ground was dry. And in the second month, on the twenty-seventh day of the month, the earth was completely dry. And God spoke to Noah, saying, "Go out of the ark, you and your wife and your sons and your sons' wives, with you. All the animals that are with you of all flesh, fowl and cattle and every crawling thing that crawls on the earth, take out with you, and let them swarm through the earth and be fruitful and multiply on the earth." And Noah went out, his sons and his wife and his sons' wives with him. Every beast, every crawling thing, and every fowl, everything that stirs on the earth, by their families, came out of the ark. And Noah built an altar to the LORD and he took from every clean cattle and every clean fowl and offered burnt offerings on the altar. And the LORD smelled the fragrant odor and the LORD said in His heart, "I will not again damn the soil on humankind's score. For the devisings of the human heart are evil from youth. And I will not again strike down all living things as I did. As long as all the days of the earth—

> seedtime and harvest
> and cold and heat
> and summer and winter
> and day and night
> shall not cease."

9. And God blessed Noah and his sons and He said to them, "Be fruitful and multiply and fill the earth. And the dread and fear of you shall be upon all the beasts of the field and all the fowl of the heavens, in all that crawls on the ground and in all the fish of the sea. In your hand they are given. All stirring things that are alive, yours shall be for food, like the green plants, I have given all to you. But flesh with its lifeblood still in it you shall not eat. And just so, your lifeblood I will requite, from every beast I will requite it, and from humankind, from every man's brother. I will requite human life.

> He who sheds human blood
>   by humans his blood shall be shed,[1]
> for in the image of God
>   He made humankind.
> As for you, be fruitful and multiply,
>   swarm through the earth, and hold sway over it."

And God said to Noah and to his sons with him, "And I, I am about to establish My covenant with you and with your seed after you, and with every living creature that is with you, the fowl and the cattle and every beast of the earth with you, all that have come out of the ark, every beast of the earth. And I will establish My covenant with you, that never again shall all flesh be cut off by the waters of the Flood, and never again shall there be a Flood to destroy the earth." And God said, "This is the sign of the covenant that I set between Me and you and every living creature that is with you, for everlasting generations: My bow I have set in the clouds to be a sign of the covenant between Me and

1. There is wordplay in the original, between 'adam, "human," and dam, "blood."

the earth, and so, when I send clouds over the earth, the bow will appear in the cloud. Then I will remember My covenant, between Me and you and every living creature of all flesh, and the waters will no more become a Flood to destroy all flesh. And the bow shall be in the cloud and I will see it, to remember the everlasting covenant between God and all living creatures, all flesh that is on the earth." And God said to Noah, "This is the sign of the covenant I have established between Me and all flesh that is on the earth."

And the sons of Noah who came out from the ark were Shem and Ham and Japheth, and Ham was the father of Canaan. These three were the sons of Noah, and from these the whole earth spread out. And Noah, a man of the soil, was the first to plant a vineyard. And he drank of the wine and became drunk, and exposed himself within his tent. And Ham the father of Canaan saw his father's nakedness and told his two brothers outside. And Shem and Japheth took a cloak and put it over both their shoulders and walked backward and covered their father's nakedness, their faces turned backward so they did not see their father's nakedness. And Noah woke from his wine and he knew what his youngest son had done to him.[2] And he said,

> "Cursed be Canaan,
> the lowliest slave shall he be
> to his brothers."[3]

And he said,

> "Blessed be the LORD
> the God of Shem,
> unto them shall Canaan be slave.
> May God enlarge Japheth,
> may he dwell in the tents of Shem,
> unto them shall Canaan be slave."

And Noah lived after the Flood three hundred and fifty years. And all the days of Noah were nine hundred and fifty years. Then he died.

From Genesis 11

[The Tower of Babel]

11. And all the earth was one language, one set of words. And it happened as they journeyed from the east that they found a valley in the land of Shinar and settled there. And they said to each other, "Come, let us bake bricks and burn them hard." And the brick served them as stone, and bitumen served them as

---

2. The text leaves it unclear what Ham has done. Perhaps simply seeing his father naked is breaking a taboo.

3. An obvious purpose of this story is to justify the idea that the Israelites, rather than the Canaanites, ought to control the land of Canaan—an important issue in later Israelite history. After antiquity, Noah's three sons were often believed to have been the ancestors of the three supposed racial groups in the world: Japheth was the ancestor of European and Asian peoples, Shem was the ancestor of the Semitic races, and Ham was the ancestor of Africans. This interpretation goes well beyond the text itself and has often been motivated, implicitly or explicitly, by racism.

mortar. And they said, "Come, let us build us a city and a tower with its top in the heavens, that we may make us a name, lest we be scattered over all the earth." And the LORD came down to see the city and the tower that the human creatures had built. And the LORD said, "As one people with one language for all, if this is what they have begun to do, now nothing they plot to do will elude them. Come, let us go down and baffle their language there so that they will not understand each other's language." And the LORD scattered them from there over all the earth and they left off building the city. Therefore it is called Babel, for there the LORD made the language of all the earth babble.[4] And from there the LORD scattered them over all the earth.

* * *

From Genesis 12, 17, 18

[God's Promise to Abraham]

12. And the LORD said to Abram,[5] "Go forth from your land and your birthplace and your father's house to the land I will show you. And I will make you a great nation and I will bless you and make your name great, and you shall be a blessing. And I will bless those who bless you, and those who damn you I will curse, and all the clans of the earth through you shall be blessed." And Abram went forth as the LORD had spoken to him and Lot went forth with him, Abram being seventy-five years old when he left Haran. And Abram took Sarai his wife and Lot his nephew and all the goods they had gotten and the folk they had bought in Haran,[6] and they set out on the way to the land of Canaan, and they came to the land of Canaan. And Abram crossed through the land to the site of Shechem, to the Terebinth of Moreh. The Canaanite was then in the land. And the LORD appeared to Abram and said, "To your seed I will give this land." And he built an altar there to the LORD who had appeared to him.

* * *

17. And Abram was ninety-nine years old, and the LORD appeared to Abram and said to him, "I am El Shaddai.[7] Walk in My presence and be blameless, and I will grant My covenant between Me and you and I will multiply you very greatly." And Abram flung himself on his face, and God spoke to him, saying, "As for Me, this is My covenant with you: you shall be father to a multitude of nations. And no longer shall your name be called Abram but your name shall be Abraham, for I have made you father to a multitude of nations.[8] And I will

4. The pun in Hebrew is between *balal*, "to mix" or "to confuse," and the Akkadian place name *Babel* (or *Babylon*), which probably originally meant "gate of heaven." The "tower" is presumably a ziggurat, the type of tall building surrounding temple complexes in many ancient Mesopotamian cultures.
5. Ten generations and hundreds of years have passed since the time of Noah. Abram is a descendant of Noah's son Shem.
6. Slaves. Slavery was a common institution in

the ancient Near East. The slave girl Hagar will play an important part in the story, since she is the mother of Abram's first son, Ishmael.
7. *El* means God; the meaning of *Shaddai* is obscure.
8. The names *Abram* and *Abraham* both mean "exalted father." Abram and Sarai (later Sarah) have to change their names, not to gain titles with new meaning but as a sign of taking on their new roles as instruments of God's purpose.

make you most abundantly fruitful and turn you into nations, and kings shall come forth from you. And I will establish My covenant between Me and you and your seed after you through their generations as an everlasting covenant to be God to you and to your seed after you. And I will give unto you and your seed after you the land in which you sojourn, the whole land of Canaan, as an everlasting holding, and I will be their God."

And God said to Abraham, "As for you, you shall keep My commandment, you and your seed after you through their generations."

* * *

18. And the LORD appeared to him in the Terebinths of Mamre[9] when he was sitting by the tent flap in the heat of the day. And he raised his eyes and saw, and, look, three men were standing before him. He saw, and he ran toward them from the tent flap and bowed to the ground. And he said, "My lord, if I have found favor in your eyes, please do not go on past your servant. Let a little water be fetched and bathe your feet and stretch out under the tree, and let me fetch a morsel of bread, and refresh yourselves. Then you may go on, for have you not come by your servant?" And they said, "Do as you have spoken." And Abraham hurried to the tent to Sarah and he said, "Hurry! Knead three *seahs* of choice semolina flour and make loaves."[1] And to the herd Abraham ran and fetched a tender and goodly calf and gave it to the lad, who hurried to prepare it. And he fetched curds and milk and the calf that had been prepared and he set these before them, he standing over them under the tree, and they ate. And they said to him, "Where is Sarah your wife?" And he said, "There, in the tent." And he said, "I will surely return to you at this very season and, look, a son shall Sarah your wife have," and Sarah was listening at the tent flap, which was behind him. And Abraham and Sarah were old, advanced in years, Sarah no longer had her woman's flow. And Sarah laughed inwardly, saying, "After being shriveled, shall I have pleasure, and my husband is old?" And the LORD said to Abraham, "Why is it that Sarah laughed, saying, 'Shall I really give birth, old as I am?' Is anything beyond the LORD? In due time I will return to you, at this very season, and Sarah shall have a son." And Sarah dissembled, saying, "I did not laugh," for she was afraid. And He said, "Yes, you did laugh."

* * *

From Genesis 21, 22

[Abraham and Isaac]

21. And the LORD singled out Sarah as He had said, and the LORD did for Sarah as He had spoken. And Sarah conceived and bore a son to Abraham in his old age at

9. Terebinths are small trees that produce turpentine; the word used here is sometimes interpreted to mean "oak trees." Mamre was the site of a cult shrine to the major Canaanite sky god.

1. A *seah* is a dry measure equal to about thirty cups; three *seah*s is almost five gallons—a lot of food for three people.

the set time that God had spoken to him. And Abraham called the name of his son who was born to him, whom Sarah bore him, Isaac.[2] And Abraham circumcised Isaac his son when he was eight days old, as God had charged him. And Abraham was a hundred years old when Isaac his son was born to him. And Sarah said,

> "Laughter has God made me,
> Whoever hears will laugh at me."

* * *

22. And it happened after these things that God tested Abraham. And He said to him, "Abraham!" and he said, "Here I am." And He said, "Take, pray, your son, your only one, whom you love, Isaac, and go forth to the land of Moriah and offer him up as a burnt offering on one of the mountains which I shall say to you." And Abraham rose early in the morning and saddled his donkey and took his two lads with him, and Isaac his son, and he split wood for the offering, and rose and went to the place that God had said to him. On the third day Abraham raised his eyes and saw the place from afar. And Abraham said to his lads, "Sit you here with the donkey and let me and the lad walk ahead and let us worship and return to you." And Abraham took the wood for the offering and put it on Isaac his son and he took in his hand the fire and the cleaver, and the two of them went together. And Isaac said to Abraham his father, "Father!" and he said, "Here I am, my son." And he said, "Here is the fire and the wood but where is the sheep for the offering?" And Abraham said, "God will see to the sheep for the offering, my son." And the two of them went together. And they came to the place that God had said to him, and Abraham built there an altar and laid out the wood and bound Isaac his son and placed him on the altar on top of the wood. And Abraham reached out his hand and took the cleaver to slaughter his son. And the Lord's messenger called out to him from the heavens and said, "Abraham, Abraham!" and he said, "Here I am." And he said, "Do not reach out your hand against the lad, and do nothing to him, for now I know that you fear God and you have not held back your son, your only one, from Me." And Abraham raised his eyes and saw and, look, a ram was caught in the thicket by its horns, and Abraham went and took the ram and offered him up as a burnt offering instead of his son. And Abraham called the name of that place YHWH-Yireh, as is said to this day, "On the mount of the Lord there is sight."[3] And the Lord's messenger called out to Abraham once again from the heavens, and He said, "By My own Self I swear, declares the Lord, that because you have done this thing and have not held back your son, your only one, I will greatly bless you and will greatly multiply your seed, as the stars in the heavens and as the sand on the shore of the sea, and your seed shall take hold of its enemies' gate. And all the nations of the earth will be blessed through your seed because you have listened to my voice." And Abraham returned to his lads, and they rose and went together to Beersheba, and Abraham dwelled in Beersheba.

* * *

2. "He who laughs."
3. The place name means "The Lord (Yaweh) sees" or "The Lord is seen."

From Exodus 19–20[1]

[Moses Receives the Law]

19. On the third new moon of the Israelites' going out from Egypt, on this day did they come to the Wilderness of Sinai. And they journeyed onward from Rephidim and they came to the Wilderness of Sinai, and Israel camped there over against the mountain. And Moses had gone up to God, and the LORD called out to him from the mountain, saying, "Thus shall you say to the house of Jacob, and shall you tell to the Israelites: 'You yourselves saw what I did to Egypt, and I bore you on the wings of eagles[2] and I brought you to Me. And now, if you will truly heed My voice and keep My covenant, you will become for Me a treasure among all the peoples, for Mine is all the earth. And as for you, you will become for Me a kingdom of priests and a holy nation.' These are the words that you shall speak to the Israelites."

And Moses came and he called to the elders of the people, and he set before them all these words that the LORD had charged him. And all the people answered together and said, "Everything that the LORD has spoken we shall do." And Moses brought back the people's words to the LORD. And the LORD said to Moses, "Look, I am about to come to you in the utmost cloud, so that the people may hear as I speak to you, and you as well they will trust for all time." And Moses told the people's words to the LORD. And the LORD said to Moses, "Go to the people and consecrate them today and tomorrow, and they shall wash their cloaks. And they shall ready themselves for the third day, for on the third day the LORD will come down before the eyes of all the people on Mount Sinai. And you shall set bounds for the people all around, saying, 'Watch yourselves not to go up on the mountain or to touch its edge. Whosoever touches the mountain is doomed to die. No hand shall touch him,[3] but He shall surely be stoned or be shot, whether beast or man, he shall not live. When the ram's horn blasts long, they[4] it is who will go up the mountain.'" And Moses came down from the mountain to the people, and he consecrated the people, and they washed their cloaks. And he said to the people, "Ready yourselves for three days. Do not go near a woman."[5] And it happened on the third day as it turned morning, that there was thunder and lightning and a heavy cloud on the mountain and the sound of the ram's horn, very strong, and all the people who were in the camp trembled. And Moses brought out the people toward God from the camp and they stationed themselves at the bottom of the mountain. And Mount Sinai was all in smoke because the LORD had come down on it in fire, and its smoke went up like the smoke from a kiln, and the whole mountain trembled greatly. And the sound of the ram's horn grew stronger and stronger. Moses would speak, and God would answer him with voice.[6] And the LORD came down on Mount Sinai, to the mountaintop, and the LORD called Moses to the mountaintop, and Moses went up. And the LORD

---

1. Translated by Robert Alter, to whose notes some of the following annotations are indebted.
2. A metaphor for salvation. "What I did to Egypt" refers to the plagues that afflicted Egypt and to the destruction of the Egyptian army, as it pursued the departing Israelites, at the Red Sea.
3. Whoever violates the ban on touching the

mountain will be impure and an outcast from the community. Therefore he has to be killed at a distance, with stones or arrows.
4. I.e., Moses and Aaron.
5. Sexual abstinence and the washing of clothes were methods of ritual purification.
6. I.e., with words.

said to Moses, "Go down, warn the people, lest they break through to the Lord to see and many of them perish. And the priests, too, who come near to the Lord, shall consecrate themselves,[7] lest the Lord burst forth against them." And Moses said to the Lord, "The people will not be able to come up to Mount Sinai, for You Yourself warned us, saying, 'Set bounds to the mountain and consecrate it.'" And the Lord said to him, "Go down, and you shall come up, you and Aaron[8] with you, and the priests and the people shall not break through to go up to the Lord, lest He burst forth against them." And Moses went down to the people and said it to them.

20. And God spoke all these words, saying: "I am the Lord your God Who brought you out of the land of Egypt, out of the house of slaves. You[9] shall have no other gods beside Me. You shall make you no carved likeness and no image of what is in the heavens above or what is on the earth below or what is in the waters beneath the earth. You shall not bow to them and you shall not worship them, for I am the Lord your God, a jealous god, reckoning the crime of fathers with sons, with the third generation and with the fourth, for My foes and doing kindness to the thousandth generation for My friends and for those who keep My commands. You shall not take the name of the Lord your God in vain, for the Lord will not acquit whosoever takes His name in vain. Remember the sabbath day to hallow it. Six days you shall work and you shall do your tasks, but the seventh day is a sabbath to the Lord your God. You shall do no task, you and your son and your daughter, your male slave and your slavegirl and your beast and your sojourner who is within your gates. For six days did the Lord make the heavens and the earth, the sea and all that is in it, and He rested on the seventh day. Therefore did the Lord bless the sabbath day and hallow it. Honor your father and your mother, so that your days may be long on the soil that the Lord your God has given you. You shall not murder. You shall not commit adultery. You shall not steal. You shall not bear false witness against your fellow man. You shall not covet your fellow man's wife, or his male slave, or his slavegirl, or his ox, or his donkey, or anything that your fellow man has."

And all the people were seeing the thunder and the flashes and the sound of the ram's horn and the mountain in smoke, and the people saw and they drew back and stood at a distance. And they said to Moses, "Speak you with us that we may hear, and let not God speak with us lest we die." And Moses said to the people, "Do not fear, for in order to test you God has come and in order that His fear be upon you, so that you do not offend." And the people stood at a distance, and Moses drew near the thick cloud where God was.

* * *

7. I.e., they are to purify themselves and remain at the bottom of the mountain as the rest of the people do.
8. Moses's closest companion and in an early tradition his brother; Aaron was Israel's first High Priest.

9. Here and throughout this passage, the Hebrew text uses the singular of "you" (formulations of law elsewhere in the Hebrew Bible use the plural). The commandments are thus addressed to each person individually.

From Job[1]

1. A man there was in the land of Uz[2] Job, his name. And the man was blameless and upright and feared God and shunned evil. And seven sons were born to him, and three daughters. And his flocks came to seven thousand sheep and three thousand camels and five hundred yokes of cattle and five hundred she-asses and a great abundance of slaves. And that man was greater than all the dwellers of the East. And his sons would go and hold a feast, in each one's house on his set day, and they would call to their sisters to eat and drink with them. And it happened when the days of the feast came round, that Job would send and consecrate them and rise early in the morning and offer up burnt offerings according to the number of them all. For Job thought, Perhaps my sons have offended and cursed God in their hearts. Thus would Job do at all times.

And one day, the sons of God[3] came to stand in attendance before the LORD, and the Adversary,[4] too, came among them. And the LORD said to the Adversary, "From where do you come?" And the Adversary answered the LORD and said, "From roaming the earth and walking about in it." And the LORD said to the Adversary, "Have you paid heed to my servant Job, for there is none like him on earth, a blameless and upright man, who fears God and shuns evil?" And the Adversary answered the LORD and said, "Does Job fear God for nothing? Have You not hedged him about and his household and all that he has all around? The work of his hands You have blessed, and his flocks have spread over the land. And yet, reach out Your hand, pray, and strike all he has. Will he not curse You to Your face? And the LORD said to the Adversary, "Look, all that he has is in your hands. Only against him do not reach out your hand." And the Adversary went out from before the LORD's presence.

And one day, his sons and his daughters were eating and drinking wine in the house of their brother, the firstborn. And a messenger came to Job and said, "The cattle were plowing and the she-asses grazing by them, and Sabeans fell upon them and took them, and the lads they struck down by the edge of the sword, and I alone escaped to tell you." This one was still speaking when another came and said, "God's fire fell from the heavens and burned among the sheep and the lads and consumed them, and I alone escaped to tell you." This one was still speaking when another came and said, "Chaldaeans set out in three bands and pounced upon the camels and took them, and the lads they struck down by the edge of the sword." This one was still speaking when another came and said, "Your sons and your daughters were eating and drinking wine in the house of their brother, the firstborn. And, look, a great wind came from beyond the wilderness and struck the four corners of the house, and it fell on the young people, and they died. And I alone escaped to tell you." And Job rose and tore his garment and shaved his head and fell to the earth and bowed down.[5] And he said,

---

1. Translated by Robert Alter, to whom some of the following notes are indebted.
2. *'Uts* (Uz) means "counsel," or "advice," so the story takes place in an unreal, fabulous landscape: the Land of Counsel.
3. This phrase reflects a premonotheistic idea of a family or council of gods.

4. "The Adversary," or "the satan" (*hasatan* in the original), means a person, thing, or set of circumstances that is an obstacle to someone. It does not mean "devil"; the modern connotations of evil are absent from the original word, and clearly this "satan" is part of God's court.
5. Gestures of mourning.

> "Naked I came out from my mother's womb,
>   and naked shall I return there.
> The LORD has given and the LORD has taken.
>   May the LORD's name be blessed."

With all this, Job did not offend, nor did he put blame on God.

2. And one day, the sons of God came to stand in attendance before the LORD, and the Adversary, too, came among them to stand in attendance before the LORD. And the LORD said to the Adversary, "From whence do you come?" And the Adversary answered the LORD and said, "From roaming the earth and walking about in it." And the LORD said to the Adversary, "Have you paid heed to My servant Job, for there is none like him on earth, a blameless and upright man, who fears God and shuns evil and still clings to his innocence, and you incited Me against him to destroy him for nothing." And the Adversary answered the LORD and said, "Skin for skin![6] A man will give all he has for his own life. Yet, reach out, pray, your hand and strike his bone and his flesh. Will he not curse You to Your face?" And the LORD said to the Adversary, "Here he is in your hands. Only preserve his life." And the Adversary went out from before the LORD's presence. And he struck Job with a grievous burning rash from the soles of his feet to the crown of his head. And he took a potsherd to scrape himself with, and he was sitting among the ashes. And his wife said to him, "Do you still cling to your innocence? Curse God and die." And he said to her, "You speak as one of the base women would speak. Shall we accept good from God, too, and evil we shall not accept?" With all this, Job did not offend with his lips.

  And Job's three companions heard of all this harm that had come upon him, and they came, each from his place—Eliphaz the Temanite and Bildad the Shuhite and Zophar the Naamathite, and they agreed to meet to grieve with him and to comfort him. And they lifted up their eyes from afar and did not recognize him, and they lifted up their voices and wept, and each tore his garment, and they tossed dust on their heads toward the heavens. And they sat with him on the ground seven days and seven nights, and none spoke a word to him, for they saw that the pain was very great.

3. Afterward, Job opened his mouth and cursed his day. And Job spoke up and he said:

> Annul the day that I was born
>   and the night that said, "A man is conceived."
> That day, let it be darkness.
>   Let God above not seek it out,
>   nor brightness shine upon it.
> Let darkness, death's shadow, foul it,
>   let a cloud-mass rest upon it,
>   let day-gloom dismay it.
> That night, let murk overtake it.
>   Let it not join in the days of the year,
>   let it not enter the number of months.

5

10

---

6. An obscure proverb, perhaps meaning that Job will truly suffer only once pain touches his own skin.

Oh, let that night be barren,
   let it have no song of joy.
Let the day-cursers hex it,
   those ready to rouse Leviathan.[7]   15
Let its twilight stars go dark.
   Let it hope for day in vain,
     and let it not see the eyelids of dawn.
For it did not shut the belly's doors
   to hide wretchedness from my eyes.   20
Why did I not die from the womb,
   from the belly come out, breathe my last?
Why did knees welcome me,
   and why breasts, that I should suck?
For now I would lie and be still,   25
   would sleep and know repose
with kings and the councilors of earth,
   who build ruins for themselves,
or with princes, possessors of gold,
   who fill their houses with silver.   30
Or like a buried stillbirth I'd be,
   like babes who never saw light.
There the wicked cease their troubling,
   and there the weary repose.
All together the prisoners are tranquil,   35
   they hear not the taskmaster's voice.
The small and the great are there,
   and the slave is free of his master.
Why give light to the wretched
   and life to the deeply embittered,   40
who wait for death in vain,
   dig for it more than for treasure,
who rejoice at the tomb,
   are glad when they find the grave?
—To a man whose way is hidden,   45
   and God has hedged him about.
For before my bread my moaning comes,
   and my roar pours out like water.
For I feared a thing—it befell me,
   what I dreaded came upon me.   50
I was not quiet, I was not still,
   I had no repose, and trouble came.

4. And Eliphaz spoke out and he said:

   If speech were tried against you, could you stand it?
     Yet who can hold back words?
   Look, you reproved many,
     and slack hands you strengthened.

---

7. Leviathan is a sea monster, representing chaos in Canaanite mythology. The "day-cursers" are
magicians.

The stumbler your words lifted up,   5
   and bended knees you bolstered.
But now it comes to you and you cannot stand it,
   it reaches you and you are dismayed.
Is not your reverence your safety,
   your hope—your blameless ways?   10
Recall, pray: what innocent man has died,
   and where were the upright demolished?
As I have seen, those who plow mischief,
   those who plant wretchedness, reap it.
Through God's breath they die,   15
   before his nostrils' breathing they vanish.
The lion's roar, the maned beast's sound—
   and the young lions' teeth are smashed.
The king of beasts dies with no prey,
   the whelps of the lion are scattered.   20
And to me came a word in secret,
   and my ear caught a tag-end of it,
in musings from nighttime's visions
   when slumber falls upon men.
Fear called to me, and trembling,   25
   and all my limbs it gripped with fear.
And a spirit passed over my face,
   made the hair on my flesh stand on end.
It halted, its look unfamiliar,
   an image before my eyes,   30
      stillness, and a sound did I hear:
Can a mortal be cleared before God,
   can a man be made pure by his Maker?
Why, His servants He does not trust,
   His agents He charges with blame.   35
All the more so, the clay-house dwellers,
   whose foundation is in the dust,
      who are crushed more quickly than moths.
From morning to eve they are shattered,
   unawares they are lost forever.   40
Should their life-thread be broken within them,
   they die, and without any wisdom.

5. Call out, pray: will any answer you,
   and to whom of the angels will you turn?
For anger kills a fool,
   and the simple, envy slays.
I have seen a fool striking root—   5
   all at once his abode I saw cursed.
His children are distant from rescue
   and are crushed in the gate—none will save.
Whose harvest the hungry eat
   and from among thorns they take it away,   10
      and the thirsty pant for their wealth.
For crime does not spring from the dust,
   nor from the soil does wretchedness sprout.

> But man is to wretchedness born
>> like sparks flying upward.   15
> Yet I search for El[8]
>> and to God I make my case,
> Who does great things without limit
>> wonders beyond all number,
> Who brings rain down on the earth   20
>> and sends water over the fields.
> Who raises the lowly on high—
>> the downcast are lifted in rescue.
> Thwarts the designs of the cunning,
>> and their hands do not perform wisely.   25
> He entraps the wise in their cunning,
>> and the crooked's counsel proves hasty.
> By day they encounter darkness,
>> as in night they go groping at noon.
> He rescues the simple from the sword,   30
>> and from the hand of the strong, the impoverished,
> and the indigent then has hope,
>> and wickedness clamps its mouth shut.
> Why, happy the man whom God corrects.
>> Shaddai's reproof do not spurn!   35
> For He causes pain and binds the wound,
>> He deals blows but His hands will heal.
> In six straits He will save you,
>> and in seven harm will not touch you.
> In famine He redeems you from death,   40
>> and in battle from the sword.
> From the scourge of the tongue you are hidden,
>> and you shall fear not assault when it comes.
> At assault and starvation you laugh,
>> and the beasts of the earth you fear not.   45
> With the stones of the field is your pact,
>> the beasts of the field leagued with you.
> And you shall know that your tent is peaceful,
>> probe your home and find nothing amiss.
> And you shall know that your seed is abundant,   50
>> your offspring like the grass of the earth.
> You shall come to the grave in vigor,
>> as grain-shocks mount in their season.
> Look, this we have searched, it is so.
>> Hear it, and you—you should know.   55

6. And Job spoke out and he said:

> Could my anguish but be weighed,
>> and my disaster on the scales be borne,
> they would be heavier now than the sand of the sea.
>> Thus my words are choked back.

8. God.

For Shaddai's arrows are in me—   5
  their venom my spirit drinks.
    The terrors of God beset me.
Does the wild ass bray over his grass,
  the ox bellow over his feed?[9]
Is tasteless food eaten unsalted,   10
  does the oozing of mallows have savor?[1]
My throat refuses to touch them.
  They resemble my sickening flesh.
If only my wish were fulfilled,
  and my hope God might grant.   15
If God would deign to crush me,
  loose His hand and tear me apart.
And this still would be my comfort,
  I shrink back in pangs—he spares not.
    Yet I withhold not the Holy One's words.   20
What is my strength, that I should hope,
  and what my end that I should endure?
Is my strength the strength of stones,
  is my flesh made of bronze?
Indeed, there is no help within me,   25
  and prudence is driven from me.
The blighted man's friend owes him kindness,
  though the fear of Shaddai he forsake.
My brothers betrayed like a wadi,[2]
  like the channel of brooks that run dry.   30
They are dark from the ice,
  snow heaped on them.
When they warm, they are gone,
  in the heat they melt from their place.
The paths that they go on are winding,   35
  they mount in the void and are lost.
The caravans of Tema looked out,[3]
  the convoys of Sheba awaited.
Disappointed in what they had trusted,
  they reached it and their hopes were dashed.   40
For now you are His.
  You see panic and you fear.
Did I say, Give for me,
  and with your wealth pay a ransom for me,
and free me from the hands of the foe,   45
  from the oppressors' hands redeem me?
Instruct me—as for me, I'll keep silent,
  and let me know where I went wrong.

---

9. Rhetorical questions. The idea is that animals do not complain when fed appropriately, and, by analogy, humans do not complain unless they are truly suffering.
1. The tasteless food may be literal (Job cannot eat because he is too upset), or metaphorical.

2. A desert ravine, which is full of water only in the rainy season; when summer comes, it runs dry.
3. For water, continuing the image of the dried-up *wadi*.

How forceful are honest words.
 Yet what rebuke is the rebuke by you?   50
Do you mean to rebuke with words,
 treat the speech of the desperate as wind?
Even for the orphan you cast lots,
 and haggle for your companion.
And now, deign to turn toward me.   55
 To your face I will surely not lie.
Relent, pray, let there be no injustice.
 Relent. I am yet in the right.
Is there injustice on my tongue?
 Does my palate not taste disasters?   60

7. Does not man have fixed service on earth,
 and like a hired worker's his days?
Like a slave he pants for shade,
 like a hired worker he waits for his pay.
Thus I was heir to futile moons,   5
 and wretched nights were allotted to me.
Lying down, I thought, When shall I rise?—
 Each evening, I was sated with tossing till dawn.
My flesh was clothed with worms and earth-clods,
 my skin rippled with running sores.   10
My days are swifter than the weaver's shuttle.
 They snap off without any hope.
Recall that my life is a breath.
 Not again will my eyes see good.
The eye of who sees me will not make me out.   15
 Your eyes are on me—I am gone.
A cloud vanishes and goes off.
 Thus, who goes down to Sheol[4] will not come up.
He will not return to his home.
 His place will not know him again.   20
As for me, I will not restrain my mouth.
 I would lament with my spirit in straits
  I would speak when my being is bitter.
Am I Yamm[5] or am I the Sea Beast,
 that You should put a watch upon me?   25
When I thought my couch would console me,
 that my bed would bear my lament,
You panicked me in dreams
 and in visions you struck me with terror.
And my throat would have chosen choking,   30
 my bones—death.
I am sickened—I won't live forever.
 Let me be, for my days are mere breath.
What is man that You make him great
 and that You pay heed to him?   35

4. The land of the dead.
5. Yamm is the sea god in Canaanite mythology, also known as Leviathan; he was subdued by Baal, the weather god, whom Job here associates with his own God.

You single him out every morning,
    every moment examine him.
How long till You turn away from me?
    You don't let me go while I swallow my spit.[6]
What is my offense that I have done to You,   40
    O Watcher of man?
Why did You make me Your target,
    and I became a burden to You?
And why do You not pardon my crime
    and let my sin pass away?   45
For soon I shall lie in the dust.
    You will seek me, and I shall be gone.

8. And Bildad the Shuhite spoke out and he said,

How long will you jabber such things?—
    the words of your mouth, one huge wind.
Would God pervert justice,
    would Shaddai pervert what is right?
If your children offended Him,   5
    He dispatched them because of their crime.
If you yourself sought out God,
    and pleaded to Shaddai,
if you were honest and pure,
    by now He would rouse Himself for you,   10
      and would make your righteous home whole.
Then your beginning would seem a trifle
    and your latter day very grand.
For ask, pray, generations of old,
    take in what their fathers found out.   15
For we are but yesterday, unknowing,
    for our days are a shadow on earth.
Will they not teach you and say to you,
    and from their heart bring out words?
Will papyrus sprout with no marsh,   20
    reeds grow grand without water?
Still in its blossom, not yet plucked,
    before any grass it will wither.
Thus is the end of all who forget God,
    and the hope of the tainted is lost.   25
Whose faith is mere cobweb,
    a spider's house his trust.
He leans on his house and it will not stand,
    he grasps it and it does not endure.
—He is moist in the sun,   30
    and his tendrils push out in his garden.
Round a knoll his roots twist,
    on a stone house they take hold.
If his place should uproot him
    and deny him—"I never saw you,"   35

6. I.e., not even for a second.

> why, this is his joyous way,
>   from another soil he will spring.
> Look, God will not spurn the blameless,
>   nor hold the hand of evildoers.
> He will yet fill your mouth with laughter   40
>   and your lips with a shout of joy.
> Your foes will be clothed in disgrace,
>   and the tent of the wicked gone.

9. And Job spoke out and he said

> Of course, I knew it was so:
>   how can man be right before God?
> Should a person bring grievance against Him,
>   He will not answer one of a thousand.
> Wise in mind, staunch in strength,   5
>   who can argue with Him and come out whole?
> He uproots mountains and they know not,
>   overturns them in His wrath.
> He makes earth shake in its setting,
>   and its pillars shudder.   10
> He bids the sun not to rise,
>   and the stars He seals up tight.
> He stretches the heavens alone
>   and tramples the crests of the sea.
> He makes the Bear and Orion,   15
>   the Pleiades and the South Wind's chambers.
> He performs great things without limit
>   and wonders without number.
> Look, He passes over me and I do not see,
>   slips by me and I cannot grasp Him.   20
> Look, He seizes—who can resist Him?
>   Who can tell him, "What do You do?"
> God will not relent his fury.
>   Beneath him Rahab's[7] minions stoop.
> And yet, as for me, I would answer Him,   25
>   would choose my words with Him.
> Though in the right, I can't make my plea.
>   I would have to entreat my own judge.
> Should I call out and He answer me,
>   I would not trust Him to heed my voice   30
> Who for a hair would crush me
>   and make my wounds many for nought.
> He does not allow me to catch my breath
>   as He sates me with bitterness.
> If it's strength—He is staunch,   35
>   and if it's justice—who can arraign Him?
> Though in the right, my mouth will convict me,
>   I am blameless, yet He makes me crooked.
> I am blameless—I know not myself,
>   I loathe my life.   40

7. Another name for the sea monster (Baal, or Leviathan).

It's all the same, and so I thought:
　　the blameless and the wicked He destroys.
If a scourge causes death in an instant,
　　He mocks the innocent's plight.
The earth is given in the wicked man's hand,　　　　　　45
　　the face of its judges He veils.
　　　　If not He—then who else?
And my days are swifter than a courier.
　　They have fled and have never seen good,
slipped away like reed ships,　　　　　　　　　　　　50
　　like an eagle swooping on prey.
If I said, I would forget my lament.
　　I would leave my grim mood and be gladdened,
I was in terror of all my suffering.
　　I knew You would not acquit me.　　　　　　　　55
I will be guilty.
　　Why should I toil in vain?
Should I bathe in snow,
　　make my palms pure with lye,
You would yet plunge me into a pit,　　　　　　　60
　　and my robes would defile me.
For He is not a man like me that I might answer Him,
　　that we might come together in court.
Would there were an arbiter between us,
　　who could lay his hand on us both,　　　　　　65
who could take from me His rod,
　　and His terror would not confound me.
I would speak, and I will not fear Him,
　　for that is not the way I am.

10. My whole being loathes my life.
Let me give vent to my lament.
　　　　Let me speak when my being is bitter.
I shall say to God: Do not convict me.
　　Inform me why You accuse me.　　　　　　　　5
Is it good for You to oppress,
　　to spurn Your own palms' labor,
　　　　and on the council of the wicked to shine?
Do You have the eyes of mortal flesh,
　　do You see as man would see?　　　　　　　　10
Are Your days like a mortal's days,
　　Your years like the years of a man,
that You should search out my crime
　　and inquire for my offense?
You surely know I am not guilty,　　　　　　　　15
　　but there is none who saves from Your hand.
Your hands fashioned me and made me,
　　and then You turn round and destroy me!
Recall, pray, that like clay You worked me,
　　and to the dust You will make me return.　　　20
Why, You poured me out like milk
　　and like cheese You curdled me.
With skin and flesh You clothed me,

with bones and sinews entwined me.
Life and kindness you gave me,   25
  and Your precepts my spirit kept.
Yet these did You hide in Your heart;
  I knew that this was with You:
If I offended, You kept watch upon me
  and of my crime would not acquit me.   30
If I was guilty, alas for me,
  and though innocent, I could not raise my head,
    sated with shame and surfeited with disgrace.
Like a triumphant lion You hunt me,
  over again wondrously smite me.   35
You summon new witnesses against me
  and swell up your anger toward me—
    vanishings and hard service are mine.
And why from the womb did You take me?
  I'd breathe my last, no eye would have seen me.   40
As though I had not been, I would be.
  From belly to grave I'd be carried.
My days are but few—let me be.
  Turn away that I may have some gladness
before I go, never more to return,   45
  to the land of dark and death's shadow,
the land of gloom, thickest murk,
  death's shadow and disorder,
    where it shines thickest murk.

11. And Zophar the Naamathite spoke out and he said:
Shall a swarm of words be unanswered,
  and should a smooth talker be in the right?
Your lies may silence folk,
  you mock and no one protests.   5
And you say: my teaching is spotless,
  and I am pure in your eyes.
Yet, if only God would speak,
  and He would open His lips against you,
would tell you wisdom's secrets,   10
  for prudence is double-edged.
    And know, God leaves some of your crime forgotten.
Can you find what God has probed,
  can you find Shaddai's last end?
Higher than heaven, what can you do,   15
  deeper than Sheol, what can you know?
Longer than earth is its measure,
  and broader than the sea.
Should He slip away or confine or assemble,
  who can resist Him?   20
For He knows the empty folk,
  He sees wrongdoing and surely takes note.
And a hollow man will get a wise heart
  when a wild ass is born a man.
If you yourself readied your heart   25

and spread out your palms to Him,
if there is wrongdoing in your hands, remove it,
   let no mischief dwell in your tents.
For then you will raise your face unstained,
   you will be steadfast and will not fear.   30
For you will forget wretchedness,
   like water gone off, recall it.
And life will rise higher than noon,
   will soar, will be like the morning.
And you will trust, for there is hope,   35
   will search, and lie secure.
You will stretch out, and none make you tremble,
   and many pay court to you.
And the eyes of the wicked will pine,
   escape will be lost to them,   40
      and their hope—a last gasp of breath.

12. And Job spoke up and he said:
Oh yes, you are the people,
   and with you wisdom will die!
But I, too, have a mind like you,
   I am no less than you,   5
      and who does not know such things?
A laughing-stock to his friend I am,
   who calls to his God and is answered,
      a laughing-stock of the blameless just man.
The smug man's thought scorns disaster,   10
   readied for those who stumble.
The tents of despoilers are tranquil,
   provokers of God are secure,
      whom God has led by the hand.
Yet ask of the beasts, they will teach you,   15
   the fowl of the heavens will tell you,
or speak to the earth, it will teach you,
   the fish of the sea will inform you.
Who has not known in all these
   that the LORD's hand has done this?   20
In Whose hand is the breath of each living thing,
   and the spirit of all human flesh.
Does not the ear make out words,
   the palate taste food?
In the aged is wisdom,   25
   and in length of days understanding.
With Him are wisdom and strength,
   He possesses counsel and understanding.
Why, He destroys and there is no rebuilding,
   closes in on a man, leaves no opening.   30
Why, He holds back the waters and they dry up,
   sends them forth and they turn the earth over.
With Him is power and prudence,
   His the duped and the duper.
He leads counselors astray   35

and judges He drives to madness.
He undoes the sash of kings
    and binds a loincloth round their waist.
He leads priests astray,
    the mighty He misleads.   40
He takes away speech from the trustworthy,
    and sense from the elders He takes,
He pours forth scorn on princes,
    and the belt of the nobles He slackens,
lays bare depths from the darkness   45
    and brings out to light death's shadow,
raises nations high and destroys them,
    flattens nations and leads them away,
stuns the minds of the people's leaders,
    makes them wander in trackless wastes—   50
they grope in darkness without light,
    He makes them wander like drunken men.

13. Why, my eye has seen all,
    my ear has heard and understood.
As you know, I, too, know.
    I am no less than you.
Yet I would speak to Shaddai,   5
    and I want to dispute with God.
And yet, you plaster lies,[8]
    you are all quack-healers.
Would that you fell silent,
    and this would be your wisdom.   10
Hear, pray, my dispute,
    and to my lips' pleas listen closely.
Would you speak crookedness of God,
    and of Him would you speak false things?
Would you be partial on His behalf,   15
    would you plead the case of God?
Would it be good that He probed you,
    as one mocks a man would you mock Him?
He shall surely dispute with you
    if in secret you are partial.   20
Will not His majesty strike you with terror,
    and His fear fall upon you?
Your pronouncements are maxims of ash,
    your word-piles, piles of clay.
Be silent before me—I would speak,   25
    no matter what befalls me.
Why should I bear my flesh in my teeth,
    and my life-breath place in my palm?
Look, He slays me, I have no hope.
    Yet my ways I'll dispute to His face.   30
Even that becomes my rescue,
    for no tainted man comes before Him.

---

8. An idiom also found in the Psalms; the idea is that the truth is "plastered over" with lies.

Hear, O hear my word
   and my utterance in your ear.
Look, pray, I have laid out my case,   35
   I know that I am in the right.
Who would make a plea against me?
   I would be silent then, breathe my last.
Just two things do not do to me,
   then would I not hide from Your presence.   40
Take Your palm away from me,
   and let Your dread not strike me with terror.
Call and I will reply,
   or I will speak, and answer me.
How many crimes and offenses have I?   45
   My offense and my wrong, inform me.
Why do You hide Your face,
   and count me Your enemy?
Would You harry a driven leaf,
   and a dry straw would You chase,   50
that You should write bitter things against me,
   make me heir to the crimes of my youth?
And You put my feet in stocks,
   watch after all my paths,
      on the soles of my feet make a mark.⁹   55

And man wears away like rot,
   like a garment eaten by moths.

14. Man born of woman,
   scant of days and sated with trouble,
like a blossom he comes forth and withers,
   and flees like a shadow—he will not stay.
Even on such You cast Your eye,   5
   and me You bring in judgment with You?
[Who can make the impure pure?
   No one.]¹
Oh, his days are decreed,
   the number of his months are with You,
      his limits You fixed that he cannot pass.   10
Turn away from him that he may cease,
   until he serves out his day like a hired man.
For a tree has hope:
   though cut down, it can still be removed,   15
      and its shoots will not cease.
Though its root grow old in the ground
   and its stock die in the dust,
from the scent of water it flowers,
   and puts forth branches like a sapling.   20
But a strong man dies defeated,
   man breathes his last, and where is he?

9. Probably a reference to branding or tattoo-
ing done to mark out a criminal.
1. This verse is bracketed because it is metri-
cally too short; many scholars think it does not
belong in the text.

Water runs out from a lake,
   and a river is parched and dries up,
but a man lies down and will not arise,   25
   till the sky is no more he will not awake
   and will not rouse from his sleep.
Would that You hid me in Sheol,
   concealed me till Your anger passed,
     set me a limit and recalled me.   30
If a man dies will he live?
   All my hard service days I shall hope
     until my vanishing comes.
Call out and I shall answer you,
   for the work of Your hand You should yearn.   35
For then You would count my steps,
   You would not keep watch over my offense.
My crime would be sealed in a packet,
   You would plaster over my guilt.
And yet, a falling mountain crumbles,   40
   a rock is ripped from its place.
Water wears away stones,
   its surge sweeps up the dust of the earth,
     and the hope of man You destroy.
You overwhelm him forever, and he goes off,   45
   You change his face and send him away.
If his sons grow great, he will not know.
   And should they dwindle, he will not notice them.
But the flesh upon him will ache,
   his own being will mourn for him.   50

*   *   *

29. And Job again took up his theme and he said:
Would that I were as in moons of yore,
   as the days when God watched over me,
when He shined his lamp over my head,
   by its light I walked in darkness,   5
as I was in the days of my prime—
   God an intimate of my tent,
when Shaddai still was with me,
   all around me my lads;
when my feet bathed in curds   10
   and the rock poured out streams of oil,
when I went out to the city's gate,
   in the square I secured my seat.[2]
Lads saw me and took cover,
   the aged arose, stood up.   15
Noblemen held back their words,
   their palm they put to their mouth.
The voice of the princes was muffled,
   their tongue to their palate stuck.

---

2. The square just inside the city gate was the town's meeting place; having a seat there would be a sign of status.

When the ear heard, it affirmed me,   20
   and the eye saw and acclaimed me.
For I would free the poor who cried out,
   the orphan with no one to help him.
The perishing man's blessing would reach me,
   and the widow's heart I made sing.   25
Righteousness I donned and it clothed me,
   like a cloak and a headdress, my justice.
Eyes I became for the blind,
   and legs for the lame I was.
A father I was for the impoverished,   30
   a stranger's cause I took up.
And I cracked the wrongdoer's jaws,
   from his teeth I would wrench the prey.
And I thought: In my nest I shall breathe my last,
   and my days will abound like the sand.   35
My root will be open to water,
   and dew in my branches abide,
My glory renewed within me,
   and my bow ever fresh in my hand.
To me they would listen awaiting   40
   and fall silent at my advice.
At my speech they would say nothing further,
   and upon them my word would drop.
They waited for me as for rain,
   and gaped open their mouths as for showers.   45
I laughed to them—they scarcely trusted—
   but my face's light they did not dim.
I chose their way and sat as chief,
   I dwelled like a king in his brigade
      when he comforts the mourning.   50

30. And now mere striplings laugh at me
   whose fathers I spurned
      to put with the dogs of my flock.
The strength of their hands—what use to me?
   From them the vigor has gone: 5
In want and starvation bereft
   they flee to desert land,
      the darkness of desolate dunes,
plucking saltwort from the bush,
   the roots of broomwood their bread.   10
From within they are banished—
   people shout over them as at thieves.
In river ravines they encamp,
   holes in the dust and crags.
Among bushes they bray,   15
   beneath thornplants they huddle.
Vile creatures and nameless, too,
   they are struck from the land.
And now I become their taunt,

I become their mocking word.   20
They despised me, were distant to me,
  and from my face they did not spare their spit.
For my bowstring they loosed and abused me,
  cast off restraint toward me.
On the right, raw youths stand up,   25
  they make me run off
    and pave against me their roadways of ruin.
They shatter my path,
  my disaster devise,
    and none helps me against them.   30
Like a wide water-burst they come,
  in the shape of a tempest they tumble.
Terror rolls over me,
  pursues my path like the wind,
    and my rescue like a cloud passes on.   35
And now my life spills out,
  days of affliction seize me.
At night my limbs are pierced,
  and my sinews know no rest.
With great power He seizes my garment,   40
  grabs hold of me at the collar.
He hurls me into the muck,
  and I become like dust and ashes.
I scream to You and You do not answer,
  I stand still and You do not observe me.   45
You become a cruel one toward me,
  with the might of Your hand You hound me.
You bear me up, on the wind make me straddle,
  break me apart in a storm.
For I know You'll return me to death,   50
  the meetinghouse of all living things.
But one would not reach out against the afflicted
  if in his disaster he screamed.
Have I not wept for the bleak-fated man,
  sorrowed for the impoverished?   55
For I hoped for good and evil came.
  I expected light and darkness fell.
My innards seethed and would not be still,
  days of affliction greeted me.
In gloom did I walk, with no sun,   60
  I rose in assembly and I screamed.
Brother I was to the jackals,
  companion to ostriches.[3]
My skin turned black upon me,
  my limbs were scorched by drought.   65
And my lyre has turned into mourning,
  my flute, a keening sound.

---

3. Known for their loud, mournful cries.

31. A pact I sealed with my eyes—
 I will not gaze on a virgin.
And what is the share from God above,
 the portion from Shaddai in the heights?
Is there not ruin for the wrongdoer,   5
 and estrangement for those who do evil?
Does He not see my way,
 and all my steps count?
Have I walked in a lie,
 has my foot hurried to deceit?   10
Let Him weigh me on fair scales,
 that God know my blamelessness.
If my stride has strayed from the way,
 and my heart gone after my eyes,
  or the least thing stuck to my palms,   15
let me sow and another shall eat,
 my offspring torn up by the roots.
If my heart was seduced by a woman,
 and at the door of my friend I lurked,
let my wife grind for another   20
 and upon her let others crouch.[4]
For that is lewdness,
 and that is a grave crime.
For it is fire that consumes to Perdition,
 and in all my yield eats the roots.   25
If I spurned the case of my slave
 or my slavegirl, in their brief against me,
what would I do when God stands up,
 and when He assays it, what would I answer?
Why, my Maker made him in the belly,   30
 and formed him in the selfsame womb.
Did I hold back the poor from his desire
 or make the eyes of the widow pine?
Did I eat my bread alone,
 and an orphan not eat from it?   35
For from my youth like a father I raised him,
 and from my mother's womb I led him.
If I saw a man failing, ungarbed,
 and no garment for the impoverished,
did his loins not then bless me,   40
 and from my sheep's shearing was he not warmed?
If I raised my hand against an orphan,
 when I saw my advantage in the gate,
let my shoulder fall out of its socket
 and my arm break off from its shaft.   45
For ruin from God is my fear,
 and His presence I cannot withstand.
If I made gold my bulwark,
 and fine gold I called my trust,

---

4. The "grinding" and "crouching" are implicit metaphors for sex.

if I rejoiced that my wealth was great   50
   and that abundance my hand had found,
if I saw light when it gleamed
   and the moon gliding grand,
and my heart was seduced in secret,
   and my hand caressed my mouth,   55
this, too, would be a grave crime,
   for I would have denied God above.[5]
If I rejoiced at my foe's disaster,
   and exulted when harm found him out—
yet I did not let my mouth offend   60
   to seek out his life in an oath.
Did the men of my tent ever say,
   "Would that we were never sated of his flesh"?
The sojourner did not sleep outside.
   My doors to the wayfarer I opened.   65
Did I hide like Adam my wrongdoings,
   to bury within me my crime,
that I should fear the teeming crowd,
   and the scorn of clans terrify me,
      fall silent and keep within doors?   70
Would that I had someone to hear me out.
   Here's my mark—let Shaddai answer me,
      and let my accuser indict his writ.
I would bear it upon my shoulder,
   bind it as a crown upon me.   75
The number of my steps I would tell Him,
   like a prince I would approach him.
If my soil has cried out against me,
   and together its furrows wept,

if I ate its yield without payment,   80
   and drove its owners to despair,
instead of wheat let nettles grow,
   and instead of barley, stinkweed.

      Here end the words of Job.

                        *   *   *

38. And the LORD answered Job from the whirlwind and He said:
   Who is this who darkens counsel
      in words without knowledge?
   Gird, pray, your loins like a man,
      that I may ask you, and you can inform Me.
   Where were you when I founded earth?   5
      Tell, if you know understanding.
   Who fixed its measures, do you know,
      or who stretched a line upon it?
   In what were its sockets sunk,
      or who laid its cornerstone,   10

---

5. Apparently refers to idolatrous worship of the sun and moon.

when the morning stars sang together,
    and all the sons of God shouted for joy?
Who hedged the sea in with doors,
    when it gushed forth from the womb,
when I made cloud its clothing, 15
    and thick mist its swaddling bands?
I made breakers upon it My limit,
    and set a bolt with double doors.
And I said, "Thus far come, no further,
    here halt the surge of your waves." 20
Have you ever commanded the morning,
    appointed the dawn to its place,
to seize the earth's corners,
    that the wicked be shaken from it?
It turns like sealing clay, 25
    takes color like a garment,
and their light is withdrawn from the wicked,
    and the upraised arm is broken.
Have you come into the springs of the sea,
    in the bottommost deep walked about? 30
Have the gates of death been laid bare to you,
    and the gates of death's shadow have you seen?
Did you take in the breadth of the earth?
    Tell, if you know it all.
Where is the way that light dwells, 35
    and darkness, where is its place,
that you might take it to its home
    and understand the paths to its house?
You know, for were you born then,
    and the number of your days is great! 40
Have you come into the storehouse of snow,
    the storehouse of hail have you seen,
which I keep for a time of strife,
    for a day of battle and war?
By what way does the west wind fan out, 45
    the east wind whip over the earth?
Who split a channel for the torrent,
    and a way for the thunderstorm,
to rain on a land without man,
    wilderness bare of humankind, 50
to sate the desolate dunes
    and make the grass sprout there?
Does the rain have a father,
    or who begot the drops of dew?
From whose belly did the ice come forth, 55
    to the frost of the heavens who gave birth?
Water congeals like stone,
    and the face of the deep locks hard.
Can you tie the bands of the Pleiades,
    or loose Orion's reins? 60
Can you bring constellations out in their season,

lead the Great Bear and her cubs?
Do you know the laws of the heavens,
    can you fix their rule on earth?
Can you lift your voice to the cloud,   65
    that the water-spate cover you?
Can you send lightning bolts on their way,
    and they will say to you, "Here we are!"?
Who placed in the hidden parts wisdom,
    or who gave the mind understanding?   70
Who counted the skies in wisdom,
    and the jars of the heavens who tilted,
when the dust melts to a mass,
    and the clods cling fast together?
Can you hunt prey for the lion,   75
    fill the king of beast's appetite,
when it crouches in its den,
    lies in ambush in the covert?
Who readies the raven's prey
    when its young cry out to God   80
        and stray deprived of food?

39. Do you know the mountain goats' birth-time,
    do you mark the calving of the gazelles?
Do you number the months till they come to term
    and know their birthing time?
They crouch, burst forth with their babes,   5
    their young they push out to the world.
Their offspring batten, grow big in the wild,
    they go out and do not return.
Who set the wild ass free,
    and the onager's reins who loosed,   10
whose home I made in the steppes,
    his dwelling-place flats of salt?
He scoffs at the bustling city,
    the driver's shouts he does not hear.
He roams mountains for his forage,   15
    and every green thing he seeks.
Will the wild ox want to serve you,
    pass the night at your feeding trough?
Bind the wild ox with cord for the furrow,
    will he harrow the valleys behind you?   20
Can you rely on him with his great power
    and leave your labor to him?
Can you trust him to bring back your seed,
    gather grain on your threshing floor?
The ostrich's wing joyously beats.   25
    Is the pinion, the plume like the stork's?
For she leaves her eggs on the ground,
    and in the dust she lets them warm.
And she forgets that a foot can crush them,
    and a beast of the field stomp on them—   30
harsh, abandons her young to a stranger,

in vain her labor, without fear.
For God made her forgetful of wisdom,
　　and He did not allot her insight.
Now on the height she races,　　　　　　　　　　　　35
　　she scoffs at the horse and its rider.
Do you give might to the horse,
　　do you clothe his neck with a mane?
Do you make his roar like locusts—
　　his splendid snort is terror.　　　　　　　　　　　40
He churns up the valley exulting,
　　in power goes out to the clash of arms.
He scoffs at fear and is undaunted,
　　turns not back before the sword.
Over him rattles the quiver,　　　　　　　　　　　　45
　　the blade, the javelin, and the spear.
With clamor and clatter he swallows the ground,
　　and ignores the trumpet's sound.
At the trumpet he says, "Aha,"
　　and from afar he scents the fray,　　　　　　　　　50
　　　the thunder of captains, the shouts.
Does the hawk soar by your wisdom,
　　spread his wings to fly away south?
By your word does the eagle mount
　　and set his nest on high?　　　　　　　　　　　　55
On the crag he dwells and beds down,
　　on the crest of the crag his stronghold.
From there he seeks out food,
　　from afar his eyes look down.
His chicks lap up blood,　　　　　　　　　　　　　60
　　where the slain are, there he is.

40. And the LORD answered Job and He said:
Will he who disputes with Shaddai be reproved?
　　Who argues with God, let him answer!
And Job answered the LORD and he said:
Look, I am worthless. What can I say back to You?　　5
　　My hand I put over my mouth.
Once have I spoken and I will not answer,
　　twice, and will not go on.
And the LORD answered Job from the whirlwind and He
　　said:
Gird, pray, your loins like a man.　　　　　　　　　10
　　Let me ask you, and you will inform Me.
Will you indeed overthrow My case,
　　hold Me guilty, so you can be right?
If you have an arm like God's,
　　and with a voice like His you can thunder,　　　　15
put on, pray, pride and preeminence,
　　and grandeur and glory don.
Let loose your utmost wrath,
　　see every proud man, bring him low.
See every proud man, make him kneel,　　　　　　　20

tramp on the wicked where they are.
Bury them in the dust together,
   shut them up in the grave.
And I on my part shall acclaim you,
   for your right hand triumphs for you.   25
Look, pray: Behemoth[6] whom I made with you,
   grass like cattle he eats.
Look, pray: the power in his loins,
   the virile strength in his belly's muscles.
He makes his tail stand like a cedar,   30
   his balls' sinews twine together.
His bones are bars of bronze,
   his limbs like iron rods.
He is the first of the ways of God.
   Let his Maker draw near him with His sword!   35
For the mountains offer their yield to him,
   every beast of the field plays there.
Underneath the lotus he lies,
   in the covert of reeds and marsh.
The lotus hedges him, shades him,   40
   the brook willows stand around him.
Look, he swallows a river at his ease,
   untroubled while Jordan pours into his mouth.
Could one take him with one's eyes,
with barbs pierce his nose?   45
Could you draw Leviathan[7] with a hook,
   and with a cord press down his tongue?
Could you put a lead-line in his nose,
   and with a fish-hook pierce his cheek?
Would he urgently entreat you,   50
   would he speak to you gentle words?
Would he seal a pact with you,
   that you take him as lifelong slave?
Could you play with him like a bird,
   and leash him for your young women?   55
Could hucksters haggle over him,
   divide him among the traders?
Could you fill his skin with darts,
   and a fisherman's net with his head?
Just put your hand upon him—   60
   you will no more recall how to battle.

41. Look, all hope of him is dashed,
   at his mere sight one is cast down.
No fierce one could arouse him,
   and who before him could stand up?
Who could go before Me in this I'd reward,   5
   under all the heavens he would be mine.
I would not keep silent about him,

---

6. The Hebrew word *behemot* simply means "beasts"; the description suggests a mythologized version of the hippopotamus, an animal the poet had presumably never seen.

7. The mythical Canaanite sea monster, here associated with the crocodile.

about his heroic acts and surpassing grace.
Who can uncover his outer garb,
   come into his double mail?   10
Who can pry open the doors of his face?
   All around his teeth is terror.
His back is rows of shields,
   closed with the tightest seal.
Each touches against the next,   15
   no breath can come between them.
Each sticks fast to the next,
   locked together, they will not part.
His sneezes shoot out light,
   and his eyes are like the eyelids of dawn.   20
Firebrands leap from his mouth,
   sparks of fire fly into the air.
From his nostrils smoke comes out,
   like a boiling vat on brushwood.
His breath kindles coals,   25
   and flame comes out of his mouth.
Strength abides in his neck,
   and before him power dances.
The folds of his flesh cling together;
   hard-cast, he will not totter.   30
His heart is cast hard as stone,
   cast hard as a nether millstone.[8]
When he rears up, the gods are frightened,[9]
   when he crashes down, they cringe.
Who overtakes him with sword, it will not avail,   35
   nor spear nor dart nor lance.
Iron he deems as straw,
   and bronze as rotten wood.
No arrow can make him flee,
   slingstones for him turn to straw.   40
Missiles are deemed as straw,
   and he mocks the javelin's clatter.
Beneath him, jagged shards,
   he draws a harrow over the mud.
He makes the deep boil like a pot,   45
   turns sea to an ointment pan.
Behind him glistens a wake,
   he makes the deep seem hoary.
He has no match on earth,
   made as he is without fear.   50
All that is lofty he can see.
   He is king over all proud beasts.

42. And Job answered the LORD and he said:
I know You can do anything,
   and no devising is beyond You.

---

8. Flour was ground between two stones; the bottom one would have to be particularly hard, to withstand the pressure.

9. "Gods" = a sign that the text is not monotheistic. Job believes that his Lord is the best and strongest but not the only god.

"Who is this obscuring counsel without knowledge?"[1]
Therefore I told but did not understand,
wonders beyond me that I did not know.   5
"Hear, pray, and I will speak
Let me ask you, that you may inform me."
By the ear's rumor I heard of You,
and now my eye has seen You.
Therefore do I recant,   10
And I repent in dust and ashes.

And it happened after the LORD had spoken these words to Job, that the LORD said to Eliphaz the Temanite: "My wrath has flared against you and your two companions because you have not spoken rightly of Me as did My servant Job. And now, take for yourselves seven bulls and seven rams and go to My servant Job, and offer a burnt-offering for yourselves, and Job My servant will pray on your behalf. To him only I shall show favor, not to do a vile thing to you, for you have not spoken rightly of Me as did my servant Job. And Eliphaz the Temanite and Bildad the Shuhite and Zophar the Naamathite went out and did according to all that the LORD had spoken to them, and the LORD showed favor to Job. And the LORD restored Job's fortunes when he prayed for his companions, and the LORD increased twofold all that Job had. And all his male and female kinfolk and all who had known him before came and broke bread with him in his house and grieved with him and comforted him for all the harm that the LORD had brought on him. And each of them gave him one kesitah[2] and one golden ring. And the LORD blessed Job's latter days more than his former days, and he had fourteen thousand sheep and six thousand camels and a thousand yoke of oxen and a thousand she-asses. And he had seven sons and three daughters. And he called the name of the first one Dove and the name of the second Cinnamon and the name of the third Horn of Eyeshade.[3] And there were no women in the land so beautiful as Job's daughters. And their father gave them an estate among their brothers. And Job lived a hundred and forty years after this, and he saw his children and his children's children, four generations. And Job died, aged and sated in years.

Psalm 8[1]

1. O Lord our Lord, how excellent is thy name in all the earth! who hast set thy glory above the heavens.

2. Out of the mouth of babes and sucklings hast thou ordained strength because of thine enemies, that thou mightest still the enemy and the avenger.

3. When I consider thy heavens, the work of thy fingers, the moon and the stars, which thou hast ordained;

4. What is man, that thou art mindful of him? and the son of man, that thou visitest him?

5. For thou hast made him a little lower than the angels, and hast crowned him with glory and honour.

---

1. I.e., giving advice in ignorance of the facts. The line is a quotation of the Lord's words to Job.
2. A valuable coin.

3. A substance used for eye makeup.
1. The text of the Psalms is that of the King James Version.

6. Thou madest him to have dominion over the works of thy hands; thou hast put all things under his feet:

7. All sheep and oxen, yea, and the beasts of the field;

8. The fowl of the air, and the fish of the sea, and whatsoever passeth through the paths of the seas.

9. O Lord our Lord, how excellent is thy name in all the earth!

Psalm 19

1. The heavens declare the glory of God; and the firmament sheweth his handywork.

2. Day unto day uttereth speech, and night unto night sheweth knowledge.

3. There is no speech nor language, where their voice is not heard.

4. Their line is gone out through all the earth, and their words to the end of the world. In them hath he set a tabernacle for the sun,

5. Which is as a bridegroom coming out of his chamber, and rejoiceth as a strong man to run a race.

6. His going forth is from the end of the heaven, and his circuit unto the ends of it: and there is nothing hid from the heat thereof.

7. The law of the Lord is perfect, converting the soul: the testimony of the Lord is sure, making wise the simple.

8. The statutes of the Lord are right, rejoicing the heart: the commandment of the Lord is pure, enlightening the eyes.

9. The fear of the Lord is clean, enduring for ever: the judgments of the Lord are true and righteous altogether.

10. More to be desired are they than gold, yea, than much fine gold: sweeter also than honey and the honeycomb.

11. Moreover by them is thy servant warned: and in keeping of them there is great reward.

12. Who can understand his errors? cleanse thou me from secret faults.

13. Keep back thy servant also from presumptuous sins; let them not have dominion over me: then shall I be upright, and I shall be innocent from the great transgression.

14. Let the words of my mouth, and the meditation of my heart, be acceptable in thy sight, O Lord, my strength, and my redeemer.

Psalm 23

1. The Lord is my shepherd; I shall not want.

2. He maketh me to lie down in green pastures: he leadeth me beside the still waters.

3. He restoreth my soul: he leadeth me in the paths of righteousness for his name's sake.

4. Yea, though I walk through the valley of the shadow of death, I will fear no evil: for thou art with me; thy rod and thy staff they comfort me.

5. Thou preparest a table before me in the presence of mine enemies: thou anointest my head with oil; my cup runneth over.

6. Surely goodness and mercy shall follow me all the days of my life: and I will dwell in the house of the Lord for ever.

Psalm 104

1. Bless the Lord, O my soul. O Lord my God, thou art very great; thou art clothed with honour and majesty.

2. Who coverest thyself with light as with a garment: who stretchest out the heavens like a curtain:

3. Who layeth the beams of his chambers in the waters: who maketh the clouds his chariot: who walketh upon the wings of the wind:

4. Who maketh his angels spirits; his ministers a flaming fire:

5. Who laid the foundations of the earth, that it should not be removed for ever.

6. Thou coveredst it with the deep as with a garment: the waters stood above the mountains.

7. At thy rebuke they fled; at the voice of thy thunder they hasted away.

8. They go up by the mountains; they go down by the valleys unto the place which thou hast founded for them.

9. Thou hast set a bound that they may not pass over; that they turn not again to cover the earth.

10. He sendeth the springs into the valleys, which run among the hills.

11. They give drink to every beast of the field: the wild asses quench their thirst.

12. By them shall the fowls of the heaven have their habitation, which sing among the branches.

13. He watereth the hills from his chambers: the earth is satisfied with the fruit of thy works.

14. He causeth the grass to grow for the cattle, and herb for the service of man: that he may bring forth food out of the earth;

15. And wine that maketh glad the heart of man, and oil to make his face to shine, and bread which strengtheneth man's heart.

16. The trees of the Lord are full of sap; the cedars of Lebanon, which he hath planted;

17. Where the birds make their nests: as for the stork, the fir trees are her house.

18. The high hills are a refuge for the wild goats; and the rocks for the conies.

19. He appointed the moon for seasons: the sun knoweth his going down.

20. Thou makest darkness, and it is night: wherein all the beasts of the forest do creep forth.

21. The young lions roar after their prey, and seek their meat from God.

22. The sun ariseth, they gather themselves together, and lay them down in their dens.

23. Man goeth forth unto his work and to his labour until the evening.

24. O Lord, how manifold are thy works! in wisdom hast thou made them all: the earth is full of thy riches.

25. So is this great and wide sea, wherein are things creeping innumerable, both small and great beasts.

26. There go the ships: there is that leviathan, whom thou hast made to play therein.

27. These wait all upon thee; that thou mayest give them their meat in due season.

28. That thou givest them they gather: thou openest thine hand, they are filled with good.

29. Thou hidest thy face, they are troubled: thou takest away their breath, they die, and return to their dust.

30. Thou sendest forth thy spirit, they are created: and thou renewest the face of the earth.

31. The glory of the Lord shall endure for ever: the Lord shall rejoice in his works.

32. He looketh on the earth, and it trembleth: he toucheth the hills, and they smoke.

33. I will sing unto the Lord as long as I live: I will sing praise to my God while I have my being.

34. My meditation of him shall be sweet: I will be glad in the Lord.

35. Let the sinners be consumed out of the earth, and let the wicked be no more. Bless thou the Lord, O my soul. Praise ye the Lord.

Psalm 137

1. By the rivers of Babylon,[1] there we sat down, yea, we wept, when we remembered Zion.

2. We hanged our harps upon the willows in the midst thereof.

3. For there they that carried us away captive required of us a song; and they that wasted us required of us mirth, saying, Sing us one of the songs of Zion.

4. How shall we sing the Lord's song in a strange land?

5. If I forget thee, O Jerusalem, let my right hand forget her cunning.

6. If I do not remember thee, let my tongue cleave to the roof of my mouth; if I prefer not Jerusalem above my chief joy.

7. Remember, O Lord, the children of Edom[2] in the day of Jerusalem; who said, Rase it, rase it, even to the foundation thereof.

8. O daughter of Babylon, who art to be destroyed; happy shall he be, that rewardeth thee as thou hast served us.

9. Happy shall he be, that taketh and dasheth thy little ones against the stones.

1. On the Euphrates River. Jerusalem was captured and sacked by the Babylonians in 586 B.C.E. The Hebrews were taken away into captivity in Babylon.

2. The Edomites helped the Babylonians capture Jerusalem.

HOMER

eighth century B.C.E.

The *Iliad* and the *Odyssey* tell the story of the clash of two great civilizations, and the effects of war on both the winners and the losers. Both poems are about the Trojan War, a mythical conflict between a coalition of Greeks and the inhabitants of Troy, a city in Asia Minor. These are the earliest works of Greek literature, composed almost three thousand years before our time. Yet they are rich and sophisticated in their narrative techniques, and they provide extraordinarily vivid portrayals of people, social relationships, and feelings, especially our incompatible desires for honor and violence, and for peace and a home.

HISTORICAL CONTEXTS

On the Greek island of Crete is an enormous palace, dominated by monumental arches adorned with fierce lions, built by the earliest Greek-speaking people: the Myceneans, who probably inspired the Trojan legends. About 2000 B.C.E., they began building big, fortified cities around central palaces in the south of Greece. The Myceneans had a form of writing now known as "Linear B"—not an alphabet but a "syllabary" (in which a symbol corresponds to each syllable, not to each letter)—as well as a centralized, tightly controlled economy and sophisticated artistic and architectural traditions. The metal they used for weapons, armor, and tools was predominantly bronze, and their time is therefore known as the Bronze Age.

After dominating the region for about six hundred years, Mycenean civilization came to an end around 1200 B.C.E. Archaeological investigations suggest that the great cities were burnt or destroyed at this time, perhaps by invasion or war. The next few hundred years are known as the Dark Ages of Greece: people seem to have been less wealthy, and the cultural knowledge of the Myceneans, including the knowledge of writing, was lost.

Greeks of this time spoke many different dialects and lived in small towns and villages scattered across a wide area. They did not regain their knowledge of reading or writing until an alphabet, invented by a trading people called the Phoenicians, was adopted in the eighth century B.C.E.

One might think that an illiterate society could have nothing like "literature," a word based on the Latin for "letters" (*litterae*). In the centuries of Greek illiteracy, however, there developed a thriving tradition of oral poetry, especially on the Ionian coast, in modern-day Turkey. Travelling bards told tales of the lost age of heroes who fought with bronze, and of the great cities besieged and destroyed by war. The Homeric poems make use of folk memories of a real conflict or conflicts between the Mycenean Greeks and inhabitants of one or more cities in Asia Minor. The world of Homer is neither historical in a modern sense nor purely fictional. Through poetry, the Greeks of the Dark Ages created and preserved their own past.

Oral poets in ancient Greece used a traditional form (a six-beat line called hexameter), fitting their own riffs into the rhythm, with musical accompaniment. They also relied on common themes, traditional stories, traditional characters, traditional descriptors (such as "swift Achilles" or "black ships"), phrases that fit the rhythm of the line, and even whole scenes that follow a set pattern, such as the way a warrior gets dressed or the way that meals are prepared. Fluent poetic ad-libbing is very difficult; these techniques gave each performer a structure, so that stories and lines did not have to be generated entirely on the spot. We know that the tradition of this type of composition must have gone back hundreds of years, because the *Iliad* and the *Odyssey* include details that would have been anachronistic by the time these poems were written down, such as the use of bronze weapons: by the eighth century, soldiers fought with iron. Details from different periods are jumbled together, so that even in the eighth century B.C.E. the heroic, mythic world of the Homeric poems must have seemed quite distant from everyday reality. In addition, the poems mix different Greek dialects, the speech of many different areas in the Greek-speaking world, into a language unlike anything anyone ever actually spoke.

There is an ancient tradition that the *Iliad* and the *Odyssey* were both composed by a blind, illiterate singer from the island of Chios, named Homer. But many scholars—in antiquity and today—have suspected that this story is more legend than fact, and it is quite possible that there was no such person as "Homer."

It is hard to understand the relation between the heroic poetry composed and sung by illiterate bards in archaic Greece, and the written texts of the *Odyssey* and the *Iliad*. The question is made all the more difficult because the poems are far longer than most instances of oral poetic performance, including that of the oral poets living in the former Yugoslavia, who were studied by classicists in the twentieth century as the closest living analogy to ancient Greek bards. Good bards may be able to keep going for an hour or two: in the Homeric poems themselves, there are accounts of singers performing for a while after dinner. But a complete performance of either of these poems would have lasted at least twenty hours. This is much too long for an audience to sit through in an evening. It would also have been difficult for any poet, even a genius, to compose at this length without the use of writing. Perhaps, then, these poems are the work of an oral poet, or poets, who became literate. Or perhaps they represent a collaboration between one or more oral poets, and a scribe. In any case, soon after the Greeks developed their alphabet, they found a way to preserve their oral tradition in two monumental written poems.

These works make use of tradition in strikingly original ways, creating just two coherent stories out of the mass of legends that surrounded the Trojan War. They are long poems about heroes, a genre that later came to be called *epic*—from the Greek for "story" or "word." Throughout the ancient world, for hundreds of years to come, everybody knew the *Iliad* and the *Odyssey*. The poems were performed aloud, illustrated in paintings on vases or on walls, read, learned by heart, remembered, reworked, and imitated by everyone in the Greek and Roman worlds, from the Athenian tragedians to the Roman poet **Virgil**.

THE *ILIAD*

The title *Iliad* suggests a work about the Trojan War, since *Ilias* is another

name for Troy. Greek readers or listeners would have been familiar with
the background myths. Paris, a prince
of Troy, son of King Priam, had to
judge which of three goddesses
should be awarded a golden apple:
Athena, goddess of wisdom; Hera, the
queen of the gods and thus a representative of power; or Aphrodite, goddess of sexual desire. He chose
Aphrodite, and as his reward she gave
him the most beautiful woman in the
world, Helen of Sparta, to be his wife.
Unfortunately, Helen already had a
husband: Menelaos (or Menelaus in
the Latin spelling), king of Sparta and
brother of the powerful general
Agamemnon. When Paris took Helen
with him back to Troy from Mycenae,
Agamemnon and Menelaos mustered
a great army, a coalition drawn from
many Greek cities, including the
great heroes Achilles, the fastest runner and best fighter, and Odysseus,
the cleverest of the Greeks. So began
a war that lasted ten years, until
Odysseus finally devised a stratagem
to enter the city walls of Troy. He
built a wooden horse, filled it with
Greek warriors, and tricked the
Trojans into taking the horse into the
city. After nightfall, the Greek soldiers leaped from the horse and killed
the male inhabitants, captured the
women, and razed the city to the
ground.

Surprisingly, none of these events
play any part in the main narrative of
the *Iliad,* which begins when the war
is already in its tenth year and ends
before the capture of the city. Moreover, the central focus is not on the
conflict between Greeks and Trojans,
but on a conflict among the Greek
commanders. The first word of the
Iliad is "Wrath," and the wrath of
Achilles—first against his comrade
Agamemnon, and only later against
the enemy Trojans—is the central

subject of the poem. In Greek, the
word used is *menis*, a term otherwise
applied only to the wrath of the gods.
Achilles' rage is an extraordinary
thing, which sets him apart from
the rest of humanity—Greeks and
Trojans. The poem tells how Achilles,
the greatest Greek hero and the son of
a goddess, becomes alienated from his
society, how his anger against the
Greeks shifts into an inhuman aggression against the Trojans, and how he
is at last willing to return to the
human world.

The *Iliad* is about war, honor, and
aggression. There are moments of
graphic violence, when we are told
exactly where the point of a spear or
sword penetrates vulnerable human
flesh: as when Achilles' friend Patroclus throws his spear at another warrior, Sarpedon, and catches him
"where the lungs close in around the
beating heart"; or when Hector rams
his spear into Patroclus, "into his
lower flank, and drove the bronze
point through"; or when Achilles'
spear "went utterly through the soft
neck" of Hector but "did not sever
the windpipe." The precise anatomi-
cal detail reminds us how vulnerable
these warriors are, because they have
mortal bodies—in contrast to the
gods, who may participate in battle
but can never die.

The plot deals with the exchange or
ransoming of human bodies. Achilles'
anger at Agamemnon is roused by a
quarrel about who owns Briseïs, a
young woman Achilles has seized as a
prize of war but whom Agamemnon
takes as recompense for the loss of his
own captive woman, Chryseïs. The
story also hinges on the ownership of
dead male bodies: the corpses, in
turn, of Sarpedon, Patroclus, and
Hector. War seems to produce its own
kind of economy, a system of
exchange: a live woman for a dead

warrior, one life for another, or death for undying fame.

The *Iliad* is a violent poem, and, on one level, the violence simply contributes to the entertainment: it is exciting to hear or read about slaughter. But it would be a mistake to see the *Iliad* as pure military propaganda. At times, the poem brings out the terrible pity of war: the city of Troy will be ruined, the people killed or enslaved, and the poet looks back with regret to "the days of peace, before the Greeks came." Some similes compare the violence on the battlefield to the events of the world of peace, where people can plow their fields, build their homes, and watch their sheep. But these similes may suggest that violence and the threat of pain and death are facts of life: even when people are at peace, there is murder, and lions or wolves leap into the fold to kill the sheep.

Within the narrow world of the battlefield, Homer's vividly imagined characters have choices to make. They cannot choose, like gods, to avoid death; but they can choose how they will die. The poem itself acknowledges that the exchange of honor for death may seem inadequate. After Agamemnon has treated him dishonorably, Achilles begins to question the whole heroic code and its system of trading death for glory: "For not worth my life is all they say I lion used to possess," he declares, since prizes of honor can always be replaced but "the life of a man does not come back." Unlike the other fighters, Achilles knows for sure—thanks to the goddess Thetis, his mother—that remaining at Troy will mean his death. But all the warriors of the *Iliad* are conscious that in fighting they risk their own deaths. Achilles' choices—to fight and die soon, in this war, or go home and live a little longer—are therefore a starker version of the decision faced by all who fight.

Fascinatingly, the *Iliad* makes the Trojans as fully human as the Greeks. The Trojan hero, Hector, seems to many readers the most likeable character in the poem, fighting not for vengeance but to protect his wife and their infant son. One of the most touching moments comes as Hector says goodbye to his tearful wife before going into battle; a deep tenderness connects Hector and his family—in

Achilles (left) slays Hector. From a red-figured volute-krater (a large ceramic wine decanter), ca. 500–480 B.C.E.

contrast to the more shallow associations of the Greeks with their female prisoners of war. As Hector reaches down to kiss his son, the child screams, frightened at seeing his father in his helmet. The parents laugh together, and Hector takes off the helmet so the baby will not be scared as he swings him in his arms. The moment is both heartwarming and chilling, since we know—and his wife knows—that this devoted father will never see his son again; the baby is right to be frightened, since he will soon be hurled headlong from the city walls by the victorious Greeks.

The *Iliad* culminates in an astonishing encounter, between Priam, king of Troy, and Achilles, who has killed his son Hector. Priam goes to plead with Achilles to return his son's body, and the two enemies end up sitting together, each weeping for those they have lost. The experience of grief is common to all humans, even those who kill each other in war. The major contrast drawn by the *Iliad* is not between Greek and Trojan, but between the humans and the immortal gods. The gods play an important role in the action of the poem, sometimes intervening to cause or prevent a hero's death or dishonor. We are told at the beginning that there is a connection between all the deaths caused by Achilles' wrath and the will of Zeus: the whole action of the poem happened as "the will of Zeus was accomplished." But the presence of the gods does not turn the human characters into puppets, controlled only by the gods or by fate. Human characters are never forced by gods to act out of character. Rather, human action and divine action work together, and the gods provide a way of talking about the elements of human experience that are otherwise incomprehensible.

Moreover, the presence of the gods—like the similes—makes us particularly aware of what is distinctive about human life in war. In the world of the gods, there are conflicts about hierarchy, just as there are on earth: sometimes the lesser gods refuse to recognize the authority of Zeus, just as some Greek chieftains sometimes refuse to bow to Agamemnon. But on Olympus, all quarrels end in laughter and drinking, not death. The most important fact about all the warriors in the *Iliad* is that they die. Moreover, before death humans have to face grief, dishonor, loss, and pain—experiences that play little or no part in any god's life. Achilles in his wrath refuses to accept the horror of loss: loss of honor, and the loss of his dearest friend, Patroclus. His anger can end, and he can eat again, only when his heart becomes "enduring," and he realizes that all humans, even the greatest warriors, have to endure unendurable loss and keep on living. The *Iliad* provides a bleak but inspiring account of human suffering as a kind of power that the gods themselves cannot achieve.

THE *ODYSSEY*

The *Odyssey* has a special place in the study of world literature, since it deals explicitly with the relationship between the people we know and those who are strange to us. It is about a journey that spans most of the world as it was known to Greeks at the time, and deals with issues that any student of world literature must confront, including the place of literature and memory in the formation of cultural identity. The poem shows us, in depth and in detail, the complex relationships between one Westerner, a Greek man, and the other cultures that he encounters—not in war, but in the course of a long journey, where the worst enemies may be found inside his own household. The poem tells the story of Odysseus's homecoming from Troy, tracing his reclamation of a household from which he has been absent for the past twenty years. It is a gripping and varied tale, which includes fantasy and magic but also focuses on domestic details and on the human need for a family and a home.

The *Odyssey* is set after the *Iliad*, and was probably produced a little later, since it seems deliberately to avoid repeating anything that had been included in the *Iliad*, and fills in many important details that had been absent from the other poem—including allusions to the actual fall of Troy, and its aftermath. The *Odyssey* creates a different but complementary vision of the Trojan War, showing how the Greeks faced further danger in the long voyage back to Greece, and in their return to homes from which they had been absent for many years.

In the Greek original, the first word of the *Odyssey*—our first clue to the poem's subject—is *andra* ("a man"). One man, Odysseus himself, is the center of the poem, in a way that no single hero, not even Achilles, is the center of the *Iliad*. The journey from war to peace requires different skills from those needed on the battlefield, and through the figure of Odysseus the poem shows us what those skills might be. He has strength and physical courage, but he also has brains: the "clear rascal" is the smartest of those who fought at Troy. He is famously adaptable, a "man who can adapt to anything," able to deal with any eventuality, no matter how difficult or unexpected. He has psychological strength, an

ability both to endure and to inflict pain without flinching; more than once, the poem connects the name *Odysseus* with the Greek word for "to be angry" or "hate" (*odyssomai*): Odysseus is the man hated by the god Poseidon. He has the patience and self-restraint required to bide his time until the moment comes for him to reveal himself to his household. Most of all, he has the will to go home, and to restore his home to its proper order. It is no accident that Odysseus's favorite weapon is not the sword or the spear but the bow, which shoots from a distance at the target of his choosing.

"Man" is also the subject of the *Odyssey* in a broader sense, because the poem has a particular interest in the diversity of cultures and ways of life. The *Iliad* is set almost exclusively on the battlefield of Troy, and is focused on the relationships among the aristocratic male warriors. By contrast, the *Odyssey* shows us a multitude of distinct worlds and cultures, including nonhuman cultures. Odysseus spends years on the luxurious island of the nymph Calypso; he encounters the sweetly singing Sirens, the monster Scylla, and the Lotus-eaters; and he disembarks on the island of the sun, with its tempting, delicious cattle, and of the witch Circe, who can turn men to pigs. He is almost killed on the island of the shepherd-giants, the Cyclopes, and he is welcomed in the magical land of Phaeacia, where fruits ripen all season long, and where he meets the king, the queen, and the princess, Nausicaa, who is out to do laundry and play ball with her girlfriends, while daydreaming about her future husband. The many cultures of the poem include both the exotic and the ordinary.

Even in the Greek world, we are

given glimpses of several distinct ways of life. In showing multiple encounters between the Greek hero and people who are very different from him, the Homeric poem invites us to think about how we ought to behave toward people who are not the same as ourselves.

The *Odyssey* is particularly concerned with the laws of hospitality, which in Greek is *xenia*—a word that covers the whole relationship between guests and hosts, and between strangers and those who take them in. Hospitality is the fundamental criterion for civilized society in this poem. Cultures may vary in other respects, but any good society will accommodate the wanderer as a guest. Odysseus encounters many strange peoples in the course of his journey. Some, like the goddess Calypso, are almost too welcoming: she invites him into her home and her bed, and keeps him there even when he longs to go home. Odysseus acknowledges that Calypso is far more beautiful than his own wife and that her island is more lush than his own stony homeland; but, movingly, he still wants to go back. This poem deals with the fundamental desire we feel for our own people and our own place, not because they are better than any other, but simply because they are ours. Similarly, Odysseus rejects the possibility of starting his life over in the hospitable land of the Phaeacians. The monstrous one-eyed Cyclops, Polyphemus, is a grotesque counterpart to the good Phaeacian hosts: instead of welcoming and feeding his guests, the Cyclops wants to eat them for dinner. This encounter is a reminder of how distinctive, and sometimes unheroic, are the skills Odysseus needs to survive the journey home. Heroes in battle, in the *Iliad*, are always concerned that their names be remembered in times to come. But Odysseus defeats Polyphemus— whose name suggests "Much-named"—by denying his own name, calling himself "Noman." The journey home has to trump even Odysseus's heroic identity.

At times, Odysseus's own men transgress the norms of hospitality, as when they kill the cattle of the Sun, which they have been expressly forbidden to touch. Hospitality is tested most severely when Odysseus arrives as a stranger back in his own home. The suitors have seized control of his house and are abusing his unwitting hospitality, in his absence, by courting his wife, devouring his food and drink, and ruining his property. There are repeated references in the *Odyssey* to the nightmare double of Odysseus's return: the homecoming of Agamemnon, who came back from Troy only to be killed in his bath by his wife, Clytemnestra, and her lover, Aegisthus. Zeus, the king of the gods, insists at the beginning of the poem that Aegisthus is hated by the gods, and he praises Agamemnon's son, Orestes, who avenges his father's death by killing the adulterous murderer.

First-time readers may be surprised that the wanderings of Odysseus, across the sea from Troy back to his stony Greek homeland, Ithaca, occupy only a short part of the whole poem. In the second half of the poem, Odysseus is back home in Ithaca, but his journey is only half complete. He arrives home as a stranger, disguised as a poor beggar. The act of homecoming seems to require several stages, beyond merely reaching a geographic location. Odysseus comes up with multiple tales to explain his presence in Ithaca; he uses his many disguises to test the loyalty of those he meets— and, as in the encounter with Polyphemus, he must show enormous self-control in his willingness to suppress his identity, at least temporarily. Throughout the poem, Odysseus has a particularly close affinity with poets and storytellers; he himself narrates his wanderings to the Phaeacians, and, once back on Ithaca, he tells a series of false stories about who he is and where he comes from. Controlling and multiplying stories is one of the most important ways in which Odysseus is a person who can "always find solutions"; he is able to see the multiplicity of the world and constantly to redefine his own place in it.

In the course of his homecoming, Odysseus passes a series of tests, and creates more tests of his own. He must show his mastery of weapons (such as the strong-bow) and his knowledge of the people who make up his household. Odysseus has to win the peace by reconnecting with each loyal member of his home: his servants, his son, his father, and—most memorably—his wife, Penelope. He tests her loyalty by refusing to reveal himself to her right away. But she shows herself a perfect match for her trickster husband, putting him to yet another test. When it is bedtime, she asks the servant to bring out the bed—the bed that, as only Odysseus himself could know, is formed from a tree growing right through the house; if Odysseus were an imposter, he would think the bed could be moved. The immovable bed is, of course, an image for the permanence of Penelope and Odysseus's marriage. When they talk in the bed that night after sex, a simile suggests that now, at last, both Odysseus and Penelope have come home; he, weeping, and she, clinging to him, are like sailors saved from drowning, "Grateful to be alive, they crawl to land." The image first seems to apply to Odysseus, and then to Penelope—a shift that suggests the dynamic intimacy between husband and wife.

The *Odyssey* has elements we associate with many other types of literature: romance, folklore, heroism, mystery, travelers' tales, magic, military exploits, and family drama. It is a text that can be enjoyed on any number of levels: as a feminized version of epic—a heroic story focused not on men fighting wars, but a journey home; as a love story; as a fantasy about fathers, sons, and patriarchy; as an account of Greek identity; as a work of primitive anthropology; as a meditation on cultural difference; as a morality tale; or as a pilgrim's progress. As the first word indicates, this is a poem about humanity. An extraordinarily rich work, as multilayered and intelligent as its hero, the *Odyssey* is enjoyable on first reading, and worth rereading over and over again.

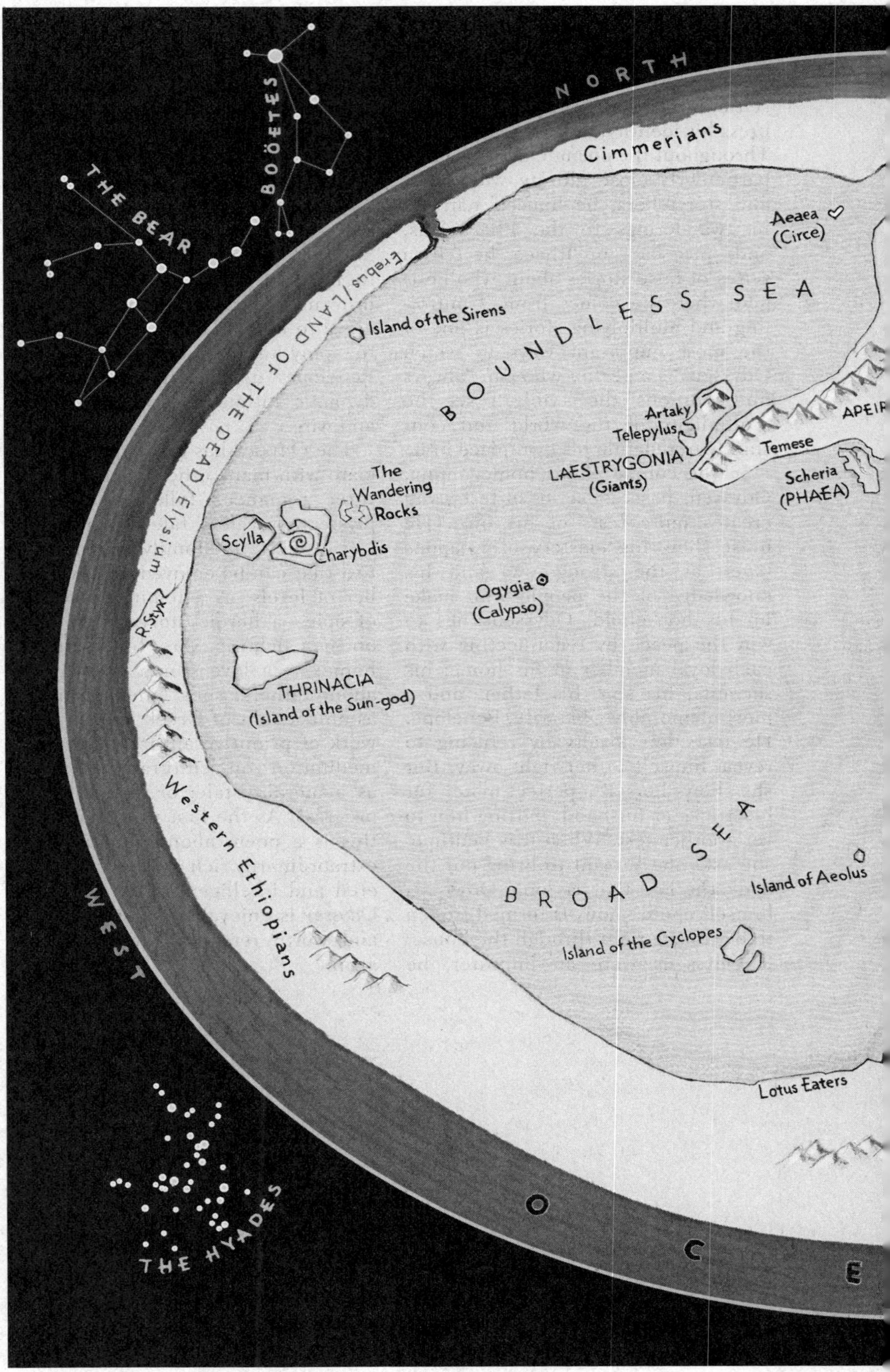
NORTH
BOÖETES
THE BEAR
Cimmerians
Aeaea
(Circe)
Erebus/LAND OF THE DEAD/Elysium
Island of the Sirens
BOUNDLESS SEA
Artaky
Telepylus
APEIR
Temese
LAESTRYGONIA
(Giants)
Scheria
(PHAEA)
The
Wandering
Rocks
Scylla
Charybdis
Ogygia
(Calypso)
R. Styx
THRINACIA
(Island of the Sun-god)
Western Ethiopians
BROAD SEA
Island of Aeolus
Island of the Cyclopes
WEST
Lotus Eaters
THE HYADES
O C E

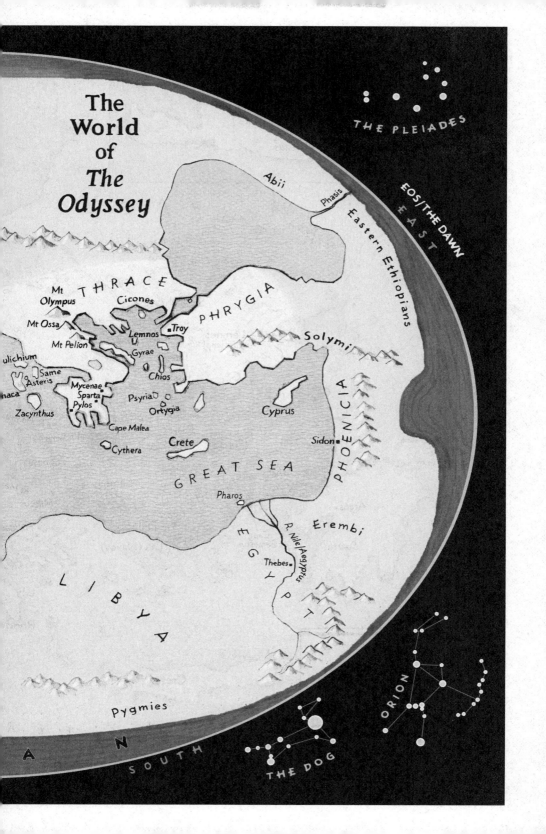

The
World
of
The
Odyssey

THE PLEIADES

Abii

Phasis

EOS/THE DAWN

E A S T

Eastern Ethiopians

THRACE

Mt
Olympus

Cicones

PHRYGIA

Mt Ossa

Lemnos

Troy

Solymi

Mt Pelion

Gyrae

ulichium

Chios

Same

Asteris

Mycenae

PHOENICIA

naca

Sparta

Psyria

Pylos

Cyprus

Zacynthus

Ortygia

Cape Malea

Sidon

Cythera

Crete

GREAT SEA

Pharos

Erembi

EGYPT

R. Nile/Aegyptus

Thebes

LIBYA

Pygmies

ORION

THE DOG

A

N

SOUTH

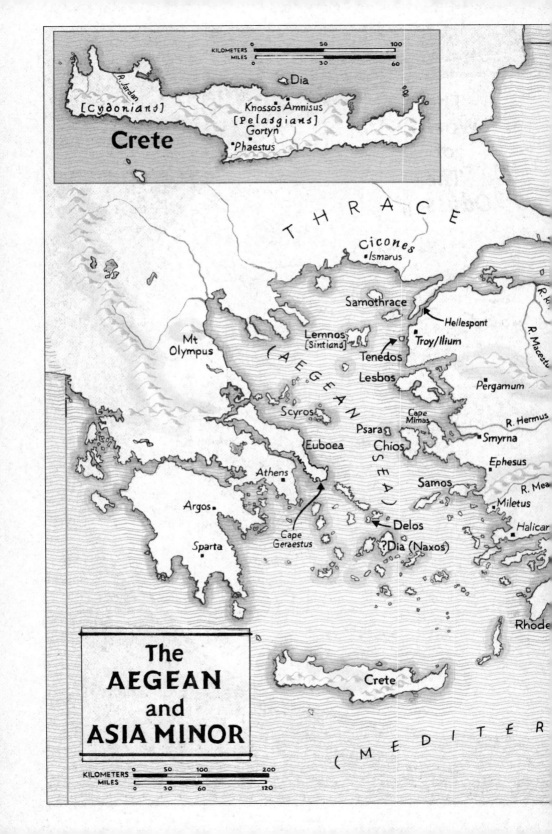

Crete

R. Jardan

[Cydonians]

Dia

Knossos Amnisus
[Pelasgians]
Gortyn
•Phaestus

KILOMETERS 0 · · · · 50 · · · · 100
MILES 0 · · · · 30 · · · · 60

T H R A C E

Cicones
•Ismarus

Samothrace

Hellespont

Lemnos
[Sintians]

Troy/Ilium

Mt
Olympus

Tenedos

Lesbos

Pergamum

Scyros

Cape
Mimas

R. Hermus

Euboea

Psara

Chios

Smyrna

Athens

Samos

Ephesus

R. Mea

Argos •

Miletus

Halicar

Sparta

Cape
Geraestus

Delos

?Dia (Naxos)

Rhode

Crete

**The
AEGEAN
and
ASIA MINOR**

KILOMETERS 0 · · · · 50 · · · · 100 · · · · 200
MILES 0 · · · · 30 · · · · 60 · · · · 120

M E D I T E R

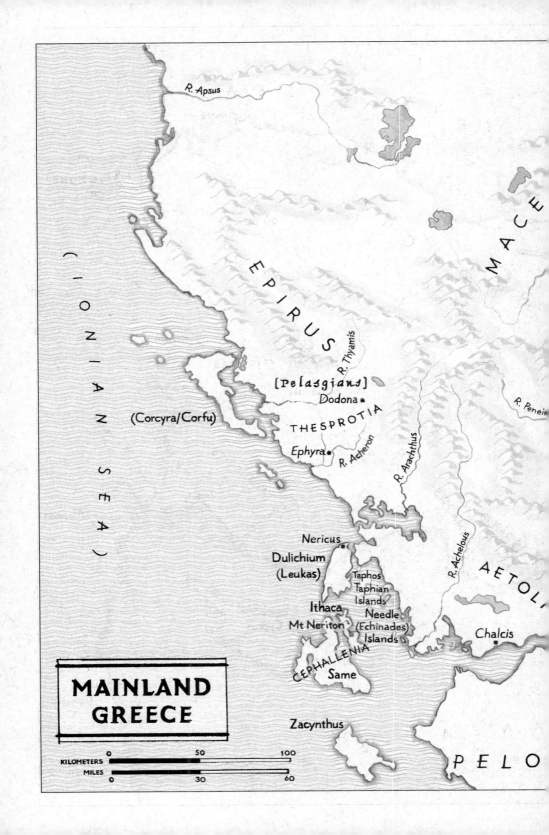

R. Apsus

MACE

EPIRUS

(IONIAN SEA)

R. Thyamis

[Pelasgians]

Dodona

THESPROTIA

R. Peneir

(Corcyra/Corfu)

Ephyra

R. Acheron

R. Arachthus

R. Achelous

AETOLI

Nericus

Dulichium
(Leukas)

Taphos
Taphian
Islands

Ithaca

Mt Neriton

Needle
(Echinades)
Islands

Chalcis

CEPHALLENIA

Same

Zacynthus

MAINLAND GREECE

PELO

KILOMETERS

0   50   100

MILES

0   30   60

THRACE

R.Arius

R. Haliacmon

NIA

PIERIA

Mt Olympus

HESSALY

Mt Ossa

Larissa

MAGNESIA

Pherae · Iolcos

Mt Pelion

Phylace ·

Myrmidons]

PHTHIA

Lemnos

(A E G E A N   S E A)

Scyros

DORIS

Aegae ·

EUBOEA

Mt Parnassus

Panopeus ·

ytho/Delphi Orchomenus · Lake

Copais

Thebes ·

BOEOTIA

Aulis ·

Euboea

Gulf of Corinth)

Athens ·

ATTICA

NNESE

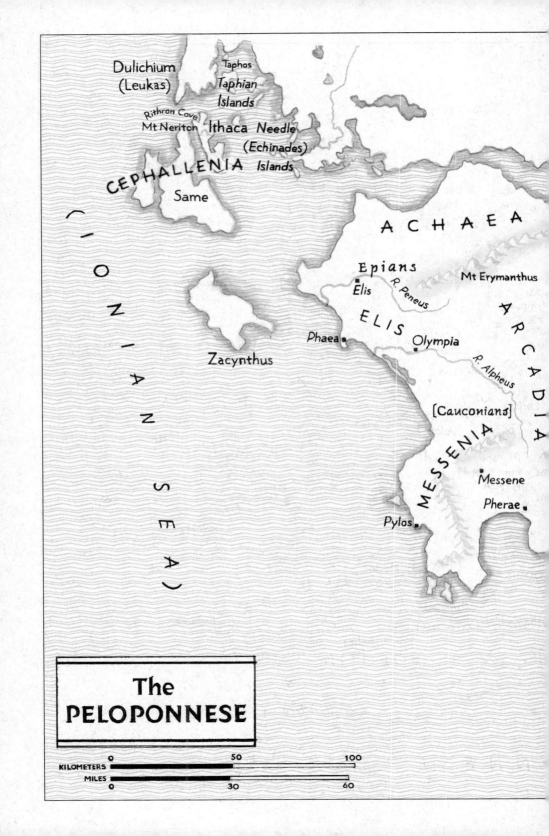

Dulichium
(Leukas)

Taphos

Taphian
Islands

Rithron Cove
Mt Neriton   Ithaca Needle
(Echinades)
Islands

CEPHALLENIA

Same

(IONIAN SEA)

ACHAEA

Epians
Elis

R. Peneus

Mt Erymanthus

ARCADIA

ELIS

Phaea

Olympia

R. Alpheus

Zacynthus

[Cauconians]

MESSENIA

Messene

Pherae

Pylos

The
PELOPONNESE

| KILOMETERS | 0 | 50 | 100 |
| MILES | 0 | 30 | 60 |

E U B O E A

Euboea

Mt Parnassus

Pytho/Delphi

Lake
Copais

Aulis

Thebes

[Cadmians]

Marathon

gae
Hyperesia (Aegira)

Eleusis

Megara

Athens

ATTICA

Mt Cyllene

Corinth

Salamis

Mycenae

A R G O

Epidaurus

Argos

Cape Geraestus

Cape Sounion

(M I R T O A N   S E A)

LACEDAEMON

Sparta

TAYGETUS MTS

Cape Malea

Cythera

From the ILIAD[1]

BOOK I

[The Wrath of Achilles]

Wrath—sing, goddess,[2] of the ruinous wrath of Peleus' son Achilles
that inflicted woes without number upon the Achaeans,
hurled forth to Hades many strong souls of warriors
and rendered their bodies prey for the dogs,
for all birds, and the will of Zeus was accomplished;   5
sing from when they two first stood in conflict—
Atreus' son, lord of men, and godlike Achilles.
        Which of the gods, then, set these two together in conflict, to fight?
Apollo, son of Leto and Zeus; who in his rage at the king
raised a virulent plague through the army; the men were dying   10
because the son of Atreus dishonored the priest Chryses.[3]
For he came to the Achaeans' swift ships
bearing countless gifts to ransom his daughter,
holding in his hands on a golden staff the wreaths of Apollo
who strikes from afar, and beseeched all the Achaeans—   15
but mostly the two sons of Atreus, marshalers of men:
        "Sons of Atreus and you other strong-greaved Achaeans,
may the gods who have homes on Olympus grant you
to plunder the city of Priam,[4] and reach your home safely;
release to me my beloved daughter, take instead the ransom,   20
revering Zeus' son who strikes from afar—Apollo."
        Then the rest of the Achaeans all shouted assent,
to respect the priest and accept the splendid ransom;
but this did not please the heart of Atreus' son Agamemnon,
and violently he sent him away and laid a powerful warning upon him: 25
"Let me not find you, old man, near our hollow ships,
either loitering now or coming again later,
lest the god's staff and wreath not protect you.
The girl I will not release; sooner will old age come upon her
in our house, in Argos,[5] far from her homeland,   30
pacing back and forth by the loom and sharing my bed.
So go, do not make me angry, and you will return the safer."
        Thus he spoke; and the old man was afraid and obeyed his word,
and he went in silence along the shore of the tumultuous sea.
And going aside, the old man fervently prayed   35
to lord Apollo, whom lovely-haired Leto bore:
"Hear me, God of the silver bow, you who stand over Chryse
and Killa most holy, you whose might rules Tenedos,[6]

---

1. Translated by Caroline Alexander.
2. Calliope, the muse who inspires epic poetry.
3. Chryses is from the town of Chryse near Troy. The Greeks had captured his daughter when they sacked Thebes (see below) and had given her to Agamemnon as his share of the booty.
4. Troy; Priam is its king. Olympus is the mountain in northern Greece that was supposed to be the home of the gods.
5. Agamemnon's home in the northeastern Peloponnesus, the southern part of mainland Greece.
6. An island off the Trojan coast. Like Chryse, Killa is a town near Troy.

God of Plague;[7] if ever I roofed over a temple that pleased you,
or if ever I burned as sacrifice to you the fatty thighbones 40
of bulls and of goats[8]—grant me this wish:
May the Danaans[9] pay for my tears with your arrows."
      Thus he prayed, and Phoebus Apollo heard him,
and set out from the heights of Olympus, rage in his heart,
with his bow on his shoulders and his hooded quiver; 45
the arrows clattered on his shoulders as he raged,
as the god himself moved; and he came like the night.
Then far from the ships he crouched, and let loose an arrow—
and terrible was the ring of his silver bow.
First he went after the mules and sleek dogs, 50
but then, letting fly a sharp arrow, he struck at the men themselves,
and the crowded pyres of the dead burned without ceasing.
      Nine days the shafts of the god flew through the army,
and on the tenth Achilles summoned the people to assembly;
the goddess of the white arms, Hera,[1] put this in his mind, 55
for she was distressed for the Danaans, since she saw them dying.
And when they were gathered together and assembled,
Achilles of the swift feet stood and addressed them:
"Son of Atreus, I now think that, staggering back,
we shall go home again—if we escape death that is— 60
if after all war and plague alike are to rout the Achaeans;
but come—let us ask some seer, or priest,
or even an interpreter of dreams, for a dream, too, is from Zeus,
who may tell us why Phoebus Apollo is so greatly angered,
if perhaps he faults our vows and sacrifice, 65
and whether receiving the burnt fat of sheep, of goats without blemish,
he may somehow be willing to avert our destruction."
      Thus Achilles spoke and sat down. Then stood among them
Calchas the son of Thestor, far the most eminent of bird-seers,
who knew things that are, and things to come, and what had gone
   before, 70
and had guided the ships of the Achaeans to Troy,
through his divination, which Phoebus Apollo gave him.
He in his wisdom spoke and addressed them:
"O Achilles, dear to Zeus, you bid me state the reason
for the wrath of Apollo, the lord who strikes from afar. 75
Then I will speak, but you listen closely and swear an oath to me
that in good earnest you will stand by me in word and strength of hand;
for I well know that I will anger a man who
has great power over the Argives, and whom the Achaeans obey.
For a king has the upper hand when he is angered with a
   base-born man; 80
if he does swallow his anger for that day,
yet he also holds resentment for later, until he brings it to fulfillment,
within his breast. You now declare whether you will protect me."

7. Apollo.
8. In sacrifice to Apollo.
9. The Greeks. Homer also calls them Achae-ans and Argives.

1. Sister and wife of Zeus; she was hostile to the Trojans and therefore favored the Greeks.

Then answering him Achilles of the swift feet spoke:
"Take courage, and speak freely of any omen you know;   85
for by Apollo beloved of Zeus, to whom you, Calchas,
pray when you reveal the gods' omens to the Danaans,
no man while I live and see light upon this earth
will lay heavy hands upon you by the hollow ships—
none of all the Danaans, not even if you speak of Agamemnon,   90
who now makes claim to be far the best man in the army."
    And then the blameless priest took courage and spoke:
"It is not with prayer, nor with sacrifice that he finds fault,
but for the sake of his priest, whom Agamemnon dishonored,
and did not release his daughter, and did not accept the ransom—   95
for that reason the god who shoots from afar has sent these sufferings,
   and will send yet more;
nor will he drive this foul plague away from the Danaans
until we give back the dark-eyed girl to her dear father
without price, without ransom, and lead a holy sacrifice
to Chryse; propitiating him in this way we might persuade him."   100
    Thus speaking he sat down; and then rose among them
the warrior son of Atreus, wide-ruling Agamemnon,
greatly distressed, his darkening heart consumed with rage,
his eyes like gleaming fires.
Glaring, he first addressed Calchas: 105
    "Prophet of evil, never yet have you spoken anything good for me,
always to prophesy evil is dear to your heart.
You have never spoken nor yet accomplished any good word;
and now you speak in assembly of the Danaans, declaiming god's will—
that for this reason, you say, the Archer who shoots from afar causes their
   affliction—   110
because I was not willing to accept his splendid ransom
for the girl Chryseïs,[2] since I greatly desire to have her
at home; for I prefer her to Clytemnestra,
my wedded wife, as she is not inferior to her,
not in figure or bearing, nor even in disposition or handiwork.   115
Yet, even so, I am willing to give her back—if this is for the best.
I wish my men to be safe rather than perish.
But make ready another prize at once, so that I alone
of the Achaeans am not unrecompensed, since that is not fitting.
For all of you are witness that my own prize goes elsewhere."   120
    Then answered him swift-footed, godlike Achilles:
"Most honored son of Atreus, of all men most covetous of possessions,
how then can the great-hearted Achaeans give you a prize?
We do not know of any great common store laid up anywhere,
but those things we carried from the cities, these have been distributed— 125
and it is not fitting to go about gathering these things again from the men.
But no, relinquish the girl to the god now; we Achaeans
will pay you back three times, four times over, if ever Zeus
gives us the well-walled city of Troy to plunder."
    Then answering him spoke powerful Agamemnon: 130

---

2. Daughter of Chryses.

"Do not in this way, skilled though you be, godlike Achilles,
try to trick me, for you will not outwit nor persuade me.
Or do you intend—while you yourself have a prize—that I just sit here
without one—are you ordering me to give the girl back?
No, either the great-hearted Achaeans will give me a prize   135
suited to my wishes, of equal value—
or if they do not give one, then I myself will go and take
either your own prize, or that of Ajax, or I will
take and carry away the prize of Odysseus;[3] and whomever I visit will be
    made angry;
but we shall consider these things later.   140
For now, come, let us drag one of our dark ships to the bright salt sea,
and assemble in it suitable rowers, and place the sacrifice in it,
and take on the girl herself, Chryseïs of the lovely cheeks;
and let there be one man in command, some man of counsel,
either Ajax or Idomeneus,[4] or noble Odysseus,   145
or you, son of Peleus, most terrifying of all men,
you might reconcile to us Apollo who works from afar, and perform
    the sacrifice."
        Then looking at him from under his brows swift-footed Achilles
    spoke:
"O wrapped in shamelessness, cunning in spirit—
how can any man of the Achaeans obey your words with good heart,   150
to journey with you or join men in violent battle?
For it was not on account of Trojan warriors I came
to wage battle here, since to me they are blameless—
never yet have they driven off my cattle, or my horses,
nor ever in Phthia,[5] where the rich earth breeds warriors,   155
have they destroyed my harvest, since there is much between us,
both shadowy mountains and clashing sea.
But we followed you, O great shameless one, for your pleasure,
to win recompense for Menelaos[6] and for you, dog-face,
from the Trojans; none of this do you pause to consider or care for.   160
And now you boast you will personally take my prize from me,
for which I suffered much hardship, which the sons of the Achaeans
    gave me!
Never do I receive a prize equal to yours when the Achaeans
sack some well-settled city of the Trojans;
it is my hands that conduct the greater part of furious war,   165
yet when it comes to division of the spoils
yours is the far greater prize, and I bearing some small thing, yet also
    prized,
make my way to my ships, wearied with fighting.
Now I am going to Phthia, since it is far better
to go home with my curved ships, and I do not intend   170
to stay here dishonored, hauling up riches and wealth for you."

3. Ajax, son of Telamon, was the bravest of
the Greeks after Achilles; Odysseus the most
crafty of the Greeks.
4. King of Crete and a prominent leader on
the Greek side.

5. Achilles' home in northern Greece.
6. Agamemnon's brother. The aim of the
expedition against Troy was to recover his wife,
Helen, who had left with with Paris, a son of
Priam.

Then Agamemnon lord of men answered him:
"Run, then, if your spirit so moves you. Nor will I
beg you to stay here for my sake. Other men stand by me,
who will pay me honor, and especially all-devising Zeus.   175
You are most hateful to me of the kings cherished by Zeus;
always contention is dear to you, and fighting and battles.
If you are so very powerful, a god doubtless gave this to you.
Go home with your ships and your companions—
be lord of the Myrmidons;[7] of you I take no account,   180
nor do I care that you are angered. But I promise you this:
As Phoebus Apollo robs me of Chryseïs,
whom I will send away, on my ship, with my companions—
so I will take Briseïs[8] of the pretty cheeks,
yes, your prize, going myself to your hut, so that you will discern   185
how much I am your better and so another man will be loath
to speak as my equal, openly matching himself with me."
          So he spoke. And anguish descended upon the son of Peleus
and the heart in his rugged breast debated two ways,
whether he should draw the sharp sword by his side   190
and scatter the men and slay and despoil the son of Atreus,
or check his anger and restrain his spirit.
While he churned these things through his heart and mind,
as he was drawing from its sheath his great sword, Athena[9] came to him
down from heaven; for Hera the goddess with white arms dispatched her,   195
who in her heart loved and cared for both men alike.
She came up behind and grabbed the son of Peleus' tawny hair,
appearing to him alone, and none of the others saw her.
Thunderstruck, Achilles turned behind him and at once recognized
Pallas Athena; for her eyes gleamed terribly.   200
And addressing her, he spoke winged words:
"Why do you come again, daughter of Zeus who wields the aegis?
Is it to witness the outrage of Agamemnon, the son of Atreus?
But I state openly to you, and I think that it will be accomplished,
that by these insolent acts he will shortly lose his life."   205
          Then the gleaming-eyed goddess addressed him:
"From heaven I have come to stop your anger, if you will heed me;
Hera the white-armed goddess sent me forth,
who in her heart loves and cares for you both alike.
Come, leave off this contention, stay your hand on your sword,   210
but rather cut him with words, telling him how things will be.
For I will tell you this, and it will be accomplished;
someday you will have three times as many shining gifts
because of this outrage; restrain yourself and obey me."
          Then in reply Achilles of the swift feet addressed her: 215
"I must obey the word of you both, goddess,

7. The contingent led by Achilles.
8. A captive woman who had been awarded to
Achilles.
9. A goddess, daughter of Zeus, and a patron of
human ingenuity and resourcefulness, whether
exemplified by handicrafts (such as carpentry or
weaving) or cunning in dealing with others. One
of her epithets is Pallas. Like Hera, she sided
with the Greeks in the war.

enraged in spirit though I am; for so is it better.
If a man heeds the gods, then they also listen to him."
He spoke and checked his powerful hand on the silver sword hilt
and back into the sheath thrust the great sword, nor did he disobey   220
the word of Athena. Then she was gone to Olympus,
to the house of Zeus who wields the aegis and the company of the other
    gods.

      And the son of Peleus once more with menacing words
addressed Agamemnon, and he did not hold back his anger:
"Wine-besotted, you who have the eyes of a dog and the heart of a deer,   225
never do you have courage to gear up for battle with your people,
nor go on ambush with the best of the Achaeans;
to you that is as death.
Far better it is, all through the broad army of the Achaeans,
to seize the gifts of the man who speaks against you.   230
King who feeds upon your people, since you rule worthless men;
otherwise, son of Atreus, this now would be your last outrage.
But I say openly to you, and I swear a great oath to it—
yes, by this scepter,[1] that never again will put forth leaves and shoots
when once it has left behind its stump in the mountains,   235
nor will it flourish again, since the bronze axe has stripped it round,
leaf and bark; and now in turn the sons of the Achaeans
busy with justice carry it around in their hands, they who
safeguard the ordinances of Zeus—this will be my great oath:
someday a yearning for Achilles will come upon the sons of the
    Achaeans,
                                                                  240
every man; then nothing will save you, for all your grief,
when at the hands of man-slaying Hector[2]
dying men fall in their multitude; and you will rip the heart within you,
raging that you paid no honor to the best of the Achaeans."

      Thus spoke the son of Peleus, and hurled the gold-studded   245
scepter to the ground, and sat down,
while the son of Atreus raged on the other side. Then between them rose
    Nestor,
the sweet-sounding, the clear speaker from Pylos,[3]
whose voice flowed from his tongue more sweetly than honey.
In his time two generations of mortal men had already   250
perished, those who were born and raised with him in days of old,
in sacred Pylos, and he was ruler among the third generation.
With kindly thoughts to both he advised and addressed them:
    "Oh look now, surely great trouble comes to the land of the
    Achaeans!
Surely Priam and the sons of Priam would be gladdened   255
and the rest of the Trojans greatly rejoiced in heart
if they were to learn you two were fighting over all this—
you who surpass the Danaans in counsel, who surpass them in fighting!

---

1. A wooden staff that symbolized authority. It was handed by a herald to whichever leader rose to speak in an assembly as a sign of his authority to speak.

2. Son of Priam; he was the foremost warrior among the Trojans.

3. A territory on the western shore of the Peloponnesus.

But hearken; you are both younger than me.
For once upon a time I banded with better   260
men even than you, and never did they slight me.
Never yet have I seen, nor shall see such men—
Peirithoös and Dryas, shepherd of his people,
and Kaineus and Exadios and Polyphemos like a god.[4]   264
These were raised to be strongest of earthly men;   266
they were the strongest and they fought with the strongest—
the Centaurs who lie in the mountains—and terribly they slaughtered
    them.
And yet with these men I kept company, coming from Pylos,
far away, from a distant land; for they summoned me.   270
And I fought by myself, I alone; against these men no
mortal now upon earth could fight.
And yet they marked my counsels and heeded my word.
Now you two heed me, since it is better to do so.
You should not, great though you are, deprive him of the girl,   275
but let her be, as it was to him the sons of the Achaeans gave her as prize;
nor you, son of Peleus, venture to contend face-to-face
with your king, since the king bearing the scepter partakes of
a very different honor, and is he to whom Zeus has given distinction.
And if you are the stronger man, and the mother who bore you a
    goddess,[5]   280
yet is this one more powerful, since he rules over more men.
Son of Atreus, restrain your spirit; for I—yes, I—
entreat you to relinquish your anger with Achilles, who is for all
Achaeans the great wall of defense against this evil war."
            Then in turn lord Agamemnon spoke: 285
"Indeed all these things, old sir, you rightly say;
but this man wants to be above all other men;
he wants to be lord over all, to rule all,
to give orders to all—which I think that one man at least will not obey.
And if the eternal gods have made him a spearman   290
they do not on that account appoint him to speak insults."
            Interrupting, godlike Achilles answered him:
"May I be called a coward and of no account
if I submit to you in everything you should say.
Give such orders to other men, but do not act as master to me.   295
For I do not think it likely I will obey you.
And I will tell you something else and put it away in your mind—
I will not fight for the girl with strength of hand,
not with you, nor with any other man, since you who take her from me
    also gave her.
But of other possessions beside my ships, swift and dark,   300

4. Heroes of an earlier generation. These are
the Lapiths from Thessaly in northern Greece.
At the wedding of Peirithoös, the mountain-
dwelling centaurs (half human, half horse)
got drunk and tried to rape the women who
were present. The Lapiths killed them after a
fierce fight. The line numbers here account
for lines that were omitted by the translator
because they may not belong to the next.
5. The sea nymph Thetis, who was married to
the mortal Peleus (Achilles' father). She later
left him and went to live with her father, Nereus,
in the depths of the Aegean Sea.

of these you can take nothing lifted against my will.
And I invite you to try, so that these men too will know—
very quickly will your dark blood gush round my spear."
    Having fought like this with words, blow for blow,
they both stood, and broke up the assembly by the ships of the Achaeans.   305
Peleus' son went to his shelter and balanced ships
with the son of Menoetius[6] and his companions.
But the son of Atreus then drew a swift ship down to the sea,
and chose twenty rowers to go in her, and put on board the sacrificial
   hecatomb
for the god, and fetching Chryseïs of the lovely cheeks   310
put her on board; and resourceful Odysseus came on as leader.
    Then, embarked, they sailed upon the watery way,
and the son of Atreus charged the men to purify themselves.
They cleansed themselves and cast the impurities into the sea,
and to Apollo they made perfect sacrificial hecatombs   315
of bulls and goats along the shore of the murmuring sea;
and the savor rose to heaven amid a swirl of smoke.
    So they attended to these tasks throughout the army; but
  Agamemnon did not
leave off the quarrel, in which he first threatened Achilles,
but spoke to Talthybios and Eurybates,   320
who were heralds and ready henchmen:
"Go to the shelter of Peleus' son Achilles;
take by the hand Briseïs of the lovely cheeks and lead her away.
And if he does not give her up, I myself will take her,
coming in force, and it will be the worse for him."   325
    So saying, he sent them forth, and enjoined on them a harsh
  command.
And they two went unwilling along the shore of the murmuring sea,
and came to the camp and ships of the Myrmidons.
They found Achilles by his shelter and dark ship,
sitting; and he did not rejoice to see them.   330
The two stood in fear and awe of the king,
and neither addressed him, nor questioned.
But Achilles understood in his heart, and spoke to them:
    "Hail heralds, messengers of Zeus, as also of men—
come close; you are not to blame in my eyes, but Agamemnon,   335
who sends you two forth on account of the girl Briseïs.
But come, Patroclus, descended from Zeus, bring out the girl
and give her to these two to take away. And let them both be witnesses
before the blessed gods and mortal men alike,
and before him, this stubborn king, if ever hereafter   340
other men need me to ward off shameful destruction.
For he surely raves in his ruinous heart,
and knows not to look ahead as well as behind
as to how the Achaeans shall fight in safety beside the ships."
    Thus he spoke and Patroclus obeyed his beloved companion,   345
and from the shelter led Briseïs of the lovely cheeks,

---

6. Patroclus, Achilles' closest friend.

and gave her to be taken away. And straightway the heralds left for the
    ships of the Achaeans.
She the young woman, unwilling, went with them. But Achilles,
weeping, quickly slipping away from his companions, sat
on the shore of the gray salt sea, and looked out to depths as dark as
    wine;   350
again and again, stretching forth his hands, he prayed to his beloved
    mother:
"Mother, since you bore me to be short-lived as I am,
Olympian Zeus who thunders on high ought to
grant me at least honor; but now he honors me not even a little.
For the son of Atreus, wide-ruling Agamemnon   355
has dishonored me; he keeps my prize, having seized it, he personally
    taking it."
        So he spoke, shedding tears, and his lady mother heard him
as she sat in the depths of the salt sea beside her aged father.
At once she rose from the clear salt sea, like mist,
and sat before him as he wept,   360
and caressed him with her hand, and spoke to him and said his name:
"Child, why do you cry? What pain has come to your heart?
Speak out, don't hide it, so that we both know."
        Groaning deeply, Achilles of the swift feet spoke to her:
"You know; why should I recount these things to you who know them all?   365
We came to Thebes, the holy city of Eëtion;[7]
we sacked it and brought everything here.
The sons of the Achaeans fairly divided the things among them,
and to the son of Atreus they gave out Chryseïs of the lovely cheeks.
Then Chryses, a priest of Apollo who strikes from afar,   370
came to the swift ships of the bronze-clad Achaeans
bearing untold ransom to set free his daughter,
holding in his hands the wreaths of Apollo who strikes from afar
on a golden staff, and beseeched all the Achaeans,
but mostly the two sons of Atreus, marshalers of men.   375
Then all the rest of the Achaeans shouted assent,
to respect the priest and take the splendid ransom;
but this did not please the heart of Atreus' son Agamemnon,
but violently he drove him away and laid a strong injunction upon him.
And in anger the old man went back; and Apollo   380
heard him when he prayed, since he was very dear to him,
and he let fly an evil arrow against the Argives; and now the men
died in quick succession as the arrows of the god ranged
everywhere through the broad army of the Achaeans. But then a seer
possessed of good knowledge publicly declared to us the wishes of the
    god who works his will.   385
Straightway I led in urging that the god be appeased;
but then anger seized the son of Atreus, and suddenly rising to speak
he declared aloud a threat, which is now fulfilled.

7. Eëtion was king of the Cilicians in Asia
Minor and father of Hector's wife, Andromache. "Thebes" (or Thebe): the Cilicians' capital city, not the Greek or Egyptian city of the
same name.

For the dark-eyed Achaeans are sending the girl on a swift ship
to the town of Chryse, taking gifts for lord Apollo; 390
just now the heralds set out from my shelter leading
the daughter of Briseus, whom the sons of the Achaeans gave to me.
But you, if you have the power, defend your son;
go to Olympus and petition Zeus, if ever in any way
in word or in deed you delighted the heart of Zeus. 395
For many times in the halls of my father I have heard you
boast when you said that from the dark-clouded son of Cronus,
alone among immortals, you warded off shameful destruction,
at that time when the other Olympians sought to bind him—
Hera and Poseidon[8] and Pallas Athena; 400
but you coming to him, goddess, released his bonds,
swiftly summoning to high Olympus the Hundred-Handed One,
whom the gods call Briareos the Strong—but all men call
Aigaion—he in turn is stronger than his father;[9]
and this one seated himself beside the son of Cronus, rejoicing in his
    glory. 405
And the blessed gods trembled before him, and did no more binding.
Now remind Zeus of these things, seat yourself beside him and clasp his
    knees
and see if he might be willing to aid the Trojans,
and to pen the Achaeans around the sterns of their ships and the sea,
dying, so that all may have profit of their king, 410
and he will know, Atreus' son, wide-ruling Agamemnon,
his delusion, when he paid no honor to the best of the Achaeans."
    Then Thetis answered him, with tears flowing down:
"Ah me, my child, why did I, bitter in childbearing, raise you?
Would that you sat by your ships without tears, without pain, 415
for indeed your measure of life is so very small, not long at all.
And now you are at once short-lived and unlucky beyond all men;
so I bore you to an unworthy fate in my halls.
To speak your request to Zeus who hurls the thunderbolt
I myself shall go to Olympus of the deep snow; perhaps he will heed me. 420
But you stay now by your fast-running ships,
nurse your wrath at the Achaeans, and leave off the war entirely.
Zeus went yesterday to the river of Ocean among the blameless
    Aethiopians,[1]
to attend a feast, and all the gods accompanied him.
On the twelfth day he will come back to Olympus, 425
and then at that time I will go for you to the bronze-floored house
    of Zeus,
and I will clasp his knees in supplication, and I think I will persuade him."
    Then speaking thus she went away and left him there,
angered in his heart on account of the fair-belted woman,
whom they were taking by force against his will. And Odysseus 430

8. Brother of Zeus and god of the sea.
9. Aigaion's father is Uranus, the Sky, husband
of Earth and the first divine ruler. He was overthrown by his son Cronus, who in turn was
overthrown by his son Zeus.
1. A people believed to live at the extreme edges
of the world. Ocean was thought of as a river
that encircled the earth.

was drawing near the town of Chryse, bearing the sacred hecatomb.
When they had come inside the deep harbor,
they furled the sails, and placed them in the dark ship,
and deftly lowering the mast by the forestays, laid it in the mast-gallows,
and rowed her to her mooring under oars;   435
then they threw the anchor stones, and made fast the stern lines,
and themselves disembarked into the broken surf,
and disembarked the hecatomb for Apollo, who strikes from afar;
and Chryseïs disembarked from the seagoing ship.
Then leading her to the altar resourceful Odysseus   440
placed her in her father's hands and addressed him:
"O Chryses, Agamemnon, lord of men, dispatched me
to lead your child to you and to perform sacred hecatombs to Phoebus
on behalf of the Danaans, so that we might propitiate lord Apollo,
who has now sent sufferings, much lamented, upon the Argives."   445
    So speaking, he placed her in the priest's arms, and he, rejoicing,
      received
his beloved daughter; and the men swiftly set up the splendid hecatomb
    for the god
in good order around the well-built altar,
then they washed their hands and took up the barley for scattering.
And Chryses prayed aloud for them, lifting his hands: 450
"Hear me, thou of the silver bow, you who stand over Chryse
and Killa most holy, you whose might rules Tenedos,
surely once before this you heard me when I prayed;
honoring me you smote hard the host of the Achaeans.
Now, as once before, fulfill this wish for me;   455
now this time ward shameful destruction from the Danaans."
Thus he spoke praying, and Phoebus Apollo heard him.
    Then when they had prayed and thrown the scattering barley
      before them,
they first drew back the heads of the sacrificial animals and cut their
      throats, and flayed them,
and cut out the thighbones and covered them over with fat   460
they had made into double folds, and placed raw flesh upon them;
the old man burned these on a cleft-stick and over them poured in libation
dark-gleaming wine; and the youths beside him held sacrificial forks in
      hand.
Then when the thighbones had been consumed by fire and they had
      tasted the entrails,
they cut up the other parts and pierced them through on spits   465
and roasted them with care, and then drew off all the pieces.
And when they had ceased their work and prepared their meal,
they feasted, nor did any man's appetite lack his due portion.
And when they had put away desire for eating and drinking,
the young men filled mixing bowls brimful with wine,   470
and after pouring libations in each cup, distributed it to all;
then all day long they sought the favor of the god in dance and song,
the young Achaean men beautifully singing a hymn of praise,
celebrating the god who works from afar; and the god rejoiced in his
      heart as he listened.

When the sun sank and dusk came on,   475
then they laid down to sleep by the stern lines of their ship;
and when dawn, born of the morning, shone forth her fingers of rosy light,
then they sailed out for the broad army of the Achaeans.
And to them Apollo who works from afar sent a following wind.
They stepped the mast and spread the glistening sails,   480
and the wind blew gusts in the middle of the sail, and around
the cutwater the bow-wave, shimmering dark, sang loud as the ship
   proceeded.
She swept over the swell, making her course.
And when they arrived at the broad army of the Achaeans,
they dragged the dark ship ashore   485
high on the sand, and splayed long struts beneath,
and themselves scattered to their ships and shelters.
      But, he, sitting idle by his fast-running ships, remained full of
   wrath—
the Zeus-descended son of Peleus,[2] Achilles of the swift feet;
never did he go to the assembly where men win glory,   490
never to war, but consumed his own heart,
biding his time there; yet he yearned for the war shout and battle.
      But when at length the twelfth dawn arose,
then all the gods who live forever went to Olympus
together, with Zeus as their leader; and Thetis did not neglect her son's   495
directives, and she rose from the heaving surface of the sea,
and at dawn ascended to towering Olympus.
She found the far-thundering son of Cronus sitting apart from the others
on the topmost peak of ridged Olympus;
and she sat before him and clasped his knees   500
with her left hand, and with her right took hold of him beneath
   his chin,[3]
and in supplication addressed lord Zeus, the son of Cronus:
"Father Zeus, if ever among the immortals I helped you
by word or by deed, accomplish this wish for me:
honor my son, who was born short-lived beyond all men,   505
and yet now the lord of men Agamemnon has
dishonored him; he holds his prize, having seized it, he personally taking it.
Do you now revenge him, Olympian Zeus, all-devising;
give strength to the Trojans until that time the Achaeans
recompense my son and exalt him with honor."   510
      So she spoke; but Zeus who gathers the clouds did not answer her,
but sat silent a long while. And as she had clasped his knees, so Thetis
now held on, clinging closely, and beseeched him again:
"Promise me faithfully, and nod your assent,
or refuse me—you have nothing to fear—so that I may learn   515
how much I am of all gods the most dishonored."
      Greatly troubled, Zeus who gathers the clouds addressed her:
"This is a deadly business, when you set me up to quarrel

---

2. Peleus was the son of Aeacus, son of Zeus.
3. She takes on the posture of the suppliant,
which physically emphasizes the desperation
and urgency of her request. Zeus was, above
all other gods, the protector of suppliants.

with Hera, when she will harass me with words of abuse.
As it is, she is always quarreling with me in the presence of the
   immortal gods,   520
and maintains, as you know, that I help the Trojans in battle.
Now go back, lest Hera notice anything;
I will make these matters my concern, to bring them to accomplishment.
Come, I will my bow my head for you, so that you may be convinced;
for among immortals this is the greatest   525
testament of my determination; for not revocable, nor false,
nor unfulfilled is anything to which I have bowed my head."
The son of Cronus spoke, and nodded with his blue-black brows,
the ambrosial mane of the lord god swept forward
from his immortal head; and he shook great Olympus.   530
       Thus the two parted after conspiring; and she
sprang into the deep salt sea from shining Olympus,
and Zeus went to his home; and all the gods rose as a body
from their seats before their father; nor did any dare
remain seated as he approached, but all stood to meet him.   535
So he took his seat there upon his throne; nor did Hera
fail to perceive at a glance that silver-footed
Thetis, the daughter of the old man of the sea, had conspired with him.
Straightway she addressed Zeus, the son of Cronus, with taunting
   words:
"Which of the gods now, O cunning schemer, has conspired with you?   540
Always you love being away from me, mulling over your secrets
to make your decisions. Never yet to me
have you willingly dared state what you are thinking."
       Then the father of gods and men answered her:
"Hera, do not hope to know all my thoughts;   545
they will be hard for you, although you are my wife.
However, that which is fitting for you to hear, no other,
of gods or men, will know before you;
but that which I may wish to consider apart from the gods—
do not press me about each and every thing, nor make inquiry."   550
       Then answered him the ox-eyed lady Hera:
"Most dread son of Cronus, what sort of word have you spoken?
Certainly before now I have neither pressed you, nor made inquiry,
and entirely without interference you devise whatever you want.
But now my heart is terribly afraid lest   555
silver-footed Thetis, daughter of the old man of the sea, won you over;
for at dawn she came to your side and clasped your knees.
And I suspect you pledged faithfully to her that you would honor
Achilles, and destroy many by the ships of the Achaeans."
       Then in answer Zeus who gathers the clouds addressed her: 560
"What possesses you? You always suspect something, I never get
   past you.
Nonetheless, you can accomplish nothing at all, but will only be
further from my heart—and it will be the worse for you.
If this is the way things are—then you may be sure this is the way that
   pleases me.
Sit down and be silent, and obey my word,   565

lest the gods in Olympus, as many as there are, be of no avail to you
   against me
as I close in, when I lay my unassailable hands upon you."
     Thus he spoke and the ox-eyed lady Hera was afraid,
and she sat down in silence, bending her own heart into submission;
and throughout the house of Zeus the heavenly gods were troubled.   570
To them Hephaestus,[4] famed for his art, began to speak,
comforting his dear mother, white-armed Hera:
"To be sure this will be a deadly business, not to be borne,
if you two quarrel this way for the sake of mortals,
carrying on this jabbering among the gods; nor   575
will there be any pleasure from our noble feast if unseemliness prevails.
I advise my mother, sensible as she is,
to be agreeable to our dear father Zeus, so that our father
will not reproach us again, and throw our feast into disorder.
For what if the Olympian wielder of lightning wished to   580
blast us from our seats—for he is much the strongest.
Rather address him with gentle words;
then straightway will the Olympian be favorable to us."
     Thus he spoke, and springing to his feet placed a
   double-handled cup
in his dear mother's hands, and addressed her: 585
"Endure, my mother, and restrain yourself, distressed though you be,
lest, dear as you are, I with my own eyes see you
struck down; then for all my grief I will have no power
to help you; for it is painful to oppose the Olympian.
For at another time before this, when I was trying to ward him
   from you,   590
he grabbed me by the foot and cast me from the threshold of heaven;
the whole day I drifted down, and as the sun set
I dropped on Lemnos,[5] and there was but little life still in me.
It was there the Sintian men quickly ministered to me after my fall."
     So he spoke and Hera, goddess of the white arms, smiled   595
and smiling accepted the cup from her son's hand.
Then to all the other gods, serving to the right,
he poured sweet nectar[6] like wine, drawing from a mixing bowl;
and unquenchable laughter broke out among the blessed gods
as they watched Hephaestus bustling through the halls.   600
     Then all day long until the sun went down,
they feasted, nor was the appetite of any stinted of fair portion—
nor stinted of the beautifully wrought lyre, which Apollo held,
or of the Muses, who sang, one following the other, with lovely voice.
Then when the sun's bright light went down,   605
they left to go to bed, each in his own house,
where the famous crook-legged god,
Hephaestus, had made a house for each with skillful understanding.
Olympian Zeus, wielder of lightning, went to his bed

---

4. The lame god of fire and the patron of crafts-
people, especially metalworkers.
5. An island in the Aegean Sea, inhabited by

the Sintians.
6. The drink of the gods.

where he was wont to retire when sweet sleep came to him;   610
here mounting his bed, he went to sleep, with Hera of the golden
    throne beside him.

Summary   As Achilles, angry with Agamemnon, stays out of the fighting, the Trojans make
a series of successful attacks against the Greek forces. They are led by the greatest of the Trojan
heroes, Hector, son of Priam and brother of Paris, who leaves behind his wife and infant son to
challenge the invading army and defend his home. When Hector brings the Trojan soldiers right up
to the Greek ships, ready to set them on fire, Agamemnon acknowledges that he made a mistake to
alienate Achilles, and sends messengers (including Odysseus) to try to persuade the hero to return
to the war. But Achilles holds out, and the fighting continues. Many men die on both sides. Finally
Achilles' friend, Patroclus, volunteers to fight in his place, borrowing Achilles' own armor. He is
killed by Hector. Hector strips Achilles' divine armor from Patroclus's corpse. A fierce fight for the
body itself ends in partial success for the Greeks; they take Patroclus's body but have to retreat to
their camp, with the Trojans at their heels.

BOOK XVIII

[*The Shield of Achilles*]

So they fought like blazing fire;
but Antilochos[7] went as swift-footed messenger to Achilles.
And he found him in front of his straight-horned ships,
foreboding in his heart those things that now had happened,
and troubled he addressed his own great-hearted spirit: 5
"Ah me, why now are the long-haired Achaeans again
driven to the ships in panicked confusion across the plain?
May the gods not have accomplished evil sufferings for my heart,
as once my mother plainly told me, and said to me
that while I yet lived, the best of Myrmidons   10
at Trojan hands would leave the light of day.
Surely Menoetius' brave son has already died,
stubborn one; and yet I told him that when he had driven off the
    blazing fire
to come back to the ships, not battle in his strength with Hector."
            While he churned these things through his mind and heart,   15
the son of noble Nestor drew close to him
shedding hot tears, and spoke his grievous message:
"Woe to me, son of brilliant Peleus, surely it is a baleful
message you will hear, would that it had never happened.
Patroclus lies dead, and they are fighting round his naked   20
body; for Hector of the shimmering helm has his armor."
            So he spoke; and a dark cloud of grief enveloped Achilles.
Taking with both hands the fire-blackened ashes,
he poured them down upon his head, and defiled his handsome face;
on his fragrant tunic the black ash settled;   25
and he lay outstretched in the dust,
a great man in his greatness, and with his own hands he defiled his hair,
    tearing at it.

7. A son of Nestor. He has been sent to tell Achilles that Patroclus is dead.

And the female slaves, whom Achilles and Patroclus had seized as plunder,
stricken at heart cried loud, and ran outside
around brilliant Achilles, and all with their hands   30
beat their breasts, and the limbs of each went slack beneath them;
on his other side Antilochos wept, pouring tears,
holding the hands of Achilles as his noble heart groaned.
For he feared lest Achilles cut his own throat with iron.
        Dreadful were Achilles' cries of grief; his lady mother heard   35
as she sat in the depths of the sea beside her aged father.
Then she wailed in turn; and all the goddesses gathered round her,
who down in the depths of the sea were daughters of Nereus.
There was Glauke, Thaleia and Kymodoke,
Nesaie and Speio, Thoë and ox-eyed Halia,   40
Kymothoë and also Aktaia, and Limnoreia,
Melite, and Iaira, Amphithoë and Agauë,
Doto, Proto and Pherousa, Dynamene,
Dexamene, Amphinome and Kallianeira;
Doris and Panope and illustrious Galateia   45
and Nemertes and Apseudes and Kallianassa;
and Klymene was there and Ianeira and also Ianassa,
Maira and Oreithyia and Amatheia of the lovely hair,
and the others who in the depths of the sea were daughters of Nereus.
And the silvery cave was filled with them; and all together   50
beat their breasts. And Thetis led the lament:
"Hear me, sister Nereids, so that all of you
may know well as you listen, how many are the sorrows in my heart.
Ay me, wretched I am—ay me, unhappy bearer of the noblest son,
since I bore a son, blameless and strong,   55
outstanding among warriors, who shot up like a young shoot,
and having nurtured him like a growing tree on the high ground of an
    orchard
I sent him forth with the curved ships to Ilion,
to go to battle against the Trojans; him I shall not welcome again
returned home into the house of Peleus.   60
So long as he lives and sees the sun's light,
he has sorrow, nor can I help him at all by going to him.
But come, so that I may see my beloved child and hear of
what sorrow has come to him while he stayed away from the fighting."
        So speaking she left the cave; and her sisters went with her   65
in tears, and the swell of the sea broke around them.
And when they reached the rich soil of Troy,
up onto the shore of the sea they went, up one after the other, where
    the ships
of the Myrmidons had been drawn up, close-pressed round swift Achilles.
And his lady mother stood beside him as he groaned deeply,   70
and keenly wailing she held her son's head,
and in lament spoke winged words:
"Child, why do you cry? What sorrow has reached your heart?
Speak out, do not hide it. Those things have been accomplished for you
through Zeus, as at that time before you prayed with uplifted hands,   75
that all the sons of the Achaeans be pinned against the sterns of their ships

and for want of you suffer deeds that shamed them."
    Then groaning deeply swift-footed Achilles answered her:
"Mother mine, these things the Olympian indeed fulfilled for me;
but what pleasure do I have in them, since my beloved companion died,   80
Patroclus, whom I revered beyond all companions,
as equal to my own life? I have lost him, and after slaying him Hector
stripped the stupendous armor, a wonder to behold,
a thing of beauty; the armor the gods gave to Peleus as splendid gifts
on that day when they placed you in the bed of a mortal man.   85
Would that you had made your home with the immortal goddesses of
    the sea,
and Peleus had taken to himself a mortal wife.
But as it is, for you too there must be grief immeasurable in heart
for the death of your son, whom you will not receive again
returned to home, since my spirit does not bid me   90
to go on living nor take my part among men, unless, before all else,
Hector, beaten beneath my spear, lose his life,
and pay the penalty for making prey of Menoetius' son Patroclus."
    Then in turn Thetis spoke to him as she shed her tear:
"Then you will die soon, my child, from what you say;   95
for your fate is prepared straightway after Hector's."
Then greatly troubled swift-footed Achilles spoke to her:
"Straightway may I die, since I was not destined to help my companion
as he was killed; and a very long way from his fatherland
he perished, and lacked me to be his defender against harm.   100
Now since I am not returning to my beloved fatherland,
nor was I in any way salvation's light to Patroclus, nor to my other
companions, who have been broken in their number by shining Hector,
but sat beside the ships a useless burden on the earth,
I who am such as no other of the bronze-clad Achaeans   105
is in battle; though in the assembly there are others better—
would that strife perish from gods and men,
and anger, which incites even a man of sense to violence,
and which, far sweeter than dripping honey,
wells like smoke in the breast of men,   110
as Agamemnon lord of men then angered me.
But let us leave these things in the past for all our distress,
subduing the spirit in our own breasts by necessity;
for now I am setting out to find the destroyer of a dear life—
Hector. I will take death at that time when   115
Zeus and the other deathless gods wish to accomplish it.
For even the mighty Heracles[8] did not escape from death,
for all that he was dearest to lord Zeus the son of Cronus,
but fate broke him and the hard anger of Hera;
so I too, if the same fate has been prepared for me,   120
shall lie when I have died. But now let me win outstanding glory,
and drive some woman of Troy, or deep-breasted Dardan[9] woman,

8. The greatest of Greek heroes, the son of Zeus by a mortal woman; pursued by the jealousy of Hera, he was forced to undertake twelve great labors and finally died in agony from the effects of a poisoned garment.
9. Trojan.

wiping with both hands from her soft cheeks
the thick-falling tears, to moan aloud,
and may they know that I stayed too long from fighting. 125
Do not detain me from battle though you love me; you will not
  persuade me."
      Then answered him Thetis of the silver feet:
"Yes, all these things, my child, you have spoken truly; nor is it shameful
to ward off sheer destruction from your afflicted comrades.
Yet your beautiful armor is held among the Trojans, 130
the brazen, glittering armor. Hector of the shimmering helm
exults in this, wearing it on his own shoulders; but I do not think
he will exult in it for long, since his slaughter is near at hand.
But do not enter in the strife of battle
until you see me returned here with your own eyes; 135
for at dawn I shall come back with the rising of the sun
carrying splendid armor from lord Hephaestus."
      Then having so spoken she took herself away from her son,
and turned to speak to her sisters of the sea:
"All of you now make your way into the broad gulf of ocean, 140
to see the old man of the sea and the halls of our father,
and to tell him everything; and I am going to high Olympus,
to the side of Hephaestus, famed for his skill, to see if he might be willing
to give to my son glorious gleaming armor."
So she spoke; and they at once plunged beneath the ocean swell; 145
and she, the goddess Thetis of the silver feet, went again to Olympus,
so that she might carry splendid armor to her beloved son.
      Her feet brought her to Olympus; meanwhile the Achaeans
fleeing with inhuman shouts before man-slaughtering Hector
reached their ships and the Hellespont. 150
But Patroclus—the strong-greaved Achaeans could not drag
the body of Achilles' henchman out from under the flying spears and
  arrow shafts;
for again the Trojan host and horses came upon him,
as did Hector son of Priam, like fire in fighting spirit.
Three times shining Hector seized the body by the feet from behind, 155
determined to drag it off, and shouted loud to spur the Trojans.
And three times the two Aiantes, mantled in their fierce courage,
beat him from the corpse. But steadfastly trusting in his battle prowess
Hector would now spring forth through the press of battle, now again
take his stand and cry aloud, nor fell back at all; 160
but as from a carcass rustic herdsmen fail to drive away
a tawny lion in his great hunger,
so the two Aiantes, fully armed, were not able
to frighten Hector son of Priam from the corpse.
      And indeed he would have dragged it away and won for himself
  glory everlasting, 165
had not swift Iris[1] with feet like the wind come to the son of Peleus
as messenger, racing from Olympus with word to prepare for battle,
in secret from Zeus and the other gods; for Hera it was who sent her;

---

1. Goddess of the rainbow and the usual messenger of the gods in the *Iliad*.

and standing close to him she spoke her winged words:
"Rise up, son of Peleus, most terrifying of men;   170
protect Patroclus, for whose sake the dread fighting
is under way before the ships—they are killing one another,
both those who fight to defend the body of he who died,
and the Trojans who rush to haul it off to windy Ilion.
Above all others shining Hector   175
is bent on dragging it away; and his heart is urgent to impale the head
upon spiked stakes, cut from its tender neck.
Come, rise up, don't lie still; shame be on your heart,
should Patrocluos become a plaything for Trojan dogs.
Yours the dishonor, if he comes mutilated to the dead."   180
        Then answered her swift-footed godlike Achilles:
"Divine Iris, which of the gods sent you as messenger to me?"
Then in turn swift Iris with feet like the wind addressed him:
"Hera sent me, the glorious wife of Zeus;
nor does the high-throned son of Cronus know, nor any other   185
of the immortals, who dwell about snow-clad Olympus."
Then answering her spoke swift-footed Achilles:
"How then am I to go among the tumult? For those others have my armor.
And my beloved mother forbade me arm for battle
before I see her coming with my own eyes;   190
for she pledged to bring splendid armor from Hephaestus.
And I do not know who else's illustrious arms I might put on,
unless it be the great shield of Telamonian Ajax.[2]
But he too, I think, is engaged among the frontline fighters,
wreaking havoc with his spear around Patroclus who lies dead."   195
Then in turn swift Iris with feet like the wind addressed him:
"We too well know that they hold your glorious armor.
But go as you are to the ditch and show yourself to the Trojans—
perhaps in dread of you they might retreat from fighting,
the Trojans, and the warrior sons of the Achaeans draw breath   200
in their extremity; for respite in war is brief."
        So speaking swift-footed Iris departed;
and Achilles beloved of Zeus arose. And Athena
cast the tasseled aegis[3] about his mighty shoulders;
she, shining among goddesses, encircled round his head a cloud of   205
gold, and from it blazed bright-shining fire.
And as when smoke rising from a city reaches the clear high air
from a distant island, which enemy men fight round,
and they the whole day long are pitted in hateful warfare
around their city walls, but with the sun's setting   210
the beacon fires blaze, torch upon torch, and flaring upward
the glare becomes visible to those who live around,
in the hope that they might come with ships as allies against destruction,
so from Achilles' head the radiance reached the clear high air.
And going away from the wall he stood at the ditch, nor did he mix with   215

2. The son of Telamon, the more famous of
the two heroes named Ajax. His distinctive
attribute in the *Iliad* is a huge shield that covers
his whole body.

3. A tasseled garment or piece of armor that
belonged to Zeus but was often carried by
Athena in poetry and art. It induced panic when
shaken at an enemy.

the Achaeans; for he observed his mother's knowing command.
And standing there he shouted, and from the distance Pallas Athena
cried out too; unspeakable was the uproar he incited in the Trojans.
As when a clarion voice is heard, when cries the trumpet
of life-destroying enemies who surround a city,   220
such then was the clarion voice of Aeacides.
      And when they heard the brazen voice of Aeacides,
the spirit in man each was thrown in turmoil; the horses with their fine
    manes
wheeled their chariots back, for in their hearts they forebode distress
    to come,
and the charioteers were struck from their senses, when they saw the
    weariless   225
terrible fire above the head of Peleus' great-hearted son
blazing; and this the gleaming-eyed goddess Athena caused to blaze.
Three times across the ditch godlike Achilles cried his great cry,
and three times the Trojans and their illustrious allies were thrown in
    panic.
Then and there perished twelve outstanding men   230
upon their own chariots and spears. And the Achaeans
with relief pulled Patroclus out from under the missiles,
and laid him on a litter; and his beloved companions stood around it
weeping, and with them followed swift-footed Achilles
shedding hot tears, when he looked upon his trusted comrade   235
lying on the bier, torn with sharp bronze,
whom he had sent forth with horses and chariots
into war, but did not welcome him returned home again.
      And ox-eyed lady Hera caused the tireless sun
to return, unwilling, into the streams of Ocean;   240
the sun set, and the glorious Achaeans ceased
from the powerful din of battle and all-leveling war.
The Trojans in their turn on the other side, withdrawing from the
mighty combat released their swift horses from under their chariots,
and gathered into assembly before taking thought for supper;   245
and the assembly took place with them standing upright, nor did any
    man dare
to take his seat; for trembling held them all, because Achilles
had appeared; he who for a long time had abandoned the painful battle.
      And to them Poulydamas, wise son of Panthoös,
was first to speak to the assembly; he alone looked both forward and
    behind him;[4]   250
he was Hector's comrade, and born in the same night,
but the one greatly excelled in speech, and the other in the spear;
he with wise intent gave counsel to them and spoke:
"Consider well, my friends; I for my part urge
you now to go to the city, and not await the bright dawn   255
on the open plain beside the ships; we are far from our ramparts.
As long as that man harbored wrath at noble Agamemnon,
so long were the Achaeans easier to fight;

---

4. I.e., he was a prophet; he knew the past and foresaw the future.

I myself used to welcome sleeping by the swift ships at night,
with the hope we would seize these double-ended ships.   260
But now terribly I dread the swift-footed son of Peleus;
such is the reckless might of that one's spirit, he will not wish
to remain upon the plain, in this middle ground where Achaeans and
   Trojans
both share between them battle's fury,
but he will fight for our city and our women.   265
Come, let us go to the city, be persuaded by me; for this is how it will be.
Now ambrosial night has curbed the swift-footed son of Peleus;
but if he finds us here
tomorrow when he rises under arms, well will a man come to know him;
and gladly will he make his way to sacred Ilion—   270
he who escapes; but the dogs and vultures will devour many
of the Trojans—but may this word never come to my hearing.
If you will be persuaded by my words, painful though they are,
this night we will harbor our strength in the place of assembly,
and our high walls and gates and the doors fitted to them—   275
the long, well-honed, barred doors—will guard our city;
and in early morning, having armed in our weapons with the dawn,
we will take up position along the ramparts. The worse for him, if he
   chooses
to come from his ships to do battle around our walls;
he will go back to the ships, when he has given his high-necked horses   280
their fill of running roundabout, as he roams beneath the city walls.
Even his courage will not permit him to storm inside,
nor will he ever sack our city. Before that the sleek dogs will devour him."
      Then looking at him from beneath his brows spoke Hector of the
   shimmering helm:
"Poulydamas, these things you declare are no longer pleasing to me,   285
you who bid us go back to cower down in the city.
Or have you all not had your fill of being penned inside the walls?
In days before, the city of Priam, as all men born of earth
were wont to say, was rich in gold, rich in bronze—
by now the splendid treasures have vanished from our houses,   290
and many possessions went for sale to Phrygia and lovely Maeonia,[5]
since mighty Zeus conceived hatred for us.
And now, at this time when the son of devious Cronus grants me
to win glory by the ships and drive the Achaeans to the sea—
you fool, no longer disclose such thoughts among the people!   295
None of the Trojans will obey you, for I will not allow it.
But come, let us all be persuaded to do as I say.
Take your meal now at your posts throughout the army
and be mindful of your watches and each of you be alert;
and whoever of the Trojans is excessively distressed for his
   possessions,   300
let him gather them together and give them to the people to consume
   as common stock;
better that one of them have profit of them than the Achaeans;

---

5. Countries in Asia Minor allied with Troy.

and in early morning, having armed in our weapons with the dawn,
by the hollow ships we shall awaken cutting war.
And if in fact Achilles the godlike has stirred himself to action by his
    ships,   305
the worse it will be for him, if he so chooses, for I will not
flee from him out of this grievous war, but I will strongly
face him—we shall see whether he will win great glory, or I.
Enyalios[6] the god of war is impartial; and often he kills the one who kills."

     Thus declared Hector, and the Trojans shouted their applause,   310
the fools, for Pallas Athena took their wits away;
all assented to Hector as he devised disaster,
but none to Poulydamas, who thought out excellent counsel.

     Then they took their meal throughout the army; but the Achaeans
through all the night groaned aloud as they mourned Patroclus.   315
And the son of Peleus led their impassioned lament,
placing his man-slaughtering hands on the breast of his companion,
groaning without ceasing, as a full-maned lion,
whose cubs a hunting man has stolen away
out from the dense forest, and who returning too late is stricken with
    grief,   320
and many is the valley he traverses, following after the footprints of
    the man,
in the hope he would find him in some quarter; for very bitter anger
    holds him;
so groaning deeply Achilles addressed the Myrmidons:
"Alas, alas, empty were the words I let fall that day
as I encouraged the warrior Menoetius within his walls;   325
I said to him that I would bring his son back to Opoeis[7] surrounded in
    glory
after sacking Ilion and receiving a share of the spoils.
But Zeus does not fulfill men's every wish;
for it was fated that we both stain the same earth
here in Troy, since I will not be returning home   330
to be received by old Peleus, the horseman, in his halls,
nor by Thetis my mother, but the earth will cover me here.
But now, Patroclus, since I am following you beneath the earth,
I shall not honor you with funeral rites, until I lay here
the armaments and head of Hector, your slayer, great-hearted one;   335
and before your pyre I shall cut the throats of twelve
noble sons of Troy, in anger for your killing.
In the meanwhile you will lie as you are by my curved ships,
and around you women of Troy and deep-breasted Dardan women
shall wail for you night and day as they shed their tears,   340
those women whom we ourselves toiled to win by force and the long spear
when we two sacked the rich cities of earth-born men."

     So speaking godlike Achilles ordered his companions
to set a great cauldron on its three-legged stand astride the fire, so that
    with all speed

---

6. Another name for Ares.
7. An ancient city near the eastern coast of the   central Greek mainland and home of Menoetius, father of Patroclus.

they could wash away the clotted blood from Patroclus; 345
and they set a cauldron for heating bathing water on the blazing fire,
then poured water in it, and took sticks of wood and kindled them
   beneath it.
And the fire caught the belly of the cauldron, and heated the water.
Then when the water had come to boil in the bright bronze,
they washed him and anointed him luxuriantly with oil, 350
and filled in his wounds with seasoned unguents;
and placing him on the bier, they covered him with soft linen
from his head to his feet, and over this with a shining mantle.
      Then nightlong the Myrmidons groaned aloud as around Achilles
of the swift feet they mourned Patroclus. 355
But Zeus addressed Hera, his sister and his wife:
"So once more, you have accomplished things your way, after all, my
   brown-eyed lady Hera,
having roused to action swift-footed Achilles. Surely the long-haired
   Achaeans
must be your own offspring!"
Then answered him ox-eyed lady Hera: 360
"Most dread son of Cronus, what sort of word have you spoken?
Surely, even a human tries to do what he can for another man,
one who is only mortal, and who does not know so many arts as we;
how then should not I—who claim to be the highest of the goddesses,
both by birth and because I am called your wife, 365
and you are lord of all the immortal gods—
how should I not contrive evil for the Trojans whom I hate?"
      Thus they were speaking such things to one another.
But silver-footed Thetis arrived at the home of Hephaestus,
imperishable, strewn with stars, conspicuous amongst the homes of the
   immortals, 370
made of bronze, which the crippled god had built himself.
And she found him dripping with sweat, twisting back and forth about
   his bellows,
hard at work; for he was forging fully twenty tripods
to stand round the inside wall of his well-built palace.
He placed golden wheels beneath the legs of each, 375
so that of their own accord they might go into the divine assembly for him
and then return back to his house again, a wonder to behold.
And they were so far finished, but the elaborate handles were not
affixed; these he was fitting and striking the rivets.
And while he toiled at these things with his skilled understanding, 380
the goddess Thetis of the silver feet approached him;
and Charis[8] of the shining headdress saw her as she was coming forward,
lovely Charis, whom the famed bent-legged god had wed,
and she clasped her hand, and spoke to her and said her name:
"Why, Thetis of the flowing robe, have you come to our house? 385
You are honored and beloved, but you have not come frequently before.
But follow me in, so that I can set all hospitality before you."
      So speaking she, shining among goddesses, led Thetis forward.

---

8. Literally, "Grace" or "Beauty," one of the Three Graces.

Then she settled her on a beautiful elaborate silver chair,
and placed a stool beneath her feet;   390
and she called Hephaestus famed for his art and spoke a word to him:
"Hephaestus, come this way; Thetis has need of something from you."
Then the renowned god of the crooked legs answered her:
"Then surely in our house is a goddess whom I hold in awe and revere.
She saved me, that time I suffered bodily pain when I was made to fall a
      long way   395
by the efforts of my dog-faced mother, who wanted
to hide me away for being lame. At that time I would have suffered many
      cares at heart,
had not Thetis taken me to her bosom,
and Eurynome the daughter of Ocean of the shifting tide.
For nine years with them I forged many intricate objects,   400
brooches and curving spirals for the hair, buds of rosettes and necklaces
in their hollow cave; and all around the boundless currents of the Ocean
with its foam flowed murmuring; nor did any other being
know of this, neither of gods nor of mortal men,
but Thetis and Eurynome knew, they who saved me.   405
Now she has come to our house; therefore I must surely
repay to Thetis of the lovely hair all the value of my life.
But you now set before her fitting hospitality,
while I put away my bellows and all my tools."

            He spoke, and the huge craftsman rose from the anvil block   410
limping, but his shrunken legs moved nimbly beneath him.
He put the bellows aside from the fire, and all the tools
with which he worked he gathered into a silver box.
And with a sponge he wiped around his face and both his arms
and powerful neck and shaggy chest,   415
and he put on a tunic, took up his thick staff, and went out the door,
limping; and supporting their master were attendants
made of gold, which seemed like living maidens.
In their hearts there is intelligence, and they have voice
and vigor, and from the immortal gods they have learned skills.   420
These bustled about supporting their master; and making his halting way
to where Thetis was, he took his seat upon a shining chair,
and clasped her hand, and spoke to her and said her name:
"Why, Thetis of the flowing robe, have you come to our house?
You are honored and beloved, but you have not come frequently before.   425
Speak what you will; my heart compels me to accomplish it,
if I am able to accomplish it, and if it can be accomplished."

            Then Thetis answered him as she let her tears fall:
"Hephaestus—who of all the goddesses on Olympus,
endures in her heart so many bitter cares,   430
as the griefs Zeus the son of Cronus has given to me beyond all?
Out of all the other goddesses of the sea he made me subject to a mortal
      husband,
Peleus son of Aeacus, and I endured the bed of a mortal man
very much unwilling; he now worn out with bitter age
lies in his halls, but there are other troubles now for me;   435
for he gave me a son to bear and to raise

outstanding among warriors, who shot up like a young shoot,
and having nurtured him like a growing tree on the high ground of an
    orchard
I sent him forth with the curved ships to Ilion,
to go to battle against the Trojans; him I shall not welcome again   440
returned home into the house of Peleus.
So long as he lives and sees the sun's light
he has sorrow, nor can I help him at all by going to him.
The girl, whom the sons of the Achaeans picked out as prize for him,
she it was, from his hands, lord Agamemnon took back;   445
and he has been consuming his heart in grief for her, while the Trojans
pinned the Achaeans against the sterns of their ships, nor
let them go forth from that place; and the Argive elders
beseeched him, and promised many splendid gifts.
At this he refused to ward off their destruction,   450
but then put his own armor about Patroclus,
and sent him to the fighting, and gave a great host with him.
All the day they battled around the Scaean gates;
and surely that same day he would have sacked the city, had not Apollo
killed the brave son of Menoetius as he was wreaking much destruction   455
among the front fighters, and gave glory to Hector.
And it is for this reason I have now come to your knees, to see if you
    would be willing
to give to my short-lived son a shield and crested helmet
and fine greaves with silver fastenings
and a breastplate; for those that were his, his trusted comrade lost   460
when he was beaten down by the Trojans; and my son lies upon the
    ground grieving at heart."
        Then answered her the famous crook-legged god:
"Have courage; do not let these matters be a care to your heart.
Would that I were so surely able to hide him away from death and its
    hard sorrow,
when dread fate comes upon him,   465
as he will have his splendid armor, such as many a man
of the many men to come shall hold in wonder, whoever sees it."
        So speaking he left her there, and went to his bellows;
and he turned them to the fire and gave them their commands to get
    to work.
And all twenty bellows began to blow into the crucibles,   470
from every angle blasting up and forth their strong-blown gusts
for him as he hurried to be now in this place, now again in that,
in whatever manner Hephaestus wished, and accomplished the job.
And he cast on the fire weariless bronze, and tin
and treasured gold and silver; and then   475
he placed his great anvil on his anvil block, and with one hand
    grasped
his mighty hammer, and with the other grasped his tongs.
        And first of all he made a great and mighty shield,
working it intricately throughout, and cast around it a shining rim
of triple thickness, glittering, and from it a silver shield-strap.   480
Five were the layers of the shield itself; and on it

he wrought with knowing genius many intricate designs.

On it he formed the earth, and the heaven, and the sea
and the weariless sun and waxing moon,
and on it were all the wonders with which the heaven is ringed,   485
the Pleiades and Hyades and the might of Orion,
and Arctos the Bear,[9] which men name the Wagon,
and which always revolves in the same place, watchful for Orion,
and alone has no part in the baths of Ocean.

And on it he made two cities of mortal men,   490
both beautiful; and in one there were weddings and wedding feasts,
and they were leading the brides from their chambers beneath the gleam
    of torches
through the city, and loud rose the bridal song;
and the young men whirled in dance and in their midst
the flutes and lyres raised their hubbub; and the women   495
standing in their doorways each watched in admiration.
And the people were thronged into the place of meeting; and there
    a dispute
had arisen, and two men were contending about the blood price
for a man who had been killed. The one was promising to pay all,
declaring so to the people, but the other refused to accept a thing;   500
and both desired the resolution be taken to a judge;
the people spoke out for both sides, favoring one or the other,
and heralds were holding the people in check. The elders
were sitting upon seats of polished stone in a sacred circle,
and holding in their hands the staves of the heralds with their ringing
    voices;   505
to these the two sides next rushed, and in turn the elders each gave
    judgment.
And there lay in their midst two talents of gold,
to give to him who might speak the straightest judgment among them.

But around the other city lay two armies of men,
shining in their armor. And they were torn between two plans,   510
either to sack the city, or to divide everything equally with its people,
as much wealth as the lovely town held within.
But the city was not yielding, and the men were secretly arming for
    ambush.
And their beloved wives and little children stood guard upon the
    ramparts
with those men whom old age held,   515
but the other men set forth; and Ares led them and Pallas Athena,
both made in gold, and the clothing on them was golden,
magnificent and mighty with their armor, like very gods,
standing out apart; and beneath them the people were smaller.
And when these arrived at the place where it seemed to them good for
    ambush,   520
on the river, at the watering place for all the grazing herds,

---

9. Ursa Major, or the Big Dipper, which never descends below the horizon (i.e., into Ocean). The Pleiades, Hyades, and Orion are all clusters of stars, or constellations. Orion was a giant hunter of Greek mythology.

there they sat down, covered in their gleaming bronze.
And at a distance from them, their two lookouts were in position
waiting for when they might see sheep and twist-horned cattle;
and these soon came in sight, with two herdsmen following with them   525
taking pleasure in their flute, and did not at all foresee the plot.
And catching sight of them ahead, the men in ambush ran toward them,
and swiftly, on both sides, cut off the herds of cattle and splendid flocks
of white-wooled sheep, and killed the shepherds for good measure.
But the other men, when they heard the great uproar from the cattle   530
as they were sitting before the place of meeting, they at once mounted
    behind their high-stepping
horses and went after them in pursuit. They reached the place swiftly,
and having arrayed the battle, began fighting by the riverbanks,
smiting one another with their bronze-headed spears.
And Strife was joining the throng of battle, and Tumult, and painful
    Death,   535
holding now a living man new-wounded, now one unharmed,
now dragging a man who had died by his feet through the press of battle;
and Death wore around her shoulders a cape crimsoned with the blood
    of men.
And they dashed in battle and fought like living men,
dragging away the bodies of those slain by one another.   540
        And on the shield he made a soft fallow field—fertile worked land
broad and thrice-plowed; and on it many plowmen
were driving their yoked teams of oxen turning up and down the field.
And when they came to the furrow end, after turning around,
then would a man come up to give into their hands a cup of   545
honey-sweet wine; and they would turn back along the row,
eager to reach the turning place of the deep fallow field.
And the earth darkened behind them, like land that has been plowed,
made of gold though it was; a wonder indeed was that which was
    wrought.
        And on the shield he placed a royal estate; and there the laborers   550
were reaping, sharp sickles in their hands.
Some sheaths were thickly falling to the ground along the row,
others the sheaf binders bundled with bands.
Three binders stood by; but behind them
children were gathering handfuls, carrying them in their arms,   555
constantly nearby. And among them the king, in silence,
staff in hand, stood near the line rejoicing in his heart.
And to one side heralds were readying a feast beneath an oak,
dressing the great ox they had slaughtered. And the women
were scattering quantities of white barley for the workers as a meal.   560
        And on the shield he put a great vineyard heavy with clumps
    of grapes,
a thing of beauty, all in gold, and the dark clusters were along it.
And it was set up on vine poles of solid silver;
and on either side he drove a ditch of blue enamel, and around it a fence
of tin. One path alone was on it,   565
on which grape bearers made their way, when they gathered in the
    vineyard.

Maidens and young men with the giddy hearts of youth
carried the honey-sweet crop in woven baskets;
and in their midst a boy played his clear-sounding lyre
with enchantment, and beautifully sang to it the mournful harvest
    song   570
in his soft voice. And the others beating time all together
with song and cries followed, skipping with their feet.
      And on it he made a herd of straight-horned cattle,
and the cows were made of gold and tin,
and lowing they hastened from the farmyard to their pasture,   575
beside a rushing river, beside the waving reeds.
Golden herdsmen accompanied the cattle,
four in all, and nine sleek dogs followed at their feet;
but two dread lions held a bellowing bull
among the foremost cattle; and he lowing loudly   580
was being dragged away, and the dogs and sturdy youths followed
    after him.
And the two lions tearing open the great bull's hide
were gulping down the entrails and dark blood; at a loss,
the herdsmen set the swift dogs in pursuit, urging them on,
but they shrank from biting the lions,   585
and standing very close bayed and stayed away.
      And on the shield the famed crook-legged god made a meadow,
a great meadow for white-fleeced sheep lying in a lovely glen,
and farmsteads and huts for the shepherds and their folds.
And on it the famed crook-legged god made a patterned place for
    dancing,   590
like that which once in broad Knossos
Daedalus created for Ariadne[1] of the lovely hair.
There the unwed youths and maidens worth many oxen as their bridal
    price
were dancing, holding each other's hands at the wrist;
and the girls were wearing finest linen, and the youths wore   595
fine-spun tunics, soft shining with oil.
And the girls wore lovely crowns of flowers, and the youths were
    carrying
golden daggers from their silver sword-belts.
And now the youths with practiced feet would lightly run in rings,
as when a crouching potter makes trial of the potter's wheel   600
fitted to his hand, to see if it speeds round;
and then another time they would run across each other's lines.
And a great crowd stood around the stirring dance
filled with delight; and among them two acrobats,   604/5
leaders of the dance, went whirling through their midst.
      And Hephaestus set on it the great might of the river Ocean,
along the outmost edge of the thick-made shield.
      And when he had made the great and massive shield,

---

1. Daughter of Minos, king of Crete. Daedalus was the prototypical craftsman who built the labyrinth to house the Minotaur and who escaped from Crete on wings with his son Icarus. Knossus was the site of Minos's great palace.

then he wrought a breastplate for Achilles more resplendent than the
   light of fire,   610
and he made a helmet for him, strong and fitted to his temples,
a thing of beauty, intricately wrought, and set a gold crest on it;
and then he made greaves for him of pliant tin.
      And when the famed crook-legged god had made all the armor
   with his toil,
lifting it up he set it before the mother of Achilles;   615
and she like a hawk leapt down from snowy summit of Olympus,
carrying the glittering armor from Hephaestus.

Summary   Achilles finally accepts gifts of restitution from Agamemnon, as he refused to do earlier. His return to the fighting brings terror to the Trojans and turns the battle into a rout in which Achilles kills every Trojan that crosses his path. As he pursues Agenor, Apollo tricks him by rescuing his intended victim (he spirits him away in a mist) and assumes Agenor's shape to lead Achilles away from the walls of Troy. The Trojans take refuge in the city, all except Hector.

BOOK XXII

[The Death of Hector]

So those who had fled terrorized like fawns into the city
dried off their sweat and drank and slaked their thirst,
slumped on the splendid ramparts. The Achaeans, however,
drew near the walls with shields inclined against their shoulders;
and there ruinous fate bound Hector to stand his ground,   5
before the Scaean gates of Ilion.
      Now Phoebus Apollo hailed Peleion:
"Why, son of Peleus, do you chase me, with those swift feet,
you a mortal, I an undying god? You must not yet know
that I am divine, you rage after me so furiously!   10
Is it of no concern, this business with the Trojans, whom you scattered
   in fear—
who are by now cowering in the city, while you slope off here?
You will never kill me; I am not marked by fate."
Then greatly stirred, swift-footed Achilles answered him:
"You have thwarted me, most malevolent of all the gods, you who strike
   from afar,   15
turning me here away from the city walls; otherwise many would
have bitten the dirt before they arrived at Ilion.
Saving them, you have robbed me of great glory,
lightly, without fear of retribution;
I would pay you back, if that power were in me."   20
So speaking, he made toward the city, intent on great things,
straining like a prizewinning horse who with his chariot
runs effortlessly, stretching over the plain—
so swiftly did Achilles move his feet and knees.
      And old Priam first beheld him with his eyes   25
as, shining like a star, Achilles streaked across the plain,

the star that comes at summer's end,[2] its clear gleaming
in the milky murk of night displayed among the multitude of stars—
the star they give the name Orion's Dog;
most radiant it is, but it makes an evil portent,   30
and brings great feverish heat on pitiful mortal men—
just so did his bronze breastplate shine about Achilles running.
The old man cried out and hammered his head with his hands,
lifting them on high; crying mightily he called,
imploring his beloved son; for before the gates Hector   35
continued to stand firm, intent on combat with Achilles.
To him the old man called piteously, reaching out his hands:
"Hector, for my sake, do not wait for this man
on your own, without allies, lest you straightway meet your fate,
broken by Peleion; since he is so much stronger,   40
he is pitiless; would that he were as dear to the gods
as he is to me—in short order would the dogs and vultures devour him
as he lay dead; and bitter pain would leave my heart.
This is the man who has bereaved me of many sons, brave sons,
killing them, or selling them to far-off islands.   45
Even now there are two, Lykaon and Polydoros,
whom I cannot see in the city of the cowering Trojans,
sons whom Altes' daughter Laothoë[3] bore me, a queen among women.
If they are alive somewhere among the army, then
I will ransom them for bronze or gold; all this is inside—   50
old, illustrious Altes endowed his daughter richly.[4]
But if they have already died and are in the house of Hades,
this is anguish to my heart and to their mother, we who bore them;
but to the rest of the people, it will be anguish shorter lived
than if you also should die, broken by Achilles.   55
Come inside the walls, my child, that you may save the
Trojan men and Trojan women, do not make a gift of glory to
the son of Peleus, who will rob you of your very life.
And on me—wretched, still feeling—have pity,
born to ill fate, whom on the threshold of old age father Zeus, son of
    Cronus,   60
will blight with my hard fate, when I have seen
the destruction of my sons, the abduction of my daughters,
my chambers ravaged, and innocent children
hurled to the ground in the terror of battle;
my daughters-in-law abducted by the wicked hands of Achaean men,   65
and I myself, last of all, at my very gates, my dogs
will rip raw, when some man with sharp bronze,
stabbing or casting, will strip the spirit from my limbs—
the dogs I raised in my halls and fed at my table as guardians of my gates,
these, maddened by the drinking of my blood,   70
will sprawl in my doorway. All is seemly for the young man

2. Sirius, or the Dog Star, the brightest star in   killed Polydorus and Lykaon in the fighting
the constellation Canis Major. In Greece it rises   outside the city (books 20 and 21).
in late summer, the hottest time of the year.   4. The dowry of Laothoë, Altes' daughter.
3. Laothoë was one of Priam's wives. Achilles

slain in war, torn by sharp bronze,
laid out dead; everything is honorable to him in death, whatever shows.
But when the dogs defile the white head and white beard
and the private parts of a dead old man—   75
this is most pitiable for wretched mortals."
So the old man spoke, and pulled his white hair with his hands,
tearing it from his head. But he did not persuade the heart of Hector.
        Now in turn his mother wailed, raining tears,
and loosening her robe, with a hand she exposed her breast   80
and raining tears addressed him with winged words:
"Hector, my child, be moved by this and have pity on me,
if ever I used to give you my breast to soothe you—
remember those times, dear child, defend yourself against this deadly man
from inside the walls; don't stand as champion against him,   85
my stubborn one. If he cuts you down, I will surely never
mourn you on your deathbed, dear budding branch, whom I bore,
nor will your worthy wife. But a long way from us
by the ships of the Achaeans the running dogs will eat you."
        Thus both of them weeping addressed their dear son,   90
repeatedly beseeching. But they did not persuade the heart of Hector,
and he awaited Achilles, who was looming huge as he drew near.
As a snake by its hole in the mountains waits for a man,
having eaten evil poisons, and a deadly anger comes upon it,
and it shoots a stinging glance, coiled by its hole,   95
so Hector keeping his spirit unquelled did not retreat,
but having leaned his shining shield against the jutting tower,
in agitation he spoke to his great-hearted spirit:
"Oh me, if I enter the gates and walls
Poulydamas will be the first to reproach me,   100
who bade me lead the Trojans to the city
that baneful night when Achilles the godlike rose,
but I was not persuaded. It would have been far better if I had.
Now since I have destroyed my people by my recklessness,
I dread the Trojan men and the Trojan women with their trailing robes,   105
lest some other man more worthless than me say:
'Hector, trusting in his strength, destroyed his people'—
thus they will speak. It would be far better, then, for me
to confront Achilles, either to kill him and return home,
or to die with honor at his hands, before my city.   110
But what if I put aside my studded shield
and my strong helmet, leaned my spear against the walls,
and going out alone approached noble Achilles,
and pledged to him Helen and the possessions with her?
All those things—as much as Alexandros carried away to Troy   115
in his hollow ships, which was the beginning of our quarrel—
to give to the sons of Atreus to lead away; and in addition
to divide everything else with the Achaeans, whatever this city holds,
and after that to make a formal oath with the Trojan council
not to hide anything, but to divide it all, equally[5]—   120

5. The line numbers here account for lines that were omitted by the translator because they may
not belong to the text.

but why does my heart debate these things? 122
I could set forth to meet him and he not pity me,
nor even respect me, but kill me naked as I was,
as if I were a woman, since I would have put off my armor. 125
It is not now possible from rock or oak, in the country way,
to chatter to him those things that a girl and youth
chatter to each other, a girl and youth—
no, it is better to engage with him straightway;
we shall see to whom the Olympians give glory." 130
          Thus his thoughts churned as he waited, and Achilles drew near,
equal to the war god, the helmet-shaking warrior,
brandishing his Pelian ash-wood spear above his right shoulder,
terrifying. The bronze glinted around him like the flare
of blazing fire or the sun rising. 135
And as he watched him, trembling took hold of Hector; and he could no
     longer endure
there to stand his ground, but left the gates behind and, terrified, he ran.
The son of Peleus charged for him, trusting in the swiftness of his feet;
as a mountain hawk, lightest of all things on wings,
easily swoops after a terror-stricken dove, 140
which, away from under, flees, but crying sharply near
he swoops continuously and his spirit drives him to take her;
so Achilles flew straight for him, ravenous, and Hector fled
under the walls of Troy, working his swift knees.
          By the watch place and the wild fig tree twisted by wind, 145
always away from the walls, along the wagon path they ran
and reached the two fair-flowing streams, where the two springs
gush forth from the whirling waters of Scamander.[6]
One flows with warm water, enveloping steam
rises from it as if from a burning fire. 150
The other even in summer runs as cold as hail,
or snow water, or ice that forms from water.
Near to these there are the broad washing hollows
of fine stone, where their lustrous clothes
the Trojan wives and their beautiful daughters washed, 155
in those days before, in peacetime, before there came the sons of the
     Achaeans.
By this place they ran, one fleeing, the other behind pursuing;
outstanding was he who fled ahead—but far better he who pursued him
swiftly; since it was not for a sacral animal, nor for an oxhide
they contended, prizes in the races of men— 160
but they ran for the life of Hector breaker of horses.
          As when prizewinning single-hoofed horses
tear around the turning post—a great prize awaits,
a tripod, or woman, in those games held when a man has died—
so three times around the city of Priam they whirled 165
in the swiftness of their feet, and all the gods looked on.
To them the father of men and gods spoke the first word:
"Alas; it is a dear man whom my eyes see

---

6. One of the two rivers in the plain of Troy.

pursued around the wall; my heart grieves
for Hector, who has burned many thigh cuts of sacral oxen to me,   170
both on the summit of Ida of the many glens, and at other times
on the heights of his citadel. But now godlike Achilles
pursues him in the swiftness of his feet around the city of Priam.
But come, you gods, consider and take counsel
whether we shall save him from death, or   175
noble though he is, break him at the hands of Achilles son of Peleus."
        Then the gleaming-eyed goddess Athena answered him:
"O father of the bright thunderbolt and black clouds, what have you said?
This man who is mortal, consigned long ago to fate—
you want to take him back and free him from the harsh sorrow of death?   180
Do so; but not all the other gods will approve."
In answer, Zeus who gathers the clouds addressed her:
"Take heart, Tritogeneia,[7] dear child. I did not now
speak in earnest, and I mean to be kind to you.
Act in whatever way your mind inclines, nor hold back any longer."   185
So speaking, he urged Athena, who had been eager even before;
and she went, slipping down from the peaks of Olympus.
        Relentlessly, swift Achilles kept driving Hector panicked before him,
as when a dog in the mountains pursues a deer's fawn
that he has started from its bed through glens and dells;   190
and though, cowering in fright, it eludes him beneath a thicket,
the dog runs on, tracking it steadily, until he finds it—
so Hector could not elude Achilles of the swift feet.
Each time he made to dash toward the Dardanian gates,
under the well-built tower,   195
in the hope that men from above might defend him with thrown missiles,
each time did Achilles, outstripping him, turn him back
toward the plain, and he himself sped ever by the city.
As in a dream a man is not able to pursue one who eludes him,
nor is the other able to escape, nor he to pursue,   200
so Achilles for all the swiftness of his feet was not able to lay hold of
    Hector, nor Hector to escape.
How then could Hector have eluded his fated death
had not Apollo for that last and final time joined closely with him
to rouse his spirit and make swift his knees?
And shining Achilles was shaking his head at his men,   205
nor allowed them to let their sharp spears fly at Hector,
lest whoever making the throw claim glory, and himself come second.
        But when for the fourth time they came to the springs,
then Zeus the father leveled his golden scales,
and placed in them two portions of death that brings enduring grief,   210
that of Achilles and that of Hector breaker of horses;
he lifted them, holding by the middle; and the measured day of Hector sank,
headed to Hades, and Phoebus Apollo abandoned him.
        Then the gleaming-eyed goddess Athena came up to the son of
    Peleus
and standing near addressed him with winged words: 215

7. Another name for Athena.

"Now I hope, illustrious Achilles, beloved of Zeus,
to carry honor for us two back to the Achaean ships,
after breaking Hector, insatiable though he be for battle;
he can no longer get clear of us,
not if Apollo the Far-Shooter should suffer countless trials for
    his sake,   220
groveling before Father Zeus who wields the aegis.
But you now stop and catch your breath, while I
make my way to Hector and convince him to fight man-to-man."
Thus spoke Athena, and Achilles obeyed and rejoiced in his heart,
and stood leaning on his bronze-flanged ash-wood spear.   225
      She left him and came up to shining Hector
in the likeness of Deïphobos,[8] in form and steady voice.
Standing close, she spoke winged words:
"My brother, swift Achilles presses you hard,
pursuing you around the city of Priam in the swiftness of his feet.   230
Come; let us take our stand and standing firm defend ourselves."
      Then great Hector of the shimmering helm addressed her in turn:
"Deïphobos, even before you were far dearest to me
of my brothers, those sons whom Hecuba and Priam bore.
Now I am minded to honor you even more in my heart—   235
you who dared for my sake, when you saw me with your eyes,
to quit the walls where the others remain inside."
      Then the gleaming-eyed goddess Athena spoke to him:
"My brother, our father and lady mother implored me greatly,
entreating in turn, and the companions about them,   240
to remain there—for so great is the dread of all;
but my inner spirit was harrowed with impotent grief.
But now let us two press straight forward and go to battle,
and let there be no restraint of our spears, so that we shall see if Achilles,
killing us both, will bear our bloodied arms   245
to his hollow ships, or if he will be broken by your spear."
Thus spoke Athena and with cunning led him on.
      And when they had advanced almost upon each other
great Hector of the shimmering helm spoke first:
"No longer, son of Peleus, shall I flee from you, as before   250
I fled three times around the great city of Priam, nor could then endure
to withstand your charge. But now my spirit stirs me
to hold firm before you. I will kill you, or be killed.
But come, let us take an oath upon our gods, for they
will be the best witnesses and protectors of agreements.   255
I will not, outrageous though you are, dishonor you if Zeus grants me
to endure, and I take your life.
But when I have stripped you of your splendid armor, Achilles,
I will give your body back to the Achaeans; and do you the same."
      Then looking at him from beneath his brows, Achilles of the
    swift feet spoke: 260
"Hector, doer of unforgettable deeds—do not to me propose agreements.
As there are no pacts of faith between lions and men,

8. Hector's brother.

nor do wolves and lambs have spirit in kind,
but they plot evil unremittingly for one another,
so it is not possible that you and I be friends, nor for us two   265
will there be oaths; before that time one of us falling
will sate with his blood the shield-bearing warrior god.
Recollect your every skill. Now the need is very great
to be a spearman and brave warrior.
There will be no further escape for you, but soon Pallas Athena   270
will break you by my spear. Now you will pay in one sum
for all the sorrows of my companions, those whom you killed, raging
   with your spear."
         He spoke, and balancing his long-shadowed spear, he let it fly.
But, holding it in his sight as it came at him, shining Hector avoided it,
for as he watched, he crouched, and the bronze spear flew over   275
and stuck in the earth; but Pallas Athena snatched it up
and gave it back to Achilles, escaping the notice of Hector, shepherd of
   the people.
And Hector addressed the noble son of Peleus:
"You missed! It was not, then, godlike Achilles,
from Zeus you knew my fate—you only thought you did;   280
and you turn out to a glib talker, cunning with words—
fearing you, you thought I would forget my strength and valor—
but you will not fix your spear in my back as I flee,
but drive it through my breast as I come at you,
if a god grants this. Now in your turn dodge my spear,   285
bronze-pointed; would that you carried the whole of it in your flesh.
Then would this war be the lighter to bear for the Trojans,
with you dead. For you are their greatest evil."
         He spoke, and balancing his long-shadowing spear, he let it fly,
and hurled at the middle of the son of Peleus' shield, nor did he miss;   290
but the spear glanced off the shield, for a long way. And Hector was angry
that his swift cast flew from his hand in vain,
and he stood dejected, nor did he have any other ash-shafted spear.
Raising his great voice he called Deïphobos of the pale shield
and asked for his long spear—but Deïphobos was not near him.   295
         And Hector understood within his heart and spoke aloud:
"This is it. The gods summon me deathward.
I thought the warrior Deïphobos was by me,
but he is inside the walls and Athena has tricked me.
Hateful death is very near me; it is no longer far away,   300
nor is there escape. And for some long time this has been pleasing
to Zeus and to Zeus' son who shoots from afar, who before this
protected me willingly enough. Yet now destiny has caught me.
Let me not die without a struggle and ingloriously,
but while doing some great thing for even men to come to hear of."   305
         So speaking he drew his sharp sword
that hung down by his side, huge and strong-made,
and collecting himself he swooped like a high-flying eagle,
an eagle that plunges through lowering clouds toward the plain
to snatch a soft Iamb or a cowering hare;   310
so Hector swooped brandishing his sharp sword.

But Achilles charged, his spirit filled with
savage passion. Before his breast he held his covering shield,
beautiful and intricately wrought, and nodded with his shining
four-ridged helmet; splendid horsehair flowed about it   315
of gold, which Hephaestus had set thickly around the helmet crest.
As a star moves among other stars in the milky murk of night,
Hesperus the Evening Star, the most beautiful star to stand in heaven,
so the light shone from the well-pointed spearhead that Achilles
was shaking in his right hand, bent upon evil for Hector,   320
surveying his handsome flesh, where it might best give way.
The rest of his body was held by brazen armor,
the splendid armor he stripped after slaying strong Patroclus—
but at that point where the collarbone holds the neck from the shoulders
    there showed
his gullet, where death of the soul comes swiftest;   325
and at this point shining Achilles drove with his spear as Hector strove
    against him,
and the spearhead went utterly through the soft neck.
Heavy with bronze though it was, the ash-spear did not sever the windpipe,
so that he could speak, making an exchange of words.
He fell in the dust. And shining Achilles vaunted: 330
"Hector, you surely thought when you stripped Patroclus
that you were safe, and you thought nothing of me as I was absent—
pitiable fool. For standing by, his far greater avenger,
I remained behind by the hollow ships—
I who have broken the strength of your knees. You the dogs and birds   335
will rip apart shamefully; Patroclus the Achaeans will honor with funeral
    rites."
        Then with little strength Hector of the shimmering helm
    addressed him:
"By your soul, by your knees, by your parents,
do not let the dogs devour me by the ships of the Achaeans,
but take the bronze and abundance of gold,   340
the gifts my father and lady mother will give you;
give my body back to go home, so that
the Trojans and the Trojan wives will give my dead body its portion of
    the fire."
        Then looking at him from under his brows Achilles of the swift
    feet answered:
"Do not, you dog, supplicate me by knees or parents.   345
Would that my passion and spirit would drive me
to devour your hacked-off flesh raw, such things you have done;
so there is no one who can keep the dogs from your head,
not if they haul here and weigh out ten times and twenty times
the ransom, and promise more,   350
not if Dardanian Priam seeks to pay your weight in gold,
not in any way will your lady mother
mourn you laid out upon your bier, the child she bore;
but the dogs and the birds will devour you wholly."
        Then, dying, Hector of the shimmering helm addressed him: 355
"Knowing you well, I divine my fate; nor will I persuade you.

Surely, the soul in your breast is iron.
Yet now take care, lest I become the cause of the god's wrath against you,
on that day when Paris and Phoebus Apollo
destroy you, great warrior though you be, at the Scaean gates."   360
Then the closure of death enveloped him as he was speaking,
and his soul flying from his limbs started for Hades,
lamenting her fate, abandoning manhood and all its young vigor.
　　　But shining Achilles addressed him, dead though he was:
"Lie dead. I will take death at that time when   365
Zeus and the other deathless gods wish to accomplish it."
He spoke and pulled his bronze spear from the dead body
and laying it aside he stripped the bloodied armor from Hector's
　　shoulders.
But the other sons of the Achaeans ran up around him
and admired Hector's physique and beauty,   370
nor was there a man who stood by him without inflicting a wound.
And thus each would speak, looking at his neighbor:
"Well, well; he is softer to handle, to be sure,
this Hector, than when he torched our ships with blazing fire."
Thus they would speak, and stabbed him as they stood by.   375
　　　But when shining Achilles of the swift feet had stripped Hector
　　of his armor,
he stood amid the Achaeans and pronounced winged words:
"O friends, leaders and counselors of the Achaeans;
since the gods gave me this man to be broken,
who committed evil deeds, more than all the other Trojans together,   380
come, let us go under arms and scout around the city
so that we may learn the disposition of the Trojans, what they have in
　　mind,
whether they will abandon their high city now this man is dead,
or desire to remain, although Hector is no longer with them—
but why does my spirit recite these things?   385
There lies by the ships a dead man, unmourned, unburied—
Patroclus. I shall not forget him as long as I am
among the living and my own knees have power in them.
And if other men forget the dead in Hades,
I will remember my beloved companion even there.   390
But come now, Achaean men, singing a victory song
let us return to our hollow ships, and bring him along.
We have achieved great glory; we have slain shining Hector,
whom the Trojans worshipped throughout their city as a god."
　　　He spoke, and conceived a shocking deed for shining Hector;   395
behind both feet he pierced the tendon
between the heel and ankle and fastened there oxhide straps,
and bound him to his chariot and let the head drag along.
Lifting his glorious armor, Achilles mounted his chariot,
and whipped the horses to begin, and they two, not unwilling, took off. 400
A cloud of dust rose as Hector was dragged, his blue-black hair
fanning around him, his head lolling wholly in the dust
that before was handsome; so Zeus gave him to his enemies
to be defiled in the land of his own fathers.
　　　His head was wholly befouled by dust; and now his mother   405

ripped her hair and flung her shining veil
far away, shrieking her grief aloud as she looked on her child.
His beloved father cried out pitiably and around them the people
were gripped by wailing and crying throughout the city—
it was as if the whole of   410
lofty Ilion, from its topmost point, were consumed with fire.
With difficulty the people restrained old Priam in his grief
as he strove to go forth from the Dardanian gates.
Thrashing in the muck, he entreated all,
calling off each man by name: 415
"Hold off, friend, for all your care for me, and let me
leave the city to go to the ships of the Achaeans.
I will entreat this reckless man of violent deeds,
if somehow he may respect my age and pity
my years. Even his father is of such years,   420
Peleus, who bore him and raised him to be the destruction
of the Trojans; and beyond all men he has inflicted hardship on me.
For so many of my flourishing sons he killed,
but for all my grief, I did not mourn as much for all of them
as for this one, bitter grief for whom will carry me down to the house of
    Hades—   425
Hector. Would that he died in my arms.
We would have glutted ourselves with crying and weeping,
his mother, she, ill-fated woman who bore him, and I."
Thus he spoke lamenting; and thereupon the people mourned.
        And Hecuba led the Trojan women in passionate lament: 430
"My child, I am nothing. Why should I live now, grievously suffering,
when you are dead? You who were night and day
my triumph through the city, a blessing to all,
to the Trojans and the Trojan women throughout the city, who
    received you
like a god; for to them you were, indeed, their glory,   435
while you lived; and now death and fate have overtaken you."
        Thus she spoke, crying. But Hector's wife knew nothing.
For no trusty messenger had come to her
announcing that her husband remained outside the walls,
and she was weaving at her loom in the corner of her high-roofed house   440
a crimson cloak of double-thickness, and working intricate figures in it.
She called through the house to her attendants with the lovely hair
to set a great tripod over the fire, so
there would be a warm bath for Hector, when he returned home from
    battle—
poor wretch, she did not know that far from all baths   445
gleaming-eyed Athena had broken him at the hands of Achilles.
Then she heard the keening and groaning from the tower
and her limbs shook, and the shuttle fell to the ground,
and she called back to her maids with the beautiful hair:
"Come, both of you follow me; I will see what trouble has happened.   450
I hear the voice of Hector's worthy mother,
the heart in my own breast leaps to my mouth, my limbs beneath me
are rigid; something evil is come near the sons of Priam.
May this word not come to my hearing; but terribly

I fear that shining Achilles has cut my bold Hector   455
from the city on his own, and driving him toward the plain
has stopped him of that fateful ardor
that possessed him, since he never remained in the ranks of men,
but rushed far to the front, yielding in his courage to no one."

     So speaking she raced through the hall like a madwoman,   460
her heart shaking; and her two maids ran with her.
But when she reached the tower and the crowd of men,
she stood on the wall, staring around her; and saw him
dragged before the city. Swift horses
dragged him, unconcernedly, to the hollow ships of the Achaeans.   465
Dark night descended over her eyes,
she fell backward and breathed out her soul;
far from her head she flung her shining headdress,
the diadem and cap and the braided binding,
and the veil, which golden Aphrodite gave her   470
on that day when Hector of the shimmering helm led her
out of the house of Eëtion, when he gave countless gifts for her dowry.
In a throng around her stood her husband's sisters and his brothers' wives,
who supported her among themselves, as she was stricken to the point of
    death.
     But when then she regained her breath and the strength in her
    breast was collected,   475
with gulping sobs she spoke with the Trojan women:
"Hector, I am unlucky. For we were both born to one fate,
you in Troy, in the house of Priam,
and I in Thebes, under forested Plakos,
in the house of Eëtion, who reared me when I was still young,   480
ill-fated he, I of bitter fate. I wish that he had not begotten me.
Now you go to the house of Hades in the depths of the earth,
leaving me in shuddering grief,
a widow in your house. The child is still only a baby,
whom we bore, you and I, both ill-fated. You will   485
be, Hector, no help to him, now you have died, nor he to you.
For even if he escapes this war of the Achaeans and all its tears,
there will always be for him pain and care hereafter.
Other men will rob him of his land;
the day of orphaning cuts a child off entirely from those his age;   490
he is bent low in all things, his cheeks are tearstained.
In his neediness, the child approaches his father's companions,
he tugs one by the cloak, another by his tunic;
pitying him, one of them offers him a little cup
and he moistens his lips, but he does not moisten his palate.   495
But a child blessed with both parents will beat him away from the feast,
striking him with his hands, reviling him with abuse:
'Get away—your father does not dine with us'—
and crying the boy comes up to his widowed mother—
Astyanax; who before on his father's knees   500
used to eat only marrow and the rich fat of sheep,
then when sleep took him and he left off his childish play,
he would slumber in bed in his nurse's embrace,

in his soft bedding, his heart filled with cheery thoughts.
Now he will suffer many things, missing his dear father— 505
'Astyanax'—'little lord of the city'—whom the Trojans called by this name,
for you alone, Hector, defended their gates and long walls.
Now beside the curved ships, away from your parents,
the writhing worms devour you when the dogs have had enough
of your naked body; yet there are clothes laid aside in the house, 510
finely woven, beautiful, fashioned by the hands of women.
Now I will burn them all in a blazing fire,
for they are no use to you, you are not wrapped in them—
I will burn them to be an honor to you in the sight of the Trojan men and
    Trojan women."
So she spoke, crying, and the women in response mourned. 515

Summary   Achilles buries Patroclus, and the Greeks celebrate the dead hero's fame with
athletic games, for which Achilles gives the prizes.

BOOK XXIV

[Achilles and Priam]

The games were dispersed, and the men scattered to go
each to his own swift ship. And they began to think about their meal
and giving themselves over to the pleasure of sweet sleep; but Achilles
wept still, remembering his beloved companion, nor did sleep,
who masters all, take hold of him, but he turned himself this side and that 5
yearning for the manly strength and noble spirit of Patroclus,
and remembered with yearning all he been through with him and all the
    woes he had suffered,
running through dangerous waves and the conflicts of men.
Recalling these things he let the warm tears fall,
as he lay now on his side, now again 10
on his back, and now face down; then starting up
he would wander in distraction along the salt-sea shore. He came to know
the dawn as she appeared over the sea and shore;
and when he had yoked his swift horses to his chariot,
he would tie Hector behind the chariot so as to drag him; 15
and after dragging him three times around the tomb of Menoetius' dead son
he would rest again in his shelter, and leave Hector
stretched in the dust upon his face. But Apollo warded off from Hector's flesh
all disfigurement, pitying the mortal man,
dead though he was, and covered him wholly round 20
with his golden aegis, so that Achilles would not tear the skin away as he
    dragged him.
        So in his rage Achilles kept outraging glorious Hector;
and as they watched, the blessed gods took pity on the son of Priam,
and kept urging sharp-sighted Hermes, Slayer of Argos, to steal him away.
And this found favor with all other gods, but not with Hera, 25
nor with Poseidon, nor with the gleaming-eyed maiden Athena,
for their hatred persisted, as at the start, for sacred Ilion,
and the people of Priam, because of the folly of Alexandros

who insulted the goddesses, when they came to his shepherd's steading,
and gave the nod to her, the goddess whose gift to him was ruinous lust.[9]   30
    But when at length the twelfth dawn rose since Hector's death,
then it was that Phoebus Apollo addressed the immortals:
"You gods are relentless, destroyers of men! Did Hector never
burn as offerings to you the thighbones of oxen and of goats without
   blemish?
And now, dead though he is, you cannot bring yourselves to rescue him,   35
for his wife to look on, for his mother, for his child,
and for his father and his people, who would with all speed
burn him upon a pyre and honor him with funeral rites;
but you gods choose to abet murderous Achilles,
in whose breast the heart knows no justice,   40
nor does his purpose bend, but his skill is in savage things, like a lion,
who giving way to his great strength and bold heart
goes for the flocks of men, to snatch his feast.
So Achilles has destroyed pity, nor has he shame,
which does great harm to men but also profits them.   45
A man surely is likely to lose someone even dearer—
a brother born of the same womb, or his own son—
but having wept and mourned, he lets it go;
for the Fates placed an enduring heart within mankind;
but Achilles, after he has stripped brilliant Hector of his life,   50
fastens him to his chariot and drags him round the tomb of his
   companion.
This is neither good for Achilles, nor is it worthy;
let him beware lest, noble though he be, we gods be angered with him.
For in his rage he outrages the senseless earth."
    Then in anger white-armed Hera addressed him: 55
"This speech of yours, you of the silver bow, might be justified
if you gods hold Achilles and Hector in the same honor.
But Hector is mortal and sucked at the breast of a woman,
while Achilles is born of a goddess, one whom I myself
nurtured and reared and gave as wife to her husband,   60
to Peleus, who was exceedingly dear to the immortals' hearts;
and all you gods took part in the wedding. And you among them
partook of the feast, lyre in hand, you companion of evil, faithless forever."
    Then answering her spoke Zeus who gathers the clouds:
"Hera, do not be angered with the gods.   65
The men will not have the same honor; yet Hector too
was dearest to the gods of all mortal men in Ilion.
For so he was to me, since he never failed to offer pleasing gifts;
my altar was never lacking its fair share of sacrifice,
of libation and the savour of burnt offering; for this honor is our due.   70
But as for stealing bold Hector away, let that go, it is in no way possible
without Achilles' notice, for always
his mother is at his side night and day alike;
but perhaps one of the gods would summon Thetis to my presence,
so that I could speak a close word to her, so that Achilles would   75

9. Aphrodite, whom Paris judged more beautiful than Athena and Hera because he found the
bribe that she offered him—Helen—the most attractive.

accept gifts from Priam and release Hector for ransom."
So he spoke; and storm-footed Iris sprang up to take his message.
Between Samothrace and rugged Imbros[1]
she leapt into the dark sea; and the sea groaned about her;
she sped to the depths of the sea like a leaden weight,   80
which mounted upon a piece of field-ox horn
goes bearing death to the fish who eat its carrion bait.
She found Thetis in a hollow cave; and gathered round her were
the other goddesses of the sea, and she in the middle
was weeping for the fate of her blameless son, who was destined   85
to perish in the rich soil of Troy, far from his fatherland.
Standing close, swift-footed Iris addressed her:
"Rise up, Thetis; Zeus whose counsels are unfailing, summons you."
Then the goddess Thetis of the silver feet answered her:
"What does he, the great god, command of me? I dread   90
mingling with the immortals; for I have sorrows without end within
    my heart.
Yet I will go, his word will not be in vain, whatever he might say."
So speaking the shining among goddesses took her blue-black
veil; and than this there is no darker garment;
and she set out, and swift Iris with feet like the wind led the way   95
before her; and on either side the waves of the sea parted for them.
Going up onto the shore, they darted to heaven;
and they found the far-thundering son of Cronus, and gathered round him
were sitting all the other blessed gods who live forever.
Then beside Zeus the father Thetis took her seat, which Athena yielded
    to her.   100
Hera placed a beautiful cup of gold into her hands
and spoke kindly words; and Thetis gave it back after drinking.
Then to them the father of gods and men began his speech:
"You have come to Olympus, divine Thetis, despite your cares,
bearing grief that cannot be forgotten in your heart; I know this.   105
But even so I will tell you the reason for which I have called you here.
For nine days a quarrel has arisen among the immortals
concerning Hector's body and Achilles, sacker of cities.
They urge sharp-sighted Hermes, Slayer of Argos, to steal the body away.
I however grant this honor to Achilles,   110
safeguarding your respect and loving friendship for time after:
go quickly to the army and lay a charge upon your son;
tell him the gods are angry,[2] and that I beyond all
immortals am provoked to rage, because in his madman's heart
he holds Hector beside his curved ships, nor has surrendered him—   115
and that perhaps in fear of me he would give Hector back.
And I will dispatch Iris to great-hearted Priam, to tell him
to obtain the release of his dear son by going to the ships of the Achaeans,
and to bear gifts for Achilles, which would soften his heart."
So he spoke; nor did the goddess Thetis of the silver feet
    disobey,   120

1. Islands in the northeast Aegean Sea.
2. Suppliants were under the protection of the gods, especially of Zeus.

and she left, darting down from the heights of Olympus,
and made her way to her son's shelter; inside she found him
groaning without cessation; around him his close companions
busily attended to him and readied the morning meal;
a great fleecy sheep had been slain by them in the shelter.   125
His lady mother sat down close beside him,
and stroked his hand, and spoke to him and said his name:
"My child, how long will you devour your heart
in weeping and grieving, mindful neither of food
nor bed? Indeed, it is good to lie with a woman   130
in lovemaking; you will not be living long with me, but already
death stands close beside you and powerful destiny.
Now, mark me at once; I bring a message for you from Zeus;
he says the gods are angry with you, and that he beyond all
immortals is provoked to rage, because in your madman's heart   135
you hold Hector beside your curved ships nor have surrendered him.
But come, give him up, and accept ransom for his body."
        Then answering her spoke swift-footed Achilles:
"Let the man appear who would bring the ransom and bear the body,
if the Olympian himself in earnest bids."   140
        So they, amid the gathering of ships, mother and son,
were speaking many things, winged words, to one another;
and the son of Cronus dispatched Iris into holy Ilion:
"Come, swift Iris, leave this Olympian seat
and bear a message to great-hearted Priam inside Ilion,   145
that he ransom his beloved son, going to the ships of the Achaeans,
and that he bear gifts for Achilles, which would soften his heart,
he alone, and let no other man of Troy go with him.
A herald may accompany him, some older man, who can drive
the mules and the strong-wheeled wagon, to bring back   150
to the city the dead man, whom godlike Achilles killed.
And let no thought of death trouble his heart, nor any fear;
for we will have Hermes, Slayer of Argos, accompany him as escort,
who will lead him, conducting him until he comes to Achilles.
And when he has led him inside Achilles' shelter,   155
Achilles himself will not kill him and he will restrain all others;
for he is not witless, nor thoughtless, nor without morals,
but with great kindness he will have mercy on the suppliant."
        So he spoke; and storm-footed Iris sprang up to take his message.
And she came to the house of Priam, and there was met with crying
    and lamentation;   160
the sons sitting about their father inside the courtyard
stained their garments with their tears, and among them the old man
was wrapped in his mantle, molded to it; much dung
was round about the neck and head of the old man,
which wallowing in he had scraped up with his own hands.   165
All through his house his daughters and the wives of his sons wailed
    in grief,
remembering those men who in such numbers and nobility
lay dead, having lost their lives at Argive hands.
And Iris, messenger of Zeus, stood by Priam and addressed him,

speaking softly; and trembling seized his limbs: 170
"Have courage in your heart, Priam son of Dardanos, nor fear at all.
For I do not come to you here bearing evil,
but with good intentions; for I am a messenger to you from Zeus,
who though far away takes great thought for and pities you.
The Olympian bids you redeem brilliant Hector by ransom,   175
and bring gifts to Achilles, which would soften his heart,
you alone, and let no other man of Troy go with you.
A herald may accompany you, some older man, who can drive
the mules and the strong-wheeled wagon, to bring back
to the city the dead man, whom godlike Achilles killed.   180
And do not let any thought of death trouble your heart, nor any fear;
for Hermes, Slayer of Argos, will follow with you as escort,
and will lead you, conducting you until he comes to Achilles.
But when he has led you inside Achilles' shelter,
Achilles himself will not kill you and will restrain all others;   185
for he is not witless, nor thoughtless, nor without morals,
but with great kindness he will have mercy on a suppliant."
        Then so speaking, Iris of the swift feet departed;
and Priam ordered his sons to prepare the strong-wheeled mule-drawn
        wagon
and to fasten upon it a wicker carrier.   190
And he went down into his storeroom, high-roofed
and fragrant with cedar, which held his many precious things.
And he called to his wife Hecuba and spoke to her:
"My poor wife, from Zeus an Olympian messenger came to me,
and bids me ransom our beloved son, going to the ships of the Achaeans,   195
to bring gifts to Achilles, which would soften his heart.
Come and tell me this—how to your mind does this seem to be?
For terribly does my spirit urge me, and my heart,
to go there to the ships, inside the broad army of the Achaeans."
        So he spoke; and his wife cried out and answered him in a word: 200
"Alas for me, where have your wits departed, for which you were
famed before, among even those from other lands, as well as those you
        ruled?
How can you wish to go to the Achaean ships alone,
into the sight of a man who killed your many and your noble
        sons? Your heart is iron.   205
For if he sets eyes upon you, and seizes you,
ravening and faithless man as he is, he will not have pity on you,
nor will he in any way respect your standing. No, let us weep now
as we sit far from Hector in our halls; thus it seems powerful Destiny
spun her fated thread[3] for him at his very birth, when I myself brought
        him to life,   210
to glut swift-footed dogs far from his parents
beside a violent man, whose liver I wish I could take hold of,
burying my teeth into its middle to eat; then would there be revenge
for my son, since he was not killed as he played the coward,
but as he took his stand in defense of the Trojans and the deep-breasted   215

3. Fate or the Fates were often pictured as spinning the thread of a person's life.

Trojan women, taking thought of neither flight nor shelter."
    And old Priam, godlike, spoke to her again:
"Do not delay me in my wish to go, nor yourself,
in my own halls, be a bird of ill omen; you will not persuade me.
For if any other person on earth had commanded me,   220
the smoke-watching seers, or priests,
we would have said it was a lie and we would turn our backs on it;
but as it is, since I myself heard the god and looked her in the face,
I am going, and her word will not be in vain. And if it is my fate
to die beside the ships of the bronze-clad Achaeans,   225
then so I wish it; let Achilles slay me at once
after I have clasped in my arms my son, when I have put away all
    desire for weeping."
    He spoke, and opened up the fine covers of his chests.
There he drew out twelve splendid robes,
and twelve single-folded woolen cloaks, and as many blankets,   230
as many mantles of white linen, and as many tunics too,
and he weighed and brought out ten full talents of gold,
and brought out two gleaming tripods, and four cauldrons,
and he brought out a splendid cup, which Thracian men gave to him
when he went to them on a mission, a magnificent possession; not   235
even this did the old man withhold, as he desired with all his heart
to ransom back his beloved son. And the Trojans, all,
he kept away from his covered halls, reviling them with shaming words:
"Be gone, outrages, disgraces; is there no weeping
in your own homes, that you have come to trouble me?   240
Or do you think it too little, that Zeus the son of Cronus has given me
    suffering,
destroying my best of sons? But you will come to know what this
    means too;
for you will be all the easier for the Achaeans
to kill now my son has died. But
before I behold with my own eyes my city sacked and ravaged,   245
may I enter in the house of Hades."
    He spoke, and drove the men off with his staff; and they went out
before the old man's urgency. And to his own sons he shouted rebuke,
railing at Helenos and Paris and brilliant Agathon
and Pammon and Antiphonos and Polites of the war cry   250
and Deïphobos and Hippothoös, too, and noble Dios.
To these nine, the old man, shouting his threats, gave orders:
"Make haste, worthless children, my disgraces. I would the pack of you
together had been slain by the swift ship instead of Hector.
Woe is me, fated utterly, since I sired the best sons   255
in broad Troy, but I say not one of them is left,
Mestor the godlike and Troilos the chariot fighter
and Hector, who was a god among men, nor did he seem to be
the son of mortal man, but of a god.
War destroyed these men, and all these things of shame are left,   260
the liars and dancers, and heroes of the dance floor,
snatchers of lambs and kids in their own land.
Will you all not prepare a wagon for me at once,

and place all these things in it, so that we can go upon our way?"
　　　　So he spoke; and they trembling before the old man's threats　　265
lifted out the strong-wheeled wagon for the mule,
a beautiful thing, newly made, and fastened the wicker carrier on it,
and took down from its peg the mule yoke
made of boxwood and with a knob upon it, well-fitted with rings to guide
　　the reins;
and they brought out the yoke strap of nine cubits length together with
　　the yoke.　　270
Then they fitted the yoke skillfully onto the well-polished wagon pole,
at the front end, and cast the ring over its peg,
and they bound the thong three times on each side to the knob, and then
secured it with a series of turns, and tucked the end under.
And carrying it from the storeroom they piled onto the polished wagon　　275
the vast ransom for the head of Hector.
They yoked the mules, strong-footed, working in harness,
which in time before the Mysians[4] gave as glorious gifts to Priam.
And for Priam they led under the yoke the horses that the old man,
keeping them for himself, tended at their well-polished manger.　　280
　　　　So the herald and Priam were having the animals yoked in the
high-roofed house, a flurry of thoughts in their minds.
And Hecuba with stricken heart drew near them,
carrying in her right hand in a cup of gold
wine that is sweet to the mind, so that they might set out after making
　　libation.　　285
She stood before the horses, and spoke to Priam and said his name:
"Here, pour an offering to Zeus the father, and pray that you come home,
back from the enemy men, since your heart drives you
to the ships, although I do not wish it.
Come, pray then to the son of Cronus of the black cloud　　290
on Ida, who looks down upon the whole of Troy,
and ask for a bird of omen, the swift messenger that for him
is most prized of birds and whose strength is greatest,
to fly to the right, so that you yourself, marking it with your eyes,
may go trusting in it to the ships of the Danaans of swift horses.　　295
But if far-thundering Zeus does not send you his messenger,
I would surely not then urge or bid you,
go to the Argive ships, for all you are determined."
　　　　Then answering her spoke godlike Priam:
"O my woman, I will not disobey what you demand;　　300
for it is good to raise one's hands to Zeus, that he might have mercy."
He spoke, and the old man called on the handmaid attendant
to pour clean water on their hands; and the maid came up beside him
holding in her hands both a water bowl and pouring jug.
And after washing his hands, Priam took the cup from his wife.　　305
Then standing in the middle of his court he prayed, and poured a wine
　　libation
as he looked toward the heavens, and lifting his voice he spoke:
"Father Zeus, ruling from Mount Ida, most glorious and greatest,

---

4. A people of central Asia Minor.

grant that I come as one welcomed to the shelter of Achilles and that he
    pity me.
And send a bird, your swift messenger, which for you yourself   310
is most prized of birds and whose strength is greatest,
to fly to the right, so that I myself, marking it with my eyes,
may go trusting in it to the ships of the Danaans of swift horses."
      So he spoke in prayer, and Zeus all-devising heard him,
and he sent at once an eagle, the surest omen of winged birds,   315
the dusky hunter men call the darkly-spangled one.
As wide as the door of a lofty room is made
in the house of a wealthy man, strong-fitted with bolts,
so wide were its wings on either side; and it appeared to them
on the right as it swept through the city. And seeing it they   320
rejoiced, and the spirit in the breasts of all was lifted.
      Then in haste the old man mounted his polished chariot,
and drove out of the gateway and echoing colonnade.
In front, drawing the four-wheeled wagon, went the mules,
which skillful Idaios the herald was driving; then the horses behind,   325
which the old man as he guided urged with his whip swiftly on
through the city. And all his dear ones followed with him
lamenting greatly, as if he were going to his death.
      Then when they descended from the city and reached the plain,
the rest, turning back, returned to Ilion,   330
the sons and the husbands of his daughters; but the two men did not
    escape the notice
of far-thundering Zeus as they came into view upon the plain, and he
    pitied the old man as he saw him
and swiftly spoke to Hermes his dear son:
"Hermes, it pleases you beyond all other gods
to act as man's companion,[5] and you listen to whomever you will;   335
go now, and lead Priam to the hollow ships of the Achaeans
in such a way that none of the other Danaans sees him,
no one notices, until he arrives at the shelter of the son of Peleus."
      So he spoke; nor did the messenger, the Slayer of Argos, disobey.
Straightway he bound beneath his feet his splendid sandals   340
immortal, golden, which carried him over the water
and over the boundless earth with the breath of the wind;
he took up his wand, with which he charms the eyes
of whichever men he wishes, and rouses them again when they have
    slumbered;
and taking this in his hands the mighty Slayer of Argos flew away.   345
Swiftly he arrived at Troy and at the Hellespont;
then he set out in the likeness of a noble youth
with his first beard, which is when early manhood is most graceful.
      And when Priam and Idaios had driven beyond the great burial
    mound of Ilos,[6]

---

5. Among his many functions, Hermes is an
escort to travelers (in particular, he guides the
souls of the dead to the underworld). He is also
a trickster and will put the guards at the Greek
wall to sleep so that Priam can pass through.
6. Priam's grandfather. The tomb was a land-
mark on the Trojan plain.

then they brought the mules and horses to a stand at the river,   350
so they could drink; for dusk by now had come upon the earth.
And as he looked, the herald caught sight of Hermes
drawing close from nearby, and raising his voice he spoke to Priam:
"Take care, son of Dardanos; there is need for a cautious mind.
I see a man, and I think we two will soon be torn to pieces.   355
Come, let us flee with the horses, or if not
let us take hold of his knees and beg, in the hope that he have mercy."
      So he spoke; and the old man's mind was in turmoil, and he was
    dreadfully afraid,
and the hair stood up on his bent limbs,
and he stood stupefied. But the Runner himself drawing near   360
and taking the old man's hand, inquired of him and addressed him:
"Whither, father, do you guide your mules and horses so
through the ambrosial night, when other mortal men are sleeping?
Do you have no fear of the Achaeans, who breathe fury,
hostile men and your enemy, who are near?   365
If any one of them should see you leading so much treasure
through the black fast-moving night, what then would be your plan?
You yourself are not young, and this man who attends you is too old
for driving men away, who might step forth in violence.
But I will do nothing to harm you, and will keep any other man   370
from you who would; for I liken you to my own father."
      Then old Priam, like a god, answered him:
"These things are much as you say, dear child.
But still one of the gods has surely stretched his hands above me,
who sent such a lucky wayfarer as you to fall in with me,   375
for such is your build and wonderful beauty,
and you have good sense in your mind; yours are blessed parents."
      Then in turn the messenger and Slayer of Argos addressed him:
"Yes, all these things, old man, you rightly say.
But come and tell me this and relate it exactly;   380
either you are sending away somewhere your many fine possessions
to men in other lands, so that they stay there safe for you,
or you are all abandoning sacred Ilion
in fear; for such a man, the best, has fallen,
your son; for he held nothing back in fight with the Achaeans."   385
      Then old Priam, like a god, answered him:
"Who are you, my good friend, and who are your parents?
How well you tell the fate of my unhappy son."
Then in turn the messenger and Slayer of Argos addressed him:
"You test me, old man, when you ask of brilliant Hector.   390
The man whom many times I saw with my own eyes
in battle where men win glory, and when he drove the Argives
to the ships and kept killing them as he slashed with his sharp bronze
    sword.
We stood by looking on in wonder; for Achilles
did not permit us to join the fight, being angered with the son of Atreus.   395
For I am a companion-in-arms of Achilles, and the same well-made ship
    brought us both.
I come from the Myrmidons, and my father is Polyktor.

He is a wealthy man, but he is old now, just as you;
He has six sons, and I am his seventh;
having shaken lots among us, it fell to me to follow here.   400
And now I have come to the plain from the ships; for at dawn
the dark-eyed Achaeans will deploy for battle round the city.
For these men have grown impatient sitting around, nor can the
Achaean kings restrain them in their eagerness for war."
      Then old Priam, like a god, answered him: 405
"If you are a companion of Peleus' son Achilles,
come and tell me the whole truth,
whether my son is still by the ships, or whether Achilles
has cut him limb from limb and already thrown him to his dogs."
      Then in turn the messenger and Slayer of Argos addressed him: 410
"O old man, the dogs have not eaten him at all, nor the birds,
but he lies there still beside Achilles' ship
among the shelters, just as he was. It is now the twelfth day
he has been lying, and his body has not decayed at all, nor have the worms
gnawed at him, which consume men slain in battle.   415
It is true Achilles drags him heedlessly around the tomb
of his companion, when the bright dawn shows forth,
but does not disfigure him; you yourself would wonder at this, going there,
how he lies fresh like the dew, and he is wholly cleansed of blood,
there is no stain anywhere; all the wounds have closed together,   420
all the wounds that he was struck; for many men drove their bronze
   weapons into him.
So do the blessed gods care for your noble son
although he is dead, since he was very dear to their hearts."
      So he spoke; and the old man rejoiced, and answered with a word:
"O child, surely it is a good thing to give the immortals   425
their proper gifts, since never did my son—if ever he was—
forget in his halls the gods who hold Olympus;
they remembered in turn these offerings even in his fated death.
But come and accept this beautiful two-handled cup from me,
and give me your protection, and with the gods escort me,   430
until I come to the shelter of the son of Peleus."
      Then in turn the messenger and Slayer of Argos addressed him:
"You make trial of my youth, old man, but you will not persuade me,
who bid me accept your gifts behind Achilles' back.
I fear him and in my heart I shrink   435
to rob him, lest something evil befall me later.
But with all kindness I would be your escort even should we go all the way
to famous Argos, whether by swift ship, or accompanying you on foot;
and no man would fight with you, making light of your escort."
      He spoke and springing onto the horse-drawn chariot the
   Runner   440
swiftly took the whip and reins into his hands,
and breathed a brave spirit into the mules and horses.
And when they reached the fortifications of the ships and the ditch—
the watch guards were just beginning to busy themselves with their
   meals—

then the messenger Argeïphontes[7] poured sleep upon them   445
all, and straightway opened the gates and pushed back the bolts,
and led in Priam and the glorious gifts upon the wagon.
    And when they came before the towering quarters of the son of
  Peleus—
which the Myrmidons had built for their lord,
cutting logs of fir, and thatched it above   450
after gathering bristling reeds from the meadow;
and all around it they built for their lord a great courtyard
with close-set stakes; a single bolt made of fir secured its door,
a bolt that three Achaean men would drive shut,
and three men would draw the great bolt back from its door,   455
three other men, but Achilles would drive it shut even on his own—
there Hermes the Runner opened it for the old man,
and brought inside the illustrious gifts for the swift-footed son of Peleus.
He descended from behind the horses to the ground and spoke:
"Old sir, I, a divine god, came to your aid;   460
I am Hermes; for my father sent me to accompany you as escort.
Yet I shall be quick to go back, nor will I enter into Achilles' sight;
for it would be cause for anger
should a mortal man entertain a god in this way, face-to-face.
But you go in and take hold of the knees of the son of Peleus;   465
and make your prayer in the name of his father and his mother of the
  lovely hair and his son, so that you stir his heart."
    Thus speaking, Hermes departed for high Olympus.
And Priam leapt from behind his horses to the ground,
and left Idaios there; and he remained   470
guarding the mules and horses. The old man went straight toward the
  quarters,
where Achilles beloved of Zeus would always sit, and found him
inside; his companions were sitting apart; two alone,
the warrior Automedon and Alkimos, companion of Ares,
were busy by him. He had just finished his meal,   475
eating and drinking, and the table still lay beside him.
Unseen by these men great Priam entered, then standing close
with his arms he clasped Achilles' knees and kissed the
terrible man-slaughtering hands, which had killed his many sons.
As when madness closes tight upon a man who, after killing someone   480
in his own land, arrives in the country of others,
at a rich man's house, and wonder grips those looking on,
so Achilles looked in wonder at godlike Priam,
and the others in wonder, too, looked each toward the other.
    And in supplication Priam addressed him: 485
"Remember your father, godlike Achilles,
The same age as I, on the ruinous threshold of old age.
And perhaps those who dwell around surround him and
bear hard upon him, nor is there anyone to ward off harm and
  destruction.

7. Literally, "Argos-slayer," another name for Hermes.

Yet surely when he hears you are living   490
he rejoices in his heart and hopes for all his days
to see his beloved son returning from Troy.
But I am fated utterly, since I sired the best sons
in broad Troy, but I say not one of them is left.
Fifty were my sons, when the sons of the Achaeans came;   495
nineteen were born to me from the womb of the same mother,
and the rest the women in my palace bore to me.
Of these furious Ares has made slack the knees of many;
he who alone was left to me, he alone protected our city and those inside it,
him it was you lately killed as he fought to defend his country,   500
Hector. And for his sake I come now to the ships of the Achaeans
to win his release from you, and I bear an untold ransom.
Revere the gods, Achilles, and have pity upon me,
remembering your father; for I am yet more pitiful,
and have endured such things as no other mortal man upon the earth,   505
drawing to my lips the hands of the man who killed my son."
          So he spoke; and he stirred in the other a yearning to weep for
    his own father,
and taking hold of his hand he gently pushed the old man away.
And the two remembered, the one weeping without cessation for
man-slaughtering Hector as he lay curled before Achilles' feet,   510
and Achilles wept for his own father, and then again for
Patroclus; and the sound of their lament was raised throughout the hall.
          But when godlike Achilles had taken his fill of lamentation
and the yearning had gone from his breast and very limbs,
he rose suddenly from his seat, and raised the old man by the hand,   515
pitying his gray head and gray beard,
and lifting his voice he addressed him with winged word:
"Poor soul, surely you have endured much evil in your heart.
How did you dare to go to the Achaean ships alone,
into the sight of a man who killed your many and your noble   520
sons? Your heart is iron.
But come and seat yourself upon the chair, and let us leave these sorrows
lying undisturbed within our hearts, grieving though we are;
for there is no profit in grief that numbs the heart.
For thus have the gods spun the thread of destiny for wretched mortals,   525
that we live in sorrow; and they themselves are free from care.
For two urns lie stored on the floor of Zeus
full of such gifts as he gives, one of evil, the other of good.
Should Zeus who delights in thunder bestow mixed lots upon a man,
he will sometimes meet with evil, another time with good;   530
but should he give to a man only from the urn of woe, he renders him the
      object of abuse,
and grinding distress drives him across the shining earth,
and he roams, esteemed by neither gods nor mortals.
Thus to Peleus too the gods gave shining gifts
from his birth; for he surpassed all men   535
in happiness and wealth, and was lord of the Myrmidons,
and to him, mortal though he was, they gave a goddess as his wife;
but to even him god gave evil, since

in his halls was born no line of lordly sons,
but he begot a single all-untimely child; nor do I care for him   540
as he grows old, since very far from my fatherland
I sit at Troy, afflicting you and your children.
And you, old man, we have heard, were blessed in time before;
as much as Lesbos, seat of Makar, contains out there within its boundaries,
and Phrygia inland and the boundless Hellespont,   545
all these, they say, old man, you surpassed in sons and wealth.
But since the gods of heaven have brought this misery to you,
there is forever fighting and the killing of men about your city.
Bear up, nor mourn incessantly in your heart;
for you will accomplish nothing in grieving for your son,   550
nor will you raise him from the dead; before that happens you will suffer
    yet another evil."
        Then old Priam, like a god, answered him:
"Do not have me sit upon a chair, god-cherished one, while Hector
lies in your shelters unburied, but quick as you can
release him, so that I may see him with my eyes, and you accept the
    many gifts   555
of ransom, which we bring for you. And have enjoyment of them, and may
you return to your fatherland, since from the first you spared me."[8]   557
        Then looking at him from under his brows swift-footed Achilles
    spoke: 559
"Provoke me no further, old man; for I myself am minded   560
to release Hector to you; from Zeus my mother came to me as messenger,
she who bore me, daughter of the old man of the sea.
I recognize, Priam, in my mind, and it does not escape me,
that some one of the gods led you to the Achaeans' swift ships;
for no mortal man, not even a young man in his prime, would dare   565
to come to our camp; nor could he have slipped by the watch guards, nor
    could he
easily force back the bolts of our doors.
Therefore do not now stir my heart further in its sorrows,
lest, old man, I do not spare even yourself within my shelter,
suppliant though you be, but transgress the commands of Zeus."   570
        Thus he spoke; and the old man was afraid and obeyed his word.
And the son of Peleus like a lion sprang out the door of his shelter,
and not alone; with him followed his two henchmen,
the warrior Automedon and Alkimos, whom beyond all other companions
Achilles honored after Patroclus died.   575
They released the horses and mules from under their yokes,
and led in the herald, crier to the old man,
and they seated him upon a bench; and from the strong-wheeled wagon
they lifted the boundless ransom for the body of Hector.
But they left two fine-spun robes and a tunic,   580
so Achilles could wrap the body and give it to be carried home.
And summoning his maids, Achilles ordered them to wash the body and
    anoint it,
after taking it to a place apart, so that Priam should not see his son,

8. The line numbers here account for lines that were omitted by the translator because they may
not belong in the text.

for fear the old man might not keep his anger hidden in his anguished heart
on seeing his son, and might stir Achilles' own heart to violence   585
and he kill Priam, and transgress the commands of Zeus.
And when then the maids had washed and anointed the body with oil,
they put around it the beautiful robe and tunic,
and Achilles himself lifted it and placed it upon a bier,
then his companions with him lifted this onto the polished wagon.   590
And Achilles groaned, and called his dear companion's name:
"Do not, Patroclus, be angered with me, if you should learn,
though you be in the house of Hades, that I released shining Hector
to his father, since the ransom he gave me was not unworthy.
And I in turn will give you a portion of it, as much as is fitting."   595
        He spoke, and godlike Achilles went back into his shelter,
and took his seat on the richly wrought chair, from which he had risen,
against the far wall, and spoke his word to Priam:
"Your son has been released to you, old man, as you bade,
and lies upon a bier; and with the dawn's appearance,   600
you will see yourself when you take him. But now let us not forget our
    supper.
For even Niobe[9] of the lovely hair did not forget her food,
she whose twelve children were destroyed in her halls,
six daughters, and six sons in the prime of manhood.
The sons Apollo slew with his silver bow   605
in his anger with Niobe, and Artemis who showers arrows slew the
    daughters,
because Niobe equalled herself to Leto of the lovely cheeks—
for she would boast that Leto bore two children, while she herself had
    borne many.
So two only though they were, they destroyed the many.
And for nine days they lay in their own blood, nor was there anyone   610
to give them burial; for the son of Cronus had turned the people into stone.
Then on the tenth day the heavenly gods gave them burial,
and Niobe bethought herself of food, when she was worn out with weeping.
And now among the rocks somewhere, in the lonely mountains
of Sipylos, where they say are the sleeping places of the immortal   615
nymphs who race beside the river Achelous,
there, stone though she is, she broods upon the cares sent her from the
    gods.[1]
But come, and let us two, illustrious old sir, take thought
of food. For you may weep for your dear son again
when you have brought him into Ilion; he will be the cause of many
    tears."   620
        He spoke, and springing to his feet swift Achilles, with a cut to
    the throat,
slaughtered a shining white sheep; his companions flayed it and with skill
    prepared it properly.

9. Wife of Amphion, one of the two founders
of the great Greek city of Thebes.
1. The legend of Niobe being turned into stone
is thought to have had its origin in a rock face of
Mount Sipylus (in Asia Minor) that resembled a
woman who wept inconsolably for the loss of
her children. The Achelous River runs near
Mount Sipylus.

They sliced the flesh skillfully and pierced it on spits
and roasted it with care, and then drew off all the pieces.
Automedon took bread to distribute around the table   625
in fine baskets; but Achilles distributed the meat;
and they reached out their hands to the good things set ready before them.
And when they had put away desire for eating and drinking,
then did Priam son of Dardanos look in wonder at Achilles,
how massive he was, what kind of man; for he was like the gods to
    look upon;   630
and Achilles looked in wonder at Dardanian Priam,
gazing on his noble face and listening to his words.
    But when they had their fill of looking upon each other,
then old Priam the godlike addressed Achilles first:
"Let me go to bed now quickly, god-cherished one, so that   635
we may have solace when we lie down beneath sweet sleep.
For not yet have my eyes closed beneath my lids,
from the time my son lost his life at your hands,
but always I groaned in lament and brooded on my sorrows without
    measure,
wallowing in dung in the enclosure of my court.   640
But now I have tasted food and let gleaming wine
down my throat; before I had tasted nothing."
    He spoke; and Achilles ordered the companions and servant women
to set out a bed under cover of the porch and to throw upon it
splendid crimson blankets to lie upon, and to spread rugs over them,   645
and to place woolen cloaks on top of all to cover them.
And the maids went from the hall bearing torches in their hands,
and working in haste soon spread two beds.
Then bantering, Achilles of the swift feet addressed Priam:
"Sleep outside, old friend, for fear one of the Achaean   650
leaders come suddenly upon us here, who forever
devise their counsels beside me, as is right and proper.
If one of them were to see you through the swift black night,
he would at once make it known to Agamemnon, shepherd of the people,
and there would be delay in the surrender of the body.   655
But come and tell me this and relate it exactly;
how many days do you desire to give funeral rites to shining Hector—
for so long I will wait and hold back the army."
    Then old Priam the godlike answered him:
"If then you are willing for me to accomplish Hector's funeral,   660
by doing as follows, Achilles, you would give me a kindness.
For you know how we are penned within the city, and it is a long way
to bring wood from the mountains; for the Trojans are greatly afraid;
nine days we would mourn him in our halls,
and on the tenth we would bury him and the people would feast,   665
and on the eleventh day we would make a tomb for him;
and on the twelfth we shall go to war, if indeed we must."
    Then in turn swift-footed godlike Achilles addressed him:
"These things, old Priam, will be as you ask;
I will suspend the war for such time, as you command."   670
And so speaking he took hold of the old man's right hand

by the wrist, lest he have any fear in his heart.
      Then they lay down to sleep there in the forecourt of the shelter,
the herald and Priam, a flurry of thoughts in their minds.
But Achilles slept in the inner recess of his well-built shelter,   675
and Briseïs of the lovely cheeks lay at his side.
      So the other gods as well as chariot-fighting men
slept through the night, overcome by soft slumber,
but sleep did not lay hold of Hermes the runner
as he turned over in his heart how he might send king Priam   680
from the ships unnoticed by the hallowed watchers of the gate.
And he stood above Priam's head and addressed him with his words:
"Old man, surely you have no thought of any evil, seeing how you sleep
in the midst of enemy men, since Achilles spared you.
And now you have won release of your beloved son, and gave many
    things for him;   685
but your sons who were left behind would give yet three times
as much ransom for you alive, should Agamemnon
the son of Atreus recognize you, and all the Achaeans."
So he spoke; and the old man was afraid, and woke up his herald.
Then Hermes yoked the mules and horses for them,   690
and himself drove swiftly through the camp; nor did anyone see.
      But when they reached the crossing of the fair-flowing stream,[2]   692
then Hermes departed for high Olympus;   694
and Dawn robed in saffron spread over all the earth;   695
the men with lamentation and groaning drove the horses on
to the city, and the mules carried the corpse. No man
saw them at first, nor any fair-belted woman,
but then Cassandra,[3] like to golden Aphrodite,
having gone up to the height of Pergamos, saw her beloved father   700
standing in the chariot and the herald and city crier;
and then she saw Hector lying upon the bier drawn by the mules.
She wailed her grief aloud, then cried out to the whole city:
"Look upon Hector, men and women of Troy! Come,
if ever before you used to rejoice when he returned alive from battle,   705
since he was the great joy of the city and all its people."
      So she spoke; nor did any man remain there in the city
nor any woman; uncontrollable grief seized all;
close by the gates they met Priam as he brought Hector's body;
at the front his beloved wife and lady mother ripped their hair in grief   710
for him, lunging at the strong-wheeled wagon,
to touch his head; and the throng surrounded him weeping.
And for the whole day long until the sun's going down they would have
mourned Hector, pouring their tears before the gates,
had not the old man spoken among them from the chariot: 715
"Make way for me to pass with the mules; later
you can sate yourselves with weeping, when I have brought him
    home."

---

2. The line numbers here account for lines that were omitted by the translator because they may not belong in the text.

3. Daughter of Priam and Hecuba; she was a prophetess and foretold the fall of Troy, but was cursed by Apollo to be disbelieved.

So he spoke; and they stood aside and made way for the wagon.
   And when they had brought him into the illustrious house, then
they laid him upon a fretted bed, and set beside it singers,   720
leaders of the dirges, who sang their mournful dirge song,
and the women keened in response.
   And white-armed Andromache led the lament among them,
holding in her arms the head of horse-breaking Hector:
"My husband, you were lost from life while young, and are leaving me
   a widow
                     725
in your halls; and the child is still just a baby,
whom we bore, you and I, ill-fated both, nor do I think
he will reach young manhood; before that this city
will be wholly ravaged; for you its watchman have perished, who used to
   guard it,
who protected its devoted wives and tender children.   730
They soon will be carried away in the hollow ships,
and I with them; and you then, my child, either you will follow with me,
and there do work unworthy of you
toiling for a harsh master—or some Achaean man
seizing you by the arm will hurl you from the ramparts, unhappy death,[4]   735
in his anger, one whose brother, perhaps, Hector slew,
or his father or even his son, since so many of the Achaeans
gripped the broad earth in their teeth at Hector's hands.
For your father was no gentle man in sad battle;
therefore the people mourn him through the city,   740
and cursed is the grief and lamentation you have laid upon your parents,
Hector. And to me beyond all others will be left painful sorrow;
for you did not reach out your hands to me from your bed as you were dying,
nor did you speak some close word to me, which I might always
remember through the nights and days as I shed my tears."   745
So she spoke, crying, and the women in response mourned.
   And Hecuba led them next in the passionate lament:
"Hector, far the dearest to my heart of all my sons,
while you were alive you were dear to the gods,
who now care for you even in your fated lot of death.   750
Other sons of mine Achilles of the swift feet would sell,
whomever he captured, beyond the murmuring salt sea,
into Samothrace, into Imbros and sea-spattered Lemnos;
but he plucked your soul from you with his tapered bronze spear,
and dragged you again and again around the tomb of his companion   755
Patroclus, whom you slew—nor did he raise him from the dead so doing—
yet now you lie as fresh as dew, unsullied in my halls,
like one whom Apollo of the silver bow
approaches and kills with his gentle arrows."
So she spoke weeping, and stirred unceasing wailing.   760
   Then third among the women, Helen led the lament:
"Hector, far dearest to my heart of all my husband's brothers;
too true, my husband is Alexandros of godlike beauty,
who led me to Troy; would that I had died before;

---

4. Astyanax was, in fact, hurled from Troy's walls after the city fell.

for this is now the twentieth year for me   765
since I set out from there and forsook my fatherland,
but never yet did I hear a harsh or abusive word from you,
but if someone else would revile me in these halls,
one of my husband's brothers, or his sisters, or one of my fine-robed
   sisters-in-law,
or my husband's mother—but my husband's father was like a kind
   father always—   770
you with soothing words would restrain them
with your gentle nature and kind speech.
Therefore I weep, grieving at heart, for you and for me, ill-fated, together;
for no longer is there anyone else in broad Troy
to be kind or friend to me, but all shudder at me."   775
So she spoke crying, and in response all the great multitude moaned.
       Then old Priam spoke his word among the people:
"Men of Troy, now fetch timber to the city. Have no fear in your heart
of cunning ambush by the Argives; for Achilles,
as he sent me from the black ships, gave orders thus,   780
that he would do no harm before the twelfth dawn comes."
So he spoke; and the men yoked the oxen and mules to the wagons,
and soon they were gathered before the city.
       For nine days they brought an immense pile of timber;
and when at length the tenth dawn showed, bringing light to mortals,   785
then, shedding tears, they carried forth bold Hector.
On the very top of the pyre they placed his body, and on it flung the fire.
       And when Dawn born of the morning showed forth her fingers
   of rosy light,
then around the pyre of illustrious Hector the people gathered;[5]   789
first they extinguished the burning pyre with dark-gleaming wine   791
entirely, all that retained the fire's strength; and then
his brothers and his comrades picked out his white bones
as they wept, and the swelling tears fell from their cheeks.
And taking the bones they placed them in a golden box,   795
after covering them round with soft purple cloth;
swiftly they placed these in a hollowed grave, and covered it
from above with great stones set close together.
Lightly they heaped up the burial mound—lookouts were set all round,
lest the strong-greaved Achaeans should attack before—   800
and when they had piled up the mound they started back. Then
having come together they duly gave a glorious feast
in the house of Priam, king nurtured by Zeus.
Thus they tended the funeral of Hector, breaker of horses.

---

5. The line numbers here account for lines that were omitted by the translator because they may
not belong in the text.

From the Odyssey[1]

BOOK I

[The Boy and the Goddess]

Tell me about a complicated man.[2]
Muse, tell me how he wandered and was lost
when he had wrecked the holy town of Troy,
and where he went, and who he met, the pain
he suffered on the sea, and how he worked   5
to save his life and bring his men back home.
He failed, and for their own mistakes, they died.
They ate the Sun God's cattle,[3] and the god
kept them from home. Now goddess, child of Zeus,[4]
tell the old story for our modern times.   10
Find the beginning.

        All the other Greeks
who had survived the brutal sack of Troy
sailed safely home to their own wives—except
this man alone. Calypso,[5] a great goddess,
had trapped him in her cave; she wanted him   15
to be her husband. When the year rolled round
in which the gods decreed he should go home
to Ithaca, his troubles still went on.
The man was friendless. All the gods took pity,
except Poseidon's[6] anger never ended   20
until Odysseus was back at home.
But now the distant Ethiopians,
who live between the sunset and the dawn,
were worshipping the Sea God with a feast,
a hundred cattle and a hundred rams.   25
There sat the god, delighting in his banquet.
The other gods were gathered on Olympus,
in Father Zeus'[7] palace. He was thinking
of fine, well-born Aegisthus, who was killed
by Agamemnon's famous son Orestes.[8]   30
He told the deathless gods,

                  "This is absurd,
that mortals blame the gods! They say we cause

---

1. Translated by Emily Wilson.
2. Odysseus, who is not named until several lines later.
3. The sun god Hyperion was, in Greek mythology, a Titan, one of the generation of gods that preceded the Olympians. The story of how Odysseus's men ate the cattle of the sun will be told in book 12.
4. The muse.
5. Daughter of the Titan Atlas, who holds up the sky.
6. Poseidon is the god of the sea, brother of Zeus.
7. Zeus is the king of the gods.
8. Agamemnon was killed on his return home by the usurper Aegisthus, with the help of Agamemnon's adulterous wife, Clytemnestra. Orestes, Agamemnon and Clytemnestra's son, killed his mother and Aegisthus.

their suffering, but they themselves increase it
by folly. So Aegisthus overstepped:
he took the legal wife of Agamemnon,   35
then killed the husband when he came back home
although he knew that it would doom them all.
We gods had warned Aegisthus; we sent down
perceptive Hermes,[9] who flashed into sight
and told him not to murder Agamemnon   40
or court his wife; Orestes would grow up
and come back to his home to take revenge.
Aegisthus would not hear that good advice.
But now his death has paid all debts."

                                              Athena[1]
looked at him steadily and answered, "Father,   45
he did deserve to die. Bring death to all
who act like him! But I am agonizing
about Odysseus and his bad luck.
For too long he has suffered, with no friends,
sea all around him, sea on every side,   50
out on an island where a goddess lives,
daughter of fearful Atlas, who holds up
the pillars of the sea, and knows its depths—
those pillars keep the heaven and earth apart.
His daughter holds that poor unhappy man,   55
and tries beguiling him with gentle words
to cease all thoughts of Ithaca; but he
longs to see even just the smoke that rises
from his own homeland, and he wants to die.
You do not even care, Olympian!   60
Remember how he sacrificed to you
on the broad plain of Troy beside his ships?
So why do you dismiss Odysseus?"[2]

"Daughter!" the Cloud God said, "You must be joking,
since how could I forget Odysseus?   65
He is more sensible than other humans,
and makes more sacrifices to the gods.
But Lord Poseidon rages, unrelenting,
because Odysseus destroyed the eye
of godlike Polyphemus, his own son,   70
the strongest of the Cyclopes—whose mother,
Thoösa, is a sea-nymph, child of Phorcys,[3]
the sea king; and she lay beside Poseidon
inside a hollow cave. The Lord of Earthquakes
prevents Odysseus from reaching home   75

---

9. Messenger god.
1. Goddess of wisdom, who favors Odysseus.
2. The word in the original for Zeus hostile

treatment of Odysseus (*odyssao*) is reminiscent
of the name "Odysseus."
3. A minor sea god. "Cyclopes": one-eyed giants.

but does not kill him. Come then, we must plan:
how can he get back home? Poseidon must
give up his anger, since he cannot fight
alone against the will of all the gods."

Athena's eyes lit up and she replied,   80
"Great Father, if the blessed gods at last
will let Odysseus return back home,
then hurry, we must send our messenger,
Hermes the giant-slayer. He must swoop
down to Ogygia right away and tell   85
the beautiful Calypso we have formed
a firm decision that Odysseus
has waited long enough. He must go home.
And I will go to Ithaca to rouse
the courage of his son, and make him call   90
a meeting, and speak out against the suitors
who kill his flocks of sheep and longhorn cattle
unstoppably. Then I will send him off
to Pylos and to Sparta, to seek news
about his father's journey home, and gain   95
a noble reputation for himself."

With that, she tied her sandals on her feet,
the marvelous golden sandals that she wears
to travel sea and land, as fast as wind.
She took the heavy bronze-tipped spear she uses   100
to tame the ranks of warriors with whom
she is enraged. Then from the mountain down
she sped to Ithaca, and stopped outside
Odysseus' court, bronze spear in hand.
She looked like Mentes now, the Taphian leader,[4]   105
a guest-friend. There she found the lordly suitors
sitting on hides—they killed the cows themselves—
and playing checkers. Quick, attentive house slaves
were waiting on them. Some were mixing wine
with water in the bowls, and others brought   110
the tables out and wiped them off with sponges,
and others carved up heaping plates of meat.
Telemachus was sitting with them, feeling
dejected. In his mind he saw his father
coming from somewhere, scattering the suitors,   115
and gaining back his honor, and control
of all his property. With this in mind,
he was the first to see Athena there.
He disapproved of leaving strangers stranded,
so he went straight to meet her at the gate,   120
and shook her hand, and took her spear of bronze,
and let his words fly out to her.

4. The Taphians were an island people from the Ionian Sea. "Mentes": a friend of Odysseus.

"Good evening,
stranger, and welcome. Be our guest, come share
our dinner, and then tell us what you need."

He led her in, and Pallas followed him.   125
Inside the high-roofed hall, he set her spear
beside a pillar in a polished stand,
in which Odysseus kept stores of weapons.
And then he led her to a chair and spread
a smooth embroidered cloth across the seat,   130
and pulled a footstool up to it. He sat
beside her on a chair of inlaid wood,
a distance from the suitors, so their shouting
would not upset the stranger during dinner;
also to ask about his absent father.   135
A girl brought washing water in a jug
of gold, and poured it on their hands and into
a silver bowl, and set a table by them.
A deferential slave brought bread and laid
a wide array of food, a generous spread.   140
The carver set beside them plates of meat
of every kind, and gave them golden cups.
The cup boy kept on topping up the wine.
The suitors sauntered in and sat on chairs,
observing proper order,[5] and the slaves   145
poured water on their hands. The house girls brought
baskets of bread and heaped it up beside them,
and house boys filled their wine-bowls up with drink.
They reached to take the good things set before them.
Once they were satisfied with food and drink,   150
the suitors turned their minds to other things—
singing and dancing, glories of the feast.
A slave brought out a well-tuned lyre and gave it
to Phemius, the man the suitors forced
to sing for them. He struck the chords to start   155
his lovely song.

        Telemachus leaned in
close to Athena, so they would not hear,
and said,

        "Dear guest—excuse my saying this—
these men are only interested in music,
a life of ease. They make no contribution.   160
This food belongs to someone else, a man
whose white bones may be lying in the rain
or sunk beneath the waves. If they saw him

---

5. There may be an implication here that the
suitors seat themselves according to some
kind of rank, with the more important ones
taking a more honorable position.

return to Ithaca, they would all pray
for faster feet, instead of wealth and gold   165
and fancy clothes. In fact, he must have died.
We have no hope. He will not come back home.
If someone says so, we do not believe it.
But come now, tell me this and tell the truth.
Who are you? From what city, and what parents?   170
What kind of ship did you here arrive on?
What sailors brought you here, and by what route?
You surely did not travel here on foot!
Here is the thing I really want to know:
have you been here before? Are you a friend   175
who visited my father? Many men
came to his house. He traveled many places."

Athena's clear bright eyes met his. She said,
"Yes, I will tell you everything. I am
Mentes, the son of wise Anchialus,   180
lord of the Taphians, who love the oar.
I traveled with my ship and my companions
over the wine-dark sea to foreign lands,
with iron that I hope to trade for copper
in Temese. My ship is in the harbor   185
far from the town, beneath the woody hill.
And you and I are guest-friends through our fathers,
from long ago—Laertes[6] can confirm it.
I hear that fine old man no longer comes
to town, but lives out in the countryside,   190
stricken by grief, with only one old slave,
who gives him food and drink when he trails back
leg-weary from his orchard, rich in vines.
I came because they told me that your father
was here—but now it seems that gods have blocked   195
his path back home. But I am sure that he
is not yet dead. The wide sea keeps him trapped
upon some island, captured by fierce men
who will not let him go. Now I will make
a prophecy the gods have given me,   200
and I think it will all come true, although
I am no prophet. He will not be gone
much longer from his own dear native land,
even if chains of iron hold him fast.
He will devise a means of getting home.   205
He is resourceful. Tell me now—are you
Odysseus' son? You are so tall!
Your handsome face and eyes resemble his.
We often met and knew each other well,
before he went to Troy, where all the best   210

---

6. Odysseus's father.

leaders of Argos sailed in hollow ships.
From that time on, we have not seen each other."

Telemachus was careful as he answered.
"Dear guest, I will be frank with you. My mother
says that I am his son, but I cannot   215
be sure, since no one knows his own begetting.
I wish I were the son of someone lucky,
who could grow old at home with all his wealth.
Instead, the most unlucky man alive
is said to be my father—since you ask."   220

Athena looked at him with sparkling eyes.
"Son of Penelope, you and your sons
will make a name in history, since you are
so clever. But now tell me this. Who are
these banqueters? And what is the occasion?   225
A drinking party, or a wedding feast?
They look so arrogant and self-indulgent,
making themselves at home. A wise observer
would surely disapprove of how they act."

Telemachus said moodily, "My friend,   230
since you have raised the subject, there was once
a time when this house here was doing well,
our future bright, when he was still at home.
But now the gods have changed their plans and cursed us,
and cast my father into utter darkness.   235
If he had died it would not be this bad—
if he had fallen with his friends at Troy,
or in his loved ones' arms, when he had wound
the threads of war to end. The Greeks would then
have built a tomb for him; he would have won   240
fame for his son. But now, the winds have seized him,
and he is nameless and unknown. He left
nothing but tears for me. I do not weep
only for him. The gods have given me
so many other troubles. All the chiefs   245
of Same, Zacynthus, Dulichium,
and local lords from rocky Ithaca,
are courting Mother, wasting our whole house.
She does not turn these awful suitors down,
nor can she end the courting. They keep eating,   250
spoiling my house—and soon, they will kill me!"

Athena said in outrage, "This is monstrous!
You need Odysseus to come back home
and lay his hands on all those shameless suitors!
If only he would come here now and stand   255
right at the gates, with two spears in his hands,
in shield and helmet, as when I first saw him!

Odysseus was visiting our house,
drinking and having fun on his way back
from sailing in swift ships to Ephyra   260
to visit Ilus. He had gone there looking
for deadly poison to anoint his arrows.
Ilus refused, because he feared the gods.
My father gave Odysseus the poison,
loving him blindly. May Odysseus   265
come meet the suitors with that urge to kill!
A bitter courtship and short life for them!
But whether he comes home to take revenge,
or not, is with the gods. You must consider
how best to drive these suitors from your house.   270
Come, listen carefully to what I say.
Tomorrow call the Achaean[7] chiefs to meeting,
and tell the suitors—let the gods be witness—
'All of you, go away! To your own homes!'
As for your mother, if she wants to marry,   275
let her return to her great father's home.
They will make her a wedding and prepare
abundant gifts to show her father's love.
Now here is some advice from me for you.
Fit out a ship with twenty oars, the best,   280
and go find out about your long-lost father.
Someone may tell you news, or you may hear
a voice from Zeus, best source of information.
First go to Pylos, question godlike Nestor;
from there, to Sparta; visit Menelaus.[8]   285
He came home last of all the Achaean heroes.
If you should hear that he is still alive
and coming home, put up with this abuse
for one more year. But if you hear that he
is dead, go home, and build a tomb for him,   290
and hold a lavish funeral to show
the honor he deserves, and give your mother
in marriage to a man. When this is done,
consider deeply how you might be able
to kill the suitors in your halls—by tricks   295
or openly. You must not stick to childhood;
you are no longer just a little boy.
You surely heard how everybody praised
Orestes when he killed the man who killed
his famous father—devious Aegisthus?   300
Dear boy, I see how big and tall you are.
Be brave, and win yourself a lasting name.
But I must go now, on my nimble ship;
my friends are getting tired of waiting for me.
Remember what I said and heed my words."   305

7. Greek.
8. Brother of Agamemnon, husband of Helen,   the woman whose abduction by Paris caused
                                               the Trojan War.

Telemachus was brooding on her words,
and said, "Dear guest, you were so kind to give me
this fatherly advice. I will remember.
I know that you are eager to be off,
but please enjoy a bath before you go,   310
and take a gift with you. I want to give you
a precious, pretty treasure as a keepsake
to mark our special friendship."

                           But the goddess
Athena met his gaze and said, "Do not
hold me back now. I must be on my way.   315
As for the gift you feel inspired to give me,
save it for when I come on my way home
and let me give you presents then as well
in fair exchange."

                       With that, the owl-eyed goddess
flew away like a bird, up through the smoke.   320
She left him feeling braver, more determined,
and with his father even more in mind.
Watching her go, he was amazed and saw
she was a god. Then godlike, he went off
to meet the suitors.

                    They were sitting calmly,   325
listening to the poet, who sang how
Athena cursed the journey of the Greeks
as they were sailing home from Troy. Upstairs,
Penelope had heard the marvelous song.
She clambered down the steep steps of her house,   330
not by herself—two slave girls came with her.
She reached the suitors looking like a goddess,
then stopped and stood beside a sturdy pillar,
holding a gauzy veil before her face.
Her slave girls stood, one on each side of her.   335
In tears, she told the holy singer,

                          "Stop,
please, Phemius! You know so many songs,
enchanting tales of things that gods and men
have done, the deeds that singers publicize.
Sing something else, and let them drink in peace.   340
Stop this upsetting song that always breaks
my heart, so I can hardly bear my grief.
I miss him all the time—that man, my husband,
whose story is so famous throughout Greece."

Sullen Telemachus said, "Mother, no,   345
you must not criticize the loyal bard
for singing as it pleases him to sing.

Poets are not to blame for how things are;
Zeus is; he gives to each as is his will.
Do not blame Phemius because he told   350
about the Greek disasters. You must know
the newest song is always praised the most.
So steel your heart and listen to the song.
Odysseus was not the only one
who did not come back home again from Troy.   355
Many were lost. Go in and do your work.
Stick to the loom and distaff. Tell your slaves
to do their chores as well. It is for men
to talk, especially me. I am the master."

That startled her. She went back to her room,   360
and took to heart her son's deliberate scolding.
She went upstairs, along with both her slaves,
and wept there for her dear Odysseus,
until Athena gave her eyes sweet sleep.
Throughout the shadowy hall the suitors clamored,   365
praying to lie beside her in her bed.
Telemachus inhaled, then started speaking.

"You suitors, you are taking this too far.
Let us enjoy the feast in peace. It is
a lovely thing to listen to a bard,   370
especially one with such a godlike voice.
At dawn, let us assemble in the square.
I have to tell you this—it is an order.
You have to leave my halls. Go dine elsewhere!
Eat your own food, or share between your houses.   375
Or if you think it easier and better
to ruin one man's wealth, and if you think
that you can get away with it—go on!
I call upon the gods; Zeus will grant vengeance.
You will be punished and destroyed, right here!"   380

He spoke, and they began to bite their lips,
shocked that Telemachus would dare to speak
so boldly. But Antinous replied,

"Telemachus, the gods themselves have taught you
such pride, to talk so big and brash in public!   385
May Zeus the son of Cronus never grant you
your true inheritance, which is the throne
of Ithaca."

          His mind alert and focused,
Telemachus replied, "Antinous,
you will not like this, but I have to say,   390
I hope Zeus does give me the throne. Do you
deny it is an honorable thing

to be a king? It brings the household wealth,
and honor to the man. But there are many
other great chiefs in sea-girt Ithaca,   395
both old and young. I know that. One of them
may seize the throne, now that Odysseus
has died. But I shall be at least the lord
of my own house and of the slaves that he
seized for my benefit."

                    Eurymachus   400
replied, "Telemachus, the gods must choose
which of us will be king of Ithaca.
But still, I hope you keep your own possessions,
and rule your house. May no man drive you out,
and seize your wealth, while Ithaca survives.   405
Now, friend, I want to ask about the stranger.
Where was he from, what country? Did he say?
Where is his place of birth, his native soil?
Does he bring news your father will come home?
Or did he come here for some other purpose?   410
How suddenly he darted off, not waiting
for us to meet him. Yet he looked important."

The boy said soberly, "Eurymachus,
my father is not ever coming home.
I do not listen now to any gossip,   415
or forecasts from the psychics whom my mother
invites to visit us. The stranger was
my father's guest-friend Mentes, son of wise
Anchialus, who rules the Taphians,
the people of the oar."

                    Those were his words,   420
but in his mind he knew she was a god.
They danced to music and enjoyed themselves
till evening, then they went back home to sleep.
Telemachus' bedroom had been built
above the courtyard, so it had a view.   425
He went upstairs, preoccupied by thought.
A loyal slave went with him, Eurycleia,
daughter of Ops; she brought the burning torches.
Laertes bought her many years before
when she was very young, for twenty oxen.   430
He gave her status in the household, equal
to his own wife, but never slept with her,
avoiding bitter feelings in his marriage.
She brought the torches now; she was the slave
who loved him most, since she had cared for him   435
when he was tiny. Entering the room,
he sat down on the bed, took off his tunic,
and gave it to the vigilant old woman.

She smoothed it out and folded it, then hung it
up on a hook beside his wooden bed,   440
and left the room. She used the silver latch
to close the door; the strap pulled tight the bolt.
He slept the night there, wrapped in woolen blankets,
planning the journey told him by Athena.

Summary   Telemachus summons a council and complains about the suitors' behavior and
the Ithacans' failure to intervene. The suitors continue to mock him. With the help of Eurycleia,
an old palace slave, but in secret from Penelope, Telemachus packs provisions and embarks on
the ship prepared for him by Athena. He travels to Pylos, where pious old Nestor welcomes him.
Then, accompanied by Nestor's youngest son, Pisistratus, Telemachus goes to Sparta, where he
is welcomed by Helen and Menelaus. Back in Ithaca, the suitors learn of Telemachus's trip and
plot to kill him when he comes back. Penelope finds out about Telemachus's journey and the
murder plot and is devastated; Athena sends a dream phantom to comfort her.

BOOK 5

[From the Goddess to the Storm]

Then Dawn rose up from bed with Lord Tithonus,[9]
to bring the light to deathless gods and mortals.
The gods sat down for council, with the great
Thunderlord Zeus. Athena was concerned
about Odysseus' many troubles,   5
trapped by the nymph Calypso in her house.

"Father, and all immortal gods," she said,
"No longer let a sceptered king be kind,
or gentle, or pay heed to right and wrong.
Let every king be cruel, his acts unjust!   10
Odysseus ruled gently, like a father,
but no one even thinks about him now.
The wretched man is stranded on an island;
Calypso forces him to stay with her.
He cannot make his way back to his country.   15
He has no ships, no oars, and no companions
to help him sail across the wide-backed sea.
His son has gone for news of his lost father,
in sandy Pylos and in splendid Sparta;
they plot to kill the boy when he returns!"   20

Smiling at her, Lord Zeus who heaps the clouds
replied, "Ah, daughter! What a thing to say!
Did you not plan all this yourself, so that
Odysseus could come and take revenge
upon those suitors? Now use all your skill: 25

9. Dawn's lover, a mortal man whom she made immortal (though not ageless) and brought to live
with her in the sky.

ensure Telemachus comes safely home,
and that the suitors fail and sail away."

Then turning to his son he said, "Dear Hermes,
you are my messenger. Go tell the goddess
our fixed intention: that Odysseus   30
must go back home—he has endured enough.
Without a god or human as his guide,
he will drift miserably for twenty days
upon a makeshift raft, and then arrive
at fertile Scheria. The magical   35
Phaeacians will respect him like a god,
and send him in a ship to his dear homeland,
with gifts of bronze and heaps of gold and clothing,
more than he would have brought with him from Troy
if he had come directly, with his share   40
of plunder. It is granted him to see
the ones he loves, beneath his own high roof,
in his own country."

               Hermes heard these words.
At once he fastened on his feet the sandals
of everlasting gold with which he flies   45
on breath of air across the sea and land;
he seized the wand he uses to enchant
men's eyes to sleep or wake as he desires,
and flew. The god flashed bright in all his power.
He touched Pieria, then from the sky   50
he plunged into the sea and swooped between
the waves, just like a seagull catching fish,
wetting its whirring wings in tireless brine.
So Hermes scudded through the surging swell.
Then finally, he reached the distant island,   55
stepped from the indigo water to the shore,
and reached the cavern where the goddess lived.

There sat Calypso with her braided curls.
Beside the hearth a mighty fire was burning.
The scent of citrus and of brittle pine   60
suffused the island. Inside, she was singing
and weaving with a shuttle made of gold.
Her voice was beautiful. Around the cave
a luscious forest flourished: alder, poplar,
and scented cypress. It was full of wings.   65
Birds nested there but hunted out at sea:
the owls, the hawks, the gulls with gaping beaks.
A ripe and verdant vine, hung thick with grapes,
was stretched to coil around her cave. Four springs
spurted with sparkling water as they laced   70
with crisscross currents intertwined together.
The meadow softly bloomed with celery

and violets. He gazed around in wonder
and joy, at sights to please even a god.
Even the deathless god who once killed Argos[1]   75
stood still, his heart amazed at all he saw.
At last he went inside the cave. Calypso,
the splendid goddess, knew the god on sight:
the deathless gods all recognize each other,
however far away their homes may be.   80
But Hermes did not find Odysseus,
since he was sitting by the shore as usual,
sobbing in grief and pain; his heart was breaking.
In tears he stared across the fruitless sea.

Divine Calypso told her guest to sit   85
upon a gleaming, glittering chair, and said,
"Dear friend, Lord Hermes of the golden wand,
why have you come? You do not often visit.
What do you have in mind? My heart inclines
to help you if I can, if it is fated.   90
For now, come in, and let me make you welcome."

At that the goddess led him to a table
heaped with ambrosia, and she mixed a drink:
red nectar.[2] So mercurial Hermes drank
and ate till he was satisfied, and then   95
the diplomat explained why he had come.

"You are a goddess, I a god—and yet
you ask why I am here. Well, I will tell you.
Zeus ordered me to come—I did not want to.
Who would desire to cross such an expanse   100
of endless salty sea? No human town
is near here, where gods get fine sacrifices.
Still, none can sway or check the will of Zeus.
He says the most unhappy man alive
is living here—a warrior from those   105
who fought the town of Priam for nine years
and in the tenth they sacked it and sailed home.
But on the journey back, they wronged Athena.
She roused the wind and surging sea against them
and all his brave companions were destroyed,   110
while he himself was blown here by the waves.
Zeus orders you to send him on his way
at once, since it is not his destiny
to die here far away from those he loves.
It is his fate to see his family   115
and come back home, to his own native land."

1. One of the standard epithets for Hermes.
2. Food of the gods.

Calypso shuddered and let fly at him.
"You cruel, jealous gods! You bear a grudge
whenever any goddess takes a man
to sleep with as a lover in her bed.   120
Just so the gods who live at ease were angry
when rosy-fingered Dawn took up Orion,[3]
and from her golden throne, chaste Artemis
attacked and killed him with her gentle arrows.
Demeter with the cornrows in her hair   125
indulged her own desire, and she made love
with Iasion in triple-furrowed fields—
till Zeus found out, hurled flashing flame and killed him.[4]
So now, you male gods are upset with me
for living with a man. A man I saved!   130
Zeus pinned his ship and with his flash of lightning
smashed it to pieces. All his friends were killed
out on the wine-dark sea. This man alone,
clutching the keel, was swept by wind and wave,
and came here, to my home. I cared for him   135
and loved him, and I vowed to to set him free
from time and death forever. Still, I know
no other god can change the will of Zeus.
So let him go, if that is Zeus' order,
across the barren sea. I will not give   140
an escort for this trip across the water;
I have no ships or rowers. But I will
share what I know with him, and gladly give
useful advice so he can safely reach
his home."

       The mediator, Zeus' servant,   145
replied, "Then send him now, avoid the wrath
of Zeus, do not enrage him, or one day
his rage will hurt you." With these words, he vanished.

Acknowledging the edict sent from Zeus,
the goddess went to find Odysseus.   150
She found him on the shore. His eyes were always
tearful; he wept sweet life away, in longing
to go back home, since she no longer pleased him.
He had no choice. He spent his nights with her
inside her hollow cave, not wanting her   155
though she still wanted him. By day he sat
out on the rocky beach, in tears and grief,
staring in heartbreak at the fruitless sea.

The goddess stood by him and said, "Poor man!
Stop grieving, please. You need not waste your life.   160

---

3. Orion was a human hunter with whom Dawn
fell in love; the huntress goddess, Artemis, shot
and killed him.

4. Demeter, goddess of the harvest, fell in love
with Iasion (and in some versions had two sons
by him); Zeus killed him with a thunderbolt.

I am quite ready now to send you off.
Using your sword of bronze, cut trunks and build
a raft, fix decks across, and let it take you
across the misty sea. I will provide
water, red wine, and food, to stop you starving,   165
and I will give you clothes, and send a wind
to blow you safely home, if this is what
those sky gods want. They are more powerful
than me; they get their way."

                              Odysseus,
informed by many years of pain and loss,   170
shuddered and let his words fly out at her.
"Goddess, you have some other scheme in mind,
not my safe passage. You are telling me
to cross this vast and terrifying gulf,
in just a raft, when even stable schooners   175
sped on by winds from Zeus would not succeed?
No, goddess, I will not get on a raft,
unless you swear to me a mighty oath
you are not planning yet more pain for me."

At that, divine Calypso smiled at him.   180
She reached out and caressed him with her hand,
saying, "You scalawag! What you have said
shows that you understand how these things work.
But by this earth, and by the sky above,
and by the waters of the Styx[5] below,   185
which is the strongest oath for blessed gods,
I swear I will not plot more pain for you.
I have made plans for you as I would do
for my own self, if I were in your place.
I am not made of iron; no, my heart   190
is kind and decent, and I pity you."

And with those words, the goddess quickly turned
and led the way; he followed in her footsteps.
They reached the cave together, man and goddess.
The chair that Hermes had been sitting on   195
was empty now; Odysseus sat there.
The goddess gave him human food and drink.
She sat and faced godlike Odysseus
while slave girls brought her nectar and ambrosia.
They reached to take the good things set before them,   200
and satisfied their hunger and their thirst.

The goddess-queen began. "Odysseus,
son of Laertes, blessed by Zeus—your plans
are always changing. Do you really want
to go back to that home you love so much?   205

5. River of the underworld.

Well then, good-bye! But if you understood
how glutted you will be with suffering
before you reach your home, you would stay here
with me and be immortal—though you might
still wish to see that wife you always pine for.   210
And anyway, I know my body is
better than hers is. I am taller too.
Mortals can never rival the immortals
in beauty."

               So Odysseus, with tact,
said "Do not be enraged at me, great goddess.   215
You are quite right. I know my modest wife
Penelope could never match your beauty.
She is a human; you are deathless, ageless.
But even so, I want to go back home,
and every day I hope that day will come.   220
If some god strikes me on the wine-dark sea,
I will endure it. By now I am used
to suffering—I have gone through so much,
at sea and in the war. Let this come too."

The sun went down and brought the darkness on.   225
They went inside the hollow cave and took
the pleasure of their love, held close together.

When vernal Dawn first touched the sky with flowers,
they rose and dressed: Odysseus put on
his cloak and tunic, and Calypso wore   230
her fine long robe of silver. Round her waist
she wrapped a golden belt, and veiled her head.
Then she prepared the journey for the man.
She gave an axe that fitted in his grip,
its handle made of finest olive wood;   235
its huge bronze blade was sharp on either side.
She also gave a polished adze. She led him
out to the island's end, where tall trees grew:
black poplar, alder, fir that touched the sky,
good for a nimble boat of seasoned timber.   240
When she had shown him where the tall trees grew,
Calypso, queen of goddesses, went home.
Odysseus began and made good progress.
With his bronze axe he cut down twenty trunks,
polished them skillfully and planed them straight.   245
Calypso brought a gimlet and he drilled
through every plank and fitted them together,
fixing it firm with pegs and fastenings.
As wide as when a man who knows his trade
marks out the curving hull to fit a ship,   250
so wide Odysseus marked out his raft.
He notched the side decks to the close-set frame
and fixed long planks along the ribs to finish.

He set a mast inside, and joined to it
a yardarm and a rudder to steer straight.   255
He heaped the boat with brush, and caulked the sides
with wickerwork, to keep the water out.
Calypso brought him fabric for a sail,
and he constructed that with equal skill.
He fastened up the braces, clews and halyards,   260
and using levers, launched her on the sea.

The work had taken four days; on the fifth
Calypso let him go. She washed and dressed him
in clothes that smelled of incense. On the raft
she put a flask of wine, a bigger flask   265
of water, and a large supply of food.
She sent him off with gentle, lukewarm breezes.
Gladly Odysseus spread out his sails
to catch the wind; with skill he steered the rudder.
No sleep fell on his eyes; he watched the stars,   270
the Pleiades, late-setting Boötes,
and Bear, which people also call the Plow,
which circles in one place, and marks Orion—
the only star that has no share of Ocean.[6]
Calypso, queen of goddesses, had told him   275
to keep the Bear on his left side while sailing.
He sailed the sea for seven days and ten,
and on the eighteenth day, a murky mountain
of the Phaeacian land appeared—it rose
up like a shield beyond the misty sea.   280

Returning from the Ethiopians,
and pausing on Mount Solyma, Poseidon,
Master of Earthquakes, saw the distant raft.[7]
Enraged, he shook his head and told himself,

"This is outrageous! So it seems the gods   285
have changed their plans about Odysseus
while I was absent! He has almost reached
Phaeacia, where it is his destiny
to flee the rope of pain that binds him now.
But I will goad him to more misery,   290
till he is sick of it."

       He gathered up
the clouds, and seized his trident and stirred round
the sea and roused the gusts of every wind,
and covered earth and sea with fog. Night stretched
from heaven. Eurus, Notus, blasting Zephyr   295

6. The idea is that the Plow (Big Dipper) is the only constellation that stays above the horizon all year round. This is not true in astronomical fact; other constellations also remain visible year round.

7. The Solymi people, and the Solyma mountain, were in Lycia, in eastern Greece; the geography requires the god to have extremely good eyesight, since Odysseus is sailing in the west.

and Boreas,[8] the child of sky, all fell
and rolled a mighty wave. Odysseus
grew weak at knees. He cried out in despair,
"More pain? How will it end? I am afraid
the goddess spoke the truth: that I will have   300
a sea of sufferings before I reach
my homeland. It is coming true! Zeus whirls
the air. Look at those clouds! He agitates
the waves, as winds attack from all directions.
I can hold on to one thing: certain death.   305
Those Greeks were lucky, three and four times over,
who died upon the plain of Troy to help
the sons of Atreus. I wish I had
died that same day the mass of Trojans hurled
their bronze-tipped spears at me around the corpse   310
of Peleus' son.[9] I would have had
a funeral, and honor from the Greeks;
but now I have to die this cruel death!"

A wave crashed onto him, and overturned
the raft, and he fell out. The rudder slipped   315
out of his hands. The winds blew all directions
and one enormous gust snapped off the mast.
The sail and yardarm drifted out to sea.
Then for a long time rushing, crashing waves
kept him submerged: he could not reach the surface.   320
The clothes Calypso gave him weighed him down.
At last he rose and spat the sour saltwater
out of his mouth—it gushed forth in a torrent.
Despite his pain and weakness, he remembered
his raft, and lunged to get it through the waves;   325
he climbed on top of it and clung to life.
The great waves carried it this way and that.
As when the thistles, clumping close together,
are borne across the prairie by the North Wind,
so these winds swept the raft across the sea.   330
The South Wind hurls it, then the North Wind grabs it,
then East Wind yields and lets the West Wind drive it.
But stepping softly, Ino,[1] the White Goddess,
Cadmus' child, once human, human-voiced,
now honored with the gods in salty depths,   335
noticed that he was suffering and lost,
with pity. Like a gull with wings outstretched
she rose up from the sea, sat on the raft
and said,

      "Poor man! Why does enraged Poseidon
create an odyssey[2] of pain for you?   340

---

8. The four winds.
9. The reference is to Achilles.
1. Ino was a human girl transformed into a sea
nymph.

2. The original uses a verb that puns on Odysseus's name: *odysat'*, which means "he hated"
or "he was angry at."

But his hostility will not destroy you.
You seem intelligent. Do as I say.
Strip off your clothes and leave the raft behind
for winds to take away. With just your arms
swim to Phaeacia. Fate decrees that there   345
you will survive. Here, take my scarf and tie it
under your chest: with this immortal veil,
you need not be afraid of death or danger.
But when you reach dry earth, untie the scarf
and throw it out to sea, away from land,   350
and turn away." With that, the goddess gave it,
and plunged back down inside the surging sea,
just like a gull. The black wave covered her.

The hero who had suffered so much danger
was troubled and confused. He asked himself,   355
"Some deity has said to leave the raft.
But what if gods are weaving tricks again?
I will not trust her yet: with my own eyes
I saw the land she said I should escape to,
and it is far away. I will do this: 360
as long as these wood timbers hold together,
I will hang on, however hard it is.
But when the waves have smashed my raft to pieces,
then I will have no choice, and I will swim."

While he was thinking this, the Lord of Earthquakes,   365
Poseidon, roused a huge and dreadful wave
that arched above his head: he hurled it at him.
As when a fierce wind ruffles up a heap
of dry wheat chaff; it scatters here and there;
so were the raft's long timbers flung apart.   370
He climbed astride a plank and rode along
as if on horseback. He took off the clothes
Calypso gave him, but he tied the scarf
around his chest, and dove into the sea,
spreading his arms to swim. The Lord of Earthquakes   375
saw him and nodded, muttering, "At last
you are in pain! Go drift across the sea,
till you meet people blessed by Zeus, the Sky Lord.
But even then, I think you will not lack
for suffering." He spurred his fine-maned horses,   380
and went to Aegae, where he had his home.

Athena, child of Zeus, devised a plan.
She blocked the path of all the other winds,
told them to cease and made them go to sleep,
but roused swift Boreas and smoothed the waves   385
in front of him, so that Odysseus
could reach Phaeacia and escape from death.

Two days and nights he drifted on the waves:
each moment he expected he would die.

But when the Dawn with dazzling braids brought day   390
for the third time, the wind died down. No breeze,
but total calm. As he was lifted up
by an enormous wave, he scanned around,
and saw the shore nearby. As when a father
lies sick and weak for many days, tormented   395
by some cruel spirit, till at last the gods
restore him back to life; his children feel
great joy; Odysseus felt that same joy
when he saw land. He swam and longed to set
his feet on earth. But when he was in earshot,   400
he heard the boom of surf against the rocks.
The mighty waves were crashing on the shore,
a dreadful belching. Everything was covered
in salty foam. There were no sheltering harbors
for ships, just sheer crags, reefs and solid cliffs.   405
Odysseus' heart and legs gave way.
Shaken but purposeful, he told himself,

"Zeus went beyond my hopes and let me see
dry land! I made it, cutting the abyss!
But I see no way out from this gray sea.   410
There are steep cliffs offshore, and all around
the rushing water roars; the rock runs sheer;
the sea is deep near shore; there is no way
to set my feet on land without disaster.
If I attempt to scramble out, a wave   415
will seize and dash me on the jagged rock;
a useless effort. But if I swim on farther,
looking for bays or coves or slanting beaches,
storm winds may seize me once again and drag me,
howling with grief, towards the fish-filled sea.   420
A god may even send a great sea-monster,
the kind that famous Amphitrite[3] rears.
I know Poseidon wants to do me harm."

As he was thinking this, the waves grew big
and hurled him at the craggy shore. His skin   425
would have been ripped away, and his bones smashed,
had not Athena given him a thought.
He grabbed a rock as he was swept along
with both hands, and clung to it, groaning, till
the wave passed by. But then the swell rushed back,   430
and struck him hard and hurled him out to sea.
As when an octopus, dragged from its den,
has many pebbles sticking to its suckers,
so his strong hands were skinned against the rocks.
A mighty wave rolled over him again.   435
He would have died too soon, in misery,

---

3. Wife of Poseidon, representative of the sea; see also 3.91.

without the inspiration of Athena.
He came up from the wave that spewed to shore
and swam towards the land, in search of beaches
with gradual slopes, or inlets from the sea.   440
He swam until he reached a river's mouth
with gentle waters; that place seemed ideal,
smooth and not stony, sheltered from the wind.
He sensed its current; in his heart he prayed,

"Unknown god, hear me! How I longed for you!   445
I have escaped the salt sea and Poseidon.
Even the deathless gods respect a man
who is as lost as I am now. I have
gone through so much and reached your flowing streams.
Pity me, lord! I am your supplicant."   450

The current ceased; the River God restrained
the waves and made them calm. He brought him safe
into the river mouth. His legs cramped up;
the sea had broken him. His swollen body
gushed brine from mouth and nostrils. There he lay,   455
winded and silent, hardly fit to move.
A terrible exhaustion overcame him.
When he could breathe and think again, he took
the goddess' scarf off, and let it go
into the river flowing to the sea;   460
strong currents swept it down and Ino's hands
took it. He crawled on land and crouched beside
the reeds and bent to kiss life-giving earth,
and trembling, he spoke to his own heart.

"What now? What will become of me? If I   465
stay up all wretched night beside this river,
the cruel frost and gentle dew together
may finish me: my life is thin with weakness.
At dawn a cold breeze blows beside the river.
But if I climb the slope to those dark woods   470
and go to rest in that thick undergrowth,
letting sweet sleep take hold of me, and losing
my cold and weariness—wild beasts may find me
and treat me as their prey."

         But he decided
to go into the woods. He found a place   475
beside a clearing, near the water's edge.
He crawled beneath two bushes grown together,
of thorn and olive.[4] No strong wet wind could blow
through them, no shining sunbeam ever strike them,

---

4. The first bush is either wild olive or fig or
evergreen thorn. The olive wood is significant
in that it is Athena's tree: the goddess is still
watching over her favorite.

no rain could penetrate them; they were growing   480
so thickly intertwined. Odysseus
crept under, and he scraped a bed together,
of leaves: there were enough to cover two
against the worst of winter. Seeing this,
the hero who had suffered for so long   485
was happy. He lay down inside and heaped
more leaves on top. As when a man who lives
out on a lonely farm that has no neighbors
buries a glowing torch inside black embers
to save the seed of fire and keep a source—   490
so was Odysseus concealed in leaves.
Athena poured down sleep to shut his eyes
so all his painful weariness could end.

BOOK 6

[A Princess and Her Laundry]

Odysseus had suffered. In exhaustion
from all his long ordeals, the hero slept.
Meanwhile, Athena went to the Phaeacians.
This people used to live in Hyperia,
a land of dancing. But their mighty neighbors,   5
the Cyclopes, kept looting them, and they
could not hold out. Their king, Nausithous,
brought them to Scheria, a distant place,
and built a wall around the town, and homes,
and temples to the gods, and plots of land.   10
He went to Hades. Then Alcinous,
who has god-given wisdom, came to power.
Bright-eyed Athena traveled to his palace,
to help Odysseus' journey home.
She went inside the decorated bedroom   15
where the young princess, Nausicaa, was sleeping,
as lovely as a goddess. Slaves were sleeping
outside her doorway, one on either side;
two charming girls with all the Graces' gifts.
The shining doors were shut, but like the wind   20
the goddess reached the bed of Nausicaa,
disguised as her best friend, a girl her age,
the daughter of the famous sailor Dymas.
Sharp-eyed Athena said,

                    "Oh, Nausicaa!
So lazy! But your mother should have taught you!   25
Your clothes are lying there in dirty heaps,
though you will soon be married, and you need
a pretty dress to wear, and clothes to give
to all your bridesmaids. That impresses people,
and makes the parents happy. When day comes,   30

we have to do the laundry. I will come
and help you, so the work will soon be done.
Surely you will not long remain unmarried.
The best young men here in your native land
already want to court you. So at dawn   35
go ask your father for the cart with mules,
to carry dresses, scarves, and sheets. You should
ride there, not walk; the washing pools are far
from town."

       The goddess looked into her eyes,
then went back to Olympus, which they say   40
is where the gods will have their home forever.
The place is never shaken by the wind,
or wet with rain or blanketed by snow.
A cloudless sky is spread above the mountain,
white radiance all round. The blessed gods   45
live there in happiness forevermore.

Then Dawn came from her lovely throne, and woke
the girl. She was amazed, remembering
her dream, and in a fine dress, went to tell
her parents, whom she found inside the hall.   50
Her mother sat beside the hearth and spun
sea-purpled yarn, her house girls all around her.
Her father was just heading out to council
with his renowned advisors, since his people
had called him to a meeting. She stood near him   55
and said,

       "Dear Daddy, please would you set up
the wagon with the big smooth wheels for me,
so I can take my fine clothes to the river
to wash them? They are dirty. And you too
should wear clean clothes for meeting your advisors,   60
dressed in your best to make important plans.
Your five sons also—two of whom are married,
but three are strapping single men—they always
want to wear nice fresh-laundered clothes when they
are going dancing. This is on my mind."   65

She said this since she felt too shy to talk
of marriage to her father. But he knew,
and answered, "Child, I would not grudge the mules
or anything you want. Go on! The slaves
can fit the wagon with its cargo rack."   70

He called the household slaves, and they obeyed.
They made the wagon ready and inspected
its wheels, led up the mules, and yoked them to it.
The girl brought out the multicolored clothes,

and put them on the cart, while in a basket   75
her mother packed nutritious food for her—
a varied meal, with olives, cheese, and wine,
stored in a goatskin. Then the girl got in.
Her mother handed her a golden flask
of oil, to use when she had had her bath.   80
Then Nausicaa took up the whip and reins,
and cracked the whip. The mules were on their way,
eager to go and rattling the harness,
bringing the clothes and girl and all her slaves.
They reached the lovely river where the pools   85
are always full—the water flows in streams
and bubbles up from underneath, to wash
even the dirtiest of laundry. There
they freed the mules and drove them to the river
to graze on honeyed grass beside the stream.   90
The girls brought out the laundry from the cart,
and brought it to the washing pools and trod it,
competing with each other. When the dirt
was gone, they spread the clothes along the shore,
where salt sea washes pebbles to the beach.   95
They bathed and rubbed themselves with olive oil.
Then they sat on the riverbank and ate,
and waited for the sun to dry the clothes.
But when they finished eating, they took off
their head-scarves to play ball. The white-armed princess   100
led them in play—like Artemis the archer,
running across the heights of Taygetus
and Erymanthus; she is glad to run
with boars and fleet-foot deer. The rustic daughters
of Zeus the Aegis King play round about her,   105
while Leto is delighted in her heart,
seeing her daughter far above the rest,
though all are beautiful. So Nausicaa
stood out above them all. But when the girl
was thinking she should head for home and yoke   110
the mules, and pack the laundry up again,
Athena's eyes flashed bright. Odysseus
must wake up, see the pretty girl, and have
an escort to the town of the Phaeacians.
The princess threw the ball towards a slave girl,   115
who missed the catch. It fell down in an eddy;
the girls all started screaming, very loudly.
Odysseus woke up, and thought things over.

"What is this country I have come to now?
Are all the people wild and violent,   120
or good, hospitable, and god-fearing?
I heard the sound of female voices. Is it
nymphs, who frequent the craggy mountaintops,
and river streams and meadows lush with grass?

Or could this noise I hear be human voices?   125
I have to try to find out who they are."

Odysseus jumped up from out the bushes.
Grasping a leafy branch he broke it off
to cover up his manly private parts.
Just as a mountain lion trusts its strength,   130
and beaten by the rain and wind, its eyes
burn bright as it attacks the cows or sheep,
or wild deer, and hunger drives it on
to try the sturdy pens of sheep—so need
impelled Odysseus to come upon   135
the girls with pretty hair, though he was naked.
All caked with salt, he looked a dreadful sight.
They ran along the shore quite terrified,
some here, some there. But Nausicaa stayed still.
Athena made her legs stop trembling   140
and gave her courage in her heart. She stood there.
He wondered, should he touch her knees, or keep
some distance and use charming words, to beg
the pretty girl to show him to the town,
and give him clothes. At last he thought it best   145
to keep some distance and use words to beg her.
The girl might be alarmed at being touched.
His words were calculated flattery.

"My lady, please! Are you divine or human?
If you are some great goddess from the sky,   150
you look like Zeus' daughter Artemis—
you are as tall and beautiful as she.
But if you live on earth and are a human,
your mother and your father must be lucky,
your brothers also—lucky three times over.   155
Their hearts must be delighted, seeing you,
their flourishing new sprout, the dancers' leader.
And that man will be luckiest by far,
who takes you home with dowry, as his bride.
I have seen no one like you. Never, no one.   160
My eyes are dazzled when I look at you.
I traveled once to Delos, on my way
to war and suffering; my troops marched with me.
Beside Apollo's altar sprang a sapling,
a fresh young palm. I gazed at it and marveled.   165
I never saw so magical a tree.
My lady, you transfix me that same way.
I am in awe of you, afraid to touch
your knees. But I am desperate. I came from
Ogygia, and for twenty days storm winds   170
and waves were driving me, adrift until
yesterday some god washed me up right here,
perhaps to meet more suffering. I think

my troubles will not end until the gods
have done their all. My lady, pity me. 175
Battered and wrecked, I come to you, you first—
and I know no one else in this whole country.
Show me the town, give me some rags to wear,
if you brought any clothes when you came here.
So may the gods grant all your heart's desires, 180
a home and husband, somebody like-minded.
For nothing could be better than when two
live in one house, their minds in harmony,
husband and wife. Their enemies are jealous,
their friends delighted, and they have great honor." 185

Then white-armed Nausicaa replied, "Well, stranger,
you seem a brave and clever man; you know
that Zeus apportions happiness to people,
to good and bad, each one as he decides.
Your troubles come from him, and you must bear them. 190
But since you have arrived here in our land,
you will not lack for clothes or anything
a person needs in times of desperation.
I will show you the town. The people here
are called Phaeacians, and I am the daughter 195
of the great King Alcinous, on whom
depends the strength and power of our people."

And then she called her slaves with braided hair.
"Wait, girls! Why are you running from this man?
Do you believe he is an enemy? 200
No living person ever born would come
to our Phaeacia with a hostile mind,
since we are much beloved by the gods.
Our island is remote, washed round by sea;
we have no human contact. But this man 205
is lost, poor thing. We must look after him.
All foreigners and beggars come from Zeus,
and any act of kindness is a blessing.
So give the stranger food and drink, and wash him
down in the river, sheltered from the wind." 210
They stopped, and egged each other on to take
Odysseus to shelter, as the princess,
the daughter of Alcinous, had told them.
They gave him clothes, a tunic and a cloak,
the olive oil in the golden flask, 215
and led him down to wash beside the river.
Odysseus politely said,

                              "Now, girls,
wait at a distance here, so I can wash
my grimy back, and rub myself with oil—
it has been quite a while since I have done it. 220

Please let me wash in private. I am shy
of being naked with you—pretty girls
with lovely hair."

          So they withdrew, and told
their mistress. Then he used the river water
to scrub the brine off from his back and shoulders,   225
and wash the crusty sea salt from his hair.
But when he was all clean and richly oiled,
dressed in the clothes the young unmarried girl
had given him, Athena made him look
bigger and sturdier, and made his hair   230
grow curling tendrils like a hyacinth.
As when Athena and Hephaestus teach
a knowledgeable craftsman every art,
and he pours gold on silver, making objects
more beautiful—just so Athena poured   235
attractiveness across his head and shoulders.
Then he went off and sat beside the sea;
his handsomeness was dazzling. The girl
was shocked. She told her slaves with tidy hair,
"Now listen to me, girls! The gods who live   240
on Mount Olympus must have wished this man
to come in contact with my godlike people.
Before, he looked so poor and unrefined;
now he is like a god that lives in heaven.
I hope I get a man like this as husband,   245
a man that lives here and would like to stay.
But, girls, now give the stranger food and drink!"

She gave her orders and the girls obeyed—
they gave Odysseus some food and drink.
He wolfed the food and drank. He was half starved;   250
it had been ages since he tasted food.
Then white-armed Nausicaa had formed a plan.
Folding the clothes, she packed them in the wagon,
and yoked the mules, and then she climbed inside.
She gave Odysseus some clear instructions.   255

"Stranger, get ready; you must go to town,
and I will have you meet the best of all
our people. You seem smart; do as I say.
While we are passing through the fields and farmlands,
you have to follow quickly with the girls   260
behind the mules, and let me lead the way.
Then we will reach the lofty city wall,
which has a scenic port on either side,
and one slim gate, where curved ships are drawn up
along the road: a special spot for each.   265
The meeting place surrounds Poseidon's shrine,
fitted with heavy stones set deep in earth.

And there the workers make the ships' equipment—
cables and sails—and there they plane the oars.
Phaeacians do not care for archery;   270
their passion is for sails and oars and ships,
on which they love to cross the dark-gray ocean.
The people in the town are proud; I worry
that they may speak against me. Someone rude
may say, 'Who is that big strong man with her?   275
Where did she find that stranger? Will he be
her husband? She has got him from a ship,
a foreigner, since no one lives near here,
or else a god, the answer to her prayers,
descended from the sky to hold her tight.   280
Better if she has found herself a man
from elsewhere, since she scorns the people here,
although she has so many noble suitors.'
So they will shame me. I myself would blame
a girl who got too intimate with men   285
before her marriage, and who went against
her loving parents' rules. But listen, stranger,
I will explain the quickest way to gain
my father's help to make your way back home.
Beside the road there is a grove of poplars;   290
it has a fountain, and a meadow round it.
It is Athena's place, where Father has
his orchard and estate,[5] as far from town
as human voice can carry. Sit down there
and wait until I reach my father's house   295
in town. But when you think I have arrived,
walk on and ask directions for the palace
of King Alcinous, my mighty father.
It will be very easy finding it;
a tiny child could guide you there. It is   300
unlike the other houses in Phaeacia.
Go through the courtyard, in the house and on
straight to the Great Hall. You will find my mother
sitting beside the hearth by firelight,
and spinning her amazing purple wool.   305
She leans against a pillar, slaves behind her.
My father has a throne right next to hers;
he sits and sips his wine, just like a god.
But pass him by, embrace my mother's knees
to supplicate. If you do this, you quickly   310
will reach your home, however far it is,
in happiness. If she is good to you,
and looks upon you kindly in her heart,
you can be sure of getting to your house,
back to your family and native land."   315

---

5. The "estate," *temenos*, is land set apart for a king or a temple precinct.

With that, she used her shining whip to urge
the mules to go. They left the river streams,
and trotted well and clipped their hooves along.
She drove an easy pace to let her slaves
and great Odysseus keep up on foot.   320
The sun was setting when they reached the grove,
the famous sanctuary of Athena.
Odysseus sat in it, and at once
he prayed to mighty Zeus' daughter.

                                        "Hear me,
daughter of Zeus! Unvanquished Queen! If ever,   325
when that earth-shaker god was wrecking me,
you helped me—may they pity me and give me
kind welcome in Phaeacia." And Athena
heard him but did not yet appear to him,
respecting her own uncle[6] in his fury   330
against Odysseus till he reached home.

BOOK 7

[A Magical Kingdom]

Odysseus sat patiently and prayed.
Meanwhile, the fine strong mules conveyed the girl
to town; she reached her father's palace gate.
Her brothers gathered round her like immortals.
They took the harness off the mules and brought   5
the clothes inside. She went to her own room.
Eurymedusa, her old slave, had lit
a fire for her. This woman had been brought
from Apeire by ship, long years before.
The people chose to give her to the king,   10
because they bowed before him like a god.
She used to babysit young Nausicaa,
and now she lit her fire and cooked her meal.

Odysseus walked briskly to the town.
Athena helpfully surrounded him   15
with mist that kept him safe from rude remarks
from people who might ask him who he was.
When he had almost reached the lovely city,
bright-eyed Athena met him, like a girl,
young and unmarried, with a water pitcher.   20
She stopped in front of him. Odysseus
said,

"Child, would you escort me to the house
of King Alcinous, who rules this land?
I have been through hard times. I traveled here

6. Poseidon.

from far away; I am a foreigner,   25
and I know no one who lives here in town
or anywhere round here."

                         With twinkling eyes
the goddess answered, "Mr. Foreigner,
I will take you to where you want to go.
The king lives near my father's home. But you   30
must walk in silence. Do not look at people,
and ask no questions. People here are not
too keen on strangers coming from abroad,
although they like to cross the sea themselves.
They know their ships go very fast. Poseidon   35
gave them this gift. Their boats can fly like wings,
or quick as thoughts."

                     The goddess led him there.
He followed closely in her skipping steps.
The seafaring Phaeacians did not see him
as he passed through the town, since that great goddess,   40
pigtailed Athena, in her care for him
made him invisible with magic mist.
He was amazed to see the ships and harbors
and meeting places of the noblemen,
and high walls set with stakes on top—a wonder!   45
They reached the splendid palace of the king.
Divine Athena winked at him and said,
"Here, Mr. Foreigner, this is the house
you wanted me to take you to. You will
find them, the king and queen, inside at dinner.   50
Do not be scared; go in. The brave succeed
in all adventures, even those who come
from countries far away. First greet the queen.
Arete is her name.[7] The king and queen
have common ancestry—Nausithous.   55
Eurymedon was long ago the king
over the Giants, who were proud and bad.
He killed them, his own people, and then he
got killed as well. His youngest daughter was
named Periboea. She was very pretty.   60
Poseidon slept with her. She had a child,
Nausithous, and he became the king
here in Phaeacia, and he had two sons,
our King Alcinous, and Rhexenor.
Apollo shot that Rhexenor when he   65
was newly married, with no son. He left
a daughter, our Arete, and her uncle,
Alcinous, made her his wife. No woman
is honored as he honors her. She is

7. The name suggests "Prayed for" or "Wanted."

precious to him, her children, and the people. 70
We look at her as if she were a goddess,
and point her out when she walks through our town.
She is extremely clever and perceptive;
she solves disputes to help the men she likes.
If she looks on you kindly in her heart, 75
you have a chance of seeing those you love,
and getting back again to your big house
and homeland."

    So bright-eyed Athena left him.
She went from lovely Scheria, across
the tireless sea, to Marathon and Athens, 80
and went inside Erechtheus' palace.[8]

Odysseus approached the royal house,
and stood there by the threshold made of bronze.
His heart was mulling over many things.
The palace of the mighty king was high, 85
and shone like rays of sunlight or of moonlight.
The walls were bronze all over, from the entrance
back to the bedrooms, and along them ran
a frieze of blue. Gold doors held safe the house.
Pillars of silver rose up from the threshold, 90
the lintel silver, and the handle, gold.
Silver and golden dogs stood at each side,
made by Hephaestus[9] with great artistry,
to guard the home of brave Alcinous—
immortal dogs, unaging for all time. 95
At intervals were seats set in the walls,
right from the doorway to the inner rooms,
with soft embroidered throws, the work of women.
Phaeacian lords and ladies sat upon them,
eating and drinking, since they lacked for nothing. 100
Boys made of gold were set on pedestals,
and they held burning torches in their hands,
lighting the hall at night for those at dinner.
The king had fifty slave girls in his house;
some ground the yellow grain upon the millstone, 105
others wove cloth and sat there spinning yarn,
with fingers quick as rustling poplar leaves,
and oil was dripping from the woven fabric.[1]
Just as Phaeacian men have special talent
for launching ships to sea, the women there 110
are expert weavers, since Athena gave them
fine minds and skill to make most lovely things.
Outside the courtyard by the doors there grows

---

8. Erechtheus was a legendary king of Athens.
9. God of fire and metalworking.
1. The oil may be from the fabric itself if it is
wool, or perhaps the women are applying olive
oil to the material to make the weaving easier.

an orchard of four acres, hedged around.
The trees are tall, luxuriant with fruit: 115
bright-colored apples, pears and pomegranate,
sweet figs and fertile olives, and the crop
never runs out or withers in the winter,
nor in the summer. Fruit grows all year round.
The West Wind always blows and makes it swell   120
and ripen: mellowing pear on mellowing pear,
apple on apple, grapes on grapes, and figs.
A fertile vineyard too is planted there.
They use the warmer side, a flattened slope,
for drying grapes in sunshine. They pick bunches   125
and trample them, while unripe clusters open
and shed their blooms, and others turn to purple.
There are two springs: one flows all through the garden,
the other gushes from the courtyard threshold,
towards the palace, and the people draw   130
freshwater. So the gods had blessed the house
of King Alcinous with lovely gifts.
Hardened, long-suffering Odysseus
stood there and stared, astonished in his heart,
then quickly strode across the palace threshold.   135
He found the lordly leaders of Phaeacia
pouring drink offerings for sharp-eyed Hermes,
to whom they give libations before bed.
Odysseus went in the house disguised
in mist with which Athena covered him,   140
until he reached Arete and the king.
He threw his arms around Arete's knees,
and all at once, the magic mist dispersed.
They were astonished when they saw the man,
and all fell silent. Then Odysseus   145
said,

    "Queen Arete, child of Rhexenor,
I have had many years of pain and loss.
I beg you, and your husband, and these men
who feast here—may the gods bless you in life,
and may you leave your children wealth and honor.   150
Now help me, please, to get back home, and quickly!
I miss my family. I have been gone
so long it hurts."

          He sat down by the hearth
among the ashes of the fire. They all
were silent till Echeneus spoke up.   155
He was an elder statesman of Phaeacia,
a skillful orator and learned man.
Wanting to help, he said,

"Alcinous,
you know it is not right to leave a stranger
sitting there on the floor beside the hearth   160
among the cinders. Everyone is waiting
for you to give the word. Make him get up,
and seat him on a silver chair, and order
wine to be poured, so we may make libations
to Zeus the Thunderlord, who loves the needy.   165
The house girl ought to bring the stranger food
out from the storeroom."

                    So Alcinous
reached for Odysseus' hand, and raised
the many-minded hero from the ashes.
He made Laodamas, his favorite son,   170
vacate his chair so he could sit beside him.
The slave girl brought him water in a pitcher
of gold to wash his hands, and poured it out
over a silver bowl, and fetched a table
of polished wood; a humble slave brought out   175
bread and an ample plateful of the meat.
Half-starved and weak, the hero ate and drank.
Majestic King Alcinous addressed
Pontonous, the wine boy.

                    "Go and mix
a bowl and serve the wine to all our guests,   180
so we may offer drink to thundering Zeus
who blesses those in need." The boy mixed up
the sweet, delicious wine, and filled the cups
for everyone, with first pour for the gods.
They made the offerings and drank as much   185
as they desired, and then Alcinous
said,

                    "Listen, lords. Hear what my heart commands.
The feast is over; go home, go to bed.
At dawn, we will call more of our best men,
and host the stranger in our halls, and offer   190
fine sacrifices to the gods, then plan
how we may help his journey, so our guest
may travel quickly, without pain or trouble,
encountering no trouble on the way,
however far away it is, until   195
he reaches home. Once there, he must endure
whatever was spun out when he was born
by Fate and by the heavy ones, the Spinners.²
But if he is immortal, come from heaven,

2. The Spinners are imagined in Greek mythology as three old female figures who construct
the thread of human destiny—associated here
with Fate, the "share" allotted to humans in life.

the gods have changed their ways, since in the past 200
they used to show themselves to us directly
whenever we would give them hecatombs.
They sit and eat among us. Even if
just one of us meets them alone, out walking,
they do not hide from us; we are close friends, 205
as are the Giants and Cyclopic peoples."

Odysseus, with careful calculation,
said,

    "No, Alcinous, please think again.
I am not like the deathless gods in heaven.
My height is normal. I look like a human. 210
In pain I am a match for any man,
whoever you may know that suffers most.
I could tell many stories of the dangers
that I have suffered through; gods willed it so.
But let me have my meal, despite my grief. 215
The belly is just like a whining dog:
it begs and forces one to notice it,
despite exhaustion or the depths of sorrow.
My heart is full of sorrow, but my stomach
is always telling me to eat and drink. 220
It tells me to forget what I have suffered,
and fill it up. At dawn tomorrow, help me
to reach my homeland, after all this pain.
May I live out my final days in sight
of my own property and slaves and home." 225

They all agreed the stranger's words made sense,
and that he should be sent back home. They poured
drink offerings to the gods, and drank as much
as they desired, then all went home to bed.
Odysseus was left there in the hall, 230
sitting beside Arete and the godlike
Alcinous. The dishes from the feast
were cleaned up by the slaves. White-armed Arete
had noticed his fine clothes, the cloak and shirt
she wove herself, with help from her slave girls. 235
Her words flew out to him as if on wings.

"Stranger, let me be first to speak to you.
Where are you from? And who gave you those clothes?
I thought you said you drifted here by sea?"

Planning his words with careful skill, he answered, 240
"It would be difficult, Your Majesty,
to tell it all; the gods have given me
so many troubles. I will tell you this.
There is an island, far out in the sea,

Ogygia, where the child of Atlas lives,   245
the mighty goddess with smooth braids, the crafty
Calypso, friend to neither gods nor mortals.
A spirit brought me to her hearth, alone,
when Zeus scooped up my ship and with bright lightning
split it apart across the wine-dark sea.   250
All of my comrades, my brave friends, were killed.
I wrapped my arms around the keel and floated
for ten days. On the tenth black night, the gods
carried me till I reached Ogygia,
home of the beautiful and mighty goddess   255
Calypso. Lovingly she cared for me,
vowing to set me free from death and time
forever. But she never swayed my heart.
I stayed for seven years; she gave me clothes
like those of gods, but they were always wet   260
with tears. At last the eighth year rolled around,
and word came down from Zeus that I must go,
and finally her mind was changed. She sent me
upon a well-bound wooden raft, equipped
with food, sweet wine, and clothes as if for gods,   265
and sent a fair warm wind. I sailed the sea
for seventeen long days; on day eighteen,
the murky mountains of your land appeared,
and I was overjoyed, but more bad luck
was hurled at me. Poseidon roused the winds   270
to block me, and he stirred the sea. I sobbed,
and clung there, going nowhere, till my raft
was smashed to pieces by the massive storm.
But I swam through this gulf of water till
the current brought me here. If I had tried   275
to land at once, I would have been swept back
against the crags. I swam a way away,
until I reached a river mouth, which seemed
a perfect spot for landing: it was sheltered
from wind, and smooth, quite free from rocks. So there   280
I flopped and tried to gather up my strength
until the holy nightfall. Then I crawled
out of the rain-fed river to the bank,
and hid inside the bushes, and I heaped
some leaves to cover me. Some god poured down   285
deep sleep. With heavy heart I slept all night
and through the dawn to noon, beneath the leaves.
Then in the afternoon, when sleep released me,
I woke, and saw girls playing on the beach—
your daughter, like a goddess, and her slaves.   290
I prayed to her. One would not think a girl
as young as her would have so much good sense;
young people are not usually so thoughtful.
She was so kind to me; she gave me food
and wine, and had them wash me in the river,   295

and let me have these clothes. Now I have told you
the truth, no matter what."

       Alcinous
said, "Just one of these things my daughter did
was not correct: she should have brought you here
to us herself, escorted by her slave girls,   300
since you had supplicated first to her."

With careful tact Odysseus replied,
"Your daughter is quite wonderful, great king.
Please do not blame her. She told me to come
here with her slaves, but I was too embarrassed,   305
and nervous. I thought you might get annoyed
at seeing me. We humans on this earth
are apt to be suspicious."

       And the king
replied, "My heart is not the type to feel
anger for no good reason. Moderation   310
is always best. Athena, Zeus, Apollo,
what a congenial man you are! I wish
you would stay here, and marry my own daughter,
and be my son. I would give you a home
and wealth if you would like to stay. If not,   315
we will not keep you here against your will.
May Zeus not have it so! As for your journey,
I give my word that you can go tomorrow.
Lying down, lulled to sleep, you will be rowed
across the peaceful sea until you reach   320
your land and home, or anywhere you want,
even beyond Euboea, which our people
saw when they carried fair-haired Rhadamanthus
to visit Tityus, the son of Gaia.[3]
It is supposed to be the farthest shore   325
on earth, but they were there and back that day,
not even tired. That shows just how fine
my ships are, and my men who stir the sea
with oars."

     At that Odysseus, who had
endured so much, was happy, and he prayed,   330

"O Father Zeus, may everything come true,
just as Alcinous has said. So may
his fame burn bright forever on the earth,
and may I reach my home."

---

3. Rhadamanthus is the mythical son of Zeus and Europa, closely associated with Crete. The story of his visit to Tityus is entirely unknown beyond this passage.

Then at these words,
white-armed Arete called to her attendants   335
to put a bed out on the porch and lay
fine purple blankets on it and to spread
covers and woolly quilts across the top.
With torches in their hands they bustled out.
They made the bed up neatly, very fast,   340
then came and called Odysseus.

                "Now guest,
get up and come outside, your bed is ready."

Odysseus was glad to go to sleep
after his long adventures, on that bed
surrounded by the rustling of the porch.   345
Alcinous was sleeping in his room,
beside his wife, who made their bed and shared it.

BOOK 8

[*The Songs of a Poet*]

Soon Dawn appeared and touched the sky with roses.
Majestic, holy King Alcinous
leapt out of bed, as did Odysseus,
the city-sacker. Then the blessed king,
mighty Alcinous, led out his guest   5
to the Phaeacian council by the ships.
They sat there side by side on polished stones.
Meanwhile, Athena walked all through the town,
appearing like the royal messenger.
To help Odysseus' journey home,   10
she stood beside each man in turn and said,

"My lord, come to the meeting place, to learn
about the visitor to our king's home.
Despite his wanderings by sea, he looks
like an immortal god."

                So she roused up   15
the hearts and minds of each, and soon the seats
of council were filled up; the men assembled.
Seeing Laertes' clever son, the crowd
marveled. Athena poured unearthly charm
upon his head and shoulders, and she made him   20
taller and sturdier, so these Phaeacians
would welcome and respect him, when he managed
the many trials of skill that they would set
to test him. When the people were assembled,
Alcinous addressed them.

"Hear me, leaders   25
and chieftains of Phaeacia. I will tell you
the promptings of my heart. This foreigner—
I do not know his name—came wandering
from west or east and showed up at my house.
He begs and prays for help to travel on.   30
Let us assist him, as we have before
with other guests: no visitor has ever
been forced to linger in my house. We always
give them safe passage home. Now let us launch
a ship for her maiden voyage on the water,   35
and choose a crew of fifty-two, the men
selected as the best, and lash the oars
beside the benches. Then return to shore,
and come to my house. Let the young men hurry
to cook a feast. I will provide supplies,   40
plenty for everyone. And I invite
you also, lords, to welcome him with me.
Do not refuse! We also must invite
Demodocus, the poet. Gods inspire him,
so any song he chooses to perform   45
is wonderful to hear."

     He led the way.
The lords went with him, and the house boy fetched
the bard. The fifty-two select young men
went to the shore, just as the king commanded.
They reached the restless salty sea, and launched   50
the black ship on the depths, set up the mast
and sails, and fastened in the oars, by tying
each to its leather thole-strap,[4] all in order.
They spread the white sails wide, and moored the ship
out in the water. Then the men walked up   55
towards the mighty palace of the king.
The halls and porticoes were thronged with people,
both old and young. To feed his many guests
Alcinous killed twelve sheep, and eight boars
with silver tusks, and two slow-lumbering cows.   60
Skinning the animals, they cooked a feast.
The house boy brought the poet, whom the Muse
adored. She gave him two gifts, good and bad:
she took his sight away, but gave sweet song.
The wine boy brought a silver-studded chair   65
and propped it by a pillar, in the middle
of all the guests, and by a peg he hung
the poet's lyre above his head and helped him
to reach it, and he set a table by him,
and a bread basket and a cup of wine   70
to drink whenever he desired. They all

---

4. Tholes are pins set in the side of a boat to keep the oar in place.

took food. When they were satisfied, the Muse
prompted the bard to sing of famous actions,
an episode whose fame has touched the sky:
Achilles' and Odysseus' quarrel—   75
how at a splendid sacrificial feast,
they argued bitterly, and Agamemnon
was glad because the best of the Achaeans
were quarreling, since when he had consulted
the oracle at Pytho, crossing over   80
the entry stone, Apollo had foretold
that this would be the start of suffering
for Greeks and Trojans, through the plans of Zeus.[5]
So sang the famous bard. Odysseus
with his strong hands picked up his heavy cloak   85
of purple, and he covered up his face.
He was ashamed to let them see him cry.
Each time the singer paused, Odysseus
wiped tears, drew down the cloak and poured a splash
of wine out of his goblet, for the gods.   90
But each time, the Phaeacian nobles urged
the bard to sing again—they loved his songs.
So he would start again; Odysseus
would moan and hide his head beneath his cloak.
Only Alcinous could see his tears,   95
since he was sitting next to him, and heard
his sobbing. So he quickly spoke.

                              "My lords!
We have already satisfied our wish
for feasting, and the lyre, the feast's companion.
Now let us go outside and set up contests   100
in every sport, so when our guest goes home
he can tell all his friends we are the best
at boxing, wrestling, high-jumping, and sprinting."

With that he led the way; the others followed.
The boy took down the lyre from its peg   105
and took Demodocus' hand to lead him
out with the crowd who went to watch the games.
Many young athletes stood there: Acroneüs,
Ocyalus, Elatreus, Nauteus,
Thoön, Anchialus, Eretmeus,   110
Anabesineus and Ponteus,
Prymneus, Proreus, Amphialus,
the son of Polynaus, son of Tecton,[6]
and Naubolus' son, Euryalus,
like Ares, cause of ruin. In his looks   115

5. Apparently the Delphic oracle ("Pytho") told Agamemnon that Troy would be destroyed when the "best of the Achaeans" were quarrel-ing.

6. These names are all invented to suggest the Phaeacians' skill in seafaring.

and strength, he was the best in all Phaeacia,
after Laodamas. Three sons of great
Alcinous stood up: Laodamas,
godlike Clytoneus, and Halius.
First came the footrace. They lined up, then dashed   120
all in an instant, right around the track
so fast they raised the dust up from the field.
Clytoneus was the best by far at sprinting:
he raced past all the others by the length
of a field plowed by mules,[7] and reached the crowd.   125
Next came the brutal sport of wrestling,
in which Euryalus was best. In jumping,
Amphialus excelled. And at the discus,
by far the best of all was Elatreus.
The prince Laodamas excelled at boxing.   130
They all enjoyed the games. When they were over,
Laodamas, Alcinous' son,
said,

    "Now my friends, we ought to ask the stranger
if he plays any sports. His build is strong;
his legs and arms and neck are very sturdy,   135
and he is in his prime, though he has been
broken by suffering. No pain can shake
a man as badly as the sea, however
strong he once was."

        Euryalus replied,
"You are quite right, Laodamas. Why not   140
call out to challenge him yourself?"

               The noble
son of Alcinous agreed with him.
He stood up in the middle of them all
and called Odysseus.

        "Come here!" he said.
"Now you, sir! You should try our games as well,   145
if you know any sports; it seems you would.
Nothing can be more glorious for a man,
in a whole lifetime, than what he achieves
with hands and feet. So try, set care aside.
Soon you will travel, since your ship is launched.   150
The crew is standing by."

            Odysseus
thought carefully—he had a plan. He answered,

---

7. The length of land that could be plowed in a day was a standard unit of measurement. The distance imagined here is probably about 200 feet (an unlikely margin for a race).

"Laodamas, why mock me with this challenge?
My heart is set on sorrow, not on games,
since I have suffered and endured so much   155
that now I only want to get back home.
I sit here praying to your king and people
to grant my wish."

         Euryalus responded
with outright taunting.

         "Stranger, I suppose
you must be ignorant of all athletics.   160
I know your type. The captain of a crew
of merchant sailors, you roam round at sea
and only care about your freight and cargo,
keeping close watch on your ill-gotten gains.
You are no athlete."

         With a scowl, he answered,   165
"What crazy arrogance from you, you stranger!
The gods do not bless everyone the same,
with equal gifts of body, mind, or speech.
One man is weak, but gods may crown his words
with loveliness. Men gladly look to him;   170
his speech is steady, with calm dignity.
He stands out from his audience, and when
he walks through town, the people look at him
as if he were a god. Another man
has godlike looks but no grace in his words.   175
Like you—you look impressive, and a god
could not improve your body. But your mind
is crippled. You have stirred my heart to anger
with these outrageous comments. I am not
lacking experience of sports and games.   180
When I was young, I trusted my strong arms
and was among the first. Now pain has crushed me.
I have endured the agonies of war,
and struggled through the dangers of the sea.
But you have challenged me and stung my heart.   185
Despite my suffering, I will compete."

With that he leapt up, cloak and all, and seized
a massive discus, heavier than that
used by the others. He spun around, drew back
his arm and from his brawny hand he hurled.   190
The stone went humming. The Phaeacians, known
for rowing, ducked down cowering beneath
its arc; it flew beyond the other pegs.
Athena marked the spot. In human guise
she spoke.

"A blind man, stranger, could discern   195
this mark by groping. It is far ahead
of all the others. You can celebrate!
You won this round, and none of them will ever
throw further—or as far!"

                Odysseus
was thrilled to realize he had a friend   200
to take his side, and with a lighter heart,
he told the young Phaeacians,

                     "Try to match this!
If you can do it, I will throw another,
as far or farther. You have made me angry,
so I will take you on in any sport.   205
Come on! In boxing, wrestling, or sprinting,
I will compete with anyone, except
Laodamas: he is my host. Who would
fight with a friend? A man who challenges
those who have welcomed him in a strange land   210
is worthless and a fool; he spites himself.
But I will challenge any of you others.
Test my ability, let me know yours.
I am not weak at any sport men practice.
I know the way to hold a polished bow.   215
I always was the first to hit my man
out of a horde of enemies, though many
comrades stood by me, arrows taking air.
At Troy, when the Achaeans shot their bows,
the only one superior to me   220
was Philoctetes. Other men who eat
their bread on earth are all worse shots than me.
But I will not compete with super-archers,
with Heracles or Eurytus, who risked
competing with the gods at archery.   225
Apollo was enraged at him and killed him
as soon as he proposed it. He died young
and did not reach old age in his own home.
And I can throw a spear beyond the shots
that others reach with arrows. I am only   230
concerned that one of you may win the footrace:
I lost my stamina and my legs weakened
during my time at sea, upon the raft;
I could not do my exercise routine."

The crowd was silent, but Alcinous   235
said, "Sir, you have expressed, with fine good manners,
your wish to show your talents, and your anger
at that man who stood up in this arena
and mocked you, as no one who understands
how to speak properly would ever do.   240

Now listen carefully, so you may tell
your own fine friends at home when you are feasting
beside your wife and children, and remember
our skill in all the deeds we have accomplished
from our forefathers' time till now. We are   245
not brilliant at wrestling or boxing,
but we are quick at sprinting, and with ships
we are the best. We love the feast, the lyre,
dancing and varied clothes, hot baths and bed.
But now let the best dancers of Phaeacia   250
perform, so that our guest may tell his friends
when he gets home, how excellent we are
at seafaring, at running, and at dancing
and song. Let someone bring the well-tuned lyre
from inside for Demodocus—go quickly!"   255

So spoke the king. The house boy brought the lyre.
The people chose nine referees to check
the games were fair. They leveled out a floor
for dancing, with a fine wide ring around.
The house boy gave Demodocus the lyre.   260
He walked into the middle, flanked by boys,
young and well trained, who tapped their feet performing
the holy dance, their quick legs bright with speed.
Odysseus was wonder-struck to see it.
The poet strummed and sang a charming song   265
about the love of fair-crowned Aphrodite
for Ares, who gave lavish gifts to her
and shamed the bed of Lord Hephaestus, where
they secretly had sex. The Sun God saw them,
and told Hephaestus—bitter news for him.[8]   270
He marched into his forge to get revenge,
and set the mighty anvil on its block,
and hammered chains so strong that they could never
be broken or undone. He was so angry
at Ares. When his trap was made, he went   275
inside the room of his beloved bed,
and twined the mass of cables all around
the bedposts, and then hung them from the ceiling,
like slender spiderwebs, so finely made
that nobody could see them, even gods: 280
the craftsmanship was so ingenious.
When he had set that trap across the bed,
he traveled to the cultured town of Lemnos,
which was his favorite place in all the world.
Ares the golden rider had kept watch.   285
He saw Hephaestus, famous wonder-worker,
leaving his house, and went inside himself;

8. Aphrodite, the goddess of sex, was married   Ares, god of war; Helius, the sun god, who
to the god Hephaestus, but had an affair with   sees whatever the sun sees, revealed the truth.

he wanted to make love with Aphrodite.
She had returned from visiting her father,
the mighty son of Cronus; there she sat.   290
Then Ares took her hand and said to her,

"My darling, let us go to bed. Hephaestus
is out of town; he must have gone to Lemnos
to see the Sintians whose speech is strange."

She was excited to lie down with him;   295
they went to bed together. But the chains
ingenious Hephaestus had created
wrapped tight around them, so they could not move
or get up. Then they knew that they were trapped.
The limping god drew near—before he reached   300
the land of Lemnos, he had turned back home.
Troubled at heart, he came towards his house.
Standing there in the doorway, he was seized
by savage rage. He gave a mighty shout,
calling to all the gods,

                    "O Father Zeus,   305
and all you blessed gods who live forever,
look! It is funny—and unbearable.
See how my Aphrodite, child of Zeus,
is disrespecting me for being lame.
She loves destructive Ares, who is strong   310
and handsome. I am weak. I blame my parents.
If only I had not been born! But come,
see where those two are sleeping in my bed,
as lovers. I am horrified to see it.
But I predict they will not want to lie   315
longer like that, however great their love.
Soon they will want to wake up, but my trap
and chains will hold them fast, until her father
pays back the price I gave him for his daughter.
Her eyes stare at me like a dog. She is   320
so beautiful, but lacking self-control."

The gods assembled at his house: Poseidon,
Earth-Shaker, helpful Hermes, and Apollo.
The goddesses stayed home, from modesty.
The blessed gods who give good things were standing   325
inside the doorway, and they burst out laughing,
at what a clever trap Hephaestus set.
And as they looked, they said to one another,

"Crime does not pay! The slow can beat the quick,
as now Hephaestus, who is lame and slow,   330
has used his skill to catch the fastest sprinter
of all those on Olympus. Ares owes
the price for his adultery." They gossiped.

Apollo, son of Zeus, then said to Hermes,
"Hermes my brother, would you like to sleep   335
with golden Aphrodite, in her bed,
even weighed down by mighty chains?"

                             And Hermes
the sharp-eyed messenger replied, "Ah, brother,
Apollo lord of archery: if only!
I would be bound three times as tight or more   340
and let you gods and all your wives look on,
if only I could sleep with Aphrodite."

Then laughter rose among the deathless gods.
Only Poseidon did not laugh. He begged
and pleaded with Hephaestus to release   345
Ares. He told the wonder-working god,

"Now let him go! I promise he will pay
the penalty in full among the gods,
just as you ask."

                   The famous limping god
replied, "Poseidon, do not ask me this.   350
It is disgusting, bailing scoundrels out.
How could I bind you, while the gods look on,
if Ares should escape his bonds and debts?"
Poseidon, Lord of Earthquakes, answered him,
"Hephaestus, if he tries to dodge this debt,   355
I promise I will pay."

                    The limping god
said, "Then, in courtesy to you, I must
do as you ask." So using all his strength,
Hephaestus loosed the chains. The pair of lovers
were free from their constraints, and both jumped up.   360
Ares went off to Thrace, while Aphrodite
smiled as she went to Cyprus, to the island
of Paphos, where she had a fragrant altar
and sanctuary. The Graces washed her there,
and rubbed her with the magic oil that glows   365
upon immortals, and they dressed her up
in gorgeous clothes. She looked astonishing.

That was the poet's song. Odysseus
was happy listening; so were they all.
And then Alcinous told Halius   370
to dance with Laodamas; no one danced
as well as them. They took a purple ball
which Polybus the artisan had made them.
One boy would leap and toss it to the clouds;
the other would jump up, feet off the ground,   375

and catch it easily before he landed.
After they practiced throwing it straight upwards,
they danced across the fertile earth, crisscrossing,
constantly trading places. Other boys
who stood around the field were beating time   380
with noisy stomping. Then Odysseus
said,

    "King of many citizens, great lord,
you boasted that your dancers are the best,
and it is true. I feel amazed to see
this marvelous show."

                     That pleased the reverend king.   385
He spoke at once to his seafaring people.
"Hear me, Phaeacian leaders, lords and nobles.
The stranger seems extremely wise to me.
So let us give him gifts, as hosts should do
to guests in friendship. Twelve lords rule our people,   390
with me as thirteenth lord. Let us each bring
a pound of precious gold and laundered clothes,
a tunic and a cloak. Then pile them up,
and let our guest take all these gifts, and go
to dinner with them, happy in his heart.   395
Euryalus should tell him he is sorry,
and give a special gift, since what he said
was inappropriate."

               They all agreed,
and each sent back a deputy to fetch
the presents. And Euryalus spoke out.   400

"My lord Alcinous, great king of kings,
I will apologize, as you command.
And I will give him this bronze sword which has
a silver handle, and a scabbard carved
of ivory—a precious gift for him."   405
With that he put the silver-studded sword
into Odysseus' hands; his words
flew out.

      "I welcome you, sir. Be our guest.
If something rude of any kind was said,
let the winds take it. May the gods allow you   410
to reach your home and see your wife again,
since you have suffered so long, far away
from those who love you."

             And Odysseus
said, "Friend, I wish you well. May gods protect you,
and may you never miss the sword you gave me."   415

With that, he strapped the silver-studded sword
across his back, and as the sun went down
the precious gifts were brought to him. The slaves
took them inside Alcinous' house.
The princes piled the lovely things beside   420
the queen, their mother. King Alcinous
led everyone inside and had them sit
on upright chairs. He told Arete,

                              "Wife,
bring out our finest chest, and put inside it
a tunic and a freshly laundered cloak.   425
Set a bronze cauldron on the fire to boil,
so he can take a bath. Then let him see
the precious gifts our noblemen have brought,
and then enjoy the banquet and the song.
I also have a gift: a splendid cup   430
of gold. I hope he always thinks of me
whenever he pours offerings to Zeus
and other gods."

                    Arete told her slaves
to quickly set a mighty pot to warm,
for washing. So upon the blazing flames   435
they set the cauldron and poured water in,
and heaped up wood. The fire licked around
the belly of the tub and warmed the water.
Arete brought from her own room a chest
to give the guest, and packed the gifts inside—   440
the clothes and gold that they had given him;
and she herself put in a cloak and tunic.
She told him,

                "Watch the lid, and tie it closed,
so nobody can rob you as you travel,
when you are lulled to sleep on your black ship."   445

Odysseus, experienced in loss,
took careful note. He shut the lid and tied
a cunning knot that he had learned from Circe.
Then right away the slave girl led him off
towards the bath to wash. He was delighted   450
to see hot water. He had not been bathed
since he had left the home of curly-haired
Calypso, who had taken care of him
as if he were a god. The slave girls washed him,
rubbed oil on him and dressed him in a tunic   455
and fine wool mantle. Freshly bathed, he joined
the men at wine. And there stood Nausicaa,
divinely beautiful, beside a pillar
that held the palace roof. She was amazed
to see Odysseus. Her words flew fast.   460

"Good-bye then, stranger, but remember me
when you reach home, because you owe your life
to me. I helped you first."

                Odysseus
replied politely, "Nausicaa, may Zeus,
husband of Hera, mighty Lord of Thunder,   465
allow me to go back and see my home.
There I shall pray to you as to a god,
forever, princess, since you saved my life."
With that he went to sit beside the king.

Now they were serving out the food and pouring   470
wine, and the steward led out to the center
Demodocus, the well-respected poet.
He sat him in the middle of the banquet,
against a pillar. Then Odysseus
thought fast, and sliced a helping from the pig,   475
all richly laced with fat. The plate of meat
had plenty left. He told the boy,

                      "Go take
this meat and give it to Demodocus.
Despite my grief, I would be glad to meet him.
Poets are honored by all those who live   480
on earth. The Muse has taught them how to sing;
she loves the race of poets."

                    So the house boy
handed it to Demodocus. He took it
gladly; and everybody took their food.
When they had had enough to eat and drink,   485
the clever mastermind of many schemes
said,

    "You are wonderful, Demodocus!
I praise you more than anyone; Apollo,[9]
or else the Muse, the child of Zeus, has taught you.
You tell so accurately what the Greeks   490
achieved, and what they suffered, there at Troy,
as if you had been there, or heard about it
from somebody who was. So sing the story
about the Wooden Horse, which Epeius
built with Athena's help. Odysseus   495
dragged it inside and to the citadel,
filled up with men to sack the town. If you
can tell that as it happened, I will say
that you truly are blessed with inspiration."

9. God associated with poetry, who carried the lyre.

A god inspired the bard to sing. He started   500
with how the Greeks set fire to their camp
and then embarked and sailed away. Meanwhile,
Odysseus brought in a gang of men
into the heart of Troy, inside the horse.
The Trojans pulled the thing up to the summit,   505
and sat around discussing what to do.
Some said, "We ought to strike the wood with swords!"
Others said, "Drag it higher up and hurl it
down from the rocks!" But some said they should leave it
to pacify the gods. So it would be.   510
The town was doomed to ruin when it took
that horse, chock-full of fighters bringing death
to Trojans. And he sang how the Achaeans
poured from the horse, in ambush from the hollow,
and sacked the city; how they scattered out,   515
destroying every neighborhood. Like Ares,
Odysseus, with Menelaus, rushed
to find Deiphobus' house,[1] and there
he won at last, through dreadful violence,
thanks to Athena. So the poet sang.   520

Odysseus was melting into tears;
his cheeks were wet with weeping, as a woman
weeps, as she falls to wrap her arms around
her husband, fallen fighting for his home
and children. She is watching as he gasps   525
and dies. She shrieks, a clear high wail, collapsing
upon his corpse. The men are right behind.
They hit her shoulders with their spears and lead her
to slavery, hard labor, and a life
of pain. Her face is marked with her despair.   530
In that same desperate way, Odysseus
was crying. No one noticed that his eyes
were wet with tears, except Alcinous,
who sat right next to him and heard his sobs.
Quickly he spoke to his seafaring people.   535

"Listen, my lords and nobles of Phaeacia!
Demodocus should stop and set aside
the lyre, since what he sings does not give pleasure
to everyone. Throughout this heavenly song,
since dinnertime, our guest has been in pain,   540
grieving. A heavy burden weighs his heart.
Let the song end, so we can all be happy,
both guest and hosts. That would be best by far.
This send-off party and these precious gifts,

---

1. After Paris was killed, Helen was appropri-
ated by Deiphobus, another Trojan prince;
Odysseus killed him and mangled his corpse,
and Menelaus reclaimed his wife.

which we give out of friendship, are for him,   545
our guest of honor. Any man of sense
will treat a guest in need like his own brother.
Stranger, now answer all my questions clearly,
not with evasion; frankness would be best.
What did your parents name you? With what name   550
are you known to your people? Surely no one
in all the world is nameless, poor or noble,
since parents give a name to every child
at birth. And also tell me of your country,
your people, and your city, so our ships,   555
steered by their own good sense, may take you there.
Phaeacians have no need of men at helm
nor rudders, as in other ships. Our boats
intuit what is in the minds of men,
and know all human towns and fertile fields.   560
They rush at full tilt right across the gulf
of salty sea, concealed in mist and clouds.
They have no fear of damages or loss.
But once I heard Nausithous, my father,
say that Poseidon hates us for the help   565
we give to take our guests across the sea,
and that one day a ship of ours would suffer
shipwreck on its return; a mighty mountain
would block our town from sight. So Father said.
Perhaps the god will bring these things to pass   570
or not, as is his will. But come now, tell me
about your wanderings: describe the places,
the people, and the cities you have seen.
Which ones were wild and cruel, unwelcoming,
and which were kind to visitors, respecting   575
the gods? And please explain why you were crying,
sobbing your heart out when you heard him sing
what happened to the Greeks at Troy. The gods
devised and measured out this devastation,
to make a song for those in times to come.   580
Did you lose somebody at Troy? A man
from your wife's family, perhaps her father
or brother? Ties of marriage are the closest
after the bonds of blood. Or else perhaps
you lost the friend who knew you best of all?   585
A friend can be as close as any brother."

BOOK 9

[A Pirate in a Shepherd's Cave]

Wily Odysseus, the lord of lies,
answered,

        "My lord Alcinous, great king,
it is a splendid thing to hear a poet
as talented as this. His voice is godlike.
I think that there can be no greater pleasure   5
than when the whole community enjoys
a banquet, as we sit inside the house,
and listen to the singer, and the tables
are heaped with bread and meat; the wine boy ladles
drink from the bowl and pours it into cups.   10
To me this seems ideal, a thing of beauty.
Now something prompted you to ask about
my own sad story. I will tell you, though
the memory increases my despair.
Where shall I start? Where can I end? The gods   15
have given me so much to cry about.
First I will tell my name, so we will be
acquainted and if I survive, you can
be my guest in my distant home one day.
I am Odysseus, Laertes' son,   20
known for my many clever tricks and lies.
My fame extends to heaven, but I live
in Ithaca, where shaking forest hides
Mount Neriton. Close by are other islands:
Dulichium, and wooded Zacynthus   25
and Same. All the others face the dawn;
my Ithaca is set apart, most distant,
facing the dark.[2] It is a rugged land,
but good at raising children. To my eyes
no country could be sweeter. As you know,   30
divine Calypso held me in her cave,
wanting to marry me; and likewise Circe,
the trickster, trapped me, and she wanted me
to be her husband. But she never swayed
my heart, since when a man is far from home,   35
living abroad, there is no sweeter thing
than his own native land and family.
Now let me tell you all the trouble Zeus
has caused me on my journey home from Troy.
A blast of wind pushed me off course towards   40
the Cicones in Ismarus.[3] I sacked

---

2. The suggestion is that Ithaca is farthest west, facing the setting sun ("the darkness"), whereas the other islands are more to the east. It is impossible to reconcile this claim with actual geography.

3. The Cicones, a Thracian people, were allies of Troy. But the passage does not suggest that Odysseus' piracy is motivated by any particular military objective.

the town and killed the men. We took their wives
and shared their riches equally among us.
Then I said we must run away. Those fools
refused to listen. They were drinking wine   45
excessively, and killing sheep and cattle
along the beach. The Cicones called out
to neighbors on the mainland, who were strong
and numerous, and skilled at horseback fighting,
and if need be, on foot. They came like leaves   50
and blossoms in the spring at dawn. Then Zeus
gave us bad luck. Poor us! The enemy
assembled round the ships and fought with swords
of bronze. And while the holy morning light
was bright and strong, we held them off, though they   55
outnumbered us. But when the sun turned round
and dipped, the hour when oxen are released,
the Cicones began to overpower
us Greeks. Six well-armed members of my crew
died from each ship. The rest of us survived,   60
and we escaped the danger. We prepared
to sail away with heavy hearts, relieved
to be alive, but grieving for our friends.
Before we launched the ships, we called aloud
three times to each of our poor lost companions,   65
slaughtered at the hands of Cicones.

The Cloud Lord Zeus hurled North Wind at our ships,
a terrible typhoon, and covered up
the sea and earth with fog. Night fell from heaven
and seized us and our ships keeled over sideways;   70
the sails were ripped three times by blasting wind.
Scared for our lives, we hoisted down the sails
and rowed with all our might towards the shore.
We stayed there for two days and nights, exhausted,
eating our hearts with pain. When bright-haired Dawn   75
brought the third morning, we set up our masts,
unfurled the shining sails, and climbed aboard.
The wind blew straight, the pilots steered, and I
would have come safely home, to my own land,
but as I rounded Malea, a current   80
and blast of wind pushed me off course, away
from Cythera. For nine days I was swept
by stormy winds across the fish-filled sea.
On the tenth day, I landed on the island
of those who live on food from luscious lotus.   85
We gathered water, and my crew prepared
a meal. We picnicked by the ships, then I
chose two men, and one slave to make the third,
to go and scout. We needed to find out
what kind of people lived there on that island.   90
The scouts encountered humans, Lotus-Eaters,

who did not hurt them. They just shared with them
their sweet delicious fruit. But as they ate it,
they lost the will to come back and bring news
to me. They wanted only to stay there,   95
feeding on lotus with the Lotus-Eaters.
They had forgotten home. I dragged them back
in tears, forced them on board the hollow ships,
pushed them below the decks, and tied them up.
I told the other men, the loyal ones,   100
to get back in the ships, so no one else
would taste the lotus and forget about
our destination. They embarked and sat
along the rowing benches, side by side,
and struck the grayish water with their oars.   105

With heavy hearts we sailed along and reached
the country of high-minded Cyclopes,
the mavericks. They put their trust in gods,
and do not plant their food from seed, nor plow,
and yet the barley, grain, and clustering wine-grapes   110
all flourish there, increased by rain from Zeus.
They hold no councils, have no common laws,
but live in caves on lofty mountaintops,
and each makes laws for his own wife and children,
without concern for what the others think.   115
A distance from this island is another,
across the water, slantways from the harbor,
level and thickly wooded. Countless goats
live there but people never visit it.
No hunters labor through its woods to scale   120
its hilly peaks. There are no flocks of sheep,
no fields of plowland—it is all untilled,
unsown and uninhabited by humans.
Only the bleating goats live there and graze.
Cyclopic people have no red-cheeked ships[4]   125
and no shipwright among them who could build
boats, to enable them to row across
to other cities, as most people do,
crossing the sea to visit one another.
With boats they could have turned this island into   130
a fertile colony, with proper harvests.
By the gray shore there lie well-watered meadows,
where vines would never fail. There is flat land
for plowing, and abundant crops would grow
in the autumn; there is richness underground.   135
The harbor has good anchorage; there is
no need of anchor stones or ropes or cables.
The ships that come to shore there can remain
beached safely till the sailors wish to leave

4. Ships were decorated with red at the prow.

and fair winds blow. Up by the harbor head   140
freshwater gushes down beneath the caves.
The poplars grow around it. There we sailed:
the gods were guiding us all through the darkness.
Thick fog wrapped round our ships and in the sky
the moon was dark and clothed in clouds, so we   145
saw nothing of the island. None of us
could see the great waves rolling in towards
the land, until we rowed right to the beach.
We lowered all the sails and disembarked
onto the shore, and there we fell asleep.   150

When early Dawn shone forth with rosy fingers,
we roamed around that island full of wonders.
The daughters of the great King Zeus, the nymphs,
drove out the mountain goats so that my crew
could eat. On seeing them, we dashed to fetch   155
our javelins and bows from on board ship.
We split into three groups, took aim and shot.
Some god gave us good hunting. All twelve crews
had nine goats each, and ten for mine. We sat there
all day till sunset, eating meat and drinking   160
our strong red wine. The ships' supply of that
had not run out; when we had sacked the holy
citadel of the Cicones, we all
took gallons of it, poured in great big pitchers.
We looked across the narrow strip of water   165
at the Cyclopic island, saw their smoke,
and heard the baaing of their sheep and goats.
The sun went down and in the hours of darkness
we lay and slept on shore beside the sea.
But when the rosy hands of Dawn appeared,   170
I called my men together and addressed them.

"My loyal friends! Stay here, the rest of you,
while with my boat and crew I go to check
who those men are, find out if they are wild,
lawless aggressors, or the type to welcome   175
strangers, and fear the gods."

        With that, I climbed
on board and told my crew to come with me
and then untie the cables of the ship.
Quickly they did so, sat along the benches,
and struck the whitening water with their oars.   180
The journey was not long. Upon arrival,
right at the edge of land, beside the sea,
we saw a high cave overhung with laurel,
the home of several herds of sheep and goats.
Around that cave was built a lofty courtyard,   185
of deep-set stones, with tall pines rising up,

and leafy oaks. There lived a massive man
who shepherded his flocks all by himself.
He did not go to visit other people,
but kept apart, and did not know the ways   190
of custom. In his build he was a wonder,
a giant, not like men who live on bread,
but like a wooded peak in airy mountains,
rising alone above the rest.

           I told
my loyal crew to guard the ship, while I   195
would go with just twelve chosen men, my favorites.
I took a goatskin full of dark sweet wine
that I was given by Apollo's priest,
Maron the son of Euanthes, who lived
inside the shady grove on Ismarus.   200
In reverence to the god, I came to help him,
and save his wife and son. He gave me gifts:
a silver bowl and seven pounds of gold,
well wrought, and siphoned off some sweet strong wine,
and filled twelve jars for me—a godlike drink.   205
The slaves knew nothing of this wine; it was
known just to him, his wife, and one house girl.
Whenever he was drinking it, he poured
a single shot into a cup, and added
twenty of water, and a marvelous smell   210
rose from the bowl, and all would long to taste it.
I filled a big skin up with it, and packed
provisions in a bag—my heart suspected
that I might meet a man of courage, wild,
and lacking knowledge of the normal customs.   215

We soon were at the cave, but did not find
the Cyclops; he was pasturing his flocks.
We went inside and looked at everything.
We saw his crates weighed down with cheese, and pens
crammed full of lambs divided up by age: 220
the newborns, middlings, and those just weaned.
There were well-crafted bowls and pails for milking,
all full of whey. My crew begged, "Let us grab
some cheese and quickly drive the kids and lambs
out of their pens and down to our swift ships,   225
and sail away across the salty water!"
That would have been the better choice. But I
refused. I hoped to see him, and find out
if he would give us gifts. In fact he brought
no joy to my companions. Then we lit   230
a fire, and made a sacrifice, and ate
some cheese, and sat to wait inside the cave
until he brought his flocks back home. He came
at dinnertime, and brought a load of wood

to make a fire. He hurled it noisily   ·   235
into the cave. We were afraid, and cowered
towards the back. He drove his ewes and nannies
inside to milk them, but he left the rams
and he-goats in the spacious yard outside.
He lifted up the heavy stone and set it   240
to block the entrance of the cave. It was
a rock so huge and massive, twenty-two
strong carts could not have dragged it from the threshold.
He sat, and all in order milked his ewes
and she-goats, then he set the lambs to suck   245
beside each bleating mother. Then he curdled
half of the fresh white milk, set that aside
in wicker baskets, and the rest he stored
in pails so he could drink it with his dinner.
When he had carefully performed his chores,   250
he lit a fire, then looked around and saw us.
'Strangers! Who are you? Where did you come from
across the watery depths? Are you on business,
or roaming round without a goal, like pirates,
who risk their lives at sea to bring disaster   255
to other people?'

       So he spoke. His voice,
so deep and booming, and his giant size,
made our hearts sink in terror. Even so,
I answered,

       'We are Greeks, come here from Troy.
The winds have swept us off in all directions   260
across the vast expanse of sea, off course
from our planned route back home. Zeus willed it so.
We are proud to be the men of Agamemnon,
the son of Atreus, whose fame is greatest
under the sky, for sacking that vast city   265
and killing many people. Now we beg you,
here at your knees, to grant a gift, as is
the norm for hosts and guests. Please, sir, my lord:
respect the gods. We are your suppliants,
and Zeus is on our side, since he takes care   270
of visitors, guest-friends, and those in need.'

Unmoved he said, 'Well, foreigner, you are
a fool, or from some very distant country.
You order me to fear the gods! My people
think nothing of that Zeus with his big scepter,   275
nor any god; our strength is more than theirs.
If I spare you or spare your friends, it will not
be out of fear of Zeus. I do the bidding
of my own heart. But are you going far
in that fine ship of yours, or somewhere near?'   280

He spoke to test me, but I saw right through him.
I know how these things work. I answered him
deceitfully.

        'Poseidon, the Earth-Shaker,
shipwrecked me at the far end of your island.
He pushed us in; wind dashed us on the rocks.   285
We barely managed to survive.'

               But he
made no reply and showed no mercy. Leaping
up high, he reached his hands towards my men,
seized two, and knocked them hard against the ground
like puppies, and the floor was wet with brains.   290
He ripped them limb by limb to make his meal,
then ate them like a lion on the mountains,
devouring flesh, entrails, and marrow bones,
and leaving nothing. Watching this disaster,
we wept and lifted up our hands in prayer   295
to Zeus. We felt so helpless. When the Cyclops
had filled his massive belly with his meal
of human meat and unmixed milk,[5] he lay
stretched out among his flocks. Then thinking like
a military man, I thought I should   300
get out my sword, go up to him and thrust
right through his torso, feeling for his liver.[6]
That would have doomed us all. On second thoughts,
I realized we were too weak to move
the mighty stone he set in the high doorway.   305
So we stayed there in misery till dawn.

Early the Dawn appeared, pink fingers blooming,
and then he lit his fire and milked his ewes
in turn, and set a lamb by every one.
When he had diligently done his chores,   310
he grabbed two men and made a meal of them.
After he ate, he drove his fat flock out.
He rolled the boulder out and back with ease,
as one would set the lid upon a quiver.
Then whistling merrily, the Cyclops drove   315
his fat flocks to the mountain. I was left,
scheming to take revenge on him and hurt him,
and gain the glory, if Athena let me.
I made my plan. Beside the pen there stood
a great big club, green olive wood, which he   320
had cut to dry, to be his walking stick.
It was so massive that it looked to us
like a ship's mast, a twenty-oared black freighter

---

5. The word for "unmixed" is usually used for wine undiluted with water. The text is making a sort of joke since milk is the equivalent of wine for this usually teetotaling character.
6. He imagines having to move by feel, since the cave is entirely dark.

that sails across the vast sea full of cargo.
I went and cut from it about a fathom,   325
and gave it to the men, and ordered them
to scrape it down. They made it smooth and I
stood by and sharpened up the tip, and made it
hard in the blazing flame. The cave was full
of dung; I hid the club beneath a pile.   330
Then I gave orders that the men cast lots
for who would lift the stake with me and press it
into his eye, when sweet sleep overtook him.
The lots fell on the men I would have chosen:
four men, and I was fifth among their number.   335

At evening he drove back his woolly flocks
into the spacious cave, both male and female,
and left none in the yard outside—perhaps
suspecting something, or perhaps a god
told him to do it. He picked up and placed   340
the stone to form a door, and sat to milk
the sheep and bleating goats in turn, then put
the little ones to suck. His chores were done;
he grabbed two men for dinner. I approached
and offered him a cup of ivy wood,   345
filled full of wine. I said,

        'Here, Cyclops! You
have eaten human meat; now drink some wine,
sample the merchandise our ship contains.
I brought it as a holy offering,[7]
so you might pity me and send me home.   350
But you are in a cruel rage, beyond
what anyone could bear. Do you expect
more guests, when you have treated us so rudely?'

He took and drank the sweet delicious wine;
he loved it, and demanded more.

         'Another!   355
And now tell me your name, so I can give you
a present as my guest, one you will like.
My people do have wine; grape clusters grow
from our rich earth, fed well by rain from Zeus.
But this is nectar, god food!'

        So I gave him   360
another cup of wine, and then two more.
He drank them all, unwisely. With the wine
gone to his head, I told him, all politeness,

---

7. The term used here is usually applied to drink offerings given to the gods.

'Cyclops, you asked my name. I will reveal it;
then you must give the gift you promised me,   365
of hospitality. My name is Noman.[8]
My family and friends all call me Noman.'
He answered with no pity in his heart,
'I will eat Noman last; first I will eat
the other men. That is my gift to you.'   370
Then he collapsed, fell on his back, and lay there,
his massive neck askew. All-conquering sleep
took him. In drunken heaviness, he spewed
wine from his throat, and chunks of human flesh.
And then I drove the spear into the embers   375
to heat it up, and told my men, 'Be brave!'
I wanted none of them to shrink in fear.
The fire soon had seized the olive spear,
green though it was, and terribly it glowed.
I quickly snatched it from the fire. My crew   380
stood firm: some god was breathing courage in us.
They took the olive spear, its tip all sharp,
and shoved it in his eye. I leaned on top
and twisted it, as when a man drills wood
for shipbuilding. Below, the workers spin   385
the drill with straps, stretched out from either end.
So round and round it goes, and so we whirled
the fire-sharp weapon in his eye. His blood
poured out around the stake, and blazing fire
sizzled his lids and brows, and fried the roots.   390
As when a blacksmith dips an axe or adze
to temper it in ice-cold water; loudly
it shrieks. From this, the iron takes on its power.
So did his eyeball crackle on the spear.
Horribly then he howled, the rocks resounded,   395
and we shrank back in fear. He tugged the spear
out of his eye, all soaked with gushing blood.
Desperately with both hands he hurled it from him,
and shouted to the Cyclopes who lived
in caves high up on windy cliffs around.   400
They heard and came from every side, and stood
near to the cave, and called out, 'Polyphemus!
What is the matter? Are you badly hurt?
Why are you screaming through the holy night
and keeping us awake? Is someone stealing   405
your herds, or trying to kill you, by some trick
or force?'

        Strong Polyphemus from inside
replied, 'My friends! Noman is killing me
by tricks, not force.'

---

8. In Greek, "Noman"—*oudeis*—sounds a little like "Odysseus."

Their words flew back to him:
'If no one hurts you, you are all alone: 410
Great Zeus has made you sick; no help for that.
Pray to your father, mighty Lord Poseidon.'

Then off they went, and I laughed to myself,
at how my name, the 'no man' maneuver, tricked him.[9]
The Cyclops groaned and labored in his pain,   415
felt with blind hands and took the door-stone out,
and sat there at the entrance, arms outstretched,
to catch whoever went out with the sheep.
Maybe he thought I was a total fool.
But I was strategizing, hatching plans,   420
so that my men and I could all survive.
I wove all kinds of wiles and cunning schemes;
danger was near and it was life or death.
The best idea I formed was this: there were
those well-fed sturdy rams with good thick fleece,   425
wool as dark as violets—all fine big creatures.
So silently I tied them with the rope
used by the giant Cyclops as a bed.
I bound the rams in sets of three and set
a man beneath each middle sheep, with one   430
on either side, and so my men were saved.
One ram was best of all the flock; I grabbed
his back and curled myself up underneath
his furry belly, clinging to his fleece;
by force of will I kept on hanging there.   435
And then we waited miserably for day.

When early Dawn revealed her rose-red hands,
the rams jumped up, all eager for the grass.
The ewes were bleating in their pens, unmilked,
their udders full to bursting. Though their master   440
was weak and worn with pain, he felt the back
of each ram as he lined them up—but missed
the men tied up beneath their woolly bellies.
Last of them all, the big ram went outside,
heavy with wool and me—the clever trickster.   445
Strong Polyphemus stroked his back and asked him,

'Sweet ram, why are you last today to leave
the cave? You are not normally so slow.
You are the first to eat the tender flowers,
leaping across the meadow, first to drink,   450
and first to want to go back to the sheepfold
at evening time. But now you are the last.

---

9. There is a pun here in the Greek that is
impossible to translate into English: *metis*
means "nobody" but also "cunning." "Maneuver" is designed to hint at the wordplay.

You grieve for Master's eye; that wicked man,
helped by his nasty henchmen, got me drunk
and blinded me. Noman will not escape!   455
If only you could talk like me, and tell me
where he is skulking in his fear of me.
Then I would dash his brains out on the rocks,
and make them spatter all across the cave,
to ease the pain that no-good Noman brought.'   460

With that, he nudged the ram away outside.
We rode a short way from the cave, then I
first freed myself and then untied my men.
We stole his nice fat animals, and ran,
constantly glancing all around and back   465
until we reached the ship. The other men
were glad to see us, their surviving friends,
but wept for those who died. I ordered them
to stop their crying, scowling hard at each.
I made them shove the fleecy flock on board,   470
and row the boat out into salty water.
So they embarked, sat on their rowing benches,
and struck their oar blades in the whitening sea.
When I had gone as far as shouts can carry,
I jeered back,

    'Hey, you, Cyclops! Idiot!   475
The crew trapped in your cave did not belong
to some poor weakling. Well, you had it coming!
You had no shame at eating your own guests!
So Zeus and other gods have paid you back.'

My taunting made him angrier. He ripped   480
a rock out of the hill and hurled it at us.
It landed right in front of our dark prow,
and almost crushed the tip of the steering oar.
The stone sank in the water; waves surged up.
The backflow all at once propelled the ship   485
landwards; the swollen water pushed us with it.
I grabbed a big long pole, and shoved us off.
I told my men, 'Row fast, to save your lives!'
and gestured with my head to make them hurry.
They bent down to their oars and started rowing.   490
We got out twice as far across the sea,
and then I called to him again. My crew
begged me to stop, and pleaded with me.

      'Please!
Calm down! Why are you being so insistent
and taunting this wild man? He hurled that stone   495
and drove our ship right back to land. We thought

that we were going to die. If he had heard us,
he would have hurled a jagged rock and crushed
our heads and wooden ship. He throws so hard!

But my tough heart was not convinced; I was   500
still furious, and shouted back again,

'Cyclops! If any mortal asks you how
your eye was mutilated and made blind,
say that Odysseus, the city-sacker,
Laertes' son, who lives in Ithaca,   505
destroyed your sight.'

              He groaned, 'The prophecy!
It has come true at last! There was a tall
and handsome man named Telemus, the son
of Eurymus, who lived among my people;
he spent his life here, soothsaying for us.   510
He told me that Odysseus' hands
would make me lose my sight. I always thought
somebody tall and handsome, strong and brave
would come to me. But now this little weakling,
this little nobody, has blinded me;   515
by wine he got the best of me. Come on,
Odysseus, and let me give you gifts,
and ask Poseidon's help to get you home.
I am his son; the god is proud to be
my father. He will heal me, if he wants,   520
though no one else, not god nor man, can do it.'

After he said these words, I answered him,
'If only I could steal your life from you,
and send you down to Hades' house below,
as sure as nobody will ever heal you,   525
even the god of earthquakes.'

              But he prayed
holding his arms towards the starry sky,
'Listen, Earth-Shaker, Blue-Haired Lord Poseidon:
acknowledge me your son, and be my father.
Grant that Odysseus, the city-sacker,   530
will never go back home. Or if it is
fated that he will see his family,
then let him get there late and with no honor,
in pain and lacking ships, and having caused
the death of all his men, and let him find   535
more trouble in his own house.'

              Blue Poseidon
granted his son's prayer. Polyphemus raised
a rock far bigger than the last, and swung,

then hurled it with immeasurable force.
It fell a little short, beside our rudder,   540
and splashed into the sea; the waves surged up,
and pushed the boat ahead, to the other shore.
We reached the island where our ships were docked.
The men were sitting waiting for us, weeping.
We beached our ship and disembarked, then took   545
the sheep that we had stolen from the Cyclops
out of the ship's hold, and we shared them out
fairly, so all the men got equal portions.
But in dividing up the flock, my crew
gave me alone the ram, the Cyclops' favorite.   550
There on the shore, I slaughtered him for Zeus,
the son of Cronus, god of Dark Clouds, Lord
of all the world. I burned the thighs. The god
ignored my offering, and planned to ruin
all of my ships and all my loyal men.   555
So all day long till sunset we were sitting,
feasting on meat and drinking sweet strong wine.
But when the sun went down and darkness fell,
we went to sleep beside the breaking waves.
Then when rose-fingered Dawn came, bright and early,   560
I roused my men and told them to embark
and loose the cables. Quickly they obeyed,
sat at their rowing benches, all in order,
and struck the gray saltwater with their oars.
So we sailed on, with sorrow in our hearts,   565
glad to survive, but grieving for our friends."

BOOK 10

[*The Winds and the Witch*]

"We reached the floating island of Aeolus,
who is well loved by all the deathless gods.
Around it, on sheer cliffs, there runs a wall
of solid bronze, impregnable. Twelve children
live with him in his palace: six strong boys,   5
and six girls. He arranged their marriages,
one sister to each brother. They are always
feasting there with their parents, at a banquet
that never ends. By day, the savor fills
the house; the court reverberates with sound.   10
At night they sleep beside the wives they love
on rope beds piled with blankets.

                              We arrived
at that fine citadel. He welcomed me
and made me stay a month, and asked for news
of Troy, the Argive ships, and how the Greeks   15
went home. I told him everything. At last

I told him he should send me on my way.
So he agreed to help me, and he gave me
a bag of oxhide leather and he tied
the gusty winds inside it. Zeus, the son   20
of Cronus, made him steward of the winds,
and he can stop or rouse them as he wishes.
He bound the bag with shining silver wire
to my curved ship, so no gust could escape,
however small, and he made Zephyr blow   25
so that the breath could carry home our ships
and us. But it was not to be. Our folly
ruined us. For nine days and nights we sailed,
and on the tenth, our native land appeared.
We were so near, we saw men tending fires.   30
Exhausted, I let sweet sleep overcome me.
I had been doing all the steering, hoping
that we would get home sooner if I did.
But while I slept my men began to mutter,
saying the great Aeolus gave me gifts—   35
silver and gold that I was taking home.
With glances to his neighbor, each complained,

'It seems that everybody loves this man,
and honors him, in every place we sail to.
He also has that loot from sacking Troy.   40
We shared the journey with him, yet we come
back home with empty hands. And now Aeolus
has made this friendly gift to him. So hurry,
we should look in the bag, and see how much
is in there—how much silver, how much gold.'   45

That bad idea took hold of them; they did it.
They opened up the bag, and all the winds
rushed out at once. A sudden buffet seized us
and hurled us back to sea, the wrong direction,
far from our home. They screamed and I woke up,   50
and wondered if I should jump off the ship
and drown, or bite my lip, be stoical,
and stay among the living. I endured it,
covered my face, and lay on deck. A blast
of storm wind whooshed the ships back to the island   55
of great Aeolus. They began to weep.
We disembarked and filled our jars with water,
and hungrily the men devoured their dinner.
When they were done, I took one slave with me
and one crew member, back to see Aeolus.   60
He was at dinner with his wife and children.
We entered and sat down beside the doorposts.
Startled, they asked,

'Why are you here again?
You had bad luck? What happened? Surely we
helped you go on your way, and meant for you   65
to reach your homeland, where you wished to go.'

I answered sadly, 'Blame my men, and blame
my stubborn urge to sleep, which ruined us.
Dear friends, you have the power to put things right.'

I hoped these words would soften them, but they   70
were silent. Then the father yelled, 'Get out!
You nasty creature, leave my island! Now!
It is not right for me to help convey
a man so deeply hated by the gods.
You godforsaken thing, how dare you come here?   75
Get out!'

        He roared and drove us from his palace.
Dispirited, we sailed away. The men
grew worn out with the agony of rowing; .
our folly had deprived us of fair winds.
We rowed six days and nights; the seventh day   80
we came to Laestrygonia—the town
of Telepylus upon the cliffs of Lamos.[1]
A herdsman there, returning to his home,
can greet another herdsman going out.[2]
A sleepless man could earn a double wage   85
by herding cows, then pasturing white sheep—
the paths of day and night are close together.[3]
We reached the famous harbor, all surrounded
by sheer rock cliffs. On each side, strips of shore
jut out and almost meet, a narrow mouth.   90
No waves rear up in there, not even small ones.
White calm is everywhere. So all the others
harbored their ships inside, crammed close together.
I was the only one who chose to moor
my ship outside the harbor, fastening   95
the cables to a rock a way away.
I disembarked and climbed a crag to scout.
I saw no sign of cattle or of humans,
except some smoke that rose up from the earth.
I picked two men, and one slave as the third,   100
and sent them to find out what people lived
and ate bread in this land. They disembarked
and walked along a smooth path, where the wagons
brought wood down from the mountains to the city.

1. Lamos is the founder of this mythical place.
2. The idea is that in this strange country
herdsmen work around the clock, a day shift
and a night shift.
3. This odd line presumably means that the

nights are almost nonexistent here, as in areas
near the Arctic Circle. Attempts to plot Laestrygonia on a real map have not been convincing; this is a fictional place, melding several
elements of actual geography.

They met a girl in front of town, out fetching   105
some water. She was heading for the fountain
of Artaky, the whole town's water source.
She was the strapping child of Antiphates,
king of the Laestrygonians. They asked her
about the king and people of the country.   110
She promptly took them to the high-roofed palace
of her own father. When they went inside
they found a woman, mountain-high. They were
appalled and shocked. The giantess at once
summoned the king her husband from the council;   115
he tried to kill my men, and grabbing one
he ate him up. The other two escaped,
back to the ship. The king's shout boomed through town.
Hearing, the mighty Laestrygonians
thronged from all sides, not humanlike, but giants.[4]   120
With boulders bigger than a man could lift
they pelted at us from the cliffs. We heard
the dreadful uproar of ships being broken
and dying men. They speared them there like fish.
A gruesome meal! While they were killing them   125
inside the harbor, I drew out my sword
and cut the ropes that moored my dark-cheeked ship,
and yelling to my men, I told them, 'Row
as fast as possible away from danger!'
They rowed at double time, afraid to die.   130
My ship was lucky and we reached the sea
beyond the overhanging cliffs. The rest,
trapped in the bay together, were destroyed.
We sailed off sadly, happy to survive,
but with our good friends lost. We reached Aeaea,   135
home of the beautiful, dreadful goddess Circe,
who speaks in human languages—the sister
of Aeetes whose mind is set on ruin.
Those two are children of the Sun who shines
on mortals, and of Perse, child of Ocean.[5]   140
Under the guidance of some god we drifted
silently to the harbor, and we moored there.
For two days and two nights we lay onshore,
exhausted and our hearts consumed with grief.
On the third morning brought by braided Dawn,   145
I took my spear and sharp sword, and I ran
up from the ship to higher ground, to look
for signs of humans, listening for voices.
I climbed up to a crag, and I saw smoke
rising from Circe's palace, from the earth   150
up through the woods and thickets. I considered

4. The giants were children of Earth, fertilized
by the blood of Uranus after his castration.
5. Perse is one of the many daughters of
Ocean; Aeetes was the cruel king of Colchis,
owner of the Golden Fleece and father of
Medea.

if I should go down and investigate,
since I had seen the smoke. But I decided
to go back down first, to the beach and ship
and feed my men, and then set out to scout.   155
When I had almost reached my ship, some god
took pity on me in my loneliness,
and sent a mighty stag with great tall antlers
to cross my path. He ran down from the forest
to drink out of the river; it was hot.   160
I struck him in the middle of his back;
my bronze spear pierced him. With a moan, he fell
onto the dust; his spirit flew away.
I stepped on him and tugged my bronze spear out,
and left it on the ground, while I plucked twigs   165
and twines, and wove a rope, a fathom's length,
well knotted all the way along, and bound
the hooves of that huge animal. I went
down to my dark ship with him on my back.
I used my spear to lean on, since the stag   170
was too big to be lugged across one shoulder.
I dumped him down before the ship and made
a comforting pep talk to cheer my men.

'My friends! We will not yet go down to Hades,
sad though we are, before our fated day.   175
Come on, since we have food and drink on board,
let us not starve ourselves; now time to eat!'

They quickly heeded my commands, and took
their cloaks down from their faces,[6] and they marveled
to see the big stag lying on the beach.   180
It was enormous. When they finished staring,
they washed their hands and cooked a splendid meal.
So all that day till sunset we sat eating
the meat aplenty and the strong sweet wine.
When darkness fell, we went to sleep beside   185
the seashore. Then the roses of Dawn's fingers
appeared again; I called my men and told them,

'Listen to me, my friends, despite your grief.
We do not know where darkness lives, nor dawn,
nor where the sun that shines upon the world   190
goes underneath the earth, nor where it rises.
We need a way to fix our current plight,
but I do not know how. I climbed the rocks
to higher ground to look around. This is
an island, wreathed about by boundless sea.   195
The land lies low. I saw smoke in the middle,
rising up through the forest and thick bush.'

6. People in Homer cover their faces in grief; the men in this small band of survivors have been grieving the loss of the other eleven ships and their crew members.

At that, their hearts sank, since they all remembered
what happened with the Laestrygonians,
their King Antiphates, and how the mighty   200
Cyclops devoured the men. They wept and wailed,
and shed great floods of tears. But all that grieving
could do no good. I made them wear their armor,
and split them in two groups. I led one,
and made Eurylochus command the other.   205
We shook the lots in a helmet made of bronze;
Eurylochus' lot jumped out. So he
went with his band of twenty-two, all weeping.
Those left behind with me were crying too.
Inside the glade they found the house of Circe   210
built out of polished stones, on high foundations.
Round it were mountain wolves and lions, which
she tamed with drugs. They did not rush on them,
but gathered around them in a friendly way,
their long tails wagging, as dogs nuzzle round   215
their master when he comes back home from dinner
with treats for them. Just so, those sharp-clawed wolves
and lions, mighty beasts, came snuggling up.
The men were terrified. They stood outside
and heard some lovely singing. It was Circe,   220
the goddess. She was weaving as she sang,
an intricate, enchanting piece of work,
the kind a goddess fashions. Then Polites,
my most devoted and most loyal man,
a leader to his peers, said,

                    'Friends, inside   225
someone is weaving on that massive loom,
and singing so the floor resounds. Perhaps
a woman, or a goddess. Let us call her.'

They shouted out to her. She came at once,
opened the shining doors, and asked them in.   230
So thinking nothing of it, in they went.
Eurylochus alone remained outside,
suspecting trickery. She led them in,
sat them on chairs, and blended them a potion
of barley, cheese, and golden honey, mixed   235
with Pramnian wine.[7] She added potent drugs
to make them totally forget their home.
They took and drank the mixture. Then she struck them,
using her magic wand, and penned them in
the pigsty. They were turned to pigs in body   240
and voice and hair; their minds remained the same.

---

7. A particular type of wine rather than from a particular location; it is described as black and harsh by the medical writer Galen. The same wine is used for the potion made in Nestor's cup, in book 11 of the *Iliad*.

They squealed at their imprisonment, and Circe
threw them some mast and cornel cherries—food
that pigs like rooting for in muddy ground.
Eurylochus ran back to our black ship,   245
to tell us of the terrible disaster
that happened to his friends. He tried to speak,
but could not, overwhelmed by grief. His eyes
were full of tears, his heart was pierced with sorrow.
Astonished, we all questioned him. At last   250
he spoke about what happened to the others.

'Odysseus, we went off through the woods,
as you commanded. In the glade we found
a beautiful tall house of polished stone.
We heard a voice: a woman or a goddess   255
was singing as she worked her loom. My friends
called out to her. She opened up the doors,
inviting them inside. Suspecting nothing,
they followed her. But I stayed there outside,
fearing some trick. Then all at once, they vanished.   260
I sat there for a while to watch and wait,
but none of them came back.'

                                  At this, I strapped
my silver-studded sword across my back,
took up my bow, and told him, 'Take me there.'
He grasped my knees and begged me tearfully,   265

'No no, my lord! Please do not make me go!
Let me stay here! You cannot bring them back,
and you will not return here if you try.
Hurry, we must escape with these men here!
We have a chance to save our lives!'

                                  I said,   270
'You can stay here beside the ship and eat
and drink. But I will go. I must do this.'
I left the ship and shore, and walked on up,
crossing the sacred glades, and I had almost
reached the great house of the enchantress Circe,   275
when I met Hermes, carrying his wand
of gold. He seemed an adolescent boy,
the cutest age, when beards first start to grow.
He took my hand and said,

                                  'Why have you come
across these hills alone? You do not know   280
this place, poor man. Your men were turned to pigs
in Circe's house, and crammed in pens. Do you
imagine you can set them free? You cannot.
If you try that, you will not get back home.

You will stay here with them. But I can help you.   285
Here, take this antidote to keep you safe
when you go into Circe's house. Now I
will tell you all her lethal spells and tricks.
She will make you a potion mixed with poison.
Its magic will not work on you because   290
you have the herb I gave you. When she strikes you
with her long wand, then draw your sharpened sword
and rush at her as if you mean to kill her.
She will be frightened of you, and will tell you
to sleep with her. Do not hold out against her—   295
she is a goddess. If you sleep with her,
you will set free your friends and save yourself.
Tell her to swear an oath by all the gods
that she will not plot further harm for you—
or while you have your clothes off, she may hurt you,   300
unmanning you.'

        The bright mercurial god
pulled from the ground a plant and showed me how
its root is black, its flower white as milk.
The gods call this plant Moly.[8] It is hard
for mortal men to dig it up, but gods   305
are able to do everything. Then Hermes
flew through the wooded island, back towards
high Mount Olympus. I went in the house
of Circe. My heart pounded as I walked.
I stood there at the doorway, and I saw her,   310
the lovely Circe with her braided hair.
I called; she heard and opened up the doors
and asked me in. I followed nervously.
She led me to a silver-studded chair,
all finely crafted, with a footstool under.   315
In a gold cup she mixed a drink for me,
adding the drug—she hoped to do me harm.
I sipped it, but the magic did not work.
She struck me with her wand and said,

                        'Now go!
Out to the sty, and lie there with your men!'   320
But I drew my sharp sword from by my thigh
and leapt at her as if I meant to kill her.
She screamed and ducked beneath the sword, and grasped
my knees, and wailing asked me,

                    'Who are you?
Where is your city? And who are your parents?   325

8. Probably an imaginary plant, though the legend may be connected to the ancient idea that garlic (which also has a white flower and dark root) can be used against bad spirits and vampires.

I am amazed that you could drink my potion
and yet are not bewitched. No other man
has drunk it and withstood the magic charm.
But you are different. Your mind is not
enchanted. You must be Odysseus,   330
the man who can adapt to anything.
Bright flashing Hermes of the golden wand
has often told me that you would sail here
from Troy in your swift ship. Now sheathe your sword
and come to bed with me. Through making love   335
we may begin to trust each other more.'

I answered, 'Circe! How can you command me
to treat you gently, when you turned my men
to pigs, and you are planning to play tricks
in telling me to come to bed with you,   340
so you can take my courage and my manhood
when you have got me naked? I refuse
to come to bed with you, unless you swear
a mighty oath that you will not form plans
to hurt me anymore.'

                When I said that,   345
at once she made the oath as I had asked.
She vowed and formed the oath, and then at last
I went up to the dazzling bed of Circe.

Meanwhile, four slaves, her house girls, were at work
around the palace. They were nymphs, the daughters   350
of fountains and of groves and holy rivers
that flow into the sea. One set fine cloths
of purple on the chairs, with stones beneath them.
Beside each chair, another pulled up tables
of silver and set golden baskets on them.   355
The third mixed up inside a silver bowl
sweet, cheering wine, and poured it in gold cups.
The fourth brought water, and she lit a fire
beneath a mighty tripod, till it boiled.
It started bubbling in the copper cauldron;   360
she took me to the bathtub, and began
to wash my head and shoulders, using water
mixed to the perfect temperature, to take
my deep soul-crushing weariness away.
After the bath, she oiled my skin and dressed me   365
in fine wool cloak and tunic, and she led me
to a silver-studded well-carved chair, and set
a footstool underneath. Another slave
brought water for my hands, in a gold pitcher,
and poured it over them, to a silver bowl.   370
She set a polished table near. The cook
brought bread and laid a generous feast, and Circe

told me to eat. But my heart was unwilling.
I sat there with my mind on other things;
I had forebodings. Circe noticed me   375
sitting, not touching food, and weighed by grief.
She stood near me and asked, 'Odysseus!
why are you sitting there so silently,
like someone mute, eating your heart, not touching
the banquet or the wine? You need not fear.   380
Remember, I already swore an oath.'

But I said, 'Circe, no! What decent man
could bear to taste his food or sip his wine
before he saw his men with his own eyes,
and set them free? If you are so insistent   385
on telling me to eat and drink, then free them,
so I may see with my own eyes my crew
of loyal men.'

       So Circe left the hall
holding her wand, and opened up the pigsty
and drove them out, still looking like fat boars,   390
large and full grown. They stood in front of her.
Majestic Lady Circe walked among them,
anointing each with some new drug. The potion
had made thick hog-hairs sprout out on their bodies.
Those bristles all flew off and they were men,   395
but younger than before, and much more handsome,
and taller. Then they recognized me. Each
embraced me tightly in his arms, and started
sobbing in desperation. So the house
rang loud with noise, and even she herself   400
pitied them. She came near to me and said,

'Odysseus, you always find solutions.
Go now to your swift ship beside the sea.
First drag the ship to land, and bring your stores
and all your gear inside the caves. Then come   405
back with your loyal men.'

       My heart agreed;
I went down to my swift ship on the shore.
I found my loyal men beside the ship,
weeping and shedding floods of tears. As when
a herd of cows is coming back from pasture   410
into the yard; and all the little heifers
jump from their pens to skip and run towards
their mothers, and they cluster round them, mooing;
just so my men, as soon as they saw me,
began to weep, and in their minds it seemed   415
as if they had arrived in their own home,
the land of rugged Ithaca, where they

were born and raised. Still sobbing, they cried out,

'Oh, Master! We are glad to see you back!
It is as if we had come home ourselves,   420
to Ithaca, our fatherland. But tell us
about how all our other friends were killed.'

I reassured them, saying, 'First we must
drag up the ship to land, and put the stores
and all our gear inside the caves; then hurry,   425
all of you, come with me, and see your friends
inside the goddess Circe's holy house,
eating and drinking; they have food enough
to last forever.'

        They believed my story,
with the exception of Eurylochus,   430
who warned them,

        'Fools! Why would you go up there?
Why would you choose to take on so much danger,
to enter Circe's house, where she will turn us
to pigs or wolves or lions, all of us,
forced to protect her mighty house for her?   435
Remember what the Cyclops did? Our friends
went to his home with this rash lord of ours.
Because of his bad choices, they all died.'

At that, I thought of drawing my long sword
from by my sturdy thigh, to cut his head off   440
and let it fall down to the ground—although
he was close family. My men restrained me,
saying to me, 'No, king, please let him go!
Let him stay here and guard the ship, and we
will follow you to Circe's holy house.'   445

So they went up, away from ship and shore.
Eurylochus did not stay there; he came,
fearing my angry scolding.

        Meanwhile Circe
had freed the other men, and in her house
she gently bathed them, rubbing them with oil.   450
She had them dressed in woolen cloaks and tunics.
We found them feasting in the hall. The men,
seeing each other face to face again,
began to weep; their sobbing filled the hall.
The goddess stood beside me and said,

        'King,   455
clever Odysseus, Laertes' son,

now stop encouraging this lamentation.
I know you and your men have suffered greatly,
out on the fish-filled sea, and on dry land
from hostile men. But it is time to eat   460
and drink some wine. You must get back the drive
you had when you set out from Ithaca.
You are worn down and brokenhearted, always
dwelling on pain and wandering. You never
feel joy at heart. You have endured too much.'   465

We did as she had said. Then every day
for a whole year we feasted there on meat
and sweet strong wine. But when the year was over,
when months had waned and seasons turned, and each
long day had passed its course, my loyal men   470
called me and said,

                              'Be guided by the gods.
Now it is time to think of our own country,
if you are fated to survive and reach
your high-roofed house and your forefathers' land.'

My warrior soul agreed. So all day long   475
till sunset we kept sitting at the feast
of meat and sweet strong wine. But when the sun
set, and the darkness came, they went to bed
all through the shadowy palace. I went up
to Circe's splendid bed, and touched her knees   480
in supplication, and the goddess listened.

'Circe,' I said, 'fulfill the vow you made
to send me home. My heart now longs to go.
My men are also desperate to leave.
Whenever you are absent, they exhaust me   485
with constant lamentation.'

                              And she answered,
'Laertes' son, great King Odysseus,
master of every challenge, you need not
remain here in my house against your will.
But first you must complete another journey.   490
Go to the house of Hades and the dreadful
Persephone,[9] and ask the Theban prophet,
the blind Tiresias, for his advice.
Persephone has given him alone
full understanding, even now in death.   495
The other spirits flit around as shadows.'

9. Hades is god of the underworld. Persephone is his wife.

That broke my heart, and sitting on the bed
I wept, and lost all will to live and see
the shining sun. When I was done with sobbing
and rolling round in grief, I said to her,   500

'But Circe, who can guide us on this journey?
No one before has ever sailed to Hades
by ship.'

         And right away the goddess answered,
'You are resourceful, King Odysseus.
You need not worry that you have no pilot   505
to steer your ship. Set up your mast, let fly
your white sails, and sit down. The North Wind's breath
will blow the ship. When you have crossed the stream
of Ocean, you will reach the shore, where willows
let fall their dying fruit, and towering poplars   510
grow in the forest of Persephone.
Tie up your ship in the deep-eddying Ocean,
and go into the spacious home of Hades.
The Pyriphlegethon and Cocytus,
a tributary of the Styx, both run   515
into the Acheron. The flowing water
resounds beside the rock. Brave man, go there,
and dig a hole a cubit[1] wide and long,
and round it pour libations for the dead:
first honey-mix,[2] then sweet wine, and the third   520
of water. Sprinkle barley, and beseech
the spirits of the dead. Vow if you reach
the barren land of Ithaca, to kill
a heifer in your halls, the best you have,
uncalved, and you will heap the fire with meat,   525
and offer to Tiresias alone
a ram, pure black, the best of all your flock.
When you have prayed to all the famous dead,
slaughter one ram and one black ewe, directing
the animals to Erebus,[3] but turn   530
yourself away, towards the gushing river.
Many will come. Then tell your men to skin
the sheep that lie there killed by ruthless bronze,
and burn them, with a prayer to mighty Hades
and terrible Persephone. Then draw   535
your sword and sit. Do not let them come near
the blood, until you hear Tiresias.
The prophet will soon come, and he will tell you
about your journey, measured out across
the fish-filled sea, and how you will get home.'   540

---

1. A unit of measure roughly equivalent to the length of a human forearm.
2. A mixture of honey with some other sub-stance, perhaps milk.
3. The underworld.

Dawn on her golden throne began to shine,
and Circe dressed me in my cloak and tunic.
The goddess wore a long white dress, of fine
and delicate fabric, with a golden belt,
and on her head, a veil. Then I walked round,   545
all through the house, and called my men. I stood
beside each one, and roused them with my words.

'Wake up! Now no more dozing in sweet sleep.
We have to go. The goddess gave instructions.'

They did as I had said. But even then   550
I could not lead my men away unharmed.
The youngest one—Elpenor was his name—
not very brave in war, nor very smart,
was lying high up in the home of Circe,
apart from his companions, seeking coolness   555
since he was drunk. He heard the noise and bustle,
the movements of his friends, and jumped up quickly,
forgetting to climb down the lofty ladder.
He fell down crashing headlong from the roof,
and broke his neck, right at the spine. His spirit   560
went down to Hades.

                    Then I told the others,
'Perhaps you think that you are going home.
But Circe says we have to go towards
the house of Hades and Persephone,
to meet Tiresias, the Theban spirit.'   565

At that, their hearts were broken. They sat down
right there and wept and tore their clothes. But all
their lamentation did no good. We went
down to our speedy ship beside the sea,
despite our grief. We shed abundant tears.   570
Then Circe came and tied up one black ewe
and one ram by the ship, and slipped away,
easily; who can see the gods go by
unless they wish to show themselves to us?"

BOOK 11

[The Dead]

"We reached the sea and first of all we launched
the ship into the sparkling salty water,
set up the mast and sails, and brought the sheep
on board with us. We were still grieving, weeping,
in floods of tears. But beautiful, dread Circe,   5
the goddess who can speak in human tongues,
sent us a wind to fill our sails, fair wind

befriending us behind the dark blue prow.
We made our tackle shipshape, then sat down.
The wind and pilot guided straight our course.   10
The sun set. It was dark in all directions.

We reached the limits of deep-flowing Ocean,
where the Cimmerians live and have their city.
Their land is covered up in mist and cloud;
the shining Sun God never looks on them   15
with his bright beams—not when he rises up
into the starry sky, nor when he turns
back from the heavens to earth. Destructive night
blankets the world for all poor mortals there.
We beached our ship, drove out the sheep, and went 20
to seek the stream of Ocean where the goddess
had told us we must go. Eurylochus
and Perimedes made the sacrifice.
I drew my sword and dug a hole, a fathom
widthways and lengthways, and I poured libations   25
for all the dead: first honey-mix, sweet wine,
and lastly, water. On the top, I sprinkled
barley, and made a solemn vow that if
I reached my homeland, I would sacrifice
my best young heifer, still uncalved, and pile   30
the altar high with offerings for the dead.
I promised for Tiresias as well
a pure black sheep, the best in all my flock.
So with these vows, I called upon the dead.
I took the sheep and slit their throats above   35
the pit. Black blood flowed out. The spirits came
up out of Erebus and gathered round.
Teenagers, girls and boys, the old who suffered
for many years, and fresh young brides whom labor
destroyed in youth; and many men cut down   40
in battle by bronze spears, still dressed in armor
stained with their blood. From every side they crowded
around the pit, with eerie cries. Pale fear
took hold of me. I roused my men and told them
to flay the sheep that I had killed, and burn them, 45
and pray to Hades and Persephone.
I drew my sword and sat on guard, preventing
the spirits of the dead from coming near
the blood, till I had met Tiresias.

First came the spirit of my man Elpenor,   50
who had not yet been buried in the earth.
We left his body in the house of Circe
without a funeral or burial;
we were too occupied with other things.
On sight of him, I wept in pity, saying,   55

'Elpenor, how did you come here, in darkness?
You came on foot more quickly than I sailed.'

He groaned in answer, 'Lord Odysseus,
you master every circumstance. But I
had bad luck from some god, and too much wine   60
befuddled me. In Circe's house I lay
upstairs, and I forgot to use the ladder
to climb down from the roof. I fell headfirst;
my neck was broken from my spine. My spirit
came down to Hades. By the men you left,   65
the absent ones! And by your wife! And father,
who brought you up from babyhood! And by
your son, Telemachus, whom you abandoned
alone at home, I beg you! When you sail
from Hades and you dock your ship again   70
at Aeaea, please, my lord, remember me.
Do not go on and leave me there unburied,
abandoned, without tears or lamentation—
or you will make the gods enraged at you.
Burn me with all my arms, and heap a mound   75
beside the gray salt sea, so in the future
people will know of me and my misfortune.
And fix into the tomb the oar I used
to row with my companions while I lived.'

'Poor man!' I answered, 'I will do all this.'   80

We sat there talking sadly—I on one side
held firm my sword in blood, while on the other
the ghost of my crew member made his speech.
Then came the spirit of my own dead mother,
Autolycus'[1] daughter Anticleia,   85
whom I had left alive when I went off
to holy Troy. On seeing her, I wept
in pity. But despite my bitter grief,
I would not let her near the blood till I
talked to Tiresias. The prophet came   90
holding a golden scepter, and he knew me,
and said,

        'King under Zeus, Odysseus,
adept survivor, why did you abandon
the sun, poor man, to see the dead, and this
place without joy? Step back now from the pit,   95
hold up your sharp sword so that I may drink
the blood and speak to you.'

---

1. Autolycus is Odysseus's maternal grandfather; the name suggests "Wolf Man."

                      At that, I sheathed
my silver-studded sword. When he had drunk
the murky blood, the famous prophet spoke.

'Odysseus, you think of going home   100
as honey-sweet, but gods will make it bitter.
I think Poseidon will not cease to feel
incensed because you blinded his dear son.
You have to suffer, but you can get home,
if you control your urges and your men.   105
Turn from the purple depths and sail your ship
towards the island of Thrinacia; there
you will find grazing cows and fine fat sheep,
belonging to the god who sees and hears
all things—the Sun God. If you leave them be,   110
keeping your mind fixed on your journey home,
you may still get to Ithaca, despite
great losses. But if you hurt those cows, I see
disaster for your ship and for your men.
If you yourself escape, you will come home   115
late and exhausted, in a stranger's boat,
having destroyed your men. And you will find
invaders eating your supplies at home,
courting your wife with gifts. Then you will match
the suitors' violence and kill them all,   120
inside your halls, through tricks or in the open,
with sharp bronze weapons. When those men are dead,
you have to go away and take an oar
to people with no knowledge of the sea,
who do not salt their food. They never saw   125
a ship's red prow, nor oars, the wings of boats.
I prophesy the signs of things to come.
When you meet somebody, a traveler,
who calls the thing you carry on your back
a winnowing fan, then fix that oar in earth   130
and make fine sacrifices to Poseidon—
a bull and stud-boar. Then you will go home
and offer holy hecatombs to all
the deathless gods who live in heaven, each
in order. Gentle death will come to you,   135
far from the sea, of comfortable old age,
your people flourishing. So it will be.'

I said, 'Tiresias, I hope the gods
spin out this fate for me. But tell me this,
and tell the truth. I saw my mother's spirit,   140
sitting in silence near the blood, refusing
even to talk to me, or meet my eyes!
My lord, how can I make her recognize
that it is me?'

                    At once he made his answer.
'That is an easy matter to explain.   145
Whenever you allow one of these spirits
to come here near the blood, it will be able
to speak the truth to you. As soon as you
push them away, they have to leave again.'

With that, Tiresias, the prophet spirit,   150
was finished; he departed to the house
of Hades. I stayed rooted there in place
until my mother came and drank the blood.
She knew me then and spoke in tones of grief.

'My child! How did you come here through the darkness   155
while you were still alive? This place is hard
for living men to see. There are great rivers
and dreadful gulfs, including the great Ocean
which none can cross on foot; one needs a ship.
Have you come wandering here, so far from Troy,   160
with ship and crew? Have you not yet arrived
in Ithaca, nor seen your wife at home?'

I answered, 'Mother, I was forced to come
to Hades to consult the prophet spirit,
Theban Tiresias. I have not yet   165
come near to Greece, nor reached my own home country.
I have been lost and wretchedly unhappy
since I first followed mighty Agamemnon
to Troy, the land of horses, to make war
upon the people there. But tell me, how   170
was sad death brought upon you? By long illness?
Or did the archer Artemis destroy you
with gentle arrows?[2] Tell me too about
my father and the son I left behind.
Are they still honored as the kings? Or has   175
another taken over, saying I
will not return? And tell me what my wife
is thinking, and her plans. Does she stay with
our son and focus on his care, or has
the best of the Achaeans[3] married her?'   180

My mother answered, 'She stays firm. Her heart
is strong. She is still in your house. And all
her nights are passed in misery, and days
in tears. But no one has usurped your throne.
Telemachus still tends the whole estate   185
unharmed and feasts in style, as lords should do,
and he is always asked to council meetings.

---

2. Artemis, goddess of hunting and childbirth,   women.
was particularly associated with the deaths of   **3.** Greeks.

Your father stays out in the countryside.
He will not come to town. He does not sleep
on a real bed with blankets and fresh sheets.   190
In winter he sleeps inside, by the fire,
just lying in the ashes with the slaves;
his clothes are rags. In summer and at harvest,
the piles of fallen leaves are beds for him.
He lies there grieving, full of sorrow, longing   195
for your return. His old age is not easy.
And that is why I met my fate and died.
The goddess did not shoot me in my home,
aiming with gentle arrows. Nor did sickness
suck all the strength out from my limbs, with long   200
and cruel wasting. No, it was missing you,
Odysseus, my sunshine; your sharp mind,
and your kind heart. That took sweet life from me.'

Then in my heart I wanted to embrace
the spirit of my mother. She was dead,   205
and I did not know how. Three times I tried,
longing to touch her. But three times her ghost
flew from my arms, like shadows or like dreams.
Sharp pain pierced deeper in me as I cried,

'No, Mother! Why do you not stay for me,   210
and let me hold you, even here in Hades?
Let us wrap loving arms around each other
and find a frigid comfort in shared tears!
But is this really you? Or has the Queen
sent me a phantom, to increase my grief?'   215

She answered, 'Oh, my child! You are the most
unlucky man alive. Persephone
is not deceiving you. This is the rule
for mortals when we die. Our muscles cease
to hold the flesh and skeleton together;   220
as soon as life departs from our white bones,
the force of blazing fire destroys the corpse.
The spirit flies away and soon is gone,
just like a dream. Now hurry to the light;
remember all these things, so you may tell   225
your wife in times to come.'

                                   As we were talking,
some women came, sent by Persephone—
the daughters and the wives of warriors.
They thronged and clustered round the blood. I wanted
to speak to each of them, and made a plan.   230
I drew my sword and would not let them come
together in a group to drink the blood.
They took turns coming forward, and each told

her history; I questioned each. The first
was well-born Tyro, child of Salmoneus,   235
and wife of Cretheus, Aeolus' son.
She fell in love with River Enipeus,
most handsome of all rivers that pour water
over the earth. She often went to visit
his lovely streams. Poseidon took his form,   240
and at the river mouth he lay with her.
Around them arched a dark-blue wave that stood
high as a mountain, and it hid the god
and mortal woman. There he loosed her belt
and made her sleep. The god made love to her,   245
and afterwards, he took her hand and spoke.

'Woman, be glad about this love. You will
bear glorious children in the coming year.
Affairs with gods always result in offspring.
Look after them and raise them. Now go home;   250
tell no one who I am. But I will tell you.
I am Poseidon, Shaker of the Earth.'
With that he sank beneath the ocean waves.

She brought two sons to term, named Pelias
and Neleus, both sturdy boys who served   255
almighty Zeus; and Pelias' home
was on the spacious dancing fields of Iolcus,
where sheep are plentiful; his brother lived
in sandy Pylos. And she bore more sons,
to Cretheus: Aeson, Pheres, Amythaeon   260
who loved war chariots.

               And after her
I saw Antiope, who said she slept
in Zeus' arms and bore two sons: Amphion
and Zethus, the first settlers of Thebes,
city of seven gates. Strong though they were,   265
they could not live there on the open plain
without defenses.

              Then I saw Alcmene,
wife of Amphitryon, who by great Zeus
conceived the lionhearted Heracles.
And I saw Megara, proud Creon's child,   270
the wife of tireless Heracles. I saw
fine Epicaste, Oedipus' mother,
who did a dreadful thing in ignorance:
she married her own son. He killed his father,
and married her. The gods revealed the truth   275
to humans; through their deadly plans, he ruled
the Cadmeans in Thebes, despite his pain.
But Epicaste crossed the gates of Hades;

she tied a noose and hung it from the ceiling,
and hanged herself for sorrow, leaving him   280
the agonies a mother's Furies bring.[4]

Then I saw Chloris, who was youngest daughter
of Amphion, who ruled the Minyans
in Orchomenus. She was beautiful,
and Neleus paid rich bride-gifts for her.   285
She was the queen in Pylos, and she bore
Chromius, Nestor, Periclymenus,
and mighty Pyro, who was such a marvel
that all the men desired to marry her.
But Neleus would only let her marry   290
a man who could drive off the stubborn cattle
of Iphicles from Phylace. The prophet
Melampus was the only one who tried,
but gods restrained him, cursing him; the herdsmen
shackled him. Days and months went by, the seasons   295
changed as the year went by, until at last
Iphicles set him free as his reward
for prophecy.[5] The will of Zeus was done.
And then I saw Tyndareus' wife,
Leda, who bore him two strong sons: the horseman   300
Castor, and Polydeuces, skillful boxer.
Life-giving earth contains them, still alive.
Zeus honors them even in the underworld.
They live and die alternately, and they
are honored like the gods.[6]

               And then I saw   305
Iphimedeia, wife of Aloeus,
who proudly said Poseidon slept with her.
She had two sons whose lives were both cut short:
Otus and famous Ephialtes, whom
the fertile earth raised up as the tallest heroes   310
after renowned Orion. At nine years,
they were nine cubits wide, nine fathoms high.
They brought the din of dreadful raging war
to the immortal gods and tried to set
Ossa and Pelion—trees, leaves and all—   315
on Mount Olympus, high up in the sky.
They might have managed it, if they had reached

4. This passage gives a version of the myth different from that of Sophocles' play, in which Oedipus's mother is called Jocasta.
5. The prophet Melampus, after his unsuccessful attempt to drive off Iphicles' cattle and win his daughter's hand, prophesied that Iphicles, who had been impotent, would be able to have more children. In reward for the good prophecy, Iphicles set Melampus free.

6. Castor and Polydeuces (also known as Pollux), the twins associated with the constellation Gemini, were given by Zeus the privilege of being alive on every other day, taking turns. According to many versions of the myth, Zeus was actually their father, having seduced Leda in the guise of a swan (so the twins are brothers of Helen and Clytemnestra).

full adulthood. Apollo, son of Zeus
by braided Leto, killed them: they were both
dead before down could grow on their young chins,   320
dead before beards could wreathe their naked faces.

Then I saw Phaedra, Procris,[7] and the lovely
daughter of dangerous Minos, Ariadne.
Theseus tried to bring her back from Crete
to Athens, but could not succeed; the goddess   325
Artemis killed her on the isle of Día,
when Dionysus spoke against her.[8] Then
came Maera, Clymene and Eriphyle:
accepting golden bribes, she killed her husband.[9]
I cannot name each famous wife and daughter   330
I saw there; holy night would pass away
before I finished. I must go to sleep
on board the ship beside my crew, or else
right here. I know the gods and you will help
my onward journey."

        They were silent, spellbound,   335
listening in the shadowy hall. White-armed
Arete spoke.

        "Phaeacians! Look at him!
What a tall, handsome man! And what a mind!
He is my special guest, but all of you
share in our rank as lords; so do not send him   340
away too fast, and when he leaves, you must
be generous. He is in need, and you
are rich in treasure, through the will of gods."

The veteran Echeneus, the oldest
man in their company, said, "Our wise queen   345
has hit the mark, my friends. Do as she says.
But first Alcinous must speak and act."

The king said, "Let it be as she has spoken,
as long as I am ruler of this nation
of seafarers. I know our guest is keen   350
to go back home, but let him stay till morning.

7. Phaedra was the elder daughter of Minos, king of Crete, who married Theseus of Athens and fell in love with his son, her stepson, with disastrous results. Procris was the daughter of Erectheus, another king of Athens, who was killed unintentionally by her husband, Cephalus.
8. Ariadne, another daughter of Minos of Crete, helped Theseus through the Cretan labyrinth to kill her half-brother, the Minotaur, and was taken off with him on his ship. In later versions of the legend, Theseus abandoned her, and she was whisked away by Dionysus. This Homeric version implies that she somehow offended Dionysus—it is unclear how, and this story is otherwise unknown.
9. Eriphyle accepted the bribe of a gold necklace to persuade her husband, Amphiaraus, king of Argos, to go on a doomed raid against Thebes.

I will give all his presents then. You men
will all help him, but I will help the most,
since I hold power here."

Odysseus

answered with careful tact, "Alcinous,   355
king over all the people, if you urged me
to stay here for a year before you gave
the parting gifts and sent me on my way,
I would be happy. It would be far better
to reach my own dear home with hands filled full   360
of treasure. So all men would honor me
and welcome me back home in Ithaca."

Alcinous replied, "Odysseus,
the earth sustains all different kinds of people.
Many are cheats and thieves, who fashion lies   365
out of thin air. But when I look at you,
I know you are not in that category.
Your story has both grace and wisdom in it.
You sounded like a skillful poet, telling
the sufferings of all the Greeks, including   370
what you endured yourself. But come now, tell me
if you saw any spirits of your friends,
who went with you to Troy and undertook
the grief and pain of war. The night is long;
it is not time to sleep yet. Tell me more   375
amazing deeds! I would keep listening
until bright daybreak, if you kept on telling
the dangers you have passed."

Odysseus

answered politely, "King Alcinous,
there is a time for many tales, but also   380
a time for sleep. If you still want to hear,
I will not grudge you stories. I will tell you
some even more distressing ones, about
my friend who managed to escape the shrieks
and battle din at Troy but perished later,   385
killed in his own home by an evil wife.
Holy Persephone dispersed the ghosts
of women and they went their separate ways.
The ghost of Agamemnon came in sorrow
with all the rest who met their fate with him   390
inside Aegisthus' house. He recognized me
when he had drunk the blood. He wept out loud,
and tearfully reached out his hands towards me,
desperate to touch. His energy and strength
and all the suppleness his limbs once had   395
were gone. I wept and my heart pitied him.
I cried out,

'Lord of men, King Agamemnon!
How did you die? What bad luck brought you down?
Was it Poseidon rousing up a blast
of cruel wind to wreck your ships? Or were you   400
killed on dry land by enemies as you
were poaching their fat flocks of sheep or cattle,
or fighting for their city and their wives?'

He answered right away, 'King under Zeus,
Odysseus—survivor! No, Poseidon   405
did not rouse up a dreadful blast of wind
to wreck my ship. No hostile men on land
killed me in self-defense. It was Aegisthus
who planned my death and murdered me, with help
from my own wife. He called me to his house   410
to dinner and he killed me, as one slaughters
an ox at manger. What a dreadful death!
My men were systematically slaughtered
like pigs in a rich lord's house for some feast,
a wedding or a banquet. You have seen   415
many cut down in war in thick of battle,
or slaughtered in a combat hand to hand;
but you would grieve with even deeper pity
if you could see us lying dead beneath
the tables piled with food and wine. The floor   420
swam thick with blood. I heard the desperate voice
of Priam's daughter, poor Cassandra,[1] whom
deceitful Clytemnestra killed beside me.
As I lay dying, struck through by the sword,
I tried to lift my arms up from the ground.   425
That she-dog turned away. I went to Hades.
She did not even shut my eyes or close
my mouth. There is no more disgusting act
than when a wife betrays a man like that.
That woman formed a plot to murder me!   430
Her husband! When I got back home, I thought
I would be welcomed, at least by my slaves
and children. She has such an evil mind
that she has poured down shame on her own head
and on all other women, even good ones.'   435

I cried out, 'Curse her! Zeus has always brought
disaster to the house of Atreus
through women. Many men were lost for Helen,
and Clytemnestra[2] formed this plot against you
when you were far away.'   440

                        At once he answered,
'So you must never treat your wife too well.

---

1. Cassandra, who had the gift of prophecy   prize of war by Agamemnon.
from Apollo, was brought back from Troy as a   2. Helen and Clytemnestra were sisters.

Do not let her know everything you know.
Tell her some things, hide others. But your wife
will not kill you, Odysseus. The wise
Penelope is much too sensible   445
to do such things. Your bride was very young
when we went off to war. She had a baby
still at her breast, who must be now a man.
He will be glad when you come home and see him,
and he will throw his arms around his father.   450
That is how things should go. My wife prevented
my eager eyes from gazing at my son.
She killed me first. I have a final piece
of sound advice for you—take heed of it.
When you arrive in your own land, do not   455
anchor your ship in full view; move in secret.
There is no trusting women any longer.
But have you any news about my son?
Is he alive? Is he in Orchomenus,
or sandy Pylos, or with Menelaus   460
in Sparta? Surely my fine son Orestes
is not yet dead.'

       I answered, 'Agamemnon,
why ask me this? I do not even know
whether he is alive or dead. It is
pointless to talk of hypotheticals.'   465

Both of us wept profusely, deeply grieving
over the bitter words we spoke. Then came
the spirits of Achilles[3] and Patroclus
and of Antilochus and Ajax,[4] who
was handsomest and had the best physique   470
of all the Greeks, next only to Achilles
the sprinter. And Achilles recognized me
and spoke in tears.

       'My lord Odysseus,
you fox! What will you think of next? How could you
bear to come down to Hades? Numb dead people   475
live here, the shades of poor exhausted mortals.'
I said, 'Achilles, greatest of Greek heroes,
I came down here to meet Tiresias,
in case he had advice for my return
to rocky Ithaca. I have not even   480
returned to Greece, my homeland. I have had
bad luck. But no one's luck was ever better
than yours, nor ever will be. In your life
we Greeks respected you as we do gods,

---

3. Best of the Greek heroes, prominent character in the *Iliad*.

4. Strong Greek hero known for defensive
fighting.

and now that you are here, you have great power   485
among the dead. Achilles, you should not
be bitter at your death.'

                But he replied,
'Odysseus, you must not comfort me
for death. I would prefer to be a workman,
hired by a poor man on a peasant farm,   490
than rule as king of all the dead. But come,
tell me about my son. Do you have news?
Did he march off to war to be a leader?
And what about my father Peleus?
Does he still have good standing among all   495
the Myrmidons? Or do they treat him badly
in Phthia and Greece, since he is old
and frail? Now I have left the light of day,
and am not there to help, as on the plains
of Troy when I was killing the best Trojans,   500
to help the Greeks. If I could go for even
a little while, with all that strength I had,
up to my father's house, I would make those
who hurt and disrespect him wish my hands
were not invincible.'

                I answered him,   505
'I have no news to tell about your father,
but I can tell you all about your son,
dear Neoptolemus. I brought him from
Scyros by ship, with other well-armed Greeks.
When we were strategizing about Troy,   510
he always spoke up first and to the purpose,
unmatched except by Nestor and myself.
And when we fought at Troy, he never paused
in the great throng of battle; he was always
fearlessly running forward, and he slaughtered   515
enormous numbers in the clash of war.
I cannot name all those he killed for us.
But with his bronze he cut down Eurypylus,
the son of Telephus, most handsome man
I ever saw, next only to great Memnon.   520
The multitude of Cetians he brought
were also killed, since Priam bribed his mother.[5]
When we, the Argive leaders, were preparing
to climb inside the Wooden Horse, it was
my task to open up and close the door.   525
The other Greek commanders were in tears;
their legs were shaking. Not your handsome boy!
I never saw his face grow pale; he had

---

5. After the death of Achilles, Priam bribed   for the Trojans.
Eurypylus's mother to persuade her son to fight

no tears to wipe away. Inside the horse,
he begged me to allow him to jump out. 530
He gripped his sword hilt and his heavy spear,
so desperate to go hurt the Trojans.
At last, when we had sacked the lofty city
of Priam, he embarked weighed down with spoils.
No sharp bronze spear had wounded him at all; 535
he was unhurt by all the skirmishes
endured in war when Ares rages blind.'

After I told him this, Achilles' ghost
took great swift-footed strides across the fields
of asphodel, delighted to have heard 540
about the glorious prowess of his son.

Other dead souls were gathering, all sad;
each told the story of his sorrow. Only
Ajax kept back, enraged because I won
Achilles' armor,[6] when the case was judged 545
beside the ships. The hero's mother, Thetis,
and sons of Troy, and Pallas, gave the arms
to me. I wish I had not won this contest!
For those arms Ajax lies beneath the earth,
whose looks and deeds were best of all the Greeks 550
after Achilles, son of Peleus.
I spoke to him to try to make it up.

'Please, Ajax, son of mighty Telamon,
can you not set aside your rage at me
about those cursed arms? Not even now, 555
in death? The gods made them to ruin us.
You were our tower; what a loss you were!
We Greeks were struck by grief when you were gone;
we mourned as long for you as for Achilles.
Blame nobody but Zeus. He ruined us, 560
in hatred for the army of the Greeks;
and that was why he brought this doom on you.
But listen now, my lord. Subdue your anger.'
He did not answer. He went off and followed
the spirits of the dead to Erebus. 565

Despite his rage, we might have spoken longer
if I had not felt in my heart an urge
to see more spirits. I saw Minos[7] there,
the son of Zeus, who holds the golden scepter
and sits in judgment on the dead. They ask 570
their king to arbitrate disputes, inside
the house of Hades, where the doors are always

---

6. Achilles' sea-goddess mother, Thetis, had   7. Legendary king of Crete.
given him armor crafted by the god Hephaestus.

wide open. I saw great Orion,[8] chasing
across the fields of asphodel the beasts
he killed when living high in lonely mountains,   575
holding his indestructible bronze club.
And I saw Tityus, the son of Gaia,
stretched out nine miles.[9] When Leto, Zeus' lover,
was traveling to Pytho, through the fields
of beautiful Panopeus, he raped her.   580
Two vultures sit on either side of him,
ripping his liver, plunging in his bowels;
he fails to push them off. I saw the pain
of Tantalus, in water to his chin,
so parched, no way to drink. When that old man   585
bent down towards the water, it was gone;
some god had dried it up, and at his feet
dark earth appeared. Tall leafy trees hung fruit
above his head: sweet figs and pomegranates
and brightly shining apples and ripe olives.   590
But when he grasped them with his hands, the wind
hurled them away towards the shadowy clouds.
And I saw Sisyphus in torment, pushing
a giant rock with both hands, leaning on it
with all his might to shove it up towards   595
a hilltop; when he almost reached the peak,
its weight would swerve, and it would roll back down,
heedlessly. But he kept on straining, pushing,
his body drenched in sweat, his head all dusty.
I saw a phantom of great Heracles.   600
The man himself is with the deathless gods,[1]
happy and feasting, with fine-ankled Hebe,[2]
the child of mighty Zeus and golden Hera.
Around his ghost, the dead souls shrieked like birds,
all panic struck. He walked like gloomy night,   605
holding his bow uncased and with an arrow
held on the string. He glowered terribly,
poised for a shot. Around his chest was strapped
a terrifying baldric made of gold,
fashioned with marvelous images of bears,   610
wild boars, and lions with fierce staring eyes,
and battles and the slaughtering of men.
I hope the craftsman who designed this scene
will never make another work like this.
This Heracles at once knew who I was,   615
and full of grief he cried,

---

8. Mythical hunter who was turned into the
constellation Orion.
9. Tityus was a Titan, one of the generation
before the Olympian gods. Gaia is the original
earth goddess.
1. Heracles, a son of Zeus, was supposed to
have been rewarded after all his labors with a
place among the Olympian gods. The confusing suggestion that his phantom is with the
dead, while his real self is with the gods, may
be a reflection of various views about whether
or not Heracles really was apotheosized.
2. "Hebe" means "youth."

'Odysseus!
Master of every circumstance, so you
are also tortured by the weight of fortune
as I was while I lived beneath the sun?
I was a son of Zeus, and yet my pain   620
was infinite. I was enslaved to someone
far less heroic than myself, who laid
harsh labors on me.[3] Once he sent me here
to bring back Cerberus,[4] since he could think
of no worse task for me. I brought the Dog   625
up out of Hades, with the help of Hermes,
and flashing-eyed Athena.'

                                   He went back
to Hades' house. I stayed, in case more heroes
who died in ancient times should come to me.
I would have seen the noble men I hoped for,   630
Pirithous and Theseus, god-born.[5]
But masses of the dead came thronging round
with eerie cries, and cold fear seized me, lest
the dreadful Queen Persephone might send
the monster's head, the Gorgon,[6] out of Hades.   635
So then I hurried back and told my men
to climb on board the ship and loose the cables.
They did so, and sat down along the benches.
The current bore the ship down River Ocean,
first with the help of oars, and then fair wind."   640

BOOK 12

[Difficult Choices]

"Our ship sailed out beyond the stream of Ocean,
across the waves of open sea, and came
to Aeaea, home of newborn Dawn, who dances
in meadows with the beams of Helius.
We beached the ship upon the sandy shore,   5
and disembarked, and there we fell asleep
while waiting for bright morning. When Dawn came,
born early, with her fingertips like petals,
I sent my men to Circe's house, to bring
the body of the dead Elpenor. Quickly   10
we chopped the wood and at the farthest headland

---

3. Eurystheus, at the behest of the goddess
Hera, laid the labors on Heracles, whom she
resented as an illegitimate son of her husband,
Zeus.
4. Guard dog of the underworld.
5. Theseus, a son of Poseidon, was a mythic

king of Athens and killer of the Minotaur. Pirithous was his best friend, a son of Zeus;
together they went to the underworld, hoping
to abduct Persephone.
6. Female monster whose gaze turns onlookers to stone.

we held a funeral for him, and wept
profusely, crying out in grief. We burned
his body and his gear, and built a mound,
and dragged a pillar onto it, and fixed   15
his oar on top—each ritual step in turn.
Circe, the well-groomed goddess, was aware
that we were back from Hades, and she hurried
to meet us with her slaves. They carried bread
and meat and bright red wine. She stood among us,   20
and said,

       'This is amazing! You all went
alive to Hades—you will be twice-dead,
when other people only die one time!
Eat now, and stay here drinking wine all day.
At dawn, sail on. I will explain your route   25
in detail, so no evil thing can stitch
a means to hurt you, on the land or sea.'

I am a stubborn man, but I agreed,
so there we sat and feasted on the meat
and strong sweet wine until the sun went down.   30
When darkness fell, the men slept by the ship.
Then Circe took my hand, and led me off
apart from them, and questioned me in detail.
I told her everything. The lady Circe
replied at last,

       'That quest is over now.   35
So listen, I will give you good instructions;
another god will make sure you remember.
First you will reach the Sirens, who bewitch
all passersby. If anyone goes near them
in ignorance, and listens to their voices,   40
that man will never travel to his home,
and never make his wife and children happy
to have him back with them again. The Sirens
who sit there in their meadow will seduce him
with piercing songs. Around about them lie   45
great heaps of men, flesh rotting from their bones,
their skin all shriveled up. Use wax to plug
your sailors' ears as you row past, so they
are deaf to them. But if you wish to hear them,
your men must fasten you to your ship's mast   50
by hand and foot, straight upright, with tight ropes.
So bound, you can enjoy the Sirens' song.
But if you beg your men to set you free,
they have to tie you down with firmer knots.
I will not give you definite instructions   55
about which route to take when you have sailed
beyond the Sirens. Let your heart decide.

There are two choices, and the first goes through
vast overhanging rocks, which Amphitrite
batters aggressively with mighty waves.   60
The blessed gods call these the Wandering Rocks.
No birds can fly through safe, not even doves,
who bring ambrosia to Zeus. One dove
is always lost in that sheer gulf of stone
and Zeus must send another to restore   65
the number of the flock. No human ship
has ever passed there. When one tries to enter,
the waves and raging gusts of fire engulf
ship timbers and the bodies of the men.
Only the famous *Argo* sailed through there   70
returning from the visit with Aeetes.
The current hurled the ship towards the rocks,
but Hera, who loved Jason, led them safe.[1]
Taking the second way, you meet two rocks:
one reaches up to heaven with its peak,   75
surrounded by blue fog that never clears.
No light comes through there, even in the summer.
No man could climb it or set foot upon it,
even if he had twenty hands and feet.
The rock is sheer, as if it had been polished.   80
Right in the middle lies a murky cave
that faces west, towards dark Erebus.
Steer your ship past it, great Odysseus.
The hollow cave is so high up, no man
could shoot it with an arrow. There lives Scylla,   85
howling and barking horribly; her voice
is puppylike, but she is dangerous;
even a god would be afraid of her.
She has twelve dangling legs and six long necks
with a gruesome head on each, and in each face   90
three rows of crowded teeth, pregnant with death.
Her belly slumps inside the hollow cave;
she keeps her heads above the yawning chasm
and scopes around the rock, and hunts for fish.
She catches dolphins, seals, and sometimes even   95
enormous whales—Queen Amphitrite, ruler
of roaring waters, nurtures many creatures.
No sailors ever pass that way unharmed.
She snatches one man with each mouth from off
each dark-prowed ship. The other rock is near,   100
enough to shoot an arrow right across.
This second rock is lower down, and on it
there grows a fig tree with thick leaves. Beneath,
divine Charybdis sucks black water down.

1. The Greek hero Jason sailed in the *Argo* to   was supposed to have taken place a generation
get the Golden Fleece from King Aeetes of Col-   before the wanderings of Odysseus. Jason was
chis. The journey of Jason and the Argonauts   the favorite of the goddess Hera.

Three times a day she spurts it up; three times   105
she glugs it down. Avoid that place when she
is swallowing the water. No one could
save you from death then, even great Poseidon.
Row fast, and steer your ship alongside Scylla,
since it is better if you lose six men   110
than all of them.'

       I answered, 'Goddess, please,
tell me the truth: is there no other way?
Or I can somehow circumvent Charybdis
and stop that Scylla when she tries to kill
my men?'

      The goddess answered, 'No, you fool!   115
Your mind is still obsessed with deeds of war.
But now you must surrender to the gods.
She is not mortal. She is deathless evil,
terrible, wild and cruel. You cannot fight her.
The best solution and the only way   120
is flight. I am afraid if you take time
to arm beside the rock, she will attack
again with all six heads and take six more.
So row away with all your might, and call
on Scylla's mother, Cratais, Great Force,   125
who bore her as a blight on humankind.
Go fast, before the goddess strikes again.
Then you will reach the island called Thrinacia,
where Helius keeps sheep and many cattle:[2]
fifty per herd, with seven herds in all.   130
They never reproduce or die, and those
who tend them are the smooth-haired goddesses,
Phaethousa and Lampetia, the shining
daughters of Helius by bright Neaira.
She brought them up, then sent them off to live   135
there in remote Thrinacia, to guard
their father's sheep and cattle. If you can
remember home and leave the cows unharmed,
you will at last arrive in Ithaca.
But if you damage them, I must foretell   140
disaster for your ship and for your crew.
Even if you survive, you will return
late and humiliated, having caused
the death of all your men.'

       The golden throne
of Dawn was riding up the sky as Circe   145
concluded, and she strode across her island.
I went back to my ship and roused the men

---

2. Helius and Hyperion are both sun gods, here confused.

to get on board and loose the sternward cables.
Embarking, they sat down, each in his place,
and struck the gray saltwater with their oars.   150
Behind our dark-prowed ship, the dreadful goddess
Circe sent friendly wind to fill the sails.
We worked efficiently to organize
the rigging, and the breeze and pilot steered.
Then with an anxious heart I told the crew,   155

'My friends, the revelations Circe shared
with me should not be kept a secret, known
to me alone. I will share them with you,
and we can die in knowledge of the truth,
or else escape. She said we must avoid   160
the voices of the otherworldly Sirens;
steer past their flowering meadow. And she says
that I alone should hear their singing. Bind me,
to keep me upright at the mast, wound round
with rope. If I beseech you and command you   165
to set me free, you must increase my bonds
and chain me even tighter.'

                    So I told them
each detail. Soon our well-built ship, blown fast
by fair winds, neared the island of the Sirens,
and suddenly, the wind died down. Calm came.   170
Some spirit lulled the waves to sleep. The men
got up, pulled down the sails, and stowed them in
the hollow hold. They sat at oar and made
the water whiten, struck by polished wood.
I gripped a wheel of wax between my hands   175
and cut it small. Firm kneading and the sunlight
warmed it, and then I rubbed it in the ears
of each man in his turn. They bound my hands
and feet, straight upright at the mast. They sat
and hit the sea with oars. We traveled fast,   180
and when we were in earshot of the Sirens,
they knew our ship was near, and started singing.

'Odysseus! Come here! You are well-known
from many stories! Glory of the Greeks!
Now stop your ship and listen to our voices.   185
All those who pass this way hear honeyed song,
poured from our mouths. The music brings them joy,
and they go on their way with greater knowledge,
since we know everything the Greeks and Trojans
suffered in Troy, by gods' will; and we know   190
whatever happens anywhere on earth.'

Their song was so melodious, I longed
to listen more. I told my men to free me.

I scowled at them, but they kept rowing on.
Eurylochus and Perimedes stood   195
and tied me even tighter, with more knots.
But when we were well past them and I could
no longer hear the singing of the Sirens,
I nodded to my men, and they removed
the wax that I had used to plug their ears,   200
and untied me. When we had left that island,
I saw a mighty wave and smoke, and heard
a roar. The men were terrified; their hands
let fall the oars—they splashed down in the water.
The ship stayed still, since no one now was pulling   205
the slender blades. I strode along the deck
pausing to cheer each man, then gave a speech
to rally all of them.

                'Dear friends! We are
experienced in danger. This is not
worse than the time the Cyclops captured us,   210
and forced us to remain inside his cave.
We got away that time, thanks to my skill
and brains and strategy. Remember that.
Come on then, all of you, and trust my words.
Sit on your benches, strike the swelling deep   215
with oars, since Zeus may grant us a way out
from this disaster also. Pilot, listen:
these are your orders. As you hold the rudder,
direct the ship away from that dark smoke
and rising wave, and head towards the rock;   220
if the ship veers the other way, you will
endanger us.'

               They promptly followed orders.
I did not mention Scylla, since she meant
inevitable death, and if they knew,
the men would drop the oars and go and huddle   225
down in the hold in fear. Then I ignored
Circe's advice that I should not bear arms;
it was too hard for me. I dressed myself
in glorious armor; in my hands I took
two long spears, and I climbed up on the forecastle.   230
I thought that rocky Scylla would appear
from that direction, to destroy my men.
So we rowed through the narrow strait in tears.
On one side, Scylla; on the other, shining
Charybdis with a dreadful gurgling noise   235
sucked down the water. When she spewed it out,
she seethed, all churning like a boiling cauldron
on a huge fire. The froth flew high, to spatter
the topmost rocks on either side. But when
she swallowed back the sea, she seemed all stirred   240
from inside, and the rock around was roaring

dreadfully, and the dark-blue sand below
was visible. The men were seized by fear.
But while our frightened gaze was on Charybdis,
Scylla snatched six men from the ship—my strongest,   245
best fighters. Looking back from down below,
I saw their feet and hands up high, as they
were carried off. In agony they cried
to me and called my name—their final words.
As when a fisherman out on a cliff   250
casts his long rod and line set round with oxhorn
to trick the little fishes with his bait;
when one is caught, he flings it gasping back
onto the shore—so those men gasped as Scylla
lifted them up high to her rocky cave   255
and at the entrance ate them up—still screaming,
still reaching out to me in their death throes.
That was the most heartrending sight I saw
in all the time I suffered on the sea.

Free from the rocks of Scylla and Charybdis   260
we quickly reached the island of the god,
Hyperion's son Helius, the Sun God.
There were his cattle, with their fine broad faces,
and many flocks of well-fed sheep. While still
out on the sea in my black ship, I heard   265
the lowing of the cattle in their pens,
and bleating of the sheep. I kept in mind
the words of blind Tiresias the prophet
and Circe. Both had given strict instructions
that we avoid the island of the Sun,   270
the god of human joy. I told the men
with heavy heart,

                        'My friends, I know how much
you have endured. But listen to me now.
Tiresias and Circe both insisted
we must avoid the island of the Sun,   275
the joy of mortals. They said dreadful danger
lurks there for us. We have to steer our ship
around it.'

               They were quite downcast by this.
Eurylochus said angrily to me,
'You are unfair to us, Odysseus.   280
You may be strong; you never seem to tire;
you must be made of iron. But we men
have had no rest or sleep; we are exhausted.
And you refuse to let us disembark
and cook our tasty dinner on this island.   285
You order us to drift around all night
in our swift ship across the misty sea.
At night, fierce storms rise up and wreck men's ships,

and how can anyone escape disaster
if sudden gusts of wind from north or west   290
bring cruel blasts to break the ship, despite
the wishes of the gods? Let us submit
to evening. Let us stay here, and cook food
beside the ship. At dawn we can embark
and sail the open sea.'

                  That was his speech.   295
The other men agreed, and then I saw
a spirit must be plotting our destruction.
My words flew out.

                  'Eurylochus! You force me
to yield, since I am one and you are many.
But all of you, swear me a mighty oath: 300
if we find any herd of cows, or flock
of sheep, do not be fool enough to kill
a single animal. Stay clear, and eat
the food provided by immortal Circe.'

They swore as I commanded. When they finished   305
making the oath, we set our well-built ship
inside the curving harbor, near freshwater.
The men got out and skillfully cooked dinner.
When they were satisfied with food and drink,
they wept, remembering their dear companions,   310
whom Scylla captured from the ship and ate.
Sweet sleep came down upon them as they cried.
When night was over, when the stars were gone,
Zeus roused a blast of wind, an eerie storm.
He covered earth and sea with fog, and darkness   315
fell down from heaven. When rose-fingered Dawn
appeared, we dragged the ship inside a cave,
a place nymphs danced in, and we moored it there.
I gave a speech to my assembled men.

'My friends, we have supplies on board. Let us   320
not touch the cattle, or we will regret it.
Those cows and fat sheep are the property
of Helius, the great Sun God, who sees
all things, and hears all things.' I told them this.
Reluctantly they yielded. But that month   325
the South Wind blew and never stopped. No other
was ever blowing, only South and East.
While the men still had food and wine, they kept
clear of the cows. They hoped to save their lives.
But when our ship's supplies ran out, the men   330
were forced to hunt; they used their hooks to catch
both fish and birds, whatever they could get,
since hunger gnawed their bellies. I strode off
to pray, in case some god would show me how

to get back home. I left my men behind,   335
and crossed the island, washed my hands, in shelter
out of the wind, and prayed to all the gods.
They poured sweet sleep upon my eyes.

                                Meanwhile,
Eurylochus proposed a foolish plan.
'Listen, my friends! You have already suffered   340
too much. All human deaths are hard to bear.
But starving is most miserable of all.
So let us poach the finest of these cattle,
and sacrifice them to the deathless gods.
If we get home to Ithaca, at once   345
we will construct a temple to the Sun God,
with treasure in it. If he is so angry
about these cows that he decides to wreck
our ship, and if the other gods agree—
I would prefer to drink the sea and die   350
at once, than perish slowly, shriveled up
here on this desert island.'

                        All the others
agreed with him. They went to poach the best
of Helius' cattle, which were grazing
beside the ship. The men surrounded them,   355
and called upon the gods. They had plucked leaves
from oak trees—on the ship there was no barley.[3]
They prayed, then killed them, skinned them, and cut off
the thighs, and covered up the bones with fat,
a double layer, with raw meat on top.   360
They had no wine to pour libations over
the burning offering, but they made do
with water, and they roasted all the innards.
And when the thighs were burned, the entrails sprinkled,
they cut the other meat up into chunks   365
for skewers.

                Sweet sleep melted from my eyes;
I rushed back to the ship beside the shore.
When I was close, the meaty smell of cooking
enfolded me. I groaned, and told the gods,

'O Zeus, and all you deathless gods! You blinded   370
my mind with that infernal sleep. My men
did dreadful things while I was gone.'

                         Meanwhile,
Lampetia in flowing skirts ran off
to tell the Sun God we had killed his cows.
Enraged, he called the other gods at once.

---

3. Barley is a component of a ritual sacrifice.

                           'Great Zeus,   375
and all you other deathless gods, you must
punish Odysseus' men. They killed
my cattle! I delighted in those cows
all through each day, when I went up to heaven
and when I turned to earth. If they do not   380
repay me, I will sink down into Hades
and bring my bright light only to the dead.'

Zeus answered, 'Helius! Please shine with us
and shine for mortals on life-giving earth.
I will immediately smite their ship   385
with my bright thunderbolt, and smash it up
in fragments, all across the wine-dark sea.'

I heard this from the beautiful Calypso,
who had been told by Hermes.

                       Back on shore
beside my ship, I scolded each of them.   390
It did no good; the cows were dead already.
The gods sent signs—the hides began to twitch,
the meat on skewers started mooing, raw
and cooked. There was the sound of cattle lowing.
For six days my men banqueted on beef   395
from Helius. When Zeus, the son of Cronus,
led in the seventh day, the wind became
less stormy, and we quickly went on board.
We set the mast up and unfurled the sails
and set out on the open sea.

                     When we   400
had left that island, we could see no other,
only the sky and sea. Zeus made a mass
of dark-blue storm cloud hang above our ship.
The sea grew dark beneath it. For a moment
the ship moved on, but then came Zephyr, shrieking,   405
noisily rushing, with torrential tempest.
A mighty gust of wind broke off both forestays;
the tacking was all scattered in the hold.
The mast was broken backwards, and it struck
the pilot in the stern; it smashed his skull.   410
His bones were crushed, his skeleton was smashed.
He fell down like a diver from the deck;
his spirit left his body. At that instant,
Zeus thundered and hurled bolts to strike the ship;
shaken, it filled with sulfur. All the men   415
fell overboard, and they were swept away
  like seagulls on the waves beside the ship.
  The gods prevented them from reaching home.

    I paced on board until the current ripped
    the ship's side from the keel. The waves bore off   420

the husk, and snapped the mast. But thrown across it
there was a backstay cable, oxhide leather.
With this I lashed the keel and mast together,
and rode them, carried on by fearsome winds.
At last the tempest ceased, the West Wind lulled.   425
I worried that the South Wind might compel me
to backtrack, to the terrible Charybdis.
All night I was swept backwards and at sunrise
I came back to the dreadful rocks of Scylla
and of Charybdis, gulping salty water,   430
and overshadowed by the fig tree's branches.
I jumped and clutched its trunk, batlike—unable
to plant my feet, or climb. The roots were down
too low; the tall long branches were too high.
So I kept clinging on; I hoped Charybdis   435
would belch my mast and keel back up. She did!
As one who spends the whole day judging quarrels
between young men, at last goes home to eat—
at that same hour, the planks came bobbing up
out of Charybdis. I let go my hands   440
and feet and dropped myself way down to splash
into the sea below, beside the timbers
of floating wood. I clambered onto them,
and used my hands to row myself away,
and Zeus ensured that Scylla did not see me,   445
or else I could not have survived. I drifted
for nine days. On the evening of the tenth,
the gods helped me to reach the island of
the dreadful, beautiful, divine Calypso.
She loved and cared for me. Why should I tell   450
the story that I told you and your wife
yesterday in your house? It is annoying,
repeating tales that have been told before."

Summary   The Phaeacians send Odysseus back to Ithaca with gifts. Athena meets him and together they plot to kill the suitors. Athena disguises Odysseus as an old beggar, and he visits Eumaeus, the old slave who takes care of his pigs. Athena goes to Telemachus and instructs him to come back home. While boarding his ship, Telemachus meets Theoclymenus, an exile who is skilled in prophecy; when they reach Ithaca, there is a good omen. Telemachus leaves Theoclymenus to stay with Pireaus.

BOOK 16

[Father and Son]

At dawn the swineherd and Odysseus
made breakfast, lit the fire, and sent the herdsmen
out with the pigs that they had rounded up.
The dogs, that as a rule would bark at strangers,
were quiet when they saw Telemachus;   5
they panted at him. When Odysseus

saw how they acted, and heard footsteps coming,
he said,

"Eumaeus, someone must be coming—
a friend or somebody you know—the dogs
are friendly, with no barking. I can hear   10
footsteps."

He hardly finished, when his son,
his own dear son, was there inside the gate.
Amazed, the swineherd jumped up, letting fall
the cups in which he had been mixing wine;
it spilled. He ran towards his master, kissed   15
his face and shining eyes and both his hands,
and wept. Just as a father, when he sees
his own dear son, his only son, his dear
most precious boy, returned from foreign lands
after ten years of grieving for his loss,   20
welcomes him; so the swineherd wrapped his arms
around godlike Telemachus and kissed him,
as if he were returning from the dead.
With tears still in his eyes he said,

"Sweet light!
You have come back, Telemachus. I thought   25
that I would never see you anymore,
after you sailed to Pylos. My dear child,
come in, let me enjoy the sight of you
now you are back. Come in! You do not often
come to the countryside to see us herders;   30
you stay in town to watch that evil horde
of suitors."

And Telemachus replied
warily, "Grandpa, yes, I will come in.
I came to see you here with my own eyes,
and hear if Mother still stays in the house,   35
or if some other man has married her
already, and Odysseus' bed
is empty, full of ugly spiderwebs."

The swineherd, the commander, said, "Indeed,
her heart is loyal. She is in your house,   40
weeping by night and sad by day."

He took
Telemachus' sword; the boy came in,
crossing the stony threshold, and his father
offered his seat. Telemachus refused,
saying, "You sit there, stranger. I can find   45
a chair around my hut. The slave can help."

Odysseus went back and sat back down.
The swineherd spread fresh brushwood and a fleece
on top, so that Telemachus could sit.
He set the bread in baskets and brought meat,   50
left over from the meal the day before.
He mixed some wine up in a wooden bowl,
and sat down opposite Odysseus.
They reached to take the good things set before them.
When they were satisfied, Telemachus   55
turned to the noble swineherd.

                "Tell me, Grandpa,
where did this stranger come from? By what route
did sailors bring him here? And who were they?
He surely did not walk to Ithaca!"

Eumaeus answered, "I will tell you, child.   60
He is from Crete. He says he wandered, lost,
through many towns—so some god spun his fate.
Now he has run away from the Thesprotians
who brought him, and arrived here on my farm.
He is all yours, your suppliant, to treat   65
however you desire."

          Telemachus
said anxiously, "This news of yours, Eumaeus,
is very worrying to me. How can I
invite him to my house? I am too young
to fight back with my fists if someone picks   70
a fight with me. My mother is unsure
if she should stay with me and show respect
towards her husband's bed and public gossip,
and keep on taking care of things at home,
or marry one of them, whichever suitor   75
asserts himself, and brings most lavish gifts.
But since this man has come here, to your house,
I will dress him in fine clothes, cloak and tunic,
and sandals for his feet, and give a sword,
and help him on his way. If you are willing,   80
keep him here in the farmhouse; care for him.
I will send you some clothes and all his food,
so he will be no bother to these men
or you. I will not let him go to meet
the suitors; they are much too violent.   85
I would be mortified if they abused him.
It would be difficult for one man, even
a strong one, to do anything to them.
They are too many."

          Then Odysseus,
frustrated, said, "My friend, it is my duty   90

to speak out when I hear the dreadful things
those suitors have been doing in your house,
against your will; it breaks my heart. You are
a good man. Tell me, did you choose to let them
bully you? Have the Ithacans been turned   95
against you by some god? Or do you blame
your brothers, who should be a man's supporters
when conflict comes? If only I had youth
to match my will! I wish I were the son
of great Odysseus—or that I were   100
the man himself come home from wandering.
We can still hope. Let someone chop my head off,
if I would not destroy them when I came
inside the palace of Odysseus!
And if I lost—since I am only one   105
against so many—I would rather die
in my own house, than watch such crimes committed!
Strangers dishonored! Slave girls dragged around,
raped in my lovely home! Men wasting wine
and bread—for nothing! For this waiting game!"   110

Telemachus said soberly, "I will
explain the situation to you, stranger.
The Ithacans are not my enemies,
and I do not have brothers I can blame.
Zeus gave my family a single line: 115
Arcesius had just one son, Laertes,
who had Odysseus, his only son,
and he had me, his only son, whom he
left back at home; he had no joy of me.
And now there are so many cruel invaders,   120
since all the toughest men from all the islands—
from Same and Dulichium and wooded
Zacynthus, and all those who hold command
in rocky Ithaca, have come to court
my mother, wasting all my wealth. She does not   125
refuse the awful prospect of remarriage,
nor can she end the courtship. They keep eating,
consuming my whole house, and soon they may
destroy me too. These things lie with the gods.
Now Grandpa, you must hurry to the queen,   130
and tell her I am safe back home from Pylos.
I will stay here while you tell her—just her;
do not let any others hear the news,
since many people want to plot my death."

Eumaeus, you replied, "I understand.   135
But tell me, on this same trip, should I go
and tell poor old Laertes? For a while
he used to watch the fields and join the slaves
for dinner at the house, when in the mood,

despite his grief for lost Odysseus.   140
But since your ship set sail away to Pylos,
they say he has stopped eating, will not drink,
and does not go to check the fields. He sits,
weeping and sobbing, worn to skin and bone."

Telemachus said calmly, "That is sad;   145
distressing news. But no, leave him alone.
If human wishes could come true, my first
would be to have my father come back home.
Take her your message, hurry back, and do not
trail round the countryside to look for him.   150
Tell Mother she should send a girl in secret
to run to old Laertes with the news."

At that, the swineherd tied his sandals on,
and started off towards the town. Athena
noticed him leaving from the yard, and stood   155
beside him as a woman, tall and skillful,
and beautiful. Odysseus could see her,
standing beside the entrance to the cottage.
Telemachus could not; the gods are not
equally visible to everyone.   160
The dogs could see her but they did not bark.
They whimpered and slunk back across the room
in fear. She raised her eyebrows, with a nod;
he understood and came out, past the wall,
and stood beside her. Then Athena told him,   165

"Odysseus, great strategist, it is
time for your son to know the truth; together
you have to plan how you will kill the suitors.
Then both of you go into town. I will
join you there soon myself; indeed I am   170
itching to fight."

                    And then Athena touched him,
using a golden wand, and dressed him up
in fine clean cloak and tunic, and she made him
taller and younger-looking. He became
tanned, and his cheeks filled out, and on his chin   175
the beard grew dark. And so her work was done,
and off she flew. Odysseus went in.
His son was startled and looked down, afraid
in case it was a god. His words flew out.

"Stranger, you look so different from before.   180
Your clothes, your skin—I think that you must be
some god who has descended from the sky.
Be kind to us, and we will sacrifice,
and give you golden treasures. Pity us!"

Long-suffering Odysseus replied,   185
"I am no god. Why would you think such things?
I am your father, that same man you mourn.
It is because of me these brutal men
are hurting you so badly."

                Then he kissed
his son and cried, tears pouring down his cheeks;   190
he had been holding back till then. The boy
did not yet trust it really was his father,
and said,

            "No, you are not Odysseus,
my father; some god must have cast a spell,
to cause me further pain. No mortal man   195
could manage such a thing by his own wits,
becoming old and young again—unless
some god appeared and did it all with ease.
You certainly were old just now, and wearing
those dirty rags. Now you look like a god."   200

Artful Odysseus said sharply, "No,
Telemachus, you should not be surprised
to see your father. It is me; no other
is on his way. I am Odysseus.
I suffered terribly, and I was lost,   205
but after twenty years, I have come home.
As for the way I look—Athena did it.
The goddess can transform me as she likes;
sometimes a homeless beggar, then she makes me
look like a young man, wearing princely clothes.   210
For heavenly gods it is not difficult
to make a mortal beautiful or ugly."

With that, he sat back down. Telemachus
hurled his arms round his father, and he wept.
They both felt deep desire for lamentation,   215
and wailed with cries as shrill as birds, like eagles
or vultures, when the hunters have deprived them
of fledglings who have not yet learned to fly.
That was how bitterly they wept. Their grieving
would have continued till the sun went down,   220
but suddenly Telemachus said,

                "Father,
by what route did the sailors bring you here,
to Ithaca? And who were they? I know
you did not walk."

           Odysseus replied,
"Son, I will tell you everything. Phaeacians,   225

famous for navigation, brought me here.
They always help their guests travel onward.
I slept as their ship sped across the ocean;
they set me down on Ithaca, still sleeping.
They brought me marvelous gifts of gold and bronze   230
and clothing, which are lying in a cave,
since gods have willed it so. Athena told me
to come here and make plans with you to kill
our enemies. How many suitors are there?
What kind of men are they? I am well-known   235
for my intelligence, and I will plot
to work out if we two alone can fight them,
or if we might need others helping us."

Telemachus considered, then said, "Father,
I always heard how excellent you are,   240
at fighting with a spear, and making plans.
But what you said just now—it is too much.
We cannot fight, the two of us, against
such strong men, and so many—there are dozens,
not just a handful. Let me tell you quickly   245
the number of the suitors. Fifty-two
came from Dulichium, all top-notch fighters,
who brought six henchmen. Twenty-four men came
from Same, twenty more from Zacynthus,
and from right here on Ithaca came twelve,   250
all strong young men. They have a house boy with them,
named Medon, and a poet, and two slaves
well trained in carving meat. If we attack
when all those men are crowded in the house,
I am afraid you will be paying back   255
their violence at all too high a price.
Think harder: can we find some kind of helper,
willing to fight for us?"

                    Odysseus
said, "Do you think Athena and her father,
Zeus, would be strong enough to keep us safe?   260
Would any other help be necessary?"

Telemachus replied, "The ones you mention
are good defenders. They sit high among
the clouds, and they control both men and gods."

The veteran Odysseus replied,   265
"Those two will quickly join the heat of battle
when we begin to grapple with the suitors,
when in my house the god of war is testing
our fighting force and theirs. Go back at dawn,
and join those overconfident young men.   270
The swineherd will escort me into town.

I will again be looking like a beggar.
If they abuse me and you see me suffer,
you must restrain yourself, repress your feelings,
even if they are pelting me with weapons,   275
and even if they grab me by the foot
to hurl me out. Just watch, and keep your temper.
Politely tell them they should stop this folly.
They will ignore you. Truly now their day
of doom is near at hand. Now listen hard.   280
Athena, my best co-conspirator,
will nudge my heart, and I will nod to you.
Then you must find all weapons in the house
that could be used for fighting; go and hide them
away inside the upstairs storage room.   285
And when the suitors ask where they have gone,
fob them off, saying, 'They were near the fire,
so I removed them from the breath of smoke,
since they were getting damaged; they were losing
the luster that they used to have, before   290
Odysseus went off to Troy. Praise Zeus!
I thought of something even more important:
if you get drunk you may start quarreling,
and hurt each other. Then your lovely dinners
and courtship will be ruined. Arms themselves   295
can prompt a man to use them.' Tell them that.
Leave out two swords, two spears, and two thick shields
for you and me to grab before we rush
to ambush them. Athena will bewitch them,
helped by sharp-witted Zeus. And one more thing: 300
if you are my true son, of my own blood,
let no one know that I am in the house.
Laertes and the swineherd must not know,
nor any of the slave girls, and not even
Penelope, until we have determined   305
the women's attitude. We also must
test the male slaves, and see who has respect
and fears me in his heart, and who does not,
and who looks up to you as you deserve."

His glowing son said, "Father, you will see   310
my courage in the moment. I am tough.
But it would take too long to go around
and test each man like that, and all the while,
the suitors would be sitting in your house,
wasting your wealth with heedless partying.   315
So reconsider. I agree you should
find out about the women—which of them
are innocent, and which dishonor you.
However, I have no desire to traipse
around to test the men; we can do that   320
later, if Zeus reveals a sign to you."

Such was their conversation. Then the ship
in which Telemachus had gone to Pylos
docked in the bay of Ithaca's main town.
They disembarked and dragged the ship onto shore.   325
The slaves brought out the splendid gifts and weapons
and took them to the house of Clytius.
A messenger was sent to tell the queen
Telemachus was back in Ithaca,
and that he said that they must come to town,   330
dragging the ship, in case she had been weeping
in her anxiety about her son.
The swineherd and this messenger met up,
on the same mission, to inform the queen.
When both of them arrived, the slave girls clustered   335
around the messenger. He said,

                            "Great queen,
your dear son has come home!"

                          And then the swineherd
took her aside and told her what her son
had ordered him to say. When he was done,
he walked out through the hall and out the courtyard,   340
leaving the palace hall to join his pigs.

The suitors were upset and down at heart.
Eurymachus the son of Polybus
said, "Friends, the journey of this upstart boy
succeeded! We were sure that he would fail.   345
We must launch our best ship, equipped with rowers,
to cross the salty sea and find the others
and tell them to come home at once."

                               His words
were hardly finished when Amphinomus
spotted a ship inside the harbor, pointed   350
away from land; the sails were being furled,
the men were carrying the oars. He laughed
triumphantly and said,

                        "No need to send
a messenger! They are already back!
Some god has told them, or they saw his ship   355
approaching, but could not catch up with it."

So leaping up, they went down to the seashore,
and dragged the black ship up onto dry land,
and servants proudly brought the weapons out.
They all went crowding to the marketplace,   360
together, and banned any other men
from joining them, both young and old. And then
Antinous addressed them.

"How amazing!
The gods have saved this man from death! For days
our scouts took turns to watch from windy cliffs.   365
And when the sun went down, we never spent
a night on shore, but sailed to wait till Dawn
at sea in ambush for Telemachus,
to make sure we would catch him. Now some god
has brought him home. We need to make new plans   370
to murder him. He must not get away.
He will obstruct our courtship if he lives,
since he is wise to us, and he will plot,
and now the people will be turned against us.
Telemachus will gather them; he must   375
be furious, and he will not postpone
action. He will stand up and tell them how
we planned to murder him, but failed to do so.
When they hear of our crimes, they will condemn us.
We may get hurt or driven from our land,   380
to foreign territories; we must stop it!
Catch him out in the countryside, away
from town, or on the road. Let us rob him,
and share his wealth and property among us—
and let his mother, and whichever man   385
marries her, keep the house. But if you think
it would be better if we let him live,
and keep his father's riches for himself,
we should stop flocking here to waste the wealth
inside his house. We should each go and court her   390
from home, by sending gifts. One day, the lady
will marry, and the lucky man will be
the one who sends the most gifts."

                              They were silent.
But then Amphinomus, the famous son
of Nisus, spoke. He had come from the wheat fields   395
and pastures of Dulichium, with others.
He was intelligent; Penelope
preferred his speeches over other men's.
Wisely he said,

              "My friends, I for my part
have no desire to kill Telemachus.   400
It is a dreadful thing to kill a person
of royal blood. So first we must discover
the gods' intentions. If great Zeus decrees it,
I will kill him myself, and urge you all
to join me. If the gods do not approve,   405
I say we must not do it."

                    So he spoke,
and they agreed with what he said. They stood,

and went back to Odysseus' house,
and sat on polished chairs.

                            Penelope
decided she must show herself to these   410
ungentlemanly suitors, since she had
found out about the plot to kill her son—
Medon had heard their plans, and he told her.
Her women at her side, she went downstairs,
into the hall, approached them and then stopped,   415
standing beside the doorpost with a veil
across her face. She told Antinous,

"You are a brute! A sneak! A criminal!
The people say you are the smartest boy
of all those your own age on Ithaca.   420
It is not true. You are insane! How could you
devise a plan to kill Telemachus?
Do you have no respect for ties created
by supplication, which Zeus watches over?
Have you forgotten that your father came here,   425
running in terror from the Ithacans,
who were enraged because he joined the pirates
of Taphos, and was hounding the Thesprotians,
our allies? So the Ithacans were eager
to kill him, rip his heart out, and devour   430
his wealth. Odysseus protected him!
Now you consume your benefactor's wealth,
and court his wife, and try to kill his son,
and you are hurting me! I tell you, stop!
And make the other suitors stop as well."   435

Eurymachys said, "Wise Penelope,
you need not worry; put all this from your mind.
No man will ever, ever hurt your boy
while I am still alive upon this earth.
I swear to you, if someone tries, my sword   440
will spill his blood! Your city-sacking husband
often would take me on his lap, and give me
tidbits of meat with his own hands, and sips
of red wine. So Telemachus is now
the man I love the most in all the world.   445
The boy is in no danger, not from us—
there is no help for death brought by the gods."

He spoke to mollify her; all the while
he was devising plans to kill her son.
She went up to her light and airy bedroom,   450
and wept for dear Odysseus, her husband,
until Athena gave her eyes sweet sleep.

As evening fell, the swineherd came back home
to find Odysseus. He and his son
had killed a year-old pig and made a meal.   455
Athena came beside Odysseus
and touched him with her wand again to make him
ragged and old, to make sure when the swineherd
came in, he would not recognize his master,
in case he told Penelope the secret.   460

He came inside. Telemachus spoke first.
"Eumaeus, you are back! What is the news
in town? Are those proud suitors in my house,
back from the ambush, or still lurking there
to catch me on my way back home?"

                                        Eumaeus   465
answered, "I did not want to trek through town
asking that question. I preferred to share
my news as fast as possible and then
come back. One of your own men went with me,
a messenger; he told your mother first.   470
I saw one more thing: as I passed the hill
of Hermes, right above the town I saw
a ship draw into harbor, full of men
and loaded up with shields and spears. I thought
it could be them, but I cannot be sure."   475

Then Prince Telemachus began to smile
and met his father's eyes; he did not let
Eumaeus see. When they were finished cooking,
they shared the dinner equally, and all
had plenty, then they took the gift of sleep.   480

BOOK 17

[Insults and Abuse]

When newborn Dawn appeared with hands of flowers,
Telemachus, Odysseus' son,
fastened his handsome sandals on his feet,
took up his sturdy spear that fit his hand,
and headed out. He told the swineherd,

                                        "Grandpa,   5
I must go into town, to see my mother.
Until we meet, I think she will not stop
her lamentations, tears, and bitter sobbing.
Now I need you to take this poor old stranger
to town to beg his supper; any man   10
who feels like it can feed him. I cannot
put up with everyone right now; I have

too many worries. If he gets annoyed,
the worse for him. I always like to tell
the honest truth."

              Odysseus replied,   15
"My friend, I do not even want to stay.
Beggars should wander round the town and country.
I will get food from charitable people.
I am too old to stay here as a farmhand,
obeying orders from an overseer.   20
This man will take me, as you told him to,
as soon as I have warmed up by the fire.
I only have these rags; the morning frost
may do me in—you say the town is far."

At that, Telemachus strode quickly out,   25
thinking about his plan to hurt the suitors.
And when he reached the royal house, he propped
his spear against a pillar, and went in,
across the stony threshold.

              Eurycleia
the nurse, was first to notice his arrival,   30
as she was laying fleeces on the chairs.
Weeping, she rushed at him. The other women
owned by strong-willed Odysseus assembled
and kissed Telemachus' head and shoulders
to welcome him. Then wise Penelope   35
came from her bedroom, looking like a goddess,
like Artemis[1] or golden Aphrodite,
and flung her arms around her darling son,
and wept. She kissed his face and shining eyes,
and through her tears her words flew out.

              "You came!   40
Telemachus! Sweet light! I was so sure
that I would never see you anymore
after you sailed to Pylos secretly,
not telling me, to get news of your father.
Tell me, what have you seen?"

              Telemachus   45
said calmly, "Mother, do not try to make me
upset, or stir my feelings. I survived
the danger. Go upstairs and take your bath,
put on clean clothes and take your women with you
into your bedroom. Sacrifice and pray   50
to all the gods, that one day Zeus may grant
revenge. Now I am going into town.

---

1. Artemis, goddess of hunting, was associated with chastity and the moon.

I will invite the stranger who arrived
right after me on Ithaca. I sent him
ahead, with my brave men, and told Piraeus   55
to take him home and treat him with all kindness
until I come."

His flying words hit home.
She washed, put on clean clothes, and prayed to all
the gods, and made them lavish sacrifices,
asking that one day Zeus would bring revenge.   60

Telemachus took up his spear and marched
out through the hall, two swift dogs at his side.
Athena poured unearthly grace upon him.
Everyone was amazed to see him coming.
The suitors gathered round and spoke to him   65
in friendly tones; at heart, they meant him harm.
Keeping away from most of them, he joined
Mentor and Antiphus and Halitherses,
who were his father's friends from long ago.
They questioned him in detail. Then Piraeus   70
approached with Theoclymenus, the stranger
whom he had brought through town towards the center.
At once Telemachus set out and rushed
to stand beside the stranger. And Piraeus
spoke first.

        "Telemachus, send women quickly   75
to my house, so I may give back the gifts
that Menelaus gave you."

        But with caution
Telemachus replied,

        "Piraeus, no.
We do not know exactly what will happen,
and if the suitors in my house by stealth   80
should kill me and divide my father's wealth
between themselves, I would prefer that you
enjoy the gifts than any of those men.
And if I kill them, planting doom among them,
bring me the gifts, and we will both be happy."   85

With this, he led the weary stranger back
to his house, where he laid their cloaks across
chairs; they went to bathe. The slave girls washed them,
rubbed them with oil, and dressed them in wool cloaks
and tunics. Then they left the baths and sat   90
on chairs. A girl brought out a golden pitcher
and poured the washing water on their hands,
over a silver bowl. She set a table

beside them, and a humble slave girl brought
a generous array from their rich stores.   95
Penelope was leaning on a chair
beside the door, facing Telemachus,
spinning fine strands of wool. They helped themselves
to food and drink. When they had had enough,
Penelope, preoccupied, spoke up.   100

"Telemachus, I will go upstairs now,
to lie down on my bed, which has become
a bed of mourning, always stained with tears,
since my Odysseus went off to Troy
with those two sons of Atreus. But you   105
have failed to tell me if you gathered news
about your father's journey home; now tell me,
before the suitors come."

                 Telemachus
answered her calmly. "Mother, I will tell you.
We went to Pylos, visiting King Nestor.   110
He made me very welcome in his palace,
under his roof, as if I were his son
returning after many years away.
He cared for me like one of his own sons.
But he said he had not heard anything   115
from anyone about Odysseus,
alive or dead. He sent me on, with horses
and carriage, to the son of Atreus,
great General Menelaus. There I saw
Helen for whose sake, by the will of gods,   120
the Greeks and Trojans suffered through the war.
When Menelaus asked why I had come
to glorious Sparta, I told him the truth
in detail, and he answered, 'Stupid cowards!
The bed they want to lie down in belongs   125
to someone truly resolute. As when
a deer lays down her newborn suckling fawns
inside the leafy den of some fierce lion,
and goes off to the slopes and grassy valleys
to graze. Then he comes back to his own bed   130
and cruelly destroys both little ones.
So will Odysseus destroy them all.
By Father Zeus, Athena, and Apollo,
I pray he is as strong as long ago,
on Lesbos, when he wrestled Philomedes   135
and hurled him to the ground, and all the Greeks
cheered. May he fight the suitors that same way,
so all of them will find their courtship ends
badly, and their lives soon. And I will answer
your questions frankly, and tell what I learned   140
from the old Sea God, who can tell no lies.

He said he saw him in distress: the nymph
Calypso has him trapped upon her island,
inside her house. He cannot come back home
to his own country, since he has no fleet   145
or crew to row across the sea's broad back.'
That was what famous Menelaus said.
My tasks accomplished, I sailed off. The gods
gave me fair wind which swiftly brought me home."

His story stirred emotions in her heart.   150
Then godlike Theoclymenus spoke up.

"My lady, wife of great Odysseus,
this news is incomplete. I will reveal
the whole truth with a prophecy. I swear
by Zeus and hospitality and by   155
the hearth of great Odysseus, the place
where I have come: he is already here
in Ithaca—at rest or on his way.
He must have learned what bad things they are doing,
and he is plotting ruin for them all.   160
I know because I saw a sign while sitting
on board the ship—I told Telemachus."

Penelope said carefully, "Well, stranger,
I hope this does come true. I would reward you
with so much warmth and generosity   165
that everyone you met would see your luck."
Meanwhile, outside Odysseus' house,
the suitors relished games of darts and discus,
playing outside as usual, with no thought
of others. Then at dinnertime, when flocks   170
of sheep were trekking home from every field,
led by their shepherds, Medon spoke. He was
the suitors' favorite slave boy, whom they always
brought to their feasts.

                        "My lords, you have enjoyed
your games. Now come inside to eat. There is   175
no harm in having meals at proper times."

They followed his advice, stood up and went
inside the palace. They spread out their cloaks
over the chairs, and killed plump goats, large rams,
some fatted pigs, and one domestic cow,   180
and cooked them for the feast.

                        Odysseus
was making haste to leave the countryside
for town. The swineherd spoke in lordly tones.

"Stranger, my master says that you can come
to town today, as you desire—though I   185
would rather leave you here to watch the farm.
But I am nervous that the master may
reproach me, and a master's curses fall
heavily on a slave. Now we must go.
The hour is late and it will soon get colder;   190
the sun is sinking low."

       Odysseus
answered, "I understand. We can go now;
you lead the way. But if you have a stick,
give it to me to lean on, since I hear
the path is slippery."

       With that, he slung   195
his bag across his shoulders by its string.
It was all tattered, full of holes. Eumaeus
gave him a serviceable stick. They left;
the dogs and herdsmen stayed to guard the farm.
The swineherd led his master into town   200
resembling a poor old beggar, leaning
upon a stick and dressed in dirty rags.
They walked along the stony path, and near
the town, they reached an ornate fountain, flowing
with clear streams, where the people came for water.   205
It had been built by Ithacus, Neritus,
and Polyctor. A circle of black poplars
grew round it, nurtured by the spring. Cool water
poured from the rocks above. There was an altar
built over it in honor of the Nymphs.   210
All passersby made offerings to them.
Melanthius the son of Dolius,
with two more herders, met them there. He was
driving the finest goats to feed the suitors.
On seeing them, he spoke abusively,   215
in brash, offensive language that enraged
Odysseus.

    "One scoundrel leads another!
Makes sense: gods join like things with like. You foul
pig-man, where are you taking this old swine?
A scrounger, who will rub on many doors,   220
demanding scraps, not gifts for warriors.
If you let me have him to guard my farm,
and muck the pens and toss the kids their fodder,
he could drink whey and fatten his stick legs.
But he does not want work. He likes to traipse   225
around the town and beg for chow to stuff
his greedy belly. I predict, if he

reaches the palace of Odysseus,
a mass of hands will hurl stools at his head,
to pelt him through the house and bruise his ribs." 230

With that, he sauntered past him, and lunged out
to kick him on the hip bone. What a fool!
Odysseus was not pushed off the path;
he stood there fixed in place, and wondered whether
to rush at him, armed with his stick, and kill him, 235
or grab him by the ears and push him down
onto the ground. Instead, he braced himself
and kept his temper. When the swineherd saw
Melanthius insulting him, he prayed,
arms high.

                    "O Fountain Nymphs, O Zeus' daughters! 240
If ever King Odysseus brought bones
of lamb and goat in luscious fat for you, then now
fulfill my prayer! May spirits guide him home!
My master will put paid to all the bluster
of this rude man, who loafs round town and lets 245
the animals be ruined by bad herders."

Melanthius the goatherd sneered at him,
"Oh, very nice! This dog knows how to talk,
and it has learned some tricks. One day I will
take him by ship and row him far away 250
from Ithaca, and get a heap of treasure
by selling him. I wish Apollo would
shoot silver arrows at Telemachus
tomorrow in his house; or that the suitors
would kill him. I am sure Odysseus 255
is far away and never coming back."

With that, he left them—they were walking slowly,
and he rushed on ahead of them. He went
inside his master's house, and sat among
the suitors, with Eurymachus, his favorite. 260
The slaves brought out a piece of meat for him,
and a submissive house girl brought him bread.
The swineherd and Odysseus went in,
and stood, surrounded by the strumming sound
of the resounding lyre that Phemius 265
was tuning for his song. Odysseus
grabbed at the swineherd's hand and said,

                                    "Eumaeus!
This is Odysseus' splendid palace.
It could be recognized among a thousand.
The rooms are all connected, and the courtyard 270
is fenced in by a wall with cornices,

and there are sturdy double doors. No man
could break through here. I notice many men
are feasting; I smell meat, and hear the lyre,
which gods have made companion to the feast." 275

Eumaeus answered, "Right! You are perceptive.
Now we must plan. Will you go inside first
to join the suitors, while I stay out here?
Or do you want to wait, and I will go?
But do not stay too long. If someone sees you, 280
you will be pelted, maybe beaten up."

Unflappable Odysseus said, "Yes,
I thought of that. You go, I will stay here.
I have been hit before. I know hard knocks.
I am resilient. I suffered war 285
and being lost at sea. So let this be.
There is no way to hide a hungry belly.
It is insistent, and the curse of hunger
is why we sail across relentless seas,
and plunder other people."

As they spoke, 290
Argos, the dog that lay there, raised his head
and ears. Odysseus had trained this dog
but with no benefit—he left too soon
to march on holy Troy. The master gone,
boys took the puppy out to hunt wild goats 295
and deer and hares. But now he lay neglected,
without an owner, in a pile of dung
from mules and cows—the slaves stored heaps of it
outside the door, until they fertilized
the large estate. So Argos lay there dirty, 300
covered with fleas. And when he realized
Odysseus was near, he wagged his tail,
and both his ears dropped back. He was too weak
to move towards his master. At a distance,
Odysseus had noticed, and he wiped 305
his tears away and hid them easily,
and said,

"Eumaeus, it is strange this dog
is lying in the dung; he looks quite handsome,
though it is hard to tell if he can run,
or if he is a pet, a table dog, 310
kept just for looks."

Eumaeus, you replied,
"This dog belonged to someone who has died
in foreign lands. If he were in good health,
as when Odysseus abandoned him

and went to Troy, you soon would see how quick 315
and brave he used to be. He went to hunt
in woodland, and he always caught his prey.
His nose was marvelous. But now he is
in bad condition, with his master gone,
long dead. The women fail to care for him. 320
Slaves do not want to do their proper work,
when masters are not watching them. Zeus halves
our value on the day that makes us slaves."

With that, the swineherd went inside the palace,
to join the noble suitors. Twenty years 325
had passed since Argos saw Odysseus,
and now he saw him for the final time—
then suddenly, black death took hold of him.

Telemachus first saw the swineherd coming.
He gave a nod to tell him to come over. 330
Glancing around, Eumaeus saw the stool
used by the boy who carved the suitors' meat.
He picked it up and set it down beside
Telemachus' table. There he sat;
the slave boy brought him meat and bread. And then 335
Odysseus approached and stepped inside,
looking like some poor homeless sad old man;
he hobbled on his stick, then slumped himself
down on the ash-wood threshold, leaning back
against the cypress doorpost, which a workman 340
had smoothed and straightened long ago. The boy
summoned the swineherd over, and picked up
a wheat loaf from the basket and as much
meat as his hands could hold, and gave it to him.
He said,

       "Please take this food out to that stranger, 345
and tell him he should walk around the hall
and beg from all the suitors; shame is not
a friend to those in need."

            The swineherd went
and told Odysseus, "Telemachus
gives you this food and says you ought to beg 350
from all these suitors; shame, he says, is not
fitting for those who have to live by handouts."

Odysseus prayed cautiously, "O Zeus,
bless this Telemachus, and may he have
all that his heart desires."

             And with both hands 355
he took the food and set it at his feet,

on top of his old ragged bag, and ate,
and listened to the singer in the hall.
As he was finishing, the music stopped;
the suitors shouted, and Athena stood   360
beside Odysseus, and prompted him
to go among the suitors, begging scraps,
to find out which of them were bad or good—
although she had no thought of saving any
out of the massacre which was to come.   365
He went around and begged from left to right,
holding his hand out, like a practiced beggar.
They gave him food in pity, and they wondered
who this man was and whereabouts he came from.
They asked each other, and Melanthius,   370
the goatherd, said,

                              "You suitors of the queen,
listen to me about this stranger here.
I saw this man before; the swineherd brought him.
I know no more; I do not know his background."

Antinous began to scold the swineherd.   375
"Pig-man! You famous idiot! Why did you
bring this man here? Do we not have already
plenty of homeless people coming here
to spoil our feasts? Is it not bad enough
that they crowd round and eat your master's wealth?   380
You had to ask this other one as well?"

Eumaeus, you replied, "Antinous,
you are a lord, but what you say is trash.
Who would invite a stranger from abroad
unless he had the skills to help the people—   385
a prophet, or a doctor, or a builder,
or poet who can sing and bring delight?
No one would ask a beggar; they bring only
their hunger. Out of all the suitors, you
are meanest to the slaves, especially me.   390
But if the prudent queen and godlike prince
still live here in this house, I do not mind."

Telemachus said, "Shush. Antinous
does not deserve an answer. He is always
picking a fight, and goading on the others."   395

Then turning to Antinous, he said,
"You care for me so nicely, like a father!
You told me I should force the stranger out.
May no god make that happen! Go to him
and give him something; I can spare the food.   400
Go on, I tell you! You should pay no heed

to Mother or the other household slaves
belonging to my father. You were not
concerned about them anyway. You want
to gorge yourself, not share with other people." 405

Antinous replied, "You little show-off!
What nasty temper! What an awful comment!
If all the suitors gave the same as me,
this house could keep him checked for three whole months."

He had a footstool underneath the table, 410
for resting his soft feet on while he feasted;
he brandished it. The others all gave food
and filled the beggar's bag. Odysseus
had finished with his test; he could have walked 415
back to the threshold, no harm done. Instead,
he stood beside Antinous and said,

"Friend, give me something. You must be the best
of all the Greeks. You look like royalty,
so you should give more food than all the rest,
and I will make you known throughout the world. 420
I used to be a rich man, with a palace.
When needy beggars came from anywhere,
no matter who they were, I gave them food.
My slaves were numberless, my wealth was great;
I had the life men say is happiness. 425
But Zeus destroyed it all; he wanted to.
He prompted me to travel with some pirates
to Egypt; that long journey spelled my ruin.
I moored my galleys in the River Nile
and told my loyal men to stay and guard them, 430
and sent out scouts to all the lookout points.
But they were too impulsive, and they sacked
the beautiful Egyptian fields, and seized
women and children, and they killed the men.
The screaming reached the town; the people heard, 435
and rushed to come and help; at dawn the plain
was all filled up with foot soldiers and horses
and flashing bronze. Then Zeus, who loves the thunder,
caused panic in my men—disastrous panic.
Danger was all around us, and not one 440
stood firm. The sharp bronze swords killed many men,
and others were enslaved as laborers.
But they gave me to somebody they met,
a foreigner named Dmetor, king of Cyprus.
I came from there. Such is my tale of woe." 445

Antinous replied, "What god imposed
this pest to spoil our feast? Stay over there,
not near my table—or you can get lost!

Get killed in Egypt or enslaved in Cyprus!
You barefaced beggar! You come up to us,   450
and these men give you treats unthinkingly;
we have so much, and people do not mind
sharing another person's wealth."

                Sharp-witted
Odysseus drew back from him and said,
"You handsome idiot! You would not give   455
a grain of salt from your own house. You sit
enjoying someone else's food, and yet
you will not give a crumb from this great banquet
to me."

       Antinous was furious,
and scowling said, "That does it! You insult me?   460
You lost the chance to leave with dignity!"
He lifted up his stool and hurled it at
Odysseus' right shoulder, near his back.
It did not knock him over; like a rock
he stood there, shook his head, and silently   465
considered his revenge. Then he went back,
sat on the threshold and set down the bag,
all full of food, and told them, "Listen, suitors
of this world-famous queen; I have to speak.
When men are fighting for their own possessions,   470
for cows or sheep, there is no shame in wounds.
But now Antinous has wounded me
because I came here hungry; hunger brings
such suffering to humans. If there are
gods of the poor, or Furies to avenge us,   475
may he be struck by death, instead of marriage!

He answered, "Stranger, shut up, or be off!
If you keep talking, we young men will drag you
across the palace by your hands and feet
and have you flayed alive!"

             But all the others   480
reproached Antinous insistently.
"You ought not to have hit a poor old beggar!
If he turns out to be a god from heaven
it will end badly! Gods disguise themselves
as foreigners and strangers to a town,   485
to see who violates their holy laws,
and who is good."

         Antinous ignored
the suitors' words. The blow increased the pain
inside Telemachus' heart, but he
let fall no tears. He calmly shook his head   490
and thought about revenge.

Penelope

heard what had happened in the hall, and said
to all her slaves,

"I hope Apollo shoots

Antinous, just as he hit the beggar!"

And old Eurynome replied, "If only   495
our prayers were answered! None of them would live
to see the Dawn ride in upon her throne."

Penelope said, "Yes, dear, they are all
our enemies and mean to do us harm.
Antinous is the worst; he is like death.   500
Some poor old stranger wandered to this house
and asked the men for food, compelled by need.
The others helped him out and filled his bag;
Antinous hurled a footstool at his shoulder."

She had this conversation in her room   505
with her attendants, while Odysseus
was eating dinner. Then she called the swineherd.

"Eumaeus! Have the stranger come to me,
so I may welcome him, and ask if he
has heard or witnessed anything about   510
long-lost Odysseus. The stranger seems
as if he must have traveled far."

Eumaeus

replied, "Your Majesty, I wish these men
would quiet down! The tales the stranger tells
would charm your heart. For three days and three nights 515
I had him stay with me. He ran away
from off a ship, and came to my house first;
he started to describe his sufferings,
and had not finished. Like a singer, blessed
by gods with skill in storytelling—people   520
watch him and hope that he will sing forever—
so this man's tale enchanted me. He says
Odysseus and he are old guest-friends
through their forefathers. This man lived in Crete,
the home of Minos,[2] and he traveled here   525
a rambling route, with dangers compassed round.
He says Odysseus is still alive
and near here, in the rich Thesprotian land,
and he is bringing home a pile of treasure."

2. Legendary king of Crete.

Penelope said, "Call him over, let him   530
tell me in person, while the suitors have
their fun here in my house or at the doors;
their mood is festive. In their homes they have
untasted food and wine, which their house slaves
devour, while they are flocking to our house   535
each day to slaughter oxen, sheep, and goats,
to feast and drink our wine, with no restraint.
Our wealth is decimated. There is no man
here like Odysseus, who could defend
the house. But if Odysseus comes back   540
to his own native land, he and his son
will soon take vengeance for their violence."

Telemachus sneezed loudly and the noise
resounded through the hall. Penelope
laughed, and she told Eumaeus,

       "Call the stranger!   545
My son just sneezed at what I said—you heard?
It is a sign of death for all the suitors;
no one can save them from their ruin now.
But listen: if I find this stranger speaking
the truth, give him nice clothes—a cloak and tunic."   550

At that, the swineherd went and stood beside
Odysseus. His words had wings.

        "Now sir,
Penelope, Telemachus' mother,
has summoned you. She feels impelled to ask
about her husband, painful though it is.   555
If you tell her the truth—and she will know—
you will get clothes; you desperately need them.
And you can ask for food all through the town,
and fill your belly. Anyone who wants
can give you scraps."

     Strong-willed Odysseus   560
answered, "Eumaeus, I will tell the truth,
the whole truth, to Penelope, and soon.
I know about Odysseus; we shared
in suffering. But I am very nervous
about the rowdy suitors. Their aggression   565
touches the iron sky. When I was walking
across the hall just now, quite harmlessly,
that man hurled something at me, and he hurt me.
Telemachus did nothing to protect me,
and nor did anybody else. So now,   570
tell her to stay right there until night falls,
however eager she may be. At dusk,
she can come nearer, sit beside the fire,

and ask about her husband's journey home.
I do have dirty clothes—you know it well,   575
since it was you I came to first for help."
The swineherd headed back; he crossed the threshold,
and sharp Penelope said,

          "Are you not
bringing the traveler? Is something wrong?
Is he too scared or shy? A homeless man   580
can ill afford such shame."

          Eumaeus answered,
"His words were common sense; he wants to stay
out of the suitors' way; they are aggressive.
He says you should stay here until sunset.
It is much better for you too, my queen,   585
to speak to him alone."

          Penelope
replied, "The stranger is no fool at least.
There never were such bullies as these men,
and they intend us harm."

          The swineherd went
back to the crowd of suitors, and approached   590
Telemachus, and tucked his head down close,
so no one else would hear. "My friend," he said,
"I have to go and watch the pigs, and all
your property, and mine. You should take care
of everything, but most of all, yourself.   595
Do not get hurt. So many mean you harm.
I pray that Zeus obliterates them all,
before they injure us!"

          Telemachus
answered, "May it be so. First eat, then go;
come back at dawn with animals for meat.   600
The rest is up to me and up to gods."
So then Eumaeus sat down on the stool,
and ate and drank, then went back to his pigs,
leaving the palace full of banqueters.
It was already late, past afternoon;   605
music and dancing entertained the suitors.

Summary   Odysseus, in disguise as a beggar, meets a professional beggar named Irus;
they fight, and Odysseus beats Irus. The suitors reward him with special meat. Odysseus warns
the nicest suitor, Amphinomus, to leave the house for his own protection, but Athena makes him
stay. Penelope, inspired by Athena, shows herself to the suitors and declares that she will marry
one of them. The young slave girl Melantho taunts Odysseus. The suitor Eurymachus throws a
footstool at him. The suitors go home to bed.

BOOK 19

[*The Queen and the Beggar*]

Odysseus was left there in the hall,
and with Athena, he was hatching plans
for how to kill the suitors. Words flew fast:

"Telemachus, we have to get the weapons
and hide them. When the suitors see them gone   5
and question you, come up with good excuses.
You can explain, 'The soot had damaged them;
when King Odysseus marched off to Troy
their metal gleamed; now they are growing dull.
I put them safe away from all that smoke.   10
Some spirit also warned me if you drink
too much and argue, you could hurt each other,
dishonoring your banquet and your courtship.
Weapons themselves can tempt a man to fight.'"

Telemachus obeyed his father's word.   15
He summoned Eurycleia, and he told her,
"Shut up the women in their rooms, while I
carry my father's weapons to the storeroom.
They have got dirty since my father left
when I was just a little boy. I want   20
to keep them safe, protected from the smoke."

The loving nurse said, "Child, I wish you would
take charge of all the household management
and guard the wealth. Which girl should bring the torch?
You said the slaves were not allowed to walk   25
in front of you."

                    He said, "This stranger will.[1]
A man who eats my bread must work for me,
even if he has come from far away."

She made no answer but locked up the doors
that led inside the hall. Odysseus   30
and his bright boy jumped up and got the helmets
and studded shields and pointed spears. Athena
stood by them with a golden lamp; she made
majestic light. Telemachus said,

                         "Father,
my eyes have noticed something very strange.   35
The palace walls, the handsome fir-wood rafters
and crossbeams and the pillars high above

---

1. Eurycleia's question implies an assumption that carrying the light is the job of a woman, a female slave; there is a momentary surprise that the answer is a man.

are visible, as if a fire were lit.
Some god from heaven must be in the house."

But cautiously Odysseus replied, 40
"Hush, no more questions, discipline your thoughts.
This is the way of gods from Mount Olympus.
You need to go to bed. I will stay here,
to aggravate the slave girls and your mother,
and make her cry, and let her question me." 45
Telemachus went through the hall, lit up
by blazing torches, to his room. Sleep came,
and there he lay till Dawn. Odysseus
stayed in the hall, still plotting with Athena
how to destroy the suitors.

       Then the queen, 50
her wits about her, came down from her room,
like Artemis or golden Aphrodite.
Slaves pulled her usual chair beside the fire;
it was inlaid with whorls of ivory
and silver, crafted by Icmalius, 55
who had attached a footstool, all in one.
A great big fleece was laid across the chair,
and pensively Penelope sat down.
The white-armed slave girls came and cleared away
the piles of bread, the tables, and the cups, 60
from which the arrogant suitors had been drinking.
They threw the embers from the braziers
onto the floor, and heaped fresh wood inside them
for light and warmth.

     And then Melantho scolded
Odysseus again. "Hey! Stranger! Will you 65
keep causing trouble, roaming round our house
at night and spying on us women here?
Get out, you tramp! Be happy with your meal!
Or you will soon get pelted with a torch!
Be off!"

    Odysseus began to scowl, 70
and made a calculated speech. "Insane!
You silly girl, why are you mad at me?
Because I am all dirty, dressed in rags,
and begging through the town? I have no choice.
That is how homeless people have to live. 75
I used to have a house, and I was rich,
respectable, and often gave to beggars;
I helped whoever came, no matter what.
I had a lot of slave girls too, and all
the things we count as wealth; the happy life. 80
Zeus ruined it. He must have wanted to.

Girl, may you never lose the rank you have
among the other slave girls—if your mistress
gets angry, or Odysseus arrives.
It might still happen. But if he is dead   85
and never coming back, his son is now
a man, praise be Apollo. He will notice
any misconduct from the women here.
He is a grown-up now."

      Penelope
had listened warily, and now she spoke   90
to scold the slave. "You brazen, shameless dog!
I see you! You will wipe away your nerve,
your grand audacity, with your own life.
You knew quite well—I told you so myself—
that I might keep the stranger in the hall   95
to question him about my missing husband.
I am weighed down by grief."

      And then she turned
to tell Eurynome, "Bring out a chair
and put a cushion on it, so this stranger
can sit and talk with me. I want to ask him   100
some questions."

     So the woman brought a chair
of polished wood, and set a cushion on it.
Odysseus knew how to bide his time.
He sat, and circumspect Penelope
began the conversation.

      "Stranger, first   105
I want to ask what people you have come from.
Who are your parents? Where is your home town?"

Cunning Odysseus said, "My good woman,[2]
no mortal on the earth would speak against you;
your glory reaches heaven. You must be   110
the daughter of a holy king who ruled
a mighty people with good laws; his rule
made the black earth grow wheat and barley; trees
were full of fruit; the sheep had lambs; the sea
provided fish, and people thrived. This is   115
your house. You have the right to question me,
but do not ask about my family
or native land. The memory will fill
my heart with pain. I am a man of sorrow.
I should not sit in someone else's house   120

2. Here and throughout the book Odysseus addresses Penelope with a word that means both
"woman" and "wife."

lamenting. It is rude to keep on grieving.
The slaves, or even you, might criticize
and say my tearfulness is caused by wine."

Penelope said cautiously, "Well, stranger,
the deathless gods destroyed my strength and beauty   125
the day the Greeks went marching off to Troy,
and my Odysseus went off with them.
If he came back and cared for me again,
I would regain my beauty and my status.
But now I suffer dreadfully; some god   130
has ruined me. The lords of all the islands,
Same, Dulichium, and Zacynthus,
and those who live in Ithaca, are courting
me—though I do not want them to!—and spoiling
my house. I cannot deal with suppliants,   135
strangers and homeless men who want a job.
I miss Odysseus; my heart is melting.
The suitors want to push me into marriage,
but I spin schemes. Some god first prompted me
to set my weaving in the hall and work   140
a long fine cloth. I said to all my suitors,
'Although Odysseus is dead, postpone
requests for marriage till I finish weaving
this sheet to shroud Laertes when he dies.
My work should not be wasted, or the people   145
in Argos will reproach me, if a man
who won such wealth should lie without a shroud.'
They acquiesced. By day I wove the web,
and in the night by torchlight, I unwove it.
I tricked them for three years; long hours went by   150
and days and months, but then, in the fourth year,
with help from my own fickle, doglike slave girls,
they came and caught me at it. Then they shouted
in protest, and they made me finish it.
I have no more ideas, and I cannot   155
fend off a marriage anymore. My parents
are pressing me to marry, and my son
knows that these men are wasting all his wealth
and he is sick of it. He has become
quite capable of caring for a house   160
that Zeus has glorified. And now, you must
reveal your ancestry. You were not born
from rocks or trees, as in a fairy tale."
The master of deception answered, "Wife
of great Odysseus, Laertes' son,   165
why will you not stop asking me about
my family? I will speak, if I must.
But you are making all my troubles worse.
It is the way of things, when someone is
away from home as long as I have been,   170

roaming through many cities, many dangers.
Still, I will tell you what you ask. My homeland
is Crete, a fertile island out at sea.
I cannot count how many people live there,
in ninety cities, and our languages   175
are mixed; there are Achaeans, native Cretans,
and long-haired Dorians and Pelasgians.
Knossos is there, a mighty city where
Minos, the intimate of Zeus, was king
for nine years,[3] and my father was his son,   180
the brave Deucalion, whose other son
was Idomeneus, who sailed to Troy
with the two sons of Atreus.[4] My name
is Aethon,[5] and I am the younger brother.
In Crete, I saw Odysseus, and gave him   185
guest-gifts. A storm had driven him off course
at Malea, and carried him to Crete,
although he yearned for Troy. He narrowly
escaped the winds and found a refuge, mooring
his ships in Amnisus, beside the cave   190
of Eileithyia.[6] He came up to town,
and asked to see my brother, who, he said,
was his good friend, a man he much admired.
But Idomeneus had sailed to Troy
ten days before. I asked him and his crew   195
inside and gave them all a lavish welcome;
our stores were ample, and I made the people
bring barley and red wine and bulls to butcher,
to satisfy their hearts. Those noble Greeks
stayed for twelve days; a mighty north wind trapped them,   200
so strong a person could not stand upright;
some spirit must have summoned it to curse them.
But on the thirteenth day, the wind died down;
they sailed away."

        His lies were like the truth,
and as she listened, she began to weep.   205
Her face was melting, like the snow that Zephyr
scatters across the mountain peaks; then Eurus
thaws it, and as it melts, the rivers swell
and flow again.[7] So were her lovely cheeks
dissolved with tears. She wept for her own husband,   210
who was right next to her. Odysseus

3. Every nine years, Minos, king of Crete, was
instructed how to rule by his father, Zeus. Deucalion, his son, succeeded him as king.
4. Agamemnon and Menelaus.
5. The name "Aethon" can suggest either
"shining" or "brown." It may suggest foxy tricks,
since the word is applied to the reddish color of
the fox in Pindar (*Olympian* 11.19).

6. Amnisus is the port of Knossos in Crete.
Eileithyia is a goddess associated with childbirth.
7. Zephyr is the West Wind, Eurus the East.
The West Wind is imagined as bringing the
snow that is melted by the East Wind of springtime.

pitied his grieving wife inside his heart,
but kept his eyes quite still, without a flicker,
like horn or iron, and he hid his tears
with artifice. She cried a long, long time,   215
then spoke again.

           "Now stranger, I would like
to set a test, to see if you did host
my husband and the men that followed him
in your own house, as you have said. Describe
his clothes, and what he looked like, and his men."   220

Odysseus the trickster said, "My lady,
that would be hard to say—his visit was
so long ago. It has been twenty years.
But I will tell the image in my mind.
Kingly Odysseus wore a purple cloak,   225
of double-folded wool, held fastened by
a golden brooch with double pins, that was
elaborately engraved. In its front paws
a dog held down a struggling dappled fawn.
All those who saw it marveled how the dog   230
could grip the fawn, and how the fawn could kick
its legs and try to get away, though both
were made of gold. I noticed his white tunic
was soft as dried-up onion peel, and shiny
as sunlight. It astonished many women.   235
But note, I do not know if he had brought
these clothes from home, or if a crew member
had given them to him on board the ship,
or some guest-friend. Odysseus had many
dear friends, since very few could match his worth.   240
And I myself gave him a sword of bronze,
a double-folded purple cloak, and tunic
edged with a fringe. I sent him off in glory
when he embarked. He had a valet with him,
I do remember, named Eurybates,   245
a man a little older than himself,
who had black skin, round shoulders, woolly hair,
and was his favorite out of all his crew
because his mind matched his."

                These words increased
her grief. She knew the signs that he had planted   250
as evidence, and sobbed; she wept profusely.
Pausing, she said, "I pitied you before,
but now you are a guest and honored friend.
I gave those clothes to him that you describe;
I took them from the storeroom, folded them,   255
and clasped that brooch for him. But I will never
welcome him home. A curse sailed on that ship

when he went off to see Evilium—
the town I will not name."[8]

                    He answered shrewdly,
"Your Majesty, Odysseus' wife,   260
stop ruining your pretty skin with tears,
and grieving for your husband, brokenhearted.
I do not blame you; any woman would
mourn for a husband by whom she had children,
even if he were not the kind of man   265
they say your husband was—a godlike hero.
But stop your crying. Listen. I will tell you
a certainty. I will be frank with you.
I heard Odysseus is coming home.
He is alive and near here, in Thesprotia.   270
By hustling, he gained a heap of treasure
that he is bringing home. He lost his ship
at sea, and let his loyal men be killed
when he had left Thrinacia; Helius
and Zeus despised Odysseus,[9] because   275
his men had killed the Cattle of the Sun.
So all those men were drowned beneath the waves,
but he himself was clinging to the rudder
and washed up in the land of the Phaeacians,
the cousins of the gods. They honored him   280
as if he were a god himself, and gave him
abundant gifts, and tried to send him home
safely. He would have been here long ago,
but he decided he should travel more
and gather greater wealth. No man on earth   285
knows better how to make a profit. Pheidon,
the king of the Thesprotians, told me this.
He poured libations and he swore to me
there was a ship already launched and crew
all set to take him home. But Pheidon said   290
good-bye to me first, as a ship of theirs
happened to be already on its way
to barley-rich Dulichium. He showed me
the treasure that Odysseus had gained—
enough to feed his children and grandchildren   295
for ten whole generations. Pheidon said
Odysseus had gone to Dodona,
to ask the rustling oak leaves whether Zeus
advised him, after all those years away,
to go home openly or in disguise.   300
I tell you, he is safe and near at hand.
He will not long be absent from his home

8. In the original, Penelope coins a compound word suggesting "Bad Troy" (Troy = Ilium).
9. The verb here, *odyssomai*, is the same one associated with the name "Odysseus" elsewhere in the poem (for example, 1.63). It means "to be angry at [somebody]" or "to hate," and it is cognate with a noun for "pain" (*odune*).

and those that love him. I swear this by Zeus,
the highest, greatest god, and by the hearth
where I am sheltering. This will come true   305
as I have said. This very lunar month,
between the waning and the waxing moon
Odysseus will come."

              Penelope
said warily, "Well, stranger, I do hope
that you are right. If so, I would reward you   310
at once with such warm generosity
that everyone you met would see your luck.
In fact, it seems to me, Odysseus
will not come home. No one will see you off
with kind good-byes. There is no master here   315
to welcome visitors as he once did
and send them off with honor. Was there ever
a man like him? Now slaves, give him a wash
and make a bed with mattress, woolen blankets
and fresh clean sheets, to keep him warm till Dawn   320
assumes her golden throne. Then bathe and oil him;
seat him inside the hall, beside my son,
and let him eat. If any of these men
is so corrupt that he would harm our guest,
the worse for him! He will get nowhere here,   325
however much he rages. Stranger, how
could you have evidence that I excel
all other women in intelligence,
if you were kept in rags, your skin all sunburnt,
in my house? Human beings have short lives.   330
If we are cruel, everyone will curse us
during our life, and mock us when we die.
The names of those who act with nobleness
are brought by travelers across the world,
and many people speak about their goodness."   335

But devious Odysseus said, "Wife
of great Odysseus, I started hating
blankets and fine clean sheets the day I rowed
from cloudy, mountainous Crete. I will lie down
as I have spent so many sleepless nights,   340
on some rough pallet, waiting for bright Dawn.
I do not care for footbaths; do not let
any of these slave women in your house
come near my feet, unless there is an old one
whom I can trust, who has endured the same   345
heartbreak and sorrow as myself. If so,
I would not mind if she should touch my feet."

Penelope said thoughtfully, "Dear guest,
how well you speak! No visitor before
who came into my house from foreign lands   350

has ever been so scrupulous. I have
a sensible old woman, who brought up
my husband. She first took him in her arms
from his own mother as a newborn child.
She is quite weak, but she can wash your feet.   355
Get up now, Eurycleia, wash your master's
age-mate.[1] By now, Odysseus himself
must have old wrinkled feet and hands like these.
We mortals grow old fast in times of trouble."

The old slave shed hot tears, and held her hands   360
across her face, and wailed,

              "Oh, child! I am
so useless to you now! Zeus hated you
beyond all other men, although you are
so god-fearing! No human ever burned
so many thigh-bones to the Lord of Thunder,   365
or sacrificed so much to him. You prayed
that you would reach a comfortable old age
and raise your son to be respected. Now
you are the only one who cannot reach
your home. And when that poor Odysseus   370
stays at the palaces of foreign kings,
I think the women slaves are mocking him
as these bad girls are hounding you. You have
refused to let them wash you, to avoid
abuse. But wise Penelope has told me   375
to wash you, and reluctantly I will,
for her sake and for yours—you move my heart.
Now listen. Many strangers have come here
in trouble and distress. But I have never
seen any man whose body, voice, and feet   380
are so much like my master's."

              He replied
shrewdly, "Old woman, everyone who sees
the two of us says we are much alike;
you were perceptive to observe the likeness."

Then the old woman took the shining cauldron   385
used for a footbath, and she filled it up
with water—lots of cold, a splash of hot.
Odysseus sat there beside the hearth,
and hurriedly turned round to face the darkness.
He had a premonition in his heart   390
that when she touched him, she would feel his scar
and all would be revealed. She kneeled beside him,
and washed her master. Suddenly, she felt

1. The original has a temporary ambiguity, where the reader or listener may wonder if Penelope has already recognized her husband and may be about to say "your master's . . . feet."

the scar. A white-tusked boar had wounded him
on Mount Parnassus long ago. He went there   395
with his maternal cousins and grandfather,
noble Autolycus,[2] who was the best
of all mankind at telling lies and stealing.
Hermes[3] gave him this talent to reward him
for burning many offerings to him.   400
Much earlier, Autolycus had gone
to Ithaca to see his daughter's baby,
and Eurycleia put the newborn child
on his grandfather's lap and said, 'Now name
your grandson—this much-wanted baby boy.'   405
He told the parents, 'Name him this. I am
disliked by many, all across the world,
and I dislike them back.[4] So name the child
'Odysseus.' And when he is a man,
let him come to his mother's people's house,   410
by Mount Parnassus. I will give him treasure
and send him home rejoicing.' When he grew,
Odysseus came there to claim his gifts.
His cousins and Autolycus embraced him,
and greeted him with friendly words of welcome.   415
His grandma, Amphithea, wrapped her arms
around him like a vine and kissed his face
and shining eyes. Autolycus instructed
his sons to make the dinner. They obeyed
and brought a bull of five years old and flayed it,   420
and chopped it all in pieces, and then sliced
the meat with skill and portioned it on skewers
and roasted it with care, and shared it out,
and everybody got the same amount.
The whole day long they feasted, till the sun   425
went down and darkness fell. Then they lay down
and took the gift of sleep. When early Dawn,
the newborn child with rosy hands, appeared,
Autolycus went hunting with his dogs
and with his sons; Odysseus went too.   430
Up the steep wooded side of Mount Parnassus
they climbed and reached its windswept folds. The sun
rose from the calmly flowing depths of Ocean
to touch the fields, just as the hunters came
into a glen. The dogs had dashed in front,   435
looking for tracks. Autolycus' sons
came after, with Odysseus who kept
close to the dogs, and brandished his long spear.
A mighty boar lurked there; its lair was thick,
protected from the wind; the golden sun   440

---

2. The name "Autolycus" suggests "Wolf Man."
3. Trickster and messenger god.
4. Autolycus uses the same verb, *odussomai*,
as in 19.275 which sounds like the name

"Odysseus" and can mean either "I am angry
at" or "I am the cause of anger (in others)." See
also the note to 1.63.

could never strike at it with shining rays,
and rain could not get in; there was a pile
of fallen leaves inside. The boar had heard
the sound of feet—the men and dogs were near.
Out of his hiding place he leapt to face them,   445
his bristles standing up, his eyes like fire,
and stood right next to them. Odysseus
was first to rush at him, his long spear gripped
tight in his hand. He tried to strike; the boar
struck first, above his knee, and charging sideways   450
scooped a great hunk of flesh off with his tusk,
but did not reach the bone. Odysseus
wounded the boar's right shoulder, and the spear
pierced through. The creature howled and fell to earth.
His life flew out. Autolycus' sons   455
bustled around and skillfully bound up
the wound received by great Odysseus,
and stopped the black blood with a charm, and took him
back to their father's house, and nursed him well,
then gave him splendid gifts, and promptly sent him   460
back home to Ithaca, and he was glad.
His parents welcomed him and asked him questions,
wanting to know how he had got the wound.
He told them he was hunting with his cousins
on Mount Parnassus, and a boar attacked him;   465
the white tusk pierced his leg.

                        The old slave woman,
holding his leg and rubbing with flat palms,
came to that place, and recognized the scar.
She let his leg fall down into the basin.
It clattered, tilted over, and the water   470
spilled out across the floor. Both joy and grief
took hold of her. Her eyes were filled with tears;
her voice was choked. She touched his beard and said,

"You are Odysseus! My darling child!
My master! I did not know it was you   475
until I touched you all around your leg."
She glanced towards Penelope, to tell her
it was her husband. But Penelope
did not look back; she could not meet her eyes,
because Athena turned her mind aside.   480
Odysseus grabbed her throat with his right hand
and with the left, he pulled her close and whispered,

"Nanny! Why are you trying to destroy me?
You fed me at your breast! Now after all
my twenty years of pain, I have arrived   485
back to my home. You have found out; a god
has put the knowledge in your mind. Be silent;
no one must know, or else I promise you,

if some god helps me bring the suitors down,
I will not spare you when I kill the rest,   490
the other slave women, although you were
my nurse."

        With calculation, Eurycleia
answered, "My child! What have you said! You know
my mind is firm, unshakable; I will
remain as strong as stone or iron. Let me   495
promise you this: if you defeat the suitors,
I will tell you which women in the palace
dishonor you, and which are free from guilt."

Odysseus already had a plan.
"Nanny, why do you mention them? No need.   500
I will myself make my own observations
of each of them. Be quiet now; entrust
the future to the gods."

          The old nurse went
to fetch more washing water; all the rest
was spilt. She washed and oiled him, and then   505
he pulled his chair beside the fire again,
to warm himself, and covered up his scar
with rags. And carefully Penelope
spoke to him.

        "Stranger, I have one small question
I want to ask you. It will soon be time   510
to lie down comfortably—at least for those
who can enjoy sweet sleep, no matter what.
But I have been afflicted by some god
with pain beyond all measure. In the day,
I concentrate on my work and my women's,   515
despite my constant grief. But when night comes,
and everybody goes to sleep, I lie
crying in bed and overwhelmed by pain;
worries and sorrows crowd into my heart.
As when the daughter of Pandareus,[5]   520
the pale gray nightingale, sings beautifully
when spring has come, and sits among the leaves
that crowd the trees, and warbles up and down
a symphony of sound, in mourning for
her son by Zethus, darling Itylus,   525
whom she herself had killed in ignorance,
with bronze. Just so, my mind pulls two directions—
should I stay here beside my son, and keep

---

5. Aedon, daughter of Pandareus, king of Crete, married Zethus, king of Thebes, and tried to kill one of the children of her sister-in-law, Niobe, in a fit of jealousy. By mistake, she killed her own son, Itylus (called Itys in other versions of the myth). She was turned into a nightingale, whose song is supposed to be a constant lament for the dead boy.

things all the same—my property, my slave girls,
and my great house—to show respect towards   530
my husband's bed and what the people say?
Or should I marry one of them—whichever
is best of all the suitors and can bring
most presents? When my son was immature,
and young, I could not leave my husband's house.   535
He would not let me. Now that he is big
and all grown-up, he urges me to go;
he is concerned that they are eating up
his property. Now how do you interpret
this dream of mine? I dreamed that twenty geese   540
came from the river to my house, and they
were eating grain and I was glad to see them.
Then a huge eagle with a pointed beak
swooped from the mountain, broke their necks, and killed them.
I wept and wailed, inside the dream; the women   545
gathered around me, and I cried because
the eagle killed my geese. Then he came back
and sitting on the jutting roof-beam, spoke
in human language, to restrain my grief.
'Penelope, great queen, cheer up. This is   550
no dream; it will come true. It is a vision.
The geese are suitors; I was once an eagle,
but now I am your husband. I have come
back home to put a cruel end to them.'
Then I woke up, looked round, and saw the geese   555
still eating grain beside the trough as they
had done before."

            Odysseus, well-known
for his intelligence, said, "My dear woman,
there is no way to wrest another meaning
out of the dream; Odysseus himself   560
said how he will fulfill it: it means ruin
for all the suitors. No one can protect them
from death."

            But shrewd Penelope said, "Stranger,
dreams are confusing, and not all come true.
There are two gates of dreams: one pair is made   565
of horn and one of ivory. The dreams
from ivory are full of trickery;
their stories turn out false. The ones that come
through polished horn come true. But my strange dream
did not come out that way, I think. I wish   570
it had, as does my son. The day of doom
is coming that will take me from the house
of my Odysseus. I will arrange
a contest with his axes. He would set them
all in a row, like ship's props. From a distance   575
he shot an arrow through all twelve of them.

I will assign this contest to the suitors.
Whoever strings his bow most readily,
and shoots through all twelve axes, will win me,
and I will follow him. I will be parted   580
from here, this lovely house, my marriage home,
so full of wealth and life, which I suppose
I will remember even in my dreams."

Scheming Odysseus said, "Honored wife
of great Odysseus, do not postpone   585
this contest. They will fumble with the bow
and will not finish stringing it or shooting
the arrow through, before Odysseus,
the mastermind, arrives."

                           She chose her words
with care: "If you would sit and entertain me,   590
guest, I would never wish to go to sleep.
But humans cannot stay awake forever;
immortal gods have set a proper time
for everything that mortals do on earth.
I will go up and lie down on my bed,   595
which is a bed of grief, all stained with tears
that I have cried since he went off to see
Evilium, the town I will not name.
I will lie there, and you lie in this house;
spread blankets on the floor, or have the slaves   600
make up a bed."

                   With that, she went upstairs,
accompanied by slave girls. In her room,
she cried for her dear husband, till sharp-sighted
Athena poured sweet sleep onto her eyes.

Summary   Odysseus itches to fight but Athena restrains him. The slaves prepare the house for the feast day. Melanthius, the goatherd, insults Odysseus. Philoetius, the cowherd, and Eumaeus, the swineherd, declare their loyalty to their old owner. The suitors pull out of the plot to kill Telemachus. They mock Odysseus in his disguise as beggar. The prophet Theoclymenus predicts their deaths.

BOOK 21

[An Archery Contest]

With glinting eyes, Athena put a thought
into the mind of wise Penelope,
the daughter of Icarius: to place
the bow and iron axes in the hall
of great Odysseus, and set the contest   5
which would begin the slaughter. She went up
to her own room. Her muscular, firm hand

picked up the ivory handle of the key—
a hook of bronze. Then with her slaves she walked
down to the storeroom where the master kept   10
his treasure: gold and bronze and well-wrought iron.
The curving bow and deadly arrows lay there,
given by Iphitus, Eurytus' son,
the godlike man he happened to befriend
at wise Ortilochus' house, far off   15
in Lacedaemon, in Messenia.[6]
Odysseus had gone to claim a debt—
some people of Messenia had come
in rowing boats and poached three hundred sheep
from Ithaca; they took their shepherds too.   20
Laertes and the other older men
had sent Odysseus to fetch them back
when he was still a boy. And Iphitus
had come there for his horses, twelve fine mares,
each suckling a sturdy mule. These horses   25
would later cause his death, when he had gone
to visit Heracles, who welcomed him,
but killed him, so that he could take the horses—[7]
betraying hospitality, and heedless
about the watchful gods. Before all that,   30
when Iphitus first met Odysseus,
he gave this bow to him, inherited
from his own father. And Odysseus
gave Iphitus a sword and spear, to mark
their bond. But Iphitus was dead before   35
the friends could visit one another's houses.
So when Odysseus' black fleet sailed
to war, he did not take the bow, but stored it
in his own house, to use in Ithaca
in memory of his friend.

                The queen had reached   40
the storeroom, and she stepped across the threshold
of polished oak; a skillful carpenter
had set it level, fixed the frame, and built
the dazzling double doors. She quickly loosed
the door-thong from its hook, pushed in the key   45
and with true aim, thrust back the fastenings.
The fine doors, as the key struck home, began
to bellow as a bull at pasture bellows.
At once, they flew apart. She stepped inside,
onto the pallet where the scented clothes   50
were stored in chests, and reached to lift the bow
down from its hook, still in its shining case.
She sat down on the floor to take it out,

---

6. Messenia is a town within Lacedaemon, the region around Sparta.

7. Heracles killed Iphitus in a dispute over the mares of Iphitus's father, Eurytus.

resting it on her lap, and started sobbing
and wailing as she saw her husband's bow.   55
At last, she dried her eyes, and in her arms
picked up the curving bow and quiver, packed
with many deadly arrows, and she went
to meet her arrogant suitors. Slaves lugged out
a chest with their master's many axes   60
of bronze and iron, for the competition.
The queen came near the suitors, and she stopped
beside a pillar with a filmy veil
across her face. Two slave girls stood with her.
She said,

      "Now listen, lords. You keep on coming   65
to this house every day, to eat and drink,
wasting the wealth of someone who has been
away too long. Your motives are no secret.
You want to marry me. I am the prize.
So I will set a contest. This great bow   70
belonged to godlike King Odysseus.
If anyone can grasp it in his hands
and string it easily, and shoot through all
twelve axes,[8] I will marry him, and leave
this beautiful rich house, so full of life,   75
my lovely bridal home. I think I will
remember it forever, even in
my dreams."

      She told Eumaeus he should set
the bow and pale-gray iron axes up
before the suitors, and in tears the swineherd   80
took them, and did as she had asked. The cowherd
wept also when he saw his master's bow.

Antinous began to scold and taunt them.
He said, "You idiots! You tactless peasants!
So thoughtless, so undisciplined! You fools,   85
your selfish crying is upsetting her!
Poor lady, she is sad enough already
at losing her beloved husband. Sit
and eat in silence, or go do your wailing
outside, and leave us suitors here to try   90
the deadly contest of the bow. I think
it will be difficult; not one of us
can match Odysseus. I saw him once
in childhood, and I still remember him."

He hoped he would be first to string the bow   95

8. The mechanics of the axe competition are debated, but it seems most likely that these are axe heads, without handles, with round, drilled holes in the end through which the wooden handle could be inserted. The axe heads are lined up in a row, with the holes all aligned straight. The goal of the contest is to shoot an arrow through all of the holes.

and shoot through all the axes. But he would
be first to taste an arrow from the hands
of great Odysseus, whom he had mocked,
urging the others on to do the same.

Then Prince Telemachus addressed them all.   100
"Zeus must have made me stupid! My dear mother,
despite her usual common sense, has said
that she will marry someone else and leave
this house. But I am laughing, and my heart
feels foolish gladness. Well, come on, you suitors.   105
You want this prize—a woman unlike any
in holy Pylos, Argos or Mycenae,
or here in Ithaca or on the mainland.
No woman in Achaea is like her.
There is no need for me to praise my mother.   110
You know her worth. So do not make excuses,
do not put off the contest of the bow.
We want to watch. And I will try myself.
If I succeed in stringing it and shooting
all through, I will no longer mind if Mother   115
goes off with someone else, and leaves me here.
Success would prove me man enough to carry
my father's arms."

                    He stood up straight and tall,
tossed off his purple cloak, unstrapped his sword,
and dug a trench to set the axes up,   120
all in a line, and trod the earth down flat.[9]
They were amazed to see him work so neatly,
though he had never seen it done before.
He stood astride the threshold and began
to try the bow. Three times he made it quiver,   125
straining to draw it back; three times he failed
to string the bow and shoot through all the axes.
He would have tried a fourth time; he was keen
to keep on pulling. But Odysseus
shook his head, stopping him. Telemachus   130
said,

     "Ugh! It seems that I will always be
too weak and useless. Or perhaps I am
too young and inexperienced at fighting
in self-defense when someone starts a quarrel.
You all are stronger than I am. You try,   135
and we can end the contest."

                    With these words,

9. If the contest is taking place in the feast
hall—which has a finished floor, not dirt—the
earth seems to be brought in and heaped up to
provide a base for the axes.

he set the bow down on the floor, propped up
against the polished, jointed double door,
and tucked the arrow up against the handle.
He sat back down where he had sat before.   140

Antinous called out, "Now, friends, get up,
from left to right, beginning with the man
next to the wine-slave!"

          They agreed. The first
was Leodes, their holy man,[1] who always
sat in the farthest corner, by the wine-bowl.   145
He was the only one who disapproved
of all their bullying. He grasped the bow
and stood astride the threshold, and he tried
to string it, but he failed. His hands were soft,
untrained by labor, and he grew worn out   150
trying to pull it back. He told the suitors,

"My friends, I cannot do it. Someone else
should have a turn. This bow will take away
courage, life-force, and energy from many
noble young men;[2] but better we should die,   155
than live and lose the goal for which we gather
in this house every day. Each man still hopes
for marriage with Odysseus' wife,
Penelope. But if one tries and fails
to string the bow, let him go use his wealth   160
to court some other fine, well-dressed Greek lady.
And after that, Penelope will marry
whichever man can bring most gifts for her—
the man whom fate has chosen."

          With these words,
he set the bow back down, and leaned it up   165
against the polished, jointed double door,
tucking the pointed arrow by the handle.
Antinous responded with a jeer.

"My goodness, Leodes! What scary words!
All your tough talk has made me really angry.   170
You cannot string the bow, so you are claiming
that it will take the life from proper men.
You surely were not born for archery.
The rest of us are actual warriors;
we will soon string this bow."

---

1. The holy man is literally a man who performs sacrifices. However, the job description is
somewhat fluid, and he also serves as a prophet
or diviner.
2. Leodes speaks in prophetic language, perhaps unconsciously. His words could suggest
only that the attempt to string the bow will
discourage those who fail, but they can also
mean that the bow will kill many men.

He told the goatherd,   175
"Melanthius, come on now, light a fire
and pull a chair beside it, with a fleece,
and bring out from the pantry a big hunk
of fat, so we young men can warm the bow,
grease it, and try it, and so end this contest."   180

Melanthius obeyed at once; he lit
a blazing fire, and pulled a chair beside it,
spreading a fleece on top, and brought the wheel
of fat. The young men warmed the bow, but still
they could not string it. They were far too weak.   185
Antinous and Eurymachus, the leaders,
strongest and most impressive of the suitors,
had still not had their turn.

Meanwhile the swineherd
and cowherd had both gone outside the house.
Odysseus himself came after them,   190
and when they were outside the gates, beyond
the courtyard, in a friendly voice he said,
"Cowherd and swineherd, I am hesitating
whether to speak out openly; my impulse
is to be frank. What if some god should guide   195
Odysseus, and suddenly, as if
from nowhere, he was here—how would you act?
Would you be with the suitors, or with him?
How are your hearts inclined?"

The cowherd said,
"O Father Zeus, please make this wish come true,   200
that he may come! May spirits guide him home!
Then you would see how well-prepared I am
to fight for him!" Eumaeus prayed in turn
that all the gods would bring Odysseus
back home. The man who thought of everything now knew   205
their minds, and said to them,

"I am here now.
I suffered terribly for twenty years,
and now I have come back to my own land.
I see that you two are the only slaves
who welcome my arrival. I have not   210
heard any others praying I would come
back to my home. I promise, if some god
brings down the noble suitors by my hands,
I will give each of you a wife and wealth,
and well-constructed houses, near my own.   215
You two will be Telemachus' brothers.
Now let me show you clearer proof, so you
can know me well and trust me. See my scar,

made by the boar's white tusk, when I had gone
to hunt on Mount Parnassus with my cousins."   220

So saying, he pulled back his rags and showed
the great big scar. They stared and studied it,
then both burst into tears. They threw their arms
around Odysseus, and kissed his face
and hugged him, overjoyed at seeing him.   225
Odysseus embraced them back and kissed them.
They would have wept till sunset, but he stopped them,
and said,

      "Stop now; if someone steps outside
and sees you crying, they may tell the men.
Go in, not both at once but taking turns,   230
first me, then you, then you. And this will be
our sign: when all the noblemen refuse
to let me have the bow and set of arrows,
then you must bring them through the hall, Eumaeus,
and put them in my hands. Command the women   235
to shut up tight the entrance to the hall,
and go to their own quarters; if they hear
men screaming or loud noises, they must not
come out, but stay there quietly, and work.
And you, Philoetius, lock up the gates   240
leading out from the courtyard with the bolt
and put the rope on too. We must move fast."

With that, he went inside, and sat back down
on the same chair he sat on earlier.
Then the two slaves went in. Eurymachus   245
was handling the bow and warming it,
turning it back and forth beside the fire.
But even after that, he could not manage
to string it, and he groaned, and yelled in fury,

"This is disastrous! For all of us!   250
I do not even mind so much about
the marriage. There are lots of other women
on Ithaca, and in the other cities.
But that we should be proven so much weaker
than King Odysseus, that we should fail   255
to string his bow! Our deep humiliation
will be well-known for many years to come!"

Antinous said, "No, Eurymachus,
it will not be like that, as you well know.
No one should shoot a bow today; it is   260
a feast day for Apollo! We should sit
calmly and leave the axe heads standing there.
No one will come and take them. Let the boy

pour wine, so we can make drink offerings,
and leave the bow for now. At dawn, call back   265
Melanthius, to bring the finest goats,
so we can make our offerings to the god,
Apollo, lord of archery, then try
the bow again, and finish up the contest."

They all agreed with him. Attendants poured   270
water to wash their hands, and boys began
to mix the wine in bowls, and poured a serving
in every cup, so they could make libations
and drink. Odysseus, the lord of lies,
had carefully considered how to fool them.   275
He said,

        "Now hear me, suitors of the Queen;
let me reveal the promptings of my heart.
Eurymachus and Lord Antinous,
I ask you specially, because you spoke
so well: now set the bow aside, and turn   280
towards the gods. At dawn, the god will choose
the victor and give him success. For now,
give me the polished bow, so I can try
my strength and find out if my hands still have
the suppleness and vigor of my youth,   285
or if it has been lost in all my years
of homelessness and poverty."

                    They bristled,
nervous in case he strung the polished bow.
Antinous said, "Foreigner! You fool!
Are you not grateful that we let you stay here   290
and eat with noblemen like us, and share
our feast, and hear us talk? No other beggars
can hear our conversation. This good wine
has made you drunk. It does have that effect
on those who gulp and fail to pace themselves.   295
Wine even turned the famous Centaur's head.[3]
When Eurytion visited the Lapiths,
inside the house of brave Pirithous
the wine made him go crazy, and he did
terrible things. The warriors were outraged,   300
and dragged him from the house. Their ruthless swords
cut off his ears and cropped his nose right off.
He wandered, still insane and blown about
by gusts of madness. From that day, the Centaurs
and humans have been enemies. His drinking   305

3. The following passage refers to the famous   dwelling people, later imagined as half-human
drunken brawl between the Lapiths, a Thes-   and half-horse.
salian tribe, and the Centaurs, a wild mountain-

was harmful to himself. If you should string
that bow, it would be worse for you. No man
will treat you kindly in our house. We will
send you by ship to Echetus, the king
of cruelty; you will find no escape.   310
Sit quietly, drink up, and do not quarrel
with younger men."

          Astute Penelope
said, "No, Antinous, it is not right
to disrespect a guest Telemachus
has welcomed to this house. And do you think   315
that if this stranger's hands were strong enough
to string the bow, he would take me away
to marry him and live with him? Of course not!
He does not even dream of such a thing.
No need to spoil the feast by worrying   320
about such things; there is no need of that."

Eurymachus said, "Shrewd Penelope,
it is indeed unlikely that this man
would marry you. But we would feel ashamed
if some rude person said, 'Those men are weak!   325
They court a fighter's wife, but cannot string
his bow! Some random beggar has shown up
and strung it easily, and shot right through
all of the axes!' They will talk like that,
and we will be humiliated!"

          Calmly,   330
Penelope replied, "Eurymachus,
people who waste the riches of a king
have lost their dignity. Why fuss at this?
The stranger is quite tall and muscular;
his father must be noble. Go on, give him   335
the bow, and let us watch. I tell you, if
he strings it by the blessing of Apollo,
I will give him a proper cloak and tunic,
fine clothes and sandals, and a two-edged sword
and dagger, sharp enough to ward away   340
both men and dogs, and I will help him go
wherever he desires to go."

          With quick
intake of breath, Telemachus replied,
"No, Mother, no one has a better right
than I to give the bow to anyone   345
or to refuse it. No one on this island
or out towards the pasturelands of Elis,
and no man in this house can force my hand,
even if I should choose to give the bow

to him to take away. Go up and work   350
with loom and distaff; tell your girls the same.
The bow is work for men, especially me.[4]
I am the one with power in this house."

She was amazed, and went back to her room,
taking to heart her son's assertive words.   355
Inside her bedroom with her girls, she wept
for her dear husband, her Odysseus,
until clear-eyed Athena let her sleep.

Meanwhile, the swineherd lifted up the bow.
The suitors made an uproar.

                 "Dirty pig-man!   360
Where are you taking it? Are you insane?
The dogs you raised yourself will eat you up
when you are out there with your pigs alone,
if we find favor with Apollo and
the other deathless gods."

                 He was afraid,   365
because there were so many people shouting
inside the hall, and set the bow he carried
down on the ground. Telemachus called out,
in forceful tones.

              "No, Grandpa! Keep on going!
Keep carrying the bow! You will soon see   370
you have to choose which master to obey.
Though I am younger than you, I am stronger;
watch out, or I will chase you to the fields,
pelting your back with stones. I wish I had
an equal edge on all those who invaded   375
my home to court my mother and make mischief.
I would soon throw them out and make them pay!"

At that, the suitors all began to laugh;
their anger at Telemachus was gone.
Eumaeus went across the hall and gave   380
the bow to competent Odysseus.
And then he summoned Eurycleia, saying,

"Telemachus gave orders you must lock
the doors into the hall and tie them fast.
If any of you women hear a noise   385
of screaming men, stay up there in your quarters;
do not come out; keep quiet and keep working."

---

4. These two lines echo the words of Hector to Andromache in book 6 of the *Iliad*: "War is a job for men, especially me."

At that, she held her tongue and locked the doors
that led into the feast-hall. Philoetius
scurried outside to bolt the outer gates   390
that led into the courtyard. On the porch
lay a fresh-knotted cable made of byblos;[5]
with that, he tied the gates, rushed in and sat
back down, and looked towards Odysseus.

The master was already handling   395
the bow and turning it this way and that,
to see if worms had eaten at the horn
while he was gone. The suitors told each other,

"He stares at it as if he were an expert
in bows. He acts the part! Perhaps he has   400
a bow like this at home or plans to make one.
See how this pitiful migrant fingers it!"
One confident young suitor said, "I hope
his future luck will match how well he does
in stringing it!"

                      So he had tricked them all.   405
After examining the mighty bow
carefully, inch by inch—as easily
as an experienced musician stretches
a sheep-gut string around a lyre's peg
and makes it fast—Odysseus, with ease,   410
strung the great bow. He held it in his right hand
and plucked the string, which sang like swallow-song,
a clear sweet note. The suitors, horrified,
grew pale, and Zeus made ominous thunder rumble.
Odysseus, who had so long been waiting,   415
was glad to hear the signal from the son
of double-dealing Cronus.[6] He took up
an arrow, which was lying on the table.
The others were all packed up in the quiver,
soon to be used. He laid it on the bridge,   420
then pulled the notch-end and the string together,
still sitting in his chair. With careful aim,
he shot. The weighted tip of bronze flew through
each axe head and then out the other side.
He told his son,

---

5. A fiber from the papyrus plant, imported to Greece from Egypt, known for its strength.
6. Cronus, leader of the Titans (divine descendants of Sky and Earth), was persuaded by his mother, Earth, to castrate his father, Sky, which he did with a sickle. Sky threatened revenge, but Cronus killed him and ruled the world with his sister/wife, Rhea; they were the parents of most of the Olympian gods. Cronus swallowed most of them, but Zeus, the sixth child, organized a war against his father, which he won, and he became king in turn.

"Telemachus, your guest   425
does you a credit. I hit all the targets
and with no effort strung the bow. I am
still strong, despite their jibes about my weakness.
Though it is daytime, it is time to feast;
and later, we can celebrate with music,   430
the joyful part of dinner."

       With his eyebrows
he signaled, and his son strapped on his sword,
picked up his spear, and stood beside his chair,
next to his father, his bronze weapons flashing.

BOOK 22

[*Bloodshed*]

Odysseus ripped off his rags. Now naked,
he leapt upon the threshold with his bow
and quiverfull of arrows, which he tipped
out in a rush before his feet, and spoke.

"Playtime is over. I will shoot again,   5
towards another mark no man has hit.
Apollo, may I manage it!"

       He aimed
his deadly arrow at Antinous.
The young man sat there, just about to lift
his golden goblet, swirling wine around,   10
ready to drink. He had no thought of death.
How could he? Who would think a single man,
among so many banqueters, would dare
to risk dark death, however strong he was?
Odysseus aimed at his throat, then shot.   15
The point pierced all the way through his soft neck.
He flopped down to the side and his cup slipped
out of his hand. A double pipe of blood
gushed from his nostrils. His foot twitched and knocked
the table down; food scattered on the ground. 20
The bread and roasted meat were soiled with blood.
Seeing him fall, the suitors, in an uproar,
with shouts that filled the hall, jumped up and rushed
to search around by all the thick stone walls
for shields or swords to grab—but there were none. 25
They angrily rebuked Odysseus.

"Stranger, you shot a man, and you will pay!
You will join no more games—you have to die!
For certain! You have killed the best young man
in all of Ithaca. Right here, the vultures 30

will eat your corpse." Those poor fools did not know
that he had killed Antinous on purpose,
nor that the snares of death were round them all.

Clever Odysseus scowled back and sneered,
"Dogs! So you thought I would not come back home   35
from Troy? And so you fleeced my house, and raped
my slave girls, and you flirted with my wife
while I am still alive! You did not fear
the gods who live in heaven, and you thought
no man would ever come to take revenge.   40
Now you are trapped inside the snares of death."

At that, pale fear seized all of them. They groped
to find a way to save their lives somehow.
Only Eurymachus found words to answer.

"If it is you, Odysseus, come back,   45
then we agree! Quite right, the Greeks have done
outrageous things to your estate and home.
But now the one responsible is dead—
Antinous! It was all his idea.
He did not even really want your wife,   50
but had another plan, which Zeus has foiled:
to lie in ambush for your son, and kill him,
then seize the throne and rule in Ithaca.
Now he is slain—quite rightly. Please, my lord,
have mercy on your people! We will pay   55
in public, yes, for all the food and drink.
We each will bring the price of twenty oxen,
and pay you all the gold and bronze you want.
Your anger is quite understandable."

Odysseus saw through him; with a glare   60
he told him, "Even if you give me all
your whole inheritance, and even more,
I will not keep my hands away from slaughter
until I pay you suitors back for all
your wickedness. You have two choices: fight,   65
or run away: just try to save your lives!
Not one of you will get away from death."

At that their knees grew weak, their hearts stopped still.
Eurymachus again addressed the suitors.
"My friends, this man will not hold back his hands.   70
Seizing the bow and arrows, he will shoot us
right from that polished threshold, till he kills
each one of us. Be quick, make plans for battle.
Draw out your swords, use tables as your shields[7]

7. In the usual arrangement, there were light   larger dining table; the suitors are to pick up
side-tables by each diner, rather than a single   their tables for self-defense.

against the deadly arrows. All together,   75
rush at him, try to drive him off the threshold,
and out of doors, then run all through the town,
and quickly call for help. This man will soon
have shot his last!"

              He drew his sharp bronze sword
and with a dreadful scream he leapt at him.   80
But that same instant, Lord Odysseus
let fly and hit his chest, beside the nipple,
and instantly the arrow pierced his liver.
The sword fell from his hand. He doubled up
and fell across the table, spilling food   85
and wine across the floor. He smashed his head
against the ground, and in his desperate pain
kicked up the chair, and darkness drenched his eyes.

Amphinomus attacked Odysseus.
He drew his sharp sword, hoping he could force him   90
to yield his place. Telemachus leapt in
and thrust his bronze spear through him from behind,
ramming it through his back and out his chest.
Face-first he crashed and thudded to the ground.
Telemachus dashed back—he left his spear   95
stuck in the body; he was terrified
that if he bent to pull it out, some Greek
would jump on him and stab him with a sword.
He ran and quickly reached his loyal father.
He stood beside him and his words flew out.   100

"Now Father, I will fetch a shield for you
and two spears and a helmet made of bronze,
and I will arm myself, and bring more arms
for our two herdsmen, since we all need weapons."

Odysseus, the master planner, answered,   105
"Run fast while I still have a stock of arrows,
before they force me from the doors—I am
fighting alone up here."

            His son obeyed.
He hurried to the storeroom for the arms,
and took eight spears, four shields, and four bronze helmets 110
each fitted out with bushy horsehair plumes.
He hurried back to take them to his father,
and was the first to strap the armor on.
The two slaves also armed themselves, and stood
flanking their brilliant, resourceful leader.   115
As long as he had arrows, he kept shooting,
and one by one he picked the suitors off,
inside his own home. Then at last the king

ran out of arrows; he set down his bow
next to the sturdy doorpost, leaning up   120
against the palace walls, all shining white.
He slung the four-fold shield across his shoulders,
and put the well-made helmet on his head.
The crest of horsehair gave a fearsome nod.
He grasped a bronze-tipped spear in either hand.   125

There was a back gate in the castle walls,
providing access to the passageway,
with tightly fitted doors. Odysseus
ordered the noble swineherd to stand there
to guard it—there was only one way out.   130
Agelaus called out to all the suitors.

"Friends, one of us should slip out through that gate
and quickly tell the people, raise alarms.
That soon would put a stop to this man's shooting."

Melanthius the goatherd answered, "No!   135
My lord, that entryway is much too narrow,
and dangerously near the palace doors.
One man, if he was brave, could keep it guarded
against us all. So I will bring you armor
out of the storeroom, which I think is where   140
those two, our enemies, have hidden it."

Melanthius the goatherd climbed up past
the arrow-slits inside the castle walls,
into the chamber. There he took twelve shields,
twelve spears and twelve bronze helmets, each one crested 145
with horsehair. Then he hurried back downstairs
and handed all the weapons to the suitors.

Odysseus could see that they had arms;
their spears were brandished. His heart stopped, his legs
trembled—he was so shocked at their presumption.   150
At once his words flew out to tell his son,

"One of the women, or Melanthius,
is waging war against us, in my house!"

Wisely Telemachus owned up at once.
"Father, it was my fault, I am to blame.   155
I left the heavy storeroom door ajar.
Someone on their side must have kept good watch.
Go there, Eumaeus, shut the door, and see
if any of the women are against us,
or else, as I suspect, Melanthius."   160

Meanwhile, Melanthius was going back
to get more weapons from the room. The swineherd
saw him and told Odysseus,

                    "My lord,
that little sneak, the man we all suspected,
is going to the stores! Odysseus,   165
you always have a plan for what to do:
so should I kill him, as I think is best,
or bring him here to you, so you can punish
his many crimes against you in your house?"

Odysseus already had a plan.   170
"Telemachus and I will keep the suitors
trapped in the hall—however much they rage.
You two, truss up his hands and feet behind him,
drag him inside the storeroom, string him up,
tying a knotted rope high on the column,   175
and hoist him to the rafters. Torture him
with hours of agony before he dies."

His word was their command; they hurried off,
and reached the weaponry. Melanthius
was unaware of them. As he was searching   180
for arms, they stopped on each side of the door
and waited. When he stepped across the threshold,
holding a lovely helmet in one hand,
and in the other hand, a rusty shield,
once carried by Laertes in his youth,   185
but now in storage, with its seams all loose,
the two men jumped on him and grabbed his hair
to drag him in and threw him on the floor,
shaking with fear. They bound his hands and feet
and yanked them painfully behind his back,   190
just as the lord of suffering had told them.
They tied him with a knotted rope and hoisted
his body up the column to the rafters.
Swineherd Eumaeus, you began to mock him:

"Keep watch the whole night through, Melanthius,   195
tucked up in this soft bed—it serves you right!
And wait there for the golden throne of Dawn
leaving the sea, that hour when you would lead
your goats to this house for the suitors' dinner."

There he was left, bound cruelly and stretched.   200
The herdsmen armed themselves and left the room,
shutting the door, and joined their cunning leader.
They stood there on the threshold, tense with purpose,
just four against so many men inside.

The child of Zeus, Athena, came to meet them; 205
her voice and looks resembled those of Mentor.
Odysseus was happy when he saw her,
and said, "Remember our old friendship, Mentor!
I have been good to you since we were boys.
So help me now!" He guessed it was Athena, 210
who rouses armies.

        From the hall, the suitors
shouted their opposition. Agelaus
called, "Mentor, do not let Odysseus
sway you to help him and to fight against us.
I think this is how things will go. When we 215
have killed this father and his son, you will
die also, if you do as you intend,
and pay with your own life for all your plots.
Our bronze will strip your life away from you,
and we will seize whatever you may own 220
and mix it with the loot we get from here.
Your sons will not survive here in these halls,[8]
nor will your wife and daughters still walk free
in Ithaca."

        At that Athena's heart
became enraged, and angrily she scolded 225
Odysseus. "Where is your courage now?
You fought nine years on end against the Trojans,
for white-armed Helen, Zeus' favorite child.[9]
You slaughtered many men when war was raging,
and formed the plan that made the city fall.[1] 230
Now you are home at last, how can you flinch
from being brave and using proper force
against these suitors? Come now, stand by me
and watch how Mentor, son of Alcimus,
will treat your enemies as recompense 235
for all your service."

        But she did not grant
decisive victory; she kept on testing
Odysseus' courage, and his son's.
She flew up like a swallow through the smoke
and nestled in the rafters of the roof. 240

Now Agelaus, Demoptolemus,
Eurynomus, Pisander, Amphimedon,
and Polybus were urging on the suitors.
Those were the most heroic of the group
who still survived and battled for their lives: 245

---

8. It is unclear in the original whether Agelaus is threatening to kill Mentor's sons or only banish them.

9. The original epithet is an unusual one, *eupatereios*, suggesting "well-fathered."

1. The trick of the Wooden Horse.

the others were defeated by the bow
and raining arrows. Agelaus told them,

"That Mentor's boasts were empty, friends! He left,
and they are all alone there at the entrance.
Now force this cruel man to stay his hands.   250
Do not hurl spears at him all in a mass,
but you six must shoot first and pray Lord Zeus
we strike Odysseus and win the fight.
Once he is down, the others will be nothing."

The six men threw their spears as he had said;   255
at once Athena made their efforts fail.
One pierced the doorpost of the palace hall,
another hit the closely fitted door,
another's spear of ash and heavy bronze
fell on the wall. The group of four avoided   260
all of the suitors' spears. Odysseus
had waited long enough.

                    "My friends," he said,
"they want to slaughter us and strip our arms!
Avenge my former wrongs, and save your lives!
Now shoot!"

                    They hurled their spears at once and hit.   265
Odysseus killed Demoptolemus;
Telemachus, Euryades; the swineherd
slaughtered Elatus, and the cowherd killed
Pisander. They all fell and bit the earth.
The other suitors huddled in a corner;   270
the four rushed up and from the corpses pulled
their spears. Again the suitors threw their weapons;
again Athena made them fail. One spear
struck at the doorpost, and another pierced
the door; another ash spear hit the wall.   275
Amphimedon's blow grazed Telemachus
right by the wrist: the bronze tore through his skin.
Ctesippus hurled his spear; it only scratched
the swineherd's shoulder, just above his shield,
flew past and fell down on the floor behind him.   280
The competent, sharp-eyed Odysseus
and his companions hurled their piercing spears
into the swarming throng. The city-sacker
skewered Eurydamas; Telemachus
slashed Amphimedon, and the swineherd struck   285
at Polybus; the cowherd sliced right through
Ctesippus' chest, and crowed,

                    "You fool! You loved
insulting us—now you have stopped your boasting.
The gods have got the last word; they have won.

This is a gift to pay you for that kick   290
you gave Odysseus when he walked through
his own house, as a homeless man in need."

Odysseus moved closer with his spear,
and pierced Agelaus; Telemachus
thrust at Leocritus, and drove his bronze   295
into his belly. He fell down headfirst,
face smashed against the floor.

               Then from the roof
Athena lifted high her deadly aegis.
The frightened suitors bolted through the hall
like cattle, roused and driven by a gadfly   300
in springtime, when the days are getting longer.
As eagles with their crooked beaks and talons
swoop from the hills and pounce on smaller birds
that fly across the fields beneath the clouds;
the victims have no help and no way out,   305
as their attackers slaughter them, and men
watch and enjoy the violence. So these
four fighters sprang and struck, and drove the suitors
in all directions. Screaming filled the hall,
as skulls were cracked; the whole floor ran with blood.   310

Leodes darted up to supplicate
Odysseus; he touched his knees.

                 "Please, mercy!
I did no wrong, I swear, in word or deed
to any of the women in the house.
I tried to stop the suitors, tried to urge them   315
to keep their hands clean, but they would not listen.
Those fools deserved their fate. But I did nothing!
I am a priest—yet I must lie with them.
Will good behavior go unrewarded?"

The calculating hero scowled at him.   320
"If, as you claim, you sacrificed for them,
you must have often prayed here in my hall
that I would not regain the joys of home,
and that my wife would marry you instead,
and bear you children. You will not escape.   325
Suffer and die!"

           Agelaus had dropped
his sword when he was killed. With his strong arm
Odysseus swung, slashed down and sliced right through
the priest's neck, and his head, still framing words,
rolled in the dust.

The poet Phemius,   330
who had been forced to sing to please the suitors,
was huddling by the back door with his lyre,
anxiously considering his choices:
to slip outside and crouch beneath the altar
of mighty Zeus, the god of home owners,   335
where his old masters burned so many thigh-bones;
or he could run towards Odysseus
and grasp him by the knees and beg for mercy.
He made his mind up: he would supplicate.
He set his hollow lyre on the ground   340
between the mixing bowl and silver chair,
and dashed to take Odysseus' knees,
beseeching him in quivering winged words.

"I beg you, Lord Odysseus! Have mercy!
Think! If you kill me now, you will be sorry!   345
I have the power to sing for gods and men.
I am self-taught—all kinds of song are planted
by gods inside my heart. I am prepared
to sing for you, as if before a god.
Wait, do not cut my throat! Just ask your son!   350
He will explain it was against my will
that I came here to sing to them after dinner.
They were too fierce and they outnumbered me.
I had no choice."

                    Then strong Telemachus
turned quickly to his father, saying, "Stop,   355
hold up your sword—this man is innocent.
And let us also save the house boy, Medon.
He always cared for me when I was young—
unless the herdsmen have already killed him,
or he already met you in your rage."   360

Medon was sensible: he had been hiding
under a chair, beneath a fresh cowhide,
in order to escape from being killed.
Hearing these words, he jumped up from the chair,
took off the cowhide and assumed the pose   365
of supplication near Telemachus,
and said,

            "Friend, here I am! Please spare my life!
Your father is too strong, and furious
against the suitors, who skimmed off his wealth
and failed to honor you. Please, talk to him!"   370

Canny Odysseus smiled down and said,
"You need not worry, he has saved your life.

So live and spread the word that doing good
is far superior to wickedness.
Now leave the hall and go outside; sit down,   375
joining the famous singer in the courtyard,
so I can finish what I have to do
inside my house."

                    The two men went outside,
and crouched by Zeus' altar, on the lookout
for death at any moment all around.   380

Odysseus scanned all around his home
for any man who might be still alive,
who might be hiding to escape destruction.
He saw them fallen, all of them, so many,
lying in blood and dust, like fish hauled up   385
out of the dark-gray sea in fine-mesh nets;
tipped out upon the curving beach's sand,
they gasp for water from the salty sea.
The sun shines down and takes their life away.
So lay the suitors, heaped across each other.
Odysseus, still scheming, told his son,   390

"I need to say something to Eurycleia.
Hurry, Telemachus, and bring her here."

Telemachus was glad to please his father.
He pushed the door ajar and called, "Come, Nanny, quick!.   395
You supervise the female palace slaves.
My father has to talk to you; come on!"

She had no words to answer him, but opened
the doors into the great and sturdy hall.
Telemachus went first and led the way.   400
Among the corpses of the slaughtered men
she saw Odysseus all smeared with blood.
After a lion eats a grazing ox,
its chest and jowls are thick with blood all over;
a dreadful sight. Just so, Odysseus   405
had blood all over him—from hands to feet.
Seeing the corpses, seeing all that blood,
so great a deed of violence, she began
to crow. Odysseus told her to stop
and spoke with fluent words.

                          "Old woman, no!   410
Be glad inside your heart, but do not shout.
It is not pious, gloating over men
who have been killed. Divine fate took them down,
and their own wicked deeds. They disrespected
all people that they met, both bad and good.   415

Through their own crimes they came to this bad end.
But tell me now about the household women.
Which ones dishonor me? And which are pure?"

The slave who loved her master answered, "Child,
I will tell you exactly how things stand.   420
In this house we have fifty female slaves
whom we have trained to work, to card the wool,
and taught to tolerate their life as slaves.[2]
Twelve stepped away from honor: those twelve girls
ignore me, and Penelope our mistress.   425
She would not let Telemachus instruct them,
since he is young and only just grown-up.
Let me go upstairs to the women's rooms,
to tell your wife—some god has sent her sleep."

The master strategist Odysseus   430
said,

        "Not yet; do not wake her. Call the women
who made those treasonous plots while I was gone."[3]
The old nurse did so. Walking through the hall,
she called the girls. Meanwhile, Odysseus
summoned the herdsmen and Telemachus   435
and spoke winged words to them.

                              "Now we must start
to clear the corpses out. The girls must help.
Then clean my stately chairs and handsome tables
with sponges fine as honeycomb, and water.
When the whole house is set in proper order,   440
restore my halls to health: take out the girls
between the courtyard wall and the rotunda.
Hack at them with long swords, eradicate
all life from them. They will forget the things
the suitors made them do with them in secret,   445
through Aphrodite."

                    Sobbing desperately
the girls came, weeping, clutching at each other.
They carried out the bodies of the dead
and piled them up on top of one another,
under the roof outside. Odysseus   450
instructed them and forced them to continue.
And then they cleaned his lovely chairs and tables

---

2. Some scholars think that *doulosune* in this line ("slavery") suggests sexual slavery and that the line (reading *doulosunes apechesthai*) should be interpreted as "to hold off against (sexual) enslavement"—i.e., to resist the kind of advances made by the suitors.

3. The Greek verb *mechanoonto* ("plotted"—with implications of cunning strategy reminiscent of Odysseus himself) suggests that these girls were deliberately hoping to work against their master—a suggestion that goes well beyond Odysseus's evidence.

with wet absorbent sponges, while the prince
and herdsmen with their shovels scraped away
the mess to make the sturdy floor all clean.   455
The girls picked up the trash and took it out.
The men created order in the house
and set it all to rights, then led the girls
outside and trapped them—they could not escape—
between the courtyard wall and the rotunda.   460
Showing initiative, Telemachus
insisted,

    "I refuse to grant these girls
a clean death, since they poured down shame on me
and Mother, when they lay beside the suitors."

At that, he wound a piece of sailor's rope   465
round the rotunda and round the mighty pillar,
stretched up so high no foot could touch the ground.
As doves or thrushes spread their wings to fly
home to their nests, but someone sets a trap—
they crash into a net, a bitter bedtime;   470
just so the girls, their heads all in a row,
were strung up with the noose around their necks
to make their death an agony. They gasped,
feet twitching for a while, but not for long.

Then the men took Melanthius outside   475
and with curved bronze cut off his nose and ears
and ripped away his genitals, to feed
raw to the dogs. Still full of rage, they chopped
his hands and feet off. Then they washed their own,
and they went back inside.

       Odysseus   480
told his beloved nurse, "Now bring me fire
and sulfur, as a cure for evil things,
and I will fumigate the house. And call
Penelope, her slaves, and all the slave girls
inside the house."

      She answered with affection,   485
"Yes, dear, all this is good. But let me bring
a cloak and shirt for you. You should not stand here,
your strong back covered only with those rags.
That would be wrong!"

      Odysseus, the master
of every cunning scheme, replied, "No, first   490
I need a fire here, to smoke the hall."
His loving slave complied and brought the fire
and sulfur, and Odysseus made smoke,
and fumigated every room inside

the house and yard. Meanwhile, the old nurse ran   495
all through the palace summoning the women.
By torchlight they came out from their apartments,
to greet Odysseus with open arms.
They kissed his face and took him by the hands
in welcome. He was seized by sweet desire   500
to weep, and in his heart he knew them all.

BOOK 23

[*The Olive Tree Bed*]

Chuckling with glee, the old slave climbed upstairs
to tell the queen that her beloved husband
was home. Her weak old knees felt stronger now;
with buoyant steps she went and stood beside
her mistress, at her head, and said,

                        "Dear child,   5
wake up and see! At long last you have got
your wish come true! Odysseus has come!
He is right here inside this house! At last!
He slaughtered all the suitors who were wasting
his property and threatening his son!"   10

But cautiously Penelope replied,
"You poor old thing! The gods have made you crazy.
They have the power to turn the sanest person
mad, or make fools turn wise. You used to be
so sensible, but they have damaged you.   15
Why else would you be mocking me like this,
with silly stories, in my time of grief?
Why did you wake me from the sleep that sweetly
wrapped round my eyes? I have not slept so soundly
since my Odysseus marched off to see   20
that cursed town—Evilium. Go back!
If any other slave comes here to wake me
and tell me all this nonsense, I will send her
back down at once, and I will not be gentle.
Your old age will protect you from worse scolding."   25

But Eurycleia answered with affection,
"Dear child, I am not mocking you. I am
telling the truth: Odysseus is here!
He is the stranger that they all abused.
Telemachus has known for quite some time,   30
but sensibly he kept his father's plans
a secret, so Odysseus could take
revenge for all their violence and pride."

Penelope was overjoyed; she jumped
from bed and hugged the nurse, and started crying.   35
Her words flew fast.

"Dear Nanny! If this is
the truth, if he has come back to this house,
how could he have attacked those shameless suitors,
when he is just one man, and there were always
so many crowded in there?"

Eurycleia   40
answered, "I did not see or learn the details.
I heard the sound of screaming from the men
as they were killed. We huddled in our room
and kept the doors tight shut, until your son
called me—his father sent him. Then I saw   45
Odysseus surrounded by dead bodies.
They lay on top of one another, sprawled
across the solid floor. You would have been
thrilled if you saw him, like a lion, drenched
in blood and gore. Now they are all piled up   50
out by the courtyard gates, and he is burning
a mighty fire to fumigate the palace,
restoring all its loveliness. He sent me
to fetch you. Come with me, so both of you
can start to live in happiness. You have   55
endured such misery. Your wish came true!
He is alive! He has come home again,
and found you and your son, and he has taken
revenge on all the suitors who abused him."

Penelope said carefully, "Do not   60
start gloating. As you know, my son and I
would be delighted if he came. We all would.
However, what you say cannot be true.
Some god has killed the suitors out of anger
at their abuse of power and their pride.   65
They failed to show respect to visitors,
both good and bad. Their foolishness has killed them.
But my Odysseus has lost his home,
and far away from Greece, he lost his life."

The nurse replied, "Dear child! How can you say   70
your husband will not come, when he is here,
beside the hearth? Your heart has always been
mistrustful. But I have clear evidence!
When I was washing him, I felt the scar
made when the boar impaled him with its tusk.   75
I tried to tell you, but he grabbed my throat
and stopped me spoiling all his plans. Come with me.
I swear on my own life: if I am lying,
then kill me."

Wise Penelope said, "Nanny,
it must be hard for you to understand   80
the ways of gods, despite your cleverness.
But let us go to meet my son, so I
can see the suitors dead, and see the man
who killed them."

So she went downstairs. Her heart
could not decide if she should keep her distance   85
as she was questioning her own dear husband,
or go right up to him and kiss his face
and hold his hands in hers. She crossed the threshold
and sat across from him beside the wall,
in firelight. He sat beside the pillar,   90
and kept his eyes down, waiting to find out
whether the woman who once shared his bed
would speak to him. She sat in silence, stunned.
Sometimes when she was glancing at his face
it seemed like him; but then his dirty clothes   95
were unfamiliar. Telemachus
scolded her.

"Mother! Cruel, heartless Mother!
Why are you doing this, rejecting Father?
Why do you not go over, sit beside him,
and talk to him? No woman in the world   100
would be so obstinate! To keep your distance
from him when he has come back after twenty
long years of suffering! Your heart is always
harder than rock!"

But thoughtfully she answered,
"My child, I am confused. I cannot speak,   105
or meet his eyes. If this is really him,
if my Odysseus has come back home,
we have our ways to recognize each other,
through secret signs known only to us two."

Hardened Odysseus began to smile.   110
He told the boy,

"You must allow your mother
to test me out; she will soon know me better.
While I am dirty, dressed in rags, she will not
treat me with kindness or acknowledge me.
Meanwhile, we must make plans. If someone murders   115
even just one man, even one who had
few friends in his community, the killer
is forced to run away and leave his homeland
and family. But we have killed the mainstay

of Ithaca, the island's best young men.   120
So what do you suggest?"

                        Telemachus
said warily, "You have to work it out.
They say you have the finest mind in all
the world; no mortal man can rival you
in cleverness. Lead me, and I will be   125
behind you right away. And I will do
my best to be as brave as I can be."

Odysseus was quick to form a plan.
He told him, "Here is what I think is best.
The three of you should wash and change your clothes,   130
and make the slave girls go put on clean dresses.
Then let the godlike singer take the lyre
and play a clear and cheerful dancing tune,
so passersby or neighbors hearing it
will think it is a wedding. We must not   135
allow the news about the suitors' murder
to spread too far until we reach the woods
of our estate, and there we can decide
the best path forward offered us by Zeus."

They did as Lord Odysseus had said.   140
They washed and changed their tunics, and the slave girls
prepared themselves. The singer took the lyre,
and roused in them desire to hear sweet music,
and dance. The house resounded with the thump
of beating feet from all the dancing men   145
and girls in pretty sashes. Those outside
who heard the noises said to one another,

"So somebody is marrying the queen
who had so many suitors! Headstrong woman!
She must have lacked the strength to wait it out   150
and keep her husband's house safe till he came."
They spoke with no idea what really happened.

Eurynome the slave woman began
to wash strong-willed Odysseus. She rubbed him
with olive oil, and dressed him in a tunic   155
and handsome cloak. And then Athena poured
attractiveness from head to toe, and made him
taller and stronger, and his hair grew thick
and curly as a hyacinth. As when
a craftsman whom Athena or Hephaestus[4]   160
has trained in metalwork, so he can make
beautiful artifacts, pours gold on silver—

---

4. Gods associated with skill in handicrafts and technology.

so she poured beauty on his head and shoulders.
After his bath he looked like an immortal.
He sat down in the same chair opposite   165
his wife and said,

               "Extraordinary woman!
The gods have given you the hardest heart.
No other wife would so reject a husband
who had been suffering for twenty years
and finally come home. Well, Nanny, make   170
a bed for me, so I can rest. This woman
must have an iron heart!"

                      Penelope
said shrewdly, "You extraordinary man!
I am not acting proud, or underplaying
this big event; yet I am not surprised   175
at how you look. You looked like this the day
your long oars sailed away from Ithaca.
Now, Eurycleia, make the bed for him
outside the room he built himself. Pull out
the bedstead, and spread quilts and blankets on it."   180
She spoke to test him, and Odysseus
was furious, and told his loyal wife,

"Woman! Your words have cut my heart! Who moved
my bed? It would be difficult for even
a master craftsman—though a god could do it   185
with ease. No man, however young and strong,
could pry it out. There is a trick to how
this bed was made. I made it, no one else.
Inside the court there grew an olive tree
with delicate long leaves, full-grown and green,   190
as sturdy as a pillar, and I built
the room around it. I packed stones together,
and fixed a roof and fitted doors. At last
I trimmed the olive tree and used my bronze
to cut the branches off from root to tip   195
and planed it down and skillfully transformed
the trunk into a bedpost. With a drill,
I bored right through it. This was my first bedpost,
and then I made the other three, inlaid
with gold and silver and with ivory.   200
I stretched ox-leather straps across, dyed purple.
Now I have told the secret trick, the token.
But woman, wife, I do not know if someone—
a man—has cut the olive trunk and moved
my bed, or if it is still safe."

                   At that,   205
her heart and body suddenly relaxed.

She recognized the tokens he had shown her.
She burst out crying and ran straight towards him
and threw her arms around him, kissed his face,
and said,

       "Do not be angry at me now,   210
Odysseus! In every other way
you are a very understanding man.
The gods have made us suffer: they refused
to let us stay together and enjoy
our youth until we reached the edge of age   215
together. Please forgive me, do not keep
bearing a grudge because when I first saw you,
I would not welcome you immediately.
I felt a constant dread that some bad man
would fool me with his lies. There are so many   220
dishonest, clever men. That foreigner[5]
would never have got Helen into bed,
if she had known the Greeks would march to war
and bring her home again. It was a goddess
who made her do it, putting in her heart   225
the passion that first caused my grief as well.
Now you have told the story of our bed,
the secret that no other mortal knows,
except yourself and me, and just one slave,
Actoris,[6] whom my father gave to me   230
when I came here, who used to guard our room.
You made my stubborn heart believe in you."

This made him want to cry. He held his love,
his faithful wife, and wept. As welcome as
the land to swimmers, when Poseidon wrecks   235
their ship at sea and breaks it with great waves
and driving winds; a few escape the sea
and reach the shore, their skin all caked with brine.
Grateful to be alive, they crawl to land.
So glad she was to see her own dear husband, 240
and her white arms would not let go his neck.
They would have wept until the rosy Dawn
began to touch the sky, but shining-eyed
Athena intervened. She held night back,
restraining golden Dawn beside the Ocean,   245
and would not let her yoke her swift young colts,
Shining and Bright. Odysseus, mind whirling,
said,

5. The foreigner is Paris, who came from Troy in the Near East to Sparta in Greece.
6. Actoris is mentioned only here, and it is possible that she has died, to be replaced by Eurynome—which would explain why Penelope is sure that Actoris has not told the stranger the secret.

"Wife, we have not come yet to the end
of all our troubles; there are more to come,
many hard labors which I must complete.   250
The spirit of Tiresias informed me,
that day I went inside the house of Hades
to ask about the journey home for me
and for my men. But come now, let us go
to bed together, wife; let us enjoy   255
the pleasure of sweet sleep."

                        Penelope,
who always thought ahead, said, "When you wish.
The bed is yours. The gods have brought you home,
back to your well-built house. But since a god
has made you speak about these future labors,   260
tell me what they involve. I will find out
eventually, and better to know now."

He answered warily, "You really are
extraordinary. Why would you make me tell you
something to cause you pain? It hurts me too,   265
but I will tell the truth, not hide it from you.
Tiresias foretold that I must travel
through many cities carrying an oar,
till I reach men who do not know the sea,
and do not eat their food with salt, or use   270
boats painted red around the prow, or oars,
which are the wings of ships. He said that I
will know I have arrived when I encounter
someone who calls the object on my back
a winnowing fan.[7] Then I must fix my oar   275
firm in the earth, and make a sacrifice
to Lord Poseidon, of a ram and ox
and stud-boar, perfect animals, then come
back home and give a hecatomb to all
the deathless gods who live above the sky.   280
If I do this, I will not die at sea;
I will grow old in comfort and will meet
a gentle death, surrounded by my people,
who will be rich and happy."

                        Sensibly
Penelope said, "If the gods allow you   285
to reach old age in comfort, there is hope
that there will be an end to all our troubles."

They talked like this. Meanwhile, the slaves were working:
Eurynome and Eurycleia laid
soft blankets on the sturdy bed by torchlight.   290

---

7. I.e., the traveler will not recognize an oar, having never seen the sea.

The nurse went off to sleep; Eurynome
picked up the torch and led them to their bed,
then went to her room. Finally, at last,
with joy the husband and the wife arrived
back in the rites of their old marriage bed.   295

Meanwhile, the herdsmen and Telemachus
stopped dancing, made the women stop, and went
to bed inside the darkened house.

                        And when
the couple had enjoyed their lovemaking,
they shared another pleasure—telling stories.   300
She told him how she suffered as she watched
the crowd of suitors ruining the house,
killing so many herds of sheep and cattle
and drinking so much wine, because of her.
Odysseus told her how much he hurt   305
so many other people, and in turn
how much he had endured himself. She loved
to listen, and she did not fall asleep
until he told it all. First, how he slaughtered
the Cicones, then traveled to the fields   310
of Lotus-Eaters; what the Cyclops did,
and how he paid him back for ruthlessly
eating his men. Then how he reached Aeolus,
who welcomed him and helped him; but it was
not yet his fate to come back home; a storm   315
snatched him and bore him off across the sea,
howling frustration. Then, he said, he came
to Laestrygonia, whose people wrecked
his fleet and killed his men. And he described
the cleverness of Circe, and his journey   320
to Hades to consult Tiresias,
and how he saw all his dead friends, and saw
his mother, who had loved him as a baby;
then how he heard the Sirens' endless voices,
and reached the Wandering Rocks and terrible   325
Charybdis, and how he had been the first
to get away from Scylla. And he told her
of how his crew devoured the Sun God's cattle;
Zeus roared with smoke and thunder, lightning struck
the ship, and all his loyal men were killed.   330
But he survived, and drifted to Ogygia.
He told her how Calypso trapped him there,
inside her hollow cave, and wanted him
to be her husband; she took care of him
and promised she could set him free from death   335
and time forever. But she never swayed
his heart. He suffered terribly, for years,
and then he reached Phaeacia, where the people

looked up to him as if he were a god,
and sent him in a ship back home again   340
to his dear Ithaca, with gifts of bronze
and gold and piles of clothes. His story ended;
sweet sleep released his heart from all his cares.

Athena, bright-eyed goddess, stayed alert,
and when she thought Odysseus had finished   345
with taking pleasure in his wife and sleep,
she roused the newborn Dawn from Ocean's streams
to bring the golden light to those on earth.
Odysseus got up and told his wife,

"Wife, we have both endured our share of trouble: 350
you wept here as you longed for my return,
while Zeus and other gods were keeping me
away from home, although I longed to come.
But now we have returned to our own bed,
as we both longed to do. You must look after   355
my property inside the house. Meanwhile,
I have to go on raids, to steal replacements
for all the sheep those swaggering suitors killed,
and get the other Greeks to give me more,
until I fill my folds. But first I will   360
go to the orchard in the countryside
to see my grieving father. Then at dawn
the news will spread that I have killed the suitors.
Your orders, wife—though you are smart enough
to need no orders—are, go with your slaves   365
upstairs, sit quietly, and do not talk
to anyone."

                    He armed himself and called
the herdsmen and Telemachus, and told them
to put on armor too—breastplates of bronze.
Odysseus led all of them outside.   370
The light was bright across the earth. Athena
hid them with night and brought them out of town.

BOOK 24

[Restless Spirits]

Then Hermes called the spirits of the suitors
out of the house. He held the golden wand
with which he casts a spell to close men's eyes
or open those of sleepers when he wants.
He led the spirits and they followed, squeaking   5
like bats in secret crannies of a cave,
who cling together, and when one becomes
detached and falls down from the rock, the rest
flutter and squeak—just so the spirits squeaked,

and hurried after Hermes, lord of healing. 10
On open roads they crossed the Ocean stream,
went past the rock of Leucas and the gates
of Helius the Sun, and skittered through
the provinces of dreams, and soon arrived
in fields of asphodel, the home of shadows 15
who have been worn to weariness by life.

They found Achilles' ghost there, and Patroclus,
and Ajax, the most handsome of the Greeks
after unmatched Achilles. Agamemnon
had just arrived to join them, in deep grief 20
for his own death, and with him came the others
killed by Aegisthus and his bodyguards.
Achilles' ghost spoke first.

               "O Agamemnon!
Men used to say that out of all the heroes,
Zeus, Lord of Lightning, favored you the most, 25
because you had command of a great army
in Troy where Greeks endured the pain of war.
But death, which no man living can avoid,
was destined to arrive at the wrong time.
If only you had died at Troy and won 30
the glory of your rank as a commander!
All of the Greeks and allies would have built
a tomb for you, and afterwards your son
would have received great honor. As it is,
it was your fate to die a dreadful death." 35

The ghost of Agamemnon answered him,
"Achilles, son of Peleus, you were
lucky to die at Troy, away from Argos.
The finest warriors of Greece and Troy
fought round your corpse and died. You lay a hero, 40
magnificent amid the whirling dust,
your days of driving chariots forgotten.[8]
We fought all day, and would have fought forever,
but Zeus sent winds to stop us. Then we brought you
back to our ships, and laid you on a bier, 45
away from battle, and we bathed your skin
in heated water and anointed you
with oil. We wept for you and cut our hair.
Your mother[9] heard the news, and with her nymphs
she came up from the waves. An eerie wailing 50
sounded across the sea. The men began

---

8. Achilles is usually known as "swift-footed," a quick sprinter on foot rather than a horseman or driver of a chariot. The most famous episode in which he uses a chariot is near the end of the *Iliad*, when he drags the body of his slaughtered enemy, Hector, around the walls of Troy—a gesture of brutality that is forgotten in Achilles' own splendid death scene.

9. Thetis, a sea goddess.

to tremble, and they would have rushed on board,
if wise old Nestor had not made them stop.
He always had the best advice for us,
and said, 'My lords, stay here. It is his mother,   55
coming with her immortal water nymphs
to find her own dead son.' At this, the Greeks
regained their courage. The old Sea King's daughters
gathered around you weeping, and they dressed you
in clothes of the immortals. All nine Muses   60
sang lamentations in their lovely voices.
No one could keep from crying at the sound,
so moving was their song. The gods and men
were mourning seventeen long nights and days
and then we gave you to the pyre, and killed   65
many fat sheep and cattle for your corpse.
You burned in clothes from gods; you were anointed
with oil and honey. Troops of warriors
on foot and horseback, fully armed, went marching
around your pyre, and made a mighty din.   70
At last Hephaestus' flame consumed your flesh.
When morning came, we gathered your white bones,
Achilles, and anointed them with oil
and unmixed wine. Your mother gave an urn
of gold with double handles, which she said   75
Hephaestus made and Dionysus gave her.
Your white bones lay inside it, Lord Achilles,
mixed with the bones of your dead friend Patroclus.
We laid the urn beside Antilochus,
the friend you most respected after him.   80
The army of Greek warriors assembled,
and with all reverence we heaped a mound
out on the headland by the Hellespont,
large enough to be visible to those
at sea, both now and in the years to come.   85
Your mother asked the gods for splendid prizes
and put them in the midst of an arena,
so the best athletes could compete for them.
You have seen many burials of heroes,
when young men tie their tunics to compete.   90
But you would have been startled at the riches
that silver-footed Thetis brought for you.
You were so dearly loved by all the gods.
You did not lose your name in death. Your fame
will live forever; everyone will know   95
Achilles. As for me, what good was it
that I wound up the war? When I came home
Aegisthus and my wicked, fiendish wife
murdered me. Zeus had planned it."

                                           While they talked,
Hermes the guide came near them, with the suitors   100

killed by Odysseus. The two great lords,
astonished at the sight, rushed up to them,
and Agamemnon's spirit recognized
the son of his old friend, Melaneus,
with whom he stayed in Ithaca. He said,   105

"Amphimedon! What happened to you all?
Why have you all come down here to the land
of darkness? You are all so young and strong;
you must have been the best boys in your town.
Maybe Poseidon raised great waves and winds   110
to wreck your fleet? Or were you all attacked
by men on land while you were poaching cows
or flocks of sheep, or fighting for a city
and women? You must tell me! We are friends.
Do you remember when I visited   115
your home, when Menelaus and myself
were trying to persuade Odysseus
to join the fleet and sail with us to Troy?
It took a whole damned month to cross the sea;
we had to work so hard to sway that man,   120
who sacked the city."[1]

          Amphimedon's spirit
answered, "Great General, Agamemnon, yes,
I do remember everything you say.
And I will tell, in every gruesome detail,
the manner of our death. Odysseus   125
was gone for many years. We came to court
his wife, who had no wish to marry us,
but would not tell us no or make an end.
She planned black death for us, and tricked us too.
She set a mighty loom up in the hall,   130
and wove a wide fine cloth, and said to us,
'Young suitors, now Odysseus is dead.
I know that you are eager for the wedding,
but wait till I am finished with this cloth,
so that my weaving will not go to waste.   135
It is a shroud for when Laertes dies,
so that the women in the town do not
blame me because a man who gained such wealth
was buried with no winding-sheet.' Her words
convinced us. So by day she wove the cloth,   140
and then at night by torchlight, she unwove it.
For three long years she fooled us; when the hours

1. According to legend, Odysseus tried to get out of going to the Trojan War by feigning madness. The usual story is that he was demonstrating his insanity by plowing his field using a donkey and an ox yoked together (animals with different strides who would not plow well together). Palamedes, a Greek who had come on the embassy with Agamemnon and Menelaus, put the newborn Telemachus in front of the plow, and Odysseus veered away from his son— thus demonstrating his sanity.

and months had passed, the fourth year rolled around,
and then a girl who knew the truth told us;
and we found her unraveling her work.   145
We made her finish it. When she had washed
the marvelous huge sheet, she showed it to us,
bright as the sun or moon. And then some spirit
of ruin brought Odysseus from somewhere
to Ithaca;[2] he went out to the fields,   150
to where the swineherd lived. His own dear son
sailed in his black ship back from sandy Pylos.
The two of them made plans to murder us.
They showed up at the palace—first the boy,
and then Odysseus propped on a stick   155
and dressed in dirty rags. He seemed to be
a poor old homeless man, who suddenly
appeared, led by the swineherd. None of us
could recognize him, even those of us
who were a little older than myself.   160
We hurled insulting words and missiles at him,
and for a while he patiently endured
abuse in his own home. But when the will
of Zeus awakened him, with his son's help,
he put the splendid weapons in the storeroom   165
and locked the door. Then came his cunning plan:
he told his wife to set for us the axes
and bow. The competition meant our doom,
the start of slaughter. None of us could string
the mighty bow—we all were far too weak.   170
But when it was his turn, we shouted out
that nobody should give the bow to him,
no matter what he said. Telemachus
alone insisted that he ought to have it.
At last Odysseus, with calm composure,   175
took it and strung it easily, and shot
all through the iron axes. Then he stood
astride the threshold with a fearsome scowl,
and started shooting fast. His arrow struck
Antinous, our leader. With sure aim   180
he shot his deadly arrows at more men;
those nearest to him fell. It was apparent
some god was helping them. Impelled by rage,
they rushed around the palace killing us
in turn. There was a dreadful noise of screaming   185
and broken skulls; the whole floor ran with blood.
So, Agamemnon, we were killed. Our bodies
still lie unburied in our killer's house.
Our families at home do not yet know.

---

2. This passage seems to reflect a different version of the story, in which Odysseus arrives on Ithaca at the exact moment that Penelope is forced to finish the weaving, and also other versions in which Odysseus and Penelope collude together to kill the suitors.

They need to wash the black blood from our wounds   190
and weep for us and lay our bodies out.
This is the honor due the dead."

                              The ghost
of Agamemnon answered, "Lucky you,
cunning Odysseus: you got yourself
a wife of virtue—great Penelope.   195
How principled she was, that she remembered
her husband all those years! Her fame will live
forever, and the deathless gods will make
a poem to delight all those on earth
about intelligent Penelope.   200
Not like my wife[3]—who murdered her own husband!
Her story will be hateful; she will bring
bad reputation to all other women,
even the good ones."

                    So they spoke together,
standing in Hades, hidden in the earth.   205

Meanwhile, Odysseus and his companions
had left the town and quickly reached the farm,
won by Laertes long ago—he fought
hard for it, and his house was there; the slaves,
who had to do his wishes, lived and slept   210
and ate their food in quarters that surrounded
the central house. One was from Sicily,
the old slave woman who took care of him
out in the countryside. Odysseus
spoke to his slaves and to his son.

                              "Go in,   215
choose the best pig and kill it for our dinner.
And I will test my father, to find out
if he will know me instantly on sight,
or not—I have been absent for so long."

At that he gave his weapons to the slaves.   220
They quickly went inside. Odysseus
walked to the fruitful orchard on his quest.
He did not find old Dolius, the steward,
nor any of his slaves or sons—he had
led them to gather rocks to build dry-walls.   235
Odysseus' father was alone,
inside the well-built orchard, digging earth
to make it level round a tree. He wore
a dirty ragged tunic, and his leggings

---

3. Clytemnestra.

had leather patches to protect from scratches.   230
He wore thick gloves because of thorns, and had
a cap of goatskin. He was wallowing
in grief. The veteran, Odysseus,
seeing his father worn by age and burdened
by desperate, heartfelt sorrow, stopped beneath   235
a towering pear tree, weeping. Then he wondered
whether to kiss his father, twine around him,
and tell him that he had come home again,
and everything that happened on the way—
or question him. He thought it best to start   240
by testing him with teasing and abuse.
With this in mind, Odysseus approached him,
as he was digging round the plant, head down.
His famous son stood at his side and said,

"Old man, you know your trade and take good care   245
of this neat garden. Every plant and vine,
and tree—the figs, the pears, the olive trees—
and bed of herbs is nicely tended. But
I have to say something—please do not get
angry at me—you do not take good care   250
of your own self. You are unkempt, old man.
Your skin is rough and dirty and your clothes
are rags. Your master is neglecting you,
although you are not lazy. In your height
and face, you seem a leader, not a slave.   255
You look like someone who would bathe and eat
and sleep on fluffy pillows and fine sheets,
as is appropriate for older people.
But tell me this: whose slave are you? Whose garden
do you take care of? Also, have I come   260
to Ithaca, as somebody I met
was telling me just now? But he was not
a helpful man: when I was asking him
about a friend of mine, an old guest-friend,
whether he is alive or dead in Hades,   265
this fellow would not say, or even listen.
A while ago, in my own native land,
I had a guest to stay with me, who was
my dearest friend of all my visitors.
He said he was from Ithaca, and that   270
Laertes was his father. I had brought him
into my house, and welcomed him with warmth;
I can afford to be quite generous.
I gave him seven heaps of golden treasure,
a bowl made all of silver and inlaid   275
with flowers, twelve unfolded cloaks, and twelve
thick blankets, twelve fine mantles, and twelve tunics.
Also I gave him four well-trained slave women,
beautiful ones, whom he picked out himself."

His father answered through his tears, "Yes, stranger,   280
you have reached Ithaca. But cruel men
have taken over here. You will receive
nothing for all those gifts. If you had found him
still living in this land, he would have matched
your gifts and welcomed you with open arms   285
before he sent you home. Initial kindness
deserves due recompense. But tell me now,
how long is it since that unlucky man
visited you? Your guest was my own son!
Perhaps fish ate him out at sea, so far   290
from home and family; or birds and beasts
ate him on land. His mother did not lay
his body out and weep for him; nor I,
his father; nor Penelope his wife,
a wise and wealthy woman. She has not   295
closed her own husband's eyes or given him
a funeral. The dead deserve this honor.
But tell me now, who are you? From what city?
Who are your parents? Do you have a ship
docked somewhere, which conveyed you here with friends   300
and crew? Or did you sail as passenger
on someone else's ship, which now is gone?"

Lying Odysseus replied, "I will
tell you the truth completely. I am from
Alybas,[4] and I have a palace there.   305
My name is Eperitus; I am son
of King Apheidas, son of Polypemon.
An evil spirit struck me and I came
from Sicily against my will. My ship
is docked away from town. It is five years   310
since poor, unfortunate Odysseus
came to my home. As he was setting out
we saw good omens—birds towards the right—
so we were hopeful we would meet again
as friends, and share more gifts."

                                 At this, a cloud   315
of black grief wrapped itself around Laertes.
He poured two handfuls of the ashy dust
over his gray old head, and started sobbing.
Odysseus felt heart-wrenched to see his own
beloved father in this state; sharp pain   320
pierced through his nostrils.[5] He rushed up to him

---

4. Alybas is probably a made-up place, perhaps coined by analogy with *alaomai*, "to wander"; ancient scholars thought it was in southern Italy. The made-up name Eperitus suggests "picked" or "chosen." The fictional father's name, Apheidas, suggests "Generous," and the grandfather, Polypemon, "Rich" or "Much Suffering."

5. The oddly specific physiological detail has been taken as metaphorical by some commentators, but it seems best to take it as entirely literal: the sudden welling up of tears puts pressure on the sinuses.

and threw his arms around him, kissing him,
and saying,

       "Father! It is me! I have
been gone for twenty years, and now am home,
in my own father's country. Stop your tears.   325
I will explain, though we do not have long.
I killed the suitors in my house; I took
revenge for all the pain they caused."

                           Laertes
answered, "If you are really my own son
Odysseus come home, show me a sign;   330
let me be sure of it."

                Odysseus
was quick to answer. "First, look here: the scar
made by the boar's white tusk when I had gone
to Mount Parnassus. You and Mother sent me,
to see my grandfather, Autolycus,   335
and get the gifts that he had promised me.
Next I will tell you all the trees that grow
in this fine orchard, which you gave to me.
When I was little, I would follow you
around the garden, asking all their names.   340
We walked beneath these trees; you named them all
and promised them to me. Ten apple trees,
and thirteen pear trees, forty figs, and fifty
grapevines which ripen one by one—their clusters
change as the weather presses from the sky,   345
sent down by Zeus."

               At that, Laertes' heart
and legs gave way; he recognized the signs
Odysseus had given as clear proof.
He threw both arms around his ruthless son,
who caught him as he fainted. When his breath   350
and mind returned, he said,

                 "O Father Zeus,
you gods are truly rulers of Olympus,
if it is true the suitors have been punished
for all the monstrous things they did. But I
am terrified the Ithacans may soon   355
attack us here, and spread the news around
to all the towns of Cephallenia."

Scheming Odysseus said, "Do not fear.
Come to the farmhouse, where I sent my boy
to go with the two herdsmen, to prepare   360
dinner as fast as possible."

With this,
the son and father walked towards the house.
They found them serving generous plates of meat
and mixing wine. The slave from Sicily
washed brave Laertes, and she rubbed his skin   365
with olive oil, and wrapped a handsome cloak
around him. Then Athena, standing near,
made him grow taller and more muscular.
When he emerged, Odysseus was shocked
to see him looking like a god. His words   370
flew fast.

       "Oh, Father! You look different!
A god has made you taller and more handsome."

Thoughtful Laertes said, "O Father Zeus,
Athena, and Apollo! If I were
as strong as when I took the sturdy fortress   375
of Nericus, out on the mainland shore,
when I was king of Cephallenia,
I would have stood beside you yesterday,
with weapons on my back, and fought with you
against the suitors who were in our house!   380
I would have brought so many of them down,
you would have been delighted!"

       So they spoke.
The work of cooking dinner was complete,
and they sat down on chairs and stools, and reached
to take the food. The old slave Dolius   385
approached them with his sons, who had been working.[6]
Their mother, the Sicilian old woman,
had gone to call them. She took care of them,
and also the old man, made weak by age.[7]
They saw Odysseus and stared, then stopped,   390
astonished. But he spoke to reassure them.

   "Old man, sit down and eat. The rest of you,
put your surprise entirely out of mind.
We have been waiting ages; we are eager
to have our dinner here."

       But Dolius   395
ran straight to him with arms outstretched, and took
Odysseus' wrist and kissed his hand,
and let his words fly out.

---

6. Dolius is also the father of Melantho and
Melanthius, who were slaughtered by Odysseus, unbeknownst to him.

7. Presumably the old man is Dolius, though
the same slave also cares for old Laertes.

"My friend! You have
come home! We are so very glad to see you!
We never thought this day would come! The gods   400
have brought you here! A heartfelt welcome to you!
I pray the gods will bless you!—Does your wife
know you have come back home? Or should I send
a message?"

But Odysseus said coolly,
"Old man, she knows already. Do not bother."   405

So Dolius sat back down on his chair.
His sons were also clustering around
their famous owner, Lord Odysseus,
to welcome him and hold him in their arms.
Then they sat down in turn beside their father.   410
They had their meal together in the farmhouse.

Meanwhile, swift Rumor spread the news all through
the city, of the suitors' dreadful murder.
When people heard, they rushed from all directions
towards the palace of Odysseus,   415
with shouts and lamentations. Then they brought
the bodies from the house and buried them.
The ones from distant towns were sent back home
by ship. The mourners gathered in the square,
heartbroken. When the people were assembled,   420
Eupeithes first stood up and spoke to them.
This man was inconsolable with grief
for his dead son Antinous, the boy
Odysseus killed first. His father wept,
tears falling as he spoke.

"This scheming man,   425
my friends, has done us all most monstrous wrongs.
First, he took many good men off to sail
with him, and lost the ships, and killed the men!
Now he has come and murdered all the best
of Cephallenia. Come on, before   430
he sneaks away to Pylos or to Elis,
we have to act! We will be shamed forever
unless we take revenge on him for killing
our sons and brothers. I would have no wish
to live; I would prefer to die and join   435
the boys already dead. We have to stop them
escaping overseas! Come on, right now!"

He spoke in tears, and pity seized them all.
But Medon and the bard had woken up;
they came outside and stood among the crowd.   440
They all were terrified, and Medon said,

"Now listen, Ithacans. Odysseus
could not have done such things without the help
of gods. I saw a god myself, disguised
as Mentor, sometimes standing at his side,   445
giving him will to fight, and sometimes rushing
all through the hall to make the suitors scatter.
They fell like flies."

        Pale terror seized them all.
Then Halitherses, an old warrior,
the only one to know both past and future,   450
stood up; he wished them well. He said to them,

"Now hear me, Ithacans. My friends, it was
because of your own cowardice this happened.
You did not listen to me, or to Mentor,
when we were telling you to stop your sons   455
from acting stupidly. They did great wrong,
through their impulsiveness; they skimmed the wealth
of an important man, and disrespected
his wife, believing he would never come.
But listen now. We must not go and fight,   460
or we will bring more ruin on our heads."

At that, some stayed there, huddling together,
but more than half jumped up with shouts. They thought
Eupeithes had the right idea. They rushed
to arms, and strapped their gleaming armor on,   465
and gathered in a mass before the town.
Eupeithes was their leader—to his cost.
He thought he would avenge his murdered son.
In fact, he would not come back home; it was
his fate to die out there.

        And then Athena   470
spoke to the son of Cronus.

        "Father Zeus,
highest of powers! Tell what hidden thoughts
lie in you. Will you now make yet more war
and bitter strife, or join the sides in friendship?"

The Gatherer of Clouds replied, "My child,   475
why ask me this? The plan was your idea,
to have Odysseus come take revenge.
Do as you wish. But here is my advice.
He has already punished all the suitors,
so let them swear an oath that he will be   480
the king forever, and let us make sure
the murder of their brothers and their sons
will be forgotten. Let them all be friends,

just as before, and let them live in peace
and in prosperity."

                Athena was   485
already eager; at these words she swooped
down from Olympus.

                Meanwhile, they had finished
dinner, and battle-scarred Odysseus
said, "Somebody must go and see if they
are coming near." A son of Dolius   490
obeyed and went. As he stepped out, he stood
across the threshold, and he saw them all
near to the house. At once his words took wings.
He told Odysseus,

                "Those men are near!
We have to arm, and fast!"

                They quickly armed.   495
Odysseus, his son and their two slaves
made four, and Dolius had his six sons.
Laertes and old Dolius were also
needed as fighters, though they had gray hair.
When all of them were dressed in gleaming bronze,   500
they opened up the gates and went outside;
Odysseus was leading them. Athena
came near, disguised as Mentor. When he saw her,
weathered Odysseus was glad and turned
towards Telemachus and said,

                "Now, son,   505
soon you will have experience of fighting
in battle, the true test of worth. You must
not shame your father's family; for years
we have been known across the world for courage
and manliness."

                Telemachus inhaled,   510
then said, "Just watch me, Father, if you want
to see my spirit. I will bring no shame
onto your family. You should not speak
of shame."

                Laertes, thrilled, cried out, "Ah, gods!
A happy day for me! My son and grandson   515
are arguing about how tough they are!"

With glinting eyes, Athena stood beside him
and said, "You are my favorite, Laertes.

Pray to the bright-eyed goddess and her father,
then lift and hurl your spear."

                  As she said this,   520
Athena breathed great energy inside him.
Laertes quickly raised and hurled the spear,
and struck Eupeithes through his bronze-cheeked helmet,
which did not stop the weapon; it pierced through.
Then with a thud he fell; his armor clanged   525
around him on the ground. Odysseus
charged the front line, his radiant son beside him;
they hacked with swords and curving spears. They would
have killed them all and made sure none of them
could go back home—but then Athena spoke.   530
Her voice held back the fighters.

                  "Ithacans!
Stop this destructive war; shed no more blood,
and go your separate ways, at once!"

                  Her voice
struck them with pale green fear and made them drop
their weapons. They were desperate to save   535
their lives, and they turned back towards the city.
Unwavering Odysseus let out
a dreadful roar, then crouched and swooped upon them,
just like an eagle flying from above.
But Zeus sent down a thunderbolt, which fell   540
in front of his own daughter, great Athena.
She looked at him with steely eyes and said,

"Odysseus, you are adaptable;
you always find solutions. Stop this war,
or Zeus will be enraged at you."

                  He was   545
glad to obey her. Then Athena made
the warring sides swear solemn oaths of peace
for future times—still in her guise as Mentor.

SAPPHO

born ca. 630 B.C.E.

Sappho is the only ancient Greek female author whose work survives in more than tiny fragments. She was an enormously talented poet, much admired in antiquity; a later poet called her the "tenth Muse." In the third century B.C.E., scholars at the great library in Alexandria arranged her poems in nine books, of which the first contained more than a thousand lines. But what we have now are pitiful remnants: one (or possibly two) complete short poems, and a collection of quotations from her work by ancient writers, supplemented by bits and pieces written on ancient scraps of papyrus found in excavations in Egypt. Yet these fragments fully justify the enthusiasm of the ancient critics; Sappho's poems (insofar as we can guess at their nature from the fragments) give us the most vivid evocation of the joys and sorrows of desire in all Greek literature.

About Sappho's life we know almost nothing. She was born about 630 B.C.E. on the fertile island of Lesbos, off the coast of Asia Minor, and spent most of her life there. Her poems suggest that she was married and had a daughter—although we should never assume that Sappho's "I" implies autobiography. It is difficult to find any evidence to answer the questions that we most want to ask. Were these poems performed for women only, or for mixed audiences? Was it common for women to compose poetry on ancient Lesbos? How did Sappho's work win acceptance in the male-dominated world of ancient Greece? We simply do not know. We also know frustratingly little about ancient attitudes toward female same-sex relationships. In the nineteenth century, Sappho's poems were the inspiration for the coinage of the modern term *lesbian*. But no equivalent term was used in the ancient world. Sappho's poems evoke a world in which girls lived an intense communal life of their own, enjoying activities and festivals in which only women took part, in which they were fully engaged with one another. Beyond the evidence of the poems themselves, however, little remains to put these works into historical context.

What we do know, and what we must always bear in mind while reading these poems, is that they were composed not to be read on papyrus or in a book but to be performed by a group of dancing, singing women and girls (a "chorus"), to the accompaniment of musical instruments. Other poets of the period composed in the choral genre, including Alcaeus, a male contemporary who was also from Lesbos. The ancient Greek equivalent of the short, nonnarrative literary form we refer to as "lyric poetry" was literally *lyric*: it was sung to the lyre or cithara, ancestors of the modern guitar. It is not really poetry but the lyrics to songs whose music is lost. These songs evoke many vivid actions, emotions, and images, which were presumably dramatized by the dancers, who might well, for example, have acted out the swift journey of Aphrodite's chariot in poem 1 ["Deathless Aphrodite of the spangled mind"], "whipping their wings down the sky."

Sappho's poems were produced almost two hundred years after the Homeric epics, and we can read them as offering a response, and perhaps a challenge, to the (mostly masculine) world of epic. The *Iliad* concentrates on the battlefield, where men fight and die, while the *Odyssey* shows us the struggles of a male warrior to rebuild his homeland in the aftermath of war. By contrast, Sappho's poems focus on women more than men, and on feelings more than actions. Like **Homer**, Sappho often refers to the physical world in vivid detail (the stars, the trees, the flowers, the sunlight), as well as to the Olympian gods, and to mythology. But she interprets these topics very differently. In poem 44, she uses the characters of the *Iliad* but concentrates on the marriage of Hector and Andromache rather than the war. Aphrodite, goddess of love and sex, seems more important to Sappho than Zeus, the father of the gods. Poem 16 offers another reinterpretation of the Trojan War, as a story not about men fighting but about a woman in love: "Helen—left behind / her most noble husband / and went sailing off to Troy." Sappho emphasizes beauty and personal choices, and suggests that love matters more than armies, and more even than home, family, parents, or children.

But Sappho's vision of love is anything but sentimental. Many of these poems evoke intense negative emotions: alienation, jealousy, and rage. In poem 31, for example, the speaker describes her overwhelming feelings as she watches the woman she loves talking to a man: she trembles, her heart races, she feels close to death. The precise clinical detail of the narrator, as she observes herself, adds to the vividness of this account of emotional breakdown. Sappho is able to describe feelings both from the outside and from the inside, and painfully evokes a sense of distance from the beloved—and from herself: "I don't know what I should do. There are two minds in me," she says in a line from a lost poem (51). In poem 58 the speaker is suffering from a different kind of alienation: watching young girls dance and sing, she stands aside, unable to participate, and bitterly regrets the loss of her own youth.

Sappho repeatedly invokes the goddess associated with sexual desire: Aphrodite. It may be tempting to read Aphrodite as simply a personification of the speaker's own desires. But Sappho presents her as a real and terrifying force in the universe, who may afflict the speaker with all the "bittersweet" agony of love, and who may also be invoked—as in poem 1—to serve her rage and aggression, acting as Sappho's own military "ally" in her desire to inflict pain on the girl who has hurt her.

Some passages of Sappho, including the famous account of jealousy, poem 31, were preserved through quotation by other ancient writers. But many of these poems survived only on scraps of papyrus, mostly dug up from the trash-heaps of the ancient Egyptian city of Oxyrhynchus. It is exciting that we have even this much Sappho: much of our present text was discovered as late as the nineteenth century. Poem 58 was discovered (supplementing a known fragment) in 2004 in the papier-mâché–type wrapping used on an Egyptian mummy. The final poems in our selection—the "Brothers" poem and the "Cypris" poem—were made public only in 2014, as a result of a new papyrus discovery. Most of the papyrus finds are torn and crumpled, so that words and whole lines are often missing from the poems. Some of these gaps can be filled in from our knowledge of Sappho's dialect and the strict meter in which she wrote. In poem 16, for instance, at the end of the third stanza and the beginning of the fourth, the mutilated papyrus tells us that someone or something led Helen astray, and there are traces of a word that seems to have described Helen. The name *Cypris* (the "Cyprian One," the love goddess Aphrodite) and phrases that mean "against her will" or "as soon as she saw him [Paris]" would fit the spaces and the meter. Uncertain as these supplements are, they could help determine our understanding of the poem. The publication of the "New Sappho" poems is an exciting reminder that there are new discoveries to be made, even in literature from over three thousand years ago. The new pieces of Sappho have also broadened our understanding of this great poet, who composed her songs about journeys, time, mythology, and family, as well as about love, alienation, and desire.

1[1]

Deathless Aphrodite of the spangled mind,[2]
child of Zeus, who twists lures, I beg you
do not break with hard pains,
    O lady, my heart

but come here if ever before   5
you caught my voice far off
and listening left your father's
    golden house and came,

yoking your car. And fine birds brought you,
quick sparrows[3] over the black earth   10
whipping their wings down the sky
    through midair—

they arrived. But you, O blessed one,
smiled in your deathless face
and asked what (now again) I have suffered and why   15
    (now again) I am calling out

and what I want to happen most of all
in my crazy heart. Whom should I persuade (now again)
to lead you back into her love? Who, O
    Sappho, is wronging you?   20

For if she flees, soon she will pursue.
If she refuses gifts, rather will she give them.
If she does not love, soon she will love
    even unwilling.

Come to me now: loose me from hard   25
care and all my heart longs
to accomplish, accomplish. You
    be my ally.

1. Translated by Anne Carson.
2. Or "of the spangled throne"; the variant manuscripts preserve both readings (in the Greek there is a single letter's difference between them). The word translated here as "spangled" usually refers to a surface shimmering with bright contrasting colors. The reader can choose whether to imagine a goddess seated in splendor on a highly wrought throne or a love goddess whose mind is shifting and fickle.
3. Aphrodite's sacred birds.

2[4]

Come to me here from Crete to this holy
temple, to your delightful grove of apple
trees, where altars smoke
      with frankincense.

16

Some say an army of horsemen, others a host of infantry,
others a fleet of ships is the most beautiful thing
on the black earth. But I say
      it's whatever you love.

It's perfectly easy to make this clear   5
to everyone. For she who surpassed
all in beauty—Helen—left behind
      her most noble husband

and went sailing off to Troy,
giving no thought at all to her child   10
or dear parents, but . . .[5]
      led her astray.

. . . for
. . . lightly
. . . reminded me now of Anactoria[6]   15
      who is not here.

I would rather see her lovely walk
and her bright sparkling face
than the chariots of the Lydians[7]
      or infantry in arms.   20

. . . not possible to happen
. . . to pray to share
. . . unexpected

---

4. This and the following Sappho poems and fragments are translated by Philip Freeman.
5. Ellipses represent places where the papyrus on which the poem is preserved is torn, and words, half-words, or whole lines are missing.
6. Presumably Anactoria is a girlfriend. The name may connote "princess," since *anax* means "leader" or "king." Anactoria was also an alternative name for the city of Miletus, a powerful city-state in Asia Minor.
7. A wealthy and powerful non-Greek people in Asia Minor, with whom Sappho, living in Lesbos just off the coast, is evidently familiar. A generation or so later, the Lydians would be absorbed into the expanding Persian Empire, but in Sappho's time they were at the height of their prosperity.

17

Come close to me, I pray,
Lady Hera, and may your graceful form appear,
you to whom the sons of Atreus prayed,
    those glorious kings,[8]

after they had accomplished many great deeds,   5
first at Troy, then on the sea.
They came to this island, but they could not
    complete their voyage home

until they called on you and Zeus the god of suppliants
and Thyone's lovely child.[9]   10
So now be kind and help me too,
    as in ancient days.

Holy and beautiful . . .
virgin . . .
around . . .   15

to be . . .
to arrive . . .

31[1]

He seems to me equal to gods that man
whoever he is who opposite you
sits and listens close
    to your sweet speaking

and lovely laughing—oh it   5
puts the heart in my chest on wings
for when I look at you, even a moment, no speaking
    is left in me

no: tongue breaks and thin
fire is racing under skin   10
and in eyes no sight and drumming
    fills ears

8. The sons of Atreus are Menelaus and Agamemnon. In the *Odyssey* (3.133ff.) we find the story of the brothers quarreling after the fall of Troy, and according to Homer, Menelaus stopped to pray to Zeus on Lesbos while Agamemnon traveled separately. Sappho's poem suggests a different legend, in which both brothers together came to her island, and prayed to Hera and Dionysos (son of Thyone) as well as Zeus.
9. Thyone is the new name given to Dionysos's mortal mother, Semele, after she was rescued from Hades by her son and became an Olympian goddess associated with frenzy.
1. Translated by Anne Carson.

and cold sweat holds me and shaking
grips me all, greener than grass
I am and dead—or almost 15
    I seem to me.

But all is to be dared, because even a person of poverty[2]

44[3]

Cyprus. . . .[4]
the herald came . . .
Idaeus, the swift messenger[5]
". . . and the rest of Asia . . . undying glory.
Hector and his companions are bringing the lively-eyed, 5
graceful Andromache from holy Thebe and ever-flowing
Placia[6] in their ships over the salty sea, along with many golden
    bracelets
and perfumed purple robes, beautifully painted ornaments
and countless silver cups and ivory."
So he spoke. Quickly Hector's dear father[7] rose up 10
and the news spread among his friends in the spacious city.
At once the sons of Ilus[8] yoked mules to the
smooth-running carts, then the whole crowd
of women and maidens with . . . ankles climbed on board.
The daughters of Priam apart . . . 15
the young men yoked horses to chariots . . .
in great style . . .
charioteers . . .
. . . like the gods
. . . holy together 20
set out . . . to Ilium
the sweet-sounding flute and the cithara mingled
and the sound of castanets. Maidens sang a holy song
and a wondrous echo reached to the sky . . .
everywhere in the streets was . . . 25
mixing-bowls and drinking cups . . .
myrrh and cassia and frankincense mingled.

2. The quotation that is our only source for this poem breaks off here, although this looks like the beginning of a new stanza.
3. This and the following Sappho poems and fragments are translated by Philip Freeman. This poem is our only surviving example of Sappho's narrative poetry. It is composed in the same meter as Homer's epics, dactylic hexameter (unlike all Sappho's other surviving work). It tells the story of the wedding of Hector, prince of Troy, and Andromache, characters famous in myth who feature in the *Iliad*. Some scholars believe this poem may have been composed for performance at a wedding.
4. The island of Cyprus was one of the most important cult centers of Aphrodite. It is not clear how the island related to the beginning of the poem, which is lost.
5. Herald of Troy, a character in the *Iliad*.
6. Homeland of Andromache, in central Greece.
7. Priam, king of Troy.
8. The Trojans; Ilus was the legendary founder of Troy, also known as Ilium.

The older women cried out with joy
and all the men erupted in a high-pitched shout
calling on Paean, far-shooting god skilled with the lyre.   30
They sang in praise of godlike Hector and Andromache.

47

Love shook my heart
like a mountain wind falling on oaks.

48

You came and I was longing for you.
You cooled my heart burning with desire.

51

I don't know what I should do. There are two minds in me

55[9]

But when you die you will lie there and there will be no memory
of you nor longing for you after, for you have no share in the roses
of Pieria.[1] But you will wander unseen in the house of Hades,[2]
flying about among the shadowy dead.

58[3]

. . . I pray
. . . now a festival
. . . under the earth
. . . having a gift of honor
. . . as I am now on the earth   5
. . . taking the sweet-sounding lyre
. . . I sing to the reed-pipe

9. This is a quotation from a lost longer poem, apparently addressed to a rich but talentless woman.
1. Birthplace of the Muses.
2. God of the dead.

3. The first part of this poem has been known since 1922 from a fragmentary papyrus, but the second part (beginning ". . . beautiful gifts") was discovered on another papyrus only in 2004.

. . . fleeing
. . . was bitten
. . . gives success to the mouth   10

. . . beautiful gifts of the violet-laden Muses, children
. . . the sweet-sounding lyre dear to song.
. . . my skin once soft is wrinkled now,
. . . my hair once black has turned to white.
My heart has become heavy, my knees   15
that once danced nimbly like fawns cannot carry me.
How often I lament these things—but what can be done?
No one who is human can escape old age.
They say that rosy-armed Dawn once took
Tithonus,[4] beautiful and young, carrying him to the   20
ends of the earth. But in time grey old age still
found him, even though he had an immortal wife.
. . . imagines
. . . might give
I love the pleasures of life . . . and this to me.   25
Love has given me the brightness and beauty of the sun.

94

. . . "I honestly wish I were dead."
Weeping she left me

with many tears and said this:
"Oh, this has turned out so badly for us, Sappho.
Truly, I leave you against my will."   5

And I answered her:
"Be happy and go—and remember me.
for you know how much we loved you.

But if not, I want to remind
you . . .   10
. . . and the good times we had.

For many crowns of violets
and roses and . . .
. . . you put on by my side,

and many woven garlands   15
made from flowers
around your soft throat,

---

4. According to myth, the goddess Dawn fell in
love with a Trojan boy called Tithonus and carried him off to be with her. She made him
immortal but could not make him immune to
old age. In some versions of the myth, he turned
into a cicada, whom the Greeks imagined as
eternally singing—a kind of insect poet.

and with much perfume
costly . . .
fit for a queen, you anointed yourself.   20

And on a soft bed
delicate . . .
you let loose your desire.

And not any . . . nor any
holy place nor . . .   25
from which we were absent.

No grove . . . no dance
. . . no sound

102

Truly, sweet mother, I cannot weave on the loom,
for I am overcome with desire for a boy because of slender Aphrodite.

104

104A

Evening, you gather together all that shining Dawn has scattered.
You bring back the sheep, you bring back the goat, you bring back
    the child to its mother.

104B

. . . most beautiful of all the stars

105[5]

105A

. . . like the sweet apple that grows red on the lofty branch,
at the very top of the highest bough. The apple-pickers have forgotten it
—no, not forgotten, but they could not reach it.

---

5. This and the next fragment may be from wedding songs. Perhaps the bride, a virgin inaccessible to men until marriage, is compared to the apple. The hyacinth may also be a reference to virginity.

105B

. . . like the hyacinth shepherds tread underfoot
in the mountains, and on the ground the purple flower

111[6]

Raise high the roof—
Hymenaeus!
Raise it up, carpenters—
Hymenaeus!
The bridegroom is coming, the equal of Ares,   5
and he's much bigger than a big man.

112

Blessed bridegroom, your wedding has been accomplished
just as you prayed and you have the maiden bride you desired.

Your form is graceful and your eyes . . .
honey-sweet. Love pours over your lovely face . . .
. . . Aphrodite has greatly honored you   5

114

"Virginity, virginity, where have you gone? You've deserted me!"
"Never again will I come to you, never again will I come."

130

Once again limb-loosening Love makes me tremble,
that bittersweet, irresistible creature.

132

I have a beautiful child who is like golden flowers
in form, my beloved Cleis,[7] for whom
I would not take all of Lydia or lovely . . .

6. This and the next two fragments are certainly from wedding songs. Hymenaeus is the
god of marriage.

7. Sadly, nothing more is known about Cleis,
beyond this fragment.

168B

The moon has set
and the Pleiades.[8] It's the middle
of the night and time goes by.
I lie here alone.

The Brothers Poem[9]

But you are always chattering that Charaxus is coming
with a full ship.[1] These things, I suppose, Zeus
knows and all the other gods. But you should not
        worry about them.

Instead send me and ask me to call on   5
and make many prayers to Queen Hera
that Charaxus return here,
   steering his ship,

and find us safe and sound. Everything else,
all of it, let us leave to the gods.   10
For fair weather comes quickly
        from great storms.

Those to whom the king of Olympus[2] wishes
to send a helpful spirit to banish toils,
these will be happy   15
  and rich in blessings.

And we—if someday his head is freed from labor
and Larichus[3] becomes a gentleman of leisure
—may we be delivered quickly
        from great heaviness of heart.   20

The Cypris Poem

How can a person not be so often distressed,
Queen Cypris,[4] about someone
you want so much to make
        your own?

8. A cluster of stars known as the Seven Sisters.
9. The Brothers Poem and the Cypris Poem
that follows were first published in 2014, from
a new papyrus find.
1. Charaxus is known from Herodotus as the
name of one of Sappho's brothers. He was supposedly a trader in Lesbian wine. This poem is
missing the first stanza or two, so the context of
the reference is hard to construct.
2. Zeus.
3. Larichus is also a brother of Sappho's, presumably younger than Charaxus.
4. Cypris is Aphrodite, goddess of love and
sex. Presumably this is a single stanza from a
much longer poem.

ANCIENT
ATHENIAN DRAMA

Modern readers usually find Athenian drama easy to appreciate, but the original performance contexts of Greek drama were radically different from anything modern readers and theatergoers have experienced. The city festivals of Athens, at which all new comedies and tragedies were first performed, involved a mixture of things we usually regard as wholly separate: politics, religion, music, poetry, serious drama, slapstick, open-air spectacles, and dance. For the combination of drama with song and dance, in a popular format performed for large audiences, our closest analogy might be the Broadway musical. But Broadway shows usually take place indoors, and have no obvious connection to politics or religion. To get a sense of the strangeness of Athenian dramatic festivals, imagine a major public political event, like the inauguration of a new American president, combine it with a major religious gathering like an evangelical rally, a papal audience, or the Hajj to Mecca, then add to the mix a Thanksgiving Day parade (with all the floats) and a grand open-air music festival. The resulting hybrid would be a modern equivalent of the two main Athenian religious occasions that included major dramatic performances: the Great Dionysia and the Lernaea. Both festivals included tragedy and comedy, although tragedy was more central to the Dionysia, while comedy played a larger role at the Lernaea.

Both festivals were held in honor of the god Dionysus, who was associated with wine and, more generally, with overturning the rules and conventions of the normal world. Dionysus was a wild figure: he rode a chariot pulled by leopards, dressed in strange, effeminate clothing and an ivy crown, and was accompanied by ecstatic, crazy women (the maenads) and hairy, half-goat men with permanent erections called satyrs. The Athenians knew him as an exotic, foreign god who originated somewhere in Asia Minor before being incorporated in the Olympian pantheon. We should remember the subversive, outsider status of this god when reading Athenian drama.

We know very little about the origins of tragedy or comedy. The word *comedy* seems to come from *komos*, a Greek word denoting a drunken procession. Aristotle tells us that *tragedy* (*tragoidia* in Greek) means "goat song," and suggests that the genre originated as part of a ritual in which a goat was sacrificed or offered as a prize. Sometime in the late sixth century B.C.E., rural celebrations in honor of Dionysus became an official, annual part of the urban festival calendar. Originally, the main entertainment was probably choruses of dancers, who sang hymns and competed for prizes; later, some form of tragedy and, later still, comedy were added to the program. Thespis, from whose name we get the term *thespian*— and about whom we know next to nothing—is traditionally said to have invented tragedy in the year 534 B.C.E. He "stepped out of the Chorus," creating a part for a single actor who could talk back to the chorus. The invention of the individual actor, distinct from the group, was enormously important: it paved the way for the whole subsequent history of Western drama.

Tragedy was something new in the late sixth century, but contests of poetry in performance had long been a part of Athenian culture. At the largest city festival, the Panathenaia ("All-Athenian," in honor of the city's goddess, Athena), performers called rhapsodes recited parts of **Homer's** *Iliad* and *Odyssey*; the best performers won prizes. The Homeric poems were an essential model for later drama. Aeschylus supposedly called his own work "slices from the feast of Homer." It was not merely the plots of Greek tragedy that were "Homeric," although like the *Iliad* and *Odyssey* many tragedies dealt with the heroes who fought in the Trojan War. Dramatists also learned from Homer how to create vivid dialogue and fast, exciting narrative, as well as sympathy for a range of different characters, Greek and foreigner alike.

Each year at the Great Dionysia, three tragic poets were chosen by the official city governor (the *archon*) to produce a tetralogy of plays for each day's entertainment. Performances began at dawn and included three tragedies, which might or might not concentrate on a linked set of stories, followed by a lighter play featuring satyrs (a "satyr play"). A rich Athenian citizen put up the money to pay for the costs of each day's performance, including purchase of costumes and masks, and training of the chorus members and actors. These producers prided themselves on their participation, and gloated if the performance they had financed won the competition: at least one backer tried to rig the results by making a night raid to destroy the gold crowns and costumes that had been ordered for his rival's chorus to wear. Before the dramatic performances began, the tribute paid to the city of Athens by her allies was heaped up in the theater for all to see, and the orphans of Athenian men killed in war in the pre-

This detail from the so-called Pronomos Vase, painted in the late fifth century B.C.E., depicts actors preparing for a satyr play.

vious year marched in front of the audience, wearing armor provided at the expense of the city. Athenian drama itself can be seen as a comparable display, a demonstration to foreigners and to the Athenians themselves of the city's artistic and intellectual riches, as well as a meditation on its vulnerability.

The only complete works of Greek drama that have survived are a small selection of the tragedies of Aeschylus, **Sophocles**, and **Euripides**, and a few comedies by Aristophanes. But of course far more people composed plays in this period, some of which were probably excellent; there were other poets—such as Agathon, a tragedian who appears in Plato's *Symposium*—who were awarded

A contemporary photograph of the remains of the theater of Dionysus in Athens.

first prize in the competitions. We have just the names of most of these other dramatists, along with some titles and some tantalizing fragments.

Similarly, the scripts are all that survive of Greek drama, and wishful thinking leads us to imagine that what we have is the most important part: we tend to think of these plays simply as "literature," words on a page. But the words must have formed only a small part of the total effect of the original performances. Those sitting in the upper areas of the theater may well not have been able to hear everything, despite the good acoustics of the theater. The music, gestures, costumes, props, and visual effects may well have had a larger impact on most audience members than any individual detail of phrasing. Writing the script was also a tiny part of the work of a dramatist. The poet was also the director, composer, and choreographer of the plays he created; in the earliest days of drama, the poets were probably also actors in their own work. The prizes were not awarded for writing, but for the work of coaching the actors and dancers: the usual phrase to

describe what a dramatist does is "to teach a chorus."

The theater of Dionysus, where the plays were performed, held at least 13,000 people, perhaps as many as 17,000—a number comparable to the seating available in New York's Madison Square Garden. This figure represents a high proportion of the male citizen body, estimated to have been about forty or sixty thousand people—although the total population of Athens, including women, children, foreigners, and slaves, may have been ten times that large.

It is possible that a few women came to the theater in the fifth century; women were almost certainly in attendance by the fourth century. We do not know whether slaves were present. In any case, the majority of the audience consisted of male citizens. In the participatory democracy of fifth-century Athens, the whole citizen body was eligible to participate in policy making, and citizens were accustomed to meet together in public to determine military and domestic policy, at least once a month and usually more often. The structure of the dramatic festival was reminiscent of

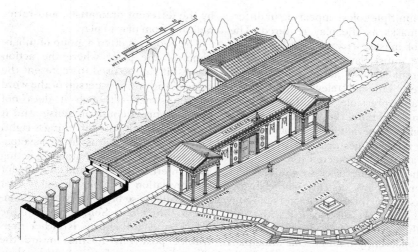

A reconstruction of the Dionysus theater by the theater and architectural scholar Richard Leacroft. An actor stands in the *orchēstra*, while another stands on the roof of the *skēnē*.

other political assemblies, where citizens sat to hear speeches on several sides of a case and made their decisions between competing sides.

The theater was an open-air venue, with seating in the round. The central space, called the *orchēstra* (which means "dancing area"), lay at the lowest point of the valley; on the slopes of the hill, spectators sat on wooden benches, surrounding the performance area on three sides. At one end of the *orchēstra* was a wooden platform or stage, with a wooden building on it (the *skēnē*), which could be used to represent whatever interior space was necessary for the play: a palace, a house, a cave, or any other type of structure. There were thus three possible ways for actors to come on and off stage: to the left or right of the stage, or through the doors of the building. Entrances and exits tend to be particularly important in Greek drama, because they took a long time; the audience would have been watching the characters make their way into the playing area before they actually reached the stage. When reading these plays, it is a good idea to pay particular attention to the moments when a new character comes on.

There were also two major structural devices that expanded the possibilities of the playing space. The *ekkuklēma* ("trolley" or "thing that rolls out") was a wooden platform on wheels, which could be trundled out from the central doors of the *skēnē*, and was conventionally used to represent the interior space. This was an essential device by which dramatists could bring the events from indoors before the eyes of the outdoor audience. The second device was the *mēchanē* ("machine" or "device"), a pulley system that allowed for the appearance and disappearance of actors in the air, above the *skēnē* building. Using the *mēchanē*, playwrights could make a god suddenly appear in the air above the palace, as a literal *deus ex māchinā* ("god from the machine"), to resolve the twists of the plot.

All the actors who performed in Athenian drama were men—including those playing female parts. All actors wore masks. Tragedy and comedy both used a tiny number of actors for the speaking parts. In the first few decades of the century, there were only two actors; later, three actors were used. This meant that the same actors had to play multiple roles, appearing in different masks as the play required. The use of masks, as well as the open-air space, must have necessitated a very different style of acting from that of modern cinema, television, or stage. Facial expressions would have been invisible behind the mask, and were therefore irrelevant; instead, actors must have relied on gestures, body language, and a strongly projected voice.

The dialogue sections of ancient Athenian plays usually show two—occasionally three—characters in confrontation or discussion with one another. Dialogue may be free-flowing and apparently natural. But dramatists made use of two important dialogue techniques. One is the *agon* ("contest" or "struggle"), in which one character makes a long, sometimes legalistic speech, arguing a particular case, and a second character replies with another speech, putting the case against. The other is *stichomythia* ("line-speech"), in which characters speak just a single line each—allowing for a fast-paced, usually argumentative exchange.

Greek drama was always composed in verse, but not in the epic meter of Homer, the hexameter (a line with a six-part pattern). The rhythm of the dialogue elements was iambic (based on a fairly flexible pattern of alternating short and long syllables), which was supposed to be the verse form closest to normal speech (like the iambic pentameter used by Shakespeare). The choral passages, by contrast, were composed in extremely complex meters, designed to be sung and accompanied by elaborate choreography. Athenian drama thus combined two very different theatrical experiences, interspersing plot-driven, character-heavy dialogue with music, poetry, and dance.

The chorus was composed of twelve—later, fifteen—masked dancers, of whom only one, the "leader," had a speaking role. This group is used in different ways by the different dramatists, and varies radically from play to play.

The chorus is often a group of inhabitants of the place where the action occurs: it can be used to represent the voice of the ordinary person or the word on the street—although it does not always express common sense, and it frequently fails to get things right. Sometimes the chorus listens sympathetically to the main characters, acting as an internal audience and allowing for the revelation of inner thoughts that might otherwise be hard for the dramatist to bring out. Sometimes, on the other hand, the chorus is either neutral or positively hostile toward the main characters. Choruses can be characters themselves, with their own biases and preoccupations.

The choral songs and dances can allow the dramatist to put the events of the play in a broader perspective: the chorus may take us back in time, looking to earlier events in the same myth, or tracing parallels between this story and others; or it may reflect on the ethical, theological, and metaphysical implications of the events at hand. The poet may also use the chorus to provide a break from the main narrative, a switch to an entirely different mood or perspective. Choral songs can increase the dramatic tension or surprise, as when a cheerful, optimistic song is followed by disaster.

Mutilation and violent death, by murder or suicide, accident, fate, or the gods, are frequent events in Greek tragedy. The threat of violence—which may or may not be averted—provides a strong element in the interest of these plays. But compared to modern television drama or action movies, there is little visible horror. Dead bodies are often displayed onstage, but the actual killing usually takes place offstage. The messenger speech is therefore one of the most important conventions of Athenian drama. Long, vivid, blow-by-blow accounts of offstage disasters allow the audience to imagine and visualize events that the dramatist cannot or will not bring onstage.

The plots of Greek tragedy focus on a few traditional story patterns, set in the distant past and in non-Athenian city-states: Argos, Thebes, or Troy. Although tragedians used preexisting stories, they felt free, within reason, to shape the myths in their own way; for instance, Aeschylus, Sophocles, and Euripides created very different plays focused on the story of Electra, daughter of the murdered Agamemnon. Tragedy was often relevant in some way to contemporary concerns, but its political and social perspectives are never as explicit as those of comedy.

Since Greek plays were always performed at a religious festival, we might expect them to be more obviously "religious" than they seem at first blush. Comedians often bring gods on stage, but they are not treated in a markedly reverent way: for instance, Dionysus in Aristophanes' *Frogs* is a craven coward with a flatulence problem. The power of the gods is usually a more serious issue in tragedy, but even here, modern readers may be surprised at how cruel and unreliable the Greek gods often seem to be. It is perhaps helpful to remember that Athenians of the fifth century—unlike most believers in modern monotheistic religions—saw no necessary connection between religion and morality. Gods are, by definition, immortal and powerful; they need not also be nice. Athenian drama was an act of service to the gods in general, and to Dionysus in particular, because it overturned the everyday world and explored the power of the imagination, showing—in Euripides' words—"how god makes possible the unexpected." By serving the gods, displaying the strange and surprising ways that divine forces operate on human lives, Athenian dramatists were also serving their audiences, creating dramas that were gripping, profound, and unpredictable: qualities that readers still appreciate in these works today.

SOPHOCLES
ca. 496–406 B.C.E.

The seven surviving plays of Sophocles are often considered the most perfect achievement of ancient Athens. They show us people—presented with psychological depth and subtlety—who stand apart from others, on the edges of their social groups. Sophocles invites us to ask what it means to be part of a family, part of a city, part of a team or an army, or part of the human race. Can we choose to embrace or reject our family, friends, and society, or do we have to accept the place to which we were born? Is it a gesture of heroism or folly to take a stand as an outsider? What should we do if forced to choose between our family and a wider social group? Sophocles' thought-provoking and compelling dramas explore themes that are just as relevant today as they were in the fifth century B.C.E., and they provide the classic treatments of mythic figures, such as Oedipus and Antigone, who have been central to later Western culture.

LIFE AND TIMES

Sophocles had an unusually long, successful, productive, and apparently happy life. He was born at the start of the fifth century, around 496 B.C.E., in the village of Colonus, which was a short distance north of Athens. His family was probably fairly wealthy—his father may have owned a workshop producing armor, a particularly marketable product at this time of war—and Sophocles seems to have been well educated. An essential element in Greek boys' education at this time was studying the Homeric poems, and Sophocles obviously learned this lesson well; in later times, he was called the "most Homeric" of the three surviving Athenian tragedians. He was a good-looking, charming boy and a talented dancer. In 480, when he was about fifteen or sixteen, he was chosen to lead a group of naked boys who danced in the victory celebrations for Athens's defeat of the Persian navy at Salamis. The beginning of his public career thus coincided with his city's period of greatest glory and international prestige.

Athens became the major power in the Mediterranean world in the middle decades of the fifth century B.C.E., a period known as the golden or classical age. The most important political figure in the newly dominant city-state was Pericles, a statesman who was also Sophocles' personal friend and who particularly encouraged the arts. Pericles seems to have instituted various legal measures to enable the theater to flourish: for instance, rich citizens were obliged to provide funding for theater productions, and the less wealthy may have had their theater tickets subsidized.

The prosperity of Sophocles' city took a sharp turn for the worse around 431 B.C.E., when the poet would have been in his mid-sixties. The Peloponnesian War, between Athens and Sparta, began at that time and would last until after Sophocles' death. Soon after the outbreak of war, Sophocles' friend Pericles died in a terrible plague that afflicted the whole city. In the last decades of the century, the city became increasingly impoverished and demoralized by war.

Sophocles worked in the Athenian theater all his life. He made some important technical changes in dramatic productions, introducing scene painting and increasing the number of chorus members from twelve to fifteen. His most important innovation was bringing in a third actor (a "tritagonist"). This allowed for three-way dialogues, and for a drama that concentrates on the complex interactions and relationships of individuals with one another. The chorus in Sophocles' dramas became far less central to the plot than it had been in Aeschylus; this is part of the reason why Sophocles' plays may seem more modern to twenty-first-century readers and audiences.

Another quality that makes Sophocles particularly accessible to modern readers is his interest in realistic characterization. Sophocles' most memorable characters are intense, passionate, and often larger than life, but always fully human. They frequently adopt positions that seem extreme, but for which they have the best of motives. Sophocles' tragedies ask us to consider when and how it is right to compromise, and to measure the slim divide between concession and selling out. Clashes between stubborn heroism and the voice of moderation are found in all Sophocles' surviving plays.

Contemporaries gave Sophocles' talent its due. He won first prize at the Great Dionysia for the first time in 468 B.C.E., defeating his older rival, Aeschylus; he was still under thirty at the time. Sophocles would defeat Aeschylus several more times in the course of his career. His output was large: he composed over a hundred and twenty plays. The seven that survive include the three

Theban plays, dealing with Oedipus and his family: *Oedipus the King*, *Antigone*, and *Oedipus at Colonus*. These were written at intervals of many years, and were never intended to be performed together. The other four surviving tragedies are *Ajax*, about a strongman hero who is driven mad by Athena; *Trachiniae*, about Heracles' agonizing death at the hands of his jealous wife Deineira (who had thought the poison she gave him was a love potion); *Electra*, which focuses on the unending grief and rage of Agamemnon's daughter after her father's murder; and *Philoctetes*, about the Greek embassy to persuade an embittered, wounded hero to return to battle in Troy. The dating of most of these plays is uncertain, although we know *Philoctetes* is a late play, composed in 409 B.C.E. The judges at the Great Dionysia loved Sophocles' work: he won first prize over twenty times, and never came lower than second.

Sophocles seems to have been equally popular as a person, known for his mellow, easygoing temperament, his religious piety, and his appreciation for the beauty of adolescent boys. We are told that he had "so much charm of character that he was loved everywhere, by everyone." He was friendly with the prominent intellectuals of his day, including the world's first historian, Herodotus. He participated in the political activity of the city; he served under Pericles as a treasurer in 443 and 442 B.C.E., and was elected as a general under him in 441. After the Sicilian disaster in 413, in which Athens lost enormous numbers of men and ships, Sophocles—then in his eighties—was one of ten men elected to an emergency group created for policy formation. Sophocles' participation in public life suggests that he was seen as a trustworthy and wise member of the community. Sophocles was married and had five sons, one of whom, Iophon, became a tragedian himself.

Sophocles lived to advanced old age and was over ninety when he died.

OEDIPUS THE KING

Many first-time readers of *Oedipus the King* will already know the shocking secret that Oedipus eventually discovers: he killed his father and married his mother, without knowing what he was doing. The mythical background to this play is familiar to readers today, and would have been well known, in its broad outlines, to Sophocles' original audience. This is a drama not of surprise but of suspense: we watch Oedipus uncover the buried truth about himself and his parentage, of which he, unlike us, is ignorant. The mystery, gradually revealed to the spectators in the course of the play, is not what the king has done, but how he will discover what he has done, and how he will respond to this terrible new knowledge.

The legend holds that Laius (Laios), son of Labdacus and king of Thebes, learned long ago from the Delphic oracle (sacred to Apollo) that his son would kill him. When Laius had a son by his wife, Jocasta (Jokasta), he gave the baby to a shepherd to be exposed on Mount Cithaeron. Exposure, a fairly common practice in the ancient world, involved leaving a baby out in some wild place, presumably to die; it allowed parents to dispose of unwanted children without incurring blood guilt. Laius increased the odds against the child's survival by piercing and binding his feet, so there was no chance he could crawl away. But the shepherd felt sorry for the boy and saved him. He was adopted by the childless king and queen of Corinth, Polybus and Merope, and grew up believing himself to be their son.

One day another oracle warned Oedipus that he would kill his father and marry his mother. Oedipus fled Corinth in the direction of Thebes, to avoid this fate. At a place where three paths crossed, he encountered his real father, Laius, without knowing who he was; they quarreled, and Oedipus killed Laius. When he reached Thebes, he found the city oppressed by a dreadful female monster, a Sphinx—part human, part lion, often also depicted in Greek art with the wings of an eagle and the tail of a snake. The Sphinx refused to let anybody into the city unless they could answer her riddle: "What walks on four legs in the morning, two legs at noon, and three legs in the evening?" She strangled and devoured all travelers who failed to answer the riddle. But Oedipus gave the right answer: "Man." (Human beings crawl on all fours in infancy, walk on two feet in adulthood, and use a cane in old age.) The Sphinx was defeated, and Oedipus was welcomed into the city as a savior. He married the newly widowed queen, Jocasta, and took over the throne.

When Sophocles' play begins, Oedipus has been ruling Thebes successfully for many years, and has four children by Jocasta, two sons and two daughters. But a new trouble is now afflicting the city. Plague has come to Thebes, and the dying inhabitants are searching for the reason why the gods are angry with the city.

The city of Athens suffered a terrible plague in 429 B.C.E., and the play may well have been composed and performed soon afterward—although the dating is uncertain and disputed. Sophocles certainly seems to invite comparisons between the real Athens and the mythical Thebes. Oedipus himself can be seen as a typical fifth-century Athenian: he is optimistic, irascible, self-confident, both pious and skeptical in his attitudes toward religion, and a committed believer in the power of human reason.

In his *Poetics*, the philosopher Aristotle describes this play as the finest of all Greek tragedies. It includes two plot patterns that he thought were essential

to good drama: a reversal of fortune (*peripeteia*), and a recognition (*anagnorisis*). Aristotle famously cites Oedipus as an example of someone whose fall into misfortune is the result not of bad deeds or evil character, but of some "mistake"—the Greek word is *hamartia*. Later critics applied the quite different concept of a "tragic flaw" to Oedipus, suggesting that we are supposed to see the disastrous events of the drama as somehow the king's own fault. An important consideration against this reading is that in *Oedipus at Colonus*, a later play about the last days of Oedipus, Sophocles makes his hero give a compelling self-defense: "How is my *nature* evil— / if all I did was to return a blow?" There is a clear distinction in Greek thought between moral culpability—which is attached to deliberate, conscious actions—and religious pollution, which may afflict even those who are morally innocent. Readers must decide for themselves how far they think Sophocles goes in presenting his Oedipus as a sympathetic or even admirable figure.

Another popular approach to the play has been to see it as a classic "tragedy of fate," in which a man is brought low by destiny or the gods. Here, we need to distinguish the myth—which can plausibly be seen as a story about the inevitable unfolding of divine will—from Sophocles' treatment of the myth in his play, which suggests a more complex relationship between destiny and human action. Before Sophocles, Aeschylus had produced a trilogy that dealt with the family of Laius and Oedipus. This does not survive, but it is likely that it showed the gradual fulfillment of an inherited curse. In Sophocles' play, our attention is focused less on the original events and their causes (the killing of Laius and the marriage to Jocasta) than on the process by which Oedipus uncovers what he has done.

Sophocles multiplies the number of oracles and messengers in the story, and Apollo—the god associated with prophecy, poetry, and interpretation, as well as with light and the sun—presides over the relentless unfolding of the truth. Oracles are only one of many types of riddling, ambiguous, or ambivalent language used in the play, which is concerned with all kinds of interpretation. Moments of dramatic irony, when the audience hears a meaning of which the speaker is unaware, are another important reminder that words may have more than one sense. For instance, Oedipus vows to fight in defense of Laius "as for my father"—speaking more truly than he knows. The interplay between literal and metaphorical meanings forms another essential technique in the play. Sophocles creates a relationship between literal and metaphorical blindness, between the light of the sun and the light of insight, between Oedipus as "father" of his people and as real father to his own siblings, and between sickness as a physical affliction and as a metaphor for pollution.

The riddle of the Sphinx defines humanity by the number of feet we use at different points in our lives. Sophocles seems to suggest that the name *Oedipus* is closely associated with feet: it can be read either as "Know-Foot" (from the verb *oida*, "to know," and *pous*, "foot"— an appropriate name for the man who solved the Sphinx's riddle), or as "Swell-Foot" (from the verb *oidao*, to swell— a reminder of the baby Oedipus's wounded feet). The first interpretation of his name makes Oedipus seem like an Everyman figure, a representative of all humanity: he is the one who truly understands the human condition. The second reminds us of the ways in which Oedipus is not like us: his feet mark the fact that he was cast out by his parents, rejected from his city, and that he has, unwittingly, done things that seem to make it impossible for him to be part of any human community.

Sigmund Freud famously claimed that the Oedipus myth represents a psychological phenomenon, the "Oedipus complex," which involves the (supposed) desire of all boys to kill their fathers and marry their mothers. But Sophocles' Oedipus does not suffer from Freud's complex: his terrible actions are committed in total ignorance, not through an unconscious desire for patricide or sex with his mother. Another way to think of Sophocles' Oedipus is as a hero who, like Odysseus, struggles to find his way back home after many wanderings and encounters with terrible monsters—but finds himself in a perverted version of the homecoming story, in which the arrival is not the end but the beginning of a nightmare.

A play whose secret you already know might seem unlikely to be interesting. But it is impossible to be bored by *Oedipus the King*. The plot races to its terrible conclusion with the twisting, breakneck pace of a thrilling murder mystery, while the contradictory figure of Oedipus himself—the blind rationalist, the polluted king, the killer of his father, the son and husband of Jocasta, the hunter and the hunted, the stranger in his own home—is a commanding presence who dominates the stage even when he can no longer see.

Oedipus the King[1]

CHARACTERS

OEDIPUS, *King of Thebes*
JOCASTA, *His Wife*
CREON, *His Brother-in-Law*
TEIRESIAS, *an Old Blind Prophet*
A PRIEST

FIRST MESSENGER
SECOND MESSENGER
A HERDSMAN
A CHORUS OF OLD MEN OF THEBES

SCENE: *In front of the palace of* OEDIPUS *at Thebes. To the right of the stage near the altar stands the* PRIEST *with a crowd of children.* OEDIPUS *emerges from the central door.*[2]

OEDIPUS   Children, young sons and daughters of old Cadmus,
   why do you sit here with your suppliant crowns?[3]
   The town is heavy with a mingled burden
   of sounds and smells, of groans and hymns and incense;
   I did not think it fit that I should hear   5
   of this from messengers but came myself,—
   I Oedipus whom all men call the Great.
      [*He turns to the* PRIEST.]
   You're old and they are young; come, speak for them.
   What do you fear or want, that you sit here
   suppliant? Indeed I'm willing to give all   10
   that you may need; I would be very hard
   should I not pity suppliants like these.
PRIEST   O ruler of my country, Oedipus,
   you see our company around the altar;
   you see our ages; some of us, like these,   15
   who cannot yet fly far, and some of us
   heavy with age; these children are the chosen
   among the young, and I the priest of Zeus.
   Within the marketplace sit others crowned
   with suppliant garlands, at the double shrine   20
   of Pallas and the temple where Ismenus[4]
   gives oracles by fire. King, you yourself
   have seen our city reeling like a wreck
   already; it can scarcely lift its prow
   out of the depths, out of the bloody surf.   25
   A blight is on the fruitful plants of the earth,
   A blight is on the cattle in the fields,
   a blight is on our women that no children

---

1. Translated by David Grene.
2. All stage directions, in italics, are inserted by the translator. Ancient Greek plays do not have these.
3. Branches twined round with wool, carried in ritual to signal that one is at the mercy of another person. "Cadmus": mythological founder and first king of Thebes.
4. River god of Thebes. "Pallas": warrior goddess, daughter of Zeus; associated with wisdom and technology.

are born to them; a god[5] that carries fire,
a deadly pestilence, is on our town,   30
strikes us and spares not, and the house of Cadmus
is emptied of its people while black Death
grows rich in groaning and in lamentation.
We have not come as suppliants to this altar
because we thought of you as of a god,   35
but rather judging you the first of men
in all the chances of this life and when
we mortals have to do with more than man.
You came and by your coming saved our city,
freed us from tribute which we paid of old   40
to the Sphinx,[6] cruel singer. This you did
in virtue of no knowledge we could give you,
in virtue of no teaching; it was a god
that aided you, men say, and you are held
with the god's assistance to have saved our lives.   45
Now Oedipus, Greatest in all men's eyes,
here falling at your feet we all entreat you,
find us some strength for rescue.
Perhaps you'll hear a wise word from some god,
perhaps you will learn something from a man   50
(for I have seen that for the skilled of practice
the outcome of their counsels live the most).
Noblest of men, go, and raise up our city,
go,—and give heed. For now this land of ours
calls you its savior since you saved it once.   55
So, let us never speak about your reign
as of a time when first our feet were set
secure on high, but later fell to ruin.
Raise up our city, save it and raise it up.
Once you have brought us luck with happy omen;   60
be no less now in fortune.
If you will rule this land, as now you rule it,
better to rule it full of men than empty.
For neither tower nor ship is anything
when empty, and none live in it together.   65

OEDIPUS   I pity you, children. You have come full of longing,
but I have known the story before you told it
only too well. I know you are all sick,
yet there is not one of you, sick though you are,

5. The University of Chicago Press's original version of the translation uses capital G for *god* here, and repeatedly (e.g., again in the other instances of the word in this speech). This has been altered to avoid the implication of monotheism; ancient Greek texts often refer to "a god" or "the god" in the singular, especially when the speaker may not know which of the many gods has been at work.

6. Winged female monster who terrorized Thebes until her riddle was finally answered by Oedipus. The riddle comes in different variants and is never cited by Sophocles, but one common version goes: "What walks on four feet in the morning, two at noon, and three at night?" Oedipus answered, "Man," because humans crawl as babies, walk as adults, and hobble with a stick in old age.

that is as sick as I myself.   70
Your several sorrows each have single scope
and touch but one of you. My spirit groans
for city and myself and you at once.
You have not roused me like a man from sleep;
know that I have given many tears to this,   75
gone many ways wandering in thought,
but as I thought I found only one remedy
and that I took. I sent Menoeceus' son
Creon, Jocasta's brother, to Apollo,
to his Pythian temple,[7]   80
that he might learn there by what act or word
I could save this city. As I count the days,
it vexes me what ails him; he is gone
far longer than he needed for the journey.
But when he comes, then, may I prove a villain,   85
if I shall not do all the god commands.
PRIEST   Thanks for your gracious words. Your servants here
    signal that Creon is this moment coming.
OEDIPUS   His face is bright. O holy Lord Apollo,
    grant that his news too may be bright for us   90
    and bring us safety.
PRIEST   It is happy news,
    I think, for else his head would not be crowned
    with sprigs of fruitful laurel.
OEDIPUS   We will know soon,
    he's within hail. Lord Creon, my good brother,   95
    what is the word you bring us from the god?
        [CREON enters.]
CREON   A good word,—for things hard to bear themselves
    if in the final issue all is well
    I count complete good fortune.
OEDIPUS   What do you mean?
    What you have said so far   100
    leaves me uncertain whether to trust or fear.
CREON   If you will hear my news before these others
    I am ready to speak, or else to go within.
OEDIPUS   Speak it to all;
    the grief I bear, I bear it more for these   105
    than for my own heart.
CREON   I will tell you, then,
    what I heard from the god.
    King Phoebus[8] in plain words commanded us
    to drive out a pollution from our land,

---

7. Apollo is the "god from the shrine of Pytho" (line 175). Pytho was the site of Apollo's oracle, and was also known as Delphi; hence the use of "Delian Healer" in line 178.

8. I.e., Apollo, the god associated with archery, sunlight, poetry, prophecy, healing, and plague. His arrows could cause disease, as they do in the beginning of the *Iliad*.

pollution grown ingrained within the land; 110
drive it out, said the god, not cherish it,
till it's past cure.
OEDIPUS   What is the rite
of purification? How shall it be done?
CREON   By banishing a man, or expiation
of blood by blood, since it is murder guilt 115
which holds our city in this destroying storm.
OEDIPUS   Who is this man whose fate the god pronounces?
CREON   My Lord, before you piloted the state
we had a king called Laius.
OEDIPUS   I know of him by hearsay. I have not seen him. 120
CREON   The god commanded clearly: let someone
punish with force this dead man's murderers.
OEDIPUS   Where are they in the world? Where would a trace
of this old crime be found? It would be hard
to guess where.
CREON   The clue is in this land; 125
that which is sought is found;
the unheeded thing escapes:
so said the god.
OEDIPUS   Was it at home,
or in the country that death came upon him,
or in another country travelling?
CREON   He went, he said himself, upon an embassy, 130
but never returned when he set out from home.
OEDIPUS   Was there no messenger, no fellow traveller
who knew what happened? Such a one might tell
something of use. 135
CREON   They were all killed save one. He fled in terror
and he could tell us nothing in clear terms
of what he knew, nothing, but one thing only.
OEDIPUS   What was it?
If we could even find a slim beginning 140
in which to hope, we might discover much.
CREON   This man said that the robbers they encountered
were many and the hands that did the murder
were many; it was no man's single power.
OEDIPUS   How could a robber dare a deed like this 145
were he not helped with money from the city,
money and treachery?
CREON   That indeed was thought.
But Laius was dead and in our trouble
there was none to help.
OEDIPUS   What trouble was so great to hinder you 150
inquiring out the murder of your king?
CREON   The riddling Sphinx induced us to neglect
mysterious crimes and rather seek solution
of troubles at our feet.

OEDIPUS   I will bring this to light again. King Phoebus   155
fittingly took this care about the dead,
and you too fittingly.
And justly you will see in me an ally,
a champion of my country and the god.
For when I drive pollution from the land   160
I will not serve a distant friend's advantage,
but act in my own interest. Whoever
he was that killed the king may readily
wish to dispatch me with his murderous hand;
so helping the dead king I help myself.   165

Come, children, take your suppliant boughs and go;
up from the altars now. Call the assembly
and let it meet upon the understanding
that I'll do everything. God will decide
whether we prosper or remain in sorrow.   170
PRIEST   Rise, children—it was this we came to seek,
which of himself the king now offers us.
May Phoebus who gave us the oracle
come to our rescue and stay the plague.
          [*Exeunt all but the* CHORUS.]
CHORUS STROPHE   What is the sweet spoken word of the god from
          the shrine of Pytho rich in gold   175
that has come to glorious Thebes?
I am stretched on the rack of doubt, and terror and trembling hold
my heart, O Delian Healer, and I worship full of fears
for what doom you will bring to pass, new or renewed in the revolving
          years.
Speak to me, immortal voice,   180
child of golden Hope.
ANTISTROPHE   First I call on you, Athene,[9] deathless daughter
          of Zeus,
and Artemis,[1] Earth Upholder,
who sits in the midst of the marketplace in the throne which
          men call Fame,
and Phoebus, the Far Shooter, three averters of Fate,   185
come to us now, if ever before, when ruin rushed upon the state,
you drove destruction's flame away
out of our land.
STROPHE   Our sorrows defy number;
all the ship's timbers are rotten;   190
taking of thought is no spear for the driving away of the plague.
There are no growing children in this famous land;
there are no women bearing the pangs of childbirth.
You may see them one with another, like birds swift on the wing,

9. I.e., Athena.
1. Sister of Apollo; goddess associated with hunting, childbirth, the moon, and protecting the weak.

quicker than fire unmastered, 195
speeding away to the coast of the western god.
ANTISTROPHE   In the unnumbered deaths
  of its people the city dies;
  those children that are born lie dead on the naked earth
  unpitied, spreading contagion of death; and grey-haired mothers
    and wives 200
  everywhere stand at the altar's edge, suppliant, moaning;
  the hymn to the healing god rings out but with it the wailing
    voices are blended.
From these our sufferings grant us, O golden Daughter of Zeus,
glad-faced deliverance.
STROPHE   There is no clash of brazen shields but our fight is with the
    war god, 205
  a war god ringed with the cries of men, a savage god who burns us;
  grant that he turn in racing course backwards out of our country's
    bounds
  to the great palace of Amphitrite or where the waves of the
    Thracian sea[2]
  deny the stranger safe anchorage.
  Whatsoever escapes the night 210
  at last the light of day revisits;
  so smite the war god, Father Zeus,
  beneath your thunderbolt,
  for you are the Lord of the lightning, the lightning that carries fire.
ANTISTROPHE   And your unconquered arrow shafts, winged by the
    golden corded bow, 215
  Lycean King,[3] I beg to be at our side for help;
  and the gleaming torches of Artemis with which she scours the
    Lycean hills,
  and I call on the god with the turban of gold, who gave his name
    to this country of ours,
  the Bacchic god[4] with the wind-flushed face,
  Evian One, who travel 220
  with the Maenad company,[5]
  combat the god that burns us
  with your torch of pine;
  for the god that is our enemy is a god unhonoured among the gods.
    [OEDIPUS returns.]
OEDIPUS   For what you ask me—if you will hear my words, 225
  and hearing welcome them and fight the plague,
  you will find strength and lightening of your load.
  Hark to me; what I say to you, I say

---

2. Northernmost part of the Aegean Sea where it borders on Thrace in northern Greece. "Amphitrite": sea goddess and consort of Poseidon, god of the seas.
3. Common epithet for Apollo.
4. Dionysus, god of wine, theater, and mad-

ness, is closely associated with Thebes, since his mother, Semele, was a princess of Thebes. He is called "Evian One" from the traditional ritual cry made by his followers: *"Evoi! Evoi!"*
5. Dionysus's wild female followers.

as one that is a stranger to the story
as stranger to the deed. For I would not   230
be far upon the track if I alone
were tracing it without a clue. But now,
since after all was finished, I became
a citizen among you, citizens—
now I proclaim to all the men of Thebes: 235
who so among you knows the murderer
by whose hand Laius, son of Labdacus,
died—I command him to tell everything
to me,—yes, though he fears himself to take the blame
on his own head; for bitter punishment   240
he shall have none, but leave this land unharmed.
Or if he knows the murderer, another,
a foreigner, still let him speak the truth.
For I will pay him and be grateful, too.
But if you shall keep silence, if perhaps   245
some one of you, to shield a guilty friend,
or for his own sake shall reject my words—
hear what I shall do then:
I forbid that man, whoever he be, my land,
my land where I hold sovereignty and throne;   250
and I forbid any to welcome him
or cry him greeting or make him a sharer
in sacrifice or offering to the gods,
or give him water for his hands to wash.
I command all to drive him from their homes,   255
since he is our pollution, as the oracle
of Pytho's god proclaimed him now to me.
So I stand forth a champion of the god
and of the man who died.
Upon the murderer I invoke this curse—   260
whether he is one man and all unknown,
or one of many—may he wear out his life
in misery to miserable doom!
If with my knowledge he lives at my hearth
I pray that I myself may feel my curse.   265
On you I lay my charge to fulfill all this
for me, for the god, and for this land of ours
destroyed and blighted, by the god forsaken.

Even were this no matter of god's ordinance
it would not fit you so to leave it lie,   270
unpurified, since a good man is dead
and one that was a king. Search it out.
Since I am now the holder of his office,
and have his bed and wife that once was his,
and had his line not been unfortunate   275
we would have common children—(fortune leaped
upon his head)—because of all these things,

I fight in his defence as for my father,
and I shall try all means to take the murderer
of Laius the son of Labdacus   280
the son of Polydorus and before him
of Cadmus and before him of Agenor.[6]
Those who do not obey me, may the gods
grant no crops springing from the ground they plough
nor children to their women! May a fate   285
like this, or one still worse than this consume them!
For you whom these words please, the other Thebans,
may Justice as your ally and all the gods
live with you, blessing you now and for ever!

CHORUS   As you have held me to my oath, I speak: 290
  I neither killed the king nor can declare
  the killer; but since Phoebus set the quest
  it is his part to tell who the man is.

OEDIPUS   Right; but to put compulsion on the gods
  against their will—no man can do that.   295

CHORUS   May I then say what I think second best?

OEDIPUS   If there's a third best, too, spare not to tell it.

CHORUS   I know that what the Lord Teiresias
  sees, is most often what the Lord Apollo
  sees. If you should inquire of this from him   300
  you might find out most clearly.

OEDIPUS   Even in this my actions have not been sluggard.
  On Creon's word I have sent two messengers
  and why the prophet is not here already
  I have been wondering.

CHORUS   His skill apart   305
  there is besides only an old faint story.

OEDIPUS   What is it?
  I look at every story.

CHORUS   It was said
  that he was killed by certain wayfarers.

OEDIPUS   I heard that, too, but no one saw the killer.   310

CHORUS   Yet if he has a share of fear at all,
  his courage will not stand firm, hearing your curse.

OEDIPUS   The man who in the doing did not shrink
  will fear no word.

CHORUS   Here comes his prosecutor:
  led by your men the godly prophet comes   315
  in whom alone of mankind truth is native.

    [Enter TEIRESIAS, led by a little boy.]

OEDIPUS   Teiresias, you are versed in everything,
  things teachable and things not to be spoken,
  things of the heaven and earth-creeping things.

---

6. Cadmus, founder and first king of Thebes, was the son of Agenor. Polydorus was Cadmus's son
and father of Labdacus, who was father of Laius.

You have no eyes but in your mind you know   320
with what a plague our city is afflicted.
My lord, in you alone we find a champion,
in you alone one that can rescue us.
Perhaps you have not heard the messengers,
but Phoebus sent in answer to our sending   325
an oracle declaring that our freedom
from this disease would only come when we
should learn the names of those who killed King Laius,
and kill them or expel from our country.
Do not begrudge us oracles from birds,   330
or any other way of prophecy
within your skill; save yourself and the city,
save me; redeem the debt of our pollution
that lies on us because of this dead man.
We are in your hands; pains are most nobly taken   335
to help another when you have means and power.

TEIRESIAS   Alas, how terrible is wisdom when
it brings no profit to the man that's wise!
This I knew well, but had forgotten it,
else I would not have come here.

OEDIPUS   What is this?   340
How sad you are now you have come!

TEIRESIAS   Let me
go home. It will be easiest for us both
to bear our several destinies to the end
if you will follow my advice.

OEDIPUS   You'd rob us
of this your gift of prophecy? You talk   345
as one who had no care for law nor love
for Thebes who reared you.

TEIRESIAS   Yes, but I see that even your own words
miss the mark; therefore I must fear for mine.

OEDIPUS   For god's sake if you know of anything,   350
do not turn from us; all of us kneel to you,
all of us here, your suppliants.

TEIRESIAS   All of you here know nothing. I will not
bring to the light of day my troubles, mine—
rather than call them yours.

OEDIPUS   What do you mean?   355
You know of something but refuse to speak.
Would you betray us and destroy the city?

TEIRESIAS   I will not bring this pain upon us both,
neither on you nor on myself. Why is it
you question me and waste your labour? I   360
will tell you nothing.

OEDIPUS   You would provoke a stone! Tell us, you villain,
tell us, and do not stand there quietly
unmoved and balking at the issue.

TEIRESIAS You blame my temper but you do not see   365
your own that lives within you;[7] it is me
you chide.

OEDIPUS Who would not feel his temper rise
at words like these with which you shame our city?

TEIRESIAS Of themselves things will come, although I hide them   370
and breathe no word of them.

OEDIPUS   Since they will come
tell them to me.

TEIRESIAS   I will say nothing further.
Against this answer let your temper rage
as wildly as you will.

OEDIPUS   Indeed I am
so angry I shall not hold back a jot   375
of what I think. For I would have you know
I think you were complotter of the deed
and doer of the deed save in so far
as for the actual killing. Had you had eyes
I would have said alone you murdered him.   380

TEIRESIAS Yes? Then I warn you faithfully to keep
the letter of your proclamation and
from this day forth to speak no word of greeting
to these nor me; you are the land's pollution.

OEDIPUS How shamelessly you started up this taunt!   385
How do you think you will escape?

TEIRESIAS   I have.
I have escaped; the truth is what I cherish
and that's my strength.

OEDIPUS   And who has taught you truth?
Not your profession surely!

TEIRESIAS   You have taught me,
for you have made me speak against my will.   390

OEDIPUS Speak what? Tell me again that I may learn it better.

TEIRESIAS Did you not understand before or would you
provoke me into speaking?

OEDIPUS   I did not grasp it,
not so to call it known. Say it again.

TEIRESIAS I say you are the murderer of the king   395
whose murderer you seek.

OEDIPUS   Not twice you shall
say calumnies like this and stay unpunished.

TEIRESIAS Shall I say more to tempt your anger more?

OEDIPUS As much as you desire; it will be said
in vain.   400

TEIRESIAS I say that with those you love best
you live in foulest shame unconsciously

7. "Temper" in the original Greek is a femi-   the one "that lives within you," i.e., Jocasta.
nine noun, and there is a veiled reference to

and do not see where you are in calamity.
OEDIPUS   Do you imagine you can always talk
   like this, and live to laugh at it hereafter?   405
TEIRESIAS   Yes, if the truth has anything of strength.
OEDIPUS   It has, but not for you; it has no strength
   for you because you are blind in mind and ears
   as well as in your eyes.
TEIRESIAS   You are a poor wretch
   to taunt me with the very insults which   410
   everyone soon will heap upon yourself.
OEDIPUS   Your life is one long night so that you cannot
   hurt me or any other who sees the light.
TEIRESIAS   It is not fate that I should be your ruin,
   Apollo is enough; it is his care   415
   to work this out.
OEDIPUS   Was this your own design
   or Creon's?
TEIRESIAS   Creon is no hurt to you,
   but you are to yourself.
OEDIPUS   Wealth, sovereignty, and skill outmatching skill
   for the contrivance of an envied life!   420
   Great store of jealousy fill your treasury chests,
   if my friend Creon, friend from the first and loyal,
   thus secretly attacks me, secretly
   desires to drive me out and secretly
   suborns this juggling, trick-devising quack,   425
   this wily beggar who has only eyes
   for his own gains, but blindness in his skill.
   For, tell me, where have you seen clear, Teiresias,
   with your prophetic eyes? When the dark singer,
   the Sphinx, was in your country, did you speak   430
   word of deliverance to its citizens?
   And yet the riddle's answer was not the province
   of a chance comer. It was a prophet's task
   and plainly you had no such gift of prophecy
   from birds nor otherwise from any god   435
   to glean a word of knowledge. But I came,
   Oedipus, who knew nothing, and I stopped her.
   I solved the riddle by my wit alone.
   Mine was no knowledge got from birds. And now
   you would expel me,   440
   because you think that you will find a place
   by Creon's throne. I think you will be sorry,
   both you and your accomplice, for your plot
   to drive me out. And did I not regard you
   as an old man, some suffering would have taught you   445
   that what was in your heart was treason.
CHORUS   We look at this man's words and yours, my king,
   and we find both have spoken them in anger.

We need no angry words but only thought
how we may best hit the god's meaning for us.   450
TEIRESIAS   If you are king, at least I have the right
no less to speak in my defence against you.
Of that much I am master. I am no slave
of yours, but Loxias',[8] and so I shall not
enroll myself with Creon for my patron.   455
Since you have taunted me with being blind,
here is my word for you.
You have your eyes but see not where you are
in sin, nor where you live, nor whom you live with.
Do you know who your parents are? Unknowing   460
you are an enemy to kith and kin
in death, beneath the earth, and in this life.
A deadly footed, double striking curse,
from father and mother both, shall drive you forth
out of this land, with darkness on your eyes,   465
that now have such straight vision. Shall there be
a place will not be harbour to your cries,
a corner of Cithaeron[9] will not ring
in echo to your cries, soon, soon,—
when you shall learn the secret of your marriage,   470
which steered you to a haven in this house,—
haven no haven, after lucky voyage?
And of the multitude of other evils
establishing a grim equality
between you and your children, you know nothing.   475
So, muddy with contempt my words and Creon's!
Misery shall grind no man as it will you.
OEDIPUS   Is it endurable that I should hear
such words from him? Go and a curse go with you!
Quick, home with you! Out of my house at once!   480
TEIRESIAS   I would not have come either had you not called me.
OEDIPUS   I did not know then you would talk like a fool—
or it would have been long before I called you.
TEIRESIAS   I am a fool then, as it seems to you—
but to the parents who have bred you, wise.   485
OEDIPUS   What parents? Stop! Who are they of all the world?
TEIRESIAS   This day will show your birth and will destroy you.
OEDIPUS   How needlessly your riddles darken everything.
TEIRESIAS   But it's in riddle answering you are strongest.
OEDIPUS   Yes. Taunt me where you will find me great.   490
TEIRESIAS   It is this very luck that has destroyed you.
OEDIPUS   I do not care, if it has saved this city.
TEIRESIAS   Well, I will go. Come, boy, lead me away.
OEDIPUS   Yes, lead him off. So long as you are here,

8. Loxias is a title of Apollo.
9. Mountain range near Thebes, where Oedipus was left to die as a baby.

you'll be a stumbling block and a vexation;   495
once gone, you will not trouble me again.

TEIRESIAS   I have said
what I came here to say not fearing your
countenance: there is no way you can hurt me.
I tell you, king, this man, this murderer
(whom you have long declared you are in search of,   500
indicting him in threatening proclamation
as murderer of Laius)—he is here.
In name he is a stranger among citizens
but soon he will be shown to be a citizen
true native Theban, and he'll have no joy   505
of the discovery: blindness for sight
and beggary for riches his exchange,
he shall go journeying to a foreign country
tapping his way before him with a stick.
He shall be proved father and brother both   510
to his own children in his house; to her
that gave him birth, a son and husband both;
a fellow sower in his father's bed
with that same father that he murdered.
Go within, reckon that out, and if you find me   515
mistaken, say I have no skill in prophecy.

   [*Exeunt separately* TEIRESIAS *and* OEDIPUS.]

CHORUS STROPHE   Who is the man proclaimed
   by Delphi's prophetic rock
   as the bloody-handed murderer,
   the doer of deeds that none dare name?   520
   Now is the time for him to run
   with a stronger foot
   than Pegasus[1]
   for the child of Zeus leaps in arms upon him
   with fire and the lightning bolt,   525
   and terribly close on his heels
   are the Fates that never miss.
ANTISTROPHE   Lately from snowy Parnassus[2]
   clearly the voice flashed forth,
   bidding each Theban track him down,   530
   the unknown murderer.
   In the savage forests he lurks and in
   the caverns like
   the mountain bull.
   He is sad and lonely, and lonely his feet   535
   that carry him far from the navel of earth;[3]
   but its prophecies, ever living,
   flutter around his head.

1. Divine winged horse.   3. Delphi was imagined to be the center of
2. Mountain in central Greece near Delphi   the earth and hence its navel.
and thus sacred to Apollo.

STROPHE The augur has spread confusion,
    terrible confusion;   540
    I do not approve what was said
    nor can I deny it.
    I do not know what to say;
    I am in a flutter of foreboding;
    I never heard in the present   545
    nor past of a quarrel between
    the sons of Labdacus and Polybus,[4]
    that I might bring as proof
    in attacking the popular fame
    of Oedipus, seeking   550
    to take vengeance for undiscovered
    death in the line of Labdacus.

ANTISTROPHE Truly Zeus and Apollo are wise
    and in human things all knowing;
    but amongst men there is no   555
    distinct judgment, between the prophet
    and me—which of us is right.
    One man may pass another in wisdom
    but I would never agree
    with those that find fault with the king   560
    till I should see the word
    proved right beyond doubt. For once
    in visible form the Sphinx
    came on him and all of us
    saw his wisdom and in that test   565
    he saved the city. So he will not be condemned by my mind.
        [*Enter* CREON.]

CREON Citizens, I have come because I heard
    deadly words spread about me, that the king
    accuses me. I cannot take that from him.
    If he believes that in these present troubles   570
    he has been wronged by me in word or deed
    I do not want to live on with the burden
    of such a scandal on me. The report
    injures me doubly and most vitally—
    for I'll be called a traitor to my city   575
    and traitor also to my friends and you.

CHORUS Perhaps it was a sudden gust of anger
    that forced that insult from him, and no judgment.

CREON But did he say that it was in compliance
    with schemes of mine that the seer told him lies?   580

CHORUS Yes, he said that, but why, I do not know.

CREON Were his eyes straight in his head? Was his mind right
    when he accused me in this fashion?

---

4. Polybus is Oedipus's adoptive father, the king of Corinth, husband of Merope.

CHORUS   I do not know; I have no eyes to see
   what princes do. Here comes the king himself.   585
      [*Enter* OEDIPUS.]
OEDIPUS   You, sir, how is it you come here? Have you so much
   brazen-faced daring that you venture in
   my house although you are proved manifestly
   the murderer of that man, and though you tried,
   openly, highway robbery of my crown?   590
   For god's sake, tell me what you saw in me,
   what cowardice or what stupidity,
   that made you lay a plot like this against me?
   Did you imagine I should not observe
   the crafty scheme that stole upon me or   595
   seeing it, take no means to counter it?
   Was it not stupid of you to make the attempt,
   to try to hunt down royal power without
   the people at your back or friends? For only
   with the people at your back or money can   600
   the hunt end in the capture of a crown.
CREON   Do you know what you're doing? Will you listen
   to words to answer yours, and then pass judgment?
OEDIPUS   You're quick to speak, but I am slow to grasp you,
   for I have found you dangerous,—and my foe.   605
CREON   First of all hear what I shall say to that.
OEDIPUS   At least don't tell me that you are not guilty.
CREON   If you think obstinacy without wisdom
   a valuable possession, you are wrong.
OEDIPUS   And you are wrong if you believe that one,   610
   a criminal, will not be punished only
   because he is my kinsman.
CREON   This is but just—
   but tell me, then, of what offense I'm guilty?
OEDIPUS   Did you or did you not urge me to send
   to this prophetic mumbler?
CREON   I did indeed,   615
   and I shall stand by what I told you.
OEDIPUS   How long ago is it since Laius . . . .
CREON   What about Laius? I don't understand.
OEDIPUS   Vanished—died—was murdered?
CREON   It is long,
   a long, long time to reckon.
OEDIPUS   Was this prophet   620
   in the profession then?
CREON   He was, and honoured
   as highly as he is today.
OEDIPUS   At that time did he say a word about me?
CREON   Never, at least when I was near him.
OEDIPUS   You never made a search for the dead man?   625
CREON   We searched, indeed, but never learned of anything.

OEDIPUS   Why did our wise old friend not say this then?

CREON   I don't know; and when I know nothing, I
usually hold my tongue.

OEDIPUS   You know this much,
and can declare this much if you are loyal.   630

CREON   What is it? If I know, I'll not deny it.

OEDIPUS   That he would not have said that I killed Laius
had he not met you first.

CREON   You know yourself
whether he said this, but I demand that I
should hear as much from you as you from me.   635

OEDIPUS   Then hear,—I'll not be proved a murderer.

CREON   Well, then. You're married to my sister.

OEDIPUS   Yes,
that I am not disposed to deny.

CREON   You rule
this country giving her an equal share
in the government?

OEDIPUS   Yes, everything she wants   640
she has from me.

CREON   And I, as thirdsman to you,
am rated as the equal of you two?

OEDIPUS   Yes, and it's there you've proved yourself false friend.

CREON   Not if you will reflect on it as I do.
Consider, first, if you think anyone   645
would choose to rule and fear rather than rule
and sleep untroubled by a fear if power
were equal in both cases. I, at least,
I was not born with such a frantic yearning
to be a king—but to do what kings do.   650
And so it is with everyone who has learned
wisdom and self-control. As it stands now,
the prizes are all mine—and without fear.
But if I were the king myself, I must
do much that went against the grain.   655
How should despotic rule seem sweeter to me
than painless power and an assured authority?
I am not so besotted yet that I
want other honours than those that come with profit.
Now every man's my pleasure; every man greets me;   660
now those who are your suitors fawn on me,—
success for them depends upon my favour.
Why should I let all this go to win that?
My mind would not be traitor if it's wise;
I am no treason lover, of my nature,   665
nor would I ever dare to join a plot.
Prove what I say. Go to the oracle
at Pytho and inquire about the answers,
if they are as I told you. For the rest,

if you discover I laid any plot 670
together with the seer kill me, I say,
not only by your vote but by my own.
But do not charge me on obscure opinion
without some proof to back it. It's not just
lightly to count your knaves as honest men, 675
nor honest men as knaves. To throw away
an honest friend is, as it were, to throw
your life away, which a man loves the best.
In time you will know all with certainty;
time is the only test of honest men, 680
one day is space enough to know a rogue.

CHORUS   His words are wise, king, if one fears to fall.
Those who are quick of temper are not safe.

OEDIPUS   When he that plots against me secretly
moves quickly, I must quickly counterplot. 685
If I wait taking no decisive measure
his business will be done, and mine be spoiled.

CREON   What do you want to do then? Banish me?

OEDIPUS   No, certainly; kill you, not banish you.[5]

CREON   I do not think that you've your wits about you. 690

OEDIPUS   For my own interests, yes.

CREON   But for mine, too,
you should think equally.

OEDIPUS   You are a rogue.

CREON   Suppose you do not understand?

OEDIPUS   But yet
I must be ruler.

CREON   Not if you rule badly.

OEDIPUS   O city, city!

CREON   I too have some share 695
in the city; it is not yours alone.

CHORUS   Stop, my lords! Here—and in the nick of time
I see Jocasta coming from the house;
with her help lay the quarrel that now stirs you.
            [Enter JOCASTA.]

JOCASTA   For shame! Why have you raised this foolish squabbling 700
brawl? Are you not ashamed to air your private
griefs when the country's sick? Go in, you, Oedipus,
and you, too, Creon, into the house. Don't magnify
your nothing troubles.

CREON   Sister, Oedipus,
your husband, thinks he has the right to do 705
terrible wrongs—he has but to choose between

---

5. Two lines omitted here owing to the confusion in the dialogue consequent on the loss of a
third line. In the omitted lines, Oedipus accuses the Chorus of being jealous, and the Chorus
accuses Oedipus of lacking trust.

two terrors: banishing or killing me.
OEDIPUS   He's right, Jocasta; for I find him plotting
with knavish tricks against my person.
CREON   That god may never bless me! May I die   710
accursed, if I have been guilty of
one tittle of the charge you bring against me!
JOCASTA   I beg you, Oedipus, trust him in this,
spare him for the sake of this his oath to god,
for my sake, and the sake of those who stand here.   715
CHORUS[6]   Be gracious, be merciful,
we beg of you.
OEDIPUS   In what would you have me yield?
CHORUS   He has been no silly child in the past.
He is strong in his oath now.   720
Spare him.
OEDIPUS   Do you know what you ask?
CHORUS   Yes.
OEDIPUS   Tell me then.
CHORUS   He has been your friend before all men's eyes; do not cast him   725
away dishonoured on an obscure conjecture.
OEDIPUS   I would have you know that this request of yours
really requests my death or banishment.
CHORUS   May the Sun god, king of gods, forbid! May I die without god's
blessing, without friends' help, if I had any such thought. But my   730
spirit is broken by my unhappiness for my wasting country; and
this would but add troubles amongst ourselves to the other
troubles.
OEDIPUS   Well, let him go then—if I must die ten times for it,
or be sent out dishonoured into exile.   735
It is your lips that prayed for him I pitied,
not his; wherever he is, I shall hate him.
CREON   I see you sulk in yielding and you're dangerous
when you are out of temper; natures like yours
are justly heaviest for themselves to bear.   740
OEDIPUS   Leave me alone! Take yourself off, I tell you.
CREON   I'll go, you have not known me, but they have,
and they have known my innocence.
        [Exit.]
CHORUS   Won't you take him inside, lady?
JOCASTA   Yes, when I've found out what was the matter.   745
CHORUS   There was some misconceived suspicion of a story, and on the
other side the sting of injustice.
JOCASTA   So, on both sides?
CHORUS   Yes.
JOCASTA   What was the story?   750

6. The meter changes in the original, marking an increase in emotional intensity, with presumably a different musical accompaniment.

CHORUS I think it best, in the interests of the country, to leave it where
it ended.

OEDIPUS You see where you have ended, straight of judgment
although you are, by softening my anger.

CHORUS Sir, I have said before and I say again—be sure that I would have   755
been proved a madman, bankrupt in sane council, if I should put
you away, you who steered the country I love safely when she
was crazed with troubles. God grant that now, too, you may
prove a fortunate guide for us.

JOCASTA Tell me, my lord, I beg of you, what was it   760
that roused your anger so?

OEDIPUS   Yes, I will tell you.
I honour you more than I honour them.
It was Creon and the plots he laid against me.

JOCASTA Tell me—if you can clearly tell the quarrel—

OEDIPUS   Creon says
that I'm the murderer of Laius.   765

JOCASTA Of his own knowledge or on information?

OEDIPUS He sent this rascal prophet to me, since
he keeps his own mouth clean of any guilt.

JOCASTA Do not concern yourself about this matter;
listen to me and learn that human beings   770
have no part in the craft of prophecy.
Of that I'll show you a short proof.
There was an oracle once that came to Laius,—
I will not say that it was Phoebus' own,
but it was from his servants—and it told him   775
that it was fate that he should die a victim
at the hands of his own son, a son to be born
of Laius and me. But, see now, he,
the king, was killed by foreign highway robbers
at a place where three roads meet—so goes the story;   780
and for the son—before three days were out
after his birth King Laius pierced his ankles
and by the hands of others cast him forth
upon a pathless hillside. So Apollo
failed to fulfill his oracle to the son,   785
that he should kill his father, and to Laius
also proved false in that the thing he feared,
death at his son's hands, never came to pass.
So clear in this case were the oracles,
so clear and false. Give them no heed, I say;   790
what god discovers need of, easily
he shows to us himself.

OEDIPUS   O dear Jocasta,
as I hear this from you, there comes upon me
a wandering of the soul—I could run mad.

JOCASTA What trouble is it, that you turn again   795
and speak like this?

OEDIPUS I thought I heard you say
that Laius was killed at a crossroads.

JOCASTA Yes, that was how the story went and still
that word goes round.

OEDIPUS Where is this place, Jocasta,
where he was murdered?

JOCASTA Phocis is the country   800
and the road splits there, one of two roads from Delphi,
another comes from Daulia.

OEDIPUS How long ago is this?

JOCASTA The news came to the city just before
you became king and all men's eyes looked to you.
What is it, Oedipus, that's in your mind?   805

OEDIPUS What have you designed, O Zeus, to do with me?

JOCASTA What is the thought that troubles your heart?

OEDIPUS Don't ask me yet—tell me of Laius—
How did he look? How old or young was he?

JOCASTA He was a tall man and his hair was grizzled   810
already—nearly white—and in his form
not unlike you.

OEDIPUS O god, I think I have
called curses on myself in ignorance.

JOCASTA What do you mean? I am terrified
when I look at you.

OEDIPUS I have a deadly fear   815
that the old seer had eyes. You'll show me more
if you can tell me one more thing.

JOCASTA I will.
I'm frightened,—but if I can understand,
I'll tell you all you ask.

OEDIPUS How was his company?
Had he few with him when he went this journey,   820
or many servants, as would suit a prince?

JOCASTA In all there were but five, and among them
a herald; and one carriage for the king.

OEDIPUS It's plain—its plain—who was it told you this?

JOCASTA The only servant that escaped safe home.   825

OEDIPUS Is he at home now?

JOCASTA No, when he came home again
and saw you king and Laius was dead,
he came to me and touched my hand and begged
that I should send him to the fields to be
my shepherd and so he might see the city   830
as far off as he might. So I
sent him away. He was an honest man,
as slaves go, and was worthy of far more
than what he asked of me.

OEDIPUS O, how I wish that he could come back quickly!   835

JOCASTA He can. Why is your heart so set on this?

OEDIPUS O dear Jocasta, I am full of fears
    that I have spoken far too much; and therefore
    I wish to see this shepherd.
JOCASTA   He will come;
    but, Oedipus, I think I'm worthy too   840
    to know what it is that disquiets you.
OEDIPUS It shall not be kept from you, since my mind
    has gone so far with its forebodings. Whom
    should I confide in rather than you, who is there
    of more importance to me who have passed   845
    through such a fortune?
    Polybus was my father, king of Corinth,
    and Merope, the Dorian, my mother.
    I was held greatest of the citizens
    in Corinth till a curious chance befell me   850
    as I shall tell you—curious, indeed,
    but hardly worth the store I set upon it.
    There was a dinner and at it a man,
    a drunken man, accused me in his drink
    of being bastard. I was furious   855
    but held my temper under for that day.
    Next day I went and taxed my parents with it;
    they took the insult very ill from him,
    the drunken fellow who had uttered it.
    So I was comforted for their part, but   860
    still this thing rankled always, for the story
    crept about widely. And I went at last
    to Pytho, though my parents did not know.
    But Phoebus sent me home again unhonoured
    in what I came to learn, but he foretold   865
    other and desperate horrors to befall me,
    that I was fated to lie with my mother,
    and show to daylight an accursed breed
    which men would not endure, and I was doomed
    to be murderer of the father that begot me.   870
    When I heard this I fled, and in the days
    that followed I would measure from the stars
    the whereabouts of Corinth—yes, I fled
    to somewhere where I should not see fulfilled
    the infamies told in that dreadful oracle.   875
    And as I journeyed I came to the place
    where, as you say, this king met with his death.
    Jocasta, I will tell you the whole truth.
    When I was near the branching of the crossroads,
    going on foot, I was encountered by   880
    a herald and a carriage with a man in it,
    just as you tell me. He that led the way
    and the old man himself wanted to thrust me

out of the road by force. I became angry
and struck the coachman who was pushing me. 885
When the old man saw this he watched his moment,
and as I passed he struck me from his carriage,
full on the head with his two-pointed goad.
But he was paid in full and presently
my stick had struck him backwards from the car 890
and he rolled out of it. And then I killed them
all. If it happened there was any tie
of kinship twixt this man and Laius,
who is then now more miserable than I,
what man on earth so hated by the gods, 895
since neither citizen nor foreigner
may welcome me at home or even greet me,
but drive me out of doors? And it is I,
I and no other have so cursed myself.
And I pollute the bed of him I killed 900
by the hands that killed him. Was I not born evil?
Am I not utterly unclean? I had to fly
and in my banishment not even see
my kindred nor set foot in my own country,
or otherwise my fate was to be yoked 905
in marriage with my mother and kill my father,
Polybus who begot me and had reared me.
Would not one rightly judge and say that on me
these things were sent by some malignant god?
O no, no, no—O holy majesty 910
of god on high, may I not see that day!
May I be gone out of men's sight before
I see the deadly taint of this disaster
come upon me.

CHORUS   Sir, we too fear these things. But until you see this man face to 915
face and hear his story, hope.

OEDIPUS   Yes, I have just this much of hope—to wait until the herdsman
comes.

JOCASTA   And when he comes, what do you want with him?

OEDIPUS   I'll tell you; if I find that his story is the same as yours, I at least 920
will be clear of this guilt.

JOCASTA   Why—what so particularly did you learn from my story?

OEDIPUS   You said that he spoke of highway *robbers* who killed Laius. Now
if he uses the same number, it was not I who killed him. One man
cannot be the same as many. But if he speaks of a man travelling
alone, then clearly the burden of the guilt inclines towards me. 925

JOCASTA   Be sure, at least, that this was how he told the story. He cannot
unsay it now, for every one in the city heard it—not I alone. But,
Oedipus, even if he diverges from what he said then, he shall
never prove that the murder of Laius squares rightly with the
prophecy—for Loxias declared that the king should be killed by 930

his own son. And that poor creature did not kill him surely,—
for he died himself first. So as far as prophecy goes, henceforward
I shall not look to the right hand or the left.

OEDIPUS   Right. But yet, send someone for the peasant to bring him here;   935
do not neglect it.

JOCASTA   I will send quickly. Now let me go indoors. I will do nothing
except what pleases you.
        [*Exeunt.*]

CHORUS STROPHE   May destiny ever find me
pious in word and deed
prescribed by the laws that live on high: 940
laws begotten in the clear air of heaven,
whose only father is Olympus;
no mortal nature brought them to birth,
no forgetfulness shall lull them to sleep;
for the god is great in them and grows not old.   945

ANTISTROPHE   Insolence[7] breeds the tyrant, insolence
if it is glutted with a surfeit, unseasonable, unprofitable,
climbs to the rooftop and plunges
sheer down to the ruin that must be,
and there its feet are no service.   950
But I pray that the god may never
abolish the eager ambition that profits the state.
For I shall never cease to hold the god as our protector.

STROPHE   If a man walks with haughtiness
of hand or word and gives no heed   955
to Justice and the shrines of gods
despises—may an evil doom
smite him for his ill-starred pride of heart!—
if he reaps gains without justice
and will not hold from impiety   960
and his fingers itch for untouchable things.
When such things are done, what man shall contrive
to shield his soul from the shafts of the god?
When such deeds are held in honour,
why should I honour the gods in the dance?[8]   965

ANTISTROPHE   No longer to the holy place,
to the navel of earth I'll go
to worship, nor to Abae
nor to Olympia,[9]
unless the oracles are proved to fit,   970
for all men's hands to point at.
O Zeus, if you are rightly called
the sovereign lord, all-mastering,

---

7. The word in Greek for "insolence" is *hybris*,
which usually connotes violence.
8. The Greek verb used here, *choreuein*, connotes "dance in a chorus," linking the mythi-

cal drama to the real theatrical performance.
9. Home to a great sanctuary of Zeus and Hera.
"The navel of earth": Delphi. "Abae": oracular
site near Thebes.

let this not escape you nor your ever-living power!
The oracles concerning Laius   975
are old and dim and men regard them not.
Apollo is nowhere clear in honour; god's service perishes.

    [*Enter* JOCASTA, *carrying garlands.*]

JOCASTA   Princes of the land, I have had the thought to go
to the gods' temples, bringing in my hand
garlands and gifts of incense, as you see.   980
For Oedipus excites himself too much
at every sort of trouble, not conjecturing,
like a man of sense, what will be from what was,
but he is always at the speaker's mercy,
when he speaks terrors. I can do no good   985
by my advice, and so I came as suppliant
to you, Lycaean Apollo,[1] who are nearest.
These are the symbols of my prayer and this
my prayer: grant us escape free of the curse.
Now when we look to him we are all afraid;   990
he's pilot of our ship and he is frightened.

    [*Enter* MESSENGER.]

MESSENGER   Might I learn from you, sirs, where is the house of Oedipus?
Or best of all, if you know, where is the king himself?

CHORUS   This is his house and he is within doors. This lady is his wife
and mother of his children.   995

MESSENGER   God bless you, lady, and god bless your household! God
bless Oedipus' noble wife!

JOCASTA   God bless you, sir, for your kind greeting! What do you want
of us that you have come here? What have you to tell us?

MESSENGER   Good news, lady. Good for your house and for your husband.   1000

JOCASTA   What is your news? Who sent you to us?

MESSENGER   I come from Corinth and the news I bring will give you
    pleasure.
Perhaps a little pain too.

JOCASTA   What is this news of double meaning?   1005

MESSENGER   The people of the Isthmus will choose Oedipus to be
    their king.
That is the rumour there.

JOCASTA   But isn't their king still old Polybus?

MESSENGER   No. He is in his grave. Death has got him.   1010

JOCASTA   Is that the truth? Is Oedipus' father dead?

MESSENGER   May I die myself if it be otherwise!

JOCASTA (*to a servant*)   Be quick and run to the king with the news!
O oracles of the gods, where are you now? It was from this man
Oedipus fled, lest he should be his murderer! And now he is dead,   1015
in the course of nature, and not killed by Oedipus.

    [*Enter* OEDIPUS.]

OEDIPUS   Dearest Jocasta, why have you sent for me?

---

1. Apollo was worshipped in rituals on Mount Lycaeon—literally, "Wolf Mountain."

JOCASTA   Listen to this man and when you hear reflect what is the outcome of the holy oracles of the gods.

OEDIPUS   Who is he? What is his message for me?   1020

JOCASTA   He is from Corinth and he tells us that your father Polybus is
dead and gone.

OEDIPUS   What's this you say, sir? Tell me yourself.

MESSENGER   Since this is the first matter you want clearly told:
Polybus has gone down to death. You may be sure of it.   1025

OEDIPUS   By treachery or sickness?

MESSENGER   A small thing will put old bodies asleep.

OEDIPUS   So he died of sickness, it seems,—poor old man!

MESSENGER   Yes, and of age—the long years he had measured.

OEDIPUS   Ha! Ha! O dear Jocasta, why should one   1030
look to the Pythian hearth? Why should one look
to the birds screaming overhead? They prophesied
that I should kill my father! But he's dead,
and hidden deep in earth, and I stand here
who never laid a hand on spear against him,—   1035
unless perhaps he died of longing for me,
and thus I am his murderer. But they,
the oracles, as they stand—he's taken them
away with him, they're dead as he himself is,
and worthless.

JOCASTA   That I told you before now.   1040

OEDIPUS   You did, but I was misled by my fear.

JOCASTA   Then lay no more of them to heart, not one.

OEDIPUS   But surely I must fear my mother's bed?

JOCASTA   Why should man fear since chance is all in all
for him, and he can clearly foreknow nothing?   1045
Best to live lightly, as one can, unthinkingly.
As to your mother's marriage bed,—don't fear it.
Before this, in dreams too, as well as oracles,
many a man has lain with his own mother.
But he to whom such things are nothing bears   1050
his life most easily.

OEDIPUS   All that you say would be said perfectly
if she were dead; but since she lives I must
still fear, although you talk so well, Jocasta.

JOCASTA   Still in your father's death there's light of comfort?   1055

OEDIPUS   Great light of comfort; but I fear the living.

MESSENGER   Who is the woman that makes you afraid?

OEDIPUS   Merope, old man, Polybus' wife.

MESSENGER   What about her frightens the queen and you?

OEDIPUS   A terrible oracle, stranger, from the gods.   1060

MESSENGER   Can it be told? Or does the sacred law
forbid another to have knowledge of it?

OEDIPUS   O no! Once on a time Loxias said
that I should lie with my own mother and
take on my hands the blood of my own father.   1065

And so for these long years I've lived away
from Corinth; it has been to my great happiness;
but yet it's sweet to see the face of parents.

MESSENGER   This was the fear which drove you out of Corinth?

OEDIPUS   Old man, I did not wish to kill my father.   1070

MESSENGER   Why should I not free you from this fear, sir,
since I have come to you in all goodwill?

OEDIPUS   You would not find me thankless if you did.

MESSENGER   Why, it was just for this I brought the news,—
to earn your thanks when you had come safe home.   1075

OEDIPUS   No, I will never come near my parents.

MESSENGER   Son,
it's very plain you don't know what you're doing.

OEDIPUS   What do you mean, old man? For god's sake, tell me.

MESSENGER   If your homecoming is checked by fears like these.

OEDIPUS   Yes, I'm afraid that Phoebus may prove right.   1080

MESSENGER   The murder and the incest?

OEDIPUS   Yes, old man;
that is my constant terror.

MESSENGER   Do you know
that all your fears are empty?

OEDIPUS   How is that,
if they are father and mother and I their son?

MESSENGER   Because Polybus was no kin to you in blood.   1085

OEDIPUS   What, was not Polybus my father?

MESSENGER   No more than I but just so much.

OEDIPUS   How can
my father be my father as much as one
that's nothing to me?

MESSENGER   Neither he nor I
begat you.   1090

OEDIPUS   Why then did he call me son?

MESSENGER   A gift he took you from these hands of mine.

OEDIPUS   Did he love so much what he took from another's hand?

MESSENGER   His childlessness before persuaded him.

OEDIPUS   Was I a child you bought or found when I   1095
was given to him?

MESSENGER   On Cithaeron's slopes
in the twisting thickets you were found.

OEDIPUS   And why
were you a traveller in those parts?

MESSENGER   I was   1100
in charge of mountain flocks.

OEDIPUS   You were a shepherd?
A hireling vagrant?

MESSENGER   Yes, but at least at that time
the man that saved your life, son.

OEDIPUS   What ailed me when you took me in your arms?

MESSENGER   In that your ankles should be witnesses.   1105

OEDIPUS   Why do you speak of that old pain?
MESSENGER   I loosed you;
  the tendons of your feet were pierced and fettered,—
OEDIPUS   My swaddling clothes brought me a rare disgrace.
MESSENGER   So that from this you're called your present name.[2]
OEDIPUS   Was this my father's doing or my mother's?   1110
  For god's sake, tell me.
MESSENGER   I don't know, but he
  who gave you to me has more knowledge than I.
OEDIPUS   You yourself did not find me then? You took me
  from someone else?
MESSENGER   Yes, from another shepherd.   1115
OEDIPUS   Who was he? Do you know him well enough
  to tell?
MESSENGER   He was called Laius' man.
OEDIPUS   You mean the king who reigned here in the old days?
MESSENGER   Yes, he was that man's shepherd.
OEDIPUS   Is he alive   1120
  still, so that I could see him?
MESSENGER   You who live here
  would know that best.
OEDIPUS   Do any of you here
  know of this shepherd whom he speaks about
  in town or in the fields? Tell me. It's time
  that this was found out once for all.   1125
CHORUS   I think he is none other than the peasant
  whom you have sought to see already; but
  Jocasta here can tell us best of that.
OEDIPUS   Jocasta, do you know about this man
  whom we have sent for? Is he the man he mentions?   1130
JOCASTA   Why ask of whom he spoke? Don't give it heed;
  nor try to keep in mind what has been said.
  It will be wasted labour.
OEDIPUS   With such clues
  I could not fail to bring my birth to light.
JOCASTA   I beg you—do not hunt this out—I beg you,   1135
  if you have any care for your own life.
  What I am suffering is enough.
OEDIPUS   Keep up
  your heart, Jocasta. Though I'm proved a slave,
  thrice slave, and though my mother is thrice slave,
  you'll not be shown to be of lowly lineage.   1140
JOCASTA   O be persuaded by me, I entreat you;
  do not do this.
OEDIPUS   I will not be persuaded to let be
  the chance of finding out the whole thing clearly.

---

2. The name "Oedipus" suggests "swollen foot."

JOCASTA   It is because I wish you well that I   1145
  give you this counsel—and it's the best counsel.
OEDIPUS   Then the best counsel vexes me, and has
  for some while since.
JOCASTA   Oedipus, may the god help you!
  God keep you from the knowledge of who you are!
OEDIPUS   Here, someone, go and fetch the shepherd for me;   1150
  and let her find her joy in her rich family!
JOCASTA   O Oedipus, unhappy Oedipus!
  that is all I can call you, and the last thing
  that I shall ever call you.
      [*Exit.*]
CHORUS   Why has the queen gone, Oedipus, in wild   1155
  grief rushing from us? I am afraid that trouble
  Will break out of this silence.
OEDIPUS   Break out what will! I at least shall be
  willing to see my ancestry, though humble.
  Perhaps she is ashamed of my low birth,   1160
  for she has all a woman's high-flown pride.
  But I account myself a child of Fortune,
  beneficent Fortune, and I shall not be
  dishonoured. She's the mother from whom I spring;
  the months, my brothers, marked me, now as small,   1165
  and now again as mighty. Such is my breeding,
  and I shall never prove so false to it,
  as not to find the secret of my birth.
CHORUS STROPHE   If I am a prophet and wise of heart
  you shall not fail, Cithaeron,   1170
  by the limitless sky, you shall not!—
  to know at tomorrow's full moon
  that Oedipus honours you,
  as native to him and mother and nurse at once;
  and that you are honoured in dancing by us, as finding favour in   1175
      sight of our king.
  Apollo, to whom we cry, find these things pleasing!
ANTISTROPHE   Who was it bore you, child? One of
  the long-lived nymphs who lay with Pan—
  the father who treads the hills?[3]   1180
  Or was she a bride of Loxias, your mother? The grassy slopes
  are all of them dear to him. Or perhaps Cyllene's king
  or the Bacchants' god that lives on the tops
  of the hills received you a gift from some
  one of the Helicon[4] nymphs, with whom he mostly plays?   1185
      [*Enter an old man, led by* OEDIPUS' *servants.*]

3. Pan was a countryside god, patron of shepherds.
4. A mountain in Boeotia, supposedly inhabited by the Muses as well as nymphs (female nature spirits). Dionysus ("the Bacchants' god"), like Pan and the messenger god, Hermes ("Cyllene's king"), haunted the wild places.

OEDIPUS   If someone like myself who never met him
   may make a guess,—I think this is the herdsman,
   whom we were seeking. His old age is consonant
   with the other. And besides, the men who bring him
   I recognize as my own servants. You   1190
   perhaps may better me in knowledge since
   you've seen the man before.
CHORUS   You can be sure
   I recognize him. For if Laius
   had ever an honest shepherd, this was he.
OEDIPUS   You, sir, from Corinth, I must ask you first,   1195
   is this the man you spoke of?
MESSENGER   This is he
   before your eyes.
OEDIPUS   Old man, look here at me
   and tell me what I ask you. Were you ever
   a servant of King Laius?
HERDSMAN   I was,—   1200
   no slave he bought but reared in his own house.
OEDIPUS   What did you do as work? How did you live?
HERDSMAN   Most of my life was spent among the flocks.
OEDIPUS   In what part of the country did you live?
HERDSMAN   Cithaeron and the places near to it.   1205
OEDIPUS   And somewhere there perhaps you knew this man?
HERDSMAN   What was his occupation? Who?
OEDIPUS   This man here,
   have you had any dealings with him?
HERDSMAN   No—
   not such that I can quickly call to mind.
MESSENGER   That is no wonder, master. But I'll make him   1210
   remember what he does not know. For I know, that he well
   knows the country of Cithaeron, how he with two flocks, I with
   one kept company for three years—each year half a year—from
   spring till autumn time and then when winter came I drove my
   flocks to our fold home again and he to Laius's steadings.   1215
   Well—am I right or not in what I said we did?
HERDSMAN   You're right—although it's a long time ago.
MESSENGER   Do you remember giving me a child
   to bring up as my foster child?
HERDSMAN   What's this?
   Why do you ask this question?
MESSENGER   Look, old man,   1220
   here he is—here's the man who was that child!
HERDSMAN   Death take you! Won't you hold your tongue?
OEDIPUS   No, no,
   do not find fault with him, old man. Your words
   are more at fault than his.
HERDSMAN   O best of masters,
   how do I give offense?   1225

OEDIPUS   When you refuse
  to speak about the child of whom he asks you.
HERDSMAN   He speaks out of his ignorance, without meaning.
OEDIPUS   If you'll not talk to gratify me, you
  will talk with pain to urge you.
HERDSMAN   O please, sir,
  don't hurt an old man, sir.   1230
OEDIPUS [*to the servants*]   Here, one of you,
  twist his hands behind him.
HERDSMAN   Why, gods help me, why?
  What do you want to know?
OEDIPUS   You gave a child
  to him,—the child he asked you of?
HERDSMAN   I did.
  I wish I'd died the day I did.   1235
OEDIPUS   You will
  unless you tell me truly.
HERDSMAN   And I'll die
  far worse if I should tell you.
OEDIPUS   This fellow
  is bent on more delays, as it would seem.
HERDSMAN   O no, no! I have told you that I gave it.   1240
OEDIPUS   Where did you get this child from? Was it your own or
  did you get it from another?
HERDSMAN   Not
  my own at all; I had it from someone.
OEDIPUS   One of these citizens? or from what house?
HERDSMAN   O master, please—I beg you, master, please   1245
  don't ask me more.
OEDIPUS   You're a dead man if I
  ask you again.
HERDSMAN   It was one of the children
  of Laius.
OEDIPUS   A slave? Or born in wedlock?
HERDSMAN   O gods, I am on the brink of frightful speech.   1250
OEDIPUS   And I of frightful hearing. But I must hear.
HERDSMAN   The child was called his child; but she within,
  your wife would tell you best how all this was.
OEDIPUS   She gave it to you?
HERDSMAN   Yes, she did, my lord.
OEDIPUS   To do what with it?
HERDSMAN   Make away with it.   1255
OEDIPUS   She was so hard—its mother?
HERDSMAN   Aye, through fear
  of evil oracles.
OEDIPUS   Which?
HERDSMAN   They said that he
  should kill his parents.
OEDIPUS   How was it that you   1260

gave it away to this old man?

HERDSMAN   O master,
  I pitied it, and thought that I could send it
  off to another country and this man
  was from another country. But he saved it
  for the most terrible troubles. If you are   1265
  the man he says you are, you're bred to misery.

OEDIPUS   O, O, O, they will all come,
  all come out clearly! Light of the sun, let me
  look upon you no more after today!
  I who first saw the light bred of a match   1270
  accursed, and accursed in my living
  with them I lived with, cursed in my killing.
      [*Exeunt all but the* CHORUS.]

CHORUS STROPHE   O generations of men, how I
  count you as equal with those who live
  not at all!   1275
  What man, what man on earth wins more
  of happiness than a seeming
  and after that turning away?
  Oedipus, you are my pattern of this,
  Oedipus, you and your fate!   1280
  Luckless Oedipus, whom of all men
  I envy not at all.

ANTISTROPHE   In as much as he shot his bolt
  beyond the others and won the prize
  of happiness complete—   1285
  O Zeus—and killed and reduced to nought
  the hooked taloned maid of the riddling speech,
  standing a tower against death for my land:
  hence he was called my king and hence
  was honoured the highest of all   1290
  honours; and hence he ruled
  in the great city of Thebes.

STROPHE   But now whose tale is more miserable?
  Who is there lives with a savager fate?
  Whose troubles so reverse his life as his?   1295
  O Oedipus, the famous prince
  for whom a great haven
  the same both as father and son
  sufficed for generation,
  how, O how, have the furrows ploughed   1300
  by your father endured to bear you, poor wretch,
  and hold their peace so long?

ANTISTROPHE   Time who sees all has found you out
  against your will; judges your marriage accursed,
  begetter and begot at one in it.   1305
  O child of Laius,
  would I had never seen you.

I weep for you and cry
a dirge of lamentation.
To speak directly, I drew my breath   1310
from you at the first and so now I lull
my mouth to sleep with your name.
      [*Enter a* SECOND MESSENGER.]

SECOND MESSENGER   O Princes always honoured by our country,
    what deeds you'll hear of and what horrors see,
    what grief you'll feel, if you as true-born Thebans   1315
    care for the house of Labdacus's sons.
    Phasis nor Ister[5] cannot purge this house,
    I think, with all their streams, such things
    it hides, such evils shortly will bring forth
    into the light, whether they will or not;   1320
    and troubles hurt the most
    when they prove self-inflicted.

CHORUS   What we had known before did not fall short
    of bitter groaning's worth; what's more to tell?

SECOND MESSENGER   Shortest to hear and tell—our glorious queen   1325
    Jocasta's dead.

CHORUS   Unhappy woman! How?

SECOND MESSENGER   By her own hand. The worst of what
      was done
    you cannot know. You did not see the sight.
    Yet in so far as I remember it
    You'll hear the end of our unlucky queen.   1330
    When she came raging into the house she went
    straight to her marriage bed, tearing her hair
    with both her hands, and crying upon Laius
    long dead—Do you remember, Laius,
    that night long past which bred a child for us   1335
    to send you to your death and leave
    a mother making children with her son?
    And then she groaned and cursed the bed in which
    she brought forth husband by her husband, children
    by her own child, an infamous double bond.   1340
    How after that she died I do not know,—
    for Oedipus distracted us from seeing.
    He burst upon us shouting and we looked
    to him as he paced frantically around,
    begging us always: Give me a sword, I say,   1345
    to find this wife no wife, this mother's womb,
    this field of double sowing whence I sprang
    and where I sowed my children! As he raved
    some god showed him the way—none of us there.
    Bellowing terribly and led by some   1350
    invisible guide he rushed on the two doors,—

---

5. Phasis is a large river in western Georgia; Ister is an ancient name for the Danube.

wrenching the hollow bolts out of their sockets,
he charged inside. There, there, we saw his wife
hanging, the twisted rope around her neck.
When he saw her, he cried out fearfully   1355
and cut the dangling noose. Then, as she lay,
poor woman, on the ground, what happened after,
was terrible to see. He tore the brooches—
the gold chased brooches fastening her robe—
away from her and lifting them up high   1360
dashed them on his own eyeballs, shrieking out
such things as: they will never see the crime
I have committed or had done upon me!
Dark eyes, now in the days to come look on
forbidden faces, do not recognize   1365
those whom you long for—with such imprecations
he struck his eyes again and yet again
with the brooches. And the bleeding eyeballs gushed
and stained his beard—no sluggish oozing drops
but a black rain and bloody hail poured down.   1370

So it has broken—and not on one head
but troubles mixed for husband and for wife.
The fortune of the days gone by was true
good fortune—but today groans and destruction
and death and shame—of all ills can be named   1375
not one is missing.
CHORUS   Is he now in any ease from pain?
SECOND MESSENGER   He shouts
for someone to unbar the doors and show him
to all the men of Thebes, his father's killer,
his mother's—no, I cannot say the word,   1380
it is unholy—for he'll cast himself
out of the land, he says, and not remain
to bring a curse upon his house, the curse
he called upon it in his proclamation. But
he wants for strength, aye, and someone to guide him;   1385
his sickness is too great to bear. You, too,
will be shown that. The bolts are opening.
Soon you will see a sight to waken pity
even in the horror of it.
          [Enter the blinded OEDIPUS.]
CHORUS   This is a terrible sight for men to see!   1390
I never found a worse!
Poor wretch, what madness came upon you!
What evil spirit leaped upon your life
to your ill-luck—a leap beyond man's strength!
Indeed I pity you, but I cannot   1395
look at you, though there's much I want to ask
and much to learn and much to see.

I shudder at the sight of you.

OEDIPUS   O, O,
   where am I going? Where is my voice
   borne on the wind to and fro?
   Spirit, how far have you sprung?

CHORUS   To a terrible place whereof men's ears
   may not hear, nor their eyes behold it.

OEDIPUS   Darkness!
   Horror of darkness enfolding, resistless, unspeakable visitant sped
      by an ill wind in haste!
   madness and stabbing pain and memory
   of evil deeds I have done!

CHORUS   In such misfortunes it's no wonder
   if double weighs the burden of your grief.

OEDIPUS   My friend,
   you are the only one steadfast, the only one that attends on me;
   you still stay nursing the blind man.
   Your care is not unnoticed. I can know
   your voice, although this darkness is my world.

CHORUS   Doer of dreadful deeds, how did you dare
   so far to do despite to your own eyes?
   what spirit urged you to it?

OEDIPUS   It was Apollo, friends, Apollo,
   that brought this bitter bitterness, my sorrows to completion.
   But the hand that struck me
   was none but my own.
   Why should I see
   whose vision showed me nothing sweet to see?

CHORUS   These things are as you say.

OEDIPUS   What can I see to love?
   What greeting can touch my ears with joy?
   Take me away, and haste—to a place out of the way!
   Take me away, my friends, the greatly miserable,
   the most accursed, whom the gods too hate
   above all men on earth!

CHORUS   Unhappy in your mind and your misfortune,
   would I had never known you!

OEDIPUS   Curse on the man who took
   the cruel bonds from off my legs, as I lay in the field.
   He stole me from death and saved me,
   no kindly service.
   Had I died then
   I would not be so burdensome to friends.

CHORUS   I, too, could have wished it had been so.

OEDIPUS   Then I would not have come
   to kill my father and marry my mother infamously.
   Now I am godless and child of impurity,
   begetter in the same seed that created my wretched self.
   If there is any ill worse than ill,

that is the lot of Oedipus.

CHORUS   I cannot say your remedy was good;
you would be better dead than blind and living.

OEDIPUS   What I have done here was best done—don't tell me   1450
otherwise, do not give me further counsel.
I do not know with what eyes I could look
upon my father when I die and go
under the earth, nor yet my wretched mother—
those two to whom I have done things deserving   1455
worse punishment than hanging. Would the sight
of children, bred as mine are, gladden me?
No, not these eyes, never. And my city,
its towers and sacred places of the gods,
of these I robbed my miserable self   1460
when I commanded all to drive *him* out,
the criminal since proved by god impure
and of the race of Laius.
To this guilt I bore witness against myself—
with what eyes shall I look upon my people?   1465
No. If there were a means to choke the fountain
of hearing I would not have stayed my hand
from locking up my miserable carcase,
seeing and hearing nothing; it is sweet
to keep our thoughts out of the range of hurt.   1470

Cithaeron, why did you receive me? Why
having received me did you not kill me straight?
And so I had not shown to men my birth.

O Polybus and Corinth and the house,
the old house that I used to call my father's—   1475
what fairness you were nurse to, and what foulness
festered beneath! Now I am found to be
a sinner and a son of sinners. Crossroads,
and hidden glade, oak and the narrow way
at the crossroads, that drank my father's blood   1480
offered you by my hands, do you remember
still what I did as you looked on, and what
I did when I came here? O marriage, marriage!
you bred me and again when you had bred
bred children of your child and showed to men   1485
brides, wives and mothers and the foulest deeds
that can be in this world of ours.

Come—it's unfit to say what is unfit
to do.—I beg of you in god's name hide me
somewhere outside your country, yes, or kill me,   1490
or throw me into the sea, to be forever
out of your sight. Approach and deign to touch me

for all my wretchedness, and do not fear.
No man but I can bear my evil doom.

CHORUS   Here Creon comes in fit time to perform   1495
or give advice in what you ask of us.
Creon is left sole ruler in your stead.

OEDIPUS   Creon! Creon! What shall I say to him?
How can I justly hope that he will trust me?
In what is past I have been proved towards him   1500
an utter liar.

> [*Enter* CREON.]

CREON   Oedipus, I've come
not so that I might laugh at you nor taunt you
with evil of the past. But if you still
are without shame before the face of men   1505
reverence at least the flame that gives all life,
our Lord the Sun, and do not show unveiled
to him pollution such that neither land
nor holy rain nor light of day can welcome.

> [*To a servant.*]

Be quick and take him in. It is most decent   1510
that only kin should see and hear the troubles
of kin.

OEDIPUS   I beg you, since you've torn me from
my dreadful expectations and have come
in a most noble spirit to a man   1515
that has used you vilely—do a thing for me.
I shall speak for your own good, not for my own.

CREON   What do you need that you would ask of me?

OEDIPUS   Drive me from here with all the speed you can
to where I may not hear a human voice.   1520

CREON   Be sure, I would have done this had not I
wished first of all to learn from the god the course
of action I should follow.

OEDIPUS   But his word
has been quite clear to let the parricide,
the sinner, die.   1525

CREON   Yes, that indeed was said.
But in the present need we had best discover
what we should do.

OEDIPUS   And will you ask about
a man so wretched?

CREON   Now even you will trust
the god.   1530

OEDIPUS   So. I command you—and will beseech you—
to her that lies inside that house give burial
as you would have it; she is yours and rightly
you will perform the rites for her. For me—
never let this my father's city have me   1535
living a dweller in it. Leave me live

in the mountains where Cithaeron is, that's called
my mountain, which my mother and my father
while they were living would have made my tomb.
So I may die by their decree who sought   1540
indeed to kill me. Yet I know this much:
no sickness and no other thing will kill me.
I would not have been saved from death if not
for some strange evil fate. Well, let my fate
go where it will.   1545
               Creon, you need not care
about my sons; they're men and so wherever
they are, they will not lack a livelihood.
But my two girls—so sad and pitiful—
whose table never stood apart from mine,
and everything I touched they always shared—   1550
O Creon, have a thought for them! And most
I wish that you might suffer me to touch them
and sorrow with them.
         [*Enter* Antigone *and* Ismene, OEDIPUS' *two daughters.*]
O my lord! O true noble Creon! Can I
really be touching them, as when I saw?   1555
What shall I say?
Yes, I can hear them sobbing—my two darlings!
and Creon has had pity and has sent me
what I loved most?
Am I right?   1560
CREON   You're right: it was I gave you this
   because I knew from old days how you loved them
   as I see now.
OEDIPUS   God bless you for it, Creon,
   and may the god guard you better on your road
   than he did me!   1565
   O children,
   where are you? Come here, come to my hands,
   a brother's hands which turned your father's eyes,
   those bright eyes you knew once, to what you see,
   a father seeing nothing, knowing nothing,   1570
   begetting you from his own source of life.
   I weep for you—I cannot see your faces—
   I weep when I think of the bitterness
   there will be in your lives, how you must live
   before the world. At what assemblages   1575
   of citizens will you make one? to what
   gay company will you go and not come home
   in tears instead of sharing in the holiday?
   And when you're ripe for marriage, who will he be,
   the man who'll risk to take such infamy   1580
   as shall cling to my children, to bring hurt
   on them and those that marry with them? What

curse is not there? "Your father killed his father
and sowed the seed where he had sprung himself
and begot you out of the womb that held him."   1585
These insults you will hear. Then who will marry you?
No one, my children; clearly you are doomed
to waste away in barrenness unmarried.
Son of Menoeceus,[6] since you are all the father
left these two girls, and we, their parents, both   1590
are dead to them—do not allow them wander
like beggars, poor and husbandless.
They are of your own blood.
And do not make them equal with myself
in wretchedness; for you can see them now   1595
so young, so utterly alone, save for you only.
Touch my hand, noble Creon, and say yes.
If you were older, children, and were wiser,
there's much advice I'd give you. But as it is,
let this be what you pray: give me a life   1600
wherever there is opportunity
to live, and better life than was my father's.
CREON   Your tears have had enough of scope; now go within the house.
OEDIPUS   I must obey, though bitter of heart.
CREON   In season, all is good.   1605
OEDIPUS   Do you know on what conditions I obey?
CREON   You tell me them,
  and I shall know them when I hear.
OEDIPUS   That you shall send me out
  to live away from Thebes.
CREON   That gift you must ask of the god.
OEDIPUS   But I'm now hated by the gods.
CREON   So quickly you'll obtain your prayer.
OEDIPUS   You consent then?
CREON   What I do not mean, I do not use to say.   1610
OEDIPUS   Now lead me away from here.
CREON   Let go the children, then, and come.
OEDIPUS   Do not take them from me.
CREON   Do not seek to be master in everything,
  for the things you mastered did not follow you throughout your life.
        [As CREON and OEDIPUS go out.]
CHORUS   You that live in my ancestral Thebes, behold this Oedipus,—   1615
  him who knew the famous riddles and was a man most masterful;
  not a citizen who did not look with envy on his lot—
  see him now and see the breakers of misfortune swallow him!
  Look upon that last day always. Count no mortal happy till
  he has passed the final limit of his life secure from pain.   1620

6. Creon is Menoeceus's son.

EURIPIDES

ca. 480–406 B.C.E.

Euripides strikes many readers as the liveliest, funniest, and most provocative of the three great Athenian tragedians whose work survives. A younger contemporary of Aeschylus and **Sophocles**, Euripides lived through most of the cultural and political turmoil of the fifth century B.C.E., and was seen as one of the most influential voices for the revolutionary new ideas that were developing in this period. Controversial in his own time for his use of colloquial language and his depictions of unheroic heroes, sexually promiscuous women, and cruel, violent gods, Euripides has lost none of his power to shock, provoke, amuse, and engage his audiences.

LIFE AND TIMES

We know little of Euripides' personal life. He seems to have been married twice, and had three sons. He was a productive but only moderately successful tragedian: he wrote over ninety plays, but won first prize only four times. He specialized in unexpected plot twists and novel approaches to his mythological material: for instance, his play about Helen of Troy (*Helen*) makes her an entirely virtuous woman who never committed adultery or ran off with Paris. There are many moments of humor in Euripides, far more than in Aeschylus or Sophocles. At the same time, his vision is often very dark. His later plays about the Trojan War (such as *Hecuba* and *Trojan Women*) can be read as terrible indictments of the suffering caused to women, children, and families by the contemporary Peloponnesian War between Athens and Sparta.

He spent most of his life in Athens, but in his old age went to visit Macedon, where he died. It has often been suggested that he left Athens in outrage at the city's failure to appreciate him, but there is no evidence for this. Euripides was probably always popular with audiences, albeit less so with the judges of the dramatic competition, who perhaps felt an obligation to uphold civic ideals. Euripides continued to be widely read, quoted, and enjoyed for generations after his death.

Medea was first performed in the spring of 431 B.C.E., immediately before the outbreak of the Peloponnesian War. It was a time of prosperity for the city: the Greeks had defeated the Persians in the year of Euripides' birth, and now the Athenian Empire extended across the Mediterranean. Athens was deeply proud of the political, artistic, and intellectual achievements of the citizens.

It was also a time of new, antitraditional ideas, brought by the Sophists, men from other societies who came to Athens to teach "cleverness" or "wisdom"—*sophia*. The Sophists were seen by some as a mark of Athens' progressive openness to new modes of thought, but by others as a dangerous influence, liable to corrupt the city's young men. The tragedies of Euripides were associated by the comic dramatist Aristophanes, and probably many others, with the iconoclasm of the Sophists. Many contemporaries found the plays shocking and controversial. Euripides uses traditional myths, but he shifts attention away from the deeds of heroes toward domestic wrangling, and shows up moral and psychological weaknesses. Euripides was seen as a cynical realist about human nature: Sophocles said that while he showed people as they ought to be, Euripides showed them as they are.

Euripides put male heroes onstage in humiliated positions: they are bedraggled and dressed in rags, or are presented as obvious cowards, liars, or brutes. Euripides' outspoken, lustful, or violent, though often sympathetic, women were found particularly outrageous by his contemporaries. Lower-class characters and slaves were prominent, and sympathetically portrayed. In religious terms, too, his plays were challenging and controversial: his characters often question the old Greek myths about the gods, and the gods themselves often seem arbitrary or cruel in their dealings with humanity. Euripides also included vivid and realistic descriptions of violence, as in the messenger speech of the *Medea*, a horrifying account of how the princess Creusa's hair was burned up by her golden crown, while her poisoned dress corroded her skin and finally ripped the flesh from her bones.

THE WORK

Medea, like almost all Greek tragedies, is based on a traditional story. According to myth, the hero Jason was told by his uncle, Pelias, that he could not claim his rightful inheritance, the throne of Iolcus, unless he could perform a seemingly impossible quest: cross the Black Sea to the distant barbarian land of Colchis, ruled by the savage king Aeetes, and bring back to Greece the Golden Fleece, which was guarded by a dragon. Jason assembled a group of the finest Greek heroes, and built the world's first ship—the *Argo*—to take them to Colchis. Once they arrived, King Aeetes set Jason the task of plowing a field with a team of fire-breathing bulls. Luckily, the king's daughter, Medea, fell in love with Jason. She was skilled in magic, and enabled him to plow the field, lull the

dragon to sleep, steal the fleece, and escape back to Greece; she killed her own brother to distract the attention of their enraged Colchian pursuers. When they arrived in Iolcus, Pelias, going back on his word, tried to hang onto power. Medea got back at him by persuading Pelias' daughters that they could make their father immortal by boiling him alive—which was, of course, untrue. After the scandal was discovered, Jason and Medea were forced into exile. The couple had children, and eventually moved to Corinth. There, Jason decided to divorce Medea and marry a native Corinthian princess instead. With that, the action of *Medea* begins.

The most well-known part of the myth was the story of the quest of the Argonauts (sailors in the *Argo*) for the Golden Fleece. But Euripides focuses not on this heroic narrative but on its squalid aftermath, and he seems to have invented certain key aspects of the story. In previous versions, the children were either murdered by Creon's family or, according to another story, accidentally killed by Medea, when she tried to use magic to make them immortal. The shocking events at the end of this play would not have been anticipated by Euripides' audience.

Euripides' concentration on the domestic troubles in Corinth, rather than the heroic quest, allows him to present Jason in a disturbingly unheroic light: as a cad who struggles to muster unconvincing strategic and rhetorical arguments to justify his shabby treatment of his first wife. Although Jason tries to talk like a Sophist, it is Medea who is the real possessor of *sophia* in the play. The term *sophia* has negative and positive connotations: it can suggest deep understanding, but it can also imply mere cleverness. The play invites us to consider which character is the smartest: Jason, with his dodges and evasions, or Medea, with her unpredictable, cruel stratagems.

Medea is strongly marked as an outsider in three crucial ways: as a woman in a male-dominated world; as a foreigner or "barbarian" in a Greek city; and as a smart person surrounded by fools. On all these grounds, the play initially seems to invite us to side with Medea. She is obviously the wronged party in her relationship with Jason; and yet, even as she expresses her devastation at the betrayal, she never presents herself as a victim. Rather, she is fierce, "like a bull or a lioness," and highly articulate in her analysis of her situation. She claims even the male values of military honor for herself and for all women, suggesting in one famous passage that women who undergo the pain and danger of childbirth are far braver than men who fight in war: "I would rather face battle / three times than go through childbirth once." It is tempting to read these lines as proto-feminist, and to see Euripides, the clever poet, as sympathetic to his clever heroine, and as a defender of the rights and dignity of women and foreigners, before an audience of Athenian male citizens.

But as the play goes on, our vision of Medea is likely to change. We may begin to see her not as strong and brave, but as frighteningly violent; not as wise, but as too clever by half. This is a disturbing play that forces readers to revise their feelings several times. Is Medea sensible in her defense of her honor and her rights, or is she driven crazy by the gods of passion? Or should we see her as an agent of the gods, imposing divine justice on oath-breaking humans? Is Euripides challenging or confirming Greek male prejudices against foreigners and women? Is he recommending new forms of wisdom, or warning against the false cleverness of upstarts and outsiders? And what does it say about the city of Athens that it is the Athenian king, Aegeus, who will welcome this terrifying figure into his community?

Thematically, the most important threads in the play include the opposition of order and chaos, and the idea of time, especially the reversal of time. The Nurse opens the play by wishing that history could be reversed, that the Argo had never set sail: the play begins with a desire to undo the beginning of the story. Medea is the granddaughter of a god, Helios, the Sun, which associates her closely with the regular passing of time, in the sun's rising and setting. Her violent revenge at the injustice done to her can be seen as an attempt to do the impossible: to undo, by violence, her life history ever since the sailing of the Argo, to regain her lost honor and resume her old self, an unmarried princess. It can also be seen as an attempt at justice, a restoration of order out of chaos—but at a terrible cost, and in violation of all moderation and humanity.

Medea is an endlessly fascinating play that seems strikingly modern in its examination of family life, infidelity, failed sexual relationships, the experience of immigrants in a foreign land, and how it feels to be an oppressed or marginalized member of society. It also points to the fear, felt by many people both ancient and modern, that the apparently weaker members of a community, such as women and resident aliens, may be smarter than their masters, and may, if pushed far enough, rise up to destroy their oppressors.

Medea[1]

CHARACTERS

MEDEA
JASON
Medea's NURSE
TUTOR of Medea and Jason's sons
CREON, King of Corinth

AEGEUS, King of Athens
MESSENGER
CHORUS of Corinthian women
Medea and Jason's Two BOYS, sons
Attendants

SETTING   Corinth, in front of the house in which Medea and Jason have
been living.

    [*Enter* Medea's NURSE *from inside the house.*]

NURSE   If only the *Argo*[2] had not slipped through
    the dark Clashing Rocks[3] and landed at Colchis,
    if only that pine tree had not been cut down
    high on Mount Pelion and made into oars
    for the heroes who went out for the Golden Fleece,   5
    sent by King Pelias. Then my mistress Medea
    would never have sailed to the towers of Iolcus,[4]
    overwhelmed by her love for Jason.
    She would not have talked the daughters of Pelias
    into killing their father,[5] then fled here to Corinth[6]   10
    with her husband and sons—where even in exile
    she has charmed the citizens of her new home,
    doing whatever she could to help out Jason.
    That is the strongest safeguard there is:
    when a wife always sides with her husband.   15
    But now they're at odds, their bond is infected.
    Deserting his children along with my mistress,
    Jason has climbed into a royal bed,
    with the daughter of Creon,[7] king of this land.
    Poor Medea feels cruelly dishonored: 20
    she keeps shouting about their oaths and bringing up
    the solemn pledge of their joined right hands;
    she keeps calling on the gods to witness
    what kind of thanks she gets from Jason.
    She stays in bed and won't eat; she hurts all over.   25

1. Translated by Sheila H. Murnaghan.
2. The first ship constructed by Jason for his
quest for the Golden Fleece.
3. Colchis, home of Medea, lay on the other
side of the Black Sea from Corinth, past the
rocks near the mouth of the Bosphorus.
4. Thessaly, in Greece.
5. Pelias, Jason's uncle, reneged on a promise
to give Jason the throne of Iolchus if he

brought back the Golden Fleece. In revenge,
Medea persuaded Pelias's daughters to boil
him alive, believing that they would make him
young again.
6. After the scandal of Pelias's murder, Jason
and Medea had to go into exile, to Corinth.
7. Creon, king of Corinth, is not the same as
the Creon (Kreon) of Thebes in Sophocles' Theban plays.

She's been weeping constantly since she heard
that she has been cast off by her husband.
She stares at the ground. When friends give advice,
she listens no more than a stone or the sea,
though sometimes she turns her pale neck away, 30
and sighs to herself about her dear father,
her homeland, her house—all those she betrayed
when she left with the man who now rejects her.
Poor thing, this disaster has made her learn
how hard it is to be cut off from home. 35
She hates her sons, gets no joy from seeing them.
I am afraid that she's planning something
[I know her: she's relentless and will not put up
with being mistreated. I can imagine
her sharpening a knife and stabbing someone, 40
sneaking into the house where the wedding bed's made,
to kill the king and his daughter's new bridegroom][8]
and will only cause herself more trouble.
She is fierce. If you get into a fight with her,
you won't come out singing a victory song. 45
  [*Enter the* TUTOR *with the two* BOYS.]
But here are the boys coming back from the track,
not thinking about their mother's problems—
young minds don't like to dwell on trouble.
TUTOR Old servant of my mistress's house,
  why do you stand here alone by the door, 50
  pouring out your troubles to yourself?
  Surely Medea doesn't want you to leave her?
NURSE Old tutor of the sons of Jason,
  when slaves are true-hearted, if their masters' luck
  takes a turn for the worse, they suffer, too. 55
  I felt so wretched about my mistress
  that I craved the relief of coming out here
  to tell her sad story to heaven and earth.
TUTOR That poor woman has not stopped lamenting?
NURSE If only! Her pain's still in its early stages. 60
TUTOR What a fool, even if she is my mistress!
  She still doesn't know her latest troubles.
NURSE What is it, old man? Don't keep it to yourself.
TUTOR No, nothing. I shouldn't have said what I did.
NURSE Please don't leave a fellow slave in the dark. 65
  If it really matters, I won't tell anyone.
TUTOR I heard someone talking, though he didn't notice.
  I was watching the old men playing checkers
  there where they sit by the spring of Peirene.[9]

8. Words in brackets here and throughout are considered by most scholars to be later additions to the text, sometimes inserted by actors, sometimes by scholars and editors [translator's note].
9. A spring in Corinth.

He said that Creon, the king here in Corinth,   70
is planning to exile these boys from the city,
along with their mother. Whether this is true
I have no idea. I certainly hope not.

NURSE   Would Jason really put his sons through that,
even if he is on bad terms with their mother?   75

TUTOR   Old loyalties are trumped by new ones;
and that man is no friend to this household.

NURSE   We're done for, if we face a new wave of troubles
when we haven't bailed ourselves out from the last.

TUTOR   But now's not the right time for her to find out.   80
So you should keep quiet. Don't say a word.

NURSE   Children, do you hear how your father treats you?
He is my master: I can't curse him. But—
it's clear he's willing to hurt his own family.

TUTOR   And who isn't? It should be clear to you   85
that all people put themselves before others
[sometimes with good reason, sometimes for gain]
if this father prefers his new wife to his children.

NURSE   Go inside, boys. It will all be fine.
Now you, make sure they are kept by themselves,   90
not near their mother while she's so distraught.
She looks at them the way a mad bull would,
as if she's about to make some move.
She won't stop raging until she crushes someone—
better her enemies than people she loves.   95

MEDEA   [from inside]   It's too much, too much to bear!
I can't take any more. I want to die!

NURSE   Boys, see what I mean! Your mother
keeps stirring up her angry heart.
Quickly, quickly, into the house,   100
but don't go near her: stay out of view.
Don't get too close, be on the watch
for her vengeful heart and her self-willed,
savage temper.
Go on inside, quick as you can.   105
Her grief is like a thundercloud
which her mounting fury will ignite.
And then what will she do,
this proud-to-the-core, uncurbable spirit
stung by sorrows?   110

[Exit the TUTOR and the BOYS into the house. Enter MEDEA.]

MEDEA   I'm abused, I'm abused, that's why I cry.
Boys, you are cursed, your mother is loathsome.
You might as well die along with your father.
Let the whole house come down!

NURSE   No, no! I don't like the sound of that.   115
Why blame your sons for their father's
offenses? Why turn on them?

Children, I'm sick with fear for you.
Our rulers have frightening tempers;
rarely governed, always in charge,   120
they can't let go of their anger.
Better to stay on a level plain.
I'd rather grow old in safety
and not lead a life of grandeur.
"Moderation" is a fine motto,   125
and we do well to live by it.
Reaching for more never brings
any real advantage in human life—
only greater ruin when an angry god
comes down on a house.   130

[*Enter the* CHORUS *of Corinthian women.*]

CHORUS   I heard a voice! I heard the cry
of that poor Colchian woman!
Tell us, old nurse, has she still not calmed down?
I'm sure I could hear through the double doors
her wailing voice.   135
I get no joy from the grief in this house.
I consider myself a friend.

NURSE   There is no house. That's all gone.
The husband's possessed by a royal bed.
The wife wastes away in the innermost room,   140
and will not be comforted
by anything a friend can say.

MEDEA   Let it come! A thunderbolt
Straight through my head!
Why stay alive? In death   145
I can rest from a life I hate.

CHORUS   O Zeus, O Earth, O Light!
Do you hear the grief
in that girl's sad song?
Why this foolish lust   150
for a fatal resting place?
You want death to hurry up?
Do not ever ask for that.
So your husband adores someone else.
You should not rage at him.   155
Zeus will stand up for you.
Do not ruin yourself mourning that man.

MEDEA   Mighty Themis! Holy Artemis![1]
Do you see what I suffer—even after
I bound my hateful husband with solemn oaths?   160

---

1. Themis, whose name means "Right" or "Lawfulness," is a female Titan associated with order and keeping promises. Artemis, a daughter of Zeus, is a goddess who protects virgins and women in childbirth.

I'd gladly watch him and his new bride
being smashed to pieces with their whole house
for the huge wrong they have done to me.
My father! My city!—shamefully lost
when I killed my brother.[2]   165
NURSE   You can hear what gods she calls on:
   unfailing Themis and great Zeus,
   who oversees the oaths of mortals.
   There is no way she'll end her anger
   with just some empty gesture.   170
CHORUS   If she would meet us
      face-to-face
      and listen to our words,
   she might let go of the rage in her heart,
   and soften her harsh temper.   175
   I am always eager
      to help a friend.
   Go bring her out of the house.
      Tell her we're on her side.
      You have to act before she can hurt   180
      those boys in there: grief spurs her on.
NURSE   I doubt I can persuade her,
   but I'll do as you ask me to,
   and make one last attempt.
   When we try to speak to her,   185
   she glares at us like a bull
   or a lioness with newborn cubs.
   I have to say our ancestors
   showed very little sense
   when they invented melodies   190
   for revels, festivals, and feasts,
   the sweetest sounds in life,
   but made no songs or harmonies
   to soothe the bitter grief
   that leads to death and devastation   195
   and brings whole houses down.
   A musical cure for that would be
   worth having. Why should people sing
   when they're gathered at a feast
   and there's joy enough already   200
   in the meal's abundance?
      [*Exit the* NURSE *into the house.*]
CHORUS   I hear the pain in her loud laments;
   she shouts out high and shrill,
   at the faithless husband who spurns her bed.

---

2. After the theft of the Golden Fleece, Jason
and Medea were pursued by the outraged Col-
chians. To slow them down, Medea killed her
brother, Aspyrtus, and threw his body parts
behind her.

She calls on Themis to hear her wrongs, 205
    daughter of Zeus, upholder of oaths.
Because of an oath, she crossed to Greece,
    sailing on the dark night waves
    of the Black Sea's watery gate.[3]

[Enter MEDEA from the house, with attendants.]

MEDEA   Women of Corinth, I have left the house 210
to avoid offending you. With many people,
you know that they're proud whether they stay home
or go out. But others are seen as aloof
just because they choose to lead quiet lives.
People aren't fair when they judge with their eyes. 215
Not taking the trouble to look inside,
they hate someone on sight who's done them no harm.
So a stranger really has to fit in.
It's not good when even a self-willed native
is out of touch and rude to fellow citizens. 220
In my case, this unexpected calamity
has crushed my spirit. I am finished, friends,
done with life's joys. I wish I were dead.
My husband, who was everything to me,
is actually, I now see, the worst of men. 225
Of all living, breathing, thinking creatures,
women are the most absolutely wretched.
First, you have to pay an enormous sum
to buy a husband who, to make things worse,
gets to be the master of your body.[4] 230
And it's a gamble: you're as likely to get
a bad one as a good one. Divorce means disgrace
for women, and you can't say no to a husband.
Finding herself among strange laws and customs,
a wife needs to be clairvoyant; she has not 235
learned at home how to deal with her mate.
If we work hard at all these things,
and our husbands don't chafe at the yoke,
then that's an enviable life. Otherwise, we're better off dead.
A man who feels oppressed by the company at home, 240
goes out and gets relief for his low spirits
[turning to a friend or someone else his age],
but we can only look to that one other person.
They tell us that we enjoy a sheltered life,
staying at home while they are out fighting. 245
How wrong they are! I would rather face battle
three times than go through childbirth once.
But it isn't the same for you as for me.
This is your city. The houses you grew up in,

3. The "gate" is the Bosphorus Strait, connecting the Black Sea to the Mediterranean.

4. In ancient Greece, the bride's family had to
pay a dowry to the husband.

all your daily pleasures, your friends, are here.   250
I am alone, without a city, disowned
by my husband, snatched from a foreign land.
I have no mother, brother, or other family
to shelter me now that disaster has struck.
So I have just one thing to ask of you: 255
if some plan or scheme occurs to me
by which I can get back at my husband
[and the king and his daughter, Jason's new wife],
say nothing. A woman is usually quite timid,
shying away from battles and weapons,   260
but if her marriage bed's dishonored,
no one has a deadlier heart.
CHORUS   I will do that. You are right to pay him back,
   Medea. I can see why you're aggrieved.
      [*Enter* CREON.]
   But here is Creon, ruler of this land,   265
   coming to announce some new decision.
CREON   You, with your scowls and your spite for your husband,
   Medea, I command you to leave this land.
   Take your two sons and go into exile—
   and no delaying. I have authority   270
   over this decree, and I'm not going home
   until I've placed you outside our borders.
MEDEA   Oh no! I am completely destroyed.
   My enemies are spreading their sails to the wind,
   and I can't disembark from disaster.   275
   But bad as things are, I have to ask:
   what's your reason, Creon, for throwing me out?
CREON   I'll come right out and say it: I'm afraid
   that you'll do my daughter some incurable harm.
   There are many signs that point to this.   280
   You are clever and skilled at causing damage,
   and you feel injured in your empty bed.
   People have told me you're threatening us all:
   the bride's father, the bridegroom, and the bride.
   So I'm acting first to protect myself.   285
   I would rather earn your hatred now
   than regret later on that I was too lenient.
MEDEA   Not again!
   Creon, the same thing keeps happening:
   my reputation gets me into trouble.   290
   No man who has his wits about him
   would raise his sons to be too clever.
   Not only will they be considered lazy,
   they'll be resented by their fellow citizens.
   When you propose a clever plan to dullards,   295
   they see you as useless rather than clever;
   and those who are thought to be sophisticated

are bothered when the people think you're smarter.
This is exactly what has happened to me.
I'm clever, so I'm envied by one group   300
[to some I'm idle, to some the reverse]
and annoy the rest—cleverness has limits.
I know you're afraid I'll do you some harm.
But why be worried? I am in no position
to go on the offensive against a king.   305
How have you wronged me? You gave your daughter
to the man you wanted to. The one I hate
is my husband. You were acting sensibly.
I don't blame you because you're doing well.
Marry her off! Best of luck to all! But—   310
just let me stay. I may have been mistreated,
but I'll keep quiet, yielding to my betters.

CREON   Your words sound pleasing, but I am afraid
that you have some evil plan in your heart.
In fact, I trust you less than I did before.   315
A hot-tempered woman—or man—is easier
to guard against than a silent, clever one.
No, you have to leave at once. Enough talking.
It is decided: you are my enemy,
and none of your tricks can keep you here.   320
    [MEDEA kneels and grasps CREON's knees and hand in a gesture of ritual
    supplication.]

MEDEA   No! By your knees! By your daughter the bride!
CREON   Your words are wasted. You will never convince me.
MEDEA   You're ignoring my prayers and driving me out?
CREON   I care about my family, not about you.
MEDEA   My lost home! I can't stop thinking about it.   325
CREON   That's what means most to me, after my children.
MEDEA   Oh, what a disaster to fall in love!
CREON   That depends, I'd say, on the circumstances.
MEDEA   Zeus, be sure to notice who's making me suffer.
CREON   Don't be a fool! Go, and take my troubles with you.   330
MEDEA   I have troubles too, far more than I need.
CREON   My guards are preparing to throw you out.
MEDEA   No, not that! Creon, I implore you.
CREON   So you're determined to make this difficult.
MEDEA   I will leave. I don't ask you to change that.   335
CREON   Then why keep pressing me? Let go of my hand.
MEDEA   Just let me stay here for one more day
so I can work out my plans for exile
and make some arrangements for my sons,
since their father is not inclined to help.   340
Show them some pity. You have children yourself;
It's only natural to wish these boys well.
I'm not worried about exile for myself
but I feel the hardship it brings my sons.

CREON   I'm really not a tyrant at heart: 345
     to my own cost, I have listened to others.
     Even though I know it's not a good idea,
     you get your wish. But I warn you,
     if tomorrow's sun finds you and your boys
     still inside the borders of this country,   350
     you will die. I say it, and I mean it.
     So stay on, if you must, for this one day;
     you won't have time to do the harm I fear.
            [*Exit* CREON. MEDEA *stands up.*]
CHORUS   Poor, poor woman,
     weighed down by troubles,   355
     where can you turn? What welcome,
     what house, what sheltering land
     [will you find]?
     Medea, some god has tossed you
        into a sea of constant trials.   360
MEDEA   It's bad all around. Who would deny that?
     But don't imagine that everything's settled.
     There are struggles ahead for the bridal pair,
     and many ordeals for the bride's father.
     Would I have fawned on him like that   365
     without something to gain or a secret plan?
     There wouldn't have been that talking and touching.
     But he is such a credulous fool:
     when he had a chance to throw me out
     and foil my plans, he gave me one more day   370
     to make corpses out of my three tormenters—
     the father, the daughter, and my own husband.
     I can think of many routes to their death;
     I'm not sure, friends, which one to try first,
     whether to set the newlyweds' house on fire,   375
     or stab someone's liver with a sharpened sword,
     silently entering the bridal bedroom.
     But there is a risk: if I am caught
     sneaking into the house, I will lose my life
     and give my enemies a chance to laugh.   380
     The safest course is the one I know best:
     to poison them with deadly drugs.
     That's it, then.
     But once they are dead—then what city
     will take me in? Where is the friend   385
     who will save my life by giving me shelter?
     Nowhere. So I will wait a little while,
     and if some tower of safety appears
     I will kill them with a hidden trick.
     But if I am forced to act in the open,   390
     I will strike with a sword. Ready to die,
     I will go to the very edge of daring.

By Hecate,[5] whom I most revere,
the goddess who is my chosen ally,
who haunts the darkest corners of my house,   395
they will not get away with causing this pain.
I will make sure they find their marriage bitter,
and bitter the tie with Creon, bitter my exile.
Now Medea, use everything you know;
you must plot and scheme as you approach   400
the dreadful act that will test your spirit.
Do you see what is being done to you?
Do not be mocked by this Sisyphean wedding;[6]
You spring from a noble father and Helios the sun.
You have the skill, and along with that   405
a woman's nature—useless for doing good
but just right for contriving evil.

CHORUS   Sacred streams are flowing backwards;
right and wrong are turned around.
It's men who do the shady scheming,   410
swear by the gods, then break their oaths.
News of this will bring us glory,
rightful honor for the female race;
women will at last be free
from the taint of ugly rumors.   415
Enough of ancient poets' legends
that tell of us as breaking faith!
The lord of song, divine Apollo,
did not grant the lyre's sweet music
for the speaking of our minds,   420
or I could have made an answer
to the stories spread by men.
Time's long record speaks on both sides.
Mad with love, you left your father.
Sailing through the briny border   425
of the double Clashing Rocks,[7]
you settled in a land of strangers.
Now your husband's left your bed;
so you're banished from this country,
a lonely exile without rights.   430

All over Greece, oaths prove hollow;
shame has melted into air.
And for you there's no safe harbor
in your lost paternal home,

5. Goddess associated with the moon and with witchcraft.
6. I.e., in the spirit of Sisyphus, a legendary Corinthian trickster, punished in Hades with the

eternal task of pushing a rock uphill only to have it roll down again [translator's note].
7. The path between the cliffs is the Bosphorus Strait.

no escaping from your troubles,⁣ 435
as you watch a royal princess
take your marriage and your house.
         [*Enter* JASON.]
JASON   This is not the first time that I've observed
how impossible a stubborn person can be.
You had the chance to stay in this country, 440
going along with what your betters had planned,
but you're being thrown out for your pointless rants,
and there's nothing I can do. Fine! Don't stop
talking about "that disgusting Jason."
But for what you've said about the rulers— 445
you are lucky that it's only exile.
The king gets more and more angry. I've tried
to calm him down, hoping you could stay.
Yet you keep up this nonsense, raving on
against the king. So you're being thrown out. 450
Still, I am not one to abandon family.
I'm here now to look out for your interests,
so you and the boys don't leave without money
or other provisions. Exile's not easy.
Maybe you can't stop hating me, 455
but I'll always want what is best for you.
MEDEA   You really are disgusting! That sums up
what I have to say about your spinelessness.
You've really come here, when you are hated
[by me and the gods and everyone else]? 460
It's not some daring noble endeavor
to look friends in the face after you've wronged them,
but the lowest and sickest of human failings:
shamelessness. Still, it is good that you came.
If I name all your appalling actions, 465
I'll get some relief, and you'll feel much worse.
Let me start at the very beginning:
I saved you, as every Greek knows
who shipped out with you on the *Argo*,
when you had to bring the fire-breathing bulls 470
under a yoke and sow a deadly field.[8]
And that serpent, which never slept
and held the Golden Fleece in winding coils,
I killed it, bringing you the light of salvation.[9]
And as for me, I cheated my father 475
and followed you to Iolcus[1] and Mt. Pelion,

8. Jason was challenged by Medea's father, King Aeetes, to plow a field with a pair of fire-breathing bulls and sow it with dragon's teeth, which would instantly grow into armed men. With Medea's help, he succeeded.

9. The Golden Fleece had hung from a tree, around which coiled a fierce dragon; Medea succeeded in defeating the dragon.
1. Ancestral kingdom of Jason.

infatuated, not thinking straight.
I made Pelias die in the most gruesome way,
at his daughters' hands; I ruined his house.
All of this I did for you, you lowlife,   480
and you have deserted me for someone new
even though we have children. If we didn't,
you could be forgiven for wanting her.
Our oaths mean nothing to you. I can't tell
if you think those gods have lost their power,   485
or imagine that the rules have changed for mortals—
since you're well aware that you broke a promise.
My right hand here—to think I let you touch it,
and to clasp my knees.[2] I was abused
by a swindler, deceived by false hopes.   490
Still, let me ask you for some friendly advice.
[But why should I think you'd help me now?
Well, if I ask you, it'll make you look worse.]
So where should I go? To my father's house
which I betrayed when I ran off with you?   495
To the poor daughters of Pelias? I'm sure
I'd be welcome there, where I killed their father.
That is how it stands: my friends at home
hate me now, and those I should have treated well
I turned into enemies by helping you.   500
For what I did, you made me the envy
of all Greek women—with such a marvelous catch,
such a loyal husband that I'm being expelled,
a miserable outcast from this country,
without any friends, alone with my sons.   505
It doesn't look so good for the bridegroom—
children out begging with the woman who saved him.
Zeus, you should have given us a touchstone
for human nature as you did for gold!
We need a way to tell from someone's looks   510
whether or not he's base on the inside.

CHORUS   There is a dreadful, incurable anger
    when former lovers fall to fighting.

JASON   It seems I'll have to be a skillful speaker,
    and, like a careful pilot, reef in my sails   515
    if I have any hope of outrunning
    the surging onslaught of your angry words.
    You make much of the help you gave me,
    but I say that it was Aphrodite[3] alone
    who assured the success of my venture.   520

---

2. Touching a person's right hand and knees was a way of asking for a favor, assuming the position of a supplicant. Medea is implying that Jason has failed to pay her back for the favors she did him.
3. Goddess of love, beauty, and sex.

You may be quick-witted, but like it or not,
I could tell how you were compelled
by Eros's sure arrows to save my life.[4]
But no need to tally this up exactly:
whatever you did was helpful enough.   525
Still, it's my view that you got much more
out of my being saved than I ever did.
First of all, you are living in Greece,
not some foreign country. Here you find justice
and the rule of law; force has no standing.   530
And all of Greece knows how clever you are;
you're famous. If you lived at the ends of the earth,
no one would ever have heard of you.
I see no point in a house full of gold,
or a gift for singing better than Orpheus,[5]   535
without the good fortune of being well known.
So—since you have turned this into a contest,
those are the things I accomplished for you.
Now, on this royal marriage that you dislike,
I can show you that I acted wisely,   540
soberly, and in the best interest
of you and the boys. Just stay calm for a moment.
When I moved here from the city of Iolcus,
I was dragged down by impossible problems.
What better solution could there be   545
for an exile like me than to marry the princess?
You are upset, but it's not what you think,
that I'm sick of you and smitten with this girl,
or want some prize for having lots of children;
I am satisfied with the ones we've got.   550
It's so we'll live well and won't be in need.
And that is important. I can tell you:
everyone steers clear of a penniless friend.
I will raise our sons as befits our family
and add some brothers to the boys you gave me.   555
Bringing them together in a single tribe,
I'll prosper. What are more children to you?
In my case, having new offspring benefits
the older ones. Is that such a bad plan?
You wouldn't say so if it weren't for the sex.   560
You women reach the point where you think
if all's well in the bedroom everything's fine;
but if some trouble arises there,
you insist on rejecting whatever's best.

4. I.e., Cupid, god of sex—the son of Aphrodite. Eros shoots arrows that inspire desire.
5. Orpheus, son of the god Apollo and the muse Calliope, was a poet-singer with semimag-ical powers: even wild animals were enchanted by his songs. Orpheus was famously devoted to his wife, Eurydice; when she died, he traveled down to the underworld to try to rescue her.

We should have some other way of getting children. 565
Then there would be no female race,
and mankind would be free from trouble.
CHORUS   Jason, you've put together a polished speech.
But, at the risk of disagreeing, I say
that you do wrong to desert your wife. 570
MEDEA   I'm clearly different from everyone else.
To me, a scoundrel who is good at speaking
should have to pay a special price for that.
Since he knows he can gloss over his crimes,
he'll try anything. But cleverness has limits. 575
That's what you are. So don't try to impress me
with clever words. A single point refutes you:
if you were so noble, you would have gotten
my consent to this marriage, not kept it secret.
JASON   Oh yes, I'm sure you would have agreed 580
if I had told you then, when even now
you can't help reacting with fury.
MEDEA   That wasn't it. You thought a foreign wife
would be an embarrassment in years to come.
JASON   You need to understand. It is not for the woman 585
that I'm taking on this royal marriage.
It's what I told you before. I only want
to give you protection and safeguard our children
by fathering royal siblings for them.
MEDEA   Spare me a life of shameful wealth 590
or a good situation that eats at my soul.
JASON   You know what you really need to pray for?
The sense not to see a good thing as shameful,
not to think you're suffering when you're doing fine.
MEDEA   Go on, be cruel. You have a safe home here, 595
while I'll be cast out with nowhere to go.
JASON   You chose that. Don't blame anyone else.
MEDEA   How? I betrayed you by marrying somebody?
JASON   By rudely cursing the royal family.
MEDEA   Well, I'll bring a curse to your house too. 600
JASON   I have had enough of squabbling with you,
but if you want some money from me
to provide for you and the boys in exile,
just say so. I want to be generous
and can contact friends who will treat you well. 605
You would be an idiot to turn me down.
You'll be better off if you forget your anger.
MEDEA   I want nothing to do with your friends.
I won't take anything you give. Don't bother.
No good comes from a bad man's gifts. 610
JASON   Well, the gods will witness how eager I am
to do what I can for you and the boys.
You are so stubborn that you reject what's good

and snub your friends. You will suffer all the more.
MEDEA   Just go! I'm sure that staying away this long   615
    has left you longing for your new bride.
    Go play the groom. And maybe I'm right to hope
    you will have a marriage that makes you weep.
        [*Exit* JASON.]
CHORUS   Overwhelming love never leads to virtue,
        or a good reputation.   620
    Just enough Aphrodite is the greatest blessing.
    Goddess, don't aim at me with your golden bow
        and arrows dipped in desire.

    I choose to be wooed by sober restraint—
        the best gift of the gods.   625
    I won't have Aphrodite stirring up quarrels
    by making me fall for a stranger. She should grant us
        harmonious marriages.

    Beloved country! Beloved home!
    May I never lose my city;   630
    that is a life without hope,
    the hardest of trials to bear.
    Better, far better to die,
    than ever come to that.
    There is no deeper pain   635
    than being cut off from home.

    I have seen it for myself;
    no one had to tell me.
    For you have no city,
    no friends who feel for you   640
    in your bitter struggles.
    Whoever doesn't honor friends
    with an open heart,
    deserves an awful death
    and is no friend of mine.   645
        [*Enter* AEGEUS.][6]
AEGEUS   Hello, Medea! And all good wishes—
    the warmest of greetings among true friends.
MEDEA   Good wishes to you, son of wise Pandion,
    Aegeus! Where are you coming from?
AEGEUS   Straight from Apollo's ancient oracle.[7]   650
MEDEA   What took you there, to the center of the earth?[8]
AEGEUS   I wanted to know how I might have children.

6. This stage direction is a modern guess, though presumably the direction of Aegeus's entrance must differ from those of all previous entrances in the play—underscoring the unex-pectedness of his arrival.
7. Delphi
8. At Delphi was a stone that was supposedly the navel of the Earth.

MEDEA	Goodness! Have you been childless all this time?
AEGEUS	Yes, childless—thanks, I am sure, to some god.
MEDEA	Do you have a wife, or do you sleep alone? 655
AEGEUS	I'm married; I have a wife who shares my bed.
MEDEA	And what did Apollo say about children?
AEGEUS	Subtler words than a man can make sense of.
MEDEA	Am I allowed to know what he said?
AEGEUS	Of course. I need the help of your clever mind. 660
MEDEA	Then if it's allowed, tell me what he said.
AEGEUS	Not to untie the foot of the wineskin . . . [9]
MEDEA	Before doing what? Or arriving where?
AEGEUS	Before I get back to my ancestral hearth.
MEDEA	And what's your reason for landing here? 665
AEGEUS	There's a man called Pittheus, king of Troezen.[1]
MEDEA	Son of Pelops,[2] said to be very pious.
AEGEUS	I want to ask him about the prophecy.
MEDEA	Yes, he's wise and knows about such things.
AEGEUS	And he's my most trusted comrade at war. 670
MEDEA	Well, good luck! I hope you get what you want.
AEGEUS	But why are you looking so red-eyed and pale?
MEDEA	It turns out I have the worst possible husband.
AEGEUS	What are you saying? Tell me what's upset you.
MEDEA	Jason mistreats me though I've given him no cause. 675
AEGEUS	What is he doing? Explain what you mean.
MEDEA	He put another woman in charge of our house.
AEGEUS	Would he do something so improper?
MEDEA	He would. So I, once prized, am now dismissed.
AEGEUS	Is he in love? Or has he fallen out with you? 680
MEDEA	So much in love that he's abandoned his family.
AEGEUS	Well, if he's that bad, forget about him.
MEDEA	He's in love with the thought of a royal match.
AEGEUS	Then tell me: who is the new wife's father?
MEDEA	Creon, who rules right here in Corinth. 685
AEGEUS	Well, I can see why you are angry.
MEDEA	Devastated. And I'm being expelled.
AEGEUS	From bad to worse! What's the reason for that?
MEDEA	Creon has declared me an exile from Corinth.
AEGEUS	And Jason accepts this? That's not right. 690
MEDEA	He protests now, but he'll gladly put up with it.

So I'm reaching out my hands to your face
and making myself your suppliant.
Take pity on me in my wretched state,

---

9. Wine was sometimes stored in animal skins, the leg being used as a spigot for dispensing drinks. The imagery suggests both "Don't get drunk" and "Don't have sex."
1. Pittheus will give his daughter Aethra to Aegeus, after getting him drunk; the Athenian hero Theseus will be conceived in this way.
2. Pelops, son of Tantalus, was served up as food to the gods by his father. The gods restored him to life, and he became the founder of the Peloponnese.

don't let me become a lonely outcast. 695
Take me into your country and your house.
Do this, and may the gods grant your wish.
May you live out the happy life you long for.
You don't know how lucky you are to find me:
I can take care of your lack of children. 700
I know the right drugs to make you a father.

AEGEUS   There are many reasons why I want to help.
First the gods, who favor suppliants,
and then the children you say I could have—
something where I'm really at a loss. 705
So, if you can get yourself to my land,
I will try to give you proper shelter.
[I should make one thing plain to you:
I'm not willing to take you away from here.]
If you leave this place on your own 710
and arrive at my house also on your own,
you will be safe. I will not hand you over.
But I can't offend my friends while I'm here.

MEDEA   Agreed. Now if you could make a formal pledge,
then I will feel you've treated me perfectly. 715

AEGEUS   You don't trust me? What's on your mind?

MEDEA   I trust you. But Pelias' family hates me,
and Creon, too. If you are bound by oaths,
you can't let them take me from your land.
If you just say yes and don't swear by the gods, 720
you might end up being gracious and giving in
to their demands. I'm completely powerless,
while they have wealth and status on their side.

AEGEUS   You clearly have this all figured out.
So if you think I should, I won't refuse. 725
This will put me in a stronger position,
with a good excuse to give your enemies,
and it helps you. Name the gods I should swear by.

MEDEA   Swear by the Earth and by the Sun, father
of my father,[3] and the entire race of gods. 730

AEGEUS   To do—or not to do—what? Say it.

MEDEA   Not ever to cast me out from your land,
and if some enemy tries to lead me away,
not to allow it while you live and breathe.

AEGEUS   I swear by the Earth and the light of the Sun, 735
and all the gods, I will do as you say.

MEDEA   Good. And the penalty if you break the oath?

AEGEUS   Whatever ungodly people have to suffer.

MEDEA   A good journey to you. All is in place.
I will come to your city soon as I can, 740
once I have fulfilled my plans and desires.

---

3. Helios, the Sun, is father of Aeetes, king of Colchis, Medea's father.

CHORUS   May Hermes,[4] guide of travelers,
  speed you to your home,
  and may you gain your heart's desire,
  for you are an honorable man, Aegeus,   745
  that is clear to me.
      [*Exit* AEGEUS.]
MEDEA   O Zeus, O Justice born of Zeus, O Sun!
  Now, friends, I know I am on the path
  to glorious victory over my enemies.
  Now I feel sure they will have to pay.   750
  I was at a loss, and then this man appeared,
  who will be a safe haven when my plots are done.
  I can fasten my mooring line to him
  when I have made my way to Athens.
  And now I will tell you what I have I mind;   755
  listen to this, though I doubt you will like it.
  I will send a trusted servant to Jason
  who will ask him to meet me face to face.
  When he comes, I will give a soothing speech
  about how I agree with him and now believe   760
  that his faithless marriage is a first-rate plan,
  advantageous and well thought through.
  Then I'll plead for the children to stay behind;
  not that I want to leave them in this hostile land
  [and have my children mistreated by enemies];   765
  it's part of a trick to kill the king's daughter.
  I'll send them to her with gifts in their hands
  [for the bride, so they won't have to leave],
  a delicate robe and a golden crown.
  Once she takes this finery and puts it on,   770
  she—and whoever touches her—will die
  because of poisons I will spread on the gifts.
  That's all there is to say on that subject.
  But the thought of what I have to do next
  fills me with grief: I need to kill the children, 775
  no one should hope to spare them that.
  Once I've torn Jason's house apart, I'll leave
  and pay no price for the poor boys' death.
  I will bring myself to this unholy act
  because I cannot let my enemies laugh.   780
  [So be it! Why should I live? I have no country,
  no home, no way of escaping my troubles.]
  It was a bad mistake to leave my home
  swayed by the words of a man from Greece,
  but with the gods' help I will punish him.   785
  He won't see the children we had grow up

4. Hermes, the messenger god, was the child of Zeus by the nymph Maia.

and he won't be able to have any more
with his brand-new bride: no, she's doomed
to an agonizing death from my drugs.
No one should think I am meek and mild   790
or passive. I am quite the opposite:
harsh to enemies and loyal to friends,
the kind of person whose life has glory.

CHORUS   Now that you have shared this plan with me,
I want to help you and to honor human law,   795
and so I say to you: don't do this thing.

MEDEA   I see why you say that, but there's no other way;
you haven't been through the troubles I have.

CHORUS   You would be able to kill your own children?

MEDEA   It is the surest way to wound my husband.   800

CHORUS   And to make yourself impossibly wretched.

MEDEA   So be it. We have done enough talking.

[MEDEA *turns to her attendants.*]

One of you servants, go bring Jason here.
And you, the friends I trust with my closest secrets,
if you respect me and have women's hearts,   805
you will say nothing about my plan.

[*Exit one of* MEDEA's *attendants.*]

CHORUS   The sons of Erechtheus,[5] long blessed with wealth,
Athenian offspring of the Olympian gods,
raised in a land untouched by war,
nourished by the glorious arts,   810
stride easily through the radiant air,
where once, it's said, the holy Muses[6]
gave birth to golden Harmony.

I've heard that Aphrodite dips her cup
in the streams of clear Cephisus,[7]   815
and sends sweet breezes through the land.
Crowned with a twining garland
of fragrant, blooming roses,
she sets Desire at Wisdom's side
to foster all that's good.   820

How can that land of sacred streams,
that open-hearted city,
be a fitting home for you,
unholy woman,
killer of children?   825

5. Athenians. Erechtheus was a legendary king
of Athens.
6. The Muses are the daughters of Zeus and
Mnemosyne (Memory). They inspire poetic
and musical creation, and their birthplace is
Pieria.
7. River in Athens.

Think what it is to strike a child!
Think who you are killing!
By every sacred thing
I beg of you:
spare those boys.   830

How can you find the will,
how can you steel your mind,
to lift your hand against your sons,
to do this awful thing?
How will you stop your tears,   835
when you see them dying?
They will huddle at your knees,
and you will not be able
to spill their blood
with a steady heart.   840
    [*Enter* JASON.]

JASON   You called me, so I've come. You may hate me,
but I won't let you down. I'm eager to hear
what you think you may need from me after all.

MEDEA   Jason, please overlook what I said before.
You should be willing to put up with my fits,   845
for the sake of the love that we once shared.
And I have been thinking all of this over
and berating myself for being obtuse.
Why turn on those who wish me well,
picking a fight with the country's rulers   850
and my husband, who serves us all
by marrying a princess and giving our sons
new royal brothers? Why be angry?
The gods will provide, so how can I lose?
Shouldn't I think of the boys? I can't forget   855
that I'm an exile and have no friends.
When I look at it that way, I can see
I've been confused and my rage was pointless.
I'm all for it now. I think you are wise
to arrange this connection. I'm the fool: 860
I should have thrown myself into these plans
and helped them along, tending the bed
and gladly serving your new bride.
It's just that women are . . . well, not quite wicked,
but anyway you shouldn't copy us   865
and get caught up in silly quarrels.
Please forgive me: I was wrong before
and now I understand much better.
Boys, boys! Come out of the house
to greet your father and talk to him.   870
    [*Enter the* TUTOR *and the two* BOYS *from the house.*]

End your anger towards one you should love
just as I, your mother, am doing.
We have made our peace, there is no more strife.
So take his hand. But oh, when I think
of all the trouble the future conceals!   875
My children, in your lives to come,
will you reach out a loving arm to me?
I am so quick to weep and full of fear.
I'm making up my quarrel with your father
but even so my eyes are filled with tears.   880
CHORUS   Tears are coming to my eyes as well.
I only hope there's nothing worse ahead.
JASON   I'm pleased with your present behavior, Medea,
and I forgive the past: of course a woman minds
if her husband decides to import a new wife.   885
But now your feelings have turned around,
and you recognize the better course at last.
That shows you are a sensible woman.
Now boys, don't think I've been a negligent father.
With the gods' help, I've secured your position.   890
I am quite sure that you will be leaders
here in Corinth, you and your new siblings.
Just be strong and stay well. I will do the rest,
along with whatever god's on our side.
I hope to see you turning into fine young men,   895
and towering over my enemies.
But you, why are your cheeks covered with tears?
Why do you look pale and turn away?
Aren't you happy with what I am saying?
MEDEA   It's nothing—just the thought of these children.   900
JASON   Don't worry. I will take care of everything.
MEDEA   You're right. I can rely on your promises.
It's just that women are made for tears.
JASON   But why are you so sad about the children?
MEDEA   I am their mother. And your hopes for their future   905
filled me with fear that those things won't happen.
Now some of what you are here to discuss
has been settled, so I'll move on to the rest:
since the rulers have decided to banish me
[and I really do see that it's for the best   910
so I won't be in your way, or theirs,
since I can't help seeming antagonistic],
I will comply and leave the country.
But the boys should stay here and be raised by you;
ask Creon to spare them this exile.   915
JASON   I may not convince him, but I will try.
MEDEA   You should get your bride to ask her father
to let the boys stay here in this country.

JASON Good idea. She'll do it if I ask her;
    she is a woman like any other.   920
MEDEA And I will be part of this effort, too.
    I will send her the most splendid gifts
    that can be found anywhere in the world
    [a delicate robe and a golden crown]
    and the boys will take them. Now servants,   925
    bring out the presents right away.
        [*Exit an attendant into the house.*]
    She will have many reasons to rejoice:
    In you she has the best of husbands
    and she will wear the ornaments
    that my grandfather Helios left to his heirs.   930
        [*Enter the attendant with the gifts.*]
    Take these wedding presents, boys,
    carry them to the happy royal bride.
    They will be perfect gifts for her.
JASON That's ridiculous! Don't deprive yourself.
    Do you think the royal house needs dresses,   935
    or gold? You should hold on to these things.
    I am sure that her high regard for me
    will matter more than material objects.
MEDEA No. They say even the gods are moved by gifts.
    For us, gold counts more than a million words.   940
    Her fortunes are high, she has a god on her side,
    she's young and has power. I'd give my life,
    and not just gold, to save the boys from exile.
    My sons, go into that fine rich house;
    appeal to your father's new wife, my mistress;   945
    ask for reprieve from a life of exile,
    and hand her the gifts. It is essential
    that she herself take them from you.
    Hurry! And bring back the good news
    that you have made your mother's wish come true.   950
        [*Exit* JASON, *the* BOYS, *and the* TUTOR.]
CHORUS No more hoping that those children will live.
    No more, for they are on the road to murder.
    The bride will reach out for the golden chains,
    poor thing, she'll reach out for her doom.
    With her own hands she will place in her hair   955
    the finery of Death.

    Lured by their lovely unearthly glow
    she'll put on the dress and the wrought-gold crown
    and make her marriage in the world below.
    That is the trap into which she will fall,   960
    poor thing, she will follow her destiny,
    inescapable Death.

And you, unlucky groom,
new member of the royal house,
you are not able to see   965
that you're leading your boys to their life's end,
and bringing a hateful death to your bride.
You have no idea of your fate.

And you, poor mother of these boys,
I also grieve for you,   970
since you are set on making them die
because of the bed which your husband left.
He thoughtlessly abandoned you
and lives with another wife.
        [*Enter the* BOYS *and the* TUTOR.]
TUTOR   Mistress! The boys are spared the fate of exile!   975
The princess gladly accepted the gifts
with her own hands. She is on their side.
But . . .
why are you upset at this good fortune?
[Why have you turned your face away?   980
Why aren't you happy with what I'm saying?]
MEDEA   Oh no!
TUTOR   That doesn't fit with the news I brought.
MEDEA   Oh no, oh no!
TUTOR   What is it that I don't understand?   985
Was I wrong to think I was bringing good news?
MEDEA   You bring the news you bring. It's not your fault.
TUTOR   But why are you crying and turning away?
MEDEA   I can't help it, old friend. Terrible plans
have been devised by the gods—and by me.   990
TUTOR   The boys' good standing here will bring you back.
MEDEA   First I, in my grief, will bring others down.
TUTOR   Other mothers have been torn from their children.
You are mortal and must accept misfortune.
MEDEA   Yes, yes, I will. Now you go inside.   995
Take care of whatever the boys might need.
        [*Exit the* TUTOR *into the house.*]
O boys, boys, you still have a city,
and a home where, leaving me for good,
you will be cut off from your unhappy mother.
I will be an exile in a foreign land   1000
without the delight of watching you thrive,
without the joy of preparing your weddings,
tending the bath and the bed, lifting the torches.[8]
How much my own strong will has cost me!
I get nothing, boys, from raising you,   1005

---

8. Torches were an important feature of ancient weddings, which took place at night.

from running myself ragged with endless work.
The birth pangs I endured were pointless.
It pains me to think what hopes I had
that you would care for me in old age
and prepare me for burial when I die—   1010
the thing that everyone wants. But now
that happy dream is dead. Deprived of you,
I will live out my life in bitter grief.
And you will embark on a different life
with no more loving eyes for your mother.   1015
But why, why, boys, are you looking at me?
Why do you smile for this one last time?
Oh, what should I do? I lost heart, my friends,
as soon as I saw their beaming faces.
I can't do it. So much for my plans!   1020
I will take the boys away from here.
Why make them suffer to hurt their father
if it means I suffer twice as much myself?
I can't do that. So much for my plans!
But wait! Can I really bear to be laughed at   1025
and let my enemies go unpunished?
I have to steel myself. I can't be weak
and let those tender thoughts take over.
Children, into the house. And anyone
who is out of place at my sacrifice   1030
can stay away. I will not spare my hand.
But oh . . .
My angry heart, do not go through with this.
For all your pain, let the children live.
They can be with you and bring you joy.   1035
And yet—by the vengeful spirits of deepest Hades—[9]
there is no way I can allow my enemies
to seize my children and to mistreat them.
[It is certain that they have to die. And so
I should kill them, since I gave them life.]   1040
It is all in place: she cannot escape;
the crown is on her head; the royal bride
revels in her new dress. I heard it clearly.
Having set out myself on the darkest road
I will send my sons down one that's even darker.   1045
I will talk to them. Give me, my children,
give me, your mother, your hands to kiss.
Oh this hand! this mouth! this face!
Oh my dear ones, my noble sons!
Be happy—but there. Your father wrecked   1050
what we had here. Oh the joy of holding them,
of their tender skin, of their sweet breath.

9. The Furies.

Go in! Go in! I can no longer bear
to look at you. My grief is too strong.
I see the horror of what I am doing,   1055
but anger overwhelms my second thoughts—
anger, boundless source of evil.
    [*Exit the* BOYS *into the house.*]
CHORUS   I have often entered into
    complicated trains of thought,
    and pursued much deeper questions   1060
    than women are supposed to tackle.
    For there's a Muse that favors me
    and confers the gift of wisdom,
    not on all, but on a few—
    [you'll find some women here and there]   1065
    who are not strangers to that Muse.
    So I can say that those who never
    find themselves producing children
    are more fortunate by far
    than those who do.   1070
    The childless never need to ask
    whether children are in the end,
    a curse or blessing in human life;
    and since they have none of their own,
    they are spared a world of trouble.   1075
    Those parents who are blessed
    with houses full of growing children
    are constantly worn out by worry:
    will they be able to raise them well
    and leave behind enough to live on?   1080
    And all along it isn't clear
    whether after all this care
    they'll turn out well or badly.
    Then there is one final drawback,
    the hardest thing of all to bear.   1085
    When the parents find a way
    to give their children what they need
    to grow up strong and honest,
    but then luck turns: death scoops them up
    and carries their bodies down to Hades.   1090
    What possible good can it do
    for the gods to impose on us
    this bitter, bitter sorrow
    as the price of having children?
MEDEA   My friends, I have been waiting a long time now   1095
    wondering how things would turn out in there.
    But now I see one of Jason's servants
    coming towards us. He is breathing hard,
    and it's clear he has something grim to report.
        [*Enter the* MESSENGER.]

MESSENGER   [Oh you have done a dreadful, lawless thing]   1100
  Run, Medea! Run! Make your escape—
  get away in a ship or overland in a carriage.
MEDEA   And what has happened that means I should flee?
MESSENGER   The royal princess has fallen down dead,
  along with her father, because of your poison.   1105
MEDEA   You have brought the most wonderful news.
  I will always think of you as a true friend.
MESSENGER   What are you saying? Are you out of your mind?
  You have desecrated the royal hearth,
  and you're glad? Not terrified at what you've done?   1110
MEDEA   I have things to say in response to that.
  But please do not rush through your report.
  How exactly did they die? You will make me
  twice as happy if they died horribly.
MESSENGER   When your boys and their father first arrived   1115
  at the new couple's house, there was much joy
  among the household slaves. We had been worried,
  but now a rumor was spreading through us
  that you and Jason had patched up your quarrel.
  One kissed their hands, another their golden heads,   1120
  and I in my happiness followed along
  into the women's rooms behind the children.
  The lady who had become our new mistress
  did not see at first that your sons were there;
  she just gazed adoringly at Jason.   1125
  But then suddenly she shut her eyes
  and turned her delicate face away,
  disgusted by the children's presence.
  But your husband mollified the girl,
  saying, "They are family, don't reject them,   1130
  let your anger go, look this way again;
  can't you treat your husband's kin as your own,
  accept their gifts, and ask your father
  to spare the boys from exile for my sake?"
  She relented when she saw those fine presents,   1135
  and granted him everything he asked.
  As soon as the boys and their father had left,
  she seized that elegant dress and put it on;
  she placed the golden crown on her head
  and arranged her hair in a shining mirror   1140
  smiling at her reflected features.
  Then she jumped up from her chair and ran
  all over the house on her little white feet,
  delighted with her presents; she kept looking down
  to see how the dress fell against her ankle.   1145
  But then we saw something truly horrible:
  her color changed; she staggered sideways
  on shaking legs; she nearly hit the ground

as she fell backwards into a chair.
An older woman, thinking at first   1150
that she was possessed by some god like Pan,[1]
raised a shout of joy. But then she saw
the foaming mouth, the skin drained of blood,
the eyeballs twisting in their sockets.
She countered that shout of joy with a shriek   1155
of woe. One slave girl rushed to the father's room;
another went straight to tell the husband
about his bride's collapse. The whole house rang
with the sound of their frantic footsteps.
In the time it would take a swift runner   1160
to cover the last lap of a footrace,
she came out of her speechless, sightless trance
with an awful, chilling cry of pain.
She was under a double assault:
the golden crown she had put in her hair   1165
spewed out a torrent of consuming flames,
while those fine robes she got from your children
were eating away at her pale flesh.
Burning in flames, she leapt up from her chair
and shook her head from side to side   1170
trying to throw off the crown. But the bands
held tight, and all of her shaking
only made the flames blaze twice as high.
She gave up the struggle and fell to the floor.
Only a parent would have known who she was.   1175
You really couldn't make out her eyes
or the shape of her face. From the top of her head
blood mixed with fire was streaming down;
the flesh flowed off her bones like pine sap,
loosened by the fangs of your unseen poison,   1180
a horrible sight. No one wanted to touch
the corpse. Her fate taught us caution.
But her poor father came in without warning;
he entered the room and found the body.
He began to wail and took it in his arms,   1185
kissed it, and spoke to it: "My poor child,
what god has destroyed you in this cruel way,
making me lose you when I'm at death's door?
All I want is to die with you, dear child."
When he stopped lamenting and tried to stand,   1190
he got tangled up in those silky robes,
like a laurel shoot encircled by ivy.
It was a horrible sort of wrestling match:
he kept struggling to get up on his legs
while she held him back. He pulled hard   1195

---

1. Half-man, half-goat, a pastoral god associated with wild, ecstatic behavior [translator's note].

but the flesh just came off his old bones.
In the end, he stopped fighting for his life,
worn out, no longer equal to the ordeal.
Two corpses lie there, the girl and her father
[nearby, a disaster that cries out for tears].   1200
I won't go into what this means for you;
you'll find out what penalty you have to pay.
The old truth comes home to me again:
human life is an empty shadow.
People who believe themselves to be   1205
the deepest thinkers are the biggest fools.
There isn't anyone who is truly blessed.
Rich people may be luckier than others
but I wouldn't really call them blessed.
          [Exit the MESSENGER.]
CHORUS   A god is giving Jason what he deserves: 1210
trouble after trouble in a single day.
[Poor girl, poor daughter of Creon,
I feel for you: you have been sent
to Hades to pay for Jason's marriage.]
MEDEA   Friends! My plan is clear: as fast as I can   1215
I will kill my sons and leave this land.
I cannot hold back and let those boys
be slaughtered by someone who loves them less.
They have to die, so it is only right
that I who gave them life should kill them.   1220
Arm yourself, my heart! Don't hesitate
to do the unavoidable awful thing.
I must pick up the sword and step across
the starting line of a painful course.
No weakening, no thoughts of the boys—   1225
how sweet they are, how you gave them birth.
Forget your children for this one day;
grieve afterwards. Even if you kill them,
they still are loved—by you, unlucky woman.
          [Exit MEDEA into the house.]
CHORUS   Look, Mother Earth and Radiant Sun,   1230
look at this deadly woman,
before she can raise her hand
to spill the blood of her children,
descendants of your golden line.
I dread to think of immortal blood   1235
shed by mortal hands!
Hold her back, Zeus-born light! Make her stop!
Get this miserable murderous Fury
out of the house!

All for nothing, your labor in childbirth,   1240
all for nothing, your dearly loved children,

you who passed through the perilous border
of the dark-faced Clashing Rocks.
Why has relentless anger
settled in your heart, 1245
why this rage for death upon death?
The stain of kindred blood weighs heavy.
The gods send the killers evil pains
to echo evil crimes.

FIRST BOY (*in the house*)   No! No! 1250
CHORUS   Do you hear? Do you hear that child's cry?
   Oh that wretched, ill-starred woman!
FIRST BOY   Help! How do I get away from our mother?
SECOND BOY   I don't know how. There's no escape.
CHORUS   Should I go in? I might prevent 1255
   those boys from dying.
FIRST BOY   Yes, by the gods, yes! Help us now!
SECOND BOY   She has us cornered with her sword.
CHORUS   Wretched woman, made of stone, made of iron!
   I see you really have it in you 1260
   to turn your deadly hand
   against the boys you bore yourself.

   I have only heard of one other woman,
   who raised her hand against her children:
   Ino, driven wild by Zeus' wife[2] 1265
   who made her wander far from home.
   Poor woman, she plunged into the sea,
   and dragged her children to unholy death.
   Stepping over the seacliff's edge,
   she died along with her two sons. 1270
   Is any awful thing impossible now?
   How much disaster has been caused
   by the pain of women in marriage!
      [*Enter* JASON.]
JASON   You women there beside the house,
   is Medea inside, the perpetrator 1275
   of these terrible crimes? Has she escaped?
   Unless she burrows deep in the earth
   or else grows wings and flies through the air,
   the royal family will make her pay.
   After she killed such powerful people, 1280
   does she think she can get away scot-free?
   Still, I'm mainly worried about the children.
   Those she abused can do the same to her,

---

2. Ino, a daughter of Cadmus, king of Thebes, was driven mad by Dionysos to participate—along with Cadmus's mother—in the dismemberment of her nephew, Pentheus. Later, she was married to King Athamas and, driven mad by Hera, she leapt into the sea with one or more of their sons.

but I am here now to save my boys.
More suffering for me if Creon's kinsmen   1285
try to punish them for their mother's crime.

CHORUS   Poor man, you don't know all of your troubles,
or you would not have said what you just did.

JASON   What is it? Does she want to kill me too?

CHORUS   The boys are dead. Their mother killed them.   1290

JASON   What are you saying? Those words are death to me.

CHORUS   Don't think of your children as among the living.

JASON   She killed them . . . where? In the house or outside?

CHORUS   If you open the doors, you will see how they died.

JASON   Servants, draw back these bolts at once,   1295
open the doors, so I can see both evils:
the slain children and the woman I will punish.

[Enter MEDEA in a winged chariot above the house, with the BOYS' bodies.]³

MEDEA   Why do you keep banging on the doors
to get at the boys and me who killed them?
Don't exert yourself. If you have something to say,   1300
I'm here, go ahead. But you'll never touch me.
This chariot from my grandfather the Sun
protects me from an enemy's hands.

JASON   You abomination, most hateful of women
to the gods, to me, to the whole human race.   1305
You were actually able to drive a sword
into sons you had borne; you've made me childless.
How can you live and see the light of the sun,
when you have committed this sacrilege
and ought to be dead? Now I see what I missed   1310
when I brought you from that barbarian place
into a Greek home. You are an evil being:
you betrayed your father and your native land.
The gods are crushing me for what you did
when you killed your brother at the family hearth   1315
before you boarded the beautiful *Argo*.
That's how you started. Then you married me,
you bore me children and you killed them
just because of some sexual grievance.
No Greek woman would ever do that.   1320
To think I bound myself to you instead
in a hateful, ruinous marriage
with an inhuman wife, a lioness
more savage than Etruscan Scylla.⁴
All the angry words I could hurl at you   1325
carry no sting, you are so brazen.

---

3. The stage mechanism used in the original production would have been the *mechane*, a crane typically used for divine appearances in Athenian tragedy.

4. Scylla is the sea monster near Etruria (modern-day Italy) who threatens Odysseus and his men in the *Odyssey*.

To hell with you, you filthy child-killer!
All that is left for me is to mourn my fate;
I have lost the joy of my new marriage;
the children that I fathered and brought up   1330
are gone. I'll never speak with them again.
MEDEA   I could refute your speech at length,
but Father Zeus already knows
how you were treated by me and what you did.
There is no way you could reject my bed   1335
and lead a happy life laughing at me,
you or the princess, no way that Creon
who arranged all this could throw me out
and not pay the price. So call me a lion,
or Scylla lurking on the Etruscan plain,   1340
I've done what I had to: I've pierced your heart.
JASON   But it hurts you too, you share in this pain.
MEDEA   The pain is worth it if it kills your laughter.
JASON   O children, what a vicious mother you had!
MEDEA   O boys, your father's disease destroyed you!   1345
JASON   It was not my hand that slaughtered them.
MEDEA   No, your arrogance and your brand-new marriage.
JASON   You really think sex was a reason to kill them?
MEDEA   You think being spurned is trivial for a woman?
JASON   Yes, if she's sensible. You resent everything.   1350
MEDEA   Well, they are gone, and that will bite deep.
JASON   Oh, but they will avenge themselves on you.
MEDEA   The gods know which of us started this trouble.
JASON   Yes, they know your mind and it disgusts them.
MEDEA   Hate all you want. I loathe the sound of your voice. 1355
JASON   And I loathe yours. We won't find it hard to part.
MEDEA   Then what's to be done? I too am eager for that.
JASON   Let me bury these bodies and weep for them.
MEDEA   Absolutely not. I will bury them myself
in the shrine of Hera of the Rocky Heights,   1360
where none of my enemies can get at them
or wreck their graves. Here in the land of Sisyphus[5]
I will institute a procession and sacred rites
as atonement for this unholy murder.[6]
Then I'll be off to the city of Erechtheus[7]   1365
to live with Aegeus, Pandion's son.
You will have a fitting death for a coward,
hit on the head by a piece of the *Argo*—
the bitter consequence of marrying me.

5. Corinth. Sisyphus was a notorious traitor, punished in the underworld for his deceitfulness by having to push a rock eternally up a hill, never managing to get it to the top without its rolling back down.
6. There was a sacred cult dedicated to "Hera of the rocky heights" at Corinth.
7. I.e., Athens.

JASON   Let a Fury rise up to avenge these boys,   1370
   and Justice that punishes bloodshed.

MEDEA   What god or spirit listens to you?
   You broke your oaths, you betrayed a friend!

JASON   Ha! Abomination! Child-killer!

MEDEA   Just go home and bury your wife.   1375

JASON   I am going, and without my children.

MEDEA   This grief is nothing. Wait till you're old.

JASON   O my children, so much loved!

MEDEA   By their mother, not by you.

JASON   And then you killed them?

MEDEA   To punish you.

JASON   Oh the misery! I just want to kiss them,   1380
   to hold them in my arms.

MEDEA   Now you want to hug them, talk to them,
   when before you shoved them aside.

JASON   By the gods,
   just let me touch their soft skin.

MEDEA   Not possible. Your words are useless.   1385

JASON   Zeus, do you hear? I am shut out,
   dismissed by this vicious animal,
   this lioness stained with children's blood.
   With all my being I grieve for them
   and summon the gods to witness   1390
   how you destroyed my children,
   and will not let me touch their bodies
   or bury them in proper tombs.
   I wish I had never fathered them
   to see them slaughtered by you.   1395
      [*Exit* MEDEA *in the chariot.*]

CHORUS   In all that Olympian Zeus watches over,
   Much is accomplished that we don't foresee.
   What we expect does not come about;
   the gods clear a path for the unexpected.
   That is how things happened here.   1400

Virgil's *Aeneid* is the greatest epic poem from ancient Rome. It has been one of the most profoundly influential works of all classical literature in the later Western cultural and literary tradition. The *Aeneid* can be described in ways that make it sound off-putting: as a work of nationalistic propaganda for a nation that no longer exists, or as a twelve-book poem about the importance of doing your duty. But such descriptions are entirely false to most readers' experience of this emotionally engaging and thought-provoking story. The *Aeneid* is an absorbing book, full of adventure, beauty, magic, dreams, love, loss, and violence. The characters make hard choices and have complex inner lives. The poem is also a profound meditation on the rights and wrongs of empire and colonialism that prompts us to ask whether civilizations, even the best of them, are ever founded without enormous personal and military cost.

LIFE AND TIMES

Virgil, whose full Roman name was Publius Vergilius Maro, was born near the peaceful northern Italian town of Mantua. His father probably owned land, and Virgil's poetry often shows a nostalgic appreciation for the quiet life of the Italian countryside. Before composing the *Aeneid*, Virgil wrote two books with a rural setting: the *Eclogues*, a set of ten poems featuring the songs and sorrows of fictional shepherds, and the *Georgics*, a four-book account of the struggles and triumphs of life on a farm. Ostensibly, neither of these texts has much to do with the subject of the *Aeneid*, which is about the quest to found an empire. But

Virgil's poetic focus is surprisingly consistent throughout his career. Whether the setting is an empire or a village garden, he is interested in the value and pathos of the human struggle to build a home, even in hostile or near-impossible conditions. The farmer in the *Georgics*, whose hard work is washed away by a violent storm, is just as much a hero as the shipwrecked Trojans in the *Aeneid*.

When Virgil was young, the world beyond Mantua saw great political and military unrest. Rome, through its impressive military discipline, had already become the dominant power in the Mediterranean world; the city had defeated its main rival, the North African state of Carthage, some two generations before (in 146 B.C.E.). Now Rome was engaged in various further wars, struggling to expand the empire both eastward and westward. These wars generated greater glory for the nation, but also greater instability at home. In Virgil's childhood, Rome was still a Republic. No single man had control of the country; instead, government was divided among the people, the magistrates, and the Senate (an assembly of councilmen). But power was shifting away from the Senate and toward the military generals responsible for Rome's victories abroad. After a series of civil wars, Julius Caesar, one of these generals, became dictator of Rome. He was assassinated in 44 B.C.E., when Virgil was twenty-six. More civil wars followed, causing disruption both at home and abroad: many country landowners—including some around Mantua, though apparently not Virgil's family—were forced to leave their homes to make room for veterans returning from war. Finally, some twelve years after the assassination, Julius Caesar's adopted great-nephew Octavian defeated the joint forces of Antony and Cleopatra, and took control of Rome. In this volatile environment, Octavian was careful not to style himself "dictator," as Julius had done. Instead, he claimed to be restoring the old ways of the Republic. He named himself "Augustus" ("The Respected One"), the "Princeps" ("First Man"), and "Emperor Caesar." Throughout his rule, Augustus was interested in controlling his public image: he knew that careful manipulation of information was essential if he were to avoid the fate of his great-uncle. In this context, it is not surprising that the emperor had a close personal relationship with the writers of Rome, who would, as Augustus knew, play an important part in shaping his public image even after his death. Augustus hoped that Virgil would provide him with a great national epic to justify, glorify, and immortalize Augustan Roman power.

We do not know how happy Augustus was with the poem that Virgil actually produced, although apparently the poet read parts of it aloud to the emperor and his sister, to great emotional effect: the sister fainted. It is possible that Augustus had hoped for a more direct account of his own glorious deeds. But perhaps he was smart enough to realize that direct propaganda never has much of a shelf life. We also do not know whether Virgil himself was satisfied with his creation. He was apparently a quiet man, moderate in his ways; thanks to Augustus's favor, he was given an expensive villa in Rome, but he seems to have preferred the quiet life of the country. He never married. As a poet, he was a perfectionist, willing to spend many hours editing his work. We are told that he compared himself to a mother bear who licks her cubs into shape. This process shows in the complex rhythms and careful patterns of Virgil's poetic style. He died of a fever at the age of fifty-one, while returning from a trip to Greece. The *Aeneid* was still incomplete, and appar-ently he gave orders from his deathbed for it to be burned. Fortunately for us, Augustus countermanded the orders, and saved the poem for posterity.

THE *AENEID*

Virgil's masterpiece is about Rome, but only indirectly. The story takes us back in time to a period well before the foundation of the city. It tells how one civilization mutates into another, finding the origins of Rome in the destruction of Troy. The poem follows the Trojan Aeneas as he escapes with his father, son, and a few companions from the smoking ruins of his home. On the journey to find a new home in the "western land," he has many adventures, including an affair with Dido, the beautiful queen of Carthage, and a trip down to the underworld, to meet his dead father. When he arrives in Italy, he struggles to establish a base in his new land—where some of the native inhabitants are far from welcoming.

The *Aeneid* deals with universal themes, including the basic human need to find, or create, a home. The story is accessible even to those who know nothing about ancient history. But readers will find it helpful to think carefully about how Virgil incorporates his own times into this mythical story. When Virgil was writing, Rome had only recently emerged from a long, terrifying period of civil war. Aeneas, like Augustus, must show strong leadership to a people traumatized by years of violence. Virgil's account of the sack of Troy, including the horrible slaughter of old king Priam before the eyes of his family, is vivid and harrowing—and many contemporary readers would have witnessed similar scenes with their own eyes. But the historical parallels in this poem are complex, and one cannot simply identify Aeneas with Augustus. The affair between Aeneas and Dido looks further back in history, to the Roman wars with Carthage. This episode also invites comparison with events of the more recent past. Like Augustus's military and political rival Antony, Aeneas falls in love with a beautiful African queen; in this interpretation, Dido foreshadows Cleopatra, who also ended up killing herself. Once Aeneas has arrived in Italy, there are further questions. Is Aeneas a foreign invader, pushing the boundaries of his empire into new lands—as Augustus did? Or are these battles between different Italian peoples more like a civil war? Virgil's evocation of historical parallels is rich and fascinating precisely because they are so hard to pin down. Moreover, temporal paradoxes are created by telling "history in the future tense": from the Roman reader's point of view, Carthage has already been defeated; but from Dido's perspective, her city has just begun to be built.

Virgil's use of literary antecedents is equally interesting. His poem combines the themes of the *Odyssey* (the wanderer in search of home) and the *Iliad* (the hero in battle). He borrows Homeric turns of phrase, similes, sentiments, and whole incidents; for instance, his Aeneas, like Odysseus, passes the land of the Cyclops, and descends alive to the world of the dead; like Achilles, he receives a new set of armor from his goddess mother, and kills in rage to avenge a dead friend. But Virgil is not playing a sterile game of copying **Homer**. Rather, Homeric parallels are part of how the poem generates meaning. Virgil often uses several Homeric allusions at the same time. For instance, Turnus—the Italian prince who is originally engaged to Lavinia, the woman who will become Aeneas's wife—is in some ways like one of the suitors in the *Odyssey*: the rival who must be defeated and killed. But on another level, Turnus is like Hector, the doomed Trojan hero of the *Iliad*, who dies defending his city and his people. From Turnus's perspective, Aeneas himself is more like the suitors of the *Odyssey*: he is a usurper in a place where he does not belong.

The *Aeneid*'s approach to storytelling is very different from that of the Homeric poems. Virgil often tells the parts of the story Homer left untold: for example, it is in Virgil, not Homer, that we get the full story of the Trojan Horse. On a more profound level, Virgil's presentation of war, peace, and human nature is quite unlike Homer's—it is both broader and deeper. Virgil is interested in communities that extend beyond the tribe or clan to the nation or the empire, and he evokes time that goes beyond the generations of a single family to the broad sweep of history. The characters, especially Aeneas, are more introspective and prone to ambivalent feelings than those in Homer; Virgil explores conflicts not just between one person and another but within an individual, between duty and the longings of the heart. In this way, Aeneas is a different kind of hero from any in Greek literature. The first time his name is mentioned, he is risking death by shipwreck and is overwhelmed by despair, wishing he could have died with his friends at Troy: he holds his hands to the sky and cries, "Three, four times blest, my comrades / lucky to die beneath the soaring walls of Troy." This is a close echo of the moment when Odysseus is shipwrecked after leaving Calypso's island and wishes he had died fighting at Troy instead of by drowning: "Those Greeks were lucky, three and four times over / who died upon the plain of Troy" (*Odyssey* 5.306–307). But the scenes are importantly different. Aeneas feels not only physical fear but also despair at being a survivor with no home to go to. We can contrast this sense of being totally lost with the first mention of Odysseus in the *Odyssey*: he longs for a home that still exists, whereas Aeneas's home has been destroyed. A little later, we see a different Aeneas when he talks to his men and tries to calm their fears, giving no hint of his own: "Call up your courage again," he tells them; "dismiss your grief and fear." From the start of the poem, Aeneas

This detail from a black figure vase by the "Louvre Painter" (6th century B.C.E.) shows Aeneas carrying his father, Anchises, on his shoulders as they escape Troy.

will be put in situations where he cannot allow himself to show or act on his deepest feelings.

Virgil also seems to question the values of the Homeric warrior code. Aeneas is not, like Achilles, a man fighting for his personal honor, against even the leaders of his own side; rather, he is, and must be, a consensus builder, a team player. Odysseus (Romanized as *Ulysses*) is presented in the *Aeneid* as a cruel brute, lacking in the mercy for the defeated that Aeneas's father, Anchises, characterizes as an essential feature of the true Roman ("to spare the defeated, break the proud in war"). Moreover, Ulysses' cleverness—epitomized by the invention of the Trojan Horse—seems in this poem to be more like wicked dishonesty. Truthfulness is an essential element in the Roman code of honor: this is partly why Dido's accusation that Aeneas has deceived and betrayed her cuts so deeply.

Aeneas is often seen as the prototype of the ideal Roman ruler, devoted above all to *pietas*—a word from which we get *pity* and *piety*, and which covers both senses, though it is often translated as "duty." But whereas *duty* may suggest adherence to a set of abstract moral principles, the Latin word connotes devotion to particular people and entities: to the gods above all, but also to one's country, leaders, community, and family, especially father and sons. An iconic moment of Aeneas's *pietas* comes as he leaves his burning city, carrying his lame old father on his shoulders, holding the images of his household gods, and leading his little son by the hand. This scene reminds us that Aeneas is struggling to hold on to a community and create continuity even from the ruins of his old home. The *pietas* that holds families and cities together is contrasted in this poem with *furor* ("rage," "fury"), the wild passion that inspires bloodlust, both in Troy and on Italian shores.

But being good is not easy, and Virgil shows that Aeneas's repression of his own feelings for the sake of devotion comes at an enormous cost. Moreover, the poem seems to suggest that duty can even be harmful to other people. Aeneas, on the instructions of the gods, abandons the great passion of his life, his love for Dido, who had convinced herself that their relationship was equivalent to marriage. In despair, she kills herself. Virgil makes us admire and sympathize with Dido, and in doing so, we are forced to question whether Aeneas's mission is worthwhile. The *Aeneid* is not merely a celebration of Roman power; it is also an analysis of the costs of empire, both to the conquered and the conquerors. Moreover, we may wonder whether Rome itself—a city famously built by Romulus, who killed his brother Remus, a city defined by foreign and civil wars—is truly a civilization in which *pietas* is the defining value. This moral ambiguity continues up to the last lines of the poem, which many first-time readers will find shocking. We are left to wonder whether moderation or violence will be the truly defining quality of the future Roman Empire.

A NOTE ON THE TRANSLATION

Translation of this complex poem often reflects the ideological biases of the translator. Some versions make Virgil sound wholeheartedly enthusiastic about imperialism, eliminating much of his ambivalence; others make him sound unrelentingly gloomy about everything. Virgil's Latin is dignified, not colloquial, and has a beautiful, musical rhythm; but trying to reproduce this effect in modern English risks sounding merely pompous.

Several excellent recent translations have steered clear of these dangers and given us readable, fast-paced versions of the *Aeneid*. We have chosen Robert Fagles's translation, because it is particularly good at evoking the psychological depth of Virgil's characters, and it allows readers to experience the sheer narrative pleasure of reading the *Aeneid*.

From the Aeneid[1]

BOOK I

[Safe Haven after Storm]

Wars and a man I sing—an exile driven on by Fate,
he was the first to flee the coast of Troy,
destined to reach Lavinian[2] shores and Italian soil,
yet many blows he took on land and sea from the gods above—
thanks to cruel Juno's[3] relentless rage—and many losses   5
he bore in battle too, before he could found a city,
bring his gods to Latium, source of the Latin race,
the Alban lords and the high walls of Rome.[4]
                                        Tell me,
Muse, how it all began. Why was Juno outraged?
What could wound the Queen of the Gods with all her power?   10
Why did she force a man, so famous for his devotion,[5]
to brave such rounds of hardship, bear such trials?
Can such rage inflame the immortals' hearts?

   There was an ancient city held by Tyrian settlers,[6]
Carthage, facing Italy and the Tiber River's mouth[7]   15
but far away—a rich city trained and fierce in war.
Juno loved it, they say, beyond all other lands
in the world, even beloved Samos,[8] second best.
Here she kept her armor, here her chariot too,
and Carthage would rule the nations of the earth   20
if only the Fates were willing. This was Juno's goal
from the start, and so she nursed her city's strength.
But she heard a race of men, sprung of Trojan blood,
would one day topple down her Tyrian stronghold,

1. Translated by Robert Fagles.
2. Lavinium is the city founded in Italy by Aeneas, near the later city of Rome. It is named after his Latin wife, Lavinia. "Lavinian" here means "Italian."
3. Juno is queen of the gods, wife of Jupiter.
4. According to legend, after Aeneas died, his son Ascanius moved from Latium and founded the city of Alba Longa; from there came Romu-

lus and Remus, who built the walls of Rome.
5. The Latin word is *pietas:* "piety," "duty," "loyalty."
6. Tyre was the main city of the Phoenicians, an ancient seafaring merchant people.
7. The Tiber runs through Rome.
8. A Greek island famous for its cult of Hera (equivalent to the Roman Juno).

breed an arrogant people ruling far and wide,   25
proud in battle, destined to plunder Libya.
So the Fates were spinning out the future . . .[9]
This was Juno's fear
and the goddess never forgot the old campaign
that she had waged at Troy for her beloved Argos.[1]   30
No, not even now would the causes of her rage,
her bitter sorrows drop from the goddess' mind.
They festered deep within her, galled her still:
the judgment of Paris, the unjust slight to her beauty,
the Trojan stock she loathed, the honors showered on Ganymede   35
ravished to the skies.[2] Her fury inflamed by all this,
the daughter of Saturn[3] drove over endless oceans
Trojans left by the Greeks and brute Achilles.[4]
Juno kept them far from Latium, forced by the Fates
to wander round the seas of the world, year in, year out.   40
Such a long hard labor it was to found the Roman people.

    Now, with the ridge of Sicily barely out of sight,
they spread sail for the open sea, their spirits buoyant,
their bronze beaks churning the waves to foam as Juno,
nursing deep in her heart the everlasting wound,   45
said to herself: "Defeated, am I? Give up the fight?
Powerless now to keep that Trojan king from Italy?
Ah but of course—the Fates bar my way.
And yet Minerva could burn the fleet to ash
and drown my Argive crews in the sea, and all for one,   50
one mad crime of a single man, Ajax, son of Oileus![5]
She hurled Jove's all-consuming bolt from the clouds,
she shattered a fleet and whipped the swells with gales.
And then as he gasped his last in flames from his riven chest
she swept him up in a cyclone, impaled the man on a crag.   55
But I who walk in majesty, I the Queen of the Gods,
the sister and wife of Jove[6]—I must wage a war,
year after year, on just one race of men!
Who will revere the power of Juno after this—
lay gifts on my altar, lift his hands in prayer?"   60

9. Refers to the Punic Wars of the third and second centuries B.C.E., in which Rome finally defeated Carthage; "Libya" is used as a generic term for the North African coast.
1. Argos is the homeland of Agamemnon and Menelaus; in the *Iliad,* Hera favors the Argives as they fight the Trojans and try to win back Helen, Menelaus's wife.
2. Paris, Prince of Troy, was asked to choose one of three goddesses: Hera, Athena (Minerva in Roman mythology), or Aphrodite (Venus to the Romans). He picked Aphrodite, and was rewarded with Helen, whom he took from her husband and led back to Troy. The second insult from the Trojans against Hera is that her husband, Zeus, once fell in love with

a Trojan boy, Ganymede, and brought him up to heaven to be his cupbearer.
3. Saturn, the Roman god of agriculture, was the father of both Jupiter and Juno.
4. The greatest Greek warrior. These survivors are the few Trojans whom Achilles has not killed.
5. In the aftermath of the Greek victory at Troy, one of the Greek soldiers, this Ajax (who is not the same as the strong hero Telemonian Ajax) raped the Trojan princess Cassandra in the temple of Minerva. The goddess took revenge by setting fire to the Greek fleet, and then overwhelming it with a storm.
6. Alternative name of Jupiter.

With such anger seething inside her fiery heart
the goddess reached Aeolia, breeding-ground of storms,
their home swarming with raging gusts from the South.
Here in a vast cave King Aeolus[7] rules the winds,
brawling to break free, howling in full gale force   65
as he chains them down in their dungeon, shackled fast.
They bluster in protest, roaring round their prison bars
with a mountain above them all, booming with their rage.
But high in his stronghold Aeolus wields his scepter,
soothing their passions, tempering their fury.   70
Should he fail, surely they'd blow the world away,
hurling the land and sea and deep sky through space.
Fearing this, the almighty Father banished the winds
to that black cavern, piled above them a mountain mass
and imposed on all a king empowered, by binding pact,   75
to rein them back on command or let them gallop free.

     Now Juno made this plea to the Lord of Winds:
"Aeolus, the Father of Gods and King of Men gave you
the power to calm the waves or rouse them with your gales.
A race I loathe is crossing the Tuscan Sea,[8] transporting   80
Troy to Italy, bearing their conquered household gods—
thrash your winds to fury, sink their warships, overwhelm them
or break them apart, scatter their crews, drown them all!
I happen to have some sea-nymphs, fourteen beauties,
Deiopea the finest of all by far . . .   85
I'll join you in lasting marriage, call her yours
and for all her years to come she will live with you
and make you the proud father of handsome children.
Such service earns such gifts."
                              Aeolus warmed
to Juno's offer: "Yours is the task, my queen,   90
to explore your heart's desires. Mine is the duty
to follow your commands. Yes, thanks to you
I rule this humble little kingdom of mine.
You won me the scepter, Jupiter's favors too,
and a couch to lounge on, set at the gods' feasts—   95
you made me Lord of the Stormwind, King of Cloudbursts."
With such thanks, swinging his spear around he strikes home
at the mountain's hollow flank and out charge the winds
through the breach he'd made, like armies on attack
in a blasting whirlwind tearing through the earth.   100
Down they crash on the sea, the Eastwind, Southwind,
all as one with the Southwest's squalls in hot pursuit,
heaving up from the ocean depths huge killer-breakers
rolling toward the beaches. The crews are shouting,
cables screeching—suddenly cloudbanks blotting out   105
the sky, the light of day from the Trojans' sight

7. Mythical king of the winds from the
Odyssey.

8. Just west of central Italy; the Trojans have
almost reached their destination.

as pitch-black night comes brooding down on the sea
with thunder crashing pole to pole, bolt on bolt
blazing across the heavens—death, everywhere
men facing instant death.   110
At once Aeneas, limbs limp in the chill of fear,
groans and lifting both his palms toward the stars
cries out: "Three, four times blest, my comrades
lucky to die beneath the soaring walls of Troy—
before their parents' eyes! If only I'd gone down   115
under your right hand—Diomedes, strongest Greek afield—
and poured out my life on the battle grounds of Troy!⁹
Where raging Hector lies, pierced by Achilles' spear,
where mighty Sarpedon lies, where the Simois River
swallows down and churns beneath its tides so many   120
shields and helmets and corpses of the brave!"¹
                              Flinging cries
as a screaming gust of the Northwind pounds against his sail,
raising waves sky-high. The oars shatter, prow twists round,
taking the breakers broadside on and over Aeneas' decks
a mountain of water towers, massive, steep.   125
Some men hang on billowing crests, some as the sea
gapes, glimpse through the waves the bottom waiting,
a surge aswirl with sand.
                    Three ships the Southwind grips
and spins against those boulders lurking in mid-ocean—
rocks the Italians call the Altars, one great spine   130
breaking the surface—three the Eastwind sweeps
from open sea on the Syrtes'² reefs, a grim sight,
girding them round with walls of sand.
                                One ship
that carried the Lycian³ units led by staunch Orontes—
before Aeneas' eyes a toppling summit of water   135
strikes the stern and hurls the helmsman overboard,
pitching him headfirst, twirling his ship three times,
right on the spot till the ravenous whirlpool gulps her down.
Here and there you can sight some sailors bobbing in heavy seas,
strewn in the welter now the weapons, men, stray spars   140
and treasures saved from Troy.
                        Now Ilioneus' sturdy ship,
now brave Achates', now the galley that carried Abas,
another, aged Aletes, yes, the storm routs them all,
down to the last craft the joints split, beams spring
and the lethal flood pours in.
                        All the while Neptune⁴   145

---

9. In the *Iliad*, Aeneas is wounded by the
Greek hero Diomedes, and is rescued by his
mother, Aphrodite.
1. Hector, the greatest Trojan hero, is killed
by Achilles in the *Iliad*. Sarpedon is another
fighter on the Trojan side, the favorite of Zeus,
who is killed by Achilles' friend Patroclus. The
Simois is the river at Troy, which in the *Iliad*

becomes thick with the blood and bodies of
those killed by Achilles.
2. A pair of shallow, sandy gulfs off the coast
of Libya.
3. Region in modern-day Turkey, allied with
Troy in the *Iliad*.
4. God of the sea (equivalent to the Greek
Poseidon).

sensed the furor above him, the roaring seas first and
the storm breaking next—his standing waters boiling up
from the sea-bed, churning back. And the mighty god,
stirred to his depths, lifts his head from the crests
and serene in power, gazing out over all his realm, 150
he sees Aeneas' squadrons scattered across the ocean,
Trojans overwhelmed by the surf and the wild crashing skies.
Nor did he miss his sister Juno's cunning wrath at work.
He summons the East- and Westwind, takes them to task:
"What insolence! Trusting so to your lofty birth? 155
You winds, you dare make heaven and earth a chaos,
raising such a riot of waves without my blessings.
You—what I won't do! But first I had better set
to rest the flood you ruffled so. Next time, trust me,
you will pay for your crimes with more than just a scolding. 160
Away with you, quick! And give your king this message:
Power over the sea and ruthless trident is mine,
not his—it's mine by lot, by destiny. His place,
Eastwind, is the rough rocks where you are all at home.
Let him bluster there and play the king in his court, 165
let Aeolus rule his bolted dungeon of the winds!"

Quicker than his command he calms the heaving seas,
putting the clouds to rout and bringing back the sun.
Struggling shoulder-to-shoulder, Triton and Cymothoë[5]
hoist and heave the ships from the jagged rocks 170
as the god himself whisks them up with his trident,
clearing a channel through the deadly reefs, his chariot
skimming over the cresting waves on spinning wheels
to set the seas to rest. Just as, all too often,
some huge crowd is seized by a vast uprising, 175
the rabble runs amok, all slaves to passion,
rocks, firebrands flying. Rage finds them arms
but then, if they chance to see a man among them,
one whose devotion and public service lend him weight,
they stand there, stock-still with their ears alert as 180
he rules their furor with his words and calms their passion.
So the crash of the breakers all fell silent once their Father,
gazing over his realm under clear skies, flicks his horses,
giving them free rein, and his eager chariot flies.

Now bone-weary, Aeneas' shipmates make a run 185
for the nearest landfall, wheeling prows around
they turn for Libya's coast. There is a haven shaped
by an island shielding the mouth of a long deep bay, its flanks
breaking the force of combers pounding in from the sea
while drawing them off into calm receding channels. 190
Both sides of the harbor, rock cliffs tower, crowned
by twin crags that menace the sky, overshadowing
reaches of sheltered water, quiet and secure.

5. Triton is a lesser sea god; Cymothoë is a sea nymph.

Over them as a backdrop looms a quivering wood,
above them rears a grove, bristling dark with shade,   195
and fronting the cliff, a cave under hanging rocks
with fresh water inside, seats cut in the native stone,
the home of nymphs. Never a need of cables here to moor
a weathered ship, no anchor with biting flukes to bind her fast.

    Aeneas puts in here with a bare seven warships   200
saved from his whole fleet. How keen their longing
for dry land underfoot as the Trojans disembark,
taking hold of the earth, their last best hope,
and fling their brine-wracked bodies on the sand.
Achates is first to strike a spark from flint,   205
then works to keep it alive in dry leaves,
cups it around with kindling, feeds it chips
and briskly fans the tinder into flame.
Then, spent as they were from all their toil,
they set out food, the bounty of Ceres,[6] drenched   210
in sea-salt, Ceres' utensils too, her mills and troughs,
and bend to parch with fire the grain they had salvaged,
grind it fine on stones.   While they see to their meal
Aeneas scales a crag, straining to scan the sea-reach
far and wide . . . is there any trace of Antheus now,   215
tossed by the gales, or his warships banked with oars?
Or Capys perhaps, or Caicus' stern adorned with shields?[7]
Not a ship in sight. But he does spot three stags
roaming the shore, an entire herd behind them
grazing down the glens in a long ranked line.   220
He halts, grasps his bow and his flying arrows,
the weapons his trusty aide Achates keeps at hand.
First the leaders, antlers branching over their high heads,
he brings them down, then turns on the herd, his shafts
stampeding the rest like rabble into the leafy groves.   225
Shaft on shaft, no stopping him till he stretches
seven hefty carcases on the ground—a triumph,
one for each of his ships—and makes for the cove,
divides the kill with his whole crew and then shares out
the wine that good Acestes,[8] princely man, had brimmed   230
in their casks the day they left Sicilian shores.

    The commander's words relieve their stricken hearts:
"My comrades, hardly strangers to pain before now,
we all have weathered worse. Some god will grant us
an end to this as well. You've threaded the rocks   235
resounding with Scylla's howling rabid dogs,
and taken the brunt of the Cyclops' boulders, too.
Call up your courage again. Dismiss your grief and fear.

---

6. Goddess of grain and harvest.
7. Names of lost Trojan leaders.

8. King in Sicily who gave the Trojans shelter
and extra supplies.

A joy it will be one day, perhaps, to remember even this.
Through so many hard straits, so many twists and turns   240
our course holds firm for Latium.[9] There Fate holds out
a homeland, calm, at peace. There the gods decree
the kingdom of Troy will rise again. Bear up.
Save your strength for better times to come."
                                        Brave words.
Sick with mounting cares he assumes a look of hope   245
and keeps his anguish buried in his heart.
The men gird up for the game, the coming feast,
they skin the hide from the ribs, lay bare the meat.
Some cut it into quivering strips, impale it on skewers,
some set cauldrons along the beach and fire them to the boil.   250
Then they renew their strength with food, stretched out
on the beachgrass, fill themselves with seasoned wine
and venison rich and crisp. Their hunger sated,
the tables cleared away, they talk on for hours,
asking after their missing shipmates—wavering now   255
between hope and fear: what to believe about the rest?
Were the men still alive or just in the last throes,
forever lost to their comrades' farflung calls?
Aeneas most of all, devoted to his shipmates,
deep within himself he moans for the losses . . .   260
now for Orontes, hardy soldier, now for Amycus,
now for the brutal fate that Lycus may have met,
then Gyas and brave Cloanthus, hearts of oak.

    Their mourning was over now as Jove from high heaven,
gazing down on the sea, the whitecaps winged with sails,   265
the lands outspread, the coasts, the nations of the earth,
paused at the zenith of the sky and set his sights
on Libya, that proud kingdom. All at once,
as he took to heart the struggles he beheld,
Venus[1] approached in rare sorrow, tears abrim   270
in her sparkling eyes, and begged: "Oh you who rule
the lives of men and gods with your everlasting laws
and your lightning bolt of terror, what crime could my Aeneas
commit against you, what dire harm could the Trojans do
that after bearing so many losses, this wide world   275
is shut to them now? And all because of Italy.
Surely from them the Romans would arise one day
as the years roll on, and leaders would as well,
descended from Teucer's[2] blood brought back to life,
to rule all lands and seas with boundless power—   280
you promised! Father, what motive changed your mind?
With that, at least, I consoled myself for Troy's demise,
that heart-rending ruin—weighing fate against fate.
But now after all my Trojans suffered, still

9. Region of central Italy, home of the Latin race.
1. Aeneas's mother; goddess of love and sex.
2. Legendary first king of Troy.

the same disastrous fortune drives them on and on.   285
What end, great king, do you set to their ordeals?

   "Antenor[3] could slip out from under the Greek siege,
then make his passage through the Illyrian gulfs and,
safe through the inlands where the Liburnians rule,
he struggled past the Timavus River's source.[4]   290
There, through its nine mouths as the mountain caves
roar back, the river bursts out into full flood,
a thundering surf that overpowers the fields.
Reaching Italy, he erected a city for his people,
a Trojan home called Padua—gave them a Trojan name,   295
hung up their Trojan arms and there, after long wars,
he lingers on in serene and settled peace.
                              "But we,
your own children, the ones you swore would hold
the battlements of heaven—now our ships are lost,
appalling! We are abandoned, thanks to the rage   300
of a single foe, cut off from Italy's shores.
Is this our reward for reverence,[5]
this the way you give us back our throne?"

   The Father of Men and Gods, smiling down on her
with the glance that clears the sky and calms the tempest,   305
lightly kissing his daughter on the lips, replied:
"Relieve yourself of fear, my lady of Cythera,[6]
the fate of your children stands unchanged, I swear.
You will see your promised city, see Lavinium's walls
and bear your great-hearted Aeneas up to the stars on high.   310
Nothing has changed my mind. No, your son, believe me—
since anguish is gnawing at you, I will tell you more,
unrolling the scroll of Fate
to reveal its darkest secrets. Aeneas will wage
a long, costly war in Italy, crush defiant tribes   315
and build high city walls for his people there
and found the rule of law. Only three summers
will see him govern Latium, three winters pass
in barracks after the Latins have been broken.
But his son Ascanius, now that he gains the name   320
of Iulus—Ilus he was, while Ilium ruled on high[7]—
will fill out with his own reign thirty sovereign years,
a giant cycle of months revolving round and round,
transferring his rule from its old Lavinian home
to raise up Alba Longa's mighty ramparts.   325

3. Trojan leader who escaped the city's sack
and settled in northern Italy.
4. Illyrium was a district, the Liburnians a
people, and Timavus a river on the coast of the
northern Adriatic sea.
5. *Pietas.*
6. Greek island where there was a cult of

Aphrodite.
7. *Ilium* is another name for Troy (hence the
title of Homer's epic poem: the *Iliad*). The
Julian family, which included Julius Caesar and
Augustus, claimed descent from Iulus (Julus),
originally name Ascanius.

There, in turn, for a full three hundred years
the dynasty of Hector will hold sway till Ilia,
a royal priestess great with the brood of Mars,
will bear the god twin sons.[8] Then one, Romulus,
reveling in the tawny pelt of a wolf that nursed him,   330
will inherit the line and build the walls of Mars
and after his own name, call his people Romans.[9]
On them I set no limits, space or time:
I have granted them power, empire without end.
Even furious Juno, now plaguing the land and sea and sky   335
with terror: she will mend her ways and hold dear with me
these Romans, lords of the earth, the race arrayed in togas.
This is my pleasure, my decree. Indeed, an age will come,
as the long years slip by, when Assaracus'[1] royal house
will quell Achilles' homeland, brilliant Mycenae too,   340
and enslave their people, rule defeated Argos.
From that noble blood will arise a Trojan Caesar,
his empire bound by the Ocean, his glory by the stars:
Julius, a name passed down from Iulus, his great forebear.
And you, in years to come, will welcome him to the skies,   345
you rest assured—laden with plunder of the East,
and he with Aeneas will be invoked in prayer.[2]
Then will the violent centuries, battles set aside,
grow gentle, kind. Vesta[3] and silver-haired Good Faith
and Romulus flanked by brother Remus will make the laws.   350
The terrible Gates of War with their welded iron bars
will stand bolted shut,[4] and locked inside, the Frenzy
of civil strife will crouch down on his savage weapons,
hands pinioned behind his back with a hundred brazen shackles,
monstrously roaring out from his bloody jaws."
                                                So   355
he decrees and speeds the son of Maia[5] down the sky
to make the lands and the new stronghold, Carthage,
open in welcome to the Trojans, not let Dido,
unaware of fate, expel them from her borders.
Down through the vast clear air flies Mercury,   360
rowing his wings like oars and in a moment
stands on Libya's shores, obeys commands
and the will of god is done.

8. Ilia, also known as Rhea Silvia, was a priest-ess sworn to religious celibacy. She was raped by Mars, the god of war, and gave birth to twins, Romulus and Remus. Her brother, jeal-ous of his own power, ordered that the babies be killed; but instead, his servant abandoned them in the wild, to be rescued by a wolf that suckled them and raised them.
9. Virgil omits the fact that Romulus killed his brother, Remus, to gain sole power over the city.
1. An early king of Troy.

2. The "Trojan Caesar" is either Julius Cae-sar, who made Rome an empire, or Augustus himself, who had plundered "the East" by defeating the Egyptian queen Cleopatra.
3. Vesta is the goddess of the hearth, repre-sentative of home life.
4. There were real Gates of War in the temple of Janus, which Augustus shut in 25 B.C.E.—the first time they had been shut since 235 B.C.E.
5. A daughter of Atlas who was impregnated by Jupiter and gave birth to Mercury (Roman version of Hermes), the messenger god.

The Carthaginians calm their fiery temper
and Queen Dido, above all, takes to heart   365
a spirit of peace and warm good will to meet
the men of Troy.
               But Aeneas, duty-bound,
his mind restless with worries all that night,
reached a firm resolve as the fresh day broke.
Out he goes to explore the strange terrain . . .   370
what coast had the stormwinds brought him to?
Who lives here? All he sees is wild, untilled—
what men, or what creatures? Then report the news
to all his comrades. So, concealing his ships
in the sheltered woody narrows overarched by rocks   375
and screened around by trees and trembling shade,
Aeneas moves out, with only Achates at his side,
two steel-tipped javelins balanced in his grip.
Suddenly, in the heart of the woods, his mother
crossed his path. She looked like a young girl,   380
a Spartan girl decked out in dress and gear
or Thracian Harpalyce tiring out her mares,
outracing the Hebrus River's rapid tides.[6]
Hung from a shoulder, a bow that fit her grip,
a huntress for all the world, she'd let her curls   385
go streaming free in the wind, her knees were bare,
her flowing skirts hitched up with a tight knot.

   She speaks out first: "You there, young soldiers,
did you by any chance see one of my sisters?
Which way did she go? Roaming the woods,   390
a quiver slung from her belt,
wearing a spotted lynx-skin, or in full cry,
hot on the track of some great frothing boar?"
So Venus asked and the son of Venus answered:
"Not one of your sisters have I seen or heard . . .   395
but how should I greet a young girl like you?
Your face, your features—hardly a mortal's looks
and the tone of your voice is hardly human either.
Oh a goddess, without a doubt! What, are you
Apollo's sister? Or one of the breed of Nymphs?   400
Be kind, whoever you are, relieve our troubled hearts.
Under what skies and onto what coasts of the world
have we been driven? Tell us, please. Castaways,
we know nothing, not the people, not the place—
lost, hurled here by the gales and heavy seas.   405
Many a victim will fall before your altars,
we'll slaughter them for you!"

6. The goddess Venus is dressed like a Spartan, a famously athletic and militaristic Greek
people, or Harpalyce, a girl who lived in the
wilds and devoted herself to hunting. The
Hebrus is a river in Thrace. In Greco-Roman
tradition, hunting was considered antithetical
to sex and marriage.

But Venus replied:
"Now there's an honor I really don't deserve.
It's just the style for Tyrian girls to sport
a quiver and high-laced hunting boots in crimson.   410
What you see is a Punic[7] kingdom, people of Tyre
and Agenor's town, but the border's held by Libyans
hard to break in war. Phoenician Dido is in command,
she sailed from Tyre, in flight from her own brother.
Oh it's a long tale of crime, long, twisting, dark,   415
but I'll try to trace the high points in their order . . .

    "Dido was married to Sychaeus, the richest man in Tyre,
and she, poor girl, was consumed with love for him.
Her father gave her away, wed for the first time,
a virgin still, and these her first solemn rites.   420
But her brother held power in Tyre—Pygmalion,
a monster, the vilest man alive.
A murderous feud broke out between both men.
Pygmalion, catching Sychaeus off guard at the altar,
slaughtered him in blood. That unholy man, so blind   425
in his lust for gold he ran him through with a sword,
then hid the crime for months, deaf to his sister's love,
her heartbreak. Still he mocked her with wicked lies,
with empty hopes. But she had a dream one night.
The true ghost of her husband, not yet buried,   430
came and lifting his face—ashen, awesome in death—
showed her the cruel altar, the wounds that pierced his chest
and exposed the secret horror that lurked within the house.
He urged her on: 'Take flight from our homeland, quick!'
And then he revealed an unknown ancient treasure,   435
an untold weight of silver and gold, a comrade
to speed her on her way.
    "Driven by all this,
Dido plans her escape, collects her followers
fired by savage hate of the tyrant or bitter fear.
They seize some galleys set to sail, load them with gold—   440
the wealth Pygmalion craved—and they bear it overseas
and a woman leads them all. Reaching this haven here,
where now you will see the steep ramparts rising,
the new city of Carthage—the Tyrians purchased land as
large as a bull's-hide could enclose but cut in strips for size   445
and called it Byrsa, the Hide, for the spread they'd bought.
But you, who are you? What shores do you come from?
Where are you headed now?"
    He answered her questions,
drawing a labored sigh from deep within his chest:
"Goddess, if I'd retrace our story to its start,   450
if you had time to hear the saga of our ordeals,
before I finished the Evening Star would close
the gates of Olympus, put the day to sleep . . .

7. I.e., Carthaginian.

From old Troy we come—Troy it's called, perhaps
you've heard the name—sailing over the world's seas   455
until, by chance, some whim of the winds, some tempest
drove us onto Libyan shores. I am Aeneas, duty-bound.
I carry aboard my ships the gods of house and home
we seized from enemy hands. My fame goes past the skies.
I seek my homeland—Italy—born as I am from highest Jove.   460
I launched out on the Phrygian sea with twenty ships,
my goddess mother marking the way, and followed hard
on the course the Fates had charted. A mere seven,
battered by wind and wave, survived the worst.
I myself am a stranger, utterly at a loss,   465
trekking over this wild Libyan wasteland,
forced from Europe, Asia too, an exile—"

    Venus could bear no more of his laments
and broke in on his tale of endless hardship:
"Whoever you are, I scarcely think the Powers hate you: 470
you enjoy the breath of life, you've reached a Tyrian city.
So off you go now. Take this path to the queen's gates.
I have good news. Your friends are restored to you,
your fleet's reclaimed. The winds swerved from the North
and drove them safe to port. True, unless my parents   475
taught me to read the flight of birds for nothing.
Look at those dozen swans triumphant in formation!
The eagle of Jove[8] had just swooped down on them all
from heaven's heights and scattered them into open sky,
but now you can see them flying trim in their long ranks,   480
landing or looking down where their friends have landed—
home, cavorting on ruffling wings and wheeling round
the sky in convoy, trumpeting in their glory.
So homeward bound, your ships and hardy shipmates
anchor in port now or approach the harbor's mouth,   485
full sail ahead. Now off you go, move on,
wherever the path leads you, steer your steps."
                                              At that,
as she turned away her neck shone with a rosy glow,
her mane of hair gave off an ambrosial fragrance,
her skirt flowed loose, rippling down to her feet   490
and her stride alone revealed her as a goddess.
He knew her at once—his mother—
and called after her now as she sped away:
"Why, you too, cruel as the rest? So often
you ridicule your son with your disguises!   495
Why can't we clasp hands, embrace each other,
speak out, and tell the truth?"

    Reproving her so, he makes his way toward town
but Venus screens the travelers off with a dense mist,

8. The eagle, king of the birds, was associated with Jupiter.

pouring round them a cloak of clouds with all her power,   500
so no one could see them, no one reach and hold them,
cause them to linger now or ask why they had come.
But she herself, lifting into the air, wings her way
toward Paphos,[9] racing with joy to reach her home again
where her temples stand and a hundred altars steam   505
with Arabian incense, redolent with the scent
of fresh-cut wreaths.
                    Meanwhile the two men
are hurrying on their way as the path leads,
now climbing a steep hill arching over the city,
looking down on the facing walls and high towers.   510
Aeneas marvels at its mass—once a cluster of huts—
he marvels at gates and bustling hum and cobbled streets.
The Tyrians press on with the work, some aligning the walls,
struggling to raise the citadel, trundling stones up slopes;
some picking the building sites and plowing out their boundaries,   515
others drafting laws, electing judges, a senate held in awe.
Here they're dredging a harbor, there they lay foundations
deep for a theater, quarrying out of rock great columns
to form a fitting scene for stages still to come.
As hard at their tasks as bees in early summer,   520
working the blooming meadows under the sun
escorting a new brood out, young adults now,
or pressing oozing honey into the combs, the nectar
brimming the bulging cells, or gathering up the plunder
workers haul back in, or closing ranks like an army,   525
driving the drones, that lazy crew, from home.
The hive seethes with life, exhaling the scent
of honey sweet with thyme.
                    "How lucky they are,"
Aeneas cries, gazing up at the city's heights,
"their walls are rising now!" And on he goes,   530
cloaked in cloud—remarkable—right in their midst
he blends in with the crowds, and no one sees him.

   Now deep in the heart of Carthage stood a grove,
lavish with shade, where the Tyrians, making landfall,
still shaken by wind and breakers, first unearthed that sign: 535
Queen Juno had led their way to the fiery stallion's head
that signaled power in war and ease in life for ages.
Here Dido of Tyre was building Juno a mighty temple,
rich with gifts and the goddess' aura of power.
Bronze the threshold crowning a flight of stairs,   540
the doorposts sheathed in bronze, and the bronze doors
groaned deep on their hinges.
                    Here in this grove
a strange sight met his eyes and calmed his fears
for the first time. Here, for the first time,

9. Greek island where there was a cult center of Aphrodite.

Aeneas dared to hope he had found some haven, 545
for all his hard straits, to trust in better days.
For awaiting the queen, beneath the great temple now,
exploring its features one by one, amazed at it all,
the city's splendor, the work of rival workers' hands
and the vast scale of their labors—all at once he sees, 550
spread out from first to last, the battles fought at Troy,
the fame of the Trojan War now known throughout the world,
Atreus' sons and Priam—Achilles, savage to both at once.[1]
Aeneas came to a halt and wept, and "Oh Achates,"
he cried, "is there anywhere, any place on earth 555
not filled with our ordeals? There's Priam, look!
Even here, merit will have its true reward . . .
even here, the world is a world of tears
and the burdens of mortality touch the heart.
Dismiss your fears. Trust me, this fame of ours 560
will offer us some haven."
            So Aeneas says,
feeding his spirit on empty, lifeless pictures,
groaning low, the tears rivering down his face
as he sees once more the fighters circling Troy.
Here Greeks in flight, routed by Troy's young ranks, 565
there Trojans routed by plumed Achilles in his chariot.
Just in range are the snow-white canvas tents of Rhesus—
he knows them at once, and sobs—Rhesus' men betrayed
in their first slumber, droves of them slaughtered
by Diomedes splattered with their blood, lashing 570
back to the Greek camp their highstrung teams
before they could ever savor the grass of Troy
or drink at Xanthus' banks.[2]
                    Next Aeneas sees
Troilus[3] in flight, his weapons flung aside,
unlucky boy, no match for Achilles' onslaught— 575
horses haul him on, tangled behind an empty warcar,
flat on his back, clinging still to the reins, his neck
and hair dragging along the ground, the butt of his javelin
scrawling zigzags in the dust.
                    And here the Trojan women
are moving toward the temple of Pallas,[4] their deadly foe, 580
their hair unbound as they bear the robe, their offering,
suppliants grieving, palms beating their breasts
but Pallas turns away, staring at the ground.
                    And Hector—
three times Achilles has hauled him round the walls of Troy

1. That is, Achilles was angry with Greeks as well as Trojans. *Atreus' sons*: Agamemnon and Menelaus, the Greek commanders in the Trojan War.
2. Rhesus, king of Thrace, came to help the Trojans, but was slaughtered by Odysseus and Diomedes in a night raid. An oracle had proclaimed that if Rhesus's horses ate Trojan grass and drank from the river Xanthus, Troy would not fall.
3. Troilus was a young son of King Priam of Troy.
4. Athena, who was hostile to Troy.

and now he's selling his lifeless body off for gold.   585
Aeneas gives a groan, heaving up from his depths,
he sees the plundered armor, the car, the corpse
of his great friend, and Priam reaching out
with helpless hands . . . [5]
                        He even sees himself
swept up in the melee, clashing with Greek captains,   590
sees the troops of the dawn and swarthy Memnon's[6] arms.
And Penthesilea leading her Amazons bearing half-moon shields[7]—
she blazes with battle-fury out in front of her army,
cinching a golden breastband under her bared breast,
a girl, a warrior queen who dares to battle men.
                                        And now   595
as Trojan Aeneas, gazing in awe at all the scenes of Troy,
stood there, spellbound, eyes fixed on the war alone,
the queen aglow with beauty approached the temple,
Dido, with massed escorts marching in her wake.
Like Diana urging her dancing troupes along   600
the Eurotas' banks or up Mount Cynthus' ridge[8]
as a thousand mountain-nymphs crowd in behind her,
left and right—with quiver slung from her shoulder,
taller than any other goddess as she goes striding on
and silent Latona[9] thrills with joy too deep for words.   605
Like Dido now, striding triumphant among her people,
spurring on the work of their kingdom still to come.
And then by Juno's doors beneath the vaulted dome,
flanked by an honor guard beside her lofty seat,
the queen assumed her throne. Here as she handed down   610
decrees and laws to her people, sharing labors fairly,
some by lot, some with her sense of justice, Aeneas
suddenly sees his men approaching through the crowds,
Antheus, Sergestus, gallant Cloanthus, other Trojans
the black gales had battered over the seas   615
and swept to far-flung coasts.
                        Aeneas, Achates,
both were amazed, both struck with joy and fear.
They yearn to grasp their companions' hands in haste
but both men are unnerved by the mystery of it all.
So, cloaked in folds of mist, they hide their feelings,   620
waiting, hoping to see what luck their friends have found.
Where have they left their ships, what coast? Why have they come?
These picked men, still marching in from the whole armada,
pressing toward the temple amid the rising din
to plead for some goodwill.

5. Having killed Hector, Achilles dragged his corpse around the city behind his chariot, until Priam came to ransom his son's body.
6. King of the Ethiopians, who fought on the Trojan side.
7. The Amazons were a race of warrior women who fought for Troy.

8. Diana (Artemis in Greek mythology) is the virgin goddess associated with hunting. She was born on Delos, the island location of Mount Cynthus; Eurotas was a river in Sparta where she was worshipped.
9. Leto, Diana's mother.

Once they had entered,   625
allowed to appeal before the queen—the eldest,
Prince Ilioneus, calm, composed, spoke out:
"Your majesty, empowered by Jove to found
your new city here and curb rebellious tribes
with your sense of justice—we poor Trojans, 630
castaways, tossed by storms over all the seas;
we beg you: keep the cursed fire off our ships!
Pity us, god-fearing men! Look on us kindly,
see the state we are in. We have not come
to put your Libyan gods and homes to the sword, 635
loot them and haul our plunder toward the beach.
No, such pride, such violence has no place
in the hearts of beaten men.
     "There is a country—
the Greeks called it Hesperia, Land of the West,
an ancient land, mighty in war and rich in soil. 640
Oenotrians[1] settled it; now we hear their descendants
call their kingdom Italy, after their leader, Italus.
Italy-bound we were when, surging with sudden breakers
stormy Orion[2] drove us against blind shoals and from the South
came vicious gales to scatter us, whelmed by the sea, 645
across the murderous surf and rocky barrier reefs:
We few escaped and floated toward your coast.
What kind of men are these? What land is this,
that you can tolerate such barbaric ways?
We are denied the sailor's right to shore— 650
attacked, forbidden even a footing on your beach.
If you have no use for humankind and mortal armor,
at least respect the gods. They know right from wrong.
They don't forget.
     "We once had a king, Aeneas . . .
none more just, none more devoted to duty, none 655
more brave in arms. If Fate has saved that man,
if he still draws strength from the air we breathe,
if he's not laid low, not yet with the heartless shades,
fear not, nor will you once regret the first step
you take to compete with him in kindness. 660
We have cities too, in the land of Sicily,
arms and a king, Acestes, born of Trojan blood.
Permit us to haul our storm-racked ships ashore,
trim new oars, hew timbers out of your woods, so that,
if we are fated to sail for Italy—king and crews restored— 665
to Italy, to Latium we will sail with buoyant hearts.
But if we have lost our haven there, if Libyan waters
hold you now, my captain, best of the men of Troy,
and all our hopes for Iulus have been dashed,
at least we can cross back over Sicilian seas, 670

---

1. An ancient Italic people.
2. This constellation marks the approach of winter.

the straits we came from, homes ready and waiting,
and seek out great Acestes for our king."

    So Ilioneus closed. And with one accord
the Trojans murmured Yes.
                          Her eyes lowered,
Dido replies with a few choice words of welcome: 675
"Cast fear to the winds, Trojans, free your minds.
Our kingdom is new. Our hard straits have forced me
to set defenses, station guards along our far frontiers.
Who has not heard of Aeneas' people, his city, Troy,
her men, her heroes, the flames of that horrendous war?   680
We are not so dull of mind, we Carthaginians here.
When he yokes his team, the Sun shines down on us as well.
Whatever you choose, great Hesperia—Saturn's fields—
or the shores of Eryx with Acestes as your king,[3]
I will provide safe passage, escorts and support   685
to speed you on your way. Or would you rather
settle here in my realm on equal terms with me?
This city I build—it's yours. Haul ships to shore.
Trojans, Tyrians: they will be all the same to me.
If only the storm that drove you drove your king   690
and Aeneas were here now! Indeed, I'll send out
trusty men to scour the coast of Libya far and wide.
Perhaps he's shipwrecked, lost in woods or towns."

    Spirits lifting at Dido's welcome, brave Achates
and captain Aeneas had long chafed to break free   695
of the mist, and now Achates spurs Aeneas on:
"Son of Venus, what feelings are rising in you now?
You see the coast is clear, our ships and friends restored.
Just one is lost. We saw him drown at sea ourselves.
All else is just as your mother promised."   700

    He'd barely ended when all at once the mist
around them parted, melting into the open air,
and there Aeneas stood, clear in the light of day,
his head, his shoulders, the man was like a god.
His own mother had breathed her beauty on her son,   705
a gloss on his flowing hair, and the ruddy glow of youth,
and radiant joy shone in his eyes. His beauty fine
as a craftsman's hand can add to ivory, or aglow
as silver or Parian marble[4] ringed in glinting gold.

    Suddenly, surprising all, he tells the queen: 710
"Here I am before you, the man you are looking for,
Aeneas the Trojan, plucked from Libya's heavy seas.
You alone have pitied the long ordeals of Troy—unspeakable—

---

3. Hesperia is "the western land," that is, Italy.
In Roman mythology, the Titan god Saturn,
when driven out by Jupiter, fled to Italy and
established the Golden Age. *Eryx*: city in Sicily.
4. That is, marble from the island of Paros; famous for its whiteness.

and here you would share your city and your home with us,
this remnant left by the Greeks. We who have drunk deep   715
of each and every disaster land and sea can offer.
Stripped of everything, now it's past our power
to reward you gift for gift, Dido, theirs as well,
whoever may survive of the Dardan[5] people still,
strewn over the wide world now. But may the gods,   720
if there are Powers who still respect the good and true,
if justice still exists on the face of the earth,
may they and their own sense of right and wrong
bring you your just rewards.
What age has been so blest to give you birth?   725
What noble parents produced so fine a daughter?
So long as rivers run to the sea, so long as shadows
travel the mountain slopes and the stars range the skies,
your honor, your name, your praise will live forever,
whatever lands may call me to their shores."
                                With that,   730
he extends his right hand toward his friend Ilioneus,
greeting Serestus with his left, and then the others,
gallant Gyas, gallant Cloanthus.
                      Tyrian Dido marveled,
first at the sight of him, next at all he'd suffered,
then she said aloud: "Born of a goddess, even so   735
what destiny hunts you down through such ordeals?
What violence lands you on this frightful coast?
Are you that Aeneas whom loving Venus bore
to Dardan Anchises on the Simois' banks at Troy?
Well I remember . . . Teucer came to Sidon once,   740
banished from native ground, searching for new realms,
and my father Belus helped him.[6] Belus had sacked Cyprus,
plundered that rich island, ruled with a victor's hand.
From that day on I have known of Troy's disaster,
known your name, and all the kings of Greece.   745
Teucer, your enemy, often sang Troy's praises,
claiming his own descent from Teucer's ancient stock.
So come, young soldiers, welcome to our house.
My destiny, harrying me with trials hard as yours,
led me as well, at last, to anchor in this land.   750
Schooled in suffering, now I learn to comfort
those who suffer too."
                   With that greeting
she leads Aeneas into the royal halls, announcing
offerings in the gods' high temples as she goes.
Not forgetting to send his shipmates on the beaches   755
twenty bulls and a hundred huge, bristling razorbacks
and a hundred fatted lambs together with their mothers:
gifts to make this day a day of joy.

---

5. Dardanus founded the city of Dardania, just above Troy; hence the Dardans or Dardanians are the Trojans.
6. After the fall of Troy, Teucer (a Trojan archer who fought on the Greek side) was exiled and later founded Salamis, a city on the island of Cyprus. (This Teucer is not the legendary founder of Troy; see line 279.)

Within the palace
all is decked with adornments, lavish, regal splendor.
In the central hall they are setting out a banquet, 760
draping the gorgeous purple, intricately worked,
heaping the board with grand displays of silver
and gold engraved with her fathers' valiant deeds,
a long, unending series of captains and commands,
traced through a line of heroes since her country's birth. 765

Aeneas—a father's love would give the man no rest—
quickly sends Achates down to the ships to take
the news to Ascanius, bring him back to Carthage.
All his paternal care is focused on his son.
He tells Achates to fetch some gifts as well, 770
plucked from the ruins of Troy: a gown stiff
with figures stitched in gold, and a woven veil
with yellow sprays of acanthus round the border.
Helen's glory, gifts she carried out of Mycenae,
fleeing Argos for Troy to seal her wicked marriage— 775
the marvelous handiwork of Helen's mother, Leda.
Aeneas adds the scepter Ilione used to bear,
the eldest daughter of Priam; a necklace too,
strung with pearls, and a crown of double bands,
one studded with gems, the other, gold. Achates, 780
following orders, hurries toward the ships.

But now Venus is mulling over some new schemes,
new intrigues. Altered in face and figure, Cupid[7]
would go in place of the captivating Ascanius,
using his gifts to fire the queen to madness, 785
weaving a lover's ardor through her bones.
No doubt Venus fears that treacherous house
and the Tyrians' forked tongues,
and brutal Juno inflames her anguish too
and her cares keep coming back as night draws on. 790
So Venus makes an appeal to Love, her winged son:
"You, my son, are my strength, my greatest power—
you alone, my son, can scoff at the lightning bolts
the high and mighty Father hurled against Typhoeus.[8]
Help me, I beg you. I need all your immortal force. 795
Your brother Aeneas is tossed round every coast on earth,
thanks to Juno's ruthless hatred, as you well know,
and time and again you've grieved to see my grief.
But now Phoenician Dido has him in her clutches,
holding him back with smooth, seductive words, 800
and I fear the outcome of Juno's welcome here . . .
She won't sit tight while Fate is turning on its hinge.
So I plan to forestall her with ruses of my own

7. Cupid (whose name means "desire") is the
son of Venus and the god of sexual desire.
8. Jupiter hurled thunderbolts at the monster

Typhoeus (Typhon), and finally trapped him
under Mount Etna.

and besiege the queen with flames,
and no goddess will change her mood—she's mine,   805
my ally-in-arms in my great love for Aeneas.

"Now how can you go about this? Hear my plan.
His dear father has just sent for the young prince—
he means the world to me—and he's bound for Carthage now,
bearing presents saved from the sea, the flames of Troy.   810
I'll lull him into a deep sleep and hide him far away
on Cythera's heights or high Idalium,[9] my shrines,
so he cannot learn of my trap or spring it open
while it's being set. And you with your cunning,
forge his appearance—just one night, no more—put on   815
the familiar features of the boy, boy that you are,
so when the wine flows free at the royal board
and Dido, lost in joy, cradles you in her lap,
caressing, kissing you gently, you can breathe
your secret fire into her, poison the queen   820
and she will never know."
                    Cupid leaps at once
to his loving mother's orders. Shedding his wings
he masquerades as Iulus, prancing with his stride.
But now Venus distils a deep, soothing sleep
into Iulus' limbs, and warming him in her breast   825
the goddess spirits him off to her high Idalian grove
where beds of marjoram breathe and embrace him with aromatic
flowers and rustling shade.
                    Now Cupid is on the move,
under her orders, bringing the Tyrians royal gifts,
his spirits high as Achates leads him on.   830
Arriving, he finds the queen already poised
on a golden throne beneath the sumptuous hangings,
commanding the very center of her palace. Now Aeneas,
the good captain, enters, then the Trojan soldiers,
taking their seats on couches draped in purple.   835
Servants pour them water to rinse their hands,
quickly serving them bread from baskets, spreading
their laps with linens, napkins clipped and smooth.
In the kitchens are fifty serving-maids assigned
to lay out foods in a long line, course by course,   840
and honor the household gods by building fires high.
A hundred other maids and a hundred men, all matched in age,
are spreading the feast on trestles, setting out the cups.
And Tyrians join them, bustling through the doors,
filling the hall with joy, to take invited seats   845
on brocaded couches. They admire Aeneas' gifts,
admire Iulus now—the glowing face of the god
and the god's dissembling words—and Helen's gown
and the veil adorned with a yellow acanthus border.

9. Another town with a temple of Venus, in Cyprus.

But above all, tragic Dido, doomed to a plague   850
about to strike, cannot feast her eyes enough,
thrilled both by the boy and gifts he brings
and the more she looks the more the fire grows.
But once he's embraced Aeneas, clung to his neck
to sate the deep love of his father, deluded father,   855
Cupid makes for the queen. Her gaze, her whole heart
is riveted on him now, and at times she even warms him
snugly in her breast, for how can she know, poor Dido,
what a mighty god is sinking into her, to her grief?
But he, recalling the wishes of his mother Venus,   860
blots out the memory of Sychaeus bit by bit,
trying to seize with a fresh, living love
a heart at rest for long—long numb to passion.
                                        Then,
with the first lull in the feast, the tables cleared away,
they set out massive bowls and crown the wine with wreaths.   865
A vast din swells in the palace, voices reverberating
through the echoing halls. They light the lamps,
hung from the coffered ceilings sheathed in gilt,
and blazing torches burn the night away.
The queen calls for a heavy golden bowl,   870
studded with jewels and brimmed with unmixed wine,
the bowl that Belus[1] and all of Belus' sons had brimmed,
and the hall falls hushed as Dido lifts a prayer:
"Jupiter, you, they say, are the god who grants
the laws of host and guest. May this day be one   875
of joy for Tyrians here and exiles come from Troy,
a day our sons will long remember. Bacchus,[2]
giver of bliss, and Juno, generous Juno,
bless us now. And come, my people, celebrate
with all goodwill this feast that makes us one!"   880

    With that prayer, she poured a libation to the gods,
tipping wine on the board, and tipping it, she was first
to take the bowl, brushing it lightly with her lips,
then gave it to Bitias—laughing, goading him on
and he took the plunge, draining the foaming bowl,   885
drenching himself in its brimming, overflowing gold,
and the other princes drank in turn. Then Iopas,
long-haired bard, strikes up his golden lyre
resounding through the halls. Giant Atlas[3]
had been his teacher once, and now he sings   890
the wandering moon and laboring sun eclipsed,
the roots of the human race and the wild beasts,
the source of storms and the lightning bolts on high,
Arcturus, the rainy Hyades and the Great and Little Bears,[4]

1. Dido's father.
2. God of wine (Dionysus in Greek mythology).
3. A Titan condemned for his defiance of

Jupiter to hold up the sky forever.
4. Stars and constellations.

and why the winter suns so rush to bathe themselves in the sea   895
and what slows down the nights to a long lingering crawl . . .
And time and again the Tyrians burst into applause
and the Trojans took their lead. So Dido, doomed,
was lengthening out the night by trading tales
as she drank long draughts of love—asking Aeneas   900
question on question, now about Priam, now Hector,
what armor Memnon, son of the Morning, wore at Troy,
how swift were the horses of Diomedes? How strong was Achilles?
"Wait, come, my guest," she urges, "tell us your own story,
start to finish—the ambush laid by the Greeks, the pain   905
your people suffered, the wanderings you have faced.
For now is the seventh summer that has borne you
wandering all the lands and seas on earth."

BOOK II

[The Final Hours of Troy]

Silence. All fell hushed, their eyes fixed on Aeneas now
as the founder of his people, high on a seat of honor,
set out on his story: "Sorrow, unspeakable sorrow,
my queen, you ask me to bring to life once more,
how the Greeks uprooted Troy in all her power,   5
our kingdom mourned forever. What horrors I saw,
a tragedy where I played a leading role myself.
Who could tell such things—not even a Myrmidon,
a Dolopian,[5] or comrade of iron-hearted Ulysses[6]—
and still refrain from tears? And now, too,   10
the dank night is sweeping down from the sky
and the setting stars incline our heads to sleep.
But if you long so deeply to know what we went through,
to hear, in brief, the last great agony of Troy,
much as I shudder at the memory of it all—   15
I shrank back in grief—I'll try to tell it now . . .

    "Ground down by the war and driven back by Fate,
the Greek captains had watched the years slip by
until, helped by Minerva's superhuman skill,
they built that mammoth horse, immense as a mountain,   20
lining its ribs with ship timbers hewn from pine.
An offering to secure safe passage home, or so
they pretend, and the story spreads through Troy.
But they pick by lot the best, most able-bodied men
and stealthily lock them into the horse's dark flanks   25
till the vast hold of the monster's womb is packed
with soldiers bristling weapons.
                            "Just in sight of Troy
an island rises, Tenedos, famed in the old songs,

5. Myrmidons and Dolopians are companions   6. Roman name for Odysseus.
of Achilles.

powerful, rich, while Priam's realm stood fast.
Now it's only a bay, a treacherous cove for ships.   30
Well there they sail, hiding out on its lonely coast
while we thought—gone! Sped home on the winds to Greece.
So all Troy breathes free, relieved of her endless sorrow.
We fling open the gates and stream out, elated to see
the Greeks' abandoned camp, the deserted beachhead.   35
Here the Dolopians[7] formed ranks—
                              "Here savage Achilles
pitched his tents—
                              "Over there the armada moored
and here the familiar killing-fields of battle.
Some gaze wonderstruck at the gift for Pallas,
the virgin never wed[8]—transfixed by the horse,   40
its looming mass, our doom. Thymoetes leads the way.
'Drag it inside the walls,' he urges, 'plant it high
on the city heights!' Inspired by treachery now
or the fate of Troy was moving toward this end.
But Capys with other saner heads who take his side,   45
suspecting a trap in any gift the Greeks might offer,
tells us: 'Fling it into the sea or torch the thing to ash
or bore into the depths of its womb where men can hide!'
The common people are split into warring factions.

    "But now, out in the lead with a troop of comrades,   50
down Laocoön[9] runs from the heights in full fury,
calling out from a distance: 'Poor doomed fools,
have you gone mad, you Trojans?
You really believe the enemy's sailed away?
Or any gift of the Greeks is free of guile?   55
Is that how well you know Ulysses? Trust me,
either the Greeks are hiding, shut inside those beams,
or the horse is a battle-engine geared to breach our walls,
spy on our homes, come down on our city, overwhelm us—
or some other deception's lurking deep inside it.   60
Trojans, never trust that horse. Whatever it is,
I fear the Greeks, especially bearing gifts.'

"In that spirit, with all his might he hurled
a huge spear straight into the monster's flanks,
the mortised timberwork of its swollen belly.   65
Quivering, there it stuck, and the stricken womb
came booming back from its depths with echoing groans.
If Fate and our own wits had not gone against us,
surely Laocoön would have driven us on, now,
to rip the Greek lair open with iron spears   70
and Troy would still be standing—
proud fortress of Priam, you would tower still!

---

7. From Dolopia, a region in Greece.   9. A Trojan priest of Neptune.
8. The goddess Athena was famously a virgin.

"Suddenly, in the thick of it all, a young soldier,
hands shackled behind his back, with much shouting
Trojan shepherds were hauling him toward the king.   75
They'd come on the man by chance, a total stranger.
He'd given himself up, with one goal in mind:
to open Troy to the Greeks and lay her waste.
He trusted to courage, nerved for either end,
to weave his lies or face his certain death.   80
Young Trojan recruits, keen to have a look,
came scurrying up from all sides, crowding round,
outdoing each other to make a mockery of the captive.
Now, hear the treachery of the Greeks and learn
from a single crime the nature of the beast . . .   85
Haggard, helpless, there in our midst he stood,
all eyes riveted on him now, and turning a wary glance
at the lines of Trojan troops he groaned and spoke:
'Where can I find some refuge, where on land, on sea?
What's left for me now? A man of so much misery!   90
Nothing among the Greeks, no place at all. And worse,
I see my Trojan enemies crying for my blood.'
                                        "His groans
convince us, cutting all our show of violence short.
We press him: 'Tell us where you were born, your family.
What news do you bring? Tell us what you trust to,   95
such a willing captive.'
                            "'All of it, my king,
I'll tell you, come what may, the whole true story.
Greek I am, I don't deny it. No, that first.
Fortune may have made me a man of misery
but, wicked as she is,   100
she can't make Sinon a lying fraud as well.
                                        "'Now,
perhaps you've caught some rumor of Palamedes,[1]
Belus' son, and his shining fame that rings in song.
The Greeks charged him with treason, a trumped-up charge,
an innocent man, and just because he opposed the war   105
they put him to death, but once he's robbed of the light,
they mourn him sorely. Now I was his blood kin,
a youngster when my father, a poor man, sent me
off to the war at Troy as Palamedes' comrade.
Long as he kept his royal status, holding forth   110
in the councils of the kings, I had some standing too,
some pride of place. But once he left the land of the living,
thanks to the jealous, forked tongue of our Ulysses—
you're no stranger to *his* story—I was shattered,
I dragged out my life in the shadows, grieving,   115
seething alone, in silence . . .
outraged by my innocent friend's demise until

1. A Greek warrior who advised the Greeks to return home from Troy. Odysseus persuaded them that he was a traitor, and had him killed. He was descended from the Egyptian king Belus.

I burst out like a madman, swore if I ever returned
in triumph to our native Argos, ever got the chance
I'd take revenge, and my oath provoked a storm of hatred. 120
That was my first step on the slippery road to ruin.
From then on, Ulysses kept tormenting me, pressing
charge on charge; from then on, he bruited about
his two-edged rumors among the rank and file.
Driven by guilt, he looked for ways to kill me, 125
he never rested until, making Calchas[2] his henchman—
but why now? Why go over that unforgiving ground again?
Why waste words? If you think all Greeks are one,
if hearing the name *Greek* is enough for you,
it's high time you made me pay the price. 130
How that would please the man of Ithaca,[3]
how the sons of Atreus would repay you!'

                       "Now, of course,
we burn to question him, urge him to explain—
blind to how false the cunning Greeks could be.
All atremble, he carries on with his tale, 135
lying from the cockles of his heart:

                      "'Time and again
the Greeks had yearned to abandon Troy—bone-tired
from a long hard war—to put it far behind and
beat a clean retreat. Would to god they had.
But time and again, as they were setting sail, 140
the heavy seas would keep them confined to port
and the Southwind filled their hearts with dread
and worst of all, once this horse, this mass of timber
with locking planks, stood stationed here at last,
the thunderheads rumbled up and down the sky. 145
So, at our wit's end, we send Eurypylus off
to question Apollo's oracle now, and back
he comes from the god's shrine with these bleak words:
"With blood you appeased the winds, with a virgin's sacrifice
when you, you Greeks, first sought the shores of Troy.[4] 150
With blood you must seek fair winds to sail you home,
must sacrifice one more Greek life in return."

   "'As the word spread, the ranks were struck dumb
and icy fear sent shivers down their spines.
Whom did the god demand? Who'd meet his doom? 155
Just that moment the Ithacan hailed the prophet,
Calchas, into our midst—he'd twist it out of him,
what was the gods' will? The army rose in uproar.
Even then our soldiers sensed that I was the one,
the target of that Ulysses' vicious schemes— 160
they saw it coming, still they held their tongues.

2. Greek prophet.
3. Greek island ruled by Ulysses.
4. Iphigeneia was sacrificed by her father,

Agamemnon, to allow the winds to blow the
fleet to Troy.

For ten days the seer, silent, closed off in his tent,
refused to say a word or betray a man to death.
But at last, goaded on by Ulysses' mounting threats
but in fact conniving in their plot, he breaks his silence   165
and dooms me to the altar. And the army gave consent.
The death that each man dreaded turned to the fate
of one poor soul: a burden they could bear.

   "'The day of infamy soon came . . .
the sacred rites were all performed for the victim,   170
the salted meal strewn, the bands tied round my head.
But I broke free of death, I tell you, burst my shackles,
yes, and hid all night in the reeds of a marshy lake,
waiting for them to sail—if only they would sail!
Well, no hope now of seeing the land where I was born   175
or my sweet children, the father I longed for all these years.
Maybe they'll wring from *them* the price for my escape,
avenge my guilt with my loved ones' blood, poor things.
I beg you, king, by the Powers who know the truth,
by any trust still uncorrupt in the world of men,   180
pity a man whose torment knows no bounds.
Pity me in my pain.
I know in my soul I don't deserve to suffer.'

   "He wept and won his life—our pity, too.
Priam takes command, has him freed from the ropes   185
and chains that bind him fast, and hails him warmly:
'Whoever you are, from now on, now you've lost the Greeks,
put them out of your mind and you'll be one of us.
But answer my questions. Tell me the whole truth.
Why did they raise up this giant, monstrous horse?   190
Who conceived it? What's it for? its purpose?
A gift to the gods? A great engine of battle?'

   "He broke off. Sinon, adept at deceit,
with all his Greek cunning lifted his hands,
just freed from their fetters, up to the stars   195
and prayed: 'Bear witness, you eternal fires of the sky
and you inviolate will of the gods! Bear witness,
altar and those infernal knives that I escaped
and the sacred bands I wore myself: the victim.
It's right to break my sworn oath to the Greeks,   200
it's right to detest those men and bring to light
all they're hiding now. No laws of my native land
can bind me here. Just keep your promise, Troy,
and if I can save you, you must save me too—
if I reveal the truth and pay you back in full.   205

   "'All the hopes of the Greeks, their firm faith
in a war they'd launched themselves
had always hinged on Pallas Athena's help.

But from the moment that godless Diomedes,
flanked by Ulysses, the mastermind of crime,   210
attacked and tore the fateful image of Pallas
out of her own hallowed shrine,[5] and cut down
the sentries ringing your city heights and seized
that holy image and even dared touch the sacred bands
on the virgin goddess' head with hands reeking blood—   215
from that hour on, the high hopes of the Greeks
had trickled away like a slow, ebbing tide . . .
They were broken, beaten men,
the will of the goddess dead set against them.
Omens of this she gave in no uncertain terms.   220
They'd hardly stood her image up in the Greek camp
when flickering fire shot from its glaring eyes
and salt sweat ran glistening down its limbs
and three times the goddess herself—a marvel—
blazed forth from the ground, shield clashing, spear brandished.   225
The prophet spurs them at once to risk escape by sea:
"You cannot root out Troy with your Greek spears unless
you seek new omens in Greece and bring the god back here"—
the image they'd borne across the sea in their curved ships.
So now they've sailed away on the wind for home shores,   230
just to rearm, recruit their gods as allies yet again,
then measure back their course on the high seas and
back they'll come to attack you all off guard.

   "'So Calchas read the omens. At his command
they raised this horse, this effigy, all to atone   235
for the violated image of Pallas, her wounded pride,
her power—and expiate the outrage they had done.
But he made them do the work on a grand scale,
a tremendous mass of interlocking timbers towering
toward the sky, so the horse could not be trundled   240
through your gates or hauled inside your walls
or guard your people if they revered it well
in the old, ancient way. For if your hands
should violate this great offering to Minerva,
a total disaster—if only god would turn it   245
against the seer himself!—will wheel down
on Priam's empire, Troy, and all your futures.
But if your hands will rear it up, into your city,
then all Asia in arms can invade Greece, can launch
an all-out war right up to the walls of Pelops.[6]   250
That's the doom that awaits our sons' sons.'

   "Trapped by his craft, that cunning liar Sinon,
we believed his story. His tears, his treachery seized

5. An oracle stated that Troy could not be
captured as long as the statue of Athena, the
Palladium (after one of Athena's titles, Pallas),
remained in place in her shrine.
6. Pelops was the grandfather of Agamemnon
and Menelaus; his walls are the walls of Argos.

the men whom neither Tydeus' son[7] nor Achilles could defeat,
nor ten long years of war, nor all the thousand ships.   255

"But a new portent strikes our doomed people
now—a greater omen, far more terrible, fatal,
shakes our senses, blind to what was coming.
Laocoön, the priest of Neptune picked by lot,
was sacrificing a massive bull at the holy altar   260
when—I cringe to recall it now—look there!
Over the calm deep straits off Tenedos swim
twin, giant serpents, rearing in coils, breasting
the sea-swell side by side, plunging toward the shore,
their heads, their blood-red crests surging over the waves,   265
their bodies thrashing, backs rolling in coil on mammoth coil
and the wake behind them churns in a roar of foaming spray,
and now, their eyes glittering, shot with blood and fire,
flickering tongues licking their hissing maws, yes, now
they're about to land. We blanch at the sight, we scatter.   270
Like troops on attack they're heading straight for Laocoön—
first each serpent seizes one of his small young sons,
constricting, twisting around him, sinks its fangs
in the tortured limbs, and gorges. Next Laocoön
rushing quick to the rescue, clutching his sword—   275
they trap him, bind him in huge muscular whorls,
their scaly backs lashing around his midriff twice
and twice around his throat—their heads, their flaring necks
mounting over their victim writhing still, his hands
frantic to wrench apart their knotted trunks,   280
his priestly bands splattered in filth, black venom
and all the while his horrible screaming fills the skies,
bellowing like some wounded bull struggling to shrug
loose from his neck an axe that's struck awry,
to lumber clear of the altar . . .   285
Only the twin snakes escape, sliding off and away
to the heights of Troy where the ruthless goddess
holds her shrine, and there at her feet they hide,
vanishing under Minerva's great round shield.
                                        "At once,
I tell you, a stranger fear runs through the harrowed crowd.   290
Laocoön deserved to pay for his outrage, so they say,
he desecrated the sacred timbers of the horse,
he hurled his wicked lance at the beast's back.
'Haul Minerva's effigy up to her house,' we shout,
'Offer up our prayers to the power of the goddess!'   295
We breach our own ramparts, fling our defenses open,
all pitch into the work. Smooth running rollers
we wheel beneath its hoofs, and heavy hempen ropes
we bind around its neck, and teeming with men-at-arms
the huge deadly engine climbs our city walls . . .   300

7. Diomedes.

And round it boys and unwed girls sing hymns,
thrilled to lay a hand on the dangling ropes
as on and on it comes, gliding into the city,
looming high over the city's heart. "Oh my country!
Troy, home of the gods! You great walls of the Dardans   305
long renowned in war!
                      "Four times it lurched to a halt
at the very brink of the gates—four times the armor
clashed out from its womb. But we, we forged ahead,
oblivious, blind, insane, we stationed the monster
fraught with doom on the hallowed heights of Troy.   310
Even now Cassandra[8] revealed the future, opening
lips the gods had ruled no Trojan would believe.
And we, poor fools—on this, our last day—we deck
the shrines of the gods with green holiday garlands
all throughout the city . . .
                      "But all the while   315
the skies keep wheeling on and night comes sweeping in
from the Ocean Stream, in its mammoth shadow swallowing up
the earth, and the Pole Star, and the treachery of the Greeks.
Dead quiet. The Trojans slept on, strewn throughout
their fortress, weary bodies embraced by slumber.   320
But the Greek armada was under way now, crossing
over from Tenedos, ships in battle formation
under the moon's quiet light, their silent ally,
homing in on the berths they know by heart—
when the king's flagship sends up a signal flare,   325
the cue for Sinon, saved by the Fates' unjust decree,
and stealthily loosing the pine bolts of the horse,
he unleashes the Greeks shut up inside its womb.
The horse stands open wide, fighters in high spirits
pouring out of its timbered cavern into the fresh air: 330
the chiefs, Thessandrus, Sthenelus, ruthless Ulysses
rappeling down a rope they dropped from its side,
and Acamas, Thoas, Neoptolemus, son of Achilles,
captain Machaon, Menelaus, Epeus himself,
the man who built that masterpiece of fraud.   335
They steal on a city buried deep in sleep and wine,
they butcher the guards, fling wide the gates and hug
their cohorts poised to combine forces. Plot complete.

     "This was the hour when rest, that gift of the gods
most heaven-sent, first comes to beleaguered mortals,   340
creeping over us now . . . when there, look,
I dreamed I saw Prince Hector before my eyes,
my comrade haggard with sorrow, streaming tears,

---

8. Daughter of King Priam. Apollo fell in love
with her and gave her the gift of unerring prophecy; but when she refused him, he turned
the gift into a curse by ensuring that nobody
would ever believe her predictions.

just as he once was, when dragged behind the chariot,
black with blood and grime, thongs piercing his swollen feet—   345
what a harrowing sight! What a far cry from the old Hector
home from battle, decked in Achilles' arms[9]—his trophies—
or fresh from pitching Trojan fire at the Greek ships.
His beard matted now, his hair clotted with blood,
bearing the wounds, so many wounds he suffered   350
fighting round his native city's walls . . .
I dreamed I addressed him first, in tears myself
I forced my voice from the depths of all my grief:
'Oh light of the Trojans—last, best hope of Troy!
What's held you back so long? How long we've waited,   355
Hector, for you to come, and now from what far shores?
How glad we are to see you, we battle-weary men,
after so many deaths, your people dead and gone,
after your citizens, your city felt such pain.
But what outrage has mutilated your face   360
so clear and cloudless once? Why these wounds?'

    "Wasting no words, no time on empty questions,
heaving a deep groan from his heart he calls out:
'Escape, son of the goddess, tear yourself from the flames!
The enemy holds our walls. Troy is toppling from her heights.   365
You have paid your debt to our king and native land.
If one strong arm could have saved Troy, my arm
would have saved the city. Now, into your hands
she entrusts her holy things, her household gods.
Take them with you as comrades in your fortunes.   370
Seek a city for them, once you have roved the seas,
erect great walls at last to house the gods of Troy!'

    "Urging so, with his own hands he carries Vesta forth
from her inner shrine, her image clad in ribbons,
filled with her power, her everlasting fire.[1]
                                          "But now,   375
chaos—the city begins to reel with cries of grief,
louder, stronger, even though father's palace
stood well back, screened off by trees, but still
the clash of arms rings clearer, horror on the attack.
I shake off sleep and scrambling up to the pitched roof   380
I stand there, ears alert, and I hear a roar like fire
assaulting a wheatfield, whipped by a Southwind's fury,
or mountain torrent in full spate, flattening crops,
leveling all the happy, thriving labor of oxen,
dragging whole trees headlong down in its wake—   385
and a shepherd perched on a sheer rock outcrop
hears the roar, lost in amazement, struck dumb.
No doubting the good faith of the Greeks now,
their treachery plain as day.

9. In the *Iliad*, Achilles' companion Patroclus
bears Achilles' arms (that is, his armor and
weapons) into battle and is killed by Hector,
who seizes them as trophies.
1. In the temple of Vesta, the hearth goddess,
was a fire that was never allowed to go out.

                    "Already, there,
the grand house of Deiphobus[2] stormed by fire,   390
crashing in ruins—
                    "Already his neighbor Ucalegon
up in flames—
                    "The Sigean straits[3] shimmering back the blaze,
the shouting of fighters soars, the clashing blare of trumpets.
Out of my wits, I seize my arms—what reason for arms?
Just my spirit burning to muster troops for battle,   395
rush with comrades up to the city's heights,
fury and rage driving me breakneck on
as it races through my mind
what a noble thing it is to die in arms!
                              "But now, look,
just slipped out from under the Greek barrage of spears,   400
Panthus, Othrys' son, a priest of Apollo's shrine
on the citadel—hands full of the holy things,
the images of our conquered gods—he's dragging along
his little grandson, making a wild dash for our doors.
'Panthus, where's our stronghold? our last stand?'—   405
words still on my lips as he groans in answer:
'The last *day* has come for the Trojan people,
no escaping this moment. Troy's no more.
Ilium, gone—our awesome Trojan glory.
Brutal Jupiter hands it all over to Greece,   410
Greeks are lording over our city up in flames.
The horse stands towering high in the heart of Troy,
disgorging its armed men, with Sinon in his glory,
gloating over us—Sinon fans the fires.
The immense double gates are flung wide open,   415
Greeks in their thousands mass there, all who ever
sailed from proud Mycenae. Others have choked
the cramped streets, weapons brandished now
in a battle line of naked, glinting steel
tense for the kill. Only the first guards   420
at the gates put up some show of resistance,
fighting blindly on.'

    "Spurred by Panthus' words and the gods' will,
into the blaze I dive, into the fray, wherever
the din of combat breaks and war cries fill the sky,   425
wherever the battle-fury drives me on and now
I'm joined by Rhipeus, Epytus mighty in armor,
rearing up in the moonlight—
Hypanis comes to my side, and Dymas too,
flanked by the young Coroebus, Mygdon's son.   430
Late in the day he'd chanced to come to Troy
incensed with a mad, burning love for Cassandra:
son-in-law to our king, *he* would rescue Troy. Poor man,
if only he'd marked his bride's inspired ravings!

2. A son of Priam.   the Sigeion promontory overlooking Troy.
3. Channel leading into the Aegean Sea, near

"Seeing their close-packed ranks, hot for battle,   435
I spur them on their way: 'Men, brave hearts,
though bravery cannot save us—if you're bent on
following me and risking all to face the worst,
look around you, see how our chances stand.
The gods who shored our empire up have left us,   440
all have deserted their altars and their shrines.
You race to defend a city already lost in flames.
But let us die, go plunging into the thick of battle.
One hope saves the defeated: they know they can't be saved!'
That fired their hearts with the fury of despair.
                                    "Now   445
like a wolfpack out for blood on a foggy night,
driven blindly on by relentless, rabid hunger,
leaving cubs behind, waiting, jaws parched—
so through spears, through enemy ranks we plow
to certain death, striking into the city's heart,   450
the shielding wings of the darkness beating round us.
Who has words to capture that night's disaster,
tell that slaughter? What tears could match
our torments now? An ancient city is falling,
a power that ruled for ages, now in ruins.   455
Everywhere lie the motionless bodies of the dead,
strewn in her streets, her homes and the gods' shrines
we held in awe. And not only Trojans pay the price in blood—
at times the courage races back in their conquered hearts
and they cut their enemies down in all their triumph.   460
Everywhere, wrenching grief, everywhere, terror
and a thousand shapes of death.
                                 "And the first Greek
to cross our path? Androgeos leading a horde of troops
and taking *us* for allies on the march, the fool,
he even gives us a warm salute and calls out: 465
'Hurry up, men. Why holding back, why now,
why drag your heels? Troy's up in flames,
the rest are looting, sacking the city heights.
But you, have you just come from the tall ships?'
Suddenly, getting no password he can trust,   470
he sensed he'd stumbled into enemy ranks!
Stunned, he recoiled, swallowing back his words
like a man who threads his way through prickly brambles,
pressing his full weight on the ground, and blindly treads
on a lurking snake and back he shrinks in instant fear   475
as it rears in anger, puffs its blue-black neck.
Just so Androgeos, seeing us, cringes with fear,
recoiling, struggling to flee but we attack,
flinging a ring of steel around his cohorts—
panic takes the Greeks unsure of their ground   480
and we cut them all to pieces.
Fortune fills our sails in that first clash
and Coroebus, flushed, fired with such success,

exults: 'Comrades, wherever Fortune points the way,
wherever the first road to safety leads, let's soldier on.   485
Exchange shields with the Greeks and wear their emblems.
Call it cunning or courage: who would ask in war?
Our enemies will arm us to the hilt.'
                                "With that he dons
Androgeos' crested helmet, his handsome blazoned shield
and straps a Greek sword to his hip, and comrades,   490
spirits rising, take his lead. Rhipeus, Dymas too
and our corps of young recruits—each fighter
arms himself in the loot that he just seized
and on we forge, blending in with the enemy,
battling time and again under strange gods,   495
fighting hand-to-hand in the blind dark
and many Greeks we send to the King of Death.
Some scatter back to their ships, making a run
for shore and safety. Others disgrace themselves,
so panicked they clamber back inside the monstrous horse,   500
burying into the womb they know so well.
                                "But, oh
how wrong to rely on gods dead set against you!
Watch: the virgin daughter of Priam, Cassandra,
torn from the sacred depths of Minerva's shrine,
dragged by the hair, raising her burning eyes   505
to the heavens, just her eyes, so helpless,
shackles kept her from raising her gentle hands.
Coroebus could not bear the sight of it—mad with rage
he flung himself at the Greek lines and met his death.
Closing ranks we charge after him, into the thick of battle   510
and face our first disaster. Down from the temple roof
come showers of lances hurled by our own comrades there,
duped by the look of our Greek arms, our Greek crests
that launched this grisly slaughter. And worse still,
the Greeks roaring with anger—we had saved Cassandra—   515
attack us from all sides! Ajax, fiercest of all and
Atreus' two sons and the whole Dolopian army,
wild as a rampaging whirlwind, gusts clashing,
the West- and the South- and Eastwind riding high
on the rushing horses of the dawn, and the woods howl   520
and Nereus[4] thrashing his savage trident, churns up
the sea exploding in foam from its rocky depths.
And those Greeks we had put to rout, our ruse
in the murky night stampeding them headlong on
throughout the city—back they come, the first   525
to see that our shields and spears are naked lies,
to mark the words on our lips that jar with theirs.
In a flash, superior numbers overwhelm us.
Coroebus is first to go,
cut down by Peneleus' right hand he sprawls   530

4. An old sea god.

at Minerva's shrine, the goddess, power of armies.[5]
Rhipeus falls too, the most righteous man in Troy,
the most devoted to justice, true, but the gods
had other plans.
                    "Hypanis, Dymas die as well,
run through by their own men—
                                        "And you, Panthus,   535
not all your piety, all the sacred bands you wore
as Apollo's priest could save you as you fell.
Ashes of Ilium, last flames that engulfed my world—
I swear by you that in your last hour I never shrank
from the Greek spears, from any startling hazard of war—   540
if Fate had struck me down, my sword-arm earned it all.
Now we are swept away, Iphitus, Pelias with me,
one weighed down with age and the other slowed
by a wound Ulysses gave him—heading straight
for Priam's palace, driven there by the outcries.   545

    "And there, I tell you, a pitched battle flares!
You'd think no other battles could match its fury,
nowhere else in the city were people dying so.
Invincible Mars[6] rears up to meet us face to face
with waves of Greeks assaulting the roofs, we see them   550
choking the gateway, under a tortoise-shell of shields,[7]
and the scaling ladders cling to the steep ramparts—
just at the gates the raiders scramble up the rungs,
shields on their left arms thrust out for defense,
their right hands clutching the gables.   555
Over against them, Trojans ripping the tiles
and turrets from all their roofs—the end is near,
they can see it now, at the brink of death, desperate
for weapons, some defense, and these, these missiles they send
reeling down on the Greeks' heads—the gilded beams,   560
the inlaid glory of all our ancient fathers.
Comrades below, posted in close-packed ranks,
block the entries, swordpoints drawn and poised.
My courage renewed, I rush to relieve the palace,
brace the defenders, bring the defeated strength.   565

    "There was a secret door, a hidden passage
linking the wings of Priam's house—remote,
far to the rear. Long as our realm still stood,
Andromache, poor woman, would often go this way,
unattended, to Hector's parents, taking the boy   570
Astyanax[8] by the hand to see grandfather Priam.
I slipped through the door, up to the jutting roof
where the doomed Trojans were hurling futile spears.

5. Minerva was a warrior goddess, often
depicted carrying weapons.
6. God of war (equivalent of the Greek Ares).
7. Position adopted by Roman soldiers: packed
tightly together, they put their shields above
their heads, making the army look like a tortoise.
8. Son of Hector and his wife, Andromache.

There was a tower soaring high at the peak toward the sky,
our favorite vantage point for surveying all of Troy   575
and the Greek fleet and camp. We attacked that tower
with iron crowbars, just where the upper-story planks
showed loosening joints—we rocked it, wrenched it free
of its deep moorings and all at once we heaved it toppling
down with a crash, trailing its wake of ruin to grind   580
the massed Greeks assaulting left and right. But on
came Greek reserves, no letup, the hail of rocks,
the missiles of every kind would never cease.

   "There at the very edge of the front gates
springs Pyrrhus, son of Achilles, prancing in arms,   585
aflash in his shimmering brazen sheath like a snake
buried the whole winter long under frozen turf,
swollen to bursting, fed full on poisonous weeds
and now it springs into light, sloughing its old skin
to glisten sleek in its newfound youth, its back slithering,   590
coiling, its proud chest rearing high to the sun,
its triple tongue flickering through its fangs.
Backing him now comes Periphas, giant fighter,
Automedon too, Achilles' henchman, charioteer
who bore the great man's armor—backing Pyrrhus,   595
the young fighters from Scyros raid the palace,
hurling firebrands at the roofs. Out in the lead,
Pyrrhus seizes a double-axe and batters the rocky sill
and ripping the bronze posts out of their sockets,
hacking the rugged oaken planks of the doors,   600
makes a breach, a gaping maw, and there, exposed,
the heart of the house, the sweep of the colonnades,
the palace depths of the old kings and Priam lie exposed
and they see the armed sentries bracing at the portals.

   "But all in the house is turmoil, misery, groans,   605
the echoing chambers ring with cries of women,
wails of mourning hit the golden stars.
Mothers scatter in panic down the palace halls
and embrace the pillars, cling to them, kiss them hard.
But on he comes, Pyrrhus with all his father's force,   610
no bolts, not even the guards can hold him back—
under the ram's repeated blows the doors cave in,
the doorposts, prised from their sockets, crash flat.
Force makes a breach and the Greeks come storming through,
butcher the sentries, flood the entire place with men-at-arms.   615
No river so wild, so frothing in spate, bursting its banks
to overpower the dikes, anything in its way, its cresting
tides stampeding in fury down on the fields to sweep
the flocks and stalls across the open plain.
I saw him myself, Pyrrhus crazed with carnage   620
and Atreus' two sons just at the threshold—

"I saw
Hecuba with her hundred daughters and daughters-in-law,[9]
saw Priam fouling with blood the altar fires
he himself had blessed.
    "Those fifty bridal-chambers
filled with the hope of children's children still to come,   625
the pillars proud with trophies, gilded with Eastern gold,
they all come tumbling down—
and the Greeks hold what the raging fire spares.

   "Perhaps you wonder how Priam met his end.
When he saw his city stormed and seized, his gates   630
wrenched apart, the enemy camped in his palace depths,
the old man dons his armor long unused, he clamps it
round his shoulders shaking with age and, all for nothing,
straps his useless sword to his hip, then makes
for the thick of battle, out to meet his death.   635
At the heart of the house an ample altar stood,
naked under the skies,
an ancient laurel bending over the shrine,
embracing our household gods within its shade.
Here, flocking the altar, Hecuba and her daughters   640
huddled, blown headlong down like doves by a black storm—
clutching, all for nothing, the figures of their gods.
Seeing Priam decked in the arms he'd worn as a young man,
'Are you insane?' she cries, 'Poor husband, what impels you
to strap that sword on now? Where are you rushing?   645
Too late for such defense, such help. Not even
my own Hector, if *he* came to the rescue now . . .
Come to me, Priam. This altar will shield us all
or else you'll die with us.'
        "With those words,
drawing him toward her there, she made a place   650
for the old man beside the holy shrine.
        "Suddenly,
look, a son of Priam, Polites, just escaped
from slaughter at Pyrrhus' hands, comes racing in
through spears, through enemy fighters, fleeing down
the long arcades and deserted hallways—badly wounded,   655
Pyrrhus hot on his heels, a weapon poised for the kill,
about to seize him, about to run him through and pressing
home as Polites reached his parents and collapsed,
vomiting out his life blood before their eyes.
At that, Priam, trapped in the grip of death,   660
not holding back, not checking his words, his rage:
'You!' he cries, 'you and your vicious crimes!
If any power on high recoils at such an outrage,
let the gods repay you for all your reckless work,

---

9. Wife of Priam, king of Troy. He had fifty sons and fifty daughters—not all by Hecuba.

grant you the thanks, the rich reward you've earned.   665
You've made me see my son's death with my own eyes,
defiled a father's sight with a son's life blood.
You say you're Achilles' son? You lie! Achilles
never treated his enemy Priam so. No, he honored
a suppliant's rights, he blushed to betray my trust,   670
he restored my Hector's bloodless corpse for burial,
sent me safely home to the land I rule!'
                              "With that
and with all his might the old man flings his spear—
but too impotent now to pierce, it merely grazes
Pyrrhus' brazen shield that blocks its way   675
and clings there, dangling limp from the boss,
all for nothing. Pyrrhus shouts back: 'Well then,
down you go, a messenger to my father, Peleus' son![1]
Tell him about my vicious work, how Neoptolemus[2]
degrades his father's name—don't you forget.   680
Now—die!'
                "That said, he drags the old man
straight to the altar, quaking, slithering on through
slicks of his son's blood, and twisting Priam's hair
in his left hand, his right hand sweeping forth his sword—
a flash of steel—he buries it hilt-deep in the king's flank.   685

    "Such was the fate of Priam, his death, his lot on earth,
with Troy blazing before his eyes, her ramparts down,
the monarch who once had ruled in all his glory
the many lands of Asia, Asia's many tribes.
A powerful trunk is lying on the shore.[3]   690
The head wrenched from the shoulders.
A corpse without a name.
                        "Then, for the first time
the full horror came home to me at last. I froze.
The thought of my own dear father filled my mind
when I saw the old king gasping out his life   695
with that raw wound—both men were the same age—
and the thought of my Creusa, alone, abandoned,
our house plundered, our little Iulus' fate.[4]
I look back—what forces still stood by me?
None. Totally spent in war, they'd all deserted,   700

1. Achilles was the son of Peleus. He was already dead, before the final storming of Troy killed by Paris with an arrow to the heel, his only vulnerability.
2. Literally, "New Warrior," another name for Pyrrhus, Achilles' son.
3. The detail that the body is left "on the shore"—which makes no narrative sense, since Priam is killed in the center of the city—is an allusion to the assassination of Pompey the Great. In the Roman civil war of 49–45 B.C.E., Pompey, representing the more aristocratic party, was defeated by the more populist Julius Caesar, and eventually assassinated; his body was famously abandoned on the beach of Egypt.
4. Creusa is Aeneas's wife; Iulus is his son.

down from the roofs they'd flung themselves to earth
or hurled their broken bodies in the flames.
                                    ["So,[5]
at just that moment I was the one man left
and then I saw her, clinging to Vesta's threshold,
hiding in silence, tucked away—Helen of Argos.   705
Glare of the fires lit my view as I looked down,
scanning the city left and right, and there she was . . .
terrified of the Trojans' hate, now Troy was overpowered,
terrified of the Greeks' revenge, her deserted husband's rage—
that universal Fury, a curse to Troy and her native land   710
and here she lurked, skulking, a thing of loathing
cowering at the altar: Helen. Out it flared,
the fire inside my soul, my rage ablaze to avenge
our fallen country—pay Helen back, crime for crime.

  "'So, this woman,' it struck me now, 'safe and sound   715
she'll look once more on Sparta, her native Greece?
She'll ride like a queen in triumph with her trophies?
Feast her eyes on her husband, parents, children too?
Her retinue fawning round her, Phrygian[6] ladies, slaves?
That—with Priam put to the sword? And Troy up in flames?   720
And time and again our Dardan shores have sweated blood?
Not for all the world. No fame, no memory to be won
for punishing a woman: such victory reaps no praise
but to stamp this abomination out as she deserves,
to punish her now, they'll sing my praise for *that*.   725
What joy, to glut my heart with the fires of vengeance,
bring some peace to the ashes of my people!'

  "Whirling words—I was swept away by fury now]
when all of a sudden there my loving mother[7] stood
before my eyes, but I had never seen her so clearly,   730
her pure radiance shining down upon me through the night,
the goddess in all her glory, just as the gods behold
her build, her awesome beauty. Grasping my hand
she held me back, adding this from her rose-red lips:
'My son, what grief could incite such blazing anger?   735
Why such fury? And the love you bore me once,
where has it all gone? Why don't you look first
where you left your father, Anchises, spent with age?
Do your wife, Creusa, and son Ascanius still survive?
The Greek battalions are swarming round them all,   740
and if my love had never rushed to the rescue,
flames would have swept them off by now or
enemy sword-blades would have drained their blood.
Think: it's not that beauty, Helen, you should hate,

5. This passage is bracketed because many scholars believe it does not belong in the poem, since it is contradicted by a passage in book VI (573–623). The contradiction may be evidence of the *Aeneid*'s unfinished status at Virgil's death. 6. That is, Trojan. Phrygia was the region of modern-day Turkey that included Troy. 7. Venus.

not even Paris, the man that you should blame, no,   745
it's the gods, the ruthless gods who are tearing down
the wealth of Troy, her toppling crown of towers.
Look around. I'll sweep it all away, the mist
so murky, dark, and swirling around you now,
it clouds your vision, dulls your mortal sight.   750
You are my son. Never fear my orders.
Never refuse to bow to my commands.
                              "'There,
yes, where you see the massive ramparts shattered,
blocks wrenched from blocks, the billowing smoke and ash—
it's Neptune himself,[8] prising loose with his giant trident   755
the foundation-stones of Troy, he's making the walls quake,
ripping up the entire city by her roots.
                      "'There's Juno,
cruelest in fury, first to commandeer the Scaean Gates,[9]
sword at her hip and mustering comrades, shock troops
streaming out of the ships.
                      "'Already up on the heights—   760
turn around and look—there's Pallas holding the fortress,
flaming out of the clouds, her savage Gorgon glaring.[1]
Even Father himself, he's filling the Greek hearts
with courage, stamina—Jove in person spurring the gods
to fight the Trojan armies!
                      "'Run for your life, my son.   765
Put an end to your labors. I will never leave you,
I will set you safe at your father's door.'

    "Parting words. She vanished into the dense night.
And now they all come looming up before me,
terrible shapes, the deadly foes of Troy,   770
the gods gigantic in power.
                      "Then at last
I saw it all, all Ilium settling into her embers,
Neptune's Troy, toppling over now from her roots
like a proud, veteran ash on its mountain summit,
chopped by stroke after stroke of the iron axe as   775
woodsmen fight to bring it down, and over and
over it threatens to fall, its boughs shudder,
its leafy crown quakes and back and forth it sways
till overwhelmed by its wounds, with a long last groan
it goes—torn up from its heights it crashes down   780
in ruins from its ridge . . .
Venus leading, down from the roof I climb
and win my way through fires and massing foes.
The spears recede, the flames roll back before me.

---

8. The god of the sea and of earthquakes
(Poseidon in Greek mythology), who was hostile to the Trojans, since Laomedon, an early
king of Troy, failed to repay him for helping to
build the city walls.

9. The main entrance to Troy.
1. Pallas Athena's shield displays the head of
a Gorgon: the monster that turns those who
look at it to stone.

"At last, gaining the door of father's ancient house,   785
my first concern was to find the man, my first wish
to spirit him off, into the high mountain range,
but father, seeing Ilium razed from the earth,
refused to drag his life out now and suffer exile.
'You,' he argued, 'you in your prime, untouched by age,   790
your blood still coursing strong, you hearts of oak,
you are the ones to hurry your escape. Myself,
if the gods on high had wished me to live on,
they would have saved my palace for me here.
Enough—more than enough—that I have seen   795
one sack of my city, once survived its capture.[2]
Here I lie, here laid out for death. Come say
your parting salutes and leave my body so.
I will find my own death, sword in hand:
my enemies keen for spoils will be so kind.   800
Death without burial? A small price to pay.
For years now, I've lingered out my life,
despised by the gods, a dead weight to men,
ever since the Father of Gods and King of Mortals
stormed at me with his bolt and scorched me with its fire.'[3]   805

"So he said, planted there. Nothing could shake him now.
But we dissolved in tears, my wife, Creusa, Ascanius,
the whole household, begging my father not to pull
our lives down with him, adding his own weight
to the fate that dragged us down.   810
He still refuses, holds to his resolve,
clings to the spot. And again I rush to arms,
desperate to die myself. Where could I turn?
What were our chances now, at this point?
'What!' I cried. 'Did you, my own father,   815
dream that I could run away and desert you here?
How could such an outrage slip from a father's lips?
If it please the gods that nothing of our great city
shall survive—if you are bent on adding your own death
to the deaths of Troy and of all your loved ones too,   820
the doors of the deaths you crave are spread wide open.
Pyrrhus will soon be here, bathed in Priam's blood,
Pyrrhus who butchers sons in their fathers' faces,
slaughters fathers at the altar. Was it for this,
my loving mother, you swept me clear of the weapons,   825
free of the flames? Just to see the enemy camped
in the very heart of our house, to see my son, Ascanius,
see my father, my wife, Creusa, with them, sacrificed,
massacred in each other's blood?

2. Troy had been sacked by Hercules, when
the previous king (Laomedon) cheated him.
3. When Anchises had his affair with Venus,
he was sworn to secrecy. He broke his word
and boasted about sleeping with the goddess,
so Jupiter hurled a thunderbolt at him as punishment, making him lame.

"'Arms, my comrades,
bring me arms! The last light calls the defeated.   830
Send me back to the Greeks, let me go back
to fight new battles. Not all of us here
will die today without revenge.'
                    "Now buckling on
my sword again and working my left arm through
the shieldstrap, grasping it tightly, just as I   835
was rushing out, right at the doors my wife, Creusa,
look, flung herself at my feet and hugged my knees
and raised our little Iulus up to his father.
'If you are going off to die,' she begged,
'then take us with you too,   840
to face the worst together. But if your battles
teach you to hope in arms, the arms you buckle on,
your first duty should be to guard our house.
Desert us, leave us now—to whom? Whom?
Little Iulus, your father and your wife,   845
so I once was called.'
                    "So Creusa cries,
her wails of anguish echoing through the house
when out of the blue an omen strikes—a marvel!
Now as we held our son between our hands
and both our grieving faces, a tongue of fire,   850
watch, flares up from the crown of Iulus' head,
a subtle flame licking his downy hair, feeding
around the boy's brow, and though it never harmed him,
panicked, we rush to shake the flame from his curls
and smother the holy fire, damp it down with water.   855
But Father Anchises lifts his eyes to the stars in joy
and stretching his hands toward the sky, sings out:
'Almighty Jove! If any prayer can persuade you now,
look down on us—that's all I ask—if our devotion
has earned it, grant us another omen, Father,   860
seal this first clear sign.'
                    "No sooner said
than an instant peal of thunder crashes on the left
and down from the sky a shooting star comes gliding,
trailing a flaming torch to irradiate the night
as it comes sweeping down. We watch it sailing   865
over the topmost palace roofs to bury itself,
still burning bright, in the forests of Mount Ida,[4]
blazing its path with light, leaving a broad furrow,
a fiery wake, and miles around the smoking sulfur fumes.
Won over at last, my father rises to his full height   870
and prays to the gods and reveres that holy star:
'No more delay, not now! You gods of my fathers,
now I follow wherever you lead me, I am with you.
Safeguard our house, safeguard my grandson Iulus!

---

4. Mountain near Troy held sacred as the birthplace of Jupiter.

This sign is yours: Troy rests in your power.   875
I give way, my son. No more refusals.
I will go with you, your comrade.'
                         "So he yielded
but now the roar of flames grows louder all through Troy
and the seething floods of fire are rolling closer.
'So come, dear father, climb up onto my shoulders!   880
I will carry you on my back. This labor of love
will never wear me down. Whatever falls to us now,
we both will share one peril, one path to safety.
Little Iulus, walk beside me, and you, my wife,
follow me at a distance, in my footsteps.   885
Servants, listen closely . . .
Just past the city walls a gravemound lies
where an old shrine of forsaken Ceres⁵ stands
with an ancient cypress growing close beside it—
our fathers' reverence kept it green for years.   890
Coming by many routes, it's there we meet,
our rendezvous. And you, my father, carry
our hearthgods now, our fathers' sacred vessels.
I, just back from the war and fresh from slaughter,
I must not handle the holy things—it's wrong—   895
not till I cleanse myself in running springs.'
                             "With that,
over my broad shoulders and round my neck I spread
a tawny lion's skin for a cloak, and bowing down,
I lift my burden up. Little Iulus, clutching
my right hand, keeps pace with tripping steps.   900
My wife trails on behind. And so we make our way
along the pitch-dark paths, and I who had never flinched
at the hurtling spears or swarming Greek assaults—
now every stir of wind, every whisper of sound
alarms me, anxious both for the child beside me   905
and burden on my back. And then, nearing the gates,
thinking we've all got safely through, I suddenly
seem to catch the steady tramp of marching feet
and father, peering out through the darkness, cries:
'Run for it now, my boy, you must. They're closing in,   910
I can see their glinting shields, their flashing bronze!'

      "Then in my panic something strange, some enemy power
robbed me of my senses. Lost, I was leaving behind
familiar paths, at a run down blind dead ends
when—
            "Oh dear god, my wife, Creusa—   915
torn from me by a brutal fate! What then,
did she stop in her tracks or lose her way?
Or exhausted, sink down to rest? Who knows?
I never set my eyes on her again.

5. Roman goddess of agriculture (equivalent to the Greek Demeter).

I never looked back, she never crossed my mind— 920
Creusa, lost—not till we reached that barrow
sacred to ancient Ceres where, with all our people
rallied at last, she alone was missing. Lost
to her friends, her son, her husband—gone forever.
Raving, I blamed them all, the gods, the human race— 925
what crueler blow did I feel the night that Troy went down?
Ascanius, father Anchises, and all the gods of Troy,
entrusting them to my friends, I hide them well away
in a valley's shelter, don my burnished gear
and back I go to Troy . . . 930
my mind steeled to relive the whole disaster,
retrace my route through the whole city now
and put my life in danger one more time.
                                   "First then,
back to the looming walls, the shadowy rear gates
by which I'd left the city, back I go in my tracks, 935
retracing, straining to find my footsteps in the dark,
with terror at every turn, the very silence makes me cringe.
Then back to my house I go—if only, only she's gone there—
but the Greeks have flooded in, seized the entire place.
All over now. Devouring fire whipped by the winds 940
goes churning into the rooftops, flames surging
over them, scorching blasts raging up the sky.
On I go and again I see the palace of Priam
set on the heights, but there in colonnades
deserted now, in the sanctuary of Juno, there 945
stand the elite watchmen, Phoenix, ruthless Ulysses
guarding all their loot. All the treasures of Troy
hauled from the burning shrines—the sacramental tables,
bowls of solid gold and the holy robes they'd seized
from every quarter—Greeks, piling high the plunder. 950
Children and trembling mothers rounded up
in a long, endless line.
                         "Why, I even dared fling
my voice through the dark, my shouts filled the streets
as time and again, overcome with grief I called out
'Creusa!' Nothing, no reply, and again 'Creusa!' 955
But then as I madly rushed from house to house,
no end in sight, abruptly, right before my eyes
I saw her stricken ghost, my own Creusa's shade.
But larger than life, the life I'd known so well.
I froze. My hackles bristled, voice choked in my throat, 960
and my wife spoke out to ease me of my anguish:
'My dear husband, why so eager to give yourself
to such mad flights of grief? It's not without
the will of the gods these things have come to pass.
But the gods forbid you to take Creusa with you, 965
bound from Troy together. The king of lofty Olympus[6]

6. Jupiter, who rules from Mount Olympus, the highest mountain in Greece.

won't allow it. A long exile is your fate . . .
the vast plains of the sea are yours to plow
until you reach Hesperian land, where Lydian Tiber[7]
flows with its smooth march through rich and loamy fields,   970
a land of hardy people. There great joy and a kingdom
are yours to claim, and a queen to make your wife.
Dispel your tears for Creusa, whom you loved.
I will never behold the high and mighty pride
of their palaces, the Myrmidons, the Dolopians,   975
or go as a slave to some Greek matron, no, not I,
daughter of Dardanus that I am, the wife of Venus' son.
The Great Mother of Gods[8] detains me on these shores.
And now farewell. Hold dear the son we share,
we love together.'
    "These were her parting words   980
and for all my tears—I longed to say so much—
dissolving into the empty air she left me now.
Three times I tried to fling my arms around her neck,
three times I embraced—nothing . . . her phantom
sifting through my fingers,   985
light as wind, quick as a dream in flight.
      "Gone—
and at last the night was over. Back I went to my people
and I was amazed to see what throngs of new companions
had poured in to swell our numbers, mothers, men,
our forces gathered for exile, grieving masses.   990
They had come together from every quarter,
belongings, spirits ready for me to lead them
over the sea to whatever lands I'd choose.
And now the morning star was mounting above
the high crests of Ida, leading on the day.   995
The Greeks had taken the city, blocked off every gate.
No hope of rescue now. So I gave way at last and
lifting my father, headed toward the mountains."

Summary of Book III *Aeneas and his fleet travel across the Mediterranean. Along their way, they meet the monstrous bird-women (Harpies) and visit Andromache, widow of Hector. Anchises dies, and the storm carries the Trojans to Carthage.*

---

7. "Hesperian" is literally "western." The River Tiber runs through Rome. "Lydian" is used as an alternative for "Etruscan," since the Etrus-
cans were thought to come from Lydia in Asia Minor (modern-day Turkey).
8. Cybele is the mother goddess.

BOOK IV

[The Tragic Queen of Carthage]

But the queen—too long she has suffered the pain of love,
hour by hour nursing the wound with her lifeblood,
consumed by the fire buried in her heart.
The man's courage, the sheer pride of his line,
they all come pressing home to her, over and over.   5
His looks, his words, they pierce her heart and cling—
no peace, no rest for her body, love will give her none.

A new day's dawn was moving over the earth, Aurora's torch
cleansing the sky, burning away the dank shade of night
as the restless queen, beside herself, confides now   10
to the sister of her soul: "Dear Anna, the dreams
that haunt my quaking heart! Who is this stranger
just arrived to lodge in our house—our guest?
How noble his face, his courage, and what a soldier!
I'm sure—I know it's true—the man is born of the gods.   15
Fear exposes the lowborn man at once. But, oh, how tossed
he's been by the blows of fate. What a tale he's told,
what a bitter bowl of war he's drunk to the dregs.
If my heart had not been fixed, dead set against
embracing another man in the bonds of marriage—   20
ever since my first love deceived me, cheated me
by his death—if I were not as sick as I am
of the bridal bed and torch,[9] this, perhaps,
is my one lapse that might have brought me down.
I confess it, Anna, yes. Ever since my Sychaeus,   25
my poor husband met his fate, and my own brother
shed his blood and stained our household gods,[1]
this is the only man who's roused me deeply,
swayed my wavering heart . . .
The signs of the old flame, I know them well.   30
I pray that the earth gape deep enough to take me down
or the almighty Father blast me with one bolt to the shades,
the pale, glimmering shades in hell, the pit of night,
before I dishonor you, my conscience, break your laws.
He's carried my love away, the man who wed me first—   35
may he hold it tight, safeguard it in his grave."

She broke off, her voice choking with tears
that brimmed and wet her breast.
                              But Anna answered:
"Dear one, dearer than light to me, your sister,
would you waste away, grieving your youth away, alone,   40
never to know the joy of children, all the gifts of love?

9. Torches were used at weddings in antiquity.
1. Sychaeus, the husband of Dido and a priest
of Hercules, was murdered by her brother
Pygmalion, the king of Tyre (a Phoenician

city-state on the coast of modern-day Lebanon).
Dido then fled and eventually used Sychaeus's
wealth to found Carthage on the North African
coast.

Do you really believe that's what the dust desires,
the ghosts in their ashen tombs? Have it your way.
But granted that no one tempted you in the past,
not in your great grief,   45
no Libyan suitor, and none before in Tyre,
you scorned Iarbas[2] and other lords of Africa,
sons bred by this fertile earth in all their triumph:
why resist it now, this love that stirs your heart?
Don't you recall whose lands you settled here,   50
the men who press around you? On one side
the Gaetulian cities, fighters matchless in battle,
unbridled Numidians—Syrtes, the treacherous Sandbanks.
On the other side an endless desert, parched earth
where the wild Barcan marauders[3] range at will.   55
Why mention the war that's boiling up in Tyre,
your brother's deadly threats? I think, in fact,
the favor of all the gods and Juno's backing drove
these Trojan ships on the winds that sailed them here.
Think what a city you will see, my sister, what a kingdom   60
rising high if you marry such a man! With a Trojan army
marching at our side, think how the glory of Carthage
will tower to the clouds! Just ask the gods for pardon,
win them with offerings. Treat your guests like kings.
Weave together some pretext for delay, while winter   65
spends its rage and drenching Orion[4] whips the sea—
the ships still battered, weather still too wild."

These were the words that fanned her sister's fire,
turned her doubts to hopes and dissolved her sense of shame.
And first they visit the altars, make the rounds,   70
praying the gods for blessings, shrine by shrine.
They slaughter the pick of yearling sheep, the old way,
to Ceres, Giver of Laws, to Apollo, Bacchus who sets us free
and Juno above all, who guards the bonds of marriage.[5]
Dido aglow with beauty holds the bowl in her right hand,   75
pouring wine between the horns of a pure white cow
or gravely paces before the gods' fragrant altars,
under their statues' eyes refreshing her first gifts,
dawn to dusk. And when the victims' chests are splayed,
Dido, her lips parted, pores over their entrails,   80
throbbing still, for signs . . . [6]
But, oh, how little they know, the omniscient seers.
What good are prayers and shrines to a person mad with love?
The flame keeps gnawing into her tender marrow hour by hour

2. King of the Berbers who granted Dido
the land on which to build her city; he then
demanded her hand in marriage, but she
refused him.
3. African groups living near Carthage.
4 Giant hunter said to stir the waves when he
walks or wades across the sea.
5. Ceres: goddess of grain and agriculture.

Apollo: god of the sun, associated with civilization. Bacchus: god of wine. Juno: queen of the
gods, goddess of marriage. All were associated
with the foundation of cities.
6. It was Roman custom to inspect the entrails
of the sacrificial victim and interpret any unusual
features as signs of the future.

and deep in her heart the silent wound lives on. 85
Dido burns with love—the tragic queen.
She wanders in frenzy through her city streets
like a wounded doe caught all off guard by a hunter
stalking the woods of Crete, who strikes her from afar
and leaves his winging steel in her flesh, and he's unaware 90
but she veers in flight through Dicte's[7] woody glades,
fixed in her side the shaft that takes her life.
                                        And now
Dido leads her guest through the heart of Carthage,
displaying Phoenician power, the city readied for him.
She'd speak her heart but her voice chokes, mid-word. 95
Now at dusk she calls for the feast to start again,
madly begging to hear again the agony of Troy,
to hang on his lips again, savoring his story.
Then, with the guests gone, and the dimming moon
quenching its light in turn, and the setting stars 100
inclining heads to sleep—alone in the echoing hall,
distraught, she flings herself on the couch that he left empty.
Lost as he is, she's lost as well, she hears him, sees him
or she holds Ascanius back and dandles him on her lap,
bewitched by the boy's resemblance to his father, 105
trying to cheat the love she dare not tell.
The towers of Carthage, half built, rise no more,
and the young men quit their combat drills in arms.
The harbors, the battlements planned to block attack,
all work's suspended now, the huge, threatening walls 110
with the soaring cranes that sway across the sky.

Now, no sooner had Jove's dear wife perceived
that Dido was in the grip of such a scourge—
no thought of pride could stem her passion now—
than Juno approaches Venus and sets a cunning trap: 115
"What a glittering prize, a triumph you carry home!
You and your boy there, you grand and glorious Powers.
Just look, one woman crushed by the craft of two gods!
I am not blind, you know. For years you've looked askance
at the homes of rising Carthage, feared our ramparts. 120
But where will it end? What good is all our strife?
Come, why don't we labor now to live in peace?
Eternal peace, sealed with the bonds of marriage.
You have it all, whatever your heart desires—
Dido's ablaze with love, 125
drawing the frenzy deep into her bones. So,
let us rule this people in common: joint command.
And let her marry her Phrygian lover, be his slave
and give her Tyrians over to your control,
her dowry in your hands!"
                            Perceiving at once 130
that this was all pretense, a ruse to shift
the kingdom of Italy onto Libyan shores,

7. Mountain in Crete.

Venus countered Juno: "Now who'd be so insane
as to shun your offer and strive with you in war?
If only Fortune crowns your proposal with success!   135
But swayed by the Fates, I have my doubts. Would Jove
want one city to hold the Tyrians and the Trojan exiles?
Would he sanction the mingling of their peoples,
bless their binding pacts? You are his wife,
with every right to probe him with your prayers.   140
You lead the way. I'll follow."
                                      "The work is mine,"
imperious Juno carried on, "but how to begin
this pressing matter now and see it through?
I'll explain in a word or so. Listen closely.
Tomorrow Aeneas and lovesick Dido plan to hunt   145
the woods together, soon as the day's first light
climbs high and the Titan's[8] rays lay bare the earth.
But while the beaters scramble to ring the glens with nets,
I'll shower down a cloudburst, hail, black driving rain—
I'll shatter the vaulting sky with claps of thunder.   150
The huntsmen will scatter, swallowed up in the dark,
and Dido and Troy's commander will make their way
to the same cave for shelter. And I'll be there,
if I can count on your own good will in this—
I'll bind them in lasting marriage, make them one.   155
Their wedding it will be!"
                                      So Juno appealed
and Venus did not oppose her, nodding in assent
and smiling at all the guile she saw through . . .

Meanwhile Dawn rose up and left her Ocean bed
and soon as her rays have lit the sky, an elite band   160
of young huntsmen streams out through the gates,
bearing the nets, wide-meshed or tight for traps
and their hunting spears with broad iron heads,
troops of Massylian[9] horsemen galloping hard,
packs of powerful hounds, keen on the scent.   165
Yet the queen delays, lingering in her chamber
with Carthaginian chiefs expectant at her doors.
And there her proud, mettlesome charger prances
in gold and royal purple, pawing with thunder-hoofs,
champing a foam-flecked bit. At last she comes,   170
with a great retinue crowding round the queen
who wears a Tyrian cloak with rich embroidered fringe.
Her quiver is gold, her hair drawn up in a golden torque
and a golden buckle clasps her purple robe in folds.
Nor do her Trojan comrades tarry. Out they march,   175
young Iulus flushed with joy.
Aeneas in command, the handsomest of them all,
advancing as her companion joins his troop with hers.
So vivid. Think of Apollo leaving his Lycian haunts

8. Hyperion, lord of the sun and one of the   9. North African tribe.
Titans (pre-Olympian gods).

and Xanthus in winter spate, he's out to visit Delos, 180
his mother's isle,[1] and strike up the dance again
while round the altars swirls a growing throng
of Cretans, Dryopians, Agathyrsians with tattoos,
and a drumming roar goes up as the god himself
strides the Cynthian ridge,[2] his streaming hair 185
braided with pliant laurel leaves entwined
in twists of gold, and arrows clash on his shoulders.
So no less swiftly Aeneas strides forward now
and his face shines with a glory like the god's.

Once the huntsmen have reached the trackless lairs 190
aloft in the foothills, suddenly, look, some wild goats
flushed from a ridge come scampering down the slopes
and lower down a herd of stags goes bounding across
the open country, ranks massed in a cloud of dust,
fleeing the high ground. But young Ascanius, 195
deep in the valley, rides his eager mount
and relishing every stride, outstrips them all,
now goats, now stags, but his heart is racing, praying—
if only they'd send among this feeble, easy game
some frothing wild boar or a lion stalking down 200
from the heights and tawny in the sun.
                              Too late—
The skies have begun to rumble, peals of thunder first
and the storm breaking next, a cloudburst pelting hail
and the troops of hunters scatter up and down the plain,
Tyrian comrades, bands of Dardans, Venus' grandson Iulus 205
panicking, running for cover, quick, and down the mountain
gulleys erupt in torrents. Dido and Troy's commander
make their way to the same cave for shelter now.
Primordial Earth and Juno, Queen of Marriage,
give the signal and lightning torches flare 210
and the high sky bears witness to the wedding,
nymphs on the mountaintops wail out the wedding hymn.
This was the first day of her death, the first of grief,
the cause of it all. From now on, Dido cares no more
for appearances, nor for her reputation, either. 215
She no longer thinks to keep the affair a secret,
no, she calls it a marriage,
using the word to cloak her sense of guilt.

Straightway Rumor flies through Libya's great cities,
Rumor, swiftest of all the evils in the world. 220
She thrives on speed, stronger for every stride,
slight with fear at first, soon soaring into the air
she treads the ground and hides her head in the clouds.
She is the last, they say, our Mother Earth produced.

1. The sun god Apollo is imagined leaving
Lycia when the river Xanthus floods, and going
to Delos, which was sacred to his mother, Leto.

2. Mount Cynthus was on Delos. Cretans and
Dryopians were Greek peoples; Agathyrsians
were a Scythian people.

Bursting in rage against the gods, she bore a sister   225
for Coeus and Enceladus:[3] Rumor, quicksilver afoot
and swift on the wing, a monster, horrific, huge
and under every feather on her body—what a marvel—
an eye that never sleeps and as many tongues as eyes
and as many raucous mouths and ears pricked up for news.   230
By night she flies aloft, between the earth and sky,
whirring across the dark, never closing her lids
in soothing sleep. By day she keeps her watch,
crouched on a peaked roof or palace turret,
terrorizing the great cities, clinging as fast   235
to her twisted lies as she clings to words of truth.
Now Rumor is in her glory, filling Africa's ears
with tale on tale of intrigue, bruiting her song
of facts and falsehoods mingled . . .
"Here this Aeneas, born of Trojan blood,   240
has arrived in Carthage, and lovely Dido deigns
to join the man in wedlock. Even now they warm
the winter, long as it lasts, with obscene desire,
oblivious to their kingdoms, abject thralls of lust."

Such talk the sordid goddess spreads on the lips of men,   245
then swerves in her course and heading straight for King Iarbas,
stokes his heart with hearsay, piling fuel on his fire.

Iarbas—son of an African nymph whom Jove had raped—
raised the god a hundred splendid temples across
the king's wide realm, a hundred altars too,   250
consecrating the sacred fires
that never died, eternal sentinels of the gods.
The earth was rich with blood of slaughtered herds
and the temple doorways wreathed with riots of flowers.
This Iarbas, driven wild, set ablaze by the bitter rumor,   255
approached an altar, they say, as the gods hovered round,
and lifting a suppliant's hands, he poured out prayers to Jove:
"Almighty Jove! Now as the Moors[4] adore you, feasting away
on their gaudy couches, tipping wine in your honor—
do you see this? Or are we all fools, Father,   260
to dread the bolts you hurl? All aimless then,
your fires high in the clouds that terrify us so?
All empty noise, your peals of grumbling thunder?
That woman, that vagrant! Here in my own land
she founded her paltry city for a pittance.   265
We tossed her some beach to plow—on my terms—
and then she spurns our offer of marriage, she
embraces Aeneas as lord and master in her realm.
And now this second Paris . . .
leading his troupe of eunuchs, his hair oozing oil,   270
a Phrygian bonnet tucked up under his chin, he revels

---

3. Titans, the first children of Earth.   4. A North African people.

in all that he has filched, while we keep bearing gifts
to your temples—yes, yours—coddling your reputation,
all your hollow show!"

                So King Iarbas appealed,
his hand clutching the altar, and Jove Almighty heard   275
and turned his gaze on the royal walls of Carthage
and the lovers oblivious now to their good name.
He summons Mercury,[5] gives him marching orders:
"Quick, my son, away! Call up the Zephyrs,[6]
glide on wings of the wind. Find the Dardan captain   280
who now malingers long in Tyrian Carthage, look,
and pays no heed to the cities Fate decrees are his.
Take my commands through the racing winds and tell him
this is not the man his mother, the lovely goddess, promised,
not for *this* did she save him twice from Greek attacks.   285
Never. He would be the one to master an Italy
rife with leaders, shrill with the cries of war,
to sire a people sprung from Teucer's noble blood[7]
and bring the entire world beneath the rule of law.
If such a glorious destiny cannot fire his spirit,   290
if he will not shoulder the task for his own fame,
does the father of Ascanius grudge his son
the walls of Rome? What is he plotting now?
What hope can make him loiter among his foes,
lose sight of Italian offspring still to come   295
and all the Lavinian fields?[8] Let him set sail!
This is the sum of it. This must be our message."

Jove had spoken. Mercury made ready at once
to obey the great commands of his almighty father.
First he fastens under his feet the golden sandals,   300
winged to sweep him over the waves and earth alike
with the rush of gusting winds. Then he seizes the wand
that calls the pallid spirits up from the Underworld
and ushers others down to the grim dark depths,
the wand that lends us sleep or sends it away,   305
that unseals our eyes in death.[9] Equipped with this,
he spurs the winds and swims through billowing clouds
till in mid-flight he spies the summit and rugged flanks
of Atlas, whose long-enduring peak supports the skies.[1]
Atlas: his pine-covered crown is forever girded   310
round with black clouds, battered by wind and rain;
driving blizzards cloak his shoulders with snow,
torrents course down from the old Titan's chin
and shaggy beard that bristles stiff with ice.

5. The messenger god; Hermes in Greek mythology.
6. Personified winds. Zephyr is usually the gentle west wind.
7. Teucer was the first king of Troy.
8. Lavinium is the city Aeneas will found in Italy.

9. Mercury is the god who guides the dead to the underworld.
1. Atlas is a Titan who was condemned by Zeus to stand holding up the sky. The Greeks and later the Romans associated Atlas with the mountains of North Africa.

Here the god of Cyllene[2] landed first,   315
banking down to a stop on balanced wings.
From there, headlong down with his full weight
he plunged to the sea as a seahawk skims the waves,
rounding the beaches, rounding cliffs to hunt for fish inshore.
So Mercury of Cyllene flew between the earth and sky   320
to gain the sandy coast of Libya, cutting the winds
that sweep down from his mother's father, Atlas.
                                    Soon
as his winged feet touched down on the first huts in sight,
he spots Aeneas founding the city fortifications,
building homes in Carthage. And his sword-hilt   325
is studded with tawny jasper stars, a cloak
of glowing Tyrian purple[3] drapes his shoulders,
a gift that the wealthy queen had made herself,
weaving into the weft a glinting mesh of gold.
Mercury lashes out at once: "You, so now you lay   330
foundation stones for the soaring walls of Carthage!
Building her gorgeous city, doting on your wife.
Blind to your own realm, oblivious to your fate!
The King of the Gods, whose power sways earth and sky—
he is the one who sends me down from brilliant Olympus,   335
bearing commands for you through the racing winds.
What are you plotting now?
Wasting time in Libya—what hope misleads you so?
If such a glorious destiny cannot fire your spirit,
[if you will not shoulder the task for your own fame,][4]   340
at least remember Ascanius rising into his prime,
the hopes you lodge in Iulus, your only heir—
you owe him Italy's realm, the land of Rome!"
This order still on his lips, the god vanished
from sight into empty air.
                            Then Aeneas   345
was truly overwhelmed by the vision, stunned,
his hackles bristle with fear, his voice chokes in his throat.
He yearns to be gone, to desert this land he loves,
thunderstruck by the warnings, Jupiter's command . . .
But what can he do? What can he dare say now   350
to the queen in all her fury and win her over?
Where to begin, what opening? Thoughts racing,
here, there, probing his options, turning
to this plan, that plan—torn in two until,
at his wits' end, this answer seems the best.   355
He summons Mnestheus, Sergestus, staunch Serestus,
gives them orders: "Fit out the fleet, but not a word.
Muster the crews on shore, all tackle set to sail,
but the cause for our new course, you keep it secret."

2. Mercury was born on Mount Cyllene, in   shells) often used to color royal vestments.
Greece.   4. Bracketed because some editors believe
3. Tyre was famed in the ancient world as the   the line does not belong in the text.
source of a rare purple dye (made from snail

Yet he himself, since Dido who means the world to him   360
knows nothing, never dreaming such a powerful love
could be uprooted—he will try to approach her,
find the moment to break the news gently,
a way to soften the blow that he must leave.
All shipmates snap to commands,   365
glad to do his orders.
                              True, but the queen—
who can delude a lover?—soon caught wind
of a plot afoot, the first to sense the Trojans
are on the move . . . She fears everything now,
even with all secure. Rumor, vicious as ever,   370
brings her word, already distraught, that Trojans
are rigging out their galleys, gearing to set sail.
She rages in helpless frenzy, blazing through
the entire city, raving like some Maenad[5]
driven wild when the women shake the sacred emblems,   375
when the cyclic orgy, shouts of "Bacchus!" fire her on
and Cithaeron echoes round with maddened midnight cries.

At last she assails Aeneas, before he's said a word:
"So, you traitor, you really believed you'd keep
this a secret, this great outrage?—steal away   380
in silence from my shores? Can nothing hold you back?
Not our love? Not the pledge once sealed with our right hands?
Not even the thought of Dido doomed to a cruel death?
Why labor to rig your fleet when the winter's raw,
to risk the deep when the Northwind's closing in?   385
You cruel, heartless—Even if you were not
pursuing alien fields and unknown homes,
even if ancient Troy were standing, still,
who'd sail for Troy across such heaving seas?
You're running away—from me? Oh, I pray you   390
by these tears, by the faith in your right hand—
what else have I left myself in all my pain?—
by our wedding vows, the marriage we began,
if I deserve some decency from you now,
if anything mine has ever won your heart,   395
pity a great house about to fall, I pray you,
if prayers have any place—reject this scheme of yours!
Thanks to you, the African tribes, Numidian warlords
hate me, even my own Tyrians rise against me.
Thanks to you, my sense of honor is gone,   400
my one and only pathway to the stars,
the renown I once held dear. In whose hands,
my guest, do you leave me here to meet my death?
'Guest'—that's all that remains of 'husband' now.
But why do I linger on? Until my brother Pygmalion   405

5. The Maenads (Bacchae) were female wor-
shippers of Bacchus, who ran wild on Mount
Cithaeron in a ritual held every other year—as
depicted in Euripides' *Bacchae*, in which one
such god-frenzied woman kills her own son.

batters down my walls? Or Iarbas drags me off, his slave?
If only you'd left a baby in my arms—our child—
before you deserted me! Some little Aeneas
playing about our halls, whose features at least
would bring you back to me in spite of all,   410
I would not feel so totally devastated,
so destroyed."
                              The queen stopped but he,
warned by Jupiter now, his gaze held steady,
fought to master the torment in his heart. At last
he ventured a few words: "I . . . you have done me   415
so many kindnesses, and you could count them all.
I shall never deny what you deserve, my queen,
never regret my memories of Dido, not while I
can recall myself and draw the breath of life.
I'll state my case in a few words. I never dreamed   420
I'd keep my flight a secret. Don't imagine that.
Nor did I once extend a bridegroom's torch
or enter into a marriage pact with you.
If the Fates had left me free to live my life,
to arrange my own affairs of my own free will,   425
Troy is the city, first of all, that I'd safeguard,
Troy and all that's left of my people whom I cherish.
The grand palace of Priam would stand once more,
with my own hands I would fortify a second Troy
to house my Trojans in defeat. But not now.   430
Grynean Apollo's oracle says that I must seize
on Italy's noble land, his Lycian lots say 'Italy!'[6]
There lies my love, there lies my homeland now.
If you, a Phoenician, fix your eyes on Carthage,
a Libyan stronghold, tell me, why do you grudge   435
the Trojans their new homes on Italian soil?
What is the crime if *we* seek far-off kingdoms too?

"My father, Anchises, whenever the darkness shrouds
the earth in its dank shadows, whenever the stars
go flaming up the sky, my father's anxious ghost   440
warns me in dreams and fills my heart with fear.
My son Ascanius . . . I feel the wrong I do
to one so dear, robbing him of his kingdom,
lands in the West, his fields decreed by Fate.
And now the messenger of the gods—I swear it,   445
by your life and mine—dispatched by Jove himself
has brought me firm commands through the racing winds.
With my own eyes I saw him, clear, in broad daylight,
moving through your gates. With my own ears I drank
his message in. Come, stop inflaming us both   450
with your appeals. I set sail for Italy—
all against my will."

6. Grynia was an Aeolian city sacred to Apollo. Lycia is another cult center of Apollo.

                                    Even from the start
of his declaration, she has glared at him askance,
her eyes roving over him, head to foot, with a look
of stony silence . . . till abruptly she cries out   455
in a blaze of fury: "No goddess was your mother!
No Dardanus sired your line, you traitor, liar, no,
Mount Caucasus fathered you on its flinty, rugged flanks
and the tigers of Hyrcania gave you their dugs to suck![7]
Why hide it? Why hold back? To suffer greater blows?   460
Did *he* groan when *I* wept? Even look at me? Never!
Surrender a tear? Pity the one who loves him?
What can I say first? So much to say. Now—
neither mighty Juno nor Saturn's son, the Father,[8]
gazes down on this with just, impartial eyes.   465
There's no faith left on earth!
He was washed up on my shores, helpless, and I,
I took him in, like a maniac let him share my kingdom,
salvaged his lost fleet, plucked his crews from death.
Oh I am swept by the Furies, gales of fire![9] Now   470
it's Apollo the Prophet, Apollo's Lycian oracles:
they're his masters now, and now, to top it off,
the messenger of the gods, dispatched by Jove himself,
comes rushing down the winds with his grim-set commands.
Really! What work for the gods who live on high,   475
what a concern to ruffle their repose!
I won't hold you, I won't even refute you—go!—
strike out for Italy on the winds, your realm across the sea.
I hope, I pray, if the just gods still have any power,
wrecked on the rocks midsea you'll drink your bowl   480
of pain to the dregs, crying out the name of Dido
over and over, and worlds away I'll hound you then
with pitch-black flames, and when icy death has severed
my body from its breath, then my ghost will stalk you
through the world! You'll pay, you shameless, ruthless—   485
and I will hear of it, yes, the report will reach me
even among the deepest shades of Death!"
                                         She breaks off
in the midst of outbursts, desperate, flinging herself
from the light of day, sweeping out of his sight,
leaving him numb with doubt, with much to fear   490
and much he means to say.
Catching her as she faints away, her women
bear her back to her marble bridal chamber
and lay her body down upon her bed.
                                    But Aeneas
is driven by duty now. Strongly as he longs   495
to ease and allay her sorrow, speak to her,

7. Dardanus was the legendary founder of Troy. The Caucasus mountains, between the Black and Caspian Seas, and Hyrcania, south of the Caspian, were notoriously wild, uncivilized regions.
8. Jupiter was the son of Saturn.
9. The Furies are spirits of vengeance who carry flaming torches.

turn away her anguish with reassurance, still,
moaning deeply, heart shattered by his great love,
in spite of all he obeys the gods' commands
and back he goes to his ships.   500
Then the Trojans throw themselves in the labor,
launching their tall vessels down along the beach
and the hull rubbed sleek with pitch floats high again.
So keen to be gone, the men drag down from the forest
untrimmed timbers and boughs still green for oars.   505
You can see them streaming out of the whole city,
men like ants that, wary of winter's onset, pillage
some huge pile of wheat to store away in their grange
and their army's long black line goes marching through the field,
trundling their spoils down some cramped, grassy track.   510
Some put shoulders to giant grains and thrust them on,
some dress the ranks, strictly marshal stragglers,
and the whole trail seethes with labor.

What did you feel then, Dido, seeing this?
How deep were the groans you uttered, gazing now   515
from the city heights to watch the broad beaches
seething with action, the bay a chaos of outcries
right before your eyes?
                        Love, you tyrant!
To what extremes won't you compel our hearts?
Again she resorts to tears, driven to move the man,   520
or try, with prayers—a suppliant kneeling, humbling
her pride to passion. So if die she must,
she'll leave no way untried.
                            "Anna, you see
the hurly-burly all across the beach, the crews
swarming from every quarter? The wind cries for canvas,   525
the buoyant oarsmen crown their sterns with wreaths.
This terrible sorrow: since I saw it coming, Anna,
I can endure it now. But even so, my sister,
carry out for me one great favor in my pain.
To you alone he used to listen, the traitor,   530
to you confide his secret feelings. You alone
know how and when to approach him, soothe his moods.
Go, my sister! Plead with my imperious enemy.
Remind him I was never at Aulis, never swore a pact
with the Greeks to rout the Trojan people from the earth![1]   535
I sent no fleet to Troy, I never uprooted the ashes
of his father, Anchises, never stirred his shade.
Why does he shut his pitiless ears to my appeals?
Where's he rushing now? If only he would offer
one last gift to the wretched queen who loves him: 540
to wait for fair winds, smooth sailing for his flight!
I no longer beg for the long-lost marriage he betrayed,

---

1. The Greek forces mustered at Aulis before sailing to Troy. It was here that Agamemnon killed his daughter to make the wind blow.

nor would I ask him now to desert his kingdom, no,
his lovely passion, Latium.[2] All I ask is time,
blank time: some rest from frenzy, breathing room   545
till my fate can teach my beaten spirit how to grieve.
I beg him—pity your sister, Anna—one last favor,
and if he grants it now, I'll pay him back,
with interest, when I die."

          So Dido pleads and
so her desolate sister takes him the tale of tears   550
again and again. But no tears move Aeneas now.
He is deaf to all appeals. He won't relent.
The Fates bar the way
and heaven blocks his gentle, human ears.
As firm as a sturdy oak grown tough with age   555
when the Northwinds blasting off the Alps compete,
fighting left and right, to wrench it from the earth,
and the winds scream, the trunk shudders, its leafy crest
showers across the ground but it clings firm to its rock,
its roots stretching as deep into the dark world below   560
as its crown goes towering toward the gales of heaven—
so firm the hero stands: buffeted left and right
by storms of appeals, he takes the full force
of love and suffering deep in his great heart.
His will stands unmoved. The falling tears are futile.[3]

                                  Then,   565
terrified by her fate, tragic Dido prays for death,
sickened to see the vaulting sky above her.
And to steel her new resolve to leave the light,
she sees, laying gifts on the altars steaming incense—
shudder to hear it now—the holy water going black   570
and the wine she pours congeals in bloody filth.[4]
She told no one what she saw, not even her sister.
Worse, there was a marble temple in her palace,
a shrine built for her long-lost love, Sychaeus.
Holding it dear she tended it—marvelous devotion—   575
draping the snow-white fleece and festal boughs.
Now from its depths she seemed to catch his voice,
the words of her dead husband calling out her name
while night enclosed the earth in its dark shroud,
and over and over a lonely owl perched on the rooftops   580
drew out its low, throaty call to a long wailing dirge.
And worse yet, the grim predictions of ancient seers
keep terrifying her now with frightful warnings.
Aeneas the hunter, savage in all her nightmares,
drives her mad with panic. She always feels alone,   585
abandoned, always wandering down some endless road,
not a friend in sight, seeking her own Phoenicians
in some godforsaken land. As frantic as Pentheus

2. Region of central Italy, land of the Latins.
3. In the Latin, as here, it is unclear who is
crying; it could be Anna, Dido, Aeneas, or all
three.
4. Dido is trying to pour libations—liquid
offerings to the gods.

seeing battalions of Furies, twin suns ablaze
and double cities of Thebes before his eyes.[5]   590
Or Agamemnon's Orestes hounded off the stage,
fleeing his mother armed with torches, black snakes,
while blocking the doorway coil her Furies of Revenge.[6]

So, driven by madness, beaten down by anguish,
Dido was fixed on dying, working out in her mind   595
the means, the moment. She approaches her grieving
sister, Anna—masking her plan with a brave face
aglow with hope, and says: "I've found a way,
dear heart—rejoice with your sister—either
to bring him back in love for me or free me   600
of love for him. Close to the bounds of Ocean,
west with the setting sun, lies Ethiopian land,
the end of the earth, where colossal Atlas turns
on his shoulder the heavens studded with flaming stars.
From there, I have heard, a Massylian priestess comes   605
who tended the temple held by Hesperian daughters.[7]
She'd safeguard the boughs in the sacred grove
and ply the dragon with morsels dripping loops
of oozing honey and poppies drowsy with slumber.
With her spells she vows to release the hearts   610
of those she likes, to inflict raw pain on others—
to stop the rivers in midstream, reverse the stars
in their courses, raise the souls of the dead at night
and make earth shudder and rumble underfoot—you'll see—
and send the ash trees marching down the mountains.   615
I swear by the gods, dear Anna, by your sweet life,
I arm myself with magic arts against my will.[8]
                     "Now go,
build me a pyre in secret, deep inside our courtyard
under the open sky. Pile it high with his arms—
he left them hanging within our bridal chamber—   620
the traitor, so devoted then! and all his clothes
and crowning it all, the bridal bed that brought my doom.
I must obliterate every trace of the man, the curse,
and the priestess shows the way!"
                     She says no more
and now as the queen falls silent, pallor sweeps her face.   625

---

5. Pentheus was the king of Thebes who, in Euripides' *Bacchae*, was driven mad so that he thought he saw two suns in the sky and was then killed by his own mother.
6. Agamemnon's son, Orestes, killed his mother in revenge for her killing his father. He was then driven mad by the Furies. The myth is the subject of Aeschylus's *Oresteia* and Euripides' *Orestes*.
7. The daughters of Hesperus, the Evening Star, tended a garden containing the golden apples that belonged to Hera. A never-sleeping dragon with a hundred heads also guarded the apples.
8. These allusions to witchcraft make Dido sound like Medea, the princess of Colchis with magical powers, who helped Jason steal the Golden Fleece from her father and escape back to Greece. Later, after several years of marriage, Jason abandoned Medea; she then, according to Euripides' *Medea*, took revenge by killing their children.

Still, Anna cannot imagine these outlandish rites
would mask her sister's death. She can't conceive
of such a fiery passion. She fears nothing graver
than Dido's grief at the death of her Sychaeus.
So she does as she is told.
630
                                   But now the queen,
as soon as the pyre was built beneath the open sky,
towering up with pitch-pine and cut logs of oak—
deep in the heart of her house—she drapes the court
with flowers, crowning the place with wreaths of death,
and to top it off she lays his arms and the sword he left
635
and an effigy of Aeneas, all on the bed they'd shared,
for well she knows the future. Altars ring the pyre.
Hair loose in the wind, the priestess thunders out
the names of her three hundred gods, Erebus, Chaos
and triple Hecate, Diana the three-faced virgin.[9]
640
She'd sprinkled water, simulating the springs of hell,
and gathered potent herbs, reaped with bronze sickles
under the moonlight, dripping their milky black poison,
and fetched a love-charm ripped from a foal's brow,
just born, before the mother could gnaw it off.
645
And Dido herself, standing before the altar,
holding the sacred grain in reverent hands—
with one foot free of its sandal, robes unbound[1]—
sworn now to die, she calls on the gods to witness,
calls on the stars who know her approaching fate.
650
And then to any Power above, mindful, evenhanded,
who watches over lovers bound by unequal passion,
Dido says her prayers.
                     The dead of night,
and weary living creatures throughout the world
are enjoying peaceful sleep. The woods and savage seas
655
are calm, at rest, and the circling stars are gliding on
in their midnight courses, all the fields lie hushed
and the flocks and gay and gorgeous birds that haunt
the deep clear pools and the thorny country thickets
all lie quiet now, under the silent night, asleep.
660
But not the tragic queen . . .
torn in spirit, Dido will not dissolve
into sleep—her eyes, her mind won't yield to night.
Her torments multiply, over and over her passion
surges back into heaving waves of rage—
665
she keeps on brooding, obsessions roil her heart:
"And now, what shall I do? Make a mockery of myself,
go back to my old suitors, tempt them to try again?
Beg the Numidians, grovel, plead for a husband—
though time and again I scorned to wed their likes?
670
What then? Trail the Trojan ships, bend to the Trojans'
every last demand? So pleased, are they, with all the help,

---

9. Erebus is Darkness, son of Chaos. Hecate,   goddess, was the goddess of witchcraft.
sometimes identified with Diana the moon   **1.** All magical practices.

the relief I lent them once? And memory of my service past
stands firm in grateful minds! And even if I were willing,
would the Trojans allow me to board their proud ships—   675
a woman they hate? Poor lost fool, can't you sense it,
grasp it yet—the treachery of Laomedon's breed?[2]
What now? Do I take flight alone, consorting
with crews of Trojan oarsmen in their triumph?
Or follow them out with all my troops of Tyrians   680
thronging the decks? Yes, hard as it was to uproot
them once from Tyre! How can I force them back to sea
once more, command them to spread their sails to the winds?
No, no, die!
                    You deserve it—
                              end your pain with the sword!
You, my sister, you were the first, won over by my tears,   685
to pile these sorrows on my shoulders, mad as I was,
to throw me into my enemy's arms. If only I'd been free
to live my life, untested in marriage, free of guilt
as some wild beast untouched by pangs like these!
I broke the faith I swore to the ashes of Sychaeus."   690

Such terrible grief kept breaking from her heart
as Aeneas slept in peace on his ship's high stern,
bent on departing now, all tackle set to sail.
And now in his dreams it came again—the god,
his phantom, the same features shining clear.   695
Like Mercury head to foot, the voice, the glow,
the golden hair, the bloom of youth on his limbs
and his voice rang out with warnings once again:
"Son of the goddess, how can you sleep so soundly
in such a crisis? Can't you see the dangers closing   700
around you now? Madman! Can't you hear the Westwind
ruffling to speed you on? That woman spawns her plots,
mulling over some desperate outrage in her heart,
lashing her surging rage, she's bent on death.
Why not flee headlong?   705
Flee headlong while you can! You'll soon see
the waves a chaos of ships, lethal torches flaring,
the whole coast ablaze, if now a new dawn breaks
and finds you still malingering on these shores.
Up with you now. Enough delay. Woman's a thing   710
that's always changing, shifting like the wind."
With that he vanished into the black night.

Then, terrified by the sudden phantom,
Aeneas, wrenching himself from sleep, leaps up
and rouses his crews and spurs them headlong on: 715
"Quick! Up and at it, shipmates, man the thwarts![3]
Spread canvas fast! A god's come down from the sky

---

2. Laomedon, father of Priam and previous
king of Troy, broke a promise to repay Apollo
and Neptune for building his city walls.
3. I.e., take up positions on the rowing benches.

once more—I've just seen him—urging us on
to sever our mooring cables, sail at once!
We follow you, blessed god, whoever you are—   720
glad at heart we obey your commands once more.
Now help us, stand beside us with all your kindness,
bring us favoring stars in the sky to blaze our way!"

Tearing sword from sheath like a lightning flash,
he hacks the mooring lines with a naked blade.   725
Gripped by the same desire, all hands pitch in,
they hoist and haul. The shore's deserted now,
the water's hidden under the fleet—they bend to it,
churn the spray and sweep the clear blue sea.
                                    By now
early Dawn had risen up from the saffron bed   730
of Tithonus,[4] scattering fresh light on the world.
But the queen from her high tower, catching sight
of the morning's white glare, the armada heading out
to sea with sails trimmed to the wind, and certain
the shore and port were empty, stripped of oarsmen—   735
three, four times over she beat her lovely breast,
she ripped at her golden hair and "Oh, by God,"
she cries, "will the stranger just sail off
and make a mockery of our realm? Will no one
rush to arms, come streaming out of the whole city,   740
hunt him down, race to the docks and launch the ships?
Go, quick—bring fire!
                    Hand out weapons!
                                    Bend to the oars!
What am I saying? Where am I? What insanity's this
that shifts my fixed resolve? Dido, oh poor fool,
is it only *now* your wicked work strikes home?   745
It should have then, when you offered him your scepter.
Look at his hand clasp, look at his good faith now—
that man who, they say, carries his fathers' gods,
who stooped to shoulder his father bent with age!
Couldn't I have seized him then, ripped him to pieces,   750
scattered them in the sea? Or slashed his men with steel,
butchered Ascanius, served him up as his father's feast?[5]
True, the luck of battle might have been at risk—
well, risk away! Whom did I have to fear?
I was about to die. I should have torched their camp   755
and flooded their decks with fire. The son, the father,
the whole Trojan line—I should have wiped them out,
then hurled myself on the pyre to crown it all!

4. The goddess Dawn had a human lover
named Tithonus, whom she had made immortal (though not ageless) and brought to live
with her.
5. These horrible possibilities have mythic
precedents. Medea, when she eloped with Jason,

ripped up her little brother's body and scattered the pieces on the sea, to distract their
father as he tried to pursue the boat. Atreus,
father of Agamemnon and Menelaus, killed
his brother's children and served them to him
at a feast.

"You, Sun, whose fires scan all works of the earth,[6]
and you, Juno, the witness, midwife to my agonies—   760
Hecate greeted by nightly shrieks at city crossroads—
and you, you avenging Furies and gods of dying Dido!
Hear me, turn your power my way, attend my sorrows—
I deserve your mercy—hear my prayers! If that curse
of the earth must reach his haven, labor on to landfall—   765
if Jove and the Fates command and the boundary stone is fixed,
still, let him be plagued in war by a nation proud in arms,
torn from his borders, wrenched from Iulus' embrace,
let him grovel for help and watch his people die
a shameful death! And then, once he has bowed down   770
to an unjust peace, may he never enjoy his realm
and the light he yearns for, never, let him die
before his day, unburied on some desolate beach![7]

"That is my prayer, my final cry—I pour it out
with my own lifeblood. And you, my Tyrians,   775
harry with hatred all his line, his race to come:
make that offering to my ashes, send it down below.
No love between our peoples, ever, no pacts of peace!
Come rising up from my bones, you avenger still unknown,
to stalk those Trojan settlers, hunt with fire and iron,   780
now or in time to come, whenever the power is yours.
Shore clash with shore, sea against sea and sword
against sword—this is my curse—war between all
our peoples, all their children, endless war!"

With that, her mind went veering back and forth—   785
what was the quickest way to break off from the light,
the life she loathed? And so with a few words
she turned to Barce, Sychaeus' old nurse—her own
was now black ashes deep in her homeland lost forever:
"Dear old nurse, send Anna my sister to me here.   790
Tell her to hurry, sprinkle herself with river water,
bring the victims marked for the sacrifice I must make.
So let her come. And wrap your brow with the holy bands.
These rites to Jove of the Styx that I have set in motion,
I yearn to consummate them, end the pain of love,   795
give that cursed Trojan's pyre to the flames."
The nurse bustled off with an old crone's zeal.
                                        But Dido,
trembling, desperate now with the monstrous thing afoot—
her bloodshot eyes rolling, quivering cheeks blotched
and pale with imminent death—goes bursting through   800
the doors to the inner courtyard, clambers in frenzy
up the soaring pyre and unsheathes a sword, a Trojan sword
she once sought as a gift, but not for such an end.

6. The sun (Helios) was sometimes personified as a god; he was the grandfather of Medea.
7. Another oblique refernce to the assassination of Pompey after he was defeated by Julius
Caesar in the civil war of 49–45 B.C.E (cf. book
II, line 690).

And next, catching sight of the Trojan's clothes
and the bed they knew by heart, delaying a moment   805
for tears, for memory's sake, the queen lay down
and spoke her final words: "Oh, dear relics,
dear as long as Fate and the gods allowed,
receive my spirit and set me free of pain.
I have lived a life. I've journeyed through   810
the course that Fortune charted for me. And now
I pass to the world below, my ghost in all its glory.
I have founded a noble city, seen my ramparts rise.
I have avenged my husband, punished my blood-brother,
our mortal foe. Happy, all too happy I would have been   815
if only the Trojan keels had never grazed our coast."
She presses her face in the bed and cries out:
"I shall die unavenged, but die I will! So—
so—I rejoice to make my way among the shades.
And may that heartless Dardan, far at sea,   820
drink down deep the sight of our fires here
and bear with him this omen of our death!"

All at once, in the midst of her last words,
her women see her doubled over the sword, the blood
foaming over the blade, her hands splattered red.   825
A scream goes stabbing up to the high roofs,
Rumor raves like a Maenad through the shocked city—
sobs, and grief, and the wails of women ringing out
through homes, and the heavens echo back the keening din—
for all the world as if enemies stormed the walls   830
and all of Carthage or old Tyre were toppling down
and flames in their fury, wave on mounting wave
were billowing over the roofs of men and gods.

Anna heard and, stunned, breathless with terror,
raced through the crowd, her nails clawing her face,   835
fists beating her breast, crying out to her sister now
at the edge of death: "Was it all for *this*, my sister?
You deceived me all along? Is this what your pyre
meant for me—this, your fires—this, your altars?
You deserted me—what shall I grieve for first?   840
Your friend, your sister, you scorn me now in death?
You should have called me on to the same fate.
The same agony, same sword, the one same hour
had borne us off together. Just to think I built
your pyre with my own hands, implored our fathers' gods   845
with my own voice, only to be cut off from you—
how very cruel—when you lay down to die . . .
You have destroyed your life, my sister, mine too,
your people, the lords of Sidon and your new city here.
Please, help me to bathe her wounds in water now,   850
and if any last, lingering breath still hovers,
let me catch it on my lips."

With those words
she had climbed the pyre's topmost steps and now,
clasping her dying sister to her breast, fondling her
she sobbed, stanching the dark blood with her own gown.   855
Dido, trying to raise her heavy eyes once more, failed—
deep in her heart the wound kept rasping, hissing on.
Three times she tried to struggle up on an elbow,
three times she fell back, writhing on her bed.
Her gaze wavering into the high skies, she looked   860
for a ray of light and when she glimpsed it, moaned.

Then Juno in all her power, filled with pity
for Dido's agonizing death, her labor long and hard,
sped Iris[8] down from Olympus to release her spirit
wrestling now in a deathlock with her limbs.   865
Since she was dying a death not fated or deserved,
no, tormented, before her day, in a blaze of passion—
Proserpina had yet to pluck a golden lock from her head
and commit her life to the Styx and the dark world below.[9]
So Iris, glistening dew, comes skimming down from the sky   870
on gilded wings, trailing showers of iridescence shimmering
into the sun, and hovering over Dido's head, declares:
"So commanded, I take this lock as a sacred gift
to the God of Death, and I release you from your body."

With that, she cut the lock with her hand and all at once   875
the warmth slipped away, the life dissolved in the winds.

Summary of Book V   The Trojans see the flames of Dido's funeral pyre as they leave.
They sail back to Sicily, where they mark the death of Anchises with funeral rites and games.
The pilot of Aeneas's ship, Palinurus, is overwhelmed by sleep at the tiller, falls into the sea, and
drowns.

BOOK VI

[The Kingdom of the Dead]

So as he speaks in tears Aeneas gives the ships free rein
and at last they glide onto Euboean Cumae's beaches.[1]
Swinging their prows around to face the sea,
they moor the fleet with the anchors' biting grip
and the curved sterns edge the bay. Bands of sailors,   5
primed for action, leap out onto land—Hesperian land.[2]
Some strike seeds of fire buried in veins of flint,

8. Iris is the goddess who sometimes acts as
messenger between heaven and earth; she
appears as a rainbow (hence "iridescence").
9. Proserpina, queen of the underworld, would
normally have taken a lock of Dido's hair to
release her life; since her death is premature,
Iris does it instead.

1. Cumae, a Greek colony on the Italian coast
(in modern Campania, near Naples), was
founded by immigrants from the island of
Euboea. It was the seat of the Sibyl, a priestess
of Apollo, for many centuries.
2. "Hesperian" means "western"; Hesperia is
also a Greek name for Italy.

some strip the dense thickets, lairs of wild beasts,
and lighting on streams, are quick to point them out.
But devout Aeneas makes his way to the stronghold   10
that Apollo rules, throned on high, and set apart
is a vast cave, the awesome Sybil's secret haunt
where the Seer of Delos[3] breathes his mighty will,
his soul inspiring her to lay the future bare.
And now they approach Diana's[4] sacred grove   15
and walk beneath the golden roofs of god.

                        Daedalus,[5]
so the story's told, fleeing the realm of Minos,
daring to trust himself to the sky on beating wings,
floated up to the icy North, the first man to fly,
and hovered lightly on Cumae's heights at last.   20
Here, on first returning to earth, he hallowed
to you, Apollo, the oars of his rowing wings
and here he built your grand, imposing temple.
High on a gate he carved Androgeos' death[6]
and then the people of Athens, doomed—so cruel—   25
to pay with the lives of seven sons. Year in, year out,
the urn stands ready, the fateful lots are drawn.

    Balancing these on a facing gate, the land of Crete
comes rising from the sea. Here the cursed lust for the bull
and Pasiphaë spread beneath him, duping both her mates,   30
and here the mixed breed, part man, part beast, the Minotaur—
a warning against such monstrous passion. Here its lair,
that house of labor, the endless blinding maze,
but Daedalus, pitying royal Ariadne's love so deep,[7]
unraveled his own baffling labyrinth's winding paths,   35
guiding Theseus' groping steps with a trail of thread.
And you too, Icarus, what part you might have played
in a work that great, had Daedalus' grief allowed it.
Twice he tried to engrave your fall in gold and
twice his hands, a father's hands, fell useless.
                            Yes,   40
and they would have kept on scanning scene by scene

if Achates, sent ahead, had not returned, bringing
Deiphobe, Glaucus' daughter, priestess of Phoebus
and Diana too, and the Sibyl tells the king:
"This is no time for gazing at the sights.   45
Better to slaughter seven bulls from a herd
unbroken by the yoke, as the old rite requires,
and as many head of teething yearling sheep."
Directing Aeneas so—and his men are quick
with the sacrifice she demands—   50
the Sibyl calls them into her lofty shrine.

    Now carved out of the rocky flanks of Cumae
lies an enormous cavern pierced by a hundred tunnels,
a hundred mouths with as many voices rushing out,
the Sibyl's rapt replies. They had just gained   55
the sacred sill when the virgin cries aloud:
"Now is the time to ask your fate to speak!
The god, look, the god!"
                              So she cries before
the entrance—suddenly all her features, all
her color changes, her braided hair flies loose   60
and her breast heaves, her heart bursts with frenzy,
she seems to rise in height, the ring of her voice no longer
human—the breath, the power of god comes closer, closer.
"Why so slow, Trojan Aeneas?" she shouts, "so slow
to pray, to swear your vows? Not until you do   65
will the great jaws of our spellbound house gape wide."
And with that command the prophetess fell silent.

    An icy shiver runs through the Trojans' sturdy spines
and the king's prayers come pouring from his heart:
"Apollo, you always pitied the Trojans' heavy labors!   70
You guided the arrow of Paris, pierced Achilles' body.[8]
You led me through many seas, bordering endless coasts,
far-off Massylian tribes, and fields washed by the Syrtes,[9]
and now, at long last, Italy's shores, forever fading,
lie within our grasp. Let the doom of Troy pursue us   75
just this far, no more. You too, you gods and goddesses,
all who could never suffer Troy and Troy's high glory,
spare the people of Pergamum now,[1] it's only right.
And you, you blessed Sibyl who knows the future,
grant my prayer. I ask no more than the realm   80
my fate decrees: let the Trojans rest in Latium,
they and their roaming gods, their rootless powers!
Then I will build you a solid marble temple,
Apollo and Diana, establish hallowed days,

8. Paris, prince of Troy, guided by Apollo,
shot an arrow that pierced Achilles' only vulnerable spot, on his heel.
9. Quicksands off the coast of North Africa.
Massylian tribes: veiled references to Carthage,
since the Massylians lived adjacent to Carthage.
1. The Trojans. (Pergamum, or Pergamea, is
the city that Aeneas founded in Crete after
fleeing Troy.)

Apollo, in your name.[2] And Sibyl, for you too,   85
a magnificent sacred shrine awaits you in our kingdom.
There I will house your oracles, mystic revelations
made to our race, and ordain your chosen priests,
my gracious lady. Just don't commit your words
to the rustling, scattering leaves—   90
sport of the winds that whirl them all away.
Sing them yourself, I beg you!" There Aeneas stopped.

    But the Sibyl, still not broken in by Apollo, storms
with a wild fury through her cave. And the more she tries
to pitch the great god off her breast, the more his bridle   95
exhausts her raving lips, overwhelming her untamed heart,
bending her to his will. Now the hundred immense
mouths of the house swing open, all on their own,
and bear the Sibyl's answers through the air:
"You who have braved the terrors of the sea,   100
though worse remain on land—you Trojans will reach
Lavinium's realm—lift that care from your hearts—
but you will rue your arrival. Wars, horrendous wars,
and the Tiber foaming with tides of blood, I see it all!
Simois, Xanthus, a Greek camp—you'll never lack them here.   105
Already a new Achilles[3] springs to life in Latium,
son of a goddess too! Nor will Juno ever fail
to harry the Trojan race, and all the while,
pleading, pressed by need—what tribes, what towns
of Italy won't you beg for help! And the cause of this,   110
this new Trojan grief? Again a stranger bride,
a marriage with a stranger once again.[4]
But never bow to suffering, go and face it,
all the bolder, wherever Fortune clears the way.
Your path to safety will open first from where   115
you least expect it—a city built by Greeks!"[5]
                                  Those words
re-echoing from her shrine, the Cumaean Sibyl chants
her riddling visions filled with dread, her cave resounds
as she shrouds the truth in darkness—Phoebus whips her on
in all her frenzy, twisting his spurs below her breast.   120
As soon as her fury dies and raving lips fall still,
the hero Aeneas launches in: "No trials, my lady,
can loom before me in any new, surprising form.
No, deep in my spirit I have known them all,
I've faced them all before. But grant one prayer.   125
Since here, they say, are the gates of Death's king
and the dark marsh where the Acheron[6] comes flooding up,

2. The Games to Apollo were established dur-
ing the Second Punic War (218–201 B.C.E.);
Augustus, Virgil's patron, built a temple to
Apollo on the Palatine.
3. Achilles: most important warrior in the *Iliad*.
Simois and Xanthus are rivers in Troy.

4. The first "stranger" or foreign bride was
Helen, for whom the Trojan War was fought
when she was taken from her husband by Paris.
5. Pallanteum, built by Arcadian Greeks and
the future site of Rome.
6. The river of grief in the Underworld.

please, allow me to go and see my beloved father,
meet him face to face.
Teach me the way, throw wide the sacred doors!   130
Through fires, a thousand menacing spears I swept him off
on these shoulders, saved him from our enemies' onslaught.
He shared all roads and he braved all seas with me,
all threats of the waves and skies—frail as he was
but graced with a strength beyond his years, his lot.   135
He was the one, in fact, who ordered, pressed me on
to reach your doors and seek you, beg you now.
Pity the son and father, I pray you, kindly lady!
All power is yours. Hecate[7] held back nothing,
put you in charge of Avernus' groves. If Orpheus   140
could summon up the ghost of his wife, trusting so
to his Thracian lyre and echoing strings; if Pollux
could ransom his brother and share his death by turns,
time and again traversing the same road up and down;
if Theseus, mighty Hercules—must I mention them?[8]   145
I too can trace my birth from Jove on high."
                So he prayed,
grasping the altar while the Sibyl gave her answer:
"Born of the blood of gods, Anchises' son,
man of Troy, the descent to the Underworld is easy.
Night and day the gates of shadowy Death stand open wide,   150
but to retrace your steps, to climb back to the upper air—
there the struggle, there the labor lies. Only a few,
loved by impartial Jove or borne aloft to the sky
by their own fiery virtue—some sons of the gods
have made their way. The entire heartland here   155
is thick with woods, Cocytus glides around it,[9]
coiling dense and dark.
But if such a wild desire seizes on you—twice
to sail the Stygian marsh, to see black Tartarus twice—[1]
if you're so eager to give yourself to this, this mad ordeal,   160
then hear what you must accomplish first.
                    "Hidden
deep in a shady tree there grows a golden bough,
its leaves and its hardy, sinewy stem all gold,
held sacred to Juno of the Dead, Proserpina.[2]
The whole grove covers it over, dusky valleys   165
enfold it too, closing in around it. No one

---

7. Diana, in her guise as goddess of magic.
8. These lines cite four mythical heroes who have preceded Aeneas in journeying to the Underworld. The first is Orpheus, the master singer, who went in search of his dead wife and used his music to persuade Hades to give her back (though he lost her again on the way up when he turned to look at her). The second is Pollux, who shared immortality with his twin brother Castor, so that they each spent six months of the year in the Underworld. The

third, Theseus, went to try to carry off Persephone, wife of Hades. The last, Heracles, had to bring back Cerberus, three-headed guard dog of Hades, as one of his Twelve Labors.
9. One of the rivers of the Underworld, the river of lamentation.
1. Tartarus is the abyss in Hades used as prison for the Titans; the Styx is another river of the Underworld (hence "Stygian").
2. Queen of the Underworld (hence, equivalent to Juno, Queen of the Upper World).

may pass below the secret places of earth before
he plucks the fruit, the golden foliage of that tree.
As her beauty's due, Proserpina decreed this bough
shall be offered up to her as her own hallowed gift.   170
When the first spray's torn away, another takes its place,
gold too, the metal breaks into leaf again, all gold.
Lift up your eyes and search, and once you find it,
duly pluck it off with your hand. Freely, easily,
all by itself it comes away, if Fate calls you on.   175
If not, no strength within you can overpower it,
no iron blade, however hard, can tear it off.

   "One thing more I must tell you.
A friend lies dead—oh, you could not know—
his body pollutes your entire fleet with death   180
while you search on for oracles, linger at our doors.
Bear him first to his place of rest, bury him in his tomb.
Lead black cattle there, first offerings of atonement.
Only then can you set eyes on the Stygian groves
and the realms no living man has ever trod."   185
Abruptly she fell silent, lips sealed tight.

   His eyes fixed on the ground, his face in tears,
Aeneas moves on, leaving the cavern, turning over
within his mind these strange, dark events.
His trusty comrade Achates keeps his pace   190
and the same cares weigh down his plodding steps.
They traded many questions, wondering, back and forth,
what dead friend did the Sibyl mean, whose body must be buried?
Suddenly, Misenus—out on the dry beach they see him,
reach him now, cut off by a death all undeserved.   195
Misenus, Aeolus'[3] son, a herald unsurpassed
at rallying troops with his trumpet's cry,
igniting the God of War with its shrill blare.
He had been mighty Hector's friend, by Hector's side
in the rush of battle, shining with spear and trumpet both. 200
But when triumphant Achilles stripped Hector's life,
the gallant hero joined forces with Dardan Aeneas,
followed a captain every bit as strong. But then,
chancing to make the ocean ring with his hollow shell,
the madman challenged the gods to match him blast for blast 205
and jealous Triton[4]—if we can believe the story—
snatched him up and drowned the man in the surf
that seethed between the rocks.
                So all his shipmates
gathered round his body and raised a loud lament,
devoted Aeneas in the lead. Then still in tears,   210
they rush to perform the Sibyl's orders, no delay,
they strive to pile up trees, to build an altar-pyre

---

3. Probably the god of the winds.   4. A sea god.

rising to the skies. Then into an ancient wood
and the hidden dens of beasts they make their way,
and down crash the pines, the ilex rings to the axe,   215
the trunks of ash and oak are split by the driving wedge,
and they roll huge rowans down the hilly slopes.

    Aeneas spurs his men in the forefront of their labors,
geared with the same woodsmen's tools around his waist.
But the same anxiety keeps on churning in his heart   220
as he scans the endless woods and prays by chance:
"If only that golden bough would gleam before us now
on a tree in this dark grove! Since all the Sibyl
foretold of you was true, Misenus, all too true."

    No sooner said than before his eyes, twin doves   225
chanced to come flying down the sky and lit
on the green grass at his feet. His mother's birds—
the great captain knew them and raised a prayer of joy:
"Be my guides! If there's a path, fly through the air,
set me a course to the grove where that rich branch   230
shades the good green earth. And you, goddess,
mother, don't fail me in this, my hour of doubt!"

    With that he stopped in his tracks, watching keenly—
what sign would they offer? Where would they lead?
And on they flew, pausing to feed, then flying on   235
as far as a follower's eye could track their flight
and once they reached the foul-smelling gorge of Avernus,
up they veered, quickly, then slipped down through the clear air
to settle atop the longed-for goal, the twofold tree, its green
a foil for the breath of gold that glows along its branch.   240
As mistletoe in the dead of winter's icy forests
leafs with life on a tree that never gave it birth,
embracing the smooth trunk with its pale yellow bloom,
so glowed the golden foliage against the ilex evergreen,
so rustled the sheer gold leaf in the light breeze.   245
Aeneas grips it at once—the bough holds back—
he tears it off in his zeal
and bears it into the vatic Sibyl's shrine.
                      All the while
the Trojans along the shore keep weeping for Misenus,
paying his thankless ashes final rites. And first   250
they build an immense pyre of resinous pitch-pine
and oaken logs, weaving into its flanks dark leaves
and setting before it rows of funereal cypress,
crowning it all with the herald's gleaming arms.
Some heat water in cauldrons fired to boiling,   255
bathe and anoint the body chill with death.
The dirge rises up. Then, their weeping over,
they lay his corpse on a litter, swathe him round
in purple robes that form the well-known shroud.

Some hoisted up the enormous bier—sad service— 260
their eyes averted, after their fathers' ways of old,
and thrust the torch below. The piled offerings blazed,
frankincense, hallowed foods and brimming bowls of oil.
And after the coals sank in and the fires died down,
they washed his embers, thirsty remains, with wine. 265
Corynaeus sealed the bones he culled in a bronze urn,
then circling his comrades three times with pure water,
sprinkling light drops from a blooming olive spray,
he cleansed the men and voiced the last farewell.
But devout Aeneas mounds the tomb—an immense barrow 270
crowned with the man's own gear, his oar and trumpet—
under a steep headland, called after the herald now
and for all time to come it bears Misenus' name.[5]
                                        The rite
performed, Aeneas hurries to carry out the Sibyl's orders.
There was a vast cave deep in the gaping, jagged rock, 275
shielded well by a dusky lake and shadowed grove.
Over it no bird on earth could make its way unscathed,
such poisonous vapors steamed up from its dark throat
to cloud the arching sky. Here, as her first step,
the priestess steadies four black-backed calves, 280
she tips wine on their brows, then plucks some tufts
from the crown between their horns and casts them
over the altar fire, first offerings, crying out
to Hecate, mighty Queen of Heaven and Hell.
Attendants run knives under throats and catch 285
warm blood in bowls. Aeneas himself, sword drawn,
slaughters a black-fleeced lamb to the Furies' mother,
Night, and to her great sister, Earth, and to you,
Proserpina, kills a barren heifer. Then to the king
of the river Styx, he raises altars into the dark night 290
and over their fires lays whole carcasses of bulls
and pours fat oil over their entrails flaming up.
Then suddenly, look, at the break of day, first light,
the earth groans underfoot and the wooded heights quake
and across the gloom the hounds seem to howl 295
at the goddess coming closer.
                                        "Away, away!"
the Sibyl shrieks, "all you unhallowed ones—away
from this whole grove! But you launch out on your journey,
tear your sword from its sheath, Aeneas. Now for courage,
now the steady heart!" And the Sibyl says no more but 300
into the yawning cave she flings herself, possessed—
he follows her boldly, matching stride for stride.
                                        You gods
who govern the realm of ghosts, you voiceless shades and Chaos—
you, the River of Fire, you far-flung regions hushed in night—

---

5. The place is still called Capo Miseno (Cape of Misenus).

lend me the right to tell what I have heard, lend your power   305
to reveal the world immersed in the misty depths of earth.

On they went, those dim travelers under the lonely night,
through gloom and the empty halls of Death's ghostly realm,
like those who walk through woods by a grudging moon's
deceptive light when Jove has plunged the sky in dark   310
and the black night drains all color from the world.
There in the entryway, the gorge of hell itself,
Grief and the pangs of Conscience make their beds,
and fatal pale Disease lives there, and bleak Old Age,
Dread and Hunger, seductress to crime, and grinding Poverty,   315
all, terrible shapes to see—and Death and deadly Struggle
and Sleep, twin brother of Death, and twisted, wicked Joys
and facing them at the threshold, War, rife with death,
and the Furies' iron chambers, and mad, raging Strife
whose blood-stained headbands knot her snaky locks.   320

There in the midst, a giant shadowy elm tree spreads
her ancient branching arms, home, they say, to swarms
of false dreams, one clinging tight under each leaf.
And a throng of monsters too—what brutal forms
are stabled at the gates—Centaurs, mongrel Scyllas,   325
part women, part beasts, and hundred-handed Briareus
and the savage Hydra of Lerna, that hissing horror,
the Chimaera armed with torches—Gorgons, Harpies
and triple-bodied Geryon, his great ghost.[6] And here,
instantly struck with terror, Aeneas grips his sword   330
and offers its naked edge against them as they come,
and if his experienced comrade had not warned him
they are mere disembodied creatures, flimsy
will-o'-the-wisps that flit like living forms,
he would have rushed them all,   335
slashed through empty phantoms with his blade.
                                                    From there
the road leads down to the Acheron's Tartarean waves.
Here the enormous whirlpool gapes aswirl with filth,
seethes and spews out all its silt in the Wailing River.[7]
And here the dreaded ferryman guards the flood,   340
grisly in his squalor—Charon . . .
his scraggly beard a tangled mat of white, his eyes
fixed in a fiery stare, and his grimy rags hang down
from his shoulders by a knot. But all on his own
he punts his craft with a pole and hoists sail   345

6. Geryon was a terrifying giant. Centaurs are half human, half horse. Scylla is a female sea monster with several doglike heads, who features in the *Odyssey*. Briareus was one of three sons of Sky and Earth (Uranus and Gaia), with a hundred arms and fifty heads. The Hydra was a multiple-headed snake, defeated by Hera-cles. The Chimaera was a fire-breathing hybrid monster, usually imagined as a mix of lion, goat, and snake. Gorgons are snakelike monsters; Harpies are female birdlike monsters.
7. Acheron, one of the Underworld rivers, led into Cocytus, river of lamentation (Wailing River).

as he ferries the dead souls in his rust-red skiff.
He's on in years, but a god's old age is hale and green.

A huge throng of the dead came streaming toward the banks:
mothers and grown men and ghosts of great-souled heroes,
their bodies stripped of life, and boys and unwed girls   350
and sons laid on the pyre before their parents' eyes.
As thick as leaves in autumn woods at the first frost
that slip and float to earth, or dense as flocks of birds
that wing from the heaving sea to shore when winter's chill
drives them over the waves to landfalls drenched in sunlight.   355
There they stood, pleading to be the first ones ferried over,
reaching out their hands in longing toward the farther shore.
But the grim ferryman ushers aboard now these, now those,
others he thrusts away, back from the water's edge.
                                              Aeneas,
astonished, stirred by the tumult, calls out: "Tell me,   360
Sibyl, what does it mean, this thronging toward the river?
What do the dead souls want? What divides them all?
Some are turned away from the banks and others
scull the murky waters with their oars!"

The aged priestess answered Aeneas briefly: 365
"Son of Anchises—born of the gods, no doubt—
what you see are Cocytus' pools and Styx's marsh,
Powers by which the gods swear oaths they dare not break.
And the great rout you see is helpless, still not buried.
That ferryman there is Charon. Those borne by the stream   370
have found their graves. And no spirits may be conveyed
across the horrendous banks and hoarse, roaring flood
until their bones are buried, and they rest in peace . . .
A hundred years they wander, hovering round these shores
till at last they may return and see once more the pools   375
they long to cross."
                    Anchises' son came to a halt
and stood there, pondering long, while pity filled his heart,
their lot so hard, unjust. And then he spots two men,
grief-stricken and robbed of death's last tribute:
Leucaspis and Orontes, the Lycian fleet's commander.   380
Together they sailed from Troy over windswept seas
and a Southern gale sprang up and
toppling breakers crushed their ships and crews.
                              Look,
the pilot Palinurus was drifting toward him now,
fresh from the Libyan run where, watching the stars,   385
he plunged from his stern, pitched out in heavy seas.
Aeneas, barely sighting him grieving in the shadows,
hailed him first: "What god, Palinurus, snatched you
from our midst and drowned you in open waters?
Tell me, please. Apollo has never lied before.   390
This is his one reply that's played me false:

he swore you would cross the ocean safe and sound
and reach Italian shores.[8] Is *this* the end he promised?"

But the pilot answered: "Captain, Anchises' son,
Apollo's prophetic cauldron has not failed you—   395
no god drowned me in open waters. No, the rudder
I clung to, holding us all on course—my charge—
some powerful force ripped it away by chance
and I dragged it down as I dropped headlong too.
By the cruel seas I swear I felt no fear for myself   400
to match my fear that your ship, stripped of her tiller,
steersman wrenched away, might founder in that great surge.
Three blustery winter nights the Southwind bore me wildly
over the endless waters, then at the fourth dawn, swept up
on a breaker's crest, I could almost sight it now—Italy!   405
Stroke by stroke I swam for land, safety was in my grasp,
weighed down by my sodden clothes, my fingers clawing
the jutting spurs of a cliff, when a band of brutes
came at me, ran me through with knives, the fools,
they took me for plunder worth the taking.   410
The tides hold me now
and the stormwinds roll my body down the shore.
By the sky's lovely light and the buoyant breeze I beg you,
by your father, your hopes for Iulus rising to his prime,
pluck me up from my pain, my undefeated captain!   415
Or throw some earth on my body—you know you can—
sail back to Velia's port.[9] Or if there's a way and
your goddess mother makes it clear—for not without
the will of the gods, I'm certain, do you strive
to cross these awesome streams and Stygian marsh—   420
give me your pledge, your hand, in all my torment!
Take me with you over the waves. At least in death
I'll find a peaceful haven."
                            So the pilot begged
and so the Sibyl cut him short: "How, Palinurus,
how can you harbor this mad desire of yours?   425
You think that you, unburied, can lay your eyes
on the Styx's flood, the Furies' ruthless stream,
and approach the banks unsummoned? Hope no more
the gods' decrees can be brushed aside by prayer.
Hold fast to my words and keep them well in mind   430
to comfort your hard lot. For neighboring people
living in cities near and far, compelled by signs
from the great gods on high, will appease your bones,
will build you a tomb and pay your tomb due rites
and the site will bear the name of Palinurus   435
now and always."
                 That promise lifts his anguish,

---

8. No such promise is mentioned earlier in   9. A bay and later a city in southern Italy.
the poem.

drives, for a while, the grief from his sad heart.
He takes delight in the cape that bears his name.[1]

So now they press on with their journey under way
and at last approach the river. But once the ferryman,   440
still out in the Styx's currents, spied them moving
across the silent grove and turning toward the bank,
he greets them first with a rough abrupt rebuke:
"Stop, whoever you are at our river's edge,
in full armor too! Why have you come? Speak up,   445
from right where you are, not one step more! This
is the realm of shadows, sleep and drowsy night.
The law forbids me to carry living bodies across
in my Stygian boat. I'd little joy, believe me,
when Hercules came and I sailed the hero over,   450
or Theseus, Pirithous,[2] sons of gods as they were
with their high and mighty power. Hercules stole
our watchdog—chained him, the poor trembling creature,
dragged him away from our king's very throne! The others
tried to snatch our queen from the bridal bed of Death!"   455

But Apollo's seer broke in and countered Charon:
"There's no such treachery here—just calm down—
no threat of force in our weapons. The huge guard
at the gates can howl for eternity from his cave,
terrifying the bloodless shades, Persephone keep   460
her chastity safe at home behind her uncle's doors.
Aeneas of Troy, famous for his devotion, feats of arms,
goes down to the deepest shades of hell to see his father.
But if this image of devotion cannot move you, here,
this bough"—showing the bough enfolded in her robes—   465
"You know it well."
                          At this, the heaving rage
subsides in his chest. The Sibyl says no more.
The ferryman, marveling at the awesome gift,
the fateful branch unseen so many years,
swerves his dusky craft and approaches shore.   470
The souls already crouched at the long thwarts—
he brusquely thrusts them out, clearing the gangways,
quickly taking massive Aeneas aboard the little skiff.
Under his weight the boat groans and her stitched seams
gape as she ships great pools of water pouring in.   475
At last, the river crossed, the ferryman lands.
the seer and hero all unharmed in the marsh,
the repellent oozing slime and livid sedge.
                                These
are the realms that monstrous Cerberus rocks with howls

---

1. There is still a Cape of Palinurus in south-eastern Italy.
2. Thessalian king, descended from Zeus; he was Theseus's best friend and accompanied Theseus on his journey to the Underworld to abduct Persephone.

braying out of his three throats,[3] his enormous bulk   480
squatting low in the cave that faced them there.
The Sibyl, seeing the serpents writhe around his neck,
tossed him a sop, slumbrous with honey and drugged seed,
and he, frothing with hunger, three jaws spread wide,
snapped it up where the Sibyl tossed it—gone.   485
His tremendous back relaxed, he sags to earth
and sprawls over all his cave, his giant hulk limp.
The watchdog buried now in sleep, Aeneas seizes
the way in, quickly clear of the river's edge,
the point of no return.
                  At that moment, cries—   490
they could hear them now, a crescendo of wailing,
ghosts of infants weeping, robbed of their share
of this sweet life, at its very threshold too:
all, snatched from the breast on that black day
that swept them off and drowned them in bitter death.   495
Beside them were those condemned to die on a false charge.
But not without jury picked by lot, not without judge
are their places handed down. Not at all.
Minos the grand inquisitor stirs the urn,
he summons the silent jury of the dead,   500
he scans the lives of those accused, their charges.
The region next to them is held by those sad ghosts,
innocents all, who brought on death by their own hands;
despising the light, they threw their lives away.
How they would yearn, now, in the world above   505
to endure grim want and long hard labor!
But Fate bars the way. The grisly swamp
and its loveless, lethal waters bind them fast,
Styx with its nine huge coils holds them captive.

Close to the spot, extending toward the horizon—   510
the Sibyl points them out—are the Fields of Mourning,
that is the name they bear. Here wait those souls
consumed by the harsh, wasting sickness, cruel love,
concealed on lonely paths, shrouded by myrtle bowers.
Not even in death do their torments leave them, ever.   515
Here he glimpses Phaedra, Procris, and Eriphyle grieving,
baring the wounds her heartless son had dealt her.[4]
Evadne, Pasiphaë, and Laodamia walking side by side,
and another, a young man once, a woman now, Caeneus,
turned back by Fate to the form she bore at first.[5]   520

3. Cerberus is the three-headed guard dog of Hades.
4. Eriphyle was bribed with a necklace to persuade her husband to join the Argive war against the Thebans, in which he was killed—their son then killed her. Phaedra, wife of Theseus, fell in love with her stepson Hippolytus and killed herself; Procris was jealous of her husband, who accidentally killed her while she was spying on him.

5. Caeneus was a woman who was changed into a man by Neptune and was changed back at death. Evadne was wife of the sacrilegious Capaneus, who was struck dead by lightning; she threw herself on his pyre. Pasiphaë was wife of Minos and the queen of Crete who fell in love with the bull and gave birth to the Minotaur. Laodamia, wife of the first Greek killed at Troy, chose to accompany him to the Underworld.

And wandering there among them, wound still fresh,
Phoenician Dido drifted along the endless woods.
As the Trojan hero paused beside her, recognized her
through the shadows, a dim, misty figure—as one
when the month is young may see or seem to see   525
the new moon rising up through banks of clouds—
that moment Aeneas wept and approached the ghost
with tender words of love: "Tragic Dido,
so, was the story true that came my way?
I heard that you were dead . . .   530
you took the final measure with a sword.
Oh, dear god, was it I who caused your death?
I swear by the stars, by the Powers on high, whatever
faith one swears by here in the depths of earth,
I left your shores, my Queen, against my will. Yes,   535
the will of the gods, that drives me through the shadows now,
these moldering places so forlorn, this deep unfathomed night—
their decrees have forced me on. Nor did I ever dream
my leaving could have brought you so much grief.
Stay a moment. Don't withdraw from my sight.   540
Running away—from whom? This is the last word
that Fate allows me to say to you. The last."

    Aeneas, with such appeals, with welling tears,
tried to soothe her rage, her wild fiery glance.
But she, her eyes fixed on the ground, turned away,   545
her features no more moved by his pleas as he talked on
than if she were set in stony flint or Parian marble rock.
And at last she tears herself away, his enemy forever,
fleeing back to the shadowed forests where Sychaeus,
her husband long ago, answers all her anguish,   550
meets her love with love. But Aeneas, no less
struck by her unjust fate, escorts her from afar
with streaming tears and pities her as she passes.

    From there they labor along the charted path
and at last they gain the utmost outer fields   555
where throngs of the great war heroes live apart.
Here Tydeus comes to meet him, Parthenopaeus
shining in arms, and Adrastus' pallid phantom.[6] Here,
mourned in the world above and fallen dead in battle,
sons of Dardanus, chiefs arrayed in a long ranked line.   560
Seeing them all, he groaned—Glaucus, Medon, Thersilochus,
Antenor's three sons and the priest of Ceres, Polyboetes,
Idaeus too, still with chariot, still with gear in hand.[7]
Their spirits crowding around Aeneas, left and right,
beg him to linger longer—a glimpse is not enough—   565
to walk beside him and learn the reasons why he's come.
But the Greek commanders and Agamemnon's troops in phalanx,

6. Three of the Argive leaders at Troy.   7. Names of Trojan warriors from the *Iliad*.

spotting the hero and his armor glinting through the shadows—
blinding panic grips them, some turn tail and run
as they once ran back to the ships, some strain   570
to raise a battle cry, a thin wisp of a cry
that mocks their gaping jaws.

    And here he sees Deiphobus too, Priam's son
mutilated, his whole body, his face hacked to pieces—
Ah, so cruel—his face and both his hands, and his ears   575
ripped from his ravaged head, his nostrils slashed,
disgraceful wound. He can hardly recognize him,
a cowering shadow hiding his punishments so raw.
Aeneas, never pausing, hails the ghost at once
in an old familiar voice: "Mighty captain,   580
Deiphobus, sprung of the noble blood of Teucer,
who was bent on making you pay a price so harsh?
Who could maim you so? I heard on that last night
that you, exhausted from killing hordes of Greeks,
had fallen dead on a mangled pile of carnage.   585
So I was the one who raised your empty tomb
on Rhoeteum Cape and called out to your shade
three times with a ringing voice. Your name and armor
mark the site, my friend, but I could not find you,
could not bury your bones in native soil   590
when I set out to sea."

    "Nothing, my friend," Priam's son replies,
"you have left nothing undone. All that's owed
Deiphobus and his shadow you have paid in full.
My own fate and the deadly crimes of that Spartan whore[8]   595
have plunged me in this hell. Look at the souvenirs she left me!
And how we spent that last night, lost in deluded joys,
you know. Remember it we must, and all too well.
When the fatal horse mounted over our steep walls,
its weighted belly teeming with infantry in arms—   600
she led the Phrygian women round the city, feigning
the orgiastic rites of Bacchus,[9] dancing, shrieking
but in their midst she shook her monstrous torch,
a flare from the city heights, a signal to the Greeks.
While I in our cursed bridal chamber, there I lay,   605
bone-weary with anguish, buried deep in sleep,
peaceful, sweet, like the peace of death itself.
And all the while that matchless wife of mine
is removing all my weapons from the house,
even slipping my trusty sword from under my pillow.   610
She calls Menelaus in and flings the doors wide open,
hoping no doubt by this grand gift to him, her lover,
to wipe the slate clean of her former wicked ways.

8. Helen.
9. Roman name for Dionysos, god of wine and frenzy.

Why drag things out? They burst into the bedroom,
Ulysses, that rouser of outrage right beside them,   615
Aeolus' crafty heir.[1] You gods, if my lips are pure,
I pray for vengeance now—
deal such blows to the Greeks as they dealt *me!*
But come, tell me in turn what twist of fate
has brought you here alive? Forced by wanderings,   620
storm-tossed at sea, or prompted by the gods?
What destiny hounds you on to visit these,
these sunless homes of sorrow, harrowed lands?"

    Trading words, as Dawn in her rose-red chariot
crossed in mid-career, high noon in the arching sky,   625
and they might have spent what time they had with tales
if the Sibyl next to Aeneas had not warned him tersely:
"Night comes on, Aeneas. We waste our time with tears.
This is the place where the road divides in two.
To the right it runs below the mighty walls of Death,   630
our path to Elysium, but the left-hand road torments
the wicked, leading down to Tartarus, path to doom."

    "No anger, please, great priestess," begged Deiphobus.
"Back I go to the shades to fill the tally out.
Now go, our glory of Troy, go forth and enjoy   635
a better fate than mine." With his last words
he turned in his tracks and went his way.
                        Aeneas
suddenly glances back and beneath a cliff to the left
he sees an enormous fortress ringed with triple walls
and raging around it all, a blazing flood of lava,   640
Tartarus' River of Fire, whirling thunderous boulders.
Before it rears a giant gate, its columns solid adamant,
so no power of man, not even the gods themselves
can root it out in war. An iron tower looms on high
where Tisiphone,[2] crouching with bloody shroud girt up,   645
never sleeping, keeps her watch at the entrance night and day.
Groans resound from the depths, the savage crack of the lash,
the grating creak of iron, the clank of dragging chains.
And Aeneas froze there, terrified, taking in the din:
"What are the crimes, what kinds? Tell me, Sibyl,   650
what are the punishments, why this scourging?
Why such wailing echoing in the air?"

    The seer rose to the moment: "Famous captain of Troy,
no pure soul may set foot on that wicked threshold.
But when Hecate put me in charge of Avernus' groves   655
she taught me all the punishments of the gods,
she led me through them all.

1. Reference to an alternative genealogy for
Ulysses (Odysseus), not as son of Laertes but
illegitimately fathered by Sisyphus, the infamous murderer and traitor, son of Aeolus.
2. One of the three Furies, divine figures of
vengeance.

Here Cretan Rhadamanthus[3] rules with an iron hand,
censuring men, exposing fraud, forcing confessions
when anyone up above, reveling in his hidden crimes,   660
puts off his day of atonement till he dies, the fool,
too late. That very moment, vengeful Tisiphone, armed
with lashes, springs on the guilty, whips them till they quail,
with her left hand shaking all her twisting serpents,
summoning up her savage sisters, bands of Furies.   665
Then at last, screeching out on their grinding hinge
the infernal gates swing wide.
                              "Can you see that sentry
crouched at the entrance? What a specter guards the threshold!
Fiercer still, the monstrous Hydra, fifty black maws gaping,
holds its lair inside.
                       "Then the abyss, Tartarus itself   670
plunges headlong down through the darkness twice as far
as our gaze goes up to Olympus rising toward the skies.
Here the ancient line of the Earth, the Titans' spawn,
flung down by lightning, writhe in the deep pit.
There I saw the twin sons of Aloeus too,[4] giant bodies   675
that clawed the soaring sky with their hands to tear it down
and thrust great Jove from his kingdom high above.

    "I saw Salmoneus[5] too, who paid a brutal price
for aping the flames of Jove and Olympus' thunder.
Sped by his four-horse chariot, flaunting torches,   680
right through the Greek tribes and Elis city's heart
he rode in triumph, claiming as *his* the honors of the gods.
The madman, trying to match the storm and matchless lightning
just by stamping on bronze with prancing horn-hoofed steeds!
The almighty Father hurled his bolt through the thunderheads—   685
no torches for him, no smoky flicker of pitch-pines, no,
he spun him headlong down in a raging whirlwind.
                                        "Tityus too:[6]
you could see that son of Earth, the mother of us all,
his giant body splayed out over nine whole acres,
a hideous vulture with hooked beak gorging down   690
his immortal liver and innards ever ripe for torture.
Deep in his chest it nestles, ripping into its feast
and the fibers, grown afresh, get no relief from pain.

    "What need to tell of the Lapiths, Ixion, or Pirithous?[7]
Above them a black rock—now, now slipping, teetering,   695

3. Brother of Minos and, like Minos, a king of
Crete.
4. The Titans, who rebelled against Jupiter
(Jove) and were destroyed.
5. King of Elis, punished for impiety because
he pretended to Jupiter's might by using torches
to imitate lightning.
6. Tityos assaulted the goddess Latona and
was punished by being stretched out and forever devoured by a vulture.
7. Pirithous, king of the Lapiths (known for
their battle against the Centaurs) and friend of
Theseus, tried to abduct Persephone and was
chained up forever. Pirithous's father, Ixion,
who assaulted Juno, was punished by being
stretched on a wheel. (The punishments of the
tottering rock and the food always out of reach
are more normally associated with Tantalus.)

watch, forever about to fall. While the golden posts
of high festal couches gleam, and a banquet spreads
before their eyes with luxury fit for kings . . .
but reclining just beside them, the oldest Fury
holds back their hands from even touching the food,   700
surging up with her brandished torch and deafening screams.

      "Here those who hated their brothers, while alive,
or struck their fathers down
or embroiled clients in fraud, or brooded alone
over troves of gold they gained and never put aside   705
some share for their own kin—a great multitude, these—
then those killed for adultery, those who marched to the flag
of civil war and never shrank from breaking their pledge
to their lords and masters: all of them, walled up here,
wait to meet their doom.   "Don't hunger to know their doom,   710
what form of torture or twist of Fortune drags them down.
Some trundle enormous boulders, others dangle, racked
to the breaking point on the spokes of rolling wheels.
Doomed Theseus sits on his seat and there he will sit forever.
Phlegyas,[8] most in agony, sounds out his warning to all,   715
his piercing cries bear witness through the darkness:
'Learn to bow to justice. Never scorn the gods.
You all stand forewarned!'

      "Here's one who bartered his native land for gold,
he saddled her with a tyrant, set up laws for a bribe,   720
for a bribe he struck them down. This one forced himself
on his daughter's bed and sealed a forbidden marriage.
All dared an outrageous crime and what they dared, they did.

      "No, not if I had a hundred tongues and a hundred mouths
and a voice of iron too—I could never capture   725
all the crimes or run through all the torments,
doom by doom."
      So Apollo's aged priestess
ended her answer, then she added: "Come,
press on with your journey. See it through,
this duty you've undertaken. We must hurry now.   730
I can just make out the ramparts forged by the Cyclops.[9]
There are the gates, facing us with their arch.
There our orders say to place our gifts."
      At that,
both of them march in step along the shadowed paths,
consuming the space between, and approach the doors.   735
Aeneas springs to the entryway and rinsing his limbs

---

8. King of the Lapiths and father of Ixion; he
was punished for setting fire to the temple of
Apollo at Delphi.

9. The entrance to Elysium (the Fortunate
Groves) was built by the god Vulcan, with help
from the Cyclopes, famous for metalworking.

with fresh pure water, there at the threshold,
just before them, stakes the golden bough.

    The rite complete at last,
their duty to the goddess performed in full,   740
they gained the land of joy, the fresh green fields,
the Fortunate Groves where the blessed make their homes.
Here a freer air, a dazzling radiance clothes the fields
and the spirits possess their own sun, their own stars.
Some flex their limbs in the grassy wrestling-rings,   745
contending in sport, they grapple on the golden sands.
Some beat out a dance with their feet and chant their songs.
And Orpheus himself, the Thracian priest with his long robes,[1]
keeps their rhythm strong with his lyre's seven ringing strings,
plucking now with his fingers, now with his ivory plectrum.   750

    Here is the ancient line of Teucer, noblest stock of all,
those great-hearted heroic sons born in better years,
Ilus, and Assaracus, and Dardanus, founder of Troy.
Far off, Aeneas gazes in awe—their arms, their chariots,
phantoms all, their lances fixed in the ground, their horses,   755
freed from harness, grazing the grasslands near and far.
The same joy they took in arms and chariots when alive,
in currying horses sleek and putting them to pasture,
follows them now they rest beneath the earth.

                                    Others, look,
he glimpses left and right in the meadows, feasting,   760
singing in joy a chorus raised to Healing Apollo,
deep in a redolent laurel grove where Eridanus River
rushes up, in full spate, and rolls through woods
in the high world above. And here are troops of men
who had suffered wounds, fighting to save their country,   765
and those who had been pure priests while still alive,
and the faithful poets whose songs were fit for Phoebus;
those who enriched our lives with the newfound arts they forged
and those we remember well for the good they did mankind.
And all, with snow-white headbands crowning their brows,   770
flow around the Sibyl as she addresses them there,
Musaeus[2] first, who holds the center of that huge throng,
his shoulders rearing high as they gaze up toward him:
"Tell us, happy spirits, and you, the best of poets,
what part of your world, what region holds Anchises?   775
All for him we have come,
we've sailed across the mighty streams of hell."

    And at once the great soul made a brief reply:
"No one's home is fixed. We live in shady groves,

---

1. Orpheus, son of Apollo, is famous both for his magical powers of song and also for his association with Orphism, the set of religious beliefs expounded by Anchises a little later in this book (line 836 ff.).
2. Legendary poet and musician.

we settle on pillowed banks and meadows washed with brooks.   780
But you, if your heart compels you, climb this ridge
and I soon will set your steps on an easy path."

So he said and walking on ahead, from high above
points out to them open country swept with light.
Down they come and leave the heights behind.   785

Now father Anchises, deep in a valley's green recess,
was passing among the souls secluded there, reviewing them,
eagerly, on their way to the world of light above. By chance
he was counting over his own people, all his cherished heirs,
their fame and their fates, their values, acts of valor.   790
When he saw Aeneas striding toward him over the fields,
he reached out both his hands as his spirit lifted,
tears ran down his cheeks, a cry broke from his lips:
"You've come at last? Has the love your father hoped for
mastered the hardship of the journey? Let me look at your face,   795
my son, exchange some words, and hear your familiar voice.
So I dreamed, I knew you'd come, I counted the moments—
my longing has not betrayed me.
Over what lands, what seas have you been driven,
buffeted by what perils into my open arms, my son?   800
How I feared the realm of Libya³ might well do you harm!"

"Your ghost, my father," he replied, "your grieving ghost,
so often it came and urged me to your threshold!
My ships are lying moored in the Tuscan sea.
Let me clasp your hand, my father, let me—   805
I beg you, don't withdraw from my embrace!"

So Aeneas pleaded, his face streaming tears.
Three times he tried to fling his arms around his neck,
three times he embraced—nothing . . . the phantom
sifting through his fingers,   810
light as wind, quick as a dream in flight.

And now Aeneas sees in the valley's depths
a sheltered grove and rustling wooded brakes
and the Lethe⁴ flowing past the homes of peace.
Around it hovered numberless races, nations of souls   815
like bees in meadowlands on a cloudless summer day
that settle on flowers, riots of color, swarming round
the lilies' lustrous sheen, and the whole field comes alive
with a humming murmur. Struck by the sudden sight,
Aeneas, all unknowing, wonders aloud, and asks: 820
"What is the river over there? And who are they
who crowd the banks in such a growing throng?"

3. Carthage.   4. River of forgetfulness.

His father Anchises answers: "They are the spirits
owed a second body by the Fates. They drink deep
of the river Lethe's currents there, long drafts   825
that will set them free of cares, oblivious forever.
How long I have yearned to tell you, show them to you,
face to face, yes, as I count the tally out
of all my children's children. So all the more
you can rejoice with me in Italy, found at last."   830

        "What, Father, can we suppose that any spirits
rise from here to the world above, return once more
to the shackles of the body? Why this mad desire,
poor souls, for the light of life?"
                                "I will tell you,
my son, not keep you in suspense," Anchises says,   835
and unfolds all things in order, one by one.
                                        "First,
the sky and the earth and the flowing fields of the sea,
the shining orb of the moon and the Titan sun, the stars:
an inner spirit feeds them, coursing through all their limbs,
mind stirs the mass and their fusion brings the world to birth.   840
From their union springs the human race and the wild beasts,
the winged lives of birds and the wondrous monsters bred
below the glistening surface of the sea. The seeds of life—
fiery is their force, divine their birth, but they
are weighed down by the bodies' ills or dulled   845
by earthly limbs and flesh that's born for death.
That is the source of all men's fears and longings,
joys and sorrows, nor can they see the heavens' light,
shut up in the body's tomb, a prison dark and deep.
                                        "True,
but even on that last day, when the light of life departs,   850
the wretches are not completely purged of all the taints,
nor are they wholly freed of all the body's plagues.
Down deep they harden fast—they must, so long engrained
in the flesh—in strange, uncanny ways. And so the souls
are drilled in punishments, they must pay for their old offenses.   855
Some are hung splayed out, exposed to the empty winds,
some are plunged in the rushing floods—their stains,
their crimes scoured off or scorched away by fire.
Each of us must suffer his own demanding ghost.
Then we are sent to Elysium's broad expanse,   860
a few of us even hold these fields of joy
till the long days, a cycle of time seen through,
cleanse our hard, inveterate stains and leave us clear
ethereal sense, the eternal breath of fire purged and pure.
But all the rest, once they have turned the wheel of time   865
for a thousand years: God calls them forth to the Lethe,
great armies of souls, their memories blank so that
they may revisit the overarching world once more
and begin to long to return to bodies yet again."

Anchises, silent a moment, drawing his son and Sibyl   870
with him into the midst of the vast murmuring throng,
took his stand on a rise of ground where he could scan
the long column marching toward him, soul by soul,
and recognize their features as they neared.
          "So come,
the glory that will follow the sons of Troy through time,   875
your children born of Italian stock who wait for life,
bright souls, future heirs of our name and our renown:
I will reveal them all and tell you of your fate.
            "There,
you see that youth who leans on a tipless spear of honor?
Assigned the nearest place to the world of light,   880
the first to rise to the air above, his blood
mixed with Italian blood, he bears an Alban name.[5]
Silvius, your son, your last-born, when late
in your old age your wife Lavinia brings him up,
deep in the woods—a king who fathers kings in turn,   885
he founds our race that rules in Alba Longa.
          "Nearby,
there's Procas, pride of the Trojan people, then come
Capys, Numitor, and the one who revives your name,
Silvius Aeneas, your equal in arms and duty,
famed, if he ever comes to rule the Alban throne.[6]   890
What brave young men! Look at the power they display
and the oakleaf civic crowns that shade their foreheads.
They will erect for you Nomentum, Gabii, Fidena town
and build Collatia's ramparts on the mountains,
Pometia too, and Inuis' fortress, Bola and Cora.   895
Famous names in the future, nameless places now.
          "Here,
a son of Mars, his grandsire Numitor's comrade—Romulus,
bred from Assaracus' blood by his mother, Ilia.[7]
See how the twin plumes stand joined on his helmet?
And the Father of Gods himself already marks him out   900
with his own bolts of honor. Under his auspices, watch,
my son, our brilliant Rome will extend her empire far
and wide as the earth, her spirit high as Olympus.
Within her single wall she will gird her seven hills,
blest in her breed of men: like the Berecynthian Mother[8]   905
crowned with her turrets, riding her victor's chariot
through the Phrygian cities, glad in her brood of gods,
embracing a hundred grandsons. All dwell in the heavens,
all command the heights.
        "Now turn your eyes this way

---

5. Aeneas's son Ascanius is destined to found
the Italian kingdom of Alba Longa; his descendants will later found the city of Rome.
6. These are all kings of Alba Longa.
7. Numitor was a king of Alba Longa. His
daughter Ilia (also known as Rhea Silvia) was

raped by the war–god Mars and gave birth to
Romulus and Remus, who were raised by a
wolf. Assaracus is a Trojan ancestor.
8. Cybele, the mother goddess, was worshipped
in the land of Troy and was depicted with a
complicated diadem.

and behold these people, your own Roman people.   910
Here is Caesar[9] and all the line of Iulus
soon to venture under the sky's great arch.
Here is the man, he's here! Time and again
you've heard his coming promised—Caesar Augustus!
Son of a god, he will bring back the Age of Gold   915
to the Latian fields where Saturn once held sway,
expand his empire past the Garamants and the Indians[1]
to a land beyond the stars, beyond the wheel of the year,
the course of the sun itself, where Atlas bears the skies[2]
and turns on his shoulder the heavens studded with flaming stars.   920
Even now the Caspian and Maeotic kingdoms quake at his coming,[3]
oracles sound the alarm and the seven mouths of the Nile
churn with fear. Not even Hercules himself could cross
such a vast expanse of earth, though it's true he shot
the stag with its brazen hoofs, and brought peace   925
to the ravaged woods of Erymanthus, terrorized
the Hydra of Lerna with his bow.[4] Not even Bacchus
in all his glory, driving his team with vines for reins
and lashing his tigers down from Nysa's soaring ridge.[5]
Do we still flinch from turning our valor into deeds?   930
Or fear to make our home on Western soil?

                              "But look,
who is that over there, crowned with an olive wreath
and bearing sacred emblems? I know his snowy hair,
his beard—the first king to found our Rome on laws,
Numa,[6] sent from the poor town of Cures, paltry land,   935
to wield imperial power.

                    "And after him comes Tullus
disrupting his country's peace to rouse a stagnant people,
armies stale to the taste of triumph, back to war again.
And just behind him, Ancus, full of the old bravado,
even now too swayed by the breeze of public favor.[7]

                                        "Wait,   940
would you like to see the Tarquin kings, the overweening
spirit of Brutus the Avenger, the fasces he reclaims?[8]

---

9. The emperor Augustus, Virgil's patron (63
B.C.E.–14 C.E.).
1. I.e., past Africa and India. Saturn (Satur-
nus) was an ancient Roman god associated
with a lost Golden Age.
2. The Titan who holds up the sky.
3. Areas inhabited by the Scythians and Parthians, at the boundaries of the Roman
Empire in Virgil's time.
4. Refers to three of the Labors of Heracles:
killing the stag of Cerynaia, the boar of Erymanthus, and the Hydra.
5. Bacchus (Dionysos), a newcomer to the set

of Olympian gods, traveled all over the world
spreading his cult, including to India (Mount
Nysa).
6. The second king of Rome, known for his
piety.
7. Tullus and Ancus: the third and fourth legendary kings of Rome.
8. The proud Tarquins, bad kings of early
Rome, were expelled from the city by Brutus
after Tarquinius Superbus raped Lucretia.
This was, in legend, the end of Roman monarchy and the origin of the Roman Republic.

The first to hold a consul's power and ruthless axes,
then, when his sons foment rebellion against the city,
their father summons them to the executioner's block   945
in freedom's noble name, unfortunate man . . .[9]
however the future years will exalt his actions:
a patriot's love wins out, and boundless lust for praise.
                                            "Now,
the Decii and the Drusi—look over there—Torquatus too,
with his savage axe, Camillus bringing home the standards.[1]   950
But you see that pair of spirits? Gleaming in equal armor,
equals now at peace, while darkness pins them down,
but if they should reach the light of life, what war
they'll rouse between them! Battles, massacres—Caesar,[2]
the bride's father, marching down from his Alpine ramparts,   955
Fortress Monaco, Pompey her husband set to oppose him
with the armies of the East.
                        "No, my sons, never inure
yourselves to civil war, never turn your sturdy power
against your country's heart. You, Caesar,[3] you
be first in mercy—you trace your line from Olympus—   960
born of my blood, throw down your weapons now!
                                        "Mummius here,
he will conquer Corinth and, famed for killing Achaeans,
drive his victor's chariot up the Capitol's heights.
And there is Paullus,[4] and he will rout all Argos
and Agamemnon's own Mycenae and cut Perseus down—
the heir of Aeacus, born of Achilles' warrior blood—   965
and avenge his Trojan kin and Minerva's violated shrine.[5]
                                            "Who,
noble Cato, could pass you by in silence? Or you, Cossus?
Or the Gracchi and their kin? Or the two Scipios,
both thunderbolts of battle, Libya's scourge?
Or you, Fabricius, reared from poverty into power?   970
Or you, Serranus the Sower, seeding your furrow?
You Fabii, where do you rush me, all but spent?
And you, famous Maximus, you are the one man
whose delaying tactics save our Roman state.[6]   975

    "Others,[7] I have no doubt,
will forge the bronze to breathe with suppler lines,

---

9. Brutus's sons tried to restore Tarquin to the
throne and thus restore the monarchy; Brutus,
in his capacity as consul, had them put to death.
1. All legendary Roman military heroes.
2. Julius Caesar, whose daughter married Pompey the Great. Pompey and Caesar fought each
other in the civil wars.
3. Augustus.
4. Aemelius Paullus defeated the king of

Macedonia (168 B.C.E.); Mummius conquered
Corinth in 146 B.C.E.
5. Refers to the rape of Cassandra by the Greek
Ajax in the temple of Minerva (Athena) at Troy.
6. Famous historical Roman figures, all
important for Rome's military success and rise
to imperial power.
7. "Others" are Greeks.

draw from the block of marble features quick with life,
plead their cases better, chart with their rods the stars
that climb the sky and foretell the times they rise.   980
But you, Roman, remember, rule with all your power
the peoples of the earth—these will be your arts:
to put your stamp on the works and ways of peace,
to spare the defeated, break the proud in war."

They were struck with awe as father Anchises paused,   985
then carried on: "Look there, Marcellus[8] marching toward us,
decked in splendid plunder he tore from a chief he killed,
victorious, towering over all. This man on horseback,
he will steady the Roman state when rocked by chaos,
mow the Carthaginians down in droves, the rebel Gauls.   990
He is only the third to offer up to Father Quirinus
the enemy's captured arms."
                                        Aeneas broke in now,
for he saw a young man walking at Marcellus' side,[9]
handsome, striking, his armor burnished bright
but his face showed little joy, his eyes cast down.   995
"Who is that, Father, matching Marcellus stride for stride?
A son, or one of his son's descendants born of noble stock?
What acclaim from his comrades! What fine bearing,
the man himself! True, but around his head
a mournful shadow flutters black as night."
                                        "My son,"   1000
his tears brimming, father Anchises started in,
"don't press to know your people's awesome grief.
Only a glimpse of him the Fates will grant the world,
not let him linger longer. Too mighty, the Roman race,
it seemed to You above, if this grand gift should last.   1005
Now what wails of men will the Field of Mars send up
to Mars' tremendous city! What a cortege you'll see,
old Tiber, flowing past the massive tomb just built!
No child of Troy will ever raise so high the hopes
of his Latin forebears, nor will the land of Romulus take   1010
such pride in a son she's borne. Mourn for his virtue!
Mourn for his honor forged of old, his sword arm
never conquered in battle. No enemy could ever
go against him in arms and leave unscathed,
whether he fought on foot or rode on horseback,   1015
digging spurs in his charger's lathered flanks.
Oh, child of heartbreak! If only you could burst
the stern decrees of Fate! You will be Marcellus.
Fill my arms with lilies, let me scatter flowers,
lustrous roses—piling high these gifts, at least,   1020
on our descendant's shade—and perform a futile rite."

8. Another military hero, successful in the
Second Punic War.
9. The young man is the Marcellus who married Augustus's daughter Julia and would have
been the heir to the empire, but died at the
age of 19, in 23 B.C.E.

So they wander over the endless fields of air,
gazing at every region, viewing realm by realm.
Once Anchises has led his son through each new scene
and fired his soul with a love of glory still to come,   1025
he tells him next of the wars Aeneas still must wage,
he tells of Laurentine peoples, tells of Latinus' city,[1]
and how he should shun or shoulder each ordeal
that he must meet.
               There are twin Gates of Sleep.
One, they say, is called the Gate of Horn   1030
and it offers easy passage to all true shades.
The other glistens with ivory, radiant, flawless,
but through it the dead send false dreams up toward the sky.
And here Anchises, his vision told in full, escorts
his son and Sibyl both and shows them out now   1035
through the Ivory Gate.
              Aeneas cuts his way
to the waiting ships to see his crews again,
then sets a course straight on to Caieta's harbor.[2]
Anchors run from prows, the sterns line the shore.

Summary of Books VII–VIII   Back in the upper world, Aeneas travels to the Trojan exiles' promised land, Latium, in central Italy. In the capital city, Laurentum, he meets Latinus, king of the Latin race, who has one daughter, Lavinia. An oracle has foretold that she must marry a stranger, and the Latin people welcome Aeneas as their future king. But Amata, Latinus's wife, had hoped her daughter would marry Turnus, leader of the rival Rutulian tribe. Juno, jealous of Trojan success, rouses the people to war and leads the native Italians against the invading Trojans. Meanwhile, Aeneas has a vision of the god of the River Tiber, who tells him that his son will found the city of Alba Longa, and that he should visit the Greek tribe of Arcadians, ruled by Evander. Evander welcomes him, and shows him the future site of Rome. Evander sends his son, Pallas, with troops of Arcadians and Etrurians, to fight with Aeneas. Meanwhile, Venus has had her husband Vulcan forge a new set of armor for Aeneas, which she brings him as he and his troops are resting, readying themselves for battle.

FROM BOOK VIII

[The Shield of Aeneas]

*   *   *

Down come captain Aeneas and all his fighters
picked for battle, water their horses well   715
and weary troops take rest.
              But the goddess Venus,
lustrous among the cloudbanks, bearing her gifts,
approached and when she spotted her son alone,
off in a glade's recess by the frigid stream,
she hailed him, suddenly there before him: "Look,   720

---

1. Latium, home of the "Laurentine peoples."   2. Modern-day Gaeta, on the west coast of Italy.

just forged to perfection by all my husband's skill:
the gifts I promised! There's no need now, my son,
to flinch from fighting swaggering Latin ranks
or challenging savage Turnus to a duel!"

   With that, Venus reached to embrace her son   725
and set the brilliant armor down before him
under a nearby oak.
                    Aeneas takes delight
in the goddess' gifts and the honor of it all
as he runs his eyes across them piece by piece.
He cannot get enough of them, filled with wonder,   730
turning them over, now with his hands, now his arms,
the terrible crested helmet plumed and shooting fire,
the sword-blade honed to kill, the breastplate, solid bronze,
blood-red and immense, like a dark blue cloud enflamed
by the sun's rays and gleaming through the heavens.   735
Then the burnished greaves of electrum,[3] smelted gold,
the spear and the shield, the workmanship of the shield,
no words can tell its power . . .
                          There is the story of Italy,
Rome in all her triumphs. There the fire-god forged them,
well aware of the seers and schooled in times to come,   740
all in order the generations born of Ascanius' stock
and all the wars they waged.
                          And Vulcan forged them too,
the mother wolf stretched out in the green grotto of Mars,
twin boys at her dugs, who hung there, frisky, suckling
without a fear as she with her lithe neck bent back,   745
stroking each in turn, licked her wolf pups
into shape with a mother's tongue.[4]
                          Not far from there
he had forged Rome as well and the Sabine women brutally
dragged from the crowded bowl when the Circus games were played
and abruptly war broke out afresh, the sons of Romulus   750
battling old King Tatius' hardened troops from Cures.[5]
Then when the same chiefs had set aside their strife,
they stood in full armor before Jove's holy altar,
lifting cups, and slaughtered a sow to bind their pacts.
                                    Nearby,
two four-horse chariots, driven to left and right, had torn   755
Mettus apart—man of Alba, you should have kept your word—
and Tullus hauled the liar's viscera through the brush
as blood-drops dripped like dew from brakes of thorns.[6]
                                    Porsenna,

---

3. Alloy of gold and silver.
4. Romulus and Remus, first builders of Rome's walls, who were suckled by the wolf.
5. At the first games in the Roman arena (the Circus), Roman men seized the Sabine women,
provoking their king, Tatius, to make war in revenge.
6. Mettus, king of Alba Longa, broke a promise to Tullus, third king of Rome, and was brutally punished.

there, commanding Romans to welcome banished Tarquin back,
mounted a massive siege to choke the city—Aeneas' heirs   760
rushing headlong against the steel in freedom's name.
See Porsenna to the life, his likeness menacing, raging,
and why? Cocles dared to rip the bridge down, Cloelia
burst her chains and swam the flood.[7]

                    Crowning the shield,
guarding the fort atop the Tarpeian Rock, Manlius   765
stood before the temple, held the Capitol's heights.
The new thatch bristled thick on Romulus' palace roof and
here the silver goose went ruffling through the gold arcades,
squawking its warning—Gauls attack the gates! Gauls
swarming the thickets, about to seize the fortress,   770
shielded by shadows, gift of the pitch-dark night.[8]
Gold their flowing hair, their war dress gold,
striped capes glinting, their milky necks ringed
with golden chokers, pairs of Alpine pikes in their hands,
flashing like fire, and long shields wrap their bodies.   775

    Here Vulcan pounded out the Salii, dancing priests of Mars,
the Luperci,[9] stripped, their peaked caps wound with wool,
bearing their body-shields that dropped from heaven,
and chaste matrons, riding in pillowed coaches,
led the sacred marches through the city.
                       Far apart   780
on the shield, what's more, he forged the homes of hell,
the high Gates of Death and the torments of the doomed,
with you, Catiline,[1] dangling from a beetling crag,
cringing before the Furies' open mouths.
                    And set apart,
the virtuous souls, with Cato[2] giving laws.
                    And amidst it all   785
the heaving sea ran far and wide, its likeness forged
in gold but the blue deep foamed in a sheen of white
and rounding it out in a huge ring swam the dolphins,
brilliant in silver, tails sweeping the crests
to cut the waves in two.
                And here in the heart   790
of the shield: the bronze ships, the battle of Actium,[3]
you could see it all, the world drawn up for war,
Leucata Headland seething, the breakers molten gold.
On one flank, Caesar Augustus leading Italy into battle,

---

7. When the Etruscan tyrant Tarquin was banished from Rome, the Etruscan general Lars Porsena attacked the city from a bridge, and took a girl—Cloelia—hostage; but a Roman, Cocles (better known as Horatius), tore down the bridge, and rescued both girl and city.
8. In 390 B.C.E. Manlius defended Rome against the invading Gauls; he was woken by geese, who were the first to hear the attack.
9. Priests of Lupercus, the Roman equivalent of Pan, the countryside god.
1. Conspirator who tried to overthrow the Roman Republic in the first century B.C.E.
2. Cato the Younger, defender of the Republic, who killed himself after the victory of Julius Caesar at Utica.
3. Site, on the northwestern Greek coast, of a major naval engagement in which Octavian (later called Augustus) defeated Antony and Cleopatra in 31 B.C.E.

the Senate and People too, the gods of hearth and home   795
and the great gods themselves. High astern he stands,
the twin flames shoot forth from his lustrous brows and
rising from the peak of his head, his father's star.
On the other flank, Agrippa[4] stands tall as he steers
his ships in line, impelled by favoring winds and gods   800
and from his forehead glitter the beaks of ships
on the Naval Crown, proud ensign earned in war.

    And opposing them comes Antony leading on
the riches of the Orient, troops of every stripe—
victor over the nations of the Dawn and blood-red shores   805
and in his retinue, Egypt, all the might of the East
and Bactra, the end of the earth, and trailing
in his wake, that outrage, that Egyptian wife![5]
All launch in as one, whipping the whole sea to foam
with tugging, thrashing oars and cleaving triple beaks   810
as they make a run for open sea. You'd think the Cyclades[6]
ripped up by the roots, afloat on the swells, or mountains
ramming against mountains, so immense the turrets astern
as sailors attack them, showering flaming tow and
hot bolts of flying steel, and the fresh blood running   815
red on Neptune's fields. And there in the thick of it all
the queen is mustering her armada, clacking her native rattles,
still not glimpsing the twin vipers hovering at her back,[7]
as Anubis[8] barks and the queen's chaos of monster gods
train their spears on Neptune, Venus, and great Minerva.   820
And there in the heart of battle Mars rampages on,
cast in iron, with grim Furies plunging down the sky
and Strife in triumph rushing in with her slashed robes
and Bellona[9] cracking her bloody lash in hot pursuit.
And scanning the melee, high on Actium's heights   825
Apollo bent his bow and terror struck them all,
Egypt and India, all the Arabians, all the Sabaeans
wheeled in their tracks and fled, and the queen herself—
you could see her calling, tempting the winds, her sails
spreading and now, now about to let her sheets run free.   830
Here in all this carnage the God of Fire forged her pale
with imminent death, sped on by the tides and Northwest Wind.
And rising up before her, the Nile immersed in mourning opens
every fold of his mighty body, all his rippling robes,
inviting into his deep blue lap and secret eddies   835
all his conquered people.
                 But Caesar[1] in triple triumph,

4. Son-in-law of Augustus, and admiral.
5. Although Actium was a battle between two Roman factions in a civil war, it is presented here as a conflict between the disciplined West and the luxurious East. The "Egyptian wife" is Cleopatra, queen of Egypt, with whom the Roman general Antony was having an affair.
6. Greek islands.
7. Anticipating her death, since Cleopatra poisoned herself with snakes.
8. Dog-headed Egyptian god.
9. Goddess of war.
1. Augustus, who took on the title "Caesar."

borne home through the walls of Rome, was paying
eternal vows of thanks to the gods of Italy:
three hundred imposing shrines throughout the city.
The roads resounded with joy, revelry, clapping hands,   840
with bands of matrons in every temple, altars in each
and the ground before them strewn with slaughtered steers.
Caesar himself, throned at brilliant Apollo's snow-white gates,
reviews the gifts brought on by the nations of the earth
and he mounts them high on the lofty temple doors   845
as the vanquished people move in a long slow file,
their dress, their arms as motley as their tongues.
Here Vulcan had forged the Nomad race, the Africans
with their trailing robes, here the Leleges, Carians,
Gelonian[2] archers bearing quivers, Euphrates flowing now   850
with a humbler tide, the Morini brought from the world's end,
the two-horned Rhine and the Dahae never conquered,
Araxes River bridling at his bridge.[3]
                Such vistas
the God of Fire forged across the shield
that Venus gives her son. He fills with wonder—   855
he knows nothing of these events but takes delight
in their likeness, lifting onto his shoulders now
the fame and fates of all his children's children.

Summary of Books IX–XI   *The war becomes bloody and violent. Jupiter orders a council
of the gods, reminding them that there was supposed to be peace between Trojans and Italians; but
he ends up renouncing responsibility: "the Fates will find the way," he declares. Pallas, son of
Evander, enters battle and is killed by Turnus. Aeneas longs to kill Turnus in revenge, but cannot
find him; Juno has spirited him away. Attempts at peace-making fail, and many are killed on both
sides, including a warrior princess named Camilla. Turnus insists on fighting Aeneas in single combat. Aeneas and King Latinus agree that if Turnus wins, the Trojans will leave, but if Turnus loses,
Aeneas will not enslave the native Italians, but will join with them on equal terms to form a new
nation. But the truce soon breaks, fighting starts again, and Aeneas is wounded. After Venus heals
him, he returns to battle in full armor, and eventually the Trojans and their allies attack Latium,
where Turnus has his stronghold. Turnus decides to fight him and again they agree to single combat;
everybody else draws back to leave space for the fight.*

FROM BOOK XII

[The Sword Decides All]

*   *   *

Latinus himself is struck that these two giant men,
sprung from opposing ends of the earth, have met,

---

2. The Lelegians and Carians were ancient
peoples of Asia Minor; the Gelonians were a
Scythian people of southern Russia.
3. Peoples and places indicating the vast extent
of the Roman Empire under Augustus: the
Euphrates is a river in Mesopotamia; the Morini

were a Gaulish tribe in modern-day Belgium,
beyond the Rhine River; the Dahae were a tribe
from east of the Caspian Sea; the Araxes River
(in modern-day Armenia) once had a bridge
built by Alexander that was swept away by
floods.

face to face, to let their swords decide.
                                    But they,
as soon as the battlefield lay clear and level,
charge at speed, rifling their spears at long range,   825
then rush to battle with shields and clanging bronze.
The earth groans as stroke after stroke they land
with naked swords: fortune and fortitude mix
in one assault. Charging like two hostile bulls
fighting up on Sila's woods or Taburnus' ridges,[4]   830
ramping in mortal combat, both brows bent for attack
and the herdsmen back away in fear and the whole herd
stands by, hushed, afraid, and the heifers wait and wonder,
who will lord it over the forest? who will lead the herd?—
while the bulls battle it out, horns butting, locking,   835
goring each other, necks and shoulders roped in blood
and the woods resound as they grunt and bellow out.
So they charge, Trojan Aeneas and Turnus, son of Daunus,[5]
shields clang and the huge din makes the heavens ring.
Jove himself lifts up his scales, balanced, trued,   840
and in them he sets the opposing fates of both . . .
Whom would the labor of battle doom? Whose life
would weigh him down to death?
                                    Suddenly Turnus
flashes forward, certain he's in the clear and
raising his sword high, rearing to full stretch   845
strikes—as Trojans and anxious Latins shout out,
with the gaze of both armies riveted on the fighters.
But his treacherous blade breaks off, it fails Turnus
in mid-stroke—enraged, his one recourse, retreat,
and swifter than Eastwinds, Turnus flies as soon   850
as he sees that unfamiliar hilt in his hand,
no defense at all. They say the captain, rushing
headlong on to harness his team and board his car
to begin the duel, left his father's sword behind
and hastily grabbed his charioteer Metiscus' blade.   855
Long as the Trojan stragglers took to their heels and ran,
the weapon did its work, but once it came up against
the immortal armor forged by the God of Fire, Vulcan,
the mortal sword burst at a stroke, brittle as ice,
and glinting splinters gleamed on the tawny sand.   860
So raging Turnus runs for it, scours the field,
now here, now there, weaving in tangled circles
as Trojans crowd him hard, a dense ring of them
shutting him in, with a wild swamp to the left
and steep walls to the right.
                                    Nor does Aeneas flag,   865
though slowed down by his wound, his knees unsteady,
cutting his pace at times but he's still in full fury,

---

4. Sila and Taburnus are mountainous, for-   5. King of Apulia.
ested areas in southern Italy.

hot on his frantic quarry's tracks, stride for stride.
Alert as a hunting hound that lights on a trapped stag,
hemmed in by a river's bend or frightened back by the ropes   870
with blood-red feathers[6]—the hound barking, closing, fast
as the quarry, panicked by traps and the steep riverbanks,
runs off and back in a thousand ways but the Umbrian hound,[7]
keen for the kill, hangs on the trail, his jaws agape—
and now, now he's got him, thinks he's got him, yes   875
and his jaws clap shut, stymied, champing the empty air.
Then the shouts break loose, and the banks and rapids round
resound with the din, and the high sky thunders back. Turnus—
even in flight he rebukes his men as he races, calling
each by name, demanding his old familiar sword.   880
Aeneas, opposite, threatens death and doom at once
to anyone in his way, he threatens his harried foes
that he'll root their city out and, wounded as he is,
keeps closing for the kill. And five full circles
they run and reel as many back, around and back,   885
for it's no mean trophy they're sporting after now,
they race for the life and the lifeblood of Turnus.

    By chance a wild olive, green with its bitter leaves,
stood right here, sacred to Faunus,[8] revered by men
in the old days, sailors saved from shipwreck.   890
On it they always fixed their gifts to the local god
and they hung their votive clothes in thanks for rescue.
But the Trojans—no exceptions, hallowed tree that it was—
chopped down its trunk to clear the spot for combat.
Now here the spear of Aeneas had stuck, borne home   895
by its hurling force, and the tough roots held it fast.
He bent down over it, trying to wrench the iron loose and
track with a spear the kill he could not catch on foot.
Turnus, truly beside himself with terror—"Faunus!"
he cried, "I beg you, pity me! You, dear Earth,   900
hold fast to that spear! If I have always kept
your rites—a far cry from Aeneas' men
who stain your rites with war."
                                 So he appealed,
calling out for the god's help, and not for nothing.
Aeneas struggled long, wasting time on the tough stump,   905
no power of *his* could loose the timber's stubborn bite.
As he bravely heaves and hauls, the goddess Juturna,[9]
changing back again to the charioteer Metiscus,
rushes in and returns her brother's sword to Turnus.

6. Hunters used ropes and nets decorated with feathers.
7. A dog breed known for its skill in hunting. (Umbria is a region of northern Italy.)
8. An old Roman god associated with the countryside and forest.
9. A nymph of Italian lakes and springs, sister of Turnus; Jupiter made her immortal after he had an affair with her.

But Venus, incensed that the nymph has had her brazen way,   910
steps up and plucks Aeneas' spear from the clinging root.
So standing tall, with their arms and fighting hearts refreshed—
one who trusted all to his sword, the other looming fiercely
with his spear—confronting each other, both men breathless,
brace for the war-god's fray.

                    Now at the same moment   915
Jove, the king of mighty Olympus, turns to Juno,
gazing down on the war from her golden cloud, and says:
"Where will it end, my queen? What is left at the last?
Aeneas the hero, god of the land: you know yourself,
you confess you know that he is heaven bound,   920
his fate will raise Aeneas to the stars.
What are you plotting? What hope can make you
cling to the chilly clouds? So, was it right
for a mortal hand to wound, to mortify a god?
Right to restore that mislaid sword to Turnus—   925
for without your power what could Juturna do?—
and lend the defeated strength? Have done at last.
Bow to my appeals. Don't let your corrosive grief
devour you in silence, or let your dire concerns come
pouring from your sweet lips and plaguing me forever.   930
We have reached the limit. To harass the Trojans
over land and sea, to ignite an unspeakable war,
degrade a royal house and blend the wedding hymn
with the dirge of grief: all that lay in your power.
But go no further. I forbid you now."

                            Jove said no more.   935
And so, with head bent low, Saturn's daughter replied:
"Because I have known your will so well, great Jove,
against my *own* I deserted Turnus and the earth.
Or else you would never see me now, alone
on a windswept throne enduring right and wrong.   940
No, wrapped in flames I would be up on the front lines,
dragging the Trojan into mortal combat. Juturna?
I was the one, I admit, who spurred her on
to help her embattled brother, true, and blessed
whatever greater daring it took to save his life,   945
but never to shower arrows, never tense the bow.
I swear by the unappeasable fountainhead of the Styx,[1]
the one dread oath decreed for the gods on high."

                                  "So,
now I yield, Juno yields, and I leave this war I loathe.
But this—and there is no law of Fate to stop it now—   950
this I beg for Latium, for the glory of your people.
When, soon, they join in their happy wedding-bonds—
and wedded let them be—in pacts of peace at last,
never command the Latins, here on native soil,

---

1. River in the Underworld; oaths sworn by the Styx could not be broken, even by the gods.

to exchange their age-old name,   955
to become Trojans, called the kin of Teucer,
alter their language, change their style of dress.
Let Latium endure. Let Alban kings hold sway for all time.
Let Roman stock grow strong with Italian strength.
Troy has fallen—and fallen let her stay—   960
with the very name of Troy!"
                    Smiling down,
the creator of man and the wide world returned:
"Now there's my sister. Saturn's second child—
such tides of rage go churning through your heart.
Come, relax your anger. It started all for nothing.   965
I grant your wish. I surrender. Freely, gladly too.
Latium's sons will retain their fathers' words and ways.
Their name till now is the name that shall endure.
Mingling in stock alone, the Trojans will subside.
And I will add the rites and the forms of worship,   970
and make them Latins all, who speak one Latin tongue.
Mixed with Ausonian[2] blood, one race will spring from them,
and you will see them outstrip all men, outstrip all gods
in reverence. No nation on earth will match the honors
they shower down on you."
                    Juno nodded assent to this,   975
her spirit reversed to joy. She departs the sky
and leaves her cloud behind.
                  His task accomplished,
the Father turned his mind to another matter, set
to dismiss Juturna from her brother's battles.
They say there are twin Curses called the Furies . . .   980
Night had born them once in the dead of darkness,
one and the same spawn, and birthed infernal Megaera,[3]
wreathing all their heads with coiled serpents,
fitting them out with wings that race the wind.
They hover at Jove's throne, crouch at his gates   985
to serve that savage king
and whet the fears of afflicted men whenever
the king of gods lets loose horrific deaths and plagues
or panics towns that deserve the scourge of war.
Jove sped one of them down the sky, commanding: 990
"Cross Juturna's path as a wicked omen!"

Down she swoops, hurled to earth by a whirlwind,
swift as a darting arrow whipped from a bowstring
through the clouds, a shaft armed by a Parthian,[4]
tipped with deadly poison, shot by a Parthian   995
or a Cretan archer—well past any cure—
hissing on unseen through the rushing dark.

2. Italian.
3. One of the Furies.

4. Parthia (a region in modern-day Iran) was
known for its skillful archers.

So raced this daughter of Night and sped to earth.
Soon as she spots the Trojan ranks and Turnus' lines
she quickly shrinks into that small bird that often,   1000
hunched at dusk on deserted tombs and rooftops, sings
its ominous song in shadows late at night. Shrunken so,
the demon flutters over and over again in Turnus' face,
screeching, drumming his shield with its whirring wings.
An eerie numbness unnerved him head to toe with dread,   1005
his hackles bristled in horror, voice choked in his throat.

   Recognizing the Fury's ruffling wings at a distance,
wretched Juturna tears her hair, nails clawing her face,
fists beating her breast, and cries to her brother:
"How, Turnus, how can your sister help you now?   1010
What's left for me now, after all I have endured?
What skill do I have to lengthen out your life?
How can I fight against this dreadful omen?
At last, at last I leave the field of battle.
Afraid as I am, now frighten me no more,   1015
you obscene birds of night! Too well I know
the beat of your wings, the drumbeat of doom.
Nor do the proud commands of Jove escape me now,
our great, warm-hearted Jove. Are these his wages
for taking my virginity? Why did he grant me life   1020
eternal—rob me of our one privilege, death?
Then, for a fact, I now could end this agony,
keep my brother company down among the shades.
Doomed to live forever? Without you, my brother,
what do I have still mine that's sweet to taste?   1025
If only the earth gaped deep enough to take me down,
to plunge this goddess into the depths of hell!"
                           With that,
shrouding her head with a gray-green veil and moaning low,
down to her own stream's bed the goddess sank away.

   All hot pursuit, Aeneas brandishes high his spear,   1030
that tree of a spear, and shouts from a savage heart:
"More delay! Why now? Still in retreat, Turnus, why?
This is no foot-race. It's savagery, swordplay cut-and-thrust!
Change yourself into any shape you please, call up
whatever courage or skill you still have left.   1035
Pray to wing your way to the starry sky
or bury yourself in the earth's deep pits!"

   Turnus shakes his head: "I don't fear you,
you and your blazing threats, my fierce friend.
It's the gods that frighten me—Jove, my mortal foe."   1040

   No more words. Glancing around he spots a huge rock,
huge, ages old, and lying out in the field by chance,
placed as a boundary stone to settle border wars.

A dozen picked men could barely shoulder it up, men
of such physique as the earth brings forth these days,   1045
but he wrenched it up, hands trembling, tried to heave it
right at Aeneas, Turnus stretching to full height, the hero
at speed, at peak strength. Yet he's losing touch with himself,
racing, hoisting that massive rock in his hands and hurling,
true, but his knees buckle, blood's like ice in his veins   1050
and the rock he flings through the air, plummeting under
its own weight, cannot cover the space between them,
cannot strike full force . . .

                    Just as in dreams
when the nightly spell of sleep falls heavy on our eyes
and we seem entranced by longing to keep on racing on,   1055
no use, in the midst of one last burst of speed
we sink down, consumed, our tongue won't work,
and tried and true, the power that filled our body
fails—we strain but the voice and words won't follow.
So with Turnus. Wherever he fought to force his way,   1060
no luck, the merciless Fury blocks his efforts.
A swirl of thoughts goes racing through his mind,
he glances toward his own Rutulians and their town,
he hangs back in dread, he quakes at death—it's here.
Where can he run? How can he strike out at the enemy?   1065
Where's his chariot? His charioteer, his sister? Vanished.

    As he hangs back, the fatal spear of Aeneas streaks on—
spotting a lucky opening he had flung from a distance,
all his might and main. Rocks heaved by a catapult
pounding city ramparts never storm so loudly, never   1070
such a shattering bolt of thunder crashing forth.
Like a black whirlwind churning on, that spear
flies on with its weight of iron death to pierce
the breastplate's lower edge and the outmost rim
of the round shield with its seven plies and right   1075
at the thick of Turnus' thigh it whizzes through,
it strikes home and the blow drops great Turnus
down to the ground, battered down on his bent knees.
The Rutulians spring up with a groan and the hillsides
round groan back and the tall groves far and wide   1080
resound with the long-drawn moan.
                    Turnus lowered
his eyes and reached with his right hand and begged,
a suppliant: "I deserve it all. No mercy, please,"
Turnus pleaded. "Seize your moment now. Or if
some care for a parent's grief can touch you still,   1085
I pray you—you had such a father, in old Anchises—
pity Daunus in his old age and send me back
to my own people, or if you would prefer,
send them my dead body stripped of life. Here,
the victor and vanquished, I stretch my hands to you,   1090
so the men of Latium have seen me in defeat.

Lavinia is your bride.
Go no further down the road of hatred."

Aeneas, ferocious in armor, stood there, still,
shifting his gaze, and held his sword-arm back,   1095
holding himself back too as Turnus' words began
to sway him more and more . . . when all at once
he caught sight of the fateful sword-belt of Pallas,[5]
swept over Turnus' shoulder, gleaming with shining studs
Aeneas knew by heart. Young Pallas, whom Turnus had overpowered,   1100
taken down with a wound, and now his shoulder flaunted
his enemy's battle-emblem like a trophy. Aeneas,
soon as his eyes drank in that plunder—keepsake
of his own savage grief—flaring up in fury,
terrible in his rage, he cries: "Decked in the spoils   1105
you stripped from one I loved—escape my clutches? Never—
Pallas strikes this blow, Pallas sacrifices you now,
makes you pay the price with your own guilty blood!"
In the same breath, blazing with wrath he plants
his iron sword hilt-deep in his enemy's heart.   1110
Turnus' limbs went limp in the chill of death.
His life breath fled with a groan of outrage
down to the shades below.[6]

---

5. Son of Evander, king of the Arcadians, who
were allied with the Trojans.

6. The same lines are used in book XI for the
death of the woman warrior, Camilla.

OVID

43 B.C.E.–17 C.E.

Ovid (whose full name was Publius Ovidius Naso) was one of the smartest, most prolific, and most consistently entertaining of the Roman poets. During his long and productive career, he wrote funny, perceptive poems about sex and relationships in contemporary Rome, as well as vivid retellings of ancient myths. His way of telling stories remains extraordinary for its subtlety and its depth of psychological understanding. His work had a massive influence on the poets and artists of the Middle Ages, the Renaissance, and beyond, and it is one of our most important and accessible sources for the rich mythology of ancient Greece and Rome.

LIFE AND TIMES

Ovid was born into an aristocratic ("equestrian") family, in the provincial Roman town of Sulmo, east of Rome. His father wanted him to become a lawyer, and therefore had him trained in rhetoric. Ovid's writing shows the influence of rhetorical technique, in its polished, witty style. But Ovid had no real interest in the law. He was a natural poet, and at the age of twenty, to his father's disappointment and disapproval, he quit his legal training. He held various minor governmental posts, but eventually became a full-time poet, with the financial aid of a rich patron called Messalla. Ovid became part of the literary circles of Rome: he knew the poets Propertius and Horace, and met **Virgil**, who was some twenty-seven years older.

Ovid married three times; he had been divorced twice before the age of thirty. His third wife seems to have had a daughter by a previous husband, but Ovid had no children of his own. Beyond that, we know little of Ovid's personal life. He wrote a great deal about extramarital sex, but emphasized that his poetic persona should not be taken as autobiography, declaring, "My Muse is slutty, but my life is chaste."

Ovid's work included various collections of poems on mythological topics, such as the *Fasti* (never finished), on the Roman calendar, and a set of poetic letters, the *Heroides*, from mythical heroines like Helen of Troy to their boyfriends. But most notorious, in his own time and later, were his two books about sex and relationships: the *Amores* and the *Ars Amatoria*. These used the tradition of Roman love elegy, which had begun with Catullus and had been developed by Ovid's friend Propertius, who evoked the desperate, abject longing of a man for a beloved and unreliable girlfriend. Ovid's love poetry focuses less on feelings than on behavior, and less on love than on sex, which he treats in a light, knowing tone. He gives, for example, a titillating account of some hot afternoon sex; tells anecdotes about his girlfriend's bad experiences with hair dye and about her attempted abortion; and offers advice about the best places to go and best lines to use for picking up a date.

All this was guaranteed to irritate the more conservative members of Roman society, who included— unfortunately for Ovid—the emperor, Augustus. Having seized power after winning the battle of Actium (in 31

B.C.E.), at the end of a long civil war, Augustus was eager to impose order on the fragmented society of Rome. A key element in his domestic strategy was to reform the morals and increase the population of the Roman elite, by promoting marriage and traditional family structures. New laws were imposed in 19–18 B.C.E. to encourage married couples to have children, and to punish adultery with exile. In this context, Ovid's *Ars Amatoria* seems deliberately calculated to enrage the emperor. The poem points up the hypocrisy of Roman sexual mores and suggests that, in fact, having lots of extramarital sex is far more traditional than Augustan family values, since the Romans have been doing it ever since the foundation of the city: it was through the rape of the Sabine women that the male inhabitants of the new city acquired wives and were able to supply Rome with future citizens.

Ovid seems to have gotten himself into even worse trouble by what he calls a mistake. We do not know exactly what happened; Ovid suggests that he saw something he should not have seen, perhaps involving the emperor's daughter, Julia, who was having an adulterous affair. Combined with the *Ars Amatoria* and Ovid's generally provocative stance toward Augustus, this mistake was the last straw; in 8 C.E., the emperor—acting, unusually, on his own initiative, without input from the Senate—condemned Ovid to permanent exile from Rome to Tomis, a remote town on the Black Sea, in modern Romania. He lived out the remaining eight years of his life in grim isolation, far from family and friends, in a cold, bleak place where, he claims, nobody even spoke Latin. Ovid wrote a series of poems from exile, mostly letters bewailing his sufferings and pleading—to friends, family, acquaintances, the general public, and to the emperor himself—to be forgiven and to be allowed back home. All were unsuccessful; Ovid died in Tomis, alone and unforgiven.

METAMORPHOSES

At the time of his exile in 8 C.E., Ovid was finishing his greatest work, the *Metamorphoses* (Greek for "changes"). It is less obviously provocative than Ovid's love poetry, but it, too, provides a radical challenge both to Augustan moral and political values and to traditional poetic norms. Virgil had written what Augustus wanted to be the official epic of the new order. For all its innovations, the *Aeneid* focused on the deeds of a single hero, and it treated its culture's dominant values (such as duty, imperial power, and military honor) with respect. The *Metamorphoses* is recognizably epic; it is the only poem Ovid wrote in the epic meter, dactylic hexameter. But it can be seen as a critical response to Virgil, even an anti-*Aeneid*. Ovid produced a series of miniature stories strung together into a long narrative of fifteen books. The transitions between them, and the connections drawn by the narrator, are often transparently contrived—perhaps in mockery of the idea of narrative unity. There is no single hero, and no moral values are presented without irony. There is, however, an element common to these stories: change; and despite its leisurely and roundabout course, the narrative has a discernible direction—as Ovid says in his introduction, "from the world's beginning to the present day." Starting with the creation of the world, the transformation of matter into living bodies (the first great metamorphosis), Ovid tells of human beings changed into animals, flowers, and trees. He proceeds through Greek myth to stories of early Rome and so to his own time, culminating in the ascension of the murdered Julius Caesar to the heavens in the form of a star and the divine promise that Augustus too, far in the future, will become a god; it is tempting to speculate that Ovid hoped—vainly—to improve his relationship with the emperor by means of these few lines. The last change of all is that of Ovid himself, who will, he declares, be transformed from a mortal man into his own immortal poem.

Change underlies both the narrative style and the vision of the world the poem projects. Virgil also told of a transformation, the new (Roman) order arising from the ruins of the old (Troy). But once the transformation was completed by the Augustan order, there was to be stability, permanence. Ovid tells of a world ceaselessly coming to be in a process that never ends. Augustan Rome is not the culminating point of history here, as it was in the *Aeneid*; indeed, the whole idea of a historical end or goal seems, in the *Metamorphoses*, impossible and absurd. Ovid's epic without a hero presents shifting perspectives and offers the reader no single point of view from which to judge his complex narratives. Against the forced imposition of political and moral unity he sets change itself.

Change is also central to the narrative manner of the *Metamorphoses*. Ovid constantly shifts his point of view, telling a story first from one character's perspective, and then from another's. One story is embedded in another, so that one narrative voice is piled on top of another, as when Venus tells Adonis the story of Atalanta. This story is set within the tale of Venus's love for Adonis and of his death, which is one of a series of stories sung by Orpheus in the poem's main narrative. In such cases, the immediate and the larger contexts give the same story different shades of meaning. And there are thematic connections between stories, so that motifs and images also change their meaning from one story

to another, or over the course of a single story. Daphne and Syrinx are turned into plants (the laurel and the reed) that are henceforth attributes of the gods who tried to rape them, a form of appropriation that substitutes for sexual violence.

A common element of many stories in books I and II is the lust of male gods for female humans. On one level, the gods' desire is presented as ridiculous: when Jupiter turns himself into a bull, the narrator comments, "Majestic power and erotic love / do not get on together very well." But these stories are also focused on rape, and, at least some of the time, the narrator shows the terror and suffering of the human victim. These stories of rape may have political implications, for rape is the ultimate imposition of control. When powerful gods force themselves on defenseless women, the reader is invited to remember how easily authority can be abused.

But male gods are not the only sexual agents in the poem: women and goddesses, too, can be overwhelmed by desire, and can themselves become sexual predators. The stories selected here from later in the *Metamorphoses* bring out the complexity of Ovid's presentation of gender and sexuality. The story of Iphis and Ianthe suggests that social gender roles for women and men are more or less arbitrary: girls usually look different from boys, but their feelings may be exactly the same. That story has a happy ending, but the tales from book X show various ways in which desire causes pain, distorts our perceptions, and ends in disaster. The tale of Pygmalion may seem an exception, but we should remember that it begins with the artist's hatred of women for their loose morals, and that the story as a whole, whatever it may say about the power of art, can also be read as a fable of man's fabrication of woman—her person and her functions—according to his desires. These stories are narrated by Orpheus, the archetypal poet, after his failure to bring Eurydice back from the underworld. The pathology of desire is fundamental to Ovid's poem, since the lover hopes to stop time, to achieve permanent possession of the beloved; but all these stories show us how impossible such a dream is. The girl is always running from the god; the boy is always running from the goddess; Orpheus's wife cannot be brought back from the land of the dead. Reaching for the body of another, the lover's own body is transformed. The closest any of these characters can get to permanence is to be transformed into a growing (living, changing) plant that will always represent their unfulfilled longings.

From Metamorphoses[1]

FROM BOOK I

[Proem]

My mind leads me to speak now of forms changed
into new bodies: O gods above, inspire
this undertaking (which you've changed as well)
and guide my poem in its epic sweep
from the world's beginning to the present day.   5

[The Creation]

Before the seas and lands had been created,
before the sky that covers everything,
Nature displayed a single aspect only
throughout the cosmos; Chaos was its name,
a shapeless, unwrought mass of inert bulk   10
and nothing more, with the discordant seeds
of disconnected elements all heaped
together in anarchic disarray.
    The sun as yet did not light up the earth,
nor did the crescent moon renew her horns,   15
nor was the earth suspended in midair,
balanced by her own weight, nor did the ocean
extend her arms to the margins of the land.
    Although the land and sea and air were present,
land was unstable, the sea unfit for swimming,   20
and air lacked light; shapes shifted constantly,
and all things were at odds with one another,
for in a single mass cold strove with warm,
wet was opposed to dry and soft to hard,
and weightlessness to matter having weight.   25
    Some god (or kinder nature) settled this
dispute by separating earth from heaven,
and then by separating sea from earth

1. Translated by Charles Martin.

and fluid aether[2] from the denser air;
and after these were separated out
and liberated from the primal heap, 30
he bound the disentangled elements
each in its place and all in harmony.
    The fiery and weightless aether leapt
to heaven's vault and claimed its citadel;
the next in lightness to be placed was air; 35
the denser earth drew down gross elements
and was compressed by its own gravity;
encircling water lastly found its place,
encompassing the solid earth entire.[3] 40
    Now when that god (whichever one it was)
had given Chaos form, dividing it
in parts which he arranged, he molded earth
into the shape of an enormous globe,
so that it should be uniform throughout. 45
    And afterward he sent the waters streaming
in all directions, ordered waves to swell
under the sweeping winds, and sent the flood
to form new shores on the surrounded earth;
he added springs, great standing swamps and lakes, 50
as well as sloping rivers fixed between
their narrow banks, whose plunging waters (all
in varied places, each in its own channel)
are partly taken back into the earth
and in part flow until they reach the sea, 55
when they—received into the larger field
of a freer flood—beat against shores, not banks.
He ordered open plains to spread themselves,
valleys to sink, the stony peaks to rise,
and forests to put on their coats of green. 60
    And as the vault of heaven is divided
by two zones on the right and two on the left,
with a central zone, much hotter, in between,
so, by the care of this creator god,
the mass that was enclosed now by the sky 65
was zoned in the same way, with the same lines
inscribed upon the surface of the earth.
Heat makes the middle zone unlivable,
and the two outer zones are deep in snow;
between these two extremes, he placed two others 70
of temperate climate, blending cold and warmth.[4]

2. A region of refined air, fiery in nature, believed to be above the "denser air" that was closer to the earth and composed the breathable atmosphere.
3. From Homer on, the ancients conceived of Ocean as a stream that surrounded the earth.
4. The sky, that is, is divided into five horizontal zones, and therefore so is the earth beneath it. On either side of the earth's uninhabitable torrid region, over which the sun passes, lies a temperate zone, and the northern one contains the inhabited, civilized lands on earth (ancient writers were vague about what the southern temperate zone contained). The two outermost zones, farthest from the sun, were too cold to live in.

Air was suspended over all of this,
proportionately heavier than aether,
as earth is heavier than water is.
He ordered mists and clouds into position,   75
and thunder, to make test of our resolve,[5]
and winds creating thunderbolts and lightning.

    Nor did that world-creating god permit
the winds to roam ungoverned through the air;
for even now, with each of them in charge   80
of his own kingdom, and their blasts controlled,
they scarcely can be kept from shattering
the world, such is the discord between brothers.

    Eurus[6] went eastward, to the lands of Dawn,
the kingdoms of Arabia and Persia,   85
and to the mountain peaks that lie below
the morning's rays; and Zephyr took his place
on the western shores warmed by the setting sun.
The frozen north and Scythia were seized
by bristling Boreas; the lands opposite,   90
continually drenched by fog and rain,
are where the south wind, known as Auster, dwells.
Above these winds, he set the weightless aether,
a liquid free of every earthly toxin.

    No sooner had he separated all   95
within defining limits, when the stars,
which formerly had been concealed in darkness,
began to blaze up all throughout the heavens;
and so that every region of the world
should have its own distinctive forms of life,   100
the constellations and the shapes of gods
occupied the lower part of heaven;
the seas gave shelter to the shining fishes,
earth received beasts, and flighty air, the birds.

    An animal more like the gods than these,   105
more intellectually capable
and able to control the other beasts,
had not as yet appeared: now man was born,
either because the framer of all things,
the fabricator of this better world,   110
created man out of his own divine
substance—or else because Prometheus[7]
took up a clod (so lately broken off
from lofty aether that it still contained
some elements in common with its kin),   115
and mixing it with water, molded it
into the shape of gods, who govern all.

    And even though all other animals

---

5. Thunder was considered an omen.
6. The east wind. Zephyr, Boreas, and
Auster were the west, north, and south winds,
respectively.

7. A god best known for stealing fire from the
gods and giving it to mortals. In some stories
he also created humans out of clay.

lean forward and look down toward the ground,
he gave to man a face that is uplifted, 120
and ordered him to stand erect and look
directly up into the vaulted heavens
and turn his countenance to meet the stars;
the earth, that was so lately rude and formless,
was changed by taking on the shapes of men. 125

* * *

[Apollo and Daphne]

Daphne,[8] the daughter of the river god
Peneus, was the first love of Apollo;
this happened not by chance, but by the cruel
outrage of Cupid; Phoebus, in the triumph 630
of his great victory against the Python,[9]
observed him bending back his bow and said,
    "What are *you* doing with such manly arms,
lascivious boy? That bow befits *our* brawn,[1] 635
wherewith we deal out wounds to savage beasts
and other mortal foes, unerringly:
just now with our innumerable arrows
we managed to lay low the mighty Python,
whose pestilential belly covered acres! 640
Content yourself with kindling love affairs
with your wee torch—and don't claim *our* glory!"
    The son of Venus[2] answered him with this:
"Your arrow, Phoebus, may strike everything:
mine will strike you: as animals to gods, 645
your glory is so much the less than mine!"
    He spoke, and soaring upward through the air
on wings that thundered, in no time at all
had landed on Parnassus'[3] shaded height;
and from his quiver drew two arrows out 650
which operated at cross-purposes,
for one engendered flight, the other, love;
the latter has a polished tip of gold,
the former has a tip of dull, blunt lead;
with this one, Cupid struck Peneus' daughter, 655
while the other pierced Apollo to his marrow.
    One is in love now, and the other one
won't hear of it, for Daphne calls it joy
to roam within the forest's deep seclusion,
where she, in emulation of the chaste 660
goddess Phoebe,[4] devotes herself to hunting;

---

8. Literally, "Laurel" (Greek).
9. The enormous snake that Apollo (Phoebus) had to kill in order to found his oracle at Delphi. "Cupid": god of sexual desire.
1. The bow was one of Apollo's attributes.

2. Goddess of love (Aphrodite in Greek).
3. Mountain in central Greece, near Delphi.
4. Diana (Artemis in Greek), Apollo's sister, virgin goddess of the hunt.

one ribbon only bound her straying tresses.
    Many men sought her, but she spurned her suitors,
loath to have anything to do with men,
and rambled through the wild and trackless groves 665
untroubled by a thought for love or marriage.
    Often her father said, "You owe it to me,
child, to provide me with a son-in-law
and grandchildren!"
             "Let me remain a virgin,
father most dear," she said, "as once before 670
Diana's father, Jove, gave her that gift."
    Although Peneus yielded to you, Daphne,
your beauty kept your wish from coming true,
your comeliness conflicting with your vow:
at first sight, Phoebus loves her and desires 675
to sleep with her; desire turns to hope,
and his own prophecy deceives the god.
    Now just as in a field the harvest stubble
is all burned off, or as hedges are set ablaze
when, if by chance, some careless traveler 680
should brush one with his torch or toss away
the still-smoldering brand at break of day—
just so the smitten god went up in flames
until his heart was utterly afire,
and hope sustained his unrequited passion. 685
    He gazes on her hair without adornment:
"What if it were done up a bit?" he asks,
and gazes on her eyes, as bright as stars,
and on that darling little mouth of hers,
though sight is not enough to satisfy; 690
he praises everything that he can see—
her fingers, hands, and arms, bare to her shoulders—
and what is hidden prizes even more.
    She flees more swiftly than the lightest breeze,
nor will she halt when he calls out to her: 695
"Daughter of Peneus, I pray, hold still,
hold still! I'm not a foe in grim pursuit!
Thus lamb flees wolf, thus dove from eagle flies
on trembling wings, thus deer from lioness,
thus any creature flees its enemy, 700
but I am stalking you because of love!
    "Wretch that I am: I'm fearful that you'll fall,
brambles will tear your flesh because of me!
The ground you're racing over's very rocky,
slow down, I beg you, restrain yourself in flight, 705
and I will follow at a lesser speed.
    "Just ask yourself who finds you so attractive!
I'm not a caveman, not some shepherd boy,
no shaggy guardian of flocks and herds—
you've no idea, rash girl, you've no idea 710
whom you are fleeing, that is why you flee!

"Delphi, Claros, Tenedos are all mine,
I'm worshiped in the city of Patara![5]
Jove is my father, I alone reveal
what was, what is, and what will come to be!   715
The plucked strings answer my demand with song!
      "Although my aim is sure, another's arrow
proved even more so, and my careless heart
was badly wounded—the art of medicine
is my invention, by the way, the source   720
of my worldwide fame as a practitioner
of healing through the natural strength of herbs.
      "Alas, there is no herbal remedy
for the love that I must suffer, and the arts
that heal all others cannot heal their lord—"   725
      He had much more to say to her, but Daphne
pursued her fearful course and left him speechless,
though no less lovely fleeing him; indeed,
disheveled by the wind that bared her limbs
and pressed the blown robes to her straining body   730
even as it whipped up her hair behind her,
the maiden was more beautiful in flight!
      But the young god had no further interest
in wasting his fine words on her; admonished
by his own passion, he accelerates,   735
and runs as swiftly as a Gallic hound[6]
chasing a rabbit through an open field;
the one seeks shelter and the other, prey—
he clings to her, is just about to spring,
with his long muzzle straining at her heels,   740
while she, not knowing whether she's been caught,
in one swift burst, eludes those snapping jaws,
no longer the anticipated feast;
so he in hope and she in terror race.
      But her pursuer, driven by his passion,   745
outspeeds the girl, giving her no pause,
one step behind her, breathing down her neck;
her strength is gone; she blanches at the thought
of the effort of her swift flight overcome,
but at the sight of Peneus, she cries,   750
"Help me, dear father! If your waters hold
divinity, transform me and destroy
that beauty by which I have too well pleased!"
      Her prayer was scarcely finished when she feels
a torpor take possession of her limbs—   755
her supple trunk is girdled with a thin
layer of fine bark over her smooth skin;
her hair turns into foliage, her arms
grow into branches, sluggish roots adhere
to feet that were so recently so swift,   760

5. All centers of Apollo's cult.   6. A hunting breed famous for speed.

her head becomes the summit of a tree;
all that remains of her is a warm glow.

Loving her still, the god puts his right hand
against the trunk, and even now can feel
her heart as it beats under the new bark;   765
he hugs her limbs as if they were still human,
and then he puts his lips against the wood,
which, even now, is adverse to his kiss.

"Although you cannot be my bride," he says,
"you will assuredly be my own tree,   770
O Laurel, and will always find yourself
girding my locks, my lyre, and my quiver too—
you will adorn great Roman generals
when every voice cries out in joyful triumph
along the route up to the Capitol;   775
you will protect the portals of Augustus,
guarding, on either side, his crown of oak;[7]
and as I am—perpetually youthful,
my flowing locks unknown to the barber's shears—
so you will be an evergreen forever   780
bearing your brilliant foliage with glory!"

Phoebus concluded. Laurel shook her branches
and seemed to nod her summit in assent.

[*Jove and Io*]

There is a grove in Thessaly,[8] enclosed
on every side by high and wooded hills: 785
they call it Tempe. The river Peneus,
which rises deep within the Pindus range,
pours its turbulent waters through this gorge
and over a cataract that deafens all
its neighbors far and near, creating clouds   790
that drive a fine, cool mist along, until
it drips down through the summits of the trees.

Here is the house, the seat, the inner chambers
of the great river; here Peneus holds court
in his rocky cavern and lays down the law   795
to water nymphs and tributary streams.

First to assemble were the native rivers,
uncertain whether to congratulate,
or to commiserate with Daphne's father:
the Sperchios, whose banks are lined with poplars,   800
the ancient Apidanus and the mild
Aeas and Amprysus; others came later—
rivers who, by whatever course they take,

---

7. The laurel tree, sacred to Apollo, was the
symbol of victory not only in athletic contests
but also in war; victorious Roman generals
honored with a triumphal procession through

the city to the Capitol wore a laurel wreath.
The oak was sacred to Jupiter.
8. A region of central Greece.

eventually bring their flowing streams,
weary of their meandering, to sea.

    Inachus[9] was the only river absent,
concealed in the recesses of his cave:
he added to his volume with the tears
he grimly wept for his lost daughter Io,
not knowing whether she still lived or not;
but since he couldn't find her anywhere,
assumed that she was nowhere to be found—
and in his heart, he feared a fate far worse.

    For Jupiter had seen the girl returning
from her father's banks and had accosted her:
"O maiden worthy of almighty Jove
and destined to delight some lucky fellow
(I know not whom) upon your wedding night,
come find some shade," he said, "in these deep woods—"
(showing her where the woods were *very* shady)
"while the sun blazes high above the earth!

    "But if you're worried about entering
the haunts of savage beasts all by yourself,
why, under the protection of a god
you will be safe within the deepest woods—
and no plebeian god, for I am he
who bears the celestial scepter in his hand,
I am he who hurls the roaming thunderbolt—
don't run from me!"

                But run she did, through Lerna
and Lyrcea,[1] until the god concealed
the land entirely beneath a dense
dark mist and seized her and dishonored her.

    Juno,[2] however, happened to look down
on Argos, where she noticed something odd:
swift-flying clouds had turned day into night
long before nighttime. She realized
that neither falling mist nor rising fog
could be the cause of this phenomenon,
and looked about at once to find her husband,
as one too well aware of the connivings
of a mate so often taken in the act.

    When he could not be found above, she said,
"Either I'm mad—or I am being had."
She glided down to earth from heaven's summit
immediately and dispersed the clouds.

    Having intuited his wife's approach,
Jove had already metamorphosed Io
into a gleaming heifer—a beauty still,
even as a cow. Despite herself,

805

810

815

820

825

830

835

840

845

---

9. A river near Argos in the northeast Peloponnesus.
1. A mountain on the border between Argos

and Arcadia to the west. "Lerna": a marsh in
the territory of Argos, near the coast.
2. Wife of Jupiter (Hera in Greek).

Juno gave this illusion her approval,   850
and feigning ignorance, asked him whose herd
this heifer had come out of, and where from;
Jove, lying to forestall all inquiries
as to her origin and pedigree,
replied that she was born out of the earth.   855
Then Juno asked him for her as a gift.

    What could he do? Here is his beloved:
to hand her over is unnatural,
but not to do so would arouse suspicion;
shame urged him onward while love held him back.   860
Love surely would have triumphed over shame,
except that to deny so slight a gift
to one who was his wife and sister both
would make it seem that this was no mere cow!

    Her rival given up to her at last,   865
Juno feared Jove had more such tricks in mind,
and couldn't feel entirely secure
until she'd placed this heifer in the care
of Argus, the watchman with a hundred eyes:
in strict rotation, his eyes slept in pairs,   870
while those that were not sleeping stayed on guard.
No matter where he stood, he looked at Io,
even when he had turned his back on her.

    He let her graze in daylight; when the sun
set far beneath the earth, he penned her in   875
and placed a collar on her indignant neck.
She fed on leaves from trees and bitter grasses,
and had no bed to sleep on, the poor thing,
but lay upon the ground, not always grassy,
and drank the muddy waters from the streams.   880

    Having no arms, she could not stretch them out
in supplication to her warden, Argus;
and when she tried to utter a complaint
she only mooed—a sound which terrified her,
fearful as she now was of her own voice.   885

    Io at last came to the riverbank
where she had often played; when she beheld
her own slack jaws and newly sprouted horns
in the clear water, she fled, terrified!

    Neither her naiad sisters[3] nor her father   890
knew who this heifer was who followed them
and let herself be petted and admired.
Inachus fed her grasses from his hand;
she licked it and pressed kisses on his palm,
unable to restrain her flowing tears.   895

    If words would just have come, she would have spoken,
telling them who she was, how this had happened,
and begging their assistance in her case;

---

3. River nymphs.

but with her hoof, she drew lines in the dust,
and letters of the words she could not speak   900
told the sad story of her transformation.
    "Oh, wretched me," cried Io's father, clinging
to the lowing calf's horns and snowy neck.
"Oh, wretched me!" he groaned. "Are you the child
for whom I searched the earth in every part?   905
Lost, you were less a grief than you are, found!
    "You make no answer, unable to respond
to our speech in language of your own,
but from your breast come resonant deep sighs
and—all that you can manage now—you *moo*!   910
    "But I—all unaware of this—was busy
arranging marriage for you, in the hopes
of having a son-in-law and grandchildren.
Now I must pick your husband from my herd,
and now must find your offspring there as well!   915
    "Nor can I end this suffering by death;
it is a hurtful thing to be a god,
for the gates of death are firmly closed against me,
and our sorrows must go on forever."
    And while the father mourned his daughter's loss,   920
Argus of the hundred eyes removed her
to pastures farther off and placed himself
high on a mountain peak, a vantage point
from which he could keep watch in all directions.
    The ruler of the heavens cannot bear   925
the sufferings of Io any longer,
and calls his son, born of the Pleiades,[4]
and orders him to do away with Argus.
    Without delay, he takes his winged sandals,
his magic, sleep-inducing wand, and cap;   930
and so equipped, the son of father Jove
glides down from heaven's summit to the earth,
where he removes and leaves behind his cap
and winged sandals, but retains the wand;
and sets out as a shepherd, wandering   935
far from the beaten path, driving before him
a flock of goats he rounds up as he goes,
while playing tunes upon his pipe of reeds.
    The guardian of Juno is quite taken
by this new sound: "Whoever you might be,   940
why not come sit with me upon this rock,"
said Argus, "for that flock of yours will find
the grass is nowhere greener, and you see
that there is shade here suitable for shepherds."
    The grandson of great Atlas takes his seat   945

4. Mercury (Hermes in Greek) was the son of
Maia, one of the Pleiades or daughters of Atlas.
They were changed into stars when the hunter
Orion was pursuing them along with their
mother Pleione, whom he wanted to rape.

and whiles away the hours, chattering
of this and that—and playing on his pipes,
he tries to overcome the watchfulness
of Argus, struggling to stay awake;
even though Slumber closes down some eyes,   950
others stay vigilant. Argus inquired
how the reed pipes, so recently invented,
had come to be, and Mercury responded:

    "On the idyllic mountains of Arcadia,[5]
among the hamadryads[6] of Nonacris,   955
one was renowned, and Syrinx[7] was her name.
Often she fled—successfully—from Satyrs,[8]
and deities of every kind as well,
those of the shady wood and fruited plain.

    "In her pursuits and in virginity   960
Diana was her model, and she wore
her robe hitched up and girt above the knees
just as her goddess did; and if her bow
had been made out of gold, instead of horn,
anyone seeing her might well have thought   965
she *was* the goddess—as, indeed, some did.

    "Wearing his crown of sharp pine needles, Pan[9]
saw her returning once from Mount Lycaeus,[1]
and began to say. . . ."

                       There remained to tell
of how the maiden, having spurned his pleas,   970
fled through the trackless wilds until she came
to where the gently flowing Ladon stopped
her in her flight; how she begged the water nymphs
to change her shape, and how the god, assuming
that he had captured Syrinx, grasped instead   975
a handful of marsh reeds! And while he sighed,
the reeds in his hands, stirred by his own breath,
gave forth a similar, low-pitched complaint!

    The god, much taken by the sweet new voice
of an unprecedented instrument,   980
said this to her: "At least we may converse
with one another—I can have that much."

    That pipe of reeds, unequal in their lengths,
and joined together one-on-one with wax,
took the girl's name, and bears it to this day.   985

    Now Mercury was ready to continue
until he saw that Argus had succumbed,
for all his eyes had been closed down by sleep.
He silences himself and waves his wand

---

5. The rustic central region of the Peloponnesus. Nonacris was a town in its northern part.
6. Tree nymphs.
7. The name means "shepherd's pipe," a
musical instrument made of reeds.
8. Woodland creatures—half man, half goat,

bald, bearded, and highly sexed.
9. A god of the wild mountain pastures and
woods, with goat's feet and horns. He was particularly associated with Arcadia.
1. A high mountain in Arcadia.

above those languid orbs to fix the spell.   990
   Without delay he grasps the nodding head
and where it joins the neck, he severs it
with his curved blade and flings it bleeding down
the steep rock face, staining it with gore.
O Argus, you are fallen, and the light   995
in all your lamps is utterly put out:
one hundred eyes, one darkness all the same!
   But Saturn's daughter[2] rescued them and set
those eyes upon the feathers of her bird,[3]
filling his tail with constellated gems.   1000
   Her rage demanded satisfaction, *now*:
the goddess set a horrifying Fury
before the eyes and the imagination
of her Grecian rival; and in her heart
she fixed a prod that goaded Io on,   1005
driving her in terror through the world
until at last, O Nile, you let her rest
from endless labor; having reached your banks,
she went down awkwardly upon her knees,
and with her neck bent backward, raised her face   1010
as only she could do it, to the stars;
and with her groans and tears and mournful mooing,
entreated Jove, it seemed, to put an end
to her great suffering.
             Jove threw his arms
around the neck of Juno in embrace,   1015
imploring her to end this punishment:
"In future," he said, "put your fears aside:
never again will you have cause to worry—
about *this* one." And swore upon the Styx.[4]
   The goddess was now pacified, and Io   1020
at once began regaining her lost looks,
till she became what she had been before;
her body lost all of its bristling hair,
her horns shrank down, her eyes grew narrower,
her jaws contracted, arms and hands returned,   1025
and hooves divided themselves into nails;
nothing remained of her bovine nature,
unless it was the whiteness of her body.
She had some trouble getting her legs back,
and for a time feared speaking, lest she moo,   1030
and so quite timidly regained her speech.
   She is a celebrated goddess now,
and worshiped by the linen-clad Egyptians.[5]
Her son, Epaphus, is believed to be
sprung from the potent seed of mighty Jove,   1035

2. Juno.
3. The peacock.
4. One of the rivers of the underworld; the gods swore solemn oaths by it.
5. Io was identified with Isis, at least by the Greeks and Romans.

and temples may be found in every city
wherein the boy is honored with his parent.

* * *

FROM BOOK II

[Jove and Europa]

When Mercury had punished her for these
impieties of thought and word,[6] he left
Athena's city, and on beating wings   1145
returned to heaven where his father Jove
took him aside and (without telling him
that his new passion was the reason) said:
  "Dear son, who does my bidding faithfully,
do not delay, but with your usual   1150
swiftness fly down to earth and find the land
that looks up to your mother[7] on the left,
called Sidon[8] by the natives; there you will see
a herd of royal cattle some way off
upon a mountain; drive them down to shore."   1155
  He spoke and it was done as he had ordered:
the cattle were immediately driven
down to a certain place along the shore
where the daughter of a great king used to play,
accompanied by maidens all of Tyre.[9]   1160
  Majestic power and erotic love
do not get on together very well,
nor do they linger long in the same place:
the father and the ruler of all gods,
who holds the lightning bolt in his right hand   1165
and shakes the world when he but nods his head,
now relinquishes authority and power,
assuming the appearance of a bull
to mingle with the other cattle, lowing
as gorgeously he strolls in the new grass.   1170
  He is as white as the untrampled snow
before the south wind turns it into slush.
The muscles stand out bulging on his neck,
and the dewlap[1] dangles on his ample chest;
his horns are crooked, but appear handmade,   1175
and flawless as a pair of matching gems.
His brow is quite unthreatening, his eye

---

6. Mercury has been in Athens, where he tried to have a love affair with Herse, daughter of King Cecrops; promised help and then betrayed by her sister Aglauros, he took his revenge on Aglauros by turning her into a statue.
7. Maia, Mercury's mother, had been transformed into a star among the Pleiades in the constellation Taurus.
8. One of the principal cities of Phoenicia (in modern Lebanon).
9. Another city of Phoenicia, but here used of Phoenicia itself.
1. A fold of loose skin hanging from the neck.

excites no terror, and his countenance
is calm.
    The daughter of King Agenor[2]
admires him, astonished by the presence   1180
of peacefulness and beauty in the beast;
yet even though he seems a gentle creature,
at first she fears to get too close to him,
but soon approaching, reaches out her hand
and pushes flowers into his white mouth.   1185
    The lover, quite beside himself, rejoices,
and as a preview of delights to come,
kisses her fingers, getting so excited
that he can scarcely keep from doing it!
    Now he disports himself upon the grass,   1190
and lays his whiteness on the yellow sands;
and as she slowly overcomes her fear
he offers up his breast for her caresses
and lets her decorate his horns with flowers;
the princess dares to sit upon his back   1195
not knowing who it is that she has mounted,
and he begins to set out from dry land,
a few steps on false feet into the shallows,
then further out and further to the middle
of the great sea he carries off his booty;   1200
she trembles as she sees the shore receding
and holds the creature's horn in her right hand
and with the other clings to his broad back,
her garments streaming in the wind behind her.

FROM BOOK V

[*Ceres and Proserpina*]

As the Muse spoke,[3] Minerva could hear wings
beating on air, and cries of greeting came
from high in the trees. She peered into the foliage,   430
attempting to discover where those sounds,
the speech of human beings to be sure,
were emanating from: why, from some birds!
Bewailing their sad fate, a flock of nine
magpies (which mimic anyone they wish to)   435
had settled in the branches overhead.
    Minerva having shown astonishment,
the Muse gave her a little goddess-chat:
"This lot has only recently been added
to the throngs of birds. Why? They lost a contest!   440

---

2. Europa. Agenor was the Phoenician king.
3. Minerva (Athena in Greek) has come to
Mount Helicon in central Greece, the home
of the nine Muses (daughters of Zeus and

Memory, they are patronesses of poetry and
the other arts). One of the Muses has told her
of an attempt recently made to trap and rape
them by the wicked Pyreneus.

Their father was Pierus, lord of Pella,[4]
their mother was Evippe of Paeonia;
nine times she called upon Lucina's[5] aid
and nine times she delivered. Swollen up
with foolish pride because they were so many,   445
that crowd of simpleminded sisters went
through all Haemonia and through Achaea[6] too,
arriving here to challenge us in song:
     "'We'll show you girls just what real class is[7]
Give up tryin' to deceive the masses   450
Your rhymes are fake: accept our wager
Learn which of us is minor and which is major
There's nine of us here and there's nine of you
And you'll be nowhere long before we're through
Nothin's gonna save you 'cuz your songs are lame   455
And the way you sing 'em is really a shame
So stop with, "Well I *never!*" and "This *can't* be real!"
We're the newest New Thing and here is our deal
If we beat you, obsolete you, then you just get gone
From these classy haunts on Mount Helicon   460
We give you Macedonia—*if* we lose
An' that's an offer you just can't refuse
So take the wings off, sisters, get down and jam
And let the nymphs be the judges of our poetry slam!'
     "Shameful it was to strive against such creatures;   465
more shameful not to. Nymphs were picked as judges,
sworn into service on their river banks,
and took their seats on benches made of tufa.
     "And then—not even drawing lots!—the one
who claimed to be their champion commenced;   470
she sang of war between the gods and Giants,
giving the latter credit more than due
and deprecating all that the great gods did;
how Typhoeus,[8] from earth's lowest depths,
struck fear in every celestial heart,   475
so that they all turned tail and fled, until,
exhausted, they found refuge down in Egypt,
where the Nile flows from seven distinct mouths;
she sang of how earthborn Typhoeus
pursued them even here and forced the gods   480
to hide themselves by taking fictive shapes:[9]
     "'In Libya the Giants told the gods to scram

4. City of Macedonia, in northern Greece. The Paeonians were a tribe living north of Macedonia.
5. Goddess of childbirth.
6. Regions of central Greece (Haemonia is another name for Thessaly). The sisters are traveling south toward Helicon.
7. Although there is no basis for it in the Latin text, the translator uses dialect and rhyme in

the speeches and song of Pierus's daughters to show how they challenge, and partially deflate, the "high-culture" assumptions and language of the Muses.
8. Monstrous son of Earth. Like the Earthborn Giants, he challenged Jupiter and the Olympian gods and was defeated.
9. An "explanation" of the Egyptian gods' animal forms.

The boss god they worship there has horns like a ram[1]
'Cuz Jupiter laid low as the leader of a flock
And Delius[2] his homey really got a shock   485
When the Giants left him with no place to go:
"Fuggedabout Apollo—make me a crow!"
And if you believe that Phoebus was a wuss
His sister Phoebe turned into a puss
Bacchus takes refuge in the skin of a goat   490
And Juno as a cow with a snow-white coat
Venus the queen of the downtown scene, yuh know what her wish is?
"Gimme a body just like a fish's"
Mercury takes on an ibis's shape
And that's how the mighty (cheep cheep) gods escape'   495
   "And then her song, accompanied on the lute,
came to an end, and it was our turn—
but possibly you haven't got the time
to listen to our song?"
                         "Oh, don't think that,"
Minerva said. "I want it word for word: 500
sing it for me just as you sang it then."
   The Muse replied: "We turned the contest over
to one of us, Calliope,[3] who rose,
and after binding up her hair in ivy
and lightly strumming a few plaintive chords,   505
she vigorously launched into her song:

   "'Ceres[4] was first to break up the soil with a curved plowshare,
the first to give us the earth's fruits and to nourish us gently,
and the first to give laws: every gift comes from Ceres.
The goddess must now be my subject. Would that I *could* sing   510
a hymn that is worthy of her, for she surely deserves it.
   "'Vigorous Sicily sprawled across the gigantic body
of one who had dared aspire to rule in the heavens;
the island's weight held Typhoeus firmly beneath it.
Often exerting himself, he strives yet again to rise up,   515
but there in the north, his right hand is held down by Pelorus,
his left hand by you, Pachynus; off in the west, Lilybaeum[5]
weighs on his legs, while Mount Etna[6] presses his head, as
under it, raging Typhoeus coughs ashes and vomits up fire.
Often he struggles, attempting to shake off the earth's weight   520
and roll its cities and mountains away from his body.
   "'This causes tremors and panics the Lord of the Silent,[7]
who fears that the earth's crust will crack and break open,
and daylight, let in, will frighten the trembling phantoms;

---

1. Ammon, the chief Egyptian god, identified
by the Greeks and Romans with Zeus/Jupiter.
He had an important oracular cult in the Libyan desert (west of the Nile valley and part of
Egypt under Roman rule).
2. Apollo, who was born on the island of
Delos.

3. "Lovely Voice," the Muse of epic poetry.
4. Goddess of grain (Demeter).
5. Mountains on the northeast, southeast, and
western promontories of Sicily, respectively.
6. The large (and still active) volcano near the
center of the east coast of Sicily.
7. Pluto or Hades, king of the dead.

dreading disaster, the tyrant left his tenebrous kingdom;   525
borne in his chariot drawn by its team of black horses,
he crisscrossed Sicily, checking the island's foundation.
   "'After his explorations had left him persuaded
that none of its parts were in imminent danger of falling,
his fears were forgotten, and Venus, there on Mount Eryx,[8]   530
observed him relaxing, and said, as she drew Cupid near her,
"My son, my sword, my strong right arm and source of my power,
take up that weapon by which all your victims are vanquished
and send your swift arrows into the breast of the deity
to whom the last part of the threefold realm[9] was allotted.   535
   "'"You govern the gods and their ruler; you rule the defeated
gods of the ocean and govern the one who rules them, too;
why give up on the dead, when we can extend our empire
into their realm? A third part of the world is involved here!
And yet the celestial gods spurn our forbearance,   540
and the prestige of Love is diminished, even as mine is.
Do you not see how Athena and huntress Diana
have both taken leave of me?[1] The virgin daughter of Ceres
desires to do likewise—and will, if we let her!
But if you take pride in our alliance, advance it   545
by joining her to her uncle!"[2]
                    "'Venus ceased speaking and Cupid
loosened his quiver, and, just as his mother had ordered,
selected, from thousands of missiles, the one that was sharpest
and surest and paid his bow the closest attention,
and using one knee to bend its horn back almost double,   550
he pierces the heart of Dis with his barb-tipped arrow.
   "'Near Henna's[3] walls stands a deep pool of water, called Pergus:
not even the river Cayster,[4] flowing serenely,
hears more songs from its swans; this pool is completely surrounded
by a ring of tall trees, whose foliage, just like an awning,   555
keeps out the sun and preserves the water's refreshing coolness;
the moist ground is covered with flowers of Tyrian purple;
here it is springtime forever. And here Proserpina
was playfully picking its white lilies and violets,
and, while competing to gather up more than her playmates,   560
filling her basket and stuffing the rest in her bosom,
Dis saw her, was smitten, seized her and carried her off;
his love was that hasty. The terrified goddess cried out
for her mother, her playmates—but for her mother most often,
since she had torn the uppermost seam of her garment,   565
and the gathered flowers rained down from her negligent tunic;
because of her tender years and her childish simplicity,
even this loss could move her to maidenly sorrow.

---

8. Mountain in western Sicily with an important cult of Venus.
9. The underworld, ruled by Pluto. The other
parts of the "threefold realm" are the sea (ruled
by Neptune) and the sky or Mount Olympus
(Jupiter).

1. Both were perpetual virgins.
2. Pluto (also called Dis) was the brother of
Jupiter, the father by Ceres of Proserpina.
3. A city in central Sicily.
4. River in Lydia in Asia Minor, famous for its
many swans.

"'Her abductor rushed off in his chariot, urging his horses,
calling each one by its name and flicking the somber,   570
rust-colored reins over their backs as they galloped
through the deep lakes and the sulphurous pools of Palike
that boil up through the ruptured earth, and where the Bacchiadae,
a race sprung from Corinth, that city between the two seas,
had raised their own walls between two unequal harbors.[5]   575
   "'There is a bay that is landlocked almost completely
between the two pools of Cyane and Pisaean Arethusa,
the residence of the most famous nymph in all Sicily,
Cyane, who gave her very own name to the fountain.
She showed herself now, emerged from her pool at waist level,   580
and recognizing the goddess, told Dis, "Go no further!
You cannot become the son-in-law of great Ceres
against her will: you should have asked and not taken!
If it is right for me to compare lesser with greater,
I accepted Anapis[6] when he desired to have me,   585
yielding to pleas and not—as in *this* case—to terror."
She spoke, and stretching her arms out in either direction,
kept him from passing. That son of Saturn could scarcely
hold back his anger; he urged on his frightening horses,
and then, with his strong right arm, he hurled his scepter   590
directly into the very base of the fountain;
the stricken earth opened a path to the underworld
and took in the chariot rushing down into its crater.
   "'Cyane, lamenting not just the goddess abducted,
but also the disrespect shown for *her* rights as a fountain,   595
tacitly nursed in her heart an inconsolable sorrow;
and she who had once been its presiding spirit,
reduced to tears, dissolved right into its substance.
You would have seen her members beginning to soften,
her bones and her fingertips starting to lose their old firmness;   600
her slenderest parts were the first to be turned into fluid:
her feet, her legs, her sea-dark tresses, her fingers
(for the parts with least flesh turn into liquid most quickly);
and after these, her shoulders and back and her bosom
and flanks completely vanished in trickling liquid;   605
and lastly the living blood in her veins is replaced by
springwater, and nothing remains that you could have seized on.
   "'Meanwhile, the terrified mother was pointlessly seeking
her daughter all over the earth and deep in the ocean.
Neither Aurora, appearing with dew-dampened tresses,   610
nor Hesperus[7] knew her to quit; igniting two torches
of pine from the fires of Etna, the care-ridden goddess
used them to illumine the wintery shadows of nighttime;
and when the dear day had once more dimmed out the bright stars,
she searched again for her daughter from sunrise to sunset.   615

5. Syracuse, on the southeastern coast of Sicily, founded by Corinthian colonists in the 8th
century B.C.E. The Bacchiadae were a leading
family who then ruled Corinth.

6. A river that empties into the sea near
Syracuse.

7. The evening star. "Aurora": goddess of the
dawn.

"'Worn out by her labors and suffering thirst, with no fountain
to wet her lips at, she happened upon a thatched hovel
and knocked at its humble door, from which there came forth
a crone who looked at the goddess, and, when asked for water,
gave her a sweet drink, sprinkled with toasted barley.   620
And, as she drank it, a boy with a sharp face and bold manner
stood right before her and mocked her and said she was greedy.
Angered by what he was saying, the goddess drenched him
with all she had not yet drunk of the barley mixture.
The boy's face thirstily drank up the spots as his arms were   625
turned into legs, and a tail was joined to his changed limbs;
so that he should now be harmless, the boy was diminished,
and he was transformed into a very small lizard.
Astonished, the old woman wept and reached out to touch him,
but the marvelous creature fled her, seeking a hideout.   630
He now has a name appropriate to his complexion,
Stellio, from the con*stella*tions spotting his body.

"'To speak of the lands and seas the goddess mistakenly searched
would take far too long; the earth exhausted her seeking;
she came back to Sicily; and, as she once more traversed it,   635
arrived at Cyane, who would have told her the story
had she not herself been changed; but, though willing in spirit,
her mouth, tongue, and vocal apparatus were absent;
nevertheless, she gave proof that was clear to the mother:
Persephone's girdle (which happened by chance to have fallen   640
into the fountain) now lay exposed on its surface.

"'Once recognizing it, the goddess knew that her daughter
had been taken, and tore her hair into utter disorder,
and repeatedly struck her breasts with the palms of both hands.
With her daughter's location a mystery still, she reproaches   645
the whole earth as ungrateful, unworthy her gift of grain crops,
and Sicily more than the others, where she has discovered
the proof of her loss; and so it was here that her fierce hand
shattered the earth-turning plows, here that the farmers and cattle
perished alike, and here that she bade the plowed fields   650
default on their trust by blighting the seeds in their keeping.
Sicilian fertility, which had been everywhere famous,
was given the lie when the crops died as they sprouted,
now ruined by too much heat, and now by too heavy a rainfall;
stars and winds harmed them, and the greedy birds devoured   655
the seed as it was sown; the harvest of wheat was defeated
by thorns and darnels and unappeasable grasses.

"'Then Arethusa[8] lifted her head from the Elean waters
and swept her dripping hair back away from her forehead,
saying, "O Mother of Grain—and mother, too, of that virgin   660
sought through the whole world—here end your incessant labors,
lest your great anger should injure the earth you once trusted,
and which, unwillingly pillaged, has done nothing ignoble;

---

8. A spring in Syracuse. Its waters are "Elean" because they were believed to originate in the
district of Pisa in Elis, a region of the western Peloponnesus in mainland Greece.

nor do I plead for my nation, since I am a guest here:
my nation is Pisa, I am descended from Elis,   665
and live as a stranger in Sicily—this land that delights me
more than all others on earth; here Arethusa
dwells with her household gods. Spare it, merciful goddess,
and when your cares and countenance both have been lightened,
there will come an opportune time to tell you the reason   670
why I was taken from home and borne off to Ortygia[9]
over a waste of waters. The earth gave me access,
showed me a path, and, swept on through underground caverns,
I raised my head here to an unfamiliar night sky.
But while gliding under the earth on a Stygian river,   675
I saw with my very own eyes your dear Proserpina;
grief and terror were still to be seen in her features,
yet she was nonetheless queen of that shadowy kingdom,
the all-powerful consort of the underworld's ruler."
    "'The mother was petrified by the speech of the fountain,   680
and stood for a very long time as though she were senseless,
until her madness had been driven off by her outrage,
and then she set out in her chariot for the ethereal regions;
once there, with her face clouded over and hair all disheveled,
she planted herself before Jove and fiercely addressed him: 685
"Jupiter, I have come here as a suppliant, speaking
for my child—and yours: if you have no regard for her mother,
relent as her father—don't hold her unworthy, I beg you,
simply because *I* am the child's other parent!
The daughter I sought for so long is at last recovered,   690
if to recover means only to lose much more surely,
or if to recover means just to learn her location!
Her theft could be borne—if only he would return her!
Then let him do it, for surely *Jove's* daughter is worthy
of a mate who's no brigand, even if *my* daughter isn't."   695
    "'Jupiter answered her, "She is indeed *our* daughter,
the pledge of our love and our common concern,
but if you will kindly agree to give things their right names,
this is not an injury requiring my retribution,
but an act of love by a son-in-law who won't shame you,   700
goddess, if you give approval; though much were lacking,
how much it is to be Jove's brother! But he lacks nothing,
and only yields to me that which the Fates have allotted.
Still, if you're so keen on parting them, your Proserpina
may come back to heaven—but only on one condition: 705
that she has not touched food, for so the Fates have required."

    "'He spoke and Ceres was sure she would get back her daughter,
though the Fates were not, for the girl had already placated
her hunger while guilelessly roaming death's formal gardens,
where, from a low-hanging branch, she had plucked without thinking   710

---

9. The island on which Syracuse was originally built and on which the Arethusan spring was
located.

a pomegranate, and peeling its pale bark off, devoured
seven of its seeds. No one saw her but Ascalaphus
(whom it is said that Orphne, a not undistinguished
nymph among those of Avernus, pregnant by Acheron,[1]
gave birth to there in the underworld's dark-shadowed forest);   715
he saw, and by his disclosure, kept her from returning.
    "'Raging, the Queen of the Underworld turned that informer
into a bird of ill omen: sprinkling the waters
of Phlegethon[2] into the face of Ascalaphus,
she gave him a beak and plumage and eyes quite enormous.   720
Lost to himself, he is clad now in yellow-brown pinions,
his head increases in size and his nails turn to talons,
but the feathers that spring from his motionless arms scarcely flutter;
a filthy bird he's become, the grim announcer of mourning,
a slothful portent of evil to mortals—the owl.   725

    "'That one, because of his tattling tongue, seems quite worthy
of punishment,—but you, daughters of Acheloüs,[3]
why do you have the plumage of birds and the faces of virgins?
Is it because while Proserpina gathered her flowers,
you, artful Sirens, were numbered among her companions?   730
No sooner had you scoured the whole earth in vain for her
than you desired the vast seas to feel your devotion,
and prayed to the gods, whom you found willing to help you,
that you might skim over the flood upon oars that were pinions,
then saw your limbs turn suddenly golden with plumage.   735
And so that your tunefulness, which the ear finds so pleasing,
should not be lost, nor your gifts of vocal expression,
your maidenly faces remain, along with your voices.

    "'But poised between his sorrowing sister and brother,
great Jove divided the year into two equal portions,   740
so now in two realms the shared goddess holds sway,
and as many months spent with her mother are spent with her husband.
She changed her mind then, and changed her expression to match it,
and now her fair face, which even Dis found depressing,
beams as the sun does, when, after having been hidden   745
before in dark clouds, at last it emerges in triumph.

    "'Her daughter safely restored to her, kindhearted Ceres
wishes to hear *your* story now, Arethusa—
what did you flee from and what changed you into a fountain?
The splashing waters are stilled: the goddess raises   750
her head from their depths and wrings dry her virid tresses,
then tells the old tale of the river Alpheus'[4] passion.
    "'"Once I was one of the nymphs who dwell in Achaea,"

---

1. Acheron ("Woe") is one of the rivers, and
Avernus a lake, in the underworld. The name
Orphne means "darkness" in Greek.
2. Fiery river of the underworld.
3. The Sirens, familiar from book 12 of the

Odyssey and often associated with death in
post-Homeric literature and art. Acheloüs is a
large river in northwest Greece.
4. River that flows past Olympia in Elis.

she said, "and none had more zeal than I for traversing
the mountain pastures or setting out snares for small game.   755
But even though I did not seek to find fame as a beauty,
men called me that, my courage and strength notwithstanding;
nor was I pleased that my beauty was lauded so often,
and for my corporeal nature (which most other maidens
are wont to take pleasure in) I blushed like a rustic,   760
thinking it wrong to please men.
                           "'"Exhausted from hunting,
I was on my way back from the Stymphalian forest,[5]
and the fierce heat of the day was doubled by my exertions.
By chance I came on a stream, gently and silently flowing,
clear to the bottom, where you could count every pebble,   765
water so still you would scarcely believe it was moving.
Silvery willows and poplars, which the stream nourished,
artlessly shaded its banks as they sloped to the water.
   "'"At once I approach and wiggle my toes in its wetness,
then wade in up to my knees—not satisfied wholly,   770
I strip off my garments and hang them up on a willow,
and, naked, merge with the waters. I strike and stroke them,
gliding below and thrashing about on the surface,
then hear a strange murmur that seems to come from the bottom,
which sends me scampering onto the near bank in terror: 775
'Why the great rush?' Alpheus cries from his waters,
then hoarsely repeating, 'Why the great rush, Arethusa?'
Just as I am, I flee without clothing (my garments
were on the bank opposite); aroused, Alpheus pursues me,
my nakedness making me seem more ripe for the taking.   780
   "'"Thus did I run, and thus did that fierce one press after,
as doves on trembling pinions flee from the kestrel,
as kestrels pursue the trembling doves and assault them.
To Orchomenus and past, to Psophis, Cyllene,
the folds of Maenalia, Erymanthus,[6] and Elis,   785
I continued to run, nor was he faster than I was;
but since Alpheus was so much stronger, I couldn't
outrun him for long, given his greater endurance.
   "'"Nonetheless, I still managed to keep on running
across the wide fields, up wooded mountains,   790
on bare rocks, steep cliffs, in wastes wild and trackless;
with the sun at my back, I could see his shadow before me,
stretched out on the ground, unless my panic deceived me;
but surely I *did* hear those frightening footsteps behind me,
and felt his hot breath lifting the hair from my shoulders.   795
   "'"Worn with exertion, I cried out, 'Help! Or I'm taken!
Aid your armoress, Diana—to whom you have often
entrusted your bow, along with your quiver of arrows!'
The goddess was moved by my plea and at once I was hidden

---

5. The woods surrounding Lake Stymphalus   6. Towns and mountains of Arcadia.
in Arcadia.

in a dense cloud of fine mist:[7] the river god, clueless,   800
circled around me, hidden in darkness, searching;
twice he unknowingly passed by the place where the goddess
had hidden me, and twice he called, 'Yo! Arethusa!'
How wretched was I? Why, even as the lamb is,
at hearing the howling of wolves around the sheepfold,   805
or as the rabbit in the briar patch who glimpses
the dog's fierce muzzle and feels too frightened to tremble.
   "'"Alpheus remained there, for as he noticed no footprints
heading away from the cloud, he continued to watch it.
An icy sweat thoroughly drenched the limbs that he looked for,   810
and the dark drops poured from every part of my body;
wherever my foot had been, there was a puddle,
and my hair shed moisture. More swiftly than I can tell it,
I turned into liquid—even so, he recognized me,
his darling there in the water, and promptly discarded   815
the human form he had assumed for the occasion,
reverting to river, so that our fluids might mingle.
Diana shattered the earth's crust; I sank down,
and was swept on through sightless caverns, off to Ortygia,
so pleasing to me because it's the goddess's birthplace;[8]   820
and here I first rose up into the air as a fountain."

   "'Here Arethusa concluded. The fruitful goddess summoned
her team of dragons and yoked them onto her chariot;
and guiding their heads with the reins, she was transported
up through the middle air that lies between earth and heaven   825
until she arrived in Athens, and, giving her carriage
to Triptolemus,[9] ordered him to go off and scatter
grain on the earth—some on land that had never been broken,
and some on land that had been a long time fallow.
   "'The young man was carried high up over Europe and Asia   830
until at last he came to the kingdom of Scythia.
Lyncus was king here; he brought him into his palace,
and asked him his name, his homeland, the cause of his journey,
and how he had come there.
                         "'"My well-known homeland," he answered,
"is Athens; I am Triptolemus; neither by ship upon water   835
nor foot upon land have I come here; the air itself parted
to make me a path on which I coursed through the heavens.
I bear you the gifts of Ceres, which, sown in your broad fields,
will yield a bountiful harvest of nourishing produce."
   "'This the barbarian heard with great envy, and wishing   840
that he himself might be perceived as the donor,
took him in as a guest, and while the young man was sleeping,
approached with a sword, and as he attempted to stab him,

7. Conventional means in ancient epic of   Diana was born, was also called Ortygia.
making someone invisible.   9. Son of the king of Eleusis, the great cult
8. The Ortygia where Arethusa ended up was   center of Demeter (Ceres) near Athens.
in Syracuse, but Delos, the Aegean island where

Ceres changed *Lyncus* to *lynx*, and ordered Triptolemus
to drive her sacred team through the air back to Athens.'   845

    "When our eldest sister had concluded
her superb performance, with one voice
the nymphs awarded victory to . . . the Muses!
    "And when the others, in defeat, reviled us,
I answered them: 'Since you display such nerve   850
in challenging the Muses, you deserve
chastisement—even more so since you've added
insult to outrage: our wise forbearance
is not without its limits, as you'll learn
when we get to the penalties, and vent   855
our righteous anger on your worthless selves.'
    "Then the Pierides[1] mock our threats,
and as they try to answer us by shouting
vulgarities and giving us the finger,
their fingers take on feathers and their arms   860
turn into pinions! Each one sees a beak
replace a sister's face, as a new bird
is added to the species of the forest;
and as they try to beat upon their breasts,
bewailing their new situation, they   865
all hang suspended, flapping in the air,
the forest's scandal—the P-Airides![2]
    "And even though they are all feathered now,
their speech remains as fluent as it was,
and they are famous for their noisiness   870
as well as for their love of argument."

FROM BOOK IX

[Iphis and Isis]

Rumor might very well have spread the news   960
of this unprecedented transformation[3]
throughout the hundred towns of Crete, if they
had not just had a wonder of their own
to talk about—the change that came to Iphis.
    For, once upon a time, there lived in Phaestus,   965
not far from the royal capital at Cnossus,
a freeborn plebeian named Ligdus, who
was otherwise unknown and undistinguished,
with no more property than fame or status,
and yet devout, and blameless in his life.   970
    His wife was pregnant. When her time had come,
he gave her his instructions with these words:
"There are two things I pray to heaven for
on your account: an easy birth and a son.

1. The daughters of Pierus.
2. The translator's pun on the name Pierides.

3. The transformation of Byblis, who loved
her brother Caunus, into a fountain.

The other fate is much too burdensome,   975
for daughters need what Fortune has denied us:
a dowry.
            "Therefore—and may God prevent
this happening, but if, by chance, it does
and you should be delivered of a girl,
unwillingly I order this, and beg   980
pardon for my impiety—*But let it die!*"
    He spoke, and tears profusely bathed the cheeks
of the instructor and instructed both.
Telethusa continued to implore
her husband, praying him not to confine   985
their hopes so narrowly—to no avail,
for he would not be moved from his decision.
    Now scarcely able to endure the weight
of her womb's burden, as she lay in bed
at midnight, a dream-vision came to her: 990
the goddess Io[4] stood (or seemed to stand)
before her troubled bed, accompanied
with solemn pomp by all her mysteries.
    She wore her crescent horns upon her brow
and a garland made of gleaming sheaves of wheat,   995
and a queenly diadem; behind her stood
the dog-faced god Anubis, and divine
Bubastis (who defends the lives of cats),
and Apis as a bull clothed in a hide
of varied colors, with Harpocrates,   1000
the god whose fingers, pressed against his lips,
command our silence; and one often sought
by his devoted worshipers—Osiris;[5]
and the asp, so rich in sleep-inducing drops.
She seemed to wake, and saw them all quite clearly.   1005
    These were the words the goddess spoke to her:
"O Telethusa, faithful devotee,
put off your heavy cares! Disobey your spouse,
and do not hesitate, when Lucina
has lightened the burden of your labor,   1010
to raise this child, whatever it will be.
I am that goddess who, when asked, delivers,
and you will have no reason to complain
that honors you have paid me were in vain."
After instructing her, the goddess left.   1015
    The Cretan woman rose up joyfully,
lifted her hands up to the stars, and prayed
that her dream-vision would be ratified.
    Then going into labor, she brought forth
a daughter—though her husband did not know it.   1020

---

4. Identified with the Egyptian Isis, goddess of fertility, marriage, and maternity, whose cult was widespread in the Roman world.

5. Husband of Isis, killed by his brother Set and restored to life by Isis; he is thus a figure of rebirth.

The mother (with intention to deceive)
told them *to feed the boy*. Deception prospered,
since no one knew the truth except the nurse.
   The father thanked the gods and named the child
for its grandfather, Iphis; since this name   1025
was given men and women both, his mother
was pleased, for she could use it honestly.
So from her pious lie, deception grew.
She dressed it as a boy—its face was such
that whether boy or girl, it was a beauty.   1030
   Meanwhile, the years went by, thirteen of them:
your father, Iphis, has arranged for you
a marriage to the golden-haired Ianthe,
the daughter of a Cretan named Telestes,
the maid most praised in Phaestus[6] for her beauty.   1035
The two were similar in age and looks,
and had been taught together from the first.
   First love came unexpected to both hearts
and wounded them both equally—and yet
their expectations were quite different: 1040
Ianthe can look forward to a time
of wedding torches and of wedding vows,
and trusts that one whom she believes a man
will be *her* man. Iphis, however, loves
with hopeless desperation, which increases   1045
in strict proportion to its hopelessness,
and burns—a maiden—for another maid!
   And scarcely holding back her tears, she cries,
"Oh, what will be the end reserved for Iphis,
gripped by a strange and monstrous passion known   1050
to no one else? If the gods had wished to spare me,
they should have; if they wanted to destroy me,
they should have given me a natural affliction.
   "Cows do not burn for cows, nor mares for mares;
the ram will have his sheep, the stag his does,   1055
and birds will do the same when they assemble;
there are no animals whose females lust
for other females! I wish that I were dead!
   "That Crete might bring forth monsters of all kinds.
Queen Pasiphaë[7] was taken by a bull,   1060
yet even *that* was male-and-female passion!
My love is much less rational than hers,
to tell the truth. At least she had the hope
of satisfaction, taking in the bull
through guile, and in the image of a cow,   1065
thereby deceiving the adulterer!
   "If every form of ingenuity
were gathered here from all around the world,

6. A city in Crete.
7. Wife of King Minos of Crete, and mother by a bull of the Minotaur.

if Daedalus[8] flew back on waxen wings,
what could he do? Could all his learnèd arts   1070
transform me from a girl into a boy?
Or could *you* change into a boy, Ianthe?

  "But really, Iphis, pull yourself together,
be firm, cast off this stultifying passion:
accept your birth—unless you would deceive   1075
yourself as well as others—look for love
where it is proper to, as a woman should!
Hope both creates and nourishes such love;
reality deprives you of all hope.

  "No watchman keeps you from her dear embrace,   1080
no husband's ever-vigilant concern,
no father's fierceness, nor does she herself
deny the gifts that you would have from her.
And yet you are denied all happiness,
nor could it have been otherwise if all   1085
the gods and men had labored in your cause.

  "But the gods have not denied me anything;
agreeably, they've given what they could;
my father wishes for me what *I* wish,
she and her father both would have it be;   1090
but Nature, much more powerful than they are,
wishes it not—sole source of all my woe!

  "But look—the sun has risen and the day
of our longed-for nuptials dawns at last!
Ianthe will be mine—and yet not mine: 1095
we die of thirst here at the fountainside.

  "Why do you, Juno, guardian of brides,
and you, O Hymen, god of marriage, come
to these rites, which cannot be rites at all,
for no one takes the bride, and both are veiled?"   1100

  She said no more. Nor did her chosen burn
less fiercely as she prayed you swiftly come,
O god of marriage.
                    Fearing what you sought,
Telethusa postponed the marriage day
with one concocted pretext and another,   1105
a fictive illness or an evil omen.
But now she had no more excuses left,
and the wedding day was only one day off.

  She tears the hair bands from her daughter's head
and from her own, and thus unbound, she prayed   1110
while desperately clinging to the altar:
"O holy Isis, who art pleased to dwell
and be worshiped at Paraetonium,
at Pharos, in the Mareotic fields,

8. Fabled craftsman who devised the heifer disguise that enabled Pasiphaë to seduce the bull and, later, built the labyrinth for the Minotaur. Forced to flee Crete, he made wings of feathers held together by wax, for himself and his son, Icarus.

and where the Nile splits into seven branches; 1115
deliver us, I pray you, from our fear!

"For I once saw thee and thy sacred emblems,
O goddess, and I recognized them all
and listened to the sound of brazen rattles[9]
and kept your orders in my memory. 1120

"And that my daughter still looks on the light,
and that I have not suffered punishment,
why, this is all your counsel and your gift;
now spare us both and offer us your aid."

Warm tears were in attendance on her words. 1125
The altar of the goddess seemed to move—
it *did* move, and the temple doors were shaken,
and the horns (her lunar emblem) glowed with light,
and the bronze rattles sounded.

               Not yet secure,
but nonetheless delighted by this omen, 1130
the mother left with Iphis following,
as was her wont, but now with longer strides,
darker complexion, and with greater force,
a keener countenance, and with her hair
shorter than usual and unadorned, 1135
and with more vigor than a woman has.

And you who were so recently a girl
are now a boy! Bring gifts to the goddess!
Now boldly celebrate your faith in her!
They bring the goddess gifts and add to them 1140
a votive tablet with these lines inscribed:

GIFTS IPHIS PROMISED WHEN SHE WAS A MAID
TRANSFORMED INTO A BOY HE GLADLY PAID

The next day's sun revealed the great wide world
with Venus, Juno, and Hymen all together 1145
gathered beneath the smoking nuptial torches,
and Iphis in possession of Ianthe.

FROM BOOK X[1]

[Pygmalion]

"Pygmalion observed how these women[2] lived lives of sordid
indecency, and, dismayed by the numerous defects
of character Nature had given the feminine spirit,
stayed as a bachelor, having no female companion. 315

---

9. Sistra, sacred rattles used in Isis's cult.
1. This selection of stories is part of the song
sung by Orpheus, the legendary singer, after he
has failed to redeem his wife, Eurydice, from
the underworld. His theme, announced in the
prologue of his song, is "young boys whom the
gods have desired, / and . . . girls seized by forbidden and blameworthy passions."
2. Orpheus has just told of the Propoetides of
Cyprus, who, as punishment for having denied
Venus's divinity, became the first women to
prostitute themselves.

"During that time he created an ivory statue,
a work of most marvelous art, and gave it a figure
better than any living woman could boast of,
and promptly conceived a passion for his own creation.
You would have thought it alive, so like a real maiden   320
that only its natural modesty kept it from moving:
art concealed artfulness. Pygmalion gazed in amazement,
burning with love for what was in likeness a body.

"Often he stretched forth a hand to touch his creation,
attempting to settle the issue: *was* it a body,   325
or was it—this he would not yet concede—a mere statue?
He gives it kisses, and they are returned, he imagines;
now he addresses and now he caresses it, feeling
his fingers sink into its warm, pliant flesh, and
fears he will leave blue bruises all over its body;   330
he seeks to win its affections with words and with presents
pleasing to girls, such as seashells and pebbles, tame birds,
armloads of flowers in thousands of different colors,
lilies, bright painted balls, curious insects in amber;
he dresses it up and puts diamond rings on its fingers,   335
gives it a necklace, a lacy brassiere and pearl earrings,
and even though all such adornments truly become her,
she does not seem to be any less beautiful naked.
He lays her down on a bed with a bright purple cover
and calls her his bedmate and slips a few soft, downy pillows 340
under her head as though she were able to feel them.

"The holiday honoring Venus has come, and all Cyprus[3]
turns out to celebrate; heifers with gilded horns buckle
under the deathblow[4] and incense soars up in thick clouds;
having already brought his own gift to the altar,   345
Pygmalion stood by and offered this fainthearted prayer:
'If you in heaven are able to give us whatever
we ask for, then I would like as my wife—' and not daring
to say, '—my ivory maiden,' said, '—one like my statue!'
Since golden Venus was present there at her altar,   350
she knew what he wanted to ask for, and as a good omen,
three times the flames soared and leapt right up to the heavens.

"Once home, he went straight to the replica of his sweetheart,
threw himself down on the couch and repeatedly kissed her;
she seemed to grow warm and so he repeated the action,   355
kissing her lips and exciting her breasts with both hands.
Aroused, the ivory softened and, losing its stiffness,
yielded, submitting to his caress as wax softens
when it is warmed by the sun, and handled by fingers,
takes on many forms, and by being used, becomes useful.   360
Amazed, he rejoices, then doubts, then fears he's mistaken,
while again and again he touches on what he has prayed for.
She is alive! And her veins leap under his fingers!

3. Island in the eastern Mediterranean sacred to Venus.
4. I.e., as they are sacrificed.

"You can believe that Pygmalion offered the goddess
his thanks in a torrent of speech, once again kissing   365
those lips that were not untrue; that she felt his kisses,
and timidly blushing, she opened her eyes to the sunlight,
and at the same time, first looked on her lover and heaven!
The goddess attended the wedding since she had arranged it,
and before the ninth moon had come to its crescent, a daughter   370
was born to them—Paphos,[5] who gave her own name to the island.

"She had a son named Cinyras, who would be regarded
as one of the blessèd, if he had only been childless.
I sing of dire events: depart from me, daughters,
depart from me, fathers; or, if you find my poems charming,   375
believe that I lie, believe these events never happened;
or, if you believe that they did, then believe they were punished.
"If Nature allows us to witness such impious misdeeds,
then I give my solemn thanks that the Thracian people
and the land itself are far away from those regions[6]   380
where evil like that was begotten: let fabled Panchaea[7]
be rich in balsam and cinnamon, costum and frankincense,
the sweat that drips down from the trees; let it bear incense
and flowers of every description: it also bears myrrh, and
too great a price was paid for that new creation.   385
"Cupid himself denies that his darts ever harmed you,
Myrrha, and swears that his torches likewise are guiltless;
one of the three sisters,[8] bearing a venomous hydra
and waving a Stygian firebrand, must have inspired your passion.
Hating a parent is wicked, but even more wicked   390
than hatred is this kind of love. Princes elected
from far and wide desire you, Myrrha; all Asia
sends its young men to compete for your hand in marriage:
choose from so many just one of these men for your husband,
so long as a certain one is not the one chosen.   395
"She understood and struggled against her perversion,
asking herself, 'What have I begun? Where will it take me?
May heaven and piety and the sacred rights of fathers
restrain these unspeakable thoughts and repel my misfortune,
if this indeed *is* misfortune; yet piety chooses   400
not to condemn this love outright: without distinctions
animals copulate; it is no crime for the heifer
to bear the weight of her father upon her own back;
daughters are suitable wives in the kingdom of horses;
the billy goats enter the flocks that they themselves sire,   405
and birds are inseminated by those who conceive them:
blessed, the ones for whom such love is permitted!
"'Human morality gives us such stifling precepts,

---

5. One of the cities of Cyprus, whose name is often used for the island as a whole.
6. A reminder that Orpheus is singing in Thrace (the region stretching along the north coast of the Aegean Sea).
7. An imaginary island near Arabia, rich in spices.
8. The Furies.

and makes indecent what Nature freely allows us!
But people say there are nations where sons and their mothers,   410
where fathers and daughters, may marry each other, increasing
the bonds of piety by their redoubled affections.
Wretched am I, who hadn't the luck to be born there,
injured by nothing more than mischance of location!
    "'Why do I obsess? Begone, forbidden desires;   415
of course he is worthy of love—but love for a father!
So, then, if I were not the daughter of great Cinyras,
I would be able to have intercourse with Cinyras:
though he is mine, he is not mine, and our nearness
ruins me: I would be better off as a stranger.   420
    "'It would be good for me to go far away from my country,
as long as I could escape from my wicked desires,
for what holds me here is the passion that I have to see him,
to touch and speak to Cinyras and give him my kisses—
if nothing more is permitted. You impious maiden,   425
what more can you imagine will ever be granted?
Are you aware how you confuse all rights and relations?
Would you be your mother's rival? The whore of your father?
Would you be called your son's sister? Your brother's own mother?
Do you not shudder to think of the serpent-coiffed sisters[9]   430
thrusting their bloodthirsty torches into the faces
of the guilty wretches that those three appear to and torture?
    "'But you, while your body is undefiled, keep your mind chaste,
and do not break Nature's law with incestuous pairing.
Think what you ask for: the very act is forbidden,   435
and he is devout and mindful of moral behavior—
ah, how I wish that he had a similar madness!'
    "She spoke and Cinyras, whom an abundance of worthy
suitors had left undecided, consulted his daughter,
ran their names by her and asked whom she wished for a husband;   440
silent at first, she kept her eyes locked on her father,
seething until the hot tears spilled over her eyelids:
Cinyras, attributing this to the fears of a virgin,
bade her cease weeping, wiped off her cheeks, and kissed her;
Myrrha rejoiced overmuch at his gesture and answered   445
that she would marry a man 'just like you.' Misunderstanding
the words of his daughter, Cinyras approved them, replying,
'May you be this pious always.' Hearing that last word,
the virgin lowers her head, self-convicted of evil.
    "Midnight: now sleep dissolves all the cares of the body;   450
Cinyras' daughter, however, lies tossing, consumed by
the fires of passion, repeating her prayers in a frenzy;
now she despairs, now she'll attempt it; now she is shamefaced,
now eager: uncertain: *What should she do now?* She wavers,
just like a tree that the axe blade has girdled completely,   455
when only the last blow remains to be struck, and the woodsman
cannot predict the direction it's going to fall in,

9. Again, the Furies.

she, after so many blows to her spirit, now totters,
now leaning in one, and now in the other, direction,
nor is she able to find any rest from her passion   460
save but in death. Death pleases her, and she gets up,
determined to hang herself from a beam with her girdle:
'Farewell, dear Cinyras: may you understand why I do this!'
she said, as she fitted the noose around her pale neck.
   "They say that, hearing her murmuring, her faithful old nurse   465
in the next chamber arose and entered her bedroom:
at sight of the grim preparations, she screams out, and striking
her breasts and tearing her garments, removes the noose from
around the girl's neck, and then, only then she collapses,
and weeping, embraces her, asking her why she would do it.   470
   "Myrrha remained silent, expressionless, with her eyes downcast,
sorrowing only because her attempt was detected.
But the woman persists, baring her flat breasts and white hair,
and by the milk given when she was a babe in the cradle
beseeches her to entrust her old nurse with the cause of her sorrow.   475
The girl turns away with a groan; the nurse is determined
to learn her secret, and promises not just to keep it:
   "'Speak and allow me to aid you,' she says, 'for in my old age,
I am not utterly useless: if you are dying of passion,
my charms and herbs will restore you; if someone wishes you evil,   480
my rites will break whatever spell you are under;
is some god wrathful? A sacrifice placates his anger.
What else could it be? I can't think of anything—Fortune
favors your family, everything's going quite smoothly,
both of your parents are living, your mother, your father—'   485
Myrrha sighed deeply, hearing her father referred to,
but not even then did the nurse grasp the terrible evil
in the girl's heart, although she felt that her darling
suffered a passion of some kind for some kind of lover.
   "Nurse was unyielding and begged her to make known her secret,   490
whatever it was, pressing the tearful girl to her bosom;
and clasping her in an embrace that old age had enfeebled,
she said, 'You're in love—I am certain! I will be zealous
in aiding your cause, never you fear—and your father
will be none the wiser!'   495
               "Myrrha in frenzy leapt up
and threw herself onto the bed, pressing her face in the pillows:
'Leave me, I beg you,' she said. 'Avoid my wretched dishonor;
leave me or cease to ask me the cause of my sorrow:
what you attempt to uncover is sinful and wicked!'
   "The old woman shuddered: extending the hands that now trembled   500
with fear and old age, she fell at the feet of her darling,
a suppliant, coaxing her now, and now attempting to scare her;
threatening now to disclose her attempted self-murder,
but pledging to aid her if she confesses her passion.
   "She lifted her head with her eyes full of tears spilling over   505
onto the breast of her nurse and repeatedly tried to
speak out, but repeatedly stopped herself short of confession,

hiding her shame-colored face in the folds of her garments,
until she finally yielded, blurting her secret:
'O mother,' she cried, 'so fortunate you with your husband!'   510
and said no more but groaned.
               "The nurse, who now understood it,
felt a chill run through her veins, and her bones shook with tremor,
and her white hair stood up in stiff bristles. She said whatever
she could to dissuade the girl from her horrible passion,
and even though Myrrha knew the truth of her warning,   515
she had decided to die if she could not possess him.
'Live, then,' the other replied, 'and possess your—' Not daring
to use the word 'father,' she left her sentence unfinished,
but called upon heaven to stand by her earlier promise.
     "Now it was time for the annual feast days of Ceres;   520
the pious, and married women clad in white vestments,
thronged to the celebration, offering garlands
of wheat as firstfruits of the season; now for nine nights
the intimate touch of their men is considered forbidden.
Among these matrons was Cenchreïs, wife of Cinyras,   525
for her attendance during these rites was required.
And so, while the queen's place in his bed was left vacant,
the overly diligent nurse came to Cinyras,
finding him drunk, and spoke to him of a maiden
whose passion for him was real (although her name wasn't)   530
and praising her beauty; when asked the age of this virgin,
she said, 'the same age as Myrrha.' Commanded to fetch her,
nurse hastened home, and entering, cried to her darling,
'Rejoice, my dear, we have won!' The unlucky maiden
could not feel joy in her heart, but only grim sorrow,   535
yet still she rejoiced, so distorted were her emotions.
     "Now it is midnight, when all of creation is silent;
high in the heavens, between the two Bears, Boötes[1]
had turned his wagon so that its shaft pointed downward;
Myrrha approaches her crime, which is fled by chaste Luna,[2]   540
while under black clouds the stars hide their scandalized faces;
Night lacks its usual fires; you, Icarus,[3] covered
your face and were followed at once by Erigone,
whose pious love of her father merited heaven.
     "Thrice Myrrha stumbles and stops each time at the omen,   545
and thrice the funereal owl sings her his poem of endings;
nevertheless she continues, her shame lessened by shadows.
She holds the left hand of her nurse, and gropes with the other
blindly in darkness: now at the bedchamber's threshold,
and now she opens the door: and now she is led within,   550
where her knees fail her; she falters, nearly collapsing,

1. The Ox-herder, a constellation that was imagined as driving Ursa Major, the Great Bear.
2. The Moon, often associated with Diana, one of whose attributes was chastity.
3. More properly Icarius, a mythic Athenian. He received Dionysus into the city, and the god rewarded him with wine, which he shared with his countrymen. Feeling its effect, they thought they had been poisoned and killed him. His daughter Erigone hanged herself in grief, and both were changed into stars.

her color, her blood, her spirit all flee together.

"As she approaches the crime, her horror increases;
regretting her boldness, she wishes to turn back, unnoticed,
but even as she holds back, the old woman leads her   555
by the hand to the high bed, where she delivers her, saying,
'Take her, Cinyras—she's yours,' and unites the doomed couple.
The father accepts his own offspring in his indecent
bed and attempts to dispel the girl's apprehensions,
encouraging her not to be frightened of him, and   560
addressing her, as it happened, with a name befitting
her years: he called her 'daughter' while she called him 'father,'
so the right names were attached to their impious actions.

"Filled with the seed of her father, she left his bedchamber,
having already conceived, in a crime against nature   565
which she repeated the following night and thereafter,
until Cinyras, impatient to see his new lover
after so many encounters, brought a light in,
and in the same moment discovered his crime and his daughter;
grief left him speechless; he tore out his sword from the scabbard;   570
Myrrha sped off, and, thanks to night's shadowy darkness,
escaped from her death. She wandered the wide-open spaces,
leaving Arabia, so rich in palms, and Panchaea,
and after nine months, she came at last to Sabaea,[4]
where she found rest from the weariness that she suffered,   575
for she could scarcely carry her womb's heavy burden.

"Uncertain of what she should wish for, tired of living
but frightened of dying, she summed up her state in this prayer:
'O gods, if there should be any who hear my confession,
I do not turn away from the terrible sentence   580
that my misbehavior deserves; but lest I should outrage
the living by my survival, or the dead by my dying,
drive me from both of these kingdoms, transform me
wholly, so that both life and death are denied me.'

"Some god *did* hear her confession, and heaven answered   585
her final prayer, for, even as she was still speaking,
the earth rose up over her legs, and from her toes burst
roots that spread widely to hold the tall trunk in position;
her bones put forth wood, and even though they were still hollow,
they now ran with sap and not blood; her arms became branches,   590
and those were now twigs that used to be called her fingers,
while her skin turned to hard bark. The tree kept on growing,
over her swollen belly, wrapping it tightly,
and growing over her breast and up to her neck; she
could bear no further delay, and, as the wood rose,   595
plunged her face down into the bark and was swallowed.

"Loss of her body has meant the loss of all feeling;
and yet she weeps, and the warm drops spill from her tree trunk;
those tears bring her honor: the distillate myrrh preserves and
will keep the name of its mistress down through the ages.   600

4. Arabia Felix, the southern tip of the Arabian Peninsula.

"But under the bark, the infant conceived in such baseness
continued to grow and now sought a way out of Myrrha;
the pregnant trunk bulged in the middle and its weighty burden
pressed on the mother, who could not cry out in her sorrow
nor summon Lucina with charms to aid those in childbirth.   605
So, like a woman exerting herself to deliver,
the tree groaned and bent over double, wet from its weeping.
Gentle Lucina stood by the sorrowing branches,
laid her hands onto the bark and recited the charms that
aid in delivery; the bark split open; a fissure   610
ran down the trunk of the tree and its burden spilled out,
a bawling boychild, whom naiads placed in soft grasses
and bathed in the tears of its mother. Not even Envy
could have found fault with his beauty, for he resembled
one of the naked cherubs depicted by artists,   615
and would have been taken as one, if you had provided
him with a quiver or else removed one from those others.

[Venus and Adonis]

"Time swiftly glides by in secret, escaping our notice,
and nothing goes faster than years do: the son of his sister
by his grandfather, the one so recently hidden   620
within a tree, so recently born, a most beautiful infant,
now is an adolescent and now a young man
even more beautiful than he was as a baby,
pleasing now even to Venus and soon the avenger
of passionate fires that brought his mother to ruin.   625
  "For while her fond Cupid was giving a kiss to his mother,
he pricked her unwittingly, right in the breast, with an arrow
projecting out of his quiver; annoyed, the great goddess
swatted him off, but the wound had gone in more deeply
than it appeared to, and at the beginning deceived her.   630
  "Under the spell of this fellow's beauty, the goddess
no longer takes any interest now in Cythera,[5]
nor does she return to her haunts on the island of Paphos,
or to fish-wealthy Cnidus or to ore-bearing Amathus;[6]
she avoids heaven as well, now—preferring Adonis,   635
and clings to him, his constant companion, ignoring
her former mode of unstrenuous self-indulgence,
when she shunned natural light for the parlors of beauty;
now she goes roaming with him through woods and up mountains
and over the scrubby rocks with her garments hitched up   640
and girded around her waist like a nymph of Diana,[7]
urging the hounds to pursue unendangering species,
hoppety hares or stags with wide-branching antlers,

---

5. Island south of the Peloponnesus, and like
Cyprus sacred to Venus.
6. All three were important centers of Venus's
cult: Paphos and Amathus were cities on the
island of Cyprus, and Cnidus was a city in Asia
Minor.
7. As a virgin and huntress, the antithesis of
Venus.

or terrified does; but she avoids the fierce wild boars and
rapacious wolves and bears armed with sharp claws,   645
and shuns the lions, sated with slaughter of cattle.
   "And she warns you also to fear the wild beasts, Adonis,
if only her warning were heeded. 'Be bold with the timid,'
she said, 'but against the daring, daring is reckless.
Spare me, dear boy, the risk involved in your courage;   650
don't rile the beasts that Nature has armed with sharp weapons,
lest I should find the glory you gain much too costly!
For lions and bristling boars and other fierce creatures
look with indifferent eyes and minds upon beauty
and youth and other qualities Venus is moved by;   655
pitiless boars deal out thunderbolts with their curved tusks,
and none may withstand the frenzied assault of the lions,
whom I despise altogether.'
                        "And when he asked why,
she said, 'I will tell you this story which will amaze you,
with its retribution delivered for ancient wrongdoing.   660
   "'But this unaccustomed labor has left me exhausted—
look, though—a poplar entices with opportune shade, and
offers a soft bed of turf we may rest on together,
as I would like to.' And so she lay down on the grasses
and on her Adonis, and using his breast as a pillow,   665
she told this story, mixing her words with sweet kisses:

   "'Perhaps you'll have heard of a maiden able to vanquish
the swiftest of men in a footrace; this wasn't a fiction,
for she overcame all contestants; nor could you say whether
she deserved praise more for her speed or her beauty.   670
She asked some god about husbands. "A husband," he answered,
"is not for you, Atalanta: flee from a husband!
But you will not flee—and losing yourself, will live on!"
   "'Frightened by his grim prediction, she went to the forest
and lived there unmarried, escaping the large and persistent   675
throng of her suitors by setting out cruel conditions;
"You cannot have me," she said, "unless you outrun me;
come race against me! A bride and a bed for the winner,
death to the losers. Those are the rules of the contest."
   "'Cruel? Indeed—but such was this young maiden's beauty   680
that a foolhardy throng of admirers took up the wager.
As a spectator, Hippomenes sat in the grandstand,
asking why anyone ever would risk such a danger,
just for a bride, and disparaging their headstrong passion.
However, as soon as he caught a glimpse of her beauty,   685
like mine or like yours would be if you were a woman,'
said Venus, 'her face and her body, both bared for the contest,
he threw up both hands and cried out, "I beg your pardons,
who only a moment ago disparaged your efforts,
but truly I had no idea of the trophy you strive for!"   690
   "'Praises ignited the fires of passion and made him
hope that no young man proved to be faster than she was

and fear that one would be. Jealous, he asked himself why he
was leaving the outcome of this competition unventured:
"God helps those who improve their condition by daring,"   695
he said, addressing himself as the maiden flew by him.
Though she seemed no less swift than a Scythian arrow,
nevertheless, he more greatly admired her beauty,
and the grace of her running made her seem even more lovely;
the breezes blew back the wings attached to her ankles   700
while her loose hair streamed over her ivory shoulders
and her brightly edged knee straps fluttered lightly; a russet
glow fanned out evenly over her pale, girlish body,
as when a purple awning covers a white marble surface,
staining its artless candor with counterfeit shadow.   705
　　"'She crossed the finish line while he was taking it in, and
Atalanta, victorious, was given a crown and the glory;
the groaning losers were taken off: end of *their* story.
But the youth, undeterred by what had become of the vanquished,
stood on the track and fixed his gaze on the maiden: 710
"Why seek such an easy victory over these sluggards?
Contend with me," he said, "and if Fortune makes me the winner,
you will at least have been beaten by one not unworthy:
I am the son of Megareus, grandson of Neptune,
my great-grandfather; my valor is no less impressive   715
than is my descent; if you should happen to triumph,
you would be famous for having beaten Hippomenes."
　　"'And as he spoke, Atalanta's countenance softened:
she wondered whether she wished to win or to *be* won,
and asked herself which god, jealous of her suitor's beauty,   720
sought to destroy him by forcing him into this marriage:
"If *I* were judging, I wouldn't think I was worth it!
Nor am I moved by his beauty," she said, "though I could be,
but I *am* moved by his youth: his boyishness stirs me—
but what of his valor? His mind so utterly fearless?   725
What of his watery origins? His relation to Neptune?
What of the fact that he loves me and wishes to wed me,
and is willing to die if bitter Fortune denies him?
　　"'"Oh, flee from a bed that still reeks with the gore of past victims,
while you are able to, stranger; marrying *me* is   730
certain destruction! No one would wish to reject you,
and you may be chosen by a much wiser young lady!
　　"'"But why should I care for you—after so many have perished?
Now *he* will learn! Let him die then, since the great slaughter
of suitors has taught him nothing! He must be weary of living!   735
So—must he die then, because he wishes to wed me,
and is willing to pay the ultimate price for his passion?
He shouldn't have to! And even though it won't be *my* fault,
my victory surely will turn the people against me!
　　"'"If only you would just give it up, or if only,   740
since you're obsessed with it, you were a little bit faster!
How very girlish is the boy's facial expression!
O poor Hippomenes! I wish you never had seen me!

You're worthy of life, and if only *my* life had been better,
or if the harsh Fates had not prevented my marriage, 745
you would have been the one I'd have chosen to marry!"
    "'She spoke, and, moved by desire that struck without warning,
loved without knowing what she was doing or feeling.
Her father and people were clamoring down at the racecourse,
when Neptune's descendent Hippomenes anxiously begged me: 750
"Cytherian Venus, I pray you preside at my venture,
aiding the fires that you yourself have ignited."
A well-meaning breeze brought me this prayer, so appealing
that, I confess, it aroused me and stirred me to action,
though I had scant time enough to bring off his rescue. 755
    "'There is a field upon Cyprus, known as Tamasus,
famed for its wealth; in olden days it was given
to me and provides an endowment now for my temples;
and there in this field is a tree; its leaves and its branches
glisten and shimmer, reflecting the gold they are made of; 760
now, as it happened, I'd just gotten back from a visit,
carrying three golden apples that I had selected:
and showing myself there to Hippomenes only,
approached him and showed him how to use them to advantage.
    "'Both of them crouched for the start; when horns gave the signal, 765
they took off together, their feet barely brushing the surface;
you would have thought they were able to keep their toes dry
while skimming over the waves, and could touch on the ripened
heads of wheat in the field without bending them under.
    "'Cries of support and encouragement cheered on the young man; 770
"Now is the time," they screamed, "go for it, go for it, hurry,
Hippomenes, give it everything that you've got now!
Don't hold back! Victory!" And I am uncertain whether
these words were more pleasing to him or to his Atalanta,
for often, when she could have very easily passed him, 775
she lingered beside, her gaze full of desperate longing,
until she reluctantly sped ahead of his features.
    "'And now Hippomenes, dry-mouthed, was breathlessly gasping,
the finish line far in the distance; he threw out an apple,
and the sight of that radiant fruit astounded the maiden, 780
who turned from her course and retrieved the glittering missile;
Hippomenes passed her: the crowd roared its approval.
    "'A burst of speed now and Atalanta makes up for lost time:
once more overtaking the lad, she puts him behind her!
A second apple: again she falls back, but recovers, 785
now she's beside him, now passing him, only the finish
remains: "Now, O goddess," he cries, "my inspiration, be with me!"
    "'With all the strength of his youth he flings the last apple
to the far side of the field: *this* will really delay her!
The maiden looked doubtful about its retrieval: I forced her 790
to get it and add on its weight to the burden she carried:
time lost and weight gained were equal obstructions: the maiden
(lest my account should prove longer than even the race was)
took second place: the trophy bride left with the victor.

"'But really, Adonis, wasn't I worthy of being   795
thanked for my troubles? Offered a gift of sweet incense?
Heedless of all I had done, he offered me neither!
Immediate outrage was followed by keen indignation;
and firmly resolving not to be spurned in the future,
I guarded against it by making this pair an example.   800
   "'Now they were passing a temple deep in the forest,
built long ago by Echion to honor Cybele,[8]
Mother of Gods, and now the length of their journey
urged them to rest here, where unbridled desire
possessed Hippomenes, moved by the strength of my godhead.   805
There was a dim and cave-like recess near the temple,
hewn out of pumice, a shrine to the ancient religion,
wherein a priest of these old rites had set a great many
carved wooden idols. Hippomenes entered that place, and
by his forbidden behavior defiled it;[9] in horror,   810
the sacred images turned away from the act, and Cybele
prepared to plunge the guilty pair in Stygian waters,
but that seemed too easy; so now their elegant pale necks
are cloaked in tawny manes; curved claws are their fingers;
arms are now forelegs, and all the weight of their bodies   815
shifts to their torsos; and now their tails sweep the arena;
fierce now, their faces; growls supplant verbal expression;
the forest now is their bedroom; a terror to others,
meekly these lions champ at the bit of the harness
on either side of the yoke of Cybele's chariot.   820
   "'My darling, you must avoid these and all other wild beasts,
who will not turn tail, but show off their boldness in battle;
flee them or else your courage will prove our ruin!'

   "And after warning him, she went off on her journey,
carried aloft by her swans; but his courage resisted   825
her admonitions. It happened that as his dogs followed
a boar they were tracking, they roused it from where it was hidden,
and when it attempted to rush from the forest, Adonis
pierced it, but lightly, casting his spear from an angle;
with its long snout, it turned and knocked loose the weapon   830
stained with its own blood, then bore down upon our hero,
and, as he attempted to flee for his life in sheer terror,
it sank its tusks deep into the young fellow's privates,
and stretched him out on the yellow sands, where he lay dying.
   "Aloft in her light, swan-driven chariot, Venus   835
had not yet gotten to Cyprus; from a great distance
she recognized the dying groans of Adonis
and turned her birds back to him; when she saw from midair
his body lying there, lifeless, stained with its own blood,

8. A fertility goddess of Asia Minor known as the Great Mother. She was often pictured wearing a crown that resembled a city wall with towers, and flanked by lions or riding in a cart drawn by them.
9. It was considered sacrilege to have sexual intercourse in the precinct of a temple.

she beat her breasts and tore at her hair and her garments, 840
and leapt from her chariot, raging, to argue with grim Fate:
   "'It will not be altogether as you would have it,'
she said. 'My grief for Adonis will be remembered
forever, and every year will see, reenacted
in ritual form, his death and my lamentation; 845
and the blood of the hero will be transformed to a flower.
Or were *you* not once allowed to change a young woman[1]
to fragrant mint, Persephone? Do you begrudge me
the transformation of my beloved Adonis?'
   "And as she spoke, she sprinkled his blood with sweet nectar, 850
which made it swell up, like a transparent bubble
that rises from muck; and in no more than an hour
a flower sprang out of that soil, blood red in its color,
just like the flesh that lies underneath the tough rind
of the seed-hiding pomegranate. Brief is its season, 855
for the winds from which it takes its name, the anemone,
shake off those petals so lightly clinging and fated to perish."

---

1. Mentha, Hades' mistress, trampled by the jealous Persephone and transformed into the mint (the meaning of her name).

II

Ancient India

The Indian subcontinent stretches from the borders of Iran and Afghanistan to those of Myanmar, and from the edges of Tibet and China to the Indian Ocean; also called South Asia, it covers an area as large as western Europe. From about the fifth century B.C.E. onward, the ancient Greeks knew this region as *Indos*, a term adapted from the Persians; after the seventh century C.E., Muslim societies came to refer to it as *al-Hind*. For much of its long history, the subcontinent has not been politically united, but it has been remarkably cohesive in its social and cultural practices: it has evolved as a distinct "cultural zone" within Asia, very different in language, religion, art, population, and ways of life from the comparable cultural zones of China and the Middle East.

THE PREHISTORIC ORIGINS OF INDIAN LITERATURE

The kinds of stories ancient Indian literature tells, the forms they take, and the themes they explore are connected to the subcontinent's past before the appearance of historical records. The earliest settled society in South Asia organized on a significant scale was that of the Indus Valley and Harappa

Kṛṣṇa battles the horse demon, Keshi. From a fifth-century C.E. terra-cotta carving.

(ca. 2600–1900 B.C.E.), which established a far-flung network of small towns and ports across what are now Pakistan and western India. This civilization had extensive contacts with Mesopotamia during the period in which the epic *Gilgamesh* was being composed in Sumerian. The Indus-Harappan people had a writing system of their own, but it remains undeciphered, even though we know a great deal about their material culture. Conquered or gradually displaced by the Indo-Aryans, or overcome by economic, political, or natural disasters, this population receded from the subcontinent's prehistory by about 1900 B.C.E., some segments perhaps surviving among the aboriginal and other ancient groups dispersed across the Indian peninsula down to modern times.

The Indo-Aryan people may have begun to arrive on the Indian subconti-nent as early as 2000 B.C.E., and to create a new settled society over the next few centuries in what are now northern Pakistan and India. Originally a nomadic pastoral people who moved with vast herds of cattle in search of grazing land, the Indo-Aryans branched off from the Indo-Iranian people, who probably migrated from the Caucasus Mountains region (modern Chechnya) to the plateau of Iran late in the third millennium B.C.E. The Indo-Iranians were themselves one of the major groups of the Indo-European people, who spread in many stages from their Caucasian homeland westward into Europe and eastward into Asia. One western Indo-European group, roughly contemporaneous with the earliest Indo-Iranians and Indo-Aryans, migrated to the Mediterranean region also around 2000 B.C.E., initially establishing the Mycenaean civilization and

An eighteenth-century watercolor depicting Kṛṣṇa protecting cowherds and cows during a fire.

subsequently emerging in history as the ancient Greeks and Romans.

When the Indo-Aryans started settling in Punjab (now divided between India and Pakistan) in the second millennium B.C.E., they established an organized agrarian village society distinct from the urban society of their Indus-Harappan predecessors, who had focused on trade. This Indo-Aryan innovation, with its economic basis in agriculture (on small family farms) and animal husbandry (mainly of the domesticated cow), has proven to be the subcontinent's enduring social form of the past 3,500 years. In the mid-twentieth century, when it still had nearly 750,000 such villages, Mahatma Gandhi famously characterized India as a "land of villages"; and, in our own times, we still invoke the "holy cow"—an image that the Indo-Aryans created in their earliest poems on the subcontinent.

The Indo-Aryans brought with them the language that eventually became Sanskrit, the medium of the largest body of Indian literature, produced continuously from approximately 1200 B.C.E. to 1800 C.E. Sanskrit is intimately related to Greek and Latin: these languages share much of their grammar, use similar sentence structures, and draw on hundreds of common roots for their vocabularies. All three languages, along with ancient Persian, may therefore have evolved from a single source called proto-Indo-European, a language (lost since antiquity) presumably used by the ancestors of the Greeks, Romans, Indo-Iranians, and Indo-Aryans a few thousand years earlier.

But the connections among these scattered peoples are not merely linguistic. When they settled at the end of their respective migrations, they began to worship pantheons of gods, establish social hierarchies, practice rituals and customs, and adopt political models that strongly resembled one another. Most important, their songs, tales, and cycles of myths seemed to invoke a common stock of older memories, images, and narratives. By the first millennium B.C.E., Greek, Sanskrit, and Latin were highly differentiated from one another, and their emerging literatures—from, respectively, **Homer** (ca. eighth century B.C.E.); **Vālmīki** (ca. sixth century B.C.E.), the author of the original *Rāmāyaṇa*; and **Virgil** (first century B.C.E.) onward—developed along independent trajectories. But they still contained remarkable echoes of one another that we cannot fully explain.

ORALITY AND WRITING IN INDIA

The first works on the subcontinent were hymns and ritual formulas (*mantras*) composed in Sanskrit, which were gathered with commentary and other theological material in four large groupings of discourse called the Vedas; these gave rise to an extensive, interconnected body of philosophy and mystical speculation called the Upaniṣads, fifty-two of which are important. Developed between approximately 1200 and 700 B.C.E., much of this literature was classified as scripture (*śruti*, revelation that is heard) and revealed knowledge (*veda*). Although the Vedic hymns are in verse, and some of them are poetry of the highest order, and even though the visionaries (*ṛṣis*) who "received them from the gods" are called *kavis* (poets), the texts themselves are not classified as *kāvya* (poetry): from this perspective, *mantras* are of divine origin and hence sacred, whereas poetry—no matter how beautiful and profound—is made by human authors and hence always mundane. Since divine revelation and knowledge need to be explained to human audiences, the Vedas and the Upaniṣads engendered many works of authoritative and specialized commentary (*śāstras*) as well as numerous compendiums and rule books (*sūtras*), which, by the latter half of the first millennium B.C.E., became part of the canon of Vedic religion and, centuries later, of classical Hinduism, one of the most important cultural forces on the subcontinent.

Although some of the essential commentaries and rule books were prepared after a writing system became available, the Hindu canon as a whole was transmitted orally throughout the ancient period. In this method of oral transmission, which is still practiced in our times, specialist priests and scholars belonging to the *brāhmaṇa* caste are trained from early childhood to memorize an entire work in multiple forms: by phoneme (sound unit), word, verse, chapter, and book; by mnemonic summaries of the whole work, and by its "indexed" words; and even by the reverse order of its verses. Taught orally for a dozen years, a good Vedic priest who specializes in the *Ṛgveda* (ca. 1000 B.C.E.), for example, can recite all 1,028 hymns in its ten books, can confirm their correct order, can reproduce any individual verse at will, and can orally list every occurrence of a given word in the text. Unlike a bard, a Vedic reciter communicates divine revelation, and hence is not free to invent, embellish, or err. In post-Vedic times (starting ca. 500 B.C.E.), this method was extended to other kinds of composition in Sanskrit. In the classical period (ca. 400–1100 C.E.), for instance, poets and literary scholars memorized entire bodies of *kāvya*, so that their literature was always at hand— a practice that also continued well into the twentieth century.

Knowledge of the early writing system of the Indus-Harappan people did not survive the end of their civilization, around 1900 B.C.E. A new system

of indigenous writing most likely reappeared around 500 B.C.E., and acquired its canonical form some 250 years later. This was the Brahmi script system, in which writing proceeds from left to right and uses alphabetical letters and diacritical marks to represent syllables (whole sounds), and hence is classified as an alpha-syllabary system, as distinct from the Greek and Latin scripts, which are strictly alphabetical. Brahmi migrated rapidly across South Asia after 250 B.C.E., spawning what would eventually become, over the next 1,500 years or so, the dozen distinct script systems in which most of the languages of the region are recorded. These include Sanskrit, Bengali, Hindi, Marathi, Kannada, and Tamil, among other languages, Urdu being among the few exceptions written in a modified Persian-Arabic script, which arrived from outside the subcontinent. During the same period, Brahmi also migrated out of India and became a transnational phenomenon of world importance: it engendered the scripts of Tibetan (Tibet), Burmese (Myanmar), Thai (Thailand), Javanese and Sumatran (Indonesia), Cham (Vietnam), and Tagalog (the Philippines), and hence launched literacy and literature across a wide swath of Asia.

By the beginning of the Common Era, professional scribes had begun to produce manuscripts with a metal stylus on prepared sheets of bark or palm leaves, tied together with string. Paper and ink first became common on the Indian subcontinent in the thirteenth century C.E.; until then, for more than a millennium, the principal form of a Sanskrit book was a palm-leaf manuscript: though highly perishable, it succeeded in recording an enormous quantity of literature, disseminating Indian epics, lyrics, stories, and plays all over the subcontinent, and well beyond its boundaries.

SOCIETY, POLITICS, AND RELIGION

The first Vedic hymns (ca. 1200 B.C.E.), and the first collection of hymns, the *Ṛg-veda saṃhitā* (ca. 1000 B.C.E.), were most likely composed in Punjab, "the land of five rivers" that are the tributaries of the Indus. Over the next few centuries, the Indo-Aryans pushed farther east, settling on the wider and equally fertile plains surrounding the Ganges river system, up to modern Bihar and Bengal. By the seventh century B.C.E., the expansion of agriculture and cattle breeding produced enough prosperity to support the first towns and cities across northern India, such as Banaras and Ayodhyā (which still flourish today). With this emerged the first recognizable political form in India: the small republic centered around an urban capital, not unlike a city-state, ruled by a lineage of hereditary monarchs. This became both the historical context and the narrative setting of the first Sanskrit epic, the *Rāmāyaṇa*, begun in the sixth century B.C.E. and composed on the central Gangetic plains.

A couple of centuries later, the small republics started to give way to bigger kingdoms that could garner sufficient surpluses from the land to maintain large armies, and control territories of several hundred square miles. Shortly after Alexander the Great invaded western and northern India, reaching Punjab in 327 B.C.E. and leaving behind a Greek colony in Gandhara (today's Peshawar and Swat Valley region, in Pakistan), the Maurya dynasty established the subcontinent's first empire—which stretched from Afghanistan to Bengal, and from the Himalayan foothills to the Deccan Plateau. Situated imaginatively in the transitional period between small republics and a vast empire, the other ancient Sanskrit epic, the *Mahabharata* (ca. 400 B.C.E.–400 C.E.), represents a world of powerful monarchies and many medium-sized kingdoms, from which the older republican ideal was beginning to fade.

This evolving world was shaped by the religion we now call Hinduism. One of the most influential ideas in Hinduism is that the universe, as it exists, is fashioned in a vast process of self-generation, in which all the primordial substance out of which it is made is godhead itself. Godhead, or "the god beyond god," is the absolute and undifferentiated original matter of the universe, and it divides itself into everything that exists; it is eternal and indestructible, and hence has no beginning or end in time. God in this view is not a creator god, or an anthropomorphic father, or a wrathful or vengeful deity; godhead is unknowable, unimaginable, and indescribable. Since everything that exists is made out of godhead (and there is no other elemental matter in the universe), god is everywhere and in everything—a view that constitutes pantheism. In some Vedic hymns, this all-pervading godhead is called *Puruṣa*, "spirit" (in the masculine gender); in the Upaniṣads, it is renamed *Brahman* (not to be confused with either *brāhmaṇa*, the priestly caste-group, or Brahmā, the later, anthropomorphic "god of creation"). The soul, spirit, or "self" (*ātman*) that animates every living creature is nothing but a piece of *Puruṣa* or *Brahman*, so it, too, is eternal and indestructible. The universe as we know it has a beginning in cosmic time, and therefore also comes to an end; since godhead cyclically differentiates itself into a particular universe, all its indestructible substance must return to it at the end of a cycle and be reintegrated into its primordial state. Any life-form's ultimate goal therefore is to be reunited with absolute godhead; for an individual soul or *ātman*, such a union with the elemental stuff of the

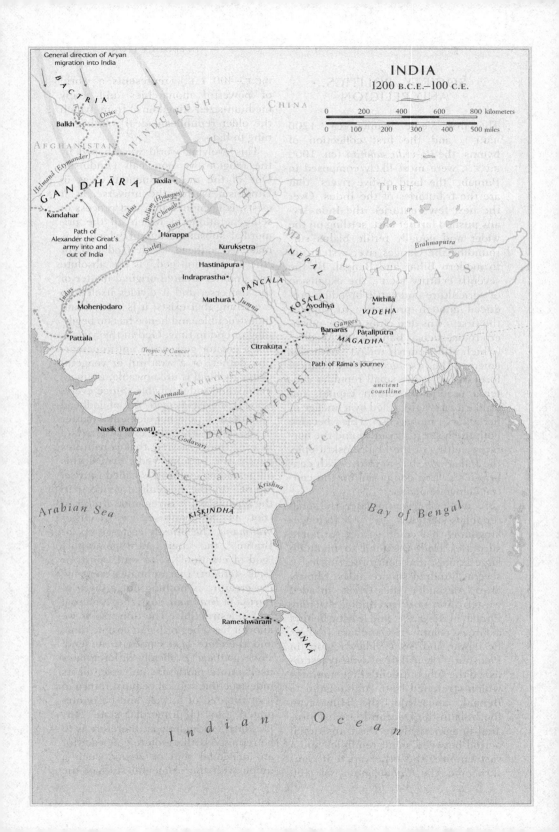

General direction of Aryan
migration into India

BACTRIA

Oxus

Balkh

AFGHANISTAN

HINDU KUSH

CHINA

INDIA
1200 B.C.E.–100 C.E.

0   200   400   600   800 kilometers
0 100 200 300 400 500 miles

Helmand (Etymander)

GANDHĀRA

Taxila

Kandahar

Path of
Alexander the Great's
army into and
out of India

Indus

Jhelum (Hydaspes)

Chenab

Ravi

Harappa

Sutlej

HIMALAYAS

TIBET

Brahmaputra

Kurukṣetra

NEPAL

Hastinapura

Indraprastha

PAÑCĀLA

Mathurā

Jumna

KOSALA

Ayodhyā

Mithilā

VIDEHA

Mohenjodaro

Indus

Pattala

Tropic of Cancer

Banaras

Ganges

Pāṭaliputra

MAGADHA

Citrakūṭa

Path of Rāma's journey

ancient
coastline

Narmada

VINDHYA RANGE

DANDAKA FOREST

Nasik (Pañcavati)

Godavari

Deccan Plateau

Krishna

Arabian Sea

KIṢKINDHĀ

Bay of Bengal

Rameshwaram

LANKĀ

Indian Ocean

A sandstone sculpture at the Temple of Śiva, Elephanta (ca. seventh–eighth centuries C.E.), depicting the "Trimurti" of Hinduism: Śiva, Viṣṇu, and Brahmā.

universe is possible only if it can achieve *mokṣa*, or "liberation," from its differentiated existence.

Works such as the *Rāmāyaṇa* and the *Mahabharata* further show us that many of Hinduism's characteristic doctrines follow from this theology of *Brahman* and *ātman*. Each of the popular gods in its pantheon becomes an aspect or a manifestation of godhead in an anthropomorphic or concrete form, which is especially useful in making divinity accessible to humans. The great gods Viṣṇu and Śiva are manifestations of godhead in equal measure; though Viṣṇu is often characterized as the god of preservation, and Śiva is distinguished as the god of destruction, each performs all the functions of creation, preservation, and destruction that only pure godhead can perform. The same is true of the anthropomorphic Brahmā, usually called the god of creation; and, by extension—because Hinduism, in the final analysis, does not attribute gender to godhead—it is equally true of the goddesses Lakṣmī, Pārvatī, and Sarasvatī (the consorts of Viṣṇu, Śiva, and Brahmā, respectively),

each of whom also is a complete embodiment of godhead. Since godhead can thus take on countless forms, there cannot be any one true representation of divinity; from its earliest phase, Hinduism therefore consistently commits itself to polytheism, the belief that there are many gods. As a result, from its very beginnings in agrarian Indo-Aryan society in northern India, Hinduism emerges as a fundamentally pluralistic religion, tolerant (in principle) of the worship of many different gods in many different ways, and of the pursuit of divergent ways of life, each of which has the potential to discover a path to *mokṣa* for an individual *ātman*.

THE RELIGIOUS CONTEXTS OF EPIC AND TALE

Within this broad matrix, India's early epics and narrative traditions develop along specific religious lines, but also in keeping with the social world shaped by Hinduism. Vālmīki's *Rāmāyaṇa*, composed and transmitted orally at the outset, is classified as the first poem in

Sanskrit because it emphasizes imaginative and aesthetic excellence outside a religious context; but it also takes the mythology of Viṣṇu and the practices of Hindu society for granted. In this framework, Viṣṇu is the "supreme god" who manifests all aspects of godhead; and Vedic rituals are essential for pleasing various gods and ensuring that individuals can pursue mokṣa. At the same time, the epic depicts a hierarchical society divided into four main caste-groups by birth: brāhmaṇas (priests), kṣatriyas (warriors), vaiśyas (traders), and śūdras (servants and cultivators). Theologically, this separation of castes is part of the primary differentiation of godhead into distinct categories of existence, and hence is divinely ordained and immutable; in most circumstances, an individual therefore cannot migrate from one caste to another on the basis of, say, talent or accomplishment. This structure is maintained by a system of endogamous marriage, in which legitimate spouses must belong to the same caste-group, so that their children are also born into their social category; in such a world, marriage is irrevocable, and miscegenation and adultery across castes can deeply destabilize not only the human order, but the cosmic moral order as well. The Rāmāyaṇa also depicts a society of villages and small republics, in which dynasties of kings do not yet pursue imperial ambitions: their role here is to preserve the divine order of things, in both the mundane world and the cosmos at large, which is populated by human beings, animal, plants, and inanimate things as well as demons, celestial beings, and gods.

In the Mahabharata, composed a little later, village society coexists with a more complex urban world: the land is now divided into many sizable dynastic kingdoms on the verge of imperial formations. The four caste-groups (varṇas) have separated into five, with the addi-

tion of "untouchables" and foreigners (such as the Greeks left behind by Alexander's army); and each caste-group is differentiated into numerous specific castes (jātīs). While the Rāmāyaṇa upholds the ideal of monogamous marriage within caste boundaries, the Mahābhārata explores multiple marriages and reproductive relationships, overlaying polygamy with polyandry and complicating issues of legitimacy, illegitimacy, and legacy by birth. Whereas the earlier epic distinguishes sharply between good and evil, the later poem adopts more complex and varying views on how action (karma) can accord with divine law (dharma); as the laws revealed by the gods in the Vedas and explained in later authoritative discourse (such as the śāstras and sūtras) are intricate, many judgments regarding the rightness and wrongness of particular actions founder in uncertainty. The **Bhagavad-gītā**, which is part of the Mahabharata, tackles the dilemmas of karma in the most difficult of situations: when is war just, how can violence and killing ever be justified, and under what circumstances can human beings even conceive of taking up arms against family and loved ones? The philosophical and theological arguments about the human and the divine, and about social and political organization, launched by the Indo-Aryans toward the end of the second millennium b.c.e., thus reach a poetic culmination in the encyclopedic structure of the Mahabharata a thousand years later.

As this historical overview suggests, for most of the ancient period the Indian subcontinent was not politically united. This pattern was to continue in the Common Era, down to modern times; since the end of British colonial rule (1757–1947), South Asia has come to be divided into seven nations, and its total population is now nearly 1.6 billion people, about three-fourths of whom live in contemporary India. The ancient period also witnessed internal religious division, with Jainism and Buddhism dissenting from Hinduism— a process that was repeated later with the arrival of other faiths, such as Zoroastrianism (ca. eleventh century) and Christianity, and the rise of Sikhism (both sixteenth century). Nevertheless, for the more than three millennia since the establishment of agrarian Indo-Aryan village society, the subcontinent has functioned as a cohesive cultural zone characterized by diversity and pluralism, which define the distinctive context of its early epics and tales.

THE RĀMĀYAŅA OF VĀLMĪKI
ca. 550 B.C.E.

The *Rāmāyaṇa* is many things to many people. It is a tale of adventure across a vast land, from palace to forest to sea; and a love story about an ideal prince and an ideal woman, whose relationship falters late in their marriage. It is a heroic epic about injustice and war, abduction and disinheritance, but also a wondrous tale involving gods, humans, animals, and demons with supernatural powers. It is a religious epic that explains the ways of the gods to human beings, and offers a model of justice and prosperity on earth. Moreover, it is great entertainment: like a roller coaster, it takes us up and down through many facets of human experience, from goodness, beauty, and romance to fear and tragedy.

CONTEXT

All we know about Vālmīki is the little he tells us about himself in his poem. He was an ascetic spiritual practitioner who had renounced normal life in human society, and lived in a small ashram, a hermit's enclave, on the banks of a river. One day he saw a pair of birds making love to each other, but a moment later a hunter shot and killed the male bird with an arrow. Incensed with this violent intrusion into a scene of great natural tenderness and beauty, Vālmīki pronounced an irrevocable curse on the hunter. Reflecting on what he had just uttered, the poet realized that he had spontaneously composed a *śloka*, an unrhymed metrical verse like a couplet, which fully expressed his compassionate grief for the slaughtered bird. Realizing that this verse form would be a perfect vehicle for story as well as song, Vālmīki set about using the *śloka* to compose the heroic and romantic tale of Rāma and Sītā, whose twin sons, Lava and Kuśa— by a twist of events—were then being raised in his ashram. Thus, the poet's life and character are fully integrated with the heroic world he creates and the tale he chooses to narrate. In the version of the epic we have inherited, and in the tradition since Vālmīki's time, he is celebrated as "the first poet," and his *Rāmāyaṇa* is known as "the inaugural poem" in Indian literature.

Vālmīki's epic tale—nearly one-and-a-half times the combined length of the *Iliad* and the *Odyssey*—was originally composed in Sanskrit around the sixth century B.C.E. By that time, a settled society had been in place in northern India for at least a thousand years. Agriculture had become the principal economic activity on the fertile plains around the Indus and Ganges rivers, and it supported a network of prosperous villages, towns, and cities. Society was organized by caste, with priests (*brāhmaṇas*), warriors (*kṣatriyas*), and traders (*vaiśyas*) comprising the three main groups, and the large populace that served them (*śūdras*) constituting the fourth category in the hierarchy. The caste structure was maintained primarily by a system of arranged marriage, in which, ideally, the bridegroom and the bride belonged to the same caste but not the same clan. Each caste-group had its own laws and moral codes (*dharma*), which defined its members' duties and obligations, but it also had to obey laws that applied to all of society. These laws were not made by human beings: they were given by the gods, and were contained in scripture.

Hinduism, which was central to upholding this social order, had been established in its early form several centuries before Vālmīki; its scriptural canon included ritual texts (the Vedas) as well as philosophy and theology (the Upaniṣads). In this system of beliefs, human beings could find "salvation" only if they accumulated "good karma" by propitiating the gods and following *dharma* precisely. But moral laws and codes of conduct are always complex and subtle, and hence easy to violate; numerous rituals are therefore necessary to keep the gods happy, maintain the moral and social orders, and make up for ethical lapses.

The world of the *Rāmāyaṇa* is structured in a similar way, but it also contains many gods, among whom three are the most important: Brahmā, primarily a benign and paternalistic god of creation; Śiva, chiefly an angry and retributive god who engenders cycles of creation and destruction; and Viṣṇu, mainly a benevolent god who preserves the moral balance of the universe. Much of the flux and dynamism of the universe is due to the perpetual struggle for supremacy between Śiva and Viṣṇu. Śiva intervenes in the human world directly, in his multifaceted anthropomorphic form; Viṣṇu, in contrast, "comes down on earth" in a series of distinct avatars or incarnations, living temporarily among mortal creatures each time for the purpose of destroying a particular source of evil. A vital feature of the *Rāmāyaṇa* is that it tells the story of Lord Viṣṇu's seventh incarnation, when he embodied himself as prince Rāma, in order to end the demonic king Rāvaṇa's reign of terror on earth and beyond.

The mundane world that Vālmīki's characters inhabit is also a deeply political one, where the two upper caste-groups, the *brāhmaṇas* (priests) and the *kṣatriyas* (warriors and rulers), dominate society. The land is divided into small, autonomous republics with prosperous cities for their capitals. The king belongs to a dynasty of warriors, but is not an absolute monarch; his power is mediated by court priests and scholarly *brāhmaṇas*. He is defined as a "protector of *dharma*," and his ideal role is to ensure that he and his subjects follow all laws. He is also fully answerable to his subjects; as their moral caretaker, he is obliged to pay attention to their needs, their voices of affirmation and protest. Moreover, the king is further constrained by life in his palace: he is usually polygamous, and has several queens; he is therefore the head of an extended family whose members participate actively in affairs of state. The warrior-dynasties in these republics follow the law of primogeniture, so that the eldest son ascends the throne in the next generation; but the inheritance of the kingdom can be complicated by the protodemocratic politics of the royal family as well as of public opinion, or by the inability of the king and his queens to beget a son. All these aspects of early Indian society, religion, and politics come into play in the dramatic narrative of the *Rāmāyaṇa*.

WORK

While Vālmīki probably composed his poem around 550 B.C.E., it was expanded and polished anonymously by others over the next five or six hundred years. Since writing systems did not exist in his society, he must have composed the epic orally, using a large repertoire of formulaic expressions. During its first few centuries, the *Rāmāyaṇa* must have been transmitted with the sophisticated methods of memorization, preservation, and reproduction already used for Hindu scripture. In its modern canonical form, the Sanskrit *Rāmāyaṇa* contains about 24,000 couplets (*slokas*) and is divided into seven books (*kāṇḍas*), each subdivided into a large number of chapters (*sargas*), most of which contain between twenty and fifty couplets. The first and last books seem to have been added later; they explicitly interpret Rāma as an avatar of Viṣṇu, and provide a multilayered narrative frame for the five books in the middle.

The English version of the *Rāmāyaṇa* reproduced here is not a translation but an adaptation and retelling of Vālmīki's poem. For the most part, it condenses the narrative of each chapter in a style that appeals to modern readers; but, in select passages, especially with important pieces of dialogue, its rendering is closer to the original. Our selection consists of excerpts from books 2, 3, and 6 that capture the key moments of the tale; together, they convey the epic's essential story as Vālmīki probably imagined it.

To understand our selection, it is necessary to know what happens in book 1, *Bāla* ("Childhood"), which is not represented here. In that book, Rāvaṇa, the brilliant and highly accomplished king of Laṅkā (an island in the south, modern Sri Laṅkā), has become invincible, demonic, and evil. Lord Viṣṇu therefore has to descend to earth in a human form and destroy him, and so takes birth as Rāma, the eldest son of Daśaratha, king of Kosala, and his principal queen, Kausalyā. Daśaratha also has two other queens, who bear him sons (Rāma's half-brothers): Kaikeyī is the mother of Bharata, whereas Sumitrā has twins, Lakṣmaṇa and Śatrughna. All four boys are trained as warriors and future rulers; Rāma and Lakṣmaṇa, inseparable since childhood, become the pupils of the sage Viśvāmitra. As teenagers, they travel with Viśvāmitra to the neighboring Videha, where Rāma wins a suitors' contest for Sītā, the foster-daughter of that republic's king but actually a child of the goddess Earth.

Our selection begins with book 2, *Ayodhyā*, where Daśaratha follows the code of primogeniture and proclaims Rāma as heir apparent to Kosala's throne, and the republic's citizens celebrate the decision enthusiastically. But following an intrigue in the extended family, Daśaratha gives in to the demand that his second son, Bharata, be made king, and that Rāma be exiled for fourteen years. We then see how Rāma responds to this development, and what decisions he, Sītā, Lakṣmaṇa, and Bharata make under the circumstances. The chapters in this book are composed in a realistic style on the whole, and they give us vivid glimpses into the thoughts and feelings of the characters involved in the struggle for power.

The excerpts from the remaining books focus on Rāma, Sītā, and Lakṣmaṇa's fourteen-year exile together, and the narrative now has the atmosphere of fairy tale and fantasy. In book 3, *Āraṇya* ("The Forest"), the trio pushes

A "Mughal"-style illustration from the *Rāmāyaṇa* dating from ca. 1600 C.E.
shows Rāma chasing a golden deer.

deeper into the vast Daṇḍaka forest,
south of the River Ganges, whose only
inhabitants are animals, ascetics, and
demons. We discover how they learn to
survive under hostile conditions, and
what kinds of dangers and temptations
they encounter. While the three are living peacefully in the Pañcavaṭī wood-
lands (in central India), Rāma and
Lakṣmaṇa unwittingly initiate a conflict
with Śūrpaṇakhā and her brother
Rāvaṇa, the demonic king of Laṅkā.
Enraged by their provocation, Rāvaṇa
decides to destroy Rāma by abducting
Sītā; how he carries out his plan constitutes a pivotal moment in the epic.

When Rāma realizes that Sītā is gone, he virtually goes mad with grief.

Books 4 and 5 (not in the anthology) follow Rāma and Lakṣmaṇa as they search desperately for Sītā. In book 4, *Kiṣkindhā* ("The Kingdom of the Monkeys"), Rāma and Lakṣmaṇa encounter a tribe of monkeys, whose citadel is at Kiṣkindhā (in southern India). Intervening in the political quarrels among their factions, the princes persuade the monkeys, and one of their powerful leaders, Hanumān, to help them look for her. In book 5, *Sundara* ("The Sundara Hill" [in Laṅkā]), Hanumān spies on Rāvaṇa's capital, and discovers where Sītā is held captive. But she refuses to escape with Hanumān for reasons that deepen the moral dimension of the story, and that leave him in a quandary. Hanumān then sets fire to Rāvaṇa's city as a warning of impending war, and returns to apprise Rāma of the situation.

In book 6, *Yuddha* ("The War"), the monkeys build a bridge or causeway across the straits to Laṅkā with remarkable inventiveness. One of Rāvaṇa's brothers betrays him and joins the princes, helping them with their battle plans. After a lengthy conflict, in which Rāvaṇa's other brothers are killed and Lakṣmaṇa is wounded, Rāma finally confronts the demon king in single combat. When he recovers Sītā, however, he finds himself deeply troubled by the question of whether she has been faithful to him during her long captivity. Resolving his dilemma with a dramatic test of fidelity, Rāma returns to Ayodhyā with Sītā and Lakṣmaṇa, and is crowned king. His reign brings peace, prosperity, and justice to the republic of Kosala, and represents the ideal of kingship.

Our selection ends on this happy note, but the canonical version of Vālmīki's epic continues further. In book 7, *Uttara* ("The Final Book"), not included here, Rāma seems set to rule happily for the rest of his days; but

people soon begin to gossip viciously about Sītā's probable infidelity with Rāvaṇa. In a misguided attempt to be morally answerable to his subjects, Rāma banishes Sītā, even though he knows that the rumors are false and that she is pregnant. Sītā takes refuge in the sage Vālmīki's ashram, where she gives birth to twin boys, Lava and Kuśa. Vālmīki composes a long poem about the life of Rāma; he trains the twins as bards, and teaches them to sing his epic beautifully. One day they sing the tale before the king, who does not know that they are his sons; when he recognizes them, he sends for his beloved queen. Overwhelmed by her suffering by then, however, Sītā asks her mother, the Earth, to take her back; the ground opens beneath her feet, and she disappears forever. Heartbroken, Rāma divides his kingdom between his sons, gives up his life on earth, and returns to heaven in his divine form as Viṣṇu, his task of destroying Rāvaṇa's evil accomplished.

Vālmīki's style in the original varies according to narrative mode. Many important events are narrated directly from an omniscient point of view; in contrast, when characters in the story tell a tale or engage in dialogue, the verse is adapted to capture their voices and personalities. In book 2, when the action is situated in the palace, the descriptions are frequently realistic; in books 3 through 5, when the action is set in the forest and focuses on animals, demons, and fantastic events—Rāvaṇa changing his form, Hanumān flying over the sea—the atmosphere and effect are often fantastic. Even in the forest scenes, however, dream-like passages can be interspersed with flashes of realism, indicating how carefully the text is crafted throughout.

Vālmīki's poem articulates a strong moral vision. It offers us the ideals of Rāma as a son, husband, and king who is serene, courageous, and circum-spect; Sītā as a vibrant, thoughtful, and selfless wife and mother; Lakṣmaṇa as a brother and brother-in-law whose first thought is always for his extended family; and Hanumān as a loyal devo-tee. All these characters are larger than life, but each of them is also flawed or suffers great injustice. Moreover, in a polygamous society, Vālmīki's epic proposes the norm of monogamous marriage based on mutual love between husband and wife; in a world of political conflict, it portrays republics that build alliances for peace, and rulers and sub-jects who live by the law, aiming for social harmony. It explicitly promotes justice, goodness, balance, and morality in forms that remain valid today, even though we may not always agree on the details from a modern perspective.

As a literary narrative with scrip-ture-like religious authority, the story of Rāma is special because it is fully integrated into the annual Hindu cal-endar, the way the story of Christ and the rituals of Christmas, Good Friday, and Easter are woven into the Chris-tian calendar. Every year, in the weeks following the autumnal equinox, the public festivals of Dusehrā and Dīvālī mark the anniversaries, respectively, of Rāma's victory over Rāvaṇa and Rāma's return to Ayodhyā. Over the nine nights preceding Dusehrā, thou-sands of local Hindu communities throughout India perform the Rāma-līlā, "the play of Rāma"; in each commu-nity, children, teenagers, and adults enact the full story of Rāma in nightly installments on an amateur stage, cul-minating in a ritual burning of gigan-tic effigies representing Rāvaṇa and his brothers. On the next night of the new moon (usually in late October), every Indian village, town, and city celebrates Dīvālī, the festival of lights, a symbolic affirmation of Rāma's coro-nation as king and the cyclical resto-ration of goodness and justice in the world.

During the past two millennia, Vālmīki's Rāmāyaṇa has spread aston-ishingly far. In India, hundreds of translations, imitations, adaptations, and retellings have appeared in the dozens of languages that gradually replaced Sanskrit after the first millen-nium C.E. Many of these local and regional versions of the epic—such as Kamban's Irāmavatāram (Tamil, twelfth century) and Tulsīdās's Rāmacaritamānasa (Avadhi/Hindi, six-teenth century)—have become literary and religious classics in their own right; and many of them are transmit-ted orally, in a form called the Rāma-kathā ("the story of Rāma"), in public readings and recitations by profes-sional performers sponsored annually by local communities. Outside India, the Rāmāyaṇa has migrated to the Per-sian, Arabic, and Chinese worlds; the central character of the Monkey King in *Journey to the West*, one of the four major classical novels in Chinese, is modeled on Hanumān. The epic has also reached every part of Southeast Asia, from Malaysia and Indonesia to the Philippines. Vālmīki's tale (origi-nally a Hindu work) reappears with variations in the Thai Rāmakien (thir-teenth century), the national epic of Thailand; in the relief sculptures at Angkor Wat, the Hindu temple com-plex in Cambodia (twelfth century onward); in Balinese classical and folk dance, dance drama, and pantomime; and in the spectacular puppet and shadow-puppet theaters of Malaysia and Indonesia (Muslim-majority soci-eties) and Thailand and Cambodia (Buddhist-majority societies). The characters and stories of Rāma and Sītā, Lakṣmaṇa and Hanumāna and Rāvaṇa, are among the best known for almost half the world's population today.

The Rāmāyaṇa of Vālmīki[1]

From Book 2

Ayodhyā

AYODHYĀ 15–16

The brāhmaṇas[2] had got everything ready for the coronation ceremonies. Gold pots of holy water from all the sacred rivers, most of them gathered at their very source, were ready. All the paraphernalia like the umbrella, the chowries,[3] an elephant and a white horse, were ready, too.

But, the king did not emerge, though the sun had risen and the auspicious hour was fast approaching. The priests and the people wondered: "Who can awaken the king, and inform him that he had better hurry up!" At that moment, Sumantra[4] emerged from the palace. Seeing them, he told them: "Under the king's orders I am going to fetch Rāma." But, on second thought, knowing that the preceptors and the priests commanded even the king's respect, he returned to the king's presence to announce that they were awaiting him. Standing near the king, Sumantra sang: "Arise, O king! Night has flown. Arise and do what should be done." The weary king asked: "I ordered you to fetch Rāma, and I am not asleep. Why do you not do as you are told to do?" This time, Sumantra hurried out of the palace and sped to Rāma's palace.

Entering the palace and proceeding unobstructed through the gates and entrances of the palace, Sumantra beheld the divine Rāma, and said to him: "Rāma, the king who is in the company of queen Kaikeyī desires to see you at once." Immediately, Rāma turned to Sītā and announced: "Surely, the king and mother Kaikeyī wish to discuss with me some important details in connection with the coronation ceremony. I shall go and return soon." Sītā, for her part, offered a heartfelt prayer to the gods: "May I have the blessing of humbly serving you during the auspicious coronation ceremony!"

As Rāma emerged from his palace there was great cheer among the people who hailed and applauded him. Ascending his swift chariot he proceeded to the king's palace, followed by the regalia. Women standing at the windows of their houses and richly adorned to express their joy, showered flowers on Rāma. They praised Kausalyā, the mother of Rāma; they praised Sītā, Rāma's consort: "Obviously she must have done great penance to get him as her husband." The people rejoiced as if they themselves were being installed on the throne. They said to one another: "Rāma's coronation is truly a blessing to all the people. While he rules, and he will rule for a long time, no one will even have an unpleasant experience, or ever suffer." Rāma too was happy to see the huge crowds of people, the elephants and the horses—indicating that people had come to Ayodhyā from afar to witness the coronation.

---

1. Translated by Swami Venkatesananda.
2. Priests, members of the highest caste.
3. Yak-tail fans used to ward off flies; kings were attended by fan bearers.

4. King Daśaratha's charioteer and chief bard. The charioteer/bard (*sūta*) composed and narrated ancient epics and sagas.

AYODHYĀ 17–18

As Rāma proceeded in his radiant chariot towards his father's palace, the people were saying to one another: "We shall be supremely happy hereafter, now that Rāma will be king. But, who cares for all this happiness? When we behold Rāma on the throne, we shall attain eternal beatitude!" Rāma heard all this praise and the people's worshipful homage to him, with utter indifference as he drove along the royal road.[5] The chariot entered the first gate to the palace. From there on Rāma went on foot and respectfully entered the king's apartments. The people who had accompanied him eagerly waited outside.

Rushing eagerly and respectfully to his father's presence, Rāma bowed to the feet of his father and then devoutly touched the feet of his mother Kaikeyī, too. "O Rāma!" said the king: he could not say anything more, because he was choked with tears and grief. He could neither see nor speak to Rāma. Rāma sensed great danger: as if he had trodden on a most poisonous serpent. Turning to Kaikeyī, Rāma asked her: "How is it that today the king does not speak kindly to me? Have I offended him in any way? Is he not well? Have I offended prince Bharata or any of my mothers? Oh, it is agonizing: and incurring his displeasure I cannot live even for an hour. Kindly reveal the truth to me."

In a calm, measured and harsh tone, Kaikeyī now said to Rāma: "The king is neither sick nor angry with you. What he must tell you he does not wish to, for fear of displeasing you. He granted me two boons. When I named them, he recoiled. How can a truthful man, a righteous king, go back on his own word? Yet that is his predicament at the moment. I shall reveal the truth to you if you assure me that you will honor your father's promise." For the first time Rāma was distressed: "Ah, shame! Please do not say such things to me! For the sake of my father I can jump into fire. And, I assure you, Rāma does not indulge in double talk. Hence, tell me what the king wants to be done."

Kaikeyī lost no time. She said: "Long ago I rendered him a great service, and he granted me two boons. I claimed them now: and he promised. I asked for these boons: that Bharata should be crowned, and that you should go away to Daṇḍaka forest now. If you wish to establish that both you and your father are devoted to truth, let Bharata be crowned with the same paraphernalia that have been got ready for you, and go away to the forest for fourteen years. Do this, O best of men, for that is the word of your father; and thus would you redeem the king."

AYODHYĀ 19–20

Promptly and without the least sign of the slightest displeasure, Rāma said: "So be it! I shall immediately proceed to the forest, to dwell there clad in bark and animal skin.[6] But why does not the king speak to me, nor feel happy in my presence? Please do not misunderstand me; I shall go, and I myself will gladly give away to my brother Bharata the kingdom, wealth, Sītā and even my own life, and it is easier when all this is done in obedience to my father's command. Let

---

5. Rāma is an equanimous hero, one who is not affected by praise or blame.
6. Hermits and ascetics who lived in forests had to wear tree bark and animal skins. Queen Kaikeyī's demands included requiring Rāma to live the austere life of a hermit.

Bharata be immediately requested to come. But it breaks my heart to see that father does not say a word to me directly."

Kaikeyī said sternly: "I shall attend to all that, and send for Bharata. I think, however, that you should not delay your departure from Ayodhyā even for a moment. Even the consideration that the father does not say so himself, should not stop you. Till you leave this city, he will neither bathe nor eat." Hearing this, the king groaned, and wailed aloud: "Alas, alas!" and became unconscious again. Rāma decided to leave at once and he said to Kaikeyī: "I am not fond of wealth and pleasure: but even as the sages are, I am devoted to truth. Even if father had not commanded me, and you had asked me to go to the forest I would have done so! I shall presently let my mother and also Sītā know of the position and immediately leave for the forest."

Rāma was not affected at all by this sudden turn of events. As he emerged from the palace, with Lakṣmaṇa, the people tried to hold the royal umbrella over him: but he brushed them aside. Still talking pleasantly and sweetly with the people, he entered his mother's apartment. Delighted to see him, Kausalyā began to glorify and bless him and asked him to sit on a royal seat. Rāma did not, but calmly said to her: "Mother, the king has decided to crown Bharata as the yuvarāja[7] and I am to go to the forest and live there as a hermit for fourteen years." When she heard this, the queen fell down unconscious and grief-stricken. In a voice choked with grief, she said: "If I had been barren, I would have been unhappy; but I would not have had to endure this terrible agony. I have not known a happy day throughout my life. I have had to endure the taunts and the insults of the other wives of the king. Nay, even he did not treat me with kindness or consideration: I have always been treated with less affection and respect than Kaikeyī's servants were treated. I thought that after your birth, and after your coronation my luck would change. My hopes have been shattered. Even death seems to spurn me. Surely, my heart is hard as it does not break into pieces at this moment of the greatest misfortune and sorrow. Life is not worth living without you; so if you have to go to the forest, I shall follow you."

AYODHYĀ 21

Lakṣmaṇa said: "I think Rāma should not go to the forest. The king has lost his mind, overpowered as he is by senility and lust. Rāma is innocent. And, no righteous man in his senses would forsake his innocent son. A prince with the least knowledge of statesmanship should ignore the childish command of a king who has lost his senses." Turning to Rāma, he said: "Rāma, here I stand, devoted to you, dedicated to your cause. I am ready to kill anyone who would interfere with your coronation—even if it is the king! Let the coronation proceed without delay."

Kausalyā said: "You have heard Lakṣmaṇa's view. You cannot go to the forest because Kaikeyī wants you to. If, as you say, you are devoted to dharma, then it is your duty to stay here and serve me, your mother. I, as your mother, am as much worthy of your devotion and service as your father is: and I do not give you permission to go to the forest. If you disobey me in this, terrible will be

7. Crown prince.

your suffering in hell. I cannot live here without you. If you leave, I shall fast unto death."

Rāma, devoted as he was to dharma, spoke: "Among our ancestors were renowned kings who earned fame and heaven by doing their father's bidding. Mother, I am but following their noble example." To Lakṣmaṇa he said: "Lakṣmaṇa, I know your devotion to me, love for me, your prowess and your strength. The universe rests on truth: and I am devoted to truth. Mother has not understood my view of truth, and hence suffers. But I am unable to give up my resolve. Abandon your resolve based on the principle of might; resort to dharma;[8] let not your intellect become aggressive. Dharma, prosperity and pleasure are the pursuit of mankind here;[9] and prosperity and pleasure surely follow dharma: even as pleasure and the birth of a son follow a dutiful wife's service of her husband. One should turn away from that action or mode of life which does not ensure the attainment of all the three goals of life, particularly of dharma; for hate springs from wealth and the pursuit of pleasure is not praiseworthy. The commands of the guru, the king, and one's aged father, whether uttered in anger, cheerfully, or out of lust, should be obeyed by one who is not of despicable behavior, with a view to the promotion of dharma. Hence, I cannot swerve from the path of dharma which demands that I should implicitly obey our father. It is not right for you, mother, to abandon father and follow me to the forest, as if you are a widow. Therefore, bless me, mother, so that I may have a pleasant and successful term in the forest."

AYODHYĀ 22–23

Rāma addressed Lakṣmaṇa again: "Let there be no delay, Lakṣmaṇa. Get rid of these articles assembled for the coronation. And with equal expedition make preparations for my leaving the kingdom immediately. Only thus can we ensure that mother Kaikeyī attains peace of mind. Otherwise she might be worried that her wishes may not be fulfilled! Let father's promise be fulfilled. Yet, so long as the two objects of Kaikeyī's desire are not obtained, there is bound to be confusion in everyone's mind. I must immediately leave for the forest; then Kaikeyī will get Bharata here and have him installed on the throne. This is obviously the divine will and I must honor it without delay. My banishment from the kingdom as well as my return are all the fruits of my own doing (kṛtānta: end of action). Otherwise, how could such an unworthy thought enter the heart of noble Kaikeyī? I have never made any distinction between her and my mother; nor has she ever shown the least disaffection for me so far. The 'end' (reaction) of one's own action cannot be foreseen: and this which we call 'daiva' (providence or divine will) cannot be known and cannot be avoided by anyone. Pleasure, pain, fear, anger, gain, loss, life and death—all these are brought about by 'daiva.' Even sages and great ascetics are prompted by the divine will to give up their self-control and are subjected to lust and anger. It is

---

8. The religious and moral law, code of righteousness.
9. The phrase "dharma, prosperity and pleasure" refers to the first three goals of life for Hindu householders: "religious acts, wealth and public life, and sexual love and family life."

unforeseen and inviolable. Hence, let there be no hostility towards Kaikeyī; she is not to blame. All this is not her doing, but the will of the divine."

Lakṣmaṇa listened to all this with mixed feelings: anger at the turn events had taken, and admiration for Rāma's attitude. Yet, he could not reconcile himself to the situation as Rāma had done. In great fury, he burst forth: "Your sense of duty is misdirected, O Rāma. Even so is your estimation of the divine will. How is it, Rāma, that being a shrewd statesman, you do not see that there are self-righteous people who merely pretend to be good for achieving their selfish and fraudulent ends? If all these boons and promises be true, they could have been asked for and given long ago! Why did they have to wait for the eve of coronation to enact this farce? You ignore this aspect and bring in your argument of the divine will! Only cowards and weak people believe in an unseen divine will: heroes and those who are endowed with a strong mind do not believe in the divine will. Ah, people will see today how my determination and strong action set aside any decrees of the divine will which may be involved in this unrighteous plot. Whoever planned your exile will go into exile! And you will be crowned today. These arms, Rāma, are not handsome limbs, nor are these weapons worn by me ornaments: they are for your service."

AYODHYĀ 24–25

Kausalyā said again: "How can Rāma born of me and the mighty emperor Daśaratha live on food obtained by picking up grains and vegetables and fruits that have been discarded? He whose servants eat dainties and delicacies—how will he subsist on roots and fruits? Without you, Rāma, the fire of separation from you will soon burn me to death. Nay, take me with you, too, if you must go."

Rāma replied: "Mother, that would be extreme cruelty towards father. So long as father lives, please serve him: this is the eternal religion. To a woman her husband is verily god himself. I have no doubt that the noble Bharata will be very kind to you and serve you as I serve you. I am anxious that when I am gone, you should console the king so that he does not feel my separation at all. Even a pious woman who is otherwise righteous, if she does not serve her husband, is deemed to be sinner. On the other hand, she who serves her husband attains blessedness even if she does not worship the gods, perform the rituals or honor the holy men."

Seeing that Rāma was inflexible in his resolve, Kausalyā regained her composure and blessed him. "I shall eagerly await your return to Ayodhyā, after your fourteen years in the forest," said Kausalyā.

Quickly gathering the articles necessary, she performed a sacred rite to propitiate the deities and thus to ensure the health, safety, happy sojourn and quick return of Rāma. "May dharma which you have protected so zealously protect you always," said Kausalyā to Rāma. "May those to whom you bow along the roads and the shrines protect you! Even so, let the missiles which the sage Viśvāmitra[1] gave you ensure your safety. May all the birds and beasts of

---

1. "Missiles" (astra) are magical weapons bestowed on worthy heroes by gods and sages. The sage Viśvāmitra had presented the young Rāma and Lakṣmaṇa with such missiles when they protected his sacrificial rites in the forest from attacks by demons (book 1, Bāla).

the forest, celestial beings and gods, the mountains and the oceans, and the deities presiding over the lunar mansions, natural phenomena and the seasons be propitious to you. May the same blessedness be with you that Indra enjoyed on the destruction of his enemy Vṛtra, that Vinatā bestowed upon her son Garuḍa, that Aditi pronounced upon her son Indra when he was fighting the demons, and that Viṣṇu enjoyed while he measured the heaven and earth.[2] May the sages, the oceans, the continents, the Vedas and the heavens be propitious to you."[3]

As Rāma bent low to touch her feet, Kausalyā fondly embraced him and kissed his forehead, and then respectfully went round him before giving him leave to go.

AYODHYĀ 26–27

Taking leave of his mother, Rāma sought the presence of his beloved wife, Sītā. For her part, Sītā who had observed all the injunctions and prohibitions connected with the eve of the coronation and was getting ready to witness the auspicious event itself, perceived her divine spouse enter the palace and with a heart swelling with joy and pride, went forward to receive him. His demeanor, however, puzzled her: his countenance reflected sorrow and anxiety. Shrewd as she was she realized that something was amiss, and hence asked Rāma: "The auspicious hour is at hand; and yet what do I see! Lord, why are you not accompanied by the regalia, by men holding the ceremonial umbrella, by the royal elephant and the horses, by priests chanting the Vedas, by bards singing your glories? How is it that your countenance is shadowed by sorrow?"

Without losing time and without mincing words, Rāma announced: "Sītā, the king has decided to install Bharata on the throne and to send me to the forest for fourteen years. I am actually on my way to the forest and have come to say good-bye to you. Now that Bharata is the yuvarāja, nay king, please behave appropriately towards him. Remember: people who are in power do not put up with those who sing others' glories in their presence: hence do not glorify me in the presence of Bharata. It is better not to sing my praises even in the presence of your companions. Be devoted to your religious observances and serve my father, my three mothers and my brothers. Bharata and Śatrughna should be treated as your own brothers or sons. Take great care to see that you do not give the least offense to Bharata, the king. Kings reject even their own sons if they are hostile, and are favorable to even strangers who may be friendly. This is my counsel."

Sītā feigned anger, though in fact she was amused. She replied to Rāma: "Your advice that I should stay here in the palace while you go to live in the

---

2. The narrative of the heroic god Indra's victory over the dragonlike demon Vṛtra is an important myth in the *Ṛg-veda*, the oldest of the Hindu scriptures. Aditi is the mother of the gods. The eagle Garuḍa is the mount of Viṣṇu, the god of preservation. In the fifth of his ten incarnations, Viṣṇu took the form of a dwarf (Vāmana), who subsequently grew into the gigantic figure Trivikrama ("the god of three strides"), spanned earth and sky with two strides, then crushed the demon Bali with his third step.
3. The four Vedas are the ancient scriptures of the Hindus. The oceans, continents, and heavens of the Hindu universe are held to have sacred powers.

forest is unworthy of a heroic prince like you, Lord. Whereas one's father, mother, brother, son and daughter-in-law enjoy their own good or misfortune, the wife alone shares the life of her husband. To a woman, neither father nor son nor mother nor friends but the husband alone is her sole refuge here in this world and in the other world, too. Hence I shall accompany you to the forest. I shall go ahead of you, clearing a path for you in the forest. Life with the husband is incomparably superior to life in a palace, or an aerial mansion, or a trip to heaven! I have had detailed instructions from my parents on how to conduct myself in Ayodhyā! But I shall not stay here. I assure you, I shall not be a burden, an impediment, to you in the forest. Nor will I regard life in the forest as exile or as suffering. With you it will be more than heaven to me. It will not be the least hardship to me; without you, even heaven is hell."

AYODHYĀ 28–29

Thinking of the great hardships they would have to endure in the forest, however, Rāma tried to dissuade Sītā in the following words: "Sītā, you come of a very wealthy family dedicated to righteousness. It is therefore proper that you should stay behind and serve my people here. Thus, by avoiding the hardships of the forest and by lovingly serving my people here, would you gladden my heart. The forest is not a place for a princess like you. It is full of great dangers. Lions dwell in the caves; and it is frightening to hear their roar. These wild beasts are not used to seeing human beings; the way they attack human beings is horrifying even to think about. Even the paths are thorny and it is hard to walk on them. The food is a few fruits which might have fallen on their own accord from the trees: living on them, one has to be contented all day. Our garments will be bark and animal skins: and the hair will have to be matted and gathered on the top of the head. Anger and greed have to be given up, the mind must be directed towards austerity and one should overcome fear even where it is natural. Totally exposed to the inclemencies of nature, surrounded by wild animals, serpents and so on, the forest is full of untold hardships. It is not a place for you, my dear."

This reiteration on the part of Rāma moved Sītā to tears. "Your gracious solicitude for my happiness only makes my love for you more ardent, and my determination to follow you more firm. You mentioned animals: they will never come anywhere near me while you are there. You mentioned the righteousness of serving your people: but, your father's command that you should go to the forest demands I should go, too; I am your half: and because of this, again I cannot live without you. In fact you have often declared that a righteous wife will not be able to live separated from her husband. And listen! This is not new to me: for even when I was in my father's house, long before we were married, wise astrologers had rightly predicted that I would live in a forest for some time. If you remember, I have been longing to spend some time in the forest, for I have trained myself for that eventuality. Lord, I feel actually delighted at the very thought that I shall at last go to the forest, to serve you constantly. Serving you, I shall not incur the sin of leaving your parents: thus have I heard from those who are well-versed in the Vedas and other scriptures, that a devoted wife remains united with her husband even after they leave this earth-plane. There is therefore no valid reason why you should wish to leave me here and go. If you still refuse to take me with you, I have no alternative but to lay down my life."

AYODHYĀ 30–31

To the further persuasive talk of Rāma, Sītā responded with a show of annoyance, courage and firmness. She even taunted Rāma in the following words: "While choosing you as his son-in-law, did my father Janaka realize that you were a woman at heart with a male body? Why, then, are you, full of valor and courage, afraid even on my account? If you do not take me with you I shall surely die; but instead of waiting for such an event, I prefer to die in your presence. If you do not change your mind now, I shall take poison and die." In sheer anguish, the pitch of her voice rose higher and higher, and her eyes released a torrent of hot tears.

Rāma folded her in his arms and spoke to her lovingly, with great delight: "Sītā, I could not fathom your mind and therefore I tried to dissuade you from coming with me. Come, follow me. Of course I cannot drop the idea of going to the forest, even for your sake. I cannot live having disregarded the command of my parents. Indeed, I wonder how one could adore the unmanifest god, if one were unwilling to obey the commands of his parents and his guru whom he can see here. No religious activity nor even moral excellence can equal service of one's parents in bestowing supreme felicity on one. Whatever one desires, and whatever region one desires to ascend to after leaving this earth-plane, all this is secured by the service of parents. Hence I shall do as commanded by father; and this is the eternal dharma. And you have rightly resolved, to follow me to the forest. Come, and get ready soon. Give away generous gifts to the brāhmaṇas and distribute the rest of your possessions to the servants and others."

Lakṣmaṇa now spoke to Rāma: "If you are determined to go, then I shall go ahead of you." Rāma, however, tried to dissuade him: "Indeed, I know that you are my precious and best companion. Yet, I am anxious that you should stay behind and look after our mothers. Kaikeyī may not treat them well. By thus serving our mothers, you will prove your devotion to me." But Lakṣmaṇa replied quickly: "I am confident, Rāma, that Bharata will look after all the mothers, inspired by your spirit of renunciation and your adherence to dharma. If this does not prove to be the case, I can exterminate all of them in no time. Indeed, Kausalyā is great and powerful enough to look after herself: she gave birth to you! My place is near you; my duty to serve you."

Delighted to hear this, Rāma said: "Then let us all go. Before leaving I wish to give away in charity all that I possess to the holy brāhmaṇas. Please get them all together. Take leave of your friends and get our weapons ready, too."

* * *

From Book 3

Āraṇya

ĀRAṆYA 14–15

Rāma, Lakṣmaṇa and Sītā were proceeding towards Pañcavaṭī.[4] On the way they saw a huge vulture. Rāma's first thought was that it was a demon in disguise. The vulture said: "I am your father's friend!" Trusting the vulture's words, Rāma asked for details of its birth and ancestry.

The vulture said: "You know that Dakṣa Prajāpati[5] had sixty daughters and the sage Kaśyapa married eight of them. One day Kaśyapa said to his wives: 'You will give birth to offspring who will be foremost in the three worlds.' Aditi, Diti, Danu and Kālaka listened attentively; the others were indifferent. As a result, the former four gave birth to powerful offspring who were superhuman. Aditi gave birth to thirty-three gods. Diti gave birth to demons. Danu gave birth to Aśvagrīva. And, Kālaka had Naraka and Kālikā. Of the others, men were born of Manu, and the sub-human species from the other wives of Kaśyapa. Tāmra's daughter was Sukī whose granddaughter was Vinatā who had two sons, Garuḍa and Aruṇa. My brother Sampāti and I are the sons of Aruṇa. I offer my services to you, O Rāma. If you will be pleased to accept them, I shall guard Sītā when you and Lakṣmaṇa may be away from your hermitage. As you have seen, this formidable forest is full of wild animals and demons, too."

Rāma accepted this new friendship. All of them now proceeded towards Pañcavaṭī in search of a suitable place for building a hermitage. Having arrived at Pañcavaṭī, identified by Rāma by the description which the sage Agastya had given, Rāma said to Lakṣmaṇa: "Pray, select a suitable place here for building the hermitage. It should have a charming forest, good water, firewood, flowers and holy grass." Lakṣmaṇa submitted: "Even if we live together for a hundred years, I shall continue to be your servant. Hence, Lord, you select the place and I shall do the needful." Rejoicing at Lakṣmaṇa's attitude, Rāma pointed to a suitable place, which satisfied all the requisites of a hermitage. Rāma said: "This is holy ground; this is charming; it is frequented by beasts and birds. We shall dwell here." Immediately Lakṣmaṇa set about building a hermitage for all of them to live in.

Rāma warmly embraced Lakṣmaṇa and said: "I am delighted by your good work and devoted service: and I embrace you in token of such admiration. Brother, you divine the wish of my heart, you are full of gratitude, you know dharma; with such a man as his son, father is not dead but is eternally alive."

Entering that hermitage, Rāma, Lakṣmaṇa and Sītā dwelt in it with great joy and happiness.

ĀRAṆYA 16

Time rolled on. One day Lakṣmaṇa sought the presence of Rāma early in the morning and described what he had seen outside the hermitage. He said: "Winter, the season which you love most, has arrived, O Rāma. There is dry

---

4. "Five banyan trees," a grove in western India, toward which Rāma has been directed by the sage Agastya.

5. A progenitor god in ancient Hindu mythology.

cold everywhere; the earth is covered with foodgrains. Water is uninviting; and fire is pleasant. The first fruits of the harvest have been brought in; and the agriculturists have duly offered some of it to the gods and the manes, and thus reaffirmed their indebtedness to them. The farmer who thus offers the first fruits to gods and manes is freed from sin.

"The sun moves in the southern hemisphere; and the north looks lusterless. Himālaya, the abode of snow, looks even more so! It is pleasant to take a walk even at noon. The shade of a tree which we loved in summer is unpleasant now. Early in the morning the earth, with its rich wheat and barley fields, is enveloped by mist. Even so, the rice crop. The sun, even when it rises, looks soft and cool like the moon. Even the elephants which approach the water, touch it with their trunk but pull the trunk quickly away on account of the coldness of the water.

"Rāma, my mind naturally thinks of our beloved brother Bharata. Even in this cold winter, he who could command the luxury of a king, prefers to sleep on the floor and live an ascetic life. Surely, he, too, would have got up early in the morning and has perhaps had a cold bath in the river Sarayū. What a noble man! I can even now picture him in front of me: with eyes like the petals of a lotus, dark brown in color, slim and without an abdomen, as it were. He knows what dharma is. He speaks the truth. He is modest and self-controlled, always speaks pleasantly, is sweet-natured, with long arms and with all his enemies fully subdued.[6] That noble Bharata has given up all his pleasures and is devoted to you. He has already won his place in heaven, Rāma. Though he lives in the city; yet, he has adopted the ascetic mode of life and follows you in spirit.

"We have heard it said that a son takes after his mother in nature: but in the case of Bharata this has proved false. I wonder how Kaikeyī, in spite of having our father as her husband, and Bharata as her son, has turned out to be so cruel."

When Lakṣmaṇa said this, Rāma stopped him, saying: "Do not speak ill of our mother Kaikeyī, Lakṣmaṇa. Talk only of our beloved Bharata. Even though I try not to think of Ayodhyā and our people there, when I think of Bharata, I wish to see him."

ĀRAṆYA 17–18

After their bath and morning prayers, Rāma, Lakṣmaṇa and Sītā returned to their hermitage. As they were seated in their hut, there arrived upon the scene a dreadful demoness. She looked at Rāma and immediately fell in love with him! He had a handsome face; she had an ugly face. He had a slender waist; she had a huge abdomen. He had lovely large eyes; she had hideous eyes. He had lovely soft hair; she had red hair. He had a lovable form; she had a terrible form. He had a sweet voice; hers resembled the barking of a dog. He was young; she was haughty. He was able; her speech was crooked. He was of noble conduct; she was of evil conduct. He was beloved; she had a forbidding appearance. Such a demoness spoke to Rāma: "Who are you, young men; and what are both of you doing in this forest, with this lady?"

---

6. A list of the conventional attributes of a handsome, brave, and virtuous warrior.

Rāma told her the whole truth about himself, Lakṣmaṇa and Sītā, about his banishment from the kingdom, etc. Then Rāma asked her: "O charming lady,[7] now tell me who you are." At once the demoness replied: "Ah, Rāma! I shall tell you all about myself immediately. I am Śūrpaṇakhā, the sister of Rāvaṇa. I am sure you have heard of him. He has two other brothers, Kumbhakarṇa and Vibhīṣaṇa.[8] Two other brothers Khara and Dūṣaṇa live in the neighborhood here. The moment I saw you, I fell in love with you. What have you to do with this ugly, emaciated Sītā? Marry me. Both of us shall roam about this forest. Do not worry about Sītā or Lakṣmaṇa: I shall swallow them in a moment." But, Rāma smilingly said to her: "You see I have my wife with me here. Why do you not propose to my brother Lakṣmaṇa who has no wife here?" Śūrpaṇakhā did not mind that suggestion. She turned to Lakṣmaṇa and said: "It is all right. You please marry me and we shall roam about happily." She was tormented by passion.

Lakṣmaṇa said in a teasing mood: "O lady, you see that I am only the slave of Rāma and Sītā. Why do you choose to be the wife of a slave? You will only become a servant-maid. Persuade Rāma to send away that ugly wife of his and marry you." Śūpaṇakha turned to Rāma again. She said: "Unable to give up this wife of yours, Sītā, you turn down my offer. See, I shall at once swallow her. When she is gone you will marry me; and we shall roam about in this forest happily." So saying, she actually rushed towards Sītā. Rāma stopped her in time, and said to Lakṣmaṇa: "What are you doing, Lakṣmaṇa? It is not right to jest with cruel and unworthy people. Look at the plight of Sītā. She barely escaped with her life. Come, quickly deform this demoness and send her away."

Lakṣmaṇa drew his sword and quickly cut off the nose and the ears of Śūpaṇakhā. Weeping and bleeding she ran away. She went to her brother Khara and fell down in front of him.

* * *

Summary   Distraught and furious, Śūrpaṇakhā asks her brothers Khara and Dūṣaṇa, who live in nearby Janasthāna, to avenge her insult by killing Rāma and Lakṣmaṇa. However, Rāma and Lakṣmaṇa kill the brothers and all their troops.

ĀRAṆYA 32–33

Śūrpaṇakhā witnessed the wholesale destruction of the demons of Janasthāna,[9] including their supreme leader Khara. Stricken with terror, she ran to Laṅkā. There she saw her brother Rāvaṇa, the ruler of Laṅkā, seated with his ministers in a palace whose roof scraped the sky.[1] Rāvaṇa had twenty arms, ten heads, was broad-chested and endowed with all the physical qualifications of a monarch. He had previously fought with the gods, even with their chief Indra. He was well versed in the science of warfare and knew the use of the celestial missiles in battle. He had been hit by the gods, even by the discus[2] of lord Viṣṇu,

7. This formulaic phrase used in addressing a lady is meant ironically here.
8. The names of the demons are suggestive: Śūrpaṇakhā means "woman with nails as large as winnowing baskets" and Kumbhakarṇa

means "pot ear." Vibhīṣaṇa means "terrifying."
9. A region near Pañcavatī.
1. A conventional description of a palace or mansion.
2. A wheel with sharp points, Viṣṇu's weapon.

but he did not die. For, he had performed breathtaking austerities for a period of ten thousand years, and offered his own heads in worship to Brahmā the creator and earned from him the boon that he would not be killed by any superhuman or subhuman agency (except by man). Emboldened by this boon, the demon had tormented the gods and particularly the sages.

Śūrpaṇakhā entered Rāvaṇa's presence, clearly displaying the physical deformity which Lakṣmaṇa had caused to her. She shouted at Rāvaṇa in open assembly: "Brother, you have become so thoroughly infatuated and addicted to sense-pleasure that you are unfit to be a king any longer. The people lose all respect for the king who is only interested in his own pleasure and neglects his royal duties. People turn away from the king who has no spies, who has lost touch with the people and whom they cannot see, and who is unable to do what is good for them. It is the employment of spies that makes the king 'far-sighted' for through these spies he sees quite far. You have failed to appoint proper spies to collect intelligence for you. Therefore, you do not know that fourteen thousand of your people have been slaughtered by a human being. Even Khara and Dūṣaṇa have been killed by Rāma. And, Rāma has assured the ascetics of Janasthāna which is your territory, that the demons shall not do them any harm. They are now protected by him. Yet, here you are; reveling in little pleasures!

"O brother, even a piece of wood, a clod of earth or just dust, has some use; but when a king falls from his position he is utterly useless. But that monarch who is vigilant, who has knowledge of everything, through his spies, who is self-controlled, who is full of gratitude and whose conduct is righteous—he rules for a long time. Wake up and act before you lose your sovereignty."

This made Rāvaṇa reflect.

ĀRAṆYA 34–35

And, Rāvaṇa's anger was roused. He asked Śūrpaṇakhā: "Tell me, who is it that disfigured you thus? What do you think of Rāma? Why has he come to Daṇḍaka forest?"

Śūrpaṇakhā gave an exact and colorful description of the physical appearance of Rāma. She said: "Rāma is equal in charm to Cupid himself. At the same time, he is a formidable warrior. When he was fighting the demons of Janasthāna, I could not see what he was doing; I only saw the demons falling dead on the field. You can easily understand when I tell you that within an hour and a half he had killed fourteen thousand demons. He spared me, perhaps because he did not want to kill a woman. He has a brother called Lakṣmaṇa who is equally powerful. He is Rāma's right-hand man and alter ego; Rāma's own life-force moving outside his body. Oh, you must see Sītā, Rāma's wife. I have not seen even a celestial nymph who could match her in beauty. He who has her for his wife, whom she fondly embraces, he shall indeed be the ruler of gods. She is a fit bride for you; and you are indeed the most suitable suitor for her. In fact, I wanted to bring that beautiful Sītā here so that you could marry her: but Lakṣmaṇa intervened and cruelly mutilated my body. If you could only look at her for a moment, you would immediately fall in love with her. If this proposal appeals to you, take some action quickly and get her here."

Rāvaṇa was instantly tempted. Immediately he ordered his flying chariot to be got ready. This vehicle which was richly adorned with gold, could move freely wherever its owner willed. Its front part resembled mules with fiendish heads. Rāvaṇa took his seat in this vehicle and moved towards the seacoast. The coastline of Laṅkā was dotted with hermitages inhabited by sages and also celestial and semi-divine beings. It was also the pleasure resort of celestials and nymphs who went there to sport and to enjoy themselves. Driving at great speed through them, Rāvaṇa passed through caravan parks scattered with the chariots of the celestials. He also drove through dense forests of sandal trees, banana plantations and cocoanut palm groves. In those forests there were also spices and aromatic plants. Along the coast lay pearls and precious stones. He passed through cities which had an air of opulence.

Rāvaṇa crossed the ocean in his flying chariot and reached the hermitage where Mārīca[3] was living in ascetic garb, subsisting on a disciplined diet. Mārīca welcomed Rāvaṇa and questioned him about the purpose of his visit.

ĀRAŅYA 36–37

Rāvaṇa said to Mārīca: "Listen, Mārīca. You know that fourteen thousand demons, including my brother Khara and the great warrior Triśira, have been mercilessly killed by Rāma and Lakṣmaṇa who have now promised their protection to the ascetics of Daṇḍaka forest, thus flouting our authority. Driven out of his country by his angry father, obviously for a disgraceful action, this unrighteous and hard-hearted prince Rāma has killed the demons without any justification. And, they have even dared to disfigure my beloved sister Śūrpaṇakhā. I must immediately take some action to avenge the death of my brother and to restore our prestige and our authority. I need your help; kindly do not refuse this time.

"Disguising yourself as a golden deer of great beauty, roam near the hermitage of Rāma. Sītā would surely be attracted, and she would ask Rāma and Lakṣmaṇa to capture you. When they go after you, leaving Sītā alone in the hermitage, I shall easily abduct Sītā." Even as Rāvaṇa was unfolding this plot, Mārīca's mouth became dry and parched with fear. Trembling with fear, Mārīca said to Rāvaṇa:

"O king, one can easily get in this world a counselor who tells you what is pleasing to you; but hard it is to find a wise counselor who tells you the unpleasant truth which is good for you—and harder it is to find one who heeds such advice. Surely, your intelligence machine is faulty and therefore you have no idea of the prowess of Rāma. Else, you would not talk of abducting Sītā. I wonder: perhaps Sītā has come into this world to end your life, or perhaps there is to be great sorrow on account of Sītā, or perhaps maddened by lust, you are going to destroy yourself and the demons and Laṅkā itself. Oh, no, you were wrong in your estimation of Rāma. He is not wicked; he is righteousness incarnate. He is not cruel-hearted; he is generous to a fault. He has not been disgraced and exiled from the kingdom. He is here to honor the promise his father had given his mother Kaikeyī, after joyously renouncing his kingdom.

"O king, when you entertain ideas of abducting Sītā you are surely playing with fire. Please remember: when you stand facing Rāma, you are standing face to face with your own death. Sītā is the beloved wife of Rāma, who is

3. An uncle of Rāvaṇa, expert in sorcery.

extremely powerful. Nay, give up this foolish idea. What will you gain by thus gambling with your sovereignty over the demons, and with your life itself? Please consult the noble Vibhīṣaṇa and your virtuous ministers before embarking upon such unwise projects. They will surely advise you against them."

* * *

ĀRAṆYA 42

Rāvaṇa was determined, and Mārīca knew that there was no use arguing with him. Hence, after the last-minute attempt to avert the catastrophe, Mārīca said to Rāvaṇa: "What can I do when you are so wicked? I am ready to go to Rāma's āśrama.[4] God help you!" Not minding the taunt, Rāvaṇa expressed his unabashed delight at Mārīca's consent. He applauded Mārīca and said: "That is the spirit, my friend: you are now the same old Mārīca that I knew. I guess you had been possessed by some evil spirit a few minutes ago, on account of which you had begun to preach a different gospel. Let us swiftly get into this vehicle and proceed to our destination. As soon as you have accomplished the purpose, you are free to go and to do what you please!"

Both of them got into the flying chariot and quickly left the hermitage of Mārīca. Once again they passed forests, hills, rivers and cities: and soon they reached the neighborhood of the hermitage of Rāma. They got down from that chariot which had been embellished with gold. Holding Mārīca by the hand, Rāvaṇa said to him: "Over there is the hermitage of Rāma, surrounded by banana plantations. Well, now, get going with the work for which we have come here." Immediately Mārīca transformed himself into an attractive deer. It was extraordinary, totally unlike any deer that inhabited the forest. It was unique. It dazzled like a huge gem stone. Each part of its body had a different color. The colors had an unearthly brilliance and charm. Thus embellished by the colors of all the precious stones, the deer which was the demon Mārīca in disguise, roamed about near the hermitage of Rāma, nibbling at the grass now and then. At one time it came close to Sītā; then it ran away and joined the other deer grazing at a distance. It was very playful, jumping about and chasing its tail and spinning around. Sītā went out to gather flowers. She cast a glance at that extraordinary and unusual deer. As she did so, the deer too, sensing the accomplishment of the mission, came closer to her. Then it ran away, pretending to be afraid. Sītā marveled at the very appearance of this unusual deer the like of which she had not seen before and which had the hue of jewels.

ĀRAṆYA 43

From where she was gathering flowers, Sītā, filled with wonder to see that unusual deer, called out to Rāma: "Come quick and see, O Lord; come with your brother. Look at this extraordinary creature. I have never seen such a beautiful deer before." Rāma and Lakṣmaṇa looked at the deer, and Lakṣmaṇa's suspicions were aroused: "I am suspicious; I think it is the same demon Mārīca

4. Hermitage.

in disguise. I have heard that Mārīca could assume any form at will, and through such tricks he had brought death and destruction to many ascetics in this forest. Surely, this deer is not real: no one has heard of a deer with rainbow colors, each one of its limbs shining resplendent with the color of a different gem! That itself should enable us to understand that it is a demon, not an animal."

Sītā interrupted Lakṣmaṇa's talk, and said: "Never mind, one thing is certain; this deer has captivated my mind. It is such a dear. I have not seen such an animal near our hermitage! There are many types of deer which roam about near the hermitage; this is just an extraordinary and unusual deer. It is superlative in all respects: its color is lovely, its texture is lovely, and even its voice sounds delightful. It would be a wonderful feat if it could be caught alive. We could use it as a pet, to divert our minds. Later we could take it to Ayodhyā: and I am sure all your brothers and mothers would just adore it. If it is not possible to capture it alive, O Lord, then it can be killed, and I would love to have its skin. I know I am not behaving myself towards both of you: but I am helpless; I have lost my heart to that deer. I am terribly curious."

In fact, Rāma was curious, too! And so, he took Sītā's side and said to Lakṣmaṇa: "It is beautiful, Lakṣmaṇa. It is unusual. I have never seen a creature like this. And, princes do hunt animals and cherish their skins.[5] By sporting and hunting kings acquire great wealth! People say that that is real wealth which one pursues without premeditation. So, let us try to get the deer or its skin. If, as you say, it is a demon in disguise, then surely it ought to be killed by me, just as Vātāpi who was tormenting and destroying sages and ascetics was justly killed by the sage Agastya.[6] Vātāpi fooled the ascetics till he met the sage Agastya. This Mārīca, too, has fooled the ascetics so far: till coming to me today! The very beauty of his hide is his doom. And, you, Lakṣmaṇa, please guard Sītā with great vigilance, till I kill this deer with just one shot and bring the hide along with me."

ĀRAṆYA 44–45

Rāma took his weapons and went after the strange deer. As soon as the deer saw him pursuing it, it started to run away. Now it disappeared, now it appeared to be very near, now it ran fast, now it seemed confused—thus it led Rāma far away from his hermitage. Rāma was fatigued, and needed to rest. As he was standing under a tree, intrigued by the actions of the mysterious deer, it came along with other deer and began to graze not far from him. When Rāma once again went for it, it ran away. Not wishing to go farther nor to waste more time, Rāma took his weapon and fitted the missile of Brahmā[7] to it and fired. This missile pierced the illusory deer-mask and into the very heart of the demon.

---

5. Hermits are required to take a vow of nonviolence, but Rāma, a warrior prince, is allowed to carry arms and to hunt.
6. The demon Vātāpi killed ascetics by tricking them. Disguising himself, he would invite innocent wayfarers to a meal. He would magically conceal himself in the food, thus entering his guests' bellies; he would then kill the men by splitting open their stomachs. The sage Agastya outwitted and killed Vātāpi by digesting his meal, and with it, the demon himself, before he could tear the sage's stomach open.
7. The creator god in the triad of Hindu great gods.

Mārīca uttered a loud cry, leapt high into the sky and then dropped dead onto the ground. As he fell, however, he remembered Rāvaṇa's instructions and assuming the voice of Rāma cried aloud: "Hey, Sītā; hey, Lakṣmaṇa."

Rāma saw the dreadful body of the demon. He knew now that Lakṣmaṇa was right. And, he was even more puzzled by the way in which the demon wailed aloud before dying. He was full of apprehension. He hastened towards the hermitage.

In the hermitage, both Sītā and Lakṣmaṇa heard the cry. Sītā believed it was Rāma's voice. She was panic-stricken. She said to Lakṣmaṇa: "Go, go quickly: your brother is in danger. And, I cannot live without him. My breath and my heart are both violently disturbed." Lakṣmaṇa remembered Rāma's admonition that he should stay with Sītā and not leave her alone. He said to her: "Pray, be not worried." Sītā grew suspicious and furious. She said to him: "Ah, I see the plot now! You have a wicked eye on me and so have been waiting for this to happen. What a terrible enemy of Rāma you are, pretending to be his brother!" Distressed to hear these words, Lakṣmaṇa replied: "No one in the three worlds can overpower Rāma, blessed lady! It was not his voice at all. These demons in the forest are capable of simulating the voice of anyone. Having killed that demon disguised as a deer, Rāma will soon be here. Fear not." His calmness even more annoyed Sītā, who literally flew into a rage. She said again: "Surely, you are the worst enemy that Rāma could have had. I know now that you have been following us, cleverly pretending to be Rāma's brother and friend. I know now that your real motive for doing so is either to get me or you are Bharata's accomplice. Ah, but you will not succeed. Presently, I shall give up my life. For I cannot live without Rāma." Cut to the quick by these terrible words, Lakṣmaṇa said: "You are worshipful to me: hence I cannot answer back. It is not surprising that women should behave in this manner: for they are easily led away from dharma; they are fickle and sharp-tongued. I cannot endure what you said just now. I shall go. The gods are witness to what took place here. May those gods protect you. But I doubt if when Rāma and I return, we shall find you." Bowing to her, Lakṣmaṇa left.

ĀRAṆYA 46

Rāvaṇa was looking for this golden opportunity. He disguised himself as an ascetic, clad in ocher robes, carrying a shell water-pot, a staff and an umbrella, and approached Sītā who was still standing outside the cottage eagerly looking for Rāma's return. His very presence in that forest was inauspicious: and even the trees and the waters of the rivers were frightened of him, as it were. In a holy disguise, Rāvaṇa stood before Sītā: a deep well covered with grass; a death-trap.

Gazing at the noble Sītā, who had now withdrawn into the cottage and whose eyes were raining tears, Rāvaṇa came near her, and though his heart was filled with lust, he was chanting Vedic hymns. He said to Sītā in a soft, tender and affectionate tone: "O young lady! Pray, tell me, are you the goddess of fortune or the goddess of modesty, or the consort of Cupid himself?" Then Rāvaṇa described her incomparable beauty in utterly immodest terms, unworthy of an anchorite whose form he had assumed. He continued: "O charming lady! You have robbed me of my heart. I have not seen such a beautiful lady, neither a divine or a semi-divine being. Your extraordinary form and your youthfulness, and your living in this forest, all these together agitate my mind. It is not right that you should live in this forest. You should stay in palaces. In the forest monkeys, lions, tigers and other wild animals live. The forest is the natural habitat of demons who roam freely. You are living alone in this dreadful forest: are you not afraid, O fair lady? Pray, tell me, why are you living in this forest?"

Rāvaṇa was in the disguise of a brāhmaṇa. Therefore, Sītā offered him the worship and the hospitality that it was her duty to offer a brāhmaṇa. She made him sit down; she gave him water to wash his feet and his hands. Then she placed food in front of him.

Whatever she did only aggravated his lust and his desire to abduct her and take her away to Laṅkā.

ĀRAṆYA 47–48

Sītā, then, proceeded to answer his enquiry concerning herself. He appeared to be a brāhmaṇa; and if his enquiry was not answered, he might get angry and curse her.[8] Sītā said: "I am a daughter of the noble king Janaka; Sītā is my name. I am the beloved consort of Rāma. After our marriage, Rāma and I lived in the palace of Ayodhyā for twelve years." She then truthfully narrated all that took place just prior to Rāma's exile to the forest. She continued: "And so, when Rāma was twenty-five and I was eighteen, we left the palace and sought the forest-life.[9] And so the three of us dwell in this forest. My husband, Rāma, will soon return to the hermitage gathering various animals and also wild fruits. Pray, tell me who you are, O brāhmaṇa, and what you are doing in this forest roaming all alone."

Rāvaṇa lost no time in revealing his true identity. He said: "I am not a brāhmaṇa, O Sītā: I am the lord of demons, Rāvaṇa. My very name strikes terror in the hearts of gods and men. The moment I saw you, I lost my heart to you; and I derive no pleasure from the company of my wives. Come with me, and be my queen, O Sītā. You will love Laṅkā. Laṅkā is my capital, it is surrounded by the ocean and it is situated on the top of a hill. There we shall live together, and you will enjoy your life, and never even once think of this wretched forest-life."

Sītā was furious to hear this. She said: "O demon-king! I have firmly resolved to follow Rāma who is equal to the god of gods, who is mighty and charming, and who is devoted to righteousness.[1] If you entertain a desire for me, his wife, it is like tying yourself with a big stone and trying to swim across the ocean: you are doomed. Where are you and where is he: there is no comparison. You are like a jackal; he the lion.[2] You are like base metal; he gold."

---

8. Priestly *brāhmaṇas* and sages have the power to curse people as well as to bestow boons.
9. Rāma must have been thirteen and Sītā six years old when they were married. The practice of "child marriage" continued in India until very recently.

1. A special epithet of Rāma. "God of gods": an epithet used for warriors, kings, and heroes. It is a reference to Indra, king of heaven and all the gods.
2. King of animals, the lion represents regal majesty and courage, while the jackal is the embodiment of cunning and deceit.

But Rāvaṇa would not give up his desire. He repeated: "Even the gods dare not stand before me, O Sītā! For fear of me even Kubera the god of wealth abandoned his chariot and ran away to Kailāsa. If the gods, headed by Indra, even sense I am angry, they flee. Even the forces of nature obey me. Laṅkā is enclosed by a strong wall; the houses are built of gold with gates of precious stones. Forget this Rāma, who lives like an ascetic, and come with me. He is not as strong as my little finger!" Sītā was terribly angered: "Surely you seek the destruction of all the demons, by behaving like this, O Rāvaṇa. It cannot be otherwise since they have such an unworthy king with no self-control. You may live after abducting Indra's wife, but not after abducting me, Rāma's wife."

ĀRAṆYA 49–50

Rāvaṇa made his body enormously big and said to Sītā: "You do not realize what a mighty person I am. I can step out into space, and lift up the earth with my arms; I can drink up the waters of the oceans; and I can kill death itself. I can shoot a missile and bring the sun down. Look at the size of my body." As he expanded his form, Sītā turned her face away from him. He resumed his original form with ten heads and twenty arms. Again he spoke to Sītā: "Would you not like to be renowned in the three worlds? Then marry me. And, I promise I shall do nothing to displease you. Give up all thoughts of that mortal and unsuccessful Rāma."

Rāvaṇa did not wait for an answer. Seizing Sītā by her hair and lifting her up with his arm, he left the hermitage. Instantly the golden chariot appeared in front of him. He ascended it, along with Sītā. Sītā cried aloud: "O Rāma." As she was being carried away, she wailed aloud: "O Lakṣmaṇa, who is ever devoted to the elder brother, do you not know that I am being carried away by Rāvaṇa?" To Rāvaṇa, she said: "O vile demon, surely you will reap the fruits of your evil action: but they do not manifest immediately." She said as if to herself: "Surely, Kaikeyī would be happy today." She said to the trees, to the river Godāvarī, to the deities dwelling in the forest, to the animals and birds: "Pray, tell Rāma that I have been carried away by the wicked Rāvaṇa." She saw Jaṭāyu and cried aloud: "O Jaṭāyu! See, Rāvaṇa is carrying me away."

Hearing that cry, Jaṭāyu woke up. Jaṭāyu introduced himself to Rāvaṇa: "O Rāvaṇa, I am the king of vultures, Jaṭāyu. Pray, desist from this action unworthy of a king. Rāma, too, is a king; and his consort is worthy of our protection. A wise man should not indulge in such action as would disgrace him in the eyes of others. And, another's wife is as worthy of protection as one's own. The cultured and the common people often copy the behavior of the king. If the king himself is guilty of unworthy behavior what becomes of the people? If you persist in your wickedness, even the prosperity you enjoy will leave you soon.

"Therefore, let Sītā go. One should not get hold of a greater load than one can carry; one should not eat what he cannot digest. Who will indulge in an action which is painful and which does not promote righteousness, fame or permanent glory? I am sixty thousand years old and you are young. I warn you. If you do not give up Sītā, you will not be able to carry her away while I am alive and able to restrain you! I shall dash you down along with that chariot."

ĀRAṆYA 51

Rāvaṇa could not brook this insult: he turned towards Jaṭāyu in great anger. Jaṭāyu hit the chariot and Rāvaṇa; Rāvaṇa hit Jaṭāyu back with terrible ferocity. This aerial combat between Rāvaṇa and Jaṭāyu looked like the collision of two mountains endowed with wings. Rāvaṇa used all the conventional missiles, the Nālikas, the Nārācas and the Vikarṇis. The powerful eagle shrugged them off. Jaṭāyu tore open the canopy of the chariot and inflicted wounds on Rāvaṇa himself.

In great anger, Jaṭāyu grabbed Rāvaṇa's weapon (a cannon) and broke it with his claws. Rāvaṇa took up a more formidable weapon which literally sent a shower of missiles. Against these Jaṭāyu used his own wings as an effective shield. Pouncing upon this weapon, too, Jaṭāyu destroyed it with his claws. Jaṭāyu also tore open Rāvaṇa's armor. Nay, Jaṭāyu even damaged the gold-plated propellers of Rāvaṇa's flying chariot, which had the appearance of demons, and thus crippled the craft which would take its occupant wherever he desired and which emitted fire. With his powerful beak, Jaṭāyu broke the neck of Rāvaṇa's pilot.

With the chariot thus rendered temporarily useless, Rāvaṇa jumped out of it, still holding Sītā with his powerful arm. While Rāvaṇa was still above the ground, Jaṭāyu again challenged him: "O wicked one, even now you are unwilling to turn away from evil. Surely, you have resolved to bring about the destruction of the entire race of demons. Unknowingly or wantonly, you are swallowing poison which would certainly kill you and your relations. Rāma and Lakṣmaṇa will not tolerate this sinful act of yours: and you cannot stand before them on the battle-field. The manner in which you are doing this unworthy act is despicable: you are behaving like a thief not like a hero." Jaṭāyu swooped on Rāvaṇa and violently tore at his body.

Then there ensued a hand-to-hand fight between the two. Rāvaṇa hit Jaṭāyu with his fist; but Jaṭāyu tore Rāvaṇa's arms away. However, new ones sprang up instantly. Rāvaṇa hit Jaṭāyu and kicked him. After some time, Rāvaṇa drew his sword and cut off the wings of Jaṭāyu. When the wings were thus cut, Jaṭāyu fell, dying. Looking at the fallen Jaṭāyu, Sītā ran towards him in great anguish, as she would to the side of a fallen relation. In inconsolable grief, Sītā began to wail aloud.

ĀRAṆYA 52–53

As Sītā was thus wailing near the body of Jaṭāyu, Rāvaṇa came towards her. Looking at him with utter contempt, Sītā said: "I see dreadful omens, O Rāvaṇa. Dreams as also the sight and the cries of birds and beasts are clear indicators of the shape of things to come.[3] But you do not notice them! Alas, here is Jaṭāyu, my father-in-law's friend who is dying on my account. O Rāma, O Lakṣmaṇa, save me, protect me!"

Once again Rāvaṇa grabbed her and got into the chariot which had been made airworthy again. The Creator, the gods and the celestials who witnessed

---

3. Dreams and omens play a comparable role in the culture of the Greeks and Romans.

this, exclaimed: "Bravo, our purpose is surely accomplished."[4] Even the sages of the Daṇḍaka forest inwardly felt happy at the thought, "Now that Sītā has been touched by this wicked demon, the end of Rāvaṇa and all the demons is near." As she was carried away by Rāvaṇa, Sītā was wailing aloud: "O Rāma, O Lakṣmaṇa."

Placed on the lap of Rāvaṇa, Sītā was utterly miserable. Her countenance was full of sorrow and anguish. The petals of the flowers that dropped from her head fell and covered the body of Rāvaṇa for a while. She was of beautiful golden complexion; and he was of dark color. Her being seated on his lap looked like an elephant wearing a golden sash, or the moon shining in the midst of a dark cloud, or a streak of lightning seen in a dense dark cloud.

The chariot streaked through the sky as fast as a meteor would. On the earth below, trees shook as if to reassure Sītā: "Do not be afraid," the waterfalls looked as if mountains were shedding tears, and people said to one another, "Surely, dharma has come to an end, as Rāvaṇa is carrying Sītā away."

Once again Sītā rebuked Rāvaṇa: "You ought to feel ashamed of yourself, O Rāvaṇa. You boast of your prowess; but you are stealing me away! You have not won me in a duel, which would be considered heroic. Alas, for a long, long time to come, people will recount your ignominy, and this unworthy and unrighteous act of yours will be remembered by the people. You are taking me and flying at such speed: hence no one can do anything to stop you. If only you had the courage to stop for a few moments, you would find yourself dead. My lord Rāma and his brother Lakṣmaṇa will not spare you. Leave me alone, O demon! But, you are in no mood to listen to what is good for your own welfare. Even as, one who has reached death's door loves only harmful objects. Rāma will soon find out where I am and ere long you will be transported to the world of the dead."

Rāvaṇa flew along, though now and then he trembled in fear.

ĀRAṆYA 54–55

The chariot was flying over hills and forests and was approaching the ocean. At that time, Sītā beheld on the ground below, five strong vānaras[5] seated and watching the craft with curiosity. Quickly, Sītā took off the stole she had around her shoulders and, removing all her jewels and putting them in that stole, bundled them all up and threw the bundle into the midst of the vānaras, in the hope that should Rāma chance to come there they would give him a clue to her whereabouts.

Rāvaṇa did not notice this but flew on. And now the craft, which shot through space at great speed, was over the ocean; a little while after that, Rāvaṇa entered Laṅkā along with his captive Sītā. Entering his own apartments, Rāvaṇa placed Sītā in them, entrusting her care to some of his chief female attendants. He said to them: "Take great care of Sītā. Let no male approach these apartments without my express permission. And, take great care to let Sītā have whatever she wants and asks for. Any neglect on your part means instant death."

4. We are reminded here that Viṣṇu incarnated himself as Rāma at the request of the gods, who wished Rāvaṇa to be killed.
5. Some scholars have suggested that *vānaras*, usually translated as "monkeys" or "apes," refers to tribal people or apelike human beings. This translator has left the word untranslated.

Rāvaṇa was returning to his own apartments: on the way he was still considering what more could be done to ensure the fulfilment of his ambition. He sent for eight of the most ferocious demons and instructed them thus: "Proceed at once to Janasthāna. It was ruled by my brother Khara; but it has now been devastated by Rāma. I am filled with rage to think that a mere human being could thus kill Khara, Dūṣaṇa and all their forces. Never mind: I shall put an end to Rāma soon. Keep an eye on him and keep me informed of his movements. You are free to bring about the destruction of Rāma." And, the demons immediately left.

Rāvaṇa returned to where Sītā was and compelled her to inspect the apartments. The palace stood on pillars of ivory, gold, crystal and silver and was studded with diamonds. The floor, the walls, the stairways—everything was made of gold and diamonds. Then again he said to Sītā: "Here at this place there are over a thousand demons ever ready to do my bidding. Their services and the entire Laṅkā I place at your feet. My life I offer to you; you are to me more valuable than my life. You will have under your command even the many good women whom I have married. Be my wife. Laṅkā is surrounded by the ocean, eight hundred miles on all sides. It is unapproachable to anybody; least of all to Rāma. Forget the weakling Rāma. Do not worry about the scriptural definitions of righteousness: we shall also get married in accordance with demoniacal wedding procedure. Youth is fleeting. Let us get married soon and enjoy life."

ĀRAṆYA 56

Placing a blade of grass between Rāvaṇa and herself,[6] Sītā said: "O demon! Rāma, the son of king Daśaratha, is my lord, the only one I adore. He and his brother Lakṣmaṇa will surely put an end to your life. If they had seen you lay your hands on me, they would have killed you on the spot, even as they laid Khara to eternal rest. It may be that you cannot be killed by demons and gods; but you cannot escape being killed at the hands of Rāma and Lakṣmaṇa. Rāvaṇa, you are doomed, beyond doubt. You have already lost your life, your good fortune, your very soul and your senses, and on account of your evil deeds Laṅkā has attained widowhood.[7] Though you do not perceive this, death is knocking at your door, O Rāvaṇa. O sinner, you cannot under any circumstances lay your hands on me. You may bind this body, or you may destroy it: it is after all insentient matter, and I do not consider it worth preserving, nor even life worth living—not in order to live a life which will earn disrepute for me."

Rāvaṇa found himself helpless. Hence, he resorted to threat. He said: "I warn you, Sītā. I give you twelve months in which to make up your mind to accept me as your husband. If within that time you do not so decide, my cooks will cut you up easily for my breakfast." He had nothing more to say to her. He turned to the female attendants surrounding her and ordered them: "Take this Sītā away to the Aśoka grove. Keep her there. Use every method of persuasion that you know of to make her yield to my desire. Guard her vigilantly. Take her and break her will as you would tame a wild elephant."

6. The magical power of Sītā's virtue allows her to use even a blade of grass as an effective barrier between herself and her abductor.

7. The ancient Indian king was considered to be the husband of the land he ruled, and kingdoms were often personified as a goddess.

The demonesses thereupon took Sītā away and confined her to the Aśoka grove, over which they themselves mounted guard day and night. Sītā did not find any peace of mind there, and stricken with fear and grief, she constantly thought of Rāma and Lakṣmaṇa.

It is said that at the same time, the creator Brahmā felt perturbed at the plight of Sītā. He spoke to Indra, the chief of gods: "Sītā is in the Aśoka grove. Pining for her husband, she may kill herself. Hence, go reassure her, and give her the celestial food to sustain herself till Rāma arrives in Laṅkā." Indra, thereupon, appeared before Sītā. In order to assure her of his identity he showed that his feet did not touch the ground and his eyes did not wink.[8] He gave her the celestial food, saying: "Eat this, and you will never feel hunger or thirst, nor will fatigue overpower you." While Indra was thus talking to Sītā, the goddess of sleep (Nidrā) had overpowered the demonesses.

ĀRAṆYA 57–58

Mārīca, the demon who had disguised himself as a unique deer, had been slain. But Rāma was intrigued and puzzled by the way in which Mārīca died, after crying: "O Sītā, O Lakṣmaṇa." Rāma sensed a deep and vicious plot. Hence he made haste to return to his hermitage. At the same time, he saw many evil omens. This aggravated his anxiety. He thought: "If Lakṣmaṇa heard that voice, he might rush to my aid, leaving Sītā alone. The demons surely wish to harm Sītā; and this might well have been a plot to achieve that purpose."

As he was thus brooding and proceeding towards his hermitage, he saw Lakṣmaṇa coming towards him. The distressed Rāma met the distressed Lakṣmaṇa; the sorrowing Rāma saw the sorrowful Lakṣmaṇa. Rāma caught hold of Lakṣmaṇa's arm and asked him, in an urgent tone: "O Lakṣmaṇa, why have you left Sītā alone and come? My mind is full of anxiety and terrible apprehension. When I see all these evil omens around us, I fear that something terrible has happened to Sītā. Surely Sītā has been stolen, killed or abducted."

Lakṣmaṇa's silence and grief-stricken countenance added fuel to the fire of anxiety in Rāma's heart. He asked again: "Is all well with Sītā? Where is my Sītā, the life of my life, without whom I cannot live even for an hour? Oh, what has happened to her? Alas, Kaikeyī's desire has been fulfilled today. If I am deprived of Sītā, I shall surely die. What more could Kaikeyī wish for? If, when I enter my hermitage, I do not find Sītā alive, how shall I live? Tell me, Lakṣmaṇa; speak. Surely, when that demon cried: 'O Lakṣmaṇa' in my voice, you were afraid that something had happened to me. Surely, Sītā also heard that cry and in a state of terrible mental agony, sent you to me. It is a painful thing that thus Sītā has been left alone; the demons who were waiting for an opportunity to hit back have been given that opportunity. The demons were sore distressed by my killing of the demon Khara. I am sure that they have done some great harm to Sītā, in the absence of both of us. What can I do now? How can I face this terrible calamity?"

Still, Lakṣmaṇa could not utter a word concerning what had happened. Both of them arrived near their hermitage. Everything that they saw reminded them of Sītā.

8. Attributes of the immortals.

ĀRAṆYA 59–60

And, once again before actually reaching the hermitage, and full of apprehension on account of Sītā, Rāma said to Lakṣmaṇa: "Lakṣmaṇa, you should not have come away like this, leaving Sītā alone in the hermitage. I had entrusted her to your care." When Rāma said this again and again, Lakṣmaṇa replied: "I have not come to you, leaving Sītā alone, just because I heard the demon Mārīca cry: 'O Lakṣmaṇa, O Sītā' in your voice. I did so only upon being literally driven by Sītā to do so. When she heard the cry, she immediately felt distressed and asked me to go to your help. I tried to calm her saying: 'It is not Rāma's voice; it is unthinkable that Rāma, who is capable of protecting even the gods, would utter the words, 'save me.' She, however, misunderstood my attitude. She said something very harsh, something very strange, something which I hate even to repeat. She said: 'Either you are an agent of Bharata or you have unworthy intentions towards me and therefore you are happy that Rāma is in distress and do not rush to his help.' It is only then that I had to leave."

In his anxiety for Sītā, Rāma was unimpressed by this argument. He said to Lakṣmaṇa: "Swayed by an angry woman's words, you failed to carry out my words; I am not highly pleased with what you have done, O Lakṣmaṇa."

Rāma rushed into their hermitage. But he could find no trace of Sītā in it. Confused and distressed beyond measure, Rāma said to himself, as he continued to search for Sītā: "Where is Sītā? Alas, she could have been eaten by the demons. Or, taken away by someone. Or, she is hidden somewhere. Or, she has gone to the forest." The search was fruitless. His anguish broke its bounds. Not finding her, he was completely overcome by grief and he began to behave as if he were mad.[9]

Unable to restrain himself, he asked the trees and the birds and the animals of the forest; "Where is my beloved Sītā?" The eyes of the deer, the trunk of the elephant, the boughs of trees, the flowers—all these reminded Rāma of Sītā. "Surely, you know where my beloved Sītā is. Surely, you have a message from her. Won't you tell me? Won't you assuage the pain in my heart?" Thus Rāma wailed. He thought he saw Sītā at a distance and going up to 'her,' he said: "My beloved, do not run away. Why are you hiding yourself behind those trees? Will you not speak to me?" Then he said to himself: "Surely it was not Sītā. Ah, she has been eaten by the demons. Did I leave her alone in the hermitage only to be eaten by the demons?" Thus lamenting, Rāma roamed awhile and ran around awhile.

ĀRAṆYA 61–62

Again Rāma returned to the hermitage, and, seeing it empty, gave way to grief again. He asked Lakṣmaṇa: "Where has my beloved Sītā gone, O Lakṣmaṇa? Or, has she actually been carried away by someone?" Again, imagining that it was all fun and a big joke which Sītā was playing, he said: "Enough of this fun, Sītā; come out. See, even the deer are stricken with grief because they do not see you." Turning to Lakṣmaṇa again, he said: "Lakṣmaṇa, I cannot live without my Sītā. I shall soon join my father in the other world. But, he may be

9. The description of the lover maddened by grief, searching for his beloved, is a theme in many literary traditions: examples include the Greek myth of Orpheus's search for Eurydice and the Persian story of Majnun ("the mad lover"), who wanders in the wilderness looking for Laila.

annoyed with me and say: 'I told you to live in the forest for fourteen years; how have you come here before that period?' Ah Sītā, do not forsake me."

Lakṣmaṇa tried to console him: "Grieve not, O Rāma. Surely, you know that Sītā is fond of the forest and the caves on the mountainside. She must have gone to these caves. Let us look for her in the forest. That is the proper thing to do; not to grieve."

These brave words took Rāma's grief away. Filled with zeal and eagerness, Rāma along with Lakṣmaṇa, began to comb the forest. Rāma was distressed: "Lakṣmaṇa, this is strange; I do not find Sītā anywhere." But Lakṣmaṇa continued to console Rāma: "Fear not, brother; you will surely recover the noble Sītā soon."

But this time, these words were less meaningful to Rāma. He was overcome by grief, and he lamented: "Where shall we find Sītā, O Lakṣmaṇa, and when? We have looked for her everywhere in the forest and on the hills, but we do not find her." Lamenting thus, stricken with grief, with his intelligence and his heart robbed by the loss of Sītā, Rāma frequently sighed in anguish, muttering: "Ah my beloved."

Suddenly, he thought he saw her, hiding herself behind the banana trees, and now behind the karnikara trees. And, he said to 'her': "My beloved, I see you behind the banana trees! Ah, now I see you behind the karnikara tree: my dear, enough, enough of this play: for your fun aggravates my anguish. I know you are fond of such play; but pray, stop this and come to me now."

When Rāma realized that it was only his hallucination, he turned to Lakṣmaṇa once more and lamented: "I am certain now that some demon has killed my beloved Sītā. How can I return to Ayodhyā without Sītā? How can I face Janaka, her father? Oh, no: Lakṣmaṇa, even heaven is useless without Sītā; I shall continue to stay in the forest; you can return to Ayodhyā. And you can tell Bharata that he should continue to rule the country."

ĀRAŅYA 63–64

Rāma was inconsolable and even infected the brave Lakṣmaṇa. Shedding tears profusely, Rāma continued to speak to Lakṣmaṇa who had also fallen a prey to grief by this time: "No one in this whole world is guilty of as many misdeeds as I am, O Lakṣmaṇa: and that is why I am being visited by sorrow upon sorrow, grief upon grief, breaking my heart and dementing me. I lost my kingdom, and I was torn away from my relations and friends. I got reconciled to this misfortune. But then I lost my father. I was separated from my mother. Coming to this hermitage, I was getting reconciled to that misfortune. But I could not remain at peace with myself for long. Now this terrible misfortune, the worst of all, has visited me.

"Alas, how bitterly Sītā would have cried while she was carried away by some demon. May be she was injured; may be her lovely body was covered with blood. Why is it that when she was subjected to such suffering, my body did not split into pieces? I fear that the demon must have cut open Sītā's neck and drunk her blood. How terribly she must have suffered when she was dragged by the demons.

"Lakṣmaṇa, this river Godāvarī was her favorite resort. Do you remember how she used to come and sitting on this slab of stone talk to us and laugh? Probably she came to the river Godāvarī in order to gather lotuses? But, no: she would never go alone to these places.

"O sun! You know what people do and what people do not do. You know what is true and what is false. You are a witness to all these. Pray, tell me, where has my beloved Sītā gone. For, I have been robbed of everything by this grief. O wind! You know everything in this world, for you are everywhere. Pray, tell me, in which direction did Sītā go?"

Rāma said: "See, Lakṣmaṇa, if Sītā is somewhere near the river Godāvarī." Lakṣmaṇa came back and reported that he could not find her. Rāma himself went to the river and asked the river: "O Godāvarī, pray tell me, where has my beloved Sītā gone?" But the river did not reply. It was as if, afraid of the anger of Rāvaṇa, Godāvarī kept silent.

Rāma was disappointed. He asked the deer and the other animals of the forest: "Where is Sītā? Pray, tell me in which direction has Sītā been taken away." He then observed the deer and the animals; all of them turned southwards and some of them even moved southwards. Rāma then said to Lakṣmaṇa: "O Lakṣmaṇa, see, they are all indicating that Sītā has been taken in a southerly direction."

ĀRAṆYA 64

Lakṣmaṇa, too, saw the animals' behavior as sure signs indicating that Sītā had been borne away in a southerly direction, and suggested to Rāma they should also proceed in that direction. As they were thus proceeding, they saw petals of flowers fallen on the ground. Rāma recognized them and said to Lakṣmaṇa: "Look here, Lakṣmaṇa, these are petals from the flowers that I had given to Sītā. Surely, in their eagerness to please me, the sun, the wind and the earth, have contrived to keep these flowers fresh."

They walked further on. Rāma saw footprints on the ground. Two of them he immediately recognized as those of Sītā. The other two were big—obviously the footprints of a demon. Bits and pieces of gold were strewn on the ground. Lo and behold, Rāma also saw blood which he concluded was Sītā's blood: he wailed again: "Alas, at this spot, the demon killed Sītā to eat her flesh." He also saw evidence of a fight: and he said: "Perhaps there were two demons fighting for the flesh of Sītā."

Rāma saw on the ground pieces of a broken weapon, an armor of gold, a broken canopy, and the propellers and other parts of a flying chariot. He also saw lying dead, one who had the appearance of the pilot of the craft. From these he concluded that two demons had fought for the flesh of Sītā, before one carried her away. He said to Lakṣmaṇa: "The demons have earned my unquenchable hate and wrath. I shall destroy all of them. Nay, I shall destroy all the powers that be who refuse to return Sītā to me. Look at the irony of fate, Lakṣmaṇa: we adhere to dharma, but dharma could not protect Sītā who has been abducted in this forest! When these powers that govern the universe witness Sītā being eaten by the demons, without doing anything to stop it, who is there to do what is pleasing to us? I think our meekness is misunderstood to be weakness. We are full of self-control, compassion and devoted to the welfare of all beings: and yet these virtues have become as good as vices in us now. I shall set aside all these virtues and the universe shall witness my supreme glory which will bring about the destruction of all creatures, including the demons. If Sītā is not immediately brought back to me, I shall destroy the three worlds—the gods, the demons and other creatures will perish, becoming targets of my most powerful missiles. When I take up my weapon in anger, O Lakṣmaṇa, no one can confront me, even as no one can evade old age and death."

ĀRAŅYA 65–66

Seeing the world-destroying mood of Rāma, Lakṣmaṇa endeavored to console him. He said to Rāma:

"Rāma, pray, do not go against your nature. Charm in the moon, brilliance in the sun, motion in the air, and endurance in the earth—these are their essential nature: in you all these are found and in addition, eternal glory. Your nature cannot desert you; even the sun, the moon and the earth cannot abandon their nature! Moreover, being king, you cannot punish all the created beings for the sin of one person. Gentle and peaceful monarchs match punishment to crime: and, over and above this, you are the refuge of all beings and their goal. I shall without fail find out the real criminal who has abducted Sītā; I shall find out whose armor and weapons these are. And you shall mete out just punishment to the sinner. Oh, no, no god will seek to displease you, O Rāma: Nor these trees, mountains and rivers. I am sure they will all eagerly aid us in our search for Sītā. Of course, if Sītā cannot be recovered through peaceful means, we shall consider other means.

"Whom does not misfortune visit in this world, O Rāma? And, misfortune departs from man as quickly as it visits him. Hence, pray, regain your composure. If you who are endowed with divine intelligence betray lack of endurance in the face of this misfortune, what will others do in similar circumstances?

"King Nahuṣa, who was as powerful as Indra, was beset with misfortune.[1] The sage Vasiṣṭha, our family preceptor, had a hundred sons and lost all of them on one day! Earth is tormented by volcanic eruptions, and earthquakes. The sun and the moon are afflicted by eclipses. Misfortune strikes the great ones and even the gods.

"For, in this world people perform actions whose results are not obvious; and these actions which may be good or evil, bear their own fruits. Of course, these fruits are evanescent. People who are endowed with enlightened intelligence know what is good and what is not good. People like you do not grieve over misfortunes and do not get deluded by them.

"Why am I telling you all this, O Rāma? Who in this world is wiser than you? However, since, as is natural, grief seems to veil wisdom, I am saying all this. All this I learnt only from you: I am only repeating what you yourself taught me earlier. Therefore, O Rāma, know your enemy and fight him."

ĀRAŅYA 67–68

Rāma then asked Lakṣmaṇa: "O Lakṣmaṇa, tell me, what should we do now?" Lakṣmaṇa replied: "Surely, we should search this forest for Sītā."

This advice appealed to Rāma. Immediately he fixed the bayonet to his weapon and with a look of anger on his face, set out to search for Sītā. Within a very short time and distance, both Rāma and Lakṣmaṇa chanced upon Jaṭāyu, seriously and mortally wounded and heavily bleeding. Seeing that enormous vulture lying on the ground, Rāma's first thought was: "Surely, this is the one that has swallowed Sītā." He rushed forward with fixed bayonet.

Looking at Rāma thus rushing towards him, and rightly inferring Rāma's mood, Jaṭāyu said in a feeble voice: "Sītā has been taken away by Rāvaṇa. I

---

1. King Nahuṣa, an ancestor of Rāma, became so powerful that he claimed the throne of Indra, king of gods, but an arrogant act soon effected his fall from his exalted position.

tried to intervene. I battled with the mighty Rāvaṇa. I broke his armor, his canopy, the propellers and some parts of his chariot. I killed his pilot. I even inflicted injuries on his person. But he cut off my wings and thus grounded me." When Rāma heard that the vulture had news of Sītā, he threw his weapon away and kneeling down near the vulture embraced it.

Rāma said to Lakṣmaṇa: "An additional calamity to endure, O Lakṣmaṇa. Is there really no end to my misfortune? My misfortune plagues even this noble creature, a friend of my father's." Rāma requested more information from Jaṭāyu concerning Sītā, and also concerning Rāvaṇa. Jaṭāyu replied: "Taking Sītā with him, the demon flew away in his craft, leaving a mysterious storm and cloud behind him. I was mortally wounded by him. Ah, my senses are growing dim. I feel life ebbing away, Rāma. Yet, I assure you, you will recover Sītā." Soon Jaṭāyu lay lifeless. Nay, it was his body, for he himself ascended to heaven. Grief-stricken afresh, Rāma said to Lakṣmaṇa: "Jaṭāyu lived a very long life; and yet has had to lay down his life today. Death, no one in this world can escape. And what a noble end! What a great service this noble vulture has rendered to me! Pious and noble souls are found even amongst subhuman creatures, O Lakṣmaṇa. Today I have forgotten all my previous misfortunes: I am extremely tormented by the loss of this dear friend who has sacrificed his life for my sake. I shall myself cremate it, so that it may reach the highest realms."

Rāma himself performed the funeral rites, reciting those Vedic mantras[2] which one recites during the cremation of one's own close relations. After this, Rāma and Lakṣmaṇa proceeded on their journey in search of Sītā.

* * *

Summary   While searching desperately for Sītā, Rāma and Laksmana encounter a tribe of monkeys, whose citadel is at Kiskindhā in southern India. Intervening in the political quarrels among their factions, the princes persuade the monkeys, and one of their powerful leaders, Hanumāna, to help them look for her. Hanumāna eventually discovers where Sītā is held captive, after spying on Rāvana's capital. Sītā refuses to escape with Hanumāna, insisting instead that Rāma himself must free her from captivity. Hanumāna sets fire to Rāvana's city as a warning of impending war, and returns to apprise Rāma of the situation. The monkey hordes build a bridge across the straits to Lankā, giving the princes and their army a passage to Lankā, where they begin to wage battle. One of Rāvana's brothers betrays him and joins Rāma and Laksmana against Rāvana. After a lengthy conflict, in which Rāvana's other brothers are killed and Laksmana is wounded, Rāma finally confronts the demon king in single combat.

From Book 6

Yuddha

YUDDHA 109–11

When Rāma and Rāvaṇa began to fight, their armies stood stupefied, watching them! Rāma was determined to win; Rāvaṇa was sure he would die: knowing this, they fought with all their might. Rāvaṇa attacked the standard on Rāma's car: and Rāma similarly shot the standard on Rāvaṇa's car. While Rāvaṇa's

2. Sacred chants, usually from the scriptures.

standard fell; Rāma's did not. Rāvaṇa next aimed at the "horses" of Rāma's car: even though he attacked them with all his might, they remained unaffected.

Both of them discharged thousands of missiles: these illumined the skies and created a new heaven, as it were! They were accurate in their aim and their missiles unfailingly hit the target. With unflagging zeal they fought each other, without the least trace of fatigue. What one did the other did in retaliation.

Rāvaṇa shot at Mātali[3] who remained unaffected by it. Then Rāvaṇa sent a shower of maces and mallets at Rāma. Their very sound agitated the oceans and tormented the aquatic creatures. The celestials and the holy brāhmaṇas witnessing the scene prayed: "May auspiciousness attend to all the living beings, and may the worlds endure forever. May Rāma conquer Rāvaṇa." Astounded at the way in which Rāma and Rāvaṇa fought with each other, the sages said to one another: "Sky is like sky, ocean is like ocean; the fight between Rāma and Rāvaṇa is like Rāma and Rāvaṇa—incomparable."

Taking up a powerful missile, Rāma correctly aimed at the head of Rāvaṇa; it fell. But another head appeared in its place. Every time Rāma cut off Rāvaṇa's head, another appeared! Rāma was puzzled. Mātali, Rāma's driver, said to Rāma: "Why do you fight like an ordinary warrior, O Rāma? Use the Brahmā-missile; the hour of the demon's death is at hand."

Rāma remembered the Brahmā-missile which the sage Agastya had given him. It had the power of the wind-god for its "feathers"; the power of fire and sun at its head; the whole space was its body; and it had the weight of a mountain. It shone like the sun or the fire of nemesis. As Rāma took it in his hands, the earth shook and all living beings were terrified. Infallible in its destructive power, this ultimate weapon of destruction shattered the chest of Rāvaṇa, and entered deep into the earth.

Rāvaṇa fell dead. And the surviving demons fled, pursued by the vānaras. The vānaras shouted in great jubilation. The air resounded with the drums of the celestials. The gods praised Rāma. The earth became steady, the wind blew softly and the sun was resplendent as before. Rāma was surrounded by mighty heroes and gods who were all joyously felicitating him on the victory.

YUDDHA 112–13

Seeing Rāvaṇa lying dead on the battlefield, Vibhīṣaṇa burst into tears. Overcome by brotherly affection, he lamented thus: "Alas, what I had predicted has come true: and my advice was not relished by you, overcome as you were by lust and delusion. Now that you have departed, the glory of Laṅkā has departed. You were like a tree firmly established in heroism with asceticism for its strength, spreading out firmness in all aspects of your life: yet you have been cut down. You were like an elephant with splendor, noble ancestry, indignation, and pleasant nature for parts: yet you have been killed. You, who were like blazing fire have been extinguished by Rāma."

Rāma approached the grief-stricken Vibhīṣaṇa and gently and lovingly said to him: "It is not right that you should thus grieve, O Vibhīṣaṇa, for a mighty warrior fallen on the battlefield. Victory is the monopoly of none: a hero is either slain in battle or he kills his opponent. Hence our ancients decreed that

---

3. Indra, king of the gods, has sent his own charioteer, Mātali, to drive Rāma's chariot in battle.

the warrior who is killed in combat should not be mourned. Get up and consider what should be done next."

Vibhīṣaṇa regained his composure and said to Rāma: "This Rāvaṇa used to give a lot in charity to ascetics; he enjoyed life; he maintained his servants well; he shared his wealth with his friends, and he destroyed his enemies. He was regular in his religious observances; learned he was in the scriptures. By your grace, O Rāma, I wish to perform his funeral in accordance with the scriptures, for his welfare in the other world." Rāma was delighted and said to Vibhīṣaṇa: "Hostility ends at death. Take steps for the due performance of the funeral rites. He is your brother as he is mine, too."

The womenfolk of Rāvaṇa's court, and his wives, hearing of his end, rushed out of the palace, and, arriving at the battlefield, rolled on the ground in sheer anguish. Overcome by grief they gave vent to their feelings in diverse heart-rending ways. They wailed: "Alas, he who could not be killed by the gods and demons, has been killed in battle by a man standing on earth. Our beloved lord! Surely when you abducted Sītā and brought her to Laṅkā, you invited your own death! Surely it was because death was close at hand that you did not listen to the wise counsel of your own brother Vibhīṣaṇa, and you ill-treated him and exiled him. Even later if you had restored Sītā to Rāma, this evil fate would not have overtaken you. However, it is surely not because you did what you liked, because you were driven by lust, that you lie dead now: God's will makes people do diverse deeds. He who is killed by the divine will dies. No one can flout the divine will, and no one can buy the divine will nor bribe it."

* * *

YUDDHA 115–16

Rāma returned to the camp where the vānara troops had been stationed. He turned to Lakṣmaṇa and said: "O Lakṣmaṇa, install Vibhīṣaṇa on the throne of Laṅkā and consecrate him as the king of Laṅkā. He has rendered invaluable service to me and I wish to behold him on the throne of Laṅkā at once."

Without the least loss of time, Lakṣmaṇa made the necessary preparations and with the waters of the ocean consecrated Vibhīṣaṇa as king of Laṅkā, in strict accordance with scriptural ordinance. Rāma, Lakṣmaṇa and the others were delighted. The demon-leaders brought their tributes and offered them to Vibhīṣaṇa who in turn placed them all at Rāma's feet.

Rāma said to Hanumān: "Please go, with the permission of king Vibhīṣaṇa, to Sītā and inform her of the death of Rāvaṇa and the welfare of both myself and Lakṣmaṇa." Immediately Hanumān left for the Aśoka-grove. The grief-stricken Sītā was happy to behold him. With joined palms Hanumān submitted Rāma's message and added: "Rāma desires me to inform you that you can shed fear, for you are in your own home as it were, now that Vibhīṣaṇa is king of Laṅkā." Sītā was speechless for a moment and then said: "I am delighted by the message you have brought, O Hanumān; and I am rendered speechless by it. I only regret that I have nothing now with which to reward you; nor is any gift equal in value to the most joyous tidings you have brought me." Hanumān submitted: "O lady, the very words you have uttered are more precious than all the jewels of the world! I consider myself supremely blessed to have witnessed Rāma's victory and Rāvaṇa's destruction." Sītā was even more delighted: she said, "Only you can utter such sweet words, O Hanumān, endowed as you are with manifold excellences. Truly you are an abode of virtues."

Hanumān said: "Pray, give me leave to kill all these demonesses who have been tormenting you so long." Sītā replied: "Nay, Hanumān, they are not responsible for their actions, for they were but obeying their master's commands. And, surely, it was my own evil destiny that made me suffer at their hands. Hence, I forgive them. A noble man does not recognize the harm done to him by others: and he never retaliates, for he is the embodiment of goodness. One should be compassionate towards all, the good and the wicked, nay even towards those who are fit to be killed: who is free from sin?" Hanumān was thrilled to hear these words of Sītā, and said: "Indeed you are the noble consort of Rāma and his peer in virtue and nobility. Pray, give me a message to take back to Rāma." Sītā replied: "Please tell him that I am eager to behold his face." Assuring Sītā that she would see Rāma that very day, Hanumān returned to Rāma.

YUDDHA 117–19

Hanumān conveyed Sītā's message to Rāma who turned to king Vibhīṣaṇa and said: "Please bring Sītā to me soon, after she has had a bath and has adorned herself." Immediately Vibhīṣaṇa went to Sītā and compelled her to proceed seated in a palanquin, to where Rāma was. Vānaras and demons had gathered around her, eager to look at Sītā. And Vibhīṣaṇa, in accordance with the tradition, wished to ensure that Sītā was not seen by these and rebuked them to go away. Restraining him, Rāma said: "Why do you rebuke them, O Vibhīṣaṇa? Neither houses nor clothes nor walls constitute a veil for a woman; her character alone is her veil. Let her descend from the palanquin and walk up to me." So she did.

Rāma said sternly: "My purpose has been accomplished, O Sītā. My prowess has been witnessed by all. I have fulfilled my pledge. Rāvaṇa's wickedness has been punished. The extraordinary feat performed by Hanumān in crossing the ocean and burning Laṅkā[4] has borne fruit. Vibhīṣaṇa's devotion has been rewarded." Rāma's heart was in a state of conflict, afraid as he was of public ridicule. Hence, he continued: "I wish to let you know that all this was done not for your sake, but for the sake of preserving my honor. Your conduct is open to suspicion, hence even your sight is displeasing to me. Your body was touched by Rāvaṇa: how then can I, claiming to belong to a noble family, accept you? Hence I permit you to go where you like and live with whom you like—either Lakṣmaṇa, Bharata, Śatrughna, Sugrīva or even Vibhīṣaṇa. It is difficult for me to believe that Rāvaṇa, who was so fond of you, would have been able to keep away from you for such a long time."

Sītā was shocked. Rāma's words wounded her heart. Tears streamed down her face. Wiping them, she replied: "O Rāma, you are speaking to me in the language of a common and vulgar man speaking to a common woman. That

---

4. When Hanumān destroys the groves of Laṅkā, Rāvaṇa's henchmen capture him and set his tail on fire. Hanumān sets fire to Laṅkā's mansions with his fiery tail and himself escapes unhurt.

which was under my control, my heart, has always been yours; how could I prevent my body from being touched when I was helpless and under another person's control? Ah, if only you had conveyed your suspicion through Hanumān when he came to meet me, I would have killed myself then and saved you all this trouble and the risk involved in the war." Turning to Lakṣmaṇa, she said: "Kindle the fire, O Lakṣmaṇa: that is the only remedy. I shall not live to endure this false calumny." Lakṣmaṇa looked at Rāma and with his approval kindled the fire. Sītā prayed: "Even as my heart is ever devoted to Rāma, may the fire protect me. If I have been faithful to Rāma in thought, word or deed, may the fire protect me. The sun, the moon, the wind, earth and others are witness to my purity; may the fire protect me." Then she entered into the fire, even as an oblation poured into the fire would. Gods and sages witnessed this. The women who saw this screamed.

YUDDHA 120–21

Rāma was moved to tears by the heart-rending cries of all those women who witnessed the self-immolation of Sītā. At the same time, all the gods, including the trinity—the Creator, the Preserver, and the Redeemer (or Transformer)[5]—arrived upon the scene in their personal forms. Saluting Rāma, they said: "You are the foremost among the gods, and yet you treat Sītā as if you were a common human being!"

Rāma replied to these divinities: "I consider myself a human being, Rāma the son of Daśaratha. Who I am, and whence I am, may you tell me!"

Brahmā the creator said: "You are verily lord Nārāyaṇa.[6] You are the imperishable cosmic being. You are the truth. You are eternal. You are the supreme dharma of the worlds. You are the father even of the chief of the gods, Indra. You are the sole refuge of perfected beings and holy men. You are the Om,[7] and you are the spirit of sacrifice. You are that cosmic being with infinite heads, hands and eyes.[8] You are the support of the whole universe. The whole universe is your body. Sītā is Lakṣmī[9] and you are lord Viṣṇu, who is of a dark hue, and who is the creator of all beings. For the sake of the destruction of Rāvaṇa you entered into a human body. This mission of ours has been fully accomplished by you. Blessed it is to be in your presence; blessed it is to sing your glories; they are truly blessed who are devoted to you, for their life will be attended with success."

As soon as Brahmā finished saying this, the god of fire emerged from the fire in his personal form, holding up Sītā in his hands. Sītā shone in all her radiance. The god of fire who is the witness of everything that takes place in the world, said to Rāma: "Here is your Sītā, Rāma. I find no fault in her. She has not erred in thought, word or deed. Even during the long period of her detention in the abode of Rāvaṇa, she did not even think of him, as her

5. The triad of the three great gods, Brahmā (Creator), Viṣṇu (Preserver), and Śiva (Redeemer or Transformer).
6. Viṣṇu in his primeval cosmic form.
7. A sacred chant (mantra) of the Vedas.
8. The cosmic being described here is Puruṣa, or "Man," a primeval being with innumerable heads, arms, and eyes who was offered as the sacrificial victim by the gods and sages in the first sacrifice, described in a hymn of the Ṛg-veda.
9. Goddess-consort of Viṣṇu.

heart was set on you. Accept her: and I command you not to treat her harshly."

Rāma was highly pleased at this turn of events. He said: "Indeed, I was fully aware of Sītā's purity. Even the mighty and wicked Rāvaņa could not lay his hands upon her with evil intention. Yet, this baptism by fire was necessary, to avoid public calumny and ridicule, for though she was pure, she lived in Laṅkā for a long time. I knew, too, that Sītā would never be unfaithful to me: for we are non-different from each other even as the sun and its rays are. It is therefore impossible for me to renounce her."

After saying so, Rāma was joyously reunited with Sītā.

YUDDHA 122–23

Lord Śiva then said to Rāma: "You have fulfilled a most difficult task. Now behold your father, the illustrious king Daśaratha who appears in the firmament to bless you and to greet you."

Rāma along with Lakṣmaṇa saw that great monarch, their father clad in a raiment of purity and shining by his own luster. Still seated in his celestial vehicle, Daśaratha lifted up Rāma and placing him on his lap, warmly embraced him and said: "Neither heaven nor even the homage of the gods is as pleasing to me as to behold you, Rāma. I am delighted to see that you have successfully completed the period of your exile and that you have destroyed all your enemies. Even now the cruel words of Kaikeyī haunt my heart; but seeing you and embracing you, I am rid of that sorrow, O Rāma. You have redeemed my word and thus I have been saved by you. It is only now that I recognize you to be the supreme person incarnated as a human being in this world in order to kill Rāvaņa."

Rāma said: "You remember that you said to Kaikeyī, 'I renounce you and your son'? Pray, take back that curse and may it not afflict Kaikeyī and Bharata." Daśaratha agreed to it and then said to Lakṣmaṇa: "I am pleased with you, my son, and you have earned great merit by the faithful service you have rendered to Rāma."

Lastly, king Daśaratha said to Sītā: "My dear daughter, do not take to heart the fire ordeal that Rāma forced you to undergo: it was necessary to reveal to the world your absolute purity. By your conduct you have exalted yourself above all women." Having thus spoken to them, Daśaratha ascended to heaven.

Before taking leave of Rāma, Indra prayed: "Our visit to you should not be fruitless, O Rāma. Command me, what may I do for you?" Rāma replied: "If you are really pleased with me, then I pray that all those vānaras who laid down their lives for my sake may come back to life. I wish to see them hale and hearty as before. I also wish to see the whole world fruitful and prosperous." Indra replied: "This indeed is an extremely difficult task. Yet, I do not go back on my word, hence I grant it. All the vānaras will come back to life and be restored to their original form, with all their wounds healed. Even as you had asked, the world will be fruitful and prosperous."

Instantly, all the vānaras arose from the dead and bowed to Rāma. The others who witnessed this marveled and the gods beheld Rāma who had all his wishes fulfilled. The gods returned to their abodes.

* * *

Summary   After crowning Vibhīsaṇa king of Laṅkā, Rāma, Lakṣmaṇa and Sītā fly to Ayodhyā in Rāvaṇa's flying chariot, accompanied by Vibhīṣaṇa, Sugrīva, Hanumān, and the monkey hordes.

YUDDHA 130

Bharata immediately made the reception arrangements. He instructed Śatrughna: "Let prayers be offered to the gods in all temples and houses of worship with fragrant flowers and musical instruments."

Śatrughna immediately gave orders that the roads along which the royal procession would wend its way to the palace should be leveled and sprinkled with water, and kept clear by hundreds of policemen cordoning them. Soon all the ministers, and thousands of elephants and men on horse-back and in cars went out to greet Rāma. The royal reception party, seated in palanquins,[1] was led by the queen-mother Kausalyā herself; Kaikeyī and the other members of the royal household followed—and all of them reached Nandigrāma.[2]

From there Bharata headed the procession with the sandals of Rāma placed on his head, with the white royal umbrella and the other regalia.[3] Bharata was the very picture of an ascetic though he radiated the joy that filled his heart at the very thought of Rāma's return to the kingdom.

Bharata anxiously looked around but saw no signs of Rāma's return! But, Hanumān reassured him: "Listen, O Bharata, you can see the cloud of dust raised by the vānaras rushing towards Ayodhyā. You can now hear the roar of the Puṣpaka flying chariot."

"Rāma has come!"—these words were uttered by thousands of people at the same time. Even before the Puṣpaka landed, Bharata humbly saluted Rāma who was standing on the front side of the chariot. The Puṣpaka landed. As Bharata approached it, Rāma lifted him up and placed him on his lap. Bharata bowed down to Rāma and also to Sītā and greeted Lakṣmaṇa. And he embraced Sugrīva, Jāmbavān, Aṅgada, Vibhīṣaṇa and others. He said to Sugrīva: "We are four brothers, and with you we are five. Good deeds promote friendship, and evil is a sign of enmity."

Rāma bowed to his mother who had become emaciated through sorrow, and brought great joy to her heart. Then he also bowed to Sumitrā and Kaikeyī. All the people thereupon said to Rāma: "Welcome, welcome back, O Lord."

Bharata placed the sandals in front of Rāma, and said: "Rāma, here is your kingdom which I held in trust for you during your absence. I consider myself supremely blessed in being able to behold your return to Ayodhyā. By your grace, the treasury has been enriched tenfold by me, as also the storehouses and the strength of the nation." Rāma felt delighted. When the entire party

1. Litters in which people were carried by bearers.
2. The village outside the city of Ayodhyā, from which Bharata ruled the kingdom on behalf of Rāma.

3. By carrying Rāma's sandals on his head, Bharata indicates his subservience to and reverence for Rāma as his sovereign, elder brother, and teacher.

had disembarked, he instructed that the Puṣpaka be returned to its original owner, Kubera.[4]

YUDDHA 131

The coronation proceedings were immediately initiated by Bharata. Skilled barbers removed the matted locks of Rāma. He had a ceremonial bath and he was dressed in magnificent robes and royal jewels. Kausalyā herself helped the vānara ladies to dress themselves in royal robes; all the queens dressed Sītā appropriately for the occasion. The royal chariot was brought; duly ascending it, Rāma, Lakṣmaṇa and Sītā went in a procession to Ayodhyā, Bharata himself driving the chariot. When he had reached the court, Rāma gave his ministers and counselors a brief account of the events during his exile, particularly the alliance with the vānara chief Sugrīva, and the exploits of Hanumān. He also informed them of his alliance with Vibhīṣaṇa.

At Bharata's request, Sugrīva despatched the best of the vānaras to fetch water from the four oceans, and all the sacred rivers of the world. The aged sage Vasiṣṭha thereupon commenced the ceremony in connection with the coronation of Rāma. Rāma and Sītā were seated on a seat made entirely of precious stones. The foremost among the sages thereupon consecrated Rāma with the appropriate Vedic chants. First the brāhmaṇas, then the virgins, then the ministers and warriors, and later the businessmen poured the holy waters on Rāma.[5] After that the sage Vasiṣṭha placed Rāma on the throne made of gold and studded with precious stones, and placed on his head the dazzling crown which had been made by Brahmā the creator himself. The gods and others paid their homage to Rāma by bestowing gifts upon him. Rāma also gave away rich presents to the brāhmaṇas and others, including the vānara chiefs like Sugrīva. Rāma then gave to Sītā a necklace of pearls and said: "You may give it to whom you like, Sītā." And, immediately Sītā bestowed that gift upon Hanumān.

After witnessing the coronation of Rāma, the vānaras returned to Kiṣkindhā. So did Vibhīṣaṇa return to Laṅkā. Rāma looked fondly at Lakṣmaṇa and expressed the wish that he should reign as the prince regent. Lakṣmaṇa did not reply: he did not want it. Rāma appointed Bharata as prince regent. Rāma thereafter ruled the earth for a very long time.

During the period of Rāma's reign, there was no poverty, no crime, no fear, and no unrighteousness in the kingdom. All the people constantly spoke of Rāma; the whole world had been transformed into Rāma. Everyone was devoted to dharma. And Rāma was highly devoted to dharma, too. He ruled for eleven thousand years.

YUDDHA 131

Rāma's rule of the kingdom was characterized by the effortless and spontaneous prevalence of dharma. People were free from fear of any sort. There were

---

4. God of wealth.
5. The *brāhmaṇas*, ministers and warriors, and businessmen represent the three highest caste-groups in Hindu society.

no widows in the land: people were not molested by beasts and snakes, nor did they suffer from diseases. There was no theft, no robbery nor any violence. Young people did not die, making older people perform funeral services for them. Everyone was happy and everyone was devoted to dharma; beholding Rāma alone, no one harmed another. People lived long and had many children. They were healthy and they were free from sorrow. Everywhere people were speaking all the time about Rāma; the entire world appeared to be the form of Rāma. The trees were endowed with undying roots, and they were in fruition all the time and they flowered throughout the year. Rain fell whenever it was needed. There was a pleasant breeze always. The brāhmaṇas (priests), the warriors, the farmers and businessmen, as also the members of the servant class, were entirely free from greed, and were joyously devoted to their own dharma and functions in society. There was no falsehood in the life of the people who were all righteous. People were endowed with all auspicious characteristics and all of them had dharma as their guiding light. Thus did Rāma rule the world for eleven thousand years, surrounded by his brothers.

This holy epic Rāmāyaṇa composed by the sage Vālmīki, promotes dharma, fame, long life and in the case of a king, victory. He who listens to it always is freed from all sins. He who desires sons gets them, and he who desires wealth becomes wealthy, by listening to the story of the coronation of Rāma. The king conquers the whole world, after overcoming his enemies. Women who listen to this story will be blessed with children like Rāma and his brothers. And they, too, will be blessed with long life, after listening to the Rāmāyaṇa. He who listens to or reads this Rāmāyaṇa propitiates Rāma by this; Rāma is pleased with him; and he indeed is the eternal lord Viṣṇu.

LAVA AND KUŚA said: Such is the glorious epic, Rāmāyaṇa. May all recite it and thus augment the glory of dharma, of lord Viṣṇu. Righteous men should regularly listen to this story of Rāma, which increases health, long life, love, wisdom and vitality.

THE BHAGAVAD-GĪTĀ
ca. fourth century B.C.E.–fourth century C.E.

The *Bhagavad-gītā* asks the most difficult of questions. What is a just war, and when can the use of armed conflict to resolve a political stalemate be justified? Under what circumstances is it possible to engage in a violent conflict with family members, clansmen, teachers, and friends—the very people who have nurtured us since infancy—and claim a victory that is morally right? What is such a victory worth if, in the name of life, wealth, or truth, it destroys what we love? As a philosophical poem, the *Bhagavad-gītā* does not provide simple answers but offers explanations that are appropriately difficult because they involve dilemmas that cannot be resolved once and for all.

CONTEXT

During the past two centuries, it has become commonplace to treat the *Bhagavad-gītā* as an independent poem, which can be read and understood by itself for its philosophical message as a meditation on universal issues. But the work is actually an integral part of the *Mahabharata*, and was originally composed as the sixty-third minor book of that epic, and included in its sixth major book, *Bhīṣma*. Since it is a poem within a poem, the *Bhagavad-gītā* is best interpreted in relation to the epic's larger narrative, setting, and background.

The *Mahabharata* is attributed to a single poet or compiler named Kṛṣṇa Dvaipāyana, but it was composed collaboratively by many generations of poets in Sanskrit between about 400 B.C.E. and 400 C.E. Its main story concerns a protracted conflict between two branches of a royal dynasty in northern India, over the inheritance of a kingdom and the succession to its throne. The embattled groups are the Kauravas and the Pāṇḍavas, who are paternal cousins; the Kauravas are one hundred brothers, led by their eldest, Duryodhana, whereas the Pāṇḍavas are five half brothers, the three eldest being Yudhiṣṭhira, Bhīma, and Arjuna. Both branches have strong and legitimate claims to the kingdom, and one possible settlement is a division of the dominion, so that each set of cousins can rule its own territory without conflict. But Duryodhana and his brothers, the Kauravas, resist such a solution; using a variety of strategies, they deny the Pāṇḍavas' claim, and send the five brothers and their shared wife (in a polyandrous marriage) into a thirteen-year exile, with the promise to restore their share of territory if they meet several conditions. The Pāṇḍavas complete their exile as required, but when they return to Duryodhana's court, he refuses to honor his word.

At this point in the main narrative, Lord Kṛṣṇa—a human avatar of Viṣṇu, the god who primarily preserves the moral order of the universe—intervenes on behalf of the Pāṇḍavas. In the course of his life in human form, Kṛṣṇa became a close friend of the third Pāṇḍava, Arjuna, in his youth; now, many years later, when Arjuna and his half brothers find themselves in an impossible situation with their cousins, Kṛṣṇa agrees to serve as their ambassador to Duryodhana. Even though Kṛṣṇa (whose divinity is evident to the other characters in the epic) offers the Kauravas a peaceable solution in accordance with *dharma* (law, morality, duty, obligation), Duryodhana refuses to give the Pāṇḍavas even five small villages as their share of the kingdom. In consultation with Kṛṣṇa, the Pāṇḍavas decide that the only way in which they can now assert their legitimate claim to the kingdom is by going to war with the Kauravas. This is a just war because their claim is based strictly on the *dharma* of succession and inheritance; and it is a justifiable war because they have exhausted every possibility of a peaceful resolution of the stalemate with the Kauravas.

The Kauravas and Pāṇḍavas then prepare for armed conflict, and their respective armies gather on the battlefield of Kurukṣetra (about sixty-five miles north of modern Delhi). Arjuna, the most skilled and feared archer of his times, enters the battlefield on a chariot, with Kṛṣṇa serving as his charioteer. But in the moments just before the battle begins, Arjuna looks at the forces arrayed on the enemy side, and sees in their midst all his cousins as well as many people he grew up with— teachers, friends, and members of his clan, people he has known and loved much of his life. Faced with the prospect of shedding their blood, he throws down his weapons and refuses to fight: he cannot imagine how any such war could possibly be good or right. But, in doing so, he immediately places himself in moral jeopardy as a warrior, because *dharma* requires that a *kṣatriya* be prepared to wage war whenever necessary, and in this case his cause is just. Caught between his fundamental duty as a warrior and his equally powerful obligation to preserve the lives of those he loves, Arjuna turns to Kṛṣṇa—his friend, aide, and counselor—and asks for his divine advice under the circumstances. The *Bhagavad-gītā* is the poetic record of that moment of crisis in Arjuna's mind, and of the conversation he has with God on the brink of war.

WORK

The *Bhagavad-gītā* is divided into eighteen chapters or cantos composed in verse, and its total length runs to seven hundred couplets. In the translation from which our selection of passages is drawn, each canto is called a "chapter"; it contains, in part, Kṛṣṇa's instruction to Arjuna about what is involved in war, violence, duty, courage, life, and death (among other things), and why it is essential to fight a just war, even if it means destroying precious lives.

The structure of the *Bhagavad-gītā* as a whole has two layers of interspersed dialogue: one between Sañjaya and Dhṛtarāṣṭra, which defines the outer frame of the book, and the other between Arjuna and Kṛṣṇa, which occurs in an inner frame. Dhṛtarāṣṭra is the father of the Kauravas and the current head of the dynasty; he is blind and old, and cannot participate in or even observe the battle. He sits in his chariot on the edge of the battlefield with his chari-oteer, a youth named Sañjaya; on the eve of the war, Dvaipāyana, the original author of the *Mahabharata*, grants Sañjaya "celestial vision," so that he can omnisciently observe everything in the past, present, and future, and everything that happens on the battlefield, in public and in private; throughout the eighteen days of the war, Sanjaya tells the blind Dhṛtarāṣṭra what happens in the war, and we, the readers, also witness the entire conflict through Sañjaya's "visionary eye." Our excerpts here mostly omit the dialogue between Sañjaya and Dhṛtarāṣṭra in the various cantos; the main exception is the passage from Chapter Eleven, which ends with a portion of Sañjaya's narrative.

In the excerpt from Chapter One we hear Arjuna's voice, explaining to Kṛṣṇa at length why he is unable to take up arms against his blood relatives, mentors, and friends. In the segments from Chapter Two, Kṛṣṇa begins his response to Arjuna's dilemma by explaining the nature of the imperishable self or soul embodied in every human being. In the portions reproduced from Chapter Three, Arjuna raises fresh questions about human action in relation to the inner self and to evil, and Kṛṣṇa teaches him the yoga or discipline of action, especially as it should be practiced by a warrior. In the next excerpt, which jumps ahead to Chapter Six, Kṛṣṇa then explains what self-discipline in general is, and what a man who establishes complete control over himself can accomplish. In the final passage, drawn from Chapter Eleven, Arjuna achieves a comprehensive, new understanding of his task as a warrior, and asks Kṛṣṇa to reveal his full divine form; Kṛṣṇa does so, but the vision is so intense that a merely human eye cannot experience it. The narrator Sanjaya, talking to King Dhṛtarāṣṭra, therefore intercedes with his extraordinary visual capacity, and reports, in part, what Kṛṣṇa reveals to Arjuna.

The passages from the *Bhagavad-gītā* reproduced here cover only a small portion of Lord Kṛṣṇa's advice to Arjuna on the battlefield of Kurukṣetra. In the course of the eighteen cantos of the book, Kṛṣṇa constructs a long argument, containing many strands, about the justification for violence in the context of a war that is morally right and in complete accordance with all applicable aspects of *dharma*. Especially when encountered in excerpts, this argument can be, and often has been, easily misunderstood. Kṛṣṇa emphatically does *not* offer a general justification for violence under all circumstances; the use of violence to settle a major dispute can be justified only when every possible option for a peaceful resolution has been explored within the full scope of the law, and all such options have failed. Moreover, in a just war, only the thoroughly trained and disciplined warrior can use violence, and even he can do so only when he is in complete control of himself, and selflessly pursues his duty as defined by *dharma*.

From The Bhagavad-gītā[1]

From CHAPTER ONE[2]

* * *

20   "Now Monkey-Bannered Arjuna,[3]
seeing his foes drawn up for war,
raised his bow, that Son of Pandu,
as the weapons began to clash.

21   "Then he said these words to Krishna:[4]
'Lord of the Earth, Unshaken One,
bring my chariot to a halt
between the two adverse armies,

22   'so I may see these men, arrayed
here for the battle they desire,
whom I am soon to undertake
a warrior's delight in fighting!

23   'I see those who have assembled,
the warriors prepared to fight,
eager to perform in battle
for Dhritarashtra's evil son!'[5]

24   "When Arjuna had spoken so
to Krishna, O Bharata,[6]
he, having brought their chariot
to a halt between the armies,

1. Translated by Gavin Flood and Charles Martin. Verse numbers run to the left of the text.
2. Most of the *Bhagavad-gītā* is narrated by Sañjaya; the double quotation marks throughout these excerpts represent Sanjaya's direct speech, addressed to Dhṛtarāṣṭra. For an explanation of these two characters, who define the outer narrative frame of the poem, see the "Work" section of the headnote. The single quotation marks represent the dialogue between Arjuna and Kṛṣṇa, which takes place within Sanjaya's narrative.
3. The third of the five sons of Pāṇḍu.
4. An incarnation of Viṣṇu, the preserver god.
5. Duryodhana, the leader of the Kauravas, who is the eldest son of Dhṛtarāṣṭra.
6. An alternate name or epithet for Dhṛtarāṣṭra, who, like his brother Pāṇḍu and their respective sons, is a descendant of Bhārata, the founder of their dynasty of kings.

25   "in the face of Bhishma, Drona,[7]
and the other Lords of the Earth,[8]
said, 'Behold, O Son of Pritha,[9]
how these Kurus[1] have assembled!'

26   "And there the son of Pritha saw
rows of grandfathers and grandsons;
sons and fathers, uncles, in-laws;
teachers, brothers and companions,

27   "all relatives and friends of his
in both of the assembled armies.
And seeing them arrayed for war,
Arjuna, the Son of Kunti,

28   "felt for them a great compassion,
as well as great despair, and said,
'O Krishna, now that I have seen
my relatives so keen for war,

29   'I am unstrung: my limbs collapse
beneath me, and my mouth is dry,
there is a trembling in my body,
and my hair rises, bristling;

30   'Gandiva, my immortal bow,[2]
drops from my hand and my skin burns,
I cannot stand upon my feet,
my mind rambles in confusion—

31   'All inauspicious are the signs
that I see, O Handsome-Haired One![3]
I foresee no good resulting
from slaughtering my kin in war!

32   'I have no wish for victory,
nor for kingship and its pleasures!
O Krishna, what good is kingship?
What good even life and pleasure?

33   'Those for whose sake we desire
kingship, pleasures and enjoyments,
are now drawn up in battle lines,
their lives and riches now abandoned:

---

7. Droṇa was the teacher or guru of both the Kauravas and the Pāṇḍavas; Bhīṣma is the granduncle of both these branches of the family.

8. "Lord of the earth" is a common epithet for a king in epic Sanskrit.

9. Another name for Kuntī, the mother of Arjuna and the Pāṇḍavas.

1. Another name for the Kauravas.

2. A powerful celestial bow of great antiquity and renown that Arjuna won from the fire god, Agni.

3. Kṛṣṇa is often depicted with long, flowing hair.

34 'fathers, grandfathers; sons, grandsons;
my mother's brothers and the men
who taught me in my youth; brothers-
and fathers-in-law: kinsmen all!

35 'Though they are prepared to slay us,
I do not wish to murder them,
not even to rule the three worlds—
how much less one earthly kingdom?

36 'What joy for us in murdering
Dhritarashtra's sons, O Krishna?
for if we killed these murderers,
evil like theirs would cling to us!

37 'So we cannot in justice slay
our kinsmen, Dhritarashtra's sons,
for, having killed our people, how
could we be pleased, O Madhava?[4]

38 'Even if they, mastered by greed,
are blind to the consequences
of the family's destruction,
of friendships lost to treachery,

39 'how are we not to comprehend
that we must turn back from evil?
The wrong done by this destruction
is evident, O Shaker of Men.

40 'For with the family destroyed,
its eternal laws must perish;
and when they perish, lawlessness
overwhelms the whole family.

41 'Whelmed by lawlessness, the women
of the family are corrupted;
from corrupted women comes
the intermingling of classes.[5]

42 'Such intermingling sends to hell
the family and its destroyers:

---

4. One of Viṣṇu's 1,008 names in Hindu ritual and mythology, meaning "the one sweet as
honey."
5. "Intermingling" here refers to miscegenation, and "classes" to caste-groups. The caste
system is based on endogamy, or marriage
within a caste-group (varṇa) or caste (jātī);
only if both partners come from the same
social category can that category be reproduced in the next generation. Here Kṛṣṇa
affirms that if two spouses belong to different
social categories (varṇa or jātī), then their children do not belong to the same category as
their parents, and hence undermine the "laws
of caste."

their ancestors fall then, deprived
of rice and water offerings.[6]

43 'Those who destroy the family,
who institute class-mingling,
cause the laws of the family
and laws of caste to be abolished.

44 'Men whose familial laws have been
obliterated, O Krishna,
are damned to dwell eternally
in hell, as we have often heard.

45 'It grieves me that as we intend
to murder our relatives
in our greed for pleasures, kingdoms,
we are fixed on doing evil!

46 'If the sons of Dhritarashtra,
armed as they are, should murder me
weaponless and unresisting,
I would know greater happiness!'

47 "And having spoken, Arjuna
collapsed into his chariot,
his bow and arrows clattering,
and his mind overcome with grief."

From CHAPTER TWO

* * *

"The Lord[7] said:

11 'Although you seem to speak wisely,
you have mourned those not to be mourned:
the wise do not grieve for those gone
or for those who are not yet gone.

12 'There was no time when I was not,
nor you, nor these lords around us,
and there will never be a time
henceforth when we shall not exist.

13 'The embodied one passes through
childhood, youth, and then old age,
then attains another body;
in this the wise are undeceived.[8]

---

6. Hindus are required to make these ritual offerings to their ancestors.
7. Lord Kṛṣṇa, who now addresses Arjuna.
8. Here Kṛṣṇa explains the process of reincarnation, emphasizing the identity of the seemingly finite embodied soul (*ātman*) with the infinite and imperishable universal spirit or godhead (*Brahman*).

14 'Contacts with matter by which we
feel heat and cold, pleasure and pain,
are transitory, come and go:
these you must manage to endure.

15 'Such contacts do not agitate
a wise man, O Bull among Men,
to whom pleasure and pain are one.
He is fit for immortality.

16 'Non-being cannot come to be,
nor can what is come to be not.
The certainty of these sayings
is known by seers of the truth.

17 'Know it as indestructible,
that by which all is pervaded;
no one may cause the destruction
of the imperishable one.

18 'Bodies of the embodied one,
eternal, boundless, all-enduring,
are said to die; the one cannot:
therefore, take arms, O Bharata!

19 'This man believes the one may kill;
That man believes it may be killed;
both of them lack understanding:
it can neither kill nor *be* killed.

20 'It is not born, nor is it ever mortal,
and having been, will not pass from existence;
ancient, unborn, eternally existing,
it does not die when the body perishes.

21 'How can a man who knows the one
to be eternal (both unborn
and without end) murder or cause
another to? Whom does he kill?

22 'Someone who has abandoned worn-out garments
sets out to clothe himself in brand-new raiment;
just so, when it has cast off worn-out bodies,
the embodied one will encounter others.

23 'This may not be pierced by weapons,
nor can this be consumed by flames;
flowing waters cannot drench this,
nor blowing winds desiccate this.

24 'Not to be pierced, not to be burned,
neither drenched nor desiccated—

eternal, all-pervading, firm,
unmoving, everlasting this!

25 'This has been called unmanifest,
unthinkable and unchanging;
therefore, because you know this now,
you should not lament, Arjuna.

26 'But even if you think that this
is born and dies time after time,
forever, O great warrior,
not even then should you mourn this.

27 'Death is assured to all those born,
and birth assured to all the dead;
you should not mourn what is merely
inevitable consequence.

28 'Beginnings are unmanifest,
but manifest the middle-state,
and ends unmanifest again;
so what is your complaint about?

29 'Somebody looks upon this as a marvel,
and likewise someone tells about this marvel,
and yet another hears about this marvel,
but even having heard it, no one knows it.

30 'The one cannot ever perish
in a body it inhabits,
O Descendent of Bharata;
and so no being should be mourned.

31 'Nor should you tremble to perceive
your duty as a warrior;
for him there is nothing better
than a battle that is righteous.

32 'And if by chance they will have gained
the wide open gate of heaven,
O Son of Pritha, warriors
rejoice in fighting such as that!

33 'If you turn from righteous warfare,
your behavior will be evil,
for you will have abandoned both
your duty and your honored name.

34 'People will speak of your disgrace
forever, and an honored man
who falls from honor into shame
suffers a fate much worse than death.

* * *

47 " 'Your concern should be with action,
never with an action's fruits;
these should never motivate you,
nor attachment to inaction.

48 'Established in this practice, act
without attachment, Arjuna,
unmoved by failure or success!
Equanimity is yoga.

49 'Action is far inferior
to the practice of higher mind;
seek refuge there, for pitiful
are those moved by fruit of action!

50 'One disciplined by higher mind
here casts off good and bad actions;
therefore, be yoked to discipline;
discipline is skill in actions.

51 'Having left the fruit of action,
the wise ones yoked to higher mind
are freed from the bonds of rebirth,
and go where no corruption is.

52 'When your higher mind has crossed
over the thicket of delusion,
you will become disenchanted
with what is heard in the *Vedas*.[9]

53 'When, unvexed by revelation,
your higher mind is motionless
and stands fixed in meditation,
then you will attain discipline.'

"Arjuna asked,

54 'Tell me, Krishna, how may I know
the man steady in his wisdom,
who abides in meditation?
How should that one sit, speak and move?'

"The Blessed Lord replied,

55 'When he renounces all desires
entering his mind, Arjuna,

---

9. Kṛṣṇa suggests here that the older ritualis-
tic knowledge embodied in the Vedas is useless for the liberation of the individual self or
soul from the bondage of karma.

and his self rests within the Self,[1]
then his wisdom is called steady.

56 'He who is not agitated
by suffering or by desires,
freed from anger, fear and passions,
is called a sage of steady mind.

57 'Who is wholly unimpassioned,
not rejoicing in the pleasant,
nor rejecting the unpleasant,
is established in his wisdom.

58 'And when this one wholly withdraws
all his senses from their objects,
as a tortoise draws in its limbs,
his wisdom is well-established.'"

* * *

From CHAPTER THREE

"Arjuna said:

1 'If you regard the intellect
as superior to action,
why urge me, O Handsome-Haired One,
into actions so appalling?

2 'By your equivocating speech,
my mind is, as it were, confused.
Tell me this one thing, and clearly:
By what means may I reach the best?'

"The Blessed Lord said:

3 'As I have previously taught,
there are two paths, O Blameless One:
there is the discipline of knowledge
and the discipline of action.

4 'Not by not acting in this world
does one become free from action,
nor does one approach perfection
by renunciation only.

5 'Not even for a moment does
someone exist without acting.

---

1. This is a play on the word *ātman*, which means both "the self" (soul) and "oneself." Kṛṣṇa now begins to describe the techniques for and effects of "withdrawing" one's senses from interaction with the external world and focusing them instead on the interior self.

Even against one's will, one acts
by the nature-born qualities.[2]

6   'He who has restrained his senses,
but sits and summons back to mind
the sense-objects, is said to be
a self-deluding hypocrite.

7   'But he whose mind controls his senses,
who undertakes the discipline
of action by the action-organs,
without attachment, is renowned.

8   'You must act as bid, for action
is better than non-action is:
not even functions of the body
could be sustained by non-action.

9   'This world is bound by action, save
for action which is sacrifice;
therefore, O Son of Kunti, act
without attachment to your deeds.

10   'When Prajāpati brought forth life,
he brought forth sacrifice as well,
saying, "By this may you produce,
may this be your wish-fulfilling cow."[3]

11   'Nourish the gods with sacrifice,
and they will nourish you as well.
By nourishing each other, you
will realize the highest good.

12   'Nourished by sacrifice, the gods
will give the pleasures you desire.
One who enjoys such gifts without
repaying them is just a thief.

13   'The good, who eat of the remains
from sacrifice, rise up faultless.
But the wicked, who cook only
for their own sakes, eat their own filth.

14   'Beings come to exist by food,
which emanates from the rain god,
who comes to be by sacrifice,
which arises out of action.

---

2. There are three such primary qualities: *sattva* (purity, light), *rajas* (passion, heat), and *tamas* (inertia, darkness).
3. In Vedic religion, Prajapati is the god (creator) of all mortal creatures. In Hindu mythology generally, *kāmadhenu* is a celestial cow who has the power to fulfill the wishes of any-one who worships her. Here Prajāpatī suggests that the act of sacrificing is itself like a wish-granting *kāmadhenu*. In the Vedic worldview, the preservation of the universe depends on the sacrifices made to the gods, and such ritual was at the center of the religion.

15 'Know that action comes from Brahman,
Brahman comes from the eternal;
so the all-pervading Brahman
is based in sacrifice forever.

16 'One who in this world does not turn
the wheel, thus setting it in motion,
lives uselessly, O Son of Pritha,
a sensual, malicious life.

17 'But the man whose only pleasure
and satisfaction is the self,
which is his sole contentment too,
has no task he must accomplish.

18 'That man finds no significance
in what has, or has not, been done;
moreover, he does not depend
on any being whatsoever.

19 'Therefore, act without attachment
in whatever situation,
for by the practice of detached
action, one attains the highest.

20 'Only by action Janaka[4]
and the others reached perfection.
In order to maintain the world,
your obligation is to act.

21 'Whatever the best leader does
the rank and file will also do;
everyone will fall in behind
the standard such a leader sets.

22 'O Son of Pritha, there is nought
that I need do in the three worlds,[5]
nor anything I might attain;
and yet I take part in action.

23 'For if I were not always to
engage in action ceaselessly,
men everywhere would soon follow
in my path, O Son of Pritha.

24 'Should I not engage in action,
these worlds would perish, utterly;
I would cause a great confusion,
and destroy all living beings.

25 'The unwise are attached to action
even as they act, Arjuna;

4. Celebrated character in the dialogues of
the *Bṛhadāraṇyaka Upaniṣad*; an exemplar of
the warrior-king who is also a man of discipline (a yogi).
5. Heaven, earth, and the underworld.

so, for the welfare of the world,
the wise should act with detachment.'"

* * *

"Arjuna said:

36 'Say what impels a man to do
such evil, Krishna, what great force
urges him, forces him into it,
even if he is unwilling?'

"The Blessed Lord said:

37 'Know that the enemy is this:
desire, anger, whose origins
are in the quality of passion,
all consuming, greatly harmful.

38 'As fire is obscured by smoke,
or by dust, a mirror's surface,
or an embryo by its membrane,
so this is covered up by that.

39 'Knowledge is constantly obscured
by this enemy of the wise,
by this insatiable fire
whose form, Arjuna, is desire.

40 'The senses, mind, and intellect
are its abode, as it is said.
Having obscured knowledge with these,
it deludes the embodied one.

41 'When you have subdued your senses,
then, O Bull of the Bharatas,
kill this demon, the destroyer
of all knowledge and discernment.

42 'Senses are said to be important,
but mind is higher than they are,
and intellect is above mind;
but Self is greater than all these.

43 'So knowing it to be supreme,
and sustaining the self with Self,
slay the foe whose form is desire,
so hard to conquer, Arjuna.'"

From CHAPTER SIX

* * *

10 "'The yogi should be self-subdued
always, and stand in solitude,

alone, controlled in thought and self,
without desires or possessions.

11 'Having established for himself
a steady seat in a pure place,
neither too high nor yet too low,
covered with grass, deer hide and cloth,

12 'with his mind sharpened to one point,
with thought and senses both subdued,
there he should sit, doing yoga
so as to purify the self,

13 'keeping his head, neck and body
aligned, erect and motionless,
gaze fixed on the tip of his nose,
not looking off distractedly,

14 'now fearless and with tranquil self,
firm in avowed celibacy,
with his thought focused on myself,
he should sit, devoted to me.

15 'Thus always chastening himself
the yogi's mind, subdued, knows peace,
whose farthest point is cessation;
thereafter, he abides in me.

16 'Yoga is not for the greedy,
nor yet for the abstemious;
not for one too used to sleeping,
nor for the sleepless, Arjuna.

17 'Yoga destroys the pain of one
temperate in his behavior,
in his food and recreation,
and in his sleep and waking too.

18 'After his thought has been subdued,
and abides only in the Self,
free from all longing and desire,
then he is said to be steadfast.

19 '"Like a lamp in a windless place
unflickering," is the likeness
of the yogi subdued in thought,
performing yoga of the Self.

20 'Where all thought comes to cease, restrained
by the discipline of yoga,
where, by the self, the Self is seen,
one is satisfied in the Self.

21 'When he knows that eternal joy
grasped only by the intellect,

beyond the senses where he dwells,
he does not deviate from truth;

22 'having attained it, he believes
there is no gain superior;
abiding there, he is unmoved
even by profound suffering.

23 'Let him know that the dissolving
of the union with suffering
is called yoga, to be practiced
with persistence, mind undaunted.

24 'Having abandoned all desires
born to satisfy intentions,
and having utterly restrained
the many senses by the mind,

25 'Gradually let him find rest,
his intellect under control,
his mind established in the Self,
not thinking about anything.

26 'Having subdued the unsteady
mind in motion, he should lead it
back from wherever it strays to,
into the domain of the Self.

27 'Supreme joy comes to the yogi
of calm mind and tranquil passion,
who has become one with Brahman
and is wholly free of evil.

28 'Constantly controlling himself,
the yogi, freed from evil now,
swiftly attains perpetual
joy of contact here with Brahman.

29 'He whose self is yoked by yoga
and who perceives sameness always,
will see the Self in all beings
and see all beings in the Self.

30 'I am not lost for someone who
perceives my presence everywhere,
and everything perceives in me,
nor is that person lost for me.

31 'The yogi firmly set in oneness
who worships me in all beings,
whatever the path that he takes,
will nonetheless abide in me.

32 'The yogi who sees all the same
analogous to his own Self

in happiness or suffering
is thought supreme, O Arjuna.'"

Summary   In Chapters Seven through Ten, Krishna explains diverse aspects of the nature of the infinite spirit, gradually unveiling the mystery of his own identity as the highest manifestation of that universal spirit and thus leading up to the revelation of his cosmic form in Chapter Eleven.

From CHAPTER ELEVEN

"Arjuna said,

1   'As a result of your kindness
in speaking of that greatest secret
recognized as the Supreme Self,
I have been left undeluded.

2   'I have, in detail, heard you speak
Of creatures' origins and ends,
and of your eternal greatness,
O One of Lotus-Petal-Eyes.

3   'This is just as you have spoken
about yourself, O Supreme Lord.
I desire to behold your
lordly form, O Supreme Spirit.

4   'If you think it is possible
for me to see this, then, O God,
O Lord of Yoga, allow me
to behold your eternal Self!'

"The Blessed Lord said,

5   'O Son of Pritha, look upon
my hundredfold, no, thousandfold
forms various and celestial,
forms of diverse shapes and colors!

6   'Behold the *Adityas* and *Vasus*,
the *Rudras*, *Ashvins* and *Maruts*,[6]
many unseen previously!
Behold these wonders, Arjuna!

7   'Here behold all the universe,
beings moving and motionless,
standing as one in my body,
and all else that you wish to see!

8   'Because you are unable to
behold me with your mortal eye,
I give you one that is divine:
Behold my majestic power!'"

---

6. Groups of Hindu deities: Adityas are sun gods; Vasus are elemental deities; Rudras are wind gods; the Ashvins are twin gods of sunrise and sunset; and the Maruts are storm gods.

Sanjaya[7] said,

9   "And after saying this, O King,
    Vishnu, the great Lord of Yoga,
    revealed his supreme, majestic
    form to him, the Son of Pritha.

10 "That form has many eyes and mouths,
    and many wonders visible,
    with many sacred ornaments,
    and many sacred weapons raised.

11 "Clothed in sacred wreaths and garments,
    with many sacred fragrances,
    and comprising every wonder,
    the infinite, omniscient god!

12 "If in the sky a thousand suns
    should have risen all together,
    the brilliance of it would be like
    the brilliance of that Great-Souled One.

13 "And then the Son of Pandu saw
    the universe standing as one,
    divided up in diverse ways,
    embodied in the god of gods."

                    *   *   *

        "Arjuna said:

43 'Father of all the world, the still and moving,
    you are what it worships and its teacher;
    with none your match, how could there be one greater
    in the three worlds, O Power-Without-Equal?

44 'Making obeisance, lying in prostration,
    I beg your indulgence, praiseworthy ruler;
    as father to son, as one friend to another,
    as lover to beloved, show your mercy!

45 'I am pleased to have seen what never has been
    seen before, yet my mind quakes in its terror:
    show me, O God, your human form; have mercy,
    O Lord of Gods, abode of all the cosmos!

46 'I wish to see you even as I did once,
    wearing a diadem, with mace and discus;
    assume that form now wherein you have four arms,
    O thousand-armed, of every form the master!'

        "The Blessed Lord said,

47 'For you, Arjuna, by my grace and favor,
    this highest form is brought forth by my power,

7. The bard who is narrating the events of the battle to King Dhṛtarāṣṭra.

of splendor made, universal, endless, primal,
and never seen before by any other.

48 'Not Vedic sacrifice nor recitation,
gifts, rituals, strenuous austerities,
will let this form of mine be seen by any
mortal but you, O Hero of the Kurus!

49 'You should not tremble, nor dwell in confusion
at seeing such a terrible appearance.
With your fears banished and your mind now cheerful,
look once again upon my form, Arjuna.'

Sanjaya said,

50 "So Krishna, having spoken to Arjuna,
stood before him once more in his own aspect;
having resumed again a gentle body,
the Great Soul calmed the one who had been frightened.

"Arjuna said,

51 'Seeing once again your gentle,
human form now, I am composed,
O Agitator of Mankind;
my mind is restored to normal.'

"The Blessed Lord said,

52 'It is difficult to see this
aspect of me that you have seen;
even the gods are forever
desirous of seeing it.

53 'Not by studying the *Vedas*,
nor even by austerities,
and not by gifts or sacrifice,
may I be seen as you saw me;

54 'but by devotion undisturbed
can I be truly seen and known,
and entered into, Arjuna,
O Scorcher of the Enemy!

55 'Who acts for me, depends on me,
devoutly, without attachment
or hatred for another being,
comes to me, O Son of Pandu!'"

III

Early Chinese Literature and Thought

Many great civilizations have perished with little consequence. What we know of them comes from the imaginative reconstructions of scholars, from inscriptions, and from the accounts of early travelers. Civilizations like those of ancient Egypt and Mesopotamia left extensive written records that were swept aside by other civilizations; the very names by which we refer to them—Egypt and Mesopotamia—are Greek. This is not the case with China, the oldest surviving civilization, whose literary tradition stretches over more than three thousand years. Its earliest literature set patterns and posed questions that shaped the actions and values of the Chinese people for thousands of years, serving as the connective tissue that gave its civilization a sense of unity and continuity.

Throughout China's long history, its territories, ruling classes, capitals, religions, and customs kept changing with the rise and fall of ruling dynasties; and its peoples have spoken a great number of widely divergent Chinese dialects as well as many non-Chinese languages from the Turkic, Mongolian, and even Indo-European language families. Thus, China might easily have become fragmented by regional interests

A contemporary rubbing made from a Han Dynasty (206 B.C.E.–220 C.E.) earthenware tile that depicts scenes of hunting and harvesting.

and linguistic differences like Europe after the fall of the Roman Empire. But whereas Rome was truly a conquest empire, a political center that ruled over many peoples, each with its own sense of distinct ethnic identity, traditional China was an idea tied to cultural values and the power of the written word. Certainly, Chinese emperors did at certain times in history conquer territories as remote as Korea, Vietnam, Tibet, and Taiwan. But China could survive periods of turmoil and even rule by non-Chinese conquerors such as the Mongols and the Manchus because peoples on the margins of the ancient heartland had for centuries been adopting China's writing, cultural values, and institutions, and had thus become "Chinese." Many times in China's history, regional identity has become subordinate to a belief in cultural and political unity.

BEGINNINGS: EARLY SAGE RULERS

Although China has always been in contact with western parts of the Eurasian landmass, it developed independently from the earlier Mesopotamian, Egyptian, and Indus Valley city civilizations. By the third millennium B.C.E. at least a dozen Neolithic (New Stone Age) cultures flourished along the Yellow River in the north and the Yangtze River in the south. By the second millennium B.C.E. most settlements had defensive walls made of rammed earth, a sign of the increasing influence of military elites, who defended the populace against other rising city-states. Later Chinese historians placed into this early period a lineage of sage rulers who laid the foundations for Chinese civilization. Fu Xi reputedly taught people how to raise silkworms. He also invented the eight trigrams, symbols consisting of three broken or unbroken (Yin and Yang) lines each, which became the basis for Chi-

na's canonical divination text, the *Classic of Changes (Yijing)*. Shennong invented the plow and instructed people in the use of medicinal herbs. Huangdi, the "Yellow Emperor," was a patron of medicine and agriculture. His scribe, Cang Jie, invented writing by creating graphs that imitated the articulate tracks of birds, realizing that the new technology "could regulate the various professions and keep under scrutiny the various kinds of people." A later sage ruler, Yao, disinherited his inept son and chose a commoner to succeed him on the throne, thus establishing the principle of virtue and merit over blood lineage. This commoner, Shun, was an ideal ruler and a model of filial piety (he remained true to his parents despite their repeated attempts to kill him). His successor, the Great Yu, showed exemplary dedication to the welfare of his people and invented irrigation, constructing channels to tame the Great Flood that occurred during his reign.

Encapsulated in this lineage of legendary rulers are fundamental values of Chinese civilization: the importance of writing and divination; an economy based on intensive agriculture and silk production; a political philosophy of virtue that emphasizes fixed social roles; and practices of self-cultivation and herbal medicine.

EARLIEST DYNASTIES: CHINA DURING THE BRONZE AGE AND THE BEGINNING OF WRITING

China's Bronze Age began around 2000 B.C.E. By 1200 B.C.E., cultures in several regions of China made ample use of bronze for the molding of more-effective weapons, for the new technology of spoke-wheel chariots, and for the production of ritual bronze vessels used in ceremonies honoring gods and ancestors. A small area in the Yellow River

This tortoiseshell, inscribed with writing dating from ca. 1200 B.C.E., was used for ceremonial divination.

basin of north-central China is the best known of these Bronze Age cultures: thanks to the groundbreaking archaeological discovery of inscriptions on tortoiseshells and cattle bones in 1898, this area could be identified as the so-called second dynasty—the Shang (ca. 1500–1045 B.C.E.). The first dynasty is traditionally identified as the Xia, whose name and list of kings are recorded in later texts, but whose existence hasn't been linked to any of the known Bronze Age archaeological sites.

The Shang was a loose confederation of city-states with a complex state system, large settlements, and, most important, a common writing system. Although it remains unclear when the Chinese script began to be developed, it appeared as a fully functional writing system during the later period of the Shang dynasty. To date, more than 48,000 fragments of inscribed shells and bones have been found. These so-called oracle bone inscriptions are usually short records of divination rituals. Ritual specialists and the Shang kings would apply heat to the bones and use the resulting cracks to interpret or predict events: determining weather, harvest, floods, or tribute payments; divining the outcome of imminent war or the birth of male offspring; or even finding the causes for the toothache of a royal family member. Thus, writing was part of ritual practices that guided political decision making and harmonized the relation between human beings and the world of unpredictable spiritual forces in the cosmos. Its use was a prerogative of the Shang king and his elites.

From the inscriptions we can see that the Shang kings paid meticulous attention to the veneration of their dead ancestors and various gods, including the highest god, Di, who also commanded rain and thunder. They used war captives as slaves and sacrificial victims and employed conscript workers for monumental labor projects. For example, the sumptuous grave site of Lady Hao, one of the prominent Shang king Wu Ding's many wives, contained hundreds of bronze objects.

Among the many objects fashioned out of bronze during the Shang Dynasty were "fangding," ritual vessels for cooking and presenting food. This fangding is the only extant example that is decorated with a human face.

THE ZHOU CONQUEST AND THE "MANDATE OF HEAVEN"

Around 1045 B.C.E. the Zhou people overthrew the Shang. The Zhou were an agrarian people and former allies of the Shang. Their justification of the conquest set the model for subsequent dynastic shifts in Chinese history. Texts recorded during the first centuries of Zhou rule claimed that a new power, "Heaven," transferred the mandate to rule to the Zhou, because the moral worth of the Shang had declined and the last Shang rulers were decadent tyrants without regard for the people. In turn, the first rulers of the Zhou, King Wen (the "cultured" or "civilized" king) and his son King Wu (the "martial" king), who completed the conquest, were praised as paragons of virtue and "sons of Heaven" deserving of the mandate. After the Zhou conquest, the claim to power in China depended on the claim to virtuous rule, which in large measure meant holding to the statutes and models of the earliest sage rulers and the virtuous early Zhou kings.

THE DECLINE OF THE EASTERN ZHOU AND THE AGE OF CHINA'S PHILOSOPHICAL MASTERS

After their conquest, the early Zhou kings rewarded their allies with gifts of land. But initially strong personal ties between the Zhou kings and their allies weakened over the centuries, and in 771 B.C.E. some vassals joined forces with nomadic tribesmen and killed the king. The Zhou court fled and moved the capital to the east. Historians thus distinguish between the Western Zhou (1045–771 B.C.E.) and the Eastern Zhou (770–256 B.C.E.) periods. The Zhou kings never regained full control over their vassals. Although its kings continued to rule for another five centuries, the Eastern Zhou Dynasty lacked strong central authority, allowing its former vassals to build up their domains into belligerent independent states. On the southern and western borders of the old Zhou domain, powerful new states arose: Chu, Wu, and Yue in the south and Qin in the west. Although many of these new kingdoms had their distinct traditions, they gradually absorbed Zhou culture, and their rulers often sought to trace their descent either from the Zhou royal house or from more ancient, northern Chinese ancestors. Just before the defeat of the Western Zhou, there were around two hundred lords with domains of varying size, all under the titular rule of the Zhou king. By the third century B.C.E., only seven powerful states were left in the struggle over supremacy, and in 256 B.C.E. the last Zhou king was killed.

The Eastern Zhou Period was one of the most formative periods in Chinese history. The Eastern Zhou rulers built new institutions, and among its vassal states a lively interstate diplomacy unfolded; new military technology revolutionized warfare, and the old aristocracy was gradually dismantled and replaced by a new class of advisers and strategists. During the earlier part of the Eastern Zhou Period, the so-called Spring and Autumn Annals Period (722–481 B.C.E., named after the court chronicle of Confucius's home state of Lu in eastern China), the old aristocracy in their chariots were still central to combat, and an honor code of military conduct was respected. Battles started with an agreement on both sides, states that were in mourning for their rulers were not attacked, and, if a state was defeated, the conqueror respectfully continued the ancestral sacrifices for the vanquished ruling lineage. This changed dramatically during the latter half of the Eastern Zhou, the so-called Warring States Period (403–221 B.C.E., named after a collection of stories about political intrigues between the Zhou states): mass infantry armies built on coercive drafts replaced the old aristocracy; raw power politics and strategic deception became the norm; the newly invented crossbow allowed soldiers to kill their enemies at greater distance, not in noble close combat; and rulers of the larger Zhou states started to call themselves kings, indicating that they not only defied the authority of the Zhou king but also intended to replace him as ruler over all of China.

It was in this climate that **Confucius**, and the philosophical masters who followed in his wake, formulated visions of how to live and govern well in a corrupt world. Chinese call this the period when "a hundred schools of thought bloomed." The Eastern Zhou Period coincides with the period when the religions and philosophies of ancient India, Greece, Persia, and Israel took shape, and scholars have compared the social and political conditions facilitating this flourishing in these different civilizations. In China, rulers of the feudal states employed able advisers, or "mas-

ters," to help them gain more resources, territory, and power, and the Chinese masters often moved between states in search for employment and patronage.

Chinese call the texts written by masters or compiled by their disciples "Masters Literature." This name derives from scenes that show a charismatic master in vivid conversation with disciples, rulers, or other contemporaries. Masters Literature flourished from the time of Confucius through the Han Dynasty (206 B.C.E.–220 C.E.). This rich corpus of texts, represented in this anthology by selections from the **Analects** and **Laozi**, reveals the broad spectrum of opinions on fundamental questions: How can we create social order in a society that is incessantly at war? How can we become exemplary, fulfilled human beings in a less-than-ideal society? How can we make use of history and existing precedents to create a better future? How should we use words,

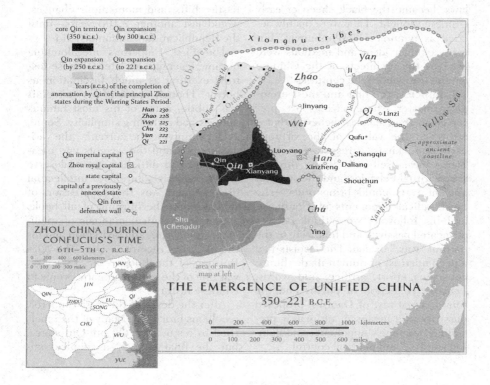

THE EMERGENCE OF UNIFIED CHINA
350–221 B.C.E.

ZHOU CHINA DURING CONFUCIUS'S TIME
6TH–5TH C. B.C.E.

and what impact can words and ideas have on social reality?

Later Chinese texts divided the masters and their followers into schools of thought, although the boundaries between their positions were often more fluid than the labels suggest. The most prominent schools were the Confucians, the Mohists (named after their master, Mozi), the Daoists, the Logicians, the Legalists, and the Yin-Yang Masters, each advocating its own programs, adopting different styles of argument, and engaging the rival camps in polemical disputes. The schools had varied degrees of success: while Confucianism and Daoism became the intellectual and religious backbone of traditional China (joined by Buddhism after it reached China from India around the Common Era), the Mohists and Logicians died out, the Yin-Yang Masters produced specialists in divination and calendrical science, and the Legalists, who advocated authoritarian rule through harsh laws, became the black sheep of early Chinese thought. They were openly decried as tyrannical and inhuman, but many of their ideas and methods were used by the architects of the Chinese empire throughout the centuries.

Confucius, the first and most exemplary master whose sayings are preserved in the *Analects*, believed that a return to the values of the virtuous early Zhou kings, a respect for social hierarchies, self-cultivation through proper ritual behavior, and the study of ancient texts could bring order. The most radical opponents of Confucius and his followers were thinkers who advocated passivity and following of the natural "way," or *dao*. The Daoists had a deep mistrust of human-made things: conscious effort, artifice, and words. *Laozi*, a collection of poems and the foundational text of Daoism, proposed passivity as a means of ultimately prevailing over one's opponents and gaining spiritual and political control.

FOUNDATIONS OF IMPERIAL CHINA: THE QIN AND THE HAN

The state of Qin, which had a reputation for ruthlessness and untrustworthiness, but whose armies were well disciplined and well supplied, destroyed the Zhou royal domain in 256 B.C.E. and conquered the last of the independent states in 221 B.C.E. That year is one of the most important dates in Chinese history. Conscious of the historical moment's weight, the king of Qin conferred the title "First Emperor of Qin" upon himself to mark the novelty of his achievement. Although the Qin was a short-lived dynasty, many of its measures—designed to create a new type of state with a strong centralized bureaucracy—were adopted and adapted by the rulers of the subsequent Han Dynasty (206 B.C.E.–220 C.E.). With the Qin unification, China was finally an empire. Imperial China, with its upheavals, dynastic shifts, and momentous changes, would last another 2,100 years—until the Republican Revolution of 1911.

The First Emperor's megalomania became legendary in later Chinese history, exerting as much fascination as horror. Though much of his statecraft was subtle, many of his most famous policies had a chilling simplicity. Some, such as unifying the currency, the various scripts, and the weights and measures used in different states, deserve credit. But his solution to intellectual disagreement was the suppression of scholars and the burning of all books except for practical manuals of medicine, agriculture, and divination and for the historical records of Qin. The "Qin Burning of the Books," of 213 B.C.E., was one of the most traumatic events in Chinese history.

After the death of the First Emperor, rebellions broke out. Many of the rebels tried to restore the old pre-Qin states, but the final winner, a simple com-

Perhaps the most illustrative symbol of the First Emperor's megalomania and imperial ambitions is the vast terra-cotta army, unearthed in 1974, that the emperor had buried with him. Over 7,000 life-size sculptures fill the burial site.

moner named Liu Bang, became the first emperor of the Han Dynasty and continued the centralized government strategy of the Qin, while eliminating its unpopular features, loosening some particularly cruel laws, cutting taxes, and refraining from the constant labor mobilizations that the Qin emperor had forced on his people.

The Han Dynasty lasted more than four hundred years. The Han was the crucial phase of imperial consolidation that set patterns for future Chinese dynasties. During this period China expanded its boundaries into Central Asia and parts of modern Korea and Vietnam. Han emperors learned to deal with the challenging threat of northern frontier tribes, developing strategies that proved effective for subsequent empires: fight them, pay them off, or appease them with marriage alliances, offering Chinese princesses as brides to the tribal chieftains.

The most influential Han ruler was Emperor Wu, whose long reign lasted from 141 to 87 B.C.E. He undertook costly campaigns to expand the empire and established government monopolies on the production of iron, salt, and liquor to finance them. He was a generous patron of the arts, of music, and of scholarship. Although he was intrigued by immortality techniques, portents, and the occult, he was the first emperor to privilege Confucian scholars, founding a state academy for the education of government officials and setting up positions for professors to teach the so-called Five Classics: the *Classic of Changes*, used for divination; the *Classic of Documents*, a collection of proclamations by early sage kings and ministers; the **Classic of Poetry**, a collection of poetry including hymns to the Zhou ancestors and ballads recounting the history of the Zhou; the *Spring and Autumn Annals*, a historical chronicle; and the *Record of Rites*,

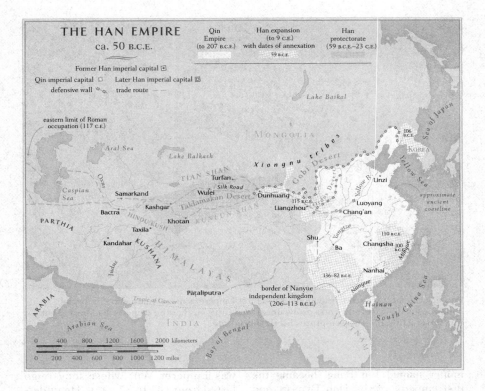

THE HAN EMPIRE
ca. 50 B.C.E.

Qin Empire (to 207 B.C.E.)
Han expansion (to 9 C.E.) with dates of annexation 59 B.C.E.
Han protectorate (59 B.C.E.–23 C.E.)

Former Han imperial capital ⊡
Qin imperial capital ▢   Later Han imperial capital ▣
defensive wall ⌒⌒   trade route ——

eastern limit of Roman occupation (117 C.E.)

the most important of several works on ritual.

Early China was a groundbreaking period of enduring influence on all subsequent periods of Chinese history. These first 1,500 years of Chinese history, from the Shang Dynasty to the end of the Han Dynasty, saw the emergence of enduring political institutions and ideologies, of moral standards and social manners. The literature produced during this period encapsulates these values and formative patterns and is still the canonical foundation of Chinese civilization.

CLASSIC OF POETRY
ca. 1000–600 B.C.E.

Standing at the beginning of China's three-millennia-long literary tradition, the *Classic of Poetry* (also known as *Book of Songs* or *Book of Odes*) is the oldest poetry collection of East Asia. Its poems reflect the breadth of early Chinese society. Some poems convey the history and values of the earlier part of the Zhou Dynasty (ca. 1045–256 B.C.E.), whose founding kings set a standard of ideal governance for later generations. Others treat themes familiar from folk ballads: courtship, marriage and love, birth and death, and the stages of the agricultural cycle such as planting and harvesting. Filled with images of nature and the plain life of an agricultural society, the *Classic of Poetry* offers a distinctive, fresh simplicity. Because of the collection's canonical status, centuries of commentary and interpretation have accrued around it, adding to its meaning and significance and endowing the simple scenes in the poems with moral or political purpose. The anthology has had a profound impact on the literatures of Korea, Japan, and Vietnam and was an important element of the traditional curriculum throughout East Asia until the beginning of the twentieth century.

THE ANTHOLOGY AND ITS SIGNIFICANCE

While other ancient literary traditions were founded on epics about gods and heroes, or sprawling legends about the origins of the cosmos, the *Classic of Poetry* provided a different sort of foundation for Chinese literature, made up of the compact and evocative form of lyric poetry. Because Chinese literature originated with the *Classic of Poetry*, short verse gained a degree of political, social, and pedagogical importance in East Asia that it has not enjoyed anywhere else in the world.

The *Classic of Poetry* contains 305 poems and consists of three parts, the "Airs of the Domains" (*Guofeng*, 160 poems), the "Odes/Elegances" (*Ya*, 105 poems), and the "Hymns" (*Song*, 40 poems). The "Hymns" are the oldest part and contain songs used in ritual performances to celebrate the Zhou royal house. Next are the "Odes," narrative ballads about memorable historical events. The youngest poems are the "Airs of the Domains," based on folk ballads from some fifteen domains of the Zhou kingdom. (The early Zhou kings gave lands to their loyal vassals and gradually built a multistate system of "domains" extending from modern-day Beijing far beyond the Yangtze River in the south.) Tradition credited **Confucius**, the most important of the early philosophical masters, with the compilation of the *Classic of Poetry*. He allegedly selected the poems in the collection from three thousand poems he found in the archives of the Zhou kingdom. Therefore, the choice and arrangement of the poems were seen as an expression of Confucius's philosophy. Confucius believed that political order depended on the ability of individuals in society to cultivate their moral virtue and thus contribute to social order. We know from the **Analects**, a collection containing Confucius's sayings, that Confucius thought highly of the *Classic of Poetry*. He advised his own son to study the *Classic of Poetry* to enhance his ability to express his opinions, he praised disciples who quoted passages from the *Classic of Poetry* to make a particular point, and he saw a comprehensive educational program in the anthology: "The *Classic of Poetry* can provide you with stimulation and with observation, with a capacity for communion, and with a vehicle for grief. At home, they [the poems] enable you to serve your father, and abroad, to serve your lord. Also, you will learn there the names of many birds, animals, plants, and trees." Confucius's high opinion of the *Classic of Poetry* led to its inclusion in the canon of "Confucian Classics." The other classics are the *Classic of Changes*, used for divination; the *Classic of Documents*, a collection of sayings by early kings and ministers; the *Spring and Autumn Annals*, a historical chronicle of Confucius's home state of Lu; and the *Record of Rites*, the most important of a few books on ritual. The Confucian Classics became the curriculum of the state academy that Emperor Wu of the Han Dynasty founded in 124 B.C.E.

As a further sign of the *Classic of Poetry*'s canonization during the Han Dynasty, a "Great Preface" written for the anthology became the single most fundamental statement about the nature and function of poetry in East Asia. Written more than half a millennium after the anthology's compilation, the "Great Preface" claimed that there were "six principles" (*liu yi*) of poetry: the three categories in which the poems were placed ("Airs of the Domains," "Odes," and "Hymns") and the three rhetorical devices of "enumeration" (*fu*), "comparison" (*bi*), and "evocative image" (*xing*). Scholars and poets have debated the usefulness and precise meaning of these principles for the last two millennia, but on a basic level the principles illuminate rhetorical patterns that distinguish the *Classic of Poetry* and even later Chinese poetry. The concept of *feng* is a good case in point: it refers to the "Airs of the Domains" section of the anthology, but it also contains a rich web of associations that grew up around its literal meaning, "wind": Like wind that causes grass to sway, the ruler can "influence" (*feng*) his people and instill virtuous behavior in them through poetry. For their part, his subjects can express their dissatisfaction with their ruler through "criticism" (*feng*). In reality, most poems in the anthology contain at best indirect criticism. But the idea that poetry and song can bridge the gulf between social classes, that they can serve as a tool for mutual "influence" and "criticism" and give the people a voice, helping them keep bad rulers in check, was central to the Confucian understanding of poetry and society. Poetry made room for social critique and created the institution of "remonstration," the duty of officials in the bureaucracy to speak out against abuses of power.

THE POEMS

Our selections come from the "Odes" section ("She Bore the Folk") and the "Airs" section (all other poems), and conclude with the "Great Preface." Although almost all poems in the *Classic of Poetry* are anonymous, they give voice to many different players in Zhou society, such as kings, aristocrats and peasants, men and women in love, and, collectively, to communities as they celebrate harvest or worship their ancestors. Poems put into the mouths of peasants or soldiers show considerable literary skill, which suggests that a member of the educated elite at the courts of the Zhou domains must have given them their final shape.

The constraints imposed by society and the conflict between individual desire and social expectations are important themes in the "Airs" section. Marriage is often praised as a sanctioned form of sexual relation, but some poems also celebrate the pleasures of transgression. "Boat of Cypress" is a remarkable outcry of a heart that refuses to bend to society's wishes. Unlike the virtuous Zhou Dynasty, the domain of Zheng and its music were associated with sensual pleasures: "Zhen and Wei," for example, depicts a festival scene along two rivers. Although its frolicking man and woman do not go beyond politely exchanging flowers as courtship gifts, the scene is highly charged with eroticism.

The protagonists in the romantic plots that appear in the poems of the "Airs of the Domains" could be from any culture past or present, but the extensive tradition of commentaries endowed these poems with specific moral and historical significance. According to the canonical "Mao commentary," "Fishhawk," the first poem of the *Classic of Poetry*, in which a young man is tormented by his desire for a girl, is not a simple romantic folk song. Instead, the commentary claims that the poem praises the consort of King Wen for being free from jealousy when her husband takes a new consort, a typical situation in traditional Chinese society, where men could have several wives. This counterintuitive reading of the poem established "Fishhawk" as a model of exemplary female behavior for all times and embedded it in the history of the early Zhou kings.

The central stylistic device of the *Classic of Poetry* is repetition with variation. Many of the poems consist of three rhyming stanzas of four or six lines with four syllables each. The stanza format encourages line repetitions, which give the poems melodic rhythm and, with the introduction of small variations, additional meaning. In "Plums Are Falling," the fruits become fewer with each repetition until the woman has finally decided whom among her suitors she wants to marry. In "Peach Tree Soft and Tender," the peach tree goes through the natural cycle of bearing blossoms, fruits, and leaves while a new bride, who it is hoped will bear many descendants for the family line, is introduced into the household. Far from being a simplistic rhetorical device, repetition with variation gives compelling shape to a suitor's intrusive desire and his lover's fear of scandal in "Zhongzi, Please." As the insolent Zhongzi systematically advances stanza by stanza from the village wall to the family's fence and through the garden towards his lover's bedchamber, the helpless woman, fearing her parents' and brothers' reproach and society's disapproval, fends her lover off by promising to keep him in her thoughts.

Among the rhetorical devices listed in the "Great Preface" to the *Classic of Poetry*, "exposition" (*fu*) and "affective image" (*xing*) are particularly interesting. Exposition, the enumeration of sequences of events in straightforward narrative fashion, structures longer odes like "She Bore the Folk," a poem on the miraculous birth of Lord Millet, the inventor of agriculture and legendary ancestor of the Zhou people. Lord Millet's birth to a resourceful mother who steps into a god's footprint and his subsequent development into the Zhous' ancestor and cultural hero are recounted through vivid enumeration. The ritual acts that the Zhou people perform to celebrate the harvest and commemorate their ancestor are also related through "exposition." Poems from the "Airs" section, by contrast, mostly employ "comparisons" (*bi*) and "affective images." Comparisons are like similes: "Huge Rat" compares an exploitative lord directly to a voracious rodent. Affective images are much more elusive and do not easily translate into any rhetorical trope in the Western tradition. *Xing*, the term rendered as "affective image," literally means "stimulus" or "excitement." *Xing* brings natural images into suggestive resonance with human situations, stimulating the imagination and pushing perception beyond a simple comparison of one thing to another. Often, the animals or plants used to evoke human situations appear in the same scene with the human protagonists, but the relation between the animals or plants and the humans is mysterious. For example, in "Dead Roe Deer" the reader sees a landscape in which a girl, a "maiden white as marble," who has just been seduced by a man, hovers next to a dead deer "wrapped in white rushes."

The resonant, elusive imagery of the *Classic of Poetry* has enticed readers through the ages. The poet and critic Ezra Pound (1885–1972), attracted to and inspired by the use of imagery in Chinese poetry, spearheaded the new movement of "imagism" in the 1910s, experimenting with the poetic power that sparse juxtaposition of images whose relation remains obscure can produce. His adoption of such poetic techniques in turn profoundly influenced modernist writers such as T. S. Eliot and James Joyce. Although Pound did not know Chinese, he eventually produced a poetic rendering of the *Classic of Poetry* in collaboration with the Harvard sinologist Achilles Fang. Because of their divergence from the wording of the originals, Pound's versions might better be conceived as English poems in their own right than translations. Yet they can come close to the Chinese originals in other ways. In Pound's version, the second stanza of "Dead Roe Deer" reads, "Where the scrub elm skirts the wood, be it not in white mat bound, as a jewel flawless found, dead as doe is maidenhood." Death hovers ominously over the deer, the woman, and her maidenhood. Here we see the drama of the distinctive Chinese trope of *xing* in full play, transposed into the English language.

The *Classic of Poetry* has left deep traces in the literary cultures of East Asia into the modern period. Because its compilation was attributed to Confucius and its traditional interpretations emphasized Confucian values, it was part and parcel of the education of political elites. Yet, despite the dominant moralizing interpretations, the poems of the *Classic of Poetry* have retained their pristine simplicity and have lost nothing of their evocative power to voice fundamental human emotions and challenges.

From the CLASSIC OF POETRY[1]

I. Fishhawk

The fishhawks sing *guan guan*
on sandbars of the stream.
Gentle maiden, pure and fair,
fit pair for a prince.

Watercress grows here and there,   5
right and left we gather it.
Gentle maiden, pure and fair,
wanted waking and asleep.

Wanting, sought her, had her not,
waking, sleeping, thought of her,   10
on and on he thought of her,
he tossed from one side to another.

Watercress grows here and there,
right and left we pull it.
Gentle maiden, pure and fair,   15
with harps we bring her company.

Watercress grows here and there,
right and left we pick it out.

1. Translated by Stephen Owen.

Gentle maiden, pure and fair,
with bells and drums do her delight.   20

VI. Peach Tree Soft and Tender

Peach tree soft and tender,
how your blossoms glow!
The bride is going to her home,
she well befits this house.

Peach tree soft and tender,   5
plump, the ripening fruit.
The bride is going to her home,
she well befits this house.

Peach tree soft and tender,
its leaves spread thick and full.   10
The bride is going to her home,
she well befits these folk.

XX. Plums Are Falling

Plums are falling,
seven are the fruits;
many men want me,
let me have a fine one.

Plums are falling,   5
three are the fruits;
many men want me,
let me have a steady one.

Plums are falling,
catch them in the basket;   10
many men want me,
let me be bride of one.

XXIII. Dead Roe Deer

A roe deer dead in the meadow,
all wrapped in white rushes.
The maiden's heart was filled with spring;
a gentleman led her astray.

Undergrowth in forest,   5
dead deer in the meadow,
all wound with white rushes,
a maiden white as marble.

Softly now, and gently, gently,
do not touch my apron, sir,
and don't set the cur to barking.

10

XXVI. Boat of Cypress

That boat of cypress drifts along,
it drifts upon the stream.
Restless am I, I cannot sleep,
as though in torment and troubled.
Nor am I lacking wine
to ease my mind and let me roam.

5

This heart of mine is no mirror,
it cannot take in all.
Yes, I do have brothers,
but brothers will not be my stay.
I went and told them of my grief
and met only with their rage.

10

This heart of mine is no stone;
you cannot turn it where you will.
This heart of mine is no mat;
I cannot roll it up within.
I have behaved with dignity,
in this no man can fault me.

15

My heart is uneasy and restless,
I am reproached by little men.
Many are the woes I've met,
and taken slights more than a few.
I think on it in the quiet,
and waking pound my breast.

20

Oh Sun! and you Moon!
Why do you each grow dim in turn?
These troubles of the heart
are like unwashed clothes.
I think on it in the quiet,
I cannot spread wings to fly away.

25

30

XLII. Gentle Girl

A gentle girl and fair
awaits by the crook of the wall;
in shadows I don't see her;
I pace and scratch my hair.

A gentle girl and comely
gave me a scarlet pipe;

5

scarlet pipe that gleams—
in your beauty I find delight.

Then she brought me a reed from the pastures,
it was truly beautiful and rare.   10
Reed—the beauty is not yours—
you are but beauty's gift.

LXIV. Quince

She cast a quince to me,
a costly garnet I returned;
it was no equal return,
but by this love will last.

She cast a peach to me,   5
costly opal I returned;
it was no equal return,
but by this love will last.

She cast a plum to me,
a costly ruby I returned;   10
it was no equal return,
but by this love will last.

LXXVI. Zhongzi, Please

Zhongzi, please
don't cross my village wall,
don't break the willows planted there.
It's not that I care so much for them,
but I dread my father and mother;   5
Zhongzi may be in my thoughts,
but what my father and mother said—
that too may be held in dread.

Zhongzi, please
don't cross my fence,   10
don't break the mulberries planted there.
It's not that I care so much for them,
but I dread my brothers;
Zhongzi may be in my thoughts,
but what my brothers said—   15
that too may be held in dread.

Zhongzi, please
don't cross into my garden,
don't break the sandalwood planted there.
It's not that I care so much for them,   20
but I dread others will talk much;

Zhongzi may be in my thoughts,
but when people talk too much—
that too may be held in dread.

XCV. Zhen and Wei

O Zhen and Wei together,
swollen now they flow.
Men and maids together,
chrysanthemums in hand.
The maid says, "Have you looked?"   5
The man says, "I have gone."
"Let's go then look across the Wei,
it is truly a place for our pleasure."
Man and maid together
each frolicked with the other   10
and gave as gift the peony.

O Zhen and Wei together,
flowing deep and clear.
Men and maids together,
teeming everywhere.   15
The maid says, "Have you looked?"
The man says, "I have gone."
"Let's go then look across the Wei,
it is truly a place for our pleasure."
Man and maid together   20
each will frolic with the other
and give as gift the peony.

CXIII. Huge Rat

Huge rat, huge rat,
eat my millet no more,
for three years I've fed you,
yet you pay me no heed.

I swear that I will leave you   5
and go to a happier land.
A happy land, a happy land,
and there I will find my place.

Huge rat, huge rat,
eat my wheat no more,   10
for three years I've fed you
and you show no gratitude.

I swear that I will leave you
and go to a happier realm.
A happy realm, a happy realm,   15
there I will find what I deserve.

Huge rat, huge rat,
eat my sprouts no more,
for three years I have fed you,
and you won't reward my toil.   20

I swear that I will leave you
and go to happy meadows.
Happy meadows, happy meadows
where none need wail and cry.

CCXLV. She Bore the Folk

She who first bore the folk—
Jiang it was, First Parent.
How was it she bore the folk?—
she knew the rite and sacrifice.
To rid herself of sonlessness   5
she trod the god's toeprint
    and she was glad.
She was made great, on her luck settled,
the seed stirred, it was quick.
She gave birth, she gave suck,   10
and this was Lord Millet.

When her months had come to term,
her firstborn sprang up.
Not splitting, not rending,
working no hurt, no harm.   15
He showed his godhead glorious,
the high god was greatly soothed.
He took great joy in those rites
and easily she bore her son.

She set him in a narrow lane,   20
but sheep and cattle warded him.
She set him in the wooded plain,
he met with those who logged the plain.
She set him on cold ice,
birds sheltered him with wings.   25
Then the birds left him
and Lord Millet wailed.
This was long and this was loud;
his voice was a mighty one.

And then he crept and crawled,   30
he stood upright, he stood straight.
He sought to feed his mouth,
and planted there the great beans.
The great beans' leaves were fluttering,
the rows of grain were bristling.   35
Hemp and barley dense and dark,
the melons, plump and round.

Lord Millet in his farming
had a way to help things grow:
He rid the land of thick grass,   40
he planted there a glorious growth.
It was in squares, it was leafy,
it was planted, it grew tall.
It came forth, it formed ears,
it was hard, it was good.   45
Its tassels bent, it was full,
he had his household there in Dai.

He passed us down these wondrous grains:
our black millets, of one and two kernels,
millets whose leaves sprout red or white,   50
he spread the whole land with black millet,
and reaped it and counted the acres,
spread it with millet sprouting red or white,
hefted on shoulders, loaded on backs,
he took it home and began this rite.   55

And how goes this rite we have?—
at times we hull, at times we scoop,
at times we winnow, at times we stomp,
we hear it slosh as we wash it,
we hear it puff as we steam it.   60
Then we reckon, then we consider,
take artemisia, offer fat.
We take a ram for the flaying,
then we roast it, then we sear it,
to rouse up the following year.   65

We heap the wooden trenchers full,
wooden trenchers, earthenware platters.
And as the scent first rises
the high god is peaceful and glad.
This great odor is good indeed,   70
for Lord Millet began the rite,
and hopefully free from failing or fault,
it has lasted until now.

From The Great Preface

"Fishhawk" is the virtue of the Queen Consort and the beginning of the "Airs"
[*Feng*, the first large section of the *Classic of Poetry*].[1] It is the means by which
the world is influenced (*feng*) and by which the relations between husband and
wife are made correct. Thus it is used in smaller communities, and it is used in

1. "The Great Preface" is attached to "Fishhawk," the first poem of the *Classic of Poetry*.
In traditional Confucian interpretations, the
poem was understood as celebrating the virtue
of the queen consort of King Wen of the Zhou
Dynasty.

larger domains. "Airs" *(Feng)* are "Influence" *(feng)*; it is to teach. By influence it stirs them; by teaching it transforms them.[2]

The poem is that to which what is intently on the mind *(zhi)* goes. In the mind, it is "being intent" *(zhi)*; coming out in language, it is a "poem."

The affections are stirred within and take on form in words. If words alone are inadequate, we speak it out in sighs. If sighing is inadequate, we sing it. If singing is inadequate, unconsciously our hands dance it and our feet tap it.[3]

Feelings emerge in sounds; when those sounds have patterning, they are called "tones." The tones of a well-managed age are at rest and happy: its government is balanced. The tones of an age of turmoil are bitter and full of anger: its government is perverse. The tones of a ruined state are filled with lament and brooding: its people are in difficulty.[4]

Thus to correctly present achievements and failures, to move Heaven and Earth, to stir the gods and spirits, there is nothing more appropriate than poetry. By it the former kings managed the relations between husbands and wives, perfected the respect due to parents and superiors, gave depth to human relations, beautifully taught and transformed the people, and changed local customs.

Thus there are six principles in the poems: (1) Airs *(Feng)*; (2) "exposition" *(fu)*; (3) "comparison" *(bi)*; (4) "affective image" *(xing)*; (5) Odes *(Ya)*; (6) Hymns *(song)*.[5]

By *feng*, those above transform those below; also by *feng*, those below criticize those above. When an admonition is given that is governed by patterning, the one who speaks it has no culpability, yet it remains adequate to warn those who hear it. In this we have *feng*.[6]

When the Way of the Kings declined, rites and moral principles were abandoned; the power of government to teach failed; the government of the domains changed; the customs of the family were altered. And at this point the changed *Feng* ("Airs") and the changed *Ya* ("Odes") were written. The historians of the domains understood clearly the marks of success and failure; they were pained by the abandonment of proper human relations and lamented the severity of punishments and governance. They sang their feelings to criticize *(feng)* those above, understanding the changes that had taken place and thinking about former customs. Thus the changed *Feng* emerge from the affections, but they go no further than rites and moral principles.

---

2. *Feng*, a central term of "The Great Preface," literally means "wind." By extension, it means "influence" (like wind bending the grasses) and "Airs," the poetry in the first part of the *Classic of Poetry* that was understood as a means to positively influence people's behavior.

3. Although *qi*, "vital breath," is not directly mentioned, the psychology of poetic composition described here relies on the notion that a release of vital breath results in ever stronger forms of outward expression: words, sighs, songs, or dance.

4. Since the poems in the *Classic of Poetry* were performed to music, the "tones" that reveal the social and political conditions under which the poems were composed became

manifest in both the words and the music.

5. The "six principles" consist of the three main parts of the *Classic of Poetry* (the "Airs," "Odes," and "Hymns") and three modes of expression ("exposition," "comparison," and "affective image"). "Exposition" describes poems with a longer narrative of events, "comparison" describes poems that use similes, and "affective image" describes poems that use natural imagery that parallels a human situation and should stir the emotions. The "six principles" became staple terms in discussions of poetry in East Asia.

6. A last addition to the many meanings of *feng*: ministers or simple people can "criticize" their rulers or superiors through this kind of poetry.

That they should emerge from the affections is human nature; that they go no further than rites and moral principles is the beneficent influence of the former kings.

Thus the affairs of a single state, rooted in the experience of a single person, are called *Feng*. To speak of the affairs of the whole world and to describe customs (*feng*) common to all places is called *Ya*. *Ya* means "proper." These show the source of either flourishing or ruin in the royal government. Government has its greater and lesser aspects: thus we have a "Greater *Ya*" and a "Lesser *Ya*." The "Hymns" give the outward shapes of praising full virtue, and they inform the spirits about the accomplishment of great deeds. These are called the "Four Beginnings" and are the ultimate perfection of the Poems.

CONFUCIUS
551–479 B.C.E.

To this day there is virtually no aspect of East Asia on which Confucius and his ideas have not had some impact. When Confucius died in 479 B.C.E., he was a relatively little-known figure, having failed to find a ruler willing to implement his philosophical vision. Although he had attracted quite a few followers and had even established a school toward the end of his life, nobody could have anticipated then how this man's legacy would shape the destiny of China, East Asia, and the world. About 350 years later, Confucian values were not only widely known and revered but had also become the basis for official Chinese state ideology during the Han Dynasty (206 B.C.E.–220 C.E.). Twenty-five hundred years later, Confucius is a national icon for China's venerable past, although Confucianism, the system of beliefs and practices that developed on the basis of Confucius's ideas, took a severe beating in mainland China during much of the twentieth century.

LIFE AND TIMES

Confucius was born in the northeastern state of Lu in today's Shandong Province. Confucius came from the lower ranks of hereditary nobility. Like other masters during the fifth to the third centuries B.C.E., a period of heated intellectual debates comparable to the contemporary flourishing of Greek philosophy, he was eager to put his talents at the disposal of an able ruler who would implement his ideas. But the rulers of Lu were often at the mercy of powerful clans whose arrogance scandalized Confucius. For example, Confucius took offence when one of the great local clans in Lu used eight rows of dancers for the ceremonies at their ancestral temple, a lavish number that only the Zhou king had the prerogative to use. In Confucius's mind, this was not a simple breach of superficial protocol but a blatant symptom of the rottenness of the political system. Disgusted with the situation in his home state, Confucius left Lu and spent many years wandering from court to court, in search of a ruler who would appreciate his talents and political vision. He finally returned to Lu and lived out his life as a teacher, gathering a considerable following.

THE ZHOU HERITAGE AND CONFUCIUS'S INNOVATION

Confucius's philosophical vision brims with admiration for the values of the early Zhou rulers. The Zhou Dynasty (ca. 1045–256 B.C.E.), by Confucius's time already five centuries old, began with two exemplary rulers, King Wen and King Wu. King Wu had destroyed the last remnants of the reputedly despised Shang Dynasty in the eleventh century B.C.E., and instituted a new government that took pride in showing concern for the people and enforcing wise policies. After King Wu's death his brother, the Duke of Zhou, conducted government affairs for the duke's young nephew, King Cheng, who was still a child. Besides King Wen, the Duke of Zhou had particular importance for Confucius, not just because he was the ancestor of the ducal family of Confucius's home state. The Duke of Zhou also protected his nephew from rebellions and challenges to the newly founded dynasty and was an exemplary regent, with an eye on the welfare of the dynasty, not on his personal ambitions. But the splendor of the dynastic founders vanished over the next half millennium, as the Zhou kings increasingly lost control over the feudal lords, who had started out as their allies in the war against the Shang. By Confucius's time the Zhou kings had only nominal power and China consisted of rival states, whose rulers competed for territory and power. In the *Analects* Confucius often sharply criticizes the irreverent behavior of the feudal lords toward the Zhou king and showcases

their corruption to explain his vision of proper government.

Although Confucius claims in the *Analects* that he is merely the "transmitter" of Zhou values and not an "innovator," he actually built a new tradition. Confucius's conviction that the political chaos he perceived around him could be avoided by returning to the moral values of the venerable founders of the Zhou Dynasty, Kings Wu and Wen and the Duke of Zhou, paid homage to tradition but was also visionary, even revolutionary. His emphasis on the importance of social roles and rituals could reinforce existing hierarchies, but at the same time it allowed individuals to develop their inner potential and find a meaningful place in society. His pedagogical program, which promoted the reading of a group of texts, later called "Confucian Classics," and their application to life's challenges, could lead to mindless memorization designed merely for career advancement, but it also enabled people to better understand and take control of their lives by following the moral models, historical precedents, and words of wisdom contained in these canonical texts.

DIVERSITY AND CORE VALUES IN THE *ANALECTS*

Confucius's vision has been extraordinarily influential over the past two and a half millennia and has profoundly shaped the societies not just of China but also of Korea, Japan, and Vietnam. The *Analects*, best translated as "Collected Sayings," convey the power of Confucius's vision. A collection of brief quotations, conversations, and anecdotes from the life of Confucius, the *Analects* were not written by the master himself, but compiled by later generations of disciples. They probably reached their current form only during the second century B.C.E., when Confucius's ideas were gaining influence and it became necessary to create a representative collection of his sayings out of the vast body of Confucius lore that circulated in various other books. Later it became the key text to understanding the great master's character and ideas. The *Analects* throw light on people, concrete situations, and above all the exemplary model of Confucius himself, instead of supplying systematic expositions of his ideas or abstract definitions of moral philosophy. When commenting on central concepts such as "goodness" or "humanity" (*ren*), "ritual" (*li*), and "respect for one's parents" (*xiao*), Confucius might utter different, even contradictory maxims: sometimes he claims that anybody who wants to can become "humane" in a moment, but at other times he turns the concept into a distant ideal. He also explains that his answers sometimes differ, because an overeager disciple needs to be held back, while a timid one needs to be encouraged. Another explanation for the widely divergent pieces of advice to be found in the *Analects* is that it was compiled over several centuries and thus includes the changing opinions of the compilers.

RITUAL

Despite the diversity of views expounded in the *Analects*, it is possible to identify a core set of values. First, there is Confucius's emphasis on ritual. Everything we do in life is a ritual, whether we greet each other with a handshake or mark life's important moments, such as birth and death, with special observances. Although Confucius briefly refers to earlier notions of the powers of Heaven and declares that he respects the gods and spirits, his concern is with our world, the world of human society. Rituals are thus used not to communicate with divine powers, but instead to make social life meaningful. One learns and perfects these rituals in one's community through continuous practice and self-cultivation. The person who has perfected himself in this manner is the *junzi*—the "superior person," or "gentleman." The word referred originally to a prince of aristocratic birth, but Confucius boldly applies it to moral, not hereditary, superiority. Although Confucius at times denies having reached the stage of *junzi* himself, he makes clear that anybody can become a *junzi*, and that everyone should strive to reach that ideal. The *Analects* also idealize historical figures whom Confucius considers models of exemplary moral conduct. Even before the sage rulers of the Zhou, there were the sage emperors of highest antiquity, including Emperor Shun, whose moral charisma was so overwhelming that it sufficed for him to sit in proper ritual position on his throne to induce spontaneous order in his empire. In Confucianism, models of proper ritual behavior are crucial to guiding one's moral self-cultivation, and book 10 of the *Analects* enshrines the master himself as such a model actor: it is the only book in which the master does not speak, but is simply shown in silent ritual action. That the compilers of the *Analects* placed this book at the heart of the *Analects*' twenty books shows that they admired Confucius not just for what he said, but for his exemplary conduct throughout his life.

SOCIAL ROLES

A second recurrent concern in the *Analects* is Confucius's attention to social roles. In his words humans owe each other "goodness" or "humanity" (*ren*)— that is, empathy and reciprocal concern, mutual respect and obligation. Some later Confucians, such as Mencius (ca. 372–289 B.C.E.), believed that this natural ability for empathy was even more important than ritual. The natural and spontaneous basis for respect is the relation between child and parent. From this experience, respect is extended to other figures, such as elder siblings, seniors, and rulers.

Although Confucius endorses social hierarchies, he abhorred any form of force and coercion. Because Confucianism and its canonical texts became the basis for the recruitment of bureaucrats and part of the ideology of government in imperial China, it is sometimes portrayed as a philosophy that, in contrast to Daoism, puts social duty over natural desires. Yet the stance of Confucius in the *Analects* is much more complex. He often navigates between the instincts of inborn nature and the need for cultivation, the power of spontaneous action and the importance of patient learning, the pleasures of a life in harmony with one's wishes and the duties of a life devoted to political service. In book 18 we see Confucius attracted to recluses, dropouts who reject life in society; another time Confucius praises the view of a disciple who values ritual celebration and joyful singing with friends over petty state service. At yet another point Confucius recommends avoiding government service unless a virtuous ruler is on the throne.

EFFICIENT ACTION

Goodness, ritual, and attention to social roles create order in society; efficient action, another major Confucian concern, helps to maintain it and to effect change in the world. One of Confucius's most attractive ideas is his promise that it is possible to harmonize one's natural impulses with social norms and thus become an efficient, harmonious agent in society. He himself apparently reached this balance only in old age: "At seventy I follow all the desires of my heart without breaking any rule." Throughout the *Analects*, Confucius is fascinated with various kinds of efficiency. Emperor Shun, facing south on his throne and thereby creating order in the world, is the prime incarnation of minimalist action put to great effect. The notion that the moral charisma of a sage ruler can be so

powerful that there is no need to resort to lowly means of war and violence became the basis of the traditional Chinese view of rulership. Confucius's admiration for efficient thinking is best exemplified by his praise of his favorite disciple Yan Hui: "When he is told one thing he understands ten." The master of efficient speech, Confucius himself seems always to know more than he says: his utterances can be so short that they verge on the obscure. Sometimes he even speaks of his desire to reject language altogether.

THE IMPORTANCE OF CANONICAL TEXTS IN CONFUCIANISM

Confucius and his followers, called *Ru*, or "traditionalist scholars," considered the study of the ancient texts that contained the legacy of the Zhou as paramount to self-cultivation. Confucius is traditionally associated with the composition of the **Classic of Poetry**, *Classic of History*, *Record of Ritual*, *Spring and Autumn Annals*, and *Classic of Changes*, which were later called the "Confucian Classics." Today hardly anybody believes that they were written or compiled by Confucius. These books became the curriculum in the first Chinese state university, founded in 124 B.C.E. by Emperor Wu of the Han Dynasty. Later the Confucian Classics and other canonical Confucian texts such as the *Analects* formed the basis for the all-important civil service examination system, which allowed hundreds of thousands of individuals to attain office in the expansive bureaucracy of the Chinese empire. For more than two millennia these texts were the backbone of the training of political and cultural elites throughout East Asia and Confucius was venerated in temples as "the foremost teacher," a deity of moral perfection and learning.

Throughout its long history, Confucianism has served many political, social, and religious causes, and it has therefore also met with strident criticism. Already in the late fifth century B.C.E., Mozi, the first forceful critic of Confucius, wrote a devastating piece, "Against the Confucians," in which he parodied Confucians as "beggars, greedy hamsters, and staring he-goats who puff themselves up like wild boars." Their clothes, cries Mozi, are hopelessly old-fashioned, and they cling to the importance of ritual only because they hope to get a good meal out of the sacrificial food prepared for the occasion.

In the twentieth century, Chinese intellectuals and the Communist Party waged mass campaigns against Confucianism, considering it the utmost evil and blaming it for everything that supposedly went wrong with China's modernization. Yet many public intellectuals in Taiwan and the United States have been propagating "Neo-Confucianism" and are convinced that it can help renew humanistic values in today's harsh and cynical world. Since the 1990s the Confucius temples in mainland China have been rebuilt. Confucius is now discussed on television talk shows in China, and the Chinese government uses his name to represent China in the world. References to Confucius hovered over the Beijing Olympics of 2008, and in the first decade of the twenty-first century the government founded several hundred "Confucius Institutes" around the world, thus using the old sage as an icon for the propagation of Chinese language and culture. The future of Confucius's legacy is as bright as ever.

From Analects[1]

From *Book I*

1.1. The Master said: "To learn something and then to put it into practice at the right time: is this not a joy? To have friends coming from afar: is this not a delight? Not to be upset when one's merits are ignored: is this not the mark of a gentleman?"

1.4. Master Zeng said: "I examine myself three times a day. When dealing on behalf of others, have I been trustworthy? In intercourse with my friends, have I been faithful? Have I practiced what I was taught?"

1.11. The Master said: "When the father is alive, watch the son's aspirations. When the father is dead, watch the son's actions. If three years later, the son has not veered from the father's way, he may be called a dutiful son indeed."

1.15. Zigong said: "'Poor without servility; rich without arrogance.' How is that?" The Master said: "Not bad, but better still: 'Poor, yet cheerful; rich, yet considerate.'" Zigong said: "In the *Poems*, it is said: 'Like carving horn, like sculpting ivory, like cutting jade, like polishing stone.' Is this not the same idea?" The Master said: "Ah, one can really begin to discuss the *Poems* with you! I tell you one thing, and you can figure out the rest."

1. Translated by Simon Leys.

From *Book II*

2.1. The Master said: "He who rules by virtue is like the polestar, which remains unmoving in its mansion while all the other stars revolve respectfully around it."

2.2. The Master said: "The three hundred *Poems*[2] are summed up in one single phrase: 'Think no evil.'"

2.4. The Master said: "At fifteen, I set my mind upon learning. At thirty, I took my stand. At forty, I had no doubts. At fifty, I knew the will of Heaven. At sixty, my ear was attuned. At seventy, I follow all the desires of my heart without breaking any rule."

2.7. Ziyou asked about filial piety. The Master said: "Nowadays people think they are dutiful sons when they feed their parents. Yet they also feed their dogs and horses. Unless there is respect, where is the difference?"

2.11. The Master said: "He who by revising the old knows the new, is fit to be a teacher."

2.19. Duke Ai[3] asked: "What should I do to win the hearts of the people?" Confucius replied: "Raise the straight and set them above the crooked, and you will win the hearts of the people. If you raise the crooked and set them above the straight, the people will deny you their support."

From *Book III*

3.5. The Master said: "Barbarians who have rulers are inferior to the various nations of China who are without."

3.21. Duke Ai asked Zai Yu which wood should be used for the local totem. Zai Yu replied: "The men of Xia used pine; the men of Yin used cypress; the men of Zhou used *fir*, for (they said) the people should *fear*."[4]

The Master heard of this; he said: "What is done is done, it is all past; there would be no point in arguing."

3.24. The officer in charge of the border at Yi requested an interview with Confucius. He said: "Whenever a gentleman comes to these parts, I always ask to see him." The disciples arranged an interview. When it was over, the officer said to them: "Gentlemen, do not worry about his dismissal. The world has been without the Way for a long while. Heaven is going to use your master to ring the tocsin."

---

2. Another name for the *Classic of Poetry*.
3. Ruler of the dukedom of Lu, Confucius's home state.
4. Zai Yu, one of Confucius's disciples, replies to the duke with a pun: in the original text the chestnut tree (*li*), translated here as "fir," puns on "fear" (*li*).

From *Book IV*

4.8. The Master said: "In the morning hear the Way; in the evening die content."

4.15. The Master said: "Shen, my doctrine has one single thread running through it." Master Zeng Shen replied: "Indeed."
    The Master left. The other disciples asked: "What did he mean?" Master Zeng said: "The doctrine of the Master is: Loyalty and reciprocity, and that's all."

From *Book V*

5.9. The Master asked Zigong: "Which is the better, you or Yan Hui?"[5]— "How could I compare myself with Yan Hui? From one thing he learns, he deduces ten; from one thing I learn, I only deduce two." The Master said: "Indeed, you are not his equal, and neither am I."

5.10. Zai Yu was sleeping during the day. The Master said: "Rotten wood cannot be carved; dung walls cannot be troweled. What is the use of scolding him?"
    The Master said: "There was a time when I used to listen to what people said and trusted that they would act accordingly, but now I listen to what they say and watch what they do. It is Zai Yu who made me change."

5.20. Lord Ji Wen[6] always thought thrice before acting. Hearing this, the Master said: "Twice is enough."

5.26. Yan Hui and Zilu were in attendance. The Master said: "How about telling me your private wishes?"
    Zilu said: "I wish I could share my carriages, horses, clothes, and furs with my friends without being upset when they damage them."
    Yan Hui said. "I wish I would never boast of my good qualities or call attention to my good deeds."
    Zilu said: "May we ask what are our Master's private wishes?"
    The Master said: "I wish the old may enjoy peace, friends may enjoy trust, and the young may enjoy affection."

From *Book VI*

6.3. Duke Ai asked: "Which of the disciples has a love of learning?" Confucius replied: "There was Yan Hui who loved learning; he never vented his frustrations upon others; he never made the same mistake twice. Alas, his allotted span of life was short; he is dead. Now, for all I know, there is no one with such a love of learning."

6.12. Ran Qiu said: "It is not that I do not enjoy the Master's way, but I do not have the strength to follow it." The Master said: "He who does not have the strength can always give up halfway. But you have given up before starting."

5. Confucius's most beloved disciple.
6. Grand officer of the state of Lu, who lived before Confucius's time.

6.13. The Master said to Zixia: "Be a noble scholar, not a vulgar pedant."

6.18. The Master said: "When nature prevails over culture, you get a savage; when culture prevails over nature, you get a pedant. When nature and culture are in balance, you get a gentleman."

6.20. The Master said: "To know something is not as good as loving it; to love something is not as good as rejoicing in it."

6.22. Fan Chi asked about wisdom. The Master said: "Secure the rights of the people; respect ghosts and gods, but keep them at a distance—this is wisdom indeed."

Fan Chi asked about goodness. The Master said: "A good man's trials bear fruit—this is goodness indeed."

6.23. The Master said: "The wise find joy on the water, the good find joy in the mountains. The wise are active, the good are quiet. The wise are joyful, the good live long."

From *Book VII*

7.1. The Master said: "I transmit, I invent nothing. I trust and love the past. In this, I dare to compare myself to our venerable Peng."[7]

7.3. The Master said: "Failure to cultivate moral power, failure to explore what I have learned, incapacity to stand by what I know to be right, incapacity to reform what is not good—these are my worries."

7.5. The Master said: "I am getting dreadfully old. It has been a long time since I last saw in a dream the Duke of Zhou."[8]

7.16. The Master said: "Even though you have only coarse grain for food, water for drink, and your bent arm for a pillow, you may still be happy. Riches and honors without justice are to me as fleeting clouds."

7.21. The Master never talked of: miracles; violence; disorders; spirits.

From *Book VIII*

8.5. Master Zeng said: "Competent, yet willing to listen to the incompetent; talented, yet willing to listen to the talentless; having, yet seeming not to have; full, yet seeming empty; swallowing insults without taking offense—long ago, I had a friend who practiced these things."

7. Identifications of this figure vary, but venerable Peng might have been a virtuous official of the Shang Dynasty (ca. 1500–1045 B.C.E.).
8. Son of King Wen, who together with King Wu founded the Zhou Dynasty (1045–256 B.C.E.). He laid the groundwork for basic institutions of the Zhou Dynasty and is the founding ancestor of the state of Lu, Confucius's home state.

8.8. The Master said: "Draw inspiration from the *Poems*; steady your course with the ritual; find your fulfillment in music."

8.13. The Master said: "Uphold the faith, love learning, defend the good Way with your life. Enter not a country that is unstable: dwell not in a country that is in turmoil. Shine in a world that follows the Way; hide when the world loses the Way. In a country where the Way prevails, it is shameful to remain poor and obscure; in a country which has lost the Way, it is shameful to become rich and honored."

8.17. The Master said: "Learning is like a chase in which, as you fail to catch up, you fear to lose what you have already gained."

From *Book IX*

9.5. The Master was trapped in Kuang. He said: "King Wen is dead: is civilization not resting now on me? If Heaven intends civilization to be destroyed, why was it vested in me? If Heaven does not intend civilization to be destroyed, what should I fear from the people of Kuang?"[9]

9.6. The Grand Chamberlain asked Zigong: "Is your Master not a saint? But then, why should he also possess so many particular aptitudes?" Zigong replied: "Heaven indeed made him a saint; but he also happens to have many aptitudes."

Hearing of this, the Master said: "The Grand Chamberlain truly knows me. In my youth, I was poor; therefore, I had to become adept at a variety of lowly skills. Does such versatility befit a gentleman? No, it does not."

9.12. The Master was very ill. Zilu organized the disciples in a retinue, as if they were the retainers of a lord. During a remission of his illness, the Master said: "Zilu, this farce has lasted long enough. Whom can I deceive with these sham retainers? Can I deceive Heaven? Rather than die amidst retainers, I prefer to die in the arms of my disciples. I may not receive a state funeral, but still I shall not die by the wayside."

9.14. The Master wanted to settle among the nine barbarian tribes of the East. Someone said: "It is wild in those parts. How would you cope?" The Master said: "How could it be wild, once a gentleman has settled there?"

9.17. The Master stood by a river and said: "Everything flows like this, without ceasing, day and night."

9.23. The Master said: "One should regard the young with awe: how do you know that the next generation will not equal the present one? If, however, by the age of forty or fifty, a man has not made a name for himself, he no longer deserves to be taken seriously."

9. Kuang was a border town where Confucius nearly fell into the hands of a lynch mob who mistook him for an adventurer who had ransacked the region. Confucius uses a pun in making his point: the name of King Wen, the founder of the Zhou Dynasty, also means "civilization" (*wen*).

From *Book X*

10.2. At court, when conversing with the under ministers, he was affable; when conversing with the upper ministers, he was respectful. In front of the ruler, he was humble yet composed.

10.4. When entering the gate of the Duke's palace, he walked in discreetly. He never stood in the middle of the passage, nor did he tread on the threshold.

When he passed in front of the throne, he adopted an expression of gravity, hastened his step, and became as if speechless. When ascending the steps of the audience hall, he lifted up the hem of his gown and bowed, as if short of breath; on coming out, after descending the first step, he expressed relief and contentment.

At the bottom of the steps, he moved swiftly, as if on wings. On regaining his place, he resumed his humble countenance.

From *Book XI*

11.9. Yan Hui died. The Master said: "Alas! Heaven is destroying me. Heaven is destroying me!"

11.10. Yan Hui died. The Master wailed wildly. His followers said: "Master, such grief is not proper." The Master said: "In mourning such a man, what sort of grief would be proper?"

11.26. Zilu, Zeng Dian, Ran Qiu, and Gongxi Chi were sitting with the Master. The Master said: "Forget for one moment that I am your elder. You often say: 'The world does not recognize our merits.' But, given the opportunity, what would you wish to do?"

Zilu rushed to reply first: "Give me a country not too small,[1] but squeezed between powerful neighbors; it is under attack and in the grip of a famine. Put me in charge: within three years, I would revive the spirits of the people and set them back on their feet."

The Master smiled. "Ran Qiu, what about you?"

The other replied: "Give me a domain of sixty to seventy—or, say, fifty to sixty leagues; within three years I would secure the prosperity of its people. As regards their spiritual well-being, however, this would naturally have to wait for the intervention of a true gentleman."

"Gongxi Chi, what about you?"

"I don't say that I would be able to do this, but I would like to learn: in the ceremonies of the Ancestral Temple, such as a diplomatic conference for instance, wearing chasuble and cap, I would like to play the part of a junior assistant."

"And what about you, Zeng Dian?"

Zeng Dian, who had been softly playing his zithern, plucked one last chord and pushed his instrument aside. He replied: "I am afraid my wish is not up to those of my three companions." The Master said: "There is no harm in that! After all, each is simply confiding his personal aspirations."

1. Literally, "a country of a thousand chariots."

"In late spring, after the making of the spring clothes has been completed, together with five or six companions and six or seven boys, I would like to bathe in the River Yi, and then enjoy the breeze on the Rain Dance Terrace, and go home singing." The Master heaved a deep sigh and said: "I am with Dian!"

The three others left; Zeng Dian remained behind and said: "What did you think of their wishes?" The Master said: "Each simply confided his personal aspirations."

"Why did you smile at Zilu?"

"One should govern a state through ritual restraint; yet his words were full of swagger."

"As for Ran Qiu, wasn't he in fact talking about a full-fledged state?"

"Indeed; have you ever heard of 'a domain of sixty to seventy, or fifty to sixty leagues'?"

"And Gongxi Chi? Wasn't he also talking about a state?"

"A diplomatic conference in the Ancestral Temple! What could it be, if not an international gathering? And if Gongxi Chi were there merely to play the part of a junior assistant, who would qualify for the main role?"

From *Book XII*

12.2. Ran Yong asked about humanity. The Master said: "When abroad, behave as if in front of an important guest. Lead the people as if performing a great ceremony. What you do not wish for yourself, do not impose upon others. Let no resentment enter public affairs; let no resentment enter private affairs."

Ran Yong said: "I may not be clever, but with your permission I shall endeavor to do as you have said."

12.5. Sima Niu was grieving: "All men have brothers; I alone have none." Zixia said: "I have heard this: life and death are decreed by fate, riches and honors are allotted by Heaven. Since a gentleman behaves with reverence and diligence, treating people with deference and courtesy, all within the Four Seas are his brothers. How could a gentleman ever complain that he has no brothers?"

12.7. Zigong asked about government. The Master said: "Sufficient food, sufficient weapons, and the trust of the people." Zigong said: "If you had to do without one of these three, which would you give up?—"Weapons."—"If you had to do without one of the remaining two, which would you give up?"—"Food; after all, everyone has to die eventually. But without the trust of the people, no government can stand."

12.11. Duke Jing of Qi asked Confucius about government. Confucius replied: "Let the lord be a lord; the subject a subject; the father a father; the son a son." The Duke said: "Excellent! If indeed the lord is not a lord, the subject not a subject, the father not a father, the son not a son, I could be sure of nothing anymore—not even of my daily food."

12.18. Lord Ji Kang was troubled by burglars. He consulted with Confucius. Confucius replied: "If you yourself were not covetous, they would not rob you, even if you paid them to."

12.19. Lord Ji Kang asked Confucius about government, saying: "Suppose I were to kill the bad to help the good: how about that?" Confucius replied: "You are here to govern, what need is there to kill? If you desire what is good, the people will be good. The moral power of the gentleman is wind, the moral power of the common man is grass. Under the wind, the grass must bend."

From *Book XIII*

13.1. Zilu asked about government. The Master said: "Guide them. Encourage them." Zilu asked him to develop these precepts. The Master said: "Untiringly."

13.3. Zilu asked: "If the ruler of Wei were to entrust you with the government of the country, what would be your first initiative?" The Master said: "It would certainly be to rectify the names." Zilu said: "Really? Isn't this a little farfetched? What is this rectification for?" The Master said: "How boorish can you get! Whereupon a gentleman is incompetent, thereupon he should remain silent. If the names are not correct, language is without an object. When language is without an object, no affair can be effected. When no affair can be effected, rites and music wither. When rites and music wither, punishments and penalties miss their target. When punishments and penalties miss their target, the people do not know where they stand. Therefore, whatever a gentleman conceives of, he must be able to say; and whatever he says, he must be able to do. In the matter of language, a gentleman leaves nothing to chance."

13.10. The Master said: "If a ruler could employ me, in one year I would make things work, and in three years the results would show."

13.11. The Master said: "'When good men have been running the country for a hundred years, cruelty can be overcome, and murder extirpated.' How true is this saying!"

13.12. The Master said: "Even with a true king, it would certainly take one generation for humanity to prevail."

13.20. Zigong asked: "How does one deserve to be called a gentleman?" The Master said: "He who behaves with honor, and, being sent on a mission to the four corners of the world, does not bring disgrace to his lord, deserves to be called a gentleman."

"And next to that, if I may ask?"

"His relatives praise his filial piety and the people of his village praise the way he respects the elders."

"And next to that, if I may ask?"

"His word can be trusted; whatever he undertakes, he brings to completion. In this, he may merely show the obstinacy of a vulgar man; still, he should probably qualify as a gentleman of lower category."

"In this respect, how would you rate our present politicians?"

"Alas! These puny creatures are not even worth mentioning!"

From *Book XIV*

14.24. The Master said: "In the old days, people studied to improve themselves. Now they study in order to impress others."

14.35. The Master said: "No one understands me!" Zigong said: "Why is it that no one understands you?" The Master said: "I do not accuse Heaven, nor do I blame men; here below I am learning, and there above I am being heard. If I am understood, it must be by Heaven."

14.38. Zilu stayed for the night at the Stone Gate. The gatekeeper said: "Where are you from?" Zilu said: "I am from Confucius's household."—"Oh, is that the one who keeps pursuing what he knows is impossible?"

14.43. Yuan Rang sat waiting, with his legs spread wide. The Master said: "A youth who does not respect his elders will achieve nothing when he grows up, and will even try to shirk death when he reaches old age: he is a parasite." And he struck him across the shin with his stick.

From *Book XV*

15.3. The Master said: "Zigong, do you think that I am someone who learns a lot of things and then stores them all up?"—"Indeed; is it not so?" The Master said: "No. I have one single thread on which to string them all."

15.5. The Master said: "Shun[2] was certainly one of those who knew how to govern by inactivity. How did he do it? He sat reverently on the throne, facing south—and that was all."

15.7. The Master said: "How straight Shi Yu was! Under a good government, he was straight as an arrow: under a bad government, he was straight as an arrow. What a gentleman was Qu Boyu![3] Under a good government, he displayed his talents. Under a bad government, he folded them up in his heart."

15.31. The Master said: "In an attempt to meditate, I once spent a whole day without food and a whole night without sleep: it was no use. It is better to study."

From *Book XVII*

17.4. The Master went to Wucheng, where Ziyou was governor. He heard the sound of stringed instruments and hymns. He was amused and said with a smile: "Why use an ox-cleaver to kill a chicken?" Ziyou replied: "Master, in the past I have heard you say: 'The gentleman who cultivates the Way loves all men; the small people who cultivate the Way are easy to govern.'" The Master said: "My friends, Ziyou is right. I was just joking."

17.9. The Master said: "Little ones, why don't you study the *Poems?* The *Poems* can provide you with stimulation and with observation, with a capacity for communion, and with a vehicle for grief. At home, they enable you to serve

2. Emperor of high antiquity known for his exemplary virtue. The throne usually faced south.

3. Shi Yu and Qu Boyu were both high officials in the state of Wei. Confucius was once hosted by Qu Boyu.

your father, and abroad, to serve your lord. Also, you will learn there the names of many birds, animals, plants, and trees."

17.19. The Master said: "I wish to speak no more." Zigong said: "Master, if you do not speak, how would little ones like us still be able to hand down any teachings?" The Master said: "Does Heaven speak? Yet the four seasons follow their course and the hundred creatures continue to be born. Does Heaven speak?"

17.21. Zai Yu asked: "Three years mourning for one's parents—this is quite long. If a gentleman stops all ritual practices for three years, the practices will decay; if he stops all musical performances for three years, music will be lost. As the old crop is consumed, a new crop grows up, and for lighting the fire, a new lighter is used with each season. One year of mourning should be enough." The Master said: "If after only one year, you were again to eat white rice and to wear silk, would you feel at ease?"—"Absolutely."—"In that case, go ahead! The reason a gentleman prolongs his mourning is simply that, since fine food seems tasteless to him, and music offers him no enjoyment, and the comfort of his house makes him uneasy, he prefers to do without all these pleasures. But now, if you can enjoy them, go ahead!"

Zai Yu left. The Master said: "Zai Yu is devoid of humanity. After a child is born, for the first three years of his life, he does not leave his parents' bosom. Three years mourning is a custom that is observed everywhere in the world. Did Zai Yu never enjoy the love of his parents, even for three years?"

From *Book XVIII*

18.5. Jieyu, the Madman of Chu, went past Confucius, singing:

> Phoenix, oh Phoenix!
> The past cannot be retrieved,
> But the future still holds a chance
> Give up, give up!
> The days of those in office are numbered!

Confucius stopped his chariot, for he wanted to speak with him, but the other hurried away and disappeared. Confucius did not succeed in speaking to him.

18.6. Changju and Jieni were ploughing together. Confucius, who was passing by, sent Zilu to ask where the ford was. Changju said: "Who is in the chariot?" Zilu said: "It is Confucius." "The Confucius from Lu?" "Himself."—"Then he already knows where the ford is."

Zilu then asked Jieni, who replied: "Who are you?"—"I am Zilu."—"The disciple of Confucius, from Lu?"—"Yes."—"The whole universe is swept along by the same flood; who can reverse its flow? Instead of following a gentleman who keeps running from one patron to the next, would it not be better to follow a gentleman who has forsaken the world?" All the while he kept on tilling his field.

Zilu came back and reported to Confucius. Rapt in thought, the Master sighed: "One cannot associate with birds and beasts. With whom should I keep company, if not with my own kind? If the world were following the Way, I would not have to reform it."

LAOZI

sixth–third centuries B.C.E.

Attributed to a master called Laozi, the *Daodejing* ("The Classic of the Way and Its Virtue") is the most often translated early Chinese text. It is also the most paradoxical, because it uses logical contradictions to articulate its vision. The *Daodejing* exhorts its readers in pithy, simple language to return to the natural way of things, to reject the corruptions of human civilization, and to adopt a productive passiveness, a stance of "nonaction," that promises unexpected success. It claims that those who understand it will preserve their lives in a dangerous world, reach their goals, and gain political power. The *Daodejing* declares at one point that its message is easy to understand, but the fact that more than seven hundred commentaries have been written on the *Daodejing* over the past 2,200 years shows that it is hardly self-explanatory. The lack of agreement among readers about the *Daodejing*'s message has only increased its popularity. It has become familiar to readers around the world thanks to the great number of translations, which sometimes differ so considerably that readers wonder whether they are all reading the same source text.

The *Daodejing* contains eighty-one short chapters written in rhythmic verse. It is divided into two main parts: one part on the "Way" (*dao*) and one part on "Virtue" (*de*). The Way refers to a natural, uncorrupted way of being that pervades everything in heaven and earth, from all beings in the cosmos to humans. Virtue is the power inherent in each thing in its natural state and the force that allows humans to reach their full potential. Both concepts were central to the intense philosophical debates initi-

ated by **Confucius** (551–479 B.C.E.), and they remained important during the so-called Warring States Period (403–221 B.C.E.), when China was divided into small rival states. During this time thinkers traveled from state to state to offer political advice to rulers hungry for territory and power. The rich corpus of so-called Masters Literature, philosophical texts centered around charismatic master figures, allows us to follow these masters' arguments in great detail. Much of the debate focused on how rulers should govern their states, and how individuals can live the best possible life. Although the thinkers of the Warring States Period did not agree about the meaning of the Way and of Virtue, they all considered these concepts important, and they discussed and debated them at length. Yet the *Daodejing* placed so much emphasis on the concept of *dao* that, together with *Zhuangzi*, it became the foundational text of Daoism, the "School of the Way." Recent excavations that produced copies of the *Daodejing* from a tomb datable to around 300 B.C.E. confirm that the text existed by that time in its more or less finished form, though the order of chapters differs.

Many Masters Texts argue for good government and a good life by referring to memorable historical events and people. But the *Daodejing* boldly projects its message beyond any specific time and place. Instead, it evokes cosmic categories such as the Way and relies on the power not of history but of universal natural imagery: the "uncarved block," the "spirit of the valley," the "gateway of the manifold secrets," or "the mysterious female." There is no identifiable speaker, except for an indefinite "I" that delivers words of wisdom as if talking from the "cosmic void." Claiming that the Way cannot be named or explained, many chapters define it negatively. They criticize conventional wisdom and elevate the values that contradict it. The *Daodejing* teaches that weakness, softness, and passivity, not force, rigidity, and assertive action, are qualities key to surviving in a dangerous world. It preaches that emptiness, not fullness; the female, not the male principle; and counterintuitive, not conventional wisdom are needed to succeed. Unlike most early Chinese texts that hurl their attacks directly against their opponents, the *Daodejing* cleverly abstains from naming rival schools of thought and thus places itself above the heated intellectual strife that surrounds it. It does not mention Confucius by name, but its polemical attack on Confucian values such as moral virtue, positive action, and refinement through education, which leads away from the state of nature, leaves no doubt that the *Daodejing* was partly written as a refutation of Confucius and his followers.

Despite its praise of weakness and nonaction, the *Daodejing* contains a powerful political philosophy and provides recipes of how to "win the empire" and how to succeed in a world of political competition and intrigue. This aspect of its message is addressed to those aspiring to become both sages and rulers: they should preserve their power by keeping the populace ignorant and manipulating them imperceptibly from above, giving the impression of not interfering but ultimately exercising absolute power.

In traditional China, the *Daodejing* was attractive because it provided a radical alternative to the Confucian vision of human morality and cultivation and was couched in poignant paradoxical formulations. Instead of arguing against the Confucian vision, it built an alternative universe that seemed to transcend the intellectual disputes of the centuries during which it was written. Although its political teachings appear abstract to the point of becoming impractical, the *Daodejing* has lost nothing of its influence. It is present in ever new editions on bookshelves around the world and variously praised as a manual of self-actualization, professional success, and leadership training in a postindustrial world.

From the Daodejing[1]

I

The way that can be spoken of
Is not the constant way;
The name that can be named
Is not the constant name.
The nameless was the beginning of heaven
    and earth;
The named was the mother of the myriad creatures.
Hence always rid yourself of desires in order to
    observe its secrets;
But always allow yourself to have desires in order
    to observe its manifestations.

5

1. Translated by D. C. Lau.

These two are the same
But diverge in name as they issue forth.   10
Being the same they are called mysteries,
Mystery upon mystery—
The gateway of the manifold secrets.

II

The whole world recognizes the beautiful as the beautiful, yet this is
    only the ugly; the whole world recognizes the good as the good,
    yet this is only the bad.
Thus Something and Nothing produce each other;
The difficult and the easy complement each other;
The long and the short off-set each other;
The high and the low incline towards each other;   5
Note and sound harmonize with each other;
Before and after follow each other.
Therefore the sage keeps to the deed that consists in taking no action
    and practises the teaching that uses no words.
The myriad creatures rise from it yet it claims no authority;
It gives them life yet claims no possession;   10
It benefits them yet exacts no gratitude;
It accomplishes its task yet lays claim to no merit.
It is because it lays claim to no merit
That its merit never deserts it.

III

Not to honor men of worth will keep the people from contention; not to
    value goods which are hard to come by will keep them from theft; not
    to display what is desirable will keep them from being unsettled of
    mind.
Therefore in governing the people, the sage empties their minds but fills
    their bellies, weakens their wills but strengthens their bones. He
    always keeps them innocent of knowledge and free from desire, and
    ensures that the clever never dare to act.
Do that which consists in taking no action, and order will prevail.

IV

The way is empty, yet use will not drain it.
Deep, it is like the ancestor of the myriad creatures.
Blunt the sharpness;
Untangle the knots;
Soften the glare;   5
Let your wheels move only along old ruts.
Darkly visible, it only seems as if it were there.
I know not whose son it is.
It images the forefather of God.

V

Heaven and earth are ruthless, and treat the myriad creatures as straw
    dogs;[2] the sage is ruthless, and treats the people as straw dogs.
Is not the space between heaven and earth like a bellows?
It is empty without being exhausted:
The more it works the more comes out.
Much speech leads inevitably to silence.   5
Better to hold fast to the void.

VI

The spirit of the valley never dies.
This is called the mysterious female.
The gateway of the mysterious female
Is called the root of heaven and earth.
Dimly visible, it seems as if it were there,   5
Yet use will never drain it.

VII

Heaven and earth are enduring. The reason why heaven and earth can be
    enduring is that they do not give themselves life. Hence they are able
    to be long-lived.
Therefore the sage puts his person last and it comes first,
Treats it as extraneous to himself and it is preserved.
Is it not because he is without thought of self that he is able to accomplish
    his private ends?

VIII

Highest good is like water. Because water excels in benefiting the myriad
    creatures without contending with them and settles where none would
    like to be, it comes close to the way.
In a home it is the site that matters;
In quality of mind it is depth that matters;
In an ally it is benevolence that matters;
In speech it is good faith that matters;   5
In government it is order that matters;
In affairs it is ability that matters;
In action it is timeliness that matters.
It is because it does not contend that it is never at fault.

XI

Thirty spokes
Share one hub.
Adapt the nothing therein to the purpose in hand, and you will have the
    use of the cart. Knead clay in order to make a vessel. Adapt the

2. Straw dogs were sometimes used in rituals. They were treated with great respect during the
ceremony, only to be trampled on and discarded afterward.

nothing therein to the purpose in hand, and you will have the use of the vessel. Cut out doors and windows in order to make a room. Adapt the nothing[3] therein to the purpose in hand, and you will have the use of the room.

Thus what we gain is Something, yet it is by virtue of Nothing that this can be put to use.

XII

The five colors make man's eyes blind;
The five notes make his ears deaf;
The five tastes injure his palate;
Riding and hunting
Make his mind go wild with excitement;   5
Goods hard to come by
Serve to hinder his progress.
Hence the sage is
For the belly
Not for the eye.   10
Therefore he discards the one and takes the other.

XVI

I do my utmost to attain emptiness;
I hold firmly to stillness.
The myriad creatures all rise together
And I watch their return.
The teeming creatures   5
All return to their separate roots.
Returning to one's roots is known as stillness.
This is what is meant by returning to one's destiny.
Returning to one's destiny is known as the constant.
Knowledge of the constant is known as discernment.   10
Woe to him who wilfully innovates
While ignorant of the constant,
But should one act from knowledge of the constant
One's action will lead to impartiality,
Impartiality to kingliness,   15
Kingliness to heaven,
Heaven to the way,
The way to perpetuity,
And to the end of one's days one will meet with no danger.

XVII

The best of all rulers is but a shadowy presence to his subjects.
Next comes the ruler they love and praise;
Next comes one they fear;
Next comes one with whom they take liberties.

---

3. "Nothing" in these instances refers to the empty spaces of wheels, vessels, and rooms.

When there is not enough faith, there is lack of good faith.   5
Hesitant, he does not utter words lightly.
When his task is accomplished and his work done
The people all say, 'It happened to us naturally.'

XVIII

When the great way falls into disuse
There are benevolence and rectitude;
When cleverness emerges
There is great hypocrisy;
When the six relations[4] are at variance   5
There are filial children;
When the state is benighted
There are loyal ministers.

XIX

Exterminate the sage, discard the wise,
And the people will benefit a hundredfold;
Exterminate benevolence, discard rectitude,
And the people will again be filial;
Exterminate ingenuity, discard profit,   5
And there will be no more thieves and bandits.
These three, being false adornments, are not enough
And the people must have something to which they
    can attach themselves:
Exhibit the unadorned and embrace the uncarved
    block,
Have little thought of self and as few desires as
    possible.   10

XX

Exterminate learning and there will no longer be worries.
Between yea and nay
How much difference is there?
Between good and evil
How great is the distance?   5
What others fear
One must also fear.
And wax without having reached the limit.
The multitude are joyous
As if partaking of the *tai lao*[5] offering   10
Or going up to a terrace in spring.
I alone am inactive and reveal no signs,
Like a baby that has not yet learned to smile,

---

4. One commentator takes them as the relation between father and son, elder and younger brother, and husband and wife.

5. A ritual feast, where three kinds of animals— ox, sheep, and pig—were sacrificed.

Listless as though with no home to go back to.
The multitude all have more than enough.   15
I alone seem to be in want.
My mind is that of a fool—how blank!
Vulgar people are clear.
I alone am drowsy.
Vulgar people are alert.   20
I alone am muddled.
Calm like the sea:
Like a high wind that never ceases.
The multitude all have a purpose.
I alone am foolish and uncouth.   25
I alone am different from others
And value being fed by the mother.

XXV

There is a thing confusedly formed,
Born before heaven and earth.
Silent and void
It stands alone and does not change,
Goes round and does not weary.   5
It is capable of being the mother of the world.
I know not its name
So I style it 'the way'.
I give it the makeshift name of 'the great'.
Being great, it is further described as receding,   10
Receding, it is described as far away,
Being far away, it is described as turning back.
Hence the way is great; heaven is great; earth is great; and the king is also
    great. Within the realm there are four things that are great, and the
    king counts as one.
Man models himself on earth,
Earth on heaven,   15
Heaven on the way,
And the way on that which is naturally so.

XXVIII

Know the male
But keep to the role of the female
And be a ravine to the empire.
If you are a ravine to the empire,
Then the constant virtue will not desert you   5
And you will again return to being a babe.
Know the white
But keep to the role of the black
And be a model to the empire.
If you are a model to the empire,   10

Then the constant virtue will not be wanting
And you will return to the infinite.
Know honor
But keep to the role of the disgraced
And be a valley to the empire.   15
If you are a valley to the empire,
Then the constant virtue will be sufficient
And you will return to being the uncarved block.
When the uncarved block shatters it becomes vessels.
The sage makes use of these and becomes the lord
    over the officials.   20
Hence the greatest cutting
Does not sever.

XXXVII

The way never acts yet nothing is left undone.
Should lords and princes be able to hold fast to it,
The myriad creatures will be transformed of their
    own accord.
After they are transformed, should desire raise its
    head,
I shall press it down with the weight of the nameless
    uncarved block.   5
The nameless uncarved block
Is but freedom from desire,
And if I cease to desire and remain still,
The empire will be at peace of its own accord.

XXXVIII

A man of the highest virtue does not keep to virtue and that is why he has
    virtue. A man of the lowest virtue never strays from virtue and that is
    why he is without virtue. The former never acts yet leaves nothing
    undone. The latter acts but there are things left undone. A man of the
    highest benevolence acts, but from no ulterior motive. A man of the
    highest rectitude acts, but from ulterior motive. A man most
    conversant in the rites acts, but when no one responds rolls up his
    sleeves and resorts to persuasion by force.
Hence when the way was lost there was virtue; when virtue was lost there
    was benevolence; when benevolence was lost there was rectitude;
    when rectitude was lost there were the rites.
The rites are the wearing thin of loyalty and good faith
And the beginning of disorder;
Foreknowledge is the flowery embellishment of the way   5
And the beginning of folly.
Hence the man of large mind abides in the thick not in the thin, in the fruit
    not in the flower.
Therefore he discards the one and takes the other.

XLII

The way begets one; one begets two; two begets three; three begets the
    myriad creatures.
The myriad creatures carry on their backs the *yin* and embrace in their
    arms the *yang* and are the blending of the generative forces of the two.
There are no words which men detest more than 'solitary', 'desolate', and
    'hapless', yet lords and princes use these to refer to themselves.
Thus a thing is sometimes added to by being diminished and diminished by
    being added to.
What others teach I also teach. 'The violent will not come to a natural end.'
    I shall take this as my precept.   5

XLVIII

In the pursuit of learning one knows more every day; in the pursuit of the
    way one does less every day. One does less and less until one does
    nothing at all, and when one does nothing at all there is nothing that is
    undone.
It is always through not meddling that the empire is won. Should you
    meddle, then you are not equal to the task of winning the empire.

LXIV

It is easy to maintain a situation while it is still
    secure;
It is easy to deal with a situation before symptoms
    develop;
It is easy to break a thing when it is yet brittle;
It is easy to dissolve a thing when it is yet minute.
Deal with a thing while it is still nothing;   5
Keep a thing in order before disorder sets in.
A tree that can fill the span of a man's arms
Grows from a downy tip;
A terrace nine storeys high
Rises from hodfuls of earth;   10
A journey of a thousand miles
Starts from beneath one's feet.
Whoever does anything to it will ruin it; whoever lays hold of it will
    lose it.
Therefore the sage, because he does nothing, never ruins anything; and,
    because he does not lay hold of anything, loses nothing.
In their enterprises the people   15
Always ruin them when on the verge of success.
Be as careful at the end as at the beginning
And there will be no ruined enterprises.
Therefore the sage desires not to desire
And does not value goods which are hard to come by;   20
Learns to be without learning
And makes good the mistakes of the multitude

In order to help the myriad creatures to be natural
and to refrain from daring to act.

LXX

My words are very easy to understand and very easy to put into practice, yet no
one in the world can understand them or put them into practice.
Words have an ancestor and affairs have a sovereign. It is because people are
ignorant that they fail to understand me.
Those who understand me are few;
Those who imitate me are honoured.
Therefore the sage, while clad in homespun, conceals on his person a
priceless piece of jade.   5

LXXVI

A man is supple and weak when living, but hard and stiff when dead. Grass and
trees are pliant and fragile when living, but dried and shrivelled when dead.
Thus the hard and the strong are the comrades of death; the supple and
the weak are the comrades of life.
Therefore a weapon that is strong will not vanquish;
A tree that is strong will suffer the axe.
The strong and big takes the lower position,
The supple and weak takes the higher position.   5

LXXXI

Truthful words are not beautiful; beautiful words are not truthful. Good words
are not persuasive; persuasive words are not good. He who knows has no
wide learning; he who has wide learning does not know.
The sage does not hoard.
Having bestowed all he has on others, he has yet more;
Having given all he has to others, he is richer still.
The way of heaven benefits and does not harm; the way of the sage is bountiful
and does not contend.   5

IV

Circling the Mediterranean: Europe and the Islamic World

The word "Mediterranean" comes from Latin, meaning "in the middle of the lands." From antiquity through the Middle Ages, the centrally located Mediterranean Sea—also called by those who lived along its shores *Mare nostrum,* or "our sea"—facilitated trade and exchange. Not only commodities but also stories and songs continually circulated from place to place, crisscrossing the water to link nations in Europe, North Africa, and the Near and Middle East. Port cities all around the Mediterranean were sites of particularly intense cultural and economic interaction, collectively making up a single complex web that knit together distant lands.

While earlier generations of historians have tended to see the diverse cultures of the Mediterranean region in monolithic terms, conceiving of an Islamic world and a Christian world that were fundamentally opposed, more recent research has unearthed the intimate links between the various cultures of the region. There was both a great deal of interaction *between* the cultural spheres conventionally marked as "Europe" and "the Islamic world" and, on the other hand, a great deal of diversity *within* each one of these apparently undifferentiated units. "Europe," as a multinational concept, almost never appeared during the Middle

A fourteenth-century image of the Venetian trader Marco Polo, embarking from Venice.

Ages; people referred to themselves as "English," "Franks," "Normans," and "Lombards," not as "Europeans." "The Islamic world" was similarly divided by rival efforts to lead the Muslim community in the caliphates of Damascus, Baghdad, and Cairo, as well as by the Mongol invasions of the thirteenth century. The opposition of "the Islamic world" and "Europe" is a modern invention: it was not the way medieval people described themselves or the world they lived in.

The false division between Europe and the Islamic world enabled a misleading view of history in which Christian Europe was seen as the sole heir to a rich legacy of Greco-Roman philosophy and literature, uncontaminated by Arabic or Persian influences—an unin-terrupted cultural bloodline, so to speak, reaching back from Aquinas to Aristotle, from **Dante** to **Virgil**. Nothing could be further from the truth. The Arabic translations of ancient Greek philosophy and science that made the work of Plato, Aristotle, and Ptolemy available to Europeans as they slowly emerged from a long period of intellectual dormancy were not just passive vessels that transmitted ancient knowledge to an awakening Europe on the cusp of the Renaissance: on the contrary, the cultural ferment of the Islamic world was an essential element in the emergence of the early modern West. The story of premodern history and literature is, therefore, above all a story of connections, interaction, and mutual influence.

This image, from an illuminated thirteenth-century Arabic manuscript, depicts the Greek philosopher Socrates discoursing with his students.

CHRISTIANITY AND PLATONISM

By the year 100, broad changes were under way in the lands circling the Mediterranean Sea. The Roman Empire, which had reached its pinnacle of cultural and military supremacy during the reign of Augustus Caesar, had expanded to the point that unrest in the eastern provinces was a perpetual worry. In the Roman-ruled province of Judea (roughly, modern Israel), the suppression by the civil authorities of a loosely organized rebellion culminated in the destruction of Jerusalem and scattering (or "diaspora") of the Jewish community in 70 C.E. Those exiled from the region included the Jewish followers of James and John who had embraced the message of the gospel, as well as those mixed Jewish and Gentile communities that took up the intensely hellenized brand of Christianity developed by Paul and his followers, which drew on the philosophy of Plato as well as of mystical Neoplatonists such as Plotinus and Porphyry. Not until about three centuries later would this heterogeneous collection of new religious orientations become codified as a single Christian doctrine, encapsulated in Jerome's production of the Latin (or "Vulgate") **Bible** and in **Augustine's** masterful synthesis of Christian doctrine and Greek philosophy.

Augustine's autobiography, the *Confessions*, pays tribute to the theologian's engagement with the philosophy and literature of the Roman world: he paraphrases Seneca and Cicero, and movingly describes the tears he shed while reading Virgil's account of Dido in the *Aeneid*. These moments illustrate the imaginative pull of classical literature, which persisted during the period of Christianity's emergence. The values of Rome, its celebration of the arts and worldly pleasures, were very much at odds with a Christian ethic that demanded a rejection of the things of this world. Music, art, and poetry were to be avoided, unless they were explicitly in the service of God: liturgical music, as part of the act of communal worship, along with painted images of the crucified Christ, the Virgin Mary, and apostles, became increasingly important in early Christianity, while the classical principles of poetic composition were applied to new types of writing such as religious hymns and saints' lives. Writers found that poetry could be made to serve Christ, in the same way that figurative parables could disseminate the eternal truths of scripture. Jesus had told illustrative anecdotes, such as the parable of the Sower or the parable of the Wise and Foolish Virgins: preachers therefore believed that they too were authorized to use fictions, as long as the effort was wholly in the service of the Lord and not intended to seduce the soul with bodily pleasures.

The yearning for a mystical faith that would provide a sense of purpose was ubiquitous in the late Roman Empire. Christianity was just one of a number of religious cults that had fashioned a kind of cultural compromise with the philosophical orientation of the period; but it thrived as no other religion did, ultimately becoming the state religion of the Roman Empire under the rule of Constantine in the fourth century. While the Italian city of Rome remained the seat of imperial power in the West, the capital city of Byzantium (modern Istanbul, in Turkey) represented Rome in the East. Renamed "Constantinople" (Constantine's city) by the Christian emperor of Rome, the city would be simply known as "al-Rum" (Rome) to speakers of Arabic and Persian. An empire stretched so widely that it had two capitals, one in the West and one in the East, was ripe for dissolution: sooner or later in the history of every

This Byzantine mosaic in the monastery church in Hosios Loukas, Greece, depicts Christ saving Adam, Eve, King David, and King Solomon, who had been confined in limbo.

empire, things fall apart. The waves of invasion of Italy by Germanic tribes came to a head in the fifth century, when Rome endured a series of weak rulers. The eastern Roman capital of Constantinople, by contrast, remained intact until the end of the Middle Ages, though during that time its character had changed very substantially from what it had been in the age of the Caesars. Both Augustine and Boethius, writing in the fifth and sixth centuries, bear witness to the decay of Rome—and to the birth of something entirely new, as a Christian culture, various and diffuse, rose out of the ashes of empire.

The diaspora—literally, "scattering" (Greek)—of Jews from Jerusalem in 70 C.E. not only facilitated the spread of Christianity throughout the Roman Em-

pire but also created a new cultural environment that would lead to the development of rabbinic Judaism. The simultaneous emergence of rabbinic Judaism and Christianity can be described as a kind of twin birth, both of them formed in the crucible of Roman aggression in the first century. Beyond the physical experience of exile, the figurative concept of diaspora—like the ancient paradigm of the mass movement of people described in Exodus, which recounts the migration of the Jewish nation from Egypt to the promised land after many years of exile—provided an enormously powerful model for thinking about the movement of peoples in the early Middle Ages. Whereas the Jewish people were thought to be consigned to a permanent state of diaspora, endlessly wandering in the desert of the wide world, other communities sometimes claimed for themselves the role of the "true Israel": for medieval Christians, thinking of themselves as the true Israel meant identifying themselves as a chosen people. But their promised land was not to be found on the earth—it was the Heavenly Jerusalem, whose pleasures would be enjoyed only in the afterlife. National histories, too, made the history of the Jewish people into a template for their own myths of origin: this can be seen in medieval chronicles that liken accounts of the Trojans, who fled the ruins of Troy to found the great city of Rome, to accounts of the Jews in the diaspora.

THE SPREAD OF ISLAM

Like the emergence of Christianity in the wake of the Jewish diaspora, the dissemination of the **Qur'an** by Muhammad and his followers in the seventh century and the subsequent formation of an Islamic community had a dramatic effect on the development of Mediterranean culture. In his account of Muhammad's life, the early biographer Ibn Ishaq describes a community struggling to form itself not only in accord with the explicit dictates found in its holy book, the Qur'an, but also in conformity with the exemplary life led by its prophet, Muhammad. These two models, the revealed book and the life perfectly led, were the religious guidelines of an empire that grew almost overnight to dominate large swathes of the Middle East and North Africa: in 750, little more than a century after Muhammad began delivering the Qur'an in 610, Islamic rule extended westward through Spain into southern France and eastward through Persia (modern Iran) into India. The spread of Islam took place not only through cultural and religious means

but also through direct military conquest, such as the assault on the Byzantine Christian empire that culminated in the Battle of Yarmūk in 636: after that time, the southern regions of Anatolia (modern Turkey) and virtually the whole of the Levant (modern Near East) were under the control of the armies of Islam. In spite of its military successes and dynamic expansion, this new empire was far from monolithic: after the fall of the Umayyad caliphate (literally, "headship") that had been based in Damascus, the Abbasid caliphate was established at Baghdad, where it endured for more than five hundred years until the Mongol invasions from Central Asia in the mid-thirteenth century. Even after their fall from power in the East, however, the Umayyads retained control in the West, where they continued to rule the Spanish provinces they had named "al-Andalus."

In addition to the political divisions centered on the caliphates, religious divisions also cut across the nations gathered under Islamic rule. The most important of these is the division of Sunni from Shi'a Islam: the former centers on a strict conformity to the exemplary life of the Prophet Muhammad and a literal reading of the Holy Book; the latter instead prescribes a special veneration of the family of the Prophet, especially his daughter Fatima, her husband (who was also the Prophet's cousin) Ali, and their sons Hasan and Hussain. The highly emotional, affective quality of Shi'a Islam is expressed in devotional stories and plays chronicling the martyrdom of the members of the Prophet's family, as well as in the later medieval emergence of Sufi mysticism; the mystics used figurative poetic language to convey the soul's experience of the divine. Both Shi'a veneration of the family of the Prophet and Sufi poetic expressions of religious devotion were regarded

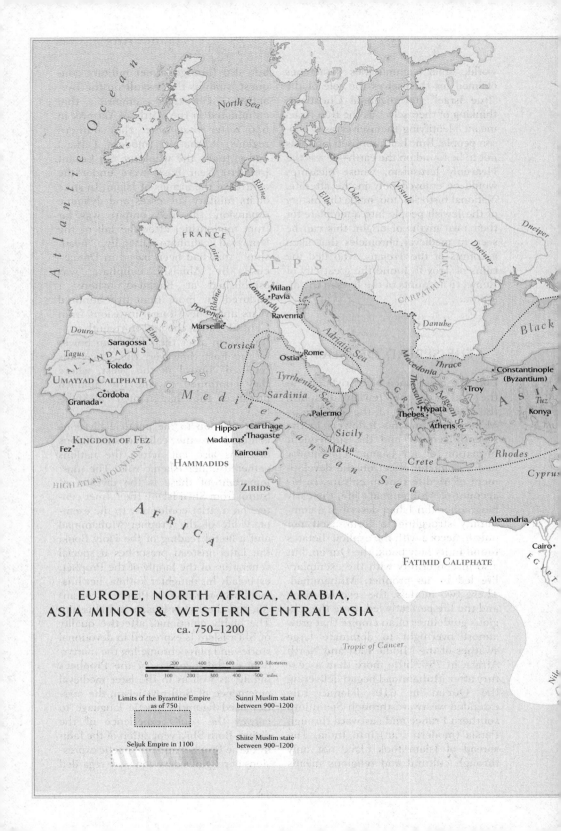

**EUROPE, NORTH AFRICA, ARABIA,
ASIA MINOR & WESTERN CENTRAL ASIA**

ca. 750–1200

				kilometers
0	200	400	600	800

					miles
0	100	200	300	400	500

Limits of the Byzantine Empire
as of 750

Sunni Muslim state
between 900–1200

Seljuk Empire in 1100

Shiite Muslim state
between 900–1200

Labels on map:

North Sea · Atlantic Ocean · Rhine · Elbe · Oder · Vistula · Dneiper · Dneister · FRANCE · ALPS · CARPATHIAN MTS. · Loire · Rhône · Provence · Marseille · Milan · Pavia · Lombardy · Ravenna · Danube · Black · PYRENEES · Douro · Ebro · Saragossa · Tagus · Toledo · AL-ANDALUS · Corsica · Adriatic Sea · Ostia · Rome · Macedonia · Thrace · Constantinople (Byzantium) · UMAYYAD CALIPHATE · Córdoba · Granada · Tyrrhenian Sea · Sardinia · Mediterranean Sea · Palermo · Thessaly · Aegean Sea · Troy · ASIA · Tuz · Konya · Hypata · Thebes · Athens · GR.. · KINGDOM OF FEZ · Fez · Hippo · Carthage · Madaurus · Thagaste · Sicily · Malta · Crete · Rhodes · Cyprus · Kairouan · HAMMADIDS · HIGH ATLAS MOUNTAINS · AFRICA · ZIRIDS · Alexandria · Cairo · EGYPT · FATIMID CALIPHATE · Nile · Tropic of Cancer

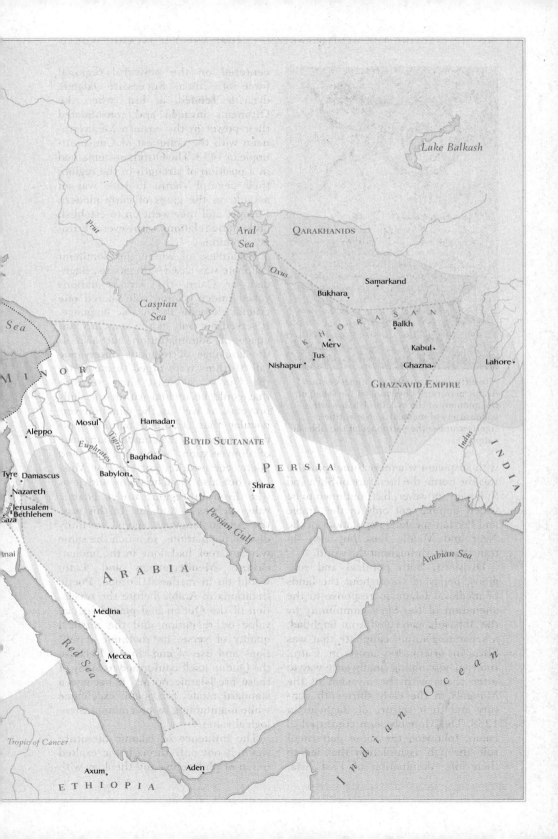

Lake Balkash

Aral
Sea

QARAKHANIDS

Oxus

Samarkand

Bukhara

Caspian
Sea

K H O R A S A N

Balkh

Merv
Tus

Kabul

Nishapur

Ghazna

Lahore

GHAZNAVID EMPIRE

Prut

Sea

MINOR

Mosul

Hamadan

Aleppo

Euphrates

Tigris

BUYID SULTANATE

PERSIA

Indus

INDIA

Baghdad

Babylon

Shiraz

Tyre Damascus

Nazareth

Persian Gulf

Jerusalem
Bethlehem

Gaza

Sinai

Arabian Sea

A R A B I A

Medina

Red Sea

Mecca

Indian Ocean

Tropic of Cancer

Axum

Aden

E T H I O P I A

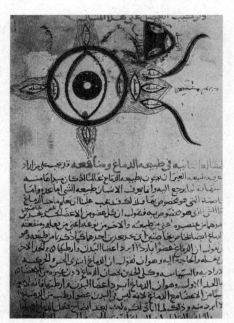

A twelfth-century copy of a ninth-century Arabic manuscript by Hunayn Ibn Ishaq on the anatomy of the eye. Ibn Ishaq wrote a wide variety of medical and scientific treatises under the patronage of the Abbasid caliphate.

with suspicion wherever Sunni practice was the norm; the literature of Shi'a and Sufi piety, however, has continued to be widely popular not only in the Arabic and Persian-speaking populations of the Near and Middle East but also—in translation—throughout the world.

Divisions, both political and religious, persisted throughout the lands of medieval Islam: in response to the alienation of the Shi'a community by the Abbasids who ruled from Baghdad, a separate Fatimid caliphate that was Shi'a in orientation arose in Cairo. Internal squabbling finally gave way to utter chaos with the invasion of the Mongols in the early thirteenth century and their seizure of Baghdad in 1258. The Mongols soon converted to Islam, following the same pattern of rule through assimilation that led to their long domination of East Asia,

centered on the powerful regional force of China. Successive Islamic dynasties ended, at last, when the Ottomans invaded and consolidated their power in the eastern Mediterranean with the conquest of Constantinople in 1453. The Ottomans remained in a position of strength in the region: their siege of Vienna in 1683 was an assault on the gates of early modern Europe, and they went on to establish diplomatic relations with several European nations.

Regardless of where the dominant caliphate was based—Damascus, Baghdad, or Cairo—the various nations yoked under Islamic rule shared one crucial element: the Arabic language. It served not only as the standard language of administration but also as the language of religious observance (all Muslims were urged to memorize the Qur'an, at least short sections that could be recited within the daily prayers), as well as the common vernacular that straddled national borders. Arabic was the standard language of conversation, administration, and poetic composition not only for Muslims but also for Christians and Jews who lived in regions under Islamic rule, such as al-Andalus. In this way, the Arabic language served to unify diverse populations, in much the same way as Greek had done in the ancient eastern Mediterranean and Latin would do in medieval Europe. Poetic traditions in Arabia before the revelation of the Qur'an had placed special value on recitation and the musical quality of verse, its rhythmic repetitions and use of end rhyme. Because the Qur'an itself conformed to many of these pre-Islamic norms, it became a standard model for poetic excellence while maintaining its preeminent theological value.

The influence of Islamic literature was felt not only through the exalted union of philosophy and theology with poetics but also on a more mundane, vernacular level. The vibrant tradition of frame-tale narratives, in which an outer layer organizes a series of nested narratives that are contained within the frame like the layers of an onion, had a long history in the Mediterranean region: writers as early as **Ovid** and Apuleius, in the first and second centuries, had relied on nested narratives. But with the arrival of more elaborate frame-tale models—especially *Kalila wa Dimna*, a series of animal fables based on the Indian *Pañcatantra*—the genre took off in Persian and Arabic literatures. Perhaps the best-known example of the frame tale, ***The Thousand and One Nights***, survives in its earliest versions in the Persian language; these were soon supplemented by a range of retellings in Arabic. The *Nights* circulated about the Mediterranean, with bits and pieces of it finding its way into other collections and its frame-tale form serving as the inspiration for many European manifestations of the genre, including **Chaucer's** ***Canterbury Tales***.

THE INVENTION OF THE WEST

For writers in the Islamic world, "the West" (*al-maghrib*) was the northern coast of Africa and al-Andalus, a region that was recognized as at once part of the Islamic sphere of influence and yet culturally and regionally distinctive. The idea of the West as a synonym for Christian Europe—which seems so natural and familiar to modern readers—did not even begin to emerge until the late Middle Ages. Medieval inhabitants of Europe instead categorized themselves in different ways: in terms of their ethnic origin or "nation," in terms of their primary language, and—above all—in terms of their religion. Unlike

in the areas under Islamic rule, where Jews and Christians were tolerated albeit subject to special taxation and restrictions (so-called *dhimmi* rule), in Christian Europe Jews were only sporadically tolerated, and Muslims were virtually unknown. We can thus infer that Europe exhibited much more religious homogeneity, at least until the first glimmerings of early Protestant reform impulses in the late fourteenth century. Uniformity of religion was further strengthened by uniformity of language, as Latin was used not only for all religious but also all political and administrative purposes, just as Arabic was in the Islamic world. Indeed, Latin's cultural hold was stronger: medieval Christians used it exclusively to compose their philosophical and scientific works, while both Arabic and Persian functioned as languages of literature and learning for Muslims. Beginning in the ninth century, however, and with increasing frequency from the twelfth century onward, vernacular languages such as English, French, German, Italian, and Spanish became more common vehicles for poetic composition.

Medieval people defined themselves first of all by their religious orientation and next by ethnic origin, relying not at all on the categories familiar to modern readers. This perspective on the place of the self in the world is well illustrated on the medieval world maps, or *mappaemundi*, that were used not as practical guides to navigation but rather as abstract overviews of both the literal shape of the world and its metaphorical meaning. Accordingly, such maps conventionally place Jerusalem at the exact center, marking the site of Christ's crucifixion as the fixed point about which the whole world revolves. The mappamundi itself is almost always oriented toward the east (Latin *oriens*), rather than toward the north as on modern maps, so that its easternmost point, the Garden of

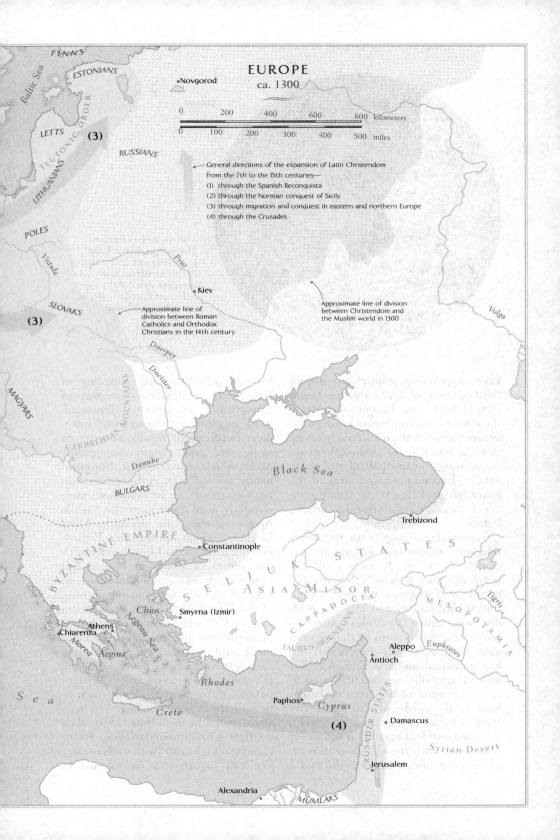

EUROPE
ca. 1300

0 · 200 · 400 · 600 · 800 kilometers

0 · 100 · 200 · 300 · 400 · 500 miles

General directions of the expansion of Latin Christendom
from the 7th to the 15th centuries—
(1) through the Spanish Reconquista
(2) through the Norman conquest of Sicily
(3) through migration and conquest in eastern and northern Europe
(4) through the Crusades

Approximate line of division between Christendom and the Muslim world in 1300

Approximate line of
division between Roman
Catholics and Orthodox
Christians in the 14th century

FINNS

ESTONIANS

Baltic Sea

LETTS

TEUTONIC ORDER

LITHUANIANS

(3)

RUSSIANS

•Novgorod

POLES

Vistula

SLOVAKS

(3)

Prut

•Kiev

Dneiper

Dneister

MAGYARS

CARPATHIAN MOUNTAINS

Danube

BULGARS

Volga

Black Sea

•Trebizond

BYZANTINE EMPIRE

•Constantinople

SELJUK STATES

ASIA MINOR

CAPPADOCIA

MESOPOTAMIA

Tigris

Chios

Smyrna (Izmir)

Athens

Chiarenza

Aegean Sea

Morea

Aegina

TAURUS MOUNTAINS

Aleppo

Euphrates

Antioch

Rhodes

Paphos•

Cyprus

•Damascus

CRUSADER STATES

(4)

S e a

Crete

Syrian Desert

•Jerusalem

Alexandria•

MUMLAKS

The so-called Hereford Mappamundi, ca. 1300. Jerusalem sits at the center of this medieval map; Asia occupies most of the top half; and Europe is in the lower-left quadrant.

Eden, appears—appropriately—as both the beginning of space and the beginning of time. Asia, Europe, and Africa, the three known continents, are depicted symmetrically on the map. Asia takes up twice as much space as the other two, dominating the top half of the world sphere; Europe is tucked away at the lower left; and "the West" (Latin *occidens*) lies, rather forlornly, at the bottom.

The medieval map, with its deeply religious imaginative geography and central focus on Jerusalem, illuminates the ways in which the repeated cycles of European warfare around the Mediterranean and into the Middle East—called "Crusades," after the cross (Latin *crux*) sewn by the warriors onto their garments—functioned not just as actual military campaigns but also as symbolic assaults designed to reclaim control of the spiritual homeland of the medieval Christian. The First Crusade, launched in 1095, included a violent assault on Jerusalem that ended with the slaughter of most of the city's inhabitants and the estab-

lishment of the "Latin Kingdom of Jerusalem": a significant outpost of Europeans occupying Jerusalem itself together with additional European fortifications in adjoining towns along the coast (most importantly Acre, which remained in European hands until 1291). Although expeditions continued to be launched intermittently until the end of the Middle Ages—including the dramatic Third Crusade, which united the English army of Richard the Lion-Hearted with the armies of Philip of France and Frederick Barbarossa of Germany—no later military successes matched those of the First Crusade that began them all. The Crusades functioned mainly as opportunities for economic development and international cooperation among the nations of Europe, helping to unify these disparate Christian nations through their shared opposition to the Muslim enemy. The passions stirred by this effort to stimulate political unity through religious fervor came at a high price: with each successive call to crusade, violent attacks

A detail from a page of the Luttrell Psalter (ca. 1300) depicts Richard I and Saladin jousting during the Third Crusade. Saladin is drawn with a grotesque blue face—a rendering that makes it all the easier for the psalter's Christian readers to see the conflict as a clearly defined battle between good and evil.

were made on the only locally available non-Christian populations within the cities of Europe—that is, the Jews. Anti-Muslim violence in the form of crusade was therefore closely linked with the persecution of Jews and the early emergence of anti-Semitism.

The opposition of Christian and non-Christian, so fundamental to the ideology of crusade, permeates the epic literature of the Middle Ages that began to emerge, originally in oral form and subsequently in written texts, by the ninth century. The Anglo-Saxon *Beowulf* describes a shadowy era in which myth and history are intertwined; for its anonymous author Christianity is an innovation applied as a veneer on a pagan Germanic past. The Germanic notion of *wyrd* or fate is aligned, by the *Beowulf*-poet, with Christian notions of divine providence, but it remains clear that the two concepts are far from identical. Epic, whether in England or in Persia, thus creates a sense of national identity by evoking a common historical origin, but it also grafts upon the rootstock of native myth new forms of identity— especially religious forms imported from outside the borders of the nation.

Epic is often opposed to romance: the former is portrayed as a masculine genre dedicated to the deeds of knights and the matter of war, the latter as a feminine genre that focuses on the relations of the lady and her lover, confined to the domestic sphere of the court. However, both genres, which rose to prominence in the twelfth century, share the idealized image of the knight: if he expresses his chivalry on the field of battle, the work is epic, but if his prowess is displayed in the private space of the bedchamber, the work is romance. The romances of Chrétien de Troyes, like the shorter romance works or *lais* of his predecessor, **Marie de France**, highlight this idealized role of the knight, which is also seen in the later medieval English, German, and Italian romances that were adapted from French originals. The French origins of the romance genre are also closely tied to the emergence of French as a literary language. Latin was unquestionably the primary language of scholarly learning, whether theological, philosophical, or scientific, but vernacular or spoken languages increasingly came to be the first choice for poetic composition. In the twelfth century, French was the first of the European languages to be elevated in this way; by the fourteenth century, other vernaculars had also begun to be widely used. Explicitly, in his treatise on languages (*De vulgari eloquentia*), and implicitly, in his **Divine Comedy**, Dante Alighieri stakes a claim for the local Florentine dialect of Italian as the "most illustrious vernacular," while Chaucer will make similar claims for English in his *Canterbury Tales*.

In spite of this ongoing shift, Latin experienced an important revival in the fourteenth century. Paradoxically at just the moment when literature in the vernacular was reaching new levels of sophistication with works such as Boccaccio's *Decameron* and Chaucer's *Canterbury Tales*, classical forms of Latin were being championed in humanistic circles under the guiding hand of **Petrarch**. Ambivalence about the competing claims of a revived classical Latin, on the one hand, and the potent spontaneity of the vernacular, on the other hand, is evident in the work of Petrarch himself: the author of several Latin treatises and a powerful advocate for classical scholarship, his exquisite lyrics in Italian would exert a powerful influence on the rise of Renaissance lyric not only in Italy but also in France and England. This paradox is reflected in modern scholarship, which tends to label Petrarch, who wrote in the early fourteenth century, as a "Renaissance" poet and his friend and disciple Boccaccio, who wrote in the mid-fourteenth

century, as a "medieval" writer. The example of these two contemporaries illustrates the ways in which period divisions, like geographical divisions, sometimes obscure the profound continuities that underlie literary history.

Though Boccaccio wrote his masterwork, the *Decameron*, in Italian, he also composed (at the encouragement of Petrarch) several treatises in Latin. Chaucer did not write in Latin, but he shared Boccaccio's consciousness of the importance of the legacy of Roman antiquity and Latin literature; he produced several English translations of Latin works, including Boethius's *Consolation of Philosophy*. In late medieval French circles too, as illustrated in the mythographic works of **Christine de Pizan** written under the influence of Boccaccio, the Greco-Roman past loomed large. In all three of these major writers, the yearning for a revival of classical antiquity reveals the extent to which the wholehearted embrace of the ancient past that we tend to associate exclusively with the Renaissance was amply foreshadowed in the work of at least some late medieval authors, especially those whose perspective was particularly cosmopolitan, rooted in the experience of the city as a cultural, economic, linguistic, and—above all—literary crossroads.

THE CHRISTIAN BIBLE:
THE NEW TESTAMENT GOSPELS

ca. first century C.E.

For some readers, the Bible is to be read as sacred history and divine revelation, as a book whose truth is grounded by religious faith. For others, it is a rich trove of cultural history, sometimes supported by archaeology and other corroborating evidence, sometimes not. Beginning in the nineteenth century, however, readers started to also think of the Bible as a work of literature, analyzing it in terms of genre and poetics and comparing it to other literary works written around the same time. The Gospels of Matthew, Mark, and Luke, for instance, all of which retell the life of Jesus, can be read as examples of Greco-Roman biography as practiced around the Mediterranean during the first century C.E. The metaphorical language of the Gospel of John reflects the strong influence of Platonic philosophy on Jewish communities within the Roman Empire. This literary approach to the Bible has inspired recent generations of modern intellectuals, writers, and artists— sometimes from a devout perspective, sometimes not. Yet it is crucial to realize that considering the Christian Bible as literature is not a modern novelty: over the past two thousand years, poets have constantly quoted and paraphrased the Gospels in order to enrich their own work with the resonant, messianic tone and powerful turns of phrase that appear in what is arguably the single most influential text of world literature.

CHRISTIAN CULTURE IN THE
ROMAN EMPIRE

Jesus was born in the town of Bethlehem, a town located in the province of Judea in the eastern part of the Roman Empire. While Latin was the language mainly used in Rome itself, in far-off Judea the language of administration was Greek. For most local inhabitants, however, the vernacular was Aramaic, a language related to Hebrew but sufficiently different from it that Aramaic speakers would not necessarily have understood Hebrew. The polyglot nature of the region was mirrored in the wide range of ethnicities and religious orientations found there. Judea and the surrounding lands had formerly been part of the vast empire established by Alexander the Great, under whose influence the local Jewish population— especially the more affluent and educated classes—had embraced Greek literature and philosophy. This religious and cultural ferment gave rise to a variety of religious groups; some became marginalized and died out, but others (including Christianity and rabbinic Judaism) would live on.

From Roman administrative records, we know that there was a historical Jesus, a disruptive rabble-rouser who attracted the attention of the local authorities and was ultimately executed. Yet the Jesus of the gospel accounts is something far more complex, more a phenomenon than a man. It is clear that the events of his life rapidly led to the establishment of not just a single community but a number of communities organized around the symbolic significance that could be assigned to this man, his words, and his deeds. These included both Jewish communities, for whom Jesus was to be identified with the long-awaited Messiah, and non-Jewish (or "Gentile") communities around the Mediterranean Sea. The dating system we use today reflects the fundamental break in time that early Christians believed had taken place. Dates in the Roman Empire were ordinarily based on the number of the year in the reign of the individual ruler, but Christians viewed Jesus as a divine lord whose authority surmounted that of any earthly kingdom or empire. Consequently, they began to number the years "A.D."— that is, *Anno Domini*, or "In the year of the Lord." Today, we more often use the more inclusive abbreviation C.E. for the Common Era, but we continue to number years from the birth of Jesus—a practice that reflects the early Christians' profound sense of a temporal rupture, the belief that a new age had dawned.

WORK

Together with the Gospel of Mark, the three books of the Bible excerpted here—the Gospels of Matthew, Luke, and John—form the core of the collection of twenty-seven books that Christians call the New Testament. This label, taken with the "Old Testament," encapsulates the Christian perspective on the relationship of Jesus' mission to the history of the Jewish people recounted in the **Hebrew Bible**, comprising the Pentateuch (the first five books, or Torah), the books of prophets and history, and the poetic books. For Christians, the old covenant established by God with Abraham and, after the flood, reestablished with Noah was merely a prefiguration, the first stage of a process that would be fulfilled only with the advent of Jesus and subsequent rise of Christianity. In some ways, this perspective honors and elevates the role of the Jewish people; in other ways, it denigrates Judaism, relegating it to a subordinate position in the divine plan for humanity.

Although the Gospels present themselves as eyewitness testimony to events in the life of Jesus, they were actually committed to written form decades after his death. The earliest of them, the Gospel of Mark, probably dates to about 70 C.E.; the latest, the Gospel of John, dates to about 100 C.E. The sequence of four gospels was established relatively early on, as was the authoritativeness of their testimony. The second-century theologian Irenaeus of Lyons declared that there are only four gospels, just as there are only four corners of the earth, and four winds in the heavens. This declaration served to exclude the many alternative accounts of the life of Jesus that were also in circulation, and to give a more specific structure to the teachings of Jesus and his authorized followers; the final result was a codified form of the New Testament and, ultimately, Christian theology. The Gospels of Matthew, Mark, and Luke are called the Synoptic Gospels, because they give a panorama or overview (synopsis) of the life of Jesus, all telling the same story but from rather distinctive perspectives. The Gospel of John also recounts the life of Jesus, but with a very different narrative line and a deep concern to integrate Platonic philosophy and mysticism into the expression of divinity in the person of Jesus Christ, identified as the Word of God.

The Synoptic Gospels have a number of episodes in common, of which the most important are the Sermon on the Mount, the Last Supper, and the crucifixion and resurrection of Jesus. Yet each of the three gospels also has its own individual character: Luke tells us the most about the childhood and parentage of Jesus, and his work is closely related to the noncanonical tradition of "infancy gospels"—stories about the life of Jesus as a child that survive in Arabic as well as in Greek and Syriac versions. Mark provides the tightest and most focused account, placing special emphasis on the death of Jesus and recounting his biography in simpler, more primitive language. Mark appears to be addressing a Gentile audience, and his gospel is sometimes associated with the early foundation of Christian communities in Rome or, at least, in the regions of the Roman Empire lying to the west of Judea. Matthew, conversely, clearly directs his biography at an audience that is quite familiar with the Hebrew Bible: he gives a very detailed account of Jesus' preaching mission and his role as the long-awaited Messiah. Matthew exhibits a special interest in the ways in which Jewish history is fulfilled in the coming of Jesus Christ, and in the ways in which the old covenant established between God and man is renewed in and superseded by the new covenant established with the sacrifice of Christ in the crucifixion.

Matthew also displays a central concern with the ways in which Jesus preached, especially his use of parables: little stories that reveal profound spiritual truths through metaphorical, even allegorical language. The excerpts presented here include parables of Jesus as recounted both by Matthew and by Luke, passages of the Gospels that are among those with the most profound literary influence on writers throughout the Middle Ages. The figurative, philosophical language of the Gospel of John would also go on to be highly influential, disseminated through a wide range of poetic evocations of the divine nature. John's account of the birth of Christ, excerpted here, seemingly describes the same transformative event narrated in the infancy chapters of Luke. Yet the two accounts could not be more different, as they represent two totally different perspectives on the nature of Jesus Christ, understood as that deepest of all paradoxes, the being who is at once both God and man. For John, Christ is the Word through which God creates all things, a mediator between matter and spirit, the temporal and the eternal. For Luke, he is Jesus of Nazareth, whose divine nature smoothly coexists with his human status, rooted in the cultural norms and social structures of first-century Judea.

The Gospels as we have them today reflect a complex and intertwined linguistic history: Jesus and his apostles would have spoken Aramaic, which we hear when Jesus cries out on the crucifix, "Eli, eli, lama sabachthani?" ("My God, my God, why have you forsaken me?" [Matthew 27.46]). However, the Gospels were written down in koine Greek, the vernacular that was the lingua franca of the eastern Mediterranean. This was a language meant to travel, and so the Gospels did: they were swiftly passed on in both oral and written form across the Mediterranean Sea, through Asia, Europe, and northern Africa. Latin translations of the Gospels soon began to be produced, and in 382 Pope Damasus asked the theologian Jerome to prepare a full, authorized translation into Latin. This version, known as the Vulgate, would become the standard version of the Bible read for more than a thousand years in the West, until new versions of the sacred text began to be produced at the dawn of the Reformation. Over the five hundred years since then, translations of the Bible have multiplied exponentially, as every spoken language has produced its own version of holy scripture. Most recently, modern writers and artists have moved the Bible into new formats such as the graphic novel, used by devout Christians to educate their children and enjoyed by a wide range of nonreligious readers.

Luke 2[1]

[The Birth and Youth of Jesus]

It happened in those days that a decree went forth from Augustus Caesar[2] that all the world should be enrolled in a census. This was the first census, when Quirinius was governor of Syria. And all went to be enrolled, each to his own city. And Joseph also went up from Galilee,[3] from the city of Nazareth, to Judaea, to the city of David[4] which is called Bethlehem, because he was of the house and family of David; to be enrolled with Mary his promised wife, who was pregnant. And it happened that while they were there her time was completed, and she bore a son, her first-born, and she wrapped him in swaddling clothes and laid him in a manger, because there was no room for them in the inn. And there were shepherds in that region, camping out at night and keeping guard over their flock. And an angel of the Lord stood before them, and the glory of the Lord shone about them, and they were afraid with a great fear. The angel said to them: Do not be afraid; behold, I tell you good news, great joy which shall be for all the people; because this day there has been born for you in the city of David a savior who is Christ the Lord. And here is a sign for you; you will find a baby wrapped in swaddling clothes and lying in a manger. And suddenly with the angel there was a multitude of the heavenly host, praising God and saying: Glory to God in the highest and peace on earth among men of good will. And it happened that after the angels had gone off from them into the sky, the shepherds began saying to each other: Let us go to Bethlehem and see this thing which has happened, which the Lord made known to us; and they went, hastening, and found Mary and Joseph, and the baby lying in the manger; and when they had seen, they spread the news about what had been told them concerning this baby. And all who heard wondered at what had been told them by the shepherds; and Mary kept in mind all these sayings as she pondered them in her heart. And the shepherds returned, glorifying and praising God over all they had heard and seen, as it had been told them.

And when eight days were past, for his circumcision, his name was called Jesus, as it was named by the angel before he was conceived in the womb.

And when the days for their purification[5] according to the Law of Moses had been completed, they took him up to Jerusalem to set him before the Lord, as it has been written in the Law of the Lord: Every male child who opens the womb shall be called sacred to the Lord; and to give sacrifice as it is stated in the Law of the Lord, a pair of turtle doves or two young pigeons. And behold, there was a man in Jerusalem whose name was Simeon, and this man was righteous and virtuous and looked forward to the consolation of Israel, and the Holy Spirit was upon him; and it had been prophesied to him by the Holy Spirit that he should

1. Gospels translated by Richmond Lattimore.
2. Gaius Julius Caesar (63 B.C.E.–14 C.E.), who took the title Augustus as the first Roman emperor.
3. The region surrounding the Sea of Galilee, in the Roman province of Judea (modern Israel).

4. Second king of Israel, according to the Hebrew Bible; he was anointed king in Bethlehem, his traditional birthplace.
5. The ritual cleansing following childbirth (prescribed in Leviticus 12).

not look upon his death until he had looked on the Lord's Anointed. And in the spirit he went into the temple; and as his parents brought in the child Jesus so that they could do for him what was customary according to the law, Simeon himself took him in his arms and blessed God and said: Now, Lord, you release your slave, in peace, according to your word; because my eyes have looked on your salvation, what you made ready in the presence of all the peoples; a light for the revelation to the Gentiles, and the glory of your people, Israel. And his father and his mother were in wonder at what was being said about him. And Simeon blessed them and said to Mary his mother: Behold, he is appointed for the fall and the rise of many in Israel; and as a sign which is disputed; and through your soul also will pass the sword; so that the reasonings of many hearts may be revealed. And there was Anna, a prophetess, the daughter of Phanuel, of the tribe of Asher. And she was well advanced in years, having lived with her husband seven years from the time of her maidenhood, and now she was eighty-four years a widow. And she did not leave the temple, serving night and day with fastings and prayers. And at this same time she came near and gave thanks to God and spoke of the child to those who looked forward to the deliverance of Jerusalem.

And when they had done everything according to the Law of the Lord, they went back to Galilee, to their own city, Nazareth.

And the child grew in stature and strength as he was filled with wisdom, and the grace of God was upon him.

Now his parents used to journey every year to Jerusalem for the feast of the Passover.[6] And when he was twelve years old, when they went up according to their custom for the festival and had completed their days there, on their return the boy Jesus stayed behind in Jerusalem, and his parents did not know it. And supposing that he was in their company they went a day's journey and then looked for him among their relatives and friends, and when they did not find him they turned back to Jerusalem in search of him. And it happened that after three days they found him in the temple sitting in the midst of the masters, listening to them and asking them questions. And all who heard him were amazed at his intelligence and his answers. And they were astonished at seeing him, and his mother said to him: Child, why did you do this to us? See, your father and I have been looking for you, in distress. He said to them: But why were you looking for me? Did you not know that I must be in my father's house? And they did not understand what he had said to them. And he returned with them and came to Nazareth, and was in their charge. And his mother kept all his sayings in her heart. And Jesus advanced in wisdom and stature, and in the favor of God and men.

---

6. The holiday (Heb. *Pesach*) commemorating the liberation of the people of Israel, led by Moses, from bondage in Egypt.

Matthew 5–7

[*The Sermon on the Mount*]

And seeing the multitudes he went up onto the mountain, and when he was seated, his disciples came to him, and he opened his mouth and taught them, saying:

Blessed are the poor in spirit, because theirs is the Kingdom of Heaven.

Blessed are they who sorrow, because they shall be comforted.

Blessed are the gentle, because they shall inherit the earth.

Blessed are they who are hungry and thirsty for righteousness, because they shall be fed.

Blessed are they who have pity, because they shall be pitied.

Blessed are the pure in heart, because they shall see God.

Blessed are the peacemakers, because they shall be called the sons of God.

Blessed are they who are persecuted for their righteousness, because theirs is the Kingdom of Heaven.

Blessed are you when they shall revile you and persecute you and speak every evil thing of you, lying, because of me. Rejoice and be glad, because your reward in heaven is great; for thus did they persecute the prophets before you.

You are the salt of the earth; but if the salt loses its power, with what shall it be salted? It is good for nothing but to be thrown away and trampled by men. You are the light of the world. A city cannot be hidden when it is set on top of a hill. Nor do men light a lamp and set it under a basket, but they set it on a stand, and it gives its light to all in the house. So let your light shine before men, so that they may see your good works and glorify your father in heaven.

Do not think that I have come to destroy the law[1] and the prophets. I have not come to destroy but to complete. Indeed, I say to you, until the sky and the earth are gone, not one iota or one end of a letter must go from the law, until all is done. He who breaks one of the least of these commandments and teaches men accordingly shall be called the least in the Kingdom of Heaven; he who performs and teaches these commandments shall be called great in the Kingdom of Heaven. For I tell you, if your righteousness is not more abundant than that of the scribes and the Pharisees,[2] you may not enter the Kingdom of Heaven.

You have heard that it was said to the ancients: You shall not murder. He who murders shall be liable to judgment. I say to you that any man who is angry with his brother shall be liable to judgment; and he who says to his brother, fool, shall be liable before the council; and he who says to his brother, sinner, shall be liable to Gehenna.[3] If then you bring your gift to the altar, and there remember that your brother has some grievance against you, leave your gift before the altar, and go first and be reconciled with your brother, and then go and offer your gift. Be quick to be conciliatory with your adversary at law when you are in the street with him, for fear your adversary may turn you over to the judge, and the judge to the officer, and you be thrown into prison. Truly I tell you, you cannot come out of there until you pay the last penny.

---

1. That is, the Torah, the five books of the law that begin the Hebrew Bible.

2. A major Jewish sect that emphasized strict observance of Jewish law; they were instrumental in the development of rabbinic Judaism.

3. Hell (Heb. *gehinnom*); figurative use of the name of a valley outside Jerusalem where children were sacrificed to pagan gods.

You have heard that it has been said: You shall not commit adultery. I tell you that any man who looks at a woman so as to desire her has already committed adultery with her in his heart. If your right eye makes you go amiss, take it out and cast it from you; it is better that one part of you should be lost instead of your whole body being cast into Gehenna. And if your right hand makes you go amiss, cut it off and cast it from you; it is better that one part of you should be lost instead of your whole body going to Gehenna. It has been said: If a man puts away his wife, let him give her a contract of divorce. I tell you that any man who puts away his wife, except for the reason of harlotry, is making her the victim of adultery; and any man who marries a wife who has been divorced is committing adultery. Again, you have heard that it has been said to the ancients: You shall not swear falsely, but you shall make good your oaths to the Lord. I tell you not to swear at all: not by heaven, because it is the throne of God; not by the earth, because it is the footstool for his feet; not by Jerusalem, because it is the city of the great king; not by your own head, because you cannot make one hair of it white or black. Let your speech be yes yes, no no; more than that comes from the evil one.

You have heard that it has been said: An eye for an eye and a tooth for a tooth. I tell you not to resist the wicked man; but if one strikes you on the right cheek, turn the other one to him also; and if a man wishes to go to law with you and take your tunic, give him your cloak also, and if one makes you his porter for a mile, go with him for two. Give to him who asks, and do not turn away one who wishes to borrow from you. You have heard that it has been said: You shall love your neighbor and hate your enemy. I tell you, love your enemies and pray for those who persecute you, so that you may be sons of your father who is in heaven, because he makes his sun rise on the evil and the good, and rains on the just and the unjust. For if you love those who love you, what reward do you have? Do not even the tax collectors do the same? And if you greet only your brothers, what do you do that is more than others do? Do not even the pagans do the same? Be perfect as your father in heaven is perfect.

Take care not to practice your righteousness publicly before men so as to be seen by them; if you do, you shall have no recompense from your father in heaven. Then when you do charity, do not have a trumpet blown before you, as the hypocrites do in the synagogues and the streets, so that men may think well of them. Truly I tell you, they have their due reward. But when you do charity, let your left hand not know what your right hand is doing, so that your charity may be in secret; and your father, who sees what is secret, will reward you. And when you pray, you must not be like the hypocrites, who love to stand up in the synagogues and the corners of the squares to pray, so that they may be seen by men. Truly I tell you, they have their due reward. But when you pray, go into your inner room and close the door and pray to your father, who is in secret; and your father, who sees what is secret, will reward you. When you pray, do not babble as the pagans do; for they think that by saying much they will be heard. Do not then be like them; for your father knows what you need before you ask him. Pray thus, then:[4] Our father in heaven, may your name be hallowed, may your kingdom come, may your will be done, as in heaven, so upon

---

4. The following verses, commonly known as the Lord's Prayer, are central to Christian religious practice.

earth. Give us today our sufficient bread, and forgive us our debts, as we also have forgiven our debtors. And do not bring us into temptation, but deliver us from evil. For if you forgive men their offenses, your heavenly father will forgive you; but if you do not forgive men, neither will your father forgive you your offenses. And when you fast, do not scowl like the hypocrites; for they make ugly faces so that men can see that they are fasting. Truly I tell you, they have their due reward. But when you fast, anoint your head and wash your face, so that you may not show as fasting to men, but to your father, in secret; and your father, who sees what is secret, will reward you.

Do not store up your treasures on earth, where the moth and rust destroy them, and where burglars dig through and steal them; but store up your treasures in heaven, where neither moth nor rust destroys them, and where burglars do not dig through or steal; for where your treasure is, there also will be your heart. The lamp of the body is the eye. Thus if your eye is clear, your whole body is full of light; but if your eye is soiled, your whole body is dark. If the light in you is darkness, how dark it is. No man can serve two masters. For either he will hate the one and love the other, or he will cling to one and despise the other; you cannot serve God and mammon.[5] Therefore I tell you, do not take thought for your life, what you will eat, or for your body, what you will wear. Is not your life more than its food and your body more than its clothing? Consider the birds of the sky, that they do not sow or harvest or collect for their granaries, and your heavenly father feeds them. Are you not preferred above them? Which of you by taking thought can add one cubit to his growth? And why do you take thought about clothing? Study the lilies in the field, how they grow. They do not toil or spin; yet I tell you, not even Solomon[6] in all his glory was clothed like one of these. But if God so clothes the grass of the field, which grows today and tomorrow is thrown in the oven, will he not much more clothe you, you men of little faith? Do not then worry and say: What shall we eat? Or: What shall we drink? Or: What shall we wear? For all this the Gentiles study. Your father in heaven knows that you need all these things. But seek out first his kingdom and his justice, and all these things shall be given to you. Do not then take thought of tomorrow; tomorrow will take care of itself, sufficient to the day is its own evil.

Do not judge, so you may not be judged. You shall be judged by that judgment by which you judge, and your measure will be made by the measure by which you measure. Why do you look at the straw which is in the eye of your brother, and not see the log which is in your eye? Or how will you say to your brother: Let me take the straw out of your eye, and behold, the log is in your eye. You hypocrite, first take the log out of your eye, and then you will see to take the straw out of the eye of your brother. Do not give what is sacred to the dogs, and do not cast your pearls before swine, lest they trample them under their feet and turn and rend you. Ask, and it shall be given you; seek, and you shall find; knock, and the door will be opened for you. Everyone who asks receives, and he who seeks finds, and for him who knocks the door will be opened. Or what man is there among you, whose son shall ask him for bread, that will give him

---

5. Wealth (an Aramaic word transliterated into Greek); the personification of Mammon as a god became a common trope in later Christian literature.

6. King of Israel and son of David, famed for his wisdom and for building the First Temple in Jerusalem.

a stone? Or ask him for fish, that will give him a snake? If then you, who are corrupt, know how to give good gifts to your children, by how much more your father who is in heaven will give good things to those who ask him. Whatever you wish men to do to you, so do to them. For this is the law and the prophets.

Go in through the narrow gate; because wide and spacious is the road that leads to destruction, and there are many who go in through it; because narrow is the gate and cramped the road that leads to life, and few are they who find it. Beware of the false prophets, who come to you in sheep's clothing, but inside they are ravening wolves. From their fruits you will know them. Do men gather grapes from thorns or figs from thistles? Thus every good tree produces good fruits, but the rotten tree produces bad fruits. A good tree cannot bear bad fruits, and a rotten tree cannot bear good fruits. Every tree that does not produce good fruit is cut out and thrown in the fire. So from their fruits you will know them. Not everyone who says to me Lord Lord will come into the Kingdom of Heaven, but he who does the will of my father in heaven. Many will say to me on that day: Lord, Lord, did we not prophesy in your name, and in your name did we not cast out demons, and in your name did we not assume great powers? And then I shall admit to them: I never knew you. Go from me, for you do what is against the law.

Every man who hears what I say and does what I say shall be like the prudent man who built his house upon the rock. And the rain fell and the rivers came and the winds blew and dashed against that house, and it did not fall, for it was founded upon the rock. And every man who hears what I say and does not do what I say will be like the reckless man who built his house on the sand. And the rain fell and the rivers came and the winds blew and battered that house, and it fell, and that was a great fall.

And it happened that when Jesus had ended these words, the multitudes were astonished at his teaching, for he taught them as one who has authority, and not like their own scribes.

Luke 15

[Parables]

All the tax collectors and the sinners kept coming around him, to listen to him. And the Pharisees and the scribes muttered, saying: This man receives sinners and eats with them. But he told them this parable, saying: Which man among you who has a hundred sheep and has lost one of them will not leave the ninety-nine in the wilds and go after the lost one until he finds it? And when he does find it, he sets it on his shoulders, rejoicing, and goes to his house and invites in his friends and his neighbors, saying to them: Rejoice with me, because I found my sheep which was lost. I tell you that thus there will be joy in heaven over one sinner who repents, rather than over ninety-nine righteous ones who have no need of repentance. Or what woman who has ten drachmas,[1] if she loses one drachma, does not light the lamp and sweep the house and search diligently until she finds it? And finding it she invites in her friends

1. Greek silver coins, each roughly equivalent in value to a manual laborer's wages for one day.

and neighbors, saying: Rejoice with me, because I found the drachma I lost. Such, I tell you, is the joy among the angels of God over one sinner who repents.

And he said: There was a man who had two sons. And the younger of them said to his father: Father, give me my appropriate share of the property. And the father divided his substance between them. And not many days afterward the younger son gathered everything together and left the country for a distant land, and there he squandered his substance in riotous living. And after he had spent everything, there was a severe famine in that country, and he began to be in need. And he went and attached himself to one of the citizens of that country, who sent him out into the fields to feed the pigs. And he longed to be nourished on the nuts that the pigs ate, and no one would give to him. And he went and said to himself: How many hired servants of my father have plenty of bread while I am dying of hunger here. I will rise up and go to my father and say to him: Father, I have sinned against heaven and in your sight, I am no longer worthy to be called your son. Make me like one of your hired servants. And he rose up and went to his father. And when he was still a long way off, his father saw him and was moved and ran and fell on his neck and kissed him. The son said to him: Father, I have sinned against heaven and in your sight, I am no longer worthy to be called your son. But his father said to his slaves: Quick, bring the best clothing and put it on him, and have a ring for his hand and shoes for his feet, and bring the fatted calf, slaughter him, and let us eat and make merry because this man, my son, was a dead man and came to life, he was lost and he has been found. And they began to make merry. His older son was out on the estate, and as he came nearer to the house he heard music and dancing, and he called over one of the servants and asked what was going on. He told him: Your brother is here, and your father slaughtered the fatted calf, because he got him back in good health. He was angry and did not want to go in. But his father came out and entreated him. But he answered and said to his father: Look, all these years I have been your slave and never neglected an order of yours, but you never gave me a kid so that I could make merry with my friends. But when this son of yours comes back, the one who ate up your livelihood in the company of whores, you slaughtered the fatted calf for him. But he said to him: My child, you are always with me, and all that is mine is yours; but we had to make merry and rejoice, because your brother was a dead man and came to life, he was lost and has been found.

From Matthew 13

[*Why Jesus Teaches in Parables*]

On that day Jesus went out of the house and sat beside the sea; and a great multitude gathered before him, so that he went aboard a ship and sat there, and all the multitude stood on the shore. And he talked to them, speaking mostly in parables: Behold, a sower went out to sow. And as he sowed, some of the grain fell beside the way, and birds came and ate it. Some fell on stony ground where there was not much soil, and it shot up quickly because there was no depth of soil, but when the sun came up it was parched, and because it had no roots it dried away. Some fell among thorns, and the thorns grew up and stifled it. But some fell upon the good soil and bore fruit, some a hundred-fold, some sixtyfold, some thirtyfold. He who has ears, let him hear. Then his disciples came to him and said: Why do you talk to them in parables? He answered them and said: Because it is given to you to understand the secrets of the Kingdom of Heaven, but to them it is not given. When a man has, he shall be given, and it will be more than he needs; but when he has not, even what he has shall be taken away from him. Therefore I talk to them in parables, because they have sight but do not see, and hearing but do not hear or understand. And for them is fulfilled the prophecy of Isaiah,[1] saying: With your hearing you shall hear and not understand, and you shall use your sight and look but not see. For the heart of this people is stiffened, and they hear with difficulty, and they have closed their eyes; so that they may never see with their eyes, or hear with their ears and with their hearts understand and turn back, so that I can heal them.

Blessed are your eyes because they see, and your ears because they hear. Truly I tell you that many prophets and good men have longed to see what you see, and not seen it, and to hear what you hear, and not heard it. Hear, then, the parable of the sower. To every man who hears the word of the Kingdom and does not understand it, the evil one comes and seizes what has been sown in his heart. This is the seed sown by the way. The seed sown on the stony ground is the man who hears the word and immediately accepts it with joy; but he has no root in himself, and he is a man of the moment, and when there comes affliction and persecution, because of the word, he does not stand fast. The seed sown among thorns is the man who hears the word, and concern for the world and the beguilement of riches stifle the word, and he bears no fruit. And the seed sown on the good soil is the man who hears the word and understands it, who bears fruit and makes it, one a hundredfold, one sixtyfold, and one thirtyfold.

He set before them another parable, saying: The Kingdom of Heaven is like a man who sowed good seed in his field. And while the people were asleep, his enemy came and sowed darnel in with the grain, and went away. When the plants grew and produced a crop, the darnel was seen. Then the slaves of the master came to him and said: Master, did you not sow good grain in your field? Where does the darnel come from? He said to them: A man who is my enemy did it. His slaves said: Do you wish us to go out and gather it? But he said: No, for fear that when you gather the darnel you may pull up the grain with it. Let them both grow until harvest time, and in the time of harvest I shall say to the harvesters: First gather the darnel, and bind it in sheaves for burning, but store the grain in my granary.

He set before them another parable, saying: The Kingdom of Heaven is like a grain of mustard, which a man took and sowed in his field; which is the smallest of all seeds, but when it grows, it is the largest of the greens and grows into a tree, so that the birds of the air come and nest in its branches.

He told them another parable: The Kingdom of Heaven is like leaven, which a woman took and buried in three measures of dough, so that it all rose.

All this Jesus told the multitudes in parables, and he did not talk to them except in parables; so as to fulfill the word spoken by the prophet, saying: I will open my mouth in parables, and pour out what has been hidden since the creation. Then he sent away the multitudes and went to the house. And his

1. See Isaiah 6.9–10.

disciples came to him and said: Make plain to us the parable of the darnel in the field. He answered them and said: The sower of the good seed is the son of man; the field is the world; the good seed is the sons of the Kingdom; the darnel is the sons of the evil one, and the enemy who sowed it is the devil; the harvest time is the end of the world, and the harvesters are angels. Then as the darnel is gathered and burned in the fire, so it is at the end of the world. The son of man will send out his angels, and they will gather from his Kingdom all that misleads, and the people who do what is not lawful, and cast them in the furnace of fire; and there will be weeping and gnashing of teeth. Then the righteous men will shine forth like the sun in the Kingdom of their father. He who has ears, let him hear. The Kingdom of Heaven is like a treasure hidden in the field, which a man found and hid, and for joy of it he goes and sells all he has and buys that field. Again, the Kingdom of Heaven is like a trader looking for fine pearls; he found one of great value, and went and sold all he had and bought it. Again, the Kingdom of Heaven is like a dragnet cast into the sea and netting every kind of fish; and when it is full they draw it out and sit on the beach and gather the good ones in baskets, but the bad they throw away. So will it be at the end of the world. The angels will go out and separate the bad from the midst of the righteous, and cast them in the furnace of fire; and there will be weeping and gnashing of teeth. Do you understand all this? They said to him: Yes. And he said to them: Therefore every scribe who is learned in the Kingdom of Heaven is like a man who is master of a house, who issues from his storehouse what is new and what is old.

Matthew 27–28

[Crucifixion and Resurrection]

When morning came, all the high priests and elders of the people held a meeting against Jesus, to have him killed. And they bound him and took him away and gave him over to Pilate the governor.[1]

Then when Judas, who had betrayed him, saw that he had been condemned, he repented and proffered the thirty pieces of silver back to the high priests and the elders, saying: I did wrong to betray innocent blood. They said: What is that to us? You look to it. And he threw down the silver pieces in the temple and went away, and when he was alone he hanged himself. The high priests took up the silver pieces and said: We cannot put them in the treasury, since it is blood money. Then they took counsel together and with the money they bought the potter's field[2] to bury strangers in. Therefore that field has been called the Field of Blood, to this day. Then was fulfilled the word spoken by Jeremiah the prophet,[3] saying: I took the thirty pieces of silver, the price of him on whom a price was set, whom they priced from among the sons of Israel, and I gave the money for the field of the potter, as my Lord commanded me.

Now Jesus stood before the governor; and the governor questioned him, saying: Are you the King of the Jews? Jesus answered: It is you who say it. And while he

---

1. Pontius Pilate, imperial administrator of the Roman province of Judea (26–36 C.E.).
2. A place where clay was dug to make pottery; after the Gospels, a common term for a burying place for the poor.

3. Alluding perhaps to the purchase of a field in Jeremiah 32, or to the potter of Jeremiah 18–19 (though the citation is to Zechariah 11.13).

was being accused by the high priests and the elders he made no answer. Then Pilate said to him: Do you not hear all their testimony against you? And he made no answer to a single word, so that the governor was greatly amazed.

For the festival, the governor was accustomed to release one prisoner for the multitude, whichever one they wished. And they had at that time a notorious man, who was called Barabbas.[4] Now as they were assembled Pilate said to them: Which one do you wish me to release for you, Barabbas, or Jesus, who is called Christ? For he knew that it was through malice that they had turned him over. Now as he was sitting on the platform, his wife sent him a message, saying: Let there be nothing between you and this just man; for I have suffered much today because of a dream about him. But the high priests and the elders persuaded the crowd to ask for Barabbas and destroy Jesus. Then the governor spoke forth and said to them: Which of the two shall I give you? They answered: Barabbas. Pilate said to them: What then shall I do with Jesus, who is called Christ? They all said: Let him be crucified. But Pilate said: Why? What harm has he done? But they screamed all the more, saying: Let him be crucified. And Pilate, seeing that he was doing no good and that the disorder was growing, took water and washed his hands before the crowd, saying: I am innocent of the blood of this man. You see to it. And all the people answered and said: His blood is upon us and upon our children. Then Pilate gave them Barabbas, but he had Jesus flogged, and gave him over to be crucified.

Then the soldiers of the governor took Jesus to the residence, and drew up all their battalion around him. And they stripped him and put a red mantle about him, and wove a wreath of thorns and put it on his head, and put a reed in his right hand, and knelt before him and mocked him, saying: Hail, King of the Jews. And they spat upon him and took the reed and beat him on the head. And after they had mocked him, they took off the mantle and put his own clothes on him, and led him away to be crucified. And as they went out they found a man of Cyrene, named Simon. They impressed him for carrying the cross.

Then they came to a place called Golgotha, which means the place of the skull, and gave him wine mixed with gall to drink. When he tasted it he would not drink it. Then they crucified him, and divided up his clothes, casting lots, and sat there and watched him. Over his head they put the label giving the charge against him, where it was written: This is Jesus, the King of the Jews. Then there were crucified with him two robbers, one on his right and one on his left. And those who passed by blasphemed against him, wagging their heads, and saying: You who tear down the temple and rebuild it in three days, save yourself, and come down from the cross, if you are the son of God. So too the high priests, mocking him along with the scribes and the elders, said: He saved others, he cannot save himself. He is King of Israel, let him come down from the cross and we will believe in him. He trusted in God, let him save him now, if he will; for he said: I am the son of God. And the robbers who were crucified with him spoke abusively to him in the same way.

But from the sixth hour there was darkness over all the earth until the ninth hour. But about the ninth hour Jesus cried out in a great voice, saying: *Elei elei*

4. Bar-Abbas, meaning "son of Abbas" (literally, "son of the Father"). John 18.40 calls Barabbas a "bandit" (*lēstēs*), a term often applied to the Jewish revolutionaries who defied Roman rule (Mark 15.7 refers to his involvement in "sedition").

lema sabachthanei?[5] Which is: My God, my God, why have you forsaken me? But some of those who were standing there heard and said: This man calls to Elijah.[6] And at once one of them ran and took a sponge, soaked it in vinegar and put it on the end of a reed, and gave it to him to drink. But the rest said: Let us see if Elijah comes to save him.

Then Jesus cried out again in a great voice, and gave up his life. And behold, the veil of the temple[7] was split in two from top to bottom, and the earth was shaken, and the rocks were split, and the tombs opened and many bodies of the holy sleepers rose up; and after his resurrection they came out of their tombs and went into the holy city, and were seen by many. But the company commander and those with him who kept guard over Jesus, when they saw the earthquake and the things that happened, were greatly afraid, saying: In truth this was the son of God. And there were many women watching from a distance there, who had followed Jesus from Galilee, waiting on him. Among them were Mary the Magdalene, and Mary the mother of James and Joseph, and the mother of the sons of Zebedee.

When it was evening, there came a rich man of Arimathaea, Joseph by name, who also had been a disciple of Jesus. This man went to Pilate and asked for the body of Jesus. Then Pilate ordered that it be given up to him. And Joseph took the body and wrapped it in clean linen, and laid it in his new tomb, which he had cut in the rock, and rolled a great stone before the door of the tomb, and went away. But Mary the Magdalene and the other Mary were there, sitting before the tomb. On the next day, which is the day after the Day of Preparation, the high priests and the Pharisees gathered in the presence of Pilate, and said: Lord, we have remembered how that impostor said while he was still alive: After three days I shall rise up. Give orders, then, that the tomb be secured until after the third day, for fear his disciples may come and steal him away and say to the people: He rose from the dead. And that will be the ultimate deception, worse than the former one. Pilate said to them: You have a guard. Go and secure it as best you can. And they went and secured the tomb, sealing it with the help of the guard.

Late on the sabbath, as the light grew toward the first day after the sabbath, Mary the Magdalene and the other Mary came to visit the tomb. And behold, there was a great earthquake, for the angel of the Lord came down from heaven and approached the stone and rolled it away and was sitting on it. His look was like lightning, and his clothing white as snow. And those who were on guard were shaken with fear of him and became like dead men. But the angel spoke forth and said to the women: Do not you fear; for I know that you look for Jesus, who was crucified. He is not here. For he rose up, as he said. Come here, and look at the place where he lay. Then go quickly and tell his disciples that he has risen from the dead, and behold, he goes before you into Galilee. There you will see him. See; I have told you. And quickly leaving the tomb, in fear and great joy, they ran to tell the news to his disciples. And behold, Jesus met them, saying: I give you greeting. They came up to him and took his feet and worshipped him.

---

5. These words are in Aramaic, a Semitic language commonly spoken in the region (closely related to Hebrew and Syriac); the rest of the gospel is in vernacular Greek.
6. The prophet who was bodily taken up to heaven in a chariot of fire (2 Kings 2.8–11);

his return was prophesied to herald the coming of the Messiah (Malachi 3.1; 4.5).
7. The veil covering the door of the inner sanctuary of the Temple (Exodus 26.31–34), where God was said to appear (Leviticus 16.2).

Then Jesus said to them: Do not fear. Go and tell my brothers to go into Galilee, and there they will see me. And as they went on their way, behold, some of the guards went into the city and reported to the high priests all that had happened. And they met with the elders and took counsel together, and gave the soldiers a quantity of money, saying: Say that the disciples came in the night and stole him away while we were sleeping. And if this is heard in the house of the governor, we shall reason with him, and make it so that you have nothing to fear. And they took the money and did as they were instructed. And this is the story that has been spread about among the Jews, to this day.

Then the eleven disciples went on into Galilee, to the mountain where Jesus had given them instructions to go; and when they saw him, they worshipped him; but some doubted. And Jesus came up to them and talked with them, saying: All authority has been given to me, in heaven and on earth. Go out, therefore, and instruct all the nations, baptizing them in the name of the Father and the Son and the Holy Spirit, teaching them to observe all that I have taught you. And behold, I am with you, all the days until the end of the world.

John 1

[*The Word*]

In the beginning was the word, and the word was with God, and the word was God. He was in the beginning, with God. Everything came about through him, and without him not one thing came about. What came about in him was life, and the life was the light of mankind; and the light shines in the darkness, and the darkness did not understand it.

There was a man sent from God; his name was John. This man came for testimony, to testify concerning the light, so that all should believe through him. He was not the light, but was to testify concerning the light. The light was the true light, which illuminates every person who comes into the world. He was in the world, and the world came about through him, and the world did not know him. He went to his own and his own people did not accept him. Those who accepted him, he gave them power to become children of God, to those who believed in his name, who were born not from blood or from the will of the flesh or from the will of man, but from God.

And the word became flesh and lived among us, and we have seen his glory, glory as of a single son from his father, full of grace and truth. John bears witness concerning him, and he cried out, saying (for it was he who was speaking): He who is coming after me was before me, because he was there before I was; because we have all received from his fullness, and grace for grace. Because the law was given through Moses; the grace and the truth came through Jesus Christ. No one has ever seen God; the only-born God who is in the bosom of his father, it is he who told of him.

And this is the testimony of John, when the Jews sent priests and Levites[1] from Jerusalem to ask him: Who are you? And he confessed, and made no

---

1. Members of the tribe of Levi (one of the sons of Jacob), who formed a hereditary subordinate priesthood (see Numbers 18.1–6).

denial, but confessed: I am not the Christ. And they asked him: What then? Are you Elijah? And he said: I am not. Are you the prophet? And he answered: No. Then they said to him: Who are you? So that we can give an answer to those who sent us. What do you say about yourself? He said: I am the voice of one crying in the desert: Make straight the way of the Lord; as Isaiah the prophet said. Now they had been sent by the Pharisees. And they questioned him and said to him: Why then do you baptize, if you are not the Christ, or Elijah or the prophet? John answered them saying: I baptize with water; but in your midst stands one whom you do not know, who is coming after me, and I am not fit to untie the fastening of his shoe. All this happened in Bethany beyond the Jordan,[2] where John was baptizing.

The next day he saw Jesus coming toward him and said: See, the lamb of God who takes away the sinfulness of the world. This is the one of whom I said: A man is coming after me who was before me, because he was there before I was. And I did not know him. But so that he might be made known to Israel, this was why I came baptizing with water. And John bore witness, saying: I have seen the Spirit descending like a dove from the sky, and it remained upon him; and I did not know him, but the one who sent me to baptize with water was the one who said to me: That one, on whom you see the Spirit descending and remaining upon him, is the one who baptizes with the Holy Spirit. And I have seen, and I have borne witness that this is the son of God.

The next day John was standing with two of his disciples, and he saw Jesus walking about and said: See, the lamb of God. His two disciples heard what he said and followed Jesus. Jesus turned about and saw them following him and said: What are you seeking? They said to him: Rabbi (which translated means master), where are you staying? He said to them: Come and see. So they came, and saw where he was staying, and stayed with him for that day. It was about the tenth hour. Andrew, one of the two who heard Jesus and followed him, was the brother of Simon Peter. He went first and found his brother Simon and said to him: We have found the Messiah (which is, translated, the Christ). He took him to Jesus. Jesus looked at him and said: You are Simon, the son of John. You shall be called Cephas[3] (which means Peter).

The next day Jesus wished to go out to Galilee. And he found Philip and said to him: Follow me. Philip was from Bethsaida, the city of Andrew and Peter. Philip found Nathanael and said to him: We have found the one of whom Moses wrote in the law, and the prophets: Jesus the son of Joseph, from Nazareth. And Nathanael said to him: Can anything good come from Nazareth? Philip said to him: Come and see. Jesus saw Nathanael coming toward him and said of him: See, a true son of Israel, in whom there is no guile. Nathanael said to him: How is it that you know me? Jesus answered and said to him: I saw you when you were under the fig tree, before Philip called you. Nathanael answered: Master, you are the son of God, you are the King of Israel. Jesus answered and said to him: Because I told you I saw you under the fig tree, you believe? You will see greater things than that. And he said to him: Truly truly I tell you, you will see the heaven open and the angels of God ascending and descending to the son of man.[4]

---

2. The river that forms the border between modern Israel and, to the east, Jordan and Syria.
3. Kêfâ (Aramaic), meaning "rock" or "stone"

(Greek petros).
4. Compare Jacob's vision of the ladder at Bethel (Genesis 28.10–17).

AUGUSTINE
354–430

When Augustine lay dying in August of 430, Vandal armies were besieging the African city of Hippo (modern Annaba, Algeria), where Augustine was the spiritual leader of a vibrant community of Christians living under the rule of the Roman Empire. Within weeks, Hippo would fall; the great city of Rome itself would be captured within thirty years. Born into the culture of antiquity but laying the foundations for the medieval millennium that was just about to begin, Augustine stands with one foot in each world. His monumental autobiography, the *Confessions*, constantly draws on the rich literature of the Roman orators and prose writers, especially Cicero. Yet it also reaches forward, innovatively exploring the ways in which the reader—like Augustine himself—might find that the Word of God has all along been lodged within his innermost soul.

LIFE AND TIMES

Augustine was a native of the northern African regions that were part of the Roman Empire. Yet the empire was in a gradual state of collapse throughout Augustine's lifetime: strong military leaders were running the government in all but name from 395 onward, and the final Roman emperor would be deposed by rebellious mercenary troops in 476. It was a transitional period—a time of great instability and, simultaneously, cultural and religious ferment. Mystery and cult religions were particularly popular, as witnessed by Augustine's account of his years with the Manichaeans. Despite the instability and uncertainty of the period, the adminis-trative and economic structures of the empire were still healthy enough to ease travel between its various parts, allow-ing Augustine to journey throughout northern Africa and Italy.

Augustine spent his early years in Africa, where there were several provin-cial cities of substantial size. Born at Thagaste (modern Souk-Ahras, Algeria), he had his first schooling at the nearby town of Madaurus and, later, at the so-phisticated cultural capital of Carthage. There, Augustine became intrigued by Manichaeanism, a dualistic religion that resembled early Christianity in empha-sizing the life of the mind and the drive toward increasing spiritual purity, though the two religions differed very significantly in their views of the nature of God. Augustine quickly rose to the top of his profession as an educator and public speaker, teaching grammar at his birthplace of Thagaste and, later, rheto-ric at Carthage. These provincial suc-cesses impelled him to Rome, where he established a school of rhetoric; he was then invited to come to Milan, which had become a capital of the Western Roman Empire, to take on the chair of rhetoric and such duties as writing hon-orific speeches to be presented at court. At Milan, Augustine entered into a very sophisticated intellectual community, where he became deeply involved in Neoplatonism both as a philosophy and as a quasi-religious form of mysticism. He also came to know Ambrose, the Roman Catholic bishop of Milan. At the time, Augustine says, he told himself that he was attending Ambrose's ser-mons simply to judge his excellence as a public speaker. In fact, Augus-tine was becoming increasingly drawn to Christianity, a religion to which his mother, Monica, had vainly tried to introduce him since he was a young child.

The bond between Augustine and Ambrose was strengthened enormously by Monica, who had followed her son to Milan and become close to Ambrose; the bishop reciprocated, constantly telling his friend Augustine what a treasure he had in his faithful and devout mother. The *Confessions* shows that Monica played a major role in her son's spiritual growth, which culminated in Augustine's conversion and baptism on Easter 386, at the age of thirty-two. This was a moment of complete change for Augustine, not just spiritually but also practically: he gave up his chair in rhetoric at the imperial court of Milan, withdrew from his engagement to marry, and went with his mother to the port of Ostia to return to Africa. But before they could sail from Italy, Monica died, as did Augustine's son, Adeodatus, who had been born in Carthage to Augustine's longtime mistress, traveled to Italy with Augustine, and undergone baptism alongside his father. Alone back in Thagaste, Augustine surrounded himself with spiritual brothers—members of the growing Christian community in the region—and transformed his family home into a monastery. When he paid a visit to a friend at Hippo in 391, Augustine found that his reputation as a spiritual leader had preceded him. The community at Hippo begged Augustine to remain with them, and he was ordained a priest at their request. By 396, he was bishop of Hippo, a position he held until his death.

WORK

Augustine probably began work on the *Confessions* in 397, when he was forty-three years old. He seems to have been suffering from a terrible case of writer's block, with several half-finished pieces of work on hand. The experience of writing the *Confessions* apparently cured it, for almost immediately after completing it Augustine went on to produce an extraordinarily large number of works. The *Confessions* is, as the name suggests, autobiographical, the story of one man's life in his own words. But it is also confessional in the sense of being a full account of one's sins; a story addressed first of all to God, the hearer who is able to forgive the transgressions that Augustine recounts. At the same time, the *Confessions* has a secondary addressee, as Augustine himself acknowledges: other would-be Christians who might be able to trace the path of their own spiritual journey as a result of having read about the struggles of another. Of the thirteen books of the *Confessions*, only the first nine are autobiographical, covering the period from Augustine's early childhood memories to his stay in Ostia in 387, as he waits for the boat that would take him home. The autobiographical genre, almost without precedent in this period, is perhaps Augustine's greatest literary legacy. We hear nothing from Augustine about his later years in Africa; instead, the final books of the *Confessions* are an analysis of the account of creation in Genesis, along with a sustained meditation on the nature of time and memory. The overall effect of the *Confessions* is to turn the reader inward, away from the individual journey of Augustine and toward the collective journey of humanity toward the divine.

Surprisingly for a book dedicated to the relationship of the soul to God, the most moving parts of the *Confessions* focus on Augustine's relationship to other human beings—not just his mother, Monica, who was so instrumental to Augustine's conversion to Christianity, but also his beloved son, Adeodatus, and the unnamed mistress who was Augustine's companion from age seventeen (when he first went to Carthage) until his mother persuaded him to enter into an arranged marriage in 385, shortly before his conversion. This woman, whom

Augustine simply calls "the One," faithfully followed him on his journeys, first to Rome and then to Milan. When Augustine finally renounced his relationship with her, she returned to Africa, "vowing before you never to know any other man." All of these human relationships, however passionate, are in the end subsumed within Augustine's all-consuming relationship with God. He addresses God familiarly throughout the Confessions, as if he were an intimate friend who knew all Augustine's secrets, but who also had the terrifying capacity to destroy, inspiring both adoration and fear.

Augustine writes frankly about his self-fashioning within the various communities to which he belonged, from his involvement in a gang of undisciplined youths to his immersion in the Manichaean community at Carthage, his time among the Neoplatonists in Milan, and his final place of rest among the Christian community at Hippo. His journey is, at a deep level, a search for the self, which he comes to find only after long struggle, and only through the companionship of others. Augustine comes

home first spiritually, with a conversion inspired by the supernatural voice of a child, and then physically, sailing from Ostia to Thagaste, where he will make a new spiritual home filled with Christian believers among the bricks and mortar of his childhood house. Desire and longing structure the narrative of the *Confessions*, from Augustine's heady days in Carthage, at the theater by day and in the arms of his mistress by night, to his patient vigil at the port of Ostia, consumed at once by sorrow for the death of Monica and joy in his discovery of Christ. Caught between his love for human beings and his longing for the divine, Augustine is never more present to us than when, shortly before his conversion, he cries out to God, "Grant me chastity and continance, only not yet." Augustine's painstaking examination of his innermost self, racked with contradictions and unexplained desires, had a profound influence not only on the medieval Christians who sought, like Augustine, to purge their souls of sin but also on the secular self-examination of early modern writers such as **Montaigne** and **Rousseau**.

From Confessions[1]

FROM BOOK I

[*Childhood*]

[6. 7]   For what do I wish to say, Lord, except that I do not know from where I came into what I call this dying life, or living death; I do not know. But the consolation of Your mercies uplifted me, as I heard from the father and mother of my flesh, out of whom and in whom You formed me at the appropriate time, for I do not remember it myself. I was embraced by the comforts of human milk, but neither my mother nor my nurses filled their own breasts for me. It was You Who through them gave me the food of my infancy according to Your ordinance and the riches spread throughout the essence of all things. You also granted me to want no more than You gave, and granted that my nurses wanted to give me what You had given them, for they sought to give me by divine ordination what they had received in abundance from You. But the good that came

---

1. Translated by Peter Constantine. Paragraph numbering throughout refers to the Latin text.

to me from them was also good for them, though it did not come from them but through them; for from You, O God, come all good things, and from my God is my entire salvation.[2] This I learned only later, when, through all the inner and outer things You bestow, You called to me; for then I only knew how to suckle, content in what was pleasurable and crying at what offended my flesh, and nothing more.

[6. 8]   Later I began to smile—first in sleep, then waking. At least that is what I was told about myself and I believe it, for this is what we see in infants, though I do not remember it about myself. Gradually I began to perceive where I was, and to want to express my needs to those who could fulfill them; but I could not express them, for the needs were inside me, and the other people outside; nor were they able with any of their senses to enter my soul. So I kicked and shouted; these were the few signs I could make that resembled my wishes, though they did not really resemble them. And when I was not obeyed, either because I was not understood or because what I wanted might harm me, I became indignant with the adults for not submitting to me, indignant with those who were not my slaves for not serving me, and avenged myself by crying. That is how infants are, as I learned from those I have been able to observe; the infants who knew nothing showing me better than my experienced nurses that I too had been like that.

* * *

[8. 13]   On my way to the present I passed from infancy to boyhood. Or is it not that boyhood came to me, succeeding infancy? Not that infancy departed, for where would it have gone? Yet suddenly it was no more, for I was no longer an infant who could not talk but had become a boy speaking.[3] This I remember; but how I learned to speak I found out only later. I was not taught to speak by adults presenting me with words in a certain fixed order, as they would do somewhat later with letters. But with the mind that You gave me, my God, I myself learned through cries and all kinds of sounds and motions of my limbs, to express the feelings of my heart so that my wishes would be fulfilled. But I was not able to express everything I wanted to express to whomever I wanted. I managed to remember whenever adults called a thing something; and when, along with their voice, they moved their bodies toward a certain object I would see and retain the sounds with which they expressed the object. Moreover, what they wanted to express was clear from their gestures, which are the natural language of all races and are expressed in the face, the eyes, and movements of the limbs, and tones of voice that indicate the state of a person's mind as it strives toward, takes hold of, rejects, or shuns a thing. In this way, by repeatedly hearing words as they were positioned in various sentences, I gradually connected them with the things they signified, and so trained my mouth to express my desires through these signs. In this way I communicated the signs of my desires to the people I was among, and so entered into the tempests of society; yet I was still dependent on the authority of my parents and the will of the adults around me.

---

2. Throughout the *Confessions* Augustine quotes liberally from the Bible. When a quotation bears on Augustine's situation, it is annotated.
3. The English word *infant* comes from the Latin *infans*, "speechless."

[9. 14]   O God, my God, what miseries I now experienced, what follies, when as a boy it was put before me that the only way of living right was to obey those who were instructing me to excel in this world by using the skill of language[4] to secure worldly honors and spurious wealth. I was sent to school to learn to read and write, the uses of which, poor wretch that I was, I did not know, and whenever I lagged in my studies I was beaten. This was extolled by adults, many previous generations having laid out the difficult path we were made to tread, increasing the toil and suffering of the sons of Adam. But, Lord, we also came upon men who prayed to You, and from them we learned, as far as we were able, to imagine You as some great being who, though we could not see You, would hear and help us. Thus I began as a boy to pray to You, my aid and refuge, and invoking You unraveled the knots of my tongue, a small boy but with great love, praying to You that I not be beaten in school.[5] And when You did not hear me—which saved me from the folly of praying to You for trifles—the adults, including my parents, laughed, though not unkindly, at the beatings I received, which at the time were a great and heavy sorrow to me.

[9. 15]   Is there anyone, O Lord, any mind so great, so close to You in powerful love? Is there anyone, I ask, so close to You in piety and magnanimous love that he will think lightly (and not because his wits are dull) of the racks and hooks[6] and other torments that men in this world pray to You with such dread to escape, but who mock the torments they so bitterly fear, just as our parents mocked the torments our tutors inflicted on us as boys? For we did not fear our torments less, nor did we pray less to You to escape them. But still we transgressed, for we wrote, read, and studied less than was demanded of us. Not that we lacked the ability or memory, O Lord, which You willed us to have in ample measure for our age. But we delighted in amusements, for which we were punished by those who also delighted in amusements—yet the amusements of adults are called "business," while those of children are punished by the adults, and no one pities either the children or the adults. Perhaps some fine arbiter might approve of my having been beaten because my playing with a ball hindered the pace of the learning that I was to use as an adult to play reprehensible games. Was he who flogged me any better? If a fellow tutor should trump him on some trifling matter, was he any the less angry or jealous than I was when a playmate beat me at ball?

* * *

[12. 19]   Yet even in childhood, when my family feared less for me than in my youth, I did not like to study, and hated being forced to do so. But I was forced, and it was good for me. Not that it was I who was doing good, because I would not have studied had I not been compelled to. No one does good when he does it against his will, even if he is doing a good thing—yet neither were they who were forcing me doing good. What was good came to me from You, my God, for they did not consider how I should later use what they forced me to learn

---

4. I.e., the study of rhetoric, which was the passport to eminence in public life.
5. Augustine recognizes the necessity of this rigorous training; that he never forgot its harshness is clear from his remark in the *City of God* (21.14): "If a choice were given him between suffering death and living his early years over again, who would not shudder and choose death?"
6. The instruments of torture and public execution.

other than to satiate the insatiable desires of an impoverished wealth and an ignominious glory. But You, Who number the hairs of our head,[7] used for my good the error of all those who urged me to learn; and You used my own error in not wanting to learn to punish me, a punishment I deserved, so small a boy and yet so great a sinner. You did me good through those who did not do good, and for my own sin You exacted a just retribution: for You have commanded, and it is so, that every disordered soul will be its own punishment.

[13. 20]   I have still not managed to fathom the reasons why I hated Greek,[8] which I studied as a boy. Yet Latin I truly loved; not what my first masters taught me, but what I later learned from the men we call grammarians. For I considered my first lessons of reading, writing, and arithmetic as great a burden and punishment as any Greek lesson. And yet, as I was flesh, a passing breath that does not return, did this not come from the sin and vanity of life? The first lessons were in fact better than the later ones, because they were more sound. Through them I acquired, and still retain, the ability to read whatever I find written and to write whatever I want; whereas in my later lessons I was forced to retain the strayings of an Aeneas[9] I did not know, forgetting my own, and to weep over a dead Dido[1] who killed herself for love; while I, without a tear, was prepared to pitiably die away from You through such works, my God, my life.

[13. 21]   What is more pitiable than a pitiful being who does not pity himself but weeps at the death of Dido for love of Aeneas; a pitiful being who does not weep over the death he is suffering because he does not love You, O God, light of my heart, bread of the mouth deep within my soul, vigor that impregnates my mind and the vessel of my thoughts. I did not love You, and fornicated against You,[2] and as I did so I heard from all around cries of "Well done! Well done!," for the friendship of this world is fornication against You; and "Well done! Well done!" is what they shout in order to shame a man who is not like them. For all this I did not weep, but wept for Dido, "who with a dagger did the lowest ends pursue,"[3] just as I, having forsaken You, pursued the lowest of Your creations, dust turning to dust. Had I been forbidden to read these works I would have suffered at not being able to read what made me suffer. And such foolishness is considered a higher and better education than that by which I learned to read and write.

[13. 22]   But now may my God call out in my soul, Your truth proclaiming to me, "This is wrong, this is wrong! Your first lessons were better by far!" For I would readily forget the strayings of Aeneas rather than forget how to read and write. The doors of the grammarians' schools are indeed hung with precious curtains,[4] but this is not so much a sign of high distinction as a cloak for their errors. Let not those whom I no longer fear cry out against me while

7. I.e., who knows and attends to the smallest detail of each life (cf. Matthew 10.30).
8. The study of Greek was important not only for gaining knowledge of Greek literature but also because it was the official language of the Eastern Roman Empire. Augustine never really mastered Greek, though his remark elsewhere that he had acquired so little Greek that it amounted to practically none is overmodest.
9. Virgil's Aeneid 3.
1. Queen of Carthage whose unrequited love

for the Trojan warrior Aeneas ended in her untimely death; Aeneas was obliged to pursue his destiny to be the founding father of Rome (Virgil, Aeneid, esp. book 4).
2. Here, metaphorically.
3. Virgil, Aeneid 6.457.
4. In Augustine's time, school entrances were covered by veils with an attendant standing by to make sure that only those who paid tuition were admitted; the veil was also a symbol of the hidden knowledge that lay beyond the threshold.

I confess to You what my soul seeks, finding peace in condemning my evil ways and loving Your good ways. Let not the sellers and buyers of high learning cry out against me. If I ask them whether it is true that Aeneas once came to Carthage, as the poet says, the less learned will reply that they do not know, while the more learned will say that he never did. But if I ask with what letters the name "Aeneas" is written, everyone who has learned this will answer me correctly, according to the agreement and decision that men have reached concerning these signs. Likewise, if I should ask which was the greater inconvenience, forgetting how to read and write or forgetting those poetic fictions, who would not know what answer someone in possession of his senses would give? Thus as a boy I sinned, preferring empty learning to learning that was more useful, going so far as to love the former and hate the latter. "One plus one is two, two plus two is four" was a hateful incantation, while the sweetest dream of my vanity was the wooden horse filled with armed men, the burning of Troy, and even the ghost of Creusa.[5]

* * *

[17. 27] Permit me, my God, also to say something about my innate talent, Your gift, and the foolishness on which I squandered it. I was set a task that greatly worried me because of the prospect of praise or shame, and the dread of being beaten: the task was to speak the words of Juno as she raged and grieved, unable as she was to "keep the Prince of Troy from seeking the shores of Italy,"[6] even though I knew she had never spoken such words. But we were forced to go astray in the footsteps of those poetic creations, and to say in plain speech what Virgil had said in verse. The declaimer who was most praised was the one who best brought forth, shrouded in the most fitting words, the grandeur of the feigned characters in their passion of rage and grief. What is it to me, my God and true life, that my declamation was applauded over that of so many of the pupils of my age and in my class? Is all this not smoke and wind? Was there nothing else on which to exercise my talent and my tongue? Your praises, Lord, Your praises through Your Scriptures, would have trellised the young vines of my heart, and foolish nonsense would not have snatched at it, vile prey for winged scavengers. There is more than one way for man to pay homage to fallen angels.

* * *

FROM BOOK II

[The Pear Tree]

[1. 1] I recall my past impurity and the carnal corruptions suffered by my soul, not because I love them but so that I may love You, my God. It is out of love for Your love that in the bitterness of my memory I seek to recall the most

---

5. While at a feast held in his honor by Dido, Aeneas tells the story of the fall of Troy and his escape from the burning city, during which he lost his wife, Creusa (Virgil, *Aeneid*, book 2, esp. 2.772).
6. Augustine was assigned the task of delivering a prose paraphrase of Juno's angry speech in *Aeneid* 1. In it she complains that her enemies, the Trojans under Aeneas, are on their way to their destined goal in Italy in spite of her resolution to prevent them. Rhetorical exercises such as this were common in the schools, because they served the double purpose of teaching both literature and rhetorical composition.

terrible things I did, so that Your sweetness will flow into me, O God, O Sweet One Who never fails, Sweet One serene and untroubled, Who gathered up the pieces into which I had been scattered when I turned away from You, the One, only to waste myself among the many. For in my youth I burned fervently to satisfy my hellish desires, wallowing in sensual and shadowy loves, my beauty wasting away; before Your eyes I was putrid, while I sought pleasure for myself and to please the eyes of others.

[2. 2] What was it that I delighted in, if not loving and being loved? But there was no path from soul to soul, no luminous links of friendship, it was only vapors rising from the slimy lusts of the flesh and the gushings of puberty that beclouded my heart, so that I was not able to discern the bright serenity of love from the hazy mists of lust. Both love and lust raged in turmoil within me, dragging me in my weak youth into the chasms of sin, plunging me into the raging abyss of disgrace. Your wrath was growing, though I did not know it. The clanking chains of my mortal flesh had rendered me deaf, punishing me for the pride of my soul, and I strayed ever further from You, and You let me. I was hurled and scattered in all directions, dissipating myself in my fornications, while You, O my belated joy, were silent! You were silent then, and in proud degradation and restless despondence I strayed ever further from You, the seed of my sorrow ever more sterile.

* * *

[2. 4] Where was I, how far was I exiled from the delights of Your House, in that sixteenth year of the age of my flesh? The madness of lust raised its scepter over me and I had relinquished myself to it entirely, condoned as it was by the turpitude of man, yet forbidden by Your laws. Meanwhile, my family did not seek through marriage to keep me from plunging into the abyss; their only concern was that I should learn to excel in discourse and be persuasive as an orator.

* * *

[4. 9] Your law punishes theft, O Lord, as does the law written in the hearts of men that even wickedness cannot erase, for what thief will gladly bear another thief robbing him, even if he is rich and the one robbing him is in need? But I wanted to steal and I did, driven not by any need, but by a lack of regard for justice and an abundance of wickedness. For I stole something of which I had plenty and far better; nor did I seek to enjoy what I had stolen, only the theft and the sin itself. Near our vineyard was a pear tree heavy with fruit that did not tempt with either color or taste. Late one night, I and some wicked youths, still seeking fun in our usual haunts, as was our foul habit, set about to shake the pears off the tree and carry them away, taking with us a huge load, not to eat, but to throw to the pigs. If we ate a few of the pears it was only to relish the wrongness of what we had done. Such was my heart, O God, such was my heart, which You took pity on in the profoundest depths of the abyss. Let my heart tell You now what it sought there, being wicked for no reason and having no cause to do ill except wickedness itself. It was detestable, but I delighted in it. I delighted in my undoing, I delighted in my eclipse, not that for which I was eclipsed but the eclipse itself, a depraved soul falling from Your firmament to its destruction, not seeking anything through my shamefulness but shame itself.

[5. 10]   Just as beauty can be seen in lovely objects, in gold and silver and such things, and just as the harmony of objects is vital to our sense of touch, each of our other senses have their own response. Transient honor too, such as the powers of ruling and command, has its splendor, which also give rises to man's urge to claim his rights. And yet in our quest for these things we must not depart from You, O Lord, nor deviate from Your law. The life we live in this world also has its appeal through a certain beauty of its own and a harmony with all the beautiful things here below, as does friendship, tied with its sweet and precious knot that unites many souls. Yet all of this can lead to sin when through an unrestrained urge for good things that are the lowest things of Your creation, forsaking things that are better and higher, forsaking You, our Lord God, Your truth, and Your law. For the lower things have their delights, but not like my God, Who made all things, and in Whom those who are righteous delight, and Who is the joy of those upright in heart.

[5. 11]   When we ask why a crime was committed, we tend not to believe the answer unless there seems to have been a desire to obtain—or a fear of losing— some of the things I have called a lower good. This lower good is beautiful and appealing, though when compared with higher and blessed good, it is base and vile. A man has committed a murder; why did he do it? Perhaps he loved the murdered man's wife, or his property, or he robbed the man to secure his livelihood, or feared that he might be robbed of his livelihood by the man he murdered; or, wronged, he burned to be avenged. Would anyone commit murder for no reason, simply delighting in murder? Who would believe such a thing? Yet it has been said[7] of a certain crazed man of boundless cruelty that he was cruel and evil without cause, though a reason was also cited: Lest through idleness his hand or heart should wilt. And yet, we should ask why was this man so cruel? It was so that through his acts of crime he might seize Rome and attain honors, power, and wealth, and free himself from fear of the laws, the dangers of poverty, and the offenses he had committed. Hence not even this man, Catiline, loved his deeds, but loved something else for the sake of which he did them.

[6. 12]   Wretch that I was, what did I love in you, my theft, O deed committed in that night of my sixteenth year? It is not that you were beautiful, for you were a theft. Are you even a thing, that I can speak to you? Beautiful were the fruits we stole, for they were Your creation, O Most Beautiful of all, Creator of all, O God that is good, God the highest Good and my true Good. Beautiful were those fruits, but it was not them that my wretched soul desired, for I had plenty better, and the ones I plucked I plucked only so that I might steal. No sooner had I plucked them than I threw them away, my sin being the only feast I rejoiced in. And the few bites of fruit that did enter my mouth were seasoned with sin. And now, O Lord my God, I ask You what it was in that theft that delighted me. It had no beauty: I do not mean beauty as in the beauty of justice or judiciousness, nor such beauty as is in the mind of man, in the memory, the senses, or blossoming life; nor as the stars are beautiful and splendid in the sky, nor as the earth and sea are filled with new life, through birth replacing what has died; not even the false beauty lurking in shadows that belongs to vice.

---

7. By the Roman historian Sallust (*Catiline* 16). Cataline was a Roman politician whose conspiracy against the state was foiled by the consul Cicero in 63 B.C.E.

[6. 13] This too is the way that pride imitates lofty elegance, whereas You alone are God, exalted above all. What does vanity seek but honors and glory, whereas You alone are to be honored and glorious in eternity. The cruelty of powerful men aims to be feared, but who is to be feared other than the one and only God? What can be seized or robbed of his power—when, where, how, or by whom? Tender caresses aim to spark love, yet nothing is more tender than Your love, nor is anything loved with more wholesomeness than Your truth, beautiful and bright above all. Curiosity poses as a desire for knowledge, whereas You Who are above all know all. Ignorance and foolishness hide behind the names of simplicity and innocence, but there is no greater simplicity than You, no greater innocence, for sinners are harmed by their own deeds. Idleness poses as a desire for calm, but what calm is there other than the Lord? Extravagance strives to be called abundance and plenty, but You are plenitude and the unfailing plenteousness of imperishable delight. Prodigality seeks to array itself in the glow of generosity, but it is You Who are the supremely abundant giver of all good. Greed seeks to possess much, but You possess all. Jealousy strives for excellence, but what is more excellent than You? Anger seeks revenge, but who avenges with greater justice than You? Fear recoils from things that are unaccustomed and unexpected, things that endanger what is beloved, and fear takes precautions for the safety of what it loves. But to You what is unaccustomed? What is unexpected? Who can take from You what You love? Where other than with You is enduring safety? Sadness pines for things lost in which cupidity delighted, insisting that nothing be taken from it, just as nothing can be taken from You.

[6. 14] Thus the soul that turns away from You fornicates, seeking outside You that which is clear and pure, but which it can only find when it returns to You. All those have erred who seek to imitate You perversely, having distanced themselves from You and extolling themselves in pride against You. But even by seeking to imitate You they admit that You are the creator of the entire universe and that it is not possible for them to distance themselves from You entirely. What then did I love in that theft, and how did I, albeit perversely and in error, imitate my Lord? Did I delight in breaking Your law at least furtively, as I lacked power, like a slave who steals with impunity, attaining a shadowy semblance of omnipotence? Behold the servant fleeing his Lord and seeking a shadow! O putridness! O monstrous life and chasm of death! Was I drawn to what was forbidden just because it was forbidden?

* * *

FROM BOOK III

[Student at Carthage]

[1. 1] I came to Carthage[8] and was immersed in a seething cauldron of illicit loves. I had not yet loved but was burning to experience love, and, consumed by an inner craving, was vexed at myself for not craving more. In love with love, I sought an object of love, but shunned a path that had no snares. I was consumed by hunger, deprived of inner food, deprived of You, my God, and yet it

8. The provincial capital city (in modern-day Tunisia), where Augustine went to study rhetoric.

was not for You that I hungered; I lacked all desire for incorruptible sustenance, not because I was sated by it, but the emptier I was the more I disdained it. And so my soul sickened, and, covered in pustules, gushed forth,
wretchedly striving to be soothed by sensual objects. Yet if these objects had
not had a soul they would not have been objects of love. To love and be loved
was all the sweeter to me if I could delight in the body of the beloved. So I sullied the clear spring of friendship with the filth of carnality, dulling its brightness with infernal lust, and though I was base and vile, in my vanity I paraded
myself as refined and urbane. So I flung myself into that love by which I so
longed to be seized. My God, my Mercy! In Your goodness how much gall
did You sprinkle on that sweetness! For I was loved, and secretly attained
the fetters of delight, rejoicing in being enmeshed in the tangle of misery, to
be scourged with the burning rods of jealousy, suspicion, fear, anger, and
contention.

[2. 2]   I was captivated by theatrical spectacles filled with images of my
miseries, which poured fuel on my fire. Why is it that man wants to sorrow by
watching distressing and tragic things that he would not want to endure? And
yet he wants to endure this sorrow as a spectator, and this sorrow is his delight.
What is this if not utter folly? Indeed, the more a man is moved by such suffering, the less free he is of it himself, for when one is suffering it is called misery,
while when one feels sympathy for the suffering of others it is called compassion. But what sort of compassion is this for things that are feigned and staged?
The spectator is not summoned to help but only to grieve, and the more he
grieves the more he applauds the actor of these representations. But if the misfortunes, whether of ancient times or invented, are acted in such a way that
the spectator does not grieve, he leaves the theater filled with disappointment
and anger, but if he does grieve he delights in his tears.

[2. 3]   Thus sorrows are also loved. But people want to enjoy themselves; no
one likes to be miserable, even if he likes to commiserate: so do we love sorrows because commiserating cannot exist without misery?

* * *

[3. 6]   My supposedly respectable studies[9] had the aim of achieving excellence in the courts of litigation, where the greater the deceit, the greater the
praise. Such is the blindness of men that they glory in blindness. And I was the
foremost pupil in the school of rhetoric. I was puffed up with pride and rejoiced
in vanity, though I was more restrained by far than my fellow students, Lord, as
You know, keeping my distance from the destructiveness of the *Destroyers*,[1] who
sported this sinister and devilish name as a sign of urbanity. I lived among them
shamelessly ashamed that I was not like them. I was with them, and at times
enjoyed their friendship, though I always abhorred the deeds with which
they shamelessly persecuted shy new students, attacking them and jeering
at them for no reason, feeding their own malicious delight. Nothing resembles
the actions of devils more than theirs, so what better name can there be for them
than "the Destroyers," destroyed and corrupted as they are by the deceitful

---

9. That is, his rhetorical studies.
1. In the Latin original *eversores*, which means
"overturners," a group of students who prided

themselves on their wild behavior and lack of
discipline.

spirits that secretly deride and waylay them with the same deeds with which they taunt and deceive others.

[4. 7] Its was among them, at my tender age, that I studied the books of eloquence by which I longed to distinguish myself, driven by delight in human vanity, a damnable and empty aim. In the course of my studies I had come upon a book by a certain Cicero, whose tongue[2] almost everyone admires, though not so much his heart. The book is called *Hortensius*,[3] and contains an exhortation to study philosophy. It altered my state of mind and my prayers, making them turn to You, Lord, changing my longings and desires. Suddenly every vanity became worthless, and with a fire raging in my heart I longed for the immortality of wisdom, rousing me to return to You. I did not immerse myself in this book to perfect my style, something I was pursuing in those days when I was nineteen with my mother's funds, as my father had died two years before. No, it was not to perfect my style, for it was not the book's style that swayed me but its words.

* * *

[5. 9] I was therefore determined to apply my mind to the Holy Scripture in order to see what it was, and what I saw was something not discernible by the proud, nor open to the young, its entrance modest but its inner halls exalted and veiled with mysteries. I was not one who was able to enter or to bow my head and proceed. I did not feel then when I approached the Scripture what I feel now, but it struck me as unworthy of comparison to the distinction of a Cicero. My strutting pride shunned the simplicity of the Scripture, my eye not keen enough to penetrate its interior. Yet the Scripture is such that it grows with those who are simple.[4] But I disdained the thought of being simple, and, swollen with pride, perceived myself as great.

* * *

FROM BOOK V

[*Augustine Leaves Carthage for Rome*]

[8. 14] You led me so that I should be persuaded to go to Rome, to teach there what I was teaching in Carthage, and I will not omit confessing to You how I was persuaded to this, because in that, too, Your most profound recesses and Your mercy most present to us must be reflected on and confessed. I did not want to go to Rome simply because my friends urged me to, assuring me that in Rome I would garner greater profit and honor, though those things did influence my mind at the time. My main, and almost my only, reason was that I had heard that young men studied there more peaceably and were subjected to more rigorous discipline, not all rushing wildly into the class of a master whose

---

2. I.e., rhetorical style. "Cicero": Marcus Tullius Cicero (106–43 B.C.E.), Roman philosopher, politician, and lawyer. Augustine's admiration of Cicero is obvious; calling him "a certain Cicero" is a rhetorical convention; Augustine uses the same formulation to refer to the Apostle Paul.
3. Cicero's *Hortensius*, written in 45 B.C.E.

and now lost, was an analysis of the sources of happiness, which Cicero concluded lay in the pursuit of wisdom.
4. A reference not only to the rhetorical simplicity of Jesus's teachings but also to his interest in teaching children; cf. Matthew 19.14: "For of such is the kingdom of heaven."

pupils they were not; in Rome they were not even admitted into a class without a master's permission. In Carthage, on the other hand, there is an uncouth and unruly excess among pupils. They brazenly interrupt classes, and with crazed rowdiness bring turmoil to the order that the masters have established for the good of their students. With surprising foolishness they wreak mayhem that would be punishable by law if custom did not protect them, and they are the more wretched in that they do as lawful what will never be lawful by Your eternal law; and they believe that they are doing this with impunity, whereas they are punished with the blindness by which they do it, and suffer incomparably worse consequences than what they wreak. Such practices, which as a student I had refused to engage in, I had to endure in others as a teacher, and so I was happy to go to a place where those who knew assured me that such things were not done. But it was in truth You, my hope and my portion in the land of the living, who wanted me to change my earthly dwelling for the salvation of my soul, and in Carthage You goaded me so that I would tear myself away from it, and for Rome You placed before me enticements that would draw me there with the advice of Manichean friends who loved a dead life, doing mad things in this life, hoping for vain things in the next. To set my steps aright, You secretly used their and my perverseness; for those who disturbed my calm were blinded by a disgraceful frenzy, while those who summoned me away loved only this world. Yet I, who detested true misery here, sought false happiness there.

[8. 15]   You knew, God, why I left Carthage and went to Rome, but You did not reveal the reason either to me or my mother, who bitterly lamented my leaving and followed me as far as the shore.[5] She clung to me in desperation, seeking either to keep me there or to come with me, but I deceived her, pretending that I had a friend I was seeing off with whom I had to wait until he had a good wind to sail. I lied to my mother—lied to such a mother—and so escaped. This too You have mercifully forgiven me, I who was filled with abhorrent foulness, preserving me from the waters of the sea for the waters of Your grace that would cleanse me[6] and dry my mother's streaming eyes, with which she daily watered before You the ground on which she stood. But she refused to return home without me, and I barely managed to persuade her to stay that night in a place near our ship where there was a sanctuary in memory of the blessed Saint Cyprian.[7] But that night I secretly departed without her as she remained behind, weeping and praying. What was she asking of You with so many tears, my God, but that You would not let me sail? Yet You, in Your high mindfulness, hearing the core of her desire, did not heed what she was asking, so that You could make out of me exactly what she had always asked. The wind blew and swelled our sails and the shore receded from our sight, and on the following morning my mother came there raving with sorrow, filling Your ears with complaints and lamentations to which You paid no heed, while You

5. Augustine's mother, Monica of Hippo (322–387), has long been venerated as a saint in the Roman Catholic Church. Here, Monica and Augustine are in the roles of Dido and Aeneas; see Virgil, *Aeneid*, book 4.
6. A reference to the ritual of immersion in water to signify the cleansing of the soul from sin; in Augustine's day, baptism was often put off until death was near, even by relatively observant Christians.
7. Bishop of Carthage, Christian writer, local martyr, and saint (ca. 200–258) who was especially popular among North African Christians.

allowed me to be transported by my desires in order to extinguish those desires, and my mother's earthly longing for me was rightly chastened by the scourge of sorrow. For she loved my being with her, as mothers do, though much more than many others, and she did not know what great joy You were preparing for her by my absence. She did not know, which is why she wept and sobbed, and through these torments she manifested the inheritance of Eve, seeking as she did with pain what with pain she had brought forth. And yet, after accusing me of deception and cruelty, she again turned to interceding for me with You, and went back home while I went on to Rome.

* * *

FROM BOOK VI

[Earthly Love]

Strong in her piety, my mother had now come to me, following me over sea and land, confident in You in every danger she faced, and even on the perilous sea she comforted the sailors, who are more used to reassuring frightened passengers unaccustomed to the sea. She promised them a safe arrival, for You had assured her of this in a vision. She found me in great peril and in despair that I would ever find truth, though when I revealed to her that I was no longer a Manichean[8] though not yet a true Christian, she did not leap with joy as if my words were unexpected. But she was now reassured concerning that part of my misery for which she had wept over me as one dead, though to be reawakened by You, and on a bier of her thoughts she offered me to You that You might say to the son of this widow, "Young man, I say to you, arise!"[9] And her son would come to life again and begin to speak, and You would deliver him to his mother.

* * *

[13. 23]   I was continually being urged to take a wife. I made a proposal and it was accepted, largely through my mother's efforts, for she hoped that once I was married baptism with its salvation would cleanse me,[1] and she was delighted that I was more receptive with every day, and she saw that her prayers and Your promises were being fulfilled in my faith. At my bidding and through her longing she begged of You every day, with cries from her heart, that You reveal to her in a vision something about my future marriage, but You never did. What she saw were empty and fantastic visions fueled by the passion of the human spirit striving for answers; she told me about these visions, discounting them, as she did not have the same confidence in them that she had when it was You Who sent them. For she said that she could discern by some

8. Augustine had for nine years been a member of this religious sect, which followed the teaching of the Babylonian mystic Mani (216–277). The Manicheans believed that the world was a battleground for the forces of good and evil; redemption in a future life would come to the elect, who renounced worldly occupations and possessions and practiced a severe asceticism (including abstention from meat). Augus-

tine's mother, Monica, was a Christian, and lamented her son's Manichean beliefs.
9. Luke 7.14, recounting one of Christ's miracles.
1. Augustine could not be baptized while living in sin with his mistress, a liaison that resulted in the birth of a son, Adeodatus, who later accompanied his father to Italy.

strange sensation, which she could not explain in words, the difference between Your revelations and the dreams of her own soul. Nevertheless, the pressure on me to marry continued and a maiden was asked for in marriage; she was two years under marriageable age, but as she was thought suitable all were prepared to wait.[2]

[14. 24]   We were a group of several friends who detested the turbulence and trouble of life, and we discussed and debated and had almost resolved to live in contemplation far removed from the bustling crowd, and this was how we intended to attain such a life: we would bring together whatever each of us was able to contribute, and from that create a single household, so that in our true friendship nothing would belong only to one person or another but would be a single possession gathered from all, and as a whole would belong to each, and all to all. We concluded that we could bring some ten men into this fellowship, some of whom were very wealthy, especially our townsman Romanianus, whom the burdensome tangle of his affairs had brought to the courts, and who from childhood had been a close friend of mine. He was the most zealous advocate of this plan, and his voice was of great weight because his wealth far exceeded that of any of us. We had also decided that two of us would be elected every year, the way magistrates are, to attend to everything, the rest of the group remaining free from such cares. But when we began to give thought as to whether wives, which some of us already had and others were hoping to attain, would agree to what we were planning with such care, it fell to pieces in our hands, and, our plans crushed, we cast them aside. And so we returned to our sighs and laments, our steps following the broad and well-trodden paths of the world,[3] for many thoughts were in our hearts, but Your counsel abides in all eternity. And yet through that counsel You laughed at our designs and prepared Your own to grant us nourishment in due season and fill our souls with blessing.

[15. 25]   In the meantime my sins were multiplying, and when the woman with whom I shared my bed was torn from my side for being an impediment to my marriage,[4] my heart that clung to her was rent and bled. She returned to Africa, vowing before You never to know any other man, leaving with me the natural son I had had by her. But wretch that I was, I could not follow that woman's example. Impatient at the delay of my marriage, since it would be two years before I could have what I wanted, I procured for myself another woman, though not a wife; for I was not a lover of marriage but a slave to lust, so that the sickness of my soul was sustained and prolonged, remaining intact, even heightened, so that my habit could be guarded and tended until I reached the state of matrimony. Nor had the wound made by the parting with my former lover healed, but after inflammation and piercing pain it festered, and though the pain dulled, it also became more desperate.

* * *

2. Under Roman law, the minimum age for marriage was twelve, so the girl that Monica arranged for Augustine to marry must have been around ten. Augustine was in his early thirties at the time.

3. Cf. Matthew 7.13: "Broad is the way that leadeth to destruction," that is, to damnation.
4. This woman had been Augustine's companion since he was seventeen and had accompanied him from Carthage to Rome.

[*Conversion*]

[11. 25]   This was how ill and tormented I was, accusing myself more bitterly than ever, twisting and wrenching to break free of my chains that were easing but still held me fast. And You, Lord, penetrated my hidden depths with severe mercy, redoubling the lashes of fear[5] and shame lest I should succumb and not break the last frail fetters that remained, allowing them to grow strong once more and bind me all the tighter. And I said to myself deep inside, "Act now, the time to act is now." In my words I was already resolved. I almost acted, but did not; however, I did not fall back into my former state, but kept close and recovered my breath. I tried once more and came even closer, and closer, I could almost touch it, almost take hold of it, yet I could not reach it, neither touching nor taking hold of it, hesitating to die to death and to live to life. Greater was the sway of the evil to which I was accustomed than the goodness to which I was unaccustomed, and the more the moment neared in which I was to become another man, the more I was struck by horror; yet horror did not strike a decisive blow, nor did it turn me away, but held me suspended.

[11. 26]   I was being held in check by vain trifles and trifling vanities, my longstanding paramours tearing at my garment of flesh and whispering: "Will you send us away? From that moment on we shall never again be with you. From that moment on you will never again be allowed this and that." And what they meant by "this and that"! What were they suggesting, my God! Let Your mercy repulse it from Your servant's soul! What filth they were proposing, what infamy! Now I less than half heard them, and they did not dare come out to contradict me openly but muttered as if behind my back, plucking at me almost furtively so I would turn and look; but they managed to hold me back and delay me from tearing myself away and shaking myself free from them, and making the leap to where I was being summoned, while the force of my habits called out to me, "Do you think you can bear being without them?"

[11. 27]   But the force of my habit said this now quite faintly, for in the direction to which I had turned my face and to which I feared to go, Continence[6] had now appeared before me, chaste and dignified, serene, cheerful though without allurements, beckoning me with sincerity to come and not to doubt, her holy hands reaching out to receive and embrace me with a profusion of honest examples: so many youths and maidens, so many people of every age, sober widows and aged virgins, and among them stood Continence herself, not barren but a fertile mother of children, with joys granted her by You, Lord, her Husband. And she smiled, both teasing and encouraging me, as if she were saying: "Can you not do what these youths and maidens can? Do you think they managed on their own without the help of the Lord their God? The Lord their God gave me to them. Why do you persist on your own where you cannot persist? Cast yourself upon Him, do not be afraid. He will not withdraw and let you fall. Cast yourself upon Him without fear—He will receive and will heal you." I truly blushed, for I was also still listening to the whisperings of frivolity, and so lingered and delayed, and again it was as if Continence were

5. Virgil, *Aeneid* 5.547.
6. Self-control or abstinence, especially with regard to sexuality; here personified as a woman.

saying: "Shut your ears to your impure limbs that are upon the earth, so that they will be mortified. They speak to you of delights, but not as does the law of the Lord your God." This dispute within my heart was merely myself battling myself, and Alypius,[7] who was at my side, waited in silence for the end of my unusual agitation.

[12. 28] From hidden depths a profound introspection had gathered together and amassed all my misery before my heart's eye, and now a violent tempest arose within me, bringing a mighty shower of tears, and I got up and hastened away from Alypius so that my storm could gush forth with all its sounds and voices. Solitude seemed to me more fit for weeping, and I moved far enough away from him so that his presence would not burden me. That was the state I was in, and Alypius sensed it, for as I got up I think I said something in which my voice was choked with tears. Confounded, Alypius remained where we had sat. I collapsed beneath a fig tree, I do not remember how, and let my tears flow, streams pouring from my eyes, an acceptable sacrifice to You, and I said many things to You, not in these exact words, but to this purpose: "But You, O Lord, for how long? For how long, Lord? Will You be angry forever? Remember not our former iniquities."[8] For I felt that these iniquities were holding me in their grip. I uttered these wretched words: "How long, how long? Ever tomorrow and tomorrow? Why not right away? Why cannot my baseness come to an end this instant?"

[12. 29] I was speaking and weeping in the most bitter contrition of my heart, when I suddenly heard from a nearby house a voice—that of a boy or a girl, I could not tell—repeating in a singsong, "Pick up and read, pick up and read." That instant, my countenance changed and I began to wonder intently whether there could be some kind of game in which children sang such words, but I could not remember there being such a game. I checked the torrent of my tears and rose, concluding that these words were clearly a divine command that I open the Book and read the first line I found. I had heard how Saint Anthony[9] had come upon a reading of the Gospel and had understood the words he heard being read out as an admonition, as if they were being spoken to him: "Go, sell all you have and give it to the poor, and you will have treasure in heaven; and come, follow me."[1] With these divine words he was immediately converted to You. So I hastened back to the place where Alypius was sitting, for it was there that I had laid down the volume of the Apostle[2] when I had arisen. I seized it, opened it, and in silence read the verse upon which my eyes first fell: "Not in revelry and drunkenness, not in lewdness and lust, not in strife and envy. But put on the Lord Jesus Christ, and make not provision for the flesh in its concupiscences." I neither wished nor needed to read further. Instantly, at the end of

7. A student of Augustine's at Carthage; he had joined the Manicheans with Augustine, followed him to Rome and Milan, and now shared his desires and doubts. After converting to Christianity along with Augustine, Alypius eventually became a bishop in North Africa in 394.
8. Cf. Psalm 79.5–8; here, Augustine compares his spiritual despair with that of captive and subjugated Israel.
9. St. Anthony the Great, also called Anthony

of the Desert (ca. 251–356), a Coptic Christian saint whose biography by Athanasius of Alexandria was widely circulated throughout the Mediterranean and was credited with many conversions.
1. Luke 18.22.
2. The Apostle Paul; Augustine is reading Paul's letter to the Romans. Compare with Dante's *Inferno* V:134–5 on p. 952.

these lines, it was as if a light of serenity was pouring into my heart, and all the darkness of uncertainty dispersed.

[12. 30]   I shut the Book, putting my finger or some other mark between the pages, and with a calm countenance told Alypius what had happened. But he also apprised me of the change within him, of which I had not been aware. He asked to see what verse I had read. I showed it to him and he read it, and read further than I had; I did not know the verse that followed. What followed was, "Receive one who is weak in the faith," and Alypius told me that he was applying this to himself. This admonition gave him strength in his pious resolution and purpose, which truly corresponded to his character, in which he had always very much differed from me for the better, and without turbulent hesitation he joined me. We go inside to my mother, we tell her, she rejoices; we recount how it had come to pass; she exults, jubilates, and praises You Who are able to do beyond that which we desire or understand. She saw that You had granted her far more for me than she had begged for in her sad and tear-filled laments to You, for You had converted me to you so that I now sought neither a wife nor any ambition of this world, and stood firm upon that rule of faith as You had shown me to my mother in a dream so many years before.[3] And You converted her mourning into joy even more abundantly than she had hoped, and in a way that was much more precious and pure than she had sought in having grandchildren of my flesh.

* * *

FROM BOOK IX

[Death of His Mother]

[8. 17]   We were together, and were resolved to dwell together in our holy cause. In seeking a place where we could serve You to the best purpose, we all decided to return to Africa. We had just reached Ostia,[4] by the mouth of the Tiber, when my mother died. I have passed over so much, as I have written in haste—receive my avowals and my gratitude, my God, for the countless things about which I have been silent—but I will not pass over all that my mind can bring forth concerning Your handmaid who brought me forth, both in the flesh so that I might be born into this temporal light, and in the soul so that I might be born to eternal light. I will not speak of her gifts, but of Your gifts to her, for neither did she create nor raise herself. It was You Who created her; nor did her father and mother know who it was that had been born to them, and it was the rod and the staff of Your Christ that had reared her in holy fear—the discipline of Your only Son—in her father's Christian household at the hand of a certain virtuous member of Your Church. She commended her mother's attentiveness for the devout training she received, but commended even more the training she received from a very old servant, who had carried her father on her back when he had been a child, in the way that children used to be carried by

3. At Carthage, when Augustine was still a Manichean, Monica had dreamed that she was standing on a wooden ruler weeping for her son and then saw that he was standing on the same ruler as herself.

4. On the southwest coast of Italy; it was the port of Rome and the point of departure for Africa.

girls who were a little older. For this reason, and because of the servant's great age and excellent morals, she was greatly respected by the masters of that Christian household, which also accounted for the daughters of the house being left in her care. This task she undertook with great diligence, disciplining the girls with ardent and holy severity when it was necessary, and training them with profound attention. For example, beyond the hours in which they were fed with great moderation at their parents' table, though they might be burning with thirst she would not allow them to drink even water, thus forestalling an evil habit and adding these wise words: "You want to drink water now because you do not have recourse to wine, but when you come to be married and are made mistresses of your own pantries and cellars, you will dislike water, but still your habit of drinking it will remain." By this kind of instruction and the authority with which she commanded, she restrained the gluttony of tender years, and tempered the very thirst of the girls to such excellent moderation that they did not strive for anything that was not seemly.

[8. 18] And yet my mother's love for wine, as she, Your handmaid, confided in me her son, her love for wine had crept up on her, for when her parents, believing her to be a temperate girl, sent her to draw wine out of the barrel, she would hold the bowl under the spigot and, before pouring the wine into the pitcher, would take a little sip with pursed lips, for more than a sip she found repellent. And yet she had not done this out of a passion for drink but out of the ebullience of youth, in which the kind of playful impulses boil over that are usually kept in check by the authority of elders. But by always adding a little more to that daily sip—for one who despises small things will fall little by little—she had fallen into the habit of drinking entire cups of unmixed[5] wine. Where then was that watchful old woman with her strict restraint? But there would have been no remedy against this hidden disease if Your healing, Lord, did not preside over us. When father, mother, and nurses are away, You are present, You Who created us, who call us, who through those placed above us induce the salvation of our souls. What did You do then, my God? How did You cure her? How did You heal her? Did You not bring forth from the soul of another a sharp reproach, like a surgeon's knife from Your secret store, and with a single slash remove all the festering putrescence? A servant with whom she used to go to the barrel happened to quarrel with her little mistress when they were alone, deriding her for her deeds with bitter insult, calling her a drunken sot. The insult stung the little girl to the quick, and she reflected on the shameful thing she had done, instantly condemning and abandoning her habit. Just as flattering friends lead to ruin, so accusing enemies often lead to reform. Yet it is not for what You do through people that You reward them, but for what people do of their own volition. The servant in her anger had sought to hurt her young mistress, not to mend her ways, and she spoke her words in secret, either in the heat of quarrel or because she might be called to account for not having said anything earlier. But You, Lord, Ruler of heaven and earth, turn to Your purposes the course of the deepest torrents, and order the turbulence of the tide of time. Through the affliction of one soul You gave health to another, and all who hear this must realize that they must not attribute a person's reform to

---

5. I.e., unmixed with water.

their own powers, when someone whom they wish to reform is reformed through words they have spoken.

[9. 19]   So my mother was brought up in modesty and sobriety, and she was made obedient by You to her parents rather than being made obedient by her parents to You, so that as soon as she was of full age to be a bride she was bestowed upon a man whom she served as her lord. And she did everything in her power to win this man over to You, speaking to him of You through the qualities by which You had made her beautiful, filling her husband with respect and love for her as well as admiration. She tolerated his infidelity so that there would never be any animosity between them, for she was awaiting Your mercy upon him, that in believing in You he might become chaste. Furthermore, he was as exceptionally kind as he was hot-tempered, but she had learned not to cross an angry husband in word or deed. It was only when his temper had settled, and he was calm and approachable, that she would explain her actions if he had happened to be too quick to flare up in anger. Many other wives who had gentler husbands bore shameful marks of beatings on their faces, and among their friends would blame their husbands' ways. But she would blame the women's tongues, giving the women as if in jest the solemn advice that the instant they had heard the marriage contract read out to them, they should have recognized that they were now slaves, and, remembering their station, it would have been more fitting for them not to take on airs before their lords. When her friends found out what a violent husband she had, they were amazed that nobody had ever heard of Patricius[6] raising his hand to her or that she never bore the marks of a beating, and that there had never been discord among them even for a day. Asked how this could be, she told her friends her custom of responding to her husband's ire which I have mentioned above. The women who followed her example were to thank her, while those who did not suffered and remained oppressed.

[9. 20]   Her mother-in-law had initially been incited against her by the insinuations of malicious servants, but was assuaged by the young wife's gentle, yielding manner and her steadfast forbearance, so that she herself revealed to her son that meddling tongues had disrupted the peace in the home, causing trouble between her and her daughter-in-law, and she insisted that he punish the wrongdoers. Patricius respected his mother's wish, ensuring that discipline and peace returned to his home, and he had the maids whipped as his mother had asked, and she promised the same payment to any servant seeking to ingratiate herself by saying evil things about her daughter-in-law. As no servant now dared speak ill of her, they all lived pleasantly and amicably together.

[9. 21]   To this good handmaid of Yours in whose womb You created me, my God, my Mercy, You granted her another great gift, that of being a peacemaker to quarreling people whenever she could. When she heard bitter words bursting forth from both sides in bilious anger, when a friend spewed out acrid rage against an absent enemy, she would only reveal to either one whatever words might lead to their reconciliation. I might have considered this a minor gift had I not had the painful experience of encountering so many people, who by some horrendous and rampant pestilence of sin not only disclose to an irate

6. Augustine's father, believed to have been a Roman citizen and a pagan until he converted to Christianity on his deathbed.

person what their irate enemy said about them, but add things that were never said, whereas it ought to be clear to any humane person that he must not incite hostility between people through hostile words, if he cannot bring himself to use benign words to extinguish the hostility. That was how she was, for You had been the inner Teacher in the school of her heart.

[9. 22] Finally, toward the very end of her husband's life on earth, she converted him to You, and once he was a believer he no longer gave her cause to lament what she had had to bear before he had become a believer. She was also the servant of Your servants, of whom all who knew her greatly praised and honored and loved You in her; they felt Your presence in her heart, which was attested by the fruits of her devout comportment, for she had been the wife of one man, had honored her debt to her parents and run her house piously, had testimony for her good works, and she had brought up children, of whom she labored as if in birth whenever she saw them straying from You.[7] Lastly she took care of all of us,[8] Your servants, Lord, for Your gift allows me to speak on behalf of us all, who, before she closed her eyes in sleep, all lived united in You since we had received the grace of Your baptism. She cared for us as though she had given birth to us all, yet served us as though she had been the daughter of every one of us.

[10. 23] With the day looming on which she was to depart this life, a day that You knew but we did not, Your hidden ways arranged that she and I would stand alone gazing out of a window that overlooked the garden of the house in which we were staying in Ostia, by the mouth of the Tiber. In this house, far from all the noise and commotion, we were recuperating from the exertions of our long journey before we set sail across the sea. She and I were talking alone, in sweet conversation, forgetting the past and reaching out for what lay ahead, she and I wondering in the presence of the Truth, which You are, what the eternal life of saints would be like, which neither eye has seen nor ear has heard, nor has it entered into the heart of man. The mouth of our hearts opened wide to drink in those celestial streams of Your fountain, the fountain of life, which is with You, so that fortified to the extent that we could be, we might to some degree contemplate such a profound matter.

[10. 24] And when in our conversation we reached the conclusion that the greatest delight of the bodily senses, the greatest corporeal light, is not worthy of comparison to the sweetness of the eternal life of saints, not worthy even of mention, we were lifted with a greater glowing love toward God, the Selfsame.[9] We rose by degrees past everything corporeal to the very heaven where sun and moon and stars shine upon the earth, and ascended even higher with our thoughts and words, with our marveling at Your works, reaching these in our minds and transcending them, coming to that region of unceasing plenty where You feed Israel in eternity with the food of truth,[1] where life is the Wisdom through which all these things are made, all things that have been and shall be. But Wisdom is not made: Wisdom is as it has been and ever shall be. For there

7. Augustine is paraphrasing Paul's description of the duties of a widow, enumerated in 1 Timothy 5.
8. I.e., Augustine and his fellow converts.
9. Reality, the divine principle. This ecstasy of Augustine and Monica is described throughout in philosophical terms in which God is Wisdom.
1. Reference to the manna that fed the Israelites in the desert during their flight from Egypt; see Exodus 16.11–35.

is no *was* or *will be* in Wisdom, only *being*, as Wisdom is eternal. For *was* and *will be* are not eternal. While we were discussing and longing for Wisdom, we touched it lightly with the most ardent effort of our hearts, and we sighed and left behind us the first-fruits of the Spirit, returning to the mere sounds of our mouths, where words have a beginning and an end, and how can these words be compared to Your Word, our Lord, who remains in Himself without age and renews all things?

[10. 25]   So we said: "If the commotion of the flesh were to fall silent in a man, silent the images of the earth and the waters and the air, and silent the heavens, and the soul were silent to itself and by not thinking of itself would surpass itself, if all dreams and imaginary revelations were silent, and silent every tongue and every sign and all that exists only transiently, since if anyone could hear these things then this is what they all would say: 'We did not make ourselves, but He who abides in eternity made us.' If having said this they fell silent, having led us to open our ears to Him who made these things, and He alone would speak through Himself and not through them so that we would hear His Word not through a tongue of flesh, nor through an Angel's voice, nor through the thundering sound from the clouds, nor through an obscure enigma,[2] but we might hear Him whom in these things we love, hear Him without these things, just as we now reached out and in swift thought touched the Wisdom that abides over all things in eternity. If this could continue, and other visions that were far inferior could be withdrawn, and could this vision ravish and absorb and envelop its beholder in inward joys, so that eternal life would be like that one moment of understanding for which we longed, then would this not mean: 'Enter into the joy of your Lord'? And when would that be? When we shall all rise again, though we shall not all be changed?"[3]

[10. 26]   Such were the things that I was saying, and even if not exactly in this way or with those words, yet, Lord, You know that it was on that day when we were speaking, and, as she and I spoke, this world with all its delights became contemptible to us, and she said, "My son, as for me, I no longer delight in anything in this life anymore. I do not know what I am still doing here, or why I am here now, since my hopes in this world have all expired. The one thing for which I wanted to linger a while longer in this life was that I might see you a true Christian before I died, but my God has granted my wish in greater abundance than I had sought, for I now see that you despise earthly happiness and have become His servant. What am I doing here?"

[11. 27]   I do not remember what I answered, but within five days, not much more, she fell sick of a fever, and one day in her illness she fainted and for a moment lost consciousness. We rushed to her side, but she was soon revived, and seeing me and my brother near her, asked, "Where was I?" And then, looking straight at us as we stood there stunned with grief, she said, "It is here that you will bury your mother." I remained silent, refraining from tears, but my brother spoke, saying he would be happier if she did not die in a strange land but in her own. Hearing his words she looked at him anxiously, her eyes

---

2. Cf. Luke 8.10: "Unto you it is given to know the mysteries of the kingdom of God: but to others in parables; that seeing they might not see, and hearing they might not understand."

3. Cf. 1 Corinthians 15.52: "the trumpet shall sound, and the dead shall be raised incorruptible, and we shall be changed," referring to the Last Judgment.

admonishing him because such things were still important to him, and then looking at me said, "Do you hear what your brother says?" and turning to us both, "Bury this body anywhere, and do not worry about such trifles. The only thing I ask of you is that wherever you may be, you will remember me at the Lord's altar." And having expressed her feeling in such words as she could still utter, she fell silent, overwhelmed by her growing illness.

[11. 28] But as I thought of Your gifts, O invisible God, which You plant in the hearts of those faithful to You and from which wondrous fruits spring, I rejoiced and gave thanks to You, recalling the worry that had burned within her about arranging and preparing a tomb next to her husband's body. Since they had lived together in great harmony, she had also wished to have this addition to that happiness and to have this commemorated among men—so slightly is the human mind able to embrace divine things—wishing that after her pilgrimage beyond the sea the same earth should cover her and her husband's earthly remains. I did not know when, through the wealth of Your goodness, these empty trifles had begun to subside in her heart, but I rejoiced, surprised at what she had divulged to me, even if in our conversation by the window, when she had said, "I do not know what I am still doing here," she no longer appeared to desire to die in her own country. I was to hear later, too, that while we were at Ostia she had one day, when I was absent, spoken with a mother's confidence to some of my friends about her contempt for this life and the goodness of death. Amazed at the courage You had given to a woman, they had asked whether she was not afraid to leave her body so far from her own city, to which she replied: "Nothing is far away from God, nor is it to be feared that at the ends of the earth He would not know from where He should resurrect me." Then on the ninth day of her illness, in the fifty-sixth year of her life and the thirty-third of mine, that pious and religious soul was freed from her body.

[12. 29] I closed her eyes, and pouring into my heart was a vast sorrow that overflowed into tears, though my eyes, under the strict command of my mind, redrank the fountain dry, the struggle causing great strife within me. At her last breath my son Adeodatus[4] broke into laments, but, checked by us all, fell silent. In the same way, the child within me strove toward weeping but was checked and silenced by the voice of my heart, for we did not think it was fitting to celebrate the funeral with tearful cries and lamentations, as in this way so many people lament the misery of the state of death, or death as complete eradication, whereas she was neither unhappy in her death, nor entirely dead: of this we were certain because of the evidence of the life she had led and her unfeigned faith.

[12. 30] What was it that was hurting me so grievously within if not the fresh wound caused by the sudden shattering of the sweetest and most beloved custom of our life together? I was delighted with her words when, in her final illness, she countered my attentions with endearments and said that I was an affectionate son, avowing with great emotion and love that she had never heard from my mouth a single harsh or reproachful word against her. And yet, my God Who has made us, what comparison could there be between the esteem I showed her and her selfless servitude to me? My soul was wounded, losing

---

4. Adeodatus was then about fifteen or sixteen years old.

such a great solace in her. It was as if my life was torn in two, since her life and mine had been as one.

[12. 31]   My son having been stopped from weeping, Euodius took up the Psalter and began to chant, our whole household answering him: "I will sing of mercy and justice to You, O Lord."[5] The news spread and many brethren and religious women gathered, and while those whose office it was began to prepare the burial, I withdrew to another part of the house where, with friends who deemed I should not be left alone, I could aptly speak about matters suitable to the moment. The balm of truth soothed my torment that was known to You but unknown to them, and they listened to me intently, supposing that I felt no sorrow. But in Your ears, where none of them could hear, I blamed the weakness of my feelings and restrained my flow of grief, which for a while ceded to my will; yet its force overcame me once more, though not as tears bursting forth or my countenance changing. But I knew what I was suppressing within my heart. I was extremely unhappy with myself that these human matters, which in the due order and lot of our condition inevitably fall to us, could have such power over me and with new grief I grieved over my grief, and so was consumed by a double sorrow.

[12. 32]   When her body was carried out for burial, we went and returned without tears. I did not weep during the prayers we poured forth to You when the sacrifice of our redemption[6] was offered for her, nor during the prayers when her body was placed beside the tomb before being interred, as is the custom; but the entire day I was profoundly sad within, and with troubled mind prayed to You as best I could that You would heal my sorrow, though You did not, impressing by this lesson upon my memory, I believe, the strength of the chains of habit upon the mind, even when it does not feed on deceit. It seemed also good to me to go and bathe, having heard that the Latin word for bath, *balneum*, had its name from the Greek *balaneion*,[7] casting anguish from the mind. This too I avow to Your mercy, Father of orphans, that I bathed and was the same as I had been before I bathed, for the bitterness of sorrow did not exude from my heart. Then I slept, woke up, but found that my grief had not softened at all. Alone as I lay in my bed, I remembered those true verses of Your Ambrose,[8] for You are

> God, Creator of all things,
> Ruler of Heaven who vests
> The day with beauteous light
> The night with reposing sleep
> Loosening man's limbs in rest
> Restoring them, refreshed for labor
> Relieving the minds of the wearied
> Untangling the sorrows of the distressed.

[12. 33]   Then gradually I returned to my former thoughts of Your handmaid, remembering her pious attachment to You and the holy helpfulness and

---

5. Cf. Psalm 101.1. "Euodius": one of Augustine's community of Christian converts.
6. Perhaps a communion service.
7. Augustine evidently derives *balaneion* ("bath") from the words *ballō* ("cast away")

and *ania* ("sorrow").
8. Ambrose (ca. 337–397), bishop of Milan and mentor to Augustine, was the author of many theological works as well as poetic hymns.

tenderness to us of which I was suddenly deprived: and I wanted to weep in Your sight for her and on her account, for myself and on my account. And I released the tears I had restrained, letting them pour forth, strewing them out so that my heart could rest in them, and my heart found repose for it was in Your ears, not in those of man who would have eyed my tears with scorn. And now, Lord, I confess this to You in writing: let him read it who will and interpret it how he may, and if he finds it to be sinful that I wept for my mother for a few minutes, the mother who was now dead to my eyes and who for many years had wept for me that I might live in Your eyes, let him not scorn me, but rather if he is a man of great love, let him weep for my sins before You, the Father of all the brethren of Your Christ.

[13. 34]   Now, my heart healed of that wound in which I could be blamed of a fleshly state of mind, before You, our God, I shed very different tears for Your maidservant, tears flowing from a spirit shaken by the thoughts of the danger every soul that dies in Adam faces,[9] though she had been made alive in Christ even before she was released from the flesh; for she had lived so that Your name would be praised in her faith and the life she led. But I do not dare claim that from the moment You regenerated her through baptism no word against Your precepts issued from her mouth. Your Son, the Truth, has said, "Whoever shall say to his brother 'you fool' shall be in danger of the fire of Gehenna."[1] And woe even to commendable lives of men, if You should examine their lives casting mercy aside. But because You do not fiercely scrutinize our sins, we hope with confidence to find some place with You. But whoever enumerates his real merits to You is merely enumerating Your gifts. If only men would know themselves to be but men, and that he who glories would glory in the Lord.

[13. 35]   Therefore, God of my heart, my Praise and my Life, laying aside for a while my mother's good deeds for which I give thanks to You with joy, I now beseech You for her sins. Hear me by the Healer of our wounds[2] Who hung upon the cross and sits at Your right hand interceding with You on our behalf! I know that she always acted with compassion, and from her heart forgave her debtors their debts. Forgive her debts too, Lord, if she contracted any in the many years since she received the water of salvation. Forgive, Lord, forgive, I beseech You, and enter not into judgment with her. May mercy exalt above justice, since Your words are true and You have promised mercy to the merciful. That the merciful be so was Your gift to them, You Who will have mercy on whom You will have mercy and will have compassion on whom You have compassion.

[13. 36]   And I believe that You have already done what I am begging of You, but accept, Lord, the willing offerings of my mouth, for as the day of her release was imminent she gave no thought to having her body sumptuously wrapped or embalmed with perfumes, nor did she ask for an excellent monument or seek to be buried in her native land. She did not enjoin us to do these things, but asked only to be remembered at Your Altar at which she had served without missing a single day, for she knew that it is there that the holy sacrifice

9. I.e., with the curse of Adam not nullified through baptism in Jesus Christ and conformity with his teachings.
1. From Matthew 5.22, Jesus's Sermon on the

Mount. He is preaching a more severe moral code than the traditional one that whoever kills shall be liable to judgment. "Gehenna": hell.
2. Jesus.

is dispensed through which the handwriting of the decree against us is blotted out.[3] It is there that the enemy summing up our sins and seeking with what to charge us is vanquished, finding nothing in Him in Whom we are victors. Who will restore to Him His innocent blood? Who will repay Him the price with which He bought us and so take us from Him? To the Sacrament of this price Your handmaid bound her soul by the bond of faith. Let none sever her from Your protection. Let neither the lion nor the dragon[4] interpose themselves by force or trickery. She will reply that she owes nothing, lest she be refuted and seized by the wily accuser. She will reply that her debts have been forgiven her by Him to Whom none can repay the price that He, Who owed nothing, paid for us.

[13. 37]   So may she rest in peace with the husband before and after whom she had no other, whom she served bringing forth with patience fruit unto You, that she might also gain him for You. Inspire, my Lord, my God, inspire Your servants my brethren, Your sons my masters, whom I serve with voice and heart and pen, that all who read this may at Your altar remember Monnica Your maidservant, with Patricius who was once her husband, by whose flesh You brought me into this life, how I do not know.[5] May they all remember with pious affection those who were my parents in this transient light and all my brethren under You our Father in our mother the Christian Church, and my fellow-citizens in that eternal Jerusalem[6] for which Your wandering people are yearning from their exodus to their return. This way my mother's last request of me will, through my confessions, be far more abundantly fulfilled by the prayers of many, than by my prayers alone.

* * *

FROM BOOK XI

[Time]

[14. 17]   Hence there was no time when you had not made something, because You had made time itself. And no times are coeternal with You, because You abide, but if they were to abide they would not be times. For what is time? Who can explain this simply and in a few words? Who can comprehend it in thought so as to express it in words? And yet, when we converse, do we ever speak of anything with greater familiarity than of time? And we know what time is when we speak of it, just as we do when we hear another speak of it. So what is time? If no one asks me this, then I know; but if I am forced to explain it to someone who asks, then I do not know, though I will boldly maintain that I do know: that if nothing passed there would be no past time, and if nothing were to come then there would be no future, and if nothing is, then there would be no present time. So how do those two times—the past and the future—exist if the past does not exist now and the future does not yet exist? As for the present, if it were always present and never passed into the past, it would be not time, but

---

3. An allusion to Christ's redemption of humanity from the curse of Adam through the Crucifixion.
4. Cf. Psalm 91.13: "Thou shalt tread upon the lion and the adder: the young lion and the dragon shalt thou trample under feet, which invokes

God's protection of the godly."
5. I.e., Augustine does not understand the seemingly miraculous process by which the fetus grows in the womb.
6. That is, heaven.

eternity. Thus if the present, in order to be time, only comes into being because it passes into the past, how can we maintain that it exists if the aim of its being is that it will not be. Can we in truth maintain that time exists because its aim is not to exist?

* * *

[18. 23]   Permit me, my Lord and my Hope, to seek further. Let not my quest be confounded. For if past and future things exist I want to know where they are, which if I am still unable to know, at least I know that wherever they are, they are not there as future or past, but as present; for if they are also there as future, they are not yet there, and if they are also there as past, they are no longer there. Thus wherever and whatever they are, they only exist as present. When true things are recounted from the past, it is not the past things themselves that are brought forth from the memory, but words generated from their images that, as they passed through the senses, were fixed as imprints in the mind. Hence my childhood, which now no longer exists, is in the past that now no longer exists: but as I recall and recount its image, I behold it in the present because it still exists in my memory. Whether there is a similar process in foretelling things of the future, if one can preview the images of things that do not yet exist, I confess, my God, I do not know. What I do know is that we often first think our future actions through, and that this thinking through is present, but the action we are thinking through does not yet exist because it is a future action. It is only once we have embarked on this action, and have begun to do what we were thinking through, that this action exists, because then it is no longer future, but present.

[18. 24]   Whatever the nature of this mysterious sensing of future things, nothing can be seen that does not exist. But what now exists is not future, but present. Thus when things of the future are said to be seen, it is not the actual things that are seen, which do not yet exist—that is, which are future—but perhaps what is seen is their causes or signs that already exist. Hence these things are not future but are present to those who see the things from which the future, being generated in the mind, is foretold. Such generated things already exist, and those who foretell the future behold them as present before them. Let me take one example from a great number of examples: I see daybreak and predict the rising of the sun. What I see is present, what I foresee is future—not the sun being future, as it already exists, but its rising, which has not yet occurred. If I could not imagine in my mind the rising itself, as I do now in speaking of it, I would not be able to foretell it. Yet the daybreak that I see in the sky is not the sunrise, though it precedes it, just as the imagining of it in my mind is not the sunrise either. Both of these are discerned as present, so that the future sunrise can be foretold. Hence future things do not yet exist, and if they do not yet exist, they do not exist and cannot be seen. But they can be foretold from things that are present, which do exist and so can be seen.

* * *

[20. 26]   What is now clear and plain is that neither future things nor things of the past exist, nor can one rightly say, "There are three times: past, present, and future," though one might rightly say, "There are three times: a present of things past, a present of things present, and a present of things future." These three do in some way exist in the mind, for I do not see them anywhere else: The present of things past is memory, the present of things present is what I am seeing, and the present of things future is expectation. If I can express myself in these terms, I see three times, and I acknowledge that there are three. But we can actually say, "There are three times: past, present, and future." It is wrong, but that is how we say it. I do not take offense or find fault with what is said in this way if it is understood to mean that neither the future nor the past are present now. There is so little that we name correctly—most things we do not—but we do manage to impart what we mean.

* * *

[26. 33] Does not my soul confess to You in all truth that I measure time? Is it, my God, that I am measuring and do not know what I am measuring? If I am measuring the movement of a body in time, am I not measuring time itself? Would I be able to measure the movement of a body, the duration of the movement, and how long it takes to move from one place to another, without measuring the time in which it moves? So how do I measure time itself? Do we use a shorter time to measure a longer time, the way we measure the length of a crossbar in cubits? We also tend to use the length of a short syllable to measure the length of a long syllable, calling it twice as long. We measure the length of poems by the length of the lines, and the length of the lines by the length of the feet, and the length of the feet by the length of the syllables, and the length of long syllables by the length of short. We do not measure the poem by its pages, for that way we would be measuring space, not time, but once we have declaimed the poem's words and they pass on, we say, "It is a long poem, because it is made up of so many lines; the lines are long, because they are made up of so many feet; they are long feet, since they stretch over so many syllables; it is a long syllable because it is twice as long as the syllable that is short." But even in this way we cannot determine a precise measurement of time, because it could be that a shorter line is spoken with more gravity and so takes up more time than a longer line declaimed with urgency. The same is true for a poem, a foot, a syllable. This has led me to believe that time is simply a distention, but of what I do not know, though it would be surprising if it were not of the mind itself. For I beseech You, my God, what is it that I am measuring, when I say either indefinitely, "This time is longer than that time," or definitely "This time is twice that"? I know that I measure time, but I do not measure the future, because it does not yet exist, nor do I measure the present, because it does not extend over any expanse, nor do I measure the past, because it no longer exists. So what is it that I am measuring? Perhaps the passing times, not those that have passed? This is what I have said before.

* * *

[31. 41] Lord my God, how deep are the recesses of Your mysteries, and how far from them have I been cast by the consequences of my errors! Heal my eyes so that with Your Light I can rejoice! If a mind existed that was graced with such great knowledge and prescience so as to know all things past and future, the way I know a well-known hymn, that mind would be most miraculous and awe-inspiring, for nothing that has taken place and nothing that is to come in future ages would elude this mind, just as when I sing that hymn it would not elude me how much of it had passed since I had begun singing, and what and how much of the hymn still remained. But far be it that You, the Creator of the universe, the Creator of minds and bodies, far be it that You should know all things future and past in that way: You know them far more wonderfully and mysteriously. Someone who sings or hears a hymn he knows will feel his perception change and expand as he anticipates the words to come and remembers the words that have past. But this is not so with You Who are unchangeably eternal, the eternal Creator of minds. Just as You knew in the Beginning the heaven and the earth without any change of Your knowledge, so You made in the Beginning the heaven and the earth without Your action expanding. Let him who understands confess to You, and let him who does not understand confess to You. How exalted You are and yet You dwell in those who are humble in heart! You raise up all who are cast down, and those whose sublimity you are do not fall.

THE QUR'AN

610–32

The word *qur'an* literally means "the recitation." For Muslims, the Qur'an is not so much a book as a living and vibrant act of speech that has been passed down through an unbroken chain of human beings from the time of Muhammad, who with his companions in seventh-century Arabia formed the first community of Muslims. At the same time, the Qur'an is also conceived of as a book: not a literal object on the shelf but a divine work that exists only in the heavenly realm of paradise. Any physical copy of the Arabic text is thought of as a pale reflection of that ideal book, a tool to enable the reader to memorize and then recite the Qur'anic text. As divine speech, moreover, the Qur'an can never be rendered perfectly in the medium of the human voice, a deficiency that testifies to its fundamental inimitability, or *i'jaz*. In accord with this view of the nature of the Qur'an, no translation into any other language is thought of as actually being the holy book itself. The most that any translation can be, for the believer, is an aid to understanding the original.

The Qur'an presents itself as the last of a sequence of revealed holy books, including the Torah (in Arabic, Tawrat), the Psalms (Zabur), and the Gospels (Injil). Similarly, Muhammad is presented as one in a lineage of prophets (that is, those who have received communications directly from God) that begins with the first man, Adam. Earlier holy books each have an associated prophet: for the Torah, Moses; for the Psalms, David; and for the Gospels, Jesus and also Mary—who, despite being female, is also recognized as part of the prophetic lineage. Indeed, a minority of classical Muslim scholars, including Ibn Hazm (d. 1065), considered her to be a prophet outright. Stories and characters from Jewish and Christian scripture reappear in the Qur'an, as seen in the chapters (or surahs) on Joseph and Mary. When hearing these verses, the earliest converts to Islam, drawn from the local Christian and Jewish communities located in Arabia, would have marveled at the different perspective brought to bear on familiar stories by this new revelation. The Qur'an recognizes the followers of other monotheistic religions, such as Jews and Christians, as "people of the Book"—those who follow the word of God as revealed by his prophets. From the point of view of Islam, the people of the Book who lived before the revelation of the Qur'an were also followers of *islam*, in the literal sense of "submission" to God's will. Those who continued to reverence their own, pre-Islamic holy books, such as Jews and Christians, could be tolerated within the Muslim community, but this inclusiveness of monotheism had its limits. Muslims generally viewed their Prophet as the last of his kind, "the seal of prophets," and the Qur'an as the last holy book that would ever be revealed to humanity. The Torah and the Gospels, while divine in their inspiration, had become corrupt over time. Only through submission to the divine will as revealed in the Qur'an, Muslims believed, could the faithful be sure they would enter into paradise and avoid the punishments of hell.

Only from the nineteenth century on has the **Bible** begun to be read as a work of literature as well as a divinely inspired text, and so too this dual focus on the Qur'an has been recent. From the Middle Ages to the twenty-first century, Western readers of the Qur'an have all too often condemned what they saw as its theological deviance and narrative incoherence. As a result, Muslims have hesitated to offer up the Qur'an for study within the framework of literary history or to allow it to move beyond the conservative framework of faith-based perspectives. This attitude has begun to change, however, because of innovative approaches to Qur'anic interpretation

on the part of Muslim communities and an increasing willingness to place the Qur'an into dialogue with other sacred scriptures. The Qur'an itself invites comparison with other literary traditions—most explicitly, the rich traditions of oral poetry found in pre-Islamic Arabia. In that context, it appears as a marvel of literature whose divine inspiration is manifest in the form of lyrical chant and resonant verse. Reading the Qur'an on the page, in translation, weakly conveys its virtue, which can be appreciated only in the musical oral recitation (*tajwid*) that reveals the rhythmic quality of the verse and the haunting repetition of syllables at the ends of successive lines. It is possible to get a sense of this music in the repeated refrain of the surah "The All-Merciful" ("Ar Rahman"), translated below.

The Qur'an is divided into 144 surahs, some of which are quite short; others are very long, resembling a biblical book in form. Each surah is made up of a number of verses (*ayat*; singular *aya*). The Qur'an is also conventionally divided up into thirty sections (*ajza'*; singular *juz'*) of roughly equal length to facilitate recitation of the entire work over the period of one month. Because of the emphasis placed on its oral recitation, which must be performed as part of the five daily prayers, Muslims begin to memorize the Qur'an at a young age; they start with the introductory surah, "The Opening" ("Al-Fatiha"), and continue on with the short Meccan surahs that are concentrated near the end of the Qur'an, including "Purity" ("Al-Ikhlas"). Instead of being arranged in the order that Muhammad received them, the surahs are arranged as Muhammad said he had been instructed by God. Some of the surahs were revealed at Mecca, when the Muslim community was starting to develop, and others at Medina, where the persecuted community took refuge; the two types tend to differ not only in length but also in subject matter and in tone. Instead of being carefully separated, however, the Meccan and Medinan surahs are intermingled, and many of the Meccan surahs dating from early in Muhammad's prophetic mission appear near the end of the text. The effect is one of fragments arranged in a mosaic—yet that mosaic has a very clearly defined form, delineated by strands running throughout. The repetition of phrases and motifs across surahs, often from different periods, creates a pattern as intricate as a woven tapestry.

With the exception of "Light" and "The All-Merciful," which were revealed at Medina, the excerpts reproduced here are Meccan surahs, which tend to be relatively short. Our aim was to provide entire chapters rather than abbreviated selections, so that the highly structured nature of the surahs could be grasped. The tightly ordered form illustrated on the level of the individual surah is also evident more generally in the Qur'an, in which the parts all contribute to make up the whole, but each part can also stand for the whole. Several of the surahs are known by another name, reflecting this part–whole relationship: "The Opening," which is the first surah, is also known as "The Mother of the Book," while surah "Ya Sin" is sometimes called "The Heart of the Qur'an." One of the last surahs, "Purity," was described by Muhammad himself as being "one-third of the Qur'an," because its highly condensed verses on the unity of God encapsulate the very core of Islamic theology. Other surahs, such as "Joseph" and "Mary," illuminate the extent to which the Qur'an is intertwined with Jewish and Christian faith traditions. Similarly, "Light" provides an Islamic vision of the divine that resonates with both the Neoplatonic concept of intellectual illumination and the Zoroastrian veneration of fire.

The Qur'an was received by Muhammad through the mediation of the angel Gabriel (Jibreel) over a period of about twenty-three years, beginning when he was forty years old and ending with his death in 632. During that time, the Qur'an existed as an oral recitation, repeated both by Muhammad himself and by the growing community of Muslims. After Muhammad's death, the community recognized the need to record the oral text to ensure that errors not creep into the recitation. The closest companions of Muhammad, under the supervision of the first caliph (or ruler) of the Muslim community, Abu Bakr, assembled the Qur'an in written form. The third caliph, Uthman, supervised the finalized version of the text, which was completed in 651, and then ordered all imperfect copies to be destroyed. It is this version of the Qur'an that we read today. Translations began to be produced almost immediately, beginning with a rendering of "The Opening" into the Persian language by Salman, one of the companions of the Prophet Muhammad. A full Persian translation of the Qur'an was made in the ninth century, attesting to the rapid embrace of Islam by the inhabitants of Persia (modern Iran). As is the case today, these translations were not made with the purpose of substituting Qur'anic verses in the local vernacular for the Arabic originals during prayer; instead, they were aids to understanding intended to enable fuller assimilation of the Arabic scripture within a new culture. Western audiences started to read the Qur'an in the Middle Ages, beginning with Robert of Ketton's Latin translation in 1143. The Qur'an is never accompanied by pictorial illustrations, in keeping with the Islamic practice of iconoclasm (the prohibition of any representation of living things, thereby avoiding the temptation of idolatry). It is, however, often rendered in elaborate calligraphy, a style of writing so ornate that it becomes art, fusing word with image in the aural masterpiece that is the Qur'an.

The Qur'an

Surah 1: The Opening[1]

1. In the Name of God,
   the All-Merciful, Ever-Merciful:[2]
2. All praise to God, Lord of the universe,[3]
3. the All-Merciful, Ever-Merciful;
4. Ruler on the Day of Reckoning
5. You alone we worship; and You alone
   we implore for help.
6. Guide us to the straight path,
7. the path of those whom You have favoured, not
   of those who have incurred Your wrath, nor
   of those who have gone astray.

Surah 12: Yusuf, or Joseph[1]

In the Name of God, the All-Merciful, Ever-Merciful

I

1. *Alif Lam Ra.*[2]
   These are the verses
   of the Manifest Book.

2. We[3] have sent it
   as an Arabic Qur'an,
   so you might
   understand.

3. We narrate to you
   the sublimest of narratives
   in revealing to you
   this Qur'an,
   though before this, you
   were indeed
   among the heedless.

---

1. Translated by M. A. R. Habib and Bruce B. Lawrence.
2. Though it appears at the outset of every chapter in the 114 chapters of the Qur'an except one (Q 9), it is only here that the *basmala*—"In the Name of God"—is treated as a verse. Its importance is underscored by its two qualifiers, "All-Merciful, Ever-Merciful" (*ar-Rahman* and *ar-Rahim*), derived from *ar-rahmah* (the mercy), which in turn derives from *ar-raham* (the womb).
3. Literally, "the worlds, or all worlds" (*'Alamin*,

pl. of *'alam*), including both Jinn and angels (see multiple references in the Qur'an, especially Q55 below on the Jinn).
1. Cf. Genesis 37.9–11.
2. *Alif Lam Ra* are an instance of what is known as the disaggregated or disconnected letters. They occur in 29 chapters, always at the beginning, and include about one half, or 14, of the 28 letters in the Arabic alphabet.
3. Throughout the Qur'an, "We" is used to express the voice of God (in Arabic "Allah").

4. When Joseph said
to his father: "My father,
I saw, in a dream, eleven stars
and the sun and moon:
I saw them bowing down
before me,"

5. he replied: "My son,
don't narrate this dream
to your brothers, lest they
plan a plot against you;
for surely Satan is
a manifest adversary
to humankind."

6. "Thus will your Lord choose you,
and teach you
the deeper meaning of events,
and perfect His favor
upon you and the family
of Jacob, as He
perfected it
before, upon your fathers
both, Abraham and Isaac[4]
for truly your Lord is
the Knowing, the Wise."

II

7. Surely, in [the story
of] Joseph and his brothers
are signs for those
who ask.

8. [His brothers] said: "Joseph
and his brother are dearer
to father than we,
though we are a larger body;
our father is in manifest error."

9. "Kill Joseph or cast him out
in some far land,
so your father will
turn his face to you alone;
and after this, you can be
a righteous community."

4. Isaac is Jacob's father, and Abraham is his grandfather; all three are recognized as prophets in Islam.

10. One of them said: "Don't kill
Joseph; if you must
act on this, throw him down
to the well's dark depth, so
some caravan will pick him up."

11. They said: "Father,
why won't you trust
us with Joseph?
For truly, we have
good will for him."

12. "Send him tomorrow with us;
so he'll enjoy himself and play,
and we'll be sure we
guard him well."

13. [Jacob] said: "It truly grieves me
that you take him, for I fear
the wolf might eat him
while you're not heeding him."

14. They said: "If the wolf
should eat him
—though we are a large body—
we would surely be among the lost."

15. So they took him,
and they all agreed
to throw him down
to the well's dark depth.
But We inspired him: "You will surely
in time apprise them of this deed of theirs
when they have grown unaware."

16. They came, then,
to their father
in the evening,
weeping.

17. They said: "Father,
we went racing, and left
Joseph with our things; then
the wolf devoured him.
You won't believe us,
even though we speak the truth.

18. They showed his shirt, soiled
with false blood. "No!" He cried,
"Your minds have enticed
you to some misdeed.
But patience is beautiful

and [I invoke] the help of God
against what you plead."

19. And a caravan came, travelers,
who sent to the well their water-carrier,
and he lowered his bucket.
"What good luck," he cried,
"Here is a boy!"
And they stowed him
in their merchandise. And God
is Aware of what they do.

20. They sold him
for a low price,
for a few silver coins,
such low regard
they had for him.

III

21. The man—Egyptian—
who bought him
told his wife: "Make easeful
his lodging; perhaps he'll
profit us or we'll
adopt him as a son."
And so We settled
Joseph in the land,
that We might teach him
the deeper meaning of events.
And so God prevails
in His affairs; but most
people do not know.

22. When he reached his prime,
We endowed him
with sound judgment and knowledge:
so We reward those who do good.

23. The woman, in whose house
he stayed, tried to seduce him;[5]
she secured the doors
and said, "Come close!"
"God forbid!" he said,
"He is my lord; he made
pleasant my lodging. Those
who do wrong will
surely not prosper."

5. Cf. Genesis 39.7–41.45.

24. She lusted
for him, and he
would have lusted for her, had he
not seen proof
from his Lord; so We kept
evil and unclean deeds
away from him, for he
was one of Our pure servants.

25. And they both raced
for the door, and she
tore his shirt from
behind, and they both
found her husband by the door.
"What penalty can there be,"
she cried, "for one
who designed evil against your wife,
but prison or torture?"

26. [Joseph] said: "It was she
who tried to seduce me."
Someone from her family
bore witness:
"If his shirt is torn
from the front, then
she speaks truthfully
and he is a liar."

27. "But if his shirt
is torn from behind,
then she is lying,
and he is truthful."

28. So when [the husband] saw his shirt
torn from behind, he said:
"This is your women's guile,
your guile is great indeed."

29. "Joseph, let this pass,
and wife, beg forgiveness
for your wrong; you
surely are a sinner."

IV

30. Women gossiped in the city:
"The governor's wife sought
to seduce her manservant
who has inflamed her
with love: we see her
openly straying."

31. When she heard
their gossip, she sent for them
and prepared for them
a banquet. She gave each of them
a knife; and said to Joseph:
"Come before them!"
When they saw him,
they so marveled at him,
they cut their hands, remarking:
"God save us! This is
no mortal—this is none other
than a noble angel!"

32. She said: "This
is the man on whose account
you reproved me!
Yes, I tried to seduce him
but he refused.
Yet, if he does not do
what I command, he'll be
thrown into prison,
ignominious."

33. He said: "My Lord,
prison is dearer to me
than what they call me to;
unless You turn away
their guile from me,
I might succumb to them,
in ignorance."

34. So his Lord answered him
and turned their guile
away from him. He is indeed
the Hearing, the Knowing.

35. Then it occurred to them,
after they had seen the signs
[of his virtue],
to imprison him awhile.

v

36. Entering the prison with him
were two young men. One of them
said: "I dreamt that I
was pressing wine." The other
said: "I dreamt that I
was carrying, on my head,
some bread, which birds
were pecking.

Tell us the deeper meaning
for we see you are
one of those who do good."

37. He said: "Surely, no food will
come to sustain you
before I inform you
of the dreams' deeper meaning.
This is part of what
my Lord has taught me.
I have left the creed
of a people who
disbelieve in God and who
deny the hereafter."

38. "And I follow the creed
of my forefathers, Abraham,
Isaac, and Jacob; it is not for us
to ascribe to God partners
of any kind—through God's
Grace upon us, and upon
humankind, though most
of humankind are ungrateful."

39. "My fellow prisoners,
which is better: many lords
differing among themselves,
or the One God,
the Omnipotent?"

40. "Besides Him, you worship nothing
but names—named by you—
you and your forefathers—
for which God has revealed
no sanction. Judgment belongs
to none but God. He
commands that you worship
none but Him. This is
the right religion, though
most of humankind
do not know.

41. "Fellow prisoners, one
of you will serve his lord
with wine; the other
will be crucified, and birds
will peck at his head.
This is the decree
in the matter on which
you both inquired."

42. And he said to the one
he thought would go free,
"Mention me to your lord."
But Satan made him forget
to mention him to his lord.
So [Joseph] remained in prison
a few years more.

VI

43. The king said:
"I saw, in a dream,
seven fat cows, which
seven lean ones devoured;
and seven ears of corn, green,
and seven others, withered.
Counselors, explain to me
my dream, if you can indeed
interpret dreams."

44. They said: "A confusing miscellany
of dreams; and we are not
versed in the deeper meaning
of dreams."

45. He, of the two, who was freed
now remembered, after all this time,
and said: "I shall disclose to you
its deeper meaning.
Dispatch me, then [to visit Joseph,
whom he then asked]:

46. "Joseph, you who
are truthful, explain
to us the meaning [of a dream]
of seven fat cows
which seven lean ones
devour, and of seven
ears of corn, green,
and seven others, withered,
so I may return
to the people, so they
may know."

47. He replied: "You will sow,
as usual, for seven years,
and what you reap, you will store,
leaving it in the ear, all
but a little, from which
you will eat."

48. "After that shall come
seven harsh years
which shall consume
what you have prepared
for them, all
but a little, which
you will preserve."

49. "Then after that shall come
a year in which the people
shall have abundant rain
and will press grapes."

VII

50. So the king said:
"Bring him to me."
But when the envoy
came to [Joseph, Joseph] said:
"Return to your lord,
and ask him the mind
of the women who
cut their hands.
Surely my Lord is
Aware of their guile."

51. The king said to the women:
"Tell me of the time
when you tried to seduce
Joseph?" They said:
"God forbid, we learned
nothing evil about him."
The governor's wife said:
"Now the truth is out:
It was I who tried to seduce him;
and he, without doubt, is telling the truth."

52. [Joseph said;][6]
"By this, my master may know
that I never was faithless to him
in his absence, and that God
will not guide the guile
of the treacherous."

53. "And I do not absolve
my own soul; the soul
is ever prone to evil,
unless my Lord affords

---

6. Some translators attribute these words to the governor's wife.

mercy. My Lord
is Forgiving,
Ever-Merciful."

54. And the king said:
"Bring him to me;
so I may keep him
for myself."
So when he had spoken
with him, he said:
"Today, we confer on you
power and trust."

55. Joseph said: "Let me
oversee the granaries
of the land: I will be
a wary custodian."

56. So We gave Joseph
power in the land, to live
wherever he wished. We bestow
Our mercy on whom
We will, nor will We forsake
the reward of those
who do good.

57. But the reward
of the Hereafter
is better, for those
who believe and are
mindful of God.

VIII

58. And the brothers of Joseph
arrived, and came before him,[7]
and he recognized them,
but they did not know him.

59. And when he had
provided them with supplies,
he said: "Bring to me
a brother of yours,
born of your own father.[8] Do you
not see that I trade fairly,
in full measure, and that I
am most gracious as a host?"

---

7. Cf. Genesis 42.3–46.7.
8. Benjamin, Joseph's full brother; his other brothers have different mothers.

60. "But if you don't
bring him to me,
you'll have no further
measure of corn from me, nor
shall you come near [me]."

61. They replied: "We'll
try to wrest him from
his father; we'll surely do that."

62. And Joseph told his servants:
"Place the goods they bartered
back in their saddle-bags,
so they'll recognize them
when they return to their people,
so they might come back."

63. And when they returned
to their father, they said:
"Father, we've been denied
any further measure of corn;
send with us our brother,
so we may procure our measure;
we'll be sure to protect him."

64. He said: "Shall I trust you
with him, as I trusted you
with his brother before?
Yet God is the Best
of Protectors, and He is
the Most Merciful
of the merciful."

65. And when they opened
their baggage, they found
their goods returned to them.
They said: "Father, what more
can we want? Our goods here
are returned to us:
we'll get food for our household,
we'll protect our brother;
and we'll get an extra camel-load
of grain, an easy load!"

66. Jacob answered: "Never
will he be sent with you,
until you make a pledge
to me—by God—that you'll bring him
to me, unless you're beseiged."
So when they had made their pledge,

he said: "God is Custodian
over all we say."

67. And: "My sons, don't
enter by one gate, but various
gates; yet I can't help you
in any way against [the Will of] God.
Judgment belongs to God alone:
in Him I put my trust,
and let all who trust
trust in Him."

68. And when they entered
from where their father
had directed, it helped them
in no way against [the Will of] God, for it was
but a need in Jacob, which
he fulfilled. For he possessed
knowledge, on account of what
We taught him. But most
of humankind does not know.

IX

69. And when they came
before Joseph, he drew
his brother to him: "I am
your own brother! So
don't grieve over
what they've been doing."

70. And while he was
preparing their supplies,
he planted a drinking cup
in his brother's saddle-bag.
Then a town-crier cried aloud:
"You, in the caravan!
You are surely thieves!"

71. They said, turning towards them:
"What are you missing?"

72. They said: "We're missing
the chalice of the king; whoever
brings it will be given
a camel-load, I pledge."

73. [The brothers] said: "By God!
You well know, we
haven't come to make mischief
in the realm, nor are we thieves!"

74. They said: "Then what
penalty should there be for this,
should you be lying?"

75. [The brothers] said:
"As penalty, the person who's
found with it in his saddle-bag,
should be held to account. That's how
we punish wrongdoers."

76. So Joseph began with
their bags, before searching
the bag of his brother; at length,
he lifted it out of his
brother's bag. So We
contrived things for Joseph, else he
could not detain his brother
within the law of the king,
without God's will. We
raise in station whom We will;
over all who know
is the All-Knowing.

77. They said: "If he has stolen,
well, he has a brother who stole
before him." But Joseph
said to himself, not
disclosing it to them:
"Your status is one
of evil,⁹ and God knows best
concerning what you claim."

78. They said: "Governor,
he has a father, truly
advanced in age; so take
one of us in his place;
for we can see, truly,
you are one of those
who do good."

79. He said: "God forbid
we detain any but the one
on whom we found our possession;
we would then be doing wrong."

X

80. So when they lost hope
with him, they conferred

---

9. Literally, "in the worst place or situation."

in private. The eldest spoke:
"Do you not know
your father took a pledge
from you, in the name of God,
and before this, you were careless
with Joseph? I shall not
leave this land until my father
gives me leave or God decrees
thus for me, for He
is the Best of Judges."

81. "[As for the rest of you]
Go back to your father,
and say, 'Father of ours, your
son has been stealing.
We are witnesses only
to what we know; and
we could hardly guard
against the unforeseen.'

82. 'Ask in the town where
we were, and the caravan
we came with; for we
are telling the truth.'"

83. [When they said this
to their father]
Jacob replied: "No, your minds
have enticed you to some
misdeed. But
patience is beautiful;
perhaps God will bring them
all back to me. For He is
the Knowing, the Wise."

84. And he turned away
from them, and sighed:
"How great is my grief
over Joseph!" His eyes
grew white in sorrow,
and he grieved inside,
in silence.

85. They said: "By God,
will you not cease
to remember Joseph
till you reach
the frailest edge of illness, or
till you are deceased?"

86. He said: "I complain only
of my grief, my sorrow,

to God, and I know from God
what you do not."

87. "My sons, go,
inquire after Joseph
and his brother, and don't
despair of God's Grace.
None despairs of God's
Grace, except unbelievers."

88. So when they came
before Joseph, they entreated:
"Governor, adversity
has touched us, our family.
We bring but meager wares, yet
remit a full measure to us,
show charity to us, for God
surely rewards the charitable."

89. He said: "Do you know
what you did with Joseph
and his brother, in your
ignorance?"

90. They said: "Are you
Joseph, really?" [He replied]:
"I am Joseph, and
this is my brother:
God has been gracious
toward us. For those
who are pious and patient,
He does not forsake
the reward of those
who do good."

91. They said: "By God!
God surely has preferred
you over us, and we
have been sinners."

92. He said: "Let no
reproach weigh upon you
this day. May God forgive you,
for He is the Most Merciful
of the merciful."

93. "Go, with this shirt of mine,
and throw it over
my father's face: sight
will light up his eyes.
Then come back with
your entire family."

XI

94. After the caravan had journeyed,
their father said: "I detect
the scent of Joseph, though you
might think me a dotard."

95. [People] said: "By God,
you're still indeed in your
old error."

96. Then, when the bearer
of good news came,
he threw [the shirt]
over Jacob's face; he regained
his vision, saying:
"Did I not say to you,
I know from God
what you do not?"

97. They said: "Father,
ask forgiveness
for our sins, for we
have done wrong."

98. He said: "I shall
ask my Lord to
forgive you, for
He is indeed
Forgiving, Ever-Merciful."

99. So when they came
before Joseph, he embraced
his parents, saying:
"Enter into Egypt, in safety,
if it be the will of God."

100. And he raised his parents, both,
on the throne, and all of them
fell down, bowing before him.
"My dear father, here is
the deeper meaning of my dream
of long ago. My Lord has brought it
into being. Truly, he was good to me
when He brought me
out of prison
and brought you
out of the desert,
after Satan had sown
discord between me
and my brothers.

My Lord is Subtle
in what He wills.
He is the Knowing, the Wise.

101. "My Lord, you have
given me dominion, and you have
taught me the deeper meaning
of events. Maker
of the heavens and earth, you are
my Protector, in this world
and the hereafter. Receive me,
as one who submits to Your will,
and unite me with the righteous."

102. This is from the chronicles
of the Unseen,[1] which we reveal
to you [Muhammad]. You were not
with them when they
concocted together
their abominable plot.

103. And most of humankind,
however ardently you strive,
will not believe.

104. And you, do not seek reward
from them for this. This is no less
than a reminder to all worlds.

XII

105. And how many signs
in the heavens and earth
do they pass by, turning
away.

106. And most of them
do not believe in God
without ascribing partners
to Him.

107. Do they feel secure, then,
from the darkening calamity
of God's punishment, or
from the sudden descending
of the Hour, while they
are unaware?

---

1. "Unseen" (Arabic *al-Ghaib*), that is, That which is is both Invisible and Unknowable.

108. Say: "This is my way;
I call to God, with clear vision,
I, and whoever follows me.
Glory be to God, that I am
not of those who ascribe
partners to Him."

109. And we sent before you
only men whom we inspired,
from the people of the cities.
Did they not travel
the earth, and behold
the end of those before them?
Surely, the abode of the hereafter
is finer for those who are
mindful of God. Will you, then,
not understand?

110. When the messengers
despaired, thinking [the people] had
denied, Our help came to them;
We saved whom We will.
But Our wrath will never be
turned from wicked people.

111. In their stories, there is
a lesson for people
of understanding. This is not
an invented tale, but confirmation
of what came before,
an exposition
of all things, a Guide
and a Mercy to
a believing people.

Surah 19: Mary

In the Name of God, the All-Merciful, Ever-Merciful

I

1. *Kaf. Ha. Ya. 'Ain. Sad.*[1]

2. A reminder of the mercy of your Lord
toward His servant Zachariah:[2]

3. When he called to his Lord
with a secret call:

---

1. See "Joseph" fn. 2, above. 2. Cf. Luke 1.5–64.

4. "My Lord, my bones are grown frail,
and my hair is ablaze with grey,
yet never has my prayer
to You, my Lord, been vain."

5. "I fear [I shall have no]
future kin, when I am gone, for
my wife is barren.
So grant me—from Yourself—
an heir

6. to bear my legacy[3]
and the legacy
of Jacob's family;
and let him, my Lord,
be well-pleasing."

7. [God said]:
"Zachariah, We give you
glad news of a son,
whose name will be John,
a name we gave
to none before him."

8. "My Lord, he said,
how can I have a son,
when my wife is barren
and I have come to wither
with age?"

9. He replied: "These are the words
of Your Lord: 'It is easy for Me.
Indeed, I created you
before, when you were nothing.'"

10. He said: "My Lord,
give me a sign."

"Your sign is this:
you will not speak
to people
for three successive nights."

11. So he ventured out
to his people
from his sanctuary,
urging them [by gestures],
to glorify God
morning and evening.

---

3. "Legacy" refers here not to wealth but prophethood.

12. "John," [We said]
Hold, steadfast, to the Book,"
and We endowed him
with sound judgment, while yet a child,

13. and with tenderness,
from Ourself,
and purity. He was
mindful of God,

14. solicitous of his parents,
and never imperious[4]
or disobedient.

15. And peace be upon him
the day he was born,
the day he dies,
and the day he
will be raised
alive.

II

16. And mention in the Book
Mary, of when she withdrew
from her people
to a place in the East.

17. She veiled herself
from them.[5] Then We sent
Our spirit, appearing
to her fully
in the form of a man.

18. She said: "I seek refuge
with the Most Merciful
from you: [withdraw][6]
if you fear Him."

19. He said: "I am only
a messenger from your Lord,
granting you a pure son."

20. "How shall I
have a son," she said, "for

4. "Imperious" (Arabic *al-Jabbar*) is also one of
the 99 names of Allah, usually translated as "The
Compeller." See also v. 32 below, where the
same attribute is negatively imputed to Jesus.
5. Literally, "She placed a screen between herself and them." In this context, the screen (Arabic *hijab*)—which refers to anything which
blocks the sight or view of something—is metaphorical, referring to Mary's seclusion from her
people.
6. The word "withdraw" is implied but not
stated in the Arabic text.

no man has touched me,
for I have not been unchaste?"

21. He replied: "This is what
your Lord has said:
'Easy it is for Me; We
will make him
a sign for humankind,
and a mercy from Us.
It is a thing
ordained.'"

22. So she conceived him,
and withdrew with him
to a place far away.

23. And the pains of labor
drove her to the trunk
of a date-palm. She cried:
"I wish I had died
before this, and been
wholly forgotten!"

24. But [a voice] called to her
from beneath: "Do not grieve;
surely your Lord
has set beneath you
a stream."

25. "And shake the trunk
of the date-palm toward you,
to let fresh, ripe dates
fall upon you."

26. "So eat and drink
and be comforted; and
if you see anyone, say:
"I have vowed to the Most Merciful
a fast, and today I shall speak
with no-one."

27. Then she came with him
to her people, carrying him.
They said: "Mary, you bring
truly an unheard-of thing."

28. "Sister of Aaron,
your father was not
a wicked man, and
your mother was not
unchaste."

29. Then she pointed to [the child];
they said: "How can we
talk with a child in the cradle?"

30. [The child] said: "I am
a servant of God;
He has given me the Book
and has made me
a prophet."

31. "And He made me blessed
wherever I may be,
and enjoined upon me
prayer and charity as long
as I live."

32. "And He made me solicitous
toward my mother, not
imperious or sullen."

33. "And peace be upon me
the day I was born,
the day I die,
and the day
I will be raised
alive."

34. This was Jesus, son
of Mary: the Word
of truth, about which
they dispute.

35. It is not for God
to bear a child. Glory be to Him:
when He decrees
something, He says
to it only "Be"
and it is.

36. For truly God is my Lord
and your Lord: therefore
worship Him. This is
the straight path.

37. But the sects differed
among themselves; and woe
will be to those who disbelieve
—from the testimony
of a momentous day.

38. How keenly will they see
and how keenly will they hear

on the Day they come
to Us. But today
the wrongdoers are
manifestly astray.

39. And warn them of the Day
of remorse, when
the matter will be decided
while they are heedless,
while they do not believe.

40. It is We who will inherit
the earth, and all those
upon it, and to Us
they will be returned.

III

41. And mention in the Book
Abraham: he was
a man of truth,
a prophet.

42. He said to his father:
"Father, why do you
worship what cannot hear
and cannot see, and can
profit you in nothing?"

43. "Father, knowledge has come
to me which has not come
to you. Therefore, follow me,
I will guide you
to a level path."

44. "Father, do not worship
Satan, for truly Satan is
a rebel against the
Most Merciful."

45. "Father, I fear
punishment will
befall you from the
Most Merciful
and you will become
an ally of Satan."

46. [His father] replied:
"Do you refuse my gods,
Abraham? If you don't desist

in this, I shall stone you.
Now be gone from me."

47. Abraham said: "Peace
be upon you; I shall ask
my Lord to forgive you,
for He has been ever Gracious
toward me."

48. "But I will turn away from
you and what you call upon
besides God, and I will call upon
my Lord. Perhaps, in
my prayer, I will not
be disappointed."

49. So when he turned away
from them and those they
worshipped besides God,
We bestowed upon him Isaac
and Jacob, and We made
each of them a prophet.

50. And We bestowed
Our Mercy upon them,
and We exalted them
in truthfulness.

IV

51. And mention in the Book
Moses: he was sincere,
and he was a messenger,
a prophet.[7]

52. And We called him
from the right side
of Mount [Sinai],
and We drew him
near for private communion.

53. And We granted him
from Our Mercy
his brother Aaron
as a prophet.

---

7. The distinction between "prophet" (*nabi*) and "messenger" (*rasul*) is still disputed: most agree that prophets were divinely inspired and taught what had already been revealed, while messengers brought forth a new scripture from God.

54. And mention in the Book
Ismail:[8] he was true
to his promise, and was
a messenger, a prophet.

55. He would always enjoin
upon his people prayer
and charity, and he would always
be pleasing to his Lord.

56. And mention in the Book
Idris:[9] he was
a man of truth, a prophet:

57. And We raised him
to an exalted rank.

58. These were among the prophets
whom God favored, from
the descendants of Adam, and
whom We carried
with Noah, and from
the descendants of Abraham and Israel,
whom We guided and chose.
When the verses of the Most Merciful
were recited to them,
they would fall prostrate,
in tears.

59. But there followed them
successors who neglected
prayer and followed their
desires. Soon, they will face
a pit of Hell.

60. Except those who turn
to repent, and believe
and do good works.
These will enter the Garden
and will not be wronged
in any way.

61. Eternal Gardens, which
the Most Merciful has promised
to His servants, in the Unseen.
His promise inexorably
will come to be.

---

8. The first son of Abraham, the older half-brother of Isaac.
9. Unlike the earlier prophets mentioned above in this surah, Idris appears in neither the Hebrew Bible nor the Gospels.

62. There, they will not hear
vain discourse, only
"Peace." And there,
will have sustenance
morning and evening.

63. This is the Garden
We shall bequeath
to our servants who were
mindful of Us.

64. [The angels say:]
"We descend only
by command of your Lord.
To Him belongs what lies
before us and what lies
behind us, and what lies
between. And your Lord
is never forgetful."

65. "Lord of the heavens
and of the earth, and of all
between them: so worship Him,
and be steadfast in His worship.
Do you know of any
equal to Him?"

v

66. Man says:
"Shall I, once dead,
be brought to life?"

67. But does not Man
recall that We created him
before, when he was
nothing?

68. So, by your Lord,
We shall surely gather them,
and the devils, around Hell,
on their knees.

69. Then We shall surely
drag out from each sect
those who were most
obdurate against
the Most Merciful.

70. Then We surely know best
those who are most worthy
to be burned there.

71. And there is not one
of you who will not
come to it: a decree
from your Lord,
destined to be.

72. But We shall save those
who were mindful of God,
and We shall leave
the wrongdoers there,
on their knees.

73. When Our clear signs
are recited to them,
the unbelievers taunt those
who believe: "Which of the two
parties is better positioned,
and superior in sway?"

74. But how many generations
before them have We
destroyed, who were
superior in possessions
and in appearance?

75. Say: "Whoever is astray,
the Most Merciful prolongs
their straying, until they see
what was promised them, either
in punishment [here] or in the [coming] Hour.
Then they will know who
is in the worse position
and weaker in force."

76. "And God increases
in guidance those who would
be guided; and enduring
good deeds
are the best rewards
in the eyes of your Lord,
and best in their
recompense."

77. Have you then seen
the person who
denies Our signs, yet
says: "I shall surely
be given wealth and children?"

78. Has he fathomed
the Unseen, or secured
with the Most Merciful
a compact?

79. No. We shall record
what he says, and We
shall prolong his
punishment.

80. We shall inherit
all that he talks of,
and he shall come
before Us
alone.

81. Yet, they have taken
gods other than
God, to empower them.

82. However, [those gods]
will reject their worship,
and become their
adversaries.

VI

83. Do you not see:
We have sent
devils against the unbelievers,
inciting them to sin?

84. So make no haste
against them, for We
are only counting
for them their term.

85. On that day We shall
gather the God-fearing to
the Most Merciful,
as an assembly.

86. And We shall drive
the sinners to hell,
like thirsty cattle
to water.

87. None shall have power
of intercession, except
whoever secures with
the Most Merciful
a compact.

88. They say: "The Most Merciful
has begotten a child."[1]

89. Assuredly, you bring forward
a monstrous thing

90. at which the heavens
might be rent apart, and
the earth burst asunder, and
the mountains collapse
in utter ruin,

91. that they ascribe a child
to the Most Merciful.

92. For it is not for the Most Merciful
to bear a child.

93. There is none in the heavens
and earth who will not come
before the Most Merciful
as a servant.

94. Most certainly, He has
taken account of them,
and counted them,
every one.

95. And every one of them
will come before Him
on the Day of Resurrection
alone.

96. Surely, on those
who believed and did good works,
the Most Merciful will bestow
Love.

97. So We have made
[the Qur'an] easy for you,
in your own tongue, so with it
you might give glad news to
the God-fearing, and with it
you might warn
a people who are
obdurate.

1. A reference not to the Christian belief that Jesus is the Son of God—a view criticized elsewhere in the Qur'an—but to the belief in pre-Islamic Arabia that the angels were the daughters of God.

98. And, before them, how many
generations have we destroyed:
can you trace even one of them
or can you hear from them
even a whisper?

Surah 24 (Excerpt): Light

35. God is the Light[1]
of the Heavens and of the Earth;
His Light is a parable, of
a lamp within a niche; the lamp within a glass,
the glass haloed as a brilliant star, lit
from an olive tree, blessèd;
whose soil is neither East nor West;
its very oil would shine forth
though untouched by fire:
Light upon Light.
God guides to His Light whom He will;
He engenders parables for humankind, He
Whose knowing encompasses all things.

36. His Light abides in houses, sanctified by God
to be raised for the adoration of His Name.

37. There is He glorified, morning and evening
by those whom neither trade nor profit can
divert from remembrance of God
or steadfastness in charity and prayer;
whose fear is for the Day
when heart and vision will turn about,

38. that God might reward their finest deeds,
giving ever more from His Grace,
for God furnishes measurelessly
those whom He will.

39. As for the unbelievers:
their deeds are like a mirage
in the burning desert: the parched man's eyes see
water in the distance; approaching, he finds
nothing; before him, he finds
God, Who will give him
his due in full: God,
whose reckoning is swift.

1. "Light" (an-Nur): that is, divine guidance, knowledge, or power. Some interpretations asso- ciate it with the believer's heart, while the lamp is viewed as the Qur'an.

40. Or, like darkness on a fathomless ocean,
wave over wave, overcast by cloud:
darkness upon darkness;
if a man stretch out his hand,
he can scarce see it.
For those whom God deprives of Light
there is no Light.

Surah 36: Ya Sin

In the Name of God, the All-Merciful, Ever-Merciful

I

1. *Ya Sin.*[1]

2. By the wise Qur'an,

3. you [Muhammad] are truly
one of the messengers

4. on a straight path.

5. It is a revelation
sent down from
the Mighty,
the Ever-Merciful,

6. that you might warn
a people whose forefathers
had no warning, and so
are heedless.

7. The sentence has been pronounced
against most of them, for
they will not believe—

8. indeed We placed
around their necks yokes
drawn up to their chins,
forcing up their heads,

9. and before them a barrier,
and behind them a barrier,
and covered them up so
they cannot see.

10. It is the same to them
whether you warn them or not:
they will not believe.

1. See "Joseph," fn. 2. *Ya Sin* has at least once been translated as "O Thou Human Being."

11. You can warn only him
who follows the Message
and fears the All-Merciful
in the Unseen. So give
glad news to him, of forgiveness
and a noble reward.

12. Truly, We bring back
to life the dead, and We transcribe
all [the deeds] they send before them
and all that they leave behind,
and We have accounted all things
in a clear record.

13. Adduce for them
a parable, of a people
to whose town there came
messengers.

II

14. When We sent to them
two messengers,[2] they denied
them both. So We
reinforced them with a third,
and they declared:
"Truly, we have been sent
as messengers to you."

15. [The people] said: "You
are merely humans, like us,
and the All-Merciful
has not sent anything. You
are only lying."

16. They said: "Our Lord knows
that truly we have been sent
as messengers to you."

17. "And what is [laid] upon us is only
the clear conveyance [of the message]."

18. [The people] said:
"We augur that you
are an evil omen. If you
don't desist, we'll surely stone you:
a painful punishment from us
will surely reach you."

2. Perhaps Moses and Jesus.

19. They replied: "Your evil omen
is within yourselves. Is it because
you have been reminded?
Surely not: you are
a transgressive people."

20. And there came from
the outskirts of the city
a man running, who said:
"My people, follow
the messengers."

21. "Follow those who ask
no reward of you, and who
are rightly guided."

22. "And why should I
not worship Him
who created me? For to Him
you will be returned."

23. "Should I take other gods
besides Him? If the All-Merciful
intended harm for me,
their intercession could not
help in any way, nor
could they save me."

24. "I would truly be
in manifest error."

25. "Truly, I believe
in your Lord; so
hear me."

26. He was told: "Enter
the Garden." He said:
"If only my people knew

27. how my Lord has
forgiven me and has
set me among the honored."

28. And We did not send down
against his people, after him,
any hosts from heaven,
nor would We deign to:

29. there was but
one single blast,
and they were vanished.

30. Alas, for [My] servants;
whichever messenger comes to them,
they mock him.

31. Don't they see how many
generations before them
We destroyed, so none
would come back to them?

32. And every one,
all together, will be brought
before Us.

III

33. A sign for them
is the dead earth:
We bring her to life,
and bring from her
grain which they eat.

34. And We placed upon her
gardens, with palm-groves
and grape-vines, and We caused
springs to burst forth there,

35. so they might eat of its fruit,
and what their hands made;
will they not, then, be thankful?

36. Glory be to Him Who
created in pairs all that
the earth yields, and
their own selves, and
also things of which they
are unaware.

37. And a sign for them
is the night: we strip away from it
the light of day, so
they are left in darkness.

38. And the sun
courses through her sure path
by decree of the Almighty,
the All-Knowing,

39. and the moon,
for whom We ordained phases,
till it returns, like
a dried date-stalk of old.

40. The sun may not outrun
the moon, nor may the night
outstrip the day. Each glides
in [its own] orbit.

41. And a sign for them
is that We carried
their offspring in the loaded Ark
[through the Flood].

42. and We have created
for them the like [ships]
in which they sail.

43. And if We willed, We could
drown them, and they would
have no helper [to hear their cry],
nor would they be saved,

44. except by Our mercy,
as a reprieve for a while.

45. When they are told,
"Have fear of what lies before you
and what lies behind you,
that you might receive mercy,"

46. they turn away
from every sign that
comes to them
from their Lord;

47. and when they are told,
"Spend [in charity] from what God
has provided you," those who
disbelieve say to those who
believe, "Should we feed those whom,
if He willed, God Himself could have fed?
You are in manifest error."

48. And they say: "When
will this promise [of resurrection] come to pass,
if you are being truthful?"

49. But [unwitting] they are waiting only
for a single blast, which will
overtake them while
they are disputing.

50. They will be unable
to disburse any bequest,

or to return to
their own people.

IV

51. The trumpet shall be sounded,
and see, how then they will
hasten from their graves
to their Lord.

52. They will say: "Woe to us!
Who has raised us
from our place of sleep?"
[A voice will answer][3]
"This is what the All-Merciful
promised: the messengers
spoke the truth."

53. It will be but
a single blast, and then
they shall be brought, all,
before Us.

54. Then, on that Day,
no soul shall be
wronged in any way,
and you shall be
requited only for
what you have done.

55. Truly, on that Day,
the people of the Garden
shall find joy in all they do,

56. they and their spouses,
in the shade, reclining
on couches.

57. There, they shall have
[every] fruit,
and they shall have
all that they call for.

58. "Peace": the word [of welcome]
from a Lord Ever-Merciful.

---

3. There is a mandatory pause here in the Arabic to indicate that the subsequent lines reply to the question just posed, shown here by the parenthetical remark.

59. [And it will be said]:
"But you who are sinners,
stand apart this Day."

60. "Did I not enjoin you,
children of Adam, not
to worship Satan, for
he is your manifest enemy,

61. and to worship Me?
—this is a straight path."

62. "But he indeed led astray
a great multitude of you:
did you not, then,
use your reason?"

63. "This is Hell, of which
you were warned."

64. "Burn in it, this Day,
for you went on disbelieving."

65. This Day, We shall seal
their mouths; but their hands
shall speak to Us, and their feet
shall bear witness to what
they earned.

66. Had We willed, We could
surely have extinguished their sight,
then they would grope to find
the path, but how should they see?

67. And had We willed, We could
have transfixed them in their place,
unable to move on or go back.

v

68. And to whomever We grant
long life, We weaken
his capacities: will they not,
then, use their reason?

69. We have not taught
[the Prophet] poetry,[4] nor
is it fitting for him. This is

---

4. Although the Qur'an uses rhyme, it stops short of being "poetry," at least in the sense of 7th-century Arabia, where poetry, and poets, were linked to public self-advancement and commercial gain.

nothing other than a reminder
and a manifest Qur'an,

70. so those who are living
might be warned, and the sentence
pronounced against the disbelieving.

71. Don't they see that
We created for them
—among the things that
Our hands have made—
livestock, over which they
have dominion,

72. and which We made
tame for them,
some to ride and others to eat?

73. And they yield further
uses, and give drink.
Will they not then
be thankful?

74. Yet still they take
other gods besides God,
hoping they might be helped.

75. [Those gods] have no power
to save them, even if they
were brought before them
as a host.

76. So do not be grieved [Muhammad]
by what they say; surely, We know
what they conceal, and
what they reveal.

77. And does not man see
that it is indeed We who created him
from a drop of semen? Yet, see,
he is an open adversary"

78. and adduces allegories
about Us, forgetting his own
creation, asking: "who can bring
life to bones that have decomposed?"

79. Say [in reply]: "He will bring
life to them, who
composed them at first,
for He knows
every creation.

80. It is He who made fire
for you from the green tree,
and see, you light from it
your own fires."

81. Is not He who created
the heavens and earth
able to create the like
of them [human beings]? Indeed,
for He is the Creator,
the All-Knowing.

82. When He intends something,
His only command is to say
to it: "Be," and it is.[5]

83. Then glory be to Him
in whose hand is dominion
over all things; and to Him
you will be returned.

Surah 55: The All-Merciful

In the Name of God, the All-Merciful, Ever-Merciful

1. The All-Merciful:
2.   He taught the Qur'an,
3.   He created man,
4.   He taught him speech.

5. Both sun and moon, exact in their span,
6.   and stars and trees, bow down, both;

7. and the sky He raised high, and set down the Balance,
8.   that you might not infract what is due in balance;
9. then set up [your] weights justly,
    and do not fall short in balance.

10. And the earth He laid out for His creatures,
11.   with her fruit and date-palms, with clustered sheaths;
12.   and corn, with husks, and scented plants.

13. Which, then, of your Lord's favors would you both deny?

14. He created humankind from dry clay like earthen pots,
15.   and Jinn He created from smokeless fire.
16. Which of your Lord's favors would you both then deny?[1]

---

5. The same phrase is used elsewhere in the Qur'an, especially regarding the birth of Jesus (e.g., Q2:116: Q3:47).
1. Although in the Arabic this refrain is repeated exactly, the wording of the modern English trans- lation varies in order to reflect the varied modes of intonation in the Arabic recitation. "Jinn": spiritual beings lower than angels and able to appear in human form (Arabic, source of English word *genie*).

17. Lord of the two Easts and Lord of the two Wests.[2]
18. And which of your Lord's favors would you both deny?

19. He let the two seas flow, so they might converge:
20.   between them a barrier, which they shall not transgress—
21. So which of your Lord's favors will you both deny?
22.   —out of them both come pearls and coral.

23. Which, then, of your Lord's favors will you both deny?

24. And His are the ships sailing high on the seas, like mountains.
25. So which of the favors of your Lord will you both deny?

26. All things upon [earth] shall perish,
27.   while the Face of your Lord abides, forever
      in Majesty and Munificence.

28. Which, then, of your Lord's favors will you both deny?

29. Whatever is in the heavens and earth beseeches Him,
      seeking each day His purpose.
30. Which of your Lord's favors will you then both deny?

31. Soon We shall settle with you, O hosts [of Jinn and humankind].
32. Then which of your Lord's favors will you both deny?
33. O company of Jinn and humankind: if you are able to pass
      beyond the realms of heaven and earth, then pass: yet you shall not pass
      without [Our] warrant.
34. And which of your Lord's favor will you both deny?
35. Against you both will be hurled a fiery flame, and smoke:
      you shall find no quarter.

36. Which, then, of your Lord's favors will you both deny?

37. When the sky is ripped asunder, turning crimson like red leather:
38. Which of your Lord's favors will you then both deny?
39. On that Day, none will be questioned about his sin,
      neither humans nor Jinn.
40. And which of your Lord's favors will you both deny?
41. The sinners shall be known by their marks, and shall be seized
      by their forelocks and feet.
42. Which, then, of your Lord's favors will you both deny?
43. This is Hell, which the sinners deny:
44.   they will wander in circles
      between it and boiling water.

45. Which, then, of your Lord's favors will you both deny?

---

2. The rising of the sun and the moon, or perhaps the farthest points of sunrise and sunset in summer and winter; an image of opposition and symmetry.

46. But for whoever fears [the Day] when he shall stand before his Lord:
     are two gardens—
47. So which of your Lord's favors will you both deny?
48.   —with spreading branches.
49. So which of your Lord's favors will you both deny?
50.   In them both will be two fountains, flowing.
51. So which of your Lord's favors will you both deny?
52.   In them both will be fruits of every kind, in pairs.
53. So which of your Lord's favors will you both deny?
54. Reclining on couches, lined in rich brocade, with fruit of both gardens
     within close reach.
55. So which of your Lord's favors will you both deny?
56.   In them will be females of modest glance, untouched before by human
     or Jinn—
57. So which of your Lord's favors will you both deny?
58.   —[In beauty] like rubies and coral.
59. So which of your Lord's favors will you both deny?
60.   What is the reward for goodness except goodness?

61. Which, then, of your Lord's favors will you both deny?
62.   And besides these two, shall be two more Gardens—[3]
63. Which, then, of your Lord's favors will you both deny?
64.   —both hued in deepest green.
65. And which of your Lord's favors will you both deny?
66.   In them both will be two fountains, overflowing.
67. Which, then, of your Lord's favors will you both deny?
68.   In them both will be fruit, date-palm, and pomegranate.
69. Which, then, of your Lord's favors will you both deny?

70.   In them will be maidens, virtuous and beauteous—
71. Which of your Lord's favors would you then both deny?
72.   —Houris,[4] dark-eyed, secluded in pavilions—
73. And which of your Lord's favors will you both deny?
74.   —untouched before by human or Jinn—
75. Which, then, of your Lord's favors will you both deny?
76.   —reclining on cushions of green and beauteous carpets.

77. Which, then, of your Lord's favors will you both deny?

78. Blessed is the Name of your Lord, forever
     in Majesty and Munificence.

---

3. The Islamic paradise has several ranks or levels, into which believers are to be placed after death according to their degree of merit; compare Dante's *Paradiso* for an adaptation of the structure of the Islamic paradise within a Christian framework.
4. Black-eyed maidens of Paradise (Arabic).

Surah 91: The Sun

In the Name of God, the All-Merciful, Ever-Merciful

1. By the sun
and her splendor;

2. by the moon
as he trails her;

3. by the day as he
displays her;

4. by the night as she
veils her;

5. by the heaven and He
Who framed her;

6. by the earth and He
Who extended her;

7. by the soul and He
Who perfected her;

8. for He inspired her
to know her [own] evil
and the piety within her;

9. he surely succeeds
who purifies her,

10. and he surely fails
who defiles her.

11. The nation of Thamud
denied [her prophet Salih],[1]
for she was a transgressor,

12. when she deputed her
most wicked offender [to denounce him].

13. God's messenger
advised them: "This is
a she-camel of God, so
provide drink for her.

---

1. This account appears in Q7:73–79, where it is compared with other histories, including that of Lot. "Thamud": ancient civilization of southern Arabia; Islamic legend holds that God sent the prophet Salih to warn the Thamudi to give up the decadence they had fallen into.

14. But they denied him
and hamstrung her.
So for their sin, their Lord
destroyed [their nation],
and levelled her.

15. Nor does He fear
what will become of her.

Surah 112: Purity [of Faith][1]

In the Name of God, the All-Merciful, Ever-Merciful

1. Say: He is God, the One,
2. God, the Absolute:
3. neither did He beget,
      nor was He begotten.
4. His like or equal there is none.

---

1. According to tradition, the Prophet Muhammad said that this chapter (surah) was equivalent to one-third of the Qur'an. The Persian poet Rumi also praises it: "Although these words are few in form, they are preferable to the lengthy chapter *Baqara* [Q2] by virtue of being to the point."

BEOWULF

ninth century

Surviving in a single tattered manuscript, its edges burned by fire, *Beowulf* provides a startlingly vivid glimpse into the early medieval past. Written in Old English, with a vocabulary that would have seemed old-fashioned even to its very first audience, the poem recalls a heroic age in which monsters stalked men by night, dragons guarded hoards of precious gems and heirloom swords, and heroes carried out great deeds of warfare that would later be commemorated by song and feasting. The bonds of family and clan give shape to the world of Beowulf and his companions, leading sometimes to the formation of new alliances, sometimes to the violent conflict of blood feud that lasted for generations. Like much Old English poetry, the poem is fundamentally elegiac, celebrating the beauty and mourning the disappearance of a culture that, by the year 1000, had already become part of the past.

The sole surviving copy of *Beowulf*

can be dated with some certainty to the years around 1000, a time of rich flowering of Anglo-Saxon literature and learning, expressed in both Old English and Anglo-Latin poetry. Yet this time was also the end of an era, just a few generations before English society would be completely transformed by the Norman Conquest of 1066. The poem thus sums up a particular form of English culture that would very soon vanish. Among the other works included in the manuscript containing *Beowulf* are saints' lives and exotic tales of the Orient: despite their varied genres, all are unified by a common theme of monsters and heroes. The three monsters of *Beowulf*—Grendel, Grendel's mother, and the dragon—and the superhuman hero who fights against them appear beside other examples of nonhuman nature, from the so-called monstrous races encountered by Alexander the Great in the extreme reaches of India to the dog-headed (or "cynocephalic") Saint Christopher. Read in this context, the poem sheds light on the nature of medieval English culture, especially on its ability to integrate pagan Germanic history within the framework of the Christian Middle Ages.

While we can date the manuscript of *Beowulf* to the years around 1000, the poem itself is almost certainly much older—a judgment based on the poem's old-fashioned vocabulary and certain genealogical allusions as well as the manuscript itself, whose copying errors suggest that a long history of transmission lies behind it. Yet the poem in its oral form is even older, drawing on a rich stock of myth and legend that was surely familiar among the northern Germanic peoples who inhabited the regions now known as Scandinavia, the Low Countries, and the British Isles. Those who read *Beowulf* or heard it recited in the eleventh century would have likely recognized allusions to ancient blood feuds and tribal clashes that are only dimly comprehensible to modern readers. The poem appears to be set in the sixth century (in particular, we can date the death of Beowulf's lord, Hygelac, to around 520), and so the story would already have seemed like ancient history to the poem's earliest hearers. To the eleventh-century reader, the events of the poem are thus doubly removed into the past. Like **Homer**'s *Iliad*, whose written text codifies a much older oral form of the poem, *Beowulf* emerges as a written work of literature only at the end of generations of transmission as song.

Although we are accustomed to thinking of *Beowulf* as an "English" poem, its subject matter is not English people at all: Beowulf himself is a member of the tribe of the Geats, who live in the south of what is now Sweden, and he goes to serve in the court of Hrothgar, king of the Danes. In the period that the poem is set, England was only beginning to be settled by Germanic tribes, which had first invaded the island around 450. For the medieval English person reading the poem around 1000, therefore, the subject matter of the poem would have been at once strange and familiar—made up of persons and places that were remote in space and time from current-day England, but connected to the poem's audience by lines of heritage and descent. This simultaneous sense of strangeness and familiarity would have been heightened by *Beowulf*'s treatment of religion. While the readers and hearers of the poem, beginning in the ninth century and almost certainly earlier, would have brought a Christian perspective to the poem, the characters clearly belong to a pre-Christian world where *wyrd* (fate) governs the events that unfold in the lives of man. Yet the text is careful to maintain ambiguity regarding the role of Christianity in the world of the poem: the monstrous Grendel is said to be one of "Cain's clan," and is thus identified as an outcast from humanity in specifically biblical terms.

Grendel is only the first of three monsters that the hero Beowulf must confront. The initial single combat against this man-beast is quickly succeeded by a similar battle—this time carried out in the watery deeps of a distant wasteland—against Grendel's mother, an even more loathsome creature. After these successes, Beowulf's heroism is acclaimed, he is richly rewarded, and he returns to his own Geatish homeland to eventually become ruler of his people. Only decades later, in that homeland, does the third episode of combat take place, which pits Beowulf against a fierce dragon guarding a buried hoard of gems and shining weapons. Once again he enters battle alone, but before the struggle ends he is aided by his kinsman and companion Wiglaf. These clashes are among the most gripping scenes of the poem. First the hero wrestles with a dreadful monster who bites through his victim's bones, drinks his blood, and swallows his flesh in great chunks, consuming him "hand and foot." The horror of the confrontation with Grendel's vengeful mother is still greater: she is a "swamp-thing from hell." In Beowulf's final monstrous encounter, the dragon "billowed and spewed" venomous fire, at once burning and poisoning his victim.

Yet Beowulf's horrific enemies are more complex than they might first appear: Grendel is both monster and man, one of the family of Cain. Like Cain himself, he is said to be "God-cursed," and his status as an outcast, cut off from the community of men, makes him seem curiously forlorn, "spurned and joyless." Although he is undoubtedly a monster, Grendel shows human emotions; he is whipped into a blind and jealous fury against those able to enjoy the bonds of family and tribe, who sleep blissfully in the communal space of Heorot's great hall. Similarly, Grendel's mother is driven not just by her monstrous nature but also by a maternal desire to avenge the death of her son—and according to the codes of Germanic tribal society, revenge was an entirely appropriate motive. Even the fight with the dragon is not cast in simple terms: when Beowulf enters his cavernous lair, it is the hero—not the monster—who is identified as the invader, and the dragon is called the "hordweard," or guardian of the hoard. Although one is a man and one is a beast, both are said to be clad in armor, the hero bearing his shield and helm, the dragon his "enameled scales." As the line that separates human from nonhuman is blurred, every violent clash, whether man against man or man against monster, is couched in terms of equivalence and balance.

As vivid as these encounters are, the poem also has an important second level, concerned with the interpersonal ties of kinship and tribe, as well as the voluntary relationship of lord and warrior. We see Beowulf take on a series of roles within this social system. He begins among the Geats as a strong fighter of somewhat marginal status as a nephew of the king, Hygelac; he then is adopted with great honor into the household of Hrothgar, king of the Danes, after defeating Grendel and his mother; and finally Beowulf becomes ruler of the Geats, when Hygelac dies without a male heir. Beowulf appears first as a warrior in the service of his lord, and later as himself a lord—in the language of the poem, a "giver of rings" as well as one who receives them. The relationship of king and warrior is reciprocal, as the warrior provides service while his lord offers protection and distributes wealth, often in the form of armbands or neck torques ("rings"). Yet perhaps the most valuable gift that the lord grants is entrance into the community itself: in *Beowulf*, as in Old English poetry more generally, no burden is heavier than involuntary solitude. The warm bonds of fellowship nurture the warrior, and to be cut off from them is unimaginably bitter. Such isolation afflicts Grendel, as we have seen, and is memorably evoked in the poem's description of how the dragon's golden hoard came into being. It was the accumulated treasure of a long-ago people, the poet says, buried for safe-keeping by the last of their line: "Death had come / and taken them all," leaving just one man "deserted and alone, lamenting his unhappiness / day and night." For the despairing survivor, there is "No trembling harp, / no tuned timber, no tumbling hawk / swerving through the hall." Bereft of the joys of the hall, the only man left alive can do little more than mourn as he waits for death.

The hall offers both the most secure and stable environment that a warrior can possibly inhabit and the culture's greatest point of vulnerability. Beowulf is given the opportunity to display his heroic nature in combat with Grendel because of the need to defend Heorot, the great hall of Hrothgar: the accursed monster has been sneaking into the hall by night, seizing and devouring warriors one by one. The threat is not simply to the lives of Hrothgar's men but to the very basis of the community, as the Danish war-riors are reduced to fearful individuals, each concerned for his own life. The great hall of Heorot is a place of communal gathering and feasting, of goodwill and social bonds, where oaths of loyalty are sworn and golden rings are distributed, where heroic deeds are sung and the genealogies of kings recounted. Yet this idyllic space, representing the unity of the king and his people, is only temporary, for the danger posed to Heorot is not erased by the death of Grendel: other threats are darkly foreshadowed in the poem through allusions to the fate of the Danes after Hrothgar's reign ended. For the poem's medieval audiences, these passing references brought to mind the full story of the tragic down-fall of Hrothgar's house and the burn-ing of Heorot.

Swords and other weaponry appear throughout the poem, not just as tools of the warfare that punctuates the nar-rative at regular intervals but as a kind of social glue that links the community of warriors both in the present and across time and space. As treasures are shared, kings disburse weapons along with golden rings, items that are as precious for their ability to create interpersonal connections as for their physical material. Hrothgar's queen, Wealhtheow, rewards Beowulf with a golden collar that marks a new bond of affinity between the Geatish hero and the ruling house of the Danes, accom-panying the sumptuous gift with the request that Beowulf do his best to support her young son in the future. The ring thus carries both material and social value, marking a bond of loyalty between persons and groups. Similarly, Hrothgar later rewards Beowulf with magnificent armor, which Beowulf goes on to deliver to his own Geatish lord, Hygelac, just as he also gives to Hygelac's queen, Hygd, the neck ring bestowed on him by Wealhtheow.

Beowulf's gifts unite the Danes and the Geats and thereby redouble his own honor. And the connections formed by heirloom weapons can extend far into the past. As Beowulf prepares to battle Grendel's mother, the Danish warrior Unferth lends him "a rare and ancient sword," and he in turn leaves his own weapon, a "sharp-honed, wave-sheened wonder-blade," with the Dane, who may keep it if he fails to return. In the muddy pool where Beowulf defeats Grendel's mother, he finds another blade, whose gold hilt is inscribed with "rune-markings" telling the name of the one "for whom the sword had first been made." This sword, "from the days of the giants," passes through time, wielded by men and by monsters, until it finally comes into the hands of Beowulf, who in turn delivers its remnants to the Danish king Hrothgar. The chain of descent confers glory on the hero, and unites the community of warriors across the ages.

Each of these three ancient swords is described as an heirloom or "ealde lafe": literally, an "old thing that is left," a remainder of past glory. The weapon is thus an instrument of warfare and a symbol of continuity, linking past, present, and future as successive men bear it. Such work of commemoration suffuses the poem, perhaps nowhere more movingly than in the songs of heroes that punctuate the communal celebrations and feasting held in Heorot. Like the "ealde lafe," the heroic song recalls figures of the past and makes them live again as the warriors listen and join in the imagined community of the tribal nation and the symbolic space of the hall. After the defeat of Grendel, Hrothgar's minstrel sings a song of the Frisian king Finn and his Danish wife Hildeburh. The story is tragic, telling of the feud that destroyed their family, but the shared experience of the minstrel's music and tale brings Hrothgar's court together—a sense of community reawakened, perhaps, for the medieval audiences who heard Beowulf performed for them.

The translation here, by Seamus Heaney, seeks to reproduce the rhythmic quality of the Old English line—made up of two half-lines, each containing two beats. Coupled with the alliteration (repeated initial consonant sounds) that is prevalent in Old English poetry, the line produces a strong sense of rhythm, a recurrent thrumming sound that gives the poem its songlike quality, impossible to ignore even in written form. To give a clearer sense of the sound of the original work, reproduced at the top of page 124 are the closing lines (2262–69) of the lament of the last survivor, who long ago buried the hoard of treasure guarded by the dragon that is Beowulf's last and most dangerous enemy. Below these lines is a very literal, rhythmic translation that conveys the lines' aural quality more emphatically than does Heaney's version.

TRIBES AND GENEALOGIES

*1. The Danes (Bright-, Half-, Ring-, Spear-, North-, East-, South-, West-Danes;
Shieldings, Honor-, Victor-, War-Shieldings: Ing's friends).*

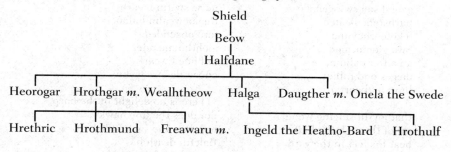

Shield
|
Beow
|
Halfdane

Heorogar   Hrothgar *m.* Wealhtheow   Halga   Daugther *m.* Onela the Swede

Hrethric   Hrothmund   Freawaru *m.*   Ingeld the Heatho-Bard   Hrothulf

2. The Geats (Sea-, War-, Weather-Geats).

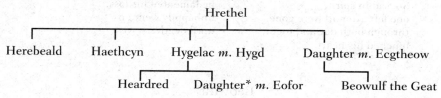

Hrethel

Herebeald   Haethcyn   Hygelac *m.* Hygd   Daughter *m.* Ecgtheow

Heardred   Daughter* *m.* Eofor   Beowulf the Geat

3. The Swedes

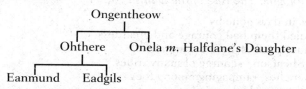

Ongentheow

Ohthere   Onela *m.* Halfdane's Daughter

Eanmund   Eadgils

*The daughter of Hygelac who was given to Eofor may have been born to him by a former wife,
older than Hygd.

4. Miscellaneous.

A. The Half-Danes (also called Shieldings) involved in the fight at Finnsburg
may represent a different tribe from the Danes described above. Their king Hoc
had a son, Hnaef, who succeeded him, and a daughter Hildeburh, who married
Finn, king of the Jutes.

B. The Jutes, or Frisians, are represented as enemies of the Danes in the fight
at Finnsburg and as allies of the Franks at the time Hygelac the Geat made the
attack in which he lost his life and from which Beowulf swam home. Also allied
with the Franks at this time were the Hetware.

C. The Heatho-Bards (i.e., "Battle-Bards") are represented as inveterate enemies of the Danes. Their king Froda had been killed in an attack on the Danes,
and Hrothgar's attempt to make peace with them by marrying his daughter
Freawaru to Froda's son Ingeld failed when the latter attacked Heorot. The
attack was repulsed, although Heorot was burned.

Beowulf, lines 2262–69[1]

	"Næs hearpan wyn,
gomen gleobeames,	ne god hafoc
geond sæl swingeð,	ne se swifta mearh
burhstede beateð.	Bealocwealm hafað
fela feorhcynna	forð onsended."
Swa giomormod	giohtho mænde,
an æfter eallum,	unbliðe hwearf
dæges ond nihtes,	oððæt deaðes wylm
hran æt heortan.	

	"There is no delight in the harp,
that joyful singing wood,	nor does the fine hawk
shoot through the hall,	nor does the swift steed
beat his feet in the yard.	Baleful death has
sent out of this world	too many of our kind."
So, sad in spirit,	he lamented his loss,
one left after all were gone,	unhappily went on
through both day and night,	until death's wave
touched his heart.	

Beowulf[1]

[Prologue: The Rise of the Danish Nation]

So. The Spear-Danes in days gone by
and the kings who ruled them had courage and greatness.
We have heard of those princes' heroic campaigns.
There was Shield Sheafson,[2] scourge of many tribes,
a wrecker of mead-benches, rampaging among foes.   5
This terror of the hall-troops had come far.
A foundling to start with, he would flourish later on
as his powers waxed and his worth was proved.
In the end each clan on the outlying coasts
beyond the whale-road had to yield to him   10
and begin to pay tribute. That was one good king.
Afterward a boy-child was born to Shield,
a cub in the yard, a comfort sent
by God to that nation. He knew what they had tholed,[3]
the long times and troubles they'd come through   15
without a leader; so the Lord of Life,
the glorious Almighty, made this man renowned.
Shield had fathered a famous son:
Beow's name was known through the north.
And a young prince must be prudent like that,   20

1. Translated by Suzanne Akbari.
1. Translated by Seamus Heaney.
2. Translates *Scyld Scefing*, which probably means "son of Sheaf." Scyld's origins are mysterious.
3. An Anglo-Saxon word that means "suf-fered, endured" and that survives in the translator's native land of Northern Ireland. In using this word, he also maintains an alliterative pattern similar to the original ("that . . . they . . . tholed").

giving freely while his father lives
so that afterward in age when fighting starts
steadfast companions will stand by him
and hold the line. Behavior that's admired
is the path to power among people everywhere. 25
  Shield was still thriving when his time came
and he crossed over into the Lord's keeping.
His warrior band did what he bade them
when he laid down the law among the Danes:
they shouldered him out to the sea's flood, 30
the chief they revered who had long ruled them.
A ring-whorled prow rode in the harbor,
ice-clad, outbound, a craft for a prince.
They stretched their beloved lord in his boat,
laid out by the mast, amidships, 35
the great ring-giver. Far-fetched treasures
were piled upon him, and precious gear.
I never heard before of a ship so well furbished
with battle-tackle, bladed weapons
and coats of mail. The massed treasure 40
was loaded on top of him: it would travel far
on out into the ocean's sway.
They decked his body no less bountifully
with offerings than those first ones did
who cast him away when he was a child 45
and launched him alone out over the waves.[4]
And they set a gold standard up
high above his head and let him drift
to wind and tide, bewailing him
and mourning their loss. No man can tell, 50
no wise man in hall or weathered veteran
knows for certain who salvaged that load.
  Then it fell to Beow to keep the forts.
He was well regarded and ruled the Danes
for a long time after his father took leave 55
of his life on earth. And then his heir,
the great Halfdane, held sway
for as long as he lived, their elder and warlord.
He was four times a father, this fighter prince:
one by one they entered the world, 60
Heorogar, Hrothgar, the good Halga,
and a daughter,[5] I have heard, who was Onela's queen,
a balm in bed to the battle-scarred Swede.
  The fortunes of war favored Hrothgar.
Friends and kinsmen flocked to his ranks, 65
young followers, a force that grew
to be a mighty army. So his mind turned

---

4. Since Shield arrived with nothing, this sentence is a litotes or understatement, a characteristic of the laconic style of old Germanic poetry.

5. The text is faulty here, and the name of Halfdane's daughter has been lost. Halfdane: according to another source, Halfdane's mother was Swedish; hence his name.

to hall-building: he handed down orders
for men to work on a great mead-hall
meant to be a wonder of the world forever;   70
it would be his throne-room and there he would dispense
his God-given goods to young and old—
but not the common land or people's lives.[6]
Far and wide through the world, I have heard,
orders for work to adorn that wallstead   75
were sent to many peoples. And soon it stood there
finished and ready, in full view,
the hall of halls. Heorot[7] was the name
he had settled on it, whose utterance was law.
Nor did he renege, but doled out rings   80
and torques[8] at the table. The hall towered,
its gables wide and high and awaiting
a barbarous burning.[9] That doom abided,
but in time it would come: the killer instinct
unleashed among in-laws, the blood-lust rampant.   85

[Heorot Is Attacked]

Then a powerful demon, a prowler through the dark,
nursed a hard grievance. It harrowed him
to hear the din of the loud banquet
every day in the hall, the harp being struck
and the clear song of a skilled poet   90
telling with mastery of man's beginnings,
how the Almighty had made the earth
a gleaming plain girdled with waters;
in His splendor He set the sun and the moon
to be earth's lamplight, lanterns for men,   95
and filled the broad lap of the world
with branches and leaves; and quickened life
in every other thing that moved.
    So times were pleasant for the people there
until finally one, a fiend out of hell,   100
began to work his evil in the world.
Grendel was the name of this grim demon
haunting the marches, marauding round the heath
and the desolate fens; he had dwelt for a time
in misery among the banished monsters,   105
Cain's clan, whom the Creator had outlawed
and condemned as outcasts.[1] For the killing of Abel

---

6. Apparently, slaves, along with pastureland used by all, were not in the king's power to give away.
7. That is, "hart," a symbol of royalty.
8. Golden bands worn around the neck.
9. The destruction by fire of Heorot—when the Heatho-Bard Ingeld attacked his father-in-law, Hrothgar—occurred at a later time than that of the poem's action. For a more detailed account of this feud and of Hrothgar's hope that it could be settled by the marriage of his daughter to Ingeld, see lines 2020–69.
1. Genesis 4.9–12.

the Eternal Lord had exacted a price:
Cain got no good from committing that murder
because the Almighty made him anathema   110
and out of the curse of his exile there sprang
ogres and elves and evil phantoms
and the giants too who strove with God
time and again until He gave them their reward.[2]
    So, after nightfall, Grendel set out   115
for the lofty house, to see how the Ring-Danes
were settling into it after their drink,
and there he came upon them, a company of the best
asleep from their feasting, insensible to pain
and human sorrow. Suddenly then   120
the God-cursed brute was creating havoc:
greedy and grim, he grabbed thirty men
from their resting places and rushed to his lair,
flushed up and inflamed from the raid,
blundering back with the butchered corpses.   125
    Then as dawn brightened and the day broke,
Grendel's powers of destruction were plain:
their wassail was over, they wept to heaven
and mourned under morning. Their mighty prince,
the storied leader, sat stricken and helpless,   130
humiliated by the loss of his guard,
bewildered and stunned, staring aghast
at the demon's trail, in deep distress.
He was numb with grief, but got no respite
for one night later merciless Grendel   135
struck again with more gruesome murders.
Malignant by nature, he never showed remorse.
It was easy then to meet with a man
shifting himself to a safer distance
to bed in the bothies,[3] for who could be blind   140
to the evidence of his eyes, the obviousness
of the hall-watcher's hate? Whoever escaped
kept a weather-eye open and moved away.
    So Grendel ruled in defiance of right,
one against all, until the greatest house   145
in the world stood empty, a deserted wallstead.
For twelve winters, seasons of woe,
the lord of the Shieldings[4] suffered under
his load of sorrow; and so, before long,
the news was known over the whole world.   150
Sad lays were sung about the beset king,

---

2. The poet is thinking here of Genesis 6.2–8,
where the Latin Bible in use at the time refers
to giants mating with women who were understood to be the descendants of Cain and
thereby creating the wicked race that God

destroyed with the flood.
3. Outlying buildings; the word is current in
Northern Ireland.
4. Hrothgar; as descendants of Shield, the
Danes are called Shieldings.

the vicious raids and ravages of Grendel,
his long and unrelenting feud,
nothing but war; how he would never
parley or make peace with any Dane   155
nor stop his death-dealing nor pay the death-price.[5]
No counselor could ever expect
fair reparation from those rabid hands.
All were endangered; young and old
were hunted down by that dark death-shadow   160
who lurked and swooped in the long nights
on the misty moors; nobody knows
where these reavers from hell roam on their errands.

   So Grendel waged his lonely war,
inflicting constant cruelties on the people,   165
atrocious hurt. He took over Heorot,
haunted the glittering hall after dark,
but the throne itself, the treasure-seat,
he was kept from approaching; he was the Lord's outcast.

   These were hard times, heartbreaking   170
for the prince of the Shieldings; powerful counselors,
the highest in the land, would lend advice,
plotting how best the bold defenders
might resist and beat off sudden attacks.
Sometimes at pagan shrines they vowed   175
offerings to idols, swore oaths
that the killer of souls might come to their aid
and save the people.[6] That was their way,
their heathenish hope; deep in their hearts
they remembered hell. The Almighty Judge   180
of good deeds and bad, the Lord God,
Head of the Heavens and High King of the World,
was unknown to them. Oh, cursed is he
who in time of trouble has to thrust his soul
in the fire's embrace, forfeiting help;   185
he has nowhere to turn. But blessed is he
who after death can approach the Lord
and find friendship in the Father's embrace.

[The Hero Comes to Heorot]

   So that troubled time continued, woe
that never stopped, steady affliction   190
for Halfdane's son, too hard an ordeal.

---

5. According to Germanic law, a slayer could achieve peace with his victim's kinsmen only by paying them *wergild* ("man-price") as compensation for the slain man.

6. The poet interprets the heathen gods to whom the Danes make offerings as different incarnations of Satan. Naturally, the pagan Danes do not think of their gods in these biblical terms, but as the poet makes clear in the following lines, they have no other recourse.

There was panic after dark, people endured
raids in the night, riven by the terror.
    When he heard about Grendel, Hygelac's thane
was on home ground, over in Geatland.   195
There was no one else like him alive.
In his day, he was the mightiest man on earth,
highborn and powerful. He ordered a boat
that would ply the waves. He announced his plan:
to sail the swan's road⁷ and seek out that king,   200
the famous prince who needed defenders.
Nobody tried to keep him from going,
no elder denied him, dear as he was to them.
Instead, they inspected omens and spurred
his ambition to go, whilst he moved about   205
like the leader he was, enlisting men,
the best he could find; with fourteen others
the warrior boarded the boat as captain,
a canny pilot along coast and currents.
    Time went by, the boat was on water,   210
in close under the cliffs.
Men climbed eagerly up the gangplank,
sand churned in surf, warriors loaded
a cargo of weapons, shining war-gear
in the vessel's hold, then heaved out,   215
away with a will in their wood-wreathed ship.
Over the waves, with the wind behind her
and foam at her neck, she flew like a bird
until her curved prow had covered the distance,
and on the following day, at the due hour,   220
those seafarers sighted land,
sunlit cliffs, sheer crags
and looming headlands, the landfall they sought.
It was the end of their voyage and the Geats vaulted
over the side, out on to the sand,   225
and moored their ship. There was a clash of mail
and a thresh of gear. They thanked God
for that easy crossing on a calm sea.
    When the watchman on the wall, the Shieldings' lookout
whose job it was to guard the sea-cliffs,   230
saw shields glittering on the gangplank
and battle-equipment being unloaded
he had to find out who and what
the arrivals were. So he rode to the shore,
this horseman of Hrothgar's, and challenged them   235
in formal terms, flourishing his spear:

7. That is, the sea. This is an example of a
"kenning," a metaphoric phrase that is used to
describe a common object. These kennings are
very common throughout Anglo-Saxon poetry.

See, for another instance, line 258, where the
poet describes a man's capacity for speech as
his "word-hoard."

"What kind of men are you who arrive
rigged out for combat in your coats of mail,
sailing here over the sea-lanes
in your steep-hulled boat? I have been stationed   240
as lookout on this coast for a long time.
My job is to watch the waves for raiders,
any danger to the Danish shore.
Never before has a force under arms
disembarked so openly—not bothering to ask   245
if the sentries allowed them safe passage
or the clan had consented. Nor have I seen
a mightier man-at-arms on this earth
than the one standing here: unless I am mistaken,
he is truly noble. This is no mere   250
hanger-on in a hero's armor.
So now, before you fare inland
as interlopers, I have to be informed
about who you are and where you hail from.
Outsiders from across the water,   255
I say it again: the sooner you tell
where you come from and why, the better."
    The leader of the troop unlocked his word-hoard;
the distinguished one delivered this answer:
"We belong by birth to the Geat people   260
and owe allegiance to Lord Hygelac.
In his day, my father was a famous man,
a noble warrior-lord named Ecgtheow.
He outlasted many a long winter
and went on his way. All over the world   265
men wise in counsel continue to remember him.
We come in good faith to find your lord
and nation's shield, the son of Halfdane.
Give us the right advice and direction.
We have arrived here on a great errand   270
to the lord of the Danes, and I believe therefore
there should be nothing hidden or withheld between us.
So tell us if what we have heard is true
about this threat, whatever it is,
this danger abroad in the dark nights,   275
this corpse-maker mongering death
in the Shieldings' country. I come to proffer
my wholehearted help and counsel.
I can show the wise Hrothgar a way
to defeat his enemy and find respite—   280
if any respite is to reach him, ever.
I can calm the turmoil and terror in his mind.
Otherwise, he must endure woes
and live with grief for as long as his hall
stands at the horizon on its high ground."   285
    Undaunted, sitting astride his horse,

the coast-guard answered: "Anyone with gumption
and a sharp mind will take the measure
of two things: what's said and what's done.
I believe what you have told me, that you are a troop   290
loyal to our king. So come ahead
with your arms and your gear, and I will guide you.
What's more, I'll order my own comrades
on their word of honor to watch your boat
down there on the strand—keep her safe   295
in her fresh tar, until the time comes
for her curved prow to preen on the waves
and bear this hero back to Geatland.
May one so valiant and venturesome
come unharmed through the clash of battle."   300
     So they went on their way. The ship rode the water,
broad-beamed, bound by its hawser
and anchored fast. Boar-shapes[8] flashed
above their cheek-guards, the brightly forged
work of goldsmiths, watching over   305
those stern-faced men. They marched in step,
hurrying on till the timbered hall
rose before them, radiant with gold.
Nobody on earth knew of another
building like it. Majesty lodged there,   310
its light shone over many lands.
So their gallant escort guided them
to that dazzling stronghold and indicated
the shortest way to it; then the noble warrior
wheeled on his horse and spoke these words: 315
"It is time for me to go. May the Almighty
Father keep you and in His kindness
watch over your exploits. I'm away to the sea,
back on alert against enemy raiders."
     It was a paved track, a path that kept them   320
in marching order. Their mail-shirts glinted,
hard and hand-linked; the high-gloss iron
of their armor rang. So they duly arrived
in their grim war-graith[9] and gear at the hall,
and, weary from the sea, stacked wide shields   325
of the toughest hardwood against the wall,
then collapsed on the benches; battle-dress
and weapons clashed. They collected their spears
in a seafarers' stook,[1] a stand of grayish
tapering ash. And the troops themselves   330
were as good as their weapons.

---

8. Images of boars—a cult animal among the
Germanic tribes and sacred to the god Freyr—
were fixed atop helmets in the belief that they
would provide protection from enemy blows.

9. "Graith" is an archaic word for equipment
or armor.
1. An archaic word for a pile or mass.

                              Then a proud warrior
questioned the men concerning their origins:
"Where do you come from, carrying these
decorated shields and shirts of mail,
these cheek-hinged helmets and javelins?   335
I am Hrothgar's herald and officer.
I have never seen so impressive or large
an assembly of strangers. Stoutness of heart,
bravery not banishment, must have brought you to Hrothgar."
    The man whose name was known for courage,   340
the Geat leader, resolute in his helmet,
answered in return: "We are retainers
from Hygelac's band. Beowulf is my name.
If your lord and master, the most renowned
son of Halfdane, will hear me out   345
and graciously allow me to greet him in person,
I am ready and willing to report my errand."
    Wulfgar replied, a Wendel[2] chief
renowned as a warrior, well known for his wisdom
and the temper of his mind: "I will take this message,   350
in accordance with your wish, to our noble king,
our dear lord, friend of the Danes,
the giver of rings. I will go and ask him
about your coming here, then hurry back
with whatever reply it pleases him to give."   355
    With that he turned to where Hrothgar sat,
an old man among retainers;
the valiant follower stood foursquare
in front of his king: he knew the courtesies.
Wulfgar addressed his dear lord: 360
"People from Geatland have put ashore.
They have sailed far over the wide sea.
They call the chief in charge of their band
by the name of Beowulf. They beg, my lord,
an audience with you, exchange of words   365
and formal greeting. Most gracious Hrothgar,
do not refuse them, but grant them a reply.
From their arms and appointment, they appear well born
and worthy of respect, especially the one
who has led them this far: he is formidable indeed."   370
    Hrothgar, protector of Shieldings, replied:
"I used to know him when he was a young boy.
His father before him was called Ecgtheow.
Hrethel the Geat[3] gave Ecgtheow

---

2. The Wendels or Vandals are another Germanic nation; it is not unusual for people to
be members of nations different from the ones
in which they reside. Hence Beowulf himself
is both a Geat and a Waegmunding.

3. The leader of the Geats prior to his son
Hygelac, who is the current leader. Note that
Ecgtheow's marriage to Hrethel's daughter
makes Beowulf part of the royal line.

his daughter in marriage. This man is their son,   375
here to follow up an old friendship.
A crew of seamen who sailed for me once
with a gift-cargo across to Geatland
returned with marvelous tales about him:
a thane,[4] they declared, with the strength of thirty   380
in the grip of each hand. Now Holy God
has, in His goodness, guided him here
to the West-Danes, to defend us from Grendel.
This is my hope; and for his heroism
I will recompense him with a rich treasure.   385
Go immediately, bid him and the Geats
he has in attendance to assemble and enter.
Say, moreover, when you speak to them,
they are welcome to Denmark."
                    At the door of the hall,
Wulfgar duly delivered the message: 390
"My lord, the conquering king of the Danes,
bids me announce that he knows your ancestry;
also that he welcomes you here to Heorot
and salutes your arrival from across the sea.
You are free now to move forward   395
to meet Hrothgar in helmets and armor,
but shields must stay here and spears be stacked
until the outcome of the audience is clear."
    The hero arose, surrounded closely
by his powerful thanes. A party remained   400
under orders to keep watch on the arms;
the rest proceeded, led by their prince
under Heorot's roof. And standing on the hearth
in webbed links that the smith had woven,
the fine-forged mesh of his gleaming mail-shirt,   405
resolute in his helmet, Beowulf spoke:
"Greetings to Hrothgar. I am Hygelac's kinsman,
one of his hall-troop. When I was younger,
I had great triumphs. Then news of Grendel,
hard to ignore, reached me at home: 410
sailors brought stories of the plight you suffer
in this legendary hall, how it lies deserted,
empty and useless once the evening light
hides itself under heaven's dome.
So every elder and experienced councilman   415
among my people supported my resolve
to come here to you, King Hrothgar,
because all knew of my awesome strength.
They had seen me boltered[5] in the blood of enemies
when I battled and bound five beasts,   420

---

4. That is, a warrior in the service of a lord like Hrethel or Hrothgar himself.   **5.** Clotted, sticky—a Northern Irish term.

raided a troll-nest and in the night-sea
slaughtered sea-brutes. I have suffered extremes
and avenged the Geats (their enemies brought it
upon themselves; I devastated them).
Now I mean to be a match for Grendel,   425
settle the outcome in single combat.
And so, my request, O king of Bright-Danes,
dear prince of the Shieldings, friend of the people
and their ring of defense, my one request
is that you won't refuse me, who have come this far,   430
the privilege of purifying Heorot,
with my own men to help me, and nobody else.
I have heard moreover that the monster scorns
in his reckless way to use weapons;
therefore, to heighten Hygelac's fame   435
and gladden his heart, I hereby renounce
sword and the shelter of the broad shield,
the heavy war-board: hand-to-hand
is how it will be, a life-and-death
fight with the fiend. Whichever one death fells   440
must deem it a just judgment by God.
If Grendel wins, it will be a gruesome day;
he will glut himself on the Geats in the war-hall,
swoop without fear on that flower of manhood
as on others before. Then my face won't be there   445
to be covered in death: he will carry me away
as he goes to ground, gorged and bloodied;
he will run gloating with my raw corpse
and feed on it alone, in a cruel frenzy
fouling his moor-nest. No need then   450
to lament for long or lay out my body:
if the battle takes me, send back
this breast-webbing that Weland[6] fashioned
and Hrethel gave me, to Lord Hygelac.
Fate goes ever as fate must."   455
    Hrothgar, the helmet of Shieldings, spoke:
"Beowulf, my friend, you have traveled here
to favor us with help and to fight for us.
There was a feud one time, begun by your father.
With his own hands he had killed Heatholaf   460
who was a Wulfing;[7] so war was looming
and his people, in fear of it, forced him to leave.
He came away then over rolling waves
to the South-Danes here, the sons of honor.
I was then in the first flush of kingship,   465
establishing my sway over the rich strongholds
of this heroic land. Heorogar,

---

6. The blacksmith of the Norse gods.   7. The Wulfings are another Germanic nation.

my older brother and the better man,
also a son of Halfdane's, had died.
Finally I healed the feud by paying: 470
I shipped a treasure-trove to the Wulfings,
and Ecgtheow acknowledged me with oaths of allegiance.
　"It bothers me to have to burden anyone
with all the grief that Grendel has caused
and the havoc he has wreaked upon us in Heorot,   475
our humiliations. My household-guard
are on the wane, fate sweeps them away
into Grendel's clutches—but God can easily
halt these raids and harrowing attacks!
　"Time and again, when the goblets passed   480
and seasoned fighters got flushed with beer
they would pledge themselves to protect Heorot
and wait for Grendel with their whetted swords.
But when dawn broke and day crept in
over each empty, blood-spattered bench,   485
the floor of the mead-hall where they had feasted
would be slick with slaughter. And so they died,
faithful retainers, and my following dwindled.
Now take your place at the table, relish
the triumph of heroes to your heart's content."   490

[Feast at Heorot]

　Then a bench was cleared in that banquet hall
so the Geats could have room to be together
and the party sat, proud in their bearing,
strong and stalwart. An attendant stood by
with a decorated pitcher, pouring bright   495
helpings of mead. And the minstrel sang,
filling Heorot with his head-clearing voice,
gladdening that great rally of Geats and Danes.
　From where he crouched at the king's feet,
Unferth, a son of Ecglaf's, spoke   500
contrary words.[8] Beowulf's coming,
his sea-braving, made him sick with envy:
he could not brook or abide the fact
that anyone else alive under heaven
might enjoy greater regard than he did: 505
"Are you the Beowulf who took on Breca
in a swimming match[9] on the open sea,
risking the water just to prove that you could win?
It was sheer vanity made you venture out

---

8. Unferth is Hrothgar's *thyle*, a kind of licensed spokesman who here engages Beowulf in a traditional "flytting" or verbal combat; see the note to line 1457. Ecglaf appears in the poem only as the father of Unferth.

9. The original Anglo-Saxon describing this contest can be interpreted in such a way that Breca and Beowulf are competing not in swimming but in rowing, which is more plausible.

on the main deep. And no matter who tried,   510
friend or foe, to deflect the pair of you,
neither would back down: the sea-test obsessed you.
You waded in, embracing water,
taking its measure, mastering currents,
riding on the swell. The ocean swayed,   515
winter went wild in the waves, but you vied
for seven nights; and then he outswam you,
came ashore the stronger contender.
He was cast up safe and sound one morning
among the Heatho-Reams,[1] then made his way   520
to where he belonged in Bronding[2] country,
home again, sure of his ground
in strongroom and bawn.[3] So Breca made good
his boast upon you and was proved right.
No matter, therefore, how you may have fared   525
in every bout and battle until now,
this time you'll be worsted; no one has ever
outlasted an entire night against Grendel."
    Beowulf, Ecgtheow's son, replied:
"Well, friend Unferth, you have had your say   530
about Breca and me. But it was mostly beer
that was doing the talking. The truth is this:
when the going was heavy in those high waves,
I was the strongest swimmer of all.
We'd been children together and we grew up   535
daring ourselves to outdo each other,
boasting and urging each other to risk
our lives on the sea. And so it turned out.
Each of us swam holding a sword,
a naked, hard-proofed blade for protection   540
against the whale-beasts. But Breca could never
move out farther or faster from me
than I could manage to move from him.
Shoulder to shoulder, we struggled on
for five nights, until the long flow   545
and pitch of the waves, the perishing cold,
night falling and winds from the north
drove us apart. The deep boiled up
and its wallowing sent the sea-brutes wild.
My armor helped me to hold out;   550
my hard-ringed chain-mail, hand-forged and linked,
a fine, close-fitting filigree of gold,
kept me safe when some ocean creature
pulled me to the bottom. Pinioned fast
and swathed in its grip, I was granted one   555

1. A people of southern Norway.
2. The Brondings are the nation to which
Breca belonged, but nothing is known of their
territory.

3. Fortified outwork of a court or castle. The
word was used by English planters in Ulster to
describe fortified dwellings they erected on lands
confiscated from the Irish [translator's note].

final chance: my sword plunged
and the ordeal was over. Through my own hands,
the fury of battle had finished off the sea-beast.
      "Time and again, foul things attacked me,
lurking and stalking, but I lashed out,   560
gave as good as I got with my sword.
My flesh was not for feasting on,
there would be no monsters gnawing and gloating
over their banquet at the bottom of the sea.
Instead, in the morning, mangled and sleeping   565
the sleep of the sword, they slopped and floated
like the ocean's leavings. From now on
sailors would be safe, the deep-sea raids
were over for good. Light came from the east,
bright guarantee of God, and the waves   570
went quiet; I could see headlands
and buffeted cliffs. Often, for undaunted courage,
fate spares the man it has not already marked.
However it occurred, my sword had killed
nine sea-monsters. Such night dangers   575
and hard ordeals I have never heard of
nor of a man more desolate in surging waves.
But worn out as I was, I survived,
came through with my life. The ocean lifted
and laid me ashore, I landed safe   580
on the coast of Finland.
                        Now I cannot recall
any fight you entered, Unferth,
that bears comparison. I don't boast when I say
that neither you nor Breca were ever much
celebrated for swordsmanship   585
or for facing danger on the field of battle.
You killed your own kith and kin,
so for all your cleverness and quick tongue,
you will suffer damnation in the depths of hell.[4]
The fact is, Unferth, if you were truly   590
as keen or courageous as you claim to be
Grendel would never have got away with
such unchecked atrocity, attacks on your king,
havoc in Heorot and horrors everywhere.
But he knows he need never be in dread   595
of your blade making a mizzle[5] of his blood
or of vengeance arriving ever from this quarter—
from the Victory-Shieldings, the shoulderers of the spear.
He knows he can trample down you Danes
to his heart's content, humiliate and murder   600

4. The manuscript is damaged here, and the
word "hell" may well be "hall": "You will suffer
condemnation in the hall" is an acceptable

translation of the line.
5. That is, drizzle.

without fear of reprisal. But he will find me different.
I will show him how Geats shape to kill
in the heat of battle. Then whoever wants to
may go bravely to mead,[6] when the morning light,
scarfed in sun-dazzle, shines forth from the south   605
and brings another daybreak to the world."
    Then the gray-haired treasure-giver was glad;
far-famed in battle, the prince of Bright-Danes
and keeper of his people counted on Beowulf,
on the warrior's steadfastness and his word.   610
So the laughter started, the din got louder
and the crowd was happy. Wealhtheow came in,
Hrothgar's queen, observing the courtesies.
Adorned in her gold, she graciously saluted
the men in the hall, then handed the cup   615
first to Hrothgar, their homeland's guardian,
urging him to drink deep and enjoy it
because he was dear to them. And he drank it down
like the warlord he was, with festive cheer.
So the Helming woman went on her rounds,   620
queenly and dignified, decked out in rings,
offering the goblet to all ranks,
treating the household and the assembled troop,
until it was Beowulf's turn to take it from her hand.
With measured words she welcomed the Geat   625
and thanked God for granting her wish
that a deliverer she could believe in would arrive
to ease their afflictions. He accepted the cup,
a daunting man, dangerous in action
and eager for it always. He addressed Wealhtheow;   630
Beowulf, son of Ecgtheow, said:
"I had a fixed purpose when I put to sea.
As I sat in the boat with my band of men,
I meant to perform to the uttermost
what your people wanted or perish in the attempt,   635
in the fiend's clutches. And I shall fulfill that purpose,
prove myself with a proud deed
or meet my death here in the mead-hall."
This formal boast by Beowulf the Geat
pleased the lady well and she went to sit   640
by Hrothgar, regal and arrayed with gold.
    Then it was like old times in the echoing hall,
proud talk and the people happy,
loud and excited; until soon enough
Halfdane's heir had to be away   645
to his night's rest. He realized
that the demon was going to descend on the hall,
that he had plotted all day, from dawn-light

---

6. An alcoholic drink made by fermenting honey and adding water.

until darkness gathered again over the world
and stealthy night-shapes came stealing forth   650
under the cloud-murk. The company stood
as the two leaders took leave of each other:
Hrothgar wished Beowulf health and good luck,
named him hall-warden and announced as follows:
"Never, since my hand could hold a shield   655
have I entrusted or given control
of the Danes' hall to anyone but you.
Ward and guard it, for it is the greatest of houses.
Be on your mettle now, keep in mind your fame,
beware of the enemy. There's nothing you wish for   660
that won't be yours if you win through alive."

[The Fight with Grendel]

Hrothgar departed then with his house-guard.
The lord of the Shieldings, their shelter in war,
left the mead-hall to lie with Wealhtheow,
his queen and bedmate. The King of Glory   665
(as people learned) had posted a lookout
who was a match for Grendel, a guard against monsters,
special protection to the Danish prince.
And the Geat placed complete trust
in his strength of limb and the Lord's favor.   670
He began to remove his iron breast-mail,
took off the helmet and handed his attendant
the patterned sword, a smith's masterpiece,
ordering him to keep the equipment guarded.
And before he bedded down, Beowulf,   675
that prince of goodness, proudly asserted:
"When it comes to fighting, I count myself
as dangerous any day as Grendel.
So it won't be a cutting edge I'll wield
to mow him down, easily as I might.   680
He has no idea of the arts of war,
of shield or sword-play, although he does possess
a wild strength. No weapons, therefore,
for either this night: unarmed he shall face me
if face me he dares. And may the Divine Lord   685
in His wisdom grant the glory of victory
to whichever side He sees fit."
Then down the brave man lay with his bolster
under his head and his whole company
of sea-rovers at rest beside him.   690
None of them expected he would ever see
his homeland again or get back
to his native place and the people who reared him.
They knew too well the way it was before,
how often the Danes had fallen prey   695
to death in the mead-hall. But the Lord was weaving

a victory on His war-loom for the Weather-Geats.
Through the strength of one they all prevailed;
they would crush their enemy and come through
in triumph and gladness. The truth is clear: 700
Almighty God rules over mankind
and always has.
              Then out of the night
came the shadow-stalker, stealthy and swift.
The hall-guards were slack, asleep at their posts,
all except one; it was widely understood   705
that as long as God disallowed it,
the fiend could not bear them to his shadow-bourne.
One man, however, was in fighting mood,
awake and on edge, spoiling for action.
   In off the moors, down through the mist-bands   710
God-cursed Grendel came greedily loping.
The bane of the race of men roamed forth,
hunting for a prey in the high hall.
Under the cloud-murk he moved toward it
until it shone above him, a sheer keep   715
of fortified gold. Nor was that the first time
he had scouted the grounds of Hrothgar's dwelling—
although never in his life, before or since,
did he find harder fortune or hall-defenders.
Spurned and joyless, he journeyed on ahead   720
and arrived at the bawn. The iron-braced door
turned on its hinge when his hands touched it.
Then his rage boiled over, he ripped open
the mouth of the building, maddening for blood,
pacing the length of the patterned floor   725
with his loathsome tread, while a baleful light,
flame more than light, flared from his eyes.
He saw many men in the mansion, sleeping,
a ranked company of kinsmen and warriors
quartered together. And his glee was demonic,   730
picturing the mayhem: before morning
he would rip life from limb and devour them,
feed on their flesh; but his fate that night
was due to change, his days of ravening
had come to an end.
              Mighty and canny,   735
Hygelac's kinsman was keenly watching
for the first move the monster would make.
Nor did the creature keep him waiting
but struck suddenly and started in;
he grabbed and mauled a man on his bench,   740
bit into his bone-lappings,[7] bolted down his blood
and gorged on him in lumps, leaving the body

---

7. That is, joints.

utterly lifeless, eaten up
hand and foot. Venturing closer,
his talon was raised to attack Beowulf   745
where he lay on the bed, he was bearing in
with open claw when the alert hero's
comeback and armlock forestalled him utterly.
The captain of evil discovered himself
in a handgrip harder than anything   750
he had ever encountered in any man
on the face of the earth. Every bone in his body
quailed and recoiled, but he could not escape.
He was desperate to flee to his den and hide
with the devil's litter, for in all his days   755
he had never been clamped or cornered like this.
Then Hygelac's trusty retainer recalled
his bedtime speech, sprang to his feet
and got a firm hold. Fingers were bursting,
the monster back-tracking, the man overpowering.   760
The dread of the land was desperate to escape,
to take a roundabout road and flee
to his lair in the fens. The latching power
in his fingers weakened; it was the worst trip
the terror-monger had taken to Heorot.   765
And now the timbers trembled and sang,
a hall-session[8] that harrowed every Dane
inside the stockade: stumbling in fury,
the two contenders crashed through the building.
The hall clattered and hammered, but somehow   770
survived the onslaught and kept standing:
it was handsomely structured, a sturdy frame
braced with the best of blacksmith's work
inside and out. The story goes
that as the pair struggled, mead-benches were smashed   775
and sprung off the floor, gold fittings and all.
Before then, no Shielding elder would believe
there was any power or person upon earth
capable of wrecking their horn-rigged hall
unless the burning embrace of a fire   780
engulf it in flame. Then an extraordinary
wail arose, and bewildering fear
came over the Danes. Everyone felt it
who heard that cry as it echoed off the wall,
a God-cursed scream and strain of catastrophe,   785
the howl of the loser, the lament of the hell-serf
keening his wound. He was overwhelmed,
manacled tight by the man who of all men

---

8. In Hiberno-English the word "session" (*seissiún* in Irish) can mean a gathering where musicians and singers perform for their own enjoyment [translator's note]. In other words, the poet is making a laconic joke, since the main function of the hall is celebration and singing.

was foremost and strongest in the days of this life.
    But the earl-troop's leader was not inclined   790
to allow his caller to depart alive:
he did not consider that life of much account
to anyone anywhere. Time and again,
Beowulf's warriors worked to defend
their lord's life, laying about them   795
as best they could, with their ancestral blades.
Stalwart in action, they kept striking out
on every side, seeking to cut
straight to the soul. When they joined the struggle
there was something they could not have known at the time,   800
that no blade on earth, no blacksmith's art
could ever damage their demon opponent.
He had conjured the harm from the cutting edge
of every weapon.⁹ But his going away
out of this world and the days of his life   805
would be agony to him, and his alien spirit
would travel far into fiends' keeping.
    Then he who had harrowed the hearts of men
with pain and affliction in former times
and had given offense also to God   810
found that his bodily powers failed him.
Hygelac's kinsman kept him helplessly
locked in a handgrip. As long as either lived,
he was hateful to the other. The monster's whole
body was in pain; a tremendous wound   815
appeared on his shoulder. Sinews split
and the bone-lappings burst. Beowulf was granted
the glory of winning; Grendel was driven
under the fen-banks, fatally hurt,
to his desolate lair. His days were numbered,   820
the end of his life was coming over him,
he knew it for certain; and one bloody clash
had fulfilled the dearest wishes of the Danes.
The man who had lately landed among them,
proud and sure, had purged the hall,   825
kept it from harm; he was happy with his nightwork
and the courage he had shown. The Geat captain
had boldly fulfilled his boast to the Danes:
he had healed and relieved a huge distress,
unremitting humiliations,   830
the hard fate they'd been forced to undergo,
no small affliction. Clear proof of this
could be seen in the hand the hero displayed
high up near the roof: the whole of Grendel's
shoulder and arm, his awesome grasp.   835

9. Grendel is magically protected from weapons.

[Celebration at Heorot]

Then morning came and many a warrior
gathered, as I've heard, around the gift-hall,
clan-chiefs flocking from far and near
down wide-ranging roads, wondering greatly
at the monster's footprints. His fatal departure   840
was regretted by no one who witnessed his trail,
the ignominious marks of his flight
where he'd skulked away, exhausted in spirit
and beaten in battle, bloodying the path,
hauling his doom to the demons' mere.[1]   845
The bloodshot water wallowed and surged,
there were loathsome upthrows and overturnings
of waves and gore and wound-slurry.
With his death upon him, he had dived deep
into his marsh-den, drowned out his life   850
and his heathen soul: hell claimed him there.
Then away they rode, the old retainers
with many a young man following after,
a troop on horseback, in high spirits
on their bay steeds. Beowulf's doings   855
were praised over and over again.
Nowhere, they said, north or south
between the two seas or under the tall sky
on the broad earth was there anyone better
to raise a shield or to rule a kingdom.   860
Yet there was no laying of blame on their lord,
the noble Hrothgar; he was a good king.
     At times the war-band broke into a gallop,
letting their chestnut horses race
wherever they found the going good   865
on those well-known tracks. Meanwhile, a thane
of the king's household, a carrier of tales,
a traditional singer deeply schooled
in the lore of the past, linked a new theme
to a strict meter.[2] The man started   870
to recite with skill, rehearsing Beowulf's
triumphs and feats in well-fashioned lines,
entwining his words.
                    He told what he'd heard
repeated in songs about Sigemund's exploits,[3]
all of those many feats and marvels,   875
the struggles and wanderings of Waels's son,
things unknown to anyone

1. A lake or pool.
2. The singer or *scop* composes extemporane-
ously in alliterative verse.
3. According to Norse legend, Sigemund, the
son of Waels (or Volsung, as he is known
in Norse), slept with his sister Sigurth, who
bore a son named Fitela; Fitela was thus also

Sigemund's nephew, as he is described here.
The singer here contrasts Sigemund's bravery
in killing a dragon with the defeat of the Danish king Heremod, who could not protect his
people. For more on Heremod as a bad king,
see lines 1709–22.

except to Fitela, feuds and foul doings
confided by uncle to nephew when he felt
the urge to speak of them: always they had been   880
partners in the fight, friends in need.
They killed giants, their conquering swords
had brought them down.
                        After his death
Sigemund's glory   grew and grew
because of his courage   when he killed the dragon,   885
the guardian of the hoard.   Under gray stone
he had dared to enter   all by himself
to face the worst   without Fitela.
But it came to pass   that his sword plunged
right through   those radiant scales   890
and drove into the wall.   The dragon died of it.
His daring had given him   total possession
of the treasure-hoard,   his to dispose of
however he liked.   He loaded a boat:
Waels's son   weighted her hold   895
with dazzling spoils.   The hot dragon melted.
*   Sigemund's name   was known everywhere.*
He was utterly valiant   and venturesome,
a fence round his fighters   and flourished therefore
after King Heremod's   prowess declined   900
and his campaigns slowed down.   The king was betrayed,
ambushed in Jutland,   overpowered
and done away with.   The waves of his grief
had beaten him down,   made him a burden,
a source of anxiety   to his own nobles: 905
that expedition   was often condemned
in those earlier times   by experienced men,
men who relied   on his lordship for redress,
who presumed that the part   of a prince was to thrive
on his father's throne   and defend the nation,   910
the Shielding land   where they lived and belonged,
its holdings and strongholds.   Such was Beowulf
in the affection of his friends   and of everyone alive.
But evil entered   into Heremod.
   Meanwhile, the Danes kept racing their mounts   915
down sandy lanes. The light of day
broke and kept brightening. Bands of retainers
galloped in excitement to the gabled hall
to see the marvel; and the king himself,
guardian of the ring-hoard, goodness in person,   920
walked in majesty from the women's quarters
with a numerous train, attended by his queen
and her crowd of maidens, across to the mead-hall.
   When Hrothgar arrived at the hall, he spoke,
standing on the steps, under the steep eaves,   925
gazing toward the roofwork and Grendel's talon:
"First and foremost, let the Almighty Father

be thanked for this sight. I suffered a long
harrowing by Grendel. But the Heavenly Shepherd
can work His wonders always and everywhere.   930
Not long since, it seemed I would never
be granted the slightest solace or relief
from any of my burdens: the best of houses
glittered and reeked and ran with blood.
This one worry outweighed all others—   935
a constant distress to counselors entrusted
with defending the people's forts from assault
by monsters and demons. But now a man,
with the Lord's assistance, has accomplished something
none of us could manage before now   940
for all our efforts. Whoever she was
who brought forth this flower of manhood,
if she is still alive, that woman can say
that in her labor the Lord of Ages
bestowed a grace on her. So now, Beowulf,   945
I adopt you in my heart as a dear son.
Nourish and maintain this new connection,
you noblest of men; there'll be nothing you'll want for,
no worldly goods that won't be yours.
I have often honored smaller achievements,   950
recognized warriors not nearly as worthy,
lavished rewards on the less deserving.
But you have made yourself immortal
by your glorious action. May the God of Ages
continue to keep and requite you well."   955
    Beowulf, son of Ecgtheow, spoke:
"We have gone through with a glorious endeavor
and been much favored in this fight we dared
against the unknown. Nevertheless,
if you could have seen the monster himself   960
where he lay beaten, I would have been better pleased.
My plan was to pounce, pin him down
in a tight grip and grapple him to death—
have him panting for life, powerless and clasped
in my bare hands, his body in thrall.   965
But I couldn't stop him from slipping my hold.
The Lord allowed it, my lock on him
wasn't strong enough; he struggled fiercely
and broke and ran. Yet he bought his freedom
at a high price, for he left his hand   970
and arm and shoulder to show he had been here,
a cold comfort for having come among us.
And now he won't be long for this world.
He has done his worst but the wound will end him.
He is hasped and hooped and hirpling[4] with pain,   975

4. That is, limping.

limping and looped in it. Like a man outlawed
for wickedness, he must await
the mighty judgment of God in majesty."
  There was less tampering and big talk then
from Unferth the boaster, less of his blather   980
as the hall-thanes eyed the awful proof
of the hero's prowess, the splayed hand
up under the eaves. Every nail,
claw-scale and spur, every spike
and welt on the hand of that heathen brute   985
was like barbed steel. Everybody said
there was no honed iron hard enough
to pierce him through, no time-proofed blade
that could cut his brutal, blood-caked claw.
  Then the order was given for all hands   990
to help to refurbish Heorot immediately:
men and women thronging the wine-hall,
getting it ready. Gold thread shone
in the wall-hangings, woven scenes
that attracted and held the eye's attention.   995
But iron-braced as the inside of it had been,
that bright room lay in ruins now.
The very doors had been dragged from their hinges.
Only the roof remained unscathed
by the time the guilt-fouled fiend turned tail   1000
in despair of his life. But death is not easily
escaped from by anyone:
all of us with souls, earth-dwellers
and children of men, must make our way
to a destination already ordained   1005
where the body, after the banqueting,
sleeps on its deathbed.
                         Then the due time arrived
for Halfdane's son to proceed to the hall.
The king himself would sit down to feast.
No group ever gathered in greater numbers   1010
or better order around their ring-giver.
The benches filled with famous men
who fell to with relish; round upon round
of mead was passed; those powerful kinsmen,
Hrothgar and Hrothulf, were in high spirits   1015
in the raftered hall. Inside Heorot
there was nothing but friendship. The Shielding nation
was not yet familiar with feud and betrayal.[5]
  Then Halfdane's son presented Beowulf

5. The poet here refers to the later history of
the Danes, when after Hrothgar's death his
nephew Hrothulf drove his son Hrethric from
the throne. For Wealhtheow's fear that this
betrayal will indeed come to pass, see lines
1168–90.

with a gold standard as a victory gift,   1020
an embroidered banner; also breast-mail
and a helmet; and a sword carried high,
that was both precious object and token of honor.
So Beowulf drank his drink, at ease;
it was hardly a shame to be showered with such gifts   1025
in front of the hall-troops. There haven't been many
moments, I am sure, when men exchanged
four such treasures at so friendly a sitting.
An embossed ridge, a band lapped with wire
arched over the helmet: head-protection   1030
to keep the keen-ground cutting edge
from damaging it when danger threatened
and the man was battling behind his shield.
Next the king ordered eight horses
with gold bridles to be brought through the yard   1035
into the hall. The harness of one
included a saddle of sumptuous design,
the battle-seat where the son of Halfdane
rode when he wished to join the sword-play:
wherever the killing and carnage were the worst,   1040
he would be to the fore, fighting hard.
Then the Danish prince, descendant of Ing,[6]
handed over both the arms and the horses,
urging Beowulf to use them well.
And so their leader, the lord and guard   1045
of coffer and strongroom, with customary grace
bestowed upon Beowulf both sets of gifts.
A fair witness can see how well each one behaved.
    The chieftain went on to reward the others:
each man on the bench who had sailed with Beowulf   1050
and risked the voyage received a bounty,
some treasured possession. And compensation,
a price in gold, was settled for the Geat
Grendel had cruelly killed earlier—
as he would have killed more, had not mindful God   1055
and one man's daring prevented that doom.
Past and present, God's will prevails.
Hence, understanding is always best
and a prudent mind. Whoever remains
for long here in this earthly life   1060
will enjoy and endure more than enough.
    They sang then and played to please the hero,
words and music for their warrior prince,
harp tunes and tales of adventure:
there were high times on the hall benches,   1065
and the king's poet performed his part
with the saga of Finn and his sons, unfolding

6. A Germanic deity and the protector of the Danes.

the tale of the fierce attack in Friesland
where Hnaef, king of the Danes, met death.[7]

Hildeburh
              had little cause   1070
to credit the Jutes:
              son and brother,
she lost them both
              on the battlefield.
She, bereft
              and blameless, they
foredoomed, cut down
              and spear-gored. She,
the woman in shock,
              waylaid by grief,   1075
Hoc's daughter—
              how could she not
lament her fate
              when morning came
and the light broke
              on her murdered dears?
And so farewell
              delight on earth,
war carried away
              Finn's troop of thanes   1080
all but a few.
              How then could Finn
hold the line
              or fight on
to the end with Hengest,
              how save
the rump of his force
              from that enemy chief?
So a truce was offered
              as follows: first   1085
separate quarters
              to be cleared for the Danes,
hall and throne
              to be shared with the Frisians.
Then, second:
              every day
at the dole-out of gifts
              Finn, son of Focwald,

---

7. This song recounts the fight at Finnsburg
between the Dane Hengest and the Jute (or
Frisian) Finn. The poet begins with the bereft
Hildeburh, daughter of the Danish king Hoc
and wife of the Jute Finn, whose unnamed son
and brother Hnaef have already been killed in
the first battle with Finn. He then tells how
Hengest, the new leader of the Danes, is offered
a truce by the weakened Finn, how together they
cremate their dead, following which Hengest
and the remaining Danes spend the winter with
Finn and the Jutes. But with the coming of
spring, the feud breaks out again and Finn and
the Jutes are slaughtered by Hengest with the
help of two other Danes, Guthlaf and Oslaf.

should honor the Danes,
                    bestow with an even   1090
hand to Hengest
            and Hengest's men
the wrought-gold rings,
                    bounty to match
the measure he gave
            his own Frisians—
to keep morale
            in the beer-hall high.
Both sides then
            sealed their agreement.   1095
With oaths to Hengest
            Finn swore
openly, solemnly,
            that the battle survivors
would be guaranteed
            honor and status.
No infringement
            by word or deed,
no provocation
            would be permitted.   1100
Their own ring-giver
            after all
was dead and gone,
            they were leaderless,
in forced allegiance
            to his murderer.
So if any Frisian
            stirred up bad blood
with insinuations
            or taunts about this,   1105
the blade of the sword
            would arbitrate it.
A funeral pyre
            was then prepared,
effulgent gold
            brought out from the hoard.
The pride and prince
            of the Shieldings lay
awaiting the flame.
            Everywhere   1110
there were blood-plastered
            coats of mail.
The pyre was heaped
            with boar-shaped helmets
forged in gold,
            with the gashed corpses
of wellborn Danes—
            many had fallen.
Then Hildeburh

                              ordered her own   1115
son's body
                              be burnt with Hnaef's
the flesh on his bones
                              to sputter and blaze
beside his uncle's.
                              The woman wailed
and sang keens,
                              the warrior went up.[8]
Carcass flame
                              swirled and fumed,   1120
they stood round the burial
                              mound and howled
as heads melted,
                              crusted gashes
spattered and ran
                              bloody matter.
The glutton element
                              flamed and consumed
the dead of both sides.
                              Their great days were gone.   1125
Warriors scattered
                              to homes and forts
all over Friesland,
                              fewer now, feeling
loss of friends.
                              Hengest stayed,
lived out that whole
                              resentful, blood-sullen
winter with Finn,
                              homesick and helpless.   1130
No ring-whorled prow
                              could up then
and away on the sea.
                              Wind and water
raged with storms,
                              wave and shingle
were shackled in ice
                              until another year
appeared in the yard
                              as it does to this day,   1135
the seasons constant,
                              the wonder of light
coming over us.
                              Then winter was gone,
earth's lap grew lovely,
                              longing woke
in the cooped-up exile

---

8. The warrior (Hildeburh's son) either goes up on the pyre or goes up in smoke. *Keens*: an Irish
   rd for funeral laments.

This painted limestone statue, discovered in Saqqara, Egypt, in 1850, depicts a scribe writing on a tablet. It dates from the third millennium B.C.E. Scribes were highly respected members of court in ancient literate societies; their work is the primary reason we have any sense of life in deep antiquity.

Clay tablets (right and top) and envelope (left) from central Turkey, dating from ca. 1850 B.C.E. These objects contain a letter, written in cuneiform, from someone named "Ashur-malik" to his brother "Ashur-idi" in which the former complains that his family has been left in Ashur without food, fuel, or clothing over the winter. The letter writer ran out of room on the large tablet and so had to continue his complaint on the little supplemental tablet.

An "oracle bone," dating from the Shang Dynasty (2nd millennium B.C.E.) in China. Oracle bones were often made of ox scapula (shoulder blades) or tortoise belly-shells and were inscribed with divinations using a bronze pin or other carving implement. These bones represent the earliest significant gathering of Chinese writing.

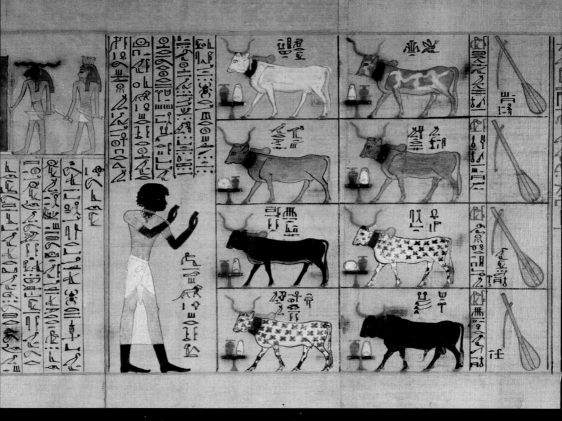

Ancient Egyptians of aristocratic status were often buried with a specially commissioned papyrus manuscript of the *Book of the Dead* that pictured them making their way to the afterlife. The manuscript here, written in hieroglyphic script and with an image of the departed at the center, is the *Book of the Dead* for an Egyptian noble of Nubian origin named Maiherperi. It dates from the reign of the pharaoh Thutmose IV, ca. fourteenth century B.C.E.

One form of writing that was a basic part of citizenship in Athens during its classical period (the fifth and fourth centuries B.C.E.) was ballot-casting. The most common medium for casting votes was broken earthenware, on which citizens would write their selection. These shards, called *ostraka*, often record a vote on the question of whether or not to banish or exile someone. This term is the source of the English word *ostracism*.

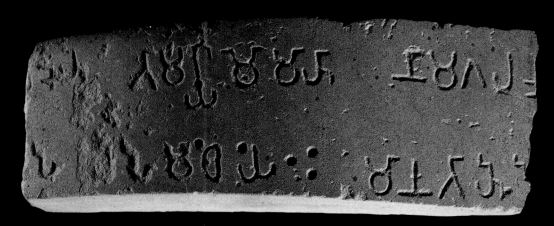

This fragment, part of the "sixth pillar edict" of King Aśoka (third century B.C.E.), shows the Brahmi script used during the Mauryan Dynasty in northern India. The Brahmi script is the ancestral source of all modern Indian scripts.

This Roman fresco painting, from a house in Pompeii whose details were preserved because of the eruption of Mount Vesuvius in 79 C.E., depicts a young woman holding a stylus and a wax tablet. Writing on wax tablets was a common means of taking notes and recording other ephemera in classical antiquity. The surface could be reused by warming and smoothing the wax to remove prior markings.

Beginning in Roman antiquity and continuing into medieval times, one of the highest-quality portable writing mediums was vellum. Made from the skin of domesticated mammals (calf, sheep, and goat skins were most common), vellum was smooth and durable and was generally reserved for special texts. Pictured here is a vellum manuscript of Homer's *Iliad* (called the *Ambrosian Iliad* or *Ilia Picta*) dating from the fifth century C.E. It is the only illustrated copy of Homer from classical antiquity to have survived.

CODICIBVS SACRIS HOSTILI CLADE PERVSTIS
ESDRA DŌ FERVENS HOC REPARAVIT OPVS

This page from the Codex Amiatinus (ca. 8th century C.E.), the earliest surviving manuscript of the Latin Vulgate Bible, depicts the Jewish scribe Ezra. Ezra is traditionally credited with reestablishing the primacy of the Law in Jewish society.

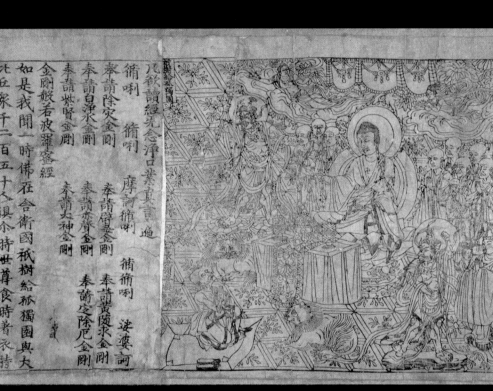

Frontispiece from the world's earliest dated printed book: a Chinese translation of the Buddhist *Diamond Sūtra*. This translation, consisting of a series of woodblock prints on a sixteen-foot scroll, was printed in 868 C.E.

A fragment of the Qur'an (specifically, the beginning of sura 33) written in Kufic script, the oldest calligraphic form of Arabic script. This parchment manuscript, decorated with designs in black and red ink and gold leaf, dates from the ninth or tenth century C.E.

The Old English poem *Beowulf* survives in only one manuscript copy, a page of which is pictured here. Though the poem is set in sixth-century Scandinavia, the date of its composition isn't known. This manuscript was copied sometime in the early eleventh century.

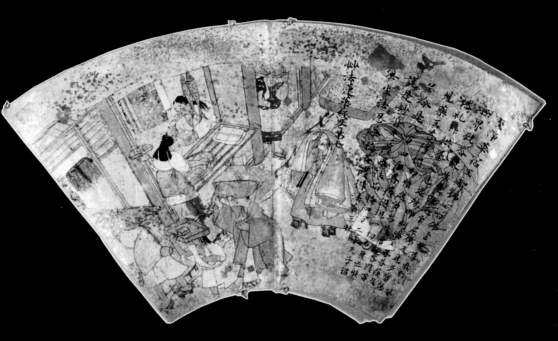

A single leaf from a fan-shaped album of excerpts from
the Buddhist *Lotus Sūtra* that was produced near the
end of the Heian Period in Japan (i.e., sometime during
the late twelfth century). In addition to the calligraphic
excerpt on the right, this page features a genre painting
of servants performing their duties. The illustrations in
these fan-shaped albums were typically unrelated to the
quoted sutra.

A page from perhaps the most famous printed book of all time: the Gutenberg Bible (ca. 1453–56). Printed in Mainz, Germany, this Bible was one of the first books (and certainly the most notable one) to be printed in Europe using a movable-type printing press. Only twenty-one copies survive.

Typographus. *Der Buchdrucker.*

Arte mea reliquas illustro Typographus artes,
  Imprimo dum varios ære micante libros.
Quæ prius aucta situ, quæ puluere plena iacebant,
Vidimus obscura nocte sepulta premi.

Hæc veterum renouo neglecta volumina Patrum
  Atq, scolis curo publica facta legi.
Artem prima nouam reperisse Moguntia fertur,
  Vrbs grauis, & multis ingeniosa modis.
Qua nihil vtilius videt, aut preciosius orbis,
  Vix melius quicquam secla futura dabunt.

C 3   Char-

A detail from the Codex Féjerváry-Mayer, a pre-Hispanic Aztec manuscript on deerskin parchment, believed to have originated in Veracruz. Pictured is an Aztec origin myth: the Nahuatl god Tezcatlipoca uses his foot as bait to lure the Earth Monster to the surface. After she swallows his foot, she is unable to sink back to her lair, and thus the surface of the earth is created by her immobilized body.

Hartmann Schedel's 1493 book, *World Chronicle* (in German, *Weltchronik*), an illustrated world history, was one of the first printed books to bring maps and illustrations to a wide readership. This page depicts the universe as it was understood at the time: with the earth at the center and other celestial bodies surrounding it. Fifty years later, the Renaissance astronomer Nicolaus Copernicus (1473–1543) overturned this model, placing the sun at the center.

Dedicatory page from Antoine du Four's *The Lives of Famous Women* (ca. 1505). The author, on bended knee, offers the book to Queen Anne of Brittany (1477–1514), who commissioned the work and for whom du Four served as confessor. The book chronicles the lives of famous women from Eve to Joan of Arc.

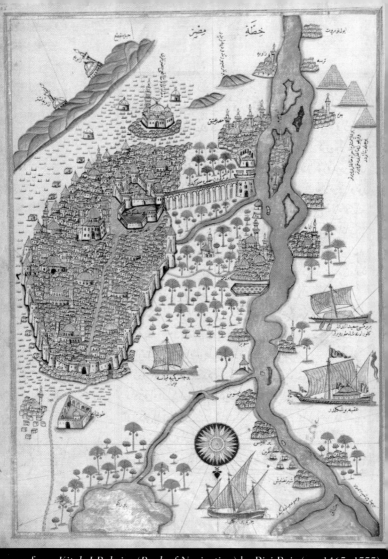

A page from *Kitab-I Bahriye* (*Book of Navigation*) by Piri Reis (ca. 1465–1555),
an Ottoman military commander, geographer, and cartographer. Published in
1521, the *Kitab-I Bahriye* is one of the most famous books of navigation from
early modernity. It provided a comprehensive and detailed overview of the known
world of the time, including the recently explored shorelines of the African
and American continents. Pictured here is a map of Egypt, with different
settlements along the Nile, including the large city of Cairo.

The Reader. A Persian miniature from an unidentified manuscript, ca. sixteenth century.

An illustration from the north Indian poetry anthology *Rasik Priya* (1591), by the Sanskrit scholar and Hindi poet Keśavdās (1555–1617). This manuscript dates from the early 17th century, after Keśavdās's death.

To the Reader.

This Figure, that thou here seest put,
　It was for gentle Shakespeare cut;
Wherein the Grauer had a strife
　with Nature, to out-doo the life :
O, could he but haue drawne his wit
　As well in brasse, as he hath hit
His face ; the Print would then surpasse
　All, that vvas euer vvrit in brasse.
But, since he cannot, Reader, looke
　Not on his Picture, but his Booke.

B. I.

Mr. WILLIAM

SHAKESPEARES

COMEDIES,
HISTORIES, &
TRAGEDIES.

Published according to the True Originall Copies.

Martin Droeshout sculpsit London.

LONDON

Printed by Isaac Iaggard, and Ed. Blount. 1623.

Frontispiece and title page of one of the most famous books of the Renaissance: the 1623 "First Folio" of the plays of William Shakespeare. The portrait by Martin Droeshout was not made from life, and yet it has fixed the public's sense of Shakespeare's appearance.

This 1645 portrait of the court jester Don Diego de Acedo is by the Spanish master Diego Velázquez (1599–1660). Intending to convey de Acedo's status and his intelligence (while also acknowledging his deformity), Velázquez poses him with a book (a traditional signal in court portraiture of gentlemanly status), notebook, stylus, and inkwell.

for a voyage home—
but more for vengeance,
   some way of bringing   1140
things to a head:
   his sword arm hankered
to greet the Jutes.
   So he did not balk
once Hunlafing[9]
   placed on his lap
Dazzle-the-Duel,
   the best sword of all,
whose edges Jutes
   knew only too well.   1145
Thus blood was spilled,
   the gallant Finn
slain in his home
   after Guthlaf and Oslaf[1]
back from their voyage
   made old accusation:
the brutal ambush,
   the fate they had suffered,
all blamed on Finn.
   The wildness in them   1150
had to brim over.
   The hall ran red
with blood of enemies.
   Finn was cut down,
the queen brought away
   and everything
the Shieldings could find
   inside Finn's walls—
the Frisian king's
   gold collars and gemstones—   1155
swept off to the ship.
   Over sea-lanes then
back to Daneland
   the warrior troop
bore that lady home.

   The poem was over,
the poet had performed, a pleasant murmur
started on the benches, stewards did the rounds   1160
with wine in splendid jugs, and Wealhtheow came to sit
in her gold crown between two good men,
uncle and nephew, each one of whom
still trusted the other;[2] and the forthright Unferth,

9. A Danish follower of Hengest.
1. Danes who seem to have gone home in order to bring reinforcements to Hengest. But it is possible that these two have been with Hengest all along and that "their voyage" is an unrelated journey.
2. See p. 864, n. 5.

admired by all for his mind and courage   1165
although under a cloud for killing his brothers,
reclined near the king.
                          The queen spoke:
"Enjoy this drink, my most generous lord;
raise up your goblet, entertain the Geats
duly and gently, discourse with them,   1170
be open-handed, happy and fond.
Relish their company, but recollect as well
all of the boons that have been bestowed on you.
The bright court of Heorot has been cleansed
and now the word is that you want to adopt   1175
this warrior as a son. So, while you may,
bask in your fortune, and then bequeath
kingdom and nation to your kith and kin,
before your decease. I am certain of Hrothulf.
He is noble and will use the young ones well.   1180
He will not let you down. Should you die before him,
he will treat our children truly and fairly.
He will honor, I am sure, our two sons,
repay them in kind, when he recollects
all the good things we gave him once,   1185
the favor and respect he found in his childhood."
She turned then to the bench where her boys sat,
Hrethric and Hrothmund, with other nobles' sons,
all the youth together; and that good man,
Beowulf the Geat, sat between the brothers.   1190
    The cup was carried to him, kind words
spoken in welcome and a wealth of wrought gold
graciously bestowed: two arm bangles,
a mail-shirt and rings, and the most resplendent
torque of gold I ever heard tell of   1195
anywhere on earth or under heaven.
There was no hoard like it since Hama snatched
the Brosings' neck-chain and bore it away
with its gems and settings to his shining fort,
away from Eormenric's wiles and hatred,   1200
and thereby ensured his eternal reward.[3]
Hygelac the Geat, grandson of Swerting,
wore this neck-ring on his last raid;[4]
at bay under his banner, he defended the booty,
treasure he had won. Fate swept him away   1205
because of his proud need to provoke
a feud with the Frisians. He fell beneath his shield,
in the same gem-crusted, kingly gear

---

3. The legend alluded to here seems to be that Hama stole the golden necklace of the Brosings from Eormenric (a historical figure, the king of the Ostrogoths, who died ca. 375), and then gave it to the goddess Freya.

4. The poet here refers to the death of Hygelac while raiding the Frisian territory of the Franks. This raid and Hygelac's death are recorded by the historian Gregory of Tours (d. 594) as having taken place about 520.

he had worn when he crossed the frothing wave-vat.
So the dead king fell into Frankish hands. 1210
They took his breast-mail, also his neck-torque,
and punier warriors plundered the slain
when the carnage ended; Geat corpses
covered the field.
      Applause filled the hall.
Then Wealhtheow pronounced in the presence of the company: 1215
"Take delight in this torque, dear Beowulf,
wear it for luck and wear also this mail
from our people's armory: may you prosper in them!
Be acclaimed for strength, for kindly guidance
to these two boys, and your bounty will be sure. 1220
You have won renown: you are known to all men
far and near, now and forever.
Your sway is wide as the wind's home,
as the sea around cliffs. And so, my prince,
I wish you a lifetime's luck and blessings 1225
to enjoy this treasure. Treat my sons
with tender care, be strong and kind.
Here each comrade is true to the other,
loyal to lord, loving in spirit.
The thanes have one purpose, the people are ready: 1230
having drunk and pledged, the ranks do as I bid."
  She moved then to her place. Men were drinking wine
at that rare feast; how could they know fate,
the grim shape of things to come,
the threat looming over many thanes 1235
as night approached and King Hrothgar prepared
to retire to his quarters? Retainers in great numbers
were posted on guard as so often in the past.
Benches were pushed back, bedding gear and bolsters
spread across the floor, and one man 1240
lay down to his rest, already marked for death.
At their heads they placed their polished timber
battle-shields; and on the bench above them,
each man's kit was kept to hand:
a towering war-helmet, webbed mail-shirt 1245
and great-shafted spear. It was their habit
always and everywhere to be ready for action,
at home or in the camp, in whatever case
and at whatever time the need arose
to rally round their lord. They were a right people. 1250

[Another Attack]

  They went to sleep. And one paid dearly
for his night's ease, as had happened to them often,
ever since Grendel occupied the gold-hall,
committing evil until the end came,
death after his crimes. Then it became clear, 1255

obvious to everyone once the fight was over,
that an avenger lurked and was still alive,
grimly biding time. Grendel's mother,
monstrous hell-bride, brooded on her wrongs.
She had been forced down into fearful waters,   1260
the cold depths, after Cain had killed
his father's son, felled his own
brother with a sword. Branded an outlaw,
marked by having murdered, he moved into the wilds,
shunned company and joy. And from Cain there sprang   1265
misbegotten spirits, among them Grendel,
the banished and accursed, due to come to grips
with that watcher in Heorot waiting to do battle.
The monster wrenched and wrestled with him,
but Beowulf was mindful of his mighty strength,   1270
the wondrous gifts God had showered on him:
he relied for help on the Lord of All,
on His care and favor. So he overcame the foe,
brought down the hell-brute. Broken and bowed,
outcast from all sweetness, the enemy of mankind   1275
made for his death-den. But now his mother
had sallied forth on a savage journey,
grief-racked and ravenous, desperate for revenge.
    She came to Heorot. There, inside the hall,
Danes lay asleep, earls who would soon endure   1280
a great reversal, once Grendel's mother
attacked and entered. Her onslaught was less
only by as much as an amazon warrior's
strength is less than an armed man's
when the hefted sword, its hammered edge   1285
and gleaming blade slathered in blood,
razes the sturdy boar-ridge off a helmet.
Then in the hall, hard-honed swords
were grabbed from the bench, many a broad shield
lifted and braced; there was little thought of helmets   1290
or woven mail when they woke in terror.
    The hell-dam was in panic, desperate to get out,
in mortal terror the moment she was found.
She had pounced and taken one of the retainers
in a tight hold, then headed for the fen.   1295
To Hrothgar, this man was the most beloved
of the friends he trusted between the two seas.
She had done away with a great warrior,
ambushed him at rest.
                Beowulf was elsewhere.
Earlier, after the award of the treasure,   1300
the Geat had been given another lodging.
    There was uproar in Heorot. She had snatched their trophy,
Grendel's bloodied hand. It was a fresh blow
to the afflicted bawn. The bargain was hard,

both parties having to pay   1305
with the lives of friends. And the old lord,
the gray-haired warrior, was heartsore and weary
when he heard the news: his highest-placed adviser,
his dearest companion, was dead and gone.
    Beowulf was quickly brought to the chamber: 1310
the winner of fights, the arch-warrior,
came first-footing in with his fellow troops
to where the king in his wisdom waited,
still wondering whether Almighty God
would ever turn the tide of his misfortunes.   1315
So Beowulf entered with his band in attendance
and the wooden floorboards banged and rang
as he advanced, hurrying to address
the prince of the Ingwins,[5] asking if he'd rested
since the urgent summons had come as a surprise.   1320
    Then Hrothgar, the Shieldings' helmet, spoke:
"Rest? What is rest? Sorrow has returned.
Alas for the Danes! Aeschere is dead.
He was Yrmenlaf's elder brother
and a soul-mate to me, a true mentor,   1325
my right-hand man when the ranks clashed
and our boar-crests had to take a battering
in the line of action. Aeschere was everything
the world admires in a wise man and a friend.
Then this roaming killer came in a fury   1330
and slaughtered him in Heorot. Where she is hiding,
glutting on the corpse and glorying in her escape,
I cannot tell; she has taken up the feud
because of last night, when you killed Grendel,
wrestled and racked him in ruinous combat   1335
since for too long he had terrorized us
with his depredations. He died in battle,
paid with his life; and now this powerful
other one arrives, this force for evil
driven to avenge her kinsman's death.   1340
Or so it seems to thanes in their grief,
in the anguish every thane endures
at the loss of a ring-giver, now that the hand
that bestowed so richly has been stilled in death.
    "I have heard it said by my people in hall,   1345
counselors who live in the upland country,
that they have seen two such creatures
prowling the moors, huge marauders
from some other world. One of these things,
as far as anyone ever can discern,   1350
looks like a woman; the other, warped
in the shape of a man, moves beyond the pale

5. The friends of the god Ing—that is, the Danes. See p. 865, n. 6.

bigger than any man, an unnatural birth
called Grendel by the country people
in former days. They are fatherless creatures, 1355
and their whole ancestry is hidden in a past
of demons and ghosts.[6] They dwell apart
among wolves on the hills, on windswept crags
and treacherous keshes, where cold streams
pour down the mountain and disappear 1360
under mist and moorland.
               A few miles from here
a frost-stiffened wood waits and keeps watch
above a mere; the overhanging bank
is a maze of tree-roots mirrored in its surface.
At night there, something uncanny happens: 1365
the water burns. And the mere bottom
has never been sounded by the sons of men.
On its bank, the heather-stepper halts:
the hart in flight from pursuing hounds
will turn to face them with firm-set horns 1370
and die in the wood rather than dive
beneath its surface. That is no good place.
When wind blows up and stormy weather
makes clouds scud and the skies weep,
out of its depths a dirty surge 1375
is pitched toward the heavens. Now help depends
again on you and on you alone.
The gap of danger where the demon waits
is still unknown to you. Seek it if you dare.
I will compensate you for settling the feud 1380
as I did the last time with lavish wealth,
coffers of coiled gold, if you come back."

[Beowulf Fights Grendel's Mother]

Beowulf, son of Ecgtheow, spoke:
"Wise sir, do not grieve. It is always better
to avenge dear ones than to indulge in mourning. 1385
For every one of us, living in this world
means waiting for our end. Let whoever can
win glory before death. When a warrior is gone,
that will be his best and only bulwark.
So arise, my lord, and let us immediately 1390
set forth on the trail of this troll-dam.
I guarantee you: she will not get away,
not to dens under ground nor upland groves
nor the ocean floor. She'll have nowhere to flee to.
Endure your troubles today. Bear up 1395
and be the man I expect you to be."

---

6. Note that Hrothgar doesn't know of the biblical genealogy of Grendel and his mother that the
poet has given us in lines 102–14.

With that the old lord sprang to his feet
and praised God for Beowulf's pledge.
Then a bit and halter were brought for his horse
with the plaited mane. The wise king mounted   1400
the royal saddle and rode out in style
with a force of shield-bearers. The forest paths
were marked all over with the monster's tracks,
her trail on the ground wherever she had gone
across the dark moors, dragging away   1405
the body of that thane, Hrothgar's best
counselor and overseer of the country.
So the noble prince proceeded undismayed
up fells and screes, along narrow footpaths
and ways where they were forced into single file,   1410
ledges on cliffs above lairs of water-monsters.
He went in front with a few men,
good judges of the lie of the land,
and suddenly discovered the dismal wood,
mountain trees growing out at an angle   1415
above gray stones: the bloodshot water
surged underneath. It was a sore blow
to all of the Danes, friends of the Shieldings,
a hurt to each and every one
of that noble company when they came upon   1420
Aeschere's head at the foot of the cliff.
   Everybody gazed as the hot gore
kept wallowing up and an urgent war-horn
repeated its notes: the whole party
sat down to watch. The water was infested   1425
with all kinds of reptiles. There were writhing sea-dragons
and monsters slouching on slopes by the cliff,
serpents and wild things such as those that often
surface at dawn to roam the sail-road
and doom the voyage. Down they plunged,   1430
lashing in anger at the loud call
of the battle-bugle. An arrow from the bow
of the Geat chief got one of them
as he surged to the surface: the seasoned shaft
stuck deep in his flank and his freedom in the water   1435
got less and less. It was his last swim.
He was swiftly overwhelmed in the shallows,
prodded by barbed boar-spears,
cornered, beaten, pulled up on the bank,
a strange lake-birth, a loathsome catch   1440
men gazed at in awe.
                Beowulf got ready,
donned his war-gear, indifferent to death;
his mighty, hand-forged, fine-webbed mail
would soon meet with the menace underwater.
It would keep the bone-cage of his body safe: 1445

no enemy's clasp could crush him in it,
no vicious armlock choke his life out.
To guard his head he had a glittering helmet
that was due to be muddied on the mere bottom
and blurred in the upswirl. It was of beaten gold,   1450
princely headgear hooped and hasped
by a weapon-smith who had worked wonders
in days gone by and adorned it with boar-shapes;
since then it had resisted every sword.
And another item lent by Unferth   1455
at that moment of need was of no small importance:
the brehon[7] handed him a hilted weapon,
a rare and ancient sword named Hrunting.
The iron blade with its ill-boding patterns
had been tempered in blood. It had never failed   1460
the hand of anyone who hefted it in battle,
anyone who had fought and faced the worst
in the gap of danger. This was not the first time
it had been called to perform heroic feats.
    When he lent that blade to the better swordsman,   1465
Unferth, the strong-built son of Ecglaf,
could hardly have remembered the ranting speech
he had made in his cups. He was not man enough
to face the turmoil of a fight under water
and the risk to his life. So there he lost   1470
fame and repute. It was different for the other
rigged out in his gear, ready to do battle.
    Beowulf, son of Ecgtheow, spoke:
"Wisest of kings, now that I have come
to the point of action, I ask you to recall   1475
what we said earlier: that you, son of Halfdane
and gold-friend to retainers, that you, if I should fall
and suffer death while serving your cause,
would act like a father to me afterward.
If this combat kills me, take care   1480
of my young company, my comrades in arms.
And be sure also, my beloved Hrothgar,
to send Hygelac the treasures I received.
Let the lord of the Geats gaze on that gold,
let Hrethel's son take note of it and see   1485
that I found a ring-giver of rare magnificence
and enjoyed the good of his generosity.
And Unferth is to have what I inherited:
to that far-famed man I bequeath my own
sharp-honed, wave-sheened wonder-blade.
With Hrunting I shall gain glory or die."   1490
    After these words, the prince of the Weather-Geats
was impatient to be away and plunged suddenly:

7. One of an ancient class of lawyers in Ireland [translator's note]. The word is used to translate
the Anglo-Saxon *thyle*.

without more ado, he dived into the heaving
depths of the lake. It was the best part of a day   1495
before he could see the solid bottom.

    Quickly the one who haunted those waters,
who had scavenged and gone her gluttonous rounds
for a hundred seasons, sensed a human
observing her outlandish lair from above.   1500
So she lunged and clutched and managed to catch him
in her brutal grip; but his body, for all that,
remained unscathed: the mesh of the chain-mail
saved him on the outside. Her savage talons
failed to rip the web of his war-shirt.   1505
Then once she touched bottom, that wolfish swimmer
carried the ring-mailed prince to her court
so that for all his courage he could never use
the weapons he carried; and a bewildering horde
came at him from the depths, droves of sea-beasts   1510
who attacked with tusks and tore at his chain-mail
in a ghastly onslaught. The gallant man
could see he had entered some hellish turn-hole
and yet the water there did not work against him
because the hall-roofing held off   1515
the force of the current; then he saw firelight,
a gleam and flare-up, a glimmer of brightness.

    The hero observed that swamp-thing from hell,
the tarn-hag[8] in all her terrible strength,
then heaved his war-sword and swung his arm: 1520
the decorated blade came down ringing
and singing on her head. But he soon found
his battle-torch extinguished; the shining blade
refused to bite. It spared her and failed
the man in his need. It had gone through many   1525
a hand-to-hand fight, had hewed the armor
and helmets of the doomed, but here at last
the fabulous powers of that heirloom failed.

    Hygelac's kinsman kept thinking about
his name and fame: he never lost heart.   1530
Then, in a fury, he flung his sword away.
The keen, inlaid, worm-loop-patterned steel
was hurled to the ground: he would have to rely
on the might of his arm. So must a man do
who intends to gain enduring glory   1535
in a combat. Life doesn't cost him a thought.
Then the prince of War-Geats, warming to this fight
with Grendel's mother, gripped her shoulder
and laid about him in a battle frenzy:
he pitched his killer opponent to the floor   1540
but she rose quickly and retaliated,
grappled him tightly in her grim embrace.

---

    8. A "tarn" is a small lake.

The sure-footed fighter felt daunted,
the strongest of warriors stumbled and fell.
So she pounced upon him and pulled out   1545
a broad, whetted knife: now she would avenge
her only child. But the mesh of chain-mail
on Beowulf's shoulder shielded his life,
turned the edge and tip of the blade.
The son of Ecgtheow would have surely perished   1550
and the Geats lost their warrior under the wide earth
had the strong links and locks of his war-gear
not helped to save him: holy God
decided the victory. It was easy for the Lord,
the Ruler of Heaven, to redress the balance   1555
once Beowulf got back up on his feet.
    Then he saw a blade that boded well,
a sword in her armory, an ancient heirloom
from the days of the giants, an ideal weapon,
one that any warrior would envy,   1560
but so huge and heavy of itself
only Beowulf could wield it in a battle.
So the Shieldings' hero hard-pressed and enraged,
took a firm hold of the hilt and swung
the blade in an arc, a resolute blow   1565
that bit deep into her neck-bone
and severed it entirely, toppling the doomed
house of her flesh; she fell to the floor.
The sword dripped blood, the swordsman was elated.
    A light appeared and the place brightened   1570
the way the sky does when heaven's candle
is shining clearly. He inspected the vault:
with sword held high, its hilt raised
to guard and threaten, Hygelac's thane
scouted by the wall in Grendel's wake.   1575
Now the weapon was to prove its worth.
The warrior determined to take revenge
for every gross act Grendel had committed—
and not only for that one occasion
when he'd come to slaughter the sleeping troops,   1580
fifteen of Hrothgar's house-guards
surprised on their benches and ruthlessly devoured,
and as many again carried away,
a brutal plunder. Beowulf in his fury
now settled that score: he saw the monster   1585
in his resting place, war-weary and wrecked,
a lifeless corpse, a casualty
of the battle in Heorot. The body gaped
at the stroke dealt to it after death:
Beowulf cut the corpse's head off.   1590
    Immediately the counselors keeping a lookout
with Hrothgar, watching the lake water,
saw a heave-up and surge of waves

and blood in the backwash. They bowed gray heads,
spoke in their sage, experienced way   1595
about the good warrior, how they never again
expected to see that prince returning
in triumph to their king. It was clear to many
that the wolf of the deep had destroyed him forever.

    The ninth hour of the day arrived.   1600
The brave Shieldings abandoned the cliff-top
and the king went home; but sick at heart,
staring at the mere, the strangers held on.
They wished, without hope, to behold their lord,
Beowulf himself.
              Meanwhile, the sword   1605
began to wilt into gory icicles
to slather and thaw. It was a wonderful thing,
the way it all melted as ice melts
when the Father eases the fetters off the frost
and unravels the water-ropes, He who wields power   1610
over time and tide: He is the true Lord.

    The Geat captain saw treasure in abundance
but carried no spoils from those quarters
except for the head and the inlaid hilt
embossed with jewels; its blade had melted   1615
and the scrollwork on it burned, so scalding was the blood
of the poisonous fiend who had perished there.
Then away he swam, the one who had survived
the fall of his enemies, flailing to the surface.
The wide water, the waves and pools,   1620
were no longer infested once the wandering fiend
let go of her life and this unreliable world.

    The seafarers' leader made for land,
resolutely swimming, delighted with his prize,
the mighty load he was lugging to the surface.   1625
His thanes advanced in a troop to meet him,
thanking God and taking great delight
in seeing their prince back safe and sound.
Quickly the hero's helmet and mail-shirt
were loosed and unlaced. The lake settled,   1630
clouds darkened above the bloodshot depths.

    With high hearts they headed away
along footpaths and trails through the fields,
roads that they knew, each of them wrestling
with the head they were carrying from the lakeside cliff,   1635
men kingly in their courage and capable
of difficult work. It was a task for four
to hoist Grendel's head on a spear
and bear it under strain to the bright hall.
But soon enough they neared the place,   1640
fourteen Geats in fine fettle,
striding across the outlying ground
in a delighted throng around their leader.

In he came then, the thanes' commander,
the arch-warrior, to address Hrothgar: 1645
his courage was proven, his glory was secure.
Grendel's head was hauled by the hair,
dragged across the floor where the people were drinking,
a horror for both queen and company to behold.
They stared in awe. It was an astonishing sight.   1650

[Another Celebration at Heorot]

    Beowulf, son of Ecgtheow, spoke:
"So, son of Halfdane, prince of the Shieldings,
we are glad to bring this booty from the lake.
It is a token of triumph and we tender it to you.
I barely survived the battle under water.   1655
It was hard-fought, a desperate affair
that could have gone badly; if God had not helped me,
the outcome would have been quick and fatal.
Although Hrunting is hard-edged,
I could never bring it to bear in battle.   1660
But the Lord of Men allowed me to behold—
for He often helps the unbefriended—
an ancient sword shining on the wall,
a weapon made for giants, there for the wielding.
Then my moment came in the combat and I struck   1665
the dwellers in that den. Next thing the damascened[9]
sword blade melted; it bloated and it burned
in their rushing blood. I have wrested the hilt
from the enemies' hand, avenged the evil
done to the Danes; it is what was due.   1670
And this I pledge, O prince of the Shieldings:
you can sleep secure with your company of troops
in Heorot Hall. Never need you fear
for a single thane of your sept[1] or nation,
young warriors or old, that laying waste of life   1675
that you and your people endured of yore."
    Then the gold hilt was handed over
to the old lord, a relic from long ago
for the venerable ruler. That rare smithwork
was passed on to the prince of the Danes   1680
when those devils perished; once death removed
that murdering, guilt-steeped, God-cursed fiend,
eliminating his unholy life
and his mother's as well, it was willed to that king
who of all the lavish gift-lords of the north   1685
was the best regarded between the two seas.
    Hrothgar spoke; he examined the hilt,
that relic of old times. It was engraved all over

9. Ornamented with inlaid designs.
1. An Irish term meaning a clan or division of a tribe.

and showed how war first came into the world
and the flood destroyed the tribe of giants.   1690
They suffered a terrible severance from the Lord;
the Almighty made the waters rise,
drowned them in the deluge for retribution.
In pure gold inlay on the sword-guards
there were rune-markings correctly incised,   1695
stating and recording for whom the sword
had been first made and ornamented
with its scrollworked hilt. Then everyone hushed
as the son of Halfdane spoke this wisdom:
"A protector of his people, pledged to uphold   1700
truth and justice and to respect tradition,
is entitled to affirm that this man
was born to distinction. Beowulf, my friend,
your fame has gone far and wide,
you are known everywhere. In all things you are even-tempered,   1705
prudent and resolute. So I stand firm by the promise of friendship
we exchanged before. Forever you will be
your people's mainstay and your own warriors'
helping hand.
                      Heremod was different,
the way he behaved to Ecgwela's sons.[2]   1710
His rise in the world brought little joy
to the Danish people, only death and destruction.
He vented his rage on men he caroused with,
killed his own comrades, a pariah king
who cut himself off from his own kind,   1715
even though Almighty God had made him
eminent and powerful and marked him from the start
for a happy life. But a change happened,
he grew bloodthirsty, gave no more rings
to honor the Danes. He suffered in the end   1720
for having plagued his people for so long:
his life lost happiness.
                      So learn from this
and understand true values. I who tell you
have wintered into wisdom.
                      It is a great wonder
how Almighty God in His magnificence   1725
favors our race with rank and scope
and the gift of wisdom; His sway is wide.
Sometimes He allows the mind of a man
of distinguished birth to follow its bent,
grants him fulfillment and felicity on earth   1730
and forts to command in his own country.
He permits him to lord it in many lands
until the man in his unthinkingness

---

2. That is, the Danes. Ecgwela was evidently a former king of the Danes.

forgets that it will ever end for him.
He indulges his desires; illness and old age   1735
mean nothing to him; his mind is untroubled
by envy or malice or the thought of enemies
with their hate-honed swords. The whole world
conforms to his will, he is kept from the worst
until an element of overweening   1740
enters him and takes hold
while the soul's guard, its sentry, drowses,
grown too distracted. A killer stalks him,
an archer who draws a deadly bow.
And then the man is hit in the heart,   1745
the arrow flies beneath his defenses,
the devious promptings of the demon start.
His old possessions seem paltry to him now.
He covets and resents; dishonors custom
and bestows no gold; and because of good things   1750
that the Heavenly Powers gave him in the past
he ignores the shape of things to come.
Then finally the end arrives
when the body he was lent collapses and falls
prey to its death; ancestral possessions   1755
and the goods he hoarded are inherited by another
who lets them go with a liberal hand.
     "O flower of warriors, beware of that trap.
Choose, dear Beowulf, the better part,
eternal rewards. Do not give way to pride.   1760
For a brief while your strength is in bloom
but it fades quickly; and soon there will follow
illness or the sword to lay you low,
or a sudden fire or surge of water
or jabbing blade or javelin from the air   1765
or repellent age. Your piercing eye
will dim and darken; and death will arrive,
dear warrior, to sweep you away.
     "Just so I ruled the Ring-Danes' country
for fifty years, defended them in wartime   1770
with spear and sword against constant assaults
by many tribes: I came to believe
my enemies had faded from the face of the earth.
Still, what happened was a hard reversal
from bliss to grief. Grendel struck   1775
after lying in wait. He laid waste to the land
and from that moment my mind was in dread
of his depredations. So I praise God
in His heavenly glory that I lived to behold
this head dripping blood and that after such harrowing   1780
I can look upon it in triumph at last.
Take your place, then, with pride and pleasure,
and move to the feast. Tomorrow morning
our treasure will be shared and showered upon you."

The Geat was elated and gladly obeyed   1785
the old man's bidding; he sat on the bench.
And soon all was restored, the same as before.
Happiness came back, the hall was thronged,
and a banquet set forth; black night fell
and covered them in darkness.
                              Then the company rose   1790
for the old campaigner: the gray-haired prince
was ready for bed. And a need for rest
came over the brave shield-bearing Geat.
He was a weary seafarer, far from home,
so immediately a house-guard guided him out,   1795
one whose office entailed looking after
whatever a thane on the road in those days
might need or require. It was noble courtesy.

[Beowulf Returns Home]

That great heart rested. The hall towered,
gold-shingled and gabled, and the guest slept in it   1800
until the black raven with raucous glee
announced heaven's joy, and a hurry of brightness
overran the shadows. Warriors rose quickly,
impatient to be off: their own country
was beckoning the nobles; and the bold voyager   1805
longed to be aboard his distant boat.
Then that stalwart fighter ordered Hrunting
to be brought to Unferth, and bade Unferth
take the sword and thanked him for lending it.
He said he had found it a friend in battle   1810
and a powerful help; he put no blame
on the blade's cutting edge. He was a considerate man.
And there the warriors stood in their war-gear,
eager to go, while their honored lord
approached the platform where the other sat.   1815
The undaunted hero addressed Hrothgar.
Beowulf, son of Ecgtheow, spoke:
"Now we who crossed the wide sea
have to inform you that we feel a desire
to return to Hygelac. Here we have been welcomed   1820
and thoroughly entertained. You have treated us well.
If there is any favor on earth I can perform
beyond deeds of arms I have done already,
anything that would merit your affections more,
I shall act, my lord, with alacrity.   1825
If ever I hear from across the ocean
that people on your borders are threatening battle
as attackers have done from time to time,
I shall land with a thousand thanes at my back
to help your cause. Hygelac may be young   1830

to rule a nation, but this much I know
about the king of the Geats: he will come to my aid
and want to support me by word and action
in your hour of need, when honor dictates
that I raise a hedge of spears around you.   1835
Then if Hrethric should think about traveling
as a king's son to the court of the Geats,
he will find many friends. Foreign places
yield more to one who is himself worth meeting."
　　Hrothgar spoke and answered him: 1840
"The Lord in his wisdom sent you those words
and they came from the heart. I have never heard
so young a man make truer observations.
You are strong in body and mature in mind,
impressive in speech. If it should come to pass   1845
that Hrethel's descendant dies beneath a spear,
if deadly battle or the sword blade or disease
fells the prince who guards your people
and you are still alive, then I firmly believe
the seafaring Geats won't find a man   1850
worthier of acclaim as their king and defender
than you, if only you would undertake
the lordship of your homeland. My liking for you
deepens with time, dear Beowulf.
What you have done is to draw two peoples,   1855
the Geat nation and us neighboring Danes,
into shared peace and a pact of friendship
in spite of hatreds we have harbored in the past.
For as long as I rule this far-flung land
treasures will change hands and each side will treat   1860
the other with gifts; across the gannet's bath,
over the broad sea, whorled prows will bring
presents and tokens. I know your people
are beyond reproach in every respect,
steadfast in the old way with friend or foe."   1865
　　Then the earls' defender furnished the hero
with twelve treasures and told him to set out,
sail with those gifts safely home
to the people he loved, but to return promptly.
And so the good and gray-haired Dane,   1870
that highborn king, kissed Beowulf
and embraced his neck, then broke down
in sudden tears. Two forebodings
disturbed him in his wisdom, but one was stronger:[3]
nevermore would they meet each other   1875
face to face. And such was his affection
that he could not help being overcome:
his fondness for the man was so deep-founded,

---

3. We are not told what the other foreboding is, but it is probably the old man's awareness of the imminence of his own death.

it warmed his heart and wound the heartstrings
tight in his breast.

     The embrace ended 1880
and Beowulf, glorious in his gold regalia,
stepped the green earth. Straining at anchor
and ready for boarding, his boat awaited him.
So they went on their journey, and Hrothgar's generosity
was praised repeatedly. He was a peerless king 1885
until old age sapped his strength and did him
mortal harm, as it has done so many.

  Down to the waves then, dressed in the web
of their chain-mail and war-shirts the young men marched
in high spirits. The coast-guard spied them, 1890
thanes setting forth, the same as before.
His salute this time from the top of the cliff
was far from unmannerly; he galloped to meet them
and as they took ship in their shining gear,
he said how welcome they would be in Geatland. 1895
Then the broad hull was beached on the sand
to be cargoed with treasure, horses and war-gear.
The curved prow motioned; the mast stood high
above Hrothgar's riches in the loaded hold.

  The guard who had watched the boat was given 1900
a sword with gold fittings, and in future days
that present would make him a respected man
at his place on the mead-bench.

     Then the keel plunged
and shook in the sea; and they sailed from Denmark.

  Right away the mast was rigged with its sea-shawl; 1905
sail-ropes were tightened, timbers drummed
and stiff winds kept the wave-crosser
skimming ahead; as she heaved forward,
her foamy neck was fleet and buoyant,
a lapped prow loping over currents, 1910
until finally the Geats caught sight of coastline
and familiar cliffs. The keel reared up,
wind lifted it home, it hit on the land.

  The harbor guard came hurrying out
to the rolling water: he had watched the offing 1915
long and hard, on the lookout for those friends.
With the anchor cables, he moored their craft
right where it had beached, in case a backwash
might catch the hull and carry it away.
Then he ordered the prince's treasure-trove 1920
to be carried ashore. It was a short step
from there to where Hrethel's son and heir,
Hygelac the gold-giver, makes his home
on a secure cliff, in the company of retainers.

  The building was magnificent, the king majestic, 1925
ensconced in his hall; and although Hygd, his queen,
was young, a few short years at court,

her mind was thoughtful and her manners sure.
Haereth's daughter[4] behaved generously
and stinted nothing when she distributed   1930
bounty to the Geats.
                        Great Queen Modthryth
perpetrated terrible wrongs.[5]
If any retainer ever made bold
to look her in the face, if an eye not her lord's[6]
stared at her directly during daylight,   1935
the outcome was sealed: he was kept bound,
in hand-tightened shackles, racked, tortured
until doom was pronounced—death by the sword,
slash of blade, blood-gush, and death-qualms
in an evil display. Even a queen   1940
outstanding in beauty must not overstep like that.
A queen should weave peace, not punish the innocent
with loss of life for imagined insults.
But Hemming's kinsman put a halt to her ways
and drinkers round the table had another tale: 1945
she was less of a bane to people's lives,
less cruel-minded, after she was married
to the brave Offa,[7] a bride arrayed
in her gold finery, given away
by a caring father, ferried to her young prince   1950
over dim seas. In days to come
she would grace the throne and grow famous
for her good deeds and conduct of life,
her high devotion to the hero king
who was the best king, it has been said,   1955
between the two seas or anywhere else
on the face of the earth. Offa was honored
far and wide for his generous ways,
his fighting spirit and his farseeing
defense of his homeland; from him there sprang Eomer,   1960
Garmund's grandson, kinsman of Hemming,[8]
his warriors' mainstay and master of the field.
    Heroic Beowulf and his band of men
crossed the wide strand, striding along
the sandy foreshore; the sun shone,   1965
the world's candle warmed them from the south
as they hastened to where, as they had heard,
the young king, Ongentheow's killer[9]

4. That is, Hygd.
5. A Danish queen whose wickedness is being used as a foil to Hygd.
6. Probably her father, although the Anglo-Saxon word can also refer to a husband.
7. A legendary king of the Angles, one of the Germanic peoples who invaded England and established a kingdom named Mercia in the north of the country prior to the composition

of *Beowulf*. Hemming is evidently a forebear of the Angles.
8. Garmund is Offa's father, Eomer his son.
9. Hygelac, king of the Geats; he led the attack against the Swedes, although a Geat named Eofor actually killed Ongentheow. This is the first reference to the feud between the Geats and the Swedes (or Shylfings); see below, lines 2379–96, 2468–89, 2922–98.

and his people's protector, was dispensing rings
inside his bawn. Beowulf's return   1970
was reported to Hygelac as soon as possible,
news that the captain was now in the enclosure,
his battle-brother back from the fray
alive and well, walking to the hall.
Room was quickly made, on the king's orders,   1975
and the troops filed across the cleared floor.
    After Hygelac had offered greetings
to his loyal thane in a lofty speech,
he and his kinsman, that hale survivor,
sat face to face. Haereth's daughter[1]   1980
moved about with the mead-jug in her hand,
taking care of the company, filling the cups
that warriors held out. Then Hygelac began
to put courteous questions to his old comrade
in the high hall. He hankered to know   1985
every tale the Sea-Geats had to tell:
"How did you fare on your foreign voyage,
dear Beowulf, when you abruptly decided
to sail away across the salt water
and fight at Heorot? Did you help Hrothgar   1990
much in the end? Could you ease the prince
of his well-known troubles? Your undertaking
cast my spirits down, I dreaded the outcome
of your expedition and pleaded with you
long and hard to leave the killer be,   1995
let the South-Danes settle their own
blood-feud with Grendel. So God be thanked
I am granted this sight of you, safe and sound."
    Beowulf, son of Ecgtheow, spoke:
"What happened, Lord Hygelac, is hardly a secret   2000
any more among men in this world—
myself and Grendel coming to grips
on the very spot where he visited destruction
on the Victory-Shieldings and violated
life and limb, losses I avenged   2005
so no earthly offspring of Grendel's
need ever boast of that bout before dawn,
no matter how long the last of his evil
family survives.
                    When I first landed
I hastened to the ring-hall and saluted Hrothgar.   2010
Once he discovered why I had come,
the son of Halfdane sent me immediately
to sit with his own sons on the bench.
It was a happy gathering. In my whole life
I have never seen mead enjoyed more   2015
in any hall on earth. Sometimes the queen

---

1. That is, Hygd.

herself appeared, peace-pledge between nations,[2]
to hearten the young ones and hand out
a torque to a warrior, then take her place.
Sometimes Hrothgar's daughter distributed   2020
ale to older ranks, in order on the benches:
I heard the company call her Freawaru
as she made her rounds, presenting men
with the gem-studded bowl, young bride-to-be
to the gracious Ingeld,[3] in her gold-trimmed attire.   2025
The friend of the Shieldings favors her betrothal:
the guardian of the kingdom sees good in it
and hopes this woman will heal old wounds
and grievous feuds.
                 But generally the spear
is prompt to retaliate when a prince is killed,   2030
no matter how admirable the bride may be.
  "Think how the Heatho-Bards are bound to feel,
their lord, Ingeld, and his loyal thanes,
when he walks in with that woman to the feast:
Danes are at the table, being entertained,   2035
honored guests in glittering regalia,
burnished ring-mail that was their hosts' birthright,
looted when the Heatho-Bards could no longer wield
their weapons in the shield-clash, when they went down
with their beloved comrades and forfeited their lives.   2040
Then an old spearman will speak while they are drinking,
having glimpsed some heirloom that brings alive
memories of the massacre; his mood will darken
and heart-stricken, in the stress of his emotion,
he will begin to test a young man's temper   2045
and stir up trouble, starting like this:
'Now, my friend, don't you recognize
your father's sword, his favorite weapon,
the one he wore when he went out in his war-mask
to face the Danes on that final day?   2050
After Withergeld[4] died and his men were doomed,
the Shieldings quickly claimed the field;
and now here's a son of one or other
of those same killers coming through our hall
overbearing us, mouthing boasts,   2055
and rigged in armor that by right is yours.'
And so he keeps on, recalling and accusing,
working things up with bitter words
until one of the lady's retainers lies

---

2. Wealhtheow, Hrothgar's queen, is called a "peace-pledge between nations" because kings attempted to end feuds by marrying their daughters to the sons of the kings of enemy nations. But as we have already seen in the case of the marriage of the Dane Hildeburh to the Jute Finn, and as we shall shortly learn again, such a strategy seems rarely to have worked.
3. King of the Heatho-Bards, whose father, Froda, was killed by the Danes.
4. A Heatho-Bard warrior.

spattered in blood, split open   2060
on his father's account.[5] The killer knows
the lie of the land and escapes with his life.
Then on both sides the oath-bound lords
will break the peace, a passionate hate
will build up in Ingeld, and love for his bride   2065
will falter in him as the feud rankles.
I therefore suspect the good faith of the Heatho-Bards,
the truth of their friendship and the trustworthiness
of their alliance with the Danes.
                          But now, my lord,
I shall carry on with my account of Grendel,   2070
the whole story of everything that happened
in the hand-to-hand fight.
                          After heaven's gem
had gone mildly to earth, that maddened spirit,
the terror of those twilights, came to attack us
where we stood guard, still safe inside the hall.   2075
There deadly violence came down on Hondscio[6]
and he fell as fate ordained, the first to perish,
rigged out for the combat. A comrade from our ranks
had come to grief in Grendel's maw:
he ate up the entire body.   2080
There was blood on his teeth, he was bloated and dangerous,
all roused up, yet still unready
to leave the hall empty-handed;
renowned for his might, he matched himself against me,
wildly reaching. He had this roomy pouch,[7]   2085
a strange accoutrement, intricately strung
and hung at the ready, a rare patchwork
of devilishly fitted dragon-skins.
I had done him no wrong, yet the raging demon
wanted to cram me and many another   2090
into this bag—but it was not to be
once I got to my feet in a blind fury.
It would take too long to tell how I repaid
the terror of the land for every life he took
and so won credit for you, my king,   2095
and for all your people. And although he got away
to enjoy life's sweetness for a while longer,
his right hand stayed behind him in Heorot,
evidence of his miserable overthrow
as he dived into murk on the mere bottom.   2100
   "I got lavish rewards from the lord of the Danes
for my part in the battle, beaten gold
and much else, once morning came

5. A Danish attendant to Freawaru, whose   6. A Geat who was accompanying Beowulf;
father killed a Heatho-Bard in the original   his name means "glove."
battle; this action is envisioned as taking place   7. The Anglo-Saxon word translated as
at Ingeld's court after the marriage.   "pouch" literally means "glove."

and we took our places at the banquet table.
There was singing and excitement: an old reciter,   2105
a carrier of stories, recalled the early days.
At times some hero made the timbered harp
tremble with sweetness, or related true
and tragic happenings; at times the king
gave the proper turn to some fantastic tale,   2110
or a battle-scarred veteran, bowed with age,
would begin to remember the martial deeds
of his youth and prime and be overcome
as the past welled up in his wintry heart.
    "We were happy there the whole day long   2115
and enjoyed our time until another night
descended upon us. Then suddenly
the vehement mother avenged her son
and wreaked destruction. Death had robbed her,
Geats had slain Grendel, so his ghastly dam   2120
struck back and with bare-faced defiance
laid a man low. Thus life departed
from the sage Aeschere, an elder wise in counsel.
But afterward, on the morning following,
the Danes could not burn the dead body   2125
nor lay the remains of the man they loved
on his funeral pyre. She had fled with the corpse
and taken refuge beneath torrents on the mountain.
It was a hard blow for Hrothgar to bear,
harder than any he had undergone before.   2130
And so the heartsore king beseeched me
in your royal name to take my chances
underwater, to win glory
and prove my worth. He promised me rewards.
Hence, as is well known, I went to my encounter   2135
with the terror-monger at the bottom of the tarn.
For a while it was hand-to-hand between us,
then blood went curling along the currents
and I beheaded Grendel's mother in the hall
with a mighty sword. I barely managed   2140
to escape with my life; my time had not yet come.
But Halfdane's heir, the shelter of those earls,
again endowed me with gifts in abundance.
    "Thus the king acted with due custom.
I was paid and recompensed completely,   2145
given full measure and the freedom to choose
from Hrothgar's treasures by Hrothgar himself.
These, King Hygelac, I am happy to present
to you as gifts. It is still upon your grace
that all favor depends. I have few kinsmen   2150
who are close, my king, except for your kind self."
Then he ordered the boar-framed standard to be brought,
the battle-topping helmet, the mail-shirt gray as hoar-frost,
and the precious war-sword; and proceeded with his speech:

"When Hrothgar presented this war-gear to me   2155
he instructed me, my lord, to give you some account
of why it signifies his special favor.
He said it had belonged to his older brother,
King Heorogar, who had long kept it,
but that Heorogar had never bequeathed it   2160
to his son Heoroward, that worthy scion,
loyal as he was.
                    Enjoy it well."
    I heard four horses were handed over next.
Beowulf bestowed four bay steeds
to go with the armor, swift gallopers,   2165
all alike. So ought a kinsman act,
instead of plotting and planning in secret
to bring people to grief, or conspiring to arrange
the death of comrades. The warrior king
was uncle to Beowulf and honored by his nephew: 2170
each was concerned for the other's good.
    I heard he presented Hygd with a gorget,
the priceless torque that the prince's daughter,
Wealhtheow, had given him; and three horses,
supple creatures brilliantly saddled.   2175
The bright necklace would be luminous on Hygd's breast.
    Thus Beowulf bore himself with valor;
he was formidable in battle yet behaved with honor
and took no advantage; never cut down
a comrade who was drunk, kept his temper   2180
and, warrior that he was, watched and controlled
his God-sent strength and his outstanding
natural powers. He had been poorly regarded
for a long time, was taken by the Geats
for less than he was worth: and their lord too   2185
had never much esteemed him in the mead-hall.
They firmly believed that he lacked force,
that the prince was a weakling; but presently
every affront to his deserving was reversed.
    The battle-famed king, bulwark of his earls,   2190
ordered a gold-chased heirloom of Hrethel's[8]
to be brought in; it was the best example
of a gem-studded sword in the Geat treasury.
This he laid on Beowulf's lap
and then rewarded him with land as well,   2195
seven thousand hides;[9] and a hall and a throne.
Both owned land by birth in that country,
ancestral grounds; but the greater right
and sway were inherited by the higher born.

---

8. Hygelac's father and, through his daughter, Beowulf's grandfather.
9. A "hide" varied in size, but was considered

to be sufficient land to support a peasant and
his family.

[The Dragon Wakes]

A lot was to happen in later days   2200
in the fury of battle. Hygelac fell
and the shelter of Heardred's shield proved useless
against the fierce aggression of the Shylfings:[1]
ruthless swordsmen, seasoned campaigners,
they came against him and his conquering nation,   2205
and with cruel force cut him down
so that afterwards
                    the wide kingdom
reverted to Beowulf. He ruled it well
for fifty winters, grew old and wise
as warden of the land
                    until one began   2210
to dominate the dark, a dragon on the prowl
from the steep vaults of a stone-roofed barrow[2]
where he guarded a hoard; there was a hidden passage,
unknown to men, but someone managed[3]
to enter by it and interfere   2215
with the heathen trove. He had handled and removed
a gem-studded goblet; it gained him nothing,
though with a thief's wiles he had outwitted
the sleeping dragon. That drove him into rage,
as the people of that country would soon discover.   2220
   The intruder who broached the dragon's treasure
and moved him to wrath had never meant to.
It was desperation on the part of a slave
fleeing the heavy hand of some master,
guilt-ridden and on the run,   2225
going to ground. But he soon began
to shake with terror; . . . . . . in shock
the wretch . . . .
      . . . . panicked and ran
away with the precious   2230
metalwork. There were many other
heirlooms heaped inside the earth-house,
because long ago, with deliberate care,
somebody now forgotten
had buried the riches of a highborn race   2235
in this ancient cache. Death had come
and taken them all in times gone by
and the only one left to tell their tale,
the last of their line, could look forward to nothing
but the same fate for himself: he foresaw that his joy   2240
in the treasure would be brief.

1. Hygelac died in the raid against the Franks (see p. 870, n. 4); Heardred died in the long feud against the Swedes or Shylfings (see p. 886, n. 9).
2. A burial mound.

3. In the single manuscript of *Beowulf*, the page containing lines 2215–31 is badly damaged, and the translation is therefore conjectural. The ellipses of lines 2227–30 indicate lines that cannot be reconstructed at all.

A newly constructed
barrow stood waiting, on a wide headland
close to the waves, its entryway secured.
Into it the keeper of the hoard had carried
all the goods and golden ware   2245
worth preserving. His words were few:
"Now, earth, hold what earls once held
and heroes can no more; it was mined from you first
by honorable men. My own people
have been ruined in war; one by one   2250
they went down to death, looked their last
on sweet life in the hall. I am left with nobody
to bear a sword or to burnish plated goblets,
put a sheen on the cup. The companies have departed.
The hard helmet, hasped with gold,   2255
will be stripped of its hoops; and the helmet-shiner
who should polish the metal of the war-mask sleeps;
the coat of mail that came through all fights,
through shield-collapse and cut of sword,
decays with the warrior. Nor may webbed mail   2260
range far and wide on the warlord's back
beside his mustered troops. No trembling harp,
no tuned timber, no tumbling hawk
swerving through the hall, no swift horse
pawing the courtyard. Pillage and slaughter   2265
have emptied the earth of entire peoples."
And so he mourned as he moved about the world,
deserted and alone, lamenting his unhappiness
day and night, until death's flood
brimmed up in his heart.   Then an old harrower of the dark   2270
happened to find the hoard open,
the burning one who hunts out barrows,
the slick-skinned dragon, threatening the night sky
with streamers of fire. People on the farms
are in dread of him. He is driven to hunt out   2275
hoards under ground, to guard heathen gold
through age-long vigils, though to little avail.
For three centuries, this scourge of the people
had stood guard on that stoutly protected
underground treasury, until the intruder   2280
unleashed its fury; he hurried to his lord
with the gold-plated cup and made his plea
to be reinstated. Then the vault was rifled,
the ring-hoard robbed, and the wretched man
had his request granted. His master gazed   2285
on that find from the past for the first time.
   When the dragon awoke, trouble flared again.
He rippled down the rock, writhing with anger
when he saw the footprints of the prowler who had stolen
too close to his dreaming head.   2290

So may a man not marked by fate
easily escape exile and woe
by the grace of God.
           The hoard-guardian
scorched the ground as he scoured and hunted
for the trespasser who had troubled his sleep.   2295
Hot and savage, he kept circling and circling
the outside of the mound. No man appeared
in that desert waste, but he worked himself up
by imagining battle; then back in he'd go
in search of the cup, only to discover   2300
signs that someone had stumbled upon
the golden treasures. So the guardian of the mound,
the hoard-watcher, waited for the gloaming
with fierce impatience; his pent-up fury
at the loss of the vessel made him long to hit back   2305
and lash out in flames. Then, to his delight,
the day waned and he could wait no longer
behind the wall, but hurtled forth
in a fiery blaze. The first to suffer
were the people on the land, but before long   2310
it was their treasure-giver who would come to grief.
    The dragon began to belch out flames
and burn bright homesteads; there was a hot glow
that scared everyone, for the vile sky-winger
would leave nothing alive in his wake.   2315
Everywhere the havoc he wrought was in evidence.
Far and near, the Geat nation
bore the brunt of his brutal assaults
and virulent hate. Then back to the hoard
he would dart before daybreak, to hide in his den.   2320
He had swinged[4] the land, swathed it in flame,
in fire and burning, and now he felt secure
in the vaults of his barrow; but his trust was unavailing.
    Then Beowulf was given bad news,
the hard truth: his own home,   2325
the best of buildings, had been burned to a cinder,
the throne-room of the Geats. It threw the hero
into deep anguish and darkened his mood:
the wise man thought he must have thwarted
ancient ordinance of the eternal Lord,   2330
broken His commandment. His mind was in turmoil,
unaccustomed anxiety and gloom
confused his brain; the fire-dragon
had razed the coastal region and reduced
forts and earthworks to dust and ashes,   2335
so the war-king planned and plotted his revenge.
The warriors' protector, prince of the hall-troop,
ordered a marvelous all-iron shield

4. That is, singed, scorched.

from his smithy works. He well knew
that linden boards would let him down   2340
and timber burn. After many trials,
he was destined to face the end of his days,
in this mortal world, as was the dragon,
for all his long leasehold on the treasure.

    Yet the prince of the rings was too proud   2345
to line up with a large army
against the sky-plague. He had scant regard
for the dragon as a threat, no dread at all
of its courage or strength, for he had kept going
often in the past, through perils and ordeals   2350
of every sort, after he had purged
Hrothgar's hall, triumphed in Heorot
and beaten Grendel. He outgrappled the monster
and his evil kin.
                One of his cruelest
hand-to-hand encounters had happened   2355
when Hygelac, king of the Geats, was killed
in Friesland: the people's friend and lord,
Hrethel's son, slaked a sword blade's
thirst for blood. But Beowulf's prodigious
gifts as a swimmer guaranteed his safety: 2360
he arrived at the shore, shouldering thirty
battle-dresses, the booty he had won.
There was little for the Hetware[5] to be happy about
as they shielded their faces and fighting on the ground
began in earnest. With Beowulf against them,   2365
few could hope to return home.
    Across the wide sea, desolate and alone,
the son of Ecgtheow swam back to his people.
There Hygd offered him throne and authority
as lord of the ring-hoard: with Hygelac dead,   2370
she had no belief in her son's ability
to defend their homeland against foreign invaders.
Yet there was no way the weakened nation
could get Beowulf to give in and agree
to be elevated over Heardred as his lord   2375
or to undertake the office of kingship.
But he did provide support for the prince,
honored and minded him until he matured
as the ruler of Geatland.
                Then over sea-roads
exiles arrived, sons of Ohthere.[6]   2380
They had rebelled against the best of all

---

5. A Frankish tribe.

6. King of the Swedes or Shylfings; after his death his sons, Eanmund and Eadgils, were driven out by their uncle Onela. They were taken in by Heardred, Hygelac's son, who was then king of the Geats, who was then in turn attacked and killed (along with Eanmund) by Onela. At this point Beowulf became king of the Geats and supported Eadgils in his successful attack on Onela.

the sea-kings in Sweden, the one who held sway
in the Shylfing nation, their renowned prince,
lord of the mead-hall. That marked the end
for Hygelac's son: his hospitality   2385
was mortally rewarded with wounds from a sword.
Heardred lay slaughtered and Onela returned
to the land of Sweden, leaving Beowulf
to ascend the throne, to sit in majesty
and rule over the Geats. He was a good king.   2390
    In days to come, he contrived to avenge
the fall of his prince; he befriended Eadgils
when Eadgils was friendless, aiding his cause
with weapons and warriors over the wide sea,
sending him men. The feud was settled   2395
on a comfortless campaign when he killed Onela.
    And so the son of Ecgtheow had survived
every extreme, excelling himself
in daring and in danger, until the day arrived
when he had to come face to face with the dragon.   2400
The lord of the Geats took eleven comrades
and went in a rage to reconnoiter.
By then he had discovered the cause of the affliction
being visited on the people. The precious cup
had come to him from the hand of the finder,   2405
the one who had started all this strife
and was now added as a thirteenth to their number.
They press-ganged and compelled this poor creature
to be their guide. Against his will
he led them to the earth-vault he alone knew,   2410
an underground barrow near the sea-billows
and heaving waves, heaped inside
with exquisite metalwork. The one who stood guard
was dangerous and watchful, warden of the trove
buried under earth: no easy bargain   2415
would be made in that place by any man.
    The veteran king sat down on the cliff-top.
He wished good luck to the Geats who had shared
his hearth and his gold. He was sad at heart,
unsettled yet ready, sensing his death.   2420
His fate hovered near, unknowable but certain:
it would soon claim his coffered soul,
part life from limb. Before long
the prince's spirit would spin free from his body.
    Beowulf, son of Ecgtheow, spoke: 2425
"Many a skirmish I survived when I was young
and many times of war: I remember them well.
At seven, I was fostered out by my father,
left in the charge of my people's lord.
King Hrethel kept me and took care of me,   2430
was openhanded, behaved like a kinsman.
While I was his ward, he treated me no worse

as a wean[7] about the place than one of his own boys,
Herebeald and Haethcyn, or my own Hygelac.
For the eldest, Herebeald, an unexpected   2435
deathbed was laid out, through a brother's doing,
when Haethcyn bent his horn-tipped bow
and loosed the arrow that destroyed his life.
He shot wide and buried a shaft
in the flesh and blood of his own brother.   2440
That offense was beyond redress, a wrongfooting
of the heart's affections; for who could avenge
the prince's life or pay his death-price?
It was like the misery felt by an old man
who has lived to see his son's body   2445
swing on the gallows. He begins to keen
and weep for his boy, watching the raven
gloat where he hangs: he can be of no help.
The wisdom of age is worthless to him.
Morning after morning, he wakes to remember   2450
that his child is gone; he has no interest
in living on until another heir
is born in the hall, now that his first-born
has entered death's dominion forever.
He gazes sorrowfully at his son's dwelling,   2455
the banquet hall bereft of all delight,
the windswept hearthstone; the horsemen are sleeping,
the warriors under ground; what was is no more.
No tunes from the harp, no cheer raised in the yard.
Alone with his longing, he lies down on his bed   2460
and sings a lament; everything seems too large,
the steadings and the fields.
                                        Such was the feeling
of loss endured by the lord of the Geats
after Herebeald's death. He was helplessly placed
to set to rights the wrong committed,   2465
could not punish the killer in accordance with the law
of the blood-feud, although he felt no love for him.
Heartsore, wearied, he turned away
from life's joys, chose God's light
and departed, leaving buildings and lands   2470
to his sons, as a man of substance will.
    "Then over the wide sea Swedes and Geats
battled and feuded and fought without quarter.
Hostilities broke out when Hrethel died.
Ongentheow's sons[8] were unrelenting,   2475

---

7. A young child [translator's note]; a Northern Irish word.
8. Ohthere and Onela, who attacked the Geats
and killed Haethcyn; Haethcyn was then
avenged by his brother Hygelac, whose attack on
the Swedes resulted in the death of Ongentheow

at the hands of the Geat Eofor (described below
in lines 2922–98). These events took place
before those of lines 2379–96, which describe
the Geats' role in the struggle between Onela
and Ohthere's two sons after Ongentheow's
death.

refusing to make peace, campaigning violently
from coast to coast, constantly setting up
terrible ambushes around Hreosnahill.[9]
My own kith and kin avenged
these evil events, as everybody knows,   2480
but the price was high: one of them paid
with his life. Haethcyn, lord of the Geats,
met his fate there and fell in the battle.
Then, as I have heard, Hygelac's sword
was raised in the morning against Ongentheow,   2485
his brother's killer. When Eofor cleft
the old Swede's helmet, halved it open,
he fell, death-pale: his feud-calloused hand
could not stave off the fatal stroke.
      "The treasures that Hygelac lavished on me   2490
I paid for when I fought, as fortune allowed me,
with my glittering sword. He gave me land
and the security land brings, so he had no call
to go looking for some lesser champion,
some mercenary from among the Gifthas[1]   2495
or the Spear-Danes or the men of Sweden.
I marched ahead of him, always there
at the front of the line; and I shall fight like that
for as long as I live, as long as this sword
shall last, which has stood me in good stead   2500
late and soon, ever since I killed
Dayraven the Frank in front of the two armies.
He brought back no looted breastplate
to the Frisian king but fell in battle,
their standard-bearer, highborn and brave.   2505
No sword blade sent him to his death:
my bare hands stilled his heartbeats
and wrecked the bone-house. Now blade and hand,
sword and sword-stroke, will assay the hoard."

[Beowulf Attacks the Dragon]

      Beowulf spoke, made a formal boast   2510
for the last time: "I risked my life
often when I was young. Now I am old,
but as king of the people I shall pursue this fight
for the glory of winning, if the evil one will only
abandon his earth-fort and face me in the open."   2515
      Then he addressed each dear companion
one final time, those fighters in their helmets,
resolute and highborn: "I would rather not
use a weapon if I knew another way

9. The place of the battle can be translated as   1. A tribe related to the Goths.
Sorrow Hill.

to grapple with the dragon and make good my boast   2520
as I did against Grendel in days gone by.
But I shall be meeting molten venom
in the fire he breathes, so I go forth
in mail-shirt and shield. I won't shift a foot
when I meet the cave-guard: what occurs on the wall   2525
between the two of us will turn out as fate,
overseer of men, decides. I am resolved.
I scorn further words against this sky-borne foe.
    "Men-at-arms, remain here on the barrow,
safe in your armor, to see which one of us   2530
is better in the end at bearing wounds
in a deadly fray. This fight is not yours,
nor is it up to any man except me
to measure his strength against the monster
or to prove his worth. I shall win the gold   2535
by my courage, or else mortal combat,
doom of battle, will bear your lord away."
    Then he drew himself up beside his shield.
The fabled warrior in his war-shirt and helmet
trusted in his own strength entirely   2540
and went under the crag. No coward path.
    Hard by the rock-face that hale veteran,
a good man who had gone repeatedly
into combat and danger and come through,
saw a stone arch and a gushing stream   2545
that burst from the barrow, blazing and wafting
a deadly heat. It would be hard to survive
unscathed near the hoard, to hold firm
against the dragon in those flaming depths.
Then he gave a shout. The lord of the Geats   2550
unburdened his breast and broke out
in a storm of anger. Under gray stone
his voice challenged and resounded clearly.
Hate was ignited. The hoard-guard recognized
a human voice, the time was over   2555
for peace and parleying. Pouring forth
in a hot battle-fume, the breath of the monster
burst from the rock. There was a rumble under ground.
Down there in the barrow, Beowulf the warrior
lifted his shield: the outlandish thing   2560
writhed and convulsed and viciously
turned on the king, whose keen-edged sword,
an heirloom inherited by ancient right,
was already in his hand. Roused to a fury,
each antagonist struck terror in the other.   2565
Unyielding, the lord of his people loomed
by his tall shield, sure of his ground,
while the serpent looped and unleashed itself.
Swaddled in flames, it came gliding and flexing
and racing toward its fate. Yet his shield defended   2570

the renowned leader's life and limb
for a shorter time than he meant it to:
that final day was the first time
when Beowulf fought and fate denied him
glory in battle. So the king of the Geats   2575
raised his hand and struck hard
at the enameled scales, but scarcely cut through:
the blade flashed and slashed yet the blow
was far less powerful than the hard-pressed king
had need of at that moment. The mound-keeper   2580
went into a spasm and spouted deadly flames:
when he felt the stroke, battle-fire
billowed and spewed. Beowulf was foiled
of a glorious victory. The glittering sword,
infallible before that day,   2585
failed when he unsheathed it, as it never should have.
For the son of Ecgtheow, it was no easy thing
to have to give ground like that and go
unwillingly to inhabit another home
in a place beyond; so every man must yield   2590
the leasehold of his days.
                              Before long
the fierce contenders clashed again.
The hoard-guard took heart, inhaled and swelled up
and got a new wind; he who had once ruled
was furled in fire and had to face the worst.   2595
No help or backing was to be had then
from his highborn comrades; that hand-picked troop
broke ranks and ran for their lives
to the safety of the wood. But within one heart
sorrow welled up: in a man of worth   2600
the claims of kinship cannot be denied.
    His name was Wiglaf, a son of Weohstan's,
a well-regarded Shylfing warrior
related to Aelfhere.[2] When he saw his lord
tormented by the heat of his scalding helmet,   2605
he remembered the bountiful gifts bestowed on him,
how well he lived among the Waegmundings,
the freehold he inherited from his father[3] before him.
He could not hold back: one hand brandished
the yellow-timbered shield, the other drew his sword—   2610
an ancient blade that was said to have belonged
to Eanmund, the son of Ohthere, the one
Weohstan had slain when he was an exile without friends.
He carried the arms to the victim's kinfolk,

---

2. Wiglaf is, like Beowulf, a member of the clan of the Waegmundings (see lines 2813–14), although both consider themselves Geats as well. See p. 850, n. 2. Nothing is known of Aelfhere.
3. Wiglaf's father is Weohstan, who, as we learn shortly, was the man who killed Eanmund, Ohthere's son, when he had taken refuge among the Geats (lines 2379–84). How Wiglaf then became a Geat is not clear, although it may have been when Beowulf helped Eanmund's brother Eadgils avenge himself on Onela, who had usurped the throne of the Swedes; Eadgils then became king.

the burnished helmet, the webbed chain-mail   2615
and that relic of the giants. But Onela returned
the weapons to him, rewarded Weohstan
with Eanmund's war-gear. He ignored the blood-feud,
the fact that Eanmund was his brother's son.[4]
Weohstan kept that war-gear for a lifetime,   2620
the sword and the mail-shirt, until it was the son's turn
to follow his father and perform his part.
Then, in old age, at the end of his days
among the Weather-Geats, he bequeathed to Wiglaf
innumerable weapons.   2625
                          And now the youth
was to enter the line of battle with his lord,
his first time to be tested as a fighter.
His spirit did not break and the ancestral blade
would keep its edge, as the dragon discovered
as soon as they came together in the combat.   2630
   Sad at heart, addressing his companions,
Wiglaf spoke wise and fluent words:
"I remember that time when mead was flowing,
how we pledged loyalty to our lord in the hall,
promised our ring-giver we would be worth our price,   2635
make good the gift of the war-gear,
those swords and helmets, as and when
his need required it. He picked us out
from the army deliberately, honored us and judged us
fit for this action, made me these lavish gifts—   2640
and all because he considered us the best
of his arms-bearing thanes. And now, although
he wanted this challenge to be one he'd face
by himself alone—the shepherd of our land,
a man unequaled in the quest for glory   2645
and a name for daring—now the day has come
when this lord we serve needs sound men
to give him their support. Let us go to him,
help our leader through the hot flame
and dread of the fire. As God is my witness,   2650
I would rather my body were robed in the same
burning blaze as my gold-giver's body
than go back home bearing arms.
That is unthinkable, unless we have first
slain the foe and defended the life   2655
of the prince of the Weather-Geats. I well know
the things he has done for us deserve better.
Should he alone be left exposed
to fall in battle? We must bond together,
shield and helmet, mail-shirt and sword."   2660
Then he waded the dangerous reek and went
under arms to his lord, saying only:

---

4. That is, Onela ignored the fact that Weohstan had killed his nephew Eanmund since he in
fact wanted Eanmund dead.

"Go on, dear Beowulf, do everything
you said you would when you were still young
and vowed you would never let your name and fame   2665
be dimmed while you lived. Your deeds are famous,
so stay resolute, my lord, defend your life now
with the whole of your strength. I shall stand by you."
    After those words, a wildness rose
in the dragon again and drove it to attack,   2670
heaving up fire, hunting for enemies,
the humans it loathed. Flames lapped the shield,
charred it to the boss, and the body armor
on the young warrior was useless to him.
But Wiglaf did well under the wide rim   2675
Beowulf shared with him once his own had shattered
in sparks and ashes.
                        Inspired again
by the thought of glory, the war-king threw
his whole strength behind a sword stroke
and connected with the skull. And Naegling snapped.   2680
Beowulf's ancient iron-gray sword
let him down in the fight. It was never his fortune
to be helped in combat by the cutting edge
of weapons made of iron. When he wielded a sword,
no matter how blooded and hard-edged the blade,   2685
his hand was too strong, the stroke he dealt
(I have heard) would ruin it. He could reap no advantage.
    Then the bane of that people, the fire-breathing dragon,
was mad to attack for a third time.
When a chance came, he caught the hero   2690
in a rush of flame and clamped sharp fangs
into his neck. Beowulf's body
ran wet with his life-blood: it came welling out.
    Next thing, they say, the noble son of Weohstan
saw the king in danger at his side   2695
and displayed his inborn bravery and strength.
He left the head alone,[5] but his fighting hand
was burned when he came to his kinsman's aid.
He lunged at the enemy lower down
so that his decorated sword sank into its belly   2700
and the flames grew weaker.
                        Once again the king
gathered his strength and drew a stabbing knife
he carried on his belt, sharpened for battle.
He stuck it deep in the dragon's flank.
Beowulf dealt it a deadly wound.   2705
They had killed the enemy, courage quelled his life;
that pair of kinsmen, partners in nobility,
had destroyed the foe. So every man should act,
be at hand when needed; but now, for the king,

---

5. That is, the dragon's flame-breathing head.

this would be the last of his many labors
and triumphs in the world. 2710
              Then the wound
dealt by the ground-burner earlier began
to scald and swell; Beowulf discovered
deadly poison suppurating inside him,
surges of nausea, and so, in his wisdom, 2715
the prince realized his state and struggled
toward a seat on the rampart. He steadied his gaze
on those gigantic stones, saw how the earthwork
was braced with arches built over columns.
And now that thane unequaled for goodness 2720
with his own hands washed his lord's wounds,
swabbed the weary prince with water,
bathed him clean, unbuckled his helmet.
   Beowulf spoke: in spite of his wounds,
mortal wounds, he still spoke 2725
for he well knew his days in the world
had been lived out to the end—his allotted time
was drawing to a close, death was very near.
   "Now is the time when I would have wanted
to bestow this armor on my own son, 2730
had it been my fortune to have fathered an heir
and live on in his flesh. For fifty years
I ruled this nation. No king
of any neighboring clan would dare
face me with troops, none had the power 2735
to intimidate me. I took what came,
cared for and stood by things in my keeping,
never fomented quarrels, never
swore to a lie. All this consoles me,
doomed as I am and sickening for death; 2740
because of my right ways, the Ruler of mankind
need never blame me when the breath leaves my body
for murder of kinsmen. Go now quickly,
dearest Wiglaf, under the gray stone
where the dragon is laid out, lost to his treasure; 2745
hurry to feast your eyes on the hoard.
Away you go: I want to examine
that ancient gold, gaze my fill
on those garnered jewels; my going will be easier
for having seen the treasure, a less troubled letting-go 2750
of the life and lordship I have long maintained."
   And so, I have heard, the son of Weohstan
quickly obeyed the command of his languishing
war-weary lord; he went in his chain-mail
under the rock-piled roof of the barrow, 2755
exulting in his triumph, and saw beyond the seat
a treasure-trove of astonishing richness,
wall-hangings that were a wonder to behold,
glittering gold spread across the ground,

the old dawn-scorching serpent's den   2760
packed with goblets and vessels from the past,
tarnished and corroding. Rusty helmets
all eaten away. Armbands everywhere,
artfully wrought. How easily treasure
buried in the ground, gold hidden   2765
however skillfully, can escape from any man!

   And he saw too a standard, entirely of gold,
hanging high over the hoard,
a masterpiece of filigree; it glowed with light
so he could make out the ground at his feet   2770
and inspect the valuables. Of the dragon there was no
remaining sign: the sword had dispatched him.
Then, the story goes, a certain man[6]
plundered the hoard in that immemorial howe,[7]
filled his arms with flagons and plates,   2775
anything he wanted; and took the standard also,
most brilliant of banners.

                   Already the blade
of the old king's sharp killing-sword
had done its worst: the one who had for long
minded the hoard, hovering over gold,   2780
unleashing fire, surging forth
midnight after midnight, had been mown down.

   Wiglaf went quickly, keen to get back,
excited by the treasure. Anxiety weighed
on his brave heart—he was hoping he would find   2785
the leader of the Geats alive where he had left him
helpless, earlier, on the open ground.

   So he came to the place, carrying the treasure
and found his lord bleeding profusely,
his life at an end; again he began   2790
to swab his body. The beginnings of an utterance
broke out from the king's breast-cage.
The old lord gazed sadly at the gold.

   "To the everlasting Lord of all,
to the King of Glory, I give thanks   2795
that I behold this treasure here in front of me,
that I have been allowed to leave my people
so well endowed on the day I die.
Now that I have bartered my last breath
to own this fortune, it is up to you   2800
to look after their needs. I can hold out no longer.
Order my troop to construct a barrow
on a headland on the coast, after my pyre has cooled.
It will loom on the horizon at Hronesness[8]
and be a reminder among my people—   2805
so that in coming times crews under sail
will call it Beowulf's Barrow, as they steer

6. That is, Wiglaf.   8. The name means "Whaleness."
7. An Irish word for dwelling.

ships across the wide and shrouded waters."
   Then the king in his great-heartedness unclasped
the collar of gold from his neck and gave it   2810
to the young thane, telling him to use
it and the war-shirt and gilded helmet well.
"You are the last of us, the only one left
of the Waegmundings. Fate swept us away,
sent my whole brave highborn clan   2815
to their final doom. Now I must follow them."
   That was the warrior's last word.
He had no more to confide. The furious heat
of the pyre would assail him. His soul fled from his breast
to its destined place among the steadfast ones.   2820

[Beowulf's Funeral]

   It was hard then on the young hero,
having to watch the one he held so dear
there on the ground, going through
his death agony. The dragon from underearth,
his nightmarish destroyer, lay destroyed as well,   2825
utterly without life. No longer would his snakefolds
ply themselves to safeguard hidden gold.
Hard-edged blades, hammered out
and keenly filed, had finished him
so that the sky-roamer lay there rigid,   2830
brought low beside the treasure-lodge.
   Never again would he glitter and glide
and show himself off in midnight air,
exulting in his riches: he fell to earth
through the battle-strength in Beowulf's arm.   2835
There were few, indeed, as far as I have heard,
big and brave as they may have been,
few who would have held out if they had had to face
the outpourings of that poison-breather
or gone foraging on the ring-hall floor   2840
and found the deep barrow-dweller
on guard and awake.
                  The treasure had been won,
bought and paid for by Beowulf's death.
Both had reached the end of the road
through the life they had been lent.
                  Before long   2845
the battle-dodgers abandoned the wood,
the ones who had let down their lord earlier,
the tail-turners, ten of them together.
When he needed them most, they had made off.
Now they were ashamed and came behind shields,   2850
in their battle-outfits, to where the old man lay.
They watched Wiglaf, sitting worn out,
a comrade shoulder to shoulder with his lord,

trying in vain to bring him round with water.
Much as he wanted to, there was no way   2855
he could preserve his lord's life on earth
or alter in the least the Almighty's will.
What God judged right would rule what happened
to every man, as it does to this day.
    Then a stern rebuke was bound to come   2860
from the young warrior to the ones who had been cowards.
Wiglaf, son of Weohstan, spoke
disdainfully and in disappointment:
"Anyone ready to admit the truth
will surely realize that the lord of men   2865
who showered you with gifts and gave you the armor
you are standing in—when he would distribute
helmets and mail-shirts to men on the mead-benches,
a prince treating his thanes in hall
to the best he could find, far or near—   2870
was throwing weapons uselessly away.
It would be a sad waste when the war broke out.
Beowulf had little cause to brag
about his armed guard; yet God who ordains
who wins or loses allowed him to strike   2875
with his own blade when bravery was needed.
There was little I could do to protect his life
in the heat of the fray, but I found new strength
welling up when I went to help him.
Then my sword connected and the deadly assaults   2880
of our foe grew weaker, the fire coursed
less strongly from his head. But when the worst happened
too few rallied around the prince.
    "So it is good-bye now to all you know and love
on your home ground, the open-handedness,   2885
the giving of war-swords. Every one of you
with freeholds of land, our whole nation,
will be dispossessed, once princes from beyond
get tidings of how you turned and fled
and disgraced yourselves. A warrior will sooner   2890
die than live a life of shame."
    Then he ordered the outcome of the fight to be reported
to those camped on the ridge, that crowd of retainers
who had sat all morning, sad at heart,
shield-bearers wondering about   2895
the man they loved: would this day be his last
or would he return? He told the truth
and did not balk, the rider who bore
news to the cliff-top. He addressed them all:
"Now the people's pride and love,   2900
the lord of the Geats, is laid on his deathbed,
brought down by the dragon's attack.
Beside him lies the bane of his life,
dead from knife-wounds. There was no way
Beowulf could manage to get the better   2905

of the monster with his sword. Wiglaf sits
at Beowulf's side, the son of Weohstan,
the living warrior watching by the dead,
keeping weary vigil, holding a wake
for the loved and the loathed.

                         Now war is looming 2910
over our nation, soon it will be known
to Franks and Frisians, far and wide,
that the king is gone. Hostility has been great
among the Franks since Hygelac sailed forth
at the head of a war-fleet into Friesland: 2915
there the Hetware harried and attacked
and overwhelmed him with great odds.
The leader in his war-gear was laid low,
fell among followers: that lord did not favor
his company with spoils. The Merovingian king 2920
has been an enemy to us ever since.
   "Nor do I expect peace or pact-keeping
of any sort from the Swedes. Remember:
at Ravenswood, Ongentheow
slaughtered Haethcyn, Hrethel's son, 2925
when the Geat people in their arrogance
first attacked the fierce Shylfings.
The return blow was quickly struck
by Ohthere's father.[9] Old and terrible,
he felled the sea-king and saved his own 2930
aged wife, the mother of Onela
and of Ohthere, bereft of her gold rings.
Then he kept hard on the heels of the foe
and drove them, leaderless, lucky to get away
in a desperate rout into Ravenswood. 2935
His army surrounded the weary remnant
where they nursed their wounds; all through the night
he howled threats at those huddled survivors,
promised to axe their bodies open
when dawn broke, dangle them from gallows 2940
to feed the birds. But at first light
when their spirits were lowest, relief arrived.
They heard the sound of Hygelac's horn,
his trumpet calling as he came to find them,
the hero in pursuit, at hand with troops. 2945
   "The bloody swathe that Swedes and Geats
cut through each other was everywhere.
No one could miss their murderous feuding.
Then the old man made his move,
pulled back, barred his people in: 2950
Ongentheow withdrew to higher ground.
Hygelac's pride and prowess as a fighter
were known to the earl; he had no confidence
that he could hold out against that horde of seamen,

9. Ongentheow.

defend his wife and the ones he loved   2955
from the shock of the attack. He retreated for shelter
behind the earthwall. Then Hygelac swooped
on the Swedes at bay, his banners swarmed
into their refuge, his Geat forces
drove forward to destroy the camp.   2960
There in his gray hairs, Ongentheow
was cornered, ringed around with swords.
And it came to pass that the king's fate
was in Eofor's hands,[1] and in his alone.
Wulf, son of Wonred, went for him in anger,   2965
split him open so that blood came spurting
from under his hair. The old hero
still did not flinch, but parried fast,
hit back with a harder stroke:
the king turned and took him on.   2970
Then Wonred's son, the brave Wulf,
could land no blow against the aged lord.
Ongentheow divided his helmet
so that he buckled and bowed his bloodied head
and dropped to the ground. But his doom held off.   2975
Though he was cut deep, he recovered again.
      "With his brother down, the undaunted Eofor,
Hygelac's thane, hefted his sword
and smashed murderously at the massive helmet
past the lifted shield. And the king collapsed,   2980
the shepherd of people was sheared of life.
Many then hurried to help Wulf,
bandaged and lifted him, now that they were left
masters of the blood-soaked battle-ground.
One warrior stripped the other,   2985
looted Ongentheow's iron mail-coat,
his hard sword-hilt, his helmet too,
and carried the graith[2] to King Hygelac,
he accepted the prize, promised fairly
that reward would come, and kept his word.   2990
For their bravery in action, when they arrived home,
Eofor and Wulf were overloaded
by Hrethel's son, Hygelac the Geat,
with gifts of land and linked rings
that were worth a fortune. They had won glory,   2995
so there was no gainsaying his generosity.
And he gave Eofor his only daughter
to bide at home with him, an honor and a bond.
      "So this bad blood between us and the Swedes,
this vicious feud, I am convinced,   3000
is bound to revive; they will cross our borders
and attack in force when they find out
that Beowulf is dead. In days gone by

1. The killing of Ongentheow by Eofor is   2. Armor.
described in lines 2486–89.

when our warriors fell and we were undefended,
he kept our coffers and our kingdom safe.   3005
He worked for the people, but as well as that
he behaved like a hero.
                          We must hurry now
to take a last look at the king
and launch him, lord and lavisher of rings,
on the funeral road. His royal pyre   3010
will melt no small amount of gold:
heaped there in a hoard, it was bought at heavy cost,
and that pile of rings he paid for at the end
with his own life will go up with the flame,
be furled in fire: treasure no follower   3015
will wear in his memory, nor lovely woman
link and attach as a torque around her neck—
but often, repeatedly, in the path of exile
they shall walk bereft, bowed under woe,
now that their leader's laugh is silenced,   3020
high spirits quenched. Many a spear
dawn-cold to the touch will be taken down
and waved on high; the swept harp
won't waken warriors, but the raven winging
darkly over the doomed will have news,   3025
tidings for the eagle of how he hoked[3] and ate,
how the wolf and he made short work of the dead."
    Such was the drift of the dire report
that gallant man delivered. He got little wrong
in what he told and predicted.
                          The whole troop   3030
rose in tears, then took their way
to the uncanny scene under Earnaness.[4]
There, on the sand, where his soul had left him,
they found him at rest, their ring-giver
from days gone by. The great man   3035
had breathed his last. Beowulf the king
had indeed met with a marvelous death.
    But what they saw first was far stranger:
the serpent on the ground, gruesome and vile,
lying facing him. The fire-dragon   3040
was scaresomely burned, scorched all colors.
From head to tail, his entire length
was fifty feet. He had shimmered forth
on the night air once, then winged back
down to his den; but death owned him now,   3045
he would never enter his earth-gallery again.
Beside him stood pitchers and piled-up dishes,
silent flagons, precious swords
eaten through with rust, ranged as they had been
while they waited their thousand winters under ground.   3050

---

3. Rooted about, a Northern Irish word [adapted from translator's note].

4. The place where Beowulf fought the dragon; it means "Eagleness."

That huge cache, gold inherited
from an ancient race, was under a spell—
which meant no one was ever permitted
to enter the ring-hall unless God Himself,
mankind's Keeper, True King of Triumphs,   3055
allowed some person pleasing to Him—
and in His eyes worthy—to open the hoard.
    What came about brought to nothing
the hopes of the one who had wrongly hidden
riches under the rock-face. First the dragon slew   3060
that man among men, who in turn made fierce amends
and settled the feud. Famous for his deeds
a warrior may be, but it remains a mystery
where his life will end, when he may no longer
dwell in the mead-hall among his own.   3065
So it was with Beowulf, when he faced the cruelty
and cunning of the mound-guard. He himself was ignorant
of how his departure from the world would happen.
The highborn chiefs who had buried the treasure
declared it until doomsday so accursed   3070
that whoever robbed it would be guilty of wrong
and grimly punished for their transgression,
hasped in hell-bonds in heathen shrines.
Yet Beowulf's gaze at the gold treasure
when he first saw it had not been selfish.   3075
    Wiglaf, son of Weohstan, spoke:
"Often when one man follows his own will
many are hurt. This happened to us.
Nothing we advised could ever convince
the prince we loved, our land's guardian,   3080
not to vex the custodian of the gold,
let him lie where he was long accustomed,
lurk there under earth until the end of the world.
He held to his high destiny. The hoard is laid bare,
but at a grave cost; it was too cruel a fate   3085
that forced the king to that encounter.
I have been inside and seen everything
amassed in the vault. I managed to enter
although no great welcome awaited me
under the earthwall. I quickly gathered up   3090
a huge pile of the priceless treasures
handpicked from the hoard and carried them here
where the king could see them. He was still himself,
alive, aware, and in spite of his weakness
he had many requests. He wanted me to greet you   3095
and order the building of a barrow that would crown
the site of his pyre, serve as his memorial,
in a commanding position, since of all men
to have lived and thrived and lorded it on earth
his worth and due as a warrior were the greatest.   3100
Now let us again go quickly

and feast our eyes on that amazing fortune
heaped under the wall. I will show the way
and take you close to those coffers packed with rings
and bars of gold. Let a bier be made   3105
and got ready quickly when we come out
and then let us bring the body of our lord,
the man we loved, to where he will lodge
for a long time in the care of the Almighty."
    Then Weohstan's son, stalwart to the end,   3110
had orders given to owners of dwellings,
many people of importance in the land,
to fetch wood from far and wide
for the good man's pyre:
                    "Now shall flame consume
our leader in battle, the blaze darken   3115
round him who stood his ground in the steel-hail,
when the arrow-storm shot from bowstrings
pelted the shield-wall. The shaft hit home.
Feather-fledged, it finned the barb in flight."
    Next the wise son of Weohstan   3120
called from among the king's thanes
a group of seven: he selected the best
and entered with them, the eighth of their number,
under the God-cursed roof; one raised
a lighted torch and led the way.   3125
No lots were cast for who should loot the hoard
for it was obvious to them that every bit of it
lay unprotected within the vault,
there for the taking. It was no trouble
to hurry to work and haul out   3130
the priceless store. They pitched the dragon
over the cliff-top, let tide's flow
and backwash take the treasure-minder.
Then coiled gold was loaded on a cart
in great abundance, and the gray-haired leader,   3135
the prince on his bier, borne to Hronesness.
    The Geat people built a pyre for Beowulf,
stacked and decked it until it stood foursquare,
hung with helmets, heavy war-shields
and shining armor, just as he had ordered.   3140
Then his warriors laid him in the middle of it,
mourning a lord far-famed and beloved.
On a height they kindled the hugest of all
funeral fires; fumes of woodsmoke
billowed darkly up, the blaze roared   3145
and drowned out their weeping, wind died down
and flames wrought havoc in the hot bone-house,
burning it to the core. They were disconsolate
and wailed aloud for their lord's decease.
A Geat woman too sang out in grief;   3150
with hair bound up, she unburdened herself

of her worst fears, a wild litany
of nightmare and lament: her nation invaded,
enemies on the rampage, bodies in piles,
slavery and abasement. Heaven swallowed the smoke. 3155

    Then the Geat people began to construct
a mound on a headland, high and imposing,
a marker that sailors could see from far away,
and in ten days they had done the work.
It was their hero's memorial; what remained from the fire 3160
they housed inside it, behind a wall
as worthy of him as their workmanship could make it.
And they buried torques in the barrow, and jewels
and a trove of such things as trespassing men
had once dared to drag from the hoard. 3165
They let the ground keep that ancestral treasure,
gold under gravel, gone to earth,
as useless to men now as it ever was.
Then twelve warriors rode around the tomb,
chieftains' sons, champions in battle, 3170
all of them distraught, chanting in dirges,
mourning his loss as a man and a king.
They extolled his heroic nature and exploits
and gave thanks for his greatness; which was the proper thing,
for a man should praise a prince whom he holds dear 3175
and cherish his memory when that moment comes
when he has to be convoyed from his bodily home.
So the Geat people, his hearth-companions,
sorrowed for the lord who had been laid low.
They said that of all the kings upon earth 3180
he was the man most gracious and fair-minded,
kindest to his people and keenest to win fame.

MARIE DE FRANCE
1150?–1200?

"Marie ai num, si sui de France" (Marie is my name, and I am from France). With these words, the author of the *Lais* tells us her name and her homeland. Yet Marie was an English writer, composing in the Anglo-Norman dialect of French that had become the mother tongue of the English ruling classes following the Norman Conquest a century before. Her short, intense stories of love and loss reflect the complex cultural encounter of Celtic folktale, Anglo-French court setting, and English landscape, and they set the stage for the flowering of the romance genre in the last decades of the twelfth century.

We know little about Marie beyond what she herself tells us in the Prologue to her *Lais*, which is reprinted here, and in the closing lines of her collection of animal fables. She is likely to have been a nun—possibly an abbess in a position of authority within her community; in offering her collection of twelve *Lais* as a gift to Henry II, King of England and Duke of Normandy, she uses terms that presume some degree of familiarity, perhaps even a family relationship. It was not uncommon in twelfth-century Europe for the illegitimate female offspring of noble or royal figures to enter convents, less because these women were pious than because it was expedient to prevent them from marrying political rivals and bearing children who might complicate the smooth order of future succession. Marie's place in the world, attached at once to the cloister and to the court, may reflect some such family history.

In addition to her *Fables*, which she claims to have translated from a now-lost text by the Anglo-Saxon king Alfred, Marie's other surviving works include the mysterious journey to the afterlife recounted in *Saint Patrick's Purgatory* (adapted from a Latin original) and an account of the life and works of the English saint Audrey. Her poems stand at the intersection of oral and written forms of literature, as well as at the crossroads of cultures—not just English and French, but Welsh or Breton as well. Celtic cultures had survived the warfare of English and French barons, both in the mountains of Wales and in Cornwall, to the north of the English Channel, and in the upper regions of Normandy and Brittany, to the south. In her Prologue, Marie describes her desire to preserve these Breton songs: having heard them sung, she writes, "I don't want to neglect or forget them." She expresses a similar sentiment in the epilogue to her *Fables*, in which she tells the reader her own name "pur remem-

brance," "for remembrance." Through the *Lais*, Marie has ensured that both she and the ancient songs she has written down will live on in memory.

The two lais included here, "Bisclavret" and "Laüstic," represent two very different types: the first, more elaborate, offers a very fully developed psychology of the main characters, while the second, shorter and jewel-like, crystallizes an essential truth about the nature of love in poetic form. In "Bisclavret," we find the tale of a man who has a secret: he spends part of each week wandering the forest in the form of a wolf, a *bisclavret*. His wife learns the truth and tricks him, condemning him to exile as an animal in the wild. Ovid's **Metamorphoses** (especially the story of Actaeon who, changed into a stag, is chased by hunting dogs) looms in the background of this tale of animal-human nature. The royal court where Bisclavret finds justice is echoed elsewhere in Marie's lais, in the court of King Arthur. Marie was the first to bring these oral Breton materials into the mainstream of European literature, setting a precedent for her French successor, Chrétien de Troyes (in his various Arthurian romances) and, later, for the anonymous English poet who wrote *Sir Gawain and the Green Knight* and Thomas Malory in his *Morte d'Arthur*.

The theme of vengeance that emerges in "Bisclavret" also haunts "Laüstic," though the final note of this short tale is the transcendence and ultimate triumph of love. The affair between a woman and her husband's friend comes to a brutal end when the beautiful nightingale, whose nighttime song fuels the dreams of lovers, is killed by the jealous husband. The body of the bird becomes a token of their forbidden passion, first wrapped by the lady in an embroidered shroud, and then preserved by her lover in a begemmed reliquary. The miniature lai, like the miniature sarcophagus, remains as a potent reminder of the power of love.

From the Lais[1]

Prologue

WHOM God has given intelligence
and the great gift of eloquence
must not conceal these, or keep still,
but share and show them with good will.   4
When much is heard of some good thing,
then comes its first fine flowering;
when many more have praise to give,
these blossoms flourish, spread, and thrive.   8
Among the ancients, custom was—
Priscian[2] can testify to this—
that in their books they made obscure
much that they wrote; this would ensure   12
that wise folk of another day,
needing to know what these texts say,
could gloss these works, and with their sense
give all the more intelligence.   16
Savants and scholars were aware
that in their strivings, more and more
they sensed the works' great subtlety
increasingly, as time went by.   20
And thus, too, they knew how to guard
from error in time afterward.
He who would keep from vice and sin
must some great arduous work begin;   24
struggle and study, strive to know,
and doing so avoid much woe,
free from great suffering and regret.
Thus I began to give some thought   28
to telling some good story, that
taken from Latin, I would put
into French; but then I would win
no glory there; so much is done!   32
I thought of lais[3] that I had heard
and did not doubt; I felt assured
that these first writers who began
these lais, who told them, made them known,   36
wished, for remembrance, to record
adventures, stories, they had heard.
I too have heard them; I do not
wish them abandoned, lost, forgot.   40
Thus I made rhymes and poetry
late into night-time, wakefully!

---

1. Translated by Dorothy Gilbert. Lines of
Marie's poetry are numbered every four lines
instead of the usual five to emphasize her use
of couplets.
2. Latin grammarian (early 6th century C.E.),
widely read in the Middle Ages.
3. Narrative poems of adventure and
romance, written in octosyllabic couplets
(French).

To honor you, most noble King,[4]
courtly and skilled in everything,   44
to whom all joy makes obeisance,
in whose heart roots all excellence,
to gather *lais* I undertook,
to rhyme, make, tell; this was my work.   48
I in my heart thought this I'd do,
fair Sire: present this work to you.
If it should please you to receive
my gift, for all the days I live   52
I shall be joyful; you shall give
great happiness. Do not believe
me proud, presumptuous; but hear
as I begin my tales; give ear.   56

Bisclavret

In crafting lays, I won't forget
—I mustn't—that of Bisclavret;
Bisclavret: so named in Breton;
But *Garwaf* in the Norman tongue.   4

One used to hear, in times gone by
—it often happened, actually—
men became werewolves, many men,
and in the forest made their den.   8
A werewolf is a savage beast;
in his blood-rage, he makes a feast
of men, devours them, does great harms,
and in vast forests lives and roams.   12
Well, for now, let us leave all that;
I want to speak of Bisclavret.

In Brittany[5] there lived a lord
—wondrous, the praise of him I've heard—   16
a good knight, handsome, known to be
all that makes for nobility.
Prized, he was, much, by his liege lord;
by all his neighbors was adored.   20
He'd wed a wife, a worthy soul,
most elegant and beautiful;
he loved her, and she loved him, too.
One thing she found most vexing, though.   24
During the week he'd disappear
for three whole days, she knew not where;
what happened to him, where he went
His household, too, was ignorant.   28
He returned home again one day;
high-spirited and happy. She

4. Henry II, king of England, who also held substantial territories in France.
5. A Celtic region of present-day northwestern France.

straightway proceeded to inquire:
    "My fair sweet friend," she said, "fair sire,   32
if I just dared, I'd ask of you
a thing I dearly wish to know,
except that I'm so full of fear
of your great anger, husband dear."   36
    When he had heard this, he embraced her,
drew her to him, clasped and kissed her.
    "Lady," he said, "come, ask away!
Nothing you wish, dear, certainly   40
I will not tell you, that I know."
    "Faith!" she said, "you have cured me so!
But I have such anxiety,
sire, on those days you part from me,   44
my heart is full of pain. I fear
so much that I will lose you, dear.
Oh, reassure me, hastily!
If you do not, I soon will die.   48
Tell me, dear husband; tell me, pray,
What do you do? Where do you stay?
It seems to me you've found another!
You wrong me, if you have a lover!"   52
    "Lady," he said, "have mercy, do!
I'll have much harm in telling you.
I'd lose your love, if I should tell
and be lost to myself, as well."   56
    Now when the wife was thus addressed,
it seemed to her to be no jest.
Oftimes she begged, with all her skill,
coaxing and flattering, until   60
at last he told her all he did,
the tale entire; kept nothing hid.
    "Dame, I become a bisclavret.
in the great forest I'm afoot,   64
in deepest woods, near thickest trees,
and live on prey I track and seize."
    When he had told the whole affair,
she persevered; she asked him where   68
his clothes were; was he naked there?
    "Lady," he said, "I go all bare."
    "Tell me, for God's sake, where you put
your clothes!"
                "Oh, I'll not tell you that: 72
I would be lost, you must believe,
if it were seen just how I live.
Bisclavret would I be, forever;
never could I be helped then, never,   76
till I got back my clothes, my own;
that's why their cache[6] must not be known."
    "Sire," said his lady in reply,
"more than all earth I love you. Why   80

6. Hiding place (French).

hide, why have secrets in your life?
Why, why mistrust your own dear wife?
That does not seem a loving thought.
What have I done? What sin, what fault   84
has caused your fear, in any way?
You must be fair! You have to say!"
  So she harassed and harried him
So much, he finally gave in.   88
  "Lady," he said, "just by the wood,
just where I enter, by the road,
there's an old chapel. Now, this place
has often brought me help and grace.   92
There is a stone there, in the brush,
hollow and wide, beneath a bush.
In brush and under bush, I store
my clothes, till I head home once more."   96
  The lady was amazed to hear:
She blushed deep red, from her pure fear.
Terror, she felt, at this strange tale.
She thought what means she could avail   100
herself of how to leave this man.
She could not lie with him again.

  In these parts lived a chevalier[7]
who had long been in love with her.   104
Much did he pray and sue, and give
largesse in service to his love;
she had not loved him, nor had she
granted him any surety   108
that she, too, loved; but now she sent
this knight the news of her intent.
  "Friend," she wrote him, "rejoice, and know
that for which you have suffered so,   112
I grant you now without delay;
I'll not hold back in any way.
My body and my love I grant;
make me your mistress, if you want!"   116
  Kindly he thanked her, and her troth
accepted; she received his oath.
She told her lover how her lord
went to the wood, and what he did,   120
what he became, once he was there.
She told in detail how and where
to find the road and clothing cache;
and then she sent him for the stash.   124
  Thus was Bisclavret trapped for life;
ruined, betrayed, by his own wife.
Because his absences were known,
people assumed he'd really gone,   128
this time, for good. They searched around,
enough, but he could not be found,

7. Knight (French).

for all their inquiries. At last
everyone let the matter rest.
The lady wed the chevalier   132
who'd been so long in love with her.

A whole year, after this event,
thus passed. The king went out to hunt,   136
went to the forest straightaway,
there where the bisclavret now lay.
The hunting dogs were now unleashed
and soon they found the changeling beast.   140
All day they flung themselves at him,
all day pursued, both dogs and men;
they almost had him. Now they'd rend
and tear him; now he'd meet his end.   144
His eye, distinguishing, could see
the king; to beg his clemency
he seized the royal stirrup, put
a kiss upon the leg and foot.   148
The king, observing, felt great fear.
Calling his men, he cried, "Come here!"
"Lords!" he said, "Come and look at this!
See what a marvel is this kiss,   152
this humble, gracious gesturing!
That's a man's mind; it begs the king
for mercy. Now, drive back the hounds!
See that none strike or give it wounds.   156
This beast has mind; it has intent.
Come, hurry up! It's time we went.
I'll give protection for this beast.
And for today, the hunt has ceased."   160

The king had turned around, at that;
following him, the bisclavret
close by; he would not lose the king,
abandon him, for anything.   164
The king then led the beast, to bring
it to the castle, marvelling,
rejoicing at it, for he'd never,
seen such a wondrous creature, ever.   168
He loved the wolf and held it dear
and he charged every follower
that, for his love, they guard it well
and not mistreat the animal.   172
No one must strike it; and, he'd said,
it must be watered and well fed.
Gladly his men now guarded it.
Among the knights, the bisclavret   176
now lived, and slept close by the king;
everyone loved it, cherishing
its noble bearing and its charm.
It never wanted to do harm,   180

and where the king might walk or ride,
there it must be, just at his side,
wherever he might go or move;
so well it showed its loyal love.   184

   What happened after that? Now, hear.
The king held court; he had appear
all barons, vassals; gave commands
to all who held from him their lands,   188
to help a festival take place,
serving with elegance and grace.
Among those chevaliers was he
—so richly dressed, so splendidly!—   192
who'd wed the wife of Bisclavret.
Little he knew or thought just yet
that he would find his foe so near!
Soon as he came, this chevalier,   196
to court, and Bisclavret could see
the man, he ran up furiously,
sank in his teeth, and dragged him close.
Many the injuries and woes   200
he would have suffered, but the king
called out commands, while brandishing
his staff. The beast rushed, twice, that day,
to bite the man; all felt dismay,   204
for none had seen the beast display
toward anyone, in any way,
such viciousness. There must be reason,
the household said, for him to seize on   208
the knight, who must have done him wrong;
the wish for vengeance seemed so strong.
   And so they let the matter rest
till the conclusion of the feast.   212
The barons took their leave, each one,
each to his castle and his home.
All my good judgment counsels me
he who was first to leave was he   216
set upon by the bisclavret.
Small wonder the beast had such hate!

   Not too long after this occurred
—such is my thought, so I have heard—   220
into the forest went the king
—so noble and so wise a being—
where he'd first found the bisclavret.
The animal was with him yet.   224
The night of this return, the king
took, in this countryside, lodging.
And this the wife of Bisclavret
well knew. Dressed fetchingly, she set   228
out to have speech with him next day;
rich gifts were part of her display.

Bisclavret saw her come. No man
had strength to hold him as he ran
up to his wife in rage and fury.   232
Hear of his vengeance! Hear the story!
He tore her nose off, then and there.
What worse could he have done to her?   236
From all sides now, and full of threat
men ran and would have killed him, but
a wise man expeditiously
spoke to the king. "Listen to me!   240
He's been with you, this animal;
there is not one man of us all
who has not, long since, had to see
and travel with him, frequently,   244
and he has harmed no one, not once
shown viciousness nor violence
save just now, as you saw him do.
And by the faith I owe to you,   248
he has some bitter quarrel with her
and with her husband, her seigneur.
She was wife to that chevalier
whom you so prized, and held so dear,   252
who disappeared some time ago.
What happened, no one seems to know.
Put her to torture. She may state
something, this dame, to indicate   256
why the beast feels for her such hate.
Force her to speak! She'll tell it straight.
We've all known marvels, chanced to see
strange events, here in Brittany."   260
    The King thought this advice was fair;
and he detained the chevalier.
The lady, too, he held; and she
he put to pain and agony.   264
Part out of pain, part out of fear,
she made her former lord's case clear:
how she had managed to betray
her lord, and take his clothes away;   268
the story he had told to her,
what he became, and how, and where;
and how, when once his clothes were gone
—stolen—he was not seen again.   272
She gave her theory and her thought:
Surely this beast was Bisclavret.
    These spoils, these clothes, the king demanded;
whether she would or no, commanded   276
that she go back and find them, get
and give them to the bisclavret.

    When they were put in front of him
he didn't seem to notice them.   280
The king's wise man spoke up once more

—the one who'd counselled him before—
"Fair sire, this will not do at all!
We can't expect this animal,   284
in front of you, sire, to get dressed
and change his semblance of a beast.
You don't grasp what this means, my king!
—or see his shame and suffering.   288
Into your room have led this beast;
with him, his clothes. Let him get dressed;
For quite some time, leave him alone.
If he's a man, that is soon known!"   292
   The king himself led the bisclavret;
and on him all the doors were shut.
They waited. And then finally
two barons, with the king, all three,   296
entered. What a discovery!
There on the king's bed, they could see
asleep, the knight. How the king ran
up to the bed, to embrace his man,   300
kiss him, a hundred times and more!
   Quickly he acted to restore
his lands, as soon as possible;
more he bestowed than I can tell.   304
His wife was banished. She was chased
out of the country, and disgraced,
and chased out, travelling with her,
her mate and co-conspirator.   308

   Quite a few children had this dame,
who in their way achieved some fame
for looks, for a distinctive face;
numbers of women of her race   312
—it's true—were born without a nose.
Noseless they lived, the story goes.

   And this same story you have heard
truly occurred; don't doubt my word.   316
I made this *lai* of Bisclavret
so no one, ever, will forget.

Laüstic

   There's an adventure, I will say,
of which the Bretons made a *lai*.
Laüstic is the name it's called
in its own country, so I'm told.   4
In French it's "Rossignol," this tale;
in proper English, "Nightingale."
   Near St. Malo[1] there was a town
that in that region had renown.   8

---

1. A seaport in northwest France, in Brittany.

There lived two knights, and side by side
their mansions, strong and fortified.
For knightly valor each had fame,
and gave their city a good name.   12
One had a wife, an excellent
lady, wise, courtly, elegant;
a marvel was she, so *soignée*,[2]
and groomed with great propriety.   16
The other of these chevaliers,
a bachelor, was by his peers
well known for prowess, and great valor.
With pleasure he did deeds of honor.   20
Much he tourneyed; with much largesse
gave of what he himself possessed.
He loved his neighbor's wife, and he
begged and sued so persistently   24
and had such qualities, that she
above all, loved him ardently;
partly, for all the good she heard;
partly, he lived close by, this lord.   28
    Well these two loved, and prudently,
and with great care and secrecy,
making sure they were not detected,
hindered, or noticed, or suspected;   32
and this they could do easily
because their dwellings lay nearby.
Nearby, their mansions and their halls,
their keeps, their dungeons. But no walls,   36
no barrier, except for one,
a great high wall of dark-hued stone.
Still, in her bedroom, when she stood
right at the window, then she could   40
talk to her love, her chevalier,
she speak to him and he to her;
they could toss tokens to each other,
throw little gifts, lover to lover.   44
Nothing displeased them in that place,
they were at ease there, face to face,
except that they could only see—
not join in pleasure utterly,   48
for when he was at home, her lord
had his wife under close, strict guard.
Still they made opportunity;
and thus by night and thus by day   52
they met; they spoke; they found a way
and none who watched could say them nay
when to their windows they would each
come, and there speak their loving speech.   56
    For a long time they loved each other,
until one summer, when the weather

2. Well groomed and elegantly dressed (French).

had made the fields and forests green
and gardens, orchards, bloom again;   60
above the flowers, with great joy
small birds sang sweetest melody.
He whose desire for love is strong
—no wonder that he heeds their song!   64
The truth about this knight, I'll tell;
he heard the song; he heard it well;
the lady, too, heard in her place;
thus they could love; court; speak, and gaze.   68
When the moon shone, the lady would
rise often from her husband's bed,
rise from beside him, while he slept
and softly, in her mantle wrapped,   72
cautiously to the window go
to see her lover, whom she knew
lived as she did, lived for her sight.
She'd stay awake most of the night.   76
    In gazing thus was their delight,
since nothing more could be their fate.
Such was the case. So often she
arose, her husband angrily   80
demanded of her, frequently,
where did she go, what for, and why?
The lady answered with this word:
    "My sire: he who has never heard   84
the nightingale, has not known joy
ever, in all this world. That's why,
that's where. So sweetly I have heard
it sing at night, enchanting bird,   88
so great my longing, my delight,
I cannot close my eyes at night."
    When he had heard her answer thus,
he laughed, enraged and furious,   92
and he resolved that without fail
he would entrap the nightingale.
Now every squire within that house
put net or snare or trap to use   96
throughout the garden. Everywhere,
on hazel, chestnut, lay a snare
or gluey bird-lime. So they got
the nightingale; so it was caught.   100
    When they had tricked and trapped the bird
alive, they brought it to the lord.
Oh, he was happy when they came!
Right to the chamber of his dame   104
he hurried. "Lady, where are you?
Come talk to us, my lady, do!
I've trapped your nightingale, the one
that's kept you sleepless for so long.   108
Now, finally, you'll sleep in peace—

these night excursions now can cease."
    She understood, as he spoke thus,
and full of grief, and furious   112
asked for the bird. But her demands
were vain; in rage, with his two hands
he broke its neck. So this seigneur,
spiteful and vicious, like a boor   116
killed it. He threw the corpse at her.
It fell on her chemise and there
bloodied her breast a little bit.
He left the room; at once went out.   120
    She gathered up the little body,
weeping vehemently. The lady
cursed those who caught the bird and laid
snares, nets, devices, all they made.   124
What joy was taken, wrenched away!
    "Alas," she said, "Oh, wretched me!
No more shall I arise at night,
go to the window for a sight   128
of my dear love and find him there.
And one thing I do know for sure:
he'll think me weak and faint of heart.
I must act now. Let me take thought.   132
I'll send my love the nightingale,
make known to him this vicious tale."
    She found a piece of samite,[3] wrought
with gold, and writing worked throughout;   136
in it she wrapped the little bird.
One of her servants she gave word,
gave him her message, and he went
to her *ami*,[4] where it was sent,   140
So to the chevalier he came
and gave him greetings from his dame,
gave the full message, told the tale,
delivered up the nightingale.   144
When the full story was made known
—he gave it good attention!—
he felt much sorrow. This knight, though,
was not a boor, nor was he slow   148
of sense. A tiny reliquary
he soon had forged, for him to carry:
not iron; not steel; pure gold, with stones
most rare and precious, lovely ones;   152
a lid that was a perfect fit.
The little bird was placed in it,
the vessel sealed. The chevalier
carried it with him everywhere.   156
    This story, more and more, got known;
it was not secret very long.
Of it the Bretons made their lay;
It's called *Laüstic* to this day.   160

---

3. Luxurious, heavy silk.   **4.** Lover (French).

DANTE ALIGHIERI
1265–1321

Midway in our life's journey, I went astray / from the straight road and woke to find myself / alone in a dark wood." With these opening words, Dante compels his reader to inhabit the point of view of a narrator who, halfway through not "my" but "our" lifetime, suddenly realizes that he is lost. His life is thus our life, and the ethical or righteous "straight road" that the narrator hopes to rediscover also comes to be the reader's own goal. Yet this identification of reader and narrator is countered, again and again in *The Divine Comedy*, by an insistence on the specific circumstances of Dante's own life: traveling into the underworld and into the other realms of the afterlife, we meet his old teacher, Brunetto Latini; the father of his close friend Guido Cavalcanti; his great-great-grandfather, Cacciaguida; and, most important, the beautiful Beatrice Portinari, whom Dante has loved (he tells us) since they were both children. In spite of the particularity of the details of this afterlife—or, perhaps, because of them—the reader constantly identifies with the narrator, experiencing the painful turns of the journey as well as the joyful expectation of heavenly bliss at the road's end.

LIFE AND TIMES

Dante Alighieri was born and raised in Florence, a northern Italian city that was at once central to his sense of identity and—as depicted in *The Divine Comedy*—a place that he loathed and despised, a degenerate community rife with corruption and discord. During the years around 1300, Florence, like other cities in northern Italy, was caught up in a large-scale confrontation between forces favoring the power of the church and those favoring the independence of city-states. Dante quickly became deeply involved with these issues, both as a member of the political governing body within the city of Florence and in his role as envoy from the city to the seat of the papal government in Rome. Dante's own view—expressed most explicitly in his *De Monarchia* (1318), a political treatise that in some ways anticipates **Machiavelli**'s *The Prince*— was that secular rule and ecclesiastical rule should be clearly divided. Dante argued that a strong ruler in the person of an idealized emperor was necessary for the church to appropriately exercise its moral and religious authority. Because it sought to place limitations on the exercise of political power by the church, *De Monarchia* was immediately condemned; it remained on the list (or "Index") of books that Catholics are forbidden to read until 1881.

Florence had taken a leading role in the disputes concerning secular and ecclesiastical power, split first into the factions of the Guelphs (who supported the pope) and the Ghibellines (who supported the Holy Roman Emperor). By the time Dante became involved in Florentine politics, the Guelphs had become dominant within the city, but an internal fracture soon developed between the Black Guelphs, who continued to support Pope Boniface VIII, and the White Guelphs, who had come to oppose his despotism. Dante was allied with the latter, and when he was in Rome on a diplomatic mission, the Black Guelphs seized control of the city. Dante was consequently forbidden from ever reentering the city of his birth, under penalty of death by burning at the stake. Even worse, the split into the White and Black parties divided Dante's family, as the Black Guelphs were led by the Donatis—relatives of his wife, Gemma Donati—and his wife and their four children remained in Florence.

Deeply embittered by the experience of exile, Dante spent the next twenty years wandering from city to city, all the while continuing with his political writing as well as his poetic efforts. The scandal arising from *De Monarchia* undoubtedly hampered Dante's efforts to return to Florence. In his *Divine Comedy*, he movingly recalls "how bitter as salt and stone / is the bread of others," and laments "how hard the way that goes / up and down / stairs that are never your own." Dante never saw his sentence of exile lifted; indeed, Florence's city council finally revoked it only in 2008. That the vote was not unanimous—the motion passed 19 to 5—suggests that the city's political divisions may have lingered for seven hundred years.

WORK

Dante himself called his monumental poem simply the *Commedia*, or "comedy"; the adjective "divine" was added later by Giovanni Boccaccio, author of *The Decameron*, the other great work of medieval Italian literature. Boccaccio thereby signaled not just the subject matter of the work—that is, the realm of the afterlife, including the domains of hell, purgatory, and heaven—but also the elevated style in which it was written. The claim of direct inspiration by God, which Dante makes explicitly throughout the work, was taken at face value by the first generations of commentators, who accepted the work as the faithful poetic record of a real visionary experience. The theological content of the *Comedy* is both dense and elaborate: perhaps the most ambitious aspect of the poem's theology centers on purgatory, a place where souls are able to do penance for their sins even after death, to which Dante devotes the second of the three parts of his work. Purgatory would not become official Christian doctrine until well after the *Comedy* was completed, but Dante was responding to contemporary popular beliefs in the ability of the prayers of the living to affect the condition of the souls of the dead. He also reflects contemporary theological views of the persistence of the union of body and soul even after death, especially in the way that the shades that populate the afterworld of *The Divine Comedy* retain their individual bodily features though their flesh has been replaced by empty form. For modern readers, the term "comedy" might seem peculiar, conditioned as we are to associate comedy with laughter, just as we associate tragedy with tears. For medieval readers, however, following classical notions of genre, a comedy was simply a story that ended on a high note, with joy and—in the case of *The Divine Comedy*—with the narrator literally being lifted up into the heavens.

The Divine Comedy is divided into three books; each charts a different realm of the afterlife, from the depths of Hell in the *Inferno*, up the mountain of Purgatory in the *Purgatorio*, and finally through the ever-higher spheres of Heaven in the *Paradiso* (only the *Inferno* is included in this Anthology). The three parts form a single path, as the narrator traverses a rugged landscape marked by hills, ravines, treacherous pathways, and difficult stairways, relying throughout on the help of a guide. For the journey through Hell and Purgatory, he follows in the footsteps of **Virgil**. The Roman poet is more than the literal guide of the wanderer within the fiction of the poem, for his *Aeneid*, the epic account of the fall of Troy and the foundation of Rome by Aeneas, is the constant poetic underpinning of Dante's own epic enterprise. But Virgil, as a pagan, cannot accompany him in Paradise: there Dante is led by Beatrice Portinari, his idealized love since childhood, who died in 1290. Both of these guides, as well as others who aid Dante along his way (such as Saint Lucy, who appears in the form of a golden eagle), are sent by a benefactor whom Dante only gradually comes to know: the *donna gentil* or "gracious lady" of Heaven, the Virgin Mary.

However important the theological message of *The Divine Comedy*, it never overshadows the essential realism and tangibility of the world Dante describes. From the horrible landscape of the ruined City of Dis seen in Hell to the brilliant light of the planets in Paradise, the reader's senses are continually stimulated. This stimulation is especially acute in the *Inferno*, where the vividness of the landscape is mirrored in the emotional affect of the narrator: he is moved to tears of pity by the sight of Paolo and Francesca, whose crime was to have given themselves over to the experience of love, but he shows contempt for the traitor Bocca degli Abati, kicking him and pulling out tufts of his hair. In keeping with Christian doctrine, the souls in this underworld have no material bodies, yet their shades retain the appearance of the bodies they had in life, and the punishments they suffer in Hell leave marks on their flesh. In the circle of schismatics, whose sin is that they have divided the community of the faithful, Dante finds Muhammad, the Prophet of Islam, his body "split . . . from his chin" down through his entrails. In this wound, the wrongful division of society, whether the body politic or the religious community, is made manifest on the canvas of the human body.

The structure of Hell, like that of Purgatory and Heaven, is highly symmetrical and full of numerical significance. *The Divine Comedy* is made up of one hundred chapters that Dante calls *cantos* (literally, "songs"), divided into three groups of thirty-three; the extra is added to the *Inferno*, which opens with an introductory canto. The numerological structure of the poem is also revealed in the landscape of each part. Hell is divided into nine circles, each containing a different category of sinners receiving their own proper form of punishment. The mountain of Purgatory is divided into nine parts as well, its seven main terraces (corresponding to the Seven Deadly Sins) surrounded by the entranceway of Ante-Purgatory and capped, at its summit, by the Earthly Paradise of Eden. Finally, the seven spheres of Heaven that lie above the mountain are brought to nine by the addition of those of the Fixed Stars and of the Primum Mobile—the first mover that imparts motion to all the other heavenly spheres. Beyond these nine are found only God and his angels. The constant play on the number three and its cube, three times three, highlights the Trinitarian theology that underlies the spiritual world of *The Divine Comedy*. Christian revelation places the earth at the center of the universe, surrounded by the spheres of the planets and of the stars and itself wounded by the cavernous pit of hell. At the base of the infernal pit, at the very center of the earth, Satan appears not wrapped in flames but rather frozen in a lake of ice. In Dante's memorable phrase, Satan is "the Great Worm of Evil / which bores through the world" as if it were a rotten apple.

Climbing over the hairy body of Satan and twisting through a narrow passageway, Dante and his guide emerge from the bowels of the earth to the base of the mountain of Purgatory. A new mood infuses the work from this point on, as the hopefulness of the narrator reflects the very different circumstances of those

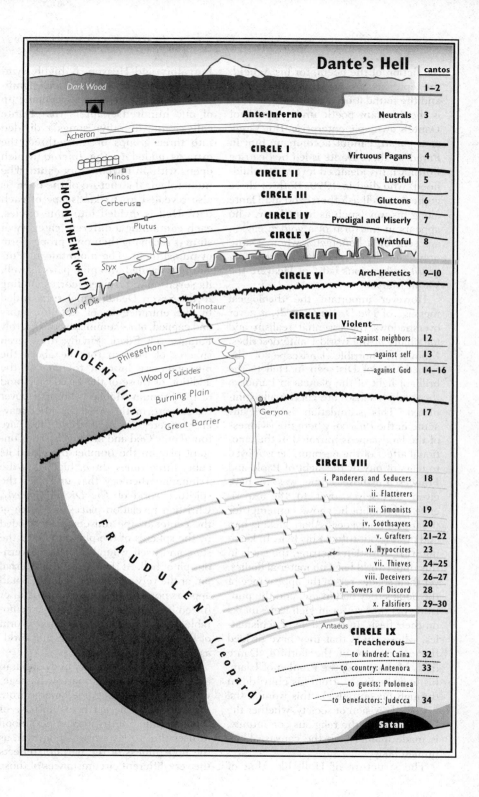

Dante's Hell

cantos

Dark Wood · 1–2

Ante-Inferno · Neutrals · 3

Acheron

CIRCLE I · Virtuous Pagans · 4

Minos

CIRCLE II · Lustful · 5

Cerberus

CIRCLE III · Gluttons · 6

Plutus

CIRCLE IV · Prodigal and Miserly · 7

CIRCLE V · Wrathful · 8

Styx

CIRCLE VI · Arch-Heretics · 9–10

City of Dis

Minotaur

CIRCLE VII · Violent—

Phlegethon · —against neighbors · 12

· —against self · 13

Wood of Suicides · —against God · 14–16

Burning Plain

Great Barrier · Geryon · 17

CIRCLE VIII

i. Panderers and Seducers · 18
ii. Flatterers
iii. Simonists · 19
iv. Soothsayers · 20
v. Grafters · 21–22
vi. Hypocrites · 23
vii. Thieves · 24–25
viii. Deceivers · 26–27
ix. Sowers of Discord · 28
x. Falsifiers · 29–30

Antaeus

CIRCLE IX · Treacherous—

—to kindred: Caïna · 32
—to country: Antenora · 33
—to guests: Ptolomea
—to benefactors: Judecca · 34

Satan

INCONTINENT (wolf)

VIOLENT (lion)

FRAUDULENT (leopard)

who suffer pain in Purgatory. Here, unlike in Hell, suffering has a purpose, gradually redeeming the inhabitants from their former state of sin and enabling their souls to rise upward. At the summit of the mountain, Dante enters the Earthly Paradise of Eden, now hidden away in Purgatory to keep it from fallen humans. Here his wonder at a magnificent procession climaxes in a moment of staggering recognition: as he puts it, "I recognize / the tokens of the ancient flame." Here Dante is met by Beatrice, his first love and the soul who will lead him the rest of the way on his upward journey.

Moving through the spheres of Paradise entails progressive dematerialization: instead of the rugged landscape of Hell, we find instead a sequence of spheres—each of which eclipses the last, each adorned with a symbolic form. In the sphere of the Crusaders, we see a mighty eagle; in the exalted spheres of the Empyrean, a celestial rose, studded with saintly souls. One of the very last of these symbolic forms is the great book "bound by love," whose "scattered leaves" make up the universe. In this vivid image, the unity of divine revelation and of the written text of *The Divine Comedy* is complete. The love that binds the book reappears in the poem's last lines, as the narrator describes the endless motion of the heavens, turned by "the Love that moves the sun and the other stars." This earth-centered image of the cosmos would, two centuries after Dante, give way to a new worldview, with the sun at its center and with humanity placed in a very different relationship to its Creator.

FROM THE DIVINE COMEDY[1]

Inferno

Canto I

THE DARK WOOD OF ERROR

Midway in his allotted threescore years and ten, Dante comes to himself with a start and realizes that he has strayed from the True Way into the Dark Wood of Error (Worldliness). As soon as he has realized his loss, Dante lifts his eyes and sees the first light of the sunrise (the Sun is the Symbol of Divine Illumination) lighting the shoulders of a little hill (The Mount of Joy). It is the Easter Season, the time of resurrection, and the sun is in its equinoctial rebirth. This juxtaposition of joyous symbols fills Dante with hope and he sets out at once to climb directly up the Mount of Joy, but almost immediately his way is blocked by the Three Beasts of Worldliness: *The Leopard of Malice and Fraud, The Lion of Violence and Ambition*, and *The She-Wolf of Incontinence*. These beasts, and especially the She Wolf, drive him back despairing into the darkness of error. But just as all seems lost, a figure appears to him. It is the shade of *Virgil*, Dante's symbol of *Human Reason*.

Virgil explains that he has been sent to lead Dante from error. There can, however, be no direct ascent past the beasts: the man who would escape them must go a longer and harder way. First he must descend through Hell (The Recognition of

1. Translated from the Italian by John Ciardi.

Sin), then he must ascend through Purgatory (The Renunciation of Sin), and only then may he reach the pinnacle of joy and come to the Light of God. Virgil offers to guide Dante, but only as far as Human Reason can go. Another guide (*Beatrice,* symbol of *Divine Love*) must take over for the final ascent, for Human Reason is self-limited. Dante submits himself joyously to Virgil's guidance and they move off.

Midway in our life's journey.[2] I went astray
    from the straight road[3] and woke to find myself
    alone in a dark wood. How shall I say   3

what wood that was! I never saw so drear,
    so rank, so arduous a wilderness!
    Its very memory gives a shape to fear.   6

Death could scarce be more bitter than that place!
    But since it came to good, I will recount
    all that I found revealed there by God's grace.   9

How I came to it I cannot rightly say,
    so drugged and loose with sleep had I become[4]
    when I first wandered there from the True Way.[5]   12

But at the far end of that valley of evil
    whose maze had sapped my very heart with fear
    I found myself before a little hill   15

and lifted up my eyes. Its shoulders glowed
    already with the sweet rays of that planet
    whose virtue leads men straight on every road,[6]   18

and the shining strengthened me against the fright
    whose agony had wracked the lake of my heart[7]
    through all the terrors of that piteous night.   21

Just as a swimmer, who with his last breath
    flounders ashore from perilous seas, might turn
    to memorize the wide water of his death—   24

---

2. Born in 1265, Dante was 35 in 1300, the fictional date of the poem. The biblical span of human life is 70 (see Psalms 90.10 and Isaiah 23.15).
3. See Proverbs 2.13–14 and 4.18–19, and also 2 Peter 2.15.
4. See Romans 13.11–12.
5. See Psalms 23.3.
6. The sun, which in the astronomical system of Dante's time was thought to be a planet that revolves around the earth.
7. This phrase refers to the inner chamber of the heart, a cavity that in the physiology of Dante's time was thought to be the location of fear. Not coincidentally, Dante's last stop in the *Inferno* ends at the lake of Cocytus (see 31.123).

so did I turn, my soul still fugitive
   from death's surviving image, to stare down
   that pass that none had ever left alive.[8]   27

And there I lay to rest from my heart's race
   till calm and breath returned to me. Then rose
   and pushed up that dead slope at such a pace   30

each footfall rose above the last.[9] And lo!
   almost at the beginning of the rise
   I faced a spotted Leopard, all tremor and flow   33

and gaudy pelt. And it would not pass, but stood
   so blocking my every turn that time and again
   I was on the verge of turning back to the wood.   36

This fell at the first widening of the dawn
   as the sun was climbing Aries with those stars
   that rode with him to light the new creation.[1]   39

Thus the holy hour and the sweet season
   of commemoration did much to arm my fear
   of that bright murderous beast with their good omen.   42

Yet not so much but what I shook with dread
   at sight of a great Lion that broke upon me
   raging with hunger, its enormous head   45

held high as if to strike a mortal terror
   into the very air. And down his track,
   a She-Wolf drove upon me, a starved horror   48

ravening and wasted beyond all belief.
   She seemed a rack for avarice, gaunt and craving.
   Oh many the souls she has brought to endless grief!   51

She brought such heaviness upon my spirit
   at sight of her savagery and desperation,
   I died from every hope of that high summit.[2]   54

---

8. This simile of Dante as the survivor of a passage through the sea invokes the story of the escape of the Israelites from Egypt through the Red Sea, a central metaphor throughout the *Comedy* (see Exodus 14). There is also probably an allusion to the opening of the *Aeneid*, where Aeneas and his men survive a storm.
9. The pilgrim is limping because he suffers from the injury of original sin.
1. In the Middle Ages it was thought that the world was created in spring, when the sun is in the constellation Aries.
2. The meaning of the leopard, lion, and "she-wolf" is open to a number of interpretations, the most plausible being that they represent the three major forms of sin found in Hell, respectively fraud, violence, and incontinence or immoderation (see Canto 11ff.). The structure of Hell indicates that the last is the least serious morally, but its role in this canto shows that it is the most difficult to overcome psychologically. Dante probably took the identities of these three beasts from a passage in Jeremiah 5.6.

And like a miser—eager in acquisition
    but desperate in self-reproach when Fortune's wheel
    turns to the hour of his loss—all tears and attrition   57

I wavered back; and still the beast pursued,
    forcing herself against me bit by bit
    till I slid back into the sunless wood.   60

And as I fell to my soul's ruin, a presence
    gathered before me on the discolored air,
    the figure of one who seemed hoarse from long silence.[3]   63

At sight of him in that friendless waste I cried:
    "Have pity on me, whatever thing you are,
    whether shade or living man." And it replied: 66

"Not man, though man I once was, and my blood
    was Lombard, both my parents Mantuan.[4]
    I was born, though late, *sub Julio*,[5] and bred   69

in Rome under Augustus in the noon
    of the false and lying gods. I was a poet
    and sang of old Anchises' noble son[6]   72

who came to Rome after the burning of Troy.
    But you—why do *you* return to these distresses
    instead of climbing that shining Mount of Joy   75

which is the seat and first cause of man's bliss?"
    "And are you then that Virgil and that fountain
    of purest speech?" My voice grew tremulous: 78

"Glory and light of poets! now may that zeal
    and love's apprenticeship that I poured out
    on your heroic verses serve me well!   81

For you are my true master and first author,
    the sole maker from whom I drew the breath
    of that sweet style whose measures have brought me honor.   84

See there, immortal sage, the beast I flee.
    For my soul's salvation, I beg you, guard me from her,
    for she has struck a mortal tremor through me."   87

---

3. The Roman poet Virgil's voice has not been heard since he died in 19 B.C.E.
4. Lombardy is the most northern area of Italy; Mantua is located to the east of Milan.
5. Virgil (70–19 B.C.E.) was born *sub Julio* (Latin), i.e., during the reign of Julius Caesar (assassinated in 44 B.C.E.), who was regarded by Dante as the founder of the Roman Empire.
6. Aeneas, the hero of Virgil's *Aeneid*. "Augustus": Julius Caesar's nephew and successor, who reigned as emperor from 27 B.C.E. to 14 C.E.

And he replied, seeing my soul in tears:
  "He must go by another way who would escape
  this wilderness, for that mad beast that fleers   90

before you there, suffers no man to pass.
  She tracks down all, kills all, and knows no glut,
  but, feeding, she grows hungrier than she was.   93

She mates with any beast, and will mate with more
  before the Greyhound comes to hunt her down.[7]
  He will not feed on lands nor loot, but honor   96

and love and wisdom will make straight his way.
  He will rise between Feltro and Feltro,[8] and in him
  shall be the resurrection and new day   99

of that sad Italy for which Nisus died,
  and Turnus, and Euryalus, and the maid Camilla.[9]
  He shall hunt her through every nation of sick pride   102

till she is driven back forever to Hell
  whence Envy first released her on the world.
  Therefore, for your own good, I think it well   105

you follow me and I will be your guide
  and lead you forth through an eternal place.
  There you shall see the ancient spirits tried   108

in endless pain, and hear their lamentation
  as each bemoans the second death of souls.[1]
  Next you shall see upon a burning mountain   111

souls in fire and yet content in fire,
  knowing that whensoever it may be
  they yet will mount into the blessed choir.[2]   114

To which, if it is still your wish to climb,
  a worthier spirit shall be sent to guide you.[3]
  With her shall I leave you, for the King of Time,   117

7. Dante's prediction of a modern political redeemer is so enigmatic that there can be no certainty of his identity. Most commentators think it is Cangrande (i.e., "Great Dog") della Scala of Verona, Dante's benefactor after his exile from Florence.
8. Feltre and Montefeltro are towns that roughly marked the limits of Cangrande's domains. But other interpretations are possible.
9. Characters in the *Aeneid* who die during Aeneas's conquest of Italy.
1. The second death is damnation; see Revelation 21.8.
2. The souls in Purgatory; the blessed are the saved in Paradise.
3. Beatrice.

who reigns on high, forbids me to come there
    since, living, I rebelled against his law.[4]
    He rules the waters and the land and air   120

and there holds court, his city and his throne.
    Oh blessed are they he chooses!" And I to him:
    "Poet, by that God to you unknown,   123

lead me this way. Beyond this present ill
    and worse to dread, lead me to Peter's gate
    and be my guide through the sad halls of Hell."   126

And he then: "Follow." And he moved ahead
in silence, and I followed where he led.

Canto II

THE DESCENT

It is evening of the first day (Friday). Dante is following Virgil and finds himself
tired and despairing. How can he be worthy of such a vision as Virgil has described?
He hesitates and seems about to abandon his first purpose.

To comfort him Virgil explains how Beatrice descended to him in Limbo and
told him of her concern for Dante. It is she, the symbol of Divine Love, who
sends Virgil to lead Dante from error. She has come into Hell itself on this errand,
for Dante cannot come to Divine Love unaided: Reason must lead him. Moreover, Beatrice has been sent with the prayers of the Virgin Mary (*Compassion*), and
of Saint Lucia (*Divine Light*). Rachel (*The Contemplative Life*) also figures in the
heavenly scene which Virgil recounts.

Virgil explains all this and reproaches Dante: how can he hesitate longer when
such heavenly powers are concerned for him, and Virgil himself has promised to
lead him safely?

Dante understands at once that such forces cannot fail him, and his spirits rise
in joyous anticipation.

The light was departing. The brown air drew down
    all the earth's creatures, calling them to rest
    from their day-roving, as I, one man alone,   3

prepared myself to face the double war
    of the journey and the pity, which memory
    shall here set down, nor hesitate, nor err.   6

O Muses! O High Genius! Be my aid!
    O Memory, recorder of the vision,
    here shall your true nobility be displayed!   9

---

4. Virgil "rebelled" against God because he was not a Christian.

Thus I began: "Poet, you who must guide me,
 before you trust me to that arduous passage,
 look to me and look through me—can I be worthy?   12

You sang how the father of Sylvius,[5] while still
 in corruptible flesh won to that other world,
 crossing with mortal sense the immortal sill.   15

But if the Adversary of all Evil
 weighing his consequence and who and what
 should issue from him, treated him so well—   18

that cannot seem unfitting to thinking men,
 since he was chosen father of Mother Rome
 and of her Empire by God's will and token.   21

Both, to speak strictly, were founded and foreknown
 as the established Seat of Holiness
 for the successors of Great Peter's throne.[6]   24

In that quest, which your verses celebrate,
 he learned those mysteries from which arose
 his victory and Rome's apostolate.   27

There later came the chosen vessel, Paul,
 bearing the confirmation of that Faith
 which is the one true door to life eternal.[7]   30

But I—how should I dare? By whose permission?
 I am not Aeneas. *I* am not Paul.
 Who could believe me worthy of the vision?   33

How, then, may I presume to this high quest
 and not fear my own brashness? You are wise
 and will grasp what my poor words can but suggest."   36

As one who unwills what he wills, will stay
 strong purposes with feeble second thoughts
 until he spells all his first zeal away—   39

so I hung back and balked on that dim coast
 till thinking had worn out my enterprise,
 so stout at starting and so early lost.   42

5. I.e., Aeneas, the father (or grandfather) of
Sylvius, who visited the underworld in *Aeneid* 6.
6. The Apostle Peter is considered by the
Roman Catholic Church to be the first pope.
7. St. Paul; see 2 Corinthians 212. Both Peter
and Paul were martyred in Rome.

"I understand from your words and the look in your eyes,"
   that shadow of magnificence answered me,
     "your soul is sunken in that cowardice   45

that bears down many men, turning their course
   and resolution by imagined perils,
     as his own shadow turns the frightened horse.   48

To free you of this dread I will tell you all
   of why I came to you and what I heard
     when first I pitied you. I was a soul   51

among the souls of Limbo, when a Lady
   so blessed and so beautiful, I prayed her
     to order and command my will, called to me.[8]   54

Her eyes were kindled from the lamps of Heaven.
   Her voice reached through me, tender, sweet, and low.
     An angel's voice, a music of its own: 57

'O gracious Mantuan whose melodies
   live in earth's memory and shall live on
     till the last motion ceases in the skies,   60

my dearest friend, and fortune's foe, has strayed
   onto a friendless shore and stands beset
     by such distresses that he turns afraid   63

from the True Way, and news of him in Heaven
   rumors my dread he is already lost.
     I come, afraid that I am too late risen.   66

Fly to him and with your high counsel, pity,
   and with whatever need be for his good
     and soul's salvation, help him, and solace me.   69

It is I, Beatrice, who send you to him.
   I come from the blessed height for which I yearn.
     Love called me here. When amid Seraphim[9]   72

I stand again before my Lord, your praises
   shall sound in Heaven.' She paused, and I began:
     'O Lady of that only grace that raises   75

feeble mankind within its mortal cycle
   above all other works God's will has placed
     within the heaven of the smallest circle;[1]   78

8. As we soon learn, the lady is Beatrice.   Paradise.
9. Angels who dwell in "the blessed height,"   1. The sphere of the moon.

so welcome is your command that to my sense,
    were it already fulfilled, it would yet seem tardy.
    I understand, and am all obedience.   81

But tell me how you dare to venture thus
    so far from the wide heaven of your joy
    to which your thoughts yearn back from this abyss.'   84

'Since what you ask,' she answered me, 'probes near
    the root of all, I will say briefly only
    how I have come through Hell's pit without fear.   87

Know then, O waiting and compassionate soul,
    that is to fear which has the power to harm,
    and nothing else is fearful even in Hell.   90

I am so made by God's all-seeing mercy
    your anguish does not touch me, and the flame
    of this great burning has no power upon me.   93

There is a Lady in Heaven[2] so concerned
    for him I send you to, that for her sake
    the strict decree is broken. She has turned   96

and called Lucia[3] to her wish and mercy
    saying: 'Thy faithful one is sorely pressed;
    in his distresses I commend him to thee.'   99

Lucia, that soul of light and foe of all
    cruelty, rose and came to me at once
    where I was sitting with the ancient Rachel,[4]   102

saying to me: 'Beatrice, true praise of God,
    why dost thou not help him who loved thee so
    that for thy sake he left the vulgar crowd?   105

Dost thou not hear his cries? Canst thou not see
    the death he wrestles with beside that river
    no ocean can surpass for rage and fury?'[5]   108

No soul of earth was ever as rapt to seek
    its good or flee its injury as I was—
    when I had heard my sweet Lucia speak—   111

---

2. The Virgin Mary.
3. St. Lucy, a third-century martyr and the
patron saint of those afflicted with poor or
damaged sight.

4. Rachel signifies the contemplative life; see
Genesis 29.16–17.
5. These are the metaphoric waters of 1.22–24.

to descend from Heaven and my blessed seat
  to you, laying my trust in that high speech
  that honors you and all who honor it.'   114

She spoke and turned away to hide a tear
  that, shining, urged me faster. So I came
  and freed you from the beast that drove you there,   117

blocking the near way to the Heavenly Height.
  And now what ails you? Why do you lag? Why
  this heartsick hesitation and pale fright   120

when three such blessed Ladies lean from Heaven
  in their concern for you and my own pledge
  of the great good that waits you has been given?"   123

As flowerlets drooped and puckered in the night
  turn up to the returning sun and spread
  their petals wide on his new warmth and light—   126

just so my wilted spirits rose again
  and such a heat of zeal surged through my veins
  that I was born anew. Thus I began: 129

"Blessèd be that Lady of infinite pity,
  and blessèd be thy taxed and courteous spirit
  that came so promptly on the word she gave thee. 132

Thy words have moved my heart to its first purpose.
  My Guide! My Lord! My Master! Now lead on:
  one will shall serve the two of us in this."   135

He turned when I had spoken, and at his back
I entered on that hard and perilous track.

Canto III

THE VESTIBULE OF HELL   *The Opportunists*

The Poets pass the Gate of Hell and are immediately assailed by cries of anguish.
Dante sees the first of the souls in torment. They are *The Opportunists*, those souls
who in life were neither for good nor evil but only for themselves. Mixed with
them are those outcasts who took no sides in the Rebellion of the Angels. They
are neither in Hell nor out of it. Eternally unclassified, they race round and round
pursuing a wavering banner that runs forever before them through the dirty air;
and as they run they are pursued by swarms of wasps and hornets, who sting
them and produce a constant flow of blood and putrid matter which trickles down
the bodies of the sinners and is feasted upon by loathsome worms and maggots
who coat the ground.

The law of Dante's Hell is the law of symbolic retribution. As they sinned so are they punished. They took no sides, therefore they are given no place. As they pursued the ever-shifting illusion of their own advantage, changing their courses with every changing wind, so they pursue eternally an elusive, ever-shifting banner. As their sin was a darkness, so they move in darkness. As their own guilty conscience pursued them, so they are pursued by swarms of wasps and hornets. And as their actions were a moral filth, so they run eternally through the filth of worms and maggots which they themselves feed.

Dante recognizes several, among them *Pope Celestine V*, but without delaying to speak to any of these souls, the Poets move on to *Acheron*, the first of the rivers of Hell. Here the newly-arrived souls of the damned gather and wait for monstrous *Charon* to ferry them over to punishment. Charon recognizes Dante as a living man and angrily refuses him passage. Virgil forces Charon to serve them, but Dante swoons with terror, and does not reawaken until he is on the other side.

I AM THE WAY INTO THE CITY OF WOE.
I AM THE WAY TO A FORSAKEN PEOPLE.
I AM THE WAY INTO ETERNAL SORROW.   3

SACRED JUSTICE MOVED MY ARCHITECT.
I WAS RAISED HERE BY DIVINE OMNIPOTENCE,
PRIMORDIAL LOVE AND ULTIMATE INTELLECT.[6]   6

ONLY THOSE ELEMENTS TIME CANNOT WEAR
WERE MADE BEFORE ME, AND BEYOND TIME I STAND.
ABANDON ALL HOPE YE WHO ENTER HERE.   9

These mysteries I read cut into stone
    above a gate. And turning I said: "Master,
    what is the meaning of his harsh inscription?"   12

And he then as initiate to novice:
    "Here must you put by all division of spirit
    and gather your soul against all cowardice.   15

This is the place I told you to expect.
    Here you shall pass among the fallen people,
    souls who have lost the good of intellect."[7]   18

So saying, he put forth his hand to me,
    and with a gentle and encouraging smile
    he led me through the gate of mystery.   21

Here sighs and cries and wails coiled and recoiled
    on the starless air, spilling my soul to tears.
    A confusion of tongues and monstrous accents toiled   24

6. I.e., God as Father, Son, and Holy Ghost.
7. "The good of intellect": i.e., God.

in pain and anger. Voices hoarse and shrill
  and sounds of blows, all intermingled, raised
  tumult and pandemonium that still 27

whirls on the air forever dirty with it
  as if a whirlwind sucked at sand. And I,
  holding my head in horror, cried: "Sweet Spirit, 30

what souls are these who run through this black haze?"
  And he to me: "These are the nearly soulless
  whose lives concluded neither blame nor praise. 33

They are mixed here with that despicable corps
  of angels who were neither for God nor Satan,
  but only for themselves.[8] The High Creator 36

scourged them from Heaven for its perfect beauty,
  and Hell will not receive them since the wicked
  might feel some glory over them." And I: 39

"Master, what gnaws at them so hideously
  their lamentation stuns the very air?"
  "They have no hope of death," he answered me, 42

"and in their blind and unattaining state
  their miserable lives have sunk so low
  that they must envy every other fate. 45

No word of them survives their living season.
  Mercy and Justice deny them even a name.
  Let us not speak of them: look, and pass on." 48

I saw a banner there upon the mist.
  Circling and circling, it seemed to scorn all pause.
  So it ran on, and still behind it pressed 51

a never-ending rout of souls in pain.
  I had not thought death had undone so many
  as passed before me in that mournful train. 54

And some I knew among them; last of all
  I recognized the shadow of that soul
  who, in his cowardice, made the Great Denial.[9] 57

8. These "angels," not mentioned in the Bible but discussed by theologians throughout the Middle Ages, were those who declined to choose either side when Satan rebelled against God.
9. This is Pope Celestine V, who was elected in July 1294 but abdicated five months later; Dante believed that this abdication ("the Great Denial") ushered in the corrupt papacy of Celestine's successor, Boniface VIII (see 19.49–57).

At once I understood for certain: these
  were of that retrograde and faithless crew
  hateful to God and to His enemies.   60

These wretches never born and never dead
  ran naked in a swarm of wasps and hornets
  that goaded them the more the more they fled,   63

and made their faces stream with bloody gouts
  of pus and tears that dribbled to their feet
  to be swallowed there by loathsome worms and maggots.   66

Then looking onward I made out a throng
  assembled on the beach of a wide river,
  whereupon I turned to him: "Master, I long   69

to know what souls these are, and what strange usage
  makes them as eager to cross as they seem to be
  in this infected light." At which the Sage: 72

"All this shall be made known to you when we stand
  on the joyless beach of Acheron."[1] And I
  cast down my eyes, sensing a reprimand   75

in what he said, and so walked at his side
  in silence and ashamed until we came
  through the dead cavern to that sunless tide.   78

There, steering toward us in an ancient ferry
  came an old man with a white bush of hair,[2]
  bellowing: "Woe to you depraved souls! Bury   81

here and forever all hope of Paradise:
  I come to lead you to the other shore,
  into eternal dark, into fire and ice.   84

And you who are living yet, I say begone
  from these who are dead." But when he saw me stand
  against his violence he began again: 87

"By other windings and by other steerage
  shall you cross to that other shore. Not here! Not here!
  A lighter craft than mine must give you passage."[3]   90

1. The first of the four rivers of Hell.
2. Charon; see *Aeneid* 6.
3. Charon knows that after death Dante will be taken not to Hell but to Purgatory in a "lighter craft" piloted by an angel; the arrival of the souls in Purgatory is described in *Purgatorio* 2.22–48. This is the first of several places in the *Commedia* where Dante predicts his own salvation.

And my Guide to him: "Charon, bite back your spleen:
   this has been willed where what is willed must be,
   and is not yours to ask what it may mean."   93

The steersman of that marsh of ruined souls,
   who wore a wheel of flame around each eye,
   stifled the rage that shook his woolly jowls.   96

But those unmanned and naked spirits there
   turned pale with fear and their teeth began to chatter
   at sound of his crude bellow. In despair   99

they blasphemed God, their parents, their time on earth,
   the race of Adam, and the day and the hour
   and the place and the seed and the womb that gave them birth.   102

But all together they drew to that grim shore
   where all must come who lose the fear of God.
   Weeping and cursing they come for evermore,   105

and demon Charon with eyes like burning coals
   herds them in, and with a whistling oar
   flails on the stragglers to his wake of souls.   108

As leaves in autumn loosen and stream down
   until the branch stands bare above its tatters
   spread on the rustling ground, so one by one   111

the evil seed of Adam in its Fall
   cast themselves, at his signal, from the shore
   and streamed away like birds who hear their call.[4]   114

So they are gone over that shadowy water,
   and always before they reach the other shore
   a new noise stirs on this, and new throngs gather.   117

"My son," the courteous Master said to me,
   "all who die in the shadow of God's wrath
   converge to this from every clime and country.   120

And all pass over eagerly, for here
   Divine Justice transforms and spurs them so
   their dread turns wish: they yearn for what they fear.   123

No soul in Grace comes ever to this crossing;
   therefore if Charon rages at your presence
   you will understand the reason for his cursing."   126

---

4. These similes are drawn from *Aeneid* 6.56–60 (all line references are to the edition in this anthology).

When he had spoken, all the twilight country
   shook so violently, the terror of it
   bathes me with sweat even in memory: 129

the tear-soaked ground gave out a sigh of wind
   that spewed itself in flame on a red sky,
   and all my shattered senses left me. Blind,   132

like one whom sleep comes over in a swoon,
I stumbled into darkness and went down.[5]

Canto IV

CIRCLE ONE: LIMBO   *The Virtuous Pagans*

Dante wakes to find himself across Acheron. The Poets are now on the brink
of Hell itself, which Dante conceives as a great funnel-shaped cave lying
below the northern hemisphere with its bottom point at the earth's center.
Around this great circular depression runs a series of ledges, each of which
Dante calls a *Circle*. Each circle is assigned to the punishment of one category of sin.

As soon as Dante's strength returns, the Poets begin to cross the *First Circle*.
Here they find the *Virtuous Pagans*. They were born without the light of Christ's
revelation, and, therefore, they cannot come into the light of God, but they are
not tormented. Their only pain is that they have no hope.

Ahead of them Dante sights a great dome of light, and a voice trumpets through
the darkness welcoming Virgil back, for this is his eternal place in Hell. Immediately the great Poets of all time appear—*Homer, Horace, Ovid,* and *Lucan*. They
greet Virgil, and they make Dante a sixth in their company.

With them Dante enters the Citadel of Human Reason and sees before his eyes
the Master Souls of Pagan Antiquity gathered on a green, and illuminated by the
radiance of Human Reason. This is the highest state man can achieve without
God, and the glory of it dazzles Dante, but he knows also that it is nothing compared to the glory of God.

A monstrous clap of thunder broke apart
   the swoon that stuffed my head; like one awakened
   by violent hands, I leaped up with a start.   3

And having risen; rested and renewed,
   I studied out the landmarks of the gloom
   to find my bearings there as best I could.   6

And I found I stood on the very brink of the valley
   called the Dolorous Abyss, the desolate chasm
   where rolls the thunder of Hell's eternal cry,   9

5. Dante is describing an earthquake, which
medieval science understood as the escape of
vapors from within the earth; it is while he is
unconscious that he crosses Acheron into Hell
proper.

so depthless-deep and nebulous and dim
   that stare as I might into its frightful pit
   it gave me back no feature and no bottom.   12

Death-pale, the Poet spoke: "Now let us go
   into the blind world waiting here below us.
   I will lead the way and you will follow."   15

And I, sick with alarm at his new pallor,
   cried out, "How can I go this way when you
   who are my strength in doubt turn pale with terror?"   18

And he: "The pain of these below us here,
   drains the color from my face for pity,
   and leaves this pallor you mistake for fear.   21

Now let us go, for a long road awaits us."
   So he entered and so he led me in
   to the first circle and ledge of the abyss.   24

No tortured wailing rose to greet us here
   but sounds of sighing rose from every side,
   sending a tremor through the timeless air,   27

a grief breathed out of untormented sadness,
   the passive state of those who dwelled apart,
   men, women, children—a dim and endless congress.   30

And the Master said to me: "You do not question
   what souls these are that suffer here before you?
   I wish you to know before you travel on   33

that these were sinless. And still their merits fail,
   for they lacked Baptism's grace, which is the door
   of the true faith *you* were born to. Their birth fell   36

before the age of the Christian mysteries,
   and so they did not worship God's Trinity
   in fullest duty. I am one of these.   39

For such defects are we lost, though spared the fire
   and suffering Hell in one affliction only:
   that without hope we live on in desire."   42

I thought how many worthy souls there were
   suspended in that Limbo, and a weight
   closed on my heart for what the noblest suffer.   45

"Instruct me, Master and most noble Sir,"
   I prayed him then, "better to understand
   the perfect creed that conquers every error: 48

has any, by his own or another's merit,
gone ever from this place to blessedness?"
He sensed my inner question and answered it:[6] 51

"I was still new to this estate of tears
when a Mighty One descended here among us,
crowned with the sign of His victorious years. 54

He took from us the shade of our first parent,[7]
of Abel, his pure son, of ancient Noah,
of Moses, the bringer of law, the obedient. 57

Father Abraham, David the King,
Israel with his father and his children,
Rachel, the holy vessel of His blessing, 60

and many more He chose for elevation
among the elect. And before these, you must know,
no human soul had ever won salvation." 63

We had not paused as he spoke, but held our road
and passed meanwhile beyond a press of souls
crowded about like trees in a thick wood. 66

And we had not traveled far from where I woke
when I made out a radiance before us
that struck away a hemisphere of dark. 69

We were still some distance back in the long night,
yet near enough that I half-saw, half-sensed,
what quality of souls lived in that light. 72

"O ornament of wisdom and of art,
what souls are these whose merit lights their way
even in Hell. What joy sets them apart?" 75

And he to me: "The signature of honor
they left on earth is recognized in Heaven
and wins them ease in Hell out of God's favor."[8] 78

And as he spoke a voice rang on the air:
"Honor the Prince of Poets; the soul and glory
that went from us returns. He is here! He is here!" 81

The cry ceased and the echo passed from hearing;
I saw four mighty presences come toward us
with neither joy nor sorrow in their bearing. 84

6. Dante's question is about the Harrowing of Hell, when, according to Christian doctrine, Christ descended into Hell after the crucifixion and rescued the souls of the righteous of Israel; see also 12.43–45.
7. Adam.
8. The "signature of honor" is "poet."

"Note well," my Master said as they came on,
　"that soul that leads the rest with sword in hand
　as if he were their captain and champion. 87

It is Homer, singing master of the earth.
　Next after him is Horace, the satirist,
　Ovid is third, and Lucan[9] is the fourth. 90

Since all of these have part in the high name
　the voice proclaimed, calling me Prince of Poets,
　the honor that they do me honors them." 93

So I saw gathered at the edge of light
　the masters of that highest school whose song
　outsoars all others like an eagle's flight. 96

And after they had talked together a while,
　they turned and welcomed me most graciously,
　at which I saw my approving Master smile. 99

And they honored me far beyond courtesy,
　for they included me in their own number,
　making me sixth in that high company. 102

So we moved toward the light, and as we passed
　we spoke of things as well omitted here
　as it was sweet to touch on there. At last 105

we reached the base of a great Citadel
　circled by seven towering battlements
　and by a sweet brook flowing round them all.[1] 108

This we passed over as if it were firm ground.
　Through seven gates I entered with those sages
　and came to a green meadow blooming round.[2] 111

There with a solemn and majestic poise
　stood many people gathered in the light,
　speaking infrequently and with muted voice. 114

Past that enameled green we six withdrew
　into a luminous and open height
　from which each soul among them stood in view. 117

9. Homer is the legendary epic poet of ancient
Greece; Horace, Ovid, and Lucan are famous
Roman poets.
1. Commentators have suggested that this is a
Castle of Fame, its seven walls symbolizing
the seven liberal arts, a system of knowledge
developed in the classical period.
2. A locale reminiscent of the classical Elysian
fields as described in *Aeneid* 6.468–73.

And there directly before me on the green
   the master souls of time were shown to me.
   I glory in the glory I have seen!   120

Electra stood in a great company
   among whom I saw Hector and Aeneas
   and Caesar in armor with his falcon's eye.[3]   123

I saw Camilla, and the Queen Amazon
   across the field. I saw the Latian King
   seated there with his daughter by his throne.[4]   126

And the good Brutus who overthrew the Tarquin:
   Lucrezia, Julia, Marcia, and Cornelia;
   and, by himself apart, the Saladin.[5]   129

And raising my eyes a little I saw on high
   Aristotle, the master of those who know,[6]
   ringed by the great souls of philosophy.   132

All wait upon him for their honor and his.
   I saw Socrates and Plato at his side
   before all others there. Democritus   135

who ascribes the world to chance, Diogenes,
   and with him there Thales, Anaxagoras,
   Zeno, Heraclitus, Empedocles.   138

And I saw the wise collector and analyst—
   Dioscorides I mean. I saw Orpheus there,
   Tully, Linus, Seneca the moralist,[7]   141

Eculid the geometer, and Ptolemy,
   Hippocrates, Galen, Avicenna,
   and Averrhoës of the Great Commentary.[8]   144

3. Julius Caesar. "Electra": the mother of Dardanus, the founder of Troy. "Hector": the leading warrior of the Trojans in the *Iliad*. "Aeneas": the hero of Virgil's Roman epic, the *Aeneid*.
4. Lavinia, heiress to King Latinus who ruled the area of Italy where Rome was later located and who married Aeneas. "Camilla": a female warrior in the *Aeneid*, where she is compared to Penthesilea, who fought for the Trojans against the Greeks.
5. Admired for his chivalry in fighting against the Crusaders, Saladin was sultan of Egypt and Syria and died in 1193. "Brutus": not the Brutus who killed Julius Caesar, but an earlier Roman who drove out the tyrant Tarquin. All four of the women mentioned were virtuous Roman matrons.
6. Aristotle (384–322 B.C.E.), Greek philosopher. The men mentioned in lines 134–38 are Greek philosophers of the 7th through the 4th centuries B.C.E.
7. Roman philosopher and dramatist, killed by Nero in 65 C.E. "Dioscorides": Greek physician (1st century C.E.). "Orpheus": mythical Greek poet. "Tully": Cicero (d. 43 B.C.E.), Roman orator.
8. Avicenna (d. 1037) and Averrhoës (d. 1198) were Islamic philosophers who wrote commentaries on Aristotle's works that were highly influential in Christian Europe. "Euclid": Greek mathematician (4th century B.C.E.). "Ptolemy": Greek astronomer and geographer (1st century C.E.) credited with devising the cosmological system that was accepted until the time of Copernicus in the 16th century (hence the term *Ptolemaic universe*). "Hippocrates and Galen": Greek physicians (4th and 2nd centuries B.C.E., respectively).

I cannot count so much nobility;
    my longer theme pursues me so that often
    the word falls short of the reality.   147

The company of six is reduced by four.
    My Master leads me by another road
    away from that serenity to the roar   150

and trembling air of Hell. I pass from light
into the kingdom of eternal night.

Canto V

CIRCLE TWO   *The Carnal*

The Poets leave Limbo and enter the *Second Circle*. Here begin the torments of
Hell proper, and here, blocking the way, sits *Minos*, the dread and semi-bestial
judge of the damned who assigns to each soul its eternal torment. He orders the
Poets back; but Virgil silences him as he earlier silenced Charon, and the Poets
move on.

They find themselves on a dark ledge swept by a great whirlwind, which spins
within it the souls of the *Carnal*, those who betrayed reason to their appetites.
Their sin was to abandon themselves to the tempest of their passions: so they are
swept forever in the tempest of Hell, forever denied the light of reason and of
God. Virgil identifies many among them. *Semiramis* is there, and *Dido*, *Cleopatra*,
Helen, *Achilles*, *Paris*, and *Tristan*. Dante sees *Paolo* and *Francesca* swept together,
and in the name of love he calls to them to tell their sad story. They pause from
their eternal flight to come to him, and Francesca tells their history while Paolo
weeps at her side. Dante is so stricken by compassion at their tragic tale that he
swoons once again.

So we went down to the second ledge alone;
    a smaller circle of so much greater pain
    the voice of the damned rose in a bestial moan.   3

There Minos sits, grinning, grotesque, and hale.
    He examines each lost soul as it arrives
    and delivers his verdict with his coiling tail.[9]   6

That is to say, when the ill-fated soul
    appears before him it confesses all,
    and that grim sorter of the dark and foul   9

decides which place in Hell shall be its end,
    then wraps his twitching tail about himself
    one coil for each degree it must descend.   12

The soul descends and others take its place:
    each crowds in its turn to judgment, each confesses,
    each hears its doom and falls away through space.   15

---

9. Minos is described as judge of the underworld in *Aeneid* 6.207–11.

"O you who come into this camp of woe,"
   cried Minos when he saw me turn away
   without awaiting his judgment, "watch where you go   18

once you have entered here, and to whom you turn!
   Do not be misled by that wide and easy passage!"
   And my Guide to him: "That is not your concern;   21

it is his fate to enter every door.
   This has been willed where what is willed must be,[1]
   and is not yours to question. Say no more."   24

Now the choir of anguish, like a wound,
   strikes through the tortured air. Now I have come
   to Hell's full lamentation, sound beyond sound.   27

I came to a place stripped bare of every light
   and roaring on the naked dark like seas
   wracked by a war of winds. Their hellish flight   30

of storm and counterstorm through time foregone,
   sweeps the souls of the damned before its charge.
   Whirling and battering it drives them on,   33

and when they pass the ruined gap of Hell
   through which we had come, their shrieks begin anew,
   There they blaspheme the power of God eternal.   36

And this, I learned, was the never-ending flight
   of those who sinned in the flesh, the carnal and lusty
   who betrayed reason to their appetite.   39

As the wings of wintering starlings bear them on
   in their great wheeling flights, just so the blast
   wherries these evil souls through time foregone.   42

Here, there, up, down, they whirl and, whirling, strain
   with never a hope of hope to comfort them,
   not of release, but even of less pain.   45

As cranes go over sounding their harsh cry,
   leaving the long streak of their flight in air,
   so come these spirits, wailing as they fly.   48

And watching their shadows lashed by wind, I cried:
   "Master, what souls are these the very air
   lashes with its black whips from side to side?"   51

---

1. I.e., is willed in Heaven by God, who has the power to accomplish whatever he wills.

"The first of these whose history you would know,"
  he answered me, "was Empress of many tongues.
  Mad sensuality corrupted her so   54

that to hide the guilt of her debauchery
  she licensed all depravity alike,
  and lust and law were one in her decree.   57

She is Semiramis[2] of whom the tale is told
  how she married Ninus and succeeded him
  to the throne of that wide land the Sultans hold.   60

The other is Dido; faithless to the ashes
  of Sichaeus, she killed herself for love.
  The next whom the eternal tempest lashes   63

is sense-drugged Cleopatra.[3] See Helen there,
  from whom such ill arose. And great Achilles,
  who fought at last with love in the house of prayer.[4]   66

And Paris. And Tristan."[5] As they whirled above
  he pointed out more than a thousand shades
  of those torn from the mortal life by love.   69

I stood there while my Teacher one by one
  named the great knights and ladies of dim time;
  and I was swept by pity and confusion.   72

At last I spoke: "Poet, I should be glad
  to speak a word with those two swept together
  so lightly on the wind and still so sad."[6]   75

And he to me: "Watch them. When next they pass,
  call to them in the name of love that drives
  and damns them here. In that name they will pause."   78

Thus, as soon as the wind in its wild course
  brought them around, I called: "O wearied souls!
  if none forbid it, pause and speak to us."   81

2. Renowned for licentiousness, a mythical queen of Assyria and wife of Ninus, the legendary founder of Ninevah. Because both the capital of Assyria and Old Cairo were known as Babylon, her land is here confused with that ruled by the sultan of Egypt.

3. Dido, whose suicide for love of Aeneas is described in *Aeneid* 4.542–942, was the widow of Sichaeus. Cleopatra killed herself after the death of her lover, Mark Antony, in 30 B.C.E.

4. The medieval version of the Troy story described Achilles as enamored of a Trojan princess, Polyxena, and killed in an ambush set by Paris when he went to meet her. Helen's seduction by Paris (see line 67) was the cause of the Trojan War.

5. The lover of Iseult, wife of his lord King Mark.

6. Francesca da Rimini and her brother-in-law Paolo Malatesta.

As mating doves that love calls to their nest
 glide through the air with motionless raised wings,
 borne by the sweet desire that fills each breast— 84

Just so those spirits turned on the torn sky
 from the band where Dido whirls across the air;
 such was the power of pity in my cry. 87

"O living creature, gracious, kind, and good,
 going this pilgrimage through the sick night,
 visiting us who stained the earth with blood, 90

were the King of Time our friend, we would pray His peace
 on you who have pitied us. As long as the wind
 will let us pause, ask of us what you please. 93

The town where I was born lies by the shore
 where the Po descends into its ocean rest
 with its attendant streams in one long murmur.[7] 96

Love, which in gentlest hearts will soonest bloom
 seized my lover with passion for that sweet body
 from which I was torn unshriven to my doom. 99

Love, which permits no loved one not to love,
 took me so strongly with delight in him
 that we are one in Hell, as we were above. 102

Love led us to one death. In the depths of Hell
 Caïna waits for him who took our lives."[8]
 This was the piteous tale they stopped to tell. 105

And when I had heard those world-offended lovers
 I bowed my head. At last the Poet spoke:
 "What painful thoughts are these your lowered brow covers?" 108

When at length I answered, I began: "Alas!
 What sweetest thoughts, what green and young desire
 led these two lovers to this sorry pass." 111

Then turning to those spirits once again,
 I said: "Francesca, what you suffer here
 melts me to tears of pity and of pain. 114

---

7. The river Po, in northern Italy, empties into the Adriatic Sea at Ravenna.

8. Caïna is the circle of Cain (described in canto 32), where those who killed their kin are punished; the lovers were killed by Gianciotto Malatesta, Francesca's husband and Paolo's brother.

But tell me: in the time of your sweet sighs
  by what appearances found love the way
  to lure you to his perilous paradise?"   117

And she: "The double grief of a lost bliss
  is to recall its happy hour in pain.
  Your Guide and Teacher knows the truth of this.   120

But if there is indeed a soul in Hell
  to ask of the beginning of our love
  out of his pity, I will weep and tell: 123

On a day for dalliance we read the rhyme
  of Lancelot,[9] how love had mastered him.
  We were alone with innocence and dim time.   126

Pause after pause that high old story drew
  our eyes together while we blushed and paled;
  but it was one soft passage overthrew   129

our caution and our hearts. For when we read
  how her fond smile was kissed by such a lover,
  he who is one with me alive and dead   132

breathed on my lips the tremor of his kiss.
  That book, and he who wrote it, was a pander.
  That day we read no further."[1] As she said this,   135

the other spirit, who stood by her, wept
  so piteously, I felt my senses reel
  and faint away with anguish. I was swept   138

by such a swoon as death is, and I fell,
  as a corpse might fall, to the dead floor of Hell.

Canto VI

CIRCLE THREE   *The Gluttons*

Dante recovers from his swoon and finds himself in the *Third Circle*. A great storm of putrefaction falls incessantly, a mixture of stinking snow and freezing rain, which forms into a vile slush underfoot. Everything about this Circle suggests a gigantic garbage dump. The souls of the damned lie in the icy paste, swollen and obscene, and *Cerberus*, the ravenous three-headed dog of Hell, stands guard over them, ripping and tearing them with his claws and teeth.

    These are the *Gluttons*. In life they made no higher use of the gifts of God than to wallow in food and drink, producers of nothing but garbage and offal. Here

9. In Arthurian legend, the lover of Arthur's wife, Guinevere.
1. Compare this line to Augustine's account in *Confessions* of his conversion by reading a passage in Paul's Epistle to the Romans.

they lie through all eternity, themselves like garbage, half-buried in fetid slush, while Cerberus slavers over them as they in life slavered over their food.

As the Poets pass, one of the speakers sits up and addresses Dante. He is *Ciacco, The Hog*, a citizen of Dante's own Florence. He recognizes Dante and asks eagerly for news of what is happening there. With the foreknowledge of the damned, Ciacco then utters the first of the political prophecies that are to become a recurring theme of the Inferno. The Poets then move on toward the next Circle, at the edge of which they encounter the monster Plutus.

My senses had reeled from me out of pity
   for the sorrow of those kinsmen and lost lovers.
   Now they return, and waking gradually,   3

I see new torments and new souls in pain
   about me everywhere. Wherever I turn
   away from grief I turn to grief again.   6

I am in the Third Circle of the torments.
   Here to all time with neither pause nor change
   the frozen rain of Hell descends in torrents.   9

Huge hailstones, dirty water, and black snow
   pour from the dismal air to putrefy
   the putrid slush that waits for them below.   12

Here monstrous Cerberus,[2] the ravening beast,
   howls through his triple throats like a mad dog
   over the spirits sunk in that foul paste.   15

His eyes are red, his beard is greased with phlegm,
   his belly is swollen, and his hands are claws
   to rip the wretches and flay and mangle them.   18

And they, too, howl like dogs in the freezing storm,
   turning and turning from it as if they thought
   one naked side could keep the other warm.   21

When Cerberus discovered us in that swill
   his dragon-jaws yawed wide, his lips drew back
   in a grin of fangs. No limb of him was still.   24

My Guide bent down and seized in either fist
   a clod of the stinking dirt that festered there
   and flung them down the gullet of the beast.   27

As a hungry cur will set the echoes raving
   and then fall still when he is thrown a bone,
   all of his clamor being in his craving,   30

2. For this creature as one of the guardians of Hell, see *Aeneid* 6.190–97.

so the three ugly heads of Cerberus,
    whose yowling at those wretches deafened them,
    choked on their putrid sops and stopped their fuss.   33

We made our way across the sodden mess
    of souls the rain beat down, and when our steps
    fell on a body, they sank through emptiness.   36

All those illusions of being seemed to lie
    drowned in the slush; until one wraith among them
    sat up abruptly and called as I passed by:[3]   39

"O you who are led this journey through the shade
    of Hell's abyss, do you recall this face?
    You had been made before I was unmade."[4]   42

And I: "Perhaps the pain you suffer here
    distorts your image from my recollection.
    I do not know you as you now appear."   45

And he to me: "Your own city, so rife
    with hatred that the bitter cup flows over
    was mine too in that other, clearer life.   48

Your citizens nicknamed me Ciacco, The Hog:
    gluttony was my offense, and for it
    I lie here rotting like a swollen log.   51

Nor am I lost in this alone; all these
    you see about you in this painful death
    have wallowed in the same indecencies."   54

I answered him: "Ciacco, your agony
    weighs on my heart and calls my soul to tears;
    but tell me, if you can, what is to be   57

for the citizens of that divided state,
    and whether there are honest men among them,
    and for what reasons we are torn by hate."   60

And he then:[5] "After many words given and taken
    it shall come to blood; White shall rise over Black
    and rout the dark lord's force, battered and shaken.   63

---

3. A Florentine named Ciacco, known only through his appearance here.
4. I.e., "You were born before I died."
5. The enigmatic "prophecy" that follows refers first to the triumph of the Whites, or "the rustic party" (to which Dante was allied), in 1300, and then their defeat by the Blacks, aided by Pope Boniface ("one now gripped by many hesitations"), in 1302, at which time Dante was exiled.

Then it shall come to pass within three suns
    that the fallen shall arise, and by the power
    of one now gripped by many hesitations   66

Black shall ride on White for many years,
    loading it down with burdens and oppressions
    and humbling of proud names and helpless tears.   69

Two are honest,[6] but none will heed them. There,
    pride, avarice, and envy are the tongues
    men know and heed, a Babel of despair."   72

Here he broke off his mournful prophecy.
    And I to him: "Still let me urge you on
    to speak a little further and instruct me: 75

Farinata and Tegghiaio, men of good blood,
    Jacopo Rusticucci, Arrigo, Mosca,
    and the others who set their hearts on doing good—[7]   78

where are they now whose high deeds might be-gem
    the crown of kings? I long to know their fate.
    Does Heaven soothe or Hell envenom them?"   81

And he: "They lie below in a blacker lair.
    A heavier guilt draws them to greater pain.
    If you descend so far you may see them there.   84

But when you move again among the living,
    oh speak my name to the memory of men!
    Having answered all, I say no more." And giving   87

his head a shake, he looked up at my face
    cross-eyed, then bowed his head and fell away
    among the other blind souls of that place.   90

And my Guide to me: "He will not wake again
    until the angel trumpet sounds the day
    on which the host shall come to judge all men.[8]   93

Then shall each soul before the seat of Mercy
    return to its sad grave and flesh and form
    to hear the edict of Eternity."   96

---

6. The identity of these two is unknown.
7. Dante asks about famous Florentines; he will find Farinata in canto 10, Tegghiaio and Rusticucci in canto 16, and Mosca in canto

28. Arrigo does not appear.
8. Virgil refers to the Last Judgment, when the dead will regain their bodies.

So we picked our slow way among the shades
    and the filthy rain, speaking of life to come.
    "Master," I said, "when the great clarion fades   99

into the voice of thundering Omniscience,
    what of these agonies? Will they be the same,
    or more, or less, after the final sentence?"   102

And he to me: "Look to your science again
    where it is written: the more a thing is perfect
    the more it feels of pleasure and of pain.   105

As for these souls, though they can never soar
    to true perfection, still in the new time
    they will be nearer it than they were before."[9]   108

And so we walked the rim of the great ledge
    speaking of pain and joy, and of much more
    that I will not repeat, and reached the edge   111

where the descent begins. There, suddenly,
we came on Plutus, the great enemy.[1]

Canto VII

| CIRCLE FOUR | *The Hoarders and the Wasters* |
| CIRCLE FIVE | *The Wrathful and the Sullen* |

Plutus menaces the Poets, but once more Virgil shows himself more powerful than the rages of Hell's monsters. The Poets enter the *Fourth Circle* and find what seems to be a war in progress.

    The sinners are divided into two raging mobs, each soul among them straining madly at a great boulder-like weight. The two mobs meet, clashing their weights against one another, after which they separate, pushing the great weights apart, and begin over again.

    One mob is made up of the *Hoarders*, the other of the *Wasters*. In life, they lacked all moderation in regulating their expenses; they destroyed the light of God within themselves by thinking of nothing but money. Thus in death, their souls are encumbered by dead weights (mundanity) and one excess serves to punish the other. Their souls, moreover, have become so dimmed and awry in their fruitless rages that there is no hope of recognizing any among them.

    The Poets pass on while Virgil explains the function of *Dame Fortune* in the Divine Scheme. As he finishes (it is past midnight now of Good Friday) they reach the inner edge of the ledge and come to a Black Spring which bubbles murkily over the rocks to form the *Marsh of Styx*, which is the *Fifth Circle*, the last station of the *Upper Hell*.

---

9. They will be more perfect because body and soul will be reunited (a principle derived from Aristotelian science), which will only increase their pain.

1. Dante combines Pluto, the classical god of the underworld, with Plutus, the classical god of wealth.

Across the marsh they see countless souls attacking one another in the foul slime. These are the *Wrathful* and the symbolism of their punishment is obvious. Virgil also points out to Dante certain bubbles rising from the slime and informs him that below that mud lie entombed the souls of the *Sullen*. In life they refused to welcome the sweet light of the Sun (Divine Illumination) and in death they are buried forever below the stinking waters of the Styx, gargling the words of an endless chant in a grotesque parody of singing a hymn.

"Papa Satán, Papa Satán, aleppy,"[2]
   Plutus clucked and stuttered in his rage;
   and my all-knowing Guide, to comfort me: 3

"Do not be startled, for no power of his,
   however he may lord it over the damned,
   may hinder your descent through this abyss."   6

And turning to that carnival of bloat
   cried: "Peace, you wolf of Hell. Choke back your bile
   and let its venom blister your own throat.   9

Our passage through this pit is willed on high
   by that same Throne that loosed the angel wrath
   of Michael on ambition and mutiny."[3]   12

As puffed out sails fall when the mast gives way
   and flutter to a self-convulsing heap—
   so collapsed Plutus into that dead clay.   15

Thus we descended the dark scarp of Hell
   to which all the evil of the Universe
   comes home at last, into the Fourth Great Circle   18

and ledge of the abyss. O Holy Justice,
   who could relate the agonies I saw!
   What guilt is man that he can come to this?   21

Just as the surge Charybdis[4] hurls to sea
   crashes and breaks upon its countersurge,
   so these shades dance and crash eternally.   24

Here, too, I saw a nation of lost souls,
   far more than were above: they strained their chests
   against enormous weights, and with mad howls   27

rolled them at one another. Then in haste
   they rolled them back, one party shouting out:
   "Why do you hoard?" and the other: "Why do you waste?"   30

---

2. Virgil apparently understands this mysterious outburst regarding Satan, but commentators have remained baffled.
3. A reference to the battle in heaven between the Archangel Michael and Satan in the form of a dragon: see Revelation 12.7–9.
4. A famous whirlpool in the Strait of Messina, between Sicily and Italy, described in *Aeneid* 3.

So back around that ring they puff and blow,
   each faction to its course, until they reach
   opposite sides, and screaming as they go   33

the madmen turn and start their weights again
   to crash against the maniacs. And I,
   watching, felt my heart contract with pain.   36

"Master," I said, "what people can these be?
   And all those tonsured[5] ones there on our left—
   is it possible they *all* were of the clergy?"   39

And he: "In the first life beneath the sun
   they were so skewed and squint-eyed in their minds
   their misering or extravagance mocked all reason.   42

The voice of each clamors its own excess
   when lust meets lust at the two points of the circle
   where opposite guilts meet in their wretchedness.   45

These tonsured wraiths of greed were priests indeed,
   and popes and cardinals, for it is in these
   the weed of avarice sows its rankest seed."   48

And I to him: "Master, among this crew
   surely I should be able to make out
   the fallen image of some soul I knew."   51

And he to me: "This is a lost ambition.
   In their sordid lives they labored to be blind,
   and now their souls have dimmed past recognition.   54

All their eternity is to butt and bray:
   one crew will stand tight-fisted, the other stripped
   of its very hair at the bar of Judgment Day.   57

Hoarding and squandering wasted all their light
   and brought them screaming to this brawl of wraiths.
   You need no words of mine to grasp their plight.   60

Now may you see the fleeting vanity
   of the goods of Fortune for which men tear down
   all that they are, to build a mockery.   63

Not all the gold that is or ever was
   under the sky could buy for one of these
   exhausted souls the fraction of a pause."   66

---

5. The tonsure—a shaving of part of the head—was a mark of clerical status.

"Master," I said, "tell me—now that you touch
  on this Dame Fortune—what *is* she, that she holds
  the good things of the world within her clutch?"   69

And he to me: "O credulous·mankind,
  is there one error that has wooed and lost you?
  Now listen, and strike error from your mind:[6]   72

That king whose perfect wisdom transcends all,
  made the heavens and posted angels on them
  to guide the eternal light that it might fall   75

from every sphere to every sphere the same.
  He made earth's splendors by a like decree
  and posted as their minister this high Dame,   78

the Lady of Permutations. All earth's gear
  she changes from nation to nation, from house to house,
  in changeless change through every turning year.   81

No mortal power may stay her spinning wheel.
  The nations rise and fall by her decree.
  None may foresee where she will set her heel: 84

she passes, and things pass. Man's mortal reason
  cannot encompass her. She rules her sphere
  as the other gods rule theirs. Season by season   87

her changes change her changes endlessly,
  and those whose turn has come press on her so,
  she must be swift by hard necessity.   90

And this is she so railed at and reviled
  that even her debtors in the joys of time
  blaspheme her name. Their oaths are bitter and wild,   93

but she in her beatitude does not hear.
  Among the Primal Beings of God's joy
  she breathes her blessedness and wheels her sphere.   96

But the stars that marked our starting fall away.
  We must go deeper into greater pain,
  for it is not permitted that we stay."[7]   99

6. Virgil now explains that each area of life is
presided over by a "guide," a kind of angel,
under the ultimate authority of God. The classical goddess Fortune—the "minister" of line
78—who was thought to distribute the world's
goods capriciously is here described as acting
under God's supervision.
7. The stars that were rising at the start of the
journey (1.37–39) are now setting: Good Friday has passed, and the time is now the early
hours of Holy Saturday.

And crossing over to the chasm's edge
    we came to a spring that boiled and overflowed
    through a great crevice worn into the ledge.   102

By that foul water, black from its very source,
    we found a nightmare path among the rocks
    and followed the dark stream along its course.   105

Beyond its rocky race and wild descent
    the river floods and forms a marsh called Styx,[8]
    a dreary swampland, vaporous and malignant.   108

And I, intent on all our passage touched,
    made out a swarm of spirits in that bog
    savage with anger, naked, slime-besmutched.   111

They thumped at one another in that slime
    with hands and feet, and they butted, and they bit
as if each would tear the other limb from limb.   114

And my kind Sage: "My son, behold the souls
    of those who lived in wrath. And do you see
    the broken surfaces of those water-holes   117

on every hand, boiling as if in pain?
    There are souls beneath that water. Fixed in slime
    they speak their piece, end it, and start again: 120

'Sullen were we in the air made sweet by the Sun;
    in the glory of his shining our hearts poured
    a bitter smoke. Sullen were we begun;   123

sullen we lie forever in this ditch.'
    This litany they gargle in their throats
    as if they sang, but lacked the words and pitch."   126

Then circling on along that filthy wallow,
    we picked our way between the bank and fen,
    keeping our eyes on those foul souls that swallow   129

the slime of Hell. And so at last we came
to the foot of a Great Tower that has no name.[9]

---

8. The second river of Hell.
9. This watchtower guards the entrance to lower Hell or the city of Dis—another name for Pluto, the classical god of the underworld, that is throughout the *Inferno* applied to Satan (see 11.65 and 34.20).

Canto VIII

CIRCLE FIVE: STYX

CIRCLE SIX: DIS

The Wrathful, Phlegyas

The Fallen Angels

The Poets stand at the edge of the swamp, and a mysterious signal flames from the great tower. It is answered from the darkness of the other side, and almost immediately the Poets see *Phlegyas*, the Boatman of Styx, racing toward them across the water, fast as a flying arrow. He comes avidly, thinking to find new souls for torment, and he howls with rage when he discovers the Poets. Once again, however, Virgil conquers wrath with a word and Phlegyas reluctantly gives them passage.

As they are crossing, a muddy soul rises before them. It is *Filippo Argenti*, one of the Wrathful. Dante recognizes him despite the filth with which he is covered, and he berates him soundly, even wishing to see him tormented further. Virgil approves Dante's disdain and, as if in answer to Dante's wrath, Argenti is suddenly set upon by all the other sinners present, who fall upon him and rip him to pieces.

The boat meanwhile has sped on, and before Argenti's screams have died away, Dante sees the flaming red towers of Dis, the Capital of Hell. The great walls of the iron city block the way to the Lower Hell. Properly speaking, all the rest of Hell lies within the city walls, which separate the Upper and the Lower Hell.

Phlegyas deposits them at a great Iron Gate which they find to be guarded by the *Rebellious Angels*. These creatures of Ultimate Evil, rebels against God Himself, refuse to let the Poets pass. Even Virgil is powerless against them, for Human Reason by itself cannot cope with the essence of Evil. Only Divine Aid can bring hope. Virgil accordingly sends up a prayer for assistance and waits anxiously for a Heavenly Messenger to appear.

Returning to my theme, I say we came
　　to the foot of a Great Tower; but long before
　　we reached it through the marsh, two horns of flame　　　3

flared from the summit, one from either side,
　　and then, far off, so far we scarce could see it
　　across the mist, another flame replied.　　　6

I turned to that sea of all intelligence
　　saying: "What is this signal and counter-signal?
　　Who is it speaks with fire across this distance?"　　　9

And he then: "Look across the filthy slew:
　　you may already see the one they summon,
　　if the swamp vapors do not hide him from you."　　　12

No twanging bowstring ever shot an arrow
　　that bored the air it rode dead to the mark
　　more swiftly than the flying skiff whose prow　　　15

shot toward us over the polluted channel
　　with a single steersman at the helm who called:
　　"So, do I have you at last, you whelp of Hell?"　　　18

"Phlegyas, Phlegyas,"[1] said my Lord and Guide,
   "this time you waste your breath: you have us only
   for the time it takes to cross to the other side."   21

Phlegyas, the madman, blew his rage among
   those muddy marshes like a cheat deceived,
   or like a fool at some imagined wrong.   24

My Guide, whom all the fiend's noise could not nettle,
   boarded the skiff, motioning me to follow:
   and not till I stepped aboard did it seem to settle   27

into the water. At once we left the shore,
   that ancient hull riding more heavily
   than it had ridden in all of time before.[2]   30

And as we ran on that dead swamp, the slime
   rose before me, and from it a voice cried:
   "Who are you that come here before your time?"   33

And I replied: "If I come, I do not remain.
   But you, who are *you*, so fallen and so foul?"
   And he: "I am one who weeps." And I then: 36

"May you weep and wail to all eternity,
   for I know you, hell-dog, filthy as you are."
   Then he stretched both hands to the boat, but warily   39

the Master shoved him back, crying, "Down! Down!
   with the other dogs!" Then he embraced me saying:
   "Indignant spirit, I kiss you as you frown.   42

Blessed be she who bore you.[3] In world and time
   this one was haughtier yet. Not one unbending
   graces his memory. Here is his shadow in slime.   45

How many living now, chancellors of wrath,
   shall come to lie here yet in this pigmire,
   leaving a curse to be their aftermath!"   48

And I: "Master, it would suit my whim
   to see the wretch scrubbed down into the swill
   before we leave this stinking sink and him."   51

And he to me: "Before the other side
   shows through the mist, you shall have all you ask.
   This is a wish that should be gratified."   54

1. A mythological figure condemned to Hell for setting fire to the temple of Apollo in revenge for the god's seduction of his daughter; Dante found him in *Aeneid* 6.714–17.

2. Because of the unaccustomed weight of the living Dante.

3. See Luke 11.27, where these words are applied to Jesus.

And shortly after, I saw the loathsome spirit
   so mangled by a swarm of muddy wraiths
   that to this day I praise and thank God for it.   57

"After Filippo Argentil"[4] all cried together.
   The maddog Florentine wheeled at their cry
   and bit himself for rage. I saw them gather.   60

And there we left him. And I say no more,
   But such a wailing beat upon my ears,
   I strained my eyes ahead to the far shore.   63

"My son," the Master said, "the City called Dis
   lies just ahead, the heavy citizens,
   the swarming crowds of Hell's metropolis."   66

And I then: "Master, I already see
   the glow of its red mosques, as if they came
   hot from the forge to smolder in this valley."   69

And my all-knowing Guide: "They are eternal
   flues to eternal fire that rages in them
   and makes them glow across this lower Hell."   72

And as he spoke we entered the vast moat
   of the sepulchre. Its wall seemed made of iron
   and towered above us in our little boat.   75

We circled through what seemed an endless distance
   before the boatman ran his prow ashore
   crying: "Out! Out! Get out! This is the entrance."   78

Above the gates more than a thousand shades
   of spirits purged from Heaven for its glory[5]
   cried angrily: "Who is it that invades   81

Death's Kingdom in his life?" My Lord and Guide
   advanced a step before me with a sign
   that he wished to speak to some of them aside.   84

They quieted somewhat, and one called, "Come,
   but come alone. And tell that other one,
   who thought to walk so blithely through death's kingdom,   87

he may go back along the same fool's way
   he came by. Let him try his living luck.
   You who are dead can come only to stay."   90

---

4. A Florentine contemporary of Dante; Dante's acquaintances recounted great enmity between them, mainly as a result of Dante's exile from Florence.
5. The rebel angels, cast out of Heaven; see Luke 10.18 and Revelation 12.9.

Reader, judge for yourself, how each black word
 fell on my ears to sink into my heart:
 I lost hope of returning to the world. 93

"O my beloved Master, my Guide in peril,
 who time and time again have seen me safely
 along this way, and turned the power of evil, 96

stand by me now," I cried, "in my heart's fright.
 And if the dead forbid our journey to them.
 let us go back together toward the light." 99

My Guide then, in the greatness of his spirit:
 "Take heart. Nothing can take our passage from us
 when such a power has given warrant for it. 102

Wait here and feed your soul while I am gone
 on comfort and good hope; I will not leave you
 to wander in this underworld alone." 105

So the sweet Guide and Father leaves me here,
 and I stay on in doubt with yes and no
 dividing all my heart to hope and fear. 108

I could not hear my Lord's words, but the pack
 that gathered round him suddenly broke away
 howling and jostling and went pouring back, 111

slamming the towering gate hard in his face.
 That great Soul stood alone outside the wall.
 Then he came back; his pain showed in his pace. 114

His eyes were fixed upon the ground, his brow
 had sagged from its assurance. He sighed aloud:
 "Who has forbidden me the halls of sorrow?" 117

And to me he said: "You need not be cast down
 by my vexation, for whatever plot
 these fiends may lay against us, we will go on. 120

This insolence of theirs is nothing new:
 they showed it once at a less secret gate[6]
 that still stands open for all that they could do— 123

the same gate where you read the dead inscription;
 and through it at this moment a Great One comes.
 Already he has passed it and moves down 126

ledge by dark ledge. He is one who needs no guide,
and at his touch all gates must spring aside."

6. A reference to Christ's descent into Hell, after the crucifixion, for the "harrowing"; see above, 4.53.

Canto IX

CIRCLE SIX

The Heretics

At the Gate of Dis the Poets wait in dread. Virgil tries to hide his anxiety from Dante, but both realize that without Divine Aid they will surely be lost. To add to their terrors *Three Infernal Furies*, symbols of Eternal Remorse, appear on a nearby tower, from which they threaten the Poets and call for *Medusa* to come and change them to stone. Virgil at once commands Dante to turn and shut his eyes. To make doubly sure, Virgil himself places his hands over Dante's eyes, for there is an Evil upon which man must not look if he is to be saved.

But at the moment of greatest anxiety a storm shakes the dirty air of Hell and the sinners in the marsh begin to scatter like frightened Frogs. *The Heavenly Messenger* is approaching. He appears walking majestically through Hell, looking neither to right nor to left. With a touch he throws open the Gate of Dis while his words scatter the Rebellious Angels. Then he returns as he came.

The Poets now enter the gate unopposed and find themselves in the Sixth Circle. Here they find a countryside like a vast cemetery. Tombs of every size stretch out before them, each with its lid lying beside it, and each wrapped in flames. Cries of anguish sound endlessly from the entombed dead.

This is the torment of the *Heretics* of every cult. By Heretic, Dante means specifically those who did violence to God by denying immortality. Since they taught that the soul dies with the body, so their punishment is an eternal grave in the fiery morgue of God's wrath.

My face had paled to a mask of cowardice
   when I saw my Guide turn back. The sight of it
   the sooner brought the color back to his.   3

He stood apart like one who strains to hear
   what he cannot see, for the eye could not reach far
   across the vapors of that midnight air.   6

"Yet surely we were meant to pass these tombs,"
   he said aloud. "If not . . . so much was promised . . .
   Oh how time hangs and drags till our aid comes!"   9

I saw too well how the words with which he ended
   covered his start, and even perhaps I drew
   a worse conclusion from that than he intended.   12

"Tell me, Master, does anyone ever come
   from the first ledge, whose only punishment
   is hope cut off, into this dreary bottom?"[7]   15

I put this question to him, still in fear
   of what his broken speech might mean; and he:
   "Rarely do any of us enter here.   18

7. I.e., "Has anyone from Limbo ever descended into lower Hell before?"

Once before, it is true, I crossed through Hell
 conjured by cruel Erichtho[8] who recalled
 the spirits to their bodies. Her dark spell   21

forced me, newly stripped of my mortal part,
 to enter through this gate and summon out
 a spirit from Judaïca. Take heart,   24

that is the last depth and the darkest lair
 and the farthest from Heaven which encircles all,[9]
 and at that time I came back even from there.   27

The marsh from which the stinking gasses bubble
 lies all about this capital of sorrow
 whose gates we may not pass now without trouble."   30

All this and more he expounded; but the rest
 was lost on me, for suddenly my attention
 was drawn to the turret with the fiery crest   33

where all at once three hellish and inhuman
 Furies[1] sprang to view, bloodstained and wild.
 Their limbs and gestures hinted they were women.   36

Belts of greenest hydras wound and wound
 about their waists, and snakes and horned serpents
 grew from their heads like matted hair and bound   39

their horrid brows. My Master, who well knew
 the handmaids of the Queen of Woe,[2] cried: "Look:
 the terrible Erinyes of Hecate's crew.   42

That is Megaera to the left of the tower.
 Alecto is the one who raves on the right.
 Tisiphone stands between." And he said no more.   45

With their palms they beat their brows, with their nails they clawed
 their bleeding breasts. And such mad wails broke from them
 that I drew close to the Poet, overawed.   48

And all together screamed, looking down at me:
 "Call Medusa[3] that we may change him to stone!
 Too lightly we let Theseus[4] go free."   51

---

8. A legendary sorceress. The story of Virgil's prior descent into Hell is apparently Dante's own invention, although in the Middle Ages Virgil had the reputation of being a magician.
9. Judecca, the last subdivision of the last circle of Hell, where Judas is punished.
1. Three mythological monsters who represent the spirit of vengeance, known in Greek as the Erinyes (see below, line 42, and lines 43–45 for their individual names); they figure promi-

nently in the *Aeneid* and other Latin poetry.
2. In classical mythology the queen of Hell is Hecate, or Proserpina, the wife of Pluto.
3. A mythological figure known as a Gorgon (line 56), so frightful in appearance that she turned those who gazed on her into stone.
4. Theseus, a legendary Athenian hero, descended into the underworld in order to try to rescue Proserpina, whom Pluto had abducted, and was rescued by Hercules.

"Turn your back and keep your eyes shut tight;
   for should the Gorgon come and you look at her,
   never again would you return to the light."   54

This was my Guide's command. And he turned me about
   himself, and would not trust my hands alone,
   but, with his placed on mine, held my eyes shut.   57

Men of sound intellect and probity,
   weigh with good understanding what lies hidden
   behind the veil of my strange allegory![5]   60

Suddenly there broke on the dirty swell
   of the dark marsh a squall of terrible sound
   that sent a tremor through both shores of Hell;   63

a sound as if two continents of air,
   one frigid and one scorching, clashed head on
   in a war of winds that stripped the forests bare,   66

ripped off whole boughs and blew them helter skelter
   along the range of dust it raised before it
   making the beasts and shepherds run for shelter.   69

The Master freed my eyes. "Now turn," he said,
   "and fix your nerve of vision on the foam
   there where the smoke is thickest and most acrid." 72

As frogs before the snake that hunts them down
   churn up their pond in flight, until the last
   squats on the bottom as if turned to stone—   75

so I saw more than a thousand ruined souls
   scatter away from one who crossed dry-shod
   the Stygian marsh into Hell's burning bowels.[6]   78

With his left hand he fanned away the dreary
   vapors of that sink as he approached;
   and only of that annoyance did he seem weary.   81

Clearly he was a Messenger from God's Throne,
   and I turned to my Guide; but he made me a sign
   that I should keep my silence and bow down.   84

Ah, what scorn breathed from that Angel-presence!
   He reached the gate of Dis and with a wand
   he waved it open, for there was no resistance.   87

5. Dante here reminds us of the need to interpret his poetry, although the lesson of this particular episode is far from self-evident.
6. This is an angel, although described in a way reminiscent of Mercury, the classical messenger of the gods. "Stygian": from the river Styx.

"Outcasts of Heaven, you twice-loathsome crew,"
    he cried upon that terrible sill of Hell,
    "how does this insolence still live in you?   90

Why do you set yourselves against that Throne
    whose Will none can deny, and which, times past,
    has added to your pain for each rebellion?   93

Why do you butt against Fate's ordinance?
    Your Cerberus, if you recall, still wears
    his throat and chin peeled for such arrogance."[7]   96

Then he turned back through the same filthy tide
    by which he had come. He did not speak to us,
    but went his way like one preoccupied   99

by other presences than those before him.
    And we moved toward the city, fearing nothing
    after his holy words. Straight through the dim   102

and open gate we entered unopposed.
    And I, eager to learn what new estate
    of Hell those burning fortress walls enclosed,   105

began to look about the very moment
    we were inside, and I saw on every hand
    a countryside of sorrow and new torment.   108

As at Arles where the Rhone sinks into stagnant marshes,
    as at Pola by the Quarnaro Gulf, whose waters
    close Italy and wash her farthest reaches,   111

the uneven tombs cover the even plain—
    such fields I saw here, spread in all directions,
    except that here the tombs were chests of pain:[8]   114

for, in a ring around each tomb, great fires
    raised every wall to a red heat. No smith
    works hotter iron in his forge. The biers   117

stood with their lids upraised, and from their pits
    an anguished moaning rose on the dead air
    from the desolation of tormented spirits.   120

And I: "Master, what shades are these who lie
    buried in these chests and fill the air
    with such a painful and unending cry?"   123

7. According to classical mythology, Hercules dragged Cerberus into the daylight.
8. Arles, located on the river Rhone in southern France, and Pola, located on the bay of Quarnero in what is now Yugoslavia, were sites of Roman cemeteries.

"These are the arch-heretics of all cults,
  with all their followers," he replied, "Far more
  than you would think lie stuffed into these vaults.   126

Like lies with like in every heresy,
  and the monuments are fired, some more, some less;
  to each depravity its own degree."   129

He turned then, and I followed through that night
between the wall and the torments, bearing right.

Canto X

CIRCLE SIX   *The Heretics*

As the Poets pass on, one of the damned hears Dante speaking, recognizes him as
a Tuscan, and calls to him from one of the fiery tombs. A moment later he
appears. He is *Farinata degli Uberti*, a great war-chief of the Tuscan Ghibellines.
The majesty and power of his bearing seem to diminish Hell itself. He asks
Dante's lineage and recognizes him as an enemy. They begin to talk politics, but
are interrupted by another shade, who rises from the same tomb.

This one is *Cavalcante dei Cavalcanti*, father of Guido Cavalcanti, a contemporary poet. If it is genius that leads Dante on his great journey, the shade
asks, why is Guido not with him? Can Dante presume to a greater genius than
Guido's? Dante replies that he comes this way only with the aid of powers Guido
has not sought. His reply is a classic example of many-leveled symbolism as well
as an overt criticism of a rival poet. The senior Cavalcanti mistakenly infers from
Dante's reply that Guido is dead, and swoons back into the flames.

Farinata, who has not deigned to notice his fellow-sinner, continues from the
exact point at which he had been interrupted. It is as if he refuses to recognize
the flames in which he is shrouded. He proceeds to prophesy Dante's banishment
from Florence, he defends his part in Florentine politics, and then, in answer to
Dante's question, he explains how it is that the damned can foresee the future
but have no knowledge of the present. He then names others who share his tomb,
and Dante takes his leave with considerable respect for his great enemy, pausing
only long enough to leave word for Cavalcanti that Guido is still alive.

We go by a secret path along the rim
  of the dark city, between the wall and the torments.
  My Master leads me and I follow him.   3

"Supreme Virtue, who through this impious land
  wheel me at will down these dark gyres,"9 I said,
  "speak to me, for I wish to understand.   6

Tell me, Master, is it permitted to see
  the souls within these tombs? The lids are raised,
  and no one stands on guard." And he to me: 9

9. Circular turns.

"All shall be sealed forever on the day
    these souls return here from Jehosaphat
    with the bodies they have given once to clay.[1]   12

In this dark corner of the morgue of wrath
    lie Epicurus[2] and his followers,
    who make the soul share in the body's death.   15

And here you shall be granted presently
    not only your spoken wish, but that other as well,
    which you had thought perhaps to hide from me."[3]   18

And I: "Except to speak my thoughts in few
    and modest words, as I learned from your example,
    dear Guide, I do not hide my heart from you."   21

"O Tuscan, who go living through this place
    speaking so decorously, may it please you pause
    a moment on your way, for by the grace   24

of that high speech in which I hear your birth,
    I know you for a son of that noble city
    which perhaps I vexed too much in my time on earth."   27

These words broke without warning from inside
    one of the burning arks. Caught by surprise,
    I turned in fear and drew close to my Guide.   30

And he: "Turn around. What are you doing? Look there:
    it is Farinata[4] rising from the flames.
    From the waist up his shade will be made clear."   33

My eyes were fixed on him already. Erect,
    he rose above the flame, great chest, great brow;
    he seemed to hold all Hell in disrespect.   36

My Guide's prompt hands urged me among the dim
    and smoking sepulchres to that great figure,
    and he said to me: "Mind how you speak to him."   39

And when I stood alone at the foot of the tomb,
    the great soul stared almost contemptuously,
    before he asked: "Of what line do you come?"   42

1. According to the Bible, the Last Judgment when the dead will again receive their bodies will take place in the Valley of Jehosaphat; see Joel 3.2 and 3.12, and Matthew 25.31–32.
2. Greek philosopher (d. 270 B.C.E.) who rejected the idea of the immortality of the soul.
3. Presumably Dante's desire to see the Florentines who inhabit this circle.
4. Farinata degli Uberti (d. 1264), a leader of the Ghibelline faction in Florence.

Because I wished to obey, I did not hide
   anything from him: whereupon, as he listened,
   he raised his brows a little, then replied: 45

"Bitter enemies were they to me,
   to my fathers, and to my party, so that twice
   I sent them scattering from high Italy."   48

"If they were scattered, still from every part
   they formed again and returned both times," I answered,[5]
"but yours have not yet wholly learned that art."[6]   51

At this another shade rose gradually,
   visible to the chin. It had raised itself,
   I think, upon its knees, and it looked around me[7]   54

as if it expected to find through that black air
   that blew about me, another traveler.
   And weeping when it found no other there,   57

turned back. "And if," it cried, "you travel through
   this dungeon of the blind by power of genius,
   where is my son? why is he not with you?"   60

And I to him: "Not by myself am I borne
   this terrible way. I am led by him who waits there,
   and whom perhaps your Guido held in scorn."[8]   63

For by his words and the manner of his torment
   I knew his name already, and could, therefore,
   answer both what he asked and what he meant.   66

Instantly he rose to his full height:
   "He *held*? What is it you say? Is he dead, then?
   Do his eyes no longer fill with that sweet light?"[9]   69

And when he saw that I delayed a bit
   in answering his question, he fell backwards
   into the flame, and rose no more from it.   72

5. Dante's family were Guelphs, who were driven out of Florence twice, in 1248 and 1260.
6. The Ghibellines were exiled in 1280, never to return.
7. This is Cavalcante de Cavalcanti, father of Dante's friend and fellow poet Guido; a Guelph, Guido married the daughter of Farinata in an unsuccessful attempt to heal the feud. In June 1300—after the fictional date of this conversation—Guido was exiled to a part of Italy where he caught the malaria from which he died in August. Dante was at that time a member of the governing body that made the decision to exile Guido.

8. The passage is ambiguous in the original Italian: as translated here, "him" refers to Virgil; but the Italian word can also be translated to refer to Beatrice, so that these two lines would then read: "that one waiting over there guides me through here, / to her whom your Guido perhaps held in scorn."
9. In line 63 Dante used a verbal form known in Italian as the remote past, which leads Cavalcante to believe, wrongly, that now, in April 1300, Guido is dead—although, ironically, in about four months he will indeed die, as Dante knew when he was writing this canto.

But that majestic spirit at whose call
   I had first paused there, did not change expression,
   nor so much as turn his face to watch him fall.   75

"And if," going on from his last words, he said,
   "men of my line have yet to learn that art,
   that burns me deeper than this flaming bed.   78

But the face of her who reigns in Hell[1] shall not
   be fifty times rekindled in its course
   before you learn what griefs attend that art.[2]   81

And as you hope to find the world again,
   tell me: why is that populace so savage
   in the edicts they pronounce against my strain?"   84

And I to him: "The havoc and the carnage
   that dyed the Arbia[3] red at Montaperti
   have caused these angry cries in our assemblage."   87

He sighed and shook his head. "I was not alone
   in that affair," he said, "nor certainly
   would I have joined the rest without good reason.   90

But I *was* alone at that time when every other
   consented to the death of Florence; I
   alone with open face defended her."   93

"Ah, so may your soul sometime have rest,"
   I begged him, "solve the riddle that pursues me
   through this dark place and leaves my mind perplexed: 96

you seem to see in advance all time's intent,
   if I have heard and understood correctly;
   but you seem to lack all knowledge of the present."   99

"We see asquint, like those whose twisted sight
   can make out only the far-off," he said,
   "for the King of All still grants us that much light.   102

When things draw near, or happen, we perceive
   nothing of them. Except what others bring us
   we have no news of those who are alive.   105

So may you understand that all we know
   will be dead forever from that day and hour
   when the portal of the Future is swung to."[4]   108

---

1. Proserpina, who is also the goddess of the moon.
2. Farinata here predicts Dante's own exile.
3. A stream near the hill of Montaperti, where the Ghibellines defeated the Guelphs in 1260.
4. The damned can see the future but not the present; after the Last Judgment, when human time is abolished, they will know nothing.

Then, as if stricken by regret, I said:[5]
　　"Now, therefore, will you tell that fallen one
　　who asked about his son, that he is not dead,　　　　　　111

and that, if I did not reply more quickly,
　　it was because my mind was occupied
　　with this confusion you have solved for me."　　　　　　114

And now my Guide was calling me. In haste,
　　therefore, I begged that mighty shade to name
　　the others who lay with him in that chest.　　　　　　117

And he: "More than a thousand cram this tomb.
　　The second Frederick[6] is here, and the Cardinal
　　of the Ubaldini.[7] Of the rest let us be dumb."　　　　　　120

And he disappeared without more said, and I
　　turned back and made my way to the ancient Poet,
　　pondering the words of the dark prophecy.[8]　　　　　　123

He moved along, and then, when we had started,
　　he turned and said to me, "What troubles you?
　　Why do you look so vacant and downhearted?"　　　　　　126

And I told him. And he replied: "Well may you bear
　　those words in mind." Then, pausing, raised a finger:
　　"Now pay attention to what I tell you here:　　　　　　129

when finally you stand before the ray
　　of that Sweet Lady[9] whose bright eye sees all,
　　from her you will learn the turnings of your way."　　　　　　132

So saying, he bore left, turning his back
　　on the flaming walls, and we passed deeper yet
　　into the city of pain, along a track　　　　　　135

that plunged down like a scar into a sink
which sickened us already with its stink.

---

5. See note 1 to line 69 above.
6. Frederick II, Holy Roman Emperor from 1215 until his death in 1250; he reputedly denied that there was life after death.
7. Ottaviano degli Ubaldini (d. 1273), who is reputed to have said, "If I have a soul, I have lost it for the Ghibellines."
8. That is, Farinata's prediction of his exile.
9. Beatrice.

Canto XI

The Heretics

The Poets reach the inner edge of the *Sixth Circle* and find a great jumble of
rocks that had once been a cliff, but which has fallen into rubble as the result of
the great earthquake that shook Hell when Christ died. Below them lies the *Seventh Circle*, and so fetid is the air that arises from it that the Poets cower for
shelter behind a great tomb until their breaths can grow accustomed to the
stench.

Dante finds an inscription on the lid of the tomb labeling it as the place in Hell
of *Pope Anastasius*.

Virgil takes advantage of the delay to outline in detail *The Division of the Lower
Hell*, a theological discourse based on *The Ethics* and *The Physics* of Aristotle
with subsequent medieval interpretations. Virgil explains also why it is that the
Incontinent are not punished within the walls of Dis, and rather ingeniously sets
forth the reasons why Usury is an act of violence against Art, which is the child of
Nature and hence the Grandchild of God. (By "Art," Dante means the arts and
crafts by which man draws from nature, i.e., Industry.)

As he concludes he rises and urges Dante on. By means known only to Virgil,
he is aware of the motion of the stars and from them he sees that it is about two
hours before Sunrise of Holy Saturday.

We came to the edge of an enormous sink
   rimmed by a circle of great broken boulders.
   Here we found ghastlier gangs. And here the stink   3

thrown up by the abyss so overpowered us
   that we drew back, cowering behind the wall
   of one of the great tombs; and standing thus,   6

I saw an inscription in the stone, and read:
   "I guard Anastasius, once Pope,
   he whom Photinus led from the straight road."[1]   9

"Before we travel on to that blind pit
   we must delay until our sense grows used
   to its foul breath, and then we will not mind it,"   12

my Master said. And I then: "Let us find
   some compensation for the time of waiting."
   And he: "You shall see I have just that in mind.   15

My son,"[2] he began, "there are below this wall
   three smaller circles, each in its degree
   like those you are about to leave, and all   18

---

1. Pope Anastasius (d. 498) was thought,
wrongly, to have accepted a heresy promoted by
the 5th-century theologian Photinus that Christ
was not divine but only human.
2. Virgil now describes the three remaining
circles of Hell: the seventh, eighth, and ninth.

The seventh is for the violent and is divided
into three parts; the eighth and ninth are for the
fraudulent—the eighth for those who deceive
generally, the ninth for those who betray those
who love them. For the scheme of Hell as a
whole, see the diagram on p. 928.

are crammed with God's accurst. Accordingly,
  that you may understand their sins at sight,
  I will explain how each is prisoned, and why.   21

Malice is the sin most hated by God.
  And the aim of malice is to injure others
  whether by fraud or violence. But since fraud   24

is the vice of which man alone is capable,
  God loathes it most. Therefore, the fraudulent
  are placed below, and their torment is more painful.   27

The first below are the violent. But as violence
  sins in three persons, so is that circle formed
  of three descending rounds of crueler torments.   30

Against God, self, and neighbor is violence shown.
  Against their persons and their goods, I say,
  as you shall hear set forth with open reason.   33

Murder and mayhem are the violation
  of the person of one's neighbor: and of his goods;
  harassment, plunder, arson, and extortion.   36

Therefore, homicides, and those who strike
  in malice—destroyers and plunderers—all lie
  in that first round, and like suffers with like.   39

A man may lay violent hands upon his own
  person and substance; so in that second round
  eternally in vain repentance moan   42

the suicides and all who gamble away
  and waste the good and substance of their lives
  and weep in that sweet time when they should be gay.   45

Violence may be offered the deity
  in the heart that blasphemes and refuses Him
  and scorns the gifts of Nature, her beauty and bounty. 48

Therefore, the smallest round brands with its mark
  both Sodom and Cahors,[3] and all who rail
  at God and His commands in their hearts' dark.   51

Fraud, which is a canker to every conscience,
  may be practiced by a man on those who trust him,
  and on those who have reposed no confidence.   54

3. In the Middle Ages, the names of Sodom (see Genesis 18.20–19.29) and Cahors, a city in southern France, became synonymous with sodomites and usurers, respectively. Usury, forbidden by the medieval church, is charging interest on loans; the logic of this prohibition—based on the argument that usury, like sodomy, is unnatural—is explained in lines 97–111 below.

The latter mode seems only to deny
   the bond of love which all men have from Nature;
   therefore within the second circle lie   57

simoniacs,[4] sycophants, and hypocrites,
   falsifiers, thieves, and sorcerers,
   grafters, pimps, and all such filthy cheats.   60

The former mode of fraud not only denies
   the bond of Nature, but the special trust
   added by bonds of friendship or blood-ties.   63

Hence, at the center point of all creation,
   in the smallest circle, on which Dis[5] is founded,
   the traitors lie in endless expiation.   66

"Master," I said, "the clarity of your mind
   impresses all you touch; I see quite clearly
   the orders of this dark pit of the blind.   69

But tell me: those who lie in the swamp's bowels,
   those the wind blows about, those the rain beats,
   and those who meet and clash with such mad howls—   72

why are *they* not punished in the rust-red city
   if God's wrath be upon them? and if it is not,
   why must they grieve through all eternity?"   75

And he: "Why does your understanding stray
   so far from its own habit? or can it be
   your thoughts are turned along some other way?   78

Have you forgotten that your *Ethics*[6] states
   the three main dispositions of the soul
   that lead to those offenses Heaven hates—   81

incontinence, malice, and bestiality?
   and how incontinence offends God least
   and earns least blame from Justice and Charity?   84

Now if you weigh this doctrine and recall
   exactly who they are whose punishment
   lies in that upper Hell outside the wall,   87

you will understand at once why they are confined
   apart from these fierce wraiths, and why less anger
   beats down on them from the Eternal Mind."   90

4. Simony is the sin of selling a spiritual good, such as a church office or a sacrament like confession, for material gain. It is named after Simon Magus, a magician who sought to buy from the Apostles the power of baptism; Acts 8.9–24.
5. Dis is Satan, who is found at the bottom of Hell (see canto 34).
6. Aristotle's *Nicomachean Ethics*.

"O sun which clears all mists from troubled sight,
    such joy attends your rising that I feel
    as grateful to the dark as to the light.   93

Go back a little further," I said, "to where
    you spoke of usury as an offense
    against God's goodness. How is that made clear?"   96

"Philosophy makes plain by many reasons,"
    he answered me, "to those who heed her teachings,
    how all of Nature,—her laws, her fruits, her seasons,—   99

springs from the Ultimate Intellect and Its art:[7]
    and if you read your *Physics*[8] with due care,
    you will note, not many pages from the start,   102

that Art strives after her by imitation,
    as the disciple imitates the master;
    Art, as it were, is the Grandchild of Creation.   105

By this, recalling the Old Testament
    near the beginning of Genesis,[9] you will see
    that in the will of Providence, man was meant   108

to labor and to prosper. But usurers,
    by seeking their increase in other ways,
    scorn Nature in herself and her followers.[1]   111

But come, for it is my wish now to go on:
    the wheel turns and the Wain lies over Caurus,
    the Fish are quivering low on the horizon,[2]   114

and there beyond us runs the road we go
down the dark scarp into the depths below."

Canto XII

CIRCLE SEVEN: ROUND ONE   *The Violent against Neighbors*

The Poets begin the descent of the fallen rock wall, having first to evade the
Minotaur, who menaces them. Virgil tricks him and the Poets hurry by.
    Below them they see the *River of Blood*, which marks the First Round of the
Seventh Circle as detailed in the previous Canto. Here are punished the *Violent
against Their Neighbors*, great war-makers, cruel tyrants, high-waymen—all who
shed the blood of their fellow men. As they wallowed in blood during their lives,

---

7. The laws of nature are determined by God.
8. Aristotle's *Physics*, which argues that human art should follow natural laws.
9. In Genesis 3.17–19, God decrees that because of the Fall people must toil, supporting themselves by the sweat of their brows.

1. The usurer makes money not from labor but from money itself, which is an unnatural and therefore illicit art.
2. The position of stars shows that it is now about 4:00 a.m. on Holy Saturday.

so they are immersed in the boiling blood forever, each according to the degree of his guilt, while fierce Centaurs patrol the banks, ready to shoot with their arrows any sinner who raises himself out of the boiling blood beyond the limits permitted him. *Alexander the Great* is here, up to his lashes in the blood, and with him *Attila, the Scourge of God*. They are immersed in the deepest part of the river, which grows shallower as it circles to the other side of the ledge, then deepens again.

The Poets are challenged by the Centaurs, but Virgil wins a safe conduct from *Chiron*, their chief, who assigns *Nessus* to guide them and to bear them across the shallows of the boiling blood. Nessus carries them across at the point where it is only ankle deep and immediately leaves them and returns to his patrol.

The scene that opened from the edge of the pit
    was mountainous, and such a desolation
    that every eye would shun the sight of it: 3

a ruin like the Slides of Mark³ near Trent
    on the bank of the Adige, the result of an earthquake
    or of some massive fault in the escarpment—   6

for, from the point on the peak where the mountain split
    to the plain below, the rock is so badly shattered
    a man at the top might make a rough stair of it.   9

Such was the passage down the steep and there
    at the very top, at the edge of the broken cleft,
    lay spread the Infamy of Crete,⁴ the heir   12

of bestiality and the lecherous queen
    who hid in a wooden cow. And when he saw us,
    he gnawed his own flesh in a fit of spleen.   15

And my Master mocked: "How you do pump your breath!
    Do you think, perhaps, it is the Duke of Athens,
    who in the world above served up your death?⁵   18

Off with you, monster; this one does not come
    instructed by your sister,⁶ but of himself
    to observe your punishment in the lost kingdom."   21

As a bull that breaks its chains just when the knife
    has struck its death-blow, cannot stand nor run
    but leaps from side to side with its last life—   24

---

3. A famous landslide on a mountain on the river Adige near Trent, a city in northern Italy.
4. The Minotaur, half man and half bull, was conceived when Pasiphaë, the wife of King Minos of Crete, had a wooden cow built within which she placed herself so as to have intercourse with a bull. The story of the Minotaur is told by Ovid, *Metamorphoses* 8.

5. Virgil is referring to Theseus, who killed the Minotaur in the labyrinth in which it was imprisoned.
6. Ariadne, daughter of Minos and Pasiphaë, who taught Theseus how to escape from the labyrinth within which the Minotaur was imprisoned.

so danced the Minotaur, and my shrewd Guide
   cried out: "Run now! While he is blind with rage!
   Into the pass, quick, and get over the side!"   27

So we went down across the shale and slate
   of that ruined rock, which often slid and shifted
   under me at the touch of living weight.   30

I moved on, deep in thought; and my Guide to me:
   "You are wondering perhaps about this ruin
   which is guarded by that beast upon whose fury   33

I played just now. I should tell you that when last
   I came this dark way to the depths of Hell,
   this rock had not yet felt the ruinous blast.   36

But certainly, if I am not mistaken,
   it was just before the coming of Him who took
   the souls from Limbo, that all Hell was shaken[7]   39

so that I thought the universe felt love
   and all its elements moved toward harmony,
   whereby the world of matter, as some believe,   42

has often plunged to chaos.[8] It was then,
   that here and elsewhere in the pits of Hell,
   the ancient rock was stricken and broke open.   45

But turn your eyes to the valley; there we shall find
   the river of boiling blood in which are steeped
   all who struck down their fellow men." Oh blind!   48

Oh ignorant, self-seeking cupidity[9]
   which spurs us so in the short mortal life
   and steeps us so through all eternity!   51

I saw an arching fosse[1] that was the bed
   of a winding river circling through the plain
   exactly as my Guide and Lord had said.   54

A file of Centaurs[2] galloped in the space
   between the bank and the cliff, well armed with arrows,
   riding as once on earth they rode to the chase.   57

---

7. Because of the earthquake that accompanied Christ's death, which occurred just before his descent to Hell and the "harrowing," Christ's rescue of the virtuous Israelites from the First Circle (see above, canto 4.52–63).
8. A reference to a theory of the Greek philosopher Empedocles that the universe is held together by alternating forces of love and hate, and that if either one predominates the result is chaos. This classical theory is not consistent with the Christian belief that the universe is created and organized by God's love.
9. Desire for wealth.
1. Ditch.
2. Mythological creatures that are half man and half horse.

And seeing us descend, that straggling band
    halted, and three of them moved out toward us,
    their long bows and their shafts already in hand.   60

And one of them cried out while still below:
    "To what pain are you sent down that dark coast?
    Answer from where you stand, or I draw the bow!"   63

"Chiron[3] is standing there hard by your side;
    our answer will be to him. This wrath of yours
    was always your own worst fate," my Guide replied.   66

And to me he said: "That is Nessus,[4] who died in the wood
    for insulting Dejanira. At his death
    he plotted his revenge in his own blood.   69

The one in the middle staring at his chest
    is the mighty Chiron, he who nursed Achilles:
    the other is Pholus,[5] fiercer than all the rest.   72

They run by that stream in thousands, snapping their bows
    at any wraith who dares to raise himself
    out of the blood more than his guilt allows."   75

We drew near those swift beasts. In a thoughtful pause
    Chiron drew an arrow, and with its notch
    he pushed his great beard back along his jaws.   78

And when he had thus uncovered the huge pouches
    of his lips, he said to his fellows: "Have you noticed
    how the one who walks behind moves what he touches?   81

That is not how the dead go." My good Guide,
    already standing by the monstrous breast
    in which the two mixed natures joined,[6] replied: 84

"It is true he lives; in his necessity
    I alone must lead him through this valley.
    Fate brings him here, not curiosity.   87

From singing Alleluia the sublime
    spirit who sends me came.[7] He is no bandit.
    Nor am I one who ever stooped to crime.[8]   90

3. A centaur renowned for wisdom who educated many legendary Greek heroes, including Achilles.
4. Nessus fell in love with Deianira, wife of Hercules, who killed him; while dying, Nessus poisoned with his own blood a robe that killed Hercules when he put it on.
5. Another centaur, killed by Hercules, whose rage is typical of these creatures.
6. When standing, Virgil reaches to the centaur's chest, where his human and animal natures join.
7. Beatrice.
8. Virgil is answering the question of lines 62–63, which assumes that they are condemned spirits.

But in the name of the Power by which I go
   this sunken way across the floor of Hell,
   assign us one of your troop whom we may follow,   93

that he may guide us to the ford, and there
   carry across on his back the one I lead,
   for he is not a spirit to move through air."   96

Chiron turned his head on his right breast
   and said to Nessus: "Go with them, and guide them,
   and turn back any others that would contest   99

their passage." So we moved beside our guide
   along the bank of the scalding purple river[9]
   in which the shrieking wraiths were boiled and dyed.   102

Some stood up to their lashes in that torrent,
   and as we passed them the huge Centaur said:
   "These were the kings of bloodshed and despoilment.   105

Here they pay for their ferocity.
   Here is Alexander. And Dionysius,
   who brought long years of grief to Sicily.[1]   108

That brow you see with the hair as black as night
   is Azzolino:[2] and that beside him, the blonde,
   is Opizzo da Esti, who had his mortal light   111

blown out by his own stepson."[3] I turned then
   to speak to the Poet but he raised a hand:
   "Let him be the teacher now, and I will listen."   114

Further on, the Centaur stopped beside
   a group of spirits steeped as far as the throat
   in the race of boiling blood, and there our guide   117

pointed out a sinner who stood alone:
   "That one before God's altar pierced a heart
   still honored on the Thames."[4] And he passed on.   120

We came in sight of some who were allowed
   to raise the head and all the chest from the river,
   and I recognized many there. Thus, as we followed   123

---

9. A river of blood, which we later learn is named Phlegethon (see 14.110).
1. Alexander the Great (d. 323 B.C.E.) and Dionysius of Syracuse in Sicily (d. 367 B.C.E.).
2. Azzolino III (d. 1259), a brutal ruler in northern Italy.
3. Opizzo II d'Este (d. 1293), another cruel northern Italian tyrant, reputedly murdered by his son, here called "stepson" either because

of the unnaturalness of the crime or because Opizzo suspected his wife of adultery.
4. Guy de Montfort (d. 1298), who killed his cousin Prince Henry of Cornwall during a church service ("before God's altar") in the Italian city of Viterbo. Nessus's image of the blood dripping from the victim's heart indicates his focus on the fact that the murder is still unavenged. "Race": flow; stream.

along the stream of blood, its level fell
    until it cooked no more than the feet of the damned.
    And here we crossed the ford to deeper Hell.   126

"Just as you see the boiling stream grow shallow
    along this side," the Centaur said to us
    when we stood on the other bank, "I would have you know   129

that on the other, the bottom sinks anew
    more and more, until it comes again
    full circle to the place where the tyrants stew.   132

It is there that Holy Justice spends its wrath
    on Sextus and Pyrrhus[5] through eternity,
    and on Attila,[6] who was a scourge on earth: 135

and everlastingly milks out the tears
    of Rinier da Corneto and Rinier Pazzo,[7]
    those two assassins who for many years   138

stalked the highways, bloody and abhorred."
And with that he started back across the ford.

Canto XIII

CIRCLE SEVEN: ROUND TWO   *The Violent against Themselves*

Nessus carries the Poets across the river of boiling blood and leaves them in the Second Round of the Seventh Circle, *The Wood of the Suicides*. Here are punished those who destroyed their own lives and those who destroyed their substance.

The souls of the Suicides are encased in thorny trees whose leaves are eaten by the odious *Harpies*, the overseers of these damned. When the Harpies feed upon them, damaging their leaves and limbs, the wound bleeds. Only as long as the blood flows are the souls of the trees able to speak. Thus, they who destroyed their own bodies are denied a human form; and just as the supreme expression of their lives was self-destruction, so they are permitted to speak only through that which tears and destroys them. Only through their own blood do they find voice. And to add one more dimension to the symbolism, it is the Harpies—defilers of all they touch—who give them their eternally recurring wounds.

The Poets pause before one tree and speak with the soul of *Pier delle Vigna*. In the same wood they see *Jacomo da Sant' Andrea*, and *Lano da Siena*, two famous *Squanderers* and *Destroyers of Goods* pursued by a pack of savage hounds. The hounds overtake *Sant 'Andrea*, tear him to pieces and go off carrying his limbs in

---

5. Sextus, the son of the Roman consul Pompey, became a pirate (1st century B.C.E.); Pyrrhus, Achilles' son, killed the aged Priam at the fall of Troy, as described in *Aeneid* 2.595–704.
6. Attila the Hun (d. 453), who led repeated

attacks against the Eastern and Western Roman Empires.
7. Both Riniers were bandits of Dante's day; they are now weeping from pain, whereas in life they never wept for their sins.

their teeth, a self-evident symbolic retribution for the violence with which these sinners destroyed their substance in the world. After this scene of horror, Dante speaks to an *Unknown Florentine Suicide* whose soul is inside the bush which was torn by the hound pack when it leaped upon Sant' Andrea.

Nessus had not yet reached the other shore
    when we moved on into a pathless wood
    that twisted upward from Hell's broken floor.   3

Its foliage was not verdant, but nearly black.
    The unhealthy branches, gnarled and warped and tangled,
    bore poison thorns instead of fruit. The track   6

of those wild beasts that shun the open spaces
    men till between Cecina and Corneto[8]
    runs through no rougher nor more tangled places.   9

Here nest the odious Harpies[9] of whom my Master
    wrote how they drove Aeneas and his companions
    from the Strophades with prophecies of disaster.   12

Their wings are wide, their feet clawed, their huge bellies
    covered with feathers, their necks and faces human.
    They croak eternally in the unnatural trees.   15

"Before going on, I would have you understand,"
    my Guide began, "we are in the second round
    and shall be till we reach the burning sand.[1]   18

Therefore look carefully and you will see
    things in this wood, which, if I told them to you
    would shake the confidence you have placed in me."   21

I heard cries of lamentation rise and spill
    on every hand, but saw no souls in pain
    in all that waste; and, puzzled, I stood still.   24

I think perhaps he thought that I was thinking
    those cries rose from among the twisted roots
    through which the spirits of the damned were slinking   27

to hide from us. Therefore my Master said:
    "If you break off a twig, what you will learn
    will drive what you are thinking from your head."[2]   30

---

8. Two towns that mark the limits of the Maremma, a desolate area in Tuscany.
9. Birds with the faces of women and clawed hands; in *Aeneid* 3 they drive the wandering Trojans from their refuge in the Strophades Islands and predict their future suffering.

1. The "burning sand" is in the third ring or "round" of the seventh circle, described in the next canto.
2. I.e., "Your thoughts that the moans come from people concealed among the trees will cease or 'break off.'"

Puzzled, I raised my hand a bit and slowly
   broke off a branchlet from an enormous thorn:
   and the great trunk of it cried: "Why do you break me?"[3]   33

And after blood had darkened all the bowl
   of the wound, it cried again: "Why do you tear me?
   Is there no pity left in any soul?   36

Men we were, and now we are changed to sticks;
   well might your hand have been more merciful
   were we no more than souls of lice and ticks."   39

As a green branch with one end all aflame
   will hiss and sputter sap out of the other
   as the air escapes—so from that trunk there came   42

words and blood together, gout by gout.
   Startled, I dropped the branch that I was holding
   and stood transfixed by fear, half turned about   45

to my Master, who replied: "O wounded soul,
   could he have believed before what he has seen
   in my verses only, you would yet be whole,[4]   48

for his hand would never have been raised against you.
   But knowing this truth could never be believed
   till it was seen, I urged him on to do   51

what grieves me now; and I beg to know your name,
   that to make you some amends in the sweet world
   when he returns, he may refresh your fame."   54

And the trunk: "So sweet those words to me that I
   cannot be still, and may it not annoy you
   if I seem somewhat lengthy in reply.[5]   57

I am he who held both keys to Frederick's heart,
   locking, unlocking with so deft a touch
   that scarce another soul had any part   60

---

3. This episode derives from *Aeneid* 3, where Aeneas and his Trojan companions, stopping in their search for a new home, discover Polydorus transformed into a bush. Sent out by Priam during the war to solicit aid from the Thracians, Polydorus had been murdered by his hosts, and the javelins with which his body had been pierced had grown into the bush from which Aeneas breaks off a branch that bleeds. See also Ovid, *Metamorphoses* 2.
4. I.e., had Dante been able to believe the story of Polydorus recounted in the *Aeneid*.
5. This is the soul of Pier della Vigna (ca. 1190–1249), who had risen to become minister to the Emperor Frederick II (on whom see n. 6 on 10.119); Frederick is referred to here as "Caesar" and "Augustus" because he sought to imitate the imperial court of Rome. Pier's name means "Peter of the Vine," probably because his father had been a simple worker in a vineyard.

in his most secret thoughts. Through every strife
   I was so faithful to my glorious office
   that for it I gave up both sleep and life.   63

That harlot, Envy, who on Caesar's face
   keeps fixed forever her adulterous stare,
   the common plague and vice of court and palace,   66

inflamed all minds against me. These inflamed
   so inflamed him that all my happy honors
   were changed to mourning. Then, unjustly blamed,   69

my soul, in scorn, and thinking to be free
   of scorn in death, made me at last, though just,
   unjust to myself.[6] By the new roots of this tree   72

I swear to you that never in word or spirit
   did I break faith to my lord and emperor
   who was so worthy of honor in his merit.   75

If either of you return to the world, speak for me,
   to vindicate in the memory of men
   one who lies prostrate from the blows of Envy."   78

The Poet stood. Then turned. "Since he is silent,"
   he said to me, "do not you waste this hour,
   if you wish to ask about his life or torment."   81

And I replied: "Question him for my part,
   on whatever you think I would do well to hear;
   I could not, such compassion chokes my heart."   84

The Poet began again: "That this man may
   with all his heart do for you what your words
   entreat him to, imprisoned spirit, I pray,   87

tell us how the soul is bound and bent
   into these knots, and whether any ever
   frees itself from such imprisonment."   90

At that the trunk blew powerfully, and then
   the wind became a voice that spoke these words:
   "Briefly is the answer given: when   93

out of the flesh from which it tore itself,
   the violent spirit comes to punishment,
   Minos assigns it to the seventh shelf.   96

---

6. I.e., "I unjustly committed suicide even though I was innocent of the accusations brought against me."

It falls into the wood, and landing there,
    wherever fortune flings it, it strikes root,
    and there it sprouts, lusty as any tare,   99

shoots up a sapling, and becomes a tree.
    The Harpies, feeding on its leaves then, give it
    pain and pain's outlet simultaneously.   102

Like the rest, we shall go for our husks on Judgment Day,
    but not that we may wear them, for it is not just
    that a man be given what he throws away.   105

Here shall we drag them and in this mournful glade
    our bodies will dangle to the end of time,
    each on the thorns of its tormented shade."   108

We waited by the trunk, but it said no more;
    and waiting, we were startled by a noise
    that grew through all the wood. Just such a roar   111

and trembling as one feels when the boar and chase
    approach his stand, the beasts and branches crashing
    and clashing in the heat of the fierce race.   114

And there on the left, running so violently
    they broke off every twig in the dark wood,
    two torn and naked wraiths went plunging by me.[7]   117

The leader cried, "Come now, O Death! Come now!"
    And the other, seeing that he was outrun,
    cried out: "Your legs were not so ready, Lano,   120

in the jousts at the Toppo."[8] And suddenly in his rush,
    perhaps because his breath was failing him,
    he hid himself inside a thorny bush   123

and cowered among its leaves. Then at his back,
    the wood leaped with black bitches, swift as greyhounds
    escaping from their leash, and all the pack   126

sprang on him; with their fangs they opened him
    and tore him savagely, and then withdrew,
    carrying his body with them, limb by limb.   129

Then, taking me by the hand across the wood,
    my Master led me toward the bush. Lamenting,
    all its fractures blew out words and blood:[9]   132

---

7. Lano of Siena and Giacomo da Sant' Andrea of Padua, two Italians of a generation earlier than Dante's; both were reputed to be spend-thrifts.

8. Lano was killed at a battle on the river Toppo in 1287.

9. Nothing is known about this suicide, who hanged himself from his own house.

"O Jacomo da Sant' Andrea!" it said,
  "what have you gained in making me your screen?
  What part had I in the foul life you led?" 135

And when my Master had drawn up to it
  he said: "Who were you, who through all your wounds
  blow out your blood with your lament, sad spirit?" 138

And he to us: "You who have come to see
  how the outrageous mangling of these hounds
  has torn my boughs and stripped my leaves from me, 141

O heap them round my ruin! I was born
  in the city that tore down Mars and raised the Baptist.[1]
  On that account the God of War has sworn 144

her sorrow shall not end. And were it not
  that something of his image still survives
  on the bridge across the Arno,[2] some have thought 147

those citizens who of their love and pain
  afterwards rebuilt it from the ashes
  left by Attila, would have worked in vain.[3] 150

I am one who has no tale to tell:
  I made myself a gibbet of my own lintel."

Canto XIV

CIRCLE SEVEN: ROUND THREE   *The Violent against God, Nature, and Art*

Dante, in pity, restores the torn leaves to the soul of his countryman and the
Poets move on to the next round, a great *Plain of Burning Sand* upon which
there descends an eternal slow *Rain of Fire*. Here, scorched by fire from above
and below, are three classes of sinners suffering differing degrees of exposure to
the fire. The *Blasphemers* (The Violent against God) are stretched supine upon
the sand, the *Sodomites* (The Violent against Nature) run in endless circles, and the
Usurers (The Violent against Art, which is the Grandchild of God) huddle on the
sands.

    The Poets find *Capaneus* stretched out on the sands, the chief sinner of that
place. He is still blaspheming God. They continue along the edge of the Wood of the
Suicides and come to a blood-red rill which flows boiling from the Wood and crosses
the burning plain. Virgil explains the miraculous power of its waters and discourses
on the *Old Man of Crete* and the origin of all the rivers of Hell.

    The symbolism of the burning plain is obviously centered in sterility (the desert
image) and wrath (the fire image). Blasphemy, sodomy, and usury are all unnatural

---

1. Florence; when the Florentines converted
to Christianity, John the Baptist replaced Mars
as patron of the city, and therefore Mars would
forever persecute the city with civil war.

2. The river that runs through Florence.
3. According to legend, Attila the Hun destroyed
Florence when he invaded Italy in the 5th
century.

and sterile actions: thus the unbearing desert is the eternity of these sinners; and thus the rain, which in nature should be fertile and cool, descends as fire. Capaneus, moreover, is subjected not only to the wrath of nature (the sands below) and the wrath of God (the fire from above), but is tortured most by his own inner violence, which is the root of blasphemy.

Love of that land that was our common source
    moved me to tears; I gathered up the leaves
    and gave them back. He was already hoarse.   3

We came to the edge of the forest where one goes
    from the second round to the third,[4] and there we saw
    what fearful arts the hand of Justice knows.   6

To make these new things wholly clear, I say
    we came to a plain whose soil repels all roots.
    The wood of misery rings it the same way   9

the wood itself is ringed by the red fosse.
    We paused at its edge: the ground was burning sand,
    just such a waste as Cato[5] marched across.   12

O endless wrath of God: how utterly
    thou shouldst become a terror to all men
    who read the frightful truths revealed to me!   15

Enormous herds of naked souls I saw,
    lamenting till their eyes were burned of tears;
    they seemed condemned by an unequal law,   18

for some were stretched supine upon the ground,
    some squatted with their arms about themselves,
    and others without pause roamed round and round.   21

Most numerous were those that roamed the plain.
    Far fewer were the souls stretched on the sand,
    but moved to louder cries by greater pain.   24

And over all that sand on which they lay
    or crouched or roamed, great flakes of flame fell slowly
    as snow falls in the Alps on a windless day.   27

Like those Alexander met in the hot regions
    of India, flames raining from the sky
    to fall still unextinguished on his legions: 30

---

4. The third ring of the seventh circle is surrounded by the second ring of the woods through which Dante has just passed and the first ring of the river of blood described in canto 12.

5. Roman general (1st century B.C.E.) who campaigned in Libya.

whereat he formed his ranks, and at their head
  set the example, trampling the hot ground
  for fear the tongues of fire might join and spread—[6]   33

just so in Hell descended the long rain
  upon the damned, kindling the sand like tinder
  under a flint and steel, doubling the pain.   36

In a never-ending fit upon those sands,
  the arms of the damned twitched all about their bodies,
  now here, now there, brushing away the brands.   39

"Poet," I said, "master of every dread
  we have encountered, other than those fiends
  who sallied from the last gate of the dead—   42

who is that wraith who lies along the rim
  and sets his face against the fire in scorn,
  so that the rain seems not to mellow him?"[7]   45

And he himself, hearing what I had said
  to my Guide and Lord concerning him, replied:
  "What I was living, the same am I now, dead.   48

Though Jupiter wear out his sooty smith[8]
  from whom on my last day he snatched in anger
  the jagged thunderbolt he pierced me with;   51

though he wear out the others one by one
  who labor at the forge at Mongibello[9]
  crying again 'Help! Help! Help me, good Vulcan!'   54

as he did at Phlegra;[1] and hurl down endlessly
  with all the power of Heaven in his arm,
  small satisfaction would he win from me."   57

At this my Guide spoke with such vehemence
  as I had not heard from him in all of Hell:
  "O Capaneus, by your insolence   60

you are made to suffer as much fire inside
  as falls upon you. Only your own rage
  could be fit torment for your sullen pride."   63

---

6. Dante is here following an account by the philosopher Albertus Magnus (d. 1280) of a legendary adventure that befell Alexander the Great in his conquest of India.
7. Capaneus, one of the seven legendary kings who besieged Thebes as described in the *Thebaid* by Statius (d. 95 C.E.). He was struck with a thunderbolt when he boasted that not even Jupiter could stop him.
8. Vulcan, Roman god of fire, volcanoes, and the forge; equivalent of Greek Hephaestus.
9. The Sicilian name for Mt. Etna, thought to be Vulcan's furnace; "the others" are the Cyclopes, Vulcan's helpers.
1. Jove defeated the rebellious Titans at the battle of Phlegra (see 31.42).

Then he turned to me more gently. "That," he said,
 "was one of the Seven who laid siege to Thebes.
 Living, he scorned God, and among the dead   66

he scorns Him yet. He thinks he may detest
 God's power too easily, but as I told him,
 his slobber is a fit badge for his breast.   69

Now follow me; and mind for your own good
 you do not step upon the burning sand,
 but keep well back along the edge of the wood."   72

We walked in silence then till we reached a rill
 that gushes from the wood; it ran so red
 the memory sends a shudder through me still.   75

As from the Bulicame[2] springs the stream
 the sinful women keep to their own use;
 so down the sand the rill flowed out in steam.   78

The bed and both its banks were petrified,
 as were its margins; thus I knew at once
 our passage through the sand lay by its side.   81

"Among all other wonders I have shown you
 since we came through the gate denied to none,
 nothing your eyes have seen is equal to   84

the marvel of the rill by which we stand,
 for it stifles all the flames above its course
 as it flows out across the burning sand."   87

So spoke my Guide across the flickering light,
 and I begged him to bestow on me the food
 for which he had given me the appetite.   90

"In the middle of the sea, and gone to waste,
 there lies a country known as Crete," he said,
 "under whose king the ancient world was chaste.[3]   93

Once Rhea chose it as the secret crypt
 and cradle of her son; and better to hide him,
 her Corybantes raised a din when he wept.[4]   96

---

2. A hot sulphurous spring that supplied water to brothels in an area of northern Italy.
3. Saturn, mythical king of Crete during the Golden Age.
4. Jupiter was hidden by his mother, Rhea, from his father, Saturn, who tried to devour all his children to thwart a prophecy that he would be dethroned by one of them. So that Saturn would not hear the infant's cries, Rhea had her servants, the Corybantes (or Bacchantes), cry out and beat their shields with their swords.

An ancient giant stands in the mountain's core.
 He keeps his shoulder turned toward Damietta,[5]
 and looks toward Rome as if it were his mirror.   99

His head is made of gold; of silverwork
 his breast and both his arms, of polished brass
 the rest of his great torso to the fork.   102

He is of chosen iron from there down,
 except that his right foot is terra cotta;
 it is this foot he rests more weight upon.[6]   105

Every part except the gold is split
 by a great fissure from which endless tears
 drip down and hollow out the mountain's pit.   108

Their course sinks to this pit from stone to stone,
 becoming Acheron, Phlegethon, and Styx.
 Then by this narrow sluice they hurtle down   111

to the end of all descent, and disappear
 into Cocytus.[7] You shall see what sink that is
 with your own eyes. I pass it in silence here."   114

And I to him: "But if these waters flow
 from the world above, why is this rill met only
 along this shelf?" And he to me: "You know   117

the place is round, and though you have come deep
 into the valley through the many circles,
 always bearing left along the steep,   120

you have not traveled any circle through
 its total round; hence when new things appear
 from time to time, that hardly should surprise you."   123

And I: "Where shall we find Phlegethon's course?
 And Lethe's?[8] One you omit, and of the other
 you only say the tear-flood is its source."   126

"In all you ask of me you please me truly,"
 he answered, "but the red and boiling water
 should answer the first question you put to me,[9]   129

---

5. A city in Egypt. The Old Man has been interpreted as an emblem of the decline of human
history.
6. The four metals and the clay represent the
degeneration of history; Dante took this image
from Daniel 2.31–35.

7. The frozen lake at the bottom of Hell: see
32.22–30 and 34.52.
8. Lethe, the river of forgetting, is crossed when
Dante passes into the Earthly Paradise on the
top of Mount Purgatory.
9. See note 9 to 12.101.

and you shall stand by Lethe, but far hence:
    there, where the spirits go to wash themselves
    when their guilt has been removed by penitence."   132

And then he said: "Now it is time to quit
    this edge of shade: follow close after me
    along the rill, and do not stray from it;   135

for the unburning margins form a lane,
and by them we may cross the burning plain."

Canto XV

CIRCLE SEVEN: ROUND THREE   *The Violent against Nature*

Protected by the marvelous powers of the boiling rill, the Poets walk along its banks across the burning plain. The *Wood of the Suicides* is behind them; the *Great Cliff* at whose foot lies the *Eighth Circle* is before them.

They pass one of the roving bands of *Sodomites*. One of the sinners stops Dante, and with great difficulty the Poet recognizes him under his baked features as *Ser Brunetto Latino*. This is a reunion with a dearly loved man and writer, one who had considerably influenced Dante's own development, and Dante addresses him with great and sorrowful affection, paying him the highest tribute offered to any sinner in the *Inferno*. *Brunetto* prophesies Dante's sufferings at the hands of the Florentines, gives an account of the souls that move with him through the fire, and finally, under Divine Compulsion, races off across the plain.

We go by one of the stone margins now
    and the steam of the rivulet makes a shade above it,
    guarding the stream and banks from the flaming snow.   3

As the Flemings in the lowland between Bruges
    and Wissant,[1] under constant threat of the sea,
crect their great dikes to hold back the deluge;   6

as the Paduans along the shores of the Brent[2]
    build levees to protect their towns and castles
    Jest Chiarentana drown in the spring torrent—   9

to the same plan, though not so wide nor high,
    did the engineer, whoever he may have been,
    design the margin we were crossing by.   12

Already we were so far from the wood
    that even had I turned to look at it,
    I could not have made it out from where I stood,   15

1. Cities that, for Dante, mark the two ends of the dike that protects Flanders from the sea.
2. A river that flows through Padua, fed by the melting snows in the mountains of the province of Chiarentana (modern Carinthia in Austria).

when a company of shades came into sight
    walking beside the bank. They stared at us
    as men at evening by the new moon's light   18

stare at one another when they pass by
    on a dark road, pointing their eyebrows toward us
    as an old tailor squints at his needle's eye.   21

Stared at so closely by that ghostly crew,
    I was recognized by one who seized the hem
    of my skirt and said: "Wonder of wonders! You?"   24

And I, when he stretched out his arm to me,
    searched his baked features closely, till at last
    I traced his image from my memory   27

in spite of the burnt crust, and bending near
    to put my face closer to his, at last
    I answered: "Ser Brunetto,[3] are you here?"   30

"O my son! may it not displease you," he cried,
    "if Brunetto Latino leave his company
    and turn and walk a little by your side."   33

And I to him: "With all my soul I ask it.
    Or let us sit together, if it please him
    who is my Guide and leads me through this pit."   36

"My son!" he said, "whoever of this train
    pauses a moment, must lie a hundred years
    forbidden to brush off the burning rain.   39

Therefore, go on; I will walk at your hem,
    and then rejoin my company, which goes
    mourning eternal loss in eternal flame."   42

I did not dare descend to his own level
    but kept my head inclined, as one who walks
    in reverence meditating good and evil.   45

"What brings you here before your own last day?
    What fortune or what destiny?" he began.
    "And who is he that leads you this dark way?"   48

"Up there in the happy life I went astray
    in a valley," I replied, "before I had reached
    the fullness of my years. Only yesterday   51

3. Brunetto Latini (ca. 1220–1294), active in Florentine politics and the author of—among other works—two books: a prose encyclopedia in French called the *Trésor*, which emphasizes the qualities needed for civic duty, and a shorter allegorical poem in Italian called the *Tesoretto*, which combines autobiography with philosophy.

at dawn I turned from it. This spirit showed
    himself to me as I was turning back,
    and guides me home again along this road."   54

And he: "Follow your star, for if in all
    of the sweet life I saw one truth shine clearly,
    you cannot miss your glorious arrival.   57

And had I lived to do what I meant to do,
    I would have cheered and seconded your work,
    observing Heaven so well disposed toward you.   60

But that ungrateful and malignant stock
    that came down from Fiesole[4] of old
    and still smacks of the mountain and the rock,   63

for your good works will be your enemy.
    And there is cause: the sweet fig is not meant
    to bear its fruit beside the bitter sorb-tree.[5]   66

Even the old adage calls them blind,
    an envious, proud, and avaricious people:
    see that you root their customs from your mind.   69

It is written in your stars, and will come to pass,
    that your honours shall make both sides hunger for you:
    but the goat shall never reach to crop that grass.[6]   72

Let the beasts of Fiesole devour their get
    like sows, but never let them touch the plant,
    if among their rankness any springs up yet,   75

in which is born again the holy seed
    of the Romans who remained among their rabble
    when Florence made a new nest for their greed."   78

"Ah, had I all my wish," I answered then,
    "you would not yet be banished from the world
    in which you were a radiance among men,   81

for that sweet image, gentle and paternal,
    you were to me in the world when hour by hour
    you taught me how man makes himself eternal,[7]   84

---

4. A hill town north of Florence whose rustic inhabitants were supposed to have joined with noble Romans in the founding of Florence, creating an unstable mixture.
5. The "bitter sorb-tree" are the Florentines descended from Fiesole; the "sweet fig" is Brunetto's term for the aristocratic Dante.

6. "I.e., Either both parties will ask you to join them or both parties will want to devour you—but keep yourself apart."
7. In the *Trésor*, Brunetto says that earthly glory gives man a second life through an enduring reputation.

lives in my mind, and now strikes to my heart;
   and while I live, the gratitude I owe it
   will speak to men out of my life and art.   87

What you have told me of my course, I write
   by another text I save to show a Lady[8]
   who will judge these matters, if I reach her height.   90

This much I would have you know: so long, I say,
   as nothing in my conscience troubles me
   I am prepared for Fortune, come what may.   93

Twice already in the eternal shade
   I have heard this prophecy; but let Fortune turn
   her wheel as she please, and the countryman his spade."[9]   96

My guiding spirit paused at my last word
   and, turning right about, stood eye to eye
   to say to me: "Well heeded is well heard."   99

But I did not reply to him, going on
   with Ser Brunetto to ask him who was with him
   in the hot sands, the best born and best known.   102

And he to me: "Of some who share this walk
   it is good to know; of the rest let us say nothing,
   for the time would be too short for so much talk.   105

In brief, we all were clerks and men of worth,
   great men of letters, scholars of renown;
   all by the one same crime defiled on earth.[1]   108

Priscian moves there along the wearisome
   sad way, and Francesco d'Accorso,[2] and also there,
   if you had any longing for such scum,   111

you might have seen that one the Servant of Servants
   sent from the Arno to the Bacchiglione
   where he left his unnatural organ wrapped in cerements.[3]   114

I would say more, but there across the sand
   a new smoke rises and new people come,
   and I must run to be with my own band.   117

---

8. Beatrice.
9. The traditional image of Fortune and her wheel is here compared to the rustic image of the peasant turning the soil with his hoe.
1. Sodomy, condemned in the Middle Ages as unnatural.
2. Priscian was a Greek grammarian (6th century C.E.); Francesco d'Accorso a Florentine law professor (d. 1293).
3. Andrea de' Mozzi, bishop of Florence (1287–95), transferred by Pope Boniface (designated here by an official title for the pope, "the Servant of [Christ's] Servants") from Florence to Vicenza; the Arno runs through Florence, the Bacchiglione through Vicenza.

Remember my *Treasure*[4], in which I still live on:
  I ask no more." He turned then, and he seemed,
  across that plain, like one of those who run   120

for the green cloth[5] at Verona; and of those,
  more like the one who wins, than those who lose.

Canto XVI

CIRCLE SEVEN: ROUND THREE   *The Violent against Nature and Art*

The Poets arrive within hearing of the waterfall that plunges over the *Great Cliff*
into the *Eighth Circle*. The sound is still a distant throbbing when three wraiths,
recognizing Dante's Florentine dress, detach themselves from their band and
come running toward him. They are *Jacopo Rusticucci, Guido Cuerra*, and *Teg-
ghiaío Aldobrandi*, all of them Florentines whose policies and personalities Dante
admired. Rusticucci and Tegghiaio have already been mentioned in a highly com-
plimentary way in Dante's talk with Ciacco (canto VI).

The sinners ask for news of Florence, and Dante replies with a passionate lament
for her present degradation. The three wraiths return to their band and the Poets
continue to the top of the falls. Here, at Virgil's command, Dante removes a *Cord*
from about his waist and Virgil drops it over the edge of the abyss. As if in answer to
a signal, a great distorted shape comes swimming up through the dirty air of the pit.

We could already hear the rumbling drive
  of the waterfall in its plunge to the next circle,
  a murmur like the throbbing of a hive,   3

when three shades turned together on the plain,
  breaking toward us from a company
  that went its way to torture in that rain.   6

They cried with one voice as they ran toward me:
  "Wait, oh wait, for by your dress you seem
  a voyager from our own tainted country."[6]   9

Ah! what wounds I saw, some new, some old,
  branded upon their bodies! Even now
  the pain of it in memory turns me cold.   12

My Teacher heard their cries, and turning to,
  stood face to face. "Do as they ask," he said,
  "for these are souls to whom respect is due;   15

and were it not for the darting flames that hem
  our narrow passage in, I should have said
  it were more fitting you ran after them."[7]   18

4. *"Treasure"*: i.e., Latini's encyclopedia, the
Trésor (French).
5. A footrace run at Verona on the first Sunday in Lent, the prize being a piece of green

cloth. For the race to be run by the Christian,
see 1 Corinthians 9.24–25.
6. Florence.
7. To hurry was considered undignified.

We paused, and they began their ancient wail
    over again, and when they stood below us
    they formed themselves into a moving wheel.   21

As naked and anointed champions do
    in feeling out their grasp and their advantage
    before they close in for the thrust or blow—[8]   24

so circling, each one stared up at my height,
    and as their feet moved left around the circle,
    their necks kept turning backward to the right.   27

"If the misery of this place, and our unkempt
    and scorched appearance," one of them began,
    "bring us and what we pray into contempt,   30

still may our earthly fame move you to tell
    who and what you are, who so securely
    set your live feet to the dead dusts of Hell.   33

This peeled and naked soul who runs before me
    around this wheel, was higher than you think
    there in the world, in honor and degree.   36

Guido Guerra[9] was the name he bore,
    the good Gualdrada's grandson. In his life
    he won great fame in counsel and in war.   39

The other who behind me treads this sand
    was Tegghiaio Aldobrandi,[1] whose good counsels
    the world would have done well to understand.   42

And I who share their torment, in my life
    was Jacopo Rusticucci;[2] above all
    I owe my sorrows to a savage wife."   45

I would have thrown myself to the plain below
    had I been sheltered from the falling fire;
    and I think my Teacher would have let me go.   48

But seeing I should be burned and cooked, my fear
    overcame the first impulse of my heart
    to leap down and embrace them then and there.   51

"Not contempt," I said, "but the compassion
    that seizes on my soul and memory
    at the thought of you tormented in this fashion— 54

---

8. The three naked Florentines form a circle and are compared to oiled wrestlers (a sport practiced in Dante's time).
9. A leading participant in the civil strife in Florence (d. 1272).
1. An ally of Guido (see 6.76).
2. An ally of Tegghiaio who blames his wife for his sodomy (see 6.77).

it was grief that choked my speech when through the scorching
   air of this pit my Lord announced to me
   that such men as you are might be approaching.   57

I am of your own land, and I have always
   heard with affection and rehearsed with honor
   your name and the good deeds of your happier days.   60

Led by my Guide and his truth, I leave the gall
   and go for the sweet apples of delight.[3]
   But first I must descend to the center of all."   63

"So may your soul and body long continue
   together on the way you go," he answered,
   "and the honor of your days shine after you—   66

tell me if courtesy and valor raise
   their banners in our city as of old,
   or has the glory faded from its days?   69

For Borsiere,[4] who is newly come among us
   and yonder goes with our companions in pain,
   taunts us with such reports, and his words have stung us."[5]   72

"O Florence! your sudden wealth and your upstart
   rabble, dissolute and overweening,
   already set you weeping in your heart!"   75

I cried with face upraised, and on the sand
   those three sad spirits looked at one another
   like men who hear the truth and understand.   78

"If this be your manner of speaking, and if you can
   satisfy others with such ease and grace,"
   they said as one, "we hail a happy man.   81

Therefore, if you win through this gloomy pass
   and climb again to see the heaven of stars;
   when it rejoices you to say 'I was,'   84

speak of us to the living." They parted then,
   breaking their turning wheel, and as they vanished
   over the plain, their legs seemed wings. "Amen"   87

could not have been pronounced between their start
   and their disappearance over the rim of sand.
   And then it pleased my Master to depart.   90

---

3. I.e., leave Hell and head for Paradise.
4. An elegant member of Florentine society.
5. An account of the recent dissension within the city, to which Dante himself was soon to fall victim.

A little way beyond we felt the quiver
   and roar of the cascade, so close that speech
   would have been drowned in thunder. As that river—   93

the first one on the left of the Apennines[6]
   to have a path of its own from Monte Veso
   to the Adriatic Sea—which, as it twines   96

is called the Acquacheta from its source
   until it nears Forli, and then is known
   as the Montone in its further course—   99

resounds from the mountain in a single leap
   there above San Benedetto dell'Alpe
   where a thousand falls might fit into the steep;   102

so down from a sheer bank, in one enormous
   plunge, the tainted water roared so loud
   a little longer there would have deafened us.   105

I had a cord bound round me like a belt[7]
   which I had once thought I might put to use
   to snare the leopard with the gaudy pelt.[8]   108

When at my Guide's command I had unbound
   its loops from about my habit, I gathered it
   and held it out to him all coiled and wound.   111

He bent far back to his right, and throwing it
   out from the edge, sent it in a long arc
   into the bottomless darkness of the pit.   114

"Now surely some unusual event,"
   I said to myself, "must follow this new signal
   upon which my good Guide is so intent."   117

Ah, how cautiously a man should breathe
   near those who see not only what we do,
   but have the sense which reads the mind beneath![9]   120

He said to me: "You will soon see arise
   what I await, and what you wonder at;
   soon you will see the thing before your eyes."   123

6. Dante compares the roar of Phlegethon to the river Montone in the Apennine Mountains of northern Italy, whose course he traces in the next nine lines.

7. While commentators disagree, it seems likely that this cord is a reference both to Job 41.1, where God says he can draw Leviathan up with a hook and bind his tongue with a cord, and to Francis of Assisi, who wore a cord as a sign of humility and obedience. As a layman, Dante may have had a connection with the Franciscan friars, a common circumstance at the time.

8. The leopard of canto 1, representing fraud.

9. Dante now realizes that Virgil can read his thoughts.

To the truth which will seem falsehood every man
  who would not be called a liar while speaking fact
  should learn to seal his lips as best he can.   126

But here I cannot be still: Reader, I swear
  by the lines of my Comedy—so may it live—
  that I saw swimming up through that foul air   129

a shape to astonish the most doughty soul,
  a shape like one returning through the sea
  from working loose an anchor run afoul   132

of something on the bottom—so it rose,
  its arms spread upward and its feet drawn close.

Canto XVII

CIRCLE SEVEN: ROUND THREE   *The Violent against Art. Geryon*

The monstrous shape lands on the brink and Virgil salutes it ironically. It is *Geryon*, the *Monster of Fraud*. Virgil announces that they must fly down from the cliff on the back of this monster. While Virgil negotiates for their passage, Dante is sent to examine the *Usurers* (The Violent against Art).

These sinners sit in a crouch along the edge of the burning plain that approaches the cliff. Each of them has a leather purse around his neck, and each purse is blazoned with a coat of arms. Their eyes, gushing with tears, are forever fixed on these purses. Dante recognizes none of these sinners, but their coats of arms are unmistakably those of well-known Florentine families.

Having understood who they are and the reason for their present condition, Dante cuts short his excursion and returns to find Virgil mounted on the back of Geryon. Dante joins his Master and they fly down from the great cliff.

Their flight carries them from the Hell of the *Violent and the Bestial* (The Sins of the Lion) into the Hell of the *Fraudulent and Malicious* (The Sins of the Leopard).

"Now see the sharp-tailed beast that mounts the brink.
  He passes mountains, breaks through walls and weapons.
  Behold the beast that makes the whole world stink."[1]   3

These were the words my Master spoke to me;
  then signaled the weird beast to come to ground
  close to the sheer end of our rocky levee.   6

The filthy prototype of Fraud drew near
  and settled his head and breast upon the edge
  of the dark cliff, but let his tail hang clear.   9

1. Geryon, the embodiment of fraud. For this figure Dante drew upon classical literature, where Geryon had not three natures—human, reptilian, and bestial—combined into one, as here, but three bodies and three heads.

His face was innocent of every guile,
   benign and just in feature and expression;
   and under it his body was half reptile.   12

His two great paws were hairy to the armpits;
   all his back and breast and both his flanks
   were figured with bright knots and subtle circlets: 15

never was such a tapestry of bloom
   woven on earth by Tartar or by Turk,
   nor by Arachne[2] at her flowering loom.   18

As a ferry sometimes lies along the strand,
   part beached and part afloat; and as the beaver,[3]
   up yonder in the guzzling Germans'[4] land,   21

squats halfway up the bank when a fight is on—
   just so lay that most ravenous of beasts
   on the rim which bounds the burning sand with stone.   24

His tail twitched in the void beyond that lip,
   thrashing, and twisting up the envenomed fork
   which, like a scorpion's stinger, armed the tip.   27

My Guide said: "It is time now we drew near
   that monster." And descending on the right
   we moved ten paces outward to be clear   30

of sand and flames. And when we were beside him,
   I saw upon the sand a bit beyond us
   some people crouching close beside the brim.   33

The Master paused. "That you may take with you
   the full experience of this round," he said,
   "go now and see the last state of that crew.   36

But let your talk be brief, and I will stay
   and reason with this beast till you return,
   that his strong back may serve us on our way."   39

So further yet along the outer edge
   of the seventh circle I moved on alone.
   And came to the sad people of the ledge.   42

Their eyes burst with their grief; their smoking hands
   jerked about their bodies, warding off
   now the flames and now the burning sands.   45

2. A woman in classical literature famous for weaving, who was turned into a spider: see Ovid, *Metamorphoses* 6.
3. Which was thought to catch fish by putting its tail into the water.
4. Accusing Germans of drunkenness was a tradition going back to the Romans.

Dogs in summer bit by fleas and gadflies,
   jerking their snouts about, twitching their paws
   now here, now there, behave no otherwise.   48

I examined several faces there among
   that sooty throng, and I saw none I knew;
   but I observed that from each neck there hung   51

an enormous purse, each marked with its own beast
   and its own colors like a coat of arms.
   On these their streaming eyes appeared to feast.[5]   54

Looking about, I saw one purse display
   azure on or, a kind of lion; another,
   on a blood-red field, a goose whiter than whey.   57

And one that bore a huge and swollen sow
   azure on field argent said to me:
   "What are you doing in this pit of sorrow?   60

Leave us alone! And since you have not yet died,
   I'll have you know my neighbor Vitaliano
   has a place reserved for him here at my side.[6]   63

A Paduan among Florentines, I sit here
   while hour by hour they nearly deafen me
   shouting: 'Send us the sovereign cavalier[7]   66

with the purse of the three goats!'" He half arose,
   twisted his mouth, and darted out his tongue
   for all the world like an ox licking its nose.   69

And I, afraid that any longer stay
   would anger him who had warned me to be brief,
   left those exhausted souls without delay.   72

Returned, I found my Guide already mounted
   upon the rump of that monstrosity.
   He said to me: "Now must you be undaunted: 75

this beast must be our stairway to the pit:
   mount it in front, and I will ride between
   you and the tail, lest you be poisoned by it."[8]   78

---

5. These are usurers, men who lent money for interest, which was forbidden by the Catholic Church in the Middle Ages (although often practiced). Each has a coat of arms on his purse by which he can be identified; all are Italians.

6. The speaker is from Padua and here maliciously identifies another Paduan who will soon be joining him.
7. A prominent Florentine banker.
8. Virgil protects Dante from Geryon's scorpion's tail.

Like one so close to the quartanary chill
　　that his nails are already pale and his flesh trembles
　　at the very sight of shade or a cool rill—   81

so did I tremble at each frightful word.
　　But his scolding filled me with that shame that makes
　　the servant brave in the presence of his lord.   84

I mounted the great shoulders of that freak
　　and tried to say "Now help me to hold on!"
　　But my voice clicked in my throat and I could not speak.   87

But no sooner had I settled where he placed me
　　than he, my stay, my comfort, and my courage
　　in other perils, gathered and embraced me.   90

Then he called out: "Now, Geryon, we are ready:
　　bear well in mind that his is living weight
　　and make your circles wide and your flight steady."   93

As a small ship slides from a beaching or its pier,
　　backward, backward—so that monster slipped
　　back from the rim. And when he had drawn clear   96

he swung about, and stretching out his tail
　　he worked it like an eel, and with his paws
　　he gathered in the air, while I turned pale.   99

I think there was no greater fear the day
　　Phaeton[9] let loose the reins and burned the sky
　　along the great scar of the Milky Way,   102

nor when Icarus,[1] too close to the sun's track
　　felt the wax melt, unfeathering his loins,
　　and heard his father cry "Turn back! Turn back!"—   105

than I felt when I found myself in air,
　　afloat in space with nothing visible
　　but the enormous beast that bore me there.   108

Slowly, slowly, he swims on through space,
　　wheels and descends, but I can sense it only
　　by the way the wind blows upward past my face.   111

Already on the right I heard the swell
　　and thunder of the whirlpool. Looking down
　　I leaned my head out and stared into Hell.   114

9. Son of Apollo, Phaeton tried to drive the
chariot of the sun, but when it got out of control
it scorched both Earth and the heavens, creating the Milky Way (Ovid, *Metamorphoses* 2).

1. Flying with wings made of wax and feathers, Icarus, the son of Daedalus, went too near
the sun and fell (Ovid, *Metamorphoses* 8).

I trembled again at the prospect of dismounting
    and cowered in on myself, for I saw fires
    on every hand, and I heard a long lamenting.   117

And then I saw—till then I had but felt it—
    the course of our down-spiral to the horrors
    that rose to us from all sides of the pit.   120

As a flight-worn falcon sinks down wearily
    though neither bird nor lure has signalled it,
    the falconer crying out: "What! spent already!"—   123

then turns and in a hundred spinning gyres
    sulks from her master's call, sullen and proud—[2]
    so to that bottom lit by endless fires   126

the monster Geryon circled and fell,
    setting us down at the foot of the precipice
    of ragged rock on the eighth shelf of Hell.   129

And once freed of our weight, he shot from there
into the dark like an arrow into air.

Canto XVIII

CIRCLE EIGHT (MALEBOLGE)	*The Fraudulent and Malicious*
BOLGIA ONE	*The Panderers and Seducers*
BOLGIA TWO	*The Flatterers*

Dismounted from Geryon, the Poets find themselves in the *Eighth Circle*, called *Malebolge* (The Evil Ditches). This is the upper half of the *Hell of the Fraudulent and Malicious*. Malebolge is a great circle of stone that slopes like an amphitheater. The slopes are divided into ten concentric ditches; and within these ditches, each with his own kind, are punished those guilty of *Simple Fraud*.

    A series of stone dikes runs like spokes from the edge of the great cliff face to the center of the place, and these serve as bridges.

    The Poets bear left toward the first ditch, and Dante observes below him and to his right the sinners of the first bolgia, the *Panderers* and *Seducers*. These make two files, one along either bank of the ditch, and are driven at an endless fast walk by horned demons who hurry them along with great lashes. In life these sinners goaded others on to serve their own foul purposes; so in Hell are they driven in their turn. The horned demons who drive them symbolize the sinners' own vicious natures, embodiments of their own guilty consciences. Dante may or may not have intended the horns of the demons to symbolize cuckoldry and adultery.

    The Poets see *Venedico Caccianemico* and *Jason* in the first pit, and pass on to the second, where they find the souls of the *Flatterers* sunk in excrement, the true

---

2. Unless it sights prey or is called back with a lure by its master, a trained falcon will continue flying until exhaustion compels it to descend.

equivalent of their false flatteries on earth. They observe *Alessio Interminelli* and *Thaïs*, and pass on.

There is in Hell a vast and sloping ground
   called Malebolge, a lost place of stone
   as black as the great cliff that seals it round. 3

Precisely in the center of that space
   there yawns a well extremely wide and deep.
   I shall discuss it in its proper place.[3] 6

The border that remains between the well-pit
   and the great cliff forms an enormous circle,
   and ten descending troughs are cut in it, 9

offering a general prospect like the ground
   that lies around one of those ancient castles
   whose walls are girded many times around 12

by concentric moats. And just as, from the portal,
   the castle's bridges run from moat to moat
   to the last bank; so from the great rock wall 15

across the embankments and the ditches, high
   and narrow cliffs run to the central well,
   which cuts and gathers them like radii. 18

Here, shaken from the back of Geryon,
   we found ourselves. My Guide kept to the left
   and I walked after him. So we moved on. 21

Below, on my right, and filling the first ditch
   along both banks, new souls in pain appeared,
   new torments, and new devils black as pitch. 24

All of these sinners were naked; on our side
   of the middle they walked toward us; on the other,
   in our direction, but with swifter stride. 27

Just so the Romans, because of the great throng
   in the year of the Jubilee,[4] divide the bridge
   in order that the crowds may pass along, 30

so that all face the Castle as they go
   on one side toward St. Peter's, while on the other,
   all move along facing toward Mount Giordano. 33

3. The last, or ninth, circle of Hell, described in cantos 31–34.
4. The year 1300 was declared the first-ever Jubilee Year by Pope Boniface, and Dante here describes the crowd control on the bridge that ran between the Castle of St. Angelo and St. Peter's Basilica in Rome.

And everywhere along that hideous track
    I saw horned demons with enormous lashes
    move through those souls, scourging them on the back.   36

Ah, how the stragglers of that long rout stirred
    their legs quick-march at the first crack of the lash!
    Certainly no one waited a second, or third!   39

As we went on, one face in that procession
    caught my eye and I said: "That sinner there:
    It is certainly not the first time I've seen that one."[5]   42

I stopped, therefore, to study him, and my Guide
    out of his kindness waited, and even allowed me
    to walk back a few steps at the sinner's side.   45

And that flayed spirit, seeing me turn around,
    thought to hide his face, but I called to him:
    "You there, that walk along with your eyes on the ground—   48

if those are not false features, then I know you
    as Venedico Caccianemico of Bologna:
    what brings you here among this pretty crew?"   51

And he replied: "I speak unwillingly,
    but something in your living voice, in which
    I hear the world again, stirs and compels me.   54

It was I who brought the fair Ghisola 'round
    to serve the will and lust of the Marquis,
    however sordid that old tale may sound.   57

There are many more from Bologna who weep away
    eternity in this ditch; we fill it so
    there are not as many tongues that are taught to say   60

'sipa'[6] in all the land that lies between
    the Reno and the Saveno, as you must know
    from the many tales of our avarice and spleen."   63

And as he spoke, one of those lashes fell
    across his back, and a demon cried, "Move on,
    you pimp, there are no women here to sell."   66

Turning away then, I rejoined my Guide.
    We came in a few steps to a raised ridge
    that made a passage to the other side.   69

---

5. This is Venedico Caccianemico, a man from Bologna who was reputed to have turned his sister Ghisolabella over to the Marquis of Este.

6. *Sipa* is a word for "yes" in the dialect spoken in the territory between the rivers Savena and Reno, which comprise the boundaries of Bologna.

This we climbed easily, and turning right
   along the jagged crest, we left behind
   the eternal circling of those souls in flight.   72

And when we reached the part at which the stone
   was tunneled for the passage of the scourged,
   my Guide said, "Stop a minute and look down   75

on these other misbegotten wraiths of sin.
   You have not seen their faces, for they moved
   in the same direction we were headed in."   78

So from that bridge we looked down on the throng
   that hurried toward us on the other side.
   Here, too, the whiplash hurried them along.   81

And the good Master, studying that train,
   said: "Look there, at that great soul that approaches
   and seems to shed no tears for all his pain—   84

what kingliness moves with him even in Hell!
   It is Jason,[7] who by courage and good advice
   made off with the Colchian Ram. Later it fell   87

that he passed Lemnos, where the women of wrath,
   enraged by Venus' curse that drove their lovers
   out of their arms, put all their males to death.   90

There with his honeyed tongue and his dishonest
   lover's wiles, he gulled Hypsipyle,
   who, in the slaughter, had gulled all the rest.   93

And there he left her, pregnant and forsaken.
   Such guilt condemns him to such punishment;
   and also for Medea is vengeance taken.   96

All seducers march here to the whip.
   And let us say no more about this valley
   and those it closes in its stony grip."   99

We had already come to where the walk
   crosses the second bank, from which it lifts
   another arch, spanning from rock to rock.   102

Here we heard people whine in the next chasm,
   and knock and thump themselves with open palms,
   and blubber through their snouts as if in a spasm.   105

---

7. Jason led the Argonauts on the voyage to the island of Colchis, where they stole the Golden Fleece. He seduced and abandoned Hypsipyle, who had hidden her father when the other women of Lemnos were killing all the males. He also married and later abandoned Medea, the daughter of the king of Colchis. For his story, see Ovid, *Metamorphoses* 7.

Steaming from that pit, a vapour rose
　　over the banks, crusting them with a slime
　　that sickened my eyes and hammered at my nose. 108

That chasm sinks so deep we could not sight
　　its bottom anywhere until we climbed
　　along the rock arch to its greatest height. 111

Once there, I peered down; and I saw long lines
　　of people in a river of excrement
　　that seemed the overflow of the world's latrines. 114

I saw among the felons of that pit
　　one wraith who might or might not have been tonsured—
　　one could not tell, he was so smeared with shit. 117

He bellowed: "You there, why do you stare at me
　　more than at all the others in this stew?"
　　And I to him: "Because if memory 120

serves me, I knew you when your hair was dry.
　　You are Alessio Interminelli da Lucca.[8]
　　That's why I pick you from this filthy fry." 123

And he then, beating himself on his clown's head:
　　"Down to this have the flatteries I sold
　　the living sunk me here among the dead." 126

And my Guide prompted then: "Lean forward a bit
　　and look beyond them, there—do you see that one
　　scratching herself with dungy nails, the strumpet 129

who fidgets to her feet, then to a crouch?
　　It is the whore Thaïs[9] who told her lover
　　when he sent to ask her, 'Do you thank me much?' 132

'Much? Nay, past all believing!' And with this
let us turn away from the sight of this abyss."

Canto XIX

CIRCLE EIGHT: BOLGIA THREE   *The Simoniacs*

Dante comes upon the *Simoniacs* (sellers of ecclesiastic favors and offices) and his
heart overflows with the wrath he feels against those who corrupt the things of
God. This *bolgia* is lined with round tube-like holes and the sinners are placed
in them upside down with the soles of their feet ablaze. The heat of the blaze is
proportioned to their guilt.

---

8. A prominent citizen of Lucca, in northern
Italy.

9. A character in a play by the Roman writer
Terence (ca. 186–ca. 159 B.C.E.).

The holes in which these sinners are placed are debased equivalents of the baptismal fonts common in the cities of Northern Italy and the sinners' confinement in them is temporary: as new sinners arrive, the souls drop through the bottoms of their holes and disappear eternally into the crevices of the rock.

As always, the punishment is a symbolic retribution. Just as the Simoniacs made a mock of holy office, so are they turned upside down in a mockery of the baptismal font. Just as they made a mockery of the holy water of baptism, so is their hellish baptism by fire, after which they are wholly immersed in the crevices below. The oily fire that licks at their soles may also suggest a travesty on the oil used in Extreme Unction (last rites for the dying).

Virgil carries Dante down an almost sheer ledge and lets him speak to one who is the chief sinner of that place, *Pope Nicholas III*. Dante delivers himself of another stirring denunciation of those who have corrupted church office, and Virgil carries him back up the steep ledge toward the *Fourth Bolgia*.

O Simon Magus![1] O you wretched crew
   who follow him, pandering for silver and gold
   the things of God which should be wedded to   3

love and righteousness! O thieves for hire,
   now must the trump of judgment sound your doom[2]
   here in the third fosse of the rim of fire!   6

We had already made our way across
   to the next grave, and to that part of the bridge
   which hangs above the mid-point of the fosse.   9

O Sovereign Wisdom, how Thine art doth shine
   in Heaven, on Earth, and in the Evil World!
   How justly doth Thy power judge and assign!   12

I saw along the walls and on the ground
   long rows of holes cut in the livid stone;
   all were cut to a size, and all were round.   15

They seemed to be exactly the same size
   as those in the font of my beautiful San Giovanni,[3]
   built to protect the priests who come to baptize;   18

(one of which, not so long since, I broke open
   to rescue a boy who was wedged and drowning in it.
   Be this enough to undeceive all men.)   21

---

1. Because in the Bible Simon Magus tried to buy spiritual power from the apostles (Acts 8.9–24), the selling of any spiritual good for material gain was known in the Middle Ages as simony. The most common form of simony was the selling of church offices.
2. Dante is here applauding the artfulness of divine justice because the simoniacs, who cared most for their purses, are here stuffed into fiery "purses" hewn into the rock; see line 69 below.
3. The baptistery in Florence where Dante himself was baptized. The subsequent personal reference has never been satisfactorily explained.

From every mouth a sinner's legs stuck out
   as far as the calf. The soles were all ablaze
   and the joints of the legs quivered and writhed about.   24

Withes and tethers would have snapped in their throes.
   As oiled things blaze upon the surface only,
   so did they burn from the heels to the points of their toes.   27

"Master," I said, "who is that one in the fire
   who writhes and quivers more than all the others?
   From him the ruddy flames seem to leap higher."[4]   30

And he to me: "If you wish me to carry you down
   along that lower bank, you may learn from him
   who he is, and the evil he has done."   33

And I: "What you will, I will. You are my lord
   and I know I depart in nothing from your wish;
   and you know my mind beyond my spoken word."   36

We moved to the fourth ridge, and turning left
   my Guide descended by a jagged path
   into the strait and perforated cleft.   39

Thus the good Master bore me down the dim
   and rocky slope, and did not put me down
   till we reached the one whose legs did penance for him.   42

"Whoever you are, sad spirit," I began,
   "who lie here with your head below your heels
   and planted like a stake—speak if you can."   45

I stood like a friar who gives the sacrament
   to a hired assassin, who, fixed in the hole,
   recalls him, and delays his death a moment.[5]   48

"Are you there already, Boniface? Are you there
   already?" he cried. "By several years the writ
   has lied. And all that gold, and all that care—   51

are you already sated with the treasure
   for which you dared to turn on the Sweet Lady[6]
   and trick and pluck and bleed her at your pleasure?"   54

4. Pope Nicholas III (r. 1277–80). He mistakenly believes that one of his successors, Boniface VIII, has come to be squeezed into the hole (line 49). Like all damned souls, Nicholas has foreknowledge, and because Boniface did not die until 1303 Nicholas is surprised at what he thinks is his appearance in 1300.
5. Hired murderers were occasionally executed by being placed head-down in a ditch and then buried alive.
6. The Church.

I stood like one caught in some raillery,
  not understanding what is said to him,
  lost for an answer to such mockery.   57

Then Virgil said, "Say to him: 'I am not he,
  I am not whom you think.'" And I replied
  as my good Master had instructed me.   60

The sinner's feet jerked madly; then again
  his voice rose, this time choked with sighs and tears,
  and said at last: "What do you want of me then?   63

If to know who I am drives you so fearfully
  that you descend the bank to ask it, know
  that the Great Mantle was once hung upon me.   66

And in truth I was a son of the She-Bear,[7]
  so sly and eager to push my whelps ahead,
  that I pursed wealth above, and myself here.   69

Beneath my head are dragged all who have gone
  before me in buying and selling holy office;
  there they cower in fissures of the stone.   72

I too shall be plunged down when that great cheat
  for whom I took you comes here in his turn.
  Longer already have I baked my feet   75

and been planted upside-down, than he shall be
  before the west sends down a lawless Shepherd[8]
  of uglier deeds to cover him and me.   78

He will be a new Jason[9] of the Maccabees;
  and just as that king bent to his high priests' will,
  so shall the French king do as this one please."   81

Maybe—I cannot say—I grew too brash
  at this point, for when he had finished speaking
  I said: "Indeed! Now tell me how much cash   84

our Lord required of Peter in guarantee
  before he put the keys into his keeping?
  Surely he asked nothing but 'Follow me!'"[1]   87

7. The arms of Nicholas's family (the Orsini) included a "she-bear."
8. Clement V (ca. 1264–1314), who became pope in 1305 after agreeing with the French king to remove the papacy to Avignon in France. He is "from the West" because he was born in western France.

9. Jason became high priest of the Jews by bribing the king: see 2 Maccabees 4.7–9.
1. See Matthew 16.18–19; the keys are the Church's power to bind (condemn) and to loose (absolve). For "follow me," see Matthew 4.18–19.

Nor did Peter, nor the others, ask silver or gold
   of Matthew when they chose him for the place
   the despicable and damned apostle sold.[2]   90

Therefore stay as you are; this hole well fits you—
   and keep a good guard on the ill-won wealth
   that once made you so bold toward Charles of Anjou.[3]   93

And were it not that I am still constrained
   by the reverence I owe to the Great Keys
   you held in life, I should not have refrained   96

from using other words and sharper still;
   for this avarice of yours grieves all the world,
   tramples the virtuous, and exalts the evil.   99

Of such as you was the Evangelist's[4] vision
   when he saw Her who Sits upon the Waters
   locked with the Kings of earth in fornication.   102

She was born with seven heads, and ten enormous
   and shining horns strengthened and made her glad
   as long as love and virtue pleased her spouse.   105

Gold and silver are the gods you adore!
   In what are you different from the idolater,
   save that he worships one, and you a score?   108

Ah Constantine,[5] what evil marked the hour—
   not of your conversion, but of the fee
   the first rich Father took from you in dower!"   111

And as I sang him this tune, he began to twitch
   and kick both feet out wildly, as if in rage
   or gnawed by conscience—little matter which.   114

And I think, indeed, it pleased my Guide: his look
   was all approval as he stood beside me
   intent upon each word of truth I spoke.   117

---

2. Matthias was chosen by lot to fill the place of Judas (Acts 1.23–26).
3. Nicholas was believed to be involved in a plot against Charles of Anjou (1226–1285), ruler of Naples and Sicily.
4. John, author of Revelation, who in the Middle Ages was identified with the author of the Gospel according to John; for this passage, which was originally interpreted as referring to pagan Rome but which Dante applies to the corrupt Church, see Revelation 17.1–18. The "seven heads" are the seven Sacraments; the "ten . . . horns," the Ten Commandments; the "spouse," God.
5. Roman emperor (r. 306–37) who was the supposed author of a document—known as the Donation of Constantine—in which he granted temporal power and the right to acquire wealth to Pope Sylvester I, "the first rich Father" of this passage. The document was proved to be a forgery in the 15th century.

He approached, and with both arms he lifted me,
   and when he had gathered me against his breast,
   remounted the rocky path out of the valley,   120

nor did he tire of holding me clasped to him,
   until we reached the topmost point of the arch
   which crosses from the fourth to the fifth rim   123

of the pits of woe. Arrived upon the bridge,
   he tenderly set down the heavy burden
   he had been pleased to carry up that ledge   126

which would have been hard climbing for a goat.
Here I looked down on still another moat.

Canto XX

       The Fortune Tellers and Diviners

Dante stands in the middle of the bridge over the *Fourth Bolgia* and looks down at the souls of the *Fortune Tellers* and *Diviners*. Here are the souls of all those who attempted by forbidden arts to look into the future. Among these damned are: *Amphiareus, Tiresias, Aruns, Manto, Eurypylus, Michael Scott, Guido Bonatti,* and *Asdente.*

   Characteristically, the sin of these wretches is reversed upon them: their punishment is to have their heads turned backwards on their bodies and to be compelled to walk backwards through all eternity, their eyes blinded with tears. Thus, those who sought to penetrate the future cannot even see in front of themselves; they attempted to move themselves forward in time, so must they go backwards through all eternity; and as the arts of sorcery are a distortion of God's law, so are their bodies distorted in Hell.

   No more need be said of them: Dante names them, and passes on to fill the canto with a lengthy account of the founding of Virgil's native city of Mantua.

Now must I sing new griefs, and my verses strain
   to form the matter of the Twentieth Canto
   of Canticle One, the Canticle of Pain.   3

My vantage point permitted a clear view
   of the depths of the pit below: a desolation
   bathed with the tears of its tormented crew,   6

who moved about the circle of the pit
   at about the pace of a litany procession.[6]
   Silent and weeping, they wound round and round it.   9

And when I looked down from their faces, I saw
   that each of them was hideously distorted
   between the top of the chest and the lines of the jaw;   12

---

6. A "litany" is a form of public prayer, often recited during stately "processions" in the church.

for the face was reversed on the neck, and they came on
    backwards, staring backwards at their lions,
    for to look before them was forbidden. Someone,   15

sometime, in the grip of a palsy may have been
    distorted so, but never to my knowledge;
    nor do I believe the like was ever seen.   18

Reader, so may God grant you to understand
    my poem and profit from it, ask yourself
    how I could check my tears, when near at hand   21

I saw the image of our humanity
    distorted so that the tears that burst from their eyes
    ran down the cleft of their buttocks. Certainly   24

I wept. I leaned against the jagged face
    of a rock and wept so that my Guide said: "Still?
    Still like the other fools? There is no place   27

for pity here. Who is more arrogant
    within his soul, who is more impious
    than one who dares to sorrow at God's judgment?[7]   30

Lift up your eyes, lift up your eyes and see
    him the earth swallowed before all the Thebans,
    at which they cried out: 'Whither do you flee,   33

Amphiareus?[8] Why do you leave the field?'
    And he fell headlong through the gaping earth
    to the feet of Minos, where all sin must yield.   36

Observe how he has made a breast of his back.
    In life he wished to see too far before him,
    and now he must crab backwards round this track.   39

And see Tiresias,[9] who by his arts
    succeeded in changing himself from man to woman,
    transforming all his limbs and all his parts;   42

later he had to strike the two twined serpents
    once again with his conjurer's wand before
    he could resume his manly lineaments.   45

---

7. This is a rebuke to Dante, who errs by showing sympathy for the damned.
8. A priest swallowed up by the Earth in a
battle against the Thebans as described in Statius's *Thebaid* (see note 7 to 14.45). For Minos,
see 5.4.

9. A soothsayer of Thebes, he struck two cou-
pling serpents with his rod and was transformed
into a woman. Seven years later he repeated the
action and was changed back into a man. See
Ovid, *Metamorphoses* 3.

And there is Aruns,[1] his back to that one's belly,
   the same who in the mountains of the Luni
   tilled by the people of Carrara's valley,   48

made a white marble cave his den, and there
   with unobstructed view observed the sea
   and the turning constellations year by year.   51

And she whose unbound hair flows back to hide
   her breasts—which you cannot see—and who also wears
   all of her hairy parts on that other side,   54

was Manto,[2] who searched countries far and near,
   then settled where I was born. In that connection
   there is a story I would have you hear.   57

Tiresias was her sire. After his death,
   Thebes, the city of Bacchus,[3] became enslaved,
   and for many years she roamed about the earth.   60

High in sweet Italy, under the Alps that shut
   the Tyrolean gate of Germany, there lies
   a lake known as Benacus[4] roundabout.   63

Through endless falls, more than a thousand and one,
   Mount Apennine from Garda to Val Camonica,[5]
   is freshened by the waters that flow down   66

into that lake. At its center is a place
   where the Bishops of Brescia, Trentine, and Verona
   might all give benediction with equal grace.   69

Peschiera,[6] the beautiful fortress, strong in war
   against the Brescians and the Bergamese,
   sits at the lowest point along that shore.   72

There, the waters Benacus cannot hold
   within its bosom, spill and form a river
   that winds away through pastures green and gold.   75

1. An Etruscan soothsayer from the city of Luni, in the area of Carrara where marble is quarried, is described by the Roman poet Lucan (39–65 C.E.) in his *Pharsalia*.
2. Another Theban soothsayer described by Roman poets.
3. Bacchus (Dionysus) was the son of Jupiter and a mortal woman, Semele, daughter of the king of Thebes.
4. The present-day Lake Garda in northern Italy, located in terms of an island where the boundaries of the three dioceses of Trent, Brescia, and Verona meet.
5. Garda is a town by the lake and Val Camonica a valley below it.
6. Peschiera is a town on the south shore of the lake; the Brescians and the Bergamese are inhabitants of two towns to the northwest of Peschiera.

But once the water gathers its full flow,
  it is called Mincius rather than Benacus
  from there to Governo,[7] where it joins the Po.   78

Still near its source, it strikes a plain, and there
  it slows and spreads, forming an ancient marsh
  which in the summer heat pollutes the air.   81

The terrible virgin, passing there by chance,
  saw dry land at the center of the mire,
  untilled, devoid of all inhabitants.   84

There, shunning all communion with mankind,
  she settled with the ministers of her arts,
  and there she lived, and there she left behind   87

her vacant corpse. Later the scattered men
  who lived nearby assembled on that spot
  since it was well defended by the fen.   90

Over those whited bones they raised the city,
  and for her who had chosen the place before all others
  they named it—with no further augury—   93

Mantua.[8] Far more people lived there once—
  before sheer madness prompted Casalodi
  to let Pinamonte play him for a dunce.[9]   96

Therefore, I charge you, should you ever hear
  other accounts of this, to let no falsehood
  confuse the truth which I have just made clear."[1]   99

And I to him: "Master, within my soul
  your word is certainty, and any other
  would seem like the dead lumps of burned out coal.   102

But tell me of those people moving down
  to join the rest. Are any worth my noting?
  For my mind keeps coming back to that alone."   105

And he: "That one whose beard spreads like a fleece
  over his swarthy shoulders, was an augur
  in the days when so few males remained in Greece   108

7. A town some 30 miles south of Peschiera. Presumably Virgil provides this detailed geography to illustrate that he is a native of this region.
8. Virgil's native city.
9. A reference to the internal intrigues of the rulers of Mantua in the 13th century.

1. Dante's Virgil contradicts the account of Mantua's founding in *Aeneid* 10.198–200. It is not clear why Dante has Virgil contradict his own poem unless he is trying to clear Virgil of any taint of himself being a magician (see note 9 to 9.20).

that even the cradles were all but empty of sons.
　He chose the time for cutting the cable at Aulis,
　and Calchas[2] joined him in those divinations.　　　　　　111

He is Eurypylus. I sing him somewhere
　in my High Tragedy; you will know the place
　who know the whole of it. The other there,　　　　　　114

the one beside him with the skinny shanks
　was Michael Scott,[3] who mastered every trick
　of magic fraud, a prince of mountebanks.　　　　　　117

See Guido Bonatti there; and see Asdente,[4]
　who now would be wishing he had stuck to his last,
　but repents too late, though he repents aplenty.　　　　　　120

And see on every hand the wretched hags[5]
　who left their spinning and sewing for soothsaying
　and casting of spells with herbs, and dolls, and rags.　　　　　　123

But come: Cain[6] with his bush of thorns appears
　already on the wave below Seville,
　above the boundary of the hemispheres;　　　　　　126

and the moon was full already yesternight,
　as you must well remember from the wood,
　for it certainly did not harm you when its light　　　　　　129

shone down upon your way before the dawn."
And as he spoke to me, we traveled on.

Canto XXI

CIRCLE EIGHT: BOLGIA FIVE　　　　　　　　　　　　*The Grafters*

The Poets move on, talking as they go, and arrive at the *Fifth Bolgia*. Here the *Grafters* are sunk in boiling pitch and guarded by *Demons*, who tear them to pieces with claws and grappling hooks if they catch them above the surface of the pitch.

　　The sticky pitch is symbolic of the sticky fingers of the Grafters. It serves also to hide them from sight, as their sinful dealings on earth were hidden from

2. Calchas and Eurypylus were prophets (or augurs) involved in the Trojan War; here Virgil says that they determined when the Greeks were to set out for the war from the island of Aulis, although *Aeneid* 2 gives a different account.
3. A famous scientist, philosopher, and astrologer from Scotland, Scott spent many years at the court of Frederick II (10.119) in Palermo and died in 1235.
4. A shoemaker famous as a soothsayer in

13th-century Italy. "Guido Bonatti": an astrologer at the court of Guido da Montefeltro (see canto 27).
5. Common soothsayers and potion makers.
6. Popular belief held that God placed Cain in the moon after the murder of Abel; "Cain with his bush of thorns" means the moon with its spots, which is now setting at the western edge of the Northern Hemisphere. Overhead, in Jerusalem, it is the dawn of Holy Saturday.

men's eyes. The demons, too, suggest symbolic possibilities, for they are armed with grappling hooks and are forever ready to rend and tear all they can get their hands on.

The Poets watch a demon arrive with a grafting *Senator of Lucca* and fling him into the pitch where the demons set upon him.

To protect Dante from their wrath, Virgil hides him behind some jagged rocks and goes ahead alone to negotiate with the demons. They set upon him like a pack of mastiffs, but Virgil secures safe conduct from their leader, *Malacoda*. Thereupon Virgil calls Dante from hiding, and they are about to set off when they discover that the *Bridge across the Sixth Bolgia* lies shattered. Malacoda tells them there is another further on and sends a squad of demons to escort them. Their adventures with the demons continue through the next canto.

These two cantos may conveniently be remembered as the *Gargoyle Cantos*. If the total *Commedia* is built like a cathedral (as so many critics have suggested), it is here certainly that Dante attaches his grotesqueries. At no other point in the *Commedia* does Dante give such free rein to his coarsest style.

Thus talking of things which my Comedy does not care
   to sing, we passed from one arch to the next
   until we stood upon its summit. There   3

we checked our steps to study the next fosse
   and the next vain lamentations of Malebolge;
   awesomely dark and desolate it was.   6

As in the Venetian arsenal,[7] the winter through
   there boils the sticky pitch to caulk the seams
   of the sea-battered bottoms when no crew   9

can put to sea—instead of which, one starts
   to build its ship anew, one plugs the planks
   which have been sprung in many foreign parts;   12

some hammer at a mast, some at a rib;
   some make new oars, some braid and coil new lines;
   one patches up the mainsail, one the jib—   15

so, but by Art Divine and not by fire,
   a viscid pitch boiled in the fosse below
   and coated all the bank with gluey mire.   18

I saw the pitch; but I saw nothing in it
   except the enormous bubbles of its boiling,
   which swelled and sank, like breathing, through all the pit.   21

And as I stood and stared into that sink,
   my Master cried, "Take care!" and drew me back
   from my exposed position on the brink.   24

7. The huge shipyard at Venice was called the Arsenal.

I turned like one who cannot wait to see
    the thing he dreads, and who, in sudden fright,
    runs while he looks, his curiosity   27

competing with his terror—and at my back
    I saw a figure that came running toward us
    across the ridge, a Demon huge and black.   30

Ah what a face he had, all hate and wildness!
    Galloping so, with his great wings outspread
    he seemed the embodiment of all bitterness.   33

Across each high-hunched shoulder he had thrown
    one haunch of a sinner, whom he held in place
    with a great talon round each ankle bone.   36

"Blacktalons of our bridge," he began to roar,
    "I bring you one of Santa Zita's Elders![8]
    Scrub him down while I go back for more: 39

I planted a harvest of them in that city:
    everyone there is a grafter except Bonturo.[9]
    There 'Yes' is 'No' and 'No' is 'Yes' for a fee."   42

Down the sinner plunged, and at once the Demon
    spun from the cliff; no mastiff ever sprang
    more eager from the leash to chase a felon.   45

Down plunged the sinner and sank to reappear
    with his backside arched and his face and both his feet
    glued to the pitch, almost as if in prayer.   48

But the Demons under the bridge, who guard that place
    and the sinners who are thrown to them, bawled out:
    "You're out of bounds here for the Sacred Face: 51

this is no dip in the Serchio:[1] take your look
    and then get down in the pitch. And stay below
    unless you want a taste of a grappling hook."   54

Then they raked him with more than a hundred hooks
    bellowing: "Here you dance below the covers.
    Graft all you can there: no one checks your books."   57

---

8. "Blacktalons" (*Malebranche*: in Italian—
"evil claws") is the generic name for the devils
in this ditch; each has a proper name as well
(lines 79, 107, 118–22). The elders of Santa
Zita in Lucca (a town near Florence) were ten
citizens who ran the government.

9. A current official in Lucca, Bonturo Datí
was in fact known as the most corrupt of all;
the devil is being ironic.
1. A river near Lucca. The Sacred Face of
Lucca was a venerated icon.

They dipped him down into that pitch exactly
    as a chef makes scullery boys dip meat in a boiler,
    holding it with their hooks from floating free.   60

And the Master said: "*You* had best not be seen
    by these Fiends till I am ready. Crouch down here.
    One of these rocks will serve you as a screen.   63

And whatever violence you see done to me,
    you have no cause to fear. I know these matters:
    I have been though this once and come back safely."[2]   66

With that, he walked on past the end of the bridge;
    and it wanted all his courage to look calm
    from the moment he arrived on the sixth ridge.   69

With that same storm and fury that arouses
    all the house when the hounds leap at a tramp
    who suddenly falls to pleading where he pauses—   72

so rushed those Fiends from below, and all the pack
    pointed their gleaming pitchforks at my Guide.
    But he stood fast and cried to them: "Stand back!   75

Before those hooks and grapples make too free,
    send up one of your crew to hear me out,
    then ask yourselves if you still care to rip me."   78

All cried as one: "Let Malacoda[3] go."
    So the pack stood and one of them came forward,
    saying: "What good does he think *this* will do?"   81

"Do you think, Malacoda," my good Master said,
    "you would see me here, having arrived this far
    already, safe from you and every dread,   84

without Divine Will and propitious Fate?
    Let me pass on, for it is willed in Heaven
    that I must show another this dread state."   87

The Demon stood there on the flinty brim,
    so taken aback he let his pitchfork drop;
    then said to the others: "Take care not to harm him!"   90

"O you crouched like a cat," my Guide called to me,
    "among the jagged rock piles of the bridge,
    come down to me, for now you may come safely."   93

---

2. Virgil may be referring to his difficulties with the devils in 8.82–128, when he and Dante tried to enter the city of Dis. **3.** "Evil-Tail."

Hearing him, I hurried down the ledge;
   and the Demons all pressed forward when I appeared,
   so that I feared they might not keep their pledge.   96

So once I saw the Pisan infantry
   march out under truce from the fortress at Caprona,
   staring in fright at the ranks of the enemy.[4]   99

I pressed the whole of my body against my Guide,
   and not for an instant did I take my eyes
   from those black fiends who scowled on every side.   102

They swung their forks saying to one another:
   "Shall I give him a touch in the rump?" and answering:
   "Sure, give him a taste to pay him for his bother."   105

But the Demon who was talking to my Guide
   turned round and cried to him: "At ease there, Snatcher!"
   And then to us: "There's no road on this side: 108

the arch lies all in pieces in the pit.[5]
   If you *must* go on, follow along this ridge;
   there's another cliff to cross by just beyond it.[6]   111

In just five hours it will be, since the bridge fell,
   a thousand two hundred sixty-six years and a day;
   that was the time the big quake shook all Hell.[7]   114

I'll send a squad of my boys along that way
   to see if anyone's airing himself below:
   you can go with them: there will be no foul play.   117

Front and center here, Grizzly and Hellken,"
   he began to order them. "You too, Deaddog.
   Curlybeard, take charge of a squad of ten.   120

Take Grafter and Dragontooth along with you.
   Pigtusk, Catclaw, Cramper, and Crazyred.
   Keep a sharp lookout on the boiling glue   123

as you move along, and see that these gentlemen
   are not molested until they reach the crag
   where they can find a way across the den."   126

---

4. A battle outside Florence in 1289, in which Dante may have taken part.
5. The bridge across the fifth ditch was smashed, as Malacoda explains, by the earthquake that occurred at the time of the crucifixion.
6. As the travelers discover, this is a lie.

7. According to medieval tradition, Christ's death on the cross occurred on Good Friday at noon, in his thirty-third year, which would be 34 c.e.; the time at which Dante and Virgil are in this fifth ditch of Malebolge is 7:00 a.m. of Holy Saturday, 1300, which is 1266 years plus one day, less five hours later.

"In the name of heaven, Master," I cried, "what sort
   of guides are these? Let us go on alone
   if you know the way. Who can trust such an escort!   129

If you are as wary as you used to be
   you surely see them grind their teeth at us,
   and knot their beetle brows so threateningly."   132

And he: "I do not like this fear in you.
   Let them gnash and knot as they please; they menace only
   the sticky wretches simmering in that stew."   135

They turned along the left bank in a line;
   but not before they had formed a single rank
   and stuck their pointed tongues out as a sign   138

to their Captain that they wished permission to pass;
and he had made a trumpet of his ass.

Canto XXII

CIRCLE EIGHT: BOLGIA FIVE   *The Grafters*

The poets set off with their escorts of demons. Dante sees the *Grafters* lying in
the pitch like frogs in water with only their muzzles out. They disappear as
soon as they sight the demons and only a ripple on the surface betrays their
presence.

   One of the Grafters, *An Unidentified Navarrese*, ducks too late and is seized by
the demons who are about to claw him, but *Curlybeard* holds them back while
Virgil questions him. The wretch speaks of his fellow sinners, *Friar Gomita* and
Michel Zanche, while the uncontrollable demons rake him from time to time with
their hooks.

   The Navarrese offers to lure some of his fellow sufferers into the hands of the
demons, and when his plan is accepted he plunges into the pitch and escapes.
Hellken and *Grizzly* fly after him, but too late. They start a brawl in mid-air and
fall into the pitch themselves. Curlybeard immediately organizes a rescue party
and the Poets, fearing the bad temper of the frustrated demons, take advantage of
the confusion to slip away.

I have seen horsemen breaking camp. I have seen
   the beginning of the assault, the march and muster,
   and at times the retreat and riot. I have been   3

where chargers trampled your land, O Aretines![8]
   I have seen columns of foragers, shocks of tourney,
   and running of tilts. I have seen the endless lines   6

march to bells, drums, trumpets, from far and near.
   I have seen them march on signals from a castle.
   I have seen them march with native and foreign gear.   9

8. The people of Arezzo, a city south of Florence.

But never yet have I seen horse or foot,
    nor ship in range of land nor sight of star,
    take its direction from so low a toot.   12

We went with the ten Fiends—ah, savage crew!—
    but "In church with saints; with stewpots in the tavern,"[9]
    as the old proverb wisely bids us do.   15

All my attention was fixed upon the pitch:
    to observe the people who were boiling in it,
    and the customs and the punishments of that ditch.   18

As dolphins surface and begin to flip
    their arched backs from the sea, warning the sailors
    to fall to and begin to secure ship—[1]   21

So now and then, some soul, to ease his pain,
    showed us a glimpse of his back above the pitch
    and quick as lightning disappeared again.   24

And as, at the edge of a ditch, frogs squat about
    hiding their feet and bodies in the water,
    leaving only their muzzles sticking out—   27

so stood the sinners in that dismal ditch;
    but as Curlybeard approached, only a ripple
    showed where they had ducked back into the pitch.   30

I saw—the dread of it haunts me to this day—
    one linger a bit too long, as it sometimes happens
    one frog remains when another spurts away;   33

and Catclaw, who was nearest, ran a hook
    through the sinner's pitchy hair and hauled him in.
    He looked like an otter dripping from the brook.   36

I knew the names of all the Fiends by then;
    I had made a note of them at the first muster,
    and, marching, had listened and checked them over again.   39

"Hey, Crazyred," the crew of Demons cried
    all together, "give him a taste of your claws.
    Dig him open a little. Off with his hide."   42

And I then: "Master, can you find out, please,
    the name and history of that luckless one
    who has fallen into the hands of his enemies?"   45

9. A popular proverb.
1. It was a common medieval belief that dolphins warned sailors of approaching storms.

My Guide approached that wraith from the hot tar
   and asked him whence he came. The wretch replied:
   "I was born and raised in the Kingdom of Navarre.[2]   48

My mother placed me in service to a knight;
   for she had borne me to a squanderer
   who killed himself when he ran through his birthright.   51

Then I became a domestic in the service
   of good King Thibault. There I began to graft,
   and I account for it in this hot crevice."   54

And Pigtusk, who at the ends of his lower lip
   shot forth two teeth more terrible than a boar's,
   made the wretch feel how one of them could rip.   57

The mouse had come among bad cats, but here
   Curlybeard locked arms around him crying:
   "While I've got hold of him the rest stand clear!"   60

And turning his face to my Guide: "If you want to ask him
   anything else," he added, "ask away
   before the others tear him limb from limb."   63

And my Guide to the sinner: "I should like to know
   if among the other souls beneath the pitch
   are any Italians?" And the wretch: "Just now   66

I left a shade who came from parts nearby.
   Would I were still in the pitch with him, for then
   these hooks would not be giving me cause to cry."   69

And suddenly Grafter bellowed in great heat:
   "We've stood enough!" And he hooked the sinner's arm
   and, raking it, ripped off a chunk of meat.   72

Then Dragontooth wanted to play, too, reaching down
   for a catch at the sinner's legs; but Curlybeard
   wheeled round and round with a terrifying frown,   75

and when the Fiends had somewhat given ground
   and calmed a little, my Guide, without delay,
   asked the wretch, who was staring at his wound: 78

"Who was the sinner from whom you say you made
   your evil-starred departure to come ashore
   among these Fiends?" And the wretch: "It was the shade   81

---

2. The identity of this sinner is not known, but he was employed in the household of Thibault II of Champagne, a man renowned for his hon- esty who was also king of Navarre, the area of Spain that is now Basque country.

of Friar Gomita of Gallura,[3] the crooked stem
  of every Fraud: when his master's enemies
  were in his hands, he won high praise from them.   84

He took their money without case or docket,
  and let them go. He was in all his dealings
  no petty bursar, but a kingly pocket.   87

With him, his endless crony in the fosse,
  is Don Michel Zanche of Logodoro;[4]
  they babble about Sardinia without pause.   90

But look! See that fiend grinning at your side!
  There is much more that I should like to tell you,
  but oh, I think he means to grate my hide!"   93

But their grim sergeant wheeled, sensing foul play,
  and turning on Cramper, who seemed set to strike,
  ordered: "Clear off, you buzzard. Clear off, I say!"   96

"If either of you would like to see and hear
  Tuscans or Lombards," the pale sinner said,
  "I can lure them out of hiding if you'll stand clear   99

and let me sit here at the edge of the ditch,
  and get all these Blacktalons out of sight;
  for while they're here, no one will leave the pitch.   102

In exchange for myself, I can fish you up as pretty
  a mess of souls as you like. I have only to whistle
  the way we do when one of us gets free."   105

Deaddog raised his snout as he listened to him;
  then, shaking his head, said, "Listen to the grafter
  spinning his tricks so he can jump from the brim!"   111

And the sticky wretch, who was all treachery:
  "Oh I am more than tricky when there's a chance
  to see my friends in greater misery."   114

Hellken, against the will of all the crew,
  could hold no longer. "If you jump," he said
  to the scheming wretch, "I won't come after you   117

at a gallop, but like a hawk after a mouse.
  We'll clear the edge and hide behind the bank:
  let's see if you're trickster enough for all of us."   120

3. A friar who was chancellor of the Gallura district on the island of Sardinia. He was hanged by his master, a lord of Pisa, when it was discovered that he had sold prisoners their freedom. 4. Little is known of this sinner, except that he too was a Sardinian.

Reader, here is new game! The Fiends withdrew
   from the bank's edge, and Deaddog, who at first
   was most against it, led the savage crew.   123

The Navarrese chose his moment carefully:
   and planting both his feet against the ground,
   he leaped, and in an instant he was free.   126

The Fiends were stung with shame, and of the lot
   Hellken most, who had been the cause of it.
   He leaped out madly bellowing: "You're caught!"   129

but little good it did him; terror pressed
   harder than wings; the sinner dove from sight
   and the fiend in full flight had to raise his breast.   132

A duck, when the falcon dives, will disappear
   exactly so, all in a flash, while he
   returns defeated and weary up the air.   135

Grizzly, in a rage at the sinner's flight,
   flew after Hellken, hoping the wraith would escape,
   so he might find an excuse to start a fight.   138

And as soon as the grafter sank below the pitch,
   Grizzly turned his talons against Hellken,
   locked with him claw to claw above the ditch.   141

But Hellken was sparrowhawk enough for two
   and clawed him well; and ripping one another,
   they plunged together into the hot stew.   144

The heat broke up the brawl immediately,
   but their wings were smeared with pitch and they could not rise.
   Curlybeard, upset as his company,   147

commanded four to fly to the other coast
   at once with all their grapples. At top speed
   the Fiends divided, each one to his post.   150

Some on the near edge, some along the far,
   they stretched their hooks out to the clotted pair
   who were already cooked deep through the scar   153

of their first burn. And turning to one side
we slipped off, leaving them thus occupied.

Canto XXIII

The Hypocrites

The Poets are pursued by the Fiends and escape them by sliding down the sloping bank of the next pit. They are now in the *Sixth Bolgia*. Here the *Hyprocrites*, weighted down by great leaden robes, walk eternally round and round a narrow track. The robes are brilliantly gilded on the outside and are shaped like a monk's habit, for the hypocrite's outward appearance shines brightly and passes for holiness, but under that show lies the terrible weight of his deceit which the soul must bear through all eternity.

The Poets talk to *Two Jovial Friars* and come upon *Caiaphas*, the chief sinner of that place. Caiaphas was the High Priest of the Jews who counseled the Pharisees to crucify Jesus in the name of public expedience. He is punished by being himself crucified to the floor of Hell by three great stakes, and in such a position that every passing sinner must walk upon him. Thus he must suffer upon his own body the weight of all the world's hypocrisy, as Christ suffered upon his body the pain of all the world's sins.

The Jovial Friars tell Virgil how he may climb from the pit, and Virgil discovers that Malacoda lied to him about the bridges over the Sixth Bolgia.

Silent, apart, and unattended we went
  as Minor Friars[5] go when they walk abroad,
  one following the other. The incident   3

recalled the fable of the Mouse and the Frog
  that Aesop tells.[6] For compared attentively
  point by point, "pig" is no closer to "hog"   6

than the one case to the other. And as one thought
  springs from another, so the comparison
  gave birth to a new concern, at which I caught   9

my breath in fear. This thought ran through my mind:
  "These Fiends, through us, have been made ridiculous,
  and have suffered insult and injury of a kind   12

to make them smart. Unless we take good care—
  now rage is added to their natural spleen—
  they will hunt us down as greyhounds hunt the hare."   15

Already I felt my scalp grow tight with fear.
  I was staring back in terror as I said:
  "Master, unless we find concealment here   18

5. Franciscan friars, who were known as "minor" or "lesser" friars because Francis of Assisi, the founder of the order, insisted upon humility.
6. The fable that Dante seems to be referring to tells how a frog offers to ferry a mouse across a river, then halfway over tries to drown him, only to be seized by a kite (a hawklike bird of prey) while the mouse escapes.

and soon, I dread the rage of the Fiends: already
   they are yelping on our trail: I imagine them
   so vividly I can hear them now." And he: 21

"Were I a pane of leaded glass, I could not
   summon your outward look more instantly
   into myself, than I do your inner thought.   24

Your fears were mixed already with my own
   with the same suggestion and the same dark look;
   so that of both I form one resolution: 27

the right bank may be sloping: in that case
   we may find some way down to the next pit
   and so escape from the imagined chase."   30

He had not finished answering me thus
   when, not far off, their giant wings outspread,
   I saw the Fiends come charging after us.   33

Seizing me instantly in his arms, my Guide—
   like a mother wakened by a midnight noise
   to find a wall of flame at her bedside   36

(who takes her child and runs, and more concerned
   for him than for herself, does not pause even
   to throw a wrap about her) raised me, turned,   39

and down the rugged bank from the high summit
   flung himself down supine onto the slope
   which walls the upper side of the next pit.   42

Water that turns the great wheel of a land-mill
   never ran faster through the end of a sluice
   at the point nearest the paddles—as down that hill   45

my Guide and Master bore me on his breast,
   as if I were not a companion, but a son.
   And the soles of his feet had hardly come to rest   48

on the bed of the depth below, when on the height
   we had just left, the Fiends beat their great wings.
   But now they gave my Guide no cause for fright;   51

for the Providence that gave them the fifth pit
   to govern as the ministers of Its will,
   takes from their souls the power of leaving it.   54

About us now in the depth of the pit we found
   a painted people, weary and defeated.
   Slowly, in pain, they paced it round and round.   57

All wore great cloaks cut to as ample a size
    as those worn by the Benedictines of Cluny.[7]
    The enormous hoods were drawn over their eyes.   60

The outside is all dazzle, golden and fair;
    the inside, lead, so heavy that Frederick's capes,
    compared to these, would seem as light as air.[8]   63

O weary mantle for eternity!
    We turned to the left again along their course,
    listening to their moans of misery,   66

but they moved so slowly down that barren strip,
    tired by their burden, that our company
    was changed at every movement of the hip.   69

And walking thus, I said: "As we go on,
    may it please you to look about among these people
    for any whose name or history may be known."   72

And one who understood Tuscan cried to us there
    as we hurried past: "I pray you check your speed,
    you who run so fast through the sick air: 75

it may be I am one who will fit your case."
    And at his words my Master turned and said:
    "Wait now, then go with him at his own pace."   78

I waited there, and saw along that track
    two souls who seemed in haste to be with me;
    but the narrow way and their burden held them back.   81

When they had reached me down that narrow way
    they stared at me in silence and amazement,
    then turned to one another, I heard one say: 84

"This one seems, by the motion of his throat,
    to be alive; and if they are dead, how is it
    they are allowed to shed the leaden coat?"   87

And then to me "O Tuscan, come so far
    to the college of the sorry hypocrites,
    do not disdain to tell us who you are."   90

And I: "I was born and raised a Florentine
    on the green and lovely banks of Arno's waters,
    I go with the body that was always mine.   93

---

7. One of the largest monasteries in Europe, located in Burgundy in France; the Benedictines are monks who follow the Rule of St. Benedict (d. 587), one of the founders of monasticism.

8. Frederick II (see note 7 to 10.119) was reported to have punished traitors by encasing them in lead and throwing them into heated cauldrons.

But who are *you*, who sighing as you go
   distill in floods of tears that drown your cheeks?
   What punishment is this that glitters so?"   96

"These burnished robes are of thick lead," said one,
   "and are hung on us like counterweights, so heavy
   that we, their weary fulcrums, creak and groan.   99

Jovial Friars and Bolognese were we.
   We were chosen jointly by your Florentines
   to keep the peace, an office usually   102

held by a single man; near the Gardingo[9]
   one still may see the sort of peace we kept.
   I was called Catalano, he, Loderingo."   105

I began: "O Friars, your evil . . ."—and then I saw
   a figure crucified upon the ground
   by three great stakes, and I fell still in awe.[1]   108

When he saw me there, he began to puff great sighs
   into his beard, convulsing all his body;
   and Friar Catalano, following my eyes,   111

said to me: "That one nailed across the road
   counselled the Pharisees that it was fitting
   one man be tortured for the public good.   114

Naked he lies fixed there, as you see,
   in the path of all who pass; there he must feel
   the weight of all through all eternity.   117

His father-in-law[2] and the others of the Council
   which was a seed of wrath to all the Jews,
   are similarly staked for the same evil."   120

Then I saw Virgil marvel for a while
   over that soul so ignominiously
   stretched on the cross in Hell's eternal exile.   123

Then, turning, he asked the Friar: "If your law permit,
   can you tell us if somewhere along the right
   there is some gap in the stone wall of the pit   126

9. A district in Florence that was destroyed by a civil war incited by their meddling in Florentine affairs. "Jovial Friars": a military and religious order in Bologna called the Knights of the Blessed Virgin Mary, or popularly the "Jovial Friars" because of the laxity of the order's rules. The members were meant to fight only in order to protect the weak and enforce peace. Cata-lano and Loderingo were two citizens of Bologna who were involved in founding the Jovial Friars in 1261.
1. This is Caiaphas, the Jewish high priest under Pontius Pilate who advised that Christ be crucified (John 11.47–52).
2. Annas: see John 18.13.

through which we two may climb to the next brink
  without the need of summoning the Black Angels
  and forcing them to raise us from this sink?" 129

He: "Nearer than you hope, there is a bridge
  that runs from the great circle of the scarp
  and crosses every ditch from ridge to ridge, 132

except that in this it is broken; but with care
  you can mount the ruins which lie along the slope
  and make a heap on the bottom." My Guide stood there 135

motionless for a while with a dark look.
  At last he said: "He lied about this business,
  who spears the sinners yonder with his hook."[3] 138

And the Friar: "Once at Bologna I heard the wise
  discussing the Devil's sins; among them I heard
  that he is a liar and the father of lies."[4] 141

When the sinner had finished speaking, I saw the face
  of my sweet Master darken a bit with anger:
  he set off at a great stride from that place, 144

and I turned from that weighted hypocrite
to follow in the prints of his dear feet.

Canto XXIV

CIRCLE EIGHT: BOLGIA SEVEN   *The Thieves*

The Poets climb the right bank laboriously, cross the bridge of the *Seventh Bolgia*
and descend the far bank to observe the Thieves. They find the pit full of monstrous reptiles who curl themselves about the sinners like living coils of rope,
binding each sinner's hands behind his back, and knotting themselves through the
loins. Other reptiles dart about the place, and the Poets see one of them fly through
the air and pierce the jugular vein of one sinner who immediately bursts into flames
until only ashes remain. From the ashes the sinner reforms painfully.

   These are Dante's first observations of the Thieves and will be carried further
in the next canto, but the first allegorical retribution is immediately apparent.
Thievery is reptilian in its secrecy; therefore it is punished by reptiles. The
hands of the thieves are the agents of their crimes; therefore they are bound
forever. And as the thief destroys his fellowmen by making their substance disappear, so is he painfully destroyed and made to disappear, not once but over
and over again.

   The sinner who has risen from his own ashes reluctantly identifies himself as
Vanni Fucci. He tells his story, and to revenge himself for having been forced to
reveal his identity he utters a dark prophecy against Dante.

---

3. See 21.111.
4. For this description of the devil, see John 8.44.

In the turning season of the youthful year,
   when the sun is warming his rays beneath Aquarius[5]
   and the days and nights already begin to near   3

their perfect balance; the hoar-frost copies then
   the image of his white sister on the ground,[6]
   but the first sun wipes away the work of his pen.   6

The peasants who lack fodder then arise
   and look about and see the fields all white,
   and hear their lambs bleat; then they smite their thighs,   9

go back into the house, walk here and there,
   pacing, fretting, wondering what to do,
   then come out doors again, and there, despair   12

falls from them when they see how the earth's face
   has changed in so little time, and they take their staffs
   and drive their lambs to feed—so in that place   15

when I saw my Guide and Master's eyebrows lower,
   my spirits fell and I was sorely vexed;
   and as quickly came the plaster to the sore: 18

for when he had reached the ruined bridge, he stood
   and turned on me that sweet and open look
   with which he had greeted me in the dark wood.   21

When he had paused and studied carefully
   the heap of stones, he seemed to reach some plan,
   for he turned and opened his arms and lifted me.   24

Like one who works and calculates ahead,
   and is always ready for what happens next—
   so, raising me above that dismal bed   27

to the top of one great slab of the fallen slate,
   he chose another saying: "Climb here, but first
   test it to see if it will hold your weight."   30

It was no climb for a lead-hung hypocrite:
   for scarcely we—he light and I assisted—
   could crawl handhold by handhold from the pit;   33

and were it not that the bank along this side
   was lower than the one down which we had slid,[7]
   I at least—I will not speak for my Guide—   36

5. January 21–February 21.
6. I.e., snow.
7. Because the whole of the eighth circle is tilted downward, the downside wall of each ditch is lower than that on the upside.

would have turned back. But as all of the vast rim
   of Malebolge leans toward the lowest well,
   so each succeeding valley and each brim   39

is lower than the last. We climbed the face
   and arrived by great exertion to the point
   where the last rock had fallen from its place.   42

My lungs were pumping as if they could not stop;
   I thought I could not go on, and I sat exhausted
   the instant I had clambered to the top.   45

"Up on your feet! This is no time to tire!"
   my Master cried. "The man who lies asleep
   will never waken fame, and his desire   48

and all his life drift past him like a dream,
   and the traces of his memory fade from time
   like smoke in air, or ripples on a stream.   51

Now, therefore, rise. Control your breath, and call
   upon the strength of soul that wins all battles
   unless it sink in the gross body's fall.   54

There is a longer ladder yet to climb:[8]
   this much is not enough. If you understand me,
   show that you mean to profit from your time."   57

I rose and made my breath appear more steady
   than it really was, and I replied: "Lead on
   as it pleases you to go: I am strong and ready."   60

We picked our way up the cliff, a painful climb,
   for it was narrower, steeper, and more jagged
   than any we had crossed up to that time.   63

I moved along, talking to hide my faintness,
   when a voice that seemed unable to form words
   rose from the depths of the next chasm's darkness.   66

I do not know what it said, though by then the Sage
   had led me to the top of the next arch;
   but the speaker seemed in a tremendous rage.   69

I was bending over the brim, but living eyes
   could not plumb to the bottom of that dark;
   therefore I said, "Master, let me advise   72

---

8. Both the climb from the pit of Hell back to Earth and then the climb up Mount Purgatory.

that we cross over and climb down the wall:[9]
    for just as I hear the voice without understanding,
    so I look down and make out nothing at all."   75

"I make no other answer than the act,"
    the Master said: "the only fit reply
    to a fit request is silence and the fact."   78

So we moved down the bridge to the stone pier
    that shores the end of the arch on the eighth bank,
    and there I saw the chasm's depths made clear;[1]   81

and there great coils of serpents met my sight,
    so hideous a mass that even now
    the memory makes my blood run cold with fright.[2]   84

Let Libya boast no longer, for though its sands
    breed chelidrids, jaculi, and phareans,
    cenchriads, and two-headed amphisbands,   87

it never bred such a variety
    of vipers, no, not with all Ethiopia
    and all the lands that lie by the Red Sea.   90

Amid that swarm, naked and without hope,
    people ran terrified, not even dreaming
    of a hole to hide in, or of heliotrope.[3]   93

Their hands were bound behind by coils of serpents
    which thrust their heads and tails between the loins
    and bunched in front, a mass of knotted torments.   96

One of the damned came racing round a boulder,
    and as he passed us, a great snake shot up
    and bit him where the neck joins with the shoulder.   99

No mortal pen—however fast it flash
    over the page—could write down *o* or *i*
    as quickly as he flamed and fell in ash;   102

and when he was dissolved into a heap
    upon the ground, the dust rose of itself
    and immediately resumed its former shape.   105

9. Into the seventh ditch.
1. They cross the bridge over the seventh ditch and then climb down the wall between the seventh and eighth ditches.
2. The following list of exotic serpents derives from a description by the Roman poet Lucan (39–65 C.E.) of the plagues of Libya.
3. I.e., bloodstone, a mineral that was believed to make the bearer invisible.

Precisely so, philosophers declare,
   the Phoenix dies and then is born again
   when it approaches its five hundredth year.[4]   108

It lives on tears of balsam and of incense;
   in all its life it eats no herb or grain,
   and nard and precious myrrh sweeten its cerements.   111

And as a person fallen in a fit,
   possessed by a Demon or some other seizure
   that fetters him without his knowing it,   114

struggles up to his feet and blinks his eyes
   (still stupefied by the great agony
   he has just passed), and, looking round him, sighs—   117

such was the sinner when at last he rose.
   O Power of God! How dreadful is Thy will
   which in its vengeance rains such fearful blows.   120

Then my Guide asked him who he was. And he
   answered reluctantly: "Not long ago
   I rained into this gullet from Tuscany.   123

I am Vanni Fucci, the beast.[5] A mule among men,
   I chose the bestial life above the human.
   Savage Pistoia was my fitting den."   126

And I to my Guide: "Detain him a bit longer
   and ask what crime it was that sent him here;
   I knew him as a man of blood and anger."   129

The sinner, hearing me, seemed discomforted,
   but he turned and fixed his eyes upon my face
   with a look of dismal shame; at length he said: 132

"That you have found me out among the strife
   and misery of this place, grieves my heart more
   than did the day that cut me from my life.   135

But I am forced to answer truthfully:
   I am put down so low because it was I
   who stole the treasure from the Sacristy,   138

4. The "phoenix" is a mythical bird that is supposed to burn to death in its own nest every five hundred years, after which either itself or its son is reborn from the ashes; for these details, including its diet of exotic herbs and its funeral preparations (lines 109–11), see Ovid, *Metamorphoses* 15. In medieval mythography the phoenix was often taken as a symbol of Christ.

5. The illegitimate son of a noble father of Pistoia, a town just north of Florence; he was known as "the beast" because of the extravagance of his misbehavior. He reputedly robbed a church in Pistoia, a crime for which a similarly named man was wrongly hanged.

for which others once were blamed. But that you may
   find less to gloat about if you escape here,
   prick up your ears and listen to what I say:[6]   141

First Pistoia is emptied of the Black,
   then Florence changes her party and her laws.
   From Valdimagra the God of War brings back   144

a fiery vapor wrapped in turbid air:
   then in a storm of battle at Piceno
   the vapor breaks apart the mist, and there   147

every White shall feel his wounds anew.
And I have told you this that it may grieve you."

Canto XXV

CIRCLE EIGHT: BOLGIA SEVEN   *The Thieves*

Vanni's rage mounts to the point where he hurls an ultimate obscenity at God,
and the serpents immediately swarm over him, driving him off in great pain. The
Centaur, *Cacus*, his back covered with serpents and a fire-eating dragon, also
gives chase to punish the wretch.

   Dante then meets *Five Noble Thieves of Florence* and sees the further retribution
visited upon the sinners. Some of the thieves appear first in human form, others as
reptiles. All but one of them suffer a painful transformation before Dante's eyes.
Agnello appears in human form and is merged with *Cianfa*, who appears as a six-
legged lizard. *Buoso* appears as a man and changes form with *Francesco*, who first
appears as a tiny reptile. Only *Puccio Sciancato* remains unchanged, though we
are made to understand that his turn will come.

   For endless and painful transformation is the final state of the thieves. In life
they took the substance of others, transforming it into their own. So in Hell their
very bodies are constantly being taken from them, and they are left to steal back
a human form from some other sinner. Thus they waver constantly between man
and reptile, and no sinner knows what to call his own.

When he had finished, the thief—to his disgrace—
   raised his hands with both fists making figs,[7]
   and cried: "Here, God! I throw them in your face!"   3

Thereat the snakes became my friends, for one
   coiled itself about the wretch's neck
   as if it were saying: "You shall not go on!"   6

6. Vanni Fucci now prophesies, in the enigmatic terms appropriate to the genre, that the
party of the Blacks (of which he was a member) will first be expelled from Pistoia by the
Whites, but that then the Whites of Florence
(Dante's party) will be defeated. The prophecy

refers to events that occurred in either 1302
or 1306.
7. An obscene gesture made by thrusting a
protruding thumb between the first and second
fingers of a closed fist.

and another tied his arms behind him again,
   knotting its head and tail between his loins
   so tight he could not move a finger in pain. 9

Pistoia! Pistoia! why have you not decreed
   to turn yourself to ashes and end your days,
   rather than spread the evil of your seed![8] 12

In all of Hell's corrupt and sunken halls
   I found no shade so arrogant toward God,
   not even him who fell from the Theban walls![9] 15

Without another word, he fled; and there
   I saw a furious Centaur race up, roaring:
   "Where is the insolent blasphemer? Where?" 18

I do not think as many serpents swarm
   in all the Maremma[1] as he bore on his back
   from the haunch to the first sign of our human form. 21

Upon his shoulders, just behind his head
   a snorting dragon whose hot breath set fire
   to all it touched, lay with its wings outspread. 24

My Guide said: "That is Cacus.[2] Time and again
   in the shadow of Mount Aventine he made
   a lake of blood upon the Roman plain. 27

He does not go with his kin by the blood-red fosse
   because of the cunning fraud with which he stole
   the cattle of Hercules. And thus it was 30

his thieving stopped, for Hercules found his den
   and gave him perhaps a hundred blows with his club,
   and of them he did not feel the first ten." 33

Meanwhile, the Centaur passed along his way,
   and three wraiths came. Neither my Guide nor I
   knew they were there until we heard them say: 36

"You there—who are you?" There our talk fell still
   and we turned to stare at them. I did not know them,
   but by chance it happened, as it often will, 39

8. The most important founder of Pistoia was
Catiline, who was a traitor against the Roman
Republic in the 1st century B.C.E.
9. Capaneus (see 14.43–69).

1. A region infested with snakes; see 13.8.
2. A monster who lived in a cave on Mount
Aventine in Rome and was killed by Hercules,
from whom he had stolen cattle; see *Aeneid* 8.

one named another. "Where is Cianfa?"[3] he cried;
  "Why has he fallen back?" I placed a finger
  across my lips as a signal to my Guide.   42

Reader, should you doubt what next I tell,
  it will be no wonder, for though I saw it happen,
  I can scarce believe it possible, even in Hell.   45

For suddenly, as I watched, I saw a lizard
  come darting forward on six great taloned feet
  and fasten itself to a sinner from crotch to gizzard.   48

Its middle feet sank in the sweat and grime
  of the wretch's paunch, its forefeet clamped his arms,
  its teeth bit through both cheeks. At the same time   51

its hind feet fastened on the sinner's thighs:
  its tail thrust through his legs and closed its coil
  over his loins. I saw it with my own eyes!   54

No ivy ever grew about a tree
  as tightly as that monster wove itself
  limb by limb about the sinner's body;   57

they fused like hot wax, and their colors ran
  together until neither wretch nor monster
  appeared what he had been when he began: 60

just so, before the running edge of the heat
  on a burning page, a brown discoloration
  changes to black as the white dies from the sheet.   63

The other two cried out as they looked on:
  "Alas! Alas! Agnello,[4] how you change!
  Already you are neither two nor one!"   66

The two heads had already blurred and blended;
  now two new semblances appeared and faded,
  one face where neither face began nor ended.   69

From the four upper limbs of man and beast
  two arms were made, then members never seen
  grew from the thighs and legs, belly and breast.   72

Their former likenesses mottled and sank
  to something that was both of them and neither;
  and so transformed, it slowly left our bank.   75

---

3. A noble Florentine, reputedly a thief.   4. Another noble Florentine thief.

As lizards at high noon of a hot day
   dart out from hedge to hedge, from shade to shade,
   and flash like lightning when they cross the way,   78

so toward the bowels of the other two,
   shot a small monster; livid, furious,
   and black as a peppercorn. Its lunge bit through   81

that part of one of them from which man receives
   his earliest nourishment; then it fell back
   and lay sprawled out in front of the two thieves.   84

Its victim stared at it but did not speak:
   indeed, he stood there like a post, and yawned
   as if lack of sleep, or a fever, had left him weak.   87

The reptile stared at him, he at the reptile;
   from the wound of one and from the other's mouth
   two smokes poured out and mingled, dark and vile.   90

Now let Lucan be still with his history
   of poor Sabellus and Nassidius,[5]
   and wait to hear what next appeared to me.   93

Of Cadmus and Arethusa[6] be Ovid silent.
   I have no need to envy him those verses
   where he makes one a fountain, and one a serpent: 96

for he never transformed two beings face to face
   in such a way that both their natures yielded
   their elements each to each, as in this case.   99

Responding sympathetically to each other,
   the reptile cleft his tail into a fork,
   and the wounded sinner drew his feet together.   102

The sinner's legs and thighs began to join:
   they grew together so, that soon no trace
   of juncture could be seen from toe to loin.   105

Point by point the reptile's cloven tail
   grew to the form of what the sinner lost;
   one skin began to soften, one to scale.   108

The armpits swallowed the arms, and the short shank
   of the reptile's forefeet simultaneously
   lengthened by as much as the man's arms shrank.   111

5. Two soldiers bitten by serpents in Lucan's *Pharsalia*.
6. See *Metamorphoses* 4.

Its hind feet twisted round themselves and grew
    the member man conceals; meanwhile the wretch
    from his one member generated two.   114

The smoke swelled up about them all the while:
    it tanned one skin and bleached the other; it stripped
    the hair from the man and grew it on the reptile.   117

While one fell to his belly, the other rose
    without once shifting the locked evil eyes
    below which they changed snouts as they changed pose   120

The face of the standing one drew up and in
    toward the temples, and from the excess matter
    that gathered there, ears grew from the smooth skin;   123

while of the matter left below the eyes
    the excess became a nose, at the same time
    forming the lips to an appropriate size.   126

Here the face of the prostrate felon slips,
    sharpens into a snout, and withdraws its ears
    as a snail pulls in its horns. Between its lips   129

the tongue, once formed for speech, thrusts out a fork;
    the forked tongue of the other heals and draws
    into his mouth. The smoke has done its work.   132

The soul that had become a beast went flitting
    and hissing over the stones, and after it
    the other walked along talking and spitting   135

Then turning his new shoulders, said to the one
    that still remained: "It is Buoso's[7] turn to go
    crawling along this road as I have done."   138

Thus did the ballast of the seventh hold
    shift and reshift; and may the strangeness of it
    excuse my pen if the tale is strangely told.   141

And though all this confused me, they did not flee
    so cunningly but what I was aware
    that it was Puccio Sciancato[8] alone of the three   144

that first appeared, who kept his old form still.
The other was he for whom you weep, Gaville.[9]

---

7. The identity of this Buoso is uncertain.
8. This third thief is also a noble Florentine.
9. The "small monster" of line 80 above is now
identified as Francesco de Cavalcanti, a Florentine nobleman who lived in Gaville, a town
south of Florence. When he was murdered by
his townsmen, his kinsmen took brutal revenge.

Canto XXVI

The Evil Counselors

Dante turns from the Thieves toward the *Evil Counselors* of the next Bolgia, and between the two he addresses a passionate lament to Florence prophesying the griefs that will befall her from these two sins. At the purported time of the Vision, it will be recalled, Dante was a Chief Magistrate of Florence and was forced into exile by men he had reason to consider both thieves and evil counselors. He seems prompted, in fact, to say much more on this score, but he restrains himself when he comes in sight of the sinners of the next Bolgia, for they are a moral symbolism, all men of gift who abused their genius, perverting it to wiles and stratagems. Seeing them in Hell he knows his must be another road: his way shall not be by deception.

So the Poets move on and Dante observes the *Eighth Bolgia* in detail. Here the *Evil Counselors* move about endlessly, hidden from view inside great flames. Their sin was to abuse the gifts of the Almighty, to steal his virtues for low purposes. And as they stole from God in their lives and worked by hidden ways, so are they stolen from sight and hidden in the great flames which are their own guilty consciences. And as, in most instances at least, they sinned by glibness of tongue, so are the flames made into a fiery travesty of tongues.

Among the others, the Poets see a great doubleheaded flame, and discover that *Ulysses* and *Diomede* are punished together within it. Virgil addresses the flame, and through its wavering tongue Ulysses narrates an unforgettable tale of his last voyage and death.

Joy to you, Florence, that your banners swell,
   beating their proud wings over land and sea,
   and that your name expands through all of Hell!   3

Among the thieves I found five who had been
   your citizens,[1] to my shame; nor yet shall you
   mount to great honor peopling such a den!   6

But if the truth is dreamed of toward the morning,
   you soon shall feel what Prato[2] and the others
   wish for you. And were that day of mourning   9

already come it would not be too soon.
   So may it come, since it must! for it will weigh
   more heavily on me as I pass my noon.   12

We left that place. My Guide climbed stone by stone
   the natural stair by which we had descended
   and drew me after him. So we passed on,   15

---

1. Cianfa (25.40), Agnello (25.65), Buoso (25.137), Puccio (25.144), and Francesco (25.149) are all Florentines.

2. A town just north of Florence, on the way to Pistoia. The reason for this threat is unclear.

and going our lonely way through that dead land
    among the crags and crevices of the cliff,
    the foot could make no way without the hand.   18

I mourned among those rocks, and I mourn again
    when memory returns to what I saw:
    and more than usually I curb the strain   21

of my genius, lest it stray from Virtue's course;
    so if some star, or a better thing, grant me merit,
    may I not find the gift cause for remorse.   24

As many fireflies as the peasant sees
    when he rests on a hill and looks into the valley
    (where he tills or gathers grapes or prunes his trees)   27

in that sweet season when the face of him
    who lights the world rides north, and at the hour
    when the fly yields to the gnat and the air grows dim.—   30

such myriads of flames I saw shine through
    the gloom of the eighth abyss when I arrived
    at the rim from which its bed comes into view.   33

As he[3] the bears avenged so fearfully
    beheld Elijah's chariot depart—
    the horses rise toward heaven—but could not see   36

more than the flame, a cloudlet in the sky,
    once it had risen—so within the fosse
    only those flames, forever passing by   39

were visible, ahead, to right, to left;
    for though each steals a sinner's soul from view
    not one among them leaves a trace of the theft.   42

I stood on the bridge, and leaned out from the edge;
    so far, that but for a jut of rock I held to
    I should have been sent hurtling from the ledge   45

without being pushed. And seeing me so intent,
    my Guide said: "There are souls within those flames;
    each sinner swathes himself in his own torment."   48

"Master," I said, "your words make me more sure,
    but I had seen already that it was so
    and meant to ask what spirit must endure   51

3. Elisha, an Old Testament prophet, was mocked by children, who were then attacked by bears. He saw the ascent to heaven of the prophet Elijah in his chariot and continued Elijah's mission: 2 Kings 2.1–25.

the pains of that great flame which splits away
 in two great horns, as if it rose from the pyre
 where Eteocles and Polynices lay?"[4]   54

He answered me: "Forever round this path
 Ulysses and Diomede[5] move in such dress,
 united in pain as once they were in wrath;   57

there they lament the ambush of the Horse
 which was the door through which the noble seed
 of the Romans[6] issued from its holy source;   60

there they mourn that for Achilles slain
 sweet Deidamia[7] weeps even in death;
 there they recall the Palladium in their pain."   63

"Master," I cried, "I pray you and repray
 till my prayer becomes a thousand—if these souls
 can still speak from the fire, oh let me stay   66

until the flame draws near! Do not deny me:
 You see how fervently I long for it!"
 And he to me: "Since what you ask is worthy,   69

it shall be. But be still and let me speak;
 for I know your mind already, and they perhaps
 might scorn your manner of speaking, since they were Greek."[8]   72

And when the flame had come where time and place
 seemed fitting to my Guide, I heard him say
 these words to it: "O you two souls who pace   75

together in one flame!—if my days above
 won favor in your eyes, if I have earned
 however much or little of your love   78

in writing my High Verses, do not pass by,
 but let one of you be pleased to tell where he,
 having disappeared from the known world, went to die."   81

4. Eteocles and his brother, Polynices, were the sons of Oedipus; cursed by their father for their imprisonment of him, they engaged in a civil war over Thebes, killed each other, and were cremated on the same pyre, the flame of which divided into two as a sign of their enmity.
5. Two of the Greek leaders in the Trojan War. They devised the trick of the Trojan horse and stole the Palladium, a statue of Pallas Athena that protected the city. Their villainy is described by Aeneas in *Aeneid* 2.
6. The Trojan survivors, who founded Rome.
7. Achilles' lover, who tried to prevent him from going to the Trojan War but was thwarted by Ulysses.
8. Virgil may assume that Greeks would disdain anyone who, like Dante, did not know Greek (and was therefore a "barbarian"); or that because he derives from the classical world he is the more appropriate interlocutor.

As if it fought the wind, the greater prong
 of the ancient flame began to quiver and hum;
 then moving its tip as if it were the tongue   84

that spoke, gave out a voice above the roar.
 "When I left Circe,"[9] it said, "who more than a year
 detained me near Gaeta long before   87

Aeneas came and gave the place that name,[1]
 not fondness for my son, nor reverence
 for my aged father, nor Penelope's[2] claim   90

to the joys of love, could drive out of my mind
 the lust to experience the far-flung world
 and the failings and felicities of mankind.   93

I put out on the high and open sea
 with a single ship and only those few souls
 who stayed true when the rest deserted me.   96

As far as Morocco and as far as Spain
 I saw both shores; and I saw Sardinia
 and the other islands of the open main.   99

I and my men were stiff and slow with age
 when we sailed at last into the narrow pass
 where, warning all men back from further voyage,[3]   102

Hercules' Pillars rose upon our sight.
 Already I had left Ceuta on the left;
 Seville now sank behind me on the right.   105

'Shipmates,' I said, 'who through a hundred thousand
 perils have reached the West, do not deny
 to the brief remaining watch our senses stand   108

experience of the world beyond the sun.
 Greeks! You were not born to live like brutes,
 but to press on toward manhood and recognition!   111

With this brief exhortation I made my crew
 so eager for the voyage I could hardly
 have held them back from it when I was through;   114

---

9. Ulysses speaks here of the sorceress Circe, who turned his shipmates into swine and took Ulysses as her lover. Dante places Circe's home near Gaeta, on the coast of Italy north of Naples. **1.** Aeneas named it after his nurse Caieta, who died there; see *Aeneid* 7. **2.** Ulysses' faithful wife.

3. The Strait of Gibraltar, with the Spanish region that includes Seville on the European side and the Spanish city of Ceüta on the African. According to myth, Hercules separated a single mountain into two to mark the point beyond which human beings should not venture.

and turning our stern toward morning, our bow toward night,
  we bore southwest out of the world of man;[4]
  we made wings of our oars for our fool's flight. 117

That night we raised the other pole ahead
  with all its stars, and ours had so declined
  it did not rise out of its ocean bed.[5] 120

Five times since we had dipped our bending oars
  beyond the world, the light beneath the moon
  had waxed and waned, when dead upon our course 123

we sighted, dark in space, a peak so tall
  I doubted any man had seen the like.[6]
  Our cheers were hardly sounded, when a squall 126

broke hard upon our bow from the new land:
  three times it sucked the ship and the sea about
  as it pleased Another to order and command. 129

At the fourth, the poop rose and the bow went down
till the sea closed over us and the light was gone."

Canto XXVII

CIRCLE EIGHT: BOLGIA EIGHT   *The Evil Counselors*

The double flame departs at a word from Virgil and behind it appears another
which contains the soul of *Count Guido da Montefeltro*, a Lord of Romagna. He
had overheard Virgil speaking Italian, and the entire flame in which his soul is
wrapped quivers with his eagerness to hear recent news of his wartorn country.
(As Farinata has already explained, the spirits of the damned have prophetic
powers, but lose all track of events as they approach.)

    Dante replies with a stately and tragic summary of how things stand in the cit-
ies of Romagna. When he has finished, he asks Guido for his story, and Guido
recounts his life, and how Boniface VIII persuaded him to sin.

When it had finished speaking, the great flame
  stood tall and shook no more. Now, as it left us
  with the sweet Poet's license, another came 3

along that track and our attention turned
  to the new flame: a strange and muffled roar
  rose from the single tip to which it burned. 6

---

4. According to the geography of Dante's day,
the Southern Hemisphere was made up entirely
of water, with the only land being Mount Purgatory. "Our bow toward night" means to follow
a westward course.
5. They had crossed the equator and could see
only the stars of the Southern Hemisphere.
6. This is Mount Purgatory.

As the Sicilian bull—that brazen spit
   which bellowed first (and properly enough)
   with the lament of him whose file had tuned it—[7]   9

was made to bellow by its victim's cries
   in such a way, that though it was of brass,
   it seemed itself to howl and agonize: 12

so lacking any way through or around
   the fire that sealed them in, the mournful words
   were changed into its language. When they found   15

their way up to the tip, imparting to it
   the same vibration given them in their passage
   over the tongue of the concealed sad spirit,   18

we heard it say:[8] "O you at whom I aim
   my voice, and who were speaking Lombard,[9] saying:
   'Go now, I ask no more,' just as I came—   21

though I may come a bit late to my turn,
   may it not annoy you to pause and speak a while:
   you see it does not annoy me—and I burn.   24

If you have fallen only recently
   to this blind world from that sweet Italy
   where I acquired my guilt, I pray you, tell me: 27

is there peace or war in Romagna? for on earth
   I too was of those hills between Urbino
   and the fold from which the Tiber springs to birth."   30

I was still staring at it from the dim
   edge of the pit when my Guide nudged me, saying:
   "This one is Italian: *you* speak to him."   33

My answer was framed already; without pause
   I spoke these words to it: "O hidden soul,
   your sad Romagna is not and never was   36

without war in her tyrants' raging blood;
   but none flared openly when I left just now.
   Ravenna's[1] fortunes stand as they have stood   39

---

7. According to classical legend, Phalaris, the tyrant of Agrigentum in Sicily, had an artisan build a brazen bull in which he roasted his victims alive, their shrieks emerging as the sounds of a bull's bellowing. His first victim was the artisan himself, Perillus.
8. The speaker is Guido da Montefeltro (d. 1298), a nobleman deeply involved in the constant warfare of 13th-century Italy but who became a friar two years before his death (see lines 64–65).
9. The dialect of northern Italy. Dante believed that since Virgil came from Mantua, his spoken language would be not Latin but this dialect.
1. The major city of Romagna, ruled at the time by the Polenta family, who also controlled the small city of Cervia.

these many years: Polenta's eagles brood
   over her walls, and their pinions cover Cervia.
   The city[2] that so valiantly withstood   42

the French, and raised a mountain of their dead,
   feels the Green Claws again. Still in Verrucchio
   the Aged Mastiff and his Pup,[3] who shed   45

Montagna's blood, raven in their old ranges.
   The cities of Lamone and Santerno[4]
   are led by the white den's Lion, he who changes   48

his politics with the compass. And as the city[5]
   the Savio washes lies between plain and mountain,
   so it lives between freedom and tyranny.   51

Now, I beg you, let us know your name;
   do not be harder than one has been to you;
   so, too, you will preserve your earthly fame."   54

And when the flame had roared a while beneath
   the ledge on which we stood, it swayed its tip
   to and fro, and then gave forth this breath: 57

"If I believed that my reply were made
   to one who could ever climb to the world again,
   this flame would shake no more. But since no shade   60

ever returned—if what I am told is true—
   from this blind world into the living light,
   without fear of dishonor I answer you.   63

I was a man of arms: then took the rope
   of the Franciscans, hoping to make amends:
   and surely I should have won to all my hope   66

but for the Great Priest[6]—may he rot in Hell!—
   who brought me back to all my earlier sins;
   and how and why it happened I wish to tell   69

in my own words: while I was still encased
   in the pulp and bone my mother bore, my deeds
   were not of the lion but of the fox: I raced   72

---

2. Forli, which defeated French invaders but then fell under the control of the tyrannical Ordelaffi family, which had green paws on its coat of arms.
3. Malatesta de Verrucchio and his son Malatestino were tyrants of Rimini who killed their enemy Montagna.
4. The cities of Faenza and Imola, on the Lamone and Santerno Rivers respectively, governed by an unreliable ruler who had a lion on a white ground on his coat of arms.
5. Cesena, located on the Savio River, was a free municipality although its politics were dominated by a single family.
6. Pope Boniface VIII.

through tangled ways; all wiles were mine from birth,
    and I won to such advantage with my arts
    that rumor of me reached the ends of the earth.   75

But when I saw before me all the signs
    of the time of life that cautions every man
    to lower his sail and gather in his lines,   78

that which had pleased me once, troubled my spirit,
    and penitent and confessed, I became a monk.
    Alas! What joy I might have had of it!   81

It was then the Prince of the New Pharisees drew
    his sword and marched upon the Lateran—
    and not against the Saracen or the Jew,[7]   84

for every man that stood against his hand
    was a Christian soul: not one had warred on Acre,[8]
    nor been a trader in the Sultan's land.   87

It was he abused his sacred vows and mine:
    his Office and the Cord I wore, which once
    made those it girded leaner.[9] As Constantine   90

sent for Silvestro to cure his leprosy,[1]
    seeking him out among Soracte's cells;
    so this one from his great throne sent for me   93

to cure the fever of pride that burned his blood.
    He demanded my advice, and I kept silent
    for his words seemed drunken to me. So it stood   96

until he said: 'Your soul need fear no wound;
    I absolve your guilt beforehand; and now teach me
    how to smash Penestrino[2] to the ground.   99

The Gates of Heaven, as you know, are mine
    to open and shut, for I hold the two Great Keys
    so easily let go by Celestine.'[3]   102

---

7. Boniface was struggling to retain the papacy against the challenge of another Roman family, the Colonnas.

8. City (now known as Akko) in the Holy Land, captured by the Crusaders and then recaptured by the Saracens.

9. Guido refers to the rough cord worn as a belt by Franciscan friars, a symbol of both obedience and poverty (hence it would make the wearer "leaner"); for another reference to this cord, see 16.106.

1. According to legend, the Emperor Constantine (r. 306–37) was cured of his leprosy by Pope Sylvester, who was hiding on Mount Soracte, some 20 miles north of Rome; see 19.109.

2. The fortress of the Colonnas.

3. The keys are those of damnation and absolution, given by Christ to Peter; see 19.85–86. Celestine V, Boniface's predecessor, resigned after five months as pope; see 3.56–57.

His weighty arguments led me to fear
   silence was worse than sin. Therefore, I said:
   'Holy Father, since you clean me here   105

of the guilt into which I fall, let it be done:
   long promise and short observance is the road
   that leads to the sure triumph of your throne.'   108

Later, when I was dead, St. Francis[4] came
   to claim my soul, but one of the Black Angels
   said: 'Leave him. Do not wrong me. This one's name   111

went into my book the moment he resolved
   to give false counsel. Since then he has been mine,
   for who does not repent cannot be absolved;   114

nor can we admit the possibility
   of repenting a thing at the same time it is willed,
   for the two acts are contradictory.'[5]   117

Miserable me! with what contrition
   I shuddered when he lifted me, saying: 'Perhaps
   you hadn't heard that I was a logician.'[6]   120

He carried me to Minos:[7] eight times round
   his scabby back the monster coiled his tail,
   then biting it in rage he pawed the ground   123

and cried: 'This one is for the thievish fire!'
   And, as you see, I am lost accordingly,
   grieving in heart as I go in this attire."   126

His story told, the flame began to toss
   and writhe its horn. And so it left, and we
   crossed over to the arch of the next fosse   129

where from the iron treasury of the Lord
the fee of wrath is paid the Sowers of Discord.

Canto XXVIII

CIRCLE EIGHT: BOLGIA NINE   *The Sowers of Discord*

The Poets come to the edge of the *Ninth Bolgia* and look down at a parade of hideously mutilated souls. These are the *Sowers of Discord,* and just as their sin was to rend asunder what God had meant to be united, so are they hacked and torn through all eternity by a great demon with a bloody sword. After each mutila-

4. Francis of Assisi (ca. 1181–1226), founder of the order of friars joined by Guido. As patron saint of Italy, Francis is venerated for his compassion and humility.
5. Guido wanted forgiveness for his sin of guile at the same time as he was committing it; in

willing the sin he showed that he was not truly repentant, the precondition for forgiveness.
6. The devil is referring to the logical law of noncontradiction.
7. For Minos, see 5.4–12.

tion the souls are compelled to drag their broken bodies around the pit and to return to the demon, for in the course of the circuit their wounds knit in time to be inflicted anew. Thus is the law of retribution observed, each sinner suffering according to his degree.

Among them Dante distinguishes three classes with varying degrees of guilt within each class. First come the *Sowers of Religious Discord.* Mahomet (Muhammad) is chief among them, and appears first, cleft from crotch to chin, with his internal organs dangling between his legs. His son-in-law, Ali, drags on ahead of him, cleft from topknot to chin. These reciprocal wounds symbolize Dante's judgment that, between them, these two sum up the total schism between Christianity and Mohammedanism. The revolting details of Mahomet's condition clearly imply Dante's opinion of that doctrine. Mahomet issues an ironic warning to another schismatic, *Fra Dolcino.*

Next come the *Sowers of Political Discord,* among them *Pier da Medicina,* the Tribune *Curio,* and *Mosca deí Lamberti,* each mutilated according to the nature of his sin.

Last of all is *Bertrand de Born, Sower of Discord Between Kinsmen.* He separated father from son, and for that offense carries his head separated from his body, holding it with one hand by the hair, and swinging it as if it were a lantern to light his dark and endless way. The image of Bertrand raising his head at arm's length in order that it might speak more clearly to the Poets on the ridge is one of the most memorable in the *Inferno.* For some reason that cannot be ascertained, Dante makes these sinners quite eager to be remembered in the world, despite the fact that many who lie above them in Hell were unwilling to be recognized.

Who could describe, even in words set free
  of metric and rhyme and a thousand times retold,
  the blood and wounds that now were shown to me!   3

At grief so deep the tongue must wag in vain;
  the language of our sense and memory
  lacks the vocabulary of such pain.   6

If one could gather all those who have stood
  through all of time on Puglia's fateful soil
  and wept for the red running of their blood   9

in the war of the Trojans;[8] and in that long war
  which left so vast a spoil of golden rings,
  as we find written in Livy,[9] who does not err;   12

along with those whose bodies felt the wet
  and gaping wounds of Robert Guiscard's[1] lances;
  with all the rest whose bones are gathered yet   15

---

8. Puglia is in southern Italy; Dante refers here to those killed when the Trojans conquered it in the *Aeneid* 7–12.

9. Roman historian (d. 17 C.E.; he chronicled the Second Punic War (218–201 B.C.E.) between Rome and Carthage under Hannibal.

After the battle of Cannae (216) the victorious Carthaginians displayed rings taken from fallen Romans.

1. A Norman conqueror (1015–1085) who fought the Greeks and Saracens for control of Sicily and southern Italy in the 11th century.

at Ceperano² where every last Pugliese
   turned traitor; and with those from Tagliacozzo³
   where Alardo won without weapons—if all these   18

were gathered, and one showed his limbs run through,
   another his lopped off, that could not equal
   the mutilations of the ninth pit's crew.   21

A wine tun when a stave or cant-bar starts
   does not split open as wide as one I saw
   split from his chin to the mouth with which man farts.   24

Between his legs all of his red guts hung
   with the heart, the lungs, the liver, the gall bladder,
   and the shriveled sac that passes shit to the bung.   27

I stood and stared at him from the stone shelf;
   he noticed me and opening his own breast
   with both hands cried: "See how I rip myself!   30

See how Mahomet's⁴ mangled and split open!
   Ahead of me walks Ali in his tears,
   his head cleft from the top-knot to the chin.   33

And all the other souls that bleed and mourn
   along this ditch were sowers of scandal and schism:
   as they tore others apart, so are they torn.   36

Behind us, warden of our mangled horde,
   the devil who butchers us and sends us marching
   waits to renew our wounds with his long sword   39

when we have made the circuit of the pit;
   for by the time we stand again before him
   all the wounds he gave us last have knit.   42

But who are you that gawk down from that sill—
   probably to put off your own descent
   to the pit you are sentenced to for your own evil?"   45

"Death has not come for him, guilt does not drive
   his soul to torment," my sweet Guide replied.
   "That he may experience all while yet alive   48

---

2. A town that the barons of Puglia were pledged to defend for Manfred, the natural son of Frederick II (10.119), but whom they betrayed; he was then killed at the battle of Benevento in 1266.
3. A town where in 1268 Manfred's nephew Conradin was defeated by the strategy rather than the brute force of Alardo de Valery.
4. Muhammad, founder of Islam (570–632), regarded by some medieval Christians as a renegade Christian and a creator of religious disunity. Ali was his nephew and son-in-law, and his disputed claim to the rulership (or caliphate) divided Islam into Sunni and Shi'a sects.

I, who am dead, must lead him through the drear
   and darkened halls of Hell, from round to round:
   and this is true as my own standing here."   51

More than a hundred wraiths who were marching under
   the sill on which we stood, paused at his words
   and stared at me, forgetting pain in wonder.   54

"And if you do indeed return to see
   the sun again, and soon, fell Fra Dolcino[5]
   unless he longs to come and march with me   57

he would do well to cheek his groceries
   before the winter drives him from the hills
   and gives the victory to the Novarese."   60

Mahomet, one foot raised, had paused to say
   these words to me. When he had finished speaking
   he stretched it out and down, and moved away.   63

Another—he had his throat slit, and his nose
   slashed off as far as the eyebrows, and a wound
   where one of his ears had been—standing with those   66

who stared at me in wonder from the pit,
   opened the grinning wound of his red gullet
   as if it were a mouth, and said through it: 69

"O soul unforfeited to misery
   and whom—unless I take you for another—
   I have seen above in our sweet Italy;   72

if ever again you see the gentle plain
   that slopes down from Vercelli to Marcabò,
   remember Pier da Medicina[6] in pain,   75

and announce this warning to the noblest two
   of Fano,[7] Messers Guido and Angiolello:
   that unless our foresight sees what is not true   78

they shall be thrown from their ships into the sea
   and drown in the raging tides near La Cattolica
   to satisfy a tyrant's treachery.   81

5. In 1300 Fra Dolcino was head of a reformist order known as the Apostolic Brothers that was condemned as heretical by the pope. He and his followers escaped to the hills near the town of Novara, but starvation forced them out and many were executed.
6. The town of Medicina lies in the Po Valley between Vercelli and Marcabò. Nothing certain is known of Pier da Medicina.
7. A town on the Adriatic coast of Italy; its two leaders—named in the same line—were drowned in 1312 by the one-eyed tyrant Malatestino of Rimini (see note 3 to 27.45) near the promontory of Focara (see line 90) after he had invited them to the town of La Cattolica for a parley.

Neptune never saw so gross a crime
   in all the seas from Cyprus to Majorca,
   not even in pirate raids, nor the Argive[8] time.   84

The one-eyed traitor,[9] lord of the demesne
   whose hill and streams one who walks here beside me
   will wish eternally he had never seen,   87

will call them to a parley, but behind
   sweet invitations he will work it so
   they need not pray against Focara's wind."   90

And I to him: "If you would have me bear
   your name to time, show me the one who found
   the sight of that land so harsh, and let me hear   93

his story and his name." He touched the cheek
   of one nearby,[1] forcing the jaws apart,
   and said: "This is the one; he cannot speak.   96

This outcast settled Caesar's doubts that day
   beside the Rubicon by telling him:
   'A man prepared is a man hurt by delay.'"   99

Ah, how wretched Curio seemed to me
   with a bloody stump in his throat in place of the tongue
   which once had dared to speak so recklessly!   102

And one among them with both arms hacked through
   cried out, raising his stumps on the foul air
   while the blood bedaubed his face: "Remember, too,   105

Mosca dei Lamberti,[2] alas, who said
   'A thing done has an end!' and with those words
   planted the fields of war with Tuscan dead."   108

"And brought about the death of all your clan!"
   I said, and he, stung by new pain on pain,
   ran off; and in his grief he seemed a madman.   111

I stayed to watch those broken instruments,
   and I saw a thing so strange I should not dare
   to mention it without more evidence   114

---

8. Cyprus and Majorca are islands at the eastern and western ends of the Mediterranean. Neptune is the classical god of the sea; Argive is another name for Greek.
9. Caius Curio, whose story is told in lines 94–102.
1. Caius Curio, a Roman of the 1st century B.C.E., was bribed by Julius Caesar to betray his friends; he urged Caesar to cross the Rubicon and invade the Roman Republic, starting a civil war.
2. A Florentine noble, who in 1215 started the civil strife that tore the city apart by advising a father to avenge the slight to his daughter by killing the man who had broken his engagement to her. Mosca's own family was a victim of the strife some 60 years later.

but that my own clear conscience strengthens me,
   that good companion that upholds a man
   within the armor of his purity.   117

I saw it there; I seem to see it still—
   a body without a head, that moved along
   like all the others in that spew and spill.   120

It held the severed head by its own hair,
   swinging it like a lantern in its hand;
   and the head looked at us and wept in its despair.   123

It made itself a lamp of its own head,
   and they were two in one and one in two;
   how this can be, He knows who so commanded.   126

And when it stood directly under us
   it raised the head at arm's length toward our bridge
   the better to be heard, and swaying thus   129

it cried:[3] "O living soul in this abyss,
   see what a sentence has been passed upon me,
   and search all Hell for one to equal this!   132

When you return to the world, remember me:
   I am Bernard de Born, and it was I
   who set the young king on to mutiny,   135

son against father, father against son
   as Achitophel set Absalom and David;
   and since I parted those who should be one   138

in duty and in love, I bear my brain
   divided from its source within this trunk;
   and walk here where my evil turns to pain,   142

an eye for an eye to all eternity:
thus is the law of Hell observed in me."[4]

Canto XXIX

CIRCLE EIGHT: BOLGIA TEN   *The Falsifers*
                                   (Class I, Alchemists)

Dante lingers on the edge of the Ninth Bolgia expecting to see one of his kinsmen, *Geri del Bello*, among the Sowers of Discord. Virgil, however, hurries him
on, since time is short, and as they cross the bridge over the *Tenth Bolgia*, Virgil

3. This is Bertran de Born, a Provençal noble- between David and his son Absalom, see 2
man and poet, who reputedly advised the son Samuel 15–17.
of Henry II of England to rebel against his **4.** In Dante's hell, the sinner is punished by
father. For Achitophel's similar scheming having to commit his sin for all of eternity.

explains that he had a glimpse of Geri among the crowd near the bridge and that
he had been making threatening gestures at Dante.

The Poets now look into the last *Bolgia* of the Eighth Circle and see *The Falsifiers*. They are punished by afflictions of every sense by darkness, stench, thirst,
fifth, loathsome diseases, and a shrieking din. Some of them, moreover, run ravening through the pit, tearing others to pieces. Just as in life they corrupted society by their falsifications, so in death these sinners are subjected to a sum of
corruptions. In one sense they figure forth what society would be if all falsifiers
succeeded—a place where the senses are an affliction (since falsification deceives
the senses) rather than a guide, where even the body has no honesty, and where
some lie prostrate while others run ravening to prey upon them.

Not all of these details are made clear until the next canto, for Dante distinguishes four classes of Falsifiers, and in the present canto we meet only the first
class, *The Alchemists*, the Falsifiers of Things. Of this class are *Griffolino D'Arezzo*
and *Capocchio*, with both of whom Dante speaks.

The sight of that parade of broken dead
　　had left my eyes so sotted with their tears
　　I longed to stay and weep, but Virgil said:　　　　　　3

"What are you waiting for? Why do you stare
　　as if you could not tear your eyes away
　　from the mutilated shadows passing there?　　　　　　6

You did not act so in the other pits.
　　Consider—if you mean perhaps to count them—
　　this valley and its train of dismal spirits　　　　　　9

winds twenty-two miles round.[5] The moon already
　　is under our feet; the time we have is short,[6]
　　and there is much that you have yet to see."　　　　　　12

"Had you known what I was seeking," I replied,
　　"you might perhaps have given me permission
　　to stay on longer." (As I spoke, my Guide　　　　　　15

had started off already, and I in turn
　　had moved along behind him; thus, I answered
　　as we moved along the cliff.) "Within that cavern　　　　18

upon whose brim I stood so long to stare,
　　I think a spirit of my own blood mourns
　　the guilt that sinners find so costly there."　　　　　　21

And the Master then: "Hereafter let your mind
　　turn its attention to more worthy matters
　　and leave him to his fate among the blind;　　　　　　24

5. The reason for this exact measurement is
not known. At 30.86 we are told that the cir-
cumference of the ninth circle is 11 miles,
showing that Hell is shaped like a funnel.

6. This means that the sun (which they cannot see) is over their heads, and the time is
about 2:00 p.m. The journey to the center of
Hell lasts 24 hours, so only 4 hours are left.

for by the bridge and among that shapeless crew
   I saw him point to you with threatening gestures,
   and I heard him called Geri del Bello.[7] You   27

were occupied at the time with that headless one
   who in his life was master of Altaforte,[8]
   and did not look that way; so he moved on."   30

"O my sweet Guide," I answered, "his death came
   by violence and is not yet avenged
   by those who share his blood, and, thus, his shame.   33

For this he surely hates his kin, and, therefore,
   as I suppose, he would not speak to me;
   and in that he makes me pity him the more."   36

We spoke of this until we reached the edge
   from which, had there been light, we could have seen
   the floor of the next pit. Out from that ledge   39

Malebolge's final cloister lay outspread,
   and all of its lay brethren might have been
   in sight but for the murk; and from those dead   42

such shrieks and strangled agonies shrilled through me
   like shafts, but barbed with pity, that my hands
   flew to my ears. If all the misery   45

that crams the hospitals of pestilence
   in Maremma, Valdichiano, and Sardinia
   in the summer months when death sits like a presence[9]   48

on the marsh air, were dumped into one trench—
   that might suggest their pain. And through the screams,
   putrid flesh spread up its sickening stench.   51

Still bearing left we passed from the long sill
   to the last bridge of Malebolge. There
   the reeking bottom was more visible.   54

There, High Justice, sacred ministress
   of the First Father, reigns eternally
   over the falsifiers in their distress.   57

I doubt it could have been such pain to bear
   the sight of the Aeginian[1] people dying
   that time when such malignance rode the air   60

---

7. First cousin to Dante's father; his death at the hands of a member of another Florentine family initiated a feud between the two families that lasted some 50 years.
8. Bertran de Born (see 28.134).
9. The region of Maremma, the river valley of Val di Chiana, and the island of Sardinia were all plagued by malaria.
1. A mythical island that was infected by Juno with a pestilence that killed all its inhabitants and was then repopulated when Jupiter turned ants into men; see Ovid, *Metamorphoses* 7.

that every beast down to the smallest worm
   shriveled and died (it was after that great plague
   that the Ancient People, as the poets affirm,   63

were reborn from the ants)—as it was to see
   the spirits lying heaped on one another
   in the dank bottom of that fetid valley.   66

One lay gasping on another's shoulder,
   one on another's belly; and some were crawling
   on hands and knees among the broken boulders.   69

Silent, slow step by step, we moved ahead
   looking at and listening to those souls
   too weak to raise themselves from their stone bed.   72

I saw two there like two pans that are put
   one against the other to hold their warmth.[2]
   They were covered with great scabs from head to foot.   75

No stable boy in a hurry to go home,
   or for whom his master waits impatiently,
   ever scrubbed harder with his currycomb[3]   78

than those two spirits of the stinking ditch
   scrubbed at themselves with their own bloody claws
   to ease the furious burning of the itch.   81

And as they scrubbed and clawed themselves, their nails
   drew down the scabs the way a knife scrapes bream[4]
   or some other fish with even larger scales.   84

"O you," my Guide called out to one, "you there
   who rip your scabby mail as if your fingers
   were claws and pincers; tell us if this lair   87

counts any Italians among those who lurk
   in its dark depths; so may your busy nails
   eternally suffice you for your work."   90

"We both are Italian whose unending loss
   you see before you," he replied in tears
   "But who are you who come to question us?"   93

"I am a shade," my Guide and Master said,
   "who leads this living man from pit to pit
   to show him Hell as I have been commanded."   96

---

2. The image is of pans leaned against one another before a kitchen fireplace.

3. A brush used to groom horses.

4. A large fish like a carp.

The sinners broke apart as he replied
    and turned convulsively to look at me,
    as others did who overheard my Guide.   99

My Master, then, ever concerned for me,
    turned and said: "Ask them whatever you wish."
    And I said to those two wraiths of misery: 102

"So may the memory of your names and actions
    not die forever from the minds of men
    in that first world, but live for many suns,   105

tell me who you are and of what city;
    do not be shamed by your nauseous punishment
    into concealing your identity."   108

"I was a man of Arezzo," one replied,
    "and Albert of Siena had me burned;
    but I am not here for the deed for which I died.[5]   111

It is true that jokingly I said to him once:
    'I know how to raise myself and fly through air';
    and he—with all the eagerness of a dunce—   114

wanted to learn. Because I could not make
    a Daedalus of him—for no other reason—
    he had his father burn me at the stake.   117

But Minos, the infallible, had me hurled
    here to the final bolgia of the ten
    for the alchemy[6] I practiced in the world."   120

And I to the Poet: "Was there ever a race
    more vain than the Sienese? Even the French,
    compared to them, seem full of modest grace."   123

And the other leper answered mockingly:[7]
    "Excepting Stricca, who by careful planning
    managed to live and spend so moderately;   126

and Niccolò, who in his time above
    was first of all the shoots in that rank garden
    to discover the costly uses of the clove;   129

---

5. Griffolino of Arezzo cheated Albero (Albert) of Siena by promising to teach him the art of Daedalus—flying. The bishop of Siena, father of the illegitimate Albero, had Griffolino burned as a heretic.

6. A practice that sought to turn base metals like lead into gold. Alchemy was not condemned outright by the Catholic Church (and in fact alchemy was practiced by many prominent clerics), but its association with the occult and with sheer greed made alchemy morally suspect.

7. The speaker is Capocchio, a Florentine burned in 1293 for alchemy, which he here admits was mere counterfeiting. The people he names were rich young noblemen of Siena who joined a "Spendthrifts' Club" and sought to outdo each other in profligacy. For another member of this club, Lano of Siena, see 13.120.

and excepting the brilliant company of talents
   in which Caccia squandered his vineyards and his woods,
   and Abbagliato displayed his intelligence.   132

But if you wish to know who joins your cry
   against the Sienese, study my face
   with care and let it make its own reply.   135

So you will see I am the suffering shadow
   of Capocchio, who, by practicing alchemy,
   falsified the metals, and you must know,   138

unless my mortal recollection strays
how good an ape I was of Nature's ways."[8]

Canto XXX

CIRCLE EIGHT: BOLGIA TEN   *The Falsifiers (The Remaining Three Classes:*
Evil Impersonators, Counterfeiters, False Witnesses)

Just as Capocchio finishes speaking, two ravenous spirits come racing through the
pit; and one of them, sinking his tusks into Capocchio's neck, drags him away like
prey. Capocchio's companion, Griffolino, identifies the two as *Gianni Schicchi* and
Myrrhe, who run ravening through the pit through all eternity, snatching at other
souls and rending them. These are the *Evil Impersonators*, Falsifiers of Persons. In
life they seized upon the appearance of others, and in death they must run with
never a pause, seizing upon the infernal apparition of these souls, while they in
turn are preyed upon by their own furies.

   Next the Poets encounter *Master Adam*, a sinner of the third class, a Falsifier of
Money, i.e., a *Counterfeiter*. Like the alchemists, he is punished by a loathsome
disease and he cannot move from where he lies, but his disease is compounded by
other afflictions, including an eternity of unbearable thirst. Master Adam identifies
two spirits lying beside him as *Potiphar's Wife* and *Sinon the Greek*, sinners of the
fourth class, *The False Witnesses*, i.e., Falsifiers of Words.

   Sinon, angered by Master Adam's identification of him, strikes him across the
belly with the one arm he is able to move. Master Adam replies in kind; and Dante,
fascinated by their continuing exchange of abuse, stands staring at them until Virgil
turns on him in great anger, for "The wish to hear such baseness is degrading."
Dante burns with shame, and Virgil immediately forgives him because of his great
and genuine repentance.

At the time when Juno took her furious
   revenge for Semele,[9] striking in rage
   again and again at the Theban royal house,

---

8. By calling himself "an ape . . . of Nature's
ways," Capocchio means that he merely imitated change in his alchemical displays rather
than actually accomplishing it.
9. Daughter of the king of Thebes, Semele
was loved by Jupiter (their union produced
Bacchus, the god of wine) and therefore incited

the wrath of Juno, who drove her brother-in-
law Athamas insane. While mad, Athamas
thought his wife, Ino, and his two sons,
Learchus and Melicertes, were a lioness and
two cubs: he killed Learchus, and Ino drowned
herself and Melicertes. See Ovid, *Metamorphoses* 4.

King Athamas, by her contrivance, grew   3
   so mad, that seeing his wife out for an airing
   with his two sons, he cried to his retinue: 6

"Out with the nets there! Nets across the pass!
   for I will take this lioness and her cubs!"
   And spread his talons, mad and merciless,   9

and seizing his son Learchus, whirled him round
   and brained him on a rock; at which the mother
   leaped into the sea with her other son and drowned.   12

And when the Wheel of Fortune spun about
   to humble the all-daring Trojan's pride[1]
   so that both king and kingdom were wiped out;   15

Hecuba—mourning, wretched, and a slave—
   having seen Polyxena sacrificed,
   and Polydorus dead without a grave;   18

lost and alone, beside an alien sea,
   began to bark and growl like a dog
   in the mad seizure of her misery.   21

But never in Thebes nor Troy were Furies seen
   to strike at man or beast in such mad rage
   as two I saw, pale, naked, and unclean,   24

who suddenly came running toward us then,
   snapping their teeth as they ran, like hungry swine
   let out to feed after a night in the pen.   27

One of them sank his tusks so savagely
   into Capocchio's neck, that when he dragged him,
   the ditch's rocky bottom tore his belly.   30

And the Aretine,[2] left trembling by me, said:
   "That incubus, in life, was Gianni Schicchi;[3]
   here he runs rabid, mangling the other dead."   33

"So!" I answered, "and so may the other one
   not sink its teeth in you, be pleased to tell us
   what shade it is before it races on."   36

---

1. Parallel to the fate of Thebes is that of Troy, which is here represented by the madness into which Queen Hecuba fell when she saw her daughter Polyxena sacrificed on Achilles' tomb and the unburied body of her betrayed son Polydorus. See Ovid, *Metamorphoses* 13.

2. Griffolino (see 29.111).
3. A Florentine who impersonated Buoso Donati (line 44), who had just died, and dictated a new will that gave him Buoso's best beast ("the fabulous lead-mare" of line 43).

And he: "That ancient shade in time above
 was Myrrha,[4] vicious daughter of Cinyras
 who loved her father with more than rightful love.   39

She falsified another's form and came
 disguised to sin with him just as that other
 who runs with her, in order that he might claim   42

the fabulous lead-mare, lay under disguise
 on Buoso Donati's deathbed and dictated
 a spurious testament to the notaries."   45

And when the rabid pair had passed from sight,
 I turned to observe the other misbegotten
 spirits that lay about to left and right.   48

And there I saw another husk of sin,
 who, had his legs been trimmed away at the groin,
 would have looked for all the world like a mandolin.   51

The dropsy's[5] heavy humors, which so bunch
 and spread the limbs, had disproportioned him
 till his face seemed much too small for his swollen paunch.   54

He strained his lips apart and thrust them forward
 the way a sick man, feverish with thirst,
 curls one lip toward the chin and the other upward.   57

"O you exempt from every punishment
 of this grim world (I know not why)," he cried,
 "look well upon the misery and debasement   60

of him who was Master Adam.[6] In my first
 life's time, I had enough to please me; here,
 I lack a drop of water for my thirst.   63

The rivulets that run from the green flanks
 of Casentino to the Arno's flood,
 spreading their cool sweet moisture through their banks,   66

run constantly before me, and their plash
 and ripple in imagination dries me
 more than the disease that eats my flesh.   69

---

4. Myrrha impersonated another woman in order to sleep with her father; see Ovid, *Metamorphoses* 10.
5. A disease in which fluid ("humors") gathers in the cells and the affected part becomes grotesquely swollen.
6. A counterfeiter, burned in 1281, who made coins stamped with the image of John the Baptist, the patron saint of Florence, that contained 21 rather than 24 carats of gold (see line 90); he worked for a noble family of Romena (individual members are mentioned in lines 76–77), a town in the Florentine district of Casentino.

Inflexible Justice that has forked and spread
   my soul like hay, to search it the more closely,
   finds in the country where my guilt was bred   72

this increase of my grief; for there I learned,
   there in Romena, to stamp the Baptist's image
   on alloyed gold—till I was bound and burned.   75

But could I see the soul of Guido here,
   or of Alessandro, or of their filthy brother,
   I would not trade that sight for all the clear   78

cool flow of Branda's fountain.[7] One of the three—
   if those wild wraiths who run here are not lying—
   is here already. But small good it does me   81

when my legs are useless! Were I light enough
   to move as much as an inch in a hundred years,
   long before this I would have started off   84

to cull him from the freaks that fill this fosse,
   although it winds on for eleven miles
   and is no less than half a mile across.   87

Because of them I lie here in this pig-pen;
   it was they persuaded me to stamp the florins
   with three carats of alloy." And I then: 90

"Who are those wretched two sprawled alongside
   your right-hand borders, and who seem to smoke
   as a washed hand smokes in winter?" He replied: 93

"They were here when I first rained into this gully,
   and have not changed position since, nor may they,
   as I believe, to all eternity.   96

One is the liar who charged young Joseph wrongly:
   the other, Sinon, the false Greek from Troy.[8]
   A burning fever makes them reek so strongly."   99

And one of the false pair, perhaps offended
   by the manner of Master Adam's presentation,
   punched him in the rigid and distended   102

belly—it thundered like a drum—and he
   retorted with an arm blow to the face
   that seemed delivered no whit less politely,   105

---

7. A fountain near Romena.
8. The "liar" is Potiphar's wife, who falsely accuses Joseph of trying to lie with her (Genesis 39.7–20); Sinon is the Greek priest who persuaded the Trojans to accept the wooden horse (*Aeneid* 2).

saying to him: "Although I cannot stir
   my swollen legs, I still have a free arm
   to use at times when nothing else will answer."   108

And the other wretch said: "It was not so free
   on your last walk to the stake, free as it was
   when you were coining." And he of the dropsy: 111

"That's true enough, but there was less truth in you
   when they questioned you at Troy." And Sinon then:
   "For every word I uttered that was not true   114

you uttered enough false coins to fill a bushel:
   I am put down here for a single crime,
   but you for more than any Fiend in Hell."   117

"Think of the Horse," replied the swollen shade,
   "and may it torture you, perjurer, to recall
   that all the world knows the foul part you played."   120

"And to you the torture of the thirst that fries
   and cracks your tongue," said the Greek, "and of the water
   that swells your gut like a hedge before your eyes."   123

And the coiner: "So is your own mouth clogged
   with the filth that stuffs and sickens it as always;
   if I am parched while my paunch is waterlogged,   126

you have the fever and your cankered brain;
   and were you asked to lap Narcissus' mirror[9]
   you would not wait to be invited again."   129

I was still standing, fixed upon those two
   when the Master said to me: "Now keep on looking
   a little longer and I quarrel with you."   132

When I heard my Master raise his voice to me,
   I wheeled about with such a start of shame
   that I grow pale yet at the memory.   135

As one trapped in a nightmare that has caught
   his sleeping mind, wishes within the dream
   that it were all a dream, as if it were not—   138

such I became: my voice could not win through
   my shame to ask his pardon; while my shame
   already won more pardon than I knew.   141

---

9. Narcissus saw his reflection in a pool of water, referred to here as a "mirror" (Ovid, *Metamorphoses* 3).

"Less shame," my Guide said, ever just and kind,
   "would wash away a greater fault than yours.
   Therefore, put back all sorrow from your mind;   144

And never forget that I am always by you
   should it occur again, as we walk on,
   that we find ourselves where others of this crew   147

fall to such petty wrangling and upbraiding.
The wish to hear such baseness is degrading."

Canto XXXI

THE CENTRAL PIT OF MALEBOLGE   *The Giants*

Dante's spirits rise again as the Poets approach the Central Pit, a great well, at the bottom of which lies Cocytus, the Ninth and final circle of Hell. Through the darkness Dante sees what appears to be a city of great towers, but as he draws near he discovers that the great shapes he has seen are the Giants and Titans who stand perpetual guard inside the well-pit with the upper halves of their bodies rising above the rim.

Among the Giants, Virgil identifies *Nimrod,* builder of the Tower of Babel; *Ephialtes* and *Briareus,* who warred against the Gods; and *Tityos* and *Typhon,* who insulted Jupiter. Also here, but for no specific offense, is *Antaeus,* and his presence makes it clear that the Giants are placed here less for their particular sins than for their general natures.

These are the sons of earth, embodiments of elemental forces unbalanced by love, desire without restraint and without acknowledgment of moral and theological law. They are symbols of the earth-trace that every devout man must clear from his soul, the unchecked passions of the beast. Raised from the earth, they make the very gods tremble. Now they are returned to the darkness of their origins, guardians of earth's last depth.

At Virgil's persuasion, Antaeus takes the Poets in his huge palm and lowers them gently to the final floor of Hell.

One and the same tongue had first wounded me
   so that the blood came rushing to my cheeks,
   and then supplied the soothing remedy.   3

Just so, as I have heard, the magic steel
   of the lance that was Achilles' and his father's
   could wound at a touch, and, at another, heal.[1]   6

We turned our backs on the valley and climbed from it
   to the top of the stony bank that walls it round,
   crossing in silence to the central pit.   9

---

1. Achilles' father, Peleus, gave him a lance that would heal any wound it inflicted.

Here it was less than night and less than day;
    my eyes could make out little through the gloom,
    but I heard the shrill note of a trumpet bray   12

louder than any thunder. As if by force,
    it drew my eyes; I stared into the gloom
    along the path of the sound back to its source.   15

After the bloody rout when Charlemagne[2]
    had lost the band of Holy Knights, Roland
    blew no more terribly for all his pain.   18

And as I stared through that obscurity,
    I saw what seemed a cluster of great towers,
    whereat I cried: "Master, what is this city?"   21

And he: "You are still too far back in the dark
    to make out clearly what you think you see;
    it is natural that you should miss the mark: 24

you will see clearly when you reach that place
    how much your eyes mislead you at a distance;
    I urge you, therefore, to increase your pace."   27

Then taking my hand in his, my Master said:
    "The better to prepare you for strange truth,
    let me explain those shapes you see ahead: 30

they are not towers but giants. They stand in the well
    from the navel down; and stationed round its bank
    they mount guard on the final pit of Hell."   33

Just as a man in a fog that starts to clear
    begins little by little to piece together
    the shapes the vapor crowded from the air—   36

so, when those shapes grew clearer as I drew
    across the darkness to the central brink,
    error fled from me; and my terror grew.   39

For just as at Montereggione[3] the great towers
    crown the encircling wall; so the grim giants[4]
    whom Jove still threatens when the thunder roars   42

2. In *The Song of Roland* (laisse 133), Roland blows his horn to alert Charlemagne to the fact that the rear guard Roland commands has been slaughtered.
3. A castle surrounded by towers, built to pro-tect Siena from attack by Florence.
4. These "giants" are the mythological Titans, monsters born of the Earth who assaulted Olympus and were defeated and imprisoned by Jupiter (Jove).

raised from the rim of stone about that well
    the upper halves of their bodies, which loomed up
    like turrets through the murky air of Hell.   45

I had drawn close enough to one already
    to make out the great arms along his sides,
    the face, the shoulders, the breast, and most of the belly.[5]   48

Nature, when she destroyed the last exemplars
    on which she formed those beasts, surely did well
    to take such executioners from Mars.   51

And if she has not repented the creation
    of whales and elephants, the thinking man
    will see in that her justice and discretion: 54

for where the instrument of intelligence
    is added to brute power and evil will,
    mankind is powerless in its own defense.   57

His face, it seemed to me, was quite as high
    and wide as the bronze pine cone in St. Peter's[6]
    with the rest of him proportioned accordingly: 60

so that the bank, which made an apron for him
    from the waist down, still left so much exposed
    that three Frieslanders[7] standing on the rim,   63

one on another, could not have reached his hair;
    for to that point at which men's capes are buckled,
    thirty good hand-spans[8] of brute bulk rose clear.   66

"Rafel mahee amek zabi almit,"[9]
    began a bellowed chant from the brute mouth
    for which no sweeter psalmody was fit.   69

And my Guide in his direction: "Babbling fool,
    stick to your horn[1] and vent yourself with it
    when rage or passion stir your stupid soul.   72

Feel there around your neck, you muddle-head,
    and find the cord; and there's the horn itself,
    there on your overgrown chest." To me he said: 75

---

5. This is Nimrod, described as "a mighty hunter before the Lord" (Genesis 10.9) and understood by medieval commentators to be a giant. He ruled over Babylon, where the tower of Babel was built (Genesis 11.1–9).
6. This bronze pine cone, over 12 feet high, stood outside St. Peter's Cathedral in Dante's time; today it can be seen in the papal gardens in the Vatican.

7. Inhabitants of the northernmost province of what is now the Netherlands, considered the tallest men of the time.
8. About 15 feet.
9. Appropriately for the builder of Babel, he speaks an incomprehensible language.
1. Nimrod has a "horn" because in the Bible he is described as a hunter (Genesis 10.9).

"His very babbling testifies the wrong
    he did on earth: he is Nimrod, through whose evil
    mankind no longer speaks a common tongue.   78

Waste no words on him: it would be foolish.
    To him all speech is meaningless; as his own,
    which no one understands, is simply gibberish."   81

We moved on, bearing left along the pit,
    and a crossbow-shot away we found the next one,²
    an even huger and more savage spirit.   84

What master could have bound so gross a beast
    I cannot say, but he had his right arm pinned
    behind his back, and the left across his breast   87

by an enormous chain that wound about him
    from the neck down, completing five great turns
    before it spiraled down below the rim.   90

"This piece of arrogance," said my Guide to me,
    "dared try his strength against the power of Jove;
    for which he is rewarded as you see.   93

He is Ephialtes, who made the great endeavour
    with the other giants who alarmed the Gods;
    the arms he raised then, now are bound forever."   96

"Were it possible, I should like to take with me,"
    I said to him, "the memory of seeing
    the immeasurable Briareus."³ And he: 99

"Nearer to hand, you may observe Antaeus⁴
    who is able to speak to us, and is not bound.
    It is he will set us down in Cocytus,   102

the bottom of all guilt. The other hulk
    stands far beyond our road. He too, is bound
    and looks like this one, but with a fiercer sulk."   105

No earthquake in the fury of its shock
    has ever seized a tower more violently,
    than Ephialtes, hearing, began to rock.   108

Then I dreaded death as never before;
    and I think I could have died for very fear
    had I not seen what manacles he wore.   111

2. This is Ephialtes, a Titan who with his twin brother Otus tried to attack Olympus by piling Mount Ossa on Mount Pelion; see *Aeneid* 6.
3. Another Titan.
4. A Titan born too late to participate in the rebellion against Jupiter and therefore not chained; he was known for eating lions (line 118) and was defeated by Hercules in a wrestling match (line 132).

We left the monster, and not far from him
   we reached Antaeus, who to his shoulders alone
   soared up a good five ells[5] above the rim.   114

"O soul who once in Zama's fateful vale—[6]
   where Scipio became the heir of glory
   when Hannibal and all his troops turned tail—   117

took more than a thousand lions for your prey;
   and in whose memory many still believe
   the sons of earth would yet have won the day   120

had you joined with them against High Olympus—
   do not disdain to do us a small service,
   but set us down where the cold grips Cocytus.[7]   123

Would you have us go to Tityos or Typhon?—[8]
   this man can give you what is longed for here:
   therefore do not refuse him, but bend down.   126

For he can still make new your memory:
   he lives, and awaits long life, unless Grace call him
   before his time to his felicity."   129

Thus my Master to that Tower of Pride;
   and the giant without delay reached out the hands
   which Hercules had felt, and raised my Guide.   132

Virgil, when he felt himself so grasped,
   called to me: "Come, and I will hold you safe."
   And he took me in his arms and held me clasped.   135

The way the Carisenda[9] seems to one
   who looks up from the leaning side when clouds
   are going over it from that direction,   138

making the whole tower seem to topple—so
   Antaeus seemed to me in the fraught moment
   when I stood clinging, watching from below   141

as he bent down; while I with heart and soul
   wished we had gone some other way, but gently
   he set us down inside the final hole   144

whose ice holds Judas and Lucifer[1] in its grip.
Then straightened like a mast above a ship.

5. About 19 feet.
6. The "vale" of the Bagradas River in Tunisia, where the Roman Scipio defeated the Carthaginian Hannibal in the battle of Zama in 202 B.C.E.
7. The frozen lake of Cocytus is in the ninth and last circle of Hell.
8. Two more Titans.
9. A leaning tower of Bologna: when a cloud passes over it, moving opposite to the tower's slant, it appears to be falling away from the sky.
1. Two of the inhabitants of Cocytus.

Canto XXXII

CIRCLE NINE: COCYTUS	*Compound Fraud*
ROUND ONE: CAÏNA	*The Treacherous to Kin*
ROUND TWO: ANTENORA	*The Treacherous to Country*

At the bottom of the well Dante finds himself on a huge frozen lake. This is *Cocytus*, the *Ninth Circle*, the fourth and last great water of Hell, and here, fixed in the ice, each according to his guilt, are punished sinners guilty of *Treachery against Those to Whom They Were Bound by Special Ties*. The ice is divided into four concentric rings marked only by the different positions of the damned within the ice.

This is Dante's symbolic equivalent of the final guilt. The treacheries of these souls were denials of love (which is God) and of all human warmth. Only the remorseless dead center of the ice will serve to express their natures. As they denied God's love, so are they furthest removed from the light and warmth of His Sun. As they denied all human ties, so are they bound only by the unyielding ice.

The first round is *Caïna*, named for Cain. Here lie those who were treacherous against blood ties. They have their necks and heads out of the ice and are permitted to bow their heads—a double boon since it allows them some protection from the freezing gale and, further, allows their tears to fall without freezing their eyes shut. Here Dante sees *Alessandro* and *Napoleone degli Alberti*, and he speaks to *Camicion*, who identifies other sinners of this round.

The second round is *Antenora*, named for Antenor, the Trojan who was believed to have betrayed his city to the Greeks. Here lie those guilty of *Treachery to Country*. They, too, have their heads above the ice, but they cannot bend their necks, which are gripped by the ice. Here Dante accidentally kicks the head of *Bocca degli Abbati* and then proceeds to treat him with a savagery he has shown to no other soul in Hell. Bocca names some of his fellow traitors, and the Poets pass on to discover two heads frozen together in one hole. One of them is gnawing the nape of the other's neck.

If I had rhymes as harsh and horrible
  as the hard fact of that final dismal hole
  which bears the weight of all the steeps of Hell,   3

I might more fully press the sap and substance
  from my conception; but since I must do
  without them, I begin with some reluctance.   6

For it is no easy undertaking, I say,
  to describe the bottom of the Universe;
  nor is it for tongues that only babble child's play.   9

But may those Ladies of the Heavenly Spring[2]
  who helped Amphion wall Thebes, assist my verse,
  that the word may be the mirror of the thing.   12

---

2. The Muses who helped the legendary musician Amphion raise the walls of Thebes with the music of his lyre.

O most miscreant rabble, you who keep
   the stations of that place whose name is pain,
   better had you been born as goats or sheep!   15

We stood now in the dark pit of the well,
   far down the slope below the Giant's feet,
   and while I still stared up at the great wall,   18

I heard a voice cry: "Watch which way you turn:
   take care you do not trample on the heads
   of the forworn and miserable brethren."   21

Whereat I turned and saw beneath my feet
   and stretching out ahead, a lake so frozen
   it seemed to be made of glass.[3] So thick a sheet   24

never yet hid the Danube's winter course,
   nor, far away beneath the frigid sky,
   locked the Don up in its frozen source: 27

for were Tanbernick[4] and the enormous peak
   of Pietrapana to crash down on it,
   not even the edges would so much as creak.   30

The way frogs sit to croak, their muzzles leaning
   out of the water, at the time and season
   when the peasant woman dreams of her day's gleaning—   33

just so the livid dead are sealed in place
   up to the part at which they blushed for shame,
   and they beat their teeth like storks.[5] Each holds his face   36

bowed toward the ice, each of them testifies
   to the cold with his chattering mouth, to his heart's grief
   with tears that flood forever from his eyes.   39

When I had stared about me, I looked down
   and at my feet I saw two clamped together
   so tightly that the hair of their heads had grown   42

together. "Who are you," I said, "who lie
   so tightly breast to breast?"[6] They strained their necks,
   and when they had raised their heads as if to reply,   45

---

3. The water for this lake derives from the crack in the Old Man of Crete (14.106–8).
4. Probably Mount Tambura, close to Mount Pietrapana in the Italian Alps. The Danube, in Central Europe, and the Don, in Russia, represent rivers of the north.

5. A harsh, clacking sound. The "part at which they blushed" is the face.
6. These are the two sons of Count Alberto degli Alberti of Florence; when he died (ca. 1280), they killed each other over politics and their inheritance.

the tears their eyes had managed to contain
   up to that time gushed out, and the cold froze them
   between the lids, sealing them shut again   48

tighter than any clamp grips wood to wood,
   and mad with pain, they fell to butting heads
   like billy goats in a sudden savage mood.   51

And a wraith who lay to one side and below,
   and who had lost both ears to frostbite, said,
   his head still bowed: "Why do you watch us so?   54

If you wish to know who they are who share one doom,
   they owned the Bisenzio's[7] valley with their father,
   whose name was Albert. They sprang from one womb,   57

and you may search through all Caïna's[8] crew
   without discovering in all this waste
   a squab more fit for the aspic than these two;   60

not him whose breast and shadow a single blow
   of the great lance of King Arthur pierced with light;[9]
   nor yet Focaccia; nor this one fastened so   63

into the ice that his head is all I see,
   and whom, if you are Tuscan, you know well—
   his name on the earth was Sassol Mascheroni.[1]   66

And I—to tell you all and so be through—
   was Camicion de' Pazzi.[2] I wait for Carlin[3]
   beside whose guilt my sins will shine like virtue."   69

And leaving him, I saw a thousand faces
   discolored so by cold, I shudder yet
   and always will when I think of those frozen places.   72

As we approached the center of all weight,[4]
   where I went shivering in eternal shade,
   whether it was my will, or chance, or fate,   75

7. A river north of Florence.
8. Named after Cain; this first of the four subdivisions of Cocytus is where those who betrayed their kin are imprisoned.
9. "Not him . . . light": This is Mordred, Arthur's nephew and son; when Arthur pierced him with a sword, he created a wound so large that the sun shone through, thus creating a hole in Mordred's shadow. Focaccia in the next line is a nobleman of Pistoia who killed his cousin.
1. A Florentine nobleman who murdered a relative.

2. A Florentine who killed his kinsman.
3. A Florentine who has betrayed a castle belonging to his party. When he dies (sometime after 1300) he will therefore be sent to the next subdivision, Antenora, for those who committed treachery against their country, city, or party—a harsher punishment, beside whose guilt Camicion says "my sins will shine like virtue."
4. The "center of all weight" is where gravity is strongest and toward which all material things are drawn.

I cannot say, but as I trailed my Guide
   among those heads, my foot struck violently
   against the face of one.[5] Weeping, it cried: 78

"Why do you kick me? If you were not sent
   to wreak a further vengeance for Montaperti,
   why do you add this to my other torment?"   81

"Master," I said, "grant me a moment's pause
   to rid myself of a doubt concerning this one,
   then you may hurry me at your own pace."   84

The Master stopped at once, and through the volley
   of foul abuse the wretch poured out, I said:
   "Who are you who curse others so?" And he: 87

"And who are *you* who go through the dead larder
   of Antenora[6] kicking the cheeks of others
   so hard, that were you alive, you could not kick harder?"   90

"I *am* alive," I said, "and if you seek fame,
   it may be precious to you above all else
   that my notes on this descent include your name."   93

"Exactly the opposite is my wish and hope,"
   he answered. "Let me be; for it's little you know
   of how to flatter on this icy slope."   96

I grabbed the hair of his dog's-ruff[7] and I said:
   "Either you tell me truly who you are,
   or you won't have a hair left on your head."   99

And he: "Not though you snatch me bald. I swear
   I will not tell my name nor show my face.
   Not though you rip until my brain lies bare."   102

I had a good grip on his hair; already
   I had yanked out more than one fistful of it,
   while the wretch yelped, but kept his face turned from me;   105

when another[8] said: "Bocca, what is it ails you?
   What the Hell's wrong? Isn't it bad enough
   to hear you bang your jaws? Must you bark too?"   108

5. Bocca degli Abati (his name is betrayed by one of the fellows damned in line 106); Bocca betrayed his party at the battle of Montaperti in 1260.
6. Dante and Virgil have moved into the second subdivision of Caïna, which is named after Antenor, a Trojan who betrayed the city to the Greeks; it is the location of those who betrayed their country.
7. The hair at the nape of the neck.
8. This is Buoso da Duera, who betrayed Manfred, the ruler of Naples, to his enemy Charles of Anjou in 1265.

"Now filthy traitor, say no more!" I cried,
  "for to your shame, be sure I shall bear back
  a true report of you." The wretch replied: 111

"Say anything you please but go away.
  And if you *do* get back, don't overlook
  that pretty one who had so much to say   114

just now. Here he laments the Frenchman's price.
  'I saw Buoso da Duera,' you can report,
  'where the bad salad is kept crisp on ice.'   117

And if you're asked who else was wintering here,
  Beccheria,[9] whose throat was slit by Florence,
  is there beside you. Gianni de' Soldanier[1]   120

is further down, I think, with Ganelon,
  and Tebaldello, who opened the gates of Faenza
  and let Bologna steal in with the dawn."   123

Leaving him then, I saw two souls together
  in a single hole, and so pinched in by the ice
  that one head made a helmet for the other.   126

As a famished man chews crusts—so the one sinner
  sank his teeth into the other's nape
  at the base of the skull, gnawing his loathsome dinner.   129

Tydeus[2] in his final raging hour
  gnawed Menalippus' head with no more fury
  than this one gnawed at skull and dripping gore.   132

"You there," I said, "who show so odiously
  your hatred for that other, tell me why
  on this condition: that if in what you tell me   135

you seem to have a reasonable complaint
  against him you devour with such foul relish,
  I, knowing who you are, and his soul's taint,   138

may speak your cause to living memory,
God willing the power of speech be left to me."

---

9. Tesauro de' Beccheria, a churchman executed for treason in Florence in 1258.
1. Gianni Soldanier was a Florentine nobleman who switched political parties; Ganelon
(line 121) is the betrayer of Roland in the *Song
of Roland*; Tebaldello (line 122) was the citi-

zen of Faenza (a town east of Florence) who
betrayed it to its enemies.
2. In the war against Thebes, Tydeus was mortally wounded by Menalippus, whom he killed
and whose skull he gnawed in fury while dying.

Canto XXXIII

CIRCLE NINE: COCYTUS   *Compound Fraud*

ROUND TWO: ANTENORA   *The Treacherous to Country*

ROUND THREE: PTOLOMEA   *The Treacherous to Guests and Hosts*

In reply to Dante's exhortation, the sinner who is gnawing his companion's head
looks up, wipes his bloody mouth on his victim's hair, and tells his harrowing story.
He is *Count Ugolino* and the wretch he gnaws is *Archbishop Ruggieri*. Both are in
Antenora for treason. In life they had once plotted together. Then Ruggieri betrayed
his fellow plotter and caused his death, by starvation, along with his four "sons." In
the most pathetic and dramatic passage of the *Inferno*, Ugolino details how their
prison was sealed and how his "sons" dropped dead before him one by one, weeping
for food. His terrible tale serves only to renew his grief and hatred, and he has hardly
finished it before he begins to gnaw Ruggieri again with renewed fury. In the immutable Law of Hell, the killer-by-starvation becomes the food of his victim.

The Poets leave Ugolino and enter *Ptolomea*, so named for the Ptolomaeus of
Maccabees, who murdered his father-in-law at a banquet. Here are punished those
who were *Treacherous against the Ties of Hospitality*. They lie with only half their
faces above the ice and their tears freeze in their eye sockets, sealing them with
little crystal visors. Thus even the comfort of tears is denied them. Here Dante
finds *Friar Alberigo* and *Branca d'Oria*, and discovers the terrible power of Ptolomea: so great is its sin that the souls of the guilty fall to its torments even before
they die, leaving their bodies still on earth, inhabited by Demons.

The sinner raised his mouth from his grim repast
    and wiped it on the hair of the bloody head
    whose nape he had all but eaten away. At last   3

he began to speak: "You ask me to renew
    a grief so desperate that the very thought
    of speaking of it tears my heart in two.   6

But if my words may be a seed that bears
    the fruit of infamy for him I gnaw,
    I shall weep, but tell my story through my tears.   9

Who you may be, and by what powers you reach
    into this underworld, I cannot guess,
    but you seem to me a Florentine by your speech.   12

I was Count Ugolino,[3] I must explain;
    this reverend grace is the Archbishop Ruggieri:
    now I will tell you why I gnaw his brain.   15

That I, who trusted him, had to undergo
    imprisonment and death through his treachery,
    you will know already. What you cannot know—   18

---

3. Ugolino, a governor of Pisa who was betrayed   His own crime is obliquely explained by his
by his enemy Archbishop Ruggieri in 1288.   narrative.

that is, the lingering inhumanity
   of the death I suffered—you shall hear in full:
   then judge for yourself if he has injured me.   21

A narrow window in that coop of[4] stone
   now called the Tower of Hunger for my sake
   (within which others yet must pace alone)   24

had shown me several waning moons already
   between its bars, when I slept the evil sleep
   in which the veil of the future parted for me.   27

This beast appeared as master of a hunt
   chasing the wolf and his whelps across the mountain[5]
   that hides Lucca from Pisa. Out in front   30

of the starved and shrewd and avid pack he had placed
   Gualandi and Sismondi and Lanfranchi[6]
   to point his prey. The father and sons had raced   33

a brief course only when they failed of breath
   and seemed to weaken; then I thought I saw
   their flanks ripped open by the hounds' fierce teeth.   36

Before the dawn, the dream still in my head,
   I woke and heard my sons, who were there with me,
   cry from their troubled sleep, asking for bread.   39

You are cruelty itself if you can keep
   your tears back at the thought of what foreboding
   stirred in my heart; and if you do not weep,   42

at what are you used to weeping?—The hour when food
   used to be brought, drew near. They were now awake,
   and each was anxious from his dream's dark mood.   45

And from the base of that horrible tower I heard
   the sound of hammers nailing up the gates:
   I stared at my sons' faces without a word.   48

I did not weep: I had turned stone inside.
   They wept. 'What ails you, Father, you look so strange,'
   my little Anselm, youngest of them, cried.   51

---

4. A cage for birds; the prison in Pisa where
Ugolino and his relatives were confined
became known as the Torre de Fame or Tower
of Hunger.
5. Mount San Giuliano lies between Pisa and
Lucca. "The wolf and his whelps": Ugolino and

his four sons. Ugolino was imprisoned with
two sons (who were grown men) and two adolescent grandsons.
6. Pisan families of the political party opposed
to that of Ugolino.

But I did not speak a word nor shed a tear:
   not all that day nor all that endless night,
   until I saw another sun appear.   54

When a tiny ray leaked into that dark prison
   and I saw staring back from their four faces
   the terror and the wasting of my own,   57

I bit my hands in helpless grief. And they,
   thinking I chewed myself for hunger, rose
   suddenly together. I heard them say: 60

'Father, it would give us much less pain
   if you ate us: it was you who put upon us
   this sorry flesh; now strip it off again.'[7]   63

I calmed myself to spare them. Ah! hard earth,
   why did you not yawn open? All that day
   and the next we sat in silence. On the fourth,   66

Gaddo, the eldest, fell before me and cried,
   stretched at my feet upon that prison floor:
   'Father, why don't you help me?'[8] There he died.   69

And just as you see me, I saw them fall
   one by one on the fifth day and the sixth.
   Then, already blind, I began to crawl   72

from body to body shaking them frantically.
   Two days I called their names, and they were dead.
   Then fasting overcame my grief and me."   75

His eyes narrowed to slits when he was done,
   and he seized the skull again between his teeth
   grinding it as a mastiff grinds a bone.   78

Ah, Pisa! foulest blemish on the land
   where "si" sounds sweet and clear,[9] since those nearby you
   are slow to blast the ground on which you stand,   81

may Caprara and Gorgona[1] drift from place
   and dam the flooding Arno at its mouth
   until it drowns the last of your foul race!   84

For if to Ugolino falls the censure
   for having betrayed your castles,[2] you for your part
   should not have put his sons to such a torture: 87

---

7. See Job 1.21.
8. See Matthew 27.46.
9. I.e., Italy, where *si* means "yes."
1. Islands belonging to Pisa that lie close to

the mouth of the Arno, which flows through Pisa.

2. In 1285 Ugolino conveyed three Pisan castles to Lucca and Florence.

you modern Thebes![3] those tender lives you spilt—
   Brigata, Uguccione, and the others
   I mentioned earlier—were too young for guilt!   90

We passed on further, where the frozen mine
   entombs another crew in greater pain;
   these wraiths are not bent over, but lie supine.[4]   93

Their very weeping closes up their eyes;
   and the grief that finds no outlet for its tears
   turns inward to increase their agonies: 96

for the first tears that they shed knot instantly
   in their eye-sockets, and as they freeze they form
   a crystal visor above the cavity.   99

And despite the fact that standing in that place
   I had become as numb as any callus,
   and all sensation had faded from my face,   102

somehow I felt a wind begin to blow,
   whereat I said: "Master, what stirs this wind?
   Is not all heat extinguished here below?"[5]   105

And the Master said to me: "Soon you will be
   where your own eyes will see the source and cause
   and give you their own answer to the mystery."   108

And one of those locked in that icy mall
   cried out to us as we passed: "O souls so cruel
   that you are sent to the last post of all,   111

relieve me for a little from the pain
   of this hard veil; let my heart weep a while
   before the weeping freeze my eyes again."   114

And I to him: "If you would have my service,
   tell me your name; then if I do not help you
   may I descend to the last rim of the ice."   117

"I am Friar Alberigo,"[6] he answered therefore,
   "the same who called for the fruits from the bad garden.
   Here I am given dates for figs full store."   120

3. In classical mythology, Thebes was notorious for its internecine violence, such as the story of Oedipus, his father, Laius, and his sons, Eteocles and Polynices (see 26.54).
4. Virgil and Dante pass into the third subdivision of Cocytus, called Ptolomea (line 124) after Ptolemy, governor of Jericho, who killed his father-in-law, Simon, and two of his sons while they were dining with him (1 Maccabees

16.11–17). In Ptolomea those who have betrayed their guests are punished.
5. Since the sun's heat was thought to cause wind, Dante wonders why he feels wind in this cold place. The answer will be given in 34.46–52.
6. A member of the Jovial Friars (see 23.100), he killed two of his relatives during a banquet at his house, signaling the assassins with an

"What! Are you dead already?" I said to him.
    And he then: "How my body stands in the world
    I do not know. So privileged is this rim   123

of Ptolomea, that often souls fall to it
    before dark Atropos[7] has cut their thread.
    And that you may more willingly free my spirit   126

of this glaze of frozen tears that shrouds my face,
    I will tell you this: when a soul betrays as I did,
    it falls from flesh, and a demon takes its place,   129

ruling the body till its time is spent.
    The ruined soul rains down into this cistern.
    So, I believe, there is still evident   132

in the world above, all that is fair and mortal
    of this black shade who winters here behind me.
    If you have only recently crossed the portal   135

from that sweet world, you surely must have known
    his body: Branca D'Oria[8] is its name,
    and many years have passed since he rained down."   138

"I think you are trying to take me in," I said,
    "Ser Branca D'Oria is a living man;
    he eats, he drinks, he fills his clothes and his bed."   141

"Michel Zanche had not yet reached the ditch
    of the Black Talons," the frozen wraith replied,
    "there where the sinners thicken in hot pitch,   144

when this one left his body to a devil,
    as did his nephew and second in treachery,
    and plumbed like lead through space to this dead level.   · 147

But now reach out your hand, and let me cry."
    And I did not keep the promise I had made,
    for to be rude to him was courtesy.   150

Ah, men of Genoa! souls of little worth,
    corrupted from all custom of righteousness,
    why have you not been driven from the earth?   153

---

order to bring the fruit. In saying that he is now being served dates instead of figs, he is ironically complimenting God for his generosity, since a date would be more valuable than a fig.
7. One of the mythological figures known as the Fates, she is the one who cuts the thread of life.
8. A nobleman of Genoa, who with a "nephew" (line 146) killed his father-in-law, Michel Zanche (line 142), at a banquet in 1275.

For there beside the blackest soul of all
   Romagna's evil plain, lies one of yours
   bathing his filthy soul[9] in the eternal   156

glacier of Cocytus for his foul crime,
   while he seems yet alive in world and time!

Canto XXXIV

NINTH CIRCLE: COCYTUS   *Compound Fraud*

ROUND FOUR: JUDECCA   *The Treacherous to Their Masters*

THE CENTER   *Satan*

"On march the banners of the King," Virgil begins as the Poets face the last
depth. He is quoting a medieval hymn, and to it he adds the distortion and perversion of all that lies about him. "On march the banners of the King—of Hell."
And there before them, in an infernal parody of Godhead, they see Satan in the
distance, his great wings beating like a windmill. It is their beating that is the
source of the icy wind of Cocytus, the exhalation of all evil.

All about him in the ice are strewn the sinners of the last round, *Judecca*, named
for Judas Iscariot. These are the *Treacherous to Their Masters*. They lie completely
sealed in the ice, twisted and distorted into every conceivable posture. It is impossible to speak to them, and the Poets move on to observe Satan.

He is fixed into the ice at the center to which flow all the rivers of guilt; and as
he beats his great wings as if to escape, their icy wind only freezes him more
surely into the polluted ice. In a grotesque parody of the Trinity, he has three
faces, each a different color, and in each mouth he clamps a sinner whom he rips
eternally with his teeth. *Judas Iscariot* is in the central mouth: *Brutus* and *Cassius*
in the mouths on either side.

Having seen all, the Poets now climb through the center, grappling hand over
hand down the hairy flank of Satan himself—a last supremely symbolic action—
and at last, when they have passed the center of all gravity, they emerge from
Hell. A long climb from the earth's center to the Mount of Purgatory awaits
them, and they push on without rest, ascending along the sides of the river Lethe,
till they emerge once more to see the stars of Heaven, just before dawn on Easter
Sunday.

"On march the banners of the King of Hell,"[1]
   my Master said. "Toward us. Look straight ahead:
   can you make him out at the core of the frozen shell?"   3

Like a whirling windmill seen afar at twilight,
   or when a mist has risen from the ground—
   just such an engine rose upon my sight   6

9. That is, Friar Alberigo (line 118); Romagna
is the part of Italy from which he and Branca
come.
1. The first few words—"On march the banners of the King"—are opening lines of a 6th-
century Latin hymn traditionally sung during
Holy Week to celebrate Christ's Passion.
Dante has added the last word, *Inferni*—"On
march the banners of the King of Hell"—in
order to apply the words to Satan.

stirring up such a wild and bitter wind
    I cowered for shelter at my Master's back,
    there being no other windbreak I could find.   9

I stood now[2] where the souls of the last class
    (with fear my verses tell it) were covered wholly;
    they shone below the ice like straws in glass.   12

Some lie stretched out; others are fixed in place
    upright, some on their heads, some on their soles;
    another, like a bow, bends foot to face.   15

When we had gone so far across the ice
    that it pleased my Guide to show me the foul creature
    that once had worn the grace of Paradise,[3]   18

he made me stop, and, stepping aside, he said:
    "Now see the face of Dis![4] This is the place
    where you must arm your soul against all dread."   21

Do not ask, Reader, how my blood ran cold
    and my voice choked up with fear. I cannot write it:
    this is a terror that cannot be told.   24

I did not die, and yet I lost life's breath:
    imagine for yourself what I became,
    deprived at once of both my life and death.   27

The Emperor of the Universe of Pain
    jutted his upper chest above the ice;
    and I am closer in size to the great mountain   30

the Titans make around the central pit,
    than they to his arms. Now, starting from this part,
    imagine the whole that corresponds to it!   33

If he was once as beautiful as now
    he is hideous, and still turned on his Maker,
    well may he be the source of every woe!   36

With what a sense of awe I saw his head
    towering above me! for it had three faces:[5]
    one was in front, and it was fiery red;   39

---

2. This is the last and lowest subdivision of Caïna, known as Judecca after Judas; the sinners here are those who betrayed their benefactors.
3. Lucifer, the "light-bearer," was the most beautiful of angels before he rebelled and was renamed Satan.
4. A classical name for Pluto, here applied to Satan (see also 11.65).
5. Satan's three faces (and much else) make him an infernal parody of the Trinity.

the other two, as weirdly wonderful,
    merged with it from the middle of each shoulder
    to the point where all converged at the top of the skull;   42

the right was something between white and bile;
    the left was about the color one observes
    on those who live along the banks of the Nile.[6]   45

Under each head two wings rose terribly,
    their span proportioned to so gross a bird:
    I never saw such sails upon the sea.   48

They were not feathers—their texture and their form
    were like a bat's wings—and he beat them so
    that three winds blew from him in one great storm: 51

it is these winds that freeze all Cocytus.
    He wept from his six eyes, and down three chins
    the tears ran mixed with bloody froth and pus.   54

In every mouth he worked a broken sinner
    between his rake-like teeth. Thus he kept three
    in eternal pain at his eternal dinner.   57

For the one in front the biting seemed to play
    no part at all compared to the ripping: at times
    the whole skin of his back was flayed away.   60

"That soul that suffers most," explained my Guide,
    "is Judas Iscariot, he who kicks his legs
    on the fiery chin and has his head inside.   63

Of the other two, who have their heads thrust forward,
    the one who dangles down from the black face
    is Brutus:[7] note how he writhes without a word.   66

And there, with the huge and sinewy arms, is the soul
    of Cassius,[8]—But the night is coming on
    and we must go, for we have seen the whole."   69

Then, as he bade, I clasped his neck, and he,
    watching for a moment when the wings
    were opened wide, reached over dexterously   72

---

6. I.e., Ethiopians (Dante refers to those who live near the Nile's source). The significance of these three colors is not certain; it has been suggested that they represent hatred, impotence, and ignorance as the opposites of the divine attributes of love, omnipotence, and wisdom (see 3.5–6).

7. One of murderers of Julius Caesar in 44 B.C.E. and thus for Dante a betrayer of the empire.

8. The other murderer of Caesar.

and seized the shaggy coat of the king demon;
　　then grappling matted hair and frozen crusts
　　from one tuft to another, clambered down.　　　　　　　75

When we had reached the joint where the great thigh
　　merges into the swelling of the haunch,
　　my Guide and Master, straining terribly,　　　　　　　78

turned his head to where his feet had been
　　and began to grip the hair as if he were climbing;
　　so that I thought we moved toward Hell again.[9]　　　81

"Hold fast!" my Guide said, and his breath came shrill
　　with labor and exhaustion. "There is no way
　　but by such stairs to rise above such evil."　　　　　84

At last he climbed out through an opening
　　in the central rock, and he seated me on the rim;
　　then joined me with a nimble backward spring.　　　87

I looked up, thinking to see Lucifer
　　as I had left him, and I saw instead
　　his legs projecting high into the air.　　　　　　　　90

Now let all those whose dull minds are still vexed
　　by failure to understand what point it was
　　I had passed through, judge if I was perplexed.　　　93

"Get up. Up on your feet," my Master said.
　　"The sun already mounts to middle tierce,[1]
　　and a long road and hard climbing lie ahead."　　　96

It was no hall of state we had found there,
　　but a natural animal pit hollowed from rock
　　with a broken floor and a close and sunless air.　　99

"Before I tear myself from the Abyss,"
　　I said when I had risen, "O my Master,
　　explain to me my error in all this:　　　　　　　　102

where is the ice? and Lucifer—how has he
　　been turned from top to bottom: and how can the sun
　　have gone from night to day so suddenly?"　　　　105

9. Virgil's reversal marks the point at which the two travelers pass from the Northern to the Southern Hemisphere. They began by climbing down Satan's body, but now reverse directions and climb up from the Earth's center (hence when they have passed through the center Dante sees Satan's legs sticking up [line 90]). Note that the travelers pass through the glassy ice, a passage that probably echoes 1 Corinthians 13.12: "For now we see through a glass, darkly; but then face to face."
1. About 7:30 a.m. on Holy Saturday. Dante has added 12 hours to his scheme so that the travelers will emerge from the Earth and arrive at the shore of Mount Purgatory just before the sunrise on the next day, Easter Sunday.

And he to me: "You imagine you are still
  on the other side of the center where I grasped
  the shaggy flank of the Great Worm of Evil   108

which bores through the world—you *were* while I climbed down,
  but when I turned myself about, you passed
  the point to which all gravities are drawn.[2]   111

You are under the other hemisphere where you stand;[3]
  the sky above us is the half opposed
  to that which canopies the great dry land.   114

Under the midpoint of that other sky
  the Man who was born sinless and who lived
  beyond all blemish, came to suffer and die.   117

You have your feet upon a little sphere
  which forms the other face of the Judecca.
  There it is evening when it is morning here.[4]   120

And this gross Fiend and Image of all Evil
  who made a stairway for us with his hide
  is pinched and prisoned in the ice-pack still.   123

On this side he plunged down from heaven's height,[5]
  and the land that spread here once hid in the sea
  and fled North to our hemisphere for fright;   126

and it may be that moved by that same fear,
  the one peak that still rises on this side
  fled upward leaving this great cavern here."   129

Down there, beginning at the further bound
  of Beelzebub's[6] dim tomb, there is a space
  not known by sight, but only by the sound   132

2. The center of the Earth, which is for Dante the center of the universe, and therefore the place where gravity is the strongest. Being furthest from Heaven, it is also the place which is most material and least spiritual.

3. I.e., under the Southern Hemisphere, exactly opposite Jerusalem where Christ ("the Man whose birth and life were free of sin") was crucified. Jerusalem is the center of the Northern Hemisphere (see Ezekiel 5.5) and is located directly over the cavity of Hell.

4. The "little sphere" upon which they stand is the other side of Judecca, which is a hollow. The sun is now over the Southern Hemisphere, and therefore it is night in the Northern, where Hell is located.

5. The land that was in the Southern Hemisphere before Satan fell fled to the Northern to avoid him; hence the Southern Hemisphere is composed of water. The exception is that when Satan plunged into the center of the world, the earth close to his body in the Northern Hemisphere moved "with that same fear" (line 127) to the Southern Hemisphere and became Mount Purgatory. The "cavern" (line 129) refers to Hell; Mount Purgatory is thus comprised of the land displaced by Satan in his fall. This elaborate explanation for medieval geography is Dante's own poetic scheme.

6. Another name for Satan.

of a little stream[7] descending through the hollow
   it has eroded from the massive stone
   in its endlessly entwining lazy flow.   135

My Guide and I crossed over and began
   to mount that little known and lightless road
   to ascend into the shining world again.   138

He first, I second, without thought of rest
   we climbed the dark until we reached the point
   where a round opening brought in sight the blest   141

and beauteous shining of the Heavenly cars.
And we walked out once more beneath the Stars.[8]

7. This stream must flow down from Purgatory, perhaps from Lethe. It finds its source in "a space" (line 131) on Mount Purgatory; thus it is "at the further bound of Beelzebub's dim tomb"—that is, it is located on the surface of the Southern Hemisphere, which since Satan is at the center of the earth is the same distance from him as Hell (his "tomb") is deep. When Dante has Virgil say that it is "down there" (line 130), he must be writing from the perspective of the Northern Hemisphere, since Mount Purgatory is at this moment above the travelers.
8. Each of the three parts of the *Divine Comedy* end with the word "stars" as an affirmation of God's benevolent order.

THE THOUSAND AND ONE NIGHTS
(ALF LAYLA WA-LAYLA)
fourteenth century

A text built from many texts, *The Thousand and One Nights* is an extraordinarily flexible and capacious storytelling machine, one that has absorbed stories from a range of cultures across Asia and North Africa and then cast them back out again into the world in many new forms, including theater, opera, film, cartoons, video games, fashion, children's toys, and, of course, other texts. Considered in light of the work's many manifestations, the "nights" are not "one thousand and one"—they are innumerable.

THE TEXT IN CONTEXT

The Thousand and One Nights was written by many unknown authors, scattered over many centuries and countries of the Middle East. The first document bearing any physical evidence of *The Thousand and One Nights* was a single piece of very rare old Syrian paper that dates from 879 C.E. Discovered in 1948 by a scholar studying in a Cairo archive, the page contained, among various other scrawls and jottings, a signature, a date, and a few words from the opening lines of the *Nights*. The next trace of the *Nights* appears in the tenth century, when Ibn al-Nadim, a book dealer in Baghdad, mentions in his catalogue a number of story collections; among them is a book of tales concerning "Shahrazad," which, he notes, is adapted from a Persian original called *Hazar Afsan*, or *Thousand Tales*. Another tenth-century writer, al-Mas'udi, also mentions Shahrazad and the now-lost Persian *Hazar Afsan*, and adds the title of the Arabic version of the work: *Alf Layla*, or *Thousand Nights*. The title that comes down to us in the earliest complete manuscript, a Syrian text dating from the fourteenth century, is the familiar *Alf Layla wa-Layla*, or *Thousand and One Nights*. The number—one thousand and one—seems precise, and in fact the first generation of Western readers took it literally, assuming that the manuscript, which contained far fewer than one thousand stories, must be incomplete. But its sense is instead symbolic: adding one more to a thousand implies an unending abundance. There is always one more tale to be told.

The Thousand and One Nights is an Arabic text, but one derived from a Persian source (reflected in the Persian names of the characters of the frame story—Shahrazad and her sister Dunyazad, King Shahrayar and his brother Shahzaman). Behind both the Arabic and the Persian texts may lie a Sanskrit original, just as the Indian *Pañcatantra* lies behind the other widely disseminated Arabic story collection, *Kalila and Dimna*; but this original, if it exists, has never been discovered. Whatever its early sources, the *Nights* quickly swelled with new stories from Arab traditions as its influence spread. One cluster of stories centers on Baghdad and its early ninth-century ruler, Harun al-Rashid, and his vizier, Ja'far al-Barmaki. Other groups of stories, which entered the collection at a later date, reflect the culture of medieval Cairo; still others allude to the itinerant heritage of the Bedouin

of the Arabian Peninsula. The text of the *Nights*—if we can call such a flexible and changeable organism a "text"— was above all an inspiration for sharing stories, and was thus subject to change with each new telling.

Though the content of the *Nights* is unique, its literary form—the frame tale—is common in Eastern and Western traditions. The frame tale is an open-ended genre, in which an outer story or "frame" provides a structure within which other, shorter stories can be told. Frame tales are among the most popular of literary forms, surviving in the major works of Boccaccio, **Chaucer, Marie de France**, and many others. The genre most likely has its origins in India, in textual traditions such as Somadeva's *Kathāsaritsāgora*. The *Pañcatantra*, a Sanskrit collection of animal stories, is among the world's best-known and oldest frame tales, and it was the inspiration for the Arabic *Kalila and Dimna*, which was quickly disseminated throughout medieval Europe. While *Kalila and Dimna* was popular in the West because of the didactic and edifying quality of the tales (they each conclude, as do Aesop's *Fables*, with a moral), *The Thousand and One Nights* were avidly read by Europeans for less noble reasons: they believed the *Nights* could offer insights into the duplicitous and irrational character of "the Oriental," and they found pleasure in the tales' sensuous details and often unrestrained sexuality. The long history of "Orientalist" approaches to *The Thousand and One Nights* in the West takes nothing away from our own enjoyment of the tales, but it is certainly a reminder of the dangers of interpreting any text as somehow embodying the culture in which it originated.

WORK

The overall frame of *The Thousand and One Nights* centers on a good king who has become a tyrant. After discovering the secret promiscuity of his wife, King Shahrayar decides that he will avoid the deception of women forever by taking a new bride every night and putting her to death in the morning. The deaths rapidly mount, the kingdom is filled with mourning parents—and to the horror and despair of the faithful royal vizier, his daughter, Shahrazad, volunteers to marry the king. He tries to dissuade her, but Shahrazad has a plan. By telling a story to the king every night, each one more marvelous and entrancing than the last, Shahrazad will continually defer the doom that awaits his bride. Yet she also has another goal, beyond self-preservation or even the salvation of her countrywomen. By telling stories that repeatedly address the problems of rule—both the rule of oneself and the rule of others—she will teach the king how to restore order in his own realm, as well as in his own soul.

Even among frame tales, *The Thousand and One Nights* is unique for its enchantingly intricate nested structure. Very often, a character in a tale will pause to tell yet another tale, with one story inside the next inside the next, like Russian nested dolls. In "The Story of the Merchant and the Demon," for example, three old men tell stories, each more fantastic than the last, to the dangerous jinn in their successful effort to purchase the merchant's freedom. This structure makes *The Thousand and One Nights* an unusually playful text, seemingly spontaneous and improvisational even on the page, and wonderfully suited to public entertainment and oral performance.

Perhaps the *Nights* is most extraordinary for the persistence of its fertile, regenerative quality even after being taken up by Western readers and rendered in a host of European and, later, American translations and adaptations. This process began in 1704, with the publication in French (by Antoine Galland) of a selection of tales from the earliest surviving complete manuscript. Readers were immediately captivated by the work: an unauthorized English translation of the French version appeared in 1706, and Galland himself quickly produced additional volumes for publication. When he ran out of tales to translate from the Syrian manuscript (which, like all the early collections, contains only about 280), Galland turned to other sets of Arabic tales, including the famous stories of Aladdin and Ali Baba. As he sought to reach the target number of one thousand and one, Galland even added some tales for which there were no written Arabic sources but only oral versions picked up from Arab visitors to Paris. The tremendous European appetite for *The Thousand and One Nights* led to the production of composite Arabic story collections in Cairo during the eighteenth and nineteenth centuries, and subsequently these versions were published in Arabic editions and translated. We can thus think of two separate lineages for the modern reception of the *Nights*: one can be traced back to the earliest complete text, the fourteenth-century Syrian manuscript translated by Galland, and the other to the later composite texts assembled in eighteenth- and nineteenth-century Cairo. The selections reproduced here come from the Syrian manuscript, but it would be wrong to think of these as the "authentic" tales and to dismiss those in the Cairo versions as unimportant innovations. Instead, the Syrian manuscript can best be thought of as a snapshot, an image captured of the *Nights* at a certain moment in time, in a certain cultural location. The Cairo manuscripts also represent a specific time and place in the life of the *Nights*—one intimately connected with the history of French and, later, British rule in Egypt.

Western reception of *The Thousand and One Nights* has been uniformly enthusiastic, and yet wildly heterogeneous—a good example of the changing fortunes in the relations between Europe and the Middle East. This heterogeneity can be seen, for example, in the nineteenth-century English translations of the *Nights*, all of which were based on the enlarged Cairo compilations. The earliest of these was by Edward Lane, an Englishman living in Cairo; it tries to conjure up an entire way of life through the medium of the *Nights*. For Lane, the stories are not so much an end in themselves as a way for him to re-create the daily experiences of a nineteenth-century Egyptian who might have listened to such stories as they were performed in the coffeehouse. The translation of the philologist John Payne, published for a very limited audience of specialists, sought to use the *Nights* to construct an ethnographic portrait of Egyptian society, while the sexually explicit, extensively footnoted, and deliberately archaic translation by the extraordinary explorer Sir Richard Burton is in a category by itself. The variety of these encounters with the *Nights*, all so different yet all produced in the same language over the span of a few decades, was wittily summed up by a nineteenth-century commentator in the *Edinburgh Review* who states that each version has "its proper destination: Galland for the nursery, Lane for the library, Payne for the study, and Burton for the sewers."

The influence of *The Thousand and One Nights* continued to spread out across the globe. Thus late nineteenth-century portrait photography in Japan shows a fascination with the "Arabian Nights" theme, which had become fashionable in stage costume and dress styles, theater and opera, music and ballet. Today, reflections of the *Nights* are visible in films and graphic novels for adults as well as cartoons and even coloring books for children. In the modern Middle East, however, attitudes toward *The Thousand and One Nights* are more ambivalent; they have even at times led to censorship, whether because of the text's graphic language or, more likely, because of the complicated history of the *Nights* in shaping European fantasies about the Orient.

While Eastern studies of the *Nights* have tended to consider the work in the context of folklore and oral storytelling, Western scholars are often preoccupied with the effort to nail down the work's point of origin. They want to know: Which is the original version? When was it composed? Is *The Thousand and One Nights* an Arab text? a Persian text? Indian? These questions ultimately slip away, because what the text *is* turns out to be much less interesting than what it *does*. *The Thousand and One Nights* has its life in transit— always becoming something new, leaving its reader in a perpetual state of anticipation. It is less a collection of stories than a machine that makes stories possible.

From The Thousand and One Nights[1]

Prologue

[*The Story of King Shahrayar and Shahrazad, His Vizier's[2] Daughter*]

It is related—but God knows and sees best what lies hidden in the old accounts of bygone peoples and times—that long ago, during the time of the Sasanid dynasty,[3] in the peninsulas of India and Indochina, there lived two kings who were brothers. The older brother was named Shahrayar, the younger Shahzaman. The older, Shahrayar, was a towering knight and a daring champion, invincible, energetic, and implacable. His power reached the remotest corners of the land and its people, so that the country was loyal to him, and his subjects obeyed him. Shahrayar himself lived and ruled in India and Indochina, while to his brother he gave the land of Samarkand[4] to rule as king.

Ten years went by, when one day Shahrayar felt a longing for his brother the king, summoned his vizier (who had two daughters, one called Shahrazad, the other Dinarzad) and bade him go to his brother. Having made preparations, the vizier journeyed day and night until he reached Samarkand. When Shahzaman heard of the vizier's arrival, he went out with his retainers to meet him. He dismounted, embraced him, and asked him for news from his older brother, Shahrayar. The vizier replied that he was well, and that he had sent him to request his brother to visit him. Shahzaman complied with his brother's request and proceeded to make preparations for the journey. In the meantime, he had the vizier camp on the outskirts of the city, and took care of his needs. He sent him what he required of food and fodder, slaughtered many sheep in his honor, and provided him with money and supplies, as well as many horses and camels.

For ten full days he prepared himself for the journey; then he appointed a chamberlain in his place, and left the city to spend the night in his tent, near the vizier. At midnight he returned to his palace in the city, to bid his wife good-bye. But when he entered the palace, he found his wife lying in the arms of one of the kitchen boys. When he saw them, the world turned dark before his eyes and, shaking his head, he said to himself, "I am still here, and this is what she has done when I was barely outside the city. How will it be and what will happen behind my back when I go to visit my brother in India? No. Women are not to be trusted." He got exceedingly angry, adding, "By God, I am king and sovereign in Samarkand, yet my wife has betrayed me and has inflicted this on me." As his anger boiled, he drew his sword and struck both his wife and the cook. Then he dragged them by the heels and threw them from the top of the palace to the trench below. He then left the city and going to the vizier ordered that they depart that very hour. The drum was struck, and they set out on their journey, while Shahzaman's heart was on fire because of what his wife had done to him and how she had betrayed him with some cook, some kitchen boy. They journeyed hurriedly, day and night, through deserts and wilds, until they reached the land of King Shahrayar, who had gone out to receive them.

---

1. All selections translated from the Arabic by Husain Haddaway except for "The Third Old Man's Tale," translated from the Arabic by Jerome W. Clinton.
2. Literally, "one who bears burdens" (Arabic):

the highest state official or administrator under a caliph or shah.
3. The last pre-Islamic dynasty (226–652).
4. A city and province in central Asia, now in Uzbekistan.

When Shahrayar met them, he embraced his brother, showed him favors, and treated him generously. He offered him quarters in a palace adjoining his own, for King Shahrayar had built two beautiful towering palaces in his garden, one for the guests, the other for the women and members of his household. He gave the guest house to his brother, Shahzaman, after the attendants had gone to scrub it, dry it, furnish it, and open its windows, which overlooked the garden. Thereafter, Shahzaman would spend the whole day at his brother's, return at night to sleep at the palace, then go back to his brother the next morning. But whenever he found himself alone and thought of his ordeal with his wife, he would sigh deeply, then stifle his grief, and say, "Alas, that this great misfortune should have happened to one in my position!" Then he would fret with anxiety, his spirit would sag, and he would say, "None has seen what I have seen." In his depression, he ate less and less, grew pale, and his health deteriorated. He neglected everything, wasted away, and looked ill.

When King Shahrayar looked at his brother and saw how day after day he lost weight and grew thin, pale, ashen, and sickly, he thought that this was because of his expatriation and homesickness for his country and his family, and he said to himself, "My brother is not happy here. I should prepare a goodly gift for him and send him home." For a month he gathered gifts for his brother; then he invited him to see him and said, "Brother, I would like you to know that I intend to go hunting and pursue the roaming deer, for ten days. Then I shall return to prepare you for your journey home. Would you like to go hunting with me?" Shahzaman replied, "Brother, I feel distracted and depressed. Leave me here and go with God's blessing and help." When Shahrayar heard his brother, he thought that his dejection was because of his homesickness for his country. Not wishing to coerce him, he left him behind, and set out with his retainers and men. When they entered the wilderness, he deployed his men in a circle to begin trapping and hunting.

After his brother's departure, Shahzaman stayed in the palace and, from the window overlooking the garden, watched the birds and trees as he thought of his wife and what she had done to him, and sighed in sorrow. While he agonized over his misfortune, gazing at the heavens and turning a distracted eye on the garden, the private gate of his brother's palace opened, and there emerged, strutting like a dark-eyed deer, the lady, his brother's wife, with twenty slave-girls, ten white and ten black. While Shahzaman looked at them, without being seen, they continued to walk until they stopped below his window, without looking in his direction, thinking that he had gone to the hunt with his brother. Then they sat down, took off their clothes, and suddenly there were ten slave-girls and ten black slaves dressed in the same clothes as the girls. Then the ten black slaves mounted the ten girls, while the lady called, "Mas'ud, Mas'ud!" and a black slave jumped from the tree to the ground, rushed to her, and, raising her legs, went between her thighs and made love to her. Mas'ud topped the lady, while the ten slaves topped the ten girls, and they carried on till noon. When they were done with their business, they got up and washed themselves. Then the ten slaves put on the same clothes again, mingled with the girls, and once more there appeared to be twenty slave-girls. Mas'ud himself jumped over the garden wall and disappeared, while the slave-girls and the lady sauntered to the private gate, went in and, locking the gate behind them, went their way.

All of this happened under King Shahzaman's eyes. When he saw this spectacle of the wife and the women of his brother the great king—how ten slaves put on women's clothes and slept with his brother's paramours and concubines and what Mas'ud did with his brother's wife, in his very palace—and pondered over this calamity and great misfortune, his care and sorrow left him and he said to himself, "This is our common lot. Even though my brother is king and master of the whole world, he cannot protect what is his, his wife and his concubines, and suffers misfortune in his very home. What happened to me is little by comparison. I used to think that I was the only one who has suffered, but from what I have seen, everyone suffers. By God, my misfortune is lighter than that of my brother." He kept marveling and blaming life, whose trials none can escape, and he began to find consolation in his own affliction and forget his grief. When supper came, he ate and drank with relish and zest and, feeling better, kept eating and drinking, enjoying himself and feeling happy. He thought to himself, "I am no longer alone in my misery; I am well."

For ten days, he continued to enjoy his food and drink, and when his brother, King Shahrayar, came back from the hunt, he met him happily, treated him attentively, and greeted him cheerfully. His brother, King Shahrayar, who had missed him, said, "By God, brother, I missed you on this trip and wished you were with me." Shahzaman thanked him and sat down to carouse with him, and when night fell, and food was brought before them, the two ate and drank, and again Shahzaman ate and drank with zest. As time went by, he continued to eat and drink with appetite, and became lighthearted and carefree. His face regained color and became ruddy, and his body gained weight, as his blood circulated and he regained his energy; he was himself again, or even better. King Shahrayar noticed his brother's condition, how he used to be and how he had improved, but kept it to himself until he took him aside one day and said, "My brother Shahzaman, I would like you to do something for me, to satisfy a wish, to answer a question truthfully." Shahzaman asked, "What is it, brother?" He replied, "When you first came to stay with me, I noticed that you kept losing weight, day after day, until your looks changed, your health deteriorated, and your energy sagged. As you continued like this, I thought that what ailed you was your homesickness for your family and your country, but even though I kept noticing that you were wasting away and looking ill, I refrained from questioning you and hid my feelings from you. Then I went hunting, and when I came back, I found that you had recovered and had regained your health. Now I want you to tell me everything and to explain the cause of your deterioration and the cause of your subsequent recovery, without hiding anything from me." When Shahzaman heard what King Shahrayar said, he bowed his head, then said, "As for the cause of my recovery, that I cannot tell you, and I wish that you would excuse me from telling you." The king was greatly astonished at his brother's reply and, burning with curiosity, said, "You must tell me. For now, at least, explain the first cause."

Then Shahzaman related to his brother what happened to him with his own wife, on the night of his departure, from beginning to end, and concluded, "Thus all the while I was with you, great King, whenever I thought of the event and the misfortune that had befallen me, I felt troubled, careworn, and unhappy, and my health deteriorated. This then is the cause." Then he grew silent. When King Shahrayar heard his brother's explanation, he shook his head, greatly amazed at the deceit of women, and prayed to God to protect him from their wickedness, saying, "Brother, you were fortunate in killing your wife and her lover, who gave you good reason to feel troubled, careworn, and ill. In my opinion, what happened to you has never happened to anyone else. By God, had I been in your place, I would have killed at least a hundred or even a thousand women. I would have been furious; I would have gone mad. Now praise be to God who has delivered you from sorrow and distress. But tell me what has caused you to forget your sorrow and regain your health?" Shahzaman replied, "King, I wish that for God's sake you would excuse me from telling you." Shahrayar said, "You must." Shahzaman replied, "I fear that you will feel even more troubled and careworn than I." Shahrayar asked, "How could that be, brother? I insist on hearing your explanation."

Shahzaman then told him about what he had seen from the palace window and the calamity in his very home—how ten slaves, dressed like women, were sleeping with his women and concubines, day and night. He told him everything from beginning to end (but there is no point in repeating that). Then he concluded, "When I saw your own misfortune, I felt better—and said to myself, 'My brother is king of the world, yet such a misfortune has happened to him, and in his very home.' As a result I forgot my care and sorrow, relaxed, and began to eat and drink. This is the cause of my cheer and good spirits."

When King Shahrayar heard what his brother said and found out what had happened to him, he was furious and his blood boiled. He said, "Brother, I can't believe what you say unless I see it with my own eyes." When Shahzaman saw that his brother was in a rage, he said to him, "If you do not believe me, unless you see your misfortune with your own eyes, announce that you plan to go hunting. Then you and I shall set out with your troops, and when we get outside the city, we shall leave our tents and camp with the men behind, enter the city secretly, and go together to your palace. Then the next morning you can see with your own eyes."

King Shahrayar realized that his brother had a good plan and ordered his army to prepare for the trip. He spent the night with his brother, and when God's morning broke, the two rode out of the city with their army, preceded by the camp attendants, who had gone to drive the poles and pitch the tents where the king and his army were to camp. At nightfall King Shahrayar summoned his chief chamberlain and bade him take his place. He entrusted him with the army and ordered that for three days no one was to enter the city. Then he and his brother disguised themselves and entered the city in the dark. They went directly to the palace where Shahzaman resided and slept there till the morning. When they awoke, they sat at the palace window, watching the garden and chatting, until the light broke, the day dawned, and the sun rose. As they watched, the private gate opened, and there emerged as usual the wife of King Shahrayar, walking among twenty slave-girls. They made their way under the trees until they stood below the palace window where the two kings sat. Then they took off their women's clothes, and suddenly there were ten slaves, who mounted the ten girls and made love to them. As for the lady, she called, "Mas'ud, Mas'ud," and a black slave jumped from the tree to the ground, came to her, and said, "What do you want, you slut? Here is Sa'ad al-Din Mas'ud." She laughed and fell on her back, while the slave mounted her and like the others did his business with her. Then the black slaves got up, washed themselves, and, putting on the same clothes, mingled with the girls. Then they walked away, entered the palace, and locked the gate behind them. As for Mas'ud, he jumped over the fence to the road and went on his way.

When King Shahrayar saw the spectacle of his wife and the slave-girls, he went out of his mind, and when he and his brother came down from upstairs, he said, "No one is safe in this world. Such doings are going on in my kingdom, and in my very palace. Perish the world and perish life! This is a great calamity, indeed." Then he turned to his brother and asked, "Would you like to follow me in what I shall do?" Shahzaman answered, "Yes. I will." Shahrayar said, "Let us leave our royal state and roam the world for the love of the Supreme Lord. If we should find one whose misfortune is greater than ours, we shall return. Otherwise, we shall continue to journey through the land, without need for the trappings of royalty." Shahzaman replied, "This is an excellent idea. I shall follow you."

Then they left by the private gate, took a side road, and departed, journeying till nightfall. They slept over their sorrows, and in the morning resumed their day journey until they came to a meadow by the seashore. While they sat in the meadow amid the thick plants and trees, discussing their misfortunes and the recent events, they suddenly heard a shout and a great cry coming from the middle of the sea. They trembled with fear, thinking that the sky had fallen on the earth. Then the sea parted, and there emerged a black pillar that, as it swayed forward, got taller and taller, until it touched the clouds. Shahrayar and Shahzaman were petrified; then they ran in terror and, climbing a very tall tree, sat hiding in its foliage. When they looked again, they saw that the black pillar was cleaving the sea, wading in the water toward the green meadow, until it touched the shore. When they looked again, they saw that it was a black demon, carrying on his head a large glass chest with four steel locks. He came out, walked into the meadow, and where should he stop but under the very tree where the two kings were hiding. The demon sat down and placed the glass chest on the ground. He took out four keys and, opening the locks of the chest, pulled out a full-grown woman. She had a beautiful figure, and a face like the full moon, and a lovely smile. He took her out, laid her under the tree, and looked at her, saying, "Mistress of all noble women, you whom I carried away on your wedding night, I would like to sleep a little." Then he placed his head on the young woman's lap, stretched his legs to the sea, sank into sleep, and began to snore.

Meanwhile, the woman looked up at the tree and, turning her head by chance, saw King Shahrayar and King Shahzaman. She lifted the demon's head from her lap and placed it on the ground. Then she came and stood under the tree and motioned to them with her hand, as if to say, "Come down slowly to me." When they realized that she had seen them, they were frightened, and they begged her and implored her, in the name of the Creator of the heavens, to excuse them from climbing down. She replied, "You must come down to me." They motioned to her, saying, "This sleeping demon is the enemy of mankind. For God's sake, leave us alone." She replied, "You must come down, and if you don't, I shall wake the demon and have him kill you." She kept gesturing and pressing, until they climbed down very slowly and stood before her. Then she lay on her back, raised her legs, and said, "Make love to me and satisfy my need, or else I shall wake the demon, and he will kill you." They replied, "For God's sake, mistress, don't do this to us, for at this moment we feel nothing but dismay and fear of this demon. Please, excuse us." She replied, "You must," and insisted, swearing, "By God who created the heavens, if you don't do it, I shall wake my husband the demon and ask him to kill you and throw you into the sea." As she persisted, they could no longer resist and they made love to her, first the older brother, then the younger. When they were done and withdrew from her, she said to them, "Give me your rings," and, pulling out from the folds of her dress a small purse, opened it, and shook out ninety-eight rings of different fashions and colors. Then she asked them, "Do you know what these rings are?" They answered, "No." She said, "All the owners of these rings slept with me, for whenever one of them made love to me, I took a ring from him. Since you two have slept with me, give me your rings, so that I may add them to the rest, and make a full hundred. A hundred men have known me under the very horns of this filthy, monstrous cuckold, who has imprisoned me in this chest, locked it with four locks, and kept me in the middle of this raging, roaring sea. He has guarded me and tried to keep me pure and chaste, not realizing that nothing can prevent or alter what is predestined and that when a woman desires something, no one can stop her." When Shahrayar and Shahzaman heard what the young woman said, they were greatly amazed, danced with joy, and said, "O God, O God! There is no power and no strength, save in God the Almighty, the Magnificent. Great is women's cunning." Then each of them took off his ring and handed it to her. She took them and put them with the rest in the purse. Then sitting again by the demon, she lifted his head, placed it back on her lap, and motioned to them, "Go on your way, or else I shall wake him."

They turned their backs and took to the road. Then Shahrayar turned to his brother and said, "My brother Shahzaman, look at this sorry plight. By God, it is worse than ours. This is no less than a demon who has carried a young woman away on her wedding night, imprisoned her in a glass chest, locked her up with four locks, and kept her in the middle of the sea, thinking that he could guard her from what God had foreordained, and you saw how she has managed to sleep with ninety-eight men, and added the two of us to make a hundred. Brother, let us go back to our kingdoms and our cities, never to marry a woman again. As for myself, I shall show you what I will do."

Then the two brothers headed home and journeyed till nightfall. On the morning of the third day, they reached their camp and men, entered their tent, and sat on their thrones. The chamberlains, deputies, princes, and viziers came to attend King Shahrayar, while he gave orders and bestowed robes of honor, as well as other gifts. Then at his command everyone returned to the city, and he went to his own palace and ordered his chief vizier, the father of the two girls Shahrazad and Dinarzad, who will be mentioned below, and said to him, "Take that wife of mine and put her to death." Then Shahrayar went to her himself, bound her, and handed her over to the vizier, who took her out and put her to death. Then King Shahrayar grabbed his sword, brandished it, and, entering the palace chambers, killed every one of his slave-girls and replaced them with others. He then swore to marry for one night only and kill the woman the next morning, in order to save himself from the wickedness and cunning of women, saying, "There is not a single chaste woman anywhere on the entire face of the earth." Shortly thereafter he provided his brother Shahzaman with supplies for his journey and sent him back to his own country with gifts, rarities, and money. The brother bade him good-bye and set out for home.

Shahrayar sat on his throne and ordered his vizier, the father of the two girls, to find him a wife from among the princes' daughters. The vizier found him one, and he slept with her and was done with her, and the next morning he ordered the vizier to put her to death. That very night he took one of his army officers' daughters, slept with her, and the next morning ordered the vizier to put her to death. The vizier, who could not disobey him, put her to death. The third night he took one of the merchants' daughters, slept with her till the morning, then ordered his vizier to put her to death, and the vizier did so. It became King Shahrayar's custom to take every night the daughter of a merchant or a commoner, spend the night with her, then have her put to death the next morning. He continued to do this until all the girls perished, their mothers mourned, and there arose a clamor among the fathers and mothers, who called the plague upon his head, complained to the Creator of the heavens, and called for help on Him who hears and answers prayers.

Now, as mentioned earlier, the vizier, who put the girls to death, had an older daughter called Shahrazad and a younger one called Dinarzad. The older daughter, Shahrazad, had read the books of literature, philosophy, and medicine. She knew poetry by heart, had studied historical reports, and was acquainted with the sayings of men and the maxims of sages and kings. She was intelligent, knowledgeable, wise, and refined. She had read and learned. One day she said to her father, "Father, I will tell you what is in my mind." He asked, "What is it?" She answered, "I would like you to marry me to King Shahrayar, so that I may either succeed in saving the people or perish and die like the rest." When the vizier heard what his daughter Shahrazad said, he got angry and said to her, "Foolish one, don't you know that King Shahrayar has sworn to spend but one night with a girl and have her put to death the next morning? If I give you to him, he will sleep with you for one night and will ask me to put you to death the next morning, and I shall have to do it, since I cannot disobey him." She said, "Father, you must give me to him, even if he kills me." He asked, "What has possessed you that you wish to imperil yourself?" She replied, "Father, you must give me to him. This is absolute and final." Her father the vizier became furious and said to her, "Daughter, 'He who misbehaves, ends up in trouble,' and 'He who considers not the end, the world is not his friend.' As the popular saying goes, 'I would be sitting pretty, but for my curiosity.' I am afraid that what happened to the donkey and the ox with the merchant will happen to you." She asked, "Father, what happened to the donkey, the ox, and the merchant?" He said:

[The Tale of the Ox and the Donkey]

There was a prosperous and wealthy merchant who lived in the countryside and labored on a farm. He owned many camels and herds of cattle and employed many men, and he had a wife and many grown-up as well as little children. This merchant was taught the language of the beasts, on condition that if he revealed his secret to anyone, he would die; therefore, even though he knew the language of every kind of animal, he did not let anyone know, for fear of death. One day, as he sat, with his wife beside him and his children playing before him, he glanced at an ox and a donkey he kept at the farmhouse, tied to adjacent troughs, and heard the ox say to the donkey, "Watchful one, I hope that you are enjoying the comfort and the service you are getting. Your ground is swept and watered, and they serve you, feed you sifted barley, and offer you clear, cool water to drink. I, on the contrary, am taken out to plow in the middle of the night. They clamp on my neck something they call yoke and plow, push me all day under the whip to plow the field, and drive me beyond my endurance until my sides are lacerated, and my neck is flayed. They work me from nighttime to nighttime, take me back in the dark, offer me beans soiled with mud and hay mixed with chaff, and let me spend the night lying in urine and dung. Meanwhile you rest on well-swept, watered, and smoothed ground, with a clean trough full of hay. You stand in comfort, save for the rare occasion when our master the merchant rides you to do a brief errand and returns. You are comfortable, while I am weary; you sleep, while I keep awake."

When the ox finished, the donkey turned to him and said, "Greenhorn, they were right in calling you ox, for you ox harbor no deceit, malice, or meanness. Being sincere, you exert and exhaust yourself to comfort others. Have you not heard the saying 'Out of bad luck, they hastened on the road'? You go into the field from early morning to endure your torture at the plow to the point of exhaustion. When the plowman takes you back and ties you to the trough, you go on butting and beating with your horns, kicking with your hoofs, and bellowing for the beans, until they toss them to you; then you begin to eat. Next time, when they bring them to you, don't eat or even touch them, but smell them, then draw back and lie down on the hay and straw. If you do this, life will be better and kinder to you, and you will find relief."

As the ox listened, he was sure that the donkey had given him good advice. He thanked him, commended him to God, and invoked His blessing on him, and said, "May you stay safe from harm, watchful one." All of this conversation took place, daughter, while the merchant listened and understood. On the following day, the plowman came to the merchant's house and, taking the ox, placed the yoke upon his neck and worked him at the plow, but the ox lagged behind. The plowman hit him, but following the donkey's advice, the ox, dissembling, fell on his belly, and the plowman hit him again. Thus the ox kept getting up and falling until nightfall, when the plowman took him home and tied him to the trough. But this time the ox did not bellow or kick the ground with his hoofs. Instead, he withdrew, away from the trough. Astonished, the plowman brought him his beans and fodder, but the ox only smelled the fodder and pulled back and lay down at a distance with the hay and straw, complaining till the morning. When the plowman arrived, he found the trough as he had left it, full of beans and fodder, and saw the ox lying on his back, hardly breathing, his belly puffed, and his legs raised in the air. The plowman felt sorry for him and said to himself, "By God, he did seem weak and unable to work." Then he went to the merchant and said, "Master, last night, the ox refused to eat or touch his fodder."

The merchant, who knew what was going on, said to the plowman, "Go to the wily donkey, put him to the plow, and work him hard until he finishes the ox's task." The plowman left, took the donkey, and placed the yoke upon his neck. Then he took him out to the field and drove him with blows until he finished the ox's work, all the while driving him with blows and beating him until his sides were lacerated and his neck was flayed. At nightfall he took him home, barely able to drag his legs under his tired body and his drooping ears. Meanwhile the ox spent his day resting. He ate all his food, drank his water, and lay quietly, chewing his cud in comfort. All day long he kept praising the donkey's advice and invoking God's blessing on him. When the donkey came back at night, the ox stood up to greet him saying, "Good evening, watchful one! You have done me a favor beyond description, for I have been sitting in comfort. God bless you for my sake." Seething with anger, the donkey did not reply, but said to himself, "All this happened to me because of my miscalculation. 'I would be sitting pretty, but for my curiosity.' If I don't find a way to return this ox to his former situation, I will perish." Then he went to his trough and lay down, while the ox continued to chew his cud and invoke God's blessing on him.

"You, my daughter, will likewise perish because of your miscalculation. Desist, sit quietly, and don't expose yourself to peril. I advise you out of compassion for you." She replied, "Father, I must go to the king, and you must give me to him." He said, "Don't do it." She insisted, "I must." He replied, "If you don't desist, I will do to you what the merchant did to his wife." She asked, "Father, what did the merchant do to his wife?" He said:

[The Tale of the Merchant and His Wife]

After what had happened to the donkey and the ox, the merchant and his wife went out in the moonlight to the stable, and he heard the donkey ask the ox in his own language, "Listen, ox, what are you going to do tomorrow morning, and what will you do when the plowman brings you your fodder?" The ox replied, "What shall I do but follow your advice and stick to it? If he brings me my fodder, I will pretend to be ill, lie down, and puff my belly." The donkey shook his head, and said, "Don't do it. Do you know what I heard our master the merchant say to the plowman?" The ox asked, "What?" The donkey replied, "He said that if the ox failed to get up and eat his fodder, he would call the butcher to slaughter him and skin him and would distribute the meat for alms and use the skin for a mat. I am afraid for you, but good advice is a matter of faith; therefore, if he brings you your fodder, eat it and look alert lest they cut your throat and skin you." The ox farted and bellowed.

The merchant got up and laughed loudly at the conversation between the donkey and the ox, and his wife asked him, "What are you laughing at? Are you making fun of me?" He said, "No." She said, "Tell me what made you laugh." He replied, "I cannot tell you. I am afraid to disclose the secret conversation of the animals." She asked, "And what prevents you from telling me?" He answered, "The fear of death." His wife said, "By God, you are lying. This is nothing but an excuse. I swear by God, the Lord of heaven, that if you don't tell me and explain the cause of your laughter, I will leave you. You must tell me." Then she went back to the house crying, and she continued to cry till the morning. The merchant said, "Damn it! Tell me why you are crying. Ask for God's forgiveness, and stop questioning and leave me in peace." She said, "I insist and will not desist." Amazed at her, he replied, "You insist! If I tell you what the donkey said to the ox, which made me laugh, I shall die." She said, "Yes, I insist, even if you have to die." He replied, "Then call your family," and she called their two daughters, her parents and relatives, and some neighbors. The merchant told them that he was about to die, and everyone, young and old, his children, the farmhands, and the servants began to cry until the house became a place of mourning. Then he summoned legal witnesses, wrote a will, leaving his wife and children their due portions, freed his slave-girls, and bid his family good-bye, while everybody, even the witnesses, wept. Then the wife's parents approached her and said, "Desist, for if your husband had not known for certain that he would die if he revealed his secret, he wouldn't have gone through all this." She replied, "I will not change my mind," and everybody cried and prepared to mourn his death.

Well, my daughter Shahrazad, it happened that the merchant kept fifty hens and a rooster at home, and while he felt sad to depart this world and leave his children and relatives behind, pondering and about to reveal and utter his secret, he overheard a dog of his say something in dog language to the rooster, who, beating and clapping his wings, had jumped on a hen and, finishing with her, jumped down and jumped on another. The merchant heard and understood what the dog said in his own language to the rooster, "Shameless, no-good rooster. Aren't you ashamed to do such a thing on a day like this?" The rooster asked, "What is special about this day?" The dog replied, "Don't you know that our master and friend is in mourning today? His wife is demanding that he disclose his secret, and when he discloses it, he will surely die. He is in this predicament, about to interpret to her the language of the animals, and all of us are mourning for him, while you clap your wings and get off one hen and jump on another. Aren't you ashamed?" The merchant heard the rooster reply, "You fool, you lunatic! Our master and friend claims to be wise, but he is foolish, for he has only one wife, yet he does not know how to manage her." The dog asked, "What should he do with her?"

The rooster replied, "He should take an oak branch, push her into a room, lock the door, and fall on her with the stick, beating her mercilessly until he breaks her arms and legs and she cries out, 'I no longer want you to tell me or explain anything.' He should go on beating her until he cures her for life, and she will never oppose him in anything. If he does this, he will live, and live in peace, and there will be no more grief, but he does not know how to manage." Well, my daughter Shahrazad, when the merchant heard the conversation between the dog and the rooster, he jumped up and, taking an oak branch, pushed his wife into a room, got in with her, and locked the door. Then he began to beat her mercilessly on her chest and shoulders and kept beating her until she cried for mercy, screaming, "No, no, I don't want to know anything. Leave me alone, leave me alone. I don't want to know anything," until he got tired of hitting her and opened the door. The wife emerged penitent, the husband learned good management, and everybody was happy, and the mourning turned into a celebration.

"If you don't relent, I shall do to you what the merchant did to his wife." She said, "Such tales don't deter me from my request. If you wish, I can tell you many such tales. In the end, if you don't take me to King Shahrayar, I shall go to him by myself behind your back and tell him that you have refused to give me to one like him and that you have begrudged your master one like me." The vizier asked, "Must you really do this?" She replied, "Yes, I must."

Tired and exhausted, the vizier went to King Shahrayar and, kissing the ground before him, told him about his daughter, adding that he would give her to him that very night. The king was astonished and said to him, "Vizier, how is it that you have found it possible to give me your daughter, knowing that I will, by God, the Creator of heaven, ask you to put her to death the next morning and that if you refuse, I will have you put to death, too?" He replied, "My King and Lord, I have told her everything and explained all this to her, but she refuses and insists on being with you tonight." The king was delighted and said, "Go to her, prepare her, and bring her to me early in the evening."

The vizier went down, repeated the king's message to his daughter, and said, "May God not deprive me of you." She was very happy and, after preparing herself and packing what she needed, went to her younger sister, Dinarzad, and said, "Sister, listen well to what I am telling you. When I go to the king, I will send for you, and when you come and see that the king has finished with me, say, 'Sister, if you are not sleepy, tell us a story.' Then I will begin to tell a story, and it will cause the king to stop his practice, save myself, and deliver the people." Dinarzad replied, "Very well."

At nightfall the vizier took Shahrazad and went with her to the great King Shahrayar. But when Shahrayar took her to bed and began to fondle her, she wept, and when he asked her, "Why are you crying?" she replied, "I have a sister, and I wish to bid her good-bye before daybreak." Then the king sent for the sister, who came and went to sleep under the bed. When the night wore on, she woke up and waited until the king had satisfied himself with her sister Shahrazad and they were by now all fully awake. Then Dinarzad cleared her throat and said, "Sister, if you are not sleepy, tell us one of your lovely little tales to while away the night, before I bid you good-bye at daybreak, for I don't know what will happen to you tomorrow." Shahrazad turned to King Shahrayar and said, "May I have your permission to tell a story?" He replied, "Yes," and Shahrazad was very happy and said, "Listen":

[The Story of the Merchant and the Demon]

THE FIRST NIGHT

It is said, O wise and happy King, that once there was a prosperous merchant who had abundant wealth and investments and commitments in every country. He had many women and children and kept many servants and slaves. One day, having resolved to visit another country, he took provisions, filling his saddlebag with loaves of bread and with dates, mounted his horse, and set out on his journey. For many days and nights, he journeyed under God's care until he reached his destination. When he finished his business, he turned back to his home and family. He journeyed for three days, and on the fourth day, chancing to come to an orchard, went in to avoid the heat and shade himself from the sun of the open country. He came to a spring under a walnut tree and, tying his horse, sat by the spring, pulled out from the saddlebag some loaves of bread and a handful of dates, and began to eat, throwing the date pits right and left until he had had enough. Then he got up, performed his ablutions, and performed his prayers.

But hardly had he finished when he saw an old demon, with sword in hand, standing with his feet on the ground and his head in the clouds. The demon approached until he stood before him and screamed, saying, "Get up, so that I may kill you with this sword, just as you have killed my son." When the merchant saw and heard the demon, he was terrified and awestricken. He asked, "Master, for what crime do you wish to kill me?" The demon replied, "I wish to kill you because you have killed my son." The merchant asked, "Who has killed your son?" The demon replied, "You have killed my son." The merchant said, "By God, I did not kill your son. When and how could that have been?" The demon said, "Didn't you sit down, take out some dates from your saddlebag, and eat, throwing the pits right and left?" The merchant replied, "Yes, I did." The demon said, "You killed my son, for as you were throwing the stones right and left, my son happened to be walking by and was struck and killed by one of them, and I must now kill you." The merchant said, "O my lord, please don't kill me." The demon replied, "I must kill you as you killed him—blood for blood." The merchant said, "To God we belong and to God we turn. There is no power or strength, save in God the Almighty, the Magnificent. If I killed him, I did it by mistake. Please forgive me." The demon replied, "By God, I must kill you, as you killed my son." Then he seized him, and throwing him to the ground, raised the sword to strike him. The merchant began to weep and mourn his family and his wife and children. Again, the demon raised his sword to strike, while the merchant cried until he was drenched with tears, saying, "There is no power or strength, save in God the Almighty, the Magnificent." Then he began to recite the following verses:

> Life has two days: one peace, one wariness,
> And has two sides: worry and happiness.
> Ask him who taunts us with adversity,
> "Does fate, save those worthy of note, oppress?
> Don't you see that the blowing, raging storms 5
> Only the tallest of the trees beset,
> And of earth's many green and barren lots,
> Only the ones with fruits with stones are hit,
> And of the countless stars in heaven's vault
> None is eclipsed except the moon and sun? 10
> You thought well of the days, when they were good,
> Oblivious to the ills destined for one.
> You were deluded by the peaceful nights,
> Yet in the peace of night does sorrow stun."

When the merchant finished and stopped weeping, the demon said, "By God, I must kill you, as you killed my son, even if you weep blood." The merchant asked, "Must you?" The demon replied, "I must," and raised his sword to strike.

But morning overtook Shahrazad, and she lapsed into silence, leaving King Shah-rayar burning with curiosity to hear the rest of the story. Then Dinarzad said to her sister Shahrazad, "What a strange and lovely story!" Shahrazad replied, "What is this compared with what I shall tell you tomorrow night if the king spares me and lets me live? It will be even better and more entertaining." The king thought to himself, "I will spare her until I hear the rest of the story; then I will have her put to death the next day." When morning broke, the day dawned, and the sun rose; the king left to attend to the affairs of the kingdom, and the vizier, Shahrazad's father, was amazed and delighted. King Shahrayar governed all day and returned home at night to his quarters and got into bed with Shahrazad. Then Dinarzad said to her sister Shahrazad, "Please, sister, if you are not sleepy, tell us one of your lovely little tales to while away the night." The king added, "Let it be the conclusion of the story of the demon and the merchant, for I would like to hear it." Shahrazad replied, "With the greatest pleasure, dear, happy King":

THE SECOND NIGHT

It is related, O wise and happy King, that when the demon raised his sword, the merchant asked the demon again, "Must you kill me?" and the demon replied, "Yes." Then the merchant said, "Please give me time to say good-bye to my family and my wife and children, divide my property among them, and appoint guardians. Then I shall come back, so that you may kill me." The demon replied, "I am afraid that if I release you and grant you time, you will go and do what you wish, but will not come back." The merchant said, "I swear to keep my pledge to come back, as the God of Heaven and earth is my witness." The demon asked, "How much time do you need?" The merchant replied, "One year, so that I may see enough of my children, bid my wife good-bye, discharge my obligations to people, and come back on New Year's Day." The demon asked, "Do you swear to God that if I let you go, you will come back on New Year's Day?" The merchant replied, "Yes, I swear to God."

After the merchant swore, the demon released him, and he mounted his horse sadly and went on his way. He journeyed until he reached his home and came to his wife and children. When he saw them, he wept bitterly, and when his family saw his sorrow and grief, they began to reproach him for his behavior, and his wife said, "Husband, what is the matter with you? Why do you mourn, when we are happy, celebrating your return?" He replied, "Why not mourn when I have only one year to live?" Then he told her of his encounter with the demon and informed her that he had sworn to return on New Year's Day, so that the demon might kill him.

When they heard what he said, everyone began to cry. His wife struck her face in lamentation and cut her hair, his daughters wailed, and his little children cried. It was a day of mourning, as all the children gathered around their father to weep and exchange good-byes. The next day he wrote his will, dividing his property, discharged his obligations to people, left bequests and gifts, distributed alms, and engaged reciters to read portions of the Qur'an in his house. Then he summoned legal witnesses and in their presence freed his slaves and slave-girls, divided among his elder children their shares of the property, appointed guardians for his little ones, and gave his wife her share, according to her marriage contract. He spent the rest of the time with his family, and when the year came to an end, save for the time needed for the journey, he performed his ablutions, performed his prayers, and, carrying his burial shroud, began to bid his family good-bye. His sons hung around his neck, his daughters wept, and his wife wailed. Their mourning scared him, and he began to weep, as he embraced and kissed his children good-bye. He said to them, "Children, this is God's will and decree, for man was created to die." Then he turned away and, mounting his horse, journeyed day and night until he reached the orchard on New Year's Day.

He sat at the place where he had eaten the dates, waiting for the demon, with a heavy heart and tearful eyes. As he waited, an old man, leading a deer on a leash, approached and greeted him, and he returned the greeting. The old man inquired, "Friend, why do you sit here in this place of demons and devils? For in this haunted orchard none come to good." The merchant replied by telling him what had happened to him and the demon, from beginning to end. The old man was amazed at the merchant's fidelity and said, "Yours is a magnificent pledge," adding, "By God, I shall not leave until I see what will happen to you with the demon." Then he sat down beside him and chatted with him. As they talked . . .

But morning overtook Shahrazad, and she lapsed into silence. As the day dawned, and it was light, her sister Dinarzad said, "What a strange and wonderful story!" Shahrazad replied, "Tomorrow night I shall tell something even stranger and more wonderful than this."

THE THIRD NIGHT

When it was night and Shahrazad was in bed with the king, Dinarzad said to her sister Shahrazad, "Please, if you are not sleepy, tell us one of your lovely little tales to while away the night." The king added, "Let it be the conclusion of the merchant's story." Shahrazad replied, "As you wish":

I heard, O happy King, that as the merchant and the man with the deer sat talking, another old man approached, with two black hounds, and when he reached them, he greeted them, and they returned his greeting. Then he asked them about themselves, and the man with the deer told him the story of the merchant and the demon, how the merchant had sworn to return on New Year's Day, and how the demon was waiting to kill him. He added that when he himself heard the story, he swore never to leave until he saw what would happen between the merchant and the demon. When the man with the two dogs heard the story, he was amazed, and he too swore never to leave them until he saw what would happen between them. Then he questioned the merchant, and the merchant repeated to him what had happened to him with the demon.

While they were engaged in conversation, a third old man approached and greeted them, and they returned his greeting. He asked, "Why do I see the two of you sitting here, with this merchant between you, looking abject, sad, and dejected?" They told him the merchant's story and explained that they were sitting and waiting to see what would happen to him with the demon. When he heard the story, he sat down with them, saying, "By God, I too like you will not leave, until I see what happens to this man with the demon." As they sat, conversing with one another, they suddenly saw the dust rising from the open country, and when it cleared, they saw the demon approaching, with a drawn steel sword in his hand. He stood before them without greeting them, yanked the merchant with his left hand, and, holding him fast before him, said, "Get ready to die." The merchant and the three old men began to weep and wail.

But dawn broke and morning overtook Shahrazad, and she lapsed into silence. Then Dinarzad said, "Sister, what a lovely story!" Shahrazad replied, "What is this compared with what I shall tell you tomorrow night? It will be even better; it will be more wonderful, delightful, entertaining, and delectable if the king spares me and lets me live." The king was all curiosity to hear the rest of the story and said to himself, "By God, I will not have her put to death until I hear the rest of the story and find out what happened to the merchant with the demon. Then I will have her put to death the next morning, as I did with the others." Then he went out to attend to the affairs of his kingdom, and when he saw Shahrazad's father, he treated him kindly and showed him favors, and the vizier was amazed. When night came, the king went home, and when he was in bed with Shahrazad, Dinarzad said, "Sister, if you are not sleepy, tell us one of your lovely little tales to while away the night." Shahrazad replied, "With the greatest pleasure":

THE FOURTH NIGHT

It is related, O happy King, that the first old man with the deer approached the demon and, kissing his hands and feet, said, "Fiend and King of the demon kings, if I tell you what happened to me and that deer, and you find it strange and amazing, indeed stranger and more amazing than what happened to you and the merchant, will you grant me a third of your claim on him for his crime and guilt?" The demon replied, "I will." The old man said:

[The First Old Man's Tale]

Demon, this deer is my cousin, my flesh and blood. I married her when I was very young, and she a girl of twelve, who reached womanhood only afterward. For thirty years we lived together, but I was not blessed with children, for she bore neither boy nor girl. Yet I continued to be kind to her, to care for her, and to treat her generously. Then I took a mistress, and she bore me a son, who grew up to look like a slice of the moon.[5] Meanwhile, my wife grew jealous of my mistress and my son. One day, when he was ten, I had to go on a journey. I entrusted my wife, this one here, with my mistress and son, bade her take good care of them, and was gone for a whole year. In my absence my wife, this cousin of mine, learned soothsaying and magic and cast a spell on my son and turned him into a young bull. Then she summoned my shepherd, gave my son to him, and said, "Tend this bull with the rest of the cattle." The shepherd took him and tended him for a while. Then she cast a spell on the mother, turning her into a cow, and gave her also to the shepherd.

When I came back, after all this was done, and inquired about my mistress and my son, she answered, "Your mistress died, and your son ran away two months ago, and I have had no news from him ever since." When I heard her, I grieved for my mistress, and with an anguished heart I mourned for my son for nearly a year. When the Great Feast of the Immolation[6] drew near, I summoned the shepherd and ordered him to bring me a fat cow for the sacrifice. The cow he brought me was in reality my enchanted mistress. When I bound her and pressed against her to cut her throat, she wept and cried, as if saying, "My son, my son," and her tears coursed down her cheeks. Astonished and seized with pity, I turned away and asked the shepherd to bring me a different cow. But my wife shouted, "Go on. Butcher her, for he has none better or fatter. Let us enjoy her meat at feast time." I approached the cow to cut her throat, and again she cried, as if saying, "My son, my son." Then I turned away from her and said to the shepherd, "Butcher her for me." The shepherd butchered her, and when he skinned her, he found neither meat nor fat but only skin and bone. I regretted having her butchered and said to the shepherd, "Take her all for yourself, or give her as alms to whomever you wish, and find me a fat young bull from among the flock." The shepherd took her away and disappeared, and I never knew what he did with her.

Then he brought me my son, my heartblood, in the guise of a fat young bull. Then my son saw me, he shook his head loose from the rope, ran toward me, and, throwing himself at my feet, kept rubbing his head against me. I was astonished and touched with sympathy, pity, and mercy, for the blood hearkened to the blood and the divine bond, and my heart throbbed within me when I saw the tears coursing over the cheeks of my son the young bull, as he dug

---

5. The moon is a symbol of beauty for men and women.
6. The Feast of Sacrifice, celebrated throughout the Muslim world at the end of the pil-
grimage to Mecca; to commemorate Abraham, who was willing to sacrifice his son Isaac when commanded by God but was allowed to offer a ram instead, Muslims sacrifice animals to God.

the earth with his hoofs. I turned away and said to the shepherd, "Let him go with the rest of the flock, and be kind to him, for I have decided to spare him. Bring me another one instead of him." My wife, this very deer, shouted, "You shall sacrifice none but this bull." I got angry and replied, "I listened to you and butchered the cow uselessly. I will not listen to you and kill this bull, for I have decided to spare him." But she pressed me, saying, "You must butcher this bull," and I bound him and took the knife . . .

But dawn broke, and morning overtook Shahrazad, and she lapsed into silence, leaving the king all curiosity for the rest of the story. Then her sister Dinarzad said, "What an entertaining story!" Shahrazad replied. "Tomorrow night I shall tell you something even stranger, more wonderful, and more entertaining if the king spares me and lets me live."

THE FIFTH NIGHT

The following night, Dinarzad said to her sister Shahrazad, "Please, sister, if you are not sleepy, tell us one of your little tales." Shahrazad replied, "With the greatest pleasure":

I heard, dear King, that the old man with the deer said to the demon and to his companions:

I took the knife and as I turned to slaughter my son, he wept, bellowed, rolled at my feet, and motioned toward me with his tongue. I suspected something, began to waver with trepidation and pity, and finally released him, saying to my wife, "I have decided to spare him, and I commit him to your care." Then I tried to appease and please my wife, this very deer, by slaughtering another bull, promising her to slaughter this one next season. We slept that night, and when God's dawn broke, the shepherd came to me without letting my wife know, and said, "Give me credit for bringing you good news." I replied, "Tell me, and the credit is yours." He said, "Master, I have a daughter who is fond of soothsaying and magic and who is adept at the art of oaths and spells. Yesterday I took home with me the bull you had spared, to let him graze with the cattle, and when my daughter saw him, she laughed and cried at the same time. When I asked her why she laughed and cried, she answered that she laughed because the bull was in reality the son of our master the cattle owner, put under a spell by his step-mother, and that she cried because his father had slaughtered the son's mother. I could hardly wait till daybreak to bring you the good news about your son."

Demon, when I heard that, I uttered a cry and fainted, and when I came to myself, I accompanied the shepherd to his home, went to my son, and threw myself at him, kissing him and crying. He turned his head toward me, his tears coursing over his cheeks, and dangled his tongue, as if to say, "Look at my plight." Then I turned to the shepherd's daughter and asked, "Can you release him from the spell? If you do, I will give you all my cattle and all my possessions." She smiled and replied, "Master, I have no desire for your wealth, cattle, or possessions. I will deliver him, but on two conditions: first, that you let me marry him; second, that you let me cast a spell on her who had cast a spell on him, in order to control her and guard against her evil power." I replied, "Do whatever you wish and more. My possessions are for you and my son. As for my wife, who has done this to my son and made me slaughter his mother, her life is forfeit to you." She said, "No, but I will let her taste what she has inflicted on others." Then the shepherd's daughter filled a bowl of water, uttered an incantation and an oath, and said to my son, "Bull, if you have been created in this image by the All-Conquering, Almighty Lord, stay as you are, but if you have been treacherously put under a spell, change back to your human form, by the will of God, Creator of the wide world." Then she sprinkled him with the water, and he shook himself and changed from a bull back to his human form.

As I rushed to him, I fainted, and when I came to myself, he told me what my wife, this very deer, had done to him and to his mother. I said to him, "Son, God has sent us someone who will pay her back for what you and your mother and I have suffered at her hands." Then, O demon, I gave my son in marriage to the shepherd's daughter, who turned my wife into this very deer, saying to me, "To me this is a pretty form, for she will be with us day and night, and it is better to turn her into a pretty deer than to suffer her sinister looks." Thus she stayed with us, while the days and nights followed one another, and the months and years went by. Then one day the shepherd's daughter died, and my son went to the country of this very man with whom you have had your encounter. Some time later I took my wife, this very deer, with me, set out to find out what had happened to my son, and chanced to stop here. This is my story, my strange and amazing story.

The demon assented, saying, "I grant you one-third of this man's life."

Then, O King Shahrayar, the second old man with the two black dogs approached the demon and said, "I too shall tell you what happened to me and to these two dogs, and if I tell it to you and you find it stranger and more amazing than this man's story will you grant me one-third of this man's life?" The demon replied, "I will." Then the old man began to tell his story, saying . . .

But dawn broke, and morning overtook Shahrazad, and she lapsed into silence. Then Dinarzad said, "This is an amazing story," and Shahrazad replied, "What is this compared with what I shall tell you tomorrow night if the king spares me and lets me live!" The king said to himself, "By God, I will not have her put to death until I find out what happened to the man with the two black dogs. Then I will have her put to death, God the Almighty willing."

THE SIXTH NIGHT

When the following night arrived and Shahrazad was in bed with King Shahrayar, her sister Dinarzad said, "Sister, if you are not sleepy, tell us a little tale. Finish the one you started." Shahrazad replied, "With the greatest pleasure":

I heard, O happy King, that the second old man with the two dogs said:

[The Second Old Man's Tale]

Demon, as for my story, these are the details. These two dogs are my brothers. When our father died, he left behind three sons, and left us three thousand dinars,[7] with which each of us opened a shop and became a shopkeeper. Soon my older brother, one of these very dogs, went and sold the contents of his shop for a thousand dinars, bought trading goods, and, having prepared himself for his trading trip, left us. A full year went by, when one day, as I sat in my shop, a beggar stopped by to beg. When I refused him, he tearfully asked, "Don't you recognize me?" and when I looked at him closely, I recognized my brother. I embraced him and took him into the shop, and when I asked him about his plight, he replied, "The money is gone, and the situation is bad." Then I took him to the public bath, clothed him in one of my robes, and took him home with me. Then I examined my books and checked my balance, and found out that I had made a thousand dinars and that my net worth was two thousand dinars. I divided the amount between my brother and myself, and said to him, "Think as if you have never been away." He gladly took the money and opened another shop.

Soon afterward my second brother, this other dog, went and sold his merchandise and collected his money, intending to go on a trading trip. We tried to dissuade him, but he did not listen. Instead, he bought merchandise and trading goods, joined a group of travelers, and was gone for a full year. Then he came back, just like his older brother. I said to him, "Brother, didn't I advise you not to go?" He replied tearfully, "Brother, it was foreordained. Now I am poor and penniless, without even a shirt on my back." Demon, I took him to the public bath, clothed him in one of my new robes, and took him back to the shop. After we had something to eat, I said to him, "Brother, I shall do my business accounts, calculate my net worth for the year, and after subtracting the capital, whatever the profit happens to be, I shall divide it equally between you and myself." When I examined my books and subtracted the capital, I found out that my profit was two thousand dinars, and I thanked God and felt very happy. Then I divided the money, giving him a thousand dinars and keeping a thousand for myself. With that money he opened another shop, and the three of us stayed together for a while. Then my two brothers asked me to go on a trading journey with them, but I refused, saying, "What did you gain from your ventures that I can gain?"

They dropped the matter, and for six years we worked in our stores, buying and selling. Yet every year they asked me to go on a trading journey with them, but I refused, until I finally gave in. I said, "Brothers, I am ready to go with you. How much money do you have?" I found out that they had eaten and drunk and squandered everything they had, but I said nothing to them and did not reproach them. Then I took inventory, gathered all I had together, and sold everything. I was pleased to discover that the sale netted six thousand dinars. Then I divided the money into two parts, and said to my brothers, "The sum of three thousand dinars is for you and myself to use on our trading journey. The other three thousand I shall bury in the ground, in case what happened to you happens to me, so that when we return, we will find three thousand dinars to reopen our shops." They replied, "This is an excellent idea." Then, demon, I divided my money and buried three thousand dinars. Of the remaining three I gave each of my brothers a thousand and kept a thousand for myself. After I closed my shop, we bought merchandise and trading goods, rented a large seafaring boat, and after loading it with our goods and provisions, sailed day and night, for a month.

---

7. Gold coins; the basic Muslim money units [translator's note].

But morning overtook Shahrazad, and she lapsed into silence. Then her sister Dinarzad said, "Sister, what a lovely story!" Shahrazad replied, "Tomorrow night I shall tell you something even lovelier, stranger, and more wonderful if I live, the Almighty God willing."

THE SEVENTH NIGHT

The following night Dinarzad said to her sister Shahrazad, "For God's sake, sister, if you are not sleepy, tell us a little tale." The king added, "Let it be the completion of the story of the merchant and the demon." Shahrazad replied, "With the greatest pleasure":

I heard, O happy King, that the second old man said to the demon:

For a month my brothers, these very dogs, and I sailed the salty sea, until we came to a port city. We entered the city and sold our goods, earning ten dinars for every dinar. Then we bought other goods, and when we got to the seashore to embark, I met a girl who was dressed in tatters. She kissed my hands and said, "O my lord, be charitable and do me a favor, and I believe that I shall be able to reward you for it." I replied, "I am willing to do you a favor regardless of any reward." She said, "O my lord, marry me, clothe me, and take me home with you on this boat, as your wife, for I wish to give myself to you. I, in turn, will reward you for your kindness and charity, the Almighty God willing. Don't be misled by my poverty and present condition." When I heard her words, I felt pity for her, and guided by what God the Most High had intended for me, I consented. I clothed her with an expensive dress and married her. Then I took her to the boat, spread the bed for her, and consummated our marriage. We sailed many days and nights, and I, feeling love for her, stayed with her day and night, neglecting my brothers. In the meantime they, these very dogs, grew jealous of me, envied me for my increasing merchandise and wealth, and coveted all our possessions. At last they decided to betray me and, tempted by the Devil, plotted to kill me. One night they waited until I was asleep beside my wife; then they carried the two of us and threw us into the sea.

When we awoke, my wife turned into a she-demon and carried me out of the sea to an island. When it was morning, she said, "Husband, I have rewarded you by saving you from drowning, for I am one of the demons who believe in God.[8] When I saw you by the seashore, I felt love for you and came to you in the guise in which you saw me, and when I expressed my love for you, you accepted me. Now I must kill your brothers." When I heard what she said, I was amazed and I thanked her and said, "As for destroying my brothers, this I do not wish, for I will not behave like them." Then I related to her what had happened to me and them, from beginning to end. When she heard my story, she got very angry at them, and said, "I shall fly to them now, drown their boat, and let them all perish." I entreated her, saying, "For God's sake, don't. The proverb advises 'Be kind to those who hurt you.' No matter what, they are my brothers after all." In this manner, I entreated her and pacified her. Afterward, she took me and flew away with me until she brought me home and put me down on the roof of my

---

8. According to the Qur'an, God created both humans and demons (jinns), some of whom accepted Islam.

house. I climbed down, threw the doors open, and dug up the money I had buried. Then I went out and, greeting the people in the market, reopened my shop. When I came home in the evening, I found these two dogs tied up, and when they saw me, they came to me, wept, and rubbed themselves against me. I started, when I suddenly heard my wife say, "O my lord, these are your brothers." I asked, "Who has done this to them?" She replied, "I sent to my sister and asked her to do it. They will stay in this condition for ten years, after which they may be delivered." Then she told me where to find her and departed. The ten years have passed, and I was with my brothers on my way to her to have the spell lifted, when I met this man, together with this old man with the deer. When I asked him about himself, he told me about his encounter with you, and I resolved not to leave until I found out what would happen between you and him. This is my story. Isn't it amazing?

The demon replied, "By God, it is strange and amazing. I grant you one-third of my claim on him for his crime."

Then the third old man said, "Demon, don't disappoint me. If I told you a story that is stranger and more amazing than the first two would you grant me one-third of your claim on him for his crime?" The demon replied, "I will." Then the old man said, "Demon, listen":

But morning overtook Shahrazad, and she lapsed into silence. Then her sister said, "What an amazing story!" Shahrazad replied, "The rest is even more amazing." The king said to himself, "I will not have her put to death until I hear what happened to the old man and the demon; then I will have her put to death, as is my custom with the others."

THE EIGHTH NIGHT

The following night Dinarzad said to her sister Shahrazad, "For God's sake, sister, if you are not sleepy, tell us one of your lovely little tales to while away the night." Shahrazad replied, "With the greatest pleasure":

[The Third Old Man's Tale][9]

The demon said, "This is a wonderful story, and I grant you a third of my claim on the merchant's life."

The third sheikh approached and said to the demon, "I will tell you a story more wonderful than these two if you will grant me a third of your claim on his life, O demon!"

To which the demon agreed.

So the sheikh began:

O sultan and chief of the demons, this mule was my wife. I had gone off on a journey and was absent from her for a whole year. At last I came to the end of my journey and returned home late one night. When I entered the house I saw a black slave lying in bed with her. They were chatting and dallying and laugh-

---

9. Translated by Jerome W. Clinton. Because the earliest manuscript does not include a story for the third sheikh, later narrators sup- plied one. This brief anecdote comes from a manuscript found in the library of the Royal Academy in Madrid.

ing and kissing and quarreling together. When she saw me my wife leaped out of bed, ran to the water jug, recited a spell over it, then splashed me with some of the water and said, "Leave this form for the form of a dog."

Immediately I became a dog and she chased me out of the house. I ran out of the gate and didn't stop running until I reached a butcher's shop. I entered it and fell to eating the bones lying about. When the owner of the shop saw me, he grabbed me and carried me into his house. When his daughter saw me, she hid her face and said, "Why are you bringing this strange man in with you?"

"What man?" her father asked.

"This dog is a man whose wife has put a spell on him," she said, "but I can set him free again." She took a jug of water, recited a spell over it, then splashed a little water from it on me, and said, "Leave this shape for your original one."

And I became myself again. I kissed her hand and said, "I want to cast a spell on my wife as she did on me. Please give me a little of that water."

"Gladly," she said, "if you find her asleep, sprinkle a few drops on her and she will become whatever you wish."

Well, I did find her asleep, and I sprinkled some water on her and said, "Leave this shape for the shape of a she-mule." She at once became the very mule you see here, oh sultan and chief of the demons."

The demon then turned to him and asked, "Is this really true?"

"Yes," he answered, nodding his head vigorously, "it's all true."

When the sheikh had finished his story, the demon shook with laughter and granted him a third of his claim on the merchant's blood.

Then the demon released the merchant and departed. The merchant turned to the three old men and thanked them, and they congratulated him on his deliverance and bade him good-bye. Then they separated, and each of them went on his way. The merchant himself went back home to his family, his wife, and his children, and he lived with them until the day he died. But this story is not as strange or as amazing as the story of the fisherman.

Dinarzad asked, "Please, sister, what is the story of the fisherman?" Shahrazad said: . . .

GEOFFREY CHAUCER
1340?–1400

While there was plenty of literature in English before Chaucer, later generations of writers would identify his *Canterbury Tales* as the foundation of the English poetic tradition. Chaucer was the first to conceive of poetry in English not as the product of an isolated, provincial nation located in an obscure corner of Europe but as a vital agent in the fourteenth-century emergence of the vernacular as a literary language. For this reason, Chaucer's models and rivals were not so much the English authors of **Beowulf** and *Sir Gawain and the Green Knight* as the Europeans **Dante**, **Petrarch**, and Boccaccio. Queen Elizabeth's tutor, Roger Ascham, recognized Chaucer's foundational role by calling him "our English **Homer**." The sentiment was reiterated by Dryden, who translated several of the tales alongside selections from **Ovid**'s *Metamorphoses*, declaring "I hold him in the same degree of veneration as the Grecians held Homer or the Romans **Virgil**." In his *Faerie Queene*, Spenser calls Chaucer the "well of English undefiled," a stream of poetic influence still visible in the opening lines of T. S. Eliot's *The Waste Land*. For these writers, Chaucer's vivid, naturalistic English was the firm ground on which they could anchor a national literature.

LIFE

Chaucer's family origins were solidly middle class. His father and grandfather had been wine merchants, and by placing the youthful Chaucer as a servant at the royal court they set in motion a social transition that would ultimately lead to the family's participation in the upper classes of English society. Chaucer's granddaughter, Alice de la Pole, married a duke, and her grandson was named as the heir to his uncle, Richard III (though he never reached the throne). Chaucer's own family history is an example of the increasing social fluidity of late medieval English culture, in which status could change dramatically over just a few generations. Unlike many premodern poets who were supported by wealthy patrons, Chaucer was obliged to hold a mundane day job for most of his career. He had the time-consuming and tedious position of record keeper at the customs authority in London, and later supervised a number of building projects in his role as clerk of public works. In his *House of Fame*, Chaucer describes poring over his financial ledgers all day, and his books of poetry and fiction all night.

Chaucer's entry into the bureaucracy of English government followed from his early placement in a series of households within the royal family, beginning as a page in the retinue of the Countess of Ulster, daughter-in-law of King Edward III. In fact, the very first documentation of the poet's existence appears in a record of clothes purchased for the then-teenage Chaucer when he was attached to the countess's household. Later in his career, Chaucer was directly rewarded for his work for the court by Edward's grandson, King Richard II, and had the support of Edward's son John of Gaunt, the Duke of Lancaster (who, through a late third marriage, also became Chaucer's brother-in-law). Chaucer had a genius for keeping on the right side of power in a difficult and competitive era, a time characterized by civil unrest, international war, and, ultimately, seizure of the throne in 1399 by John of Gaunt's son and Richard II's cousin, Henry IV. Chaucer appears to have seamlessly transferred his loyalty from Richard to the new king, addressing one of his final lyrics, "A Complaint to His Purse," to the "conqueror of Brutus's Albion, who by lineage and free election is the true king." His subtle and politically astute poetry is as much the product of social and economic turmoil as is **Dante**'s *Divine Comedy*: unlike Dante, however, who ended his days in exile, Chaucer knew how to play all sides against each other in order to protect himself.

As a soldier in the Hundred Years' War and, later, a diplomatic envoy for the English government, Chaucer traveled repeatedly to France, Spain, and—most importantly—Italy; there he encountered the work of Dante, Petrarch, and Boccaccio, which became central to his own writing. French literature had already had a strong impact on English writers of the period, but Italian literature was something new and exciting: through Chaucer, the humanist tradition championed by Petrarch began to be felt in England, along with the high allegorical mode of Dante and the story collections of Boccaccio. While the exact chronology of Chaucer's works is uncertain, they are often divided roughly into three periods: the so-called French phase, which includes the *Book of the Duchess*, an elegiac dream vision that owes much to the *Romance of the Rose* and the poetry of Machaut and Froissart; the Italian phase, which features the *Parliament of Fowls* and the *House of Fame*, both of which refer explicitly to Dante's *Divine Comedy*; and the English phase, during which Chaucer composed his *Canterbury Tales*. This sequence has many faults—most seriously, it tends to privilege the final, culminating period of the poet's career as specifically "English." Yet despite simplifying, it provides a use-

ful way to contextualize a series of major works, each of which represents a significant innovation beyond what had come before.

In addition to the literature of his French and Italian contemporaries, Chaucer was deeply indebted to the major classical authors, especially Ovid and Virgil. A more particular influence, however, was the late antique philosophical poem of Boethius, the *Consolation of Philosophy*. Chaucer was a penetrating reader of the *Consolation*, which he translated into English, and he repeatedly turned to Boethian themes such as the competing roles of Fortune and Providence, the place of free will in the human soul, and the role of love as source of both chaos and order. In his dream visions and *Troilus and Criseyde*, Chaucer ostentatiously displays his classical learning and makes continual reference to the poems of his French and Italian contemporaries. But in the *Canterbury Tales*, Chaucer suddenly begins to wear his learning much more lightly: allusions become indirect and often parodic, and the focus of the poetry shifts instead to the landscape of society and, especially, to the relationship between the nature of a storyteller and the story he or she tells.

TIMES

Chaucer's England was the crucible of Reformation: the last years of the fourteenth century witnessed the emergence of religiously unorthodox communities loosely grouped under the term "Lollardy," an originally derogatory term used to identify such would-be reformers as dangerous heretics who sowed discord in the church. Lollard preachers argued that the Bible should be available in the vernacular language so that each person could know scripture at first hand, that images were really idols leading away from rather than toward God, and that pilgrimages were nothing more than social gatherings thinly disguised as devotional practice. In Chaucer's day, such unorthodox views were regarded with suspicion but were not yet as energetically suppressed as they would be just a few years after his death, when those suspected of Lollardy might be burned in the public square along with their unauthorized translations. Chaucer's Parson, who recounts a penitential treatise as the concluding story of the *Canterbury Tales*, is mocked by the Host, who exclaims, "I smell a Lollard in the wind." This kind of mockery, still just barely playful in the last decade of the fourteenth century, would soon evolve into denunciation and persecution. After this violent suppression, the aims of the Lollards would reemerge more successfully in the sixteenth century.

The same impulse that led medieval English men and women to want to read the **Bible** in English also led to other expressions of religious piety, including the tremendously popular stories of the lives of saints (two of which appear in the *Canterbury Tales*, in the Prioress's Tale and the Second Nun's Tale) and autobiographies of devout women such as Julian of Norwich and Margery Kempe. Chaucer's Wife of Bath is far less focused on heavenly goals than were these women: for her, pilgrimage is less about retracing the pathway to God than about "wandering by the way." Like Margery Kempe, however, the Wife of Bath is a strong female representative of the emerging bourgeois class whose wealth was built on local industries such as brewing (Margery Kempe) and weaving (the Wife of Bath), and whose independence was expressed physically through the act of travel both within England and abroad. Chaucer's pilgrims exemplify the late medieval English eagerness to find the right path to God, whether through the unmediated experience of scripture, as advocated by the Lollards,

or through the highly overdetermined mediation of pardons (certificates from Rome that guaranteed the devout buyer a shorter stay in purgatory).

The same instability that had come to threaten the church's control of the Christian flock in England, through the rise of Lollardy, also affected the smooth working of government. The reign of Richard II, who had ascended the throne as a child in 1377 following the death of his grandfather Edward III, was marked by capricious rule, discord between the king's advisers and the major lords of the realm, and repeated heavy taxation necessitated by the ongoing war between England and France. Discord within the capital city of London itself was particularly intense, as the burghers of the city became increasingly involved in the disputes between Parliament and the king. The greatest disruption took place in 1381, as a popular uprising broke out in the countryside in response to the imposition of yet another heavy tax. The Peasants' Revolt, as it was later called, moved rapidly through the towns and fields outside London, entering the city with violence. When the archbishop of Canterbury confronted the mob, urging the peasants to return to their homes, he was decapitated and his head impaled on a pike on London Bridge. The peasants rampaged through the streets, sacking and burning the palace of the king's uncle and chief adviser, John of Gaunt. Gaunt was connected to Chaucer both as his main patron and through family ties, but the revolt struck still closer to home for Chaucer: the mob slaughtered a group of Flemish immigrant workers in a London street where Chaucer had lived as a boy, and it entered the city through a major gate— Aldgate—above which Chaucer had his lodgings. Although Chaucer must have witnessed this violence at first hand, his allusions to social unrest are always oblique and, above all, cautious.

WORK

The Canterbury Tales is a frame-tale poem; like **The Thousand and One Nights** and Boccaccio's *Decameron*, it has a beginning and ending within which a series of tales are related. Unlike *The Thousand and One Nights*, which has (for the most part) a single storyteller, and the *Decameron*, which has a relatively homogenous company of noble young narrators, *The Canterbury Tales* revels in the extraordinary range of possible tales and possible tale-tellers. From the humble Miller to the chivalric Knight, from the bossy Wife of Bath to the effete Pardoner, Chaucer's diverse pilgrims span the range of medieval English life. The pilgrims are, in a way, types or ideals of each manner of life available to the individual: the company includes a nun, a lawyer, a squire, a sailor, and so on. But each teller is also an individual, characterized as such not only in the prefatory prologues that introduce each tale but also in the manner in which the tale itself is told. Petty rivalries, as between the Miller and the Reeve or between the Friar and the Summoner, are played out during the interludes between tales; tale-tellers pay back or "quite" one another by telling stories that indirectly comment on their fellows, causing sometimes argument and discord, sometimes laughter, or sometimes—as at the end of the Pardoner's Tale—both.

Chaucer's Wife of Bath is endowed with a vivid personality and a complex inner life that she herself tells us all about. In her Prologue, she sets her female experience against the misogynist stereotypes of women as lawless, sexually voracious, and manipulative creatures, a view promoted by certain traditions of medieval religious thought. Yet the reader is forced to ask if the Wife's frank celebration of her own sexuality, and her account of the torment she has inflicted on her three old husbands, does not in fact confirm those stereotypes. An answer is suggested by the Wife's claim that she is only playing: indeed, at one point she speaks as if she were showing her almost exclusively male audience how she would conduct a kind of school for wives. She seems, in other words, to be putting on a performance, pretending to reveal to her fascinated audience the secrets that women share among themselves and thereby letting men witness the intimate life of a woman. Yet as the Prologue proceeds we feel that her playful dramatics give way to a more serious, more authentic self-revelation. We learn that not only have her husbands suffered in marriage but that she has too, that she is unavoidably (if cheerfully) aware of her advancing years, and that what she seems to value most is neither money nor the sex she so aggressively celebrates but the companionship and love she comes finally to share with her fifth husband. In the same way, her tale gradually reveals itself to be more than simply a nostalgic wish fulfillment for the return of youth and beauty. When the criminal knight tries to learn what women most desire, he is offered a series of misogynist answers; but when forced to marry he discovers, through the moral lecture his old wife delivers, that she possesses a wisdom that he himself lacks. This is why he leaves the final decision about what form she will assume up to her, and in granting her mastery he is rewarded not merely with youth and beauty but with a marriage of mutual affection. It is through this experience, then, rather than by relying on the authority of time-honored opinions, that the knight comes to learn about the true nature of women.

CHAUCER'S LANGUAGE

Chaucer's Middle English strikes the present-day reader as both familiar and strange, separated from Modern English by peculiarities of pronunciation and word order, but recognizable as its ancestor through names and terms that have remained essentially unchanged. Unlike the Old English of *Beowulf*, which must be learned as though it were a foreign language, Middle English is usually approached as if it were a dialect or an idiom—close to home, but still uncannily strange. We reproduce below the first eighteen lines of the General Prologue to the *Tales*, not only to illustrate the gap between English of the fourteenth century and the twenty-first, and to provide a frame of reference for the modern English translation that follows, but also to give a taste of the unfamiliar familiar tongue of the father of English poetry.

Whan that Aprill with his shoures soote
The droghte of March hath perced to the roote,
And bathed every veyne in swich licour
Of which vertu engendred is the flour;
Whan Zephirus eek with his sweete breeth
Inspired hath in every holt and heeth
The tender croppes, and the yonge sonne
Hath in the Ram his halve cours yronne,
And smale foweles maken melodye,
That slepen al the nyght with open ye
(So priketh hem nature in hir corages);
Thanne longen folk to goon on pilgrimages,
And palmeres for to seken straunge strondes,
To ferne halwes, kowthe in sondry londes;
And specially from every shires ende
Of Engelond to Caunterbury they wende,
The hooly blissful martir for to seke,
That hem hath holpen whan that they were seeke.

FROM THE CANTERBURY TALES[1]

The General Prologue

Here begins the Book of the Tales of Canterbury.

When April comes and with its showers sweet
Has, to the root, pierced March's drought complete,
And then bathed every vein in such elixir
That, by its strength, engendered is the flower;
When Zephirus[2] with his sweet breath   5
Inspires life anew, through grove and heath,
In tender shoots, and when the spring's young sun
Has, in the Ram,[3] full half its course now run,

---

1. Translated from Middle English by Sheila Fisher.
2. Zephyr, the west wind.

3. Aries, the first sign of the zodiac in the solar year (March 21–April 20).

And when small birds begin to harmonize
That sleep throughout the night with open eyes   10
(So nature, stirring them, pricks up their courage),
Then folks, too, long to go on pilgrimage,
And palmers hope to seek there, on strange strands,[4]
Those far-off shrines well known in many lands;
And especially, from every shire's end   15
Of England, to Canterbury they wend;
The holy, blessed martyr[5] they all seek,
Who has helped them when they were sick and weak.
      It happened, in that season, on a day
In Southwark,[6] at the Tabard as I lay   20
Ready to start out on my pilgrimage
To Canterbury, with true, devoted courage,
At night, there came into that hostelry,[7]
Fully nine-and-twenty in a company
Of sundry folks, as chance would have them fall   25
In fellowship, and pilgrims were they all,
Who, toward Canterbury, wished to ride.
The chambers and the stables were all wide,
And we were put at ease with all the best.
And, shortly, when the sun went to its rest,   30
I had so spoken with them, every one,
That I was in their fellowship anon,
And to rise early I gave them my vow,
To make our way, as I will tell you now.
      But, nonetheless, while I have time and space,   35
Before much further in this tale I pace,
It seems quite right and proper to relate
To you the full condition and the state
Of each of them, just as they seemed to me,
And what they were, and of what degree,   40
And also of the clothes they were dressed in,
And with a knight, then, I will first begin.
      A Knight there was, and that, a worthy man,
Who, from the time when he first began
To ride to war, he loved most chivalry,   45
Truth and honor, largesse and courtesy.
Full worthy he, to fight in his lord's war,
No other man had ridden half so far,
As much in Christian as in heathen lands,
And all honor his worthiness commands;   50

---

4. Shores, beaches. "Palmers": pilgrims who had returned from the Holy Land (they carried palm fronds in imitation of Jesus and his apostles during their entry into Jerusalem).
5. St. Thomas Becket (ca. 1118–1170), killed by assailants loyal to King Henry II of England as he stood before the altar of his church at Canterbury; until the Reformation, the site was something of a national center of religious devotion.
6. A suburb of London, south of the Thames, where theaters, brothels, and other businesses of dubious repute set up shop beyond the reach of the city's laws.
7. I.e., the Tabard.

At Alexandria[8] he was, when it was won.
At banquets, he was many times the one
Seated with honor above all knights in Prussia;
In Lithuania, he'd raided, and in Russia,
Unrivalled among knightly Christian men.   55
In Granada, at the siege, he'd also been
Of Algeciras; he rode at Belmarin.
At Ayas and at Adalia he had been
When they fell; and then in the Great Sea[9]
At fine armed conquests, he fought worthily.   60
In fifteen mortal battles had he been,
And thrice he fought for God at Tlemcen
Alone in lists, and always slew his foe.
And this same worthy knight had been also
At one time fighting alongside Balat's lord   65
Against another Turkish heathen horde;
And always was his fame a sovereign prize.
Not only was he was worthy, he was wise,
And in his bearing, meek as is a maid.
In all his life, no rude word had he said   70
To any man, however much his might.
He was a true and perfect gentle knight.
But now to tell you about his array,
His horse was good, but his dress was not gay.
His tunic was of fustian, coarse and plain,   75
Which by his rusty mailcoat was all stained,
For just lately he'd come from his voyage,
And now he went to make his pilgrimage.
　　With him there was his son, a young SQUIRE,
A lover and in arms, a bachelor,   80
His locks waved like they'd seen a curling press.
About twenty years of age he was, I guess.
In his stature, he was of average length,
And wonderfully deft, and of great strength.
He'd ridden sometimes with the cavalry   85
In Flanders, in Artois, and Picardy,[1]
And fared quite well, within small time and space,
In hope of standing in his lady's grace.
Embroidered was he, as if he were a bed
All full of fresh spring flowers, white and red.   90
Singing he was, or fluting, all the day;
He was as fresh as is the month of May.
Short was his gown, its sleeves hung long and wide.
Well could he sit his horse, and nicely ride.
And also he wrote songs, both verse and note,   95

---

8. A city in northern Egypt, sacked by Peter I of Cyprus in 1365. The following places named, ranging from eastern Europe to the Muslim-held regions in southern Spain and North Africa, demonstrate both the large number and the wide variety of the Knight's campaigns.

9. The Mediterranean.

1. Regions in modern Belgium and northern France.

He jousted and he danced, he drew and wrote.
So hotly loved he that when nighttime came,
The nightingale and he slept both the same.[2]
Courteous and meek, to serve, quite able,
He carved before his father at the table.[3]   100
    A YEOMAN[4] had he—no servants beside,
For at this time, that's how he chose to ride,
And he was clad in coat and hood of green.
A sheaf of peacock arrows, bright and keen,
Under his belt, he bore quite properly   105
(For he could tend his gear quite yeomanly;
His arrows did not droop with feathers low),
And in his hand he bore a mighty bow.
A close-cropped head had he, a face well browned.
No man more skilled in woodcraft might be found.   110
Upon his arm he wore a gay wrist guard,
And by his side a small shield and a sword,
By his other side, a bright, gay dagger fell,
As sharp as a spear's point, and sheathed up well;
On his breast, a silver Christopher[5] was seen.   115
He bore a horn, its baldric was of green;
A forester, he was, truly, as I guess.
    There was also a Nun, a PRIORESS,
Who in her smiling was simple and gracious;
Her greatest oath was "by Saint Eligius";[6]   120
And she was known as Madame Eglentine.[7]
Quite well she sang the liturgy divine,
Intoning it in her nose quite properly;
And French she spoke quite well and elegantly,
After the school of Stratford-at-the-Bow,[8]   125
Because Parisian French she did not know.
In dining, she was well taught overall;
She let no morsel down from her lips fall,
Nor wet her fingers in her sauce so deep;
Deftly she could lift up a bite, and keep   130
A single drop from falling on her breast.
In courtesy, she found what pleased her best.
Her upper lip she wiped so nice and clean
That in her cup no single speck was seen
Of grease, because she drank her drink so neat.   135
Quite daintily, she reached out for her meat.
And truthfully, she was so very pleasant,
And amiable, her manners excellent;
She pained herself to imitate the ways

2. That is, not at all. In Persian, Arabic, Occitan, and French poetry, the nightingale was a symbol of erotic love.
3. One of the duties of a squire, and also a sign of obedience and loyalty.
4. A superior grade of servant in a noble household.

5. A medal bearing the image of the patron saint of travelers.
6. The patron saint of goldsmiths, said to have been a remarkably attractive man.
7. The name of a kind of wild rose (more appropriate to a romance heroine than a nun).
8. A village 2 miles from London.

Of court, and to be stately all her days, 140
And to be held worthy of reverence.
But, now, to speak about her conscience,
She was so full of pity and charity,
That she'd cry for a mouse that she might see
Caught in a trap, if it bled or was dead. 145
With her, she had her small hounds, which she fed
With roasted flesh, or milk and pure white bread.[9]
Sorely she wept if one of them were dead,
Or if men smote it so hard it would smart;
With her, all was conscience and tender heart. 150
Quite properly, her pleated wimple draped,
Her eyes blue gray as glass, her nose well-shaped,
Her mouth quite small, and also soft and red.
But, certainly, she had a fair forehead;
It was almost a span[1] in breadth, I own; 155
For, truth to tell, she was not undergrown.
Quite elegant, her cloak, I was aware.
Made of small corals on her arm she'd bear,
A rosary, set off with beads of green,
And thereon hung a broach of golden sheen, 160
On which the letter "A," inscribed and crowned
With "Amor vincit omnia"[2] was found.
          Another NUN riding with her had she,
Who was her secretary, and priests three.
          A MONK there was, the handsomest to see, 165
An outrider, who most loved venery,[3]
A manly man, to be an abbot able.
Many a striking horse had he in stable,
And when he rode, men might his bridle hear
Jingling in a whistling wind as clear 170
And just as loud as tolls the chapel bell
Of the house where he was keeper of the cell.
The rule of Saints Maurus and Benedict,[4]
Because it was so old and somewhat strict—
This same Monk let the old things pass away 175
And chose the new ways of the present day.
For that text he'd not give you one plucked hen
That said that hunters are not holy men,
Or that a monk who disobeys his order
Is likened to a fish out of the water— 180
That is to say, a monk out of the cloister.
But that text, he held not worth an oyster.
And I said his opinion was good.

9. A diet enjoyed only by the wealthy; in this period, most ate black or brown bread, with little meat.
1. A handspan (a wide forehead was a sign of beauty).
2. "Love conquers all" (Latin).
3. Hunting; also, sexual pleasure (Latin, *ven-*

eria). "Outrider": here, the monk whose duty was to look after the lands belonging to the monastery.
4. The founder (d. 547) of the Benedictine order; Maurus (d. 584) was his disciple and founded an abbey in France.

What! Should he study, and make himself mad should
He, always poring over books in cloister,   185
Or should he work with his hands and labor
As Augustine bids?[5] How shall the world be served?
For Augustine, let this work be reserved!
A fine hard-pricking spursman he, all right;
He had greyhounds as swift as birds in flight;   190
In pricking and in hunting for the hare,
Lay all his lust; for no cost would he spare.
I saw his sleeves were fur lined at the hand
With rich, gray squirrel, the finest in the land;
And to fasten his hood beneath his chin,   195
He had, all wrought from gold, a fancy pin;
A love knot on the larger end was cast.
His head was bald, and it shone just like glass,
His face shone, too, as though he'd been anointed.
He was a lord full fat and well appointed;   200
His eyes rolled in his head and shone as bright
As fires under furnace pots, cast light;
His boots were supple, his horses strong and fit;
Now, certainly, he was a fair prelate;
He was not pale like a tormented ghost.   205
A fat swan[6] loved he best of any roast.
His palfrey was as brown as is a berry.
        A FRIAR there was, a wanton one, and merry,
A limitor,[7] quite an important man.
In all four orders[8] is no one who can   210
Talk quite so smoothly, with such winning speech.
Many marriages made he in the breach
For young women and at his own expense.
In him, his order found a fine defense.
Quite well beloved and on close terms was he   215
With the franklins[9] all throughout his country,
And with all the town's most worthy women,
For he had the right to hear confession,
As he said, more than a curate surely,
For, by his order, he was licensed fully.   220
So, quite sweetly, would he hear confession,
And quite pleasant was his absolution:
He was an easy man in giving penance,
Where he knew he'd get more than a pittance.
If to a poor order one has given,   225
It's a sure sign that one's been well shriven;
If a man gave, he knew well what it meant:
He dared to boast that this man would repent.

5. The rule of St. Augustine of Hippo (354–
430), author of the *Confessions*, requires that
monks engage in manual labor.
6. An expensive and rare delicacy; ordinarily,
monks abstained from eating meat.
7. A friar licensed to beg in a specific territory.

8. In the 14th century, Franciscans, Augus-
tinians, Carmelites, and Dominicans. Friars,
unlike monks, circulated among the people.
9. Upper-middle-class landowners, ranked below
the gentry.

For many a man is just so hard of heart,
He may not weep, though he may sorely smart.   230
Therefore, instead of giving tears and prayers,
Men must yield up their silver to poor friars.
His hood's tip always was stuffed full of knives
And pins, for him to give out to fair wives.
Certainly his merry voice was pleasing: 235
And he could play the fiddle well and sing;
For ballads, he took first prize utterly.
His neck was white as is the fleur-de-lis.[1]
A strong champion was he in a brawl.
The taverns in each town, he knew them all;   240
Each in keeper and every barmaid, too,
More than lepers[2] or beggar girls, he knew,
Because, for such a worthy man as he,
It would not do, with his ability,
With sick lepers to have an acquaintance.   245
It is not right; it hardly can advance
Him if he has to spend time with the poor,
Just with the rich and victualers, for sure.
And over all, where profit should arise,
Polite was he, and served in humble guise.   250
No man was so effective anywhere:
He was, in his house, the best beggar there.
For private begging turf, he laid out rent;
None of his brothers came there where he went;
And although one were a shoeless widow,   255
So charming was his "In principio,"[3]
A farthing he would get before he went.
His income was much higher than his rent.
And he could rage just like a little whelp.
On love-days,[4] like a judge, well could he help,   260
For there, he was not like a cloisterer
In a threadbare cloak, like a poor scholar,
But like a master or the pope as well.
Of double worsted, rounded as a bell
Fresh from the casting, was his short, rich cloak.   265
With affectation, he lisped when he spoke,
To make his English sweet upon his tongue;
In his harping, whenever he had sung,
His eyes would twinkle in his head as bright
As do the stars upon a frosty night.   270
This worthy limitor was named Huberd.
      A MERCHANT was there, too, with a forked beard,
In mixed-hued clothes; high on his horse he sat;
Upon his head, a Flemish beaver hat,

1. A lily (in heraldry, the royal arms of France).
2. Shunned through antiquity and the Middle
Ages, but healed by Jesus (see Mark 1.40–45;
Luke 17.11–19).
3. "In the beginning" (Latin), the opening

words of the Vulgate translation of the Gospel
of John, whose first fourteen verses were used
by friars in devotions and in greetings.
4. Days when disputes were judged out of
court.

And his fair boots were fastened stylishly.   275
He uttered his ideas quite solemnly,
Sounding always increase in his winning.
He wished the sea safe, more than anything,
Between the ports of Middleburgh and Orwell.[5]
Well could he in exchange his florins sell.[6]   280
This worthy man quite deftly used his wit:
Were he in debt, no one would know of it,
So stately was he in his management
Of borrowing, buying, selling where he went.
Surely, he was a worthy man, in all,   285
But, truth to say, I don't know what he's called.
    A CLERK from Oxford[7] was with us also,
Whose work in logic started long ago.
As skinny was his horse as is a rake,
And he was not so fat, I undertake;   290
He looked hollow, and thus, grave and remote.
Quite threadbare was his outermost short coat;
He had as yet no clerical appointment,
And wasn't made for secular employment.
For he would rather have, at his bed's head,   295
Twenty books, all well bound in black or red,
Of Aristotle[8] and his philosophy
Than rich robes, or fiddle, or gay psaltery.
But, for all that he was a philosopher,
He had little gold piled in his coffer;[9]   300
For, anything that his friends to him lent,
On books and on his learning, it got spent.
Busily, for the souls of them he prayed
Who, so that he could go to school, had paid.
Of his studies, he took most care and heed.   305
Not one word spoke he more than he had need,
And that was said with dignity and respect,
And short, and quick, and full of intellect;
Resounding in moral virtue was his speech,
And gladly would he learn, and gladly teach.   310
    A SERGEANT OF THE LAW,[1] wary and wise,
Who often in Saint Paul's court[2] did advise,
There was also, quite rich in excellence.
Dignified and judicious in each sense—
Or he seemed such, his words were all so wise.   315
He was often a judge at the assize,[3]

5. Cities in the Netherlands and England, respectively.
6. I.e., he also profited in currency exchange. Florins were gold coins minted in Florence, Italy.
7. A student.
8. The rediscovered works of Aristotle (384–322 B.C.E.) were widely read and commented on in medieval universities, especially his works on logic and science.
9. A joke that relies on understanding "philosopher" as also meaning "alchemist" (one who sought to create gold out of base metals).
1. A judge.
2. By St. Paul's Cathedral, a meeting place for lawyers and their clients.
3. Circuit court, presided over by itinerant judges.

With full commission—and through royal consent.
For all his learning and his fame's extent,
Fees and robes, he did have, many a one.
So great a land buyer elsewhere was none: 320
He would directly buy up the estate;
His purchase, no one could invalidate.
Nowhere was such a busy man as he;
He seemed busier than he was, actually.
He knew the precedents for everything   325
The law had done since William was the king.[4]
Fine legal texts, thus could he draft and draw
In which no one could find a single flaw;
Every statute, he could recite by rote.
He rode there in a simple mixed-hued coat.   330
A striped silk belt around his waist he wore;
About his dress, I won't tell any more.
        A FRANKLIN rode there in his company,
And his beard was white as is the daisy;
His mood was sanguine,[5] his face rosy red.   335
Well loved he, in the morning, wine-soaked bread;
To live in sheer delight was his one care,
For he was Epicurus's[6] own heir,
Who thought that to lead life in all its pleasure
Was true perfect bliss beyond all measure.   340
A householder, and a full great one, was he;
A Saint Julian[7] he was, in his country.
His bread, his ale, were always very fine;
No other man had better stocks of wine.
His house was never lacking in baked meat,   345
Or fish or flesh, in plenty so complete
That it snowed, in his house, with food and drink,
With any dainties of which men could think.
According to the seasons of the year,
New dishes on his table would appear.   350
Fat partridges in coops, when he did like;
He kept his fish pond stocked with bream and pike.
And woe unto his cook if he'd not got
His gear set and the sauce, spicy and hot.
Covered and ready did his table stay   355
Set up for meals within the hall all day.
At county courts, he was the lord and sire;
And went to Parliament to serve his shire.
A two-edged dagger and a purse of silk
Hung from his girdle, white as morning's milk.   360
A sheriff had he been, an auditor,[8]

4. I.e., since modern law was established by William I, the Norman who conquered England in 1066.

5. In medieval physiology, the dominance of blood (one of the four bodily humors), indicated by his red face, was believed to explain a cheerful disposition.

6. Greek philosopher (340–270 B.C.E.), viewed in the Middle Ages as a proponent of hedonism.

7. The legendary patron saint of innkeepers.

8. An official responsible for verifying accounts.

And nowhere such a worthy landholder.
    A HABERDASHER and a CARPENTER,
A WEAVER, DYER, and a TAPESTRY MAKER—
They were all clothed in the same livery   365
Of one great parish guild fraternity.[9]
All fresh and newly furbished was their gear;
On their knives no brass mountings were found here,
But only silver; fashioned just as fit,
Their girdles and their purses, every bit.   370
Each of them seemed such a worthy burgess[1]
He might sit in the guildhall on the dais.
And each, with all the wisdom that he can,
Was suited to be made an alderman.
Income had they enough, and property,   375
To this their wives would certainly agree;
Or else, quite surely, they would all be blamed.
It is quite nice "My Lady" to be named,
At feasts and vigils, to march first in line,
And have, borne royally, a mantel[2] fine.   380
    For this trip, a COOK rode with them then
To boil the marrowbones up with the hens,
Along with spices tart and galingale.[3]
Well did he know a draught of London ale.
He could both roast and simmer, boil and fry,   385
Make stews and hash and also bake a pie.
But it was a real shame, it seemed to me,
That on his shin, a pus-filled sore had he.
A milky pudding made he with the best.
    A SHIPMAN was there, who lived in the west;   390
He came from Dartmouth,[4] for all that I guessed.
To ride a packhorse he did try his best,
In a gown of coarse wool cloth cut to the knee.
A dagger hanging on a strap had he
Around his neck, under his arm coming down.   395
The hot summer had turned his skin all brown.
And certainly, he was a good fellow.
So many draughts of fine wine from Bordeaux[5]
Had he drawn, while the merchants were asleep.
In a good conscience, small stock did he keep.   400
If, when he fought, he had the upper hand,
He sent them all, by water, back to land.
But in the art of reckoning the tides,
The currents and all perils near, besides,
The moon and piloting and anchorage,   405

9. A trade group whose purposes were social, religious, and economic.
1. Propertied citizen.
2. I.e., a mantle (Chaucer's spelling, now obsolete).
3. Aromatic root, also used as a powder.
4. Port on the southwest coast of England.
5. A center of the wine trade, in southwest France.

No one was so skilled from Hull to Carthage.[6]
Hardy and wise in what was undertaken,
With many tempests had his beard been shaken.
He knew well all the harbors that there were,
Stretching from Gotland to Cape Finisterre,[7]   410
And each inlet from Brittany to Spain;
His sailing ship was called the "Magdalene."[8]

    With us was a DOCTOR OF MEDICINE;
No one was like him, all the world within,
To speak of medicine and surgery,   415
For he was schooled well in astrology.
Through natural magic,[9] he gave patients hope
By keeping close watch on their horoscope.
He could divine when planets were ascendant
To aid the star signs governing his patient.   420
Of every malady, he knew the source
In humors hot, cold, moist, or dry, of course,
And where they were engendered, from which humor.[1]
He was a perfect, true practitioner.
The cause and root known of the malady,   425
At once he gave the sick their remedy.
Quite ready had he his apothecaries
To send him their drugs and electuaries,[2]
For each made profit for the other one—
Their friendship had not recently begun.   430
Well knew he his old Aesculapius,[3]
Dioscorides, and also Rufus,
Old Hippocrates, Hali, and Galen,
Rhazes, Avicenna, Serapion,
Averroes, Damascien, Constantinus,   435
Bernard, Gaddesden, Gilbertus Anglicus.
Of his own diet, moderate was he,
For it contained no superfluity,
But was nourishing and digestible.
His study was but little on the Bible.   440
In blood red and in blue he was all clad,
A lining of two kinds of silk he had.
Yet he was quite cautious with expenses;
He saved what he earned in pestilences.
In medicine, gold[4] works well for the heart,   445

6. I.e., from northern England to North Africa (Carthage) or Spain (Cartagena; Chaucer has "Cartage"); the Shipman is widely traveled.
7. From an island off the coast of Sweden to the west coast of Spain.
8. Named after Mary Magdalen, Jesus's disciple; according to a French tradition, she, her brother Lazarus, and some companions came to the port city of Marseille in the south of France and converted all of Provence.
9. As opposed to black magic.

1. According to humoral physiology, illness was caused by imbalance in the four humors—the different combinations of the four qualities (hot, cold, moist, dry).
2. Medicinal pastes.
3. Greek god of healing. The list that follows names medical authors from ancient Greece, the Arabic world (including Avicenna), and medieval England (John of Gaddesden [d. 1348/49] and Gilbert the Englishman [d. ca. 1250]).
4. Used as a medicine in the Middle Ages.

Therefore, he'd loved gold from the very start.
    A good WIFE was there from nearby to BATH;
It was a pity she was deaf by half.
In cloth-making she had such a talent
She far passed those from Ypres and from Ghent.[5]   450
And throughout all her parish, there was no
Wife who might first to the offering go
Before her; if one did, so mad was she
That she lost any sense of charity.
Her coverchiefs of fine linen were found;   455
I dare swear that they weighed a full ten pounds,
The ones that, Sundays, sat upon her head.
Her stockings were all fine and scarlet red,
Quite tightly laced, her shoes quite soft and new.[6]
Bold was her face, and fair, and red of hue.   460
All her life, she was a worthy woman,
Husbands at the church door, she'd had five then,
Not counting other company in youth—
No need to speak of that now, to tell the truth.
And thrice she had been to Jerusalem;[7]   465
Many a foreign sea, she'd covered them;
At Rome she'd been, and also at Boulogne,
At Saint James in Galicia and Cologne.
She knew much of wandering by the way.
Gap toothed[8] she was, it is the truth to say.   470
Quite easily on her ambling horse, she sat,
Wearing a wimpled headdress and a hat
Like a buckler or a shield as broad and round;
A foot-mantle about her large hips wound,
And on her feet a pair of sharp spurs poked.   475
In fellowship, quite well she laughed and joked.
The remedies of love she knew by heart,
For of that old dance, she knew all the art.
    A good man was there of religion,
Of a town, he served as the poor PARSON.   480
But he was rich in holy thought and work.
He was also a learned man, a clerk,
And Christ's gospel truthfully he would preach;
His parishioners devoutly he would teach.
Gracious he was, a wonder of diligence,   485
And in adversity, he had such patience,
And in this, he had often tested been.
For tithes, he found it loathsome to curse men,
But he would rather give, there is no doubt,
To his poor parishioners, round about,   490

---

5. Two cities in Flanders (modern Belgium) renowned for cloth production.
6. I.e., of good quality, supple leather.
7. The major pilgrimage site for medieval Christians; lesser popular pilgrimage sites—in Italy, France, Spain, and Germany, respectively—follow.
8. According to medieval lore, a sign of a tendency to wander, associated especially with sexual excess.

From Mass offerings and his own pay, too.
With little, he could easily make do.
Wide was his parish, the houses far asunder,
But he would not leave them, for rain or thunder,
If sickness or if trouble should befall   495
The farthest in his parish, great or small,
He'd go on foot; his staff in hand he'd keep.
This noble example he gave to his sheep:
That first he wrought, and afterward, he taught.
Out of the Gospels, those words he had caught,   500
And his own metaphor he added, too:
If gold should rust, then what will iron do?
For if a priest is foul, in whom we trust,
No wonder that a foolish man should rust;
And it's a shame, if care he does not keep—   505
A shepherd to be shitty with clean sheep.
Well should a priest a good example give,
By his own cleanness, how his sheep should live.
His parish, he would not put out for hire
And leave his sheep encumbered in the mire   510
To run to London to Saint Paul's⁹ to switch
And be a chantry priest¹ just for the rich,
Nor by guild brothers would he be detained;²
But he stayed home and with his flock remained,
So that the wolf would not make it miscarry;   515
He was a shepherd, not a mercenary.
And though he holy was, and virtuous,
To sinners, he was not contemptuous,
Not haughty nor aloof was he in speech,
With courtesy and kindness would he teach.   520
To draw folks up to heaven with his fairness,
By good example: this was all his business.
But if there were a person who was stubborn,
Whoever he was, high or low rank born,
Then he would scold him sharply, at the least.   525
There is nowhere, I know, a better priest.
He waited for no pomp or reverence;
For him, no finicky, affected conscience,
But the words of Christ and his apostles twelve
He taught: but first, he followed them himself.   530
    With him, his brother who was a PLOWMAN rode;
Of dung, this man had hauled out many a load;
A true laborer, and a good one was he,
Living in peace and perfect charity.
God loved he best with all of his whole heart   535
At all times, though it caused him joy or smart,

9. The largest cathedral in medieval England.   members).
1. A priest supported by an endowment to   2. I.e., he would not take the lucrative posi-
say daily mass for the souls of particular indi- tion of priest for a guild.
viduals (usually wealthy men or their family

And next, his neighbor, just as he loved himself.
He would thresh, dig ditches, and also delve,
For Christ's sake and the sake of each poor man,
And without pay, he'd do all that he can.   540
His tithes, with all due fairness, he'd not shirk,
But paid from what he owned and with his work.
In a workman's smock, he rode on a mare.
   A REEVE and a MILLER were also there,
A SUMMONER and then a PARDONER,   545
A MAN and myself—that's all there were.
   The MILLER was a stout churl, it is true;
Quite big he was in brawn, and in bones, too.
That stood him in good stead; for where he came,
He'd win the ram[3] in every wrestling game.   550
He was short necked and broad, a thick-thewed thug;
There was no door around he couldn't lug
Right off its hinges, or break with his head.
His beard, just like a sow or fox, was red,[4]
And also broad, as though it was a spade.   555
Right up atop his nose's ridge was laid
A wart; on it, a tuft of hairs grew now,
Red as the bristles in ears of a sow;
His nostrils were quite black, and also wide.
A sword and buckler bore he by his side.   560
His mouth was as great as a great cauldron.
A jangling goliard, he was quite the one—
Of sin and harlotries, he most would tell.
He made three times his pay and stole corn well;
And yet, he had a thumb of gold, all right.[5]   565
A blue hood wore he, and a coat of white.
A bagpipe he knew how to blow and play.
And sounding it, he led us on our way.
   A good MANCIPLE[6] did business for a law school;
All food buyers could follow well his rule   570
For prudent buying; it would earn them merit;
For, whether he paid straight or took on credit,
In buying, he watched carefully and waited,
So he was in good shape and well ahead.
Now, is it not from God a sign of grace   575
That this unlearned man's wit can outpace
The wisdom of a heap of learned men?
Of his masters, he had more than thrice ten,
Who were quite skilled and expert in the law,

---

3. I.e., the prize for the winner of a village wrestling contest.
4. His coloration, together with the description of his nostrils and mouth, would suggest to medieval readers a temperament given to strong displays of temper or rage.
5. "An honest miller has a golden thumb" was a proverb expressing the general belief that all millers were dishonest (either because no such miller existed or because millers cheated their customers with a heavy thumb on the scale).
6. Agent responsible for buying supplies and paying bills, especially for a college or monastery.

And in that house, a full dozen one saw 580
Worthy to be stewards of rents and land
For any lord who dwells now in England,
To make him live within the means he had
In debtless honor (unless he were mad),
Or as frugally as he could desire, 585
And able thus to help out all the shire
In any circumstance that may befall:
And yet this Manciple hoodwinked them all.
    The REEVE was a slender, choleric[7] man.
He shaved his beard as closely as one can; 590
His hair, short and up by his ears, he'd crop,
And, like a priest's, he'd dock it on the top.
Quite long his legs were; they were also lean,
And just like sticks; no calf was to be seen.
He could well guard the granary and bin; 595
No auditor around could with him win.
He knew well, by the drought and by the rain,
The yieldings of his seed and of his grain.
His lord's sheep, his cattle, and his dairy,
His swine and horses, his livestock and poultry 600
Were wholly under this Reeve's governing,
And by his contract, he gave reckoning,
Because his lord, in age, was twenty years.
No man alive could bring him in arrears.[8]
No bailiff, herdsman, worker there might be 605
But he knew all their tricks and treachery;
As they feared death, of him they were all scared.
His dwelling place upon a heath was fair;
All shaded with green trees on every hand.
He could, much better than his lord, buy land. 610
Quite richly had he stocked up, privately.
And he could please his lord so cleverly
That he'd lend to him from his lord's own goods,
And have his thanks, then, plus a coat and hood.
When he was young, he had learned a fine trade, 615
A good wright, a skilled carpenter he made.
The Reeve on his stout farm horse sat that day,
Which was called Scot and was a dapple gray.
His overcoat was long, of darkish blue,
And by his side, a rusty blade hung, too. 620
From Norfolk[9] was this Reeve, of whom I tell,
From near a town that men call Baldeswell.
Like a friar's, he tucked his coat up fast.
In our company, he always rode the last.
    A SUMMONER[1] was with us in that place, 625

---

7. Dominated by choler, the humor associated with irascibility. "Reeve": farm or estate manager.
8. I.e., convict him of having unpaid debts.

9. County northeast of London.
1. An officer of the ecclesiastical courts who served summonses to individuals charged with offenses against canon law.

Who had a fiery-red cherubic face,
Pimply was he, with eyes swollen and narrow.
Hot he was and lecherous as a sparrow,[2]
With scabbed black brows; his beard had lost some hair.
And of his visage, children were quite scared.   630
Not lead monoxide, mercury, or sulphur,
Not borax, white lead, or cream of tartar—
No single ointment that would cleanse or bite—
Could help him to remove those pustules white,
Nor cure the pimples sitting on his cheeks.   635
Well loved he garlic, onions, also leeks,[3]
And drinking blood red wine, strongly fermented;
Then he would speak and cry as though demented.
And when of this good wine he'd drunk his fill,
No words but Latin from his mouth would spill.   640
A few such terms he knew, like two or three,
That he had learned by hearing some decree—
It's no wonder, for he heard it all day;
And thus you know full well how any jay[4]
Can call out "Walter" as well as the pope.   645
But whoever might on other matters grope,
Then his philosophy was spent thereby;
Always, "Questio quid iuris,"[5] cry he would.
He was a noble rascal in his kind;
A better fellow men would never find.   650
And he would suffer, for a quart of wine,
A good fellow to have his concubine
A full year, and excuse him thus completely;
For he himself could pluck a finch[6] discreetly.
If he found a good fellow anywhere,   655
Then he would quickly teach to him that there
Was no need to fear archdeacons' curses,[7]
Unless men's souls were found in their purses;
For in their purses, they will punished be.
"The purse is the archdeacon's hell," said he.   660
He downright lied, I know, in what he said;
Excommunication guilty men should dread.
Absolving saves, but cursing slays indeed;
Of *Significavit*,[8] men should well take heed.
Under his thumb, he had, as it did please   665
Him, the young girls there of the diocese;
He counseled all who told him things in secret.

---

2. A proverbially lecherous bird; this behavior is a manifestation of the Summoner's "hot" temperament.
3. These foods, according to medieval medicine, would increase the heat of the body and thus also cause lust, outbursts of fury, and outbreaks of the skin.
4. A popinjay, or parrot.
5. "The question [is], what [point] of law [applies]" (Latin); a phrase familiar to the Summoner from the ecclesiastical courts.
6. To trick or blackmail; to have sexual relations.
7. I.e., excommunication.
8. Literally, "he has signified" (Latin): the writ issued for the arrest of an excommunicated person.

A garland he had fashioned and then set,
Big as an ale-house sign, upon his head.
He'd made a buckler from a loaf of bread. 670
      With him, there rode a gentle PARDONER
Of Roncevalles,[9] and good, close friends they were.
He'd come straight from the papal court at Rome,
And loudly sang, "Come hither, love, to me!"
With a stiff bass, the Summoner sang along; 675
No trumpet's sound was ever half so strong.
This Pardoner had hair yellow as wax,
But smooth it hung as does a hank of flax;
In skinny strands, the locks hung from his head,
And with them, he his shoulders overspread; 680
But thin it lay; its strands hung one by one.
For stylishness, a hood he would wear none,
Since it was trussed up within his wallet.
He thought he wore the latest fashions yet;
With loose hair, his head save for his cap was bare. 685
Such staring eyes he had, just like a hare.
A veronica[1] he'd sewn on his cap.
His wallet lay before him in his lap,
With pardons hot from Rome stuffed to the brim.
A voice high as a goat's came out of him. 690
No beard had he, nor should he wait for one;
His face smooth like his shaving'd just been done.
I think he was a gelding or a mare.
But, in his craft, from Berwick down to Ware,[2]
No pardoner like him in all the land. 695
In his bag was a pillowcase on hand,
And he declared it was Our Lady's[3] veil;
He said he had a big piece of the sail
Saint Peter used upon his boat when he,
Before Christ took him, had gone out to sea. 700
He had a fake gold cross bedecked with stones,
A glass he had that carried some pig bones.[4]
But with these relics, whenever he spied
A poor parson out in the countryside,
On that day, much more money would he make 705
Than, in two months, the poor parson might take;
And thus, with his feigned flattery and japes,
He made the parson and people his apes.
But to tell the whole truth, now, finally,

9. A church-affiliated hospital in London, supported in part by the sale of pardons—papal indulgences purchased to shorten the time spent by souls in purgatory.
1. A reproduction of Jesus's features, as were said to have been miraculously impressed on the cloth offered to him by St. Veronica on his way to his crucifixion. The veronica was also a key point of reference for medieval artists who wished to claim a divine origin for their craft.
2. I.e., from northernmost England to the south.
3. The Virgin Mary.
4. The Pardoner has a variety of false saints' relics; such relics were believed to possess the saints' spiritual power and thus found eager buyers.

In church, a noble ecclesiastic was he.   710
Well could he read a lesson or a story,
But best of all, he sang the offertory;
For well he knew, when that song had been sung,
Then he must preach and smoothly file his tongue
To win his silver, as quite well could he;   715
Therefore, he sang quite loud and merrily.
    Now, I have told you truly, in a clause,
The rank, the dress, the number, and the cause
That brought together all this company
In Southwark, at this noble hostelry   720
That's called the Tabard, next door to the Bell.
But now it's time that to you I should tell
How that we all behaved on that same night
When we should in that hostelry alight;
Afterward, I will tell of our voyage   725
And all the rest about our pilgrimage.
But first I pray you, by your courtesy,
That you not blame my own vulgarity,
Although I might speak plainly in this matter,
When I tell you their words and their demeanor,   730
Or if I speak their words, exact and true.
For this you all know just as well as I do:
Whoever tells a tale after a man,
He must repeat, as closely as he can,
Every last word, if that is his duty,   735
Even if he has to speak quite rudely,
Or otherwise, he makes his tale untrue,
Or makes things up, or finds words that are new.
He may not spare, though that man were his brother;
He might as well say one word as another.   740
Christ himself plainly spoke in Holy Writ;
You know no vulgarity is in it.
And Plato says, whoever can him read,
That words must be the cousin to the deed.[5]
Also, I pray you that you will forgive me   745
Although I've not ranked folks by their degree
Here in this tale, the way that they should stand.
My wit is short, you may well understand.
    Our Host put us at ease with his great cheer;
At once, he set up supper for us here.   750
He served us all with victuals that were fine;
It pleased us well to drink his good, strong wine.
An impressive man our HOST was, all in all;
He could have been a marshal in a hall.
A large man he, with eyes both bright and wide—   755
No fairer burgess anywhere in Cheapside[6]—

---

5. Apparently an allusion to Plato's *Timaeus* 29B, borrowed by Chaucer from Boethius's *Consolation of Philosophy* (ca. 525 C.E.) or from the *Roman de la Rose* (ca. 1275).
6. A major business district in London.

Bold in his speech, and wise, and quite well taught.
And in his manhood, he did lack for naught.
Moreover, he was quite a merry man;
After supper, to amuse us, he began,   760
And spoke of pleasure, among other things,
When we had settled up our reckonings.
He then said thus: "Now, my good lords, truly,
To me, you are quite welcome, heartily;
For, by my word, if that I shall not lie,   765
So merry a company, this whole year, I
Have not seen in this inn, as I see now.
I'd gladly make you happy, knew I how.
I've just thought what would be entertaining;
It'd please you, and it wouldn't cost a thing.   770
      You go to Canterbury—bless the Lord,
May the blissful martyr pay you your reward!
I know well, as you travel by the way,
You all intend to tell tales and to play;
For truly, comfort and mirth both have flown   775
If you ride on the way dumb as a stone;
Now, I know a way I can divert you,
As I have said, and give you comfort, too.
And if it pleases you to give assent
So you all agree to trust my judgment,   780
And to do according to what I say,
Tomorrow, when you all ride by the way,
Now, by the soul of my father who is dead,
Unless you're merry, I'll give you my head!
Hold up your hands, now, without further speech."   785
      All our assent took not long to beseech.
It did not seem worthwhile to make a fuss,
For we did not need more time to discuss,
And we told him to give his verdict then.
"My lords," said he, "this plan is best. Now, listen.   790
But take it not, I pray you, with disdain.
This is the point, to speak now, short and plain:
Each one of you, to help shorten our way,
Along this journey, two tales you will say,
Toward Canterbury, as I mean you to,   795
And homeward, you'll tell us another two,
Of adventures that in old times did befall.
The one who bears himself the best of all—
That is to say, the one of you who might
Tell tales that have most meaning and delight—   800
Shall have a supper paid for by us all,
Sitting right near this post here in this hall,
When we all come again from Canterbury.
And to make you all even more merry,
I will myself quite gladly with you ride,   805
Right at my own expense, and be your guide.
Whoever will my judgment now gainsay

Shall pay for all we spend along the way.
If it be so, and all of you agree,
Without more words, at once, now you tell me,   810
And I'll make myself ready long before."
    This thing was granted, and our oaths we swore
With quite glad hearts, and we prayed him also
That he fully would agree to do so,
And that he would become our governor,   815
And of our tales, the judge and record keeper,
And set the supper at a certain price,
And we would all be ruled by his advice
In all respects; and thus, with one assent
We were all accorded with his judgment.   820
And thereupon, the wine was fetched in fast;
We drank, and to our rest we went at last,
Without us any longer tarrying.
    In the morning, as day began to spring,
Up rose our Host, and was, for us, the cock,   825
And gathered us together in a flock;
With slow gait, we started on our riding,
Till we came to Saint Thomas's Watering;[7]
And there, our Host began to stop his horse
And said, "Lords, listen—if you please, of course.   830
Let me remind you that you gave your word.
If evening-song and morning-song accord,[8]
Let see now who shall tell us the first tale.
As ever may I drink of wine or ale,
Whoso now rebels against my judgment   835
Shall pay for all that by the way is spent.
Now let's draw straws, and then we shall depart;
Whoever has the shortest straw will start.
Sir Knight, my master and my lord," he said,
"Now you draw first, for thus I have decided.   840
Come near," said he, "my lady Prioress.
And you, sir Clerk, leave off your bashfulness.
Don't study now. Lay hands to, every man!"
At once, to draw straws, everyone began;
To quickly tell the way it did advance,   845
Were it by fortune or by luck or chance,
The truth is this: the draw fell to the Knight,
For which we were quite glad, as it was right;
By agreement and arrangement, now he must
Tell us his tale, as it was only just,   850
As you have heard; what more words need be spent?
And when this good man saw the way it went,
Because he wise was, and obedient
To keep the word he gave by free assent,
He said, "Now, since I shall begin the game,   855
What, welcome is this straw, in the Lord's name!

---

7. A spring dedicated to St. Thomas (not far from the inn).

8. I.e., if your intention at night matches what you promised in the morning.

Now, let us ride, and hearken what I say."
And with that word, we rode forth on our way,
And he began with then a merry cheer
His tale at once, and said as you may hear.   860

The Wife of Bath's Prologue and Tale

The Wife of Bath's Prologue

"Experience, though no authority
Were in this world, is right enough for me
To speak of the woe that is in marriage;
For, my lords, since I was twelve years of age,[1]
Thanks be to God, eternally alive,   5
Husbands at the church door, I have had five—
If quite so often I might wedded be—
And all were worthy men in their degree.
But it was told me not so long ago,[2]
That since just once our Christ did ever go   10
To a wedding, in Cana in Galilee,[3]
That by that same example, he taught me
That only one time I should wedded be.
Lo, listen, what a sharp word then spoke he,
Beside a well when Jesus, God and man,   15
Spoke in reproof of the Samaritan:[4]
"Thou hast had five husbands,' then said he,
'And that same man here who now hath thee
Is not thy husband,' said he by the well.
But what he meant thereby, I cannot tell;   20
Except I ask, why is it the fifth man
Was not husband to the Samaritan?
How many might she have in marriage?
Yet I've never heard tell, in all my age,
About this, any number definite.   25
Up and down, men gloss[5] and guess about it,
But well I know, expressly, it's no lie,
That God bade us to wax and multiply;[6]
This gentle text, I can well understand.
Also, well I know, he said my husband   30
Should leave mother and father and cleave to me.[7]
But of no number a mention made he,
Of bigamy, or of octogamy;[8]
Why then should men speak of it villainy?

---

1. The minimum age of marriage, in canon law.
2. Many of the biblical sources cited by the Wife of Bath in the argument that follows can be found in St. Jerome's *Adversus Jovinianum* (392 c.e.), a polemical diatribe that is highly critical of both women and marriage.
3. See John 2.2.
4. A woman from Samaria (see John 4.7–18).
5. Interpret.
6. Genesis 1.28.
7. Genesis 2.24.
8. Marriage to two or to eight. Usually, *bigamy* involves concurrent marriages (as below, in references to biblical figures), but the Wife of Bath often instead means consecutive marriages.

Lo, here is the wise king, Don[9] Solomon;   35
I think he had some wives, well more than one.
Now would to God it lawful were for me
To be refreshed here half so much as he!
A gift from God had he with all his wives!
No man has such a gift who's now alive.   40
This noble king, God knows, as I would judge it,
That first night had many a merry fit
With each of them, so well was he alive.
Blessèd be God that I have wedded five!
Of whom I have picked out the very best,   45
For both their nether purse[1] and money chest.
Different schools can turn out perfect clerks,
And different practices in sundry works
Make the workman perfect, it's no lie;
From my five husbands, studying am I.   50
Welcome the sixth, when he shall come along.
In truth, I won't keep chaste for very long.
And when my husband from this world has passed,
Another Christian man will wed me fast;
Then the apostle[2] says that I am free   55
To wed, by God, where it most pleases me.
He says to be wedded is not sinning;
Better to be wedded than be burning.
What do I care if folks speak villainy
About accursed Lamech's bigamy?[3]   60
Abraham was a holy man, I know;
And as I understand it, Jacob also;
And each of them had wives now, more than one,
As many other holy men have done.
Where, can you say, in any kind of age,   65
That our high God has forbidden marriage
Expressly, in a word? I pray, tell me.
Or where did he command virginity?
I know as well as you, or else you should,
The apostle, when he speaks of maidenhood,   70
Said that a precept for it he had none.[4]
Men may counsel a woman to be one,
But counseling does not make a commandment.
All of it he left to our own judgment;
For if our God commanded maidenhood,   75
Then wedding with the deed, he'd damn for good.
And surely, if no seed were ever sown,
From what, then, would virginity be grown?
And at the least, Paul never dared demand

9. Master. The biblical king Solomon was proverbially renowned for his great wisdom and for his hundreds of wives and concubines (see 1 Kings 11.3).
1. I.e., scrotum.
2. St. Paul; see 1. Corinthians 7.39, 9.

3. See Genesis 4.19. Lamech (cursed as a murderer) is the first man in the Bible said to have had more than one wife (or a wife and a concubine) at the same time, but he was hardly the last, as the Wife of Bath points out.
4. 1 Corinthians 7.25.

A thing that his own Master won't command.   80
The prize is set up for virginity;
Catch it who may; who runs the best, let's see.
    To everyone, this word does not apply,
But only where God's might wants it to lie.
I know the apostle was a virgin;   85
Nonetheless, although he wrote and said then
He wished that everyone was such as he,
This is but counsel to virginity.[5]
He gave me leave to be a wife, all the same,
With his permission, so it is no shame,   90
If my mate dies, to go then and wed me,
Without objections about bigamy.
Though it may be good not to touch women[6]—
In his bed or on his couch, he meant then—
Fire and flax together make peril so—   95
What this example resembles, you all know.
The sum is this: he held virginity
More perfect than to wed from frailty.
Frailty I call it, unless he and she
Wished to lead all their lives in chastity.   100
    I grant it well that I have no envy,
Though maidenhood's preferred to bigamy.
To be clean pleases them, body and spirit;
Of my state, I make no boast about it,
For you well know, a lord in his household,   105
He has not every vessel made of gold;[7]
Some come from wood, and serve their lord withal.
In sundry ways, folks to him God does call,
Each has God's special gift while he must live,
Some this, some that, it pleases God to give.[8]   110
    Virginity thus is great perfection,
And also continence spurred by devotion,
But Christ, who of perfection is the well,
Bade not that every person should go sell
All that he has and give it to the poor,   115
And follow in his footsteps thus, for sure.
He spoke to those who would live perfectly,[9]
And my lords, by your leave, that is not me.
I will bestow the flower of my life
In married acts and fruits, and be a wife.   120
    Tell me, for what purpose and conclusion
Were the members[1] made for generation,
And by so perfectly wise a maker wrought?
Trust it well now: they were not made for nought.
Say what you will, or hedge it by glossing,   125
That they were made simply for the purging

5. 1 Corinthians 7.8.
6. 1 Corinthians 7.1.
7. See 2 Timothy 2.20.

8. See 1 Corinthians 7.7.
9. See Matthew 19.21.
1. I.e., sexual organs.

Of urine; and both our small things also
Were made so male from female we could know,
And for no other cause—do you say no?
Experience well knows it is not so.   130
So the clerks will not be angry at me,
They were made for both: I say this truly.
That is, to do our business and for ease
In engendering, where God we don't displease.
Why should men otherwise in their books set   135
It down that man should yield his wife her debt?[2]
Now how to her should he make his payment,
Unless he'd used his silly[3] instrument?
Thus, they were bestowed upon a creature
To purge urine, and so we could engender.   140
     But I don't say that each one's obligated,
Who has the harness that I've just related,
To go and use it for engendering.
Then for chastity, men wouldn't care a thing.
Christ was a maiden and shaped like a man,   145
And many saints, since first the world began;
They lived forever in perfect chastity.
I won't envy any virginity.
Let them be bread of wheat that's been refined,
As barley bread, let us wives be defined;   150
And yet, with barley bread, as Mark can tell,
Our Lord has refreshed many men quite well.[4]
In whatever rank God's called to us,
I'll persevere; I'm not fastidious.
In wifehood, I will use my instrument   155
As freely as my Maker has it sent.
If I'm aloof, then God send me dismay!
My husband can well have it, night and day,
When it pleases him to come and pay his debt.
A husband I will have—I won't stop yet—   160
Who shall be both my debtor and my slave,
With tribulation, unless he behaves,
Upon his flesh while I may be his wife.
I have the power, during all my life
Over his own body, and not he.   165
Thus the Apostle has told this to me,
And bade our husbands they should love us well.[5]
This meaning, I like more than I can tell"—
     Up the Pardoner starts, immediately;
"Now, Madame, by God and Saint John," said he,   170
"You are a noble preacher on this strife.
Alas! I was about to wed a wife.
Why on my flesh now pay a price so dear?"

2. The marital debt, mutually owed; see 1 Corinthians 7.3–4.
3. Innocent.
4. See not Mark but John 6.9–13.
5. Ephesians 5.25.

I'd rather not wed any wife this year!"
    "Just wait! My tale is not begun," said she.   175
"No, you'll drink from another cask, you'll see,
Before I go, that will taste worse than ale.
And when I will have told you all my tale
Of the tribulation that's in marriage—
About which I'm an expert in my age—   180
That is to say that I have been the whip—
Then you can choose if you might want to sip
Out of the cask that I will open here.
Beware of it, before you come too near;
For I shall give examples, more than ten.   185
'Whoever won't be warned by other men,
By him will other men corrected be.'
Those same words were written by Ptolemy;[6]
Read his *Almageste,* and there you'll find it still."
    "Madame, I pray you, if it be your will,"   190
Said this Pardoner, "now as you began,
Tell forth your tale, and don't spare any man;
Teach us young men all about your practice."
    "Gladly," said she, "since you might well like this;
But yet I pray to all this company,   195
If I speak after my own fantasy,
Do not be aggrieved by what I say,
For my intent is only now to play.
    And now, sir, now I'll tell on with my tale.
As ever I might drink of wine or ale,   200
I'll tell the truth; those husbands that I had,
Some three of them were good, and two were bad.
The three who were good men were rich and old;
And so they barely could the statute hold
Through which they all had bound themselves to me.   205
By God, you know what I mean, certainly!
So help me God, I laugh to remember
How pitifully at night I made them labor!
In faith, I set no store by their pleasure.
To me, they had given land and treasure;   210
No longer need I use my diligence
To win their love or do them reverence.
They loved me so well that, by God above,
I set no value then upon their love!
A wise woman will be the busy one   215
To get herself love, yes, where she has none.
But since I had them wholly in my hand,
And since to me they'd given all their land,
Why should I take care that I should them please
Unless it were for my profit and my ease?   220

---

6. Greek astronomer and mathematician (2nd century C.E.); his textbook, the *Almagest,* dominated astronomy for more than a thousand years; a preface containing proverbial wisdom attributed to Ptolemy was later added to the text.

I set them so to hard work, by my lights,
That they sung "Wey-la-way!" on many nights.
I don't think the bacon was meant for them now
That some men win in Essex at Dunmowe.[7]
I governed them so well, after my law,   225
That each of them was eager, as I saw,
To bring me home some gay things from the fair.
They were glad when my speech to them was fair;
I scolded them, as God knows, spitefully.
        Now, listen how I acted properly,   230
You wise wives, who can so well understand.
Thus should you accuse falsely, out of hand.
For half so boldly knows no living man
How to swear and lie just as a woman can.
This statement about wise wives, I don't make—   235
Unless it be when they've made some mistake.
A wise wife, who knows what's good for her,
Will swear the tattling crow is mad for sure,[8]
And make sure that her maid has assented
As her witness. But hear now what I said: 240
        'Sir old dotard, is this your array?
Why is it that my neighbor's wife's so gay?
She is honored everywhere she goes;
I sit at home; I have no decent clothes.
What do you do at my neighbor's house there?   245
Are you so amorous? Is she so fair?
What do you whisper to our maid? Bless me!
Sir old lecher, now let your jokes be!
If, without guilt, I have a chum or friend,
Just like a fiend, you scold me without end   250
If I should play or walk down to his house!
But you come home as drunken as a mouse,
And then preach from your bench, no proof from you!
And it's great mischief, as you tell me too,
A poor woman to wed, for the expense;   255
If she's rich and born to lofty parents,
Then you say that a torment it will be
To bear her pride and sullen melancholy.
And if she should be fair, you horrid cur,
You say every lecher soon will have her;   260
For she can't long in chastity abide,
Who is always assailed on every side.
        You say some folk want us for our richness,
Some for our figure, and some for our fairness,
Some because she can either dance or sing,   265
Some for gentility and socializing;

---

7. A village ca. 35 miles northeast of London. In the 13th century, the custom began of awarding a side of bacon to the couple who swore not to have quarreled or regretted their marriage during the first year after their wedding.

8. The talking bird who reveals a wife's infidelity by repeating words it has heard is a common motif in folktales.

And some because their hands and arms are small;
By your lights, to the devil thus goes all.
You say men cannot defend a castle wall
When it's so long assailed by large and small.   270
      And if she should be ugly, you say she
Will covet every man that she may see,
For like a spaniel, she will on him leap
Until she finds a man to buy her cheap.
No goose goes out there on the lake so gray   275
That she will be without a mate, you say.
You say it's hard for men to have controlled
A thing that no man willingly would hold.
Thus you say, scoundrel, when you go to bed,
That no wise man has any need to wed,   280
Nor one who toward heaven would aspire.
With wild thunder claps and lightning's fire
May your old withered neck break right in two!
      You say that leaky houses, and smoke too,
And scolding wives all cause a man to flee   285
Out of his own house; ah now, God bless me!
What can ail such an old man, who must chide?
You say that we wives will our vices hide
Till we're hitched, and then we show them to you—
Well may that be the proverb of a shrew!   290
      You say horses, hounds, asses, and oxen
At different times can be tried out by men;
Wash bowls and basins, spoons and stools, you say,
All household things men try before they pay;
The same thing goes for clothes and gear and pots;   295
But to try out a wife, a man may not
Till they are wedded—you old dotard shrew!—
And then we show our vices, so say you.
      You say also that it displeases me
Unless you will always praise my beauty,   300
Or else always pore over my face,
And call me "Fair Madame" in every place.
Unless you make a feast upon the day
That I was born, and dress me fresh and gay;
Unless to my nurse, you do all honor,   305
And to the chambermaid within my bower,[9]
And to my father's folk and kin all day—
Old barrelful of lies, all this you say!
      Yet of Jenkin, who is our apprentice,
Whose curly hair shines just like gold—for this,   310
And because he will squire me around,
A cause for false suspicions, you have found.
I don't want him, though you should die tomorrow!
      Tell me: why do you hide, to my sorrow,
The keys now of your chest[1] away from me?   315

9. Bedroom.   1. Strongbox.

They are my goods as well as yours, bless me!
Will you make an idiot of your dame?
Now, by that good lord who is called Saint James,
You will not, though it might make you crazy,
Be master of both my goods and body;   320
One of them you'll forgo, to spite your eyes.
What good is it to ask around and spy?
I think you want to lock me in your chest!
You should say, "Wife, go where you think is best;
Enjoy yourself; I'll believe no tales of this.   325
I know you for my own true wife, Dame Alice."
We love no man who will take heed or charge
Of where we go; we want to be at large.
          And of all men, quite blessèd must he be,
That wise astrologer, Don Ptolemy,   330
Who says this proverb in his *Almageste,*
"Of all men, his wisdom is the highest
Who never cares who holds the world in hand."
By this proverb, you should well understand,
If you have enough, why then should you care   335
How merrily some other folks might fare?
For certainly, old dotard, by your leave,
You'll have some quaint things sure enough come eve.
He is too great a niggard who would spurn
A man to light a candle at his lantern;   340
By God, from that, he doesn't have less light.
If you've enough, complaining isn't right.
          You also say if we make ourselves gay
With our clothing and with precious array,
That it is peril to our chastity;   345
Woe to you—you then enforce it for me,
And say these words in the Apostle's name:
"In clothing made from chastity and shame
You women all should dress yourselves," said he,
"Not with well-coifed hair and with gay jewelry,   350
Not with rich clothes, with pearls, or else with gold."[2]
With your text and your rubric,[3] I don't hold,
Or follow them as much as would a gnat.
          You said this: that I was just like a cat;
Whoever wanted to singe a cat's skin   355
He could be sure the cat would then stay in;
And if the cat's skin were so sleek and gay,
She'd not stay in the house for half a day;
Forth she'd go, before the day was dawning,
To show her skin and to go caterwauling.   360
That is to say, if I am gay, sir shrew,
I'll run to put my poor old clothes on view.
          Sir old fool, what help is it if you spy?

---

2. See I Timothy 2.9–10.   3. Direction written in red.

Though you prayed Argus[4] with his hundred eyes
To be my bodyguard, as he'd know best,   365
He'd not guard me till I let him, I'll be blessed.
I'd hoodwink him, as I am prospering!
    Yet you also say that there are three things,
And that these same things trouble all this earth,
And that no man might yet endure the fourth.[5]   370
Oh, dear sir shrew, Jesus shorten your life!
Yet you will preach and say a hateful wife
Is one of these misfortunes that you reckon.
Aren't there other kinds of comparison
That, for all your parables, you could use,   375
Unless a poor wife were the one you'd choose?
    You liken, too, a woman's love to hell,
To barren land where water may not dwell.
You liken it also to a wild fire;
The more it burns, the more it has desire   380
To consume everything that burned will be.
You say that just as worms destroy a tree,
A wife destroys her husband, you have found;
This, they well know who to wives have been bound.'
    My lords, right thus, as you can understand,   385
I stiffly[6] kept my old husbands in hand
And swore they said thus in their drunkenness;
And all was false; except I took witness
On Jenkin there, and on my niece, also.
Oh Lord! The pain I did them and the woe.   390
And, by God's sweet pain, they were not guilty!
For, like a horse, I could bite and whinny.
I knew how to complain well even when
I had the guilt, or I'd been ruined then.
Whoever comes first to the mill, first grinds;   395
Complaining first, our war stopped, I did find.
They were glad to excuse themselves quite quickly
For things of which they never had been guilty.
Of wenches, I'd accuse them out of hand
When, in their sickness, they could hardly stand.   400
    Yet it tickled his heart, because then he
Thought that I had for him such great fancy!
I swore that all my walking out at night
Was to spy on wenches he was holding tight;
Using that cover, I enjoyed much mirth.   405
For all such wit is given us at birth;
Deceit, weeping, and spinning God did give
To women by nature, all the time they live.
And thus of one thing, I can surely boast:
In the end, I'm the one who won the most   410

---

4. In classical myth, a monster used by
Hera/Juno, queen of the gods, to watch over
one of her husband's paramours.

5. See Proverbs 30.21–23.
6. Firmly.

By tricks or force or by some other thing
As much as constant grumbling and grousing.
Namely, then, they would have bad luck in bed:
I did them no pleasure, and I chided;
I would no longer in the bed abide, 415
If I felt his arm come over my side,
Till he had paid his ransom down to me;
Then I'd suffer him to do his foolery.
Therefore, to every man this tale I tell:
Win whoso may, for all is there to sell; 420
With empty hands men may no hawks then lure.
For profit, I would all their lust endure,
And I would fake it with feigned appetite;
And yet in bacon,[7] I had no delight.
That was the reason I would always chide them, 425
For though the pope were sitting right beside them,
At their own table, I would never spare.
In truth, I repaid them word for word there.
So help me, oh true God omnipotent,
If now I made my will and testament, 430
There was not one unpaid word I did owe.
By my own wit, I brought it all about so
That they must give it up, and for the best,
Or otherwise, we never would have rest;
Though he looked as crazy as a lion, 435
He would fail at gaining his conclusion.
     Then I would say to him, 'Sweetheart, take heed—
See how meek our sheep Willie looks, indeed!
Come near, my spouse, and let me kiss your cheek!
Truly you should be all patient and meek, 440
And have, too, a carefully spiced conscience,
Since you always preach about Job's patience.[8]
Suffer always, since you can so well preach;
Unless you do, for sure we shall you teach
That it's nice to have a wife in peace now. 445
Doubtless, one of the two of us must bow,
And so, since man is more reasonable
Than woman, to suffer you are able.
What ails you now that thus you grouse and groan?
Do you just want my quaint thing[9] for your own? 450
Why, take it all! Lo, have it through and through!
You love it well, by Peter,[1] curse on you;
For if I wanted to sell my *belle chose*,[2]
Then I could walk as fresh as is a rose;
But I will keep it just for your own tooth. 455
You are to blame, by God! I tell the truth.'
These are the kinds of words I had on hand.

---

7. I.e., preserved (old) meat; or perhaps a reference to the prize at Dunmow.
8. Proverbial; see the book of Job.

9. Genitals.
1. St. Peter.
2. Pretty thing (French).

And now I will speak of my fourth husband.
    My fourth husband was a reveler—
That is to say, he had a paramour—   460
And young and full of wantonness was I,
Stubborn, strong and jolly as a magpie.
How I'd dance when the small harp was playing;
Like a nightingale's was all my singing,
When I had drunk my draught of fine sweet wine!   465
Metellius, the foul churl, the swine,
Who, with a staff, bereft his wife of life,
Because she drank wine,[3] if I were his wife,
He wouldn't frighten me away from drink!
And after wine, on Venus[4] I must think,   470
For just as sure as cold engenders hail,
A lecherous mouth must have lecherous tail.
In wine-drunk women, there is no defence—
This, lechers know from their experience.
    But—Lord Christ!—when memories come back to me,   475
About my youth and all my jollity,
It tickles me right down to my heart's root.
To this day, it does my heart good, to boot,
That I have had my world right in my time.
But age, alas, that poisons what is prime,   480
Has bereft me of my beauty and my pith.[5]
Let it go. Farewell! The devil go therewith!
The flower's gone; there is no more to tell;
The bran, as I best can, now must I sell;
But yet to be right merry I have planned.   485
And now I will tell of my fourth husband.
    I say, I had in my heart a great spite
That he in any other took delight.
By God and Saint Judocus,[6] he's repaid!
Of the same wood, a cross for him I made;   490
Not in a foul manner with my body,
But I made folks such cheer that certainly
I made him fry enough in his own grease
Because his jealous anger would not cease.
By God, on earth I was his purgatory,   495
For which, I hope his soul will be in glory.
God knows, he often sat and sang "Alack"
When his shoe so bitterly pinched him back.
There was no man who knew, save God and he,
In what ways I twisted him so sorely.   500
When I came from Jerusalem, he died;
Buried beneath the cross's beam,[7] he lies.

3. One of the historical anecdotes compiled in the rhetorical handbook by Valerius Maximus (1st century c.e.), which presents Metellius's act as justified.
4. Roman goddess of love.
5. Energy.

6. St. Judoc or Josse, a 7th-century Breton saint (never canonized) whose emblem was the pilgrim's staff.
7. I.e., in a place of honor within the church itself.

His tomb is not fancy or curious
As was the sepulcher of Darius,
Which Appelles had formed so skillfully;[8]   505
A waste to bury him expensively.
Let him fare well. God rest his soul, I ask it!
He is now in his grave and in his casket.
  Now of my fifth husband I will tell.
May God let his soul never go to hell!   510
Yet to me he was the biggest scoundrel;
On my whole row of ribs, I feel it still,
And ever shall until my dying day.
But in our bed, he was so fresh and gay,
And he knew so well just how to gloss me   515
When he wanted my *belle chose,* as you'll see;
Although he'd beaten me on every bone,
Quickly he'd win back my love for his own.
I believe that I loved him best since he
Could be standoffish with his love for me.   520
We women have, and no lie this will be,
In this matter, our own quaint[9] fantasy:
Whatever thing won't lightly come our way,
Then after it we'll cry and crave all day.
Forbid us something, and that desire we;   525
Press on us fast, and then we're sure to flee.
With standoffishness, we spread out all our wares;
Great crowds at market make the goods dear there,
Too great a bargain isn't thought a prize;
And this knows every woman who is wise.   530
  My fifth husband—now God his soul should bless—
Whom I took for love and not for richness,
Formerly, he was a clerk at Oxford,
And had left school, and went back home to board
With my close friend who in our town did dwell.   535
God save her! Her name's Alison, as well.
She knew both my heart and my privacy
More than our parish priest did, so help me!
With her, I shared my secrets one and all.
For had my husband pissed upon a wall,   540
Or done a thing that should have cost his life,
To her and to another worthy wife,
And to my niece, whom I did love so well,
All of his secrets I'd be sure to tell.
God knows too that I did this quite often   545
So I made his face both red and hot then
From shame itself. He blamed himself that he
Had ever shared with me his privacy.

---

8. According to the (fictional) account in Walter of Châtillon's 12th-century Latin epic *Alexandreis*, the famous painter Apelles (4th c. B.C.E.) decorated the tomb of the Persian king Darius (d. 486 B.C.E.).

9. "Queynt," meaning "quaint" in the modern English sense and also a pun on the slang word for the female sex organ; the pun is especially likely coming a few lines after the last reference to Wife's *"belle chose"* (510).

And so it happened that one time in Lent—
For often times to my close friend I went,　　　　　　550
Because I always did love being gay,
And to walk out in March, April, and May,
From house to house, and sundry tales to hear—
Jenkin the clerk, Alison, my friend dear,
And I myself, into the fields all went.　　　　　　555
My husband was at London all that Lent;
More leisure for my playing, I then had,
To see and to be seen (and I was glad)
By lusty folks. Did I know where good grace
Was destined to find me, or in what place?　　　　　　560
Therefore, I made all my visitations
To vigils and also to processions,
To preachings and to these pilgrimages,
To miracle plays[1] and to marriages,
And always wore my gowns of scarlet bright.　　　　　　565
Neither the worms nor moths nor any mites,
On my soul's peril, had my gowns abused.
Do you know why? Because they were well used.
　　　Now I'll tell you what happened then to me.
I say that out into the fields walked we,　　　　　　570
Till truly, we had such a flirtation,
This clerk and I, that I made due provision
And spoke to him, and said to him how he,
Were I a widow, should be wed to me.
For certainly—and I'm not boasting here—　　　　　　575
I have not ever lacked provisions clear
For marriage, or for such things, so to speak.
I hold a mouse's heart not worth a leek
Who's only got one hole where it can run,
And if that fails, then everything is done.　　　　　　580
　　　I made him think he had enchanted me—
My mother taught me all that subtlety—
And said I had dreamed this of him all night:
As I lay on my back he'd slain me quite,
And I dreamed full of blood then was my bed;　　　　　　585
'But yet I hope you'll do me good,' I said,
'For blood betokens gold, as was taught me.'
And all was false; I had no dream, you see,
But I always followed my mother's lore,
In this as well as other things before.　　　　　　590
　　　But now, sirs, let's see what I shall say then.
Aha! By God, I've got my tale again.
　　　When my fourth husband lay up on his bier,
I wept quite long and made a sorry cheer,
As wives must, for it is common usage.　　　　　　595
With my coverchief, I hid my visage,

1. Medieval dramas focused on the lives and acts of the saints or on events from the Bible (also called "mystery plays"); performed in the vernacular, they were extremely popular.

But since I was provided with my next mate,
I didn't weep much—this to you I'll state.
    To church was my husband borne next morning
With the neighbors, who for him were mourning;   600
And there Jenkin, our clerk, was one of those.
So help me God, when I saw how he goes
Behind the bier, I thought he had a pair
Of legs and feet that were so clean and fair,
I gave him all my heart for him to hold.   605
He was, I think, just twenty winters old,
And I was forty, if I tell the truth;
But yet I always had a coltish tooth[2]
Gap toothed was I, and that became me well;
With Venus's seal[3] I'm printed, I can tell.   610
So help me God, I was a lusty one,
And fair and rich and young and well begun,
And truly, as my husbands all told me,
I had the best *quoniam*[4] there might be.
For certainly, I'm all Venerian   615
In feeling, and my heart is Martian.[5]
Venus gave me my love and lecherousness,
And Mars gave me my sturdy hardiness;
My ascendant sign's Taurus,[6] with Mars therein.
Alas! Alas! That ever love was sin!   620
I always followed my inclination
By virtue of my stars' constellation;
Thus I could not withdraw—I was made so—
My chamber of Venus from a good fellow.
Yet I have Mars's mark[7] upon my face,   625
And also in another private place.
For as God so wise is my salvation,
I have never loved in moderation,
But I always followed my appetite,
Should he be long or short or black or white;   630
I took no heed, so long as he liked me,
Of how poor he was, or of what degree.
    What should I say, but at the month's end, he,
This pretty clerk, this Jenkin, so handy,[8]
Has wedded me with great solemnity,   635
And I gave him all the land and property
That ever had been given me before.
But after, I was made to rue that sore;
My desires he would not suffer to hear.
By God, he hit me once upon the ear,   640
Because, out of his book, a leaf I rent,

---

2. I.e., youthful appetites.
3. An alluring birthmark.
4. Literally, "whereas" (Latin): another slang form for female genitals.
5. Belonging to Mars, the Roman god of war.

6. Sign of the zodiac (April 21–May 20) in which Venus is dominant.
7. Probably a red birthmark.
8. Clever; courteous.

And from that stroke, my ear all deaf then went.
But, like a lionness, I was stubborn,
And with my tongue, I was a jangler[9] born,
And I would walk around, as I once did,   645
From house to house, although he did forbid;
Because of this, quite often he would preach,
And from old Roman stories, he would teach;
How one Simplicius Gallus[1] left his wife,
And her forsook for the rest of his life,   650
Because one day, and for no reason more,
Bareheaded she was looking out the door.
     Another Roman he told me by name,
Who, since his wife was at a summer's game
Without his knowledge, he then her forsook.   655
And then he would into his Bible look
For the proverb of Ecclesiasticus[2]
Where he commands, and he does forbid thus:
That man shall not suffer wife to roam about.
Then would he say right thus, without a doubt: 660
     'Whoever builds his house up all from willow
And pricks his blind horse over fields so fallow,
And lets his wife go seeking shrines so hallowed,
Is worthy to be hanging on the gallows!'
But all for nought: I didn't give a straw   665
For all his old proverbs or for his saws,
Nor by him would I then corrected be.
I hate him who my vices tells to me,
And so do more of us, God knows, than me.
This drove him mad about me, utterly;   670
For I wouldn't bear with any of this.
     I'll tell you the truth now, by Saint Thomas,[3]
Why once out of his book a leaf I rent,
For which he hit me so that deaf I went.
     He had a book that, gladly, night and day,   675
For his pleasure, he would be reading always;[4]
It's called Valerius and Theophrastus;
He always laughed as he read it to us.
And also there was once a clerk at Rome,
A cardinal, who was called Saint Jerome,   680
Who made a book against Jovinian;

9. Chatterer.
1. This story and the next (lines 647–49) are found in Valerius Maximus.
2. See Ecclesiasticus 25.25–26.
3. Thomas Becket, to whose shrine the pilgrims are traveling.
4. This single anthology contains a number of works, all hostile or cast as hostile to women: *Letter of Valerius Concerning Not Marrying*, by Walter Map (12th century); *Against Jovinian* (a 4th-century monk), by the Church Father

Jerome (d. 420), which mentions a lost *Golden Book of Marriage* by the Greek philosopher Theophrastus (d. 285 B.C.E.) and writings by the Church Father Tertullian (d. ca. 220) and Crisippus (otherwise unknown); Trotula, a legendary 11th-century Italian female doctor; Heloise (d. 1164), a participant in a scandalous love affair who wrote that philosophers should never marry; the biblical book of Proverbs; and the *Art of Love* by Ovid (43 B.C.E.–17 C.E.), a how-to book on seduction.

In which book was also Tertullian,
Crisippus, Trotula, and Heloise,
An abbess near to Paris, if you please,
And too the Parables of Solomon,   685
Ovid's *Ars*, and more books, many a one,
And all of these in one volume were bound,
And every night and day, some time he found
When he had some leisure and vacation
From his other worldly occupation,   690
To read then in this book of wicked wives.
He knew of them more legends and more lives
Then there are of good wives in the Bible.
For trust it well, it is impossible
For any clerk to speak some good of wives,   695
Unless he speaks about holy saints' lives:
This for no other women will he do.
Now who painted the lion, tell me who?[5]
By God, if women had written stories,
Like clerks do within their oratories,   700
They would have written of men more wickedness
Than all the mark of Adam could redress.
The children of Venus and Mercury[6]
In their actions are always contrary;
Mercury loves both wisdom and science;   705
Venus, revelry and extravagance.
Because of their different dispositions,
Each falls in the other sign's exaltation.
And thus, God knows, Mercury's despondent
In Pisces,[7] when Venus is ascendant,   710
And Venus falls where Mercury is raised.
Therefore, no woman by a clerk is praised.
The clerk, when he is old and may not do
Of Venus's work what's worth his old shoe,
Then he sits down and writes in his dotage   715
That women cannot keep up their marriage!
    But now to my purpose, why I told you
That I was beaten for a book, it's true!
One night Jenkin, who was our lord and sire,
Read in this book, as he sat by the fire,   720
Of Eve first: because of her wickedness,
All mankind was brought into wretchedness,
And thus Jesus Christ himself was slain then,
Who bought us with his own heart's blood again.
Lo, here, expressly, of woman you find   725
That woman was the loss of all mankind.
    He read to me how Samson lost his hair:

5. In one of Aesop's fables, a lion argues that
the representation of a man killing a lion did
not prove the man's superiority: if a lion could
create an artwork, it would depict the opposite.

6. Winged messenger of the Roman gods, the
god of commerce and trickery.
7. Sign of the zodiac (February 20–March 20).

His lover cut it while he did sleep there;
And through this treason, he lost both his eyes.[8]
 And then he read to me, if I don't lie,   730
About Dianyra and Hercules;[9]
She made him set himself on fire, if you please.
 Nor forgot he the woe throughout his life
That Socrates[1] endured from his two wives,
How Xantippa cast piss upon his head.   735
This foolish man sat still like he were dead;
He wiped his head and no more dared say plain,
But 'Before thunder stops, there comes the rain!'
 Of Pasiphaë, who was the queen of Crete,
From evilness, the tale seemed to him sweet;   740
Fie! Speak no more—it is a grisly thing—
Of her lust and horrible desiring.[2]
 Of Clytemnestra, who, from lechery,
Falsely made her husband die,[3] you see,
He read out that tale with great devotion.   745
 He told me also on what occasion
Amphiaraus at Thebes had lost his life.[4]
My husband had a legend of his wife,
Eriphyle, who, for a brooch of gold
Has privately unto the Greeks then told   750
Where her husband had kept his hiding place,
And thus at Thebes he suffered sorry grace.
 Of Livia and Lucia,[5] then heard I:
How both of them had made their husbands die,
The one for love, the other one for hate.   755
This Livia, for sure, one evening late,
Poisoned her husband for she was his foe;
Lecherous Lucia loved her husband so
That, to make sure he'd always on her think,
She gave to him such a kind of love-drink   760
He was dead before it was tomorrow;
And thus, always, husbands have had sorrow.
 Then he told me how one Latumius
Complained once to his fellow Arrius
That in his garden there grew such a tree   765
On which, he said, that all of his wives three

---

8. See Judges 13–16 for the story of Delilah and Samson, whose superhuman strength lay in his hair.
9. The greatest hero of classical mythology, who died because his wife unwittingly gave him a poisoned cloak. (Many of the following exempla are drawn from myth.)
1. The Greek philosopher (469–399 B.C.E.) immortalized in the dialogues of his pupil Plato; Xantippa is protrayed as a shrew in ancient biographies.
2. The union of Pasiphaë with a bull produced the Minotaur.

3. Conspiring with her lover, the queen of Mycenae murdered her husband, Agamemnon, when he returned from leading the Greeks in the Trojan War.
4. He was forced to join the war against Thebes, whose disastrous outcome he foresaw, by his wife, who had been bribed.
5. According to Jerome, Livia, who had a lover, deliberately poisoned her husband, Drusus (d. 23 C.E.), whose father later became the Roman emperor Tiberius, and Lucia (Lucilla) accidentally poisoned her husband, the poet Lucretius (d. 55 B.C.E.), with a love potion.

Hung themselves with spite, one then another.
Said this Arrius, 'Beloved brother,
Give me a shoot from off that blessèd tree,
And in my garden, planted it will be.'[6]   770
       And later on, about wives he has read,
And some had slain their husbands in their bed,
And let their lechers hump them all the night,
While on the floor the corpses lay upright.
And some have driven nails into the brain,   775
While they did sleep, and thus they had them slain.
And some did give them poison in their drink.
He spoke more slander than the heart can think,
And on top of it, he knew more proverbs
Than in this world there can grow grass and herbs.   780
'Better,' he said, 'that your habitation
Be either with a lion or foul dragon,
Than with a woman who is used to chide.
Better,' said he, 'high on the roof abide,
Than down in the house with an angry wife;[7]   785
They're so wicked and contrary all their lives,
That they hate what their husbands love always.'
He said, 'A woman casts her shame away,
When she casts off her shift.' He spoke more so:
'A fair woman, unless she's chaste also,   790
Is just like a gold ring in a sow's nose.'[8]
Who would imagine, or who would suppose
The woe that in my heart was, and the pain?
       And when I saw he never would refrain
From reading on this cursèd book all night,   795
Then suddenly, three leaves I have ripped right
Out of his book, as he read, and also
With my fist, I took him on the cheek so
That backward in our fire, right down fell he.
He starts up like a lion who's gone crazy,   800
And with his fist, he hit me on the head
So on the floor I lay like I were dead.
And when he saw how still it was I lay,
He was aghast, and would have fled away,
Till, at last, out of my swoon I awoke.   805
'Oh! Hast thou slain me, false thief?' then I spoke,
'And for my land, hast thou now murdered me?
Before I'm dead, yet will I still kiss thee.'
       And fairly he knelt down when he came near,
And he said, 'Alison, my sister dear,   810
Never more will I hit you, in God's name!
If I've done so, you are yourself to blame.
I pray you, your forgiveness now I seek.'
And right away, I hit him on the cheek,

---

6. A story told in the *Letter of Valerius*.   8. Proverbs 11.22.
7. Proverbs 21.9.

And said, 'Thief, now this much avenged am I;   815
I may no longer speak, now I will die.'
But then, at last, after much woe and care,
We two fell into an agreement there,
He gave me all the bridle in my hand
To have the governing of house and land,   820
And of his tongue, and of his hands, then, too;
I made him burn his book without ado.
And when I had then gotten back for me,
By mastery, all the sovereignty,
And when he said to me, 'My own true wife,   825
Do as you like the rest of all your life;
Keep your honor, and keep my rank and state'—
After that day, we never had debate.
God help me so, there's no wife you would find
From Denmark to India who was so kind,   830
And also true, and so was he to me.
I pray to God, who sits in majesty,
To bless his soul with all his mercy dear.
Now will I tell my tale, if you will hear."

Behold the words between the Summoner and the Friar.

The Friar laughed, when he had heard all this;   835
"Madame," said he, "so have I joy or bliss,
This is a long preamble to a tale!"
The Summoner had heard his windy gale,
"By God's two arms," the Summoner said, "lo!
Always will a friar interfere so.   840
Lo, good men, a fly and then a friar
Will both fall in every dish and matter.
Of preambulation, what's to say of it?
What! Amble, trot, keep still, or just go sit!
You're hindering our sport in this manner."   845
"You say so, sir Summoner?" said the Friar;
"Now, by my faith, I shall, before I go,
Tell a tale of a summoner, you know,
That all the folks will laugh at in this place."
"Now, elsewise, Friar, I do curse your face,"   850
Said this Summoner. "And I curse myself, too,
Unless I tell some tales, at least a few,
Of friars before I come to Sittingbourne⁹
So that, be sure, I will make your heart mourn.
I know full well that you're out of patience."   855
Our Host cried out, "Peace now! And that at once!"
And he said, "Let the woman tell her tale.
You act like folks who are all drunk on ale.
Do, madame, tell your tale, and all the rest."
"All ready, sir," said she, "as you think best,   860

9. A town on the road to Canterbury, 40 miles from London.

If I have license of this worthy Friar."
　"Yes, madame," said he, "tell on. I will hear."

Here the Wife of Bath ends her Prologue.

The Wife of Bath's Tale

Here begins the Tale of the Wife of Bath.

　　In the olden days of good King Arthur,
Of whom Britons still speak with great honor,
This whole land was all filled up with fairies. 865
The elf queen, with her pretty company,
Went dancing then through many a green mead.
I think this was the old belief, indeed;
I speak of many hundred years ago.
But now no one sees elves and fairies go, 870
For now all the charity and prayers
Of limitors[1] and other holy friars,
Who haunt through every land and every stream
As thick as motes floating in a sun beam,
Blessing halls and chambers, kitchens, bowers, 875
Cities, boroughs, castles, and high towers,
Barns and villages, cowsheds and dairies—
This is the reason why there are no fairies.
For there where once was wont to walk an elf,
Now there the begging friar walks himself 880
In the afternoons and in the mornings,
He says his matins[2] and his holy things
As he walks all throughout his begging grounds.
Now women may go safely all around.
In every bush and under every tree, 885
There is no other incubus[3] but he,
And he'll do them no harm but dishonor.
　　So it happened that this good King Arthur
Once had a lusty knight, a bachelor,
Who, one day, came riding from the river, 890
And it chanced that, as he was born, alone,
He saw a maiden walking on her own,
From which maid, then, no matter what she said,
By very force, he took her maidenhead;
This oppressive violence caused such clamor, 895
And such a suit for justice to King Arthur
That soon this knight was sentenced to be dead,
By the course of law, and should have lost his head—
By chance that was the law back long ago—

1. Friars licensed to beg in a specific territory.
2. I.e., morning prayers.
3. An evil spirit believed to have sex with women as they sleep.

Except the queen and other ladies also   900
So long had then prayed to the king for grace
Till he had granted his life in that place,
And gave him to the queen, to do her will,
To choose whether she would him save or kill.
     The queen then thanked the king with all her might,   905
And after this, thus spoke she to the knight,
When, on a day, she saw that it was time.
"You stand," she said, "in this state for your crime:
That of your life, you've no security.
I grant you life, if you can tell to me   910
What thing it is that women most desire.
Keep your neck-bone from the ax now, sire!
And if, at once, the answer you don't know,
Still, I will give you leave so you can go
A twelvemonth and a day, to search and learn   915
Sufficient answer before you return;
Before you leave, I'll have security
That here you'll surrender up your body."
     Woe was this knight, and he sighs sorrowfully;
But what! He can't do all he likes completely.   920
And at last, he decided that he'd wend
His way and come back home at the year's end,
With such an answer as God would convey;
He takes his leave and goes forth on his way.
     He seeks in every house and every place   925
Where he has hopes that he'll find some good grace
To learn the thing that women love the most,
But he could not arrive on any coast
Where he might find out about this matter,
Two creatures who agreed on it together.   930
     Some said that all women best loved richness,
Some said honor, and some said jolliness,
Some, rich array, and some said lust in bed,
And often times to be widowed and wed.
     Some said that our hearts were most often eased   935
When we could be both flattered and well pleased.
He got quite near the truth, it seems to me.
A man shall win us best with flattery,
Solicitude, and eager busyness.
Thus we are captured, both the more and less.   940
     And some said that the best of all love we
To do what pleases us, and to be free,
And that no man reproves us for our folly,
But says that we are wise and never silly.
For truly, there is not one of us all,   945
If any one will claw us where it galls,
That we won't kick when what he says is true.
Try, and he'll find it so who will so do;
For, be we ever so vicious within,
We want to be held wise and clean of sin.   950

And some say that we find it very sweet
To be thought dependable and discreet,
And in one purpose steadfastly to dwell,
And not betray a thing that men us tell.
A rake handle isn't worth that story.   955
We women can't keep secrets, by God's glory;
See Midas—will you hear the tale withal?[4]
      Once Ovid, among some other things small,
Said Midas covered up with his long hair,
On his head two ass's ears that grew there,   960
And this flaw he did hide as best he might
Quite cleverly from every mortal's sight,
So that, save for his wife, no one did know.
He loved her most, and trusted her also;
He prayed her that to no other creature   965
She would tell how he was so disfigured.
      She swore to him, "No"; all this world to win,
She would not do that villainy or sin,
To make her husband have so foul a name.
She wouldn't tell because of her own shame.   970
But, nonetheless, it seemed to her she died
Because so long she must that secret hide;
She thought it swelled so sorely near her heart
That some word from her must, by needs, depart;
Since she dared not tell it to any man,   975
Down to the marsh that was nearby, she ran—
Until she got there, her heart was on fire—
And as a bittern[5] bellows in the mire,
Down by the water, she did her mouth lay:
"Thou water, with your sound do not betray: 980
To thee I tell, and no one else," she said,
"My husband has long ass ears on his head!
Now is my heart all whole; now is it out.
I could no longer keep it, without doubt."
Here you see, if a time we might abide,   985
Yet it must out; we can no secret hide.
If of this tale you want to hear the rest,
Read Ovid, and there you will learn it best.
      This knight, about whom my tale is concerned,
Seeing that the answer he'd not learned—   990
That is to say, what women love the best—
Sorrowful was the spirit in his breast.
But home he goes; no more might he sojourn;
The day had come when homeward he must turn.
And on his way, it happened he did ride,   995
With all his cares, near to a forest's side,
Where he saw come together for a dance,
Some four and twenty ladies there by chance;

4. See Ovid, *Metamorphoses* 11.172–93 (where   by his wife).
Midas's secret is discovered by a servant, not   5. A wading bird with a deep, booming call.

Toward which dance he eagerly did turn,
In hopes some wisdom from them he might learn.   1000
But truly, before he had arrived there,
The dancing ladies vanished—who knew where.
No creature saw he left there who bore life,
Save on the green, he saw sitting a wife[6]—
A fouler creature, none imagine might.   1005
This old wife then arose to meet the knight.
"Sir knight, there's no road out of here," said she.
"What you are seeking, by your faith, tell me.
Perhaps, then, you'll be better prospering."
She said, "These old folks can know many things."   1010
        "Beloved mother," said this knight, "it's fate
That I am dead unless I can relate
What thing it is that women most desire.
Could you tell me, I'd well repay your hire."
        "Pledge me your troth," said she, "here in my hand,   1015
And swear to me the next thing I demand,
You shall do it if it lies in your might,
And I'll tell you the answer before night."
        "I grant," he said, "you have this pledge from me."
        "Then, sire, I dare well boast to you," said she,   1020
"Your life is safe, and I will stand thereby;
Upon my life, the queen will say as I.
Let see who is the proudest of them yet
Who wears either a coverchief or hairnet
Who dares say 'Nay' to what I will you teach.   1025
Let us go forth without a longer speech."
Then she whispered a message in his ear,
And bade him to be glad, and have no fear.
        When they came to the court, this knight did say
That, as he'd pledged, he had held to his day,   1030
And he said his answer was ready then.
Many noble wives and many maidens
And many widows, because wise are they,
With the queen sitting as the judge that day,
Were all assembled, his answer to hear;   1035
And then this knight was told he should appear.
        It was commanded that there should be silence
And that the knight should tell in audience
The thing that worldly women love the best.
The knight did not stand like a beast at rest;   1040
At once to his question then he answered
With manly voice, so all the court it heard:
        "My liege lady, generally," said he,
"Women desire to have sovereignty
As well over their husbands as their loves,   1045
And to be in mastery them above.
This is your greatest desire, though me you kill.

6. A woman.

Do as you like; I am here at your will."
In all the court, there was no wife or maiden
Nor widow who denied what he had said then,   1050
But they said he was worthy of his life.
And with that word, then, up jumps the old wife,
Whom the knight had seen sitting on the green:
"Mercy," said she, "my sovereign lady queen!
Before your court departs, by me do right.   1055
I taught this very answer to this knight;
For which he pledged to me his troth and hire,
So that the first thing I'd of him require,
This he would do, if it lay in his might.
Before the court, then I pray you, sir knight,"   1060
Said she, "that you now take me for your wife,
For well you know that I have saved your life.
Upon my faith, if I say false, say 'nay.' "
        This knight answered, "Alas, and well away!
I know that was my promise, I'll be blessed.   1065
But for God's love now, choose a new request!
Take all my goods, and let my body go."
        "Oh no," said she, "I curse us both then so!
For though I may be foul and poor and old,
I'd not want all the metal, ore, or gold   1070
That's buried in the earth or lies above,
Unless I were your lady and your love."
        "My love?" said he, "oh, no, my damnation!
Alas, that one of my birth and station
Ever should so foully disparaged be!"   1075
But all for naught; the end is this, that he
Constrained was here; by needs, he must her wed,
And take his old wife, and go off to bed.
        Now here some men would want to say perhaps
That I take no care—so it is a lapse—   1080
To tell you all the joy and the array
That at the wedding feast was on that day:
To which, my answer here is short and small:
I say there was no joy or feast at all.
Only sorrow and heaviness, I say.   1085
For privately he wedded her next day,
And all day after, he hid like an owl,
For woe was he that his wife looked so foul.
        Great was the woe the knight had in his thoughts,
When he was with his wife to their bed brought;   1090
He wallows and he writhes there, to and fro.
His old wife just lay smiling, even so,
And said, "Oh husband dear, God save my life!
Like you, does every knight fare with his wife?
Is this the law here in the house of Arthur?   1095
Is each knight to his wife aloof with her?
I am your own love, and I am your wife;
And I am she who has just saved your life.
Surely, toward you I have done only right;

Why fare you thus with me on this first night? 1100
You're faring like a man who's lost his wits,
What's my guilt? For love of God, now tell it,
And it will be amended if I may."
    "Amended?" said this knight, "Alas! No way!
It will not be amended, this I know. 1105
You are so loathly, and so old also,
And come from such low lineage, no doubt,
Small wonder that I wallow and writhe about.
I would to God my heart burst in my breast!"
    "Is this," said she, "the cause of your unrest?" 1110
    "Yes," said he, "no wonder is, that's certain."
    "Sir," said she, "I could mend this again,
If I liked, before there'd passed days three,
If you might now behave well toward me.
    But since you speak now of such gentleness[7] 1115
As descends to you down from old richness,
So that, because of it, you're gentle men,
Such arrogance is just not worth a hen.
See who is most virtuous all their lives,
In private and in public, and most strives 1120
To always do what gentle deeds he can:
Now take him for the greatest gentle man.
Christ wills we claim from him our gentleness,
Not from our elders and from their old richness.
Though they leave us their worldly heritage, 1125
And we claim that we're from high lineage,
Yet they may not bequeath a single thing
To us here of their virtuous living,
Which is what made them be called gentle men;
This is the path they bade us follow then. 1130
    Well can he, the wise poet of Florence,
Who's named Dante,[8] speak forth with this sentence.
Lo, Dante's tale is in this kind of rhyme:
'Seldom up his family tree's branches climbs
A man's prowess, for God, in his goodness, 1135
Wills that from him we claim our gentleness';
For, from our elders, we may no thing claim
But temporal things that may hurt us and maim.
    And every man knows this as well as me,
If gentleness were planted naturally 1140
In a certain lineage down the line, yet
They'd not cease in public or in private,
From gentleness, to do their fair duty;
They might not then do vice or villainy.
    Take fire and bring it in the darkest house, 1145
From here to mountains of the Caucasus,[9]

---

7. Gentility; nobility.
8. Dante Alighieri (1265–1321), Florentine poet whose *Divine Comedy* had a significant influence on Chaucer; the following lines echo *Purgatorio* 7.121–23.
9. The mountain range on the southwest border of Russia, between the Black and Caspian Seas.

And let men shut the doors and go return;
Yet still the fire will lie as fair and burn
Like twenty thousand men might it behold;
Its natural duty it will always hold,   1150
On my life, till extinguished it may be.
    Here, may you well see how gentility
Is not connected to one's possessions,
Since folks don't follow its operation
Always, as does the fire, lo, in its kind.   1155
For, God knows it, men may well often find
That a lord's son does shame and villainy;
And he who wants praise for his gentility,
Since a gentle house he was born into,
And had elders full of noble virtue,   1160
And who will not himself do gentle deeds,
And dead gentle ancestors hardly heeds,
He is not gentle, be he duke or earl;
A villain's sinful deeds do make a churl.
For such gentleness is only fame   1165
From your elders' high goodness and their name,
Which is a thing your person does not own.
Your gentleness must come from God alone.
Thus our true gentleness must come from grace;
It's not a thing bequeathed us with our place.   1170
    Think how noble, as says Valerius,
Was this one Tullius Hostillius,[1]
Nobility did poverty succeed.
Read Seneca, and Boethius[2] read;
There you shall see expressly that, indeed,   1175
The man is gentle who does gentle deeds.
And therefore, my dear husband, I conclude:
Though my ancestors were humble and rude,
Yet may the high God, and for this I pray,
Grant me grace to live virtuously each day.   1180
I am gentle, whenever I begin,
To live virtuously and to waive sin.
    You reproach me for poverty, indeed,
High God above, on whom we base our creed,
In willing poverty did live his life.   1185
And certainly each man, maiden, or wife
May understand that Jesus, heaven's king,
Would not choose a vicious way of living.
Glad poverty's an honest thing, it's true;
Thus Seneca and other clerks say, too.   1190
He who sees he's well paid by poverty,

---

1. Third king of Rome (7th century B.C.E.); according to legend, he began life as a herdsman.
2. Christian Roman philosopher (d. 474), whose *Consolation of Philosophy*, written in prison before his execution, was translated from Latin by Chaucer. Seneca the Younger (d. 65 C.E.), Roman Stoic moralist and dramatist who committed suicide by order of the emperor Nero.

Though he had no shirt, he seems rich to me.
He is a poor man who can only covet,
For he wants what he lacks power to get;
He who has naught, and does not covet, too,   1195
Is rich, though he a peasant seems to you.
True poverty, it sings out properly;
Now Juvenal[3] says of it merrily:
'The poor man, when he should go by the way,
Before the thieves, this man can sing and play.'   1200
Poverty is a hateful good, I guess,
A great encouragement to busyness;
Great improver of wisdom and good sense
For him who can suffer it with patience.
Poverty, though miserable seems its name,   1205
Is a possession no one else will claim.
Poverty often, when a man is low,
Can make him both his God and himself know.
Poverty's an eyeglass, it seems to me,
Through which he might his good and true friends see.   1210
And sire, now, if I don't grieve you, therefore
For poverty don't blame me anymore.
      Now, sire, with old age you have reproached me;
And truly, sire, though no authority
Were in books, you gentlemen of honor   1215
Say folks to an old man should show favor
And call him father, in your gentleness;
And I shall find authorities, I guess.
      Now, since you say that I am foul and old,
You don't have to fear to be a cuckold;   1220
For filth and age, so far as I can see,
Are great wardens upon one's chastity.
But, nonetheless, since I know your delight,
I shall fulfill your worldly appetite.
      Choose now," said she, "of these things, one of two: 1225
Till I die, to have me foul and old, too,
And be to you a true and humble wife,
And never displease you in all my life,
Or else you can have now a fair, young thing,
And take your chances with the visiting   1230
That happens at your house because of me,
Or in some other place, as well may be.
Choose yourself whichever one will please you."
      This knight now ponders and sighs sorely, too,
But finally, he said in this way here: 1235
"My lady and my love and wife so dear,
I put myself in your wise governing;
Choose yourself which one may be most pleasing
And most honor to both you and me too.
I do not care now which one of the two;   1240

---

3. Roman poet (d. ca. 120 C.E.); the quotation is from *Satire* 10.22.

What pleases you suffices now for me."
  "Then have I got mastery from you," said she,
"Since I may choose and govern all the rest?"
  "Yes, truly, wife," said he, "I think it best."
  "Kiss me," said she, "we are no longer angry,   1245
  For, by my troth,[4] to you I will both be—
Yes, now both fair and good, as will be plain.
I pray to God that I might die insane,
Unless to you I'm also good and true
As any wife's been, since the world was new.   1250
Unless tomorrow I'm as fair to see
As any queen or empress or lady,
Who is between the east and then the west,
Do with my life and death as you think best.
Cast up the curtain; how it is, now see."   1255
  And when the knight saw all this verily,
That she now was so fair and so young, too,
For joy he seized her within his arms two,
His heart was all bathed in a bath of bliss.
A thousand times in a row, he did her kiss,   1260
And she obeyed him then in everything
That was to his pleasure or his liking.
  And thus they both lived until their lives' end
In perfect joy; and Jesus Christ us send,
Husbands meek and young and fresh in bed,   1265
And the grace to outlive those whom we wed;
I pray that Jesus may shorten the lives
Of those who won't be governed by their wives;
And old and stingy niggards who won't spend,
To them may God a pestilence soon send!   1270

4. I.e., "I swear."

CHRISTINE DE PIZAN

ca. 1364–ca. 1431

"My head bowed as if in shame and my eyes full of tears, I sat slumped against the arm of my chair with my cheek resting on my hand. All of a sudden, I saw a beam of light, like the rays of the sun, shine down into my lap." Christine de Pizan's best-known allegory, *The Book of the City of Ladies*, opens with the narrator lamenting her female nature: she has been reading book after book about the character of women, learning that she, like all of her kind, is unfit for pursuing study, unable to perform meaningful work, and particularly likely to sin. Comforted by three crowned women, shining "goddesses" who embody Reason, Rectitude, and Justice, the narrator relearns the history of mankind—this time, through the lens of the feminine. From the stories of women of ancient times such as Dido and Lucrece to the lives of medieval saints, the goddesses work with the narrator to build the City of Ladies, stone by shining stone.

LIFE AND TIMES

Although Christine de Pizan lived almost her whole life in and around Paris, and wrote all of her works in the French language, she always remained (as she puts it in her *Book of Deeds of Arms and Chivalry*) "an Italian woman." Christine was the daughter of Tommaso da Pizzano, a doctor of medicine and of astrology, who moved from Italy to France to serve at the royal court of Charles V, and thus her fortunes were from childhood dependent on the favor and financial support of the ruling family. (The name "de Pizan," sometimes also spelled "de Pisan," reflects the family's landholdings in the town of Pizzano, on the outskirts of Bologna.) Her relationship to the royal household was reinforced after she wed Etienne de Castel, who worked as an administrative secretary and aide at the court. The marriage seems to have been a success: in her autobiographical writings, Christine refers to those ten years as the happiest of her life, and describes their abrupt end as the shattering of a ship tossed by a storm upon the rocks. Her ship had lost its "captain," and Christine had lost her "dearest friend." At the age of twenty-five, Christine found herself obliged to support herself, her three young children, a niece, and her widowed mother, at a time when few opportunities for paid work were available to women. Her solution: to live by her pen, becoming the first known female professional writer in European history.

The years around 1400 were tumultuous ones, especially for those near the royal court of France: the popular and effective ruler Charles V had died two decades before, leaving a son, Charles VI, who was at best erratic and at times descended into mental instability. His queen, Isabeau of Bavaria, attempted to maintain stable rule, aided by one of the king's brothers, but her efforts were thwarted by her own foreign birth and by rivalry on the part of other family members (especially Charles VI's uncle, the Duke of Burgundy). At the same time, the nation was engaged in repeated conflicts with England, in the course of the Hundred Years' War (1337–1453), and repeated bouts of plague following the devastating outbreak of the mid-fourteenth century roiled the country. Christine represents this political and social instability throughout her works, nowhere more memorably than in *Christine's Vision*, in which the "Crowned Dame" who represents the French nation laments the wicked children who tear her clothing and wound her body. By writing books of counsel and advice for the royal court, as well as works praising the virtues of the past king Charles V and the present queen Isabeau of Bavaria, Christine hoped to do her part in healing the body politic.

THE BOOK OF THE CITY OF LADIES

Christine de Pizan produced an extraordinary volume of writings, even compared with the prodigious output of her contemporaries **Petrarch**, Boccaccio, and **Chaucer**. She wrote hundreds of poems, both short lyrics and narrative works; allegorical visions, often incorporating autobiographical accounts of her life and times; and encyclopedic surveys of history and of myth. *The Book of the City of Ladies* is her most mature work, combining a remarkable ability to compile large amounts of information into a memorable form with the poetic gifts of metaphor and allegory: the city of ladies is a monumental edifice, built up piece by piece with "stones" made up of tales of individual women. Instead of being lofty, abstract figures, the goddesses of Reason, Rectitude, and Justice give Christine practical advice, urging her to wield "the pick of understanding" to dig out the badly shaped stones—that is, texts that describe women as ignorant and sinful—and instead to lay the foundations with the straight stones that are stories of great women of the past.

The three books of the *City of Ladies*, each supervised by a different goddess, demarcate progressive levels of the city-building project, moving upward from the foundations of book 1 to the walls of book 2 and finally to the houses and roofs of book 3. The first book, which is excerpted here, features women who ruled cities and empires, including Dido of Carthage and Semir-amis of Babylon: these women, who had been condemned as lascivious and unstable by writers such as Virgil and **Dante**, become for Christine exemplars of the female ability to rule. Figures of myth also appear throughout book 1 as models for women's behavior: Ovid's Io, for example, is transformed from a foolish cow to a brilliant woman who gave the gift of learning and language to the Egyptians, while Minerva appears not as a goddess but as a woman who taught the Greeks their alphabet and ruled the city of Athens, where classical civilization flowered. The later books include historical examples of notable women of Christine's own time, both the lofty and the humble: not just duchesses and princesses but also Novella, the woman who sometimes lectured in the legal classroom of her father at the University of Bologna, and Anastasia, a brilliant painter of manuscript illustrations in medieval Paris.

Christine's works were quickly translated into other languages, and an English translation of the *City of Ladies* was read at the Tudor court. It is tempting to think of Christine's "city" as a hospitable home for the queens Mary I and Elizabeth, who would soon sit on the English throne. Although Christine's works were extremely popular during her lifetime and for more than a century after her death, they fell into neglect in subsequent generations. In the early 1970s, however, readers began to search out female authors of the premodern past. Along with **Marie de France**, Christine de Pizan is one of a long-forgotten generation of medieval foremothers who laid the foundations for women writers of today.

From The Book of the City of Ladies[1]

FROM *PART ONE*

1. *Here begins* The Book of the City of Ladies

One day, I was sitting in my study surrounded by many books of different kinds, for it has long been my habit to engage in the pursuit of knowledge. My mind had grown weary as I had spent the day struggling with the weighty tomes of various authors whom I had been studying for some time. I looked up from my book and decided that, for once, I would put aside these difficult texts

---

1. Translated from the French by Rosalind Brown-Grant.

and find instead something amusing and easy to read from the works of the poets. As I searched around for some little book, I happened to chance upon a work which did not belong to me but was amongst a pile of others that had been placed in my safekeeping. I opened it up and saw from the title that it was by Matheolus.[2] With a smile, I made my choice. Although I had never read it, I knew that, unlike many other works, this one was said to be written in praise of women. Yet I had scarcely begun to read it when my dear mother called me down to supper, for it was time to eat. I put the book to one side, resolving to go back to it the following day.

The next morning, seated once more in my study as is my usual custom, I remembered my previous desire to have a look at this book by Matheolus. I picked it up again and read on a little. But, seeing the kind of immoral language and ideas it contained, the content seemed to me likely to appeal only to those who enjoy reading works of slander and to be of no use whatsoever to anyone who wished to pursue virtue or to improve their moral standards. I therefore leafed through it, read the ending, and decided to switch to some more worthy and profitable work. Yet, having looked at this book, which I considered to be of no authority, an extraordinary thought became planted in my mind which made me wonder why on earth it was that so many men, both clerks and others, have said and continue to say and write such awful, damning things about women and their ways. I was at a loss as to how to explain it. It is not just a handful of writers who do this, nor only this Matheolus whose book is neither regarded as authoritative nor intended to be taken seriously. It is all manner of philosophers, poets and orators too numerous to mention, who all seem to speak with one voice and are unanimous in their view that female nature is wholly given up to vice.

As I mulled these ideas over in my mind again and again, I began to examine myself and my own behaviour as an example of womankind. In order to judge in all fairness and without prejudice whether what so many famous men have said about us is true, I also thought about other women I know, the many princesses and countless ladies of all different social ranks who have shared their private and personal thoughts with me. No matter which way I looked at it and no matter how much I turned the question over in my mind, I could find no evidence from my own experience to bear out such a negative view of female nature and habits. Even so, given that I could scarcely find a moral work by any author which didn't devote some chapter or paragraph to attacking the female sex, I had to accept their unfavourable opinion of women since it was unlikely that so many learned men, who seemed to be endowed with such great intelligence and insight into all things, could possibly have lied on so many different occasions. It was on the basis of this one simple argument that I was forced to conclude that, although my understanding was too crude and ill-informed to recognize the great flaws in myself and other women, these men had to be in the right. Thus I preferred to give more weight to what others said than to trust my own judgement and experience.

I dwelt on these thoughts at such length that it was as if I had sunk into a deep trance. My mind became flooded with an endless stream of names as

2. The French poet's Latin poem *Liber Lamentationum* (ca. 1295), which became enormously popular in its French translation by Jean le Fèvre as *The Lamentations of Matheolus* (ca. 1320), attacked women and marriage.

I recalled all the authors who had written on this subject. I came to the conclusion that God had surely created a vile thing when He created woman. Indeed, I was astounded that such a fine craftsman could have wished to make such an appalling object which, as these writers would have it, is like a vessel in which all the sin and evil of the world has been collected and preserved. This thought inspired such a great sense of disgust and sadness in me that I began to despise myself and the whole of my sex as an aberration in nature.

With a deep sigh, I called out to God: 'Oh Lord, how can this be? Unless I commit an error of faith, I cannot doubt that you, in your infinite wisdom and perfect goodness, could make anything that wasn't good. Didn't you yourself create woman especially and then endow her with all the qualities that you wished her to have? How could you possibly have made a mistake in anything? Yet here stand women not simply accused, but already judged, sentenced and condemned! I just cannot understand this contradiction. If it is true, dear Lord God, that women are guilty of such horrors as so many men seem to say, and as you yourself have said that the testimony of two or more witnesses is conclusive, how can I doubt their word? Oh God, why wasn't I born a male so that my every desire would be to serve you, to do right in all things, and to be as perfect a creature as man claims to be? Since you chose not to show such grace to me, please pardon and forgive me, dear Lord, if I fail to serve you as well as I should, for the servant who receives fewer rewards from his lord is less obligated to him in his service.'

Sick at heart, in my lament to God I uttered these and many other foolish words since I thought myself very unfortunate that He had given me a female form.

2. The three ladies

Sunk in these unhappy thoughts, my head bowed as if in shame and my eyes full of tears, I sat slumped against the arm of my chair with my cheek resting on my hand. All of a sudden, I saw a beam of light, like the rays of the sun, shine down into my lap. Since it was too dark at that time of day for the sun to come into my study, I woke with a start as if from a deep sleep. I looked up to see where the light had come from and all at once saw before me three ladies, crowned and of majestic appearance, whose faces shone with a brightness that lit up me and everything else in the place. As you can imagine, I was full of amazement that they had managed to enter a room whose doors and windows were all closed. Terrified at the thought that it might be some kind of apparition come to tempt me, I quickly made the sign of the cross on my forehead.

With a smile on her face, the lady who stood at the front of the three addressed me first: 'My dear daughter, don't be afraid, for we have not come to do you any harm, but rather, out of pity on your distress, we are here to comfort you. Our aim is to help you get rid of those misconceptions which have clouded your mind and made you reject what you know and believe in fact to be the truth just because so many other people have come out with the opposite opinion. You're acting like that fool in the joke who falls asleep in the mill and whose friends play a trick on him by dressing him up in women's clothing. When he wakes up, they manage to convince him that he is a woman despite all evidence to the contrary! My dear girl, what has happened to your sense? Have you forgotten that it is in the furnace that gold is refined, increasing in value the more it is beaten and fashioned into different shapes? Don't know that it's the very finest things which are the subject of the most intense discussion? Now, if you turn your mind to the very highest realm of all, the realm of abstract ideas, think for a moment whether or not those philosophers whose views against women you've been citing have ever been proven wrong. In fact, they are all constantly correcting each other's opinions, as you yourself should know from reading Aristotle's *Metaphysics* where he discusses and refutes both their views and those of Plato and other philosophers.[3] Don't forget the Doctors of the Church either, and Saint Augustine[4] in particular who all took issue with Aristotle himself on certain matters, even though he is considered to be the greatest of all authorities on both moral and natural philosophy. You seem to have accepted the philosophers' views as articles of faith and thus as irrefutable on every point.

'As for the poets you mention, you must realize that they sometimes wrote in the manner of fables which you have to take as saying the opposite of what they appear to say. You should therefore read such texts according to the grammatical rule of *antiphrasis*, which consists of interpreting something that is negative in a positive light, or vice versa. My advice to you is to read those passages where they criticize women in this way and to turn them to your advantage, no matter what the author's original intention was. It could be that Matheolus is also meant to be read like this because there are some passages in his book which, if taken literally, are just out-and-out heresy. As for what these authors—not just Matheolus but also the more authoritative writer of the *Romance of the Rose*[5]—say about the God-given, holy state of matrimony, experience should tell you that they are completely wrong when they say that marriage is insufferable thanks to women. What husband ever gave his wife the power over him to utter the kind of insults and obscenities which these authors claim that women do? Believe me, despite what you've read in books, you've never actually *seen* such a thing because it's all a pack of outrageous lies. My dear friend, I have to say that it is your naivety which has led you to take what they come out with as the truth. Return to your senses and stop worrying your head about such foolishness. Let me tell you that those who speak ill of women do more harm to themselves than they do to the women they actually slander.'

3. Christine recounts how the lady who had spoken to her told her who she was, what her function and purpose was, and how she prophesied that Christine would build a city with the help of the three ladies

On receiving these words from the distinguished lady, I didn't know which of my senses was the more struck by what she said: whether it was my ears as I took in her stirring words, or my eyes as I admired her great beauty and

---

3. The influential Greek philosophers Plato (429–347 B.C.E.) and his student Aristotle (384–322 B.C.E.) were widely read in Latin translation in the Middle Ages.
4. Augustine of Hippo (354–430). Doctors of the Church: title given in the Middle Ages to certain saints who were also outstanding

theologians.
5. A very popular French allegorical romance, written in two parts—by Guillaume de Lorris (ca. 1237) and by Jean de Meun (ca. 1275); Christine's objections are mainly to the continuation, which includes a number of misogynistic passages.

dress, her noble bearing and face. It was the same for the other ladies too: my gaze darted back and forth from one to the other since they were all so alike that you could hardly tell them apart. All except for the third lady, who was no less imposing than the other two. This lady had such a stern face that whoever glanced into her eyes, no matter how brazen they were, would feel afraid of committing some misdeed since she seemed to threaten punishment to all wrongdoers. Out of respect for the ladies' noble appearance, I stood up before them but was far too dumbfounded to utter a single word. I was extremely curious to know who they were and would have dearly loved to dare ask them their names, where they were from, why they had come, and what the priceless symbols were that each of them held like a sceptre in her right hand. Yet I didn't think myself worthy to put these questions to such honourable ladies as these, so I held my tongue and carried on gazing at them. Though still frightened, I was also in part reassured, for the lady's words had already begun to assuage my fears.

Presently, the wise lady who had addressed me first seemed to read my mind and began to answer my unspoken questions with these words: 'My dear daughter, you should know that it is by the grace of God, who foresees and ordains all things, that we, celestial creatures though we may be, have been sent down to earth in order to restore order and justice to those institutions which we ourselves have set up at God's command. All three of us are His daughters, for it was He who created us. My task is to bring back men and women when they drift away from the straight and narrow. Should they go astray but yet have the sense to know me when they see me, I come to them in spirit and speak to their conscience, instructing them in the error of their ways and showing them how exactly it is that they have done wrong. Then I teach them to follow the correct road and to avoid doing what is undesirable. Because it is my role to light their way to the true path and to teach both men and women to acknowledge their flaws and weaknesses, you see me here holding up a shining mirror like a sceptre in my right hand. You can be sure that whoever looks into this mirror, no matter who they may be, will see themselves as they truly are, such is its great power. Not for nothing is it encrusted with precious stones, as you can see. With the help of this mirror, I can determine the nature, quantity and essence of all things and can take full measure of them. Without this mirror, nothing can come to good. Since you obviously want to know what function my two sisters perform, each of them will shortly speak to you in turn and will add her weight to my words by giving you a clear explanation of both her name and her powers.

'First, however, I will tell you exactly why we are here. I want you to know that, as we do nothing without good reason, our appearance here today has a definite purpose. Though we do not attempt to be known in all places, since not everyone strives to acquaint themselves with us, we have none the less come to visit you, our dear friend. Because you have long desired to acquire true knowledge by dedicating yourself to your studies, which have cut you off from the rest of the world, we are now here to comfort you in your sad and dejected state. It is your own efforts that have won you this reward. You will soon see clearly why it is that your heart and mind have been so troubled.

'Yet we also have a further, more important reason for coming to visit you, which we'll now go on to tell you about. Our wish is to prevent others from falling into the same error as you and to ensure that, in future, all worthy ladies and valiant women are protected from those who have attacked them. The female sex has been left defenceless for a long time now, like an orchard without a wall, and bereft of a champion to take up arms in order to protect it. Indeed, this is because those trusty knights who should by right defend women have been negligent in their duty and lacking in vigilance, leaving womankind open to attack from all sides. It's no wonder that women have been the losers in this war against them since the envious slanderers and vicious traitors who criticize them have been allowed to aim all manner of weapons at their defenceless targets. Even the strongest city will fall if there is no one to defend it, and even the most undeserving case will win if there is no one to testify against it. Out of the goodness and simplicity of their hearts, women have trusted in God and have patiently endured the countless verbal and written assaults that have been unjustly and shamelessly launched upon them. Now, however, it is time for them to be delivered out of the hands of Pharaoh.[6] For this reason, we three ladies whom you see before you have been moved by pity to tell you that you are to construct a building in the shape of a walled city, sturdy and impregnable. This has been decreed by God, who has chosen you to do this with our help and guidance. Only ladies who are of good reputation and worthy of praise will be admitted into this city. To those lacking in virtue, its gates will remain forever closed.'

4. How, before the lady revealed her name, she spoke at greater length about the city which Christine was destined to build, and explained that she was entrusted with the task of helping her to construct the enclosure and external walls

'So you see, my dear daughter, that you alone of all women have been granted the honour of building the City of Ladies. In order to lay the foundations, you shall draw fresh water from us three as from a clear spring. We will bring you building materials which will be stronger and more durable than solid, uncemented marble. Your city will be unparalleled in splendour and will last for all eternity.

'Haven't you read that King Tros founded the city of Troy with the help of Apollo, Minerva and Neptune,[7] whom the people of that time believed to be gods? Haven't you also heard of Cadmus, who created the city of Thebes at the gods' command?[8] Yet, in the course of time, even these cities fell into ruin and decay. However, in the manner of a true sibyl, I prophesy to you that this city which you're going to build with our help will never fall or be taken. Rather, it will prosper always, in spite of its enemies who are racked by envy. Though it may be attacked on many sides, it will never be lost or defeated.

---

6. Like the Isrelites from Egypt; in this comparison, Christine is implicitly cast as Moses.
7. According to classical myth, the city of Troy (in modern-day Turkey) was founded by the son of Tros, aided by Apollo (god of the sun, prophecy, and music), Athena (called by the Romans Minerva, goddess of wisdom and war), and Poseidon (Neptune, god of the sea).

8. According to myth, the earliest inhabitants of the new city were men who grew from the dragon's teeth that Cadmus had sown in the ground on the instructions of Athena. Christine would have been most familiar with the verson of the story told in Ovid, *Metamorphoses* 3.1–137.

'In the past, as the history books tell you, certain courageous ladies who refused the yoke of servitude founded and established the realm of Amazonia.[9] For many years afterwards, this realm was maintained under the rule of various queens, all of whom were noble ladies chosen by the women themselves, and who governed well and wisely, making every effort to keep their country safe. These women were very strong and powerful, having extended their rule over many of the lands of the east and having subjugated to their will all the neighbouring countries. They were feared by everyone, even the Greeks, who were the bravest nation in the world at that time. None the less, even the Amazons' power began to crumble in due course, as is the way with all earthly rulers. Now, the only trace that is left of that proud realm is its name.

'By contrast, the city which you're going to build will be much more powerful than these. As has been decided amongst the three of us, it is my task to help you begin by giving you tough, indestructible cement which you will need to set the mighty foundations and to support the great walls that you must raise all around. These walls should have huge high towers, solid bastions surrounded by moats, and outer forts with both natural and manmade defences. This is what a powerful city must have in order to resist attack. On our advice, you will sink these foundations deep in order to make them as secure as possible, and you will construct such high walls that the city inside will be safe from assault. Dear Christine, I have now told you all about why we have come. However, in order to convince you to give greater weight to my words, I'm going to reveal my name to you. The very sound of it should reassure you that, if you follow my instructions, you will find me to be an infallible guide to you in all your endeavours. I am called Lady Reason, so rest assured that you are in good hands. For the moment, I will say no more.'

* * *

14. More discussion and debate between Christine and Reason

'My lady, you have truly spoken well, and your words are like music to my ears. Yet, despite what we've said about intelligence, it's undeniable that women are by nature fearful creatures, having weak, frail bodies and lacking in physical strength. Men have therefore argued that it is these things that make the female sex inferior and of lesser value. To their minds, if a person's body is defective in some way, this undermines and diminishes that person's moral qualities and thus it follows that he or she is less worthy of praise.'

Reason's reply was, 'My dear daughter, this is a false conclusion which is completely untenable. It is definitely the case that when Nature fails to make a body which is as perfect as others she has created, be it in shape or beauty, or in some strength or power of limb, she very often compensates for it by giving that body some greater quality than the one she has taken away. Here's an example: it's often said that the great philosopher Aristotle was very ugly, with one eye lower than the other and a deformed face. Yet, if he was physically misshapen, Nature certainly made up for it by endowing him with extraordinary intellectual

---

9. The country believed to be inhabited only by Amazons, the warrior women featured in several Greek myths; its location, a matter of dispute, was usually held to be somewhere near the Black Sea.

powers, as is attested by his own writings. Having this extra intelligence was worth far more to him than having a body as beautiful as that of Absalom.

'The same can be said of the emperor Alexander the Great,[1] who was extremely short, ugly and sickly, and yet, as is well known, he had tremendous courage in his soul. This is also true of many others. Believe me, my dear friend, it doesn't necessarily follow that a fine, strong body makes for a brave and courageous heart. Courage comes from a natural, vital force which is a gift from God that He allows Nature to implant in some rational beings more than in others. This force resides in the mind and the heart, not in the bodily strength of one's limbs. You very often see men who are well built and strong yet pathetic and cowardly, but others who are small and physically weak yet brave and tough. This applies equally to other moral qualities. As far as bravery and physical strength are concerned, neither God nor Nature has done the female sex a disservice by depriving it of these attributes. Rather, women are lucky to be deficient in this respect because they are at least spared from committing and being punished for the acts of appalling cruelty, the murders and terrible violent deeds which men who are equipped with the necessary strength have performed in the past and still do today. It probably would have been better for such men if their souls *had* spent their pilgrimage through this mortal life inside the weak body of a woman. To return to what I was saying, I am convinced that if Nature decided not to endow women with a powerful physique, she none the less made up for it by giving them a most virtuous disposition: that of loving God and being fearful of disobeying His commandments. Women who don't act like this are going against their own nature.

'However, dear Christine, you should note that God clearly wished to prove to men that, just because *all* women are not as physically strong and courageous as men generally are, this does not mean that the entire female sex is lacking in such qualities. There are in fact several women who have displayed the necessary courage, strength and bravery to undertake and accomplish extraordinary deeds which match those achieved by the great conquerors and knights mentioned in books. I'll shortly give you an example of such a woman.

'My dear daughter and beloved friend, I've now prepared a trench for you which is good and wide, and have emptied it of earth which I have carried away in great loads on my shoulders. It's now time for you to place inside the trench some heavy, solid stones which will form the foundations of the walls for the City of Ladies. So take the trowel of your pen and get ready to set to with vigour on the building work. Here is a good, strong stone which I want you to lay as the first of your city's foundations. Don't you know that Nature herself used astrological signs to predict that it should be placed here in this work? Step back a little now and let me put it into position for you.'

* * *

19. About Queen Penthesilea and how she went to the rescue of the city of Troy

'This Queen Orithyia lived for a long time and died at a fine old age, having kept the realm of Amazonia in a flourishing state and expanded its dominion. The Amazons crowned as her successor her own daughter, the brave Penthesilea,

---

1. The greatest Greek general of antiquity (356–323 B.C.E.), renowned in the Middle Ages as an ideal of knighthood and the power to rule.

who surpassed all others in intelligence, courage, prowess and virtue. She too was forever eager to take up arms and fight, increasing the Amazons' power further than ever before in her relentless pursuit of territory. She was so feared by her enemies that none dared approach her and so proud that she never slept with a man but preferred to remain a virgin all her life.

'It was during her reign that the terrible war between the Greeks and the Trojans broke out.[2] Because of the name that the great Hector had made for himself as the finest, bravest and most highly skilled knight in the world, Penthesilea, who was naturally drawn to him since they shared the same qualities, heard so much about him that she began to love him with a pure and noble heart and desired above all else to go and see him. In order to fulfil this wish, she left her country with a great host of noble ladies and maidens all expert in the arts of war and richly armed, setting off to the city of Troy which lay a great distance away. However, distances always seem shorter when one's heart is filled with a strong desire.

'Unfortunately, when Penthesilea arrived in Troy, it was already too late: she discovered that Hector had been killed by Achilles during a battle in which the flower of Trojan chivalry had been wiped out. Penthesilea was received with all honours by the Trojans—King Priam, Queen Hecuba and all the barons—yet she was inconsolable and heartbroken to find that Hector was dead. The king and queen, who never left off grieving for the death of their son, offered to show her his body since they had been unable to let her see him alive. They took her to the temple where his tomb had been prepared, truly the very noblest and finest sepulchre that has ever been recorded in the history books. There, in a beautiful, sumptuous chapel all decorated with gold and precious stones, sat the embalmed and robed body of Hector on a throne in front of the main altar dedicated to the gods. He appeared to be more alive than dead as he brandished a naked sword in his hand and his haughty face still seemed to be throwing out a challenge to the Greeks. He was draped in a long, full garment which was woven with fine gold and trimmed and embroidered with jewels. This garment came down to the floor, covering the lower half of his body, which lay completely immersed in a precious balm that gave off a most delicious scent. The Trojans worshipped this body, bathed in the dazzling light of hundreds of candles, as if it were one of their gods. A costlier tomb surely never was seen. Here they brought Queen Penthesilea, who no sooner glimpsed the body through the open chapel door than she fell on her knees in front of Hector and greeted him as if he were still alive. She then went up close towards him and gazed deeply on his face. Through her tears she cried out: "O flower of chivalry, the very epitome and pinnacle of bravery: who can dare to call themselves valiant or even strap on a sword now that the finest and most shining example of knighthood has gone? Alas, cursed be the day that he whose vile hand deprived the world of its greatest treasure was ever born! Most noble prince, why was Fortune so contrary as to prevent me from being by your side when this traitor was plotting your downfall? This never would have happened because I would not have allowed it. If your killer were still alive, I would surely avenge your death and thus extinguish the great sorrow and anger which are burning up my heart as I see you lifeless before me and unable to speak to me, as was my only desire.

2. The Trojan War, a central theme of classical literature; it was the subject of Homer's *Iliad* and the backdrop of Virgil's *Aeneid*. Hector was the greatest warrior among the Trojans; Achilles, the greatest among the Greeks.

Yet, since Fortune decreed that it should be so and I can do nothing to gainsay her, I swear by the very highest gods of our faith and solemnly promise you, my dear lord, that as long as I have breath in my body I will make the Greeks pay for your death." As she knelt before the corpse, Penthesilea's words reached the great crowd of barons, knights and ladies who were all gathered there and moved them to tears. She could barely drag herself away from the tomb but, finally, she kissed his hand that was holding the sword and took her leave, saying: "Most excellent knight, what must you have been like when you were alive, given that the mere image of you in death is so full of majesty!"

'Weeping tender tears, she left his side. As soon as she could, she put on her armour and, with her army of noble ladies, dashed out of the city to attack the Greeks who were holding Troy in a state of siege. To make a brief tale of it, she and her army set to with such vigour that, if she had lived longer, no Greek would ever again have set foot in Greece. She struck down and nearly killed Pyrrhus, Achilles's son, who was a very fine soldier. It was only with great difficulty that his men were able to rescue him and drag him, half-dead, back to safety. Thinking that he was unlikely to survive, the Greeks were distraught, for he had been their greatest hope. If Penthesilea felt hatred for the father, she certainly didn't spare the son.

'In short, though Penthesilea performed the most extraordinary feats, she finally succumbed after having spent several days with her army in the thick of battle. When the Greeks were at their lowest ebb, Pyrrhus, who had recovered from his wounds but was overcome with shame and sorrow that she had done him such grievous harm, ordered his valiant men to concentrate solely on surrounding Penthesilea and separating her from her companions. He wanted to kill her with his own hands and would pay a handsome reward to anyone who managed to trap her. Pyrrhus's men took a long time to do his bidding because Penthesilea dealt out such fearsome blows that they were extremely afraid of approaching her. However, in the end, after an enormous amount of effort on their part, they finally managed to encircle her one day and isolate her from her ladies. The Greeks attacked the other Amazons so fiercely that they were powerless to help their queen and Penthesilea herself was exhausted after having accomplished more in that time than even Hector himself could have done. Despite the astonishing strength with which she defended herself, the Greeks were able to smash all her weapons and tear off a good part of her helmet. When Pyrrhus saw her bare blonde head, he struck her such a blow that he split her whole skull in two. Thus died the great and good Penthesilea, a huge loss both to the Trojans and to her own countrywomen, who were immediately plunged into grief, which was understandable since from that day forth the Amazons never knew any other queen to rival her. With heavy hearts, they carried her dead body back home.

'So, you have now heard how the realm of Amazonia was founded and how it lasted for over eight hundred years. You can work this out by checking in the history books for the length of time it took from the beginning of their reign up to when Alexander the Great conquered the entire world, at which point they were still reckoned to be a powerful nation. The accounts of his exploits tell how he went to their country and was received by the queen and her ladies. Alexander lived a long time after the destruction of Troy and more than four hundred years after the founding of Rome,[3] which itself postdated the fall of Troy by a great deal. So, if you make the effort to compare these histories and calculate the timescale

3. Generally given in legend as 753 B.C.E.

involved, you will see that the reign of the Amazons was extremely long-lived. You'll also realize that, of all the kingdoms that lasted this long, there is none that could boast such a large number of illustrious rulers who accomplished such extraordinary deeds as this great nation could of its queens and ladies.'

* * *

37. About all the great good that these ladies have brought into the world

'My lady, I'm delighted to hear from your lips that so much good has been brought into the world thanks to the intelligence of women. Yet there are still those men who go around claiming that women know nothing of any worth. It's also a common way to mock someone for saying something foolish by telling them that they're thinking like a woman. On the whole, men seem to hold the view that women have never done anything for humankind but bear children and spin wool.'

Reason's reply was: 'Now can you understand the terrible ingratitude of those men who say such things? It's as if they're enjoying all the benefits without having any idea of where they come from or whom they should thank for them. You can clearly see how God, who does nothing without good cause, wanted to show men that they should no more denigrate the female sex than they should their own sex. He chose to endow women's minds with the capacity not simply to learn and grasp all kinds of knowledge but also to invent new ones by themselves, discovering sciences which have done more good and have been more useful to humanity than any others. Just take the example of Carmentis, whom I told you about before. Her invention of the Latin alphabet pleased God so much that He wished it to replace the Hebrew and Greek alphabets which had been so prestigious. It was by His will that the alphabet spread throughout most of Europe, a vast expanse of land, where it is used in countless books and volumes in all disciplines which recall and preserve for ever the glorious deeds of men and the marvellous workings of God, in addition to all the arts and sciences. But don't let it be said that I'm telling you these things out of bias: these are the words of Boccaccio himself and thus the truth of them is indisputable.

'One could sum up by saying that the good things that this Carmentis has done are truly infinite, since it is thanks to her that men have been brought out of their ignorant state and become civilized, even if they themselves have not acknowledged this fact. Thanks to her, men possess the art of encoding their thoughts and wishes into secret messages which they can send all over the world. They have the means to make their desires known and understood by others, and they have access to knowledge of past and present events as well as to some aspects of the future. Moreover, thanks to this lady's invention, men can draw up treaties and strike up friendships with people in faraway places; through their correspondence back and forth, they can get to know each other without ever meeting face to face. In short, it is impossible to count up all the advantages that the invention of the alphabet has brought: it is writing which allows us to describe and to know God's will, to understand celestial matters, the sea, the earth, all individuals and all objects. I ask you, then, was there ever a man who did more good than this?'

38. More on the same topic

'One might also ask if any man ever did as much for the benefit of humankind as this noble Queen Ceres,[4] whom I was telling you about before. Who could ever deserve more praise than she who led men, who were no better than savage primitives, out of the woods where they were roaming like wild beasts without any laws, and instead took them to dwell in towns and cities and taught them how to live a law-abiding existence? It was she who introduced men to far better nourishment than their previous diet of acorns and wild apples, giving them wheat and corn which makes their bodies more beautiful, their complexions clearer and their limbs stronger and more supple. This is much more suitable and substantial food for human beings to eat. It was she who showed men how to clear the land which was full of thistles, thorns, scrubby bushes and wild trees, and to plough the earth and sow seed by which means agriculture became a sophisticated rather than a crude process and could be used for the common good of all. It was she who enriched humankind by turning coarse primitives into civilized citizens and by transforming men's minds from being lazy, unformed and shrouded in ignorance to being capable of more suitable meditations and of the contemplation of higher matters. Finally, it was she who sent men out into the fields to work the land, men whose efforts sustain the towns and cities and provide for those inhabitants who are freed up to perform other tasks which are essential for human existence.

'Isis[5] is a similar example in terms of horticulture. Who could ever match the enormous benefits which she brought into the world when she discovered how to grow trees which bear fine fruit and to cultivate other excellent herbs which are so suitable for a human diet?

'Minerva too used her wisdom to endow human beings with many vital things such as woollen clothing, instead of the animal pelts which were all there was previously to wear. For the benefit of humankind, she invented carts and chariots to relieve men of the burden of carrying their possessions from place to place in their arms. Not to mention, my dear Christine, what she gave to noblemen and knights when she taught them the art and skill of making armour to give their bodies greater protection in battle, armour which was stronger, more practical and much finer than the leather hides which they had had to put on in the past.'

I answered Reason, saying, 'Indeed, my lady, from what you're telling me I've now realized the full extent to which those men who attack women have failed to express their gratitude and acknowledgement. They have absolutely no grounds for criticizing women: it's not just that every man who is born of woman receives so much from her, but also that there is truly no end to the great gifts which she has so generously showered on him. Those clerks who slander women, attacking them either verbally or in their writings, really should shut their mouths once and for all. They and all those who subscribe to their views should bow their heads in shame for having dared to come out with such things, considering that the reality is utterly different from what they've claimed. Indeed, they owe a huge debt of thanks to this noble lady Carmentis, for having used her fine mind to instruct them like a teacher with her pupils—

---

4. The Roman goddess of agriculture—the equivalent of Demeter, one of the most important of the Greek deities (described in a chapter not included here).

5. One of the principal Egyptian deities, the goddess of earth; she was credited with teaching the Egyptians how to cultivate wheat and barley.

a fact which they can't deny—and to endow them with the knowledge that they themselves hold in the highest regard, which is the noble Latin alphabet.

'But what about all the many noblemen and knights who go against their duty by launching their sweeping attacks on women? They too should hold their tongues, given that all their skills in bearing arms and fighting in organized ranks, of which they're so inordinately proud, have come down to them from a woman. More generally, does any man who eats bread and lives in a civilized fashion in a well-ordered city or who cultivates the land have the right to slander and criticize women, as so many of them do, seeing all that has been done for them? Certainly not. It is women like Minerva, Ceres and Isis who have brought them so many advantages which they will always be able to live off and which will for ever enhance their daily existence. Are these things to be taken lightly? I think not, my lady, for it seems to me that the teachings of Aristotle, which have so greatly enriched human knowledge and are rightly held in such high esteem, put together with all those of every other philosopher who ever lived, are not worth anything like as much to humankind as the deeds performed by these ladies, thanks to their great ingenuity.'

Reason replied to me, 'These ladies were not the only ones to do so much good. There have been many others, some of whom I'll now go on to tell you about.'

* * *

46. About the good sense and cleverness of Queen Dido

'As you yourself pointed out earlier, good judgement consists of weighing up carefully what you wish to do and working out how to do it. To prove to you that women are perfectly able to think in this way, even about the most important matters, I'll give you a few examples of some high-born ladies, the first of whom is Dido.[6] As I'll go on to tell you, this Dido, whose name was originally Elissa, revealed her good sense through her actions. She founded and built a city in Africa called Carthage and was its queen and ruler. It was in the way that she established the city and acquired the land on which it was built that she demonstrated her great courage, nobility and virtue, qualities which are indispensable to anyone who wishes to act prudently.

'This lady was descended from the Phoenicians, who came from the remotest regions of Egypt to settle in Syria where they founded and built several fine towns and cities. Amongst these people was a king named Agenor, who was a direct ancestor of Dido's father. This king, who was called Belus, ruled over Phoenicia and conquered the kingdom of Cyprus. He had only two children: a son, Pygmalion, and a daughter, Dido.

'On his deathbed, Belus ordered his barons to honour his children and be loyal to them, making them swear an oath that they would do so. Once the king was dead, they crowned his son Pygmalion and married the beautiful Elissa to a duke named Acerbas Sychaea, or Sychaeus, who was the most powerful lord in the country after the king. This Sychaeus was a high priest in the temple dedicated to Hercules, whom they worshipped, as well as being an extremely wealthy man. He and his wife loved each other very deeply and led a happy life

6. The legendary founder of Carthage (a city that was located northeast of modern Tunis, in Tunisia); the dominant version of her story focuses on her love for the Trojan refugee Aeneas and her suicide after he leaves her to fulfill his destiny as forefather of the Roman people (see Virgil's *Aeneid*, esp. book 4).

together. But King Pygmalion was an evil man, the cruellest and most envious person you ever saw, whose greed knew no bounds. Elissa, his sister, was all too aware of what he was like. Seeing how rich her husband was and how well known for his fabulous wealth, she advised Sychaeus to be on his guard against the king and to put his treasure in a safe place where her brother couldn't lay his hands on it. Sychaeus followed his wife's advice but failed to watch his own back against possible attack from the king as she had told him to do. Thus it happened that, one day, the king had him killed in order to steal his great riches from him. Elissa was so distraught at his death that she nearly died of grief. For a long time, she gave herself over to weeping and wailing for the loss of her beloved lord, cursing her brute of a brother for having ordered his murder. However, the wicked king, whose wishes had been thwarted since he had only managed to recover a tiny part of Sychaeus's wealth, bore a deep grudge against his sister, whom he suspected of having hidden it all away.

'Realizing that her own life was in danger, Elissa's good sense told her to leave her native land and live elsewhere. Her mind made up, she carefully considered all that she needed to do and then steeled herself to put her plans into effect. This lady knew very well that the king did not enjoy the full support of his barons or his subjects because of his great cruelty and the excessive burdens he imposed on them. She therefore rallied to her cause some of the princes, townspeople and even the peasants. Having sworn them to secrecy, she outlined her plans to them in such persuasive terms that they declared their loyalty to her and agreed to go with her.

'As quickly and as quietly as she could, Elissa had her ship prepared. In the dead of night, she set sail with all her treasure and her many followers aboard, urging the sailors to make the ship go as fast as possible. Yet this lady's cleverness didn't end there. Knowing that her brother would send his men after her as soon as he learnt of her flight, she had great chests, trunks and boxes secretly filled up with heavy, worthless objects to make it look as if they contained treasure. The idea was that she would give these chests and boxes to her brother's men if they would only leave her alone and let her continue on her course. It all happened just as she planned, for they had not long been at sea when a whole host of the king's men came racing after her to stop her. In measured tones, she pointed out to them that as she was only setting out on a pilgrimage, they should allow her to sail on unhindered. However, seeing that they remained unconvinced by her explanation, she declared that if it was her treasure her brother was after, she would be prepared to give it to him, even though he had no right to interfere with her wishes. The king's men, who knew that this was his sole desire, forced her to part with it as that way they could do the king's bidding and she could appease her brother. With a sad face, as if it cost her dear, the lady made them load up all the chests and boxes on to their ships. Thinking that they had done well and that the king would be delighted with the news, his men immediately went on their way.

'Uttering not a single word of protest, the queen's only thoughts were of setting sail once more. They journeyed on, by day and night, until they came to the island of Cyprus, where they stopped for a short while to refresh themselves. As soon as she had made her sacrifices to the gods, the lady went back to the ship, taking with her the priest from the temple of Jupiter and his family. This priest had predicted that a lady would come from the land of the Phoenicians and that he would leave his country to join her. Casting off again, they left the island of

Crete behind them and passed the island of Sicily on their right. They sailed along the whole length of the coast of Massylia until they finally arrived in Africa, where they landed. No sooner had they docked than the people living there rushed down to see the ship and to find out where those aboard were from.

'When they saw the lady and realized that she and her people had come in peace, they went and brought them food in abundance. Elissa talked to them in a very friendly way, explaining to them that she had heard such good things about their country that she wished to make her home there, if they had no objections. They replied that they were happy for her to do so. Insisting that she didn't want to establish a large colony on this foreign soil, the lady asked them to sell her a piece of land by the coast which was no bigger than what could be covered by the hide of a cow. Here she would build some dwellings for herself and her people. They granted her wishes and, as soon as the terms of the deal had been agreed upon, her cleverness and good sense came to the fore. Taking the cowhide, the lady had it cut into the tiniest strips possible, which were then tied together to form a rope. This rope was laid out on the ground by the seashore where it enclosed a huge plot of land. Those who had sold her the land were amazed and stunned by her cunning ruse, yet they had to abide by the deal they had struck with her.

'So it was that this lady took possession of all this territory in Africa. On her plot of land, a horse's head was discovered. This head, along with the movements and noises of the birds in the sky, they interpreted as prophetic signs that the city which they were about to found would be full of warriors who would excel themselves in the pursuit of arms. The lady immediately sent all over for workmen and spent her wealth freely to pay for their labour. The place which she had built was a magnificent and mighty city called Carthage, the citadel and main fortress of which were called Byrsa, which means "cowhide."[7]

'Just as she was beginning to build her city, she received news that her brother was coming after her and her followers for having made a fool of him and tricked him out of his treasure. She told his messengers that she had most definitely given the treasure to the king's men for them to take back to him, but that perhaps it was they who had stolen it and replaced it with worthless objects instead. It was possibly even the gods who had decided to metamorphose the treasure and stop the king from having it because of the sin he had committed in ordering her husband's murder. As for her brother's threats, she had faith that, with the help of the gods, she could defend herself against him. Elissa therefore assembled all her fellow Phoenicians together and told them that she wanted no one to stay with her against their will nor suffer any harm for her sake. If any or all of them wanted to return home, she would reward them for their hard work and let them go. They all replied with one voice that they would live and die by her side, and would never leave her even for a single day.

'The messengers departed and the lady worked as fast as she could to finish the city. Once it was completed, she established laws and rules for her people to live an honest and just existence. She conducted herself with such wisdom and prudence that her fame spread all over the world and talk of her was on everyone's lips. Thanks to her bold and courageous actions and her judicious rule, she became so renowned for her heroic qualities that her name was changed to Dido,

7. In Greek.

which means *"virago"*[8] in Latin: in other words, a woman who has the virtue and valour of a man. She lived a glorious life for many years, one which would have lasted even longer had Fortune not turned against her. As this goddess is wont to be envious of those she sees prosper, she concocted a bitter brew for Dido to drink, which I'll tell you about all in good time.'

* * *

48. About Lavinia, daughter of King Latinus

'Lavinia, queen of the Laurentines,[9] was similarly renowned for her good sense. Descended from the same Cretan king, Saturn, whom I've just mentioned, she was the daughter of King Latinus. She later wed Aeneas, although before her marriage she had been promised to Turnus, king of the Rutulians. Her father, who had been informed by an oracle that she should be given to a Trojan prince, kept putting off the wedding despite the fact that his wife, the queen, was very keen for it to take place. When Aeneas arrived in Italy, he requested King Latinus's permission to enter his territory. He was not only granted leave to do so but was immediately given Lavinia's hand in marriage. It was for this reason that Turnus declared war on Aeneas, a war which caused many deaths and in which Turnus himself was killed. Having secured the victory, Aeneas took Lavinia as his wife. She later bore him a son, even though he himself died whilst she was still pregnant. As her time grew near, she became very afraid that a man called Ascanius, Aeneas's elder son by another woman,[1] would attempt to murder her child and usurp the throne. She therefore went off to give birth in the woods and named the newborn baby Julius Silvius. Vowing never to marry again, Lavinia conducted herself with exemplary good judgement in her widowhood and managed to keep the kingdom intact, thanks to her astuteness. She was able to win her stepson's affection and thus defuse any animosity on his part towards her or his stepbrother. Indeed, once he had finished building the city of Alba, Ascanius left to make his home there. Meanwhile, Lavinia ruled the country with supreme skill until her son came of age. This child's descendants were Romulus and Remus, who later founded the city of Rome. They in turn were the ancestors of all the noble princes who came after them.

'What more can I tell you, my dear Christine? It seems to me that I've cited sufficient evidence to make my point, having given enough examples and proofs to convince you that God has never criticized the female sex more than the male sex. My case is conclusive, as you have seen, and my two sisters here will go on to confirm this for you in their presentation of the facts. I think that I have fulfilled my task of constructing the enclosure walls of the City of Ladies, since they're all now ready and done. Let me give way to my two sisters: with their help and advice you'll soon complete the building work that remains.'

END OF THE FIRST PART OF THE BOOK OF THE CITY OF LADIES.

8. Literally, "manlike woman" (Latin), in a heroic sense; while the English word sometimes retains this meaning, it also (and more often) came to mean "a shrew."
9. Inhabitants of Laurentum, on the coast of Latium just south of the mouth of the Tiber, where Aeneas and his men are said to have landed in Italy.
1. Aeneas's wife Creusa, who had died during the Greek sack of Troy.

V

Medieval China

The "Middle" in the European "Middle Ages" signifies the time between the Roman Empire and the Renaissance, a transitional period that has often been seen as a time of relative intellectual and cultural stagnation. In the case of China the situation is quite the reverse. If we use Western period terms, the *middle* of a Chinese "Middle Age" would mean "central." It is a period when Chinese thought and literature reached what many regard as their highest forms. During the medieval Period of Disunion (third through sixth centuries), a notoriously tumultuous age of political division, Buddhism, which had spread from India to China, took deep root in Chinese society, stimulating renewed interest in Daoist philosophy and the rise of religious Daoism. During the following two great medieval Chinese dynasties, the Tang and the Song (seventh through thirteenth centuries), classical Chinese poetry and prose reached an unprecedented height to which later ages would look back with awe and a sense that the achievements of its greatest writers could never be matched.

THE TANG DYNASTY

The long Tang Dynasty (618–907) was an age of cultural confidence and, initially, of expansion, as Tang armies pushed outward at every frontier. Particularly important was the expansion to the

A Southern Song Dynasty hand scroll, "Streams and Mountains Under Fresh Snow," attributed to Liu Songnian, twelfth century.

northwest and control of the trade routes to the west. Chang'an, an old capital now clothed in new splendor, mirrored the cosmopolitan empire it controlled. It was laid out on a grid pattern, with a mighty walled palace city at its north and two bustling markets to the south. The city teemed with foreigners, who came to the Chinese capital by the Central Asian land routes or the South Asian maritime trade routes as merchants, diplomatic envoys, pilgrims, monks, or adventurers. Nestorian Christians, Zoroastrians, Jews, and Arab merchants mingled with Japanese monks and Persian doctors. The people of Chang'an quickly adopted new hairstyles, new games such as polo, and new musical instruments, importing exotic melodies and dances from China's Central Asian "west."

The Tang was an age of innovation. Tea became a major commercial crop, and its consumption spread from China to East Asia via monks who used it to stay awake during long hours of meditation and sutra recitation. New Buddhist schools appeared, such as Chan (better known in its Japanese form, "Zen"), an iconoclastic form of Buddhism that espoused mind-to-mind transmission of truth, claiming that the study of scriptures was of no use.

The most influential invention during the Tang Dynasty was printing. A printed copy of the Buddhist Diamond Sutra, dated 868, is considered the world's oldest printed book. Sealed in a cave in remote Dunhuang, a Silk Road oasis in northwest China some 1100 miles from Chang'an, it was discovered by archaeologists in the early twentieth century.

The Tang period is most famous for its poetry. The civil service examination used by the Tang in recruiting its elites for government service came to require the composition of poetry, and it also became an integral part of social life—a medium of social exchange. In few other places in the world has lyric poetry ever enjoyed such centrality, and a number of major poets emerged whose works have made them renowned in China to this day. A great poem might deal with large philosophical issues, but it was just as likely to describe a meeting with an old friend. Poetry was seen as a way to record both an individual's personality and a country's historic moments. The writings of Wang Wei, **Li Bo**, and **Du Fu** came to exemplify poetic perfection, in different styles.

In the 750s, the confidence of the Tang Dynasty was broken during the reign of one its most splendid emperors, Xuanzong. Xuanzong gave military governors in frontier regions great powers, hoping thereby to strengthen the defense of the empire. An able administrator, patron of the arts, and even scholar in his own right—he wrote a commentary on *Laozi* and set up a school for examinations in Daoist scriptures—Xuanzong was greatly devoted to a concubine of lower status, Yang Guifei (or "Prized Consort Yang"), whose family increasingly began to occupy strategic official positions. An Lushan, an associate of Yang's kinsmen, rebelled in 755, took Chang'an, and put the emperor to flight. Threatened by his own armies, Xuanzong was forced to witness the execution of his beloved concubine. Although the rebellion was soon put down, the dynasty never quite regained its former authority.

TANG POETRY

The poetry of the Tang Dynasty is generally considered the high point of China's three-millennia-old history of poetry. Much compelling verse was written after the period, not least

Women under the Tang Dynasty were riding horses and even playing polo. This painting, inspired by a painting by Zhang Xuan, a court painter flourishing during the reign of Emperor Xuanzong, presumably depicts an outing of court women led by Lady Guo Guo. She was a sister of the emperor's beloved Prized Consort Yang.

because the poetic giants of the Tang inspired later poets to write with self-conscious sophistication and skill. But later poets generally agreed that **Du Fu**, **Li Bo**, and their contemporaries had set a standard that could not be surpassed. For many centuries the elegant urgency and technical virtuosity with which these poets captured the world, as well as the scope of their poetic visions and themes, formed the basis for later poetic training and inspiration. The primacy of Tang poetry in the Chinese poetic canon continued until the early twentieth century, when Chinese intellectuals launched a revolutionary movement to replace the classical written idiom with vernacular spoken language. Today traditional poetry is popular once again, and the accomplishments of the Tang poets remain the high-water mark of what poetry can do.

Every educated Chinese during the Tang Dynasty was expected to be able to spontaneously dash off a poem with grace, or at least technical competence. Poetry was a form of social communication, not an arcane and highbrow art. The sheer mass of Tang

poems still extant—close to 50,000, by some 2,200 authors—clearly indicates how common poetry was in everyday life. Many of those whose poems survived spent their lives in some official government position, after taking the civil service examination that qualified them for office. Whenever these scholar-officials were sent to a new post in the vast territory of the Tang Empire they would take leave from their colleagues and friends with a "farewell" poem and expect a poetic gift in return. In their new province, they would make friends by going on pleasure excursions or visiting temples and invariably writing poems about their journeys. They could also write poems to praise the imperial court or to criticize its policies. Poetry thus was a cultural custom, a craft that taught people how to pay attention to and share the significant moments in their lives—to find something lovely in a scene; to convey feelings about separation and friendship, painful and pleasurable events; to thank a host for a splendid evening party; or simply to express what would otherwise be awkward or impossible to say. Though the

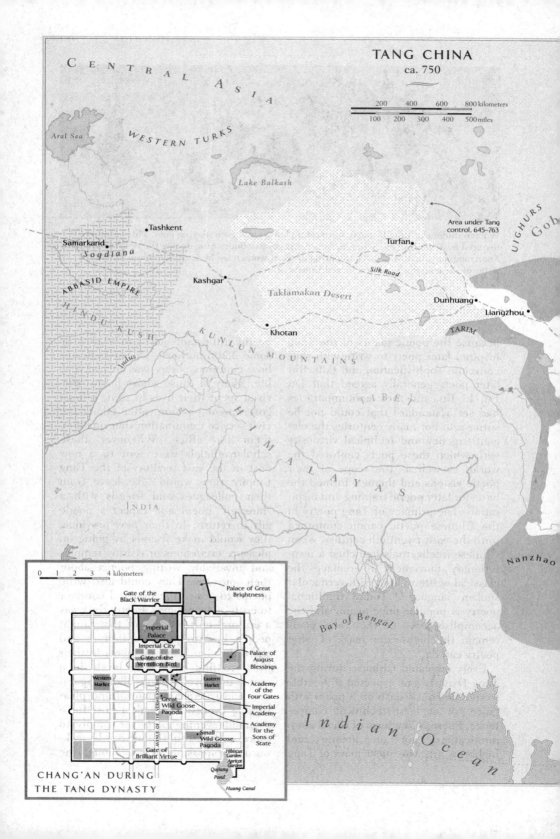

TANG CHINA
ca. 750

200   400   600   800 kilometers
100   200   300   400   500 miles

C E N T R A L   A S I A

W E S T E R N   T U R K S

Aral Sea

Lake Balkash

UIGHURS

Gobi

Area under Tang
control, 645–763

Tashkent

Samarkand

Sogdiana

Turfan

Silk Road

ABBASID EMPIRE

Kashgar

Taklamakan Desert

Dunhuang

Liangzhou

H I N D U   K U S H

Indus

K U N L U N   M O U N T A I N S

Khotan

TARIM

H I M A L A Y A S

I N D I A

Nanzhao

Bay of Bengal

I n d i a n   O c e a n

0   1   2   3   4 kilometers

Gate of the
Black Warrior

Palace of Great
Brightness

Imperial
Palace

Imperial City

Gate of the
Vermilion Bird

Palace of
August
Blessings

Western
Market

Eastern
Market

Academy
of the
Four Gates

AVENUE OF THE VERMILION BIRD

Great
Wild Goose
Pagoda

Imperial
Academy

Academy
for the
Sons of
State

Small
Wild Goose
Pagoda

Gate of
Brilliant Virtue

Hibiscus
Garden

Apricot
Garden

Qujiang
Pond

Huang Canal

CHANG'AN DURING
THE TANG DYNASTY

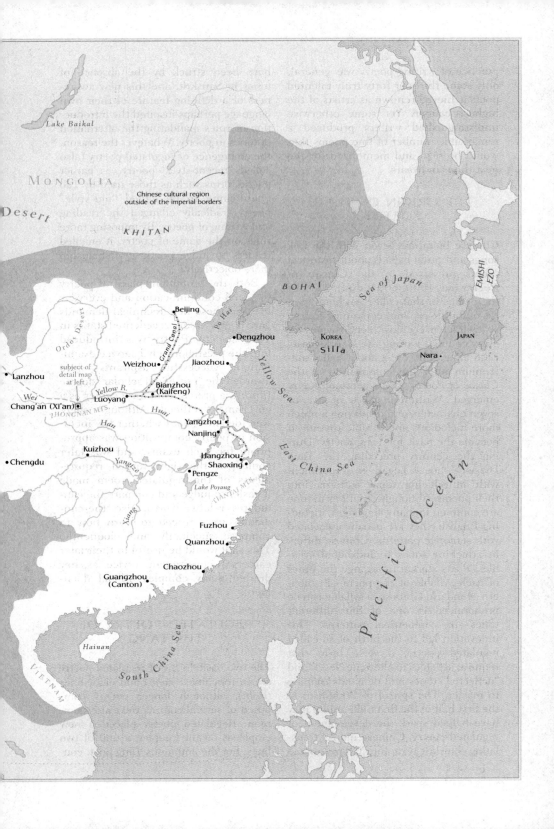

Lake Baikal

MONGOLIA

Desert

KHITAN

Chinese cultural region
outside of the imperial borders

BOHAI

Sea of Japan

EMISHI
EZO

Ordos Desert

Po Hai

Grand Canal

Beijing

Dengzhou

KOREA
Silla

JAPAN

Nara

subject of
detail map
at left.

Weizhou

Jiaozhou

Yellow R.

Bianzhou
(Kaifeng)

Lanzhou

Wei

Yellow Sea

Chang'an (Xi'an)

ZHONGNAN MTS.

Luoyang

Huai

Han

Han

Yangzhou

Nanjing

East China Sea

Kuizhou

Chengdu

Yangzze

Hangzhou
Shaoxing

Xiang

Pengze

Lake Poyang

TIANTAI MTS.

Fuzhou

Quanzhou

Pacific   Ocean

Chaozhou

Guangzhou
(Canton)

Hainan

VIETNAM

South China Sea

South China Sea

practice of writing poetry was general, only some thirty or forty truly talented poets achieved renown as artists of the highest caliber. Yet some otherwise undistinguished writers produced a remarkable number of fine poems that would be read and memorized for the next thousand years.

THE ORIGIN OF TANG POETRY

Chinese literature began with the folk songs and ritual ballads about historical events preserved in the *Classic of Poetry* (ca. 1000–600 B.C.E.). Most of the poems in that collection have stanzas of four to six lines containing four to six characters each, with end rhymes for every couplet. During the Han Dynasty (206 B.C.E.–220 C.E.), about half a millennium after the compilation of the *Classic of Poetry*, a new genre of poetry emerged. Written in lines of five or seven characters and displaying a much more melodious and flexible rhythm, it became the basis for Tang poetry. During the century preceding the Tang Dynasty, poets began to experiment with introducing tonal patterns into their poems. Although variations in tone are common in many languages, including English, they are usually associated with sentence patterns. Chinese differs in attaching tones to individual syllables. Poets started to arrange the tones of each syllable of the poem—in modern Mandarin Chinese, a syllable can be pronounced in one of four different tones—in symmetrical patterns. This innovation led to the birth of so-called regulated poetry, a verse form that requires syllables to alternate "level" and "deflected" tones and demands training to master. The spread of Buddhism in the first half of the first millennium may have helped spark the development of regulated poetry. Chinese monks translating Sanskrit texts into Chinese must have been struck by the absence of tones in Sanskrit, and this new awareness of a defining feature of their own language perhaps inspired the introduction of rules mandating the alternation of tones in poetry. Whatever the reason, the emergence of regulated poetry (also called "recent-style" poetry, as earlier poetic forms such as those used by Tao Qian came to be called "old-style" poetry) radically changed the reading and writing of poetry. By imposing more rules on the game of poetry, it enabled readers to judge poetic craftsmanship more objectively.

Both the prominent place of poetry in social communication and everyday life and these new technical demands gave poetry an unprecedented status in Tang society. Poetry was introduced into the prestigious civil service examination; successful aspirants were awarded the "presented scholar" degree (*jinshi*), a prerequisite for a career as a government official. Although there were debates about whether the inclusion of poetry composition was appropriate for such exams, and was later abolished, the tight formal requirements of the regulated poem made it easier to judge and compare the candidates' relative worth. Also, the candidates were forced to learn how to compose succinctly and eloquently. This skill would be useful in their later careers in government service, as they drafted many complex official documents.

REGULATED POETRY OF THE TANG

The two basic forms of regulated poetry are in four lines (*jueju*) and eight lines (*lüshi*), although longer poems composed of several stanzas were also common. Regulated poetry placed a new emphasis on the couplet, a unit of two lines. For the ambitious Tang poet, couplets provided an opportunity to display virtuosity, as they provided a showcase for the parallelism required of the regulated poem. Consider **Du Fu's "Spring Prospect**," which describes the fall of the Tang capital to rebels in 755 and the destruction of the great Tang Empire against the backdrop of innocent spring:

> The nation shattered, mountains and rivers remain;
> city in spring, grass and trees burgeoning.
> Feeling the times, blossoms draw tears;
> hating separation, birds alarm the heart.
> Beacon fires three months in succession,
> a letter from home worth ten thousand in gold.
> White hairs, fewer for the scratching,
> soon too few to hold a hairpin up.

Let us examine how this five-syllable regulated poem reads in classical Chinese. Some of the rhymes and tones are hardly recognizable in the modern Mandarin pronunciation of the characters given here, but they did rhyme and tonally harmonize during the Tang Dynasty. "Level tones" are marked with a hyphen (–); "deflected tones," with a straight line (|):

					FIRST COUPLET
國	破	山	河	在	(Chinese characters)
guó	pò	shān	hé	zài	(modern Mandarin pronunciation)
|	|	–	–	|	(tonal pattern)
nation	shattered	mountain	river	remain	(word-for-word translation)
城	春	草	木	深	
chéng	chūn	cǎo	mù	shēn ^(rhyme word)	
–	–	|	|	–	
city	spring	grass	tree	grow thick	
感	時	花	濺	淚	*SECOND COUPLET*
gǎn	shí	huā	jiàn	lèi	
|	–	–	|	|	
feel	time	blossom	shed	tear	
恨	別	鳥	驚	心	

hèn	bié	niǎo	jīng	xīn (rhyme word)
—	|	|	—	—
hate	separation	bird	alarm	heart

烽　火　連　三　月　　**THIRD COUPLET**

fēng	huǒ	lián	sān	yuè
|	|	—	—	|
beacon	fire	in succession	3	months

家　書　抵　萬　金

jiā	shū	dǐ	wàn	jīn (rhyme word)
—	—	|	|	—
home	letter	worth	10,000	gold

白　頭　搔　更　短　　**FOURTH COUPLET**

bái	tóu	sāo	gèng	duǎn
—	—	—	|	|
white	head	scratch	even	shorter

渾　欲　不　勝　簪

hún	yù	bù	shēng	zān (rhyme word)
|	|	|	—	—
simply	want	not	hold	hairpin

The poem consistently relies on parallelism as it poignantly contrasts the stability of the natural cycle with the abrupt changes brought about by the rebellion. In the first couplet the capital Chang'an is taken by rebel forces, the emperor has fled to Sichuan Province and abdicated, and the "nation is shattered," yet, perversely, we see the "city in spring," untouched by the disaster of historic proportion. In the second couplet, even blossoms and birds appear startled by the human tragedy. The third couplet shows the economic costs of the rebellion: the rebels have cordoned off the capital so tightly that letters have become almost priceless, smuggled in and out only at risk of one's life. The last couplet lacks precise parallelisms but ends with thematic resonances and shows the poet in despair: the hairpin no longer secures his official cap to his head, because he has become too old and the dynasty he wanted to serve has fallen on hard times.

Parallelism in Tang poetry functioned on many levels beyond the grammatical, including thematic parallelism and contrast between lines or in the poem as a whole. Thus Tang writings on poetry distinguish many types. The parallel couplet was the central device of regulated poetry, and during the Tang people would write out their favorite couplets in lavish calligraphy on little hanging scrolls, which they could carry when traveling. Indeed, Tang poets compiled entire anthologies containing only beautiful couplets excerpted from famous poems. The emphasis on fashioning beautiful couplets created a huge market for practical manuals that explained how to avoid violating the tonal rules and how to come up with an impressive parallel. This approach later drew criticism from poets who saw artistic ambition and inspiration, rather than craft and training, as the keys to good poetry. But the attraction of Tang poetry lies precisely in the felicitous match of craft with inspiration. It was solid training in the rules of regulated poetry that enabled Tang poets to capture their experience of the world in memorable words. The ultimate art of Tang poetry is that it often hides its artfulness under the serene surface of natural imagery.

LI BO

701–762

Although Li Bo (also known as Li Po and Li Bai) was raised in Sichuan in western China, speculations about his Turkic family background have enhanced his image as an exotic eccentric. Li Bo never attempted to take the civil service examination, which was the primary but not sole venue for advancement. Thanks to his connection with an influential Daoist at court, Li Bo gained a post at the eminent Hanlin Academy, an institution founded by Emperor Xuanzong to support unconventional intellectuals and literary talents. But Li Bo's drinking habits and unusual personality led to his dismissal only two years later. During the An Lushan Rebellion he joined the cause of a prince who attempted to establish an independent regime in southeast China, and after the rebellion was suppressed he was arrested for treason. Sentenced to exile, he was pardoned before he reached his remote destination; he died a few years later.

There are many legends about Li Bo's life, encouraged by the nonchalant poses projected in his poetry: according to one such legend, he drowned while trying to embrace the moon's reflection on the water. For someone who claimed in his poetry to converse and drink with the moon such an end was not implausible, though overindulgence in alcohol and Daoist longevity elixirs, which often contained mercury, might have played a role.

Much Tang poetry tends to treat the world at hand; Li Bo supplies an additional dimension by describing Daoist worlds beyond the world, evoking moments of history and legend, and even transforming everyday occasions into something miraculous. Because of his flair and capacity to see the world with fresh eyes, his contemporaries called him "the banished immortal"—an ethereal heaven-dwelling being exiled for a lifetime in the world of mortals as punishment for some extravagant misdemeanor.

Li Bo cultivated this reputation by writing poems that tell of encounters with immortals and of cloud-climbing excursions through the heavens.

Of the thousand-some poems by Li Bo that survive, many are written in the old verse form popular before the rise of regulated poetry during the Tang. Li Bo particularly liked to imitate folk songs and infuse his poetry with colloquial and bold language. In this way he could sometimes give voice to the common people's hardships: in "South of the Walls We Fought," for example, he echoes an older anonymous lament of soldiers fallen in battle, turning it into bitter criticism of the constant warfare of his time on the northern and northwestern frontier of Tang China against peoples such as the Tibetans.

Li Bo and **Du Fu** are considered the most important Tang poets, and readers and critics over the past millennium have devoted considerable effort to debating their relative merits and shortcomings. Quite apart from the greatness of their poetry, they made a particularly fitting couple, because they embody the two poles of poetic creativity that have been of greatest concern in the Chinese literary tradition: while Du Fu became the poet who captured, chronicled, and criticized reality within its limits, Li Bo came to stand for the poet who dedicated himself to breaking free from social convention and from the limits imposed by reality.

The Sun Rises and Sets[1]

The sun comes up from its nook in the east,
Seems to rise from beneath the earth,
Passes on through Heaven,
   sets once again in the western sea,
And where, oh, where, can its team of six dragons   5
   ever find any rest?
Its daily beginnings and endings,
   since ancient times never resting.
And man is not made of its Primal Stuff—
   how can he linger beside it long?   10
Plants feel no thanks for their flowering in spring's wind,
Nor do trees hate losing their leaves
   under autumn skies:
Who wields the whip that drives along
   four seasons of changes—   15
The rise and the ending of all things
   is just the way things are.

Xihe! Xihe![2]
Why must you always drown yourself
   in those wild and reckless waves?   20
What power had Luyang[3]

---

1. Translated by Stephen Owen.
2. Goddess who drove the sun's carriage.
3. According to legend, the lord of Luyang stopped the sun so that he could continue to fight in combat.

That he halted your course by shaking his spear?
This perverts the Path of things,
    errs from Heaven's will—
So many lies and deceits!   25
I'll wrap this Mighty Mudball of a world
    all up in a bag
And be wild and free like Chaos itself!

South of the Walls We Fought[4]

We fought last year at the Sanggan's source,
this year we fight on the Cong River road.
We washed weapons in the surf of Tiaozhi,
grazed horses on grass in Sky Mountain's snow.[5]
Thousands of miles ever marching and fighting: 5
until all the Grand Army grows frail and old.

The Xiongnu[6] treat slaughter as farmers treat plowing;
since bygone days only white bones are seen
    in their fields of yellow sand.
The House of Qin built the wall   10
    to guard against the Turk;
for the House of Han the beacon fires
    were blazing still.

Beacon fires blaze without ceasing,
the marching and battle never end.   15
They died in fighting on the steppes,
their vanquished horses neigh,
    mourning to the sky.
Kites and ravens peck men's guts,
fly with them dangling from their beaks   20
    and hang them high
        on boughs of barren trees.
The troops lie mud-smeared in grasses,
and the general acted all in vain.
Now I truly see that weapons   25
    are evil's tools:
the Sage will use them only
    when he cannot do otherwise.

---

4. Translated by Stephen Owen.
5. Four locations of Tang campaigns in the
north and northwest.

6. Formidable enemies of the Han Empire
(206 B.C.E.–220 C.E.).

Bring in the Wine[7]

Look there!
   The waters of the Yellow River,
   coming down from Heaven,
   rush in their flow to the sea,
   never turn back again   5
Look there!
   Bright in the mirrors of mighty halls
   a grieving for white hair,
   this morning blue-black strands of silk,
   now turned to snow with evening.   10
For satisfaction in this life
   taste pleasure to the limit,
And never let a goblet of gold
   face the bright moon empty.
Heaven bred in me talents,   15
   and they must be put to use.
I toss away a thousand in gold,
   it comes right back to me.
So boil a sheep,
   butcher an ox,   20
      make merry for a while,
And when you sit yourself to drink, always
   down three hundred cups.
   Hey, Master Cen,
   Ho, Danqiu,[8]   25
   Bring in the wine!
   Keep the cups coming!
And I, I'll sing you a song,
You bend me your ears and listen—
The bells and the drums, the tastiest morsels,   30
   it's not these that I love—
All I want is to stay dead drunk
   and never sober up.
The sages and worthies of ancient days
   now lie silent forever,   35
And only the greatest drinkers
   have a fame that lingers on!
Once long ago
   the prince of Chen
      held a party at Pingle Lodge.[9]   40
A gallon of wine cost ten thousand cash,
   all the joy and laughter they pleased.
      So you, my host,
How can you tell me you're short on cash?
Go right out!   45

---

7. Translated by Stephen Owen.
8. Two friends of Li Bo.
9. The scene of merry parties described by the

poet Cao Zhi (192–232), the brother of Cao Pi,
the author of "A Discourse on Literature."

Buy us some wine!
   And I'll do the pouring for you!
Then take my dappled horse,
   Take my furs worth a fortune,
Just call the boy to get them,   50
   and trade them for lovely wine,
And here together we'll melt the sorrows
   of all eternity!

Question and Answer in the Mountains[1]

They ask me why I live in the green mountains.
I smile and don't reply; my heart's at ease.
Peach blossoms flow downstream, leaving no trace—
And there are other earths and skies than these.

Summer Day in the Mountains[2]

Lazily waving a fan of white feathers,
Stripped naked here in the green woods,
I take off my headband, hang it on a cliff,
My bare head splattered by wind through pines.

Drinking Alone with the Moon[3]

A pot of wine among the flowers.
I drink alone, no friend with me.
I raise my cup to invite the moon.
He and my shadow and I make three.

The moon does not know how to drink;   5
My shadow mimes my capering;
But I'll make merry with them both—
And soon enough it will be Spring.

I sing—the moon moves to and fro.
I dance—my shadow leaps and sways.   10
Still sober, we exchange our joys.
Drunk—and we'll go our separate ways.

Let's pledge—beyond human ties—to be friends,
And meet where the Silver River ends.

1. Translated by Vikram Seth.   3. Translated by Vikram Seth.
2. Translated by Stephen Owen.

The Hardships of Traveling the Road I[4]

Clear wine in golden goblets, at ten thousand a peck:
Prized delicacies on jade plates, worth a myriad cash.
But I stopped the cup, threw down the chopsticks, was unable to eat:
I took out my sword, stared all around, my heart was blindly lost.
I wanted to cross the Yellow River, but ice blocked the waterway: 5
Was about to climb the Taihang range, but snow darkened the sky.
At my ease I let fall a line, sitting by the side of a stream;
Longed to be aboard ship again and dreamt of the realm of the sun.

   The hardships of traveling the road—hardships of traveling the road:
   So many branching roads!—and where now am I?   10
The long wind will smite the waves, and surely will come a time,
To hang straight the cloudy sail and cross the gray-blue sea!

Seeing Off Meng Haoran at Yellow Crane Tower,
on His Way to Guangling[5]

My old friend bids farewell in the west at Yellow Crane Tower.[6]
Amid misty blossoms of the third month goes down to Yangzhou.
His lone sail's far shadow vanishes in the deep-blue void.
Now I see only the Long River flowing to the edge of the sky.

In the Quiet Night[7]

The floor before my bed is bright:
Moonlight—like hoarfrost—in my room.
I lift my head and watch the moon.
I drop my head and think of home.

Sitting Alone by Jingting Mountain[8]

The flocks of birds have flown high and away,
A solitary cloud goes off calmly alone.
We look at each other and never get bored—
Just me and Jingting Mountain.

---

4. Translated by Paul W. Kroll.
5. Translated by Paul W. Kroll.
6. A famous scenic spot in the southeastern

city of Hangzhou.
7. Translated by Vikram Seth.
8. Translated by Stephen Owen.

A Song on Visiting Heaven's Crone Mountain in a Dream: On Parting[9]

Seafarers speak of that isle of Ying[1]—
but in blurred expanses of breakers and mist
   it is hard indeed to find.

Yue men tell of Heaven's Crone,[2]
appearing, then gone, it may be seen   5
   in the clouds and colored wisps.

Heaven's Crone reaches to sky
   and sideways runs to the sky,
its force stands over the Five Great Peaks,
   it casts Redwall in the shade.   10
Mount Tiantai[3] is forty and eight
   thousand yards high,
yet facing this it seems to tip,
   sagging southeastwardly.

And I, wishing to reach that place,   15
   once dreamed of Wu and Yue,
I spent a whole night flying across
   the moon in Mirror Lake.

The lake moon caught my reflection,
and went with me on to Shan Creek.   20
The place where Lord Xie spent the night
   is still to be found there now,
where green waters are ruffled in ripples,
   and the gibbon's wail is clear.

I put on the clogs of Lord Xie,[4]   25
and scaled that ladder into blue clouds.
Halfway up cliffside I saw sun in sea,
and heard in the air the Heaven-Cock crow.

A thousand peaks and ten thousand turns,
   my path was uncertain;   30
I was lost among flowers and rested on rock,
   when suddenly all grew black.

Bears roared and dragons groaned,
   making the cliff-streams quake,
the deep forests were shivering,—tiered ridges shook,   35

9. Translated by Stephen Owen.
1. One of the islands of immortals.
2. A mountain near the ancient southern state of Yue.
3. A sacred Buddhist mountain in southeast-

ern China (modern Zhejiang Province).
4. A 5th-century poet renowned for his land-scape poetry, he was also famous for supposedly inventing special mountain-climbing shoes.

clouds hung blue,—portending rain,
troubled waters rolled,—giving off mists.

Thunder-rumbling in Lightning Cracks,
hill ridges split and fell;
then the stone doors of Caves to Heaven   40
swung open with a crash.
A billowing vast blue blackness
    whose bottom could not be seen,
where sun and moon were gleaming
    on terraces silver and gold.   45

Their coats were of rainbow,—winds were their steeds,
the lords of the clouds—came down in their hosts.
Tigers struck harps,—phoenixes drew coaches in circles,
those who are the Undying—stood in ranks like hemp.
All at once my soul was struck,—and my spirit shuddered, 50
I leapt up in dazed alarm,—and gave a long sigh.
I was aware only—of this moment's pillow and mat,
I had lost those mists and bright wisps—that had been here just
    before.

All pleasures in our mortal world   55
    are also just like this,
whatever has happened since ancient times
    is the water flowing east.

When I leave you now, you go,—when will you ever return?
just set a white deer out to graze   60
    upon green mountainsides,
and when I must go, I'll ride it
    to visit mountains of fame.

How can I pucker my brows and break my waist
    serving power and prestige?—   65
it makes me incapable
    of relaxing heart or face.

DU FU

712–770

Du Fu failed in his political ambitions, and his poetry was not widely read during his lifetime. But during the Song Dynasty he rose to the top of the poetic canon because of his versatility and ability to capture the dramatic historical events and spirit of his age. Ever since that time, Du Fu, together with **Li Bo,** has maintained the reputation as the greatest of Chinese poets.

Du Fu was the grandson of a prominent court poet. Although he dreamed of an official career, that dream was dashed after he twice failed the civil service examination. When An Lushan rebelled in 755, the imperial court escaped but Du Fu was left behind in the capital. Eventually he slipped through the enemy lines and made his way to the court of the new emperor in exile. There he briefly held one of the court positions he had so much desired; but following the recapture of the capital, he was exiled to a minor provincial post. He soon quit in disgust and embarked on a lifetime of travels. He first went to seek the help of relatives in northwest China, and then took up residence in Chengdu in Sichuan Province. In his later years Du Fu moved to Kuizhou, where he produced his most admired poetry sequence, the "Autumn Meditations."

Du Fu is considered the "poet-historian" of Chinese literature, carrying out the Confucian duty to chronicle and criticize the events of his time. Prophetically, he grasped that the An Lushan Rebellion was an event of major historical proportions. But it was his ability to capture the rebellion's impact on his life and on the lives of the people around him that gave depth to his voice. In "Moonlight Night" Du Fu imagines his wife, whom he had managed to send to safety while he remained trapped in the occupied capital, watching the moon and worrying about him; "Qiang Village" conveys the riveting scene of reunion, after Du Fu has finally escaped from the capital and is reunited with his family. But the effects of the rebellion linger on even after it is quashed: a decade later, he devotes "Ballad of the Firewood Vendors" to the local working women in his new home in Kuizhou who despair that the loss of life has destroyed the marriage prospects of an entire generation.

The greatness of Du Fu's poetry lies in its extraordinary range of themes, styles, and observations. His poetic mastery is particularly visible in his preferred verse form, the regulated poem, in which he can be not just witty but also prophetic and visionary. Even when he is sober and humble, his everyday observations can reach cosmic proportions and take the unsuspecting reader by surprise.

Painted Hawk[1]

Wind-blown frost rises from plain white silk,
a gray falcon—paintwork's wonder.

Body strains, its thoughts on the cunning hare,
its eyes turn sidelong like a Turk in despair.

1. Translated by Stephen Owen.

You could pinch the rays glinting on tie-ring,   5
its stance, to be called to the column's rail.

When will it strike the common birds?—
bloody feathers strewing the weed-covered plain.

Moonlight Night[2]

From her room in Fuzhou tonight,
all alone she watches the moon.

Far away, I grieve that her children
can't understand why she thinks of Chang'an.

Fragrant mist in her cloud hair damp,   5
clear lucence on her jade arms cold—

when will we lean by chamber curtains
and let it light the two of us, our tear stains dried?

Spring Prospect[3]

The nation shattered, mountains and rivers remain;
city in spring, grass and trees burgeoning.

Feeling the times, blossoms draw tears;
hating separation, birds alarm the heart.

Beacon fires three months in succession,   5
a letter from home worth ten thousand in gold.

White hairs, fewer for the scratching,
soon too few to hold a hairpin up.[4]

Qiang Village I[5]

Lofted and lifted, west of the clouds of red,
The trek of the sun descends to the level earth.
By the brushwood gate songbirds and sparrows chaffer,
And the homebound stranger from a thousand li[6] arrives.
Wife and children marvel that I am here: 5
When the shock wears off, still they wipe away tears.

2. Translated by Burton Watson. This poem
was written in 756, when Du Fu was held captive in the fallen capital of Chang'an during
the An Lushan Rebellion and his wife and family had fled to safety in Fuzhou in the north.
3. Translated by Burton Watson. This poem
was written when Du Fu was still a captive in
Chang'an.

4. Officials used hairpins to keep their caps in
place.
5. Translated by Paul W. Kroll. This poem was
written in 757, when Du Fu finally rejoined
his family after their separation during the turmoil of the An Lushan Rebellion.
6. About 250 miles.

In the disorders of the age was I tossed and flung;
That I return alive is a happening of chance.
Neighbors swarm up to the tops of the walls,
Touched and sighing, even they sob and weep.   10
The night wastes on, and still we hold the candle,
Across from another, as if asleep and in a dream.

My Thatched Roof Is Ruined by the Autumn Wind[7]

In the high autumn skies of September
 the wind cried out in rage,
Tearing off in whirls from my rooftop
 three plies of thatch.
The thatch flew across the river,   5
 was strewn on the floodplain,
The high stalks tangled in tips
 of tall forest trees,
The low ones swirled in gusts across ground
 and sank into mud puddles.   10
The children from the village to the south
 made a fool of me, impotent with age,
Without compunction plundered what was mine
 before my very eyes,
Brazenly took armfuls of thatch,   15
 ran off into the bamboo,
And I screamed lips dry and throat raw,
 but no use.
Then I made my way home, leaning on staff,
 sighing to myself.   20
A moment later the wind calmed down,
 clouds turned dark as ink,
The autumn sky rolling and overcast,
 blacker towards sunset,
And our cotton quilts were years old   25
 and cold as iron,
My little boy slept poorly,
 kicked rips in them.
Above the bed the roof leaked,
 no place was dry,   30
And the raindrops ran down like strings,
 without a break.
I have lived through upheavals and ruin
 and have seldom slept very well,
But have no idea how I shall pass   35
 this night of soaking.
Oh, to own a mighty mansion
 of a hundred thousand rooms,
A great roof for the poorest gentlemen
 of all this world,   40

7. Translated by Stephen Owen.

a place to make them smile,
A building unshaken by wind or rain,
    as solid as a mountain,
Oh, when shall I see before my eyes
    a towering roof such as this?   45
Then I'd accept the ruin of my own little hut
    and death by freezing.

I Stand Alone[8]

A single bird of prey beyond the sky,
a pair of white gulls between riverbanks.

Hovering wind-tossed, ready to strike;
the pair, at their ease, roaming to and fro.

And the dew is also full on the grasses,   5
spiders' filaments still not drawn in.

Instigations in nature approach men's affairs—
I stand alone in thousands of sources of worry.

Spending the Night in a Tower by the River[9]

A visible darkness grows up mountain paths,
I lodge by river gate high in a study,

Frail cloud on cliff edge passing the night,
The lonely moon topples amid the waves.

Steady, one after another, a line of cranes in flight;   5
Howling over the kill, wild dogs and wolves.

No sleep for me. I worry over battles.
I have no strength to right the universe.

Thoughts while Travelling at Night[1]

Light breeze on the fine grass.
I stand alone at the mast.

Stars lean on the vast wild plain.
Moon bobs in the Great River's spate.

Letters have brought no fame.   5
Office? Too old to obtain.

Drifting, what am I like?
A gull between earth and sky.

8. Translated by Stephen Owen.   1. Translated by Vikram Seth.
9. Translated by Stephen Owen.

Ballad of the Firewood Vendors[2]

Kuizhou women, hair half gray,
forty, fifty, and still no husbands;
since the ravages of rebellion, harder than ever
   to marry—
a whole life steeped in bitterness and long sighs.   5
Local custom decrees that men sit, women stand;
men mind the house door, women go out and work,
at eighteen, nineteen, off peddling firewood,
with money they get from firewood, making
   ends meet.   10
Till they're old, hair in two buns dangling to the neck,
stuck with wild flowers, a mountain leaf, a silver pin,
they struggle up the steep paths, flock to the market gate,
risk their lives for extra gain by dipping from salt wells.
Faces powdered, heads adorned, sometimes a trace   15
   of tears,
cramped fields, thin clothing, the weariness of
   stony slopes—
But if you say all are ugly as the women of Witch's
   Mountain,   20
how to account for Zhaojun,[3] born in a village to
   the north?

Autumn Meditations IV[4]

I've heard them say, Chang'an's like a chessboard;
sad beyond bearing, the happenings of these
   hundred years!
Mansions of peers and princes, all with new
   owners now;   5
in civil or martial cap and garb, not the same as before.
Over mountain passes, due north, gongs and
   drums resound;
wagons and horses pressing west speed the
   feather-decked dispatches.[5]   10
Fish and dragons sunk in sleep, autumn rivers cold;
old homeland, those peaceful times, forever in
   my thoughts!

2. Translated by Burton Watson. This poem, written in 766, describes local customs in Kuizhou, set on steep hillsides along the Yangzi River, where Du Fu had settled.
3. Wang Zhaojun, a stunningly beautiful court lady of the Han Dynasty (206 B.C.E.–220 C.E.) who embodied the suffering of exile, because she was married off to a tribal chief of the fierce Xiongnu tribes as part of Han diplo-macy on the unruly northern frontier. "Witch's Mountain": Wushan, near Kuizhou.
4. Translated by Burton Watson. This poem comes from Du Fu's most famous poetic cycle, "Autumn Meditations."
5. Feathers attached to military dispatches marked the message as urgent; Uighurs were threatening from the north and Tibetans from the west.

VI

Japan's Classical Age

Although Japan consists of the four main islands of Hokkaidō, Honshū, Shikoku, and Kyūshū and about a thousand smaller islets, its contacts with the continent have always been close. In fact, much of what makes Japanese culture distinctive stems from the creative ways in which the Japanese adapted Chinese and Korean culture to their own circumstances. For example, the Japanese imported the Chinese writing system, but used it to produce their own distinct literature. They produced literature in two literary languages, one vernacular and the other Chinese-style, which differed strikingly in themes, rhetoric, and the gender of their authors. Some of the greatest works of Japanese literature were written by women in the vernacular language.

Much like the Romans confronting the older and more established civilization of the Greeks, early Japanese writers faced the challenging task of building their own literature on the sophisticated precedents of their mother culture while asserting their own originality. In addition to literature, Japan adopted crucial institutions and cultural practices from

Illustrated Biography of Prince Shōtoku, painted in 1069 by Hata no Chitei. This is part of a series of ten panels that depict the life of Prince Shōtoku (574–622), founder of Buddhism in Japan.

China, such as the concept of a state headed by a divine monarch, a government system based on administrative statutes and laws, Buddhism used as a state religion protecting the people's welfare, city planning, temple architecture, sacred sculpture, religious rituals, court music and elegant dances, imperial excursions, medicine, the culture of painting, calligraphy, and tea. But whereas Rome had conquered Greece and had its young elite educated by Greek slaves, early Japanese had relatively little actual contact with China and knew it mostly from books, thus feeling less self-conscious about their cultural identity. They believed in the numinous power of their language and their gods and were proud of the pristine simplicity of their earliest literature. Unlike parts of Korea and Vietnam, which at certain points in their history were conquered by China, Japan was never directly colonized by China; its inhabitants could admire their old neighbor at a safe distance.

CONTINENTAL CULTURE AND BI-LITERACY

The cultural dialogue with China resulted in one of the world's most complex literary traditions. Writing was invented in China some eighteen centuries before the Japanese learned how to read and write. Unlike Koreans and Vietnamese, who exclusively used Chinese-style writing for centuries, the Japanese used the Chinese writing system to produce texts in two literary languages: vernacular Japanese and Chinese-style writing (also called "Sino-Japanese," *kanbun*, or simply "Literary Chinese"). Chinese-style writing was transnational, enabling the Japanese court to participate in the diplomatic and cultural exchange with China and other states in the Chinese sphere of influence such as Korea and Vietnam; playing a

role similar to that of Latin in medieval Europe, it became the official language of the imperial administration and the Buddhist clergy, and was thus associated with high status, serious purpose, and male authorship. Although vernacular literature, in particular poetry, could serve similarly prestigious purposes at court, it became the preferred medium for emotional intimacy, romance, psychological sophistication, and fiction, all of which were associated with female sensibility.

Because the Chinese and Japanese languages belong to radically different language families, adopting Chinese characters to write Japanese required complex adjustments. Chinese is a noninflected language, with a "subject–predicate–object" word order; and literary Chinese is largely monosyllabic, meaning that most words consist of one or at most two syllables. Japanese, in contrast, is agglutinative, meaning that it strings short semantic elements together into long, complex words. It has highly inflected verbs and adjectives, which can carry a number of suffixes; these qualify such things as the mood, probability, or duration of an action or the social status of an agent. Moreover, Japanese has a "subject–object–predicate" word order and is polysyllabic—indeed, one word can sometimes fill an entire line of poetry. Chinese-style writing was written according to the Chinese word order and used the Chinese characters "logographically" for their meaning, each character representing a word. When Chinese-style writing was read out loud, the Japanese reader would perform a translation of sorts, adjusting the Chinese-style phrase to Japanese word order and adding inflections as needed. In contrast, vernacular Japanese writing mixed characters used for meaning with characters used "phonographically," for their sound value only. These characters functioned basically like a syllabic alphabet. As a result, in phonographic writing one word could require many Chinese characters.

Despite this complexity, Japan was not a bilingual culture; very few people learned spoken Chinese in addition to their native tongue. Japanese readers voiced Chinese texts in Japanese pronunciation. Their East Asian neighbors would be able to read the same text but would pronounce it in their languages and dialects. This led to a fascinating communicative paradox that can occur only in cultures with nonalphabetic writing systems. The Japanese ambassadors who visited China in order to present tribute gifts and bring home the newest law codes, Buddhist texts, musical instruments, and poetry collections could usually not ask for directions or the simplest things. Yet they could write sophisticated Chinese-style poetry for their Chinese hosts and communicate through so-called "brush talk": conversations through written messages in the shared Chinese script.

HEIAN COURT CULTURE (794–1185)

As the result of struggles between the imperial court and the Buddhist clergy, the court moved from Nara to a new capital in 794: Heian-kyō ("the Capital of Peace"), modern-day Kyoto. Despite centuries of warrior rule and occasional civil wars, Kyoto would remain the seat of the imperial court until 1868. The four centuries of the Heian Period, when Kyoto was the sole political and cultural center of Japan, became in retrospect a golden age, viewed by subsequent ages as the pinnacle of culture. The literature produced by Kyoto's court aristocracy defined all later standards of taste and embodied a refinement of sensibilities that had timeless appeal.

Heian literature was mostly produced by and for the capital elite. There are descriptions of travel in the provinces, but Heian aristocrats found the countryside at best rustic and charming, at worst

The Tōdaiji Temple complex in Nara, Japan, was built in the eighth century and has been frequently repaired and reconstructed over the centuries. The building here, the "Great Buddha Hall," is today one of the largest wooden buildings in the world.

This detail from a twelfth-century illustrated hand scroll of Lady Murasaki's diary gives us a glimpse of the dress and domestic situation of women at the Heian court.

embarrassing and primitive. The capital was the center of all ambitions and hopes: aristocrats eagerly awaited the promotion ceremonies that could secure them a higher rank and better post in the extensive court bureaucracy. In their court diaries, written in Chinese-style, they meticulously recorded the daily court routine. These diaries show mostly the official side of Heian life. For a picture of Heian after nightfall, we need to look at vernacular tales and women's diaries. Here we learn that men often had several wives and carried on several romantic affairs at once. They visited their lovers in the women's homes, plying them with allusive poetry or the tasteful calligraphy of a "morning-after note," written on a paper of just the right shade and adorned with just the right twig or blossom in season.

We get a remarkable close-up of the everyday lives, pleasures, and anxieties of Heian aristocratic women from works such as **Murasaki Shikibu**'s *The Tale of Genji* and **Sei Shōnagon**'s *The Pillow Book*. Heian women were dressed in a dozen layers of clothing whose shades carefully matched the season and occasion. They were hidden from view, spending their days in the dimly lit interiors of their residences waiting for welcome distractions: the banter of servants, an occasional outside caller with whom to exchange the latest gossip (if it was a man, the lady hid behind a screen as they talked), a love letter, or, even better, festivals or pilgrimages to nearby temples that broke the daily routine. Aristocratic women usually received a thorough education in *waka* poetry (classical Japanese verse composed in the set pattern of 5-7-5-7-7 syllables). They were also trained in music, dance, and often even the Chinese Classics, although Chinese scholarship was traditionally a male domain. Heian elite women had ample time to read and write and developed a subtle sense of propriety and distinction in social relations, clothing decorum, the delicate psychology of romantic affairs, and poetry exchanges.

By the tenth century, *waka* poetry was enshrined as the canonical court

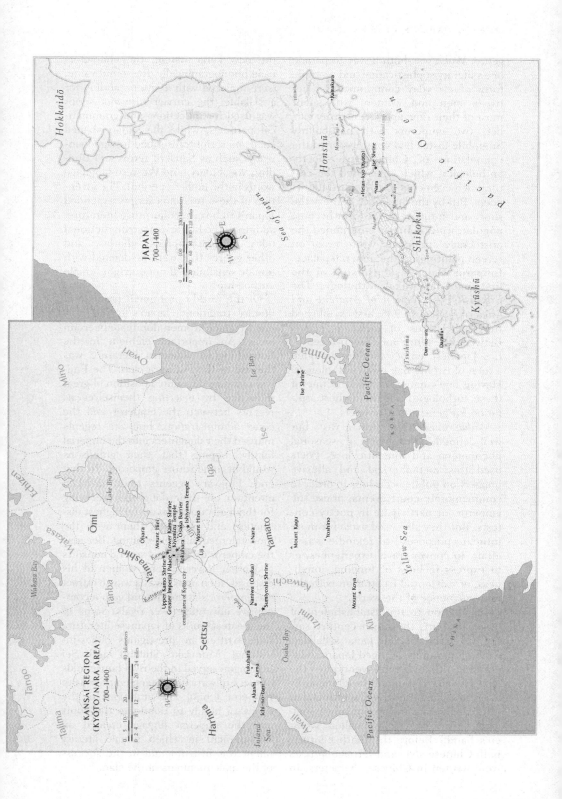

JAPAN
700–1400

0 50 100 200 kilometers
0 20 40 60 80 100 120 miles

Hokkaidō

Honshū

Sea of Japan

Kamakura

Mount Fuji

Suruga

Hitachi

Heian-kyō (Kyōto)

Nara

Ōmi

Yamato

Ise Shrine

Ise

area of detail map

Mount Kōya

Shikoku

Tosa

Iyo

Kyūshū

Dazaifu

Dan-no-ura

Tsushima

KOREA

Inland Sea

Pacific Ocean

KANSAI REGION
(KYŌTO/NARA AREA)
700–1400

0 5 10   20   40 kilometers
0 2 4 8   12 16 20   24 miles

Tango

Tajima

Tamba

Wakasa Bay

Wakasa

Echizen

Ōmi

Lake Biwa

Mino

Owari

Ōhara

Mount Hiei

Yamashiro

Upper Kamo Shrine
Lower Kamo Shrine
Greater Imperial Palace
central area of Kyōto city
Katsura
Kamo
Ōsaka Barrier
Kiyomizu Temple
Kōkuhara
Uji
Ishiyama Temple
Mount Hino

Iga

Ise

Ise Bay

Ise Shrine

Shima

Pacific Ocean

Settsu

Yodo

Naniwa (Ōsaka)
Sumiyoshi Shrine

Kawachi

Izumi

Kii

Nara

Mount Kagu

Yoshino

Mount Kōya

Yamato

Harima

Awaji

Inland Sea

Ichi-no-tani
Akashi
Sumi
Fukuhara

Ōsaka Bay

Pacific Ocean

genre. *Waka* was both a way to parade one's literary sophistication and a simple form of everyday communication between men and women, who spent most of their time apart. A century earlier, two emperors with particularly Sinophile tastes had commissioned the compilation of Chinese-style poetry anthologies, which celebrated the cultural achievements of the court and its poets. But by the late ninth century the short and intimate *waka* form became popular: *waka* contests entertained the aristocracy and poets wrote *waka* on screen paintings in the imperial palace. Emperor Daigo's sponsorship of the first imperial *waka* anthology, *The Kokinshū (Collection of Ancient and Modern Poems)*, in 905, first established the high status of *waka* at court. Between the tenth and fifteenth centuries Japanese emperors commissioned a total of twenty-one *waka* anthologies. Having one's name included in one of these anthologies was the highest aspiration for generations of poets.

Waka relied heavily on a vast, but well-defined, vocabulary of seasonal phenomena and romantic love. Poets used this metaphorical and allusive imagery on public occasions in order to commemorate court events, praise the emperor, or participate in poetry contests. But they also used *waka* for more intimate purposes—to rekindle a love affair, to convey travel experiences, or to express feelings of longing, loneliness, or existential frustration with the impermanence of the world.

In addition to the establishment of *waka* at court, the ninth century saw the invention of the kana syllabary, which profoundly changed Japanese literature. Although the invention of the kana syllabary did not fundamentally alter how Japanese wrote, it introduced a script that became specifically associated with women: it was called "women's hand." Before the tenth century, both Chinese-style and vernacular texts were written in Chinese characters. In the new kana system, the characters used phonographically, for sound value, were replaced with a letter standing for a syllable: the curvier *hiragana* script was used for inflections and grammatical particles, while the square-shaped *katakana* script transcribed foreign loanwords such as Sanskrit terms and Buddhist vocabulary (and Western-language words in the modern period). The invention of these two kana scripts expanded Japan's rich vernacular prose literature, adding to the literary spectrum fictional tales, autobiographical diaries, and other genres that were associated with female sensibility, if not outright female authorship.

Of the world's prominent premodern literary traditions, Japan's is the only one in which women dominated certain areas. An important element in the flourishing of women's literature was the rise of the Fujiwara clan. The Fujiwara managed to gain a position of great influence by inserting themselves as regents between the emperor and the court administration. Fujiwara regents married their daughters into the imperial family, hoping that their grandsons would become future emperors. To that end, Fujiwara regents often lavished attention on their daughters, securing for them an education of the highest distinction and providing them with the most talented ladies-in-waiting. Because the emperor usually had several consorts and other lower-ranking women at his disposal, such polish was a way to attract the emperor's attention and gain a competitive advantage over rivals. Some of the greatest works of Japanese literature were written by prestigious ladies-in-waiting: Murasaki Shikibu and Sei Shōnagon served in the rival households of two Fujiwara daughters, empresses to Emperor Ichijō. The ambitions of the Fujiwara family to dominate the court and the imperial lineage created an environment in which female literary talent was instrumental in the success of the male members of the clan.

SEI SHŌNAGON

ca. 966–1017

The gifted coterie of women writers who served as ladies-in-waiting to the Japanese imperial consorts of the late tenth and early eleventh centuries produced a number of superlative literary works that today stand at the center of the canon of Japanese literature. Next to **Murasaki Shikibu's** *The Tale of Genji* is *The Pillow Book* by Sei Shōnagon, who earned no kind words from Shikibu. In her diary she grumbled that Shōnagon was "dreadfully conceited" and "thought herself so clever, littering her writings with Chinese characters, but if one examined them closely, they left much to be desired." Shikibu was annoyed by Shōnagon's pretensions to break into the domain of Chinese learning, reserved at the time for male aristocrats. As ladies-in-waiting to two imperial consorts who maintained competing literary salons, Shikibu and Shōnagon were themselves engaged in an intense rivalry that spurred them to produce works to which later generations would look up with nostalgic awe. In design, form, and purpose, the two books are polar opposites. *The Tale of Genji* is an extensive, intricate, patient work of fiction. *The Pillow Book* is a slender catchall of personal observation, impressionistic and highly opinionated. Shōnagon has a sharp tongue, a keen eye, and a brush that moves masterfully between capturing lyrical moods and making pithy points. That she is both a supreme embodiment and a critical arbiter of Heian courtly tastes gives *The Pillow Book* a delightful depth.

SEI SHŌNAGON AND THE HEIAN COURT

Sei Shōnagon, whose actual name was probably Kiyohara Nagiko, was the daughter of a provincial governor noted for his poetry (in Heian Japan names were context-dependent, and a gentlewoman was usually named after the court title of a male relative). Although Shōnagon's father was a middle-ranking courtier with an appointment in the provinces, she seems to have spent all her life in the capital, the seat of the imperial court. Between 993 and 1000 she served Empress Teishi (977–1000), one of the consorts of Emperor Ichijō (980–1011). What we know about Shōnagon's life is mostly contained in *The Pillow Book*, which does not mention a husband or children, but other sources of the period suggest that she was briefly married to an undistinguished man named Tachibana no Norimitsu and had at least one child. In *The Pillow Book* Sei Shōnagon repeatedly mocks Norimitsu as a hopeless boor who lacks poetic sensibility, and the marriage apparently did not last long.

Shōnagon lived during the middle of the Heian Period, which was named after its capital, Heian-kyō, the "Capital of Peace and Tranquility" (present-day Kyoto). The Heian court, centered on the symbolic figure of the emperor, followed a complex aristocratic system. The large bureaucratic apparatus of ministries and offices reflected a strict hierarchy based on rank as well as an educational system whose focus was the study of the Chinese Classics. Although aristocratic women like Shōnagon received an excellent training in Chinese literature, they produced literature written only in vernacular Japanese; Chinese-style genres, which stood at the top of the literary hierarchy, were largely the domain of male aristocrats. Shōnagon particularly relished the moments when she succeeded in using her Chinese learning to outdo a man, even if she was bound to use vernacular Japanese and the vernacular *kana* script (called "woman's hand") in her sophisticated responses to his letters.

In the Heian court, where men and women were strictly segregated, letters exchanged between lovers, relatives, or friends played a crucial role in social relations. Although they spent their days participating in an extensive array of court ceremonies, receiving visitors and engaging in witty conversation, the women were generally hidden away, secured in their residences in spaces behind paper doors and screens through which they would usually speak with their visitors unseen. Writing provided an outlet, enabling them both to dispel their boredom and to express private sentiments that transcended or critiqued the swirl of rumors, whispers, and intrigue that defined their lives.

Aristocratic men enjoyed considerably more freedom. Men usually lived in or near the living quarters of their wives' parents, but they often pursued romantic interests elsewhere; they took several wives and installed them in separate residences, visited at their whim. Marriage arrangements were loose. Marriages could be established by a man's frequent visits; a cessation in visiting was equivalent to a divorce. If his visits became increasingly sporadic as he was drawn to romantic adventures elsewhere, the woman was left waiting and worrying about the future of their relationship.

Daughters were crucial pawns in the marriage politics of the Heian imperial court. Beginning in the latter half of the tenth century, the northern branch of the powerful Fujiwara clan controlled the imperial succession through the so-called regent system. It became customary for a Fujiwara regent to rule on behalf of a child emperor and to marry his daughters into the imperial family. Thus, the Fujiwara regents became uncles and grandfathers of future emperors and were often more powerful than those emperors. Shōnagon lived during one of the most successful regencies of the Heian Period, that of Fujiwara no Michinaga (966–1027). Michinaga had his eldest daughter Shōshi appointed consort of Emperor Ichijō, to whom she bore two later emperors. While Murasaki Shikibu served in Shōshi's lively entourage, which featured several other prominent women writers, Shōnagon was lady-in-waiting to Shōshi's cousin, Teishi. Teishi was the daughter of Fujiwara no Michitaka, an elder brother and rival of Michinaga, who became regent in 990. After Michitaka unexpectedly died in an epidemic in 995 and, in the following year, Teishi's brother Korechika was sent into exile on the urging of their increasingly powerful uncle, Teishi lost her footing at court. Michinaga's daughter Sōshi advanced to the position of highest consort, and Teishi had to leave the palace. Although Shōnagon continued to serve Teishi until the young empress died in childbirth in 1000, these last few years must have been painful and humiliating, in stark contrast to the earlier, happier times at court that *The Pillow Book* evokes so vividly.

THE PILLOW BOOK AND HEIAN LITERATURE

The Pillow Book chronicles with wit and humor the moments of glamour and ennui, the obsessions and trivia, of Heian court life. It centers on questions of aristocratic taste, the paramount importance of learning and education, and the pleasures of experiencing the world through the refined languages of literature, art, and music. Over the course of *The Pillow Book*, as Shōnagon expounds on why some kinds of carriages should move faster than others, why priests should be handsome, or how a lover should make his good-byes, she emerges as an impatient and imperious figure. She is every inch the aristocrat, whose fastidious standards brook no slipshod behavior. So deft is she at homing in on human foibles and skewering the offender that the effect of her sharp sallies can be shattering. We chuckle at her delicious wit, but we are glad we are not the objects of her scrutiny. *The Pillow Book* is written in a compact and forceful style, which favors brevity and compression and produces surprising effects by means of unusual juxtapositions. Shōnagon's literary persona favors witty repartee, sly self-promotion, and occasional cutting insults. Her candor in admitting her hypercritical nature, and her display of ruthless honesty toward others and herself, gives her an irrepressible, magnetic voice. She is a presence.

The exact date of composition and the title of *The Pillow Book* have been subjects of much debate. It was probably finished around 1005, after Empress Teishi's death. Writing *The Pillow Book* in memory of her late patroness, Shōnagon focused exclusively on those happy years when Teishi's standing at court was at its height. That she was painfully aware, as she was composing the book, of the tragic fall that lay in store for Teishi and herself makes the work all the more poignant.

In the last section of our selections Shōnagon wants us to know that even the paper on which she wrote her original *Pillow Book* came from that happy period, before Teishi lost her place at court. Paper was a rare commodity and Teishi's brother Korechika, before his ignominious exile, had brought the empress a stack from the supply being used in the palace for copying the *Historical Records* by the Chinese historian Sima Qian. We can be sure that this connection to China's canonical history—written eleven centuries earlier—certainly pleased her. Just as Sima Qian had chronicled the history of China up until his own time, the Han Dynasty, so Shōnagon understood herself as a chronicler of Heian court life.

Even more contested than *The Pillow Book*'s date and title is its original format. The more than three hundred separate sections can be grouped into three basic types: diary-style entries describing datable events at court, catalogues of objects or attributes, and essayistic jottings on general topics. This mélange is unusual. Some moments in *The Pillow Book* exhibit the intimacy of a typical Heian women's diary, others evoke scenes that look as if they were taken from a Heian romantic tale such as *The Tale of Genji*, and yet other parts resemble the philosophical musings of the later essay genre (such as Yoshida Kenkō's famous *Essays in Idleness*). That *The Pillow Book* contains such variety in one book, sometimes even a single section, makes it unique. It is also a uniquely jumbled text: the earliest surviving copy of *The Pillow Book* dates to several hundred years after Shōnagon's time, and the text has come down to the present in four manuscript lineages that differ both in content and in the arrangement of individual sections. Two versions group the entries by type, while the version now considered more authentic and canonical (represented in the selection here) freely mixes the diary entries, catalogues, and essayistic sections.

Shōnagon's brush follows the rhythms of Heian court life with its cycle of annual festivals—occasions for sumptuous display for men and women alike—and its keen awareness of questions of rank and propriety. Section 2, "Times of Year," takes us through some of the annual highlights. In section 6, "The Emperor's Cat," a cat receives court rank and the poor dog Okinamaro receives a beating, is expelled, and returns in humiliation. This story is often read as an allegory for Kore-chika's exile, throwing a critical light on the cruel workings of court politics and intrigue. The story in section 20 about an imperial consort who knew the entire *Kokinshū* (*Collection of Ancient and Modern Poems*) by heart shows the pleasures and pressures of court life: the ability to recite a famous poem, to render it in beguiling callig-raphy, or to adapt it to a new occa-sion when poetry composition was a key aspect of living at court and to maintaining one's reputation. Shōnagon enjoys reporting the occasions when she succeeded in coming up with a witty solution to an unexpected chal-lenge, though she often emphasized how badly things could have turned out without the stroke of her genius at the right moment. There can be no doubt that Shōnagon liked to emerge triumphant: in section 82, her over-confident claim that a snow mountain they had built in the garden of the pal-ace would survive for an impossibly long time forces her to take hilarious measures in seeking to win her dispute with the Empress.

To receive favorable judgment and to pass astute judgment were highly desir-able in the Heian court. Therefore, the vocabulary of judgment and taste is particularly central to *The Pillow Book*. The most important term is *okashi*, which can mean anything from "de-lightful," "intriguing," or "charming" to "engaging" or just "interesting" and occurs more than four hundred times in *The Pillow Book*. The word is so per-vasive that the translator of our selec-tions renders it nearly thirty different ways. In the book's famous opening section alone—"In spring, the dawn— when the slowly paling mountain rim is tinged with red, and wisps of faintly crimson-purple cloud float in the sky"—it appears three times. Shōna-gon's frequent outcries of *okashi* are

much more than an indulgence in superficial pleasure or beauty. There is a delicacy in *The Pillow Book* that helps us see, hear, and feel the world around us with superior nuance. Whether rep-resenting changes in robes to match the cherry blossom season, a cuckoo's cry so faint that the hearer wonders whether it is actually heard or only imagined, or the thoughts piqued by various insects, the details in *The Pil-low Book* capture the sensuous variety of life. *The Pillow Book* seems to prescribe a restrained cultivation of feeling—a responsiveness to the emo-tional environment—along with physi-cal grace and a genuine appreciation of shape, proportion, color, and tone: an appreciation that includes the power to make subtle distinctions.

This cultivated aestheticism isn't always focused on things that are beauti-ful. In a world that values the matching of tastes, Shōnagon is quick to pinpoint moments when they clash. Ugly and repellent details—fleas dancing under ladies' skirts, houseflies alighting with their "damp little feet," silver tweezers that can pull out unsightly hair, or a slovenly looking woman making out in broad daylight with a "scrawny man with hair sprouting from his face"—also make occasional appearances in *The Pil-low Book*. These mismatches appear not just in the list of "dispiriting" and "dis-tressing things," or in "things that can-not be compared," but also in the diary section: Shōnagon's tale about the argu-ment over the snow mountain is sugges-tively intertwined with the story of a bawdy begging nun who occasionally intrudes and scandalizes the company. In the midst of her sublime expressions of courtly taste and beauty, Shōnagon is also attracted to the grotesque, even as she castigates it.

Unlike other Heian classics such as *The Kokinshū*, *The Tales of Ise*, and *The Tale of Genji*, *The Pillow Book* did not become a canonical text in the medieval period. Its relative neglect is attributable in part to its containing far less poetry—the main focus of those studying these texts—than the other three works. In the early modern period it became the subject of parodies. *The Mongrel Pillow Book* of 1606 apes *The Pillow Book*'s aesthetics of lists: "Things that have ones hair stand on end . . . Putting on armor in winter without underclothes . . . Malaria. The pros-pect of an evening spent in conversation with one's boy favorite."

Shōnagon continues to fascinate readers, and its large number of translations and adaptations have made *The Pillow Book* into a favored work of world literature. Today Shōnagon's strong female voice inspires in her readers a kind of empathy with the world of an eleventh-century Japanese gentlewoman that she herself could never have dreamed of.

From The Pillow Book[1]

1 *In spring, the dawn*—when the slowly paling mountain rim is tinged with red, and wisps of faintly crimson-purple cloud float in the sky.

In summer, the night—moonlit nights, of course, but also at the dark of the moon, it's beautiful when fireflies are dancing everywhere in a mazy flight. And it's delightful too to see just one or two fly through the darkness, glowing softly. Rain falling on a summer night is also lovely.

In autumn, the evening—the blazing sun has sunk very close to the mountain rim, and now even the crows, in threes and fours or twos and threes, hurrying to their roost, are a moving sight. Still more enchanting is the sight of a string of wild geese in the distant sky, very tiny. And oh how inexpressible, when the sun has sunk, to hear in the growing darkness the wind, and the song of autumn insects.

In winter, the early morning—if snow is falling, of course, it's unutterably delightful, but it's perfect too if there's a pure white frost, or even just when it's very cold, and they hasten to build up the fires in the braziers and carry in fresh charcoal. But it's unpleasant, as the day draws on and the air grows warmer, how the brazier fire dies down to white ash.

2 *Times of year*—The first month; the third, fourth and fifth months; the seventh, eighth and ninth; the eleventh and twelfth—in fact every month according to its season, the year round, is delightful.

On the first day of the year, the sky is gloriously fresh and spring mists hang in the air. It's quite special and delightful the way people everywhere have taken particular care over their clothing and makeup, and go about exchanging New Year felicitations.

On the seventh day, people pluck the new shoots of herbs that have sprung up in the patches of bare earth amidst the snow[2]—they're wonderfully green and fresh, and it's charming just what a fuss is made over these herbs, which

1. Translated by and with notes adapted from Meredith McKinney.
2. In this passage Shōnagon describes some of the court festivals of the first four months of the year. The seventh day of the First Month is the Festival of Young Herbs, when various herbs are made into a gruel that is supposed to ward off evil spirits and to protect one's health throughout the year.

normally aren't to be seen at such close quarters. Those of good family who live outside the palace brighten up their carriages and set off to see the Parading of the Blue Roans. It's fun how, when the carriages are pulled over the big ground beam of the central palace gate, all the ladies' heads are jolted together so that your hair combs tumble out and can easily break if you aren't careful, and everybody laughs. I remember seeing a large group of senior courtiers and others standing about near the Left Gate Watch guardhouse, gaily snatching the attendants' bows and twanging them to startle the horses—also, peeping through the carriage blinds and delightedly glimpsing groundswomen and other serving ladies coming and going near one of the lattice fences further in. Witnessing such a scene, of course you sigh and wonder just what sort of people they must be, to manage to be so at ease in the 'nine-fold palace.' But when I actually saw them at such close quarters at the palace, the attendants' faces were all dark and blotchy where their white powder hadn't covered the skin properly, precisely like black patches of earth showing through where snow has half melted—a truly horrible sight. The horses' rearing and lunging was quite terrifying, so I retreated to the depths of the carriage, where I could no longer really see.

On the eighth day, there's a special thrill in the noise of all the carriages hurtling about as everyone who's received a promotion does the rounds to exchange felicitations.

On the fifteenth day, the day of the full moon, a delightful scene always takes place in the houses of the nobility after the festival food is served. Both the senior and junior gentlewomen of the house go about looking for a chance to strike each other with gruel sticks,[3] constantly glancing behind them to make sure they aren't hit themselves. It's marvellous fun when someone manages somehow to get in a strike, and everyone bursts into delighted peals of laughter—though you can certainly see why the poor victim herself feels upset.

A young man has recently begun to call on his new wife.[4] Now it's time for him to set off for the palace, and lurking in the background peeping out is one of her gentlewomen, gleefully self-important and struggling to contain herself till he leaves. The gentlewomen who are sitting gathered around the girl all smile, realizing perfectly well what's going on, but she secretly motions them to stay quiet. Meanwhile, the girl sits there innocently, seeming to have noticed nothing. Then up comes the gentlewoman, with some excuse such as 'I'll just pick this up,' darts over and strikes her and runs off, while everyone collapses in laughter. The young man doesn't take it amiss but smiles amiably, and as for the girl, it's quite charming to see that though she doesn't seem particularly surprised, she is nevertheless blushing slightly.

The gentlewomen strike each other too, and I gather men even get struck sometimes. It's also amusing to witness someone for some reason lose her temper and burst into tears, and roundly abuse whoever has struck her. Even the more exalted people in the palace join in the day's fun.

There's a charming scene in the palace at the time of the Spring Appointments List.[5] It's snowing and everything's icy, and men of the fourth and fifth ranks are walking about holding their letters requesting promotion. The youthful, high-spirited ones inspire you with confidence in them, but there are also old white-haired fellows who go around confiding in people, in hopes that this will improve their chances. They approach some gentlewoman and obliviously set about singing their own praises to her, and they can have no idea that some of the younger gentlewomen are busy imitating them and laughing behind their back. 'Do please mention me favourably to the Emperor or Empress,' they implore us—and it's a fine thing if they actually gain the post they want, but really most pathetic when they fail.

The third day of the third month is full of the soft sunshine of spring. Now is the time when the peach trees begin to bloom, and of course the willows too are particularly lovely at this time. It's charming to see the buds still cocooned in their sheaths like silkworms—but on the other hand, once the leaves have opened they're rather unpleasant.

If you break off a branch of splendidly flowering cherry and arrange it in a large flower vase, the effect is delightful. And it's particularly charming if a gentleman, be it one of Her Majesty's brothers or a normal guest, is seated nearby engaged in conversation, wearing a cloak in the cherry-blossom combination with undersleeves displayed.

And how delightful it all is at the time of the Festival in the fourth month![6] The court nobles and senior courtiers in the festival procession are only distinguishable by the different degrees of colour of their formal cloaks, and the robes beneath are all of a uniform white, which produces a lovely effect of coolness. The leaves of the trees have not yet reached their full summer abundance but are still a fresh young green, and the sky's clarity, untouched by either the mists of spring or autumn's fogs, fills you with inexplicable pleasure. And when it clouds a little in the evening or at night, how unbearably lovely then to hear from far in the distance the muted call of a *hototogisu*,[7] sounding so faint you almost doubt your ears.

It's delightful, as the day of the Festival approaches, to see the attendants going to and fro carrying tight rolls of dark leaf-green or lavender fabric,[8] wrapped lightly in just a touch of paper. Patterning effects such as graded dye and dapple dye strike you as unusually beautiful at this time.

The little girls who will be in the procession are also enchanting. They've already washed their hair and done it nicely, but they may still be wearing their everyday threadbare and rumpled clothes, and they trot around full of excited anticipation, crying 'Rethread my high clogs for me!' or 'Sew up the soles of my shoes!' But for all their boisterous posturing and prancing, once they're dressed up in their festival finery they suddenly begin parading about with great solemnity, like self-important priests at the head of some dignified procession, no doubt starting to feel thoroughly nervous. It's also touching to see, in the festival procession, a parent or aunt or perhaps an older sister accompanying the little girls and carefully tending their clothing as they walk.

When you see a man who's set his heart on becoming Chamberlain, but who's in no position to achieve his goal just yet, dressed specially in the Chamberlain's

---

6. The Kamo Festival, still one of the most important festivals of Kyoto; it includes a large procession through the city from and back to the Kamo Shrines.

7. A kind of cuckoo whose call is much praised by Japanese poets.
8. Used to make up the robes worn at the festival.

green formal cloak[9] for the day of the Festival, you wish for his sake he didn't have to take it off again. It's a pity that it isn't damask like the real one, however.

* * *

4 *It breaks my heart to think* of parents sending a beloved son into the priesthood. Poor priests, they're not the unfeeling lumps of wood that people take them for. They're despised for eating that dreadful monastic food, and their sleeping arrangements are no better. A young priest must naturally be full of curiosity, and how could he resist the forbidden urge to peep into a room, especially if there's a woman in there? But this is criticized as disgraceful too.

Exorcist priests have an even harder life.[1] If they ever nod off, exhausted from their long labours, people complain that they do nothing but sleep. How constrained and miserable this must make them feel!

Well, this is how things used to be, anyway. These days, in fact, priests lead a much easier life.

* * *

6 *The Emperor's cat* had received the fifth rank, and was given the appropriate title-name 'Myōbu.' It was a charming creature, and the Emperor was quite devoted to it.

One day its carer, Muma no Myōbu,[2] found it lying basking on the veranda. 'How vulgar!' she scolded. 'Back you come inside.' But the cat continued to lie there asleep in the sun, so she decided to give it a fright. 'Okinamaro!' she cried to the dog. 'Here, boy! Come and get Myōbu!' The foolish dog couldn't believe its ears, and came rushing over, whereupon the terrified cat fled inside through the blind.

The Emperor was at that time in the Breakfast Room, and he witnessed this event with astonishment. He tucked the cat into the bosom of his robe, and summoned his men. When the Chamberlains Tadataka and Narinaka appeared, the Emperor ordered them, 'Give Okinamaro a thorough beating and banish him to Dog Island! Be quick about it!'

Everyone gathered and a noisy hunt ensued. The Emperor went on to chastise Muma no Myōbu, declaring that he would replace her as Myōbu's carer as she was completely untrustworthy, and thenceforth she no longer appeared in his presence. Meanwhile, they rounded up the dog, and had the guards drive it out.

We all pitied the poor thing. 'Oh dear,' we said, 'and to think how he used to swagger about the place as if he owned it.'

'Remember how on the third of the third month the Secretary Controller decked him out with a garland of willow and a peach-flower comb, and tied a branch of cherry blossom on his back? Who'd have guessed then that he'd meet with such a fate?'

'And the way he always attended Her Majesty at meal times. How we'll miss him!'

Then around noon three or four days later, we heard a dog howling dreadfully. What dog could be howling on and on like this? we wondered, and as we

9. Usually only the Chamberlain could wear the color green, which was permitted to members of his office of lesser rank on this occasion.
1. Exorcizing a tenacious possession required that incantations and spells be performed for

many hours.
2. A title for a gentlewoman of fifth rank. It was also applied to cats, and only cats of fourth and fifth rank were permitted in the emperor's palace.

listened dogs gathered from everywhere to see what was afoot. One of the cleaning women came running in. 'Oh, it's dreadful! Two of the Chamberlains are beating the dog! It's bound to die! His Majesty banished it, but apparently it came back, so they're teaching it a lesson.'

Alas, poor creature! It was Okinamaro. 'It's Tadataka and Sanefusa doing it,' someone said.

We sent someone to stop them, but at that point the dog finally ceased its howling. 'It's dead,' came the report, 'so they've thrown it outside the guardhouse.'

That evening as we were sorrowing over poor Okinamaro, up staggered a miserable trembling creature, terribly swollen and looking quite wretched. Can it be Okinamaro? we wondered. What other dog could be wandering around at this hour in such a state?

We called his name, but he didn't respond. 'It's him,' some of us declared, while others maintained that it wasn't, till Her Majesty said, 'Send for Ukon. She would recognize him.' We duly did so, and when she came Her Majesty showed her the dog and asked if it was indeed Okinamaro.

'There's certainly a likeness,' replied Ukon, 'but this dog looks simply revolting. And you only have to say his name and Okinamaro bounds happily up, but this dog doesn't respond at all. It must be a different dog. And they did say they'd killed him and thrown out the corpse, didn't they? How could he have survived after two men had beaten him like that?' This moved Her Majesty to fresh sorrow.

It grew dark. We gave the dog some food, but it didn't eat it, so we decided that it was indeed a different dog and left it at that.

The next morning, Her Majesty had performed her ablutions and had her hair combed, and I was holding the mirror for her to check that all was in order when I spied the dog, still there, crouching at the foot of a pillar. Seeing it I said aloud to myself, 'Oh poor Okinamaro, what a terrible beating he got yesterday! It's so sad to think he must be dead. I wonder what he'll be reborn as next time. How dreadful he must have felt!'

At this the dog began to tremble, and tears simply poured from its eyes. How extraordinary! I realized it was indeed Okinamaro! It was pitiful to recall how he'd avoided revealing himself the night before, but at the same time the whole thing struck me as quite marvellous. I set down the mirror and said, 'So you're Okinamaro, are you?' and he threw himself on the ground, whimpering and weeping.

Her Majesty laughed with relief, and sent for Ukon and told her the story. There was a great deal of laughter over it all, and the Emperor heard and came in to see what was happening. He laughed too, and observed, 'Isn't it odd to think a dog would have such fine feelings.' His gentlewomen also heard of it and gathered round, and this time when we called the dog he got up and came.

'His poor face is all swollen!' I cried. 'I do wish I could do something for it.'

'Now you're wearing your heart on your sleeve,' everyone teased me.

Tadataka heard from the Table Room, and sent saying, 'Is it really him? I must come and have a look.'

'Oh dear no, how awful!' I declared. 'Tell him it's not Okinamaro at all!'

'He's bound to be found out sooner or later,' came Tadataka's reply. 'You can't go on hiding him forever.'

Well, in due course Okinamaro was pardoned, and everything returned to normal. Now has there ever been such a delightful and moving moment as when Okinamaro began to tremble and weep at those pitying words of mine? Humans may cry when someone speaks to them sympathetically—but a dog?

* * *

20   *The sliding panels that close off the north-east corner* of the Seiryōden, at the northern end of the aisle, are painted with scenes of rough seas, and terrifying creatures with long arms and legs.[3] We have a fine time complaining about how we hate coming face to face with them whenever we open the door from the Empress's room.

On this particular day, a large green porcelain vase had been placed at the foot of the nearby veranda railing, with a mass of absolutely gorgeous branches of flowering cherry, five feet long or more, arranged in it with the flowers spilling out over the railing. His Excellency Korechika,[4] the Grand Counsellor, arrived around noon. He was wearing a rather soft and supple cloak in the cherry-blossom combination, over deep violet gathered trousers of heavy brocade and white under-robes, and he had arranged the sleeves of his wonderfully glowing deep scarlet-purple damask cloak for display. The Emperor was present, so His Excellency placed himself on the narrow veranda outside the door to converse.

Inside the blinds, we gentlewomen sat with our cherry-blossom combination Chinese jackets worn draped loosely back from the shoulders. Our robes were a fine blend of wisteria and kerria-yellow and other seasonal combinations, the sleeves all spilling out on display below the blinds that hung from the little half-panel shutters.

Suddenly, from the direction of the Imperial Day Chamber came the loud pounding of the attendants' feet as they arrived to deliver His Majesty's meal. The sound of the cry 'Make way!' reverberating through the scene of this gloriously serene spring day was utterly delightful. Then the Chamberlain arrived to report that he had delivered the last tray and the meal was in place, and His Majesty departed by the central door.

Korechika saw His Majesty on his way along the corridor, then returned to seat himself by the vase of blossoms once more. Her Majesty now moved aside her standing curtain and came out to the edge of the threshold near him to talk, and all those present were simply overcome with the sheer splendour of the scene. At this point Korechika languidly intoned the lines from the old poem:

'The months and years may pass,
but let this remain unchanging
as Mount Mimoro . . .'[5]

—and most enchanting it was, for seeing her splendour we did indeed long for Her Majesty to continue just like this for a thousand years.

No sooner had those in charge of serving the Emperor's meal called the men to remove the trays than His Majesty returned.

3. The frightening scenes from Chinese legends painted on the panels in the emperor's private residence, the Seiryōden, served as a protective device, required because the northeast was considered unlucky in geomancy.
4. The brother of Empress Teishi, whom Shōnagon served.
5. Part of a poem from *The Manyōshū*. Mount Mimoro, the site of an ancient Shinto shrine associated with the imperial line, figures here as an auspicious image of continuity.

Her Majesty now turned to me and asked me to grind some ink, but I was so agog at the scene before me that I could barely manage to keep the inkstick steady in its holder. Then Her Majesty proceeded to fold a piece of white paper, and said to us, 'Now I want each of you to write here the first ancient poem that springs to mind.'

I turned for help to the Grand Counsellor, who was sitting just outside. 'What on earth can I write?' I begged him, but he only pushed the paper back to me, saying, 'Quick, write something down yourself for Her Majesty. It's not a man's place to give advice here.'

Her Majesty provided us with the inkstone. 'Come on, come on,' she scolded, 'don't waste time racking your brains. Just quickly jot down any ancient poem that comes to you on the spur of the moment. Even something hackneyed will do.' I've no idea why we should have felt so daunted by the task, but we all found ourselves blushing deeply, and our minds went quite blank. Despite their protestations, some of the senior gentlewomen managed to produce two or three poems on spring themes such as blossoms and so forth, and then my turn came. I wrote down the poem:

> With the passing years
> My years grow old upon me
> yet when I see
> this lovely flower of spring
> I forget age and time.[6]

but I changed 'flower of spring' to 'your face, my lady.'

Her Majesty ran her eye over the poems, remarking, 'I just wanted to discover what was in your hearts.'

'In the time of Retired Emperor Enyū,'[7] she went on, 'His Majesty ordered the senior courtiers each to write a poem in a bound notebook, but it proved fearfully difficult, and some of them begged to be excused from the task. The Emperor reassured them that it didn't matter whether their calligraphy was skilful or otherwise, nor whether the poem was appropriate to the occasion, and finally after a great deal of trouble they all managed to produce something. Our present Regent,[8] who was Captain Third Rank at the time, wrote the following poem:

> "As the tide that swells
> in Izumo's Always Bay
> so always and always
> oh how my heart swells and fills
> deep with love to think of you."

but he changed the last line to read "deep with trust in you, my lord," and His Majesty was full of praise for him.'

When I heard this, I felt a sudden sweat break out all over me. I do think, though, that that poem of mine isn't the sort of thing a young person could

---

6. Shōnagon cleverly adapts an old poem to the situation at hand. The original poem was written by an admiring father to his daughter; Shōnagon makes it into a compliment to the empress.

7. The father of the present emperor, Teishi's husband.
8. Michitaka, the father of Teishi and Kore-chika.

have come up with. Even people who can usually turn out a fine poem found themselves for some reason at a loss that day, and several made mistakes in their writing.

There was also the occasion when Her Majesty placed a bound book of *Kokin-shū* poems in front of her, and proceeded to read out the opening lines of various poems and ask us to complete them. Why on earth did we keep stumbling over the answers, even for poems we'd engraved on our memories day in and day out? Saisho only managed about ten. Others could produce only five or six, and really, you'd think they could simply have admitted that they couldn't recall them. But no, they kept agonizing over the task. 'But we can't be so rude as to refuse point-blank to answer,' they wailed, 'when Her Majesty has been so good as to put the question to us,' which I found rather amusing.

Her Majesty then read out the complete poem for each of those that nobody had been able to answer, marking them with a bookmark, and everyone groaned, 'Oh of course I knew that one! Why am I being so stupid today?' Some of us had copied out the *Kokinshū* many times, and should really have known it all by heart.

'As I'm sure you are all aware,' Her Majesty began, 'the lady known as the Senyōden Consort, High Consort in the reign of Emperor Murakami,[9] was the daughter of the Minister of the Left, of the Smaller Palace of the First Ward. When she was still a girl, her father gave her the following advice: "First, you must study calligraphy. Next, you must determine to outshine everyone in your skill on the seven-stringed *kin*.[1] And you must also make it your study to commit to memory all the poems in the twenty volumes of the *Kokinshū*."

'Now the Emperor had learned of this, so one day, when he was kept from his usual duties by an abstinence,[2] he took a copy of the *Kokinshū* to the High Consort's quarters, and set up a standing curtain between them. She found this unusual behaviour rather odd, and when he opened a book and began asking her to recite the poem that so-and-so had written on such-and-such a date and occasion, she was intrigued to realize what he was up to—though on the other hand, she would also have been dreadfully nervous that there might be some which she would forget or misquote. He called in two or three of his gentlewomen who were well-versed in poetry, and had them extract the answers from her, and keep count of her mistakes with *go* counters. It must have been a wonderful scene to witness. I do envy them all, even the people who were merely serving on this occasion.

'Well, he pressed her to go on answering, and she went through them making not a single mistake, though she cleverly gave just enough of each poem to show she knew it, and didn't try to complete them. His Majesty decided he would call a halt just as soon as she made a mistake, and as she went on and on he even began to get rather irritated, but they reached the tenth volume and still she hadn't made a single slip. "This has been quite futile," he finally declared, and he put a marker in the book and retired to another room to sleep. All very wonderful it was.

'When he awoke many hours later, he decided that it would never do to leave the matter hanging, and moreover it had better be done that day, since she might refresh her memory with another copy of the work if he left it till tomorrow.

9. That is, 946–61; this story serves as an example of how admirable people were "in the old days."

1. A zitherlike instrument of the koto family,

particularly difficult to play; by Shōnagon's time it was somewhat old-fashioned.

2. A period of forced seclusion, prescribed by divination, to avoid evil influences.

So he produced the remaining ten volumes, had the lamps lit and proceeded to work his way through the rest of the poems until long into the night. But she never made a single mistake.

'Meanwhile, word was sent to her father that the Emperor had returned to her quarters and that the test was continuing. The Minister flew into a panic with worry that she might fail the test; he ordered numerous sutras to be said for her,[3] while he placed himself facing the direction of the palace and spent the entire night in heartfelt prayer. Altogether a fascinating and moving story,' Her Majesty remarked in conclusion.

His Majesty too heard the tale with admiration. 'I wouldn't be able to manage more than three or four volumes myself,' he remarked.

'In the old days, even the most inconsequential people were impressive. You don't hear such stories these days, do you,' everyone agreed, and all the Empress's gentlewomen, and those who served the Emperor and were permitted to visit the Empress's quarters, gathered round and began talking. It was indeed a scene to fill the heart with ease and delight.

* * *

30 *A priest who gives a sermon should be handsome.* After all, you're most aware of the profundity of his teaching if you're gazing at his face as he speaks. If your eyes drift elsewhere you tend to forget what you've just heard, so an unattractive face has the effect of making you feel quite sinful. But I'll write no further on this subject. I may have written glibly enough about sinful matters of this sort in my younger days, but at my age the idea of sin has become quite frightening.

I must say, however, from my own sinful point of view, it seems quite uncalled-for to go around as some do, vaunting their religious piety and rushing to be the first to be seated wherever a sermon is being preached.

An ex-Chamberlain never used to take up the vanguard of imperial processions, and once he retired from the post you'd no longer see him about the palace. These days things are apparently different. The so-called 'Chamberlain fifth-ranker' is actually kept in reasonably busy service, but privately he must nevertheless miss the prestige of his former post and feel at a loss how to fill his days, so once he tries going to these places and hears a few sermons he'll no doubt develop a taste for it and start to go along on a regular basis.

You'll find him turning up there with his summer under-robe prominently displayed beneath his cloak even in baking summer weather, and the hems of his pale lavender or blue-grey gathered trousers loose and trodden. He has an abstinence tag[4] attached to his lacquered cap, and he no doubt intends to draw attention to the fact that although it's an abstinence day and he shouldn't leave the house, this doesn't apply to him since his outing is of a pious nature. He chats with the officiating priest, even goes so far as to help oversee the positioning of the ladies' carriages, and is generally completely at home in the situation. When some old crony of his whom he hasn't seen recently turns up, he's consumed with curiosity. Over he goes, and they settle down together and proceed to talk and nod and launch into interesting stories, spreading out their

---

3. That is, chanted by a priest to ensure her success.
4. A label attached to the hat to signify that

the wearer is under abstinence taboo (see p. 1218, n. 2).

fans and putting them to their mouths when they laugh, groping at their ornately decorated rosaries and fiddling with them as they talk, craning to look here and there, praising and criticizing the carriages, discussing how other priests did things this way or that in other Lotus Discourses[5] and sutra dedication services they've been to, and so on and so forth—and not listening to a word of the actual sermon they're attending. Indeed they would have heard it all so often before that they'd gain nothing from it anyway.

And then there's another type. The preacher has already seated himself when after a while up rolls a carriage, accompanied by only a couple of outriders. It draws to a halt, and the passengers step out—three or four slender young men, dressed perhaps in hunting costume or in cloaks more delicately gauzy than a cicada's wing, gathered trousers and gossamer silk shifts, and accompanied by a similar number of attendants. Those already seated move themselves along a little to make way for them when they enter. They seat themselves by a pillar near the preacher's dais and set about softly rubbing their rosaries as they listen to the sermon, and the preacher, who no doubt feels rather honoured to have them there, throws himself with fresh vigour into the task of putting his message across. The young men, however, far from casting themselves extravagantly to the floor as they listen, instead decide to leave after a decent amount of time has passed, and as they go they throw glances in the direction of the women's carriages and comment to each other, and you'd love to know what it was they were saying. It's funny how you find yourself watching them as they depart, interestedly identifying the ones you know, and speculating on the identity of those you don't.

Some people really take things to extremes, though. If someone mentions having been to a Lotus Discourse or other such event, another will say, 'And was so and so there?' and the reply is always, 'Of course. How could he not be?' Mind you, I'm not saying one should never show up at these places. After all, even women of low standing will apparently listen to sermons with great concentration. Actually, when I first started attending sermons, I never saw women going about here and there on foot to them. Occasionally you would find women in travelling attire, elegantly made up, but they were out as part of another excursion to some temple or shrine. You didn't often hear of women attending sermons and the like in this costume, though. If the ladies who went to sermons in those days had lived long enough to see the way things are today, I can just imagine how they would have criticized and condemned.

* * *

39 *Refined and elegant things*—A girl's over-robe of white on white over pale violet-grey. The eggs of the spot-billed duck. Shaved ice with a sweet syrup, served in a shiny new metal bowl. A crystal rosary. Wisteria flowers. Snow on plum blossoms. An adorable little child eating strawberries.

40 *Insects*—The bell cricket. The cicada. Butterflies. Crickets. Grasshoppers. Water-weed shrimps. Mayflies. Fireflies.

The bagworm[6] is a very touching creature. It's a demon's child, and the mother fears it must have the same terrible nature as its parent, so she dresses it in ragged clothes and tells it to wait until she returns for it when the autumn

---

5. Formal debates by priests on the Lotus Sutra, held on special ceremonial occasions.
6. A small insect thought to resemble a demon and to utter cries of despair.

wind blows. The poor little thing doesn't realize that its mother has deserted it, and when it hears the autumn winds begin in the eighth month, it sets up a pitiable little tremulous cry for her.

The snap-beetle is also touching. Though it's a mere insect, it has apparently dedicated itself to the Buddhist Way, for it continually touches its forehead to the ground in prayer as it walks along. It's fascinating the way you find it wandering about in astonishingly dark places, making that clicking sound.

Nothing is more unlovely than a fly, and it properly belongs in the list of infuriating things. Flies aren't big enough to make them worth bothering to hate, but just the way they settle all over everything in autumn, and their damp little feet when they land on your face . . . And I hate the way the word is used in people's names.[7]

Summer insects[8] are quite enchanting things. I love the way they'll fly round above a book when you've drawn the lamp up close to look at some tale. Ants are rather horrible, but they're wonderfully light creatures, and it's intriguing to see one running about over the surface of the water.

*   *   *

68 *Things that can't be compared*—Summer and winter. Night and day. Rainy days and sunny days. Laughter and anger. Old age and youth. White and black. People you love and those you hate. The man you love and the same man once you've lost all feeling for him seem like two completely different people. Fire and water. Fat people and thin people. People with long hair and those with short hair.

The noisy commotion when crows roosting together are suddenly disturbed by something during the night. The way they tumble off their perches, and flap awkwardly about from branch to branch, squawking sleepily, makes them seem utterly different from daytime crows.

*   *   *

71 *Rare things*—A son-in-law who's praised by his wife's father. Likewise, a wife who's loved by her mother-in-law.

A pair of silver tweezers that can actually pull out hairs properly.

A retainer who doesn't speak ill of his master.

A person who is without a single quirk. Someone who's superior in both appearance and character, and who's remained utterly blameless throughout his long dealings with the world.

*   *   *

82 *Once when Her Majesty was in residence* in the Office of the Empress's Household, a Continuous Sutra Reading[9] took place in the western aisle. A scroll of the Buddha's image was set up, and of course the monks were seated as usual.

Two days into the ceremony, we heard below the veranda a queer voice saying, 'Would there be any distribution of the offerings[1] for me?' and a monk was

---

7. Sometimes "fly" (*hae*) was used in the names of people of the lower classes.
8. Insects such as moths or mayflies that are attracted to flames.

9. A ritual recitation that would continue through several days and nights.
1. Offerings of food on Buddhist altars were generally handed out after the ceremony.

heard to reply, 'Come come, what can you be thinking? The ceremony's not over yet.'

Wondering who this person was, I went over to have a look, and discovered the voice belonged to a nun well past her prime, dressed in horribly grimy clothes and looking like a little monkey.

'What is it she wants?' I asked.

At this, she replied herself in a carefully affected tone, 'I am a disciple of the Buddha, come to ask for the altar offerings, and these monks are refusing to give them to me.'

Her voice was remarkably bright and elegant for a beggar. What a pity someone like her should have sunk to this, I thought, yet at the same time I couldn't help feeling there was something unpleasantly pretentious and flamboyant about her, given her circumstances.

'So altar offerings are the only thing you'll eat, are they? This is wonderfully pious of you,' I remarked.

She was reading me carefully. 'No one's saying I won't eat other things,' she said slyly. 'It's because there's nothing else that I'm asking for offerings.'

I put together some snacks and rice cakes and gave the bundle to her, whereupon she became extremely friendly, and began to chatter about all manner of things.

Some young gentlewomen then came out, and all set about questioning the woman about where she lived, and whether she had a man, and children. She produced such entertaining replies, elaborating them with jokes and suchlike, that everyone kept drawing her out with endless questions, such as whether she sang and danced, until she set about singing,

> 'Who oh who shall I sleep with tonight?
> I think I'll sleep with "Hitachi no Suke"
> for I love the silk touch of her skin in bed . . .'

with much more besides. She also sang,

> 'The peak of Man Mountain[2] stands proud in fame.
> Its scarlet tip has quite a name!'

waving her head about as she sang in a manner that was utterly grotesque. The ladies all laughed in disgust and cried, 'Away with you! Away with you!'

'Poor thing,' I said. 'What shall we give her?'

At this point Her Majesty intervened. 'You've been making the woman act in a way that I've really found very difficult to have to overhear. I simply had to block my ears. Give her this gown[3] and send her on her way immediately.'

'Here's a generous gift from Her Majesty. Your own gown's filthy, so make yourself nice and clean with this one,' we said, and tossed the gown to her. She abased herself in thanks, and then lo and behold she proceeded to drape the gown over her shoulder and perform a dance! She really was disgusting, so we all withdrew inside again and left her to it.

---

2. A mountain outside the capital, famous for its autumn colors. The "peak" here refers both to the mountain and to the tip of a penis.

3. Payments or gifts were usually made in clothing.

This apparently gave her a taste for visiting, because after this she was often to be seen wandering about drawing attention to herself. We took to calling her 'Hitachi no Suke,' after her song. Far from wearing the nice clean gown, she still went about in her filthy one, which made us wonder with considerable annoyance what she'd done with the one we gave her.

One day Ukon paid us a visit, and Her Majesty told her about the woman. 'They have tamed her and more or less installed her. She's always coming around now,' she said, and she had Kohyōe take up the tale and give an imitation of Hitachi no Suke.

'I'd love to see her,' said Ukon, laughing. 'Do show her to me. You all seem to be great fans of hers. I promise I won't entice her away from you.'

A little later, another much more refined beggar nun turned up at the palace. We called her over and questioned her in the same way, and were touched by how shamefaced and piteous she was. Her Majesty gave her a gown, and she abased herself in thanks and retreated, overcome with tears of joy. This was all very well, but Hitachi no Suke happened to come along and catch sight of her as she was leaving. After that, Hitachi no Suke didn't show up again for a long time, and none of us would have given her a second thought I'm sure.

Towards the middle of the twelfth month there was a great fall of snow. The maids collected a large mound of it on the veranda, so then we ladies decided we should have a real snow mountain built out in the garden. We summoned the servants and set them all to work under Her Majesty's orders. The groundsmen who had come in to clean got involved as well, and together they all set about creating an absolutely towering snow mountain. Some of the senior officials from the Empress's Office also gathered to give advice and enjoy the scene. The original three or four groundsmen had soon swelled to around twenty. Her Majesty even sent to ask the servants who were at home to come and help, informing them that everyone involved would receive three days extra pay, and the same amount would be deducted from all those who didn't come; some who heard this came running hastily to join in, though the message couldn't reach those whose homes were more distant.

When the construction was finally completed, the officials from the Empress's Office were summoned and each was given two large bundles of silk rolls. These they spread out on the veranda, and everyone in turn came and took a roll, bowed and tucked it into his belt, and retired. The senior courtiers, who were dressed in informal hunting costume for the job instead of their usual formal cloaks, remained behind.

'How long do you think it will last?' Her Majesty asked everyone. One guessed ten days, another suggested a little longer. Everyone gave opinions ranging over a week or two.

'What do you think?' Her Majesty then asked me.

'I think it will stay there until beyond the tenth day of the first month,' I replied.

Even Her Majesty thought this highly unlikely, and all the ladies were unanimous in declaring that it couldn't last beyond the end of the year at the very latest.

'Oh dear,' I thought privately, 'I've probably overestimated. I suppose it can't really last as long as that. I should have said something like the first day of the new year instead'—but I decided that even if I turned out to be wrong, I should stand by what I said, and I stubbornly continued to argue my case.

On the twentieth day it rained, but there was no sign of the snow mountain melting away. All that happened was that it lost a little of its height. I was beside myself with fervent prayers to the Kannon of White Mountain[4] to preserve it from melting.

On the day when the snow mountain was made, the Aide of Ceremonial Tadataka came to call. I put out a cushion for him, and during our talk he remarked, 'You know, there's not a place in the palace that hasn't built a snow mountain today. His Majesty has ordered one made in his garden, and they're busy making them in the Crown Prince's residence and in the Kōkiden and Kyōgokudono[5] as well.'

I then had someone nearby convey to him the following poem.

> Our singular snow mountain
> we thought was so uniquely ours
> has multiplied abroad
> and become merely commonplace
> as the common snow that falls.

He sat tilting his head admiringly over it for a while, then he finally said, 'It would be merely flippant of me to attempt to sully this marvellous poem with one in response. I shall simply tell the tale of it to everyone when we're gathered before His Majesty,' and he rose and departed. I must say this diffidence struck me as rather odd, in someone with his reputation for being a great poetry-lover.

When I told Her Majesty, she remarked, 'He must certainly have been deeply impressed with it.'

As the month drew to a close, the snow mountain seemed to have shrunk a little, but it still remained very high. One day around midday we'd gone out to sit on the veranda, when Hitachi no Suke suddenly appeared again.

'Why are you back?' we asked. 'We haven't seen you here for ages.'

'Well, the fact is I met with a misfortune,' she replied.

'What was it?' we asked.

'I shall tell you my thoughts at the time in question,' she said, and then she proceeded to recite, in ponderously drawn-out tones,

> 'Alas I am awash
> with envy at the gifts whose burden
> weights her till she limps—
> who is that "deep-sea fisher girl"
> to whom so many things are given?'

and with that she gave a nasty laugh. When no one deigned to look in her direction, she clambered on to the snow mountain and walked about for some time before she finally left.

After she had gone we sent word to Ukon telling her what had happened, and she made us laugh all over again when she replied, 'Why didn't you get someone

---

4. A sacred mountain famous for its perpetual snow. On its summit was an important shrine to Kannon, the Bodhisattva of Mercy who hears people in need.

5. The home of Teishi's rival Shōshi, another wife of Emperor Ichijō; one of her ladies-in-waiting was Murasaki Shikibu, the author of *The Tale of Genji*.

to accompany her and bring her over here? What a shame! She must have climbed the snow mountain and walked round like that because you were ignoring her.'

The year ended without any change to our snow mountain. On the night of the first day of the new year, there was a great fall of snow.

Excellent! I thought. There'll be a fresh pile of snow for the mountain—but then Her Majesty decided that this wasn't fair. 'We must brush off the new snow and leave the original heap as it was,' she declared.

Next morning when I went to my room very early, the chief retainer of the Office of the Empress's Household arrived, shivering with cold. On the sleeve of his night-watch cloak, which was a deep, almost cirron-leaf green, he held something wrapped in green paper, attached to a sprig of pine needles.

'Who is this from?' I inquired, and when he replied that it came from the Kamo High Priestess, I was filled with sudden delighted awe, and took it and carried it straight back to Her Majesty.

Her Majesty was still asleep when I arrived, and in order to get in I tugged a go-board table over to the lattice shutter facing her curtained dais, and stood on it while I struggled to raise the shutter. It was extremely heavy, and because I was only lifting one end of it, it grated against the next one, which woke Her Majesty.

'Why on earth are you doing that?' she inquired.

'A message from the Kamo High Priestess has arrived,' I replied. 'I simply had to get the shutter open so you would have it as early as possible.'

'Well, this certainly is early,' she said, getting up. She opened the package, and found two hare-mallets, the heads wrapped in imitation of hare-wands, decorated prettily with sprigs of mountain orange, creeping fern and mountain sedge. But there was no letter.

'I can't believe there would be no message,' said Her Majesty, searching, and then she discovered on one of the little pieces of paper that wrapped the mallet heads the following poem.

> When I went searching
> the mountain for the echoing ring
> of the woodsman's axe
> I found the tree he cut was for
> the festive hare-wands of this day.[6]

A delightful poem, and delightful too was the scene of Her Majesty composing her reply. In all her letters and replies to the High Priestess, you could see just how much trouble she took from the number of problems she had with her writing. To the man who had brought the message she gave a white-weave shift, and another of maroon which was I think in the plum combination, and it was lovely to see him making his way back through the snowy landscape with the robes over his shoulder. It's only a pity that I never discovered what Her Majesty wrote in reply.

As for the snow mountain, it showed no sign of melting away but continued to stand there, just as if it really was Koshi's famous snowy mountain. It now looked quite black with dirt, and was not a sight to please the eye, but I nevertheless felt elated at the thought of being proved right, and prayed that it could

6. The first hare day of the year, when decorated sticks and poles were presented to members of the court and hung in rooms to ward off evil spirits.

somehow be made to survive until the middle of the month. Everyone declared that it couldn't last beyond the end of the first week, and we were all waiting anxiously to witness the final outcome, when it was suddenly decided on the third day that Her Majesty would return to the imperial palace. I was terribly disappointed at the thought that I'd have to leave without ever knowing the moment of my mountain's final end, and others also said it was a great shame to have to leave now. Her Majesty agreed, and indeed I'd very much wanted her to witness that my guess had been right. But we had to leave and that was that.

There was great upheaval for the move, with Her Majesty's effects and all the other things being carried out, and in the midst of this I managed to call over to the veranda one of the gardeners who was living under a lean-to roof he had set up against the garden wall, and have a confidential word with him. 'You must take great care of this snow mountain, and make sure no children climb on it and destroy it. Keep a firm watch on it until the fifteenth. If it lasts till then, Her Majesty intends to reward you with a special gift, and you'll get high praise from me personally as well,' I said, and to persuade him further I heaped on him various leftovers, fruit and so on, though this would have enraged the kitchen maids and servants, who disliked him.

All this made him beam with pleasure. 'That's very easily done,' he assured me. 'I'll guard it carefully. The children will be sure to try and climb it.'

'You must forbid it,' I warned him, 'and if there's anyone who won't obey then let me know.'

I accompanied Her Majesty on her move to the palace, and stayed there until the seventh day, when I went home.

I was so anxious about my snow mountain while I was at the palace that I was constantly sending servants of various sorts, from the toilet cleaner to the head housekeeper, to keep the gardener up to the mark. On the seventh day I even sent along some of the leftovers from the Festival of Young Herbs feast, and everyone laughed at the tale of how reverently he'd received them.

Once I was back home the snow mountain continued to obsess me, and the first thing I did every morning was send someone over, just to keep him reminded of how very important it was. On the tenth day I was delighted to hear that enough still remained to last until the fifteenth. Day and night my constant stream of messengers continued, but then on the night of the thirteenth there was a terrific downpour of rain. I was beside myself, convinced that this would finally finish off my mountain. All that night I stayed up, lamenting that it couldn't possibly last another day or two. Those around me laughed and declared that I really had lost my mind. When one of our party left I leapt up and tried to rouse the servants, and flew into a rage when they refused to get up, but finally one emerged and I sent her off to bring a report.

'It's down to the size of a round cushion,' she reported. 'The gardener has looked after it most assiduously, and he hasn't let the children near it. He says it should last till tomorrow morning, and he's looking forward to his reward.' I was absolutely thrilled. I could hardly wait till the next day, when I decided I would compose a suitable poem and send it to Her Majesty with a container full of the snow. The anticipation was becoming quite unbearable.

The next morning I got up while it was still dark. I gave one of the servants a box and sent her off with the order to choose the whitest of the snow to put in it, and be careful to scrape away any that was dirty. But she was no sooner gone than back she came, dangling the empty container, to report that the last of the snow mountain had already disappeared. I was devastated. The clever poem that I had laboured and groaned over, and that I'd looked forward to being on everyone's lips, was to my horror suddenly quite worthless.

'How on earth could this have happened?' I said miserably. 'There was all that snow still there yesterday, and it's disappeared overnight!'

'The gardener was wringing his hands in despair,' replied the maid. 'He said that it was there until late last night, and he'd been so looking forward to getting his reward.'

In the midst of all the fuss, word arrived from Her Majesty, inquiring whether there was any snow left today. Thoroughly mortified, I replied, 'Please tell Her Majesty that I consider it a great victory that it was still there until yesterday evening, despite the fact that everyone predicted it couldn't last beyond the end of the year. But after all, my prediction would have been altogether too impressive if the snow had remained until the very day I guessed. During the night some spiteful person must have destroyed the last of it.'

This was the first subject I raised in Her Majesty's presence when I went back to the palace on the twentieth. I related to her how appalled I'd been to see the maid return with the empty container dangling from her hand—like the wandering performer's act with the empty lid, when he came on announcing 'the Buddha's thrown his body off Snow Mountain and all that's left is his hat'[7]— and I went on to explain how I'd planned to make a miniature snow mountain in the lid and send a poem with it, written exquisitely on white paper. Her Majesty laughed a great deal at my story, as did everyone else present.

'I fear I've committed a grave sin by destroying something you had so set your heart on,' Her Majesty then told me. 'To tell the truth, on the night of the fourteenth I sent some retainers there to remove it. When I read your message, I thought you were wonderfully clever to have guessed something like this had happened.'

The fellow apparently emerged wringing his hands and pleading, but he was told that it was an order from the Empress, and was forbidden to tell anyone from my place about it, on pain of having his house destroyed. They threw all the snow away near the south wall of the Left Palace Guards Office, and I gather they reported that it was packed down very hard, and there was a great deal of it. Her Majesty admitted that it would actually have lasted through even as far as the twentieth, and would no doubt have received some added snow from the first snowfall of the spring, too. Then she went on to relate that His Majesty had also heard about it, and had remarked to the senior courtiers that a great deal of thought had obviously gone into this contest of ours. 'Well then,' she said in conclusion, 'tell us the poem you'd prepared. After all, I've made my confession, and as you can see, you actually won your bet.'

The ladies added their voices to Her Majesty's request, but I replied sulkily, 'I don't see why I should be expected to turn around and tell you my poem, after the depressing things I've just heard'—and in truth I was by this time feeling thoroughly miserable.

At this point His Majesty arrived, and he said to me teasingly, 'I've always believed you were a favourite with Her Majesty, but I must say this has made me wonder.' This only served to depress me even more deeply, and by now I was close to tears.

7. A comic image of absence, apparently referring to an act based on the well-known story that the Buddha threw himself off Snow Mountain in exchange for enlightenment.

'Oh dear, oh dear,' I moaned, 'life's so hard! And to think how overjoyed I was, too, about the snow that fell after we'd built the mountain, and then Her Majesty decided it shouldn't count, and ordered it removed.'

Then His Majesty smiled and remarked, 'I suppose she just didn't want to see you win.'

* * *

104 *Things that are distressing to see*—Someone wearing a robe with the back seam hitched over to one side, or with the collar falling back to reveal the nape of the neck.

A woman who emerges with a child slung on her back to greet a special visitor.

A priest acting as Yin-Yang master, who conducts his purification ceremony with that little white paper cap[8] stuck on his forehead.

I do hate the sight of some swarthy, slovenly-looking woman with a hairpiece, lying about in broad daylight with a scrawny man with hair sprouting from his face. What kind of a picture do they think they make, lounging there for all to see? Of course this is not to say they should stay sitting upright all night for fear people will find them disgusting—no one can see them when it's dark, and besides, everyone else indulges in the same thing at night. The decent thing to do is to get up early once it's morning. No doubt it doesn't look quite as bad for people of high station to take daytime naps in summer, but anyone less than attractive will emerge from a nap with a face all greasy and bloated with sleep, and sometimes even a squashed cheek. How dreary for two such people to have to look each other in the face when they get up!

It's most distressing to see someone thin and swarthy dressed in a see-through gossamer-silk shift.

* * *

144 *Endearingly lovely things*—A baby's face painted on a gourd. A sparrow coming fluttering down to the nest when her babies are cheeping for her.

A little child of two or three is crawling rapidly along when his keen eye suddenly notices some tiny worthless thing lying nearby. He picks it up in his pretty little fingers, and shows it to the adults. This is very endearing to see. It's also endearing when a child with a shoulder-length 'nun's cut' hairstyle[9] that's falling into her eyes doesn't brush it away but instead tilts her head to tip it aside as she examines something.

A very young son of a noble family walking about dressed up in ceremonial costume. An enchanting little child who falls asleep in your arms while you're holding and playing with it is terribly endearing.

Things children use in doll play. A tiny lotus leaf that's been picked from a pond. A tiny *aoi*[1] leaf. In fact, absolutely anything that's tiny is endearing.

A very white, plump child of around two, who comes crawling out wearing a lavender silk-gauze robe with the sleeves hitched back, or a child walking about in a short robe that looks more long sleeves than robe. All these are endearing. And it's very endearing when a boy of eight or ten reads something aloud in his childish voice.

8. A Buddhist priest should not wear the white paper cap of a Yin-Yang diviner in a Shinto ceremony.
9. That is, with long bangs, resembling the hair of women who shaved the crown of their head in a tonsure.
1. A plant used in Japanese heraldry.

It's also enchanting to see a pretty little white chick, its lanky legs looking like legs poking out from under a short robe, cheeping loudly as it runs and pauses here and there around someone's feet. Likewise, all scenes of chicks running about with the mother hen. The eggs of a spot-billed duck. A green-glass pot.

* * *

257 *Things that give you pleasure*—You've read the first volume of a tale you hadn't come across before, and are longing to go on with it—then you find the other volume. The rest of it can sometimes turn out to be disappointing, however.

Piecing back together a letter that someone has torn up and thrown away, and finding that you can read line after line of it.

It's extremely pleasing when you've had a puzzling dream which fills you with fear at what it may portend, and then you have it interpreted and it turns out to be quite harmless.

It's also wonderfully pleasing when you're in a large company of people in the presence of someone great, and she's talking, either about something in the past or on a matter she's only just heard about, some topic of the moment, and as she speaks it's you she singles out to look at.

Then there's the pleasing moment when you've heard that someone who matters a lot to you and who's far from you—perhaps in some distant place, or even simply elsewhere in the capital—has been taken ill, and you're worrying and wringing your hands over the uncertainty, when news arrives that the illness has taken a turn for the better.

Someone you love is praised by others, and some high-ranking person comments that his talents are 'not inconsiderable.'

When a poem that you've composed for some event, or in an exchange of poems, is talked of by everyone and noted down when they hear it. This hasn't yet happened to me personally, but I can imagine how it would feel.

It's very pleasing when someone you don't know well mentions an old poem or story that you haven't heard of, and then it comes up again in conversation with someone else. If you come across it later in something you're reading, there's the delightful moment when you cry, 'Oh is *that* where it comes from!', and you enjoy recalling the person's mention of it.

Managing to lay hands on some Michinoku or any good quality paper.

You feel very pleased with yourself when a person who rather overawes you asks you to supply the beginning or end of some bit of poem they quote, and you suddenly recall it. It so often happens that as soon as anyone asks you, even something you know perfectly well goes clean out of your head.

Finding something you need in a hurry.

How could you fail to feel pleased when you win at a matching game,[2] or some other kind of competition?

Managing to get the better of someone who's full of themselves and overconfident. This is even more pleasing if it's a man, rather than one of your own circle of gentlewomen. It's fun to be constantly on your guard because you're expecting him to try to get even with you, and it's also fun to have been fooled into relaxing your guard over time, as he continues to act quite unconcerned and pretend nothing's happened.

---

2. A popular diversion in which participants competed in matching objects such as shells, flowers, or paintings.

When someone you don't like meets with some misfortune, you're pleased even though you know this is wicked of you.

You've sent out your robes to be freshly glossed[3] for some event, and are holding your breath to see how they come out, when they're delivered looking absolutely beautiful. A comb that's come up delightfully with polishing is also pleasing. There are a lot of other things of this sort too.

It's very pleasing when you've finally recovered from a nasty illness that's plagued you day in, day out for months. This is even more the case when it's not your own illness but that of someone you love.

And it's wonderfully pleasing when a crowd of people are packed into the room in Her Majesty's presence, and she suddenly spies someone who's only just arrived at court, sitting rather withdrawn by a distant pillar, and beckons her over, whereupon everyone makes way and the girl is brought up and ensconced very close to Her Majesty.

* * *

529 *I have written in this book* things I have seen and thought, in the long idle hours spent at home, without ever dreaming that others would see it. Fearing that some of my foolish remarks could well strike others as excessive and objectionable, I did my best to keep it secret, but despite all my intentions I'm afraid it has come to light.

Palace Minister Korechika one day presented to the Empress a bundle of paper. 'What do you think we could write on this?' Her Majesty inquired. 'They are copying *Records of the Historian*[4] over at His Majesty's court.'

'This should be a "pillow,"[5] then,' I suggested.

'Very well, it's yours,' declared Her Majesty, and she handed it over to me.

I set to work with this boundless pile of paper to fill it to the last sheet with all manner of odd things, so no doubt there's much in these pages that makes no sense.

Overall, I have chosen to write about the things that delight, or that people find impressive, including poems as well as things such as trees, plants, birds, insects and so forth, and for this reason people may criticize it for not living up to expectations and only going to prove the limits of my own sensibility. But after all, I merely wrote for my personal amusement things that I myself have thought and felt, and I never intended that it should be placed alongside other books and judged on a par with them. I'm utterly perplexed to hear that people who've read my work have said it makes them feel humble in the face of it. Well, there you are, you can judge just how unimpressive someone is if they dislike things that most people like, and praise things that others condemn. Anyway, it does upset me that people have seen these pages.

When Captain of the Left Tsunefusa was still Governor of Ise, he came to visit me while I was back at home, and my book disconcertingly happened to be on the mat from the nearby corner that was put out for him. I scrambled to try and retrieve it, but he carried it off with him, and kept it for a very long time before returning it.

That seems to have been the moment when this book first became known—or so it is written.

---

3. Silk was made shiny by being beaten on special blocks.
4. The *Historical Records* by Sima Qian.
5. This concluding section explains the ori-gins of *The Pillow Book* and of its title. A "pillow" might simply be a notebook for daily jottings kept at hand in some private place.

MURASAKI SHIKIBU

ca. 978–ca. 1014

The Tale of Genji is the undisputed masterpiece of Japanese prose and often considered the first great novel in the history of world literature. That it was written by an eleventh-century court lady is even more extraordinary. Virginia Woolf, who reviewed its first complete English translation—the masterful rendering by Arthur Waley—in 1925, responded to Murasaki Shikibu with the lonely empathy of an early twentieth-century woman author: "There was Sappho and a little group of women all writing poetry on a Greek island six hundred years before the birth of Christ. They fall silent. Then about the year 1000 we find a certain court lady, the Lady Murasaki, writing a very long and beautiful novel in Japan." Although originally written for a narrow circle of court aristocrats in Kyoto, *The Tale of Genji* has had unparalleled success in engaging generations of passionate readers and it is now uniquely representative of Japanese literature. Vast in scale and peopled by hundreds of characters, this thousand-page tale depicts the lives and loves of a former prince—Genji—who dies two-thirds through the book, and the lives and loves of his descendants. On a deeper level, *The Tale of Genji* is about the human ability to be touched by other people and by the outside world, about the tantalizing line between love and lust, and about the vulnerability of women in a male-dominated world. It celebrates the power of poetry, music, and dance to shape society and give depth to human life. Revered for its psychological insight, it captures a world that, however remote from our own, has always retained the sharp authenticity of real life. At its most basic, it chronicles the struggle with the most fundamental of human experiences: love, art, and death.

LIFE AND TIMES

The actual name of the author of *The Tale of Genji* is unknown. It was common at the time to name women after the office held by a male relative. "Shikibu" refers to the appointment her father held at the "Ministry of Ceremonial." The nickname "Murasaki" ("lavender," "purple") is based either on the heroine Murasaki in *The Tale of Genji* or on the color of wisteria, the emblematic flower of her clan. Murasaki Shikibu's ancestors had belonged to a branch of the Fujiwara ("wisteria fields") clan, which had managed since the tenth century to dominate the throne by ruling as regents on behalf of young emperors and marrying their daughters into the imperial family. Despite Murasaki's distinguished ancestry, her family eventually declined to the level of provincial governors. Her father had a mediocre career in the court administration, although he was known as a poet and scholar of Chinese literature. Through him Murasaki got a glimpse of life outside the Heian-era capital of Kyoto, when in her teens she accompanied him for a couple of years on one of his appointments in the provinces. After returning to the capital, Murasaki was briefly married to the much older Fujiwara no Nobutaka, a middle-ranking aristocrat. When he died in 1001, Murasaki was in her early twenties, now a widow with a two-year-old daughter. Murasaki probably started writing *The Tale of Genji* after the death of her husband. These early chapters won her a growing reputation and led to an invitation from Empress Shōshi around 1006 to serve as lady-in-waiting at the imperial court, where she remained until her death around 1014.

The flourishing of female literature during this time was in no small part a result of the efforts of the Fujiwara regents to fill the ranks of their daughters' entourages with the most talented and educated women. Shōshi was one of the consorts of Emperor Ichijō, and she was far more successful than her rival, Empress Teishi, whom **Sei Shōnagon**, the author of *The Pillow Book*, served. She bore Ichijō two emperors and her fortunes reflected the power of her father, the regent Fujiwara no Michinaga. Employment as ladies-in-waiting gave Heian women writers the financial support and leisure to produce literature that commanded the attention of society in the capital.

Murasaki had broad learning in Japanese vernacular literature—*waka* poetry, women's diaries, and tales—but also acquired a profound understanding of the Chinese classics (canonical texts) and Chinese poetry. While aristocratic women at the time were often knowledgeable in Chinese literature, they did not produce Chinese-style texts in the authoritative idiom of the male court bureaucracy and the Buddhist clergy, writing instead in the vernacular language. In her diary Murasaki confesses:

> When my brother, the Secretary at the Ministry of Ceremonial, was young and studied the Chinese classics, I used to listen to him and became unusually good at understanding those passages which he found too difficult to grasp. My father, a most learned man, was always lamenting this fact: "Just my luck!" he would say. "What a pity that she was not born a man!"

A father's admiration for his daughter's academic brilliance cannot conceal the fact that in Heian society, Chinese learning was truly valuable only for men.

In Heian Japan, men and women were strictly segregated and women's lives were extremely circumscribed. The role of a lady was to marry and bear children; and if she came from a suitably good family, she was apt to find herself a pawn in the marriage politics of the imperial court. A noblewoman's days were spent behind curtains and screens, hidden from the world (or from the male world). A man's first marriage often took place when he was still a boy of twelve or thirteen; women were even a year or two younger. Because of the ages of the spouses and the likelihood of the first marriage in particular being a political and economic arrangement, both husband and wife tended eventually to seek love elsewhere, although only men could have multiple marriage partners. The purpose of marriage was procreation, continuation of the family line, and the creation of advantageous alliances with other families. Ordinarily a man's several wives lived in different establishments. His first wife would typically remain in her parents' house. Initially, the young husband might take up residence there or merely visit. Sometimes her parents would furnish the newlyweds with a house of their own, though doing so was less common when the couple married at a young age and the maternal grandparents would be expected to assume many of the child-rearing duties. If in time a man took a second or third wife, he would usually live with his first (and main) wife and commute between the separate residences. It was in this world of gender asymmetries that Heian women's literature thrived. At the same time, Heian women used the status they had as female authors to voice how women suffered from their dependence on their husbands, lovers, and patrons.

An early sixteenth-century illustrated calligraphic excerpt from chapter 17, "The Picture Contest," of *The Tale of Genji*. The artwork is attributed to Reizei Tamehiro.

THE TALE OF GENJI

Although Genji's women play an important role in the tale, it is named after its male protagonist. He is the son of the reigning emperor and his beloved but low-ranking consort, Kiritsubo ("Paulownia Pavilion"). Her favor with the emperor makes her a target of vicious rivalry among the emperor's higher-ranking women, such as the Kokiden Consort, his principal wife. Genji's mother dies in despair when he is in his third year, and his father is eventually forced to remove him from the imperial line to protect him from the ill will of his other consorts. He makes the boy a commoner, bestowing the family name "Genji" on him. As Genji grows up his brilliance elicits sighs of admiration wherever he appears, and he is soon being called "the Radiant Prince." The emperor dotes on his remarkable son, who reminds him all the more painfully of his former favorite consort. He eventually finds solace in the young Fujitsubo, daughter of a previous emperor, who resembles Kiritsubo but is of highest rank.

With even more determination than his father, Genji embarks on a search for women who can replace the mother he barely remembers. His fatal attraction to Fujitsubo leads to one of his greatest transgressions. Fujitsubo gives birth to a son who later becomes emperor and whom everybody believes to be the son of Genji's father. Later, Fujitsubo's niece Murasaki becomes Genji's great love. Sometimes Genji's escapades with women of very high rank lead to disaster: after his affair with Oborozukiyo, who is the younger sister of his father's principal wife, the Kokiden consort (and thus his mortal enemy), he is forced into exile to the rustic countryside. Sometimes inattention, rather than sexual transgression, brings about disaster: Genji's failure to respond to the jealous passion of the lady at Rokujō, widow of a former crown prince, leads inexorably to the death of some of the most important women in his life.

Genji is charismatic, irresistible, and tantalizingly flawed. Charming and handsome, brilliant and ardent, rakish but faithful in his own way (unlike other men, he never abandons any woman he has loved), he is an extraordinary literary figure. Readers may hate Genji or adore him, but we can hardly deny that his creator has fashioned a character who is both larger than life and believably human.

The fifty-four-chapter tale falls broadly into three parts. The first thirty-three chapters describe Genji's career from his birth through his exile and his eventual glorious return to the capital. They focus on the various women with whom he becomes involved in his younger years. Chapters 34 through 41 treat the waning years of Genji's life, concluding with the death of Murasaki and Genji's own death. The remaining thirteen chapters, including the last ten so-called Uji chapters, move to the world of Kaoru, supposedly Genji's son by the Third Princess, and his friend Prince Niou, the son of Genji's daughter, the Akashi Empress. Featuring the two young men's rivalry over several women living in Uji, south of the capital of Kyoto, they draw the reader from the elegant capital to the countryside. Lacking the radiance of Genji's presence, this world is populated with compromised protagonists, darker entanglements with life's sufferings, and thinner hopes for salvation.

Though *The Tale of Genji* is a coherent whole, it can also be appreciated as a collection of interrelated episodes revolving around Genji, his women, and their descendants, in part because of how the work was composed. Since Murasaki wrote it over a span of a dozen years, probably starting with what eventually became chapter 5 ("Little Purple Gromwell," included here), the tale developed in thematic sequences. It first circulated in various shorter installments—single chapters or sequences—among Kyoto's court aristocracy. The sequences show how Murasaki's protagonists, interests, and narrative techniques evolved over time. The "Broom Cypress Sequence," for example, which includes chapters 2,

4, 6, and sequels in chapters 15 and 16, was apparently inserted later. Whereas the core chapters of the tale's first part show Genji dangerously in love with high-ranking women who were close to the emperor, in the "Broom Cypress Sequence" he pursues women of the middle and lower aristocracy. The key prelude to Genji's later conquests occurs in chapter 2 ("Broom Cypress," included here), when the seventeen-year-old Genji and his friends while away a rainy night in his quarters at the palace debating what makes the perfect woman. In the process, the young men trade stories of their experiences with women. Although Genji dozes off now and then, he takes away the lessons from that night and applies them to his pursuit of women in the following chapters of the sequence.

In *The Tale of Genji* Murasaki sometimes relied on conventions from earlier tales, so-called *monogatari*. A typical plot element was an illustrious aristocrat's discovery of a heroine in humble circumstances. This describes the situation of Genji's mother, and also many of Genji's own exploits. Liaisons between high-ranking men and humble women were far more popular in literary romances than in Heian-era reality. A real-life Genji would probably never have married somebody like the character Murasaki, orphaned and without appropriate family background. But in romantic tales, the total infatuation of an aristocrat with a lower-ranking woman was an expression of passion and emotional depth; for female readers it perhaps even inspired hope that they might find salvation and social mobility through the power of romantic love. Because of the social gap between Genji and his lovers, the tale's low-ranking heroines spend considerable energy agonizing about their lowly position and trying to cope with social marginalization. Another typical plot element of earlier tales is the pursuit of love in unexpected or forbidden places. There is no lack of such episodes in Genji's career; he strongly resembles the real-life Ariwara no Narihira (825–880), the epitome of a romantic lover and hero of the earlier *monogatari The Tales of Ise*.

The Tale of Genji displays the remarkable blend of Murasaki's talents. She was a gifted poet, inserting several hundred poems in the tale. Where modern readers might expect Genji and his lovers to exchange love letters in prose, Murasaki has them communicate through elaborate poems. Indeed, most of the protagonists are named after imagery from those poems, and until the early modern period readers studied *The Tale of Genji* to enhance their skills in poetry composition. Also, Murasaki was a perceptive reader of women's confessional diaries and a masterful prose stylist, relying on the nuanced expression of interiority developed by women diarists before her for the intimate psychological portrayal of *The Tale of Genji*'s fictional protagonists. Lastly, her expertise in Chinese literature inspired her to enrich recurring motifs with resonant references to Chinese poetry. In the first chapter she evokes "The Song of Lasting Regret" by the Tang poet Bo Juyi, which tells of the tragic love between a Chinese emperor and a low-ranking concubine, as a poignant analogy to the fate of Genji's mother; like a motif in music, Bo Juyi's gripping ballad keeps reappearing throughout the novel in various guises.

In its day *The Tale of Genji* was just another vernacular tale that, in the estimation of the learned elite, stood far below the Chinese-style writing by Heian men. Chinese learning—a coveted quality for a male aristocrat—was a dubious asset for a court lady. In her diary Murasaki tells how angry she was when somebody teased her for her Chinese learning and gave her the nickname "Our Lady of the Chronicles." But in fact this title should have pleased her: in "Fireflies" (chapter 25, included here) Genji discusses the worth of romantic tales with Tamakazura, his best friend's daughter, and she inspires him to argue that fiction is in some way more truthful than official Chinese-style histories such as the venerable *Chronicles of Japan*: vernacular tales tell the real stories that are left out of the Chinese-style histories.

Whether meant as a playful jibe or a serious polemical claim, Murasaki's bold comparison of popular vernacular tales to canonical Chinese-style histories facilitated the canonization of *The Tale of Genji* in later ages. *The Tale of Genji* became the subject of erudite scholastic commentaries; it inspired screen paintings and illustrated hand scrolls, Noh and puppet plays, poetry handbooks, parodies, and, more recently, woodblock prints, films, and manga (comic book) versions. This "Genji cult" is in part a result of the late-nineteenth-century promotion of *The Tale of Genji* from the status of a brilliant masterpiece to that of a modern national classic said to encapsulate Japanese sensibility. But leaving politics aside, one of the many reasons for *The Tale of Genji*'s timeless appeal is that it is a grand meditation on the emotional and psychological dynamics of love and loss. It seduces the reader with its extensive depictions of courtship and passion, but its ultimate theme is the deeper longing to find a common language through which to connect with another person.

MAIN CHARACTERS IN *THE TALE OF GENJI*

AKASHI EMPRESS, *daughter of Genji and the Akashi Lady; becomes empress by marrying one of Emperor Suzaku's sons, the last reigning emperor to appear in the tale*

AKASHI LADY, *daughter of the Akashi Novice; meets Genji during his exile and bears him a daughter who eventually becomes empress*

AKASHI NOVITIATE, *former governor of Harima, father of the Akashi Lady*

ASSISTANT HANDMAID, *Genji's aged and coquettish admirer*

BISHOP, *Murasaki's great-uncle, a distinguished Buddhist cleric*

EMPEROR SUZAKU, *Genji's elder half brother, son of the Kokiden Consort; succeeds the Kiritsubo Emperor on the throne*

EMPEROR REIZEI, *son of Genji and Fujitsubo, but believed to be the son of Genji's father; succeeds Suzaku as emperor*

FUJITSUBO, *daughter of an earlier emperor; Genji's father's empress with whom Genji has a son, the later Emperor Reizei*

GENJI'S WIFE, *daughter of the Minister of the Left; marries Genji at age 16, when Genji is 12*

HACHINOMIYA, *"Eighth Prince"; younger brother of Genji who lives as a saintly ascetic in Uji and is the father of the "Uji princesses" and Ukifune*

HIGH PRIESTESS OF ISE, *Akikonomu, the daughter of the Lady at Rokujō*

KAORU, *son of the Third Princess, Genji's wife, by Kashiwagi; friend of Niou and central protagonist of the "Uji chapters," named after his mysterious natural "fragrance"*

KASHIWAGI, *eldest son of Tō no Chūjō and actual father of Kaoru, believed to be Genji's son; his affair with the Third Princess leads to his early death*

KIRITSUBO EMPEROR, *Genji's father*

KOKIDEN CONSORT, *daughter of the Minister of the Right; mother of Emperor Suzaku and archenemy of Genji*

KOREMITSU, *Genji's foster brother and confidant*

LADY AT ROKUJŌ, *daughter of a Minister and widow of a deceased Heir Apparent; Genji's neglect of her has fatal consequences*

MINISTER OF THE LEFT, *father of Genji's wife and of Tō no Chūjō, Genji's friend*

MINISTER OF THE RIGHT, *father of the Kokiden Consort and Oborozukiyo*

MURASAKI, *unrecognized daughter of Prince Hyōbu and niece of Fujitsubo; raised by Genji, who later marries her*

NIOU, *imperial prince and son of the Akashi Empress, Genji's daughter, and the last reigning emperor to appear in the tale; friend of Kaoru and central protagonist of the "Uji chapters," named after his memorable "perfume"*

OBOROZUKIYO, *daughter of the Minister of the Right and younger sister of Kokiden; enters the service of Suzaku; Genji's affair with her leads to his exile*

PRINCE HYŌBU, *Fujitsubo's elder brother, Murasaki's father*

SOCHINOMIYA, *also "Prince Hotaru," Genji's half brother, who unsuccessfully courts Tamakazura*

TAMAKAZURA, *daughter of Tō no Chūjō by a low-ranking mistress; discovered by Genji, who installs her into his mansion and passes her off as his own daughter*

THIRD PRINCESS, *third daughter of Emperor Suzaku, who marries her to Genji; mother of Kaoru, whom people believe to be Genji's son, but whose actual father is Kashiwagi, the eldest son of Tō no Chūjō, with whom she has an affair*

TŌ NO CHŪJŌ, *son of the Minister of the Left and brother of Aoi; his name is the title of a post he occupies*

UJI PRINCESSES, *daughters of Hachinomiya, the younger brother of Genji who lives in Uji; the older of the princesses is also known as "Oigimi," the younger as "Naka no kimi"*

UKIFUNE, *unrecognized daughter of Hachinomiya and half-sister of the "Uji Princesses"*

YOKAWA BISHOP, *bishop at the large Enryakuji temple complex on Mount Hiei, northeast of Kyoto; discovers Ukifune and ordains her as a nun*

From The Tale of Genji[1]

From Chapter I

Kiritsubo

THE LADY OF THE PAULOWNIA-COURTYARD CHAMBERS

In whose reign was it that a woman of rather undistinguished lineage captured the heart of the Emperor and enjoyed his favor above all the other imperial wives and concubines? Certain consorts, whose high noble status gave them a sense of vain entitlement, despised and reviled her as an unworthy upstart from the very moment she began her service. Ladies of lower rank were even more vexed, for they knew His Majesty would never bestow the same degree of affection and attention on them. As a result, the mere presence of this woman at morning rites or evening ceremonies seemed to provoke hostile reactions among her rivals, and the anxiety she suffered as a consequence of these ever-increasing displays of jealousy was such a heavy burden that gradually her health began to fail.

His Majesty could see how forlorn she was, how often she returned to her family home. He felt sorry for her and wanted to help, and though he could scarcely afford to ignore the admonitions of his advisers, his behavior eventually became the subject of palace gossip. Ranking courtiers and attendants found it difficult to stand by and observe the troubling situation, which they viewed as deplorable. They were fully aware that a similarly ill-fated romance had thrown the Chinese state into chaos.[2] Concern and consternation gradually spread through the court, since it appeared that nothing could be done. Many considered the relationship scandalous, so much so that some openly referred to the example of the Prize Consort Yang. The only thing that made it possible for the woman to continue to serve was the Emperor's gracious devotion.

The woman's father had risen to the third rank as a Major Counselor before he died. Her mother, the principal wife of her father, was a woman of old-fashioned upbringing and character who was well trained in the customs and rituals of the court. Thus, the reputation of her house was considered in no way inferior and did not suffer by comparison with the brilliance of the highest nobility. Unfortunately, her family had no patrons who could provide political support, and after her father's death there was no one she could rely on. In the end, she found herself at the mercy of events and with uncertain prospects.

Was she not, then, bound to the Emperor by some deep love from a previous life? For in spite of her travails, she eventually bore him a son—a pure radiant gem like nothing of this world. Following the child's birth His Majesty had to wait impatiently, wondering when he would finally be allowed to see the boy.

---

1. Translated by Dennis Washburn. Except where indicated, all notes are his. Murasaki Shikibu often alludes directly to works of poetry (both Chinese and Japanese), fiction, history, and court records. Most of these allusions are to Japanese poems compiled in imperial anthologies during the 10th and early 11th centuries. Notes throughout this selection cite the source of only some of these allusions.

2. The courtiers are referring to "Song of Lasting Regret" by the Tang Dynasty poet Bai Juyi (722–846). The poem recounts the infatuation of the Emperor Xuanzong (685–762) with Yang Guifei, which caused him to neglect affairs of state. His army revolted, and he was forced to execute his lover.

As soon as it could be ritually sanctioned, he had the infant brought from the home of the woman's mother, where the birth had taken place,[3] and the instant he gazed on the child's countenance he recognized a rare beauty.

Now, as it so happened, the Crown Prince[4] had been born three years earlier to the Kokiden Consort, who was the daughter of the Minister of the Right. As the unquestioned heir to the throne, the boy had many supporters and the courtiers all treated him with the utmost respect and deference. He was, however, no match for the radiant beauty of the newborn Prince; and even though the Emperor was bound to acknowledge the higher status of his older son and to favor him in public, in private he could not resist treating the younger Prince as his favorite and lavishing attention upon him.

The mother of the newborn Prince did not come from a family of the highest rank, but neither was she of such low status that she should have been constantly by the Emperor's side like a common servant. Certainly her reputation was flawless, and she comported herself with noble dignity, but because His Majesty obsessively kept her near him, willfully demanding that they not be separated, she had to be in attendance at all formal court performances or elegant entertainments. There were times when she would spend the night with him and then be obliged to continue in service the following day. Consequently, as one might expect, other courtiers came to look down on her not only as a person of no significance, but also as a woman who lacked any sense of propriety. Moreover, because the Emperor treated her with special regard following the birth of his second son, the Kokiden Consort and her supporters grew anxious; they worried about the effect of such an infatuation on the prospects of the Crown Prince and wondered if the younger Prince might not surpass his half brother in favor and usurp his position. The Kokiden Consort had been the Emperor's first wife. She had arrived at the palace before all the other women, and so His Majesty's feelings of affection for her were in no way ordinary. He considered her protests troubling, but he also had to acknowledge that she was deserving of sympathy, since she had given him two imperial princesses in addition to the Crown Prince.

Even though the mother of the newborn Prince relied on the Emperor's benevolence for protection, many of the ladies at court scorned her. She grew physically weak, and because she felt powerless and had no one to turn to for help, she suffered greatly because of his love.

Her chambers at the palace were in the Kiritsubo—named for its courtyard, which was graced with paulownia trees. Because the Kiritsubo was in the northeast corner of the palace, and thus separated from the Emperor's quarters in the Seiryōden, he would have to pass by the chambers of many of the other court ladies on his frequent visits to her. Their resentment of these displays was not at all unreasonable, and so it was decided that the woman herself would have to go more often to the Seiryōden. The more she went, however, the more her rivals would strew the covered passageways connecting the various parts of the palace with filth. It was an absolutely intolerable situation, for the hems of the robes of the accompanying attendants would be soiled. On other occasions,

---

3. It was customary for births to take place outside the palace in order to avoid defilement. A period of confinement for ritual purification usually followed a birth, which is why the Emperor has to wait to see his son.

4. Genji's half brother Suzaku [editor's note].

when the woman could not avoid taking the interior hallways, her rivals would arrange for the doors at both ends to be closed off so that she could neither proceed forward nor turn back, trapping her inside and making her feel utterly wretched. As the number of these cruel incidents mounted, His Majesty felt sorry that his beloved should have to suffer so and ordered that she be installed in the chambers of the Kōrōden, a hall next to the Seiryōden. To do so, however, he had to move the lady who had resided there from the very beginning of her service at court to other quarters, causing her to nurse a deep resentment that proved impossible to placate.

When the young Prince turned three, the court observed the ceremony of the donning of his first trousers. Employing all the treasures from the Imperial Storehouse and the Treasury, the event was every bit as lavish as the ceremony for the Crown Prince. Numerous objections were raised as a consequence of this ostentatious display, and everyone censured the ceremony as a breach of protocol. Fortunately, as the young Prince grew, his graceful appearance and matchless temperament became a source of wonder to all, and it was impossible for anyone to entirely resent him. Discerning courtiers who possessed the most refined sensibility could only gaze in amazement that such a child should have been born into this world.

During the summer of the year the young Prince turned three, his mother's health began to fail. She asked for permission to leave the court and return to her family home, but the Emperor would not hear of it and refused to let her go. She had been sickly and frail for some time, and so His Majesty had grown accustomed to seeing her in such a condition. "Wait a little while," he simply told her, "and let's see how you feel." Then, over the course of the next five or six days, she became seriously ill. The woman made a tearful entreaty, and at last she received permission to leave the palace. Even under these dire circumstances she was very careful to avoid any behavior that could be criticized as untoward or inappropriate. She decided to retire from the court in secret, leaving her young son behind.

Resigned to the fact that the life of his true love was approaching its end and mindful of the taboo against defiling the palace with death, His Majesty was nonetheless grief-stricken beyond words that the dictates of protocol prevented him from seeing her off. The woman's face, with its lambent beauty conveying that air of grace so precious to him, was now thin and wasted. She had tasted the sorrows of the world to the full, but as she slipped in and out of consciousness, she could not convey to him even those feelings that might have been put into words. The Emperor, who now realized that his beloved was on the verge of death, lost control and made all sorts of tearful vows to her, no longer able to distinguish past from future. She, however, could not respond to him. The expression of weariness in her eyes made her all the more alluringly vulnerable as she lay there in a semiconscious state. The Emperor was beside himself and had no idea what he should do. He had granted her the honor of leaving in a carriage drawn by servants, but when he returned to her chambers again, he simply could not bring himself to let her go.

"Didn't we swear an oath to journey together on the road to death? No matter what, I cannot let you abandon me," he said.

She was deeply moved by his display of sorrowful devotion. Though breathing with great difficulty, she still managed to compose a verse for him:

> Now in deepest sorrow as I contemplate
> Our diverging roads, this fork where we must part
> How I long to walk the path of the living

"Had I known that things would turn out like this . . ."

She evidently wanted to say more to him, but her breathing was labored. She was so weak and in such pain the Emperor longed to keep her at the palace and see it through to the end, come what may. But when he received an urgent message informing him that the most skilled of priests had been called to her family home to chant the requisite prayers of healing for her that evening, His Majesty at last agreed that his beloved should leave the palace, unbearable as it was for him to make that decision.

His heart was full and he could not sleep as he impatiently waited for the short summer night to end. The messenger he sent had barely had time to get to the woman's home and return with news of her condition, yet His Majesty was assailed by a sense of dark foreboding.

As it turned out, when the messenger arrived at the woman's residence, he found the family distraught and weeping. "She passed away after midnight," they informed him. The messenger returned to the palace in a state of shock. The Emperor, stunned and shaken by the news, was so upset that he shut himself away from the rest of the court.

His Majesty desperately wanted to see the young Prince his beloved had left behind at the palace, but there was no precedent for permitting anyone to serve at court while having to wear robes of mourning. So it was decided that the boy should be sent from the palace to his mother's residence. Too young to fully comprehend what was going on, he knew from the way people around him were behaving, and from the Emperor's ceaseless tears, that something was terribly wrong. The death of loved ones is always a source of grief, but the little boy's puzzled expression only added to the unspeakable sadness of it all.

* * *

The days passed in a meaningless blur for the Emperor, who dutifully observed each of the seven-day ceremonies leading up to the forty-ninth day after the funeral. Despite the passage of time, His Majesty was so lost in grief he could find no comfort. He was indifferent to the consorts and ladies-in-waiting who attended him in the evenings and instead passed his days and nights distracted and disconsolate. For all who observed his grief, it was truly an autumn drenched by a dew of tears.

Over in the chambers of the Kokiden the mother of the Crown Prince and her faction remained implacably unforgiving. "Is he still so in love with her," she complained, "that even after her death he doesn't consider the feelings of others?" And indeed it was true that whenever the Emperor looked at the Crown Prince, his thoughts would inevitably drift in yearning to the younger Prince, and he would then dispatch his most trusted ladies-in-waiting or nurses to the family home of his late beloved to inquire after the boy.

* * *

The soughing of the wind, the chirring of insects . . . these brought only sadness to him. The quarters of the Kokiden Consort were close by on the north side of his private chambers in the Seiryōden. It had been a long time since she last came to serve him here, and on this particular evening, with the moon in full splendor, he could hear her indulging in musical entertainment to pass the night. The Emperor was appalled and found it quite unpleasant. The courtiers and ladies-in-waiting who observed his countenance at that moment listened uneasily as well. The Kokiden Consort was a proud and haughty woman who behaved as though she couldn't care less about His Majesty's grief.

* * *

The days and months passed, and the young Prince finally came back to the palace. He had grown so splendid and handsome that he no longer seemed to belong to this mortal world. His worried father, knowing that the beautiful die young, took the boy's good looks as an unlucky omen.

In the spring of the following year the time came for the Emperor to formally designate the heir apparent. He was seized by a desire to pass over the presumed Crown Prince, his son by the Kokiden Consort, and appoint his favored younger son instead, but he knew that the little Prince had no supporters and that the court would never accept such a move, which might prove dangerous to the boy. So in the end he went against his personal wishes and confirmed the Crown Prince as his heir apparent, all the while keeping his true feelings concealed. The courtiers remarked among themselves that no matter how much His Majesty preferred the younger son, he knew there were limits to his affection. When the Kokiden Consort caught wind of these rumors, she felt both relief and satisfaction.

The grandmother of the young Prince had long been sunk in a deep depression, and finding no means to console herself, she finally passed away. Was her death the answer to her prayers to be allowed to go to her daughter? The Emperor was once more plunged into grief beyond the measure of ordinary mortals. By this time the young Prince was almost six and was old enough now to understand what was happening. Deeply attached to his grandmother, he wept inconsolably. As she neared death, she recognized how accustomed her grandson had grown to being with her through the years, and she repeated over and over how sad she was to leave him alone in the world.

With both his mother and grandmother gone, the young Prince moved back to the palace for good. When he turned seven he underwent the ceremony of the First Reading, which initiated him into the study of the Chinese classics. The court had never known a child so precociously intelligent, and His Majesty, knowing how others felt and believing that talent and beauty die young, could not help but view such abilities with alarm.

"How could anyone possibly resent him now?" the Emperor declared. "Because he has lost his mother, I want him treated with affection."

Eventually even the Kokiden Consort and her attendants were won over, and whenever the young Prince accompanied his father to the Kokiden chambers, he would be permitted entry behind the curtains where the ladies-in-waiting were serving His Majesty. The fiercest warriors and most implacable enemies would have smiled had they seen him, and the ladies of the court were reluctant to let him out of their sight. The Kokiden Consort had given the Emperor two princesses as well, but neither of them could compare in beauty to this boy. The other consorts and ladies felt no inhibitions around him—indeed, they allowed him to catch glimpses of their faces—and his own appearance was so elegant that they would experience an embarrassed excitement whenever they saw him. All the courtiers considered him exceptionally splendid, a playmate to be treated with special deference.

His formal training included instruction on the koto and flute, and word of his talents echoed throughout the palace—though if I were to go into all the details about his abilities my account would seem exaggerated, and he would come across as too good to be true.

The Emperor learned that among the members of a mission from the Korean kingdom of Koryō was a diviner skilled at the art of physiognomy. An old edict by the Emperor Uda had forbidden the presence of foreigners within the palace, so His Majesty discreetly arranged to have the young Prince meet with this man at the Kōrōkan, the residence provided for foreign missions. The Major Controller of the Right assumed the role of guardian and accompanied the boy to the mission under the pretense that he was the father of the child. The diviner was both puzzled and astounded. He tilted his head back and forth, unable to believe that this child could really be the Major Controller's son.

"The young man's features tell me he is destined to be ruler of this country," the diviner declared, "and will perhaps even attain the supreme position of Emperor. Yet if that is what fate has in store for him, I foresee chaos and great sorrow for the court. On the other hand, if his destiny is to ascend to a position such as Chancellor and act as a guardian of imperial rule, then it appears he will be a great benefactor to the state. Still, I must say that judging by his features alone, the path leading to the Chancellorship seems less likely."

The Major Controller was himself a scholar of considerable learning and discernment, and his conversations with the men of the Korean mission were deeply engaging. The party composed and exchanged verses in Chinese, and because the mission planned to leave for home in a day or two, one of the diviner's poems expressed the joy at having met such a remarkable boy face-to-face and the sorrow of having to part from him so soon. In response to the heartfelt expression of this poem, the young Prince composed an accomplished verse of his own. The diviner praised his effort as auspicious and bestowed lavish gifts on him. In return, the diviner received splendid presents from the imperial household. Naturally, news of this encounter spread through the court. His Majesty did not let on that he knew anything about it, but the grandfather of the Crown Prince, who happened to be the Minister of the Right, caught wind of the gossip and, not knowing quite what to make of it, grew suspicious.

The Emperor in his wisdom had earlier sought out the opinion of a Japanese diviner, whose reading of the boy's physiognomy accorded with his own thinking at the time. His Majesty had been holding back on installing the young Prince in the line of succession, and was thus impressed by the perspicacity of the Korean diviner, who recognized the boy's imperial lineage. Even so, he could not be sure how long his own reign would last, and he hesitated to appoint his son prince-without-rank. He anxiously wondered whether the boy, who lacked support from his mother's family, would not end up precariously adrift once he was no longer in the line of succession. For that reason he determined that the boy's prospects might be better if he were made to serve as a loyal subject of the imperial court, and so he had his son tutored accordingly in the arts and in various fields of learning. The boy was so exceptionally bright it seemed a shame to demote him to commoner status, but the Emperor knew that designating his son heir apparent would invite the calumny and scorn of the court. He consulted yet another diviner who was wise in the ways of Indic astrology, and when this new reading proved to be in line with the others and with His Majesty's own thoughts on the matter as well, he decided to confer on the boy the clan name of Minamoto—Genji[5]—thereby making him a commoner.

Months and years passed, but there was never a moment when the Emperor forgot his love for the lady who had resided in the chambers looking out on the paulownia courtyard. Thinking he might find someone who could assuage his grief, he had women of appropriate breeding and talents brought before him. But it was all in vain, for where in the world could he expect to find her equal? Just when he had reached the point where he found everything tiresome and was contemplating retiring from the world, an Assistant Handmaid informed him of a young woman, the Fourth Princess of the previous Emperor, whose beauty was matchless, whose reputation at court was beyond reproof, and whose mother had raised her with extraordinary care and devotion. Since this Assistant Handmaid had once served at the court of the previous Emperor, she was familiar with the mother of this young woman and accustomed to waiting on her. In the course of her service she had been able to observe the Fourth Princess as she grew from childhood, and even now would occasionally see her.

"I have served at court for three successive reigns," she told the Emperor, "and I have never before seen anyone who even closely resembles the late lady of the Kiritsubo. The daughter of the former Empress, however, definitely puts me in mind of her. She is a woman of exquisite refinement and beauty."

Could this really be true? His Majesty, who could barely contain himself, began to make some discreet inquiries.

The mother of the Fourth Princess warned her daughter about the situation at the palace. "The Kokiden Consort is a vindictive woman. Just look at the unfortunate example of the lady in the Kiritsubo. The treatment she suffered was truly appalling." Unable to decide if she should allow her daughter to go to the palace, the mother was still struggling with the Emperor's request when suddenly she passed away.

Thinking that the Princess was now helpless and alone, His Majesty again approached the young lady. "I will think of you as an equal to my own daughters," he assured her. Her ladies-in-waiting, her supporters from her mother's family, and her older brother, Prince Hyōbu, who served in the Ministry of War, were all of the opinion that attending the Emperor would bring solace to her—and in any case it certainly would be preferable to remaining in her current wretched circumstances.

So it was that she was sent to the palace and installed in the Higyōsha, which was also called the Fujitsubo because its chambers looked out onto a courtyard graced with wisteria. The young woman was thereafter referred to as "Fujitsubo," and truly in face and figure she bore an uncanny resemblance to the deceased lady of the Kiritsubo. Fujitsubo, however, was of undeniably higher birth, and that status protected her from criticism, since the courtiers were predisposed to judge her a superior woman. Since she lacked no qualifications, the Emperor did not feel constrained in his relationship with her. The court had never accepted

5. The name "Genji" is the reading of the characters for Minamoto (*gen*) and "family name" (*shi/ji*).

His Majesty's love for the lady of the Kiritsubo, and so his affection for her was viewed as inappropriate and inopportune. The Emperor never wavered in his undying love for the lady of the paulownia-courtyard chambers, but it is a poignant fact of human nature that feelings change over time. Inevitably his attention shifted toward Fujitsubo, who, it seems, brought comfort to his heart.

Because the young Genji was always at his father's side, he was constantly in the presence of the women who attended His Majesty most frequently. These women grew familiar with the boy and gradually came to feel that they did not have to be reserved around him. Of course, none of the consorts considered herself inferior to the others, but even though each one was very attractive in her own individual way, there was no denying that they all had passed, or were on the verge of passing, the peak of their charms . . . all but Fujitsubo, that is. She still possessed the loveliness of youthful beauty and, try as she might to keep herself hidden away behind her screens, Genji, who was always nearby, would catch glimpses of her figure. He had no memory of his mother, and when he heard the head of the imperial household staff say that Fujitsubo looked just like her, his young heart ached with wistful longing—if only he could always be close to his father's new consort!

Genji and Fujitsubo were the two most precious people to the Emperor. "Do not be shy around the boy," His Majesty told Fujitsubo. "It may seem strange and curious, but I feel as though it is fitting for him to think of you as his mother. Do not think him discourteous, but cherish him for my sake. His face and expressions are so like his mother's . . . and since you resemble her so closely, you can hardly blame him for thinking of you the way he does."

After the Emperor made this request, Genji, in his boyish emotions, would try everything—even references to the transient blossoms of spring or the blazing leaves of autumn—to gain Fujitsubo's recognition of his yearning affection for her. When the Kokiden Consort learned of the unprecedented favoritism His Majesty was displaying toward these two, she once more grew cold and distant toward Fujitsubo and her retinue. Moreover, her earlier ominous dislike of Genji and his mother flared up again, and she found the boy repellent. Her son, the Crown Prince, was considered flawlessly handsome, and his reputation was above reproach. Nonetheless, he was no match for the lustrous beauty of Genji, who possessed an aura that prompted the courtiers to call him "the Radiant Prince." Because Fujitsubo was his equal in looks and in the affections of the Emperor, she came to be referred to as "the Princess of the Radiant Sun."

It pained the Emperor that his son would eventually grow out of his youthful good looks, but when Genji turned twelve, preparations were made for the coming-of-age ceremony in which his hair would be done up and his clothes and cap worn in the style of an adult. His Majesty personally tended to every little detail of the ceremony, adding touches that went beyond custom and set a new standard. The ceremony that had initiated the Crown Prince into manhood had been a spectacular affair held in the Shishinden, the great ceremonial hall of the palace. The Emperor wanted Genji's ceremony to be just as majestic and proper. He had various offices—including the Treasury and the Imperial Granaries—make formal preparations for the many banquets and celebrations that would follow the ceremony, and he left special instructions that no expense should be spared and that his directives should be carried out so as to make the occasion one of utmost splendor.

His Majesty was seated facing east under the eastern eaves of his residence in the Seiryōden, and the seats for Genji and the minister who would bestow the cap were located in front of him. Genji appeared before the Emperor at around four in the afternoon, during the Hour of the Monkey.[6] The lambent glow of his face, which was still framed on either side by the twin loops of his boyish hairdo, made his father feel all the more regretful about the change in appearance that was about to take place. The honor of trimming back Genji's hair fell to the Minister of the Treasury, whose face betrayed the pain he felt the moment he cut Genji's beautiful locks. The Emperor had a hard time keeping his emotions in check. *If only his mother were here to see this ceremony,* he thought, struggling to maintain his composure.

The capping ritual followed, and when that was finished, Genji withdrew to an antechamber to rest and change into the formal attire of an adult: an outer robe with the underarm vents sewn up. Stepping down into the garden east of the Seiryōden, he faced his father and performed obeisance, placing his ceremonial wand on the ground, rising and bowing left, right and left again, then sitting and repeating his actions to show his gratitude. He cut such a magnificent figure that all in attendance were moved to tears. As might be expected, the Emperor found it harder than the others to hide his feelings. At that moment the sad events of the past, which he normally kept himself from dwelling on, came flooding back. Since Genji was still at a tender age, His Majesty had fretted that cutting his locks and putting his hair up in the style of an adult man would spoil his looks. To his amazement the ceremony only added to Genji's aura of masculine beauty.

The Minister of the Left, who performed the capping ritual, had taken the younger sister of the Emperor as his principal wife. She gave him a daughter, whom he doted upon, raising her with the utmost care. The Minister was troubled when he learned that the Crown Prince evidently desired his daughter, because he was secretly planning to arrange a match for her with Genji. And so in the days leading up to the ceremony, he approached the Emperor with his proposal.

"I see," His Majesty replied. "Well . . . given that the boy seems to have no patrons for his coming-of-age ceremony, and since we have to select an aristocratic young woman to sleep with him on the night of his initiation, let's choose your daughter." Thus encouraged, the Minister followed through with his plans.

After the ceremony, Genji withdrew into the attendant's antechamber. As the party was making a celebratory toast in his honor, the Emperor gave permission for Genji, who had no rank, to sit at a place below the imperial princes but above the ministers. The Minister of the Left, who was seated next to him, casually dropped a few hints about his daughter, but Genji, who was still at an age when he felt diffident and embarrassed about such matters, did not respond.

An attendant from the imperial household staff brought a message from the Emperor to the Minister, requesting his presence. The Minister went to the imperial quarters, where a senior lady-in-waiting presented him with the appropriate gifts that custom demanded: a white oversized woman's robe made especially for this presentation, along with a set of three robes. His Majesty vented his pent-up emotions, presenting a cup of rice wine to the Minister and reminding him of his responsibilities toward Genji:

6. In premodern Japan the hours of the day, like the months, were designated by the signs of the Chinese zodiac. The Hour of the Monkey was about 3–5 p.m. [editor's note].

>   *When you with purple cords first bound his hair*
>   *Did you not also bind your heart and swear*
>   *Eternal vows to give him your daughter*

The Minister composed this reply:

>   *So long as the deep purple of these cords that bind*
>   *Our hearts as tightly as your son's hair never fade*
>   *So our mutual vow will retain its deep hue*

He stepped down from the long bridge that connected the imperial residence in the Seiryōden and the Ceremonial Court in the Shishinden and performed obeisance in the east garden. There he received a horse from the Left Division of the Imperial Stables and a falcon caged in a mew from the Office of the Chamberlain. Princes and nobles lined up along the foot of the stairs leading down from the Seiryōden into the east garden, and they each received gifts appropriate to their rank.

Decorative boxes of thin cypress wood filled with delicacies and baskets of fruit were among the items prepared for the Emperor that day. The Major Controller of the Right, who had acted earlier as Genji's guardian, had been put in charge of the presentations. The garden overflowed with trays stacked with rice cakes flavored with various fillings and with four-legged chests of Chinese-style lacquer stuffed with presents for the lower-ranking attendants—so many that their numbers surpassed even the presentations made at the coming-of-age ceremony held for the Crown Prince. Indeed, it was an incomparably magnificent affair.

That evening, Genji departed for the residence of the Minister of the Left, which was located on Sanjō Avenue. The ceremony welcoming Genji as groom and solemnizing his wedding was conducted with unprecedented attention to proper form. Feeling a touch of dread, the Minister was captivated by the masculine beauty of Genji, who still looked quite boyish. In contrast his daughter, who at sixteen was four years older than her new husband, was put off by Genji's youthfulness and considered their match inappropriate.

The Minister enjoyed the full confidence of the Emperor. After all, his principal wife, the mother of the bride, was His Majesty's full sister. Thus, the bride came from a distinguished line on both sides of her family. Moreover, the addition of Genji to the Minister's family diminished the prestige of his rival the Minister of the Right, who as grandfather of the Crown Prince would eventually assume power as Chancellor. The Minister of the Left had numerous children by several wives. His principal wife had given him, in addition to Genji's bride, a son who was now Middle Captain in the Inner Palace Guard. This young man, Tō no Chūjō,[7] was exceptionally handsome, and the Minister of the Right could hardly ignore such a promising prospect, even though he was not on good terms with the Minister of the Left, his main rival for power. He therefore arranged to marry the young Tō no Chūjō to his fourth daughter, who

---

7. I am following custom and using this name for Genji's close friend, brother-in-law, and rival. The name Tō no Chūjō refers to his positions as Middle Captain in the Inner Palace Guard (*Chūjō*) and in the Office of the Cham- berlain. Like most of the male characters, he is identified by his position at court through- out the narrative, but since his positions and ranks change over time, it is easier to refer to him throughout by this initial appellation.

was his greatest treasure in the world. His regard for his son-in-law was every bit as strong as that given to Genji by the Minister of the Left. For their part, the two young men forged an ideal friendship.

Because the Emperor was always summoning him, Genji found it difficult to live at his wife's residence.[8] In his heart, he was obsessed with the matchless beauty of the Fujitsubo Consort, who seemed to be exactly the kind of woman he wanted to take as his wife. *Is there no one else like her?* he wondered. He found his bride to be a woman of great charm and proper training, but he was not really attracted to her. He had been drawn to Fujitsubo when he was a child, and the torment caused by his feelings for her was excruciating. Now that he was an adult, he was no longer permitted behind the curtains of the consorts. Whenever there was a musical entertainment, he would play the flute in accompaniment to Fujitsubo's koto, his notes subtly conveying his true feelings for her. The sound of her soft voice was a comfort to him, and the only time he felt happy was when he was at the palace. He would serve there for five or six days in succession, occasionally spending a mere two or three days at his wife's residence. His father-in-law attributed Genji's behavior to his youth and did not fault him for it, but instead continued to do all he could to offer support at court. He chose only the most exceptional ladies-in-waiting to serve his son-in-law and daughter, and he went out of his way to put on the musical entertainments that Genji so enjoyed and to show him every favor.

When Genji stayed at the palace, he took up residence in the Kiritsubo. The women who had once served his mother had not been dismissed and scattered, and so they were now assigned to wait on him. Orders were sent down to the Office of Palace Repairs and to the Bureau of Skilled Artisans to rebuild and expand the former residence of Genji's mother, a villa on Nijō Avenue. The project was to be carried out so splendidly that there would be no other villa like it. The setting of the surrounding woods and hills was already unparalleled, and when the garden pond was enlarged, the result was so eye-catching that it created a stir. Genji thought wistfully that such a villa would be the perfect residence for a wife who had all the qualities of his ideal woman, Fujitsubo.

It is said that it was the Korean diviner who, in his admiration, first bestowed on Genji the sobriquet Radiant Prince.

From Chapter II

Hahakigi

BROOM CYPRESS

The Radiant Prince—a splendid, if somewhat bombastic, title. In fact, his failings were so numerous that such a lofty sobriquet was perhaps misleading. He engaged in all sorts of flings and dalliances, but he sought to keep them secret out of fear that he would become fodder for gossips who delighted in circulat-

---

8. Uxorilocal marriage arrangements were widespread in the Heian period, and thus it was common for a young nobleman to make his father-in-law's residence his primary abode [editor's note].

ing rumors about him and end up leaving to later generations a reputation as a careless, frivolous man. Genji was keen to avoid the censure of the court and, thus constrained, went about feigning a serious and earnest demeanor for a time, abstaining from all elegantly seductive or charming affairs. No doubt the Lesser Captain of Takano, that legendary lover, would have been amused.[9]

Genji was serving as Middle Captain in the Palace Guard at the time, and in fact he preferred being stationed there. Consequently, his visits to his wife, who resided at the estate of her father, the Minister of the Left, all but ceased. Although people expressed their suspicions about him, wondering if his heart wasn't in wild turmoil over a secret lover, Genji was not the sort who carried on common affairs impulsively or brazenly. There were rare occasions, however, when he strayed from his professed path of moderation, and he had an unfortunate tendency to become obsessed with relationships that brought him stress and pain, giving himself over entirely to behavior that could hardly be called proper.

During a stretch in the rainy season when there was no break in the clouds, a directional taboo[1] forced Genji to stay on and attend the Emperor for a longer than normal period. The members of the household of the Minister of the Left grew anxious and resentful at Genji's neglect of his wife, but they continued to arrange every detail of his wardrobe so that he would cut a remarkable figure at court. Moreover, the sons of the Minister, Genji's brothers-in law, would spend all their free time in Genji's palace quarters when they happened to be in service. One of these sons, Tō no Chūjō, was a Middle Captain who also served in the Office of the Chamberlain. He was a full sibling to Genji's wife—he and his sister had both been born to Princess Ōmiya—and of all the Minister's children he was closest to Genji and could behave in a more intimate and relaxed manner in his friend's presence at entertainments and amusements. Tō no Chūjō preferred the company of Genji because the residence that his own father-in-law, the Minister of the Right, had painstakingly provided and maintained for him and his wife was a dreary, uninspiring place. It must be added that he was fond of having affairs with other women.

Tō no Chūjō also had dazzlingly furnished quarters at his father's residence at Sanjō, but he was always accompanying Genji on his comings and goings. They were constantly together, day and night, pursuing the same interests and diversions, and he in no way lagged behind the Radiant Prince in his accomplishments. Because they were inseparable, it was natural that they did not stand on ceremony with one another. They never kept their innermost feelings hidden, but displayed an easygoing harmony whenever they spoke.

They had endured an especially tedious day, having spent the time in idleness on account of the interminable rain, and because the palace seemed practically deserted during the early evening hours, Genji's quarters took on a more relaxed atmosphere than usual. Drawing an oil lamp beside him, Genji perused some Chinese classics. Tō no Chūjō pulled out some letters written on paper of vari-

---

9. The tale of the amorous Lesser Captain of Takano referred to here has not survived.
1. A directional taboo, or prohibition, required a person to avoid traveling in a certain direction so as not to disturb gods whose movements over time were predictable (based on Chinese zodiacal and calendrical practices) and could be charted by the Bureau of Divination. Such prohibitions were often used as a convenient excuse for a gentleman to avoid meeting his wife or lover [editor's note].

ous hues from a small cabinet near him and was seized by the desire to read them. Genji would not allow that, but he did say, "I'll let you look at a few of the more appropriate ones . . . there are several I'd be ashamed for you to read."

Tō no Chūjō resented his friend's refusal. "But it's just those letters you don't feel free to share with me that I'm curious to see. I've exchanged many letters of the most common variety with ladies of all ranks, and at the time we were corresponding I couldn't wait to read them. Yet when I reread them now, the only ones really worthwhile were written when the women were being petulant or impatient with me for keeping them waiting."

Despite his protests, he knew full well that Genji would never have letters from high-ranking ladies—letters that had to be kept strictly confidential—lying scattered about in a commonplace cabinet like this where anyone could see them. Genji would certainly hide his most intriguing missives in a secret location, and would be comfortable sharing only those from easygoing ladies of decidedly second-rate backgrounds.

"Well, you certainly have a lot of them, don't you?" said Tō no Chūjō, who went on to interrogate Genji about the author of each of the missives. He found it amusing that his suppositions and guesses about the letters were sometimes right on the money, and other times wildly off the mark. Still, Genji gave very little away, and, by leading his friend on, he managed to disguise the identities of the letter writers.

"You must have a great number of letters at your place," said Genji. "I'd really like to take a peek at them. If you let me, I'll gladly open this cabinet to you."

"I have very few worth looking at," Tō no Chūjō answered. "You see, I've come to the realization that as far as women are concerned, there aren't many who are flawless enough to make you think *she's the one*. I've come across many who have passable skills in the arts, who can write flowing characters that create an impression of superficial elegance, who show a kind of facile understanding of how to respond in verse on certain occasions. Yet even when one chooses a woman on the basis of such accomplishments, she almost always fails to live up to the expectations created by her talents and disappoints in the end. She'll swell with pride, going on and on about her own accomplishments, looking down on others and, all in all, behaving rather foolishly. Her parents are always waiting on her, spoiling her with affection and lavishing attention, keeping their precious little princess hidden away in the recesses of their estates until some man hears about her extraordinary gifts and gets all worked up. Beautiful, young, and carefree, with little to distract her, she'll follow the lead of others, dedicate herself to some trivial diversion, and as a result acquire and perfect some skill. Naturally, those who look after her keep silent about her flaws, keeping up appearances and spreading plausible-sounding rumors that make her seem better than she really is. Since such rumors are all a man has to go on, can he really afford to assume the worst about her without actually meeting her? So a man goes about, wondering if she's the genuine article, and when they finally meet . . . well, it's rare that a woman actually lives up to her reputation."

Listening to Tō no Chūjō's lament, which gave the impression of a world-weary man who had experienced the shame of such disappointments, Genji smiled wryly. Although he knew that his friend's account of women was hardly the whole of the matter, he had had a few affairs that matched Tō no Chūjō's experiences.

"Can there really be women," Genji asked, "who lack even the most trivial merits?"

"I'm not saying that," Tō no Chūjō responded. "Who would be foolish enough to be drawn to a woman with absolutely no talent? A woman who has nothing to recommend her is as rare as one who is perfect in every way. My point is that a woman who is born into the nobility is raised with the greatest care, which includes concealing her many faults. So of course she's going to look superior to other women. A woman born into a family of middling rank will reveal her sensibility and habits of mind with a style and personality all her own, and so you would expect to discover various things that distinguish her from others. As for women of the lowest class . . . well, I'm not especially interested in learning anything about them."

Genji's curiosity was piqued by the worldly posture his friend had assumed. "I wonder about your standards. Can you really classify all women on the basis of just three levels? How do you discriminate between a woman born of a noble family . . . say rank three or above . . . whose social position has been ruined and whose rank has fallen so that it is indistinguishable from others, and a woman of less distinguished background . . . say rank four or lower . . . whose family has so prospered at court that they can now lavishly furnish her residence and adopt a smug attitude that proclaims their daughter inferior to no one?"

Just as Genji posed his question, the Warden of the Left Mounted Guard and the Junior Secretary from the Ministry of Rites showed up, explaining that directional prohibitions for that day were keeping them confined to the palace. They both had reputations as elegant lovers, and since they were also eloquent speakers—fluent, logical, and precise—Tō no Chūjō was eager to detain them and get their opinions on his idea of classifying women according to three levels. Their subsequent conversation touched upon topics of a highly questionable and even slightly disreputable nature.

The Warden addressed the matter straightaway. "A woman who is a parvenu will likely be judged by court society as inferior despite her rise in status, especially if her pedigree is not appropriate to her rank. On the other hand, a woman who may have a distinguished pedigree, but who lacks the means to make her way at court, will see her fortunes and position diminish over time, and her prospects and reputation crumble away until she cannot maintain her status in spite of her pride. Events will then conspire to make her situation more and more untenable. Looking at each of these types of women, I'm afraid we have to relegate them both to your middle category. Provincial governors toil away, tied up with petty people and affairs, but even among that lot, consigned to a middling station in life, there are various gradations that distinguish them. We live in an age when we sometimes find governors who are really not at all inferior, even though they come from the middle ranks. Actually, there are some of the fourth rank who are qualified to serve as a counselor, who have unsullied reputations and comfortable fortunes and prospects, and who are easier to take than some inexperienced or immature nobility of higher rank. There are many instances of such men who maintain splendid households where their daughters are nurtured with the utmost care. Nothing is lacking, nothing held back, no expense spared to raise them in the most dazzling manner . . . and as a result they grow into excellent young ladies who are beyond reproach. These women go into court service and many of them find unexpected good fortune, marrying above their station."

Genji smiled at that. "I guess that when all is said and done, the key is finding a girl from a rich family."

Tō no Chūjō responded petulantly. "Now you're talking nonsense. Such a remark is not worthy of you."

The Warden continued his disquisition: "The highborn lady who brings together both pedigree and public reputation, yet who in private lacks personal breeding and manners, is eccentric and not worth discussing. She's the type who makes you wonder in disappointment how she could have been brought up like that. Of course, it strikes you as perfectly natural when a woman's pedigree and reputation are in harmony and her character is flawless. So you assume that's the way things ought to be and aren't surprised by her, even though such a woman is a rarity. But perhaps I should set aside any discussion of the highest-ranking ladies, for someone as lowly as I could never be on their level.

"Beyond these types, you sometimes unexpectedly come across an adorable, defenseless girl whose existence is unknown to court society. She lives in a lonely, sublimely dilapidated residence shut away from the world behind a gate overgrown with weeds, and so of course you think of her as an exceptionally rare find. You're mysteriously drawn to her, your imagination stimulated by the things that make her different, and you wonder how she could have ended up in a place like that. Her father is likely to be some pathetic, overweight old man, her brothers probably all have unpleasant faces, and there in the women's quarters in the inner recesses of the residence . . . which, no matter how you try to imagine it, is nothing out of the ordinary . . . is a fiercely proud lady with all the refined demeanor of one who has somehow managed to acquire some accomplishments, even if she is not of the first rank and thus not all that much to talk about. And yet because you would never expect to find a woman like that in such a place, how could you not find her alluring? Of course, you can't compare the discovery of a woman like that to opting for a flawless woman of superior rank, but by the same token it is difficult to simply toss her aside."

The Warden glanced knowingly at the Junior Secretary, who, interpreting the expression as a subtle reference to the flawless reputation of his own sister, kept his counsel on the matter.

Genji seemed lost in thought: *I wonder about all this. Are there really women like that out in the world? After all, when I consider my wife, there don't seem to be any perfect women among the highest classes.*

Genji was dressed in an intentionally casual manner in an informal robe, minus trousers, over soft white under-robes. He had neglected to tie up the cords of his outer robes, and as he half-reclined amidst his books and papers in the dim shadows cast by the lamp, he cut such an attractive figure that the other men felt a desire to see him as a woman. He was so beautiful that pairing him with the very finest of the ladies at the court would fail to do him justice.

During the course of the young men's discussion of various types of women, the Warden remarked, "There are women who are flawless enough for a commonplace affair, but when the time comes to take a wife, you find it impossible to decide even if you have a large number of women to choose from. The same is true of men who serve at court and are expected to be rock-solid pillars of society. It proves quite difficult to produce a man of true worth and ability, and so no matter how gifted or clever he may be, in the end there will never be more than one or two who are fit to govern. That's why superior people command their inferiors, and inferiors follow their superiors, mutually accommodating each other to carry out public affairs.

"Now then, just consider the person who is to take charge of the private affairs of your household. It wouldn't do at all if she doesn't have the proper qualifications. That being the case, a man is naturally going to look around because he knows that a woman may possess some good qualities while lacking others. After all, it is rare to find one who, though maybe not perfect, is at least acceptable . . . and even a man who is not inclined to compare the appearance of one woman to another is going to take great care in making his decision, since the one he chooses will be his mate for life. All things being equal, he will take someone whose tastes match his own and who does not have the kind of flaws he must spend all his time correcting and setting in order. Well, this is all very hard, and a woman is not necessarily going to fulfill all of a man's expectations. That's why a man who does not allow his affections to stray, who focuses his attention on one woman and does not discard the karmic bonds of his first marriage vows, will always be seen as sincere, honest, and loyal. And a woman who is able to keep her husband from straying is the one we take to be refined and attractive.

"Given all that—how should I put this?—having observed all sorts of relationships in society, I can't help having doubts as to whether there is any woman who is perfectly elegant, or who can live up to the ideals in a man's heart. In the case of your lordships, what kind of woman could ever be worthy enough to meet your exalted standards? No doubt she would have to be young and beautiful and beyond reproach in every way. She would be well versed in composition, but her choice of words would be modest and her brushstrokes light and delicate, leaving you a little agitated and longing for a more revealing response. You are forced to wait, feeling unbearably impatient until that moment when you can get close enough to her to make your advances and exchange a few words. But she will say very little, speaking under her breath in a faint voice that shows how adept she is at concealing her flaws. Just when you think she is most pliant and feminine, she starts to fret about whether or not you really love her. And then when you humor her, she becomes flirtatious. This has to be the worst fault in women.

"Above all, a wife must never neglect her duty to assist her husband. A husband can get along well enough if a woman is not too emotionally demanding, does not make a big fuss over niceties, and doesn't give herself over to fashion. Of course, a man doesn't want a wife who is too serious, who busies herself with supporting her husband and managing the household to the extent that she keeps her hair swept back all the time, exposing her ears and making herself unattractive. A man who goes to work in the morning and returns home in the evening doesn't want to have to go to the trouble of talking with a stranger about the odd behavior of people he has encountered in public and private or about the good and bad things he has seen and heard. If he has a wife who is close to him and will listen to his stories and understand him, then doesn't he assume he should be able to discuss such matters with her? Maybe he suddenly recalls something and smiles, or perhaps tears come to his eyes, or maybe he relives some feeling of righteous indignation at something that happened to someone. Or he might have feelings that he just cannot keep to himself and thinks he might share them with her and ask her opinion. But if she is unattractive or too preoccupied to understand, he ends up turning away from her in disillusionment. Remembering something he has kept inside, a thought that makes him laugh or let out an audible sigh, he will mention it, almost as if speaking to himself, and all she will do is look up with a blank expression and reply, 'Did you just say something?' What man wouldn't regret marrying someone like that?

"When all is said and done, we men really should consider picking a completely childlike, compliant woman . . . a woman we can mold into an acceptable and flawless wife. Even when she gives you some cause for concern, you still have the feeling that there is some value in disciplining her. When you are with such a woman face to face, she is truly vulnerable and precious to you, and you are compelled to view her faults through forgiving eyes. Even so, there will be occasions when you have to be apart, and you tell her about something important that must be done, or give her some task, trivial or practical, that must be carried out to the letter. It will turn out that she cannot act on her own and is unable to do things as you instructed. This is really quite annoying and her unreliability will cause you no end of trouble. Why does it always seem that it's the cold, distant, slightly unpleasant woman who, depending on the occasion, is able to perform well in front of others and bring honor to your house?"

The Warden had tried to cover all aspects of the subject, but he was unable to come to any firm conclusions. Instead, he finished his analysis by heaving a great sigh. "Considering all of this," he continued, "you can't choose a wife solely on the basis of her family background, and certainly not on the basis of her looks alone. If you can find a woman who is not so strange or demure as to make you regret your choice, if she is serious through and through and has a quiet personality, then you ought to consider her dependable. Should she have any talents beyond these basic qualifications or be sweet-tempered, you should count yourself lucky. Even if she is deficient in certain respects, you shouldn't make unreasonable demands for her to improve. So long as she is morally upright and not fretful or jealous, then she will over time acquire an outward grace. Her comportment will be modest, she will protect her honor, and she will endure things she has a right to complain about, hiding her resentment behind feigned ignorance or pretending to be nonchalant.

"Unfortunately, there are cases where a woman can no longer suppress the emotions that have been building up inside her heart, and she will leave behind some fierce words that chill your soul, or compose a moving poem to which she has attached a memento that will remind you of her, then hide herself away in some village deep in the mountains or on a deserted strand along the shore. When I was a child I would hear stories like that, which the ladies-in-waiting would read aloud, and I found them so touching I was moved to tears. Now, when I think back on it, their tales seem frivolous and overly dramatic. A woman who casts aside a man who has deep feelings for her and runs off to hide in utter disregard of the husband's feelings, even when she has just cause for being upset, will stir anxieties that last a lifetime. The whole affair is extremely tiresome. Some people will praise her actions, saying how exquisitely profound her emotions are, and as a result her feelings of sad regret will accumulate to the point where she decides to become a nun. Having made up her mind, her heart seems pure and serene and she can no longer even consider returning to her former life. Her acquaintances come to call on her, telling her how melancholy it is that things should have come to this. When her husband hears of this he weeps, and the messenger and older ladies-in-waiting tell her what a shame it is and how sad that her husband has such deep feelings. The woman, who still has lingering affection for him, will then realize she had no reason to throw away his love. She will gather together the hair she had clipped from her forehead when she took vows as a nun and, feeling forlorn and helpless now that there is no turning back, will break down and cry. Though she had kept her emotions in check up to that moment, once she gives in to her feelings she is no longer able to hold back her tears whenever she considers her situation. Because she now seems to have so many regrets, the Buddha himself must look at her as one whose heart is tainted by base attachments. Halfhearted devotion to the Buddha is an even more certain path to Hell than being mired in the five evils of earthly existence.[2] Even if the marital bond was deep enough that the husband takes her back before she renounces the world, is there any couple that would not harbor at least some resentment upon recalling such an incident? For better or worse they live together as husband and wife, and their relationship is based on a deep karmic bond and shared emotions that can weather almost anything that might happen. Yet whenever a wife runs away, can any couple ever completely put aside their feelings of mutual reproach?

"It is folly for a wife to resent her husband, display her anger, and quarrel obsessively over some little affair he has had on the side. A man's affections may stray, but so long as he is still capable of the kind of feelings he had for her when they were first married, then she has good reason to think that their relationship has strong emotional bonds. If she makes a big fuss over his dalliances, however, those bonds may be cut for good.

"In general, then, a woman should be modest in all things. She should give a gentle hint when she knows something is going on that justifies her resentment. Or she should imply, without being spiteful, that there have been some occasions that have bothered her. If she behaves in such a way, her husband's regard for her will surely increase. Most of the time a man's wandering heart can be calmed by the guidance of his wife. A woman who is too lenient and turns a blind eye to her husband's behavior may in contrast seem easygoing and lovable, but in the end she will be dismissed as frivolous. As Bai Juyi put it, 'Who can tell where an unmoored ship will drift?'[3] Isn't that the truth?"

Tō no Chūjō nodded and replied, "Staying on the same subject, it's a serious matter when a person you like for their charm and sensitivity gives you cause to wonder if they can be trusted. Although people may choose to put up with their partner's wayward behavior and even fool themselves into believing they see some improvement, that doesn't mean that the wayward partner has reformed. In any case, when an indiscretion brings discord to a marriage, there is probably no better recourse than to calmly ignore it." His remarks described perfectly the situation of his own sister, which was no doubt his intention, and

2. In Buddhism the five evils are lust, wrath, greed, worldly attachment, and pride (ego).

3. A reference to a poem on marriage included in the collected writings of Bai (Bo) Juyi.

so it irritated him that her husband, Genji, was not joining in the discussion but was pretending to nod off instead.

The Warden, who now found himself regarded as the expert on such matters, whinnied on and on. Tō no Chūjō, who wanted to hear what he had to say, assumed the role of disciple and listened eagerly.

"Compare women to artisans, if you will," the Warden continued. "For example, a woodworker may indulge his imagination and create all sorts of items . . . toys meant for a moment's diversion, objects not based on any model or pattern. These things look fashionable and amaze you with the cleverness of their construction, and insofar as they are new and different and in keeping with the times, they attract attention as modern and up-to-date and so have a certain charm. Yet when one has something of true beauty made properly . . . formal furnishings, say, or some decorative object for your residence that has a conventional form . . . the distinction between a maker of novelties and a master craftsman is plain for all to see. To take another example, there are many skilled painters at the palace, but when you have to pick one to do basic sketching for a work, it's hard to tell at a glance which ones are the truly skilled artists. Paintings that present startling scenes of the mountains on the Isle of Hōrai where the immortals dwell, or that show the stern visages of beasts from exotic lands or the faces of demons no man has ever seen, all give play to the imagination and astonish our eyes, since they bear no resemblance to the real world. Such works are fine, given what they are, and any painter should be able to execute them. But when it comes to realistically depicting scenes in the everyday world . . . mountain vistas, flowing streams, the appearance of our dwellings . . . what matters is the attention to detail and technique a master painter brings to his representation of both serenely commonplace objects and steep, rugged landscapes. Whether creating the impression that one is far removed from society by piling up layer upon layer of thick foliage, or giving one a sense of familiarity and comfort by foregrounding a garden enclosed by a bamboo fence, all such effects require a special power and grace far beyond the skills of an ordinary artist.

"Or take calligraphy. Even a person with no real knowledge of the art can add a flourish here and there to create the impression . . . at least at a cursory glance . . . that he has great talent, while a person who can in fact write with true skill and care may appear to lack the ability of a master. But when you compare the works of such people side by side, you can see that the latter is closer to the genuine thing. So it is with all trivial matters of art and pleasure. I know that when it comes to human emotions, it is even more the case that you cannot trust the affected elegance a woman puts on for show on a special occasion. Shall I tell you how I came by this knowledge, though I may have to speak indiscreetly about an affair?" He shifted a little closer, and Genji woke up. Tō no Chūjō was sitting across from him, his chin cupped in his hands, listening in earnest anticipation. It made for a charming tableau, resembling a scene in which a learned priest expounds on the ways of the world. It was the kind of moment, however, when young men find it hard to keep their relationships secret.

"Some time ago," the Warden resumed, "when I was still a very low-ranking official, I was quite taken with a young woman. But, as I presumed to mention to Your Highnesses earlier, she was not exceptionally beautiful, and so I deci-

ded in my youthful, fickle heart that I would not take her as my main wife.
Though I thought of her as someone I could always turn to and rely on, there
was something lacking, and I was sure I could do better. So I played around
and cheated on her, and when she became distressingly jealous, she lost favor
with me. I kept hoping that she would not be like that, and wanted her to be a
little less sensitive. While I found it irksome that she was so unforgiving and
suspicious, I was also puzzled that she had lost patience with a man of such a
low rank as I. At the same time, I couldn't understand why she still had feelings for me. I often felt sorry for her, and so I eventually brought my tendency
to stray under control.

"Her temperament was such that somehow or another she contrived to do
her best for me, even in matters for which she had no innate ability. She prodded herself, ashamed of faults she didn't want others to see, and she earnestly
supported me in every way, trying her best never to go against my wishes in even
the slightest matter. At the beginning I had thought of her as a strong-willed
woman, but in the end she was yielding and accommodating. She worried that
she might put me off if she did not make herself attractive, and whenever she
allowed herself to be seen by someone not close to her, she would fret about it,
feeling that perhaps she had shamed her husband. She did her utmost to maintain her wifely virtue, and as we grew accustomed to living as husband and wife,
I was not at all ill disposed toward her except for that one detestable flaw . . .
her jealousy, which she could not control.

"At the time she seemed so absurdly obedient and fearful, I thought I should
teach her a lesson . . . you know, shake her up a little so she would stop being
jealous and mend her ways. So I pretended I was truly fed up and that we should
break off our relationship. Since she had previously shown only a submissive
attitude to me, I thought for sure I could teach her a lesson and intentionally
treated her with wretched callousness. When, as usual, she got angry, I told
her that if she were going to be so willful and disagreeable, I would put an end
to our marriage and not meet her again despite the deep bond we shared as
husband and wife. I said, 'If you really want us to separate, just keep harboring
your baseless suspicions. But if you want us to have a long future together, then
you have to accept that there will be hardships and try to not let things bother
you. Rid yourself of your twisted disposition, and I will find you endearing. As
soon as I work my way up at court and achieve respectable status, no other
woman will ever compete with you for my devotion.' I thought I was being so
clever in straightening her out with such assertive words, but she just smiled
vaguely and replied, 'It doesn't bother or worry me that you are in a period in
your life when you have neither status nor distinction, nor am I waiting impatiently for you to achieve success. But I find it painfully unbearable to have to
always hide my feeling of wretchedness and rely on the uncertain hope that as
the months and years go by the day will finally arrive when you reform your
behavior. So the time has come when we must go our separate ways.' Her spiteful words made me very angry and I said a number of hateful things to her. At
that point the woman, unable to control her passions, grabbed my hand and bit
one of my fingers. I put on a show of outrage and, holding out my crooked finger, stalked out. 'Now that you've disfigured me like this,' I threatened, 'how
can I possibly show myself at court? You yourself said I'm of no consequence,
so now that you've done this, how do you expect me to get ahead? If this is how

things are, then it looks like we really are through once and for all.' I composed a poem:

> As I bend my wounded fingers counting
> The times I called on you, your flaws it seems
> Are not confined to jealousy alone

'You won't have me to resent anymore,' I said, and as expected she burst into tears and shot back:

> Having counted in my heart the times
> I showed restraint at your behavior
> Now I have to take my hand from yours

"She challenged me in this manner, and even though I did not believe our relationship would really change, I drifted about seeing women here and there and let many days pass without once communicating with her. Then one night, near the end of the eleventh month, I was detained at the palace in order to rehearse music and dance for the Rinji Festival at the Kamo Shrine. A miserable sleet was falling that night, and as I was saying goodbye to my companions, who were going their separate ways, it occurred to me that I had no other place to go but hers. Sleeping at the palace seemed a dreary prospect, and the thought of visiting some woman who puts on an air of refined elegance chilled me to the bone. And so, all the while wondering what she thought about me, I went to peek in on her and see how she was faring. As I brushed the snow off myself, I felt constrained by feelings of embarrassment, and yet I hoped that perhaps tonight her icy resentment had thawed. The lamps had been dimmed and turned toward the walls, and softly padded robes had been plumped up and hung over a large filigree basket to be warmed and perfumed. The blinds were raised just as they were supposed to be, and the room gave the appearance that she had been waiting for me to return that very evening. Since everything was prepared just to my liking, I felt a swelling pride until I noticed she was nowhere to be found. Only the women who served her were there, as I had expected, and they told me she had gone to her parents' residence for the evening. She had left no elegant poem to rouse my interest, no word at all that she was anxious to see me. She had simply left and locked herself away, showing no consideration for me. I was quite let down and couldn't help wondering if her unyielding spitefulness wasn't implicitly signaling to me that I should go ahead and hate her if I wanted. The rooms gave no indication she was having an affair . . . was her aim to make me angry and suspicious of her? Yet the hues and stitching of the robes she had laid out for me were prepared with more than normal care, just as I would have wished. Clearly she was taking care to look after me even though she now assumed I had abandoned her.

"Things being the way they were, I figured she would never cut me off completely, and so I tried to downplay our spat and make up with her. And though she did not defy me by hiding herself away and making me run around looking for her or by replying in a way that would cause me embarrassment, still she told me, 'I cannot continue putting up with you the way you are now. If you reform and develop a more steady disposition, then maybe we can see each other.' Even though she spoke to me like that, I was convinced she could never leave me, and so I thought I'd let her stew a while longer to punish her. 'All right, then, let's do as you suggest,' I told her, showing her just how stubborn I could be. She suffered so much during that time that at last she died. I knew then that I should never have made light of her, and I can't help thinking now that it's good enough for a man if his wife is someone who is wholly dependable. It was always worthwhile talking to her, regardless of whether we were discussing some trivial, passing matter or an important issue. She was so skilled at dyeing cloth that it's no exaggeration to compare her to the goddess of fall foliage, Princess Tatsuta herself. And when it came to weaving, she was as skillful as the Celestial Weaver Maid we celebrate at Tanabata.[4] Gifted in such ways, she was an exceptional wife."

The Warden felt a keen sorrow at the memory. Tō no Chūjō tried to console him, saying, "Her weaving may have been unsurpassed, but her real virtue was following the example of the Celestial Weaver Maid, who faithfully keeps her vow of love with the Herdsman. The fact is, you cannot expect to find someone again whose weaving compares with that of Princess Tatsuta. When the passing flowers or autumn foliage are not in harmony with the hues of the season, they do not stand out as brightly, and their beauty dissipates. Women are just like that . . . their beauty passing out of season. That's why it's so difficult in this hard life to decide upon a wife."

These words acted as encouragement to the Warden, who promptly resumed his discussion. "After she died, I started calling on a woman whose family lineage was peerless and who seemed to have an exquisitely refined temperament. She wrote poetry in a flowing hand, was well trained in the plucking style of the koto, and sang like a master. I couldn't find any flaws in anything I saw or heard of her. She was also passably good-looking, and so even while I continued to be on familiar terms with the woman who bit my finger, I was also secretly visiting this other woman and eventually grew very attracted to her. After the death of my wife, while I was grieving and wondering what I should do, I came to the realization that nothing could be done for those who have died and started visiting the other woman more frequently. After I became familiar with her, I began to notice that she was somewhat ostentatious . . . and flirtatious. Since she did not seem to be the sort of woman I could trust, I began to keep my distance a little, and when I did so she started meeting another man in secret.

"It was an autumn evening during the tenth month. The moon was bright and seductive, and as I set out from the palace I encountered a certain high-ranking courtier. We got into my carriage together, and though I was intending to stay the night at the home of my father, who was a Major Counselor at the time, this courtier told me he was quite eager to stop by a certain place where a woman was waiting for him. Because the house he mentioned happened to be on the way to my father's house, I caught a glimpse of its garden through the fence and saw the moon shimmering on the surface of the pond. Finding it hard to pass by a dwelling where even the moon seemed to have taken up residence, I dismounted the

---

4. Tanabata is a festival on the seventh day of the seventh lunar month that celebrates the annual meeting of the young lovers Orihime (the Celestial Weaver Maid, i.e., the star Vega) and Hikoboshi (the Celestial Oxherd, i.e., the star Altair). Because their love distracted them from their heavenly responsibilities, they were separated by the Milky Way and are allowed to meet only once a year, crossing over a bridge formed by the wings of a flock of magpies. Princess Tatsuta (Tatsuta-hime) is the goddess of fall who weaves the brocade of autumn foliage on Mount Tatsuta. She is thus the patron goddess of weaving and dyeing.

carriage with the man. He apparently had had this sort of rendezvous before and seemed very excited when he sat down on the widely spaced boards of an open veranda near the inner gate. He struck a dashing pose as he gazed up at the moon. Chrysanthemums, their colors faded by the autumn frost, were arrayed gorgeously, and the scarlet profusion of scattered maple leaves rustling in the breeze looked magnificent. The man took out a flute from the breast fold of his robe and began to play various popular *saibara* such as 'The Shade Is Good.'[5] He also sang a few verses: 'Let us tarry awhile at the well of Asuka, the shade is good, the waters cool, the grasses inviting . . .' The woman inside accompanied him skillfully, having apparently readied her six-string koto. Her instrument reverberated clearly, and she played it flawlessly, softly, having tuned it to a folksy minor key, and the sound that wafted from the other side of the bamboo blinds seemed quite fashionably modern, a perfect accompaniment to the pure autumn moon. The man was charmed and impressed and moved closer to the blind. Alluding to a poem about visiting the abode of a beautiful woman, he tried to get a response from her, saying, 'I see no trace of anyone having disturbed the fallen leaves in your garden.' He picked some chrysanthemums and composed a poem:

> *How lovely are the peerless moon*
> *And music here . . . yet do they draw*
> *None but coldhearted men to you*

'I hear you have spoken ill of me. But never mind. Let me have one more song. When a person you want to encourage to listen is present, you should put all your skills on display.' The woman replied to his brazen bantering, affecting a disinterested voice:

> *A leaf can never hope to stay the autumn breeze*
> *Any more than words or music could make tarry*
> *This flutist who accompanies the bitter wind*

"She responded seductively, unaware that I was witness to her distasteful forwardness. She then switched to a larger thirteen-string koto tuned to the *banshiki* mode,[6] darker in tone and thus appropriate for the season. Her style of plucking was lively and contemporary, and yet even though her playing sparkled, listening to her left me feeling unsettled and embarrassed. When a lady you are seeing intimately from time to time goes out of her way to be fashionably elegant, she is certainly very alluring, at least on those infrequent occasions when you actually meet. But if on one of your rare visits a woman you are considering as a possible mate behaves too voluptuously, then you begin to grow wary and worry she might not be reliable after all. On the basis of what I observed that evening, I decided to end my affair with that lady.

"Though I was young and inexperienced at the time, when I look back and compare those two women, their capriciousness made them seem inscrutable and unreliable to me. And from now on I will likely be even more inclined to

---

5. The genre of music referred to here, the *saibara*, was a popular form in which the lyrics of folk songs (usually) were set to Chinese music. Lines from various *saibara* appear throughout the narrative.

6. This is one of six modes (or keys) used in *gagaku*, Japanese court music, which is based largely on the court music of Tang China. The various modes usually had seasonal or poetic associations.

feel that way about women. Your lordships may take delight only in the pleasures of those fragile and fleeting charms of a young lady whom poets would
liken to the dew on bush clover that scatters when you pluck the flower, or to
sleet on leaves of dwarf bamboo that melts away at your touch. But though you
may feel that way now, just wait another seven years, and when you reach my
age you will think the same way I do. Please take my poor, humble advice and
be careful with women who lead you on. They'll cheat on you and make you
look foolish in the eyes of others."

And so he advised them.

Tō no Chūjō continued to nod his head.

Genji smiled faintly, apparently agreeing with the Warden, then remarked,
"It seems in both cases your romantic escapades were awkward and unlucky."
They all had a good laugh.

Tō no Chūjō spoke up next: "I'd like to tell you about a foolish woman I knew.
I started seeing her in secret, and because it looked as though I would have to
keep seeing her on the sly, I didn't think our affair would last. But as we grew
intimate I came to have deeper feelings for her, and even though I could not
meet her very often, I simply couldn't get her out of my mind. Eventually our
relationship reached the stage where I could see she trusted me, and many times
I honestly thought if she depends on me so much, then there must be things I
do that upset her. If there were, however, she never let on about them. Even
when I did not visit her for long stretches, she did not jealously resent me or
think me inconsiderate. Instead, she kept up appearances morning and night,
as if she expected me every day. She was so meek and docile that I was moved
to pity and assured her that she could always rely on me.

"She had no parents and was quite lonely and helpless. That's why I found
it touching that she apparently thought of me as her provider. She was so
quiet and unassuming that I was unconcerned and let my guard down. But
then, during one of those long stretches when I did not call on her, she
received some rather deplorable messages from my wife's household . . . messages that implied threats against her. Unfortunately, I heard about that only
much later.

"I was unaware there had been such unpleasantness, and even though I had
not forgotten her, we went so long without exchanging a word that she grew
despondent. She was so wretched worrying over the baby girl I had fathered by
her that she sent me a wild pink, suggesting, I suppose, that the child was like
the flower, hidden from sight and easy to overlook." Tears welled up in Tō no
Chūjō's eyes.

"And the letter that accompanied the flower?" asked Genji.

"Nothing special, really," he replied. "She sent this poem:

> *The hedge around the hut of the mountain peasant*
> *Grows untended now . . . let fall your tender mercy*
> *Let it fall like dew and settle on this wild pink*[7]

---

7. The word I have translated as "wild pink" is
nadeshiko. In the two poems that follow immediately below, the word for wild pink is
tokonatsu. Although the two names refer to

the exact same flower, Murasaki Shikibu uses
both in this sequence of poems to distinguish
between mother and child. In the first poem,
nadeshiko refers to Tō no Chūjō's child by his

"With her verse fresh in my mind, I went to see her. She was as faithful and uncomplaining as ever, but her face was worn with care. It was autumn, and as she gazed out from her dilapidated house at the overgrown garden drenched in dew, her tearful expression seemed to vie in sadness with the melancholy chirring of the bell crickets. I felt as though I were part of some old romance:

> *I cannot judge which of these flowers is fairest*
> *Their colors mingling in never-ending summer*
> *But there is none dearer than my little wild pink*

"I turned my attention from the child and comforted the lady by reminding her of the old poem in which a lover promises to visit always, so that dust never settles on their bed.[8] She replied with this.

> *Autumn arrives and rough winds shake*
> *Dew from wild pinks and tears from sleeves*
> *That wipe dust from my lonely bed*

"She spoke casually, giving no hint that she harbored any serious resentment. Even when she wept, she seemed ashamed and awkward and tried to hide her face from me. It pained her to think that I might view her suffering as accusatory, and that attitude so reassured me about our relationship that I did not visit her again for a long time. During that interval she ran off, disappearing without a trace.

"She may still be alive somewhere, but her situation must be precarious and uncertain. If only she had given me some indication of how strongly attached she was to me at that moment when I was so moved by her plight, then she would never have had to run away like that. I would never have neglected her as I did but would have treated her properly, just like any other woman I called on, and looked after her forever. I cherished that little wild pink and so assumed I would always be able to visit her. But now I am unable to track her whereabouts. Certainly this woman is an example of the unreliable type you mentioned earlier. She appeared so unruffled, never letting on that she found my treatment of her cruel, but in the end my feelings for her, which had never waned, turned out to be nothing more than a futile, one-sided love. Now, even as I am slowly getting her out of my heart, I sometimes think about her, imagining that she has not forgotten me altogether . . . that there are evenings when

---

lover, while in the second and third poems *tokonatsu* refers to the woman. Both *nadeshiko* and *tokonatsu* may be identified as other flowers (e.g., a carnation or a gillyflower), but both are generic names for pinks. I have chosen to use the name "wild pink" to suggest the well-worn theme in the tradition of Japanese literature that Murasaki Shikibu drew on of a beautiful lover who is discovered by a man in an out-of-the-way place, like a wildflower growing in a hidden spot. The two poems below also play on the word *tokonatsu*, which is a homophone for "never-ending summer," and

which has an element, *toko*, that is a homophone for "bed." [The mother appears in chapter 4 (*Yūgao*) as Genji's lover, the lady of the Evening Faces. The little girl is the future Tamakazura, who will later be taken in by Genji. In chapter 25, included below, she discusses with Genji the virtues and vices of romantic tales—Editor's note].

8. *Kokinshū* 167 (Ōshikōchi no Mitsune): "I long to stop even a mote of dust from settling on this bed of pinks that have come into bloom since first you and I lay on our bed."

she realizes she cannot blame anyone else for her predicament and her heart smolders with regret. She is certainly the type of woman you cannot rely on or hold to for very long.

"Although a difficult woman is memorable, and thus hard to get out of your mind, when things do not go well and you find it troublesome to continue seeing her . . . as you found with the woman who bit your finger . . . you tire of the relationship. And a talented woman like your koto player is almost certain to be burdened by the sin of infidelity. As for the woman I spoke of, she was so utterly lacking in character that I have doubts about her as well. So I have reached the point where I find it impossible to choose which type of woman is best. It has proven difficult to compare each respective relationship between men and women in this manner. Where is the woman who could combine the virtues of the three women we discussed without inevitably bringing with her all their unmanageable flaws? Set your sights on the beautiful goddess of fortune, Kichijōten,[9] and not only will her holiness bore you stiff, but you'll end up reeking of incense to boot!"

The young men all laughed at that.

"But come now," Tō no Chūjō prodded the Junior Secretary from the Ministry of Rites. "There must be a few unusual affairs going on around your place. Tell us a little about them."

"Do you honestly think anything worth discussing happens in a place as lowly as mine?" the young man asked.

Tō no Chūjō remained insistent, however. He declared that he was waiting for a response, and so the Junior Secretary wracked his brain to come up with some tale.

"When I was still a student of letters in the Bureau of Education,[1] I happened to be calling on a clever young woman. Like the woman the Warden mentioned, she was a good companion. I could discuss official matters with her, and she was also deeply prudent when it came to the conduct of household affairs. Her brilliance would put an unprepared scholar to shame, and so it was hard to hold my own with her in any conversation we had.

"I began to attend an academy to study Chinese with a certain scholar who just happened to have many daughters. As things turned out, I became intimate with one of them, and when her father found out, he brought out some ceremonial sake cups and spoke to me in an overly suggestive tone, reciting a line from Bai Juyi's poem in praise of marriage: 'Listen while I recite a poem about the two paths of life.' You know the poem . . . the one that extols the virtues of a wife who comes from an impoverished home and urges the husband to cherish her. I hadn't actually fallen head over heels for the woman or anything like that, but I was mindful of her father's feelings. In any case I was beholden to him, and she was a kind and considerate support to me. Even during our pillow talk she would impart her knowledge of Chinese, teaching many crucial things

9. Images of Kichijōten were common in Buddhist temples, and it was said that monks often fell in love with her [editor's note].
1. This official academy or university was loosely based on Chinese bureaucratic models and used to train young men for positions in the government. The course of study largely emphasized the Confucian canon and focused on the fields of Chinese classics, law, ethics, and letters (primarily history and poetry). It also provided instruction in practical fields such as mathematics and yin-yang studies (i.e., divination) [editor's note].

I would need for my official position. Her own writing was clear, almost mannish. She employed a precise, rational diction and never mixed the more feminine *kana* script with her Chinese characters. Naturally I couldn't break off the relationship, because with her as my teacher I was able to learn how to write halting verses in Chinese. Even now I can't forget the debt I owe her . . . but then again, for a man like me who has no intellectual talents at all to have to rely on a woman I was intimate with and have her witness my pathetic performances . . . well, it was too shameful. Your lordships, of course, would never need such an efficient and rigorous helpmate. As for me, even though our relationship strikes me as trivial and regrettable now, at the same time she was someone I was drawn to, perhaps as a result of a karmic bond from a former life. It seems that men are really the feckless ones."

The moment he finished, both Genji and Tō no Chūjō cajoled him, saying, "Well, well, a most intriguing lady indeed," in order to get him to finish up his story. Knowing he was being led on, the Junior Secretary feigned distaste, a comical sneer crinkling his nose as he continued.

"Now then, I did not go to see her for the longest time, and when I finally dropped in on some errand, she was not at all the relaxed, familiar woman she had once been, but instead stayed behind a bothersome screen when we met. It seemed to me she was being peevish, which was foolish behavior, and so I thought this might be the perfect opportunity to break up with her. Yet I knew that such an intelligent woman would never hold a grudge for a frivolous reason. She understood the ways of the world and would not be resentful. She spoke in a voice that sounded rushed and breathy. 'These past few months I have been indisposed by a severe malady and prescribed a regimen of herbal tonic concocted mainly of garlic. This has rendered me extremely malodorous and incapable of meeting you tête-à-tête. Though we cannot meet directly, I would be pleased to undertake any miscellaneous tasks you might request of me.' Her words were so admirably learned, and so . . . manly. When I got up to leave she was perhaps feeling anxious and restless, for she added in a screechy voice, 'Please do come by when this odor has dissipated!' I felt very sorry to leave without responding to her, but there was no reason to hang around and, to tell the truth, the odor was getting to me. So I had no choice but to cast an imploring look at her as if to excuse myself. I sent this poem:

> *On a night when the spider's busy spinning*
> *Foretold my arrival, why insist I wait*
> *And put me off till the smell of garlic fades*

"'What sort of excuse are you giving me?' I asked. The words had barely left my lips, and I was on the verge of making my escape, when her reply came chasing me down:

> *If my love could bring you every night,*
> *Why then should the daytime be so blinding*
> *Or this smell of garlic so offensive*[2]

---

2. The poem plays on the word *hiru*, meaning either "daytime" or "garlic." This wordplay explains the Junior Secretary's admiration of her quick wit [editor's note].

"You have to admit that she was certainly quick." He spoke so calmly that the young nobles found the whole account implausibly sordid.

"A complete fabrication," they said, laughing. "Where could anyone ever find a woman like that? You might just as easily have gone off to meet a demon. The whole thing is unpleasantly weird." Flicking their thumbs with the nail of their index finger to indicate their pique, they chided the Junior Secretary and pressured him to tell them something better than that. But the young man just sat there and replied, "How can I serve you up anything stranger than that?"

The Warden interceded.

"Generally speaking," he said, "it is really pathetic how people of no importance, men or women, think they have to show off every last little thing they have learned. A woman who acquires knowledge of Chinese and has read the Three Histories or the Five Classics lacks all feminine charm. But then again, why should we assume that a woman, just because she's a woman, would go through life without acquiring any knowledge at all of public and private affairs? Though she may not receive any formal education, a woman who has even a modicum of intelligence will retain many things she sees and hears. Through such knowledge she may learn to write cursive Chinese characters, and the next thing you know she is sending stiffly written letters half-filled with Chinese script to other ladies who don't have a clue what to do with them. When you see such a woman you're filled with chagrin, wondering why she couldn't be a bit more soft-spoken and ladylike. She may not have intended to show off her learning in the letter, but of course as it is being read aloud in a halting, strained voice the whole thing seems calculated. There are many examples of this sort of behavior among the upper ranks of court ladies.

"A woman with aspirations to being a poet will become so obsessed with the art of composition that she'll insert allusions to felicitous old phrases even in the opening lines of her correspondence. She'll send off a poem at the most inopportune moments, which can be quite offputting. If the man doesn't reply, he's inconsiderate, and if he can't come up with an equally learned allusion, he looks ridiculous. For instance, at some seasonal festival, when a man is really busy . . . let's say on the morning of the Sweet Flag Festival in the fifth month when you don't have a moment to think calmly about anything . . . she whips out a poem with some fabulous allusion playing on the words 'sweet flag' and 'sweet eyes,' or some such nonsense. Or maybe it's the Chrysanthemum Festival, when you have no time at all to wrack your brains to come up with some difficult poem in Chinese as the occasion demands, and here she is sending you a lamentation that strains to play on the words 'chrysanthemum' and 'dew.'[3] The poem is not only unsuitable to the time and place but also a downright nuisance. What otherwise might have seemed a charming or moving poem at a subsequent reading ends up being totally inappropriate and not worth a second glance because of the manner in which it was sent. Composing a poem with no forethought is not very tactful.

3. The Sweet Flag Festival, which fell on the fifth day of the Fifth Month, was celebrated at the court with equestrian and archery competitions. The Chrysanthemum Festival was observed on the ninth day of the Ninth Month; chrysanthemums were thought to possess properties that ensured a long life, and so on that day, the flowers were wrapped in thin cotton cloths that, once dampened with dew, were rubbed over the body to take advantage of chrysanthemums' supposed life-prolonging properties [editor's note].

"It is far easier to deal with a woman who has no talent for discerning the proper moment or season to compose, who does not put on airs and try to act refined in a way that leaves you wondering why she did what she did. In all cases a woman should pretend to be ignorant, even if she has a little learning. And when she has something to say, she should just focus on a couple of points and skip the rest."

While the Warden was droning on, Genji was preoccupied with thoughts of one particular woman. Comparing her to the women he had heard about this evening, he was moved to an even greater admiration, since she seemed to be that rare type who was neither extravagant nor lacking in any way.

There was no conclusion to their discussion, and in the end as daybreak neared their ramblings came to include some rather queer and disreputable stories.

*　*　*

From Chapter V

Wakamurasaki

LITTLE PURPLE GROMWELL

*　*　*

With no one to talk to and idle time to kill after the healing rites were completed, he stepped out under cover of the heavy evening mist and set off with Koremitsu toward the fence he had spotted earlier. Peering at the bishop's residence through gaps in the fence, he could see into a room on the near side that faced Amida's Pure Land[4] in the west. The blinds had been raised slightly, which allowed him to observe a nun performing religious devotions before her own personal image of Amida Buddha. She was apparently making an offering of flowers. Leaning against one of the central pillars, she had placed a sutra scroll on top of an armrest and was struggling to read the scripture. She did not look like a common woman. She was probably over forty, her complexion exceptionally fair and graceful. Though she was thin, her cheeks were plump, and the strands of her hair, which had been cut attractively to neatly frame the area around her eyes, struck Genji as more distinctively fashionable than the long hair that was the common style. Watching her, he was touched by her appearance.

Two pretty adult attendants, also neatly turned out, were with her, and some young girls were playing there, running in and out of the room. One of them, who must have been about ten years old, was wearing a white singlet under a soft, crinkled outer robe dyed the rich yellow of mountain rose and lined with a yellow fabric. She didn't look like the other girls at all; her features were so attractive that Genji could tell at once that she would grow up to be a woman of surpassing beauty. Her hair flowed out behind her, spreading open in the shape of a fan as she stood there, her face red from brushing tears away.

---

4. Devotees of Pure Land Buddhism believe that they will be reborn in the "Western Paradise" of the Buddha Amitabha [editor's note].

"What happened?" the nun asked her. "Did you get into a quarrel with the other girls?"

When the nun looked up to speak, Genji could see the resemblance in their faces and assumed that they must be mother and daughter.

"Inuki let my baby sparrow out of the cage and it flew away." The girl was pouting.

One of the young women sitting there said, "Careless as usual. Inuki's in for a real scolding this time. What a nuisance she is! So where did the sparrow go? It's such a darling little thing; it would be horrid if the crows get to it."

She stood up and went out, her hair quite long and luxuriant. *Certainly easy on the eyes,* Genji thought. Apparently her name was Shōnagon, and she was the nurse who looked after the little girl.

"How childish!" the nun said. "Really, this whole thing is just too petty. You pay no heed to me, even though I could pass away any day now, and instead go running about chasing after sparrows. How many times have I told you it's a sin in the sight of Buddha to capture living creatures. It's deplorable. Come over here!"

The girl knelt down beside her. Her face was remarkably sweet, her unplucked eyebrows 'had the most charming air about them, and the cut of her hair and the look of her forehead, with those bangs swept up so innocently, were unbearably cute. Genji couldn't stop gazing at her. *I'd really love to see her when she's grown up,* he mused. It occurred to him that his desire to see her grown up was kindled by her uncanny resemblance to Fujitsubo, the woman to whom his heart was eternally devoted. It was thus natural that his gaze would be drawn to the girl, and tears came to his eyes.

Stroking the child's hair, the nun told her, "You may not be fond of combing your hair, but it's so lovely. You're such a silly girl, and your childishness weighs heavily on my mind. Other children your age don't act like this. Even though your mother was only ten when her father passed away, she still understood everything going on around her. It won't be long before I die and you'll be left completely alone in the world. How will you ever manage to get by?"

Seeing the nun weep so bitterly, Genji felt a pang of sympathetic sorrow. The girl, with her childish emotions, stared at her grandmother, then hung her head and stared at the floor. Her hair came cascading down around her face. It was splendidly lustrous.

Just then the nun composed a verse:

> The evanescent dewdrop tarries, reluctant
> To disappear into the sky and abandon
> The tender shoot of grass to its uncertain fate

The other young woman, who was still sitting in the room, was now crying. "How true!" she said, and composed this reply:

> How could the dewdrop disappear
> Without knowing the destiny
> Of the shoot of grass it clings to

Just then the bishop entered and said, "What are you doing? You're clearly visible from the outside. Why, today of all days, are you out on the veranda? I just found out from the ascetic who lives up the mountain that His Lordship, Captain Genji, has arrived to receive treatment for his fever. He arrived in such secrecy that I knew nothing about it. I've been here all this time and didn't pay my respects to him."

"How awful," the nun said, lowering the blinds. "Has anyone seen us like this? We're not at all presentable."

"Don't you want to take this opportunity," asked the bishop, "to catch a glimpse of the Radiant Genji? After all, he has such a noble reputation at the court. His looks are enough to make even the heart of a monk who has renounced society forget the sorrows of life and desire to live on in this world. I shall send him a letter."

Upon hearing the bishop stand up to leave, Genji also retired, delighted at the thought that he had discovered such a gorgeous child under these circumstances. His amorous companions were always going out, and so they were skilled at finding the kind of unusual woman that one rarely meets at court. Genji, however, could only go out occasionally, and so he was even more delighted to have the unexpected good fortune to stumble across a girl like this. She was certainly lovely, but her beauty made him curious. Who was she? She resembled Fujitsubo so closely that he was completely taken with the notion that he might be able to make her a replacement for the woman he loved, keeping the girl by him mornings and evenings as a comfort to his heart.

Genji had withdrawn and was lying down and resting when a disciple of the bishop called out for Koremitsu. They were close by, so Genji could hear everything they said. The disciple was apparently reading aloud the bishop's message:

"I just now learned that His Lordship has passed by my residence, and though I was caught by surprise, I still should have called on you. However, as you know, I have secluded myself in this temple, and so I regret that you have traveled here in secret, for I could have made my abode, rough and humble though it is, ready for you. I feel this is truly unfortunate, for it was in no way my intention to slight you."

Genji sent back a reply:

"Starting around the tenth of this month I began suffering repeated bouts of ague. The attacks were so frequent I found them hard to bear, and so on the advice of others I came discreetly to see the ascetic here. I chose to keep my journey a strict secret, because if the ascetic's spells were ineffective for me, it would certainly damage his reputation. It would be a much greater pity if such a venerable ascetic were to fail than it would be if the healer were some ordinary priest, and so I wanted to exercise some caution. I shall go to your residence presently."

The bishop himself appeared soon after. Even though he was a priest, he had a reputation at court as a man of flawless breeding and dignity, and his bearing was enough to put people to shame. Genji, who was dressed in humble fashion, felt awkward before him. The bishop spoke of the time he had spent in seclusion here, and then insisted repeatedly that Genji pay him a visit.

"My house is but a rustic hut," he said, "not all that different from this abode here, but at least it will provide you a view of the cool stream there."

Genji felt embarrassed as he recalled the fawning manner in which the bishop had described his radiant looks to the women, who had never seen him. Still, he was eager to learn more about the lovely little girl, and so he went with the bishop.

Just as the bishop said, the garden at his residence exuded an air of elegance. The trees and grasses, which were familiar varieties, had been cultivated with special care. Because it was the night of the new moon, cressets had been set along the banks of the stream, the light from their fires reflecting in the water, and oil lamps were hung beneath the eaves. The room facing south at the front of the house had been cleaned and neatly prepared. The refined scent of incense wafted out from the interior and mingled with the scent of the ritual incense offered to the Buddha, suffusing the entire area around the residence. Genji's perfumed robes carried their own special scent, which the people in the house could not help but notice.

The reverend bishop instructed Genji on the evanescence of this world and on the worlds to come. Genji, with some trepidation, was forced to acknowledge to himself the gravity of his sin of loving Fujitsubo, and it was torment knowing he could do nothing about the one thing preoccupying his heart. It seemed that he was doomed to suffer obsessively on account of his sin for the rest of this life; and what made it worse for him was always imagining the kinds of terrible retribution that awaited him in future lives. He thought he would like to leave the base temptations of this world and retreat to a humble abode like this, but then he found it hard to concentrate on the bishop's lesson, since the alluring vision of that young girl he had spied on during the day lingered in his heart alongside the image of the woman, Fujitsubo, the girl so resembled.

"Who lives here?" Genji asked. "Upon arriving today, I was reminded of a dream I wanted to ask you about."

The bishop smiled. "So you want to suddenly change the subject to your dreams, do you? Well, you can ask, but I'm afraid I'll disappoint you. You probably didn't know the former Major Counselor, since he passed away some time ago, but his primary wife is my younger sister. After he died, she took religious vows and left her household to become a nun. She's been suffering from a variety of ailments recently, and since I no longer go back to the capital she has decided to go into seclusion, using my residence as her haven."

Genji said, "I've heard that the Major Counselor had a daughter. My motive in asking about her, by the way, is quite sincere. It is *not* frivolous curiosity."

"He did indeed. One daughter. Let's see . . . it's been more than ten years now since she died. The late Counselor intended to send her into service at the court, and so he raised her with the greatest care. When he passed away before he could realize his hopes and dreams, my sister ended up raising her daughter by herself. When the girl reached womanhood Prince Hyōbu, who was Minister of War at the time,[5] was able to conduct a clandestine affair with her, using one of her scheming ladies-in-waiting as his go-between. Prince Hyōbu's primary wife, however, was a woman of impeccable birth, and as a result my niece suffered various insults that brought worry and grief. She grew increasingly despondent day by day, until at last she died. I have witnessed with my own eyes how sick from worry a person can get."

Genji gathered from the bishop's story that the little girl he had seen was the granddaughter of the nun. The Prince in question was the older brother of Fujitsubo, which explained the resemblance between the woman Genji loved and

5. The name Prince Hyōbu is taken from the Ministry of War (*Hyōbushō*). Since this prince is identified by his position, I am using this name as a matter of convenience.

the little girl. Now he felt an even stronger desire to see the girl and make the child his own. She was possessed of both a noble lineage and extraordinary beauty, but she also had an obedient temperament and was not impudent or forward. He wanted to get close to her, raise and train her in accordance with his own desires and tastes, and then make her his wife.

"A sad tale, indeed," Genji remarked. Since he wanted to find out for sure what had become of the little girl he had seen earlier, he added, "Did your niece leave any children behind to remember her by?"

The bishop told him, "A child was born just before my niece died . . . a girl. The child is the cause of terrible worry for my sister, who as death approaches fears she will leave her granddaughter in an unsettled situation."

So she's the one I was looking at, Genji thought.

"I know this will sound like a bizarre request, but would you do me the kindness of asking the girl's grandmother to consider allowing me to take charge of the child? I have good reasons for this request. I do call upon my primary wife from time to time, but we really don't get along so well, and I live alone for the most part. You may not consider her the proper age for such an arrangement, and you may think I am motivated by some common, base desire. But if you do, you are being unkind and dishonoring my intentions."

"Such a proposition would normally be met with great joy, but the girl is still so innocent it would be difficult, would it not, to take her as a wife—even if the whole thing was done in jest? A woman becomes an adult when a husband looks after her, and so it is not my place to deal with the details concerning such a matter. If I may, I will consult with her grandmother and try to obtain an answer for you."

The bishop was so forbiddingly sincere and stiffly formal in his manner of speech that it made Genji's youthful spirit feel small, and he was unable to come up with a clever response.

"It's time," continued the bishop, "to perform my devotions before the shrine of Amida Buddha in the prayer hall. I have not finished early evening services yet, but I will call on you again when they are over."

The bishop left and Genji was feeling ill. It had started to rain, bringing a cooling breeze. Moreover, the water in the pool of a nearby waterfall had risen with the spring runoff, and the roar was clearly audible. He could just barely make out the sound of sleepy voices reciting sutras, a sound that sent chills through him. The atmosphere of the place would have affected even the most insensitive of people, and, coupled with his preoccupation with both Fujitsubo and the girl, it prevented him from getting any sleep at all. The bishop had told him that he was off to early evening devotions, but it was already late at night. Genji could clearly sense that the women who resided in the interior of the house were not asleep, and though they were trying to be quiet he could make out the clicking of rosary beads rubbing against an armrest and the elegant, inviting rustle of robes. Because they were near him, he slid open ever so slightly the center panels of the screens that had been set up outside his room and lightly tapped the palm of his hand with a fan in order to draw their attention. Apparently they thought it unlikely that anyone would be there, but at the same time they couldn't very well ignore his summons. He heard one of the women moving over toward him.

Apparently confused, she retreated a bit and said, "That's odd. I thought I heard something. I must be deluded."

Genji spoke up. "They say the guiding voice of the Buddha will never delude you or lead you astray, even in the darkest places."

His voice was so youthful and aristocratic that her own voice sounded hesitant and embarrassed in response. "Guiding to where?" she asked. "I'm not sure I understand you."

"You probably think something is amiss, which is reasonable, since I called out so suddenly. Please present the following to your mistress."

> Glimpsing that sweet child so like a shoot of spring grass
> The sleeves of my traveling robes never dry out
> Damp as they are from dew and my own endless tears

The woman responded, "You surely must know there's no one here who would accept that kind of message. To whom should I give it?"

"It so happens," Genji explained, "that I have reasons for my entreaty, and so I ask for your understanding."

The woman retreated back into the interior of the house and spoke with the nun, who was confused by the request. It was, after all, shocking in so many respects.

"Really, these young people and their modern ways!" she grumbled. "Apparently this lord is under the misapprehension that the girl is old enough to understand the relationship between men and women. And how did he come to hear about our poems that referred to her as 'spring grass'?"

She was confused but realized it would be rude to take an inordinately long time to respond. So she sent the following:

> Are you comparing the dew-soaked pillow
> Of a single night's journey to these sleeves
> Covered by the moss of ancient mountains

"Unlike your robes," she added, "it seems that mine will never dry."

"I'm not very experienced at communicating this way through a messenger," Genji answered. "Please forgive me, but I would be grateful if you would allow me a moment to speak with you about a serious matter."

The nun turned to her attendants. "I'm afraid he's mistakenly heard that the girl is older than she is. He seems such a high-ranking lord that I feel humbled before him. How should I respond?"

"You must answer him," one of her women advised. "It would be a pity if you made him feel awkward."

"Yes, I suppose you're right," the nun relented. "But if I were still a young woman, I'd find it rather improper to meet him. His words are so earnest they make me feel unworthy."

She rose and moved nearer to him.

"I realize that this is all quite sudden for you," Genji said, "and that under these circumstances you must think my request rash and immoderate. But I assure you, I have no base desires in my heart, and swear to you that the Amida Buddha himself understands the depths of my feelings, which you seem to find incomprehensible."

He spoke in a very respectful manner, since he himself was feeling awkward about raising the subject so directly in the presence of her quiet dignity.

"I must admit I never imagined that we would meet," the nun responded, "but that doesn't mean I consider the karmic bond between us to be shallow. Why should I, since we are speaking to one another like this?"

"I was moved when I heard about the painful struggles the girl has endured," Genji continued, "and wondered if you would consider me a substitute for the mother who has passed away. I was at a very tender age myself when I lost my mother and grandmother, the ones who should have looked after me most closely. As the months and years have passed I feel I have been living in a peculiar, drifting state. The girl's situation is so similar to my own that I sincerely ask permission to be her companion. Because I'm concerned about how you will interpret my request, I feel constrained in bringing it up. However, I'll have very few opportunities to approach you."

"I know I should be overjoyed by your request, but I'm reluctant to grant it. I don't know what you've heard about the girl, but isn't it possible that you are misinformed about how old she is? Insignificant though I am, the girl who lives here is completely dependent on me for support, and she's so young, I couldn't possibly agree to your request."

"I know all about her," Genji pressed his case. "If you'll just consider the depths of my feelings, which are anything but common, you will put your reservations aside."

In spite of his insistent pleadings, the nun was convinced that Genji was unaware of the inappropriateness of the request and would not give her assent. When the bishop returned, Genji at once closed up the folding screen. *Well, at least I've pleaded my case. At least I can feel relieved about that.*

With the arrival of dawn the sound of monks confessing their sins in the hall where they devotedly chanted the *Lotus Sutra* came drifting down the mountainside. Their voices mingled nobly with the roar of the waterfall.

Genji sent a verse to the bishop:

> *Voices of atonement waft down the mountain . . .*
> *As I awake from dreams and earthly desires*
> *The sound of falling waters calls forth my tears*

The bishop replied:

> *Purified in these mountain waters*
> *My own heart is unmoved by the sound*
> *That calls forth those tears that soak your sleeves*

"Have my own ears grown accustomed to the falling waters?" he added.

The sky brightened to reveal an overcast day. The continuous crying of mountain birds mingled together so that Genji could not tell from which direction they were coming. The various blossoms on the trees and grasses, whose names he did not know, were scattering in wild profusion, making it look as though someone had spread a brocade cloth over the landscape. He looked on in wonder at the deer ambling about, pausing here and there as they moved along. The scene was a diversion from his illness.

Normally, the old healer wasn't able to get out and about very easily, but somehow he managed to make his way to the bishop's residence and performed a protective spell. He was hoarse and missing so many teeth that his pronunciation was a little off, but he read the *dharani*[6] in a voice that possessed the august quality appropriate to a priest of great distinction and merit.

The party that would escort Genji back to the capital arrived and, after offering their congratulations on his cure, presented him with a message conveying best wishes from the Emperor. The bishop busily prepared delicacies not normally served at court, offering unusual types of fruits and nuts that had been harvested from various places, including the deep valley below.

"I have made a solemn vow to remain here for the year," the bishop told Genji, offering him some rice wine, "and so I will not be able to see you off. Ironically, my vow is now making me regret having to part with you."

"The waters of this mountain will remain in my heart. I have been undeservedly blessed by a gracious message from His Majesty, who is anxiously awaiting my return. However, I shall come here again before the season of spring blossoms has passed."

> Returning to court, I shall tell them
> You must go see the mountain cherries
> Before the breeze scatters their petals

Genji's manner of speaking and the tenor of his voice were dazzling.

The bishop replied:

> The udumbara blooms once in three thousand years
> When a perfect lord appears[7] . . . having looked on you
> I no longer have eyes for those mountain cherries

Genji smiled and sagely remarked, "The *Lotus Sutra* teaches that the flower of the udumbara blooms only once and in its proper time, which is quite rare. You flatter me."

The healer received the winecup and looked at Genji in tearful reverence:

> The pine door waiting deep in the mountains
> Has now been opened so that I may see
> The face of a flower ne'er glimpsed before

As a memento of their meeting, he presented Genji with a *tokko*.[8] The metal rod, with its diamond-shaped points at both ends, was one of the implements he used in his esoteric rituals to symbolize the strength and wisdom needed to break free of earthly desires.

The bishop also presented several appropriate gifts. One was a rosary made of embossed seeds from the fruit of the bodhi tree that the famed Prince Shōtoku had acquired from the Korean kingdom of Paekche. The rosary had been placed in a Chinese-style box that was wrapped up in a gauze pouch and attached to a

---

6. *Dharani* are spells or incantations used for meditation, healing, or protection. They consist of a phrase or line originally in Sanskrit that encapsulates a central teaching of a sacred text in Buddhism. Often the syllables in the phrase had no semantic force, but *dharani* were used as an aid in meditation and, in this case, as a protective spell.

7. A Buddhist belief (the udumbara is a variety of fig) [editor's note].

8. This is an abbreviation of *tokkosho* (Sanskrit, *vajra*), a Buddhist ritual implement [editor's note].

branch of five-needle pine. Another gift was a set of medicine jars made of lapis lazuli, which were filled with medicines and attached to branches of wisteria and cherry.

Genji had arranged to have gifts and offerings brought from the capital for the healer and for the monks who had chanted sutras for him. He presented the required gifts to everyone there, even the woodcutters who lived in the vicinity, and after making an offering for continued sutra readings, he prepared to leave.

The bishop went inside with Genji's message and conveyed it directly to the nun. She replied to him, "No matter what he says, I couldn't possibly give him an answer now. If his heart is really set on the girl, then maybe we can consider it in four or five years."

The bishop agreed with her and told Genji how matters stood. Genji was deeply dissatisfied that the nun had thwarted his desires and responded by having one of the pages serving at the bishop's residence take a note to her:

> As I travel home through morning mists
> Having seen the flowers hue at dusk
> How painful to have to leave it now

Though the nun dashed off her reply, the brushstrokes were elegant and her characters truly graceful:

> It may be hard for the mist to leave the flower
> But gazing at the sky obscured by morning haze
> I can judge neither what it portends nor your aims

Just as Genji was about to board his carriage, a crowd of people, including his brothers-in-law, arrived from the palace to greet him.

"You left without bothering to tell any of us where you were going!" Tō no Chūjō complained.

He and his brothers had wanted to accompany Genji, and so they vented their grievances: "We would have loved to join you on your excursion here, but you heedlessly abandoned us. It would be a shame to return to the capital without resting for a while in the shade of these stunningly beautiful blossoms."

They all sat down on the moss in the shade of some craggy outcroppings and passed around the winecups. The cascading waterfall behind them made an elegant backdrop.

Tō no Chūjō pulled a flute from the breastfold of his robe and began to play clear, dulcet notes. Sachūben kept time by tapping a fan on the palm of his left hand and sang the line "West of the temple at Toyora" from the *saibara* "Kazuraki." The men in the party were all extraordinarily handsome, but Genji, still listless from his fever and leaning against a boulder, was incomparable. His looks were so awesomely superior that no one could take their eyes off him. Tō no Chūjō was gifted at playing the flute, so he had made certain to bring with him attendants who could accompany him on the double-reed *hichiriki* and the seventeen-pipe *shō*.[9]

9. The *hichiriki* is a type of flageolet. The *shō* is a mouth organ, similar to panpipes, made of bamboo.

The bishop brought out his own seven-string koto and insisted that Genji play it: "Please, just one song for us. I'd like to give the birds in the mountains a surprise."

Genji demurred, saying, "I'm not feeling all that strong."

Still, he managed to pluck out a not uncharming tune before they all set off.

Even the humblest monks and pages wept tears of regret that Genji should be leaving so soon. Within the bishop's residence some of the older nuns, having never before seen a man of such extraordinary appearance, remarked, "He surely cannot be a person of this world."

The bishop wiped away a tear and said, "Ahh, it makes me terribly sad to think that such an impressive, handsome man should have been destined by his karma to be born during the final period of the Dharma in this troubled realm of the rising sun."[1]

To the little girl's innocent heart, Genji seemed a paragon of beauty.

"He is even more splendid than my father, the Captain of the Guards," she gushed.

"If that's how you feel," said one of the female attendants, "then why don't you become his child?"

The girl nodded, thinking how wonderful it would be if only she could. Subsequently, whenever she played with her Hina dolls[2] or drew pictures of the court, she pretended that the lord was the Radiant Genji, and she would dress him in the finest attire and treat him most solicitously.

Genji first went straight to the palace to inform his father of all that had happened in recent days. The Emperor thought his son looked thin and haggard and worried that it might be something serious. He asked Genji about the effectiveness of the venerable healer, and, on hearing the details, remarked graciously, "We must promote him to a more senior rank as a priest. He has apparently accumulated much merit through years of austerities, so why have we never heard of him before?"

The Minister of the Left arrived at the palace as well and spoke to his son-in-law: "I thought about coming to meet you, but since you had gone off in secret I hesitated, not knowing what you were doing. Why don't you come and spend a leisurely day or two at my residence? I can escort you there right away."

Genji did not feel much like going with him and left the palace reluctantly. The Minister had his own carriage brought around and humbled himself by getting in second. His deferential gesture was a polite way of showing the care and consideration with which he was treating his son-in-law, but it made Genji feel uncomfortable.

Once they arrived at the Minister's residence, Genji could see that they had made preparations for his visit. It had been a long time since they had last seen him, and in the interim they had refurbished everything, adding decorations so that the place shone like a burnished jewel. As usual, Genji's wife stayed in her

1. A reference to the doctrine of *mappō*, one of the Three Ages of Buddhism. *Mappō*, the age when the law or Dharma is corrupted, is the final historical stage of Buddhism. Although various timelines were given, the most widely accepted view was that *mappō* would begin 2,000 years after Sakyamuni Buddha's passing and last for 10,000 years. The first two ages are the age of the correct Dharma/Law and the age of the imitated Dharma. This doctrine was extremely influential during the Heian period, when it was believed that *mappō* would begin in the year 1052 C.E.

2. Dolls dressed as highborn men and women [editor's note].

quarters and did not come out to meet him. She finally appeared only after her father had coaxed her repeatedly. Genji watched as she sat there stiffly, not moving a muscle, so prim and proper, arranged like some fairy-tale princess in a painting.

I doubt if it would do any good to tell her what's in my heart, he brooded, *or to speak about my trip to the mountains, but it would be wonderful if she would just respond to me in a pleasant manner. Still, the plain truth is that she remains cold and remote in my presence, and we're becoming increasingly distant and estranged as the years go by.*

He considered the situation unfair and intolerable.

"Just once in a while I'd like to see you acting like a normal wife. I've been quite ill recently, but you couldn't be bothered to even ask how I was. I know that such callous behavior isn't rare for you, but I resent it all the same."

She paused for a moment, then responded, "Yes, I know how you feel. As the poet put it, 'How hurtful it is to be ignored.'" She cast a sidelong glance at him— an expression that gave her face an air of extreme reticence and an affect of grace and beauty.

"You so rarely speak to me," Genji shot back, "so why is it that when you do, you have to say such strange and unpleasant things? You cite the line 'How hurtful it is to be ignored,' but that poem referred to lovers having an affair, not to married couples. What a deplorable thing to say! You're always doing things to put me off, to make me feel awkward. And all the while I've tried various things hoping that the time will come when your attitude toward me changes. But now I see that you have grown even more distant. All right then, perhaps some day, in some life to come . . ."

He withdrew to their bedchamber for the night, but she did not follow after him. He couldn't bring himself to call for her, and so he sighed and lay down. He pretended to fall asleep, even though he was thoroughly disgruntled, his mind troubled by all the difficulties that may arise in relationships between men and women.

He couldn't get the girl out of his mind, and he was curious to see what that little shoot of grass would look like when she was fully grown. The nun, acting as the girl's grandmother, had not been at all unreasonable in thinking that the child was not an appropriate age for him. It would thus be difficult to make any hurried advances at this stage. So how could he contrive to bring her with him and always have her as a comfort and joy? The girl's father, Prince Hyōbu, was certainly a refined and graceful man, but his looks did not possess her lambent sheen. So how could it be that the girl bore such a striking family resemblance to Fujitsubo? Was it because the girl's father and aunt were both born to the same imperial consort? Mulling over these points, the family connections made him feel closer to her, and somehow his desires became more urgent.

The day after returning from his mountain retreat, Genji sent letters to the house in Kitayama. His letter to the bishop merely implied what his intentions were. In the letter to the nun he wrote:

> Awed and constrained by your august countenance, I was unable to express my thoughts clearly and openly to you. I would be overjoyed if you could at least understand that my decision to address you in this manner is evidence of the depth of my feelings and the sincerity of my motives.

He enclosed a letter to the girl as well, which he had folded up in a knot:

> The vision of the mountain cherry
> Continues lingering inside me
> Though I left my feelings there with you

"As Prince Motoyoshi put it, 'I fear the wind that blows in the night.'[3] I too worry that the wind might scatter the blossoms so that I may no longer view them."

The handwriting was of course magnificent, and even though the letter had been wrapped casually, to the eyes of the older people there it was startlingly beautiful. They were troubled and perplexed by the situation, unsure how to respond.

The nun sent a reply:

> I did not give your proposition any serious consideration after you left, and now, even though you have so graciously written to us, I have no idea how to respond. She is not even capable of writing the *Naniwazu*[4] in *kana* yet, and so even though she now has your letter, it really does no good.

> You left your heart just before
> The mountain blossoms scatter
> Short-lived like your devotion

"I am now all the more concerned," she added.

The bishop's reply was essentially the same, and Genji was frustrated. After a few days he sent Koremitsu off with the following instuctions: "There should be a person there, a nurse named Shōnagon. Meet her and find out what you can."

It's his nature, I suppose, Koremitsu thought. *He can never let anything go.* Koremitsu had caught only the briefest glimpse of the girl—and thought she looked very young—but it was pleasant to recall the moment he had seen her.

Receiving yet another letter of proposal from Genji, the bishop thanked Koremitsu, who then met with Shōnagon and conveyed Genji's wishes. He spoke in detail about Genji's feelings and told her about his status and circumstances. He was a smooth, glib talker and was able to put together quite a convincing case for his lord. For all that, the girl was absurdly young to be married off, and everyone there felt that the request was somehow ominous, even distasteful, and they wondered what Genji had in mind.

Genji had poured his soul into his letter, which was written with deep sincerity, and as he had done before, he included a folded note for the little girl:

"I know you do not yet write in cursive style, but still I long to see those characters you practice when you copy the lines: *My love for you is not shallow like the reflection of Mount Asaka you see when you peek into the mountain spring.*"[5]

---

3. *Shūishū* 29: "Anxious that the wind during the night may have scattered the blossoms of plum, I rise early to view them."
4. The *Naniwazu* refers to a poem in the *kana* preface to the *Kokinshū* that children in particular used, along with the poem on Mount Asaka that appears below, as a text to practice writing the *kana* syllabary: "The trees in bloom at the inlet of Naniwa announce that winter is over, spring has arrived! The trees in bloom!"
5. The place name Asaka plays on the homophone *asa*, meaning "shallow." The poem Genji cites that the girl would have practiced writing is from the *Man'yōshū*. The poems that follow make variations on similar lines in the *Kokin rokujō*, a *waka* anthology.

> *What does shallow Mount Asaka have to do*
> *With these deep feelings . . . why is the reflection*
> *Of your face in the mountain spring so distant*

The nun replied for the girl:

> *They say one feels regret after drawing water*
> *From a mountain spring . . . so how could you see the face*
> *Of a lover in a spring as shallow as this*

Before Koremitsu returned to Genji, Shōnagon, the girl's nurse, told him, "Once we have spent some time here and my young lady's grandmother is feeling better, we will travel to the capital and definitely be in touch with you then."

Genji was irritated and dissatisfied when he learned from Koremitsu's report that his proposal had been rejected.

Fujitsubo was ill and had withdrawn from the palace to her home. Genji could see his father's anxious, grieving expression, which aroused great feelings of pity. Yet he also considered it an opportunity, and was soon lost in a reverie, as if his spirit had drifted out of his body. He stopped calling on his various women and instead idled away the days at the palace or at his own villa, dreamily gazing out until evening, when he would then pester one of Fujitsubo's ladies-in-wating, Ōmyōbu, to intercede on his behalf. It is not clear how she managed to arrange a tryst, but after some truly outrageous and exhausting machinations she pulled it off, and Genji was able at last to be with the woman he considered perfect. His meetings with her were so brief, however, they merely intensified the pain of his lonely yearnings. Were these trysts real, or were they a dream? He could no longer tell.

Her Highness was in a state of constant distraction, for she was all too aware that her unimaginable affair with Genji was genuinely shocking. She was determined to put an end to their relationship, since she found the prospect of continuing to meet him extremely unpleasant and depressing, and her appearance betrayed just how difficult it was for her to cope with the situation. Still, she somehow managed to maintain a sweet and familiar attitude toward Genji, and her dignified demeanor and discretion put him to shame. Her behavior only made him realize that there was no one like her in the world, that he could find no flaws in her—and that realization gave rise to a wistful anguish as he was left to wonder why it was that the woman who turned out to be his ideal was forbidden to him.

How could he possibly tell her all the things he wanted to say? He wished he might reside in obscurity in the perpetual darkness of the Kurabu Mountains. Unfortunately, his nights were short, and brought him nothing but sorrow and pain.

> *Though I am with you here and now*
> *So rare are these nights that I long*
> *To lose myself inside this dream*

He was sobbing now.

Feeling pity for him, she replied:

> *Will we not be forever the stuff of gossip . . .*
> *No one has ever suffered the anguish I feel*
> *Trapped in a dream from which I never awaken*

Fujitsubo's turmoil was understandable, and he felt ashamed before her. Ōmyōbu gathered up his robes and brought them to him.

Genji returned to his residence and spent a tearful day in bed. When he was told that Fujitsubo would no longer accept his messages, even though he knew she had always refused to read them anyway, he was hurt and could not focus his thoughts. He did not appear at court but locked himself away for two or three days. His Majesty was worried by his son's absence and wondered if something was wrong, if he had fallen ill again. In the face of what Genji had done with Fujitsubo, his father's concern terrified him.

Fujitsubo was distressed by her plight, and her illness, which had prompted her to withdraw from the palace in the first place, worsened. Messengers arrived one after another urging her to return, but she refused. There could be no doubt that she was not feeling normal, but no one knew what was wrong with her. As it turned out, she had already secretly surmised her condition, and the shock of realizing that she was expecting a child upset her. She was now panicked and confused. *What will become of me?* More and more, as the summer progressed, she refused to get up. She was now in her third month, and her condition was obvious. Her ladies-in-waiting observed this and grew worried and suspicious. She lamented that she should have to suffer such a strange and unhappy fate.

Because no one guessed what had actually happened, Fujitsubo's attendants were surprised to learn that their lady had said nothing to His Majesty until now. Only Fujitsubo knew, in her heart of hearts, what had happened. Her closest attendants, Ōmyōbu and Ben, the daughter of Fujitsubo's nurse, tended to her intimately in the bath, and so they had clearly seen her condition and recognized what was happening. They were troubled, because they knew they did not dare discuss the situation between themselves. Ōmyōbu in particular felt sad that her lady's inescapable karmic destiny had brought her to this pass. In order to explain the delay in reporting the pregnancy, they had no choice but to tell the Emperor that they had been beguiled by a spirit and had not recognized their mistress's condition right away. The women who served Fujitsubo all assumed that that was indeed the case, and the Emperor, overwhelmed with even more feelings of pity and concern, was constantly sending messengers to ask how she was doing. Their visits, however, only kept her in a constant state of dread and depression.

One night Genji had a weird and terrifying dream. He summoned a diviner who interpreted the dream to mean that Genji would become the father of an Emperor. This was shocking and unthinkable.

The diviner added, "Your dream also means that your fortunes are crossed and that you must exercise caution and good behavior."

Genji felt awkward, and so he told the diviner, "This isn't my dream. I have merely relayed to you what someone of very high rank told me. So until the dream actually comes true, don't say anything to anyone about it."

Genji was trying to make sense of things in his own mind, but when he heard that Fujitsubo was pregnant, he realized that her child might be what his dream portended. He sent increasingly desperate messages to Fujitsubo, but Ōmyōbu was now having second thoughts. Communicating like this was extremely risky and difficult, and she found that she could no longer act as a go-between for Genji. Even her brief one-line replies, which had always been infrequent at best, stopped altogether.

Fujitsubo returned to the palace in the seventh month. Because he had not seen her for so long, His Majesty's desire had only grown stronger, and he lavished his gracious affection on her. She was now a little plump, and her face had grown thin and careworn, but her appearance was truly, incomparably lovely. As he had done before, the Emperor would spend the whole day in her chambers. The early autumn sky signaled to them that it was the appropriate season for musical diversions, and so His Majesty was constantly calling for Genji, who had a talent for performance, to come and play various pieces on the koto or the flute. Genji had to struggle to keep his emotions in check on these occasions, though there were moments when his expression betrayed the feelings he found so hard to suppress. For her part, Fujitsubo would obsess over things she wished had turned out differently.

The health of the nun who had been staying at the mountain temple in Kitayama improved, and she finally returned to her residence in the capital. Genji inquired after her and sent her letters from time to time. It did not surprise him that in her replies she continued to refuse his proposition, but it didn't bother him that much because he was preoccupied by his concern with Fujitsubo and had little time to think much about other matters.

By the ninth month, as the end of autumn was approaching, Genji was lonely and depressed. A gorgeous moonlit evening inspired him at last to go to the place of a woman he had been secretly visiting. But then the weather changed—it turned stormy and a chill evening rain began to fall. The lady lived in the vicinity of Rokujō and Kyōgoku, and as he left the palace her place began to seem a little too distant. On the way he saw a weather-beaten house standing in the gloomy shade of an ancient grove of trees.

Koremitsu, who was accompanying Genji as usual, said, "That used to be the house of the late Major Counselor. I guess you should know that I visited it recently and learned that the nun has taken a turn for the worse. They have no idea what to do for her."

"What a pity," Genji replied. "I must pay her a visit. Why didn't you tell me about this earlier? Have a message taken to her."

Koremitsu sent one of the attendants in with instructions to say that Genji had arrived with the express purpose of calling on the nun. When the messenger entered and announced his lord's visit, the women were caught off guard.

One of them said, "This is most awkward. Our lady has been feeling much worse these last few days and couldn't possibly meet your lord."

It would have been rude and uncouth to send him away, however, so they prepared a space on the veranda under the eaves on the south side of the house and invited Genji to enter there.

"Frightfully untidy, I'm afraid," another of the women remarked, "but my lady wanted to show some gratitude for your visit. Your arrival was so unexpected, however, that you caught us unprepared. So please forgive the dark and gloomy atmosphere of this chamber."

The place did strike Genji as quite odd, but he answered, "I've been meaning to visit you all this time, but I refrained from doing so because I've been treated in such a way as to make me believe nothing would come of it. I'm anxious about you, having just learned that your illness has taken a turn for the worse."

"My ailments are no worse than usual, though I do sense now that I am nearing my end," the nun told him. "You have been gracious enough to call on me, but I'm not able to greet you directly. With regards to your proposal, the girl is still at an innocent age and lacks judgment, but once she is a little more mature, by all means think of her as you would any other woman and take her as one of your own. I'm so worried about leaving her behind in this world, isolated and helpless, that my anxiety creates a burden of attachment for me that will surely be a hindrance on the path to the salvation I pray for."

Because she was in a room close by, Genji could catch fragments of her weary voice.

"We are not worthy of this, and should be grateful for his attentions," she added. "If only the girl were old enough to be able to thank him properly."

Genji was keenly moved.

"If my feelings for the girl were truly shallow, then why would I embarrass myself by coming here and possibly looking lecherous? The moment I recognized there was some kind of karmic bond between us, I was deeply attracted to the girl and convinced to an almost mystical degree that our bond was not something that belonged to this world."

He turned to one of the attendants and continued, "My visit here may have been in vain, but may I ask for a word with the girl herself?"

"Oh, I don't know about that," one of the nun's attendants interjected. "She has been kept in the dark about all of this, and is now fast asleep."

Just as the woman spoke these words, the girl's voice could be heard from inside.

"Grandmama, Lord Genji is here . . . you know, the man who visited us at the temple? So why haven't you gone out to meet him?"

The women were all mortified and tried to hush the girl, but she protested, "Didn't Grandmama say that the sight of him was always a comfort to her?"

She spoke as if she were informing them of something that would benefit her grandmother. Genji was utterly charmed, but he had to be considerate of the bruised feelings of the flustered women there, and so he pretended he hadn't heard a thing. After politely bidding farewell and leaving his best wishes for them, he made his way home. *She may be a little girl,* he thought, *but I can't wait to see her after she's been properly trained.*

The next day Genji sent a most solicitous letter inquiring after the health of the nun. As always, he included a small folded letter for the girl:

> Hearing a young crane cry I long to go to it
> But my boat tangled among the reeds is hindered
> And I cannot leave this inlet to tend its needs

"As the poet put it, 'I always yearn to go back to the same person.'"[6]

Genji deliberately composed his note in a childish hand that was so delightful the women told the girl to imitate it in her copybook.

Shōnagon replied, "Our lady may not make it through the day, and we are preparing to take her back to the temple in Kitayama. She may not be able to express in this world her gratitude for your visit and your expressions of concern."

Genji felt very sad when he heard this.

---

6. *Kokinshū* 732 (Anonymous): "I always yearn to go back to the same person, like a little boat that has made its way through the channel and comes rowing home."

One autumn evening, when he was more preoccupied than ever with his long-ing for Fujitsubo, the woman who constantly tormented his heart, he felt his seemingly perverse desire to possess her little niece growing even stronger. He remembered a line from the nun's poem—"The evanescent dewdrop tarries, reluctant to disappear into the sky"—and thought lovingly of the girl. At the same time he was anxious and unsure, thinking that she might not live up to his expectations. An image of *wakamurasaki*[7]—a little purple gromwell—popped into his head:

> *How I yearn to quickly pluck up and make my own*
> *That little purple gromwell sprouting in the wild*
> *With roots that share their color with wisteria*

During the tenth month His Majesty decided to plan a visit to the Suzaku Palace. The dancers for the day of departure were to be selected from among sons of aristocratic families, high-ranking officials, and courtiers who had tal-ents suitable for the occasion. From princes and ministers on down, each and every one practiced their skills. It was a hectic, busy time.

Because of all the preparations, it occurred to Genji that he had not contacted the nun in her mountain temple for some time. When at last he sent a mes-senger there, he received the following reply from the bishop:

"I am sorry to report that she passed away on the twentieth of last month. I know it is the reality of this world that we must all die, but still I cannot help mourning her."

After reading this, Genji experienced the poignant sorrow of the evanescent world and wondered what would become of the girl who had been the source of such worry for the nun. The girl was so young, she must be pining for her grand-mother. Genji had vague memories of being left behind by his own mother, and so he sent his deepest condolences. Shōnagon composed a sympathetic reply.

Genji learned that after the twenty-day period of mourning and confinement was over, the girl came back to the capital and was now at the late nun's resi-dence. He waited until a seemly period of time passed, then went to call on her one evening when he had some free time. The place was run-down and deso-late, and there were few people about—the kind of place that would surely frighten a child. Genji was shown to the same space on the south side of the residence that they had used on his previous visit. He was moved to tears by Shōnagon's heartbreaking account of her mistress's final days.

"There is talk that the girl's father would have her come to his villa," Shōnagon told him. "But the nun was quite concerned about that prospect. After all, her own daughter, this child's late mother, found that household unbearably cruel and depressing. The girl is now at that in-between stage, no longer a child, but

---

7. The Japanese species of gromwell is a small plant that produces white flowers in the sum-mer. Its purple roots were used to make dye for clothing. As in other cultures, purple was asso-ciated with royalty, and so I have translated *murasaki* as "purple gromwell" to indicate both the rustic image of the word and its imperial associations. The Japanese name for wisteria is *fuji*, alluding to the girl's aunt, Fujitsubo, and suggesting by way of the color purple shared by the two plants the nature of their relation-ship. That is, since *murasaki* (or *wakamura-saki*) is the smaller, more rustic plant, Genji's poem acknowledges a difference in their rela-tive status. His poem alludes to *Kokinshū* 867 (Anonymous): "Because of this one purple gromwell, I look on all the grasses in Musash-ino with tender feelings."

not old enough to really understand the motives of other people. And with all the other children at her father's residence, she is not likely to be welcomed with open arms, but will instead be belittled and treated as a stepchild. With so many indications that the girl will be badly served there, we are grateful for your passing words of kind consideration. Still, we cannot fathom your future intentions, and even though we should feel happy on occasions like this when you visit us, we remain extremely hesitant about your proposal . . . after all, the girl is simply not appropriate for you. Her character is immature and undeveloped, even for someone her age."

"Why do you continue to waver when I have repeatedly opened up to you like this? I know in my heart that my feelings of longing and pity, which her innocence stirs in me, are signs of a special bond between us from a former life. If I may, I would like to speak with her directly and tell her how I feel."

> Seeing the young tangled seaweed struggle to grow
> Amidst reeds in the bay of Wakanoura
> Can the wave, once it has drawn near, recede again

"It would be too hateful for the wave to have to withdraw now," Genji concluded.

Shōnagon answered, "You are truly gracious, my lord, but . . ."

> If the algae at Wakanoura yielded
> Without knowing the true intentions of the wave
> Would it not be set adrift upon the shallows[8]

"It just isn't reasonable."

The polished manner of her verse made it almost possible for Genji to forgive her refusal.

"Why does the day when we may finally meet never come?"[9] he murmured. The younger women in the house shivered in delight and admiration.

The little girl had been lying down, crying and grieving for her grandmother until her playmates told her, "A lord dressed in court robes has arrived. Perhaps it is the Prince, your father!"

She got up and went out to see for herself, calling out, "Shōnagon! Where is the nobleman in court robes? Is my father here?"

Her voice sounded achingly sweet as she approached.

"I'm not your father," said Genji, "but that doesn't mean you should treat me as a stranger. Come over here."

The girl immediately recognized his voice and realized that this was the splendid lord who had called on them before. Embarrassed that she had spoken improperly, she went over to her nurse and said, "I want to go now. I'm sleepy."

"Why do you want to hide from me? Please come over here and rest at my knees. Please, come closer."

"As you can see," said Shōnagon, pushing the girl toward him, "she really knows very little about the world."

8. Both poems play on the homophone *waka*, meaning "youthful."
9. Compare this *waka* poem by Fujiwara no Koremasa: "Though I keep my impatience a secret, as the years go by, why is it so hard to pass beyond the barrier gate of Ōsaka, the slope where we may finally meet?"

The girl sat innocently on the other side of the blinds from Genji, who put his hand through to search around for her. Her lustrous hair was draped over soft, rumpled robes, and even though he did not have a clear view of her, when he touched the rich thickness of the strands he imagined how attractive she must really be. When he tried to hold her hand she was put off that a stranger should have come so close to her and pulled away in fright.

"I told you I was sleepy," she said to Shōnagon.

At that moment Genji slipped inside the curtains and told her, "You must think of me now as the one you will rely upon. So please don't be distant or afraid."

His actions were upsetting to Shōnagon, who exclaimed, "What are you thinking, my lord, impetuously barging in here like this during a period of mourning? It's outrageous. You can talk to her all you like, but it won't do you any good. She's just too young to understand."

"You may be right," Genji answered, "but just what do you think I'm going to do with someone so young? Carefully observe the sincerity of my feelings, the purity of my heart, and you will realize that they are peerless, that you will find nothing like them in this world."

The wind was blowing violently and hail began to fall. It was a lonely, terrifying night.

"Why," Genji asked, tears in his eyes, "should she have to spend any more time in this isolated, deserted house?"

He couldn't stand the idea of going home and abandoning them here.

"Lower the shutters. It looks like it will be a frightful evening," he ordered. "I shall stand guard for you tonight. Please, everyone, gather closer to me."

With a remarkable air of familiarity about him, he went inside the curtained area where the girl slept. The women found his behavior shockingly abnormal, but they did not know what to do and did not even try to move from where they were sitting. Shōnagon couldn't stand it. She was beside herself, but she couldn't very well offer vehement objections or make a scene, and so she stayed put as well, sighing in lament.

The girl, not knowing what was going on, was truly scared and trembling. Genji felt sorry for her, thinking that her beautiful figure was shivering because of the cold, and he had a singlet brought in and wrapped around her. Genji knew perfectly well that his behavior was not normal, and so he spoke sensitively to the girl.

"You really must come with me. There are many gorgeous paintings at my residence and Hina court dolls to play with." His manner was kind and intimate as he spoke of things he was sure would appeal to her childish heart and allay her fears. Nonetheless, she still found it hard to sleep, and spent the night tossing and turning.

As the night wore on, the wind continued to gust and the women whispered among themselves:

"How forlorn we would have been had he not come here. If only they were a little closer in age, it would be so wonderful."

Shōnagon, worried about her charge, hovered just outside the curtains the whole time. When the wind began to die down a little, Genji got ready to go home. It was still dark, and he had a knowing look on his face, as if he were leaving some romantic tryst.

"Now that I've witnessed her situation with my own eyes," Genji said, "it's all too pathetic, and I will now be more anxious about her than ever. She should be moved to my residence, where I spend my days and nights in solitary reverie. How can she remain here like this? It's a wonder she isn't in a constant state of terror."

Shōnagon replied, "Prince Hyōbu has hinted that he would come for her, but that won't happen until after the forty-nine-day period of purification is complete."

"He *is* the one who really ought to look after her," Genji agreed, "but they have grown accustomed to living apart and the girl most likely regards him as much a stranger to her as I am. I may have only just met her today, but my feelings and motives are not shallow—indeed, they are far more worthy than her father's."

Genji stroked the girl's hair, then glanced back repeatedly at her as he made his way out.

* * *

Genji experienced a swirl of conflicting emotions. There would be gossip about what was going on,[1] and he would undoubtedly gain a reputation as a lecher. If the girl were of an age when she could understand these matters and consent to the relationship, then people would understand, and it would all seem normal. But she was not of that age, and if her father were to come searching for her, then Genji's own actions would be seen as wild and rash. Yet despite his reservations, if he were to let this opportunity slip away, he would have bitter regrets. And so he departed while it was still dark. His wife remained her usual sullen and distant self.

"I just remembered some pressing matters I have to attend to," Genji told her. "I shall return shortly."

After going to his own quarters in the house at Sanjō and changing his robes, he set off alone with Koremitsu, who was riding alongside the carriage on his horse. He left before the women attendants even realized he was gone.

He knocked on the gate and someone who had been apprised of the situation opened it. Genji had his carriage drawn inside quietly. Koremitsu tapped at the double doors in the corner of the main hall, then coughed as a signal. On hearing this, Shōnagon knew who was there and came out.

"My lord has arrived," Koremitsu announced.

"The girl is resting inside," Shōnagon told him. "Why have you come out so late at night?" She assumed they were stopping by on the way back from their previous rendezvous at the palace.

"I have something I must tell her before she is moved to her father's residence," Genji replied.

"Whatever would that be? And how could she possibly give you a clear answer?" Shōnagon laughed and began to withdraw.

Genji suddenly barged in, and Shōnagon was completely taken aback. "The older women are in there! They are absolutely unpresentable!"

1. That is, Genji's intentions to take away the girl [editor's note].

"She's not awake yet, is she?" Genji said. "Well, then, I suppose I shall have to get her up. How can she remain asleep, oblivious to this lovely morning mist?"

He barged straight into the girl's sleeping quarters. Shōnagon was so flabbergasted that neither she nor her women could utter a peep in protest.

Genji picked up the girl, who was sleeping innocently, and woke her in his arms. She was still half asleep, and so she thought her father had come for her. Stroking her tangled hair, Genji said to her, "Come with me. I'm acting as a messenger for your father."

When she saw that it wasn't her father holding her, she was startled and fearful. "Come now, is that any way to act? I am just the same as your father." As he was carrying the girl out, Koremitsu, Shōnagon and the others all asked him what was happening.

"I told you I was worried about not being able to come here very often, and so I want to move her to my residence, which is much safer and more comfortable. If she were cruelly taken away to her father's villa, it would be that much more difficult for us to communicate. One of you may accompany me if you wish."

Shōnagon, who was now frantic, replied, "But today is the worst possible time you could have chosen. What should I say when her father comes for her? If it is, as you say, truly fated for her to be your wife, then surely that is how things will turn out later on. As it is now, she is just too young, and you have given us no time to think about things, which is putting all of the attendants in an awkward position."

"Very well, then," Genji responded, "some of you may follow later."

He had his carriage brought around. Everyone there was stunned and at a loss as to what to do. The girl, who did not understand what was happening, was frightened and started to cry.

With no way to stop him, Shōnagon brought out the clothes she had been sewing the previous night and, changing into a not altogether unattractive robe herself, got into the carriage with him.

Genji's residence in Nijō was close by, and so they arrived before first light. The carriage was drawn up to the west hall and Genji alighted. He easily swept the girl up in his arms and brought her out.

Shōnagon wavered: "This is all like a dream. What should I be doing?"

"That's entirely up to you. Now that I've brought the young lady here, you may return if you wish. I'll be happy to have someone escort you back."

Shōnagon smiled bitterly at his words, for she had no choice but to resign herself to the situation. She got out of the carriage. This had all been so sudden and outrageous that nothing could be done about it. She could not calm her heart. *What will her father say? And what about my young mistress? What will become of her? To have been left behind by all the people who loved her . . . it's just too much to bear.*

She could hardly hold back her tears, but she found a way to restrain herself, knowing that it would bring bad luck to cry on a momentous occasion like this.

The west hall was not usually inhabited, and there were no curtains or furnishings. Genji summoned Koremitsu and ordered him to have curtains, screens, and the like placed here and there where he indicated. He had the silk blinds hanging between the pillars around the inner chamber removed, and he had his attendants straighten up the room. When they were finished, he sent for robes and bedding from the east hall, then went in to rest. The girl now found the scene genuinely menacing and, uncertain about Genji's intentions, she began to tremble. Still, she managed not to cry out loud.

"I want to sleep with Shōnagon," she whimpered in a girlish voice.

"You must no longer sleep with her," Genji instructed, and the girl fell prostrate, weeping and feeling completely forlorn. Her nurse couldn't sleep either and stayed up all night lost in her thoughts.

As the dawn broke, Shōnagon studied her new surroundings. The residence and furnishings gave off a resplendent air—even the sand in the garden looked like jewels scattered all around. She remained hesitant, but it appeared that there were no other women serving in this hall. It was a pavilion where Genji would receive less intimate guests who called infrequently.

There were male servants just outside the bamboo blinds, and one of the men, who had heard that his lord had brought a woman here, was whispering to the others, "I wonder who she is? She must be someone extraordinary."

Cooked rice and water for their morning ablutions were brought in, and the sun was already high when they finally got up. Genji said, "This won't do at all. We have no one in service here. Choose those women at your former residence you would like to have as attendants for your young lady and I will send for them this evening."

Genji next summoned some page girls from the east hall, then told his servants, "Have these pages select several younger girls to serve over here."

Presently four captivating little girls appeared. The young lady was still asleep, her robes wrapped around her. Genji made her get up.

"This pouting and cold behavior will not do!" Genji scolded. "Would a man who is wild at heart have done all this for you? A woman must be kindhearted and obedient."

And with those words, from that moment on, her training began.

Her features were even more beautiful than when he had seen her from a distance. He spoke warmly to her, telling her stories and showing her all sorts of delightful pictures and playthings, which he had brought in for her, and did everything he could to soothe her feelings. Eventually she got up and inspected her quarters. She was wearing her dark mourning robes, soft and rumpled, and looked so adorable as she sat there with her innocent smile that Genji couldn't help smiling himself as he watched her.

Genji left for the east hall, and the young lady went over to the edge of the veranda and peeked out at the pond and the trees in the garden. She was fascinated by the grasses, which had been withered by the frost so that they looked like something out of a painting. A crowd of male courtiers of the fourth or fifth rank, none of whom she knew, bustled in and out, making her feel that she had come to some splendid world. She examined the captivating pictures on the folding screens and door panels, and with her childish disposition she was able quickly to comfort herself.

Genji did not go to the palace for two or three days so that he could spend time talking with the girl and making her feel at ease in her new surroundings. He wrote poems and drew pictures, presenting them to her with the thought that they might serve as a model for her own practice. He put them together to make a very charming collection. One of the poems, which he copied on purple-colored paper, was taken from *Kokin rokujō*:

> *I've never been there but lament my fate*
> *Each time I hear the name "Musashino" . . .*
> *The place where little* murasaki *grows*

The girl took up the sheet of paper and studied the unusual, exquisite brush-strokes. In smaller characters Genji had added his own verse:

> *Unable to cross Musashino's dewy plains*
> *I've yet to see the purple roots of the gromwell . . .*
> *How I long for the wisteria's little kin*

"Why don't you try writing something?" Genji encouraged her, though Fujit-subo was still obviously on his mind.

"But I can't write well," she protested, looking up at him. She was so lovely he couldn't help but smile.

"Even if you can't write well, you must at least try. You won't get better if you don't write anything. Let me show you."

He found it charming the way she held her brush and how she turned away from him when she wrote, and he thought it strange that he should have such feelings.

"I've made a mistake," she said, trying to keep him from seeing what she wrote. But he made her show it to him anyway.

> *I worry, unsure why you grieve . . .*
> *Tell me again which plant is it*
> *The one I am related to*

Her writing was quite immature, but he could see at once that she had the talent to be accomplished in composition. The lines of her brushstrokes were rich and gentle, and they resembled the hand of her late grandmother. If she practiced more modern models, he knew that she would be able to write very well.

He had court dolls and dollhouses made especially for her, and as they passed the time together he was able to distract himself from his painful longing for Fujitsubo.

The women who had remained behind at the girl's former residence were flustered and embarrassed when Prince Hyōbu came back and asked for his daughter, for they did not know what they should say to him. Genji had told them not to let anyone know what had happened—at least not for a while. Because Shōnagon agreed with him, she insisted that it was best to keep the matter quiet. Thus, all they could say to the father was that Shōnagon had taken his daughter into hiding, without telling them where.

Prince Hyōbu assumed that nothing could be done at this point, and he resigned himself to the situation. *Her grandmother was opposed to sending the girl to my residence, and so Shōnagon was moved to carry out her wishes, even if it meant going to this extreme. But why couldn't she just gently tell me that it would be too unbearable to move the girl, rather than willfully spiriting her away?*

When he left the house he said tearfully, "Let me know if you hear any news of her." This troubled the women.

He sent an inquiry to the bishop as well, but the bishop had no clue as to her whereabouts. Prince Hyōbu suffered longing and regret over the child's beauty, which would now go to waste. The enmity his primary wife had harbored toward the girl's mother had abated, and even she regretted that she would not be able to raise the child as she had hoped.

Gradually attendants arrived and gathered in the quarters of the girl—whom Genji called his little Murasaki. As a couple they possessed a rare, modern look. The youngest attendants and the little girls who were her playmates passed the time together without a care. Although there were lonely evenings when Genji was away and she cried out of yearning for her grandmother, she gave no thought at all to her father. From the beginning she had grown accustomed to not having him around, and she was now exceedingly close to the man who was her new father. Whenever he returned, she would be the first to go out to greet him. They would talk together lovingly, and she never felt distant or embarrassed when he held her to his bosom. Insofar as they looked like a father and a daughter, their behavior was quite endearing.

If a woman has a calculating heart and a troublesome disposition that makes an issue of everything, then a man has to take care that he not allow her emotions to lead her astray and keep her from fulfilling his desires. She will tend to be jealous and resentful, and difficulties he never imagined, such as a separation, will naturally arise. Murasaki, however, was an absolutely captivating companion for Genji. A real daughter, when she had reached this age, would not have been able to behave so intimately, to have gone to sleep or risen in such close proximity to him. Genji came to feel that his young Murasaki was a rare hidden treasure, his precious plaything.

From Chapter VII

Momiji no ga

AN IMPERIAL CELEBRATION OF AUTUMN FOLIAGE

The procession to the Suzaku Palace was set to take place sometime after the tenth day of the tenth month. Because it promised to be an unusually lavish event, the imperial consorts and ladies, who were not permitted to leave the palace, complained bitterly that they would not be able to see it. His Majesty was also disappointed that Fujitsubo would not be able to view the procession, and so he had the musicians and dancers perform a dress rehearsal in front of his living quarters in the Seiryōden.

Genji, a Captain in the Palace Guard, performed a dance called "Waves of the Blue Sea." His partner was Tō no Chūjō, who, as son of the Minister of the Left, was unquestionably superior to other men in terms of his looks and training. Performing next to Genji, however, he seemed like some nondescript tree deep in the mountains growing beside a cherry in full bloom. As the bright slanting rays of the setting sun shone down on them, the music swelled and the performance reached its climax. Genji was carefully following the prescribed form of the dance, but his movements and expressiveness were without peer. The music paused and he recited the accompanying verse in Chinese by Ono no Takamura in a voice as sweet and ethereal as the cry of the Buddha's heavenly Kalavínka bird.[2] The Emperor was so moved by the performance that he brushed away a tear, while all the upper-ranking courtiers and princes were weeping. At the conclusion of Genji's recitation, the lively music, which had paused for him, started up again. Genji had twirled the sleeves of his robe around his arms at the very end of the verse, and he was now readjusting them, his face flushed, looking even more radiant than usual.

As auspiciously splendid as Genji's dance had been, the Kokiden Consort found it strangely disturbing and remarked, "His looks are enough to captivate the gods in the heavens. It seems weirdly unpleasant."

The younger women deplored her unkind words.

Fujitsubo might have enjoyed viewing the dance more had it not been for the terrible guilt she felt at having received the Emperor's gracious gift of ordering this rehearsal for her benefit. To make matters worse, she had to watch a dance performed by the very man with whom she had conducted her outrageous affair. The whole thing seemed like a dream to her. That evening she was in service to the Emperor in his chambers.

"Waves of the Blue Sea" had swept everything before it at the rehearsal that day.

"What did you think of it?" His Majesty asked Fujitsubo. She struggled to answer, but managed to stammer out, "It was certainly a special performance."

"Genji's partner did not look bad either," the Emperor continued. "When it comes to form and gesture, good breeding will out. Professional dancers, those who have some reputation, are no doubt skillful, but they cannot display the same natural, unaffected beauty and grace that we saw today. The two men performed so magnificently, I have to admit I'm worried that when they dance under the autumn foliage on the day of the procession, it might be a bit of a letdown. But never mind . . . I so wanted you to see the performance that I had them prepare for it."

The following morning Genji sent a note to Fujitsubo:

"How did I look yesterday? As I danced, my heart was being torn apart by an unrequited love such as the world has never known."

> I should never have danced in your presence
> With thoughts so troubled . . . did you understand
> When, in wild abandon, I twirled my sleeves

"I feel uncertain before your grace."

Unable to shake the captivating sight of his face and elegant dancing figure, Fujitsubo could not very well pretend she had not seen his note, and so she replied:

> Chinese dancers conceived the "Waves of the Blue Sea"
> Twirling their sleeves so long ago and far away . . .
> But your every gesture touched me here and now

---

2. A bird mentioned in Buddhist sutras for its surpassingly beautiful voice, to which the Buddha's voice is often compared [editor's note].

"My heart is overflowing."

Genji had not expected a reply, and so he was ecstatic. Smiling, he thought that her words, which displayed knowledge of ancient dance and foreign courts, showed she had already acquired the dignity expected of a future Empress. He unrolled the letter and pored over it as if it were some treasured sutra.

On the day of the procession the princes of the blood and all members of the court participated. Genji's older half brother, the Crown Prince, accompanied the Emperor. As custom demanded, two boats were rowed around the lake at the site of the performance. One boat, adorned with the head of a dragon, held performers playing Chinese court music, while the other boat, adorned with the head of a blue heron, carried performers playing Korean court music.[3] There were many varieties of Chinese and Korean dance, and the sound of musical instruments and drums reverberated in all directions. Genji had looked so spectacular at the rehearsal the previous evening that the Emperor's old fears that his son might be fated to die young were revived, and he had sutras read for Genji at various temples around the capital to ward off evil. Everyone at the court who heard about this was sympathetic and thought it a reasonable precaution—everyone, that is, except the Kokiden Consort, mother of the Crown Prince, who spitefully remarked: "Isn't this really taking things a bit too far?"

The Emperor had gathered and selected the most distinguished players from among courtiers of both high and low rank to serve as the flutists and drummers who would accompany "Waves of the Blue Sea." He had the performers divided into sides—those playing Chinese music on the left, those playing Korean music on the right. He then chose two Consultants from the Council of State, men who also served as the directors of the Left and Right Gate Guards, to conduct the Chinese and Korean music respectively. Prior to this performance each aristocratic house had sought out the most skilled dance instructors and secluded themselves away to practice under their tutelage.

The intermittent soughing of the wind in the pines mingled with the indescribably polished sound of forty musicians playing in the shade of tall trees in autumn foliage. Truly it sounded like a breeze blowing down from the deepest mountains, and amidst the multihued leaves that had fallen all around, the dazzling performance of "Waves of the Blue Sea" was sublime. The autumn leaves that had adorned Genji's headdress at the outset had dropped off as the dance proceeded. Having lost a little of its luster, the headdress was now suffering in comparison with Genji's lambent face. So the Consultant who was conducting the musicians of the Left plucked some of the chrysanthemums that had been placed in front of the Emperor and inserted them into the headdress.

As the day drew to a close, a chill evening drizzle began to fall, as if the scene had moved the very sky itself. The color of the chrysanthemums now adorning Genji's spectacular figure had faded slightly with the frost, and their beauty was beyond the power of words to describe. Genji himself was putting all his skill into his performance, dancing in a way that would never be equaled again. As he executed the final movements, retracing his steps just before he exited with a flourish, it seemed that an unearthly chill coursed through all of the spectators. Lower-class people

---

3. The term for these boats is *ryōtōgekisu* (dragon head, blue heron head). In China it referred to a single boat with a carving of a dragon's head at the prow and one of a blue heron's head at the stern, but in Japan it referred to a pair of boats.

were also watching from the shade of craggy rocks, or from beneath the leaves falling from the mountain trees, and though one would hardly have imagined that they had the sensitivity to appreciate the performance, they were able to dimly recognize the sadness of transient beauty and wept accordingly.

The Fourth Prince, the Emperor's son by the Shōkyōden Consort, was still a boy. Nonetheless, his performance of "Dance of the Autumn Wind" proved to be the most spectacular event after Genji's dance. Because those two performances were so dazzling, everything that followed seemed bland by comparison, which put a damper on the whole affair.

That evening, both Genji and Tō no Chūjō were promoted—Genji to the senior third rank, which was rather an extraordinary rise given his previous status, and Tō no Chūjō to the lower division of the senior fourth rank, which was also an unusual rise. Other high-ranking courtiers had reason to rejoice as well, since those who deserved promotions received them. Since they had all benefited from Genji's success—his own rise having helped pull everyone up with him—it makes one curious to know just what virtue from a previous life now endowed him with the qualities that drew everyone's admiring eyes and caused hearts to be joyful.

At around the time of the procession Fujitsubo left the court and withdrew to her own residence. As always, Genji sought out every opportunity to see her, and consequently he was subjected to complaints from the Minister of the Left's household that he never visited his wife. Moreover, he learned that his wife was more distressed than usual because one of her attendants had reported to her that Genji had plucked a certain "wild grass"—meaning his little Murasaki—and that "he was keeping her in his villa at Nijō."

It's natural she would feel upset, Genji thought, *since she knows nothing at all about the situation or how young Murasaki is. Even so, why can't she just tell me how she feels and vent her resentments like a normal woman? I could then speak without reserve, tell her all the things I feel in my heart and put her mind at ease. But no, she has to be so damnably suspicious all the time. It's no wonder I find myself conducting these illicit affairs.*

Still, he had to admit that there were no flaws in his wife's appearance or manners that made him feel dissatisfied. And even though she did not understand his feelings for her, she was the first woman he had known, and so he could not help but regard her with special tenderness. He was sure that over time her attitude toward him would change and she would come to understand. After all, he had faith that, given her gentle and serious nature, she would naturally come around to him. The feelings he had for her were special and different from those he had for other women.

Murasaki was now comfortable with Genji. Possessed of both a virtuous character and attractive looks, she would innocently follow after Genji, clinging to him. For the moment, he was inclined not to give the people in his residence too much information about her, and he kept her in a separate wing of the villa, which he had done up in a lavish manner. He would visit her mornings and evenings, instructing her in all manner of things, copying out books for her to emulate in her writing practice. It made him feel as though he had taken in a daughter from some aristocratic household. He gave special care to setting up the household office and choosing the staff to serve her, so that she would never have cause for worry or complaint. Apart from Koremitsu, Genji kept everyone else in the dark about this woman he was treating so solicitously. Her father, Prince Hyōbu, had been unable to discover what had happened to her.

Murasaki would often reflect on the past, and she missed her grandmother terribly. For that reason Genji would try to divert her whenever he was at Nijō, and he even spent the night with her on occasion. Yet he was busy traveling here and there, visiting his many other women and going out during the evening, and so there were times when she would call after him and tell him how she ached to be with him. He found her unbearably sweet at those moments. Whenever he returned from two or three days of service at the palace, or from a visit with his wife at Sanjō, she would always look depressed. He found this distressing, and because he sometimes felt as though he were caring for a motherless child, he was no longer comfortable going out on his nighttime escapades. Upon hearing how well Genji was caring for the girl, the bishop at Kitayama was relieved and happy, even though he still considered the arrangement abnormal. Each time he conducted a memorial service for his sister, the late nun, Genji never failed to provide him with solemn, elaborate offerings.

Genji very much wanted to find out how Fujitsubo was doing. She had withdrawn to her own villa on Sanjō Avenue, and so he called on her there. He was met by several of her ladies-in-waiting—Ōmyōbu, Chūnagon and Nakatsukasa—and it bothered him that they acted so formally, clearly treating him as if he were a stranger. He stayed calm, keeping his feelings to himself as he exchanged pleasantries and court gossip with the women. Just then the Minister of War, Prince Hyōbu, arrived. When he learned that Genji was there as well, he granted him an audience. The Prince's elegant looks and bearing bespoke his high breeding, and Genji found his softly erotic, seductive manner so appealing that he imagined that the Prince would be a very alluring partner were he a woman. What's more, because the Prince was the older brother of Fujitsubo and the father of Murasaki, Genji felt a surge of intimacy with the man, speaking to him in a relaxed, warmly familiar way. Noticing that Genji was kindly opening up to him more than usual, the Prince found him quite enchanting. Unaware that Genji was now his son-in-law, he had a similar fantasy, imagining what Genji would be like as a woman.

Being Fujitsubo's older brother, he had the right to go in behind her curtains to speak to her when evening came. Genji was jealous of him, recalling the times when, as a little boy, he would be permitted to accompany his father behind Fujitsubo's curtains and address her face-to-face with no intermediaries. When he thought of the pain their separation caused him, he could hardly stand it.

"Though I should visit you more often," Genji said, "I normally don't have any reason to come here, so naturally I have neglected to stay in touch. Still, it would make me happy if you would send word should you ever need me to take care of something."

His manner was serious and he made no pretense of showing the usual charming warmth as he left Fujitsubo's residence. Ōmyōbu had been useless to Genji in arranging a meeting with Fujitsubo, and it was clear that Fujitsubo now regretted more than ever the karmic destiny that had brought them together. In the face of her mistress's coldhearted attitude, Ōmyōbu felt so ashamed, so at a loss, that as the days went by she found she was no longer able to help Genji in any way. Mutually lost in their unending torment, Fujitsubo and Genji realized how evanescent their bond had been.

Murasaki's nurse, Shōnagon, observed the wonderful though completely unexpected rapport that had developed between Genji and her young mistress and was convinced that their relationship was a blessing from the Buddha, to whom the old nun had constantly prayed and made hopeful offerings. Yet Shōnagon continued to be assailed with doubts about Murasaki's future.

Genji's wife is a woman of unquestionably high status and breeding, and he is involved with a number of other women as well. Surely when the girl comes of age someone will cause problems for her, will they not?

It was only because Genji seemed so devoted to Murasaki that Shōnagon felt she could trust him.

Murasaki was told that three months was an appropriately long period to wear robes of mourning for her grandmother, and so she put them away at the end of the twelfth month, just in time for the New Year. Having known no parent other than her grandmother, she was influenced by the old nun's tastes and continued to wear modest robes of plain crimson, purple, or yellow. In spite of these preferences, she was lovely—indeed, it could even be said that she was rather chic.

On the morning of the first day of the New Year, Genji peeked in on Murasaki's quarters on his way to court to attend the ceremony offering congratulations to the Emperor.

"Your change of attire makes you look more grown up than usual," he laughed, exuding a dazzlingly gentle and affectionate appeal.

Before he knew it, Murasaki was absorbed in arranging her Hina court dolls, setting out various accessories on a series of three-foot-long shelves and spreading the little dollhouses that had been made for her all around the room until it was overflowing with her playthings.

"That Inuki!" Murasaki grumbled. "Last night during the demon purification ritual, she was following the exorcist and got so excited by his mask and lance that she broke this. I've been trying to fix it."

Clearly she regarded this as a major crisis.

"She really is inconsiderate, isn't she?" Genji responded. "I'll have it repaired for you. You just remember that there is no crying or pouting today—it would bring bad luck."

His dashing looks, together with the grand size of his retinue, made his departure for court seem so ceremonious that the women attendants at his residence came out onto the veranda to see him off. Murasaki also stepped outside to watch him leave, then went back inside and dressed up her Genji doll to match the attire he was wearing to the palace.

"I hope you'll start acting a little more mature this year," Shōnagon scolded her charge. "Here you are, already past your tenth birthday, and you're still playing with these dolls. It just won't do. You have a husband now, and you really must start behaving more like a proper wife and looking more like a lady for him. You still can't stand for me to fix up your hair."

Shōnagon scolded Murasaki in order to shame the girl for always being so absorbed in her playthings. But the effect of her admonition was to make Murasaki finally understand her circumstances for the first time.

So he's my husband, is he? The attendants here all have husbands, but they're really ugly. Mine, on the other hand, is a dashing, handsome young man.

It may have been true that she was still attached to her playthings, but her newfound awareness of her relationship with Genji signaled that she was now a year older. The people who served at Genji's mansion had found her childish behavior, which could be quite pronounced at times, awkward and inappropriate, and yet they had no idea that she was in fact a wife in name only, for Genji had not had sex with her even though they slept together.

Following the ceremony at the palace, Genji went to the Minister of the Left's residence on Sanjō. His wife, as always, presented an icy, beautiful perfection that emitted not the slightest hint of demureness or endearing warmth. He felt uncomfortable in her presence.

"How happy it would make me if—this year, at least—you could change your attitude toward me so that we might have a little more normal relationship as husband and wife."

She, however, was in no mood for reconciliation. Having heard that he had set up another woman at his villa—evidently someone of great value worthy of his special attentions—she could not help feeling depressed and awkward around him. She struggled to act nonchalant, to pretend that she knew nothing about what was going on, and she found it hard, whenever he was intimate and unreserved, to remain stubborn and refuse to open up to him. Indeed, the gentle way she always responded had a special quality that set her apart from other women. Four years older than her husband, she was, at the age of twenty-two, now in her prime, and this was a problem for Genji because her flawless beauty and manners made him lose confidence when he was in her presence. There was nothing lacking in her, no flaws that he could detect anyway, and when he reflected on his own behavior he had to admit that her resentment was justified, since it was caused by those inexcusable affairs his fickle heart led him to pursue. After all, she was the only daughter of the Minister of the Left—a man who of all the nobles of similar rank had the weightiest reputation at court— and Princess Ōmiya, who was the younger sister of the Emperor. The greatest care had been lavished on his wife's upbringing, which meant that her sense of pride was exceptionally strong and that she would take even the most trivial slight or indiscretion as a serious and unpleasant injustice. This in turn made Genji resentful, wondering why it was that he was the one who always had to humor her pride. And so their hearts remained distant and unreconciled.

The Minister of the Left was disturbed by his son-in-law's fickleness, and yet whenever he saw Genji he would always forget his resentments, treat him deferentially, and do everything in his power to look after him. The following morning, as Genji was dressing and preparing to leave for court, the Minister dropped by to look in on him. Now that Genji had been promoted to the third rank, his father-in-law had ordered the servants to bring in a famous obi sash made of lacquered leather studded with gemstones that would show at the back of his robe and indicate his new status. He also had his servants straighten up the back of Genji's robes and was so particular about the choice of shoes it was almost as if he were putting them on Genji's feet himself. His solicitous behavior was somehow both touching and a little pathetic.

"Should I wear this on official occasions?" Genji asked. "The privy banquet will be held soon, on the Day of the Rat . . . is it the twenty-first or the twenty-third this year? Either way, I have to practice my Chinese verse for the event."

"I have better obi for events like that," the Minister sniffed. "This one just struck me as rather unusual-looking. That's all."

He pressed Genji to put it on, being almost religiously devoted to looking after him any way he could. Genji's appearances at Sanjō were certainly infrequent, but just to see this remarkable young man coming and going from his residence was a source of great joy and pride for the Minister.

Genji set off to make his New Year's round of visits. He did not have all that many places to call on: he paid his respects to the Emperor, to the Crown Prince, and to the former Emperor. He also dropped by Fujitsubo's villa on Sanjō.

"He's more remarkable than ever today. It's thrilling to realize that as he grows older, he's becoming even more handsome."

Fujitsubo's women were praising him up and down, and so she could not resist peeking through the gaps between her curtains to steal a glimpse. Immediately she was lost in her own troubled thoughts.

Her pregnancy was a source of considerable anxiety. Would she survive it? She was supposed to have given birth during the twelfth month, but here it was the New Year already. Her attendants were in a state of anticipation, thinking that surely their mistress would give birth sometime this month. Even His Majesty was having preparations made at court. But the first month passed with no indication that the birth was imminent, and rumors were now flying around court society. Was this delay the fault of some malign spirit? Such gossip made Fujitsubo feel even more miserable, for just as she was frightened by the possibility that she might die in childbirth, she was just as deathly afraid that the secret of her affair with Genji would be exposed. Her mental anguish eventually made her physically ill.

It was now increasingly clear to Genji that he was the father, and so to ward off evil spirits he discreetly ordered esoteric rites to be performed at various temples around the capital. He fully understood the evanescent nature of the world, but he could not help torturing himself with the thought that his relationship with Fujitsubo would end too soon and come to naught.

Then, sometime after the tenth of the second month, Fujitsubo gave birth to a Prince. The Emperor and all the people at Fujitsubo's residence in Sanjō were relieved and excited by this auspicious event, even if Genji and Fujitsubo were not. His Majesty had been praying for her to live a long life, yet now the thought of a long life was a burden to Fujitsubo, given all her cares. When rumors reached her that the Kokiden Consort had tried to curse her by praying for an unlucky birth, she realized that news of her death would have served as a source of amusement to some at the court. She drew strength and determination from that thought, and gradually her health and spirits improved.

The Emperor's desire to see the child as quickly as possible was boundless. Genji, who was keeping his feelings to himself, was also extremely anxious to see the child to confirm whether or not he was the father. Choosing a time when he knew there would be no one else around, he paid a visit to Fujitsubo.

"My father is eagerly waiting to see the child," Genji told her. "I thought I might take a look at the baby and then report to the Emperor."

"That's out of the question . . . he was just born and is not presentable in his present condition."

Fujitsubo quite reasonably refused, for there was no denying that the baby bore a shocking, almost otherworldly resemblance to Genji—a living reproduction.

Suffering from the demon of guilty conscience, Fujitsubo was convinced that anyone who saw the baby would instantly recognize the sin that she had committed with Genji. Since sanctimonious people were always eager to discover and condemn even the most minor of faults, what would they say about this? What would happen to her reputation? Dwelling on such possibilities, Fujitsubo was deeply distressed, body and soul.

Genji would meet with Ōmyōbu once in a while, doing his utmost through her to plead his case with Fujitsubo. Not surprisingly, his pleas fell on deaf ears.

He continually pestered her about the young Prince until finally Ōmyōbu told him, "Why must you insist on seeing him? You'll have your chance in due time." Even though she tried to reassure him, she seemed as troubled at heart as he.

Constrained by his surroundings, Genji could not speak frankly with Ōmyōbu. "Will there ever be a time or conditions when I can speak directly to Fujitsubo, without having to rely on an intermediary?"

It was heartbreaking to see him on the verge of tears.

> What karmic bond forged in a former life
> Destined us to meet again in this world
> Only to find ourselves always apart

"I cannot understand these things," he lamented.

Having witnessed the torments her lady was experiencing, Ōmyōbu found it impossible, in the face of Genji's sadness, to curtly refuse him. She recalled the poem by Fujiwara no Kanesuke that evoked the "hearts of parents lost in darkness," and replied:

> The one looking on the child suffers regret
> The one who cannot see the child suffers grief . . .
> Must all parents wander lost in such darkness

"How sad that the birth of this child should keep your hearts from finding peace," she murmured.

With no means of communicating with Fujitsubo, Genji returned to his residence. Troubled by the possibility of idle chatter at the court, Fujitsubo told Ōmyōbu that she could no longer tolerate her leading Genji here; that was how she really felt. Wary that Ōmyōbu might bring Genji to her, she was no longer able to trust her lady-in-waiting as she had in the past, and stopped treating her as a confidante. She continued to treat Ōmyōbu kindly, so that no one would suspect anything was amiss, but there were times now when she appeared displeased by Ōmyōbu's conduct. Aware that she was estranged from Fujitsubo, Ōmyōbu felt sad that things had not turned out as she had expected.

The baby was taken to the palace during the fourth month. Larger than usual for a baby that age, the boy was already able to turn himself over. His face bore a striking resemblance to Genji's, but it never occurred to the Emperor that Genji might be the child's true father. Rather, he assumed that people who shared unparalleled good looks would naturally resemble one another. His affection and care for the baby were boundless. His affection for Genji also knew no limits, but the lack of recognition and support for Genji among the high-ranking courtiers had made it impossible for him to install Genji in the line of succession. He constantly regretted his decision, and it was a source of pain for him to now look on his son's mature bearing and features and have to think what a waste it was to have removed Genji from the imperial line. It was thus a source of consolation for him that Fujitsubo, the fourth daughter of the previous Emperor and a woman of unimpeachable status, had given him a son who possessed the same radiant beauty as Genji. He considered the child a flawless jewel and lavished the greatest care on him—attention that, for Fujitsubo, merely added to the guilt and anxiety filling her heart.

One day, when Genji decided to pass the time performing music in Fujitsubo's quarters at the palace, as was his wont, His Majesty joined them. He was carrying the infant Prince in his arms.

"I have many, many children," he remarked to Genji, "but you were the only one I was able to be with all day from the time you were this one's age. Maybe it's because this little one brings those days back to me that I think he looks so much like you. I wonder if all children look the same when they are very young?"

It was obvious that the Emperor found the child adorable.

Genji felt himself blanch. Fear, shame, elation, pity . . . all these emotions over whelmed him to the point that he felt he was going to cry. The baby prattled and smiled, and looked almost preternaturally cute. Was it all that unreasonable or vain of Genji to think—assuming he really did resemble this child during his own infancy—that he himself must indeed have been incredibly precious? Fujitsubo could hardly stand to be there—she was so mortified that she began to perspire. At the same time Genji, who had been so eager to see the child, was unnerved in his presence, and the turmoil in his heart forced him to withdraw from Fujitsubo's quarters.

Genji returned to his Nijō villa, and after resting for a while to calm his nerves, he decided that he should pay a visit to his wife. Pinks were brightly blooming amidst the vibrant green of the plantings that seemed to cover the entire front garden, so he had one of them picked and sent to Ōmyōbu. There were so many things he had to write to Fujitsubo:

> Though I see you in him, the one so like this little pink,
> I cannot tell you so, and thus my heart knows no comfort
> My tears heavier than the dew on this flower's petals

"No matter how much I long to see the little one bloom, because our relationship was not meant to last in this vain world . . ."

His note must have been delivered at an opportune moment. Ōmyōbu showed it to Fujitsubo and encouraged her lady to write back:

"You really should answer him, even if, as Ōshikōchi no Mitsune put it, your response is no more than a mote of dust on the petal of a pink."[4]

Fujitsubo was deeply moved and sent back a simple poem written in the faintest of hands. Her characters looked as though she had pulled the brush away before finishing each stroke:

4. *Kokinshū* 167 (Ōshikōchi no Mitsune): "I long to stop even a mote of dust from settling on this bed of pinks that have come into bloom since first you and I lay on our bed." Mitsune's poem is alluded to in the *Hahakigi* chapter.

> *Though I may consider it the source*
> *Of the heavy dew that soaks my sleeves*
> *How could I discard this precious pink*

Ōmyōbu was overjoyed that her lady had responded, and she promptly delivered the poem to Genji. At that moment Genji was lying languidly, absently lost in melancholy thoughts, sure that his poem had been in vain and that no reply would be coming back to him. But as soon as he saw Ōmyōbu, his heart beat wildly and he was so happy he wept.

Feeling that it was not good for him to just lie around and mope, absorbed in his cares, he decided he should go to the west hall to see the one person who was his solace. His hair was mussed, he had carelessly tossed on a loose robe, and he was playing a sweetly nostalgic air on his flute when he looked in on Murasaki. She was reclining on an armrest, her elegant appearance calling to mind the image of pinks drenched in dew—perfectly lovely and cute. As enchanting as she looked, it turned out that she was nursing a new grudge against Genji. This was unusual for her, but there she was, sitting with her back toward him, annoyed that he had not come to see her sooner even though he had been in his quarters for some time. Genji moved over to the veranda at the edge of the room and knelt there.

"Come over here," Genji coaxed her, but she ignored him and continued to sulk.

She expressed her resentment toward him by murmuring lines from the *Man'yōshū*: "Is he like seaweed on the shore at high tide, which I long for so much, but see so seldom?"

She covered her mouth with the sleeve of her robe, apparently embarrassed at her own precociousness. Her gesture made her all the more adorable.

"Ahh, that's unfortunate . . . you've already learned how to complain just like an adult. Well, then, let me remind you of this poem: 'Were I to see you morning and night, just as often as the divers at Ise see the seaweed, would I not grow weary of you?'"[5]

He summoned a servant and had her bring in a thirteen-string koto for Murasaki to play.

"This instrument is difficult because the second string closest to you is thin and easily broken," Genji told her. He then tuned the instrument to a lower key to reduce the tension on the strings. He played a few short songs to test the tuning and then pushed the koto over in front of her. Murasaki found it impossible to continue sulking, and she played beautifully. She was still so small that she had to raise herself up and stretch to reach the strings, but he found the movements of her left hand, as she pressed the strings to make the instrument reverberate, delightfully refined. He instructed her by accompanying her on the flute. She had a quick memory and could pick up even the difficult keys in just one try. Clever, possessed of a sweet disposition, she was everything he had long hoped for in a woman. The court song "Hosoroguseri" may have had a peculiar-sounding title, but as Genji focused on playing it in his inimitable style, Murasaki

---

5. *Kokinshū* 683 (Anonymous).

accompanied him, skillfully keeping time to the rhythm even though she was so young.

Oil lamps were brought in and they passed the time poring over paintings together. He had mentioned earlier to his retinue that he intended to go out, and so a member of his escort began to cough to signal it was time to go.

"It looks like it might rain . . ." one of his guards remarked, and Murasaki at once became sullen and depressed, as she always did when Genji was about to leave.

She pushed the paintings away and lay facedown. Genji found her so endearing that he began to stroke her hair, which was spilling abundantly over her shoulders.

"I suppose you miss me when I'm away?" he asked her.

She nodded.

"I hate going even a single day without seeing you," Genji tried to comfort her, adding, "But since you are still a child, I have to ask you to be patient a little while longer and to not worry so. I have such fond feelings for you, but I must also consider the feelings of others and not offend those who may be jealous and resentful. Those women are troublesome, and that's why, for the present at least, I have to visit them as I do. When you are grown up I won't have to go out anymore, but for now I want to avoid the harm that might arise as a result of the jealousy of other women so that we might live a long life and be together as much as we desire."

Murasaki felt embarrassed to hear Genji speak about their relationship in such detail, and so she did not answer him. She drew herself up onto Genji's lap and went to sleep.

Genji felt terribly sorry for her and told his attendants, "I'll not be going out this evening." They all rose and withdrew, and he had his dinner, which he normally ate in his own rooms, brought to her quarters instead.

He woke Murasaki and told her, "I'm not going out after all."

Her mood at once improved and she got up. They ate together, but Murasaki was still anxious about his plans and merely picked at her food.

"If you're not going out," she suggested, "then why not sleep here tonight?"

If it is so difficult for us to part at a moment like this, Genji mused, *then how much more difficult will it be when we have to part on the inevitable road of death?*

* * *

From Chapter IX

Aoi

LEAVES OF WILD GINGER

The court changed when His Majesty abdicated and the Crown Prince took the throne as Emperor Suzaku. The Kokiden faction, headed by the Minister of the Right, was now in ascendance, and Genji began to feel that everything was more difficult for him. Just before His Majesty stepped down, he had promoted his favored son to Major Captain of the Right—a rise in status that required the Radiant Prince, in keeping with the dignity of his new position, to begin showing more restraint in pursuing his frivolous nightly adventures. The result was that his many lovers began to complain more and more of his heartlessness. Was it in retribution for causing all these lamentations that Genji suffered from what he saw as the unending cruelty of Fujitsubo, who kept her distance from him? Now, more than ever, she served at the side of the Retired Emperor—almost as if she were some low-ranking attendant. This did not sit well with the Kokiden Consort, but she was now Imperial Mother and had to serve exclusively at the palace—an arrangement that was a source of considerable relief to Fujitsubo.

Depending on the occasion, the Retired Emperor would sponsor musical entertainments so lavish and spectacular that they became the talk of court society. He seemed more content now than when he had held power. The only thing lacking for him was Fujitsubo's little son, the new Crown Prince. He yearned to see the boy, who could not be by his side. Having long worried that Fujitsubo's son had no supporters at court, he asked Genji to look after the boy's affairs—a request that was of course awkward for Genji, but one that also made him happy.

At this point I must bring up another, entirely separate matter. At the time Emperor Suzaku ascended the throne, an imperial princess was appointed as the new High Priestess for the Imperial Shrine at Ise. The mother of this princess was the lady at Rokujō—the woman Genji had long been visiting discreetly—while the father was an imperial prince who had actually been ahead of Suzaku in the line of succession, but who had died before he could take the throne. Because the Princess was appointed High Priestess under these circumstances, the lady at Rokujō, who no longer had any confidence in the reliability of Genji's feelings, was greatly worried about her daughter's future. The girl was, after all, only thirteen and would be alone in Ise. Thus, the lady at Rokujō had for some time been giving serious consideration to leaving the capital herself and accompanying her daughter to the Imperial Shrine. When the Retired Emperor heard about her plans to leave, he was extremely upset and spoke sharply to Genji about the matter.

"Do I need to remind you," he scolded, "that she was the first wife of my late brother and would have been an Imperial Consort? He had special affection for her, but now I hear rumors about how carelessly you treat her, as if she were some ordinary woman. It's pathetic. I look on her daughter, the High Priestess, as one of my own, and so you must put an end to this frivolous behavior—not just for her sake, but for mine as well. If you persist in playing these irresponsible little games, then don't be surprised when your reputation is in ruins."

Genji could not deny that his father was speaking the truth. Thoroughly chastened, he refrained from answering, whereupon the Retired Emperor added, his tone a little softer, "Never do anything to dishonor or shame a woman. Treat them all gently and give them no cause to resent you."

With that admonition ringing in his ears, Genji humbly withdrew from his father's presence, terrified at the thought that a day might come when his father learned the truth about Genji's wildly reckless affair with Fujitsubo.

If his father was lecturing him about it, then obviously gossip about his affair with the lady at Rokujō had spread through the court. His promiscuity had damaged her honor and his own reputation. He could just imagine how terribly she must be suffering, but there was simply no way he could formally acknowledge their relationship. For one thing, the lady herself was embarrassed that at the age of twenty-nine she was having an affair with a man seven years younger. Moreover, she always tried to appear distant and aloof, and so Genji had grown more reserved with her. Now, however, everyone at court, even the Retired Emperor, knew what was going on, and she lamented that Genji's feelings for her were so shallow.

Genji had long been pursuing the daughter of Prince Shikibu—a lady he knew as Asagao, his Princess of the bellflowers. His efforts had so far proven futile, however, and when Princess Asagao heard rumors of his affair, she resolved never to end up like the lady at Rokujō and refused to give even the most perfunctory of replies to his vain entreaties. Even so, she showed a proper attitude and conducted herself in a way that would give no offense to Genji, and so he continued to consider her a woman of superior qualities.

Needless to say, the household of the Minister of the Left was not amused by Genji's restless disposition, but then again, since he showed no qualms about carrying on so openly, it would have been useless to have complained to him about it. His wife, for one, did not harbor any deep resentment toward him, not least because she was now pregnant and suffering most pitifully not only from morning sickness but also from anxiety over the dangers posed by the coming birth. Genji thought the pregnancy remarkable, and for the first time felt sympathy for his wife. Because everyone was so overjoyed for her, there was a concern that such happiness could invite bad fortune, and so various prayers and rituals of abstinence[6] were commissioned in order to ensure safe delivery for mother and child. With all these things going on, Genji had less and less time to even consider the feelings of his other women. He was especially mindful of the feelings of the lady at Rokujō, but despite his best intentions not to neglect her, his visits practically ceased altogether.

The High Priestess of the Kamo Shrine also stepped down at about that time, and her successor was the third daughter of the Retired Emperor by the Kokiden Consort. This girl was a special favorite of both parents, and it bothered them that unlike her siblings she would have to live isolated from court life. Unfortunately, there were no other princesses appropriate for the position. Although the rituals of investiture were austere, as was customary with Shinto shrines, they would nonetheless be solemn and grand. The Festival of the Kamo Shrine, which was held in the fourth month, was always a major event in the capital; those who accompanied the High Priestess's procession would decorate their carriages and headdresses with heart-shaped leaves of wild ginger[7] Because this year marked the new Priestess's inaugural procession, many attractions would be added to the public events already scheduled, and the festival, in keeping with the special status of the High Priestess, would be an especially glorious one.

A few days before the start of the Kamo Festival, twelve high-ranking officials were required to attend the Priestess during the procession to her ritual of

6. That is, periods of seclusion [editor's note].
7. *Aoi*, the Japanese name for wild ginger, is also a homophone for the words *au hi*, which means "the day we will meet." The combination of the heart-shaped leaves of the plant, which is an evergreen, and the romantic impli-

cations of its name are played on later in this chapter in an exchange of poems between Genji and the older lady, Naishi, who appeared in the *Momiji no ga* chapter. Because much of this chapter centers on Genji's wife, she has been identified traditionally as Aoi.

purification, which took place on the banks of the Kamo River. Given the auspicious nature of the event, only men with honorable prospects and good looks were chosen for this task, and every detail of their appearance was carefully considered—from the color of the trains on their robes and the pattern of their trousers to the choice of horses and saddles. By special order of Emperor Suzaku, Genji was chosen to participate, and when those who planned to view the procession heard about this decision, they gave extra thought in advance to preparing and positioning their carriages along the route.

The thoroughfare of Ichijō was crammed with carriages and bustling with people. Viewing platforms had been erected at various sites and decorated with great care. Those decorations, together with the sleeves of the court ladies' robes, which trailed out from beneath the blinds set up on the platforms, created their own splendid spectacle.

Genji's wife rarely left her father's residence to go view events like this. Moreover, she had given no thought at all of going to view this particular procession, since she was feeling ill and nervous. Her younger attendants, however, all complained to her.

"What is my lady thinking? How could we ever hope to enjoy the beauty of the procession if we have to sneak off just to take a peak?"

"Ordinary folk, even the lowest woodcutters and hunters who have no connection with anyone in the procession, will be there to take in the sights. They'll especially want to catch a glimpse of your husband."

"People from distant provinces will bring their wives and children to take a look. So it's just not fair that we have to miss it!"

Princess Ōmiya, who, as the younger sister of the Retired Emperor, truly understood the importance of such matters, heard these complaints and urged her daughter to go.

"You've been feeling better recently, and your attendants will feel left out and dissatisfied if you don't."

And with that, all the women were suddenly informed, to their joy, that their lady would be going out after all.

Because the sun was already well up, they left without formally preparing the carriages in a manner befitting the status of the Minister's household. By the time they arrived, Ichijō Avenue was already packed with carriages lining both sides of the street, and it was difficult finding a place to park the imposing and dignified vehicles, unhitch the oxen, and set the shafts on their supports. Many noblewomen already had their carriages positioned there, and the male guards escorting Genji's wife decided to clear a space by pushing aside those that had no guardsmen protecting them.

Among the carriages that had been lined up in that space, two of them exuded a special air of refinement—informal in style, with roofs and blinds made of *hinoki*[8] wicker, slightly worn, but adorned with silk curtains. The women inside had obviously intended to remain inconspicuous. The fresh, vibrant colors of the cuffs of their sleeves, the hems of their skirts, and the ends of their singlets all peeked out coyly from beneath the blinds. The guards escorting Genji's wife were explicitly told not to touch these two carriages and warned, "This is not a carriage you can just push aside as you wish!" Unfortunately, the young men in

---

8. A Japanese evergreen used for various building purposes [editor's note].

both parties had been drinking too much, and in the end there was no way to prevent the situation from getting out of control. The older retainers from the Minister's household commanded the young men to desist, but they were unable to stop a fight from breaking out.

The lady at Rokujō, whose daughter would soon go off to serve as the Ise Priestess, had been thinking she might find relief from her tormented feelings about Genji by coming discreetly to view the procession for the Purification Ritual. Her attendants, aware of her desire to remain incognito, did not reveal her identity, but it was obvious to the men accompanying Genji's wife whose carriages they were moving.

"Don't let them talk to us like that," several of the men shouted. "They must think they can still rely on Lord Genji!"

Several of Genji's attendants had been assigned to accompany his wife's party. They all regarded this incident as most regrettable, but it would have been extremely awkward for them to intervene, and so they looked the other way. In the end, the carriages of Genji's wife and her attendants were positioned in the spaces that had been cleared away, and the carriages of the lady at Rokujō had been relegated to a place behind them, where she could neither see nor be seen. She was in an agony of anger and indignation, and now that her identity had been revealed, after having gone to such great lengths to conceal it out of concern that her shameful feelings for Genji might be exposed, there was no limit to the feelings of chagrin and remorse she suffered. Because the stands for her carriage shafts had been broken in the melee, they had to be propped up on the wheel hubs of some unknown carriages next to hers. It must have looked unsightly, and she was mortified, wondering vainly why she had ever decided to come here.

She no longer wanted to view the procession and wished instead to go home, but there was no space to move her carriage. Just then cries rang out from the crowd:

"They're on their way!"

Her resolve weakened, and now she wanted to wait until her cruel lover had passed. She recalled an ancient poem in which the Goddess of Ise asks a man to stop his horse at Sasanokuma to let it drink from the Hinokuma River—all so that she might have the chance to gaze upon him.[9] Anxious, she wondered if Genji would stop to acknowledge her . . . but no, he continued on, coldly passing by without so much as a glance in her direction. The turmoil in her heart was greater than ever. Genji feigned disinterest in the many carriages that lined the way, even though they were more splendidly decorated than usual, with the hems of robes spilling out from beneath the blinds as though the occupants were in competition with one another. Still, he did occasionally smile and give a sly, sidelong glance at certain carriages, and when he recognized the carriages of his father-in-law, he assumed a solemn expression as he passed. The men in his escort silently bowed to show their deep respect for Genji's wife. The Rokujō lady, overwhelmed by this display, which clearly demonstrated the inferiority of her status, could not have felt more wretched.

9. A sacred song for the Sun Goddess from *The Kokinshū*.

How cruel of those chill waters of lustration
To grant but a glimpse of your reflected image
Reminding me all the more of my wretched fate

She knew it would be disgraceful to weep in front of her women, so she comforted herself with the thought that she would have regretted passing up the opportunity to witness the radiance of his appearance and the beauty of his countenance on such a dazzling occasion.

The high-ranking nobles who accompanied the Kamo Priestess on the procession were superbly decked out in fine robes, each in keeping with his status at court, and attended by magnificent-looking escorts. The appearance of those of the highest rank was especially breathtaking, and yet, as remarkable as they were, they seemed to pale in comparison with Genji's radiance. One of the eight men in his retinue, which had been assembled just for this event, was a man of the sixth rank, a Lesser Captain in the Right Imperial Guard. It was most unusual to assign someone of his status to this kind of duty, but he was so remarkably good-looking that he was chosen anyway. The other men in Genji's escort were also dazzlingly resplendent, and Genji's appearance, which was always esteemed by the court, was so awe-inspiring that the very trees and grasses seemed to bow before him. Normally, it would be considered improper and unsightly for ladies of rank who, for the sake of modesty, wore veils beneath their deep-brimmed hats, or for nuns who had renounced the world to literally fall over one another in an effort to catch a glimpse of him. Today, however, was different, and no one reproved them. Women of the lower classes—their mouths drawn in where they were missing teeth, their hair tucked modestly inside their robes—jostled each other and made fools of themselves, clasping their hands to their foreheads in supplication to Genji. Vulgar men were grinning stupidly from ear to ear, unaware of how ridiculous their faces looked. Daughters of minor provincial officials, whom Genji would never so much as glance at, had arrived in their lavishly decorated carriages, hopelessly preening and posturing because they knew Genji would be passing by. So many amusing things to observe—including the many women who, having been favored by a covert visit from Genji, were now lamenting to themselves that they no longer belonged among the blessed few he favored.

Prince Shikibu, the Minister of Ceremonials, was viewing the procession from one of the platforms, and when he saw Genji, ominous thoughts came to him: *He has matured so, and his appearance is so truly spectacular that I fear he will attract the attention of gods and demons.*

Prince Shikibu's daughter, Princess Asagao, had exchanged many letters with Genji over several years and so she knew his sensibilities were anything but ordinary. Now that she was seeing his beauty for the first time, her heart was deeply moved.

A woman can be touched be a man's sincerity, she told herself, *even if he is rather ordinary-looking. How much more appealing, then, is the sincerity of a man whose looks are as stunning as his?*

Despite these sentiments, she was not inclined to allow her relationship with Genji to become any more familiar or intimate. Her younger attendants were all praising him so much they sounded uncouth, and she found it irritating to listen to them.

When the Kamo Festival proper was held a few days later, no one from the Minister of the Left's residence came out to view it. Genji had been informed of the quarrel between the carriages, and he felt sorry for the lady at Rokujō. He was also offended by his wife's conduct.

"It's a shame," he remarked, "that such a dignified person should show so little sympathy or kindness toward others. She probably never intended for such a thing to happen, and yet her temperament prevents her from even considering the possibility that women who share the kind of relationship she and the lady do should be mutually affectionate and supportive. No wonder her subordinates, who lack judgment and status, acted as outrageously as they did. As for the lady who suffered this insult, she has such a superior upbringing and is so sensitive to any slight that the whole sordid incident must have been terribly unpleasant for her."

Genji felt such pity that he went to Rokujō to visit the lady. She, however, was reluctant to meet him. Her daughter, after all, was still living in the residence while undergoing the rites of purification that would prepare her to serve as the High Priestess at Ise. Branches of the sacred *sakaki* tree[1] had been placed at all the corners and gates, and thus the lady did not feel comfortable letting Genji in to see her, since that would run the risk of defilement. Genji thought her precaution perfectly reasonable, but he still muttered to himself, "Why must things always be like this? Why do women have to flash their horns and quarrel?"

Genji retreated to his own residence at Nijō. On the day of the Kamo Festival he went with Murasaki to view the festivities. After ordering Koremitsu to prepare their carriages, he went over to the west hall.

"Will all your little ladies be going as well?" he teasingly asked, referring to Murasaki's playmates.

Observing her outfit and makeup, which exuded an exceptionally graceful air, he couldn't help smiling.

"Very well, then, shall we be going? Let's go view the festival together."

He stroked her hair, which looked even more lustrous than usual, and added, "It's been a while since you've had the ends trimmed. Today would be an auspicious time to do it." He summoned a scholar from the Bureau of Divination and asked him which hours that day would be lucky or unlucky for trimming hair. He then told Murasaki, "Have your little ladies come forth." He looked them over and found their childish figures delightfully charming. Their hair had been trimmed gorgeously and hung down in sharp relief over the outer trousers of their festive robes . . . altogether adorable. "I'll cut your hair," Genji said to Murasaki. "It's really thick, isn't it? What would become of it if you just let it grow out?" He found trimming her hair a little difficult. "Ladies with very long hair tend to cut the sidelocks that frame their foreheads a little shorter than the rest. I don't think you would look as attractive without short locks." When he finished with the trimming, Genji offered the obligatory benediction, expressing the hope that her hair might grow "a thousand fathoms."

Murasaki's nurse, Shonagon, had been watching them, her heart filled with gratitude. Genji composed and recited a verse:

1. *Sakaki* is a flowering evergreen tree native to Japan. It is sacred in the Shinto religion, and branches of *sakaki*, decorated with slips or streamers of paper, are used for ritual offerings and purifications.

> *I shall protect you, watching your hair grow*
> *Like strands of rippling seaweed stretching up*
> *From the thousand-fathomed depths of the sea*

Murasaki chose to write out her reply:

> *You swear love as deep as the thousand-fathomed sea*
> *Yet how am I to know that's true, since you wander*
> *Coming and going like uncertain, restless tides*

Such clever wit, and such youthful beauty. She's perfect, Genji thought.

So many sightseeing carriages had arrived for the Kamo Festival that there were not enough spaces to park them all this day as well. Because they were having trouble finding a place to stop, they pulled up near the parade grounds and pavilion where the Mounted Guard held their archery competition during the fifth month of each year.

"So many high-ranking officials have brought their carriages here, the area is really bustling," Genji said, sounding a little confounded and irritable. He had his carriage pause for a moment next to a lady's carriage that was not at all inelegant. The carriage was filled with occupants, and a fan was thrust out beckoning him over to them.

"Would you like to set your carriage here?" a woman asked. "We could make some space for you."

Genji was somewhat taken aback, wondering what kind of woman could be so coquettish. This spot, however, was an excellent place from which to view the festival parade, and so he decided to accept the invitation.

"How did you manage to come by this space?" he asked. "It's good enough to make people resent you, so I'll take you up on your offer."

The lady in the carriage then broke off a section of her stylish folding fan and wrote out the following:

> *Heart-shaped leaves of wild ginger adorn another*
> *Though their name promises some day we'll meet . . . vainly*
> *I waited for the Kamo gods to bless this day*

"I cannot pass beyond the ropes marking off that sacred space."

Genji recognized the handwriting. It was the old Assistant Handmaid, Naishi no suke. He found it shocking that someone her age should be flirting like a young woman. He was genuinely displeased and sent back a curt reply:

> *The feelings of one adorned with those heart-shaped leaves*
> *Are certainly fickle, since she can "meet this day"*
> *Any man she wants from among the eighty clans*

Naishi was filled with resentment when she received Genji's cruel response:

> *A bitter adornment, this wild ginger*
> *With its empty promise of meeting you . . .*
> *Mere leaves signifying vain and false hopes*

Many women, not just Naishi, experienced pangs of jealousy as they tried to guess the identity of the lady riding with Genji. They resented that for her sake he chose to keep his blinds down, because it denied them an opportunity to catch a glimpse of him. The women gossiped among themselves:

"He was so splendid-looking the day of the procession."

"Yes, but today's he's going about rather informally, don't you think?"

"Who is that riding with him? I wonder. She must be a special woman."

Genji remained disgruntled, thinking, *What a complete waste of time, exchanging verses that play on a subject like leaves of wild ginger.*

Anyone else would certainly have refrained from sending a note out of respect for the lady riding with him—but not someone as impudent as Naishi.

For her part, the lady at Rokujō had never in all her life experienced the kind of torment brought on recently by her dark, obsessive thoughts. She had, it is true, resigned herself to Genji's cruel neglect, but the thought of leaving him behind in order to go with her daughter to Ise brought on agonizing loneliness. She was also fully aware that she would be an object of derision at the court. Whenever she thought, wistfully, that perhaps she ought to stay behind in the capital, she would become anxious, for she knew that if she stayed she would expose herself to even more extreme levels of ridicule. Her days and nights were so filled with troubled thoughts that she couldn't help but recall the *Kokinshū* poem: "Am I a float on the line of the fisherman of Ise that my heart should be adrift like this, bobbing on the waves?"[2] Finding no relief from her obsessive, insecure state of mind, she fell ill.

Genji wasn't in the least concerned about her stated desire to accompany her daughter to Ise, and he never once tried to dissuade her by telling her that it was out of the question. Instead he remarked, rather sarcastically, "I understand. It's perfectly reasonable for you to find repugnant the prospect of continuing a relationship with a man as worthless as I. Yet no matter how unpleasant it may be for you now, if you were to stay with me to the end, your choice would prove that you're a woman of uncommonly deep sensibility, would it not?"

On hearing such hateful words, the lady withdrew even deeper into her dark thoughts. Distressed and depressed, she had decided to go see the procession only because she wanted some relief from her insecurity and indecisiveness. And then, when she did go, she found herself buffeted about, as if she were adrift on the violent rapids of the river of lustration.

While all of this was taking place, a malignant spirit was causing concern for everyone at the Minister of the Left's Sanjō residence. Genji's wife was suffering terribly, and under the circumstances it was not appropriate for him to be going around visiting his other women. Indeed, during this period he only rarely went to his own residence in Nijō. True, he had never warmed to his wife much, but he did consider her someone of special importance to him. He was wracked with grief that she should now be suffering so much as a consequence of her remarkable pregnancy, and he had prayers and rites performed for her in his own quarters at his father-in-law's residence.

Many souls of the deceased and spirits of living persons were exorcised and forced to reveal their names. One particular spirit, however, resisted all attempts to move it into the body of a medium and persisted in clinging fast to Genji's

---

2. Anonymous poem from *The Kokinshū*.

wife. It did no real harm, but it would not leave her body, even for a few moments. The deeply obsessive nature of this spirit, which would not obey the holiest of exorcists, made it clear that this was no commonplace possession. The attendants considered the various women Genji called on and whispered among themselves:

"Only the ladies at Rokujō and Nijō have a special place in his heart—perhaps their resentment is especially strong."

Diviners were brought in to confirm these suspicions, but they failed to do so. Whenever they questioned the spirits, they learned nothing that would suggest any of them was driven by revenge or hatred. There was the spirit of a former nurse and spirits that had haunted the families of the Minister and Princess Ōmiya for generations, but these had appeared simply because their daughter was in a fragile condition. None of them were really malicious but seemed to have shown up at random. Why, then, was Genji's wife constantly shouting out and weeping? She was always nauseous or had choking sensations, and she would writhe around as if in unbearable agony. Genji and her parents were frightened and upset, wondering how this would all turn out and worrying that she might die.

Because the Retired Emperor repeatedly sent messages of concern and graciously ordered prayers and rituals, her death would be all the more lamentable. Upon hearing that everyone at the court was worried, the lady at Rokujō was afflicted with the troubling thought that she was being diminished as sympathy for her rival grew. She had always had a jealous, competitive streak, but until that absurd quarrel over the carriages had unsettled her heart, it had never been as pronounced as it was now, and she felt a degree of resentment that no one at the Minister's household could have ever imagined.

The lady knew, as a result of her confused emotions, that her condition was not normal, and so she decided to undergo esoteric Buddhist healing rites. However, she had to move out of her residence and have the rites performed elsewhere in order to avoid defiling her daughter, who was still preparing to be the High Priestess of Ise. Genji heard about her plans and, moved to pity as he wondered how she was feeling, went to call on her. Because she was not at her usual residence in Rokujō, he had to be exceptionally discreet when he visited. He repeatedly asked her to overlook the way he had neglected her recently, pointing out that it was due to circumstances beyond his control. He even tried to elicit her sympathy by describing the terrible suffering of his wife.

"I'm not all that concerned about her myself," he said, "but I do feel sorry for her parents, who are upset and making rather too much of a fuss about it. So while she is in this condition, I really should stay close by her. If you could take all of these things into account, I would be very grateful."

Genji pleaded with her, but he could see from the expression on her face that she was suffering even more than usual, and he felt terribly sorry for her.

The lady had been moody and withdrawn that night, but when—in the welter of her yearnings and resentments—she saw how ravishing he looked as he prepared to leave at the crack of dawn, she was tempted to reconsider her decision to leave the capital with her daughter. At the same time, the lady was realistic enough to know that Genji, who already held that wife of his in high esteem, would feel even greater affection and lavish his attentions solely on *her* once the child was born. And when that happened, *she* would be left waiting, fretting impatiently over whether Genji would ever show up and knowing that whenever he did come to see her, it would be out of some lukewarm sense of duty or pity. Her tangled emotions opened her eyes afresh to the reality of her situation. After waiting all day for his morning-after letter, it finally arrived that evening—a short, curt note with no poem attached:

"Her condition had been improving recently, but now she has suffered a relapse, and I really must stay here."

She read the note and thought it was just another of his typical excuses. Even so, she sent a response:

> Intimate with love's path where dew has soaked my sleeves
> I followed too far . . . now my sad fate is to end
> Like a peasant planting fields, my robes soaked in mud

"Perhaps it is fitting to remind you of the old poem about the water of the mountain well. The poet, having tried to draw water from a well so shallow, regrets that she too gets nothing but damp sleeves."[3]

Genji pored over her response, marveling at the beauty of her script, which was far superior to everyone else's, and wondered why the world had to be so damnably complicated. He felt painfully torn—on the one hand, he couldn't simply abandon a woman of her sensibility and looks, and, on the other, there was no way he could settle on just one woman. He sent his reply well after dark:

"What do you mean that only your sleeves are damp? Your feelings for me must not be very deep."

> How shallow the path of love you follow
> That you merely dampen your sleeves with dew
> While I drench myself where the mud is deep

He added, among other things, "Do you imagine that my feelings for you are insincere, that I would not reply to you in person were my wife's condition not truly serious?"

At the Minister's residence the obsessive spirit was appearing more persistently and causing Genji's wife great distress. The lady at Rokujō then heard gossip to the effect that it was either her own living spirit or that of her late father. She gave the rumors careful consideration. Even though she had never wished ill fortune to befall others, she had often lamented her own bad luck, and she was aware that the living spirit of a person who is preoccupied with personal desires and attachments might wander from the body. She had lived for so many years convinced that she had suffered as much grief and anxiety as it was possible for one person to suffer, and now it was as if her soul had been torn asunder. That day when the foolish incident with the carriages occurred, she had been treated disdainfully, and *that woman*, Genji's wife, had in effect ignored her as though she were beneath contempt. After the procession to the Purification Ritual was over, her heart and mind lost their moorings and drifted, all on account of that one incident, and she found it truly difficult to calm her nerves.

Lately, whenever she dozed off, she began having a recurring dream. She would find herself in the beautifully appointed, luxurious quarters of some

3. Anonymous poem from an earlier *waka* anthology, the *Kokin waka rokujō*.

woman—Genji's wife, she assumed—and would then watch in horror as her living spirit, so completely different from her waking self, would move around the woman, pulling and tugging at her, and then, driven by menacingly obsessive emotions, violently striking and shaking her. Because of this recurring dream, the lady had many moments when she believed she was losing her grip on reality.

Ah, how horrible this is! What they say is true after all. A person's living spirit really can leave the body and wander about.[4] *And even if it isn't true in my case, people at the court prefer to speak ill of others, and this situation will provide fodder to those who relish spreading malicious gossip.*

Fearing that she would be notorious, the lady made a resolution to herself: *They say it's common for people to leave behind their obsessive attachments and resentments when they die. I've always considered such a thing deeply sinful and ominous, even when it has happened to people with whom I have no connections. But now there are rumors that it's my living spirit that's acting in such a grotesque, unearthly way. It must be retribution for the sins of a former life. I must never give another thought to that cruel man.*

She resolved over and over to put him out of her mind, but, try as she might, her resolutions were just another way to think about *him*.

As part of a series of purification rites in preparation for her departure for Ise, the daughter of the lady at Rokujō was to have moved during the previous year into a detached residence at the palace called the Shosai-in, which served as the pavilion of the First Lustration. However, there had been a number of complications, and so it was decided that she would not move into the pavilion until the autumn. Thereafter, in the ninth month, the Ise Priestess would move again, undergoing the Second Lustration at a temporary shrine built for this purpose on the plains of Sagano, famous for its lovely autumn vistas. The attendants in the residence at Rokujō thus had to make preparations for two purification rites, one right after the other. Their mistress, alas, was distracted and depressed and lying prone in her suffering, unable to rouse herself. This was no trivial matter for the ladies-in-waiting to the Priestess, since her mother's illness could be defiling, and so they commissioned prayers and rites. In truth, the lady didn't really seem all that sick, and as the days and months passed no one was sure exactly what was wrong or how serious it was. Genji was constantly inquiring after the lady's health, but because his wife—who was far more important to him—was suffering so much, he was burdened with seemingly endless concerns.

Because they assumed it was not yet time for Genji's wife to give birth, everyone at the Sanjō residence was caught off guard when she went into labor and appeared to be on the verge of delivering the child. More and more malignant spirits were drawn to her as the moment of the birth neared, and the number and intensity of the prayers and rites meant to assure a safe childbirth increased. Still, that one stubborn, obsessive spirit remained, more intransigent than ever. Even the most venerable of the priests found this spirit abnormal, and they were unable to exorcise it. As they tried to make the spirit show itself, their prayers finally forced it to speak to them through Genji's wife.

The spirit, in a weeping voice wracked with pain, pleaded with the priests, "Please stop for a moment. I have something I must say to Lord Genji."

4. *Kokinshū* 977 (Ōshikōchi Mitsune): "It must have wandered off, abandoning my body . . . this heart of mine that goes its own way, doing things I do not intend."

The attendants at once whispered among themselves, "Just as we thought; there's some reason for this after all."

Genji was shown in to where his wife was lying behind her curtains. Because she seemed to be near death, her parents withdrew a short distance away in case their daughter had some last words for her husband. The priests ceased their prayers and lowered their voices as they chanted the Kannon chapter of the *Lotus Sutra*. Their murmuring created an atmosphere at once uncanny and sublime. Genji lifted the curtains and looked in on his wife. There was something alluring about her as she lay there, her belly large and distended. Even someone with whom she had no connection at all would have been distracted gazing at her, so it was natural for Genji to feel overwhelmed with regret and sorrow. Her long, luxuriant black hair, which had been pulled back and tied up, stood out in vivid contrast to the white of her maternity robes. She was always so prim and proper that Genji had never found her special elegance all that attractive. Now, for the first time, as she lay there in her vulnerable, helpless condition, she struck him as not just precious but voluptuous. He took her hand.

"How terrible this is. Must you cause me to grieve so?"

He began to cry and could speak no further. She weakly raised her head and gazed at him with that expression that had hitherto always made him feel uncertain and inadequate in her presence. Tears filled her eyes, and when he gazed back at her—a woman who now seemed so accessible to him—how could he not be deeply touched?

Because she was crying so intensely, Genji assumed she was thinking of her poor, anxious parents and, on seeing him here like this, regretting that they would soon part.

"You mustn't brood so much about everything," Genji comforted her. "You don't feel well now, but you'll get better. And even if death should separate us, remember that husbands and wives are destined to meet in the next world. You have a deep bond with your father and mother, and no matter how many times you are reborn, that bond is never-ending. I am sure there will be a time when you will see them again."

"No, no, that's not why I'm crying. I'm crying because the exorcists' prayers hurt me so. I asked for you to come here so that I might have a moment of relief from them. I never imagined that I would come here in this form, but now I know the truth. The spirit of a person lost in obsessive longing will actually wander from the body." The voice that came from his wife's lips had a gentle, seductive familiarity. "Just as they did in ancient times . . ."

> Bind the hems of my robes
> To keep my grieving soul
> From wandering the skies

As he was listening to the voice, his wife's appearance changed and she no longer looked like herself. Genji was trying to comprehend this inexplicable, eerie phenomenon when he suddenly realized he was gazing on the countenance of the lady at Rokujō. He was horrified. He had dismissed out of hand the rumors claiming the spirit possessing his wife was the lady's, considering them nothing more than the idle gossip of vulgar, insensitive people. But he was witnessing the possession with his own eyes and understood now that such things did happen in this world. It was uncanny. *How wretched*, he thought. He then answered her, saying, "You sound like someone I know, but I'm not certain. Tell me who you are."

The spirit replied in a way that left no doubt it was *she*. To say that he was shocked would not do justice to the sense of horror he experienced. At the same time, the presence of the attendants made him feel awkward and embarrassed, since they might recognize that the spirit was the lady's.

When the voice grew a little more subdued, Genji's mother-in-law, thinking that her daughter was feeling more comfortable, brought in a hot medicinal infusion. The attendants raised his wife from behind and supported her in a squatting posture. She gave birth to a boy.

The joy everyone felt was boundless. In contrast, the malign spirits that had been forced into the mediums were raising a tremendous fuss, since they resented the safe delivery. There was still the afterbirth to worry about, but thanks to the numerous prayers and supplications to the Buddha, it was a normal birth. The abbot of the Enryakuji Temple on Mount Hiei and the other distinguished priests quickly withdrew, wiping the sweat from their proud, satisfied faces. All the women in the household were finally able to relax a little after so many days of worry and devoted service. They were sure that the worst was over; and even though new prayers and rites for the mother were ordered, for the moment the baby became the center of attention. Everyone let their guard down as they were absorbed in helping out with the remarkable child. The Retired Emperor, princes of the blood, and the highest-ranking officials all attended, without fail, the traditional banquets held on the third, fifth, seventh, and ninth nights following the birth. In joyous celebration, they brought with them exquisite and remarkable gifts of food and clothing, and because the child was a boy, the celebrations were all the more lively and auspicious.

When the lady at Rokujō learned about all of this, she grew agitated. She had heard that Genji's wife had been in a precarious state, but now, apparently, everything was fine, and she felt both jealous and disappointed. She continued to feel weird, as though she were not herself, and her robes reeked of the smell of the poppy seeds that exorcists burn to drive out a lingering spirit. Strangely, the smell would not dissipate, but continued to permeate her body no matter how often she tried washing her hair and changing her robes. She was disgusted with herself and worried what others might say or think. She couldn't very well discuss this with anyone, so she was forced to suffer in isolation, which only made her emotional turmoil worse. Genji was feeling somewhat calmer, but whenever he recalled the unpleasant moment when the lady's spirit had addressed him unbidden in that weird and shocking manner, he was reminded of the pain she was experiencing because he had not called on her in such a long time. He vacillated, thinking that perhaps he should visit her in person. But then every time he considered the idea of a visit, he couldn't help worrying that he might be appalled, wondering how she could have fallen into such a state. After considering all the options, he decided it would be best for her if he just sent a message.

Everyone was worried about the prognosis for Genji's wife, who had suffered so grievously, and kept a vigilant watch over her. Naturally, Genji stopped going out on his nightly amorous excursions, even though his wife was still quite sick and unable to see her husband in the customary manner. The baby boy was exceptionally handsome, and because there were worries that his looks might attract the resentful attention of malignant spirits, every effort was made from the moment of his birth to protect him and bring him up with the greatest care. Genji's father-in-law was tremendously pleased, since things had worked out as he had hoped. Though he continued to show concern over his daughter, who had not yet fully recovered, he assumed that her condition was simply the aftereffect of having been so ill and that there was no reason to be unduly alarmed.

On seeing the beauty of the eyes and features of the baby, who bore a striking resemblance to Fujitsubo's child, Genji thought lovingly of his other, unacknowledged son, the new Crown Prince, and he was seized with an unbearable desire to go to the palace to visit him.

"I've not been to the palace for some time, and that concerns me. Since my confinement ends today, I had better go there." He then added, with some resentment, "I wonder if I might speak to my wife directly, without a curtain between us? Why do we always have to be so formal with one another, especially now?"

"As you wish, my lord," one of the women responded. "Your relationship with my lady need not be so formal and distant. Though she is terribly weakened by her ordeal, there is no need to separate the two of you with screens or curtains."

The attendants brought in a cushion for him and placed it close to where his wife was lying. He went in, sat down, and began speaking to her. She answered from time to time, but she still seemed very weak. He remembered the state she had been in at that moment when he had been certain she was about to die. He now felt as if it had all been a dream. He spoke of the period when she had been in mortal danger, and it made his heart ache to think that she had been on the point of death, and to recall how she had stopped breathing, but then recovered and spoke to him so urgently.

"There is so much I want to tell you, but they say you are too weak and not up to it, so I'll let it go for now," he said. He reminded her to drink her medicine and showed her consideration in other ways as well. Her attendants were deeply impressed by his ministrations, amazed that he had learned such things.

Her appearance as she lay there was heartbreakingly sweet, so weak and pale that he could hardly tell if she were dead or alive. Her abundant hair was properly done up, and the strands that were lying across the pillow were incomparably elegant. He gazed possessively at her, feeling strange that in all their time together he should ever have found her deficient in any way.

"I must go visit my father, but I shall return quickly," Genji told her. "How happy it would make me if I could always gaze on you as I'm doing now. But your mother is constantly nearby, so out of deference to her I have refrained from seeing you directly, lest I be considered rash. You must do all you can to get well, then move back to your own chambers. One reason you are not improving may be that you have become too childishly dependent on others."

With these words he took his leave, put on splendid robes and went out. In the past she rarely saw him off, but this time she lay there watching him in rapt attention.

The Autumn Ceremonial for Court Promotions was scheduled for that evening, and because the Minister of the Left had to preside over the event, he too left his daughter at his Sanjō residence and headed for the palace. Each of his

sons was hoping to receive a promotion, and since they didn't want to be separated from their father on this particular day, they all left with him.

As a result, there were very few people at the Minister's residence that
evening, and while the villa was deserted a malignant spirit suddenly assaulted
Genji's wife. The choking sensation she experienced made breathing difficult,
and she was in great distress. She stopped breathing before there was time to
inform those who had gone to the ceremony.

On hearing the news, everyone was stunned, and they left the palace not knowing
where their feet were taking them. Though it was the evening of the Autumn Ceremonial, in the face of such a tragedy it would not have been appropriate to continue the event. The crisis had arisen in the middle of the night, and so they were
unable to call for the abbot at Mount Hiei, or even for a distinguished priest. They
had all relaxed and let their guard down, assuming that the worst was over, and
because her death was so unexpected, the attendants at the Minister's residence were in a panic—confused, stumbling about, bumping into things. Messengers bearing condolences from various noble houses crowded into the
residence at Sanjō, but there was no one to take their messages, and the whole
house was shaking from the uproar. It was frightening to see how upset everyone was.

Because so many malignant spirits had possessed her, they followed prescribed
custom and left her body lying there. They didn't disturb her or move the position of her pillow, lest her soul fail to find its way back should it try to return.
They kept watch over her for two or three days, but when her appearance began
to change, they realized they had reached the end, that she was indeed gone,
and were overwhelmed by grief.

With his wife's tragic death coming on the heels of his shocking encounter
with the living spirit of the lady at Rokujō, Genji was preoccupied with thoughts
of the tiresome nature of this world, and as a result he felt put off by the words
of condolences he received from people—even from women with whom he had
a special relationship. Genji's father-in-law, the Minister of the Left, was deeply
honored to receive condolences directly from the Retired Emperor. It was an
honor that brought a moment of relief to his unremitting sorrow, and it left him
crying tears of both joy and grief. On the advice of others, the Minister spared
no expense or effort in commissioning mystery rites intended to revive his
daughter, and though it was evident for all to see that her body was decaying
away, in his distracted state he vainly persisted until there was nothing more to
be done. When at last they took his daughter's body to be cremated on the plains
of Toribeno, there were many heart-rending moments along the way.

* * *

At the Nijō villa his men and women were preparing for his arrival, cleaning
and polishing. The senior attendants all appeared before him, and they vied to
outdo one another in the splendor of their clothing and makeup. Genji couldn't
help but be touched by the lively scene before him, which contrasted so starkly
with the lonely, melancholy scene he had left behind at the Sanjō residence.
He changed out of his mourning robes and went over to Murasaki's quarters
in the west hall. The clothing and furnishings there had been changed with
the advent of winter, and the rooms had a bright, fresh look to them. The out-
fits of the pretty women and girls there were pleasing to his eyes, and Murasa-

ki's nurse, Shōnagon, had made sure that all the preparations had been carried out to his complete satisfaction. Indeed, everything looked wonderful to him.

Murasaki was sweetly done up . . . truly lovely.

"It's been a long time," Genji began. "You've become quite the young lady."

He raised the lower half of the curtains to peek in on her, and when he did so she shyly turned away from him. Even so, he could see that her beauty was perfection itself. Glimpsing her profile in the lamplight, he could tell from her eyes and face that she looked exactly like Fujitsubo, the woman who had so possessed his heart, and he was overjoyed. He moved closer to her and spoke of all the things that had happened, and of how anxious he had been, wondering how she had fared during his period of mourning.

"I want to talk to you at leisure, tell you stories of all that took place while I was away. For the time being, however, I'll sleep in the east hall. Having just come out of mourning, it might be bad luck for me to stay here just now. But soon we will have all the time in the world to be together . . . so much so that you may come to regard me as a nuisance."

Shōnagon, who was listening in on them, was delighted by his words, but then she immediately began having anxious thoughts about the precarious position of her young charge. After all, Genji discreetly visited many highborn ladies, and it was also possible that he would be drawn to some new lady who might appear on the scene and take the place of his late wife. Shōnagon's suspicious nature was an unattractive trait, but her doubts were understandable, since her primary responsibility was to look after Murasaki.

Genji returned to his own chambers. One of his female attendants, Chūjō no kimi, massaged his legs, and he was finally able to relax and fall asleep. The next morning he sent a letter to his little son at Sanjō. The melancholy reply, obviously written for him by the boy's grandmother, filled him with inexhaustible grief.

With little to occupy him, Genji would lose himself in reveries of longing. Yet because he was reluctant to wander about on some random nocturnal adventure, he could not rouse himself to go out. His little Murasaki was now grown up and ideal in all respects. She looked spectacular, and he felt that now was the appropriate time to consummate their relationship. From time to time he would casually drop hints about their marriage, but she seemed to have no idea what he was talking about.

They whiled away the hours, relieving their tedium by playing Go or word games like *hentsugi*, writing down radicals or parts of a Chinese character and trying to guess which one it was. Murasaki had a clever and engaging personality, and she would demonstrate endearing talents in even the most trivial of pastimes. For several years he had driven all thoughts of taking her as a wife out of his mind, dismissing her talents as nothing more than the accomplishments of a precocious child. Now he could no longer control his passion—though he did feel pangs of guilt, since he was painfully aware of how innocent she was.

Her attendants assumed he would consummate their relationship at some point, but because he had always slept with her, there was simply no way for them to know when that moment would come. One morning Genji rose early, but Murasaki refused to get up. Her behavior worried her attendants.

"What's wrong?' they whispered. "She seems unusually out of sorts today."

Right before Genji returned to his own quarters, he placed just inside her curtains a box filled with inkstones, brushes, and paper, which she was to use for the customary morning-after letter.[5] When there was no one else around, Murasaki finally lifted her head and found his betrothal note folded in a love knot at her pillow. Still in a daze, she opened the letter.

> *How strange that we have stayed apart so long*
> *Though we slept together night after night*
> *With only the robes we wore between us*

The poem was written in a playful, spontaneous manner, as if he had allowed his emotions to carry him along. It had never crossed her mind that he might be the kind of man who harbored such thoughts about her, and she burned with shame when she recalled their sordid first night: *How could I have been so naive? How could I have ever trusted a man with such base intentions?*

Genji returned to her quarters at midday, peeking in through her curtains.

"Something seems to be bothering you . . . are you not well? It would be quite tedious for me if we weren't able to play Go today."

Murasaki was still lying face down. She pulled the bedding up over her face so that she would not have to look at him. When her attendants withdrew, Genji went over to her.

"Why are you acting so despondent? Are you displeased with me? I never imagined that you could be so cold. Your women must think this is all very queer."

He tugged her bedding away. She was bathed in perspiration, and tears had soaked the hair framing her forehead.

"Now this won't do at all!" Genji was put out. "Tears on the first day of your marriage? It's ominous . . . very inauspicious." He tried all sorts of things to cheer her up, but she thought him utterly horrid and refused to speak.

"All right, then, have it your way," he told her spitefully. "I won't come here any more if you insist on putting me to shame!"

He opened the box with the writing implements and checked inside. There was no reply note. *She's still a child after all*, he thought ruefully. He now felt sorry for her and decided to stay with her inside the curtains for the rest of the day. He passed the whole time trying to comfort her, but this proved difficult. Her refusal to warm up to him, however, merely made her look all the more precious to him.

It was the First Day of the Boar in the tenth month, when the moon rose in the north-northwest. The custom was to serve cakes made of pounded rice on this day, so as evening wore on and they reached the Hour of the Boar a little after 9:00 p.m., Genji had rice cakes shaped to look like baby pigs brought in to him and Murasaki. The boar was a symbol of fertility, but the First Day of the Boar was not an auspicious time for marriage. Moreover, Genji was still in mourning, and so he made sure their celebration was subdued, serving the rice cakes in Murasaki's quarters only. Observing the various colors of the rice cakes, which were flavored with beans, or chestnuts, or poppy, among other things, and nestled in cypress boxes, Genji remembered that he had to have white rice

---

5. After a couple's first night together the man was supposed to leave the woman a poem, to which she should respond [editor's note].

cakes prepared for tomorrow evening, the Third Night of their marriage. He stepped out and summoned Koremitsu.

"Have rice cakes brought here tomorrow," he ordered, "though not as many as today. This was not a particularly auspicious day for such things."

Seeing Genji's wry smile, Koremitsu caught on immediately. He did not press his lord on the matter, but simply replied with a perfectly serious expression on his face.

"Of course, my lord. It's most reasonable of you to choose an auspicious day to serve rice cakes." He then added, rather drolly, "Let's see . . . tomorrow is the Day of the Rat. Shall I tell them you're having rice cakes in the shape of baby mice to celebrate the event? And just how many will you need?"

"I suppose a third as many as we had today . . . that should be enough," Genji answered. And with that Koremitsu, who knew just what to do, withdrew. *He's certainly an experienced hand*, thought Genji. Koremitsu spoke of this to no one else, and had the rice cakes prepared at his own residence, without telling anyone why he needed them. He was so discreet, in fact, it was almost as if he had made them himself.

Genji was finding it so difficult to comfort Murasaki that he was at a loss. At the same time he was delighted when it occurred to him that, for the first time in her life, she must have felt like a stolen bride. With that realization came another.

She has been precious to me for many years, but my feelings for her during all that time were nothing compared to what I feel for her now. The heart is a peculiar thing. Now I find it impossible to be apart from her, even for a single night.

Koremitsu stealthily brought a box filled with the rice cakes Genji had ordered late the previous night. Deeply considerate and sensitive to the situation, Koremitsu thought it might be embarrassing for Murasaki if he asked her nurse, Shōnagon, to take the box into her chambers. So instead he summoned Shōnagon's daughter, Ben.

"Take this to your young mistress, and don't let anyone see you." He handed her an incense jar, inside of which he had hidden the box of rice cakes. "Now listen to me. This is a gift to celebrate an auspicious event, so you must set it beside her pillow. Be very careful. You must carry out my instructions to the letter." Ben thought that this request was suspicious, but she took the jar anyway.

"I have never," she insisted, "been unfaithful in serving my lady."

He cut her short.

"Don't use the word 'unfaithful.' The very uttering of it on an occasion like this is bad luck."

Ben considered the whole affair very odd, but she was young and really had no idea what Koremitsu was talking about. She placed the jar inside her lady's curtains next to her pillow. Genji, as he always did, explained the significance of the rice cakes to Murasaki.

Murasaki's attendants had known nothing about this. It wasn't until the next morning, when Genji had the box of rice cakes taken away, that they finally realized their lord had formally taken their young mistress as his wife. When could all of the dishes have been brought in? The stands on which the plates rested looked fabulous, their legs intricately carved in the shape of flowers. Various kinds of rice cakes had been specially prepared, and everything used for the

Third Night celebration—the silver plates, silver chopsticks, silver chopstick rests—had been exquisitely arranged. Shōnagon wondered, *Has he actually gone so far as to recognize her as his wife?* And when she saw it was true, she was profoundly grateful and wept at this proof of Genji's honorable intentions.

The other women were disappointed that they had not been let in on the secret, and they grumbled among themselves. "Of course it's wonderful that things have turned out like this, but why did our lord have to keep it secret? And that Koremitsu . . . whatever could he have been thinking?"

Following his marriage to Murasaki, Genji would feel so anxious about her whenever he went to the palace or called on the Retired Emperor, even for a short visit, that a vision of her would come to him and he would see her face. He found his own attraction to her mysterious. He received resentful letters from his other women enticing him to visit, and their notes did make him feel bad for them. But the very thought that such visits would be hard on his new bride troubled him. He recalled a line from an old *Man'yōshū* poem: "How can I endure a single night apart from you?"[6] He simply could not bring himself to go out on his nocturnal forays, but instead pretended he wasn't feeling well and was indisposed. He passed the time sending replies to his ladies along the lines of "I've been preoccupied of late with thoughts of the sad evanescence of this world. Once this mood of mine has passed, we shall, I assure you, meet again."

Oborozukiyo, the lady Genji associated with that evening of the misty moon, could not get him out of her mind. Her older sister, the Kokiden Consort, who was now the Imperial Mother, was extremely displeased to learn about this infatuation, and was further annoyed when her own father, the Minister of the Right, dismissed her concerns.

"Why should I be bothered about this?" he said. "If she realizes her heart's desire and becomes one of Genji's wives, I won't complain. After all, the woman who was most significant to him has apparently died."

The Kokiden Consort replied, "And what's wrong with her entering service in the women's quarters?" She seemed to have her heart firmly set on sending her younger sister to court to serve her son, Emperor Suzaku.

For his part, Genji did not consider Oborozukiyo just another woman, and he thought it a shame that she should be sent into service at the palace. At the present moment, however, he was not inclined to divide his attention among his women. He wanted to focus on Murasaki alone.

I'd better let it be, he thought. *Murasaki is good enough. Life is brief, and so I should just settle down with her. I must never again stir resentment in a woman.*

This train of thought brought back the incident with the lady at Rokujō. He had learned a fearful lesson. He was sorry for her, but now he could never feel comfortable recognizing her formally as a wife. *If she could be satisfied with continuing to meet as we have over the years, if she could go on being my companion, a woman who could talk with me on those occasions when it's natural and proper to do so, if we could just be a comfort to one another . . .*

As he mulled over their relationship, he realized that no matter how difficult she might be, she was someone he could not easily abandon.

* * *

6. Poem from *Man'yōshū*: "Now that we are betrothed, sharing a pillow of new grasses, how can I endure a single night apart from you?"

From Chapter X

Sakaki

A BRANCH OF SACRED EVERGREEN

The day of departure for the new High Priestess of Ise was drawing near, and her mother's heart was filled with melancholy and loneliness. Following the death of Genji's wife, whose special status the lady at Rokujō had found such an affront to her dignity, rumors spread around the court to the effect that now, at last, Genji would surely make her his primary wife. Even her own ladies-in-waiting were atwitter with anticipation at the possibility. Contrary to expectations, however, Genji's visits to the lady abruptly ceased altogether, and upon experiencing his shockingly cold behavior, the lady realized that something must have happened to truly upset him. She therefore resolved to abandon her lingering attachments and strengthened her resolve to accompany her daughter to Ise.

There was no precedent for a parent to accompany the High Priestess to Ise, but the lady, who wanted to distance herself from her troubled relationship with Genji, explained that she couldn't be separated from her daughter because the girl was simply too young to be on her own outside the capital. Hearing that the lady had decided to leave, Genji felt a twinge of remorse and exchanged with her a series of elegantly touching letters. The lady, however, was convinced that it was now too late for them and that they should not meet face to face. Genji would almost certainly consider her refusal hateful, but she was firmly resolved, heart and mind, for she knew it was inappropriate to do anything that would further disturb her troubled spirit and cause her more pain and suffering.

She would return occasionally to her villa on Rokujō, but she did so infrequently and in such secrecy that Genji was never able to learn when she was in residence there. Since she had moved out to the compound of the temporary shrine on the plains of Sagano—a place difficult for him to visit no matter how much he longed to go—they remained apart as days and months passed, even though he continued to be deeply concerned about her. On top of everything else, Genji's father was from time to time troubled by various ailments, which was unusual, and these additional worries burdened his heart and gave him no rest. Still, Genji was shamed by the prospect that the lady might think him cold and that people who heard about their relationship might consider him heartless, and so in spite of his travails he decided to go to the temporary shrine in Sagano. It was already the seventh day of the ninth month, and he assumed that their departure for Ise was imminent—perhaps in the next day or two. The lady was feeling restless, pressured by the numerous preparations she had to make for the departure. Now, on top of everything else, Genji was sending note after note begging to meet, if only for a moment. He told her that he would even stand outside her blinds. She struggled, unsure what to do, until she finally concluded that it would be excessively unfriendly not to meet him. She agreed to have him visit her secretly, but with a screen between them.

Once he had set out to cross the broad plains of Sagano, he was moved to sorrowful compassion. The autumn flowers were withering, and the lonely sound of the wind in the pine trees harmonized with the rasping cries of insects coming from the sere thickets of satin-tail grass. Faint notes of music, gentle and tender, were wafting faintly on the wind, though he could not quite make out the song or the kind of koto being played.

An escort of ten or so of Genji's most trusted guards accompanied him. In an effort to avoid attracting attention, his men had eschewed wearing formal robes. Genji, on the contrary, had not bothered to disguise himself, but had taken special care in preparing his attire. Because he looked so resplendent, he made the sophisticated, urbane young men traveling with him appreciate the profound beauty of the setting.

Why did I wait until now to come here? Genji reflected, bitterly regretting the time that had been lost.

A scattering of temporary dwellings roofed with wood-plank shingles stood inside a low, fragile, rustic-looking enclosure of brushwood. The *torii*[7] gate was made of logs that had not been stripped of their bark, creating an atmosphere of solemnity that, given the purpose of his visit, made him hesitate to enter such sacred ground. Here and there several Shinto clerics were coughing or clearing their throats in order to signal that Genji had arrived, and another group of priests stood talking amongst themselves. It was a different world altogether, one that struck Genji as strange and unfamiliar. The building where the ceremonial fire was kept constantly blazing was glowing faintly, and, since there were so few people about, stillness had settled over the compound. Genji felt a stab of keen sorrow when it occurred to him just how many days and months she had spent in isolation here, lost in her obsessive longings.

He withdrew, moving out of sight to what he assumed was the appropriate building on the north side of the main hall, and sent in a message to the lady announcing his arrival. He could hear intriguing sounds of people bustling about, but received only a reply from an intermediary. It irritated Genji that his lady showed no inclination to meet face to face, and so with great sincerity he spoke to her.

"If you could just appreciate how difficult and inappropriate it is for someone of my position to be coming here in secret like this, then you would not keep yourself apart from me, as if you had drawn a sacred straw rope between us. I wish to clear away the dark feelings and resentments that cloud my heart."

At that point her attendants interceded for him.

"Truly it would be a pity to leave him standing outside, looking so forlorn."

What should I do? the lady fretted. *I risk being shamed if I go out to meet him now, especially with my women watching . . . and even he might think it inappropriate for someone of my age.*

But as reluctant as she was to see him, she didn't want to seem cold or willfully aloof. In the end, the impression she made on his heart when she went out and sat behind her blind with much sighing and hesitation was one of magnificent refinement.

"May I be permitted to come up onto the veranda?" he asked, and stepped up.

His handsome figure and graceful movements gave off an incomparable radiance in the evening moonlight, which shone clearly into the space. They had reached the point in their relationship where he felt embarrassed to try to give some plausible excuse for all the months he had ignored her, so instead he presented her with a small branch of *sakaki*, the sacred evergreen, which he had

---

7. Gateway to a Shinto shrine [editor's note].

broken off on his way here. "Having made a signpost of my feelings, which, like the color of this sacred branch will never fade, I have entered this holy compound. And yet, how unfeeling you remain."

She responded with a poem:

> *With no cedar trees to serve as signpost*
> *To guide you to this sacred enclosure*
> *Have you in error brought sakaki here*[8]

Genji replied as follows:

> *Thinking you might be where the shrine maiden dwells*
> *In longing I plucked this branch along the way*
> *Drawn by the fragrance of sacred evergreens*

He felt constrained by the atmosphere of their surroundings, but he entered just inside her blind and leaned against one of the tie beams around the entrance.

During all those years when Genji ought to have followed the dictates of his heart and bestowed visits on her—a period during which the lady also thought longingly of him—his complacency, born of self-conceit, prevented him from feeling any sense of guilt or urgency about their relationship. Then, after he had been convinced in his heart that she was frighteningly flawed, his passion for her cooled to the point that now they were estranged. Yet as memories of their affair came back to him on the occasion of this extraordinary meeting, his heart was roiled by powerful emotions of sorrow and pity. Thinking of all that had happened and of all that was to come, he wept, brokenhearted. Although the lady seemed to be trying to steel herself, since she did not want her true feelings to show, she was unable to hold her emotions in check, and the sight of her struggling became more and more difficult for him to bear. As she looked at him, his appearance seemed to be telling her to reconsider her plans to leave the capital for Ise. Gazing into the sublime beauty of the sky—was it the early setting of the moon that made it seem so lovely?—his complaints spilled forth as he pleaded with her not to spurn his love. His pleas should have been enough to make the numerous hurts and resentments that had accumulated in her heart vanish. Indeed, even though she had finally resolved to make a clean break with him, now that they were meeting again her resolve began to crumble, and she found herself wavering.

Young noblemen accompanied one another on visits to this temporary shrine, and they cut remarkably splendid figures as they wandered about the garden there—a place they found difficult to leave. The scene before Genji and the lady was thus perfect, and there is simply no way to convey in writing all the words and feelings that these two, who had tasted sorrow to the full, shared with each other.

The sky was gradually growing light—its appearance seemed to have been made especially for them. Genji, who was finding it difficult to depart, took her hand and hesitated, overwhelmed by feelings of intimacy.

8. Anonymous poem from *The Kokinshū*: "If you truly long for me, come to the foot of Mount Miwa, to my hut . . . to the gate where the sacred cedars stand."

Partings at the break of dawn are always
Soaked by the dew . . . but never have I known
So sorrowful an autumn sky as this

A chill wind was blowing, and the raspy, mournful voices of bell crickets seemed to capture the mood of the moment. No one—not even a person untroubled by sad thoughts—could have passed by this scene without having been deeply affected. That being the case, it is hardly surprising, then, that the two of them, who were so distraught, found it hard to find the words for their poems of parting. Finally, she was able to reply:

Parting in autumn is sorrow enough . . .
Let me not hear as well the mournful cries
Of bell crickets in fields of withered grass

Though he was filled with frustrations and regrets, it was no use obsessing over them; and so, wishing to avoid the gaze of others, Genji departed. His path was drenched in dew and tears.

The lady, unable to maintain a stoic bearing, was lost in melancholy reverie, staring sadly at the place where Genji had been just moments earlier. His visage, which had been faintly visible in the moonlight, and the lingering fragrance of his perfumed robes, made a deep impression on the young women in attendance, and their praise for him perhaps went beyond the bounds of what was proper. "Is any journey worth abandoning a man like this?" they tearfully whispered among themselves, unaware of all that had taken place between Genji and their mistress.

His letter the next morning provided an unusually detailed account of his feelings, and though she found it difficult to resist his blandishments, she could not reverse herself and be indecisive once again. Thus, his letter came to naught. Genji was a man capable of unparalleled eloquence in expressing romantic emotions—even for affairs that didn't mean all that much to him—and so for a relationship that he could never have considered ordinary, it must have been all the more painful to have her reject him this way. He had magnificent robes and furnishings and goods of all sorts prepared and sent to her and her attendants for their journey, but she felt neither joy nor resentment at his show of concern. She was leaving behind a reputation as a frivolous and cruel woman, and as the day of departure drew near, she was now constantly regretting her situation, as if she were aware for the first time of the consequences of her actions. Her daughter, the High Priestess, had a youthful outlook on things, and she was happy that the departure date, which had been unsettled, was now firmly fixed. Naturally, gossip about the mother's unprecedented decision to accompany her daughter swirled about the court—some of it sympathetic, some sharply critical because of her relationship with Genji.

People whose status is such that they are never subjected to the barbed comments of others seem to have an easier time in life. Unfortunately, for those of high status who stand out in society, there are also many constraints on their behavior.

On the sixteenth day the Rite of Purification for the Ise Priestess was conducted at the Katsura River to the west of the capital. The ceremony was grander than most, in part because it was customary to choose men of high status and splendid reputations—a Consultant, for example, or a Middle Counselor—to serve as a member of her imperial escort. All of this of course reflected the interest that the Retired Emperor was taking in the matter.

Just as they were departing, a letter arrived from Genji revealing all the emotions he had not yet been able to fully express. He had addressed it "To the High Priestess, with Humble Reverence" and bound it with a ritual cord made of paper mulberry bark. "They say," he had written, "that the god of thunder himself has never sundered a relationship between lovers."[9]

> O Gods of the land of the Eight Isles
> If you feel pity, then judge kindly
> Two who taste in full parting's sorrow

"Thinking about you, I cannot help but feel depressed and dissatisfied."

Although she was extremely busy with her preparations, the High Priestess replied. Her Head of Household wrote out the response:

> Were the gods of our land to judge you
> Would they not first and foremost condemn
> The thoughtlessness of your heart and words

Genji was curious about the Ceremony of Parting and wanted to go to the palace, but he decided against it because he thought it would look pathetic for a man to be seeing off a lover who had rejected him. So, with nothing to occupy him, he was lost in his own thoughts. The High Priestess's reply poem was so mature that he had to smile as he read it. *She must be alluring beyond her years,* he thought, aroused to abnormal fantasies about her not as a Priestess but as a woman. His disposition always drew him toward relationships that were unusual and problematic.

How unfortunate that I wasn't able to see her when she was a child, he mused, *when I might have been able to get a good look at her. Oh well, nothing in this world is fixed forever, and so I should be able to meet her at some point.*

On the day of the Ceremony of Parting a large number of carriages lined up to view the procession, since it featured the presence of a lady and a daughter of exceptional beauty and breeding. At the Hour of the Monkey, around four o'clock in the afternoon, the procession arrived at the palace. The lady had last come here borne in a palanquin when she was to have become Empress. Her father had always aimed for her to reach the pinnacle of court society, but then her circumstances, which he had nurtured so carefully, suddenly changed. Upon seeing the palace now, after the collapse of her father's dreams, she was reminded of the mutability of all things in this world—a thought that moved her profoundly. She had come as the bride of the Crown Prince when she was sixteen and left the palace at twenty when he died. Now she was thirty, and upon seeing the ninefold palace again she composed a poem to herself:

> On this day, as much as I try to suppress
> Memories of all that happened long ago
> Unbearable sorrow lingers in my heart

9. Anonymous poem from *The Kokinshū*: "Would even the thunder-spirit who stomps and rages in the high plains of the heavens ever try to rend our love?"

The Ise Priestess had turned fourteen. She was exquisite, and her figure, properly attired for this occasion, was so stunningly beautiful that it raised concerns that she might draw the attention of gods or demons. The Emperor Suzaku was smitten by her, and when he placed the Comb of Parting in her hair, he could not hold back his emotions, and tears welled up in his eyes.

The carriages of the ladies accompanying the High Priestess to Ise were lined up along the compound of buildings housing the Eight Ministries under the Council of State. As they awaited departure the variegated hues of the sleeves of those ladies seated inside were spilling out from under the blinds, giving off a fresh appearance and vivacious charm. Many lords were feeling wistful regret, each of them seeing this moment as his own personal farewell to his parting lover.

The party set off after dark, and when they turned at Nijō Avenue onto the boulevard of Tōin, they passed by Genji's villa. Feeling great pity, Genji attached a poem to a branch of *sakaki* and sent it to the lady.

> *When you depart today will your sleeves be dampened*
> *By the Eighty Rapids at Suzuka River . . .*
> *Or by tears of regret for leaving me behind*

It was already quite dark when his letter arrived, and the lady was feeling rushed and flustered. Her reply, which she sent from the barrier gate at Ōsaka, did not reach him until the following day.

> *I cannot tell if my sleeves were dampened*
> *By the rapids at Suzuka River . . .*
> *Do your thoughts escort me to far Ise*

Though terse and hastily written, her calligraphy was interestingly elegant. Even so, he felt she should have written something that showed a little more depth of feeling for him. A thick fog had settled over everything, and as he stared out achingly at the misty early dawn, he whispered a poem to himself:

> *I gaze in longing toward the path you travel*
> *Hoping from afar that this year the autumn fog*
> *Will not hide Mount Osaka, where lovers meet*

He did not go over to the west hall to see Murasaki, but kept to himself, sunk in lonely, distracted thoughts. Compared to him, however, the lady on the road to Ise must surely have been suffering an even more exquisite agony.

Genji's father was ill, and by the tenth month his condition had become serious. Everyone in court society was concerned and grieving. Emperor Suzaku was so troubled that he personally called on his father. Although weakened by illness, the Retired Emperor asked repeatedly after the Crown Prince. He then spoke about Genji.

"When I'm gone I want you to continue thinking of him as an adviser in all matters of state, both great and small, just as when I was alive. In my opinion, you should not hesitate at all to entrust the government to him just because he is young. As the Korean diviner predicted, he is a man destined to rule the court. For that reason I was afraid that conflict might arise, and so I took him out of the line of succession and made him a commoner, with the idea that he would be of service to the throne. Do not go against my wishes on this matter."

Although there were numerous heartrending last requests, these are not the sort of things a woman should be relating, and I feel awkward having mentioned what little I have here. Emperor Suzaku was moved to sadness and gave repeated assurances that he would carry out his father's final instructions. He was so glorious in appearance and mature in demeanor that the Retired Emperor looked on him with joy and a sense of trust. Because the audience with his father was formal and public, Suzaku felt constrained, and he soon returned to the palace, regretting that many things had been left unsaid.

The Crown Prince had wanted to accompany Suzaku on his visit, but because it would have been too much excitement for the Retired Emperor, his visit was changed to another day. The boy was graceful and mature-looking beyond his years, and his longing to see his father had been building all throughout the illness. He was, in his innocence of the true circumstances of his birth, overjoyed when he was finally allowed to visit, and the scene of them together was touching. When the Retired Emperor saw Fujitsubo weeping disconsolately, his heart was filled with conflicting emotions. He spoke to the Crown Prince about all the things he should expect as future sovereign, but the boy was at such a tender age that the Retired Emperor couldn't help looking on him with a mix of concern and pity, and he repeatedly admonished Genji to be vigilant in attending to affairs of state and in looking after the interests of the Crown Prince. It was late at night when the boy left, and the tumultuous scene of his procession, which included virtually all of the upper ranking courtiers, was so grandly solemn that it was indistinguishable from that of Emperor Suzaku's. The Retired Emperor was sorry to see the boy go and dissatisfied that they had not had enough time together.

The Kokiden Consort also wanted to pay a visit, but the presence of Fujitsubo made her hesitate . . . and while she was vacillating, trying to decide what to do, the Retired Emperor passed away peacefully and with dignity. Many at the court were caught off guard and panicked. Even though the Retired Emperor had abdicated, he had maintained control of political power so the court would continue to function as it had during his reign. Suzaku, however, was still young, and his maternal grandfather, the Minister of the Right, was shallow, impulsive, and spiteful. Senior ministers and high-ranking nobles all fretted over what would become of the court under his control.

Fujitsubo and Genji had cause to be more distraught and uneasy than anyone. Observing that Genji's filial devotion in carrying out the subsequent memorial rites was much greater than that shown by the other princes, courtiers looked on him with pity and awe. Even in the unadorned robes of mourning, the extraordinary purity of his appearance stirred sympathy in onlookers. He had encountered misfortunes in consecutive years, and so he came to consider the world of the court vain and tedious. It occurred to him that the death of his father provided the perfect opportunity for him to withdraw from society and take religious vows, but because he was still bound by many relationships, he was not ready to do so just yet.

* * *

From Chapter XII

Suma

EXILE TO SUMA

* * *

Oborozukiyo[1] returned to court service in the seventh month. Suzaku had a strong lingering affection for her, and so he kept her near him as he had always done, acting as though he knew nothing of the imprecations directed at her by certain courtiers. He would on occasion reproach her for one reason or another while also offering tender vows of love. In both looks and bearing Suzaku possessed a youthful grace and elegance, and Oborozukiyo was certainly grateful for, and embarrassed by, his show of noblesse oblige. Yet her heart had room only for memories of Genji.

On one occasion, during a musical performance, Suzaku remarked, "It's at times like this that I miss Genji the most. I venture to say that there are many here who miss him even more than I. It seems as if the light has gone out of everything." He then added, "I have acted contrary to my father's wishes. I shall come to regret my sin." Tears welled up in his eyes, and at that moment Oborozukiyo could no longer restrain her own.

"I have learned from experience that the world is a tiresome place," he continued, "and no longer feel that I want to remain in it much longer. If I were no longer here, how would you feel about it? It makes me bitter to think that my death would not affect you nearly as much as the absence of one who still lives nearby. The poet who wrote the line 'while I am in this world'[2] did not express noble sentiments." His manner was so gentle, and his words suffused with such profound emotion, that tears began to stream down Oborozukiyo's cheeks.

"For whom do you weep?" Suzaku asked. "It makes me sad that you have yet to give me a child . . . it's as if something were missing in my life. I have considered adopting the Crown Prince as my father instructed me, but, given the enmity between my mother and the Fujitsubo Consort, it would cause too much trouble to do so."

Certain people were conducting affairs of state in a manner contrary to his wishes, but he was too young and weak-willed to resist, even though he was disappointed and bothered by many things, including Genji's exile, that had been carried out in his name.

At Suma the winds of autumn—the "season of anxious grief"[3]—were intensifying. Though his villa was some distance from the shore, each night the waves, which Middle Counselor Yukihira observed were stirred by winds blowing through the barrier pass, sounded as if they were breaking quite close. Genji had never experienced anything as affecting as the autumn in this place.

---

1. Genji's affair with her, described in pages not included here, forced him to leave the capital and go into exile to rustic Suma [editor's note].
2. Poem from an imperial *waka* collection, the *Shūishū* (Ōtomo no Momoyo): "What good would it do to die of longing? I want to be with my love for those days I am alive." The line *ikeru hi* ("those days I am alive") is misquoted in the text as *ikeru yo* (literally, "the world I live in").
3. Anonymous poem from *The Kokinshū*: "Looking upon the light of the moon filtering through the trees, I see that autumn, season of anxious grief, has arrived."

He had only a few attendants with him. Because they were all asleep, he was lying awake by himself, his head propped up on his pillow, listening to the winds howling from every direction. Feeling as though the waves were crashing near his residence, tears welled up instinctively—so many that it seemed his pillow might float away. He tried playing his seven-string koto a little, but the music just made him feel even more frightened and alone, and so he abruptly stopped and murmured the following poem:

> Does the wind blow from where my loved ones mourn
> For I seem to hear in the sound of waves
> Voices crying in pain from loneliness

Hearing his poem, his attendants were startled awake. Seeing how splendid Genji looked, they were overcome by emotion, and as they arose unsteadily they were quietly wiping their noses to disguise their tears.

Genji wondered, *How must my attendants feel? For my sake alone they have come wandering with me to this sorry existence, having left behind their comfortable, familiar homes and parted with parents and siblings from whom even the briefest absence would be hard to bear.*

Such musings made him miserable, but then he realized that it must make his attendants feel forlorn to see him so downhearted like this. And so, during the days that followed, he diverted them with playful banter, and in moments of idle leisure he would make scrolls by gluing together pieces of paper of various hues and practice writing poems. He also drew remarkable-looking sketches and paintings on rare Chinese silk of patterned weave and used them to decorate the front panels of folding screens. Before he came to Suma he had heard about the views of the sea and mountains here, and he had imagined from afar what they looked like. Now that they were right before his eyes, he depicted those rocky shores—their incomparable beauty truly surpassed anything he had imagined—in charcoal sketches of unrivaled skill. A member of his escort remarked with impatient frustration, "If only we could summon the great masters Chieda and Tsunenori[4] and have them color in your sketches . . ." Genji's gentle, familiar behavior and splendid bearing helped his attendants forget the cares of the world. Four or five were in constant attendance, and they were overjoyed to be able to serve him in such close proximity.

One pleasant evening, when the garden flowers near the veranda were a riot of colors, Genji stepped out into a passageway that framed a view of the sea. As he stood there motionless for a few moments, he didn't look like an earthly being, given the odd juxtaposition of his beauty and the setting, and so the divine splendor of his appearance was eerily unsettling. His loose purple trousers, cinched at the ankles, were lined with a pale green; his robe was a soft white silk twill. His dark blue cloak was loosely tied, giving him a casual air as he began reciting in hushed tones the opening lines of his ritual devotions: "I, a disciple of Sakyamuni Buddha . . ."

He slowly chanted a sutra in a voice so sonorous that it too seemed like nothing of this world. From boats in the offing came voices of fishermen singing as they rowed over the waves. Viewed from a distance, the vague outlines of the

---

4. Tsunenori flourished during the reign of Emperor Murakami (946–67). Not much is known about Chieda.

boats resembled little birds floating on the sea, creating a lonesome effect. Just then a line of migrating geese flew overhead, their cries like the creaking of the oars, and Genji gazed out at the scene in rapt silence, his hands, white and lambent in contrast to the dark beads of his rosary, moving almost imperceptibly to brush away the tears running down his cheeks. His magnificent appearance gave comfort to his retainers, all of whom were yearning for their loved ones back home. Genji composed a verse:

> Is it because these wild geese, the first of autumn
> Were with the loved ones I miss in the capital
> That their cries echo mournfully across the skies

Yoshikiyo responded:

> Though not companions of mine from the past
> These geese crying out still stir memories
> One after another of my old life

Koremitsu also responded:

> Am I to consider these geese as companions
> On my exile when they willingly chose to leave
> Familiar homes for distant realms beyond the clouds

The Lesser Captain of the Right Palace Guard—the young man whose loyalty cost him a promising career—composed yet another poem:

> Even wild geese who leave familiar homes
> To migrate through distant skies find comfort
> So long as they are with their companions

"What would become of me if I were to lose sight of my companions?"

Although the Lesser Captain's father, who had once been Vice Governor of Iyo, had recently been appointed Vice Governor of Hitachi, the young man had decided not to accompany him, but went into exile with Genji instead. The choice must have caused him great distress, but he put on a brave front and pretended that nothing bothered him.

The full moon rose vivid and bright, bringing back memories to Genji. "That's right . . . tonight is the fifteenth." Staring up at the face of the moon, he lovingly imagined the music that would be playing on a night like this at the palace, with all the ladies gazing out at the night sky. When he murmured a line from Bai Juyi—"Feelings for acquaintances of old, now two thousand leagues distant"[5]—his attendants could not restrain their tears. With indescribable yearning he recalled the poem Fujitsubo sent him complaining about how the "ninefold mists" kept her from the palace. As memories of this and other moments came to him, he wept aloud. He heard a voice saying, "The hour is late." However, he could not bring himself to retire.

---

5. She is mentioned in passing in the *Hanachirusato* chapter.

> *As I gaze at the moon I am at peace*
> *Even if only briefly, for it shines*
> *On the distant palace I long to see*

He had warm recollections of a certain night when he had talked intimately with Emperor Suzaku about times past. *How closely he resembles our late father!* Genji whispered a line from a poem in Chinese by the exiled Sugawara no Michizane: "The robe bestowed on me by the Emperor is now with me here."[6] Truly the robe never left his sight but was always near him.

> *My sleeves both right and left are wet with tears*
> *Tears of bitter resentment on the one*
> *Tears of longing for you on the other*

* * *

As the days and months passed, there were many occasions back in the capital when the courtiers, Emperor Suzaku first among them, experienced pangs of wistful longing for Genji. The Crown Prince in particular constantly shed tears whenever he thought of him, so that his nurses, especially Myōbu, looked on with pity.

Fujitsubo, who had always been fearful about her son's position, was beside herself with anxiety now that Genji was not there to look after his interests. At the beginning of his exile the princes who were his half brothers and other high-ranking noblemen who had been close to him would send sympathetic notes inquiring how he was faring. Many at the court deemed these exchanges of heartfelt correspondence, which included poetry in Chinese, extraordinarily felicitous. When the Kokiden Consort learned about these letters, however, she harshly disparaged them.

"One might expect a man who has incurred official censure to find it a daily struggle just to savor the taste of food as he would like . . . but not Genji. He resides in an attractive villa, writing letters critical of the court, and like that traitorous official in the Qin dynasty, gets his sycophants to go along with everything he says. Why, they'd call a deer a horse if he told them to!"[7] When word spread of what she said and the asperity with which she spoke, people at the court were afraid, and no one wrote to Genji anymore.

The passage of time brought no comfort to Murasaki. When the women who had been serving Genji in the east hall moved to her quarters in the west hall, they had been skeptical of her, wondering why their lord would have brought such a young lady to his villa. But after they got to know her—her charming, endearing looks, her steady, sincere personality, her kindness and deep sensitivity—not one of them chose to leave. Those ladies-in-waiting of higher status and greater discernment were able once in a while to catch a glimpse of her behind her screens, and when they did they saw that their lord's preference for her over his other ladies was perfectly justified.

---

6. A line from a Chinese-style poem that Sugawara no Michizane wrote in exile when he looked at a robe he had received from the emperor while still at court. The poetry of famous Chinese and Japanese exiles, such as Bai (Bo) Juyi and Michizane, keeps Genji company during his own time in exile [editor's note].

7. This anecdote is related in Sima Qian's *Historical Records* [editor's note].

The longer Genji stayed at Suma, the more living apart from Murasaki became intolerable. Despite his torment, he rejected the idea of having her come to live with him in a place completely unsuitable for her: *How could I have her live in a place I myself consider retribution for past sins?* Everything in this province was so different from the capital. He had never before been exposed to the sight of lower-class people, who had no inkling of who he was, and they were a shock to his sensibilities—naturally he found them uncouth and beneath him. From time to time smoke would rise quite near his villa, and at first he imagined it was from the fires the fishermen used to extract salt. Later he learned it was smoke from smoldering brush that had been cleared on the mountain behind the villa. It was all such a marvel to him that he composed a poem:

> *Like brush burning at the huts of rustics*
> *My heart smolders with my constant yearnings*
> *For tidings from my loved one back at home*

* * *

Just when life was feeling most tiresome, Tō no Chūjō suddenly paid a visit. He may have been the son of the Minister of the Left, but he was also the husband of the younger sister of the Kokiden Consort, and so his career had not suffered. He was a man of sterling character and, having been promoted to Consultant at the third rank, he now possessed an impeccable reputation. Despite his good fortune, however, the palace was a dreary place for him with Genji gone, and at every event he found himself longing for his old friend. It finally reached the point where he no longer cared that he might become the subject of malicious gossip and censure, and he decided to venture to Suma. The moment he laid eyes on Genji he experienced a joy, mingled with a few tears, that he had not savored in a long time.

In Tō no Chūjō's eyes, the villa at Suma had a vaguely Chinese style about it. The setting was like something out of a painting, and the effect created by the fence of bamboo wattle, the stone steps, the pine pillars, all as rustic and simple as Bai Juyi's hut, was peculiarly charming. Eschewing royal colors, Genji was dressed without ostentation, wearing dark bluish-gray hunting cloak and trousers, cinched at the ankles, over a humble light red robe, creating the impression that he was a mountain peasant. Though Genji was intentionally dressed like a provincial, his looks were so dazzling that Tō no Chūjō couldn't help smiling. The personal effects he kept close at hand were simple and humble-looking, and his sitting room was completely exposed to view from the outside. The boards for Go and backgammon, the furnishings, and the pieces used for playing *tagi*[8] had all been fashioned intentionally to have an appropriately countrified look, while the implements used for the Buddhist rituals he practiced showed signs of his wholehearted devotion. Even the meal provided was prepared in an intriguing way in harmony with the setting.

Tō no Chūjō, spotting some fishermen carrying shellfish they had just harvested, summoned them over and asked them what it was like to live for so many years on these shores. They told him about the various hardships and worries that they had experienced, and though their babbling speech was in a rough dia-

8. A game that is similar to tiddlywinks, except that the object is to flip stones onto a board instead of counters into a cup.

lect he found hard to follow, he was nonetheless moved as he observed them—they made him realize that all people, no matter what their status, experienced similar emotions and were not that different. As a reward for the shellfish, he adorned them with robes and other gifts, and the honor he bestowed on them made them think, if only for a moment, that the world was their oyster.

Genji's horses were stabled close by, and Tō no Chūjō watched in amazement as someone brought rice stalks from a strange-looking storehouse in the distance—apparently some kind of granary—to feed them. The scene reminded him of a line from the *saibara* "Asukai," from which he sang the words "the grasses are inviting." He then told Genji all that had happened during the months he had been away, alternately crying and laughing.

"My father," he said, "is always fretting over your son, and it makes him feel sad that the little one should be so innocent about what is happening in the world." Genji could hardly bear to think about the boy.

There is no way for me to record all that was said between them, and I can't even do justice to a small part of their conversation. They did not sleep that night but passed the time composing Chinese poetry until dawn. Still, even Tō no Chūjō had to be mindful of the consequences of rumors at the court, and so he hurried back to the capital at daybreak. Such haste made his departure all the harder for Genji to take. They took up their cups of wine and toasted one another, reciting together a line of verse composed by Bai Juyi to bid farewell to his friend, Yuan Zhen, who had visited the poet in exile: "Into the winecup in spring pour tears of drunken sorrow." All their companions wept with them, apparently in bitter regret that the two friends should have to part after so short a time together.

A formation of wild geese flew across the dimly lit sky. Genji composed the following:

> In what spring will I be allowed at last
> To go and view the capital again . . .
> How I envy these geese returning home

Tō no Chūjō could hardly bring himself to leave.

> Will not the wild geese that leave unsated
> From this enchanting abode lose their way
> On the road to the capital in bloom

The gifts from the capital were elegant and in good taste. In seeing off his guests, Genji showed his appreciation for them by making a present of a black horse.

"You may think it inauspicious to receive a memento from someone in exile," he said, "but, like me, this horse misses home, for he tends to neigh whenever he feels a breeze coming from the direction of the capital."[9] It was an exceptionally fine-looking steed.

"Keep these in remembrance of us," Tō no Chūjō replied, presenting Genji with several items, including a remarkable flute that had a reputation at court for its pure tonal qualities. All the same, he was careful not to give presents

9. Allusion to a Chinese poem in *Selections of Refined Literature* [editor's note].

that might invite censure. By now the sun was rising. Because it was already late to be starting off, he hurried away, flustered, glancing back over and over. How forlorn Genji looked as he saw the party off. "When will I see you again? Surely your exile won't last much longer."

Genji replied with a poem:

> O crane, you who can soar so near the clouds
> Above the palace . . . look on one whose life
> Is pure and spotless as a day in spring

"While I fully expect to return, it is difficult for people who suffer the misfortune of exile, even the wisest sages of the past, to mingle again successfully in court society, and so . . . well, I don't feel as though I want to see the capital again."

To no Chūjō answered with a verse of his own:

> Longing for the companion who flew beside him
> Wing to wing, the solitary crane with no guide
> To help cries out within the clouds and the palace

"Your absence is so painful, I now regret the good fortune of being your close friend." They had not had time to converse at their leisure, and his departure left such a void that Genji spent the rest of the day sunk in melancholy reverie.

On the Day of the Serpent, which fell during the first ten days of the third month, one of Genji's attendants, a person who took pride in his knowledge of such things, told him, "This is a day when a person who has the sort of cares that trouble you should perform rites of purification." And so Genji, who had wanted to go view the shore in any case, headed down to the sea. He had some simple soft blinds erected to create a temporary enclosure for himself, then summoned a diviner, a master of the way of yin-yang who traveled back and forth between the capital and this province. As part of the Purification Ritual, a large doll to which all defilements and malign spirits had been transferred was placed in a boat and set adrift on the waves. Watching it float away, Genji was reminded of his own fate.

> Like a ritual doll drifting out
> Into an unknown expanse of sea
> I am overwhelmed by my sorrow

Sitting in the midst of the bright, cheerful scenery, he looked indescribably handsome. The surface of the sea was serenely calm and gave no sign as to which way the currents were flowing, but as he pondered the flow of his own life, his past and his future, he composed another poem:

> Surely the myriad deities
> Must take pity on me . . . after all
> Is what I have done truly a crime

The wind suddenly picked up, and the skies darkened. People began bustling to get ready to leave, even though the Purification Ritual was not finished. Rain fell suddenly and violently, and his attendants were so flustered that they were unable to raise their parasols as they made their way back to the residence. The party had not prepared for this kind of storm; the wind, unlike anything they had seen before, blew away everything around them, and the waves broke with terrifying power, forcing everyone to flee before their fury. With each flash of lightning and crash of thunder, the surface of the sea shimmered like a silk quilt spread out before them. While the party struggled, barely managing to make it back, they feared they might be struck by lightning at any moment.

"I've never gone through anything like this!" said one of the attendants.

"Usually you see some signs that the wind is going to pick up. This is a shockingly rare occurrence," replied another.

Even as they spoke, stunned and dismayed, the thunder continued unabated, and the torrential rain fell so hard it seemed as though it would pierce through whatever it struck. *Is the world coming to an end?* they all wondered, feeling forlorn and confounded. All the while Genji was calmly reciting a sutra. The thunder lessened somewhat when darkness fell, but the wind howled on throughout the night.

When it seemed that the storm was subsiding, one of the attendants remarked, "Surely this is a sign of the power of all the prayers I've been offering."

"If it had gone on much longer," his companion added, "we would have been swallowed up by the waves for sure."

"I've heard that a tsunami can kill a person in an instant," someone else chimed in, "but I never knew anything like this could happen."

When dawn approached, everyone was finally able to fall asleep. Genji was also able to rest a little, but as he dozed off, someone—a person whose features he could not make out very clearly—approached him in a dream. "You have been summoned to the palace," the figure demanded, "so why have you not made an appearance?" The figure was walking about, apparently searching for him. Seeing this, Genji was startled awake. The Dragon King in the sea was known to be a connoisseur of genuine beauty, and so Genji realized he must have caught the deity's eye. The dream gave him such a horrifying, uncanny sensation that he could no longer stand residing in this abode by the sea.

From Chapter XIII

Akashi

THE LADY AT AKASHI

Several days passed, but the rain and wind did not let up, and the thunder did not abate. These endless hardships made Genji increasingly lonely and miserable, and under such circumstances, facing a dark past and bleak future, he could no longer put on a brave front.

What should I do? he asked himself as he pondered his situation. *If this storm drives me back to the capital before I receive a pardon, I'll be a laughingstock. Perhaps it would be best to leave here and seek out some abode deep in the mountains, leaving no trace of myself in the world.* But then he had second thoughts. *Even if I were to leave for the mountains, people would still gossip about me, saying that I retreated in a panic, driven off by the wind and waves. Later generations would consider me utterly contemptible.*

These thoughts weren't the only thing troubling him. The dream he had a few nights earlier, during which he had seen that foreboding figure, kept recurring. Day after day went by without a break in the clouds, and he grew increasingly anxious, fretting about what was happening in the capital and thinking abjectly that, if things continued like this, he would be cast utterly adrift. Yet because it was too stormy to even poke one's head outside, no one arrived from the capital to see him.

At last a messenger arrived from his Nijō villa. The man, who had rashly braved the weather, was soaked to the point of looking weird and unearthly. He was also of very humble station—had Genji passed such a person on the road at an earlier point in his life, he would not have recognized him as human and would have had his servants brush him aside. The fact that Genji now felt a deep kinship with such a man brought home just how far he had come down in the world and how much his self-esteem had collapsed.

The man carried a letter from Murasaki:

"This terrible, tedious storm goes on without end, making me feel as though the skies were closing me off from you even more than before, for now I cannot even gaze in your direction."

> *How fiercely must the winds blow across those strands*
> *During this time when endless waves drench the sleeves*
> *Of one who is longing for you from afar*

The account she gave of her anguish affected him greatly. After opening her letter, his mood turned to dark despair, and he felt like the poet whose river of tears "overflowed its banks."[1]

"Even in the capital," the messenger informed him, "people are viewing this storm as an eerie omen, and I've heard that they plan to hold a ritual congregation of the *Sutra for Benevolent Rulers* to protect against a disaster.[2] High-ranking officials who usually attend the palace to conduct affairs of state cannot do so because the roads are all blocked."

The messenger's way of speaking was stiff and unclear, but because Genji was curious about court matters, he was eager to learn more. He summoned the man to appear before him and questioned him further.

"Day after day the rain falls with no letup and the winds continue to gust," the messenger said. "Everyone is alarmed and amazed by this extraordinary weather. Of course, we haven't seen anything like what you've had here at Suma, what with hail falling so hard it drills into the ground and with this constant rumbling of thunder."

The expression on the man's face, which told of his surprise and fear of the terrible conditions at Suma, sharpened all the more the sense of isolation felt by Genji's attendants.

---

1. Poem from Ki no Tsurayuki's *Tosa Diary* included in this volume: "The river of tears has overflowed its banks and further dampens the sleeves of both the one who goes and the one who stays behind."
2. This congregation, called *Ninnōe*, was held in the palace in the fall and spring or in times of emergency to protect the realm.

As the storm raged on and on, Genji began to wonder if this might not be the end of the world . . . but then, the following morning, the wind picked up with even greater intensity, the tide surged, and waves broke violently on the shore, looking as if they might sweep away even the rocky crags and hills. No words could describe the booming thunder or the flashing lightning, which seemed to be crashing down right on top of them. Everyone was frightened out of his wits.

"What misdeed did we commit," bemoaned one retainer, "that we should suffer this tragic destiny? Must we die without seeing our parents again, without looking on the beloved faces of our wives and children?"

Genji regained his composure, resolute in the conviction that having committed no great crime his life would not end on these shores. Still, his attendants were in such a state of panic that he had an offering of multicolored strips of cloth made to the gods of the sea. He also made numerous supplications: "O deity of Sumiyoshi,"[3] he intoned, "you who calm and protect these nearby shores, if truly you are a manifestation of the Buddha taken form as the guardian divinity of this region, then deliver us from harm!" His attendants were deeply distressed by the prospect that not only they themselves but their lord as well would be swept into the sea and perish in this unheard-of fashion. A few of them gathered their courage as best they could and, regaining a sense of propriety, joined their voices in praying to the Buddha and the gods, each offering his own life in exchange for the safety of their lord. Turning in the direction of the Sumiyoshi Shrine, they made their supplications.

"Our lord was reared in the bosom of the Emperor's palace and had every sort of pleasure lavished upon him. Yet has not his profound compassion spread throughout this great realm of eight islands, lifting up and saving many who were mired in sin and impiety? What crime has he committed that he must now suffer retribution by drowning here amidst these foul, unjust waves and wind? You gods of Heaven and of Earth, show us clearly that you discern right from wrong! Though guiltless, he has been charged with crimes, stripped of office and rank, separated from home, driven into exile. Grieving anxiously morning and night, he has suffered this tragic fate . . . is he about to lose his life as well because of some sin in a former life, or some crime committed in this one? Gods and Buddha, if you are just, then put an end to our lordship's suffering!"

Genji once more offered prayers to the Dragon King and to the myriad gods of the sea, but the thunder only crashed all the more loudly, and lightning struck the gallery connecting Genji's quarters to the rest of the villa. Flames leapt up and the passageway caught on fire, throwing everyone into a state of panic. No one had enough wits about him to be able to deal with the situation, and so they had their lord move to the rear of the residence to a room that, from the looks of it, must have been the kitchen. Everyone, irrespective of rank, crowded into the space, and the thunder could barely be heard above the tumultuous din of the crying and shouting there. As the day ended, the sky was black as an inkstone.

Finally the winds gradually subsided, the rain tapered off, and sparkling stars were visible. Genji's attendants felt embarrassed for their lord, thinking it was an affront to his dignity to remain in a place as strange and disreputable as this,

---

3. A Shinto shrine near Osaka [editor's note].

and so they wanted to try to move him back to the main hall. They hesitated, however, debating what they should do.

One of them declared, "Even the quarters that escaped the fire have an ominous air about them. The people over there are in a state of shock, noisily stomping about, and the blinds have all been blown away."

Another attendant replied, "In that case, let's wait until morning."

All the while Genji was meditating and softly invoking the name of the Buddha. Feeling unsettled and restless, he mulled over all that had happened. After the moon rose he could make out clearly just how close to the villa the tide had surged. Pushing open a door of rough wattle and glancing outside, he gazed off toward the shore at the roiling surf left in the wake of the storm. No one in the immediate vicinity possessed the qualifications—sensitivity, proper judgment, ability to divine past and future—needed to make sense of all this and reliably sort things out. Instead, the only people to make their way to the villa were those strange, lowly fisherfolk, who gathered at a residence where they had heard a nobleman resides, babbling away in an unfamiliar dialect. Even though Genji considered them exceedingly bizarre, he couldn't very well have them chased away.

One of his attendants remarked, "If the wind hadn't subsided for a while, the high tide would have left nothing behind. The mercy of the gods is boundless!"

Feeling forlorn, he composed a verse:

> Had the gods of the sea shown no mercy
> Then the tide surging from all directions
> Would surely have swept me into the deep

Genji had maintained his composure throughout the tumult of the storm, but it had been terribly nerve-wracking and exhausting, and he began to doze off in spite of himself. The room he was using as a temporary shelter was so crude and rough that he could not lie down, so he slept while propping himself up against a pillar. As he did so, his late father came to him in a dream and stood before him, looking just as he did when he was alive.

"Why do you remain in such a strange, unseemly place as this?" His father took his hand and, pulling Genji to his feet, exhorted him: "Hurry now! Board a boat and leave these shores, following wherever the deity of Sumiyoshi may lead you!"

Genji felt overjoyed. "From the moment I was separated from your august presence," he said, "I have been beset with all manner of sorrows, so that now I feel I ought to end my life on this shore."

"Such rash thoughts simply will not do! All these trials are a mere trifle . . . retribution for some minor misdeeds. Though I committed no serious breach of conduct during my reign, I was unknowingly guilty of some misdeeds and have spent all my time after death atoning for them[4] without once giving any thought to matters of this world. But then I saw how deeply mired you are in your troubles here, and I could not bear it. I entered the sea and rose up to these shoals. Though I am now utterly exhausted, I must take this opportunity and hurry on

---

4. This statement by Genji's father is an apparent reference to a vision by the monk Nichizō, who saw the historical Emperor Daigo suffering the torments of Hell.

to the capital, where I will speak to Suzaku on your behalf." With that he rose to leave.

Genji was upset that his father was going away so soon, and because he wanted to accompany him, he began to weep. He looked up, but there was no one there—only the shining face of the moon. It had all felt so real, it hadn't felt like a dream at all. The lingering presence of his father remained, so palpable that Genji was profoundly moved by the sight of the wispy lines of clouds trailing across the night sky like traces of his father's ghostly presence. He had not seen his father's figure for many years, not even in his dreams. Now, even though he had glimpsed for only a few fleeting moments the face he had been longing so impatiently to see, the image continued to linger, hovering before his mind's eye. The poignant sense of gratitude he felt toward his father, who had flown to aid him when his life had reached its nadir and he was in despair and contemplating the end of his life, also made him look at the storm in a different, more positive light. The aftereffect of his dream was a boundless sense of happiness and relief that someone was looking out for him. His heart was full of conflicting emotions, and even though he had seen his father only in a dream, the turmoil in his heart distracted him from the sorrows of the waking world. He wanted to go back to sleep in hopes of seeing his father again, but the irritation he felt at himself for not responding to his father in more detail kept him from being able to close his eyes, and he stayed awake until dawn.

A small boat approached the shore and several men came toward the exile's abode. When one of Genji's retainers asked them to identify themselves, they answered, "The former Governor of Harima Province, a novitiate who has recently taken his vows, had this boat readied, and we journeyed here from the bay at Akashi. If Yoshikiyo, the Minamoto Lesser Counselor, is here, our lord would like to meet and discuss some matters at length."

Yoshikiyo was startled by their arrival and seemed not to know what to make of it.

"I was familiar with the man before he was a novitiate and still Governor of Harima and had opportunities to converse with him over the course of several years. However, we had a mutual falling-out over some trifling matter, and so it has been a long time since we exchanged any correspondence of a particularly personal nature. What business would bring him here over such rough seas?"

Genji's dream, especially his father's exhortation, was still vivid in his mind, and he told Yoshikiyo to hurry up and meet with the novitiate. So Yoshikiyo went down to the boat, scarcely believing that it had set out during the storm amidst such violent waves and wind.

"Earlier this month," the novitiate explained, "a remarkable-looking figure came to me in a dream and told me something incredible. 'On the thirteenth of this month,' he announced, 'I will give you a clear sign, so have a boat prepared and no matter what happens, make for Suma when the wind and waves subside.' Because he had informed me in advance, I did as instructed and had a boat ready. I waited as long as I could, until the ferocity of the rain and wind and thunder alarmed me and made me worry for the safety of your lord. Then it hit me that there have been many examples, even in other lands, in which a person who acted on his belief in a dream saved the state. Though your lord may have no use for my message, I could not let the appointed day spoken of in my dream pass without reporting these tidings to him. So I set out in the boat, and a miraculously favorable wind blew it along until we arrived at this strand. Truly this can only be a sign of divine favor. Is it possible that some sign was given to your lord here as well? If so, then please convey my words to him, ashamed though I am to beg your indulgence."

Yoshikiyo discreetly reported what he had heard.

Genji mulled over the information, turning over in his mind all things past and future—disturbing things he had seen in both his dreams and his waking life— that might be taken as signs from the gods: *If I hesitate out of fear that gossips will ruin my reputation by criticizing me for following after some eccentric novitiate, I could end up rejecting what might be genuine divine assistance. If that happened, I'd be an even greater laughingstock. It is hard enough to turn away from the advice of men . . . how much harder, then, to defy the gods. It's proper that I should be deferential, even in minor matters, and yield to the views of those higher in rank who are older, respected and trustworthy. A sage of old once advised that "one cannot be censured for following." In truth, I failed to heed those words, and as a result I've had to undergo many bitter, unprecedented hardships, including this life-threatening storm. In the face of all that, salvaging my reputation for posterity no longer seems so important. What's more, my father did admonish me in my dream, so why should I have any doubts about the novitiate's story?*

After deliberating in this way, Genji sent his reply: "Though I have encountered unheard-of difficulties in this unfamiliar province, no one from the capital has inquired after me. I have gazed after the sun and moon coursing through the sky to who knows where, and thought of them as my only companions from home . . . but now, to my great joy, a fisherman's boat arrives.[5] Is there a retreat on the shores of Akashi, some place where I might withdraw in peace?"

The novitiate's delight knew no bounds, and he expressed his deep gratitude.

"This is all fine and well," said a member of Genji's escort, "but our lord should go aboard before dawn so that he will not be seen."

Genji boarded the boat accompanied by the usual retinue of four or five of his most trusted attendants. The miraculous breeze that had brought the boat here picked up again, and they arrived at Akashi so quickly it was as if they had flown there. The shores of Suma and Akashi were separated by only a few miles, and so the journey would have been short in any case. Even so, the willfulness of the breeze seemed uncanny all the same.

What Yoshikiyo had told him years earlier was true—the scenery on the shores of Akashi was truly spectacular. For Genji, who was hoping for a peaceful sanctuary, the only distraction was the large number of people bustling about. The novitiate's estate extended from the waterfront up into the recesses of the hills, and he had brought together on his land all sorts of attractive buildings constructed with an eye to how well they suited the seasons and the topography—a thatched-roof cottage near the shore that would intensify the pleasures of viewing the four seasons, a magnificent meditation hall standing beside a stream flowing down out of the hills on a site perfect for performing ritual devotions and focusing one's thoughts on the next world, a row of granaries built to provide for the needs of this world and filled with the bountiful harvests of autumn

---

5. Poem by Ki no Tsurayuki: "To my great joy a fisherman's boat arrives, borne by a breeze that blows on one who has been soaked by waves."

in order to sustain the novitiate throughout his remaining years of life. Fearful of the recent tidal surges, the novitiate had moved his daughter and her entourage to a residence at the foot of the hills, allowing Genji to comfortably occupy the villa near the sea.

The sun was rising just as Genji was moving from the boat to a carriage. As soon as the novitiate caught a glimpse of him in the dim early morning light, he immediately forgot about his own advancing years and felt as though his life had been extended. With a beaming smile, he at once offered a prayer to the deity of Sumiyoshi. It seemed to him that he had been allowed to grasp the light of the sun and the moon in his hands, and so it seemed perfectly natural that he should busy himself tending to Genji's needs.

To capture the scene in a painting—not just the beauty of the setting, which goes without saying, but also the elegance of the buildings, the indescribable appearance of the grove of trees surrounding them, the rocks and plants in the gardens, the waters of the inlet—seemed impossible for anyone but the most inspired of artists. The residence here was much brighter and more cheerful than the villa at Suma Genji had occupied these many months, and the utterly charming furnishings brought back fond memories. The novitiate's lifestyle was, as Yoshikiyo had reported, no different from that enjoyed at the most distinguished aristocratic houses in the capital; indeed, the blinding brilliance of his lifestyle appeared, if anything, to be superior.

* * *

It was now the fourth month, and with the change of the seasons Genji was provided with superb new robes and silk curtains to hang around the dais in his sleeping quarters. He found the tendency of his host to obsess over every last detail when serving him somewhat pathetic and overdone. But, at the same time, he observed that the old man's proud dignity revealed a nobility of character, and so he allowed the novitiate to have his way in such matters.

Murasaki continued to send messages as frequently as ever. One quiet, calm moonlit evening, when a cloudless sky spread far into the distance over the sea, the scene brought to mind the water in the garden pond at his Nijō villa. He was filled with an ineffable yearning—a yearning for what or for whom he could not articulate. Before his eyes, off in the distance, was the island of Awaji. "Ah, how far away it seems . . . ,"[6] he murmured.

> *This moon illuminates the poignant beauty*
> *Of Awaji Island . . . ahh, how far it seems*
> *Bringing painful longings for my distant home*

He took his seven-string koto from its cover and plucked a few notes. He had not touched it for some time, and the sight of him aroused restless emotions in his attendants, who found their lord troublingly sad and beautiful.

Genji performed a tune titled "Kōryō,"[7] utilizing all his skills to produce an immaculate rendition. The music mingled with the rustling of the pines and

6. Poem by Ōshikōchi no Mitsune: "Ah, how far away it seemed . . . the moon I viewed at Awaji. Is it the special atmosphere of the setting here this evening that makes it look so near?"
7. A "secret" song composed by the legendary musician Reirin for the Yellow Emperor.

the rippling sound of the waves and wafted toward the lady's residence at the foot of the hill, sending shivers of delight through the refined young ladies-in-waiting there. The rustic denizens of that shore, who certainly were unable to recognize the song, walked along the beach feeling exhilarated, even though they ran the risk of catching cold in the sea breeze. Unable to restrain himself, the novitiate relaxed his devotions and hurried over to Genji's residence.

"It would seem I am still driven by memories to return to the world I supposedly left behind when I took my vows," he said, tears welling up. "The atmosphere conjured by your music, which draws me here this evening, is surely a harbinger of the Pure Land paradise I pray for in the coming life."

Memories came flooding back to Genji's heart as well . . . the musical entertainments celebrating various seasons at court . . . so-and-so playing the koto . . . such-and-such on the flute . . . the sound of voices singing in chorus . . . courtiers praising him lavishly for his own musical skills. How wonderful was the honor and respect shown to him by everyone from the Emperor on down; and of course how grand were the circumstances of those he loved and his own status back then. He felt like he was in a dream, and the overtones his koto produced as he played in that trancelike state conveyed an unearthly, frightening loneliness.

The novitiate could not help feeling maudlin, and he sent for a *biwa* lute[8] and a thirteen-string koto from the villa at the base of the hill. Playing the role of an itinerant priest performing on the lute, he played a couple of very charming, unusual tunes. He presented the thirteen-string koto to Genji, who played a little on the instrument. The novitiate marveled at how brilliantly talented the young lord was in a variety of arts. Even an instrument that does not produce an especially distinct timbre may, depending on the occasion, sound quite superior. As the music drifted across the waters stretching interminably into the distance, the stirring cry of a Water Rail—so like the rapping of some paramour at the gate of his beloved—rang out amidst the shadows of trees in rampant foliage more vivid and fresh than even the blossoms of spring or the leaves of autumn at their peak.

Genji was impressed by the novitiate's koto, which produced such unique tones, and by his host's own sweetly charming skills. "The thirteen-string koto is most delightful when played in a relaxed, informal style by a woman who exudes a gentle and intimate grace." Genji was referring to women in general, but the old novitiate, misinterpreting his intent, smiled and replied, "I'm not sure that any woman, no matter how gentle or graceful, could play better than Your Lordship. I myself learned to play under the tutelage of a disciple of the Engi period Emperor, Daigo,[9] but as you can see I'm not especially gifted, and so I've cast aside the things of this world. Still, whenever I was depressed I would play a little, and as a result there is someone here who learned the instrument by imitating me, and so her style naturally resembles Emperor Daigo's. Of course, I am just a humble mountain rustic, hard of hearing, and it may be that I am so used to the sound of the wind rustling in the pines that I can no longer tell the difference between it and the sound of the koto. Even so, would you

8. A four-stringed pear-shaped Japanese lute [editor's note].
9. Daigo (885–930) ruled 897–930 c.e. and

his reign included the Engi period, from 901 to 923 c.e.

permit me to arrange for you to hear her in private?" His voice was tremulous, and he seemed to be on the verge of breaking down in tears.

"I should have known that in a place such as this, where people are accustomed to the superior music of nature, my performance would not sound like a koto. All very regrettable . . ." Genji pushed the instrument away. "It's odd, really, but since ancient times the thirteen-string koto has been considered a woman's instrument. Emperor Saga[1] passed down the techniques, and it is said that his daughter, the Fifth Princess, was the most skillful virtuoso of her age, though no one remains in her lineage to pass along that style of performance. Nowadays, for the most part, those who have achieved a reputation as master of the koto choose to approach this instrument superficially, as a pleasant diversion and no more. Thus, it's fascinating that an older style of performance should have survived, hidden away in a place like this. How will I manage to hear this person you spoke of?"

"There is nothing to prevent you from listening to her," the novitiate said. "You could even summon her. After all, if I may point to the story handed down by Bai Juyi, there was a woman, the wife of a merchant, who won praise for her talent with the lute . . . and what you said of the koto is true of the lute as well. In ancient times there were very few people who could calmly strum that instrument and reveal its true nature, but the lady I mentioned can play it exceptionally well, with a gentle charm and few hesitations. I'm not sure how she managed to learn the lute as well, but when I hear her music mingling with the sound of the waves, it sometimes brings on feelings of melancholy. At other times it provides a respite from my accumulating sorrows."

Delighted that the old man was a true connoisseur, Genji swapped instruments with him, exchanging the thirteen-string koto for the lute. As expected, the novitiate's skill on the koto was well above average. He played tunes in a style no longer heard in the modern world. His spectacular fingering showed a touch of continental flair, and the vibrato he produced with his left hand was deep and clear. Though they were not at Ise, Genji had one of his men, who had a fine voice, sing the line "Shall we pick up shells along the pristine shore?" from the *saibara* "The Sea at Ise," while he himself kept rhythm by using flat wooden clappers. From time to time he joined in the singing, and the novitiate would often pause to praise him. As the night wore on, the old man had unusual delicacies brought out and pressed wine upon everyone so that they would naturally forget the cares of the world.

The late night breeze off the shore was chilly, and the light of the setting moon seemed intensely clear. As the world grew quiet the novitiate opened up to Genji, telling him one small anecdote after another about all that had happened in his life—the burdens he had assumed when he first moved to Akashi and how he had devoted himself single-mindedly to his religious practice with the next life in mind. He even brought up, without prompting, his daughter's situation. Genji was amused by this show of paternal devotion, but at the same time he was also touched by the young lady's predicament.

"I hesitate to mention it," the old man continued, "but I wonder if your move to a strange province such as this—temporary though it may be—isn't the work of the gods and the Buddha who, by troubling your heart for a brief period, are

1. Ruled 809–23 C.E.

showing kindness and pity toward an old priest like me who has prayed to them for so long. I say this because it has been eighteen years since I first placed my faith in the deity of Sumiyoshi. From the time my daughter was a little girl I had ambitions for her, and so each spring and autumn, without fail, I go to pray at the Sumiyoshi Shrine. I practice my devotions day and night at each of the six prescribed times. But, rather than concentrating my prayers on the wish to be reborn on a lotus in the Pure Land, I ask that my ambitions for my daughter be fulfilled and that she be granted a noble position at court. Regrettably, sins from a previous life have brought me misfortune in this one, and I've become the miserable mountain peasant you see before you. My father was able to rise in status as a Minister of State, but I have ended up a rustic provincial. It grieves me to imagine what might become of my descendants, how low they might sink should my family's decline continue; that is why from the moment my daughter was born, I've invested all my hopes and expectations in her. As a consequence of my deep resolve to present her by any means possible to a high-ranking nobleman in the capital, I've rejected many suitors who wished to take her as a wife. Some of those suitors were men whose status was higher than mine, and I've suffered harsh treatment on account of their resentment of me. However, I don't consider that a hardship, and I admonish my daughter by reminding her that as long as I'm alive I'll look after her, even though, as you can see from the narrow cut of my sleeves, I don't have much wealth to give her. And I've told her that if I die while she is still young and unmarried, she should throw herself into the sea."

He broke down sobbing. He said so many other things besides, it is impossible to relate them all here. Genji was listening to all this during a period in his own life when he had been beset constantly with various problems, and so the old man's story invited tears of sympathy.

"Accused without basis and cast adrift in an unfamiliar land," Genji responded, "I have wracked my brain trying vainly to identify the misdeed I supposedly committed. But now, on hearing your tale this evening and reconsidering the matter, I'm deeply moved by the realization that we truly share a bond from a previous life that is anything but shallow. Why did you not tell me earlier that you knew all this? Once I had departed the capital I lost my attachments and came to find the fickleness of the world insipid and tiresome, and while passing the days and months pursuing only religious austerities, I grew disconsolate and melancholy. I heard faint reports about your daughter, but because it seemed likely that you would reject as inauspicious the suit of an exile without status, I had no confidence to even try. Now it appears that you are beckoning me to her quarters. To have her share my lonely bed would be a comfort."

The young lady's father was thrilled beyond measure at these words.

> Do you know as well what it means to sleep alone
> Then perhaps you understand the boredom she feels
> Waiting for the dawn on Akashi's lonely strand

"You may well appreciate," he added, "how much greater my own sense of melancholy has been, wearied as I am from years of concern over her." Now that he had finally spoken of his daughter, his body was trembling in agitation—though he did not lose his air of refinement and dignity.

"That may be," Genji replied, "but those who are accustomed to living on this bay may not appreciate how lonely it is for someone like me . . ."

In lonely travel robes, on a pillow of grass
I wait in sleepless grief for dawn at Akashi
Unable to weave a dream and join my lover[2]

Genji was in dishabille; there is simply no way to describe how charming he looked at that moment.

The novitiate talked on and on at length about all sorts of things, but it would be annoying to record them all here. However, because I have not written down everything exactly as it happened or was spoken, I may have accentuated some of the man's more eccentric and stubborn characteristics.

With things going more or less as he had hoped, the novitiate felt as though a burden had been lifted from him. At around noon the following day, Genji sent a letter to the lady's residence at the base of the hill. He had given careful attention to the letter, thinking that the lady seemed on the one hand like someone of dauntingly superior talent who would be hard to approach, and on the other, like an unexpected find hidden away in this obscure location. He prepared the letter with exquisite care, writing on light brown Korean paper.

Gazing sadly at the sky, is it near or far . . .
How I want to pay a visit to those treetops
At the abode obscured by mist and faint rumor

"My longing for you has overwhelmed my secret love."[3] Was that the full extent of his letter?

The novitiate had already arrived at his daughter's residence and was waiting with secret anticipation. Things were working out as expected, and by the time the letter arrived he had already arranged for refreshments for the messenger, plying him with wine until the man was embarrassingly drunk.

The lady took a long time to compose her reply. Her father entered her quarters and pressed her to answer, but she refused to listen to him. Intimidated by the brilliant wit of Genji's letter, she felt inadequate and ashamed to set her own hand to paper, which would expose the truth about her. Comparing his status to hers, it was obvious that the gulf separating them was enormous. She withdrew to lie down, telling her father that she wasn't feeling well. Unable to persuade his daughter and with his patience now exhausted, the novitiate wrote the reply for her:

"For a woman whose sleeves have about them the rustic air of the provinces, your graciousness brings a surfeit of happiness that is too much for her to bear. She is too overwhelmed even to read your letter, but observing her . . ."

---

2. This poem, like the one it answers, plays primarily on the word *akashi*—referring to the place name and to dawn breaking. Lovers would share robes as part of their bedding, and it was believed that this act ensured that they would meet in their dreams. Travel robes convey an image of sleeping alone, thus making it impossible to meet one's lover in a dream and intensifying the sense of loneliness.

3. Anonymous poem from *The Kokinshū*: "Though I never wanted to let the colors of my love show, my longing for you has overwhelmed my secret."

Lost in lonely thoughts, gazing sadly
At the same sky you are viewing now
Are not her feelings the same as yours

"Is my view of her perhaps too romantic?"

The note was written on Michinokuni paper, which lent it an old-fashioned aura, but Genji was a little surprised, shocked even, at the seductive allure of the calligraphy, which was embellished with refined flourishes. The novitiate had presented Genji's messenger with, among other things, an exceptionally fine set of women's robes.

The following day Genji sent another note:

"I've never seen a letter by proxy before."[4]

How wretched my uncertain heart
Knowing there is no one who asks
"Do tell me, how are things with you"

"The difficulty of speaking of my feelings to one I have not yet seen . . ."

This time he used an extremely soft, thin paper, and his calligraphy was exquisite. Only a young lady who was excessively shy and introverted would have failed to appreciate it, and indeed when the Akashi lady saw it, she was amazed. Still, she remained convinced that the immeasurable difference in status between them made any relationship hopelessly unsustainable, and it made her cry to know that he was courting her even though she was of such inferior rank. She remained outwardly impassive, but this time she did as she was told and replied to him. Writing on heavily perfumed paper of light purple hue, her brush-strokes were thick and bold in some places, thin and wispy in others—a technique she employed to disguise any flaws in her hand.

How could you ever declare such feelings
To me, a person you have never met
Can rumors really trouble you so much

Her calligraphy and phrasing had an aristocratic flair not at all inferior to those of the most distinguished ladies.

Remembering all the exchanges he had engaged in with women back in the capital, Genji regarded the lady's letter with delight. Of course, he was mindful of prying eyes and of the censure he would surely suffer if he wrote too often, so he would let two or three days lapse between letters, and even then he corresponded only when he guessed that she might be experiencing emotions similar to his own—on an early evening passed in the quiet diversion of solitary idleness, for example, or a dawn that provided a scene of poignant beauty. Her replies on these occasions were always appropriate, and after thinking about her responses he concluded that she was a lady of discretion and noble character, and thus someone he very much wanted to meet. He asked Yoshikiyo to describe her and reacted with some distaste at the look on the young man's face as he did so—a look that seemed to say, *she belongs to me*—and he felt a

---

4. The word Genji uses, *senjigaki*, refers to a letter dictated by the emperor or by an aristocrat.

twinge of pity that his retainer's aspirations to win the lady for himself, which he had harbored for many years, would be thwarted right before his eyes. Genji believed, however, that he could justify his actions so long as the lady encouraged him to pursue a relationship. The problem was that she was proving even more aloof and proud than most highborn women. Genji found this kind of behavior damnably irritating, and so as time passed they began to engage in a contest of wills.

After crossing the barrier pass at Suma, his anxiety about Murasaki back in the capital only grew worse, and many times his resolve weakened as he wondered what to do—after all, being apart made it difficult to "bear this foolish game."[5] Should he have her come in secret to Akashi? Each time he asked himself this question, he ended up thinking better of it. No matter what happened, he believed that he would not spend many more years like this in exile, and so if he brought her here now, he would be criticized.

That same year the court witnessed many uncanny omens and disturbing incidents. On the evening of the thirteenth day of the third month—that is, the very day of the storm at Suma—thunder and lightning crashed, and wind and rain raged at the palace. During the night Emperor Suzaku dreamed that his father, the late Emperor, appeared below the steps leading out to the garden on the east side of the imperial quarters in the Seiryōden. His father was glaring at him, obviously in a foul mood, and so Suzaku sat up in a formal posture to show his respect. His father told him many things, and so must have said something about Genji. Suzaku was extremely frightened, but he was also moved to pity at the realization that his father's spirit had not yet been reborn in the Pure Land. Later, when he discussed his dream with his mother, the Kokiden Consort, she told him, "On nights when it rains and storms it's natural for you to dream of things that preoccupy your mind. A sovereign mustn't allow such trivial matters to upset him."

For some reason—perhaps because he had looked directly into his father's furious gaze—Suzaku began to have trouble with his eyes. His suffering was beyond endurance, and purification rites and exorcisms were performed constantly at both the palace and the residence of the Kokiden Consort.

Other incidents also brought grief to the palace. Suzaku's grandfather, the Minister of the Right who served as his Chancellor, suddenly died. Being advanced in years, his death was not unexpected or strange, but it was still a shock all the same, coming as it did after everything else that had happened. Then, on top of all this, the Kokiden Consort began to suffer from an unknown malady, and she grew weaker over time.

Occasionally Suzaku would give voice to his concerns, telling his mother, "If Genji has been exiled without just cause, then there is no escaping the conclusion that all of these problems are the result of karmic retribution. I think the time has come to restore him to his former rank."

The Kokiden Consort brushed aside his concerns and strongly admonished her son. "If you do that, you'll be criticized for lacking substance and lose respect. If you permit a man who has been expelled from the capital to return after less

5. Anonymous poem from *The Kokinshū*: "When I try to stay away and not meet you, just to see what will happen, my yearning is so great that I can no longer bear this foolish game."

than three years, what will people say?" Her words made Suzaku waver, but as the days and months continued to go by, the afflictions that he and his mother suffered grew ever more severe.

With the coming of autumn to Akashi, the sea breezes began to blow, stirring melancholy thoughts that were especially poignant. Genji was still sleeping in his solitary bed, but his loneliness was unbearable. He often spoke to the novitiate, telling the old man, "One way or another you will have to devise some pretext to have your daughter come here." Genji was convinced that it would be improper for him to go to her, and in any case the lady had shown no indication that she was inclined to meet him.

Only a provincial woman whose circumstances were utterly wretched, she thought, would frivolously exchange vows as my father has encouraged me to do on the basis of some flimsy, seductive flattery from a man of the capital who has come here for a brief stay. He would never respect me or consider me one of his wives, and if I were to yield to him it would only add to my misery and woe, would it not? During this period of my life, while I remain a young, unmarried woman, my parents, who harbor these unattainable ambitions for me, seem to have placed their extravagant expectations for the future on very uncertain supports. And even if he did take me as a wife, wouldn't that merely add to their worries? So long as Genji remains at Akashi, the happiness I feel just exchanging letters with him is fortune enough for me. For many years I heard reports about him, and now I'm able to catch brief, indirect signs of his presence at a place where I never imagined I might meet such a man. I was told that his skill on the koto was peerless, and when I hear the notes from his instrument wafting to me on the breeze, I can guess what he is doing during the day. Now he has gone so far as to recognize my existence by courting me like this, and that is too great an honor, much more than someone like me, someone whose circumstances have been reduced to the status of the fisherfolk here, could ever deserve.

As these thoughts raced through her mind, she felt more and more ashamed, and could not bring herself to even contemplate the possibility that she might have an intimate relationship with Genji.

Although the lady's parents were confident that the prayers they had offered over so many years would surely be answered, they also began to have ominous misgivings as they imagined how much sorrow they would experience if, having thoughtlessly rushed to give their daughter to Genji, there came a time when he no longer cared for her or counted her among his wives. They had heard how great and magnanimous he was, and yet how bitter would be their misery were he to abandon her! Relying upon the unseen Buddha and gods with no sign or proof of their blessing, knowing nothing of Genji's intentions or of their own daughter's karmic destiny, they tortured themselves with their obsessive worrying.

Genji was constantly pressing the novitiate. "If only I could hear the sound of her koto mingling with the sound of the autumn waves . . . what a waste, not to be able to listen to her play in this perfect season."

The novitiate ignored his wife's concerns and, without a word to his servants, secretly chose a propitious day to arrange a tryst. He went about busily sprucing up his daughter's quarters so that her rooms looked resplendent. Then, on the thirteenth day of the eighth month, with a nearly full moon shining gloriously, he sent a message to Genji that consisted of nothing more than a single line of verse: "On an evening too precious to waste."[6] Though Genji considered the wily old man a rather elegant pander, that didn't stop him from donning an informal cloak and setting out very late that night. A stylish carriage had been provided for him, but he thought it was too ostentatious for an occasion such as this and set out on horseback instead. His escort, which included only Koremitsu and a few attendants, was modest. He realized for the first time that the villa at the foot of the hill was farther away than he thought. From the road he could see all around the shore, and the moonlight reflecting off the inlets brought to mind an old verse describing such a scene as one to be viewed with "dear companions."[7] The words "dear companions" at once brought his beloved Murasaki to mind, and he immediately felt the urge to ride on past the villa and continue on to the capital. Instinctively, he muttered a poem to himself:

> *Take flight, my stallion, with autumn moon reflecting*
> *Off your lustrous coat . . . carry me through cloudy skies*
> *So I may meet my love, if but for a moment*

The villa of the Akashi lady, a stylish structure with many admirable touches, was set deep in a grove of trees. Whereas the residence near the shore that Genji was using was grand and attractive, the villa here was the kind of place where a person would lead a forlorn, solitary existence. Genji experienced a sweet, sublime sorrow at the thought that living here would allow him to contemplate to the full the sadness of life. The novitiate's handbell sounded a note of profound melancholy as it reverberated faintly from the meditation hall nearby and mingled with the soughing of the pines. The roots of the pine trees growing on the craggy rocks created a tasteful backdrop, and the chirruping of insects filled the garden. Genji glanced about, surveying the scene. The lady's quarters had been burnished with special care, and the door, made of exceptional wood, had been left open a crack so that the moonlight could stream in.

Genji stood uncertainly, hesitating before finally saying a few words of courtship. The lady, however, had been determined not to allow her relationship with him to become as intimate as this, and so she grew sullen and depressed, displaying a cold disposition that signaled she would not permit him to have his way.

She's getting above herself with these superior airs. Genji was irritated and resentful. *When a courtship has gone as far as ours, it is customary for the woman, even one whose high status makes her difficult to approach, to set aside her stubborn willfulness and yield. Could it be that she is belittling me for my loss of status? It would hardly be appropriate under the circumstances to force myself on her, but to lose a battle of wills with her would make me look pathetic.*

If only his handsome figure, confused and resentful, could have been displayed to a woman who was truly sensitive to beauty!

A curtain close by rustled and one of the silk streamers decorating it brushed lightly across the strings of a koto. The faint notes conjured in Genji's mind a pleasant image of the lady plucking the instrument, looking relaxed and unguarded. "Is this the koto I've heard so much about?" He asked her this and many other things besides, all trying to persuade her to play.

6. Poem by Minamoto no Saneakira: "On an evening too precious to waste, if only I could show the moon and the blossoms to one who understands, as I do, true beauty."

7. The source is not clear. An early commentary cites the following poem: "Shall we go to view it, dear companions . . . the moon's visage in the depths of the inlets at Tamatsushima?"

> *If there were someone I could talk to*
> *Intimately, would I awaken*
> *From the dream that is this world of woe*

She replied:

> *Wandering just as I am, lost in the darkness*
> *Of a night without end, how could I speak to you*
> *Not knowing what is dream, what is reality*

The dignified bearing of her figure, which he could barely make out in the dim light, put him very much in mind of the lady at Rokujō, who was now in Ise with her daughter.

Apparently the Akashi lady had not been prepared for his visit and, unaware of her father's machinations, had been caught off guard. It had never occurred to her that Genji might make such outrageous advances like this, and so she was quite flustered and upset. Moving into a room just off her private chambers, she somehow managed to securely latch the sliding door from the inside. Genji had no intention, it seemed, of trying to force the door open. Then again, how could he simply leave things as they were? The lady was aristocratic and tall, and her sense of propriety and dignity made Genji feel embarrassed and uncertain. Thinking about how their relationship had been destined by these strange circumstances, he was moved by the depth of the bond ordained by their karma. Surely his love for her would grow stronger the more intimate they became with one another.

He had come to loathe the long nights of autumn, which dragged on tediously for him in his solitary bed. But this night seemed to be rushing toward dawn, and so, mindful as ever that prying eyes might catch sight of his visit, he hurriedly left her, murmuring sweetly gentle words to her.

He discreetly dispatched the customary morning-after letter. His secrecy makes one wonder: was he bothered by a guilty conscience? The Akashi lady, worried about gossip, was equally careful to keep their affair secret, even from the others at her villa at the foot of the hill, and so she did not show the messenger bearing Genji's letter any special treatment or give him any lavish gifts. Her father deplored her aloof behavior.

Following this initial tryst, Genji would from time to time call on the lady in strictest secrecy. Their residences were separated by some distance, and there were nights when he was reluctant to venture out, concerned that he might encounter some of the local fishermen, who were by nature loquacious and prone to gossip. On those nights when he did not visit, the lady would be upset, taking his absence as proof that—just as she had imagined all along—his feelings for her were not sincere. Her father, seeing his daughter suffer and knowing that she had good reason for feeling the way she did, worried about how it would all turn out. He forgot about his devotions and his prayers for rebirth in paradise, unable to focus on anything besides waiting and listening for indications that Genji was calling on his daughter. It was truly pathetic that the heart of a man who had ostensibly taken religious vows could be so troubled by worldly affairs.

* * *

From Chapter XXV

Hotaru

FIREFLIES

[*In omitted chapters, Genji is summoned back from exile, Reizei, Genji's son by Fujitsubo, becomes emperor, and the Akashi lady gives birth to a little girl, the future Akashi Empress. Genji finally persuades the Akashi Lady to move from the provinces to the capital and has Murasaki rear their daughter. Genji builds a mansion in the Rokujō area to accommodate his various women. He also takes in Tamakazura, the lost daughter of Tō no Chūjō, and is caught between fatherly and romantic feelings.*]

* * *

The rainy season continued for longer than usual this year, and because the women at Rokujō were bored and had no way to brighten either the skies or their mood, they passed the days and nights amusing themselves with illustrated tales. The Akashi lady prepared some stylish and interesting works of that type and sent them over to the quarters of her daughter, the Akashi Princess.[8]

Meanwhile, the lady in the west hall, Tamakazura, was more intrigued than the others by these stories, which she found fascinating and strange, perhaps because she had come from the provinces. Whatever the reason, she was utterly absorbed in reading them day and night. Quite a few of the young women who had been assigned to her quarters were proficient at reading and copying, and so she was able to collect quite a few texts describing the personal circumstances of a variety of remarkable characters. She couldn't tell if those stories were true or mere fiction, and, moreover, she couldn't find a single character whose circumstances were similar to her own. It appeared as though the heroine Princess in *The Tale of Sumiyoshi*[9] experienced many remarkable incidents considered unusual as much in her own day as in the present. She compared the heroine's narrow escape from a forced marriage to the Chief Auditor to her own experience with the loathsome Taifu no Gen.

Genji couldn't avoid seeing these illustrated tales, which were left scattered all around Tamakazura's quarters.

"Ahh . . . how tedious," he chided. "Women are by nature blithely content to allow others to deceive them. You know full well these tales have only the slightest connection to reality, and yet you let your heart be moved by trivial words and get so caught up in the plots that you copy them out without giving a thought to the tangled mess your hair has become in this humid weather."

Genji smiled. "Of course, if we didn't have these old tales to read," he continued, "we'd have nothing to divert us in our idle hours. What's more, even among this mass of falsehoods we find some stories that are properly written and exhibit enough sensitivity to make us imagine that they really happened. On the one hand, we may know that it's all silly, but we're still fascinated and affected by the fiction. When we read about some lovely princess lost in troubled thoughts, we're drawn to her story . . . or, when we encounter a tale that makes us wonder uncertainly if what it describes is really plausible or proper, we're nonetheless

---

8. Genji's daughter by the Akashi lady [editor's note].

9. A well-known tale in the author's time [editor's note].

surprised and amazed that it could be told with such marvelous exaggeration. Of course, later on, when we come back to the tale in a calmer state of mind, we might dislike it or think it inappropriate . . . yet even then there may be aspects of the story that seem as charming to us as when we first read it. Recently, whenever I overhear one of the ladies-in-waiting reading to my little daughter, I'm struck by the realization that there are without doubt skilled storytellers in this world and that such tales must come from the mouths of people accustomed to spinning lies . . . but perhaps that is not the case?"

As soon as he spoke those words, Tamakazura shot back, "There is certainly no doubt that someone practiced at lying would be inclined to draw such a conclusion . . . for all sorts of reasons. I remain convinced, however, that these stories are quite truthful."

She pushed her inkstone away, and, when she did, Genji responded, "Have I been speaking rudely of your stories? Tales have provided a record of events in the world since the age of the gods, but histories of Japan like the *Nihongi*[1] give only partial accounts of the facts. The type of tales you are reading provide detailed descriptions that make more sense and follow the way of history."

Genji smiled again before continuing.

"A story may not relate things exactly as they happened out of consideration for the circumstances of its characters. Yet there are moments when one wants to pass on to later generations the appearance and condition of people living in the present—both the good and the bad. These are the subjects that people never tire of, no matter how many times they read about them. Thus, it's hard to keep such matters to oneself, and so you begin to tell stories about them. If you want to be upright and proper, then you will select only the good details to relate. Or, if you want to play to people's baser interests, then you will compile the strange and wondrous details of bad behavior. But in either case, you will always be speaking about things of this world. Styles of storytelling may differ in other lands, and even in Japan tales from the past certainly differ from those of the present . . . and of course there are distinctions between deep and shallow topics and themes. For that reason, the narrow-minded conclusion that all tales are falsehoods misses the heart of the matter. Even the Dharma, which was explicated for us through Sakyamuni's[2] splendidly pure heart, contains *hōben*, those parables that he told to illustrate the truth of the Law. There are many contradictory parts in the sutras that raise doubts in the mind of an unenlightened person. However, if you carefully consider the matter, you realize that all of the sutras have a single aim. The distinction between enlightenment and suffering is really no different from the distinction between the good and the bad in tales such as these. In the end, the correct view of the matter is that nothing is worthless." Genji was now claiming that tales were beneficial.

"Tell me, then," he concluded, "have you found any stories of piously foolish men like me among all your old scrolls? There couldn't possibly be any fictional princesses in this world who are as extremely aloof and heartless as you . . . who pretend not to notice anything. So, how about it? Shall we make a story unlike any other that has ever been told and pass it on to later generations?"

---

1. *Chronicles of Japan.* One of the two 8th-century chronicles of Japan, written in Sino-Japanese and modeled on the Chinese official histories, that told the history of the Japanese islands from the Age of the Gods to recent times [editor's note].

2. The Buddha (literally, "Sage of the Sakyas") [editor's note].

Genji sidled over to her. Tamakazura turned away from him, hiding her face in her collar, and said, "Even if we don't make a story together, the relationship we do have is so bizarre and unbelievable that it will likely never become the subject of court gossip."

"You think it's bizarre? Truly, there has never been a daughter as cruel as you." He had moved even closer, and his behavior was much too forward.

> Having a surfeit of cares and longings
> I seek answers for them in tales of old
> But find there no child as unfilial

"Even the teachings of Buddha admonish unfilial children," he added. When she refused to show her face, he began stroking her hair. As he did so, her resentment led her to reply:

> Though I have searched through all these ancient tales
> Truly I find no models in this world
> For parental feelings resembling yours

He felt ashamed when he heard her poem and went no further than stroking her hair. Given her situation, whatever would become of her?

Murasaki was also reading illustrated tales under the pretext that the Akashi Princess had requested them, and she was finding it hard to put them down. Looking at an illustration from *Tales of Kumano*[3] she remarked, "This is quite skillfully rendered." She gazed at the little girl, who was innocently taking a nap, and remembered when she was that age.

Genji studied the illustration. "How precocious children were back then. I was quite reserved by comparison when I was their age . . . a model of behavior, really." In truth, he was fond of being the model for all sorts of unheard-of behavior.

"You shouldn't be reading love stories in front of her," he continued. "She may not be all that intrigued by some young girl holding a secret love in her heart, but she is destined to be Empress, and it would be most unfortunate if she grew to accept the idea that it was normal for such affairs to actually take place." Had Tamakazura heard what he just said, she certainly would have taken umbrage at the difference in the way he treated his daughter and the way he treated her.

"People with shallow minds may imitate the behavior they read about in these stories, but they look rather pathetic when they do," Murasaki replied. "In *The Tale of the Hollow Tree*, the young Fujiwara Princess, Atemiya, is a prudent, dignified woman who never goes astray. However, her manner is stiff and unyielding, she lacks feminine grace, and her story ends up being just as bad an influence."

"People in real life seem to be the same," Genji said. "Everyone has their own way of doing things, but it's hard to strike a proper balance. A woman who has been brought up with the greatest care by parents who are not without breeding may grow up to be innocent and childlike, but the fact that she may also have many flaws will, sad to say, lead people to wonder what her parents were up to

---

3. This work has been lost.

and how they went about raising their daughter. On the other hand, when you see a young woman who in appearance and behavior is exactly what she should be for someone of her status, clearly her parents' efforts have paid off, and she brings honor to their house. If a young lady's nurses or attendants praise her to an absurd degree, then when her actions or words don't match her puffed-up reputation she will not seem as attractive. Parents should never let people who lack taste and judgment go about praising their daughters." He was determined to do everything in his power to ensure that his own daughter would avoid criticism.

Many of the tales depicted mean, vindictive stepmothers. He worried that the Akashi Princess might get the idea that all stepmothers were like those she read about. As a result, he took extra precaution when selecting stories and having clean copies and illustrations of them made for her.

* * *

From Chapter XL

Minori

RITES OF THE SACRED LAW

* * *

The following day she[4] was in pain and unable to get up, perhaps because she had overexerted herself by staying up throughout the dedication ceremony. At every similar event that she had attended over the years, she would wonder if *this day* would be the last time she would see the faces and figures of those who had gathered, the last time she would see them display their various talents or hear them play the koto or the flute. On such occasions, she would be moved even by the sight of faces normally beneath her notice. Her feelings were, of course, even stronger whenever she observed the other ladies at Rokujō. They were, after all, women with whom she shared both gentle rivalry and mutual affection, especially when they appeared together at some concert or diversion held in the summer or winter. Although no one can expect to remain for very long in this world, the thought that she would soon leave the other ladies behind, going forth all alone to an unknown destination, brought home to Murasaki the poignant sorrow of the evanescence of life.

When the dedication ceremony ended and each of the guests had begun to make his or her way home, she felt a twinge of regret that this would likely be the last time that she saw any of them. She sent a poem to Hanachirusato:[5]

> *While my life, like these rites, must soon come to an end*
> *We may rely on the truth of the sacred law*
> *That karma will bind us through all the worlds to come*[6]

---

4. Murasaki [editor's note].
5. One of Genji's ladies, also living in his Rokujō mansion [editor's note].
6. This poetic exchange gives the chapter its title. It should be noted, however, that the word

minori, which clearly means "rites" here, also refers to the Law (the Dharma), that is, the truth of the Buddha's teachings. That double sense operates implicitly in both poems.

Hanachirusato replied:

> *Even had these rites not been this magnificent*
> *They would still have forged a lasting bond between us*
> *Undeserving though I am, with little time left*

Immediately after the dedication ceremony, other solemn rites, such as the continuous reading of the *Lotus Sutra* and the ritual of confession and penance, were attentively performed. The esoteric healing rites that had been carried out every day over a long period showed no signs of helping Murasaki recover. Genji commissioned additional services at various holy sites and temples known for the efficaciousness of their prayers.

When summer arrived, Murasaki's fainting spells increased even though the weather was no hotter than usual. There were no alarming symptoms that one could point to as the source of her malaise. She was simply growing weaker, without ever suffering the sort of pain that caused others distress. Worried about what was to become of their mistress if she continued to weaken, her attendants observed her condition with regret and sorrow and fell into dark despair.

Because Murasaki's health was slowly failing, the Akashi Empress[7] withdrew from the palace and went to the Nijō villa. She was to take up residence in the east hall, and so Murasaki waited there to receive her. The ceremony greeting Her Majesty's arrival was nothing out of the ordinary, but Murasaki found everything about it moving, since she knew that she would never witness it again. She listened attentively as the name of each nobleman who had escorted the Akashi Empress—a very large group of senior officials indeed—was read out.

Since the two women had not seen each other for a long time, they seized this moment as a rare opportunity to speak intimately and at length. Genji arrived and said, "I feel like a bird evicted from its own nest. It's obvious that I'm of absolutely no use this evening. I'll take my leave and retire for the night." He went back to his quarters feeling quite happy to see Murasaki up and about—it was, however, only a brief moment of comfort for him.

"Since we will be staying in separate quarters," Murasaki said, "I would be deeply honored to have Your Majesty come to see me in the west hall. I know it is presumptuous of me to make such a request, but it is a considerable strain on me to leave my residence to visit you here." She stayed a while longer, and when the Akashi lady joined them, they continued their quiet, heartfelt conversation.

Murasaki had many things on her mind, but wisely she did not broach the subject of what would happen after her death. She calmly made a few passing references to the ephemeral nature of life, but the serious manner in which she talked made it clearer than any words she might have spoken just how sad and forlorn she felt. When she saw all of the children of the Akashi Empress, tears welled up and her face blushed with a most lovely glow. "I had so wanted to see each of them grow up . . . it would seem my heart regrets having so little time left."

Her Majesty wept as well and wondered why Murasaki had to be so fixated on death. The subject of their conversation shifted, providing Murasaki the

7. As noted above, Genji's daughter, the Akashi Princess who becomes the Kiritsubo Consort, has been elevated to the title of empress. The narrative does not explain when this event took place. From this point on, I will identify Genji's daughter as the Akashi Empress.

chance to speak about the ladies-in-waiting who had served her closely over the years. She did her best to avoid saying anything inauspicious, as if she were making last requests, but she felt sorry for her attendants, who would have nowhere else to turn once she was gone. "When I am no longer around," she remarked, "please remember to look after them." A sutra reading[8] was about to begin, and so Murasaki retired to her own quarters in the west hall.

As he walked around the villa, Niou, the Third Prince, had the most charming appearance of all Her Majesty's many children. During those intervals when Murasaki was feeling a little better, she would have him sit next to her and, when no one was around, ask him, "Would you remember me if I were not here?"

"I would miss you very much, Grandmama. You are much more important to me than Father or Mother! If you weren't here, I'd feel awful!" The way he rubbed his eyes to hide his tears was so adorable that she had to smile despite her sadness.

"When you are all grown up, you are to live here. And when the red plum and the cherry tree that grow in front of the west hall are in bloom in their respective seasons, you must not forget to view and enjoy them. At the appropriate times, you must make offerings of their branches to the Buddha in my memory."

The little boy nodded solemnly, then stared into Murasaki's face. Just as he was about to cry, he stood up and scampered off. She had raised him and the Third Princess with special consideration, and it filled her with pity and regret to know that she would not be able to help raise them to adulthood.

The heat of summer was so oppressive, she couldn't wait for the cool of autumn to arrive; and when it did, her spirits revived a little. Still, this was but a temporary respite, for even though the chill autumn winds were not yet blowing—cutting winds that bring only sorrows[9]—she was already spending her days in dewy tears.

The Akashi Empress was preparing to return to the palace. Murasaki wanted to ask her to stay on a little longer, even though such a request would overstep the bounds of propriety. It would also have been awkward, since His Majesty was now sending one messenger after another urging her to return. In the end, she didn't ask, and because she was so weak, she was unable to go to the east hall to see Her Majesty off. That was when the Empress took the extraordinary step of calling on her in the west hall. Murasaki was humbled and shamed that the Empress would deign to visit her, but she thought that it would have been senseless not to meet. Thus, she had special seating and furnishings prepared to receive her exalted guest.

Despite the fact that she was terribly emaciated, Murasaki still looked remarkable; the loss of weight had, if anything, distilled her beauty, which now possessed a boundless nobility and grace. Once, in the glorious flowering of her prime, her looks exuded to an almost excessive degree a lambent glow that was like the bright fragrance of blossoms. Now her infinitely cherished appearance,

---

8. This reading may be the *Sutra of Great Wisdom* (*Daihannyakyō*), which an empress would normally have performed during the second and eighth months (though the reading could be held on special occasions as well). However, the timing does not seem right here, and it is likely that the sutra reading is part of the healing rites for Murasaki.

9. Poem by Izumi Shikibu: "What sort of wind is it, this wind that blows in autumn . . . how cutting it is, bringing only sorrow."

which brought to mind the transient nature of the mortal world, possessed a deeper loveliness, one that evoked incomparable feelings of compassion and sweet sorrow.

At dusk, a terrible, chilling wind began to blow, and just as she propped herself up on an armrest, thinking that she would gaze out at her garden, she saw Genji arriving.

"How good that you're able to get up today! Her Majesty's visit has apparently cheered you, has it not?"

She felt bad for him—he looked so happy whenever she was briefly feeling better that it moved her to imagine how devastated he would be when the end came.

> How brief the moment when you see me sitting up
> As brief as the time that dew clings to bush clover
> Before being blown off and scattered by the wind[1]

It was an apt comparison, for the dew clung precariously to the stems of bush clover in her garden that bent and sprang back with each gust of wind. Genji gazed out at the scene, and the melancholy desolation that accompanied this season was unbearable.

> Our lives are like fragile dewdrops vying
> To disappear . . . would that no time elapse
> Between the first one to go and the last

He could not brush all the tears from his eyes.

The Akashi Empress replied:

> Who can look at this world, so like the droplets
> That cannot resist the blasts of autumn winds
> And think that only dew on the top leaves fades

As they exchanged poems, Genji treasured the sight of these two women, ideal beauties both. Though he wished he could go on gazing at them like this for a thousand years, his heart ached, knowing that such a dream could never be fulfilled, for he had no way to keep his beloved from dying.

"You should leave now. I'm feeling very ill," Murasaki said. "It's terribly rude of me to say that I'm too ill to do anything for you." She pulled a standing curtain over and lay down so that they would not have to see her suffering. This time, it did not appear she would recover.

"What's wrong?" The Akashi Empress took Murasaki's hand and watched her tearfully. She looked every bit like a dewdrop fading away, and so they hurriedly sent off countless messengers to commission more sutra readings. There had been episodes like this in the past from which she had always recovered, but Genji suspected that the malignant spirit of the Rokujō lady might still be at work; accordingly, he did everything he could to protect Murasaki, ordering prayers and services to be held throughout the night. His efforts were in vain, however, for just as dawn approached her spirit vanished and she passed away.

---

1. Murasaki's poem plays on two senses of the word *oku*—"to be up/sit up" and "to settle."

The Akashi Empress thought it a sign of the boundless karmic bond she shared with Murasaki that she had not returned to the palace and was with the woman who had raised her until the very end. Neither she nor Genji could accept that her death was part of the natural order of things, that such partings were common to all. To them, her passing was singular and overwhelming, and so they felt as if they were wandering lost in the sort of dream one has in that twilight time between night and the dawn. No one there could make a rational judgment about anything. The attendants and other servants were completely stunned.

Genji suffered the most. Because he was upset and not thinking clearly, he summoned his son,[2] who was in attendance nearby, and had him move over in front of Murasaki's curtain.

"It appears that this is the end," he said. "It would be a great shame to go against her wishes at this point and not carry out what she had desired for so many years. The holy men who performed the healing rites and the priests reading scripture have all gone silent and have probably left, but some of them may still be here; tell one of them to cut her hair like a nun's. It won't do any good for her in this life, but if she shows a mark of her devotion to the Buddha, then at least she may rely on his mercy to comfort her on the dark path she is to follow. Is there some priest suitable for the task?"

Judging by his expression as he spoke, Genji was trying to be strong, but the color had drained from his face, and unable to bear his loss, he could not stop his tears. His son looked on in sympathy, thinking that his father's grief was perfectly understandable.

"Sometimes a malignant spirit will do this kind of thing just to torment the bereaved ones," said Genji's son. "What I mean is, the spirit may be making it appear that she is not breathing . . . that may be what's happening here. If that's the case, then it would be best to do what she wanted in any case, since according to the *Contemplation Sutra*,[3] making vows to uphold the precepts for even one day and night will lead to rebirth in Amida's Pure Land. Of course, if she *is* dead, simply cutting her hair at this point would have little benefit . . . it won't provide a light to guide her in the next world and would make the grief of those who look at her even worse. I wonder if it's for the best?"

He wanted to do all he could to make arrangements for the funeral and period of confinement, and so he summoned several priests from among those who had not yet withdrawn and were willing to serve during the weeks ahead. He also saw to all other necessary preparations.

Although he had longed for Murasaki for years after catching a glimpse of her on that morning after the autumn tempest, Genji's son had never harbored any improper or presumptuous fantasies about her. *In what world to come will I ever see her again as I did on that morning long ago? I never did hear her speak . . . not even a faint whisper.* Not a day had gone by since then when she hadn't been on his mind. *As it turns out, I will never hear her voice . . . and if*

2. Genji's oldest child from his first marriage. Long ago this son once caught an enthralling glimpse of his stepmother Murasaki, but has had no chance since to satisfy his yearning to see her again [editor's note].

3. The *Kanmuryōjukyō* is one of the three major scriptures of Pure Land Buddhism, along with the *Sutra of Infinite Life*, which is also known as the *Larger Pure Land Sutra*, and the *Amida Sutra*.

I'm ever to satisfy my hope of seeing her again, the only time to do so is right now, even if it means gazing at her lifeless form. He had been trying to control himself, since it would look odd if he exhibited excessive grief, but these thoughts brought him to tears. The attendants were loudly weeping and wailing, and Genji's son scolded them. "Really now, be still for a while!" As he spoke, he lifted one of the panels of Murasaki's standing curtain and peered inside. Because it was difficult to make things out in the dim light of early dawn, Genji had placed a lamp near Murasaki's bed and was gazing at her. He so regretted that such a lovely face would soon be no more—a face infinitely dear to him, one possessing such noble grace—it seemed that he no longer had the will to even try to hide his beloved from the gaze of his son, who was peeking in on this scene.

"Here she is, her face looking the same as ever . . . and yet it's obvious that she's no longer with us." Genji covered his face with his sleeves. His son, blinded by tears, could not see very well. To clear his vision, he closed his eyes tight and then opened them so that he could look at her; when he did, he was overcome by a feeling of sadness unlike anything he had ever known. He feared that he would lose his composure completely. Her hair was stretched out beside her, left just as it was when she died, incomparably lustrous and beautiful with not one strand of those thick, cascading tresses out of place. It no longer mattered to her that she was exposed to his gaze. In the bright glare of the lamplight, her complexion had an alabaster glow, and her face, needless to say, looked more pure and spotless than when she was alive, since she had always avoided being seen and concealed her real appearance under makeup. Gazing on her unique, extraordinary beauty, he wished that her soul, which had already departed, would soon return to her body—though he knew such a wish was unreasonable.

The women who had been her closest attendants were too overcome by grief to think clearly, and so Genji forced himself to calm down and set about making arrangements for the funeral. Although he had witnessed many sorrowful events in the past, he had no experience handling such matters directly himself. Undertaking this sad responsibility was like nothing else he had ever done in the past or would do in the future.

* * *

From Chapter XLI

Maboroshi

SPIRIT SUMMONER

Observing the bright cheer of the New Year season only served to make Genji's mood darker and more disordered. The sorrow that had completely overtaken his heart did not dissipate over time as might have been expected. Outside his quarters people were gathering for the customary seasonal visit, but he chose to remain inside his blinds, offering the excuse that he was not well. When Sochinomiya[4] arrived, Genji sent out a message saying that he preferred to meet in a private room in the interior of the residence. He included a poem with his note:

4. Genji's half brother, who unsuccessfully courts Tamakazura [editor's note].

> *The one who always lavished praise*
> *Upon these blossoms here is gone*
> *Why should spring care to visit me*

Tears welled up in Sochinomiya's eyes, and he replied:

> *Does the spring seek in vain the fragrance*
> *Of the red plum . . . are you suggesting*
> *It comes for common blossoms only*

Genji experienced a sense of deep nostalgia as he watched his younger brother strolling beneath the red plum trees. *Does anyone appreciate such beauty as deeply as Sochinomiya?* The blossoms were just barely open, and their fragrant glow was delightful. There was no music or entertainment this year—indeed, the celebrations were very different in form.

The ladies-in-waiting who had been in Murasaki's service for many years made no effort to change their wardrobes with the advent of the new season. Instead, they continued to wear dark robes of mourning. Their grief was hard to assuage, but since they remained devoted to Murasaki, they continued to serve Genji. It gave them a measure of comfort that he chose to stay with them in his quarters at the Nijō villa, where they could be near him, rather than going off to call on his other ladies at the Rokujō estate. After Murasaki died and Genji began sleeping by himself, he treated even those women whom he had previously regarded as lovers the same as any other attendant—though, to be sure, his relationship with them had never really been all that serious. He even had the women who served on duty at night withdraw to a spot some distance away from his sleeping chambers.

Whenever Genji was bored, he would reminisce about the old days. Though his devotion to following the path of Buddha had deepened and he had purged all traces of his former, fickle disposition, he would nevertheless recall things from the years he spent with Murasaki—especially the way she looked when her jealousy flared up over one of his passing affairs. *I suppose it made no difference whether my affairs were serious or mere dalliances . . . either way, they hurt her. Why did I have to be so impulsive? She got used to my pecadilloes as time went on and adopted an attitude of tolerance that allowed her to deal with them and to understand the true depth of my devotion to her. Though she never grew resentful or bore a grudge, she must have suffered from the turmoil in her heart, wondering with each passing affair what would become of her.* He was overcome by feelings of remorse and pity, and his heart was filled to bursting with shame and regret. Some of the women who most closely served him knew how their departed lady felt about Genji's betrayals, but they were circumspect about the subject, and would only discuss it with him in the most delicate terms.

Murasaki's face had betrayed no hint of her emotions when he brought the Third Princess[5] to Rokujō. Still, thinking back on it, he recalled how grief-stricken she looked during those moments when she sadly contemplated her wearisome existence. One time in particular—that snowy dawn following the Third Night with the Princess when Murasaki's spirit appeared at his pillow and he rushed

---

5. Third daughter of Emperor Suzaku, who marries her to Genji, much to Murasaki's dismay [editor's note].

back to her quarters—he remembered how he had tapped at her lattice shutter and was kept standing outside because no one could hear him; he had waited so long he thought he was going to freeze. Beneath those glowering skies, she had received him so sweetly and gently, hiding her tear-soaked sleeves from his view and doing everything she could to divert his attention from her own sorrow.

Every night until dawn, one thought ran through his mind over and over even in his dreams: *When will I be able to see her again . . . in what future world will we meet?* In the faint light of dawn Genji overheard a woman who must have been returning to his attendants' quarters saying, "My . . . it snowed heavily last night, didn't it?" Those words transported him back to that dawn long ago, and the loneliness that swept over him when he realized his beloved was not lying there beside him was shattering.

> *I long to melt like snow, to disappear*
> *From this world of sadness . . . but snow still falls*
> *And I still live on against my wishes*

To distract himself from sorrowful thoughts, Genji called for water to cleanse his hands and, as was now his custom, performed his devotions. The attendants stirred up the charcoal embers in the brazier, and then moved it closer to him. Two of the women, Chūnagon and Chūjō, sat nearby and talked with him. "Sleeping by myself last night, I felt lonelier than ever," Genji told them. "I still seem to be caught up in my attachments to this world, which I ought to understand well enough to renounce." He gazed off, lost in reverie. Then, as he glanced around, it occurred to him how sad these women would be and how much more grief they would have to endure were he to turn his back on the world. He privately continued his devotions out of sight, and anyone who heard the sublime beauty of his voice reading the sutras would have been moved to weep. One can only imagine the overwhelming feelings of those who were with him all the time, day and night. Their compassion for him was so great that they would not have been able to hold back the flood of tears even if their sleeves had been weirs.

"I was born into such a high station in life that I have lacked for nothing in this world," Genji remarked. "Yet I've always had the feeling that I was destined to experience more misfortune and regret than the average person. The Buddha has determined that I must know the truth about this world . . . that it is an ephemeral realm of woe. Throughout my long life, I pretended to ignore that truth. However, as I approach my final years and have had to experience the ultimate sorrow of witnessing my beloved's death, I now fully appreciate the nature of my karma and the limits of my desires. Since the fragile, dewlike bonds that tied me to this world have disappeared, I'm at peace. Still, I've grown closer to you now than when you were serving your late mistress, and so when it comes time to say my farewells I know that my heart will be in even greater agony than it is now. Our lives and loves are so fleeting . . . my mind is not right, for it is wrong of me to have such attachments."

He wiped his eyes in an effort to hide his tears, but he could not hold them back and they fell in spite of him. The women who witnessed his grief could not help but weep themselves. They each wanted to tell him how sorry they would be if he abandoned them, but their hearts were too full to say anything, and the conversation ended.

In moments of quiet solitude, Genji would have Murasaki's women sit nearby and converse with him either at dawn, following a sleepless night filled with regrets, or at dusk, following a day spent gazing off in pensive reverie. He did not look down on them as ordinary in any way; in fact, he had known one of the women, Chūjō, from the time she was a child. She had once been an object of his desire, and it must have been awkward for her when she first came to attend Murasaki, for soon after she began keeping her distance from Genji. For his part, he remembered how much Murasaki favored Chūjō over the other ladies-in-waiting, and it touched him to think of her now as a memento of his late beloved. Though he no longer considered her a sexual intimate, she had retained her attractive looks and personality. Indeed, because she resembled Murasaki a little, she was a living memorial, an evergreen planted beside a grave, and thus dearer to him than the other ladies-in-waiting.

Genji stopped meeting people with whom he felt no close affinity. Senior officials who were on good terms with him or his imperial brothers would often call on him at his estate, but he rarely met them directly. He even stayed behind his blinds when he spoke to his son.

If I agree to meet people, he had reasoned, *I risk exposing just how feeble-minded I've become over the past few months. Even if I'm in command of my faculties and keep my emotions in check. I'm likely to say something foolish, embarrass myself, and leave a bad reputation to later generations. I suppose that if people gossip about me and claim that I refuse to see anyone because I've grown senile, the effect on my reputation will be much the same. Still, it's far worse to have people witness my infirmities with their own eyes than to have them merely speculate about them.*

Genji was not yet ready to turn his back on the world. Biding his time and composing himself, he felt that he should wait to take vows, even during this period when people must be gossiping about how much he had changed. Whenever he made a rare, brief visit to one of his ladies—Akashi or Hanachirusato—he would be so overcome with emotion that tears would fall like rain. This was too shameful for him to bear and, consequently, he would let so much time elapse between visits or letters that the two ladies were always fretting about him.

The Akashi Empress returned to the palace, leaving the Third Prince, Niou, to comfort his lonely grandfather. "Grandmama Murasaki told me to give special attention to this tree," the boy announced, carefully tending the red plum in the garden that fronted the west hall of the Nijō villa. Genji was very touched watching him. It was the second month and the tops of the plum trees were in full bloom. Spring mists provided a delightful cover to those trees not yet in blossom. Hearing the cheerful voice of a warbler singing in the red plum tree just outside the west hall—a tree that also served as a memento of Murasaki—Genji stepped out to have a look. Walking about, he murmured a poem:

> *Feigning ignorance of her passing, the warbler*
> *Still comes to the house of the lady who planted*
> *This red plum tree and admired its fragrant blossoms*

It was now deep into the spring season, and the garden at the southeast residence at Rokujō looked just as spectacular as it did when Murasaki was still alive. However, Genji could no longer savor its beauty; just to look at it unsettled him and brought back all sorts of heartrending memories. His desire to go off to a remote spot deep in the mountains far removed from this world of woe—a place where he would not hear even the cry of a bird to remind him of spring[6]—only intensified. The sight of mountain roses and other flowers blooming in wild profusion suddenly brought dewy tears to his eyes.

The single-petal cherry blossoms had scattered already, the double-petal blossoms were past their peak, and the mountain cherries were now in bloom. The wisteria apparently darkened in color later than the cherries . . . Murasaki had had a good understanding of the plants in her garden, knowing which ones bloomed early, which ones late, and she had planted many varieties so that every season of the year would be filled with fragrant splendor. "My cherry is in bloom," Niou declared, referring to the one Murasaki had planted. "I'd hate it if the petals fell! There has to be some way to protect them . . . I know! I'll put a curtain around the tree, and so long as the cloth stays up, the wind won't be able to touch it!" The little boy's face showed just how clever he considered his plan to be. He was so precious-looking that Genji couldn't help but smile. "That's quite a good idea," he told his grandson. "You're much cleverer than the man who wanted to cover the sky with his sleeves!"[7] Genji considered this Prince his sole pleasure in life.

"We won't have much time to get to know one another. Life being what it is, regardless of how much time we may have together, the day will come when I'm no longer with you." Seeing his sentimental grandfather tear up as he was so wont to do recently, the boy was put off. "Grandmama Murasaki was always talking that way . . . I don't like it." Niou turned his face away, fingering his sleeves as he tried to hide his own tears.

Genji would often lean on the railing of the veranda just outside the corner of Murasaki's old quarters, lost in reverie as he gazed longingly around her garden or into the interior spaces beyond her blinds. Some of her women were still wearing mourning robes as a remembrance of their mistress; others wore robes of more everyday colors, though the pattern of their silks was plain and subdued. His own cloak was dyed an everyday hue, but its pattern was drab and inconspicuous. The furnishings and decorations were extremely austere—not much craftsmanship had gone into them, and they had such a forlorn air that he composed the following:

> After I have renounced this world of woe
> Will it fall to ruin, this springtime hedge
> My departed love tenderly nurtured

No one was forcing him to take vows, but, even so, his decision made him terribly sad.

Bored and with time on his hands, Genji went to pay a call on the Third Princess. Niou, carried by an attendant, accompanied him, and when they arrived, he ran around playing with the Third Princess's little boy, Kaoru. Still very much a child, it seemed that Niou had forgotten all about the scattering cherry blossoms that had so worried him earlier.

6. Anonymous poem from *The Kokinshū*: "Does she not know my feelings are as deep as those mountain recesses, where not even the cries of birds can be heard?"

7. Anonymous poem from the imperial anthology *The Gosenshū*: "If only I had sleeves wide enough to cover the heavens, I would not leave spring blossoms to the mercy of the wind."

The Third Princess was reading a sutra before the altar. She did not strike Genji as being especially devoted to the religious life, nor did she appear troubled at heart or regretful at having taken vows. She practiced her devotions quietly, without distraction, and Genji envied her ability to single-mindedly distance herself from the world. He deplored the fact that his own resolve to follow the religious life should be inferior to this shallow woman's. The flowers decorating the altar possessed a beguiling beauty in the dim twilight of dusk, prompting Genji to remark, "Now that the woman who was so attracted to the spring is gone, the colors of the blossoms have lost their charms for me. But seeing those flowers adorning the Buddha, I can't help finding them lovely. I've never seen the mountain roses in her garden bloom like they have this year . . . their petals are enormous! It's not a flower that one usually associates with refined elegance, but their vibrant colors are so exquisite and charming! How sad that they should be so much more lush and fragrant this spring, as if they were heedless of the fact that the one who planted them is gone."

The Third Princess offhandedly replied, "No spring comes to this dark valley . . ."[8]

Couldn't she have put it another way? Genji found her allusion tasteless and insensitive. It occurred to him that even at casual moments like this, Murasaki never once said or did anything that would cause him to think, I wish she hadn't done that. He tried conjuring up her appearance at different stages of her life, beginning from the time she was a child. A succession of images of her on various occasions in the past came to him one after another, reminding him of the wit and charm that had characterized her attitude, her behavior, and her manner of speech. Genji, who was now susceptible to teary sentimentality, was embarrassed that his memories should cause him to weep in the presence of the Third Princess.

The dusk, made indistinct by shimmering mists, was lovely to behold, and he decided to call on the Akashi lady. Since he had not looked in on her for some time, she was not expecting this visit and was caught by surprise. Still, she managed to receive him with grace and charm, which, to his eyes, made her look every bit the superior lady she was; and yet, try as he might, he could not control the natural inclination to compare her with Murasaki and note the differences in their personalities and talents. Recalling images of Murasaki ought to have brought some relief to him, but instead it merely increased his longing and sorrow, making it all the more difficult for him to find consolation.

The atmosphere of the quarters of his Akashi lady was very different from that of the apartments of the Third Princess, and Genji felt that here he could speak at ease about the old days. "I learned long ago that obsessing sorrowfully over a woman was certainly not proper, and in all my relationships I have tried to avoid attachments to this world. During the period of my life leading up to my exile—a time when people at the court were convinced that my fortunes were in decline—I thought things over carefully and concluded that there was nothing in particular to stop me from wandering off deep into the fields and mountains where I could take it on myself to abandon this world. But now in my

8. Poem by Kiyowara no Fukayabu from *The Kokinshū*: "Because spring comes not to this valley where no light shines, there are no lamentations for the scattering of blossoms."

twilight years, as I near the end of my life. I find myself entangled in bonds that will prove a hindrance to salvation. How frustrating to be weak-willed!"

Though he was speaking of his sorrows in general, the Akashi lady understood with pained sympathy the real reason why he was in such a mood. At that moment he seemed especially miserable to her.

"Even a person," she began, "who in the eyes of ordinary people appears to have nothing at all to regret, may in fact keep many bonds hidden away in their hearts. How could such a person possibly abandon those relationships with an easy conscience? Such ill-advised action would invite criticism for being frivolous and rash. When it comes to making a decision about a matter as serious as renouncing the world, it is best, in my opinion, to take your time, so that in the end you will make a deeply considered choice and bring peace and calm to your heart and mind. From what I know of past examples, they say it is never proper to renounce the world when your heart and mind are unsettled, when things have gone against your wishes and you find the world detestable. In your case, you should resist the impulse to take vows and hold off making such a life-changing decision until the children of the Akashi Empress are grown up and their positions truly secure. I would feel more at ease and happier if you would wait." The Akashi lady looked magnificent as she offered him her mature, sensible advice.

"You may be right," Genji replied, "but the deep wisdom that recommends taking time to think it over before renouncing the world may in fact prove the shallower choice." He went on to share with her things that had been on his mind for a long time. "The spring Fujitsubo passed away I felt just like the poet who wrote about those cherry trees blooming on the plains of Fukakusa.[9] I felt that way because I had seen her when I was young and was deeply moved by her beauty, which was apparent even to the court at large. Being more familiar with her than others, my grief was of course greater at the time of her death, but the special loss I felt was not due simply to our relationship as a man and woman . . . it grew out of feelings that were more complex than that. Now Murasaki has preceded me in death, and it is so hard to forget her that I find no way to console my heart. In this case, too, my grief is not simply the kind that comes when death severs a relationship between husband and wife. No, when I think back over the circumstances that led me to want to raise her from childhood, the way we grew old together, and how, in the end, I was left behind, the grief I feel arises out of all that happened between us and possesses a special quality that makes it too hard to bear. With all of the things that we experienced together—the sad and the sublime, the exquisite and the elegant, the amusing and the delightful—with such memories filling my thoughts, how could my grief be shallow?"

Genji shared his memories and talked about current happenings at the court until late that night. It occurred to him that he should stay with the Akashi lady until dawn, but instead he returned to his own quarters in the southeast residence. She could not help but be moved to sorrow and pity. For his part, he startled himself when he realized what a peculiar change had come over him.

9. Poem by Kamitsuke no Mineo from *The Kokinshū*: "If the cherry trees on the plains of Fukakusa have any feelings at all, for this year only let them put forth blossoms of mourning gray."

He set about his regular devotions, and in the middle of the night moved to his daytime quarters and lay down temporarily. When morning came, he sent a letter to the Akashi lady:

> *Crying on and on, wild geese head north, longing to return . . .*
> *I weep as well, longing to return, but in this sad world*
> *Nothing remains as it was and there is no place to rest*

She had resented his leaving her early the previous night, but seeing how much pain he was in, she realized that he was no longer himself. She put her own feelings aside, tears welling up in her eyes.

> *The water in the seedling paddy*
> *Where wild geese once gathered disappears*
> *And with it the flower's reflection*

Her calligraphy was lovely as ever.

For some reason, Genji recalled, Murasaki had never taken to her, though in her final years the two of them recognized their mutual interests and grew friendlier. Still, even after they realized that they were not a threat to each other and were able to establish a trusting relationship, Murasaki remained uncomfortable around her . . . and I was the only one who ever noticed how stiff and formal she was.

Whenever his loneliness became too much for him, Genji would suddenly drop in on the Akashi lady just to talk about everyday matters. Now, however, nothing remained of his former passion, and he showed no inclination to spend the night with her.

From her quarters in the northeast residence Hanachirusato sent new summer robes for the change of season. A poem was attached:

> *This day brings the start of the season . . .*
> *Will your heart be filled with memories*
> *As your old robes are exchanged for new*

Genji replied:

> *From this day forward, each time I put on these robes*
> *Diaphanous as cicada wings, the sorrows*
> *Of this fragile, fleeting world will only deepen*

During the fourth month, on the day of the Kamo Festival, the atmosphere at the Rokujō estate was so tedious that Genji told his female attendants, "It would make all of you feel better if you were to go off to see the sights today." Recalling how the Kamo Shrine looked during the festival, he added, "You will likely feel left out if you don't go. Perhaps it would be best if you returned discreetly to your family homes and then went to the festival from there."

Chūjō was taking a nap on the eastern side of Genji's quarters. When he stepped out and saw her lying there she got up, looking very dainty and adorable. The expression on her face was fresh and bright, and her hair, mussed from sleep, cascaded down and hid her face in a most charming fashion. Her trousers were dyed a scarlet hue tinged with yellow; her singlet was burnt orange and over it was an outer robe of dark gray and black. Her robes were not properly layered, since she had just got up from her nap, and her train and jacket had slipped down. While she casually pulled them back up, Genji picked up some of the sprigs of wild ginger that she had set aside in preparation for the festival. "What are these called?" he asked. "I've completely forgotten their name." Chūjō responded with a poem:

> *Gods do not reveal themselves in a vessel choked with weeds*
> *Nor do you show yourself . . . so I adorned my hair with leaves*
> *That promise a tryst, only to find you forgot their name*[1]

She seemed embarrassed as she spoke. Genji realized that what she said was true and felt sorry for her.

> *Having now forsaken the things of this world*
> *Including the ways of love, is it sinful*
> *Of me to pluck off these leaves of wild ginger*

Apparently Chūjō alone remained an object of Genji's affection.

With nothing else to do during the fifth month but gaze out at the endless rains of the season, Genji, sinking ever deeper into his brooding thoughts, was overcome with a sense of desolation. It was the tenth day of the month, and Genji's son was in attendance that evening. There was a rare break in the clouds, and the instant the bright moonlight broke through, the mandarin orange tree, which was then in full bloom, stood out vividly before their eyes. The fragrance of the tree wafted toward them on the breeze, stirring nostalgic memories. As they waited in anticipation for the sound of "the cuckoo's voice, which calls out for a thousand years,"[2] the clouds gathered again and suddenly took on an ominous appearance. They were startled when a driving rain began to fall and the wind accompanying the rain caused the lamps to flicker and nearly extinguished them. The sky seemed to have turned black. "The sound of the rain at the window."[3] Genji murmured these and other rather trite, common lines of old verse. Perhaps it was due to the atmosphere of the moment, but his son fervently wished that Murasaki had been there to hear his father's voice—truly a voice to be heard, as the old poem had it, "from my beloved's hedge."[4]

"Things aren't all that different now that I'm living by myself," Genji remarked, "but still, I feel strangely alone. Having grown accustomed to this solitary life, I wonder . . . even if I were to live in a hut deep in the mountains, would my heart really grow pure and tranquil?" He then called out to his attendants: "Bring

---

1. In addition to the oft-used play on the word *aoi,* the poem refers to a *yorube,* a sacred vessel containing water used in Shinto rituals to draw a god to its reflection. The comparison of Genji to a deity in this context is sexually suggestive: though the original text is coy, it leaves no doubt that he accepts the invitation, for in his reply poem he plays on the word *tsumi,* which means both "sin" and "to pluck."

2. Anonymous poem from *The Gosenshū:* "I hear the cuckoo's voice, which calls out for a thousand years amidst the orange blossoms, whose colors remain forever the same."
3. A reference to a poem included in the collected writings of Bo Juyi, the Tang Poet [editor's note].
4. The source of the poem is uncertain. It is cited in later commentaries.

food and refreshments here! I suppose it's much too late to summon some men to join us."

Genji's son could tell from the expression on his father's face as he gazed up distractedly toward the skies that the old man was in no mood for entertainment.[5] It was painful to see him in such a state, and he worried that his father's inability to take his mind off Murasaki was a lingering attachment that would make it difficult for him to purify and calm his heart. It occurred to him that if he himself found it so hard to forget Murasaki after only the briefest glimpse of her, how much more difficult must it be for his father?

"It seems like she left us only yesterday," he said, "but the first anniversary is already upon us. What sort of memorial service have you planned?"

Genji replied, "I don't plan to do anything out of the ordinary. This would be the right time to dedicate the mandala of Amida's paradise that she commissioned. She also had a large number of sutras prepared, and before she died she explained what she wanted done for the dedication to that bishop . . . I've forgotten his name . . . anyway, he knows what to do. If there are other details that need to be seen to, I'll just have to go along with whatever bishop what's-his-name recommends."

"She put a lot of thought into arranging these things ahead of time, and they'll certainly be a comfort to her in the afterlife. When I think back on it now, she was destined not to live long in this world, which makes it all the more regrettable that she left behind no children to remember her by."

"That may be," Genji said, "but of all my women, even those who are destined to live a long life, only a few gave me children. In that regard, I consider myself unlucky. It is you, my son, with all of your daughters, who will ensure that our family line flourishes."

Cognizant of his own tendency to break down over every little thing—a weakness he found difficult to conceal—Genji tried to avoid bringing up the past very often. Just then, the cuckoo that they had been waiting for gave a faint cry. Upon hearing it, Genji was unusually moved and whispered a line of verse: "How could it have known?"

> *Is it yearning for the one who is gone*
> *That leads you back here, O mountain cuckoo*
> *Soaked by a sudden evening shower*

Genji looked up ever more intently into the sky.
   His son replied:

> *Take this message with you, mountain cuckoo*
> *To one who is beloved of me . . . tell her*
> *The orange tree at home is in full bloom*

Many of the women in attendance also composed poems, but I shall refrain from setting them down here. Genji's son stayed on in service—a task that he

---

5. Poem by Sakai no Hitozane from *The Kokinshū*: "The vaulting heavens are no memento for the lady I loved . . . why then, should I gaze distractedly up at the sky each time I long for you?"

assumed from time to time because he felt sorry that his lonely father was now sleeping by himself. He had many memories associated with these bedchambers—a place familiar to him now, but one that had been off limits while Murasaki was alive.

The following month, during the hottest season of the year, Genji stayed in a room cooled by the nearby pond. Looking at the lotus blooming profusely, the dew covering the many flowers brought back a line from a poem by Lady Ise: "How can there be so many tears?" He remained distracted, lost in his thoughts until the sun went down. Amidst the shrill cries of the cicadas, he sat by himself observing the pinks in the garden, which were aglow in the slanting light at sunset.[6] But they were no comfort to him.

> *Do these cicadas take this summer day*
> *A day I pass in idleness and tears*
> *As a pretext for incessant crying*

Swarms of fireflies reminded Genji of a line spoken by the Emperor in Bai Juyi's *Song of Everlasting Sorrow:*[7] "Here in the evening pavilion fireflies flit about, and I long for Yang Guifei." Reciting lines like this from old Chinese verse had now become habitual for him.

> *They at least know it is night, these flickering fireflies . . .*
> *But because my grief and sorrow are with me always*
> *I can no longer distinguish between night and day*

The seventh day of the seventh month arrived, and with it the festival of Tanabata. Genji did not have the heart to celebrate with the customary composition of verses in Chinese and Japanese. He did not call for music, but instead whiled away the time by gazing outside in idle reverie. There were no attendants to observe the meeting of the two celestial lovers, the weaver maiden and the oxherd. Late at night, Genji arose by himself in the dark and pushed open the hinged door at the corner of the hall. Dew had drenched the garden just below the veranda. He passed through the door into the walkway and, after looking around, went outside.

> *I look up to observe the heavenly lovers*
> *But their tryst belongs to a world beyond the clouds*
> *In this garden of parting, only dew remains*

* * *

---

6. Poem by Sosei from *The Kokinshū*: "Am I the only one who finds them moving . . . these Japanese pinks aglow in the light of sunset when crickets cry?"

7. Known in this anthology as "The Song of Lasting Regret."

From Chapter XLV

Hashihime

THE DIVINE PRINCESS AT UJI BRIDGE

In those days a certain aging prince of the blood, Hachinomiya[8] was living in obscurity, no longer counted as a member of court society. His mother was from a most distinguished family, and at one point there was hope that he might be named Crown Prince and attain the heights of glory. His circumstances, however, changed with the coming of a new sovereign, and as a consequence of certain incidents, he was censured and the court turned its back on him. All traces of his earlier aspirations faded. In the end, his supporters withdrew one after another, their hearts filled with bitter resentment, and he was left with no one to turn to either in public or in private. It seemed that he was utterly abandoned.

His principal wife was the daughter of a Minister who served long ago. Hachinomiya's many trials and tribulations left her feeling sad and forlorn whenever she recalled the ambitions her parents had for her, and yet she found comfort from the woes of the world in the intimate, unrivaled bond she shared with her husband over the years. Their mutual devotion was truly extraordinary.

Though they were married for many years, they had no children, and Prince Hachinomiya would often wistfully express his hope that somehow they might have an adorable child to relieve their loneliness and boredom. Then, miraculously, a beautiful little girl was born to them. Their joy was boundless, and they did everything they could to love and care for her. Soon after, Hachinomiya's wife was pregnant again; and though they wanted their second child to be a boy, they had another girl. Sadly, the mother suffered terribly from the effects of the birth and died. Her husband was in a state of shock and grief.

I have lived in a world that has brought me nothing but a surfeit of unbearable sorrows, Hachinomiya told himself, *but my attachment to the beauty and grace of the woman I loved kept me fettered to it . . . and now it's come to this. I'm on my own again, and the loneliness and tedium I suffer will be more intense than ever. Trying to raise two small daughters, constrained by my position as a Prince . . . I shall look a proper fool, utterly pathetic!*

He considered acting on his deepest wish by taking vows and renouncing the world, but he struggled terribly with the decision, hesitant to leave behind two girls who had no one to look after them. As he wavered, the months and years passed, and before he knew it, his daughters had grown to womanhood, lovely and ideal in looks and demeanor and a constant source of comfort to him.

The attendants who waited on the younger child did not serve her with whole-hearted devotion and were always whispering among themselves, "Really now, her birth was so inauspicious!" Her mother, however, had been deeply concerned over the little girl's future, which preoccupied her thoughts even when she was on the verge of death, fading in and out of consciousness. "Have pity and look on her

---

8. *Hachinomiya* means "the Eighth Prince." It is not in the original text at this point, but appears later when more of Hachinomiya's background is explained. I am introducing the name here in this fashion as a matter of convenience.

as a memento of me," she pleaded with her husband over and over. Thus, despite his resentment that the birth of the child had broken the karmic bond he shared with his wife from a previous life, he accepted that his beloved's death was meant to be. Remembering that his wife had begged him to the very end to look after and cherish the girl, he treated his second daughter as a precious treasure.

This younger girl was truly beautiful—so much so that it made people uneasy, since her looks might be ill-omened. Her older sister was quiet and thoughtful by nature, nobly refined and attractive in both appearance and manner. Of the two, the younger sister created the stronger impression as a woman of distinguished aristocratic lineage—a lady whom people were inclined to treat with tender favor. Their father, however, looked after each of them with equal consideration, though there were many things that he could not do for them given his straitened circumstances. As the years went by, his residence grew increasingly desolate, and the attendants, despairing of the bleak prospects facing their young mistresses, found the situation intolerable and began to leave one after another, scattering to other households. The younger sister's nurse, who had been selected without much consideration during the turmoil that followed the death of the mother, was a woman of shallow sensibility—as one might have expected given her breeding and low status—and she abandoned her charge when the girl was still quite young. As a result, the Prince had to bring her up entirely on his own.

The Prince's estate at the time was extensive and eye catching, and the vistas created by the pond and the landscaped hills in the garden remained as lovely as ever—except that now the garden was terribly overgrown. He would spend his idle days gazing out in reverie at the scene, but because there was no longer anyone on his household staff who could properly take care of the grounds, they were neglected. Lush green grasses and weeds grew in thick profusion while *shinobugusa* ferns,[9] whose very name makes one long for the past, spread under the eaves as though they were taking possession of the place. The colors and fragrances of the flowers of each season or of the autumn foliage often brought him comfort, since he had once enjoyed them with his beloved wife. However, as his estate grew ever more deserted and lonely and there were fewer and fewer people he could rely upon, he began to spend all of his time on his religious devotions, fastidiously looking after the decorations for the altar in his meditation hall.

He was frustrated that his circumstances bound him to the world against his wishes, and could only assume that the obstacles he faced in fulfilling his desire to renounce it all were the effects of his karmic destiny. As time went by, he grew ever more detached from relationships with women. *At this point in my life*, he wondered, *why should I act like other men and marry again?* He became a hermit in spirit. After losing his beloved wife, it never occurred to him—not even as an idle fancy—to give himself over to normal human emotions.

There were some who reproached him for his behavior: "Why must you insist on remaining alone? You certainly experienced more than a normal share of grief when your wife passed away, but to continue to dwell on your loss after all this time . . . well, you ought to show consideration for others and remarry like any

9. Literally, "ferns of nostalgic longings."

other man. If you did, your neglected villa, which is an unsightly mess, would be in good shape in no time." He had many such reasonable suggestions from people here and there hoping to establish a connection with an imperial prince, but he paid no attention to any of their proposals.

Between periods of meditation and prayer, Hachinomiya would relax with his daughters; because they were getting older, he taught them how to play the koto and engaged them in trivial pastimes such as Go and *hentsugi*.[1] Observing the character of his daughters, he could see that the older sister was refined, serious and contemplative. The younger girl was sweet and gentle, and her shy, deferential air was most endearing. Each had distinctive merits.

* * *

A saintly ascetic who was a master of esoteric Buddhism lived in the mountains at Uji. He had a reputation as a most learned man, but he remained secluded and hardly ever appeared at court. When he learned that a prince of the blood was living alone nearby, doing noble religious practices and studying sutras, he thought him admirable and visited regularly. The ascetic elucidated the deeper meaning of the texts that Prince Hachinomiya had been studying for many years, bringing him to greater awareness of the vain mutability of the world. Despite his spiritual progress, Hachinomiya had to explain to the ascetic why he had not chosen the path of renunciation. "Though my heart is set on rebirth in the next world, where I may take my seat on the lotus and dwell in the unsullied pond of paradise, I am too anxious about leaving behind my young daughters to take priestly vows just yet."

As it turned out, this very same ascetic would, from time to time, travel to the capital to teach Retired Emperor Reizei about scripture and doctrinal matters. On one such occasion, after answering questions Reizei posed concerning the profound sutras they were reading, he took advantage of the opportunity to mention Hachinomiya.

"The Prince is very wise," the ascetic remarked, "and has gained a deep understanding of the teachings of the Buddha.[2] I believe he was truly born to follow the path of enlightenment . . . a saintly man who is sincerely dedicated to his devotions."

"But is it true that he has not yet become a priest?" Reizei asked. "The young men here refer to him as the earthbound saint . . . a most poignant situation."

Kaoru happened to be in service to Reizei at that moment and privately pondered what was being discussed: *I myself know full well the insipid nature of the world, but my practice of religious austerities is hardly enough to draw the attention of others. To my shame, I thoughtlessly let the time pass.* He listened intently to the conversation, wondering how it was that a man could become saintly while still living in this vulgar world.

"He originally intended to take priestly vows," the ascetic remarked, "but, as he once lamented to me, some trivial matters held him back, and now he finds that he cannot possibly abandon his poor daughters." Holy man though he was

1. This game is mentioned in the *Aoi* chapter. It involves writing down radicals or parts of a Chinese character and trying to guess the whole character.
2. The text uses the word *naikyō*, literally,

"inner teachings," to distinguish Buddhism from the "outer teachings," *gaikyō*, which refers mainly to Confucian works. The use of this word reinforces Hachinomiya's political fecklessness and his otherworldly preoccupations.

the ascetic was a connoisseur of the finer things. "When his daughters perform in concert," he added, "their captivating music vies with the sound of the rapids, putting one in mind of paradise!"

This praise of the young princesses had an old-fashioned ring to it that made Reizei smile.

"One would imagine that having grown up in the house of such a saintly man they would have been completely unfamiliar with secular diversions," he said. "What a delight to hear otherwise. He can't very well abandon them, being so worried about their future . . . apparently, he has a very difficult problem on his hands. If it happens that I should outlive him, even for a brief time, I wonder . . . would he give his daughters to me?"

Reizei was—or so people thought—the tenth son of the old Emperor, and thus Hachinomiya's younger half brother. He recalled the example of the cloistered Third Princess, whose father, Suzaku, had placed her in Genji's care. *If only I could have his daughters . . . they would be companions to me in my idleness.*

Kaoru's thoughts were focused not on the two princesses at Uji, as might have been expected of a young man, but on their father. He now wanted more than ever to meet and observe someone whose state of mind seemed so utterly devoted to religious practices. As the ascetic was preparing to return to his mountain retreat, Kaoru spoke to him and requested his help in arranging a visit. "I very much want to go there and study under Prince Hachinomiya's guidance, so please make some discreet inquiries on my behalf."

Reizei sent a message to Hachinomiya: "I have heard through an intermediary about the conditions in which you are living and have been greatly moved."

> *Though my heart, weary of this tiresome world*
> *Travels to the Uji mountains, the veil*
> *Of eightfold clouds you've drawn obscures my view*

The ascetic sent Reizei's messenger on ahead, and so the man reached Hachinomiya first. It was a rare occurrence for anyone, let alone a messenger from such a distinguished figure, to visit this humble abode in the shadow of the mountains. Hachinomiya was overjoyed and welcomed the man in a suitable manner, plying him with wine and local delicacies. He then composed his reply:

> *I did not cut all ties to purify my heart*
> *It's just that I grew weary of this world of woe*
> *And made a home of this but in Ujiyama*[3]

Because Hachinomiya refused to consider himself an enlightened holy man, it was clear that he harbored lingering resentments against the world. Reizei was deeply affected by the reply.

The ascetic conveyed to Hachinomiya Kaoru's profound desire to follow the path of the Buddha: "The young man told me that he has had an abiding inter-

3. Hachinomiya's poem alludes to a poem by Kisen from *The Kokinshū.* The play on Uji/ ushi will become a dominant, recurring element throughout the final chapters of the narrative. However, this poem also suggests that Hachinomiya did not voluntarily choose to follow the religious path at Uji and thus hints at a lingering bitterness that Reizei picks up on immediately [editor's note].

est since childhood in acquiring knowledge of the holy scriptures, but so long as he remains unavoidably caught up in the mundane world, he will be kept busy day and night with public and private matters. He said that someone as unimportant as he should have no cause to feel constrained about turning his back on the world, shutting himself away and studying. And yet his current life-style naturally causes him to neglect his devotions and give himself up to worldly diversions. That's why he spoke so earnestly to me, saying that after hearing about the admirable life you lead, he was eager to turn to you for reli-gious guidance."

Hachinomiya replied at length: "Normally, the realization of the truth of muta-bility and the beginnings of an aversion to this world can be traced to some moment when a person suffers a reversal of fortune that makes him resentful and motivates him to pursue the path of religious devotion. It is thus remark-able that a young man like Kaoru, who has everything he wants, who has known no disappointments, should be so focused on the afterlife. In my case, perhaps it was destined that I should come to detest the world and turn to religion, as though the Buddha were giving me special encouragement. In the course of things, I was able to fulfill my wish to quietly practice my devotions; but now I sense that my life will soon come to an end without ever achieving any true spiritual enlightenment after all this time. Kaoru will be a companion in the study of the Dharma, but one who will put me to shame, since I'm all too aware that I've learned nothing of the past and future." He exchanged letters with Kaoru, and the young man set out to visit him.

In truth, the scene was even more poignantly desolate than what the ascetic had described. The villa was so simple and severe that it reminded Kaoru of a hermit's temporary grass hut. Other residences may be referred to in similar terms as mountain villas, but those are places of repose with their own special charms. Here, the violent roar of the rapids and crashing of waves made it seem impossible that one could forget one's cares, and with the fierce howling of the wind at night, there would not have been a moment to dream peaceful dreams. The appearance of the place moved Kaoru to speculate that Hachinomiya, who was determined to find enlightenment, may have found it easier to renounce the world in this environment, which had nothing appealing about it that might distract his attention from his devotions. *But what do his daughters think about it? It's certainly a far remove from the gentle, feminine places where princesses usually reside.*

A single sliding door separated the chapel from the daughters' quarters. Given the alluring atmosphere, a young man of amorous proclivities would have wanted to make advances to see how the young women might respond and thus find out what they were like. Kaoru, however, checked himself, thinking that to engage in suggestively playful banter would undermine the true purpose of his visit. After all, he had come to this place deep in the mountains with the intention of turn-ing away from worldly desires. Thus, he sensitively focused on expressing his concern for Hachinomiya's difficult circumstances, and continued thereafter to visit again and again. Despite maintaining his connection with the vulgar world, Hachinomiya had gained profound insight from pursuing religious studies and austerities in his mountain retreat, and, just as Kaoru had hoped, he humbly shared his wisdom without ever flaunting his knowledge.

There are many holy men and learned priests in the world, but virtuous men at the rank of bishop or abbot are often officious and aloof. They are always busy, and so they tend to be curt and blunt in manner. Kaoru found them much too pompous and overweening to ask them to clearly explain the meanings and workings of things in the world. There were also disciples of Buddha, men at a much lower rank who had accrued great merit by practicing austerities and upholding the Precepts, but they were usually vulgar in appearance, rough in speech and uncouthly familiar in comportment. Kaoru was usually occupied with official duties during the daytime and had time to reflect on profound subjects only during the quiet evening hours. He thus found it altogether unpleasant to summon such boorish disciples close to his bedchambers to discuss the teachings. In contrast, Hachinomiya was truly refined and ennobled by his suffering. The words and expressions he used when discussing the teachings of the Buddha that the bishops and disciples lectured on were simpler and more familiar to Kaoru. Moreover, though he had not achieved an especially profound understanding of the scriptures, as a man whose karmic destiny was to be born a prince of the blood he had an unusually fine, innate grasp of the true nature of the world. The two men gradually grew closer. Kaoru began to wish he could be with his mentor all the time and longed to meet him during those periods when he was busy at court and could not go to Uji.

Reizei could see how highly Kaoru esteemed Prince Hachinomiya, and so he too began sending a constant stream of messages to Uji. Hardly a word had been spoken about Hachinomiya for years, but now gradually more and more visitors found their way to his lonely, desolate abode. Reizei would on appropriate occasions honor him with messages inquiring after his well-being, and Kaoru would take every opportunity to be of faithful service, seeing to both elegant celebrations and more serious, practical matters. In this way, three years passed.

It happened in late autumn, The seasonal Invocation of the Holy Name was at hand, and because the roar of the rapids at the fishing weir had been especially grating recently, Hachinomiya went up to the meditation hall at the temple where the ascetic lived to spend a week practicing his devotions.

While their father was gone, the two sisters felt more forlorn, bored, and depressed than ever. Kaoru, remembering that he had not called at Uji in some time, very discreetly set out during the wee hours of the night just as the predawn moon was rising. He had a very small escort and was dressed in a manner that would disguise his identity.

Because Hachinomiya's villa was on the near bank of the river, there was no need to arrange for a boat. Kaoru traveled on horseback; the closer he got to Uji, the denser the fog grew. As he made his way through undergrowth thick enough to obscure the path, he struggled against a fierce wind that shook the dew from the leaves of the trees. He was thoroughly soaked and chilled to the bone, but he couldn't complain, since he was the one who decided to come here. Having hardly ever set out on this sort of adventure, he felt sad and exhilarated at the same time.

> How much stranger than the dew dropping from leaves
> Helpless in the blasts sweeping down the mountain
> Are these tears of mine that fall so easily

He ordered his escort to be quiet lest they awaken some meddlesome mountain peasant. He also took care to minimize the clopping of his horse as he cut through fences of brush wattle or waded through murmuring streams. However, for all his caution, he could not disguise his fragrance, which was carried on the wind. At house after house people startled awake, wondering, *Whose fragrance do I smell?*[4]

As they neared the villa they heard chillingly sublime music, though they could not tell what the instruments were. *I have heard that Hachinomiya always plays in this manner, but I have never had the chance to hear his koto, so famous for its tonal beauty. What a stroke of luck that I should arrive at this moment!* With such thoughts in mind, Kaoru entered and realized that he had been hearing a *biwa* lute. The instrument was tuned to the *ōshiki* mode,[5] and though the song was an ordinary prelude used for tuning, in such a setting it had an otherworldly feel: the sound produced by the plectrum was pure and enchanting. A thirteen-string koto could be heard accompanying the *biwa* intermittently, and its graceful, feminine tone was deeply affecting.

He had concealed himself since he wanted to listen a while longer, but then a man—a guard or watchman of some sort who had clearly heard Kaoru's arrival—stepped out brusquely. "My lord has gone into retreat for certain reasons," the man said. "I shall have a messenger inform him that you are here."

"There's no need to bother with that." Kaoru replied. "I really mustn't intrude on him during the limited number of days he has to practice his devotions. It would, however, be a shame if after having drenched my robes getting here I should have to go back disappointed that it was all for naught. Please inform your mistresses about my situation . . . it would be some consolation to hear at least a word of pity from them."

A knowing smile spread over the man's unattractive face. "As you wish, my lord," he said, and started back inside.

"Wait a moment!" Kaoru called the man back. "I've heard from various people over the years how well the Prince's daughters play together and have been eager to hear them. This is a welcome chance for me. Is there no hidden corner nearby where I might conceal myself for a short time? I don't want my unexpected appearance to make them stop."

Even someone of rough, common sensibilities like the watchman could recognize from Kaoru's features and overall appearance that he was a remarkably impressive person—this despite his being dressed in hunting robes.

"They play all the time," the watchman informed him, "mornings and evenings when no one is around to hear them. But whenever someone calls from the capital, even a person of lower rank, they refuse to play at all. In fact, our lord has largely kept the presence of his daughters a secret, and he has made it clear that he does not want us to tell anyone that they live here."

Kaoru smiled and replied, "It's deplorable of Prince Hachinomiya to hide them away. Everyone praises him as a rare exemplar of virtue, yet here he is, behaving secretively. Be that as it may, take me to where I may listen to them. My intentions are strictly honorable. How very strange that they should be living like this . . . in truth, they can hardly be considered normal."

4. Poem by Sosei from *The Kokinshū*: "Whose fragrance do I smell? Someone has hung his purple trousers over mistflowers in the autumn fields."
5. This mode is equivalent to the key of A.

"As you wish, my lord. Were I to refuse, I would be criticized afterward as a man of no judgment." So saying, he showed Kaoru to a spot in the garden in front of the residence that was closed off by a fence made of a lattice of bamboo. The watchman then called the escort into a gallery in the west hall and received them there himself.

A gate in the wattle fence appeared to lead to the residence beyond, and so Kaoru pushed it open a crack and peeked through. Gazing across the misty garden, enchanting in the pale light of the moon, he could see the two sisters sitting just inside their raised blinds. A page girl was seated on the veranda, looking thin and cold in her soft, shabby robe. Several grown-up attendants were sitting there as well, dressed in a similar manner. The sisters were seated inside in the aisle room. One of them was partially hidden behind a pillar. A *biwa* lute was set out in front of her and she was turning over the plectrum with her fingertips, toying with it. When the moon suddenly emerged from behind a cloud and brightly lit up the scene, she said, "I may not have a fan, but I can still call forth the moon with this."[6] The lovely glow of her face, which peeked out from behind the plectrum, was utterly adorable.

The other sister, who was reclining nearby, was leaning over a koto. "I've heard of people calling forth the setting sun,"[7] she said, "but you are certainly prone to some peculiar notions!" She was smiling, and her figure seemed a little more dignified and modestly refined.

"Even if this plectrum can't call forth the moon," her sister retorted, "that doesn't mean the *biwa* and the moon aren't connected!"[8] Their silly, sisterly exchanges touched Kaoru with their warmth and charm. They were not at all what he had imagined earlier from his distant vantage. Though he would on occasion hear younger ladies-in-waiting reading romances handed down from the past—stories that invariably included scenes involving characters like these two sisters—he himself had always remained skeptical, doubtful that such things could ever actually take place in real life. Yet here he was, finding himself irresistibly drawn to these young women. *It's true . . . remarkable things really do occur in out-of-the-way places in this world!*

Because the fog was thick, he could not make the princesses out all that clearly. Just as he was hoping the moon would emerge from behind the clouds

6. Quotation from the *Japanese and Chinese Poems for Recitation* 587: "We raise a fan to call forth the moon, hidden behind mountain ranges; winds blow through the empty heavens, and we know them by the swaying trees." This allusion is especially noteworthy because the source of the verse is the *Zhi guan* (*On Cessation and Contemplation*) by the Chinese monk Chih-I (538–597), which was an important Tendai Buddhist text on meditation. The moon and wind stand for truth, which may be blocked from view or invisible to humankind until some evidence, expedient teaching, or symbol (such as a moon-shaped fan, or in this case a plectrum) makes them evident. Murasaki Shikibu is remarkably consistent in fitting poetic allusions to a narrative situation, and here she has the younger daughter cite a verse that reveals the extent of the unusual influence of her religious father.

7. The playful reference here is to a Chinese-style *bugaku* dance called "The Masked Warrior King" (cf. the *Wakana* chapter, Part 2). As part of the dance a rod or baton was lifted toward the sun.

8. The plectrum could be stored by slipping it into a space between the tailpiece (*fukuju*, the piece of the instrument on the bottom front of the soundboard where the strings are attached) and the face of the soundboard. Beneath the tailpiece was a round acoustic hole called the "hidden moon" or "dark moon" (*ingetsu*), and so the younger sister is defending her poetic allusion by stressing a figurative relationship between the plectrum and the moon.

again, it appeared that someone stepped out from the interior of the residence and announced the arrival of a visitor, for the blinds were lowered immediately and everyone moved back inside. Neither sister look flustered; their quiet, gentle movements as they concealed themselves without so much as a rustle of their robes created an impression of endearing feminine softness, and he found their extreme elegance and courtly grace alluring.

Kaoru silently withdrew and then had a messenger rush back to the capital with orders to bring a carriage.

"I came at an inconvenient time," he told the homely watchman, "but as things turned out, my visit has given me joy and some small comfort from my cares. Inform your lord's daughters that I have arrived . . . and do be sure to let them know just how soaked I am as a result of my exertions." The man went off and delivered the message.

The two princesses, who never imagined that they might be spied on like this, were terribly embarrassed when they realized that Kaoru had possibly overheard their casual conversation. The breeze had earlier carried in a mysteriously wonderful fragrance, but because they had noticed it at an hour when a visitor was unlikely, they had not been at all alarmed. Their carelessness made them feel ashamed, and they didn't know what to do.

The attendant who was to deliver his message requesting an audience with the princesses struck Kaoru as much too young and inexperienced for the task. He thought that timing was crucial in all matters, and because the fog had not cleared yet, he took advantage of the moment to stride over to a spot in front of the blinds and kneel there. The unsophisticated young attendants had no idea what to say to him and seemed ill at ease even offering a cushion.

"It's discomfiting to be left outside these blinds," Kaoru said. "If my heart were really impulsive and shallow, would I have bothered traveling the rugged mountain path all the way here? This is a most peculiar welcome, I must say. Still, I would hope that if I were to come through the drenching dews over and over, you might at least recognize the sincerity of my feelings." He spoke in a genuinely earnest manner.

Not one of the younger attendants was capable of a smooth, coherent response—indeed, they felt so awkward and embarrassed that they wanted to disappear. As a result, some time passed while they went to wake up the more experienced women. The older sister, uncomfortable that the delay in replying would create the impression that they were teasing Kaoru, spoke up at last. "We are, as you can tell, inexperienced in such matters, so how could we pretend to know how to answer you?" She spoke in a hushed, reserved tone, her voice noble and gracious.

"I realize that it's customary for a woman to pretend that she knows nothing of the aching sorrow in a man's heart, even when she is all too aware of his feelings. But it's especially disappointing that you in particular should feign complete ignorance about me. I imagine that, since you reside in the house of a remarkable, enlightened man, you too have a clear understanding of the world. Thus, it would be best to use your wisdom to judge the depth or shallowness of my feelings, which are too powerful for me to keep hidden any longer. Must you cut me off, believing I am driven by wanton passions? There are some who have urged me to be more amorously inclined, but I stalwartly refuse to yield to such temptations. Reports about me must no doubt have reached you. How happy it would make me if I could turn to you as a companion, one who would listen in sympathy to my stories about tedious court society, or if you would come to trust me enough that I in turn could provide a diversion from your feelings of isolation and brooding sorrow." He said many other things besides. She, being diffident, found it hard to answer him and left it instead to an old attendant who had just been roused from sleep to respond in her place.

This older woman, who was known as Bennokimi, was anything but reticent.

"Really, now . . . this is unacceptable. How rude to leave his lordship seated in such a spot! He should be seated *inside* the blinds! These young women . . . they know nothing about protocol."

The two sisters felt ill at ease, since the voice speaking so bluntly was that of an old woman.

"It is exceedingly strange, you see," Bennokimi continued, "but due to the circumstances of my young mistresses' father, who is no longer counted as one who resides in this world, we receive neither visits nor expressions of concern from those people one might assume would still remember him. That's why your unexpected devotion to my lord is so moving, even to the heart of someone as insignificant as I am. My young mistresses feel grateful to you as well . . . it's just that they are shy and have a hard time expressing their emotions."

* * *

From Chapter XLVII

Agemaki

A BOWKNOT TIED IN MAIDEN'S LOOPS

* * *

Bennokimi informed Kaoru of all her mistress had said. *What is driving the Princess to turn her back on the world like this?* he wondered. *Did she learn the truth of the world's mutability at the side of her saintly father?* Because her heart seemed all the more in tune with his own, he could not despise her as someone who was making a pretense of her wisdom. "If that's how she feels," he said, "then naturally she would think it improper to see me now, even with a blind or curtain between us. But, come now . . . find some place where I may discreetly enter her private chambers." On hearing his words, Bennokimi set about complying with his orders. She dismissed most of the attendants early and told those ladies-in-waiting who were in on the plot to make preparations.

A little later that evening, the wind suddenly picked up and blew violently, causing the crude, rickety shutters to rattle and squeak. Kaoru was certain that the Princess would not be able to hear him enter her chambers because of all the noise, and so Bennokimi stealthily led him there. The old attendant was concerned that the Middle Counselor might make a mistake, since her mistresses were in the same room. However, the princesses were accustomed to sleeping together, and it might have seemed odd to ask them to retire to separate quarters. Besides, Bennokimi assumed that Kaoru was well enough acquainted with the sisters not to confuse them.

As it turned out, the older Princess was wide awake, fearful that something was afoot. As soon as she heard Kaoru enter, she quietly got up to make her escape, hurriedly slipping out through the curtains around her bedding. She felt terrible for her sister, who was innocently sleeping away, and it broke her heart to imagine what would happen. *If only we could hide together*, she thought—but it was too late to go back now. Trembling, she looked on in the dim, flickering lamplight as Kaoru, wearing only a single under robe, lifted one of the panels on the standing curtains and entered their bedchamber with an impudent expression, as if the place belonged to him. *How dreadful! What must my sister be thinking?*

With these thoughts running through her mind, she opened up a folding screen along the front of a crumbling wall and withdrew behind it, where she sat feeling miserable and uncomfortable. It was deeply upsetting to think that her sister, who had vehemently deplored the very idea of a future as wife of the Middle Counselor, might now mistakenly think she had planned this shocking tryst and hate her for it. As she reflected sadly that all of their troubles stemmed from having been left behind in this world with no one to support them, she had the sensation that she had last seen her father's figure departing for his retreat up the mountain only just this evening. She was filled with longing and grief.

When Kaoru entered the chambers and saw a woman sleeping alone, his heart leapt with joy, since it appeared that everything was going according to plan. But then it gradually became apparent that the woman was not the Princess he desired, but someone slightly more beautiful and alluring in appearance. Her shock and desperation as she startled from her slumbers made it clear that she had absolutely no idea what was happening, and he was moved to sympathy at her plight. At the same time, he was extremely angry, provoked by the callous behavior of the older sister who had fled into hiding. Though he could hardly deny that he was attracted to the younger Princess and did not want her to go to another man, he was nonetheless frustrated that his true desires were being denied. *I don't want the Princess to think I'm a man of fickle, shallow character, but I have no choice but to spend the night here. If it's my destiny after all to end up with the younger sister instead, well . . . it's not as though she's a complete stranger to me.* With those thoughts in mind, he regained his composure and, behaving the same way he did that earlier night with the Princess he loved, he did not force himself on her sister, but passed the time engaging in gentle, courtly conversation until dawn broke.

The older attendants, thinking that they had given the couple more than ample time, were just then questioning one another:

"Where has our younger mistress gone? This is very strange!"

"Oh well . . . she must have gone off for some reason. I'm sure she's fine."

Marriage proposals aside, Kaoru's remarkably splendid, attractive features and figure were enough to make the attendants feel their wrinkles would disappear just by gazing at him. One old woman, a toothless hag given to making unpleasant remarks, said, "Why must our older mistress be so aloof toward him? Perhaps she's been possessed by one of those fearsome gods that people always seem to be going on about."

"Really, now, watch what you say . . . such inauspicious words! Why would some spirit possess her? She acts like this because she was brought up far removed from people. With no one to advise her on how to behave appropriately, she feels awkward interacting with others. Just wait . . . once she gets used to having him around, she'll naturally warm to him soon enough."

"I just hope that she warms to him soon . . . I do so wish for her to fulfill her ideal destiny."

While the attendants were talking, they fell asleep one by one, and soon the discordant sounds of snoring and other noises reverberated.

A poet once claimed that the length of an autumn's night is "determined by one's companion."[9] Though this particular night had been awkward, unlike any other he had experienced, Kaoru still felt that the dawn arrived much too quickly. As he gazed at the younger Princess, who looked so fresh and lustrous that he could no longer decide which of the sisters was more attractive to him, he did not want to leave with his desires unsated. "Think lovingly of me as I think of you . . . and never emulate the behavior of one who is cold and heartless." He promised her as he left that they would meet again. It was all like a strange dream to him; while he was composing himself, thinking that he wanted to try again to be with the older Princess who had cruelly rejected him, he returned to his room, just as he had before, and lay down.

Bennokimi entered. "This is most peculiar," she remarked. "Where has my lady gone?" The younger Princess, mortified and dazed, continued to lie there trying to understand how all of this had come about. Recalling what had been said to her the day before, she was bitterly aggrieved by her sister's cruel scheming.

With the coming light of day the "cricket" emerged from her hiding place in the wall. She pitied her sister and was all too aware of how she must feel. The two of them could not bring themselves to speak to one another. The older Princess's thoughts were in chaos. *Now that we've both been exposed to his gaze, we've lost our air of mystery . . . what misery! From now on, we will never be able to relax or let down our guard.*

Bennokimi went over to the room where Kaoru was staying and learned about her mistress's shockingly stubborn rejection. The lady was too particular, given to brooding too deeply over her situation—so much so, indeed, that she made herself hateful. Bennokimi was stunned and most sorry for the Middle Counselor.

"Even when she rejected me before," Kaoru said, "I took comfort in thinking that there was still some hope that I might somehow persuade her . . . but what happened last night was utter humiliation. I ought to throw myself in the river. After observing just how troubled Hachinomiya was by the prospect of abandoning his daughters and leaving them on their own, I decided it wouldn't do for me to turn my back on this world and abandon them as well. Well, what's done is done . . . I shall never again consider either one of them an object of romantic interest. In return, they must never forget the anguish and bitterness they have caused me to suffer. Prince Niou remains unabashed in his pursuit of the younger sister, and if she were to yield to him I would fully understand

9. Poem by Ōshikōchi Mitsune from *The Kokinshū*: "How long and endless an autumn night feels has since ancient times been determined by one's companion."

her decision—all things being equal, it seems perfectly natural for her to seek out someone of the highest rank. In fact, her attitude is reasonable, which is why I feel ashamed and have no intention of subjecting myself ever again to the unpleasant, mocking gaze of the women here. I must insist, however, that you never divulge to anyone what a fool I've been." He vented his frustrations, then hurried off much earlier than normal.

"How sad for the both of them," the attendants whispered among themselves.

What happened with him? What if he grows spiteful and turns against my sister as well? The older Princess was brokenhearted, in utter misery. She deplored and resented the meddlesome ways of her women, who always acted against her wishes. While she was turning over these various thoughts in her mind, a letter arrived. She was bemused to find herself so uncharacteristically happy and grateful to receive a message from him. Almost as if he were unaware of the season, he had attached it to a bough covered almost entirely in green leaves, with only a single sprig displaying the crimson foliage of autumn.

> *How I long to ask the mountain goddess*
> *Who dyed the same branch different colors*
> *Which one of these two hues is the deeper*

He had controlled the angry resentment that had seemed so evident when he left, concealing it beneath a few words written on a letter wrapped up with an outer sheet of paper. It was obvious that he was prepared to let the incident pass as if nothing had happened, but she felt agitated and uneasy all the same. Her ladies-in-waiting were annoyingly insisting that she must respond, but she was in a quandary and found it difficult to write anything. It was too unpleasant to ask her younger sister to reply, since that would have been a tacit acknowledgment of last night's tryst with the Middle Counselor. And yet, if she herself wrote back, it would be as good as acknowledging her own affair with him. She finally managed the following:

> *I know not why the mountain goddess dyed this branch*
> *With two colors . . . but surely the leaves that have changed*
> *Hold the deeper hue that attracts your changing heart*

Though she had casually scribbled her reply, Kaoru was charmed, and his grudge against her faded away.

She has indicated to me over and over that even though as sisters they are two, at heart they are one, and she wants to yield and have me take the younger Princess in her place. Apparently, she's unhappy that I would not accept such an arrangement, and so she devised the scheme that she carried out last night. If her plans come to naught and I remain indifferent toward her younger sister, she may well come to pity her and think me cruelly insensitive . . . if that happens, it will be all the more difficult to win the lady I've truly wanted from the very beginning. Even the old lady-in-waiting who has served as my intermediary will very likely consider me rash and thoughtless. How I regret letting my heart be stained by love's passion . . . I resolved to renounce all attachments to this world, yet I was unable to achieve what I most desired.

Kaoru realized how ridiculous he would look to others. No, it was worse than that . . . he resembled some common lover who rows his laughable little boat back and forth to see the same woman over and over.[1] He spent the entire night lost in such reflections. The next morning, beneath a delightful dawn sky, he went to call on Niou.

After the Sanjō residence of the Third Princess burned down, Kaoru moved with his mother back to the Rokujō estate; because his quarters there were near the rooms Niou used when not at his Nijō villa, he was able to visit the Prince regularly. This arrangement pleased Niou very much. His residence at Rokujō, which was ideal for living a leisurely life untroubled by distractions, looked out from the veranda onto a front garden unlike any other—the same types of flowers grew there as elsewhere, the trees and grasses swayed in similar fashion, and yet somehow their shapes and elegant movements had a special appeal. Even the reflection of pure, clear moonlight in the garden stream looked like something out of an illustration.

Knowing Niou's fondness for such scenes, Kaoru had assumed that his friend would still be up when he arrived, and sure enough, he was. When Kaoru's distinctive scent came wafting in on the breeze, a startled Niou noted his arrival immediately and, putting on a court cloak, properly arranged himself before stepping out to greet his guest. Kaoru showed his respect by stopping partway up the front steps. Niou at once leaned against the railing and, without so much as a word inviting his friend to come up to the veranda, began making small talk. As they were chatting, something reminded Niou of the Uji villa, and he complained bitterly about how his proposal was being handled. His reproaches were a bit much for Kaoru, who was finding it so difficult to satisfy his own desires. Then it occurred to him that having Niou get his way might also work to his advantage by removing an obstacle to courting the older Princess, and so he spoke more openly than usual about what needed to be done.

Fog settled at a most inopportune moment in the predawn darkness. The sky took on a chill aspect, misty clouds obscured the moon, and the shadows of the trees presented an elegant gloominess in the faint light. Reminiscing about the poignant beauty of the Uji villa, Niou insisted to his friend, "You must take me there again in the very near future." Observing the obvious reluctance in Kaoru's expression, he playfully composed the following:

> *Are you so petty that you'd rope off*
> *Those wide fields where maidenflowers bloom*
> *In order to keep others away*

Kaoru replied in kind:

> *Maidenflowers blooming in morning fields*
> *Covered in deep mists may only be seen*
> *By those whose hearts are truly drawn to them*[2]

1. Anonymous poem from *The Kokinshū*: "I always yearn to go back to the same person, like a little boat that has made its way through the channel and comes rowing home."
2. Poem by Mibu no Tadamine from *The Kokinshū*: "Is it because maidenflowers find it painful to be viewed by men that they bloom hidden in the autumn mists?" Kaoru's poem mentions the place name Ashitanohara (in modern Nara Prefecture), which I have rendered according to its literal meaning, "morning fields," in keeping with the setting of this scene as a whole. Ashitanohara was famous for maidenflowers, but it was also associated with morning fog.

"These are no ordinary flowers," he added, as if intentionally trying to get a rise out of his friend—and, indeed, Niou was thoroughly irritated, exclaiming, "Ahh . . . how cheeky you are!"[3]

Niou had been talking like this about the younger Uji Princess for several years. Until last night Kaoru had been concerned about her looks, but now he considered it unlikely that Niou would be disappointed in her charms. He had also worried that her breeding and character might not meet expectations when seeing her up close, but evidently she had no flaws that might give cause for regret. He felt sorry for the older Princess, since it seemed unkind to undercut the plans that she was secretly making, but, regardless, he felt that he simply could not transfer his feelings from one sister to the other. *If I yield the younger Princess to Niou, neither he nor the woman I love will have any cause to resent me.*

Niou, who had no idea what Kaoru was secretly planning in his heart, was railing on about how his friend was selfishly intending to keep both Uji Princesses for himself. Kaoru found this amusing and couldn't resist tweaking his friend by assuming the role of father to the sisters. "It would be most unfortunate were you to cause her to suffer on account of your incorrigible tendency to pursue frivolous affairs."

"All right, then . . . I'll show you," Niou replied earnestly. "I've never been more devoted to anyone."

"That's all fine and well, but neither princess has shown the slightest indication that she's willing to give herself to you. This will be an excruciatingly difficult task to carry out," Kaoru said, then explained in detail just what needed to be done when they traveled together to Uji.

The twenty-eighth day of the month—the final day of the Equinox Festival—happened to be an auspicious one on the calendar. Kaoru, after privately making arrangements, decided that it would be the perfect time to make a secret excursion with Niou to the Uji villa. Niou's heart was so set on the younger Princess that there would have been no end of trouble had his mother, the Akashi Empress, found out about this adventure, for she certainly would have forbidden it. With that risk in mind, Kaoru went about the tricky task of planning the trip, all the while maintaining a nonchalant air, as if nothing out of the ordinary was afoot. The country estate of Genji's son was in the vicinity of Uji, and they had to be cautious and not attract attention when ferrying across the river. The need for secrecy also prompted Kaoru to forego staying over at some grand residence on the way. He chose instead to take Niou quietly to an inconspicuous residence of one of his retainers at a nearby manor, and then to go on to the Uji villa by himself. It was highly unlikely that anyone would notice them, but Kaoru did not want to give away the slightest hint of what he was up to—not even to that homely watchman who occasionally patrolled the grounds of the Uji villa.

As they always did whenever the arrival of the Middle Counselor was announced, the attendants bustled about preparing themselves to receive him. The princesses considered this something of a nuisance, with the older sister thinking, *I've made it abundantly clear that he should turn his fragrant atten-*

3. Poem by Bishop Henjō from *The Kokinshū*: "Ahh, how cheeky you are, you maidenflowers standing in autumn fields flaunting your seduc- tive charms . . . but blossoms too will soon fade."

tions to my sister . . . to the leaf that has changed colors. Will he finally come to understand? Meanwhile, the younger sister's thoughts were of a different order. I'm not the one he truly desires, so what does his visit today have to do with me? Still, she felt that she had to be on her guard, since she could no longer just blithely trust her sister—not after what had happened the night the Middle Counselor stole into her bedchambers. Indeed, her distrust was so great, she no longer spoke directly to the older Princess, but communicated through an intermediary. Her women were upset by this break between siblings, and they fretted over how it all might end.

Kaoru had Niou ride to the Uji villa on horseback. He then led him inside under cover of a dark, moonless night and summoned Bennokimi. "I must have a word with your older mistress," he said. "The way she insists on keeping her distance from me is deeply humiliating, but I cannot bring myself to just slink away and leave things between us as they are. I want you to show me to her chambers later this evening, just as you did before." His words struck Bennokimi as sincere, and he seemed to have no hidden motives. Thus, she agreed to go in and speak with the older Princess—after all, from her perspective it hardly mattered which of her mistresses he chose to take for his wife.

When the older Princess was informed of Kaoru's request, she was at once pleased and relieved. Just as I thought . . . he now prefers my sister. She had all of the sliding panel doors between the main chamber and the surrounding aisle rooms securely locked—all of them, that is, except for the ones that led to her younger sister's quarters. After taking that precaution, she received him.

"I must speak briefly with you," Kaoru began, "but it's awkward to have to speak as loudly as this, since others may hear what I have to say. Won't you open the panels just a bit? This is truly maddening."

"I can hear you perfectly well," she replied, leaving the doors locked.

But then she reconsidered. He must feel that he owes it to me to say something, since he has undergone a change of heart and doesn't want to offend me. What harm could it do at this point to see him? It's not like I haven't met him face to face before. It would be unkind of me to let the night pass without responding. With those thoughts in mind, she moved toward him and opened the panels.

At that moment, he reached through, grasped her sleeve, and while pulling on it to keep her from escaping, gave voice to all his complaints. She was mortified and immediately regretted her decision. How dreadful! Why did I ever agree to meet him? Still, she kept her wits and used all of her wiles to try to cajole and convince him to go to her sister instead. "You must not make a distinction, but consider us as one and the same." Kaoru found her demeanor, so sweet and pitiful as she pleaded earnestly with him, deeply affecting.

Niou, meanwhile, was doing just as he had been instructed. He drew near the door that Kaoru had used that earlier night, and then signaled Bennokimi by opening his fan. She showed him the way in, and as he entered he found it delightfully charming that she should be guiding him along a familiar path that another had obviously taken before him.

The older Princess, of course, knew nothing about Niou's presence, and so she continued trying to persuade Kaoru to go to her sister. Kaoru was amused but, at the same time, he felt sorry for her. He also recognized that if he said nothing about what was going on now, she would later come to resent his deception, and he would have no way to absolve himself of blame. He thus concluded that it was best to apprise her of the situation. "Prince Niou followed me tonight, and I was unable to turn him away. Evidently, he was able to enter furtively, without making a sound. That scheming old lady-in-waiting of yours, Bennokimi, has no doubt been speaking with him. Now that I've been rejected by both you and your sister, I'm destined to become a laughingstock at court."

The Princess was blindsided by this appalling turn of events, for it had never crossed her mind that something like this might occur. "I had no idea," she said, "just how far you were willing to go to carry out such an outrageous scheme. My lack of caution makes it obvious how feckless and naive I truly am, and you must take me for an utter fool." She was at a loss for words to describe her feelings at that moment.

"Nothing I say would make any difference now," Kaoru replied. "Even if I offer repeated explanations and apologies, they would not be enough. Go ahead . . . pinch and scratch me if you wish. Apparently, you were holding out hopes for a man of more distinguished lineage than I, but, as I know all too well, karmic destiny does not always work out exactly as our hearts might wish. That's why I sympathize with you now that Prince Niou has bestowed his affections on your sister . . . for I too am acquainted with the hopelessness that comes with being rejected and cast adrift with no haven. What is to be will be, and you should resign yourself to your fate. No matter how securely you may fasten these panels, no one believes our relationship is pure and chaste. Do you really imagine that the man who asked me to bring him to your sister is, at this moment, bothered by a conscience as full and troubled as ours?"

She was upset beyond words. Nonetheless, as it appeared that he might force the sliding panels open any moment, she maintained her composure, determined to calm his passions. "This 'karmic destiny' you speak of . . . it's not something tangible, not something I can see with my own eyes. I can't follow what you mean by such words, no matter how much I try. I feel as though a mist arising from tears of uncertainty[4] obscures and obstructs my path ahead. Trying to fathom your intentions toward me is unpleasant, like a bad dream. If future generations should ever speak of my sister and me, no doubt they will cite our story as an example of the foolishness of those easily deceived women who appear so often in ancient tales. Does Prince Niou possess the same degree of judgment and sincerity as someone who's capable of scheming the way you have? You've caused enough anguish and grief . . . don't confound me further. I don't expect to live much longer, but if I do, I shall speak to you when I'm feeling somewhat calmer. For now I must retire, since I'm really quite ill . . . it feels as though darkness has swept over me. Let go of my sleeves."

The reasonableness with which she pleaded with him despite being extremely upset made Kaoru feel at once ashamed of himself and protective. "I have gone to extraordinary lengths to respect and obey your wishes, my beloved . . . so much so that I've become obsessed, fixated on you. It seems that you find me inexpressibly despicable and unpleasant, and so there's nothing I can say to you. More and more, I've come to feel that I no longer want to live in this world."

4. Poem by Minamoto no Wataru from *The Gosenshū*: "That tears of uncertainty, of not knowing what the future brings, are sorrowful is due simply to the fact that they fall in plain sight".

He paused for a moment, then continued." Very well, then, since you are ill I shall let go . . . but please let me speak with you through your blinds. Do not completely abandon me."

When he released her sleeves, the Princess withdrew toward the interior of the room, but not all the way. Kaoru was moved by her gesture and said, "I shall spend the night here taking consolation from the fact that you have remained this near to me. It is more than I dared dream of, and so I swear I shall do nothing untoward." The roar of the rapids kept him awake, and a storm that raged in the middle of the night made him feel like a pheasant sleeping apart from his mate.[5] In that state of mind, he spent the night sleepless till dawn.

* * *

When the older Princess overheard her women gossiping, she felt her chest tighten in despair. *My sister's bond with Prince Niou is broken for good. So long as he had yet to decide on some distinguished lady to be his principal wife, he was probably content to use my sister as his plaything. He was no doubt mindful of what Kaoru and others might think of him, and so he offered up an endless string of pretty words professing his deep devotion.* She was convinced of Niou's deceitfulness. But that hardly mattered now, for who was she to resent his cruelty, given her own failures? More and more, she felt that there was no haven for her in this world, and she collapsed facedown, weeping.

In her frail condition, the Princess increasingly felt as though she should no longer go on living in this world. Although her attendants were not of such high status that she was ever constrained or awkward in their presence, it would be too painful to bear if they knew that she had overheard their gossip about Prince Niou's marriage. And so she lay down to sleep, pretending that she had heard nothing.

The younger Princess was napping, which apparently is something one does when longing for someone. It was adorable the way she slept with her arm as a pillow, her hair gathered at her head. The older Princess continued gazing at her sister's surpassing features; she grieved as her father's words of warning came back repeatedly: *Father, you surely have not sunk to those depths that await the deeply sinful . . . but, if you are not in Hell, then just where are you? Please come for us, call us to wherever you may be. You left us to our suffering and will not appear even in our dreams.*

The chill rain gave a terrifyingly lonely cast to the winter sky at dusk, and the sound of the wind blowing around the base of the trees was ineffable. Reclining on an armrest, pondering the past and the future, she cut an incomparably dignified and graceful figure. Even though her hair had not been properly groomed for a long time, perfect tresses draped down over her white robes.[6] She had a slight pallor from days of illness, but this merely added an alabaster glow to her complexion. The gentle curve of her eyes and forehead as she gazed

---

5. *Yamadori* (literally, "bird of the mountain") refers to a species of pheasant. The male and female supposedly roosted on separate slopes at the peak of a mountain, and so they became a poetic symbol of loneliness.

6. White robes were worn at times of illness or confinement. An example of this is found in the "Leaves of Wild Ginger" chapter at the time Genji's wife gives birth to his son. Page girls and ladies-in-waiting might wear white robes as well if they were in attendance at night.

pensively outside made one wish to show her to any man sensitive enough to appreciate such sublime beauty.

The younger Princess was startled out of her nap by a violent gust of wind. Her layers of clothing, which included robes in the mountain-rose style of fallen-leaf gold with a pale violet lining, as well as robes of pale blue lined with white, were bright and vibrant. Her face had a special glow as if it had been tinted, and she looked as if she didn't have a care in the world.

"I dreamed of our father just now," she said. "He appeared briefly just over there. He seemed terribly worried."

"After Father died," the older Princess replied, her grief now greater than ever, "I had so hoped that I would see him in my dreams . . . but he has never once appeared to me."

They both broke down and wept. The older Princess contemplated the world to come. *Of late Father has been on our minds constantly, and so he was bound to appear in a dream. How I long to go to him . . . but as a woman, I'm too deeply sinful.* She desperately wanted to obtain the magical incense from China that, when burned, enabled one to see the spirits of the dead.[7]

A messenger from Niou arrived late that night when it was pitch-black outside. The letter should have been a comfort to them, coming as it did when they were feeling so forlorn, but the younger Princess would not look at it right away.

"You must reply to him in a sweet, gentle manner," her older sister advised. "I am in a fragile condition and may not be around much longer, and so I worry that some someone even more cruel and inconsiderate than Prince Niou may appear and deal with you as he wishes. So long as the Prince thinks of you once in a while, no matter how rarely, I'm sure that no other man would dare have such evil designs on you. I know that it's difficult for you to accept this situation, but at least you can count on him for support and protection."

"Are you planning to abandon me? How horrible of you!" She pulled her sleeves completely over her face.

"The term of life is fixed, and death awaits us all," the older sister replied. "When Father died, I didn't want to live on after him for even a few brief moments. Despite my wishes, I lived on anyway. I know not if death will come tomorrow,[8] but even though I accept that the world is fleeting, I still grieve. After all, for whose sake do I value my life, if not for yours?"[9]

They pulled an oil lamp over and read the letter. As always, it was long and detailed.

> *The clouds that we sadly gaze at are the same*
> *As any other clouds . . . so why should these rains*
> *Increase my anxious yearning this winter night*

7. Poem 160 from *Collected Writings of Bo Juyi*. Bai (Bo) Juyi's poem retells the famous story of how, during the early Han dynasty, Emperor Wu, following the death of his imperial wife Li, had a Taoist adept prepare a special magical incense that when burned enabled Wu to see the figure of his beloved Li faintly in the smoke.
8. Poem by Ki no Tsurayuki, written on the death of Ki no Tomonori: "Though I may reflect on life, not knowing if death will come on the morrow, I grieve for one who did not live to see the evening of this day."
9. Poem from the personal collection of Lady Ise: "Scooping up water from a mountain spring gushing forth from rocky crags, I realize, for whose sake do I value my life if not for yours?"

Apparently, he had added conventional phrases such as "sleeves that have never been as drenched in my tears as they are now,"[1] but they were nothing more than common clichés. With the letter looking as if it had been scribbled out like some tiresome chore that Niou had to perform, the older Princess's resentment grew even greater. Still, his looks and figure were so splendid and his demeanor so elegant that it was natural that the younger Princess was still attracted to him. Indeed, the longer his absences, the more she missed him. In any case, Niou had made so many extravagant vows that she knew in her heart that he would never stop calling on her. For that reason alone her anger waned, and she remained devoted to him.

The messenger remarked, "I must be returning this evening," and pressed for a reply. The younger Princess gave him a poem and not a single word more.

> The skies that I gaze upon from this village
> Pelted by hail, deep in mountain recesses
> Are, mornings and nights, ever dark and cloudy

It was the final day of the tenth month, and Niou was disturbed to realize that yet another month had passed by since he last saw his love. Night after night, he kept telling himself that this was the night to go. However, something always prevented him, and he began to feel like a small boar caught up in countless reeds.[2] For one thing, the Gosechi Festival would be held early this year,[3] and as a result there were many stylish diversions throughout the palace that kept him occupied. Even though he did not deliberately neglect his Uji Princess, he allowed more time to slip, and she was left to suffer the unbearable loneliness of waiting for him. Nonetheless, even when he was having a passing affair with one of the ladies at court, she was constantly on his mind.

His mother, the Akashi Empress, brought up the matter of his engagement to the Minister's daughter, Roku no kimi. "If there's someone you love and want to call on, then once you have secured the steady support that a marriage like this promises, bring her in discreetly as one of your ladies and treat her with honor and respect."

"Let's wait awhile. I have things to consider," he replied, cutting her off.

Niou was concerned that his bride might truly end up suffering the indignity of becoming one of his "ladies," as his mother put it, and he wanted to avoid that outcome. But the anxious princesses at Uji did not know what was in his heart. As the days and months passed, they could only languish after him.

Appearances to the contrary, Niou is not the serious, trustworthy man that I took him to be. In his heart, Kaoru was sorry he ever vouched for the Prince, and now he very rarely visited Niou's quarters. He sent message after message

---

1. A poem from which this line is taken is cited in a later commentary, but the source is unknown.
2. Poem by Kakinomoto Hitomaro: "Unable to meet my love these days, I feel like a small boat trying to make port caught up in countless reeds."
3. The Gosechi Festival was held during the eleventh month. In most years, it was scheduled around the middle of the month on the second of the three Days of the Ox that occurred during that month (zodiacal days cycled around once every twelve days). However, in some years there were only two Days of the Ox, and, when that occurred, the festival was held on the first of those days.

to the Uji villa inquiring after the older Princess and learned that her condition had improved a little around the beginning of the eleventh month. Subsequently, during this busy season at the court, his time was entirely taken up with both public and private responsibilities, and he did not dispatch anyone for five or six days. Then, suddenly, he had an alarming premonition about the Princess's health; having no other recourse available to him, Kaoru dropped everything that he was supposed to do and went to Uji.

He had left orders that healing rites were to be conducted thoroughly with no letup, but the Princess had sent the ascetic back to his mountain retreat, insisting that she was feeling much better. There were few people attending her when Kaoru arrived, and so, as always, he summoned Bennokimi and asked about her mistress's condition.

"Her symptoms are vague," the old woman informed him, "and she doesn't seem to be suffering from anything serious . . . it's just that she won't eat anything, my lord. She's always been extremely delicate compared to most women, but ever since our young mistress's affair with Prince Niou began, her mood has darkened and she goes on refusing to even glance at the slightest piece of fruit. She's shockingly emaciated, and her condition seems hopeless now. I've experienced so much sorrow in my long life, but to have to witness this horror . . . I only hope that I may die first, before my mistress . . ." Understandably, words failed her and she broke down in tears.

"This is hard for me to hear. Why didn't you let me know sooner? I've been very busy recently at both the palace and the villa of Retired Emperor Reizei, and I was worried at not being able to ask after her for several days." He went into the Princess's chambers and sat down near her pillow. He tried to speak with her, but she was unable to answer, as if she had lost her voice.

"No one, not one person informed me that you have taken a turn for the worse," he said reprovingly. "It's deplorable! I was so worried, I left specific instructions to look after you, but what good did it do . . . it's too late now." He sent for the ascetic again and also summoned a large number of priests and healers who had a good reputation for the efficacy of their prayers. The healing rites and sutra readings were set to begin early the following morning, and so he ordered a great many of his own retainers and staff to come to Uji to assist with preparations. Soon the villa was bustling with people of both high and low station, and the attendants there took heart and felt reassured as all traces of their feeling of isolation faded.

When evening came, Kaoru was offered a simple meal of steamed rice gruel and then asked to retire to the guest rooms that he always used. He protested, insisting, "I want to stay close by to help nurse the Princess." Because the priests were seated in the aisle room to the south, he set up a folding screen in a space on the east side of his beloved's bedchamber, very near to her. The younger Princess was troubled by his presence, but her attendants had all concluded that the relationship between their older mistress and the Middle Counselor was far from ordinary; they could not bring themselves to cruelly keep him away from her. After the priests started the early evening services, they began a continuous reading of the *Lotus Sutra*. The twelve priests chanting the sutra all had sonorous voices, and the effect was nobly inspiring.

With lamps lit in the space on the south side, the interior of the Princess's room was dark. Kaoru lifted up one of the panels on her standing curtain and slipped just inside to look at his beloved. When he did so, two or three older attendants shifted closer to her. The younger sister quickly hid herself from his sight and, with so few people about, lay down feeling lonely and helpless.

"Why will you not speak to me?" Kaoru pleaded, taking her hand and startling her awake.

"I would like to talk to you, but it hurts whenever I talk," she said quietly, speaking under her breath. "You didn't come here for so long that I was worried. I would have regretted it had I passed away without being able to see you again."

"That I should have kept you waiting for me this long . . ." Kaoru began sobbing. He gently placed his hand on her forehead. She was a little feverish. "What sin did you commit to bring about this illness? It must be retribution for having made someone suffer," he said, speaking softly in her ear. As he went on to tell her all of the things that he felt for her, she began to find his words troublesome and embarrassing and covered her face. He gazed down at her frail, delicate body and felt his chest tighten at the thought of what it would feel like to have to look on her lifeless figure.

"I'm sure that it has been terribly trying for you to have to look after her for so long," he said to the younger sister. "Tonight I shall stand watch, so please try to get some rest."

She was concerned, but withdrew a short distance away on the assumption that the Middle Counselor must have reason to want to speak privately to his beloved.

Kaoru should not have addressed her face to face, but when he drew closer to look at her, the Princess, despite her embarrassment and discomfort, accepted that their relationship was destined by a bond they shared in a previous life. She also recognized his noble virtues. After all, compared to Prince Niou, the Middle Counselor was exceptionally kind, gentle and trustworthy. No . . . she simply couldn't be so cruel as to send him away now, for she did not want him to remember her after she died as willful or thoughtless.

All through the night, Kaoru ordered her women to prepare medicinal infusions, but she refused to take even a sip. Aghast at the situation, he was desperate beyond words, wondering if there was anything he could do to save her life.

The ascetic, who was napping after having performed services during the night, was startled by the sublime voices of the priests who arrived in the predawn hours and took over the continuous reading of the *Lotus Sutra*. Now awake, he chanted a *dharani* spell in a voice that, despite being hoarse and cracked from age, sounded mature and truly efficacious.

"How did the Princess get along last night?" he asked, and then began to reminisce tearfully about the late Hachinomiya, all the while blowing his nose over and over. "Which realm does he inhabit now? I always imagined that he would end up in paradise, despite the lingering attachment of his concern for his daughters, but recently I saw him in a dream . . . he was dressed in earthly robes and spoke quite distinctly to me. 'Because I detested the world and was deeply estranged from it,' he said. 'I had no desire to tarry in it for long. Yet, at the time of my death, some trivial worries distracted me from focusing on my salvation. To my bitter regret, the realm that I had hoped to attain still remains beyond me. Perform memorial rites to hasten my entry into paradise.' I couldn't think of what to do right away, and so I asked five or six of my disciples who happened to be performing services just then to chant the holy name. Then another idea occurred to me, and I sent them out in all directions to perform the Never-Disparaging austerity to teach that all people may attain Buddhahood."[4]

Kaoru wept bitterly as the ascetic spoke. The older Princess, who was already troubled, realized that she had committed a grave sin by hindering her father's salvation and wanted more than ever to just disappear completely. As she lay there listening to the ascetic, she thought, *Somehow I want to find Father's spirit while his destination is still unsettled and go together with him to the same place.*

The ascetic withdrew without saying much more. The priests who had been sent off a few days earlier to perform the Never-Disparaging austerity had gone to villages in the vicinity and even as far as the capital, but after laboring through rough winds at dawn, they sought out the place where the ascetic had summoned them. Kneeling at the center gate, they continued the reading of the *Lotus Sutra* in a most venerable manner. The final lines of the scripture, with their invocation to do good deeds for all sentient beings who are destined to become Buddhas, were especially moving. Kaoru, whose heart had long been drawn toward the path of enlightenment, found the scene unbearably affecting. The rustling of silk told him that the younger Princess, nervous and fretful about her sister's condition, had moved tentatively behind the standing curtain at the back of the room. He straightened himself up and assumed a more formal posture.

"How do those abject voices that never disparage sound to you?" Kaoru asked. "They may not have carried out an abject practice, but their humility is noble and awe-inspiring."

> *Plovers cry mournfully at the water's edge*
> *Amidst an icy frost glinting bright and clear*
> *How desolate a sound in predawn twilight*

He did not intone his verse, but spoke it as if he were simply conversing with her.

Something in his manner reminded the younger Princess of her cruel lover, prompting her to compare the two men in her mind. However, she found it difficult to reply directly to Kaoru, and so she gave her reply to Bennokimi to pass to him:

> *Plovers calling out in the early dawn*
> *As they brush away the frost from their wings*
> *Do they understand my sad, pensive heart*

---

4. This extreme religious austerity is called *jōfukyō* (literally, "never treat lightly"). Jōfukyō is the Japanese name of the bodhisattva Sadāparibhūta, who appears in the *Lotus Sutra*. Sadāparibhūta was the name of Sakyamuni in one of his previous lifetimes as a bodhisattva. He recognized the truth that all living beings could attain Buddhahood, and so he practiced humility before all he met (and suffered persecution as a result), saying that he could never disparage them because they possess the Buddha nature. Priests sent out on this austerity would go out and abject themselves before those they met, regardless of the person's status, as a way to teach this truth.

The old attendant was hardly an appropriate stand-in for her mistress, but she conveyed the poem with stylish grace. A trivial exchange, to be sure, but her response was warm and sensitive, even if she was retiring by nature. It disturbed him to wonder how he would feel if he had to be separated from her following the death of her sister.

Kaoru contemplated Prince Hachinomiya's appearance in the ascetic's dream, and after imagining what the troubled figures of the princesses must look like from their father's vantage on high, he commissioned sutra readings at the mountain temple above where Hachinomiya used to go into retreat. He also dispatched messengers to various temples here and there with requests for prayers and sent letters requesting leave from all of his public and private affairs. No rite of purification, prayer ceremony, or exorcism was overlooked in his effort to heal the Princess. Nonetheless, because her illness was not the result of some sinful behavior, nothing seemed to work.

If the Princess herself prayed to the Buddha for her recovery, she might have improved, but her thoughts were on different matters. *I must take this infirmity as my opportunity to die. He has now attended to me so closely—seen my face, touched me—that there is no longer any distance between us; now I have no excuse to treat him as anything other than my husband. Of course, even if he were to take me as his wife, the ardor that has driven him to treat me with such kindness would surely cool over time as we both grew familiar with one another, and I would be left in the end with nothing but uncertainty and heartache. No . . . if it turns out that I'm forced to live on, then I will use my illness as a pretext to take vows and become a nun. That is the only way to ensure that we stay together to the end, that our hearts remain as one forever.*

She was convinced that she must fulfill her wish one way or another, but she couldn't bring up the matter in such detail that others would catch on to her plans. Thus, she said to her sister, "I feel that my condition is more and more hopeless, but I've heard that taking vows to uphold the Precepts is very effective for healing and may extend my life. Would you please speak to the ascetic? He is a master of esoteric rites."

Her attendants wept and objected vociferously. "It's unthinkable," they told her. "The Middle Counselor is at his wits' end, frantic over your illness. He would be devastated if you did such a thing!" To the Princess's chagrin, they all found the idea outrageous and would not even mention it to the man they relied on for support.

Because Kaoru had withdrawn from the court and gone into seclusion like this, word spread and gentlemen soon arrived from the court to inquire after him. Seeing how concerned he was over the princess's illness, his retainers and those members of his staff who were close to him grieved for their lord, each offering prayers for her recovery.

When he realized that today was *Toyo no Akari*—"the Feast of the Glowing Harvest"—Kaoru's thoughts turned toward the capital. The winds at Uji were frightful, and the snow swirled about madly. The weather in the capital wouldn't be like this at all, and yet, while he himself had chosen to stay here to be with his beloved, his loneliness was unbearable. He gazed outside, lost in wistful thoughts. *Is she destined to die while the two of us remain strangers, never consummating our relationship? It's hard for me to accept such a fate, but I will not give voice to any bitterness. If only she could recover a little, display once more her sweet and gentle disposition even for a brief time, I would share with her all my thoughts and feelings!*

Evening fell at last on a gloomy, sunless day. He whispered the following to himself:

> *Deep in the mountains, beneath cloudy skies*
> *I see no sunlight, no festive headbands*
> *A season indeed to darken my heart*[5]

The attendants were all encouraged that the Middle Counselor remained with them like this. He was seated as always near her pillow; when the rough winds caused the standing curtains to flutter, the younger Princess withdrew to a room in the interior to avoid being seen. Her unsightly old attendants followed after, their faces flushed in embarrassment as they too scurried to hide themselves. As they did so, Kaoru moved closer and spoke tearfully to his beloved. "How are you feeling? I have prayed for you with all my heart and soul, but none of it seems to be doing any good. It makes me feel desolate, not having heard even a word from you . . . I shall suffer terribly if you leave me behind."

Although the Princess was slipping in and out of consciousness, she still made sure that she kept her face hidden. "If I were feeling a little better, there is much I would like to tell you, but I regret for your sake that I must soon pass on."

Her demeanor told of the deep compassion that she felt for him, and he found it harder than ever to hold back his tears. He was reluctant to show any signs of sorrow, knowing that would be inauspicious, but he began sobbing anyway.

He kept watch over her, reflecting on their relationship. *What sort of bond did we share in a previous life? Despite my boundless love, I must be parted from her having tasted only a surfeit of bitter hardships. If she would reveal at least some small imperfection in herself, it might help temper the longings I will feel for her after she's gone.* To his eyes, she seemed more precious than ever, radiant and lovely. Her arms were terribly thin, her body wraithlike, but her complexion was still lustrous, pale, and graceful. In her soft white robes, with her bedcovers pushed to the side, she gave the impression of a court doll, hollow inside its robes, lying asleep. Her hair, which was not excessively thick or long, had been laid out just as it was. It spilled down over her pillow in shimmering undulations that had a delightfully charming air.

What will become of her in the end? Is there no possibility that she may live on? Must her beauty pass from the world? He would never again experience such profound regrets. She had been ill for so long and had not been properly groomed or dressed all that time, yet her looks were still far superior even to a woman who endlessly fusses over herself and remains unapproachable, lest someone see her unprepared. As he studied his beloved's face, he could not calm his fear that her spirit would soon slip away.

"If you should abandon me after all," he said, "I doubt that I will survive much longer myself. And if by chance I should live on for many years, I shall withdraw from the world and go off somewhere deep in the mountains. The one thing that might hold me back are the hardships your sister would face on her own." He was hoping to get some sort of response by mentioning her sister.

---

5. The poem plays on the word *hikage*, meaning "sunlight" and "headband" (referring to the headband worn by Gosechi dancers at the Feast of the Glowing Harvest).

The Princess pulled her sleeves away from her face a little.

"I always knew that my life would be brief, and so I could not accept your proposal. I don't want to die and leave you with memories of me as willful and unkind, but there was nothing else I could do. That's why I suggested that you think of the sister I leave behind in the same way you think of me. If you had not defied my wishes, I might have been at peace now . . . it is the one lingering regret that may yet keep me attached to this world and hinder my salvation."

"Am I fated to suffer the extremes of sorrow? I am by nature different from others . . . I was never attracted to worldly affairs of any kind. You're the only one that I have ever loved, so I simply could not do as you requested and take your sister instead. I regret that now and feel bad for you, but you need not worry about her."

Kaoru did his best to comfort and reassure her, but when her suffering seemed to grow more intense, he summoned the ascetic and other venerable priests and had them use all of their powers to perform healing rites and prayers. He himself offered heartfelt prayers to the Buddha.

Is it to encourage the rejection of this world that the gods and Buddha expressly allow so much grief and anguish in it? As he sat there gazing at her, she vanished before his eyes, fading like withering grasses in winter. He was mad with grief, frantically stamping his feet in frustration at not being able to call her back, oblivious to how others might view his behavior.

When the younger Princess realized that the end had come, she too was stunned and distraught at being left behind. Her attendants, who as usual were acting wise and in control, could see that their mistress was not in her right mind and escorted her out of the room, saying that it would bring bad luck if she were to remain near a defiling corpse.

This simply can't be happening, Kaoru told himself. *It must be a dream.* He brought the lamp closer to her face, which was still partly hidden by her sleeves. She looked as if she were asleep: nothing about her had changed, and she was lying there as beautiful as in life. He thought wistfully, *If only I could go on like this, looking upon her as I would the empty shell of a cicada!*[6]

In order to prepare the body for the funeral rites, her women combed and arranged her hair; the air around them was suffused with the warm, rich perfume that had always scented her hair when she was alive. Kaoru prayed to the Buddha. *She was a superior woman, unrivaled in this world. Is there nothing ordinary about her that would make it easier for me to accept her death . . . some small flaw at least? If you really are the guide who will show me how to renounce this world, then let me see something other than her beauty—something fearful and offputting about her corpse that will lessen my regrets and assuage my grief.*

His prayer served no purpose, however, for his yearning only grew more intense the more he gazed at her. Knowing that soon her body would have to be consigned to the flames, he set about making the proper arrangements for the services—but it was all much too much for him. He felt unsteady, drifting along as though he was walking through the air. When the last feeble-looking

---

6. Poem by Bishop Shōen from *The Kokinshū* composed after the burial of the Horikawa chancellor, Fujiwara no Mototsune, at Mount Fukakusa: "One finds comfort in gazing on the body, an empty shell of a cicada . . . send up at least a plume of smoke, Mount Fukakusa!"

traces of the pyre disappeared, so few plumes of smoke had risen to the sky that he was left feeling defeated and hopeless. He returned to the villa in a daze.

Many attendants secluded themselves at the villa for the period of confinement and mourning. Though their presence helped to relieve the loneliness a little, the younger Princess was so depressed and ashamed at how others viewed her that she herself did not seem to be among the living any more. Niou sent one message after another, but the Princess could not forget that her sister had died never wavering in her attitude that his neglect was unforgivably cruel. It was her woeful lot to be married to such an awful man.

Kaoru now found the world thoroughly wearisome, but though he was inclined finally to fulfill his most cherished wish and follow the path of the Buddha, he couldn't bring himself to take that step just yet. For one thing, he had his mother, the Third Princess, to consider. For another, he was troubled by the heartrending circumstances of the Princess at Uji. He mulled over the situation. *I should have done as the late Princess requested . . . I should have taken her sister as my wife and looked on her as a memento. But at the time she asked, I felt in my heart that I could never shift my affections, even though my beloved insisted that her heart was one with her sister's. Had I known that I would cause the younger Princess such misery by bringing Niou here, I would have married her instead. Had I done that, I might have found in my visits here some consolation for my unrequited love.*

He didn't go back to the capital for even a brief visit. Because he had thoroughly cut himself off and remained inconsolable in his seclusion, people at the court concluded that his affection for the late Princess had been anything but ordinary, and everyone, from the palace on down, sent letters expressing their condolences.

Empty days passed by. Kaoru arranged for the memorial services held every seven days, and he made sure they were each conducted in a most solemn and dignified manner. He showed extraordinary devotion to her memory, but since they had not been married, there were limits on what he could do. Forbidden by custom to change the color of his clothing, he would steal mournful glances at the black robes worn by those women who had been closest to their late mistress.

> It is useless for one not permitted to mourn
> To shed these blood-red tears, for they can never dye
> My crimson cloak gray in memory of my love

Kaoru cut a youthful, dashingly handsome figure as he gazed out lost in reverie, soaking his sleeves with his endless tears; the light crimson cloak he was permitted to wear seemed to glisten like melting ice. The attendants, peeking in to observe him, were all in tears.

"What's done is done, and I suppose it's useless now to lament the loss of our mistress . . . but it's truly regrettable that the Middle Counselor, who has been so close to this household over the years, will soon become an outsider to us all."

"What a strange, unexpected destiny has befallen him!"

"That a man as deeply thoughtful and kind as he should have been rejected by both of our ladies . . ."

Kaoru spoke to the younger Princess. "I think of you as a memento of the past, and from now on I hope that we might be able to speak freely with one another and that I may still call on you and be of service. Do not be aloof and treat me as a stranger."

The Princess, however, was still overwhelmed by her misfortunes and was too shy to meet or talk with him. She had always struck him as a little innocent and child-like, more open and noble compared to her sister, and yet to him she lacked the gentle warmth and beauty of spirit of the woman who had so touched his heart.

One day, when the skies were darkened by heavy snowfall, Kaoru passed the time from morning until evening staring blankly outside. That night the clouds cleared away, and the moon of the twelfth month—the moon that people always invoke as a symbol of chill desolation—shone clear and bright. He rolled up the blinds on the veranda to look up at it. The distant sound of the bell at the mountain temple echoed from high above, and as he strained to listen at his pillow, he heard it tolling out the close of day.[7]

> Not wishing to be left behind, to linger on
> I would follow the moon in its course . . . for this world
> Is not a realm I shall reside in forever

A stronger wind began to blow. When Kaoru got up to lower the shutters again, he glanced out into the garden. The ice at the water's edge, which was reflecting the image of the snow-covered mountains all around, sparkled brilliantly in the light of the moon. He could refurbish his villa on Sanjō in the capital all he liked, but nothing he could add to it would ever equal the scene before him.

If only she could come back to me, even for a moment, he thought, *I would talk with her about this sublime beauty!* His obsessive longing was simply too much to keep inside his breast.

> In my anguish over the loss of my beloved
> I long to vanish into the Snowy Mountains
> Leaving no trace while seeking the potion of death

If only there were some demon to teach me the second part of that verse of scripture, then I might well have an excuse to toss myself from some great height like that youth in the Snowy Mountains.[8] For someone who supposedly aspired to enlightenment in this way, his motivations were certainly less than pure.

7. Poem 978 from *Collected Writings of Bo Juyi:* "Straining to listen at my pillow, I hear the sound of the temple bell. I roll up the blinds and look out at the snow on the peaks." Anonymous poem from *The Shūishū:* "In grief and sorrow I listen to the sound of the temple bell as it tolls out the close of day."
8. In his poem and in this statement, Kaoru alludes to the story of Sessen Dōji (Youth of the Snow Mountains) that appears in the *Mahāparinirvāna Sutra* (the Nirvana sutra). Sessen Dōji, who was Sakyamuni in a previous life, is a young man seeking enlightenment by practicing austerities in the Himalaya Mountains (the Snowy Mountains). The deity Śakra (Indra) decides to test the young man and approaches him disguised as a demon. He gives Sessen Dōji the first half of a Buddhist verse ("All is fleeting, nothing is constant/this is the law of birth and death") and offers the second half in exchange for his flesh and blood. The young man agrees, carves the verse into the stone wall of the cave that serves as his hermitage, then throws himself from a high place to fulfill the bargain. At that moment, Śakra changes back to his real form and saves Sessen Dōji.

Kaoru would summon the attendants and speak with them. At such times, he struck them as a paragon of noble virtue, gentle and deeply thoughtful. The younger ladies-in-waiting were completely smitten and thought him magnificent. The older women could only look at him and regret all the more what might have been.

"Our late mistress realized that Prince Niou was not trustworthy, and she was distressed at the prospect of being ridiculed. That's what made her ill."

"Yes, but she didn't want to let our young mistress know how worried she was, and so she kept her bitterness locked inside her heart and refused to eat anything—not even the smallest piece of fruit. She just grew weaker and weaker."

"On the surface she never gave any indication that she was deeply concerned about such things, but deep down she must have brooded endlessly over their situation."

"Her suffering began when all her hopes for her sister's future went awry and she realized that she had failed to live up to her father's admonition."

They went on sharing stories, relating what the late Princess had said on this or that occasion. With each anecdote, they invariably ended up breaking down and weeping.

Kaoru blamed his own folly for these tragedies and wanted to go back to the past and redo it. The world was unbearably trying to him, and he would spend sleepless nights immersing himself in prayer and meditation until dawn. Late one night as a heavy snow was falling, the shouts of men and the neighing of horses broke in on the freezing darkness. The venerable priests who had been commissioned for evening services were startled. Just as they were wondering what sort of men could have made their way here through the snow in the dead of night, Niou arrived, disguised in hunting robes and thoroughly soaked through. Kaoru knew by the impetuous rapping at the gate that it was the Prince, and so he withdrew and hid in a private space in the interior of the villa. The period of mourning and confinement had not yet passed, but Niou had been so fretful and impatient to see his Uji Princess that he had traveled all night long to get to her, struggling to make his way through the blizzard.

* * *

From Chapter XLIX

Yadoriki

TREES ENCOILED IN VINES OF IVY

* * *

The Uji Princess had never forgotten that peculiar night they spent together; having observed the workings of Kaoru's sincere, sensitive character—so unlike other men—did she wistfully imagine what might have been? A woman her age was no longer an inexperienced young girl, and when she compared the Middle Counselor to the man who had given her cause for resentment, she realized that Kaoru was far superior in all respects. Was that why, on this particular night, she took pity on him for having always kept her distance and, perhaps worried that she might come across as cold and inconsiderate, allowed him to be seated in the aisle room inside the veranda blinds? A standing curtain was set up inside the blinds of the main chambers, and she received him after withdrawing to the interior of the room.

"Although I did not receive an explicit invitation, I'm very happy to have been granted this rare permission to call on you," Kaoru began. "I wanted to come right away, but then I learned that the Prince might be returning and worried that it might prove awkward if I were here. So I decided to come today instead. Is it possible that, after all these years, you're showing some inclination to at last reward my earnest devotion to you? You've taken the remarkable step of relaxing your guard a little and allowing me inside your blinds."

The Princess still seem reserved toward him and had difficulty finding words to express what she wanted to say, but she finally replied with an air of modesty:

"It made me glad to hear about the memorial services the other day, and I would have regretted it if, as I always do, I simply kept my feelings to myself and let the occasion pass without somehow letting you know how much I appreciate all you've done." Because she had withdrawn so far back in her room, he could only catch faint snatches of her soft voice.

Feeling impatient and dissatisfied, he said, "You sound so distant. I should like permission to speak seriously with you about a certain worldly matter."

She thought his request reasonable, and his heart suddenly raced again at the sound of her moving closer toward him. He nonetheless exerted great self-control and maintained a nonchalant attitude. His manner of speech made it clear that he considered Niou's behavior inconsiderate. He criticized Niou and offered her words of comfort, talking to her soothingly on all sorts of subjects.

The Uji Princess could not openly voice her discontent with her marriage. Instead, she hinted indirectly, with few words, that she did not blame her misfortune on Niou so much as on her own karmic destiny.[9] She also expressed her heartfelt desire to go to the Uji villa for a brief visit.

"I'm afraid I can't decide on my own to help you," Kaoru replied. "It would be best to approach Prince Niou honestly and modestly with your request, and then do as he wishes. If you don't do that, he might misinterpret your motives a little, and it would be most unfortunate if he were then to consider you frivolous and untrustworthy. Once it's clear to him that he has nothing to be concerned about, then nothing will prevent me from accompanying you to Uji, and I will do all I can to be of service. The Prince knows full well that I am not like other men and that he can trust me completely."

While he was speaking with her, however, Kaoru did not for a moment forget his regrets, and he mentioned that he would like to go back to the past: "If only I could do it all over again."

It was growing dark, and the Princess was troubled that Kaoru showed no inclination to leave. "I'm not feeling all that well," she told him, "and so perhaps we might talk again some other time when I'm better."

He could tell from her movements that she was preparing to withdraw; because he desperately wanted her to stay, he said, as if to mollify her, "So tell me,

9. The source of this line has not been definitively identified, but a later commentary cites the following poem: "Is my misfortune due to my woeful destiny or to his cruelty? I recall the little shrimp that live amid the seaweed the fishermen harvest and know it is my own fault." The poem plays on the word *warekara*, which may be read as the name of a species of shrimp or as a phrase meaning "I'm to blame."

then . . . when were you thinking of going to Uji? The paths must be terribly overgrown, and I shall have to have them cleared before then."

She stopped and paused for a moment. "This month will soon be over, so I was thinking perhaps the first of next month. But still, it seems best to keep the trip secret. If I were to ask Prince Niou for permission, it might lead to all sorts of troublesome complications."

Her voice was sweet and soft—so like her older sister's! He was assailed by memories and longings and could no longer restrain himself. He quietly stretched his arm through the blinds hanging next to the pillar he was leaning against and gently took hold of her sleeves.

Was this his intention all along? Ahh . . . how horrid he is! Not knowing what to say, she did not reply. Instead, she tried to move further back into the interior of the room. When she did so, he slipped further through the blinds—as if he had the run of the place!—and lay down beside her. "You have me all wrong, do you not?" he complained. "I was delighted when you said that you thought it best to travel to Uji secretly, and I entered because I wanted to ask if perhaps I hadn't misheard you. How unpleasant you are! You have no reason to be so cold and aloof."

She did not feel up to replying to him. Shocked by his behavior, she now detested him, though she remained sufficiently in control of her emotions to admonish his actions: "I never expected this sort of thing from you. What will my attendants think? Your behavior is atrocious!"

She was on the verge of tears—and with just cause. But though he felt sorry for her, he continued to plead his case: "Am I so outrageous that people would censure me? Meeting you face to face like this brings back memories of that night we spent together. A meeting your late sister approved, I might add. You think me shocking and atrocious, but your reaction is deeply offensive to me. You may rest assured that my intentions are in no way lascivious." He was very calm and gentle, but he talked on and on, telling her how keenly he felt the pain caused by the feelings of remorse he had kept inside himself for so many months.

She did not know what to do, since there was no indication that he was going to let go of her sleeves. It is difficult for me to convey just how frightened and disturbed she was. She felt more awkward and disgusted with him than she would have with a man who was a total stranger. When, at last, she began to cry, Kaoru said, "Why are you carrying on so? You're being childish, you know." She was adorable beyond words, and he felt bad for her, but at the same time her demeanor was so deeply thoughtful and prudent that it made him feel ashamed. He could see that she was even more mature and lovely than in the old days at Uji.

The yearnings that unsettle my heart this way are all the result of having given her up of my own volition to another man. Overwhelmed by self-reproach, he broke down in tears, sobbing.

Only two ladies-in-waiting were in close attendance that evening. Still, they would have been vigilant and would have been suspicious had a man with no relationship to the Princess—and thus no reason to be there—entered the main chamber. They would have drawn nearer, wondering what was happening. The Middle Counselor, however, had been a confidant of their mistress for a long time, and if he was on familiar-enough terms to be allowed to speak directly and intimately with her, then the situation seemed perfectly acceptable. Indeed, given the circumstances at that moment, they felt uncomfortable being so near and pretended not to notice anything. They quietly withdrew, which made the

Princess feel even more wretched. As for Kaoru, he was finding it extremely difficult to suppress the overpowering regrets he harbored for all that had happened in the past. Nonetheless, his matchless prudence, a virtue he had possessed since his youth, kept his passions in check, and he did not do as he wished with the Uji Princess. It wouldn't do to describe this scene in any greater detail. For Kaoru, the visit had proven completely pointless; because he was reluctant to be seen by others he withdrew, reflecting remorsefully on all he had done.

Kaoru had been under the impression that it was still early evening, but in fact dawn was approaching. He grew anxious that censorious eyes might see him leaving at this hour, worried not for his own reputation, but for that of the Uji Princess. *I'd heard rumors of late that she hasn't been feeling well, and now I understand why. She was extremely embarrassed that I saw her pregnancy belt,*[1] *and her reaction made me feel so bad that I did not take her. What a fool I am . . . as usual.*

Other thoughts, however, tempered these reflections. *And yet I never intended to do anything cruel. If, in a moment of weakness, I had given in to my baser instincts and forced myself on her, I'd never be able to feel at ease meeting her after that. Even if we carried on an affair, it would take tremendous effort on my part to arrange our secret trysts, and that would cause her to suffer the torment of constant dread.*

Despite these seemingly wise rationalizations, he could not completely repress his desires, and his unbeatable yearnings for her in the present moment[2] left him feeling utterly helpless. Come what may, he had to see her again, and yet his was a desire that would never be truly sated. He could not get the image of her out of his mind—the elegantly refined, enchanting figure that was even more willowy than in the old days at Uji. As a result, he had the sensation that she was always with him, and he could think of nothing else.

She very much wants to go back to Uji, and I would like to escort her there, but Niou would never permit such a thing. And if we went in secret against his wishes, it might well end in calamity. Is there any way I can get what I want without destroying our reputations? He lay there staring out blankly, lost in these pensive thoughts.

His letter to the Uji Princess arrived early in the morning in the predawn darkness. Just like his previous letters, it was folded so as to resemble a formal missive rather than a love note.

> *All for naught did I travel o'er*
> *That dew-drenched path, the autumn sky*
> *Stirring memories of the past*

"Not understanding the reasons for your cruelty only makes it all the more intolerable. There are no words to describe how I feel."

Since she always replied to his letters, her women would surely take notice and think something amiss if she did not do so this time. However, it was too arduous a task for her to write a letter, and so she simply scribbled a note: "I received your letter. I am much too ill right now and cannot reply." When Kaoru read it, he was let down by its brevity. He longingly recalled her alluring air.

---

1. This belt was a kind of sash (*obi*) worn low on the belly to provide support during pregnancy.
2. Anonymous poem from *The Gosenshū*: "How

must they have been, those times before ever we met? For when I cannot see you in the present moment, I yearn for you."

Now a little wiser in the ways of men and women, the Uji Princess did not consider Kaoru's behavior entirely shocking or despicable. For his part, when he recalled her demeanor at the moment she saw him off—her gentle kindness and humility, her complete lack of coldness, the warm familiarity with which she spoke—envy and sadness assailed his heart and he was disconsolate, tormented by conflicting emotions. He thought her far superior in every way from the young woman she was when he first saw her at Uji.

If, for some reason, Niou should ever be estranged from her, he fantasized, *I would likely be the only person she could turn to for support. Yet even if that happened, it would not be easy for me to visit her openly. Instead, I would have to meet her in secret, and she would be my haven, the lasting object of my heart's desire, the woman I would love above all others.*

How truly despicable that his heart should have been so fixated on her! Men may exude an air of kindness and sagacity, but they are cruelly fickle. Kaoru was sure that the sorrow over his lost love could never be assuaged, and yet here he was, suffering much worse over his love for her younger sister. Her attractiveness was all he could think about; when he heard someone mention that Niou would be returning to the Nijō villa that day, all his altruistic impulses to act as her support disappeared as his chest burned with jealous rancor.

* * *

From Chapter LIII

Tenarai

PRACTICING CALLIGRAPHY

In those days, there was an exceptionally pious priest residing at Yokawa on Mount Hiei[3]—a certain bishop whose name slips my mind. He had a mother who was over eighty years old and a younger sister who was in her fifties. Both of these women had become nuns, and together they undertook a pilgrimage to Hatsuse in fulfillment of a long-standing vow they had made to Kannon. Their traveling party included one of the bishop's closest and most highly regarded disciples, an ascetic who accompanied them in order to perform the dedication of sutras and images of the Buddha.

After completing numerous acts of devotion, they started for home. Unfortunately, just as they were crossing the hills on the slope of Narasaka, the mother fell ill. Her condition caused tremendous apprehension among the attendants, who worried that their mistress might not be able to complete her pilgrimage. Thinking it best to rest for a day, the party stopped in the vicinity of Uji at the house of an acquaintance of the bishop. But then the old woman took a turn for the worse, and a messenger was immediately dispatched to Yokawa.

His Holiness had made a firm vow to remain in retreat for the year and not leave Mount Hiei. Nonetheless, he rushed to his aged mother's side, disturbed

---

3. Yokawa, along with Tōdō (east pagoda) and Saitō (west pagoda), was one of three extensive compounds that comprised the important and influential monastic center of Enryakuji. Part of this temple's prestige derived from geomantic practices. Mount Hiei is located northeast of Kyoto. Northeast was considered a permanently unlucky direction, and it was thus believed that a holy site like Enryakuji protected the capital from evil influences.

by the possibility that she might die on the road. Although his mother had lived such a long life that there would have been no need to feel any special regret about her passing, the bishop himself, along with his most efficacious disciples, raised a tremendous clamor as they performed healing rites.

The master of the house where they were lodging listened to this uproar with a worried expression: *What effect will the defiling presence of an ill, very old woman have as I purify myself in preparation for a pilgrimage to Mitake? What if she should die here?*

Upon hearing these concerns, the bishop recognized that his host had good reason to be anxious, and he felt sorry for being such an imposition. Moreover, the house was quite small and inconvenient. For these reasons, he decided that he would move his mother little by little whenever she felt well enough to travel. His plan, however, was thwarted when he learned that the direction to his mother's house was prohibited to them, blocked by the presence of the Middle Deity. He then remembered that an old imperial villa formerly used by the late Emperor Suzaku was nearby, just north of the Uji River.[4] Since His Holiness knew the steward who oversaw that estate, he sent a note requesting permission to stay there for a day or two.

"The steward and all the members of his household left yesterday on a pilgrimage to Hatsuse," reported the messenger, who had brought back with him the caretaker of the villa, an eccentric, ragged-looking old man.

"Yes, that's right," the caretaker affirmed. "The main hall is empty at the moment, so you must come right away before anyone else arrives. You see, pilgrims are always stopping by to lodge there."

"That sounds perfect," the bishop replied. "I know it's an imperial residence, but if no one is using it right now, we'll be able to rest at our leisure."

His Holiness sent some members of the party to inspect the site. The old caretaker was accustomed to looking after people who needed lodging, since visitors arrived regularly, and so he had already arranged to have plain and simple furnishings set out for the guests. The bishop then made his way over to the villa ahead of his mother and sister. The place had fallen into disrepair, and when His Holiness observed its frighteningly eerie atmosphere, he ordered his most saintly disciples to begin chanting sutras. The ascetic and one other disciple—a priest of equal rank and eminence—expressed their concern that something uncanny might happen in such a setting. Both men had experience with situations like this, and so they ordered the lighting of torches, a task they assigned to some lower-ranking monks whose burly appearance made them the appropriate choice for driving off lingering spirits.

The monks took up their torches and immediately set off to inspect the grounds behind the main hall, a neglected spot that people rarely approached. Warily peering into an eerie stand of trees that resembled a sacred grove at a shrine, they spotted something white amidst the undergrowth.

"What could that be?" The party froze in its tracks. Raising their torches higher, the men could make out the seated figure of a young lady.

"It must be a fox spirit in human form. Abhorrent creature! I'll make it show its true shape," one of the monks said, taking a few steps closer to the figure.

---

4. This may be a reference to the real-life Emperor Suzaku (923–952), who used a villa near Uji as a retreat from the capital. However, since the association of fictional characters with real-life figures is a recurring feature of Murasaki Shikibu's narrative technique, it may be that the author is simply introducing new information about her character, Suzaku.

"Don't be rash! It could be a malevolent spirit," warned another who, just to be safe, was keeping his eyes fixed on the strange apparition and displaying the mudra[5] used to ward off evil. Had there been any hair on his head, he felt sure it would have been standing on end.

The fearless monk was undeterred, however, and moved closer to the strange figure to get a better look. It was a young lady with long, lustrous hair leaning against the thick gnarly roots of a tree. She was weeping most piteously.

"This is passing strange," he said. "I should like for His Holiness to have a look."

"Yes, indeed . . . exceedingly weird," replied one of his companions, who hurried off to inform the bishop of the unearthly discovery.

"I have long heard of fox spirits taking on human form, but I've never witnessed such a thing personally." So saying, the bishop left the main hall with the express intent of investigating the matter himself.

The bishop's mother and sister were now on their way to the villa, and the menial servants were busy tending to their responsibilities in the kitchen and living quarters as they hastened to make preparations for the arrival of their guests. As a result, the area behind the main hall remained deserted except for the four or five monks who were keeping an eye on the strange creature. They observed no change in its condition. Hours passed as they watched in doubtful wonder.

It will soon be dawn, and finally we shall see if it's human or something else. With that thought in mind, they recited the proper incantations in their hearts and formed the correct mudras. While they were doing so, the true nature of the creature became evident to the bishop.

"It's not a fox spirit, it's a young woman. She's human. Approach her and find out her name. She's obviously not dead. Probably someone left her body here thinking she had passed away, and she revived after they left. That must be what happened here, wouldn't you agree?"

"Why would anyone abandon a woman like this at an imperial villa?" one of the monks asked.

"Even if she *is* human, maybe she was bewitched by a fox spirit or wood sprite and tricked into following it here," suggested another.

"Either way, this is most unfortunate. Her presence defiles this place, and your mother is just about to arrive."

The monks shouted for the caretaker. The echoing of their voices was eerily disturbing.

The disheveled old man emerged from the main hall, pushing the unkempt hair on his forehead back up under his cap.

"Does a young woman live close by? Look at what we've found," one of the monks said, pointing to the young lady.

"Must be the work of a fox," the caretaker replied. "Queer things happen from time to time in this grove. Why, just the year before last, in the autumn, a fox took a little child who lives on the estate . . . barely two years old, mind you . . . and left him in these woods. Nothing to be shocked about, really."

"Did the child die?"

"No, no, he's fine. Foxes like to alarm folks, but they don't do any real harm." The caretaker seemed utterly nonchalant about the matter, as if being bewitched

5. Mudras were an important practice in Shingon Buddhism. Shingon esoteric practices during the Heian period were influential and had an impact on other Buddhist sects, including the Tendai Monastery at Enryakuji on Mount Hiei.

by a fox spirit was the most natural thing in the world. Apparently, he was more preoccupied with preparing food for all the visitors who had arrived in the middle of the night.

"In that case," the bishop said, "we'd better check again to see if that's what befell this young lady."

The fearless monk who had confronted the apparition earlier approached once again and began tugging on one of the sleeves of the young lady's robes.

"Be you demon or deity, be you fox or woodland sprite, you cannot hope to conceal your identity in the presence of these most eminent priests. Announce yourself! Tell us your name!"

The woman buried her face in her sleeves and wept all the harder.

"Come now, insolent sprite or demon! Do you really think you can keep your true shape hidden?"

Though he was determined to get a better look at her face, the monk was steeling himself just in case this was one of those female demons with no eyes or nose that he had read about in ancient tales. Still, he felt that he had to put on a brave front with the bishop watching him, and so he tried to pull the woman's sleeves back. Whereupon she threw herself facedown, sobbing loudly.

The intrepid monk remained convinced that anything so unusual and suspicious could not be a creature of this world and that it would be best for them to continue observing it to see if any transformation took place. However, the weather was changing and there was no time for that. "A heavy storm is coming," he said. "If we leave the creature here like this, it will surely die and defile the residence. We should drive it away, outside the enclosure."

"She's obviously human," the bishop reassured him, "and it would be cruel to knowingly abandon her while she's alive. After all, it's natural for us to feel bad if we do nothing to help the fish that swim in the lakes or the deer that cry in the mountains when such creatures have been caught and are about to die. Human life is all too fleeting as it is, and so even if this young lady is destined to survive only a day or two more, we shouldn't begrudge her the time she has left. Perhaps a god or a demon possessed her, or maybe she was driven from her home, or deceived by someone plotting against her. Whatever the case, even if it seems that she's fated to die in this strange, pathetic manner, the Buddha would certainly show mercy to one in her situation. It is our duty to do no less. At the very least, we must try to help her. Give her medicinal infusions for a while. If she passes away after that, then I suppose there's not much more we could have done for her."

The bishop ordered the ascetic to pick up the young lady and carry her inside the villa. Some of the monks objected: "But Your Holiness . . . that's out of the question. To take a foul creature like this inside the villa will surely have a baleful effect on your mother, who's suffering enough as it is."

Others showed greater sympathy: "But if she *has* been bewitched by a shapeshifter, then it would be a grave sin to leave a living being out in this rain and allow her to pass away before our very eyes."

The menials would have raised a tremendous fuss and said all sorts of crude things had the monks brought the young lady into the main hall, and so they laid her down in an inconspicuous corner where people wouldn't be bustling in and out.

The carriages bearing the bishop's mother and his sister arrived at the villa. As soon as the women alighted, a clamor arose when, to everyone's alarm, it was discovered that the mother was feeling worse as a result of the strain of the journey. Only after things had settled down did the bishop turn his attention once more to the young lady.

"How's she doing?"

"Lethargic and unresponsive," one of the monks reported. "She doesn't even seem to be breathing at times. It's as if she's been possessed by a malevolent spirit and is no longer aware of herself or her surroundings."

"What are you two talking about?" asked the bishop's sister, who had overheard their conversation.

"I've witnessed many strange occurrences in my lifetime," the bishop answered, "but in all my sixty-plus years, this has to be one of the most unusual I've ever encountered."

Tears came to the nun's eyes as she listened to her brother explain what had happened.

"When we were staying at the temple in Hatsuse," she said, "I had a dream about a young lady. Could you describe this woman to me? May I see her?"

"By all means, go to her at once," the bishop replied. "She's resting just beyond the sliding doors on the east side."

The nun hurried over and peeked into the room. There wasn't a servant in sight. A woman was lying there, alone and abandoned. She seemed very young, but exuded an air of refined beauty. Dressed in crimson trousers over a singlet of white damask that was suffused with an ethereal scent, her appearance gave the impression of boundless grace and nobility.

"Why . . . she's the very image of my late lamented daughter," the nun gasped. Unable to stop her tears, she summoned her attendants and had them pick up the young lady and carry her to chambers further inside the villa. Of course, the attendants could not tell just by looking what tribulations this woman had endured, and so they carried out the nun's orders without fear or hesitation.

The young lady appeared to be lifeless, but then she opened her eyes ever so slightly.

"Say something," the nun implored. "Tell me who you are and how you ended up like this."

The young lady was silent. It seemed as though the nun's words were incomprehensible to her.

The nun picked up a cup containing a medicinal infusion and, with her own hands, tried to get the patient to drink. The lady, however, did not have the strength to take the medicine and seemed to be on the verge of breathing her last.

At that moment the nun turned in desperation to the saintly ascetic. "This infusion is no use. Her condition is worse than ever. She's going to die if we don't do something. Please, please perform a healing rite for her!"

"This is exactly what I was worried about," the ascetic replied. "I advised His Holiness against getting involved with such a strange and hopeless case." Despite these misgivings, the ascetic began chanting the *Heart Sutra* in order to appease the local deities before he commenced with the healing rites.[6]

6. The *Heart Sutra* is a central scripture of Mahāyāna Buddhism. The syncretic nature of religious belief at the time meant that even Buddhist priests had to be respectful of Shinto practices. The desire to maintain a proper balance between different religious systems is depicted at several points in the narrative.

The bishop stuck his head in and asked again, "How is she doing? Try to find out what sort of spirit is possessing her so that we may exorcise it."

The young lady was extremely weak, and it looked as if she might expire at any moment. "I don't think she'll last much longer," one of the attendants remarked.

"What a nuisance. If she dies, then we'll have to go into retreat. And all because of an unexpected defilement," grumbled another.

"You're right. It really *will* be a nuisance. What's more, she looks like she comes from a distinguished noble family, so even after we know for sure that she's dead, we won't be able to dispose of her body right away!"

"Be still," the nun scolded, "and make sure that no one hears about this matter! Any kind of gossip about this is bound to stir up trouble."

The nun kept constant vigil and was so preoccupied by her desire to save the young lady that she seemed to others to be more concerned about the threat to the well-being of a stranger than she was about the illness afflicting her own mother. Still, even though the young lady *was* an outsider, she was so extraordinarily beautiful that all of the attendants who saw her thought it would be terrible to just let her die. So moved, they fussed over her, doing all they could to be of assistance.

Weak as she was, she managed to open her eyes from time to time. Whenever she did, an endless stream of tears would pour forth.

"Ahh . . . how heartbreaking," cried the nun. "I believe the Buddha has brought you to me as a replacement for the beloved daughter whose death I continue to mourn. If you should die as well and this all comes to naught, then our chance encounter will have left me with nothing but one more bitter, painful memory. We must have been destined to meet. Perhaps we share a bond from a previous life. Please . . . won't you at least speak to me a little?"

The nun continued to plead in this fashion until, finally, the young lady replied in a thin whisper: "I may have survived, but I'm a woman of no importance, and my life is worthless. Don't let anyone else see me. This evening, after darkness falls, throw me back into the river."

"You've uttered hardly a word to me since you were brought here, and so I suppose I should be thrilled to hear your voice. But what fearful things you say! Whatever could possess you to speak like that? And how did you come to be in those woods behind the villa?"

The young lady did not respond. The nun examined her body, looking for wounds or any sign of strange anomalies. Finding nothing out of the ordinary, she was at once shocked and saddened by the sight of such unblemished beauty, for it caused her to have doubts about the young lady, who might truly be a shape-shifter come to bewitch people and lead their hearts astray.

The bishop's party remained in retreat at the villa for two full days, and the unceasing reverberation of voices chanting prayers and healing rites for the two afflicted women left everyone on edge and feeling uneasy about the strange, suspicious events that had occurred.

A number of peasants living in the vicinity of the villa had once been in service to the bishop. When they learned that His Holiness was staying there, they came to pay their respects and express condolences for his mother's illness.

As the bishop was listening to them prattle on and on about trivial, everyday matters, one of the peasants offered an apology to him: "We're sorry that we couldn't be of service to you earlier, but you see, Lady Ukifune, a daughter of the late Prince Hachinomiya, died suddenly, without any prior indication that she was ill. Well, this lady was being courted by the Major Captain of the Right, and so I can assure you that her death caused quite a stir. We were so busy yesterday taking care of the funeral arrangements that we couldn't get away to see you until now."

The man's story got the bishop to thinking about the young lady who had been found in the grove behind the villa: *Is it possible that a demon snatched the soul of Hachinomiya's daughter and brought it here? Similar cases have been known to occur in the past.* His doubts were prompted by his observations over the past couple of days, for no matter how often he checked in on her, he never got the sense that she was really alive. There was something alarmingly sinister about her that greatly disturbed him—a precarious, ephemeral quality, as if she might suddenly disappear.

Several people questioned the peasant's story: "But the smoke and flames we observed last night didn't seem big enough for a proper funeral pyre."

"The rites were kept simple on purpose," the man explained. "If you ask me, it wasn't much of a ceremony." The peasants, who had been defiled by their proximity to death, were kept standing outside and were eventually sent away.

Some in the bishop's party began to gossip among themselves.

"The Major Captain was once enamored of Hachinomiya's eldest daughter, but she passed away several years ago. I wonder who that menial could have been referring to?"

"Now that the Major Captain has wed the Fujitsubo Princess,[7] do you really think it likely that he would give his heart to another woman?"

With his mother's condition improving and the direction toward her home no longer prohibited, the bishop decided that the party should make its way back, especially given how awkward it was to remain any longer in such a dreary, haunted place.

Several people wondered aloud about the decision: "But the young lady is still in such a delicate state," they pointed out. "Is she really up to the journey? The poor little thing may suffer terribly on the way."

Despite these concerns, two carriages were readied. The bishop's mother rode in the lead carriage and was accompanied by two other nuns who had been assigned to care for her. The young lady was placed in the second carriage and was accompanied by the bishop's sister and an attendant who stayed by her side throughout the trip.

Progress was slow and fitful, mainly because the party had to make frequent stops in order to prepare medicine for the young lady. Since the nuns resided in Ono on the lower slopes of Mount Hiei, their journey was a long one.

"We should have arranged to stop somewhere along the way," someone complained; and indeed, it was very late at night when they finally arrived.

The bishop looked after his mother, while his sister, the nun, tenderly cared for the young lady, whose identity remained unknown. Each of the nun's attendants took turns assisting her, taking the woman from the carriage and carrying her inside to rest. The bishop's mother was constantly beset by the infirmities of old age, and for a time her condition worsened as a result of the lingering effects

---

7. This "Second Princess" is the second daughter of the present emperor and is married to Kaoru. She resides in the "Chambers of the Wisteria Court" (Fujitsubo) [editor's note].

of the journey. Nonetheless, she eventually recovered, and His Holiness was able to retire back up the mountain to his temple at Yokawa.

It was rather scandalous for a priest to be traveling in the company of a young woman, and so the bishop spoke not a word about his trip to those disciples who had not been with him to witness what had taken place. For her part, his sister made all of her attendants swear an oath of silence, for she feared that someone might come looking for the young lady.

How is it possible that someone who seems to be of such high status should have fallen so low and ended up in a place inhabited by rustics? The nun imagined several possibilities. *Did she fall ill while traveling on a pilgrimage, only to be betrayed and abandoned by a duplicitous stepmother? She has uttered nothing apart from that horrid request to be thrown into the river.*

The nun was extremely anxious, hoping that the patient would soon recover her health and faculties. Sadly, the young lady made no effort to get up, but remained lethargic and disoriented. Her condition was so alarming that survival seemed unlikely. Still, the nun couldn't bear the unpleasant thought of giving up, and so she revealed to others the dream she saw on her pilgrimage at Hatsuse. She also discreetly contacted the ascetic who had granted her pleas for healing rites when they were staying at the imperial villa in Uji and asked him to burn poppy seeds in an effort to exorcise any malicious spirits that might be lingering.

The rites of exorcism continued to be performed throughout the fourth and fifth months. Saddened and perplexed that nothing seemed to be helping, the nun sent a letter to the bishop:

> Please come down to us again. Help this woman. That she has managed to hold on this long shows that it is not her destiny to die at this time. Whatever spirit or demon has possessed her will not let go. My dear brother, I know that you vowed to stay in retreat and not venture out, not even to the capital, but can there be any harm, would you really be breaking your vow, in coming to Ono?

After reading this heartrending message, His Holiness decided to leave his mountain retreat and descend to Ono. *What a curious affair! The young lady has survived so long . . . what if I had made a snap judgment to abandon her at that villa? My discovery of her there must have been the workings of a shared karmic bond, and so I must do my utmost to save her. If I fail, then I'll have to assume that she was fated to die after all.*

Receiving her brother with reverence and joy, the nun described to him the young lady's condition over the past few months: "A patient who's been ill as long as this would normally show the unpleasant effects, but she hasn't deteriorated at all. You can see that she's as youthful and lovely as ever . . . nothing of her appearance shows any sign of disfigurement. True, she does appear to be nearing death, and yet she continues to cling to life." The nun spoke with sincere intensity, weeping the whole time.

"From the moment I first saw her," the bishop replied, "I knew there was something out of the ordinary. Well . . . I shall see what I can do." He peeked in on the young lady, and then added, "She really is quite beautiful, isn't she! No doubt she was born with such features as a reward for good deeds performed in a previous life. What trespass could she have possibly committed to deserve this cruel fate? Have you heard anything that might explain what happened?"

"I've heard nothing . . . no rumors or gossip. I'm convinced that she's merciful Kannon's answer to my prayers."

"No, no, that's not right. There must exist some prior bond between people for karmic destiny to bring them together. Nothing happens by accident, so how could you think it possible, absent some necessary cause, for Kannon to have brought you someone who has no connection to you?" After voicing his priestly doubts about his sister's interpretation of events, he at once set about performing an exorcism.

The nun, who for her own reasons wanted to keep the young lady's presence a secret, felt that it would be awkward if word got out that her brother, who had declined to interrupt his vows even when summoned by the palace, had inexplicably left his mountain temple to go to the trouble of performing prayers and rites for a woman like this. The other priests in attendance shared the nun's concern, and they advised His Holiness to perform the rites quietly in order to keep them secret.

"I will hear no more of this, my noble disciples," the bishop replied. "I've proven to be a shameless priest, for I have broken many of the prohibitions that I'd sworn to uphold. Still, when it comes to women, I've never defiled myself or done anything that would merit censure. I'm over sixty now, and if at this point in my life I'm condemned for trying to save a young woman, then so be it. I would simply consider that my karmic destiny."

"But whenever vulgar rumormongers spread vicious gossip about a holy man of your high repute, that damages the Buddha's sacred teachings," the disciples said, voicing their displeasure.

The bishop made a gravely solemn vow: "If she shows no signs of improving while I am performing these incantations, then I swear I shall never do them again!" He persevered with the rites all through the night, and at dawn succeeded in driving out the stubborn spirit and forcing it into the body of a medium. The bishop and his disciple, the ascetic, wondered just what kind of creature had possessed the young lady, and they took turns continuing the rites in the hopes of pressing the spirit to reveal its situation and motives.

The spirit, which had for several months resisted revealing anything at all about its true nature, was finally overcome and began to shout and curse: "Once, my status was such that no one would ever have expected a man like me to end up in a place like this, subdued in this fashion. You see, long ago I was a monk who practiced austerities, but as a result of some petty resentments I harbored toward the world, I was unable to break free of my attachments and achieve salvation. While wandering adrift in the limbo between realms of existence, I came upon a place where several beautiful sisters resided, and I managed to steal the life of the eldest. Sometime later, I heard the young lady who lies here before you bemoaning her fate and insisting day and night that she wanted to die. One night, when she was alone in the pitch darkness, I took advantage of her despair to possess her. Alas, merciful Kannon protected her, allowing this saintly bishop to defeat me in the end. I shall leave you now!"

"Who are you? Announce yourself," the bishop demanded. However, the spirit's words were no longer intelligible, perhaps because the medium was exhausted.

Her mind and soul restored, the young lady regained her senses a little and glanced around the room. Surrounded by a throng of wizened old monks, she didn't recognize a single face. The sensation of having arrived in some strange, unknown land was profoundly unsettling. She tried recalling details from her past, but couldn't remember anything clearly—not the place where she lived, not even her own name.

All I remember is that I decided to throw myself in the river because it was unbearable to go on living. But where am I now? She struggled to make sense of fragmentary memories. *I was suffering dreadfully, lost in hopeless sorrow, but everyone around me was asleep. Stepping out through the hinged doors at the corner of some room, I felt the wind blowing wildly and heard the violent roar of a river. Frightened and alone, oblivious to past and future, I collapsed on the edge of the veranda and pondered uncertainly which way I should go. Having come this far, I felt ambivalent about going back inside, and as I sat there brooding, I kept telling myself that I should be resolute and leave this world behind once and for all, that it would be better to be devoured by demons than have anyone see me looking so foolish and pathetic. And then, at that moment, a radiantly handsome man approached and said, "Come with me, come to my home." I recall the feeling of being embraced in his arms, and then, just as I recognized him as the man whom people addressed as "Your Lordship,"*[8] *I must have fallen into a trance. When I came to and looked around, I was in an unfamiliar grove and the man had disappeared without a trace. I remember weeping bitterly as I realized that I had not, in the end, been able to die as I had wished. After that, I can't recall what happened, no matter how hard I try. I gather from what people have been saying that many days have passed since then. And to think, what a wretched-looking figure I must have presented to these strangers who were caring for me all that time.*

During those days when she was sunk in that trancelike state, she had eaten at least a few morsels of food on occasion. Now, however, because she was ashamed and filled with remorse at the thought of having been resuscitated in this way, she fell into a deep depression and refused everything, even her medicine.

"Why must you remain so weak, seemingly unwilling to let us help you?" the nun tearfully pleaded. "I was so happy when your fever finally broke and you seemed to be feeling more yourself, but now . . ."

The nun kept a constant bedside vigil, lavishing attention on her patient. The attendants in residence also did everything they could to help, thinking it would be most regrettable if the young lady were to die under their care, especially seeing how fair and graceful of face and figure she was.

The young lady was grateful, but in her heart she continued to long for death. Still, she had managed to come back from the brink, clinging to life despite her ordeal, and because of her youthful vitality, she gradually regained the strength to raise her head, and eventually began to eat and take her medicine again. Despite this improvement, she also continued to lose weight, and her face looked increasingly gaunt.

The nun was happily anticipating a speedy recovery when the young lady said to her, "You must make me a nun. Otherwise, I can no longer go on living."

"It would be a great pity to alter such beauty as yours," the nun protested. "How can you ask me to do such a thing?"

---

8. Although he is not explicitly named in the text, the implication is that Ukifune is recalling her relationship with Niou, who is depicted several times in the *Ukifune* chapter embracing her.

As a compromise, the bishop snipped a few wisps of hair from the top of the young lady's head and had her take an oath swearing to uphold the Five Precepts.[9] This did not satisfy her, but being passive and yielding by nature, she couldn't bring herself to insist on being allowed to take the full formal vows that would make her a nun.

Setting off back up the mountain, the bishop gave instructions to his sister as he parted: "Let's leave it at this for now and focus on nursing her back to health."

The nun was overjoyed to have been entrusted with the care of this young lady, who seemed like a dream come true to her.[1] In her zeal, she would have her charge sit up and personally see to combing her hair, which, although it had been braided in a rather unsightly fashion and carelessly left that way during the long ordeal of spirit possession, was not especially tangled. By the time the nun finished, the young lady's tresses had a vibrant, lovely sheen. The presence of such beauty in a place with so many gray-haired nuns who all seemed to be just a year shy of one hundred[2] made everyone feel as though a dazzling, wondrous angel had descended from the heavens. This stirred a sense of foreboding in the nun, who pressed the young lady to tell her more.

"Why do you seem so cold, keeping your distance from me even though I fret so terribly over you? Who are you? Where are you from? How did you end up in that grove?"

Feeling deeply ashamed at what the nun must think of her, the young lady replied, "I must have lost my memory while I was in that weird trance, for I have almost no recollection of anything that happened before that spirit possessed me. The only thing I can vaguely recall is sitting at the edge of a veranda, gazing blankly at a garden and thinking that I no longer wanted to live in this world. Suddenly, a man stepped out from beneath a large tree nearby. I have the feeling that he took me with him somewhere. After that, I can't remember a thing . . . I can't even remember who I am."

Her manner of speaking was sweetly endearing. She then broke down in tears as she added, "Whatever happens, I don't want anyone to find out that I'm still alive. It would be too much to bear if someone were to come looking for me."

Realizing how painful her questions must be, the nun felt that she could press the young lady no further. She was even more astounded than the old bamboo cutter must have been when he discovered the moon princess, Kaguyahime, inside a stalk of bamboo,[3] Knowing how that story ended, the nun was uneasy, wondering if this young lady like Kaguyahime, might disappear, like moonlight slipping through some narrow gap.

Now, the bishop's mother had come from a distinguished background, while his sister, the nun, had been the principal wife of a high-ranking official. The nun had given her husband a daughter, but when he passed away she was left to raise their only child on her own. She did everything she could for the girl, eventually arranging a promising marriage to a young groom of exceptional

---

9. The Five Precepts constitute a vow against killing, stealing, lying, promiscuity, and intemperance. The vows to become a true nun are more numerous.

1. The phrasing of this line calls to mind the dream the nun had at Hatsuse, implying that her prayers were answered.

2. *Tales of Ise,* section 63: "The grizzled lady who is just a year shy of one hundred seems to be yearning for me, for the image of her face appears before my eyes."

3. The divine protagonist of the *Tale of the Bamboo Cutter* who, after her adventures on Earth, ascends to heaven again [editor's note].

breeding. But then her daughter died as well. Heartbroken and despondent at being a childless widow, she took vows and withdrew to begin life at her mountain retreat in Ono.

Lamenting the tedium of her forlorn existence, the nun desperately wanted to find someone comparable in age and looks to her lost daughter—a keepsake of the one she mourned day and night. And then, quite unexpectedly, she was granted this young lady, who in face and figure was even lovelier than her own daughter. Hardly able to believe this was really happening, the nun was at once astonished and overjoyed. Although she herself was now in her fifties, she had retained a graceful beauty and dignified demeanor.

* * *

It may be awkward, but I must be brave and take advantage of this opportunity to ask His Holiness to administer vows to me. There's almost no one here to stop me, so the timing couldn't be better. With that in mind, Ukifune arose and addressed the bishop's mother.

"I'm seriously ill, so when your son, His Holiness, arrives, please inform him that I would like to take the vows that will make me a nun."

The senile old woman nodded in vague agreement.

Ukifune returned to her usual quarters. The nun was the only person who was permitted to comb her hair—Ukifune couldn't stand having anyone else touch it—and because she couldn't dress it herself, she simply loosened the cords and let it hang down a little. It made her sad to think that it was by her choice and no one else's that her mother would never again see her the way she looked now. She had been under the impression that her hair had thinned out as a result of the terrible ordeal she had been through, and yet, far from falling out, it was if anything thicker, a full six feet in length, and beautiful all the way to the ends. Each strand was fine and gave off a lovely sheen.

Ukifune recited a snatch of verse to herself: ". . . hoping that it would come to this."[4]

The bishop arrived at dusk. The aisle room facing south had been cleaned and cleared away, and soon a host of round shaven heads were scurrying about raising an alarming uproar that disturbed the normally quiet atmosphere of the place. His Holiness went over to his mother's quarters to ask after her.

"How have you been doing these past few months? I see that the rooms on the east side are vacant. Has my sister already left on her pilgrimage? Is that young lady still in residence here?"

"She is," the old nun replied. "She decided to remain here. She told me to tell you that she's not feeling well and that she wants to become a nun. She wants you to administer the vows."

The bishop arose and went over to the young lady's chambers. "Excuse me, are you in here?"

Because she was sitting behind a standing curtain when he called out, she moved closer to him by way of reply, her demeanor quiet and demure.

"From the moment I first met you under those startling circumstances, I felt certain that there must be a bond between us from some previous life. Since

4. *The Gosenshū* 1240 (Bishop Henjō, written when he first took the tonsure): "Surely my mother never stroked my pitch-black hair hoping that it would come to this."

then, I have prayed devotedly for you. Of course, as a priest, it wouldn't do for me to call on you or send you letters without some reason to do so, and so naturally I have not kept in touch. How has it been, living among old women who have renounced the world? They must look frightfully strange to you, no?"

"It's depressing for me. Despite my desire to end my life, I continue to survive for reasons that remain a mystery. Please don't get me wrong . . . there's no way someone as foolish as I can adequately express the gratitude I feel for all the kindness you've shown on my behalf. It's just that I can no longer lead the sort of life expected of a woman. Please make me a nun. Even if I were to return to society, someone in my situation would never be able to settle into a normal relationship."

"But you have such a long future ahead of you," the bishop counseled her. "Why is your heart so firmly fixed on this one desire? Becoming a nun may instead lead to regrets and attachments that will only increase your sins. You may think yourself strong enough at the time you stir your heart to action and make the decision, but being a woman, your resolve will waver as the years go by, and you will face many impediments to salvation."

"From the time I was a child," Ukifune replied, "I knew only heartache and misfortune, and for that reason my mother even told me once that she had thought about making me a nun. Later, after I came to understand things a little better, I had no desire to live as a normal woman, but increasingly focused my thoughts and placed my hopes on the world to come. Now I feel as if I'm on the verge of collapse and that death is gradually drawing nearer. So I ask you again . . . please . . ." She was crying as she spoke.

It makes no sense. What could have made someone so beautiful despise her life so much? Even the spirit that possessed her said that she wanted to die. Making this connection, the bishop considered her request. *She certainly has good cause to feel the way she does. In fact, it's amazing that she's managed to live this long. Having been possessed once by such an evil creature, she's in terrible danger.*

"Despite my reservations, the Buddha himself[5] would praise the merits of your stated resolve. So who am I, a priest, to stand in your way? It is no trouble to administer the vows to you, but because I've been called out on an urgent matter, I have to go to the palace tonight. Starting tomorrow I must undertake healing rites for the First Princess. It will take about seven days to complete, and when I withdraw from the palace, I'll drop by here on the way back and perform the ceremony for you."

Ukifune was bitterly disappointed to hear that, for she knew that if the nun were back by then, she would most certainly object.

"I'm suffering just as much as when you administered to me the vows to uphold the Five Precepts. If my condition worsens, I fear that taking vows to become a nun will do no good at all. I would be grateful if you could do the ceremony today."

She was weeping so violently that she moved his pious heart to pity. "It's late, isn't it? In the old days I never gave a thought to going up and down this mountain, but as the years pass by it's getting harder for me to bear the strain, and so I thought I should rest here on my way to the palace. If you're really in such a hurry to take your vows, then I'll carry them out today."

---

5. The text uses the phrase "the Three Treasures" (*sanbō*—the Buddha, the Dharma/Law, the priesthood), but in this context the word refers to the Buddha.

Ukifune was overjoyed. She picked up a pair of scissors and pushed the lid of a comb box toward the bishop.

"Come here, my noble disciples," he called out.

The two monks who had first discovered the young lady happened to be accompanying the bishop, and when they entered the room he told them, "Prepare to cut her hair."

The ascetic thought this was a reasonable course of action. *She was in such a terrible state when we found her, it would seem cruel to force her to remain in society as a laywoman.* Nevertheless, the length of hair that she had laid out through the gaps in the curtain panels was so beautiful that he hesitated for a moment, reluctant to use the scissors.

At that moment, Shōshō was in her own room talking with her older brother, who was also an ascetic, while Saemon was receiving another of the priests who was a personal acquaintance of hers.[6] Because visits from people close to the nuns were so rare at this out-of-the-way place, both women were preoccupied entertaining their guests, leaving the page girl, Komoki, as the only one attending the young lady. When Komoki reported to them what was happening, Shōshō rushed in a panic over to Ukifune's chambers, where she found the bishop helping the young lady, who did not have proper religious attire, put on one of his own outer robes and a surplice for the ceremony.

"This is merely for the sake of form," he said. "Now, please face in the direction of your parents and pay obeisance to them."

Ukifune had no idea which way to turn, and with the memory of her mother being too much for her to bear, she wept.

"Oh my dear . . . how distressing!" Shōshō exclaimed. "Why are you taking such an ill-advised step? What will my mistress say when she returns?"

We've already begun the ceremony, His Holiness thought, *and now that we've come this far, such talk will only serve to upset the young lady and put her in the wrong frame of mind.* He admonished Shōshō, preventing her from saying anything more or coming any closer to interfere.

"Turning round and round, wandering through the Three Realms where all is in flux . . . ," the bishop chanted.

At last, I've cut myself off from all obligations and attachments, Ukifune mused. Still, as she recalled the debt she owed her mother, taking this step made her sad.

The bishop's disciple was having difficulty cutting her hair. "In a quiet moment," the ascetic said, "have the nuns trim it up for you."

His Holiness clipped the locks around her forehead. "Never regret the change in your appearance," he told the young lady, and then instructed her in the noble truths. They had all advised against rushing into this, but how happy she felt to have finally renounced the world. She felt that only by taking this step did she have a sign from the Buddha that surviving had been worthwhile after all.

The bishop and his entourage departed for the capital and the residence fell silent. As the evening breeze rustled outside, the nuns let the young woman know of their disappointment. "You've been living in this forlorn house for some time, and given your situation, we were expecting that you would soon be leading an auspicious life with the Middle Captain. But now that you've taken this

---

6. Two attendants to whom the nun had entrusted Ukifune [editor's note].

drastic action, how do you plan to spend the many years of life that remain to you? It makes even those of us who are old and decrepit sad to think that a normal life is over for a woman when she becomes a nun."

Despite their comments, at that moment Ukifune felt only relief and joy. She had come to the point where she couldn't imagine having to live on in this world and so, for her, becoming a nun was a wonderful thing, one that brightened her mood and lifted her burdens.

Early the next morning, however, she was ashamed to see her changed appearance, in part because no one around her had agreed with her decision, which they considered thoughtless. The ends of her hair had been cut so carelessly that they had suddenly gone all wild and uneven. Ukifune wanted someone to come in—preferably without making any snide or disapproving comments—and dress her hair properly, but because she was by nature shy and timid, she remained in her room with the blinds down to keep it dark.

She had never been able to express her most private feelings easily. Moreover, she now had no confidante to whom she could open up. Thus, all she could do when her emotions were too much for her to hold in was sit down in front of her ink-stone and pour her heart into the poems she would scribble out under the pretext of practicing her calligraphy.

> Yet again have I turned my back on this world . . .
> A world I once renounced, thinking of myself
> And those I knew as not among the living

"By taking these vows, I've made an end of it at last," she wrote. Still, looking at her own poem, her heart was filled with sorrow and pity.

> Over and over have I turned my back
> On a world that I have been determined
> To make an end of once and for all time

As she sat scribbling other poems that expressed similar sentiments, a letter from the Middle Captain arrived. The old nuns had been shocked and stunned about what had happened, and in the midst of the uproar someone had sent word to the Middle Captain. He thought it a great shame, but he was also filled with regret and disappointment. *She was deeply determined to take this step, and that must be why she kept her distance and refused to reply to me, since she probably wanted to avoid any frivolous exchanges. But even so, what a drastic thing to do! The night I mentioned how much I wanted to get a closer look at her hair, which seemed so alluring that time I caught a glimpse of it, I was told, "All in due time."* He sent off a reply: "I don't know what to say to you."

> I must make haste, for I do not wish to be late
> And fail to board the fishing boat that from this world
> Rows away, bearing a nun to that distant shore[7]

---

7. This poem (and the reply that follows) plays on the word *ama*, which can mean both "fisherman (or diver)" and "nun."

Ukifune made an exception and agreed to read his note. In that moment of intense emotion, how must she have felt, moved by the thought that now, indeed, it was over? Along the edge of a mere scrap of paper, she wrote the following, again under the pretense of practicing her calligraphy:

> *Though her heart is leaving behind the shore*
> *Of this woeful world, the destination*
> *Of the nun's drifting bark remains unknown*

Shōshō wrapped the poem up to send to the Middle Captain.

"You should make a cleaner copy of it first," Ukifune said.

"But I might make an error if I do that," Shōshō replied, and sent it off just as it was.

It was a rare sight indeed to see a reply in the young lady's own hand. There are no words that can adequately describe the anguish the Middle Captain experienced.

The bishop's sister returned from her pilgrimage only to be deeply distressed to find out what had happened. "I'm aware that a woman in my position should be encouraging you for taking this step," she said to the young lady, "but you have so many years ahead of you, how are you going to get by? I have no idea how much longer I will live—I could pass away today or tomorrow—and so all my thoughts have been on ensuring that your future is secure once I'm gone. That's why I went to Hatsuse to pray to Kannon."

The nun was prostrate, writhing in grief. Ukifune found her extremely pitiful, but then she thought of her true mother and felt her heart break as she imagined just how terrible it must have been for a parent who had been left without even a body to mourn.

As usual, Ukifune was unresponsive and sat with her back to the nun. Because she looked so very tender and lovely, the nun couldn't hold back her tears as she remarked, "You certainly are a passive, fragile little thing!" She then made arrangements to provide her with the appropriate religious attire. A short outer robe and a surplice were tailored in the dark gray cloth that the nuns were accustomed to wearing. As the women there stitched the robes and tried them on the young lady, they vented their disappointment.

"She unexpectedly brought a radiant light to this mountain abode, and it was a joy to look at her every morning and evening. What a shame it's come to this!"

The women also expressed their resentment of the bishop and bitterly criticized his actions.

* * *

When the First Princess had completely recovered, the bishop returned to Yokawa. On the way he dropped by the residence in Ono, where he was met with a bitter outburst from his sister.

"You may have intended to set her on the path to salvation in the next life, but she is still young and beautiful, and if she comes to regret her decision, your rash actions will stir lingering attachments that will surely add to the burden of her sins. Why didn't you consult with me first? It's incomprehensible!" The nun's complaints, however, were useless at this point.

"You must now concentrate solely on your devotions," the bishop told Ukifune. "No one, neither the old nor the young, knows how long they have to live. The fact that you have rejected this world as a fleeting illusion is the proper frame of mind for someone in your situation."

His words were mortifying to Ukifune, for they were reminders that he had earlier witnessed her wretched condition.

The bishop brought out the damask, gauze and silk cloth he had received from Her Majesty as a reward for his services. "Take these," he told Ukifune, "and have a new habit made for you. So long as I'm alive, I'll do what I can to assist you. Nothing need worry you. We're all born creatures of this vulgar world, and insofar as we're pressured by our attachments and desire for its glories, it seems that all people find renunciation difficult. Why would anyone in your position, pursuing religious devotions in the midst of this forest, ever have cause to feel regret or shame?"

And so he instructed her, finishing with two lines from Bai Juyi: "Life is as thin and fragile as a leaf on a tree. The moon wanders through the sky until dawn breaks over the pines at the gate."[8] He may have been a monk, but to Ukifune, who sat there listening to him speak in his formidably elegant and erudite manner, he was saying things that she very much wanted to hear.

The wind, which blew all day long, sounded forlorn and melancholy. She heard the bishop saying, "On a day like this, even a hermit in the mountains is moved to weep aloud."

Am I not also a hermit now? Ukifune asked herself. *That must be the reason why I cannot stop my tears.*

She stood up and moved toward the edge of the veranda. Looking out at the valley spreading off into the distance, she saw a hunting party of men dressed in robes of various hues. Although they were heading up Mount Hiei, it was unusual for anyone to travel along the path that ran past the residence here. Once in a great while she might catch sight of a monk walking along from the direction of Kurodani, but to see a layperson out here was rarer still. Then she realized that the party belonged to the Middle Captain, who had been so aggrieved by her behavior.

He was visiting with the intent of making yet another of his complaints— useless though they were now—but because the autumn foliage was so delightful, having turned a deeper crimson here than in other places, he was enchanted, his mind distracted, from the moment he entered the valley.

How astonishing it would be to come across a beautiful woman in a place like this, he thought.

"I had some free time," he told the nun, "and feeling bored, I took to imagining how lovely the autumn leaves must look right now. Even your trees seem to beckon me to lodge for the night beneath their sheltering shade."

He was seated on the south-facing veranda, gazing around at the view. The nun, lachrymose as ever, composed the following:

> *The chill blasts of late autumn sweep*
> *The mountain's base, wither the trees*
> *Leave no sheltering shade for you*

8. Poem from *Collected Writings of Bo Juyi* [editor's note].

The Middle Captain replied:

> *I know no one awaits me, but gazing*
> *At the treetops in this mountain village*
> *It is hard for me to just pass them by*

He continued talking on and on about the young lady, though words could do nothing to win her now. "Do let me steal a glance of her to see how her appearance has changed," he pleaded with Shōshō. "You can at least do that much, as a token of the promise you once made to me."

Because he pressed her this way, Shōshō went inside, and when she saw how beautiful Ukifune looked, she felt the urge to do anything she could to show the young lady to the Middle Captain. Wearing subtly figured robes of simple, serene colors—light gray over pale orange-brown—she had a dainty physique, lithe and elegant, her face had a bright, modern appeal, and the ends of her hair, thick and abundant, spread across her back and shoulders like an opened multiribbed fan. Her fine complexion and delicate features gave off a lambent, rosy glow, as if she had applied her makeup with exquisite care.

Shōshō wanted to paint a picture to capture the scene of Ukifune performing her devotions, absorbed in reading a sutra with a rosary hanging from the frame of the standing curtain next to her.

Each time I see her like this, Shōshō reflected, *I'm moved to tears. And if I feel that way, how much more intense would be the reaction of a man whose heart was drawn to her?* Thinking that perhaps this was the appropriate moment to act, she let the Middle Captain know that there was a small opening just beneath the latch on the sliding door, and then moved aside the standing curtain that might otherwise have obstructed his view.

Seeing the young lady for the first time, the Middle Captain was filled with regret, resentment and sorrow, as if he himself were somehow to blame for what had happened. *I never once imagined that she was this beautiful. For a woman so extraordinary, so perfect in all respects, to have become a nun . . .* He could not contain his emotions and so he withdrew before she could hear him weeping madly, as if he had taken leave of his senses.

* * *

VII

Islam and Pre-Islamic Culture in North Africa

The Prophet Muhammad and the emergence of Islam united disparate Arab tribes over the course of the seventh century, turning them into a potent cultural and political force. Islam initially spread as the religion of a dynamic Arab state that took advantage of the weakness of the Byzantine and Persian Empires in the Middle East, and soon extended its political boundaries even further, to Spain, Central Asia, and Afghanistan. Once conquests slowed down and political boundaries were consolidated, traders carried the religion even further, to West Africa and China, as well as South and Southeast Asia. Arab traders established an increasingly far-flung network of cities and trading posts, facilitating an extraordinary exchange of goods. In Cordoba, the center of Muslim Spain, one had access to goods coming from Delhi, the Sultanate in northern India, and from what is now Bulgaria in eastern Europe to Sudan. Along with commodities, what traveled along these trade routes were armies. Islam became the religion of the ruling classes in the different empires. However, unlike Christianity, Islam did not seek converts, which meant that it often allowed local religious practices to exist alongside Islam, thus creating multicultural societies in

A contemporary photograph of the Grand Mosque at Djenne, Mali, which was first built in the thirteenth century.

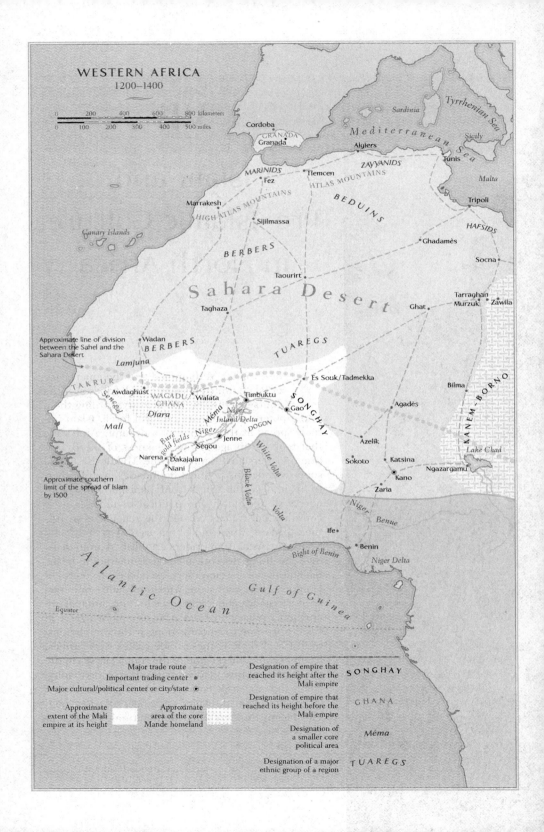

WESTERN AFRICA
1200–1400

0   200   400   600   800 kilometers
0   100   200   300   400   500 miles

Canary Islands

Tyrrhenian Sea

Sardinia

Cordoba
GRANADA
Granada

Mediterranean Sea

Sicily

Malta

Algiers

Tunis

MARINIDS
Fez

Tlemcen

ZAYYANIDS

ATLAS MOUNTAINS

BEDUINS

Tripoli

HAFSIDS

Marrakesh

HIGH ATLAS MOUNTAINS

Sijilmassa

Ghadamès

Socna

BERBERS

Taourirt

Tarraghan
Murzuk   Zawila

S a h a r a   D e s e r t

Taghaza

Ghat

Approximate line of division
between the Sahel and the
Sahara Desert

Wadan
BERBERS

Lamjuna

TUAREGS

Es Souk/Tadmekka

Bilma

KANEM–BORNO

TAKRUR

Awdaghust

WAGADU/
GHANA   Walata   Timbuktu

Agadès

Senegal

Diara

Méma
Niger
Inland Delta

SONGHAY
Gao

Azelik

Lake Chad

Mali

Buré
gold fields

Niger

DOGON

Jenne

Sokoto

Katsina

Ngazargamu

Narena   Dakajalan
Niani

Ségou

White Volta

Kano

Zaria

Approximate southern
limit of the spread of Islam
by 1500

Black Volta

Niger

Benue

Volta

Ife

Benin

Bight of Benin

Niger Delta

A t l a n t i c   O c e a n

Gulf of Guinea

Equator

Major trade route
Important trading center •
Major cultural/political center or city/state ⊛

Approximate
extent of the Mali
empire at its height

Approximate
area of the core
Mande homeland

Designation of empire that
reached its height after the
Mali empire

SONGHAY

Designation of empire that
reached its height before the
Mali empire

GHANA

Designation of
a smaller core
political area

Méma

Designation of a major
ethnic group of a region

TUAREGS

which different religions existed side by side.

The same pattern held true of culture. Far from seeking to export a homogeneous notion of culture, the various Islamic empires were places of vibrant cultural exchange, in which art and ideas traveled as freely as goods and armies. Writing was especially enriched by the interchange; new literary forms that blended imported styles with existing local ones emerged throughout the Islamic world. Oral literature, such as the Mali epic *Sunjata*, continued to flourish, while incorporating Islamic elements, much as the pre-Christian epic *Beowulf* had received a late Christian layer or veneer to make the traditional story compatible with the new dominant religion. The result was a fascinating encounter of cultures and religions, whose products are presented here.

Between 640 and 700 C.E., North Africa was occupied by Arab invaders seeking to expand the growing sphere of influence of an Arab world increasingly united by Islam. One far-reaching result of the Arab conquest was that it led to an economic revolution by combining the faltering economy of late Roman North Africa with the desert and savannah lands of West Africa into a vast commercial network that extended from the Atlantic to East Asia and from the equator throughout northern Europe. By the latter half of the eighth century, most of the native Berber peoples of the Maghreb (Northwest Africa) had been converted to Islam. Owing to increasingly dynamic market forces to the north of the desert and the spread of camel-herding in the desert itself, Muslim Berber merchants became engaged in the systematic development of trans-Saharan trade.

The ninth-century Arab occupation of southern Morocco gave rise to a string of oasis cities south of the High Atlas Mountains. These included the bustling market town of Sijilmasa, which became the northern counterpart of the commercial centers of Tadmekka and Awdaghust on the southern edge of the Sahara. By the end of the tenth century, the southern trading centers had been colonized by Muslim (mostly Berber) immigrants from the north. They were merchants eager to trade with the markets of desert-edge kingdoms like Ghana, Takrur, and Gao, and especially to extract wealth from parts of the western Sudan described by Arab travelers as "the land of gold."

Thus, Islam arrived in West Africa via Muslim traders, and by 1068 the respected Arab geographer Al-Bakri was writing that there were significant Muslim populations occupying towns of the Mande peoples, which included the Maninka of the Upper Niger region who became founders of the Mali Empire in the thirteenth century.

But Islam was not only an economic force; it also reshaped the cultural landscape. By the thirteenth century Islam had become a common, though not universal, aspect of Mande culture. Far from imposing onto North Africa, including the Mali Empire, its own conception of art, Islam was gradually integrated into Mande culture, with Mande bards (*jeliw*) assimilating elements of Islamic tradition. Some of the stories told by Muslim clerics and by pilgrims returning from Mecca were adapted to local narrative repertoires. The Prophet Muhammad and various characters from his life and times were borrowed by Mande bards and incorporated into their most important oral traditions, including the epic *Sunjata*, which tells the story of the thirteenth-century hero who is credited with the founding of the Mali Empire.

SUNJATA: A WEST AFRICAN EPIC OF THE MANDE PEOPLES

late thirteenth–early fourteenth century

The West African epic named after its central hero, Sunjata, is an essential part of Mande culture. The heartland of Mande territory is located in what is now northeastern Guinea and southern Mali, but the Mande peoples are found throughout a much larger portion of sub-Saharan West Africa, speaking various related languages and dialects. The Mande, also known as "the people of Manden," who include the Bamana of Mali and the Maninka of Guinea, are heirs to a vibrant historical legacy, the high point of which was the Mali Empire that flourished from the mid-thirteenth to the early fifteenth century. The epic narrative of Sunjata and his contemporaries illustrates the Mande peoples' own view of this glorious past both before and after Islam began to influence their culture, and it rightfully credits their ancestors with establishing one of the great empires of the medieval world.

In Mande culture, oral tradition is the domain of bards popularly known as griots, but as *jeliw* or *jelilu* (sing. *jeli*) to their own people. They are the hereditary oral artists responsible for relating the alleged deeds of the early ancestors, keeping them and their exploits alive in the community's memory. For many centuries the *jeliw* have served as genealogists, musicians, praise-singers, spokespersons, and diplomats. As the principal narrators of oral tradition, the bards have been responsible for preserving narratives that express what peoples of the Mande cultural heartland believe to have happened in the distant past. For centuries, stories of the ancestors have passed from one generation of *jeliw* to the next, and the principal Mande clans frame their identities in terms of descent from the ancestors described in epic tradition.

As specialists in maintaining the oral traditions of their culture, *jeliw* are known to their people as guardians of "The Word." In early times they served as the spokespersons of chiefs (*dugu-tigiw*) and kings (*mansaw*), and were thus responsible for their patrons' reputations in the community. Generations of *jeli* families were permanently attached to leading households and ruling dynasties, who supported the bards in exchange for their services in the verbal arts. The *jeliw* encouraged their patrons to strive for ambitious goals by reminding them of the examples set by their heroic ancestors, as described in the epic narratives. They pointed out mistakes through the use of proverbs, and admonished their patrons when they seemed likely to fail in their duties. At the same time, the bards' own security depended on their rulers' political power and social prestige, so the stories they told tended to be biased in favor of their patrons' own ancestors.

In Mande societies, all matters involving family, clan, and ethnic kinship are of supreme importance. People are identified by their *jamu*—the family name or patronymic associated with famous ancestors remembered for important deeds alleged to have occurred around the beginning of the thirteenth century. Thanks to regular exposure to live or locally taped performances by *jeliw* that are played privately or heard regularly on local radio broadcasts, general awareness of the heroes and heroines of ancient times, like those in *Sunjata*, enters the people's consciousness in childhood and grows there throughout their lives. Memories of the ancestors are constantly evoked in praise songs and narrative episodes that are sung or recited by the bards on virtually any occasion that calls for entertainment. When elders meet in village council, the ancestral spirits are felt to be present because, according to tradition, it was they who established the relative status of everyone present, as well as the administrative protocols to be followed and the values underpinning every decision. The ancestors who are described in *kuma koro* or "ancient speech" define the identity of virtually everyone of Mande origin.

The performance of *Sunjata* would often be accompanied by musical instruments: a small lute (*nkoni*), a twenty-one-string calabash harp (*kora*), or a Malian xylophone (*bala*). Even without music, Mande oral poetry incorporates a kind of call-and-response rhythm through the repeated assent of the *"naamu-sayer"* (responding person) to each line sung by the *jeli*. The *naamus* of this secondary performer might be translated as "yes" or "We hear you." Common interjections include *tinye* ("it's true") in the indigenous language, as well as terms borrowed from Arabic and reflecting the influence of Islam, such as *walahi* ("I swear") and *amina* ("amen"). In all cases, the community hears not only the poem but an enthusiastic, repeated approbation of it. The *jeli*'s own language when narrating the stories of the ancestors is also distinct from everyday speech, as he turns to *kuma koro* ("ancient speech") for the performance. Even the most central names in the story may vary according to the pronunciation of the individual *jeliw* and to regional differences, so that Sunjata, for example, may appear as Son-Jara, So'olon Jara, or Sunjara.

Oral literature that has been passed down from generation to generation is difficult to date. The epic material feeding this version of the *Sunjata* epic was narrated and recorded only in the late twentieth century, although it retells stories that go back centuries. Djanka Tassey Condé, the *jeli* who narrated this version, lived his entire life in the small village of Fadama near the Niandan River in northeastern Guinea. Nominally a Muslim like most people in today's Mande society, Tassey was descended from a lineage of Condé bards who trace their ancestry to forebears who lived before the arrival of Islam in the land of Dò ni Kiri as it is described in the Mande epic. Even among other bardic Manden families, the Condé of Fadama are respected for their vast knowledge of Mande epic tradition. In the 1970s and 1980s, Tassey's brother Mamadi Condé was *belentigi* (chief bard) of Fadama, and one of the best-known Manden orators, distinguished for his depth of knowledge. When Mamadi died in 1994, his brother Tassey became the *belentigi*. Several months later, David C. Conrad, who edited this version of *Sunjata*, began a collaborative relationship with Tassey Condé that lasted until that great bard's death in 1997.

The passages collected here are from the rendering by Tassey Condé of this communal, epic story. The narrative is episodic and often disjunct, full of magic (*dalilu*) and humor, as the *jeli* gives his own version of a story familiar to his listeners. The epic tells of the great expectation surrounding the birth of Sunjata, whose heroism has long been foretold. Foreigners come to defeat a wild buffalo that has been decimating Mande lands, and their first achievement is to recognize the buffalo woman Dò Kamissa as the culprit. They tame her with kindness, claiming that she resembles their mother, until she relents and offers them her wisdom. Urging them to look beyond appearances, she commends to them the deformed Sogolon, who will be the mother of Sunjata. When Sunjata is finally born, into a world full of sorcery and treachery, he barely escapes the many plots against him, and is eventually driven into exile by the jealousy of his stepbrother. His greatest achievement comes with the defeat of the tyrannous Sumaworo to liberate Manden, which the text recognizes as a foundational imperial gesture. *Sunjata* also emphasizes, however, that the hero's exalted stature comes at a great cost to the community: while Sumaworo furiously seeks the man who is fated to succeed him, we are told, the Mande people suffer his violent attacks.

Like most epics, *Sunjata* is a relation of the hero's many trials, which he surmounts through his courage, tenacity, and piety. Yet the singular hero is also deeply ensconced in his community: in order to lead he must find allies, cultivate friends, and honor his family. Part of the charm of *Sunjata* lies in its attention to detail, and its fresh humor as it relates the interactions of legendary heroes with the very concrete world around them. This is a poem about the power struggles that can lead to war, certainly, but it is also about people's relationship to a place and a landscape. Land takes on a concrete quality beyond its political significance as Sunjata pleads for a plot in which to bury his mother when she dies in exile. In its vivid re-creation of the hero's experience, *Sunjata* knits together the mythic and the everyday, the ancestral and the contemporary, providing for its Mande listeners a recognizable, living history, and for everyone else rich insight into the culture of a once-glorious empire.

From Sunjata[1]

The Search for a Special Wife

When Maghan Konfara[2] was a *mansa* in Manden, he had power, he had wealth, he was popular, and he had *dalilu*—but he had no child. Maghan Konfara, Sunjata's father, craved a child. Though his friends had begun to have children, he still had no child. But then his *dalilu*[3] showed that he would finally have a child. His *moriw*,[4] his sand diviners, and his pebble diviners[5] all said, "Simbon, you will sire a child who will be famous." Everybody he consulted said the same thing. "But try to marry a light-skinned woman," they told him. "If you marry a light-skinned woman, she will give birth to the child that has been foreseen." Because Maghan Konfara was powerful, he married nine light-skinned women. But aside from Flaba Naabi, none of them gave him a child. He was perplexed. From the

---

1. Translated from the Maninka by David C. Conrad. All notes were made by the translator unless otherwise indicated. In an excerpted section, the narrator, Tassey Condé, introduces the birth of the seventh king (*mansa*) Sunjata by recalling the lineage of kings born before Sunjata. He declares that he will not start from the very beginning since the listeners and the Mande people are all Adam's descendants.
2. Maghan Knofara is the father of Sunjata, also referred to as Simbon (Master Hunter) and *Mansa* (ruler) [editor's note].

3. Magic, occult, or secret power; in everyday use, any means used to achieve a goal.
4. Nominal Muslims who, in oral tradition, often perform divination.
5. Seers and healers who identify the source of all kinds of problems by spreading a pile of sand and reading symbols in it, or casting multiple objects such as pebbles or cowrie shells and reading the configurations in which they land. Diviners then prescribe appropriate sacrifices to remedy the problem.

last Wednesday of the month of Jomènè[6] to the same time the following year, Maghan Konfara did not sire a child. (If you want to know about Sunjata, then you have to learn what Sunjata's father and the people of Manden had to endure!)

He sent the *moriw* back into retreat, telling them, "I need a child, so do your best. It's said that if I sire the child that has been foreseen, that child will rule Manden. I must sire this child." The *moriw*, all of whom were present, went back into retreat. When they returned, they told him, "Simbon, marry somebody who is a mulatto." So he married nine mulatto women. But aside from Marabajan Tarawelé, none of those mulatto women gave birth. From that time of the year to the same time the following year, none of those women who were with him in the house bore any male children. Simbon was frustrated. Maghan Konfara sent the *moriw* back into retreat. He said, "Tell me the truth. Ah! If you see that I will not have any children, tell me. A child is something that only God can provide; it cannot be bought in the market." This time the *moriw* told him, "Very well, marry a black woman. Find a black woman who has a white heart." This time he married nine black women. But aside from Nyuma Damba Magasuba, none of them bore any children.

Maghan Konfara was frustrated. His *moriw* told him again, "Very well, man, free one of your slave girls and marry her." (In those days they still practiced slavery.) He liberated and married nine slave girls. But aside from Jonmusoni Manyan, none of the slave girls bore him any children. Frustrated, Simbon gathered the people of Konfara together on the last Wednesday of Jomènè.

When the people of Konfara had gathered, he separated the *moriw*, the sand diviners, and the pebble diviners into groups and sent them all into retreat. He said, "I told you not to hesitate. If you see that I won't have a child, tell me. Go into the house. If you do not tell me the truth, I'll kill all of you and replace you." When the *moriw* came out of retreat, they told him, "Simbon, you will sire a child. Make one of your *jelimusow*[7] happy. Marry her so she will give birth." He made nine *jelimusow* happy, but aside from Tunku Manyan Diawara, none of them ever gave birth.

Now all of Manden was frustrated. (It's hard to give birth to a child who will be famous!) And when all of Manden became frustrated, the diviners were ashamed of themselves. They met and swore an oath: "Any one of us who has broken a taboo should confess it. Maybe this is our fault. If we don't get together and tell this man the truth, the feet of our descendants will not be able to even break an egg in Manden." They went into retreat and came back out, telling Simbon, "Someone will come from the East. He will be coming from the land of the white-skinned people. This much has been revealed to us. Let this man pray to God for a solution to your problem. If you let this man pray to God on the matter of your son, anything he tells you will be God's word. We won't be able to accomplish this ourselves. God has shown us a good man."

While they waited there in Farakoro,[8] Manjan Bereté arrived. Manjan Bereté was the first Muslim leader of Manden; he opened the door[9] to the

6. The first month of the year.
7. Female bards (sing. *jelimuso*).
8. Sometimes shortened to "Farako." Evidently the hometown of Sunjata's father, located in the territory (*jamana*) of Konfura [editor's note]. Farakoro appears in the longer

version of Maghan Konfura's name, as he was known to Tassey Condé and his ancestral bards of Fadama: Farako Manko Farakonken.
9. That is, he was instrumental in the introduction of Islam.

Mande people. (He is also the ancestor of the Bereté in Manden. The home of the Bereté people is Farisini Hejaji,[1] a region in the land of Mecca; the Bereté are Suraka.[2]) Bereté packed up some books and came from Farisi to the land of Manden because it was a powerful place. If he found someone in the land of Manden who would join him, who would work with the Koran, then his blessings would be great. Because he could not get used to the food here, Manjan Bereté brought Sansun Bereté, his little sister, with him when he came to meet Simbon. He brought his sister so she could prepare his food until he became better acquainted with the Mande people.

Manjan Bereté came and lived with Simbon. He said, "You need the religion practiced in my homeland. The Prophet has said nobody should take up swords in the religion again, that we should now be gentle with one another. Let us win people over with kindness, so we can awaken their minds and they can join the religion. The blessings will be great for anyone who accomplishes this."

[*In an omitted passage, Konfara suggests that Bereté's sister is his destined wife. Bereté forbids this union, but his fathers and brothers convince him that Konfara can have his sister if he converts to Islam. Bereté's sister gives birth to a son, but it is not the foretold son.*]

Simbon said, "How do I get that son? Pray to God for me to have that son. Will I get that son?"

"Yes, you will get that son."

"Very well, pray to God for that."

Manjan Bereté prayed to God. He said, "Simbon, you will get this child. When I was praying, God revealed to me that there are others like me who will come. They too will come from the land of the white-skins. Those people will not bring any woman with them when they come. But they will tell you the name of the place that is their destination, and if you ask them to, they will bring you a woman from that place. She will bear that child."

[*In an omitted passage, the narrator describes the Moroccan background of two brothers, Abdu Karimi and Abdu Kassimu, who will travel to the land of Dò ni Kiri to hunt a buffalo that is devastating the countryside, and will eventually become known as Danmansa Wulanni and Danmansa Wulanba.*]

Two Hunters Arrive in Manden

Abdu Karimi and Abdu Kassimu came to Manden from Morocco. When they got here they walked all night and all the following day, and were already under the three *nkiliki* trees of Manden by the evening of that second day. When Abdu Karimi and Abdu Kassimu arrived under the trees, they measured out their food, cooked their meal, ate, and slept there.

(People used to rest under those three *nkiliki* trees when traveling to and from Dò ni Kiri, the home of the Condé. Travelers of Manden, from the home of the Mansaré, used to rest there, as did travelers from Negeboriya, the home of the Koroma. Travelers from Soso, from the home of the Kanté, also used to rest under those trees. People could get the news of the world there.)

---

1. "Farisi" is from Fars, a region in Persia. "Hejaji" is from Hejaz, a region that was the ancient cradle of Islam, including the Red Sea coast of Arabia and the cities of Mecca, Medina, and others.

2. A Maninka and Bamana term for the local perception of "Arab," which includes "Moors" and North Africans in general.

Abdu Karimi and Abdu Kassimu, who were Arab *kamalenw*,[3] were worried, for they did not know where they were headed. They found a place where some traders had left their cooking pots. After eating, the Arab *kamalenw* said, "Let's lie down here and wait for these traders to return. We'll soon learn our next destination."

While Abdu Karimi and Abdu Kassimu were sleeping, some traders who were on their way from Manden arrived. Some traders also arrived from Negeboriya, home of the Koroma. They all greeted one another.

The Arab *kamalenw* asked, "Is everything all right with the people of Manden?"

The traders replied, "There is nothing wrong with them."

"Is everything all right with the Koroma of Negeboriya?"

The traders said, "Nothing is troubling them." They too measured out their food; then they went to sleep.

While the brothers were lying there, some traders who were on their way from Soso arrived. These traders had visited Dò ni Kiri and found it in turmoil. Upon meeting Abdu Karimi and Abdu Kassimu, they asked, "Where are you from?"

The *kamalenw* said, "We are from Morocco."

"Where are you going?"

The *kamalenw* replied, "We were on our way to the land of the Condé, but we don't know the way."

The traders said, "The *mansa* of Dò ni Kiri is Donsamogo Diarra; he is quarreling with his sister."

I just told you about this sister, called Dò Kamissa, the first daughter of Ma'an Solonkan. She and her brother, Donsamogo Diarra, were quarreling over the issue of the legacy left by Ma'an Solonkan, their mother.

Dò Kamissa said, "Donsamogo Diarra, if you refuse to share our mother's legacy with me, I'll take it myself."

The Condé elders said to her, "Go ahead and *try* to take a share for yourself; you are too headstrong."

"You think I can't take it for myself?"

"Yes, that's right." They did not know she had the power to transform herself into different things.

Dò Kamissa left the town and stayed in a farm hamlet near Dò ni Kiri. At that time, the place known as Dò ni Kiri included the twelve towns of Dò, the four towns of Kiri, and the six towns on the other side of the river. At the break of day, Dò Kamissa transformed herself into a buffalo and began to kill the people living in those places.

It became a bad time for Dò ni Kiri.

Donsamogo Diarra said, "This buffalo has killed all of the hunters that I requested from Manden." He sent a message to the Koroma of Negeboriya, but the buffalo killed all of the hunters who came from there. He sent for the hunters of Soso, but when they came the buffalo killed them all, too.

Donsamogo Diarra was at a loss. He sent out the word from Dò ni Kiri. He said, "People have died because of me. Anyone who kills this buffalo will get to choose a wife from three age sets[4] of Dò ni Kiri's girls." Everybody who visited Dò ni Kiri

3. *Kamalenw*: plural form of *kamalen*, a circumcised youth 15–25 years old.
4. Children born within the same span of about three years are identified as a single group or age set that grows up together, going through the various initiation rituals into adulthood.

was told about this. And when the traders returned to the camp under the *nkiliki* tree, they told Abdu Karimi and Abdu Kassimu about the turmoil in Dò ni Kiri.

The traders said, "Things in Dò ni Kiri have become very bad. Donsamogo Diarra's quarrel with his sister has resulted in many deaths. Hunger has come to Kiri because no one can go in or out. The paths to the village and farms have been closed. There is no way for crops to be brought home, for the buffalo is blocking the way. The Condé say that anyone who kills this buffalo will get to choose a wife from three sets of Dò ni Kiri girls."

The Arab *kamalenw* were still camped there. The younger brother, Abdu Karimi, said, "Big brother, do you hear what they are saying?"

Abdu Kassimu replied, "I hear it."

Together they said, "Let us go to Dò ni Kiri."

The elder brother said, "Hey, little brother, what about these things they are talking about? Suppose the buffalo kills us?"

Abdu Karimi replied, "If the buffalo kills us, at least we'll die for the sake of the Condé. They are having a bad time in Dò ni Kiri. I feel bad for them. Remember how our fathers told us the story of the Condé ancestor Samasuna?[5] Before the Prophet could make any progress, God told him to fight at Kaïbara.[6] The Condé ancestor Samasuna took a thousand of his sons to go and help our ancestors fight at the battle of Kaïbara, and there he lost all thousand of his sons. No matter how difficult the fight at Dò ni Kiri will be, it can't be more difficult than the battle at Kaïbara.

"The thousand sons that the Condé ancestor Samasuna gave all died on the battleground of our ancestors' war at Kaïbara. If the two of us should die for the sake of the Condé, will our deaths be equal to the deaths of those thousand men? If it's our time to die, we should die for a good cause. We do not equal a thousand men. But if we should die for the sake of the Condé, we will only be doing what the thousand men did for those ancestors. So let us go to Dò ni Kiri. Knowing what the Condé ancestors suffered for our sake at Kaïbara, we would be bastards if we retreated now, after hearing that the Condé are suffering." Thus Abdu Karimi encouraged his elder brother.

Abdu Kassimu now had the courage to go to Dò ni Kiri. But first the brothers packed their belongings and went straight to Konfara. They bypassed Dò ni Kiri and went straight to Manden.

When the brothers arrived in Manden, Manjan Bereté was sitting in a circle near Maghan Konfara. The two men were playing *wari*.[7] Manjan Bereté was sitting in the circle near Simbon, with prayer beads in his hands, praying to God: "May God not let me be embarrassed by my prediction." They remained sitting when they saw Abdu Karimi and Abdu Kassimu approaching. When the two brothers arrived, all of the men met in that same circle, and Manjan Bereté and Maghan Konfara stopped playing *wari*.

---

5. Samson (Shamsūn in Arabic) is not mentioned in the Qur'an, but according to other sources of Muslim tradition (e.g., al-Tha'labi and al-Tabari), he dedicated his life to God and continually fought against idolators.
6. Maninka usage of Khaybar, an oasis ninety-five miles from Medina, Arabia, the site of a famous battle fought by the Prophet Muhammad and his army.
7. A popular game played with two rows of shallow holes, usually in a carved wooden board, with small stones or cowrie shells used as counters.

Abdu Karimi said, "My respected *karamogo*, we have come to God, we have come to the Mande people, and we have come to Simbon. What makes us walk fast will also make us talk fast."

After greeting the brothers, the Mande people asked them, "Where did you come from?"

The Arab *kamalenw* said, "We come from Morocco."

"What is your family?"

"We are Sharifu."[8]

The Mande people saluted them, "You Haidara,"[9] to which the *kamalenw* replied, "Marahaba."[1]

The Mande people said, "The honor is yours, the honor is Simbon's."

The Arab *kamalenw* said, "We come from Morocco. We are children of Abdu Sharifu. We are descendants of Saïdina Ali."[2]

The *kamalenw* explained, "We have heard that the Condé are suffering, that they are quarreling with their sister who has transformed herself into a buffalo. Every morning the buffalo has killed people in all of the twelve towns of Dò, the four towns of Kiri, and the six towns across the river. That is why we have come. We want to go to Dò ni Kiri, to help the Condé with their trouble. We want you to perform the sand divination for us. If our sand is sweet, we will go to Dò ni Kiri. And if our sand is not sweet, we will still go to Dò ni Kiri."

[*In an omitted passage, the narrator recounts that the sand is indeed sweet and a sacrifice must accompany the divination. Before the hunters leave, Maghan Konfara asks for a wife but the younger brother refuses. The narrator introduces the buffalo's female genie companion, who advises the brothers on how to respond to abusive women they will meet, and how to approach Dò Kamissa, the Buffalo Woman, and avoid being killed by her.*]

Dò Kamissa the Buffalo Woman

After walking for one kilometer, the brothers passed into the land of Konfara, and from there crossed into the land of the Condé. There they met a woman who had borne one child, just as the female genie had told them. The genie had said, "You will not see me again. But if you don't heed the advice I give you, the buffalo will kill you."

When they greeted this woman who had borne one child, she spoke abusively to them. She said, "Eh! Is it the woman who should greet first, or is it the man? You do not pass by a beautiful woman without greeting her!" She said every possible bad word to them.

---

8. Contraction of the longer plural form Sharifulu from the Arabic Shurafa' (sing. Sharīf), a lineage claiming descent from the family of the Prophet Muhammad.
9. A prestigious Muslim family name in Manden, here used in a greeting as the equivalent of Sharifu.
1. Response to a greeting that honors people by saluting their ancestors with the family name

or *jamu* (patronymic, identity). From Arabic *mrehba* ("welcome").
2. 'Alī ibn Abī Tālib, cousin and son-in-law of the Prophet Muhammad, and one of the first converts to Islam; renowned as a warrior during Islam's struggle for survival, he took part in most of the Prophet's expeditions and displayed legendary courage at the battles of Badr and Khaybar.

They said, "M'ba.[3] We are children of the road. We do not know anything about women or men. We have never been to this country. We speak to everyone we meet, so they can help us."

She replied, "Am I the one who is supposed to help you?"

Huh! They passed on by her without quarreling further.

After they passed that woman, they walked another kilometer and met the full-breasted girl. When they met this girl they said, "Lady, we greet you, God is great."

Ah! She abused them. She said every bad word to them.

The younger brother said, "Aaah, you do not understand. A beautiful woman like you will pass by a man like that? You do not know what is happening." (No matter how proud a girl is, once you call her "beautiful," she will soften.)

After the hunters passed by the full-breasted girl, she went on her way. (Humility really comes only with death, but men act humbly until they get what they want.)

After walking on for another kilometer, they heard the pounding of the mortars and pestles[4] of Dò ni Kiri, and there they met Dò Kamissa herself. She carried a hoe on her shoulder and a walking staff served as her third leg.

When they said, "Greetings mother." Heeeh! She cursed their father. After that, she cursed their grandfather. Then she cursed their mother.

"You are calling me mother? Was I the one who gave birth to your father or your mother?" She said every bad word to them.

Abdu Karimi said, "Big brother, don't you think this lady resembles our mother?"

[*In an omitted passage, the brothers help the buffalo woman feed her chickens before they arrive in Dò ni Kiri and are given lodging. They set out on their plan, treating the buffalo woman as they would treat their mother. After three failed attempts at forming a bond, she finally invites them into her home for a conversation.*]

Dò Kamissa's Revelations

Dò Kamissa the Buffalo Woman said, "You have outdone me. No one can get the better of people like you. You are polite. You were brought up well. Eh! Despite everything you were told, you were not discouraged. You favor me? Now I will cooperate with you. Were it not for you, I would have wiped out Dò ni Kiri.

"You know that Donsamogo Diarra, with whom I am quarreling, is my brother. I was the firstborn of my father's children. When I reached puberty, I said, 'My Lord God, I will give the largest of the two gold earrings that are on my ears to whoever brings me the news that my father has had a son. My Lord God, I will also give the beautiful outer one of the two wrappers I am wearing to the person that brings me such good news.' I was the first to offer a sacrifice for my brother. So who does he think he is, telling me that women shouldn't have property? Huh!

"I would have wiped out Donsamogo's entire lineage. But you Sharifu, you have outdone me. I will cooperate with you and give you my life, for I know that if you kill me, you will bury me; you will not let my body go to God as a bad body.

---

3. Contraction of *marahaba*, a response to a greeting that honors people by saluting their ancestors with the family name or jamu (patronymic, identity). From Ar. mrehba ("welcome").

4. The mortar is a large wooden receptacle in which women pound grain with a heavy, wooden, dub-shaped pestle that can be as long as five feet.

"Before I give myself up to you, though, I will ask you to do three things for me. If you agree to do those three things, then I will cooperate with you. But if you do not agree to those three things, I will keep after you until you do."

The *kamalenw* said, "Ma, tell us the three things you want us to do for you."

She said, "Here's the first: Don't go to town immediately after killing the buffalo; come to this hamlet instead. You'll find me dead. Because I am the only one who knows what I have done,[5] my brother must not see my corpse. When you arrive here, you'll see that I have poured water on the fire. There will be a hoe; there will also be an axe. Take the axe and cut down a *toro* tree. Take the hoe and dig my grave. After you have laid me in it, fire the musket. At no point can my brother, my father's son, see my body; nor can my body be carried to Dò ni Kiri. I have not done any good for them. I have wiped out their children, I have wiped out their wives, I have widowed their husbands; this is all my doing.

"That's the first thing you must do. Now, you know that whoever kills me will be rewarded with the choice of a wife from three sets of Dò ni Kiri's girls. The second thing you must do for me is refuse all of the fine young girls they bring out for you. Do not choose any of those girls as your wife, because they would be forcing my father's last-born to remain in the house. Five sets of girls have gone to their husbands, but she has not married, and if you do not marry her, she will never be married. She holds something special in her breast for whoever marries her. You, Sharifu, must marry her.

"She is very ugly. She's the 'Short Sogolon' you've heard about, the one who is so very ugly. I damaged one of her tear ducts and now her eyes water all the time. Her head is bald, she has a humped back, her feet are twisted, and when she walks, she limps this way and that. I, Dò Kamissa, did all of that to her.

"How could I make her so ugly when I loved her so much? I put my far-seeing mask[6] on her face before she was old enough to wear it, and, in doing so, cut her tear duct, caused her hair to fall out, and put a hump on her back. By putting her on my sorcery horse when she was too young, I twisted her feet, stretched her tendons, and made her knock-kneed. All of this is my fault. I take the blame, and if she does not get married, it will be my curse.

"So, when the men of Dò ni Kiri bring those beautiful Condé women to you, do not accept any of them. Choose my father's last-born. Some call her 'Humpbacked Sogolon.' Some call her 'Ugly Sogolon.' Everybody used to call her whatever they felt like. But the real name of that last-born child is Sogolon Wulen Condé. There will be something special in her breast for you because she'll have all the *dalilu*.[7]

"If you choose her over all the beautiful daughters they offer you and are not satisfied with the way she looks, then cut off the buffalo's tail when you kill it. The tail is heavy with gold and silver, because I took the gold and silver earrings of every Dò ni Kiri woman I killed and hung them from the hair of my tail. I have a lot of hair on my tail, and it is heavy with the gold and silver ear jewelry of the Dò ni Kiri women. If you exchange some of that gold, you can go and marry a beautiful woman somewhere else, a wife to have along with Sogolon Condé. But do not refuse to take Sogolon! Then there will be no problems. Will you do this, or not?"

---

5. Contrary to what the narrator has previously indicated.
6. A magic object allowing the wearer to see unimaginable distances. The concept might have entered oral tradition when Europeans were observed using telescopes and binoculars, but there also could have been an indigenous mask imbued with such power.
7. The mother's physical deformities signal her possession of special occult powers that she will pass on to her child.

The Sharifu said, "We agree to that."

She said, "That is the second thing you must do. Here's the third thing: the dead buffalo's carcass must not be taken to the town."

"Eh, Condé woman! We have agreed to your other demands, but we might not be able to do this. What if we can't convince the people of Dò ni Kiri not to take the carcass back to town? What if they force us? We'll be powerless to fight them off or to take the carcass from them."

"Oh, you will do your best to heed what I have said. If you can do the other things, then forget about that last request. But you must respect my other two wishes."

"Very well."

As the brothers were about to leave, she said to them, "Sit down." Once they were sitting, she said, "The weapons you brought won't do anything to me. The arrows and quivers you brought won't do anything either. I am in control of my own life."

She put her hand in her basket of cleaned cotton, pulled out the spindle, and handed it to them. Then, putting her hand in her storage basket, she took out the distaff that usually holds the thread, and gave it to them, saying, "Put this in your bow and shoot the buffalo with it. It will stop the buffalo. If you do not shoot the buffalo with it—if you shoot a big arrow at the buffalo instead—then the buffalo will kill you."

[In an omitted passage, Dò Kamissa provides the brothers with various enchanted objects that will help them kill her buffalo wraith.]

Death of the Buffalo

The brothers left the town and went into the bush, past the lake of Dò ni Kiri and into the forest. They crossed another open space and entered more forest. There, before going any further, they saw the buffalo.

(Before they came to the bush that day, the brothers' name was Sharifu. But afterwards they were called Diabaté or Tarawèlè. They left their Sharifu identity behind in Manden[8] and came to be known as Tarawèlè and Diabaté. We will soon come to the reason for this.)

There was the buffalo. Abdu Karimi, the younger brother, said to Abdu Kassimu, "Big brother! You should be the one to take the magic dart and shoot the buffalo, because the killing of this buffalo will make history. The person who kills this buffalo will be mentioned in all of the future generations' histories, right up until the trumpet is blown on Judgment Day. You are my big brother, so you kill the buffalo."

Abdu Kassimu said, "Little brother, a job must be left to the experts. Yes, I was the first to be born. But I know what *dalilu* you have—and I know you must be the one to kill the buffalo." He handed the magic dart to his younger brother.

Abdu Karimi told his elder brother to go on ahead. Crawling through the grass, Abdu Karimi came ever closer to the buffalo. He remembered what the old woman had told him: that he should not try to kill the buffalo until he was in its

---

8. Only after the buffalo is mortally wounded does Tassey begin to use the names by which the brothers are usually known, Danmansa Wulanni and Danmansa Wulanba. These prob-ably originated as praise names based on the brothers' exploits, e.g., Danmansa Wulanba can be roughly translated as "Big Lord of the Solitary Forest Buffalo."

shadow. She'd said, "Do not miss me! If you miss the buffalo, I'll kill you." The younger brother crawled until he reached the buffalo's shadow. He took the distaff and put it on the spindle. He pulled the string of his bow back, back, back, he pulled it still harder, and he could feel that he had something very powerful in his hand. When he'd pulled the bowstring back to his shoulder, he let the spindle go, *pow*! It shot right into the buffalo's chest.

The buffalo was startled when the spindle pierced its chest. It raised its head, saw Abdu Karimi, and bellowed, *hrrr*! And there, while he was still right beside the wounded buffalo, Abdu Karimi told his elder brother, "Run!" for the buffalo had been shot and the struggle between them had begun.

(It's said that greatness will not be acquired without hardship. We've been telling you about the hardship Manden had to endure before the country could know peace. Sunjata would not have been born without this hardship, and without Sunjata, Manden would never have been sweet. And if Manden was never sweet, we Mande people would never have known ourselves!)

Bellowing, the buffalo began to chase the *kamalenw*, it came up behind Abdu Karimi, who was trying to catch up with his elder brother. Abdu Karimi dropped the bamboo stick, which instantly sprouted into a grove of bamboo, and before the buffalo could get through it, the *kamalenw* were far ahead.

Once it was clear of the bamboo, the buffalo started chasing them again. When it came up behind them and bellowed, the brothers dropped the hot charcoal. In those days, the Mande bush had been there a long time and had never been burned. So when the *kamalenw* dropped the hot charcoal, the bush caught on fire, stopping the buffalo and forcing it back while they dashed ahead through the grass.

When the fire died out, the buffalo jumped into the ashes and started chasing them again. But by the time it reached them and bellowed, they were already at the lake of Dò ni Kiri. There Abdu Karimi dropped the egg, which turned the ground into deep mud. The buffalo got stuck in the mud. (This is the mud referred to in the Condé song "Dala Kombo Kamba":

> "Condé drinker of big lake water,
> Those who drank the big lake water,
> They did not stop to clean it.
> Those who clean the big lake,
> They did not drink its big water."

It was Danmansa Wulanba and Danmansa Wulanni[9] who cleaned the water of the big lake.)

By the time the mud started to dry, it was too late for the buffalo: the spindle wounds were letting water into its intestines, and it fell down. When the buffalo fell, Danmansa Wulanni said, "Big brother, look behind you! The buffalo has fallen."

A new family lineage was created at the moment the elder brother looked back and saw that the buffalo was dying. Going back, he put his foot on the buffalo's body. He said, "Ah, little brother! You have given me a name. Ah, little brother! You were sired by Abdu Mutulu Budulaye, Abdu Mutulu Babatali. Aba Alibi's own son is Sedina Alia, to whom God gave a sword, and you were sired by Alia. Sedina Alia's son is Hassana Lonsani, and you were sired by him. Hassana Lonsani's son

---

9. The elder brother is Wulanba, the younger Wulanni.

is Sissi; Sissi's son is Kèmo; Kèmo's son is Kèmomo Tènè; Kèmo Tènè's son is Sharifu—and you were sired by Sharifu. Aah, Karimi! You have given us names."

After hearing this praise, the younger brother said, "Eh, big brother! If you were a praise-singer or *jeli*, no one could surpass you (*i jèmba tè*)!"

That was the beginning of the *jeli* family known as Diabaté;[1] that was the origin of the lineage. "Diabaté" was first said in Manden, in the Mande language, when the buffalo was killed in the bush.

Once the buffalo was dead, the brothers saw that its tail was heavy with gold and silver.

In cutting off the buffalo's tail, the brothers were able to take for themselves all of the gold and silver in its hair. The *kamalenw* were also able to use the tail as proof that they really had killed the buffalo. As soon as they showed the tail, people knew that the business was finished, because the tail of Dò Kamissa's buffalo wraith could only be cut off if the buffalo was dead. Ahuh! (And this was the beginning of the custom of removing the tails of dead game.)

[*In an omitted passage, Danmansa Wulanba and Danmansa Wulanni try to respect Dò Kamissa's wish that her wraith be buried in the bush, but the towns-people insist on retrieving the buffalo carcass and dragging it into town to be desecrated.*]

Sogolon Wulen Condé of Dò Ni Kiri

After the buffalo was dead, the people of Dò ni Kiri started beating the ceremonial drum. All of the people living in the twelve towns of Dò, the four towns of Kiri, and the six towns across the river were expected to attend, and they all came. When the twenty-two towns were all present, the people said, "What did we say? We said that we'll bring out three age sets of girls for the hunter that kills this buffalo, and that he can choose any girl from among them to be his wife. Bring your daughters forward." (Huh! If you bring out three age sets of daughters from twenty-two towns, you should bring out the oldest set first, then the next oldest, then the youngest set.)

The villagers brought out the beautiful Condé girls, formed them into three circles, and told the boys to choose. The people said, "Even if you choose ten or twenty girls, they will be your wives. Or if you choose only one girl, she will be your wife. You have delivered us from disaster! And everyone here wants to have their daughters married to you two boys.

"You Sharifu, we don't go back on our promises. Take a look at these girls, and take any one that pleases you." The two men followed one another, walking around, around, around the circle. When they had returned to where they started they said, "Where are the rest of the girls?"

The Condé ancestor said, "You young men search every house, so that no one can hide his daughter."

---

1. The singing or chanting of praises is an occupational specialty of *jeliw*. This is a popular etymology explaining how the Diabaté *jeliw* acquired their family name. When the younger brother killed the buffalo and the elder brother praised his courage by reciting their family genealogy, this was the way a *jeli* would do it. When the younger brother said, "no one could surpass you," the phrase *jèmba tè* evolved through repetition into "Diabaté" which, along with "Kouyaté," is one of the two names exclusive to traditional bards.

The villagers searched the entire town but found no other girls. Everybody wanted to marry their daughter to the brothers!

When the searchers returned they said, "There is nobody left."

A bystander said, "What about the bad old woman who was just killed? She has her father's last-born still in her house."

Somebody said, "Eeh, man! Heeeye, can we show that one to the strangers?"

Danmansa Wulanni said, "Go and get that woman you're talking about. Has she been married to another man?"

They said, "No."

"Has she been married before?"

"No."

The brothers said, "Well, if she is unmarried, go get her."

The people said, "Out of five age sets of girls that have found husbands, only she has remained unmarried."

The brothers said, "If she is an unmarried girl, go get her."

Ma Dò Kamissa had told them that the door of Sogolon Wulen Condé's father's house was the one facing the town's meeting ground. She'd also told them, "When Sogolon is coming from my father's house to go into the town meeting ground, a little black cat will come from behind her and pass in front of her; the little black cat will go from in front of her and pass behind her. If you see that happening to anyone, then you'll know that she is the girl I am talking about."

They sent for Sogolon, and as she was being brought out of the house—just as she reached the edge of the town meeting ground—a black cat came from behind her and passed in front of her; it went from in front of her and passed behind her.

As soon as the brothers saw Sogolon, they said, "This is the one we've been talking about."

They heard people go, "Wooo!"

They were asked, "Is this really the one you were talking about?"

To which the brothers replied, "Yes, this is the one we have been talking about."

Ancestor Donsamogo Diarra said to them, "You Sharifu, is this the one you want?"

To which they replied, "Yes, this is the one we want."

"Are you *sure* this is the one you want?"

"This is the one we want."

He said, "This one is even more powerful than my sister, whom you killed, and you know how much *dalilu* she had. This one has *really* powerful *dalilu*. But if you say that you want her, I'll give her to you. Go ahead and take her with you. If you're not compatible, just bring her back. I'll return her to where you found her, and I'll give you another wife.

"Now, I don't want to contradict myself, but just take another look at these other girls. We'll give you up to three months. If, after three months, you're not compatible with my sister, come back and I will give you one of these girls. I will put my sister back where she came from."

The brothers said, "Very well."

She was Sogolon, the woman who was given to them, the mother of Simbon. Simbon, whose birth was foretold and who united Manden—this is the child about to be born. We can talk about Turama'an, we can talk about Kankejan, or of Tombonon Sitafa Diawara, of Fakoli, Sumaworo, or of Tabon Wana Faran

Kamara; but the one who organized them all, united them into one place and called it Manden, well, the person who did all those things was Sunjata, and this is how his mother was married.

[*In an omitted passage, both brothers try to consummate the marriage but are unsuccessful. They reach Konfara and offer Sogolon to Maghan Konfara. While Simbon prepares for their meeting, the community shows the new bride a mixed welcome. At the threshold of the new couple's home, Sogolon and Konfara test each other with three magical back-and-forth attacks before Sogolon acquiesces to her role as a traditional bride. On their wedding night, she uses sorcery to watch the other women dancing, making them wary of her.*]

Sogolon was still a virgin when she came to Maghan Konfara. After three days, her bloody virgin cloth was taken out. The following month, she became pregnant with Sunjata. That is how Sunjata was conceived.

The co-wives said, "We won't be able to do anything against this woman." She had gone to her husband almost at the end of the lunar month, and for the rest of that month, she did not see the other moon. She had conceived.

When the women of Manden heard this, they went outside the town and held a meeting under a baobab tree. They said, "Getting pregnant is one thing, delivering is another. Make miscarriage medicine, anything that will spoil the belly with a touch. Everyone must prepare her own."

Sogolon Condé also had very powerful *dalilu*. When her belly started to expand, the other wives would visit her, saying, "Younger sister, this is the medicine we use here in Manden for pregnant women. Aah, all of the women here wanted a child, but we have not been able to conceive. You may be the lucky one bearing our husband's child—but the child belongs to all of us. Here, M'ma,[2] dilute this medicine in water and drink it."

Heh, Sogolon, the Condé woman, diluted that medicine in water and drank it. She drank it and drank it, for seven years. And each time she drank it, her belly would shrink away, *jè*!

After seven years of this, Sogolon Condé went outside the town.

She prayed to God. She said, "M'mari! That is enough! Enough of what those Mande people have done to me. I come to you, God. I am only a stranger here, and the men who brought me here cannot help."

[*In an omitted passage, the narrator describes his own family's relationship with characters in the narrative, and with ancestors from Arab tradition.*]

The Childhood of Ma'an Sunjata

God made Ma'an Sunjata into a person, made him into a human fetus and brought him into the world.

When the Mande women heard the news of Ma'an Sunjata's birth, they again gathered together under the Mande baobab tree. They said, "It is one thing to give birth to a son, but another thing for him to survive."

Then what did they do to him? Through sorcery they stretched the tendons of his two feet. They lamed him and forced him to crawl on the ground for one year!

---

2. Affectionate greeting to a woman, equivalent to the masculine "M'ba" [editor's note].

Two years!
Three years!
Four years!
Five years!
Six years!

Then, in Sunjata's seventh year, the co-wives provoked Sogolon to anger. (Because we are walking on a straight path, we cannot wander from one side to the other. We have to take the main road, so we will know how Manden was built.)

One day, in Sunjata's seventh year, Maramajan Tarawèlè was picking some leaves from the same baobab tree that we've already mentioned. As Maramajan Tarawèlè was on her way back to the villiage, Ma Sogolon Wulen Condé, who was sitting under the eaves of the house she shared with Ma'an Sunjata, asked, "Big sister Maramajan Tarawèlè, won't you give me a few of your baobab leaves?"

Maramajan Tarawèlè said, "Ah! Younger sister, you are the only one of us to have a son. Why would you ask us for baobab leaves? Your lame son is sitting right there inside the house. If you want baobab leaves, why don't you tell your son to stand up and go get some?"

Ma Sogolon Wulen Condé said, "Ah, that is not what I meant. I thought I could depend on the help of my sisters. I didn't know you were upset because I had this child."

The two women didn't know Sunjata was listening to them.

Afterwards, when Ma Sogolon Condé walked by, Sunjata said, "Mother! Mother!" She did not answer because she knew he had overheard them.

He said, "Mother, what are they saying?"

"Forget about that talk."

"Ah, how can I ignore that? Mother, I'll walk today. They insult you by saying you have a lame person in your house, and yet you beg them for a baobab leaf? I'll walk today. Go and get my father's *sunsun*[3] staff, and bring it to me. I'll walk today."

Ma Sogolon Condé went and got the *sunsun* staff and brought it to Simbon. When he attempted to stand by thrusting the *sunsun* staff firmly into the ground and holding on to it, the *sunsun* staff broke.

Sunjata said to Sogolon, "Ah, mother. They say you have a lame son in the house, but you gave birth to a real son. Nothing happens before its time. Go and bring my father's iron staff." But when she gave him the iron staff, he broke it, too.

He said, "Go and tell my father's blacksmith to forge an iron staff so I can walk." The blacksmith carried one load of iron to the bellows, forged it, and made it into an iron staff. But when Sunjata thrust that iron staff into the ground and tried to stand, the staff bent. (That iron staff, the one they say was bent by Sunjata into a bow, is now in Narena.)

Sunjata broke both of his father's staffs and an iron one that was forged for him. Therefore, when he stood, he did it on his own, first lifting one foot, then the other foot, then the other one, and so on.

His mother said, "Simbon has walked!"

The *jeliw* sang this song:

3. An extremely hard wood called "false ebony" or "West African ebony" [editor's note].

"Has walked,
Jata has walked.
Has walked,
Jata has walked."

Thus it was his mother's rivalry with her co-wives, and their humiliation of her, that caused Jata to walk. (That is why I can't believe it when I hear people saying they do not love their mother! Heh! Jelimoril[4] Your father belongs to everyone, but your mother belongs only to you. When you meet people for the first time, they don't ask you about your father; they ask about your mother.)

After that, God gave Sunjata feet. Sunjata went into the house, took his father's bow and quiver, and left town. (Some people say he made the bent iron staff into his bow, but don't repeat that.)

When he reached the baobab tree, he shook it, uprooted it, and put it on his shoulder. He carried it into his mother's yard and said, "Now everyone will come here for baobab leaves."

So it was that when the Mande women next saw Sogolon they said, as they picked the baobab leaves, "Aah, Sogolon Condé! We knew this would happen for you. The prayers and sacrifices we made on your behalf have been answered." (Now, when you are having a hard time, everyone abuses you. But when things are going well for you, people say, "We knew this would happen for you." May God help us persevere!)

Sogolon eventually had three more children. After So'olon Ma'an was born— but before he could walk—his younger brother So'olon Jamori was born. Then, while So'olon Ma'an was still crawling on the ground, Manden Bori was born. Finally after So'olon Ma'an walked, So'olon Kolonkan was born.

[*In an omitted passage, Sunjata's enemies conspire with nine sorceresses to kill him, but one sorceress warns him and reveals that the sorceresses agreed to kill him only because the reward is a dead bull and the sorceresses crave meat. Sunjata suggests that he provide the meat instead and that they spare his life. He upholds his end of the compromise and the sorceresses vow that no female, human or animal or otherwise, will ever hurt him. Dankaran Tuman and his mother conspire to have Sunjata murdered in his sleep. Meanwhile, Sunjata spends a rainy day playing the hunter's harp while he waits for the weather to change so he can go hunting.*]

Mistaken Murder and the Question of Exile

As So'olon Ma'an waited for the rain to stop so he could go hunting, he sat in his hammock with his six-stringed hunter's harp and sang to himself. (His younger brothers Manden Bori and So'olon Jamori were also harp players.) After playing "Kulanjan"[5] for a while, Sunjata changed tunes and played "Sori."[6]

Some youths passing by So'olon Ma'an's door heard him singing in a low, sweet voice and stopped in his door to listen. One of these youths was an apprentice hunter. He said, "I will listen to Sunjata until the rain stops."

---

4. During performances, *jeliw* occasionally speak to people in the audience, commenting on something in the narrative.
5. One of the oldest melodies in the bards'

repertory; often dedicated to hunters, Sumaworo is praised as "Kulanjan."
6. A lesser-known melody dedicated to hunters.

While the youth stood at the door, Sunjata put some snuff into his mouth. When the snuff was wet, he stopped playing the harp and went to spit out the door, where he noticed the young man. Sunjata said, "Who's there?"

The youth said, "Brother So'olon Ma'an, it is me."

"Ah, what are you doing here?"

"Your brother sent a message that we should bring him some food and supplies. So that's what I'm doing. But it is raining, and a slave with wet clothes does not enter the house of his betters. I am an apprentice hunter at the farm. I stopped under your eaves when I heard your music. Let me keep listening to you until the rain stops."

(Meanwhile, the musket[7] of conspiracy was being loaded in town.)

So'olon Ma'an said to the youth, "Come into the house."

The young man entered the house and sat on the edge of the bed. Simbon was playing the harp. When he played certain parts, the young man would tap his feet, because the harp music was so sweet. But the youth was also tired, and the warm room felt good to him. He became sleepy and started to nod. Ma'an Sunjata told him, "Lie on the bed." When the young man was asleep on the bed, Simbon stood up and covered the young man with a blanket. When the rain stopped, Sunjata—who forgot about the young man sleeping there—stood up, put on his crocodile-mouth hat, took his hunter's hammock, his quiver, bow, and fly whisk,[8] shut the front door, and went out the back. Taking a deep breath, he went into the bush.

While Simbon was in the bush, Dankaran Tuman came and stood under the eaves of the house, where he heard the young man snoring. He did not know that Ma'an Sunjata had left the house.

Dankaran Tuman went and told the seven young men, "Didn't I tell you that Sunjata sleeps anytime it rains into the evening? He's sleeping now; go get your clubs."

After getting their clubs, the seven young men came to Simbon's door. But they were afraid of him. To each other they said, "Man, don't you know who So'olon Ma'an is? One man can't outdo him, two men can't outdo him, even the seven of us together can't outdo him. When we go in, listen carefully for the sound of his breathing, and be sure to hit him on the head. If we only hit him on the back, he'll be sure to capture us." They went in and surrounded the young man. When they located the source of his breathing, they raised their clubs and hit him on the head. They beat him until his body went cold.

When the body was cold, they left to tell Dankaran Tuman that they'd finished the work he had given them. Dankaran Tuman told his mother, "Ahah, Mother. The bad thing is now off our backs. He is dead." (No matter how good you think you are, you'll always do something bad to your enemy!)

"Eh! Dankaran Tuman," she said, "has he died?"

"Yes! The son of the Condé woman has died today!"

---

7. Maninka *morifa*. The first firearms did not arrive in West Africa until the 16th century, but the *jeliw* frequently speak of muskets in the time of Sunjata. Linear chronology is not a pressing issue in their views of the distant past, but what is of interest is the imagery of a formidable weapon and a hero's power to repel any iron projectile.

8. Ideally made from the tail of a dangerous wild animal and possibly symbolizing the one cut from the slain Buffalo of Dò, although elephant tails were highly prized for this essential hunters' device carrying occult protective qualities.

"Ah, my son! Now I will not be the failure in my husband's home. Now my heart is cool. If you have killed Ma'an Sunjata, *aagba*! Manden Bori and So'olon Jamori can't stand up to you. The only brother I was worried about has been killed."

They did not sleep that night.

Sansun Bereté said, "Heee, just wait until Sogolon Condé knows about this."

When day broke, Dankaran Tuman and his mother went to spy on Sogolon.

"Huh!" they whispered. "Don't say or do anything! When he's slept for a long time, his mother will go and open the door on him."

Sansun Bereté said, "If you don't say anything, no one will guess that you are the one who killed him."

As the soft morning sun rose on them, they saw Sunjata, Danama Yirindi[9]—yes, the son of the Condé woman—walking along, carrying three dead animals; one was hanging over his left shoulder, one was hanging over his right shoulder, and one was on his head.

When they saw him, Sansun Bereté said, "Dankaran Tuman! Didn't you say that Sunjata was dead?"

Dankaran Tuman replied, "Mother, we really killed him."

"Then who is this coming? Who is coming?"

"It is Sunjata who is coming."

When they saw that it really was Sunjata, Dankaran Tuman peed in his pants.

Walking up to them, Sunjata said to Sansun Bereté, "Big mother, here is some wild game for you." Then, laying another animal before his step-brother, he said, "Big brother, here is one for you."

There was nothing they could say.

Sunjata carried the last animal to his mother's place and said, "Mother, here is your animal."

His mother said, "Ah, my son, thank you."

When he returned to his house and pushed the door open, there were flies all over the stinking body—wooooo!

Sunjata shouted, "Mother, Mother! Come here! I'll kill someone today. Ever since I was born, I've never done anything bad like this. My brother did this, and I'll take revenge."

Ma Sogolon Condé came to the door.

Sunjata said, "You see this? I went to the bush and forgot about the young man you see lying here. My brother's men beat him to death with their clubs. I'll kill for this young man. I know this is Dankaran Tuman's boy, but he died my death. I'll prove to them that I am not the one who died."

Ma Sogolon Condé knew that Konfara would be destroyed by So'olon Ma'an's revenge, because he would kill anyone known to be one of Dankaran Tuman's supporters.

Sunjata dashed out of the house. When he reached for his iron staff, his mother ran and called Jelimusoni Tunku Manyan Diawara.

Sogolon said, "Sunjata is going to kill someone right now if you don't stop him."

Jelimusoni Tunku Manyan Diawara went and took hold of Simbon.

She said, "Simbon, won't you think about your mother? Simbon! Won't you think of me? Won't you leave this to God? Don't you realize that Dankaran Tuman has poked himself in the eye?" Sunjata tried and tried to break away, but she would not let go. Ha! She was able to hold him.

9. A praise-name for Sunjata that can be translated as "superhero."

Then Ma Sogolon Condé said, "My son Sunjata, your popularity is your biggest problem. If they have started murdering people because of you, shouldn't we go away?"

This is why they went into exile. (One never sells his father's homeland, but it can be pawned!)

Departure for Exile

[*In an omitted passage, Sunjata repeatedly refuses to flee from his step-brother, but Sogolon argues that neither he nor Dankaran Tuman can understand the special circumstances of her background in Dò ni Kiri and how she was brought to their father because of Sunjata's destiny. She convinces Sunjata that even if they go away, he will eventually take over the leadership of Manden.*]

Ma Sogolon Condé then set out to visit Sansamba Sagado, the Somono[1] ancestor. (This is the Sansamba Sagado you always hear about in the histories of Manden. He was involved with the organization of Manden, and those towns along the bank of the river—Jelibakoro, Sansando, and Baladugu—are populated with his Mande descendants. If you talk about Manden without talking about Sansamba Sagado, you have not covered the subject of Manden.)

Saying, "Sansamba Sagado," Sogolon removed her silver wrist and ankle bracelets and gave them to the Somono ancestor as the price for a future river crossing. This way, he would take her children across the river whenever they needed to cross, at any time of day or night, without anybody in Manden knowing that he'd done so.

The days passed. Then, one day, at three o'clock in the morning, Sogolon woke up her children and said, "The time has come for what we talked about."

They left together. When they came to the riverbank, she took the path to Sansamba Sagado's house. Waking him, she said, "This is the day we talked about."

He was not a man to break his promise. Taking his bamboo pole and his paddle, he left to meet Sogolon and her children in the bushes by the bank of the river. The water was rising; it nearly touched the leaves on the bushes. Sansamba Sagado's canoe was attached to a *npeku* tree; he untied it and brought it to them, saying, "Get in!"

Ma Sogolon Condé, her daughter Ma Kolonkan, Manden Bori, and So'olon Jamori got into the canoe. But when they told Sunjata to get in, he refused.

Ma Sogolon Condé said, "Ah, Sunjata! Do you want to make me suffer?"

He said, "Mother, if I told you that I will go with you, then I will go. You take the canoe now; I will join you later."

They crossed the river in the canoe, and before they could reach the other side, they saw Sunjata sitting on the bank. He had brought his *dalilu* with him.

A Visit to Soso

[*In an omitted passage, Sogolon decides to stop in Soso to ask for the help of Sumaworo, a powerful sorcerer who, in his youth, had been her husband's hunting apprentice. Meanwhile, Sumaworo's personal oracle informs him that the man who will eventually take Soso and Manden away from him has not*

---

1. Maninka- or Bamana-speaking specialists in fishing, canoeing, boating, and the water-borne transport of people and goods.

only been born, but has grown up into a hunter and will be identifiable as the one who violates Sumaworo's taboo.]

They were now in Soso.

Sogolon Condé arrived and said, "Eh, Soso *mansa*. These are the children of your former master. Their relationship with their brother is strained, and murder has been committed as a result. The death of one of two friends[2] does not spoil the friendship; the one who survives continues the friendship. I've come to put Ma'an Sunjata and his younger siblings under your protection. You should train them to be hunters, people who can kill their own game." (Oh! She did not know that Dankaran Tuman had sent a message ahead of them to Soso!)[3]

Sumaworo said, "Condé woman, that pleases me. I agree to care for them and take them under my protection, so long as they do not interfere with my sacred totem."

"God willing, they will never spoil your totem."

"Well, if they do not interfere with my totem, then I agree to protect them."

They spent the day there. That evening Ma Sogolon Condé said that she had brought a small amount of cotton she wanted to spin at night, and asked the children of Soso to collect a pile of dried cow dung she could use to light her lantern of conversation.[4] The children brought her the cow dung she needed. Sumaworo owned all the musical instruments, and he brought all of them—except for the *bala*[5]—out for the first time that night. He brought out the *kèrèlèng-kèngbèng*,[6] the *kòwòro*,[7] the *donso nkoni*,[8] the three-stringed *bolon*,[9] the *soron*,[1] and the *kora*.[2] (The *kora* was the last of the instruments to be brought out; that is why they call it *ko la*, which means "the last one."[3] Eventually it came to be called *kora*. It is played in Kita and Senegal.)

Taking out his *nkoni*,[4] Sumaworo sat down by the people who were talking. Sunjata and his siblings came and sat down too. Contented, Ma Sogolon Condé said, "Wait. I will sing three songs." They said, "Very well." When anybody sang, Sumaworo would accompany them on the *nkoni*.

For Ma Sogolon Condé's first song, she sang:

> "Big ram,
> The pen where the rams are kept,
> The leopard must not enter,
> Big ram.

---

2. Sumaworo and Sunjata's father.
3. Offering a reward to kill Sunjata.
4. When villagers gather after dark to socialize and play music, they do it around a lantern to avoid burning valuable fuel needed for cooking fires.
5. An indigenous xylophone.
6. Named from the sound it makes (i.e., onomatopoeic), this child's instrument consists of a tin can resonator (or a tiny gourd) and a stick for a neck that supports a single string.
7. More commonly known as *dan*, an inverted open calabash instrument with a neck for each of its six strings; technically known as a pentatonic pluriac.
8. The hunters' harp, a large animal-skin–covered calabash with a single neck and six

strings, played to praise hunters.
9. The harp used to praise warriors; larger and deeper toned than the hunters' harp, an animal-skin–covered calabash with a single neck supporting three or four strings.
1. A large, rarely seen harp of northeastern Guinea, similar to the *kora* but with twelve strings.
2. With twenty-one strings, the largest of the calabash harps.
3. *Ko la* = literally "later on," another popular etymology.
4. Bamana *ngoni*; a traditional lute consisting of four to five strings attached to a single neck on a wooden, trough-shaped body covered with animal skin.

The pen where the rams are kept,
The leopard must not enter."

Sumaworo's *nkoni* was in harmony with her song.
After that, what else did she sing? She sang:

"Pit water,
Don't compare yourself with clear water flowing over
rocks,
The pure white rocks.
Pit water,
Don't compare yourself with clear water flowing over
rocks,
The pure white rocks."

Again, Sumaworo's *nkoni* was in harmony with her song.
The third song she sang was:

"Big vicious dog,
If you kill your vicious dog,
Somebody else's will bite you,
Vicious dog.
If you kill your vicious dog,
Somebody else's will bite you."

Sumaworo's *nkoni* was still in harmony with her song.
Then the gathering broke up.

[*In omitted passages, Sumaworo performs a ritual to identify his rival for power,
learns that it is Sunjata, and resolves to kill him. Sunjata intentionally violates a
taboo by sitting in Sumaworo's sacred hammock, confirming that he is the rival
described by the oracle. In an episode about Sumaworo's youthful rebelliousness
and leadership, he invents different stringed musical instruments at various
stages of his youth. The narrator describes Fakoli's birth by his father's second
wife, Kosiya Kante, who was also the sister of Sumaworo. During his hunting
apprenticeship, Sumaworo encounters a group of genies and their instruments.
Sumaworo covets the* bala, *but when he hears that the price would be people,
four members of his family, he refuses. Kosiya, upon hearing this, decides to sacrifice herself, and Fakoli is raised by his father's first wife, who carries him to the
sacred sites of Manden to receive protective devices and become a hunter.*

*The scene then shifts back to Soso at the time of Sogolon's visit with her
children, when Sumaworo is in power. Sumaworo interprets the meaning of the
songs sung earlier by Sogolon. Sunjata violates Sumaworo's sacred taboo, the two
men engage in the deadly snuff-taking ritual, and Sunjata is banished from Soso.
Continuing the journey into exile, Sunjata violates sacred taboos in each of the
places they stop, including Nema, where they remain.*]

Sumaworo's Tyranny over Manden

When Sogolon and her children were staying with ancestor Faran Tunkara at
Kuntunya in Nema, he sometimes sent Sunjata on journeys out between the
edges of the village and the place where the sun sets. Whenever war broke out,
the village sent for Sunjata, who would come and join the Kuntunya army, march-

ing along with them. Whenever he captured three prisoners, he kept one for himself. Whenever he captured five prisoners, he kept two. Whenever he captured ten prisoners, he kept four as his share. (The other six captives were given to the Kuntunya *mansa*.) This is how Sunjata collected his own band of men.

Sunjata stayed in Kuntunya for twenty-seven years, and before the end of the twenty-seventh year, well, things turned very bad in Manden. Things were terrible in Manden! Sumaworo, who was looking for Sunjata, had sent his warriors to Manden. Whenever Sumaworo consulted Nènèba, his oracle, it would say, "Your successor has grown."

Before consulting Nènèba, Sumaworo first had to have three age sets of young men pile wood beneath Nènèba's cauldron; this had to be done morning and evening, for the oracle always said, "Fire, fire, fire, fire, fire, fire." Then Sumaworo would bathe in the cauldron's medicines whenever he went to visit Nènèba. And Nènèba would tell Sumaworo what to sacrifice before setting out to war.

Every morning Nènèba told Sumaworo, "Sumaworo, only God knows the day. Your successor has grown up."

Sumaworo asked the Mande people, "Has Ma'an Sunjata returned to Manden?" Meanwhile, he laid waste to Manden nine times. The Mande people struggled and rebuilt their villages nine times during Sumaworo's failed search for Sunjata.

Whenever Sumaworo killed some Mande villagers, he would tell his men to search among the bodies for the Condé woman's son. But his men never found Sunjata; instead, they would return saying, "The Mande people do not know the whereabouts of the Condé woman's son."

Sumaworo then summoned all of the Mande villagers to Kukuba. He killed all of the men who attended this meeting except for the leaders Turama'an and Kankejan, who could disappear in broad daylight, and Fakoli, who could stand and vanish instantly. The people who had that kind of *dalilu* were the only ones he did not kill; he killed all of the other men. The people of Manden mourned and wept. But Ma'an Sunjata and his brothers were not there.

After another month had passed, Sumaworo summoned his men to Bantamba, saying, "I have to finish off the Mande. If I do that, I'll find my successor. If I kill all the human beings, my successor will be among them."

So he called the Mande to a meeting in Bantamba. After looking them over he said to his men, "Kill them all." Only those who had the power to disappear in broad daylight escaped. Again Manden wept.

He summoned the Mande to Nyèmi-Nyèmi, and they wept there, too.

Every time Mande people were summoned by Sumaworo, it ended in mourning. Sumaworo was killing the people of Manden, searching among the bodies for his successor. After every massacre, he would go to his Nènèba. (The Kantés now have that Nènèba in Balandugu, the only town they established. Sumaworo's descendants did not establish any other towns, because he was so ruthless.) The Nènèba would say, "Sumaworo, uh heh. You still haven't found him yet? You've killed so many, yet the one you want is not among them."

Sumaworo asked, "What should I do?" To which the oracle replied, "Keep searching for him. He has reached maturity."

When the Mande people were summoned again, this time to Kambasiga, Fakoli went to see Kani Simbon, the Kulubali ancestor.

He said, "Simbon. Manden is about to be wiped out. We must sit down together and find a solution to this problem in Manden. Manden will be reduced to being Soso's peanut farm, because Sumaworo has said two things. He has said, 'Manden's reputation is better than Manden itself,' and 'The Mande women are better than the Mande men.' By this he meant that Manden has only women because he's killed all the men. He said these things to provoke Sunjata, who he now knows to be his successor, into responding." Having said that, Fakoli then returned to Manden and said, "Let us build a council hall at the edge of town, and let the surviving men of Manden hold meetings there. If we don't get together, Manden is doomed." So the men worked hard and built a council hall. Afterwards, they sat in front of the council hall while Fakoli addressed them.

He said, "We have finished building this council hall, which belongs to all of us—except for the one who wants to destroy Manden. If you are a man of courage, this is your council hall. If you are a man of truth, this is your council hall. If you are a master of sorcery, this is your council hall. If you have love for Manden in your heart, this is your council hall."

The Expedition to Find Sunjata and Return Him to Manden

[*In an omitted passage, the assembled elders decide to summon diviners to learn who will be the liberator of Manden, and where he can be found. After an extended period of divination it is determined that Ma'an Sunjata is the one who was foreseen, and that a special delegation must be sent to find Sogolon and her children. Volunteering for this delegation are the Muslim diviners Manjan Bereté and Siriman Kanda Touré, as well as the female bard Tunku Manyan Diawara and the female slave Jonmusoni Manyan. They plan to visit distant markets with special sauce ingredients that can only be found in Manden, as a way of finding the people they seek.*]

Manjan Bereté laid down his prayer skin[5] as soon as he'd left town, and made two invocations to God: he asked that no one would see the travelers leave, and that they would meet no one on the road. He said, "Siriman Kanda Touré, we mustn't be seen on the road. It doesn't matter whether you are a man or a woman: every one of us must use their *dalilu*." When he'd finished making his two invocations. Manjan Bereté shook hands with his companions, who asked where they would sleep that night.

"Ahhh," said Manjan Bereté, "let us try to reach Soso today. Because tomorrow is Soso's market day."

As a result of his two invocations, each of his companions became invisible when Manjan Bereté shook their hands. When he gave his hand to one of his companions and withdrew it, the person became invisible. Then Manjan Bereté circled his prayer skin and became invisible himself.

They traveled on to the outskirts of Soso, where they spent the night. At daybreak Manjan Bereté said, "Take the things to the market." They set their goods out in the Soso market, but nobody wanted them. They went on to the market of Tabon; but no one wanted what they had. They went to the market of Kirina; no one was interested.

On Thursday they took the road to Kuntunya and slept outside that town to be ready for the market on Friday.

Meanwhile, at a house in that same town, Ma Sogolon Condé was saying to her daughter, "Ma Kolonkan, *aaaoy*! My stomach is hurting me because it's been

---

5. His Muslim prayer rug, the hide of a goat or sheep.

twenty-seven years since I last had *dado*[6] in Manden. Tomorrow morning, do not wash the dishes, do not scrub the pots; instead, be the first one into the market, my child, and get me some *dado* to eat." (When a *dado* eater goes for a long time without having any, their stomach hurts; this is why Ma Sogolon Condé was complaining all night to Ma Kolonkan. It was a good thing that the Mande people spending the night outside of town had brought *dado*!)

As soon as the sun started to show its face the next morning, Manjan Bereté said, "Take the things into the market." The two women went and sat outside the covered part of the market. They had the *dado* there, along with some *namugu* and some *nèrè* seeds[7] they had on display.

Ma So'olon Wulen Condé said to Ma Kolonkan, "Go early to the market so you can get the *dado* I want." As soon as she'd arrived at the market, Kolonkan saw two women standing there with *dado*. She clapped her hands, saying, "From the time we came from Manden, my mother has not said anything about *dado*, nothing at all. It was only yesterday that she suddenly spoke of *dado*—and here it is! Heh! My mother has *dalilu*." She did not even stop to greet the *dado* seller; she immediately reached for the *dado* and put some in her mouth.

Jelimusoni Tunku Manyan Diawara said, "Eh! You, girl, are impolite! Don't touch our merchandise without greeting us or asking us first."

"Eeeh, I was so surprised! My mother told me to come to the market today to see if I could find *dado*. She said she's gone for so long without eating the old things of Manden that her stomach hurts. We haven't seen *dado* since we arrived here; we haven't even seen anyone who sells it. I just wanted to taste it because it is something we always used to have."

Tunku Manyan Diawara asked, "Who are you? Where do you come from?"

"Ah, mother, we come from Manden."

"Who is with you here?"

"I am here with my mother Sogolon Wulen Condé, my elder brother Ma'an Sunjata, and my elder brother So'olon Jamori."

"Aaah! You are the people we have come for! Our road has been good. Let us go to your house."

[*In omitted passages Kolonkan conducts the Mande delegation to her house for a joyful reunion with Sogolon. Manjan Bereté announces that they have been sent to ask Sogolon to return to Manden because her children are needed there. Sogolon explains that her sons are hunting in the bush and concerns herself with providing the customary hospitality to the guests.*

Kolonkan goes out of town to find meat for the guests from Manden and discovers animals killed by her brothers. Her brother Manden Bori is enraged that she has removed the animals' internal organs, and they fight. Kolonkan's curse on his descendants—they will not be able to decide on a ruler until the final trumpet is blown—still affects them in today's Hamana region of Guinea. Tassey Condé mentions a childhood experience with his famous father, Babu Condé, toward the end of the colonial era and describes how he, Tassey, became the spokesman for

---

6. Dried hibiscus blossoms and/or leaves, used as a condiment in sauces.
7. *Namugu* is powdered leaves of the baobab tree, used as an ingredient in sauces. *Nèrè*:

Parkia biglobosa; the seeds are pounded into a paste that is fermented and rolled into balls to make a pungent condiment called *sumbala*.

the bards of Fadama. Reverting to his story, Tassey describes Sogolon's great happiness at the prospect of her sons' returning to Manden. The next episode describes a momentous family meeting of Sogolon and her children, in which the rarely mentioned brother Jamori plays a conspicuous part.]

Sogolon Bestows the Legacy of Maghan Konfara

Sogolon said to her children, "Let us go outside the town. I want to give you my final words." They left the Mande delegation behind and went out of town. When they arrived there, Ma So'olon Condé said to Manden Bori, "Break off that termite mound."[8]

When Manden Bori broke off the termite mound, Sogolon said, "Pick some leaves." He picked some leaves.

She said, "Lay them on the termite mound."

When they were laid on it, she said, "Ma'an Sunjata, you sit on that."[9]

Then she said, "Go and break off another termite mound." So Manden Bori went and broke another one and put leaves[1] on it.

She said, "So'olon Jamori, you sit on that. Now go and break off another one for you to sit on." Manden Bori broke off another termite mound and brought it over.

The three men sat, but Ma So'olon Condé stood up. Ma Kolonkan stood behind her. Women would usually be seated during a hunter's ceremony,[2] but here they did not sit down.

While they were standing, Ma So'olon Wulen Condé said, "Manden Bori! What I say to you is also for So'olon Jamori and for Ma'an Sunjata[3] to hear. The people of Manden have come for you; they are calling you to war.

"When your father died, Dankaran Tuman wanted your father's gold and silver; he also wanted your father's *dalilu* but did not know where to find it. That's why he has plotted against you all this time: he thought that when he killed you, he could take your father's legacy, his *dalilu*.

"But my sons, you do not have your father's *dalilu*; Dankaran Tuman does not have it either. I have your father's *dalilu* here. If you are seeing that a man's *dalilu* went to his last wife,[4] it is because my husband trusted me. When my husband was dying, he gave his *dalilu* to me so that I could keep it safe and give it to you when you reached maturity. I have brought you here now to give you your father's *dalilu*, because the Mande people have come to take you to war. But what worries me is that there are three things in your father's *dalilu*, and they cannot be separated. They can only go to one person. Ah! There are three things, but your father had three sons. These three

---

8. As the youngest of three sons, Manden Bori is ordered to perform the menial tasks.
9. Of the many kinds of termite mounds (some well over six feet tall), the type referred to here is approximately one to two feet high, shaped like a hard clay mushroom, and the larger ones could be used as stools.
1. For a soft and clean seat.
2. If present at a hunters' meeting, women would be seated in the background. In this and the following line, the bard explains that mother and daughter remain standing because

Sogolon is in charge of this solemn occasion.
3. On occasions where oral communication must be precise, it is customary for an important speaker's words to be repeated several times by various people in the presence of the person addressed. When a *jeli* is available the speaker addresses the bard, who repeats and validates what was just heard. At Sogolon's secret meeting, the youngest son serves to repeat and reaffirm her words.
4. The legacy would normally go to the first (senior) wife.

things would not be of any benefit to you if we were to divide them up amongst you.

"The Mande messengers have come for your brother Ma'an Sunjata. You must allow him to be given the three things, because the three things—the sorcery horse, the sorcery bow, and the sorcery mask—all work together: when you sit on the sorcery horse, you must also wear the sorcery mask and take up the sorcery bow. Then you are ready for combat against all comers.

"If you mount the sorcery horse without carrying the sorcery bow, or without wearing the sorcery mask, then somebody will strike you down while the horse is galloping. If you put on the sorcery mask without carrying the sorcery bow and you are not on the horse, you will not be able to kill the enemies you see. If you take up the sorcery bow without wearing the mask and without being on the horse, what good is that? The three things must go to one person: please, allow me to give them to Ma'an Sunjata."

So'olon Jamori said, "Manden Bori, tell our mother that I do not agree to what she is saying. Ah! She herself says there are three things. There are three of us. They are easily divided.

"Have you not heard the Mande saying that if you cannot take your father's legacy on your head, you must at least drag part of it behind you? If I cannot carry it, I will drag it behind me. Let her bring the three things out and divide them between the three of us."

Ma So'olon Condé said, "Eh, So'olon Jamori my son! Eh, So'olon Jamori! I was afraid you'd cause trouble; that is why I wanted to bring you out of the town. Did you not hear me say that there are three things, but they can only solve one problem? Will you not be agreeable?"

Manden Bori said, "Big brother So'olon Jamori,[5] will you not have pity on our mother, who is so worried about this? Let us agree to give the *dalilu* to brother So'olon Maghan."

Ah! Jamori said if Manden Bori did not shut his mouth, he would slap his ears.

Manden Bori said, "You can't slap my ears. Why should you slap my ears for this? Don't you know our brother can battle Soso with or without our father's legacy?

"And who used up our mother's legacy? You and I did; our brother did not take part in that. Our mother took her gold earring and silver bracelet and gave them to Sansamba Sagado, the Somono ancestor, as a future day's river-crossing fee. And how many of us got into the canoe that day, when we left Manden by crossing the river? The canoe our mother paid for with her legacy? Our mother went in the canoe, our little sister got into the canoe, you got into the canoe, and I got into the canoe. Did our brother get in? Hah! Didn't our brother say he was not getting in? Didn't my mother weep? Didn't he say that we should go ahead and he would follow? And by the time we got to the other side of the river, didn't we see our brother already sitting there?

"The *dalilu* with which our brother crossed the river was our father's legacy, and Sunjata can battle Sumaworo with that. But you say you will slap my ears? Why didn't you slap my ears on the riverbank?"

Ma'an Sunjata said, "Manden Bori, be quiet. Tell my mother that we will not quarrel. If you see somebody taking your friend's share of the sauce, your own

---

5. In many variants of the epic, Sogolon's son Jamori is not mentioned at all, and the claim here that Manden Bori was the youngest of the three brothers is an especially rare detail.

sauce cannot satisfy you. Does she think I will quarrel with this foolish person? I will never quarrel with So'olon Jamori over our father's legacy. Even if he were to ask me to give it all to him, I would do it. Tell my mother to bring out the legacy.

"But mother, we will never forget the two things you have done for us. First, we were legitimately born, and it is because of our legitimacy that the Mande people came to find us. Second, my father married fifty women—fifty wives!—and two other women, none of whom gave birth to a child. Sansun Bereté was one of the other two women: she gave birth to Dankaran Tuman and Nana Triban.

"But you! You were the fifty-second wife. Eh! Out of all his wives, why did my father give his legacy to you? Because of your devotion, and it was for us you were so devoted. I trust in God. Even if you do not give me the legacy, I will vanquish Sumaworo because of your devotion. Bring out the legacy."

Ma So'olon Wulen Condé said, "I am pleased with that, now excuse me." She pushed her hand into her abdomen. When she did that, *ho!* The *dalilu* fell out. When the three *dalilu* were piled together, Ma'an Sunjata laughed.

He started to say, "So'olon Jamori," but suddenly his mother began to shake. So'olon Ma'an held his mother until her dizziness passed. When the dizziness left her eyes, Sunjata said, "Manden Bori, tell our mother that she should tell So'olon Jamori he should choose one of the things. Aheh! My little brother and I will not quarrel over my father's legacy."

So'olon Jamori said that he chose the sorcerer's mask. They asked, "Is that your choice?" And he replied, "Uhuh, that is mine." They said, "Very well, take it."

Sunjata said, "Manden Bori, choose one."

Manden Bori said, "I will not take a share in this legacy. I am holding your shirt-tail, and so long as I hold your shirt-tail, nothing will happen to me in the war with Soso. When you die, Sunjata, your legacy will come to me anyway. It was my father's legacy, but you are my father now, and so it belongs to you. Take both my share and your share."

Ma'an Sunjata said, "Is that your word?"

"Uhuh. It is your name, not mine or So'olon Jamori's, that will become attached to the bow and *mansaya*[6] we are quarreling over." (That is why, when people go outside town for a private meeting, they say, "Let us speak with the truth of Manden Bori.")

Manden Bori, the youngest of the brothers, had his oldest brother's blessing. Ma So'olon Wulen Condé spoke. She said, "Manden Bori, is that your word? Come here."

Taking Manden Bori behind a bush, Sogolon said, "Manden Bori, you've honored me, and so now God will honor you. Nobody will ever dishonor you. If you'd acted the way So'olon Jamori acted, then all of the Mande people would know that your father's *dalilu* had been divided—and if your rival knows your secret, he will vanquish you. You preferred to keep all of this secret so I would not be shamed.

"Come and let me give you my legacy. My legacy is something that did not come from here, in Nema, or Manden. It came from Dō ni Kiri, the home of my brothers. I will give this ring to you. So long as you live, it will protect you from genies or enemies that might threaten you; it will also keep you safe in the bush. If you find yourself in trouble, look at this ring and say, 'Ah, mother!' If you do that, God will protect you. If you look at it and say, 'Ah, genie!' God will save you

6. The bow and quiver were symbolic of Mande kingship (*mansaya*).

from genies. If you look at it and say, 'Genie and man!' God will spare you from both." (That was the first of the brass rings hunters now wear on their fingers. Some people call such a ring "genie and man.") Sogolon said, "This is your keep-sake." Then they all returned to town.

[*In the next scene, Sogolon suddenly dies and Sunjata tells Manden Bori to request a plot of land for her burial.*]

The Burial of Sogolon and Departure from Nema

On the path to town, Manden Bori met with Faran Tunkara, the *mansa* of Nema. He said, "Mansa, my brother says that I should come and tell you that my mother is dead. He'd like you to agree to give him some land he can use for her burial."

Now, Faran Tunkara had been unhappy to see the messengers from Manden arrive in Nema. From the time Sunjata arrived in Nema, he'd helped the Kuntunya people win every single battle they'd faced, and he returned with slaves from every campaign. But Faran Tunkara could not keep Sunjata in Nema, because Sogolon and her family had arrived there by choice. He decided to start a quarrel so he could detain Sunjata.

So Nema Faran Tunkara said, "Manden Bori, go and tell your brother that I, Nema Faran Tunkara, say that I own all the land here. Unless you brought a piece of land with you from Manden to bury your corpse in, you should load her body on your head and carry it back to Manden the same way you brought her. Tell him that if you bury her in my land, I will blast her out of the ground with gunpowder. Go and tell your brother that."

Manden Bori returned on the path and relayed Nema Faran Tunkara's message to Sunjata. When he heard what Manden Bori reported, Manjan Bereté said, "What kind of man is Nema Faran Tunkara? Simbon, let me go and give him a real 'message.'"

"Eee," said Sunjata, "just leave it alone. Don't worry, he'll provide the land. I've spent twenty-seven years here; I'm in his army. And he says I should carry my mother's body back to Manden? He'll soon provide the land."

To Manden Bori, Sunjata said, "Go back and tell Nema Faran Tunkara that I, the son of the Condé woman, say he should give me some land in which I can bury my mother. Tell him it is I who say so."

When Tunkara was told this, he said to Manden Bori, "I do not want ever to see you here again. From the minute you first arrived here, I knew that you're a hotheaded man. Go and tell your brother that I don't go back on what I've said twice. Tell him I have no land for him here."

Manden Bori went and told this to Ma'an Sunjata. Manjan Bereté and Siriman Kanda Touré became angry. They were all brave men; they all had *dalilu*, and they all knew how to fight. But when they started to leave the house to find Nema Faran Tunkara, Ma'an Sunjata said, "Be patient and take your seats. He will soon provide the land."

Sunjata took the path that passed behind the house. Along the way, he picked up a fragment of old clay pot, a piece of old calabash, the feather of a guinea fowl, and a partridge feather. To these things he added a stick of bamboo. He gave all of these things to Manden Bori, and said, "Tell Tunkara that I say he should give me land to bury my mother in. If he's asking a price for his land, well, tell him I'll pay his fees with these things. Tell him he must agree to let me lay my mother in the ground."

As he gave Faran Tunkara these things from Sunjata, Manden Bori said, "My brother says this is payment for your land, and that you should agree to let him bury his mother."

Faran Tunkara said, "Is this what you pay for land in your country? Huh, Manden Bori? I do not ever want to see you here again. Take these things and go away."

But Tunkara's *jeli* man, who was sitting there beside him, said, "He should not take those things away from here. Heh! Sunjata has sent you an important message.

"M'ba, when these people came to Nema, didn't I say you should kill Sunjata? And didn't you reply that Sunjata had come to place himself in your care, and that therefore you must not do anything to him? Ahuh! Well, now he has said something to you; there's a message in these things he sent. Since you do not understand the message, I will tell you what these things mean."

To which Faran Tunkara replied, "All right, tell me what they mean."

The *jeli* said, "This piece of bamboo means that you should give him land so he can bury his mother in it. If you do not give him land, the Mande people will come and take it for themselves. If he should be named king after he finishes fighting that war for Manden, he will bring the Mande army here to Nema, and he will break Nema like this old clay pot or this old calabash. Then the guinea fowls and the partridges will take their dust baths in the ruins of Nema. See? These are the feathers of those guinea fowls and partridges. Nothing will grow in the ruins of Nema but weeds; that's what this piece of bamboo stick means."

Now, Mansa Tunkara was a good debater, and he always won arguments. So he said, "I am right."

The *jeli* said, "How can you be right about this?"

"I am right," said Faran Tunkara, "because these people have been here for twenty-seven years. During the time those three brothers served in my army, I lost no battles. They never cheated me, were never disobedient to me; I never had to discipline them for chasing women. Now their mother has died. Are they going to do the right thing and say the corpse is mine, or are they just going to demand that I give them land?"

Everyone agreed that the three brothers should have observed the custom of saying, "This is your corpse."

Faran Tunkara said, "Ah! This is why I refused. Eh! If they were raised correctly as children, they should have said that God has made this my opportunity, and that this is my corpse. But did they show me the proper respect? Should they be looking for land to lay their mother in?"

Everybody said, "You are right!" Even Manjan Bereté himself came and said, "You are right."

"Very well," said Faran Tunkara. "If I am right, give her to me and I will conduct the funeral."

Even though she was a woman, the people of Nema gave Sogolon a man's funeral. They killed cows, fired their guns, and beat the special drum. (This tradition started with Ma So'olon Wulen Condé's funeral.) Then they took her body to the town of Kuntunya, and on Thursday they buried her.

When they were finished with the burial, Simbon asked for Faran Tunkara's permission to leave Nema. Because all debts had now been settled between the two men, Sunjata was able to say, "I will leave tomorrow."

Faran Tunkara said, "Go with my blessing. I give you the road." But once Sunjata and his brothers had returned to their house, Faran Tunkara summoned his warriors, telling them, "I cannot allow Sunjata to leave with his men, because those men are rightfully mine; Sunjata had no men of his own until he arrived here. Prepare yourselves and go on ahead to cut them off. Go ahead as far as the second village and wait for them there; attack them when they arrive, and try to capture them. If you bring them back, they will never leave Nema again."

Faran Tunkara's warriors left, passing the first village and preparing their attack at the second. And when Sunjata and his companions arrived at the second village, they were attacked. So'olon Jamori did not survive the attack! He died there; he did not live to reach Manden. So the three parts of his father's legacy were combined and given to Simbon. (That is why we say that if a *kamalen* of the Mansaré lineage becomes selfish, do not bother to curse him. He won't live long.)

Sunjata and his men escaped that ambush, and Sunjata added the captives they took from among Faran Tunkara's warriors to his own troops.

[*The narrator explains that despite the ambush that killed So'olon Jamori, Faran Tunkara sent troops to support Manden's campaign against Soso, and Sunjata never attacked Nema. Claiming that he wants to notify Sumaworo of his return so he will not be accused of sneaking back into Manden, Sunjata stops in Soso. Sumaworo issues a series of warnings to Sunjata that he must not attack Soso. They engage in a traditional boasting contest, concluding with Sunjata's vow to return and Sumaworo's reply that he will be waiting.*]

The Return of Sunjata

Sunjata took the road toward home. When they arrived at the edge of town, the townspeople could hear *nege* music[7] played by Jelimusoni Tunku Manyan Diawara.

She sang to Manden:

"The *danama yirindi*[8] that we have been looking for,
He is at the edge of town.
Come, let us go.
For the sake of the Condé woman's son,
Come, let us go.
The person that Manden was busy searching for,
Known as So'olon Ma'an,
Come, let us go."

Sansamba Sagado crossed the river with his canoe that day. He put the canoe into the river without a pole or paddle, and as soon as he untied the canoe, it headed straight for Sunjata and his men—*prrrr*, just as if it had a motor.

Sunjata loaded his men into the canoe and said, "You will now see the power of my *dalilu*." He struck the water, the canoe went *prrrr*, and they landed on the

---

7. *Nege* = iron; also a synonym for the *nkarin-yan*, a rhythm instrument consisting of a notched iron tube seven to eight inches long, held in one hand and scraped with a thin metal rod.
8. Roughly translated as "superhero."

riverbank in Manden, where Simbon stepped out. His fathers, brothers, and all the men of Manden were there to greet and embrace him. (The shade tree under which the people of Manden welcomed Sunjata home is still living today.) When he arrived, Manden was jubilant, Manden celebrated. They named that place Nyani, the town of happiness, the town of rejoicing, *ko anyè nyani so*.[9]

As the people of Manden welcomed Sunjata and his men, they said, "Manjan Bereté, you are welcome; Siriman Kanda Touré, you are welcome; Tunku Man-yan Diawara, you are welcome; Jonmusoni Manyan, you are welcome. You have brought a gift for Manden: you have found Simbon! We knew that someday the son of Farako Manko Farakonken and the Condé woman would return. But Manden suffered while he was away; we have suffered so much at Sumaworo's hands. Let Sunjata see for himself how many of those he knew here have been killed by Sumaworo. The only people left here are those with *dalilu*, and Suma-woro has even caused those who have *dalilu* to suffer.

"When we knew Sunjata was returning, we carried out divinations and swore oaths and saw that only he could receive ancestor Mamadi Kani's legacy. And now that he has come, heh! We all—the Kulubali, the Konaté, and the Douno—say that he should accept the legacy and help Manden. Simbon, you have been called to take the legacy." (This saying—"Take your legacy," or *ko ila kè ta*—came to be spoken as "Keita.")

[*In the following brief departure from his narrative, the bard (who is traditionally expected to instruct as well as entertain) reiterates his view of human origins and explains who really built Paris. In the omitted passage, the bard explains the power of the Condé people, their descent from Isiaaka, and the equality of all humans as children of God.*]

Fakoli Reveals His Power

While the Mande men were in a meeting, a message from Sumaworo arrived. He said that he'd been waiting a long time for a message from the Mande. He said it had been a long time since their *mansa* arrived, and that he'd not seen any Mande messengers. Finally, Sumaworo said that since So'olon Ma'an had now returned home, he wanted to see all of the Mande people at Dakajalan on the fourteenth of the new month. The battle had now been set.

As soon as he heard Sumaworo's message, So'olon Ma'an replied by having his people beat the signal drum, calling everyone to the council hall. On his way to the council hall, Fakoli was thinking, "We are going to march against Soso!" But his mother and Sumaworo had suckled at the same breast, and he wondered if it was right for him to join the Mande people in attacking Sumaworo. He decided, "As soon as I get to the council hall, I will ask the Mande people to let me go to Soso. Let Manden come and fight both me and my uncle."

But before Fakoli had the chance to say this to the men gathered in the council hall, Manden Bori laughed at him. Manden Bori always ridiculed Fakoli whenever he entered the council hall. When he heard Manden Bori laughing at him, Fakoli became angry and said, "Turama'an, let me give you a message for Simbon. Tell Simbon to ask his younger brother why he always laughs at me. Of all the people that enter the council hall, it's me

9. This and the following line comprise a popular etymology.

that Manden Bori laughs at. Why does he laugh at me? What have I done to him?"

When Ma'an Sunjata was given this message, he said, "Manden Bori, stop laughing at Fakoli. Didn't you hear him saying that you are shaming him? Why do you laugh at him?"

Manden Bori replied, "Big brother, the tall men always duck their heads as they enter the council hall. Though Fakoli is only one and a half arm-spans tall, he also ducks his head when he comes in. That is what makes me laugh. Aaah, that Fakoli, heh, heh."

Fakoli said, "Turama'an, tell Simbon that he should tell his younger brother that short Mande people can do things that tall Mande people cannot do. And he'd better believe it."

Manden Bori said, "I won't believe that until I see it. Really, do you believe that? I don't."

Fakoli picked up his goatskin rug and, placing it in the center of the council hall, sat down on it. He waved his hand and grunted. He raised the roof from the house! The sun shone in on everybody. He said, "Well, Manden Bori, what about that?"

Manden Bori said, "You spoke the truth."

(They were fair about crediting one another with the truth, for there was respect among those with *dalilu*.)

The people asked Fakoli to put the roof back where it belonged. They said, "No tall Mande man has ever done such a thing."

Then Fakoli placed his hand in the middle of the council hall floor. He crouched there and wrinkled his face. Wrinkled his face and wrinkled his face! He squeezed everyone against the wall. That was the origin of the song "Nyari Gbasa," which goes:

> "Fakoli, our arms will break,
> Fakoli, our heads will burst,
> Fakoli, our stomachs will rupture."

(That song belongs to the Koroma family.)

The people said, "Fakoli, stop! No tall Mande man has done such a thing."

Fakoli Explains His Dilemma and Takes His Leave from Manden

After performing these feats, Fakoli spoke to the assembled elders. He said, "Turama'an, Simbon, and everyone in the council hall: Sumaworo has sent a message that we should meet at Dakajalan. But my mother and Sumaworo were the children of the three Touré women, and it would be shameful for me to participate in Manden's attack on my uncle. I ask that you give me leave to go to Soso. I should be at my uncle's side when you come to attack him."

Ma'an Sunjata heard what Fakoli said, even though Manden Bori refused to repeat it to him. To Manden Bori, Sunjata said, "Haven't I told you? Fakoli is right. You and I have uncles whose home is Dò ni Kiri. What if we knew that Dò ni Kiri would be attacked? Would we stay here and do nothing?"

Manden Bori said, "Would anyone dare to attack Dò ni Kiri?"

"That's not the point. If Fakoli says he is going to help his mother's kinsman, leave him alone and let him go." Then, turning to Fakoli, Sunjata said, "Fakoli, you have done well by Manden. You helped us during Sumaworo's nine invasions of Manden, and our nine efforts to rebuild our homeland. So if you should say that you are going to help your uncle, very well; we won't stop you. But remember that if we meet on the battlefield there will be no brotherhood, no friendship between us. Don't think us ungrateful. But there's no gratitude when the guns start firing. That is all I have to say."

Fakoli said, "Bisimillahi,"[1] and returned to his house for the night.

The next morning Fakoli bathed in the water of his seven medicine pots. Taking his battle-axe on his shoulder, he brought out his horse and mounted it. His groom, Nyana Jukuduma,[2] was with him. He lifted up his wife, Keleya Konkon, and sat her behind him on his horse; then he took the ends of his scarf and tied them together, saying, "Because I know the kind of man my uncle is, he might wait for me on the road."[3]

While he was preparing to leave, another message from Sumaworo arrived. Sumaworo said that he'd been informed of Fakoli's plan to help him fight against Manden, and that Fakoli must not go to Soso. Sumaworo said he'd learned that if the Mande were successful in defeating him, they planned to replace Sumaworo with Fakoli as ruler of Soso. When the people of Soso heard this, they promised to cut off Fakoli's head, just as the Mande people already wanted to. Thus, one way or another, said Sumaworo, Fakoli's "feet would be bringing his head" if he dared to come to Soso. Fakoli laughed, "I'm not going to die for anyone—not Sunjata, and not Sumaworo." (Even today, that expression is often quoted.)

Fakoli said, "Go and tell my uncle that I'll soon be there. If I were really planning to get myself killed, then I'd let him carry out his threats against me. But since I don't intend to die, I'll go to Soso today. Tell him to get ready."

[*In an omitted passage, Sumaworo deploys soldiers to intercept Fakoli and kill him, but Fakoli makes himself and his companions invisible and arrives unscathed at the gates of Soso.*]

Fakoli Finds Trouble in Soso

When Sumaworo learned that Fakoli was accompanied only by his wife and his slave, he told Bala Fasali,[4] "Take the *bala* and welcome my nephew."

Bala Fasali took up the *bala* and sang the song we now call "Janjon":[5]

> "Eh, Fakoli!
> You became a son.
> If death is inevitable,
> A formidable child should be born.
> The Mande people said
> That if you came, they would wait for you on the road.
> The people of Soso said
> That if you came, your feet would bring your head.
> Knowing that, you still had no fear.
> If death is inevitable,
> A formidable child should be born."

---

1. Literally, "in the name of Allah" (Arabic), a traditional Muslim invocation spoken at the outset of an undertaking [editor's note].
2. A slave that cared for his horse.
3. To ambush him.
4. An unusual pronunciation of this famous bard's name, which is usually given as Bala Fasaké, or a variant thereof.
5. One of the oldest and most famous songs of Manden, said to have been originally composed for Fakoli, but in later times played to honor any distinguished personage.

Sumaworo welcomed Fakoli by standing and raising his elephant tail in salute. Fakoli sat down and explained why he had come to Soso. He said, "Bala Fasali, you take part in this.[6] Let Sumaworo hear what I have to say. I have come because Sumaworo has done many things, and though I was invisible as I traveled, I come in good faith.

"The three Touré women gave birth to my mother and to Sumaworo. I have been thinking about my mother ever since war was declared between Soso and Manden. Had my mother been a man, she would have fought in this war alongside Sumaworo, her brother. That is why I decided to come: to fight in place of my mother. I have come to Sumaworo through the will of God; let us unite and fight the coming war together."

Sumaworo replied, "Bala Fasali, I'll tell you what to say to Fakoli. Tell him that I appreciate his words, and that I am pleased he has come."

After this meeting, Fakoli was taken to meet Sumaworo's wives. Sumaworo had three hundred and thirty-three wives. Fakoli had only one wife, Keleya Konkon.

To his three hundred and thirty-three wives, Sumaworo said: "Fakoli has arrived just as I am going to war. The oracle Nènèba says that in order to win this war I must offer three hundred and thirty-three different dishes as sacrifice. I want these dishes to be prepared the day after tomorrow, on Friday. I mention this because Fakoli should know about this sacrifice if we are to be allies."

Fakoli said, "Fine. Since I have come to take the place of my mother, my wife will cook the one bowl of food my mother would have provided."

When the Soso women heard Fakoli say that, they said, "Paki! We'll show that Mande woman how much better a Soso woman's cooking is." This was insulting to Keleya Konkon, who said, "I'm going to build my fire near theirs. Fakoli, go and find a cooking pot for me. Those Soso women want to brag? They'll soon learn that Mande women can also cook. They will realize that Manden has kitchens, too." Fakoli left to find a cooking pot for Keleya Konkon.

Among the three hundred and thirty-three dishes prepared by Sumaworo's wives were beans, rice, fonio, cereal paste, millet wafers, wheat meal, cassava, and porridge: all of these different foods were included in the sacrifice.

Fakoli's wife said to him, "Bring me rice, pounded cassava, and fonio for my pot. God willing, I'm going to cook a meal that the *jelilu* will sing about for years to come."

Keleya Konkon put her one pot on the fire. Whenever she saw the Soso women who were cooking rice put some into their pots, she would put rice in her one pot, then sit down. Whenever she saw the Soso women who were cooking fonio put some into their pots, she would add some fonio in her one pot then sit down.

When the women who were cooking *monie*[7] were rolling their *monie* balls, Keleya Konkon also rolled *monie* balls. When the women put the *monie* balls into their pots, Keleya Konkon would put *monie* balls into her pot too, then take her seat. When the women who were baking *takura*[8] were putting their *takura* balls into their pots, Keleya Konkon also put *takura* balls into her pot, then sat down.

---

6. Custom dictated that the dignitary, in this case Fakoli, would speak to the *jeli*, who would then add weight to the message by repeating it to the person addressed.
7. A millet porridge made with small balls of

millet flour flavored with tamarind or lemon.
8. A millet cake made with five balls of soaked millet flour and baked or steamed in a clay pot buried in the ground; one of the preferred foods for sacrifice or alms-giving.

So Keleya Konkon put into her one pot all of the same things the Soso women put into their three hundred and thirty-three pots. Then, when the women started dishing out rice, she took her rice bowl and dished out the rice from her pot. When the women started dishing out the fonio, she took her fonio bowl and dished out her fonio from the same pot.

Sumaworo's wives produced three hundred and thirty-three dishes—but Fakoli's wife also produced three hundred and thirty-three dishes, and all from her one pot! The wives couldn't get the best of her.

Some scandalmongers went to Sumaworo and told him what had happened, adding, "Didn't we tell you that Fakoli came to take your place? You have three hundred and thirty-three wives, who have cooked you three hundred and thirty-three dishes. Your nephew has only one wife, but she has also prepared three hundred and thirty-three dishes! In fact, Keleya Konkon's servings are bigger than yours! Everything that you have, Fakoli now also has. He came to take your place. If you don't take this Fakoli business seriously, he will take Soso away from you even before you go to war."

Sumaworo said, "Huh? Oho!" And he called his people together. Sumaworo sent the scandalmonger to go and bring Fakoli to the meeting.

Instead of going to find Fakoli, the scandalmonger simply went and stood on the road, then returned to Sumaworo, saying, "I have called him." A lot of time passed; Fakoli did not come to see Sumaworo. When Sumaworo sent for someone, he expected that person to arrive one minute after the messenger returned.

"Ah!" said Sumaworo. "Did you not see my nephew?"

To which the scandalmonger replied, "I saw him."

"Ah, did you not call him?"

"I called him."

"All right, go and tell him I am waiting for him."

The scandalmonger went and stood in the road again. Returning to Sumaworo, he said, "I have called him."

More time passed and still Fakoli did not appear. Now very angry, Sumaworo sent another messenger to get Fakoli. He said, "You go and tell Fakoli that I am waiting for him."

That messenger did find Fakoli. He said, "Fakoli, this is the third time you have been called. Why didn't you come when we called? Who do you think you are?"

Fakoli said, "Me? Was I called three times?"

"Yes, the message came and came again."

"Me? M'ba, I refuse."

That messenger ran back and told Sumaworo, "Your nephew refuses to come."

Sumaworo said, "*Paki!* That's it! Fakoli dares tell me, Sumaworo, 'I refuse'?"

Once Sumaworo's last messenger had gone, Fakoli put on his hat with the three hundred birds' heads. He put his axe on his shoulder and tied his head-band around his head, because he knew there was going to be trouble.

When Sumaworo saw Fakoli approaching, he stood up in his royal seat and said, "Fakoli, am I the one to whom you said, 'I refuse'?"

Fakoli replied, "I refuse," for he believed it would be cowardly to explain himself to Sumaworo.

Again, Sumaworo asked, "Am I the one to whom you said, 'I refuse'?"

"I refuse."

"Why?"

"I refuse."

"Ah, very well." Sumaworo said. "What they told me is the truth. You claim that you came to help me. But you have not come to help me. You know what you came for. I have three hundred and thirty-three wives who have prepared three hundred and thirty-three dishes for me. You have only one wife, yet she also produced three hundred and thirty-three dishes for you.

"Did you come to help me? Were you told that your head and my head are equal? I gave you this wife you're so proud of—the one with your mother's name[9]—and now I am taking her back. You can't brag about what you don't have anymore! This Kosiya Kanté that you have, she is my daughter,[1] so now I am taking her back."

Fakoli said, "Ah! Uncle, have matters between us sunk so low? Has our dispute come to the point of taking back a wife? You can have her! I don't even want her now, at least not until the smoke from our battle with the Mande people at Dakajalan has settled. Until then, I don't want her!"

He brought out his blanket and tore off a strip, *prrrr*! He threw it to Keleya Konkon and told her to use it for a mourning veil, saying, "I will not marry you again until I've defeated your brother[2] in gunsmoke. I am returning to Manden."

Turning his back on Keleya Kondon, he gave the tail of his horse to Nyana Jukuduma,[3] and the two men took the road to Manden, where the diviners were still praying to God.

When Fakoli got back to Manden, he went and stood at the door of the council hall. He said, "Simbon, my uncle and I have quarreled. He has taken my wife from me. I will not take back Keleya Konkon until I do it in gunsmoke."

"Huh," Ma'an Sunjata laughed.

Manjan Bereté and Siriman Kanda Touré also laughed. They said, "Manden is now complete." They said they had put their trust in Turama'an. (This is why you sometimes hear a person say that they put their trust in Turama'an instead of Fakoli.[4] The people gave their trust to Turama'an while Fakoli was off visiting his uncle.)

Still standing on the threshold of the council hall, Fakoli said, "Simbon, I do not want a wife from Manden or Negeboriya. Send a message to your uncles in Dò ni Kiri, and ask them to give you your 'nephew wife.'[5] Then give that wife to me. I want to have that woman before we go to the battle at Dakajalan. Then, regardless of what happens, no one will be able to blame my actions in battle on the fact that I have no wife. If I don't have a wife before going into battle, the

---

9. Fakoli's mother was Kosiya, so his wife Keleya was not exactly her namesake.

1. Family relationships among Manding peoples are perceived on several levels, or "paths." Keeping in mind that this is the storyteller's viewpoint, this is probably meant in the sense that the wife Sumaworo provided for Fakoli was a classificatory "daughter" of Sumaworo. In Manding societies, the children of one's cousins are considered to be one's own children.

2. In the same way that Keleya Konkon could be a classificatory "daughter" of Sumaworo, she could also be a classificatory "sister." Indeed, on one path a person can be classified as one's sibling, while on another path the same person can be referred to as one's father, uncle, mother, or aunt. This reflects the polygymous practice of men marrying wives of the same age as their children.

3. The slave would run behind the horse, hanging on to its tail.

4. Turama'an had acquired a leadership position or military command that was formerly held by Fakoli.

5. In Maninka and Bamana society, it is claimed, both jokingly and seriously, that it is the uncle's duty to give his nephew a wife, the so-called nephew wife. The obligation of this uncle–nephew bond is implied in the Bamana proverb: "When your uncle fails to give you a wife, he is no longer your uncle but your mother's brother."

people will say I fought well because I was trying to get myself a wife—that I was afraid of staying a bachelor. So let me have your 'nephew wife' before we leave for the war." Ma'an Sunjata sent a message to his uncle (our ancestor!) in Dò ni Kiri, who sent Ma Sira Condé to Sunjata as his nephew wife. Ma'an Sunjata then gave this wife to Fakoli.

At that time, Fakoli was feeling bitter. Having refused to live in Negeboriya, Manden, and Soso, he'd built his own hamlet and remained there until it was time for the battle at Dakajalan. The people all said, "Eeeh, Fakoli is bitter! He has refused to live with us; he's built his own hamlet." (That hamlet, built in Manden, became Bambugu, and it was there that Sira Condé was brought to Fakoli.)

A Visit to Kamanjan in Sibi

Dressed in his ritual attire, Sunjata said to Fakoli, "Before she died, my mother asked God to help me earn the support of a Mande elder whose *dalilu* is greater than mine, and I believe I must not go to war without having first accomplished this. Now that you're settled, Fakoli, I ask you—just as I'm asking Turama'an, Kankejan, Tombonon Sitafa Diawara, and all the Simbons—please give me sixty men so I can greet Kamanjan, because I esteem him above all other elders."

Kamanjan was much older than Sunjata; Kamanjan and Sunjata's father, Maghan Konfara, were born at the same time. Kamanjan never committed a shameful deed in his entire life, and anyone who commanded an army would seek his advice. This is why Sunjata said, "Let's go to greet Kamanjan."

With sixty men, Sunjata went to salute Kamanjan at the battle site called Kalassa, near Sibi Mountain, where Kamanjan liked to hold torchlit meetings at night. It was a special honor to be asked by Kamanjan to extinguish the torches at the end of such meetings; only those *kamalenw* he knew to be special in their towns would be allowed to put out the flames.

Sunjata arrived as Kamanjan was having one of his nighttime meetings, and all of the torches were lit. With his hand, Sunjata extinguished them all. Then he used a little thing to reignite them, *kan!* Suddenly everything was illuminated again. The people at the meeting said, "As soon as Sunjata put out the torches, he lit his own torch."

(Sunjata's own light was as powerful as the light from a pressure lamp, and the little town where Sunjata extinguished the torches is called Kalassa, which is near Tabon on the Bamako road. The Konaté live there.)

After relighting the torches, Sunjata saluted Kamanjan and explained the purpose of his visit, saying, "I left here with my mother; now I have returned."

Kamanjan said, "Simbon! Have you come?"

"Yes, I have come."

"Ah, are you the one that Manden will send against Sumaworo?"

"Uhuh. That is why I have come to greet you, father Kamanjan. The last person to be told you're leaving on a trip must be the first person you greet upon your return."

"Sunjata, what *dalilu* did you bring with you? Hm? Sumaworo is a bad one. Haven't you heard people sing his praises? They sing:

'Transforms in the air,
Sumaworo,
Transforms on the ground,

Sumaworo.
Manden pi-pa-pi,
Whirlwind of Manden,
Kukuba and Bantamba,
Nyemi-Nyemi and Kambasiga,
Sege and Babi'?"

Sunjata said, "Yes, Father Kamanjan, I've heard that."

"Then what kind of *dalilu* did you bring to use against him?"

"Ah, father Kamanjan, that is why I have come to greet you and tell you my thoughts."

"Well, I've become old since we last met here. I can't go to war again, nor can I ask anyone else to do that. All those who attacked Sumaworo have been defeated, and this is Manden's fault; it was Manden that made it possible for Sumaworo to become what he is. It was a mistake for us to give him the four *jamanaw*.[6] Not satisfied with that, he now wants to add Manden to Soso. That is what we must fight to avoid."

Kamanjan and Sunjata were talking beneath the tree that is called *balansan*[7] in Manden, and when Kamanjan said, "Ah!" the *balansan* flipped upside down onto its top branches.

When Sunjata also said, "Ah!" the *balansan* flipped back over onto its roots. (It's true, *binani tinima*!)

Kamanjan said, "Ah!" a second time, and the *balansan* flipped back over onto its top branches.

Before Sunjata could say, "Ah," again, his sister whispered in his ear, "Big brother, this is not what my mother told you to do. Let Kamanjan do this. Our mother prayed that you would be blessed by an elder with *dalilu* stronger than yours. Kamanjan is trying to demonstrate to you how strong his *dalilu* is. If you beat him with your own *dalilu*, he will not give you anything. Let him do this, and he will flip the tree back once he's satisfied. If you add his *dalilu* to what you already have, maybe you will win the war against Sumaworo. You should act like you do not know anything, so Kamanjan will give you his *dalilu*."

A Strategic Alliance: Kolonkan's Marriage

The battle that followed Sunjata's meeting with Kamanjan did not go well for Manden, and the town was filled with sorrow. But Kamanjan didn't let Sunjata leave him empty-handed. Kamanjan said, "Simbon, I see that your sister has matured since we last met. Yes, she has matured, and you should give her to me so I can marry her. Though your sister spent twenty-seven years at Nema, your mother—who was of the best stock—said she would never be given to a man there. You yourself agreed that your sister would only be married here in Manden. So give her to me."

---

6. The four main provinces of Soso that commonly appear in praise-lines to Sumaworo (though rarely identified in the same way): Kukuba, Bantamba, Nyemi-Nyemi, and Kambasiga. This comment, which the bard attributes to a contemporary of Sunjata's father, appears to imply a failed policy of appeasement toward Sumaworo.

7. *Acacia albida*; in Mande lore, one of the many trees, including the baobab and the dubalen, that carry strong associations with the spirit world.

Ma'an Sunjata said, "Eh! Father Kamanjan, that won't be possible. If I give you my younger sister, I would be embarrassed to discuss certain subjects with you. There are things I could discuss with you so long as there's no marriage between us. Now that my mother and father are both dead, I'm depending on your counsel on such matters. But a marriage between us would make it embarrassing for me to do so.[8] Besides that, you are a battle commander. If we do something to displease you, if you become offended, we might quarrel."

Kamanjan said, "Ah, give her to me."

"Well, I'll give her to you if you will command the Kamara people to show respect for the Mansaré people. Tell the Kamara people to show respect for my people and for me. The Kamara should respect us, *Kamaralu yé dan a na.*" (The Dannalu, who take their name from that saying, live between Balia and Wulada. Now, because of Ma Kolonkan's marriage to Kamanjan, the Dannalu must be mentioned whenever the Kamara are discussed.) Ma Kolonkan was given to Kamanjan Kamara as soon as he made this promise to Sunjata. Kamanjan entered her, and she eventually gave birth to his son Fadibali.

The Battle of Negeboriya

Kamanjan said, "Simbon, I respect you, and believe you'll be successful in the war against Sumaworo. But listen: don't go to Dakajalan yet. Go to Negeboriya first and pay your respects to Fakoli's relatives. Though Fakoli is from Negeboriya, not Manden, he has done much for us. Besides, haven't you ever heard the saying, 'Negeboriya Maghan, Kayafaya Maghan'?[9] The Negeboriyans are our in-laws.

"Fakoli has said, 'The Mande people are wrong if they think I am helping them only because I want to win the *mansaya* for myself,' and we believe him. After all, none of the Koroma living in our Mansaré towns have ever tried to take the *mansaya* for themselves.

"Fakoli has also said, 'I am only helping Manden because of Ma Tenenba Condé; it was she who raised and blessed me. Tenenba Condé's sister is So'olon Wulen Condé, and So'olon Wulen Condé's son is Ma'an Sunjata. So I am not helping you because of personal ambition. If you listen to the Mande people's gossip about me now, you'll be ashamed to face me later.'

"Turama'an and Kankejan have said the same sorts of things. So go and pay your respects to the people of Negeboriya."

Taking their leave from Tabon, Ma'an Sunjata and his companions mounted their horses and rode straight to Negeboriya. But Sumaworo had built a wall around that town by the time they arrived. In fact, Sumaworo had built walls around many towns of Manden and was occupying them with his troops.

When Sumaworo's men heard that So'olon Ma'an and his troops were coming to pay their respects to the people of Negeboriya, they lined their musket barrels along the top of the wall and waited. When Sunjata and his men arrived, the muskets fired and fired and fired at them!

Forced to retreat, Sunjata returned to find Manden in mourning over his defeat at the Battle of Negeboriya. But Sunjata's powerful army was not destroyed, and

---

8. In this case of *buranya* ("having an older in-law"), Sunjata would have to practice great restraint and lack of familiarity toward his sister's husband, and would no longer be able to appeal to him for help or advice.

9. Kayafaya is said to have been a *jamana*, or province, attached to Negeboriya under the Koroma ruling lineage.

Sumaworo had lost his sacred drum Dunun Mutukuru during the battle. (That drum, the Dunun Mutukuru, was never found; only the *bala* was saved.)

[*In omitted passages, back in Manden two rams that are named for Sunjata and Sumaworo, respectively, fight one another in a symbolic preview of the battle to come. Preparing for the Battle of Dakajalan, Sunjata calls for volunteers. The army of Manden is divided into companies of men who possess occult powers, companies of those who have no magic, and one unit made up of famous ancestral figures with the power to become invisible. In a secret meeting with Manjan Bereté, Sunjata learns the elaborate strategy he must adopt to defeat Sumaworo. He exchanges his sorcery horse for the sorcery mare of the jelimuso Tunku Manyan Diawara. He also sends a messenger to his sister, Nana Triban, who is in Soso, to retrieve from her the dibilan medicine that she steals from the tail of Sumaworo's horse*]

Trading Insults and Swearing Oaths

Manden mourned after each of their battles against Sumaworo. He made many women widows. He made shirts and pants from the skins of Mande and Soso people. He sewed a hat of human skin. He even made shoes of human skin and then ordered the surviving Mande people to come and name them. If one of the people tried to name the shoes "Finfirinya Shoes," Sumaworo would say, "That is not the name." If someone tried "Dulubiri shoes," he would say, "That is not the name." Finally, the people asked him, "All right, Sumaworo, what are your shoes called?" He said, "My human-skin shoes are called 'Take the Air, take the Ground from the Chief.' I wear your skins because the Mande people will always be around me, Sumaworo. You will always be in my power."

After both sides had made their preparations, the war began. Briefly, here's what happened:

The three Mande divisions—including those men who could become invisible in the daytime and the five *mori* diviners—arrived at the first battle. Simbon was placed in the middle of his men, with Manjan Bereté directly in front of him. The men were packed so tightly that the head of one man's horse touched the tail of the horse in front of him. Sanbari Mara Cissé and Siriman Kanda Touré were there, as were Kòn Mara and Djané, Manden Bori, Tombonon Sitafa Diawara, Turama'an, Kankejan, and Fakoli. Sunjata ordered them to maintain their positions on the battlefield, so they marched back and forth in a line, like an army of ants. Simbon was in the middle!

When they arrived at the battlefield, Ma'an Sunjata said, "Men of Manden, wait here," and crossed the field with his masked flag bearers, headed for Sumaworo's camp. Sumaworo's troops were also there, waiting in position. Sumaworo sat astride his horse, surrounded by his corps of personal guards.

As he approached Sumaworo, Sunjata said, "Father Sumaworo, good morning." (True bravery is revealed by the mouth!)

Sumaworo said, "Marahaba, good morning. Where are the Mande troops?"

"Ah, Father Sumaworo, they are over on the Mande side."

"Ah, is that how you usually arrange your troops?"

Sunjata said, "Well, I am new at this. This is our first encounter in battle. If I brought my men over here, they'd mingle with your troops, and we'd be unable to tell whose men are whose.[1] You can see them standing over there on the Mande side."

"Ah, So'olon Ma'an, this is not the usual procedure."

Feeling bold, Sunjata said, "Well, you killed all of the other leaders; there was nobody left to lead the Mande troops."

Sumaworo said, "I say to you, Bala Fasali, tell Simbon that I am doing him a favor by inviting him to meet here on the battlefield. I understand that the Mande people sent for Sunjata so he could be their commander in battle. But apparently they did not tell him about anything that happened while he was away.

"This is why I have invited him to come and meet in the field: so that I can tell him what I have to say, and he can tell me what is on his mind. Then I will do to him what I planned to do—or he can try to do to me what he wants to."

Simbon said, "I appreciate the invitation. Ah! You are my respected elder. The person who has helped one's father is also one's father. But let me tell you something, father Sumaworo: people may refuse peanuts, but not the ones that have been placed right in front of them."

Sumaworo said, "M'ba, give me some snuff from Manden."[2]

"Ah! Father Sumaworo, it is more appropriate for the master to give snuff to his apprentice, rather than for the apprentice to give snuff to his master. Give me some snuff from Soso, so that I will know I have met my master."

Sumaworo took out his snuffbox and handed it to Sunjata. Simbon put some snuff in his palm, took a pinch and snorted it, took another pinch and snorted it, and put some in his mouth. He closed the snuffbox and gave it back to Sumaworo. The snuff did not even make Sunjata's tongue quiver.

Sumaworo was surprised. Anybody who took that snuff would immediately fall over. It was poison! But So'olon Ma'an sucked on the snuff and didn't even cough. He spit the snuff on the ground.

Then Sumaworo said, "Give me some Mande snuff." Simbon reached in his pocket, took out his snuffbox, and handed it to Sumaworo, who put some in his palm. He took a pinch of snuff and snorted it, took some more and snorted it, and put the rest in his mouth. That was specially prepared snuff, too, but it did not do anything to him.

Sumaworo said to him, "I asked you to meet with me because the Mande people seem to think you are their *mansa*, and it's true that you would not be here if you didn't have some *dalilu*. But your *dalilu* will do no good against me. I told you before, when you passed through Soso, that if the Mande people tried to send you to fight me, you should refuse. As you now know, I have become hot ashes surrounding Manden and Soso; any toddler who tries to cross me will be burned up to his thighs. And yet here you are."

"Ah, father Sumaworo, as I told you, this is my father's home, not yours. You are not from here: your grandfather came from Folonengbe; your father was a latecomer to Manden. You are only the second generation of your people in Manden. But we have been here for eight generations: our ancestor Mamadi

1. The problem of distinguishing between ally and enemy in the heat of battle was a serious concern. In an episode not included in this book, the narrator describes how Kamanjan Kamara introduced facial scarification for that purpose.

2. This request commences a standard ritual called *sigifili*, conducted between opposing commanders before a battle; it involved boasting about one's powers and swearing oaths while taking a poisonous snuff that would kill a liar.

Kani first came here from Hejaji. After him came Mamadi Kani's son, Kani Simbon, Kani Nyogo Simbon, Kabala Simbon, Big Simbon Mamadi Tanyagati, Balinene, Bele, and Belebakòn, and Farako Manko Farakonken. Now I am Farako Manko Farakonken's son, the eighth generation. My people have been here all along; you only arrived yesterday, your dawn is just breaking today.

"Huh!" continued Sunjata. "And you say that I have just arrived? M'ba, huh! You are my respected elder, so I will not be the first to make a move. You invited me here to tell me that I'm a disrespectful child? You just go ahead and show what you've got."

Sumaworo said, "Bisimillahi."

The Battle of Dakajalan and Fakoli's Revenge

When something is filled to the brim, it will overflow.

When Sumaworo took his sword and struck at Sunjata, his blade flexed like a whip. Sunjata also struck with his sword; the blade of his sword also bent. Sumaworo raised his musket and fired, but nothing touched So'olon Ma'an. So'olon Ma'an then fired his musket at Sumaworo but failed to wound him.

With that, the *dalilu* was finished, and the two men just stood there. Sumaworo reached into his saddlebag and took his whip. As he raised his hand like this, So'olon Ma'an seized his reins like this—*Clap!*—and dashed away.

The two armies were waiting, Soso on one side, Manden on the other. Everybody was watching the commanders on the battlefield. Fakoli stood off to one side of Sunjata; Turama'an was on his other side. Sumaworo was also flanked by his men.

Blu, blu! Sunjata, Sumaworo, and their men dashed across the field and up the hill. Near the top of the hill, they faded from sight; even their dust disappeared. Soon they reached the edge of a very deep ravine. Gathering all her strength, Sunjata's sorcery mare (Tunku Manyan Diawara's horse) jumped the ravine and landed on the other side. When Sumaworo's horse tried to jump the ravine, it tumbled to the bottom.[3] Fakoli and Turama'an—whose horses safely jumped the ravine—turned and, with Sunjata, went to look down at Sumaworo who was trapped at the bottom of the ravine.

Sunjata called down, "Sumaworo, what is the matter?"

"So'olon Ma'an, kill me here; do not carry me to the town. Do not bring such shame to me. God controls all time. Please do not take me back."

Sumaworo removed his *dalilu* and dropped his horse-whip. He stripped completely, taking off his human-skin shirt and trousers.

Sunjata said, "I am not going to finish you off. No one can climb out of that ravine; you're stuck. I do not want your shirt of human skin, because it is the skin of my father's relatives. I will not take it." Turning to his companions he said, "Come, let's go home."

They had gone some distance when Fakoli made a decision, turned, and went back to the ravine. When he arrived there, he said to Sumaworo, "What did I tell you? When you took back your sister,[4] what did I say?" Taking his axe from his shoulder, Fakoli struck Sumaworo on the head, *poh!* He said, "This will be men-

---

3. Though not usually seen in versions of the Sunjata epic, the incident of the horse tumbling into a ravine is a popular motif in *jeli* storytell-ing, a favorite way of disposing of the hero's enemy.

4. Fakoli's wife, Keleya Konkon.

tioned in Ma'an Sunjata's praise song." (And he was right! Though we sing, "Head-breaking Mari Jata," it was Fakoli who broke Sumaworo's head.)[5]

Fakoli started to leave. But he was still angry, so he went back to the ravine again and struck Sumaworo on the leg, *gbao!* Fakoli broke Sumaworo's leg, saying, "This will also be mentioned in Ma'an Sunjata's praise song." (That is why we sing, "Leg-Breaking Mari Jata.")

With his axe, Fakoli returned to the ravine a third time and broke Sumaworo's arm, saying, "This, too, will be mentioned in Ma'an Sunjata's praise song." (And so we sing, "Arm-Breaking Mari Jata." Aheh! It was not Jata who broke it! It was Fakoli who broke it.)

Finally Sunjata and his men went home. Laughter returned to Manden, and eventually Soso joined in.

[*In omitted passages, the narrator describes how, following the defeat of Suma-woro, the people of Soso dispersed and eventually settled in various communities along the Atlantic coast. Meanwhile, Sunjata begins to initiate reforms and orga-nize the newly unified Mali Empire.*]

The Campaign against Jolofin Mansa

After the war was over, Ma'an Sunjata said, "My fathers and my brothers: now that the war has ended and the *mansaya* has come to us, the Mansaré, let's send our horse-buyers to Senu to replace the many Mande horses killed by Sumaworo. We should buy enough horses for each of our elders and warriors to have one."

So the horse-buyers went to Senu and bought hundreds of horses. On the way back to Manden, the horse-buyers stopped at the *jamana* of Jolofin Mansa, and there Jolofin Mansa robbed the buyers of their horses; he then took the horse-buyers captive and beheaded all but two. Jolofin Mansa sent the two survivors to tell Ma'an Sunjata that even though Ma'an Sunjata had taken over the power—that Sunjata had recently received the Mande *mansaya*—he knew the Mande walked on all fours like dogs, and that they should leave horse-riding to others.

The two horse-buyers arrived in Manden and gave the message to Ma'an Sun-jata, who said, "Jolofin Mansa has extended an invitation to me. I myself will lead the campaign against Jolofin Mansa."

His younger brother Manden Bori said, "Elder brother, are you going to lead us in that campaign? Give me the command, and I will do the fighting."

"I am not giving you command of the army."

Fakoli said, "Simbon, give me the army! We will not stay here while you lead the army. Give the army to me, Fakoli, so I can go after Jolofin Mansa."

Simbon said, "I will not give you the army. I will go myself."

Meanwhile, Turama'an was digging his own grave. He cut some *tòrò* branches, laid them on his grave, and had his shroud sewn. Then he said to Ma'an Sunjata, "Simbon, I'll kill myself if you do not give me the army. Would you really leave us

---

5. It is unusual for a *jeli* to describe the death of Sumaworo, as Tassey Condé does here. In many versions, Sumaworo flees to the mountain at Koulikoro where he disappears. The Kouyaté and Diabaté *jeliw*, among others, are usually careful not to say that Sumaworo was slain by Sunjata, Fakoli, or anybody else. Such things arc taken seriously in modern times, because Maninka and Bamana identify with the ances-tors whose names they carry. The version trans-lated here was recorded in a private performance in the narrator's own house, but in a public per-formance, giving details of a humiliating defeat (even one alleged to have occurred more than seven centuries ago) risks embarrassing any people in the audience who regard themselves as descendants of the defeated ancestor.

behind while you lead the army to go after Jolofin Mansa? Give me the army. If you don't, if you go after Jolofin Mansa yourself, you will lose me, for I'll kill myself."

"Ah," said Simbon. "I did not know you felt so strongly, Turama'an. Your *dalilu* and my *dalilu* are tied together: my mother was given to your fathers, who killed the buffalo of Dò ni Kiri. If your father and my mother had gotten along, my mother would have stayed with your father. Because my mother did not get along with your fathers, your fathers brought my mother to my father, and I was born out of that marriage, as were my younger brothers Manden Bori and So'olon Jamori.

"My father took my younger siblings Nana Triban and Tenenbajan, and gave them to Danmansa Wulanni and Danmansa Wulanba, your fathers. You, Turama'an, are the son of Danmansa Wulanni. Considering what you have said, you and I are equal in this war, and I will let you take the army."

So Sunjata gave Turama'an command of the army, and Turama'an prepared the army for war. With the campaign underway, they marched to Jolofin Mansa's land.

(You know Jolofin Mansa, he was one of the Mansaré. The son of Latali Kalabi, the Mansaré ancestor, was Danmatali Kalabi; Danmatali Kalabi then also named his son Latali Kalabi. This second Latali sired Kalabi Doman and Kalabi Bomba, and Kalabi Doman sired Mamadi Kani. Mamadi Kani sired Kani Simbon, Kani Nyogo Simbon, Kabala Simbon, Big Simbon Madi Tanyagati, and M'balinene; M'balinene sired Bele, Bele sired Belebakon, Belebakon sired Maghan Konfara, and this Farako Manko Farakonken was Ma'an Sunjata's father.

So Jolofin *Mansa* and Ma'an Sunjata both descended from the same person. And Jolofin's people—the *Jolofin na mò'òlu*—became known as the Wolofo.[6] Have you heard people calling the Wolofo "little Mande people"? That's because they all came from Manden.)

Turama'an marched the army of Manden to Jolofin Mansa's land and there destroyed Jolofin Mansa's place like it was an old clay pot; Turama'an broke it like an old calabash. He also captured those who were supposed to be captured, killed those who were supposed to be killed.

Though his soldiers had been defeated, Jolofin Mansa had not been captured, so he fled with Turama'an in pursuit. Jolofin Mansa headed for the big river.[7]

At that time, no one knew that Jolofin Mansa could transform himself into a crocodile, living on land or under water. When he came to the big river, Jolofin Mansa plunged in and swam into a cave; there he transformed himself into a crocodile and lay down to wait.

Standing above the cave, Turama'an and his men said, "Jolofin Mansa went in here." The Mande men were good warriors, but they were not used to water fighting. All of the battle commanders standing there were dressed for fighting on land; they were all wearing hunting clothes and carried quivers and bows. Until they stood at the entrance to that cave, the Mande people did not know that they had a warrior who could fight under water.

Turama'an said, "Jolofin Mansa has changed himself into a crocodile and gone into that cave. We can't leave him there, for if we destroy the war *mansa*'s home without killing the war *mansa* himself, we have not won the battle. But who will go after him?"

Everybody kept quiet, *lele!*

6. Maninka pronunciation attaches an extra vowel. The Wolof, who call their country Jolof (see previous sentence), arc mainly in Senegal (the narrator's "Senu"), and they speak a lan-guage that is not interintelligible with Manding languages.
7. The Senegal River.

Again Turama'an asked, "Who will go after him?" Nobody spoke up, so Turama'an asked a third time, "Who will follow this man?"

The Diawara chief, whose name was Tombonon Sitafa Diawara, stepped out from among the soldiers. He said, "Turama'an, tell the Mande people that if they agree, I, Sitafa Diawara, will go after Jolofin Mansa. But also tell them that I am not doing this to prove my manhood. I'm doing it because we can't return home to Simbon having only destroyed Jolofin Mansa's home. If we return home without also having killed Jolofin Mansa himself, Simbon will wonder why we told him to stay home."

(That is why, if you are a real man, you should stay low to the ground when you are among the *kamalenw*. You should only reveal the kind of man you are when somebody challenges your group.)

Meanwhile, Jolofin Mansa's crocodile wraith was lying in the cave, its mouth open wide. The upper jaw reached to the top of the entrance, the lower jaw reached to the bottom. Anybody who went after the crocodile would end up in its stomach, and the crocodle would just close his mouth. Eh! There would be no need to chew.

Sitafa Diawara said, "I'll give you two signs when I get down to where the crocodile is. If, while the water is bubbling and churning and turning the color of blood, you see a pelican flying from where the sun sets to where it rises, Manden should weep, for you'll know that Jolofin Mansa has defeated me. But if, while the water is bubbling and churning and turning the color of blood, the pelican flies from where the sun rises to where it sets, you Mande people should be happy, for it will mean I have honored you and God. Those are the signs I've given you."

Diawara put on his medicine clothes and gathered all his *dalilu*. He had a small knife fastened to his chest, and a short Bozo[8] fish-spear hung from his waist.

To the other warriors Diawara said, "Excuse me. We may meet in this world or we may meet in God's kingdom. If I'm successful, we'll meet in this world; I'll come back and find you here. But if I'm overcome by the crocodile, we'll meet in God's kingdom." Then he dove into the water and swam into the cave, unaware that he was actually swimming straight into the crocodile's stomach. The crocodile closed its mouth on him.

As the crocodile closed its mouth on him, Diawara the hunter demonstrated his *dalilu*. Though he was trapped inside the crocodile, he was still alive, as comfortable as if he were in his own house. Taking his spear from his side, he stabbed the crocodile here, *pu!*; he stabbed it there, *pu!* The crocodile went *kututu*. Diawara speared the crocodile over and over again.

The water bubbled, and blood came to the surface. As the water around him turned bloody, Diawara reached for the knife on his chest. He sliced a hole in the crocodile's belly and swam out of it. Then, still under the water, he twisted the crocodile's front legs and tied them together.

As Diawara swam to the surface with the crocodile, a pelican flew by, squawking, from east to west. Manden laughed. As they hauled the crocodile wraith up onto the riverbank, Jolofin Mansa himself appeared. He was captured, tied up, and taken to Sunjata, the *mansa*.

Turama'an, who was the commander at that battle, brought Jolofin Mansa's treasure to Ma'an Sunjata. Manden was at last free, and the war was over.

---

8. An ethnic group of the Middle Niger, specializing in fishing and boating occupations, mainly located between Sansanding and Lake Debo in Mali.

VIII

Europe and the New World

"All the world's a stage, / And all the men and women merely players." **William Shakespeare**'s famous comparison of human beings to actors playing their various roles in the great theater of the world conjures up the exhilarating liberty and mobility we associate with the memorable characters of Renaissance literature. Because "merely" meant, in Shakespeare's day, "wholly" and "entirely," the line evokes a lively sense of the men and women of that world performing their roles with the gusto of actors. Their social roles as princes, clowns, thieves, or housewives appear, from one angle, as exciting opportunities for the characters to explore. Yet such roles are also clearly confining: Renaissance men and women were born into societies that strictly regulated their actions and even their clothing—only actors had the right to vary their garb and dress above their station. Whether Renaissance subjects relished the pleasures of playing or resented the constraints of their social roles is a subject often taken up in the literature of the day.

The most memorable characters of Renaissance literature enjoy greater autonomy and more fully realized personalities, and are much more prone to introspection than their medieval predecessors. Characters like **Cervantes'** idealistic but mad Don

A detail from Hans Holbein's 1533 painting commonly called *The Ambassadors*.

Quixote; Shakespeare's hesitant Hamlet; and Milton's "domestic" Adam and "adventurous" Eve are frequently presented in acts of thought, fantasy, planning, doubt, and internal debate. Deliberating with others and themselves about what to do seems at least as important to these characters as putting their plans into action.

One reason for this shift toward internal, mental, and psychological portraiture is that Renaissance authors, like the characters they invent, inhabited a world of such widespread revolutionary change that they could not passively receive the traditional wisdom of previous ages. The stage on which they played was transformed and expanded by both the scientific and the geographical advances of the age. When Nicolaus Copernicus (1473–1543) discovered that the earth moves around the sun and when Galileo Galilei (1564–1642) turned his telescope up to the heavens, the nature of the universe and creation had to be reconceived. When Christopher Columbus (1451–1506) sailed to what he thought were the Indies, he introduced a New World to Europe, which began for the first time to think of itself as the Old World. Around the time that Columbus was sailing to America, humanist thinkers in Italy began to use new scholarly methods that gave them fuller access to the cultural legacy of ancient Greece and Rome as well as a new sense of their own place in history. On scientific, geographical, and scholarly fronts, the world of Renaissance Europe was undergoing revolutionary change.

After Johannes Gutenberg's invention of the printing press in 1439, the new ideas and controversies of the age reached a broader audience than ever before. Texts of all sorts were printed widely, and the spread of the printing press across Europe meant that writers could often avoid local censorship by having texts printed elsewhere, as occurred with Protestant Bibles in local languages that circulated widely despite Catholic prohibitions, or works like the biting satire *Lazarillo de Tormes*, which the Inquisition banned in Spain but which were printed and reprinted in the Netherlands or Italy. Despite censorship, the average person's access to information increased dramatically.

The new discoveries, rapidly circulating, were avidly resisted in some quarters, as when the Inquisition forced Galileo to repudiate the Copernican theory that the earth rotates around the sun. At the same time, they led to an unprecedented sense of possibility. In his dialogue *The City of the Sun* (1602) Galileo's friend and supporter Tommasso Campanella (1568–1639) optimistically asserted that the three great inventions of his day—the compass, the printing press, and the gun—were "signs of the union of the entire world."

As the two great powers of the age, Habsburg Spain and the Ottoman Empire, grew ever more dominant, this "union of the world" could also seem threatening. With the defeat of the Muslim stronghold of Granada in 1492, and the expulsion of the Jews in the same year, Spain emerged as a centralized, militantly Christian state. Spain's modernized army effectively replaced older chivalric forms of combat with new troops armed with guns and cannons, making great inroads into Italy and France. Charles, king of Spain, was crowned Holy Roman Emperor in 1519, consolidating many of the great dynastic houses of Europe. Soon the Habsburg domains extended across the globe, from Europe to the New World in the west to Asia, in an empire without precedent.

ENCOUNTERING THE NEW WORLD

As emperor, Charles V took for his emblem the Pillars of Hercules, which for the ancients had signaled the end of the known world at the Straits of Gibraltar. But Charles reversed the motto that accompanied the emblem, from the forbidding "Ne Plus Ultra" (*no further*, Latin) to the endlessly ambitious "Plus Ultra," which encouraged going *ever further*. So the Spanish did across the globe, all while battling the Ottomans' own expansion into the Mediterranean and North Africa.

The new discoveries challenged European centrality in the world and in creation. Contact with New World peoples forced Europeans to consider as never before what counted as culture, civilization, and even humanity, casting into doubt the authority of the classics that scholars had recently embraced with a new fervor. In an ironic exchange on Prospero's island in Shakespeare's *The Tempest*, Miranda exclaims, "Oh brave new world, that has such people in it," only to suffer her father's devastating correction: "Tis new to thee." Although Columbus considered the New World a *tabula rasa*—a clean slate ready to be imprinted with Christianity and European ways—by the time the conquerors Hernán Cortés (1485–1547) and Francisco Pizarro (1478–1541) encountered the great civilizations of the Aztecs and the Incas in the 1520s and 1530s, Europe was forced to grapple with other versions of what culture could mean.

As the explorers contemplated complex societies that had been completely unknown to the Old World, the arbitrariness of European social arrangements became visible to many thoughtful observers. Thomas More (1478–1535) was inspired by reports of new social arrangements to imagine his own island of *Utopia*, a wry fantasy nonetheless full of hope for reform. In one of his skeptical, probing *essais* (called "**Of Cannibals**") **Michel de Montaigne** (1533–1592) elaborated on Jean de Léry's detailed and even-handed ethnography of the Tupinamba Indians in Brazil, to ask larger questions about European society, whose peculiarities proved as unintelligible to the "cannibals" as Tupinamba society was to Europeans.

Europeans assumed that the New World existed for their profit and delectation—an idea expressed everywhere from the famous engraving by Jan van der Straet that depicted America as a seductive woman welcoming the explorer Amerigo Vespucci with open arms, to John Donne's poem "To his mistress going to bed," in which he exclaims as he finally manages to peel off her clothes, "Oh, my America, my new found land." Yet these assumptions were quickly challenged in the New World, both by an impregnable landscape and by the continued resistance of the native population. New World authors both indigenous and *mestizo* (born of the union of a European and an Indian), such as Inca Garcilaso de la Vega or Guaman Poma, demonstrated that America had its own history, far predating the encounter, and decried the abuses of the conquest as they argued for their own role in governing their societies. Spanish reformers such as Bartolomé de las Casas (1484–1566) also took up the cause of the Indians, promoting legal protections that ultimately failed to stop abuses that occurred far from the metropole. As the New World yielded untold mineral wealth, Spain set up an elaborate political structure to control it, while other European nations mounted their own expeditions or turned to piracy in efforts to rival Spanish successes. Meanwhile, the tremendous influx of wealth from the New World had a destabilizing effect across Europe, leading to persistent inflation and new possibilities of social mobility.

CONFLICTS IN EUROPE

If the New World proved difficult to control from across the ocean, Europe was no less riven by conflict. Not even

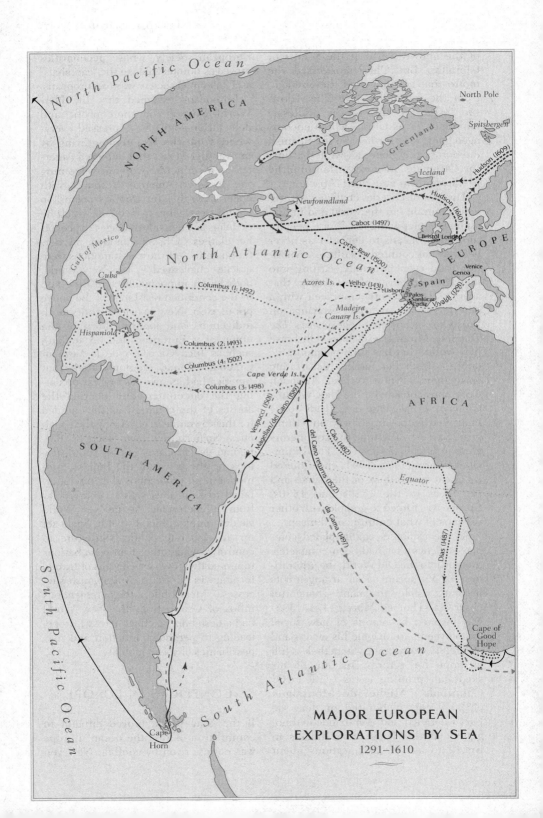

North Pacific Ocean

NORTH AMERICA

North Pole

Spitsbergen

Greenland

Iceland

Hudson (1609)

Hudson (1610)

Newfoundland

Cabot (1497)

Bristol London

Gulf of Mexico

North Atlantic Ocean

Corte-Real (1500)

EUROPE

Cuba

Columbus (1: 1492)

Azores Is.

Velho (1431)

Lisbon

Spain

Venice

Genoa

Palos

Sanlucar

Cadiz

Vivaldi (1291)

Hispaniola

Columbus (2: 1493)

Madeira

Canary Is.

Columbus (4: 1502)

Cape Verde Is.

Columbus (3: 1498)

AFRICA

SOUTH AMERICA

Vespucci (1501)

Magellan/del Cano (1519)

del Cano returns (1522)

Cão (1482)

Equator

da Gama (1497)

Dias (1487)

South Pacific Ocean

Cape of Good Hope

Cape Horn

South Atlantic Ocean

MAJOR EUROPEAN
EXPLORATIONS BY SEA
1291–1610

From Jan van der Straet, *Vespucci Discovering America*, 1589. The fertility of the New World is represented as a sexualized female body.

the threat of "the Turk," as the Europeans referred to the Ottoman expansion, could paper over the serious rifts that divided the continent. The Protestant Reformation, which initially targeted the abuses and corruption of the Catholic Church, quickly became a political as well as a religious crisis. Movements originally intended to reform the Church—such as those led by Martin Luther (1483–1546) and John Calvin (1509–1564)—were rapidly adopted by Renaissance princes bridling under papal authority. The reformers' attacks on the Pope, who wielded enormous political and military as well as spiritual power, provided an opportunity for rulers across Europe to increase their own sway. Henry VIII of England famously broke with the Catholic Church and declared himself head of the Church of England, and the pattern of contesting or breaking with papal authority was repeated throughout Europe. By nationalizing religious authority, monarchs claimed for themselves more and more rights that traditionally had belonged to the Pope or that had been shared by parliaments. Securing these rights from these other institutions brought monarchs closer to the absolutist rule that they craved. And yet, the Protestant Reformation had so emboldened subjects to challenge religious and political authority that the advantage enjoyed by European monarchs in the later sixteenth century would occasionally give way to a violent overthrow, as it did during the English Civil War (1642–51), when Charles I, a king reviled for his dismissal of Parliament and for failure to grant religious liberties to the more extreme Protestants among his subjects, was beheaded and the monarchy temporarily abolished.

Given the political force of the Catholic Church and the Protestant Reformation, it is no wonder that the Renaissance often appears to be more preoccupied with earthly princes and empires than

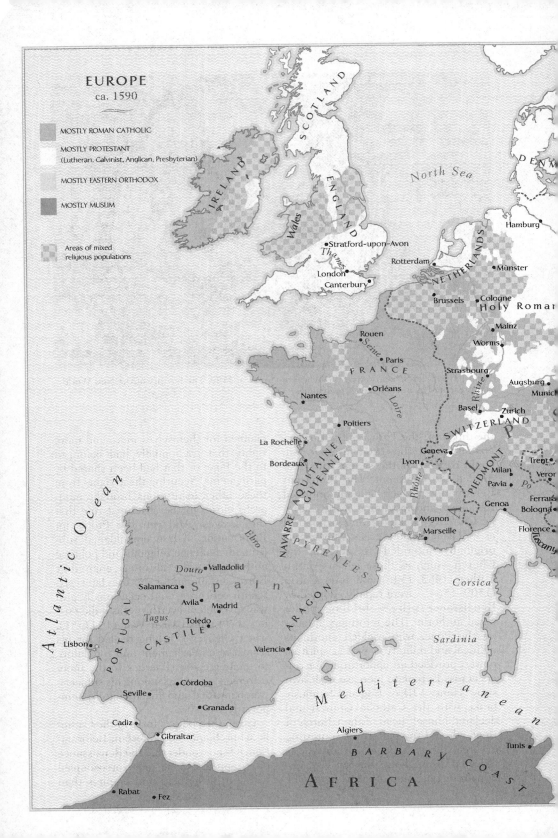

EUROPE
ca. 1590

MOSTLY ROMAN CATHOLIC

MOSTLY PROTESTANT
(Lutheran, Calvinist, Anglican, Presbyterian)

MOSTLY EASTERN ORTHODOX

MOSTLY MUSLIM

Areas of mixed
religious populations

North Sea

SCOTLAND

IRELAND

ENGLAND

Wales

• Stratford-upon-Avon
Thames
London •
• Canterbury

DENM

Hamburg •

Rotterdam •
NETHERLANDS
• Münster

Brussels • • Cologne
Holy Roman

• Mainz
Worms •

Rouen •
Seine
• Paris

FRANCE

Strasbourg •

Rhine

Augsburg •
Munich •

Nantes •

• Orléans
Loire

Basel •
Zurich •
SWITZERLAND

ALP

Poitiers •

La Rochelle •

Bordeaux •

AQUITAINE /
GUIENNE

Geneva •
Lyon •
Rhône

PIEDMONT

Milan •
Pavia •
Po

Trent •
Veror

Genoa •
Avignon •
Marseille •

Ferrar
Bologna •
Florence •
Tuscany

NAVARRE
PYRENEES

Atlantic Ocean

Ebro

Douro
• Valladolid

Salamanca •
S p a i n

Avila •
• Madrid

ARAGON

Corsica

Tagus
PORTUGAL
• Toledo
CASTILE

Lisbon •

• Córdoba

Valencia •

Sardinia

Seville •
• Granada

M e d i t e r r a n e a n

Cadiz •
• Gibraltar

Algiers •

B A R B A R Y   C O A S T

Tunis •

A F R I C A

• Rabat • Fez

with the heavenly King. In this new world of politics, the role of the Renaissance prince and his courtiers was instrumental. **Niccolò Machiavelli's** revolutionary treatise *The Prince* underscored the importance of the strong ruler—or at least a ruler who always appeared strong—as the head of his state. Dispelling with all pieties in favor of practical advice and placing ruthless effectiveness over morality, Machiavelli broke with a long tradition of advisors who preached moral behavior to their rulers, recognizing instead the exigencies of his time and the importance of projecting strength and authority. In his *Book of the Courtier*, Baldassare Castiglione (1478–1529) explained how to comport oneself with courtly grace, suggesting in the process that nobility could be learned. In an uncertain and rapidly changing world, performance and self-improvement were intertwined.

HUMANISM

The new Renaissance consciousness of how individuals could fashion themselves through their actions was in part due to the influence of the classics. Humanism, the intellectual movement that championed the return to the culture of Greece and Rome as a way to renew Europe, sought civic and moral guidance as well as aesthetic inspiration in the ancient texts. As the modern European rulers took on cadres of secretaries, ambassadors, and advisors, humanist pedagogy made education a road to power and privilege as never before.

The literal meaning of the word *renaissance*—"rebirth"—casts the great intellectual and artistic achievements of the period as a reprise of ancient culture. The artists and intellectuals of the Renaissance imagined the world of antiquity "reborn" through their work, in a vigorous renewal comparable to the thrilling discoveries of their own age. The degree to which European intellectuals of the period engaged with the writings of the ancient world is difficult for the average modern reader to realize. For these writers, references to classical mythology, philosophy, and literature are not ornaments or affectations. Along with references to the Scriptures, they are a major part of their mental equipment and way of thinking. Every cultivated person wrote and spoke Latin, with the result that a Western community of intellectuals could exist, a spiritual "republic of letters" above individual nations.

The archetypal humanist is often said to be the poet and scholar **Francis Petrarch** (1304–1374), who anticipated certain ideals of the high Renaissance: a lofty conception of the literary art, a taste for the good life, and a strong sense of the memories and glories of antiquity. In this last respect, what should be emphasized is the imaginative quality, the visionary impulse with which the writers of the period looked at those memories—the same vision and imagination with which they regarded such contemporary heroes as the great navigators and astronomers.

The vision of an ancient age of glorious intellectual achievement that is "now" brought to life again implies, of course, however roughly, the idea of an intervening "middle" age, by comparison ignorant and dark. The hackneyed, vastly inaccurate notion that the "light" of the Renaissance broke through a long "night" of the Middle Ages was not devised by subsequent centuries; it was held by the humanist scholars of the Renaissance themselves. Petrarch imagined himself living in "sad times": "It were better to be born either earlier or much later, for there was once and perhaps will be again a happier age. In the middle, you see, in our time, squalor and baseness have flowed together." Addressing his book, Petrarch expresses his longing for a new age: "But if you, as is my wish and ardent hope, shall live on after me, a more propitious age will come again: this Lethean stupor surely can't endure forever. Our posterity, perchance, when the shadows have lifted, may enjoy once more the radiance the ancients knew." The combination of self-deprecation, aspiration, and arrogance aptly characterizes the period's sense of its own superiority over not only the New World but also the recent past.

Despite the fractured political and religious landscape of Europe, especially in the sixteenth century, the great intellectual innovations of the Renaissance expanded across all boundaries. The movement had its inception in Italy with Petrarch, and developed most remarkably in the visual arts, made its way across Europe to Spain, France, and England, where its main achievements were in literature, particularly the drama. The intellectual fervor of humanism, like the poetic conventions of Petrarchism, gradually expanded into multiple languages and national traditions. Their dissemination led to new genres and to playful recombinations of older ones, inaugurating a period of great innovation in all forms of literature.

Definitions of the Renaissance must take account of the period's preoccupation with this life rather than with the life beyond. Though an oversimplification, one might say that an ideal medieval man or woman, whose mode of action is basically oriented toward the thought of the afterlife (and who therefore conceives of life on earth as transient and preparatory) contrasts with an ideal Renaissance man or woman, whose enthusiasm for earthly interests is actually enhanced by the knowledge that one's time on earth is fleeting. Once again, Petrarch provides the best example: the *Rime Sparse* (Scattered Rhymes), the extensive sequence of love poems for which he is best known, are full of renunciation, as the poet searches in vain for religious consolation for the travails of earthly desire. Yet in the process of charting the futility of earthly love, the poems paint an incredibly detailed portrait of the poet-lover in all his earthly variations, rendering his interior life both immediate and engrossing.

THE WELL-LIVED LIFE

The emphasis on the immediate and tangible is reflected in the earthly, amoral, and aesthetic character of what we may call the Renaissance code of behavior. Human action is judged not in terms of right and wrong, of good and evil (as it is judged when life is viewed as a moral "test," with reward or punishment in the afterlife), but in terms of its present concrete validity and effectiveness, of the delight it affords, of its memorability and its beauty. Much of what is typical of the Renaissance, then, from architecture to poetry, from sculpture to rhetoric, may be related to a taste for the harmonious and the memorable, for the spectacular effect, for the successful striking of a pose. Individual human action, seeking in itself its own reward, finds justification in its formal appropriateness; in its being a well-rounded achievement, perfect of its kind; in the zest and gusto with which it is, here and now, performed; and, finally, in its proving worthy of remaining as a testimony to the performer's power on earth. In this sense, the purpose of life is the unrestrained and self-sufficient practice of one's "virtue," the competent and delighted exercise of one's skill.

The leaders of the period saw in a work of art the clearest instance of beautiful, harmonious, and self-justified performance. To create such a work became the valuable occupation par excellence, the most satisfactory display of virtue. The Renaissance view of antiquity exemplifies this attitude. The artists and intellectuals of the period not only drew on antiquity for certain practices and forms but also found there a recognition of the place of the arts among outstanding modes of human action. In this way, the concepts of "fame" and "glory" became particularly associated with the art of poetry because the Renaissance drew from antiquity the idea of the poet as celebrator of high deeds, the "dispenser of glory."

At the same time, there is no reason to forget that such virtues and skills are God's gift. Renaissance intellectuals, artists, aristocrats, and princes did not lack in abiding religious faith or fervor. Machiavelli, Rabelais, and Cervantes take for granted the presence of God in their own and in their heroes' lives. For many, the Protestant Reformation and the growth of mysticism within the Catholic Church led to a more intimate and individualized relationship with the divine. Much about the religious temper of the age is expressed in its art, particularly in Italian painting, where Renaissance Madonnas celebrate earthly beauty even as they inspire thoughts of the divine.

SKEPTICISM AND MELANCHOLY

Especially where there is a close association between the practical and the intellectual—as in the exercise of political power, the act of scientific discovery, the creation of works of art—the Renaissance assumption is that there are things here on earth that are highly worth doing, and that by doing them, humanity proves its privileged position in creation and therefore incidentally follows God's intent. The often-cited phrase "the dignity of man" describes this positive, strongly affirmed awareness of the intellectual and physical "virtues" of the human being, and of the individual's place in creation. And yet, alongside the delight of earthly achievement, there

Madonna and Child, ca. 1465, by Fra Filippo Lippi. The object of the painting's devotions is somewhat unclear: is our eye focused on the baby Jesus, or on the beauty of Mary's face?

lurked in many Renaissance minds nagging doubts: What is the purpose or ultimate worth of all this activity? What meaningful relation does it bear to any all-inclusive, cosmic pattern? The Renaissance coincided with, and perhaps to some extent occasioned, a loss of firm belief in the final unity and the final intelligibility of the universe. In the wake of the geographic and scientific discoveries, thinkers such as Montaigne and Descartes became skeptics, doubting and questioning received knowledge.

For some Renaissance writers and artists, the sense of uncertainty became so strong as to paralyze their aspiration to power or thirst for knowledge or delight in beauty. The resulting attitude we may call Renaissance melancholy. It was sometimes openly expressed (as by some characters in Elizabethan drama) and other times

Young Man Holding a Skull, 1519, by Lucas van Leyden. This young nobleman, a paragon of Renaissance fashion, points to a skull that he cradles in his left arm, reminding the viewer of the inevitable fate that even the best-dressed courtier will face.

merely provided an undercurrent of sadness or wise resignation to a work (as in Montaigne's *Essays*). Thus while on one, and perhaps the better-known, side of the picture, human intellect in Renaissance literature enthusiastically illuminates the realms of knowledge and unveils the mysteries of the universe, on the other it is beset by puzzling doubts and a profound mistrust of its own powers.

Doubts about the value of human action within the scheme of eternity did not, however, diminish the outpouring of ideas about the ideal order-ing of this world. Renaissance poets and intellectuals tested ideas about the ideal prince, courtier, councilor, and humble subject as well as the ideal court and society. More's *Utopia* imagines a perfectly ordered society, as improbable as it is optimistic, while Machiavelli proposes his amoral ideas about the effective (rather than ideal) prince. Shakespeare's *Hamlet* gives us a prince far from ideal, confronting the effects of private violations on the public realm. In all these works, Renaissance writers can be seen tirelessly examining the nature of their own world, the problem of power, and the vexed relations between the absolute authority of the prince and the rights and liberties of the people. Its zeal for defining the social contract partly explains why the Renaissance is often viewed as the "early modern" period; the "rebirth" and flourishing of antiquity also heralded ideas that we associate with the modern political world.

The joining of philosophical and imaginative thinking in literary expression is characteristic of the Renaissance, which cultivated the idea of "serious play." Throughout the literature of the period, we see the creative and restless mind of the Renaissance intellectual "freely ranging," as Sir Philip Sidney put it, "only in the zodiac of his own wit," creating fictional characters and worlds that might, if the poet is sufficiently persuasive, be put into practice and change the nature of the real world.

FRANCIS PETRARCH

1304–1374

Although Petrarch, a contemporary of **Dante**, lived and died in the Middle Ages, he did everything in his power to distinguish himself and his scholarship from the period he dismissed as the "Dark Ages." Petrarch dedicated himself to the recovery of classical learning in a spirit commonly associated with a later period, in which humanist scholars zealously pursued the rebirth of antiquity. Yet Petrarch's status as a precursor of the Renaissance is primarily due to an aspect of his work that neither he nor his contemporaries regarded as a lasting contribution: his 366 lyric poems in the vernacular, mostly dedicated to his frustrated desire for an elusive woman named Laura. Petrarch's experience of love and sense of his own fragmented and fluid self set the standard for the lyric expression of subjective and erotic experience in the Renaissance. His efforts to scrutinize himself intently and at times unflatteringly and to capture his own elusive inner workings in verse inspired a poetic tradition that has influenced lyric sequences from **Shakespeare**'s sonnets to Walt Whitman's *Leaves of Grass* to contemporary pop lyrics.

Francis Petrarch was born in Arezzo on July 20, 1304, three years after his father and Dante Alighieri were exiled from Florence. In 1314, Petrarch's father moved his family to Avignon, the new seat of the papacy (1309–77), where he became prosperous in the legal profession. Petrarch himself initially trained as a law student, but chose instead to pursue the study of classical culture and literature. He soon came to the attention of the pow-erful Colonna family, whose patronage launched his career as a diplomat-scholar and allowed him to travel widely and move in the intimate circles of European princes and scholars. He refused the offices of bishop and papal secretary, preferring instead to ground his growing prestige in his humanistic scholarship. Imaginative conversation with the ancients, like imitation of their poetry, brought him into contact with the past: his research into classical history and arts profoundly influenced his sense of himself and his own cultural moment. He died in 1374 near Padua, his head resting on a volume of his beloved **Virgil**.

Petrarch's most famous work, the *Rime Sparse* (Scattered Rhymes) or *Rerum Fragmenta Vulgarium* (Fragments in the Vernacular), is a collection of 366 songs and sonnets (based on the calendar year associated with the liturgy) of extraordinary technical virtuosity and variety. Written in Italian and woven into a highly introspective narrative, the lyric collection takes the poet himself as its object of study. The poems painstakingly record how his thoughts and identity are scattered and transformed by the experience of love for a beautiful, unattainable woman named Laura. Even some of his friends suspected that Laura was merely the theme and emblem of his lyric poetry and not a historical woman; she appears to have been both. On the flyleaf of his magnificent copy of Virgil, Petrarch inscribed a note on her life:

> Laura, illustrious through her own virtues, and long famed through my

verses, first appeared to my eyes in my youth, in the year of our Lord 1327, on the sixth day of April, in the church of St. Clare in Avignon, at matins; and in the same city, also on the sixth day of April, at the same first hour, but in the year 1348, the light of her life was withdrawn from the light of day, while I, as it chanced, was in Verona, unaware of my fate. * * * Her chaste and lovely form was laid to rest at vesper time, on the same day on which she died in the burial place of the Brothers Minor. I am persuaded that her soul returned to the heaven from which it came, as Seneca says of Africanus. I have thought to write this, in bitter memory, yet with a certain bitter sweetness, here in this place that is often before my eyes, so that I may be admonished, by the sight of these words and by the consideration of the swift flight of time, that there is nothing in this life in which I should find pleasure; and that it is time, now that the strongest tie is broken, to flee from Babylon; and this, by the prevenient grace of God, should be easy for me, if I meditate deeply and manfully on the futile cares, the empty hopes, and the unforeseen events of my past years.

(Translated by E. H. Wilkins)

Petrarch's note illuminates the powerful role that Laura plays in his personal struggles between spiritual aspirations and earthly attachments. Thoughts of Laura return him to the problem of his own will, torn between spiritual and sensual desires, always delaying worldly renunciation. Even when he expresses disgust with earthly rewards and pleasures, it is conditional: he will choose the right course of action, Petrarch writes, *if* he meditates "deeply and manfully" on the disappointments and failures of his past and denies memory's seductively bittersweet pleasures.

In the *Rime Sparse*, Laura's ambiguous position between divine guide and earthly temptress contrasts sharply with the role that Beatrice played in Dante's spiritual pilgrimage, the **Divine Comedy**. Whereas Dante's love finally leads him to paradise, it is never clear to Petrarch whether he is pursuing heavenly or earthly delights and whether he will safely reach any destination or "port" (in the nautical image of sonnet 189). When Dante looks into Beatrice's eyes on Mount Purgatory, he sees a reflection of the heavens; when Petrarch gazes into Laura's eyes, he sees himself. Not even his use of the liturgical year (especially the anniversaries of Christ's death and resurrection) to structure his account of their relationship guarantees that a spiritual conversion will follow Petrarch's self-analysis or "confession" of his life. In a contrary and skeptical mood at the end of one of his most philosophical poems (song 264), Petrarch asserts, "I see the better, but choose the worse."

The lyric collection's first sonnet, in which Petrarch solicits compassion as well as pardon from his readers, establishes the *Rime Sparse*'s close relationship to confessional narrative. Its themes of conversion, memory, and forgetfulness (of God and oneself) evoke the model of **St. Augustine** and raise the question of whether Petrarch will follow suit: will he ultimately transcend his attachment to a woman's physical beauty, his love of language and poetic figures, and his narcissistic preoccupation with himself? In dramatic opposition to the transcendent model of Augustine is **Ovid** of the **Metamorphoses**, the classical counterepic that artfully uses fragmentation, fluid change, and scattering to describe the effects of power—divine, political, or erotic—on bodies and on minds. Petrarch refers to a variety of Ovidian figures in the *Rime Sparse*, including Narcissus and Echo, Actaeon and Diana, Medusa, and Pygmalion. His chief Ovidian model, however, is the story of Apollo, the god who "invents" the genre of lyric during his amorous chase of the nymph Daphne. While running, Apollo describes her various beauties—eyes, figure, and hair—and imaginatively embellishes what he sees. When Daphne eludes him through her transformation into the laurel, Apollo claims her as his tree, if not his lover, and declares that the laurel will be the sign of triumph in letters and warfare. The prominence of this tale in the *Rime Sparse* suggests that if Laura had not lived, Petrarch would have had to invent her. Her name interweaves key attributes of Petrarch's poetic imagination: *lauro* and *alloro* ("laurel"), *oro* ("gold," for her tresses and value), *l'aura* ("breeze" and "inspiration," which etymologically relates to "breath"), *laus* or *lauda* ("praise"). Such wordplay suggests the selective, even obsessive character of Petrarch's poetic style. Like Apollo, Petrarch also "translates" his beloved's elusive body into the more tangible figures of rhetoric.

Petrarch's great legacy to Renaissance European literature is the *Rime Sparse*'s language of self-description, which starts from the conventional hyperbole, antithesis, and oxymoron (rhetorical exaggeration and opposition) that characterized troubadour songs, provençal lyric, and classical love elegy: *I freeze and burn, love is bitter and sweet, my sighs are tempests and my tears are floods, I am in ecstasy and agony, I am possessed by memories of her and I am in exile from myself.* Petrarch transformed such rhetorical figures or tropes of love into a powerful language of intro-

spection and self-fashioning that swept through European literature. Although it soon became so popular that writers endlessly repeated and even trivialized it, Petrarchism had serious dimensions that helped articulate growing questions about the self: is it determined by God or flexible and in the shaping hands of humankind? Do culture, history, and force of will compose and transform it?

Petrarchism offered rich formal possibilities as well: although Petrarch often wrote in other meters, the *sonnet* became in his hands an extraordinarily supple metrical form. A *Petrarchan sonnet*, as the form is now known, is a fourteen-line poem with a break after line eight. The *octet* is usually broken into two stanzas of four lines each, with a rhyme scheme of *abba*, and the *sestet* is made up of two three-line stanzas, rhyming *cdc*. The sonnet proved remarkably flexible, allowing poets to express themselves in a compact and striking manner. The sestet and the octet may contrast formally or semantically, as may the stanzas within a section of the sonnet, while its rhyme can reinforce or contradict meaning. The possibilities are virtually endless, as Petrarch's many imitators were to demonstrate.

Across sixteenth- and seventeenth-century Europe, writers turned to Petrarch as a beacon of Italian humanism who offered a powerful intellectual and formal toolkit for introspection. Through their own poems, they made Petrarchism into an international language, adapting it to various national traditions and rehearsing it in countless iterations.

Rime Sparse

1[1]

You who hear in scattered rhymes the sound of those sighs with
which I nourished my heart during my first youthful error,[2] when
I was in part another man from what I am now:

for the varied style in which I weep and speak between vain
hopes and vain sorrow, where there is anyone who understands   5
love through experience, I hope to find pity, not only pardon.

But now I see well how for a long time I was the talk of the
crowd, for which often I am ashamed of myself within;[3]

and of my raving, shame is the fruit, and repentance, and the
clear knowledge that whatever pleases in the world is a brief   10
dream.

3[4]

It was the day when the sun's rays turned pale with grief for his
Maker[5] when I was taken, and I did not defend myself against it,
for your lovely eyes, Lady, bound me.

It did not seem to me a time for being on guard against Love's
blows; therefore I went confident and without fear, and so my   5
misfortunes began in the midst of the universal woe.[6]

Love found me altogether disarmed, and the way open through
my eyes to my heart, my eyes which are now the portal and
passageway of tears.

Therefore, as it seems to me, it got him no honor to strike me   10
with an arrow in that state,[7] and not even to show his bow to
you, who were armed.

---

1. Translated by Robert M. Durling.
2. Mental and physical "wandering" as well as a
moral "mistake." "Scattered rhymes": reference
to the sonnet collection's title, *Rime Sparse*.
3. The Italian, *di me medesmo meco mi ver-
gogno*, suggests intense self-consciousness.
4. Translated by Robert M. Durling.

5. The anniversary of Christ's crucifixion.
Elsewhere (sonnet 211 and a note in Petrarch's
copy of Virgil) given as April 6, 1327.
6. The communal Christian grief that contrasts with Petrarch's private woes.
7. State of grief over the crucifixion.

34[8]

Apollo, if the sweet desire is still alive that inflamed you beside
the Thessalian waves,[9] and if you have not forgotten, with the
turning of the years, those beloved blond locks;

against the slow frost and the harsh and cruel time that lasts as
long as your face is hidden, now defend the honored and holy   5
leaves where you first and then I were limed;

and by the power of the amorous hope that sustained you in
your bitter life, disencumber the air of these impressions.[1]

Thus we shall then together see a marvel[2]—our lady sitting on the
grass and with her arms making a shade for herself.   10

62[3]

Father in heaven, after each lost day,
Each night spent raving with that fierce desire
Which in my heart has kindled into fire
Seeing your acts adorned for my dismay;

Grant henceforth that I turn, within your light[4]   5
To another life and deeds more truly fair,
So having spread to no avail the snare
My bitter foe[5] might hold it in despite.

The eleventh year,[6] my Lord, has now come round
Since I was yoked beneath the heavy trace   10
That on the meekest weighs most cruelly.

Pity the abject plight where I am found;
Return my straying thoughts to a nobler place;
Show them this day you were on Calvary.

---

8. Translated by Robert M. Durling.
9. Petrarch links his love of Laura to the love
of Apollo for Daphne in Ovid's *Metamorphoses*. Daphne, daughter of the god of the Peneus
River in Thessaly, was pursued by Apollo, the
god of poetry. She begged her father to change
her form, which had "given too much pleasure," and was transformed into the laurel
tree. Apollo, whom Petrarch associates with

the sun god, claimed the laurel as his personal
emblem.
1. Grief, cloudy weather, and aging.
2. Supernatural and highly meaningful
spectacle.
3. Translated by Bernard Bergonzi.
4. Of grace.
5. Satan.
6. I.e., 1338.

126[7]

Clear, fresh, sweet waters,[8] where she who alone seems lady
to me rested her lovely body,
    gentle branch where it pleased her (with sighing I remember)
to make a column for her lovely side,
    grass and flowers that her rich garment covered along with   5
her angelic breast, sacred bright air where Love opened my heart
with her lovely eyes: listen all together to my sorrowful dying
words.

    If it is indeed my destiny and Heaven exerts itself that Love
close these eyes while they are still weeping,   10
    let some grace bury my poor body among you and let my soul
return naked to this its own dwelling;
    death will be less harsh if I bear this hope to the fearful pass,
for my weary spirit could never in a more restful port or a more
tranquil grave flee my laboring flesh and my bones.   15

    There will come a time perhaps when to her accustomed
sojourn the lovely, gentle wild one will return
    and, seeking me, turn her desirous and happy eyes toward
where she saw me on that blessed day,
    and oh the pity! seeing me already dust amid the stones,   20
Love will inspire her to sigh so sweetly that she will win mercy
for me and force Heaven, drying her eyes with her lovely veil.

    From the lovely branches was descending (sweet in
memory) a rain of flowers over her bosom,
    and she was sitting humble in such a glory,[9] already covered   25
with the loving cloud;
    this flower was falling on her skirt, this one on her blond
braids, which were burnished gold and pearls to see that day;
this one was coming to rest on the ground, this one on the water,
this one, with a lovely wandering, turning about seemed to say: 30
"Here reigns Love."[1]

    How many times did I say to myself then, full of awe: "She was
surely born in Paradise!"
    Her divine bearing and her face and her words and her sweet
smile had so laden me with forgetfulness   35
    and so divided me from the true image, that I was sighing:
"How did I come here and when?" thinking I was in Heaven, not
there where I was. From then on this grass has pleased me so that
elsewhere I have no peace.

    If you had as many beauties as you have desire, you could   40
boldly leave the wood and go among people.[2]

---

7. Translated by Robert M. Durling.
8. Of the river Sorgue.
9. An image associated with the Virgin Mary.
1. Amor (Cupid) or Christ. The floral and
bejeweled images associate Laura's body with
the bride of the Song of Songs, whose erotic
chastity is celebrated as an "enclosed garden"
and "fountain sealed."
2. The last two lines are addressed to the
poem.

189[3]

My ship laden with forgetfulness passes through a harsh sea, at
midnight, in winter, between Scylla and Charybdis, and at the
tiller sits my lord, rather my enemy;[4]

each oar is manned by a ready, cruel thought that seems to scorn
the tempest and the end; a wet, changeless wind of sighs, hopes,   5
and desires breaks the sail;

a rain of weeping, a mist of disdain wet and loosen the already
weary ropes, made of error twisted up with ignorance.

My two usual sweet stars[5] are hidden; dead among the waves are
reason and skill; so that I begin to despair of the port.   10

333[6]

Go, grieving rimes of mine, to that hard stone
Whereunder lies my darling, lies my dear,
And cry to her to speak from heaven's sphere.
Her mortal part with grass is overgrown.

Tell her, I'm sick of living; that I'm blown   5
By winds of grief from the course I ought to steer,
That praise of her is all my purpose here
And all my business; that of her alone

Do I go telling, that how she lived and died
And lives again in immortality,   10
All men may know, and love my Laura's grace.

Oh, may she deign to stand at my bedside
When I come to die; and may she call to me
And draw me to her in the blessèd place!

3. Translated by Robert M. Durling.
4. Love. Scylla and Charybdis are the twinned
oceanic dangers through which Odysseus, in
Homer's *Odyssey*, and Aeneas, in Virgil's *Aeneid*, must chart a middle course. Forgetfulness
of oneself and of God is sinful in Augustinian
terms. The ship, captained by Reason, is a traditional figure for the embodied soul.
5. Laura's eyes.
6. Translated by Morris Bishop.

NICCOLÒ MACHIAVELLI

1469–1527

Widely vilified and secretly admired, Niccolò Machiavelli attempted to teach the rulers of his time how to get power and hold on to it. With his mix of clear-eyed, pragmatic observation and humanist idealism, Machiavelli transformed our conception of political power. Sharply contrasting traditional morality to the pragmatic necessities of ruling, Machiavelli tried to address the painful fragmentation and constant warfare of the many states that then made up what is today Italy. His solution—a strong, effective prince unconstrained by moral pieties—struck his contemporaries as a terrifying prescription for the use of force and deception, even though Machiavelli always stressed the ruler's need for popular support. Seeking to discuss the conduct of political affairs from a new rational basis, Machiavelli has been credited with having turned politics into a science.

LIFE AND TIMES

The son of a lawyer, Machiavelli was born to a well-connected but not wealthy family in the city-state of Florence, ruled by the beloved Lorenzo di Medici. He received a modest education, and was introduced to the scholarly circles around the ruler. Machiavelli's adult life was closely bound up with the political fortunes of his city-state. Renaissance Italy was a fractured collection of polities, constantly overrun by the armies of France, Spain, and the Holy Roman Empire, all of which took advantage of Italian fragmentation to expand their territorial claims. When Machiavelli was a young man, Florence experienced

its own profound political upheavals: after Lorenzo's death in 1492, the Medici were expelled from power and Florence was ruled by the Dominican preacher Savonarola. When Savonarola's regime collapsed, the city returned to republican government, and Machiavelli embarked on a distinguished career of public service, serving a city-state whose government was the most widely representative of its time. From 1498 to 1512, Machiavelli was secretary to the Second Chancery, charged with internal and war affairs. He also served as a diplomatic envoy (his low rank meant he could not be an ambassador), and, during the conflict between Florence and Pisa, he dealt with military problems firsthand. His many missions to some of the most powerful rulers of his time—King Louis XII of France, Cesare Borgia, Pope Julius II, the Emperor Maximilian—allowed him to observe up close their methods for gaining and maintaining political power; this led to two books—*Portraits*—of the affairs of their territories, written in 1508 and 1510. Machiavelli noted what made for effective conquest and rule, and contrasted the ruthlessness of a figure like Borgia to the slow deliberations of the consensus-based government in his own city. The constant threats and emergencies faced by Florence and other Italian states made Machiavelli's ideal leader— the hardheaded, strong prince—seem an appealing figure as a possible savior against foreign invasions.

As a student of politics and an acute observer of historical events, Machiavelli tried to apply his experience of other states to strengthening his own. He noted that one weakness of the

Italian city-states was their reliance on mercenary soldiers, who were ever ready to change sides for higher pay. Instead, following Cesare Borgia's example, he set out in 1505 to establish an army of Florentine citizens, animated by their love for their country, which achieved some surprising victories. Yet the republican forces were not enough to fend off all attackers, and, in 1512, in a moment of military weakness, the Medici faction regained power. With the end of the republic, Machiavelli lost his post. The Medici accused him unjustly of conspiracy and had him imprisoned and tortured. Once released, he retreated from the city to his family's farm, with his wife, Marietta Corsini, and their five children. There, in a study where he imagined himself in conversation with the classical writers he most admired (as detailed in the "Letter to Francesco Vettori," also included in this anthology), Machiavelli produced his major works: a study of republican government, the *Discourses on the First Ten Books of Livy* (1513–21), and one on statecraft, *The Prince*, written in 1513 with the hope that the Medici would ultimately grant him a public office. As his exile grew longer, he also wrote a number of literary works, including the much-applauded comedy *La mandragola* (The Mandrake), first performed in 1520. That same year Machiavelli was commissioned to write a history of Florence, which he presented in 1525 to Pope Clement VII (Giulio de' Medici).

After a reconciliation of sorts with the ruling Medicis, Machiavelli was entrusted with the upkeep of military fortifications in Florence. Here, too, he served the city well, presenting a strong enough defense that when the Holy Roman Empire invaded Italy in 1527, Florence avoided being attacked. Instead, the imperial forces sacked Rome with incredible violence. For Florence, which had long benefited from the strength of a series of Medici popes in Rome, the result was the collapse of Medici domination and, once more, the return of republican government. Despite Machiavelli's long history of service to the republic, however, he was now regarded as a Medici sympathizer and passed over for public office. This last disappointment may have accelerated his demise. He died on June 22, 1527, and was buried in the church of Santa Croce.

THE PRINCE

Although he wrote widely across many genres, Machiavelli's reputation—and his notoriety—is based on *The Prince*. This "handbook" on how to obtain and keep political power consists of twenty-six chapters. The first eleven deal with different types of dominions and how they are acquired and preserved—the early title of the whole book, in Latin, was *De principatibus* (Of Princedoms)—while the twelfth through fourteenth chapters focus on problems of military power. The book's astounding fame, however, is based on the final part (from chapter fifteen to the end), which deals primarily with the attributes and "virtues" of the prince himself.

Traditional manuals for rulers—a genre often referred to as the "mirror of princes"—couched their advice in the language of Christian morality. Their point was to remind the ruler to remain virtuous as they educated him and gave him advice. Erasmus's roughly contemporary *The Education of a Christian Prince* (1516), for example, which he presented to the future Charles V of Spain and also to Henry VII of England, held that what the prince most needed was "the best possible understanding of Christ." Machiavelli's point, by stark contrast, is to make the ruler effective by giving him advice on how to stay in power. For Machiavelli, the end of political stability justifies the means, even if those means include deception and violent force.

The view of humanity in Machiavelli is not cheerful. Indeed, the pessimistic notion that humanity is evil is not so much Machiavelli's conclusion about human nature as his premise, the point of departure for the course a ruler should follow: "A prudent ruler . . . cannot and should not observe faith when such observance is to his disadvantage and the causes that made him give his promise have vanished. If men were all good, this advice would not be good, but since men are wicked and do not keep their promises to you, you likewise do not have to keep yours to them." The idealism of Christian morality is checked by realism, by the facts on the ground. Machiavelli sees humanity as it is, not as it should be, and indicates the rules of the game as his experience shows it must, under the circumstances, be played. This kind of bald assessment did not sit well with European Christians invested in moral absolutes and in the idea that it was God who bestowed power to rulers.

Yet despite his emphasis on ruthlessly preserving power, Machiavelli stresses over and over again the importance for a ruler of preserving the goodwill of his subjects. In Machiavelli's view, a ruthless leader such as Cesare Borgia would at least avoid the weakness of lords who "plundered their subjects rather than governed them" and allowed "thefts, brawls, and every sort of excess." It is better for a prince to be thought stingy, he explains, than for him to grow poor through lavishness and then be forced to rob his subjects.

Machiavelli's pragmatism, his emphasis on fact, on how the real world works rather than on lofty ideals, contrasts with his own idealization of the strong ruler. His picture of the perfectly efficient ruler shows the Renaissance tendency toward "perfected" form. In this, he is closer than one might suspect to that more obvious treatise of political idealism, Thomas More's *Utopia* (1516), in which the desires and venality of humankind are curbed by a strong ruler and the rules he bequeaths to society. Most clearly at the end of the book, Machiavelli abandons complex reality in favor of an ideal vision and he offers the conclusion to his many lessons: the ideal ruler, now technically equipped by Machiavelli's lessons, is to undertake a mission—the liberation of Italy. The realistic method described throughout now appears directed toward an ideal task. Instead of technical political considerations (choice of the opportune moment, evaluation of military power), Machiavelli invokes religious and ancient precedents, calling for a new Moses to lead Italy out of bondage: "Everything is now fully disposed for the work . . . if only your House adopts the methods of those I have set forth as examples. Moreover, we have before our eyes extraordinary and unexampled means prepared by God. The sea has been divided. A cloud has guided you on your way. The rock has given forth water. Manna has fallen."

Although *The Prince* did not succeed in winning Machiavelli the favor of the Medici, or, for that matter, in achieving the unification of Italy, it was hugely influential throughout Europe. The work circulated widely in manuscript before being published in 1532, and the response to it was unmitigated outrage. Whatever truths readers recognized in Machiavelli's little book, it was tempting to accuse him of provoking the amorality (or immorality) that in some cases he simply described. "Machiavellian" became an insult denoting amorality in the service of *Realpolitik*, and the intricacies of Machiavelli's study of political power were overlooked. A careful reading of *The Prince* offers a very different impression, however, as the acute realism of the political observer gives way to the humanist dreaming of ancient glories.

From The Prince[1]

[New Princedoms Gained with Other Men's Forces and through Fortune]

From CHAPTER 7

* * *

[*Cesare Borgia*][2]

Cesare Borgia, called by the people Duke Valentino, gained his position through his father's Fortune and through her lost it, notwithstanding that he made use of every means and action possible to a prudent and vigorous man for putting down his roots in those states that another man's arms and Fortune bestowed on him. As I say above, he who does not lay his foundations beforehand can perhaps through great wisdom and energy lay them afterward, though he does so with trouble for the architect and danger to the building. So on examining all the steps taken by the Duke, we see that he himself laid mighty foundations for future power. To discuss these steps is not superfluous; indeed I for my part do not see what better precepts I can give a new prince than the example of Duke Valentino's actions. If his arrangements did not bring him success, the fault was not his, because his failure resulted from an unusual and utterly malicious stroke of Fortune.[3]

[*Pope Alexander VI Attempts to Make Cesare a Prince*]

Alexander VI,[4] in his attempt to give high position to the Duke his son, had before him many difficulties, present and future. First, he saw no way in which he could make him lord of any state that was not a state of the Church, yet if the Pope tried to take such a state from the Church, he knew that the Duke of Milan and the Venetians[5] would not allow it because both Faenza and Rimini were already under Venetian protection. He saw, besides, that the weapons of Italy, especially those of which he could make use, were in the hands of men who had reason to fear the Pope's greatness; therefore he could not rely on them, since they were all among the Orsini and the Colonnesi[6] and their allies. He therefore was under the necessity of disturbing the situation and embroiling the states of Italy so that he could safely master part of them. This he found easy since, luckily for him, the Venetians, influenced by other reasons, had set out to get the French to come again into Italy. He did not merely oppose their coming; he made it easier by dissolving the early marriage of King Louis.[7] The King then marched into Italy with the Venetians' aid and Alexander's consent; and he was no sooner in Milan than the Pope got soldiers from him for an attempt on Romagna; these the King granted for the sake of his own reputation.[8]

---

1. Translated by Allan H. Gilbert.
2. Son of Pope Alexander VI and duke of Valentinois and Romagna. His skillful and merciless subjugation of the local lords of Romagna occurred between 1499 and 1502.
3. Ill health.
4. Rodrigo Borgia (ca. 1431–1503), pope (1492–1503), father of Cesare and Lucrezia Borgia.

5. The Venetian Republic opposed the expansion of the papal states. "Duke of Milan": Ludovico Il Moro, the flamboyant duke of the Sforza family.
6. Powerful Roman families.
7. Louis XII, king of France (d. 1515).
8. According to his agreement with Pope Alexander VI.

[Borgia Determines to Depend on Himself]

Having taken Romagna, then, and suppressed the Colonnesi, the Duke, in attempting to keep the province and to go further, was hindered by two things: one, his own forces, which he thought disloyal; the other, France's intention. That is, he feared that the Orsini forces which he had been using would fail him and not merely would hinder his gaining but would take from him what he had gained, and that the King would treat him in the same way. With the Orsini, he had experience of this when after the capture of Faenza he attacked Bologna, for he saw that they turned cold over that attack. And as to the King's purpose, the Duke learned it when, after taking the dukedom of Urbino, he invaded Tuscany—an expedition that the King made him abandon. As a result, he determined not to depend further on another man's armies and Fortune.

[The Duke Destroys His Disloyal Generals]

The Duke's first act to that end was to weaken the Orsini and Colonnesi parties in Rome by winning over to himself all their adherents who were men of rank, making them his own men of rank and giving them large subsidies; and he honored them, according to their stations, with military and civil offices, so that within a few months their hearts were emptied of all affection for the Roman parties, and it was wholly transferred to the Duke. After this, he waited for a good chance to wipe out the Orsini leaders, having scattered those of the Colonna family; such a chance came to him well and he used it better. When the Orsini found out, though late, that the Duke's and the Church's greatness was their ruin, they held a meeting at Magione, in Perugian territory. From that resulted the rebellion of Urbino, the insurrections in Romagna, and countless dangers for the Duke, all of which he overcame with the aid of the French. Thus having got back his reputation, but not trusting France or other outside forces, in order not to have to put them to a test, he turned to trickery. And he knew so well how to falsify his purpose that the Orsini themselves, by means of Lord Paulo,[9] were reconciled with him (as to Paulo the Duke did not omit any sort of gracious act to assure him, giving him money, clothing and horses) so completely that their folly took them to Sinigaglia into his hands. Having wiped out these leaders, then, and changed their partisans into his friends, the Duke had laid very good foundations for his power, holding all the Romagna along with the dukedom of Urbino, especially since he believed he had made the Romagna his friend and gained the support of all those people, through their getting a taste of well-being.

[Peace in Romagna; Remirro de Orco]

Because this matter is worthy of notice and of being copied by others, I shall not omit it. After the Duke had seized the Romagna and found it controlled by weak lords who had plundered their subjects rather than governed them, and had given them reason for disunion, not for union, so that the whole province was full of thefts, brawls, and every sort of excess, he judged that if he intended

9. Member of the Orsini.

to make it peaceful and obedient to the ruler's arm, he must of necessity give it good government. Hence he put in charge there Messer[1] Remirro de Orco, a man cruel and ready, to whom he gave the most complete authority. This man in a short time rendered the province peaceful and united, gaining enormous prestige. Then the Duke decided there was no further need for such boundless power, because he feared it would become a cause for hatred; so he set up a civil court in the midst of the province, with a distinguished presiding judge, where every city had its lawyer. And because he knew that past severities had made some men hate him, he determined to purge such men's minds and win them over entirely by showing that any cruelty which had gone on did not originate with himself but with the harsh nature of his agent. So getting an opportunity for it, one morning at Cesena he had Messer Remirro laid in two pieces in the public square with a block of wood and a bloody sword near him. The ferocity of this spectacle left those people at the same time gratified and awe-struck.

[Princely Virtues]

From CHAPTER 15

On the Things for Which Men, and Especially Princes, Are Praised or Censured

* * * Because I know that many have written on this topic, I fear that when I too write I shall be thought presumptuous, because, in discussing it, I break away completely from the principles laid down by my predecessors. But since it is my purpose to write something useful to an attentive reader, I think it more effective to go back to the practical truth of the subject than to depend on my fancies about it. And many have imagined republics and principalities that never have been seen or known to exist in reality. For there is such a difference between the way men live and the way they ought to live, that anybody who abandons what is for what ought to be will learn something that will ruin rather than preserve him, because anyone who determines to act in all circumstances the part of a good man must come to ruin among so many who are not good. Hence, if a prince wishes to maintain himself, he must learn how to be not good, and to use that ability or not as is required.

Leaving out of account, then, things about an imaginary prince, and considering things that are true, I say that all men, when they are spoken of, and especially princes, because they are set higher, are marked with some of the qualities that bring them either blame or praise. To wit, one man is thought liberal, another stingy (using a Tuscan word, because *avaricious* in our language is still applied to one who desires to get things through violence, but *stingy* we apply to him who refrains too much from using his own property); one is thought open-handed, another grasping; one cruel, the other compassionate; one is a breaker of faith, the other reliable; one is effeminate and cowardly,

1. My lord (from the French *monsieur*).

the other vigorous and spirited; one is philanthropic, the other egotistic; one is lascivious, the other chaste; one is straightforward, the other crafty; one hard, the other easy to deal with; one is firm, the other unsettled; one is religious, the other unbelieving; and so on.

And I know that everybody will admit that it would be very praiseworthy for a prince to possess all of the above-mentioned qualities that are considered good. But since he is not able to have them or to observe them completely, because human conditions do not allow him to, it is necessary that he be prudent enough to understand how to avoid getting a bad name because he is given to those vices that will deprive him of his position. He should also, if he can, guard himself from those vices that will not take his place away from him, but if he cannot do it, he can with less anxiety let them go. Moreover, he should not be troubled if he gets a bad name because of vices without which it will be difficult for him to preserve his position. I say this because, if everything is considered, it will be seen that some things seem to be virtuous, but if they are put into practice will be ruinous to him; other things seem to be vices, yet if put into practice will bring the prince security and well-being.

CHAPTER 16

On Liberality and Parsimony

Beginning, then, with the first of the above-mentioned qualities, I assert that it is good to be thought liberal. Yet liberality, practiced in such a way that you get a reputation for it, is damaging to you, for the following reasons: If you use it wisely and as it ought to be used, it will not become known, and you will not escape being censured for the opposite vice. Hence, if you wish to have men call you liberal, it is necessary not to omit any sort of lavishness. A prince who does this will always be obliged to use up all his property in lavish actions; he will then, if he wishes to keep the name of liberal, be forced to lay heavy taxes on his people and exact money from them, and do everything he can to raise money. This will begin to make his subjects hate him, and as he grows poor he will be little esteemed by anybody. So it comes about that because of this liberality of his, with which he has damaged a large number and been of advantage to but a few, he is affected by every petty annoyance and is in peril from every slight danger. If he recognizes this and wishes to draw back, he quickly gets a bad name for stinginess.

Since, then, a prince cannot without harming himself practice this virtue of liberality to such an extent that it will be recognized, he will, if he is prudent, not care about being called stingy. As time goes on he will be thought more and more liberal, for the people will see that because of his economy his income is enough for him, that he can defend himself from those who make war against him, and that he can enter upon undertakings without burdening his people. Such a prince is in the end liberal to all those from whom he takes nothing, and they are numerous; he is stingy to those to whom he does not give, and they are few. In our times we have seen big things done only by those who have been looked on as stingy; the others have utterly failed. Pope Julius II,[2] though he made use of a

---

2. Pope Julius II (r. 1503–13) was known as the "Warrior Pope" and led efforts to drive French forces from Italy.

reputation for liberality to attain the papacy, did not then try to maintain it, because he wished to be able to make war. The present King of France[3] has carried on great wars without laying unusually heavy taxes on his people, merely because his long economy has made provision for heavy expenditures. The present King of Spain,[4] if he had continued liberal, would not have carried on or completed so many undertakings.

Therefore a prince ought to care little about getting called stingy, if as a result he does not have to rob his subjects, is able to defend himself, does not become poor and contemptible, and is not obliged to become grasping. For this vice of stinginess is one of those that enables him to rule. Somebody may say: Caesar, by means of his liberality, became emperor, and many others have come to high positions because they have been liberal and have been thought so. I answer: Either you are already prince, or you are on the way to become one. In the first case liberality is dangerous; in the second it is very necessary to be thought liberal. Caesar was one of those who wished to attain dominion over Rome. But if, when he had attained it, he had lived for a long time and had not moderated his expenses, he would have destroyed his authority. Somebody may answer: Many who have been thought very liberal have been princes and done great things with their armies. I answer: The prince spends either his own property and that of his subjects or that of others. In the first case he ought to be frugal; in the second he ought to abstain from no sort of liberality. When he marches with his army and lives on plunder, loot, and ransom, a prince controls the property of others. To him liberality is essential, for without it his soldiers would not follow him. You can be a free giver of what does not belong to you or your subjects, as were Cyrus, Caesar, and Alexander,[5] because to spend the money of others does not decrease your reputation but adds to it. It is only the spending of your own money that hurts you.

There is nothing that eats itself up as fast as does liberality, for when you practice it you lose the power to practice it, and become poor and contemptible, or else to escape poverty you become rapacious and therefore are hated. And of all the things against which a prince must guard himself, the first is being an object of contempt and hatred. Liberality leads you to both of these. Hence there is more wisdom in keeping a name for stinginess, which produces a bad reputation without hatred, than in striving for the name of liberal, only to be forced to get the name of rapacious, which brings forth both bad reputation and hatred.

From CHAPTER 17

On Cruelty and Pity, and Whether It Is Better to Be Loved or to Be Feared, and Vice Versa

Coming then to the other qualities already mentioned, I say that every prince should wish to be thought compassionate and not cruel; still, he should be careful not to make a bad use of the pity he feels. Cesare Borgia was considered cruel, yet this cruelty of his pacified the Romagna, united it, and changed its

---

3. Louis XII (r. 1498–1515), mocked for his economy.
4. Ferdinand the Catholic (1452–1516), king of Aragon, whose marriage to Isabel of Castile unified Spain.

5. Great conquerors and imperial leaders of the classical world: Cyrus the Great, founder of the Achaemenid (Persian) Empire; Julius Caesar, Roman general and statesman; and Alexander the Great, king of Macedonia.

condition to that of peace and loyalty. If the matter is well considered, it will be seen that Cesare was much more compassionate than the people of Florence, for in order to escape the name of cruel they allowed Pistoia to be destroyed.[6] Hence a prince ought not to be troubled by the stigma of cruelty, acquired in keeping his subjects united and faithful. By giving a very few examples of cruelty he can be more truly compassionate than those who through too much compassion allow disturbances to continue, from which arise murders or acts of plunder. Lawless acts are injurious to a large group, but the executions ordered by the prince injure a single person. The new prince, above all other princes, cannot possibly avoid the name of cruel, because new states are full of perils. Dido in Virgil puts it thus: "Hard circumstances and the newness of my realm force me to do such things, and to keep watch and ward over all my lands."[7]

All the same, he should be slow in believing and acting, and should make no one afraid of him, his procedure should be so tempered with prudence and humanity that too much confidence does not make him incautious, and too much suspicion does not make him unbearable.

All this gives rise to a question for debate: Is it better to be loved than to be feared, or the reverse? I answer that a prince should wish for both. But because it is difficult to reconcile them, I hold that it is much more secure to be feared than to be loved, if one of them must be given up. The reason for my answer is that one must say of men generally that they are ungrateful, mutable, pretenders and dissemblers, prone to avoid danger, thirsty for gain. So long as you benefit them they are all yours; as I said above, they offer you their blood, their property, their lives, their children, when the need for such things is remote. But when need comes upon you, they turn around. So if a prince has relied wholly on their words, and is lacking in other preparations, he falls. For friendships that are gained with money, and not with greatness and nobility of spirit, are deserved but not possessed and in the nick of time one cannot avail himself of them. Men hesitate less to injure a man who makes himself loved than to injure one who makes himself feared, for their love is held by a chain of obligation, which, because of men's wickedness, is broken on every occasion for the sake of selfish profit; but their fear is secured by a dread of punishment which never fails you.

Nevertheless the prince should make himself feared in such a way that, if he does not win love, he escapes hatred. This is possible, for to be feared and not to be hated can easily coexist. In fact it is always possible, if the ruler abstains from the property of his citizens and subjects, and from their women. And if, as sometimes happens, he finds that he must inflict the penalty of death, he should do it when he has proper justification and evident reason. But above all he must refrain from taking property, for men forget the death of a father more quickly than the loss of their patrimony. Further, causes for taking property are never lacking, and he who begins to live on plunder is always finding cause to seize what belongs to others. But on the contrary, reasons for taking life are rarer and fail sooner.

6. Pistoia was a city under Florentine rule, riven by quarrels among its aristocratic families, which Cesare Borgia attempted to conquer. Machiavelli was Florence's envoy to Pistoia on several occasions in 1501–2, and wrote a memorandum on its problems. Here, he condemns what he considers Florence's insufficiently decisive actions against the leaders of the rival factions in Pistoia.
7. Virgil, *Aeneid* 1.563–4. Dido, queen of Carthage, is building her city as Aeneas arrives on her shores.

But when a prince is with his army and has a great number of soldiers under his command, then above all he must pay no heed to being called cruel, because if he does not have that name he cannot keep his army united or ready for duty. It should be numbered among the wonderful feats of Hannibal[8] that he led to war in foreign lands a large army, made up of countless types of men, yet never suffered from dissension, either among the soldiers or against the general, in either bad or good fortune. His success resulted from nothing else than his inhuman cruelty, which, when added to his numerous other strong qualities, made him respected and terrible in the sight of his soldiers. Yet without his cruelty his other qualities would not have been adequate. So it seems that those writers have not thought very deeply who on one side admire his accomplishment and on the other condemn the chief cause for it.

* * *

Returning, then, to the debate on being loved and feared, I conclude that since men love as they please and fear as the prince pleases, a wise prince will evidently rely on what is in his own power and not on what is in the power of another. As I have said, he need only take pains to avoid hatred.

CHAPTER 18

In What Way Faith Should Be Kept by Princes

Everybody knows how laudable it is in a prince to keep his faith and to be an honest man and not a trickster. Nevertheless, the experience of our times shows that the princes who have done great things are the ones who have taken little account of their promises and who have known how to addle the brains of men with craft. In the end they have conquered those who have put their reliance on good faith.

You must realize, then, that there are two ways to fight. In one kind the laws are used, in the other, force. The first is suitable to man, the second to animals. But because the first often falls short, one has to turn to the second. Hence a prince must know perfectly how to act like a beast and like a man. This truth was covertly taught to princes by ancient authors, who write that Achilles and many other ancient princes were turned over for their upbringing to Chiron[9] the centaur, that he might keep them under his tuition. To have as teacher one who is half beast and half man means nothing else than that a prince needs to know how to use the qualities of both creatures. The one without the other will not last long.

Since, then, it is necessary for a prince to understand how to make good use of the conduct of the animals, he should select among them the fox and the lion, because the lion cannot protect himself from traps, and the fox cannot protect himself from the wolves. So the prince needs to be a fox that he may know how to deal with traps, and a lion that he may frighten the wolves. Those who act like

8. Carthaginian leader who fought against Rome in the Second Punic War (218–201 B.C.E.). He famously marched his army, including war elephants, across the Alps into Italy.
9. In Greek myth, Chiron was the wisest of the centaurs (half men, half horses). He was renowned as the teacher of gods and heroes, including the great warrior Achilles, the Greek champion in the Trojan War.

the lion alone do not understand their business. A prudent ruler, therefore, cannot and should not observe faith when such observance is to his disadvantage and the causes that made him give his promise have vanished. If men were all good, this advice would not be good, but since men are wicked and do not keep their promises to you, you likewise do not have to keep yours to them. Lawful reasons to excuse his failure to keep them will never be lacking to a prince. It would be possible to give innumerable modern examples of this and to show many treaties and promises that have been made null and void by the faithlessness of princes. And the prince who has best known how to act as a fox has come out best. But one who has this capacity must understand how to keep it covered, and be a skilful pretender and dissembler. Men are so simple and so subject to present needs that he who deceives in this way will always find those who will let themselves be deceived.

I do not wish to keep still about one of the recent instances. Alexander VI[1] did nothing else than deceive men, and had no other intention; yet he always found a subject to work on. There never was a man more effective in swearing that things were true, and the greater the oaths with which he made a promise, the less he observed it. Nonetheless his deceptions always succeeded to his wish, because he thoroughly understood this aspect of the world.

It is not necessary, then, for a prince really to have all the virtues mentioned above, but it is very necessary to seem to have them. I will even venture to say that they damage a prince who possesses them and always observes them, but if he seems to have them they are useful. I mean that he should seem compassionate, trustworthy, humane, honest, and religious, and actually be so; but yet he should have his mind so trained that, when it is necessary not to practice these virtues, he can change to the opposite, and do it skilfully. It is to be understood that a prince, especially a new prince, cannot observe all the things because of which men are considered good, because he is often obliged, if he wishes to maintain his government, to act contrary to faith, contrary to charity, contrary to humanity, contrary to religion. It is therefore necessary that he have a mind capable of turning in whatever direction the winds of Fortune and the variations of affairs require, and, as I said above, that he should not depart from what is morally right, if he can observe it, but should know how to adopt what is bad, when he is obliged to.

A prince, then, should be very careful that there does not issue from his mouth anything that is not full of the above-mentioned five qualities. To those who see and hear him he should seem all compassion, all faith, all honesty, all humanity, all religion. There is nothing more necessary to make a show of possessing than this last quality. For men in general judge more by their eyes than by their hands; everybody is fitted to see, few to understand. Everybody sees what you appear to be; few make out what you really are. And these few do not dare to oppose the opinion of the many, who have the majesty of the state to confirm their view. In the actions of all men, and especially those of princes, where there is no court to which to appeal, people think of the outcome. A prince needs only to conquer and to maintain his position. The means he has used will always be judged honorable and will be praised by everybody, because the crowd is always caught by

---

1. Pope Rodrigo Borgia (r. 1492–1503), father of Cesare Borgia, was widely considered worldly and corrupt.

appearance and by the outcome of events, and the crowd is all there is in the world; there is no place for the few when the many have room enough. A certain prince of the present day,[2] whom it is not good to name, preaches nothing else than peace and faith, and is wholly opposed to both of them, and both of them, if he had observed them, would many times have taken from him either his reputation or his throne.

From CHAPTER 19
On Avoiding Contempt and Hatred

But because I have spoken of the more important of the qualities above, I wish to cover the others briefly with this generality. To wit, the prince should give his attention, as is in part explained above, to avoiding the things that make him hateful and contemptible. As long as he escapes them, he will have done his duty, and will find no danger in other injuries to his reputation. Hatred, as I have said, comes upon him chiefly from being rapacious and seizing the property and women of his subjects. He ought to abstain from both of these, for the majority of men live in contentment when they are not deprived of property or honor. Hence the prince has to struggle only with the ambition of the few which can be restrained in many ways and with ease. Contempt is his portion if he is held to be variable, volatile, effeminate, cowardly, or irresolute. From these a prince should guard himself as from a rock in the sea. He should strive in all his actions to give evident signs of greatness, spirit, gravity, and fortitude. Also in the private affairs of his subjects he should make it understood that his opinion is irrevocable. In short he should keep up such a reputation that nobody thinks of trying to deceive him or outwit him.

The prince who makes people hold that opinion has prestige enough. And if a prince has a high reputation, men hesitate to conspire against him and hesitate to attack him, simply because he is supposed to be of high ability and respected by his subjects. For a prince must needs have two kinds of fear: one within his state, because of his subjects; the other without, because of foreign rulers. From these dangers he defends himself with good weapons and good friends. And if his weapons are good, he will always have good friends. Conditions within the state, too, will always remain settled when those without are settled, if they have not already been unsettled by some conspiracy. And when things without are in movement, if he has ruled and lived as I have said, and does not fail himself, he will surely repel every attack, as I said Nabis the Spartan did.[3]

But with respect to his subjects, when there is no movement without, he has to fear that they will make a secret conspiracy. From this the prince protects himself adequately if he avoids being hated and despised and keeps the people satisfied with him. The latter necessarily follows the former, as was explained above at length. Indeed one of the most potent remedies the prince can have against conspiracies is not to be hated by the majority of his subjects. The reason for this is that a man who conspires always thinks he will please the people by killing the

2. Ferdinand the Catholic, king of Spain.
3. Last ruler (d. 192 B.C.E.) of independent Sparta, a Greek city-state. A controversial figure, he was known for ably maintaining his power in a time of war, but was also reviled in classical sources for his use of mercenaries and abuse of power.

prince; but when he thinks he will offend them by it, he does not pluck up courage to adopt such a plan, because the difficulties that fall to the portion of conspirators are numerous. Experience shows that there have been many conspiracies and that few have come out well. They fail because the conspirator cannot be alone, and he can get companions only from those who, he thinks, are discontented. But as soon as you have revealed your purpose to a malcontent, you have given him an opportunity to become contented, because he evidently can hope to gain every advantage from his knowledge. Such is his position that, seeing on the one hand certain gain, and on the other gain that is uncertain and full of danger, he must needs be a rare friend, or, at any rate, an obstinate enemy of the prince, if he keeps faith with you. To put the thing briefly, I say that on the part of those who conspire there is nothing but fear, jealousy, and the expectation of punishment, which terrifies them. But on the part of the prince are the majesty of his high office, the laws, the power of his friends and his party that protects him. Evidently when the popular goodwill is joined to all these things, it is impossible that anybody can be so foolhardy as to conspire against him. Ordinarily the conspirator must be afraid before the execution of his evil deed, but in this case he also has reason to fear after his transgression, because he will have the people against him and therefore cannot hope for any escape.

* * * *

I conclude, therefore, that a prince need not pay much attention to conspiracies when the people are well disposed to him. But when they are unfriendly and hate him, he must fear everything and everybody. Further, well-organized governments and wise princes have striven with all diligence not to make the upper classes feel desperate, and to satisfy the populace and keep them contented. In fact this is one of the most important matters a prince has to deal with.

Among the kingdoms well organized and well governed in our times is France. In this country there are numerous good institutions on which depend the liberty and security of the king. The first of these is the parliament and its authority. He who organized this kingdom set up the parliament because he knew the ambition of the nobles and their arrogance, and judged it necessary that the nobility should have a bit in its mouth to restrain it. On the other hand, he knew the hatred, founded on fear, of the generality of men for the nobles, and intended to secure the position of the latter. Yet he did not wish this to be the special concern of the king, because he wished to relieve the king from the hatred he would arouse among the great if he favored the people, and among the people if he favored the nobles. Therefore he set up a third party as judge, to be the one who, without bringing hatred on the king, should restrain the nobles and favor the people. This institution could not be better or more prudent, nor could there be a stronger cause for the security of the king and the realm. From this can be deduced another important idea: to wit, princes should have things that will bring them hatred done by their agents, but should do in person those that will give pleasure. Once more I conclude that a prince should esteem the nobles but should not make himself hated by the populace.

* * *

It should here be observed that hate is gained through good deeds as well as bad ones. Therefore, as I said above, if a prince wishes to keep his position, he is often obliged not to be good. For if that large body, whether made up of people or soldiers or grandees, whose support you believe you need to maintain yourself, is corrupt, you must feed its humor in order to satisfy it. In such conditions, good deeds are enemies to you. But let us come to Alexander. He was of such goodness that among the other matters for which he is praised is this, that, in the fourteen years during which he held the empire, no one was ever put to death by him without trial. All the same, since he was thought to be under the influence of women, and a man who allowed his mother to govern him, he came to be despised. Then the army plotted against him and killed him.

* * *

I say that the princes of our times are less troubled than the emperors were by the necessity of making their conduct satisfy the soldiers above all others. It is true that they do have to give their troops some consideration, yet it is quickly settled, because none of these princes have armies already formed that have grown old along with the governments and administrations of the provinces, as did the armies of the Roman Empire. If, therefore, it was then necessary to satisfy the soldiers rather than the people, it was because the soldiers were more powerful than the people. Now it is more necessary to princes, except the Turk and the Soldan,[4] to satisfy the people rather than the soldiers, for the people are the more powerful. I make an exception of the Turk, who always keeps about him twelve thousand infantry and fifteen thousand cavalry, on whom depend his security and the strength of his kingdom. So it is necessary that, giving second place to any other consideration, that lord should keep the friendship of his soldiers. Since the kingly authority of the Soldan is likewise entirely in the hands of the soldiers, it is needful for him to have them as his friends, without regard for the people. You should observe that this government of the Soldan is unlike all other principates; it is like the Christian papacy, which can be called neither a hereditary principality nor a new one. The sons of the old prince are not heirs and do not carry on a line of princes, but the successor is he who is chosen to that rank by those who have the right to do so. And yet, since this method of government has long been used, it cannot be called a new principality, because it encounters none of the difficulties of new ones. Even if the ruler is new, the institutions of the state are old and arranged to receive him as though he were their hereditary lord.

[The Best Defense]

From CHAPTER 20

Whether Fortresses and Other Things That Princes Employ Every Day Are Useful or Useless

Some princes, in order to hold their positions securely, have disarmed their subjects. Others have kept their subject territories divided. Some have nourished enmities against themselves. Yet others, by a change in policy, have tried

---

4. "Turk": ruler of the Ottoman Empire, supported by a corps of Janissaries (elite infantry troops); Soldan: sultan of Egypt, supported by a corps of Mamluks (slave soldiers).

to gain to their side those they suspected at the beginnings of their reigns. Some have built fortresses. Some have dismantled and destroyed them. From all these things it is not possible to educe a final decision, without coming to the particulars of those states where matters like these must be decided. Hence I shall speak in the general manner that the material in itself justifies.

It has never been true, then, that a new prince has disarmed his subjects. On the contrary, when he has found them disarmed, he has always armed them, because, when you arm them, their arms become your own; those whom you have suspected become faithful; those who were faithful are kept so, and instead of your subjects they become your partisans. It is impossible to arm all your subjects, yet if you benefit those you arm, you can deal much more securely with those who are left unarmed. The very diversity of procedure which the favored ones see applied to them, binds them to you. The others excuse you, holding it necessary that those should have more favor who undergo the most danger and have the greatest obligation. But when you disarm new subjects you get their ill will; for you show that you distrust them either for their worthlessness or their lack of fidelity. Either one of these beliefs rouses hatred against you. And because you are not able to remain unarmed, you are obliged to turn to mercenary soldiers * * *. Even if mercenaries were good, they could not be sufficient to defend you from hostile rulers and untrustworthy subjects. Hence, as I have said, a new prince, in a new principate, has always organized armies there. Histories are full of examples of this.

But when a prince acquires a new state that he joins as a member to his old one, then it is necessary to disarm the new state, except for those who have been your partisans in gaining it. And even these it is necessary to render soft and effeminate as time and opportunity permit; and you must arrange things in such a way that the arms of your whole state are in the hands of your own soldiers, who live in your old state close to you.

* * *

There is no doubt that princes become great when they overcome difficulties and opposition. Therefore Fortune avails herself of this, especially when she wishes to bestow greatness on a new prince, who has more need to acquire reputation than a hereditary one. For she causes enemies to rise up against him, and makes him undertake campaigns against them, that he may have an opportunity to conquer them, and rise high by ascending the ladder provided by his enemies. Hence many think that a wise prince, whenever he has opportunity for it, should craftily nourish some hatreds against himself, in order that by overthrowing them he may increase his greatness.

Princes, and especially new ones, sometimes find more fidelity and helpfulness in those whom they have distrusted at the beginning of their rule, than in those who at first were attached to them. Pandolfo Petrucci,[5] prince of Siena, ruled his state more with those he distrusted than with the others. But of this thing it is not possible to speak in general because it varies according to the individual case. I shall say only this. Those men who are unfriendly in the early days of a reign, and are of such a kind that they have need of support if they are to maintain themselves, are always to be gained by the prince with the greatest

5. Ruler of the Italian Republic of Siena (1452–1512).

ease, and they are obliged to serve him faithfully, in proportion as they know it is needful for them to cancel with their deeds the unfavorable opinion he had of them. Hence the prince always derives more profit from them than from those who feel too secure in his service, and as a result neglect his affairs.

And because the subject demands it, I do not wish to omit a reminder to princes who have secured a brand-new state by means of the favor of persons within it. They should consider well what cause moved those who favored the change to do so. If it is not natural affection for the new ruler, but merely discontent with the government as it was, a prince will succeed in keeping them as his friends only with effort and great difficulty, because it is impossible for him to satisfy them. And if he will examine the cause of this, with the aid of examples derived from ancient and modern affairs, he will see that it is much easier to gain the friendship of the men who had been contented with the earlier government, and therefore were his enemies, than to gain that of those who became his friends and favored his occupation merely because they were not contented.

In order to hold their positions more securely, princes have been in the habit of building fortresses, which serve as bridle and bit for those who plan to act against them; princes also wish to have secure places of refuge from sudden assaults. I praise this method, because it has been used from ancient times. Nonetheless, Messer Niccolò Vitelli,[6] in our times, has been seen dismantling two fortresses in Città di Castello, in order to keep that state. Guido Ubaldo,[7] duke of Urbino, when he returned into his dominions after Cesare Borgia had been driven out of them, completely ruined all the fortresses of that province, and believed that without them it would be more difficult for him to lose that territory again. The Bentivogli,[8] when they returned to Bologna, employed similar methods.

Fortresses, then, are useful or not according to the times. If they benefit you in some circumstances, they will damage you in others. This matter can be considered as follows: a prince who has more fear of the people than of foreigners ought to build fortresses; but he who has more fear of foreigners than of his people should leave them out of his plans. The castle of Milan, which Francesco Sforza[9] built there, has done and will do more damage to the house of Sforza than any other cause of trouble in that state. Therefore not to be hated by the people is the best fortress there is. Even if you have fortresses, and the people hate you, you will not be safe, because, when the people have taken arms, foreigners who will assist them are never lacking. * * * Considering all these things, then, I praise him who builds fortresses and him who does not build them. I blame any prince who, trusting in his castles, thinks it of little importance that his people hate him.

6. Military ruler of the Italian city-state of Città di Castello (1414–1486).
7. Ruler of the Italian city-state of Urbino (1472–1508).
8. Ruling family of the Italian city-state of Bologna during the Renaissance.
9. Duke of Milan (1401–1466), founder of the Sforza dynasty that ruled the city-state of Milan from 1450–1535.

[Ferdinand of Spain, Exemplary Prince]

CHAPTER 21

What Is Necessary to a Prince That He May Be Considered Excellent

Nothing gives a prince so much respect as great undertakings and unusual examples of his own ability. In our day we have Ferdinand of Spain. He can be called, as it were, a new king, because, though at the beginning he was weak, he has become the first king of the Christians in fame and glory. If you will consider his actions, you will find them all great and some of them extraordinary. In the beginning of his reign he attacked Granada,[1] and that undertaking was the foundation of his power. In the first place, he carried it on when he was without other occupation and had no fear of being impeded; he used it to occupy the minds of the barons of Castile, who, when they were thinking about that war, did not think of rebelling. By this means he gained reputation and control over them without their realizing it. He was able to support armies with the money of the Church and the people, and, by means of that long war, to lay a foundation for his army, which later did him honor. Besides this, in order to undertake greater enterprises, he availed himself of religion and turned to a pious cruelty, hunting down the Moors and driving them out of his kingdom. Nothing can be more wretched or more unusual than this example of his ability. Cloaked with this same mantle, he attacked Africa; he undertook his enterprise in Italy; and finally he assailed France. And so he has always kept the minds of his subjects in suspense and wonder, and concerned with the outcome of his deeds. And his actions have begun in such a way, one coming from another, that between any two of them, he has never given men time enough to enable them to work quietly against him.

It is also to the profit of a prince to give unusual examples of his ability in internal affairs, like those that are related of Messer Bernabò of Milan.[2] I mean when he has an opportunity because someone does something extraordinary, either good or bad, in ordinary life, and the prince takes a method of rewarding or punishing him that will be widely talked of. And above all, a prince should endeavor in all his actions to show that he deserves fame as a great man and one of high mental capacity.

A prince is also esteemed when he is a true friend or a true enemy; that is, when without any reservation he shows himself favorable to one ruler and against another. This procedure is always more profitable than to remain neutral, because if two potentates, your neighbors, come to grips, they are such that when one of them conquers, you either will have to be afraid of the conqueror, or you will not. In either of these two cases, it will be better for you to make your policy plain and put up a good fight. In the first of them, if you do not adopt an open policy, you will always be the prey of the conqueror, to the pleasure and satisfaction of him who is conquered. You can give no reason why anybody should protect you and receive you, and will find

---

1. City in southern Spain that was the seat of Nasrid rule in Spain for centuries before it was conquered by Ferdinand and Isabella of Spain in 1492.

2. Bernabò Visconti, ruler of Milan from 1354 to 1385.

nobody to do it. The one who conquers does not wish friends whom he suspects and who will not aid him in adversity, and the loser will not receive you because you have not been willing to share his fortunes with arms in your hands.

When Antiochus[3] led his army into Greece, summoned there by the Aetolians to drive out the Romans, he sent ambassadors to the Achaeans, who were friends of the Romans, to advise them to remain neutral. On the other side, the Romans tried to persuade them to take arms with them. This matter came up for decision in the council of the Achaeans, where the agent of Antiochus advised them to remain neutral. The Roman legate answered: "As to what the others say about not getting yourselves into the war, nothing is less advantageous to you; without thanks, without dignity, you will be the reward of the victor."

It will always come about that he who is not your friend will ask you to be neutral, and he who is friendly to you will ask you to come out clearly with arms. Princes of irresolute character, in order to escape the perils of the moment, generally take the way of neutrality, and generally go to smash. But when a prince comes out vigorously in favor of one side, if the one you have joined wins, even though he is powerful and you are at his discretion, he is under obligation to you, and has formed a friendship for you. Moreover, men are never so dishonorable that they will give so great an example of ingratitude as to oppress you. And then victories are never so decided that the victor is not subject to qualifications, and especially with regard to justice. But if the one to whom you adhere loses, you are received by him, he aids you as long as he can, and you are the companion of a fortune that may rise again.

In the second case, when those who fight are of such a sort that you do not need to fear whichever one conquers, it is so much the more prudent for you to join your friend, because you go to the ruin of one neighbor with the aid of another who, if he were wise, would protect him. If your ally is victorious he is at your discretion, and it is impossible that with your aid he will not win.

Here it may be observed that a prince should be careful not to join company with one more powerful than himself, in order to attack someone, except when necessity constrains him, in the way mentioned above. If your powerful ally conquers, you remain his prisoner. And princes should avoid, as much as they can, being at the discretion of others. The Venetians joined the King of France against the Duke of Milan, when they were able to avoid making that alliance, and it resulted in their ruin. But when such an alliance cannot be avoided (as happened to the Florentines when the Pope and the King of Spain went with their armies to attack Lombardy), then a prince should join in for the reasons I have given. No state should believe it can always make plans certain of success; it should rather expect to make only doubtful ones. For the course of human events teaches that man never attempts to avoid one disadvantage without running into another. Prudence, therefore, consists in the power to recognize the nature of disadvantages and to take the less disagreeable as good.

A prince should also show himself a lover of excellence by giving preferment to gifted men and honoring those who excel in some art. Besides, he should encourage his citizens by giving them a chance to exercise their functions qui-

---

3. Antiochus III "the Great" (ca. 241–187 B.C.E.), ruler of the Seleucid Empire in Asia Minor.

etly, in trade and agriculture and every other occupation of man. A citizen should not hesitate to increase his property for fear it will be taken away from him, or to open a new business for fear of taxes. On the contrary the prince should offer rewards to those who undertake to do these things, and to anybody who thinks of improving in any way his city or his dominion. Besides this, at suitable times of the year he should engage the attention of the people with festivals and shows. And because every city is divided into gilds or wards, he should take account of these bodies, meet with them sometimes, and give in person an example of humanity and generosity. At the same time he should always preserve the dignity befitting his rank, for this ought never to be lacking in any circumstances.

[Good Counsel vs. Flattery]

From CHAPTER 23

In What Way Flatterers Are to Be Avoided

I do not wish to omit an important subject and an error from which princes with difficulty protect themselves, if they are not unusually prudent, or if they are not able to choose well. I refer to flatterers, of whom courts are full. Men are generally so well pleased with their own abilities and so greatly deceived about them that they protect themselves with difficulty from this plague, and when they do endeavor to protect themselves, they run the risk of becoming contemptible, for the reason that there is no way of protecting yourself from flattery except to have men understand that they do not offend you by speaking the truth to you; but when anyone can speak the truth to you, you do not receive proper respect. Hence a prudent prince must adopt a third method. He should choose wise men in his state, and to them alone he should give full power to speak the truth freely, but only on the matters he asks about, and on nothing else. Yet he should ask them about everything, and heed their opinions. Then he should make up his mind in private, at his leisure. With these pieces of advice, and with every one of them, he should conduct himself in such a way that each adviser may know that he will be so much the more in favor in proportion as he speaks more freely. But the prince should not consent to listen to anyone except these advisers, should carry out what he decides on, and should be firm in his decisions. He who does otherwise is either ruined by flatterers, or changes often, because of the varied opinions he listens to. As a result, he receives little respect.

* * *

A prince, therefore, should always take advice, but he should do it when he pleases and not when someone else pleases. On the contrary he should not let anyone dare to advise him when he does not ask for advice. But he should be a big asker, and a patient listener to the truth about the things asked. Still further, he should be angry if for any reason anybody should not tell him the truth. Many think that if a prince gives the impression of being prudent, he should be thought so not because of his own natural gifts but because of the good advice he has at hand; but without question they are wrong. For this is a general rule that never fails: a prince who is not wise himself cannot be well advised, unless by chance he gives himself over to one man who entirely directs him, and that man is exceedingly prudent. In this instance the prince surely would be, but such a condition would not last long, because in a short time that tutor of his would take away his throne. As a matter of fact, an unwise prince who asks counsel from more than one man will never receive unified advice, nor will he be able to unify it unaided. Each of the advisers will think about what concerns himself, and the prince will not be able to control them or to understand them. It cannot be otherwise; men are always wicked at bottom, unless they are made good by some compulsion. Hence I conclude that good counsels, whatever their source, necessarily result from the prudence of the ruler, and not the prudence of the ruler from good counsels.

[Why Princes Fail]

CHAPTER 24

Why the Princes of Italy Have Lost Their Authority

The things written above, if they are prudently carried into effect, will make a new prince seem to be an old one, and will immediately make him safer and firmer in his realm than if he had grown old in it. For the actions of a new prince are more closely watched than those of a hereditary one; and when they are seen to show great ability they influence men more and attach them to the prince more closely than ancient blood can, for men are much more impressed with present things than with past ones, and when in the present they find something good, they enjoy it and seek for nothing further. In fact, they will take every means of defending such a prince, if only he does not fail himself in other things. And thus he will secure a double glory: that of having begun a new princedom, and of having enriched and strengthened it with good laws, good arms, and good examples. On the contrary, he is doubly disgraced who, though born a prince, loses his dominion because he is not prudent.

And if those lords are examined who have lost their positions in Italy in our times, such as the King of Naples, the Duke of Milan, and others, they will exhibit first a common defect in their armies, for the reasons that have been discussed at length above. Further, it will be seen that some of them either had the people as enemies, or they had the friendship of the people, but had not been able to secure themselves against the upper classes. For realms without these defects are not lost if the prince has strength enough to keep an army in the field. Philip of Macedon,[4] not the father of Alexander but the one who was conquered by Titus Quintus, did not have a large realm, in comparison with the greatness of the Romans and the Greeks who attacked him. Nevertheless, because he was a warrior, and knew how to deal with his people and to secure himself against the upper classes, he kept up the war for several years. Even

---

4. Philip V (238–179 B.C.E.), king of Macedonia, defeated in 197 B.C.E. by a Roman army led by Titus Quintus Flaminius.

though at the end he lost control of some cities, he nevertheless retained his royal authority.

Therefore these princes of ours who have been many years in their positions should blame for the loss of them not Fortune, but their own worthlessness. In good weather they never thought of change (it is a common defect of men not to reckon on a storm when the sea is calm). Hence when times of adversity came, they thought about running away and not about defending themselves; and they hoped that the people, disgusted by the insolence of the conquerors, would call them back. This plan, when there are no others, is good, but it is a bad thing to abandon other resources for this one. A prince should not be willing to fall, just because he believes he will find somebody to set him up again; that may not come about, or if it does, it cannot bring you security, because such an expedient for defence is base and does not depend on yourself. Only those means of security are good, are certain, are lasting, that depend on yourself and your own vigor.

["Fortune is a woman"]

From CHAPTER 25

The Power of Fortune in Human Affairs, and to What Extent She Should Be Relied On

It is not unknown to me that many have been and still are of the opinion that the affairs of this world are so under the direction of Fortune and of God that man's prudence cannot control them; in fact, that man has no resource against them. For this reason many think there is no use in sweating much over such matters, but that one might as well let Chance take control. This opinion has been the more accepted in our times, because of the great changes in the state of the world that have been and now are seen every day, beyond all human surmise. And I myself, when thinking on these things, have now and then in some measure inclined to their view. Nevertheless, because the freedom of the will should not be wholly annulled, I think it may be true that Fortune is arbiter of half of our actions, but that she still leaves the control of the other half, or about that, to us.

I liken her to one of those raging streams that, when they go mad, flood the plains, ruin the trees and the buildings, and take away the fields from one bank and put them down on the other. Everybody flees before them; everybody yields to their onrush without being able to resist anywhere. And though this is their nature, it does not cease to be true that, in calm weather, men can make some provisions against them with walls and dykes, so that, when the streams swell, their waters will go off through a canal, or their currents will not be so wild and do so much damage. The same is true of Fortune. She shows her power where there is no wise preparation for resisting her, and turns her fury where she knows that no walls and dykes have been made to hold her in. And if you consider Italy—the place where these variations occur and the cause that has set them in motion—you will see that she is a country without dykes and without any wall of defence. If, like Germany, Spain, and France, she had

had a sufficient bulwark of military vigor, this flood would not have made the great changes it has, or would not have come at all.

And this, I think, is all I need to say on opposing oneself to Fortune, in general. But limiting myself more to particulars, I say that a prince may be seen prospering today and falling in ruin tomorrow, though it does not appear that he has changed in his nature or any of his qualities. I believe this comes, in the first place, from the causes that have been discussed at length in preceding chapters. That is, if a prince bases himself entirely on Fortune, he will fall when she varies. I also believe that a ruler will be successful who adapts his mode of procedure to the quality of the times, and likewise that he will be unsuccessful if the times are out of accord with his procedure. Because it may be seen that in things leading to the end each has before him, namely glory and riches, men proceed differently. One acts with caution, another rashly; one with violence, another with skill; one with patience, another with its opposite; yet with these different methods each one attains his end. Still further, two cautious men will be seen, of whom one comes to his goal, the other does not. Likewise you will see two who succeed with two different methods, one of them being cautious and the other rash. These results are caused by nothing else than the nature of the times, which is or is not in harmony with the procedure of men. It also accounts for what I have mentioned, namely, that two persons, working differently, chance to arrive at the same result; and that of two who work in the same way, one attains his end, but the other does not.

On the nature of the times also depends the variability of the best method. If a man conducts himself with caution and patience, times and affairs may come around in such a way that his procedure is good, and he goes on successfully. But if times and circumstances change, he is ruined, because he does not change his method of action. There is no man so prudent as to understand how to fit himself to this condition, either because he is unable to deviate from the course to which nature inclines him, or because, having always prospered by walking in one path, he cannot persuade himself to leave it. So the cautious man, when the time comes to go at a reckless pace, does not know how to do it. Hence he comes to ruin. Yet if he could change his nature with the times and with circumstances, his fortune would not be altered.

Pope Julius II proceeded rashly in all his actions, and found the times and circumstances so harmonious with his mode of procedure that he was always so lucky as to succeed. Consider the first enterprise he engaged in, that of Bologna, while Messer Giovanni Bentivogli[5] was still alive. The Venetians were not pleased with it; the King of Spain felt the same way; the Pope was debating such an enterprise with the King of France. Nevertheless, in his courage and rashness Julius personally undertook that expedition. This movement made the King of Spain and the Venetians stand irresolute and motionless, the latter for fear, and the King because of his wish to recover the entire kingdom of Naples. On the other side, the King of France was dragged behind Julius, because the King, seeing that the Pope had moved and wishing to make him a friend in order to put down the Venetians, judged he could not refuse him soldiers without doing him open injury. Julius, then, with his rash movement, attained what

5. Of the ruling family Bentivogli. The pope undertook to dislodge him from Bologna in 1506.

no other pontiff, with the utmost human prudence, would have attained. If he had waited to leave Rome until the agreements were fixed and everything arranged, as any other pontiff would have done, he would never have succeeded, for the King of France would have had a thousand excuses, and the others would have raised a thousand fears. I wish to omit his other acts, which are all of the same sort, and all succeeded perfectly. The brevity of his life did not allow him to know anything different. Yet if times had come in which it was necessary to act with caution, they would have ruined him, for he would never have deviated from the methods to which nature inclined him.

I conclude, then, that since Fortune is variable and men are set in their ways, they are successful when they are in harmony with Fortune and unsuccessful when they disagree with her. Yet I am of the opinion that it is better to be rash than over-cautious, because Fortune is a woman and, if you wish to keep her down, you must beat her and pound her. It is evident that she allows herself to be overcome by men who treat her in that way rather than by those who proceed coldly. For that reason, like a woman, she is always the friend of young men, because they are less cautious, and more courageous, and command her with more boldness.

[The Roman Dream]

From CHAPTER 26

An Exhortation to Take Hold of Italy and Restore Her to Liberty from the Barbarians

Having considered all the things discussed above, I have been turning over in my own mind whether at present in Italy the time is ripe for a new prince to win prestige, and whether conditions there give a wise and vigorous ruler occasion to introduce methods that will do him honor, and bring good to the mass of the people of the land. It appears to me that so many things unite for the advantage of a new prince, that I do not know of any time that has ever been more suited for this. And, as I said, if it was necessary to make clear the ability of Moses that the people of Israel should be enslaved in Egypt, and to reveal Cyrus's greatness of mind that the Persians should be oppressed by the Medes, and to demonstrate the excellence of Theseus that the Athenians should be scattered, so at the present time, in order to make known the greatness of an Italian soul, Italy had to be brought down to her present position, to be more a slave than the Hebrews, more a servant than the Persians, more scattered than the Athenians; without head, without government; defeated, plundered, torn asunder, overrun; subject to every sort of disaster.

And though before this, certain persons[6] have showed signs from which it could be inferred that they were chosen by God for the redemption of Italy, nevertheless it has afterwards been seen that in the full current of action they have been cast off by Fortune. So Italy remains without life and awaits the man, whoever he may be, who is to heal her wounds, put an end to the plundering of Lombardy and the tribute laid on Tuscany and the kingdom of

---

6. Possibly Cesare Borgia and Francesco Sforza, who were discussed earlier in the book.

Naples, and cure her of those sores that have long been suppurating. She may be seen praying God to send some one to redeem her from these cruel and barbarous insults. She is evidently ready and willing to follow a banner, if only some one will raise it. Nor is there at present anyone to be seen in whom she can put more hope than in your illustrious House, because its fortune and vigor, and the favor of God and of the Church, which it now governs,[7] enable it to be the leader in such a redemption. This will not be very difficult, as you will see if you will bring to mind the actions and lives of those I have named above. And though these men were striking exceptions, yet they were men, and each of them had less opportunity than the present gives; their enterprises were not more just than this, nor easier, nor was God their friend more than he is yours. Here justice is complete. "A way is just to those to whom it is necessary, and arms are holy to him who has no hope save in arms."[8] Everything is now fully disposed for the work, and when that is true an undertaking cannot be difficult, if only your House adopts the methods of those I have set forth as examples. Moreover, we have before our eyes extraordinary and unexampled means prepared by God. The sea has been divided. A cloud has guided you on your way. The rock has given forth water. Manna has fallen.[9] Everything has united to make you great. The rest is for you to do. God does not intend to do everything, lest he deprive us of our free will and the share of glory that belongs to us.

It is no wonder if no one of the above-named Italians[1] has been able to do what we hope your illustrious House can. Nor is it strange if in the many revolutions and military enterprises of Italy, the martial vigor of the land always appears to be exhausted. This is because the old military customs were not good, and there has been nobody able to find new ones. Yet nothing brings so much honor to a man who rises to new power, as the new laws and new methods he discovers. These things, when they are well founded and have greatness in them, make him revered and worthy of admiration. And in Italy matter is not lacking on which to impress forms of every sort. There is great vigor in the limbs if only it is not lacking in the heads. You may see that in duels and combats between small numbers, the Italians have been much superior in force, skill, and intelligence. But when it is a matter of armies, Italians cannot be compared with foreigners. All this comes from the weakness of the heads, because those who know are not obeyed, and each man thinks he knows. Nor up to this time has there been a man able to raise himself so high, through both ability and fortune, that the others would yield to him. The result is that for the past twenty years, in all the wars that have been fought when there has been an army entirely Italian, it has always made a bad showing. Proof of this was given first at the Taro, and then at Alessandria, Capua, Genoa, Vailà, Bologna, and Mestri.[2]

If your illustrious House, then, wishes to imitate those excellent men who redeemed their countries, it is necessary, before everything else, to furnish

---

7. Pope Leo X (1475–1521) was a Medici (Giovanni de' Medici). "House": of Medici. *The Prince* was first meant for Giuliano de' Medici. After Giuliano's death it was dedicated to his nephew Lorenzo, later duke of Urbino.

8. Livy's *History* 9.1, para. 10.
9. Another allusion to Moses.
1. Perhaps another reference to Borgia and Sforza.
2. Sites of battles occurring between the end of the 15th century and 1513.

yourself with your own army, as the true foundation of every enterprise. You cannot have more faithful, nor truer, nor better soldiers. And though every individual of these may be good, they become better as a body when they see that they are commanded by their prince, and honored and trusted by him. It is necessary, therefore, that your House should be prepared with such forces, in order that it may be able to defend itself against the foreigners with Italian courage.

And though the Swiss and the Spanish infantry are properly estimated as terribly effective, yet both have defects. Hence a third type would be able not merely to oppose them but to feel sure of overcoming them. The fact is that the Spaniards are not able to resist cavalry, and the Swiss have reason to fear infantry, when they meet any as determined in battle as themselves. For this reason it has been seen and will be seen in experience that the Spaniards are unable to resist the French cavalry, and the Swiss are overthrown by Spanish infantry. And though of this last a clear instance has not been observed, yet an approach to it appeared in the battle of Ravenna,[3] when the Spanish infantry met the German battalions, who use the same methods as the Swiss. There the Spanish, through their ability and the assistance given by their shields, got within the points of the spears from below, and slew their enemies in security, while the Germans could find no means of resistance. If the cavalry had not charged the Spanish, they would have annihilated the Germans. It is possible, then, for one who realizes the defects of these two types, to equip infantry in a new manner, so that it can resist cavalry and not be afraid of foot-soldiers; but to gain this end they must have weapons of the right sorts, and adopt varied methods of combat. These are some of the things which, when they are put into service as novelties, give reputation and greatness to a new ruler.[4]

This opportunity, then, should not be allowed to pass, in order that after so long a time Italy may see her redeemer. I am unable to express with what love he would be received in all the provinces that have suffered from these foreign deluges; with what thirst for vengeance, what firm faith, what piety, what tears! What gates would be shut against him? what peoples would deny him obedience? what envy would oppose itself to him? what Italian would refuse to follow him? This barbarian rule stinks in every nostril. May your illustrious House, then, undertake this charge with the spirit and the hope with which all just enterprises are taken up, in order that, beneath its ensign, our native land may be ennobled, and, under its auspices, that saying of Petrarch may come true: "Manhood[5] will take arms against fury, and the combat will be short, because in Italian hearts the ancient valor is not yet dead."

---

3. Between Spain and France in April 1512.
4. Machiavelli was subsequently the author of the treatise *Art of War* (1521).

5. An etymological translation of the original *virtù* (from the Latin *vir*, "man"). The quotation is from the canzona "My Italy."

MARGUERITE DE NAVARRE

1492–1549

The French "discovered" Italy in the latter part of the fifteenth century, both through travel and, starting in 1494, through military invasions. Eager to imitate more sophisticated Italian city-states, French rulers and aristocrats adapted Italian artistic, literary, and social values to their own culture. Marguerite de Navarre, one of the most influential members of French courtly society, played a significant part in bringing about this transformation. As a writer and a patron of artists, she also responded seriously to the spiritual and intellectual challenge to Christian faith brought about by the Reformation. Her lively collection of stories, the *Heptameron*, gives voice to characters whose different positions afford them starkly different views of the world.

LIFE AND TIMES

Marguerite was born in 1492 into the French royal family. Her brother, the future King Francis I, was born two years later. From her earliest years, Marguerite received an exceptionally good education, including instruction in Latin, Italian, Spanish, and German; later in life she also studied Greek and Hebrew. At seventeen she was married to Charles, duke of Alençon, a feudal lord who was intellectually not her match. When her brother succeeded Louis XII to the French throne in 1515, Marguerite became one of the most influential women at the royal court, where she advised the king and received dignitaries and ambassadors as well as eminent men of letters. Under Francis I, the French court flourished culturally, hiring Ital-

ian artists as famous as Leonardo da Vinci (1452–1519) and Benvenuto Cellini (1500–1571).

Francis I continued the Italian wars, the complicated conflicts fought on Italian soil between his forces and those of the Holy Roman Emperor, Charles V. His defeat in the crucial battle of Pavia in 1525 was a double blow for Marguerite: her brother was taken to Madrid as a prisoner and her husband died of battle wounds. Marguerite went to Madrid to assist her sick brother and helped negotiate with Charles V for his release.

The year following her husband's death, Marguerite became "queen of Navarre" when she married Henri d'Albret, the king of Navarre in title only, since most of that domain had been annexed by Spain in 1516. Eleven years younger than Marguerite, Henri d'Albret was a dashing, flighty, and intellectually disappointing husband—and is thought to be the prototype for the philandering and misogynistic character of Hircan in the *Heptameron*. Their only daughter, Jeanne, born in 1527, was the mother of the future King Henry IV of France.

Marguerite continued to be involved in her royal brother's activities, participating in diplomacy and peace talks. Her interest, however, was increasingly focused on intellectual and literary pursuits and on religious meditation and debate. Erasmus, John Calvin, and Pope Paul III were among her numerous correspondents. Throughout her life she was a protector of writers and thinkers accused or suspected of Protestant leanings, including Rabelais, who dedicated the third book of *Gargantua and Pantagruel* to her. Her first published work, *The Mirror of the Sinful Soul* (1531), was found by the theologians of the Sorbonne to contain elements of Protestant "heresy"; the edition of 1533, containing an additional "Dialogue in the Form of a Night Vision" on the theological problem of salvation, was condemned. The king had to intervene on behalf of his sister and her chaplain. Later it became more difficult for Francis I to manage the rivalry between Catholics and Protestants, which was a political and military matter as much as it was a religious dispute. Protestants and their sympathizers were persecuted, and several prominent intellectuals went into prudent exile or were burned at the stake. Marguerite, who had an intellectual and mystical faith, appears never to have abandoned Catholicism but to have hoped for internal reform.

After the death of her brother in 1547, she published her *Marguerite de la Marguerite des Princesses* (with a play on the word *marguerite*, which in French means both "pearl" and "daisy"), a collection including long devotional poems and theatrical pieces ranging from allegory to farce. In 1549 she retired to Navarre and died in the castle of Odos on December 21.

THE *HEPTAMERON*

Marguerite's greatest literary achievement is the *Heptameron*, which was not published until 1559, a decade after her death. A collection of seventy stories told over seven days, it is framed by a larger narrative that reveals the storytellers' characters and relationships with each other. We do not know the exact circumstances of its production, and there are doubts that Marguerite herself authored all of its parts. Some scholars have concluded that Marguerite collected or commissioned tales for the narrative, and perhaps composed only the frame narrative—in many ways the work's most compelling feature. In the prologue, five men and five women, all nobles, are brought together in the Pyrenees when natural and criminal forces—including a flood, bandits, a bear, and murderers—prevent them from returning home. They arrive independently at an abbey, where, at the suggestion of Parlamente, thought to represent Marguerite herself, they agree to tell stories each day until they are able to return home. The stories deal above all with the antagonism between the sexes, particularly concerning issues of marital fidelity and the status of women. The *Heptameron* pays considerable attention to ideas of masculinity and to ideals and stereotypes about women. Class tensions are somewhat more muted, although the stories often pit powerful lords and husbands against those whose only weapon is their cleverness. The courtly men and women who narrate and hear the stories are, to say the least, unafraid to disagree with each other about the tales' significances, both in the frame and through their stories, which implicitly debate such issues as the just desserts for the philandering husband or the clever wife.

The *Heptameron* belongs to a tradition of framed storytelling that includes **The Thousand and One Nights**, **Chaucer's Canterbury Tales**, and Boccaccio's *Decameron*. In the prologue, Parlamente overtly ties the storytelling game to the *Decameron* and a recent translation into French (commissioned by Marguerite) that drew, she says, the admiration of the French court. In writing a French *Decameron*, however, the group proposed, "they should not write any story that was not truthful." The relationship between language and truth therefore becomes a dominant theme. Unable to devote themselves entirely to religious pursuits, the characters choose "truthful" stories as a worthwhile pastime.

By truthfulness, Marguerite means stories that are honest about social tensions. When the characters comment—in the frame and in their own stories—on each others' tales, they reveal how social factors influence their view of the world. Divine "truth" gives way to individual and social perspective: age, gender, social standing, education, marital status, and religious disposition form the grounds for rivalry and dispute among the group members.

The story reproduced here, story 8, shows a strong female character managing male desire. A wise wife protects her chambermaid and foils her philandering husband at the same time, exposing the blindness of his sexual infatuation.

The "amusing and virtuous" pastime of a privileged group of storytellers forced into reclusion becomes in these pages a lively debate on gender roles, true virtue, and the force of society's disapproval. Balanced between the court and broader social concerns, between older certainties and new challenges, the *Heptameron* presents a lively and complex portrait of Marguerite de Navarre's changing world. At the same time, it offers an enduring account of the gendered division of experience, exploring how men and women manage and mismanage their desires.

From the Heptameron[1]

From *Prologue*

* * *

Parlamente, the wife of Hircan,[2] was not one to let herself become idle or melancholy, and having asked her husband for permission, she spoke to the old Lady Oisille.[3]

"Madame," she said. "you have had much experience of life, and you now occupy the position of mother in regard to the rest of us women, and it surprises me that you do not consider some pastime to alleviate the boredom and distress that we shall have to bear during our long stay here. Unless we have some amusing and virtuous way of occupying ourselves, we run the risk of [falling]
[4] sick."

Longarine,[5] the young widow, added, "What is worse, we'll all become miserable and disagreeable—and that's an incurable disease. There isn't a man or woman amongst us who hasn't every cause to sink into despair, if we consider all that we have lost."

Ennasuite[6] laughed and rejoined, "Not everyone's lost a husband, like you, you know. And as for losing servants, no need to despair about that—there are

---

1. Translated by P. A. Chilton.
2. Hircan is variously described, in the book itself and by its commentators, as brilliant, flighty, sensual, capable of sarcasm and grossness. The name is related to Hircania, an imaginary and proverbially wild region in classical literature; the root is that of *hircus*, Latin for "goat" (cf. English *hircine*: libidinous). Parlamente probably represents Marguerite, whose name can be construed as *perle amante*, "loving pearl," or as *parlementer*, which refers to eloquent speaking.
3. The oldest, most authoritative, and most evangelical of the storytellers; she seems to be named for Louise—either Louise of Savoy,

Marguerite's mother, or her lady-in-waiting, Louise de Daillon.
4. Brackets indicate translator's interpolations.
5. A young and wisely talkative widow, often identified with one of Marguerite's ladies-in-waiting, who among her titles had that of lady of Langrai (hence her name, which is also interpreted as a play on *langue orine*, meaning "tongue of gold").
6. *Enna* may stand for "Anne," and *suite* means "retinue"; so the character is identifiable with Anne de Vivonne, one of the ladies in Marguerite's entourage who collaborated on the *Heptameron* project at court. Her attitude toward men can be bitter and sharply ironic.

plenty of men ready to do service! All the same, I do agree that we ought to have something to amuse us, so that we can pass the time as pleasantly as we can."

Her companion Nomerfide[7] said that this was a very good idea, and that if she had to spend a single day without some entertainment, she would be sure to die the next.

All the men supported this, and asked the Lady Oisille if she would kindly organize what they should do.

"My children," replied Oisille, "when you ask me to show you a pastime that is capable of delivering you from your boredom and your sorrow, you are asking me to do something that I find very difficult. All my life I have searched for a remedy, and I have found only one—the reading of holy Scripture, in which one may find true and perfect spiritual joy, from which proceed health and bodily repose. And if you ask what the prescription is that keeps me happy and healthy in my old age, I will tell you. As soon as I rise in the morning I take the Scriptures and read them. I see and contemplate the goodness of God, who for our sakes has sent His son to earth to declare the holy word and the good news by which He grants remission of all our sins, and payment of all our debts, through His gift to us of His love, His passion and His merits. And my contemplations give me such joy, that I take my psalter, and with the utmost humility, sing the beautiful psalms and hymns that the Holy Spirit has composed in the heart of David and the other authors. The contentment this affords me fills me with such well-being that whatever the evils of the day, they are to me so many blessings, for in my heart I have by faith Him who has borne these evils for me. Likewise, before supper, I withdraw to nourish my soul with readings and meditations. In the evening I ponder in my mind everything I have done during the day, so that I may ask God forgiveness of my sins, and give thanks to Him for His mercies. And so I lay myself to rest in His love, fear and peace, assured against all evils. And this, my children, is the pastime that long ago I adopted. All other ways have I tried, but none has given me spiritual contentment. I believe that if, each morning, you give one hour to reading, and then, during mass, say your prayers devoutly, you will find even in this wilderness all the beauty a city could afford. For, a person who knows God will find all things beautiful in Him, and without Him all things will seem ugly. So I say to you, if you would live in happiness, heed my advice."

Then Hircan spoke: "Madame, anyone who has read the holy Scriptures— as indeed I think we all have here—will readily agree that what you have said is true. However, you must bear in mind that we have not yet become so mortified in the flesh that we are not in need of some sort of amusement and physical exercise in order to pass the time. After all, when we're at home, we've got our hunting and hawking to distract us from the thousand and one foolish thoughts that pass through one's mind. The ladies have their housework and their needlework. They have their dances, too, which provide a respectable way for them to get some exercise. All this leads me to suggest, on behalf of the men here, that you, Madame, since you are the oldest among us, should read to us every morning about the life of our Lord Jesus Christ, and the great and wonderful things He has done for us. Between dinner and ves-

---

7. The youngest member of the group, who generally views life with joyful optimism.

pers I think we should choose some pastime, which, while not being prejudicial to the soul, will be agreeable to the body. In that way we shall spend a very pleasant day."

Lady Oisille replied that she herself found it so difficult to put behind her the vanities of life, that she was afraid the pastime suggested by Hircan might not be a good choice. However, the question should, she thought, be judged after an open discussion, and she asked Hircan to put his point of view first.

"Well, my point of view wouldn't take long to give," he began, "if I thought that the pastime I would really like were as agreeable to a certain lady among us as it would be to me. So I'll keep quiet for now, and abide by what the others say."

Thinking he was intending this for her, his wife, Parlamente, began to blush. "It may be, Hircan," she said, half angrily and half laughing, "that the lady you think ought to be the most annoyed at what you say would have ways and means of getting her own back, if she so desired. But let's leave on one side all pastimes that require only two participants, and concentrate on those which everybody can join in."

Hircan turned to the ladies. "Since my wife has managed to put the right interpretation on my words," he said, "and since private pastimes don't appeal to her, I think she's in a better position than anyone to know which pastime all of us will be able to enjoy. Let me say right now that I accept her opinion as if it were my own."

They all concurred in this, and Parlamente, seeing that it had fallen to her to make the choice, addressed them all as follows.

"If I felt myself to be as capable as the ancients, by whom the arts were discovered, then I would invent some pastime myself that would meet the requirements you have laid down for me. However, I know what lies within the scope of my own knowledge and ability—I can hardly even remember the clever things other people have invented, let alone invent new things myself. So I shall be quite content to follow closely in the footsteps of other people who have already provided for your needs. For example, I don't think there's one of us who hasn't read the hundred tales by Boccaccio,[8] which have recently been translated from Italian into French, and which are so highly thought of by the [most Christian] King Francis I, by Monseigneur the Dauphin, Madame the Dauphine[9] and Madame Marguerite. If Boccaccio could have heard how highly these illustrious people praised him, it would have been enough to raise him from the grave. As a matter of fact, the two ladies I've mentioned, along with other people at the court, made up their minds to do the same as Boccaccio. There was to be one difference—that they should not write any story that was not truthful. Together with Monseigneur the Dauphin the ladies promised to produce ten stories each, and to get together a party of ten people who were qualified to contribute something, excluding those who studied and were men of letters. Monseigneur the Dauphin didn't want their art brought in, and he was afraid that rhetorical ornament would in part falsify the truth of the account. A number of things led to the project being completely forgotten—the major affairs of state that subsequently

---

8. The *Decameron*.
9. The future queen Catherine de Médici.

"Monseigneur the Dauphin": the future Henry II, nephew of Marguerite.

overtook the King, the peace treaty between him and the King of England, the confinement of Madame the Dauphine and several other events of sufficient importance to keep the court otherwise occupied. However, it can now be completed in the ten days of leisure we have before us, while we wait for our bridge to be finished. If you so wished, we could go each afternoon between midday and four o'clock to the lovely meadow that borders the Gave de Pau, where the leaves on the trees are so thick that the hot sun cannot penetrate the shade and the cool beneath. There we can sit and rest, and each of us will tell a story which he has either witnessed himself, or which he has heard from somebody worthy of belief. At the end of our ten days we will have completed the whole hundred. And if, God willing, the lords and ladies I've mentioned find our endeavors worthy of their attention, we shall make them a present of them when we get back, instead of the usual statuettes and beads. I'm sure they would find that preferable. In spite of all this, if any of you is able to think of something more agreeable, I shall gladly bow to his or her opinion."

But every one of them replied that it would be impossible to think of anything better, and that they could hardly wait for the morrow. So the day came happily to a close with reminiscences of things they had all experienced in their time.

As soon as morning came they all went into Madame Oisille's room, where she was already at her prayers. When they had listened for a good hour to the lesson she had to read them, and then devoutly heard mass, they went, at ten o'clock, to dine, after which they retired to their separate rooms to attend to what they had to do. At midday they all went back as arranged to the meadow, which was looking so beautiful and fair that it would take a Boccaccio to describe it as it really was. Enough for us to say that a more beautiful meadow there never was seen. When they were all seated on the grass, so green and soft that there was no need for carpets or cushions, Simontaut[1] said: "Which of us shall be [the one in charge]?"

* * *

Story 8

In the county of Alès there was once a man by the name of Bornet, who had married a very decent and respectable woman. He held her honor and reputation very dear, as I am sure all husbands here hold the honor and reputation of *their* wives dear. He wanted her to be faithful to him, but was not so keen on having the rule applied to them both equally. He had become enamored of his chambermaid, though the only benefit he got from transferring his affections in this way was the sort of pleasure one gets from varying one's diet. He had a neighbor called Sendras, who was of similar station and temperament to himself—he was a tailor and a drummer. These two were such close friends that, with the exception of the wife, there was nothing that they did not share

1. Identified with François de Bourdeille, the husband of Anne of Vivonne. He is the long-standing *serviteur* to Parlamente: "According to the *serviteur*'s practice, as the *Heptameron* presents it, a married aristocratic woman has the right to maintain several devoted knights in her service. . . . Since it is supposed to be chaste, the *serviteur*'s relationship, this remnant of courtly and chivalrous love, can coexist with faithful marriage. . . . Nevertheless, there is evidently considerable anxiety about the institution as such" [From the translator's introduction]. His name punningly alludes to masculinity (*monte haut*: rises high).

between them. Naturally he told him that he had designs on the chamber-maid.

Not only did his friend wholeheartedly approve of this, but did his best to help him, in the hope that he too might get a share in the spoils.

The chambermaid herself refused to have anything to do with him, although he was constantly pestering her and in the end she went to tell her mistress about it. She told her that she could not stand being badgered by him any lon-ger, and asked permission to go home to her parents. Now the good lady of the house, who was really very much in love with her husband, had often had occasion to suspect him, and was therefore rather pleased to be one up on him, and to be able to show him that she had found out what he was up to. So she said to her maid: "Be nice to him dear, encourage him a little bit, and then make a date to go to bed with him in my dressing-room. Don't forget to tell me which night he's supposed to be coming, and make sure you don't tell anyone else."

The maid did exactly as her mistress had instructed. As for her master, he was so pleased with himself that he went off to tell his friend about his stroke of luck, whereupon the friend insisted on taking his share afterwards, since he had been in on the business from the beginning. When the appointed time came, off went the master, as had been agreed, to get into bed, as he thought, with his little chambermaid. But his wife, having abandoned her position of authority in order to serve in a more pleasurable one, had taken her maid's place in the bed. When he got in with her, she did not act like a wife, but like a bashful young girl, and he was not in the slightest suspicious. It would be impossible to say which of them enjoyed themselves more—the wife deceiving her husband, or the husband who thought he was deceiving his wife. He stayed in bed with her for some time, not as long as he might have wished (many years of marriage were beginning to tell on him), but as long as he could manage. Then he went out to rejoin his accomplice, and tell him what a good time he had had. The lustiest piece of goods he had ever come across, he declared. His friend, who was younger and more active than he was, said: "Remember what you promised?"

"Hurry up, then," replied the master, "in case she gets up, or my wife wants her for something."

Off he went and climbed into bed with the supposed chambermaid his friend had just failed to recognize as his wife. *She* thought it was her husband again, and did not refuse anything he asked for (I say "asked," but "took" would be nearer the mark, because he did not dare open his mouth). He made a much longer business of it than the husband, to the surprise of the wife, who was not used to these long nights of pleasure. However, she did not complain, and looked forward to what she was planning to say to him in the morning, and the fun she would have teasing him. When dawn came, the man got up, and fon-dling her as he got out of bed, pulled off a ring she wore on her finger, a ring that her husband had given her at their marriage. Now the women in this part of the world are very superstitious about such things. They have great respect for women who hang on to their wedding rings till the day they die, and if a woman loses her ring, she is dishonored, and is looked upon as having given her faith to another man. But she did not mind him taking it, because she thought it would be sure evidence against her husband of the way she had hoodwinked him.

The husband was waiting outside for his friend, and asked him how he had got on. The man said he shared the husband's opinion, and added that he would have stayed longer, had he not been afraid of getting caught by the daylight. The pair of them then went off to get as much sleep as they could. When morning came, and they were getting dressed together, the husband noticed that his friend had on his finger a ring that was identical to the one he had given his wife on their wedding day. He asked him where he had got it, and when he was told it had come from the chambermaid the night before, he was aghast. He began banging his head against the wall, and shouted: "Oh my God! Have I gone and made myself a cuckold without my wife even knowing about it?"

His friend tried to calm him down. "Perhaps your wife had given the ring to the girl to look after before going to bed?" he suggested. The husband made no reply, but marched straight out and went back to his house.

There he found his wife looking unusually gay and attractive. Had she not saved her chambermaid from staining her conscience, and had she not put her husband to the ultimate test, without any more cost to herself than a night's sleep? Seeing her in such good spirits, the husband thought to himself: "She wouldn't be greeting me so cheerfully if she knew what I'd been up to."

As they chatted, he took hold of her hand and saw that the ring, which normally never left her finger, had disappeared. Horrified, he stammered: "What have you done with your ring?"

She was pleased that he was giving her the opportunity to say what she had to say.

"Oh! You're the most dreadful man I ever met! Who do you think you got it from? You think you got it from the chambermaid, don't you? You think you got it from that girl you're so much in love with, the girl who gets more out of you than I've ever had! The first time you got into bed you were so passionate that I thought you must be about as madly in love with her as it was possible for any man to be! But when you came back the *second* time, after getting up, you were an absolute devil! Completely uncontrolled you were, didn't know when to stop! You miserable man! You must have been blinded by desire to pay such tribute to my body—after all you've had me long enough without showing much appreciation for my figure. So it wasn't because that young girl is so pretty and so shapely that you were enjoying yourself so much. Oh no! You enjoyed it so much because you were seething with some depraved pent-up lust—in short the sin of concupiscence was raging within you, and your senses were dulled as a result. In fact you'd worked yourself up into such a state that I think any old nanny-goat would have done for you, pretty or otherwise! Well, my dear, it's time you mended your ways. It's high time you were content with me for what I am—your own wife and an honest woman, and it's high time that you found *that* just as satisfying as when you thought I was a poor little erring chambermaid. I did what I did in order to save you from your wicked ways, so that when you get old, we can live happily and peacefully together without anything on our consciences. Because if you go on in the way you have been, I'd rather leave you altogether than see you destroying your soul day by day, and at the same time destroying your physical health and squandering everything you have before my very eyes! But if you will acknowledge that you've been in the wrong, and make up your mind to live according to the ways of God and His commandments, then I'll overlook all your past misbehavior, even as I hope God will forgive me *my* ingratitude to Him, and failure to love Him as I ought."

If there was ever a man who was dumbfounded and despairing, it was this poor husband. There was his wife, looking so pretty, and yet so sensible and so chaste, and he had gone and left her for a girl who did not love him. What was worse, he had had the misfortune to have gone and made her do something wicked without her even realizing what was happening. He had gone and let another man share pleasures which, rightly, were his alone to enjoy. He had gone and given himself cuckold's horns and made himself look ridiculous for evermore. But he could see she was already angry enough about the chambermaid, and he did not dare tell her about the other dirty trick he had played. So he promised that he would leave his wicked ways behind him, asked her to forgive him and gave her the ring back. He told his friend not to breathe a word to anybody, but secrets of this sort nearly always end up being proclaimed from the [roof-tops], and it was not long before the facts became public knowledge. The husband was branded as a cuckold without his wife having done a single thing to disgrace herself.

"Ladies, it strikes me that if all the men who offend their wives like that got a punishment like that, then Hircan and Saffredent ought to be feeling a bit nervous."

"Come now, Longarine," said Saffredent, "Hircan and I aren't the only married men here, you know."

"True," she replied, "but you're the only two who'd play a trick like that."

"And just when have you heard of us chasing our wives' maids?" he retorted.

"If the ladies in question were to tell us the facts," Longarine said, "then you'd soon find plenty of maids who'd been dismissed before their pay-day!"

"Really," intervened Geburon, "a fine one you are! You promise to make us all laugh, and you end up making these two gentlemen annoyed."

"It comes to the same thing," said Longarine. "As long as they don't get their swords out, their getting angry makes it all the more amusing."

"But the fact remains," said Hircan, "that if our wives were to listen to what this lady here has to say, she'd make trouble for every married couple here!"

"I know what I'm saying, and who I'm saying it to," Longarine replied. "Your wives are so good, and they love you so much, that even if you gave them horns like a stag's, they'd still convince themselves, and everybody else, that they were garlands of roses!"

Everyone found this remark highly amusing, even the people it was aimed at, and the subject was brought to a close. Dagoucin,[2] however, who had not yet

---

2. The most philosophical member of the group, described elsewhere (story 11) as "so wise that he would rather die than say some-thing foolish." He is also the saintliest; our translator indicates that his name is "a fairly obvious pun: *de goûts saints* (of saintly tastes)."

said a word, could not resist saying: "When a man already has everything he needs in order to be contented, it is very unreasonable of him to go off and seek satisfaction elsewhere. It has often struck me that when people are not satisfied with what they already have, and think they can find something better, then they only make themselves worse off. And they do not get any sympathy, because inconstancy is one thing that is universally condemned."

"But what about people who have not yet found their other half?" asked Simontaut. "Would you still say it was inconstancy if they seek her wherever she may be found?"

"No man can know," replied Dagoucin, "where his other half is to be found, this other half with whom he may find a union so equal that between [the parts] there is no difference; which being so, a man must hold fast where Love constrains him and, whatever may befall him, he must remain steadfast in heart and will. For if she whom you love is your true likeness, if she is of the same will, then it will be your own self that you love, and not her alone."

"Dagoucin, I think you're adopting a position that is completely wrong," said Hircan. "You make it sound as if we ought to love women without being loved in return!"

"What I mean, Hircan, is this. If love is based on a woman's beauty, charm and favors, and if our aim is merely pleasure, ambition, or profit, then such love can never last. For if the whole foundation on which our love is based should collapse, then love will fly from us and there will be no love left in us. But I am utterly convinced that if a man loves with no other aim, no other desire, than to love truly, he will abandon his soul in death rather than allow his love to abandon his heart."

"Quite honestly, Dagoucin, I don't think you've ever really been in love," said Simontaut, "because if you had felt the fire of passion, as the rest of us have, you wouldn't have been doing what you've just been doing—describing Plato's republic, which sounds all very fine in writing, but is hardly true to experience."

"If I have loved," he replied, "I love still, and shall love till the day I die. But my love is a perfect love, and I fear lest showing it openly should betray it. So greatly do I fear this, that I shrink to make it known to the lady whose love and friendship I cannot but desire to be equal to my own. I scarcely dare think my own thoughts, lest something should be revealed in my eyes, for the longer I conceal the fire of my love, the stronger grows the pleasure in knowing that it is indeed a perfect love."

"Ah, but all the same," said Geburon, "I don't think you'd be sorry if she did return your love!"

"I do not deny it. But even if I were loved as deeply as I myself love, my love could not possibly increase, just as it could not possibly decrease if I were loved less deeply than I love."

At this point, Parlamente, who was suspicious of these flights of fancy, said: "Watch your step, Dagoucin. I've seen plenty of men who've died rather than speak what's in their minds."

"Such men as those," he replied, "I would count happy indeed."

"Indeed," said Saffredent, "and worthy to be placed among the ranks of the Innocents—of whom the Church chants '*Non loquendo, sed moriendo confessi sunt*'![3] I've heard a lot of talk about these languishing lovers, but I've never seen a single one actually die. I've suffered enough from such torture, but I got over it in the end, and that's why I've always assumed that nobody else ever really dies from it either."

"Ah! Saffredent, the trouble is that you desire your love to be returned," Dagoucin replied, "and men of your opinions never die for love. But I know of many who *have* died, and died for no other cause than that they have loved, and loved perfectly."

3. "Not by speaking but by dying they confessed" (Latin), a line recited during the Feast of the Holy Innocents.

MICHEL DE MONTAIGNE
1533–1592

The probing, skeptical essays of Michel Eyquem de Montaigne show a Renaissance mind exploring its own workings. The first writer to ask "Who am I?" and pursue the question with extraordinary honesty and rigor, Montaigne at times appears surprisingly modern in his outlook. He pays unflinching attention to the embarrassing realities of his own body and mind, even as he considers the most abstract questions. His radical break with traditional forms of writing and thinking is particularly striking in that Montaigne was an avid student of the classical even as he also paved the way for the modern form of the essay.

LIFE AND TIMES

Montaigne was born on February 28, 1533, in the castle of Montaigne, to a Catholic father and a Protestant mother of Spanish-Jewish descent. His father, Pierre Eyquem, was for two terms mayor of Bordeaux and had fought in Italy under Francis I. Though no man of learning, Pierre had unconventional ideas of upbringing: Michel was awakened in the morning by the sound of music and was taught Latin as his mother tongue. At six Michel went to the famous Collège de Guienne at Bordeaux; later he studied law; and in 1557 he became a member of the Bordeaux parliament. In 1565 he married Françoise de la Chassaigne, daughter of a man who, as one of Montaigne's colleagues in the Bordeaux parliament, was a member of the new legal nobility.

Perhaps because of disappointed political ambitions, Montaigne retired from politics in 1570 at the age of thirty-eight: he sold his post as magistrate and retreated to his castle of Montaigne, which he had inherited two years earlier. There he devoted himself to meditation and writing. Although Montaigne spent, as he put it, "most of his days, and most hours of the day" in his library on the third floor of a round tower, the demands of his health and France's tumultuous politics often drew him out of retirement. For the sake of his health (he suffered from gallstones), in 1580 he took a journey through Switzerland, Germany, and Italy. While in Italy he received news that he had been appointed mayor of Bordeaux, an office that he held for two terms (1581–85).

His greatest political distractions, however, concerned the Catholic and Protestant factions that violently divided the court and France itself. French politics profoundly influenced the attitudes toward warfare, political resistance, and mercy expressed in Montaigne's *Essays*. When Henry II died in a jousting accident in 1559 and left the fifteen-year-old Francis II to succeed him, the Huguenots (French Reformers in the tradition of John Calvin), recognized the opportunity to influence the weakened royal government. Catherine de Médicis, the queen mother, seized power when Francis II died in 1560 (his successor, Charles IX, was only ten years old). Her policy of limited religious toleration satisfied neither the Catholic nor the Huguenot factions, and from 1562 to 1598 France repeatedly fell into civil war. In the infamous St. Bartholomew's Day Massacre of August 24, 1572, noblemen, municipal authorities, and the Parisian mobs indiscriminately slaughtered the Protestants in Paris. The slaughter was imitated in other French cities, and the civil wars once again broke out.

Throughout his country's political struggles, Montaigne sympathized with the unfanatical Henry of Navarre, leader of the Protestants, but his attitude was neutral and conservative. He expressed his joy when Henry of Navarre became King Henry IV and turned Catholic to do so: "Paris," Henry memorably observed, "is well worth a Mass." Montaigne, who died on September 13, 1592, did not live to see Henry's triumphal entrance into Paris.

ESSAYS

Montaigne's *Essays*, which began as a collection of interesting quotations, observations, and recordings of remarkable events, slowly developed into its final form of three large books. The essays are at once highly personal and outward looking; they present a curious mind investigating history, the complex and changing sociopolitical world, and the mind's own slightly mysterious workings. To *essay*—from the French *essayer*, meaning to attempt or try out—is Montaigne's characteristic intellectual operation, as he carefully examines his topics from a variety of possible angles. The literary result of that operation is the *essay*, the common noun that, in the wake of Montaigne, describes a short piece of highly personal and exploratory writing.

Though fascinated by the complexities of self-understanding, Montaigne explores far more than his own circumstances or thoughts. "I am a man," he says, quoting the Roman playwright Terence, and "I consider nothing human to be alien to me." As an ethnographer and historian, Montaigne studies geographically and historically distant cultures, insisting that cultural norms are relative and should be free from judgment by sixteenth-century European standards. As a psychologist, he is drawn to the stranger thoughts and experiences of himself and his countrymen. His method is not didactic or moralizing, and his criticism, which he reserves for fellow Europeans, emerges largely through subtle ironies that he leaves readers to detect.

When Montaigne looks inward, he does not aggrandize or justify himself but tries to understand how the mind works. Far from prizing his capacity for reason and judgment, for example, he neutrally observes, "My judgment floats, it wanders." Montaigne is, in fact, disarmingly modest: "Reader, I am myself the subject of my book; it is not reasonable to expect you to waste your leisure on a matter so frivolous and empty." Although massively learned, he emphasizes not what he knows but rather, like his revered model, Plato's Socrates, the ways that knowledge reveals how little he truly knows.

Although he refuses certainty and mocks vanity, Montaigne's stance is skeptical, not cynical. Thus when he "essays" or probes the human capacity to act purposefully and coherently, he does not aim to prove that action is futile. Instead, he resists granting the mind a coherence it does not possess; to Montaigne, the Stoic ideal of the "constant man," unmoved by emotion or circumstance, is an impoverished version of humankind. Instead, he emphasizes the strangeness and instability of the self: "There is as much difference between us and ourselves as between us and others." This idea became highly influential in Renaissance thinking and shaped such haunting insights as John Donne's observation that "ourselves are what we know not." For Renaissance thinkers who embraced Montaigne's doubt, the difficult philosophical imperative of Socrates, "know thyself," seemed unattainable.

Montaigne charts the elusive "self" through a wide range of anecdotes, both contemporary and classical. A slippery or indefinable historical character intrigues him far more than a monolithic or single-minded one. The legendary warrior Alexander the Great is rendered frighteningly transparent by his obsession with power and conquest: he wants nothing less than to be a god. Emperor Augustus, on the other hand, rewards study precisely because his character has "escaped" the willful reductions of historians bent on "fashioning a consistent and solid fabric" of his character.

Why was Montaigne so unusually able to suspend the self-interest and bias he considered ingrained in human nature in order to analyze himself, and his culture? As his life in politics indicates, the violent instability of French history taught him tolerance, skepticism about human self-interest, and hatred of dogmatic positions: "It demands a great deal of self-love and presumption, to take one's own opinions so seriously as to disrupt the peace in order to establish them, introducing so many inevitable evils, and so terrible a corruption of manners as civil wars and political revolutions with them." His hatred of political radicalism influenced much of what he saw in ancient history and in contemporary accounts of New World discovery and conquest. Alienated from his own political context, Montaigne developed a rich double perspective, both ethnographic (outward-looking and impartial) and self-critical (introspective and moral). As he reflects on the ancient and new worlds, he pays special attention to how human beings respond to adversity, oppression, and physical torture.

In the best known of the selections included here, "Of Cannibals" (which influenced **Shakespeare**'s reflections in *The Tempest* on the ideal commonwealth, colonialism, and the nature of savages), Montaigne compares the behavioral codes of Brazilian cannibals and those of "ourselves" (Europeans) and concludes that "each man calls barbarism whatever is not his own practice." Once he has asserted the relativity of customs, Montaigne is able to praise elements of the savages' culture that he regards as superior to Europe's. He admires the savages' courage, for instance, in which "the honor of valor consists in combating, not in beating." Moreover, he finds in the positive example of the Brazilian cannibals an implicit criticism of violence by Europeans both at home and in the New World.

As an ethnographer, Montaigne is able to grapple with a distinct and alien culture without passing judgment; but when he reflects on France, he becomes a moralist. Central to "Of Cannibals" is the invocation of the Catholics' torture and burning of fellow citizens. Montaigne juxtaposes two kinds of savagery: that which appears foreign (cannibalism) and that which has grown too familiar (religious persecution). His own country's civil strife enables him to transcend smug cultural bias, making him a powerful critic of European culture and allowing him to imagine communities other than his own. Like the world of antiquity, which also riveted his imagination, the idea of America allowed Montaigne to explore alternate worlds for their own sake and for their illumination of his own.

The genre that Montaigne inaugurated quickly made its way into the English tradition, with the *Essays* of Francis Bacon (1597). Yet its larger influence reached much further: with the advent of the Enlightenment and the rise of periodicals, the essay enabled the intellectual exchange of carefully considered, highly personal opinions in the public realm and thus shapes our own thinking and writing to this day.

From Essays[1]

To the Reader

This book was written in good faith, reader. It warns you from the outset that in it I have set myself no goal but a domestic and private one. I have had no thought of serving either you or my own glory. My powers are inadequate for such a purpose. I have dedicated it to the private convenience of my relatives and friends, so that when they have lost me (as soon they must), they may recover here some features of my habits and temperament, and by this means keep the knowledge they have had of me more complete and alive.

If I had written to seek the world's favor, I should have bedecked myself better, and should present myself in a studied posture. I want to be seen here in my simple, natural, ordinary fashion, without straining or artifice; for it is myself that I portray. My defects will here be read to the life, and also my natural form, as far as respect for the public has allowed. Had I been placed among those nations which are said to live still in the sweet freedom of nature's first laws, I assure you I should very gladly have portrayed myself here entire and wholly naked.

Thus, reader, I am myself the matter of my book; you would be unreasonable to spend your leisure on so frivolous and vain a subject.

So farewell. Montaigne, this first day of March, fifteen hundred and eighty.

---

1. Translated by Donald Frame.

Of Cannibals

When King Pyrrhus[2] passed over into Italy, after he had reconnoitered the formation of the army that the Romans were sending to meet him, he said: "I do not know what barbarians these are" (for so the Greeks called all foreign nations), "but the formation of this army that I see is not at all barbarous." The Greeks said as much of the army that Flaminius brought into their country, and so did Philip, seeing from a knoll the order and distribution of the Roman camp, in his kingdom, under Publius Sulpicius Galba.[3] Thus we should beware of clinging to vulgar opinions, and judge things by reason's way, not by popular say.

I had with me for a long time a man who had lived for ten or twelve years in that other world which has been discovered in our century, in the place where Villegaignon landed, and which he called Antarctic France.[4] This discovery of a boundless country seems worthy of consideration. I don't know if I can guarantee that some other such discovery will not be made in the future, so many personages greater than ourselves having been mistaken about this one. I am afraid we have eyes bigger than our stomachs, and more curiosity than capacity. We embrace everything, but we clasp only wind.

Plato brings in Solon,[5] telling how he had learned from the priests of the city of Saïs in Egypt that in days of old, before the Flood, there was a great island named Atlantis, right at the mouth of the Strait of Gibraltar, which contained more land than Africa and Asia put together, and that the kings of that country, who not only possessed that island but had stretched out so far on the mainland that they held the breadth of Africa as far as Egypt, and the length of Europe as far as Tuscany, undertook to step over into Asia and subjugate all the nations that border on the Mediterranean, as far as the Black Sea; and for this purpose crossed the Spains, Gaul, Italy, as far as Greece, where the Athenians checked them; but that some time after, both the Athenians and themselves and their island were swallowed up by the Flood.

It is quite likely that that extreme devastation of waters made amazing changes in the habitations of the earth, as people maintain that the sea cut off Sicily from Italy—

> 'Tis said an earthquake once asunder tore
> These lands with dreadful havoc, which before
> Formed but one land, one coast
>
> VIRGIL[6]

—Cyprus from Syria, the island of Euboea from the mainland of Boeotia; and elsewhere joined lands that were divided, filling the channels between them with sand and mud:

---

2. King of Epirus (in Greece) who fought the Romans in Italy in 280 B.C.E.
3. Both Titus Quinctius Flaminius and Publius Sulpicius Galba were Roman statesmen and generals who fought Philip V of Macedon in the early years of the 2nd century B.C.E.
4. In Brazil. Villegaignon landed there in 1557.
5. In his *Timaeus*.
6. *Aeneid* 3.414–15.

A sterile marsh, long fit for rowing, now
Feeds neighbor towns, and feels the heavy plow.
HORACE[7]

But there is no great likelihood that that island was the new world which we have just discovered; for it almost touched Spain, and it would be an incredible result of a flood to have forced it away as far as it is, more than twelve hundred leagues; besides, the travels of the moderns have already almost revealed that it is not an island, but a mainland connected with the East Indies on one side, and elsewhere with the lands under the two poles; or, if it is separated from them, it is by so narrow a strait and interval that it does not deserve to be called an island on that account.

It seems that there are movements, some natural, others feverish, in these great bodies, just as in our own. When I consider the inroads that my river, the Dordogne, is making in my lifetime into the right bank in its descent, and that in twenty years it has gained so much ground and stolen away the foundations of several buildings, I clearly see that this is an extraordinary disturbance; for if it had always gone at this rate, or was to do so in the future, the face of the world would be turned topsy-turvy. But rivers are subject to changes: now they overflow in one direction, now in another, now they keep to their course. I am not speaking of the sudden inundations whose causes are manifest. In Médoc, along the seashore, my brother, the sieur d'Arsac, can see an estate of his buried under the sands that the sea spews forth; the tops of some buildings are still visible; his farms and domains have changed into very thin pasturage. The inhabitants say that for some time the sea has been pushing toward them so hard that they have lost four leagues of land. These sands are its harbingers; and we see great dunes of moving sand that march half a league ahead of it and keep conquering land.

The other testimony of antiquity with which some would connect this discovery is in Aristotle, at least if that little book *Of Unheard-of Wonders* is by him. He there relates that certain Carthaginians, after setting out upon the Atlantic Ocean from the Strait of Gibraltar and sailing a long time, at last discovered a great fertile island, all clothed in woods and watered by great deep rivers, far remote from any mainland; and that they, and others since, attracted by the goodness and fertility of the soil, went there with their wives and children, and began to settle there. The lords of Carthage, seeing that their country was gradually becoming depopulated, expressly forbade anyone to go there any more, on pain of death, and drove out these new inhabitants, fearing, it is said, that in course of time they might come to multiply so greatly as to supplant their former masters and ruin their state. This story of Aristotle does not fit our new lands any better than the other.

This man I had was a simple, crude fellow—a character fit to bear true witness; for clever people observe more things and more curiously, but they interpret them; and to lend weight and conviction to their interpretation, they cannot help altering history a little. They never show you things as they are, but bend and disguise them according to the way they have seen them; and to give credence to their judgment and attract you to it, they are prone to add something to their matter, to stretch it out and amplify it. We need a man

7. Horatius Flaccus (65–8 B.C.E.), great poet of Augustan Rome; *Art of Poetry*, lines 65–66.

either very honest, or so simple that he has not the stuff to build up false inventions and give them plausibility; and wedded to no theory. Such was my man; and besides this, he at various times brought sailors and merchants, whom he had known on that trip, to see me. So I content myself with his information, without inquiring what the cosmographers say about it.

We ought to have topographers who would give us an exact account of the places where they have been. But because they have over us the advantage of having seen Palestine, they want to enjoy the privilege of telling us news about all the rest of the world. I would like everyone to write what he knows, and as much as he knows, not only in this, but in all other subjects; for a man may have some special knowledge and experience of the nature of a river or a fountain, who in other matters knows only what everybody knows. However, to circulate this little scrap of knowledge, he will undertake to write the whole of physics. From this vice spring many great abuses.

Now, to return to my subject, I think there is nothing barbarous and savage in that nation, from what I have been told, except that each man calls barbarism whatever is not his own practice; for indeed it seems we have no other test of truth and reason than the example and pattern of the opinions and customs of the country we live in. *There* is always the perfect religion, the perfect government, the perfect and accomplished manners in all things. Those people are wild, just as we call wild the fruits that Nature has produced by herself and in her normal course; whereas really it is those that we have changed artificially and led astray from the common order, that we should rather call wild. The former retain alive and vigorous their genuine, their most useful and natural, virtues and properties, which we have debased in the latter in adapting them to gratify our corrupted taste. And yet for all that, the savor and delicacy of some uncultivated fruits of those countries is quite as excellent, even to our taste, as that of our own. It is not reasonable that art should win the place of honor over our great and powerful mother Nature. We have so overloaded the beauty and richness of her works by our inventions that we have quite smothered her. Yet wherever her purity shines forth, she wonderfully puts to shame our vain and frivolous attempts:

> Ivy comes readier without our care;
> In lonely caves the arbutus grows more fair;
> No art with artless bird song can compare.
> PROPERTIUS[8]

All our efforts cannot even succeed in reproducing the nest of the tiniest little bird, its contexture, its beauty and convenience; or even the web of the puny spider. All things, says Plato,[9] are produced by nature, by fortune, or by art; the greatest and most beautiful by one or the other of the first two, the least and most imperfect by the last.

These nations, then, seem to me barbarous in this sense, that they have been fashioned very little by the human mind, and are still very close to their original naturalness. The laws of nature still rule them, very little corrupted by ours; and they are in such a state of purity that I am sometimes vexed that they were unknown earlier, in the days when there were men able to judge them better

---

8. *Elegies* 1.2.10–12.   9. See his *Laws*.

than we. I am sorry that Lycurgus[1] and Plato did not know of them; for it seems to me that what we actually see in these nations surpasses not only all the pictures in which poets have idealized the golden age and all their inventions in imagining a happy state of man, but also the conceptions and the very desire of philosophy. They could not imagine a naturalness so pure and simple as we see by experience; nor could they believe that our society could be maintained with so little artifice and human solder. This is a nation, I should say to Plato, in which there is no sort of traffic, no knowledge of letters, no science of numbers, no name for a magistrate or for political superiority, no custom of servitude, no riches or poverty, no contracts, no successions, no partitions, no occupations but leisure ones, no care for any but common kinship, no clothes, no agriculture, no metal, no use of wine or wheat.[2] The very words that signify lying, treachery, dissimulation, avarice, envy, belittling, pardon—unheard of. How far from this perfection would he find the republic that he imagined: *Men fresh sprung from the gods* [Seneca].[3]

> These manners nature first ordained.
>
> VIRGIL[4]

For the rest, they live in a country with a very pleasant and temperate climate, so that according to my witnesses it is rare to see a sick man there; and they have assured me that they never saw one palsied, bleary-eyed, toothless, or bent with age. They are settled along the sea and shut in on the land side by great high mountains, with a stretch about a hundred leagues wide in between. They have a great abundance of fish and flesh which bear no resemblance to ours, and they eat them with no other artifice than cooking. The first man who rode a horse there, though he had had dealings with them on several other trips, so horrified them in this posture that they shot him dead with arrows before they could recognize him.

Their buildings are very long, with a capacity of two or three hundred souls; they are covered with the bark of great trees, the strips reaching to the ground at one end and supporting and leaning on one another at the top, in the manner of some of our barns, whose covering hangs down to the ground and acts as a side. They have wood so hard that they cut with it and make of it their swords and grills to cook their food. Their beds are of a cotton weave, hung from the roof like those in our ships, each man having his own; for the wives sleep apart from their husbands.

They get up with the sun, and eat immediately upon rising, to last them through the day; for they take no other meal than that one. Like some other Eastern peoples, of whom Suidas[5] tells us, who drank apart from meals, they do not drink then; but they drink several times a day, and to capacity. Their drink is made of some root, and is of the color of our claret wines. They drink it only lukewarm. This beverage keeps only two or three days; it has a slightly sharp taste, is not at all heady, is good for the stomach, and has a laxative effect upon those who are not used to it; it is a very pleasant drink for anyone who is

---

1. The half-legendary Spartan lawgiver (9th century B.C.E.).
2. This passage is always compared with Shakespeare's *The Tempest* 2.1.147 ff.
3. Roman tragedian (ca. 4 B.C.E.–65 C.E.), philosopher, and political leader, *Epistles* 90.
4. *Georgics* 2.20.
5. A Byzantine lexicographer.

accustomed to it. In place of bread they use a certain white substance like pre-served coriander. I have tried it; it tastes sweet and a little flat.

The whole day is spent in dancing. The younger men go to hunt animals with bows. Some of the women busy themselves meanwhile with warming their drink, which is their chief duty. Some one of the old men, in the morning before they begin to eat, preaches to the whole barnful in common, walking from one end to the other, and repeating one single sentence several times until he has completed the circuit (for the buildings are fully a hundred paces long). He recommends to them only two things: valor against the enemy and love for their wives. And they never fail to point out this obligation, as their refrain, that it is their wives who keep their drink warm and seasoned.

There may be seen in several places, including my own house, specimens of their beds, of their ropes, of their wooden swords and the bracelets with which they cover their wrists in combats, and of the big canes, open at one end, by whose sound they keep time in their dances. They are close shaven all over, and shave themselves much more cleanly than we, with nothing but a wooden or stone razor. They believe that souls are immortal, and that those who have deserved well of the gods are lodged in that part of heaven where the sun rises, and the damned in the west.

They have some sort of priests and prophets, but they rarely appear before the people, having their home in the mountains. On their arrival there is a great feast and solemn assembly of several villages—each barn, as I have described it, makes up a village, and they are about one French league[6] from each other. The prophet speaks to them in public, exhorting them to virtue and their duty; but their whole ethical science contains only these two articles: resoluteness in war and affection for their wives. He prophesies to them things to come and the results they are to expect from their undertakings, and urges them to war or holds them back from it; but this is on the condition that when he fails to prophesy correctly, and if things turn out otherwise than he has predicted, he is cut into a thousand pieces if they catch him, and condemned as a false prophet. For this reason, the prophet who has once been mistaken is never seen again.

Divination is a gift of God; that is why its abuse should be punished as imposture. Among the Scythians, when the soothsayers failed to hit the mark, they were laid, chained hand and foot, on carts full of heather and drawn by oxen, on which they were burned. Those who handle matters subject to the control of human capacity are excusable if they do the best they can. But these others who come and trick us with assurances of an extraordinary faculty that is beyond our ken, should they not be punished for not making good their promise, and for the temerity of their imposture?

They have their wars with the nations beyond the mountains, further inland, to which they go quite naked, with no other arms than bows or wooden swords ending in a sharp point, in the manner of the tongues of our boar spears. It is astonishing what firmness they show in their combats, which never end but in slaughter and bloodshed; for as to routs and terror, they know nothing of either.

Each man brings back his trophy the head of the enemy he has killed, and sets it up at the entrance to his dwelling. After they have treated their prisoners well for a long time with all the hospitality they can think of, each man who has a pris-oner calls a great assembly of his acquaintances. He ties a rope to one of the

6. About 2.49 miles.

prisoner's arms, by the end of which he holds him, a few steps away, for fear of being hurt, and gives his dearest friend the other arm to hold in the same way; and these two, in the presence of the whole assembly, kill him with their swords. This done, they roast him and eat him in common and send some pieces to their absent friends. This is not, as people think, for nourishment, as of old the Scythians used to do; it is to betoken an extreme revenge. And the proof of this came when they saw the Portuguese, who had joined forces with their adversaries, inflict a different kind of death on them when they took them prisoner, which was to bury them up to the waist, shoot the rest of their body full of arrows, and afterward hang them. They thought that these people from the other world, being men who had sown the knowledge of many vices among their neighbors and were much greater masters than themselves in every sort of wickedness, did not adopt this sort of vengeance without some reason, and that it must be more painful than their own; so they began to give up their old method and to follow this one.

I am not sorry that we notice the barbarous horror of such acts, but I am heartily sorry that, judging their faults rightly, we should be so blind to our own. I think there is more barbarity in eating a man alive than in eating him dead; and in tearing by tortures and the rack a body still full of feeling, in roasting a man bit by bit, in having him bitten and mangled by dogs and swine (as we have not only read but seen within fresh memory, not among ancient enemies, but among neighbors and fellow citizens, and what is worse, on the pretext of piety and religion),[7] than in roasting and eating him after he is dead.

Indeed, Chrysippus and Zeno, heads of the Stoic sect, thought there was nothing wrong in using our carcasses for any purpose in case of need, and getting nourishment from them; just as our ancestors,[8] when besieged by Caesar in the city of Alesia, resolved to relieve their famine by eating old men, women, and other people useless for fighting.

> The Gascons once, 'tis said, their life renewed
> By eating of such food.
>
> JUVENAL[9]

And physicians do not fear to use human flesh in all sorts of ways for our health, applying it either inwardly or outwardly. But there never was any opinion so disordered as to excuse treachery, disloyalty, tyranny, and cruelty, which are our ordinary vices.

So we may well call these people barbarians, in respect to the rules of reason, but not in respect to ourselves, who surpass them in every kind of barbarity.

Their warfare is wholly noble and generous, and as excusable and beautiful as this human disease can be; its only basis among them is their rivalry in valor. They are not fighting for the conquest of new lands, for they still enjoy that natural abundance that provides them without toil and trouble with all necessary things in such profusion that they have no wish to enlarge their boundaries. They are still in that happy state of desiring only as much as their natural needs demand; anything beyond that is superfluous to them.

They generally call those of the same age, brothers; those who are younger, children; and the old men are fathers to all the others. These leave to their

---

7. The allusion is to the spectacles of religious warfare that Montaigne himself had witnessed in his time and country.
8. The Gauls.

9. Decimus Junius Juvenal (fl. early 2nd century C.E.), last great Roman satirist; *Satires* 15.93–94.

heirs in common the full possession of their property, without division or any other title at all than just the one that Nature gives to her creatures in bringing them into the world.

If their neighbors cross the mountains to attack them and win a victory, the gain of the victor is glory, and the advantage of having proved the master in valor and virtue; for apart from this they have no use for the goods of the vanquished, and they return to their own country, where they lack neither anything necessary nor that great thing, the knowledge of how to enjoy their condition happily and be content with it. These men of ours do the same in their turn. They demand of their prisoners no other ransom than that they confess and acknowledge their defeat. But there is not one in a whole century who does not choose to die rather than to relax a single bit, by word or look, from the grandeur of an invincible courage; not one who would not rather be killed and eaten than so much as ask not to be. They treat them very freely, so that life may be all the dearer to them, and usually entertain them with threats of their coming death, of the torments they will have to suffer, the preparations that are being made for the purpose, the cutting up of their limbs, and the feast that will be made at their expense. All this is done for the sole purpose of extorting from their lips some weak or base word, or making them want to flee, so as to gain the advantage of having terrified them and broken down their firmness. For indeed, if you take it the right way, it is in this point alone that true victory lies:

> It is no victory
> Unless the vanquished foe admits your mastery.
>   CLAUDIAN[1]

The Hungarians, very bellicose fighters, did not in olden times pursue their advantage beyond putting the enemy at their mercy. For having wrung a confession from him to this effect, they let him go unharmed and unransomed, except, at most, for exacting his promise never again to take up arms against them.

We win enough advantages over our enemies that are borrowed advantages, not really our own. It is the quality of a porter, not of valor, to have sturdier arms and legs; agility is a dead and corporeal quality; it is a stroke of luck to make our enemy stumble, or dazzle his eyes by the sunlight; it is a trick of art and technique, which may be found in a worthless coward, to be an able fencer. The worth and value of a man is in his heart and his will; there lies his real honor. Valor is the strength, not of legs and arms, but of heart and soul; it consists not in the worth of our horse or our weapons, but in our own. He who falls obstinate in his courage, *if he has fallen, he fights on his knees* [Seneca].[2] He who relaxes none of his assurance, no matter how great the danger of imminent death; who, giving up his soul, still looks firmly and scornfully at his enemy—he is beaten not by us, but by fortune; he is killed, not conquered.

The most valiant are sometimes the most unfortunate. Thus there are triumphant defeats that rival victories. Nor did those four sister victories, the fairest that the sun ever set eyes on—Salamis, Plataea, Mycale, and Sicily[3]—ever dare

---

1. *Of the Sixth Consulate of Honorius,* lines 248–49.
2. *Of Providence* 2.

3. References to the famous Greek victories against the Persians and (at Himera, Sicily) against the Carthaginians in or about 480 B.C.E.

match all their combined glory against the glory of the annihilation of King Leonidas and his men at the pass of Thermopylae.[4]

Who ever hastened with more glorious and ambitious desire to win a battle than Captain Ischolas to lose one? Who ever secured his safety more ingeniously and painstakingly than he did his destruction? He was charged to defend a certain pass in the Peloponnesus against the Arcadians. Finding himself wholly incapable of doing this, in view of the nature of the place and the inequality of the forces, he made up his mind that all who confronted the enemy would necessarily have to remain on the field. On the other hand, deeming it unworthy both of his own virtue and magnanimity and of the Lacedaemonian name to fail in his charge, he took a middle course between these two extremes, in this way. The youngest and fittest of his band he preserved for the defense and service of their country, and sent them home; and with those whose loss was less important, he determined to hold this pass, and by their death to make the enemy buy their entry as dearly as he could. And so it turned out. For he was presently surrounded on all sides by the Arcadians, and after slaughtering a large number of them, he and his men were all put to the sword. Is there a trophy dedicated to victors that would not be more due to these vanquished? The role of true victory is in fighting, not in coming off safely; and the honor of valor consists in combating, not in beating.

To return to our story. These prisoners are so far from giving in, in spite of all that is done to them, that on the contrary, during the two or three months that they are kept, they wear a gay expression; they urge their captors to hurry and put them to the test; they defy them, insult them, reproach them with their cowardice and the number of battles they have lost to the prisoners' own people.

I have a song composed by a prisoner which contains this challenge, that they should all come boldly and gather to dine off him, for they will be eating at the same time their own fathers and grandfathers, who have served to feed and nourish his body. "These muscles," he says, "this flesh and these veins are your own, poor fools that you are. You do not recognize that the substance of your ancestors' limbs is still contained in them. Savor them well; you will find in them the taste of your own flesh." An idea that certainly does not smack of barbarity. Those that paint these people dying, and who show the execution, portray the prisoner spitting in the face of his slayers and scowling at them. Indeed, to the last gasp they never stop braving and defying their enemies by word and look. Truly here are real savages by our standards; for either they must be thoroughly so, or we must be; there is an amazing distance between their character and ours.

The men there have several wives, and the higher their reputation for valor the more wives they have. It is a remarkably beautiful thing about their marriages that the same jealousy our wives have to keep us from the affection and kindness of other women, theirs have to win this for them. Being more concerned for their husbands' honor than for anything else, they strive and scheme to have as many companions as they can, since that is a sign of their husbands' valor.

Our wives will cry "Miracle!" but it is no miracle. It is a properly matrimonial virtue, but one of the highest order. In the Bible, Leah, Rachel, Sarah, and Jacob's wives gave their beautiful handmaids to their husbands; and Livia seconded the appetites of Augustus to her own disadvantage; and Stratonice, the

---

4. The Spartan king Leonidas's defense here also took place in 480 B.C.E., during the war against the Persians.

wife of King Deiotarus,[5] not only lent her husband for his use a very beautiful young chambermaid in her service, but carefully brought up her children, and backed them up to succeed to their father's estates.

And lest it be thought that all this is done through a simple and servile bondage to usage and through the pressure of the authority of their ancient customs, without reasoning or judgment, and because their minds are so stupid that they cannot take any other course, I must cite some examples of their capacity. Besides the warlike song I have just quoted, I have another, a love song, which begins in this vein: "Adder, stay; stay, adder, that from the pattern of your coloring my sister may draw the fashion and the workmanship of a rich girdle that I may give to my love; so may your beauty and your pattern be forever preferred to all other serpents." This first couplet is the refrain of the song. Now I am familiar enough with poetry to be a judge of this: not only is there nothing barbarous in this fancy, but it is altogether Anacreontic.[6] Their language, moreover, is a soft language, with an agreeable sound, somewhat like Greek in its endings.

Three of these men, ignorant of the price they will pay some day, in loss of repose and happiness, for gaining knowledge of the corruptions of this side of the ocean; ignorant also of the fact that of this intercourse will come their ruin (which I suppose is already well advanced: poor wretches, to let themselves be tricked by the desire for new things, and to have left the serenity of their own sky to come and see ours!)—three of these men were at Rouen, at the time the late King Charles IX was there. The king talked to them for a long time; they were shown our ways, our splendor, the aspect of a fine city. After that, someone asked their opinion, and wanted to know what they had found most amazing. They mentioned three things, of which I have forgotten the third, and I am very sorry for it; but I still remember two of them. They said that in the first place they thought it very strange that so many grown men, bearded, strong, and armed, who were around the king (it is likely that they were talking about the Swiss of his guard) should submit to obey a child, and that one of them was not chosen to command instead. Second (they have a way in their language of speaking of men as halves of one another), they had noticed that there were among us men full and gorged with all sorts of good things, and that their other halves were beggars at their doors, emaciated with hunger and poverty; and they thought it strange that these needy halves could endure such an injustice, and did not take the others by the throat, or set fire to their houses.

I had a very long talk with one of them; but I had an interpreter who followed my meaning so badly, and who was so hindered by his stupidity in taking in my ideas, that I could get hardly any satisfaction from the man. When I asked him what profit he gained from his superior position among his people (for he was a captain, and our sailors called him king), he told me that it was to march foremost in war. How many men followed him? He pointed to a piece of ground, to signify as many as such a space could hold; it might have been four or five thousand men. Did all this authority expire with the war? He said that this much remained, that when he visited the villages dependent on him, they made paths for him through the underbrush by which he might pass quite comfortably.

All this is not too bad—but what's the use? They don't wear breeches.

---

5. Tetrarch of Galatia, in Asia Minor.
6. Worthy of Anacreon (572?–488? B.C.E.), major Greek writer of amatory lyrics.

MIGUEL DE CERVANTES
1547–1616

Often described as the first novel, Miguel de Cervantes' *Don Quixote* uses the conventions of fiction to question the accepted truths of his own society. What happens when readers take books at their word, or try to live out ideal versions of the world around them, as does the would-be knight Don Quixote? How does life in early modern Spain fall short of the wishful fictional version? In *Don Quixote*, the narrative breaks off and leaves the reader hanging, characters reflect on what it means to exist in print, and a complicated cast of antagonistic narrators all quarrel over the *real* truth, as Cervantes ironically surveys his world while examining the nature of fiction.

LIFE

The author of Don Quixote's extravagant adventures himself had a most unusual and adventurous life. As a student, soldier, captive, and tax collector, he witnessed his contemporaries at their best and at their worst. His skeptical, ironic perspective on both the literary and political pieties of his day is combined in his works with a profound sympathy for human striving. The son of an apothecary, Miguel de Cervantes Saavedra was born in Alcalá de Henares, a university town near Madrid. Almost nothing is known of his childhood and early education. Only in 1569 is he mentioned as a favorite pupil by a Madrid humanist, Juan López. Records indicate that by the end of that year he had left Spain and was living in Rome, for a time in the service of a future cardinal. He enlisted in the Spanish fleet under the command of Don John of Austria and took part in the struggle of the allied forces of Christendom against the Ottomans. He was at the crucial Battle of Lepanto (1571), where in spite of fever he fought valiantly and received three gunshot wounds, one of which permanently impaired the use of his left hand, "for the greater glory of the right." After further military action at Palermo and Naples, he and his brother Rodrigo, bearing testimonials from Don John and from the viceroy of Sicily, began the journey back to Spain, where Miguel hoped to obtain a captaincy. In September 1575 their ship was captured near Marseille by Barbary pirates, and the two brothers were taken as prisoners to Algiers. Cervantes' captors, considering him a person of some consequence because of the letters he carried, held him as a slave for a high ransom. His daring and fortitude as he attempted repeatedly to escape excited the admiration of Hassan Pasha, the viceroy of Algiers, who bought him for five hundred crowns after five years of captivity.

Cervantes was finally ransomed on September 15, 1580, and reached Madrid in December of that year, though his experience of captivity would remain with him throughout his literary career. That career began rather inauspiciously; he wrote some ten to twenty plays, with middling success, and in 1585 published *Galatea*, a pastoral romance that anticipates the formal experimentation of *Don Quixote* but ends inconclusively. None of these established his reputation or, more important, allowed him to live from his writing. At about this time he had a daughter with Ana Franca de Rojas, and during the same period married Catalina de Salazar, who was eighteen years his junior. Seeking nonliterary employment, he obtained a position in the navy, requisitioning and collecting supplies for the "Invincible Armada." Irregularities in his administration, for which he was held responsible if not directly guilty, caused him to spend more time in prison. In 1590 he was denied colonial employment in the New World. Later he served as tax collector in the province of Granada but was dismissed from government service in 1597.

The following years of Cervantes' life are the most obscure; there is a legend that *Don Quixote* was first conceived and planned while its author was in prison in Seville. In 1604 he was in Valladolid, then the temporary capital of Spain, living in sordid surroundings with the numerous women of his family (his wife, daughter, niece, and two sisters). It was in Valladolid, in late 1604, that he obtained the official license for the publication of *Don Quixote* (Part I). The book appeared in 1605 and was a popular success. Cervantes followed the Spanish court when it returned to Madrid, where he continued to live poorly in spite of a popularity with readers that quickly made proverbial figures of his heroes. A false sequel to his book appeared, prompting him to write his own continuation, *Don Quixote*, Part II, published in 1615. His *Exemplary Novellas* had appeared in 1613. He died on April 23, 1616. *Persiles and Sigismunda*, his last novel, was published posthumously in 1617.

TIMES

Cervantes' Spain was a great empire, with huge possessions in the New World, in Italy, and in Flanders, sustained by an equally enormous army of disciplined soldiers organized in infantry battalions—the famous *tercios españoles*. It was ruled by Philip II, the devout Habsburg monarch who became known as "the prudent king" for his careful administration. In 1580, Philip annexed the Portuguese crown and its commercial empire in Asia, Africa, and the New World, rendering Spain a truly global power. At the same time, the enormous influx of gold from the Americas led to inflation and widespread poverty, and to the general perception that everything and everyone could be bought. As the vivacious gypsy Preciosa jokes to an impoverished official in one of Cervantes' novellas, if he only took bribes as everyone expects him to do, he would not be so poor. Both as a tax collector and as a convict, Cervantes had ample experience of a down-and-out, picaresque Spain that held the law in small regard, a world depicted in colorful detail in the earthier episodes of *Don Quixote*.

Overburdened with military expenses and foreign debt, the Crown experienced repeated bankruptcies despite the heavy taxes it imposed on its subjects. In 1588, it suffered the added indignity of the Armada's defeat by the English navy, and Spain entered a long period of decline and disillusion. Philip's death in 1598 signaled the end of an era. Cervantes marked the occasion with a devastating sonnet on the king's funerary monument. Its greatness, the poem suggests, is but an illusion: as soon as the admiring glances of the impressionable viewers wander, king, reign, and monument are reduced to nothingness.

Meanwhile, the Counter-Reformation led to an increased emphasis on religious orthodoxy, and heightened suspicions of the humanist reform traditions that had shaped Cervantes' thought. Increasingly, his society scrutinized not only people's religious practices but also their roots, stigmatizing them for Jewish or Muslim forebears and holding all *conversos* and *Moriscos* (converts from Judaism and Islam, respectively) suspect. Cervantes' own fortunes may have been complicated by his origins: we cannot be sure whether he came from a line of *conversos*, but his family connections to the medical profession, the denial of his request for New World employment, and the refusal of the authorities to reward his heroic military service and captivity with any real preferment all suggest a striking disregard for his services. If he was in fact descended from Jews, Cervantes would have been barred from many honors and privileges in his time, however sincere his own Christian faith. Cervantes mocked the Inquisitorial and popular anxiety about origins in his dramatic interlude *The Miracle Show*. In this satire of Spanish obsessions with honor, legitimacy, and "blood purity," rascally entertainers trick village notables by convincing them that only those who are legitimate and free of the Jewish "taint" can actually see their marvelous show. In his version of "The Emperor's New Clothes," Cervantes holds up a sly theatrical mirror to his own society's prejudices.

During Cervantes' life, Spain faced challenges to both its political power and its religious orthodoxy. Protestants across Europe and humanist reformers within the Catholic Church constantly defied the strictures of the Counter-Reformation. The Ottoman Empire, which encroached on Italy, the Mediterranean, and North Africa, represented the greatest geopolitical threat to Spain, and also the religious threat of Islam as a competing faith. In its own territories, Spain struggled to incorporate the descendants of its Muslim subjects. Though this population had been forcibly converted to Christianity, their place and that of their descendants within a belligerently Christian nation were increasingly threatened. Their customs and language were forbidden by law, in an attempt to enforce acculturation. Beginning in 1609, the Moriscos,

though Christians, were forcibly expelled from Spain, prompting widespread condemnation by Church authorities across Europe. Cervantes comments directly on the situation of the Moriscos in *Don Quixote*. In "The Captive's Tale" of Part I, he considers how Spanish society might receive a hugely sympathetic young woman, a fresh convert from Islam, who had saved a Spanish captive much like the author himself. In Part II, published after the expulsions, in a section not included in this anthology, Sancho Panza, Don Quixote's earthy sidekick, runs into his Morisco former neighbor, Ricote, now back in Spain disguised as a German pilgrim. They proceed to share a communal meal, with plenty of wine to go around. Thus Cervantes turns again and again to his own experience of captivity and to the Morisco problem within Spain, to explore how a newly unified and forcibly homogenized nation might include those it had led to Christianity.

DON QUIXOTE

The Ingenious Gentleman Don Quixote de la Mancha was a popular success from the time Part I was published in 1605, although it was only later recognized as an important work of literature. This delay was due partly to the fact that in a period of established and well-defined literary genres such as the epic, the tragedy, and the pastoral romance (Cervantes himself had tried his hand at some of these forms), the unconventional combination of elements in *Don Quixote* resulted in a work of considerable novelty, with the serious aspects hidden under a mocking surface.

The proclaimed purpose of the book was to satirize the romances of chivalry. In those long yarns—based on the Carolingian and Arthurian legends, and full of supernatural deeds of valor, implausible and complicated adventures, duels, and enchantments—the literature that had expressed the medieval spirit of chivalry and romance had become conventional and formulaic (much as, in our day, certain literary conventions have become "pulp" fiction and film melodrama). Up to a point, then, what Cervantes set out to do was to produce a parody, a caricature of a hugely popular literary type. But he did not limit himself to such a relatively simple and direct undertaking. To expose the silliness of the romances of chivalry, he showed to what extraordinary consequences they would lead a man insanely infatuated with them, once this man set out to live "now" according to their patterns of action and belief. While the anachronism of Don Quixote makes him a figure of fun, it also allows Cervantes to examine the realities of his own time: an impoverished Spain full of underemployed noblemen; an overextended empire burdened by too many modern, impersonal wars; widespread anxiety about religious and political conformity, as well as genealogical "purity."

So what we have is not mere parody or caricature, for there is a great deal of difference between presenting a remote and more or less imaginary world and presenting an individual deciding to live by the standards of that world in a modern and realistic context. The first consequence is a mingling of genres. Don Quixote sees the world through the lens of medieval chivalry as its authors had portrayed it, and often the narrator echoes his vision, albeit in an ironic mode. The chivalric world is continuously jostled by elements of contemporary life evoked by the narrator—the realities of landscape and speech, peasants and nobles, inns and highways. The hero attempting to recreate the world of the romances is not, as we know, a cavalier; he is an impoverished country gentleman who embraces that code in the "modern"

world. His squire, the peasant Sancho Panza, is only too happy to point out Don Quixote's delusions. Nevertheless, he too becomes invested in the quest, in search of material wealth and aggrandizement. The exchanges between Don Quixote and Sancho pit a gentleman against a peasant, yet more often than not the two find common ground in their conviction that they can improve their lot through their own actions.

Don Quixote soon finds that he is not the only one modeling his life after books. Other characters follow their own idealizing genres, such as the pastoral romance to which Don Quixote and his friends will turn at the end. All must make their peace with the reality of the world that surrounds them. That debased world, in turn, produces its own stories, such as the picaresque "life" that the rascally Ginés de Pasamonte has written in prison (Part I, chapter 22), and the mix of recent history and romance that is the "Captive's Tale," related by its protagonist at the inn.

Along the way, Cervantes casts doubt on the possibility of reconstructing history from written sources. The facts about Don Quixote are never fully available to the primary narrator, who confesses to the many gaps in his knowledge and keeps losing track of the story. While the prologue describes the text as the author's "child," the narrator is not even certain of his protagonist's name. More spectacularly, the first part of the novel breaks off entirely at the end of chapter 8, leaving both characters and readers in suspense. The problem of finding more text then leads to one of Cervantes' most interesting narrative games: a second author, Cid Hamete Benengeli, who just happens to be an "Arabic historian," and whose disheveled account must be translated from a forbidden language by a "Spanish-speaking Moor"—a

Morisco. The entire story from this point forth is thus supposedly written by a Moor, the traditional enemy of a Spanish knight, and translated by a marginalized contemporary Morisco. Don Quixote and his narrator both worry about the implications of such authorship for the story on which they are embarked: will the Moorish author distort Don Quixote's adventures, or diminish his greatness? Part I also moves away from Don Quixote and Sancho to present a number of other stories that play with generic conventions—of lovelorn shepherds and the shepherdesses who puncture their illusions, young lovers who fall prey to ignoble lords, friendships undone by sexual jealousy, and captives redeemed by mysterious ladies. The narrative games are fully fleshed out in Part II, when Don Quixote and Sancho, now famous from Part I, must confront their own celebrity and grapple with the selves that the printing press has given them, while the authorial voice of Cide Hamete intervenes more and more frequently to make sure that the reader gets the "right" story.

Generally speaking, the encounters between the ordinary world and Don Quixote confront reality with illusion, and reason with imagination. Among the first adventures are some that have most contributed to the popularity of the Don Quixote legend: he sees windmills and decides they are giants, country inns become castles, and flocks of sheep become armies. Though the conclusions of such episodes often have the ludicrousness of slapstick comedy, there is a powerfully imposing quality about Don Quixote's insanity; his madness always has method, a commanding persistence and coherence. And there is perhaps an inevitable sense of moral grandeur in the spectacle of anyone remaining so unflinchingly faithful to his or her own vision. The world of "reason" may win in point of fact, but we come to wonder whether from a moral point of view Quixote is not the victor.

Yet at the same time the novel explores the deterioration of the chivalric ideals that inspire its protagonist—for instance, the notion of love as devoted "service." Don Quixote loves a purely fantastic lady, Dulcinea, so remote and unattainable that she does not even exist. Other plots interwoven through the text, and not included in our selection, show lovers struggling with problems of class and religious difference, and pervasive sexual jealousy. *Don Quixote* also examines the anachronism of individual heroics: new forms of warfare had rendered knights passé in more than the literary sense—battles are now fought with artillery and squadrons of infantry. The episode of the lions (Part II, chapter 17) features the knight, crowned with cottage cheese, seeking a challenge at all costs. That challenge comes in the ironic form of a caged animal being sent to the king, and who has no intention of engaging in battle. Unwilling to confront the futility of the knight in an age of gunpowder, Don Quixote will take what he can get in the form of challenges. The ridiculousness of the situation is counterbalanced by the basic seriousness of Quixote's motives; his notion of courage for its own sake appears, and is recognized, as singularly noble, a sort of generous display of integrity in a world usually ruled by lower standards. Thus the distinction between reason and madness, truth and illusion, becomes, to say the least, ambiguous. The hero's delusions are indeed exposed when they come up against hard facts, but the authority of such facts is seen to be morally questionable. A similar ambiguity colors a later episode where he frees a group of thuggish galley slaves (Part I, chapter 22). Don Quixote, comically anachronistic, ignores the existence of a centralized state with its own justice system, which has tried the men and found them guilty. Yet his intervention and his determination to hear out the prisoners raises more basic questions of social justice, and insists on the imagination, however anachronistic, as a basic tool for rethinking the status quo.

Don Quixote has been intensely read and reread, since its first publication, for its broad humor and its slippery ironies alike. Both parts of the novel were immediately translated across Europe, giving rise to such rewritings and imitations as the Jacobean comedy *The Knight of the Burning Pestle* (1607), the early feminist novel *The Female Quixote* (1752), and, more recently, the Broadway musical *Man of la Mancha* (1964). In Spain, *Don Quixote* has long been embraced as the symbol of a kind of national idealism; the philosopher Miguel de Unamuno in his *Life of* Don Quixote *and Sancho* (1905) argued that the novel was the true "Spanish Bible," a degree of respect that might well have amused the more irreverent Cervantes.

From Don Quixote[1]

From Part I

[*Prologue*]

Idling reader, you may believe me when I tell you that I should have liked this book, which is the child of my brain, to be the fairest, the sprightliest, and the cleverest that could be imagined; but I have not been able to contravene the law of nature which would have it that like begets like. And so, what was to be expected of a sterile and uncultivated wit such as that which I possess if not an offspring that was dried up, shriveled, and eccentric: a story filled with thoughts that never occurred to anyone else, of a sort that might be engendered in a prison where every annoyance has its home and every mournful sound its habitation?[2] Peace and tranquillity, the pleasures of the countryside, the serenity of the heavens, the murmur of fountains, and ease of mind can do much toward causing the most unproductive of muses to become fecund and bring forth progeny that will be the marvel and delight of mankind.

It sometimes happens that a father has an ugly son with no redeeming grace whatever, yet love will draw a veil over the parental eyes which then behold only cleverness and beauty in place of defects, and in speaking to his friends he will make those defects out to be the signs of comeliness and intellect. I, however, who am but Don Quixote's stepfather, have no desire to go with the current of custom, nor would I, dearest reader, beseech you with tears in my eyes as others do to pardon or overlook the faults you discover in this book; you are neither relative nor friend but may call your soul your own and exercise your free judgment. You are in your own house where you are master as the king is of his taxes, for you are familiar with the saying, "Under my cloak I kill the king."[3] All

---

1. Translated by Samuel Putnam.
2. Cervantes was imprisoned in Seville in 1597 and 1602.
3. I.e., the king does not own your body.

of which exempts and frees you from any kind of respect or obligation; you may say of this story whatever you choose without fear of being slandered for an ill opinion any more than you will be rewarded for a good one.

I should like to bring you the tale unadulterated and unadorned, stripped of the usual prologue and the endless string of sonnets, epigrams, and eulogies such as are commonly found at the beginning of books. For I may tell you that, although I expended no little labor upon the work itself, I have found no task more difficult than the composition of this preface which you are now reading. Many times I took up my pen and many times I laid it down again, not knowing what to write. On one occasion when I was thus in suspense, paper before me, pen over my ear, elbow on the table, and chin in hand, a very clever friend of mine came in. Seeing me lost in thought, he inquired as to the reason, and I made no effort to conceal from him the fact that my mind was on the preface which I had to write for the story of Don Quixote, and that it was giving me so much trouble that I had about decided not to write any at all and to abandon entirely the idea of publishing the exploits of so noble a knight.

"How," I said to him, "can you expect me not to be concerned over what that venerable legislator, the Public, will say when it sees me, at my age, after all these years of silent slumber, coming out with a tale that is as dried as a rush, a stranger to invention, paltry in style, impoverished in content, and wholly lacking in learning and wisdom, without marginal citations or notes at the end of the book when other works of this sort, even though they be fabulous and profane, are so packed with maxims from Aristotle and Plato and the whole crowd of philosophers as to fill the reader with admiration and lead him to regard the author as a well read, learned, and eloquent individual? Not to speak of the citations from Holy Writ! You would think they were at the very least so many St. Thomases[4] and other doctors of the Church; for they are so adroit at maintaining a solemn face that, having portrayed in one line a distracted lover, in the next they will give you a nice little Christian sermon that is a joy and a privilege to hear and read.

"All this my book will lack, for I have no citations for the margins, no notes for the end. To tell the truth, I do not even know who the authors are to whom I am indebted, and so am unable to follow the example of all the others by listing them alphabetically at the beginning, starting with Aristotle and closing with Xenophon, or, perhaps, with Zoilus or Zeuxis, notwithstanding the fact that the former was a snarling critic, the latter a painter. This work will also be found lacking in prefatory sonnets by dukes, marquises, counts, bishops, ladies, and poets of great renown; although if I were to ask two or three colleagues of mine, they would supply the deficiency by furnishing me with productions that could not be equaled by the authors of most repute in all Spain.

"In short, my friend," I went on, "I am resolved that Señor Don Quixote shall remain buried in the archives of La Mancha until Heaven shall provide him with someone to deck him out with all the ornaments that he lacks; for I find myself incapable of remedying the situation, being possessed of little learning or aptitude, and I am, moreover, extremely lazy when it comes to hunting up authors who will say for me what I am unable to say for myself. And if I am in

---

4. Thomas Aquinas (1225–1274), Italian philosopher and theologian, venerated by Roman Catholics as a "Doctor of the Church."

a state of suspense and my thoughts are woolgathering, you will find a sufficient explanation in what I have just told you."

Hearing this, my friend struck his forehead with the palm of his hand and burst into a loud laugh.

"In the name of God, brother," he said, "you have just deprived me of an illusion. I have known you for a long time, and I have always taken you to be clever and prudent in all your actions; but I now perceive that you are as far from all that as Heaven from the earth. How is it that things of so little moment and so easily remedied can worry and perplex a mind as mature as yours and ordinarily so well adapted to break down and trample underfoot far greater obstacles? I give you my word, this does not come from any lack of cleverness on your part, but rather from excessive indolence and a lack of experience. Do you ask for proof of what I say? Then pay attention closely and in the blink of an eye you shall see how I am going to solve all your difficulties and supply all those things the want of which, so you tell me, is keeping you in suspense, as a result of which you hesitate to publish the history of that famous Don Quixote of yours, the light and mirror of all knight-errantry."

"Tell me, then," I replied, "how you propose to go about curing my diffidence and bringing clarity out of the chaos and confusion of my mind?"

"Take that first matter," he continued, "of the sonnets, epigrams, or eulogies, which should bear the names of grave and titled personages: you can remedy that by taking a little trouble and composing the pieces yourself, and afterward you can baptize them with any name you see fit, fathering them on Prester John of the Indies or the Emperor of Trebizond, for I have heard tell that they were famous poets; and supposing they were not and that a few pedants and bachelors of arts should go around muttering behind your back that it is not so, you should not give so much as a pair of maravedis[5] for all their carping, since even though they make you out to be a liar, they are not going to cut off the hand that put these things on paper.

"As for marginal citations and authors in whom you may find maxims and sayings that you may put in your story, you have but to make use of those scraps of Latin that you know by heart or can look up without too much bother. Thus, when you come to treat of liberty and slavery, jot down:

Non bene pro toto libertas venditur auro.[6]

And then in the margin you will cite Horace or whoever it was that said it. If the subject is death, come up with:

*Pallida mors aequo pulsat pede pauperum tabernas
Regumque turres.*[7]

If it is friendship or the love that God commands us to show our enemies, then is the time to fall back on the Scriptures, which you can do by putting yourself out very little; you have but to quote the words of God himself:

5. Coin worth a thirty-fourth of a *real*; that is, even two *maravedíes* were worth very little. "Prester John": in medieval and early modern European folklore, the priest-monarch of a lost Christian kingdom in Asia or Africa. "Trebizond": successor state to the Byzantine Empire in modern-day Turkey; it flourished from the 13th to the 15th century.

6. Freedom is not bought by gold (Latin); from the anonymous *Aesopian Fables* 3.14.

7. Pale death knocks at the cottages of the poor and the palaces of kings with equal foot (Latin); from Horace, *Odes* 1.4.13–14.

Ego autem dico vobis: diligite inimicos vestros.[8]

If it is evil thoughts, lose no time in turning to the Gospels:

De corde exeunt cogitationes malae.[9]

If it is the instability of friends, here is Cato for you with a distich:

Donec eris felix multos numerabis amicos;
Tempora si fuerint nubila, solus eris.[1]

With these odds and ends of Latin and others of the same sort, you can cause yourself to be taken for a grammarian, although I must say that is no great honor or advantage these days.

"So far as notes at the end of the book are concerned, you may safely go about it in this manner: let us suppose that you mention some giant, Goliath let us say; with this one allusion which costs you little or nothing, you have a fine note which you may set down as follows: *The giant Golias or Goliath. This was a Philistine whom the shepherd David slew with a mighty cast from his sling-shot in the valley of Terebinth, according to what we read in the Book of Kings,* chapter so-and-so where you find it written.[2]

"In addition to this, by way of showing that you are a learned humanist and a cosmographer, contrive to bring into your story the name of the River Tagus, and there you are with another great little note: *The River Tagus was so called after a king of Spain; it rises in such and such a place and empties into the ocean, washing the walls of the famous city of Lisbon; it is supposed to have golden sands,* etc. If it is robbers, I will let you have the story of Cacus,[3] which I know by heart. If it is loose women, there is the Bishop of Mondoñedo,[4] who will lend you Lamia, Laïs, and Flora, an allusion that will do you great credit. If the subject is cruelty, Ovid will supply you with Medea; or if it is enchantresses and witches, Homer has Calypso and Vergil Circe. If it is valorous captains, Julius Caesar will lend you himself, in his *Commentaries,* and Plutarch will furnish a thousand Alexanders. If it is loves, with the ounce or two of Tuscan that you know you may make the acquaintance of Leon the Hebrew,[5] who will satisfy you to your heart's content. And in case you do not care to go abroad, here in your own house you have Fonseca's *Of the Love of God,*[6] where you will encounter in condensed form all that the most imaginative person could wish upon this subject. The short of the matter is, you have but to allude to these names or touch upon those stories that I have mentioned and leave to me the business of the notes and citations; I will guarantee you enough to fill the margins and four whole sheets at the back.

"And now we come to the list of authors cited, such as other works contain but in which your own is lacking. Here again the remedy is an easy one; you

---

8. But I say unto you, love your enemies (Latin); Matthew 5.44.
9. For out of the heart proceed evil thoughts (Latin); Matthew 15.19.
1. As long as you are happy, you will count many friends, but if times become clouded, you will be alone (Latin); not from Cato but instead Ovid, *Sorrows* 1.9.5–6.
2. 1 Samuel 17.48–49.

3. Gigantic thief defeated by Hercules in Virgil's *Aeneid* 8.
4. Father Antonio de Guevara (ca. 1481–1545).
5. Judah Leon Abravanel, known as León Hebreo (ca. 1465–ca. 1523), Neoplatonic author of the *Dialogues of Love* (1535).
6. Cristóbal de Fonseca, *Treatise of the Love of God* (1592).

have but to look up some book that has them all, from A to Z as you were say-ing, and transfer the entire list as it stands. What if the imposition is plain for all to see? You have little need to refer to them, and so it does not matter; and some may be so simple-minded as to believe that you have drawn upon them all in your simple unpretentious little story. If it serves no other purpose, this imposing list of authors will at least give your book an unlooked-for air of authority. What is more, no one is going to put himself to the trouble of verify-ing your references to see whether or not you have followed all these authors, since it will not be worth his pains to do so.

"This is especially true in view of the fact that your book stands in no need of all these things whose absence you lament; for the entire work is an attack upon the books of chivalry of which Aristotle never dreamed, of which St. Basil has nothing to say, and of which Cicero had no knowledge; nor do the fine points of truth or the observations of astrology have anything to do with its fanciful absurdities; geometrical measurements, likewise, and rhetorical argu-mentations serve for nothing here; you have no sermon to preach to anyone by mingling the human with the divine, a kind of motley in which no Christian intellect should be willing to clothe itself.

"All that you have to do is to make proper use of imitation in what you write, and the more perfect the imitation the better will your writing be. Inasmuch as you have no other object in view than that of overthrowing the authority and prestige which books of chivalry enjoy in the world at large and among the vul-gar, there is no reason why you should go begging maxims of the philosophers, counsels of Holy Writ, fables of the poets, orations of the rhetoricians, or mir-acles of the saints; see to it, rather, that your style flows along smoothly, pleas-ingly, and sonorously, and that your words are the proper ones, meaningful and well placed, expressive of your intention in setting them down and of what you wish to say, without any intricacy or obscurity.

"Let it be your aim that, by reading your story, the melancholy may be moved to laughter and the cheerful man made merrier still; let the simple not be bored, but may the clever admire your originality; let the grave ones not despise you, but let the prudent praise you. And keep in mind, above all, your purpose, which is that of undermining the ill-founded edifice that is constituted by those books of chivalry, so abhorred by many but admired by many more; if you succeed in attaining it, you will have accomplished no little."

Listening in profound silence to what my friend had to say, I was so impressed by his reasoning that, with no thought of questioning them, I decided to make use of his arguments in composing this prologue. Here, gentle reader, you will perceive my friend's cleverness, my own good fortune in coming upon such a counselor at a time when I needed him so badly, and the profit which you your-selves are to have in finding so sincere and straightforward an account of the famous Don Quixote de la Mancha, who is held by the inhabitants of the Campo de Montiel region to have been the most chaste lover and the most valiant knight that had been seen in those parts for many a year. I have no desire to enlarge upon the service I am rendering you in bringing you the story of so notable and honored a gentleman; I merely would have you thank me for having made you acquainted with the famous Sancho Panza, his squire, in whom, to my mind, is to be found an epitome of all the squires and their droll-eries scattered here and there throughout the pages of those vain and empty books of chivalry. And with this, may God give you health, and may He be not unmindful of me as well. VALE.[7]

["I Know Who I Am, and Who I May Be, If I Choose"]

CHAPTER I

Which treats of the station in life and the pursuits of the famous gentleman, Don Quixote de la Mancha.

In a village of La Mancha[1] the name of which I have no desire to recall, there lived not so long ago one of those gentlemen who always have a lance in the rack, an ancient buckler, a skinny nag, and a greyhound for the chase. A stew with more beef than mutton in it, chopped meat for his evening meal, scraps for a Saturday, lentils on Friday, and a young pigeon as a special delicacy for Sunday, went to account for three-quarters of his income. The rest of it he laid out on a broadcloth greatcoat and velvet stockings for feast days, with slippers to match, while the other days of the week he cut a figure in a suit of the finest homespun. Living with him were a housekeeper in her forties, a niece who was not yet twenty, and a lad of the field and marketplace who saddled his horse for him and wielded the pruning knife.

This gentleman of ours was close on to fifty, of a robust constitution but with little flesh on his bones and a face that was lean and gaunt. He was noted for his early rising, being very fond of the hunt. They will try to tell you that his surname was Quijada or Quesada—there is some difference of opinion among those who have written on the subject—but according to the most likely conjectures we are to understand that it was really Quejana. But all this means very little so far as our story is concerned, providing that in the telling of it we do not depart one iota from the truth.

You may know, then, that the aforesaid gentleman, on those occasions when he was at leisure, which was most of the year around, was in the habit of reading books of chivalry with such pleasure and devotion as to lead him almost wholly to forget the life of a hunter and even the administration of his estate. So great was his curiosity and infatuation in this regard that he even sold many acres of tillable land in order to be able to buy and read the books that he loved, and he would carry home with him as many of them as he could obtain.

Of all those that he thus devoured none pleased him so well as the ones that had been composed by the famous Feliciano de Silva,[2] whose lucid prose style and involved conceits were as precious to him as pearls; especially when he came to read those tales of love and amorous challenges that are to be met with in many places, such a passage as the following, for example: "The reason of the unreason that afflicts my reason, in such a manner weakens my reason that I with reason lament me of your comeliness." And he was similarly affected when his eyes fell upon such lines as these: ". . . the high Heaven of your divin-

---

7. Farewell (Latin).
1. Efforts at identifying the village have proved inconclusive. La Mancha is a region of central Spain south of the capital, Madrid.

2. Author of romances (16th century); the lines that follow are from his *Don Florisel de Niguea*.

ity divinely fortifies you with the stars and renders you deserving of that desert your greatness doth deserve."

The poor fellow used to lie awake nights in an effort to disentangle the meaning and make sense out of passages such as these, although Aristotle himself would not have been able to understand them, even if he had been resurrected for that sole purpose. He was not at ease in his mind over those wounds that Don Belianís[3] gave and received; for no matter how great the surgeons who treated him, the poor fellow must have been left with his face and his entire body covered with marks and scars. Nevertheless, he was grateful to the author for closing the book with the promise of an interminable adventure to come; many a time he was tempted to take up his pen and literally finish the tale as had been promised, and he undoubtedly would have done so, and would have succeeded at it very well, if his thoughts had not been constantly occupied with other things of greater moment.

He often talked it over with the village curate, who was a learned man, a graduate of Sigüenza,[4] and they would hold long discussions as to who had been the better knight, Palmerin of England or Amadis of Gaul; but Master Nicholas, the barber of the same village, was in the habit of saying that no one could come up to the Knight of Phoebus,[5] and that if anyone *could* compare with him it was Don Galaor, brother of Amadis of Gaul, for Galaor was ready for anything—he was none of your finical knights, who went around whimpering as his brother did, and in point of valor he did not lag behind him.

In short, our gentleman became so immersed in his reading that he spent whole nights from sundown to sunup and his days from dawn to dusk in poring over his books, until, finally, from so little sleeping and so much reading, his brain dried up and he went completely out of his mind. He had filled his imagination with everything that he had read, with enchantments, knightly encounters, battles, challenges, wounds, with tales of love and its torments, and all sorts of impossible things, and as a result had come to believe that all these fictitious happenings were true; they were more real to him than anything else in the world. He would remark that the Cid Ruy Díaz had been a very good knight, but there was no comparison between him and the Knight of the Flaming Sword, who with a single backward stroke had cut in half two fierce and monstrous giants. He preferred Bernardo del Carpio, who at Roncesvalles had slain Roland despite the charm the latter bore, availing himself of the stratagem which Hercules employed when he strangled Antaeus,[6] the son of Earth, in his arms.

He had much good to say for Morgante[7] who, though he belonged to the haughty, overbearing race of giants, was of an affable disposition and well brought up. But, above all, he cherished an admiration for Rinaldo of Montalbán,[8] espe-

3. The allusion is to a romance by Jerónimo Fernández.
4. Ironic, for Sigüenza was the seat of a minor and discredited university.
5. Or Knight of the Sun. Heroes of romances customarily adopted emblematic names and also changed them according to circumstances. "Palmerin . . . Amadis": each a hero of a very famous chivalric romance, as are those mentioned in the following paragraphs.
6. The mythological Antaeus was invulnerable as long as he maintained contact with his mother, Earth. Hercules killed him while hold-

ing him raised in his arms. "Charm": the magic gift of invulnerability.
7. In Pulci's *Morgante Maggiore* (1483), a comic-epic poem of the Italian Renaissance.
8. Roland's cousin in Boiardo's *Roland in Love* (*Orlando Innamorato*) and Ariosto's *Roland Mad* (*Orlando Furioso*), romantic and comic-epic poems of the Italian Renaissance. Roland (or Orlando) was a military leader under the Frankish king Charlemagne in the 8th century; in legend he became the hero of many popular romances.

cially as he beheld him sallying forth from his castle to rob all those that crossed his path, or when he thought of him overseas stealing the image of Mohammed which, so the story has it, was all of gold. And he would have liked very well to have had his fill of kicking that traitor Galalón,[9] a privilege for which he would have given his housekeeper with his niece thrown into the bargain.

At last, when his wits were gone beyond repair, he came to conceive the strangest idea that ever occurred to any madman in this world. It now appeared to him fitting and necessary, in order to win a greater amount of honor for himself and serve his country at the same time, to become a knight-errant and roam the world on horseback, in a suit of armor; he would go in quest of adventures, by way of putting into practice all that he had read in his books; he would right every manner of wrong, placing himself in situations of the greatest peril such as would redound to the eternal glory of his name. As a reward for his valor and the might of his arm, the poor fellow could already see himself crowned Emperor of Trebizond at the very least; and so, carried away by the strange pleasure that he found in such thoughts as these, he at once set about putting his plan into effect.

The first thing he did was to burnish up some old pieces of armor, left him by his great-grandfather, which for ages had lain in a corner, moldering and forgotten. He polished and adjusted them as best he could, and then he noticed that one very important thing was lacking: there was no closed helmet, but only a morion, or visorless headpiece, with turned-up brim of the kind foot soldiers wore. His ingenuity, however, enabled him to remedy this, and he proceeded to fashion out of cardboard a kind of half-helmet, which, when attached to the morion, gave the appearance of a whole one. True, when he went to see if it was strong enough to withstand a good slashing blow, he was somewhat disappointed; for when he drew his sword and gave it a couple of thrusts, he succeeded only in undoing a whole week's labor. The ease with which he had hewed it to bits disturbed him no little, and he decided to make it over. This time he placed a few strips of iron on the inside, and then, convinced that it was strong enough, refrained from putting it to any further test; instead, he adopted it then and there as the finest helmet ever made.

After this, he went out to have a look at his nag; and although the animal had more *cuartos*, or cracks, in its hoof than there are quarters in a real,[1] and more blemishes than Gonela's steed which *tantum pellis et ossa fuit*,[2] it nonetheless looked to its master like a far better horse than Alexander's Bucephalus or the Babieca of the Cid.[3] He spent all of four days in trying to think up a name for his mount; for—so he told himself—seeing that it belonged to so famous and worthy a knight, there was no reason why it should not have a name of equal renown. The kind of name he wanted was one that would at once indicate what the nag had been before it came to belong to a knight-errant and what its present status was; for it stood to reason that, when the master's worldly condition changed, his

9. Ganelón, the villain in the Charlemagne legend who betrayed the French at Roncesvalles.
1. A silver coin worth about $16 in today's US currency. "Cuarto": copper coin worth four *maravedíes*.
2. Was so much skin and bones (Latin, from Plautus, *Andalucia* 3.6). "Gonela": legendary fool in the 15th-century court of Ferrara.
3. The Chief (Spanish)—that is, Ruy Díaz, celebrated hero of *Poema del Cid* (12th century). "Bucephalus": the horse of Alexander the Great.

horse also ought to have a famous, high-sounding appellation, one suited to the new order of things and the new profession that it was to follow.

After he in his memory and imagination had made up, struck out, and discarded many names, now adding to and now subtracting from the list, he finally hit upon "Rocinante," a name that impressed him as being sonorous and at the same time indicative of what the steed had been when it was but a hack,[4] whereas now it was nothing other than the first and foremost of all the hacks in the world.

Having found a name for his horse that pleased his fancy, he then desired to do as much for himself, and this required another week, and by the end of that period he had made up his mind that he was henceforth to be known as Don Quixote, which, as has been stated, has led the authors of this veracious history to assume that his real name must undoubtedly have been Quijada, and not Quesada as others would have it. But remembering that the valiant Amadis was not content to call himself that and nothing more, but added the name of his kingdom and fatherland that he might make it famous also, and thus came to take the name Amadis of Gaul, so our good knight chose to add his place of origin and become "Don Quixote de la Mancha"; for by this means, as he saw it, he was making very plain his lineage and was conferring honor upon his country by taking its name as his own.

And so, having polished up his armor and made the morion over into a closed helmet, and having given himself and his horse a name, he naturally found but one thing lacking still: he must seek out a lady of whom he could become enamored; for a knight-errant without a ladylove was like a tree without leaves or fruit, a body without a soul.

"If," he said to himself, "as a punishment for my sins or by a stroke of fortune I should come upon some giant hereabouts, a thing that very commonly happens to knights-errant, and if I should slay him in a hand-to-hand encounter or perhaps cut him in two, or, finally, if I should vanquish and subdue him, would it not be well to have someone to whom I may send him as a present, in order that he, if he is living, may come in, fall upon his knees in front of my sweet lady, and say in a humble and submissive tone of voice, 'I, lady, am the giant Caraculiambro, lord of the island Malindrania, who has been overcome in single combat by that knight who never can be praised enough, Don Quixote de la Mancha, the same who sent me to present myself before your Grace that your Highness may dispose of me as you see fit'?"

Oh, how our good knight reveled in this speech, and more than ever when he came to think of the name that he should give his lady! As the story goes, there was a very good-looking farm girl who lived near by, with whom he had once been smitten, although it is generally believed that she never knew or suspected it. Her name was Aldonza Lorenzo, and it seemed to him that she was the one upon whom he should bestow the title of mistress of his thoughts. For her he wished a name that should not be incongruous with his own and that would convey the suggestion of a princess or a great lady; and, accordingly, he resolved to call her "Dulcinea del Toboso," she being a native of that place. A musical name to his ears, out of the ordinary and significant, like the others he had chosen for himself and his appurtenances.

---

4. In Spanish, *rocín*. The suffix *"ante"* is comically taken for *"antes"* (Spanish, before).

CHAPTER II

*Which treats of the first sally that the ingenious Don Quixote
made from his native heath.*

Having, then, made all these preparations, he did not wish to lose any time in putting his plan into effect, for he could not but blame himself for what the world was losing by his delay, so many were the wrongs that were to be righted, the grievances to be redressed, the abuses to be done away with, and the duties to be performed. Accordingly, without informing anyone of his intention and without letting anyone see him, he set out one morning before daybreak on one of those very hot days in July. Donning all his armor, mounting Rocinante, adjusting his ill-contrived helmet, bracing his shield on his arm, and taking up his lance, he sallied forth by the back gate of his stable yard into the open countryside. It was with great contentment and joy that he saw how easily he had made a beginning toward the fulfillment of his desire.

No sooner was he out on the plain, however, than a terrible thought assailed him, one that all but caused him to abandon the enterprise he had undertaken. This occurred when he suddenly remembered that he had never formally been dubbed a knight, and so, in accordance with the law of knighthood, was not permitted to bear arms against one who had a right to that title. And even if he had been, as a novice knight he would have had to wear white armor, without any device on his shield, until he should have earned one by his exploits. These thoughts led him to waver in his purpose, but, madness prevailing over reason, he resolved to have himself knighted by the first person he met, as many others had done if what he had read in those books that he had at home was true. And so far as white armor was concerned, he would scour his own the first chance that offered until it shone whiter than any ermine. With this he became more tranquil and continued on his way, letting his horse take whatever path it chose, for he believed that therein lay the very essence of adventures.

And so we find our newly fledged adventurer jogging along and talking to himself. "Undoubtedly," he is saying, "in the days to come, when the true history of my famous deeds is published, the learned chronicler who records them, when he comes to describe my first sally so early in the morning, will put down something like this: 'No sooner had the rubicund Apollo spread over the face of the broad and spacious earth the gilded filaments of his beauteous locks, and no sooner had the little singing birds of painted plumage greeted with their sweet and mellifluous harmony the coming of the Dawn, who, leaving the soft couch of her jealous spouse, now showed herself to mortals at all the doors and balconies of the horizon that bounds La Mancha—no sooner had this happened than the famous knight, Don Quixote de la Mancha, forsaking his own downy bed and mounting his famous steed, Rocinante, fared forth and began riding over the ancient and famous Campo de Montiel.'"[5]

And this was the truth, for he was indeed riding over that stretch of plain.

"O happy age and happy century," he went on, "in which my famous exploits shall be published, exploits worthy of being engraved in bronze, sculptured in marble, and depicted in paintings for the benefit of posterity. O wise magician,

5. The scene of a battle in 1369.

whoever you be, to whom shall fall the task of chronicling this extraordinary history of mine! I beg of you not to forget my good Rocinante, eternal companion of my wayfarings and my wanderings."

Then, as though he really had been in love: "O Princess Dulcinea, lady of this captive heart! Much wrong have you done me in thus sending me forth with your reproaches and sternly commanding me not to appear in your beauteous presence. O lady, deign to be mindful of this your subject who endures so many woes for the love of you."

And so he went on, stringing together absurdities, all of a kind that his books had taught him, imitating insofar as he was able the language of their authors. He rode slowly, and the sun came up so swiftly and with so much heat that it would have been sufficient to melt his brains if he had had any. He had been on the road almost the entire day without anything happening that is worthy of being set down here; and he was on the verge of despair, for he wished to meet someone at once with whom he might try the valor of his good right arm. Certain authors say that his first adventure was that of Puerto Lápice, while others state that it was that of the windmills; but in this particular instance I am in a position to affirm what I have read in the annals of La Mancha; and that is to the effect that he went all that day until nightfall, when he and his hack found themselves tired to death and famished. Gazing all around him to see if he could discover some castle or shepherd's hut where he might take shelter and attend to his pressing needs, he caught sight of an inn not far off the road along which they were traveling, and this to him was like a star guiding him not merely to the gates, but rather, let us say, to the palace of redemption. Quickening his pace, he came up to it just as night was falling.

By chance there stood in the doorway two lasses of the sort known as "of the district"; they were on their way to Seville in the company of some mule drivers who were spending the night in the inn. Now, everything that this adventurer of ours thought, saw, or imagined seemed to him to be directly out of one of the storybooks he had read, and so, when he caught sight of the inn, it at once became a castle with its four turrets and its pinnacles of gleaming silver, not to speak of the drawbridge and moat and all the other things that are commonly supposed to go with a castle. As he rode up to it, he accordingly reined in Rocinante and sat there waiting for a dwarf to appear upon the battlements and blow his trumpet by way of announcing the arrival of a knight. The dwarf, however, was slow in coming, and as Rocinante was anxious to reach the stable, Don Quixote drew up to the door of the hostelry and surveyed the two merry maidens, who to him were a pair of beauteous damsels or gracious ladies taking their ease at the castle gate.

And then a swineherd came along, engaged in rounding up his drove of hogs— for, without any apology, that is what they were. He gave a blast on his horn to bring them together, and this at once became for Don Quixote just what he wished it to be: some dwarf who was heralding his coming; and so it was with a vast deal of satisfaction that he presented himself before the ladies in question, who, upon beholding a man in full armor like this, with lance and buckler, were filled with fright and made as if to flee indoors. Realizing that they were afraid, Don Quixote raised his pasteboard visor and revealed his withered, dust-covered face.

"Do not flee, your Ladyships," he said to them in a courteous manner and gentle voice. "You need not fear that any wrong will be done you, for it is not in accordance with the order of knighthood which I profess to wrong anyone, much less such highborn damsels as your appearance shows you to be."

The girls looked at him, endeavoring to scan his face, which was half hidden by his ill-made visor. Never having heard women of their profession called damsels before, they were unable to restrain their laughter, at which Don Quixote took offense.

"Modesty," he observed, "well becomes those with the dower of beauty, and, moreover, laughter that has not good cause is a very foolish thing. But I do not say this to be discourteous or to hurt your feelings; my only desire is to serve you."

The ladies did not understand what he was talking about, but felt more than ever like laughing at our knight's unprepossessing figure. This increased his annoyance, and there is no telling what would have happened if at that moment the innkeeper had not come out. He was very fat and very peaceably inclined; but upon sighting this grotesque personage clad in bits of armor that were quite as oddly matched as were his bridle, lance, buckler, and corselet, mine host was not at all indisposed to join the lasses in their merriment. He was suspicious, however, of all this paraphernalia and decided that it would be better to keep a civil tongue in his head.

"If, Sir Knight," he said, "your Grace desires a lodging, aside from a bed—for there is none to be had in this inn—you will find all else that you may want in great abundance."

When Don Quixote saw how humble the governor of the castle was—for he took the innkeeper and his inn to be no less than that—he replied, "For me, Sir Castellan,[6] anything will do, since

> Arms are my only ornament,
> My only rest the fight, etc."

The landlord thought that the knight had called him a castellan because he took him for one of those worthies of Castile, whereas the truth was, he was an Andalusian from the beach of Sanlúcar, no less a thief than Cacus[7] himself, and as full of tricks as a student or a page boy.

"In that case," he said,

> "Your bed will be the solid rock,
> Your sleep: to watch all night.

This being so, you may be assured of finding beneath this roof enough to keep you awake for a whole year, to say nothing of a single night."

With this, he went up to hold the stirrup for Don Quixote, who encountered much difficulty in dismounting, not having broken his fast all day long. The knight then directed his host to take good care of the steed, as it was the best piece of horseflesh in all the world. The innkeeper looked it over, and it did not impress him as being half as good as Don Quixote had said it was. Having stabled the animal, he came back to see what his guest would have and found the latter

6. The Spanish *castellano* means both "castellan" and "Castilian" (i.e., a native of Castile, or, more generally, of Spain).
7. In Roman mythology, Cacus stole some of Hercules' cattle, concealing the theft by having them walk backward into his cave; he was finally discovered and slain.

being relieved of his armor by the damsels, who by now had made their peace with the new arrival. They had already removed his breastplate and backpiece but had no idea how they were going to open his gorget or get his improvised helmet off. That piece of armor had been tied on with green ribbons which it would be necessary to cut, since the knots could not be undone, but he would not hear of this, and so spent all the rest of that night with his headpiece in place, which gave him the weirdest, most laughable appearance that could be imagined.

Don Quixote fancied that these wenches who were assisting him must surely be the chatelaine and other ladies of the castle, and so proceeded to address them very gracefully and with much wit:

> "Never was knight so served
> By any noble dame
> As was Don Quixote
> When from his village he came,
> With damsels to wait on his every need
> While princesses cared for his hack . . ."

"By hack," he explained, "is meant my steed Rocinante, for that is his name, and mine is Don Quixote de la Mancha. I had no intention of revealing my identity until my exploits done in your service should have made me known to you; but the necessity of adapting to present circumstances that old ballad of Lancelot has led to your becoming acquainted with it prematurely. However, the time will come when your Ladyships shall command and I will obey and with the valor of my good right arm show you how eager I am to serve you."

The young women were not used to listening to speeches like this and had not a word to say, but merely asked him if he desired to eat anything.

"I could eat a bite of something, yes," replied Don Quixote. "Indeed, I feel that a little food would go very nicely just now."

He thereupon learned that, since it was Friday, there was nothing to be had in all the inn except a few portions of codfish, which in Castile is called *abadejo*, in Andalusia *bacalao*, in some places *curadillo*, and elsewhere *truchuella* or small trout. Would his Grace, then, have some small trout, seeing that was all there was that they could offer him?

"If there are enough of them," said Don Quixote, "they will take the place of a trout, for it is all one to me whether I am given in change eight reales or one piece of eight. What is more, those small trout may be like veal, which is better than beef, or like kid, which is better than goat. But however that may be, bring them on at once, for the weight and burden of arms is not to be borne without inner sustenance."

Placing the table at the door of the hostelry, in the open air, they brought the guest a portion of badly soaked and worse cooked codfish and a piece of bread as black and moldy as the suit of armor that he wore. It was a mirth-provoking sight to see him eat, for he still had his helmet on with his visor fastened, which made it impossible for him to put anything into his mouth with his hands, and so it was necessary for one of the girls to feed him. As for giving him anything to drink, that would have been out of the question if the inn-keeper had not hollowed out a reed, placing one end in Don Quixote's mouth while through the other end he poured the wine. All this the knight bore very patiently rather than have them cut the ribbons of his helmet.

At this point a gelder of pigs approached the inn, announcing his arrival with four or five blasts on his horn, all of which confirmed Don Quixote in the belief that this was indeed a famous castle, for what was this if not music that they were playing for him? The fish was trout, the bread was of the finest, the wenches were ladies, and the innkeeper was the castellan. He was convinced that he had been right in his resolve to sally forth and roam the world at large, but there was one thing that still distressed him greatly, and that was the fact that he had not as yet been dubbed a knight; as he saw it, he could not legitimately engage in any adventure until he had received the order of knighthood.

CHAPTER III

Of the amusing manner in which Don Quixote had himself dubbed a knight.

Wearied of his thoughts, Don Quixote lost no time over the scanty repast which the inn afforded him. When he had finished, he summoned the landlord and, taking him out to the stable, closed the doors and fell on his knees in front of him.

"Never, valiant knight," he said, "shall I arise from here until you have courteously granted me the boon I seek, one which will redound to your praise and to the good of the human race."

Seeing his guest at his feet and hearing him utter such words as these, the innkeeper could only stare at him in bewilderment, not knowing what to say or do. It was in vain that he entreated him to rise, for Don Quixote refused to do so until his request had been granted.

"I expected nothing less of your great magnificence, my lord," the latter then continued, "and so I may tell you that the boon I asked and which you have so generously conceded me is that tomorrow morning you dub me a knight. Until that time, in the chapel of this your castle, I will watch over my armor, and when morning comes, as I have said, that which I so desire shall then be done, in order that I may lawfully go to the four corners of the earth in quest of adventures and to succor the needy, which is the chivalrous duty of all knights-errant such as I who long to engage in deeds of high emprise."

The innkeeper, as we have said, was a sharp fellow. He already had a suspicion that his guest was not quite right in the head, and he was now convinced of it as he listened to such remarks as these. However, just for the sport of it, he determined to humor him; and so he went on to assure Don Quixote that he was fully justified in his request and that such a desire and purpose was only natural on the part of so distinguished a knight as his gallant bearing plainly showed him to be.

He himself, the landlord added, when he was a young man, had followed the same honorable calling. He had gone through various parts of the world seeking adventures, among the places he had visited being the Percheles of Málaga, the Isles of Riarán, the District of Seville, the Little Market Place of Segovia, the Olivera of Valencia, the Rondilla of Granada, the beach of Sanlúcar, the Horse Fountain of Cordova, the Small Taverns of Toledo,[8] and numerous other

---

8. All reputed to be haunts of robbers and rogues.

localities where his nimble feet and light fingers had found much exercise. He had done many wrongs, cheated many widows, ruined many maidens, and swindled not a few minors until he had finally come to be known in almost all the courts and tribunals that are to be found in the whole of Spain.

At last he had retired to his castle here, where he lived upon his own income and the property of others; and here it was that he received all knights-errant of whatever quality and condition, simply out of the great affection that he bore them and that they might share with him their possessions in payment of his good will. Unfortunately, in this castle there was no chapel where Don Quixote might keep watch over his arms, for the old chapel had been torn down to make way for a new one; but in case of necessity, he felt quite sure that such a vigil could be maintained anywhere, and for the present occasion the courtyard of the castle would do; and then in the morning, please God, the requisite ceremony could be performed and his guest be duly dubbed a knight, as much a knight as anyone ever was.

He then inquired if Don Quixote had any money on his person, and the latter replied that he had not a cent, for in all the storybooks he had never read of knights-errant carrying any. But the innkeeper told him he was mistaken on this point: supposing the authors of those stories had not set down the fact in black and white, that was because they did not deem it necessary to speak of things as indispensable as money and a clean shirt, and one was not to assume for that reason that those knights-errant of whom the books were so full did not have any. He looked upon it as an absolute certainty that they all had well-stuffed purses, that they might be prepared for any emergency; and they also carried shirts and a little box of ointment for healing the wounds that they received.

For when they had been wounded in combat on the plains and in desert places, there was not always someone at hand to treat them, unless they had some skilled enchanter for a friend who then would succor them, bringing to them through the air, upon a cloud, some damsel or dwarf bearing a vial of water of such virtue that one had but to taste a drop of it and at once his wounds were healed and he was as sound as if he had never received any.

But even if this was not the case, knights in times past saw to it that their squires were well provided with money and other necessities, such as lint and ointment for healing purposes; and if they had no squires—which happened very rarely—they themselves carried these objects in a pair of saddlebags very cleverly attached to their horses' croups in such a manner as to be scarcely noticeable, as if they held something of greater importance than that, for among the knights-errant saddlebags as a rule were not favored. Accordingly, he would advise the novice before him, and inasmuch as the latter was soon to be his godson, he might even command him, that henceforth he should not go without money and a supply of those things that have been mentioned, as he would find that they came in useful at a time when he least expected it.

Don Quixote promised to follow his host's advice punctiliously; and so it was arranged that he should watch his armor in a large barnyard at one side of the inn. He gathered up all the pieces, placed them in a horse trough that stood near the well, and, bracing his shield on his arm, took up his lance and with stately demeanor began pacing up and down in front of the trough even as night was closing in.

The innkeeper informed his other guests of what was going on, of Don Quixote's vigil and his expectation of being dubbed a knight; and, marveling greatly at so extraordinary a variety of madness, they all went out to see for themselves and stood there watching from a distance. For a while the knight-to-be, with tranquil mien, would merely walk up and down; then, leaning on his lance, he would pause to survey his armor, gazing fixedly at it for a considerable length of time. As has been said, it was night now, but the brightness of the moon, which well might rival that of Him who lent it, was such that everything the novice knight did was plainly visible to all.

At this point one of the mule drivers who were stopping at the inn came out to water his drove, and in order to do this it was necessary to remove the armor from the trough.

As he saw the man approaching, Don Quixote cried out to him, "O bold knight, whoever you may be, who thus would dare to lay hands upon the accouterments of the most valiant man of arms that ever girded on a sword, look well what you do and desist if you do not wish to pay with your life for your insolence!"

The muleteer gave no heed to these words—it would have been better for his own sake had he done so—but, taking it up by the straps, tossed the armor some distance from him. When he beheld this, Don Quixote rolled his eyes heavenward and with his thoughts apparently upon his Dulcinea exclaimed, "Succor, O lady mine, this vassal heart in this my first encounter; let not your favor and protection fail me in the peril in which for the first time I now find myself."

With these and other similar words, he loosed his buckler, grasped his lance in both his hands, and let the mule driver have such a blow on the head that the man fell to the ground stunned; and had it been followed by another one, he would have had no need of a surgeon to treat him. Having done this, Don Quixote gathered up his armor and resumed his pacing up and down with the same calm manner as before. Not long afterward, without knowing what had happened—for the first muleteer was still lying there unconscious—another came out with the same intention of watering his mules, and he too was about to remove the armor from the trough when the knight, without saying a word or asking favor of anyone, once more adjusted his buckler and raised his lance, and if he did not break the second mule driver's head to bits, he made more than three pieces of it by dividing it into quarters. At the sound of the fracas everybody in the inn came running out, among them the innkeeper; whereupon Don Quixote again lifted his buckler and laid his hand on his sword.

"O lady of beauty," he said, "strength and vigor of this fainting heart of mine! Now is the time to turn the eyes of your greatness upon this captive knight of yours who must face so formidable an adventure."

By this time he had worked himself up to such a pitch of anger that if all the mule drivers in the world had attacked him he would not have taken one step backward. The comrades of the wounded men, seeing the plight those two were in, now began showering stones on Don Quixote, who shielded himself as best he could with his buckler, although he did not dare stir from the trough for fear of leaving his armor unprotected. The landlord, meanwhile, kept calling to them to stop, for he had told them that this was a madman who would be sure to go free even though he killed them all. The knight was shouting louder than ever, calling them knaves and traitors. As for the lord of the castle, who allowed knights-errant to be treated in this fashion, he was a lowborn villain, and if he, Don Quixote, had but received the order of knighthood, he would make him pay for his treachery.

"As for you others, vile and filthy rabble, I take no account of you; you may stone me or come forward and attack me all you like; you shall see what the reward of your folly and insolence will be."

He spoke so vigorously and was so undaunted in bearing as to strike terror in those who would assail him; and for this reason, and owing also to the persuasions of the innkeeper, they ceased stoning him. He then permitted them to carry away the wounded, and went back to watching his armor with the same tranquil, unconcerned air that he had previously displayed.

The landlord was none too well pleased with these mad pranks on the part of his guest and determined to confer upon him that accursed order of knighthood before something else happened. Going up to him, he begged Don Quixote's pardon for the insolence which, without his knowledge, had been shown the knight by those of low degree. They, however, had been well punished for their impudence. As he had said, there was no chapel in this castle, but for that which remained to be done there was no need of any. According to what he had read of the ceremonial of the order, there was nothing to this business of being dubbed a knight except a slap on the neck and one across the shoulder, and that could be performed in the middle of a field as well as anywhere else. All that was required was for the knight-to-be to keep watch over his armor for a couple of hours, and Don Quixote had been at it more than four. The latter believed all this and announced that he was ready to obey and get the matter over with as speedily as possible. Once dubbed a knight, if he were attacked one more time, he did not think that he would leave a single person in the castle alive, save such as he might command be spared, at the bidding of his host and out of respect to him.

Thus warned, and fearful that it might occur, the castellan brought out the book in which he had jotted down the hay and barley for which the mule drivers owed him, and, accompanied by a lad bearing the butt of a candle and the two aforesaid damsels, he came up to where Don Quixote stood and commanded him to kneel. Reading from the account book—as if he had been saying a prayer—he raised his hand and, with the knight's own sword, gave him a good thwack upon the neck and another lusty one upon the shoulder, muttering all the while between his teeth. He then directed one of the ladies to gird on Don Quixote's sword, which she did with much gravity and composure; for it was all they could do to keep from laughing at every point of the ceremony, but the thought of the knight's prowess which they had already witnessed was sufficient to restrain their mirth.

"May God give your Grace much good fortune," said the worthy lady as she attached the blade, "and prosper you in battle."

Don Quixote thereupon inquired her name, for he desired to know to whom it was he was indebted for the favor he had just received, that he might share with her some of the honor which his strong right arm was sure to bring him. She replied very humbly that her name was Tolosa and that she was the daughter of a shoemaker, a native of Toledo who lived in the stalls of Sancho Bienaya.[9] To this the knight replied that she would do him a very great favor if

9. An old square in Toledo.

from then on she would call herself Doña Tolosa, and she promised to do so. The other girl then helped him on with his spurs, and practically the same conversation was repeated. When asked her name, she stated that it was La Molinera and added that she was the daughter of a respectable miller of Antequera. Don Quixote likewise requested her to assume the "don" and become Doña Molinera and offered to render her further services and favors.

These unheard-of ceremonies having been dispatched in great haste, Don Quixote could scarcely wait to be astride his horse and sally forth on his quest for adventures. Saddling and mounting Rocinante, he embraced his host, thanking him for the favor of having dubbed him a knight and saying such strange things that it would be quite impossible to record them here. The innkeeper, who was only too glad to be rid of him, answered with a speech that was no less flowery, though somewhat shorter, and he did not so much as ask him for the price of a lodging, so glad was he to see him go.

CHAPTER IV

Of what happened to our knight when he sallied forth from the inn.

Day was dawning when Don Quixote left the inn, so well satisfied with himself, so gay, so exhilarated, that the very girths of his steed all but burst with joy. But remembering the advice which his host had given him concerning the stock of necessary provisions that he should carry with him, especially money and shirts, he decided to turn back home and supply himself with whatever he needed, and with a squire as well; he had in mind a farmer who was a neighbor of his, a poor man and the father of a family but very well suited to fulfill the duties of squire to a man of arms. With this thought in mind he guided Rocinante toward the village once more, and that animal, realizing that he was homeward bound, began stepping out at so lively a gait that it seemed as if his feet barely touched the ground.

The knight had not gone far when from a hedge on his right hand he heard the sound of faint moans as of someone in distress.

"Thanks be to Heaven," he at once exclaimed, "for the favor it has shown me by providing me so soon with an opportunity to fulfill the obligations that I owe to my profession, a chance to pluck the fruit of my worthy desires. Those, undoubtedly, are the cries of someone in distress, who stands in need of my favor and assistance."

Turning Rocinante's head, he rode back to the place from which the cries appeared to be coming. Entering the wood, he had gone but a few paces when he saw a mare attached to an oak, while bound to another tree was a lad of fifteen or thereabouts, naked from the waist up. It was he who was uttering the cries, and not without reason, for there in front of him was a lusty farmer with a girdle who was giving him many lashes, each one accompanied by a reproof and a command, "Hold your tongue and keep your eyes open"; and the lad was saying, "I won't do it again, sir; by God's Passion, I won't do it again. I promise you that after this I'll take better care of the flock."

When he saw what was going on, Don Quixote was very angry. "Discourteous knight," he said, "it ill becomes you to strike one who is powerless to defend himself. Mount your steed and take your lance in hand"—for there was a lance leaning against the oak to which the mare was tied—"and I will show you what a coward you are."

The farmer, seeing before him this figure all clad in armor and brandishing a lance, decided that he was as good as done for. "Sir Knight," he said, speaking very mildly, "this lad that I am punishing here is my servant; he tends a flock of sheep which I have in these parts and he is so careless that every day one of them shows up missing. And when I punish him for his carelessness or his roguery, he says it is just because I am a miser and do not want to pay him the wages that I owe him, but I swear to God and upon my soul that he lies."

"It is you who lie, base lout," said Don Quixote, "and in my presence; and by the sun that gives us light, I am minded to run you through with this lance. Pay him and say no more about it, or else, by the God who rules us, I will make an end of you and annihilate you here and now. Release him at once."

The farmer hung his head and without a word untied his servant. Don Quixote then asked the boy how much his master owed him. For nine months' work, the lad told him, at seven reales the month. The knight did a little reckoning and found that this came to sixty-three reales; whereupon he ordered the farmer to pay over the money immediately, as he valued his life. The cowardly bumpkin replied that, facing death as he was and by the oath that he had sworn—he had not sworn any oath as yet—it did not amount to as much as that; for there were three pairs of shoes which he had given the lad that were to be deducted and taken into account, and a real for two blood-lettings when his servant was ill.

"That," said Don Quixote, "is all very well; but let the shoes and the blood-lettings go for the undeserved lashes which you have given him; if he has worn out the leather of the shoes that you paid for, you have taken the hide off his body, and if the barber let a little blood for him when he was sick,[1] you have done the same when he was well; and so far as that goes, he owes you nothing."

"But the trouble is, Sir Knight, that I have no money with me. Come along home with me, Andrés, and I will pay you real for real."

"I go home with him!" cried the lad. "Never in the world! No, sir, I would not even think of it; for once he has me alone he'll flay me like a St. Bartholomew."

"He will do nothing of the sort," said Don Quixote. "It is sufficient for me to command, and he out of respect will obey. Since he has sworn to me by the order of knighthood which he has received, I shall let him go free and I will guarantee that you will be paid."

"But look, your Grace," the lad remonstrated, "my master is no knight; he has never received any order of knighthood whatsoever. He is Juan Haldudo, a rich man and a resident of Quintanar."

"That makes little difference," declared Don Quixote, "for there may well be knights among the Haldudos, all the more so in view of the fact that every man is the son of his works."

"That is true enough," said Andrés, "but this master of mine—of what works is he the son, seeing that he refuses me the pay for my sweat and labor?"

"I do not refuse you, brother Andrés," said the farmer. "Do me the favor of coming with me, and I swear to you by all the orders of knighthood that there are in this world to pay you, as I have said, real for real, and perfumed at that."

---

1. Barbers were also surgeons.

"You can dispense with the perfume," said Don Quixote; "just give him the reales and I shall be satisfied. And see to it that you keep your oath, or by the one that I myself have sworn I shall return to seek you out and chastise you, and I shall find you though you be as well hidden as a lizard. In case you would like to know who it is that is giving you this command in order that you may feel the more obliged to comply with it, I may tell you that I am the valorous Don Quixote de la Mancha, righter of wrongs and injustices; and so, God be with you, and do not fail to do as you have promised, under that penalty that I have pronounced."

As he said this, he put spurs to Rocinante and was off. The farmer watched him go, and when he saw that Don Quixote was out of the wood and out of sight, he turned to his servant, Andrés.

"Come here, my son," he said. "I want to pay you what I owe you as that righter of wrongs has commanded me."

"Take my word for it," replied Andrés, "your Grace would do well to observe the command of that good knight—may he live a thousand years; for as he is valorous and a righteous judge, if you don't pay me then, by Roque,[2] he will come back and do just what he said!"

"And I will give you my word as well," said the farmer; "but seeing that I am so fond of you, I wish to increase the debt, that I may owe you all the more." And with this he seized the lad's arm and bound him to the tree again and flogged him within an inch of his life. "There, Master Andrés, you may call on that righter of wrongs if you like and you will see whether or not he rights this one. I do not think I have quite finished with you yet, for I have a good mind to flay you alive as you feared."

Finally, however, he unbound him and told him he might go look for that judge of his to carry out the sentence that had been pronounced. Andrés left, rather down in the mouth, swearing that he would indeed go look for the brave Don Quixote de la Mancha; he would relate to him everything that had happened, point by point, and the farmer would have to pay for it seven times over. But for all that, he went away weeping, and his master stood laughing at him.

Such was the manner in which the valorous knight righted this particular wrong. Don Quixote was quite content with the way everything had turned out; it seemed to him that he had made a very fortunate and noble beginning with his deeds of chivalry, and he was very well satisfied with himself as he jogged along in the direction of his native village, talking to himself in a low voice all the while.

"Well may'st thou call thyself fortunate today, above all other women on earth, O fairest of the fair, Dulcinea del Toboso! Seeing that it has fallen to thy lot to hold subject and submissive to thine every wish and pleasure so valiant and renowned a knight as Don Quixote de la Mancha is and shall be, who, as everyone knows, yesterday received the order of knighthood and this day has righted the greatest wrong and grievance that injustice ever conceived or cruelty ever perpetrated, by snatching the lash from the hand of the merciless foeman who was so unreasonably flogging that tender child."

At this point he came to a road that forked off in four directions, and at once he thought of those crossroads where knights-errant would pause to consider which path they should take. By way of imitating them, he halted there for a while; and when he had given the subject much thought, he slackened Rocinante's rein and

2. The origin of this oath is unknown.

let the hack follow its inclination. The animal's first impulse was to make straight for its own stable. After they had gone a couple of miles or so Don Quixote caught sight of what appeared to be a great throng of people, who, as was afterward learned, were certain merchants of Toledo on their way to purchase silk at Murcia. There were six of them altogether with their sunshades, accompanied by four attendants on horseback and three mule drivers on foot.

No sooner had he sighted them than Don Quixote imagined that he was on the brink of some fresh adventure. He was eager to imitate those passages at arms of which he had read in his books, and here, so it seemed to him, was one made to order. And so, with bold and knightly bearing, he settled himself firmly in the stirrups, couched his lance, covered himself with his shield, and took up a position in the middle of the road, where he paused to wait for those other knights-errant (for such he took them to be) to come up to him. When they were near enough to see and hear plainly, Don Quixote raised his voice and made a haughty gesture.

"Let everyone," he cried, "stand where he is, unless everyone will confess that there is not in all the world a more beauteous damsel than the Empress of La Mancha, the peerless Dulcinea del Toboso."

Upon hearing these words and beholding the weird figure who uttered them, the merchants stopped short. From the knight's appearance and his speech they knew at once that they had to deal with a madman; but they were curious to know what was meant by that confession that was demanded of them, and one of their number who was somewhat of a jester and a very clever fellow raised his voice.

"Sir Knight," he said, "we do not know who this beauteous lady is of whom you speak. Show her to us, and if she is as beautiful as you say, then we will right willingly and without any compulsion confess the truth as you have asked of us."

"If I were to show her to you," replied Don Quixote, "what merit would there be in your confessing a truth so self-evident? The important thing is for you, without seeing her, to believe, confess, affirm, swear, and defend that truth. Otherwise, monstrous and arrogant creatures that you are, you shall do battle with me. Come on, then, one by one, as the order of knighthood prescribes; or all of you together, if you will have it so, as is the sorry custom with those of your breed. Come on, and I will await you here, for I am confident that my cause is just."

"Sir Knight," responded the merchant, "I beg your Grace, in the name of all the princes here present, in order that we may not have upon our consciences the burden of confessing a thing which we have never seen nor heard, and one, moreover, so prejudicial to the empresses and queens of Alcarria and Estremadura,[3] that your Grace will show us some portrait of this lady, even though it be no larger than a grain of wheat, for by the thread one comes to the ball of yarn; and with this we shall remain satisfied and assured, and your Grace will likewise be content and satisfied. The truth is, I believe that we are already so much of your way of thinking that though it should show her to be blind of one eye and distilling vermilion and brimstone from the other, nevertheless, to please your Grace, we would say in her behalf all that you desire."

"She distills nothing of the sort, infamous rabble!" shouted Don Quixote, for his wrath was kindling now. "I tell you, she does not distill what you say at all,

---

3. Ironic, because both were known as particularly backward regions.

but amber and civet[4] wrapped in cotton; and she is neither one-eyed nor hunch-backed but straighter than a spindle that comes from Guadarrama. You shall pay for the great blasphemy which you have uttered against such a beauty as is my lady!"

Saying this, he came on with lowered lance against the one who had spoken, charging with such wrath and fury that if fortune had not caused Rocinante to stumble and fall in mid-career, things would have gone badly with the merchant and he would have paid for his insolent gibe. As it was, Don Quixote went rolling over the plain for some little distance, and when he tried to get to his feet, found that he was unable to do so, being too encumbered with his lance, shield, spurs, helmet, and the weight of that ancient suit of armor.

"Do not flee, cowardly ones," he cried even as he struggled to rise. "Stay, cravens, for it is not my fault but that of my steed that I am stretched out here."

One of the muleteers, who must have been an ill-natured lad, upon hearing the poor fallen knight speak so arrogantly, could not refrain from giving him an answer in the ribs. Going up to him, he took the knight's lance and broke it into bits, and then with a companion proceeded to belabor him so mercilessly that in spite of his armor they milled him like a hopper[5] of wheat. The merchants called to them not to lay on so hard, saying that was enough and they should desist, but the mule driver by this time had warmed up to the sport and would not stop until he had vented his wrath, and, snatching up the broken pieces of the lance, he began hurling them at the wretched victim as he lay there on the ground. And through all this tempest of sticks that rained upon him Don Quixote never once closed his mouth nor ceased threatening Heaven and earth and these ruffians, for such he took them to be, who were thus mishandling him.

Finally the lad grew tired, and the merchants went their way with a good story to tell about the poor fellow who had had such a cudgeling. Finding himself alone, the knight endeavored to see if he could rise; but if this was a feat that he could not accomplish when he was sound and whole, how was he to achieve it when he had been thrashed and pounded to a pulp? Yet nonetheless he considered himself fortunate; for as he saw it, misfortunes such as this were common to knights-errant, and he put all the blame upon his horse; and if he was unable to rise, that was because his body was so bruised and battered all over.

CHAPTER V

In which is continued the narrative of the misfortune that befell our knight.

Seeing, then, that he was indeed unable to stir, he decided to fall back upon a favorite remedy of his, which was to think of some passage or other in his books; and as it happened, the one that he in his madness now recalled was the story of Baldwin and the Marquis of Mantua, when Carloto left the former wounded upon the mountainside,[6] a tale that is known to children, not unknown to young men, celebrated and believed in by the old, and, for all of that, not any truer than the miracles of Mohammed. Moreover, it impressed

---

4. A musky substance used in perfume, imported from Africa in cotton packings.
5. Funnel-shaped container for grain.

6. The allusion is to an old ballad about Charlemagne's son Charlot (Carloto) wounding Baldwin, nephew of the Marquis of Mantua.

him as being especially suited to the straits in which he found himself; and, accordingly, with a great show of feeling, he began rolling and tossing on the ground as he feebly gasped out the lines which the wounded knight of the wood is supposed to have uttered:

> "Where art thou, lady mine,
> That thou dost not grieve for my woe?
> Either thou art disloyal,
> Or my grief thou dost not know."

He went on reciting the old ballad until he came to the following verses:

> "O noble Marquis of Mantua,
> My uncle and liege lord true!"

He had reached this point when down the road came a farmer of the same village, a neighbor of his, who had been to the mill with a load of wheat. Seeing a man lying there stretched out like that, he went up to him and inquired who he was and what was the trouble that caused him to utter such mournful complaints. Thinking that this must undoubtedly be his uncle, the Marquis of Mantua, Don Quixote did not answer but went on with his recitation of the ballad, giving an account of the Marquis' misfortunes and the amours of his wife and the emperor's son, exactly as the ballad has it.

The farmer was astounded at hearing all these absurdities, and after removing the knight's visor which had been battered to pieces by the blows it had received, the good man bathed the victim's face, only to discover, once the dust was off, that he knew him very well.

"Señor Quijana," he said (for such must have been Don Quixote's real name when he was in his right senses and before he had given up the life of a quiet country gentleman to become a knight-errant), "who is responsible for your Grace's being in such a plight as this?"

But the knight merely went on with his ballad in response to all the questions asked of him. Perceiving that it was impossible to obtain any information from him, the farmer as best he could relieved him of his breastplate and backpiece to see if he had any wounds, but there was no blood and no mark of any sort. He then tried to lift him from the ground, and with a great deal of effort finally managed to get him astride the ass, which appeared to be the easier mount for him. Gathering up the armor, including even the splinters from the lance, he made a bundle and tied it on Rocinante's back, and, taking the horse by the reins and the ass by the halter, he started out for the village. He was worried in his mind at hearing all the foolish things that Don Quixote said, and that individual himself was far from being at ease. Unable by reason of his bruises and his soreness to sit upright on the donkey, our knight-errant kept sighing to Heaven, which led the farmer to ask him once more what it was that ailed him.

It must have been the devil himself who caused him to remember those tales that seemed to fit his own case; for at this point he forgot all about Baldwin and recalled Abindarráez, and how the governor of Antequera, Rodrigo de Narváez, had taken him prisoner and carried him off captive to his castle. Accordingly, when the countryman turned to inquire how he was and what was troubling him, Don Quixote replied with the very same words and phrases that the captive Abindarráez used in answering Rodrigo, just as he had read in the story *Diana* of Jorge de Montemayor,[7] where it is all written down, applying them very aptly to the present circumstances as the farmer went along cursing his luck for having to listen to such a lot of nonsense. Realizing that his neighbor was quite mad, he made haste to reach the village that he might not have to be annoyed any longer by Don Quixote's tiresome harangue.

"Señor Don Rodrigo de Narváez," the knight was saying, "I may inform your Grace that this beautiful Jarifa of whom I speak is not the lovely Dulcinea del Toboso, in whose behalf I have done, am doing, and shall do the most famous deeds of chivalry that ever have been or will be seen in all the world."

"But, sir," replied the farmer, "sinner that I am, cannot your Grace see that I am not Don Rodrigo de Narváez nor the Marquis of Mantua, but Pedro Alonso, your neighbor? And your Grace is neither Baldwin nor Abindarráez but a respectable gentleman by the name of Señor Quijana."

"I know who I am," said Don Quixote, "and who I may be, if I choose: not only those I have mentioned but all the Twelve Peers of France and the Nine Worthies[8] as well; for the exploits of all of them together, or separately, cannot compare with mine."

With such talk as this they reached their destination just as night was falling; but the farmer decided to wait until it was a little darker in order that the badly battered gentleman might not be seen arriving in such a condition and mounted on an ass. When he thought the proper time had come, they entered the village and proceeded to Don Quixote's house, where they found everything in confusion. The curate and the barber were there, for they were great friends of the knight, and the housekeeper was speaking to them.

"Señor Licentiate Pero Pérez," she was saying, for that was the manner in which she addressed the curate, "what does your Grace think could have happened to my master? Three days now, and not a word of him, nor the hack, nor the buckler, nor the lance, nor the suit of armor. Ah, poor me! I am as certain as I am that I was born to die that it is those cursed books of chivalry he is always reading that have turned his head; for now that I recall, I have often heard him muttering to himself that he must become a knight-errant and go through the world in search of adventures. May such books as those be consigned to Satan and Barabbas,[9] for they have sent to perdition the finest mind in all La Mancha."

The niece was of the same opinion. "I may tell you, Señor Master Nicholas," she said, for that was the barber's name, "that many times my uncle would sit reading those impious tales of misadventure for two whole days and nights at a stretch; and when he was through, he would toss the book aside, lay his hand on his sword, and begin slashing at the walls. When he was completely exhausted, he would tell us that he had just killed four giants as big as castle towers, while the sweat that poured off him was blood from the wounds that he

---

7. The reference is to *The Abencerraje*, the tale of the love of Abindarráez, a captive Moor, for the beautiful Jarifa.
8. In a tradition originating in France, the Nine Worthies consisted of three biblical, three classical, and three Christian figures (David, Hector, Alexander, Charlemagne, and so on). In French medieval epics, the Twelve

Peers (Roland, Oliver, and so on) were warriors all equal in rank, forming a kind of guard of honor around Charlemagne.
9. The thief whose release, rather than that of Jesus, the crowd requested when Pilate, conforming to Passover custom, was ready to have one prisoner set free.

had received in battle. He would then drink a big jug of cold water, after which he would be very calm and peaceful, saying that the water was the most precious liquid which the wise Esquife, a great magician and his friend, had brought to him. But I blame myself for everything. I should have advised your Worships of my uncle's nonsensical actions so that you could have done something about it by burning those damnable books of his before things came to such a pass; for he has many that ought to be burned as if they were heretics."

"I agree with you," said the curate, "and before tomorrow's sun has set there shall be a public *auto de fe*,[1] and those works shall be condemned to the flames that they may not lead some other who reads them to follow the example of my good friend."

Don Quixote and the farmer overheard all this, and it was then that the latter came to understand the nature of his neighbor's affliction.

"Open the door, your Worships," the good man cried. "Open for Sir Baldwin and the Marquis of Mantua, who comes badly wounded, and for Señor Abindarráez the Moor whom the valiant Rodrigo de Narváez, governor of Antequera, brings captive."

At the sound of his voice they all ran out, recognizing at once friend, master, and uncle, who as yet was unable to get down off the donkey's back. They all ran up to embrace him.

"Wait, all of you," said Don Quixote, "for I am sorely wounded through fault of my steed. Bear me to my couch and summon, if it be possible, the wise Urganda to treat and care for my wounds."

"There!" exclaimed the housekeeper. "Plague take it! Did not my heart tell me right as to which foot my master limped on? To bed with your Grace at once, and we will take care of you without sending for that Urganda of yours. A curse, I say, and a hundred other curses, on those books of chivalry that have brought your Grace to this."

And so they carried him off to bed, but when they went to look for his wounds, they found none at all. He told them it was all the result of a great fall he had taken with Rocinante, his horse, while engaged in combating ten giants, the hugest and most insolent that were ever heard of in all the world.

"Tut, tut," said the curate. "So there are giants in the dance now, are there? Then, by the sign of the cross, I'll have them burned before nightfall tomorrow."

They had a thousand questions to put to Don Quixote, but his only answer was that they should give him something to eat and let him sleep, for that was the most important thing of all; so they humored him in this. The curate then interrogated the farmer at great length concerning the conversation he had had with his neighbor. The peasant told him everything, all the absurd things their friend had said when he found him lying there and afterward on the way home, all of which made the licentiate more anxious than ever to do what he did the following day,[2] when he summoned Master Nicholas and went with him to Don Quixote's house.

---

1. Literally, "act of faith" (Portuguese); the act of publicly burning a heretic at the stake by the Spanish Inquisition.

2. He and the barber burned most of Don Quixote's library.

[Fighting the Windmills and a Choleric Biscayan]

From CHAPTER VII

Of the second sally of our good knight,
Don Quixote de la Mancha.

* * *

After that he remained at home very tranquilly for a couple of weeks, without giving sign of any desire to repeat his former madness. During that time he had the most pleasant conversations with his two old friends, the curate and the barber, on the point he had raised to the effect that what the world needed most was knights-errant and a revival of chivalry. The curate would occasionally contradict him and again would give in, for it was only by means of this artifice that he could carry on a conversation with him at all.

In the meanwhile Don Quixote was bringing his powers of persuasion to bear upon a farmer who lived near by, a good man—if this title may be applied to one who is poor—but with very few wits in his head. The short of it is, by pleas and promises, he got the hapless rustic to agree to ride forth with him and serve him as his squire. Among other things, Don Quixote told him that he ought to be more than willing to go, because no telling what adventure might occur which would win them an island, and then he (the farmer) would be left to be the governor of it. As a result of these and other similar assurances, Sancho Panza forsook his wife and children and consented to take upon himself the duties of squire to his neighbor.

Next, Don Quixote set out to raise some money, and by selling this thing and pawning that and getting the worst of the bargain always, he finally scraped together a reasonable amount. He also asked a friend of his for the loan of a buckler and patched up his broken helmet as well as he could. He advised his squire, Sancho, of the day and hour when they were to take the road and told him to see to laying in a supply of those things that were most necessary, and, above all, not to forget the saddlebags. Sancho replied that he would see to all this and added that he was also thinking of taking along with him a very good ass that he had, as he was not much used to going on foot.

With regard to the ass, Don Quixote had to do a little thinking, trying to recall if any knight-errant had ever had a squire thus asininely mounted. He could not think of any, but nevertheless he decided to take Sancho with the intention of providing him with a nobler steed as soon as occasion offered; he had but to appropriate the horse of the first discourteous knight he met. Having furnished himself with shirts and all the other things that the innkeeper had recommended, he and Panza rode forth one night unseen by anyone and without taking leave of wife and children, housekeeper or niece. They went so far that by the time morning came they were safe from discovery had a hunt been started for them.

Mounted on his ass, Sancho Panza rode along like a patriarch, with saddlebags and flask, his mind set upon becoming governor of that island that his master had promised him. Don Quixote determined to take the same route and road over the Campo de Montiel that he had followed on his first journey; but he was not so uncomfortable this time, for it was early morning and the sun's rays fell upon them slantingly and accordingly did not tire them too much.

"Look, Sir Knight-errant," said Sancho, "your Grace should not forget that island you promised me; for no matter how big it is, I'll be able to govern it right enough."

"I would have you know, friend Sancho Panza," replied Don Quixote, "that among the knights-errant of old it was a very common custom to make their squires governors of the islands or the kingdoms that they won, and I am resolved that in my case so pleasing a usage shall not fall into desuetude. I even mean to go them one better; for they very often, perhaps most of the time, waited until their squires were old men who had had their fill of serving their masters during bad days and worse nights, whereupon they would give them the tide of count, or marquis at most, of some valley or province more or less. But if you live and I live, it well may be that within a week I shall win some kingdom with others dependent upon it, and it will be the easiest thing in the world to crown you king of one of them. You need not marvel at this, for all sorts of unforeseen things happen to knights like me, and I may readily be able to give you even more than I have promised."

"In that case," said Sancho Panza, "if by one of those miracles of which your Grace was speaking I should become king, I would certainly send for Juana Gutiérrez, my old lady, to come and be my queen, and the young ones could be infantes."

"There is no doubt about it," Don Quixote assured him.

"Well, I doubt it," said Sancho, "for I think that even if God were to rain kingdoms upon the earth, no crown would sit well on the head of Mari Gutiérrez,[3] for I am telling you, sir, as a queen she is not worth two maravedis. She would do better as a countess, God help her."

"Leave everything to God, Sancho," said Don Quixote, "and he will give you whatever is most fitting; but I trust you will not be so pusillanimous as to be content with anything less than the title of viceroy."

"That I will not," said Sancho Panza, "especially seeing that I have in your Grace so illustrious a master who can give me all that is suitable to me and all that I can manage."

CHAPTER VIII

Of the good fortune which the valorous Don Quixote had in the terrifying and never-before-imagined adventure of the windmills, along with other events that deserve to be suitably recorded.

At this point they caught sight of thirty or forty windmills which were standing on the plain there, and no sooner had Don Quixote laid eyes upon them than he turned to his squire and said, "Fortune is guiding our affairs better than we could have wished; for you see there before you, friend Sancho Panza, some thirty or more lawless giants with whom I mean to do battle. I shall deprive them of their lives, and with the spoils from this encounter we shall begin to enrich ourselves; for this is righteous warfare, and it is a great service to God to remove so accursed a breed from the face of the earth."

"What giants?" said Sancho Panza.

"Those that you see there," replied his master, "those with the long arms some of which are as much as two leagues in length."

---

3. Sancho's wife, Juana Gutiérrez.

"But look, your Grace, those are not giants but windmills, and what appear to be arms are their wings which, when whirled in the breeze, cause the millstone to go."

"It is plain to be seen," said Don Quixote, "that you have had little experience in this matter of adventures. If you are afraid, go off to one side and say your prayers while I am engaging them in fierce, unequal combat."

Saying this, he gave spurs to his steed Rocinante, without paying any heed to Sancho's warning that these were truly windmills and not giants that he was riding forth to attack. Nor even when he was close upon them did he perceive what they really were, but shouted at the top of his lungs, "Do not seek to flee, cowards and vile creatures that you are, for it is but a single knight with whom you have to deal!"

At that moment a little wind came up and the big wings began turning.

"Though you flourish as many arms as did the giant Briareus,"[4] said Don Quixote when he perceived this, "you still shall have to answer to me."

He thereupon commended himself with all his heart to his lady Dulcinea, beseeching her to succor him in this peril; and, being well covered with his shield and with his lance at rest, he bore down upon them at a full gallop and fell upon the first mill that stood in his way, giving a thrust at the wing, which was whirling at such a speed that his lance was broken into bits and both horse and horseman went rolling over the plain, very much battered indeed. Sancho upon his donkey came hurrying to his master's assistance as fast as he could, but when he reached the spot, the knight was unable to move, so great was the shock with which he and Rocinante had hit the ground.

"God help us!" exclaimed Sancho, "did I not tell your Grace to look well, that those were nothing but windmills, a fact which no one could fail to see unless he had other mills of the same sort in his head?"

"Be quiet, friend Sancho," said Don Quixote. "Such are the fortunes of war, which more than any other are subject to constant change. What is more, when I come to think of it, I am sure that this must be the work of that magician Frestón, the one who robbed me of my study and my books,[5] and who has thus changed the giants into windmills in order to deprive me of the glory of overcoming them, so great is the enmity that he bears me; but in the end his evil arts shall not prevail against this trusty sword of mine."

"May God's will be done," was Sancho Panza's response. And with the aid of his squire the knight was once more mounted on Rocinante, who stood there with one shoulder half out of joint. And so, speaking of the adventure that had just befallen them, they continued along the Puerto Lápice highway; for there, Don Quixote said, they could not fail to find many and varied adventures, this being a much traveled thoroughfare. The only thing was, the knight was exceedingly downcast over the loss of his lance.

"I remember," he said to his squire, "having read of a Spanish knight by the name of Diego Pérez de Vargas, who, having broken his sword in battle, tore from an oak a heavy bough or branch and with it did such feats of valor that day, and pounded so many Moors, that he came to be known as Machuca,[6] and he and his descendants from that day forth have been called Vargas y Machuca.

---

4. In Greek mythology, a giant with a hundred arms.
5. Don Quixote had promptly attributed the ruin of his library to magical intervention (see p. 1564, n. 2).
6. "The Crusher," the hero of a folk ballad.

I tell you this because I too intend to provide myself with just such a bough as the one he wielded, and with it I propose to do such exploits that you shall deem yourself fortunate to have been found worthy to come with me and behold and witness things that are almost beyond belief."

"God's will be done," said Sancho. "I believe everything that your Grace says; but straighten yourself up in the saddle a little, for you seem to be slipping down on one side, owing, no doubt, to the shaking-up that you received in your fall."

"Ah, that is the truth," replied Don Quixote, "and if I do not speak of my sufferings, it is for the reason that it is not permitted knights-errant to complain of any wound whatsoever, even though their bowels may be dropping out."

"If that is the way it is," said Sancho, "I have nothing more to say; but, God knows, it would suit me better if your Grace did complain when something hurts him. I can assure you that I mean to do so, over the least little thing that ails me—that is, unless the same rule applies to squires as well."

Don Quixote laughed long and heartily over Sancho's simplicity, telling him that he might complain as much as he liked and where and when he liked, whether he had good cause or not; for he had read nothing to the contrary in the ordinances of chivalry. Sancho then called his master's attention to the fact that it was time to eat. The knight replied that he himself had no need of food at the moment, but his squire might eat whenever he chose. Having been granted this permission, Sancho seated himself as best he could upon his beast, and, taking out from his saddlebags the provisions that he had stored there, he rode along leisurely behind his master, munching his victuals and taking a good, hearty swig now and then at the leather flask in a manner that might well have caused the biggest-bellied tavernkeeper of Málaga to envy him. Between draughts he gave not so much as a thought to any promise that his master might have made him, nor did he look upon it as any hardship, but rather as good sport, to go in quest of adventures however hazardous they might be.

The short of the matter is, they spent the night under some trees, from one of which Don Quixote tore off a withered bough to serve him as a lance, placing it in the lance head from which he had removed the broken one. He did not sleep all night long for thinking of his lady Dulcinea; for this was in accordance with what he had read in his books, of men of arms in the forest or desert places who kept a wakeful vigil, sustained by the memory of their ladies fair. Not so with Sancho, whose stomach was full, and not with chicory water. He fell into a dreamless slumber, and had not his master called him, he would not have been awakened either by the rays of the sun in his face or by the many birds who greeted the coming of the new day with their merry song.

Upon arising, he had another go at the flask, finding it somewhat more flaccid than it had been the night before, a circumstance which grieved his heart, for he could not see that they were on the way to remedying the deficiency within any very short space of time. Don Quixote did not wish any breakfast; for, as has been said, he was in the habit of nourishing himself on savorous memories. They then set out once more along the road to Puerto Lápice, and around three in the afternoon they came in sight of the pass that bears that name.

"There," said Don Quixote as his eyes fell upon it, "we may plunge our arms up to the elbow in what are known as adventures. But I must warn you that even though you see me in the greatest peril in the world, you are not to lay hand upon your sword to defend me, unless it be that those who attack me are rabble and men of low degree, in which case you may very well come to my aid; but if they be gentlemen, it is in no wise permitted by the laws of chivalry that you should assist me until you yourself shall have been dubbed a knight."

"Most certainly, sir," replied Sancho, "your Grace shall be very well obeyed in this; all the more so for the reason that I myself am of a peaceful disposition and not fond of meddling in the quarrels and feuds of others. However, when it comes to protecting my own person, I shall not take account of those laws of which you speak, seeing that all laws, human and divine, permit each one to defend himself whenever he is attacked."

"I am willing to grant you that," assented Don Quixote, "but in this matter of defending me against gentlemen you must restrain your natural impulses."

"I promise you I shall do so," said Sancho. "I will observe this precept as I would the Sabbath day."

As they were conversing in this manner, there appeared in the road in front of them two friars of the Order of St. Benedict, mounted upon dromedaries— for the she-mules they rode were certainly no smaller than that. The friars wore travelers' spectacles and carried sunshades, and behind them came a coach accompanied by four or five men on horseback and a couple of mule-teers on foot. In the coach, as was afterwards learned, was a lady of Biscay,[7] on her way to Seville to bid farewell to her husband, who had been appointed to some high post in the Indies. The religious were not of her company although they were going by the same road.

The instant Don Quixote laid eyes upon them he turned to his squire. "Either I am mistaken or this is going to be the most famous adventure that ever was seen; for those black-clad figures that you behold must be, and without any doubt are, certain enchanters who are bearing with them a captive princess in that coach, and I must do all I can to right this wrong."

"It will be worse than the windmills," declared Sancho. "Look you, sir, those are Benedictine friars and the coach must be that of some travelers. Mark well what I say and what you do, lest the devil lead you astray."

"I have already told you, Sancho," replied Don Quixote, "that you know little where the subject of adventures is concerned. What I am saying to you is the truth, as you shall now see."

With this, he rode forward and took up a position in the middle of the road along which the friars were coming, and as soon as they appeared to be within earshot he cried out to them in a loud voice, "O devilish and monstrous beings, set free at once the highborn princesses whom you bear captive in that coach, or else prepare at once to meet your death as the just punishment of your evil deeds."

The friars drew rein and sat there in astonishment, marveling as much at Don Quixote's appearance as at the words he spoke. "Sir Knight," they answered him, "we are neither devilish nor monstrous but religious of the Order of St. Benedict who are merely going our way. We know nothing of those who are in that coach, nor of any captive princesses either."

"Soft words," said Don Quixote, "have no effect on me. I know you for what you are, lying rabble!" And without waiting for any further parley he gave spur to Rocinante and, with lowered lance, bore down upon the first friar with such

7. The Basque region in northern Spain and southwestern France.

fury and intrepidity that, had not the fellow tumbled from his mule of his own accord, he would have been hurled to the ground and either killed or badly wounded. The second religious, seeing how his companion had been treated, dug his legs into his she-mule's flanks and scurried away over the countryside faster than the wind.

Seeing the friar upon the ground, Sancho Panza slipped lightly from his mount and, falling upon him, began stripping him of his habit. The two mule drivers accompanying the religious thereupon came running up and asked Sancho why he was doing this. The latter replied that the friar's garments belonged to him as legitimate spoils of the battle that his master Don Quixote had just won. The muleteers, however, were lads with no sense of humor, nor did they know what all this talk of spoils and battles was about; but, perceiving that Don Quixote had ridden off to one side to converse with those inside the coach, they pounced upon Sancho, threw him to the ground, and proceeded to pull out the hair of his beard and kick him to a pulp, after which they went off and left him stretched out there, bereft at once of breath and sense.

Without losing any time, they then assisted the friar to remount. The good brother was trembling all over from fright, and there was not a speck of color in his face, but when he found himself in the saddle once more, he quickly spurred his beast to where his companion, at some little distance, sat watching and waiting to see what the result of the encounter would be. Having no curiosity as to the final outcome of the fray, the two of them now resumed their journey, making more signs of the cross than the devil would be able to carry upon his back.

Meanwhile Don Quixote, as we have said, was speaking to the lady in the coach.

"Your beauty, my lady, may now dispose of your person as best may please you, for the arrogance of your abductors lies upon the ground, overthrown by this good arm of mine; and in order that you may not pine to know the name of your liberator, I may inform you that I am Don Quixote de la Mancha, knight-errant and adventurer and captive of the peerless and beauteous Doña Dulcinea del Toboso. In payment of the favor which you have received from me, I ask nothing other than that you return to El Toboso and on my behalf pay your respects to this lady, telling her that it was I who set you free."

One of the squires accompanying those in the coach, a Biscayan, was listening to Don Quixote's words, and when he saw that the knight did not propose to let the coach proceed upon its way but was bent upon having it turn back to El Toboso, he promptly went up to him, seized his lance, and said to him in bad Castilian and worse Biscayan,[8] "Go, *caballero*, and bad luck go with you; for by the God that created me, if you do not let this coach pass, me kill you or me no Biscayan."

Don Quixote heard him attentively enough and answered him very mildly, "If you were a *caballero*,[9] which you are not, I should already have chastised you, wretched creature, for your foolhardiness and your impudence."

"Me no *caballero*?" cried the Biscayan. "Me swear to God, you lie like a Christian. If you will but lay aside your lance and unsheath your sword, you will soon

---

8. Castilian is the language of Castile; Biscayan is the Basque language.   9. Knight, gentleman (Spanish).

see that you are carrying water to the cat![1] Biscayan on land, gentleman at sea, but a gentleman in spite of the devil, and you lie if you say otherwise."

"'"You shall see as to that presently," said Agrajes,'"[2] Don Quixote quoted. He cast his lance to the earth, drew his sword, and, taking his buckler on his arm, attacked the Biscayan with intent to slay him. The latter, when he saw his adversary approaching, would have liked to dismount from his mule, for she was one of the worthless sort that are let for hire and he had no confidence in her; but there was no time for this, and so he had no choice but to draw his own sword in turn and make the best of it. However, he was near enough to the coach to be able to snatch a cushion from it to serve him as a shield; and then they fell upon each other as though they were mortal enemies. The rest of those present sought to make peace between them but did not succeed, for the Biscayan with his disjointed phrases kept muttering that if they did not let him finish the battle then he himself would have to kill his mistress and anyone else who tried to stop him.

The lady inside the carriage, amazed by it all and trembling at what she saw, directed her coachman to drive on a little way; and there from a distance she watched the deadly combat, in the course of which the Biscayan came down with a great blow on Don Quixote's shoulder, over the top of the latter's shield, and had not the knight been clad in armor, it would have split him to the waist.

Feeling the weight of this blow, Don Quixote cried out, "O lady of my soul, Dulcinea, flower of beauty, succor this your champion who out of gratitude for your many favors finds himself in so perilous a plight!" To utter these words, lay hold of his sword, cover himself with his buckler, and attack the Biscayan was but the work of a moment; for he was now resolved to risk everything upon a single stroke.

As he saw Don Quixote approaching with so dauntless a bearing, the Biscayan was well aware of his adversary's courage and forthwith determined to imitate the example thus set him. He kept himself protected with his cushion, but he was unable to get his she-mule to budge to one side or the other, for the beast, out of sheer exhaustion and being, moreover, unused to such childish play, was incapable of taking a single step. And so, then, as has been stated, Don Quixote was approaching the wary Biscayan, his sword raised on high and with the firm resolve of cleaving his enemy in two; and the Biscayan was awaiting the knight in the same posture, cushion in front of him and with uplifted sword. All the bystanders were trembling with suspense at what would happen as a result of the terrible blows that were threatened, and the lady in the coach and her maids were making a thousand vows and offerings to all the images and shrines in Spain, praying that God would save them all and the lady's squire from this great peril that confronted them.

But the unfortunate part of the matter is that at this very point the author of the history breaks off and leaves the battle pending, excusing himself upon the ground that he has been unable to find anything else in writing concerning the exploits of Don Quixote beyond those already set forth.[3] It is true, on the other hand, that the second author of this work could not bring himself to believe

---

1. An inversion of a proverbial phrase: "carrying the cat to the water."
2. A violent character in the romance *Amadís de Gaula*. His challenging phrase is the conventional opener of a fight.

3. "The author" is Cervantes himself, adopting here—with tongue in cheek—a device used in the romances of chivalry to create suspense.

that so unusual a chronicle would have been consigned to oblivion, nor that the learned ones of La Mancha were possessed of so little curiosity as not to be able to discover in their archives or registry offices certain papers that have to do with this famous knight. Being convinced of this, he did not despair of coming upon the end of this pleasing story and Heaven favoring him, he did find it, as shall be related in the second part.

CHAPTER IX

In which is concluded and brought to an end the
stupendous battle between the gallant Biscayan and the
valiant Knight of La Mancha.

In the first part of this history we left the valorous Biscayan and the famous Don Quixote with swords unsheathed and raised aloft, about to let fall furious slashing blows which, had they been delivered fairly and squarely, would at the very least have split them in two and laid them wide open from top to bottom like a pomegranate; and it was at this doubtful point that the pleasing chronicle came to a halt and broke off, without the author's informing us as to where the rest of it might be found.

I was deeply grieved by such a circumstance, and the pleasure I had had in reading so slight a portion was turned into annoyance as I thought of how difficult it would be to come upon the greater part which it seemed to me must still be missing. It appeared impossible and contrary to all good precedent that so worthy a knight should not have had some scribe to take upon himself the task of writing an account of these unheard-of exploits; for that was something that had happened to none of the knights-errant who, as the saying has it, had gone forth in quest of adventures, seeing that each of them had one or two chroniclers, as if ready at hand, who not only had set down their deeds, but had depicted their most trivial thoughts and amiable weaknesses, however well concealed they might be. The good knight of La Mancha surely could not have been so unfortunate as to have lacked what Platir and others like him had in abundance. And so I could not bring myself to believe that this gallant history could have remained thus lopped off and mutilated, and I could not but lay the blame upon the malignity of time, that devourer and consumer of all things, which must either have consumed it or kept it hidden.

On the other hand, I reflected that inasmuch as among the knight's books had been found such modern works as *The Disenchantments of Jealousy* and *The Nymphs and Shepherds of Henares*, his story likewise must be modern, and that even though it might not have been written down, it must remain in the memory of the good folk of his village and the surrounding ones. This thought left me somewhat confused and more than ever desirous of knowing the real and true story, the whole story, of the life and wondrous deeds of our famous Spaniard, Don Quixote, light and mirror of the chivalry of La Mancha, the first in our age and in these calamitous times to devote himself to the hardships and exercises of knight-errantry and to go about righting wrongs, succoring widows, and protecting damsels—damsels such as those who, mounted upon their palfreys and with riding-whip in hand, in full possession of their virginity, were in the habit of going from mountain to mountain and from valley to valley; for unless there were some villain, some rustic with an ax and hood, or some monstrous giant to force them, there were in times past maiden ladies who at the end of eighty years, during all which time they had not slept for a single day beneath a roof, would go to their graves as virginal as when their mothers had borne them.

If I speak of these things, it is for the reason that in this and in all other respects our gallant Quixote is deserving of constant memory and praise, and even I am not to be denied my share of it for my diligence and the labor to which I put myself in searching out the conclusion of this agreeable narrative; although if heaven, luck, and circumstance had not aided me, the world would have had to do without the pleasure and the pastime which anyone may enjoy who will read this work attentively for an hour or two. The manner in which it came about was as follows:

I was standing one day in the Alcaná, or market place, of Toledo when a lad came up to sell some old notebooks and other papers to a silk weaver who was there. As I am extremely fond of reading anything, even though it be but the scraps of paper in the streets, I followed my natural inclination and took one of the books, whereupon I at once perceived that it was written in characters which I recognized as Arabic. I recognized them, but reading them was another thing; and so I began looking around to see if there was any Spanish-speaking Moor near by who would be able to read them for me. It was not very hard to find such an interpreter, nor would it have been even if the tongue in question had been an older and a better one.[4] To make a long story short, chance brought a fellow my way; and when I told him what it was I wished and placed the book in his hands, he opened it in the middle and began reading and at once fell to laughing. When I asked him what the cause of his laughter was, he replied that it was a note which had been written in the margin.

I besought him to tell me the content of the note, and he, laughing still, went on, "As I told you, it is something in the margin here: 'This Dulcinea del Toboso, so often referred to, is said to have been the best hand at salting pigs of any woman in all La Mancha.'"

No sooner had I heard the name Dulcinea del Toboso than I was astonished and held in suspense, for at once the thought occurred to me that those notebooks must contain the history of Don Quixote. With this in mind I urged him to read me the title, and he proceeded to do so, turning the Arabic into Castilian upon the spot: *History of Don Quixote de la Mancha, Written by Cid Hamete Benengeli,*[5] *Arabic Historian.* It was all I could do to conceal my satisfaction and, snatching them from the silk weaver, I bought from the lad all the papers and notebooks that he had for half a real; but if he had known or suspected how very much I wanted them, he might well have had more than six reales for them.

The Moor and I then betook ourselves to the cathedral cloister, where I requested him to translate for me into the Castilian tongue all the books that had to do with Don Quixote, adding nothing and subtracting nothing; and I offered him whatever payment he desired. He was content with two arrobas of raisins and two fanegas[6] of wheat and promised to translate them well and faithfully and

---

4. I.e., Hebrew.
5. Citing some ancient chronicle as the author's source and authority is very much in the tradition of the romances. "*Benengeli*": eggplant

(Arabic).
6. About fifty pounds. "Two arrobas": three bushels.

with all dispatch. However, in order to facilitate matters, and also because I did not wish to let such a find as this out of my hands, I took the fellow home with me, where in a little more than a month and a half he translated the whole of the work just as you will find it set down here.

In the first of the books there was a very lifelike picture of the battle between Don Quixote and the Biscayan, the two being in precisely the same posture as described in the history, their swords upraised, the one covered by his buckler, the other with his cushion. As for the Biscayan's mule, you could see at the distance of a crossbow shot that it was one for hire. Beneath the Biscayan there was a rubric which read: "Don Sancho de Azpeitia," which must undoubtedly have been his name; while beneath the feet of Rocinante was another inscription: "Don Quixote." Rocinante was marvelously portrayed: so long and lank, so lean and flabby, so extremely consumptive-looking that one could well understand the justness and propriety with which the name of "hack" had been bestowed upon him.

Alongside Rocinante stood Sancho Panza, holding the halter of his ass, and below was the legend: "Sancho Zancas." The picture showed him with a big belly, a short body, and long shanks, and that must have been where he got the names of Panza y Zancas[7] by which he is a number of times called in the course of the history. There are other small details that might be mentioned, but they are of little importance and have nothing to do with the truth of the story—and no story is bad so long as it is true.

If there is any objection to be raised against the veracity of the present one, it can be only that the author was an Arab, and that nation is known for its lying propensities; but even though they be our enemies, it may readily be understood that they would more likely have detracted from, rather than added to, the chronicle. So it seems to me, at any rate; for whenever he might and should deploy the resources of his pen in praise of so worthy a knight, the author appears to take pains to pass over the matter in silence; all of which in my opinion is ill done and ill conceived, for it should be the duty of historians to be exact, truthful, and dispassionate, and neither interest nor fear nor rancor nor affection should swerve them from the path of truth, whose mother is history, rival of time, depository of deeds, witness of the past, exemplar and adviser to the present, and the future's counselor. In this work, I am sure, will be found all that could be desired in the way of pleasant reading; and if it is lacking in any way, I maintain that this is the fault of that hound of an author rather than of the subject.

But to come to the point, the second part, according to the translation, began as follows:

As the two valorous and enraged combatants stood there, swords upraised and poised on high, it seemed from their bold mien as if they must surely be threatening heaven, earth, and hell itself. The first to let fall a blow was the choleric Biscayan, and he came down with such force and fury that, had not his sword been deflected in mid-air, that single stroke would have sufficed to put an end to this fearful combat and to all our knight's adventures at the same time; but fortune, which was reserving him for greater things, turned aside his adversary's blade in such a manner that, even though it fell upon his left shoulder, it did him no other damage than to strip him completely of his armor on that side,

7. Paunch and Shanks (Spanish).

carrying with it a good part of his helmet along with half an ear, the headpiece clattering to the ground with a dreadful din, leaving its wearer in a sorry state.

Heaven help me! Who could properly describe the rage that now entered the heart of our hero of La Mancha as he saw himself treated in this fashion? It may merely be said that he once more reared himself in the stirrups, laid hold of his sword with both hands, and dealt the Biscayan such a blow, over the cushion and upon the head, that, even so good a defense proving useless, it was as if a mountain had fallen upon his enemy. The latter now began bleeding through the mouth, nose, and ears; he seemed about to fall from his mule, and would have fallen, no doubt, if he had not grasped the beast about the neck, but at that moment his feet slipped from the stirrups and his arms let go, and the mule, frightened by the terrible blow, began running across the plain, hurling its rider to the earth with a few quick plunges.

Don Quixote stood watching all this very calmly. When he saw his enemy fall, he leaped from his horse, ran over very nimbly, and thrust the point of his sword into the Biscayan's eyes, calling upon him at the same time to surrender or otherwise he would cut off his head. The Biscayan was so bewildered that he was unable to utter a single word in reply, and things would have gone badly with him, so blind was Don Quixote in his rage, if the ladies of the coach, who up to then had watched the struggle in dismay, had not come up to him at this point and begged him with many blandishments to do them the very great favor of sparing their squire's life.

To which Don Quixote replied with much haughtiness and dignity, "Most certainly, lovely ladies, I shall be very happy to do that which you ask of me, but upon one condition and understanding, and that is that this knight promise me that he will go to El Toboso and present himself in my behalf before Doña Dulcinea, in order that she may do with him as she may see fit."

Trembling and disconsolate, the ladies did not pause to discuss Don Quixote's request, but without so much as inquiring who Dulcinea might be they promised him that the squire would fulfill that which was commanded of him.

"Very well, then, trusting in your word, I will do him no further harm, even though he has well deserved it."

CHAPTER X

Of the pleasing conversation that took place between
Don Quixote and Sancho Panza, his squire.

By this time Sancho Panza had got to his feet, somewhat the worse for wear as the result of the treatment he had received from the friars' lads. He had been watching the battle attentively and praying God in his heart to give the victory to his master, Don Quixote, in order that he, Sancho, might gain some island where he could go to be governor as had been promised him. Seeing now that the combat was over and the knight was returning to mount Rocinante once more, he went up to hold the stirrup for him; but first he fell on his knees in front of him and, taking his hand, kissed it and said, "May your Grace be pleased, Señor Don Quixote, to grant me the governorship of that island which you have won in this deadly affray; for however large it may be, I feel that I am indeed capable of governing it as well as any man in this world has ever done."

To which Don Quixote replied, "Be advised, brother Sancho, that this adventure and other similar ones have nothing to do with islands; they are affairs of the crossroads in which one gains nothing more than a broken head or an ear the less. Be patient, for there will be others which will not only make you a governor, but more than that."

Sancho thanked him very much and, kissing his hand again and the skirt of his cuirass, he assisted him up on Rocinante's back, after which the squire bestraddled his own mount and started jogging along behind his master, who was now going at a good clip. Without pausing for any further converse with those in the coach, the knight made for a nearby wood, with Sancho following as fast as his beast could trot; but Rocinante was making such speed that the ass and its rider were left behind, and it was necessary to call out to Don Quixote to pull up and wait for them. He did so, reining in Rocinante until the weary Sancho had drawn abreast of him.

"It strikes me, sir," said the squire as he reached his master's side, "that it would be better for us to take refuge in some church; for in view of the way you have treated that one with whom you were fighting, it would be small wonder if they did not lay the matter before the Holy Brotherhood[8] and have us arrested; and faith, if they do that, we shall have to sweat a-plenty before we come out of jail."

"Be quiet," said Don Quixote. "And where have you ever seen, or read of, a knight being brought to justice no matter how many homicides he might have committed?"

"I know nothing about omecils,"[9] replied Sancho, "nor ever in my life did I bear one to anybody; all I know is that the Holy Brotherhood has something to say about those who go around fighting on the highway, and I want nothing of it."

"Do not let it worry you," said Don Quixote, "for I will rescue you from the hands of the Chaldeans, not to speak of the Brotherhood. But answer me upon your life: have you ever seen a more valorous knight than I on all the known face of the earth? Have you ever read in the histories of any other who had more mettle in the attack, more perseverance in sustaining it, more dexterity in wounding his enemy, or more skill in overthrowing him?"

"The truth is," said Sancho, "I have never read any history whatsoever, for I do not know how to read or write; but what I would wager is that in all the days of my life I have never served a more courageous master than your Grace; I only hope your courage is not paid for in the place that I have mentioned. What I would suggest is that your Grace allow me to do something for that ear, for there is much blood coming from it, and I have here in my saddlebags some lint and a little white ointment."

"We could well dispense with all that," said Don Quixote, "if only I had remembered to bring along a vial of Fierabrás's[1] balm, a single drop of which saves time and medicines."

"What vial and what balm is that?" inquired Sancho Panza.

"It is a balm the recipe for which I know by heart; with it one need have no fear of death nor think of dying from any wound. I shall make some of it and

---

8. A tribunal instituted by Ferdinand and Isabella at the end of the 15th century to punish highway robbers.
9. In Spanish, a wordplay on *homocidios* (homicides) / *omecillos* (grudges). In English,

omecils appears only in this passage of *Don Quixote*.
1. A giant Saracen healer in the medieval epics of the Twelve Peers (see p. 1563, n. 7).

give it to you; and thereafter, whenever in any battle you see my body cut in two—as very often happens—all that is necessary is for you to take the part that lies on the ground, before the blood has congealed, and fit it very neatly and with great nicety upon the other part that remains in the saddle, taking care to adjust it evenly and exactly. Then you will give me but a couple of swallows of the balm of which I have told you, and you will see me sounder than an apple in no time at all."

"If that is so," said Panza, "I herewith renounce the governorship of the island you promised me and ask nothing other in payment of my many and faithful services than that your Grace give me the recipe for this wonderful potion, for I am sure that it would be worth more than two reales the ounce anywhere, and that is all I need for a life of ease and honor. But may I be so bold as to ask how much it costs to make it?"

"For less than three reales you can make something like six quarts," Don Quixote told him.

"Sinner that I am!" exclaimed Sancho. "Then why does your Grace not make some at once and teach me also?"

"Hush, my friend," said the knight, "I mean to teach you greater secrets than that and do you greater favors; but, for the present, let us look after this ear of mine, for it is hurting me more than I like."

Sancho thereupon took the lint and the ointment from his saddlebags; but when Don Quixote caught a glimpse of his helmet, he almost went out of his mind and, laying his hand upon his sword and lifting his eyes heavenward, he cried, "I make a vow to the Creator of all things and to the four holy Gospels in all their fullness of meaning that I will lead from now on the life that the great Marquis of Mantua did after he had sworn to avenge the death of his nephew Baldwin: not to eat bread off a tablecloth, not to embrace his wife, and other things which, although I am unable to recall them, we will look upon as understood—all this until I shall have wreaked an utter vengeance upon the one who has perpetrated such an outrage upon me."

"But let me remind your Grace," said Sancho when he heard these words, "that if the knight fulfills that which was commanded of him, by going to present himself before my lady Dulcinea del Toboso, then he will have paid his debt to you and merits no further punishment at your hands, unless it be for some fresh offense."

"You have spoken very well and to the point," said Don Quixote, "and so I annul the vow I have just made insofar as it has to do with any further vengeance, but I make it and confirm it anew so far as leading the life of which I have spoken is concerned, until such time as I shall have obtained by force of arms from some other knight another headpiece as good as this. And do not think, Sancho, that I am making smoke out of straw; there is one whom I well may imitate in this matter, for the same thing happened in all literalness in the case of Mambrino's helmet[2] which cost Sacripante so dear."

"I wish," said Sancho, "that your Grace would send all such oaths to the devil, for they are very bad for the health and harmful for the conscience as well. Tell me, please: supposing that for many days to come we meet no man

2. The enchanted helmet of Mambrino, a Moorish king, is stolen by Dardinel (not Sacripante, as Don Quixote mistakenly recalls) in Boiardo's *Roland in Love*.

wearing a helmet, then what are we to do? Must you still keep your vow in spite of all the inconveniences and discomforts, such as sleeping with your clothes on, not sleeping in any town, and a thousand other penances contained in the oath of that old madman of a Marquis of Mantua, an oath which you would now revive? Mark you, sir, along all these roads you meet no men of arms but only muleteers and carters, who not only do not wear helmets but quite likely have never heard tell of them in all their livelong days."

"In that you are wrong," said Don Quixote, "for we shall not be at these crossroads for the space of two hours before we shall see more men of arms than came to Albraca to win the fair Angélica."[3]

"Very well, then," said Sancho, "so be it, and pray God that all turns out for the best so that I may at last win that island that is costing me so dearly, and then let me die."

"I have already told you, Sancho, that you are to give no thought to that; should the island fail, there is the kingdom of Denmark or that of Sobradisa, which would fit you like a ring on your finger, and you ought, moreover, to be happy to be on *terra firma*.[4] But let us leave all this for some other time, while you look and see if you have something in those saddlebags for us to eat, after which we will go in search of some castle where we may lodge for the night and prepare that balm of which I was telling you, for I swear to God that my ear is paining me greatly."

"I have here an onion, a little cheese, and a few crusts of bread," said Sancho, "but they are not victuals fit for a valiant knight like your Grace."

"How little you know about it!" replied Don Quixote. "I would inform you, Sancho, that it is a point of honor with knights-errant to go for a month at a time without eating, and when they do eat, it is whatever may be at hand. You would certainly know that if you had read the histories as I have. There are many of them, and in none have I found any mention of knights eating unless it was by chance or at some sumptuous banquet that was tendered them; on other days they fasted. And even though it is well understood that, being men like us, they could not go without food entirely, any more than they could fail to satisfy the other necessities of nature, nevertheless, since they spent the greater part of their lives in forests and desert places without any cook to prepare their meals, their diet ordinarily consisted of rustic viands such as those that you now offer me. And so, Sancho my friend, do not be grieved at that which pleases me, nor seek to make the world over, nor to unhinge the institution of knight-errantry."

"Pardon me, your Grace," said Sancho, "but seeing that, as I have told you, I do not know how to read or write, I am consequently not familiar with the rules of the knightly calling. Hereafter, I will stuff my saddlebags with all manner of dried fruit for your Grace, but inasmuch as I am not a knight, I shall lay in for myself a stock of fowls and other more substantial fare."

"I am not saying, Sancho, that it is incumbent upon knights-errant to eat only those fruits of which you speak; what I am saying is that their ordinary sustenance should consist of fruit and a few herbs such as are to be found in the fields and with which they are well acquainted, as am I myself."

---

3. Another allusion to *Roland in Love*.
4. Solid earth (Latin, literal trans.), here referring to Firm Island, a legendary final des- tination for the squires of knights-errant. "Sobradisa": an imaginary realm.

"It is a good thing," said Sancho, "to know those herbs, for, so far as I can see, we are going to have need of that knowledge one of these days."

With this, he brought out the articles he had mentioned, and the two of them ate in peace, and most companionably. Being desirous, however, of seeking a lodging for the night, they did not tarry long over their humble and unsavory repast. They then mounted and made what haste they could that they might arrive at a shelter before nightfall; but the sun failed them, and with it went the hope of attaining their wish. As the day ended they found themselves beside some goatherds' huts, and they accordingly decided to spend the night there. Sancho was as much disappointed at their not having reached a town as his master was content with sleeping under the open sky; for it seemed to Don Quixote that every time this happened it merely provided him with yet another opportunity to establish his claim to the title of knight-errant.

[Of Goatherds, Roaming Shepherdesses, and Unrequited Loves]

CHAPTER XI

Of what happened to Don Quixote in the company of certain goatherds.

He was received by the herders with good grace, and Sancho having looked after Rocinante and the ass to the best of his ability, the knight, drawn by the aroma, went up to where some pieces of goat's meat were simmering in a pot over the fire. He would have liked then and there to see if they were done well enough to be transferred from pot to stomach, but he refrained in view of the fact that his hosts were already taking them off the fire. Spreading a few sheepskins on the ground, they hastily laid their rustic board and invited the strangers to share what there was of it. There were six of them altogether who belonged to that fold, and after they had urged Don Quixote, with rude politeness, to seat himself upon a small trough which they had turned upside down for the purpose, they took their own places upon the sheep hides round about. While his master sat there, Sancho remained standing to serve him the cup, which was made of horn. When the knight perceived this, he addressed his squire as follows:

"In order, Sancho, that you may see the good that there is in knight-errantry and how speedily those who follow the profession, no matter what the nature of their service may be, come to be honored and esteemed in the eyes of the world, I would have you here in the company of these good folk seat yourself at my side, that you may be even as I who am your master and natural lord, and eat from my plate and drink from where I drink; for of knight-errantry one may say the same as of love: that it makes all things equal."

"Many thanks!" said Sancho, "but if it is all the same to your Grace, providing there is enough to go around, I can eat just as well, or better, standing up and alone as I can seated beside an emperor. And if the truth must be told, I enjoy much more that which I eat in my own corner without any bowings and scrapings, even though it be only bread and onions, than I do a meal of roast turkey where I have to chew slowly, drink little, be always wiping my mouth, and can neither sneeze nor cough if I feel like it, nor do any of those other things that you can when you are free and alone.

"And so, my master," he went on, "these honors that your Grace would confer upon me as your servant and a follower of knight-errantry—which I am, being your Grace's squire—I would have you convert, if you will, into other things that will be of more profit and advantage to me; for though I hereby acknowledge them as duly received, I renounce them from this time forth to the end of the world."

"But for all that," said Don Quixote, "you must sit down; for whosoever humbleth himself, him God will exalt."[5] And, laying hold of his squire's arm, he compelled him to take a seat beside him.

The goatherds did not understand all this jargon about squires and knights-errant; they did nothing but eat, keep silent, and study their guests, who very dexterously and with much appetite were stowing away chunks of meat as big as your fist. When the meat course was finished, they laid out upon the sheep-skins a great quantity of dried acorns and half a cheese, which was harder than if it had been made of mortar. The drinking horn all this while was not idle but went the rounds so often—now full, now empty, like the bucket of a water wheel—that they soon drained one of the two wine bags that were on hand. After Don Quixote had well satisfied his stomach, he took up a handful of acorns and, gazing at them attentively, fell into a soliloquy.

"Happy the age and happy those centuries to which the ancients gave the name of golden, and not because gold, which is so esteemed in this iron age of ours, was then to be had without toil, but because those who lived in that time did not know the meaning of the words 'thine' and 'mine.' In that blessed era all things were held in common, and to gain his daily sustenance no labor was required of any man save to reach forth his hand and take it from the sturdy oaks that stood liberally inviting him with their sweet and seasoned fruit. The clear-running fountains and rivers in magnificent abundance offered him palatable and transparent water for his thirst; while in the clefts of the rocks and the hollows of the trees the wise and busy honey-makers set up their republic so that any hand whatever might avail itself, fully and freely, of the fertile harvest which their fragrant toil had produced. The vigorous cork trees of their own free will and grace, without the asking, shed their broad, light bark with which men began to cover their dwellings, erected upon rude stakes merely as a protection against the inclemency of the heavens.

"All then was peace, all was concord and friendship; the crooked plowshare had not as yet grievously laid open and pried into the merciful bowels of our first mother, who without any forcing on man's part yielded her spacious fertile bosom on every hand for the satisfaction, sustenance, and delight of her first sons. Then it was that lovely and unspoiled young shepherdesses, with locks that were sometimes braided, sometimes flowing, went roaming from valley to valley and hillock to hillock with no more garments than were needed to cover decently that which modesty requires and always has required should remain covered. Nor were their adornments such as those in use today—of Tyrian purple and silk worked up in tortured patterns; a few green leaves of burdock or of ivy, and they were as splendidly and as becomingly clad as our ladies of the court with all the rare and exotic tricks of fashion that idle curiosity has taught them.

"Thoughts of love, also, in those days were set forth as simply as the simple hearts that conceived them, without any roundabout and artificial play of words

5. Matthew 23.12.

by way of ornament. Fraud, deceit, and malice had not yet come to mingle with truth and plain-speaking. Justice kept its own domain, where favor and self-interest dared not trespass, dared not impair her rights, becloud, and persecute her as they now do. There was no such thing then as arbitrary judgments, for the reason that there was no one to judge or be judged. Maidens in all their modesty, as I have said, went where they would and unattended; whereas in this hateful age of ours none is safe, even though she go to hide and shut herself up in some new labyrinth like that of Crete; for in spite of all her seclusion, through chinks and crevices or borne upon the air, the amorous plague with all its cursed importunities will find her out and lead her to her ruin.

"It was for the safety of such as these, as time went on and depravity increased, that the order of knights-errant was instituted, for the protection of damsels, the aid of widows and orphans, and the succoring of the needy. It is to this order that I belong, my brothers, and I thank you for the welcome and the kindly treatment that you have accorded to me and my squire. By natural law, all living men are obliged to show favor to knights-errant, yet without being aware of this you have received and entertained me; and so it is with all possible good will that I acknowledge your own good will to me."

This long harangue on the part of our knight—it might very well have been dispensed with—was all due to the acorns they had given him, which had brought back to memory the age of gold; whereupon the whim had seized him to indulge in this futile harangue with the goatherds as his auditors. They listened in open-mouthed wonderment, saying not a word, and Sancho himself kept quiet and went on munching acorns, taking occasion very frequently to pay a visit to the second wine bag, which they had suspended from a cork tree to keep it cool.

It took Don Quixote much longer to finish his speech than it did to put away his supper; and when he was through, one of the goatherds addressed him.

"In order that your Grace may say with more truth that we have received you with readiness and good will, we desire to give you solace and contentment by having one of our comrades, who will be here soon, sing for you. He is a very bright young fellow and deeply in love, and what is more, you could not ask for anything better than to hear him play the three-stringed lute."

Scarcely had he done saying this when the sound of a rebec[6] was heard, and shortly afterward the one who played it appeared. He was a good-looking youth, around twenty-two years of age. His companions asked him if he had had his supper, and when he replied that he had, the one who had spoken to Don Quixote said to him, "Well, then, Antonio, you can give us the pleasure of hearing you sing, in order that this gentleman whom we have as our guest may see that we of the woods and mountains also know something about music. We have been telling him how clever you are, and now we want you to show him that we were speaking the truth. And so I beg you by all means to sit down and sing us that love-song of yours that your uncle the prebendary composed for you and which the villagers liked so well.

"With great pleasure," the lad replied, and without any urging he seated himself on the stump of an oak that had been felled and, tuning up his rebec, soon began singing, very prettily, the following ballad:

6. Three-stringed instrument played with a bow.

THE BALLAD THAT ANTONIO SANG

I know well that thou dost love me,
My Olalla, even though
Eyes of thine have never spoken—
Love's mute tongues—to tell me so.

Since I know thou knowest my passion,
Of thy love I am more sure;
No love ever was unhappy
When it was both frank and pure.

True it is, Olalla, sometimes
Thou a heart of bronze hast shown,
And it seemed to me that bosom,
White and fair, was made of stone.

Yet in spite of all repulses
And a chastity so cold,
It appeared that I Hope's garment
By the hem did clutch and hold.

For my faith I ever cherished;
It would rise to meet the bait;
Spurned, it never did diminish;
Favored, it preferred to wait.

Love, they say, hath gentle manners:
Thus it is it shows its face;
Then may I take hope, Olalla,
Trust to win a longed-for grace.

If devotion hath the power
Hearts to move and make them kind,
Let the loyalty I've shown thee
Plead my cause, be kept in mind.

For if thou didst note my costume,
More than once thou must have seen,
Worn upon a simple Monday
Sunday's garb so bright and clean.

Love and brightness go together.
Dost thou ask the reason why
I thus deck myself on Monday?
It is but to catch thine eye.

I say nothing of the dances
I have danced for thy sweet sake;
Nor the serenades I've sung thee
Till the first cock did awake.

Nor will I repeat my praises
Of that beauty all can see;
True my words but oft unwelcome—
Certain lasses hated me.

One girl there is, I well remember—
She's Teresa on the hill—
Said, "You think you love an angel,
But she is a monkey still.

"Thanks to all her many trinkets
And her artificial hair

> *And her many aids to beauty,*
> *Love's own self she would ensnare."*
>   *She was lying, I was angry,*
> *And her cousin, very bold,*
> *Challenged me upon my honor;*
> *What ensued need not be told.*
>   *Highflown words do not become me;*
> *I'm a plain and simple man.*
> *Pure the love that I would offer,*
> *Serving thee as best I can.*
>   *Silken are the bonds of marriage,*
> *When two hearts do intertwine;*
> *Mother Church the yoke will fasten;*
> *Bow your neck and I'll bow mine.*
>   *Or if not, my word I'll give thee,*
> *From these mountains I'll come down—*
> *Saint most holy be my witness—*
> *Wearing a Capuchin⁷ gown.*

With this the goatherd brought his song to a close, and although Don Quixote begged him to sing some more, Sancho Panza would not hear to this as he was too sleepy for any more ballads.

"Your Grace," he said to his master, "would do well to find out at once where his bed is to be, for the labor that these good men have to perform all day long does not permit them to stay up all night singing."

"I understand, Sancho," replied Don Quixote. "I perceive that those visits to the wine bag call for sleep rather than music as a recompense."

"It tastes well enough to all of us, God be praised," said Sancho.

"I am not denying that," said his master; "but go ahead and settle yourself down wherever you like. As for men of my profession, they prefer to keep vigil. But all the same, Sancho, perhaps you had better look after this ear, for it is paining me more than I like."

Sancho started to do as he was commanded, but one of the goatherds, when he saw the wound, told him not to bother, that he would place a remedy upon it that would heal it in no time. Taking a few leaves of rosemary, of which there was a great deal growing thereabouts, he mashed them in his mouth and, mixing them with a little salt, laid them on the ear, with the assurance that no other medicine was needed; and this proved to be the truth.

CHAPTER XII

Of the story that one of the goatherds told to Don Quixote and the others.

Just then, another lad came up, one of those who brought the goatherds their provisions from the village.

"Do you know what's happening down there, my friends?" he said.

"How should we know?" one of the men answered him.

---

7. An austere order of Franciscan friars.

"In that case," the lad went on, "I must tell you that the famous student and shepherd known as Grisóstomo died this morning, muttering that the cause of his death was the love he had for that bewitched lass of a Marcela, daughter of the wealthy Guillermo—you know, the one who's been going around in these parts dressed like a shepherdess."

"For love of Marcela, you say?" one of the herders spoke up.

"That is what I'm telling you," replied the other lad. "And the best part of it is that he left directions in his will that he was to be buried in the field, as if he were a Moor, and that his grave was to be at the foot of the cliff where the Cork Tree Spring is; for, according to report, and he is supposed to have said so himself, that is the place where he saw her for the first time. There were other provisions, which the clergy of the village say cannot be carried out, nor would it be proper to fulfill them, seeing that they savor of heathen practices. But Grisóstomo's good friend, the student Ambrosio, who also dresses like a shepherd, insists that everything must be done to the letter, and as a result there is great excitement in the village.

"Nevertheless, from all I can hear, they will end by doing as Ambrosio and Grisóstomo's other friends desire, and tomorrow they will bury him with great ceremony in the place that I have mentioned. I believe it is going to be something worth seeing; at any rate, I mean to see it, even though it is too far for me to be able to return to the village before nightfall."

"We will all do the same," said the other goatherds. "We will cast lots to see who stays to watch the goats."

"That is right, Pedro," said one of their number, "but it will not be necessary to go to the trouble of casting lots. I will take care of the flocks for all of us; and do not think that I am being generous or that I am not as curious as the rest of you; it is simply that I cannot walk on account of the splinter I picked up in this foot the other day."

"Well, we thank you just the same," said Pedro.

Don Quixote then asked Pedro to tell him more about the dead man and the shepherd lass; to which the latter replied that all he knew was that Grisóstomo was a rich gentleman who had lived in a near-by village. He had been a student for many years at Salamanca[8] and then had returned to his birthplace with the reputation of being very learned and well read; he was especially noted for his knowledge of the science of the stars and what the sun and moon were doing up there in the heavens, "for he would promptly tell us when their clips was to come."

"Eclipse, my friend, not clips," said Don Quixote, "is the name applied to the darkening-over of those major luminaries."

But Pedro, not pausing for any trifles, went on with his story. "He could also tell when the year was going to be plentiful or estil—"

"Sterile, you mean to say, friend—"

"Sterile or estil," said Pedro, "it all comes out the same in the end. But I can tell you one thing, that his father and his friends, who believed in him, did just as he advised them and they became rich; for he would say to them, 'This year, sow barley and not wheat'; and again, 'Sow chickpeas and not barley'; or, 'This season there will be a good crop of oil,[9] but the three following ones you will not get a drop.'"

8. Town west of Madrid that is home to Spain's oldest university, founded in 1134.

9. I.e., olive oil.

"That science," Don Quixote explained, "is known as astrology."

"I don't know what it's called," said Pedro, "but he knew all this and more yet. Finally, not many months after he returned from Salamanca, he appeared one day dressed like a shepherd with crook and sheepskin jacket; for he had resolved to lay aside the long gown that he wore as a scholar, and in this he was joined by Ambrosio, a dear friend of his and the companion of his studies. I forgot to tell you that Grisóstomo was a great one for composing verses; he even wrote the carols for Christmas Eve and the plays that were performed at Corpus Christi by the lads of our village, and everyone said that they were the best ever.

"When the villagers saw the two scholars coming out dressed like shepherds, they were amazed and could not imagine what was the reason for such strange conduct on their part. It was about that time that Grisóstomo's father died and left him the heir to a large fortune, consisting of land and chattels, no small quantity of cattle, and a considerable sum of money, of all of which the young man was absolute master; and, to tell the truth, he deserved it, for he was very sociable and charitably inclined, a friend to all worthy folk, and he had a face that was like a benediction. Afterward it was learned that if he had changed his garments like this, it was only that he might be able to wander over the wastelands on the trail of that shepherdess Marcela of whom our friend was speaking, for the poor fellow had fallen in love with her. And now I should like to tell you, for it is well that you should know, just who this lass is; for it may be—indeed, there is no maybe about it—you will never hear the like in all the days of your life, though you live to be older than Sarna."

"You should say *Sarah*," Don Quixote corrected him; for he could not bear hearing the goatherd using the wrong words all the time.[1]

"The itch," said Pedro, "lives long enough; and if, sir, you go on interrupting me at every word, we'll never be through in a year."

"Pardon me, friend," said Don Quixote, "it was only because there is so great a difference between Sarna and Sarah that I pointed it out to you; but you have given me a very good answer, for the itch does live longer than Sarah; and so go on with your story, and I will not contradict you anymore."

"I was about to say, then, my dear sir," the goatherd went on, "that in our village there was a farmer who was richer still than Grisóstomo's father. His name was Guillermo, and, over and above his great wealth, God gave him a daughter whose mother, the most highly respected woman in these parts, died in bearing her. It seems to me I can see the good lady now, with that face that rivaled the sun and moon; and I remember, above all, what a friend she was to the poor, for which reason I believe that her soul at this very moment must be enjoying God's presence in the other world.

"Grieving for the loss of so excellent a wife, Guillermo himself died, leaving his daughter Marcela, now a rich young woman, in the custody of one of her uncles, a priest who holds a benefice in our village. The girl grew up with such beauty as to remind us of her mother, beautiful as that lady had been. By the time she was fourteen or fifteen no one looked at her without giving thanks to God who had created such comeliness, and almost all were hopelessly in love

---

1. Actually in this case the goatherd is not really wrong, for *sarna* means "itch" and "older than the itch" was a proverbial expression. ("Sarah" is a reference to the wife of Abraham in the Old Testament.)

with her. Her uncle kept her very closely shut up, but, for all of that, word of her great beauty spread to such an extent that by reason of it, as much as on account of the girl's wealth, her uncle found himself besought and importuned not only by the young men of our village, but by those for leagues around who desired to have her for a wife.

"But he, an upright Christian, although he wished to marry her off as soon as she was of age, had no desire to do so without her consent, not that he had any eye to the gain and profit which the custody of his niece's property brought him while her marriage was deferred. Indeed, this much was said in praise of the good priest in more than one circle of the village; for I would have you know, Sir Knight, that in these little places everything is discussed and becomes a subject of gossip; and you may rest assured, as I am for my part, that a priest must be more than ordinarily good if his parishioners feel bound to speak well of him, especially in the small towns."

"That is true," said Don Quixote, "but go on. I like your story very much, and you, good Pedro, tell it with very good grace."

"May the Lord's grace never fail me, for that is what counts. But to go on: Although the uncle set forth to his niece the qualities of each one in particular of the many who sought her hand, begging her to choose and marry whichever one she pleased, she never gave him any answer other than this: that she did not wish to marry at all, since being but a young girl she did not feel that she was equal to bearing the burdens of matrimony. As her reasons appeared to be proper and just, the uncle did not insist but thought he would wait until she was a little older, when she would be capable of selecting someone to her taste. For, he said, and quite right he was, parents ought not to impose a way of life upon their children against the latters' will. And then, one fine day, lo and behold, there was the finical Marcela turned shepherdess; and without paying any attention to her uncle or all those of the village who advised against it, she set out to wander through the fields with the other lasses, guarding flocks as they did.

"Well, the moment she appeared in public and her beauty was uncovered for all to see, I really cannot tell you how many rich young bachelors, gentlemen, and farmers proceeded to don a shepherd's garb and go to make love to her in the meadows. One of her suitors, as I have told you, was our deceased friend, and it is said that he did not love but adored her. But you must not think that because Marcela chose so free and easy a life, and one that offers little or no privacy, that she was thereby giving the faintest semblance of encouragement to those who would disparage her modesty and prudence; rather, so great was the vigilance with which she looked after her honor that of all those who waited upon her and solicited her favors, none could truly say that she had given him the slightest hope of attaining his desire.

"For although she does not flee nor shun the company and conversation of the shepherds, treating them in courteous and friendly fashion, the moment she discovers any intentions on their part, even though it be the just and holy one of matrimony, she hurls them from her like a catapult. As a result, she is doing more damage in this land than if a plague had fallen upon it; for her beauty and graciousness win the hearts of all who would serve her, but her disdain and the disillusionment it brings lead them in the end to despair, and then they can only call her cruel and ungrateful, along with other similar epithets that reveal all too plainly the state of mind that prompts them. If you were to stay here some time, sir, you would hear these uplands and valleys echo with the laments of those who have followed her only to be deceived.

"Not far from here is a place where there are a couple of dozen tall beeches, and there is not a one of them on whose smooth bark Marcela's name has not been engraved; and above some of these inscriptions you will find a crown, as if by this her lover meant to indicate that she deserved to wear the garland of beauty above all the women on the earth. Here a shepherd sighs and there another voices his lament. Now are to be heard amorous ballads, and again despairing ditties. One will spend all the hours of the night seated at the foot of some oak or rock without once closing his tearful eyes, and the morning sun will find him there, stupefied and lost in thought. Another, without giving truce or respite to his sighs, will lie stretched upon the burning sands in the full heat of the most exhausting summer noontide, sending up his complaint to merciful Heaven.

"And, meanwhile, over this one and that one, over one and all, the beauteous Marcela triumphs and goes her own way, free and unconcerned. All those of us who know her are waiting to see how far her pride will carry her, and who will be the fortunate man who will succeed in taming this terrible creature and thus come into possession of a beauty so matchless as hers. Knowing all this that I have told you to be undoubtedly true, I can readily believe this lad's story about the cause of Grisóstomo's death. And so I advise you, sir, not to fail to be present tomorrow at his burial; it will be well worth seeing, for he has many friends, and the place is not half a league from here."

"I will make a point of it," said Don Quixote, "and I thank you for the pleasure you have given me by telling me so delightful a tale."

"Oh," said the goatherd, "I do not know the half of the things that have happened to Marcela's lovers; but it is possible that tomorrow we may meet along the way some shepherd who will tell us more. And now it would be well for you to go and sleep under cover, for the night air may not be good for your wound, though with the remedy that has been put on it there is not much to fear."

Sancho Panza, who had been sending the goatherd to the devil for talking so much, now put in a word with his master, urging him to come and sleep in Pedro's hut. Don Quixote did so; and all the rest of the night was spent by him in thinking of his lady Dulcinea, in imitation of Marcela's lovers. As for Sancho, he made himself comfortable between Rocinante and the ass and at once dropped off to sleep, not like a lovelorn swain but, rather, like a man who has had a sound kicking that day.

CHAPTER XIII

In which is brought to a close the story of the shepherdess
Marcela, along with other events.

Day had barely begun to appear upon the balconies of the east when five or six goatherds arose and went to awaken Don Quixote and tell him that if he was still of a mind to go see Grisóstomo's famous burial they would keep him company. The knight, desiring nothing better, ordered Sancho to saddle at once, which was done with much dispatch, and then they all set out forthwith.

They had not gone more than a quarter of a league when, upon crossing a footpath, they saw coming toward them six shepherds clad in black sheepskins and with garlands of cypress and bitter rosebay on their heads. Each of them carried a thick staff made of the wood of the holly, and with them came two gentlemen on horseback in handsome traveling attire, accompanied by three lads on foot. As the two parties met they greeted each other courteously, each inquiring as to the other's destination, whereupon they learned that they were all going to the burial, and so continued to ride along together.

Speaking to his companion, one of them said, "I think, Señor Vivaldo, that we are going to be well repaid for the delay it will cost us to see this famous funeral; for famous it must surely be, judging by the strange things that these shepherds have told us of the dead man and the homicidal shepherdess."

"I think so too," agreed Vivaldo. "I should be willing to delay our journey not one day, but four, for the sake of seeing it."

Don Quixote then asked them what it was they had heard of Marcela and Grisóstomo. The traveler replied that on that very morning they had fallen in with those shepherds and, seeing them so mournfully trigged out, had asked them what the occasion for it was. One of the fellows had then told them of the beauty and strange demeanor of a shepherdess by the name of Marcela, her many suitors, and the death of this Grisóstomo, to whose funeral they were bound. He related, in short, the entire story as Don Quixote had heard it from Pedro.

Changing the subject, the gentleman called Vivaldo inquired of Don Quixote what it was that led him to go armed in that manner in a land that was so peaceful.

"The calling that I profess," replied Don Quixote, "does not permit me to do otherwise. An easy pace, pleasure, and repose—those things were invented for delicate courtiers; but toil, anxiety, and arms—they are for those whom the world knows as knights-errant, of whom I, though unworthy, am the very least."

No sooner had they heard this than all of them immediately took him for a madman. By way of assuring himself further and seeing what kind of madness it was of which Don Quixote was possessed, Vivaldo now asked him what was meant by the term knights-errant.

"Have not your Worships read the annals and the histories of England that treat of the famous exploits of King Arthur, who in our Castilian balladry is always called King Artús? According to a very old tradition that is common throughout the entire realm of Great Britain, this king did not die, but by an act of enchantment was changed into a raven; and in due course of time he is to return and reign once more, recovering his kingdom and his scepter; for which reason, from that day to this, no Englishman is known to have killed one of those birds. It was, moreover, in the time of that good king that the famous order of the Knights of the Round Table was instituted; and as for the love of Sir Lancelot of the Lake and Queen Guinevere, everything took place exactly as the story has it, their confidante and go-between being the honored matron Quintañona; whence comes that charming ballad that is such a favorite with us Spaniards:

> Never was there a knight
> So served by maid and dame
> As the one they call Sir Lancelot
> When from Britain be came—

to carry on the gentle, pleasing course of his loves and noble deeds.

"From that time forth, the order of chivalry was passed on and propagated from one individual to another until it had spread through many and various parts of the world. Among those famed for their exploits was the valiant Amadis of Gaul, with all his sons and grandsons to the fifth generation; and there was also the brave Felixmarte of Hircania, and the never sufficiently praised Tirant lo Blanch; and in view of the fact that he lived in our own day, almost, we came near to seeing, hearing, and conversing with that other courageous knight, Don Belianís of Greece.[2]

"And that, gentlemen, is what it means to be a knight-errant, and what I have been telling you of is the order of chivalry which such a knight professes, an order to which, as I have already informed you, I, although a sinner, have the honor of belonging; for I have made the same profession as have those other knights. That is why it is you find me in these wild and lonely places, riding in quest of adventure, being resolved to offer my arm and my person in the most dangerous undertaking fate may have in store for me, that I may be of aid to the weak and needy."

Listening to this speech, the travelers had some while since come to the conclusion that Don Quixote was out of his mind, and were likewise able to perceive the peculiar nature of his madness, and they wondered at it quite as much as did all those who encountered it for the first time. Being endowed with a ready wit and a merry disposition and thinking to pass the time until they reached the end of the short journey which, so he was told, awaited them before they should arrive at the mountain where the burial was to take place, Vivaldo decided to give him a further opportunity of displaying his absurdities.

"It strikes me, Sir Knight-errant," he said, "that your Grace has espoused one of the most austere professions to be found anywhere on earth—even more austere, if I am not mistaken, than that of the Carthusian monks."

"Theirs may be as austere as ours," Don Quixote replied, "but that it is as necessary I am very much inclined to doubt. For if the truth be told, the soldier who carries out his captain's order does no less than the captain who gives the order. By that I mean to say that the religious, in all peace and tranquility, pray to Heaven for earth's good, but we soldiers and knights put their prayers into execution by defending with the might of our good right arms and at the edge of the sword those things for which they pray; and we do this not under cover of a roof but under the open sky, beneath the insufferable rays of the summer sun and the biting cold of winter. Thus we become the ministers of God on earth, and our arms the means by which He executes His decrees. And just as war and all the things that have to do with it are impossible without toil, sweat, and anxiety, it follows that those who have taken upon themselves such a profession must unquestionably labor harder than do those who in peace and tranquility and at their ease pray God to favor the ones who can do little in their own behalf.

"I do not mean to say—I should not think of saying—that the state of knight-errant is as holy as that of the cloistered monk; I merely would imply, from what I myself endure, that ours is beyond a doubt the more laborious and arduous calling, more beset by hunger and thirst, more wretched, ragged, and ridden with lice. It is an absolute certainty that the knights-errant of old

2. Each of the knights praised here is the fictitious hero of a romance popular in Cervantes' time.

experienced much misfortune in the course of their lives; and if some by their might and valor came to be emperors, you may take my word for it, it cost them dearly in blood and sweat, and if those who rose to such a rank had lacked enchanters and magicians to aid them, they surely would have been cheated of their desires, deceived in their hopes and expectations."

"I agree with you on that," said the traveler, "but there is one thing among others that gives me a very bad impression of the knights-errant, and that is the fact that when they are about to enter upon some great and perilous adventure in which they are in danger of losing their lives, they never at that moment think of commending themselves to God as every good Christian is obliged to do under similar circumstances, but, rather, commend themselves to their ladies with as much fervor and devotion as if their mistresses were God himself; all of which to me smacks somewhat of paganism."

"Sir," Don Quixote answered him, "it could not by any means be otherwise; the knight-errant who did not do so would fall into disgrace, for it is the usage and custom of chivalry that the knight, before engaging in some great feat of arms, shall behold his lady in front of him and shall turn his eyes toward her, gently and lovingly, as if beseeching her favor and protection in the hazardous encounter that awaits him, and even though no one hears him, he is obliged to utter certain words between his teeth, commending himself to her with all his heart; and of this we have numerous examples in the histories. Nor is it to be assumed that he does not commend himself to God also, but the time and place for that is in the course of the undertaking."

"All the same," said the traveler, "I am not wholly clear in this matter; for I have often read of two knights-errant exchanging words until, one word leading to another, their wrath is kindled; whereupon, turning their steeds and taking a good run up the field, they whirl about and bear down upon each other at full speed, commending themselves to their ladies in the midst of it all. What commonly happens then is that one of the two topples from his horse's flanks and is run through and through with the other's lance; and his adversary would also fall to the ground if he did not cling to his horse's mane. What I do not understand is how the dead man would have had time to commend himself to God in the course of this accelerated combat. It would be better if the words he wasted in calling upon his lady as he ran toward the other knight had been spent in paying the debt that he owed as a Christian. Moreover, it is my personal opinion that not all knights-errant have ladies to whom to commend themselves, for not all of them are in love."

"That," said Don Quixote, "is impossible. I assert there can be no knight-errant without a lady; for it is as natural and proper for them to be in love as it is for the heavens to have stars, and I am quite sure that no one ever read a story in which a loveless man of arms was to be met with, for the simple reason that such a one would not be looked upon as a legitimate knight but as a bastard one who had entered the fortress of chivalry not by the main gate, but over the walls, like a robber and a thief."

"Nevertheless," said the traveler, "if my memory serves me right, I have read that Don Galaor, brother of the valorous Amadis of Gaul, never had a special lady to whom he prayed, yet he was not held in any the less esteem for that but was a very brave and famous knight."

Once again, our Don Quixote had an answer. "Sir, one swallow does not make a summer. And in any event, I happen to know that this knight was secretly very much in love. As for his habit of paying court to all the ladies that caught his fancy, that was a natural propensity on his part and one that he was unable to resist. There was, however, one particular lady whom he had made the mistress of his will and to whom he did commend himself very frequently and privately; for he prided himself upon being a reticent knight."

"Well, then," said the traveler, "if it is essential that every knight-errant be in love, it is to be presumed that your Grace is also, since you are of the profession. And unless it be that you pride yourself upon your reticence as much as did Don Galaor, then I truly, on my own behalf and in the name of all this company, beseech your Grace to tell us your lady's name, the name of the country where she resides, what her rank is, and something of the beauty of her person, that she may esteem herself fortunate in having all the world know that she is loved and served by such a knight as your Grace appears to me to be."

At this, Don Quixote heaved a deep sigh. "I cannot say," he began, "as to whether or not my sweet enemy would be pleased that all the world should know I serve her. I can only tell you, in response to the question which you have so politely put to me, that her name is Dulcinea, her place of residence El Toboso, a village of La Mancha. As to her rank, she should be at the very least a princess, seeing that she is my lady and my queen. Her beauty is superhuman, for in it are realized all the impossible and chimerical attributes that poets are accustomed to give their fair ones. Her locks are golden, her brow the Elysian Fields, her eyebrows rainbows, her eyes suns, her cheeks roses, her lips coral, her teeth pearls, her neck alabaster, her bosom marble, her hands ivory, her complexion snow-white. As for those parts which modesty keeps covered from the human sight, it is my opinion that, discreetly considered, they are only to be extolled and not compared to any other."

"We should like," said Vivaldo, "to know something as well of her lineage, her race and ancestry."

"She is not," said Don Quixote, "of the ancient Roman Curtii, Caii, or Scipios, nor of the modern Colonnas and Orsini, nor of the Moncadas and Requesenses of Catalonia, nor is she of the Rebellas and Villanovas of Valencia, or the Palafoxes, Nuzas, Rocabertis, Corellas, Lunas, Alagones, Urreas, or Gurreas of Aragon, the Cerdas, Manriques, Mendozas, or Guzmanes of Castile, the Alencastros, Pallas, or Menezes of Portugal; but she is of the Tobosos of La Mancha, and although the line is a modern one, it well may give rise to the most illustrious families of the centuries to come. And let none dispute this with me, unless it be under the conditions which Zerbino has set forth in the inscription beneath Orlando's arms:

> *These let none move*
> *Who dares not with Orlando his valor prove.*"[3]

"Although my own line," replied the traveler, "is that of the Gachupins of Laredo, I should not venture to compare it with the Tobosos of La Mancha, in view of the fact that, to tell you the truth, I have never heard the name before."

---

3. From Ludovico Ariosto's *Orlando Furioso*, 24.57.

"How does it come that you have never heard it!" exclaimed Don Quixote.

The others were listening most attentively to the conversation of these two, and even the goatherds and shepherds were by now aware that our knight of La Mancha was more than a little insane. Sancho Panza alone thought that all his master said was the truth, for he was well acquainted with him, having known him since birth. The only doubt in his mind had to do with the beauteous Dulcinea del Toboso, for he knew of no such princess and the name was strange to his ears, although he lived not far from that place.

They were continuing on their way, conversing in this manner, when they caught sight of some twenty shepherds coming through the gap between two high mountains, all of them clad in black woolen garments and with wreaths on their heads, some of the garlands, as was afterward learned, being of cypress, others of yew. Six of them were carrying a bier covered with a great variety of flowers and boughs.

"There they come with Grisóstomo's body," said one of the goatherds, "and the foot of the mountain yonder is where he wished to be buried."

They accordingly quickened their pace and arrived just as those carrying the bier had set it down on the ground. Four of the shepherds with sharpened picks were engaged in digging a grave alongside the barren rock. After a courteous exchange of greetings, Don Quixote and his companions turned to look at the bier. Upon it lay a corpse covered with flowers, the body of a man dressed like a shepherd and around thirty years of age. Even in death it could be seen that he had had a handsome face and had been of a jovial disposition. Round about him upon the bier were a number of books and many papers, open and folded.

Meanwhile, those who stood gazing at the dead man and those who were digging the grave—everyone present, in fact—preserved an awed silence, until one of the pallbearers said to another, "Look well, Ambrosio, and make sure that this is the place that Grisóstomo had in mind, since you are bent upon carrying out to the letter the provisions of his will."

"This is it," replied Ambrosio; "for many times my unfortunate friend told me the story of his misadventure. He told me that it was here that he first laid eyes upon that mortal enemy of the human race, and it was here, also, that he first revealed to her his passion, for he was as honorable as he was lovelorn; and it was here, finally, at their last meeting, that she shattered his illusions and showed him her disdain, thus bringing to an end the tragedy of his wretched life. And here, in memory of his great misfortune, he wished to be laid in the bowels of eternal oblivion."

Then, turning to Don Quixote and the travelers, he went on, "This body, gentlemen, on which you now look with pitying eyes was the depository of a soul which heaven had endowed with a vast share of its riches. This is the body of Grisóstomo, who was unrivaled in wit, unequaled in courtesy, supreme in gentleness of bearing, a model of friendship, generous without stint, grave without conceit, merry without being vulgar—in short, first in all that is good and second to none in the matter of misfortunes. He loved well and was hated, he adored and was disdained; he wooed a wild beast, importuned a piece of marble, ran after the wind, cried out to loneliness, waited upon ingratitude, and his reward was to be the spoils of death midway in his life's course—a life that was brought to an end by a shepherdess whom he sought to immortalize that she might live on in the memory of mankind, as those papers that you see there would very plainly show if he had not commanded me to consign them to the flames even as his body is given to the earth."

"You," said Vivaldo, "would treat them with greater harshness and cruelty than their owner himself, for it is neither just nor fitting to carry out the will of one who commands what is contrary to all reason. It would not have been a good thing for Augustus Caesar to consent to have them execute the behests of the divine Mantuan in his last testament.[4] And so, Señor Ambrosio, while you may give the body of your friend to the earth, you ought not to give his writings to oblivion. If out of bitterness he left such an order, that does not mean that you are to obey it without using your own discretion. Rather, by granting life to these papers, you permit Marcela's cruelheartedness to live forever and serve as an example to the others in the days that are to come in order that they may flee and avoid such pitfalls as these.

"I and those that have come with me know the story of this lovesick and despairing friend of yours; we know the affection that was between you, and what the occasion of his death was, and the things that he commanded be done as his life drew to a close. And from this lamentable tale anyone may see how great was Marcela's cruelty; they may behold Grisóstomo's love, the loyalty that lay in your friendship, and the end that awaits those who run headlong, with unbridled passion, down the path that doting love opens before their gaze. Last night we heard of your friend's death and learned that he was to be buried here, and out of pity and curiosity we turned aside from our journey and resolved to come see with our own eyes that which had aroused so much compassion when it was told to us. And in requital of that compassion, and the desire that has been born in us to prevent if we can a recurrence of such tragic circumstances, we beg you, O prudent Ambrosio!—or, at least, I for my part implore you—to give up your intention of burning these papers and let me carry some of them away with me."

Without waiting for the shepherd to reply he put out his hand and took a few of those that were nearest him.

"Out of courtesy, sir," said Ambrosio when he saw this, "I will consent for you to keep those that you have taken; but it is vain to think that I will refrain from burning the others."

Vivaldo, who was anxious to find out what was in the papers, opened one of them and perceived that it bore the title "Song of Despair."

Hearing this, Ambrosio said, "That is the last thing the poor fellow wrote; and in order, sir, that you may see the end to which his misfortunes brought him, read it aloud if you will, for we shall have time for it while they are digging the grave."

"That I will very willingly do," said Vivaldo.

And since all the bystanders had the same desire, they gathered around as he in a loud clear voice read the following poem.

---

4. Virgil (born near Mantua in 70 B.C.E.) had left instructions that his Roman epic, the *Aeneid*, should be burned.

CHAPTER XIV

*In which are set down the despairing verses of the deceased
shepherd, with other unlooked-for happenings.*

Grisóstomo's Song

Since thou desirest that thy cruelty
Be spread from tongue to tongue and land to land,
The unrelenting sternness of thy heart
Shall turn my bosom's hell to minstrelsy
That all men everywhere may understand
The nature of my grief and what thou art.
And as I seek my sorrows to import,
Telling of all the things that thou hast done,
My very entrails shall speak out to brand
Thy heartlessness, thy soul to reprimand,
Where no compassion ever have I won.
Then listen well, lend an attentive ear;
This ballad that thou art about to hear
Is not contrived by art; 'tis a simple song
Such as shepherds sing each day throughout the year—
Surcease of pain for me, for thee a prong.
Then let the roar of lion, fierce wolf's cry,
The horrid hissing of the scaly snake,
The terrifying sound of monsters strange,
Ill-omened call of crow against the sky,
The howling of the wind as it doth shake
The tossing sea where all is constant change,
Bellow of vanquished bull that cannot range
As it was wont to do, the piteous sob
Of the widowed dove as if its heart would break,
Hoot of the envied owl,[5] ever awake,
From hell's own choir the deep and mournful throb—
Let all these sounds come forth and mingle now.
For if I'm to tell my woes, why then, I vow,
I must new measures find, new modes invent,
With sound confusing sense, I may somehow
Portray the inferno where my days are spent.
The mournful echoes of my murmurous plaint
Father Tagus shall not hear as he rolls his sand,
Nor olive-bordered Betis;[6] my lament shall be
To the tall and barren rock as I acquaint
The caves with my sorrow; the far and lonely strand
No human foot has trod shall hear from me
The story of thine inhumanity
As told with lifeless tongue but living word.
I'll tell it to the valleys near at hand
Where never shines the sun upon the land;

---

5. Envied by other birds as the only one that witnessed the Crucifixion.

6. The river Guadalquivir. "Father Tagus": the river Tagus, the Iberian Peninsula's longest river.

By venomous serpents shall my tale be heard
On the low-lying, marshy river plain.
And yet, the telling will not be in vain;
For the reverberations of my plight,
Thy matchless austerity and this my pain,
Through the wide world shall go, thee to indict.
   Disdain may kill; suspicion false or true
May slay all patience; deadliest of all
Is jealousy; while absence renders life
Worse than a void; Hope lends no roseate hue
Against forgetfulness or the dread call
Of death inevitable, the end of strife.
Yet—unheard miracle!—with sorrows rife,
My own existence somehow still goes on;
The flame of life with me doth rise and fall.
Jealous I am, disdained; I know the gall
Of those suspicions that will not be gone,
Which leave me not the shadow of a hope,
And, desperate, I will not even grope
But rather will endure until the end,
And with despair eternally I'll cope,
Knowing that things for me will never mend.
   Can one both hope and fear at the same season?
Would it be well to do so in any case,
Seeing that fear, by far, hath the better excuse?
Confronting jealousy, is there any reason
For me to close my eyes to its stern face,
Pretend to see it not? What is the use,
When its dread presence I can still deduce
From countless gaping wounds deep in my heart?
When suspicion—bitter change!—to truth gives place,
And truth itself, losing its virgin grace,
Becomes a lie, is it not wisdom's part
To open wide the door to frank mistrust?
When disdain's unveiled, to doubt is only just.
O ye fierce tyrants of Love's empery!
Shackle these hands with stout cord, if ye must.
My pain shall drown your triumph—woe is me!
   I die, in short, and since nor life nor death
Yields any hope, to my fancy will I cling.
That man is freest who is Love's bond slave:
I'll say this with my living-dying breath,
And the ancient tyrant's praises I will sing.
Love is the greatest blessing Heaven e'er gave.
What greater beauty could a lover crave
Than that which my fair enemy doth show
In soul and body and in everything?
E'en her forgetfulness of me doth spring
From my own lack of grace, that I well know.
In spite of all the wrongs that he has wrought,
Love rules his empire justly as he ought.

Throw all to the winds and speed life's wretched span
By feeding on his self-deluding thought.
No blessing holds the future that I scan.
   Thou whose unreasonableness reason doth give
For putting an end to this tired life of mine,
From the deep heart wounds which thou mayest plainly see,
Judge if the better course be to die or live.
Gladly did I surrender my will to thine,
Gladly I suffered all thou didst to me;
And now that I'm dying, should it seem to thee
My death is worth a tear from thy bright eyes,
Pray hold it back, fair one, do not repine,
For I would have from thee no faintest sign
Of penitence, e'en though my soul thy prize.
Rather, I'd have thee laugh, be very gay,
And let my funeral be a festive day—
But I am very simple! knowing full well
That thou art bound to go thy blithesome way,
And my untimely end thy fame shall swell.
   Come, thirsting Tantalus from out Hell's pit;
Come, Sisyphus with the terrifying weight
Of that stone thou rollest; Tityus, bring
Thy vulture and thine anguish infinite;
Ixion[7] with thy wheel, be thou not late;
Come, too, ye sisters ever laboring;[8]
Come all, your griefs into my bosom fling,
And then, with lowered voices, intone a dirge,
If dirge be fitting for one so desperate,
A body without a shroud, unhappy fate!
And Hell's three-headed gateman,[9] do thou emerge
With a myriad other phantoms, monstrous swarm,
Beings infernal of fantastic form,
Raising their voices for the uncomforted
In a counterpoint of grief, harmonious storm.
What better burial for a lover dead?
   Despairing song of mine, do not complain,
Nor let our parting cause thee any pain,
For my misfortune is not wholly bad,
Seeing her fortune's bettered by my demise.
Then, even in the grave, be thou not sad.

Those who had listened to Grisóstomo's poem liked it well enough, but the one who read it remarked that it did not appear to him to conform to what had been told him of Marcela's modesty and virtue, seeing that in it the author

---

7. In Greek myth, all four are proverbial images of mortals punished by the Gods with different forms of torture: Tantalus, craving water and fruit which he always fails to reach; Sisyphus, forever vainly trying to roll a stone upward to the top of a hill; Tityus, having his liver devoured by a vulture; and Ixion, being bound to a revolving wheel.

8. In classical mythology, the three Fates (*Moerae* to the Greeks, *Parcae* to the Romans), spinners of man's destiny.

9. Cerberus, a doglike three-headed monster, the mythological guardian of Hell.

complains of jealousy, suspicion, and absence, all to the prejudice of her good name. To this Ambrosio, as one who had known his friend's most deeply hidden thoughts, replied as follows:

"By way of satisfying, sir, the doubt that you entertain, it is well for you to know that when the unfortunate man wrote that poem, he was by his own volition absent from Marcela, to see if this would work a cure; but when the enamored one is away from his love, there is nothing that does not inspire in him fear and torment, and such was the case with Grisóstomo, for whom jealous imaginings, fears, and suspicions became a seeming reality. And so, in this respect, Marcela's reputation for virtue remains unimpaired; beyond being cruel and somewhat arrogant, and exceedingly disdainful, she could not be accused by the most envious of any other fault."

"Yes, that is so," said Vivaldo.

He was about to read another of the papers he had saved from the fire when he was stopped by a marvelous vision—for such it appeared—that suddenly met his sight; for there atop the rock beside which the grave was being hollowed out stood the shepherdess Marcela herself, more beautiful even than she was reputed to be. Those who up to then had never seen her looked on in silent admiration, while those who were accustomed to beholding her were held in as great a suspense as the ones who were gazing upon her for the first time.

No sooner had Ambrosio glimpsed her than, with a show of indignation, he called out to her, "So, fierce basilisk[1] of these mountains, have you perchance come to see if in your presence blood will flow from the wounds of this poor wretch whom you by your cruelty have deprived of life?[2] Have you come to gloat over your inhuman exploits, or would you from that height look down like another pitiless Nero upon your Rome in flames and ashes?[3] Or perhaps you would arrogantly tread under foot this poor corpse, as an ungrateful daughter did that of her father Tarquinius?[4] Tell us quickly why you have come and what it is that you want most; for I know that Grisóstomo's thoughts never failed to obey you in life, and though he is dead now, I will see that all those who call themselves his friends obey you likewise."

"I do not come, O Ambrosio, for any of the reasons that you have mentioned," replied Marcela. "I come to defend myself and to demonstrate how unreasonable all those persons are who blame me for their sufferings and for Grisóstomo's death. I therefore ask all present to hear me attentively. It will not take long and I shall not have to spend many words in persuading those of you who are sensible that I speak the truth.

"Heaven made me beautiful, you say, so beautiful that you are compelled to love me whether you will or no; and in return for the love that you show me, you would have it that I am obliged to love you in return. I know, with that natural understanding that God has given me, that everything beautiful is lov-

---

1. A mythical lizardlike creature whose gaze and breath were supposed to be lethal.
2. According to folklore, the corpse of a murdered person was supposed to bleed in the presence of the murderer.
3. In tale and proverb, the Roman emperor Nero is supposed to have been singing while from a tower he observed the burning of Rome

in 64 C.E.
4. The inaccurate allusion is to Tullia, actually the wife of the last of the legendary kings of early Rome, Tarquinius; she let the wheel of her carriage trample over the body of her father—the previous king, Servius Tullius—whom her husband Tarquinius had liquidated.

able; but I cannot see that it follows that the object that is loved for its beauty must love the one who loves it. Let us suppose that the lover of the beautiful were ugly and, being ugly, deserved to be shunned; it would then be highly absurd for him to say, 'I love you because you are beautiful; you must love me because I am ugly.'

"But assuming that two individuals are equally beautiful, it does not mean that their desires are the same; for not all beauty inspires love, but may sometimes merely delight the eye and leave the will intact. If it were otherwise, no one would know what he wanted, but all would wander vaguely and aimlessly with nothing upon which to settle their affections; for the number of beautiful objects being infinite, desires similarly would be boundless. I have heard it said that true love knows no division and must be voluntary and not forced. This being so, as I believe it is, then why would you compel me to surrender my will for no other reason than that you say you love me? But tell me: supposing that Heaven which made me beautiful had made me ugly instead, should I have any right to complain because you did not love me? You must remember, moreover, that I did not choose this beauty that is mine; such as it is, Heaven gave it to me of its grace, without any choice or asking on my part. As the viper is not to be blamed for the deadly poison that it bears, since that is a gift of nature, so I do not deserve to be reprehended for my comeliness of form.

"Beauty in a modest woman is like a distant fire or a sharp-edged sword: the one does not burn, the other does not cut, those who do not come near it. Honor and virtue are the adornments of the soul, without which the body is not beautiful though it may appear to be. If modesty is one of the virtues that most adorn and beautify body and soul, why should she who is loved for her beauty part with that virtue merely to satisfy the whim of one who solely for his own pleasure strives with all his force and energy to cause her to lose it? I was born a free being, and in order to live freely I chose the solitude of the fields; these mountain trees are my company, the clear-running waters in these brooks are my mirror, and to the trees and waters I communicate my thoughts and lend them of my beauty.

"In short, I am that distant fire, that sharp-edged sword, that does not burn or cut. Those who have been enamored by the sight of me I have disillusioned with my words; and if desire is sustained by hope, I gave none to Grisóstomo or any other, and of none of them can it be said that I killed them with my cruelty, for it was rather their own obstinacy that was to blame. And if you reproach me with the fact that his intentions were honorable and that I ought for that reason to have complied with them, I will tell you that when, on this very spot where his grave is now being dug, he revealed them to me, I replied that it was my own intention to live in perpetual solitude and that only the earth should enjoy the fruit of my retirement and the spoils of my beauty; and if he with all this plain-speaking was still stubbornly bent upon hoping against hope and sailing against the wind, is it to be wondered at if he drowned in the gulf of his own folly?

"Had I led him on, it would have been falsely; had I gratified his passion, it would have been against my own best judgment and intentions; but, though I had disillusioned him, he persisted, and though I did not hate him, he was driven to despair. Ask yourselves, then, if it is reasonable to blame me for his woes! Let him who has been truly deceived complain; let him despair who has been cheated of his promised hopes; if I have enticed any, let him speak up; if I have accepted the attentions of any, let him boast of it; but let not him to whom I have promised nothing, whom I have neither enticed nor accepted, apply to me such terms as cruel and homicidal. It has not as yet been Heaven's will to destine me to love any man, and there is no use expecting me to love of my own free choice.

"Let what I am saying now apply to each and every one of those who would have me for their own, and let it be understood from now on that if any die on account of me, he is not to be regarded as an unfortunate victim of jealousy, since she that cares for none can give to none the occasion for being jealous; nor is my plain-speaking to be taken as disdain. He who calls me a wild beast and a basilisk, let him leave me alone as something that is evil and harmful; let him who calls me ungrateful cease to wait upon me; let him who finds me strange shun my acquaintance; if I am cruel, do not run after me; in which case this wild beast, this basilisk, this strange, cruel, ungrateful creature will not run after them, seek them out, wait upon them, nor endeavor to know them in any way.

"The thing that killed Grisóstomo was his impatience and the impetuosity of his desire; so why blame my modest conduct and retiring life? If I choose to preserve my purity here in the company of the trees, how can he complain of my unwillingness to lose it who would have me keep it with other men? I, as you know, have a worldly fortune of my own and do not covet that of others. My life is a free one, and I do not wish to be subject to another in any way. I neither love nor hate anyone; I do not repel this one and allure that one; I do not play fast and loose with any. The modest conversation of these village lasses and the care of my goats is sufficient to occupy me. Those mountains there represent the bounds of my desire, and should my wishes go beyond them, it is but to contemplate the beauty of the heavens, that pathway by which the soul travels to its first dwelling place."

Saying this and without waiting for any reply, she turned her back and entered the thickest part of a nearby wood, leaving all present lost in admiration of her wit as well as her beauty. A few—those who had felt the powerful dart of her glances and bore the wounds inflicted by her lovely eyes—were of a mind to follow her, taking no heed of the plainly worded warning they had just had from her lips; whereupon Don Quixote, seeing this and thinking to himself that here was an opportunity to display his chivalry by succoring a damsel in distress, laid his hand upon the hilt of his sword and cried out, loudly and distinctly, "Let no person of whatever state or condition he may be dare to follow the beauteous Marcela under pain of incurring my furious wrath. She has shown with clear and sufficient reasons that little or no blame for Grisóstomo's death is to be attached to her; she has likewise shown how far she is from acceding to the desires of any of her suitors, and it is accordingly only just that in place of being hounded and persecuted she should be honored and esteemed by all good people in this world as the only woman in it who lives with such modesty and good intentions."

Whether it was due to Don Quixote's threats or because Ambrosio now told them that they should finish doing the things which his good friend had desired should be done, no one stirred from the spot until the burial was over and Grisóstomo's papers had been burned. As the body was laid in the grave, many tears were shed by the bystanders. Then they placed a heavy stone upon it until the slab which Ambrosio was thinking of having made should be ready, with an epitaph that was to read:

> *Here lies a shepherd by love betrayed,*
> *His body cold in death,*
> *Who with his last and faltering breath*
> *Spoke of a faithless maid.*
> *He died by the cruel, heartless hand*
> *Of a coy and lovely lass,*
> *Who by bringing men to so sorry a pass*
> *Love's tyranny doth expand.*

They then scattered many flowers and boughs over the top of the grave, and, expressing their condolences to the dead man's friend, Ambrosio, they all took their leave, including Vivaldo and his companions. Don Quixote now said good-bye to the travelers as well, although they urged him to come with them to Seville, assuring him that he would find in every street and at every corner of that city more adventures than are to be met with anywhere else. He thanked them for the invitation and the courtesy they had shown him in offering it, but added that for the present he had no desire to visit Seville, not until he should have rid these mountains of the robbers and bandits of which they were said to be full.

Seeing that his mind was made up, the travelers did not urge him further but, bidding him another farewell, left him and continued on their way; and the reader may be sure that in the course of their journey they did not fail to discuss the story of Marcela and Grisóstomo as well as Don Quixote's madness. As for the good knight himself, he was resolved to go seek the shepherdess and offer her any service that lay in his power; but things did not turn out the way he expected.* * *

[*Fighting the Sheep*]

From CHAPTER XVIII

In which is set forth the conversation that Sancho Panza had with his master, Don Quixote, along with other adventures deserving of record.

*   *   *

Don Quixote caught sight down the road of a large cloud of dust that was drawing nearer.

"This, O Sancho," he said, turning to his squire, "is the day when you shall see the boon that fate has in store for me; this, I repeat, is the day when, as well as on any other, shall be displayed the valor of my good right arm. On this day I shall perform deeds that will be written down in the book of fame for all centuries to come. Do you see that dust cloud rising there, Sancho? That is the dust stirred up by a vast army marching in this direction and composed of many nations."

"At that rate," said Sancho, "there must be two of them, for there is another one just like it on the other side."

Don Quixote turned to look and saw that this was so. He was overjoyed by the thought that these were indeed two armies about to meet and clash in the middle of the broad plain; for at every hour and every moment his imagination was filled with battles, enchantments, nonsensical adventures, tales of love, amorous challenges, and the like, such as he had read of in the books of chivalry, and every word he uttered, every thought that crossed his mind, every act he performed, had to do with such things as these. The dust clouds he had sighted were raised by two large droves of sheep coming along the road in opposite directions, which by reason of the dust were not visible until they were close at hand, but Don Quixote insisted so earnestly that they were armies that Sancho came to believe it.

"Sir," he said, "what are we to do?"

"What are we to do?" echoed his master. "Favor and aid the weak and needy. I would inform you, Sancho, that the one coming toward us is led and commanded by the great emperor Alifanfarón, lord of the great isle of Trapobana. This other one at my back is that of his enemy, the king of the Garamantas, Pentapolín of the Rolled-up Sleeve, for he always goes into battle with his right arm bare."

"But why are they such enemies?" Sancho asked.

"Because," said Don Quixote, "this Alifanfarón is a terrible pagan and in love with Pentapolín's daughter, who is a very beautiful and gracious lady and a Christian, for which reason her father does not wish to give her to the pagan king unless the latter first abjures the law of the false prophet, Mohammed, and adopts the faith that is Pentapolín's own."

"Then, by my beard," said Sancho, "if Pentapolín isn't right, and I am going to aid him all I can."

"In that," said Don Quixote, "you will only be doing your duty; for to engage in battles of this sort you need not have been dubbed a knight."

"I can understand that," said Sancho, "but where are we going to put this ass so that we will be certain of finding him after the fray is over? As for going into battle on such a mount, I do not think that has been done up to now."

"That is true enough," said Don Quixote. "What you had best do with him is to turn him loose and run the risk of losing him; for after we emerge the victors we shall have so many horses that even Rocinante will be in danger of being exchanged for another. But listen closely to what I am about to tell you, for I wish to give you an account of the principal knights that are accompanying these two armies; and in order that you may be the better able to see and take note of them, let us retire to that hillock over there which will afford us a very good view."

They then stationed themselves upon a slight elevation from which they would have been able to see very well the two droves of sheep that Don Quixote took to be armies if it had not been for the blinding clouds of dust. In spite of this, however, the worthy gentleman contrived to behold in his imagination what he did not see and what did not exist in reality.

Raising his voice, he went on to explain, "That knight in the gilded armor that you see there, bearing upon his shield a crowned lion crouched at the feet of a damsel, is the valiant Laurcalco, lord of the Silver Bridge; the other with the golden flowers on his armor, and on his shield three crowns argent on an azure field, is the dread Micocolembo, grand duke of Quirocia. And that one on Micocolembo's right hand, with the limbs of a giant, is the ever undaunted Brandabarbarán de Boliche, lord of the three Arabias. He goes armored in a serpent's skin and has for shield a door which, so report has it, is one of those from the temple that Samson pulled down, that time when he avenged himself on his enemies with his own death.

"But turn your eyes in this direction, and you will behold at the head of the other army the ever victorious, never vanquished Timonel de Carcajona, prince of New Biscay, who comes with quartered arms—azure, vert, argent, and or[5]— and who has upon his shield a cat or on a field tawny, with the inscription *Miau*, which is the beginning of his lady's name; for she, so it is said, is the peerless Miulina, daughter of Alfeñiquén, duke of Algarve. And that one over there, who weights down and presses the loins of that powerful charger, in a suit of snow-white armor with a white shield that bears no device whatever— he is a novice knight of the French nation, called Pierres Papin, lord of the baronies of Utrique. As for him you see digging his iron spurs into the flanks of that fleet-footed zebra courser and whose arms are vairs azure, he is the mighty duke of Nervia, Espartafilardo of the Wood, who has for device upon his shield an asparagus plant with a motto in Castilian that says '*Rastrea mi suerte*.'"[6]

In this manner he went on naming any number of imaginary knights on either side, describing on the spur of the moment their arms, colors, devices, and mottoes; for he was completely carried away by his imagination and by this unheard-of madness that had laid hold of him.

Without pausing, he went on, "This squadron in front of us is composed of men of various nations. There are those who drink the sweet waters of the famous Xanthus; woodsmen who tread the Massilian plain; those that sift the fine gold nuggets of Arabia Felix; those that are so fortunate as to dwell on the banks of the clear-running Thermodon, famed for their coolness; those who in many and diverse ways drain the golden Pactolus; Numidians, whose word is never to be trusted; Persians, with their famous bows and arrows; Medes and Parthians, who fight as they flee; Scythians, as cruel as they are fair of skin; Ethiopians, with their pierced lips; and an infinite number of other nationalities whose visages I see and recognize although I cannot recall their names.

"In this other squadron come those that drink from the crystal currents of the olive-bearing Betis; those that smooth and polish their faces with the liquid of the ever rich and gilded Tagus; those that enjoy the beneficial waters of the divine Genil; those that roam the Tartessian plains with their abundant pasturage; those that disport themselves in the Elysian meadows of Jerez; the men of La Mancha, rich and crowned with golden ears of corn; others clad in iron garments, ancient relics of the Gothic race; those that bathe in the Pisuerga, noted for the mildness of its current; those that feed their herds in the widespreading pasture lands along the banks of the winding Guadiana, celebrated for its underground course;[7] those that shiver from the cold of the wooded Pyrenees or dwell amid the white peaks of the lofty Apennines—in short, all those whom Europe holds within its girth."

So help me God! How many provinces, how many nations did he not mention by name, giving to each one with marvelous readiness its proper attributes; for he was wholly absorbed and filled to the brim with what he had read in those lying books of his! Sancho Panza hung on his words, saying nothing, merely turning his head from time to time to have a look at those knights and

---

5. Heraldic terms for, respectively, blue, green, silver, and gold.

6. Probably a pun on *rastrear* (Spanish for "to track" or "to drag"). The meaning of the motto may be either "On Fortune's track" or "My

Fortune creeps." "Arms": i.e. coat of arms, heraldic device.

7. The Guadiana does run underground part of the way through La Mancha.

giants that his master was pointing out to him; but he was unable to discover any of them.

"Sir," he said, "may I go to the devil if I see a single man, giant, or knight of all those that your Grace is talking about. Who knows? Maybe it is another spell, like last night."[8]

"How can you say that?" replied Don Quixote. "Can you not hear the neighing of the horses, the sound of trumpets, the roll of drums?"

"I hear nothing," said Sancho, "except the bleating of sheep."

And this, of course, was the truth; for the flocks were drawing near.

"The trouble is, Sancho," said Don Quixote, "you are so afraid that you cannot see or hear properly; for one of the effects of fear is to disturb the senses and cause things to appear other than what they are. If you are so craven as all that, go off to one side and leave me alone, and I without your help will assure the victory to that side to which I lend my aid."

Saying this, he put spurs to Rocinante and, with his lance at rest, darted down the hillside like a flash of lightning.

As he did so, Sancho called after him, "Come back, your Grace, Señor Don Quixote; I vow to God those are sheep that you are charging. Come back! O wretched father that bore me! What madness is this? Look you, there are no giants, nor knights, nor cats, nor shields either quartered or whole, nor vairs azure or bedeviled. What is this you are doing, O sinner that I am in God's sight?"

But all this did not cause Don Quixote to turn back. Instead, he rode on, crying out at the top of his voice, "Ho, knights, those of you who follow and fight under the banners of the valiant Pentapolín of the Rolled-up Sleeve; follow me, all of you, and you shall see how easily I give you revenge on your enemy, Alifanfarón of Trapobana."

With these words he charged into the middle of the flock of sheep and began spearing at them with as much courage and boldness as if they had been his mortal enemies. The shepherds and herdsmen who were with the animals called to him to stop; but seeing it was no use, they unloosed their slings and saluted his ears with stones as big as your fist.

Don Quixote paid no attention to the missiles and, dashing about here and there, kept crying, "Where are you, haughty Alifanfarón? Come out to me; for here is a solitary knight who desires in single combat to test your strength and deprive you of your life, as a punishment for that which you have done to the valorous Pentapolín Garamanta."

At that instant a pebble from the brook struck him in the side and buried a couple of ribs in his body. Believing himself dead or badly wounded, and remembering his potion, he took out his vial, placed it to his mouth, and began to swallow the balm; but before he had had what he thought was enough, there came another almond, which struck him in the hand, crushing the tin vial and carrying away with it a couple of grinders from his mouth, as well as badly mashing two of his fingers. As a result of these blows the poor knight tumbled from his horse. Believing that they had killed him, the shepherds hastily collected their flock and, picking up the dead beasts, of which there were more than seven, they went off down the road without more ado.

8. The inn where they had spent the previous night had been pronounced by Don Quixote to be an enchanted castle.

Sancho all this time was standing on the slope observing the insane things that his master was doing; and as he plucked savagely at his beard he cursed the hour and minute when luck had brought them together. But when he saw him lying there on the ground and perceived that the shepherds were gone, he went down the hill and came up to him, finding him in very bad shape though not unconscious.

"Didn't I tell you, Señor Don Quixote," he said, "that you should come back, that those were not armies you were charging but flocks of sheep?"

"This," said Don Quixote, "is the work of that thieving magician, my enemy, who thus counterfeits things and causes them to disappear. You must know, Sancho, that it is very easy for them to make us assume any appearance that they choose; and so it is that malign one who persecutes me, envious of the glory he saw me about to achieve in this battle, changed the squadrons of the foe into flocks of sheep. If you do not believe me, I beseech you on my life to do one thing for me, that you may be undeceived and discover for yourself that what I say is true. Mount your ass and follow them quietly, and when you have gone a short way from here, you will see them become their former selves once more; they will no longer be sheep but men exactly as I described them to you in the first place. But do not go now, for I need your kind assistance; come over here and have a look and tell me how many grinders are missing, for it feels as if I did not have a single one left."

* * *

["To Right Wrongs and Come to the Aid of the Wretched"]

CHAPTER XXII

Of how Don Quixote freed many unfortunate ones who, much against their will, were being taken where they did not wish to go.

Cid Hamete Benengeli, the Arabic and Manchegan[9] author, in the course of this most grave, high-sounding, minute, delightful, and imaginative history, informs us that, following the remarks that were exchanged between Don Quixote de la Mancha and Sancho Panza, his squire, as related at the end of Chapter XXI, the knight looked up and saw coming toward them down the road which they were following a dozen or so men on foot, strung together by their necks like beads on an iron chain and all of them wearing handcuffs. They were accompanied by two men on horseback and two on foot, the former carrying wheel-lock muskets while the other two were armed with swords and javelins.

"That," said Sancho as soon as he saw them, "is a chain of galley slaves, people on their way to the galleys where by order of the king they are forced to labor."

"What do you mean by 'forced'?" asked Don Quixote. "Is it possible that the king uses force on anyone?"

"I did not say that," replied Sancho. "What I did say was that these are folks who have been condemned for their crimes to forced labor in the galleys for his Majesty the King."

9. Of La Mancha.

"The short of it is," said the knight, "whichever way you put it, these people are being taken there by force and not of their own free will."

"That is the way it is," said Sancho.

"Well, in that case," said his master, "now is the time for me to fulfill the duties of my calling, which is to right wrongs and come to the aid of the wretched."

"But take note, your Grace," said Sancho, "that justice, that is to say, the king himself, is not using any force upon, or doing any wrong to, people like these, but is merely punishing them for the crimes they have committed."

The chain of galley slaves had come up to them by this time, whereupon Don Quixote very courteously requested the guards to inform him of the reason or reasons why they were conducting these people in such a manner as this. One of the men on horseback then replied that the men were prisoners who had been condemned by his Majesty to serve in the galleys, whither they were bound, and that was all there was to be said about it and all that he, Don Quixote, need know.

"Nevertheless," said the latter, "I should like to inquire of each one of them, individually, the cause of his misfortune." And he went on speaking so very politely in an effort to persuade them to tell him what he wanted to know that the other mounted guard finally said, "Although we have here the record and certificate of sentence of each one of these wretches, we have not the time to get them out and read them to you; and so your Grace may come over and ask the prisoners themselves, and they will tell you if they choose, and you may be sure that they will, for these fellows take a delight in their knavish exploits and in boasting of them afterward."

With this permission, even though he would have done so if it had not been granted him, Don Quixote went up to the chain of prisoners and asked the first whom he encountered what sins had brought him to so sorry a plight. The man replied that it was for being a lover that he found himself in that line.

"For that and nothing more?" said Don Quixote. "And do they, then, send lovers to the galleys? If so, I should have been rowing there long ago."

"But it was not the kind of love that your Grace has in mind," the prisoner went on. "I loved a wash basket full of white linen so well and hugged it so tightly that, if they had not taken it away from me by force, I would never of my own choice have let go of it to this very minute. I was caught in the act, there was no need to torture me, the case was soon disposed of, and they supplied me with a hundred lashes across the shoulders and, in addition, a three-year stretch in the *gurapas*, and that's all there is to tell."

"What are *gurapas*?" asked Don Quixote.

"*Gurapas* are the galleys," replied the prisoner. He was a lad of around twenty-four and stated that he was a native of Piedrahita.

The knight then put the same question to a second man, who appeared to be very downcast and melancholy and did not have a word to say. The first man answered for him.

"This one, sir," he said, "is going as a canary—I mean, as a musician and singer."

"How is that?" Don Quixote wanted to know. "Do musicians and singers go to the galleys too?"

"Yes, sir; and there is nothing worse than singing when you're in trouble."

"On the contrary," said Don Quixote, "I have heard it said that he who sings frightens away his sorrows."

"It is just the opposite," said the prisoner; "for he who sings once weeps all his life long."

"I do not understand," said the knight.

One of the guards then explained. "Sir Knight, with this *non sancta*[1] tribe, to sing when you're in trouble means to confess under torture. This sinner was put to the torture and confessed his crime, which was that of being a *cuatrero*, or cattle thief, and as a result of his confession he was condemned to six years in the galleys in addition to two hundred lashes which he took on his shoulders; and so it is he is always downcast and moody, for the other thieves, those back where he came from and the ones here, mistreat, snub, ridicule, and despise him for having confessed and for not having had the courage to deny his guilt. They are in the habit of saying that the word *no* has the same number of letters as the word *sí*, and that a culprit is in luck when his life or death depends on his own tongue and not that of witnesses or upon evidence; and, in my opinion, they are not very far wrong."

"And I," said Don Quixote, "feel the same way about it." He then went on to a third prisoner and repeated his question.

The fellow answered at once, quite unconcernedly. "I'm going to my ladies, the *gurapas*, for five years, for the lack of five ducats."[2]

"I would gladly give twenty," said Don Quixote, "to get you out of this."

"That," said the prisoner, "reminds me of the man in the middle of the ocean who has money and is dying of hunger because there is no place to buy what he needs. I say this for the reason that if I had had, at the right time, those twenty ducats your Grace is now offering me, I'd have greased the notary's quill and freshened up the attorney's wit with them, and I'd now be living in the middle of Zocodover Square in Toledo instead of being here on this highway coupled like a greyhound. But God is great; patience, and that's enough of it."

Don Quixote went on to a fourth prisoner, a venerable-looking old fellow with a white beard that fell over his bosom. When asked how he came to be there, this one began weeping and made no reply, but a fifth comrade spoke up in his behalf.

"This worthy man," he said, "is on his way to the galleys after having made the usual rounds clad in a robe of state and on horseback."[3]

"That means, I take it," said Sancho, "that he has been put to shame in public."

"That is it," said the prisoner, "and the offense for which he is being punished is that of having been an ear broker, or, better, a body broker. By that I mean to say, in short, that the gentleman is a pimp, and besides, he has his points as a sorcerer."

"If that point had not been thrown in," said Don Quixote, "he would not deserve, for merely being a pimp, to have to row in the galleys, but rather should be the general and give orders there. For the office of pimp is not an indifferent one; it is a function to be performed by persons of discretion and is most necessary in a well-ordered state; it is a profession that should be followed only by the wellborn, and there should, moreover, be a supervisor or examiner as in the case of other offices, and the number of practitioners should be fixed by law as is done

---

1. Unholy (Latin).
2. Gold or silver coins minted in Spain and elsewhere in Europe to facilitate trade.

3. I.e., after having been flogged in public, with all the ceremony that accompanied that punishment.

with brokers on the exchange. In that way many evils would be averted that arise when this office is filled and this calling practiced by stupid folk and those with little sense, such as silly women and pages or mountebanks with few years and less experience to their credit, who, on the most pressing occasions, when it is necessary to use one's wits, let the crumbs freeze between their hand and their mouth and do not know which is their right hand and which is the left.

"I would go on and give reasons why it is fitting to choose carefully those who are to fulfill so necessary a state function, but this is not the place for it. One of these days I will speak of the matter to someone who is able to do something about it. I will say here only that the pain I felt at seeing those white hairs and this venerable countenance in such a plight, and all for his having been a pimp, has been offset for me by the additional information you have given me, to the effect that he is a sorcerer as well; for I am convinced that there are no sorcerers in the world who can move and compel the will, as some simple-minded persons think, but that our will is free and no herb or charm can force it.[4] All that certain foolish women and cunning tricksters do is to compound a few mixtures and poisons with which they deprive men of their senses while pretending that they have the power to make them loved, although, as I have just said, one cannot affect another's will in that manner."

"That is so," said the worthy old man; "but the truth is, sir, I am not guilty on the sorcery charge. As for being a pimp, that is something I cannot deny. I never thought there was any harm in it, however, my only desire being that everyone should enjoy himself and live in peace and quiet, without any quarrels or troubles. But these good intentions on my part cannot prevent me from going where I do not want to go, to a place from which I do not expect to return; for my years are heavy upon me and an affection of the urine that I have will not give me a moment's rest."

With this, he began weeping once more, and Sancho was so touched by it that he took a four-real piece from his bosom and gave it to him as an act of charity.

Don Quixote then went on and asked another what his offense was. The fellow answered him, not with less, but with much more, briskness than the preceding one had shown.

"I am here," he said, "for the reason that I carried a joke too far with a couple of cousins-german[5] of mine and a couple of others who were not mine, and I ended by jesting with all of them to such an extent that the devil himself would never be able to straighten out the relationship. They proved everything on me, there was no one to show me favor, I had no money, I came near swinging for it, they sentenced me to the galleys for six years, and I accepted the sentence as the punishment that was due me. I am young yet, and if I live long enough, everything will come out all right. If, Sir Knight, your Grace has anything with which to aid these poor creatures that you see before you, God will reward you in Heaven, and we here on earth will make it a point to ask God in our prayers to grant you long life and good health, as long and as good as your amiable presence deserves."

---

4. Here Don Quixote despises charms and love potions, although often elsewhere, in his own vision of himself as a knight-errant, he accepts enchantments and spells as part of his world of fantasy.
5. First cousins.

This man was dressed as a student, and one of the guards told Don Quixote that he was a great talker and a very fine Latinist.

Back of these came a man around thirty years of age and of very good appearance, except that when he looked at you his eyes were seen to be a little crossed. He was shackled in a different manner from the others, for he dragged behind him a chain so huge that it was wrapped all around his body, with two rings at the throat, one of which was attached to the chain while the other was fastened to what is known as a keep-friend or friend's foot, from which two irons hung down to his waist, ending in handcuffs secured by a heavy padlock in such a manner that he could neither raise his hands to his mouth nor lower his head to reach his hands.

When Don Quixote asked why this man was so much more heavily chained than the others, the guard replied that it was because he had more crimes against him than all the others put together, and he was so bold and cunning that, even though they had him chained like this, they were by no means sure of him but feared that he might escape from them.

"What crimes could he have committed," asked the knight, "if he has merited a punishment no greater than that of being sent to the galleys?"

"He is being sent there for ten years," replied the guard, "and that is equivalent to civil death. I need tell you no more than that this good man is the famous Ginés de Pasamonte, otherwise known as Ginesillo de Parapilla."

"Señor Commissary," spoke up the prisoner at this point, "go easy there and let us not be so free with names and surnames. My just name is Ginés and not Ginesillo; and Pasamonte, not Parapilla as you make it out to be, is my family name. Let each one mind his own affairs and he will have his hands full."

"Speak a little more respectfully, you big thief, you," said the commissary, "unless you want me to make you be quiet in a way you won't like."

"Man goes as God pleases, that is plain to be seen," replied the galley slave, "but someday someone will know whether my name is Ginesillo de Parapilla or not."

"But, you liar, isn't that what they call you?"

"Yes," said Ginés, "they do call me that; but I'll put a stop to it, or else I'll skin their you-know-what. And you, sir, if you have anything to give us, give it and may God go with you, for I am tired of all this prying into other people's lives. If you want to know anything about my life, know that I am Ginés de Pasamonte whose life story has been written down by these fingers that you see here."

"He speaks the truth," said the commissary, "for he has himself written his story, as big as you please, and has left the book in the prison, having pawned it for two hundred reales."

"And I mean to redeem it," said Ginés, "even if it costs me two hundred ducats."

"Is it as good as that?" inquired Don Quixote.

"It is so good," replied Ginés, "that it will cast into the shade *Lazarillo de Tormes*[6] and all others of that sort that have been or will be written. What I

6. A picaresque or rogue novel, published anonymously about the middle of the 16th century.

would tell you is that it deals with facts, and facts so interesting and amusing that no lies could equal them."

"And what is the title of the book?" asked Don Quixote.

"The Life of Ginés de Pasamonte."

"Is it finished?"

"How could it be finished," said Ginés, "when my life is not finished as yet? What I have written thus far is an account of what happened to me from the time I was born up to the last time that they sent me to the galleys."

"Then you have been there before?"

"In the service of God and the king I was there four years, and I know what the biscuit and the cowhide are like. I don't mind going very much, for there I will have a chance to finish my book. I still have many things to say, and in the Spanish galleys I shall have all the leisure that I need, though I don't need much, since I know by heart what it is I want to write."

"You seem to be a clever fellow," said Don Quixote.

"And an unfortunate one," said Ginés; "for misfortunes always pursue men of genius."

"They pursue rogues," said the commissary.

"I have told you to go easy, Señor Commissary," said Pasamonte, "for their Lordships did not give you that staff in order that you might mistreat us poor devils with it, but they intended that you should guide and conduct us in accordance with his Majesty's command. Otherwise, by the life of—But enough. It may be that someday the stains made in the inn will come out in the wash. Meanwhile, let everyone hold his tongue, behave well, and speak better, and let us be on our way. We've had enough of this foolishness."

At this point the commissary raised his staff as if to let Pasamonte have it in answer to his threats, but Don Quixote placed himself between them and begged the officer not to abuse the man; for it was not to be wondered at if one who had his hands so bound should be a trifle free with his tongue. With this, he turned and addressed them all.

"From all that you have told me, my dearest brothers," he said, "one thing stands out clearly for me, and that is the fact that, even though it is a punishment for offenses which you have committed, the penalty you are about to pay is not greatly to your liking and you are going to the galleys very much against your own will and desire. It may be that the lack of spirit which one of you displayed under torture, the lack of money on the part of another, the lack of influential friends, or, finally, warped judgment on the part of the magistrate, was the thing that led to your downfall; and, as a result, justice was not done you. All of which presents itself to my mind in such a fashion that I am at this moment engaged in trying to persuade and even force myself to show you what the purpose was for which Heaven sent me into this world, why it was it led me to adopt the calling of knighthood which I profess and take the knightly vow to favor the needy and aid those who are oppressed by the powerful.

"However, knowing as I do that it is not the part of prudence to do by foul means what can be accomplished by fair ones, I propose to ask these gentlemen, your guards, and the commissary to be so good as to unshackle you and permit you to go in peace. There will be no dearth of others to serve his Majesty under more propitious circumstances; and it does not appear to me to be just to make slaves of those whom God created as free men. What is more, gentlemen of the guard, these poor fellows have committed no offense against you. Up there, each of us will have to answer for his own sins; for God in Heaven will not fail to punish the evil and reward the good; and it is not good for self-respecting men to be executioners of their fellow-men in something that does not concern them. And so, I ask this of you, gently and quietly, in order that, if you comply with my request, I shall have reason to thank you; and if you do not do so of your own accord, then this lance and this sword and the valor of my arm shall compel you to do it by force."

"A fine lot of foolishness!" exclaimed the commissary. "So he comes out at last with this nonsense! He would have us let the prisoners of the king go free, as if we had any authority to do so or he any right to command it! Be on your way, sir, at once; straighten that basin that you have on your head, and do not go looking for three feet on a cat."[7]

"You," replied Don Quixote, "are the cat and the rat and the rascal!" And, saying this, he charged the commissary so quickly that the latter had no chance to defend himself but fell to the ground badly wounded by the lance blow. The other guards were astounded by this unexpected occurrence; but, recovering their self-possession, those on horseback drew their swords, those on foot leveled their javelins, and all bore down on Don Quixote, who stood waiting for them very calmly. Things undoubtedly would have gone badly for him if the galley slaves, seeing an opportunity to gain their freedom, had not succeeded in breaking the chain that linked them together. Such was the confusion that the guards, now running to fall upon the prisoners and now attacking Don Quixote, who in turn was attacking them, accomplished nothing that was of any use.

Sancho for his part aided Ginés de Pasamonte to free himself, and that individual was the first to drop his chains and leap out onto the field, where, attacking the fallen commissary, he took away that officer's sword and musket; and as he stood there, aiming first at one and then at another, though without firing, the plain was soon cleared of guards, for they had taken to their heels, fleeing at once Pasamonte's weapon and the stones which the galley slaves, freed now, were hurling at them. Sancho, meanwhile, was very much disturbed over this unfortunate event, as he felt sure that the fugitives would report the matter to the Holy Brotherhood, which, to the ringing of the alarm bell, would come out to search for the guilty parties. He said as much to his master, telling him that they should leave at once and go into hiding in the nearby mountains.

"That is all very well," said Don Quixote, "but I know what had best be done now." He then summoned all the prisoners, who, running riot, had by this time despoiled the commissary of everything that he had, down to his skin, and as they gathered around to hear what he had to say, he addressed them as follows:

"It is fitting that those who are wellborn should give thanks for the benefits they have received, and one of the sins with which God is most offended is that of ingratitude. I say this, gentlemen, for the reason that you have seen and had manifest proof of what you owe to me; and now that you are free of the yoke which I have removed from about your necks, it is my will and desire that you should set out and proceed to the city of El Toboso and there present yourselves before the lady Dulcinea del Toboso and say to her that her champion,

7. I.e., looking for the impossible ("five feet" is the more usual form of the proverb).

the Knight of the Mournful Countenance, has sent you; and then you will relate to her, point by point, the whole of this famous adventure which has won you your longed-for freedom. Having done that, you may go where you like, and may good luck go with you."

To this Ginés de Pasamonte replied in behalf of all of them, "It is absolutely impossible, your Grace, our liberator, for us to do what you have commanded. We cannot go down the highway all together but must separate and go singly, each in his own direction, endeavoring to hide ourselves in the bowels of the earth in order not to be found by the Holy Brotherhood, which undoubtedly will come out to search for us. What your Grace can do, and it is right that you should do so, is to change this service and toll that you require of us in connection with the lady Dulcinea del Toboso into a certain number of Credos and Hail Marys which we will say for your Grace's intention, as this is something that can be accomplished by day or night, fleeing or resting, in peace or in war. To imagine, on the other hand, that we are going to return to the fleshpots of Egypt, by which I mean, take up our chains again by setting out along the highway for El Toboso, is to believe that it is night now instead of ten o'clock in the morning and is to ask of us something that is the same as asking pears of the elm tree."

"Then by all that's holy!" exclaimed Don Quixote, whose wrath was now aroused, "you, Don Son of a Whore, Don Ginesillo de Parapilla, or whatever your name is, you shall go alone, your tail between your legs and the whole chain on your back."

Pasamonte, who was by no means a long-suffering individual, was by this time convinced that Don Quixote was not quite right in the head, seeing that he had been guilty of such a folly as that of desiring to free them; and so, when he heard himself insulted in this manner, he merely gave the wink to his companions and, going off to one side, began raining so many stones upon the knight that the latter was wholly unable to protect himself with his buckler, while poor Rocinante paid no more attention to the spur than if he had been made of brass. As for Sancho, he took refuge behind his donkey as a protection against the cloud and shower of rocks that was falling on both of them, but Don Quixote was not able to shield himself so well, and there is no telling how many struck his body, with such force as to unhorse and bring him to the ground.

No sooner had he fallen than the student was upon him. Seizing the basin from the knight's head, he struck him three or four blows with it across the shoulders and banged it against the ground an equal number of times until it was fairly shattered to bits. They then stripped Don Quixote of the doublet which he wore over his armor, and would have taken his hose as well, if his greaves had not prevented them from doing so, and made off with Sancho's greatcoat, leaving him naked; after which, dividing the rest of the battle spoils amongst themselves, each of them went his own way, being a good deal more concerned with eluding the dreaded Holy Brotherhood than they were with burdening themselves with a chain or going to present themselves before the lady Dulcinea del Toboso.

They were left alone now—the ass and Rocinante, Sancho and Don Quixote: the ass, crestfallen and pensive, wagging its ears now and then, being under the impression that the hurricane of stones that had raged about them was not yet over; Rocinante, stretched alongside his master, for the hack also had been felled by a stone; Sancho, naked and fearful of the Holy Brotherhood; and Don

Quixote, making wry faces at seeing himself so mishandled by those to whom he had done so much good.

[A Story of Captivity in North Africa, Told to Don Quixote at the Inn]

From CHAPTER XXXIX

In which the captive narrates the events of his life.[8]

"It was in a village in the mountains of León[9] that the line of which I come had its beginnings, a family more favored by nature than by fortune, although amid the poverty that prevailed in that region my father had the reputation of being a rich man and indeed might have been one, had he displayed the same skill in conserving his property that he did in squandering it. His inclination to liberal spending came from his having been a soldier in his youth, for that is a school in which the miser becomes generous and the generous becomes prodigal; if there are some soldiers that are parsimonious, they may be said to be freaks such as are rarely to be met with.

"My father went beyond the bounds of liberality and came close to prodigality, which is not a profitable thing for a married man with children to bring up who are to succeed him and carry on his name. He had three of them, all of them males and of an age to decide upon their calling in life. Accordingly, when he saw that, as he put it, there was no use in his trying to overcome his natural propensity, he made up his mind to rid himself of the instrument and cause of his lavish spending; in other words, he would get rid of his property, for without his fortune Alexander himself would have appeared in straitened circumstances. And so, calling the three of us together one day and closing himself alone with us, he proceeded to address us somewhat in the following manner:

"'My sons, there is no need of my telling you that I have your welfare at heart; it is enough to know and state that you are my sons. On the other hand, the fact that I am unable to control myself when it comes to preserving your estate may well give you a contrary impression. For this reason, in order that you may be assured from now on that I love you as a father should and have no desire to ruin you as a stepfather might, I have decided to do for you something that I have long had in mind and to which I have given the most mature consideration. You are of an age to enter upon your professions in life, or at least to choose the ones which, when you are older, will bring you profit and honor.

"'What I have thought of doing is to divide my estate into four parts, three of which I will turn over to you so that each has that which is his by right, while the fourth part I will retain for my own livelihood and support for the rest of

---

8. Chapters 39–41 show Don Quixote once again listening to other characters' interpolated stories, in this case, that of a former captive who had arrived at the inn with a mysterious veiled woman. Cervantes himself spent five years as a captive in North Africa, and the captive's marvelous narrative is full of precise details about piracy in the Mediterranean, life in captivity, and the complicated connections across the Christian–Muslim divide.

9. A region in northern Spain, associated with Christian resistance to the Muslim invasion of the peninsula.

the time that Heaven shall be pleased to grant me. But after each of you has had his due share of the property, I would have you follow one of the courses that I shall indicate. We have here in Spain a proverb which to my mind is a very true one, as indeed they all are, being wise maxims drawn from long experience. This one runs, "The Church, the sea, or the Royal Household," which in plainer language is equivalent to saying, "He who would make the most of himself and become a rich man, let him become a churchman, or go to sea and be a merchant, or enter the service of kings in their palaces." For there is another saying, "Better a king's crumb than a lord's favor."

"'I tell you this because it is my wish that one of you follow the profession of letters, that another go into trade, and that the third serve his king as a soldier, seeing that it is a difficult thing to obtain service in his household; for if the military life does not bring much wealth, it does confer fame and high esteem. Within a week, I will give you your shares in money, without defrauding you of a single penny, as you shall see in due course. Tell me, then, if you feel inclined to follow my advice and precepts in relation to what I have suggested.'

"He then called upon me as the eldest to answer; and after having told him that he ought not to rid himself of his property in that manner but should spend as much of it as he wished, since we were young and able to make our own way, I ended by assuring him that I would do as he desired, my own choice being to follow the profession of arms and thus serve God and my king. My second brother, having made a similar declaration, announced his intention of going to the Indies and investing his share in commerce. The youngest one, and in my opinion the wisest, said that he preferred to enter the Church or to go to Salamanca[1] to complete the course of study that he had already begun.

"When we had made our choice of callings, my father embraced us all, and within the brief space of time mentioned he carried out his promise by giving each of us his share, which as I remember amounted to three thousand ducats in currency; for an uncle of ours had purchased the estate and paid for it in cash in order to keep it in the family. On that same day the three of us took leave of our goodhearted father; but inasmuch as it seemed to me an inhuman thing for him to be left with so little money in his old age, I prevailed upon him to take two of my three thousand ducats, since the remainder would be sufficient to meet my wants as a soldier. Moved by my example, my two brothers each gave him a thousand, so that he had in all four thousand, plus the three thousand which, as it appeared, his share of the estate was worth; for he did not care to dispose of his portion but preferred to keep it in land.

"And so, then, as I was saying, we took our leave of him and of our uncle, not without much feeling and many tears on the part of all. They charged us to let them know, whenever it was possible for us to do so, as to how we were faring and whether we were meeting with prosperity or adversity, and we promised them that we would. When he had embraced us and given us his benediction, we all departed, one setting out for Salamanca, another for Seville,[2] while I made for Alicante, where I had heard there was a Genoese craft taking on a cargo of wool for that city.

1. Site of the oldest and most prestigious university in Spain.
2. Seville was the port city for trade and travel to the New World; Alicante was a port for Mediterranean trade.

"It is now twenty-two years since I left my father's house, and although in the course of that time I have written a number of letters, I have had no word either of him or of my brothers. As to my own experiences during those years, I shall relate them for you briefly. Embarking at Alicante, I had a fair voyage to Genoa, and from there I went on to Milan, where I fitted myself out with arms and a few accessories. For it was my intention to take service in the Piedmont, and I was already on my way to Alessandria dell Paglia when I heard that the great Duke of Alva was starting for Flanders. I then changed my plan and, joining his army, served with him in the three campaigns that he waged. I was present at the deaths of the Counts of Egmont and Hoorne and rose to the rank of ensign under a famous captain of Guadalajara, Diego de Urbina by name. After I had been in Flanders for some while, news came of the league which his Holiness, Pope Pius V of blessed memory, had formed with Venice and Spain against the common enemy, the Turk, who about that time had taken, with his fleet, the famous island of Cyprus, which was then under the rule of the Venetians.[3] This was a serious loss and one truly to be deplored.

"It was known for a fact that the commanding general of this league was to be his Most Serene Highness, John of Austria, brother of our good King Philip, and there was much talk of the great and warlike preparations that he was making. I was deeply stirred by all this and felt a desire to take part in the coming campaign; and although I had prospects and almost certain promises of being promoted to captain where I then served, on the first occasion that offered, I chose to leave all this and return to Italy. And as it happened, John of Austria had just arrived in Genoa on his way to Naples to join the Venetian fleet, as he afterward did at Messina.

"In short, I may tell you that I was soon taking part in that most fortunate campaign,[4] having already been made a captain of infantry, an honor that I owed to my good fortune rather than to my merits. And on that day that was so happy a one for all Christendom, since it revealed to all the nations of the world the error under which they had been laboring in believing that the Turks were invincible at sea—on that day, I repeat, in which the haughty Ottoman pride was shattered, among all the happy ones that were there (and those Christians that died were even happier than those that remained alive and victorious), I alone was wretched; for in place of a naval crown[5] such as I might have hoped for had it been in Roman times, I found myself on the night that followed that famous day with chains on my feet and manacles on my hands.

"The way in which it came about was this: El Uchali,[6] King of Algiers, a bold and successful corsair, had attacked and captured the flagship of Malta, on which only three knights were left alive and those three badly wounded; where-

3. All the figures mentioned here are historical. The Captive fights for Habsburg Spain on various fronts: in Flanders, where the Spanish general Fernando Alvarez de Toledo, Duke of Alba (1507–1582) was charged with putting down the revolt of the Northern Provinces, and in the Mediterranean, where Spain joined in a "Holy League" with the papacy and Venice to combat the Ottoman Empire ("the Turk"). "Counts of Egmont and Hoorne": Belgian nobles executed for their rebellion in 1568. "Diego de Urbina":

Cervantes served under this captain at the naval battle of Lepanto, where the Ottomans were defeated.
4. I.e., the battle of Lepanto, fought in the Ionian Sea near Corinth, Greece.
5. Awarded to the first man to board the enemy ship during battle.
6. Uluch Ali (1519–1587), viceroy of Algiers (an Ottoman protectorate) and commander of the Ottoman fleet, defeated the Maltese flagship at Lepanto.

upon the ship of Giovanni Andrea[7] on which I and my company were stationed, came to its assistance. Doing what was customary under the circumstances, I leaped aboard the enemy galley, which, by veering off from the attacking vessel, prevented my men from following me. Thus I was alone among the enemy, who so greatly outnumbered me that any hope of resistance was vain; and the short of it is, after I had been badly wounded, they captured me. As you know, gentlemen, El Uchali and all his fleet made their escape, so that I was left a prisoner in his hands; and that is the reason why it was that only I was miserable among so many who were happy, and a captive among so many who were free. For there were fifteen thousand Christians slaving at the oars in the Turkish fleet who that day obtained their liberty.[8]

"They took me to Constantinople, where the Grand Turk Selim[9] made my master commander at sea for having done his duty in battle so well and displayed his bravery by carrying off the standard of the Order of Malta.[1] The following year, which was '72, I was in Navarino, rowing in the flagship with the three lanterns, and there I saw and noted how the opportunity was lost for capturing the entire Turkish fleet in the harbor; for all the sailors and Janizaries[2] were convinced that they would be attacked while in port and had their clothing and their *passamaques*, or shoes, in readiness in order that they might be able to flee overland without waiting to give combat, so great was the fear that our fleet inspired in them. But Heaven ordained otherwise, not because of any fault or carelessness on the part of our commander, but as a punishment for the sins of Christendom, since it is God's will that we should have with us always the agents of his wrath.

"The upshot of it was, El Uchali withdrew to Modon, which is an island near Navarino, and there, disembarking his men, he proceeded to fortify the mouth of the harbor, after which he waited quietly until John retired. On this voyage one of the galleys, called the *Prize*, whose captain was a son of the famous corsair Barbarossa, was captured by the Neapolitan craft known as the *She-Wolf*, commanded by that thunderbolt of war, that father to his men, the fortunate and never-vanquished captain, Don Alvaro de Bazán, Marquis of Santa Cruz.

"I must not omit telling you what took place in connection with this capture. Barbarossa's son was so cruel and treated his captives so badly that the moment the rowers saw the *She-Wolf* bearing down and gaining upon them, they all at one and the same time dropped their oars and seized the captain, who was standing upon the gangway platform, urging them to row faster. Laying hold of him, they passed him on from bench to bench and from poop to prow, and so bit and chewed him that before he had gone much farther than the ship's mast his soul had already gone to Hell. Such, as I have said, was the cruelty with which he treated them and the hatred that they had for him.

"We then returned to Constantinople, and the next year, which was '73, we learned how John had captured Tunis, driven the Turks out of that kingdom,

7. The Genoese admiral Giovanni Andrea Doria (1539–1606), who led the forces of the Holy League at Lepanto.
8. Captives on either side of the Habsburg–Ottoman conflict were primarily put to work as oarsmen in Mediterranean galleys.
9. Selim II (1524–1574, r. 1566–74), sultan of the Ottoman Empire.
1. I.e., the flag of the militant Christian religious order based on the island of Malta, in the Mediterranean, from where they attacked North African ships.
2. Ottoman soldiers; originally an elite corps made up of captured Christian boys.

and placed Muley Hamet on the throne, thus cutting short the hopes that Muley Hamida,[3] bravest and cruelest Moor in all the world, had of returning to rule there. The Great Turk felt this loss very keenly and, having resort to the cunning which all those of his line possess, he made peace with the Venetians, who desired it much more than he did; and the following year, in '74, he attacked the Goleta[4] and the Fort near Tunis which John had left in a state of semi-completion.

"During all this time I was at the oar, with no hope whatever of gaining my freedom. At least I had no hope of ransom, for I was determined not to write the news of my misfortune to my father. Both the Goleta and the Fort finally fell, for in front of them were massed seventy-five thousand Turkish regulars, while the number of Moors and Arabs from all over Africa was in excess of four hundred thousand; and this enormous force was equipped with so many munitions and engines of war and accompanied by so many sappers that the latter might readily have buried both their objectives under handfuls of earth.

"The Goleta, which had previously been looked upon as inexpugnable, was the first to succumb; and if it was lost, this was not the fault of its defenders, who did all that they should and could have done. It was rather due to the fact that, as experience showed, it was easy to throw up entrenchments in the desert sand; for water was commonly found there at a depth of two palms, but the Turks went down for a depth of two *varas*[5] without striking any, and as a result, piling their sandbags one on top of another, they were able to raise ramparts so high that they could command the walls of the fort and fire upon them as from a bastion, so that it was impossible to make a stand or put up a defense.

* * *

From CHAPTER XL

In which the captive's story is continued.

* * *

"Well, then, the Goleta and the Fort having fallen, the Turks ordered the former stronghold dismantled, there being nothing left of the Fort to raze; and in order to accomplish the task more speedily and with less labor, they mined three-quarters of it, but by no device could they succeed in blowing up what appeared to be the weakest part, namely the old walls. On the other hand, all that remained of the new fortifications that the Little Friar[6] had built was brought to the ground with the greatest of ease.

"Finally, the victorious fleet returned in triumph to Constantinople, and a few months afterward my master, El Uchali, died, the one who was known as 'Uchali Fartax,' which in the Turkish tongue means 'scurvy renegade'; for that is what he was, and it is the custom of the Turks to bestow names that signify some fault or virtue. This is for the reason that they have only four surnames

---

3. Muley Hamet (Muley Mohammed) became ruler of Tunis in 1573, but was captured by the Ottomans the following year. His brother Muley Hamida (Ahmed Sultan) had joined the attack on Tunis by John of Austria.

4. Fortress at the mouth of Tunis's harbor.
5. One *vara* is a measure equivalent to about 2.8 feet.
6. Nickname for the Italian architect Giacome Paleazzo, who served Philip II.

altogether, which apply to those descended from the Ottoman line, the others, as I started to say, take their names and surnames from bodily defects or moral characteristics. And this Scurvy One, being a slave of the Grand Seignior's, had slaved at the oar for fourteen years, being then more than thirty-four years of age when he turned renegade. The way it came about was this: as he was rowing one day a Turk had dealt him a blow, and in order to be revenged on the fellow he renounced his faith. After that, his valor proved to be so outstanding that he did not have to resort to the usual underhanded ways and means by which the Great Turk's favorites rise at court, but was made king of Algiers and later commander at sea, which is the office that is third in rank in that seigniory.

"El Uchali was a Calabrian by birth and a man of moral principle who treated his captives with great humanity. He came to have three thousand of them, and after his death they were divided in accordance with the provisions of his will between the Grand Seignior (who is heir to all who die and who shares with the offspring left by the deceased) and his renegades. I fell to a Venetian renegade who, as a cabin boy aboard a ship, had been captured by Uchali. His master grew so fond of him that the youth became his prime favorite, and he also came to be the cruelest one of his kind that was ever seen. His name was Hassan Aga,[7] and, amassing great wealth, he rose to be king of Algiers. I accompanied him there from Constantinople and was somewhat pleased at being so near to Spain. Not that I intended to write to anyone there concerning my misfortunes; but I wished to see if fortune would be more favorable to me here than it had been in Turkey, where I had unsuccessfully essayed a thousand different means of escape. In Algiers I thought to find other ways of attaining what I desired; for never once did the hope leave me of achieving my freedom; and when my plottings and schemings did not come up to expectations and my attempts were unsuccessful, I did not at once abandon myself to despair but began to look for or invent some fresh hope to sustain me, however faint and weak it might be.

"In this way I managed to keep myself alive, shut up in a prison or house which the Turks call a bagnio, in which they confine their Christian captives, both those of the king and those belonging to certain private individuals, and also those that are referred to as being *del Almacen*, that is to say, captives that belong to the Council and serve the city in public works and other employment. It is very difficult for these last to obtain their freedom, for inasmuch as they are held in common and have no individual for a master, there is no one with whom to treat regarding their ransom even where they have the means for purchasing their liberation. In these bagnios, as I have said, they are accustomed to place captives belonging to certain private citizens of the town, chiefly the ones that are to be ransomed, since there they may keep them in safety and leisure. For the king's captives do not go out to labor with the rest of the galley crew, unless their ransom be late in coming, in which case, by way of inducing them to write for it more urgently, they put them to work and send them to gather wood with the others, which is no small task.

"I, then, was one of this group; for when they discovered that I was a captain, although I told them that I had no fortune and few prospects, they neverthe-

---

7. Hasan Aga, or Hasan the Venetian, was captured at a young age and converted to Islam. A protegé of Uluch Ali, he ruled Algiers from 1577 to 1578.

less insisted upon placing me among those gentlemen and others who were waiting for ransom. They put a chain upon me, but more as a mark of my status than in order to keep me from escaping; and thus I spent my days in that bagnio along with many important personages who had been designated and were being held for the purpose I have mentioned. And although we were at times harassed by hunger and the want of clothing, nothing distressed us so much as what we almost constantly saw and heard of the cruelties, such as never before were heard of or seen, which my master practiced upon the Christians. Each day he hanged his man, impaled one, cut off the ear of another; and all this with so little excuse, or with none at all, that the Turks had to admit he did it simply to be doing it, inasmuch as their natural bent toward the entire human race is a homicidal one.

"The only person who made out well with him was a Spanish soldier by the name of Saavedra,[8] for although this man had done things which will remain in the memory of that people for years to come, and all by way of obtaining his liberty, yet the Moor never dealt him a blow nor ordered him flogged; as a matter of fact, he never even gave him so much as a harsh word. And for the least of the many things that Saavedra did, we were all afraid that he would be impaled, and he himself feared it more than once. If time permitted, which unfortunately it does not, I could tell you here and now something of that soldier's exploits which would interest and amaze you much more than my own story.

"To continue: Overlooking the courtyard of our prison were the windows of a wealthy Moor of high rank. These, as is usually the case, more nearly resembled peepholes and were, moreover, covered with very thick and tightly drawn blinds. It happened, then, that one day I and three companions were on the prison terrace, amusing ourselves by seeing how far we could leap with our chains on; and, since we were alone, all the rest of the Christians having gone out to labor, I chanced to raise my eyes, when through one of those closed windows I saw a reed appear with a piece of linen cloth attached to the end of it, and it was moving and waving as if signaling for us to come and take it. As we stood gazing up at it, one of those who was with me went over and placed himself directly beneath the reed to see if it would be released or what would happen; but the moment he did so, it was raised and moved from side to side as if someone were saying no by shaking the head. The Christian then came back, and at once it was lowered again and the person above began making exactly the same motions with it as before. Another of my companions repeated the performance, and the same thing happened with him. And a third man had a similar experience.

"Seeing this, I could not resist the temptation to try my luck, and as soon as I was beneath the reed, it was dropped. It fell at my feet there in the bagnio, and I immediately hastened to untie the linen cloth, whereupon I found knotted in it ten cianis, which are gold coins of base alloy in use among the Moors, each being worth ten reales in our money. I need not tell you how happy I was over this windfall, and my happiness was equaled by my wonder as to how it had come to us, and to me in particular, since the unwillingness of the donor to release the reed to anyone other than me showed clearly that I was the one for whom the favor was intended. Taking the welcome money, I broke the reed

8. Cervantes refers to himself here; his full name was Miguel de Cervantes Saavedra.

and went back to the terrace, where I once more gazed up at the window. Then it was I saw a very white hand emerge, which opened and closed very quickly; and by this we understood or were led to imagine that it was some woman who lived in that house who had shown us this act of kindness. By way of thanking her, we salaamed after the fashion of the Moors, which is done by bowing the head, bending the body at the waist, and crossing the arms upon the bosom.

"Shortly afterward, through the same window, there came a little cross made of reeds, only to be at once withdrawn. This strengthened us in the belief that some Christian woman must be a captive in that house, and that it was she who had done us the favor; but the whiteness of the hand and the Moorish bracelets of which we had caught a glimpse inclined us to think otherwise, although we fancied that it might be some fair renegade, for such women are commonly taken as lawful wives by their masters, who are glad to do this, since they esteem them more highly than those of their own race.

"In all our discussions about the matter, however, we were very far from the truth; but from that time forth we were solely concerned with looking up at that window from which the reed had appeared, as if it had been our north star. Two weeks went by in which we had no further sight of it, nor of the hand, nor any signal whatsoever. And although during that time we did our best to find out who lived in the house and if there was any renegade Christian woman in it, we found no one who could tell us any more about the matter than that the house belonged to a rich and prominent Moor by the name of Hadji Morato, a former alcaide of La Pata, which is a very important office with them.[9]

"But just as we had given up hope of a second rain of cianis, we unexpectedly saw the reed appear again with another knotted cloth on the end of it, a thicker one this time. This happened at an hour when the bagnio was all but deserted, as it had been on the previous occasion, and we made the same test, each of the others in turn going to stand beneath the window before I did, but it was only when I came up that the reed was released and dropped. I undid the knot and found forty Spanish gold crowns and a message written in Arabic with the sign of the cross beneath it. I kissed the cross, took the crowns, and returned to the terrace, where we all again salaamed. Then the hand appeared once more, and I made signs that we would read the message, after which the window was closed. We were at once pleased and bewildered by what had occurred, and as none of us understood Arabic, great was our curiosity to know what the message contained, and greater still our difficulty in finding someone who could read it for us.

"Finally, I decided to take a certain renegade into my confidence. He was a native of Murcia who professed to be a good friend of mine and who had promised to keep any secret that I might entrust to him; for it is the custom of some renegades, when they intend to return to Christian territory, to carry about with them testimonials of one sort or another from important captives to the effect that So-and-So is a good man, has always shown kindness to Christians, and is anxious to flee at the first opportunity that offers. There are those who procure these certificates with a proper object in mind, and there are others who cunningly misemploy them in case of need. The latter, when they go to commit depredations on Christian soil, if perchance they are lost or captured, will pro-

---

9. Hajji Murad, a Slavonian who converted to Islam and became a powerful official in Algiers. "Alcaide": commander of a fortress or garrison, in this case the city of al-Batha.

duce their affidavits as evidence of the purpose for which they came: namely, that of remaining in a Christian land; and they will assert that it was for this reason they joined the Turks. In such a manner they escape the immediate consequences of their act and are reconciled with the Church before it can punish them; and then, as soon as they are able to do so, they return to Barbary to become what they were before. But, as has been said, there are others who make honest use of these certificates and actually do remain with their coreligionists.

"It was one of these renegades who was my friend. He had testimonials from all of us in which we expressed our confidence in him as forcefully as we could, and if the Moors had found him with these papers on his person, they would have burned him alive. He was known to be well versed in Arabic, being able not only to speak it but to write it as well. And so, before I unbosomed myself to him, I asked him to read the message for me, telling him that I had accidentally come upon it in a hole in my cell. He opened it and studied it for some little time, muttering to himself all the while. I asked him if he understood it, and he assured me that he did, very well, and that if I wished him to give it to me word for word, I should provide him with pen and ink, as he could do it better that way. We gave him what he asked for, and he translated the message little by little. When he had finished he said, 'You will find set down here in Spanish absolutely everything that is written on this paper; and you are to remember that where it says Lela Marien, that means Our Lady the Virgin Mary.'

"Following is the message as he had transcribed it:

"When I was young, my father had a slave girl who taught me the Christian *zala*[1] in my language, and she also told me many things about Lela Marien. The Christian woman died, and I know that she did not go to the fire but is with Allah, for twice afterward I saw her and she told me to make my way to the land of the Christians to see Lela Marien, who loved me a great deal. I do not know how to do so. I have seen many Christians from this window, and only you have seemed to me to be a gentleman. I am very young and beautiful and have much money to take with me. See if you can arrange for us to go, and there you may be my husband if you wish. If you do not wish it so, it will not matter to me, for Lela Marien will provide someone to marry me. I myself have written this; have a care as to whom you give it to read; do not trust any Moor, for they are all treacherous. I am deeply concerned lest you show this to someone, for if my father knew of it, he would cast me into a well and cover me with stones. On the reed I shall put a thread. Attach your reply to it, and in case you have no one who can write Arabic for you, tell me by means of signs and Lela Marien will make me understand. May She and Allah and this cross protect you. The cross I kiss many times, as the Christian slave woman bade me.

"You can imagine, gentle folk, how astonished and pleased we were by the contents of this message. Indeed, we showed our feelings so openly that the renegade realized it was not by chance that this paper had been found but that it was in reality addressed to one of our number. He accordingly now asked us if his suspicions were true, telling us that we should confide everything to him, as he would be willing to risk his life for our freedom. Saying this, he brought forth from his bosom a metal crucifix and with many tears swore by the God

1. Salaam, here with the sense of prayer or ceremony.

whom that image represented and in whom he, though a wicked sinner, still fully and faithfully believed, that he would loyally guard all the secrets we might see fit to reveal to him; for he felt—indeed, he was almost certain—that through the one who had written that message he and all of us would be able to gain our freedom and it would be possible for him to fulfill his dearest wish, that of returning to the bosom of Holy Mother Church, from which like a rotten limb he had been severed and separated through ignorance and sin.

"So many tears did the renegade shed, and so many signs of repentance did he show, that we all of us unanimously consented and agreed to tell him the truth of the matter; and so we proceeded to give him an account of everything, keeping nothing hidden. We pointed out to him the little window through which the reed had appeared, and he then and there made note of the house and announced his intention of taking special pains to find out who lived in it. We also decided that it would be well to reply to the Moorish damsel's note, and, seeing that we had someone there who was capable of doing this, the renegade at once wrote out the words that I dictated to him, which were exactly as I shall give them to you; for nothing of any importance that happened to me in the course of this adventure has slipped my memory, nor shall it escape me as long as I live. This was the reply that we sent to the Moorish lady:

"May the true Allah protect you, my lady, and that blessed Mary who is the true Mother of God and who has put it in your heart to go to the land of the Christians, because she loves you well. Pray to her to show you how you may carry out her command, for she is well disposed and will assuredly do so. Do not fail to write and advise me of your plans, and I will always let you have an answer. The great Allah has given us a Christian captive who knows how to read and write your language, as you can plainly see from this message. Thus, with nothing to fear, we shall be able to know your wishes. You say that if you go to the land of the Christians, you will be my wife, and I as a good Christian promise you that you shall be, and you know that Christians keep their promises better than Moors. May Allah and Mary His Mother watch over you, my lady.

"Having written and sealed this message, I waited two days until the bagnio was deserted as usual, and then I went out to my accustomed place on the terrace to see if the reed would appear, which it did very shortly. As soon as I caught sight of it, although I could not see who was letting it down, I held up the paper as a sign the person above should attach the thread. This had already been done, however, and I now fastened the paper to it, and shortly thereafter our star once more made its appearance with the white banner of peace in the form of a little bundle. It fell at my feet, and, upon picking it up, I found in the cloth all sorts of gold and silver coins, more than fifty crowns, which more than fifty times doubled our happiness and strengthened our hope of obtaining our liberty.

"That same night our renegade came back and told us what he had learned. The one who lived in that house was the same Moor whose name, Hadji Morato, had been mentioned to us. He was enormously rich and had one daughter, the only heir to all his wealth; and it was the general opinion in the city that she was the most beautiful woman in Barbary. Many of the viceroys who came there had sought her hand in marriage, but she had been unwilling to wed; and it was also known that she had had a female slave who was a Christian and who was now dead. All of which bore out what was said in the note. We then took counsel with the renegade as to what we should do in order to rescue the Moorish damsel and make our escape to the land of Christians, and it was finally agreed that we should wait until we had further word from Zoraida, which was the name of the one who now wishes to be known as Maria.[2] For we saw plainly enough that she and no other would be able to provide a way out of all these difficulties. When we had reached this decision, the renegade told us not to worry, that he would set us at liberty or lose his life in the attempt.

"For four days the bagnio was full of people, and as a result the reed did not appear, but at the end of that period, when the place was once more empty, the bundle was again let down, so pregnant-looking as to promise a very happy birth. The reed and the cloth descended to me, and I found in the latter a message and a hundred gold crowns, with no other money whatsoever. The renegade being present, we gave him the note to read inside our cell, and he translated it for us as follows:

"Sir, I do not know how to arrange for us to go to Spain, nor has Lela Marien told me, although I have asked it of her. The thing that can be done is for me to give you for this venture much money in gold. Ransom yourself and your friends with it, and let one of you go ahead to the land of the Christians, purchase a boat there, and return for the others. He will find me in my father's garden, which is at the Babazón gate[3] near the seashore. I expect to be there all this summer with my father and my servants. You will be able to take me away from there by night and carry me to the boat with nothing to fear. And remember that you are to be my husband, or I shall ask Mary to punish you. If you can trust no one to go for the boat, ransom yourself and go; for I know that you are more trustworthy than any other, being a gentleman and a Christian. Make it a point to become familiar with the garden; and, meanwhile, when I see you out for a stroll, I shall know that the bagnio is empty and will give you much money. Allah protect you, my lord.

"Such were the contents of the second note; and when all had heard it read, each offered to be the ransomed one, promising to go and return with all haste; and I myself made the same offer. But the renegade opposed all this, saying he would by no means consent for anyone to go free until we all went together; for experience had taught him that men when freed were lax about keeping the word they had given in captivity. He added that many times certain important captives had had recourse to this expedient and had ransomed one of their number to go to Valencia or Majorca, providing him with sufficient money to fit out a boat and return for them, but he had never come back. For, the renegade observed, liberty recovered and the dread of losing it again would erase from their memories all the obligations that there are. By way of showing us the truth of this statement, he briefly related for us what had recently happened to some Christian gentlemen, one of the strangest cases that had ever been heard of in those parts where the most astonishing and terrifying things are all the time occurring.

"In short, he told us that what we could and should do was to give him the ransom money intended for one of us Christians, and he would buy a boat

---

2. Zoraida is based on a historical figure. Hajji Murad had a daughter named Zahara, who married first Abd al-Malik, future sultan of Morocco, and then, after his death, Hasan Pasha, with whom she moved to Constantinople.
3. Bab Azoun, gate to the city of Algiers.

there in Algiers under pretext of turning merchant and trading with Tetuan and along the coast in that region. Being a ship's master, it would be easy for him to hit upon a way of rescuing us from the bagnio and putting us all aboard, especially if the Moorish lady, as she said, was to provide the money for ransoming the entire lot of us. As free men, it would be the easiest thing in the world to embark, even at midday. The greatest obstacle lay in the fact that the Moors would not permit any renegade to buy or own a boat, unless it was a vessel to go on pillaging expeditions; for they feared that if he purchased a small one, especially if he was a Spaniard, he merely wanted it for the purpose of escaping to Christian territory. He, our friend, could readily overcome this difficulty, however, by taking a Tagarin Moor[4] into partnership with him in the purchase of the boat and the profits to be derived from it, and under cover of this arrangement he could become master of the craft; and with that he regarded the rest of it as something already accomplished.

"Although it seemed to me and to my comrades that it would have been better to send to Majorca for the boat as the Moorish lady had suggested, we did not dare oppose him, being fearful that if we did not do as he said he would reveal our plans and put us in danger of losing our lives when our dealings with Zoraida were discovered, for whose life we would all have given our own. We accordingly determined to leave the matter in the hands of God and in those of the renegade, and we therewith replied to Zoraida that we would do all that she had counseled us, since the advice she had given us was as good as if it had come from Lela Marien herself, adding that it remained for her to decide as to whether the project was to be postponed or put into execution at once. I also, once more, made an offer to marry her. And so it came about that the next day, when there was no one in the bagnio, she on various occasions by means of the reed and the cloth conveyed to us two thousand gold crowns and a message in which she informed us that on the next *Jumá*, that is to say, Friday, she was leaving for her father's summer place and that before she left she would give us more money. In case this was not enough, we were to let her know and we might have anything we asked for; for her father had so much that he would never miss it, and, what was more, she held the keys to everything.

"We at once gave the renegade fifteen hundred crowns with which to buy the boat, while I took eight hundred to procure my own ransom, giving the money to a merchant of Valencia who was in Algiers at the time and who had the king release me on the promise that, when the next boat arrived from home, he would pay the ransom fee; for if he were to pay it at once, the king might suspect that the funds had been in Algiers for some time and that the merchant for his own profit had kept the matter secret. Moreover, my master was so captious that I on no account dared pay him immediately. And so, on the Thursday before the Friday that the beauteous Zoraida had fixed as the day for going to her father's summer place, she gave us another thousand crowns, at the same time advising us of her departure and requesting me, in case I was ransomed, to make myself acquainted with the site or, in any event, to seek to procure an opportunity for going there to see her. I replied in a few words that

4. Term used in North Africa for a Muslim who had lived among Christians, particularly in the kingdom of Aragon.

I would do this, urging her to be sure and commend us to Lela Marien by making use of all those prayers that the slave woman had taught her.

"When this had been done, it was arranged that my three companions likewise should be ransomed, so that they would be able to leave the bagnio; since if they saw me set at liberty while they remained behind, despite the fact that there was sufficient money to ransom them, they might create a disturbance and the devil might put it into their heads to do something that would injure Zoraida. It was true that, in view of their rank, I could feel reasonably safe in this regard, but, nevertheless, I did not wish to imperil the undertaking, and so I had them released at the same time as myself, paying over all the money to the merchant in order that he might with confidence and security pledge his word, although we never once divulged to him our secret plan, as there would have been too much danger in doing so."

CHAPTER XLI

In which the captive's story is still further continued.

"A fortnight had not gone by before our renegade had bought a boat capable of carrying more than thirty persons; and by way of rendering the project safer and allaying suspicion, he made a voyage, as he had suggested, to a place called Shershel which is thirty leagues from Algiers in the direction of Oran and which does a large trade in dried figs. Two or three times he did this in the company of the Tagarin Moor I have mentioned; for *Tagarinos* is the name given in Barbary to the Moors of Aragon, while those of Granada are called *Mudéjares*; but in the kingdom of Fez the *Mudéjares* are termed *Elches*, and they are the ones whom that king chiefly employs in war.

"To go on with my story, then: Each time that he passed with his boat he anchored in a cove that was not two crossbow shots from the house where Zoraida was waiting, and there, with the two little Moors that served him as oarsmen, he would deliberately station himself, either to say his prayers or by way of acting out the part he was later to perform in earnest. Thus, he would go to Zoraida's garden and beg fruit, and her father would give it to him without recognizing him. As he told me afterward, he would have liked to have a word with Zoraida herself so he could tell her he was there on my orders to bear her off to the land of the Christians and at the same time urge her to feel safe and happy.

"This, however, was impossible, for Moorish ladies do not permit themselves to be seen by any of their own race or by any Turk unless their husband or father so commands them. With Christian captives, on the other hand, they are allowed to converse and have dealings to a rather surprising extent. For my part, I was just as glad that he had not spoken to her, for she might have been disturbed to find her plan being discussed by renegades.

"But God in any case had ordained otherwise, and our renegade did not have an opportunity of gratifying his laudable desire. Seeing how safely he was able to go to Shershel and return and anchor where he chose, and perceiving that the Tagarin, his companion, was wholly compliant with his wishes and that all that was needed now was a few Christians to man the oars, he told me to look about for some that I might take with me in addition to those that were being ransomed and to engage them for the following Friday, which was the date he had set for our departure. I accordingly spoke to a dozen Spaniards, all of them powerful rowers. They were chosen from among those that were best in a position to leave the city, and it was no small task finding so many of them at that particular moment, since there were then twenty ships at sea and they had taken all the available oarsmen.

"I should not have been able to find them if it had not been that their master that summer was not going on a cruise but was occupied with completing the construction of a galiot which he had on the stocks. All that I told these men was that the next Friday afternoon they should steal out one by one and wait for me in the vicinity of Hadji Morato's garden. I gave these directions to each one separately, instructing them that if they saw any other Christians in the neighborhood, all they were to say to them was that I had ordered them to stay there until I came.

"Having attended to this, I had something else to do that was still more important, and that was to let Zoraida know how far our plans had progressed in order that she might be forewarned and not be caught off guard if we suddenly decided to abduct her before, as she would think, the Christian's boat would have had time to return. I therefore resolved to go to the garden and see if I could speak with her; so on a day before my departure I went there under pretense of gathering a few herbs, and the first person I encountered was her father, who addressed me in the language that throughout Barbary and even in Constantinople is in use between captives and Moors, and which is neither Moorish nor Castilian nor the tongue of any other nation, but a mixture of all of them by means of which we manage to understand one another. It was in this language that he asked me who I was and what I was doing in his garden. I replied that I was Arnaut Mami's[5] slave—because I knew for a certainty that Arnaut Mami was a very great friend of his—and that I was looking for herbs to make him a salad. He then inquired as to whether I was a ransomed man or not and what price my master wanted for me.

"As I was thus engaged in answering his questionings, the lovely Zoraida came out of the garden house. She had caught sight of me some while before; and since Moorish women, as I have said, are not at all prudish about showing themselves to Christians and do not avoid their company, she thought nothing of coming up to where her father stood conversing with me. In fact, when her father saw her slowly approaching, he called to her to come. It would be too much for me to undertake to describe for you now the great beauty, the air of gentle breeding, the rich and elegant attire with which my beloved Zoraida presented herself to my gaze. I shall merely tell you that more pearls hung from her comely throat, her ears, her hair than she has hairs on her head. On her feet, which, as is the custom, were bare, she wore two *carcajes*—for that is what they call bracelets for the ankles in the Moorish tongue—made of purest gold and set with many diamonds whose value, as she told me afterward, her father estimated at ten thousand doblas,[6] while those upon her wrist were worth fully as much as the others.

"The pearls also were numerous, for the way that Moorish women have of displaying their magnificence is by decking themselves out in this manner. And

5. The corsair captain who captured Cervantes himself in 1575.   6. Gold coin worth six reales.

so it is you find more pearls of one kind or another among the Moors than all the other nations combined have to show, and Zoraida's father was reputed to have an abundance of them and the best that there were in Algiers. In addition, he had more than two hundred thousand Spanish crowns, and the fair one I now call mine was mistress of all this wealth.

"If you would form an idea of how beautiful she was in her prosperous days and when so adorned, you have but to observe how much of beauty is left her now after all that she has suffered. For it is a well-known fact that the beauty of some women has its day and season and is diminished or heightened by accidental causes. It is, moreover, a natural thing that the passions of the mind should add to or detract from it, and most often they destroy it utterly. What I am trying to say is that, as she came toward me that day, she impressed me as being, both in herself and in her adornments, the most dazzling creature that I had ever seen, and when I thought of all that I owed to her, it seemed to me that I had before me a goddess from Heaven who had come to earth for my delight and comfort.

"As she came up, her father told her in their language that I was the captive of his friend, Arnaut Mami, and that I had come to look for a salad. She gave me her hand and, in that admixture of tongues that I have described, asked me if I was a gentleman and why it was I had not been ransomed. I replied that I already had been, and that from the price paid she could see the esteem in which my master held me, for the sum of one thousand five hundred soltanis[7] had been put up for me. To which she answered, 'In truth, had you been my father's slave, I would not have permitted him to let you go for twice as much, for you Christians always lie in everything you say and make yourselves out to be poor in order to cheat the Moors.'

"'That may be, lady,' I said, 'but I dealt truthfully with my master, as I do and shall do with everybody in this world.'

"'And when are you going?' Zoraida asked.

"'Tomorrow, I expect; for there is a vessel here from France that sets sail then and I intend to go on it.'

"'Would it not be better,' said Zoraida, 'to wait for one from Spain, seeing that the French are not your friends?'

"'No,' I told her, 'although if I were certain that a ship from Spain was on the way, I would wait for it. It is more likely, however, that I shall go tomorrow, for the desire I have to see my native land and my loved ones is such that I cannot bear to wait for another opportunity, even though a better one, if it be late in coming.'

"'You no doubt have a wife in your own country,' she said, 'and I suppose you are anxious to see her.'

"'No,' I assured her, 'I am not married, but I have promised to wed as soon as I return.'

"'And is the lady to whom you have given this promise beautiful?'

"'She is so beautiful,' I replied, 'that by way of praising her and telling the simple truth, I will say that she very much resembles you.'

"Her father laughed heartily at this. 'In Allah's name, Christian,' he said, 'she must be beautiful indeed if she is like my daughter, who is the most beautiful in all this realm. If you do not believe me, look at her well and tell me if I do not speak the truth.'

7. Ottoman coin worth seventeen reales.

"Throughout the greater part of this conversation, Zoraida's father acted as our interpreter, being the more adept at languages; for while she spoke the bastard tongue that, as I have said, is in use there, she expressed her meaning by signs rather than by words.

"As we were discussing these and other subjects, a Moor came running up, crying in a loud voice that four Turks had leaped the garden railing or wall and were picking the fruit although it was not yet ripe. Both the old man and Zoraida were alarmed at this; for the fear that the Moors have of the Turks is a common and, so to speak, an instinctive thing. They are especially afraid of Turkish soldiers, who treat their Moorish subjects more haughtily, insolently, and cruelly than if the latter were their slaves.

"Zoraida's father then said to her, 'Daughter, retire to the house and shut yourself in while I speak to these dogs. As for you, Christian, gather your herbs and go in peace, and may Allah bring you safely to your own country.'

"I bowed, and he went away to look for the Turks, leaving me alone with Zoraida, who made as if to go back into the house as her father had commanded her. He had no sooner disappeared among the garden trees, however, than she, her eyes brimming with tears, turned to me and said, '*Tamejí*, Christian, *tamejí?*' Which means, 'Are you going, Christian, are you going?'

"And I answered her, 'Yes, lady, but under no condition without you. Wait for me next *Jumá*, and do not be frightened when you see us, for we are surely going to the land of the Christians.'

"I said this in such a way that she understood everything very well; and, throwing her arm about my neck, she began with faltering step to walk toward the house. But as luck would have it—and it would have been very unlucky indeed for us if Heaven had not ordered it otherwise—as we were going along in this manner, her father, who was coming back from his encounter with the Turks, caught sight of us, and we knew that he had seen us and had seen her arm about me. But Zoraida, cleverly on her guard, did not remove her arm; instead, she clung to me more than ever and laid her head upon my bosom, swaying at the knees a little and giving every evidence of having fainted, while I pretended to be supporting her against my will. The old man ran up to us and, seeing his daughter in this condition, asked her what the matter was.

"'Undoubtedly,' he said, when he received no reply, 'it was those dogs coming into the garden that did this to her.' And, taking her off my bosom, he pressed her to his own, as she, her eyes not yet dry from her tears, sighed deeply and said, '*Amejí*, Christian, *amejí!*'[8]

"'It is not necessary, my daughter, for the Christian to go,' her father said. 'He has done you no harm, and the Turks have left. There is no cause for you to be frightened, for nothing is going to hurt you, since the Turks at my request have gone back to where they belong.'

"'It is true, sir, as you have said,' I told him, 'that they have given her a fright; but since she says for me to go, I would not cause her any annoyance; and so, peace be with you, and with your permission I will return to this garden for herbs, if I find it necessary, for my master says there are no better ones for salad than those that grow here.'

---

8. "Go, Christian, go."

"'Come back for all that you need,' replied Hadji Morato. 'My daughter does not say this because you or any of the other Christians annoy her. She either meant that the Turks should go, not you, or else that it was time you were looking for your herbs.'

"With this, I at once took my leave of both of them, and Zoraida, who appeared to be suffering deeply, went away with her father, while I, under pretense of gathering my salad, was able to roam the garden at will. I carefully noted the entrances and exits, the means they used to secure the house, and everything that might facilitate our plan; after which, I went to give an account of what had happened to the renegade and my companions. In the meanwhile, I looked forward to the time when I should be able to enjoy undisturbed the boon which fate had bestowed upon me in the person of the beauteous and charming Zoraida.

"Time went by, and at length the day came that meant so much to us. With all of us following the plan which, after many long discussions and the most careful consideration, we had decided upon, we met with the success that we longed for. On the next Friday after the day on which I had spoken to Zoraida in the garden, our renegade at nightfall anchored his boat almost directly opposite the house where she was, the Christians who were to man the oars having been notified in advance that they might hide themselves in various places round about. As they waited for me, they were all of them anxious and elated, eager to board the vessel on which their gaze was fixed; for they were unaware of the arrangement with the renegade and thought that they would have to gain their freedom by force of arms, through slaying the Moors who were on the boat.

"Accordingly, as soon as I and my companions showed ourselves, those who were in hiding sighted us and came up. This was at an hour when the gates of the city were closed, and in the whole of the countryside not a soul was to be seen. When we were all together, we discussed the question as to whether it would be better to go first for Zoraida or to make prisoners of the Moorish oarsmen. Before we had reached a decision, our renegade arrived and asked us what was the cause of our delay, for it was now time, all the Moors being off guard and most of them asleep. I told him why we were hesitating, and he replied that the most important thing was to capture the vessel first of all, which could be done very easily and with no danger whatever, and after that we could go for Zoraida. We all agreed with him, and so, without waiting any longer and with him as our guide, we went to the vessel, where he was the first to leap aboard. Laying a hand on his cutlass, he cried in the Moorish tongue, 'None of you stir from here or it will cost you your lives!'

"By this time nearly all the Christians were aboard; and the Moors, who were possessed of little courage, upon hearing their captain address them in this manner, were thoroughly terrified. None of them dared reach for his weapons, and for that matter, they had few if any; and so, without saying a word, they let themselves be shackled by the Christians, who accomplished this very quickly, threatening them that if they raised any kind of outcry they would all die by the knife.

"When this had been achieved, with half our number remaining behind to guard the prisoners, the rest of us, again with the renegade as our guide, made our way to Hadji Morato's garden; and it was our good fortune that, as we went to try the gate, it swung open as readily as if it had not been locked. We then, very quietly and saying nothing, went on to the house without our presence being discovered by anyone. Zoraida, fairest of the fair, was waiting for us at a window, and as soon as she heard the sound of people below, she asked in a low voice if we were *Nizarani*, that is to say, Christians. I answered in the affirmative, saying that she should come down. Recognizing me, she did not hesitate for a moment, but without a word she came down instantly and, opening the door, appeared there in the sight of all, so beautiful and so richly clad that I cannot possibly tell you how she looked.

"As soon as I saw her, I took one of her hands and began kissing it, and the renegade and my two comrades did the same, while the others, being unacquainted with the circumstances, followed our example, since it seemed to them that we were merely recognizing and thanking her as the lady who was responsible for our going free. The renegade asked in Moorish if her father was in the house, and she replied that he was sleeping.

"'Then it will be necessary to wake him,' he said, 'for we must take him with us and everything of value that there is in this beautiful summer place.'

"'No,' she answered, 'you must by no means lay hands on my father. In this house there is nothing for you save that which I bring with me, and it is enough to make you all rich and happy. Wait a moment and you will see.'

"She then went back into the house, saying she would return at once and bidding us meanwhile not to make any noise. I took this opportunity of asking the renegade what had passed between them, and when he told me, I made it clear to him that under no condition was he to go beyond Zoraida's wishes. She now reappeared with a small trunk filled with gold crowns, so heavy that she could hardly carry it. At that instant, unfortunately, her father awoke and, hearing a noise in the garden, came to the window and looked out. Recognizing us all as Christians, he began bawling at the top of his lungs in Arabic, 'Christians! Christians! Thieves! Thieves!' This frightened us very much and threw us into confusion; but the renegade, perceiving the danger we were in and how important it was to go through with our undertaking before being detected, ran up as fast as he could to where Hadji Morato was, being accompanied by some of the rest of us. As for myself I did not dare leave Zoraida unprotected, for she, half fainting, had fallen in my arms.

"In brief, those who went up handled the matter so expeditiously that in a moment they were back, bringing with them Hadji Morato, his hands bound and with a napkin over his mouth so that he could not speak a word—and they threatened him that if he tried to speak it would cost him his life. When his daughter saw him, she put her hands over her eyes, and her father in turn was horrified at sight of her, not knowing that she had placed herself in our hands of her own free will. But it was essential now for us to be on our way, and so we hastily but with due care boarded the ship, where those that we had left behind were waiting for us, fearful that some untoward accident had befallen us.

"It was a little after two in the morning by the time we were all on the vessel. They then untied Hadji Morato's hands and removed the napkin from his mouth, but the renegade again warned him not to say anything or they would kill him. As the old man looked at his daughter, he began sighing mournfully, especially when he saw her held tightly in my embrace, and when he observed that she did not struggle, protest, or attempt to escape me; but he nonetheless remained silent lest they carry out the renegade's threat.

"Finding herself on the boat now and perceiving that we were about to row away while her father and the other Moors remained bound, Zoraida spoke to the renegade, requesting him to do her the favor of releasing the prisoners, particularly her father, as she would rather cast herself into the sea than have a parent who loved her so dearly carried away captive in front of her eyes and through her fault. The renegade repeated to me what she had said, and, for my part, I was quite willing. He, however, replied that this was not the wise thing to do, for the reason that, if they were left behind, they would alarm the entire city and countryside, whereupon some fast-sailing craft would put out in pursuit of us and so comb the sea and land that there would be no possibility of our escaping. What we might do, he added, was to give them their freedom as soon as we set foot on Christian soil. We all agreed to this, and when the matter was explained to Zoraida, along with the reasons why we could not comply with her wishes, she also was satisfied. And then, gladly and silently, cheerfully and with alacrity, each one of our powerful rowers took up his oar, as, commending ourselves with all our hearts to God, we set out on our voyage to the island of Majorca, which is the nearest Christian territory.

"However, inasmuch as the tramontane wind[9] was blowing a little and the sea was a bit rough, it was impossible for us to follow the route to Majorca, and we were compelled to hug the coast in the direction of Oran. This worried us considerably, for we feared that we would be discovered from the town of Shershel, which is about seventy miles from Algiers. And we also were afraid that we might encounter in those waters one of the galiots that commonly ply the coast with merchandise of Tetuán, although each of us secretly felt that if we did meet with a merchant vessel of that sort, providing it was not a cruiser, we not only should not be captured but, rather, should be able to come into possession of a craft in which we could more safely complete our voyage. In the meantime, as we were sailing along, Zoraida buried her face in my hands in order not to see her father, and I could hear her calling on Lela Marien to come to our aid.

"We must have gone a good thirty miles when dawn came, and we found ourselves at a distance of something like three musket shots off land. The shore was deserted, and we saw no one who might descry us, but, nevertheless, by rowing as hard as we could we put out a little more to the open sea, which was now somewhat calmer. When we were about two leagues from the coast, the order was given to row by turns so that we could have a bite to eat, the ship being well stocked with food; but those at the oars said it was not yet time for them to take a rest—the others might eat, but they themselves did not wish on any account to relax their efforts. We were starting to do as they had suggested when a strong wind came up, which obliged us to leave off rowing and set sail at once for Oran, that being the only course left us. All this was done very quickly, and with the sail we made more than eight miles an hour, with no fear other than that of falling in with a vessel that was out cruising.

"We gave the Moorish rowers some food, and the renegade consoled them by telling them they were not captives but would be given their freedom at the first opportunity. He said the same to Zoraida's father, who replied, 'If you promised me anything else, O Christian, I might believe it and hope for it by reason of the generous treatment you have accorded me, but when it comes to setting me free, do not think that I am so simple-minded as to put any credence in that; for you would never have incurred the risk of depriving me of my liberty only to restore

9. I.e., wind from beyond the mountains (in this case the Alps), hence north wind.

it to me so freely, especially since you know who I am and the profit you may derive from releasing me. Indeed, if you wish to name the sum, I hereby offer you whatever you ask for me and for this unfortunate daughter of mine, or for her alone, for she is the greater and better part of my soul.'

"As he said this, he began weeping so bitterly that we were all moved to compassion, and Zoraida could not resist stealing a glance at him. When she saw him weeping, she was so touched that she rose from my feet and went over to embrace him, and as she laid her cheek against his the two of them shed so many tears that a number of us could not but join them in their weeping. But when her father perceived that she was in festive attire and decked out in all her jewels, he spoke to her in their own language.

"'How does it come, my daughter,' he said, 'that last night, at dusk, before this terrible thing happened to us, I saw you clad in ordinary household garb; and now, without your having had time to dress, and without my having brought you any good news to celebrate by thus adorning and bedecking your person, I nonetheless behold you wearing the best garments with which I was able to provide you when fortune smiled upon us? Answer me this, for I am even more astonished and bewildered by it than I am by this misfortune that has come to us.'

"The renegade informed us of all that the Moor had said to his daughter, who did not utter a word in reply. And when the old man saw, over at one side of the boat, the small trunk in which she was in the habit of keeping her jewels, he was more bewildered than ever; for he knew very well that he had not brought it to the summer place but had left it in Algiers. He thereupon asked her how the trunk had come into our hands and what was inside it; and then the renegade, without giving Zoraida time to answer, spoke up.

"'You need not trouble, sir, to ask your daughter Zoraida so many questions, for I can give you one answer that will serve for all. I would have you know that she is a Christian, and that it is she who has filed our chains for us and set us free from our captivity. She goes of her own free will and, I fancy, is as happy about it as one who emerges from darkness into light, from death into life, or from the pains of hell into glory everlasting.'

"'Is it true, my daughter, what this man says?' asked the Moor.

"'It is,' said Zoraida.

"'So you are a Christian,' said the old man, 'and it is you who have placed your father in the hands of his enemies?'

"'As to my being a Christian,' she told him, 'that is true enough, but it is not true that I am responsible for your being in this situation; for I never had any desire to leave you or to do you harm, but only to do good to myself.'

"'And what good have you done yourself, daughter?'

"'Put that question,' she said, 'to Lela Marien, for she can tell you better than I.'

"No sooner had he heard this than the Moor, with an incredibly swift movement, hurled himself head foremost into the sea; and he would undoubtedly have drowned if the long and cumbersome robe that he wore had not tended to bear him up. Zoraida screamed for someone to rescue him, whereupon we all ran forward and, seizing him by his robe, hauled him in, half drowned and unconscious, at which his daughter was so distressed that she wept over him as bitterly and mournfully as if he were already dead. We turned him face downward and he disgorged much water, and after a couple of hours he was himself once more.

"Meanwhile, the wind had changed and we had to make for land, exerting all our strength at the oars in order not to be driven ashore. Luck was with us, and we were able to put into a cove alongside a promontory or cape which the Moors call *Cava Rumia*, signifying in our language 'the wicked Christian woman'; for it is a tradition among them that La Cava, through whom Spain was lost, is buried in that spot, *'cava'* in their tongue meaning 'bad woman,' while *'rumia'* is 'Christian.'[1] They regard it as bad luck to be compelled to drop anchor there, and they never do so unless it is absolutely necessary. But for us it was not the 'bad woman's' shelter; rather, it was a haven in distress, as the sea was now raging.

"Stationing our sentinels on land and never once relinquishing the oars, we ate what the renegade had provided and prayed to God and Our Lady with all our hearts that they would favor and aid us in order that we might bring to a happy conclusion an undertaking that had begun so propitiously. Upon Zoraida's request, the order was given to set her father and all the other Moors ashore, for her tender heart could not bear to see her father thus bound and her fellow countrymen held prisoners in front of her very eyes. We promised her that this should be done as soon as it came time for us to depart; for we ran no risk by leaving them in this deserted place. Our prayers were not in vain; for, Heaven favoring us, the wind changed and the sea grew calm, inviting us to resume with cheerful hearts the voyage that we had begun.

"We then unbound the Moors and, one by one, set them on land, at which they were greatly astonished; but when it came to disembarking Zoraida's father, who had by now completely recovered his senses, he gave us a piece of his mind.

"'Why do you think, Christians,' he said, 'that this wicked female is happy at your giving me my liberty? Do you imagine that it is out of filial affection? Assuredly not. It is only because my presence is an impediment to the carrying out of her base designs. And do not think that what has led her to change her religion is a belief that yours is better than ours; it is because she knows that in your country immodesty is more freely practiced than in ours.'

"As her father spoke, another Christian and I held Zoraida's arms that she might not be tempted to some foolish act. The old man now turned upon her.

"'O infamous and ill-advised maiden! Where do you think you are going, so blindly and foolishly, with these dogs, our natural enemies? Cursed be the hour in which I begot you, and cursed all the luxury in which I have reared you!'

"Seeing that he was likely to go on in this way for some while, I hastened to put him ashore; and from there he kept on shouting at us, pursuing us with his curses and lamentations as he implored Mohammed to pray to Allah that we be destroyed, confounded, and brought to an end. And when, having set sail, we could no longer hear his words, we could still see his gestures, could see him plucking out his beard, tearing his hair, and rolling on the ground. At one point he raised his voice to such a pitch that we could make out what he said.

"'Return, my beloved daughter, return to land, and I will forgive you everything. Give those men the money that is yours and come back to comfort your

---

1. Legend had it that Rodrigo, the last Visigothic king of Iberia, seduced Florinda ("La Cava"), the daughter of Count Julián. Her father took revenge on Rodrigo by betraying Spain to the invading Moors in 711.

brokenhearted father, who, if you leave him now, will leave his bones on these deserted sands.'

"Zoraida heard all this and was deeply grieved by it. Weeping, she could only say to him in reply, 'O my father, may it please Allah that Lela Marien, who has been the cause of my turning Christian, console you in your sorrow! Allah well knows that I could have done nothing other than what I did. These Christians are in no wise to blame, for even had I not wished to come with them, even had I chosen to remain at home, it would have been impossible, so eagerly did my soul urge me to do that which to me seems as good, my dear father, as it seems evil to you.'

"When she said this, her father could no longer hear her, for we had lost him from view; and so, while I comforted Zoraida, we all of us turned our attention to the voyage, as we now had a wind so favorable that we firmly expected to be off the coast of Spain by dawn the next day.

"Blessings, however, are almost never unmixed with some evil that, without our having foreseen it, comes to disturb them. It may have been simply our misfortune, or it may have been those curses that the Moor had heaped upon his daughter (for a curse of that kind is always to be dreaded, whatever the father may be like), but, in any event, our luck now changed. We were on the high seas, and the night was a little more than three hours gone. We were proceeding at full sail with the oars lashed, since the wind had relieved us of the necessity of using them, when by the light of the moon, which was shining brightly, we sighted alongside us a square-rigged vessel with all sails set that was luffing a little and standing across our course. It was so close upon us that we had to strike sail in order not to run foul of her, while they swung their prow about to give us room to pass.

"They now came to the ship's rail to ask us who we were, from where we came, and where we were going. When these questions were put to us in French, our renegade said, 'Let no one answer, for they are undoubtedly French pirates who plunder everything in sight.' As a result of this warning, no one said a word in reply. We were a little ahead, and the other vessel was lying to leeward, when suddenly they fired two pieces of artillery, both of them, as it seemed, loaded with chain-shot; for with one they cut our mast in half and brought both mast and sail down into the sea, while the other cannon, discharged at the same moment, sent a shot into the middle of our craft, laying it wide open but doing no further damage to it. As we saw ourselves sinking, we began crying out for help, imploring those on the other ship to come to our aid as we were filling with water. They then struck their own sails, and, lowering a skiff or boat, as many as a dozen Frenchmen, all well armed, with matchlocks and matches lighted, came alongside us. When they saw how few we were and how our craft was going down, they took us in, telling us that this had come about through our discourtesy in not answering them.

"Our renegade, then, without anyone's seeing what he did, took the trunk containing Zoraida's wealth and dumped it into the sea. To make a long story short, we all went aboard with the Frenchmen, who, after they had learned everything they wished to know about us, proceeded to despoil us of all that we possessed as if we had been their deadly enemies. They even took Zoraida's anklets, but this did not grieve me as much as it did her. What I feared more was that, having deprived her of her exceedingly rich and precious gems, they would go on to steal that jewel that was worth more than all the others and which she most esteemed. Their desires, however, did not go beyond money, in which regard they were insatiable in their covetousness. They would even have taken the garments their captives wore if these had been of any use to them. Some of them were for wrapping us all in a sail and tossing us into the sea; for it was their intention, by passing themselves off as Bretons, to put in at certain Spanish ports, and if they brought us in alive they would be punished when the theft was discovered.

"But the captain, who was the one who had despoiled my beloved Zoraida, said that he was content with the prize that he had and did not wish to stop at any port in Spain. Instead, he preferred to slip through the Strait of Gibraltar at night, or any way he could, and go on to La Rochelle, the port from which he had put out. Accordingly, they agreed to let us take their small boat and all that we needed for the brief voyage that remained for us. This they did the next day, within sight of the Spanish coast, a sight that caused us wholly to forget all our sufferings and hardships, which were as if they had never been, so great is the joy that comes from recovering one's lost freedom.

"It may have been around midday when they put us in the boat, giving us two kegs of water and some biscuit. And as the lovely Zoraida went to embark, the captain, moved by some sympathetic impulse or other, gave her as many as twenty gold crowns and would not permit his men to take from her those same garments that she is now wearing. As we entered the small boat, we thanked them for their kindness, our manner being one of gratitude rather than indignation, and they then put out to sea, making for the Strait, while we, needing no other compass than the land that lay ahead of us, bent to the oars so lustily that by sundown we were, as we thought, near enough to be able to reach it before the night was far gone.

"But as there was no moon and the sky was darkened over and we were ignorant of our exact whereabouts, it did not seem wise to attempt a landing, although many of us thought that we should do so, saying that it would be better to run ashore even if it were on some rocks, far from any inhabited place, since in that way we would assure ourselves against the very likely danger of Tetuán corsairs, who at night are in Barbary and by morning off the coast of Spain, where they commonly take some prize and then return to sleep in their own houses. There were a number of conflicting suggestions, but the one that was finally adopted was that we should gradually draw near the shore and, if the sea was calm enough to permit it, land wherever we were able.

"This was the plan followed, and shortly before midnight we came to the foot of an enormous and very high mountain that was not so near the sea but that it afforded a convenient space for a landing. We ran up on the sand and leaped ashore, kissing the ground on which we stood and shedding many joyful tears as we gave thanks to God, Our Lord, for the incomparable blessing that He had conferred upon us. Removing the provisions from the boat, we drew it ashore and then went a long way up the mountain; for even here we could not feel in our hearts or bring ourselves to believe that the land beneath our feet was Christian soil. The sun, it seemed to me, came up more slowly than we could have wished, and in the meanwhile we had climbed the entire mountainside in an effort to see if we could discover any village or even a few shepherds' huts; but however much we strained our eyes, we were able to descry no village, no human being, no path, no road.

"Nevertheless, we determined to keep on and go farther inland, since surely we could not fail to come upon someone who could give us our bearings. What distressed me more than anything else was seeing Zoraida go on foot over this rough country; for though I once tried carrying her on my shoulders, my weariness wearied her more than she was rested by her repose, and so she would not again consent to my making the exertion but went along very cheerfully and patiently, her hand in mine. We had gone, I imagine, a little less than a quarter of a league when there reached our ears the sound of a little bell, which showed plainly that we must be near some flock or herd, and as we all gazed about us attentively to see if we could discern any, we saw at the foot of a cork tree a young shepherd who very calmly and unconcernedly was engaged in whittling a stick with his knife.

"We called to him, and he, raising his head, got to his feet very nimbly. As we afterward learned, the first persons that he caught sight of among us were the renegade and Zoraida, and seeing them in Moorish costume, he thought that all Barbary must have descended upon him. Dashing with amazing swiftness into a nearby wood, he began raising a terrible din as he shouted, 'Moors! Moors! The Moors have landed! Moors! Moors! To arms! To arms!'

"We were quite perplexed by all this, not knowing what to do; but, reflecting that the shepherd's cries would arouse the countryside and that the mounted coast guard would soon be along to find out what the trouble was, we decided that the renegade should take off his Turkish clothes and put on a captive's jacket, which one of us now gave him though he himself was left with only his shirt. And then, commending ourselves to God, we proceeded along the same path that the shepherd had taken, expecting that the guard would be upon us at any moment. In this we were not wrong, for two hours had not gone by when, as we were coming out of a thicket onto a plain, we caught sight of all of fifty horsemen coming toward us at top speed.

"As soon as we saw them, we stopped and watched them, and they, when they came up and found, in place of the Moors they were seeking, a handful of poor Christians, were very much surprised. One of them asked if it was we who had caused the shepherd to sound the call to arms. 'Yes,' I replied, and was about to go on and tell him our story, who we were and from whence we came, when one of our number happened to recognize the horseman who had put the question and, without giving me a chance to reply, spoke up and said, 'Thanks be to God, sirs, for having brought us into such good hands; for unless I am mistaken, this region where we now are is in the neighborhood of Vélez Málaga—unless all the years of my captivity have so deprived me of my memory that I cannot recall that you, sir, who have just asked us our names, are Pedro de Bustamente, my uncle.'

"The Christian captive had no sooner said this than the horseman dismounted and came up to embrace the young fellow. 'My dearest nephew!' he cried. 'I recognize you now. I and my sister—your mother—and all your relatives who are still alive have wept for you as dead, and now it appears that God has been pleased to prolong their lives that they might have the pleasure of seeing you again. We had heard that you were in Algiers, but from the look of your garments and those of all this company I realize that you have been miraculously liberated.'

"'That,' replied the young man, 'is the truth, and there will be time to tell you all about it.'

"As soon as the guardsmen realized that we were Christian captives, they dismounted, and each then offered us his own horse to carry us to the city of Vélez Málaga, which was a league and a half from there. We told them where we had left the boat, and some of them went back to get it and take it to the town. Others mounted behind us on the cruppers, Zoraida going with the young man's uncle.

"The entire town came out to receive us, for someone had ridden ahead and told them of our coming. They were not the kind of folk to be astonished at seeing captives free or Moors held prisoner, being quite accustomed to such a sight. What they rather marveled at was Zoraida's beauty. Despite the fact that she was weary from the journey, she looked her loveliest at that moment, so joyful was she at finding herself on Christian soil with nothing to fear any longer. Happiness had put so much color into her face that—unless it can be that my love for her deceived me—I shall venture to say that there never was a more beautiful creature in all this world, none that I have ever seen, at any rate.

"We went directly to the church to thank God for his mercy; and as soon as Zoraida entered the portals, she remarked that there were faces there that resembled that of Lela Marien. We informed her that these were images of the Virgin, and the renegade to the best of his ability then went on to explain what their meaning was and how she might worship them as if each were the same Lela Marien who had spoken to her. Being possessed of a good, clear mind, she understood all this very readily. After that, they took us to various houses in the town, and the Christian who had come with us brought the renegade, Zoraida, and me to the home of his parents, who were people in moderately comfortable circumstances and who entertained us with as great a show of affection as they did their own son.

"We were in Vélez for six days, at the end of which time the renegade, having ascertained what he had to do, departed for Granada in order that, through the mediation of the Holy Inquisition, he might be restored to the sacred bosom of the Church. Each of the other liberated Christians went his own way, Zoraida and I being left with no other means than the crowns which the French captain had courteously given her. With them I purchased the beast on which she now rides; and with me serving her up to now as father and squire, not as husband, we are at present on our way to see if my own father is still alive or if one of my brothers has prospered to a greater extent than I.

"Seeing that Heaven has seen fit to give her to me as my companion, I can imagine no other fortune, however good, that might come to me which I should hold to be of greater worth. The patience with which she endures the hardships that poverty brings with it, and her desire to become a Christian, are such as to fill me with admiration and induce me to serve her all my life long. My happiness, however, at knowing that I am hers and she is mine is marred by the fact that I am at a loss where to find a nook in my own country in which to shelter her. For it may be that time and death have wrought such changes in the life and fortunes of my father and my brothers that, if they should not be there, I shall hardly find anyone who is acquainted with me.

"Gentle folk, that is all there is to my story. As to whether it be a pleasing and a curious one, that is for you in your good judgment to decide. For my own part, I may say that I should like to have told it more briefly, although, as it is, the fear of tiring you has led me to omit a number of incidents."

["*Set Free at Once That Lovely Lady*"]

CHAPTER LII

*Of the quarrel that Don Quixote had with the goatherd, together with
the rare adventure of the penitents, which the knight by the sweat of
his brow brought to a happy conclusion.*[2]

* * *

The goatherd stared at Don Quixote, observing in some astonishment the
knight's unprepossessing appearance.

"Sir, he said, turning to the barber who sat beside him, "who is this man who
looks so strange and talks in this way?"

"Who should it be," the barber replied, "if not the famous Don Quixote de la
Mancha, righter of wrongs, avenger of injustices, protector of damsels, terror
of giants, and champion of battles?"

"That," said the goatherd, "sounds to me like the sort of thing you read of in
books of chivalry, where they do all those things that your Grace has mentioned
in connection with this man. But if you ask me, either your Grace is joking or
this worthy gentleman must have a number of rooms to let inside his head."

"You are the greatest villain that ever was!" cried Don Quixote when he heard
this. "It is you who are the empty one; I am fuller than the bitch that bore you ever
was." Saying this, he snatched up a loaf of bread that was lying beside him and
hurled it straight in the goatherd's face with such force as to flatten the man's
nose. Upon finding himself thus mistreated in earnest, Eugenio, who did not
understand this kind of joke, forgot all about the carpet, the tablecloth, and the
other diners and leaped upon Don Quixote. Seizing him by the throat with both
hands, he would no doubt have strangled him if Sancho Panza, who now came
running up, had not grasped him by the shoulders and flung him backward over
the table, smashing plates and cups and spilling and scattering all the food and
drink that was there. Thus freed of his assailant, Don Quixote then threw himself
upon the shepherd, who, with bleeding face and very much battered by Sancho's
feet, was creeping about on his hands and knees in search of a table knife with
which to exact a sanguinary vengeance, a purpose which the canon and the curate
prevented him from carrying out. The barber, however, so contrived it that the
goatherd came down on top of his opponent, upon whom he now showered so
many blows that the poor knight's countenance was soon as bloody as his own.

As all this went on, the canon and the curate were laughing fit to burst, the
troopers[3] were dancing with glee, and they all hissed on the pair as men do at
a dog fight. Sancho Panza alone was in despair, being unable to free himself of
one of the canon's servants who held him back from going to his master's aid.
And then, just as they were all enjoying themselves hugely, with the exception

---

2. Last chapter of Part I. Through various
devices, including the use of Don Quixote's own
belief in enchantments and spells, the curate
and the barber have persuaded the knight to let
himself be taken home in an oxcart.
3. A canon from Toledo who has joined Don
Quixote and his guardians on the way; conversing about chivalry with the knight, he has had

cause to be "astonished at Don Quixote's well-
reasoned nonsense." Eugenio, a very literate
goatherd they have met on the way, has just
told them the story of his unhappy love for
Leandra. The girl, instead of choosing one of
her local suitors, had eloped with a flashy and
crooked soldier; robbed and abandoned by him,
she had been put by her father in a convent.

of the two who were mauling each other, the note of a trumpet fell upon their ears, a sound so mournful that it caused them all to turn their heads in the direction from which it came. The one who was most excited by it was Don Quixote; who, very much against his will and more than a little bruised, was lying pinned beneath the goatherd.

"Brother Demon," he now said to the shepherd, "for you could not possibly be anything but a demon, seeing that you have shown a strength and valor greater than mine, I request you to call a truce for no more than an hour; for the doleful sound of that trumpet that we hear seems to me to be some new adventure that is calling me."

Tired of mauling and being mauled, the goatherd let him up at once. As he rose to his feet and turned his head in the direction of the sound, Don Quixote then saw, coming down the slope of a hill, a large number of persons clad in white after the fashion of penitents; for, as it happened, the clouds that year had denied their moisture to the earth, and in all the villages of that district processions for prayer and penance were being organized with the purpose of beseeching God to have mercy and send rain. With this object in view, the good folk from a nearby town were making a pilgrimage to a devout hermit who dwelt on these slopes. Upon beholding the strange costumes that the penitents wore, without pausing to think how many times he had seen them before, Don Quixote imagined that this must be some adventure or other, and that it was for him alone as a knight-errant to undertake it. He was strengthened in this belief by the sight of a covered image that they bore, as it seemed to him this must be some highborn lady whom these scoundrelly and discourteous brigands were forcibly carrying off; and no sooner did this idea occur to him than he made for Rocinante, who was grazing not far away.

Taking the bridle and his buckler from off the saddletree, he had the bridle adjusted in no time, and then, asking Sancho for his sword, he climbed into the saddle, braced his shield upon his arm, and cried out to those present, "And now, valorous company, you shall see how important it is to have in the world those who follow the profession of knight-errantry. You have but to watch how I shall set at liberty that worthy lady who there goes captive, and then you may tell me whether or not such knights are to be esteemed."

As he said this, he dug his legs into Rocinante's flanks, since he had no spurs, and at a fast trot (for nowhere in this veracious history are we ever told that the hack ran full speed) he bore down on the penitents in spite of all that the canon, the curate, and the barber could do to restrain him—their efforts were as vain as were the pleadings of his squire.

"Where are you bound for, Señor Don Quixote?" Sancho called after him. "What evil spirits in your bosom spur you on to go against our Catholic faith? Plague take me, can't you see that's a procession of penitents and that lady they're carrying on the litter is the most blessed image of the Immaculate Virgin? Look well what you're doing, my master, for this time it may be said that you really do not know."

His exertions were in vain, however, for his master was so bent upon having it out with the sheeted figures and freeing the lady clad in mourning that he did not hear a word, nor would he have turned back if he had, though the king himself might have commanded it. Having reached the procession, he reined in Rocinante, who by this time was wanting a little rest, and in a hoarse, excited voice he shouted, "You who go there with your faces covered, out of shame, it may be, listen well to what I have to say to you."

The first to come to a halt were those who carried the image; and then one of the four clerics who were intoning the litanies, upon beholding Don Quixote's weird figure, his bony nag, and other amusing appurtenances, spoke up in reply.

"Brother, if you have something to say to us, say it quickly, for these brethren are engaged in macerating their flesh, and we cannot stop to hear anything, nor is it fitting that we should, unless it is capable of being said in a couple of words."

"I will say it to you in one word," Don Quixote answered, "and that word is the following: 'Set free at once that lovely lady whose tears and mournful countenance show plainly that you are carrying her away against her will and that you have done her some shameful wrong. I will not consent to your going one step farther until you shall have given her the freedom that should be hers.'"

Hearing these words, they all thought that Don Quixote must be some madman or other and began laughing heartily; but their laughter proved to be gunpowder to his wrath, and without saying another word he drew his sword and fell upon the litter. One of those who bore the image, leaving his share of the burden to his companions, then sallied forth to meet the knight, flourishing a forked stick that he used to support the Virgin while he was resting; and upon this stick he now received a mighty slash that Don Quixote dealt him, one that shattered it in two, but with the piece about a third long that remained in his hand he came down on the shoulder of his opponent's sword arm, left unprotected by the buckler, with so much force that the poor fellow sank to the ground sorely battered and bruised.

Sancho Panza, who was puffing along close behind his master, upon seeing him fall cried out to the attacker not to deal another blow, as this was an unfortunate knight who was under a magic spell but who had never in all the days of his life done any harm to anyone. But the thing that stopped the rustic was not Sancho's words; it was, rather, the sight of Don Quixote lying there without moving hand or foot. And so, thinking that he had killed him, he hastily girded up his tunic and took to his heels across the countryside like a deer.

By this time all of Don Quixote's companions had come running up to where he lay; and the penitents, when they observed this, and especially when they caught sight of the officers of the Brotherhood with their crossbows, at once rallied around the image, where they raised their hoods and grasped their whips as the priests raised their tapers aloft in expectation of an assault; for they were resolved to defend themselves and even, if possible, to take the offensive against their assailants, but, as luck would have it, things turned out better than they had hoped. Sancho, meanwhile, believing Don Quixote to be dead, had flung himself across his master's body and was weeping and wailing in the most lugubrious and, at the same time, the most laughable fashion that could be imagined; and the curate had discovered among those who marched in the procession another curate whom he knew, their recognition of each other serving to allay the fears of all parties concerned. The first curate then gave the second a very brief account of who Don Quixote was, whereupon all the penitents came up to see if the poor knight was dead. And as they did so, they heard Sancho Panza speaking with tears in his eyes.

"O flower of chivalry,"[4] he was saying, "the course of whose well-spent years has been brought to an end by a single blow of a club! O honor of your line, honor and glory of all La Mancha and of all the world, which, with you absent

---

4. Note how Sancho has absorbed some of his master's speech mannerisms.

from it, will be full of evildoers who will not fear being punished for their deeds! O master more generous than all the Alexanders, who after only eight months of service presented me with the best island that the sea washes and surrounds! Humble with the proud, haughty with the humble, brave in facing dangers, long-suffering under outrages, in love without reason, imitator of the good, scourge of the wicked, enemy of the mean—in a word, a knight-errant, which is all there is to say."

At the sound of Sancho's cries and moans, Don Quixote revived, and the first thing he said was, "He who lives apart from thee, O fairest Dulcinea, is subject to greater woes than those I now endure. Friend Sancho, help me onto that enchanted cart, as I am in no condition to sit in Rocinante's saddle with this shoulder of mine knocked to pieces the way it is."

"That I will gladly do, my master," replied Sancho, "and we will go back to my village in the company of these gentlemen who are concerned for your welfare, and there we will arrange for another sally and one, let us hope, that will bring us more profit and fame than this one has."

"Well spoken, Sancho," said Don Quixote, "for it will be an act of great prudence to wait until the present evil influence of the stars has passed."

The canon, the curate, and the barber all assured him that he would be wise in doing this; and so, much amused by Sancho Panza's simplicity, they placed Don Quixote upon the cart as before, while the procession of penitents re-formed and continued on its way. The goatherd took leave of all of them, and the curate paid the troopers what was coming to them, since they did not wish to go any farther. The canon requested the priest to inform him of the outcome of Don Quixote's madness, as to whether it yielded to treatment or not; and with this he begged permission to resume his journey. In short, the party broke up and separated, leaving only the curate and the barber, Don Quixote and Panza, and the good Rocinante, who looked upon everything that he had seen with the same resignation as his master. Yoking his oxen, the carter made the knight comfortable upon a bale of hay, and then at his customary slow pace proceeded to follow the road that the curate directed him to take. At the end of six days they reached Don Quixote's village, making their entrance at noon of a Sunday, when the square was filled with a crowd of people through which the cart had to pass.

They all came running to see who it was, and when they recognized their townsman, they were vastly astonished. One lad sped to bring the news to the knight's housekeeper and his niece, telling them that their master had returned lean and jaundiced and lying stretched out upon a bale of hay on an oxcart. It was pitiful to hear the good ladies' screams, to behold the way in which they beat their breasts, and to listen to the curses which they once more heaped upon those damnable books of chivalry, and this demonstration increased as they saw Don Quixote coming through the doorway.

At news of the knight's return, Sancho Panza's wife had hurried to the scene, for she had some while since learned that her husband had accompanied him as his squire; and now, as soon as she laid eyes upon her man, the first question she asked was if all was well with the ass, to which Sancho replied that the beast was better off than his master.

"Thank God," she exclaimed, "for all his blessings! But tell me now, my dear, what have you brought me from all your squirings? A new cloak to wear? Or shoes for the young ones?"

"I've brought you nothing of the sort, good wife," said Sancho, "but other things of greater value and importance."

"I'm glad to hear that," she replied. "Show me those things of greater value and importance, my dear. I'd like a sight of them just to cheer this heart of mine which has been so sad and unhappy all the centuries that you've been gone."

"I will show them to you at home, wife," said Sancho. "For the present, be satisfied that if, God willing, we set out on another journey in search of adventures, you will see me in no time a count or the governor of an island, and not one of those around here, but the best that is to be had."

"I hope to Heaven it's true, my husband, for we certainly need it. But tell me, what is all this about islands? I don't understand."

"Honey," replied Sancho, "is not for the mouth of an ass. You will find out in good time, woman; and you're going to be surprised to hear yourself called 'my Ladyship' by all your vassals."

"What's this you are saying, Sancho, about ladyships, islands, and vassals?" Juana Panza insisted on knowing—for such was the name of Sancho's wife, although they were not blood relatives, it being the custom in La Mancha for wives to take their husbands' surnames.

"Do not be in such a hurry to know all this, Juana," he said. "It is enough that I am telling you the truth. Sew up your mouth, then; for all I will say, in passing, is that there is nothing in the world that is more pleasant than being a respected man, squire to a knight-errant who goes in search of adventures. It is true that most of the adventures you meet with do not come out the way you'd like them to, for ninety-nine out of a hundred will prove to be all twisted and crosswise. I know that from experience, for I've come out of some of them blanketed and out of others beaten to a pulp. But, all the same, it's a fine thing to go along waiting for what will happen next, crossing mountains, making your way through woods, climbing over cliffs, visiting castles, and putting up at inns free of charge, and the devil take the maravedi that is to pay."

Such was the conversation that took place between Sancho Panza and Juana Panza, his wife, as Don Quixote's housekeeper and niece were taking him in, stripping him, and stretching him out on his old-time bed. He gazed at them blankly, being unable to make out where he was. The curate charged the niece to take great care to see that her uncle was comfortable and to keep close watch over him so that he would not slip away from them another time. He then told them of what it had been necessary to do in order to get him home, at which they once more screamed to Heaven and began cursing the books of chivalry all over again, praying God to plunge the authors of such lying nonsense into the center of the bottomless pit. In short, they scarcely knew what to do, for they were very much afraid that their master and uncle would give them the slip once more, the moment he was a little better, and it turned out just the way they feared it might.

* * *

From Part II

[Prologue]

To the Reader

God bless me, gentle or, it may be, plebeian reader, how eagerly you must be awaiting this prologue, thinking to find in it vengeful scoldings and vituperations directed against the author of the second Don Quixote—I mean the one who, so it is said, was begotten in Tordesillas and born in Tarragona.[1] The truth is, however, that I am not going to be able to satisfy you in this regard; for granting that injuries are capable of awakening wrath in the humblest of bosoms, my own must be an exception to the rule. You would, perhaps, have me call him an ass, a crackbrain, and an upstart, but it is not my intention so to chastise him for his sin. Let him eat it with his bread and have done with it.

What I cannot but resent is the fact that he describes me as being old and one-handed, as if it were in my power to make time stand still for me, or as if I had lost my hand in some tavern instead of upon the greatest occasion that the past or present has ever known or the future may ever hope to see.[2] If my wounds are not resplendent in the eyes of the chance beholder, they are at least highly thought of by those who know where they were received. The soldier who lies dead in battle has a more impressive mien than the one who by flight attains his liberty. So strongly do I feel about this that even if it were possible to work a miracle in my case, I still would rather have taken part in that prodigious battle than be today free of my wounds without having been there. The scars that the soldier has to show on face and breast are stars that guide others to the Heaven of honor, inspiring them with a longing for well-merited praise. What is more, it may be noted that one does not write with gray hairs but with his understanding, which usually grows better with the years.

I likewise resent his calling me envious; and as though I were some ignorant person, he goes on to explain to me what is meant by envy; when the truth of the matter is that of the two kinds, I am acquainted only with that which is holy, noble, and right-intentioned.[3] And this being so, as indeed it is, it is not likely that I should attack any priest, above all, one that is a familiar of the Holy Office.[4] If he made this statement, as it appears that he did, on behalf of a certain person, then he is utterly mistaken; for the person in question is one whose genius I hold in veneration and whose works I admire, as well as his constant industry and powers of application. But when all is said, I wish to thank this gentlemanly author for observing that my *Novels*[5] are more satirical than exemplary, while admitting at the same time that they are good; for they could not be good unless they had in them a little of everything.

1. A continuation of *Don Quixote* was published by a writer who gave himself the name of Avellaneda and claimed to come from Tordesillas. The mood of the second prologue is grim in comparison to the optimistic and witty prologue to Part I.
2. Cervantes received three gunshot wounds in the battle of Lepanto (1571); one of them cost him the use of his left hand.

3. *Jealousy* and *zealousness* are etymologically related.
4. An allusion to the Spanish playwright Lope de Vega (1562–1635), who had been made a priest and appointed an official of the Spanish Inquisition. Avellaneda accused Cervantes of envying Lope's enormous popularity.
5. *Exemplary Novels* (1613).

You will likely tell me that I am being too restrained and overmodest, but it is my belief that affliction is not to be heaped upon the afflicted, and this gentleman must be suffering greatly, seeing that he does not dare to come out into the open and show himself by the light of day, but must conceal his name and dissemble his place of origin, as if he had been guilty of some treason or act of lese majesty. If you by chance should come to know him, tell him on my behalf that I do not hold it against him; for I know what temptations the devil has to offer, one of the greatest of which consists in putting it into a man's head that he can write a book and have it printed and thereby achieve as much fame as he does money and acquire as much money as he does fame; in confirmation of which I would have you, in your own witty and charming manner, tell him this tale.

There was in Seville a certain madman whose madness assumed one of the drollest forms that ever was seen in this world. Taking a hollow reed sharpened at one end, he would catch a dog in the street or somewhere else; and, holding one of the animal's legs with his foot and raising the other with his hand, he would fix his reed as best he could in a certain part, after which he would blow the dog up, round as a ball. When he had it in this condition he would give it a couple of slaps on the belly and let it go, remarking to the bystanders, of whom there were always plenty, "Do your Worships think, then, that it is so easy a thing to inflate a dog?" So you might ask, "Does your Grace think that it is so easy a thing to write a book?" And if this story does not set well with him, here is another one, dear reader, that you may tell him. This one, also, is about a madman and a dog.

The madman in this instance lived in Cordova. He was in the habit of carrying on his head a marble slab or stone of considerable weight, and when he met some stray cur he would go up alongside it and drop the weight full upon it, and the dog in a rage, barking and howling, would then scurry off down three whole streets without stopping. Now, it happened that among the dogs that he treated in this fashion was one belonging to a capmaker, who was very fond of the beast. Going up to it as usual, the madman let the stone fall on its head, whereupon the animal set up a great yowling, and its owner, hearing its moans and seeing what had been done to it, promptly snatched up a measuring rod and fell upon the dog's assailant, flaying him until there was not a sound bone left in the fellow's body; and with each blow that he gave him he cried, "You dog! You thief! Treat my greyhound like that, would you? You brute, couldn't you see it was a greyhound?" And repeating the word "greyhound" over and over, he sent the madman away beaten to a pulp.

Profiting by the lesson that had been taught him, the fellow disappeared and was not seen in public for more than a month, at the end of which time he returned, up to his old tricks and with a heavier stone than ever on his head. He would go up to a dog and stare at it, long and hard, and without daring to drop his stone, would say, "This is a greyhound; beware." And so with all the dogs that he encountered: whether they were mastiffs or curs, he would assert that they were greyhounds and let them go unharmed.

The same thing possibly may happen to our historian; it may be that he will not again venture to let fall the weight of his wit in the form of books which, being bad ones, are harder than rocks.

As for the threat he has made to the effect that through his book he will deprive me of the profits on my own,[6] you may tell him that I do not give a rap.

---

6. Avellaneda asserted that his second part would earn the profits Cervantes might have expected from a continuation of his own.

Quoting from the famous interlude, *La Perendenga*,[7] I will say to him in reply, "Long live my master, the Four-and-twenty,[8] and Christ be with us all." Long live the great Count of Lemos, whose Christian spirit and well-known liberality have kept me on my feet despite all the blows an unkind fate has dealt me. Long life to his Eminence of Toledo, the supremely charitable Don Bernardo de Sandoval y Rojas.[9] Even though there were no printing presses in all the world, or such as there are should print more books directed against me than there are letters in the verses of *Mingo Revulgo*,[1] what would it matter to me? These two princes, without any cringing flattery or adulation on my part but solely out of their own goodness of heart, have taken it upon themselves to grant me their favor and protection, in which respect I consider myself richer and more fortunate than if by ordinary means I had attained the peak of prosperity. The poor man may keep his honor, but not the vicious one. Poverty may cast a cloud over nobility but cannot wholly obscure it. Virtue of itself gives off a certain light, even though it be through the chinks and crevices and despite the obstacles of adversity, and so comes to be esteemed and as a consequence favored by high and noble minds.

Tell him no more than this, nor do I have anything more to say to you, except to ask you to bear in mind that this *Second Part of Don Quixote*, which I herewith present to you, is cut from the same cloth and by the same craftsman as Part I. In this book I give you Don Quixote continued and, finally, dead and buried, in order that no one may dare testify any further concerning him, for there has been quite enough evidence as it is. It is sufficient that a reputable individual should have chronicled these ingenious acts of madness once and for all without going into the matter again; for an abundance even of good things causes them to be little esteemed, while scarcity may lend a certain worth to those that are bad.

I almost forgot to tell you that you may look forward to the Persiles on which I am now putting the finishing touches, as well as Part Second of the *Galatea*.[2]

["*Put into a Book*"]

CHAPTER III

*Of the laughable conversation that took place between
Don Quixote, Sancho Panza, and the bachelor Sansón Carrasco.*

Don Quixote remained in a thoughtful mood as he waited for the bachelor Carrasco,[3] from whom he hoped to hear the news as to how he had been put into a book, as Sancho had said. He could not bring himself to believe that any such

---

7. No interlude by this name has survived.
8. Municipal authorities of Seville, Cordova, and Granada.
9. Archbishop of Toledo, uncle of the duke of Lerma, and patron of Cervantes.
1. Long verse satire, well known in Cervantes' time; it is alluded to again in Part II, chapter LXXIII (see p. 1685).
2. *The Trials of Persiles and Sigismunda* was published in 1617, two years after Part II of *Don Quixote*. A second part of *The Galatea*

was never published.
3. I.e., the bachelor of arts Sansón Carrasco, an important new character who appears at the beginning of Part II and will play a considerable role in the story with his attempts at "curing" Don Quixote. In the preceding chapter he has been telling Sancho about a book relating the adventures of Don Quixote and his squire, by which the two have been made famous; the book is, of course, *Don Quixote*, Part I.

history existed, since the blood of the enemies he had slain was not yet dry on the blade of his sword; and here they were trying to tell him that his high deeds of chivalry were already circulating in printed form. But, for that matter, he imagined that some sage, either friend or enemy, must have seen to the printing of them through the art of magic. If the chronicler was a friend, he must have undertaken the task in order to magnify and exalt Don Quixote's exploits above the most notable ones achieved by knights-errant of old. If an enemy, his purpose would have been to make them out as nothing at all, by debasing them below the meanest acts ever recorded of any mean squire. The only thing was, the knight reflected, the exploits of squires never were set down in writing. If it was true that such a history existed, being about a knight-errant, then it must be eloquent and lofty in tone, a splendid and distinguished piece of work and veracious in its details.

This consoled him somewhat, although he was a bit put out at the thought that the author was a Moor, if the appellation "Cid" was to be taken as an indication,[4] and from the Moors you could never hope for any word of truth, seeing that they are all of them cheats, forgers, and schemers. He feared lest his love should not have been treated with becoming modesty but rather in a way that would reflect upon the virtue of his lady Dulcinea del Toboso. He hoped that his fidelity had been made clear, and the respect he had always shown her, and that something had been said as to how he had spurned queens, empresses, and damsels of every rank while keeping a rein upon those impulses that are natural to a man. He was still wrapped up in these and many other similar thoughts when Sancho returned with Carrasco.

Don Quixote received the bachelor very amiably. The latter, although his name was Sansón, or Samson, was not very big so far as bodily size went, but he was a great joker, with a sallow complexion and a ready wit. He was going on twenty-four and had a round face, a snub nose, and a large mouth, all of which showed him to be of a mischievous disposition and fond of jests and witticisms. This became apparent when, as soon as he saw Don Quixote, he fell upon his knees and addressed the knight as follows:

"O mighty Don Quixote de la Mancha, give me your hands; for by the habit of St. Peter that I wear[5]—though I have received but the first four orders—your Grace is one of the most famous knights-errant that ever have been or ever will be anywhere on this earth. Blessings upon Cid Hamete Benengeli who wrote down the history of your great achievements, and upon that curious-minded one who was at pains to have it translated from the Arabic into our Castilian vulgate for the universal entertainment of the people."

Don Quixote bade him rise. "Is it true, then," he asked, "that there is a book about me and that it was some Moorish sage who composed it?"

"By way of showing you how true it is," replied Sansón, "I may tell you that it is my belief that there are in existence today more than twelve thousand copies of that history. If you do not believe me, you have but to make inquiries in Portugal, Barcelona, and Valencia, where editions have been brought out, and there is even a report to the effect that one edition was printed at Antwerp. In short, I feel certain that there will soon not be a nation that does not know it or a language into which it has not been translated."

4. The allusion is to Cid Hamete Benengeli (see p. 1573, n. 5). The word *cid* is of Arabic derivation.

5. The dress of one of the minor clerical orders.

"One of the things," remarked Don Quixote, "that should give most satisfaction to a virtuous and eminent man is to see his good name spread abroad during his own lifetime, by means of the printing press, through translations into the languages of the various peoples. I have said 'good name,' for if he has any other kind, his fate is worse than death."

"If it is a matter of good name and good reputation," said the bachelor, "your Grace bears off the palm from all the knights-errant in the world; for the Moor in his tongue and the Christian in his have most vividly depicted your Grace's gallantry, your courage in facing dangers, your patience in adversity and suffering, whether the suffering be due to wounds or to misfortunes of another sort, and your virtue and continence in love, in connection with that platonic relationship that exists between your Grace and my lady Doña Dulcinea del Toboso."

At this point Sancho spoke up. "Never in my life," he said, "have I heard my lady Dulcinea called 'Doña,' but only 'la Señora Dulcinea del Toboso'; so on that point, already, the history is wrong."

"That is not important," said Carrasco.

"No, certainly not," Don Quixote agreed. "But tell me, Señor Bachelor, what adventures of mine as set down in this book have made the deepest impression?"

"As to that," the bachelor answered, "opinions differ, for it is a matter of individual taste. There are some who are very fond of the adventure of the windmills— those windmills which to your Grace appeared to be so many Briareuses and giants. Others like the episode at the fulling mill. One relishes the story of the two armies which took on the appearance of droves of sheep, while another fancies the tale of the dead man whom they were taking to Segovia for burial. One will assert that the freeing of the galley slaves is the best of all, and yet another will maintain that nothing can come up to the Benedictine giants and the encounter with the valiant Biscayan."

Again Sancho interrupted him. "Tell me, Señor Bachelor," he said, "does the book say anything about the adventure with the Yanguesans, that time our good Rocinante took it into his head to go looking for tidbits in the sea?"

"The sage," replied Sansón, "has left nothing in the inkwell. He has told everything and to the point, even to the capers which the worthy Sancho cut as they tossed him in the blanket."

"I cut no capers in the blanket," objected Sancho, "but I did in the air, and more than I liked."

"I imagine," said Don Quixote, "that there is no history in the world, dealing with humankind, that does not have its ups and downs, and this is particularly true of those that have to do with deeds of chivalry, for they can never be filled with happy incidents alone."

"Nevertheless," the bachelor went on, "there are some who have read the book who say that they would have been glad if the authors had forgotten a few of the innumerable cudgelings which Señor Don Quixote received in the course of his various encounters."

"But that is where the truth of the story comes in," Sancho protested.

"For all of that," observed Don Quixote, "they might well have said nothing about them; for there is no need of recording those events that do not alter the veracity of the chronicle, when they tend only to lessen the reader's respect for the hero. You may be sure that Aeneas was not as pious as Vergil would have us believe, nor was Ulysses as wise as Homer depicts him."

"That is true enough," replied Sansón, "but it is one thing to write as a poet and another as a historian. The former may narrate or sing of things not as they were but as they should have been; the latter must describe them not as they should have been but as they were, without adding to or detracting from the truth in any degree whatsoever."

"Well," said Sancho, "if this Moorish gentleman is bent upon telling the truth, I have no doubt that among my master's thrashings my own will be found; for they never took the measure of his Grace's shoulders without measuring my whole body. But I don't wonder at that; for as my master himself says, when there's an ache in the head the members have to share it."

"You are a sly fox, Sancho," said Don Quixote. "My word, but you can remember things well enough when you choose to do so!"

"Even if I wanted to forget the whacks they gave me," Sancho answered him, "the welts on my ribs wouldn't let me, for they are still fresh."

"Be quiet, Sancho," his master admonished him, "and do not interrupt the bachelor. I beg him to go on and tell me what is said of me in this book."

"And what it says about me, too," put in Sancho, "for I have heard that I am one of the main presonages in it—"

"*Personages*, not *presonages*, Sancho my friend," said Sansón.

"So we have another one who catches you up on everything you say," was Sancho's retort. "If we go on at this rate, we'll never be through in a lifetime."

"May God put a curse on *my* life," the bachelor told him, "if you are not the second most important person in the story; and there are some who would rather listen to you talk than to anyone else in the book. It is true, there are those who say that you are too gullible in believing it to be the truth that you could become the governor of that island that was offered you by Señor Don Quixote, here present."

"There is still sun on the top of the wall," said Don Quixote, "and when Sancho is a little older, with the experience that the years bring, he will be wiser and better fitted to be a governor than he is at the present time."

"By God, master," said Sancho, "the island that I couldn't govern right now I'd never be able to govern if I lived to be as old as Methuselah.[6] The trouble is, I don't know where that island we are talking about is located; it is not due to any lack of noddle on my part."

"Leave it to God, Sancho," was Don Quixote's advice, "and everything will come out all right, perhaps even better than you think; for not a leaf on the tree stirs except by His will."

"Yes," said Sansón, "if it be God's will, Sancho will not lack a thousand islands to govern, not to speak of one island alone."

"I have seen governors around here," said Sancho, "that are not to be compared to the sole of my shoe, and yet they call them 'your Lordship' and serve them on silver plate."

"Those are not the same kind of governors," Sansón informed him. "Their task is a good deal easier. The ones that govern islands must at least know grammar."

6. In the Bible's Book of Genesis, a man who lived 969 years.

"I could make out well enough with the *gram*," replied Sancho, "but with the *mar* I want nothing to do, for I don't understand it at all. But leaving this business of the governorship in God's hands—for He will send me wherever I can best serve Him—I will tell you, Señor Bachelor Sansón Carrasco, that I am very much pleased that the author of the history should have spoken of me in such a way as does not offend me; for, upon the word of a faithful squire, if he had said anything about me that was not becoming to an old Christian, the deaf would have heard of it."

"That would be to work miracles," said Sansón.

"Miracles or no miracles," was the answer, "let everyone take care as to what he says or writes about people and not be setting down the first thing that pops into his head."

"One of the faults that is found with the book," continued the bachelor, "is that the author has inserted in it a story entitled *The One Who Was Too Curious for His Own Good*. It is not that the story in itself is a bad one or badly written; it is simply that it is out of place there, having nothing to do with the story of his Grace, Señor Don Quixote."[7]

"I will bet you," said Sancho, "that the son of a dog has mixed the cabbages with the baskets."[8]

"And I will say right now," declared Don Quixote, "that the author of this book was not a sage but some ignorant prattler who at haphazard and without any method set about the writing of it, being content to let things turn out as they might. In the same manner, Orbaneja,[9] the painter of Ubeda, when asked what he was painting would reply, 'Whatever it turns out to be.' Sometimes it would be a cock, in which case he would have to write alongside it, in Gothic letters, 'This is a cock.' And so it must be with my story, which will need a commentary to make it understandable."

"No," replied Sansón, "that it will not; for it is so clearly written that none can fail to understand it. Little children leaf through it, young people read it, adults appreciate it, and the aged sing its praises. In short, it is so thumbed and read and so well known to persons of every walk in life that no sooner do folks see some skinny nag than they at once cry, 'There goes Rocinante!' Those that like it best of all are the pages; for there is no lord's antechamber where a *Don Quixote* is not to be found. If one lays it down, another will pick it up; one will pounce upon it, and another will beg for it. It affords the pleasantest and least harmful reading of any book that has been published up to now. In the whole of it there is not to be found an indecent word or a thought that is other than Catholic."

"To write in any other manner," observed Don Quixote, "would be to write lies and not the truth. Those historians who make use of falsehoods ought to be burned like the makers of counterfeit money. I do not know what could have led the author to introduce stories and episodes that are foreign to the subject matter when he had so much to write about in describing my adventures. He must, undoubtedly, have been inspired by the old saying, 'With straw or with hay . . .'[1] For, in truth, all he had to do was to record my thoughts, my

---

7. The story, a tragic tale about a jealousy-ridden husband, occupies several chapters of Part I. Here, as elsewhere in this chapter, Cervantes echoes criticism currently aimed at his book.

8. I.e., has jumbled together things of differ-ent kinds.

9. This painter, possibly Cervantes' invention, has never been identified.

1. The proverb concludes either "the mattress is filled" or "I fill my belly."

sighs, my tears, my lofty purposes, and my undertakings, and he would have had a volume bigger or at least as big as that which the works of El Tostado[2] would make. To sum the matter up, Señor Bachelor, it is my opinion that, in composing histories or books of any sort, a great deal of judgment and ripe understanding is called for. To say and write witty and amusing things is the mark of great genius. The cleverest character in a comedy is the clown, since he who would make himself out to be a simpleton cannot be one. History is a near-sacred thing, for it must be true, and where the truth is, there is God. And yet there are those who compose books and toss them out into the world as if they were no more than fritters."

"There is no book so bad," opined the bachelor, "that there is not some good in it."

"Doubtless that is so," replied Don Quixote, "but it very often happens that those who have won in advance a great and well-deserved reputation for their writings, lose it in whole or in part when they give their works to the printer."

"The reason for it," said Sansón, "is that, printed works being read at leisure, their faults are the more readily apparent, and the greater the reputation of the author the more closely are they scrutinized. Men famous for their genius, great poets, illustrious historians, are almost always envied by those who take a special delight in criticizing the writings of others without having produced anything of their own."

"That is not to be wondered at," said Don Quixote, "for there are many theologians who are not good enough for the pulpit but who are very good indeed when it comes to detecting the faults or excesses of those who preach."

"All of this is very true, Señor Don Quixote," replied Carrasco, "but, all the same, I could wish that these self-appointed censors were a bit more forbearing and less hypercritical; I wish they would pay a little less attention to the spots on the bright sun of the work that occasions their fault-finding. For if *aliquando bonus dormitat Homerus*,[3] let them consider how much of his time he spent awake, shedding the light of his genius with a minimum of shade. It well may be that what to them seems a flaw is but one of those moles which sometimes add to the beauty of a face. In any event, I insist that he who has a book printed runs a very great risk, inasmuch as it is an utter impossibility to write it in such a manner that it will please all who read it."

"This book about me must have pleased very few," remarked Don Quixote.

"Quite the contrary," said Sansón, "for just as *stultorum infinitus est mumerus*,[4] so the number of those who have enjoyed this history is likewise infinite. Some, to be sure, have complained of the author's forgetfulness, seeing that he neglected to make it plain who the thief was who stole Sancho's gray;[5] for it is not stated there, but merely implied, that the ass was stolen; and, a little further on, we find the knight mounted on the same beast, although it has not made its reappearance in the story. They also say that the author forgot to tell us what Sancho did with those hundred crowns that he found in the valise on the Sierra Morena, as nothing more is said of them and there are

---

2. Alonso de Madrigal (ca. 1400–1455), bishop of Ávila, a prolific author of devotional works.
3. Good Homer sometimes nods too (Latin)—

Horace, *Art of Poetry*, l. 359.
4. Infinite is the number of fools (Latin).
5. In Part I, chapter 23.

many who would like to know how he disposed of the money or how he spent it. This is one of the serious omissons to be found in the work."

To this Sancho replied, "I, Señor Sansón, do not feel like giving any account or accounting just now; for I feel a little weak in my stomach, and if I don't do something about it by taking a few swigs of the old stuff, I'll be sitting on St. Lucy's thorn.[6] I have some of it at home, and my old woman is waiting for me. After I've had my dinner, I'll come back and answer any questions your Grace or anybody else wants to ask me, whether it's about the loss of the ass or the spending of the hundred crowns."

And without waiting for a reply or saying another word, he went on home. Don Quixote urged the bachelor to stay and take potluck with him, and Sansón accepted the invitation and remained. In addition to the knight's ordinary fare, they had a couple of pigeons, and at table their talk was of chivalry and feats of arms. Carrasco was careful to humor his host, and when the meal was over they took their siesta.

[A Victorious Duel]

CHAPTER XII

Of the strange adventure that befell the valiant Don Quixote with the fearless Knight of the Mirrors.[7]

The night following the encounter with Death was spent by Don Quixote and his squire beneath some tall and shady trees,[8] the knight having been persuaded to eat a little from the stock of provisions carried by the gray.

"Sir," said Sancho, in the course of their repast, "how foolish I'd have been if I had chosen the spoils from your Grace's first adventure rather than the foals from the three mares.[9] Truly, truly, a sparrow in the hand is worth more than a vulture on the wing."[1]

"And yet, Sancho," replied Don Quixote, "if you had but let me attack them as I wished to do, you would at least have had as spoils the Empress's gold crown and Cupid's painted wings;[2] for I should have taken them whether or no and placed them in your hands."

"The crowns and scepters of stage emperors," remarked Sancho, "were never known to be of pure gold; they are always of tinsel or tinplate."

6. I.e., I shall be weak and exhausted (proverbial).
7. Until he earns this title (in chapter 15), he will be referred to as the Knight of the Wood.
8. Don Quixote and his squire are now in the woody region around El Toboso, Dulcinea's hometown. Sancho has been sent to look for his knight's lady and has saved the day by pretending to see the beautiful damsel in a "village wench, and not a pretty one at that, for she was round-faced and snub-nosed." But by his imaginative lie he has succeeded, as he had planned, in setting in motion Don Quixote's belief in spells and enchantments: enemy

magicians, envious of him, have hidden his lady's splendor only from his sight. While the knight was still under the shock of this experience, farther along their way he and his squire have met a group of itinerant players dressed in their proper costumes for a religious play, *The Parliament of Death*.
9. Don Quixote has promised them to Sancho as a reward for bringing news of Dulcinea.
1. I.e., a bird in the hand is worth two in the bush.
2. The Empress and Cupid are characters in *The Parliament of Death*.

"That is the truth," said Don Quixote, "for it is only right that the accessories of a drama should be fictitious and not real, like the play itself. Speaking of that, Sancho, I would have you look kindly upon the art of the theater and, as a consequence, upon those who write the pieces and perform in them, for they all render a service of great value to the State by holding up a mirror for us at each step that we take, wherein we may observe, vividly depicted, all the varied aspects of human life; and I may add that there is nothing that shows us more clearly, by similitude, what we are and what we ought to be than do plays and players.

"Tell me, have you not seen some comedy in which kings, emperors, pontiffs, knights, ladies, and numerous other characters are introduced? One plays the ruffian, another the cheat, this one a merchant and that one a soldier, while yet another is the fool who is not so foolish as he appears, and still another the one of whom love has made a fool. Yet when the play is over and they have taken off their players' garments, all the actors are once more equal."

"Yes," replied Sancho, "I have seen all that."

"Well," continued Don Quixote, "the same thing happens in the comedy that we call life, where some play the part of emperors, others that of pontiffs—in short, all the characters that a drama may have—but when it is all over, that is to say, when life is done, death takes from each the garb that differentiates him, and all at last are equal in the grave."

"It is a fine comparison," Sancho admitted, "though not so new but that I have heard it many times before. It reminds me of that other one, about the game of chess. So long as the game lasts, each piece has its special qualities, but when it is over they are all mixed and jumbled together and put into a bag, which is to the chess pieces what the grave is to life."

"Every day, Sancho," said Don Quixote, "you are becoming less stupid and more sensible."

"It must be that some of your Grace's good sense is sticking to me," was Sancho's answer. "I am like a piece of land that of itself is dry and barren, but if you scatter manure over it and cultivate it, it will bear good fruit. By this I mean to say that your Grace's conversation is the manure that has been cast upon the barren land of my dry wit; the time that I spend in your service, associating with you, does the cultivating; and as a result of it all, I hope to bring forth blessed fruits by not departing, slipping, or sliding, from those paths of good breeding which your Grace has marked out for me in my parched understanding."

Don Quixote had to laugh at this affected speech of Sancho's, but he could not help perceiving that what the squire had said about his improvement was true enough; for every now and then the servant would speak in a manner that astonished his master. It must be admitted, however, that most of the time when he tried to use fine language, he would tumble from the mountain of his simple-mindedness into the abyss of his ignorance. It was when he was quoting old saws and sayings, whether or not they had anything to do with the subject under discussion, that he was at his best, displaying upon such occasions a prodigious memory, as will already have been seen and noted in the course of this history.

With such talk as this they spent a good part of the night. Then Sancho felt a desire to draw down the curtains of his eyes, as he was in the habit of saying when he wished to sleep, and, unsaddling his mount, he turned him loose to graze at will on the abundant grass. If he did not remove Rocinante's saddle, this was due to his master's express command; for when they had taken the field and were not sleeping under a roof, the hack was under no circumstances to be stripped. This was in accordance with an old and established custom which knights-errant faithfully observed: the bridle and saddlebow might be removed, but beware of touching the saddle itself! Guided by this precept, Sancho now gave Rocinante the same freedom that the ass enjoyed.

The close friendship that existed between the two animals was a most unusual one, so remarkable indeed that it has become a tradition handed down from father to son, and the author of this veracious chronicle even wrote a number of special chapters on the subject, although, in order to preserve the decency and decorum that are fitting in so heroic an account, he chose to omit them in the final version. But he forgets himself once in a while and goes on to tell us how the two beasts when they were together would hasten to scratch each other, and how, when they were tired and their bellies were full, Rocinante would lay his long neck over that of the ass—it extended more than half a yard on the other side—and the pair would then stand there gazing pensively at the ground for as much as three whole days at a time, or at least until someone came for them or hunger compelled them to seek nourishment.

I may tell you that I have heard it said that the author of this history, in one of his writings, has compared the friendship of Rocinante and the gray to that of Nisus and Euryalus and that of Pylades and Orestes;[3] and if this be true, it shows for the edification of all what great friends these two peace-loving animals were, and should be enough to make men ashamed, who are so inept at preserving friendship with one another. For this reason it has been said:

> There is no friend for friend,
> Reeds to lances turn . . . [4]

And there was the other poet who sang:

> Between friend and friend the bug . . . [5]

Let no one think that the author has gone out of his way in comparing the friendship of animals with that of men; for human beings have received valuable lessons from the beasts and have learned many important things from them. From the stork they have learned the use of clysters; the dog has taught them the salutary effects of vomiting as well as a lesson in gratitude; the cranes have taught them vigilance, the ants foresight, the elephants modesty, and the horse loyalty.[6]

Sancho had at last fallen asleep at the foot of a cork tree, while Don Quixote was slumbering beneath a sturdy oak. Very little time had passed when the knight was awakened by a noise behind him, and, starting up, he began looking about him and listening to see if he could make out where it came from. Then he caught sight of two men on horseback, one of whom, slipping down from the saddle, said to the other, "Dismount, my friend, and unbridle the horses; for there seems to be plenty of grass around here for them and sufficient silence and solitude for my amorous thoughts."

Saying this, he stretched himself out on the ground, and as he flung himself down the armor that he wore made such a noise that Don Quixote knew at once,

---

3. Famous examples of friendship in Virgil's *Aeneid* and in Greek tradition and drama.
4. From a popular ballad.
5. The Spanish expression "a bug in the eye"

implies keeping a watchful eye on somebody.
6. All folkloristic beliefs about the virtues of animals. "Clysters": enemas.

for a certainty, that he must be a knight-errant. Going over to Sancho, who was still sleeping, he shook him by the arm and with no little effort managed to get him awake.

"Brother Sancho," he said to him in a low voice, "we have an adventure on our hands."

"God give us a good one," said Sancho. "And where, my master, may her Ladyship, Mistress Adventure, be?"

"Where, Sancho?" replied Don Quixote. "Turn your eyes and look, and you will see stretched out over there a knight-errant who, so far as I can make out, is not any too happy; for I saw him fling himself from his horse to the ground with a certain show of despondency, and as he fell his armor rattled."

"Well," said Sancho, "and how does your Grace make this out to be an adventure?"

"I would not say," the knight answered him, "that this is an adventure in itself, but rather the beginning of one, for that is the way they start. But listen; he seems to be tuning a lute or guitar, and from the way he is spitting and clearing his throat he must be getting ready to sing something."

"Faith, so he is," said Sancho. "He must be some lovesick knight."

"There are no knights-errant that are not lovesick," Don Quixote informed him. "Let us listen to him, and the thread of his song will lead us to the yarn-ball of his thoughts; for out of the abundance of the heart the mouth speaketh."

Sancho would have liked to reply to his master, but the voice of the Knight of the Wood, which was neither very good nor very bad, kept him from it; and as the two of them listened attentively, they heard the following:

SONNET

> Show me, O lady, the pattern of thy will,
> That mine may take that very form and shape;
> For my will in thine own I fain would drape,
> Each slightest wish of thine I would fulfill.
> If thou wouldst have me silence this dread ill
> Of which I'm dying now, prepare the crape!
> Or if I must another manner ape,
> Then let Love's self display his rhyming skill.
> Of opposites I am made, that's manifest:
> In part soft wax, in part hard-diamond fire;
> Yet to Love's laws my heart I do adjust,
> And, hard or soft, I offer thee this breast:
> Print or engrave there what thou may'st desire,
> And I'll preserve it in eternal trust.

With an Ay! that appeared to be wrung from the very depths of his heart, the Knight of the Wood brought his song to a close, and then after a brief pause began speaking in a grief-stricken voice that was piteous to hear.

"O most beautiful and most ungrateful woman in all the world!" he cried, "how is it possible, O most serene Casildea de Vandalia,[7] for you to permit this captive knight of yours to waste away and perish in constant wanderings, amid

---

7. The Knight of the Wood's counterpart to Don Quixote's Dulcinea del Toboso.

rude toils and bitter hardships? Is it not enough that I have compelled all the knights of Navarre, all those of León, all the Tartessians and Castilians, and, finally, all those of La Mancha, to confess that there is no beauty anywhere that can rival yours?"

"That is not so!" cried Don Quixote at this point. "I am of La Mancha, and I have never confessed, I never could nor would confess a thing so prejudicial to the beauty of my lady. The knight whom you see there, Sancho, is raving; but let us listen and perhaps he will tell us more."

"That he will," replied Sancho, "for at the rate he is carrying on, he is good for a month at a stretch."

This did not prove to be the case, however; for when the Knight of the Wood heard voices near him, he cut short his lamentations and rose to his feet.

"Who goes there?" he called in a loud but courteous tone. "What kind of people are you? Are you, perchance, numbered among the happy or among the afflicted?"

"Among the afflicted," was Don Quixote's response.

"Then come to me," said the one of the Wood, "and, in doing so, know that you come to sorrow's self and the very essence of affliction."

Upon receiving so gentle and courteous an answer, Don Quixote and Sancho as well went over to him, whereupon the sorrowing one took the Manchegan's arm.

"Sit down here, Sir Knight," he continued, "for in order to know that you are one of those who follow the profession of knight-errantry, it is enough for me to have found you in this place where solitude and serenity keep you company, such a spot being the natural bed and proper dwelling of wandering men of arms."

"A knight I am," replied Don Quixote, "and of the profession that you mention; and though sorrows, troubles, and misfortunes have made my heart their abode, this does not mean that compassion for the woes of others has been banished from it. From your song a while ago I gather that your misfortunes are due to love—the love you bear that ungrateful fair one whom you named in your lamentations."

As they conversed in this manner, they sat together upon the hard earth, very peaceably and companionably, as if at daybreak they were not going to break each other's heads.

"Sir Knight," inquired the one of the Wood, "are you by any chance in love?"

"By mischance I am," said Don Quixote, "although the ills that come from well-placed affection should be looked upon as favors rather than as misfortunes."

"That is the truth," the Knight of the Wood agreed, "if it were not that the loved one's scorn disturbs our reason and understanding; for when it is excessive scorn appears as vengeance."

"I was never scorned by my lady," said Don Quixote.

"No, certainly not," said Sancho, who was standing near by, "for my lady is gentle as a ewe lamb and soft as butter."

"Is he your squire?" asked the one of the Wood.

"He is," replied Don Quixote.

"I never saw a squire," said the one of the Wood, "who dared to speak while his master was talking. At least, there is mine over there; he is as big as your father, and it cannot be proved that he has ever opened his lips while I was conversing."

"Well, upon my word," said Sancho, "I have spoken, and I will speak in front of any other as good—but never mind; it only makes it worse to stir it."

The Knight of the Wood's squire now seized Sancho's arm. "Come along," he said, "let the two of us go where we can talk all we like, squire fashion, and leave these gentlemen our masters to come to lance blows as they tell each other the story of their loves; for you may rest assured, daybreak will find them still at it."

"Let us, by all means," said Sancho, "and I will tell your Grace who I am, so that you may be able to see for yourself whether or not I am to be numbered among the dozen most talkative squires."

With this, the pair went off to one side, and there then took place between them a conversation that was as droll as the one between their masters was solemn.

CHAPTER XIII

In which is continued the adventure of the Knight of the Wood, together with the shrewd, highly original, and amicable conversation that took place between the two squires.

The knights and the squires had now separated, the latter to tell their life stories, the former to talk of their loves; but the history first relates the conversation of the servants and then goes on to report that of the masters. We are told that, after they had gone some little distance from where the others were, the one who served the Knight of the Wood began speaking to Sancho as follows:

"It is a hard life that we lead and live, *Señor mio*, those of us who are squires to knights-errant. It is certainly true that we eat our bread in the sweat of our faces, which is one of the curses that God put upon our first parents."[8]

"It might also be said," added Sancho, "that we eat it in the chill of our bodies, for who endures more heat and cold than we wretched ones who wait upon these wandering men of arms? It would not be so bad if we did eat once in a while, for troubles are less where there is bread; but as it is, we sometimes go for a day or two without breaking our fast, unless we feed on the wind that blows."

"But all this," said the other, "may very well be put up with, by reason of the hope we have of being rewarded; for if a knight is not too unlucky, his squire after a little while will find himself the governor of some fine island or prosperous earldom."

"I," replied Sancho, "have told my master that I would be satisfied with the governorship of an island, and he is so noble and so generous that he has promised it to me on many different occasions."

"In return for my services," said the Squire of the Wood, "I'd be content with a canonry. My master has already appointed me to one—and what a canonry!"

"Then he must be a churchly knight," said Sancho, "and in a position to grant favors of that sort to his faithful squire; but mine is a layman, pure and simple, although, as I recall, certain shrewd and, as I see it, scheming persons

8. Cf. Genesis 3.19: "In the sweat of thy face shalt thou eat bread, till thou return unto the ground."

did advise him to try to become an archbishop. However, he did not want to be anything but an emperor. And there I was, all the time trembling for fear he would take it into his head to enter the Church, since I was not educated enough to hold any benefices. For I may as well tell your Grace that, though I look like a man, I am no more than a beast where holy orders are concerned."

"That is where you are making a mistake," the Squire of the Wood assured him. "Not all island governments are desirable. Some of them are misshapen bits of land, some are poor, others are gloomy, and, in short, the best of them lays a heavy burden of care and trouble upon the shoulders of the unfortunate one to whose lot it falls. It would be far better if we who follow this cursed trade were to go back to our homes and there engage in pleasanter occupations, such as hunting or fishing, for example; for where is there in this world a squire so poor that he does not have a hack, a couple of greyhounds, and a fishing rod to provide him with sport in his own village?"

"I don't lack any of those," replied Sancho. "It is true, I have no hack, but I do have an ass that is worth twice as much as my master's horse. God send me a bad Easter, and let it be the next one that comes, if I would make a trade, even though he gave me four fanegas[9] of barley to boot. Your Grace will laugh at the price I put on my gray—for that is the color of the beast. As to greyhounds, I shan't want for them, as there are plenty and to spare in my village. And, anyway, there is more pleasure in hunting when someone else pays for it."

"Really and truly, Sir Squire," said the one of the Wood, "I have made up my mind and resolved to have no more to do with the mad whims of these knights; I intend to retire to my village and bring up my little ones—I have three of them, and they are like oriental pearls."

"I have two of them," said Sancho, "that might be presented to the Pope in person, especially one of my girls that I am bringing up to be a countess, God willing, in spite of what her mother says."

"And how old is this young lady that is destined to be a countess?"

"Fifteen," replied Sancho, "or a couple of years more or less. But she is tall as a lance, fresh as an April morning, and strong as a porter."

"Those," remarked the one of the Wood, "are qualifications that fit her to be not merely a countess but a nymph of the verdant wildwood. O whore's daughter of a whore! What strength the she-rogue must have!"

Sancho was a bit put out by this. "She is not a whore," he said, "nor was her mother before her, nor will either of them ever be, please God, so long as I live. And you might speak more courteously. For one who has been brought up among knights-errant, who are the soul of courtesy, those words are not very becoming."

"Oh, how little your Grace knows about compliments, Sir Squire!" the one of the Wood exclaimed. "Are you not aware that when some knight gives a good lance thrust to the bull in the plaza, or when a person does anything remarkably well, it is the custom for the crowd to cry out, 'Well done, whoreson rascal!' and that what appears to be vituperation in such a case is in reality high praise? Sir, I would bid you disown those sons or daughters who do nothing to cause such praise to be bestowed upon their parents."

---

9. One fanega is about 1.6 bushels, or 56 liters.

"I would indeed disown them if they didn't," replied Sancho, "and so your Grace may go ahead and call me, my children, and my wife all the whores in the world if you like, for everything that they say and do deserves the very highest praise. And in order that I may see them all again, I pray God to deliver me from mortal sin, or, what amounts to the same thing, from this dangerous calling of squire, seeing that I have fallen into it a second time, decoyed and deceived by a purse of a hundred ducats that I found one day in the heart of the Sierra Morena.[1] The devil is always holding up a bag full of doubloons in front of my eyes, here, there—no, not here, but there—everywhere, until it seems to me at every step I take that I am touching it with my hand, hugging it, carrying it off home with me, investing it, drawing an income from it, and living on it like a prince. And while I am thinking such thoughts, all the hardships I have to put up with serving this crackbrained master of mine, who is more of a madman than a knight, seem to me light and easy to bear."

"That," observed the Squire of the Wood, "is why it is they say that avarice bursts the bag. But, speaking of madmen, there is no greater one in all this world than my master; for he is one of those of whom it is said, 'The cares of others kill the ass.' Because another knight has lost his senses, he has to play mad too[2] and go hunting for that which, when he finds it, may fly up in his snout."

"Is he in love, maybe?"

"Yes, with a certain Casildea de Vandalia, the rawest[3] and best-roasted lady to be found anywhere on earth; but her rawness is not the foot he limps on, for he has other and greater schemes rumbling in his bowels, as you will hear tell before many hours have gone by."

"There is no road so smooth," said Sancho, "that it does not have some hole or rut to make you stumble. In other houses they cook horse beans, in mine they boil them by the kettleful.[4] Madness has more companions and attendants than good sense does. But if it is true what they say, that company in trouble brings relief, I may take comfort from your Grace, since you serve a master as foolish as my own."

"Foolish but brave," the one of the Wood corrected him, "and more of a rogue than anything else."

"That is not true of my master," replied Sancho. "I can assure you there is nothing of the rogue about him; he is as open and aboveboard as a wine pitcher and would not harm anyone but does good to all. There is no malice in his makeup, and a child could make him believe it was night at midday. For that very reason I love him with all my heart and cannot bring myself to leave him, no matter how many foolish things he does."

"But, nevertheless, good sir and brother," said the Squire of the Wood, "with the blind leading the blind, both are in danger of falling into the pit. It would be better for us to get out of all this as quickly as we can and return to our old haunts; for those that go seeking adventures do not always find good ones."

Sancho kept clearing his throat from time to time, and his saliva seemed rather viscous and dry; seeing which, the woodland squire said to him, "It looks

---

1. When Don Quixote retired there in Part I, chapter 23.
2. In the Sierra Morena, Don Quixote had decided to imitate Amadis de Gaula and Ariosto's Roland "by playing the part of a desperate and raving madman" as a consequence of love.
3. The Spanish has a pun on *crudo*, meaning both "raw" and "cruel."
4. Meaning that his misfortunes always come in large quantities.

to me as if we have been talking so much that our tongues are cleaving to our palates, but I have a loosener over there, hanging from the bow of my saddle, and a pretty good one it is." With this, he got up and went over to his horse and came back a moment later with a big flask of wine and a meat pie half a yard in diameter. This is no exaggeration, for the pasty in question was made of a hutch-rabbit of such a size that Sancho took it to be a goat, or at the very least a kid.

"And are you in the habit of carrying this with you, Señor?" he asked.

"What do you think?" replied the other. "Am I by any chance one of your wool-and-water[5] squires? I carry better rations on the flanks of my horse than a general does when he takes the field."

Sancho ate without any urging, gulping down mouthfuls that were like the knots on a tether, as they sat there in the dark.

"You are a squire of the right sort," he said, "loyal and true, and you live in grand style as shown by this feast, which I would almost say was produced by magic. You are not like me, poor wretch, who have in my saddlebags only a morsel of cheese so hard you could crack a giant's skull with it, three or four dozen carob beans, and a few nuts. For this I have my master to thank, who believes in observing the rule that knights-errant should nourish and sustain themselves on nothing but dried fruits and the herbs of the field."

"Upon my word, brother," said the other squire, "my stomach was not made for thistles, wild pears, and woodland herbs. Let our masters observe those knightly laws and traditions and eat what their rules prescribe; I carry a hamper of food and a flask on my saddlebow, whether they like it or not. And speaking of that flask, how I love it! There is scarcely a minute in the day that I'm not hugging and kissing it, over and over again."

As he said this, he placed the wine bag in Sancho's hands, who put it to his mouth, threw his head back, and sat there gazing up at the stars for a quarter of an hour. Then, when he had finished drinking, he let his head loll on one side and heaved a deep sigh.

"The whoreson rascal!" he exclaimed, "that's a fine vintage for you!"

"There!" cried the Squire of the Wood, as he heard the epithet Sancho had used, "do you see how you have praised this wine by calling it 'whoreson'?"

"I grant you," replied Sancho, "that it is no insult to call anyone a son of a whore so long as you really do mean to praise him. But tell me, sir, in the name of what you love most, is this the wine of Ciudad Real?"[6]

"What a winetaster you are! It comes from nowhere else, and it's a few years old, at that."

"Leave it to me," said Sancho, "and never fear, I'll show you how much I know about it. Would you believe me, Sir Squire, I have such a great natural instinct in this matter of wines that I have but to smell a vintage and I will tell you the country where it was grown, from what kind of grapes, what it tastes like, and how good it is, and everything that has to do with it. There is nothing so unusual about this, however, seeing that on my father's side were two of the best winetasters La Mancha has known in many a year, in proof of which, listen to the story of what happened to them.

---

5. I.e., lowly or paltry.
6. The main town in La Mancha and the center of a wine-producing region.

"The two were given a sample of wine from a certain vat and asked to state its condition and quality and determine whether it was good or bad. One of them tasted it with the tip of his tongue while the other merely brought it up to his nose. The first man said that it tasted of iron, the second that it smelled of Cordovan leather. The owner insisted that the vat was clean and that there could be nothing in the wine to give it a flavor of leather or of iron, but, nevertheless, the two famous wine-tasters stood their ground. Time went by, and when they came to clean out the vat they found in it a small key attached to a leather strap. And so your Grace may see for yourself whether or not one who comes of that kind of stock has a right to give his opinion in such cases."

"And for that very reason," said the Squire of the Wood, "I maintain that we ought to stop going about in search of adventures. Seeing that we have loaves, let us not go looking for cakes, but return to our cottages, for God will find us there if He so wills."

"I mean to stay with my master," Sancho replied, "until he reaches Saragossa, but after that we will come to an understanding."

The short of the matter is, the two worthy squires talked so much and drank so much that sleep had to tie their tongues and moderate their thirst, since to quench the latter was impossible. Clinging to the wine flask, which was almost empty by now, and with half-chewed morsels of food in their mouths, they both slept peacefully; and we shall leave them there as we go on to relate what took place between the Knight of the Wood and the Knight of the Mournful Countenance.

CHAPTER XIV

Wherein is continued the adventure of the Knight of the Wood.

In the course of the long conversation that took place between Don Quixote and the Knight of the Wood, the history informs us that the latter addressed the following remarks to the Manchegan:

"In short, Sir Knight, I would have you know that my destiny, or, more properly speaking, my own free choice, has led me to fall in love with the peerless Casildea de Vandalia. I call her peerless for the reason that she has no equal as regards either her bodily proportions or her very great beauty. This Casildea, then, of whom I am telling you, repaid my worthy affections and honorable intentions by forcing me, as Hercules[7] was forced by his stepmother, to incur many and diverse perils; and each time as I overcame one of them she would promise me that with the next one I should have that which I desired; but instead my labors have continued, forming a chain whose links I am no longer able to count, nor can I say which will be the last one, that shall mark the beginning of the realization of my hopes.

"One time she sent me forth to challenge that famous giantess of Seville, known as La Giralda,[8] who is as strong and brave as if made of brass, and who without moving from the spot where she stands is the most changeable and fickle woman in the world. I came, I saw, I conquered her. I made her stand still

---

7. In Greek mythology, the hero son of Zeus and Alcmena; he was persecuted by Zeus's wife, Hera.
8. Actually the bell tower of the cathedral of Seville, originally built as a minaret.

and point in one direction only, and for more than a week nothing but north winds blew. Then, there was that other time when Casildea sent me to lift those ancient stones, the mighty Bulls of Guisando,[9] an enterprise that had better have been entrusted to porters than to knights. On another occasion she commanded me to hurl myself down into the Cabra chasm[1]—an unheard-of and terribly dangerous undertaking—and bring her back a detailed account of what lay concealed in that deep and gloomy pit. I rendered La Giralda motionless, I lifted the Bulls of Guisando, and I threw myself into the abyss and brought to light what was hidden in its depths; yet my hopes are dead—how dead!—while her commands and her scorn are as lively as can be.

"Finally, she commanded me to ride through all the provinces of Spain and compel all the knights-errant whom I met with to confess that she is the most beautiful woman now living and that I am the most enamored man of arms that is to be found anywhere in the world. In fulfillment of this behest I have already traveled over the greater part of these realms and have vanquished many knights who have dared to contradict me. But the one whom I am proudest to have overcome in single combat is that famous gentleman, Don Quixote de la Mancha; for I made him confess that my Casildea is more beautiful than his Dulcinea, and by achieving such a conquest I reckon that I have conquered all the others on the face of the earth, seeing that this same Don Quixote had himself routed them. Accordingly, when I vanquished him, his fame, glory, and honor passed over and were transferred to my person.

> The brighter is the conquered one's lost crown,
> The greater is the conqueror's renown.[2]

Thus, the innumerable exploits of the said Don Quixote are now set down to my account and are indeed my own."

Don Quixote was astounded as he listened to the Knight of the Wood, and was about to tell him any number of times that he lied; the words were on the tip of his tongue, but he held them back as best he could, thinking that he would bring the other to confess with his own lips that what he had said was a lie. And so it was quite calmly that he now replied to him.

"Sir Knight," he began, "as to the assertion that your Grace has conquered most of the knights-errant in Spain and even in all the world, I have nothing to say, but that you have vanquished Don Quixote de la Mancha, I am inclined to doubt. It may be that it was someone else who resembled him, although there are very few that do."

"What do you mean?" replied the one of the Wood. "I swear by the heavens above that I did fight with Don Quixote and that I overcame him and forced him to yield. He is a tall man, with a dried-up face, long, lean legs, graying hair, an eagle-like nose somewhat hooked, and a big, black, drooping mustache. He takes the field under the name of the Knight of the Mournful Countenance, he has for squire a peasant named Sancho Panza, and he rides a famous steed called Rocinante. Lastly, the lady of his heart is a certain Dulcinea del Toboso, once upon a time known as Aldonza Lorenzo, just as my own lady, whose name

9. Statues representing animals and supposedly marking a place where Caesar defeated Pompey.
1. Possibly an ancient mine in the Sierra de

Cabra near Cordova.
2. From Alonso de Ercilla y Zúñiga's *Araucana*, a poem about the Spanish struggle against the Araucanian Indians of Chile.

is Casildea and who is an Andalusian by birth, is called by me Casildea de Vandalia. If all this is not sufficient to show that I speak the truth, here is my sword which shall make incredulity itself believe."

"Calm yourself, Sir Knight," replied Don Quixote, "and listen to what I have to say to you. You must know that this Don Quixote of whom you speak is the best friend that I have in the world, so great a friend that I may say that I feel toward him as I do toward my own self; and from all that you have told me, the very definite and accurate details that you have given me, I cannot doubt that he is the one whom you have conquered. On the other hand, the sight of my eyes and the touch of my hands assure me that he could not possibly be the one, unless some enchanter who is his enemy—for he has many, and one in particular who delights in persecuting him—may have assumed the knight's form and then permitted himself to be routed, by way of defrauding Don Quixote of the fame which his high deeds of chivalry have earned for him throughout the known world. To show you how true this may be, I will inform you that not more than a couple of days ago those same enemy magicians transformed the figure and person of the beauteous Dulcinea del Toboso into a low and mean village lass, and it is possible that they have done something of the same sort to the knight who is her lover. And if all this does not suffice to convince you of the truth of what I say, here is Don Quixote himself who will maintain it by force of arms, on foot or on horseback, or in any way you like."

Saying this, he rose and laid hold of his sword, and waited to see what the Knight of the Wood's decision would be. That worthy now replied in a voice as calm as the one Don Quixote had used.

"Pledges," he said, "do not distress one who is sure of his ability to pay. He who was able to overcome you when you were transformed, Señor Don Quixote, may hope to bring you to your knees when you are your own proper self. But inasmuch as it is not fitting that knights should perform their feats of arms in the darkness, like ruffians and highway-men, let us wait until it is day in order that the sun may behold what we do. And the condition governing our encounter shall be that the one who is vanquished must submit to the will of his conqueror and perform all those things that are commanded of him, provided they are such as are in keeping with the state of knighthood."

"With that condition and understanding," said Don Quixote, "I shall be satisfied."

With this, they went off to where their squires were, only to find them snoring away as hard as when sleep had first overtaken them. Awakening the pair, they ordered them to look to the horses; for as soon as the sun was up the two knights meant to stage an arduous and bloody single-handed combat. At this news Sancho was astonished and terrified, since, as a result of what the other squire had told him of the Knight of the Wood's prowess, he was led to fear for his master's safety. Nevertheless, he and his friend now went to seek the mounts without saying a word, and they found the animals all together, for by this time the two horses and the ass had smelled one another out. On the way the Squire of the Wood turned to Sancho and addressed him as follows:

"I must inform you, brother, that it is the custom of the fighters of Andalusia, when they are godfathers in any combat, not to remain idly by, with folded hands, while their godsons fight it out. I tell you this by way of warning you that while our masters are settling matters, we, too, shall have to come to blows and hack each other to bits."

"That custom, Sir Squire," replied Sancho, "may be all very well among the fighters and ruffians that you mention, but with the squires of knights-errant it is not to be thought of. At least, I have never heard my master speak of any such custom, and he knows all the laws of chivalry by heart. But granting that it is true and that there is a law which states in so many words that squires must fight while their masters do, I have no intention of obeying it but rather will pay whatever penalty is laid on peaceable-minded ones like myself, for I am sure it cannot be more than a couple of pounds of wax,[3] and that would be less expensive than the lint which it would take to heal my head—I can already see it split in two. What's more, it's out of the question for me to fight since I have no sword nor did I ever in my life carry one."

"That," said the one of the Wood, "is something that is easily remedied. I have here two linen bags of the same size. You take one and I'll take the other and we will fight that way, on equal terms."

"So be it, by all means," said Sancho, "for that will simply knock the dust out of us without wounding us."

"But that's not the way it's to be," said the other squire. "Inside the bags, to keep the wind from blowing them away, we will put a half-dozen nice smooth pebbles of the same weight, and so we'll be able to give each other a good pounding without doing ourselves any real harm or damage."

"Body of my father!" cried Sancho, "just look, will you, at the marten and sable and wads of carded cotton that he's stuffing into those bags so that we won't get our heads cracked or our bones crushed to a pulp. But I am telling you, Señor mio, that even though you fill them with silken pellets, I don't mean to fight. Let our masters fight and make the best of it, but as for us, let us drink and live; for time will see to ending our lives without any help on our part by way of bringing them to a close before they have reached their proper season and fall from ripeness."

"Nevertheless," replied the Squire of the Wood, "fight we must, if only for half an hour."

"No," Sancho insisted, "that I will not do. I will not be so impolite or so ungrateful as to pick any quarrel however slight with one whose food and drink I've shared. And, moreover, who in the devil could bring himself to fight in cold blood, when he's not angry or vexed in any way?"

"I can take care of that, right enough," said the one of the Wood. "Before we begin, I will come up to your Grace as nicely as you please and give you three or four punches that will stretch you out at my feet; and that will surely be enough to awaken your anger, even though it's sleeping sounder than a dormouse."

"And I," said Sancho, "have another idea that's every bit as good as yours. I will take a big club, and before your Grace has had a chance to awaken my anger I will put yours to sleep with such mighty whacks that if it wakes at all it will be in the other world; for it is known there that I am not the man to let my face be mussed by anyone, and let each look out for the arrow.[4] But the best thing to do

3. In some confraternities, penalties for being absent were paid in wax, presumably to make church candles.
4. A proverbial expression from archery: let each one take care of his or her own arrow. Other obviously proverbial expressions follow, as is typical of Sancho's speech.

would be to leave each one's anger to its slumbers, for no one knows the heart of any other, he who comes for wool may go back shorn, and God bless peace and curse all strife. If a hunted cat when surrounded and cornered turns into a lion, God knows what I who am a man might not become. And so from this time forth I am warning you, Sir Squire, that all the harm and damage that may result from our quarrel will be upon your head."

"Very well," the one of the Wood replied, "God will send the dawn and we shall make out somehow."

At that moment gay-colored birds of all sorts began warbling in the trees and with their merry and varied songs appeared to be greeting and welcoming the fresh-dawning day, which already at the gates and on the balconies of the east was revealing its beautiful face as it shook out from its hair an infinite number of liquid pearls. Bathed in this gentle moisture, the grass seemed to shed a pearly spray, the willows distilled a savory manna, the fountains laughed, the brooks murmured, the woods were glad, and the meadows put on their finest raiment. The first thing that Sancho Panza beheld, as soon as it was light enough to tell one object from another, was the Squire of the Wood's nose, which was so big as to cast into the shade all the rest of his body. In addition to being of enormous size, it is said to have been hooked in the middle and all covered with warts of a mulberry hue, like eggplant; it hung down for a couple of inches below his mouth, and the size, color, warts, and shape of this organ gave his face so ugly an appearance that Sancho began trembling hand and foot like a child with convulsions and made up his mind then and there that he would take a couple of hundred punches before he would let his anger be awakened to the point where he would fight with this monster.

Don Quixote in the meanwhile was surveying his opponent, who had already adjusted and closed his helmet so that it was impossible to make out what he looked like. It was apparent, however, that he was not very tall and was stockily built. Over his armor he wore a coat of some kind or other made of what appeared to be the finest cloth of gold, all bespangled with glittering mirrors that resembled little moons and that gave him a most gallant and festive air, while above his helmet were a large number of waving plumes, green, white, and yellow in color. His lance, which was leaning against a tree, was very long and stout and had a steel point of more than a palm in length. Don Quixote took all this in, and from what he observed concluded that his opponent must be of tremendous strength, but he was not for this reason filled with fear as Sancho Panza was. Rather, he proceeded to address the Knight of the Mirrors, quite boldly and in a highbred manner.

"Sir Knight," he said, "if in your eagerness to fight you have not lost your courtesy, I would beg you to be so good as to raise your visor a little in order that I may see if your face is as handsome as your trappings."

"Whether you come out of this emprise the victor or the vanquished, Sir Knight," he of the Mirrors replied, "there will be ample time and opportunity for you to have a sight of me. If I do not now gratify your desire, it is because it seems to me that I should be doing a very great wrong to the beauteous Casildea de Vandalia by wasting the time it would take me to raise my visor before having forced you to confess that I am right in my contention, with which you are well acquainted."

"Well, then," said Don Quixote, "while we are mounting our steeds you might at least inform me if I am that knight of La Mancha whom you say you conquered."

"To that our[5] answer," said he of the Mirrors, "is that you are as like the knight I overcame as one egg is like another; but since you assert that you are persecuted by enchanters, I should not venture to state positively that you are the one in question."

"All of which," said Don Quixote, "is sufficient to convince me that you are laboring under a misapprehension; but in order to relieve you of it once and for all, let them bring our steeds, and in less time than you would spend in lifting your visor, if God, my lady, and my arm give me strength, I will see your face and you shall see that I am not the vanquished knight you take me to be."

With this, they cut short their conversation and mounted, and, turning Rocinante around, Don Quixote began measuring off the proper length of field for a run against his opponent as he of the Mirrors did the same. But the Knight of La Mancha had not gone twenty paces when he heard his adversary calling to him, whereupon each of them turned halfway and he of the Mirrors spoke.

"I must remind you, Sir Knight," he said, "of the condition under which we fight, which is that the vanquished, as I have said before, shall place himself wholly at the disposition of the victor."

"I am aware of that," replied Don Quixote, "not forgetting the provision that the behest laid upon the vanquished shall not exceed the bounds of chivalry."

"Agreed," said the Knight of the Mirrors.

At that moment Don Quixote caught sight of the other squire's weird nose and was as greatly astonished by it as Sancho had been. Indeed, he took the fellow for some monster, or some new kind of human being wholly unlike those that people this world. As he saw his master riding away down the field preparatory to the tilt, Sancho was alarmed; for he did not like to be left alone with the big-nosed individual, fearing that one powerful swipe of that protuberance against his own nose would end the battle so far as he was concerned and he would be lying stretched out on the ground, from fear if not from the force of the blow.

He accordingly ran after the knight, clinging to one of Rocinante's stirrup straps, and when he thought it was time for Don Quixote to whirl about and bear down upon his opponent, he called to him and said, "*Señor mio*, I beg your Grace, before you turn for the charge, to help me up into that cork tree yonder where I can watch the encounter which your Grace is going to have with this knight better than I can from the ground and in a way that is much more to my liking."

"I rather think, Sancho," said Don Quixote, "that what you wish to do is to mount a platform where you can see the bulls without any danger to yourself."

"The truth of the matter is," Sancho admitted, "the monstrous nose on that squire has given me such a fright that I don't dare stay near him."

"It is indeed of such a sort," his master assured him, "that if I were not the person I am, I myself should be frightened. And so, come, I will help you up."

While Don Quixote tarried to see Sancho ensconced in the cork tree, the Knight of the Mirrors measured as much ground as seemed to him necessary and then, assuming that his adversary had done the same, without waiting for sound of trumpet or any other signal, he wheeled his horse, which was no swifter nor any more impressive-looking than Rocinante, and bore down upon

---

5. Note the dignified, "majestic" plural form.

his enemy at a mild trot; but when he saw that the Manchegan was busy helping his squire, he reined in his mount and came to a stop midway in his course, for which his horse was extremely grateful, being no longer able to stir a single step. To Don Quixote, on the other hand, it seemed as if his enemy was flying, and digging his spurs with all his might into Rocinante's lean flanks he caused that animal to run a bit for the first and only time, according to the history, for on all other occasions a simple trot had represented his utmost speed. And so it was that, with an unheard-of fury, the Knight of the Mournful Countenance came down upon the Knight of the Mirrors as the latter sat there sinking his spurs all the way up to the buttons without being able to persuade his horse to budge a single inch from the spot where he had come to a sudden standstill.

It was at this fortunate moment, while his adversary was in such a predicament, that Don Quixote fell upon him, quite unmindful of the fact that the other knight was having trouble with his mount and either was unable or did not have time to put his lance at rest. The upshot of it was, he encountered him with such force that, much against his will, the Knight of the Mirrors went rolling over his horse's flanks and tumbled to the ground, where as a result of his terrific fall he lay as if dead, without moving hand or foot.

No sooner did Sancho perceive what had happened than he slipped down from the cork tree and ran up as fast as he could to where his master was. Dismounting from Rocinante, Don Quixote now stood over the Knight of the Mirrors, and undoing the helmet straps to see if the man was dead, or to give him air in case he was alive, he beheld—who can say what he beheld without creating astonishment, wonder, and amazement in those who hear the tale? The history tells us that it was the very countenance, form, aspect, physiognomy, effigy, and image of the bachelor Sansón Carrasco!

"Come, Sancho," he cried in a loud voice, "and see what is to be seen but is not to be believed. Hasten, my son, and learn what magic can do and how great is the power of wizards and enchanters."

Sancho came, and the moment his eyes fell on the bachelor Carrasco's face he began crossing and blessing himself a countless number of times. Meanwhile, the overthrown knight gave no signs of life.

"If you ask me, master," said Sancho, "I would say that the best thing for your Grace to do is to run his sword down the mouth of this one who appears to be the bachelor Carrasco; maybe by so doing you would be killing one of your enemies, the enchanters."

"That is not a bad idea," replied Don Quixote, "for the fewer enemies the better." And, drawing his sword, he was about to act upon Sancho's advice and counsel when the Knight of the Mirrors' squire came up to them, now minus the nose which had made him so ugly.

"Look well what you are doing, Don Quixote!" he cried. "The one who lies there at your feet is your Grace's friend, the bachelor Sansón Carrasco, and I am his squire."

"And where is your nose?" inquired Sancho, who was surprised to see him without that deformity.

"Here in my pocket," was the reply. And, thrusting his hand into his coat, he drew out a nose of varnished pasteboard of the make that has been described. Studying him more and more closely, Sancho finally exclaimed, in a voice that was filled with amazement, "Holy Mary preserve me! And is this not my neighbor and crony, Tomé Cecial?"

"That is who I am!" replied the de-nosed squire, "your good friend Tomé Cecial, Sancho Panza. I will tell you presently of the means and snares and falsehoods that brought me here. But, for the present, I beg and entreat your master not to lay hands on, mistreat, wound, or slay the Knight of the Mirrors whom he now has at his feet; for without any doubt it is the rash and ill-advised bachelor Sansón Carrasco, our fellow villager."

The Knight of the Mirrors now recovered consciousness, and, seeing this, Don Quixote at once placed the naked point of his sword above the face of the vanquished one.

"Dead you are, knight," he said, "unless you confess that the peerless Dulcinea del Toboso is more beautiful than your Casildea de Vandalia. And what is more, you will have to promise that, should you survive this encounter and the fall you have had, you will go to the city of El Toboso and present yourself to her in my behalf, that she may do with you as she may see fit. And in case she leaves you free to follow your own will, you are to return to seek me out— the trail of my exploits will serve as a guide to bring you wherever I may be— and tell me all that has taken place between you and her. These conditions are in conformity with those that we arranged before our combat and they do not go beyond the bounds of knight-errantry."

"I confess," said the fallen knight, "that the tattered and filthy shoe of the lady Dulcinea del Toboso is of greater worth than the badly combed if clean beard of Casildea, and I promise to go to her presence and return to yours and to give you a complete and detailed account concerning anything you may wish to know."

"Another thing," added Don Quixote, "that you will have to confess and believe is that the knight you conquered was not and could not have been Don Quixote de la Mancha, but was some other that resembled him, just as I am convinced that you, though you appear to be the bachelor Sansón Carrasco, are another person in his form and likeness who has been put here by my enemies to induce me to restrain and moderate the impetuosity of my wrath and make a gentle use of my glorious victory."

"I confess, think, and feel as you feel, think, and believe," replied the lamed knight. "Permit me to rise, I beg of you, if the jolt I received in my fall will let me do so, for I am in very bad shape."

Don Quixote and Tomé Cecial the squire now helped him to his feet. As for Sancho, he could not take his eyes off Tomé but kept asking him one question after another, and although the answers he received afforded clear enough proof that the man was really his fellow townsman, the fear that had been aroused in him by his master's words—about the enchanters' having transformed the Knight of the Mirrors into the bachelor Sansón Carrasco—prevented him from believing the truth that was apparent to his eyes. The short of it is, both master and servant were left with this delusion as the other ill-errant knight and his squire, in no pleasant state of mind, took their departure with the object of looking for some village where they might be able to apply poultices and splints to the bachelor's battered ribs.

Don Quixote and Sancho then resumed their journey along the road to Saragossa, and here for the time being the history leaves them in order to give an account of who the Knight of the Mirrors and his long-nosed squire really were.

CHAPTER XV

Wherein is told and revealed who the Knight of the Mirrors and his squire were.

Don Quixote went off very happy, self-satisfied, and vainglorious at having achieved a victory over so valiant a knight as he imagined the one of the Mirrors to be, from whose knightly word he hoped to learn whether or not the spell which had been put upon his lady was still in effect; for, unless he chose to forfeit his honor, the vanquished contender must of necessity return and give an account of what had happened in the course of his interview with her. But Don Quixote was of one mind, the Knight of the Mirrors of another, for, as has been stated, the latter's only thought at the moment was to find some village where plasters were available.

The history goes on to state that when the bachelor Sansón Carrasco advised Don Quixote to resume his feats of chivalry, after having desisted from them for a while, this action was taken as the result of a conference which he had held with the curate and the barber as to the means to be adopted in persuading the knight to remain quietly at home and cease agitating himself over his unfortunate adventures. It had been Carrasco's suggestion, to which they had unanimously agreed, that they let Don Quixote sally forth, since it appeared to be impossible to prevent his doing so, and that Sansón should then take to the road as a knight-errant and pick a quarrel and do battle with him. There would be no difficulty about finding a pretext, and then the bachelor knight would overcome him (which was looked upon as easy of accomplishment), having first entered into a pact to the effect that the vanquished should remain at the mercy and bidding of his conqueror. The behest in this case was to be that the fallen one should return to his village and home and not leave it for the space of two years or until further orders were given him, it being a certainty that, once having been overcome, Don Quixote would fulfill the agreement, in order not to contravene or fail to obey the laws of chivalry. And it was possible that in the course of his seclusion he would forget his fancies, or they would at least have an opportunity to seek some suitable cure for his madness.

Sansón agreed to undertake this, and Tomé Cecial, Sancho's friend and neighbor, a merry but featherbrained chap, offered to go along as squire. Sansón then proceeded to arm himself in the manner that has been described, while Tomé disguised his nose with the aforementioned mask so that his crony would not recognize him when they met. Thus equipped, they followed the same route as Don Quixote and had almost caught up with him by the time he had the adventure with the Cart of Death. They finally overtook him in the wood, where those events occurred with which the attentive reader is already familiar; and if it had not been for the knight's extraordinary fancies, which led him to believe that the bachelor was not the bachelor, the said bachelor might have been prevented from ever attaining his degree of licentiate, as a result of having found no nests where he thought to find birds.

Seeing how ill they had succeeded in their undertaking and what an end they had reached, Tomé Cecial now addressed his master.

"Surely, Señor Sansón Carrasco," he said, "we have had our deserts. It is easy enough to plan and embark upon an enterprise, but most of the time it's hard to get out of it. Don Quixote is a madman and we are sane, yet he goes away sound and laughing while your Grace is left here, battered and sorrowful. I wish you would tell me now who is the crazier: the one who is so because he cannot help it, or he who turns crazy of his own free will?"

"The difference between the two," replied Sansón, "lies in this: that the one who cannot help being crazy will be so always, whereas the one who is a madman by choice can leave off being one whenever he so desires."

"Well," said Tomé Cecial, "since that is the way it is, and since I chose to be crazy when I became your Grace's squire, by the same reasoning I now choose to stop being insane and to return to my home."

"That is your affair," said Sansón, "but to imagine that I am going back before I have given Don Quixote a good thrashing is senseless; and what will urge me on now is not any desire to see him recover his wits, but rather a thirst for vengeance; for with the terrible pain that I have in my ribs, you can't expect me to feel very charitable."

Conversing in this manner they kept on until they reached a village where it was their luck to find a bonesetter to take care of poor Sansón. Tomé Cecial then left him and returned home, while the bachelor meditated plans for revenge. The history has more to say of him in due time, but for the present it goes on to make merry with Don Quixote.

CHAPTER XVI

*Of what happened to Don Quixote upon his meeting with
a prudent gentleman of La Mancha.*

With that feeling of happiness and vainglorious self-satisfaction that has been mentioned, Don Quixote continued on his way, imagining himself to be, as a result of the victory he had just achieved, the most valiant knight-errant of the age. Whatever adventures might befall him from then on he regarded as already accomplished and brought to a fortunate conclusion. He thought little now of enchanters and enchantments and was unmindful of the innumerable beatings he had received in the course of his knightly wanderings, of the volley of pebbles that had knocked out half his teeth, of the ungratefulness of the galley slaves and the audacity of the Yanguesans whose poles had fallen upon his body like rain. In short, he told himself, if he could but find the means, manner, or way of freeing his lady Dulcinea of the spell that had been put upon her, he would not envy the greatest good fortune that the most fortunate of knights-errant in ages past had ever by any possibility attained.

He was still wholly wrapped up in these thoughts when Sancho spoke to him.

"Isn't it strange, sir, that I can still see in front of my eyes the huge and monstrous nose of my old crony, Tomé Cecial?"

"And do you by any chance believe, Sancho, that the Knight of the Mirrors was the bachelor Sansón Carrasco and that his squire was your friend Tomé?"

"I don't know what to say to that," replied Sancho. "All I know is that the things he told me about my home, my wife and young ones, could not have come from anybody else; and the face, too, once you took the nose away, was the same as Tomé Cecial's, which I have seen many times in our village, right next door to my own house, and the tone of voice was the same also."

"Let us reason the matter out, Sancho," said Don Quixote. "Look at it this way: how can it be thought that the bachelor Sansón Carrasco would come as a knight-errant, equipped with offensive and defensive armor, to contend with me? Am I, perchance, his enemy? Have I given him any occasion to cherish a grudge against me? Am I a rival of his? Or can it be jealousy of the fame I have acquired that has led him to take up the profession of arms?"

"Well, then, sir," Sancho answered him, "how are we to explain the fact that the knight was so like the bachelor and his squire like my friend? And if this was a magic spell, as your Grace has said, was there no other pair in the world whose likeness they might have taken?"

"It is all a scheme and a plot," replied Don Quixote, "on the part of those wicked magicians who are persecuting me and who, foreseeing that I would be the victor in the combat, saw to it that the conquered knight should display the face of my friend the bachelor, so that the affection which I bear him would come between my fallen enemy and the edge of my sword and might of my arm, to temper the righteous indignation of my heart. In that way, he who had sought by falsehood and deceits to take my life, would be left to go on living. As proof of all this, Sancho, experience, which neither lies nor deceives, has already taught you how easy it is for enchanters to change one countenance into another, making the beautiful ugly and the ugly beautiful. It was not two days ago that you beheld the peerless Dulcinea's beauty and elegance in its entirety and natural form, while I saw only the repulsive features of a low and ignorant peasant girl with cataracts over her eyes and a foul smell in her mouth. And if the perverse enchanter was bold enough to effect so vile a transformation as this, there is certainly no cause for wonderment at what he has done in the case of Sansón Carrasco and your friend, all by way of snatching my glorious victory out of my hands. But in spite of it all, I find consolation in the fact that, whatever the shape he may have chosen to assume, I have laid my enemy low."

"God knows what the truth of it all may be," was Sancho's comment. Knowing as he did that Dulcinea's transformation had been due to his own scheming and plotting, he was not taken in by his master's delusions. He was at a loss for a reply, however, lest he say something that would reveal his own trickery.

As they were carrying on this conversation, they were overtaken by a man who, following the same road, was coming along behind them. He was mounted on a handsome flea-bitten mare and wore a hooded great-coat of fine green cloth trimmed in tawny velvet and a cap of the same material, while the trappings of his steed, which was accoutered for the field, were green and mulberry in hue, his saddle being of the *jineta*[6] mode. From his broad green and gold shoulder strap there dangled a Moorish cutlass, and his half-boots were of the same make as the baldric. His spurs were not gilded but were covered with highly polished green lacquer, so that, harmonizing as they did with the rest of his apparel, they seemed more appropriate than if they had been of purest gold. As he came up, he greeted the pair courteously and, spurring his mare, was about to ride on past when Don Quixote called to him.

"Gallant sir," he said, "if your Grace is going our way and is not in a hurry, it would be a favor to us if we might travel together."

6. I.e., it has a high pommel and short stirrups.

"The truth is," replied the stranger, "I should not have ridden past you if I had not been afraid that the company of my mare would excite your horse."

"In that case, sir," Sancho spoke up, "you may as well rein in, for this horse of ours is the most virtuous and well mannered of any that there is. Never on such an occasion has he done anything that was not right—the only time he did misbehave, my master and I suffered for it aplenty. And so, I say again, your Grace may slow up if you like; for even if you offered him your mare on a couple of platters, he'd never try to mount her."

With this, the other traveler drew rein, being greatly astonished at Don Quixote's face and figure. For the knight was now riding along without his helmet, which was carried by Sancho like a piece of luggage on the back of his gray, in front of the packsaddle. If the green-clad gentleman stared hard at his new-found companion, the latter returned his gaze with an even greater intensity. He impressed Don Quixote as being a man of good judgment, around fifty years of age, with hair that was slightly graying and an aquiline nose, while the expression of his countenance was half humorous, half serious. In short, both his person and his accouterments indicated that he was an individual of some worth.

As for the man in green's impression of Don Quixote de la Mancha, he was thinking that he had never before seen any human being that resembled this one. He could not but marvel at the knight's long neck, his tall frame, and the leanness and the sallowness of his face, as well as his armor and his grave bearing, the whole constituting a sight such as had not been seen for many a day in those parts. Don Quixote in turn was quite conscious of the attentiveness with which the traveler was studying him and could tell from the man's astonished look how curious he was; and so, being very courteous and fond of pleasing everyone, he proceeded to anticipate any questions that might be asked him.

"I am aware," he said, "that my appearance must strike your Grace as being very strange and out of the ordinary, and for that reason I am not surprised at your wonderment. But your Grace will cease to wonder when I tell you, as I am telling you now, that I am a knight, one of those

> *Of whom it is folks say,*
> *They to adventures go.*[7]

I have left my native heath, mortgaged my estate, given up my comfortable life, and cast myself into fortune's arms for her to do with me what she will. It has been my desire to revive a knight-errantry that is now dead, and for some time past, stumbling here and falling there, now throwing myself down headlong and then rising up once more, I have been able in good part to carry out my design by succoring widows, protecting damsels, and aiding the fallen, the orphans, and the young, all of which is the proper and natural duty of knights-errant. As a result, owing to my many valiant and Christian exploits, I have been deemed worthy of visiting in printed form nearly all the nations of the world. Thirty thousand copies of my history have been published, and, unless Heaven forbid, they will print thirty million of them.

"In short, to put it all into a few words, or even one, I will tell you that I am Don Quixote de la Mancha, otherwise known as the Knight of the Mournful

---

7. These two verses, which recall medieval popular romance ballads, appear in a Spanish translation of Petrarch's allegorical poem, the *Triumphs*, although they are not in the original.

Countenance. Granted that self-praise is degrading, there still are times when I must praise myself, that is to say, when there is no one else present to speak in my behalf. And so, good sir, neither this steed nor this lance nor this buckler nor this squire of mine, nor all the armor that I wear and arms I carry, nor the sallowness of my complexion, nor my leanness and gauntness, should any longer astonish you, now that you know who I am and what the profession is that I follow."

Having thus spoken, Don Quixote fell silent, and the man in green was so slow in replying that it seemed as if he was at a loss for words. Finally, however, after a considerable while, he brought himself to the point of speaking.

"You were correct, Sir Knight," he said, "about my astonishment and my curiosity, but you have not succeeded in removing the wonderment that the sight of you has aroused in me. You say that, knowing who you are, I should not wonder any more, but such is not the case, for I am now more amazed than ever. How can it be that there are knights-errant in the world today and that histories of them are actually printed? I find it hard to convince myself that at the present time there is anyone on earth who goes about aiding widows, protecting damsels, defending the honor of wives, and succoring orphans, and I should never have believed it had I not beheld your Grace with my own eyes. Thank Heaven for that book that your Grace tells me has been published concerning your true and exalted deeds of chivalry, as it should cast into oblivion all the innumerable stories of fictitious knights-errant with which the world is filled, greatly to the detriment of good morals and the prejudice and discredit of legitimate histories."

"As to whether the stories of knights-errant are fictitious or not," observed Don Quixote, "there is much that remains to be said."

"Why," replied the gentleman in green, "is there anyone who can doubt that such tales are false?"

"I doubt it," was the knight's answer, "but let the matter rest there. If our journey lasts long enough, I trust with God's help to be able to show your Grace that you are wrong in going along with those who hold it to be a certainty that they are not true."

From this last remark the traveler was led to suspect that Don Quixote must be some kind of crackbrain, and he was waiting for him to confirm the impression by further observations of the same sort; but before they could get off on another subject, the knight, seeing that he had given an account of his own station in life, turned to the stranger and politely inquired who his companion might be.

"I, Sir Knight of the Mournful Countenance," replied the one in the green-colored greatcoat, "am a gentleman, and a native of the village where, please God, we are going to dine today. I am more than moderately rich, and my name is Don Diego de Miranda. I spend my life with my wife and children and with my friends. My occupations are hunting and fishing, though I keep neither falcon nor hounds but only a tame partridge[8] and a bold ferret or two. I am the owner of about six dozen books, some of them in Spanish, others in Latin, including both histories and devotional works. As for books of chivalry, they have not as yet crossed the threshold of my door. My own preference is for profane[9] rather than devotional writings, such as afford an innocent amusement, charming us by

8. Used as a decoy.   9. I.e., secular, nonreligious.

their style and arousing and holding our interest by their inventiveness, although I must say there are very few of that sort to be found in Spain.

"Sometimes," the man in green continued, "I dine with my friends and neighbors, and I often invite them to my house. My meals are wholesome and well prepared and there is always plenty to eat. I do not care for gossip, nor will I permit it in my presence. I am not lynx-eyed and do not pry into the lives and doings of others. I hear mass every day and share my substance with the poor, but make no parade of my good works lest hypocrisy and vainglory, those enemies that so imperceptibly take possession of the most modest heart, should find their way into mine. I try to make peace between those who are at strife. I am the devoted servant of Our Lady,[1] and my trust is in the infinite mercy of God Our Savior."

Sancho had listened most attentively to the gentleman's account of his mode of life, and inasmuch as it seemed to him that this was a good and holy way to live and that the one who followed such a pattern ought to be able to work miracles, he now jumped down from his gray's back and, running over to seize the stranger's right stirrup, began kissing the feet of the man in green with a show of devotion that bordered on tears.

"Why are you doing that, brother?" the gentleman asked him. "What is the meaning of these kisses?"

"Let me kiss your feet," Sancho insisted, "for if I am not mistaken, your Grace is the first saint riding *jineta* fashion that I have seen in all the days of my life."

"I am not a saint," the gentleman assured him, "but a great sinner. It is you, brother, who are the saint; for you must be a good man, judging by the simplicity of heart that you show."

Sancho then went back to his packsaddle, having evoked a laugh from the depths of his master's melancholy and given Don Diego fresh cause for astonishment.

Don Quixote thereupon inquired of the newcomer how many children he had, remarking as he did so that the ancient philosophers, who were without a true knowledge of God, believed that mankind's greatest good lay in the gifts of nature, in those of fortune, and in having many friends and many and worthy sons.

"I, Señor Don Quixote," replied the gentleman, "have a son without whom I should, perhaps, be happier than I am. It is not that he is bad, but rather that he is not as good as I should like him to be. He is eighteen years old, and for six of those years he has been at Salamanca studying the Greek and Latin languages. When I desired him to pass on to other branches of learning, I found him so immersed in the science of Poetry (if it can be called such) that it was not possible to interest him in the Law, which I wanted him to study, nor in Theology, the queen of them all. My wish was that he might be an honor to his family; for in this age in which we are living our monarchs are in the habit of highly rewarding those forms of learning that are good and virtuous, since learning without virtue is like pearls on a dunghill. But he spends the whole day trying to decide whether such and such a verse of Homer's *Iliad* is well conceived or not, whether or not Martial is immodest in a certain epigram, whether certain lines of Vergil are to

1. The Virgin Mary, mother of Jesus.

be understood in this way or in that. In short, he spends all his time with the books written by those poets whom I have mentioned and with those of Horace, Persius, Juvenal, and Tibullus. As for our own moderns, he sets little store by them, and yet, for all his disdain of Spanish poetry, he is at this moment racking his brains in an effort to compose a gloss on a quatrain that was sent him from Salamanca and which, I fancy, is for some literary tournament."

To all this Don Quixote made the following answer:

"Children, sir, are out of their parents' bowels and so are to be loved whether they be good or bad, just as we love those that gave us life. It is for parents to bring up their offspring, from the time they are infants, in the paths of virtue, good breeding, proper conduct, and Christian morality, in order that, when they are grown, they may be a staff to the old age of the ones that bore them and an honor to their own posterity. As to compelling them to study a particular branch of learning, I am not so sure as to that, though there may be no harm in trying to persuade them to do so. But where there is no need to study *pane lucrando*[2]— where Heaven has provided them with parents that can supply their daily bread—I should be in favor of permitting them to follow that course to which they are most inclined; and although poetry may be more pleasurable than useful, it is not one of those pursuits that bring dishonor upon those who engage in them.

"Poetry in my opinion, my dear sir," he went on, "is a young and tender maid of surpassing beauty, who has many other damsels (that is to say, the other disciplines) whose duty it is to bedeck, embellish, and adorn her. She may call upon all of them for service, and all of them in turn depend upon her nod. She is not one to be rudely handled, nor dragged through the streets, nor exposed at street corners, in the market place, or in the private nooks of palaces. She is fashioned through an alchemy of such power that he who knows how to make use of it will be able to convert her into the purest gold of inestimable price. Possessing her, he must keep her within bounds and not permit her to run wild in bawdy satires or soulless sonnets. She is not to be put up for sale in any manner, unless it be in the form of heroic poems, pity-inspiring tragedies, or pleasing and ingenious comedies. Let mountebanks keep hands off her, and the ignorant mob as well, which is incapable of recognizing or appreciating the treasures that are locked within her. And do not think, sir, that I apply that term 'mob' solely to plebeians and those of low estate; for anyone who is ignorant, whether he be lord or prince, may, and should, be included in the vulgar herd.

"But," Don Quixote continued, "he who possesses the gift of poetry and who makes the use of it that I have indicated, shall become famous and his name shall be honored among all the civilized nations of the world. You have stated, sir, that your son does not greatly care for poetry written in our Spanish tongue, and in that I am inclined to think he is somewhat mistaken. My reason for saying so is this: the great Homer did not write in Latin, for the reason that he was a Greek, and Vergil did not write in Greek since he was a Latin. In a word, all the poets of antiquity wrote in the language which they had imbibed with their mother's milk and did not go searching after foreign ones to express their loftiest conceptions. This being so, it would be well if the same custom were to be adopted by all nations, the German poet being no longer looked down upon

2. Earning one's bread (Latin).

because he writes in German, nor the Castilian or the Basque for employing his native speech.

"As for your son, I fancy, sir, that his quarrel is not so much with Spanish poetry as with those poets who have no other tongue or discipline at their command such as would help to awaken their natural gift; and yet, here, too, he may be wrong. There is an opinion, and a true one, to the effect that 'the poet is born,' that is to say, it is as a poet that he comes forth from his mother's womb, and with the propensity that has been bestowed upon him by Heaven, without study or artifice, he produces those compositions that attest the truth of the line: 'Est deus in nobis,' etc.[3] I further maintain that the born poet who is aided by art will have a great advantage over the one who by art alone would become a poet, the reason being that art does not go beyond, but merely perfects, nature; and so it is that, by combining nature with art and art with nature, the finished poet is produced.

"In conclusion, then, my dear sir, my advice to you would be to let your son go where his star beckons him; for being a good student as he must be, and having already successfully mounted the first step on the stairway of learning, which is that of languages, he will be able to continue of his own accord to the very peak of humane letters, an accomplishment that is altogether becoming in a gentleman, one that adorns, honors, and distinguishes him as much as the miter does the bishop or his flowing robe the learned jurisconsult. Your Grace well may reprove your son, should he compose satires that reflect upon the honor of other persons; in that case, punish him and tear them up. But should he compose discourses in the manner of Horace, in which he reprehends vice in general as that poet so elegantly does, then praise him by all means; for it is permitted the poet to write verses in which he inveighs against envy and the other vices as well, and to lash out at the vicious without, however, designating any particular individual. On the other hand, there are poets who for the sake of uttering something malicious would run the risk of being banished to the shores of Pontus.[4]

"If the poet be chaste where his own manners are concerned, he will likewise be modest in his verses, for the pen is the tongue of the mind, and whatever thoughts are engendered there are bound to appear in his writings. When kings and princes behold the marvelous art of poetry as practiced by prudent, virtuous, and serious-minded subjects of their realm, they honor, esteem, and reward those persons and crown them with the leaves of the tree that is never struck by lightning[5]—as if to show that those who are crowned and adorned with such wreaths are not to be assailed by anyone."

The gentleman in the green-colored greatcoat was vastly astonished by this speech of Don Quixote's and was rapidly altering the opinion he had previously held, to the effect that his companion was but a crackbrain. In the middle of the long discourse, which was not greatly to his liking, Sancho had left the highway to go seek a little milk from some shepherds who were draining the udders of their ewes near by. Extremely well pleased with the knight's sound sense and excellent reasoning, the gentleman was about to resume the conversation when,

---

3. There is a god in us (Latin); Ovid's *Fasti* 6.5.
4. As the poet Ovid was by the Roman emperor Augustus in 8 C.E.
5. An ancient folk belief about the laurel.

raising his head, Don Quixote caught sight of a cart flying royal flags that was coming toward them down the road and, thinking it must be a fresh adventure, began calling to Sancho in a loud voice to bring him his helmet. Whereupon Sancho hastily left the shepherds and spurred his gray until he was once more alongside his master, who was now about to encounter a dreadful and bewildering ordeal.

[*"For I Well Know the Meaning of Valor"*]

CHAPTER XVII

Wherein Don Quixote's unimaginable courage reaches its highest point, together with the adventure of the lions and its happy ending.

The history relates that, when Don Quixote called to Sancho to bring him his helmet, the squire was busy buying some curds from the shepherds and, flustered by his master's great haste, did not know what to do with them or how to carry them. Having already paid for the curds, he did not care to lose them, and so he decided to put them into the headpiece, and, acting upon this happy inspiration, he returned to see what was wanted of him.

"Give me that helmet," said the knight; "for either I know little about adventures or here is one where I am going to need my armor."

Upon hearing this, the gentleman in the green-colored greatcoat looked around in all directions but could see nothing except the cart that was approaching them, decked out with two or three flags which indicated that the vehicle in question must be conveying his Majesty's property. He remarked as much to Don Quixote, but the latter paid no attention, for he was always convinced that whatever happened to him meant adventures and more adventures.

"Forewarned is forearmed," he said. "I lose nothing by being prepared, knowing as I do that I have enemies both visible and invisible and cannot tell when or where or in what form they will attack me."

Turning to Sancho, he asked for his helmet again, and as there was no time to shake out the curds, the squire had to hand it to him as it was. Don Quixote took it and, without noticing what was in it, hastily clapped it on his head; and forthwith, as a result of the pressure on the curds, the whey began running down all over his face and beard, at which he was very much startled.

"What is this, Sancho?" he cried. "I think my head must be softening or my brains melting, or else I am sweating from head to foot. If sweat it be, I assure you it is not from fear, though I can well believe that the adventure which now awaits me is a terrible one indeed. Give me something with which to wipe my face, if you have anything, for this perspiration is so abundant that it blinds me."

Sancho said nothing but gave him a cloth and at the same time gave thanks to God that his master had not discovered what the trouble was. Don Quixote wiped his face and then took off his helmet to see what it was that made his head feel so cool. Catching sight of that watery white mass, he lifted it to his nose and smelled it.

"By the life of my lady Dulcinea del Toboso!" he exclaimed. "Those are curds that you have put there, you treacherous, brazen, ill-mannered squire!"

To this Sancho replied, very calmly and with a straight face, "If they are curds, give them to me, your Grace, so that I can eat them. But no, let the devil eat them, for he must be the one who did it. Do you think I would be so bold as to soil your Grace's helmet? Upon my word, master, by the understanding that God has given me, I, too, must have enchanters who are persecuting me as your Grace's creature and one of his members, and they are the ones who put that filthy mess there to make you lose your patience and your temper and cause you to whack my ribs as you are in the habit of doing. Well, this time, I must say, they have missed the mark; for I trust my master's good sense to tell him that I have neither curds nor milk nor anything of the kind, and if I did have, I'd put it in my stomach and not in that helmet."

"That may very well be," said Don Quixote.

Don Diego was observing all this and was more astonished than ever, especially when, after he had wiped his head, face, beard, and helmet, Don Quixote once more donned the piece of armor and, settling himself in the stirrups, proceeded to adjust his sword and fix his lance.

"Come what may, here I stand, ready to take on Satan himself in person!" shouted the knight.

The cart with the flags had come up to them by this time, accompanied only by a driver riding one of the mules and a man seated up in front.

"Where are you going, brothers?" Don Quixote called out as he placed himself in the path of the cart. "What conveyance is this, what do you carry in it, and what is the meaning of those flags?"

"The cart is mine," replied the driver, "and in it are two fierce lions in cages which the governor of Oran is sending to court as a present for his Majesty. The flags are those of our lord the King, as a sign that his property goes here."

"And are the lions large?" inquired Don Quixote.

It was the man sitting at the door of the cage who answered him. "The largest," he said, "that ever were sent from Africa to Spain. I am the lionkeeper and I have brought back others, but never any like these. They are male and female. The male is in this first cage, the female in the one behind. They are hungry right now, for they have had nothing to eat today; and so we'd be obliged if your Grace would get out of the way, for we must hasten on to the place where we are to feed them."

"Lion whelps against me?" said Don Quixote with a slight smile. "Lion whelps against me? And at such an hour? Then, by God, those gentlemen who sent them shall see whether I am the man to be frightened by lions. Get down, my good fellow, and since you are the lionkeeper, open the cages and turn those beasts out for me; and in the middle of this plain I will teach them who Don Quixote de la Mancha is, notwithstanding and in spite of the enchanters who are responsible for their being here."

"So," said the gentleman to himself as he heard this, "our worthy knight has revealed himself. It must indeed be true that the curds have softened his skull and mellowed his brains."

At this point Sancho approached him. "For God's sake, sir," he said, "do something to keep my master from fighting those lions. For if he does, they're going to tear us all to bits."

"Is your master, then, so insane," the gentleman asked, "that you fear and believe he means to tackle those fierce animals?"

"It is not that he is insane," replied Sancho, "but, rather, foolhardy."

"Very well," said the gentleman, "I will put a stop to it." And going up to Don Quixote, who was still urging the lionkeeper to open the cages, he said, "Sir Knight, knights-errant should undertake only those adventures that afford some hope of a successful outcome, not those that are utterly hopeless to begin with; for valor when it turns to temerity has in it more of madness than of bravery. Moreover, these lions have no thought of attacking your Grace but are a present to his Majesty, and it would not be well to detain them or interfere with their journey."

"My dear sir," answered Don Quixote, "you had best go mind your tame partridge and that bold ferret of yours and let each one attend to his own business. This is my affair, and I know whether these gentlemen, the lions, have come to attack me or not." He then turned to the lionkeeper. "I swear, Sir Rascal, if you do not open those cages at once, I'll pin you to the cart with this lance!"

Perceiving how determined the armed phantom was, the driver now spoke up. "Good sir," he said, "will your Grace please be so kind as to let me unhitch the mules and take them to a safe place before you turn those lions loose? For if they kill them for me, I am ruined for life, since the mules and cart are all the property I own."

"O man of little faith!" said Don Quixote. "Get down and unhitch your mules if you like, but you will soon see that it was quite unnecessary and that you might have spared yourself the trouble."

The driver did so, in great haste, as the lionkeeper began shouting, "I want you all to witness that I am being compelled against my will to open the cages and turn the lions out, and I further warn this gentleman that he will be responsible for all the harm and damage the beasts may do, plus my wages and my fees. You other gentlemen take cover before I open the doors; I am sure they will not do any harm to me."

Once more Don Diego sought to persuade his companion not to commit such an act of madness, as it was tempting God to undertake anything so foolish as that; but Don Quixote's only answer was that he knew what he was doing. And when the gentleman in green insisted that he was sure the knight was laboring under a delusion and ought to consider the matter well, the latter cut him short.

"Well, then, sir," he said, "if your Grace does not care to be a spectator at what you believe is going to turn out to be a tragedy, all you have to do is to spur your flea-bitten mare and seek safety."

Hearing this, Sancho with tears in his eyes again begged him to give up the undertaking, in comparison with which the adventure of the windmills and the dreadful one at the fulling mills—indeed, all the exploits his master had ever in the course of his life undertaken—were but bread and cakes.

"Look, sir," Sancho went on, "there is no enchantment here nor anything of the sort. Through the bars and chinks of that cage I have seen a real lion's claw, and judging by the size of it, the lion that it belongs to is bigger than a mountain."

"Fear, at any rate," said Don Quixote, "will make him look bigger to you than half the world. Retire, Sancho, and leave me, and if I die here, you know our ancient pact: you are to repair to Dulcinea—I say no more."

To this he added other remarks that took away any hope they had that he might not go through with his insane plan. The gentleman in the green-colored greatcoat was of a mind to resist him but saw that he was no match for the knight in the matter of arms. Then, too, it did not seem to him the part of wisdom to fight it out with a madman; for Don Quixote now impressed him as being quite mad in every way. Accordingly, while the knight was repeating his threats to the lionkeeper, Don Diego spurred his mare, Sancho his gray, and the driver his mules, all of them seeking to put as great a distance as possible between themselves and the cart before the lions broke loose.

Sancho already was bewailing his master's death, which he was convinced was bound to come from the lions' claws, and at the same time he cursed his fate and called it an unlucky hour in which he had taken it into his head to serve such a one. But despite his tears and lamentations, he did not leave off thrashing his gray in an effort to leave the cart behind them. When the lionkeeper saw that those who had fled were a good distance away, he once more entreated and warned Don Quixote as he had warned and entreated him before, but the answer he received was that he might save his breath as it would do him no good and he had best hurry and obey. In the space of time that it took the keeper to open the first cage, Don Quixote considered the question as to whether it would be well to give battle on foot or on horseback. He finally decided that he would do better on foot, as he feared that Rocinante would become frightened at sight of the lions; and so, leaping down from his horse, he fixed his lance, braced his buckler, and drew his sword, and then advanced with marvelous daring and great resoluteness until he stood directly in front of the cart, meanwhile commending himself to God with all his heart and then to his lady Dulcinea.

Upon reaching this point, the reader should know, the author of our veracious history indulges in the following exclamatory passage:

"O great-souled Don Quixote de la Mancha, thou whose courage is beyond all praise, mirror wherein all the valiant of the world may behold themselves, a new and second Don Manuel de León,[6] once the glory and the honor of Spanish knighthood! With what words shall I relate thy terrifying exploit, how render it credible to the ages that are to come? What eulogies do not belong to thee of right, even though they consist of hyperbole piled upon hyperbole? On foot and singlehanded, intrepid and with greathearted valor, armed but with a sword, and not one of the keen-edged Little Dog make,[7] and with a shield that was not of gleaming and polished steel, thou didst stand and wait for the two fiercest lions that ever the African forests bred! Thy deeds shall be thy praise, O valorous Manchegan; I leave them to speak for thee, since words fail me with which to extol them."

Here the author leaves off his exclamations and resumes the thread of the story.

Seeing Don Quixote posed there before him and perceiving that, unless he wished to incur the bold knight's indignation there was nothing for him to do but release the male lion, the keeper now opened the first cage, and it could be seen at once how extraordinarily big and horribly ugly the beast was. The first thing the recumbent animal did was to turn round, put out a claw, and stretch himself all over. Then he opened his mouth and yawned very slowly, after

---

6. Don Manuel Ponce de León, a paragon of gallantry and knightly courtesy, from the time of Ferdinand and Isabella.

7. The trademark of a famous armorer of Toledo and Saragossa.

which he put out a tongue that was nearly two palms in length and with it licked the dust out of his eyes and washed his face. Having done this, he stuck his head outside the cage and gazed about him in all directions. His eyes were now like live coals and his appearance and demeanor were such as to strike terror in temerity itself. But Don Quixote merely stared at him attentively, waiting for him to descend from the cart so that they could come to grips, for the knight was determined to hack the brute to pieces, such was the extent of his unheard-of madness.

The lion, however, proved to be courteous rather than arrogant and was in no mood for childish bravado. After having gazed first in one direction and then in another, as has been said, he turned his back and presented his hind parts to Don Quixote and then very calmly and peaceably lay down and stretched himself out once more in his cage. At this, Don Quixote ordered the keeper to stir him up with a stick in order to irritate him and drive him out.

"That I will not do," the keeper replied, "for if I stir him, I will be the first one he will tear to bits. Be satisfied with what you have already accomplished, Sir Knight, which leaves nothing more to be said on the score of valor, and do not go tempting your fortune a second time. The door was open and the lion could have gone out if he had chosen; since he has not done so up to now, that means he will stay where he is all day long. Your Grace's stoutheartedness has been well established; for no brave fighter, as I see it, is obliged to do more than challenge his enemy and wait for him in the field; his adversary, if he does not come, is the one who is disgraced and the one who awaits him gains the crown of victory."

"That is the truth," said Don Quixote. "Shut the door, my friend, and bear me witness as best you can with regard to what you have seen me do here. I would have you certify: that you opened the door for the lion, that I waited for him and he did not come out, that I continued to wait and still he stayed there, and finally went back and lay down. I am under no further obligation. Away with enchantments, and God uphold the right, the truth, and true chivalry! So close the door, as I have told you, while I signal to the fugitives in order that they who were not present may hear of this exploit from your lips."

The keeper did as he was commanded, and Don Quixote, taking the cloth with which he had dried his face after the rain of curds, fastened it to the point of his lance and began summoning the runaways, who, all in a body with the gentleman in green bringing up the rear were still fleeing and turning around to look back at every step. Sancho was the first to see the white cloth.

"May they slay me," he said, "if my master hasn't conquered those fierce beasts, for he's calling to us."

They all stopped and made sure that the one who was doing the signaling was indeed Don Quixote, and then, losing some of their fear, they little by little made their way back to a point where they could distinctly hear what the knight was saying. At last they returned to the cart, and as they drew near Don Quixote spoke to the driver.

"You may come back, brother, hitch your mules, and continue your journey. And you, Sancho, may give each of them two gold crowns to recompense them for the delay they have suffered on my account."

"That I will, right enough," said Sancho. "But what has become of the lions? Are they dead or alive?"

The keeper thereupon, in leisurely fashion and in full detail, proceeded to tell them how the encounter had ended, taking pains to stress to the best of his ability the valor displayed by Don Quixote, at sight of whom the lion had been so cowed that he was unwilling to leave his cage, though the door had been left open quite a while. The fellow went on to state that the knight had wanted him to stir the lion up and force him out, but had finally been convinced that this would be tempting God and so, much to his displeasure and against his will, had permitted the door to be closed.

"What do you think of that, Sancho?" asked Don Quixote. "Are there any spells that can withstand true gallantry? The enchanters may take my luck away, but to deprive me of my strength and courage is an impossibility."

Sancho then bestowed the crowns, the driver hitched his mules, and the lionkeeper kissed Don Quixote's hands for the favor received, promising that, when he reached the court, he would relate this brave exploit to the king himself.

"In that case," replied Don Quixote, "if his Majesty by any chance should inquire who it was that performed it, you are to say that it was the Knight of the Lions; for that is the name by which I wish to be known from now on, thus changing, exchanging, altering, and converting the one I have previously borne, that of Knight of the Mournful Countenance; in which respect I am but following the old custom of knights-errant, who changed their names whenever they liked or found it convenient to do so."

With this, the cart continued on its way, and Don Quixote, Sancho, and the gentleman in the green-colored greatcoat likewise resumed their journey. During all this time Don Diego de Miranda had not uttered a word but was wholly taken up with observing what Don Quixote did and listening to what he had to say. The knight impressed him as being a crazy sane man and an insane one on the verge of sanity. The gentleman did not happen to be familiar with the first part of our history, but if he had read it he would have ceased to wonder at such talk and conduct, for he would then have known what kind of madness this was. Remaining as he did in ignorance of his companion's malady, he took him now for a sensible individual and now for a madman, since what Don Quixote said was coherent, elegantly phrased, and to the point, whereas his actions were nonsensical, foolhardy, and downright silly. What greater madness could there be, Don Diego asked himself, than to don a helmet filled with curds and then persuade oneself that enchanters were softening one's cranium? What could be more rashly absurd than to wish to fight lions by sheer strength alone? He was roused from these thoughts, this inward soliloquy, by the sound of Don Quixote's voice.

"Undoubtedly, Señor Don Diego de Miranda, your Grace must take me for a fool and a madman, am I not right? And it would be small wonder if such were the case, seeing that my deeds give evidence of nothing else. But, nevertheless, I would advise your Grace that I am neither so mad nor so lacking in wit as I must appear to you to be. A gaily caparisoned knight giving a fortunate lance thrust to a fierce bull in the middle of a great square makes a pleasing appearance in the eyes of his king. The same is true of a knight clad in shining armor as he paces the lists in front of the ladies in some joyous tournament. It is true of all those knights who, by means of military exercises or what appear to be such, divert and entertain and, if one may say so, honor the courts of princes. But the best showing of all is made by a knight-errant who, traversing deserts and solitudes, crossroads, forests, and mountains, goes seeking dangerous adventures with the intention of bringing them to a happy and successful conclusion, and solely for the purpose of winning a glorious and enduring renown.

"More impressive, I repeat, is the knight-errant succoring a widow in some unpopulated place than a courtly man of arms making love to a damsel in the city. All knights have their special callings: let the courtier wait upon the ladies and lend luster by his liveries to his sovereign's palace; let him nourish impoverished gentlemen with the splendid fare of his table; let him give tourneys and show himself truly great, generous, and magnificent and a good Christian above all, thus fulfilling his particular obligations. But the knight-errant's case is different.

"Let the latter seek out the nooks and corners of the world; let him enter into the most intricate of labyrinths; let him attempt the impossible at every step; let him endure on desolate highlands the burning rays of the midsummer sun and in winter the harsh inclemencies of wind and frost; let no lions inspire him with fear, no monsters frighten him, no dragons terrify him, for to seek them out, attack them, and conquer them all is his chief and legitimate occupation. Accordingly, I whose lot it is to be numbered among the knights-errant cannot fail to attempt anything that appears to me to fall within the scope of my duties, just as I attacked those lions a while ago even though I knew it to be an exceedingly rash thing to do, for that was a matter that directly concerned me.

"For I well know the meaning of valor: namely, a virtue that lies between the two extremes of cowardice on the one hand and temerity on the other. It is, nonetheless, better for the brave man to carry his bravery to the point of rashness than for him to sink into cowardice. Even as it is easier for the prodigal to become a generous man than it is for the miser, so is it easier for the foolhardy to become truly brave than it is for the coward to attain valor. And in this matter of adventures, you may believe me, Señor Don Diego, it is better to lose by a card too many than a card too few, and 'Such and such a knight is temerarious and overbold' sounds better to the ear than 'That knight is timid and a coward.'"

"I must assure you, Señor Don Quixote," replied Don Diego, "that everything your Grace has said and done will stand the test of reason; and it is my opinion that if the laws and ordinances of knight-errantry were to be lost, they would be found again in your Grace's bosom, which is their depository and storehouse. But it is growing late; let us hasten to my village and my home, where your Grace shall rest from your recent exertions; for if the body is not tired the spirit may be, and that sometimes results in bodily fatigue."

"I accept your offer as a great favor and an honor, Señor Don Diego," was the knight's reply. And, by spurring their mounts more than they had up to then, they arrived at the village around two in the afternoon and came to the house that was occupied by Don Diego, whom Don Quixote had dubbed the Knight of the Green-colored Greatcoat.

[Last Duel]

CHAPTER LXIV

Which treats of the adventure that caused Don Quixote the most sorrow of all those that have thus far befallen him.[8]

* * *

One morning, as Don Quixote went for a ride along the beach, clad in full armor—for, as he was fond of saying, that was his only ornament, his only rest the fight and, accordingly, he was never without it for a moment—he saw approaching him a horseman similarly arrayed from head to foot and with a brightly shining moon blazoned upon his shield.

As soon as he had come within earshot the stranger cried out to Don Quixote in a loud voice, "O illustrious knight, the never to be sufficiently praised Don Quixote de la Mancha, I am the Knight of the White Moon, whose incomparable exploits you will perhaps recall. I come to contend with you and try the might of my arm, with the purpose of having you acknowledge and confess that my lady, whoever she may be, is beyond comparison more beautiful than your own Dulcinea del Toboso. If you will admit the truth of this fully and freely, you will escape death and I shall be spared the trouble of inflicting it upon you. On the other hand, if you choose to fight and I should overcome you, I ask no other satisfaction than that, laying down your arms and seeking no further adventures, you retire to your own village for the space of a year, during which time you are not to lay hand to sword but are to dwell peacefully and tranquilly, enjoying a beneficial rest that shall redound to the betterment of your worldly fortunes and the salvation of your soul. But if you are the victor, then my head shall be at your disposal, my arms and steed shall be the spoils, and the fame of my exploits shall go to increase your own renown. Consider well which is the better course and let me have your answer at once, for today is all the time I have for the dispatching of this business."

Don Quixote was amazed at the knight's arrogance as well as at the nature of the challenge, but it was with a calm and stern demeanor that he replied to him.

"Knight of the White Moon," he said, "of whose exploits up to now I have never heard, I will venture to take an oath that you have not once laid eyes upon the illustrious Dulcinea; for I am quite certain that if you had beheld her you would not be staking your all upon such an issue, since the sight of her would have convinced you that there never has been, and never can be, any beauty to compare with hers. I do not say that you lie, I simply say that you are mistaken; and so I accept your challenge with the conditions you have laid down, and at once, before this day you have fixed upon shall have ended. The only exception I make is with regard to the fame of your deeds being added to my renown, since I do not know what the character of your exploits has been and am quite content

---

8. Don Quixote and Sancho, after a great many encounters and experiences (of which the most prominent have been Don Quixote's descent into the cave of Montesinos and their residence at the castle of the playful ducal couple who give Sancho the "governorship of an island" for ten days), are now in Barcelona. Famous as they are, they meet the viceroy and the nobles; their host is Don Antonio Moreno, "a gentleman of wealth and discernment who was fond of amusing himself in an innocent and kindly way."

with my own, such as they are. Take, then, whichever side of the field you like, and I will take up my position, and may St. Peter bless what God may give."

Now, as it happened, the Knight of the White Moon was seen by some of the townspeople, who informed the viceroy that he was there, talking to Don Quixote de la Mancha. Believing this to be a new adventure arranged by Don Antonio Moreno or some other gentleman of the place, the viceroy at once hastened down to the beach, accompanied by a large retinue, including Don Antonio, and they arrived just as Don Quixote was wheeling Rocinante to measure off the necessary stretch of field. When the viceroy perceived that they were about to engage in combat, he at once interposed and inquired of them what it was that impelled them thus to do battle all of a sudden.

The Knight of the White Moon replied that it was a matter of beauty and precedence and briefly repeated what he had said to Don Quixote, explaining the terms to which both parties had agreed. The viceroy then went up to Don Antonio and asked him if he knew any such knight as this or if it was some joke that they were playing, but the answer that he received left him more puzzled than ever; for Don Antonio did not know who the knight was, nor could he say as to whether this was a real encounter or not. The viceroy, accordingly, was doubtful about letting them proceed, but inasmuch as he could not bring himself to believe that it was anything more than a jest, he withdrew to one side, saying, "Sir Knights, if there is nothing for it but to confess or die, and if Señor Don Quixote's mind is made up and your Grace, the Knight of the White Moon, is even more firmly resolved, then fall to it in the name of God and may He bestow the victory."

The Knight of the White Moon thanked the viceroy most courteously and in well-chosen words for the permission which had been granted them, and Don Quixote did the same, whereupon the latter, commending himself with all his heart to Heaven and to his lady Dulcinea, as was his custom at the beginning of a fray, fell back a little farther down the field as he saw his adversary doing the same. And then, without blare of trumpet or other warlike instrument to give them the signal for the attack, both at the same instant wheeled their steeds about and returned for the charge. Being mounted upon the swifter horse, the Knight of the White Moon met Don Quixote two-thirds of the way and with such tremendous force that, without touching his opponent with his lance (which, it seemed, he deliberately held aloft) he brought both Rocinante and his rider to the ground in an exceedingly perilous fall. At once the victor leaped down and placed his lance at Don Quixote's visor.

"You are vanquished, O knight! Nay, more, you are dead unless you make confession in accordance with the conditions governing our encounter."

Stunned and battered, Don Quixote did not so much as raise his visor but in a faint, wan voice, as if speaking from the grave, he said, "Dulcinea del Toboso is the most beautiful woman in the world and I the most unhappy knight upon the face of this earth. It is not right that my weakness should serve to defraud the truth. Drive home your lance, O knight, and take my life since you already have deprived me of my honor."

"That I most certainly shall not do," said the one of the White Moon. "Let the fame of my lady Dulcinea del Toboso's beauty live on undiminished. As for me, I shall be content if the great Don Quixote will retire to his village for a year or until such a time as I may specify, as was agreed upon between us before joining battle."

The viceroy, Don Antonio, and all the many others who were present heard this, and they also heard Don Quixote's response, which was to the effect that, seeing nothing was asked of him that was prejudicial to Dulcinea, he would fulfill all the other conditions like a true and punctilious knight. The one of the White Moon thereupon turned and with a bow to the viceroy rode back to the city at a mild canter. The viceroy promptly dispatched Don Antonio to follow him and make every effort to find out who he was; and, in the meanwhile, they lifted Don Quixote up and uncovered his face, which held no sign of color and was bathed in perspiration. Rocinante, however, was in so sorry a state that he was unable to stir for the present.

Brokenhearted over the turn that events had taken, Sancho did not know what to say or do. It seemed to him that all this was something that was happening in a dream and that everything was the result of magic. He saw his master surrender, heard him consent not to take up arms again for a year to come as the light of his glorious exploits faded into darkness. At the same time his own hopes, based upon the fresh promises that had been made him, were whirled away like smoke before the wind. He feared that Rocinante was maimed for life, his master's bones permanently dislocated—it would have been a bit of luck if his madness also had been jolted out of him.[9]

Finally, in a hand litter which the viceroy had them bring, they bore the knight back to town. The viceroy himself then returned, for he was very anxious to ascertain who the Knight of the White Moon was who had left Don Quixote in so lamentable a condition.

From CHAPTER LXV

Wherein is revealed who the Knight of the White Moon was,
with the freeing of Don Gregorio and other events.

The Knight of the White Moon was followed not only by Don Antonio Moreno, but by a throng of small boys as well, who kept after him until the doors of one of the city's hostelries had closed behind him. A squire came out to meet him and remove his armor, for which purpose the victor proceded to shut himself up in a lower room, in the company of Don Antonio, who had also entered the inn and whose bread would not bake until he had learned the knight's identity. Perceiving that the gentleman had no intention of leaving him, he of the White Moon then spoke.

"Sir," he said, "I am well aware that you have come to find out who I am; and, seeing that there is no denying you the information that you seek, while my servant here is removing my armor I will tell you the exact truth of the matter. I would have you know, sir, that I am the bachelor Sansón Carrasco from the same village as Don Quixote de la Mancha, whose madness and absurdities inspire pity in all of us who know him and in none more than me. And so, being convinced that his salvation lay in his returning home for a period of rest in his own house, I formed a plan for bringing him back.

"It was three months ago that I took to the road as a knight-errant, calling myself the Knight of the Mirrors, with the object of fighting and overcoming him without doing him any harm, intending first to lay down the condition that

---

9. The original Spanish has an untranslatable pun on *deslocado*, which means "out of joint" ("dislocated") and also "cured of madness" (from *loco*, "mad").

the vanquished was to yield to the victor's will. What I meant to ask of him—
for I looked upon him as conquered from the start—was that he should return
to his village and not leave it for a whole year, in the course of which time he
might be cured. Fate, however, ordained things otherwise; for he was the one
who conquered me and overthrew me from my horse, and thus my plan came
to naught. He continued on his wanderings, and I went home, defeated, humiliated, and bruised from my fall, which was quite a dangerous one. But I did not
for this reason give up the idea of hunting him up once more and vanquishing
him as you have seen me do today.

"Since he is the soul of honor when it comes to observing the ordinances of
knight-errantry, there is not the slightest doubt that he will keep the promise
he has given me and fulfill his obligations. And that, sir, is all that I need to tell
you concerning what has happened. I beg you not to disclose my secret or
reveal my identity to Don Quixote, in order that my well-intentioned scheme
may be carried out and a man of excellent judgment be brought back to his
senses—for a sensible man he would be, once rid of the follies of chivalry."

"My dear sir," exclaimed Don Antonio, "may God forgive you for the wrong
you have done the world by seeking to deprive it of its most charming madman!
Do you not see that the benefit accomplished by restoring Don Quixote to his
senses can never equal the pleasure which others derive from his vagaries? But
it is my opinion that all the trouble to which the Señor Bachelor has put himself will not suffice to cure a man who is so hopelessly insane; and if it were not
uncharitable, I would say let Don Quixote never be cured, since with his return
to health we lose not only his own drolleries but also those of his squire, Sancho Panza, for either of the two is capable of turning melancholy itself into joy
and merriment. Nevertheless, I will keep silent and tell him nothing, that I may
see whether or not I am right in my suspicion that Señor Carrasco's efforts will
prove to have been of no avail."

The bachelor replied that, all in all, things looked very favorable and he
hoped for a fortunate outcome. With this, he took his leave of Don Antonio,
after offering to render him any service that he could; and, having had his
armor tied up and placed upon a mule's back, he rode out of the city that same
day on the same horse on which he had gone into battle, returning to his native
province without anything happening to him that is worthy of being set down
in this veracious chronicle.

* * *

[Homecoming and Death]

CHAPTER LXXIII

*Of the omens that Don Quixote encountered upon entering
his village, with other incidents that embellish and lend credence
to this great history.*

As they entered the village, Cid Hamete informs us, Don Quixote caught sight
of two lads on the communal threshing floor who were engaged in a dispute.

"Don't let it worry you, Periquillo," one of them was saying to the other;
"you'll never lay eyes on it again as long as you live."

Hearing this, Don Quixote turned to Sancho. "Did you mark what that boy said, my friend?" he asked. "'You'll never lay eyes on it[1] again . . .'"

"Well," replied Sancho, "what difference does it make what he said?"

"What difference?" said Don Quixote. "Don't you see that, applied to the one I love, it means I shall never again see Dulcinea."

Sancho was about to answer him when his attention was distracted by a hare that came flying across the fields pursued by a large number of hunters with their greyhounds. The frightened animal took refuge by huddling down beneath the donkey, whereupon Sancho reached out his hand and caught it and presented it to his master.

"*Malum signum, malum signum,*"[2] the knight was muttering to himself. "A hare flees, the hounds pursue it, Dulcinea appears not."

"It is very strange to hear your Grace talk like that," said Sancho. "Let us suppose that this hare *is* Dulcinea del Toboso and the hounds pursuing it are those wicked enchanters that transformed her into a peasant lass; she flees, I catch her and turn her over to your Grace, you hold her in your arms and caress her. Is that a bad sign? What ill omen can you find in it?"

The two lads who had been quarreling now came up to have a look at the hare, and Sancho asked them what their dispute was about. To this the one who had uttered the words "You'll never lay eyes on it again as long as you live," replied that he had taken a cricket cage from the other boy and had no intention of returning it ever. Sancho then brought out from his pocket four cuartos and gave them to the lad in exchange for the cage, which he placed in Don Quixote's hands.

"There, master," he said, "these omens are broken and destroyed, and to my way of thinking, even though I may be a dunce, they have no more to do with what is going to happen to us than the clouds of yesteryear. If I am not mistaken, I have heard our curate say that sensible persons of the Christian faith should pay no heed to such foolish things, and you yourself in the past have given me to understand that all those Christians who are guided by omens are fools. But there is no need to waste a lot of words on the subject; come, let us go on and enter our village."

The hunters at this point came up and asked for the hare, and Don Quixote gave it to them. Continuing on their way, the returning pair encountered the curate and the bachelor Carrasco, who were strolling in a small meadow on the outskirts of the town as they read their breviaries. And here it should be mentioned that Sancho Panza, by way of sumpter cloth, had thrown over his gray and the bundle of armor it bore the flame-covered buckram robe in which they had dressed the squire at the duke's castle, on the night that witnessed Altisidora's[3] resurrection; and he had also fitted the miter over the donkey's head, the result being the weirdest transformation and the most bizarrely appareled ass that ever were seen in this world. The curate and the bachelor

1. The pronoun *it* is the same as *her* in the Spanish, because the boy's reference is to a cricket cage, which is a feminine noun. (In Spanish, all nouns are either masculine or feminine.) Hence Don Quixote's inference that the boys are discussing Dulcinea.

2. An ill omen (Latin)—that is, meeting a

hare is considered a bad sign.

3. A girl in the duke's castle, where Don Quixote and Sancho were guests for a time. She dramatically pretended to be in love with Don Quixote. "Sumpter cloth": decorative or protective covering for a pack animal.

recognized the pair at once and came forward to receive them with open arms. Don Quixote dismounted and gave them both a warm embrace; meanwhile, the small boys (boys are like lynxes in that nothing escapes them), having spied the ass's miter, ran up for a closer view.

"Come, lads," they cried, "and see Sancho Panza's ass trigged out finer than Mingo,[4] and Don Quixote's beast is skinnier than ever!"

Finally, surrounded by the urchins and accompanied by the curate and the bachelor, they entered the village and made their way to Don Quixote's house, where they found the housekeeper and the niece standing in the doorway, for the news of their return had preceded them. Teresa Panza, Sancho's wife, had also heard of it, and, half naked and disheveled, dragging her daughter Sanchica by the hand, she hastened to greet her husband and was disappointed when she saw him, for he did not look to her as well fitted out as a governor ought to be.

"How does it come, my husband," she said, "that you return like this, tramping and footsore? You look more like a vagabond than you do like a governor."

"Be quiet, Teresa,"[5] Sancho admonished her, "for very often there are stakes where there is no bacon. Come on home with me and you will hear marvels. I am bringing money with me, which is the thing that matters, money earned by my own efforts and without harm to anyone."

"You just bring along the money, my good husband," said Teresa, "and whether you got it here or there, or by whatever means, you will not be introducing any new custom into the world."

Sanchica then embraced her father and asked him if he had brought her anything, for she had been looking forward to his coming as to the showers in May. And so, with his wife holding him by the hand while his daughter kept one arm about his waist and at the same time led the gray, Sancho went home, leaving Don Quixote under his own roof in the company of niece and housekeeper, the curate and the barber.

Without regard to time or season, the knight at once drew his guests to one side and in a few words informed them of how he had been overcome in battle and had given his promise not to leave his village for a year, a promise that he meant to observe most scrupulously, without violating it in the slightest degree, as every knight-errant was obliged to do by the laws of chivalry. He accordingly meant to spend that year as a shepherd,[6] he said, amid the solitude of the fields, where he might give free rein to his amorous fancies as he practiced the virtues of the pastoral life; and he further begged them, if they were not too greatly occupied and more urgent matters did not prevent their doing so, to consent to be his companions. He would purchase a flock sufficiently large to justify their calling themselves shepherds; and, moreover, he would have them know, the most important thing of all had been taken care of, for he had hit upon names that would suit them marvelously well. When the curate asked him what these names were, Don Quixote replied that he himself would be known as "the

---

4. The allusion is to the opening lines of *Mingo Revulgo* (15th century), a satire: "Hey! Mingo Revulgo, hey! What have you done with your blue cloth doublet? Do you not wear it on Sundays?"

5. Sancho's wife, here referred to as Teresa, is earlier named Juana.

6. Because the knight-errant's life has been forbidden him by his defeat, Don Quixote for a time plans to live according to another and no less "literary" code, that of the pastoral. The following paragraphs, especially through the bachelor Carrasco, refer humorously to some of the conventions of pastoral literature.

shepherd Quixotiz," the bachelor as "the shepherd Carrascón," the curate as "the shepherd Curiambro," and Sancho Panza as "the shepherd Pancino."

Both his listeners were dismayed at the new form which his madness had assumed. However, in order that he might not go faring forth from the village on another of his expeditions (for they hoped that in the course of the year he would be cured), they decided to fall in with his new plan and approve it as being a wise one, and they even agreed to be his companions in the calling he proposed to adopt.

"What's more," remarked Sansón Carrasco, "I am a very famous poet, as everyone knows, and at every turn I will be composing pastoral or courtly verses or whatever may come to mind, by way of a diversion for us as we wander in those lonely places; but what is most necessary of all, my dear sirs, is that each one of us should choose the name of the shepherd lass to whom he means to dedicate his songs, so that we may not leave a tree, however hard its bark may be, where their names are not inscribed and engraved as is the custom with lovelorn shepherds."

"That is exactly what we should do," replied Don Quixote, "although, for my part, I am relieved of the necessity of looking for an imaginary shepherdess, seeing that I have the peerless Dulcinea del Toboso, glory of these brookside regions, adornment of these meadows, beauty's mainstay, cream of the Graces—in short, one to whom all praise is well becoming however hyperbolical it may be."

"That is right," said the curate, "but we will seek out some shepherd maids that are easily handled, who if they do not square with us will fit in the corners."

"And," added Sansón Carrasco, "if we run out of names we will give them those that we find printed in books the world over: such as Fílida, Amarilis, Diana, Flérida, Galatea, and Belisarda; for since these are for sale in the market place, we can buy them and make them our own. If my lady, or, rather, my shepherdess, should by chance be called Ana, I will celebrate her charms under the name of Anarda; if she is Francisca, she will become Francenia; if Lucía, Luscinda; for it all amounts to the same thing. And Sancho Panza, if he enters this confraternity, may compose verses to his wife, Teresa Panza, under the name of Teresaina."

Don Quixote had to laugh at this, and the curate then went on to heap extravagant praise upon him for his noble resolution which did him so much credit, and once again he offered to keep the knight company whenever he could spare the time from the duties of his office. With this, they took their leave of him, advising and beseeching him to take care of his health and to eat plentifully of the proper food.

As fate would have it, the niece and the housekeeper had overheard the conversation of the three men, and as soon as the visitors had left they both descended upon Don Quixote.

"What is the meaning of this, my uncle? Here we were thinking your Grace had come home to lead a quiet and respectable life, and do you mean to tell us you are going to get yourself involved in fresh complications—

> Young shepherd, thou who comest here,
> Young shepherd, thou who goest there . . . [7]

7. From a pastoral ballad.

For, to tell the truth, the barley is too hard now to make shepherds' pipes of it."[8]

"And how," said the housekeeper, "is your Grace going to stand the midday heat in summer, the winter cold, the howling of the wolves out there in the fields? You certainly cannot endure it. That is an occupation for robust men, cut out and bred for such a calling almost from their swaddling clothes. Setting one evil over against another, it is better to be a knight-errant than a shepherd. Look, sir, take my advice, for I am not stuffed with bread and wine when I give it to you but am fasting and am going on fifty years of age: stay at home, attend to your affairs, go often to confession, be charitable to the poor, and let it be upon my soul if any harm comes to you as a result of it."

"Be quiet, daughters," said Don Quixote. "I know very well what I must do. Take me up to bed, for I do not feel very well; and you may be sure of one thing: whether I am a knight-errant now or a shepherd to be, I never will fail to look after your needs as you will see when the time comes."

And good daughters that they unquestionably were, the housekeeper and the niece helped him up to bed, where they gave him something to eat and made him as comfortable as they could.

From CHAPTER LXXIV

*Of how Don Quixote fell sick, of the will that he made,
and of the manner of his death.*

Inasmuch as nothing that is human is eternal but is ever declining from its beginning to its close, this being especially true of the lives of men, and since Don Quixote was not endowed by Heaven with the privilege of staying the downward course of things, his own end came when he was least expecting it. Whether it was owing to melancholy occasioned by the defeat he had suffered, or was, simply, the will of Heaven which had so ordained it, he was taken with a fever that kept him in bed for a week, during which time his friends, the curate, the bachelor, and the barber, visited him frequently, while Sancho Panza, his faithful squire, never left his bedside.

Believing that the knight's condition was due to sorrow over his downfall and disappointment at not having been able to accomplish the disenchantment and liberation of Dulcinea, Sancho and the others endeavored to cheer him up in every possible way. The bachelor urged him to take heart and get up from bed that he might begin his pastoral life, adding that he himself had already composed an eclogue that would cast in the shade all that Sannazaro[9] had ever written, and had purchased with his own money from a herdsman of Quintanar two fine dogs to guard the flock, one of them named Barcino and the other Butrón. All this, however, did not serve to relieve Don Quixote's sadness; whereupon his friends called in the doctor, who took his pulse and was not very well satisfied with it. In any case, the physician told them, they should attend to the health of his soul as that of his body was in grave danger.

Don Quixote received this news calmly enough, but not so his housekeeper, niece, and squire, who began weeping bitterly, as if he were already lying dead

---

8. A proverb.
9. Jacopo Sannazaro (1456–1530), Italian poet

whose *Arcadia* is one of the milestones in the pastoral tradition.

in front of them. It was the doctor's opinion that melancholy and depression were putting an end to his patient's life. The knight then requested them to leave him alone as he wished to sleep a little, and they complied. He slept for more than six hours at a stretch, as the saying is, and so soundly that the housekeeper and niece thought he would never wake.

At last he did, however, and at once cried out in a loud voice, "Blessed be Almighty God who has given me so many blessings! Truly His mercy is boundless and is not limited or restrained by the sins of men."

The niece listened carefully to what her uncle said, and it seemed to her that he was speaking more rationally than was his wont, at least during his illness.

"Sir," she said to him, "what does your Grace mean? Has something occurred that we know nothing about? What is this talk of mercy and sins?"

"The mercy that I speak of," replied Don Quixote, "is that which God is showing me at this moment—in spite of my sins, as I have said. My mind now is clear, unencumbered by those misty shadows of ignorance that were cast over it by my bitter and continual reading of those hateful books of chivalry. I see through all the nonsense and fraud contained in them, and my only regret is that my disillusionment has come so late, leaving me no time to make any sort of amends by reading those that are the light of the soul. I find myself, niece, at the point of death, and I would die in such a way as not to leave the impression of a life so bad that I shall be remembered as a madman; for even though I have been one, I do not wish to confirm it on my deathbed. And so, my dear, call in my good friends: the curate, the bachelor Sansón Carrasco, and Master Nicholas the barber; for I want to confess my sins and make my last will and testament."

The niece, however, was relieved of this errand, for the three of them came in just then.

"I have good news for you, kind sirs," said Don Quixote the moment he saw them. "I am no longer Don Quixote de la Mancha but Alonso Quijano, whose mode of life won for him the name of 'Good.' I am the enemy of Amadis of Gaul and all his innumerable progeny; for those profane stories dealing with knight-errantry are odious to me, and I realize how foolish I was and the danger I courted in reading them; but I am in my right senses now and I abominate them."

Hearing this, they all three were convinced that some new kind of madness must have laid hold of him.

"Why, Señor Don Quixote!" exclaimed Sansón. "What makes you talk like that, just when we have received news that my lady Dulcinea is disenchanted? And just when we are on the verge of becoming shepherds so that we may spend the rest of our lives in singing like a lot of princes, why does your Grace choose to turn hermit? Say no more, in Heaven's name, but be sensible and forget these idle tales."

"Tales of that kind," said Don Quixote, "have been the truth for me in the past, and to my detriment, but with Heaven's aid I trust to turn them to my profit now that I am dying. For I feel, gentlemen, that death is very near; so, leave all jesting aside and bring me a confessor for my sins and a notary to draw up my will. In such straits as these a man cannot trifle with his soul. Accordingly, while the Señor Curate is hearing my confession, let the notary be summoned."

Amazed at his words, they gazed at one another in some perplexity, yet they could not but believe him. One of the signs that led them to think he was dying was this quick return from madness to sanity and all the additional things he had to say, so well reasoned and well put and so becoming in a Christian that none of them could any longer doubt that he was in full possession of his faculties. Sending the others out of the room, the curate stayed behind to confess him, and before long the bachelor returned with the notary and Sancho Panza, who had been informed of his master's condition, and who, finding the housekeeper and the niece in tears, began weeping with them. When the confession was over, the curate came out.

"It is true enough," he said, "that Alonso Quijano the Good is dying, and it is also true that he is a sane man. It would be well for us to go in now while he makes his will."

At this news the housekeeper, niece, and the good squire Sancho Panza were so overcome with emotion that the tears burst forth from their eyes and their bosoms heaved with sobs; for, as has been stated more than once, whether Don Quixote was plain Alonso Quijano the Good or Don Quixote de la Mancha, he was always of a kindly and pleasant disposition and for this reason was beloved not only by the members of his household but by all who knew him.

The notary had entered along with the others, and as soon as the preamble had been attended to and the dying man had commended his soul to his Maker with all those Christian formalities that are called for in such a case, they came to the matter of bequests, with Don Quixote dictating as follows:

"ITEM. With regard to Sancho Panza, whom, in my madness, I appointed to be my squire, and who has in his possession a certain sum of money belonging to me: inasmuch as there has been a standing account between us, of debits and credits, it is my will that he shall not be asked to give any accounting whatsoever of this sum, but if any be left over after he has had payment for what I owe him, the balance, which will amount to very little, shall be his, and much good may it do him. If when I was mad I was responsible for his being given the governorship of an island, now that I am of sound mind I would present him with a kingdom if it were in my power, for his simplicity of mind and loyal conduct merit no less."

At this point he turned to Sancho. "Forgive me, my friend," he said, "for having caused you to appear as mad as I by leading you to fall into the same error, that of believing that there are still knights-errant in the world."

"Ah, master," cried Sancho through his tears, "don't die, your Grace, but take my advice and go on living for many years to come; for the greatest madness that a man can be guilty of in this life is to die without good reason, without anyone's killing him, slain only by the hands of melancholy. Look you, don't be lazy but get up from this bed and let us go out into the fields clad as shepherds as we agreed to do. Who knows but behind some bush we may come upon the lady Dulcinea, as disenchanted as you could wish. If it is because of worry over your defeat that you are dying, put the blame on me by saying that the reason for your being overthrown was that I had not properly fastened Rocinante's girth. For the matter of that, your Grace knows from reading your books of chivalry that it is a common thing for certain knights to overthrow others, and he who is vanquished today will be the victor tomorrow."

"That is right," said Sansón, "the worthy Sancho speaks the truth."

"Not so fast, gentlemen," said Don Quixote. "In last year's nests there are no birds this year. I was mad and now I am sane; I was Don Quixote de la Mancha, and now I am, as I have said, Alonso Quijano the Good. May my repentance and the truth I now speak restore to me the place I once held in your esteem. And now, let the notary proceed:

"ITEM. I bequeath my entire estate, without reservation, to my niece Antonia Quijana, here present, after the necessary deductions shall have been made from the most available portion of it to satisfy the bequests that I have stipulated. The first payment shall be to my housekeeper for the wages due her, with twenty ducats over to buy her a dress. And I hereby appoint the Señor Curate and the Señor Bachelor Sansón Carrasco to be my executors.

"ITEM. It is my will that if my niece Antonia Quijana should see fit to marry, it shall be to a man who does not know what books of chivalry are; and if it shall be established that he is acquainted with such books and my niece still insists on marrying him, then she shall lose all that I have bequeathed her and my executors shall apply her portion to works of charity as they may see fit.

"ITEM. I entreat the aforementioned gentlemen, my executors, if by good fortune they should come to know the author who is said to have composed a history now going the rounds under the title of *Second Part of the Exploits of Don Quixote de la Mancha*, to beg his forgiveness in my behalf, as earnestly as they can, since it was I who unthinkingly led him to set down so many and such great absurdities as are to be found in it; for I leave this life with a feeling of remorse at having provided him with the occasion for putting them into writing."

The will ended here, and Don Quixote, stretching himself at length in the bed, fainted away. They all were alarmed at this and hastened to aid him. The same thing happened very frequently in the course of the three days of life that remained to him after he had made his will. The household was in a state of excitement, but with it all the niece continued to eat her meals, the housekeeper had her drink, and Sancho Panza was in good spirits; for this business of inheriting property effaces or mitigates the sorrow which the heir ought to feel and causes him to forget.

Death came at last for Don Quixote, after he had received all the sacraments and once more, with many forceful arguments, had expressed his abomination of books of chivalry. The notary who was present remarked that in none of those books had he read of any knight-errant dying in his own bed so peacefully and in so Christian a manner. And thus, amid the tears and lamentations of those present, he gave up the ghost; that is to say, he died. Perceiving that their friend was no more, the curate asked the notary to be a witness to the fact that Alonso Quijano the Good, commonly known as Don Quixote, was truly dead, this being necessary in order that some author other than Cid Hamete Benengeli might not have the opportunity of falsely resurrecting him and writing endless histories of his exploits.

Such was the end of the Ingenious Gentleman of La Mancha, whose birthplace Cid Hamete was unwilling to designate exactly in order that all the towns and villages of La Mancha might contend among themselves for the right to adopt him and claim him as their own, just as the seven cities of Greece did in the case of Homer. The lamentations of Sancho and those of Don Quixote's niece and his housekeeper, as well as the original epitaphs that were composed for his tomb, will not be recorded here, but mention may be made of the verses by Sansón Carrasco:

Here lies a gentleman bold
Who was so very brave
He went to lengths untold,
And on the brink of the grave
Death had on him no hold.
By the world he set small store—
He frightened it to the core—
Yet somehow, by Fate's plan,
Though he'd lived a crazy man,
When he died he was sane once more.

* * *

POPOL VUH
transcribed 1554–58

A compendium of stories cherished by the ancient, the colonial, and even the modern Quiché Maya people of Guatemala, the sixteenth-century Popol Vuh has been compared to the *Odyssey* of the Greeks and the *Mahābhārata* of India. Woven together, its stories form an epic narrative that leads from the creation of the world and of humankind to the time of the text's writing, amid the violence of the Spanish Conquest. Inevitably, following the conquest of Mexico in 1521, Spanish imperialism cast its eye toward Guatemala, and in 1524, after a brief struggle, Quiché fell to Spanish and Mexican troops under the command of Pedro de Alvarado (called "the sun" by native people). By the 1530s, Quiché scribes, presumably including the Popol Vuh author, were being trained to use alphabetic writing. The book thus represents the cultural and intellectual mix born of the encounter: it is written in the Quiché language but in the Roman alphabet, and translates into book form what may have been an earlier text. In the narrative itself the anonymous author hints at the existence of a certain "council book" (*popol vuh*), presumably a pre-Columbian screen-fold that served him as a source. The Maya were the only civilization in the New World to have developed a full writing system, based on an elaborate system of glyphs.

The sixteenth-century Quiché were well acquainted with "council books," some dating from the classic period of Maya culture (100–900 C.E.), which saw the rise of such imposing centers as Tikal, Copán, and Palenque. By the time of European contact those important sites, abandoned in the mysterious collapse of Maya civilization ca. 900 C.E., lay in ruins. But Maya learning survived in southern Guatemala among the Quiché and their neighbors, and in the northern part of the Yucatán peninsula. Mayanists conclude that although the Popol Vuh is not an actual transcription of ancient screen-folds, it no doubt borrows from them. The modern text survives thanks to a copy made by a Dominican friar in the early eighteenth century, but it may have lost accompanying illustrations or hieroglyphs, which were standard for Mayan writings.

Stylistically, the text is fascinated by numbers, as evidenced in the pairing, tripling, and quadrupling of phrases. Major characters and deities also are paired, occasionally tripled, with a strong suggestion that they are the same. The work has a repeating structure, fitted to a traditional pattern of four successive worlds, or creations: the first three are said to have ended in failure; our own is the fourth. Yet against the background of this formal pattern, the hero-gods appear as light-hearted boys, even as tricksters. Their adventures, which are sometimes quite bawdy, have a playful, anecdotal quality.

As the author plainly states in the preamble that begins part 1, "We shall write about this now amid the preaching of God, in Christendom now." Admittedly, then, the Popol Vuh is written after the conquest, but the question of how much of it was influenced by Christian missionaries is not easy to settle. Most critics have assumed that the account of the Earth's creation that immediately follows the preamble owes something to the **Book of Genesis**. If so, the material has been thoroughly assimilated to the Maya pantheon and to the Native American concept of primordial water. The text may be as easily compared to Aztec accounts of creation, in which the gods deliberate, then place the Earth on the surface of a preexisting sea, as to Genesis.

Part 1 continues with a description of the first three efforts at creating humans, in line with a widespread pattern shared by Aztec and other Meso-american traditions. As part 1 ends, the narrative moves on to the exploits of the divine heroes Hunahpu and Xbalanque. The work of these two heroes may be said to prepare the world for society and for the well-being of individuals within society when they bring low the over-proud Seven Macaw, while part 3, the most celebrated portion of the Popol Vuh, confronts the scourge of death.

In the cycle of tales that comprises part 3, Hunahpu and Xbalanque vanquish the lords of the Maya underworld, called Xibalba (a term of obscure etymology, provisionally translated "place of fright"). This material is quintessentially Mayan: scenes from the story are preserved on painted vases of the classic period, recovered by archaeologists from Maya burial chambers. The story told here must have aided the Maya in their journey through the realms of death somewhat as the *Book of the Dead* comforted the ancient Egyptians. Parts 4 and 5 complete the vast epic, relating the connected stories of the origin of humans, the discovery of corn, the birth of the sun, and the history of the Quiché tribes and their royal lineages down to the time of the Spanish Conquest and, subsequently, to the 1550s.

Old as the stories are, they are also new. Narratives of the origin and destruction of early humans can still be heard in traditional Maya storytelling sessions. The tale of the discovery of corn continues to be widely told; and the exploits of the trickster Zipacna and the hero twins also persist in shorter versions. Beyond the native community, knowledge of the Popol Vuh among Central Americans is not only widespread but taken for granted. For the Salvadoran novelist Manlio Argueta (*Cuzcatlán*, 1986) the story of the origin of humans from corn as told in the Popol Vuh is a reminder, in Argueta's words, that "the species will not perish." The theme appears also in the 1949 novel *Men of Maize* by the Guatemalan Nobel laureate Miguel Angel Asturias, inspired by the same source.

In the translation printed here, wherever the text solidifies into a string of three or more couplets, the passage is set apart as though it were a poem. This is a device of the translator. It is not meant to imply that the lines were chanted but rather to show off the more pronounced moments of formalism in a prose that borders on oratory.

Popol Vuh[1]

FROM PART I

[Prologue, Creation]

THIS IS THE BEGINNING OF THE ANCIENT WORD, here in this place called Quiché. Here we shall inscribe, we shall implant the Ancient Word, the potential and source for everything done in the citadel of Quiché, in the nation of Quiché people.

And here we shall take up the demonstration, revelation, and account of how things were put in shadow and brought to light by

> the Maker, Modeler,
> named Bearer, Begetter,
> Hunahpu Possum, Hunahpu Coyote,
> Great White Peccary,
> Sovereign Plumed Serpent,
> Heart of the Lake, Heart of the Sea,
> plate shaper,
> bowl shaper,[2] as they are called,
> also named, also described as
> the midwife, matchmaker
> named Xpiyacoc, Xmucane,
> defender, protector,[3]
> twice a midwife, twice a matchmaker,

as is said in the words of Quiché. They accounted for everything—and did it, too—as enlightened beings, in enlightened words. We shall write about this now amid the preaching of God, in Christendom now. We shall bring it out because there is no longer

> a place to see it, a Council Book,
> a place to see "The Light That Came from
>   Beside the Sea,"
> the account of "Our Place in the Shadows,"
> a place to see "The Dawn of Life,"

as it is called. There is the original book and ancient writing, but the one who reads and assesses it has a hidden identity.[4] It takes a long performance and account to complete the lighting of all the sky-earth:

> the fourfold siding, fourfold cornering,
> measuring, fourfold staking,
> halving the cord, stretching the cord

---

1. Translated by Dennis Tedlock.
2. All thirteen names refer to the Creator or to a company of creators, a designation applicable clearly to the first four names and *Sovereign Plumed Serpent. Heart of the Lake* and *Heart of the Sea* also apply, since the creators will later be described as "in the water," and somewhat obscurely, so does the last pair of names (*plate* and *bowl* may be read as "earth" and "sky," respectively). *Hunahpu Pos-*

sum, Hunahpu Coyote, Great White Peccary, and *Coati* refer specifically to the grandparents of the gods, usually called Xpiyacoc and Xmucane.
3. Four names for Xpiyacoc and Xmucane.
4. The hieroglyphic source (*Council Book*) was suppressed by missionaries; it was said to have been brought to Quiché in ancient times from the far side of a lagoon (*Sea*). The reader hides his identity to avoid the missionaries.

in the sky, on the earth,
the four sides, the four corners,[5]
by the Maker, Modeler,
mother-father of life, of humankind,
giver of breath, giver of heart,
bearer, upbringer in the light that lasts
of those born in the light, begotten in the light;
worrier, knower of everything, whatever there is:
sky-earth, lake-sea.

THIS IS THE ACCOUNT, here it is:

Now it still ripples, now it still murmurs, ripples, it still sighs, still hums, and it is empty under the sky.

Here follow the first words, the first eloquence:

There is not yet one person, one animal, bird, fish, crab, tree, rock, hollow, canyon, meadow, forest. Only the sky alone is there; the face of the earth is not clear. Only the sea alone is pooled under all the sky; there is nothing whatever gathered together. It is at rest; not a single thing stirs. It is held back, kept at rest under the sky.

Whatever there is that might be is simply not there: only the pooled water, only the calm sea, only it alone is pooled.

Whatever might be is simply not there: only murmurs, ripples, in the dark, in the night. Only the Maker, Modeler alone, Sovereign Plumed Serpent, the Bearers, Begetters are in the water, a glittering light. They are there, they are enclosed in quetzal feathers, in blue-green.

Thus the name, "Plumed Serpent." They are great knowers, great thinkers in their very being.

And of course there is the sky, and there is also the Heart of Sky. This is the name of the god, as it is spoken.

And then came his word, he came here to the Sovereign Plumed Serpent, here in the blackness, in the early dawn. He spoke with the Sovereign Plumed Serpent, and they talked, then they thought, then they worried. They agreed with each other, they joined their words, their thoughts. Then it was clear, then they reached accord in the light, and then humanity was clear, when they conceived the growth, the generation of trees, of bushes, and the growth of life, of humankind, in the blackness, in the early dawn, all because of the Heart of Sky, named Hurricane. Thunderbolt Hurricane comes first, the second is Newborn Thunderbolt, and the third is Sudden Thunderbolt.[6]

So there were three of them, as Heart of Sky, who came to the Sovereign Plumed Serpent, when the dawn of life was conceived:

"How should the sowing be, and the dawning? Who is to be the provider, nurturer?"[7]

"Let it be this way, think about it: this water should be removed, emptied out for the formation of the earth's own plate and platform, then should come the

---

5. As though a farmer were measuring and staking a cornfield.
6. Alternate names for Heart of Sky, the deity who cooperates with Sovereign Plumed Serpent. The triple naming adapts the Christian trinity to native theology, perhaps more in the spirit of defiant preemption than of conciliation.
7. That is, humanity, which alone is capable of *nurturing* the gods with sacrifices.

sowing, the dawning of the sky-earth. But there will be no high days and no bright praise for our work, our design, until the rise of the human work, the human design," they said.

And then the earth arose because of them, it was simply their word that brought it forth. For the forming of the earth they said "Earth." It arose suddenly, just like a cloud, like a mist, now forming, unfolding. Then the mountains were separated from the water, all at once the great mountains came forth. By their genius alone, by their cutting edge[8] alone they carried out the conception of the mountain-plain, whose face grew instant groves of cypress and pine.

And the Plumed Serpent was pleased with this:

"It was good that you came, Heart of Sky, Hurricane, and Newborn Thunderbolt, Sudden Thunderbolt. Our work, our design will turn out well," they said.

And the earth was formed first, the mountain-plain. The channels of water were separated; their branches wound their ways among the mountains. The waters were divided when the great mountains appeared.

Such was the formation of the earth when it was brought forth by the Heart of Sky, Heart of Earth, as they are called, since they were the first to think of it. The sky was set apart, and the earth was set apart in the midst of the waters.

Such was their plan when they thought, when they worried about the completion of their work.[9]

FROM PART 2

[The Twins Defeat Seven Macaw]

HERE IS THE BEGINNING OF THE DEFEAT AND DESTRUCTION OF THE DAY OF SEVEN MACAW by the two boys, the first named Hunahpu and the second named Xbalanque.[1] Being gods, the two of them saw evil in his attempt at self-magnification before the Heart of Sky.

* * *

This is the great tree of Seven Macaw, a nance,[2] and this is the food of Seven Macaw. In order to eat the fruit of the nance he goes up the tree every day. Since Hunahpu and Xbalanque have seen where he feeds, they are now hiding beneath the tree of Seven Macaw, they are keeping quiet here, the two boys are in the leaves of the tree.

And when Seven Macaw arrived, perching over his meal, the nance, it was then that he was shot by Hunahpu. The blowgun shot went right to his jaw, breaking his mouth. Then he went up over the tree and fell flat on the ground. Suddenly Hunahpu appeared, running. He set out to grab him, but actually it was the arm

---

8. ...Refers to the cutting of flesh with a knife....In the present context, it implies that "the mountains were separated from the water" through an act resembling the extraction of the heart (or other organs) from a sacrifice [translator's note].

9. That is, the creation of humans; an account of the first three, unsuccessful, attempts at creating humans occupies the remainder of part 1.

1. First mention of the twin hero gods (their origin is recounted in part 3). Here they confront the false god Seven Macaw, who has arisen during the time of primordial darkness, boasting, "My eyes are of metal; my teeth just glitter with jewels, and turquoise as well.... I am like the sun and the moon." Note that all the characters in parts 1, 2, and 3 are supernatural; humans are not created until part 4.

2. A pickle tree (Byrsonima crassifolia).

of Hunahpu that was seized by Seven Macaw. He yanked it straight back, he bent it back at the shoulder. Then Seven Macaw tore it right out of Hunahpu. Even so, the boys did well: the first round was not their defeat by Seven Macaw.

And when Seven Macaw had taken the arm of Hunahpu, he went home. Holding his jaw very carefully, he arrived:

"What have you got there?" said Chimalmat, the wife of Seven Macaw.

"What is it but those two tricksters! They've shot me, they've dislocated my jaw.[3] All my teeth are just loose, now they ache. But once what I've got is over the fire—hanging there, dangling over the fire—then they can just come and get it. They're real tricksters!" said Seven Macaw, then he hung up the arm of Hunahpu.

Meanwhile Hunahpu and Xbalanque were thinking. And then they invoked a grandfather, a truly white-haired grandfather, and a grandmother, a truly humble grandmother—just bent-over, elderly people. Great White Peccary is the name of the grandfather, and Great White Coati is the name of the grandmother.[4] The boys said to the grandmother and grandfather:

"Please travel with us when we go to get our arm from Seven Macaw; we'll just follow right behind you. You'll tell him:

'Do forgive us our grandchildren, who travel with us. Their mother and father are dead, and so they follow along there, behind us. Perhaps we should give them away, since all we do is pull worms out of teeth.' So we'll seem like children to Seven Macaw, even though *we're* giving *you* the instructions," the two boys told them.

"Very well," they replied.

After that they approached the place where Seven Macaw was in front of his home. When the grandmother and grandfather passed by, the two boys were romping along behind them. When they passed below the lord's house, Seven Macaw was yelling his mouth off because of his teeth. And when Seven Macaw saw the grandfather and grandmother traveling with them:

"Where are you headed, our grandfather?" said the lord.

"We're just making our living, your lordship," they replied.

"Why are you working for a living? Aren't those your children traveling with you?"

"No, they're not, your lordship. They're our grandchildren, our descendants, but it is nevertheless *we* who take pity on *them*. The bit of food they get is the portion we give them, your lordship," replied the grandmother and grandfather. Since the lord is getting done in by the pain in his teeth, it is only with great effort that he speaks again:

"I implore you, please take pity on me! What sweets can you make, what poisons[5] can you cure?" said the lord.

"We just pull the worms out of teeth, and we just cure eyes. We just set bones, your lordship," they replied.

"Very well, please cure my teeth. They really ache, every day. It's insufferable! I get no sleep because of them—and my eyes. They just shot me, those two tricksters! Ever since it started I haven't eaten because of it. Therefore take pity on me! Perhaps it's because my teeth are loose now."

---

3. This is the origin of the way a macaw's beak looks, with a huge upper mandible and a small, retreating lower one [translator's note].
4. Animal names of the divine grandparents,

Xpiyacoc and Xmucane, who are also the twins' genealogical grandparents.
5. Play on words as *qui* is translated as both "sweet" and "poison."

"Very well, your lordship. It's a worm, gnawing at the bone.[6] It's merely a matter of putting in a replacement and taking the teeth out, sir."

"But perhaps it's not good for my teeth to come out—since I am, after all, a lord. My finery is in my teeth—and my eyes."

"But then we'll put in a replacement. Ground bone will be put back in." And this is the "ground bone": it's only white corn.

"Very well. Yank them out! Give me some help here!" he replied.

And when the teeth of Seven Macaw came out, it was only white corn that went in as a replacement for his teeth—just a coating shining white, that corn in his mouth. His face fell at once, he no longer looked like a lord. The last of his teeth came out, the jewels that had stood out blue from his mouth.

And when the eyes of Seven Macaw were cured, he was plucked around the eyes, the last of his metal came off.[7] Still he felt no pain; he just looked on while the last of his greatness left him. It was just as Hunahpu and Xbalanque had intended.

And when Seven Macaw died, Hunahpu got back his arm. And Chimalmat, the wife of Seven Macaw, also died.

Such was the loss of the riches of Seven Macaw: only the doctors got the jewels and gems that had made him arrogant, here on the face of the earth. The genius of the grandmother, the genius of the grandfather did its work when they took back their arm: it was implanted and the break got well again. Just as they had wished the death of Seven Macaw, so they brought it about. They had seen evil in his self-magnification.

After this the two boys went on again. What they did was simply the word of the Heart of Sky.

FROM PART 3

[Victory over the Underworld]

AND NOW WE SHALL NAME THE NAME OF THE FATHER OF HUNAHPU AND XBAL-ANQUE. Let's drink to him, and let's just drink to the telling and accounting of the begetting of Hunahpu and Xbalanque. We shall tell just half of it, just a part of the account of their father. Here follows the account.

These are the names: One Hunahpu and Seven Hunahpu,[8] as they are called.

* * *

AND ONE AND SEVEN HUNAHPU WENT INSIDE DARK HOUSE.[9]

And then their torch was brought, only one torch, already lit, sent by One and Seven Death, along with a cigar for each of them, also already lit, sent by the lords. When these were brought to One and Seven Hunahpu they were

---

6. The present-day Quiché retain the notion that a toothache is caused by a worm gnawing at the bone [translator's note].

7. This is clearly meant to be the origin of the large white and completely featherless eye patches and very small eyes of the scarlet macaw [translator's note].

8. Twin sons of Xpiyacoc and Xmucane; the elder of these twins, One Hunahpu, will become the father of Hunahpu and Xbalanque. "As for Seven Hunahpu," according to

the text, "he has no wife. He's just a partner and just secondary; he just remains a boy."

9. The first of the "test" houses in Xibalba (the underworld) to which One and Seven Hunahpu, avid ballplayers, have been lured by the underworld lords, One and Seven Death; the lords have promised them a challenging ball game. The Mesoamerican ball game, remotely comparable to both basketball and soccer, was played on a rectangular court, using a ball of native rubber.

cowering, here in the dark. When the bearer of their torch and cigars arrived, the torch was bright as it entered; their torch and both of their cigars were burning. The bearer spoke:

"'They must be sure to return them in the morning—not finished, but just as they look now. They must return them intact,' the lords say to you," they were told, and they were defeated. They finished the torch and they finished the cigars that had been brought to them.

And Xibalba is packed with tests, heaps and piles of tests.

This is the first one: the Dark House, with darkness alone inside.

And the second is named Rattling House, heavy with cold inside, whistling with drafts, clattering with hail. A deep chill comes inside here.

And the third is named Jaguar House, with jaguars alone inside, jostling one another, crowding together, with gnashing teeth. They're scratching around; these jaguars are shut inside the house.

Bat House is the name of the fourth test, with bats alone inside the house, squeaking, shrieking, darting through the house. The bats are shut inside; they can't get out.

And the fifth is named Razor House, with blades alone inside. The blades are moving back and forth, ripping, slashing through the house.

These are the first tests of Xibalba, but One and Seven Hunahpu never entered into them, except for the one named earlier, the specified test house.

And when One and Seven Hunahpu went back before One and Seven Death, they were asked:

"Where are my cigars? What of my torch? They were brought to you last night!"

"We finished them, your lordship."

"Very well. This very day, your day is finished, you will die, you will disappear, and we shall break you off. Here you will hide your faces: you are to be sacrificed!" said One and Seven Death.

And then they were sacrificed and buried. They were buried at the Place of Ball Game Sacrifice,[1] as it is called. The head of One Hunahpu was cut off; only his body was buried with his younger brother.

"Put his head in the fork of the tree that stands by the road," said One and Seven Death.

And when his head was put in the fork of the tree, the tree bore fruit. It would not have had any fruit, had not the head of One Hunahpu been put in the fork of the tree.

This is the calabash tree, as we call it today, or "the skull of One Hunahpu," as it is said.

And then One and Seven Death were amazed at the fruit of the tree. The fruit grows out everywhere, and it isn't clear where the head of One Hunahpu is; now it looks just the way the calabashes look. All the Xibalbans see this, when they come to look.

The state of the tree loomed large in their thoughts, because it came about at the same time the head of One Hunahpu was put in the fork. The Xibalbans said among themselves:

---

1. Probably not a place name, but rather a name for the altar where losing ball players were sacrificed [translator's note].

"No one is to pick the fruit, nor is anyone to go beneath the tree," they said. They restricted themselves; all of Xibalba held back.

It isn't clear which is the head of One Hunahpu; now it's exactly the same as the fruit of the tree. Calabash came to be its name, and much was said about it. A maiden heard about it, and here we shall tell of her arrival.

AND HERE IS THE ACCOUNT OF A MAIDEN, the daughter of a lord named Blood Gatherer.[2]

And this is when a maiden heard of it, the daughter of a lord. Blood Gatherer is the name of her father, and Blood Moon is the name of the maiden.

And when he heard the account of the fruit of the tree, her father retold it. And she was amazed at the account:

"I'm not acquainted with that tree they talk about. '"Its fruit is truly sweet!" they say,' I hear," she said.

Next, she went all alone and arrived where the tree stood. It stood at the Place of Ball Game Sacrifice:

"What? Well! What's the fruit of this tree? Shouldn't this tree bear something sweet? They shouldn't die, they shouldn't be wasted. Should I pick one?" said the maiden.

And then the bone spoke; it was here in the fork of the tree:

"Why do you want a mere bone, a round thing in the branches of a tree?" said the head of One Hunahpu when it spoke to the maiden. "You don't want it," she was told.

"I do want it," said the maiden.

"Very well. Stretch out your right hand here, so I can see it," said the bone.

"Yes," said the maiden. She stretched out her right hand, up there in front of the bone.

And then the bone spit out its saliva, which landed squarely in the hand of the maiden.

And then she looked in her hand, she inspected it right away, but the bone's saliva wasn't in her hand.

"It is just a sign I have given you, my saliva, my spittle. This, my head, has nothing on it—just bone, nothing of meat. It's just the same with the head of a great lord: it's just the flesh that makes his face look good. And when he dies, people get frightened by his bones. After that, his son is like his saliva, his spittle, in his being, whether it be the son of a lord or the son of a craftsman, an orator. The father does not disappear, but goes on being fulfilled. Neither dimmed nor destroyed is the face of a lord, a warrior, craftsman, orator. Rather, he will leave his daughters and sons. So it is that I have done likewise through you. Now go up there on the face of the earth; you will not die. Keep the word. So be it," said the head of One and Seven Hunahpu—they were of one mind when they did it.

This was the word Hurricane, Newborn Thunderbolt, Sudden Thunderbolt had given them. In the same way, by the time the maiden returned to her home, she had been given many instructions. Right away something was generated in her belly, from the saliva alone, and this was the generation of Hunahpu and Xbalanque.

2. Fourth-ranking lord of Xibalba, whose commission is to draw blood from people.

And when the maiden got home and six months had passed, she was found out by her father. Blood Gatherer is the name of her father.

* * *

AND THEY CAME TO THE LORDS.[3] Feigning great humility, they bowed their heads all the way to the ground when they arrived. They brought themselves low, doubled over, flattened out, down to the rags, to the tatters. They really looked like vagabonds when they arrived.

So then they were asked what their mountain[4] and tribe were, and they were also asked about their mother and father:

"Where do you come from?" they were asked.

"We've never known, lord. We don't know the identity of our mother and father. We must've been small when they died," was all they said. They didn't give any names.

"Very well. Please entertain us, then. What do you want us to give you in payment?" they were asked.

"Well, we don't want anything. To tell the truth, we're afraid," they told the lord.

"Don't be afraid. Don't be ashamed. Just dance this way: first you'll dance to sacrifice yourselves, you'll set fire to my house after that, you'll act out all the things you know. We want to be entertained. This is our heart's desire, the reason you had to be sent for, dear vagabonds. We'll give you payment," they were told.

So then they began their songs and dances, and then all the Xibalbans arrived, the spectators crowded the floor, and they danced everything: they danced the Weasel, they danced the Poorwill,[5] they danced the Armadillo. Then the lord said to them:

"Sacrifice my dog, then bring him back to life again," they were told.

"Yes," they said.

> When they sacrificed the dog
>> he then came back to life.
> And that dog was really happy
>> when he came back to life.
> Back and forth he wagged his tail
>> when he came back to life.

And the lord said to them:

"Well, you have yet to set my home on fire," they were told next, so then they set fire to the home of the lord. The house was packed with all the lords, but they were not burned. They quickly fixed it back again, lest the house of One Death be consumed all at once, and all the lords were amazed, and they went on dancing this way. They were overjoyed.

And then they were asked by the lord:

"You have yet to kill a person! Make a sacrifice without death!" they were told.

"Very well," they said.

And then they took hold of a human sacrifice.

---

3. Forced to flee the underworld the maiden (Blood Moon) finds refuge on earth with Xmucane. There she gives birth to the twins, who, like their father and uncle, become ballplayers and are enticed to the underworld. Surviving the Dark House and other tests, they disguise themselves as vagabonds and earn a reputation as clever entertainers among the denizens of Xibalba; as such they are summoned to entertain the high lords.
4. A metonym for almost any settlement, but especially a fortified town or citadel, located on a defensible elevation [translator's note].
5. The goatsucker. The dances apparently were imitations of these animals and birds.

And they held up a human heart on high.

And they showed its roundness to the lords.

And now One and Seven Death admired it, and now that person was brought right back to life. His heart was overjoyed when he came back to life, and the lords were amazed:

"Sacrifice yet again, even do it to yourselves! Let's see it! At heart, that's the dance we really want from you," the lords said now.

"Very well, lord," they replied, and then they sacrificed themselves.

AND THIS IS THE SACRIFICE OF HUNAHPU BY XBALANQUE. One by one his legs, his arms were spread wide. His head came off, rolled far away outside. His heart, dug out, was smothered in a leaf,[6] and all the Xibalbans went crazy at the sight.

So now, only one of them was dancing there: Xbalanque.

"Get up!" he said, and Hunahpu came back to life. The two of them were overjoyed at this—and likewise the lords rejoiced, as if they were doing it themselves. One and Seven Death were as glad at heart as if they themselves were actually doing the dance.

And then the hearts of the lords were filled with longing, with yearning for the dance of little Hunahpu and Xbalanque, so then came these words from One and Seven Death:

"Do it to us! Sacrifice us!" they said. "Sacrifice both of us!" said One and Seven Death to Hunahpu and Xbalanque.

"Very well. You ought to come back to life. What is death to you?[7] And aren't we making you happy, along with the vassals of your domain?" they told the lords.

And this one was the first to be sacrificed: the lord at the very top, the one whose name is One Death, the ruler of Xibalba.

And with One Death dead, the next to be taken was Seven Death. They did not come back to life.

And then the Xibalbans were getting up to leave, those who had seen the lords die. They underwent heart sacrifice there, and the heart sacrifice was performed on the two lords only for the purpose of destroying them.

As soon as they had killed the one lord without bringing him back to life, the other lord had been meek and tearful before the dancers. He didn't consent, he didn't accept it:

"Take pity on me!" he said when he realized. All their vassals took the road to the great canyon, in one single mass they filled up the deep abyss. So they piled up there and gathered together, countless ants, tumbling down into the canyon, as if they were being herded there. And when they arrived, they all bent low in surrender, they arrived meek and tearful.

Such was the defeat of the rulers of Xibalba. The boys accomplished it only through wonders, only through self-transformation.

* * *

Such was the beginning of their disappearance and the denial of their worship.

---

6. As a tamale is wrapped. In the typical Mesoamerican heart sacrifice, the victim's arms and legs were stretched wide and the heart was excised and offered to a deity.

7. Evident sarcasm.

Their ancient day was not a great one,
these ancient people only wanted conflict,
their ancient names are not really divine,
but fearful is the ancient evil of their faces.

They are makers of enemies, users of owls,[8]
they are inciters to wrongs and violence,
they are masters of hidden intentions as well,
they are black and white,[9]
masters of stupidity, masters of perplexity,

as it is said. By putting on appearances they cause dismay.

Such was the loss of their greatness and brilliance. Their domain did not return to greatness. This was accomplished by little Hunahpu and Xbalanque.

FROM PART 4

[Origin of Humanity, First Dawn]

AND HERE IS THE BEGINNING OF THE CONCEPTION OF HUMANS, and of the search for the ingredients of the human body. So they spoke, the Bearer, Begetter, the Makers, Modelers named Sovereign Plumed Serpent:

"The dawn has approached, preparations have been made, and morning has come for the provider, nurturer, born in the light, begotten in the light. Morning has come for humankind, for the people of the face of the earth," they said. It all came together as they went on thinking in the darkness, in the night, as they searched and they sifted, they thought and they wondered.

And here their thoughts came out in clear light. They sought and discovered what was needed for human flesh. It was only a short while before the sun, moon, and stars were to appear above the Makers and Modelers. Split Place, Bitter Water Place is the name: the yellow corn, white corn came from there.

And these are the names of the animals who brought the food: fox, coyote, parrot, crow. There were four animals who brought the news of the ears of yellow corn and white corn. They were coming from over there at Split Place, they showed the way to the split.[1]

And this was when they found the staple foods.

And these were the ingredients for the flesh of the human work, the human design, and the water was for the blood. It became human blood, and corn was also used by the Bearer, Begetter.

And so they were happy over the provisions of the good mountain, filled with sweet things, thick with yellow corn, white corn, and thick with pataxte and cacao, countless zapotes, anonas, jocotes, nances, matasanos,[2] sweets—the rich foods filling up the citadel named Split Place, Bitter Water Place. All the edible fruits were there: small staples, great staples, small plants, great plants. The way was shown by the animals.

---

8. The lords had used owls as messengers to lure the ballplayers to Xibalba.
9. Contradictory, duplicitous.
1. In the widespread Mesoamerican story of the discovery of corn, one or more animals reveal that corn and other foods are hidden within a rock or a mountain, accessible through a cleft; in some versions the mountain is split apart by lightning.
2. Quincelike fruits of the tree *Casimiroa edulis*. Pataxte (*Theobroma bicolor*) is a species of cacao that is inferior to cacao proper (*T. cacao*). Zapotes are fruits of the sapota tree (*Lucuma mammosa*). Anonas are custard apples (genus *Anona*). Jocotes are yellow plumlike fruits of the tree *Spondias purpurea*.

And then the yellow corn and white corn were ground, and Xmucane did the grinding nine times. Corn was used, along with the water she rinsed her hands with, for the creation of grease; it became human fat when it was worked by the Bearer, Begetter, Sovereign Plumed Serpent, as they are called.

After that, they put it into words:

> the making, the modeling of our first mother-father,
> with yellow corn, white corn alone for the flesh,
> food alone for the human legs and arms,
> for our first fathers, the four human works.

It was staples alone that made up their flesh.

THESE ARE THE NAMES OF THE FIRST PEOPLE WHO WERE MADE AND MODELED.

> This is the first person: Jaguar Quitze.
> And now the second: Jaguar Night.
> And now the third: Not Right Now.
> And the fourth: Dark Jaguar.[3]

And these are the names of our first mother-fathers.[4] They were simply made and modeled, it is said; they had no mother and no father. We have named the men by themselves. No woman gave birth to them, nor were they begotten by the builder, sculptor, Bearer, Begetter. By sacrifice alone, by genius alone they were made, they were modeled by the Maker, Modeler, Bearer, Begetter, Sovereign Plumed Serpent. And when they came to fruition, they came out human:

> They talked and they made words.
> They looked and they listened.
> They walked, they worked.

They were good people, handsome, with looks of the male kind. Thoughts came into existence and they gazed; their vision came all at once. Perfectly they saw, perfectly they knew everything under the sky, whenever they looked. The moment they turned around and looked around in the sky, on the earth, everything was seen without any obstruction. They didn't have to walk around before they could see what was under the sky; they just stayed where they were.

As they looked, their knowledge became intense. Their sight passed through trees, through rocks, through lakes, through seas, through mountains, through plains. Jaguar Quitze, Jaguar Night, Not Right Now, and Dark Jaguar were truly gifted people.

And then they were asked by the builder and mason:

"What do you know about your being? Don't you look, don't you listen? Isn't your speech good, and your walk? So you must look, to see out under the sky. Don't you see the mountain-plain clearly? So try it," they were told.

And then they saw everything under the sky perfectly. After that, they thanked the Maker, Modeler:

> "Truly now,
> double thanks, triple thanks
> that we've been formed, we've been given
> our mouths, our faces,

---

3. The four original Quiché males.
4. That is, parents, although only the first three founded lineages; Dark Jaguar had no son.

> we speak, we listen,
> we wonder, we move,
> our knowledge is good, we've understood
> what is far and near,
> and we've seen what is great and small
> under the sky, on the earth.
> Thanks to you we've been formed,
> we've come to be made and modeled,
> our grandmother, our grandfather,"

they said when they gave thanks for having been made and modeled. They understood everything perfectly, they sighted the four sides, the four corners in the sky, on the earth, and this didn't sound good to the builder and sculptor:

"What our works and designs have said is no good:

'We have understood everything, great and small,' they say." And so the Bearer, Begetter took back their knowledge:

"What should we do with them now? Their vision should at least reach nearby, they should see at least a small part of the face of the earth, but what they're saying isn't good. Aren't they merely 'works' and 'designs' in their very names? Yet they'll become as great as gods, unless they procreate, proliferate at the sowing, the dawning, unless they increase."

"Let it be this way: now we'll take them apart just a little, that's what we need. What we've found out isn't good. Their deeds would become equal to ours, just because their knowledge reaches so far. They see everything," so said

> the Heart of Sky, Hurricane,
> Newborn Thunderbolt, Sudden Thunderbolt,
> Sovereign Plumed Serpent,
> Bearer, Begetter,
> Xpiyacoc, Xmucane,
> Maker, Modeler,

as they are called. And when they changed the nature of their works, their designs, it was enough that the eyes be marred by the Heart of Sky. They were blinded as the face of a mirror is breathed upon. Their vision flickered. Now it was only from close up that they could see what was there with any clarity.

And such was the loss of the means of understanding, along with the means of knowing everything, by the four humans. The root was implanted.

And such was the making, modeling of our first grandfather, our father, by the Heart of Sky, Heart of Earth.

AND THEN THEIR WIVES AND WOMEN CAME INTO BEING. Again, the same gods thought of it. It was as if they were asleep when they received them, truly beautiful women were there with Jaguar Quitze, Jaguar Night, Not Right Now, and Dark Jaguar. With their women there they really came alive. Right away they were happy at heart again, because of their wives.

Red Sea Turtle is the name of the wife of Jaguar Quitze.

Prawn House is the name of the wife of Jaguar Night.

Water Hummingbird is the name of the wife of Not Right Now.

Macaw House is the name of the wife of Dark Jaguar.

So these are the names of their wives, who became ladies of rank, giving birth to the people of the tribes, small and great.

* * *

AND HERE IS THE DAWNING AND SHOWING OF THE SUN, MOON, AND STARS. And Jaguar Quitze, Jaguar Night, Not Right Now, and Dark Jaguar were overjoyed when they saw the sun carrier.[5] It came up first. It looked brilliant when it came up, since it was ahead of the sun.

After that they unwrapped their copal[6] incense, which came from the east, and there was triumph in their hearts when they unwrapped it. They gave their heartfelt thanks with three kinds at once:

Mixtam Copal is the name of the copal brought by Jaguar Quitze.

Cauiztan Copal, next, is the name of the copal brought by Jaguar Night.

Godly Copal, as the next one is called, was brought by Not Right Now.

The three of them had their copal, and this is what they burned as they incensed the direction of the rising sun. They were crying sweetly as they shook their burning copal,[7] the precious copal.

After that they cried because they had yet to see and yet to witness the birth of the sun.

And then, when the sun came up, the animals, small and great, were happy. They all came up from the rivers and canyons; they waited on all the mountain peaks. Together they looked toward the place where the sun came out.

So then the puma and jaguar cried out, but the first to cry out was a bird, the parrot by name. All the animals were truly happy. The eagle, the white vulture, small birds, great birds spread their wings, and the penitents and sacrificers knelt down.

FROM PART 5

[Prayer for Future Generations]

AND THIS IS THE CRY OF THEIR HEARTS, HERE IT IS:

> "Wait! On this blessed day,
> thou Hurricane, thou Heart of the Sky-Earth,
> thou giver of ripeness and freshness,
> and thou giver of daughters and sons,
> spread thy stain, spill thy drops
> of green and yellow;[8]
> give life and beginning
> to those I bear and beget,
> that they might multiply and grow,
> nurturing and providing for thee,
> calling to thee along the roads and paths,
> on rivers, in canyons,
> beneath the trees and bushes;
> give them their daughters and sons.
>
> "May there be no blame, obstacle, want or misery;
> let no deceiver come behind or before them,
> may they neither be snared nor wounded,
> nor seduced, nor burned,

---

5. The morning star.
6. Resin used as incense.
7. Note that the Mesoamerican pottery censer must be shaken or swayed back and forth to keep the incense burning.
8. The imagery, denoting human offspring, alludes to semen and plant growth.

nor diverted below the road nor above it;
may they neither fall over backward nor stumble;
keep them on the Green Road, the Green Path.

"May there be no blame or barrier for them
through any secrets or sorcery of thine;
may thy nurturers and providers be good
before thy mouth and thy face,
thou, Heart of Sky; thou, Heart of Earth;
thou, Bundle of Flames;[9]
and thou, Tohil, Auilix, Hacauitz,[1]
under the sky, on the earth,
the four sides, the four corners;
may there be only light, only continuity within,
before thy mouth and thy face, thou god."

9. A sacred relic left to the Quiché lords by Jaguar Quitze; like the sacred bundles of the North American peoples, a cloth-wrapped ark with mysterious contents [translator's note].
1. Patron deities of the Quiché lineages.

WILLIAM SHAKESPEARE
1564–1616

Hamlet portrays the doubts and fears of a conflicted prince whose dead father places on him the most burdensome of obligations: to avenge the king's murder by none other than his brother, Hamlet's uncle Claudius, who has married the recently widowed queen, Gertrude. Hamlet's personal tragedy is also that of Denmark, a state left rudderless by the domestic and familial conflicts of the play. Rich though it may be in plot, the most striking thing about *Hamlet* is its representation of the main character's interiority. Balancing the public and the private, Shakespeare gives the audience intimate access to the prince's mind, by transforming his thoughts into powerful dialogue and unprecedented soliloquies. Using older dramatic forms such as revenge tragedy, Shakespeare forged an entirely new type of play that depicts the inner doubts and hesitations of his quintessential protagonist.

LIFE AND TIMES

William Shakespeare was born in the rural community of Stratford-upon-Avon in Warwickshire. His father, John Shakespeare, was a glover and, when William was born, prominent in the town's government. Little is known of Shakespeare's early life, although it is likely that he received an education at the good local grammar school. He married Anne Hathaway, about seven years his senior, when he was eighteen. The couple had three children, Susanna (1583) and the twins Judith and Hamnet (1585).

Shakespeare lived in a period of great nationalist fervor. Under Queen Elizabeth I (1533–1603, ruled 1558–1603), a successful and much beloved ruler, England solidified its sense of itself as a small but heroic Protestant nation valiantly resisting the encroachment of Spain and other enemies. In 1587, fearing a Catholic conspiracy, Elizabeth put to death her cousin, Mary Queen of Scots, who had sought refuge in England in 1568. Even after a powerful storm scattered the Spanish Armada, the fleet sent to invade England in 1588, the nation continued to fear Spanish invasion and Catholic plots against Elizabeth. The sense of a state under siege in *Hamlet* would thus have echoed powerfully for the English, just as they would have recognized the public tragedy of a nation undone by its rulers' outsized appetites for power. The play's reliance on the truth spoken by a ghost trapped in Purgatory—Catholic notions rejected by Protestantism—is also striking in a period that saw both the strong official repudiation of Catholicism and an enduring popular attachment to its rituals.

After a youth spent in the provinces, by 1592 Shakespeare had made his way to the burgeoning city of London. There he rapidly became the "greatest shake-scene" around, in the irritated words of a rival who envied Shakespeare's ability to impress audiences despite his lack of a university education. Shakespeare soon became a shareholder in a prominent players' company that claimed the Lord Chamberlain as patron and the tragic actor Richard Burbage and the comedian Will Kempe as members. Shakespeare's company originally performed at the theatre, north of the city of London, where its actor-owner, James Burbage, faced steady opposition from puritanical city officials who sought to close the theaters, which they considered to be hotbeds of immorality. Burbage conceived of a means to escape civic legislation against theatrical performances, and secretly moved the boards of his playhouse across the river Thames to the south bank; with these planks he constructed the Globe, the theater most often associated with Shakespeare's name.

The Globe was open to all social classes: anyone who wished could enter the theater by paying a penny, and at the cost of another, get a bench, cushion, and protection (in the boxes) from inclement weather. This mixing of social classes in his audience was echoed in Shakespeare's plays: rather than submitting to the stricter forms of classical drama, Shakespeare mixed comic routines with tragic soliloquies, the speech of common soldiers and bawds with the elegant language of the court. The Globe used almost no scenery and few stage props, so Shakespeare had to evoke the scene through language and deploy stage props sparingly. Only the costumes were lavish and constituted one of the most valuable possessions of the company. Shakespeare knew the theater inside out and his plays used its resources to the fullest, including sudden entrances and concealed eavesdroppers, brutal swordfights and touching love scenes, and witty asides and striking double entendres.

Although he began his career as a player, Shakespeare found his calling as a playwright and his fortune as a shareholder in his company. His financial successes enabled him to purchase the title of gentleman for his father, a purchase that made Shakespeare himself officially a "gentleman born," and a fine house in Stratford to which he eventually retired. Despite the unparalleled success of his plays, Shakespeare seems to have valued them only in performance, and never sought to have them printed. Early versions of the plays were often published in unauthorized versions, in some cases on the basis of actors' recollections of their lines. After Shakespeare's death in 1616, his friends published most of his plays in the collection we know as the "First Folio" (1623), the basis for most later editions.

HAMLET

Shakespeare's plays constitute the most important body of dramatic work in the modern world, and no character in literature is more familiar to audiences around the globe than Hamlet. Beyond the impact of the protagonist, *Hamlet* has commanded a leading place in our literary heritage for juxtaposing political obligation and human limitations, idealized virtue and actual experience. Though it is a drama about characters of superior station and the conflicts and problems associated with men and women of high degree, it reveals these problems in a particular family, but presents the domestic conflict within the larger world of politics— like the plays of antiquity that deal with the Theban myth, such as **Oedipus the King** or *Antigone*. Shakespeare underscores the humanity and frailty of rulers, providing a window into their interiority, whether it be the portrayal of a villainous king in *Richard III* or of a frail and diminished one in *King Lear*. The vulnerability of Hamlet, the disproportion between the heroism demanded of him and the response he can muster, and his acute awareness of how he fails all make him a singularly compelling figure. Leavened with odd moments of black humor, the portrayal of Hamlet's exquisitely self-conscious dilemma amid the increasingly dangerous and opaque machinations of his uncle's court is gripping and casts doubt on dynastic rule itself.

Based on a medieval Scandinavian legend, Shakespeare's play brings the figure of the hero who feigns madness much closer to his own time. In spite of the Danish locale and the relatively remote period of the action, the setting of *Hamlet* is plainly a Renaissance court.

There is a ruler holding power, and much of the action is related to questions concerning the nature of that power—the way in which he had acquired it and the ways in which it can be preserved. Around the king are several courtiers, among whom Hamlet, the heir apparent, is only the most prominent. The sense of outside dangers and internal disruption everywhere frames the personal story of Hamlet, of his revenge, and of Claudius's crime. These individual stories are signs of a general societal breakdown. The play charts a kingdom and a society going to pieces, and the realization by its most privileged subjects that it has already crumbled. Lurking behind it all is a sense of the vanity of those forms of human endeavor and power of which the kingdom and the court are symbols.

The tone Shakespeare wants to establish is evident from the opening scenes: the night air is full of premonitions; sentinels turn their eyes toward the threatening outside world; meanwhile, the Ghost has already made his appearance, a sinister omen. The kingdom is presented in terms that are an almost point-by-point reversal of the ideal. Claudius, whether we believe the Ghost's indictment or not (Hamlet does not necessarily, and some of his famous indecision has been attributed to his seeking evidence of the Ghost's truthfulness before acting), has by marrying the queen committed an act that by Elizabethan standards is incestuous. There is an overwhelming sense of disintegration in the body of the state, evident in the first court assembly and in all subsequent ones. Instead of supporting the throne, the two most promising courtiers, Hamlet and Laertes, are restless presences, contemplating departure from a troubled scene.

Decadent and overwrought, the court is marked by semblance instead of substance. Thus Polonius, who after Hamlet is the major figure in the king's retinue, is presented satirically in his empty formalities and conventional behavior. Often, as with the minor figure of Osric, manners are replaced by mannerisms. Courtly life as depicted in the play suggests always the hollow, the fractured, and the crooked. The traditional forms and institutions of gentle living and all the pomp and solemnity of the court are marred by corruption and distortion. Courtship and love are reduced to Hamlet's mockery of Ophelia, and all but undone by the punning undercurrents of bawdiness. In the famous play-within-the-play, the theater, a traditional institution of court life, is used by the hero as a device to expose the king's crime. There are elements of macabre caricature in Shakespeare's treatment of the solemn theme of death, as in the black comedy of Polonius's death, or the clownish talk of the gravediggers. Finally, the arms tournament, the typical occasion for the display of courtiers' gallantry in front of their king, is here turned by the scheming of the king himself into an almost farcical scene of carnage.

This sense of corruption and decadence dominates the temper of the play and situates Hamlet, his indecision, and his sense of vanity and disenchantment with the world in which he must live. In Hamlet the relationship between thought and deed, intent and realization, is confused, while all around him the norms and institutions that regulate a well-ordered court have been replaced by duplicity and dissimulation. He and the king are "mighty opposites," and it can be argued that against Hamlet's indecision and negativism the king presents a more positive scheme of action, at least in the purely Machiavellian sense, at the level of practical power politics. On various occasions the king shows a high and competent conception of his office: a culminating instance is the courageous and cunning way in which he confronts and handles

Laertes' wrath. Since his life is obviously threatened by Hamlet (who was seeking to kill him when by mistake he killed Polonius instead), one might argue that the king acts within a legitimate pattern of politics in wanting to have Hamlet liquidated. Yet this argument cannot be carried so far as to demonstrate that he represents a fully positive attitude toward life and the world, even in the strictly amoral terms of political technique. For in fact his action is corroded by the vexations of his own conscience. Despite his energy and his extrovert qualities, he too becomes part of the negative picture of disruption and lacks concentration of purpose. The images of decay and putrescence that characterize his court extend to his own speech: his "offense," in his own words, "smells to heaven."

Hamlet as a Renaissance tragedy presents a world particularly "out of joint," a world that, having long ago lost the sense of a grand timeless design that was so important in medieval times (to Hamlet the thought of the afterlife is even more puzzling and dark than that of this life), looks with an even greater sense of disenchantment at the temporal world symbolized by the kingdom and the court. They could have given individual action a purposeful meaning. Yet now their order has been destroyed, and ideals that once had power and freshness have lost their vigor under the impact of satiety, doubt, and melancholy.

Because communal values are so degraded, it is natural to ask in the end whether some alternative attempt at a settlement could be imagined, with Hamlet—like other Renaissance heroes—adopting an individual code of conduct, however extravagant. On the whole, Hamlet seems too steeped in his own hopelessness and in the courtly mechanism to which he inevitably belongs to be able to find personal intellectual and moral compromise or his own version of escape. Still, the tone of his brooding and often moralizing speech, his melancholy and dissatisfaction, his very desire for revenge imply a nostalgia for a world—associated with his father—of loyal allegiances and ideals of honor. Yet in *Hamlet* the political world turns out to offer no protection for the values—friendship, loyalty, and honesty—that Hamlet himself most cherishes. This is perhaps the reason why Hamlet has struck many later readers as a representative modern, someone forced to make his way in a world no longer ordered by traditional institutions.

The influence of Shakespeare's plays on the course of English literature is matched only by the King James translation of the Bible. In his time, Shakespeare garnered the interest of two British monarchs (Elizabeth I and James I), the love of popular audiences, and the respect of such tough critics as the poet and playwright Ben Jonson, who saw him as "the Soule of the Age" yet recognized that he was "Not of an age, but for all time!" *Hamlet* has always been one of Shakespeare's best loved and most widely produced plays. A tantalizing window into an inscrutable interiority, the play has fascinated thinkers and writers from Sigmund Freud, who offered it as an example of the Oedipal complex, to Tom Stoppard, who portrayed the absurdity of the minor characters with great humor in his *Rosencrantz and Guildenstern Are Dead* (1966).

Hamlet, Prince of Denmark

CHARACTERS

Claudius, KING *of Denmark*
HAMLET, *son to the late, and nephew to the present king*
POLONIUS, *lord chamberlain*
HORATIO, *friend to Hamlet*
LAERTES, *son of Polonius*
PRIEST
SERVANT
MARCELLUS, ⎱ *officers*
BERNARDO, ⎰
FRANCISCO, *a soldier*
REYNALDO, *servant to Polonius*
PLAYERS
TWO CLOWNS, *grave-diggers*
FORTINBRAS, *prince of Norway*
CAPTAIN

VOLTIMAND,
CORNELIUS,
ROSENCRANTZ,
GUILDENSTERN, ⎬ *courtiers*
OSRIC,
GENTLEMEN,
ENGLISH AMBASSADORS
Gertrude, QUEEN *of Denmark, and mother to Hamlet*
OPHELIA, *daughter of Polonius*
LORDS, *Ladies, Officers, Soldiers,* SAILORS, MESSENGERS, *and Other Attendants*
GHOST *of Hamlet's father*
DANES

[SCENE: *Denmark.*]

Act 1

SCENE I

[SCENE: *Elsinore. A platform before the castle.*]

[FRANCISCO *at his post. Enter to him* BERNARDO.]

BERNARDO Who's there?
FRANCISCO Nay, answer me: stand, and unfold yourself.

BERNARDO   Long live the king!

FRANCISCO   Bernardo?

BERNARDO   He.   5

FRANCISCO   You come most carefully upon your hour.

BERNARDO   'Tis now struck twelve; get thee to bed, Francisco.

FRANCISCO   For this relief much thanks: 'tis bitter cold,
And I am sick at heart.

BERNARDO   Have you had quiet guard?

FRANCISCO   Not a mouse stirring.   10

BERNARDO   Well, good night.
If you do meet Horatio and Marcellus,
The rivals[1] of my watch, bid them make haste.

FRANCISCO   I think I hear them. Stand, ho! Who is there?

     [*Enter* HORATIO *and* MARCELLUS.]

HORATIO   Friends to this ground.

MARCELLUS   And liegemen to the Dane.[2]   15

FRANCISCO   Give you good night.

MARCELLUS   O, farewell, honest soldier:
Who hath relieved you?

FRANCISCO   Bernardo hath my place.
Give you good night.

     [*Exit.*]

MARCELLUS   Holla! Bernardo!

BERNARDO   Say,
What, is Horatio there?

HORATIO   A piece of him.

BERNARDO   Welcome, Horatio; welcome, good Marcellus.   20

MARCELLUS   What, has this thing appeared again to-night?

BERNARDO   I have seen nothing.

MARCELLUS   Horatio says 'tis but our fantasy,
And will not let belief take hold of him
Touching this dreaded sight, twice seen of us: 25
Therefore I have entreated him along
With us to watch the minutes of this night,
That if again this apparition come,
He may approve our eyes[3] and speak to it.

HORATIO   Tush, tush, 'twill not appear.

BERNARDO   Sit down a while;   30
And let us once again assail your ears,
That are so fortified against our story,
What we have two nights seen.

HORATIO   Well, sit we down,
And let us hear Bernardo speak of this.

BERNARDO   Last night of all,   35
When yond same star that's westward from the pole
Had made his course to illume that part of heaven

---

1. Partners.
2. The king of Denmark.

3. Confirm what we saw.

Where now it burns, Marcellus and myself,
The bell then beating one,—

    [Enter GHOST.*]*

MARCELLUS   Peace, break thee off; look, where it comes again!   40

BERNARDO   In the same figure, like the king that's dead.

MARCELLUS   Thou art a scholar; speak to it, Horatio.

BERNARDO   Looks it not like the king? mark it, Horatio.

HORATIO   Most like it: it harrows me with fear and wonder.

BERNARDO   It would be spoke to.

MARCELLUS   Question it, Horatio.   45

HORATIO   What art thou, that usurp'st this time of night,
Together with that fair and warlike form
In which the majesty of buried Denmark[4]
Did sometimes[4] march? by heaven I charge thee, speak!

MARCELLUS   It is offended.

BERNARDO   See, it stalks away!   50

HORATIO   Stay! speak, speak! I charge thee, speak!

    [Exit GHOST.*]*

MARCELLUS   'Tis gone, and will not answer.

BERNARDO   How now, Horatio! you tremble and look pale:
Is not this something more than fantasy?
What think you on 't?   55

HORATIO   Before my God, I might not this believe
Without the sensible and true avouch
Of mine own eyes.

MARCELLUS   Is it not like the king?

HORATIO   As thou art to thyself:
Such was the very armor he had on   60
When he the ambitious Norway[5] combated;
So frown'd he once, when, in an angry parle,
He smote the sledded[6] Polacks on the ice.
'Tis strange.

MARCELLUS   Thus twice before, and jump[7] at this dead hour,   65
With martial stalk hath he gone by our watch.

HORATIO   In what particular thought to work I know not;
But, in the gross and scope of my opinion,[8]
This bodes some strange eruption to our state.

MARCELLUS   Good now, sit down, and tell me, he that knows,   70
Why this same strict and most observant watch
So nightly toils the subject[9] of the land,
And why such daily cast of brazen cannon,
And foreign mart for implements of war;
Why such impress of shipwrights,[1] whose sore task   75
Does not divide the Sunday from the week;

4. Formerly, "Denmark": the king of Denmark.
5. The king of Norway (the elder Fortinbras).
6. They travel in sledges. "Parle": parley.
7. Just.
8. Taking a general view.
9. The people.
1. Ship carpenters. "Mart": trading. "Impress": pressing into service.

What might be toward,[2] that this sweaty haste
Doth make the night joint-laborer with the day:
Who is't that can inform me?

HORATIO   That can I;
At least the whisper goes so. Our last king,   80
Whose image even but now appear'd to us,
Was, as you know, by Fortinbras of Norway,
Thereto pricked on by a most emulate pride,
Dared to the combat; in which our valiant Hamlet—
For so this side of our known world esteem'd him—   85
Did slay this Fortinbras; who by a seal'd compact
Well ratified by law and heraldry,[3]
Did forfeit, with his life, all those his lands
Which he stood seized of, to the conqueror:
Against the which, a moiety competent   90
Was gagèd[4] by our king; which had returned
To the inheritance of Fortinbras,
Had he been vanquisher; as, by the same covenant
And carriage[5] of the article design'd,
His fell to Hamlet. Now, sir, young Fortinbras,   95
Of unimprovèd metal hot and full,
Hath in the skirts[6] of Norway here and there
Shark'd up a list of lawless resolutes,
For food and diet, to some enterprise
That hath a stomach in 't:[7] which is no other—   100
As it doth well appear unto our state—
But to recover of us, by strong hand
And terms compulsatory, those foresaid lands
So by his father lost: and this, I take it,
Is the main motive of our preparations,   105
The source of this our watch and the chief head
Of this post-haste and romage[8] in the land.

BERNARDO   I think it be no other but e'en so:
Well may it sort,[9] that this portentous figure
Comes armèd through our watch, so like the king   110
That was and is the question of these wars.

HORATIO   A mote it is to trouble the mind's eye.
In the most high and palmy state of Rome,
A little ere the mightiest Julius fell,
The graves stood tenantless, and the sheeted dead   115
Did squeak and gibber in the Roman streets:
As stars with trains of fire and dews of blood,
Disasters in the sun; and the moist star,

---

2. Impending.
3. Duly ratified and proclaimed through heralds.
4. Pledged. "Seized": possessed. "Moiety competent": equal share.
5. Purport.

6. Outskirts, border regions. "Unimprovèd": untested.
7. Calls for courage.
8. Bustle. "Head": origin, cause.
9. Fit with the other signs of war.

Upon whose influence Neptune's empire stands,[1]
Was sick almost to doomsday with eclipse: 120
And even the like precurse[2] of fierce events,
As harbingers preceding still the fates
And prologue to the omen coming on,
Have heaven and earth together demonstrated
Unto our climatures[3] and countrymen. 125
      [*Re-enter* GHOST.]
But soft, behold! lo, where it comes again!
I'll cross it, though it blast me. Stay, illusion!
If thou hast any sound, or use of voice,
Speak to me:
If there be any good thing to be done, 130
That may to thee do ease and grace to me,
Speak to me:
If thou art privy to thy country's fate,
Which, happily, foreknowing may avoid,
O, speak! 135
Or if thou hast uphoarded in thy life
Extorted treasure in the womb of earth,
For which, they say, you spirits oft walk in death,
Speak of it: stay, and speak! [*The cock crows.*] Stop it, Marcellus.
MARCELLUS   Shall I strike at it with my partisan? 140
HORATIO   Do, if it will not stand.
BERNARDO   'Tis here!
HORATIO   'Tis here!
      [*Exit* GHOST.]
MARCELLUS   'Tis gone!
We do it wrong, being so majestical,
To offer it the show of violence;
For it is, as the air, invulnerable, 145
And our vain blows malicious mockery.
BERNARDO   It was about to speak, when the cock crew.
HORATIO   And then it started like a guilty thing
Upon a fearful summons. I have heard
The cock, that is the trumpet to the morn, 150
Doth with his lofty and shrill-sounding throat
Awake the god of day, and at his warning,
Whether in sea or fire, in earth or air,
The extravagant[4] and erring spirit hies
To his confine: and of the truth herein 155
This present object made probation.[5]
MARCELLUS   It faded on the crowing of the cock.
Some say that ever 'gainst[6] that season comes

1. The moon (*moist star*) regulates the sea's
tides. "Disasters": ill omens.
2. Foreboding.
3. Regions.

4. Wandering out of its confines.
5. Gave proof.
6. Just before.

Wherein our Saviour's birth is celebrated,
The bird of dawning singeth all night long: 160
And then, they say, no spirit dare stir abroad,
The nights are wholesome, then no planets strike,
No fairy takes nor witch hath power to charm,
So hallowèd and so gracious[7] is the time.
HORATIO   So have I heard and do in part believe it.   165
But look, the morn, in russet mantle clad,
Walks o'er the dew of yon high eastward hill:
Break we our watch up; and by my advice,
Let us impart what we have seen to-night
Unto young Hamlet; for, upon my life,   170
This spirit, dumb to us, will speak to him:
Do you consent we shall acquaint him with it,
As needful in our loves, fitting our duty?
MARCELLUS   Let's do 't, I pray; and I this morning know
Where we shall find him most conveniently.   175
    [*Exeunt.*]

SCENE 2

[SCENE: *A room of state in the castle.*]

    [*Flourish. Enter the* KING, QUEEN, HAMLET, POLONIUS, LAERTES,
    VOLTIMAND, CORNELIUS, LORDS, *and attendants.*]

KING   Though yet of Hamlet our dear brother's death
The memory be green, and that it us befitted
To bear our hearts in grief and our whole kingdom
To be contracted in one brow of woe,
Yet so far hath discretion[8] fought with nature   5
That we with wisest sorrow think on him,
Together with remembrance of ourselves.
Therefore our sometime sister, now our queen,
The imperial jointress to this warlike state,
Have we, as 'twere with a defeated joy,—   10
With an auspicious and a dropping eye,
With mirth in funeral and with dirge in marriage,
In equal scale weighing delight and dole,—
Taken to wife: nor have we herein barr'd[9]
Your better wisdoms, which have freely gone   15
With this affair along. For all, our thanks.
Now follows, that[1] you know, young Fortinbras,
Holding a weak supposal of our worth,
Or thinking by our late dear brother's death
Our state to be disjoint and out of frame,   20
Colleaguèd with this dream[2] of his advantage,

---

7. Full of blessing. "Strike": exercise evil
influence (compare *moonstruck*). "Fairy takes":
bewitches.
8. Restraint (on grief).

9. Ignored. "Dole": grief.
1. What.
2. Combined with this fantastic notion.

He hath not failed to pester us with message,
Importing the surrender of those lands
Lost by his father, with all bonds of law,
To our most valiant brother. So much for him   25
Now for ourself, and for this time of meeting:
Thus much the business is: we have here writ
To Norway, uncle of young Fortinbras,—
Who, impotent and bed-rid, scarcely hears
Of this his nephew's purpose,—to suppress   30
His further gait herein; in that the levies,
The lists and full proportions,[3] are all made
Out of his subject: and we here dispatch
You, good Cornelius, and you, Voltimand,
For bearers of this greeting to old Norway,   35
Giving to you no further personal power
To business with the king more than the scope
Of these delated[4] articles allow.
Farewell, and let your haste commend your duty.

CORNELIUS
VOLTIMAND   } In that and all things will we show our duty.   40

KING   We doubt it nothing: heartily farewell.
      [*Exeunt* VOLTIMAND *and* CORNELIUS.]
And now, Laertes, what's the news with you?
You told us of some suit; what is 't, Laertes?
You cannot speak of reason to the Dane,
And lose your voice: what wouldst thou beg, Laertes, 45
That shall not be my offer, not thy asking?
The head is not more native to[5] the heart,
The hand more instrumental to the mouth,
Than is the throne of Denmark to thy father.
What wouldst thou have, Laertes?

LAERTES   My dread lord,   50
Your leave and favor to return to France,
From whence though willingly I came to Denmark,
To show my duty in your coronation,
Yet now, I must confess, that duty done,
My thoughts and wishes bend again toward France   55
And bow them to your gracious leave and pardon.

KING   Have you your father's leave? What says Polonius?
POLONIUS   He hath, my lord, wrung from me my slow leave
By laborsome petition, and at last
Upon his will I sealed my hard consent: 60
I do beseech you, give him leave to go.

KING   Take thy fair hour, Laertes; time be thine,
And thy best graces spend it at thy will!
But now, my cousin Hamlet, and my son,—

---

3. Amounts of forces and supplies. "Gait":   4. Detailed.
proceeding.   5. Naturally bound to.

HAMLET [*Aside.*]   A little more than kin, and less than kind.   65
KING   How is it that the clouds still hang on you?
HAMLET   Not so, my lord; I am too much i' the sun.[6]
QUEEN   Good Hamlet, cast thy nighted color off,
And let thine eye look like a friend on Denmark.
Do not for ever with thy vailèd[7] lids   70
Seek for thy noble father in the dust:
Thou know'st 'tis common; all that lives must die,
Passing through nature to eternity.
HAMLET   Aye, madam, it is common.
QUEEN   If it be,
Why seems it so particular with thee?   75
HAMLET   Seems, madam! nay, it is; I know not "seems."
'Tis not alone my inky cloak, good mother,
Nor customary suits of solemn black,
Nor windy suspiration of forced breath,
No, nor the fruitful river in the eye,   80
Nor the dejected havior of the visage,
Together with all forms, moods, shapes of grief,
That can denote me truly: these indeed seem,
For they are actions that a man might play:
But I have that within which passeth show;   85
These but the trappings and the suits of woe.
KING   'Tis sweet and commendable in your nature, Hamlet,
To give these mourning duties to your father:
But, you must know, your father lost a father,
That father lost, lost his, and the survivor bound   90
In filial obligation for some term
To do obsequious[8] sorrow: but to persevere
In obstinate condolement is a course
Of impious stubbornness; 'tis unmanly grief:
It shows a will most incorrect[9] to heaven,   95
A heart unfortified, a mind impatient,
An understanding simple and unschool'd:
For what we know must be and is as common
As any the most vulgar thing to sense,
Why should we in our peevish opposition   100
Take it to heart? Fie! 'tis a fault to heaven,
A fault against the dead, a fault to nature,
To reason most absurd, whose common theme
Is death of fathers, and who still hath cried,
From the first corse till he that died to-day,   105
"This must be so." We pray you, throw to earth
This unprevailing[1] woe, and think of us

6. The cue to Hamlet's irony is given by the King's "my cousin . . . my son" (line 64). Hamlet is punning on *son.*
7. Downcast.

8. Dutiful, especially concerning funeral rites (obsequies).
9. Not subdued.
1. Useless.

As of a father: for let the world take note,
You are the most immediate to our throne,
And with no less nobility of love   110
Than that which dearest father bears his son
Do I impart toward you. For your intent
In going back to school in Wittenberg,
It is most retrograde[2] to our desire:
And we beseech you, bend you to remain   115
Here in the cheer and comfort of our eye,
Our chiefest courtier, cousin and our son.
QUEEN   Let not thy mother lose her prayers, Hamlet:
    I pray thee, stay with us; go not to Wittenberg.
HAMLET   I shall in all my best obey you, madam.   120
KING   Why, 'tis a loving and a fair reply:
    Be as ourself in Denmark. Madam, come;
    This gentle and unforced accord of Hamlet
    Sits smiling to my heart: in grace whereof,
    No jocund health that Denmark drinks to-day,   125
    But the great cannon to the clouds shall tell,
    And the king's rouse the heaven shall bruit[3] again,
    Re-speaking earthly thunder. Come away.
        [Flourish. Exeunt all but HAMLET.]
HAMLET   O, that this too too sullied flesh would melt,
    Thaw and resolve itself into a dew!   130
    Or that the Everlasting had not fixed
    His canon[4] 'gainst self-slaughter! O God! God!
    How weary, stale, flat and unprofitable
    Seem to me all the uses of this world!
    Fie on 't! ah fie! 'tis an unweeded garden,   135
    That grows to seed; things rank and gross in nature
    Possess it merely. That it should come to this!
    But two months dead! nay, not so much, not two:
    So excellent a king; that was, to this,
    Hyperion to a satyr: so loving to my mother,   140
    That he might not beteem[5] the winds of heaven
    Visit her face too roughly. Heaven and earth!
    Must I remember? why, she would hang on him,
    As if increase of appetite had grown
    By what it fed on: and yet, within a month—   145
    Let me not think on't—Frailty, thy name is woman!—
    A little month, or ere those shoes were old
    With which she followed my poor father's body,
    Like Niobe,[6] all tears:—why she, even she,—

2. Opposed. "Wittenberg": the seat of a university; at the peak of fame in Shakespeare's time because of its connection with Martin Luther.
3. Proclaim, echo. "Rouse": carousal, revel.
4. Law.
5. Allow. "Hyperion": the sun god.

6. A proud mother who boasted of having more children than Leto; her seven sons and seven daughters were slain by Apollo and Artemis, children of Leto. The grieving Niobe was changed by Zeus into a continually weeping stone.

O God! a beast that wants discourse[7] of reason 150
Would have mourned longer,—married with my uncle,
My father's brother, but no more like my father
Than I to Hercules: within a month;
Ere yet the salt of most unrighteous tears
Had left the flushing in her gallèd[8] eyes, 155
She married. O, most wicked speed, to post
With such dexterity to incestuous sheets![9]
It is not, nor it cannot come to good:
But break, my heart, for I must hold my tongue!

       [*Enter* HORATIO, MARCELLUS, *and* BERNARDO.]

HORATIO   Hail to your lordship!
HAMLET   I am glad to see you well: 160
   Horatio,—or I do forget myself.
HORATIO   The same, my lord, and your poor servant ever.
HAMLET   Sir, my good friend; I'll change[1] that name with you:
   And what make you from Wittenberg, Horatio?
   Marcellus? 165
MARCELLUS   My good lord?
HAMLET   I am very glad to see you. [*To* BERNARDO.] Good even, sir.
   But what, in faith, make you from Wittenberg?
HORATIO   A truant disposition, good my lord.
HAMLET   I would not hear your enemy say so, 170
   Nor shall you do my ear that violence,
   To make it truster of your own report
   Against yourself: I know you are no truant.
   But what is your affair in Elsinore?
   We'll teach you to drink deep ere you depart. 175
HORATIO   My lord, I came to see your father's funeral.
HAMLET   I pray thee, do not mock me, fellow-student;
   I think it was to see my mother's wedding.
HORATIO   Indeed, my lord, it followed hard upon.
HAMLET   Thrift, thrift, Horatio! the funeral baked-meats 180
   Did coldly furnish forth the marriage tables.
   Would I had met my dearest[2] foe in heaven
   Or ever I had seen that day, Horatio!
   My father!—methinks I see my father.
HORATIO   O where, my lord?
HAMLET   In my mind's eye, Horatio. 185
HORATIO   I saw him once; he was a goodly king.
HAMLET   He was a man, take him for all in all,
   I shall not look upon his like again.
HORATIO   My lord, I think I saw him yesternight.
HAMLET   Saw? who? 190

---

7. Lacks the faculty.
8. Inflamed.
9. According to principles that Hamlet accepts,

marrying one's brother's widow is incest.
1. Exchange.
2. Bitterest.

HORATIO   My lord, the king your father.

HAMLET   The king my father!

HORATIO   Season your admiration[3] for a while
   With an attent ear, till I may deliver,
   Upon the witness of these gentlemen,
   This marvel to you.

HAMLET   For God's love, let me hear.   195

HORATIO   Two nights together had these gentlemen,
   Marcellus and Bernardo, on their watch,
   In the dead vast and middle of the night,
   Been thus encountered. A figure like your father,
   Armed at point exactly, cap-a-pe,[4]   200
   Appears before them, and with solemn march
   Goes slow and stately by them: thrice he walked
   By their oppressed and fear-surprisèd eyes,
   Within his truncheon's length; whilst they, distilled
   Almost to jelly with the act of fear,   205
   Stand dumb, and speak not to him. This to me
   In dreadful secrecy impart they did;
   And I with them the third night kept the watch:
   Where, as they had delivered, both in time,
   Form of the thing, each word made true and good,   210
   The apparition comes: I knew your father;
   These hands were not more like.

HAMLET   But where was this?

MARCELLUS   My lord, upon the platform where we watched.

HAMLET   Did you not speak to it?

HORATIO   My lord, I did.
   But answer made it none: yet once methought   215
   It lifted up its head and did address
   Itself to motion, like as it would speak:
   But even then the morning cock crew loud,
   And at the sound it shrunk in haste away
   And vanished from our sight.

HAMLET   'Tis very strange.   220

HORATIO   As I do live, my honored lord, 'tis true,
   And we did think it writ down in our duty
   To let you know of it.

HAMLET   Indeed, indeed, sirs, but this troubles me.
   Hold you the watch to-night?

MARCELLUS }
BERNARDO }   We do, my lord.   225

HAMLET   Armed, say you?

MARCELLUS }
BERNARDO }   Armed, my lord.

---

3. Restrain your astonishment.   4. From head to foot. "At point": completely.

HAMLET   From top to toe?

MARCELLUS   ⎱
BERNARDO   ⎰   My lord, from head to foot.

HAMLET   Then saw you not his face?

HORATIO   O, yes, my lord; he wore his beaver[5] up.

HAMLET   What, looked he frowningly?   230

HORATIO   A countenance more in sorrow than in anger.

HAMLET   Pale, or red?

HORATIO   Nay, very pale.

HAMLET   And fixed his eyes upon you?

HORATIO   Most constantly.

HAMLET   I would I had been there.

HORATIO   It would have much amazed you.   235

HAMLET   Very like, very like. Stayed it long?

HORATIO   While one with moderate haste might tell[6] a hundred.

MARCELLUS   ⎱
BERNARDO   ⎰ Longer, longer.

HORATIO   Not when I saw 't.

HAMLET   His beard was grizzled?[7] no?

HORATIO   It was, as I have seen it in his life,   240
A sable silvered.[8]

HAMLET   I will watch to-night;
Perchance 'twill walk again.

HORATIO   I warrant it will.

HAMLET   If it assume my noble father's person,
I'll speak to it, though hell itself should gape
And bid me hold my peace. I pray you all,   245
If you have hitherto concealed this sight,
Let it be tenable in your silence still,[9]
And whatsoever else shall hap to-night,
Give it an understanding, but no tongue:
I will requite your loves. So fare you well: 250
Upon the platform, 'twixt eleven and twelve,
I'll visit you.

ALL   Our duty to your honor.

HAMLET   Your loves, as mine to you: farewell.

      [*Exeunt all but* HAMLET.]

My father's spirit in arms! all is not well;
I doubt[1] some foul play: would the night were come!   255
Till then sit still, my soul: foul deeds will rise,
Though all the earth o'erwhelm them, to men's eyes.

      [*Exit.*]

---

5. Visor.
6. Count.
7. Gray.

8. Black and white.
9. Consider it still a secret.
1. Suspect.

SCENE 3

[SCENE: *A room in Polonius's house.*]

[*Enter* LAERTES *and* OPHELIA.]

LAERTES   My necessaries are embarked: farewell:
And, sister, as the winds give benefit
And convoy² is assistant, do not sleep,
But let me hear from you.
OPHELIA   Do you doubt that?
LAERTES   For Hamlet, and the trifling of his favor,   5
Hold it a fashion, and a toy in blood,
A violet in the youth of primy nature,
Forward,³ not permanent, sweet, not lasting,
The perfume and suppliance of a minute;
No more.   10
OPHELIA   No more but so?
LAERTES   Think it no more:
For nature crescent does not grow alone
In thews and bulk; but, as this temple⁴ waxes,
The inward service of the mind and soul   15
Grows wide withal. Perhaps he loves you now;
And now no soil nor cautel⁵ doth besmirch
The virtue of his will: but you must fear,
His greatness weighed,⁶ his will is not his own;
For he himself is subject to his birth: 20
He may not, as unvalued persons do,
Carve for himself, for on his choice depends
The safety and health of this whole state,
And therefore must his choice be circumscribed
Unto the voice and yielding⁷ of that body   25
Whereof he is the head. Then if he says he loves you,
It fits your wisdom so far to believe it
As he in his particular act and place
May give his saying deed; which is no further
Than the main voice of Denmark goes withal.⁸   30
Then weigh what loss your honor may sustain,
If with too credent ear you list his songs,
Or lose your heart, or your chaste treasure open
To his unmastered importunity.
Fear it, Ophelia, fear it, my dear sister,   35
And keep you in the rear of your affection,
Out of the shot and danger of desire.
The chariest maid is prodigal enough

2. Conveyance, means of transport.
3. Early. "Fashion": passing mood. "Primy": early, young.
4. The body. "Crescent": growing.

5. No foul or deceitful thoughts.
6. When you consider his rank. "Will": desire.
7. Assent.
8. Goes along with, agrees. "Main": powerful.

If she unmask her beauty to the moon:
Virtue itself 'scapes not calumnious strokes: 40
The canker galls the infants of the spring
Too oft before their buttons be disclosed,
And in the morn and liquid dew of youth
Contagious blastments⁹ are most imminent.
Be wary then; best safety lies in fear: 45
Youth to itself¹ rebels, though none else near.
OPHELIA   I shall the effect of this good lesson keep,
As watchman to my heart. But, good my brother,
Do not, as some ungracious pastors do,
Show me the steep and thorny way to heaven,   50
Whilst, like a puffed and reckless libertine,
Himself the primrose path of dalliance treads
And recks not his own rede.²
LAERTES   O, fear me not.
I stay too long; but here my father comes.
[*Enter* POLONIUS.]
A double blessing is a double grace;   55
Occasion smiles upon a second leave.
POLONIUS   Yet here, Laertes! Aboard, aboard, for shame!
The wind sits in the shoulder of your sail,
And you are stayed for. There; my blessing with thee!
And these few precepts in thy memory   60
See thou character.³ Give thy thoughts no tongue,
Nor any unproportioned⁴ thought his act.
Be thou familiar, but by no means vulgar.
Those friends thou hast, and their adoption tried,
Grapple them to thy soul with hoops of steel,   65
But do not dull thy palm⁵ with entertainment
Of each new-hatched unfledged comrade. Beware
Of entrance to a quarrel; but being in,
Bear 't, that the opposèd may beware of thee.
Give every man thy ear, but few thy voice: 70
Take each man's censure,⁶ but reserve thy judgment.
Costly thy habit as thy purse can buy,
But not expressed in fancy; rich, not gaudy:
For the apparel oft proclaims the man;
And they in France of the best rank and station   75
Are of a most select and generous chief⁷ in that.
Neither a borrower nor a lender be:
For loan oft loses both itself and friend,
And borrowing dulls the edge of husbandry.⁸
This above all: to thine own self be true,   80

9. Blights.
1. Against its better self.
2. Does not follow his own advice.
3. Engrave in your memory.
4. Unsuitable.

5. Make the palm of your hand callous (by the indiscriminate shaking of hands).
6. Opinion.
7. Preeminence.
8. Thriftiness.

And it must follow, as the night the day,
Thou canst not then be false to any man.
Farewell: my blessing season[9] this in thee!

LAERTES   Most humbly do I take my leave, my lord.
POLONIUS   The time invites you; go, your servants tend.[1]   85
LAERTES   Farewell, Ophelia, and remember well
What I have said to you.
OPHELIA   'Tis in my memory locked,
And you yourself shall keep the key of it.
LAERTES   Farewell.
          [Exit.]
POLONIUS   What is 't, Ophelia, he hath said to you?
OPHELIA   So please you, something touching the Lord Hamlet.   90
POLONIUS   Marry, well bethought:
'Tis told me, he hath very oft of late
Given private time to you, and you yourself
Have of your audience been most free and bounteous:
If it be so—as so 'tis put on me,   95
And that in way of caution—I must tell you,
You do not understand yourself so clearly
As it behoves my daughter and your honor.
What is between you? give me up the truth.
OPHELIA   He hath, my lord, of late made many tenders   100
Of his affection to me.
POLONIUS   Affection! pooh! you speak like a green girl,
Unsifted[2] in such perilous circumstance.
Do you believe his tenders, as you call them?
OPHELIA   I do not know, my lord, what I should think.   105
POLONIUS   Marry, I'll teach you: think yourself a baby,
That you have ta'en these tenders for true pay,
Which are not sterling. Tender[3] yourself more dearly;
Or—not to crack the wind of the poor phrase,
Running it thus—you'll tender me a fool.[4]   110
OPHELIA   My lord, he hath importuned me with love
In honorable fashion.
POLONIUS   Aye, fashion you may call it; go to, go to.
OPHELIA   And hath given countenance[5] to his speech, my lord,
With almost all the holy vows of heaven.   115
POLONIUS   Aye, springes to catch woodcocks. I do know,
When the blood burns, how prodigal the soul
Lends the tongue vows: these blazes, daughter,
Giving more light than heat, extinct in both,
Even in their promise, as it is a-making,   120
You must not take for fire. From this time
Be something scanter of your maiden presence;

9. Ripen.
1. Wait.
2. Untested.
3. Regard.

4. You'll furnish me with a fool (a foolish daughter).
5. Authority.

Set your entreatments[6] at a higher rate
Than a command to parley. For Lord Hamlet,
Believe so much in him, that he is young,   125
And with a larger tether may he walk
Than may be given you: in few, Ophelia,
Do not believe his vows; for they are brokers,
Not of that dye which their investments[7] show,
But mere implorators of unholy suits,   130
Breathing like sanctified and pious bawds,
The better to beguile. This is for all:
I would not, in plain terms, from this time forth,
Have you so slander any moment[8] leisure,
As to give words or talk with the Lord Hamlet.   135
Look to 't, I charge you: come your ways.
OPHELIA   I shall obey, my lord.
        [*Exeunt.*]

                        SCENE 4

[SCENE: *The platform.*]

        [*Enter* HAMLET, HORATIO, *and* MARCELLUS.]
HAMLET   The air bites shrewdly; it is very cold.
HORATIO   It is a nipping and an eager[9] air.
HAMLET   What hour now?
HORATIO   I think it lacks of twelve.
MARCELLUS   No, it is struck.
HORATIO   Indeed? I heard it not: it then draws near the season   5
        Wherein the spirit held his wont to walk.
        [*A flourish of trumpets, and ordnance shot off within.*]
        What doth this mean, my lord?
HAMLET   The king doth wake to-night, and takes his rouse,
        Keeps wassail, and the swaggering up-spring reels;
        And as he drains his draughts of Rhenish[1] down,   10
        The kettle-drum and trumpet thus bray out
        The triumph of his pledge.[2]
HORATIO   Is it a custom?
HAMLET   Aye, marry, is 't:
        But to my mind, though I am native here
        And to the manner born, it is a custom   15
        More honored[3] in the breach than the observance.
        This heavy-headed revel east and west
        Makes us traduced and taxed of other nations:
        They clepe us drunkards, and with swinish phrase
        Soil our addition;[4] and indeed it takes   20

6. Conversation, company.
7. Clothes. "Brokers": procurers, panders.
8. Use badly any momentary.
9. Sharp.

1. Rhine wine. "Up-spring reels": wild dances.
2. In downing the cup in one draught.
3. Honorable.
4. Reputation. "Taxed": blamed. "Clepe": call.

From our achievements, though performed at height,[5]
The pith and marrow of our attribute.[6]
So, oft it chances in particular men,
That for some vicious mole of nature in them,
As, in their birth,—wherein they are not guilty,   25
Since nature cannot choose his origin,—
By the o'ergrowth of some complexion,[7]
Oft breaking down the pales and forts of reason,
Or by some habit that too much o'er-leavens[8]
The form of plausive[9] manners, that these men,—   30
Carrying, I say, the stamp of one defect,
Being nature's livery, or fortune's star,—
Their virtues else[1]—be they as pure as grace,
As infinite as man may undergo—
Shall in the general censure take corruption   35
From that particular fault: the dram of evil
Doth all the noble substance often dout
To his own scandal.[2]
      [*Enter* GHOST.]
HORATIO   Look, my lord it comes!
HAMLET   Angels and ministers of grace defend us!
Be thou a spirit of health or goblin damned,
Bring with thee airs from heaven or blasts from hell,   40
Be thy intents wicked or charitable,
Thou comest in such a questionable shape
That I will speak to thee: I'll call thee Hamlet,
King, father, royal Dane: O, answer me!   45
Let me not burst in ignorance; but tell
Why thy canónized bones, hearsèd in death,
Have burst their cerements; why the sepulchre,
Wherein we saw thee quietly inurned,
Hath oped his ponderous and marble jaws,   50
To cast thee up again. What may this mean,
That thou, dead corse, again, in complete steel,
Revisit'st thus the glimpses of the moon,
Making night hideous; and we fools of nature
So horridly to shake our disposition   55
With thoughts beyond the reaches of our souls?
Say, why is this? Wherefore? what should we do?
      [GHOST *beckons* HAMLET.]
HORATIO   It beckons you to go away with it,
As if it some impartment did desire
To you alone.   60
MARCELLUS   Look, with what courteous action
It waves you to a more removèd ground:

5. Done in the best possible manner.
6. Reputation.
7. Excess in one side of their temperament.
8. Modifies, as yeast changes dough.

9. Agreeable.
1. The rest of their qualities.
2. To its own harm. "Dout": extinguish, nullify.

But do not go with it.
HORATIO   No, by no means.
HAMLET   It will not speak; then I will follow it.
HORATIO   Do not, my lord.
HAMLET   Why, what should be the fear?   65
I do not set my life at a pin's fee;
And for my soul, what can it do to that,
Being a thing immortal as itself?
It waves me forth again: I'll follow it.
HORATIO   What if it tempt you toward the flood, my lord,   70
Or to the dreadful summit of the cliff
That beetles o'er[3] his base into the sea,
And there assume some other horrible form,
Which might deprive your sovereignty of reason
And draw you into madness? think of it: 75
The very place puts toys[4] of desperation,
Without more motive, into every brain
That looks so many fathoms to the sea
And hears it roar beneath.
HAMLET   It waves me still.
Go on; I'll follow thee.   80
MARCELLUS   You shall not go, my lord.
HAMLET   Hold off your hands.
HORATIO   Be ruled; you shall not go.
HAMLET   My fate cries out,
And makes each petty artery in this body
As hardy as the Nemean lion's nerve.[5]
Still am I called, unhand me, gentlemen;   85
By heaven, I'll make a ghost of him that lets[6] me:
I say, away! Go on; I'll follow thee.
        [*Exeunt* GHOST *and* HAMLET.]
HORATIO   He waxes desperate with imagination.
MARCELLUS   Let's follow; 'tis not fit thus to obey him.
HORATIO   Have after. To what issue will this come?   90
MARCELLUS   Something is rotten in the state of Denmark.
HORATIO   Heaven will direct it.
MARCELLUS   Nay, let's follow him.
        [*Exeunt.*]

SCENE 5

[SCENE: *Another part of the platform.*]

        [*Enter* GHOST *and* HAMLET.]
HAMLET   Whither wilt thou lead me? speak; I'll go no further.
GHOST   Mark me.
HAMLET   I will.

3. Juts over.   Hercules as one of his twelve labors.
4. Fancies.   6. Hinders.
5. Sinew, muscle. "Nemean lion": slain by

GHOST   My hour is almost come,
When I to sulphurous and tormenting flames[7]
Must render up myself.
HAMLET   Alas, poor ghost!
GHOST   Pity me not, but lend thy serious hearing   5
To what I shall unfold.
HAMLET   Speak; I am bound to hear.
GHOST   So art thou to revenge, when thou shalt hear.
HAMLET   What?
GHOST   I am thy father's spirit;
Doomed for a certain term to walk the night,   10
And for the day confined to fast in fires,
Till the foul crimes done in my days of nature
Are burnt and purged away. But that I am forbid
To tell the secrets of my prison-house,
I could a tale unfold whose lightest word   15
Would harrow up thy soul, freeze thy young blood,
Make thy two eyes, like stars, start from their spheres,[8]
Thy knotted and combinèd locks to part
And each particular hair to stand on end,
Like quills upon the fretful porpentine: 20
But this eternal blazon[9] must not be
To ears of flesh and blood. List, list, O, list!
If thou didst ever thy dear father love—
HAMLET   O God!
GHOST   Revenge his foul and most unnatural murder.   25
HAMLET   Murder!
GHOST   Murder most foul, as in the best it is,
But this most foul, strange, and unnatural.
HAMLET   Haste me to know 't, that I, with wings as swift
As meditation or the thoughts of love,   30
May sweep to my revenge.
GHOST   I find thee apt;
And duller shouldst thou be than the fat weed
That roots itself in ease on Lethe[1] wharf,
Wouldst thou not stir in this. Now, Hamlet, hear:
'Tis given out that, sleeping in my orchard,   35
A serpent stung me; so the whole ear of Denmark
Is by a forgèd process of my death
Rankly abused: but know, thou noble youth,
The serpent that did sting thy father's life
Now wears his crown.
HAMLET   O my prophetic soul!   40
My uncle!

---

7. Of purgatory.
8. Transparent revolving shells in each of which, according to Ptolemaic astronomy, a planet or other heavenly body was placed.

9. Publication of the secrets of the other world (of eternity). "Porpentine": porcupine.
1. The river of forgetfulness in Hades.

GHOST   Aye, that incestuous, that adulterate beast,
   With witchcraft of his wit, with traitorous gifts,—
   O wicked wit and gifts, that have the power
   So to seduce!—won to his shameful lust   45
   The will of my most seeming-virtuous queen:
   O Hamlet, what a falling-off was there!
   From me, whose love was of that dignity
   That it went hand in hand even with the vow
   I made to her in marriage; and to decline   50
   Upon a wretch, whose natural gifts were poor
   To those of mine!
   But virtue, as it never will be moved,
   Though lewdness court it in a shape of heaven,[2]
   So lust, though to a radiant angel linked,   55
   Will sate itself in a celestial bed
   And prey on garbage.
   But, soft! methinks I scent the morning air;
   Brief let me be. Sleeping within my orchard,
   My custom always of the afternoon.   60
   Upon my secure hour thy uncle stole,
   With juice of cursed hebenon[3] in a vial,
   And in the porches of my ears did pour
   The leperous distilment; whose effect
   Holds such an enmity with blood of man   65
   That swift as quicksilver it courses through
   The natural gates and alleys of the body;
   And with a sudden vigor it doth posset
   And curd, like eager[4] droppings into milk,
   The thin and wholesome blood: so did it mine;   70
   And a most instant tetter barked about,[5]
   Most lazar-like,[6] with vile and loathsome crust,
   All my smooth body.
   Thus was I, sleeping, by a brother's hand
   Of life, of crown, of queen, at once dispatched: 75
   Cut off even in the blossoms of my sin,
   Unhouseled, disappointed, unaneled;[7]
   No reckoning made, but sent to my account
   With all my imperfections on my head:
   O, horrible! O, horrible! most horrible!   80
   If thou hast nature in thee, bear it not;
   Let not the royal bed of Denmark be
   A couch for luxury and damned incest.
   But, howsoever thou pursuest this act,
   Taint not thy mind, nor let thy soul contrive   85

2. A heavenly, angelic form.
3. Henbane, a poisonous herb.
4. Sour. "Posset": coagulate.
5. The skin immediately became thick like the bark of a tree.

6. Leper-like (from the beggar Lazarus, "full of sores," in Luke 16.20).
7. Without sacrament, unprepared, without extreme unction.

Against thy mother aught: leave her to heaven,
And to those thorns that in her bosom lodge,
To prick and sting her. Fare thee well at once!
The glow-worm shows the matin to be near,
And 'gins to pale his uneffectual fire: 90
Adieu, adieu, adieu! remember me.
    [*Exit.*]
HAMLET   O all you host of heaven! O earth! what else?
And shall I couple hell? O, fie! Hold, hold, my heart;
And you, my sinews, grow not instant old,
But bear me stiffly up. Remember thee!   95
Aye, thou poor ghost, while memory holds a seat
In this distracted globe. Remember thee!
Yea, from the table[8] of my memory
I'll wipe away all trivial fond records,
All saws of books, all forms, all pressures past,   100
That youth and observation copied there:
And thy commandment all alone shall live
Within the book and volume of my brain,
Unmixed with baser matter: yes, by heaven!
O most pernicious woman!   105
O villain, villain, smiling, damnèd villain!
My tables,—meet it is I set it down,
That one may smile, and smile, and be a villain;
At least I'm sure it may be so in Denmark.
    [*Writing.*]
So, uncle, there you are. Now to my word;   110
It is "Adieu, adieu! remember me."
I have sworn 't.
HORATIO
            } [*Within.*] My lord, my lord!
MARCELLUS
    [*Enter* HORATIO *and* MARCELLUS.]
MARCELLUS   Lord Hamlet!
HORATIO   Heaven
                               secure him!
HAMLET   So be it!
MARCELLUS   Illo,[9] ho, ho, my lord!   115
HAMLET   Hillo, ho, ho, boy! come, bird, come.
MARCELLUS   How is't, my noble lord?
HORATIO   What news, my lord?
HAMLET   O, wonderful!
HORATIO   Good my lord, tell it.
HAMLET   No; you will reveal it.
HORATIO   Not I, my lord, by heaven.

---

8. Writing tablet; used in the same sense in line 107. "Globe": head.   9. A falconer's call.

MARCELLUS   Nor I, my lord.   120
HAMLET   How say you, then; would heart of man once think it?
　　But you'll be secret?
HORATIO   ⎫
MARCELLUS   ⎬   Aye, by, heaven, my lord.
HAMLET   There's ne'er a villain dwelling in all Denmark
　　But he's an arrant knave.
HORATIO   There needs no ghost, my lord, come from the grave   125
　　To tell us this.
HAMLET   Why, right; you are i' the right;
　　And so, without more circumstance[1] at all,
　　I hold it fit that we shake hands and part:
　　You, as your business and desire shall point you;
　　For every man hath business and desire,   130
　　Such as it is; and for my own poor part,
　　Look you, I'll go pray.
HORATIO   These are but wild and whirling words, my lord.
HAMLET   I'm sorry they offend you, heartily;
　　Yes, faith, heartily.
HORATIO   There's no offense, my lord.   135
HAMLET   Yes, by Saint Patrick, but there is, Horatio,
　　And much offense too. Touching this vision here,
　　It is an honest[2] ghost, that let me tell you:
　　For your desire to know what is between us,
　　O'ermaster 't as you may. And now, good friends,   140
　　As you are friends, scholars and soldiers,
　　Give me one poor request.
HORATIO   What is 't, my lord? we will.
HAMLET   Never make known what you have seen tonight.
MARCELLUS   ⎫
HORATIO   ⎬   My lord, we will not.
HAMLET   Nay, but swear 't.
HORATIO   In faith,
　　My lord, not I.
MARCELLUS   Nor I, my lord, in faith.   145
HAMLET   Upon my sword.
MARCELLUS   We have sworn, my lord, already.
HAMLET   Indeed, upon my sword, indeed.
GHOST [Beneath.]   Swear.
HAMLET   Ah, ha, boy! say'st thou so? art thou there, true-penny?[3]
　　Come on: you hear this fellow in the cellarage:
　　Consent to swear.
HORATIO   Propose the oath, my lord.   150

1. Ceremony.   3. Honest fellow.
2. Genuine.

HAMLET   Never to speak of this that you have seen,
   Swear by my sword.
GHOST [*Beneath.*]   Swear.
HAMLET   Hic et ubique?[4] then we'll shift our ground.
   Come hither, gentlemen,   155
   And lay your hands again upon my sword:
   Never to speak of this that you have heard,
   Swear by my sword.
GHOST [*Beneath.*]   Swear.
HAMLET   Well said, old mole! canst work i' the earth so fast?   160
   A worthy pioner![5] Once more remove, good friends.
HORATIO   O day and night, but this is wondrous strange!
HAMLET   And therefore as a stranger give it welcome.
   There are more things in heaven and earth, Horatio,
   Than are dreamt of in your philosophy.   165
   But come;
   Here, as before, never, so help you mercy,
   How strange or odd soe'er I bear myself,
   As I perchance hereafter shall think meet
   To put an antic[6] disposition on,   170
   That you, at such times seeing me, never shall,
   With arms encumbered[7] thus, or this head-shake,
   Or by pronouncing of some doubtful phrase,
   As "Well, well, we know," or "We could, an if we would,"
   Or "If we list to speak," or "There be, an if they might,"   175
   Or such ambiguous giving out, to note
   That you know aught of me: this not to do,
   So grace and mercy at your most need help you,
   Swear.
GHOST [*Beneath.*]   Swear.   180
HAMLET   Rest, rest, perturbèd spirit!
      [*They swear.*]
   So, gentlemen,
   With all my love I do commend[8] me to you:
   And what so poor a man as Hamlet is
   May do, to express his love and friending to you,   185
   God willing, shall not lack. Let us go in together;
   And still your fingers on your lips, I pray,
   The time is out of joint: O cursèd spite,
   That ever I was born to set it right!
   Nay, come, let's go together.   190
      [*Exeunt.*]

4. Here and everywhere (Latin).
5. Miner.
6. Odd, fantastic.
7. Folded.
8. Entrust.

Act 2

SCENE I

[SCENE: *A room in Polonius's house.*]

[*Enter* POLONIUS *and* REYNALDO.]

POLONIUS   Give him this money and these notes, Reynaldo.
REYNALDO   I will, my lord.
POLONIUS   You shall do marvelous wisely, good Reynaldo,
Before you visit him, to make inquire
Of his behavior.
REYNALDO   My lord, I did intend it.   5
POLONIUS   Marry, well said, very well said. Look you, sir,
Inquire me first what Danskers are in Paris,
And how, and who, what means, and where they keep,⁹
What company, at what expense, and finding
By this encompassment¹ and drift of question   10
That they do know my son, come you more nearer
Than your particular demands will touch it:
Take you, as 'twere, some distant knowledge of him,
As thus, "I know his father and his friends,
And in part him": do you mark this, Reynaldo?   15
REYNALDO   Aye, very well, my lord.
POLONIUS   "And in part him; but," you may say, "not well:
But if 't be he I mean, he's very wild,
Addicted so and so"; and there put on him
What forgeries you please; marry, none so rank   20
As may dishonor him; take heed of that;
But, sir, such wanton, wild and usual slips
As are companions noted and most known
To youth and liberty.
REYNALDO   As gaming, my lord.
POLONIUS   Aye, or drinking, fencing, swearing, quarreling,   25
Drabbing:² you may go so far.
REYNALDO   My lord, that would dishonor him.
POLONIUS   Faith, no; as you may season it in the charge.³
You must not put another scandal on him,
That he is open to incontinency;   30
That's not my meaning: but breathe his faults so quaintly⁴
That they may seem the taints of liberty,
The flash and outbreak of a fiery mind,
A savageness in unreclaimèd blood,
Of general assault.⁵
REYNALDO   But, my good lord,—   35

---

9. Dwell. "Danskers": Danes.
1. Roundabout way.
2. Whoring.
3. Qualify it in making the accusation.

4. Delicately, skillfully. "Incontinency": extreme sensuality.
5. Assailing all. "Unreclaimèd": untamed.

POLONIUS   Wherefore should you do this?
REYNALDO   Aye, my lord,
   I would know that.
POLONIUS   Marry, sir, here's my drift,
   And I believe it is a fetch of warrant:[6]
   You laying these slight sullies on my son,
   As 'twere a thing a little soiled i' the working,   40
   Mark you,
   Your party in converse, him you would sound,
   Having ever seen in the prenominate[7] crimes
   The youth you breathe of guilty, be assured
   He closes with you in this consequence;[8]   45
   "Good sir," or so, or "friend," or "gentleman,"
   According to the phrase or the addition[9]
   Of man and country.
REYNALDO   Very good, my lord.
POLONIUS   And then, sir, does he this—he does—what was I about to
   say? By the mass, I was about to say something: where did I leave?   50
REYNALDO   At "closes in the consequence," at "friend or so," and
   "gentleman."
POLONIUS   At "closes in the consequence," aye, marry;
   He closes with you thus: "I know the gentleman;
   I saw him yesterday, or t' other day,   55
   Or then, or then, with such, or such, and, as you say,
   There was a' gaming, there o'ertook in 's rouse,[1]
   There falling out at tennis": or perchance,
   "I saw him enter such a house of sale,"
   Videlicet,[2] a brothel, or so forth.   60
   See you now;
   Your bait of falsehood takes this carp of truth:
   And thus do we of wisdom and of reach,[3]
   With windlasses and with assays of bias,[4]
   By indirections find directions out: 65
   So, by my former lecture and advice,
   Shall you my son. You have me, have you not?
REYNALDO   My lord, I have.
POLONIUS   God be wi' ye; fare ye well.
REYNALDO   Good my lord!
POLONIUS   Observe his inclination in yourself.[5]   70
REYNALDO   I shall, my lord.
POLONIUS   And let him ply his music.
REYNALDO   Well, my lord.

6. Allowable stratagem.
7. Aforementioned. "Having ever": if he has
ever.
8. You may be sure he will agree in this
conclusion.
9. Title.
1. Intoxicated in his reveling.

2. Namely.
3. Wise and far-sighted.
4. Sending the ball indirectly (in bowling),
devious attacks. "Windlasses": winding ways,
round-about courses.
5. Ways of procedure by yourself.

POLONIUS   Farewell!
     [*Exit* REYNALDO. —*Enter* OPHELIA.]
  How now, Ophelia! what's the matter?
OPHELIA   O, my lord, I have been so affrighted!   75
POLONIUS   With what, i' the name of God?
OPHELIA   My lord, as I was sewing in my closet,
  Lord Hamlet, with his doublet[6] all unbraced,
  No hat upon his head, his stockings fouled,
  Ungartered and down-gyvèd[7] to his ankle;   80
  Pale as his shirt, his knees knocking each other,
  And with a look so piteous in purport
  As if he had been loosèd out of hell
  To speak of horrors, he comes before me.
POLONIUS   Mad for thy love?
OPHELIA   My lord, I do not know,   85
  But truly I do fear it.
POLONIUS   What said he?
OPHELIA   He took me by the wrist and held me hard;
  Then goes he to the length of all his arm,
  And with his other hand thus o'er his brow,
  He falls to such perusal of my face   90
  As he would draw it. Long stayed he so;
  At last, a little shaking of mine arm,
  And thrice his head thus waving up and down,
  He raised a sigh so piteous and profound
  As it did seem to shatter all his bulk   95
  And end his being: that done, he lets me go:
  And with his head over his shoulder turned,
  He seemed to find his way without his eyes;
  For out o' doors he went without their help,
  And to the last bended their light on me.   100
POLONIUS   Come, go with me: I will go seek the king.
  This is the very ecstasy of love;
  Whose violent property fordoes itself[8]
  And leads the will to desperate undertakings
  As oft as any passion under heaven   105
  That does afflict our natures. I am sorry.
  What, have you given him any hard words of late?
OPHELIA   No, my good lord, but, as you did command,
  I did repel his letters and denied
  His access to me.
POLONIUS   That hath made him mad.
  I am sorry that with better heed and judgment   110
  I had not quoted him: I fear'd he did but trifle
  And meant to wreck thee; but beshrew my jealousy![9]

6. Jacket. "Closet": private room.   madness.
7. Pulled down like fetters on a prisoner's leg.   9. Curse my suspicion. "Quoted": noted.
8. Which, when violent, destroys itself. "Ecstasy":

By heaven, it is as proper to our age
To cast beyond ourselves[1] in our opinions   115
As it is common for the younger sort
To lack discretion. Come, go we to the king:
This must be known; which, being kept close, might move
More grief to hide than hate to utter love.[2]
Come.   120
    [*Exeunt.*]

SCENE 2

[SCENE: *A room in the castle.*]

    [*Flourish. Enter* KING, QUEEN, ROSENCRANTZ, GUILDENSTERN, *and
    attendants.*]
KING   Welcome, dear Rosencrantz and Guildenstern!
  Moreover that we much did long to see you,
  The need we have to use you did provoke
  Our hasty sending. Something have you heard
  Of Hamlet's transformation; so call it,   5
  Sith[3] nor the exterior nor the inward man
  Resembles that it was. What it should be,
  More than his father's death, that thus hath put him
  So much from the understanding of himself,
  I cannot dream of: I entreat you both,   10
  That, being of so young days brought up with him
  And sith so neighbored to his youth and behavior,
  That you vouchsafe your rest[4] here in our court
  Some little time: so by your companies
  To draw him on to pleasures, and to gather   15
  So much as from occasion you may glean,
  Whether aught to us unknown afflicts him thus,
  That opened[5] lies within our remedy.
QUEEN   Good gentlemen, he hath much talked of you,
  And sure I am two men there are not living   20
  To whom he more adheres.[6] If it will please you
  To show us so much gentry[7] and good will
  As to expend your time with us awhile
  For the supply and profit of our hope,
  Your visitation shall receive such thanks   25
  As fits a king's remembrance.
ROSENCRANTZ   Both your majesties
  Might, by the sovereign power you have of us,
  Put your dread pleasures more into[8] command

---

1. Overshoot, go too far.
2. If Hamlet's love is revealed. "To hide": if
kept hidden.
3. Since.
4. Consent to stay.

5. Once revealed.
6. Is more attached.
7. Courtesy.
8. Give your sovereign wishes the form of.

Than to entreaty.
GUILDENSTERN   But we both obey,
  And here give up ourselves, in the full bent⁹   30
  To lay our service freely at your feet,
  To be commanded.
KING   Thanks, Rosencrantz and gentle Guildenstern.
QUEEN   Thanks, Guildenstern and gentle Rosencrantz:
  And I beseech you instantly to visit   35
  My too much changèd son. Go, some of you,
  And bring these gentlemen where Hamlet is.
GUILDENSTERN   Heavens make our presence and our practices
  Pleasant and helpful to him!
QUEEN   Aye, amen!
    [*Exeunt* ROSENCRANTZ, GUILDENSTERN, *and some attendants.* —*Enter*
    POLONIUS.]
POLONIUS   The ambassadors from Norway, my good lord,   40
  Are joyfully returned.
KING   Thou still¹ hast been the father of good news.
POLONIUS   Have I, my lord? I assure my good liege,
  I hold my duty as I hold my soul,
  Both to my God and to my gracious king: 45
  And I do think, or else this brain of mine
  Hunts not the trail of policy so sure
  As it hath used to do, that I have found
  The very cause of Hamlet's lunacy.
KING   O, speak of that; that do I long to hear.   50
POLONIUS   Give first admittance to the ambassadors;
  My news shall be the fruit to that great feast.
KING   Thyself do grace² to them, and bring them in.
    [*Exit* POLONIUS.]
  He tells me, my dear Gertrude, he hath found
  The head and source of all your son's distemper.   55
QUEEN   I doubt it is no other but the main;
  His father's death and our o'erhasty marriage.
KING   Well, we shall sift him.
    [*Re-enter* POLONIUS, *with* VOLTIMAND *and* CORNELIUS.]
                        Welcome, my good friends!
  Say, Voltimand, what from our brother Norway?
VOLTIMAND   Most fair return of greetings and desires.   60
  Upon our first,³ he sent out to suppress
  His nephew's levies, which to him appeared
  To be a preparation 'gainst the Polack,
  But better looked into, he truly found
  It was against your highness: whereat grieved,   65
  That so his sickness, age and impotence

---

9. Bent (as a bow) to the limit.   2. Honor. "Fruit": dessert.
1. Always.   3. As soon as we made the request.

Was falsely borne in hand,[4] sends out arrests
On Fortinbras; which he, in brief, obeys,
Receives rebuke from Norway, and in fine[5]
Makes vow before his uncle never more   70
To give the assay[6] of arms against your majesty.
Whereon old Norway, overcome with joy,
Gives him three thousand crowns in annual fee
And his commission to employ those soldiers,
So levied as before, against the Polack: 75
With an entreaty, herein further shown,
    [*Giving a paper.*]
That it might please you to give quiet pass
Through your dominions for this enterprise,
On such regards of safety and allowance
As therein are set down.
KING   It likes us well,   80
And at our more considered time we'll read,
Answer, and think upon this business.
Meantime we thank you for your well-took labor:
Go to your rest; at night we'll feast together:
Most welcome home!
    [*Exeunt* VOLTIMAND *and* CORNELIUS.]
POLONIUS   This business is well ended.   85
My liege, and madam, to expostulate
What majesty should be, what duty is,
Why day is day, night night, and time is time,
Were nothing but to waste night, day and time.
Therefore, since brevity is the soul of wit   90
And tediousness the limbs and outward flourishes,
I will be brief. Your noble son is mad:
Mad call I it; for, to define true madness,
What is 't but to be nothing else but mad?
But let that go.
QUEEN   More matter, with less art.   95
POLONIUS   Madam, I swear I use no art at all.
That he is mad, 'tis true: 'tis true 'tis pity,
And pity 'tis 'tis true: a foolish figure;[7]
But farewell it, for I will use no art.
Mad let us grant him then: and now remains   100
That we find out the cause of this effect,
Or rather say, the cause of this defect,
For this effect defective comes by cause:
Thus it remains and the remainder thus.
Perpend.[8]   105
I have a daughter,—have while she is mine,—

4. Deceived, deluded.   7. Of speech.
5. Finally.   8. Consider.
6. Test.

Who in her duty and obedience, mark,
Hath given me this: now gather and surmise.
[*Reads.*] "To the celestial, and my soul's idol, the most beautified
Ophelia,"—That's an ill phrase, a vile phrase; "beautified" is a vile   110
phrase; but you shall hear. Thus:
   [*Reads.*] "In her excellent white bosom, these," &c.
QUEEN Came this from Hamlet to her?
POLONIUS Good madam, stay awhile; I will be faithful.
     [*Reads.*] "Doubt thou the stars are fire; 115
        Doubt that the sun doth move;
       Doubt truth to be a liar;
       But never doubt I love.
"O dear Ophelia, I am ill at these numbers;[9] I have not art to reckon
my groans: but that I love thee best, O most best, believe it. Adieu.   120
    "Thine evermore, most dear lady, whilst this
      machine is to him,[1] HAMLET."
This in obedience hath my daughter shown me;
And more above,[2] hath his solicitings,
As they fell out by time, by means and place,   125
All given to mine ear.
KING   But how hath she
Received his love?
POLONIUS   What do you think of me?
KING As of a man faithful and honorable.
POLONIUS I would fain prove so. But what might you think,
When I had seen this hot love on the wing,—   130
As I perceived it, I must tell you that,
Before my daughter told me,—what might you,
Or my dear majesty your queen here, think,
If I had played the desk or table-book,[3]
Or given my heart a winking,[4] mute and dumb,   135
Or looked upon this love with idle sight;
What might you think? No, I went round[5] to work,
And my young mistress thus I did bespeak:
"Lord Hamlet is a prince, out of thy star;[6]
This must not be": and then I prescripts gave her,   140
That she should lock herself from his resort,
Admit no messengers, receive no tokens.
Which done, she took the fruits of my advice;
And he repulsed, a short tale to make,
Fell into a sadness, then into a fast,   145
Thence to a watch, thence into a weakness,
Thence to a lightness,[7] and by this declension
Into the madness wherein now he raves

9. Verses.   4. Shut my heart's eye.
1. Body is attached.   5. Straight.
2. Moreover.   6. Sphere.
3. If I had acted as a desk or notebook (in 7. Light-headedness. "Watch": insomnia.
keeping the matter secret).

And all we mourn for.

KING   Do you think this?

QUEEN   It may be, very like.   150

POLONIUS   Hath there been such a time, I'd fain know that,
    That I have positively said "'tis so,"
    When it proved otherwise?

KING   Not that I know.

POLONIUS [*Pointing to his head and shoulder.*]   Take this, from this,
    if this be otherwise: 155
    If circumstances lead me, I will find
    Where truth is hid, though it were hid indeed
    Within the center.[8]

KING   How may we try it further?

POLONIUS   You know, sometimes he walks for hours together
    Here in the lobby.

QUEEN   So he does, indeed.   160

POLONIUS   At such a time I'll loose my daughter to him:
    Be you and I behind an arras then;
    Mark the encounter: if he love her not,
    And be not from his reason fall'n thereon,[9]
    Let me be no assistant for a state,   165
    But keep a farm and carters.

KING   We will try it.

QUEEN   But look where sadly the poor wretch comes reading.

POLONIUS   Away, I do beseech you, both away:
    I'll board him presently.[1]

      [*Exeunt* KING, QUEEN, *and attendants.* —*Enter* HAMLET, *reading.*]
    O, give me leave: how does my good Lord Hamlet?   170

HAMLET   Well, God-a-mercy.

POLONIUS   Do you know me, my lord?

HAMLET   Excellent well; you are a fishmonger.[2]

POLONIUS   Not I, my lord.

HAMLET   Then I would you were so honest a man.   175

POLONIUS: Honest, my lord!

HAMLET   Aye, sir; to be honest, as this world goes, is to be one man
    picked out of ten thousand.

POLONIUS   That's very true, my lord.

HAMLET   For if the sun breed maggots in a dead dog, being a good   180
    kissing carrion[3]—Have you a daughter?

POLONIUS   I have, my lord.

HAMLET   Let her not walk i' the sun: conception is a blessing; but as
    your daughter may conceive,—friend, look to 't.

POLONIUS [*Aside.*]   How say you by that? Still harping on my daughter: 185
    yet he knew me not at first; he said I was a fishmonger: he is far
    gone: and truly in my youth I suffered much extremity for love; very

---

8. Of the earth.   2. Fish seller, but also slang for procurer.
9. For that reason.   3. Good bit of flesh for kissing.
1. Approach him at once.

near this. I'll speak to him again.—What do you read, my lord?

HAMLET   Words, words, words.

POLONIUS   What is the matter,[4] my lord?   190

HAMLET   Between who?

POLONIUS   I mean, the matter that you read, my lord.

HAMLET   Slanders, sir: for the satirical rogue says here that old men
have gray beards, that their faces are wrinkled, their eyes purging
thick amber and plum-tree gum, and that they have a plentiful lack   195
of wit, together with most weak hams: all which, sir, though I most
powerfully and potently believe, yet I hold it not honesty to have it
thus set down; for yourself, sir, shall grow old as I am, if like a crab
you could go backward.

POLONIUS [Aside.]   Though this be madness, yet there is method in   200
't.—Will you walk out of the air, my lord?

HAMLET   Into my grave.

POLONIUS   Indeed, that's out of the air.

   [Aside.]

How pregnant sometimes his replies are! a happiness[5] that often
madness hits on, which reason and sanity could not so prosperously   205
be delivered of. I will leave him, and suddenly contrive the means of
meeting between him and my daughter.—My honorable lord, I will
most humbly take my leave of you.

HAMLET   You cannot, sir, take from me any thing that I will more willingly part withal: except my life, except my life, except my life.   210

POLONIUS   Fare you well, my lord.

HAMLET   These tedious old fools.

   [Re-enter ROSENCRANTZ and GUILDENSTERN.]

POLONIUS   You go to seek the Lord Hamlet; there he is.

ROSENCRANTZ [To POLONIUS.]   God save you, sir!

   [Exit POLONIUS.]

GUILDENSTERN   My honored lord!   215

ROSENCRANTZ   My most dear lord!

HAMLET   My excellent good friends! How dost thou, Guildenstern? Ah,
Rosencrantz! Good lads, how do you both?

ROSENCRANTZ   As the indifferent[6] children of the earth.

GUILDENSTERN   Happy, in that we are not over-happy;   220
On Fortune's cap we are not the very button.[7]

HAMLET   Nor the soles of her shoe?

ROSENCRANTZ   Neither, my lord.

HAMLET   Then you live about her waist, or in the middle of her
favors?   225

GUILDENSTERN   Faith, her privates[8] we.

HAMLET   In the secret parts of Fortune? O, most true; she is a strumpet.
What's the news?

---

4. The subject matter of the book. Hamlet
responds as if he referred to the subject of a
quarrel.
5. Aptness of expression.

6. Average.
7. Top.
8. Ordinary men (with obvious play on the
sexual term *private parts*).

ROSENCRANTZ   None, my lord, but that the world's grown honest.

HAMLET   Then is doomsday near: but your news is not true. Let   230
me question more in particular: what have you, my good friends,
deserved at the hands of Fortune, that she sends you to prison
hither?

GUILDENSTERN   Prison, my lord!

HAMLET   Denmark's a prison.   235

ROSENCRANTZ   Then is the world one.

HAMLET   A goodly one; in which there are many confines, wards[9] and
dungeons, Denmark being one o' the worst.

ROSENCRANTZ   We think not so, my lord.

HAMLET   Why, then, 'tis none to you; for there is nothing either good   240
or bad, but thinking makes it so: to me it is a prison.

ROSENCRANTZ   Why, then your ambition makes it one; 'tis too narrow
for your mind.

HAMLET   O God, I could be bounded in a nut-shell and count myself
a king of infinite space, were it not that I have bad dreams.   245

GUILDENSTERN   Which dreams indeed are ambition; for the very substance of the ambitious is merely the shadow of a dream.

HAMLET   A dream itself is but a shadow.

ROSENCRANTZ   Truly, and I hold ambition of so airy and light a quality
that it is but a shadow's shadow.   250

HAMLET   Then are our beggars bodies, and our monarchs and outstretched heroes the beggars' shadows. Shall we to the court? for,
by my fay, I cannot reason.

ROSENCRANTZ   }
                  We'll wait upon you.
GUILDENSTERN   }

HAMLET   No such matter: I will not sort you[1] with the rest of my   255
servants; for, to speak to you like an honest man, I am most dreadfully
attended. But, in the beaten way of friendship, what make you at
Elsinore?

ROSENCRANTZ   To visit you, my lord; no other occasion.

HAMLET   Beggar that I am, I am even poor in thanks; but I thank you: 260
and sure, dear friends, my thanks are too dear a halfpenny.[2] Were
you not sent for? Is it your own inclining? Is it a free visitation?
Come, deal justly[3] with me: come, come; nay, speak.

GUILDENSTERN   What should we say, my lord?

HAMLET   Why, any thing, but to the purpose. You were sent for; and   265
there is a kind of confession in your looks, which your modesties
have not craft enough to color: I know the good king and queen
have sent for you.

ROSENCRANTZ   To what end, my lord?

HAMLET   That you must teach me. But let me conjure you, by the   270
rights of our fellowship, by the consonancy of our youth, by the
obligation of our ever-preserved love, and by what more dear

---

9. Cells. "Confines": places of confinement.
1. Put you together.

2. If priced at a halfpenny.
3. Honestly.

a better proposer[4] could charge you withal, be even and direct
with me, whether you were sent for, or no.

ROSENCRANTZ [*Aside to* GUILDENSTERN.]   What say you?   275

HAMLET [*Aside.*]   Nay then, I have an eye of[5] you.—If you love me,
hold not off.

GUILDENSTERN   My lord, we were sent for.

HAMLET   I will tell you why; so shall my anticipation prevent your
discovery,[6] and your secrecy to the king and queen moult no feather.   280
I have of late—but wherefore I know not—lost all my mirth, forgone
all custom of exercises; and indeed it goes so heavily with my
disposition that this goodly frame, the earth, seems to me a sterile
promontory; this most excellent canopy, the air, look you, this brave
o'erhanging firmament, this majestical roof fretted[7] with golden fire,   285
why, it appears no other thing to me than a foul and pestilent congregation of vapors. What a piece of work is a man! how noble in
reason! how infinite in faculty! in form and moving how express[8] and
admirable! in action how like an angel! in apprehension how like a
god! the beauty of the world! the paragon of animals! And yet, to me,   290
what is this quintessence of dust? man delights not me; no, nor
woman an neither, though by your smiling you seem to say so.

ROSENCRANTZ   My lord, there was no such stuff in my thoughts.

HAMLET   Why did you laugh then, when I said "man delights not me"?

ROSENCRANTZ   To think, my lord, if you delight not in man, what   295
lenten entertainment the players shall receive from you: we coted[9]
them on the way; and hither are they coming, to offer you service.

HAMLET   He that plays the king shall be welcome; his majesty shall
have tribute of me; the adventurous knight shall use his foil and
target; the lover shall not sigh gratis; the humorous[1] man shall end   300
his part in peace; the clown shall make those laugh whose lungs are
tickle o' the sere,[2] and the lady shall say her mind freely, or the blank
verse shall halt for 't. What players are they?

ROSENCRANTZ   Even those you were wont to take such delight in, the
tragedians of the city.   305

HAMLET   How chances it they travel? their residence, both in reputation
and profit, was better both ways.

ROSENCRANTZ   I think their inhibition comes by means of the late
innovation.[3]

HAMLET   Do they hold the same estimation they did when I was in the   310
city? are they so followed?

ROSENCRANTZ   No, indeed, are they not.

HAMLET   How comes it? do they grow rusty?

ROSENCRANTZ   Nay, their endeavor keeps in the wonted pace: but

---

4. Speaker.
5. On.
6. Precede your disclosure.
7. Adorned.
8. Precise.
9. Overtook.

1. Eccentric, whimsical.
2. Ready to shoot off at a touch.
3. The introduction of the children (line 315),
as Rosencrantz explains in his subsequent
replies to Hamlet. "Inhibition": prohibition.

there is, sir, an eyrie of children, little eyases,[4] that cry out on the 315
top of question[5] and are most tyrannically clapped for 't: these are
now the fashion, and so berattle[6] the common stages—so they call
them—that many wearing rapiers are afraid of goose-quills,[7] and
dare scarce come thither.

HAMLET   What, are they children? who maintains 'em? how are they 320
escoted?[8] Will they pursue the quality[8] no longer than they can sing?
will they not say afterwards, if they should grow themselves to
common players—as it is most like, if their means are no better,—
their writers do them wrong, to make them exclaim against their
own succession?[9] 325

ROSENCRANTZ   Faith, there has been much to-do on both sides, and
the nation holds it no sin to tarre[1] them to controversy: there was
for a while no money bid for argument unless the poet and the player
went to cuffs in the question.[2]

HAMLET   Is 't possible? 330

GUILDENSTERN   O, there has been much throwing about of brains.

HAMLET   Do the boys carry it away?[3]

ROSENCRANTZ   Aye, that they do, my lord; Hercules and his load too.[4]

HAMLET   It is not very strange; for my uncle is king of Denmark,
and those that would make mows[5] at him while my father lived, give 335
twenty, forty, fifty, a hundred ducats a-piece, for his picture in little.
'Sblood, there is something in this more than natural, if philosophy
could find it out.

[Flourish of trumpets within.]

GUILDENSTERN   There are the players.

HAMLET   Gentlemen, you are welcome to Elsinore. Your hands, come 340
then: the appurtenance of welcome is fashion and ceremony: let me
comply with you in this garb, lest my extent[6] to the players, which,
I tell you, must show fairly outwards, should more appear like
entertainment[7] than yours. You are welcome: but my uncle-father
and aunt-mother are deceived. 345

GUILDENSTERN   In what, my dear lord?

HAMLET   I am but mad north-north-west: when the wind is southerly
I know a hawk from a handsaw.[8]

[Re-enter POLONIUS.]

POLONIUS   Well be with you, gentlemen!

HAMLET   Hark you, Guildenstern; and you too: at each ear a hearer: 350

---

4. Nestling hawks. "Eyrie": nest.
5. Above others on matter of dispute.
6. Berate.
7. Gentlemen are afraid of pens (that is, of poets satirizing the "common stages").
8. Profession of acting. "Escoted": financially supported.
9. Recite satiric pieces against what they are themselves likely to become, common players.
1. Incite.
2. No offer to buy a plot for a play if it did not

contain a quarrel between poet and player on that subject.
3. Win out.
4. The sign in front of the Globe Theater showed Hercules bearing the world on his shoulders.
5. Faces, grimaces.
6. Welcoming behavior. "Garb": style.
7. Welcome.
8. A hawk from a heron as well as a kind of ax from a handsaw.

that great baby you see there is not yet out of his swaddling clouts.[9]

ROSENCRANTZ   Happily he's the second time come to them; for they
say an old man is twice a child.

HAMLET   I will prophesy he comes to tell me of the players; mark it.
You say right, sir: o' Monday morning; 'twas so, indeed.[1]   355

POLONIUS   My lord, I have news to tell you.

HAMLET   My lord, I have news to tell you. When Roscius[2] was an actor
in Rome,—

POLONIUS   The actors are come hither, my lord.

HAMLET   Buz, buz![3]   360

POLONIUS   Upon my honor,—

HAMLET   Then came each actor on his ass,—

POLONIUS   The best actors in the world, either for tragedy, comedy,
history, pastoral, pastoral-comical, historical-pastoral, tragical-
historical, tragical-comical-historical-pastoral, scene individable,   365
or poem unlimited:[4] Seneca cannot be too heavy, nor Plautus too
light. For the law of writ and the liberty,[5] these are the only men.

HAMLET   O Jephthah,[6] judge of Israel, what a treasure hadst thou!

POLONIUS   What a treasure had he, my lord?

HAMLET   Why,   370
        "One fair daughter, and no more,
            The which he lovèd passing well."[7]

POLONIUS   [Aside.]   Still on my daughter.

HAMLET   Am I not i' the right, old Jephthah?

POLONIUS   If you call me Jephthah, my lord, I have a daughter that I   375
love passing well.

HAMLET   Nay, that follows not.

POLONIUS   What follows, then, my lord?

HAMLET   Why,
        "As by lot, God wot."
and then you know,   380
        "It came to pass, as most like it was,"—
the first row of the pious chanson will show you more; for look, where
my abridgment[8] comes.
        [Enter four or five PLAYERS.]
You are welcome, masters; welcome, all. I am glad to see thee well.
Welcome, good friends. O, my old friend! Why thy face is valanced[9]   385
since I saw thee last; comest thou to beard me in Denmark? What,
my young lady and mistress! By'r lady, your ladyship is nearer to

9. Clothes.
1. Hamlet, for Polonius's sake, pretends he is deep in talk with Rosencrantz.
2. A famous Roman comic actor (ca. 126–62 B.C.E.).
3. An expression used to stop the teller of a stale story.
4. For plays governed and those not governed by classical rules.
5. Possibly, for both written and extempo-

rized plays. Seneca (after 4 B.C.E.–65 C.E.) was a Roman who wrote tragedies. Plautus (ca. 254–184 B.C.E.) was a Roman who wrote comedies.
6. Who was compelled to sacrifice a dearly beloved daughter (2 Judges).
7. From an old ballad about Jephthah.
8. That is, the players interrupting him. "Row": stanza. "Chanson": song.
9. Draped (with a beard).

heaven than when I saw you last, by the altitude of a chopine. Pray God, your voice, like a piece of uncurrent gold, be not cracked within the ring.[1] Masters, you are all welcome. We'll e'en to 't like French falconers, fly at any thing we see: we'll have a speech straight: come, give us a taste of your quality; come, a passionate speech.   390

FIRST PLAYER   What speech, my good lord?

HAMLET   I heard thee speak me a speech once, but it was never acted; or, if it was, not above once; for the play, I remember, pleased not   395 the million; 'twas caviare to the general:[2] but it was—as I received it, and others, whose judgments in such matters cried in the top of mine[3]—an excellent play, well digested in the scenes, set down with as much modesty as cunning. I remember, one said there were no sallets in the lines to make the matter savory, nor no matter in the   400 phrase that might indict the author of affection;[4] but called it an honest method, as wholesome as sweet, and by very much more handsome than fine.[5] One speech in it I chiefly loved: 'twas Aeneas' tale to Dido; and thereabout of it especially, where he speaks of Priam's slaughter:[6] it live in your memory, begin at this line; let me   405 see, let me see;

"The rugged Pyrrhus, like th' Hyrcanian beast,"[7]—
It is not so: it begins with "Pyrrhus."
"The rugged Pyrrhus, he whose sable arms,
Black as his purpose, did the night resemble   410
When he lay couchèd in the ominous horse,[8]
Hath now this dread and black complexion smeared
With heraldry more dismal: head to foot
Now is he total gules; horridly tricked[9]
With the blood of fathers, mothers, daughters, sons,   415
Baked and impasted with the parching streets,
That lend a tyrannous[1] and a damnèd light
To their lord's murder: roasted in wrath and fire,
And thus o'er-sizèd[2] with coagulate gore,
With eyes like carbuncles, the hellish Pyrrhus   420
Old grandsire Priam seeks."
So, proceed you.

POLONIUS   'Fore God, my lord, well spoken, with good accent and good discretion.

FIRST PLAYER   'Anon he finds him   425
Striking too short at Greeks; his antique sword,
Rebellious to his arm, lies where it falls,

---

1. A pun on the *ring* of the voice and the *ring* around the king's head on a coin. "Chopine": a thick-soled shoe. "Uncurrent": unfit for currency.
2. A delicacy wasted on the general public.
3. Were louder (more authoritative than) mine.
4. Affectation. "Sallets": salads (that is, relish, spicy passages).
5. More elegant than showy.

6. The story of the fall of Troy, told by Aeneas to Queen Dido. Priam was the king of Troy.
7. Tiger. "Pyrrhus": Achilles' son (also called Neoptolemus).
8. The wooden horse in which Greek warriors were smuggled into Troy.
9. Adorned. "Gules": heraldic term for red.
1. Savage.
2. Glued over.

Repugnant to command: unequal matched,
Pyrrhus at Priam drives; in rage strikes wide;
But with the whiff and wind of his fell sword   430
The unnervèd father falls. Then senseless Ilium,[3]
Seeming to feel this blow, with flaming top
Stoops to his base, and with a hideous crash
Takes prisoner Pyrrhus's ear: for, lo! his sword,
Which was declining on the milky[4] head   435
Of reverend Priam seemed i' the air to stick:
So, as a painted tyrant, Pyrrhus stood,
And like a neutral to his will and matter,
Did nothing.
But as we often see, against some storm,   440
A silence in the heavens, the rack[5] stand still,
The bold winds speechless and the orb below
As hush as death, anon the dreadful thunder
Doth rend the region, so after Pyrrhus's pause
Aroused vengeance sets him new a-work;   445
And never did the Cyclops'[6] hammers fall
On Mars's armor, forged for proof[7] eterne,
With less remorse than Pyrrhus's bleeding sword
Now falls on Priam.
Out, thou strumpet, Fortune! All you gods,   450
In general synod take away her power,
Break all the spokes and fellies from her wheel,
And bowl the round nave[8] down the hill of heaven
As low as to the fiends!
POLONIUS   This is too long.   455
HAMLET   It shall to the barber's, with your beard. Prithee, say on: he's
   for a jig[9] or a tale of bawdry, or he sleeps: say on: come to Hecuba.
FIRST PLAYER   "But who, O, who had seen the mobled[1] queen—"
HAMLET   "The mobled queen?"
POLONIUS   That's good; "mobled queen" is good.   460
FIRST PLAYER   "Run barefoot up and down, threatening the flames
   With bisson rheum; a clout[2] upon that head
   Where late the diadem stood; and for a robe,
   About her lank and all o'er-teemèd loins,[3]
   A blanket, in the alarm of fear caught up: 465
   Who this had seen, with tongue in venom steeped
   'Gainst Fortune's state[4] would treason have pronounced:
   But if the gods themselves did see her then,
   When she saw Pyrrhus make malicious sport

3. Troy's citadel.
4. White-haired.
5. Clouds. "Against": just before.
6. The gigantic workmen of Hephaestus (Vulcan), god of blacksmiths and fire.
7. Protection.
8. Hub. "Fellies": rims.

9. Ludicrous sung dialogue, short farce.
1. Muffled.
2. Cloth. "Bisson rheum": blinding moisture, tears.
3. Worn out by childbearing.
4. Government.

In mincing with his sword her husband's limbs,   470
The instant burst of clamor that she made,
Unless things mortal move them[5] not at all,
Would have made milch the burning eyes of heaven[6]
And passion in the gods."

POLONIUS   Look, whether he has not turned his color and has tears in   475
'␣s eyes. Prithee, no more.
HAMLET   'Tis well; I'll have thee speak out the rest of this soon. Good
my lord, will you see the players well bestowed?[7] Do you hear, let
them be well used, for they are the abstracts and brief chronicles
of the time: after your death you were better have a bad epitaph than   480
their ill report while you live.
POLONIUS   My lord, I will use them according to their desert.
HAMLET   God's bodykins,[8] man, much better: use every man after his
desert, and who shall 'scape whipping? Use them after your own
honor and dignity: the less they deserve, the more merit is in your   485
bounty. Take them in.
POLONIUS   Come, sirs.
HAMLET   Follow him, friends: we'll hear a play to-morrow. [Exit
POLONIUS with all the PLAYERS but the first.] Dost thou hear me, old
friend; can you play the Murder of Gonzago?   490
FIRST PLAYER   Aye, my lord.
HAMLET   We'll ha 't to-morrow night. You could, for a need, study a
speech of some dozen or sixteen lines, which I would set down and
insert in 't, could you not?
FIRST PLAYER   Aye, my lord.   495
HAMLET   Very well. Follow that lord; and look you mock him not.
[Exit FIRST PLAYER.] My good friends, I'll leave you till night: you are
welcome to Elsinore.
ROSENCRANTZ   Good my lord!
HAMLET   Aye, so, God be wi' ye! [Exeunt ROSENCRANTZ and GUIL-   500
DENSTERN.] Now I am alone.
   O, what a rogue and peasant slave am I!
Is it not monstrous that this player here,
But in a fiction, in a dream of passion,
Could force his soul so to his own conceit   505
That from her[9] working all his visage wanned;
Tears in his eyes, distraction in 's aspect,
A broken voice, and his whole function[1] suiting
With forms to his conceit? and all for nothing!
For Hecuba![2]   510
What's Hecuba to him, or he to Hecuba,
That he should weep for her? What would he do,

5. The gods.
6. The stars. "Milch": moist (milk-giving).
7. Taken care of, lodged.
8. By God's little body.

9. His soul's.
1. Bodily action.
2. Queen of Troy, Priam's wife. "Conceit":
imagination, conception of the role played.

Had he the motive and the cue for passion
That I have? He would drown the stage with tears
And cleave the general air with horrid speech,   515
Make mad the guilty and appal the free,
Confound the ignorant, and amaze indeed
The very faculties of eyes and ears.
Yet I,
A dull and muddy-mettled rascal, peak,[3]   520
Like John-a-dreams, unpregnant of my cause,[4]
And can say nothing; no, not for a king,
Upon whose property and most dear life
A damn'd defeat was made. Am I a coward?
Who calls me villain? breaks my pate across?   525
Plucks off my beard, and blows it in my face?
Tweaks me by the nose? gives me the lie i' the throat,
As deep as to the lungs? who does me this?
Ha!
'Swounds, I should take it: for it cannot be   530
But I am pigeon-livered and lack gall
To make oppression bitter, or ere this
I should have fatted all the region kites[5]
With this slave's offal: bloody, bawdy villain!
Remorseless, treacherous, lecherous, kindless[6] villain!   535
O, vengeance!
Why, what an ass am I! This is most brave,
That I, the son of a dear father murdered,
Prompted to my revenge by heaven and hell,
Must, like a whore, unpack my heart with words,   540
And fall a-cursing, like a very drab,
A scullion!
Fie upon 't! About,[7] my brain! Hum, I have heard
That guilty creatures, sitting at a play,
Have by the very cunning of the scene   545
Been struck so to the soul that presently
They have proclaimed their malefactions;
For murder, though it have no tongue, will speak
With most miraculous organ. I'll have these players
Play something like the murder of my father   550
Before mine uncle: I'll observe his looks;
I'll tent him to the quick: if he but blench,[8]
I know my course. The spirit that I have seen
May be the devil; and the devil hath power

---

3. Mope. "Muddy mettled": of poor metal
(spirit, temper), dull-spirited.
4. Not really conscious of my cause, unquick-
ened by it. "John-a-dreams": a dreamy, absent-
minded character.

5. Kites (hawks) of the air.
6. Unnatural.
7. To work!
8. Flinch. "Tent": probe.

To assume a pleasing shape; yea, and perhaps   555
Out of my weakness and my melancholy,
As he is very potent with such spirits,
Abuses me to damn me. I'll have grounds
More relative⁹ than this. The play's the thing
Wherein I'll catch the conscience of the king.   560
    [Exit.]

Act 3

SCENE I

[SCENE: *A room in the castle.*]

    [*Enter* KING, QUEEN, POLONIUS, OPHELIA, ROSENCRANTZ, *and*
    GUILDENSTERN.]
KING   And can you, by no drift of circumstance,¹
  Get from him why he puts on this confusion,
  Grating so harshly all his days of quiet
  With turbulent and dangerous lunacy?
ROSENCRANTZ   He does confess he feels himself distracted,   5
  But from what cause he will by no means speak.
GUILDENSTERN   Nor do we find him forward to be sounded;
  But, with a crafty madness, keeps aloof,
  When we would bring him on to some confession
  Of his true state.
QUEEN   Did he receive you well?   10
ROSENCRANTZ   Most like a gentleman.
GUILDENSTERN   But with much forcing of his disposition.
ROSENCRANTZ   Niggard of question, but of our demands
  Most free in his reply.
QUEEN   Did you assay² him
  To any pastime?   15
ROSENCRANTZ   Madam, it so fell out that certain players
  We o'er-raught³ on the way: of these we told him,
  And there did seem in him a kind of joy
  To hear of it: they are about the court,
  And, as I think, they have already order   20
  This night to play before him.
POLONIUS   'Tis most true:
  And he beseeched me to entreat your majesties
  To hear and see the matter.
KING   With all my heart; and it doth much content me
  To hear him so inclined.   25
  Good gentlemen, give him a further edge,⁴
  And drive his purpose on to these delights.

9. Relevant.
1. Turn of talk, or roundabout way.
2. Try to attract him.

3. Overtook.
4. Incitement.

ROSENCRANTZ   We shall, my lord.
    [*Exeunt* ROSENCRANTZ *and* GUILDENSTERN.]
KING   Sweet Gertrude, leave us too;
  For we have closely[5] sent for Hamlet hither,
  That he, as 'twere by accident, may here   30
  Affront Ophelia:
  Her father and myself, lawful espials,
  Will so bestow[6] ourselves that, seeing unseen,
  We may of their encounter frankly judge,
  And gather by him, as he is behaved,   35
  If 't be the affliction of his love or no
  That thus he suffers for.
QUEEN   I shall obey you:
  And for your part, Ophelia, I do wish
  That your good beauties be the happy cause
  Of Hamlet's wildness: so shall I hope your virtues   40
  Will bring him to his wonted way again,
  To both your honors.
OPHELIA   Madam, I wish it may.
    [*Exit* QUEEN.]
POLONIUS   Ophelia, walk you here. Gracious, so please you,
  We will bestow ourselves. [*To* OPHELIA.] Read on this book;
  That show of such an exercise may color[7]   45
  Your loneliness. We are oft to blame in this,—
  'Tis too much proved—that with devotion's visage
  And pious action we do sugar o'er
  The devil himself.
KING [*Aside.*]   O, 'tis too true!
  How smart a lash that speech doth give my conscience!   50
  The harlot's cheek, beautied with plastering art,
  Is not more ugly to the thing that helps it
  Than is my deed to my most painted word:
  O heavy burthen!
POLONIUS   I hear him coming: let's withdraw, my lord.   55
    [*Exeunt* KING *and* POLONIUS.—*Enter* HAMLET.]
HAMLET   To be, or not to be: that is the question:
  Whether 'tis nobler in the mind to suffer
  The slings and arrows of outrageous fortune,
  Or to take arms against a sea of troubles,
  And by opposing end them. To die: to sleep;   60
  No more; and by a sleep to say we end
  The heart-ache, and the thousand natural shocks
  That flesh is heir to, 'tis a consummation[8]
  Devoutly to be wished. To die, to sleep;
  To sleep: perchance to dream: aye, there's the rub;[9]   65

---

5. Privately.   8. Final settlement.
6. Place. "Affront": confront. "Espials": spies. 9. The impediment (a bowling term).
7. Excuse.

For in that sleep of death what dreams may come,
When we have shuffled off this mortal coil,[1]
Must give us pause: there's the respect
That makes calamity of so long life;[2]
For who would bear the whips and scorns of time,   70
The oppressor's wrong, the proud man's contumely,
The pangs of despisèd love, the law's delay,
The insolence of office, and the spurns
That patient merit of the unworthy takes,
When he himself might his quietus make   75
With a bare bodkin? who would fardels[3] bear,
To grunt and sweat under a weary life,
But that the dread of something after death,
The undiscovered country from whose bourn[4]
No traveler returns, puzzles the will,   80
And makes us rather bear those ills we have
Than fly to others that we know not of?
Thus conscience does make cowards of us all,
And thus the native hue of resolution
Is sicklied o'er with the pale cast of thought,   85
And enterprises of great pitch[5] and moment
With this regard their currents turn awry
And lose the name of action. Soft you now!
The fair Ophelia! Nymph, in thy orisons[6]
Be all my sins remembered.

OPHELIA   Good my lord,   90
How does your honor for this many a day?
HAMLET   I humbly thank you: well, well, well.
OPHELIA   My lord, I have remembrances of yours,
    That I have longed to re-deliver;
    I pray you, now receive them.
HAMLET   No, not I;   95
    I never gave you aught.
OPHELIA   My honored lord, you know right well you did;
    And with them words of so sweet breath composed
    As made the things more rich: their perfume lost,
    Take these again; for to the noble mind   100
    Rich gifts wax poor when givers prove unkind.
    There, my lord.
HAMLET   Ha, ha! are you honest?
OPHELIA   My lord?
HAMLET   Are you fair?   105
OPHELIA   What means your lordship?
HAMLET   That if you be honest and fair, your honesty should admit
    no discourse to your beauty.

1. Have rid ourselves of the turmoil of mortal
life.
2. So long-lived. "Respect": consideration.
3. Burdens. "Bodkin": poniard, dagger.
4. Boundary.
5. Height.
6. Prayers.

OPHELIA   Could beauty, my lord, have better commerce[7] than with
honesty?   110

HAMLET   Aye, truly; for the power of beauty will sooner transform
honesty from what it is to a bawd than the force of honesty can
translate beauty into his[8] likeness: this was sometime a paradox,
but now the time gives it proof.[9] I did love you once.

OPHELIA   Indeed, my lord, you made me believe so.   115

HAMLET   You should not have believed me; for virtue cannot so
inoculate our old stock, but we shall relish[1] of it: I loved you not.

OPHELIA   I was the more deceived.

HAMLET   Get thee to a nunnery: why wouldst thou be a breeder of
sinners? I am myself indifferent honest; but yet I could accuse me   120
of such things that it were better my mother had not borne me:
I am very proud, revengeful, ambitious; with more offenses at my
beck than I have thoughts to put them in, imagination to give them
shape or time to act them in. What should such fellows as I do
crawling between heaven and earth! We are arrant knaves all; believe   125
none of us. Go thy ways to a nunnery. Where's your father?

OPHELIA   At home, my lord.

HAMLET   Let the doors be shut upon him, that he may play the fool
no where but in 's own house. Farewell.

OPHELIA   O, help him, you sweet heavens!   130

HAMLET   If thou dost marry, I'll give thee this plague for thy dowry:
be thou as chaste as ice, as pure as snow, thou shalt not escape
calumny. Get thee to a nunnery, go: farewell. Or, if thou wilt needs
marry, marry a fool; for wise men know well enough what monsters[2]
you make of them. To a nunnery, go; and quickly too. Farewell.   135

OPHELIA   O heavenly powers, restore him!

HAMLET   I have heard of your paintings too, well enough; God hath
given you one face, and you make yourselves another: you jig, you
amble, and you lisp, and nick-name God's creatures, and make your
wantonness your ignorance.[3] Go to, I'll no more on 't; it hath made   140
me mad. I say, we will have no more marriages: those that are
married already, all but one, shall live; the rest shall keep as they are.
To a nunnery, go.
        [Exit.]

OPHELIA   O, what a noble mind is here o'erthrown!
The courtier's, soldier's, scholar's, eye, tongue, sword: 145
The expectancy and rose of the fair state,
The glass of fashion and the mould of form.[4]
The observed of all observers, quite, quite down!
And I, of ladies most deject and wretched,
That sucked the honey of his music vows,   150

---

7. Intercourse.
8. Its.
9. In his mother's adultery.
1. Retain the flavor of. "Inoculate": graft itself onto.
2. Cuckolds bear imaginary horns and "a

horned man's a monster" (*Othello* 4.1).
3. Misname (out of affectation) the most natural things, and pretend that this is due to ignorance instead of affectation.
4. The mirror of fashion and the model of behavior.

Now see that noble and most sovereign reason,
Like sweet bells jangled, out of tune and harsh;
That unmatched form and feature of blown[5] youth
Blasted with ecstasy: O, woe is me,
To have seen what I have seen, see what I see! 155

[*Re-enter* KING *and* POLONIUS.]

KING Love! his affections do not that way tend;
Nor what he spake, though it lacked form a little,
Was not like madness. There's something in his soul
O'er which his melancholy sits on brood,
And I do doubt[6] the hatch and the disclose 160
Will be some danger: which for to prevent,
I have in quick determination
Thus set it down:—he shall with speed to England,
For the demand of our neglected tribute:
Haply the seas and countries different 165
With variable objects shall expel
This something-settled matter in his heart,
Whereon his brains still beating puts him thus
From fashion of himself.[7] What think you on 't?
POLONIUS It shall do well: but yet do I believe 170
The origin and commencement of his grief
Sprung from neglected love. How now, Ophelia!
You need not tell us what Lord Hamlet said;
We heard it all. My lord, do as you please;
But, if you hold it fit, after the play, 175
Let his queen mother all alone entreat him
To show his grief: let her be round[8] with him;
And I'll be placed, so please you, in the ear
Of all their conference. If she find him not,
To England send him, or confine him where 180
Your wisdom best shall think.
KING   It shall be so:
Madness in great ones must not unwatched go.
[*Exeunt.*]

SCENE 2

[SCENE: *A hall in the castle.*]

[*Enter* HAMLET *and* PLAYERS.]

HAMLET Speak the speech, I pray you, as I pronounced it to you,
trippingly on the tongue: but if you mouth it, as many of your players
do, I had as lief the town-crier spoke my lines. Nor do not saw
the air too much with your hand, thus; but use all gently: for in the
very torrent, tempest, and, as I may say, whirlwind of your passion, 5

---

5. In full bloom.
6. Fear.

7. Makes him behave unusually.
8. Direct.

you must acquire and beget a temperance that may give it smoothness. O, it offends me to the soul to hear a robustious periwig-pated fellow tear a passion to tatters, to very rags, to split the ears of the groundlings,[9] who, for the most part, are capable of nothing but inexplicable dumb-shows and noise: I would have such a fellow whipped for o'er doing Termagant;[1] it out-herods Herod: pray you, avoid it.

FIRST PLAYER   I warrant your honor.

HAMLET   Be not too tame neither, but let your own discretion be your tutor: suit the action to the word, the word to the action; with this special observance, that you o'erstep not the modesty[2] of nature: for anything so overdone is from the purpose of playing, whose end, both at the first and now, was and is, to hold, as 'twere, the mirror up to nature; to show virtue her own feature, scorn her own image, and the very age and body of the time his form and pressure.[3] Now this overdone or come tardy off, though it make the unskillful laugh, cannot but make the judicious grieve; the censure of the which one must in your allowance o'erweigh a whole theater of others. O, there be players that I have seen play, and heard others praise, and that highly, not to speak it profanely,[4] that neither having the accent of Christians nor the gait of Christian, pagan, nor man, have so strutted and bellowed, that I have thought some of nature's journeymen had made men, and not made them well, they imitated humanity so abominably.

FIRST PLAYER   I hope we have reformed that indifferently[5] with us, sir.

HAMLET   O, reform it altogether. And let those that play your clowns speak no more than is set down for them: for there be of them that will themselves laugh, to set on some quantity of barren[6] spectators to laugh too, though in the mean time some necessary question of the play be then to be considered: that's villainous, and shows a most pitiful ambition in the fool that uses it. Go, make you ready.

[*Exeunt* PLAYERS. —*Enter* POLONIUS, ROSENCRANTZ, *and* GUILDENSTERN.]

How now, my lord! will the king hear this piece of work?

POLONIUS   And the queen too, and that presently.

HAMLET   Bid the players make haste.

[*Exit* POLONIUS.]

Will you two help to hasten them?

ROSENCRANTZ
GUILDENSTERN   } We will, my lord.

[*Exeunt* ROSENCRANTZ *and* GUILDENSTERN.]

HAMLET   What ho! Horatio!

[*Enter* HORATIO.]

HORATIO   Here, sweet lord, at your service.

---

9. Spectators in the pit, where admission was cheapest.
1. God of the Muslims in old romances and morality plays; he was portrayed as being noisy and excitable.
2. Moderation.

3. Impress, shape. "Feature": form. "His": its.
4. Hamlet apologizes for the profane implication that there could be men not of God's making.
5. Pretty well.
6. Silly.

HAMLET   Horatio, thou art e'en as just a man
  As e'er my conversation coped withal.[7]   45
HORATIO   O, my dear lord,—
HAMLET   Nay, do not think I flatter;
  For what advancement may I hope from thee,
  That no revenue hast but thy good spirits,
  To feed and clothe thee? Why should the poor be flattered?
  No, let the candied tongue lick absurd pomp,   50
  And crook the pregnant hinges of the knee
  Where thrift may follow fawning.[8] Dost thou hear?
  Since my dear soul was mistress of her choice,
  And could of men distinguish, her election
  Hath sealed thee for herself: for thou hast been   55
  As one, in suffering all, that suffers nothing;
  A man that fortune's buffets and rewards
  Hast ta'en with equal thanks: and blest are those
  Whose blood and judgment[9] are so well commingled
  That they are not a pipe for fortune's finger   60
  To sound what stop she please.[1] Give me that man
  That is not passion's slave, and I will wear him
  In my heart's core, ay, in my heart of heart,
  As I do thee. Something too much of this.
  There is a play to-night before the king;   65
  One scene of it comes near the circumstance
  Which I have told thee of my father's death:
  I prithee, when thou sees that act a-foot,
  Even with the very comment of thy soul[2]
  Observe my uncle: if his occulted guilt   70
  Do not itself unkennel in one speech
  It is a damned ghost that we have seen,
  And my imaginations are as foul
  As Vulcan's stithy.[3] Give him heedful note;
  For I mine eyes will rivet to his face,   75
  And after we will both our judgments join
  In censure of his seeming.[4]
HORATIO   Well, my lord:
  If he steal aught the whilst this play is playing,
  And 'scape detecting, I will pay the theft.
HAMLET   They are coming to the play: I must be idle:[5]   80
  Get you a place.
      [*Danish march. A flourish. Enter* KING, QUEEN, POLONIUS, OPHELIA,
      ROSENCRANTZ, GUILDENSTERN, *and other* LORDS *attendant, with the*
      guard carrying torches.]

---

7. As I ever associated with.
8. Material profit may be derived from cringing. "Pregnant hinges": supple joints.
9. Passion and reason.
1. For Fortune to put her finger on any wind-

hole of the pipe she wants.
2. With all your powers of observation.
3. Smithy.
4. To judge his behavior.
5. Crazy.

KING How fares our cousin Hamlet?

HAMLET Excellent, i' faith; of the chameleon's dish: I eat the air,[6] promise-crammed: you cannot feed capons so.

KING I have nothing with this answer, Hamlet; these words are not mine.[7] 85

HAMLET No, nor mine now. [*To* POLONIUS.] My lord, you played once i' the university, you say?

POLONIUS That did I, my lord, and was accounted a good actor.

HAMLET What did you enact? 90

POLONIUS I did enact Julius Caesar: I was killed i' the Capitol; Brutus killed me.

HAMLET It was a brute part of him to kill so capital a calf there. Be the players ready?

ROSENCRANTZ Aye, my lord: they stay upon your patience. 95

QUEEN Come hither, my dear Hamlet, sit by me.

HAMLET No, good mother, here's metal more attractive.

POLONIUS [*To the* KING.] O, ho! do you mark that?

HAMLET Lady, shall I lie in your lap? [*Lying down at* OPHELIA's *feet.*]

OPHELIA No, my lord. 100

HAMLET I mean, my head upon your lap?

OPHELIA Aye, my lord.

HAMLET Do you think I meant country matters?

OPHELIA I think nothing, my lord.

HAMLET That's a fair thought to lie between maids' legs. 105

OPHELIA What is, my lord?

HAMLET Nothing.[8]

OPHELIA You are merry, my lord.

HAMLET Who, I?

OPHELIA Aye, my lord. 110

HAMLET O God, your only jig-maker.[9] What should a man do but be merry? for, look you, how cheerfully my mother looks, and my father died within 's two hours.

OPHELIA Nay, 'tis twice two months, my lord.

HAMLET So long? Nay then, let the devil wear black, for I'll have a 115
suit of sables.[1] O heavens! die two months ago, and not forgotten yet? Then there's hope a great man's memory may outlive his life half a year: but, by 'r lady, he must build churches then; or else shall he suffer not thinking on, with the hobby-horse,[2] whose epitaph is, "For, O, for, O, the hobby-horse is forgot." 120

[*Hautboys play. The dumb-show enters. —Enter a King and a Queen very lovingly; the Queen embracing him and he her. She kneels, and makes show of protestation unto him. He takes her up, and declines his head upon her neck; lays him down upon a bank of flowers: she, seeing him asleep,*]

6. The chameleon was supposed to feed on air.

7. Have nothing to do with my question.

8. A sexual pun: no thing.

9. Maker of comic songs.

1. Hamlet notes sarcastically the lack of mourning for his father in the fancy dress of court and king.

2. A figure in the old May Day games and Morris dances.

leaves him. Anon comes in a fellow, takes off his crown, kisses it, and pours poison in the King's ears, and exits. The Queen returns; finds the King dead, and makes passionate action. The Poisoner, with some two or three Mutes comes in again, seeming to lament with her. The dead body is carried away. The Poisoner woos the Queen with gifts: she seems loath and unwilling awhile, but in the end accepts his love. —Exeunt.]

OPHELIA What means this, my lord?

HAMLET Marry, this is miching mallecho;³ it means mischief.

OPHELIA Belike this show imports the argument of the play.

[*Enter* PROLOGUE.]

HAMLET We shall know by this fellow: the players cannot keep counsel;⁴ they'll tell all.   125

OPHELIA Will he tell us what this show meant?

HAMLET Aye, or any show that you'll show him: be not you ashamed to show, he'll not shame to tell you what it means.

OPHELIA You are naught,⁵ you are naught: I'll mark the play.

PROLOGUE For us, and for our tragedy,   130
　　　　　Here stooping to your clemency,
　　　　　We beg your hearing patiently.

HAMLET Is this a prologue, or the posy⁶ of a ring?

OPHELIA 'Tis brief, my lord.

HAMLET As woman's love.   135

[*Enter two* PLAYERS, KING *and* QUEEN.]

PLAYER KING Full thirty times hath Phœbus's cart⁷ gone round
Neptune's salt wash and Tellus's orbed ground,
And thirty dozen moons with borrowed sheen
About the world have times twelve thirties been,
Since love our hearts and Hymen did our hands   140
Unite commutual in most sacred bands.

PLAYER QUEEN So many journeys may the sun and moon
Make us again count o'er ere love be done!
But, woe is me, you are so sick of late,
So far from cheer and from your former state,   145
That I distrust you.⁸ Yet, though I distrust,
Discomfort you, my lord, it nothing must:
For women's fear and love holds quantity,⁹
In neither aught, or in extremity.
Now, what my love is, proof hath made you know,   150
And as my love is sized, my fear is so:
Where love is great, the littlest doubts are fear,
Where little fears grow great, great love grows there.

PLAYER KING Faith, I must leave thee, love, and shortly too;
My operant powers their functions leave¹ to do: 155
And thou shalt live in this fair world behind,

---

3. Sneaking misdeed.
4. A secret.
5. Naughty, improper.
6. Motto, inscription.

7. The chariot of the sun.
8. I am worried about you.
9. Maintain mutual balance.
1. Cease.

Honored, beloved; and haply one as kind
For husband shalt thou—
PLAYER QUEEN   O, confound the rest!
   Such love must needs be treason in my breast:
   In second husband let me be accurst!   160
   None wed the second but who killed the first.
HAMLET [*Aside.*]   Wormwood, wormwood.
PLAYER QUEEN   The instances that second marriage move
   Are base respects of thrift,[2] but none of love:
   A second time I kill my husband dead,   165
   When second husband kisses me in bed.
PLAYER KING   I do believe you think what now you speak,
   But what we do determine oft we break.
   Purpose is but the slave to memory,
   Of violent birth but poor validity: 170
   Which now, like fruit unripe, sticks on the tree,
   But fall unshaken when they mellow be.
   Most necessary 'tis that we forget
   To pay ourselves what to ourselves is debt:
   What to ourselves in passion we propose,   175
   The passion ending, both the purpose lose.
   The violence of either grief or joy
   Their own enactures[3] with themselves destroy:
   Where joy most revels, grief doth most lament;
   Grief joys, joy grieves, on slender accident.   180
   This world is not for aye, nor 'tis not strange
   That even our loves should with our fortunes change,
   For 'tis a question left us yet to prove,
   Whether love lead fortune or else fortune love.
   The great man down, you mark his favorite flies;   185
   The poor advanced makes friends of enemies:
   And hitherto doth love on fortune tend;
   For who not needs shall never lack a friend,
   And who in want a hollow friend doth try
   Directly seasons[4] him his enemy.   190
   But, orderly to end where I begun,
   Our wills and fates do so contrary run,
   That our devices still are overthrown,
   Our thoughts are ours, their ends none of our own:
   So think thou wilt no second husband wed,   195
   But die thy thoughts when thy first lord is dead.
PLAYER QUEEN   Nor earth to me give food nor heaven light!
   Sport and repose lock from me day and night!
   To desperation turn my trust and hope!
   An anchor's cheer in prison be my scope!   200
   Each opposite, that blanks[5] the face of joy,

2. Considerations of material profit. "Instances": motives.
3. Their own fulfillment in action.

4. Matures.
5. Makes pale. "Anchor's cheer": hermit's, or
anchorite's, fare.

Meet what I would have well and it destroy!
Both here and hence pursue me lasting strife,
If, once a widow, ever I be wife!

HAMLET   If she should break it now!   205

PLAYER KING   'Tis deeply sworn. Sweet, leave me here a while;
My spirits grow dull, and fain I would beguile
The tedious day with sleep.
    [*Sleeps.*]

PLAYER QUEEN   Sleep rock thy brain;
And never come mischance between us twain!
    [*Exit.*]

HAMLET   Madam, how like you this play?   210

QUEEN   The lady doth protest[6] too much, methinks.

HAMLET   O, but she'll keep her word.

KING   Have you heard the argument?[7] Is there no offense in 't?

HAMLET   No, no, they do but jest, poison in jest; no offense i' the
world.   215

KING   What do you call the play?

HAMLET   The Mouse-Trap. Marry, how? Tropically.[8] This play is the
image of a murder done in Vienna: Gonzago is the duke's name; his
wife, Baptista: you shall see anon; 'tis a knavish piece of work; but
what o' that? your majesty, and we that have free souls, it touches   220
us not: let the galled jade wince, our withers are unwrung.[9]
    [*Enter* LUCIANUS.]
This is one Lucianus, nephew to the king.

OPHELIA   You are as good as a chorus, my lord.

HAMLET   I could interpret[1] between you and your love, if I could see
the puppets dallying.   225

OPHELIA   You are keen,[2] my lord, you are keen.

HAMLET   It would cost you a groaning to take off my edge.

OPHELIA   Still better and worse.

HAMLET   So you must take[3] your husbands. Begin, murderer; pox,
leave thy damnable faces, and begin. Come: the croaking raven doth   230
bellow for revenge.

LUCIANUS   Thoughts black, hands apt, drugs fit, and time agreeing;
Confederate season, else no creature seeing;
Thou mixture rank, of midnight weeds collected,
With Hecate's ban[4] thrice blasted, thrice infected,   235
Thy natural magic and dire property,
On wholesome life usurp immediately.
    [*Pours the poison into the sleeper's ear.*]

HAMLET   He poisons him i' the garden for his estate. His name's

---

6. Promise.
7. Plot of the play in outline.
8. By a trope, figuratively.
9. Not wrenched. "Galled jade": injured horse. "Withers": the area between a horse's shoulders.
1. Act as interpreter (regular feature in puppet shows).

2. Bitter, but Hamlet chooses to take the word sexually.
3. That is, for better or for worse, as in the marriage service—but in fact you "mis-take," deceive them.
4. Goddess of witchcraft's curse. "Confederate": favorable.

Gonzago: the story is extant, and written in very choice Italian: you shall see anon how the murderer gets the love of Gonzago's wife.

OPHELIA The king rises.

HAMLET What, frighted with false fire![5]

QUEEN How fares my lord?

POLONIUS Give o'er the play.

KING Give me some light. Away!

POLONIUS Lights, lights, lights!

[*Exeunt all but* HAMLET *and* HORATIO.]

HAMLET Why, let the stricken deer go weep,
The hart ungallèd play;
For some must watch, while some must sleep:
Thus runs the world away.

Would not this, sir, and a forest of feathers—if the rest of my fortunes turn Turk with me—with two Provincial roses on my razed shoes, get me a fellowship in a cry[6] of players, sir?

HORATIO Half a share.

HAMLET A whole one, I.
For thou dost know, O Damon dear,
This realm dismantled was
Of Jove himself; and now reigns here
A very, very—pajock.

HORATIO You might have rhymed.[7]

HAMLET O good Horatio, I'll take the ghost's word for a thousand pound. Didst perceive?

HORATIO Very well, my lord.

HAMLET Upon the talk of the poisoning?

HORATIO I did very well note him.

HAMLET Ah, ha! Come, some music! come, the recorders!
For if the king like not the comedy,
Why then, belike, he likes it not, perdy.[8]
Come, some music!

[*Re-enter* ROSENCRANTZ *and* GUILDENSTERN.]

GUILDENSTERN Good my lord, vouchsafe me a word with you.

HAMLET Sir, a whole history.

GUILDENSTERN The king, sir—

HAMLET Aye, sir, what of him?

GUILDENSTERN Is in his retirement marvelous distempered.

HAMLET With drink, sir?

GUILDENSTERN No, my lord, rather with choler.[9]

HAMLET Your wisdom should show itself more richer to signify this to the doctor; for, for me to put him to his purgation would perhaps plunge him into far more choler.

GUILDENSTERN Good my lord, put your discourse into some frame, and start not so wildly from my affair.

5. Blank shot.
6. Company; a term generally used with hounds. "Turk with": betray. "Razed shoes": sometimes worn by actors.
7. *Ass* would have rhymed. "Pajock": peacock.
8. By God (*per Dieu*).
9. Bile, anger.

HAMLET I am tame, sir: pronounce.

GUILDENSTERN The queen, your mother, in most great affliction of spirit, hath sent me to you.

HAMLET You are welcome. 285

GUILDENSTERN Nay, good my lord, this courtesy is not of the right breed. If it shall please you to make me a wholesome[1] answer, I will do your mother's commandment: if not, your pardon and my return shall be the end of my business.

HAMLET Sir, I cannot. 290

GUILDENSTERN What, my lord?

HAMLET Make you a wholesome answer; my wit's diseased: but, sir, such answer as I can make, you shall command; or rather, as you say, my mother: therefore no more, but to the matter: my mother, you say,— 295

ROSENCRANTZ Then thus she says; your behavior hath struck her into amazement and admiration.[2]

HAMLET O wonderful son, that can so astonish a mother! But is there no sequel at the heels of this mother's admiration? Impart.

ROSENCRANTZ She desires to speak with you in her closet, ere you go to bed. 300

HAMLET We shall obey, were she ten times our mother. Have you any further trade with us?

ROSENCRANTZ My lord, you once did love me.

HAMLET So I do still, by these pickers and stealers.[3] 305

ROSENCRANTZ Good my lord, what is your cause of distemper? you do surely bar the door upon your own liberty, if you deny your griefs to your friend.

HAMLET Sir, I lack advancement.[4]

ROSENCRANTZ How can that be, when you have the voice of the king 310 himself for your succession in Denmark?

HAMLET Aye, sir, but "while the grass grows,"[5]—the proverb is something musty.

[Re-enter PLAYERS with recorders.]

O, the recorders! let me see one. To withdraw with you:—why do you go about to recover the wind of me, as if you would drive 315 me into a toil?[6]

GUILDENSTERN O, my lord, if my duty be too bold, my love is too unmannerly.

HAMLET I do not well understand that. Will you play upon this pipe?

GUILDENSTERN My lord, I cannot. 320

HAMLET I pray you.

GUILDENSTERN Believe me, I cannot.

HAMLET I do beseech you.

---

1. Sensible.
2. Confusion and surprise.
3. The hands.
4. Hamlet pretends that the cause of his "distemper" is frustrated ambition.

5. The proverb ends: "oft starves the silly steed."
6. Snare. "Withdraw": retire, talk in private. "Recover the wind of": get to the windward.

GUILDENSTERN   I know no touch of it, my lord.

HAMLET   It is as easy as lying: govern these ventages[7] with your fingers   325
and thumb, give it breath with your mouth, and it will discourse most
eloquent music. Look you, these are the stops.

GUILDENSTERN   But these cannot I command to any utterance of
harmony; I have not the skill.

HAMLET   Why, look you now, how unworthy a thing you make of me!   330
You would play upon me; you would seem to know my stops; you
would pluck out the heart of my mystery; you would sound me from
my lowest note to the top of my compass: and there is much music,
excellent voice, in this little organ; yet cannot you make it speak.
'Sblood, do you think I am easier to be played on than a pipe? Call   335
me what instrument you will, though you can fret[8] me, yet you cannot
play upon me.

    [Re-enter POLONIUS.]

God bless you, sir!

POLONIUS   My lord, the queen would speak with you, and presently.

HAMLET   Do you see yonder cloud that's almost in shape of a camel?   340

POLONIUS   By the mass, and 'tis like a camel, indeed.

HAMLET   Methinks it is like a weasel.

POLONIUS   It is backed like a weasel.

HAMLET   Or like a whale?

POLONIUS   Very like a whale.   345

HAMLET   Then I will come to my mother by and by. They fool me to
the top of my bent. I will come by and by.

POLONIUS   I will say so.

    [Exit POLONIUS.]

HAMLET   "By and by" is easily said. Leave me, friends.

    [Exeunt all but HAMLET.]

'Tis now the very witching time of night,   350
When churchyards yawn, and hell itself breathes out
Contagion to this world: now could I drink hot blood,
And do such bitter business as the day
Would quake to look on. Soft! now to my mother.
O heart, lose not thy nature; let not ever   355
The soul of Nero[9] enter this firm bosom:
Let me be cruel, not unnatural:
I will speak daggers to her, but use none;
My tongue and soul in this be hypocrites;
How in my words soever she be shent,   360
To give them seals[1] never, my soul, consent!

    [Exit.]

---

7. Windholes.

8. Vex, with a pun on *frets*, the ridges placed
across the finger board of a guitar to regulate
the fingering.

9. A Roman emperor (37–68 C.E.) who murdered his mother.

1. Ratify them by action. "Shent": reproached.

SCENE 3

[SCENE: *A room in the castle.*]

[*Enter* KING, ROSENCRANTZ, *and* GUILDENSTERN.]

KING   I like him not, nor stands it safe with us
To let his madness range. Therefore prepare you;
I your commission will forthwith dispatch,
And he to England shall along with you:
The terms of our estate[2] may not endure   5
Hazard so near us as doth hourly grow
Out of his lunacies.

GUILDENSTERN   We will ourselves provide:
Most holy and religious fear it is
To keep those many many bodies safe
That live and feed upon your majesty.   10

ROSENCRANTZ   The single and peculiar[3] life is bound
With all the strength and armor of the mind
To keep itself from noyance; but much more
That spirit upon whose weal depends and rests
The lives of many. The cease[4] of majesty   15
Dies not alone, but like a gulf doth draw
What 's near it with it; it is a massy wheel,
Fixed on the summit of the highest mount,
To whose huge spokes ten thousand lesser things
Are mortised[5] and adjoined; which, when it falls,   20
Each small annexment, petty consequence,
Attends the boisterous ruin. Never alone
Did the king sigh, but with a general groan.

KING   Arm you, I pray you, to this speedy voyage,
For we will fetters put about this fear,   25
Which now goes too free-footed.

ROSENCRANTZ } We will haste us.
GUILDENSTERN

[*Exeunt* ROSENCRANTZ *and* GUILDENSTERN. —*Enter* POLONIUS.]

POLONIUS   My lord, he's going to his mother's closet:
Behind the arras I'll convey myself,
To hear the process: I'll warrant she'll tax him home:[6]   30
And, as you said, and wisely was it said
'Tis meet that some more audience than a mother,
Since nature makes them partial, should o'erhear
The speech, of vantage.[7] Fare you well, my liege:
I'll call upon you ere you go to bed,   35
And tell you what I know.

KING   Thanks, dear my lord.

[*Exit* POLONIUS.]

O, my offense is rank, it smells to heaven;

---

2. My position as king.
3. Individual.
4. Decease, extinction.

5. Fastened.
6. Take him to task thoroughly.
7. From a vantage point.

It hath the primal eldest curse[8] upon 't,
A brother's murder. Pray can I not,
Though inclination be as sharp as will: 40
My stronger guilt defeats my strong intent,
And like a man to double business bound,
I stand in pause where I shall first begin,
And both neglect. What if this cursed hand
Were thicker than itself with brother's blood,   45
Is there not rain enough in the sweet heavens
To wash it white as snow? Whereto serves mercy
But to confront the visage of offense?[9]
And what's in prayer but this twofold force,
To be forestalled ere we come to fall,   50
Or pardoned being down? Then I'll look up;
My fault is past. But O, what form of prayer
Can serve my turn? "Forgive me my foul murder?"
That cannot be, since I am still possessed
Of those effects for which I did the murder,   55
My crown, mine own ambition and my queen.
May one be pardoned and retain the offense?[1]
In the corrupted currents of this world
Offense's gilded hand may shove by justice,
And oft 'tis seen the wicked prize itself   60
Buys out the law:[2] but 'tis not so above;
There is no shuffling, there the action lies
In his[3] true nature, and we ourselves compelled
Even to the teeth and forehead of our faults
To give in evidence. What then? what rests?[4]   65
Try what repentance can: what can it not?
Yet what can it when one can not repent?
O wretched state! O bosom black as death!
O limèd soul, that struggling to be free
Art more engaged! Help, angels! make assay![5]   70
Bow, stubborn knees, and, heart with strings of steel,
Be soft as sinews of the new-born babe!
All may be well.
    [*Retires and kneels. —Enter* HAMLET.]
HAMLET   Now might I do it pat,[6] now he is praying
And now I'll do 't: and so he goes to heaven: 75
And so am I revenged. That would be scanned;[7]
A villain kills my father; and for that,
I, his sole son, do this same villain send
To heaven.

8. The curse of Cain.
9. Guilt.
1. The things obtained through the offense.
2. The wealth unduly acquired is used for
bribery.
3. Its.

4. What remains?
5. Make the attempt! "Limèd": caught as with
birdlime.
6. Conveniently.
7. Would have to be considered carefully.

O, this is hire and salary, not revenge.   80
He took my father grossly, full of bread,
With all his crimes broad blown, as flush as May;
And how his audit[8] stands who knows save heaven?
But in our circumstance and course of thought,
'Tis heavy with him: and am I then revenged,   85
To take him in the purging of his soul,
When he is fit and seasoned[9] for his passage?
No.
Up, sword, and know thou a more horrid hent:[1]
When he is drunk asleep, or in his rage,   90
Or, in the incestuous pleasure of his bed;
At game, a-swearing, or about some act
That has no relish of salvation in 't;
Then trip him, that his heels may kick at heaven
And that his soul may be as damned and black   95
As hell, whereto it goes. My mother stays:
This physic but prolongs thy sickly days.
    [*Exit.*]
KING [*Rising.*]   My words fly up, my thoughts remain below:
Words without thoughts never to heaven go.
    [*Exit.*]

SCENE 4

[SCENE: *The Queen's closet.*]

[*Enter* QUEEN *and* POLONIUS.]
POLONIUS   He will come straight. Look you lay home to him:
Tell him his pranks have been too broad[2] to bear with,
And that your grace hath screen'd and stood between
Much heat and him. I'll sconce me even here.
Pray you, be round[3] with him.
HAMLET [*Within.*]   Mother, mother, mother!   5
QUEEN   I'll warrant you; fear me not. Withdraw,
I hear him coming.
    [POLONIUS *hides behind the arras. —Enter* HAMLET.]
HAMLET   Now, mother, what's the matter?
QUEEN   Hamlet, thou hast thy father much offended.
HAMLET   Mother, you have my father much offended.
QUEEN   Come, come, you answer with an idle tongue.   10
HAMLET   Go, go, you question with a wicked tongue.
QUEEN   Why, how now, Hamlet!
HAMLET   What's the matter now?
QUEEN   Have you forgot me?
HAMLET   No, by the rood,[4] not so:
You are the queen, your husband's brother's wife;   15

8. Account. "Broad blown": in full bloom.   lesson.
9. Ripe, ready.   3. Straightforward.
1. Grip.   4. Cross.
2. Unrestrained. "Lay home": give him a stern

And—would it were not so!—you are my mother.
QUEEN   Nay, then, I'll set those to you that can speak.
HAMLET   Come, come, and sit you down; you shall not budge:
You go not till I set you up a glass[5]
Where you may see the inmost part of you.   20
QUEEN   What wilt thou do? thou wilt not murder me?
Help, help, ho!
POLONIUS [*Behind.*]   What, ho! help, help, help!
HAMLET [*Drawing.*]   How now! a rat? Dead, for a ducat, dead!
        [*Makes a pass through the arras.*]
POLONIUS [*Behind.*]   O, I am slain!
        [*Falls and dies.*]
QUEEN   O me, what hast thou done?   25
HAMLET   Nay, I know not: is it the king?
QUEEN   O, what a rash and bloody deed is this!
HAMLET   A bloody deed! almost as bad, good mother,
As kill a king, and marry with his brother.
QUEEN   As kill a king!
HAMLET   Aye, lady, 'twas my word.   30
        [*Lifts up the arras and discovers* POLONIUS.]
Thou wretched, rash, intruding fool, farewell!
I took thee for thy better: take thy fortune;
Thou find'st to be too busy[6] is some danger.
Leave wringing of your hands: peace! sit you down,
And let me wring your heart: for so I shall,   35
If it be made of penetrable stuff;
If damned custom have not brassed it so,
That it be proof and bulwark against sense.[7]
QUEEN   What have I done, that thou darest wag thy tongue
In noise so rude against me?
HAMLET   Such an act   40
That blurs the grace and blush of modesty,
Calls virtue hypocrite, takes off the rose
From the fair forehead of an innocent love,
And sets a blister there; makes marriage vows
As false as dicers' oaths: O, such a deed   45
As from the body of contraction[8] plucks
The very soul, and sweet religion makes
A rhapsody of words: heaven's face doth glow;[9]
Yea, this solidity and compound mass,
With tristful visage, as against the doom,[1]   50
Is thought-sick at the act.
QUEEN   Aye me, what act,
That roars so loud and thunders in the index?[2]
HAMLET   Look here, upon this picture, and on this,
The counterfeit presentment[3] of two brothers.   55

5. Mirror.
6. Too much of a busybody.
7. Feeling.
8. Duty to the marriage contract.

9. Blush with shame.
1. Doomsday. "Tristful": sad.
2. Prologue, table of contents.
3. Portrait.

See what a grace was seated on this brow;
Hyperion's curls, the front of Jove himself,
An eye like Mars, to threaten and command;
A station[4] like the herald Mercury
New-lighted on a heaven-kissing hill; 60
A combination and a form indeed,
Where every god did seem to set his seal
To give the world assurance of a man:
This was your husband. Look you now, what follows:
Here is your husband; like a mildewed ear,[5] 65
Blasting his wholesome brother. Have you eyes?
Could you on this fair mountain leave to feed,
And batten[6] on this moor? Ha! have you eyes?
You cannot call it love, for at your age
The hey-day in the blood is tame, it's humble, 70
And waits upon[7] the judgment: and what judgment
Would step from this to this? Sense sure you have,
Else could you not have motion: but sure that sense
Is apoplexed: for madness would not err,
Nor sense to ecstasy was ne'er so thralled 75
But it reserved some quantity of choice,
To serve in such a difference. What devil was 't
That thus hath cozened you at hoodman-blind?[8]
Eyes without feeling, feeling without sight,
Ears without hands or eyes, smelling sans[9] all, 80
Or but a sickly part of one true sense
Could not so mope.[1]
O shame! where is thy blush? Rebellious hell,
If thou canst mutine in a matron's bones,
To flaming youth let virtue be as wax 85
And melt in her own fire: proclaim no shame
When the compulsive ardor gives the charge,[2]
Since frost itself as actively doth burn,
And reason panders[3] will.

QUEEN   O Hamlet, speak no more:
Thou turn'st mine eyes into my very soul, 90
And there I see such black and grained spots
As will not leave their tinct.[4]

HAMLET   Nay, but to live
In the rank sweat of an enseamèd[5] bed,
Stew'd in corruption, honeying and making love
Over the nasty sty,—

QUEEN   O, speak to me no more; 95
These words like daggers enter in my ears;

4. Posture.
5. Of corn.
6. Gorge, fatten. "Leave": cease.
7. Is subordinated to.
8. Blindman's buff. "Cozened": tricked.
9. Without.

1. Be stupid.
2. Attack.
3. Becomes subservient to.
4. Lose their color. "Grained": dyed in.
5. Greasy.

No more, sweet Hamlet!

HAMLET   A murderer and a villain;
A slave that is not twentieth part the tithe[6]
Of your precédent lord; a vice of kings;
A cutpurse[7] of the empire and the rule,   100
That from a shelf the precious diadem stole
And put it in his pocket!

QUEEN   No more!

HAMLET   A king of shreds and patches—
          [*Enter* GHOST.]
Save me, and hover o'er me with your wings,
You heavenly guards! What would your gracious figure?   105

QUEEN   Alas, he's mad!

HAMLET   Do you not come your tardy son to chide,
That, lapsed in time and passion, lets go by
The important acting of your dread command?
O, say!

GHOST   Do not forget: this visitation   110
Is but to whet thy almost blunted purpose.
But look, amazement on thy mother sits:
O, step between her and her fighting soul:
Conceit[8] in weakest bodies strongest works:
Speak to her, Hamlet.

HAMLET   How is it with you, lady?   115

QUEEN   Alas, how is 't with you,
That you do bend your eye on vacancy
And with the incorporal air do hold discourse?
Forth at your eyes your spirits wildly peep;
And, as the sleeping soldiers in the alarm,   120
Your bedded hairs, like life in excrements,[9]
Start up and stand on end. O gentle son,
Upon the heat and flame of thy distemper
Sprinkle cool patience. Whereon do you look?

HAMLET   On him, on him! Look you how pale he glares!   125
His form and cause conjoined, preaching to stones,
Would make them capable.[1] Do not look upon me,
Lest with this piteous action you convert
My stern effects:[2] then what I have to do
Will want true color; tears perchance for[3] blood.   130

QUEEN   To whom do you speak this?

HAMLET   Do you see nothing there?

QUEEN   Nothing at all; yet all that is I see.

HAMLET   Nor did you nothing hear?

QUEEN   No, nothing but ourselves.

HAMLET   Why, look you there! look, how it steals away!

---

6. Tenth.
7. Pickpocket. "Vice": clown, from the custom in the old morality plays of having a buf-
foon take the part of Vice or of a particular
vice.

8. Imagination.
9. Outgrowths. "Alarm": call to arms.
1. Of feeling.
2. You make me change my purpose.
3. Instead of.

My father, in his habit as he lived!   135
Look, where he goes, even now, out at the portal!
    [*Exit* GHOST.]
QUEEN   This is the very coinage of your brain:
  This bodiless creation ecstasy
  Is very cunning in.
HAMLET   Ecstasy!
  My pulse, as yours, doth temperately keep time,   140
  And makes as healthful music: it is not madness
  That I have uttered: bring me to the test,
  And I the matter will re-word, which madness
  Would gambol from. Mother, for love of grace,
  Lay not that flattering unction to your soul,   145
  That not your trespass but my madness speaks:
  It will but skin and film the ulcerous place,
  Whiles rank corruption, mining all within,
  Infects unseen. Confess yourself to heaven;
  Repent what's past, avoid what is to come,   150
  And do not spread the compost on the weeds,
  To make them ranker. Forgive me this my virtue,
  For in the fatness of these pursy[4] times
  Virtue itself of vice must pardon beg.
  Yea, curb[5] and woo for leave to do him good.   155
QUEEN   O Hamlet, thou hast cleft my heart in twain.
HAMLET   O, throw away the worser part of it,
  And live the purer with the other half.
  Good night: but go not to my uncle's bed;
  Assume a virtue, if you have it not.   160
  That monster, custom, who all sense doth eat,
  Of habits devil, is angel yet in this,
  That to the use of actions fair and good
  He likewise gives a frock or livery,
  That aptly is put on.[6] Refrain to-night,   165
  And that shall lend a kind of easiness
  To the next abstinence; the next more easy;
  For use almost can change the stamp[7] of nature,
  And either curb the devil, or throw him out
  With wondrous potency. Once more, good night: 170
  And when you are desirous to be blest,
  I'll blessing beg of you. For this same lord,
    [*Pointing to* POLONIUS.]
  I do repent: but heaven hath pleased it so,
  To punish me with this, and this with me,
  That I must be their scourge and minister.   175
  I will bestow[8] him, and will answer well
  The death I gave him. So, again, good night.

---

4. Swollen from pampering.
5. Bow.
6. I.e., habit, although like a devil in establishing evil ways in us, is like an angel in doing the same for virtues. "Aptly": easily.
7. Cast, form. "Use": habit.
8. Stow away. "Minister": agent of punishment.

I must be cruel, only to be kind:
Thus bad begins, and worse remains behind.
One word more, good lady.
QUEEN   What shall I do?   180
HAMLET   Not this, by no means, that I bid you do:
Let the bloat⁹ king tempt you again to bed;
Pinch wanton on your cheek, call you his mouse;
And let him, for a pair of reechy¹ kisses,
Or paddling in your neck with his damned fingers,   185
Make you to ravel all this matter out,
That I essentially am not in madness,
But mad in craft.² 'Twere good you let him know;
For who, that's but a queen, fair, sober, wise,
Would from a paddock, from a bat, a gib,   190
Such dear concernings³ hide? who would do so?
No, in despite of sense and secrecy,
Unpeg the basket on the house's top,
Let the birds fly, and like the famous ape,⁴
To try conclusions, in the basket creep   195
And break your own neck down.
QUEEN   Be thou assured, if words be made of breath
And breath of life, I have no life to breathe
What thou hast said to me.
HAMLET   I must to England; you know that?
QUEEN   Alack,   200
I had forgot: 'tis so concluded on.
HAMLET   There's letters sealed: and my two schoolfellows,
Whom I will trust as I will adders fanged,
They bear the mandate; they must sweep my way,
And marshal me to knavery. Let it work;   205
For 'tis the sport to have the enginer
Hoist with his own petar:⁵ and 't shall go hard
But I will delve one yard below their mines,
And blow them at the moon: I, 'tis most sweet
When in one line two crafts directly meet.   210
This man shall set me packing:
I'll lug the guts into the neighbor room.
Mother, good night. Indeed this councillor
Is now most still, most secret and most grave,⁶
Who was in life a foolish prating knave.   215
Come, sir, to draw toward an end with you.
Good night, mother.
         [*Exeunt severally;* HAMLET *dragging in* POLONIUS.]

---

9. Bloated with drink.
1. Fetid.
2. Simulation.
3. Matters with which one is closely concerned. "Paddock": toad. "Gib": tomcat.
4. The ape in the unidentified animal fable to which Hamlet alludes; apparently the animal saw birds fly out of a basket and drew the conclusion that by placing himself in a basket he could fly, too.
5. Petard, a variety of bomb. "Marshal": lead. "Enginer": military engineer. "Hoist": blow up.
6. Hamlet is punning on the word.

Act 4

SCENE I

[SCENE: *A room in the castle.*]

[*Enter* KING, QUEEN, ROSENCRANTZ, *and* GUILDENSTERN.]

KING There's matter in these sighs, these profound heaves:
You must translate: 'tis fit we understand them.
Where is your son?

QUEEN Bestow this place on us[7] a little while.

[*Exeunt* ROSENCRANTZ *and* GUILDENSTERN.]

Ah, mine own lord, what have I seen to-night!   5

KING What, Gertrude? How does Hamlet?

QUEEN Mad as the sea and wind, when both contend
Which is the mightier: in his lawless fit,
Behind the arras hearing something stir,
Whips out his rapier, cries "A rat, a rat!"   10
And in this brainish apprehension[8] kills
The unseen good old man.

KING   O heavy deed!
It had been so with us, had we been there:
His liberty is full of threats to all,
To you yourself, to us, to every one.   15
Alas, how shall this bloody deed be answered?
It will be laid to us, whose providence
Should have kept short,[9] restrained and out of haunt,
This mad young man: but so much was our love,
We would not understand what was most fit,   20
But, like the owner of a foul disease,
To keep it from divulging, let it feed
Even on the pith of life. Where is he gone?

QUEEN To draw apart the body he hath killed:
O'er whom his very madness, like some ore   25
Among a mineral[1] of metals base,
Shows itself pure; he weeps for what is done.

KING O Gertrude, come away!
The sun no sooner shall the mountains touch,
But we will ship him hence: and this vile deed   30
We must, with all our majesty and skill,
Both countenance[2] and excuse. Ho, Guildenstern!

[*Re-enter* ROSENCRANTZ *and* GUILDENSTERN.]

Friends both, go join you with some further aid:
Hamlet in madness hath Polonius slain,
And from his mother's closet hath he dragged him: 35
Go seek him out; speak fair, and bring the body
Into the chapel. I pray you, haste in this.

[*Exeunt* ROSENCRANTZ *and* GUILDENSTERN.]

7. Leave us alone.   1. Mine. "Ore": gold.
8. Imaginary notion.   2. Recognize.
9. Under close watch.

Come, Gertrude, we'll call up our wisest friends;
And let them know, both what we mean to do,
And what's untimely done. . . .[3] 40
Whose whisper o'er the world's diameter
As level as the cannon to his blank[4]
Transports his poisoned shot, may miss our name
And hit the woundless air. O, come away!
My soul is full of discord and dismay. 45
        [*Exeunt.*]

SCENE 2

[SCENE: *Another room in the castle.*]

        [*Enter* HAMLET.]
HAMLET   Safely stowed.
ROSENCRANTZ } [*Within.*] Hamlet! Lord Hamlet!
GUILDENSTERN }
HAMLET   But soft, what noise? who calls on Hamlet?
   O, here they come.
        [*Enter* ROSENCRANTZ *and* GUILDENSTERN.]
ROSENCRANTZ   What have you done, my lord, with the dead body? 5
HAMLET   Compounded[5] it with dust, whereto 'tis kin.
ROSENCRANTZ   Tell us where 'tis, that we may take it thence
   And bear it to the chapel.
HAMLET   Do not believe it.
ROSENCRANTZ   Believe what? 10
HAMLET   That I can keep your counsel and not mine own. Besides, to
   be demanded of a sponge! what replication[6] should be made by the
   son of a king?
ROSENCRANTZ   Take you me for a sponge, my lord?
HAMLET   Aye, sir; that soaks up the king's countenance,[7] his rewards, 15
   his authorities. But such officers do the king best service in the end:
   he keeps them, like an ape, in the corner of his jaw; first mouthed,
   to be last swallowed: when he needs what you have gleaned, it is but
   squeezing you, and sponge, you shall be dry again.
ROSENCRANTZ   I understand you not, my lord. 20
HAMLET   I am glad of it: a knavish speech sleeps in a foolish ear.
ROSENCRANTZ   My lord, you must tell us where the body is, and go
   with us to the king.
HAMLET   The body is with the king, but the king is not with the body.
   The king is a thing— 25
GUILDENSTERN   A thing, my lord?
HAMLET   Of nothing: bring me to him. Hide fox, and all after.[8]
        [*Exeunt.*]

---

3. This gap in the text has been guessingly filled
in with "So envious slander."
4. His target.
5. Mixed.

6. Formal reply. "Demanded": questioned by.
7. Favor.
8. A children's game.

SCENE 3

[SCENE: *Another room in the castle.*]

        [*Enter* KING, *attended.*]

KING   I have sent to seek him, and to find the body.
  How dangerous is it that this man goes loose!
  Yet must not we put the strong law on him:
  He's loved of the distracted multitude,
  Who like not in their judgment, but their eyes;   5
  And where 'tis so, the offender's scourge is weighed,
  But never the offense. To bear[9] all smooth and even,
  This sudden sending away must seem
  Deliberate pause: diseases desperate grown
  By desperate appliance[1] are relieved,   10
  Or not at all.

        [*Enter* ROSENCRANTZ.]
          How now! what hath befall'n?

ROSENCRANTZ   Where the dead body is bestowed, my lord,
  We cannot get from him.

KING   But where is he?

ROSENCRANTZ   Without, my lord; guarded, to know your pleasure.

KING   Bring him before us.   15

ROSENCRANTZ   Ho, Guildenstern! bring in my lord.

        [*Enter* HAMLET *and* GUILDENSTERN.]

KING   Now, Hamlet, where's Polonius?

HAMLET   At supper.

KING   At supper! where?

HAMLET   Not where he eats, but where he is eaten: a certain convocation   20
  of public worms are e'en at him. Your worm is your only emperor for
  diet:[2] we fat all creatures else to fat us, and we fat ourselves for
  maggots: your fat king and your lean beggar is but variable service,[3]
  two dishes, but to one table: that's the end.

KING   Alas, alas!   25

HAMLET   A man may fish with the worm that hath eat of a king, and
  eat of the fish that hath fed of that worm.

KING   What dost thou mean by this?

HAMLET   Nothing but to show you how a king may go a progress[4]
  through the guts of a beggar.   30

KING   Where is Polonius?

HAMLET   In heaven; send thither to see: if your messenger find him
  not there, seek him i' the other place yourself. But indeed, if you
  find him not within this month, you shall nose[5] him as you go up
  the stairs into the lobby.   35

KING   [*To some attendants.*] Go seek him there.

HAMLET   He will stay till you come.

---

9. Conduct. "Scourge": punishment.
1. Treatment. "Deliberate pause": the result of careful argument.
2. Possibly a punning reference to the Diet

(assembly) of the Holy Roman Empire at Worms.
3. That is, the service varies, not the food.
4. Royal state journey.
5. Smell.

[*Exeunt attendants.*]

KING   Hamlet, this deed, for thine especial safety,
  Which we do tender,[6] as we dearly grieve
  For that which thou hast done, must send thee hence   40
  With fiery quickness: therefore prepare thyself;
  The bark is ready and the wind at help,
  The associates tend, and every thing is bent
  For England.
HAMLET   For England?
KING   Aye, Hamlet.
HAMLET   Good.
KING   So is it, if thou knew'st our purposes.   45
HAMLET   I see a cherub that sees them. But, come; for England!
  Farewell, dear mother.
KING   Thy loving father, Hamlet.
HAMLET   My mother: father and mother is man and wife; man and
  wife is one flesh, and so, my mother. Come, for England!   50
      [*Exit.*]
KING   Follow him at foot;[7] tempt him with speed aboard;
  Delay it not; I'll have him hence to-night:
  Away! for every thing is sealed and done
  That else leans on[8] the affair: pray you, make haste.
      [*Exeunt* ROSENCRANTZ *and* GUILDENSTERN.]
  And, England,[9] if my love thou hold'st at aught—   55
  As my great power thereof may give thee sense,
  Since yet thy cicatrice looks raw and red
  After the Danish sword, and thy free awe
  Pays homage to us—thou mayst not coldly set[1]
  Our sovereign process; which imports at full,   60
  By letters conjuring[2] to that effect,
  The present death of Hamlet. Do it, England;
  For like the hectic[3] in my blood he rages,
  And thou must cure me; till I know 'tis done,
  Howe'er my haps, my joys were ne'er begun.   65
      [*Exit.*]

SCENE 4

[SCENE: *A plain in Denmark.*]

[*Enter* FORTINBRAS, *a* CAPTAIN, *and soldiers, marching.*]

FORTINBRAS   Go, captain, from me greet the Danish king;
  Tell him that by his license Fortinbras
  Craves the conveyance[4] of a promised march
  Over his kingdom. You know the rendezvous.
  If that his majesty would aught with us,   5

6. Care for.
7. At his heels.
8. Pertains to.
9. The king of England.

1. Regard with indifference.
2. Enjoining.
3. Fever.
4. Convoy.

We shall express our duty in his eye;[5]
And let him know so.
CAPTAIN   I will do 't, my lord.
FORTINBRAS   Go softly on.

[*Exeunt* FORTINBRAS *and soldiers.* —*Enter* HAMLET, ROSENCRANTZ,
GUILDENSTERN, *and others.*]

HAMLET   Good sir, whose powers[6] are these?
CAPTAIN   They are of Norway, sir.   10
HAMLET   How purposed, sir, I pray you?
CAPTAIN   Against some part of Poland.
HAMLET   Who commands them, sir?
CAPTAIN   The nephew to Old Norway, Fortinbras.
HAMLET   Goes it against the main[7] of Poland, sir,   15
Or for some frontier?
CAPTAIN   Truly to speak, and with no addition,
We go to gain a little patch of ground
That hath in it no profit but the name.
To pay five ducats, five, I would not farm it;   20
Nor will it yield to Norway or the Pole
A ranker rate, should it be sold in fee.[8]
HAMLET   Why, then the Polack never will defend it.
CAPTAIN   Yes, it is already garrisoned.
HAMLET   Two thousand souls and twenty thousand ducats   25
Will not debate the question of this straw!
This is the imposthume[9] of much wealth and peace,
That inward breaks, and shows no cause without
Why the man dies. I humbly thank you, sir.
CAPTAIN   God be wi' you, sir.
[*Exit.*]
ROSENCRANTZ   Will 't please you go, my lord?   30
HAMLET   I'll be with you straight. Go a little before.
[*Exeunt all but* HAMLET.]
How all occasions do inform against[1] me,
And spur my dull revenge! What is a man,
If his chief good and market[2] of his time
Be but to sleep and feed? a beast, no more.   35
Sure, he that made us with such large discourse,[3]
Looking before and after, gave us not
That capability and god-like reason
To fust[4] in us unused. Now, whether it be
Bestial oblivion, or some craven scruple   40
Of thinking too precisely on the event,[5]—
A thought which, quartered, hath but one part wisdom
And ever three parts coward,—I do not know
Why yet I live to say "this thing's to do,"

5. Presence.
6. Armed forces.
7. The whole of.
8. For absolute possession. "Ranker": higher.
9. Ulcer.

1. Denounce.
2. Payment for, reward.
3. Reasoning power.
4. Become moldy, taste of the cask.
5. Outcome.

Sith I have cause, and will, and strength, and means,   45
To do 't. Examples gross as earth exhort me:
Witness this army, of such mass and charge,[6]
Led by a delicate and tender prince,
Whose spirit with divine ambition puffed
Makes mouths[7] at the invisible event,   50
Exposing what is mortal and unsure
To all that fortune, death, and danger dare,
Even for an egg-shell. Rightly to be great
Is not to stir without great argument,
But greatly to find quarrel in a straw   55
When honor's at the stake. How stand I then,
That have a father killed, a mother stained,
Excitements of my reason and my blood,
And let all sleep, while to my shame I see
The imminent death of twenty thousand men,   60
That for a fantasy and trick[8] of fame
Go to their graves like beds, fight for a plot
Whereon the numbers cannot try the cause,[9]
Which is not tomb enough and continent[1]
To hide the slain? O, from this time forth,   65
My thoughts be bloody, or be nothing worth!
       [*Exit.*]

SCENE 5

[SCENE: *Elsinore. A room in the castle.*]

       [*Enter* QUEEN, HORATIO, *and a* GENTLEMAN.]
QUEEN   I will not speak with her.
GENTLEMAN   She is importunate, indeed distract:
    Her mood will needs be pitied.
QUEEN   What would she have?
GENTLEMAN   She speaks much of her father, says she hears
    There's tricks i' the world, and hems and beats her heart,   5
    Spurns enviously at straws;[2] speaks things in doubt,
    That carry but half sense: her speech is nothing,
    Yet the unshapèd use of it doth move
    The hearers to collection; they aim[3] at it,
    And botch[4] the words up fit to their own thoughts;   10
    Which, as her winks and nods and gestures yield them,
    Indeed would make one think there might be thought,
    Though nothing sure, yet much unhappily.
HORATIO   'Twere good she were spoken with, for she may strew
    Dangerous conjectures in ill-breeding minds.[5]   15

6. Cost.
7. Laughs at.
8. Trifle.
9. So small that it cannot hold the men who fight for it.
1. Container.

2. Gets angry at trifles.
3. Guess. "Collection": gathering up her words and trying to make sense of them.
4. Patch.
5. Minds breeding evil thoughts.

QUEEN Let her come in.
[*Exit* GENTLEMAN.]
[*Aside.*] To my sick soul, as sin's true nature is,
Each toy seems prologue to some great amiss:
So full of artless jealousy⁶ is guilt,
It spills itself in fearing to be spilt.   20
[*Re-enter* GENTLEMAN, *with* OPHELIA.]
OPHELIA Where is the beauteous majesty of Denmark?
QUEEN How now, Ophelia!
OPHELIA [*Sings.*]   How should I your true love know
From another one?
By his cockle hat and staff   25
And his sandal shoon.⁷

QUEEN Alas, sweet lady, what imports this song?
OPHELIA Say you? nay, pray you, mark.
[*Sings.*]   He is dead and gone, lady,
He is dead and gone;
At his head a grass-green turf,   30
At his heels a stone.
Oh, oh!
QUEEN Nay, but Ophelia,—
OPHELIA   Pray you, mark.
[*Sings.*]   White his shroud as the mountain snow,—   35
[*Enter* KING.]
QUEEN Alas, look here, my lord.
OPHELIA [*Sings.*]   Larded⁸ with sweet flowers;
Which bewept to the grave did—not—go
With true-love showers.
KING How do you, pretty lady?   40
OPHELIA Well, God 'ild⁹ you! They say the owl was a baker's daughter.
Lord, we know what we are, but know not what we may be.¹ God be
at your table!
KING Conceit upon her father.
OPHELIA Pray you, let's have no words of this; but when they ask you   45
what it means, say you this:
[*Sings.*]   To-morrow is Saint Valentine's day
All in the morning betime,
And I a maid at your window,
To be your Valentine.   50
Then up he rose, and donned his clothes,
And dupped² the chamber-door;
Let in the maid, that out a maid
Never departed more.

6. Uncontrolled suspicion. "Toy": trifle. "Amiss": misfortune.
7. Shoes. These are all typical signs of pilgrims traveling to places of devotion.
8. Garnished.
9. Yield—that is, repay.
1. An allusion to a folk tale about a baker's daughter changed into an owl for having shown no charity to those in need.
2. Opened.

KING   Pretty Ophelia!   55
OPHELIA   Indeed, la, without an oath, I'll make an end on 't:
   [*Sings.*]   By Gis³ and by Saint Charity,
            Alack, and fie for shame!
         Young men will do 't, if they come to 't;
            By Cock,⁴ they are to blame.   60
         Quoth she, before you tumbled me,
            You promised me to wed.
   He answers:

            So would I ha' done, by yonder sun,
            An thou hadst not come to my bed.   65
KING   How long hath she been thus?
OPHELIA   I hope all will be well. We must be patient: but I cannot
   choose but weep, to think they should lay him i' the cold ground.
   My brother shall know of it: and so I thank you for your good counsel.
   Come, my coach! Good night, ladies; good night, sweet ladies; good   70
   night, good night.
         [*Exit.*]
KING   Follow her close; give her good watch, I pray you.
         [*Exit* HORATIO.]
   O, this is the poison of deep grief; it springs
   All from her father's death. O Gertrude, Gertrude,
   When sorrows come, they come not single spies,   75
   But in battalions! First, her father slain:
   Next, your son gone; and he most violent author
   Of his own just remove: the people muddied,⁵
   Thick and unwholesome in their thoughts and whispers,
   For good Polonius' death; and we have done but greenly   80
   In hugger-mugger⁶ to inter him: poor Ophelia
   Divided from herself and her fair judgment,
   Without the which we are pictures, or mere beasts:
   Last, and as much containing as all these,
   Her brother is in secret come from France,   85
   Feeds on his wonder,⁷ keeps himself in clouds,
   And wants not buzzers⁸ to infect his ear
   With pestilent speeches of his father's death;
   Wherein necessity, of matter beggared,⁹
   Will nothing stick our person to arraign¹   90
   In ear and ear. O my dear Gertrude, this,
   Like to a murdering-piece,² in many places
   Gives me superfluous death.

---

3. By Jesus.
4. Corruption of *God*, but with a sexual
undermeaning.
5. Confused, their thoughts made turbid (as
water by mud).
6. Hasty secrecy. "Greenly": foolishly.
7. Broods, keeps wondering.

8. Lacks not tale-bearers.
9. The necessity to build up a story without
the materials for doing so.
1. Will not hesitate to accuse me.
2. A variety of cannon that scattered its shot
in many directions.

[*A noise within.*]

QUEEN   Alack, what noise is this?

KING   Where are my Switzers?[3] Let them guard the door.

      [*Enter another* GENTLEMAN.]

   What is the matter?

GENTLEMAN   Save yourself, my lord: 95

   The ocean, overpeering of his list,[4]

   Eats not the flats with more impetuous haste

   Than young Laertes, in a riotous head,[5]

   O'erbears your officers. The rabble call him lord;

   And, as the world were now but to begin,   100

   Antiquity forgot, custom not known,

   The ratifiers and props of every word,

   They cry "Choose we; Laertes shall be king!"

   Caps, hands and tongues applaud it to the clouds,

   "Laertes shall be king, Laertes king!"   105

QUEEN   How cheerfully on the false trail they cry!

   O, this is counter,[6] you false Danish dogs!

      [*Noise within.*]

KING   The doors are broke.

      [*Enter* LAERTES, *armed*; DANES *following.*]

LAERTES   Where is this king? Sirs, stand you all without.

DANES   No, let's come in.

LAERTES   I pray you, give me leave.   110

DANES   We will, we will.

      [*They retire without the door.*]

LAERTES   I thank you: keep the door. O thou vile king,

   Give me my father!

QUEEN   Calmly, good Laertes.

LAERTES   That drop of blood that's calm proclaims me bastard;

   Cries cuckold to my father; brands the harlot   115

   Even here, between the chaste unsmirchèd brows

   Of my true mother.

KING   What is the cause, Laertes,

   That thy rebellion looks so giant-like?

   Let him go, Gertrude; do not fear[7] our person

   There's such divinity doth hedge a king,   120

   That treason can but peep to what it would,[8]

   Acts little of his[9] will. Tell me, Laertes,

   Why thou art thus incensed: let him go, Gertrude

   Speak, man.

LAERTES   Where is my father?

KING   Dead.

QUEEN   But not by him.   125

KING   Let him demand his fill.

---

3. Swiss guards.
4. Overflowing above the high-water mark.
5. Group of rebels.
6. Following the scent in the wrong direction.

7. Fear for.
8. Look from a distance at what it desires.
9. Its.

LAERTES   How came he dead? I'll not be juggled with
   To hell, allegiance! vows, to the blackest devil!
   Conscience and grace, to the profoundest pit
   I dare damnation: to this point I stand,   130
   That both the worlds I give to negligence,[1]
   Let come what comes; only I'll be revenged
   Most thoroughly for my father.
KING   Who shall stay you?
LAERTES   My will, not all the world
   And for my means, I'll husband them so well,   135
   They shall go far with little.
KING   Good Laertes,
   If you desire to know the certainty
   Of your dear father's death, is 't writ in your revenge
   That, swoopstake,[2] you will draw both friend and foe,
   Winner and loser?   140
LAERTES   None but his enemies.
KING   Will you know them then?
LAERTES   To his good friends thus wide I'll ope my arms;
   And, like the kind life-rendering pelican,[3]
   Repast them with my blood.
KING   Why, now you speak
   Like a good child and a true gentleman.   145
   That I am guiltless of your father's death,
   And am most sensibly in grief for it,
   It shall as level to your judgment pierce
   As day does to your eye.
DANES [*Within.*]   Let her come in.
LAERTES   How now! what noise is that?   150
     [*Re-enter* OPHELIA.]
   O heat, dry up my brains! tears seven times salt,
   Burn out the sense and virtue[4] of mine eye!
   By heaven, thy madness shall be paid with weight,
   Till our scale turn the beam. O rose of May!
   Dear maid, kind sister, sweet Ophelia!   155
   O heavens! is 't possible a young maid's wits
   Should be as mortal as an old man's life?
   Nature is fine in love, and where 'tis fine
   It sends some precious instance[5] of itself
   After the thing it loves.   160
OPHELIA [*Sings.*]   They bore him barefaced on the bier
             Hey non nonny, nonny, hey nonny
             And in his grave rained many a tear,—
   Fare you well, my dove!

1. I don't care what may happen to me in either this world or the next.
2. Without making any distinction, as the winner takes the whole stake in a card game.
3. In myth, the pelican is supposed to feed its young with its own blood.
4. Power, faculty.
5. Sample, token. "Fine": refined.

LAERTES   Hadst thou thy wits, and didst persuade revenge,   165
  It could not move thus.
OPHELIA [*Sings.*]   You must sing down a-down,
              An you call him a-down-a.
  O, how the wheel becomes it! It is the false steward,[6] that stole his
  master's daughter.   170
LAERTES   This nothing's more than matter.[7]
OPHELIA   There's rosemary, that's for remembrance: pray you, love,
  remember: and there is pansies, that's for thoughts.
LAERTES   A document[8] in madness; thoughts and remembrance fitted.
OPHELIA   There's fennel for you, and columbines: there's rue for you: 175
  and here's some for me: we may call it herbs of grace o' Sundays: O,
  you must wear your rue with a difference. There's a daisy: I would
  give you some violets,[9] but they withered all when my father died:
  they say he made a good end,—
  [*Sings.*]   For bonnie sweet Robin is all my joy.   180
LAERTES   Thought and affliction, passion, hell itself,
  She turns to favor[1] and to prettiness.
OPHELIA [*Sings.*]   And will he not come again?
              And will he not come again?
                No, no, he is dead,   185
                Go to thy death-bed,
              He never will come again.
              His beard was as white as snow,
              All flaxen was his poll
                He is gone, he is gone,   190
                And we cast away moan
              God ha' mercy on his soul!
  And of all Christian souls, I pray God. God be wi' you.
        [*Exit.*]
LAERTES   Do you see this, O God?
KING   Laertes, I must commune with your grief,   195
  Or you deny me right. Go but apart,
  Make choice of whom your wisest friends you will.
  And they shall hear and judge 'twixt you and me:
  If by direct or by collateral hand
  They find us touched,[2] we will our kingdom give,   200
  Our crown, our life, and all that we call ours,
  To you in satisfaction; but if not,
  Be you content to lend your patience to us,
  And we shall jointly labor with your soul
  To give it due content.

---

6. An allusion (probably to a lost ballad) further expressing Ophelia's preoccupation with betrayal, lost love, and death. "How the wheel becomes it": that is, how well the refrain fits.
7. This nonsense is more indicative than sane speech.
8. Lesson. Traditionally, flowers and herbs have symbolic meanings. Here rosemary is the symbol for remembrance and pansies symbolize thoughts.
9. Violets symbolize faithfulness. Fennel stands for flattery, columbines for cuckoldom, and rue for sorrow and repentance (compare the verb *rue*).
1. Charm.
2. Involved (in the murder). "Collateral": indirect.

LAERTES   Let this be so;   205
  His means of death, his obscure funeral,
  No trophy, sword, nor hatchment[3] o'er his bones,
  No noble rite nor formal ostentation,
  Cry to be heard, as 'twere from heaven to earth,
  That I must call 't in question.
KING   So you shall;   210
  And where the offense is let the great axe fall.
  I pray you, go with me.
     [Exeunt.]

SCENE 6

[SCENE: *Another room in the castle.*]

     [*Enter* HORATIO *and a* SERVANT.]
HORATIO   What are they that would speak with me?
SERVANT   Sea-faring men, sir: they say they have letters for you.
HORATIO   Let them come in.
     [*Exit* SERVANT.]
  I do not know from what part of the world
  I should be greeted, if not from Lord Hamlet.   5
     [*Enter* SAILORS.]
FIRST SAILOR   God bless you, sir.
HORATIO   Let him bless thee too.
FIRST SAILOR   He shall, sir, an 't please him.
  There's a letter for you, sir; it comes from the ambassador that was
  bound for England; if your name be Horatio, as I am let to know   10
  it is.
HORATIO [*Reads.*]   "Horatio, when thou shalt have overlooked[4] this,
  give these fellows some means to the king: they have letters for him.
  Ere we were two days old at sea, a pirate of very warlike appointment
  gave us chase. Finding ourselves too slow of sail, we put on a compelled   15
  valor, and in the grapple I boarded them: on the instant they
  got clear of our ship; so I alone became their prisoner. They have
  dealt with me like thieves of mercy:[5] but they knew what they did;
  I am to do a good turn for them. Let the king have the letters I have
  sent; and repair thou to me with as much speed as thou wouldst fly   20
  death. I have words to speak in thine ear will make thee dumb; yet
  are they much too light for the bore[6] of the matter. These good
  fellows will bring thee where I am. Rosencrantz and Guildenstern
  hold their course for England: of them I have much to tell thee.
  Farewell.   25
     "He that thou knowest thine, HAMLET."
  Come, I will make you way for these your letters;
  And do 't the speedier, that you may direct me
  To him from whom you brought them.
     [*Exeunt.*]

---

3. Coat of arms.
4. Read over.

5. Merciful.
6. Caliber, that is, importance.

SCENE 7

[SCENE: *Another room in the castle.*]

    [*Enter* KING *and* LAERTES.]

KING   Now must your conscience my acquittance seal,
  And you must put me in your heart for friend,
  Sith you have heard, and with a knowing ear,
  That he which hath your noble father slain
  Pursued my life.
LAERTES   It well appears: but tell me   5
  Why you proceeded not against these feats,
  So crimeful and so capital in nature,
  As by your safety, wisdom, all things else,
  You mainly[7] were stirred up.
KING   O, for two special reasons,
  Which may to you perhaps seem much unsinewed,[8]   10
  But yet to me they're strong. The queen his mother
  Lives almost by his looks; and for myself—
  My virtue or my plague, be it either which—
  She's so conjunctive[9] to my life and soul,
  That, as the star moves not but in his sphere,   15
  I could not but by her. The other motive,
  Why to a public count I might not go,
  Is the great love the general gender[1] bear him;
  Who, dipping all his faults in their affection,
  Would, like the spring that turneth wood to stone,   20
  Convert his gyves[2] to graces; so that my arrows,
  Too slightly timber'd for so loud a wind,
  Would have reverted to my bow again
  And not where I had aim'd them.
LAERTES   And so have I a noble father lost;   25
  A sister driven into desperate terms,
  Whose worth, if praises may go back again,
  Stood challenger on mount of[3] all the age
  For her perfections: but my revenge will come.
KING   Break not your sleeps for that: you must not think   30
  That we are made of stuff so flat and dull
  That we can let our beard be shook with danger
  And think it pastime. You shortly shall hear more:
  I loved your father, and we love ourself;
  And that, I hope, will teach you to imagine—   35
    [*Enter a* MESSENGER, *with letters.*]
  How now! what news?
MESSENGER   Letters, my lord, from Hamlet:
  This to your majesty; this to the queen.
KING   From Hamlet! who brought them?

---

7. Powerfully.
8. Weak.
9. Closely joined.

1. Common people. "Count": accounting, trial.
2. Leg irons (shames).
3. Above. "Go back": to what she was before her madness.

MESSENGER   Sailors, my lord, they say; I saw them not:
They were given me by Claudio; he received them   40
Of him that brought them.
KING   Laertes, you shall hear them.
Leave us.
        [*Exit* MESSENGER.]
[*Reads.*] "High and mighty, you shall know I am set naked on your
kingdom. To-morrow shall I beg leave to see your kingly eyes: when
I shall, first asking your pardon thereunto, recount the occasion of   45
my sudden and more strange return.   HAMLET."
What should this mean? Are all the rest come back?
Or is it some abuse, and no such thing?[4]
LAERTES   Know you the hand?
KING   'Tis Hamlet's character.[5] "Naked!"   50
And in a postscript here, he says "alone."
Can you advise me?
LAERTES   I'm lost in it, my lord. But let him come;
It warms the very sickness in my heart,
That I shall live and tell him to his teeth,   55
"Thus diddest thou."
KING   If it be so, Laertes,—
As how should it be so? how otherwise?—
Will you be ruled by me?
LAERTES   Aye, my lord;
So you will not o'errule me to a peace.
KING   To thine own peace. If he be now returned,   60
As checking[6] at his voyage, and that he means
No more to undertake it, I will work him
To an exploit now ripe in my device,
Under the which he shall not choose but fall:
And for his death no wind of blame shall breathe;   65
But even his mother shall uncharge the practice,[7]
call it accident.
LAERTES   My lord, I will be ruled;
The rather, if you could devise it so
That I might be the organ.[8]
KING   It falls right.
You have been talked of since your travel much,   70
And that in Hamlet's hearing, for a quality
Wherein, they say, you shine; your sum of parts[9]
Did not together pluck such envy from him,
As did that one, and that in my regard
Of the unworthiest siege.[1]
LAERTES   What part is that, my lord?   75
KING   A very riband in the cap of youth,

---

4. A delusion, not a reality.
5. Handwriting.
6. Changing the course of, refusing to
continue.

7. Not recognize it as a plot.
8. Instrument.
9. The sum of your gifts.
1. Seat, that is, rank.

Yet needful too; for youth no less becomes[2]
The light and careless livery that it wears
Than settled age his sables and his weeds,[3]
Importing health and graveness. Two months since   80
Here was a gentleman of Normandy:—
I've seen myself, and served against, the French,
And they can well on horseback: but this gallant
Had witchcraft in 't; he grew unto his seat,
And to such wondrous doing brought his horse   85
As had he been incorpsed and demi-natured[4]
With the brave beast: so far he topped my thought
That I, in forgery of shapes and tricks,[5]
Come short of what he did.
LAERTES   A Norman was 't?
KING   A Norman.   90
LAERTES   Upon my life, Lamord.
KING   The very same.
LAERTES   I know him well: he is the brooch[6] indeed
And gem of all the nation.
KING   He made confession of you,
And gave you such a masterly report,   95
For art and exercise in your defense,[7]
And for your rapier most especial,
That he cried out, 'twould be a sight indeed
If one could match you: the scrimers[8] of their nation,
He swore, had neither motion, guard, nor eye,   100
If you opposed them. Sir, this report of his
Did Hamlet so envenom with his envy
That he could nothing do but wish and beg
Your sudden coming o'er, to play with him.
Now, out of this—
LAERTES   What out of this, my lord? 105
KING   Laertes, was your father dear to you?
Or are you like the painting of a sorrow,
A face without a heart?
LAERTES   Why ask you this?
KING   Not that I think you did not love your father,
But that I know love is begun by time,   110
And that I see, in passages of proof,[9]
Time qualifies[1] the spark and fire of it.
There lives within the very flame of love
A kind of wick or snuff[2] that will abate it;

---

2. Is the appropriate age for. "Riband": ribbon, ornament.
3. Furs (also meaning "blacks," dark colors) and robes.
4. Incorporated and split his nature in two.
5. In imagining methods and skills of horsemanship.
6. Ornament.
7. Report of your mastery in the theory and practice of fencing.
8. Fencers.
9. Instances that prove it.
1. Weakens.
2. Charred part of the wick.

And nothing is at a like goodness still,   115
For goodness, growing to a plurisy,[3]
Dies in his own too much: that we would do
We should do when we would; for this "would" changes
And hath abatements and delays as many
As there are tongues, are hands, are accidents,   120
And then this "should" is like a spendthrift sigh,
That hurts by easing.[4] But, to the quick o' the ulcer:
Hamlet comes back: what would you undertake,
To show yourself your father's son in deed
More than in words?

LAERTES   To cut his throat i' the church.   125
KING   No place indeed should murder sanctuarize;
Revenge should have no bounds. But, good Laertes,
Will you do this, keep close within your chamber.
Hamlet returned shall know you are come home:
We'll put on[5] those shall praise your excellence   130
And set a double varnish on the fame
The Frenchman gave you; bring you in fine together
And wager on your heads: he, being remiss,[6]
Most generous and free from all contriving,
Will not peruse[7] the foils, so that with ease,   135
Or with a little shuffling, you may choose
A sword unbated, and in a pass of practice[8]
Requite him for your father.

LAERTES   I will do 't;
And for that purpose I'll anoint my sword.
I bought an unction of a mountebank,[9]   140
So mortal that but dip a knife in it,
Where it draws blood no cataplasm so rare,
Collected from all simples[1] that have virtue
Under the moon, can save the thing from death
That is but scratched withal: I'll touch my point   145
With this contagion, that, if I gall[2] him slightly,
It may be death.

KING   Let's further think of this;
Weigh what convenience both of time and means
May fit us to our shape: if this should fail,
And that our drift look through[3] our bad performance,   150
'Twere better not assayed: therefore this project
Should have a back or second, that might hold
If this did blast in proof.[4] Soft! let me see:

3. Excess. "Still": constantly.
4. A sigh that gives relief but is harmful
(according to an old notion that it draws
blood from the heart).
5. Instigate.
6. Careless. "In fine": finally.
7. Examine closely.
8. Treacherous thrust. "Unbated": not blunted

(as a rapier for exercise ordinarily would be).
9. Ointment of a peddler of quack medicines.
1. Healing herbs. "Cataplasm": plaster.
2. Scratch.
3. Our design should show through. "Shape":
plan.
4. Burst (like a new firearm) once it is put to
the test.

We'll make a solemn wager on your cunnings:
I ha 't: 155
When in your motion you are hot and dry—
As make your bouts more violent to that end—
And that he calls for drink, I'll have prepared him
A chalice for the nonce;[5] whereon but sipping,
If he by chance escape your venomed stuck,[6]   160
Our purpose may hold there. But stay, what noise?
      [*Enter* QUEEN.]
How now, sweet queen!
QUEEN   One woe doth tread upon another's heel,
  So fast they follow: your sister's drowned, Laertes.
LAERTES   Drowned! O, where?   165
QUEEN   There is a willow grows aslant[7] a brook,
  That shows his hoar leaves in the glassy stream;
  There with fantastic garlands did she come
  Of crow-flowers, nettles, daisies, and long purples,
  That liberal shepherds give a grosser name,   170
  But our cold maids do dead men's fingers call them:
  There, on the pendent boughs her coronet weeds
  Clambering to hang, an envious sliver[8] broke;
  When down her weedy trophies and herself
  Fell in the weeping brook. Her clothes spread wide,   175
  And mermaid-like a while they bore her up:
  Which time she chanted snatches of old tunes,
  As one incapable of[9] her own distress,
  Or like a creature native and indued[1]
  Unto that element: but long it could not be   180
  Till that her garments, heavy with their drink,
  Pulled the poor wretch from her melodious lay
  To muddy death.
LAERTES   Alas, then she is drowned!
QUEEN   Drowned, drowned.
LAERTES   Too much of water hast thou, poor Ophelia,   185
  And therefore I forbid my tears: but yet
  It is our trick;[2] nature her custom holds,
  Let shame say what it will: when these are gone,
  The woman[3] will be out. Adieu, my lord:
  I have a speech of fire that fain would blaze,   190
  But that this folly douts[4] it.
      [*Exit.*]
KING   Let's follow, Gertrude:
  How much I had to do to calm his rage!
  Now fear I this will give it start again;

---

5. For that particular occasion.
6. Thrust.
7. Across.
8. Malicious bough.
9. Insensitive to.

1. Adapted, in harmony with.
2. Peculiar trait.
3. The softer qualities, the woman in me.
4. Extinguishes.

Therefore let's follow.
    [*Exeunt.*]

Act 5

SCENE I

[SCENE: *A churchyard.*]

    [*Enter two* CLOWNS, *with spades, etc.*]

FIRST CLOWN   Is she to be buried in Christian burial that willfully seeks her own salvation?

SECOND CLOWN   I tell thee she is; and therefore make her grave straight: the crowner[5] hath sat on her, and finds it Christian burial.

FIRST CLOWN   How can that be, unless she drowned herself in her own   5 defense?

SECOND CLOWN   Why, 'tis found so.

FIRST CLOWN   It must be "se offendendo";[6] it cannot be else. For here lies the point: if I drown myself wittingly, it argues an act: and an act hath three branches; it is, to act, to do, to perform: argal,[7] she   10 drowned herself wittingly.

SECOND CLOWN   Nay, but hear you, goodman delver.

FIRST CLOWN   Give me leave. Here lies the water; good: here stands the man; good: if the man go to this water and drown himself, it is, will he, nill he,[8] he goes; mark you that; but if the water come to   15 him and drown him, he drowns not himself: argal, he that is not guilty of his own death shortens not his own life.

SECOND CLOWN   But is this law?

FIRST CLOWN   Aye, marry, is 't; crowner's quest[9] law.

SECOND CLOWN   Will you ha' the truth on 't? If this had not been a   20 gentlewoman, she should have been buried out o' Christian burial.

FIRST CLOWN   Why, there thou say'st: and the more pity that great folk should have countenance[1] in this world to drown or hang themselves, more than their even[2] Christian. Come, my spade. There is no ancient gentlemen but gardeners, ditchers and gravemakers: they hold   25 up Adam's profession.

SECOND CLOWN   Was he a gentleman?

FIRST CLOWN   A' was the first that ever bore arms.

SECOND CLOWN   Why, he had none.

FIRST CLOWN   What, art a heathen? How dost thou understand the   30 Scripture? The Scripture says Adam digged: could he dig without arms? I'll put another question to thee: if thou answerest me not to the purpose, confess thyself—

SECOND CLOWN   Go to.

FIRST CLOWN   What is he that builds stronger than either the mason,   35 the shipwright, or the carpenter?

---

5. Coroner. "Straight": right away.
6. The Clown's blunder for *se defendendo*: "in self-defense" (Latin).
7. Blunder for *ergo*: "therefore" (Latin).

8. Willy-nilly.
9. Inquest.
1. Sanction.
2. Fellow.

SECOND CLOWN   The gallows-maker; for that frame outlives a thousand
tenants.

FIRST CLOWN   I like thy wit well, in good faith: the gallows does well;
but how does it well? it does well to those that do ill: now, thou dost   40
ill to say the gallows is built stronger than the church: argal, the
gallows may do well to thee. To 't again, come.

SECOND CLOWN   "Who builds stronger than a mason, a shipwright, or
a carpenter?"

FIRST CLOWN   Aye, tell me that, and unyoke.[3]   45

SECOND CLOWN   Marry, now I can tell.

FIRST CLOWN   To 't.

SECOND CLOWN   Mass, I cannot tell.

[Enter HAMLET and HORATIO, afar off.]

FIRST CLOWN   Cudgel thy brains no more about it, for your dull ass
will not mend his pace with beating, and when you are asked this   50
question next, say "a grave-maker": the houses that he makes last till
doomsday. Go, get thee to Yaughan; fetch me a stoup[4] of liquor.

[Exit SECOND CLOWN. —FIRST CLOWN digs and sings.]
      In youth, when I did love, did love,
         Methought it was very sweet,
      To contract, O, the time, for-a my behove,   55
         O, methought, there-a was nothing-a meet.[5]

HAMLET   Has this fellow no feeling of his business that he sings at
grave-making?

HORATIO   Custom hath made it in him a property of easiness.[6]

HAMLET   'Tis e'en so: the hand of little employment hath the daintier[7]   60
sense.

FIRST CLOWN [Sings.]   But age, with his stealing steps,
         Hath clawed me in his clutch,
      And hath shipped me intil[8] the land,
         As if I had never been such.   65

[Throws up a skull.]

HAMLET   That skull had a tongue in it, and could sing once: how the
knave jowls it to the ground, as if it were Cain's jaw-bone, that did
the first murder! It might be the pate of a politician,[9] which this ass
now o'er-reaches;[1] one that would circumvent God, might it not?

HORATIO   It might, my lord.   70

HAMLET   Or of a courtier, which could say, "Good morrow, sweet lord!
How dost thou, sweet lord?" This might be my lord such-a-one, that
praised my lord such-a-one's horse, when he meant to beg it; might
it not?

HORATIO   Aye, my lord.   75

HAMLET   Why, e'en so: and now my Lady Worm's; chapless, and
knocked about the mazzard[2] with a sexton's spade: here's fine revolution,

3. Call it a day.
4. Mug. "Yaughan": apparently a tavern keeper's name.
5. Fitting. "Contract": shorten. "Behove": profit.
6. Has made it a matter of indifference to
him.
7. Finer sensitivity. "Of little employment":

that does little labor.
8. Into.
9. In a pejorative sense. "Jowls": knocks. "First
murder": possibly an allusion to the legend
that Cain slew Abel with an ass's jawbone.
1. Outwits.
2. Pate. "Chapless": the lower jawbone missing.

an we had the trick to see 't. Did these bones cost no more
the breeding, but to play at loggats[3] with 'em? mine ache to think
on 't.   80
FIRST CLOWN [*Sings.*]   A pick-axe, and a spade, a spade,
                                    For a shrouding sheet:
                                    O, a pit of clay for to be made
                                    For such a guest is meet.
            [*Throws up another skull.*]
HAMLET   There's another: why may not that be the skull of a lawyer?   85
Where be his quiddities now, his quillets, his cases, his tenures,[4] and
his tricks? why does he suffer this rude knave now to knock him
about the sconce with a dirty shovel, and will not tell him of his
action of battery?[5] Hum! This fellow might be in 's time a great buyer
of land, with his statutes, his recognizances,[6] his fines, his double   90
vouchers, his recoveries: is this the fine[7] of his fines and the recovery
of his recoveries, to have his fine pate full of fine dirt? will his vouchers
vouch him no more of his purchases, and double ones too, than the
length and breadth of a pair of indentures? The very conveyances[8] of
his lands will hardly lie in this box; and must the inheritor himself   95
have no more, ha?
HORATIO   Not a jot more, my lord.
HAMLET   Is not parchment made of sheep-skins?
HORATIO   Aye, my lord, and of calf-skins too.
HAMLET   They are sheep and calves which seek out assurance[9] in that.   100
I will speak to this fellow. Whose grave's this, sirrah?
FIRST CLOWN   Mine, sir.
    [*Sings.*]   O, a pit of clay for to be made
                        For such a guest is meet.
HAMLET   I think it be thine indeed, for thou liest in 't.   105
FIRST CLOWN   You lie out on 't, sir, and therefore 'tis not yours: for my
part, I do not lie in 't, and yet it is mine.
HAMLET   Thou dost lie in 't, to be in 't and say it is thine: 'tis for the dead,
not for the quick;[1] therefore thou liest.
FIRST CLOWN   'Tis a quick lie, sir; 'twill away again, from me to you.   110
HAMLET   What man dost thou dig it for?
FIRST CLOWN   For no man, sir.
HAMLET   What woman then?
FIRST CLOWN   For none neither.
HAMLET   Who is to be buried in 't?   115
FIRST CLOWN   One that was a woman, sir; but, rest her soul, she's dead.
HAMLET   How absolute the knave is! we must speak by the card,[2] or
equivocation will undo us. By the Lord, Horatio, these three years I

3. A game resembling bowls. "Trick": faculty.
4. Real estate holdings. "Quiddities": subtle
definitions. "Quillets": quibbles.
5. Assault. "Sconce": head.
6. Varieties of bonds. This passage contains
legal terms relating to the transfer of estates.
7. End. Hamlet is punning on the legal and
nonlegal meanings of the word.
8. Deeds. "Indentures": contracts drawn in

duplicate on the same piece of parchment; the
two copies were separated by an indented line.
9. Security; another pun, because the word is
also a legal term.
1. Living.
2. By the chart, that is, exactness. "Absolute":
positive.

have taken note of it; the age is grown so picked[3] that the toe of the
peasant comes so near the heel of the courtier, he galls his kibe.[4] How   120
long hast thou been a grave-maker?

FIRST CLOWN   Of all the days i' the year, I came to 't that day that our
last King Hamlet o'ercame Fortinbras.

HAMLET   How long is that since?

FIRST CLOWN   Cannot you tell that? every fool can tell that: it was that   125
very day that young Hamlet was born: he that is mad, and sent into
England.

HAMLET   Aye, marry, why was he sent into England?

FIRST CLOWN   Why, because a' was mad; a' shall recover his wits there:
or, if a' do not, 'tis no great matter there.   130

HAMLET   Why?

FIRST CLOWN   'Twill not be seen in him there; there the men are as mad
as he.

HAMLET   How came he mad?

FIRST CLOWN   Very strangely, they say.   135

HAMLET   How "strangely?"

FIRST CLOWN   Faith, e'en with losing his wits.

HAMLET   Upon what ground?

FIRST CLOWN   Why, here in Denmark: I have been sexton here, man and
boy, thirty years.   140

HAMLET   How long will a man lie i' the earth ere he rot?

FIRST CLOWN   I' faith, if a' be not rotten before a' die—as we have many
pocky corses now-a-days, that will scarce hold the laying in[5]—
a' will last you some eight year or nine year: a tanner will last you
nine year.   145

HAMLET   Why he more than another?

FIRST CLOWN   Why, sir, his hide is so tanned with his trade that a' will
keep out water a great while; and your water is a sore decayer of
your whoreson dead body. Here's a skull now: this skull has lain in
the earth three and twenty years.   150

HAMLET   Whose was it?

FIRST CLOWN   A whoreson mad fellow's it was: whose do you think it
was?

HAMLET   Nay, I know not.

FIRST CLOWN   A pestilence on him for a mad rogue! a' poured a flagon   155
of Rhenish on my head once. This same skull, sir, was Yorick's skull,
the king's jester.

HAMLET   This?

FIRST CLOWN   E'en that.

HAMLET   Let me see. [*Takes the skull.*] Alas, poor Yorick! I knew him,   160
Horatio: a fellow of infinite jest, of most excellent fancy: he hath
borne me on his back a thousand times; and now how abhorred in
my imagination it is! my gorge rises at it. Here hung those lips that
I have kissed I know not how oft. Where be your gibes now? your
gambols? your songs? your flashes of merriment, that were wont to   165

3. Choice, fastidious.
4. Hurts the chilblain on the courtier's heel.

5. Hold together till they are buried. "Pocky":
with marks of disease (from "pox").

set the table on a roar? Not one now, to mock your own grinning? quite chop-fallen?[6] Now get you to my lady's chamber, and tell her, let her paint an inch thick, to this favor[7] she must come; make her laugh at that. Prithee, Horatio, tell me one thing.

HORATIO What's that, my lord? 170

HAMLET Dost thou think Alexander looked o' this fashion i' the earth?

HORATIO E'en so.

HAMLET And smelt so? pah!

[*Puts down the skull.*]

HORATIO E'en so, my lord.

HAMLET To what base uses we may return, Horatio! Why may not imagi- 175
nation trace the noble dust of Alexander, till he find it stopping a bung-
hole?

HORATIO 'Twere to consider too curiously, to consider so.

HAMLET No, faith, not a jot; but to follow him thither with modesty
enough[8] and likelihood to lead it: as thus: Alexander died, Alexander 180
was buried, Alexander returneth into dust; the dust is earth; of earth
we make loam; and why of that loam, whereto he was converted, might
they not stop a beer-barrel?

Imperious Caesar, dead and turned to clay,
Might stop a hole to keep the wind away: 185
O, that that earth, which kept the world in awe,
Should patch a wall to expel the winter's flaw!

But soft! but soft! aside: here comes the king.

[*Enter* PRIESTS *etc., in procession; the Corpse of* OPHELIA, LAERTES,
and mourners following; KING, QUEEN, *their trains, etc.*]

The queen, the courtiers: who is this they follow?
And with such maimèd rites?[9] This doth betoken 190
The corse they follow did with desperate hand
Fordo its own life: 'twas of some estate.[1]
Couch we awhile, and mark.

[*Retiring with* HORATIO.]

LAERTES What ceremony else?

HAMLET That is Laertes, a very noble youth: mark. 195

LAERTES What ceremony else?

FIRST PRIEST Her obsequies have been as far enlarged
As we have warranty: her death was doubtful;
And, but that great command o'ersways the order[2]
She should in ground unsanctified have lodged 200
Till the last trumpet; for[3] charitable prayers,
Shards, flints and pebbles should be thrown on her:
Yet here she is allowed her virgin crants,
Her maiden strewments and the bringing home[4]
Of bell and burial. 205

6. The lower jaw fallen down, hence dejected.
7. Appearance.
8. Without exaggeration.
9. Incomplete, mutilated ritual.
1. Rank. "Fordo": destroy.
2. The king's command prevails against ordi-

nary rules. "Doubtful": of uncertain cause
(that is, accident or suicide).
3. Instead of.
4. Laying to rest. "Crants": garlands. "Strewments": strews the grave with flowers.

LAERTES   Must there no more be done?
FIRST PRIEST   No more be done:
   We should profane the service of the dead
   To sing a requiem and such rest to her
   As to peace-parted souls.
LAERTES   Lay her i' the earth:
   And from her fair and unpolluted flesh   210
   May violets spring! I tell thee, churlish priest,
   A ministering angel shall my sister be,
   When thou liest howling.
HAMLET   What, the fair Ophelia!
QUEEN [*Scattering flowers.*]   Sweets to the sweet: farewell!
   I hoped thou shouldst have been my Hamlet's wife;   215
   I thought thy bride-bed to have decked, sweet maid,
   And not have strewed thy grave.
LAERTES   O, treble woe
   Fall ten times treble on that cursed head
   Whose wicked deed thy most ingenious sense
   Deprived thee of! Hold off the earth a while,   220
   Till I have caught her once more in mine arms.
         [*Leaps into the grave.*]
   Now pile your dust upon the quick and dead,
   Till of this flat a mountain you have made
   To o'ertop old Pelion[5] or the skyish head
   Of blue Olympus.
HAMLET [*Advancing.*]   What is he whose grief   225
   Bears such an emphasis? whose phrase of sorrow
   Conjures the wandering stars and makes them stand
   Like wonder-wounded hearers? This is I,
   Hamlet the Dane.
         [*Leaps into the grave.*]
LAERTES   The devil take thy soul!
         [*Grappling with him.*]
HAMLET   Thou pray'st not well.   230
   I prithee, take thy fingers from my throat;
   For, though I am not splenitive[6] and rash,
   Yet have I in me something dangerous,
   Which let thy wisdom fear. Hold off thy hand.
KING   Pluck them asunder.
QUEEN   Hamlet, Hamlet!
ALL   Gentlemen,—   235
HORATIO   Good my lord, be quiet.
         [*The attendants part them, and they come out of the grave.*]
HAMLET   Why, I will fight with him upon this theme
   Until my eyelids will no longer wag.
QUEEN   O my son, what theme?

5. The mountain on which the Aloadae, two   Olympus.
rebellious giants in Greek mythology, piled   6. Easily moved to anger.
up Mount Ossa in their attempt to reach

HAMLET   I loved Ophelia: forty thousand brothers   240
   Could not, with all their quantity of love,
   Make up my sum. What wilt thou do for her?
KING   O, he is mad, Laertes.
QUEEN   For love of God, forbear him.
HAMLET   'Swounds, show me what thou 'lt do: 245
   Woo 't weep? woo 't fight? woo 't fast? woo 't tear thyself?
   Woo 't drink up eisel?[7] eat a crocodile?
   I'll do 't. Dost thou come here to whine?
   To outface me with leaping in her grave?
   Be buried quick with her, and so will I: 250
   And, if thou prate of mountains, let them throw
   Millions of acres on us, till our ground,
   Singeing his pate against the burning zone,
   Make Ossa like a wart! Nay, an thou 'lt mouth,
   I'll rant as well as thou.
QUEEN   This is mere madness: 255
   And thus a while the fit will work on him;
   Anon, as patient as the female dove
   When that her golden couplets are disclosed,[8]
   His silence will sit drooping.
HAMLET   Hear you, sir;
   What is the reason that you use me thus?   260
   I loved you ever: but it is no matter;
   Let Hercules himself do what he may,
   The cat will mew, and dog will have his day.
      [Exit.]
KING   I pray thee, good Horatio, wait upon him.
      [Exit HORATIO.]
   [To LAERTES.] Strengthen your patience in our last night's speech;   265
   We'll put the matter to the present push.[9]
   Good Gertrude, set some watch over your son.
   This grave shall have a living monument:
   An hour of quiet shortly shall we see;
   Till then, in patience our proceeding be.   270
      [Exeunt.]

SCENE 2

[SCENE: A hall in the castle.]

      [Enter HAMLET and HORATIO.]
HAMLET   So much for this, sir: now shall you see the other;
   You do remember all the circumstance?

---

7. Vinegar (the bitter drink given to Christ).   8. Twins are hatched.
"Woo't": wilt thou.   9. We'll push the matter on immediately.

HORATIO   Remember it, my lord?

HAMLET   Sir, in my heart there was a kind of fighting,
That would not let me sleep: methought I lay   5
Worse than the mutines in the bilboes.[1] Rashly,
And praised be rashness for it, let us know,
Our indiscretion sometime serves us well
When our deep plots do pall;[2] and that should learn us
There's a divinity that shapes our ends,   10
Rough-hew them how we will.

HORATIO   That is most certain.

HAMLET   Up from my cabin,
My sea-gown scarfed about me, in the dark
Groped I to find out them; had my desire,
Fingered their packet, and in fine withdrew   15
To mine own room again; making so bold,
My fears forgetting manners, to unseal
Their grand commission; where I found, Horatio,—
O royal knavery!—an exact command,
Larded with many several sorts of reasons,   20
Importing[3] Denmark's health and England's too,
With, ho! such bugs and goblins in my life,
That, on the supervise, no leisure bated,[4]
No, not to stay the grinding of the axe,
My head should be struck off.

HORATIO   Is 't possible?   25

HAMLET   Here's the commission: read it at more leisure.
But wilt thou hear now how I did proceed?

HORATIO   I beseech you.

HAMLET   Being thus be-netted round with villainies,—
Ere I could make a prologue to my brains,   30
They had begun the play,—I sat me down;
Devised a new commission; wrote it fair:
I once did hold it, as our statists[5] do,
A baseness to write fair, and labored much
How to forget that learning; but, sir, now   35
It did me yeoman's service:[6] wilt thou know
The effect of what I wrote?

HORATIO   Aye, good my lord.

HAMLET   An earnest conjuration from the king,
As England was his faithful tributary,
As love between them like the palm might flourish,   40
As peace should still her wheaten garland wear

---

1. Mutineers in iron fetters.
2. Become useless.
3. Concerning.
4. As soon as the message was read, with no
time subtracted for leisure. "Bugs": imaginary
horrors to be expected if I lived.
5. Statesmen.
6. Excellent service.

And stand a comma[7] 'tween their amities,
And many such-like "As"es of great charge,[8]
That, on the view and knowing of these contents,
Without debatement further, more or less, 45
He should the bearers put to sudden death,
Not shriving-time[9] allowed.
HORATIO   How was this sealed?
HAMLET   Why, even in that was heaven ordinant.[1]
I had my father's signet in my purse,
Which was the model of that Danish seal: 50
Folded the writ up in the form of the other;
Subscribed it; gave 't the impression;[2] placed it safely,
The changeling never known. Now, the next day
Was our sea-fight; and what to this was sequent
Thou know'st already. 55
HORATIO   So Guildenstern and Rosencrantz go to 't.
HAMLET   Why, man, they did make love to this employment;
They are not near my conscience; their defeat
Does by their own insinuation[3] grow:
'Tis dangerous when the baser nature comes 60
Between the pass and fell[4]-incensèd points
Of mighty opposites.
HORATIO   Why, what a king is this!
HAMLET   Does it not, think'st thee, stand me now upon[5]—
He that hath killed my king, and whored my mother;
Popped in between the election and my hopes; 65
Thrown out his angle for my proper life,[6]
And with such cozenage—is't not perfect conscience,
To quit[7] him with this arm? and is't not to be damned,
To let this canker of our nature come
In further evil? 70
HORATIO   It must be shortly known to him from England
What is the issue of the business there.
HAMLET   It will be short: the interim is mine;
And a man's life's no more than to say "One."
But I am very sorry, good Horatio, 75
That to Laertes I forgot myself;
For, by the image of my cause, I see
The portraiture of his: I'll court his favors:

---

7. Connecting element.
8. "'As'es": a pun on *as* and *ass*, which extends
to "of great charge," signifying both "moral
weight" and "ass's burden."
9. Time for confession and absolution.
1. Ordaining.
2. Of the seal.

3. Meddling. "Defeat": destruction.
4. Fiercely. "Baser": lower in rank than the
king and Prince Hamlet. "Pass": thrust.
5. Is it not my duty now?
6. An angling line for my own life.
7. Pay back.

But, sure, the bravery[8] of his grief did put me
Into a towering passion.
HORATIO   Peace! who comes here?   80
      [*Enter* OSRIC.]
OSRIC   Your lordship is right welcome back to Denmark.
HAMLET   I humbly thank you, sir. Dost know this waterfly?
HORATIO   No, my good lord.
HAMLET   Thy state is the more gracious, for 'tis a vice to know him. He
hath much land, and fertile: let a beast be lord of beasts, and his crib   85
shall stand at the king's mess: 'tis a chough,[9] but, as I say, spacious in
the possession of dirt.
OSRIC   Sweet lord, if your lordship were at leisure, I should impart a thing
to you from his majesty.
HAMLET   I will receive it, sir, with all diligence of spirit. Put your bonnet   90
to his right use; 'tis for the head.
OSRIC   I thank your lordship, it is very hot.
HAMLET   No, believe me, 'tis very cold; the wind is northerly.
OSRIC   It is indifferent[1] cold, my lord, indeed.
HAMLET   But yet methinks it is very sultry and hot, or my complexion—   95
OSRIC   Exceedingly, my lord; it is very sultry, as 'twere,—I cannot tell
how. But, my lord, his majesty bade me signify to you that he has laid
a great wager on your head: sir, this is the matter—
HAMLET   I beseech you, remember—
      [HAMLET *moves him to put on his hat.*]
OSRIC   Nay, good my lord; for mine ease, in good faith. Sir, here is newly   100
come to court Laertes; believe me, an absolute gentleman, full of most
excellent differences, of very soft society and great showing:[2] indeed,
to speak feelingly of him, he is the card or calendar of gentry,[3] for
you shall find in him the continent of what part[4] a gentleman would
see.   105
HAMLET   Sir, his definement suffers no perdition in you; though, I
know, to divide him inventorially would dizzy the arithmetic[5] of memory, and yet but yaw neither, in respect of his quick sail.[6] But in the
verity of extolment, I take him to be a soul of great article, and his
infusion[7] of such dearth and rareness, as, to make true diction of him,   110
his semblable is his mirror, and who else would trace him, his umbrage,[8]
nothing more.
OSRIC   Your lordship speaks most infallibly of him.
HAMLET   The concernancy, sir? why do we wrap the gentleman[9] in our

---

8. Ostentation, bravado.
9. Jackdaw. "Mess": table.
1. Fairly.
2. Agreeable company, handsome in appearance. "Differences": distinctions.
3. Chart and model of gentlemanly manners.
4. Whatever quality. "Continent": container.
5. Arithmetical power. "Definement": definition. "Perdition": loss. "Inventorially": make

an inventory of his virtues.
6. And yet would only be able to steer unsteadily
(unable to catch up with the *sail* of Laertes's
virtues).
7. The virtues infused into him. "Verify of
extolments": to prize Laertes truthfully. "Article": importance.
8. Keep pace with him, his shadow.
9. Laertes. "Concernancy": meaning.

more rawer breath? 115

OSRIC Sir?

HORATIO Is 't not possible to understand in another tongue?[1] You will
do 't, sir, really.

HAMLET What imports the nomination of this gentleman?

OSRIC Of Laertes? 120

HORATIO His purse is empty already; all's golden words are spent.

HAMLET Of him, sir.

OSRIC I know you are not ignorant—

HAMLET I would you did, sir; yet, in faith, if you did, it would not much
approve me.[2] Well, sir? 125

OSRIC You are not ignorant of what excellence Laertes is—

HAMLET I dare not confess that, lest I should compare with him in
excellence; but, to know a man well, were to know himself.[3]

OSRIC I mean, sir, for his weapon; but in the imputation laid on him by
them, in his meed he's unfellowed.[4] 130

HAMLET What's his weapon?

OSRIC Rapier and dagger.

HAMLET That's two of his weapons: but, well.

OSRIC The king, sir, hath wagered with him six Barbary horses: against
the which he has imponed, as I take it, six French rapiers and poniards, 135
with their assigns,[5] as girdle, hanger, and so: three of the carriages,
in faith, are very dear to fancy, very responsive[6] to the hilts, most
delicate carriages, and of very liberal conceit.[7]

HAMLET What call you the carriages?

HORATIO I knew you must be edified by the margent[8] ere you had 140
done.

OSRIC The carriages, sir, are the hangers.

HAMLET The phrase would be more germane to the matter if we could
carry a cannon by our sides:[9] I would it might be hangers till then.
But, on: six Barbary horses against six French swords, their assigns, 145
and three liberal-conceited carriages; that's the French bet against
the Danish. Why is this "imponed," as you call it?

OSRIC The king, sir, hath laid, sir, that in a dozen passes between
yourself and him, he shall not exceed you three hits: he hath laid on
twelve for nine; and it would come to immediate trial, if your lordship 150
would vouchsafe the answer.[1]

1. In a less affected jargon or in the same jargon when spoken by another (that is, Hamlet's)
tongue.
2. Be to my credit.
3. To know others one has to know oneself.
4. In the reputation given him by his weapons, his merit is unparalleled.
5. Appendages. "Imponed": wagered.
6. Closely matched. "Carriages": ornamented straps by which the rapiers hung from the

belt. "Very dear to fancy": agreeable to the taste.
7. Elegant design.
8. Instructed by the marginal note.
9. Hamlet is playfully criticizing Osric's affected application of the term *carriage*, more properly used to mean "gun carriage."
1. The terms of this wager have never been satisfactorily clarified.

HAMLET   How if I answer "no"?

OSRIC   I mean, my lord, the opposition of your person in trial.

HAMLET   Sir, I will walk here in the hall: if it please his majesty, it is the breathing time[2] of day with me; let the foils be brought, the gentleman willing, and the king hold his purpose, I will win for him an I can; if not, I will gain nothing but my shame and the odd hits.   155

OSRIC   Shall I redeliver you e'en so?[3]

HAMLET   To this effect, sir, after what flourish your nature will.

OSRIC   I commend my duty to your lordship.   160

HAMLET   Yours, yours. [*Exit* OSRIC.] He does well to commend it himself; there are no tongues else for's turn.

HORATIO   This lapwing[4] runs away with the shell on his head.

HAMLET   He did comply with his dug before he sucked it. Thus has he— and many more of the same breed that I know the drossy[5] age dotes on—only got the tune of the time and outward habit of encounter; a kind of yesty[6] collection, which carries them through and through the most fond and winnowed opinions;[7] and do but blow them to their trial, the bubbles are out.   165

[*Enter a* LORD.]

LORD   My lord, his majesty commended him[8] to you by young Osric, who brings back to him, that you attend him in the hall: he sends to know if your pleasure hold to play with Laertes, or that you will take longer time.   170

HAMLET   I am constant to my purposes; they follow the king's pleasure: if his fitness speaks, mine is ready; now or whensoever, provided I be so able as now.   175

LORD   The king and queen and all are coming down.

HAMLET   In happy time.

LORD   The queen desires you to use some gentle entertainment[9] to Laertes before you fall to play.   180

HAMLET   She well instructs me.

[*Exit* LORD.]

HORATIO   You will lose this wager, my lord.

HAMLET   I do not think so; since he went into France, I have been in continual practice; I shall win at the odds. But thou wouldst not think how ill all's here about my heart: but it is no matter.   185

HORATIO   Nay, good my lord,—

HAMLET   It is but foolery; but it is such a kind of gaingiving[1] as would perhaps trouble a woman.

HORATIO   If your mind dislike anything, obey it. I will forestall their

---

2. Time for exercise.
3. Is that the reply you want me to carry back?
4. A bird supposedly able to run as soon as it is out of its shell.
5. Degenerate. "Comply": use ceremony.
6. Frothy.

7. Makes them pass the test of the most refined judgment.
8. Sent his regards.
9. Kind word of greeting.
1. Misgiving.

repair[2] hither, and say you are not fit.   190

HAMLET   Not a whit; we defy augury: there is special providence in the
fall of a sparrow. If it be now, 'tis not to come; if it be not to come, it
will be now; if it be not now, yet it will come: the readiness is all; since
no man has aught of what he leaves, what is 't to leave betimes?[3]
Let be.   195

[*Enter* KING, QUEEN, LAERTES, *and* LORDS, OSRIC *and other attendants with
foils and gauntlets; a table and flagons of wine on it.*]

KING   Come, Hamlet, come, and take this hand from me.

[*The* KING *puts* LAERTES' *hand into* HAMLET's.]

HAMLET   Give me your pardon, sir: I've done you wrong;
But pardon't, as you are a gentleman.
This presence[4] knows,
And you must needs have heard, how I am punished   200
With sore distraction. What I have done,
That might your nature, honor and exception[5]
Roughly awake, I here proclaim was madness.
Was't Hamlet wronged Laertes? Never Hamlet:
If Hamlet from himself be ta'en away,   205
And when he's not himself does wrong Laertes,
Then Hamlet does it not, Hamlet denies it.
Who does it then? His madness: if 't be so,
Hamlet is of the faction that is wronged;
His madness is poor Hamlet's enemy.   210
Sir, in this audience,
Let my disclaiming from a purposed evil
Free me so far in your most generous thoughts,
That I have shot mine arrow o'er the house,
And hurt my brother.

LAERTES   I am satisfied in nature,   215
Whose motive, in this case, should stir me most
To my revenge: but in my terms of honor[6]
I stand aloof, and will no reconcilement,
Till by some elder masters of known honor
I have a voice and precedent of peace,   220
To keep my name ungored.[7] But till that time
I do receive your offered love like love
And will not wrong it.

HAMLET   I embrace it freely,
And will this brother's wager frankly play.
Give us the foils. Come on.

LAERTES   Come, one for me.   225

---

2. Coming.

3. What is wrong with dying early (leaving
betimes), because man knows nothing of life
(*what he leaves*)?

4. Audience.

5. Objection.

6. "Nature" is Laertes' natural feeling toward
his father. "Honor" is the code of honor with its
conventional rules.

7. Unwounded. "A voice and": an opinion
based on.

HAMLET I'll be your foil,[8] Laertes: in mine ignorance
 Your skill shall, like a star i' the darkest night,
 Stick fiery off[9] indeed.
LAERTES   You mock me, sir.
HAMLET No, by this hand.
KING Give them the foils, young Osric. Cousin Hamlet,   230
 You know the wager?
HAMLET   Very well, my lord;
 Your grace has laid the odds o' the weaker side.
KING I do not fear it; I have seen you both:
 But since he is bettered, we have therefore odds.
LAERTES This is too heavy; let me see another.   235
HAMLET This likes me well. These foils have all a length?
  [*They prepare to play.*]
OSRIC Aye, my good lord.
KING Set me the stoups[1] of wine upon that table.
 If Hamlet give the first or second hit,
 Or quit in answer of the third exchange,[2]   240
 Let all the battlements their ordnance fire;
 The king shall drink to Hamlet's better breath;
 And in the cup an union[3] shall he throw,
 Richer than that which four successive kings
 In Denmark's crown have worn. Give me the cups; 245
 And let the kettle[4] to the trumpet speak,
 The trumpet to the cannoneer without,
 The cannons to the heavens, the heaven to earth,
 "Now the king drinks to Hamlet." Come, begin;
 And you, the judges, bear a wary eye.   250
HAMLET Come on, sir.
LAERTES   Come, my lord.
  [*They play.*]
HAMLET   One.
LAERTES   No.
HAMLET   Judgment.
OSRIC A hit, a very palpable hit.
LAERTES   Well; again.
KING Stay; give me drink. Hamlet, this pearl is thine;
 Here's to thy health.
  [*Trumpets sound, and cannon shot off within.*]
      Give him the cup.
HAMLET I'll play this bout first; set it by awhile.   255
 Come. [*They play.*] Another hit; what say you?

---

8. A pun, because "foil" means both "rapier"
and "a thing that sets off another to advantage" (as gold leaf under a jewel).
9. Stand out brilliantly.
1. Cups.

2. Requite, or repay (by scoring a hit) on the
third bout.
3. A large pearl.
4. Kettledrum.

LAERTES   A touch, a touch, I do confess.

KING   Our son shall win.

QUEEN   He's fat and scant of breath.
Here, Hamlet, take my napkin,[5] rub thy brows:
The queen carouses to thy fortune, Hamlet.   260

HAMLET   Good madam!

KING   Gertrude, do not drink.

QUEEN   I will, my lord; I pray you, pardon me.

KING [*Aside.*]   It is the poisoned cup; it is too late.

QUEEN   Come, let me wipe thy face.

LAERTES   My lord, I'll hit him now.

KING   I do not think 't.   265

LAERTES [*Aside.*]   And yet it is almost against my conscience.

HAMLET   Come, for the third, Laertes: you but dally;
I pray you, pass with your best violence;
I am afeard you make a wanton[6] of me.

LAERTES   Say you so? come on.
    [*They play.*]

OSRIC   Nothing, neither way.   270

LAERTES   Have at you now!
    [LAERTES *wounds* HAMLET; *then, in scuffling, they change rapiers, and* HAMLET
    wounds LAERTES.]

KING   Part them; they are incensed.

HAMLET   Nay, come, again.
    [*The* QUEEN *falls.*]

OSRIC   Look to the queen there, ho!

HORATIO   They bleed on both sides. How is it, my lord?

OSRIC   How is 't, Laertes?

LAERTES   Why, as a woodcock to mine own springe,[7] Osric;   275
I am justly killed with mine own treachery.

HAMLET   How does the queen?

KING   She swounds to see them bleed.

QUEEN   No, no, the drink, the drink,—O my dear Hamlet,—
The drink, the drink! I am poisoned.   280
    [*Dies.*]

HAMLET   O villainy! Ho! let the door be locked:
Treachery! seek it out.
    [LAERTES *falls.*]

LAERTES   It is here, Hamlet: Hamlet, thou art slain;
No medicine in the world can do thee good,
In thee there is not half an hour of life;   285
The treacherous instrument is in thy hand,
Unbated and envenomed: the foul practice[8]
Hath turned itself on me; lo, here I lie,
Never to rise again: thy mother's poisoned:

---

5. Handkerchief. "Fat": sweaty, or soft, because   7. Snare.
out of training.   8. Plot.
6. Weakling, spoiled child.

I can no more: the king, the king's to blame. 290
HAMLET   The point envenomed too!
   Then, venom, to thy work.
       [*Stabs the* KING.]
ALL   Treason! treason!
KING   O, yet defend me, friends; I am but hurt.
HAMLET   Here, thou incestuous, murderous, damnèd Dane, 295
   Drink off this potion: is thy union here?
   Follow my mother.
       [KING *dies.*]
LAERTES   He is justly served;
   It is a poison tempered[9] by himself.
   Exchange forgiveness with me, noble Hamlet:
   Mine and my father's death come not upon thee, 300
   Nor thine on me!
       [*Dies.*]
HAMLET   Heaven make thee free of it! I follow thee.
   I am dead, Horatio. Wretched queen, adieu!
   You that look pale and tremble at this chance,
   That are but mutes or audience to this act, 305
   Had I but time—as this fell sergeant, death,
   Is strict in his arrest—O, I could tell you—
   But let it be. Horatio, I am dead;
   Thou livest; report me and my cause aright
   To the unsatisfied.
HORATIO   Never believe it: 310
   I am more an antique Roman than a Dane:
   Here's yet some liquor left.
HAMLET   As thou'rt a man,
   Give me the cup: let go; by heaven, I'll have 't.
   O good Horatio, what a wounded name,
   Things standing thus unknown, shall live behind me! 315
   If thou didst ever hold me in thy heart,
   Absent thee from felicity a while,
   And in this harsh world draw thy breath in pain,
   To tell my story.
       [*March afar off, and shot within.*]
               What warlike noise is this?
OSRIC   Young Fortinbras, with conquest come from Poland, 320
   To the ambassadors of England gives
   This warlike volley.
HAMLET   O, I die, Horatio;
   The potent poison quite o'er-crows[1] my spirit:
   I cannot live to hear the news from England;
   But I do prophesy the election lights 325
   On Fortinbras: he has my dying voice;

---

9. Compounded.   1. Overcomes.

So tell him, with the occurrents, more and less,
Which have solicited.[2] The rest is silence.
　　　[*Dies.*]
HORATIO　　Now cracks a noble heart. Good night sweet prince,
And flights of angels sing thee to thy rest;　　　　　　　　　　330
　　　[*March within.*]
Why does the drum come hither?
　　　[*Enter* FORTINBRAS, *and the* ENGLISH AMBASSADORS, *with drum, colors, and attendants.*]
FORTINBRAS　　Where is this sight?
HORATIO　　　　　　　　　　　　　What is it you would see?
If aught of woe or wonder, cease your search.
FORTINBRAS　　This quarry cries on havoc.[3] O proud death,
What feast is toward[4] in thine eternal cell,　　　　　　　　335
That thou so many princes at a shot
So bloodily hast struck?
FIRST AMBASSADOR　　　　　　　The sight is dismal;
And our affairs from England come too late:
The ears are senseless that should give us hearing,
To tell him his commandment is fulfilled,　　　　　　　　340
That Rosencrantz and Guildenstern are dead:
Where should we have our thanks?
HORATIO　　　　　　　　　　　　　Not from his mouth
Had it the ability of life to thank you:
He never gave commandment for their death.
But since, so jump upon[5] this bloody question,　　　　　345
You from the Polack wars, and you from England
Are here arrived, give order that these bodies
High on a stage be placèd to the view;
And let me speak to the yet unknowing world
How these things came about; so shall you hear　　　　　350
Of carnal, bloody and unnatural acts,
Of accidental judgments, casual slaughters,
Of deaths put on[6] by cunning and forced cause,
And, in this upshot, purposes mistook
Fall'n on the inventors' heads: all this can I　　　　　　355
Truly deliver.
FORTINBRAS　　　Let us haste to hear it,
And call the noblest to the audience.
For me, with sorrow I embrace my fortune:
I have some rights of memory in this kingdom,
Which now to claim my vantage[7] doth invite me.　　　　360

2. Which have brought all this about. "Occurrents": occurrences.
3. This heap of corpses proclaims a carnage.
4. Imminent.

5. So immediately on.
6. Prompted. "Casual": chance.
7. Advantageous position, opportunity. "Have some rights of memory": am still remembered.

HORATIO   Of that I shall have also cause to speak,
  And from his mouth whose voice will draw on more:[8]
  But let this same be presently performed,
  Even while men's minds are wild; lest more mischance
  On[9] plots and errors happen.
FORTINBRAS   Let four captains   365
  Bear Hamlet, like a soldier, to the stage;
  For he was likely, had he been put on,[1]
  To have proved most royal: and, for his passage,[2]
  The soldiers' music and the rites of war
  Speak loudly for him.   370
  Take up the bodies: such a sight as this
  Becomes the field, but here shows much amiss.
  Go, bid the soldiers shoot.
    [*A dead march. Exeunt, bearing off the bodies: after which a peal
    of ordnance is shot off.*]

---

8. More voices.   1. Tried (as a king).
9. Following on.   2. Death.

Selected Bibliographies

I. Ancient Mediterranean and Near Eastern Literature

On the early history of writing, an excellent starting point is Walter Ong, *Orality and Literacy: Technologizing of the Word* (1982), which teases out the cultural and psychological implications of the shift from an oral to a literate culture. Those with a particular interest in Near Eastern cultures can begin with James Pritchard's classic anthology of texts in translation, containing many illustrations: *The Ancient Near East: An Anthology of Texts and Pictures* (reissued 2010). A good illustrated survey of Greek and Roman culture by a number of different specialists is John Boardman, Jasper Griffin, and Oswyn Murray, *The Oxford History of the Classical World* (1986). Introductory texts that combine discussion of Greek, Roman, and Near Eastern cultures include *An Introduction to the Ancient World* (2008), by Lukas de Blois and R. J. van der Spek, and the less scholarly but lively *The History of the Ancient World: From the Earliest Accounts to the Fall of Rome*, by Susan Wise Bauer (2007). Reliable general introductions to Greek and Roman literature include Albin Lesky, *Greek Literature* (reissued 1996), and G. B. Conte, *Latin Literature: A History* (reissued 1999). For more information about the ancient world, including images of ancient art, architecture, and artifacts, as well as ancient Greek and Roman texts, a wonderful resource is Tufts University's website *Perseus* (www.perseus.tufts.edu).

Ancient Athenian Drama

A good introduction to the genre of Athenian tragedy, which includes discussions of all the extant plays and is particularly strong on social context, is Edith Hall, *Greek Tragedy: Suffering under the Sun* (2010). Marianne McDonald and J. Michael Walton, eds., *Cambridge Companion to Greek and Roman Theatre* (2007), includes essays on both tragedy and comedy, and also has some discussion of staging. Another fine collection of introductory essays, on tragedy, comedy, and satyr plays, is Ian C. Storey and Arlene Allan, *A Guide to Ancient Greek Drama* (2005). Further information on performance contexts, in the fifth century and also in modern revivals, can be found in David Wiles, *Mask and Performance in Greek Tragedy: From Ancient Festival to Modern Experimentation* (2007). Many pieces of visual evidence of Greek theater, including vase paintings, statues, and photographs of remaining theater sites, are collected in Richard Green and Eric Handley, *Images of the Greek Theater* (1995).

Euripides

A good collection of scholarly essays on Euripides is Judith Mossman, ed., *Euripides* (2003). For representations of "barbarians" in tragedy, including in *Medea*, see Edith Hall, *Inventing the Barbarian: Greek Self-Definition through Tragedy* (1989). Ruby Blondell, ed., *Women on the Edge: Four Plays* (1999), includes a translation of *Medea* and three other Euripides plays focused on women, as well as a useful introduction that discusses representations of gender in these plays. A good general introduction to Euripides, with brief discussions of all nineteen extant plays and a focus on their reception after ancient times is Michael Walton, *Euripides Our Contemporary* (2010). William Allan, *Euripides: Medea* (2002), surveys the most important literary themes of the play.

Gilgamesh

The most recent scholarly translations of *The Epic of Gilgamesh* are Stephanie Delany, *Myths from Mesopotamia: Creation, the Flood, Gilgamesh, and Others* (1989); Maureen Kovacs, *The Epic of Gilgamesh* (1989); Andrew George, *The Epic of Gilgamesh: The Babylonian Epic Poem and Other Texts in Akkadian and Sumerian* (1999) and *The Babylonian Gilgamesh Epic: Introduction, Critical Edition, and Cuneiform Texts* (2003); and Benjamin Foster, *The Epic of Gilgamesh* (2001). They contain ample commentary and important introductory articles that aid in the interpretation of the epic. The poet Stephen Mitchell's *Gilgamesh: A New English Version* (2004) is a smooth verse retelling of the epic. David Ferry, *Gilgamesh: A New Rendering into English Verse* (1992) is also recommended. For a study of the evolution of the story over time, see Geffrey Tigay, *The Evolution of the Gilgamesh Epic* (1982). Alexander Heidel shows the importance of *Gilgamesh* for biblical studies in *The Gilgamesh Epic and Old Testament Parallels* (1963). Rivkah Harris, *Gender and Aging in Mesopotamia: The Gilgamesh Epic and Other Ancient Literature* (2000), discusses the gender dynamic in the epic in the light of other ancient texts. John Maier, *Gilgamesh: A Reader* (1997), contains seminal articles on *Gilgamesh* and an extensive bibliography. David Damrosch, *The Buried Book: The Loss and Rediscovery of the Great Epic of Gilgamesh* (2007), tells the story of the colonial adventurers, scholars, and contemporary writers involved in the rediscovery of *Gilgamesh*.

For those wishing to discover the riches of Mesopotamian literature beyond *Gilgamesh*, Benjamin Foster's voluminous *Before the Muses: An Anthology of Akkadian Literature* (1993, 2005) and *From Distant Days: Myths, Tales, and Poetry of Ancient Mesopotamia* (1995) contain a wealth of material. Jack Sasson et al., *Civilizations of the Ancient Near East* (1995), vol. 4, is devoted to languages and literatures of the region. For vivid presentations of Mesopotamian civilization, see Jean Bottéro, *Mesopotamia: Writing, Reasoning, and the Gods* (1992); J. N. Postgate, *Early Mesopotamia: Society and Economy at the Dawn of History* (1992); and Benjamin Foster and Karen Polinger Foster, *Civilizations of Ancient Iraq* (2009).

The Hebrew Bible

Richard Elliott Friedman, *Who Wrote the Bible?* (1987), is a clear introduction to the idea that each of the first books of the Bible is composed from several narrative strands (the "documentary hypothesis"). The *Anchor Bible*, in multiple volumes, has useful introductions and notes to each book of the Bible, including historical information. More on the historicity of the Bible can be found in Ronald Hendel, *Remembering Abraham: Culture, History and Memory in Ancient Israel* (2004). Robert Alter and Frank Kermode, eds., *The Literary Guide to the Bible* (1987), has useful essays on approaching the stylistic and narrative structures of the Bible. James L. Crenshaw, *Defending God: Biblical Responses to the Problem of Evil* (2005), is an interesting attempt to grapple with the central moral problems raised by the Hebrew Bible.

Homer

The first chapter of Erich Auerbach's *Mimesis: The Representation of Reality in Western Literature* (1953), trans. Willard Trask, gives a stimulating account of how Homeric narrative technique might differ from that of the Hebrew Bible. Essential works on the relation of the Homeric poems to the Greek oral tradition include Albert Lord, *The Singer of Tales* (1960), and Milman Parry, *The Making of Homeric Verse* (1973). Jenny Strauss Clay, *The Wrath of Athena: Gods and Men in the Odyssey* (1983), provides a useful overview of the gods in the epic. Female characters, human and divine, are discussed in Beth Cohen, ed., *The Distaff Side: Representing the Female in Homer's Odyssey* (1995). A good collection of classic essays on the *Odyssey* is Seth Schein, ed., *Reading the Odyssey: Selected Interpretative Essays* (1996). Those interested in the history of Homeric Greece will find useful information in M. I. Finley, *Early Greece: The Bronze and Archaic Ages* (1981). James Tatum, *The Mourner's Song: War and Remembrance from the Iliad to Vietnam* (2003), is a moving account of the *Iliad* in the context of later representations of war. Sheila Murnaghan's introductory essays to Stanley Lombardo's translations of the *Odyssey* (2000) and the *Iliad* (1997) provide rich interpretations of important literary themes, such as disguise, hospitality, heroism, and death.

Ovid

Sarah Mack, *Ovid* (1988), is a good general introduction, with a long chapter on the *Metamorphoses*. Philip Hardie, *Ovid's Poetics of Illusion* (2002), is an important guide to Ovid's poetic technique; metapoetic aspects are also discussed in R. A. Smith, *Poetic Allusion and Poetic Embrace in Ovid and Virgil* (1997), which includes a fine reading of the Pygmalion episode. Garth Tissol, *The Face of Nature* (1997), provides a useful close reading of the poem, including discussion of Ovid's puns, and looks in particular at the Myrrha episode. Charles Martindale, *Ovid Renewed: Ovidian Influences on Literature and Art from the Middle Ages to the Twentieth Century* (1988), gives some idea of the importance of Ovid for later literature.

Sappho

A useful collection of scholarly essays is Ellen Greene, ed., *Reading Sappho: Contemporary Approaches* (1996). Marguerite Johnson, *Sappho* (2007), is a clear, short introduction to some important literary themes in the poet's work. Sappho is read alongside two male, contemporary lyric poets in A. P. Burnett, *Three Archaic Poets: Archilochus, Alcaeus, Sappho* (1983). The reception of Sappho is particularly interesting; Margaret Reynolds, ed., *The Sappho Companion* (2000), is a collection of translations, imitations, and adaptations of Sappho's poems by postclassical poets and writers.

Sophocles

A good literary introduction to Sophocles, which draws on psychoanalytic and anthropological ideas to emphasize pairs of concepts (such as civilization versus wildness) is Charles Segal, *Tragedy and Civilization: An Interpretation of Sophocles* (1981). Important essays by various scholars on *Oedipus the King*, including a classic article by E. R. Dodds on common student misinterpretations of the play, are collected in Michael O'Brien,

ed., *Twentieth-Century Interpretations of* Oedipus Rex (1968). Mary Blundell, *Helping Friends and Harming Enemies* (1989), reads Sophocles through the maxim of Greek popular morality alluded to in its title; one chapter is devoted to *Antigone*. The city of Thebes in Greek tragedy in general, and in these plays in particular, is discussed by Froma Zeitlin in her essay in Zeitlin and John J. Winkler, eds., *Nothing to Do with Dionysos?* (1990). In two editions of the plays in Greek, scholars have written introductions that are accessible and useful even to the nonspecialist reader: R. D. Dawe on *Oedipus Tyrannos*, and Mark Griffith on *Antigone* (1982 and 1999 respectively). The political dimensions of the plays are particularly difficult for modern readers to grasp; an interesting attempt to apply the specifics of Athenian political history to the plays is Michael Vickers, *Sophocles and Alcibiades: Athenian Politics in Ancient Greek Literature* (2008). Both plays have been adapted in many different ways for the modern stage; one important example is Seamus Heaney's version of *Antigone*, set in Northern Ireland, *The Burial at Thebes* (2004).

Virgil

The structure of the whole poem is discussed in David O. Ross, *Virgil's Aeneid: A Reader's Guide* (2007). S. Harrison, ed., *Oxford Readings in Virgil's* Aeneid (1990) has useful articles on many aspects of the poem. A good literary introduction to the whole poem is Michael C. J. Putnam, *Virgil's* Aeneid: *Interpretation and Influence* (1995). Yasmin Syed, *Virgil's* Aeneid *and the Roman Self* (2005), gives an interesting account of how the poem participated in, and formed, Roman cultural values. A good short discussion of Virgilian allusion to earlier literature, why it works and why it matters, is R. O. A. M. Lyne, *Further Voices in Virgil's* Aeneid (1987). S. Quinn, ed., *Why Virgil?* (2000), includes literary essays and some examples of modern literature imitating or responding to Virgil. David Quint, *Epic and Empire* (1993), provides an important model for reading Virgil and later epics in terms of the losers and winners of history.

II. Ancient India

Burton Stein, *A History of India* (1998), and Stanley Wolpert, *A New History of India* (2008), offer good, complementary historical overviews of ancient India; Upinder Singh, *A History of Ancient and Early Medieval India* (2009), provides a more detailed, up-to-date account. Romila Thapar, *Cultural Pasts: Essays in Early Indian History* (2000), contains the best critical analyses of specific aspects of the ancient period. Thomas R. Trautmann, *The Aryan Debate* (2005), surveys recent controversies on India's prehistory, and includes a selection of important texts from the eighteenth century onward. Patrick Olivelle, *Upaniṣads* (1996), provides an excellent overview of Vedic religion, with translations of some canonical texts; Gavin Flood, *An Introduction to Hinduism* (1996), explains both early and later forms of the religion. Peter Harvey, *An Introduction to Buddhism* (1990), covers history, doctrine, and practice, with a focus on Mahayana Buddhism; Joseph M. Kitagawa and Mark D. Cummings, *Buddhism and Asian History* (1989), offers greater depth as well as a broader sweep, with specialist essays by many scholars.

The Bhagavad-gītā
Among the world's canonical religious texts, the *Bhagavad-gītā* is second only to the Bible in the number of times it has been translated, and the range of languages into which it has been rendered. Of the many modern translations available in English, Barbara Stoler Miller, *The Bhagavad-gītā: Krishna's Counsel in Time of War* (1986), is one of the most reliable and accessible. R. C. Zaehner, *The Bhagavad-gītā* (1969), includes the original Sanskrit text in English transcription, along with a literal rendering, a more polished version, and a commentary on each verse. The most useful Indian translation into English is S. Radhakrishnan's older *The Bhagavad-gītā*—1948 and later editions. For a discussion of Indian interpretations of the poem, see Robert Minor, *Modern Interpreters of the Bhagavadgītā* (1986); and for an account of its reception in the West, consult Eric Sharpe, *The Universal Gītā: Western Images of the* Bhagavad Gītā, *a Bicentennial Survey* (1985).

The Rāmāyaṇa of Vālmīki
The Rāmāyaṇa of Vālmīki: An Epic of Ancient India (1984–), translated, annotated, and introduced by various scholars led by Robert Goldman, is the best recent version in English; five volumes, representing books 1 through 5, have appeared so far. Swami Venkatesanand, *The Concise Rāmāyaṇa* (1988), the source of our text, is a condensed prose version, which emphasizes the religious message of Vālmīki's epic, interpreted from a conservative modern perspective. A particularly readable literary prose rendering of Kamban's twelfth-century Tamil version of the poem appears in R. K. Narayan, *The Rāmāyaṇa* (1972). Important scholarly essays on most aspects of "the story of Rāma" are collected in Paula Richman, *Many Rāmāyaṇas: The Diversity of a Narrative Tradition in South Asia* (1991).

III. Early Chinese Literature and Thought

Jacques Gernet, *A History of Chinese Civilization* (1982), is a commanding survey history of China. Patricia Ebrey, Anne Walthall, and James Palais, *Pre-Modern East Asia to 1800: A Cultural, Social and Political History* (2009), is an excellent shorter account of Chinese history in the broader context of East Asia. Michael Loewe and Edward Shaughnessy, eds., *The Cambridge History of Ancient China* (1999), is a comprehensive reference work for early Chinese history and culture. For a vivid account of thought and society in early imperial China, see Mark Lewis, *The Early Chinese Empires: Qin and Han* (2007). For a comprehensive history of Chinese Literature refer to Kang-i Sun Chang and Stephen Owen, eds.,

The Cambridge History of Chinese Literature (2010). Wiebke Denecke, Waiyee Li, and Xiaofei Tian, eds., *The Oxford Handbook of Classical Chinese Literature (1000 BCE–900 CE)* (2017) gives a comprehensive thematic, topical, and cross-cultural overview of Chinese literature during its first two millennia.

For those wishing to explore more early Chinese texts, Stephen Owen, *Anthology of Chinese Literature, Beginnings to 1911* (1996), presents a rich selection of Chinese literature with ample introductory material and commentary. Cyril Birch, *Anthology of Chinese Literature* (1965), and Victor Mair, *The Columbia Anthology of Traditional Chinese Literature* (1994), which is organized by genre and not chronology, are also recommended. For early Chinese thought and religion, see William Theodore de Bary, *Sources of Chinese Tradition* (2nd ed. 1999), a two-volume anthology covering a broad variety of original texts in translation from the beginnings to the modern period.

For broader explorations of Chinese Masters Literature, see Benjamin Schwartz, *The World of Thought in Ancient China* (1985); A. C. Graham, *Disputers of the Tao: Philosophical Argument in Ancient China* (1989); Chad Hansen, *A Daoist Theory of Chinese Thought: A Philosophical Interpretation* (1992); and Wiebke Denecke, *The Dynamics of Masters Literature: Early Chinese Thought from Confucius to Han Feizi* (2010). To explore comparisons between Ancient Greece and China, see Lisa Raphals, *Knowing Words: Wisdom and Cunning in the Classical Traditions of China and Greece* (1992), and Steven Shankman and Stephen Durrant, *The Siren and the Sage: Knowledge and Wisdom in Ancient Greece and China* (2000).

Classic of Poetry
Other translations for comparison include Arthur Waley, *The Book of Songs* (1937), and Ezra Pound, *The Classic Anthology Defined by Confucius* (1954). Anecdotes by the Han Dynasty scholar Han Ying (fl. 150 B.C.E.) that show how poems from the *Classic of Poetry* were applied to concrete situations and moral questions can be found in James R. Hightower, *Han Shih Wai Chuan: Han Ying's Illustrations of the Didactic Application of the Classic of Songs* (1952). For stimulating studies of the anthology and its interpretation, see Steven Van Zoeren, *Poetry and Personality: Reading, Exegesis and Hermeneutics in Traditional China* (1991), and Haun Saussy, *The Problem of a Chinese Aesthetic* (1993). Pauline Yu, *The Reading of Imagery in the Chinese Poetic Tradition* (1987), is a compelling study of imagery in the *Classic of Poetry* and other Chinese texts. For the "Great Preface" of the *Classic of Poetry* and Chinese poetics in general, Stephen Owen's *Readings in Chinese Literary Thought* (1992) gives a captivating introduction to major works of Chinese literary thought and provides a bilingual translation of the original texts with detailed commentary. James Liu's *Chinese Theories of Literature* (1975) sketches major Chinese paradigms of the concept of literature. To explore literary thought in more recent times, see *Modern Chinese Literary Thought: Writings on Literature, 1893–1945*, ed. Kirk Denton (1996). For scholarly essays on Chinese literary criticism in general, see *Chinese Aesthetics and Literature: A Reader*, ed. Corinne H. Dale (2004). For a broader exploration of literary interpretation in Chinese and Western literatures, see Longxi Zhang's *The Tao and the Logos: Literary Hermeneutics, East and West* (1992).

Confucius
There are many translations of the *Analects*. The selections in this anthology are from Simon Leys's complete translation, *The Analects of Confucius* (1997). Arthur Waley's resonant translation of 1938 has recently been reprinted with an explanatory introduction by Sarah Allan (2000). D. C. Lau, *Analects* (1979), is a solid translation and contains a lucid introduction to Confucius and his ideas. Roger T. Ames and Henry Rosemont, *The Analects of Confucius: A Philosophical Translation* (1998), provides the classical Chinese text alongside an English version. For an overview of early Chinese philosophy and thought, read A. C. Graham,

Disputers of the Tao: Philosophical Argument in Ancient China (1989), and Wiebke Denecke, *The Dynamics of Masters Literature. Early Chinese Thought from Confucius to* Hanfeizi (2011). Herbert Fingarette, *Confucius—The Secular as Sacred* (1972), remains one of the most persuasive accounts of the appeal of the *Analects*. David L. Hall and Roger T. Ames, *Thinking through Confucius* (1987), is an innovative reading of the *Analects* inspired by American pragmatic philosophy. John Makeham, *Transmitters and Creators: Chinese Commentators and Commentaries on the* Analects (2003), gives insight into later commentators' understanding of the *Analects*. For a compelling account of early Confucianism, see Robert Eno, *The Confucian Creation of Heaven: Philosophy and the Defense of Ritual Mastery* (1990). Thomas A. Wilson, *On Sacred Grounds: Culture, Society, Politics, and the Formation of the Cult of Confucius* (2002), is a collection of articles about the religious dimensions of Confucianism and the Confucius cult. Lionel Jensen, *Manufacturing Confucianism: Chinese Traditions and Universal Civilization* (1997), discusses how the image of Confucianism created by European missionaries working in China during the sixteenth and seventeenth centuries has influenced modern understandings. John Makeham, *Lost Soul: "Confucianism" in Contemporary Chinese Academic Discourse* (2008), surveys the significance of Confucianism in today's intellectual debates.

Laozi

Among the many translations of the *Daodejing*, D. C. Lau, *Tao Te Ching* (1963); Roger Ames and David L. Hall, *Daodejing—Making This Life Significant—A Philosophical Translation* (2003); and Red Pine, *Lao-tzu's Taote-*ching: *With Selected Commentaries of the Past 2000 Years* (1997), are especially recommended. Robert G. Henricks, *Lao-Tzu's Tao Te Ching: A New Translation Based on the Recently Discovered Ma-wang-tui Texts* (1989) and *Lao Tzu's Tao Te Ching: A Translation of the Startling New Documents Found at Guodian* (2000), are based on excavated manuscripts of the *Daodejing* and are interesting to compare to the received text. For an overview of early Chinese philosophy and thought, read A. C. Graham, *Disputers of the Tao: Philosophical Argument in Ancient China* (1989), and Wiebke Denecke, *The Dynamics of Masters Literature. Early Chinese Thought from Confucius to* Hanfeizi (2011).

For a broader view on the *Daodejing* within the context of Early Chinese intellectual debates, see the chapters on the *Daodejing* in the books on Chinese Masters Literature indicated in the regional introduction to "Early Chinese Thought and Literature." Arthur Waley, *The Way and Its Power: A Study of the* Tao Te Ching *and Its Place in Chinese Thought* (1958), is still a classic study of the *Daodejing*. Michael LaFargue, *Tao and Method: A Reasoned Approach to the* Tao Te Ching (1994), is a compelling reconstruction of what the text might have meant to its earliest readers. For interpretations of one of the most influential commentators of the *Daodejing*, see Rudolf Wagner, *The Craft of the Chinese Commentator: Wang Bi on the* Laozi (2000) and *A Chinese Reading of the* Daodejing: *Wang Bi's Commentary on the* Laozi *with Critical Text and Translation* (2003). For views on the *Daodejing* and its relation to the *Laozi* and Daoism, see Livia Kohn and Michael LaFargue, *Lao-tzu and the* Tao-te-ching (1998), and Mark Csikszentmihalyi and Philip J. Ivanhoe, *Religious and Philosophical Aspects of the* Laozi (1999).

IV. Circling the Mediterranean: Europe and the Islamic World

On the idea of the Mediterranean, see the classic 1949 study by Fernand Braudel, *The Mediterranean and the Mediterranean World in the Age of Philip II*, trans. Siân Reynolds (1972–1973; rpt., 1996), as well as the increasingly influential work of Peregrine Horden and Nicholas Purcell, *The Corrupting Sea: A Study of Mediterranean History* (2000). On late antiquity and the early Middle Ages, see Peter Brown, *The World of Late Antiquity: From Marcus Aurelius to Muhammad* (1989), and Averil Cameron, *The Mediterranean World in Late Antiquity*, A.D. *395–600* (1993).

For an overview of medieval Islamic history, see John Esposito, *Oxford History of Islam* (2000); Albert Hourani, *A History of the Arab Peoples* (2002); Seyyed Hossein Nasr, *Islam: Religion, History and Civilization* (2003). Information on almost any subject can be found in P. J. Bearman et al., eds., *Encyclopaedia of Islam*, 12 vols. (2nd ed., 1960–2005). A useful account of Persian poetics is offered by Julie Scott Meisami, *Medieval Persian Court Poetry* (1987).

For a survey of Europe's history from the fall of Rome to the beginnings of the Renaissance, three classic and still valuable studies are R. W. Southern, *The Making of the Middle Ages* (1953); Charles Homer Haskins, *The Renaissance of the Twelfth Century* (1927); and J. W. Huizinga, *The Autumn of the Middle Ages* (1919), trans. Rodney J. Payton and Ulrich Mammitzsch (1996). For information on almost any topic pertaining to medieval Europe, see *The Dictionary of the Middle Ages*, gen. ed. Joseph Strayer, 13 vols. (1989), with *Supplement 1*, ed. William Chester Jordan (2003).

Classic overviews of medieval European literary history and its place within the discipline of world literature can be found in Ernst Robert Curtius, *European Literature and the Latin Middle Ages* (1948), trans. Willard Trask (1953), and Erich Auerbach, *Mimesis: The Representation of Reality in Western Literature* (1946), trans. Willard Trask (1953; rpt., 2003). On the literary interactions of the Islamic world and medieval Europe, see María Rosa Menocal, *The Arabic Role in Medieval Literary History* (1987), and the reappraisal of Menocal's work in *A Sea of Languages: Literature and Culture in the Pre-modern Mediterranean*, ed. Suzanne Conklin Akbari and Karla Mallette (2011).

Augustine

A wonderful introduction and detailed notes can be found in the translation by Henry Chadwick (1991) and also the 3-volume edition and commentary by James J. O'Donnell (1992), both titled *Confessions*. O'Donnell's text is available online from the Stoa Consortium in cooperation with the Perseus Project at www.stoa.org/hippo/. For an account of Augustine's life by the foremost historian of early Christianity in the Roman Empire, see Peter Brown, *Augustine of Hippo: A Biography* (1967; 2nd ed., 2000). A provocative and engaging life of the bishop and saint appears in James J. O'Donnell, *Augustine: A New Biography* (2005). On Augustine's own reading practices and the reading communities that formed in his wake, see Brian Stock, *Augustine the Reader: Meditation, Self-Knowledge and the Ethics of Interpretation* (1996). A collection of scholarly essays that contextualize Augustine and his works in theological, historical, and cultural terms is *A Companion to Augustine* (2012) by Mark Vessey, with the assistance of Shelley Reid, ed.

Beowulf

See the invaluable guide to the poem by Andy Orchard, *A Critical Companion to 'Beowulf'* (2003). A useful collection of essays is Robert Bjork and John Niles, eds., *A Beowulf Handbook* (1997). For a broad view of Anglo-Saxon literature and culture, see Malcolm Godden and Michael Lapidge, eds., *The Cambridge Companion to Old English Literature* (1991).

The Christian Bible

A full text with useful notes can be found in *The New Oxford Annotated Bible: New Revised Standard Version*, ed. Michael D. Coogan, Marc Z. Brettler, Carol Newsom, and Pheme Perkins (4th ed., 2010). For a brief overview of the historical background of the Bible and the diverse reading communities that have made it their own, see John Riches, *The Bible: A Very Short Introduction* (2000). The poetic and artistic qualities of scripture are on view in *The Literary Guide to the Bible*, ed. Robert Alter and Frank Kermode (1987). A more idiosyncratic reading of the Bible, rooted in a deep knowledge of history but with the profound inquisitiveness of a science fiction writer, appears in Isaac Asimov, *Asimov's Guide to the Bible: The Old and New Testaments* (1981; rpt., 1988). An intriguing interpretation of the Bible as graphic novel is Siku's *The Manga Bible: From Genesis to Revelation* (2008).

Geoffrey Chaucer

The most complete edition of Chaucer's poetry, with authoritative notes and commentary, is *The Riverside Chaucer*, ed. Larry D. Benson (3rd ed., 1987). An engaging portrait of Chaucer and his times can be found in Donald R. Howard, *Chaucer: His Life, His Works, His World* (1987). On the manuscript history of the *Canterbury Tales* in historical context, see Derek Pearsall, *The Canterbury Tales* (1985), and for an art-historical perspective focused on the poem's interlocking structure, see V. A. Kolve, *Chaucer and the Imagery of Narrative: The First Five Canterbury Tales* (1984). On Chaucer's role in the premodern invention of the subject, see Lee Patterson, *Chaucer and the Subject of History* (1991). On sexuality and gender, including influential readings of the Wife of Bath and the Pardoner, see Carolyn Dinshaw, *Chaucer's Sexual Poetics* (1989).

Christine de Pizan

A full translation of Christine de Pizan's *City of Ladies* appears in Rosalind Brown-Grant, trans., *The Book of the City of Ladies* (1999); another popular translation of the same title is by Earl Jeffrey Richards (1982). *Christine de Pizan: Her Life and Works* (1984), by Charity Cannon Willard, is a highly readable biography of the author by a scholar who played a crucial role in reawakening modern readers' interest in Christine's writings. Well-chosen excerpts from Christine's numerous works of prose and poetry, accompanied by influential critical essays, appear in Renate Blumenfeld-Kosinski and Kevin Brownlee, ed. and trans., *The Selected Writings of Christine de Pizan* (1997). For an insightful study of the interrelation of the text and illuminated miniatures in Christine's manuscripts, see Sandra Hindman, *Christine de Pizan's "Epistre Othéa": Painting and Politics at the Court of Charles VI* (1986). A study of Christine de Pizan's *City of Ladies* in the light of premodern feminism is Maureen Quilligan's *The Allegory of Female Authority: Christine de Pizan's "Cité des Dames"* (1991).

Dante Alighieri

Charles Singleton's annotated translation of Dante's *Divine Comedy*, with facing-page Italian text, is unsurpassed (6 vols., 1970–1975; rpt., 1990–1991). See also Singleton's groundbreaking and still stimulating short studies *Commedia: Elements of Structure* (1954) and *Journey to Beatrice* (1958). Short articles on a range of topics appear in *The Dante Encyclo-pedia*, gen. ed. Richard Lansing (2000), and a synoptic view of the encyclopedic quality of the *Comedy* is given in Giuseppe Mazzotta, *Dante's Vision and the Circle of Knowledge* (1993). The influence of Singleton remains strong in recent generations of Dante scholarship. Robert Pogue Harrison responds to Singleton's *Journey* in his *Body of Beatrice* (1988), while Teodolinda Barolini pushes back against the theologizing impulse of Singleton's work in *The Undivine Comedy: Detheologizing Dante* (1992). On Dante's relationship to his poetic forebears, from Virgil to the Occitan troubadours, see Teodolinda Barolini, *Dante's Poets: Textuality and Truth in the "Comedy"* (1984).

Marie de France

A full collection of Marie's lais appears in Dorothy Gilbert, trans., *Marie de France: Poetry* (2015). A still useful overview of her work is Emanuel J. Mickel, Jr., *Marie de France* (1974); for an insightful reading of Marie within the framework of medieval gender categories, see R. Howard Bloch, *The Anonymous Marie de France* (2003). An influential study of Marie's ouvre is Sharon Kinoshita and Peggy McCracken, *Marie de France: A Critical Companion* (2012).

The Qur'an

An extraordinarily readable translation of the Qur'an with good annotations is M. A. S. Abdel Haleem, *The Qur'an: A New Translation* (2004). See also his *Understanding the Qur'an: Themes and Style* (1999). A scholarly collection of essays appears in Jane Dammen McAuliffe, ed., *The Cambridge Companion to the Qur'an* (2009); for detailed information on specific topics, see also McAuliffe, ed., *The Encyclopaedia of the Qur'an*, 5 vols. (2001–2006). A useful overview is W. Montgomery Watt and Richard Bell, *Introduction to the Qur'an* (rev. ed., 2001). To get a sense of the rhythm and musicality of Qur'anic recitation, see Michael Sells, "Sound, Spirit, and Gender in the Qur'an" (1991), reprinted as an appendix to his *Approaching the Qur'an: The Early Revelations* (2nd ed., 2007), which includes a CD.

The Thousand and One Nights

The best short overview of the history of the *Nights'* composition and translation is Dwight F. Reynolds, "A Thousand and One Nights: A History of the Text and Its Reception," in *Arabic Literature in the Post-classical Period*, ed. Roger Allen and D. S. Richards (2006). The novelist Robert Irwin has published a widely available (but not always consistently reliable) guide called *The Arabian Nights: A Companion* (1994; rpt., 2004). The two best collections on the *Nights* focus respectively on the formation of the work and on its reception. The first is *The Arabian Nights Reader*, ed. Ulrich Marzolph (2006), which includes many of the crucial, groundbreaking scholarly articles on the *Nights* by such authors as Muhsin Mahdi, the modern editor of the Arabic text, and Nabia Abbott, the discoverer of the ninth-century manuscript fragment that is the first evidence of the work; the second, which offers some very useful correctives to Irwin, is *The Arabian Nights in Historical Context: Between East and West*, ed. Saree Makdisi and Felicity Nussbaum (2008).

Fruitful literary analyses of the *Nights* include Sandra Naddaff, *Arabesque: Narrative Structure and the Aesthetics of Repetition in the 1001 Nights* (1991), which features a comparative and theoretical literary analysis of the Porter and the Three Ladies group of tales, and David Pinault, *Story-telling Techniques in the Arabian Nights* (1992), which offers an excellent comparative analysis of the Syria and Cairo compilations of the *Nights* and their historical contexts. Provocative food for thought on the *Nights'* role in modern fiction, especially in magical realism, can be found in Jorge Luis Borges, "The Translators of *The Thousand and One Nights*" (1934), trans. Esther Allen, in *Selected Non-fictions* (in paperback as *The Total Library: Non-fiction, 1922–86*), ed. Eliot Weinberger (1999), and in *The Translation Studies Reader*, ed. Lawrence Venuti (2nd ed., 2004). Finally, http://journalofthenights.blogspot.com/ provides an appropriately abundant and fertile overview of everything imaginable responding to the *Nights*—adaptations (music, opera, theatre, film, video games, toys, etc.), recently published studies and articles, new translations, political issues (especially censorship), et cetera.

V. Medieval China

Two books by Mark Lewis, *China between Empires: The Northern and Southern Dynasties* (2009) and *China's Cosmopolitan Empire: The Tang Dynasty* (2009), provide lively depictions of China's medieval world. Edward H. Schafer's *The Golden Peaches of Samarkand: A Study of T'ang Exotics* (1963) vividly evokes the multiethnic atmosphere of Tang culture.

For a general survey of medieval literature, see the relevant chapters in *The Cambridge History of Chinese Literature*, ed. Stephen Owen and Kang-i Sun Chang, 2 vols. (2010). On medieval poetry in particular, see Stephen Owen, *The Making of Early Chinese Classical Poetry* (2006); Kang-i Sun Chang, *Six Dynasties Poetry* (1986); and Kōjirō Yoshikawa, *An Introduction to Sung Poetry*, trans. Burton Watson (1967). Xiaofei Tian's *Beacon Fire and Shooting Star: The Literary Culture of the Liang (502–557)* (2008) is a compelling study of literary court culture in the South during the Period of Disunion.

Tang Poetry

Stephen Owen's *Traditional Chinese Poetry and Poetics: Omen of the World* (1985) provides a general introduction to Chinese poetry. For an anthology of guided readings in various genres of Chinese poetry, see Zongqi Cai's *How to Read Chinese Poetry: A Guided Anthology* (2008). To further explore the breadth and development of Tang poetry, see Stephen Owen's four magisterial studies: *The Poetry of the Early T'ang* (1977), *The Great Age of Chinese Poetry: The High T'ang* (1981), *The End of the Chinese 'Middle Ages': Essays in Mid-Tang Literary Culture* (1996), and *The Late Tang: Chinese Poetry of the Mid-Ninth Century (827–860)* (2006).

For translations of Li Bo's poetry, see Vikram Seth's *Three Chinese Poets: Translations of Poems by Wang Wei, Li Bai, and Du Fu* (1992). Paul W. Kroll's *Studies in Medieval Taoism and the Poetry of Li Po* (2009) and Paula Varsano's *Tracking the Banished Immortal: The Poetry of Li Bo and Its Critical Reception* (2003) are compelling studies of the poetry; Arthur Waley's *The Poetry and Career of Li Po, 701–762 A.D.* (1950) is a biography.

Among translations of Du Fu, David Hawkes's *A Little Primer of Tu Fu* (1967), an introductory bilingual edition of a few of the poems, is particularly recommended. For a complete bilingual translation of Du Fu's poetry see Stephen Owen's *The Poetry of Du Fu*, 6 volumes (2016).

See also Burton Watson's *The Selected Poems of Du Fu* (2002). For studies of Du Fu's life and legacy see David McCraw's *Du Fu's Laments from the South* (1992) and Eva Shan Chou's *Reconsidering Tu Fu: Literary Greatness and Cultural Context* (1995).

VI. Japan's Classical Age

To further explore early and medieval Japanese history see Conrad Schirokauer, David Lurie, and Suzanne Gay's *A Brief History of Japanese Civilization* (2nd ed., 2006) For a shorter treatment of Japanese history in the context of East Asia, Patricia Buckley Ebrey, Anne Walthall, and James B. Palais, *East Asia: A Cultural, Social, and Political History* (2nd ed., 2009), is recommended.

Traditional Japanese Literature: An Anthology, Beginnings to 1600, ed. Haruo Shirane (2007), and Donald Keene's *Anthology of Japanese Literature: From the Earliest Era to the Mid-Nineteenth Century* (1955) are great treasure troves of original early and medieval Japanese texts in English translation; see also *Traditional Japanese Poetry: An Anthology*, trans. Steven D. Carter (1991), and *Classical Japanese Prose: An Anthology*, ed. Helen Craig McCullough (1990). Lovers of travel literature will appreciate Donald Keene's *Travelers of a Hundred Ages: The Japanese as Revealed through 1,000 Years of Diaries* (rev. ed., 1999). Keene presents a sweeping history of premodern Japanese literature in *Seeds in the Heart: Japanese Literature from Earliest Times to the Late Sixteenth Century* (1993). For a comprehensive history of Japanese literature see *Cambridge History of Japanese Literature* (2016), edited by Haruo Shirane, Tomi Suzuki, and David Lurie.

Earl Miner, Hiroko Odagiri, and Robert E. Morrell's *The Princeton Companion to Classical Japanese Literature* (1985) is a reliable reference work to the world of Japanese literature. Groundbreaking studies of the interplay between Chinese and Japanese cultural traditions in Japanese literature include David Pollack, *The Fracture of Meaning: Japan's Synthesis of China from the Eighth through the Eighteenth Centuries* (1986); Thomas LaMarre, *Uncovering Heian Japan: An Archaeology of Sensation and Inscription* (2000); and Atsuko Sakaki, *Obsessions with the Sino-Japanese Polarity in Japanese Literature* (2005). Tomiko Yoda's *Gender and National Literature: Heian Texts in the Constructions of Japanese Modernity* (2004) is a compelling study of how Heian texts have influenced modern Japanese identity and self-understanding.

Murasaki Shikibu

This anthology uses a new translation by Dennis Washburn; the three previous English translations of *The Tale of Genji* all have their partisans. The first English translation was published by Arthur Waley in installments between 1925 and 1933. Edward G. Seidensticker's *The Tale of Genji* (1976) is a beautiful translation, more faithful than Waley's. The translation by Royall Tyler (2001) is yet more faithful.

For a glimpse into the life of the author, see *Murasaki Shikibu: Her Diary and Poetic Memoirs*, trans. Richard Bowring (1982). Ivan Morris, *The World of the Shining Prince: Court Life in Ancient Japan*, with a new introduction by Barbara Ruch (1964; rpt., 1994), is a colorful account of the world that Murasaki and her characters inhabit.

The best brief introduction to the tale is Richard Bowring, *Murasaki Shikibu: "The Tale of Genji"* (1988). Two excellent longer studies are Norma Field, *The Splendor of Longing in the "Tale of Genji"* (1987), and Haruo Shirane, *The Bridge of Dreams: A Poetics of "The Tale of Genji"* (1987). *Envisioning "The Tale of Genji": Media,*

Gender, and Cultural Production (2008), a collection of articles edited by Shirane, gives fascinating glimpses of how *The Tale of Genji* influenced later literature, art, and popular culture.

Sei Shōnagon
The selections printed in this anthology are taken from a complete translation by Meredith McKinney, *The Pillow Book* (2006). Other important translations include the pioneering translation of Arthur Waley, *The Pillow-Book of Sei Shōnagon* (1928); Ivan Morris, *The Pillow Book of Sei Shōnagon*, 2 vols. (1967) (the second volume contains useful notes and appendices); and the sampling in Helen Craig McCullough, *Classical Japanese Prose: An Anthology* (1990). Ivan Morris's *The World of the Shining Prince: Court Life in Ancient Japan* (1964), a colorful portrayal of the Heian period, will be helpful to readers of both *The Pillow Book* and *The Tale of Genji*.

VII. Islam and Pre-Islamic Culture in North Africa

David Conrad's *Empires of Medieval West Africa* (rev. ed., 2010) provides a broad introduction to West Africa, as does Nehemia Levtzion's *Ancient Ghana and Mali* (1980). Levtzion and J. F. P. Hopkins's *Corpus of Early Arabic Sources for West African History* (1981) is an excellent source book for the study of the region. For the history of Islam in West Africa, consult Levtzion and R. L. Pouwels's *The History of Islam in Africa* (2000) and Levtzion and Jay Spaulding's *Medieval West Africa: Views from Arab Scholars and Merchants* (2003).

Sunjata
Musical performances involving the singing of stories and praises about Sunjata are called *Sunjata fasa,* and the prose narrative in its many versions is known as *Manden maana,* or *Manden tariku.* The version excerpted here was collected and translated by David C. Conrad; his *Sunjata* (2004) offers a detailed introduction. Conrad's *Epic Ancestors of the Sunjata Era: Oral Tradition from the Maninka of Guinea* collects seven variants of the Sunjata epic. Laye Camara's *The Guardian of the Word* (1984) is a prose variant in novel form, based on the narrative by Babu Condé of Fadama, Guinea, recorded in 1963. But it was another prose variant, Djibril Tamsir Niane's *Sundiata: An Epic of Old Mali* (1965) that first drew worldwide attention to this epic. The three versions edited by Gordon Innes in *Sunjata* (1974) were narrated in the Mandinka dialect of the Gambia, and the one published by John Johnson in 1986 as *Son-Jara* third edition (2003) represents the Kita region of Mali. Eric Charry's *Mande Music* (2000) describes the musical instruments involved in performing the epic, while Stephen Belcher, *Epic Traditions of Africa* (1999), and Marloes Janson, *The Best Hand is the Hand that Always Gives: Griottes and their Profession in Eastern Gambia* (2002), provide broad context and analytical insight.

VIII. Europe and the New World

Eugene Rice with Anthony Grafton, *The Foundations of Early Modern Europe*, second edition (1994), is the finest introduction to the contexts in which Renaissance or early modern literature was produced. William Bouwsma, *A Usable Past: Essays in European Cultural History* (1990), especially the chapter "Anxiety and the Formation of Early Modern Culture," also offers illuminating perspectives on the intellectual character of the period. Constance Jordan, *Renaissance Feminism: Literary Texts and Political Models* (1990), is a recommended study of the place of women in history and political thought. William Kerrigan and Gordon Braden, *The Idea of the Renaissance* (1989), offers a helpful and direct analysis of the critical construction of the Renaissance as a concept. Harry Berger Jr., *Second World and Green World: Studies in Renaissance Fiction-Making* (1988), especially the title essay, is a dense but recommended study of the aims of fiction making. Stephen Greenblatt,

Renaissance Self-Fashioning (1980), describes the construction of identity in the period. J. H. Elliott's *The Old World and the New: 1492–1650* (1992) and *Imperial Spain: 1492–1716*, second edition (2002) provide good introductions.

Miguel de Cervantes

William Byron, *Cervantes: A Biography* (1978), is thorough. Ruth El Saffar, ed., *Critical Essays on Cervantes* (1986), and Anne Cruz and Carroll Johnson, eds., *Cervantes and his Postmodern Constituencies* (1998) offer interesting essays by eminent scholars. Vladimir Nabokov, *Lectures on Don Quixote* (1983), presents an elegant engagement with Cervantes' fiction. More technical studies include Carroll Johnson, *Cervantes and the Material World* (2000) and David Quint, *Cervantes' Novel of Modern Times: A New Reading of* Don Quixote (2003).

Niccolò Machiavelli

Peter E. Bondanella focuses on the literary aspects of Machiavelli's works in *Machiavelli and the Art of Renaissance History* (1973). Sebastian de Grazia, *Machiavelli in Hell* (1989), on politics in *The Prince*, contains indexes and a bibliography. J. R. Hale's biography, *Machiavelli and Renaissance Italy* (1972), places Machiavelli in a historical perspective. A political analysis is provided by Anthony Parel in *The Political Calculus: Essays on Machiavelli's Political Philosophy* (1972). Roberto Ridolfi, *The Life of Niccolò Machiavelli* (1963), is still considered the best and most accurate biography. Silvia Ruffo-Fiore, *Niccolò Machiavelli* (1982), is a useful comprehensive guide for the beginning student. Victoria Kahn, *Machiavellian Rhetoric: From the Counter-Reformation to Milton* (1994), and Wayne A. Rebhorn, *Foxes and Lions: Machiavelli's Confidence Men* (1988), are recommended.

Marguerite de Navarre

P. A. Chilton's justly praised translation of the *Heptameron* (1984) has an excellent introduction. John D. Lyons and Mary B. McKinley, eds., *Critical Tales: New Studies of the Heptameron and Early Modern Culture* (1993), contains useful essays on the *Heptameron*. B. J. Davis, *The Storytellers in Marguerite de Navarre's Heptameron* (1978), presents detailed discussions of the narrators. Timothy Hampton, *Literature and Nation in the Sixteenth Century: Inventing Renaissance France* (2001) offers a historical reading of story 10. Samuel Putnam, *Marguerite de Navarre* (1935), is an informative and readable biography. Barbara M. Stephenson, *The Power and Patronage of Marguerite de Navarre* (2004), uses Marguerite's letters to trace her involvement in politics and in religious reform.

Michel de Montaigne

Hugo Friedrich, *Montaigne* (1991), is a careful historical study of the author. David Quint, *Montaigne and the Quality of Mercy* (1998) analyzes the political and ethical goals of the *Essays*. Judith Shklar, *Ordinary Vices* (1984), and Edwin Duval, "Lessons of the New World: Design and Meaning in Montaigne's 'Des Cannibales' (I:31) and 'Des coches' (III:6)," in *Montaigne: Essays in Reading*, ed. Gerard Defaux, *Yale French Studies* 64 (1983): 95–112, provide excellent studies of Montaigne that include, but are not limited to, his New World contexts. Marcel Tetel, *Montaigne,* updated edition (1990), and Richard Sayce, *The Essays of Montaigne: A Critical Exploration* (1972), are excellent introductions designed for the general reader.

Francis Petrarch

Ernest Hatch Wilkins's biography, *Life of Petrarch* (1961), is informative, but tends to take Petrarch's autobiographical writings at face value. Giuseppe Mazzotta, *The Worlds of Petrarch* (1993), is an encyclopedic introduction to Petrarch's work and times. Victoria Kirkham and Armando Maggi have compiled the useful *Petrarch: A Critical Guide to the Complete Works* (2009). Robert Durling's introduction to *Petrarch's Lyric Poems* (1976) provides a rich overview of his poetry. Diana Vickers, "Diana Described: Scattered Woman and Scattered Rhyme," *Writing and Sexual Difference,* ed. Elizabeth Abel (1982), is the central feminist reading of Petrarch's lyric. In *Unrequited Conquests* (2000), Roland Greene reads Petrarchism in relation to early modern imperialism.

Popol Vuh

Dennis Tedlock's translation, satisfyingly annotated, is published as *Popol Vuh: The Mayan Book of the Dawn of Life* (1985; revised 1996). The text in this volume is from the 1996 edition. Older translations with useful introductions are Adrián Recinos, Delia Goetz, and Sylvanus Morley, *Popol Vuh: The Sacred Book of the Ancient Quiché Maya* (1950); and Munro S. Edmonson. *The Book of Counsel: The Popol Vuh of the Quiché Maya of Guatemala* (1971). Edmonson's is the only Quiché-English edition. Essays on the Popol Vuh and related topics are in Tedlock's *The Spoken Word and the Work of Interpretation* (1983).

William Shakespeare

Recent biographies placing Shakespeare in his social and intellectual context include Stephen Greenblatt, *Will in the World: How Shakespeare Became Shakespeare* (2004) and Jonathan Bate, *Soul of the Age: A Biography of the Mind of William Shakespeare* (2009). Marjorie Garber, *Shakespeare After All* (2005), provides a lively introduction, with individual essays on all the plays. Paul Arthur Cantor, *Shakespeare, "Hamlet"* (1989), is an in-depth study of the tragedy. Valuable studies are to be found in Harry Levin, *The Question of "Hamlet"* (1959) and Margreta de Grazia, *"Hamlet" without Hamlet* (2007).

Permissions Acknowledgments

Beowulf: From BEOWULF, trans. by Seamus Heaney. Copyright © 2000 by Seamus Heaney. Used by permission of W. W. Norton & Company, Inc.

Bhagavad-gītā: From THE BHAGAVAD-GITA: A NEW TRANSLATION, trans. by Gavin Flood & Charles Martin. Copyright © 2012 by Gavin Flood and Charles Martin. Used by permission of W. W. Norton & Company, Inc.

Geoffrey Chaucer: From THE SELECTED CANTERBURY TALES: A NEW VERSE TRANSLATION, trans. by Sheila Fisher. Copyright © 2011 by Sheila Fisher. Used by permission of W. W. Norton & Company, Inc.

The Christian Bible: Excerpts from THE FOUR GOSPELS AND THE REVELATION by Richmond Lattimore. Copyright © 1979 by Richmond Lattimore. Reprinted by permission of Farrar, Straus and Giroux.

Classic of Poetry: From "Classic of Poetry" from AN ANTHOLOGY OF CHINESE LITERATURE: BEGINNINGS TO 1911 ed. and trans. by Stephen Owen. Copyright © 1996 by Stephen Owen and The Council for Cultural Planning and Development of the Executive Yuan of the Republic of China. Used by permission of W. W. Norton & Company, Inc.

Confucius: From THE ANALECTS OF CONFUCIUS, trans. by Simon Leys. Copyright © 1997 by Pierre Ryckmans. Used by permission of W. W. Norton & Company, Inc.

Dante Alighieri: "Inferno" from THE DIVINE COMEDY, trans. by John Ciardi. Copyright © 1954, 1957, 1959, 1960, 1961, 1965, 1967, 1970 by the Ciardi Family Publishing Trust. Used by permission of W. W. Norton & Company, Inc.

Miguel de Cervantes: Excerpts from DON QUIXOTE: Two Volumes In One, trans. by Samuel Putnam, translation copyright © 1949 by The Viking Press, Inc. Used by permission of Viking Books, an imprint of Penguin Publishing Group, a division of Random House LLC. All rights reserved. Any third-party use of this material, outside of this publication, is prohibited. Interested parties must apply directly to Penguin Random House LLC for permission.

Marie de France: From MARIE DE FRANCE: POETRY (Norton Critical Edition), ed. and trans. by Dorothy Gilbert. Copyright © 2015 by W. W. Norton & Company, Inc. Translation copyright © 2015 by Dorothy Gilbert. Used by permission of W. W. Norton & Company, Inc.

Marguerite de Navarre: From THE HEPTAMERON, trans. with an introduction by P. A. Chilton (Penguin Classics 1984). Copyright © 1984 P. A. Chilton. Reproduced by permission of Penguin Books Ltd.

Christine de Pizan: From THE BOOK OF THE CITY OF LADIES, trans. by Rosalind Brown-Grant (Penguin Classics 1999). Translation copyright © 1999 by Rosalind Brown-Grant. Reproduced with permission of Penguin Books Ltd.

Du Fu: "Qiang Village 1," translated by Paul W. Kroll. Reprinted by permission of Paul W. Kroll. "Thoughts While Travelling at Night" from THREE CHINESE POETS: TRANSLATIONS OF POEMS BY WANG WEI, LI BAI, AND DU FU (1992), trans. by Vikram Seth. Copyright © 1992 by Vikram Seth. Reprinted by permission of David Godwin Associates Ltd. "My Thatched Roof is Ruined by the Autumn Wind" and "Spending the Night in a Tower by the River," trans. by Stephen Owen from THE GREAT AGE OF CHINESE POETRY. Copyright © 1981 by Yale University. Reprinted by permission of Yale University Press. "Moonlight Night," "Spring Prospect," "Ballad of the Firewood Vendors," and "Autumn Meditations IV" from SELECTED POEMS OF DU FU, trans. by Burton Watson. Copyright © 2002 by Columbia University Press. Reprinted by permission of the publisher. "Painted Hawk" and "I Stand Alone," trans. by Stephen Owen from AN ANTHOLOGY OF CHINESE LITERATURE: BEGINNINGS TO 1911, ed. and trans. by Stephen Owen. Copyright © 1996 by Stephen Owen and The Council for Cultural Planning and Development of the Executive Yuan of the Republic of China. Used by permission of W. W. Norton & Company, Inc.

Euripides: From MEDEA: A NORTON CRITICAL EDITION, ed. and trans. by Sheila Murnaghan. Copyright © 2018 by W. W. Norton & Company, Inc. Used by permission of W. W. Norton & Company, Inc.

Gilgamesh: From THE EPIC OF GILGAMESH, trans. by Benjamin R. Foster. Copyright © 2001 by W. W. Norton & Company, Inc. Used by permission of W. W. Norton & Company, Inc.

Sunjata: From SUNJATA: A NEW PROSE VERSION, ed. and trans. by David C. Conrad. Copyright © 2016 by the Hackett Publishing Company, Inc. Reprinted with the permission of Hackett Publishing Company. All rights reserved.

The Thousand and One Nights: From THE ARABIAN NIGHTS: THE THOUSAND AND ONE NIGHTS, trans. by Husain Haddawy. Copyright © 1990 by W. W. Norton & Company, Inc. Used by permission of W. W. Norton & Company, Inc. [The Third Old Man's Tale], trans. by Jerome W. Clinton is reprinted by permission of Jerome W. Clinton.

Virgil: "Book One: Safe Haven After Storm," "Book Two: The Final Hours of Troy," "Book Four: The Tragic Queen of Carthage," "Book Six: The Kingdom of the Dead," from "Book Eight: The Shield of Aeneas," and from "Book Twelve: The Sword Decides All" from THE AENEID, trans. by Robert Fagles, translation copyright © 2006 by Robert Fagles. Used by permission of Viking Books, an imprint of Penguin Publishing Group, a division of Penguin Random House LLC. All rights reserved. Any third-party use of this material, outside of this publication, is prohibited. Interested parties must apply directly to Penguin Random House LLC for permission.

IMAGES

2–3 bpk Bildagentur/Antikensammlung, Staatliche Museen, Berlin, Germany/Art Resource, NY; 4 The Metropolitan Museum of Art, Raymond and Beverly Sackler Gift, 1988 (1988.433.1); 6 DEA/G. Dagli Orti/De Agostini/Getty Images; 8 DEA Picture Library/De Agostini/Getty Images; 11 De Agostini Picture Library/De Agostini/Getty Images; 12 Scala/Art Resource, NY; 16 Alinari/Bridgeman Images; 20 Werner Forman/Art Resource, NY; 125 © The Trustees of the British Museum/Art Resource, NY; 391 Scala/Art Resource, NY; 392 Marie Mauzy/Art Resource, NY; 476 © RMN-Grand Palais/Art Resource, NY; 620–1 Image copyright © The Metropolitan Museum of Art. Image source: Art Resource, NY; 622 V&A Images, London/Art Resource, NY; 627 Werner Forman/Art Resource, NY; 632 Angelo Hornak/Corbis via Getty Images; 688–9 GRANGER/GRANGER—All rights reserved; 691 (top) © RMN-Grand Palais/Art Resource, NY; 691 (bottom) Bridgeman-Giraudon/Art Resource, NY; 695 HIP/Art Resource, NY; 732–3 bpk Bildagentur/Bodleian Library, Oxford, Great Britain/Photo: Hermann Buresch/Art Resource, NY; 734 Bridgeman-Giraudon/Art Resource, NY; 736 Erich Lessing/Art Resource, NY; 740 SSPL/Science Museum/Art Resource, NY; 744 Wikimedia Commons, public domain; 745 HIP/Art Resource, NY; 1178–9 Image copyright © The Metropolitan Museum of Art. Image source: Art Resource, NY; 1181 akg-images/Pictures From History; 1200–1 De Agostini Picture Library/Bridgeman Images; 1203 JTB Photo/UIG via Getty Images; 1204 Gianni Dagli Orti/REX/Shutterstock; 1233 © Harvard Art Museum/Art Resource, NY; 1418–9 Gavin Hellier/Getty Images; 1468–9 © National Gallery, London/Art Resource, NY; 1473 Bridgeman-Giraudon/Art Resource, NY; 1478 bpk Bildagentur/Alte Pinakothek, Bayerische Staatsgemaeldesammlungen, Munich, G/Art Resource, NY; 1479 © The Trustees of the British Museum/Art Resource, NY

COLOR INSERT

C1 Erich Lessing/Art Resource, NY; C2 © The Trustees of the British Museum/Art Resource, NY; C3 With permission of the Royal Ontario Museum © ROM; C4 DEA/S.Vannini/De Agostini/Getty Images; C5 Scala/Art Resource, NY; C6 © The Trustees of the British Museum/Art Resource, NY; C7 © Vanni Archive/Art Resource, NY; C8 HIP/Art Resource, NY; C9 Scala/Art Resource; C10 © British Library Board/Robana/Art Resource, NY; C11 bpk Bildagentur/Museum fuer Islamische Kunst, Staatliche Museen, Berlin, German/Photo: Georg Niedermeiser/Art Resource, NY; C12 © British Library Board/Robana/Art Resource, NY; C13 Burstein Collection/CORBIS/Getty Images; C14 © Lebrecht Music & Arts; C15 © The Trustees of the British Museum/Art Resource, NY; C16 Digital Image © 2017 Museum Associates/LACMA. Licensed by Art Resource, NY; C17 Werner Forman/Art Resource, NY; C18 bpk Bildagentur/Germanisches Nationalmuseum, Nuremberg, Germany/Photo: Lutz Braun/Art Resource, NY; C19 © DeA Picture Library/Art Resource, NY; C20 Art Collection 2/Alamy Stock Photo; C21 Erich Lessing/Art Resource, NY; C22 bpk Bildagentur/Museum fuer Asiatische Kunst, Staatliche Museen, Berlin, Germany/Art Resource, NY; C23 © British Library Board. All Rights Reserved/Bridgeman Images; C24 Erich Lessing/Art Resource, NY

Index